# Feenin

# Feenin

*(a novel)*

## NANE QUARTAY

A

**SBI**

**PUBLICATION**

A STREBOR BOOKS INTERNATIONAL LLC PUBLICATION
DISTRIBUTED BY SIMON & SCHUSTER, INC.

Published by

Strebor Books International LLC
P.O. Box 10127
Silver Spring, MD 20914
*http://www.streborbooks.com*

ISBN 0-9711953-7-4
LCCN 2002114446

Distributed by Simon & Schuster, Inc.
1230 Avenue of the Americas
New York, NY 10020
1-800-223-2336

*Cover illustration: André Harris*
*Typesetting and interior design: Kris Tobiassen*

First Printing June 2003
Manufactured and Printed in the United States
10  9  8  7  6  5  4  3  2  1

# Acknowledgements

To all of my friends! Those who helped me with encouragement as I dreamed a little dream of a novel. You helped keep the ebon in my flow. Thanks to Bernard Moseby, Linda, Terry T, Carolyn Corbin and Lisa Cannon for being the first to read my story, even when it was raggedy. To Stephanie Kelly, Cheryl R, Kendall Rhodes, Norma Chapman, John, John and John for letting me flip the script whenever I wanted to trip. It was mad fun!

I also wish to express my many thanks to the writers for allowing my words to wander in their intellectual space. You all helped me dot the 'i's' and cross the 't's' of my imagination. I owe you all. Black Inkwell, Albany Writer's Group and my fair and honest backbreaking critics at Barnes and Noble.

It takes a village to raise a child. It took a tribe to raise mine. There are going to be friends that I have missed but just know that it wasn't my intention.

Peace!
NANE Q

# Prologue

Tokus Stone stood looking out the window at nothing, wondering what would happen next . . . and he wanted to say good-bye. "Peace" to the violence that lay outside, on the desolate streets below. "Later" to the hunger that plucked at his insides, that gnawed at him until his soul went raw. "See ya" to the cold harshness of people, to their salty numbness that dripped like bitter syrup into their eyes and mouths. He felt them all . . . and he dealt with the barren landscape as hell. An entity that was very, very real. He brought the binoculars to his eyes and looked down at the street from the eighth-floor apartment. A people watcher in the ghetto. All the despair of a sixteen-year-old, saddened by abuse and devoid of love, arose in him as he watched his people and listened to his drunken stepfather rage at his mother.

"You just a lyin' ass ho," his stepfather spit out. Tokus' fertile young mind conjured images of the hookers he passed downtown every day. They wore outfits that stirred his imagination into hard places. They'd let you feel 'em up and everything for two dollars, but Tokus kept that to a minimum. That

wasn't his mother though, and he could gladly kill his stepfather whenever that word came out his lying, drunken mouth.
He looked down at the people crawling on the street far
below.

The nothingness of the big city glared back at young
Tokus, invading him, filling him with emptiness. I'm gonna
get outta here, he thought. Education would be his rescuer,
his lifeline out of the ghetto. One day he wanted to own his
own business, be his own boss. Take care of his mother and
help her cast off the line of losers she always seemed to reel
in, present husband included, and leave this street life
behind them. Soon he would enter his junior year in high
school, and if he kept his grades where they were, he was sure
he would be able to get a grant to attend the university. Yes,
he would "learn" his way out of the projects, and nothing
could stop him.

The usual suspects were hanging out on the corner. A
coarse sky loomed over the drab neighborhood, spreading
dreary light over the mundane existence known as the slums.
There was a corner store with bars on the windows, and various colored brick buildings lined the rest of the block.
Morning, noon and night the desolation was the same; poor
people crammed on top of poor people with the only common
denominator being pain and hunger and devising a means to
get beyond and above the cycle of sleeping and waking. With
no hope in between. Everything is fair when ya' living in the
city, Tokus mused.

He watched through his binoculars as a Black Jesus stumbled around the corner, running down the street as if the devil

were after him. He wore a tattered pair of shorts and a tiny vest a few sizes too small. On his back was a cross made of cheap wood and printed in big, white letters on a placard attached to the top of it was the word "America." His eyes bulged in fear as he pumped his fists, snatching at momentum, frantically reaching for speed to add to his cumbersome frame. Black Jesus wasn't made for running. A carload of teenagers came screeching around the corner after him with automatic weapons pointed out the windows. Tokus watched the usual suspects sprint for cover as rapid gunfire spit forth, showering the sidewalk. The first shot caught Black Jesus in the leg and spun him around as the car pulled up beside him. The second shot pierced his side and slammed him against the wall. The third bullet hit Black Jesus in the chest, and he danced, dead against the cold, brick building. He slumped to the ground, lifeless. "America" was stained with his blood.

"Why you always got to wait till you get drunk to come in here with your mess?" his mother asked the drunk. She didn't yell. "Crazed people yell," she had once told Tokus, "and I ain't crazed!" Tokus loved her for her understanding, but he just wished she would leave her husband and move on. He had long ago stopped asking his mother why she stayed, and at some point, Tokus had stopped caring. She had chosen her path and she walked it with determination. She could walk it alone as far as he was concerned, but something, somewhere had to change.

The harsh reality of his stepfather's wrath was an early lesson for Tokus. From the age of four until he was nine there were savage belts and wicked belt buckles. From ten to twelve there were stinging electrical cords and big, thick-handled straw brooms. But at fourteen, Tokus developed into a strong, muscular banger, and his stepfather resorted to using fists. He delivered solid heavyweight punches that overpowered the boy, laying him out, leaving him flat on his back, looking up at a twisted face, flared nostrils and bulging jaws that snorted air with a twisted disposition. Sweat poured angrily down the wild man's face. Yellow teeth showed unevenly as he sneered, standing over the fallen child, cursing the day of Tokus' conception. Tokus had taken many beatings, but as he grew in mental and physical strength, a lifetime of fear was replaced by a burning desire for payback. He waited. His time would come.

A piercing scream, a chorus of pain came down the hallway. Tokus winced inside and ran toward its source. He came to a stop in the bedroom doorway, catching his breath in horror. His stepfather knelt between his mother's legs. Her skirt was hiked way up over her thighs and her blouse was ripped open. Her breasts flopped out lewdly, exposed as the man reached out and pawed them. Then he slapped her in the face.

"You don't tell me 'no,' you lying slut!" he screamed. "You! Don't! Tell! Me! No!" he growled, punctuating each word with a backhand. "You just open your legs and get ready!" he finished. His chest heaved from mixing alcohol with physical exertion. He never saw Tokus charging toward him with his shoulder aimed like a battering ram.

Tokus saw his chance and hit harder than he had ever hit anyone on the football field and sent the man sprawling, face first, into the nightstand near the bedside. Tokus sprang to his feet in a defensive stance. The fading afternoon sunlight streamed through the window behind him, bathing him in ninja shadows. The stepfather rolled onto his back. The skin on his face puckered where he had been cut. The blood leaked down his face as he climbed to his feet, wobbled a bit, then threw his head back and screamed like a banshee. Tokus waited as his stepfather rushed toward him, a bulldozer with bared teeth.

Reality slowed for Tokus and he entered the "zone," a place where everything and everyone moved in surreal, slow motion. As his stepfather covered the few feet between them, Tokus realized that pound for pound, body-to-body, he would get steamrolled, so he went low, throwing his shoulders at the older man's knees. The stepfather went sailing, flailing into the curtains behind Tokus and crashing through the window. He grasped a handful of curtain and clung, pulling the fabric behind him and ripping the curtain rods out of the wall. The thin, aluminum rods wedged into the corner of the window and held for a second but the weight of the stepfather quickly snapped them in half. Tokus heard a desperate scream before the rods went clattering out the bedroom window, eight stories to the ground below.

Tokus looked at the window, shocked! For a second. Then he went over to the window to see where the creep had landed.

"Help!" came a panicked cry.

Tokus looked down, surprised to see that his stepfather was hanging on the window ledge. Shards of glass were biting into his fingers and blood leaked out onto the ledge. He was holding on with both hands, but Tokus wondered, for how long?

"Help me!" he screamed at Tokus.

"Help me, who?" Tokus asked.

"Help me, Tokus!"

"Mr. Tokus."

"Mr. Tokus! Mr. Tokus! Mr. Damn Tokus! Now pull me up! Please!" The glass bit deeper into the tender flesh of his fingers. Tokus' mother hurried over to the window, saw her husband hanging there and got frantic.

"Oh, my God!" she shrilled. "Oh! My! God! Tokus, pull him, pull him up!" she ordered and began to cry, her fingers dug deeply into the soft flesh of his shoulder.

Tokus leaned his head out the window. "You gonna die."

"Please, Tokus! Please?" The dangling stepfather kicked frantically at the building, his fingers pressed farther into the bits of glass as he fought against the fall.

"You know," Tokus began. "When you fall? Before you hit the ground? You gonna feel like I feel when you hit me. When you hit Ma."

"I won't do it no mo'!" the stepfather cried. His fingers slipped a fraction, and tiny squirts of blood shot against the windowsill. He moaned in pain and his arms tensed, tightening, gripping against the gravity that was pulling his body toward the hard concrete.

"Never no mo'! Promise! I promise! Please, Tokus!" the dying man cried for his life.

"A feelin' of nothin'," Tokus continued. "Nothin' you can do about it. As you fall. Nothin' you can hold on to. Nothin'."

"Tokus! Pull me up!" the stepfather begged.

"Tokus, help! Pull! Help him up!" his mother sobbed and collapsed to the floor, whimpering.

"Tokus, don't kill me! Don't let me die!" his stepfather yelled. Then he lost his grip.

Tokus lunged forward and caught his stepfather's hand. The momentum almost pulled Tokus out the window, but he held strongly to the wall with his free hand as the flailing, screaming man struggled against him. It took all his strength to pull the big man back up. His stepfather seemed to be fighting his efforts, twisting and turning, screaming and crying, but after a minute they both tumbled inside and sprawled on the floor, exhausted.

His mother rushed to her husband and fussed over him, ministering with a soft, gentle hand while she cried with relief and happiness. Tokus sat opposite the pair and looked into the man's eyes, surprised at the anger and fear he saw there. His stepfather was a changed man. There would be no more abuse.

The next day passed uneventfully. On the contrary, not a single word was exchanged in the strangely quiet, dysfunctional household. Hollow silence echoed ominously off the thin, plaster walls within the tenement as the three of them avoided each other in the small, two-bedroom apartment. Nothing mentioned, nothing gained.

Two days later, Tokus' mother and stepfather went away forever, leaving him alone in a man's world to fend for himself.

Tokus stood looking out the window at nothing, wondering what would happen next.

# Mistress of IT

She stood, deliriously trembling, at the entrance to the park. The young girl searched frantically; her addiction screamed out for satisfaction and her flesh moved in chronic surrender. Long gone were the days when drug use was recreational fun, a fad. Times were now hard-core bouts of having and not having, getting and getting got over, even worse, acts that were once theatric drama were now hellish scenes in which she starred. Control of her life had been violently wrested from her and abused by a blizzard of white powder that enslaved her mind and spirit. Yet she loved her master. Her deeds were the proof. So she searched, following a voice only she could hear. The call of yearning.

She had to feed It. It was her habit. A greedy insatiable monster who stomped across the landscape of her soul. It talked to her often. It knew where the drugs were and was well versed in all the ingenious ways in which to procure the precious substance.

The park loomed before her, threatening in the darkness of the late hour, sinister in its rolling, grassy slopes. An alarm went off somewhere in her mind, warning of danger, but that was drowned out by the thunder of It.

"Go," It said and she obediently shuffled down the man-made pathway as It grew heavy with urgency. The sights of the park held no interest to her. The beauty of nature's multi-colored leaves of the tall trees, the picturesque shores on either side of the Hudson River were a mere blur, as she set about her mission. She passed the small, outdoor amphi-theater with hillside seating and the area known as The Shade, where tall trees stood with their leaves clasping together overhead, casting cool, shadowed refuge during the burning midday hours. The park was deserted—not a soul was in sight—but It guided her. She blindly obeyed. A monument saluting the Buffalo Soldiers was around the bend, hidden from her side of the path by the sloping land. The statue was huge. One soldier stood tall, rifle at the ready, while another kneeled to help a fallen comrade. This part of history meant nothing to her. It only had eyes for the three men who leaned against the tall, stone wall encrypted with the story of the all-black regiment known as the Buffalo Soldiers.

"Look!" It exclaimed as she rounded the curved pathway. She saw a light-skinned man with a big nose put a crack pipe to his lips. Reflexively, she inhaled with him and It pin-pricked her brain with a glimpse of false euphoria. She put on her best sexy, crack smile and floated over to where the men stood between the soldiers and the wall.

The big-nosed smoker started rapping:

Take two and pass,
take two and pass,
take two and pass
so the rock will last.

A dark-skinned man had the pipe. He took two hits and passed the pipe when he spotted the girl approaching.

"H-h-hold up! Waitaminute!" one of the men stuttered, looking the girl over. He recognized the type. "W-w-we got us a trick baby here. Y-y-you out here trickin', baby girl? Huh?"

The big-nosed man broke out with another rhyme:

All men are created equal.
That's why corrupt governments
Kill innocent people.
With chemical warfare
They created crack and AIDS.
Got the public thinkin'
These are things that Black folks made.

"Ask!" It commanded.

"Let me get a hit?" she asked.

"You t-t-trippin'," came the reply.

"Give me some," she said seductively.

"Yeah. You out here trickin'," the man said.

"Well," the big-nose spoke up, "I don't need no pussy, so get on, trick! I don't need no pussy."

"That's cause you smokin' that shit!" the dark man said. "You don't need no orgasm cause in your brain you already done got off. Skeeted ever' which-a-way!" He turned back to the girl. She could feel It agitating her. The hunger in her eyes was deepening. Her skin . . . her blood cried out for cocaine.

The dark man pulled a pebble-sized rock of crack cocaine out of his pocket. It's heart skipped a beat.

"You want some?" the dark man asked. She nodded her assent, mute with It.

"I give you some . . . if you take all your clothes off."

"No!" she shouted without consulting with It.

"What?" It said.

"No! No! Hell no!" she sang. It got angry. It was real ugly when provoked.

"Let me show you something," It said and began flashing scenes across her mind. Scenes from another time, another life. She was on her knees in the back seat of an old abandoned car with three teenaged boys. She'd spit them out the window. Then a German shepherd hunched over her, the dog's paws on her back, its hot breath on her neck. A group of men stood around watching, drinking beer and laughing at the girl who would do anything to get high.

"You will," It said and suddenly she felt the call of cocaine pulling, tearing at every fiber of her being.

"We outside," she said to the man, fighting It.

"Ain't nobody out here but us," the man and It replied in unison. Slowly, she looked around the park. In the thick stillness, she felt eyes everywhere. But there were no other people, not a one.

"Where at?" she asked.

"Here," the dark man replied, mirthfully. He leaned back against the stone wall with a knowing look.

"Go ahead," It said. "Do it. Now!" A blinding high pushed through her flesh, beamed directly into her brain that sent her mind on a spinning, flashing plateau that was miles above the cosmic reach of common thought, a teasing glimpse that quickly dissipated. She sobbed aloud and with trembling fingers, she peeled off her dirty, ripped shirt, exposing the holey, rusty bra underneath.

"Yeah!" It shouted. The three men smoked as they watched, eyeing her small pointy breasts as she removed her bra.

"The rest," said the dark man, wisps of smoke escaping from his lips. She stepped out of her pants and stood naked before them. She extended her arm, palm outward, seeking payment.

"Naw!" the dark man said. "Naw, you got to do more than that, baby!"

"You said naked," she cried.

"I know what I said!" he barked. "But let me see you crawl. Crawl to me. On your hands and knees. But sexy though! Like on TV," he finished. It brought her to her knees. She was openly crying now, and she began to crawl.

"Be sexy!" It warned.

Her sobs were alarming as she fought It. Cries of pain racked her body and she shook with the effort of trying to control herself-to lift herself from her knees, get up, get dressed and escape. She was fed up. It surged to life in response, shocking her with the overpowering need for crack, but she had reached the point of emotional saturation. She collapsed in a heap, mourning her searing desires and the pain It had wrought. The agony of living the white lie.

"She buggin' out," the big-nose said.

"Yeah," said the dark man with a mischievous grin. "Let's take her clothes." The three men gathered up her clothes and ran, laughing with chemical glee, leaving her naked and alone in the park.

Tokus was taking the shortcut to Heath Street when he spotted the naked woman, shivering in the shadows of the old abandoned bridge that passed over the park. She huddled there, soaked in tears, another victim of the rock laid bare by the addiction to the altered state of mind. Her pain, her shame was something that no longer touched Tokus. He had seen her condition many times in many guises, but he attributed their plight to weak-mindedness. Some people just have addictive personalities, he reasoned.

Life had forced Tokus into a lifestyle that suited his need to survive a lifestyle just outside the word of the law. He hated the effect of drugs on people and the victims beyond the addicts. But drugs were a crutch people sought with a need, heedless of its impending, destructive effects. No matter, Tokus thought, 'cause I got dreams. Sadly, he looked at the naked girl, turned and walked away, headed back to his favorite street corner. The best drug spot in the city. He fingered the plastic-wrapped pieces of crack in his pocket and mentally prepared himself for a night of selling drugs in a world where dreams die first.

# Wall Street

Tokus emerged from his office, a dark, dilapidated alleyway that stank of urine and spilled wine into the still night air on Heath Street. A wad of money was hidden in his underwear, taped to his thigh. The distinct sounds and smells of the money market washed over him in waves. Traffic was heavy as customers moved from broker to broker-curious, inquisitive and careful. Now this, Tokus thought, is a seller's market.

Mentally, he checked the stats of the Underground Index.

Crack cocaine was at twenty dollars a share. A real keeper. Crack has a bright future in America. It feeds on itself.

Marijuana was strong and holding. A solid investment with good returns. This commodity suffered a minor setback when crack burst onto the scene but has since undergone a full recovery.

Alcohol was deceptively steady, an old blue blood's legacy to society. Liquor stores, which endured the ups and downs of economics, stood on both ends of the block. A few doors down from the package store was the neighborhood church. A fortress of God in a sea of iniquity.

These were the numbers, the real numbers, on the poor man's Wall Street on Addict Aisle.

Buyers lined the street. Their need, popping in their veins like popcorn, was as real as water is to life. But they were cautious, scared that their future was dependent upon today's decisions. The buy. That's what it was all about. A bad choice, like buying a piece of soap or a white pebble would leave a buyer in no-man's land, alone and abandoned, with no help in sight. So addicts worked hard at being good, knowledgeable consumers.

Tokus spotted a couple, a man and a woman, coming down the Aisle.

They looked tired. Both wore torn jeans and T-shirts run over with multicolored dirt, their eyes alight with anticipation. They started across the street toward Tokus. The couple stopped in the middle of the street, purposeful, oblivious to the traffic and the crowds. The nappy-headed, dirty-faced man unzipped his pants and urinated, blind to the world. It was only fair. The world was blind to him. He stood back, zipped his pants and admired his work with the woman beside him, rapt, intent, as the liquid ran along the ground. A finger trail pointed in the direction of a young hood off to Tokus' left and, armed with this inside information, the buyers went off eagerly to purchase their shares.

"It gets wild," Tokus muttered as he scanned the Aisle for his regulars. He saw Fiction lounging in the doorway of one of the old abandoned buildings across the street. Fiction was a skinny fella who wore Coke-bottle glasses that seemed too heavy for his face. He was called Fiction because only the truth could be stranger than him. There was a girl with him. Tokus guessed she was sixteen, seventeen tops, who didn't care for truth or Fiction, only the nether world to which she sought entrance. Tokus imagined they were discussing stock options when they turned and disappeared inside the building. It seemed they had agreed on a merger when they appeared silhouetted in the shattered window. The girl went down on her knees, groping for Fiction's zipper. Ah, Tokus mused, insider trading. Services for shares.

A group of buyers turned the corner from Highwater Street onto the Aisle, coming to a halt on the perimeter of the frenzied activities. They stopped to observe the action while passing a joint and a forty ounce of malt liquor among themselves while they plotted and schemed.

The bedlam surrounding Tokus registered as normality. Addict Aisle was a body with the heart cut out, open and bleeding with desperation. He reflected on the drug industry and its place in every society, every city and its thriving, flourishing future.

"We need two bumpies."

Tokus was startled out of his fruitless mental wanderings, automatically reaching into his pocket while checking out his customers. He withdrew his hand, empty, upon seeing the two children who were trying to buy crack to get high.

"Get outta my face." Tokus dismissed them.

"Two!" the other kid said.

"No," Tokus answered.

"We want two bumps," the boy demanded.

"You get shit from me." Tokus turned on them. "Now get the fuck outta my face, kid!" he yelled menacingly and the two youngsters scampered down the street. Damn! Tokus shook his head ruefully. Farther down the Aisle, a dealer took the kids' money and discreetly passed them the coke.

"Damn!" Tokus exclaimed again. He looked at his watch. He usually quit dealing at twelve on school nights, but Tokus had decided to put the "closed" sign in the window early, permanently shutting down his business. Tonight was the first night of the rest of his life.

Usually his schedule had never varied. It was a discipline that had gotten Tokus through high school, after his mother and stepfather had abandoned him, and that structure served him well in college. The university had been a lot tougher on his abilities and his resolve, but in a few short weeks it was finally "G" day. Graduation. The whole idea of graduating from college and moving into the legal way of life brought a smile to his face. But he needed his nights free to concentrate on studying for the final exams. He had enough money saved to sustain him for a few weeks, so Tokus had decided to stop dealing. In a few minutes he would be free. His days of selling drugs to functioning zombies would be forever in the past. Tokus smiled inwardly. A few more and I'm outta here.

An old man pushing a shopping cart ambled over and gave his bottle and can collection money to Tokus for the phantom dream.

"Quit," Tokus said as he handed the man the rock. The old man looked at Tokus with disdain. This was his last night on the corner so Tokus was going to tell everyone to quit. The looks he received indicated how far over the crack edge the users had fallen. The old man snorted derisively and hobbled off slowly as he groped in his pocket for a pipe.

A shiny, jet-black Lexus drove up to the curb with a distinguished-looking gentleman behind the wheel. Tokus wondered what the story was with that guy. Obviously, the man had money; yet success didn't seem to fulfill him. As high as he had climbed, he still needed to fly.

"Quit," Tokus said.

The rock was piped and lit before the car pulled away from the sidewalk headed back to the suburbs-the nice part of town.

A bum ambled over to him, smiling, shuffling, doing his best Chris Rock, begging for free dope. He was the worst kind of crack head-a broke one. Tokus chased him away.

A well-dressed older man with a secret came to Tokus for a vial of poison. Tokus knew his secret. She lived on Barrett Street, three blocks east of the Aisle. Minutes away from the church where this guy preached. His name was Deaugood.

"Let me have one," the man said simply.

Tokus' eyebrows arched in a question. "How many?"

"One."

"For who?"

"Myself," the man said to the sidewalk. Tokus shook his head in wonder as he felt around in his pocket for a rock of crack.

"Quit," he said, placing the pebble in the preacher's hand. The preacher looked at Tokus, wide-eyed, with a comment just behind his lips. Instead his teeth clenched and his look went from one of incredulity to one of intense pain. His hand clenched around the crack cocaine in a fist that suddenly clutched at his heart. He swayed a bit, a rickety swoon that led into a stumble as he staggered into Tokus "office." Tokus' brow furrowed in alarmed. Oh, no, he panicked, not tonight. I just wanna get outta here. The preacher was leaning against a building trying to breathe, catching air in raspy wheezes.

"What's wrong, old man?" Tokus asked from the sidewalk, determined not to get any nearer.

"You better not die here, preacher," Tokus whispered harshly, as he quickly glanced up and down the Aisle. No one was paying the incident the least bit of attention.

Tokus glared back into the alley.

The preacher was slouched against a building. His body trembled while his lungs hacked for air to feed his drumming heart. The preacher's body was spewing up pain and panic in his face, but Tokus didn't see any fear there. The preacher had danced with this convulsion before and he knew the intricate steps. Soon the coughs eased and Deaugood slowly began to gather himself.

When Tokus saw the preacher straighten up, he regarded him with a twinkle in his eye. "You know, preacher man-ah," Tokus began in his best Southern, Sunday go-to-meetin' voice. "You got to hold on to God's unchangin' hand." Tokus hopped toward the preacher on one foot with one finger raised in the air. The minister, who was now standing with his fist closed around the rock, looked on, stunned, as Tokus went on with his sermon.

"He can be your Kryptonite-ah, when the woman-ah, with the cooty-cat-ah. Come round. I say the cooty-cat-ah, with the cape-ah, with the silver 'S' hanging out of it come round."

The two men stood face to face. Serious.

Finally Tokus said, "Quit."

The preacher walked away, head bowed. Lust chased him down the street and around the corner to the house where his mistress waited hungrily.

Midnight is the hour of sin and pain on Addict Aisle and Tokus decided to leave and be rid of both. Glancing up and down the Aisle, he silently said good-bye to what had been his life, before turning his back and walking away from it all. With a smile.

When he turned the corner onto Highwater Street, Tokus ran headfirst into hell. Dressed in black.

# Nemesis

On the corner of Heath and Highwater, Bug Minnon's life was changed forever. On a warm, cloudless night he came face-to-face with his enemy. A nemesis who had been a life-long companion, a monster who stomped around the land-scape of his soul, leaving a poison that seeped into his heart. Sometimes it even showed its hideous face for all the world to see.

"I can read miiiinds, man!" Bug crazily exclaimed.

Moose stood with his head turned skyward, an upturned nose sniffing the air.

"You smell rain?" his voice wafted down to the smallish man. Bug was so zooted he simply floated himself up to where he could hear better.

"Naw, man," Bug answered. But yo' ass always smellin' rain, he thought, cause of that metal-plated brain you got. If Bug ever told anyone about Moose's weakness they would both be dead. First Moose would kill him and then someone else would kill Moose. Hell, people would fight to draw straws to see who'd get the first shot at the big man. Bug's mind twirled the idea around in the haze of his stupor, toyed with the notion of betraying his best friend, of having power over a giant. But then he discarded the idea, tossing it into the mushy mist of his smoke-filled brain. Moose kept him fed. With brain food. Mind candy. Manna. Because of Moose, Bug could look into people's thoughts.

"I can read miiiinds, man!" Bug repeated. Moose stopped sniffing the air and arched an eyebrow at Bug.

"Here we go," Moose groaned.

"For real!" Bug said. "One rock! If I smoke me some . . . I can read people's minds. Tha's right. That's the kind of high I gets," Bug finished triumphantly.

Moose was quiet. He was in one of his moods, Bug determined. Danger! Danger! The thought flitted across Bug's mind making him giggle fiendishly. Boy, he felt good! Moose turned to him and raised his arm, pointing across the street.

"What's that man thinkin'?" Moose asked with a devilish glint in his eye.

"Who?" Bug squeaked.

"Him," Moose thundered, jabbing his finger in the direction of a man in a wheelchair. Bug squinted in the darkness, focusing, channeling his powers. The old man sat in his wheelchair. Both his legs were amputated at the knees and he was filthy. He sat facing a water fountain fashioned of stone angels and granite doves spouting dirty yellowish liquid. Behind him was a playground with two children playing on the swings, laughing carelessly and living young. Their laughter washed over the grim, crippled figure as he stared blankly at the large structure of intended serenity. A large dog sat behind the man, steadily chewing on the rubber wheel of his chair. The man sat motionless, a living statue, hardened, transfixed, with a mongrel gnawing on his "leg."

Bug went into a trance. "He's thinkin'," Bug droned. "If I could crawl around inside the inconsequential, the indignities of life would hold no meaning." Bug turned to look at Moose. "And I could stab this dog in his eye," he finished. Moose regarded Bug, surprised.

"Told you!" Bug exclaimed. Moose's eyes clicked before he turned and began walking down the street.

"Come on," he called over his shoulder. "Let's go down to the Aisle and cop."

Bug hurried after Moose, and they headed for the red-light district; the best stuff was down there.

Drug traffic on Heath Street was like shopping at the mall but without the ornamental finery. Heath Street was a collection of rundown, abandoned buildings. The gutted houses had no windows, just black holes that beckoned no-dared one to enter. The streets were littered with the used paraphernalia of chronic drug use-needles, pipes, rubber straps and such. There was even a version of a drug drive-thru as dealers did their business from open car windows.

The dealers themselves were bold and brazen, kings ruling over all who reside on the Aisle of Addicts. They all wore similar expressions, a defiant look that dared and a scowl that warned. Expressions that became a part of their lives as card-carrying chemical distribution reps. The citizens of Addict Aisle shuffle around obediently in their empty, lifeless husks of bodies, their very existence like wisps of smoke born of their habit. The men, bedraggled and beaten, in search of the next fix. The women, some old, some decrepit, having sold the last of their material goods are now selling the one commodity left to them. The drug denying them the ability to see what they have become-walking sperm banks with a habit.

Numbed to the elements of street life, Moose and Bug looked neither left nor right. Sights of the city made some people cry but, for them, it was emotionally effortless. As they hurried down Highwater Street, Bug took a moment to consider the man he called a friend. Moose was frightening. He cut an imposing figure, in dress as well as in manner. He was clad in a tight, black T-shirt with the word "Hell" splattered across his chest in red, burning letters with the evil image of the devil hidden in the flames. Moose was a roughneck, one of the roughest necks around and he always seemed anxious for a fight because he thought there wasn't a man on the planet who could handle him.

And with good reason. Moose's chassis was built on a massive core, an eighteen-wheeler with sledgehammer fists powered by steel ribbon biceps. A big, strapping, brooding man with a fast-burning fuse, Moose was the image of a man on a dark mission, to be avoided, or failing that, appeased at all times and at all costs.

Earlier in the evening, Bug and Moose had been up on Judson Street getting high on some shit that Moose boosted from a corner hood. The young pusher had been frightened into bravado until Moose put his finger in the middle of the kid's forehead and pushed. Hard! Then the thug dropped all pretense and offered Moose everything that he had on him.

Moose took it, and punished the hood with raging fists to the head, twice when the boy was knocked out.

Moose was a fearless man, but like other supermen, failed to take into account the infirmities of mere mortals. Bug was snapped back to reality as they rounded the corner onto Heath Street when a young hood went crashing, face first into Moose's chest. Bug gasped.

The man stumbled backwards onto Heath Street and looked up to see what he had run into.

"'Scuse me, my man," he pardoned.

Oh, hell! Bug's mind set off an alarm. That's Tokus. Tokus the drug dealer.

"'Scuse me, hell, bitch!" Moose spat.

Tokus' eyes went dark-dead, dead like the sea, dead like death, and the darkness of the night surrounded him like a comforting blanket. Tokus glared at Moose.

"I said 'excuse me,'" he replied flatly.

"You gonna 'scuse me' what you got in your pocket, little man," Moose said.

The two men eyed each other, assessing, measuring. Moose was much taller than Tokus, yet they met eye-to-eye, neither man flinching. Tokus reached into his pocket, took out a large baggie full of white powder and smiled at Moose. A dangerous smile.

"You want this?" Tokus asked. "Take it."

The street grew eerily silent as they faced each other. The air grew heavy with tension. The night pulsed with the quickening of the crowd as they gathered around, drugs forgotten, chemical euphoria delayed.

"That's mine," Moose stated, laying claim to the big bag of cocaine while he took his shirt off, revealing a heavily muscled chest. Bug counted the scars of two gunshot wounds and at least three knife wounds.

"Oh, yeah," Moose cried. "That's mine, little man."

Tokus, who had been taking his shirt off, paused, dropped his shirt to the ground and stepped toward Moose, his body tensing, his face clouding over with midnight madness. Moose suddenly reached out with both hands and grabbed Tokus by the head, pulled him close and noisily kissed him on the lips. Then he shoved him roughly away. "Bitch," he sneered. Moose assumed a boxing stance, his eyes aglitter with the excitement of a veteran prizefighter. Tokus just looked mad.

They circled each other until Moose moved in, fast and fierce, rushing Tokus with all his weight and power behind a vicious right hand. Bug had seen many a man fall victim to that blow. Moose called it his money punch, but Tokus dodged it with ease. Instinctively, Moose followed with a sharp left. Again, Tokus avoided the blow. Going with the momentum from the misguided left, Moose shot his foot at the side of Tokus' head. Tokus sidestepped as Moose stumbled past him, tried to regain his balance and failed, falling hard and landing on one knee. Tokus came in swinging, landing a thundering right, complete with thunderclap, to the top of Moose's head.

"Ahhhh, damn!" Tokus screamed and clutched his fist.

The big man crumbled into the street in a heap while Tokus winced and cradled his hand as if a worm of pain was wriggling up his arm. Tokus shook his fist as if it had hit a solid metal brick and his fingers seemed to swell with pain. His fist had hit something harder than bone. Moose wasn't getting up.

Tokus stepped back, breathing heavily. The rise and fall of his chest echoed loudly into the silence of the night as the fiends of Addict Aisle looked on.

Sensing that the fight was over, a few of the druggies got brave. Moose had victimized most of them at one time or another.

"Get up!"

"Come on, you ole punk ass! Get up!"

"You pussy man!"

"Strictly butt!"

"Strictly dickly is what you mean!"

"Yeah!"

Amazingly, Moose got one hand underneath himself and began struggling to his feet. His eyes rolled crazily in his head and one side of his face ticked madly. Tokus stepped toward Moose, his fist curled and cocked, when Bug leapt between them.

"Naw, man! Naw!" Bug cried. "My man is out! He's out! You can see that! He's out, man!"

"Not if he gets up," Tokus growled. Moose had made it to one knee, but his entire body was shaking. Saliva trailed in a long string from the corner of his mouth and his eyes had turned a bright red. Specks of blood dotted his head where Tokus had punched him. Bug turned back to Tokus.

"He's done. Why you gonna hurt him again, man?"

"He kissed me," Tokus roared.

"So kiss him back then!" Bug replied desperately. Moose moaned.

"Get out of the way or take his place," Tokus warned.

Bug looked at Tokus and knew there was no question of his intent. Here lay his best friend and Bug had a decision to make. Unbidden, memories came rushing at him like scarlet ghosts and the ugly monster reared his head and roared. Ninth-grade study hall. A football player, a senior twice his size had stood over him, threatening. His heart had raced in epileptic spurts. Like now. A thin sheen of sweat had broken out on his brow. Like now. His body had felt fragile, as if one touch would send it bursting into bloody, boneless pieces. Like now. Then, horribly, he had bowed his head, turned and run away. Like now.

Bug didn't wait to see if his best friend made it to his feet or not, but the sound of Moose screaming followed him down the block and around every corner for the rest of his life.

His nemesis had won again.

# New Stiles

Bug scurried from the painful screams that coursed through his brain and reverberated inside him. Growing in intensity instead of fading with the distance that he put between himself and the horror of his life-he was a coward in flight. He slammed into the park, past the Shade and the Buffalo Soldiers into the darkness under the bridge. His soul found comfort in the dark. A place where he could become invisible while he shed real, bitter tears. And the tears came in torrents. His high from the crack was gone and he felt it. It was a thing called reality, a hard cold thud of an unclouded mind whispering with conscience and crying with shame.

He collapsed against the brick wall and slid to the ground with his face buried in his hands, his heart wrestling with the flow of thin blood that coursed through its chambers. His chest heaved from exertion from the hurried flight he had taken down Highwater Street as he tried to outrun an intangible part of himself. The need to run a marathon crept upon him and Bug shrieked out loud as he realized that the race would require a few additional miles and he would still lose.

This demon wasn't even a thing of the past. It was horrifyingly now.

Moose was far from the best of men, but he and Bug had called each other friend. Leaving him when he needed help desperately was the ultimate in cowardice and Bug knew it. Felt it at the core of what pure heart he had left. But morality had no meaning in his life. He had given that away the minute he sucked on the glass dick and inhaled the newest of poisons: crack. Rat poison, rubbing alcohol and cocaine stirred together into a coarse paste and married by flame to the hungry walls of Bug's brain. He cried at his weakness.

Time was immaterial to him and Bug had no sense of how long he had been under the bridge when he noticed a subtle movement in the dark. The thick blackness in the air seemed impenetrable but Bug hadn't been paying any particular attention to his surroundings. The bridge spanned a narrow finger of the Hudson River but from underneath it arched largely into the night. A parking lot was tarred under the bridge and connected to parking lots on either side. The hard, black surfaces stopped short of the shoreline, which had been paved with a walkway, interspersed with well-kept plots of grass. This was one of the safest places outdoors to get high and publicly intoxicated.

Bug often did both.

Alarmed, Bug squinted to focus in the darkness and when his eyes adjusted he almost jumped at the sight. There was a naked woman huddled in the darkness. She sobbed and inched away from Bug in fear. That was when he saw her eyes. And in her eyes Bug instantly knew what the deal was. Why she was outside buck-assed naked. He had seen it before. A nasty, crackhead ho that had run into a brainblasted smoker who didn't want her services. Trickin' a trick.

But Bug had his own pain. His pain came from an internal wellspring that just kept gushing and frothing. An affliction that knew no mercy. Just like hers.

So who was he to judge?

"Hey," Bug gently called her. "You gonna be alright?"

She screamed hysterically at him. Stupid question.

"Listen," Bug stood up and began unbuttoning his shirt. She screeched again. "I know," Bug said softly. "I know. Look, just take my shirt and cover yourself up, girl. Here." Bug tossed the shirt to her without approaching her. She made no move to catch it and it floated to the ground. Bug paused as a truck passed noisily overhead. The still, night air amplified the rumbling of the big rig as it pounded over the bridge, and as Bug waited, he heard the gears shift before the truck picked up speed.

"Come on, now," Bug pled. "How you gonna get home all naked and everything? Just put it on and you can run straight to your house."

She eyed Bug warily, but some of what he said seemed to have reached her. Slowly she reached out and pulled the shirt to her.

Bug stood, waiting while she buttoned up the shirt. As the girl slowly covered herself, Bug pondered the meaning of the simple act of clothing himself. Of having fabric, a barrier, between his naked self and the world, hiding the imperfections because, after all, they were his faults and not for the world's prying eyes. Of protecting what was his and his alone, to be bared only at his discretion. Life could be like that sometimes. Life could be a shirt with no heart or brain or any other vital organ adorning the sleeves.

"You know what?" Bug asked her as the girl buttoned the shirt up. "I ain't smokin' no more. Fuck it. I'm leaving that shit alone. Look what it did to me. Fuck it." Idly he pulled at the sleeve of the ragged tee shirt that he wore as the girl stood and watched him.

"Fuck it," she repeated, her voice sounding small and defeated.

Bug nodded his head. "You live around here?"

"No," she replied. "I don't live nowhere."

"Oh," was all Bug responded. He looked at her. Standing there wearing his shirt, she didn't look that bad. Her hair was nappy and filthy, and her face was streaked with tear-tracked dirt. But underneath all that, Bug saw something. Maybe it was time to hope.

Bug looked up at the bridge that ran overhead, linking one side of the city with the other. He remembered reading a book about a man named Stiles. His name meant "a bridge between two pastures," a point of crossing over to a new land. It was time for him to seek new stiles. A better way. A better life.

Another truck rumbled overhead and Bug listened expectantly for the shifting of gears that would signal a change of speed. When he heard the ratchet of the engine, Bug made a decision.

"You want to 'fuck it' with me? You know, quit this smokin' shit?"

She paused for a moment, regarding Bug. Then, slowly, she nodded her head in agreement.

"First things first. What's your name? I'm Bug."

"Pharren," she said softly. "My name is Pharren."

"Pharren." Bug tried the name on for size. "We really got to do this. 'Cause I'm serious. Okay?"

"Okay," Pharren answered.

"Okay," Bug agreed. "I live over on Orange Street. You ready?"

"Yeah. I'm ready. Let's go."

"My son lives with me," Bug told her as they began walking. "His name is Monday."

Together they went off. Halfway there, he took her hand.

# We in Here

Tokus sat down and ordered barbecued ribs and collard greens with a distinct disregard for cholesterol counters and heart monitors. This was soul food at its finest; food for the spirit. That's what fatback seasoning and ham hocks meant: a gateway to the cure for what ails ya'. A balm in the season of discontent with a dash of hot sauce in case your vision got watered down and led astray. Death weighed heavily on his soul, so Tokus needed a stain lifter, a vanisher to let him know that he was still real. A solid commodity that needed to be given succor in the throes of being alive and striving.

His plate came with a flourish-black-eyed peas on the side with a dash of black pepper gently caressing the tops of the pods. Steam was still rising from the plate so Tokus looked around at the surroundings, hoping to spot something new, something to signify the dawn of a new beginning. All he wanted was a life without murder and avarice to feed upon so that he could begin anew in a world of justice. That was all he wanted. A world in which he could receive all that was meant for him. Love and happiness.

Tokus recalled a movie he had seen called The Best Part
Yet. It was about a guy who had spent his first twenty years
waiting for the best part yet, the shining moment of his life.
He thought he saw it a few times: once in a job that paid him
lots of money; once when he learned the joy of the slots; and
again in the arms of a woman and her body with its love melting all over him in tides of pleasure. But they were just fleet-
ing glimpses. The slots cost him his job and the woman took
her body away . . . along with its allure. In the end the desperate man had held a pistol to his head as he wondered aloud, to
no one at all, "Now this is the best part yet," before he pulled
the trigger.

If he only knew, Tokus mused.

His thoughts were interrupted when the tall, white cop
walked in the door. The cop stood in the doorway for a
moment, looking over the customers with an unsettling stare,
searching. His haunted, gray eyes settled on Tokus for a split
second too long before he went over to the counter and
placed an order. The hum of conversations died down when
the law walked in the door; all talk faded to whispers. It's
never known what is expected when a white cop bothers to
invite himself into a world where he fits like rat hair in a hot
dog.

Lika's Place was a neighborhood restaurant with good
food and reasonable prices. Usually this meal was a splurge for
Tokus, spiritual spending, so to speak. After dining on some
good down-home cooking, he was always left with a full stomach and a sense of contentment. It was quiet and peaceful at
Lika's. Lika herself had an unusual sense of drama. She had

decorated the dining area with an African motif: paintings, drawings and even a small sculpture of a falling African with a heavy chain around his wrist. There were also photos of great African-Americans affixed to the wall. They were all dead now. Malcolm X, Martin Luther the King, W.E.B. DuBois and Richard Wright.

Tokus fixated on a poster of an older black man that hung directly in his line of vision. Thinning, gray hair was dotted with blood on one side of his head, his lip was busted, and one eye was swollen shut. Small streaks of blood flowed from the intrusions to the man's flesh and his open eye cried in pain as it swelled with hatred. The caption underneath read, "Thirty years of police force."

The night's events crept back into Tokus' thoughts, frightened memories that fluttered here and there, causing panic wherever they fled. He ate a forkful of greens and forced himself to look up at the television screen that hung from the ceiling over the serving counter.

It was playing an old seventies flick, one of the many blaxploitation films that happened to be a hard-core, action movie that touched the grit of life. An old man was sitting in a chair with a shotgun nestled in his arms talking to his young nephew who was hiding from the cops. The old man stood up and peeked out the window. The nephew shook his head and said, "But, Big Daddy, they don't even know that we in here." Big Daddy frowned scornfully at him. "We in here. They out there. We don't know what they know . . . and don't know!" Seconds later, an amplified voice blared out, "This is the police. You have five minutes to come out-or we're coming in."

The face of Five-O blocked the television when he came over and said with an evil grin, "Tokus Stone. The man. Ruler of Zamunda. King of the streets. Can we talk?"

Five-O didn't wait for an answer. He put his plate down on the table, opposite Tokus, and pulled up a chair. He sat heavily and reached for the hot sauce in the middle of the table to sprinkle over the fried chicken and macaroni and cheese piled on his plate.

"Did you hear about what happened up on the Aisle the other night?" Five-O asked Tokus.

Tokus didn't answer.

Five-O paused with the bottle of cayenne pepper in mid-shake. "Did you?"

A look passed between them.

"Let's make this simple," Tokus replied. "Just what in the hell do you want from me, Mr. Joe P. Law? Ruler of the Blue Klan. Scum of New York."

Five-O sprinkled the red sauce liberally over the heaping plate of food and put the bottle back on the table before he spoke.

"Aah," he answered. "Direct. I like that in a slave. And believe me, Tokus, that is exactly what you are . . . my slave. From this point forward you will do exactly what I tell you, exactly when I tell you to do it. When I say, 'shit,' you say, 'what color?' Is that straight with you?"

A phone rang. Five-O gulped down a mouthful of the macaroni and held up a finger to Tokus as he chewed. He reached into his pocket, pulled out a cellular phone and barked into it.

"Yeah!"

Five-O listened and his face grew dark.

"What! And how do you know that?"

He listened longer this time.

"Well, I'm taking care of that. If you let me!"

Another pause.

"At this very moment," Five-O growled and fixed Tokus with his stare.

"Give me a fuckin' break, will ya! What are you doing, watching me through your precious glass wall?"

As Five-O listened, his mouth twisted into a sneer, an angry curl. He gripped the phone tightly and closed his eyes before he responded.

"Yeah. Yeah. Yeah. All right. It's done." He punched the button to hang up and turned to face Tokus.

Five-O knew about Moose. There was no doubt of that now. Tokus realized it when the cop seated himself and spoke to him by name. Now it was time to find out precisely what Five-O had in mind. Calmly, Tokus regarded the policeman who was sitting in a soul food restaurant, eating fried chicken, in front of a poster indicting a police state. He looked up at the poster again. The red spots of blood that dotted the coarse gray hair; the bloody, busted lip; and the dark, swollen, angry eye. Was that face the result of taking life head-on?

"Excuse me," Tokus said softly. "It's probably my fault. I probably didn't ask the right question. Let me rephrase. What, exactly, do you want from me, you fucking dick?"

"Simple," Five-O answered, picking up a chicken leg from his plate. "I want you to kill a man."

Tokus tried to hide his shock.

"Now why would I kill someone for you?"

Thirty years of police force, the poster screamed.

"Because I checked your resume," Five-O replied. "And I see you have experience in the field."

"No, I don't," Tokus responded. "Who told you that? Noooo!" Tokus had learned a long time ago to never admit anything. Even when, deep in your brain, you knew that you were "it," you always "tag off." "It" was always someone else. Deny, deny, deny!

"Who's bullshitting now, huh?" Five-O groaned with his mouth full of chicken. "What do you need . . . pictures? Or will an oral report be good enough for you?"

"Tell me . . . something!" Tokus said.

"No, no, no," Five-O swallowed. "I'm the master, remember?"

Five-O stood from the table, his meal unfinished. "Meet me tomorrow at the church up on the Aisle. Make it around noonish, okay? See you later, buddy."

With that he turned on his heel and walked out the door.

Tokus heard his future fade away with the hollow echoes of the cop's dying footsteps.

# Exorcist Marbles

The church stood out like a pimple against the face of the ghetto, an unwanted sentry with evil at its doors. Holiness Baptist Church was carved into the façade in a holy arc above the doorway, reaching out in both directions, gathering lost souls into its bosom. A muted, soft light shone through the stained glass portrait of a Black Jesus with open, welcoming arms.

From across the street Tokus studied the building ruefully, fighting the urge to turn tail and run. His life would be changed forever if he walked through those church doors. Tokus felt it. Was certain of it. What was even more certain, and more immediate, was what would happen if he didn't go inside. If the law wanted him in church, Tokus knew, he had better be in church. Helplessly, he crossed the street and went through the tall, wooden doors.

Once inside, Tokus saw that it was indeed a "holiness" church. Rows of benches formed a funneling aisle that led to the pulpit. The pulpit itself was raised a few steps from the

floor, with room to the left for the choir, room to the right for
the piano, and in the middle, the dais from which the minis-
ters flung the "word" at the congregation. Directly behind the
dais was a big, soft chair with two smaller ones on either side.
This was church! He could almost feel the many Sunday ser-
mons, the hand clapping and the joyous shouts echoing from
the walls. They floated over Tokus like alien ghosts, which he
shook off with animosity.

Spirits had no place in his life.

All his life had been a bitter taste that he kept spitting out
into the wind.

And now the devil himself wanted to meet him in a church.

Tokus slid into the nearest pew and waited.

Five-O wanted Tokus to kill a man. Tokus was determined
not to do it. Not that he was a stranger to the many faces of
death. He had seen it in various forms, and it no longer
impressed him with the fear of what would come next. Death
was just a void. Something he would live through when he
got there.

Death had spoiled him from God. Tokus didn't flee God;
he just didn't know Him.

A side door that Tokus hadn't noticed opened slowly and
out stepped Reverend Deaugood, head bowed, reading the
Bible. Deaugood hardly looked up as he made his way to the
pulpit and Tokus stretched out on the pew-a caustic observer.
The aged, wooden pew emitted a loud squeak, causing the
Reverend's head to snap up at the sound. Smiling, he began
walking toward Tokus with a greeting. "Brother! Welcome to

Holiness . . ." Deaugood's voice trailed off as he recognized Tokus.

Tokus smiled and folded his arms across his chest. "Hello, Reverend Deaugood! Can I call you Reverend? Well! You sure look different than you did the other night. Bent over in the alleyway with a rock squeezed tight in your hand and having a heart attack. You was snortin' air like the devil was trying to get out!"

Tokus stood from the bench.

"That was you, wasn't it, Reverend?"

It was more a statement than a question and Deaugood took it at its value. He looked at Tokus carefully, then turned and looked at the pulpit for a moment before turning back to Tokus. When he spoke, his voice was calm, rational. "Listen to me, young man. The fact that you judge me; that don't bother me. You're young. You think you got it all figured out anyway. The fact that you think that I'm not a man of God, couldn't be a man of God . . ." Deaugood groped. "Well, that . . . that kinda dismays me a bit."

Deaugood paused and fixed Tokus with a stare. "No matter what you think I do, don't ever assume that I can't do this," he finished, indicating the Bible he held in his hand.

Tokus snorted in response. "You know what, Deaugood? Long time ago, I knew this man. He was an older dude . . . about your age. He ain't have no kids so he became a big brother to this little knuckle-headed boy. But soon the man became a father figure. He provided discipline, morality and respect for a little boy who was looking for a father to teach him the meaning of these things."

In the front of the church, a dark figure emerged, unseen, and slid into a shadowy corner. He peeked around the corner at the two men and listened.

Tokus went on. "One day the man passed away. You know what the little boy said at 'dad's' wake? He read a poem: 'His life was an extension of his God-in its livelihood and in its meaning. Inevitable in his life was the specter of death with its claim on his last breath. Between the first breath and the last, the first day and the last, the first joy and the last; he rose above the small and became the epitome of God's intentions." Tokus looked meaningfully at the pulpit, nodded his head in agreement and sat down. "Now that is what you are supposed to be, Deaugood-the epitome of God's intentions."

Five-O stepped from his hiding place. "Very nice," he said. Both men turned as Five-O sauntered toward them. A cigarette dangled from the corner of his mouth, unlit. His face was all angles and hard lines. Straight-back eyebrows clung to a sharply angled forehead that off-ramped into a slightly tilted nose. His eyes looked like the devil had been playing with exorcist marbles. They jellied before they turned evil.

He tilted his head at Tokus with a reproving look. "Don't you know you never get a second chance to make a first impression?"

Tokus waited.

"All right," Five-O said finally. "I don't have much time. You two . . . sit down."

Neither man moved.

"I said sit down!" Five-O barked. They sat.

"All right," Five-O said as he fished a lighter out of his pocket and lit his cigarette. Angles and lines danced over his face through the flickering flame.

"Now," Five-O began. "Reverend, this guy over here . . . is a drug dealer. But you already know that, don't you? Anyway, I want Tokus here to do something for me . . . a favor, you know! But he doesn't want to do it. Can you believe that, Rev! Astounding, right? But Rev, you heard about that guy who was found dead up on Highwater Street? Guess who did it? Go ahead! Guess! I'll give you a clue. The killer is in this room. Now Rev, I'm a cop. If I kill someone, it's not murder, so it had to be one of you."

Five-O looked from Tokus to Deaugood. "Did you guess? Do you know? It was Tokus Stone! Mr. Man here. Yes, sirree! Hit that big black buck in the top of his head . . ." Five-O turned to Tokus. "Didn't know that guy had a metal plate in his head, didja? You hit him so hard that you drove that metal right into his brain. It was a slow, painful death. Painful."

The tip of the cigarette glowed as the cop took a hit and spoke to the preacher. "Tokus could go away for life. Would you like that, Reverend? Probably, right? But I've given him an out. All he has to do is poison someone for me. Put the poison in a rock of cocaine, sell it to the mark and the guy will go away, way up high. He probably wouldn't even know he was dead till he came down."

The cigarette glowed again.

"So basically, Reverend, it's take a life or do 'life.' And make no mistake, Tokus, I'll push hard, very hard, to make sure that you never get out."

Five-O let the threat hang there, deadly in its silence.

Deaugood clutched his Bible, cleared his throat and looked questioningly at the cop.

"Excuse me," he said. "But why do I need to hear all this? It has nothing to do with me."

Five-O puffed on his cigarette as if it were bubble gum-flavored.

"Because . . . you have a story to tell, Reverend, and I can't wait to hear the ending."

# Useless Freedom

"You know, everybody in America, this great country of mine, has freedom. But the way you people live, it's a useless freedom . . . and that's when shit happens."

Five-O paused to take a drag off his cigarette, dumping ashes on the church floor while Tokus and Deaugood waited. Five-O's presence shattered the serenity of the church. He corrupted the spirit with his manner, his stance and the stale, pungent smoke that wafted from the cancer stick in his hand. He did the devil's work and cloaked it in a blue uniform-smile. Joy in other's pain; pain in other's limbs-that was his motto.

The wooden pew was becoming uncomfortable to Tokus. He shifted to the left, wishing that this twisted nightmare would hurry to its conclusion.

"So Rev," Five-O said. "You gonna tell us the story of your useless freedom?"

Deaugood looked exasperated, as if he didn't have the slightest clue what Five-O was talking about. Tokus wanted to choke him.

"Come on," Five-O urged.

"What you mean?" Deaugood cried.

"What you mean!" Five-O said mockingly. "What you mean!" He dropped his cigarette on the church floor and ground it out with his foot. He walked over to where Tokus sat and leaned against the raised back of the bench. Tokus glanced at the cop, hoping he would slip and fall on his ass. A smile played at the corner of Five-O's lips. "You know, 'back in the day,' as the local coloreds would say, when I was a teenager, my brother was a cop. That's why I'm a cop . . . 'cause of my brother. See, my brother was a man. A man with power. A man with a badge. So sometimes he would blur the lines. You know, mix the black and the white and make gray. Everything was gray to him. But he had this badge, so gray was good. My brother also had this thing for black women."

Five-O paused to look at Deaugood. "By the way, is that a myth about black women?"

Deaugood didn't respond.

"All right," Five-O went on. "Well, then my brother took a fancy to this young girl. She was only about sixteen but that didn't matter to him. See, back then there wasn't no such thing as raping a nigger girl so he could do whatever he wanted to. He could take it or leave it."

Tokus shifted in his seat again, irritated. The way that Five-O was objectifying black women was getting under his skin.

The soft, muffled ringing of a telephone echoed through the church. Five-O held the two men with an upheld finger as he reached into his pocket for his cellular phone.

"Yeah!" he barked. He listened for a minute.

"What is your malfunction, mister?" Five-O roared. His face had turned a dark crimson before he turned away and began whispering harshly into the phone. "Look, I've been doing this for years. It's my job, for Christ's sakes! I know what to do and I know how to do it. So I don't need your shit and I don't need you on my back."

Five-O listened. He didn't utter another word into the phone. He just grunted and punched the button to hang up. The devil was playing with those evil marbles again. His eyes jellied as he glared.

"Is this story going anyplace, you fucking maggot?" Tokus spat at Five-O. A slow silence followed and hung in the air, oddly, by an evil smile that spread slowly across the cop's face.

"Sure," Five-O sang. "Sure. See, my brother had a problem."

"No shit!" Tokus pitched in.

"No shit," Five-O answered. "Yes, yes, yes. See, his problem was that a young, black buck beat him to the punch. Boy was somewhat like you, Tokus. He was out on the streets peddling dope. Marijuana at first . . . that was the thing back then. Then he moved up to heroin and LSD. Chemicals."

Five-O paused to light up another cigarette. Tokus glanced at Deaugood. The Reverend slouched on the bench, eyes downcast and nodding his head almost imperceptibly. Five-O puffed on his smoke a few times to get it burning good and resumed his tale.

"So one day, my brother answers a call for an assault and when he gets there . . . it's the girl. She's sitting on the street corner . . . just sitting there. Doesn't look like anything's wrong except her dress is all ripped up. She doesn't have on any underwear, and she's a basket case. My brother tries to help her but she won't say a word. She won't even acknowledge his presence. So he reaches out and helps her to her feet. He puts her in the squad car and as he gets in, he sees bloodstains on the ground where the girl had been sitting." Five-O walked across the aisle to Deaugood. "See, Tokus, the girl had been raped. By the drug-dealing punk. My brother found out who did it, but the girl still wasn't talking."

"Stop!" Deaugood leapt to his feet and the word came out with a hard edge. Five-O ignored his plea.

"That drug dealer . . ."

"Please! God! Stop!"

"Was the good Reverend Mister Deaugood."

Tokus tried to hide his disgust. "Surprise, surprise."

"That's not the real surprise though," Five-O crowed. "There's more, there's more, there's more! The girl got pregnant! The day my brother found out, he went looking for Deaugood. Caught him with a stash in his pocket. Deaugood was hot. He had heroin, LSD and cocaine on him. The good Reverend went away for six long years-hard time. That's where he met Jesus and he came out of prison a Holy Roller."

Deaugood dropped back into his seat, apparently stunned by Five-O's knowledge and the shameful revelation of his past. He looked sorrowfully from Tokus to Five-O and back to Tokus.

"That was over twenty years ago," Deaugood said apologetically. "It's not real to me anymore. That's not me now. It's not real."

Five-O sneered. "It was about twenty-three years ago and it was-and still is-very, very real. Okay? See, 'cause that girl had that baby, a little baby boy, dropped out of school and lived with dead insides for the rest of her life." Five-O turned to Tokus. "Now this is as real as it gets. The girl's name . . . was Rosetta Stone."

Tokus' jaw dropped and his life went slack.

"Your mother," Five-O roared with laughter.

# Then Speechless

Five-O faced the two men, intently watching as they squirmed under his jaundiced eye. The diaphanous sounds of life seeped inside the church as he waited. He smiled as he waited for the explosion that accompanied unexpected, painful revelations.

Tokus sat on the hard bench and listened to the tear roll down his face-a tear for himself and the man who had fathered him. He heard the harshness of the years roll away into oblivion. The echoes of childhood reverberated painfully in his soul and then cascaded away in a wash of painful renewal. This is it, he reflected. This is me.

Deaugood sat across the aisle from Tokus, watching and waiting, unable to voice a comforting word that would compensate for a lifetime of non-existence. No words would suffice. No voice could encompass, and no actions could speak to the darkness of what now existed. Tokus looked into the preacher's eyes. For a sign. Guilt, shame, hypocrisy-anything that would help him gauge the lunacy of Deaugood's actions. The preacher's eyes held no remorse. In fact, there seemed to be a hint of defiance, a smirk of daring, a glint of dangerous liberation from the constraints of his religion. Sin.

Deaugood laid his Bible down.

"I didn't . . ." he began.

"Didn't what?" Tokus barked.

"I mean . . ."

"Mean what?" Tokus growled. Deaugood was standing with his hands held outward, imploring.

"Look here, old man," Tokus said bitterly. "There's only one thing you can say to me. Say that it's a lie. Tell me I'm not on this earth because you decided to rape my mother! Say it!"

"I . . . I . . . I can't," Deaugood sputtered.

Five-O laughed loudly and stepped forward, the devil's enjoyment written all over his face. "As much as I enjoy these little family reunions, I think I'll leave you two alone. Give you some quality time together. But Tokus, you have forty-eight hours to take care of that little assignment I gave you." He pulled a small plastic bag out of his pocket and tossed it to Tokus.

"Here," Five-O said. "That's strychnine. Melt it down and rock it up and give my friend a dose. Remember. Forty-eight hours." Tokus stared numbly at the package in his hand.

"Why?" Tokus said in a raspy voice.

"Yours is not to question why," Five-O answered as he began walking toward the door. "Why do I have to go all the way out to the mall to get my girlfriend some body oils when my wife buys it from the corner store? Why! Why! Why!"

Five-O bustled out the door.

The church filled with a silence that bristled with anger and anxiety. Neither man knew how to break it yet were apprehensive about filling the void. Tokus started for the door.

"Wait," Deaugood cried.

"No," Tokus stated calmly.

"Let me explain," Deaugood pled.

"You know, Deaugood," Tokus answered. "I should just punch your face in. That would give me such joy. Just to watch your face break, watch you drop. Like a piece of rotten . . ."

"Would you please . . . just give me a chance to explain."

"Look here, Deaugood," Tokus said. "The only explanation you owe will be the one you have to give when you open your eyes in hell. The hell that your Bible has ready for you."

Tokus walked to the door, opened it and paused to look back at Deaugood. "You don't owe me a damned thing," he said and stepped out of the church.

Deaugood went home that night with a heavy heart. A weight had been thrust upon him. For years he had carried it inside until it had become a silent episode of a long-gone dream gone bad. Now it blossomed full weight and everything inside him bowed in an attempt to bear the freshness of the scars. His wife noticed it upon his back, too. When she asked him what was wrong he said, "Nothing," and kissed her. What would she say if she knew? What would she do? What would his congregation do?

Deaugood looked in on his daughter. Doria looked up from the book she was reading and smiled at him. The smile faded when she saw the worry etched into his face. When she asked him what was wrong, he smiled and said, "Nothing, baby girl, nothing," and went to his room and closed the door. He wondered where his son Bug was. He wished that he could see him right then. Maybe they could talk. Find answers. Forgive and forget.

Deaugood lay down on his bed. He was weary.

His heart twinged. Deaugood closed his eyes.

His chest tightened and his heartbeat gathered speed. Deaugood clenched his teeth and rode the wave of pain that gripped him. It hurt. He had never felt the pain like this. Deep inside, somewhere, he felt calm . . . and joy! The pain took him, his vision blurred, his heart pelted against his chest but Deaugood simply hissed. No one could hear him.

"Father, forgive me," he prayed. A light beckoned to him from beyond and Deaugood followed it forever. Never to return.

# Zero to Infinity

The color and the detail of the small African warriors on the shelf caught Pharren by surprise, holding her in their stare as she examined them with delicate fingers. Bug's apartment was small but it was comfortable compared to some of the places she had laid her head to rest. The furnishings were sparse with barely the necessities, but it looked lived in. She could make it better . . . in time. She sat on the well-worn couch with the tiny figurine standing gingerly in her palm.

"That's an Undamo Warrior," Bug said from the bedroom doorway. He had a blanket in his hand for Pharren. She would be sleeping on the couch.

"Things from the past," Pharren said, a bit sadly.

She had taken a bath, cleaned off the dirt and grime, and now wore a long gray shirt and an old, baggy pair of Bug's pants. All of his clothes were too big for her, making her seem small and timid. She was in unfamiliar surroundings and her nervousness showed in her face. Bug walked over and sat next to her on the couch. He said nothing, just looked intently at her face. He found her face interesting. Soulful. She blushed beneath his stare.

"What's wrong?" she asked, her eyes downcast.

"Nothin'," Bug replied. "This is just the first time I really got to look at your face. All I saw at first was your eyes."

She looked up at Bug. He touched her cheek. Pharren's hair was combed straight back and tied in a ponytail, pushing her face to the fore. She had passionate features. Bug could imagine enjoying them. Touching them. Kissing them.

"Your skin is smooth, and I like the way your face is made. Your lips, the shape of your face, cute little nose and a round forehead. I like the round forehead."

Pharren giggled.

"I'm serious. You look like the kind of woman that I could have somethin' with. That makes it all better. If you want somethin'."

"You know you inspectin' me like I'm a piece of meat," Pharren said lightly.

"No. I handle you like a piece of art."

They were silent for a moment.

"Anyway," Bug said. "Things from our past . . . are our past. We live now. For now on. Okay?"

"For now on," Pharren repeated.

"Plus, we can do this. Together. Draw strength from each other. And my son, Monday. He's eight years old now."

Pharren looked around the room. "Where is your son? Can I meet him?"

"I don't know where he's at," Bug replied. "He'll be home soon though."

"He might be with his mother?" Pharren asked. Bug regarded her for a moment before answering.

"I never met his mother."

"What?"

"I never met his mother," Bug stated. "Long time ago, before I started smokin', I was hustlin'. You know, whatever I had to do to get some dead presidents. Benjamins, Washingtons, Lincolns, whatever. Well, one day I was gonna rob this store, so I hid in the back, near the trash thing . . . the dumpster . . . 'bout closin' time. Right when they started turnin' the lights off in the store, I heard some noise. I ain't quite hear it at first 'cause I was all hyped up and everything, but I knew I heard somethin'. I had to see what it was before I did anything else. A rustlin' noise. Like paper movin'. I ain't know what it was but right then I heard somebody at the back door of the store. So I lifted the lid of the trash thing and climbed in. So I was bein' real quiet, listenin' as the man from the store came out the back door and walked around outside. And that was when I saw him."

"Saw who?"

"The baby. He was layin' on top of a trash bag. Naked. He couldna been even a few days old. So I'm all stooped down, hopin' that he don't start cryin'. And you know what he did? He smiled at me. I swear! He smiled right at me! Like we wasn't in the stinkin' ass garbage together."

Bug paused and looked away. Pharren gently touched his hand.

"I chilled there for a minute. Just lookin' at him. Then he reached for me. I never did rob that store. I took him home with me."

"So you named him 'Monday.'" Pharren prodded gently.

Bug nodded his head. "That's the day I found him."

"He better be glad you didn't find him on Sunday." Pharren smiled.

Bug laughed. "Right!" he agreed. "But I gotta set some new rules for him. He can't be stayin' out late like this. Not anymore."

Pharren looked down at the figurine she still held in her hand.

"These are pretty," she said.

"Undamo. They were assassins. In Africa."

A knock at the door interrupted Bug as he was about to launch into the history lesson that he had given to Monday many times. It was rare for anyone to come knocking on his door and never at this time of night. Instantly, Bug thought of his son and wondered where he was and why he wasn't home. He was alarmed. He crossed the room to the door, tossing the blanket to Pharren before calling out. "Who?"

"Police. Open up."

"What is it, officer?" Bug asked.

"This the police. Open the door."

"For what, officer?" Bug asked.

"I have your son out here." The voice boomed. "Now open up."

Bug opened the door. Five-O was standing there with Monday, Bug's eight-year-old son, glaring with the intensity of "right." The law. Bug was familiar with Five-O and his tactics, and he knew this wasn't good. Five-O was a snake, a devil. Someone to be avoided, someone who couldn't solve

most problems without a violent or otherwise painful solution. Monday came in the doorway and threw his arms
around Bug, holding him tight, scared.

"This yours?" Five-O asked, pointing at Monday with his
nightstick.

"My son," Bug replied.

"We found your son outside," Five-O said, motioning
toward the open door. Harsh moonlight framed Five-O as he
stood with his baton in his hand.

"He was hustling a little earlier in the mall parking lot,
collecting money for charity. Probably you," Five-O continued.

Bug started to protest but Five-O shut him down with a
raised voice. "Just where were you, crackhead, while your son
was running the streets?"

Bug flinched under the accusation, clutching Monday
even closer to him as Five-O began his cop stroll, back and
forth, taking in the surroundings and slamming the nightstick
into his palm. Bug watched the baton apprehensively. He was
very familiar with the stick and the sickening joy Five-O
derived from swinging it. Five-O had beaten him once,
behind a building over on Clinton Avenue for peeing outside.

"If I ever catch you pissing outside again, I'll rip your dick
off and show it to you from the other end," Five-O had told
him as he lay in a quivering heap with blood steaming from
cuts in his head.

The memory of it was painfully vivid.

Five-O turned to Bug. "You know I hate people like you,"
he spat. Pharren got up from the couch and went over to Bug

and gently took Monday's hand. She looked to Five-O for permission. Five-O waited as she led the child from the room.

"People like you give humanity a bad name," Five-O continued. He began slapping one end of the baton into the palm of his hand, punctuating sentences with loud slaps.

Slap! Slap! "You know what that means, smoker? Humanity?"

Bug tensed at the harsh sound.

Slap! "It means taking care of you and yours."

The pain and the threat of Five-O echoed off the walls.

Slap! Slap! "It means knowing right from wrong."

Bug's eyes narrowed defiantly. He knew it was going to happen. The hurt.

Slap! "It means manhood. Being a man."

But not the shame. Not this time.

Slap! "Are you, you little rock monster?"

Bug sputtered, "Am I what?"

"A man!" Five-O barked. The bedroom door squeaked open a crack and Pharren peeked out, wide-eyed, at the two men.

"Yes, I am," Bug replied.

"My ass, you're not!" Five-O bellowed. "A man takes care of his own. Where were you tonight while your son ran the streets? I know where you were. Fiending. Smoking."

"Fuck you, Five-O! Fuck you!"

Five-O bore down on Bug until his face was inches away. He spoke in anger and spittle. "Actually, you wasn't smokin' though. No, you wasn't. In reality . . . you know, reality that place that you try to escape all the time . . . in reality you were at the bottom of nowhere on a springboard, mister. Borderline bitch!"

Five-O paused. He seemed to be struggling within, fighting the good, the bad and the ugly. Finally he spoke, "You are zero to infinity. The real nowhere man."

Slap! The baton started again.

Bug cowered.

Slap! "If I find your son like I found him tonight! Once! Just one more time again; I will lock you up and find someone who will take care of the kid. Someone who gives a damn."

Five-O turned for the door. He paused to glance back at Bug. Pharren, and now Monday, were both watching.

"You got me, stupid man?" Five-O hissed.

Bug lowered his head. Five-O didn't see the tear in Bug's eye. Nor did he notice his clenched fist.

# Mind Power

Anger pelted Bug in a harsh shower in his darkness. His personal unending pit.

Five-O had left something rancid behind when he had slammed his way out of Bug's house. Something that remained inside Bug's heart. Something that hardened and reached and exploded and damaged. Bug felt himself go black. A soft click accompanied the carefully closed bedroom door as Pharren and Monday left him alone with his anguish.

They had seen. They had heard it all.

Bug's home, his domain, had been shattered, burned to the ground by stinging, fiery arrows that Five-O had thrown at him.

In front of Monday. His son.

Monday was the anchor in Bug's life, the laughter in the rain, the innocence in a spotted world. In Monday's eyes the sun rose high in the sky so that they two, father and son, would have a place together. Two against the world. For Bug, there was nothing so precious in a cold world than having a warm heart waiting for him when he came home from the war called survival.

Five-O had brought frost to a warm heart.

Bug knew he needed to talk to Monday-maybe explain, as best he could-about the policeman's visit. But any explanation that came to mind was only a pathetic excuse for not being there. Briefly, it occurred to Bug that maybe he should try telling Monday the truth about what happened that night. That he had gotten high off crack with Moose and that they were going to get another fix when they ran into Tokus. That Tokus and Moose had fought until Moose was seriously hurt. That he had run away in fear, leaving Moose to suffer.

Bug discarded that idea.

He stopped with his hand on the knob of the bedroom door, steeling himself with resolve he didn't feel when the sound of muted sobs echoed from within. It was Monday. Pharren was soothing him.

"It's all right, baby. Shh. Shh."

"But I ain't try to . . ."

"Shh, baby. Come on now. Shh."

Bug backed away from the door. This was supposed to be a new beginning for him. A new start. A chance to start all over. Five-O had no idea. No one did. His change had come from within, from his heart and now he couldn't share it with his son. He had been emasculated. Yet he wore the cloth of hope for a better life. One that Five-O could never enter with his stick of intimidation and pain.

Bug looked at the front door and his bravado abandoned him. Five-O could come into his home at any time and tear it apart any time he desired to spill dark blood. Whup! Whup! That's the sound of the police.

Anger welled up in Bug. At his helplessness. At his vagueness. Bug moved away from the door to the mantel where the tiny Undamo warriors stood, the miniature wooden figures he had collected to teach Monday about that part of his heritage. The Undamo. Assassins.

It had taken Bug months to amass his collection of the Undamo tribe. He had found each one of the dozen figurines in the unexpected places. He had felt as if each one had been calling to him. One under a pile of knick-knacks in a bookstore. Its vibrant earth colors caught his eye and its red, black and green mask appealed to him with meaning. After his initial discovery, the remainder of the tribe seemed to gather at his will: garage sales, flea markets. He even found one at a swap meet.

Bug whispered to them.

"Lies! They lie! They lie like they know," Bug ranted. "But they don't know. They don't know."

He paused to pick up one of the Undamo Warriors and spoke directly to it. "I am a man. A father. For my son . . . I gotta step up. Stand tall." With a sob, Bug flopped down into a chair.

"Shit," he exclaimed. The night's events crept into his thoughts. Tokus and Moose. The fearful flight down the street. The pain of cowardice. Pharren under the bridge. Five-O in the doorway.

"Why do lies have to be so . . . so . . . real?" Bug asked the Undamo. "Something inside me ain't right. Some cold where

I should be strong. Some weak where there's supposed to be fight. 'Cause if I can't fight this . . . shit! That's what it is! Shit! Then I can't fight for Monday. I gots to get my life back."

Bug leaned his head back and closed his eyes. "I gots to," he mumbled. Soon he fell off the ledge of consciousness into sleep.

"Your life will not tremble."

A voice in the darkness called out. Bug had heard voices in his sleep before, but they would always be gone in the morning.

"Look to me, Undamo."

That word got his attention and Bug felt his vision search the blackness for the calling voice. Suddenly, there were colors-red, black and green-but Bug knew he was dreaming. I ain't answerin', Bug thought fearfully. Hell, no. Nope.

"Look to me, Undamo."

Who would mistake him for an Undamo! The darkness shifted and Bug saw. It was the warrior he had held in his hand, the one he had talked to. The Undamo's eyes looked into Bug, inside his soul. The place where he lay hidden, away from the world, huddled in close, cramped quarters. There was strength and compassion in the assassin's eyes, a comforting sense of surety that gave Bug a jolt of clarity. The Undamo held his hand out to him, palm upward. Small replicas of Bug floated above the Undamo's splayed fingers, revolving slowly, bathed in a soft, blue light.

"This is T'challa," the Undamo spoke.

"No. That's me," Bug heard himself say.

"You are T'challa," the Undamo stated and motioned toward the replica's forehead. Bug's body jerked in response. The head of the replica began to glow a bright orange, and Bug felt his brain begin to burn as he watched. The Undamo made another movement over the front of the tiny head, over the cerebrum, the center of judgment and emotion. Bug felt a hot slashing in his head and calmness washed over him: He wasn't afraid. It was liberating. Then the Undamo really went to work, paring and reinforcing. Shearing off the useless, inhibiting pieces of Bug's psyche, while placing bundles of ambrosia at the doors of the once hidden fortress of his mind. The pons varolli, which controls sensations, speech and vision; the cerebellum, which coordinates movement; the medulla oblongata, which monitors breathing heartbeat. They were all reborn and made better, stronger. When the Undamo was finished, a new man was made.

"Thank you," Bug whispered. The Undamo nodded his head once and made another motion. This time it was over the replica's heart. The operation was complete.

"Your life will not tremble," the Undamo commanded.

"As a man," Bug replied and resumed his sleep.

Pharren gently shook Bug, trying to wake him.

"Bug," she called. "Get up. Wake up."

His eyes opened.

"Bug," Pharren said.

"My name," he stated, "is T'challa."

# Poisoned Ambrosia

The loneliness of Tokus' apartment was good company, compared to the friends he didn't have, and the life he wasn't living. The thoroughness of it all, from birth to manhood, sadly amused him. There was his stepfather, an electrical extension cord with teeth and the power of the world, who stung Tokus with unbridled anger and pure hatred. There was the death of Moose on his hands, all over his fingers and up under his skin, vibrating with the reminder of living. Then along came Five-O, a bastard in a prick suit with an assassination and a death warrant all rolled up in a bag of poison. Surely, Tokus thought, this was a full plate. With a bag of chips on the side.

His father was a rapist.

Settling back on the couch, Tokus reached for the remote control and hit the power button. The sound came in before the picture fuzzed to life, bathing the living room of the small apartment in an eerie, alien light. Tokus had the normal bachelor's pad. A medium-sized bedroom was located just beyond the tiny, thin kitchen. A moderate pile of dishes was stacked in the sink but otherwise it was relatively clean. The bathroom was in a little nook off to the left, exactly one step past the hall closet. It was functional and reasonably well kept. The front room was comfortable with the basic living room set-matching couch, love seat and chair. It was strong, comfortable furniture. He really didn't want to buy any more, and Tokus tried to be as neat and as careful as possible. The walls were bare. There were no pictures or giant posters or cheap art or paintings-no, just the plain white walls and a battery-powered clock that Tokus bought at a garage sale for fifty cents. It worked perfectly. He didn't need much. A forty-ounce of malt liquor sat on one of the two end tables that Tokus had found on the sidewalk one day. Next to the bottle was a bag of weed, killer ganja, that he fully intended to smoke and get high and away from earthly troubles. He needed to escape. Get zooted.

It should be so easy.

Deaugood was dead. Word traveled at light speed in the ghetto. The much-adored reverend Skellum Deaugood had passed away in his sleep. A man whose good works would live on as he watched from up above.

"Hell is up there, too," Tokus growled as he lifted the forty-ounce of beer from the end table to his lips and took a good, solid swig. A nasty thought rushed down his throat, pursued by the ale, taking form as it went to the bottom. He belched.

The wake was being held today.

Tokus wondered if Deaugood's family knew that the great Reverend was a rapist. Smiling, he took another swig. The picture would be perfect, the drama complete. He had the power to hurt and destroy an entire family in the blink of an eye. It would be so nasty to walk up to the microphone and look out at the mournful, expectant crowd and prepare to shock them out of their sadness and into angry denial. Together maybe they could all go over and spit on Deaugood's casket.

There came a knock on his door.

A voice blared out. It was Peanut, a neighbor from across the hall.

"Yo, man," Peanut said. "I got that for you. I got it from the store."

Tokus rose and opened the door. Peanut stood in the doorway with a cigar in one hand and a beer in the other, waiting for Tokus to invite him in. Peanut was alcohol, and alcohol was him. It was in his red eyes, his drunken conversation; it was even his walk.

Tokus took the cigar from Peanut, paused and said, "Come in."

Peanut limped into the room, looking around with a herky-jerky motion of his head. He sniffled his nose a few times, emitted a loud screech and turned to Tokus. Tokus shut the door, pointed Peanut to the couch and went over to sit in the chair. It was best to keep distance from Peanut sometimes. Peanut relaxed on the couch as he watched Tokus unwrap the cigar, a blunt, and then slice it down the middle with a small knife that he pulled from his pocket. He dumped the tobacco out on the tabletop, laid the tobacco wrapper beside the pile and reached for the bag of weed. After prying the bag open, Tokus poured the marijuana evenly into the tobacco skin and rolled it up nice and snug. He wet the edge of the rolled cigar with his tongue to make it adhere, and the blunt was complete. Peanut popped the top of his can of beer, took a sip and sniffled a few more times before he spoke.

"Yo! You know you and me gonna be all right . . . when I get my money."

Tokus eyed Peanut while he lit the weed-packed cigar. Peanut was crazy. He had a lawsuit against the three major networks for contributory negligence. According to Peanut, the sound of rapid gunfire, which each television station broadcast nightly, had given him breast cancer. Ten million dollars would cure it just fine, but he would settle for two million. When that money came through, Peanut and Tokus would get amazingly high and stupidly inebriated. Peanut's treat.

Breast cancer! Tokus shook his head. Peanut was crazy.

The combination of tobacco and weed produced a strong smoke that bitterly relaxed his mind to the point of uncaring fun. He took a long pull of the blunt, held the smoke in and passed it to Peanut.

"Peanut, if you smoke a strong blunt . . . your breast cancer will be gone," Tokus said without exhaling. "You know cannabis is medicinal."

"Naw, man, naw," Peanut replied. "Blunts just get you high, man." He took another hit. "You heard about that preacher who died yesterday? Heart attack." He passed the blunt.

Tokus nodded yes. Peanut went on.

"I bet that shit hurt! Man, your heart just gettin' all tight on ya' . . . then your lungs ain't workin' right. Then you probably die with your eyes open. Tryin' to take some light with ya."

Peanut shook his head ruefully, "I ain't gonna go out like that. Peaceful. That's how you go. Peacful."

Tokus' thoughts were elsewhere. He pondered confronting the Reverend's wife and family at the funeral and making the announcement. Maybe tell them of the two lives that her husband ruined. About his mother, a torn woman, both mentally and physically, who suffered so deeply that she would abandon her son to follow a man whose only love was the power of pain. Or maybe he would take the grieving widow down the spiraling pathway of the life that was created on a lonely, violent day. The day his mother was taken away forever. He would tell them! Loud and clear!

Deaugood's life was poisoned ambrosia; may it rot the ground where it lay.

"Ha!" Tokus laughed aloud, a short bark that held no enjoyment. Peanut sprang to his feet, startled.

"Whew, boy, I thought that was some gunfire or somethin'."

"Peanut, you are flippin'."

"For real! I felt my cancer actin' up. Don't bust out like that, baby! Laugh like regular folks."

Tokus passed the blunt to Peanut, smiling at the "regular" man. Peanut sat down, happily puffin' on the cigar with one hand held over his chest. Tokus took a long drink of beer, slammed the bottle down on the table with a loud "bang" and reached for the remote control. Peanut sprang to his feet again.

"So you got breast cancer, right?" Tokus asked.

Peanut nodded his head. "Yeah."

"And you got it from the evening news?" Tokus prodded.

"Yeah."

"From the 'bang-bang' of gunfire?"

"Yeah. And I got proof, see . . ."

"And gunfire is all over the news . . . right?" Tokus cut off the reply.

"Yeah," Peanut replied warily.

"So I could kill you," Tokus said as he grinned drunkenly. "Right now."

"What you talkin 'bout . . ." Peanut stammered.

"Because," Tokus paused to beer burp. "I . . . I . . . I got cable. CNN. News, twenty-four, seven." Tokus aimed the remote control at the television set. He was smiling but Peanut was shaking. He was afraid. Tokus watched him, realizing that the fear was real and the emotion was strong as Peanut dropped the blunt and began to plead. His pleas fell on deaf ears as Tokus began racing through channels. Peanut shrieked.

Tokus reeled as he weighed the experience of feeling power, of having someone in his grip, under his thumb without mercy. Manipulation of the powerless reveals the weakness of truth and the touching and feeling of men's souls. There was at once the satisfaction of lust spent and the tainting of a heart in this vindictiveness.

Peanut was crying.

# Big Ma

Tokus stood way back, behind a huge, scarred oak tree, watching the pained procession of the bereaved at the shattered funeral. Deaugood's family, his wife, his son and his daughter stood in a grieving line with pain settling differently on each face. The mother was sadly stricken. Hers was a face that had seen many a black horror-the dogs of the civil rights movement, riots and Jim Crow-but the agony seemed to come from a different place. The difference could be heard in the wrenching sobs that rang out into the stone garden. Her cries put a pall on the still grayness of the day. A sadness hung about her.

Tokus thought about his mother. About the good things. Then he wished. On the good things.

The daughter stood next to her mother, holding the older woman's hand, offering a sad comfort and haunted warmth. She wore an expression of shocked disbelief that her father was gone, as if the naked soul of Reverend Skellum Deaugood wasn't sprawled inside the steel blue coffin that rested on slats above its six-foot-deep destination. To her, his spirit was alive, moving with warmth that said "father." Always would. She pulled her mother closer.

The son was different. Tokus looked closer at the young man who stood apart from the grieving family. A hint of recognition bothered Tokus as he studied him but he couldn't put a name to the passing twinge. He knew that face. From somewhere.

Tokus moved in closer. He caused no undue attention as he stepped forward. His intentions were still unclear, yet the angry motive was harsh and driving him mercilessly. The Reverend must have been a good man, Tokus thought, as he took lot of the large crowd attending the service. They looked sad. Tokus felt bitter.

An elderly woman walked over to Tokus and stopped him. She looked into his eyes with kindness of age.

"What is it?" she asked, taking his hand in hers. "You look so hurt, young man."

Tokus looked down at the aged hands that held him so kindly, so safely and he couldn't speak. There was only one purpose for Tokus at the funeral: to announce to the congregation that his father, the rapist, was being buried. Dirt forever. He wasn't prepared for compassion.

"The Reverend was a good man," the old woman said. "He taught me how to see the heart of a person. Their spirit. And you know what? I see yours."

"Come on." She patted Tokus' hand. "Come with me."

She pulled Tokus through the crowd of people, past the well-dressed men and women who murmured in hushed, mournful conversations, to a spot with a clear view of the casket and the grieving family.

"Some would question why the good Lord would take a man like Reverend Deaugood from us. From the church and from his family." The old woman indicated the bereaved with a nod of her head.

"Some might not," Tokus blurted and the old lady recoiled a bit. Tokus instantly regretted his outburst but could see no way to reach out and pull the hurtful words back.

The woman paused a moment, as if contemplating the full weight of death and circumstance, of life and challenge, of struggling to overcome the tangible and the intangible, only to end up in a casket, waiting to be lowered slowly into the earth.

"Young man, the Reverend did a good work with his family, seeing as where he came from," she began. "And he came a long ways . . . yes, he did. He had to reach, I mean reach high, 'cause he didn't have no example. You know, nobody to follow. What they call role models nowadays. He did good."

Tokus looked at the old lady, indecisive with his secret, hesitant, but realizing it still had power. I should tell her about the nastiness of drug dealing, rape and jail.

But what purpose would be served?

This woman was dear to life-the world was a better place with her in it. Someone like her was what was missing from his frame of reference for family. A nurturer. A grandma to visit, to be pampered by. The one woman who would always make everything all right. Gently, he squeezed her hand in understanding. She looked up at Tokus.

"Baby," she began, "I know . . ."

"Big Ma," a small voice softly interrupted. "Bianca keep pinchin' me. I tol' her to stop but she keep on pinchin' me."

Big Ma was gentle. "Hush, child. Tell her I said she better behave 'fore I have to come over there. Go on, now!" The little girl hurried off to deliver the message.

"That's my granddaughter," she said as she turned to Tokus. "One of them. Family is about all I have left. But it's all that really matters though. In this world. In this time."

The image of the widow and her children again caused Tokus a nagging discomfort. The vague feeling of having met the son persisted.

"Everybody's looking for a place," Big Ma continued.

"Get out of the way or take his place." The words flashed through his mind and Tokus suddenly remembered the young, black man. Deaugood's son was the crackhead who was with Moose that fateful night of the fight that had ended in death. Deaugood's son had tried to stop Tokus but had failed miserably. If only Tokus had listened.

"So are you," Big Ma said. Tokus turned to her. "You lookin' for a place. And I know where it is."

"You do?" Tokus asked.

"Yes. 'Cause I know who you are."

Tokus smiled grimly. "So do I."

"Do you?" she asked cryptically. "Listen to me, a long time ago the Reverend was a young man runnin' the streets. I knew him all his life. From a little baby to a hard-headed hustler. And he was hard-headed! He wouldn't listen to nobody! Nobody! His mother, his father. Even the police. You know how ya'll young folks get."

Big Ma heaved. "But then Skellum did something that I couldn't forgive. One night he took his girlfriend, his widow now . . . he took her home and then it was back to the streets, hustling, where he met this other girl. He said he loved her, but the girl wouldn't have him while he had a girlfriend. So Skellum took her. Took her womanhood. It was so evil of him to take a life and change it that way. Forever. I hated him for that. I guess Skellum hated himself, too. His smile, that happy smile, was gone. It went somewhere cold and dark, 'cause he didn't care anymore. Next thing I know . . . he's in jail. And the girl turned up pregnant. She had the baby while Skellum was in jail. A little boy. I went to her. I tried to talk to her but she was so scared . . . so different. I couldn't help her hurt . . . her pain. It was everywhere."

Tokus stared at her. She seemed to be reliving a personal nightmare. Tokus touched her shoulder as his own anger subsided. Big Ma blinked back a tear. "She had a baby boy. She named him Tokus. That ain't a regular name."

She looked Tokus squarely in the eyes. "That's your name."

Tokus returned her stare. "Yes."

"Ma Deaugood," a young man interrupted. "My condolences. Your son was a good man."

"Thank you so much." She looked at Tokus wonderingly. "So . . . why are you here?"

"I . . . I . . . don't know," Tokus stammered.

# Fishouse Fat

Fishouse Fat was kind of skinny. Tough skinny with a hide of toughened leather from nearly sixty years of suffering the afflictions of blindness and blackness. A nonentity in a painfully physical world. A harsh wisdom had resulted from his journey through the maze of life. And something else. It clung to him while reaching out to anyone around. Fishouse was called a psychic but he, himself, held none of those beliefs. He considered himself a poor man.

But Fishouse Fat smiled. He wore happiness like a coat that should have been bitter to the touch. Instead he exuded an aura of a well-kept man with a soft shoulder, bearing the world. It was a comfortable glow that he welcomed others to share.

Fishouse Fat could usually be found sitting in the park on his favorite bench facing the river. Tokus found the man a joy to talk to, always willing to share his wisdom. He was a source of sound, practical advice. Tokus tiptoed up behind Fishouse, trying to surprise him-something that had never worked on the blind man before. Tokus was barely a step away from him when Fishouse yelled out.

"Don't even try it, young fella!"

"Man!" Tokus exclaimed. "How do you do that every time? I can't ever sneak up on you."

"Tokus, you know you can't . . . on my worst day. But you won't quit, will ya'?"

Tokus grinned at him.

A smile spread across Fishouse's face. "I like that. You, uhh," Fishouse motioned with his hands. "You, uhh . . . figure you gonna grow some standin' there?"

Tokus took a seat on the bench next to him. It was a moment before Fishouse spoke.

"You in trouble, ain't ya?"

"Could be," Tokus responded.

Fishouse laughed, a chuckle that rumbled inside him, its echo barely audible. But Tokus knew he was laughing. "You know why you can't sneak up on me?" he asked Tokus. "'Cause of your brow."

"My brow?"

"Yeah. Your brow. Up there above your eye. Your brow. I can feel what's on there. I can feel the pain, the joy, the mean, the worry . . . all that. So you couldn't sneak up on me 'fore; don't try to sneak up on me now."

Tokus said nothing.

"Yo' call," Fishouse said. "Just don't burn too fast, young fella. Don't burn too fast."

"I ain't tryin' to burn, Fishouse."

"It's more than you though, Tokus," Fishouse argued. "It ain't just one person. It's reform. Reformin' yo' self. Stone gardens is fulla people who fail to recognize."

Fishouse turned and firmly fixed Tokus with an upheld finger.

"Nothing dictates your life. If you take aim at somethin', your life writes itself. But you got to aim at some good shit. Not the shit out here today. Most of the stuff these young boys out here doin' is garbage. Zero, two or three times over. Just bullshit that got thrown at a black wall to see if it would stick. Chillun these days just reach up there and grab whatever's left. But it's all bullshit."

Fishouse counted off with his fingers.

"Drugs! Bullshit!"

"Guns! Bullshit!"

"Jheri curls! Bullshit!"

Fishouse paused, catching himself.

"But I can't say nothing about Jheri curls, though." His hand went to the thin copse of hair that clung stubbornly to his scalp. "'Cause I'm right there on Jheri Curl Street."

"On the corner of Jheri and Curl," Tokus offered.

"On the street," Fishouse finished. "But you see what I mean?"

"On one level, yes, I understand. But on another level, you're looking from the mountaintop while I'm looking up at a monster. You've been to war . . . you're a warrior. You've been battle-tested while I'm just a soldier going into war."

"But it all boils down to one thing," Fishouse Fat answered. "Fast fuse, young fella. Fast fuse. Kids today live like they ain't 'spectin' to make it past the age of twenny. That's a fast fuse. A short line on a short time. Burnin'. Burnin' quick. And your lives . . . no sooner'n you started it . . . it's gone."

Fishouse stared into the darkness through sightless eyes. "Watching thoughts" is what he called it. The gray, dark waters of the Hudson River splashed and twirled as the current whirled the toxic wastes just under the surface. Tokus always imagined that if someone dove into that water he would surface with three green eyes and an extra warped limb. He wondered if the river had ever been a clear, beautiful blue. Over on the opposite shore, Tokus saw two men fishing.

"Tokus," Fishouse began, "it's time for you to make that stand in your life. You only get one chance. You got to know now how you burn. Make the right choice, son. Make the right choice."

Tokus regarded the blind man for a moment. Everything Tokus wanted in life was so close. Graduation. A career with no drugs. Happiness. So close. All he had to do was make the right decision. No easy task.

"Thanks, Fishouse," Tokus said, rising to his feet from the bench. "Much respect. Much love."

"Much love!" Fishouse exclaimed. "Much love for what I said or much love for what you heard?"

"Much love," Tokus responded, "for knowing that I burn."

# Hey Killer!

Tokus had a family, a brother and a sister. A revelation that needed exploring. Developing. He was determined to get to know his newfound siblings, though they were strangers to him. His grandmother, Big Ma, had told him many things about Bug and Doria but she had taught him so much more. About family. He had left Deaugood's funeral with a sense of how beautiful it could be to have a grand relative and the warmth of belonging.

His brother, Bug, lived on Orange Street with his eight-year-old son, Monday.

His sister, Doria, was a junior in high school. A straight "A" student with a good head on her shoulders, according to Big Ma. "That girl got common sense," Big Ma had told him.

Tokus' mind went 'round and 'round with the possibilities of what could be, but after the glow of wonder died to a pulsing ember, there were questions. And no easy answers.

Tokus just wanted to meet them. Doria first. Bug could be a problem but Tokus hoped and wished they could at least talk. About anything. They weren't too old or too grown up that they couldn't become brothers.

The funeral had been days ago yet Tokus couldn't muster the courage to meet his newfound siblings. Rejection would hurt much more than he cared to admit, and he would rather remain silent than face their rejection or cope with their denial.

Tokus meandered down Raymar Avenue amongst the unusual quiet that brushed through the leaves of the trees that lined lawn edges. It was an affluent, quiet section of the city that accommodated rich, white people, tweeting birds and swimming pools. Tokus was headed over to Orange Street. He had been there a few times, standing outside Bug's house, trying to gather up the courage to confront his brother. But he had always ended up just walking away. Issues unresolved; brother unmet.

At the end of Raymar Avenue there was a shortcut, an alleyway, that Tokus usually took. It let out a block away from Bug's house. Actually it was three connecting alleyways, with each corridor equal in length to a city block. It was a strange location for a back way. Dank shadows and dark hideaways contrasted with the security of this prosperous neighborhood. But there was still enough distance to separate the "haves" from the "have nots." Tokus' footsteps echoed in the still, smooth air, crunching gravel from heel to toe as he turned the corner from Raymar into the shadows of the alley. Behind him was the idyllic life that education, perseverance and desire were meant to achieve. And in a world of great and distant dreams, Tokus saw his place at the feast, back there, in that neighborhood, somewhere.

Tokus never heard the dark sedan that pulled into the alley behind him.

Five-O quietly pulled alongside Tokus in an unmarked car. A growl was strewn across his face. The solitude of the back street now took on the makings of a dark trap.

"Hey, killer," Five-O barked at him. Tokus kept walking.

"Hey, killer," Five-O barked louder. "I suggest you stop and get your black ass over here!"

Tokus stopped and turned. Five-O inched the car forward.

"Did you complete the assignment?" he asked.

Tokus shrugged.

Five-O spat. "Just say 'no' because I just saw the old, rubbery bastard an hour ago!"

Five-O beat the steering wheel with his fists and grit his teeth so hard that Tokus thought he heard them cracking. Five-O looked like a madman-stone, cold crazy.

"Now tell me, what the hell is your malfunction, boy? I asked you to do one thing for yourself. One thing! And you want to do it on c.p. time, right? Colored people's time. You want to do everything late, don't you?"

Five-O paused, waiting for a response. Tokus was speechless.

"Well, you don't have late, nigger man," Five-O hissed. "You don't even have now! Come on . . ."

Five-O sprang out of the car and stomped over to Tokus. His first punch caught Tokus in the stomach, doubling him over, forcing the air from his body in one, shocking instant.

His next blow landed squarely on Tokus' jaw, sending him crashing to the ground.

"Oh, yeah!" Five-O growled through clenched teeth as he calmly looked up and down the alley. "I see I have to treat you like the bitch that you are, huh?"

He launched a vicious kick to the ribs that lifted Tokus from his knees over onto his back. Tokus looked up at the cop through a haze of pain. His ribs were on fire and his lungs ached with every breath. He knew that there was much more to come. Blue-clan violence was nothing new; it just had never happened to him before. He could only hope that he wouldn't die in an alley.

"One fucking thing," Five-O ranted. "Just one fucking thing. And you can't do it. Just one fucking thing."

Tokus looked up at him.

"Fuck you!"

Five-O stomped him in the face.

"No, you are the one about to be royally fucked," Five-O roared.

Suddenly, Five-O cried out and began brushing at his neck. A small dart pushed through his skin. It had entered Five-O's flesh with a hard "snick," and he yelled out as he reached for the tiny missile. Five-O plucked at it but it didn't budge. Angrily, he yelled and snatched it from his neck. Small strands of flesh clung to three tiny barbs that protruded along the thin shaft of the needle. Five-O threw it on the ground and stepped forward. His head was on a swivel, searching for the shooter. He felt his neck and his hand come away with a spot of blood as he scanned the alleyway. There was no one.

"Good for your ass." Tokus coughed in pain.

Five-O ignored him, wavering as he bellowed. "Someone's there!" He staggered forward. "You just stay your ass there! Your black ass better not move. I'll be right back."

A man stepped into view from behind a trimmed hedge on the lawn of a large white, two-storied house not twenty feet away on Raymar Avenue.

Five-O laughed with glee when he saw him.

Tokus couldn't believe his eyes.

It was Bug. Half his face was painted in an African mask-red, black and green, primeval, a stark contrast to the pristine surroundings but Tokus recognized him. Bug held a bamboo stick in one hand as he stood defiantly in the open sunlight staring at Tokus. He didn't move a muscle when Five-O yelled, "Freeze," jumped into his car, squealed it into a U-turn and raced up onto the lawn. The wheels of the car spewed up thick slabs of sod. Bug's eyes were locked on Tokus. Five-O braked his car a few feet in front of Bug, jumped out and drew his revolver. "Get those hands up, bitch!"

Bug turned to face the law.

Five-O put his gun back in its holster. "Oh, it's you," he began. "You shot me in the neck! With that! Now I'm gonna stomp a mud hole in your . . ."

Five-O faltered in mid-stride, grasping at his stomach. Slowly, he fell to the ground in a trembling heap as painful gasps of air escaped from his body. Convulsions wracked him as he simultaneously tried to swallow his tongue and vomit. Deathly grunts emanated from somewhere within the tortured frame of Five-O and in seconds it got worse.

Bug looked down at the fallen figure of authority that had threatened him, at the man who was no longer a maiming insult. When death had finally made its claim, Bug turned and disappeared into the plush foliage of serenity that was God's property.

Tokus watched Bug leave. Escaping a surreal slow-motion nightmare marked by murder. The dart that Five-O had brushed from his neck lay on the ground accusingly. It took Tokus a few minutes to compose himself. There was agonizing pain in his ribs and his jaw, but eventually he was able to rise. He struggled over to where the dart lay, carefully picked it up and staggered down the alley. Tokus threw the poisoned bamboo missile down the sewer somewhere on Orange Street.

His brother would be free.

# Oval Trust

Somewhere inside his private life, Tokus made the decision that it was time to unite with his brother and sister. To be together, or apart, forever. Inside, Tokus felt enormous, as if he would burst with his secret knowledge, and he wanted to share it. With them.

Gingerly, he touched his jaw. It was still tender from where Five-O had hit him. He thought it might have been broken, but the pain had slowed to a dull ache. He was experiencing a mild discomfort when he took deep breaths, but the kick to his ribs had only bruised them at worst. The anxiety of waiting for the police to come knocking at his door troubled Tokus more than any physical ailment and filled him with a sense of urgency. He had decided to handle his dilemma as he had dealt with any other problem that was beyond his control. He would wait it out. Ignore the problem and it would go away. It had worked before and he could only hope it would net him the same positive results. For the first time in years, Tokus had prayed.

He decided to approach Doria first and let truth step into the light. Tokus just wished that Doria would be able to see beyond the obvious, beyond the harsh negatives and anger, and peep into what he wanted, what he needed.

Plano High School stood three stories tall, in a nondescript fashion, about fifty yards back off Common Street, where Tokus stood waiting for the afternoon bell to ring. He pictured Doria running out with a happy, energetic smile. Like a picture. Oh, yeah, Tokus mused. Right! Kids didn't smile in school nowadays. They mostly ducked and dodged the bullets and the drugs. Thick, plush grass carpeted the ground from the street all the way to the driveway in front of the school, where buses waited to load the raucous teenagers and cart them home. Tokus walked across the lawn to the side of the brick building by the concrete steps, hoping that Doria would use these exits when school was dismissed. He had brought some of his books with him to avoid looking so obviously out of place as he scanned the crowd of crackling, energetic beings known as teenagers, hoping to spy his sister.

There it was. That word. Sister. Tokus liked the sound of it. Its meaning was clear in his mind, even in his heartbeat, as it began to pound loudly-counting off the seconds to the moment that could change his life forever. The school bell went off and Tokus involuntarily tensed as the wait began. Instantly, kids were bursting through the doors in hordes of hustle and noise. They were already late for basketball courts, street corners and home. Tokus remembered the feeling. Three girls pushed out the third exit door. Tokus spied Doria.

She was a beautiful girl. She smiled at one of the other girls and the picture was complete. Her light, slightly burnished skin and pretty, brown eyes seemed uniquely in place. She wore her hair curled down to her shoulders with touches of gold running through it. She probably drove the boys crazy. The three girls were coming straight toward him and Tokus resisted the urge to duck behind the side of the building. Instead, he turned his head in the other direction, away from them, as they neared. They giggled as they passed and when Tokus turned to watch them, he exhaled heavily before he began to follow.

The group of girls walked past the rapidly filling school buses and down the sidewalk to Common Street in a carefree burst of youth and energy, the world passing them by with the promise of a trouble-free tomorrow. Tokus followed at a discreet distance. The moment of truth was upon him and suddenly all his plans seemed faulty. Every reason, every explanation that came to him echoed flatly in his mind. Every word seemed destined to fall on deaf ears, the victim of a sham uncovered. Tokus knew he was running out of room. This was the end of the road . . . or the beginning. He quickened his pace while his mind raced, closing the gap between himself and the girls while his insides reverberated panic.

"Doria," Tokus called. The three girls turned in unison as Tokus hurriedly caught up to them. Doria watched him with a cautiously questioning eye.

Tokus fidgeted. "You don't know me, but my name is Tokus. Tokus Stone. I need to talk to you about your brother, Bug."

"Tokus!" one of Doria's friends exclaimed. "What kind of name is Tokus? Swahili?"

The other girl said, "No, girl, that's Zulu!" She flirted closer to Tokus. "You look like a Zulu, uh-huh." Both of the girls wore jean overalls with the suspenders hanging down, and Tokus noticed they looked like twins. He looked past them at Doria.

"It's important," he said. "Very important."

"About my brother?" Doria wondered. "Important how?"

Tokus looked at the other girls. "Well, it's important and it's private. It concerns Bug and your father."

"What about my father?" Doria was instantly defensive.

"In private. Please?"

Doria watched Tokus for a minute. She seemed doubtful but curious. The mention of her father had drawn her. She turned to her girls. "Wait for me a minute, okay? I'll be back. Don't go anywhere."

"Are you coming back, too, Zulu?" one of the girls asked.

"It's Swahili!" the other girl squealed. "We'll be right here, Doria."

Tokus and Doria paced a discreet distance and turned to face each other. Doria was very pretty-the beauty of almond smooth skin, shaped gently by an oval trust and kindness that reached up into the corners of her eyes. She was a sister that he would always protect and cherish. Tokus looked her in the eye and began the lie.

"Someone is looking for your brother," he began.

"And?" Doria shrugged.

"Well," Tokus said, "I hate to alarm you . . ."

Doria was taken aback. "But you are, aren't you?"

Tokus paused. Doria had struck a counterpoint in his plan. Big Ma had told him that Doria was a bright girl who didn't miss much, so he had better be careful with his game of deceit. It was time to improvise.

"Well," Tokus began again, "like I said, this matter concerns you, Bug and your father. The Reverend. And you both need to know. You and Bug."

Doria studied him suspiciously. He could almost hear the gears turning in her pretty little head.

Finally she said, "What is it? What do we need to know? What is so important?"

"I'd rather tell you both together. Then you'll understand."

"Uh-uh," Doria answered. "I don't need my brother with me to hear what you have to say. You might even be the person who is out here looking for him. So tell me."

"Doria, please!" Tokus cried.

"Forget you then." She turned away.

"All right! Okay, then! Damn!" Tokus conceded. His heart beat nervously as he gathered his will to face the moment of truth. Now that it had arrived, Tokus found himself groping for elusive words and meanings that were bound to hammer at his sister's life with the force of a dark unknown . . . about her father.

"Doria . . ." Tokus stalled. "Before I tell you anything, I have to ask you to hear me out before you go reacting all over the place. Okay?"

"I can't promise that."

"Promise to try."

"Will you please just spit it out?!"

Tokus did just that. For Doria he used the word "date" and left out the part about rape but everything else was hung out there for her. Considering the severity of the news, Doria handled it relatively well. She stood there, slack-jawed with an incredulous look, rejecting the entire idea immediately.

"I guess you just expect me to believe this?"

"I have no reason to lie," Tokus answered.

"My father would have told us. He didn't keep secrets."

"Everybody has secrets. And you're talking to one now."

Doria had more questions, heavy ones, but she was soon softened by the sincerity of Tokus' entreaties.

"And I just came here to ask you if you would be my sister. If I could be your brother," Tokus finished hopefully.

Doria looked at him numbly. "I guess we had better get over to my brother's house. We were walking past his house on the way home anyway."

She turned toward her friends who were still waiting patiently and said, "Come on, Tokus."

They began walking in silence, the girls quieted by the serious expression on Doria's face. They had never seen her switch moods so suddenly, and all their attempts at conversation were met with curt responses.

After a few blocks had rolled by, Doria looked over at Tokus.

"Oh, yeah," she said. "If you don't know . . . my brother calls himself T'Challa now."

"T'Challa?" Tokus repeated.

"Now you know," Doria said.

# T'Challa

The man who stood before Tokus with his arms folded across his chest was not the same man who had run away leaving his friend, fleeing in fear from the screams of pain. More than his name had changed and it showed in his eyes. In his stance. Tokus wondered if T'Challa, his brother, could put that night in its proper perspective. In the past. A forgotten space and time in a life long ago, a dark creature who didn't have to live again.

It had taken a sincere entreaty from Doria before T'Challa would allow Tokus entrance into his home. Tokus took a seat on the beaten, living room couch, as the two men eyed each other warily, each with a brotherly secret of death of which the sister could never be made aware. Doria sat on the arm of the far end of the couch facing T'Challa.

Five-O was gone. Dead. Ghost. T'Challa had taken him out with cold, hard anger, openly defiant in the harsh sunlight. Tokus didn't approve of murder, but he was still breathing a sigh of relief that the threat of the law no longer loomed over him and he could now move forward with his life. Starting here. Starting now.

An awkward, tense silence hung over the room. Doria squirmed in her seat.

"T'Challa," she began. "Tokus gotta tell you something."

"Must be important," T'Challa answered. "You brung him here. All right. What?"

Tokus paused and looked around the room for the first time since he had entered. A woman was sitting at a table in the kitchen. Seated across from her was a small boy. That must be Monday, Tokus reasoned, T'Challa's little boy. Monday was openly curious and Tokus smiled at him. A tiny grin creased his small face and he gave a little wave and chirped, "Hi."

Tokus smiled his "hi" in return.

The apartment was small. It looked like two bedrooms with a closed door just off the kitchen and another one directly behind T'Challa. The kitchen itself was ghetto issue— a room with a sink, refrigerator, stove and brown cabinet.

"I thought we could speak privately," Tokus said. "The three of us."

"What is it?" T'Challa pressed. "What do you want?"

"It's not so important. It's just personal."

"Yeah," Doria piped up. "Very personal. For real T'Challa. For real."

T'Challa nodded. He called Pharren. "Ya'll go in the bedroom for a minute. Gone."

After the door closed behind them, T'Challa looked at Tokus. "You killed him."

"Who killed who?" Doria jumped up.

"It was an accident," Tokus replied.

"Who did you kill?"

"I didn't murder anybody! I got in a fight. It was an accident."

Doria stepped back, eyes widened in disbelief.

"Look, Doria," Tokus explained. "That guy was trying to
kill me. And he had the nerve to kiss me first! On the lips! It
was an unprovoked attack. Next thing I know, I hit him and
he was on the ground, bleeding. I didn't touch him again after
that."

Tokus turned to T'Challa.

"I swear, I never touched him again after he went down. I
didn't find out that he died until hours later."

"But why did he jump on you?" Doria asked.

Tokus averted his eyes. He couldn't look at her. "For
drugs. I was a drug dealer. It was my last night sellin'. I used to
deal up on the Aisle."

"You killed him," T'Challa stated.

"I didn't mean to. But he was trying to rob me. That's not
in my best interest. Even if it was in yours!"

T'Challa's eyes darkened. Hard. Tokus wished he could
have that last sentiment back. This wasn't going as planned.

"Listen," Tokus said, "I shouldn't have said that. I didn't
come here to argue. There's something you need to know."

Tokus proceeded to relate the family secret to a bemused
T'Challa. When he finished, T'Challa leaned forward with a
thoughtful look.

"That's a good one," he said. "That's a good story."

"He admitted it to me," Tokus said.

T'Challa paused to mull that one over. After a minute Doria's voice came soft and slow. "I believe him, T'Challa."

Tokus looked at Doria gratefully.

"Why?" T'Challa asked.

Doria turned a trusting look at Tokus. In her eyes Tokus saw everything that a sister could be . . . and he hoped that she saw a brother's reflection. A real brother.

"Who would want to be my brother, unless he was?"

"Or," T'Challa countered. "why would someone want to be my brother . . . unless he had to be?"

T'Challa was suspicious. The two men knew each other beyond Doria's realm of knowledge. The streets were their common denominator and they both understood that the man on the streets was a menace, not a brother.

"Doria," T'Challa said. "Go in the room with my son. Tokus and me . . . we gotta talk."

Doria started to object but one look from T'Challa and she pulled up short, rose from her seat and left the room. T'Challa stood and regarded Tokus coolly, then turned and walked across the room. When he was standing in front of the Undamo display he faced Tokus and spoke sternly.

"You left something out," he uttered.

"Left what out of what?" Tokus replied.

"You're older than me," T'Challa answered. "If Deaugood got your mother pregnant, why didn't he marry her?"

"I guess they didn't get along," Tokus answered.

"No," T'Challa replied. "Get along or not get along didn't matter back then. If you got along good enough to do the bump and grind, you were friends enough to take care of your kids. So stop lying."

Tokus hesitated before deciding on the truth.

"Okay," he said. "The good Reverend Minister Deaugood . . . raped my mother. Bam! There it is. Okay! The cold hard fact. He raped my mother."

T'Challa stared at him stonily.

"So violence begot violence, huh?"

Tokus eyes snapped. "That was low."

"What else did you lie about?" T'Challa snapped.

"Nothing else."

"Now I'm supposed to believe that, right?"

"What did you expect?" Tokus whispered harshly. "You want me to tell Doria that her father raped my mother? Get real, my man. Get real!"

T'Challa walked over and took the seat directly across from Tokus. "You killed Moose."

"It was an accident. Self-defense." Tokus was defensive. "He was trying to rob me and you knew it!"

T'Challa didn't answer. They were quiet for a moment.

"You killed Five-O," Tokus stated.

"I had to. Anyway, it looked like he was trying to kill you."

"Yeah," Tokus replied. "But what about the police? You don't even care if they come for you, do you?"

"Five-O won't," T'Challa replied.

"You left that dart there for the police to find," Tokus said.

"I know," T'Challa admitted.

"No, you don't know. I picked it up and threw it in a sewer about five blocks away. They'll never find it."

T'Challa gave him a searching stare before going over to
the bedroom door and calling for Doria. As the door opened
T'Challa turned to Tokus and said, "We'll see."

Doria came into the room and then they talked, the three
of them. Soon Monday and Pharren joined them. Tokus felt
as if they were making progress, even though they really had
no starting point and no guidance, no rule or reason. Their
journey took place on a narrow path with an unending free
fall threatening on each side. The process of getting to know
each other was a sometimes awkward, extra sensitive, precari-
ous balance on the precipice of a burgeoning relationship
with arms and legs flailing to maintain the perch. Perfect balance was the ultimate goal . . . the state of "ooommm." The
tranquil state of "ooommm" eluded them, but there was a
crack of light at the end of the trek.

Tokus also took stock of Pharren. She seemed shy but there
was also a quiet strength he sensed there, as if she had brought
that quality to T'Challa's life, for Tokus saw it in his brother,
too. And Monday was a sheer joy. They connected instantly.
He sat next to Tokus on the couch and looked at him happily.

"So you my uncle now?" Monday asked.

Tokus looked at T'Challa before he answered.

"Yes, I am."

"Uncle Tokus?"

"Well, maybe just Tokus, okay?"

"Okay," Monday said and jumped into Tokus' arms. Tokus
grinned so hard his face hurt before he released his nephew.

They talked well into the night until, finally, Tokus and
Doria had to leave.

"T'Challa," Tokus said as he reached into his pocket. "Doria. I would be so proud if you both would come to my graduation."

He pulled the invitations from his pocket and extended them to the surprised pair.

"I graduate from the university after the final exams," Tokus explained. "Will you be there for me?"

Doria took the invitations. T'Challa nodded in agreement.

# BOOK II:
# The Arrival of the Lie

# Echo of Her Eyes

He could almost feel it, the echo of her eyes, as they moved closer, consuming him. Red fire burned in their wake. Streaks of white heat danced in the blazing tendrils, and they called him like a bandit to come steal away and take illicit pleasures. John Zabriski hid behind a dark pair of shades from a world that was oblivious to his existence, his eyes warped from the drug that sent his mind on a sinuous journey of heat and love. With a smile, he leaned back in his seat and spoke to the echoes. His words were a whisper against the humming of the plane's engines, but each syllable was clear and precise.

"You are my baby. Absolutely. My baby."

The eyes had him forever. They belonged to him, the eyes were a mere reflection of the feline quality of his own hazy pupils, both elongated and burning. For as long as desire ached in him, for as long as the drug lasted, John Zabriski was in the dubious position of owning and being owned by his new precious creation.

The pills! His hand flew to his breast pocket, anxiously checking for his small bottle of tablets. The label read it contained a prescription for arrhythmia but John's heart was fine. Settling back into the cushioned comfort of his first-class seat aboard the huge airliner, his heart was beating quite lovely at the moment.

"Me and my baby," John sighed.

"And you love your baby, don't you?"

A deep, menacing voice rumbled in John's ear. He had forgotten that his huge, burly companion, Bossman, was seated next to him. Bossman was sinister. John had felt it the moment he had met his new business partner. He was a clothed ape with speaking ability, as far as John was concerned, but he needed Bossman to start the operation in motion, to get the ball rolling. John Zabriski planned on becoming a rich man.

The echo of her eyes caused ripples in his mind, warming John, as they became tides that began lapping and cresting. Bossman faded from his wakefulness as John waited, steadying himself, poised for the perfect wave. And when he caught it, he rode it hard. Blue, translucent eyes hovered in front of him as he rose to the peak of his mind play, his personal ocean where he could frolic barefoot without a surfboard, both balanced and steady as the eyes turned and slowly, slowly melded with his.

He felt a physical blue all over his body. As pure as the clear sky that lingered outside the window of the plane, as blue as fantasy and agony combining to form a hue that was as transparent as lust. John had found her and she pulsated with pleasure. She absolutely resonated a climax that stretched over time and place taking John on a journey that would never end.

Suddenly, he came down. It was a jarring crash that caused him to gasp as he watched the eyes quickly fade from view.

"Hold on," John hissed. "I'm coming."

He pulled the bottle of pills from his pocket, wrestled frantically with the childproof cap and finally, gratefully, popped a white capsule into his mouth. The pill rushed John Zabriski in sparks and flares, bursting into flame halfway down his throat.

The echo of her eyes returned, along with the shifting of his own. He felt his eyes twist and stretch as they went vertical. Feline. Straight up and down. As the tingling glow began spreading through his body, John thought about how much America would love his invention.

"Feenin," he sighed.

That's what he called the white, granular powder he had perfected in the German labs that were now mere images in his rearview mirror. It was just as well that the foreigners were no longer a factor in his plans. "Addictive" and "dangerous" were two words that had been used to describe his product, but they were wrong. After all, he was a scientist.

John had secretly paid a few college students to be his guinea pigs and found positive, stunning results. Physical addictiveness was nil and there was no evidence of any bodily damage that resulted from usage, unlike the poisons that plagued society, tearing at its very fabric. Mental addiction, well, that couldn't be helped. Some people were just born to be addicts of one thing or another. Life is like that sometimes: a trick baby doing what he knows best.

One of the test subjects, a young man, quickly flew out of control with his usage. He had actually come to John's office demanding dose upon dose of the drug as payment for being a lab rat. John had pulled him into his office and given him a few special doses, pure Feenin laced with hydrochloric acid that he kept in his desk for occasions such as this. There couldn't be any wild cards in his deck-the stakes were too high-and after the student swallowed those pills, his brain had done a slow stir-fry. Walking zombies told no tales.

"Aren't you taking too many of those?"

John snapped back into real time when he was interrupted by the gravelly voice of Bossman. John glanced over at the big man, thankful to be wearing the dark, tinted shades, as a strange paranoia crept upon him. He felt Bossman's eyes probing into his thoughts. His pupils felt strange. Bossman's head had taken on a strange shape. It was taller. Straight up and down.

He would be happy to be rid of Bossman, who was looking at him with a severe, studious glare. As soon as the plane landed, when the money started piling up, he planned on never setting eyes on the face of Bossman again.

Feenin would go nationwide. Maybe even worldwide. Everything was in place. Way Jalon would supply the capital to get the venture off the ground, while John provided the product and Bossman set up the mechanics that would ensure the smooth operation of the new machine: the labs, chemicals, distribution and all the other illegalities. John had no intentions of getting his hands dirty or exposing himself to the stains of incrimination.

"Aren't you taking too many of those?" Bossman repeated.

John clutched the bottle of pills to his chest. "No, I'm not. Feenin is not addictive. I've been taking them for over a week . . . and I'm not hooked. They're just incredibly effective."

Bossman waited as a flight attendant walked past them. There were only a handful of people in the cabin-none close enough to overhear them, but Bossman was nothing if not careful. Brute strength had gained him a fortune, he had told John, but discretion was also golden.

"Listen, Zabriski, there isn't a drug in the world, that when introduced to the human body, doesn't have an adverse effect on the system. The body is, in effect, in an altered state thereafter."

"Let me guess," John said. "You don't drink. You don't smoke. And you probably breathe once every thirty-five minutes to help preserve the ozone layer, right?"

"Oh, don't get me wrong, Zabriski. I have my fun. I do the things I do. I'm just not into denial. I don't delude myself into thinking that if I stuff powder up my nose that I'm in the same state of mind that I was before I snorted."

Bossman grunted as John turned to look out the window of the plane.

"Those little pills that you're popping in your mouth are drugs. They are what they are, so face the reality clearly. Don't wait until you get 'walleyed' and then extol the virtue of drugs to me."

Bossman looked down at his watch.

"You popped two of those pills in less than twenty minutes."

"What are you doing? Writing a book or something?"

"Maybe."

"Well, skip that chapter 'cause it's none of your business," John replied brazenly.

"Really," Bossman replied calmly. "I just like to time things. Minutes. Seconds. Hours. Time is the only constant. It's utterly reliable."

The flight attendant came over to them, smiling. "Can I get you two gentlemen something to drink?"

"Do you have any chocolate chicken?" John asked.

The woman stared. John guffawed and slapped his knee. He cracked himself up. Bossman and the flight attendant waited.

"Can I have a soda?" John exclaimed after his giggles subsided. "Chocolate chicken." John slapped his knee again as she turned to Bossman.

"I'd like a beer," Bossman said. John looked at Bossman in feigned shock.

"A beer! Are you going to alter your state?"

"Just slightly," Bossman answered.

When the drinks arrived, Bossman looked down at his watch again.

"One minute and sixteen seconds," he told her. "Impressive."

She flashed Bossman a puzzled smile and walked away. John stared wondrously at the drink in front of him, watching the carbonated bubbles rush to the top of the plastic cup. He leaned forward to take a sip and felt the weight of the computer disks in his pocket press against his ribcage. The three disks were his little secret, his life insurance against an untimely death. He had determined to never reveal his formula, but there was just too much data pertaining to the chemical makeup of Feenin for his brain to retain, so he had encoded the information on the disks. If the existence of the disks were ever discovered, John knew he would become expendable.

He needed another pill . . . but not in front of Bossman.

"Rest room," he said and sprang from his seat. He quickly strode down the aisle and bustled into the small lavatory. After sliding the door shut and locking the "occupied" sign in place, he popped a pill and phased out with the rush for a few minutes, leaning against the wall in the confined space. He splashed purple and blue water from the faucet on his face, looked in the mirror and stared in his eyes, fell in love for a few minutes before he opened the door to go back to his seat.

"I bet you feel better now, Zabriski," Bossman growled. John took his seat and picked up his soda. Now wasn't the time for words . . . it was drinking time. One long, lovely swallow of all that color, the oranges and the reds, and those briskly moving bubbles.

"Shut up," John said and raised the beverage to his lips. Gently, he put the drink on the small shelf in front of him. It was half-empty. Or half-full.

"I'll do you one better," Bossman said. "I'll shut up forever."

Bossman reached inside his breast pocket and pulled out a vial that had traces of a white powder clinging to the bottom.

"See this?" Bossman began. "This stuff seriously alters your state of mind. It's unusually fast acting . . . takes about one minute to do you in. When ingested it makes its way directly to the heart, tightens it with every beat but never lets it expand again. You just drank a good quantity of it about-" Bossman consulted his watch. "-forty-five seconds ago. So now . . . I'm shutting up."

Zabriski started to reply when he felt a tension in his lungs. He clawed at his chest as he felt the clamping of his heart. The slowed beating was beginning to echo louder in his mind. He pursed his lips as he tried to yell out, but a hiss was all he managed. Fifteen seconds later, Zabriski's body bucked a few times before he left the world on a jet plane, following the eyes that still beckoned to him, even in death, with a quiet twinkle and burning tendrils.

"Foolish man," Bossman muttered as he searched the dead man for the Feenin and the three disks. He put them in his pocket and arranged Zabriski in his seat and fastened the seat belt around his waist. He wedged a pillow under Zabriski's dead head and turned it toward the window, making him appear to be asleep. The plane would be landing soon and Bossman planned on being the first man to depart before the body was discovered. It really didn't matter in the end because it would take quite some time before the cause of death was discovered. If it was discovered at all.

Bossman leaned back in his seat and relaxed, the dead man next to him now a forgotten casualty of the high stake game of monopoly. Now only two players remained: him and Way Jalon. Bossman liked the new odds and could only see success for himself in the future. Losing was not on his agenda.

He thought back to the look on Zabriski's face as he had popped those pills. The Feenin was what he had called it, and Bossman wondered about the high. He pulled the bottle out of his pocket as the pilot announced that the plane was beginning its descent into JFK Airport. He had a connecting shuttle directly from the city to Albany where Way Jalon was waiting for him.

Before the wheels of the aircraft touched down, Bossman felt the warmth of her touch. And felt her breath rush down his ear. A blue wind that carried her voice with the softest, electric touch. The azure zephyr brushed a wing gently against his brain . . . and he saw them. He couldn't help but stare. He was lost as he gazed deeply into the echo of her eyes.

# Pause Awakens

Pause always awoke from the recurring dream in a start, surprised by the intensity of its grip. A subtle tinge of animosity trembled through her at the callousness of her life, at what she would never be in an existence that was dictated by what she had become: death.

Yet she dreamed.

Little Eva hid from her father in her sister's closet, between a box of folded clothes and one filled with dirty laundry. His temper rampaged around the household on a daily basis, differing only in severity and form. Abuse wasn't a syndrome back then. It was only a formality, a consequence of being born female in a masculine world. It had been hours since her father had stomped around the house searching for her, angrily calling her name. Little Eva had prayed in her silence. Begged her higher power to stop him from finding her. Hitting her. Touching her.

She thought she heard the loud click of the front door downstairs, that maybe her father had left but she was afraid to leave her hiding place. She had made that mistake once before. Her father had gone to the front door and slammed it as if leaving. When she emerged from her hiding place, he was standing there, waiting. He strapped her to the bed, naked, and beat her until angry, red welts covered her bare behind. Then he touched her and stroked her while she cried, violating her while he told her what a bad girl she had been.

One by one, her illusions of happiness had been shattered by the truth of her father's brutality, by the pain of his voice and the fear of his footsteps.

Now she found comfort in the darkness of her sister's closet, safety in the quiet, and soon she was lulled to sleep.

She awoke to the sounds of creaking bedsprings and synchronized grunts. She froze. Listening. She couldn't identify the sounds. Or the voices.

She listened harder.

"Gentle at first. Mmmm!"

That voice registered. It was her sister.

"I know what I'm doing, baby . . . right there. Right?"

Who was that?! Little Eva inched the door open a crack. She could just see the bottom edge of the bed. The mattress was rocking, doing a strange dance to the sounds of moans and groans that seemed to crowd the room, getting louder and longer. But Little Eva couldn't see into the bed, couldn't see who was in the bed making those sounds. Doing whatever he was doing to her sister. All she saw was feet. Four feet. Twenty toes. Pointed downward. They stuck out over the edge of the bed and from her vantagepoint, Little Eva noticed a big toe that was black and germy. It was nasty. It looked as if a coat of dark smut had plastered itself to the nail and stayed there. Little Eva eyed it, fascinated, as she slowly rose to her feet. Careful to be quiet, Little Eva stood with her eyes opened wide in wondrous expectation, her senses sharpened. She felt the grooves in the wood as her fingers trailed up the wall. Her pupils widened and from darkness there came vision. The pants and groans grew in proportions and fell into the rhythm of time and place.

Little Eva saw.

She didn't know what it was, but she saw.

Kelly, her sister, was on the bed, naked, with a naked man. Kelly was on her hands and knees with the naked man kneeling behind her. With one hand, Kelly reached back and pulled the man closer. The man thrust harder and Kelly tilted her head back and groaned. The man leaned forward and kissed her neck, licked her ear. From the closet, Little Eva could see their tongues wrestling like pale snakes, and soon the two bodies found a new rhythm. Little Eva covered her eyes with her fingers, as her mind screamed, No! No! No!

"Fuck me, baby!"

Little Eva's eyes popped open and she looked again.

"Come on," she heard her sister cry. "Fuck me! A . . . little . . . harder."

So now it had a name. Fuck. That was a bad word. Well, not baaad, bad. It was sometimes bad. Little Eva couldn't help but think of all the times that she wanted to call her father that word. He used it so often, Little Eva considered it generic. It just seemed to fit him most of the time. Like a snakeskin.

Suddenly the room grew quiet, causing Little Eva to focus on the silence, straining, trying to see what her sister was doing in the bed. Then she heard a scratching sound. A flame flickered to life in the man's hand. He put the fire to the tip of a funny, twisted looking cigarette. He put the cigarette to his lips, inhaled and pushed his hips forward as he exhaled. Kelly looked back over her shoulder and pursed her lips. The man held the cigarette to her lips. She inhaled, then smiled and ground her hips back into him as the smoke escaped from her nose in small, billowing wisps.

The acrid smell of marijuana soon filled the room, catching Little Eva by surprise. It was an odor she had smelled before, at school in the dark corners of the playground. In secret. Her best friend, Susie, called it "mind benders" because some of the kids who did it sometimes came back from recess, bent. All silly and giggling with eyes as red as fire.

But why would her sister want to be bent? Little Eva had long ago given up trying to understand her sister. It wasn't that she and Kelly shared any real sisterly closeness; in fact, Kelly considered her more of a nuisance than anything. Kelly was a wild child, rebellious. She defied their father, even though the consequences could be painful, and dared to be free from his iron rule. Little Eva envied her sister's bravery.

"You know what to do, baby," she heard her sister moan.

The cigarette was gone but they hadn't changed their position. Kelly was still kneeling with the man behind her. She rocked gently as she spoke.

"You're good! But you're wild. C'mon. Give it to me." The man responded with a grunt and a thrust, meeting Kelly in the middle. Little Eva noticed the heaving of the man's chest, the rise and fall of it, as he rubbed his hand over her sister's body. He seemed to be trying to touch everything!

"You high?" he asked Kelly.

"Yes," she replied and the man suddenly picked up the pace. He bucked faster and faster. The bed squeaked frantically, trying to keep up with the staccato slapping of flesh against flesh. Little Eva watched as Kelly gritted her teeth and then traced her tongue over her lips. She closed her eyes and reached back for the man again.

"All of it! All of it! Mm, mm, mm," she groaned. Kelly put one hand against the headboard of the bed and pushed back frantically, meeting the man's thrusts. Her head was bowed with her long hair dangling down, obscuring her face.

A flash of silver danced in a sliver of moonlight that shone through the bedroom window, reflecting directly into Little Eva's eyes. Her mind pitched in panic when she saw the serrated edge of a knife in the man's hand. It was raised high over his head, and he brought it down in a vicious arc toward her sister's neck. Little Eva felt herself falling away in shock but her legs were wooden and her body was firmly frozen in place as her eyes remained riveted on the sight that her young mind told her was not happening.

The knife came down on the back of Kelly's neck and the point came out the other side. Eva heard a surprised gurgle escape from her sister's body even as the blade was savagely ripped from her throat. Kelly fell face-first on the bed, her naked body obscene from the intimate violence. Blood flowed in a thick stream through her clasping fingers, spreading dark stains over the sheets.

"Yeah, bitch!" the man yelled as he turned her body over. His eyes were big and mad. Little Eva's were, too.

"Never again," he cried and brought the knife down again, driving it into her chest over and over in a fanatical fit. It seemed like ages had passed before the man calmed himself enough to notice the splattered blood coating his naked body.

Kelly's chest was split wide open. The opening grew in proportion until it was a fissure, a chasm that glowed a hellish pin-blue. The man stepped away from the bed, taken aback at the strange cold that emanated from his victim. An eerie frost filled the room as Little Eva, more curious now than frightened, stared at the unreal drama that she witnessed. A chilling noise emitted from the hole in her dead sister's chest and Little Eva saw a slight movement. Suddenly, a frozen tiny hand reached out of the hole. Something quickly climbed out. It was a golem, a doll-sized man. He was very small but Little Eva saw his face in close-up. The miniature black man limped forward and looked Little Eva in the face. His eyes were slightly twisted and Little Eva noticed that his entire stomach was missing. She saw completely through him. A tiny white man was next out of the hole. He had garret marks around his neck and jelly for a right eye. After him came a dark-haired lady, but she looked perfectly fine. No bruises or cuts were visible on her body.

She had been poisoned. There was a toxicant substance inside the woman that had eaten its way into her stomach, lungs and heart and burned them into death.

Little Eva didn't know this fact.

Adult Eva did.

A dove flew out of the glowing opening of her sister's chest. It was a frozen blue-black color with a white face. It turned to look at Eva . . . and she felt her soul harden. On the dove's face . . . was a single, blue tear that froze midway down its face.

Pause always awoke from this night terror with a shout, sweat covering her body and soaking the sheets. It was a recurring dream that always seemed to shake her to the core. But once awake it meant nothing to her, its meaning a drowsy back-wash. It could be overcome, just as any other obstacle that threatened her path. She found joy in repetition.

Little Eva, even Adult Eva, only existed at the periphery of her memory now. They died a lifetime ago along with her father, her sister and her hopes for love. Everything is nothing and now there is only Pause. And a Pause would kill.

# You Sweat, You Live

He was going to have to be careful with that stuff, that Feenin. Having a modicum of control was of the utmost importance to Bossman, and he would never let any drug overcome his drive or threaten his well being. Harmful urges, the lusts of life, had been purged from his mind since the day he had become bull-headed and tightened his sphincter to the point where only air threatened to escape. No drug could change that.

But the Feenin was a strangely beautiful lady crying out in the night. She had beckoned him to the skies as the plane touched down, and he had risen from his seat and raised his arms to the heavens-he could fly! The flight attendant had brought him back down, breaking the siren-call of the beautiful lady, when she had said in a strange voice, "Are you okay, Sir?"

"Just stretching," he had answered without turning to face her.

Bossman walked down State Street among the tall, government buildings that seemed to have been designed with squares and transparency in mind. He turned south on Madison Avenue. The twin towers of the plaza loomed before him. They were big, blue structures of glass and steel that stretched across a four-lane street, connected by an overhead tunnel that funneled the privileged to and fro, eliminating the need to mingle with regular folk. A testament to money and the ego it sometimes bred.

Soon, Bossman contemplated, he would get himself an office on one of the higher floors-a huge one with a bathroom and a bedroom. A nice little spot to entertain women. Perhaps help enhance their performance. The thought excited him. He decided to go downtown and get himself a hooker after the meeting. The sixteenth floor would be an ideal location to live that life. Bossman knew, his instincts screamed, that the Feenin would explode. The same way that it exploded inside his brain when he had tried it. All of his blood had rushed out of him and into some secret place and in its stead, his heart had pumped pleasure, physical euphoria all over his body. Of course, his mind had to shift to an altered reality to handle such bliss and, amazingly, it landed on a spiritual plane that was parallel with his vibrating self. Bossman shook his head in wonder at the memory and thought, it's a good thing I'm not hooked on that shit.

On the fifteenth floor of the Plaza was the office of Way Jalon, the man who waited for Bossman to deliver the disks with the formula encoded on them. Way Jalon was money, old money, untouchable and defined by the power that went along with that stature. The Jalon fortune reached back in time to the Schuylers and Cornings-wealth that spanned generations and became imbedded by history into the very soil of Albany, New York. The Jalon family made its fortune in everything from shipping, hauling slave cargo and moving forward into the prosperous heyday of the city's industrial revolution to its modern-day ownership of a multitude of companies. There were stories of the founding father, William Jalon, that told of a ruthless and devious man who eschewed honor for money. It seemed to be a trait that was passed down through generations to Way Jalon.

Bossman knew the old badger was up there now, staring out of that glass wall of his. Every time that Bossman had been to Way Jalon's office, the self-proclaimed King of the City was always standing in front of that glass, staring out. Bossman imagined pulling him back to earth and then taking his place on the pedestal reserved for the powerful.

Rows of people crowded the street leading up to the huge, glass doors that accessed the concourse of the Plaza. Bossman plowed along with them down under the archway and on through the wall of glass doors that led into the Plaza concourse. He strode directly to the elevators and waited, looking up at the glowing numbers as the elevators went from floor to floor, all four of them avoiding the bottom landing.

The plane ride coasted into his thoughts.

Bossman had left John Zabriski dead in first class, with his seat belt securely buckled. He had made his getaway, leisurely checked through Customs and escaped to his waiting car. Zabriski had been a foolish man. He actually had believed that Bossman wasn't aware of the existence of the disks or the information encoded upon them. To add insult to injury, the poor man had the audacity to keep the disks in his possession. On him! Sometimes the smartest people-the brainiacs-could do the dumbest things. Zabriski had downloaded the information onto disks three days ago. Bossman had had him under surveillance for the previous five days. It had been too easy to take everything from him . . . his disks and his life.

Feenin had that effect. Feenin, that's what Zabriski had called it. It made the mind lazy. It was very disconcerting. One dose and there was a hot, sexy flash followed by an agitating hunger that would explode into tiny, bursting emotions. And it was all good. Bossman had caught sensitivity by the tail, saddled it and went splattering in every direction.

Yes. Bossman knew.

Ten minutes after Zabriski had gasped into death, curiosity had toyed with Bossman, challenged him into a gray zone, a no-man's land, a "sometimes" place where some people sometimes went and sometimes never returned. Bossman had popped one of the pills and took a trip without the luggage. His first journey sent him soaring to the north and he went for miles and miles before he returned, regretfully, to his body. Another pill . . . and Bossman raced west. He went east. South. Southeast. Northsouth. Westsouth. Bossman went every which way before the plane touched down. But when they landed, he didn't take another. There were still a few pills left in the bottle in his pocket.

The elevator arrived and when the door slid open, Bossman piled in with the crush of people who jammed themselves inside. He wouldn't touch the Feenin again, he resolved, because he could control his primal urges. Those destructive whims that tended to deprive the sane of what should be theirs. His iron will, his drive, was the reason he was Bossman.

The car stopped at the fifteenth floor and Bossman wedged his wide body toward the door. He occupied looming space as he moved forward. His presence preceded his mass as the other passengers turned and twisted to give him room to exit. A determined demeanor furrowed his brow, a single-mindedness that hid his intellectual capability. He stepped from the elevator and turned to his right, passing the door-ways of buzzing secretaries and vain, male drones.

Bossman snorted. They were nothing to him. College-educated and alumni-appointed with no real purpose in life. They were plodders, trudging from day to day, watching the grand picture of life on a two inch screen. They had no power. Power was the thing buried deep in Bossman's pocket. Computer disks with numbers and symbols, inscribed with a formula that might soon change the world.

He stopped at beveled glass doors that announced that these were the offices of Way Jalon, president of Jalon Holdings. Bossman stepped into a large room. A secretary sat behind a small desk at the farthest point from the door. She looked up at Bossman and reached for the phone. She mouthed a few words into the receiver, hung up and spoke to Bossman.

"Mr. Jalon will see you now." She indicated the huge wooden doors behind her. Bossman passed her without a glance and went inside.

Way Jalon stood in a far corner of his office, looking out of a huge wall of glass that overlooked the city, his back to Bossman. The office was rich. There was a wet bar to the left of Way Jalon, fully stocked, Bossman noted, which stood facing a set of futons that looked like a year's salary. The futons were plush, with big, stuffed cushions surrounded by leather. They each sat across from a lavish, high-backed, wooden chair that was obviously reserved for the great Way Jalon, a simple reminder of exactly who ran the ship, an unspoken confirmation of who held the reins of power. There were also two huge doors on that side of the room. Bossman had never seen them open nor had he ever seen anyone allowed past them. He wondered what secrets those rooms held.

When Way Jalon turned to face Bossman, a hint of a smile tugged at the corners of his mouth.

"How was your flight?" he asked.

"Successful," Bossman said simply.

"So," Way Jalon motioned to a chair facing the desk in the center of the room while he took his seat behind it, "can we proceed with the operation?"

"Absolutely," Bossman said as he settled into the hard, wooden chair.

Way Jalon was old money, what Bossman considered unearned income, accompanied by unearned respect. Way rose from his chair and strode over to the wet bar while Bossman took a moment to consider his new partner. Bossman saw an Armani suit, tailored to fit a forty-something-year-old back. A businessman with a cloying ability to smell where the money was to be made and a ruthless demeanor that would serve them both well. Here was a man who had transcended mere money and taken the giant step to magnate.

They had reached an agreement of mistrust immediately.

"Drink?" Way Jalon offered.

"No thanks."

Way Jalon came back with a Scotch in a fluted snifter and took his seat.

"So," he began, "where are we now?"

"I have the disks," Bossman replied. "That's my end of it. From this point forward there are only two players. You and I. There will never be a third party present whenever we meet. Acceptable?"

"Absolutely."

"Good. Is distribution in place?"

"On request. All that remains is the manufacture of the product." Way took a sip of his drink and waited.

Bossman paused but finally reached inside his pocket and produced the disks.

"Everything you need is on here." Bossman passed the disks across the desk. "I think we have a winner here. The profit will surpass your wildest dreams. That is, if this endeavor is handled correctly."

Way Jalon held the disks with the reverence of gold.

"There are two things that I never do," he said. "One is dream; the other is fail. That's where you come in. I need you to spearhead the day-to-day operations."

Bossman shot forward in his seat. This wasn't part of the deal, but Way Jalon stopped him with a raised finger.

"Don't worry. You will not have any official capacity. Your name will never appear on any books, anywhere. I want to minimize mistakes and maximize profits both quickly and quietly. You have a vested interest in this venture which should ensure your motivation and provide me with a degree of insurance also."

Bossman regarded Way Jalon with the suspicious eye of a trapped rat who suddenly realizes that there is no way out of a gilded snare.

"Is that really necessary?" Bossman asked.

"It's imperative."

"Well, I don't think it is."

"It's really quite simple," Way began. "You see, I don't trust people who have nothing to lose. Someone who has no reason to sweat will never be cognizant of the real value of water. No water, no life."

Way Jalon paused to look Bossman in the eye. "You sweat, you live."

"That's all well and good," Bossman replied. "Philosophically. But in realistic terms, I don't know if you've ever experienced a sweaty emotion in your entire lifetime, so I question your method."

Bossman looked around the lavish office at the expensive frills and perks and privileges before he spoke.

"But I don't question your abilities. Or the results you achieve. Let's make progress."

"You'll find that 'progress' is a pseudonym for success," Way Jalon said. "At least in my realm of expertise. My expertise . . . my knowledge . . . is what you need. It's what my fifty percent of this arrangement is costing you. So let me inform you of what you are paying for. Our success is dependent upon blind obedience. Specifically, your blind obedience, your ability to carry out any objective that I issue. No questions asked. Secondly, and this is of major importance, is that you must never let yourself become vulnerable to anyone or anything."

Way Jalon drained the remainder of his drink and walked over to the bar to pour another. He half-turned to speak to Bossman.

"Obviously, if a situation develops where you become a pawn to another, then you become my albatross and I simply cannot allow that."

Bossman watched intently as Way returned to his seat with his drink.

"If that happens, rest assured, you will go down in flames," Way Jalon finished, leaving no doubt about his warning. Bossman leaned back in his chair with unworried ease.

"But you know," he began, "anyone can catch fire and burn. Even you."

Way Jalon leaned forward. "So we have an agreement?"

"Agreed."

"Then let's move forward," Way replied. "This is how we move into the rarefied air of tax-free millions . . ."

Approximately one hour later Bossman made his way out of the Plaza with a grudging respect for Way Jalon's business acumen and a gnawing suspicion that he had just jumped from the frying pan headlong into the fire.

# Ten Letters

Way Jalon stood by the window, looking out over his city. The window ran the entire length of one wall of his office on the fifteenth floor of the Plaza. The glass, clear and thick, was tinted blue by its width. Strong and safe, it would almost hold up to the force of a bullet. This was just one of the perks granted to him as one of the most powerful men in the city. There had been problems with the construction. The glass wasn't up to code-it wasn't nearly thick enough, but Way Jalon could change codes. Zip codes, if necessary. So he had his wall.

Way Jalon was a man of success, a descendant of wealth. The first Jalon touched the shores of New York along with the Schuylers and Livingstons and Van Rensselaers. William Jalon came up the Hudson River by boat and straggled off the pier into the woods. He walked up to the biggest tree he could find and flung his arms as far around the thick trunk as he could. He looked skyward and proclaimed, "You are all mine!"

Way Jalon paused to reflect on his family's history, a city's history for all intents and purposes. He looked through the glass to the south. Downtown, past North Pearl Street, exit ramps looped up into the sky over the Hudson River and came down in East Greenbush and Rensselaer. The long and winding river snaked narrowly between Albany and the eastern side of the state at this juncture before it wiggled and twisted its way down to New York City.

Way could almost see William Jalon embracing a huge birch tree while anointing himself king. That birch tree would become part of the first ship William Jalon put underway. William Jalon amassed a fortune in a hurry, beginning with shipping, transporting anything that fit on board. He built whaling ships that operated out of Hudson, a small town that thrived from the fishing industry.

From there, William Jalon prospered. As his fortune grew he began to hunger for something more. Power. He wanted a city. He wanted his name stamped on a map. He spent the rest of his life gobbling up anything money could buy and destroying what it couldn't in his drive to rule over all.

William Jalon bestowed his dream upon his two sons, Seth and Blaize, who carried it on wholeheartedly. The two brothers stepped their father's goals up to a new level. They dreamed bigger. They were industrious and greedy-an effective combination-and together they reached into the guts of the workingman's life, via politics and pocketbooks. They bought mayors, they shaped laws and enforced their bottom line. Their whims became facts-laws that had force every day on every street in Albany.

They had what they wanted but they still yearned for more.

The Jalon brothers kissed fate when they stumbled into the slave trade. They had an abundant fleet that could move the human cargo quickly and efficiently, which led them to open offices in every state on the East Coast.

The Jalon brothers raked the money in by the shipload, and the legacy grew as it was passed from generation to generation, down to the present Jalon: Way.

Way Jalon wanted to add his own chapter to the story.

The glass wall was indicative of his stature, as was his office. It was huge. Bigger than some homes, and at times Way had spent weeks on end there. There was a bed in a comfortable-sized room through a set of double oak doors adjacent to a fully-stocked wet bar in the far corner. An assemblage of two futons and a high-backed wooden chair sat directly across from the bar, which was where Way Jalon negotiated his most important business matters. Over drinks, drugs, women . . . whatever it took, terms were set and agreements were made there. In front of the window-wall sat a huge desk. A small, uncomfortable chair faced the desk, a seat for his subjects as they came begging favors. The entrance to his office stood some fifteen feet away over a solitary expanse of carpet. It was a horribly long and lonely distance to cover, a walk which gave Way a chance to intimidate the peasants by staring intently at them as they approached his kingly throne. He usually had a plan in mind before they reached him, and as he extended his hand to greet them, he had already decided their fate.

The window-wall afforded Way Jalon the chance to oversee what he owned, his land, his empire. Way saw the big picture, which was why he needed a big window. His vision was wide, panoramic, encompassing large pieces of the puzzle that smaller-minded people failed to grasp, even if he glued it to their fingers. But the pieces always fit. His many businesses spread over the city like a suffocating blanket, but Way knew that he alone was the only man who could make it breathe. With but a touch and a command.

But Way felt the urge to go higher. Scale bigger mountains. So naturally he couldn't let this opportunity slip by. Not on his life. This was going to be pure, worldwide power. Feenin. A drug so new it wasn't illegal yet, and by the time it became a crime to use it, its destructive effects would be evident and its momentum too strong to stop. And Feenin didn't cost much to manufacture. The expense had been cut down to almost fifty-five cents per pound! Way Jalon introduced the Feenin to the world, well, not the world, but to a test market of drug users, at fifteen dollars a pop, thereby undercutting the twenty-dollar cost of crack, and the fiends came running. And it was surprising to identify some of the worst fiends. The affluent were expected. The poor, again, were expected. But the middle ground was terrible. Terrible eyes. Terrible needs. Wonderful money.

Feenin was hot. It had spread beyond the sample users like wildfire and now Way Jalon had to adjust and move his plan slightly ahead of schedule. Positive adjustments were easy for him to accommodate and a joy to implement. He sometimes whistled while he did this work.

Way Jalon smiled out the window-wall and thought, I have their lives. He turned from the wall of glass and looked down at the sheet of paper on his desk. A name was scribbled on it that represented the first squashed bug that he would step on as he climbed to the top. His mind pointed and counter-pointed any difficulties that might arise from that hastily-sprawled name. He had left nothing to chance. Everything and everyone connected to that name was a bit in the data banks of Way's brain. The name was a man, and the man is an animal. The male animal was the most difficult to predict when no rules and regulations existed. When the male animal sensed the absence of protocol, his whim became law and the consequence became survival of the fittest. His very ferocity toward life made him the most unpredictable and wildest in his own jungle.

While Way Jalon had a grudging respect for the man behind the name-those people surely had courage-it was a respect tinged with animosity. Way glanced at the huge oak doors next to the wet bar. He kept his anger there, behind closed doors where his expression could be free. A forbidden room that housed a haunting portion of his legacy, handed down through generations in hushed tones and kept alive by its legitimacy. Way shared his secret with no one and guarded it with fervency. Entrance through those doors was prohibited and no mistakes of entry were tolerated.

Way thought about the man who would become a part of the legacy. The ten letters. Yet there was no room in his regard for any type of underestimation. Herbert Mulne had held the man in low esteem, and had paid with his life. Not that Way attached any significance to the intellect of Herbert Mulne, known as Five-O to the criminal element that he moved amongst. He was a greedy, unimaginative little man whom Way had known since his college days. Herbert's pathetic, little intellect had ended up on a cop's payroll, stealing and swiping when he could, while Way had gone on to amass a fortune. Herbert had thought he was untouchable, because he was a cop, but he had paid the devil's fortune. Years of payoffs; taking drug dealers' money before sending them to jail; physically abusing the defenseless; just to let off steam, had all come back to visit him and left him lifeless. He had been found dead beside his car on someone's lawn. How appropriate.

Way hadn't really liked Herbert but he didn't need to. They conducted business with a mutual disrespect and a harsh dislike for one another, yet they got things done. Herbert had come through again with the delivery of this man, the ten letters that were spelled out across the paper on Way's desk. Way looked down again. This guy was perfect. He would take a big fall and be speechless, defenseless and completely dumbfounded when he heard the giant splat.

Way had a plan. First, Way intended to remove the man from his habitat, his element, get him away from the ghetto. Take him, body and soul, from his lifestyle of bleakness and hopelessness to a morning of roses and fresh pussy and watch his instincts fall away with the finality of a warm death. Way would attack the animal at the base of his confidence, at his very existence. His strength.

Way stared at the name. It was an important component of the plan.

Phase One included appointing this man as the head of operations and distribution of Stoneway Incorporated, unaware that he would be a high-tech drug dealer with all the trimmings . . . and all of the accountability.

Phase Two involved preparing the Feenin for nationwide distribution. Way had converted two warehouses into labs in order to manufacture the drug in massive quantities if needed and they were up and running. Since only two labs were in production, distribution was an integral component of the operation, a vital part, and there was no room for miscalculations.

Way had decided to go all out. He would move the product in massive quantities by every available means-trucks, planes, couriers-and he would even do a few special deliveries. At the moment Feenin had a nonlegal status, no laws were being broken. But that loophole wouldn't stay open long and Way Jalon had to be prepared for the sly manipulation of the law. Authority didn't really apply to him. No court could hold him, but it could be so predictable that it could often create surprise out of the mundane. Ask O.J. He had escaped the monotonous long arm of the law with a painful backhand to the face of America, with a force that sung, aimed at its unjust justice system.

Way Jalon read the name again. Ten letters. He counted his at worse; he only had eight letters. Maybe, Way figured, he should use someone else. Someone like Chris Rock, or maybe Clarence Thomas . . . Nooo! That would be too easy. These ten letters had heart. His story was one of sheer determination. His man had started selling drugs at the age of seventeen, in the streets all hours of the night, and yet he had still managed to graduate near the top of his class in high school.

His parents were nowhere to be found but he survived, utterly alone, as he moved with direction into college. What Way Jalon found amazing was that the young man had never been caught. He had absolutely no criminal record, not even a misdemeanor charge. At the university, the young man seemed to surge even higher. He went through college as if he had caught the tail of a tiger, tearing through four years at one of the best universities in the state. His nightlife remained the same, however; he sold drugs to the drugged.

That was where Herbert had found him. On a street corner selling drugs. Herbert had done a background check and brought him to Way Jalon's attention. Now that Herbert Mulne was dead, Way had to carry out the remainder of his plan himself. He would have to meet the target and offer him the biggest break of his life, a chance to move into a higher tax bracket. Way hated to get personally involved but this time it was unavoidable. The fewer people involved, the better.

Way Jalon would take this man.

Studies proved that he couldn't stand. For anything! The numbers were there and statistics are the basis of reality. A professional baseball player who can hit three out of every ten pitches is hitting three hundred percent. Miss seven out of ten balls and make millions. It's all basis.

Numbers don't lie.

There are more African-American men in America's prisons than there are in America's colleges.

They wear numbers.

In this great country of his, a Negro has never been counted among the fifty richest people in the nation.

Not one.

Most black people wore handcuffs on the evening news. Nightly.

Way Jalon would take this man.

When he had briefed Bossman on the architecture of the operation, its two levels- legal and illegal-he hadn't told him about this man. He saw no reason to mention it. Strike one on Bossman.

Way Jalon would use one business to power the other. Nationwide, if necessary.

Stoneway Incorporated would have its hand in everything. From stationery-letters packed with Feenin-to grain-trucks designed to carry flour would instead be loaded with white pills. The culprit of Stoneway Incorporated had already been hand picked and investigated. He was perfect. A former drug dealer with a college education. Someone who could always be pointed at with an accusing finger. Way picked the piece of paper off the desk and smiled at the name, scrawled there, like fate. Ten letters.

The first five read, T-O-K-U-S.

# Snapshot

The blinking light of his private line caught Way's eye. He reached for the phone expecting to hear a familiar voice. "Way," he said into the mouthpiece.

"Pause," a female voice answered.

Pause was a sexy, sick woman. Her beauty, the deep blue eyes that held men stiff, the sensual figure that moved with the promise of a pleasure pulled slowly from deep within and the powerful air of femininity that she wore like expensive perfume, was truly beguiling. She wore her long, blond hair in a variety of styles, each appealing and complementing a face that held the eye just a fraction of a second longer than the libido needed. What she was blessed with on the outside only hid the curse that bred inside of her. She was a cold-hearted, twisted killer behind a stiffened, skin-toned mask. She was the perfect assassin . . . with a deadly smile. Way thought it best to keep her at a distance. That was why she was one of the few people allowed to use his private line. Pause affected him. She disrupted his mind with lust. It was a craving Way recognized and knew there was no controlling, so he dealt with her over the phone as much as possible.

"What have you found?" Way asked. Sounds of street traffic droned on the background so he knew she was at a pay phone. Pause preferred public phones. She felt she could speak freely in the open spaces they provided.

Way Jalon had assigned Pause to watch Bossman. Way was suspicious by nature, but in Bossman he saw an especially evil intent which always led to downfall. Besides, anyone who dared to attempt to play on an even field with Way became a target of ill will. Way considered himself a polished professional and Bossman a complete brute. An animal. And like any beast, Way figured, he would be intoxicated by physical sensations-be it booze, drugs, skydiving, fire-walking . . . whatever. Bossman would live through the rush, the glow of feeling, the joy of pleasure and plunge headlong into the next kaleidoscope of tingles, flushed with excitement and looking for more. Now Way's intuition was proving true.

She had been watching him for the past two days and this was her first report. Pause was a heavy hitter. Insidiously psychotic, she loved to hit things and make them die. He had hired her many times.

"You and Bossman must have a really sweet deal," she said. Way heard the loud squeal of a big vehicle braking to a stop.

"And that concerns you?" Way demanded. She was overstepping.

"It's just that Bossman has been on a drugging and whoring binge since I got on him," Pause answered. "I figured you sent him to drugs and whores, whores and drugs until he dropped."

"Did he drop?" Way asked hopefully.

"No," Pause answered. "But he does talk quite a bit. Hold on." Way listened as Pause growled at someone.

"No!"

"I can tell! I see you!" Way heard a feminine voice exclaim.

"I said, 'no!'" Pause repeated.

"I just wanted to meet you. We can do it," the voice pled.

"If you don't get the fuck away from me, I'll hurt you! Now fuck off!"

Pause returned, "Okay."

Here it comes, Way thought. The real reason Pause had buzzed him on his urgent private line, the real situation that would probably result in the setting free of someone's soul. Strike two, Bossman.

"What is he talking about?" Way asked.

"I caught up to the hooker Bossman had last night and I paid her to do me. Afterwards, I asked her about Bossman. She said he liked to get high. She said he had some different kind of drug . . . not cocaine. It looked like cocaine but she knew a coke high and this wasn't it. It felt different, tasted different when it drained back down her nostrils into her mouth. But when Bossman snorted it, he got freaky deaky on her. She said they were rutting like animals. He put her on top and grabbed her by the ass and just started poking up in her and grunting and friction and she thought he started barking, so she started barking and . . ."

"Get to the point, will you!" Psychotic bitch, Way thought.

"Well, I enjoyed the moment," Pause said. "Anyway, she said that right in the middle of the rutting, Bossman would stop bucking and start talking. He told her about this new drug called Feenin and about how it was coming soon to a theater near you. And if she had a snapper, if her sex was good enough, she could clamp it onto his rod and ride to the top with him."

Way didn't even think about it.

"Take him," he ordered.

Pause gasped with joy.

"But I don't want a mess on this one," he amended. Pause could sometimes get carried away with her work. "Don't let it come back on us. And make sure the police never find a trace of the Feenin. The product isn't ready for public exposure. Clear?"

Pause hesitated. Way waited patiently, listening to the street sounds that seeped from the city into the phone to his ear. He knew Pause had trouble with orders that required restraint.

"Clear?" Way repeated.

"Clear," she sighed.

"And Pause? Try to be gentle," Way added oddly.

"Like a snapshot," came the reply.

"While you're at it, take out the whore, too."

"Already did," Pause answered before she hung up.

# Simpleton Brick

Way strode confidently through the halls of the university up to Convention Hall in time to watch the newest crop of graduates cross the stage. He had a singular purpose for being there, a grand design that had caused him to leave his office and ride the long stretch of Washington Avenue to the university-to observe Tokus Stone. Tokus Stone needed to be handled personally and delicately, gently steered and manipulated. Way Jalon left nothing to chance.

As diplomas were being handed out, Way came through the huge double doors and stood off to the side, watching and listening, amused as the gaiety of the event hovered thickly in the air. A celebration bubbled slightly under the surface of the moment, waiting for a signal to vent itself late into the night. The smiles of happiness would fade into oblivion if those young people knew of the harsh jungle they were entering. A wilderness with teeth, for some, while others would ascend mountains, but each would come at a cost that would leave deep, serpentine marks. After all, a diploma was just a piece of paper that hung unread on the office wall.

"Tokus Stone," an amplified voice announced.

Out stepped the object of Way's desire. Way put Tokus at about six feet, two inches tall, approximately two hundred pounds. Two-ten maybe. His face held a rugged determination that suggested graduation was only the beginning, that the stage he walked across was the starting line, not the finish. There was no hint of the foolish joy that was usually exhibited at a moment like this. None of the dancing and yelling that the other graduates saved for center stage. This was just a secondary triumph. He knows, Way mused. He knows that society is out there, waiting for him with a blindfold in one hand and a dagger in the other, smiling.

Soon, they would meet face-to-face.

After the caps were tossed into the air and the crowd had settled into a reasonable hubbub of excited activity, Way Jalon searched the throng for his quarry. He spotted Tokus standing alone in a far corner of the auditorium and began nudging people aside as he made a beeline in that direction.

Way cornered Tokus and greeted him with congratulations.

"Mr. Stone, may I be the first to add my 'well done' to your list of accomplishments." He offered his hand.

Tokus looked at him, surprised, recovered and shook his hand firmly. "Thank you."

"Mr. Stone," Way continued. "My name is Way Jalon, president of Jalon Holdings . . . I'm sure you've heard the name before. I'm here to make you an offer."

Tokus turned his full gaze upon the distinguished-looking man who stood before him. An air of money and power clung to him, those things no longer a privilege but a birthright.

"My company, Jalon Holdings, has been watching your progress at the University for the past two years, and we were impressed with your tenacity and decision-making. Your degree is well-earned. Your grades are excellent, and you have the presence of leadership that, combined with a thinking man's ability, impressed us greatly."

"Well . . ." Tokus seemed at a loss. "Thank you."

"Combine those talents with another factor that we require and you are, by far, our best candidate."

"What factor is that?"

"You are a black man."

Tokus rocked back, his eyes narrowed. He looked Way Jalon in the eye before he answered.

"The blackness is a plus, huh?"

"Yes." Way looked at Tokus. "I'm sure you have some idea of the complex world of high finance, it's high pressure, high income, and immensely diverse. Indeed, it is mostly a separate entity from the rest of the world. It's also very, very exclusive."

Way paused importantly, measuring his words with a casualty that belied his purpose.

"You see, Tokus, even in the rarefied air of the 'haves,' we are still subject to the whims of public opinion, the 'have nots.' Affirmative action is one of those flights of fancy. So we comply. In our concession, however, we have only one certainty that allows us to proceed with surety. That certainty is ability. Your ability, Tokus. As I said, we've been watching you and we are quite sure that you have what it takes to get the job done."

Tokus was silent.

"Listen," Way continued. "Tonight is your night to celebrate and I've taken up enough of your time, so here's my card. I'll be expecting to hear from you soon. You come to my office and we'll talk more."

Tokus took the business card and put it in his pocket.

Way extended his hand to Tokus. "Once again, congratulations."

Tokus shook his hand firmly and looked him in the eye. "I appreciate your candor. And I'll give this a lot of thought."

"That's all I can ask." Way smiled, turned and walked away.

T'Challa and Doria, with Monday in tow, passed Way as they approached Tokus.

T'Challa looked into Way's eyes and felt the frost of privileged insensitivity bred by voluntary isolation from a warm, passionate world. Instinctively, he reached for Monday as they walked toward Tokus. Doria rushed into Tokus' arms with a big hug. "You did it," she cried. "You made it."

"Was that the man?" T'Challa asked, indicating the retreating figure of Way Jalon.

"He offered me a job," Tokus replied.

"You da man!" Monday squealed. Tokus squatted so that he was eye level with his nephew.

"No, you da man!"

"You da man!"

"No, you da man!"

"UH-UH. You. Da. Man!"

Tokus extended his fist toward the little boy.

"Slap my hand, black soul man," he said. They tapped fists and Monday rushed into his arms. T'Challa detected a tear in his brother's eye before Tokus released his son. T'Challa was surprised at how quickly Doria and Monday had accepted Tokus as part of the family. Tokus seemed so genuine in his feelings toward them with his yearning for a family, that when the affection was returned, it all seemed like a natural fit.

"You gonna take the job?" T'Challa asked.

"Maybe."

"The man."

"Yeah. You felt it, too?"

"What kinda job did he offer?" T'Challa asked.

"We didn't get into specifics," Tokus said. "It wasn't an official interview."

"The man," T'Challa repeated.

"Yeah," Tokus agreed. "But he was kinda straight with me. He needs a token black to balance his ledger."

T'Challa mulled that one over for a minute.

"Just don't let him hit you in the head with a simpleton brick," he advised.

"That's not possible," Tokus replied.

"Remember, they don't have to play you," T'Challa said. "But they can play everybody around you like a Milli Vanilli song and then drop you like a bad bag of dope."

"True that," Tokus replied. "True that."

# A Pause Can Kill

Bossman was high. High on life. Greed. Pleasure. And Feenin.

Every time he used Feenin he discovered new attributes that elated him with wonder. Dollar signs floated past his twisted, bloodshot eyes-so many that he had stopped counting hours ago.

Bossman had a bag of powdered Feenin on the nightstand next to the bed. He had gotten it from a warehouse that had been converted for the production of Feenin. It was coming out of there by the pound. Any day now they would be going into full distribution and the windfall would be large. He was sampling large amounts of the drug on a daily basis; an ounce here, an ounce there. He didn't have to answer to anyone and all his jaded eyes could spy success, looming on the horizon.

Way Jalon had chosen well when he decided to manufacture Feenin in a row of warehouses that moved product constantly. Every day, all day, huge trucks would leave the many buildings carrying all manner of Feenin-packed merchandise.

The shipments took place on a fairly, normal business day, on a fairly normal schedule.

He felt a movement next to him in the huge, canopied bed that was part of the honeymoon suite he had reserved. The room was huge and elegant. Bossman wondered what the rest of the suite looked like. He had taken the woman from the door directly to the bed without a glance in either direction and taken her warm body until it glowed as red hot as he was.

He felt the girl next to him stir. Bossman stirred, too, when his mind replayed the things this girl-what is her name?-had done to him last night.

"Mmmm," she purred as she reached for Bossman. He smiled at her and reached over to the nightstand for the bag of granulated Feenin and scooped some up his nose. Two sniffs sped to his brain and everything opened. He had an idea.

The girl was sitting up now, her eyes aglitter and focused on the freakish substance.

"Let's do what we did," she pouted, "last night."

"No," Bossman said. "Let's go a little higher." His pupils were turning strangely vertical, straight up and down, as he eyed the girl anew, wondering where he had gotten her but ecstatic that he had her. She was thick, like a black woman-breasts standing proud, hips, waist, ass, all pliable and plush.

"Are you sure you don't have any nigger in you, girl?" He reached under the covers and cupped her ass.

"No," she answered. She looked at Bossman, then at the bag in his hand and back at him again.

"So what do you think about my product?" Bossman asked the girl. "How do you like it?"

"What is it?"

"I call it Feenin. It's synthetic. I made it myself. It's fucking great, isn't it? I even like it myself. But unlike the junk that's out there now, this substance doesn't damage your body. There are no side effects."

He paused to scoop a tiny spoonful out of the bag, and waited with his hand in midair.

"It comes in powdered form, liquid or 'rocked' into pill form. But for you . . ." Bossman put the spoon over his pubic hair and tapped the powder out. He continued, "It can be ingested, smoked or sniffed." The spoon came out of the bag again as the girl went into action, her tongue eagerly darting here and there in his hair, then on him. Bossman sniffed the powder and relaxed as he watched her work. Inch by inch, warm friction enveloped him and from there she worked by feel and instinct. She moved slowly, carefully and smoothly, pausing to get every speck of the soft, white powder. Finally, she seemed satisfied that it was all gone, and with a sensuous stare, she began a touching crawl up to his chest. The feel of her skin on his bare flesh pulsed wherever she touched and when she kissed him, her tongue demanded submission. She traced her tongue over his lips.

"Bitchin,'" Bossman whispered, smiling at the girl who sat astride him. "You will be gentle with me, right?"

"If you are," she replied.

"I'll hold you to that."

Bossman dipped the spoon again and brought it to her nose. She took the hit. Bossman snorted the rest in one shot. She paused a moment, waiting for her brain to ignite, and when it did, she smiled and reached back to guide Bossman inside her. Once inside, Bossman went deep, but only once as he grabbed her around the waist and held her there. She groaned and bit his shoulder, leaving a mark. She started sucking the mark. Then they rocked. Slowly. Gently. Bossman felt her sheer walls come tumbling down like Jericho and the speed of her hips start moving much faster than "gentle." He had to slow her down. He grabbed her by both ass cheeks and held her motionless. His fingers sank into the firm, round lobes, and he couldn't help but linger there a moment. The urge for a nipple crept upon him and soon his lips found one. He kneaded and nibbled. Sucked and licked. He looked up at her and said, "Now this is foreplay," before returning to his milking post. She placed her hand on the back of his head and guided him with squeezes and taps and rubs. Bossman leaned back and peered between their bodies and watched, enraptured by the clash of the sexes. A hard, moist, warm exchange that brought an inkling. The inkling tripped an alarm inside him. She swayed and plunged on top of him; she was on fire. Inside. A fire that twisted in a circular urgency. Her muscles gripped him with a lustful, hot crush.

Suddenly, Bossman felt red, hot flame rushing from his stomach back up his throat. He coughed and felt the burn whistling in his nasal cavity, past his eardrums and straight to his brain. The girl began to gag. Her lustful cries became agonizing fits of convulsions as she sat atop Bossman and dug her fingernails into his neck. Bossman mouthed a "What the . . ." But the words came out in a fetid rush of dead air. His heart began beating in jackhammer sequence and his body tightened. Immobility seized him, except for the staccato tics of a retarded spasm, and bile rushed to the back of his mouth with every burst of his speeding heart. His bowels released. His last thought before dying was of what he had lost. His money, not his life.

A dark, slim figure darted into Bossman's hotel room, quietly closing the door behind her, listening for any sounds, and watching for any movement. When satisfied that nothing was stirring, the figure moved softly to the nightstand at the side of the bed. A shaft of light peeked into the room and illuminated her darkened face. She seemed unfazed by the horrid surroundings. The bed was full of squalor. It smelled of the chaos of vomit, blood, sex and seared guts, all straining to stain the satin sheets in a deathly art motif. A bloody tear ran from the corner of the girl's eyes. Murder was strange art. Calmly, she surveyed the filth and naked death sprawled before her. The dead no longer held surprise.

Now she worked quickly. She replaced the tainted bag of Feenin with a large bag of pure cocaine. She had poisoned the Feenin with an exotic, rare, crystalline substance that was virtually undetectable and mimicked the symptoms of a heart attack. Tenderly, she lifted Bossman's dead hand and forced the bag into it, effectively fingerprinting the bag and placing it on the table. She stopped to look down at the bloody tear on the girl's face and smiled. Not everyone appreciated art, its powerful emotion, with the proper respect. But Pause did. The Feenin, she put in her pocket. Visually, she checked for any spots where the Feenin might have fallen but she saw none. The silver spoon lay on the bed near Bossman. That also went into her pocket. Done, she thought and headed for the door. She eased into the hallway, checking in both directions and sauntered next door to her room.

Once inside, she picked up the phone and punched in seven digits. It was picked up on the second ring.

"Way," the voice said.

"Pause," she answered.

The phone went dead in her hand.

# Stoneway

Way Jalon stood looking out the window of his office as the sun shone down with favor on his property, the entire city of Albany, New York. He had a drink in his hand, a victory splash in the morning to celebrate the winning of the day. In a few moments, Mr. Tokus Stone would come walking into his office and become the biggest pawn that Way had ever played in his economic game of rape and plunder.

Tokus Stone of Stoneway, Inc.

That had a melodic ring to it and Way was sure that Tokus would hear the musical notes in the title. Blacks are creative that way.

Stoneway, Inc. would be a commercial hub, moving product from here to there with Tokus Stone at the helm. All types of product, from high-tech components to potato chips, would move with a Tokus Stone thought.

But the Feenin belonged to Way, the synthetic substance was the wave of the future and he owned the entire beach, from sea to shining sea. Nothing illegal about it . . . yet!

Therein lay the reason for the need of a Tokus Stone, a nigger, a jigaboo with high-falutin' ideas. Basic in his existence and necessary only by some big mistake.

Feenin was an unknown quantity that would soon be renowned for its smell, taste, feel and name. When it became a physical entity-a bad habit with a name-someone would have to take the fall for the phenomenon that would sweep the streets of the nation. It would be Tokus Stone of Stoneway, Inc.

Had a nice ring to it, actually.

The phone on his desk beeped. His secretary's voice came through the box. "Mr. Jalon, your nine o'clock is here."

Way pressed the button. "Give me a moment."

He strode over and put his drink on the wet bar, gave his city one last look over, went back to the desk and pressed the button.

"Okay, Connie," Way Jalon said. "Caveat Emptor."

The secretary turned to Tokus Stone, who was looking around the room. "Mr. Jalon will see you now."

"Thanks," Tokus said and pushed through the office door.

Way Jalon watched the young man as he approached, noting a determined stride and the set of the bright eye that had been turned on, machinelike. The eye that saw and heard everything. Way was sure he had made the correct choice in Tokus Stone.

They shook hands and exchanged amenities before getting down to business.

"Do you remember our first meeting, Mr. Stone?"

"Explicitly," Tokus replied.

"And you can see the advantages of joining our corporation as an executive of Stoneway? This would be your baby, from birth to infinity, with all the controls in place."

"Sounds like a perfect setup," Tokus said. "As long as it's not a setup to fail."

"Mr. Stone. Tokus. I don't, I repeat, do not want you to fail. Success is imperative. I'm not in the business of losing money. When I spoke to you of our needs for a black man for this position, I did not mean to imply that a black man would just 'have' this position. Tokenism is, after all, just a word. Not a faith. Not a belief. Not some anonymous creed to live by. It's just a word. Business comes in one hue, one color. Not black, not white. Just good old-fashioned green. Green moves obstacles and constructs mountains out of molehills-thousands of them. The question is: Can you build a mountain of your own?"

"I've been climbing them all my life," Tokus answered coldly. "The biggest obstacle I've ever encountered have been the sub-humans."

Way arched an eyebrow in question.

Tokus continued. "Ahh . . . I see you aren't familiar with that particular race of people. Let me enlighten you. The sub-humans are a race of people with concept problems. Their vision is skewered. They can't see. When they look at a man, any man that is different from them, they see something evil . . . something inferior. They see something other than what is so painfully obvious. They don't see a man. They see the skin he's in."

Tokus leaned forward and looked Way Jalon in the eye. "I need to meet every key man that you have on staff. If you've hired any sub-humans, I want to shake them loose. Is that acceptable to you?"

Way paused only for a fraction of a second before answering. "It's your show, Tokus. Whatever you want. Whatever you feel is necessary."

Now Way leaned forward behind his huge desk and gave Tokus the hard eye. "Just don't waste my money."

They had reached an agreement.

Way went on to give Tokus the lay of the land, bare bones information about structure and personnel, procedure and company policies, projections and profits. Way was grudgingly impressed with Tokus' intellect. He had an astutely curious mind that soaked in knowledge and logically placed it into its proper context. Tokus had a competent hand.

Way was determined to see if he could shake it.

They had been talking for hours and lunch was fast approaching. Way leaned back in his chair with his fingers steepled under his chin.

"Tell me something, Tokus," he began. "When I find something fascinating, I have to ask questions and this is something only you can answer. Enlighten me. Exactly how does it feel to be a black man in America?"

Tokus waited.

Way raised a hand in supplication. "Don't misinterpret my question. I ask it with honest curiosity and no evil intentions . . . I'm not being deceptive. But African-Americans are really in the most unique position of any race in this country."

Tokus waited quietly.

Way continued. "I must admit, though, you are the first black man I've ever spoken more than two words with. I see them on the news and they don't look hospitable. Sometimes they even have cuffs on . . . negative images abound! But I'm a logical man and I know this can't be factual, so I wonder. Again, enlighten me."

A moment passed between the two men before Tokus spoke.

"Mr. Jalon," Tokus replied. "I'd best describe being a black man in America as being an apple hanging on a tree. It's a big orchard, so basically it's just a matter of hanging out with all the other apples waiting for the man to come and pluck you. When that doesn't happen, if that doesn't happen, you just hold on, hanging there until you rot off. If you drop . . . you're apple cider. The tragedy occurs to you right before the inevitable 'splat.' It comes in a flash. This had to happen."

"Well, that's a pretty dire existence," Way responded.

Tokus chuckled. "No, Mr. Jalon. What's dire is the idea that someone could explain their existence in a few sentences. Explain their life and ideals and their sense of right and wrong in five minutes or less. Me? I'm strictly new generation, Mr. Jalon. Bred on mind power and strength of heart-I don't just hold on. And tragedy! Tragedy is a story told by the victorious."

Tokus paused to fix Way Jalon in his stare.

"I'm sure you could tell your share of tragedies, Mr. Jalon. And I'm also sure that you have no shortage of apple cider."

# Vertical Eyes

Tokus looked down at the mark on the floor. It read: "The bull starts here." And he toed the line and threw a dart. He didn't care what he scored; he just felt happy and prosperous. Stoneway, Inc. had been under his guidance for a scant three months and Tokus felt fully in control. The only fly in his ointment had been Way Jalon, the man himself. In a few instances, he had found himself being second-guessed and his orders overridden by Way Jalon. That in itself wasn't that bothersome-he supposed that the man with the most to lose would be the one with the most nits to pick-but the very nature of Way's demands were contradictory and seemed counterproductive to what needed to be done.

On occasion, Tokus felt that he had come close to stepping over the line with Way Jalon. Way wanted to send out forty-eight of the fifty trucks from the warehouse in Industrial Park on one of his "private deals," their destination unknown. Way had done the same on a few separate runs, each time setting Tokus further and further behind schedule. But this deal would cost Tokus dearly and he refused to allow it. He stormed into Way's office and made demands.

"Either one of two things will happen: I succeed, or you fire me. But I won't lose because you won't let me do my job. I need those trucks. They're mine."

Way was furious but in the end he relented.

For the most part, however, Way Jalon had remained true to his word and let Tokus deal with a free hand.

Success had finally found him and Tokus intended to hold on to it for dear life.

He felt that a celebration was in order, a kiss to the fulfillment of optimistic dreams, to the fruition of hope. Tokus ended up at a corner bar, playing darts and drinking beer, enjoying himself in silent triumph . . . and a second beer buzz.

"You can't beat me." A sultry voice, one that demanded attention, pulled Tokus in its direction and his eyes feasted while his heart raced to keep pace. She was a picture. The kind of woman that was a figment of the imagination and had to be sketched on paper before the illusion slipped away. She wore a black miniskirt that fit her snugly, not too revealing, and a beige top with a plunging neckline that held a promise that begged to be whispered. Her eyes were wonderful; sexy and deep and Tokus found himself at a loss, speechless for the first time in recent memory.

"Holy smokes and gees, girl," he stammered.

She laughed.

"Did I say that out loud?" Tokus asked her.

She smiled and nodded her head. She was one beautiful black woman. Chocolate. Her hair hung in curls almost down to her shoulders, framing her face, eyes and full, lush lips. He imagined she could drain a man of pain and anger and then fill him with the pleasure of having her. Especially if she was touched in the most intimate way.

"What's your name?" Tokus asked.

"Parise," she answered sweetly.

"Can I buy you a drink? Maybe engage you in some thrilling conversation?"

"Got one already, see?"

"Okay." Tokus smiled. "Then I guess you won't take this ass whuppin' personally, right?"

Parise laughed and gestured for Tokus to go right ahead and take his turn. She sat at a nearby table and watched as he threw three darts that netted him eight points. Tokus walked to the dartboard, pulled the darts out, walked back to Parise and said, "So . . . so . . . so there! See if you can beat that!"

She gave him a ridiculous look and stepped to the line. Tokus was more than happy for the view as she stood there. He would give anything just to be able to touch her. She turned to him and closed her eyes before she released a dart and scored twenty. She smiled at him. He appreciated it.

"What's your name?" she asked him.

"Tokus," he responded.

"Well, Tokus," Parise began. "Where did you learn how to play darts?"

Tokus took a swallow of his beer before answering. "Never did. I just need activity. A happy mind is a terrible thing to waste."

"Happy?" she asked.

"Ecstatic," Tokus replied and tipped his beer up for another swallow.

"That's good," she said.

Tokus nodded his head and they were silent for a moment. Something about this woman pulled at him, drawing him toward a silken trap that he would clamp around himself with no desire to escape. Suddenly, Parise stepped closer and looked him in the eye.

"Tokus," she said. "You're looking at me like you don't have a woman."

"No woman, no cry," Tokus replied.

"No cry?" she said.

"No cry, bumba clot, Rasta," Tokus sang.

She laughed. And Tokus fell for her smile. He knew he shouldn't. Now was not the right time. It was Parise's fault for looking at him that way, with an invitation.

The hint of high times pinched the outer edges of the smoke-filled bar, its few patrons capturing the rhythm of the music from the jukebox in toe taps and head nods. Tables lined the wall from the doorway to the dance floor, which was a tiny, twenty-foot square of hardwood that was dimly lit. The long L-shaped bar faced the wall and formed a corridor guarded by an old, drunk, white man who wore a dirty tank-top tee shirt. His exposed skin was covered with tattoos-his arms, shoulders and even his bald head. He lingered over his drink, looked into the top of the glass and broke out into a huge grin before picking it up and tossing it down in one long gulp. He waved impatiently at the bartender for another.

Tokus rolled the three darts in his palm as he watched Parise. She was much better at this than he was.

"You know something?" Tokus said. Parise looked at him. "I've never lost. At anything."

"Oh, yeah?"

"Oh, yeah. So let's make a bet."

The tattooed drunk rose from his stool and staggered toward them.

"Hey, young people," he said in a voice gruff with alcohol. "You know, you two make a nice lookin' couple. I mean that. I do." To Tokus he said, "If I was your age, let me tell you . . ."

Parise cut him off. "That sure is a lot of 'skin art' you've got goin' on. Even on your skull."

The old man said, "Yeah. Yeah. Look, I got a lot of them, all over. I even got one on my pecker." They looked at the boozer, mildly taken aback. He rambled on, "Know what it says? It says 'Ti.' But when it gets hard, it says 'Ticonderoga'!"

Laughter exploded spontaneously. The drunk wobbled over to the table next to them and, still laughing at his own joke, put his drink down and took a seat. Parise turned back to Tokus.

"What kind of bet?" she asked.

"If I win this game," Tokus said. "And I will win! You go out with me. Deal?"

"But you're not going to win." Parise laughed.

"I never lose. Bet me."

"Okay. Bet." Parise agreed.

Tokus took a drink of his beer while Parise prepared the

game. He noticed the drunk sitting at the table with his back to the bar, a dollar bill folded lengthwise in his hand. Tokus didn't need to look to know that the old man was getting ready to sniff cocaine out of it. Parise had the game ready and Tokus turned and picked his darts up from the table, giving her a confident look before he took his turn.

Halfway into the game, Tokus was being crushed. Parise had tripled his score with a giggle and a well-curved figure.

"You know," Tokus cried. "You really should have some mercy. The gloating and giggling and stuff . . . well, that is not attractive, girl."

Parise sauntered over to him. "So, I'm not attractive?"

"Yeah, you're attract . . . I didn't mean . . ."

Parise watched him wriggle.

"Listen," Tokus took a deep breath. "You are a beautiful woman. Beyond attractive. I see you as a 'Soul Kiss.'"

Parise looked at him skeptically. "A 'soul kiss?'"

"Yeah, a 'Soul Kiss.'"

"You mean that I could kiss your soul?"

Tokus looked deeply into her eyes.


I'm a man on a mission,
in search of a Soul Kiss.
To find that special someone,
Who knows that emotion is this.
Satisfaction is forever a moment,
Your toes will never uncurl.
Touching deep inside the woman,
And from there, comes the girl.

Parise and Tokus looked into each other's eyes. In silence they almost touched and in that moment they had each other, inside where feelings were real.

"That was beautiful." Parise touched his hand.

Tokus held her hand and said nothing, not trusting his voice at the moment.

The tattooed drunk rose from his chair and began shimmying from side to side, doing a trembling dance. He threw his head back and yelled, "OOOO, OWWW," and began doing a spastic catwalk-waddle toward them. The old man stopped in front of Tokus with another yell and stared drunkenly. His red eyes were oddly shifting and Tokus noticed a strange dilation of the pupils. Tokus felt as if he were looking into the eyes of a cat. Feline eyes glowed at him from a bald-headed mask of tattoos, wide, open and green. Haunting in a strange, alien way . . . unless cats with huge, bloodshot eyeballs were common. There wasn't the laser beam dot of cocaine high in his eyes, nor was there the soft fuzziness of a marijuana excursion. The pupils seemed to glow, grow and warp. They were vertical eyes. Straight up and down.

Just as suddenly as it began, the old man seemed to shut down and a smile creased his face. He sang, "Hi, neighbor," turned and danced his way back to his table. Tokus wondered what kind of drug was inside that old man!

"What in the hell is his problem?" Tokus said aloud.

Parise shrugged. "I wonder my mys-"

A chair came flying through the air, crashing into the wall directly behind Tokus. He spun around and saw the old man standing there with that stupid grin on his face.

"Hi, neighbor," he sang. Tokus calmed himself and reached for his beer. The bottle lay broken on the floor. Tokus growled and stepped toward the old man. Parise stopped him with a restraining hand on his arm.

"He's just an old drunk," she reasoned. "The bartender will take care of him." The bartender, a large, stonefaced woman, came around the counter to Tokus. "You all right, man?"

Tokus nodded curtly.

"All right, Bernie," the bartender yelled. "You ain't gots to go home but you will get the hell up outta here!"

The drunk started singing a protest. "We shall overdrii-ink. We shall overdriiiink."

"Go! Now!" commanded the barkeep. The drunk muttered his way out the door.

"Let me get you another beer," the bartender told Tokus. "On the house."

Tokus and Parise sat at another table and talked well into the night. But Tokus was distracted. Something about the old drunk had unnerved him. What could make an old drunk behave so badly . . . so totally out of control? A man who had at least twenty years of drug use on his resume. He had probably tried everything from corn liquor to cocaine without the effects that Tokus had witnessed. The thought nagged at him.

Parise sensed his distraction. She gently touched his cheek and said softly, "Tokus, it was just an old drunk."

That was when Tokus realized it was his eyes. His vertical eyes.

# Dead 'Em

Way Jalon stood looking out at the city from his fifteenth-floor office, drawing the lines that divided his sphere of influence. Albany was nearly all his now and soon, with the launching of his newest product, there would be a new order. A new city: Way, New York.

Pause watched Way intently while she waited patiently. She knew that conceit was the result of success and she sensed in Way Jalon the ultimate pride. He would be God . . . if he could. Even Way had limitations. Pause found him intriguing physically- he was a richly handsome man-and psychologically. As far as men went, Pause had a talent for being able to identify their deepest drive-that one peccadillo, that one destructive urge, and tease it with a magical touch that would help her "dead 'em."

But Way was different.

He didn't vary much from mortal man. Her talent had proven itself again. She had found his inner love, but his was a vainglorious obsession that was beyond even her ability to manipulate. Way Jalon loved his children. There were two, both of them male: Money and Power. They were adopted, of course, born and bred by men long dead, but they belonged to Way now and he huddled them against his bosom and reveled in their scent. Openly.

Though Pause had completed many assignments for Way Jalon, this was just her third time in his office. They usually handled business over the phone or via a pager, but this time she was being given the privilege of waiting, while he looked out of that egotistical wall of glass. From the street one would look up to see Way, standing there, keeping watch over his children. Men! They deserved labor pains twice a day.

Way turned from the window to face Pause.

"I have an important assignment for you." He walked over to his chair behind his desk. He sat while Pause took the chair that faced him across the expanse of polished desk. Way opened a drawer, moved his gun aside, a pistol he always kept loaded, and pulled out a large, glossy photo that he pushed across the desk to Pause. It was a picture of Tokus Stone.

"Watch him," Way said.

"That's easy," Pause replied, looking at the picture. "He's handsome."

Way smiled at her. "I want him controlled. I don't want any wild cards in my deck or wild hairs up my ass. Understood?"

"This guy is a wild hair?" Pause asked doubtfully. "I mean, just looking at him I could tell you some things about him. Most of which, I bet, are probably true."

"Like what?" Way wondered.

"For one, I would say that he is a hard worker with a lot of brains. 'Smooth' is a word that comes to mind. Secondly, I'd say he is probably happier than a faggot in boys town just to have a job working for you and making the big bucks."

"Very good," Way said. "Yes, he is very intelligent. I've seen that firsthand, but he's bucking up against me now. I've given him the impression that he matters. I want you to keep that illusion alive but with a little twist."

"Well," Pause replied, her interest piqued. "How do you want him?"

"Compliant. Submissive. The only word he should utter is 'yes.' To whatever I say. The fool nearly cost me a good deal of money recently and that is simply not allowed. I only need him for a little while."

Way saw no need to tell Pause about the incident that had taken place between Tokus and him. Tokus would have quit on him if he hadn't given in on the trucking shipment issue. Way was sure of it. Tokus definitely would have quit. Way had needed those trucks badly. He had scheduled the forty-eight trailers to be packed with full loads of Feenin and shipped to destinations in fifteen different cities. He had wanted to hit America with a bang.

But Way needed Tokus more than any grand plans.

Way would work around him . . . for now.

"So he lives," Pause stated.

"Yes," Way replied. "He lives."

"No dead 'em," Pause prodded.

"No dead 'em," Way repeated.

Pause regarded Way thoughtfully. She wondered if he ever imagined a hint of her motivation, of the urge she had to bend him, break him and watch him grovel, subservient at her feet with the fear of death trembling his knees. The things she would do to him. The very thought of it made her center heat up as she crossed one leg over the other and squeezed. She looked at the picture of Tokus Stone again.

Way regarded her critically. "Now listen, Tokus Stone was once a drug dealer and one night he encountered a man called Moose . . ."

Way Jalon related every detail he knew about the night of Moose's murder, everything that was in the file kept by Herbert Mulne, the rogue cop know as Five-O. When he finished, Pause looked down at the picture again.

"I've got it," she said. "The means and the method."

"Do it." Way rose from his desk and walked over to the wall to look over his real estate. Pause had been dismissed.

She stared at Way Jalon. She didn't like being treated as if she were an under-thought, an insignificant, pesky insect. She wanted to rattle his cage.

"Way Jalon," she called in a sweet voice. "How come you never let anybody into that room back there?" She indicated the two oak doors over by the bar. Way Jalon didn't turn around.

"None of your business," he hissed.

"What's back there? Some freaky shit, I bet!"

"You have your assignment," Way growled. "Now get to it. Because I promise you, you don't want to find out."

Pause glared angrily at his back . . . and she thought of Delton. She had seduced Delton and drugged him. When he awoke he was hog-tied with a piano wire looped around his neck. The other end of the wire was tied to a wooden curl bar about three feet long. Curling that bar, with a foot squarely planted between the man's shoulder blades, was Pause, straining with effort as she pulled.

As the wire began cutting into Delton's neck he tried to scream around the gag crammed in his mouth as his body bucked violently. Pause eased up on the wire and walked around to face the bleeding man. She knelt down close to his face.

"You're crying," she said softly. "Ohhhh, baby. Poor baby." Pause made kissing noises, smacking her lips loudly, soothing him. The man whimpered through the gag. Pause rose to her feet.

"Bitch!" she yelled, before she gave the wire one last powerful pull.

Pause threw the photograph on the desk and got up to leave. She had a burning desire to see a man in pain, and Tokus Stone would wear napalm burns on his back.

# Imande'

A silent warmth had developed between Tokus and T'Challa over the course of the past few months, a bond that was strengthened by a mutual respect and understanding. Without knowing it, they had become brothers, rooted in the same earth, branches on the same tree.

It had taken Tokus a little while to adjust to T'Challa, to reconcile the fact that his brother was a different man than the cowardly crackhead who had fled down Heath Street one dark night. T'Challa was a strong man, small in size but giant in presence, who would give rugged affection, and then, only to a select few. He spoke his few words carefully but he usually said volumes; his actions a strong reflection of the man he had become.

T'Challa had filed "fear" somewhere distant, banished it forevermore from his being. There was nothing or no one that he wouldn't stand up to. It was now only a matter of how much he wanted to fight. Tokus saw it in T'Challa's eyes whenever the hint of an insult came near.

Tokus turned the corner from Lark Street onto Orange Street and headed toward his brother's house. He was going to offer T'Challa a job at Stoneway. A better paying job than the gigs T'Challa had been getting recently. It was tough surviving on a janitor's pay, and flipping burgers didn't leave much room for a budget. Neither job turned out to be steady, permanent work. Tokus understood his brother's need to be his own man, to stand on his own two feet to support Pharren and Monday, but he hoped that T'Challa would relent on this one. It wasn't that T'Challa would be indebted or anything, but what good was success if it couldn't be shared with family!

Tokus offered T'Challa a job at Stoneway once before and had been flatly refused.

"No," T'Challa had answered.

"Why not?" Tokus asked.

"I ain't qualified. I don't fit."

"You don't have to fit."

"Yes, I do."

Tokus hadn't asked again. T'Challa would fit. Tokus knew it. His brother had instinct, raw intellect and savvy-all assets that could drive any career upward. T'Challa had just lost a job that he badly needed, so Tokus figured that the time was right to renew the offer.

T'Challa lived on the first floor of an old, blue, two-story house with a cinderblock porch composed of three steps and a rickety handrail that threatened to fall off at any given moment. It was one in a block of identical houses, the only variation being the color. People were sitting out on their porches-ghetto patios-just lounging, enjoying a seasonably warm day.

Tokus mounted the steps and knocked. Pharren opened the door with a worried look on her face.

"Tokus," she said loudly. "Come in." She closed the door behind him and hurried off to the bedroom, mumbling something Tokus couldn't understand. Tokus walked over to the mantel where the Undamo Assassins were on display. One of them looked familiar. Tokus looked closer. Its face was painted red, black and green with intricate designs on the right side. In his mind's eye, Tokus saw that same design on his brother's face as he stood on a lawn on Raymar Avenue with Five-O lying at his feet.

"Tokus," T'Challa called to him. He stood in the bedroom doorway with his arms folded across his chest.

"What's up, my brother?" Tokus greeted him.

"Nothin'," T'Challa replied. "I got Monday in the bed though. He's sick."

"What's wrong with him?" Tokus came alert.

"Don't know. I might have to take him to the hospital if he don't get any better though."

"Can I see him?"

"Yeah. Come on."

Monday was lying on the bed with his head in Pharren's lap. She was brushing his forehead with a damp cloth and holding him tightly. The boy shook violently and mumbled incoherently with his eyes wide open. Tokus watched him closely. His pupils were swollen and vibrating vertically. Tokus recoiled, alarmed. He had seen those eyes before.

Those vertical eyes. Feline eyes. Long and hazy. They were the eyes of a blathering drunk on a rampage fueled by a chemical reaction in a chemist's lab-the man's brain. This drug was something foreign to Tokus, something new, and he knew it was something that shouldn't be ravaging the body of an eight-year-old.

Concern etched deeply into T'Challa's face as he watched his son thrash and fight against the sickness that punished his young body. He turned to Tokus with a bewildered expression before he made a decision. "Let's take him to the emergency room."

"T'Challa," Tokus rasped. "No."

T'Challa spoke to Pharren. "Where are his shoes?"

She pointed to the floor at T'Challa's feet.

"We got to take him to the hospital." T'Challa worried as he picked up the child's shoes. "Find out what's wrong with him."

"T'Challa," Tokus said louder. "You can't take him to the hospital."

T'Challa sat down on the bed and grabbed Monday's foot, trying to put on the shoe. He reached for the right one.

"Yes, I am. He's hurtin'."

"You can't," Tokus pleaded.

T'Challa paused with the shoe in midair. "Are you blind to all this or can't you see! My boy is hurtin'."

"I know T'Challa," Tokus cried. "I know . . ."

Suddenly, Monday began tossing wildly in Pharren's arms, bucking her back against the headboard of the bed. "Imande'! Imande'!" Monday chanted as Pharren wrestled with him.

T'Challa stared openmouthed at his son until the fits began to subside and Monday's body calmed to a low moan. Pharren looked worn and ragged.

"We better go," she said.

"T'Challa," Tokus said. "You can't take Monday to the hospital."

"Why you keep sayin' that?" T'Challa demanded.

"Because there would be too many questions."

"They had better ask questions," T'Challa growled.

"They'd ask questions because . . ."

"Can't you see I don't give a fat, rat ass right about now?"

"Because I think Monday has some drugs in him!" Tokus exclaimed. "Some new shit. Some new kind of drug. I saw this same type of reaction a couple of days ago. The same eyes. It's some new shit . . . I just don't know what it is though."

T'Challa dropped Monday's shoe and stood facing Tokus.

"Drugs?" he whispered harshly.

"Yes, drugs," Tokus said carefully. "If I'm right, we just need to wait this out. Maybe an hour or two."

"Drugs?" T'Challa didn't want to believe it.

"Yeah," Tokus responded gently. "I saw this old drunk the other night, you know, one of those fifty-year users, and he was buggin' out. Really trippin'. His eyes . . . his pupils . . . they were long. Vertical. Just like Monday's eyes. It made me wonder, so I asked around . . . trying to find out what's up. There's a new drug out there. They call it Feenin but that was about all I could find out. A name. It seems like it will take addiction to a new level."

T'Challa looked at his son, tossing and turning in Pharren's arms. "We gonna find out who gave this stuff to my son, yo! And when I do! I got something for that ass . . . whoever it was!"

Monday began to chant anew, "Imande'! Imande'!"

"Let's wait this out," Tokus said. "Give it an hour. If we take him to the hospital, there would be too many questions to answer. The authorities are trouble. You know that as well as I do."

T'Challa looked from Tokus to Monday before making his decision. A thin sheen of sweat had broken across the child's forehead and he seemed to be calming down, coming out of it.

"Imande'!" The voice came again. "Imande'!"

T'Challa turned to Tokus. "Imande' is an Undamo word."

"What does it mean?"

"It means 'avenge,'" T'Challa replied.

# Passion's Turn

Pause decided to make him burn-to light him and watch as he melted into a mound of chocolate, spiral-shaped shit. Her game had changed from one of physical terror to one of mental intimidation, but manipulation had its own joyful quirks and kinks. And Pause felt real kinky.

She had spotted Tokus coming out of his brother's house on Orange Street. She sat behind the wheel of a jet-black Chevy Blazer with tinted windows, watching, as he emerged with a solemn expression on his face. He had been inside the house for hours but Pause was on assignment, so patience was mandatory. She looked at her watch. It was nearing midnight.

She followed Tokus to a bar called The Branch, a local club where college kids partied. She pulled into a far corner of the parking lot and reached into the back seat for a large handbag. Inside was a makeup kit. Pause could be many a woman due to the contents of her kit. She could be a beautiful mermaid or a snarling harpy. All her parts were parts.

Tonight, she decided, she would use her sexy, come-bed-me persona. She brushed her long, blond hair straight back, letting it fall in a cascade over her shoulders, framing her face. She wouldn't need much makeup, just lipstick, because Pause was a natural beauty. Her looks were a key component of what made her the best at what she did.

Pause checked herself one last time in the rearview mirror-everything about her said "come-on." Perfect, she thought, before she got out and walked inside the club. Sounds of drunken revelry shook the building, music blared and people bounced, rocking and rolling. Groups of people stood by the bar. Others edged the dance floor, screaming independent yells of triumph and guzzling alcohol in mass amounts that went down like happy juice, instantly obliterating inhibitions.

Pause waited for her eyes to adjust to the darkness and the strobing lights. She scanned the room, searching the dance floor and the booths that lined the far wall for her target. She spotted him sitting alone at the bar, tossing down a drink.

"Hey, let's dance." A young man hopped up to her, moving up and down in a pale imitation of a dance he had seen on Soul Train. Pause gave him a frosty glare and walked away. She slid onto the stool next to her victim. The bartender hustled right over. She ordered a drink and observed Tokus discreetly in the mirrored wall that ran the length of the bar while she waited. He wore a faraway expression, his mind in other places. One corner of his mouth was slightly down, curled in a sneer, the product of angry thoughts. He had both hands clamped tightly around his drink. Tokus Stone looked like he could use a friend. Problem was, he wasn't giving Pause a glance. That was highly unusual in itself. She had presence.

"Hi." A dark-haired man sidled up to her. "Care to dance a little?"

"No," Pause replied curtly. He started to rephrase his question when Pause turned on him with a scowl that looked like spit in his eyes. He walked away. Her drink arrived and she tossed her head back and downed it in one gulp. The swift motion caught her target's eye as she watched him observe her in the mirror. She saw a glint of interest flicker in his eyes. Their mirrored eyes met.

"Another," Tokus motioned to the bartender. Pause repeated the motion. The bartender brought two glasses and placed one in front of each of them. Vodka on the rocks. Tokus lifted his glass in the air in a toast and waited for Pause to join him. She did.

"And I wanna taste her, straight, no chaser," he sang and tossed his drink down his gullet in one swift motion. Pause smiled at him, looking deep into his eyes before she tilted her glass and quickly drained hers too. They watched each other intently for a second while the alcohol burned its way down to their bellies. They motioned to the bartender and two more drinks appeared.

Pause picked up her drink and looked over at Tokus.

"Are you drinking happy or drinking sad?"

"I'm drinking pissed!" Tokus replied.

"Well, I'm drinking drunk," Pause said. "What are you pissed about?"

"My nephew's sick, is all." Tokus sipped his drink.

"Oh. Listen. Tonight, drink drunk with me."

Tokus bit his upper lip as he watched her. Pause knew what response was coming. A smile slowly spread across Tokus' face.

"Tonight?" he grinned.

She playfully pushed his arm. "You know what I mean. Come on."

"How about if I drink 'don't care.' Cool?" Tokus asked.

"That's cool."

Tokus raised his drink. "Salud."

They chugged down the drinks. Pause fought the irritating burn that charged down her throat and slammed the glass down on the bar.

"Enough!" she announced.

"They ran out of liquor?" Tokus stammered.

"Let's ask," Pause gasped. They signaled the bartender who looked at them warily before coming over. The alcohol had taken full effect then, as they both began talking to the bartender in languages that were somewhat based in English, with drunken dialect slurring all over the vowels. After two minutes of that, the bartender held up one finger, silencing them.

"We got no more. Fuckin'. Liquor," he pronounced.

They exchanged looks and burst out laughing.

"A beer then," Tokus ordered.

"Me, too," Pause echoed.

After the beers arrived, Tokus and Pause looked at each other.

Pause sipped her beer. "Is that a myth about black men?"

Tokus burped. "Excuse me. Which one?"

"About sex."

"What about sex?"

"About the black male size."

"What about the size?"

"You know," Pause said, exasperated. "You're going to make me say it, huh?"

"No. You don't have to say it." He took a sip of his beer. "You know what? That is one myth I would never shatter. Yes, it's true. It's even strapped to my ankle as we speak." He smiled drunkenly at her. "At least, I think that's my ankle."

Pause returned his smile. "All right," she said. "Tell me this. Do you date white women?"

"I'm not dating anyone."

"But do you like white women?"

"Depends."

"On what?"

"If she can forgive herself for loving a black man."

They watched each other for a moment before returning to their beers. After the tension drained, Pause built some more.

"My name's Eva," she said.

"Tokus," he said, offering his hand. She took it.

"Forgiveness isn't on my agenda," Pause said with a gleam in her eye. "Just pure, physical fun. Sex." She inched closer to Tokus and whispered, "With you."

Tokus didn't answer. Instead, he turned the glass up and gulped the rest of his beer. He looked over at Pause, whose eyes scorched him with hot promises and passion's turn. He nodded his head "yes" and ordered another beer.

Pause smiled.

# Full Fire

Tokus awoke with nylon ropes tied to his wrists and ankles as he attempted to filter sunlight through his pained eyelids. Eva sat at the foot of the bed, naked, watching him. The strange sensation of waking up in an unknown bed disoriented him, causing him to flinch as he replayed the past twenty-four hours trying to locate himself. He saw Eva through the strange shadows of his hangover.

"It's good to see that some myths are true." She looked down at him.

The woman from last night was gone. Tokus shook his head, trying to clear it, but that only made him wince in pain as his alcohol-swollen brain banged against his skull. He narrowed his eyes and focused. Eva sat on the bed with her legs crossed under her. Her hair was pulled back in a tight, severe bun. She had an officious look in her eye. She was still a beautiful woman but her pale skin, which had been soft to look at, was now legally tight. Tokus was groggy, his head hurt and a raw soreness was pushing its way into his consciousness; but he still registered her eyes.

"Yo." Tokus' throat was raw. "Yo. What did we do last night? Ropes!"

He held his arms in the air, looking at the loose ends of the ropes dangling in front of his bloodshot eyes.

"Ropes? Damn, woman!" He smiled at her. "I was all right . . . right?"

"Very," Pause answered shortly.

"Hope so. All this and I didn't come off correctly . . . my head is killing me. I'll never drink again."

"You were so good last night that I want you to do something for me," Pause said. "We are going to have sex."

"We are?" Tokus slowly sat up in the bed, ignoring his nakedness.

"Yes. Whenever I want it and however I want it."

"Listen, Eva . . ." Tokus began untying the rope around his wrist. "Listen, Eva . . ."

"Leave that!" Pause commanded.

"I really would like to, but I need the bathroom. My stomach is boiling. I hate alcohol." He had one wrist untied before Pause spoke.

"Read this." She handed him a card. Tokus squinted at the card. It seemed to be moving and fading, but after the initial struggle, he read it. He cast a puzzled eye at her. She definitely had a plan.

"You're a lawyer?" he asked.

"Yes, I'm a lawyer. An attorney with a firm downtown. In that office, we have a file on a Mr. Tokus Stone. The long and the short of it is we know what you did. It wouldn't take much to put you down and away for quite some time."

Tokus regarded her carefully. She still hadn't said anything specific. His gut instinct told him she was bluffing. That voice might have just been the alcohol talking.

Pause leaned forward. Her breasts, which had seemed perfect in the moonlight, swung ominously toward him.

"I know all about you," she whispered.

"So what?" Tokus replied. "I know all about me, too. So what?"

"I know that you are a once-upon-a-time drug dealer with blood on his hands. 'Moose' blood, if I recall correctly."

Tokus nodded and focused on her face. So, this is the thing called "life," what everyone had warned him about. The fate of the fearless and the reckless running in circles and circumstance, never free to rest. He knew this was just the beginning.

"So, is this the new wave of rehabilitation?" Tokus snorted. "Instead of jail, I get a good roll in the sack with a white woman?"

"Not exactly," Pause said.

"Well, what, exactly, do you want Eva? Damn!"

"Two things," she began. "First, I want information on your boss, Way Jalon. Whatever moves he makes, we want to know about them. He's making moves and we want specifics."

"Who is this 'we' you keep referring to?"

"Don't ask questions. Secondly, I want that," she said, prodding his penis. "And I want it when I want it, how I want it."

"I'm not a slab of meat, Eva," Tokus replied, untying the rope from his other wrist.

"Yes, you are."

"No, I'm not. So let's be real. What is this all about? Money? Control? Is this the way it is up here? On the hill where the power brokers play? We had a night together. That's all. Now we have complications. Why? Why are you so suddenly in my life?"

Pause looked stonily at Tokus before she spoke. "Doesn't matter in the end, does it? Your fate is always just a phone call away. Three digits. Nine. One. One."

Tokus stared at her in disbelief. Pause reached up to the back of her head and her hair cascaded down around her face. She shook it into place and her beauty returned.

"Now this is how I want you . . ."


Later that night, Tokus lay in Pause's bed with his hands chained to the bedposts and his feet shackled. She stood over him, enjoying his naked helplessness. She wore a judge's robe with nothing underneath it. He wore an old pair of tattered pants that reached only to his knees with the crotch cut out. He was flaccid.

"Get it up, boy!" she thundered.

"I can't, Your Honor." Tokus spoke his line.

"Then the judge will have to get you up." She pounced on the bed. "I'll get him up." She took him in her mouth. Tokus felt himself responding as the blood began rushing to engorge him. He succumbed to his rage as she engulfed him with warmth. Inch by inch, friction slid down the length of his shaft and, inch by inch, his body was unable to deny his base instincts. His mind told him "no" while his body reacted with a thoughtless "yes." His wrath would bend her, twist her to the tune of the pain she was inflicting on him. Red rage. He focused on that. The anger.

She climbed atop him and mounted his manhood. She began violently bucking and grunting. Her face was grim as she leaned forward and raked her fingers across his chest, upward until her hand gripped his throat. She began to tighten her fingers around his windpipe.

"Don't stop, Mandingo," she growled between bucks. "Don't! You! Dare! Stop!"

Pause groaned and went off somewhere by herself, faster and faster. She twisted her pelvis and Tokus felt small tears rip across the flesh of his shaft. It hurt. She was oblivious to the anger that spewed out of Tokus' eyes, a full fire of hate and venom. He watched her as she raped him and his fingers felt his chains. Slowly, he began to pull.

# Watching Thoughts

Tokus and T'Challa saw Feenin up close. From green vertical eyes to brown feline eyes to red burning slits that ran straight up and down. It was a twisting, vibrating path that the addicts were dancing upon, all to their own rhythm of life. Tokus and T'Challa had spent the better part of the day scouring the city, seeking answers, but a definitive solution had eluded them. The two brothers were no more informed than when they had set out that morning to find out about the newest drug to hit the streets. A drug that had left T'Challa's son worn and frightened after a bad trip down an acid highway.

Night fell quietly on Tokus and T'Challa as they combed the neighborhood, watching and prowling, searching for the one bit of evidence that would lead them to the person responsible for giving Monday a dose of poison. Tokus saw a raw determination in T'Challa that was frightening and driven by the anger of watching his child do the junkie jig, a dance that T'Challa had banished from his life by changing the music. He was seething with anger and the intent of finding the person who had introduced Monday to this new drug and its deadly, musical stylings.

But they had come up empty. Feenin was quickly becoming the high of choice, but its origins were still a mystery. No one was talking and Tokus was sure someone knew where the drug was coming from, but since the addicts were tripping, he couldn't push the issue. As far as they were concerned, they had found a new gravy train and if you weren't on board, you would have to find your ticket elsewhere. A junkie's secret. Who would've ever believed that could happen? It was scary.

Tokus had one last straw to grasp. They were going to see Fishouse Fat. His ears were always open to the sounds of the street that floated his way and he usually heard more than what was said. All was quiet as they walked the long, winding pavement through the park around a sloping, grass hill, toward the monument of the Buffalo Soldiers.

Fishouse Fat was sitting on his bench facing the river, "watching thoughts" through sightless eyes that were hidden behind his blind man's shades, seemingly frozen in time. When they drew near, Fishouse Fat turned to them and smiled.

"Tokus!" he greeted. Tokus had been trying to sneak up on the sightless, old man for years, but Fishouse always knew who he was.

"Fishouse. Fishouse, my brother is with me. This is T'Challa."

Fishouse turned his head toward T'Challa-as if seeing him-with a look of surprise and excitement.

"Whoa, boy!" he exclaimed. "Undamo! You Undamo!"

T'Challa looked on, openmouthed.

"I can see it," Fishouse continued. "They came to you at night. They changed you. Inside."

"Yeah!" T'Challa wondered aloud. "But how you know all that?" T'Challa looked from Tokus to Fishouse back to Tokus with an incredulous question.

Fishouse said, "I can see it! Tokus, I think I can see! I think I got vision! I mean, I ain't never seen befo' so I ain't 'xactly sure, but I see shapes and lightness. And it's deep. Real deep."

He turned to T'Challa. "Imande'."

T'Challa fell silent. Something inside him seemed to grow. Fishouse's words appeared to be a confirmation, a sign, something foretold of life, of his life and what he needed to do with it.

T'Challa breathed his reply. "Imande'."

Fishouse looked out into the silence. Watching thoughts. Waiting for sights. After a moment, Tokus spoke.

"Fishouse. Look, I need to ask you about something. And it's really important."

"Feenin," Fishouse said. "It's new junk. A high that's brand-new and hard to duplicate. Stuff that's mixed up in a lab-a-tory. It makes things open up. Like my eyes."

"Where's it coming from? Who makes it?"

"Your eye," Fishouse said. "Tokus, watch out for your eye."

"Okay, Fishouse," Tokus replied. "I'll watch out for my eye. But we need to know . . . where are the drugs coming from?"

"They got a little 'ping' to 'em. Feenin. It does! It goes 'ping.' Ping hurts." Fishouse sang, "It's a thin liiiine . . ."

"Fishhouse," Tokus interrupted.

"Between love and pain . . . my cryin' blues."

"Fishouse!" Tokus cried.

"Boy . . ." Fishouse smiled. "Ain't many songs I can sang, but . . ." He sang again, "It's a thin liiiine . . . between love and pain." He shook his head, chuckling to himself.

"I don't know where they comin' from, Tokus. But I know some come from that big buildin' over on Industrial Park. They ain't been open long but they ship candy and tayta chips and soda and stuff out to the stores. They ship Feenin, too. On the down-low, you know."

Tokus' face darkened as he listened. "Are you sure about this, Fishouse?"

"Yeah. Real sure. Sure as sure can be."

"Son-of-a-fuckin' bitch!" Tokus exploded. He marched backed and forth in front of the park bench ranting. "Damn! Damn! Damn!"

"What's wrong?" T'Challa watched him. "What's up?"

"Fuck! Fuck! Fuck!" Tokus yelled. He spun on his heel and cursed the sky. His fists were clenched so tightly that cords stood out on his forearms.

T'Challa waited patiently. When the stream of curses dried up, Tokus turned back to the stunned pair with a drained look on his face.

He spoke softly, "Thanks, Fishouse." He motioned to T'Challa, "Come on."

Tokus was steamed. Anger slipped from beneath the mask of control he had pulled over his face. His shoulders were squared in a hulking mode.

Fishouse called out, "Tokus! Watch ya' eye! Watch ya' eye! Hell, you can even watch mine." With that, Fishouse took his shades off and for the first time ever, Tokus saw his eyes. The pupils were vertical. Feline. Straight up and down.

"I think I see," Fishouse said. "But it hurts."

Tokus wanted to reproach him for using Feenin, but he couldn't. Drugs happened to people, anyone could succumb, as he and T'Challa had seen.

"You can see, Fishouse," Tokus replied. "Better than most people can. I'll get with you later, okay? T'Challa, let's roll."

Tokus strode from the park without another word, anger etched deeply into his face. When they turned onto Central Avenue, T'Challa tapped him on the arm.

"What's up?" he said. "Somethin's on your mind. What?"

"I'll show you," Tokus answered shortly.

They crossed the street and went downtown. Bistros and restaurants lined the street in this section of the city. Establishments of fine dining with entrees, minus the prices and definitely no cheeseburgers or French fries on the menu.

"Tell me," T'Challa said. "Now!"

Tokus stopped to look at his brother. So many things had changed about him. Once he had run away; now he was making demands. Tokus felt a surge of pride.

"You know that building that Fishouse was talking about?" Tokus said. "The one that the Feenin is coming from? That's a Stoneway building. My building. That's where we're going now."

Tokus reminded himself to inform Eva about these developments when they met for her slave sex game. The

demented bitch. If something illegal was happening, Tokus
wanted to implicate her with the knowledge of wrongdoing.
He had to play her game but he could make up his own rules.
Tokus had never felt such hatred for another human being as
he did for Eva. She raped him while she despised him. Well, if
the law came knocking, she was going down with him
because Tokus knew she would never work within the frame-
work of the law. Her brain was illegal. Sick woman.

A noisy crowd of people were gathered across the street in
front of an eatery that advertised "high dining in French cui-
sine." The front of the building was constructed entirely of
tall, black glass embroidered with intricate gold designs. An
old, dark Mexican man stood facing the glass with a brick in
each hand.

"Here come the cops!" someone yelled.

"I 'on't care," the Mexican yelled back. "Look in my
eyes. You don't see no fuck in there. I don't give a fuck." His
eyes were feline and hazy. "They took my job. They took my
'partment. I got nowhere to live. I wanna go to jail." He
reared back and threw the brick at the dark glass. It shattered the storefront explosively. The entire wall came crashing noisily to the ground. And in that instant, that heartbeat, Tokus himself, was watching thoughts. He saw
snatches of his life through the falling shards of glass that
dropped in tingling, dark raindrops in the background of his
memories.

The image of Five-O in a church popped into his mind.
His eyes were exorcist marbles that glinted as he barked into a
cell phone.

"What are you doing? Watching me through your precious glass wall?"

He saw the mental image of Way Jalon standing in front of the window-wall in his office. That thought was stamped onto Tokus' brain, but the picture faded away only to be replaced by a glimpse of Eva's face through the falling glass. His mind raced back to a hotel room. Eva sat on the edge of the bed, looking down on his naked body.

"Moose blood, if I recall correctly," Eva whispered through a foggy haze. How did she know Moose? In Arbor Hill, he was Moose; in society he would be Billy Badass or some such shit. But "Moose!" No. But she knew him as "Moose."

These thoughts were a glimpse, a solid imprint in Tokus' mind when the old Mexican man shattered the dark glass of the restaurant, explosively bringing the entire wall tumbling down.

These thoughts were inspired by the slingshot of fate that flung a rock at a glass house and shattered a secret. Way Jalon was sitting at what had been a private table a second earlier. He wore a stoic look of a man whose evening had been interrupted by a fly in his soup. Across from him sat his dinner companion, Eva, a flirtatious smile adorning her face.

As the cops came and dragged the Mexican away, Way Jalon looked up and saw Tokus. Their eyes locked. Everything clicked into place for Tokus Stone in that brief moment of contact. It all made sense. Way Jalon was setting him up. No one else could move Feenin through Stoneway without Tokus' knowledge.

Five-O had been working for Way Jalon! But why?

And Eva, if that was her real name, was extra flavoring, the proof in the pudding, probably one of Way's checks and balances for which he was infamous. That was how she knew about Moose. Way had told her. He truly left nothing to chance.

Five-O's manipulations had been the result of Way's commands.

Eva's demented sex games were one of Way's countermeasures.

Feenin.

But Way Jalon had made two miscalculations. Selecting Tokus for the fall guy was one. The next would be his arrogance.

Tokus turned to T'Challa. When he spoke, his voice was tight with the slightest hint of anger coiled in his throat. "Come on. Let's bounce."

They walked away. Tokus had a meeting to attend. In the office of Way Jalon.

# I Hate the Moor

The Plaza loomed before them and Tokus peered at the light from the single window on the fifteenth floor, the office of Way Jalon. He imagined he saw the silhouette of the great overseer as he stood there, looking out. Watching. Waiting. The tall, modernistic structure stood fifty stories high, reflecting images of a dark city back into nowhere, the lone light shining like a beacon.

Tokus glanced at T'Challa before they went through the double glass doors. They hopped down a few steps to the marble landing, walked down the escalator over to a bank of elevators and waited.

T'Challa turned to Tokus. "What floor is his office on?"

T'Challa wore a pair of dark, baggy pants and a slightly darker shirt with an African flag emblazoned on the right shoulder. He stood with his feet slightly spread, his eyes focused, determined. He was definitely hyped, fully prepared, and almost overeager, yet he still seemed tightly controlled.

"Fifteen," Tokus answered. He was dressed in a severe casual suit, no tie with a high collar that fit comfortably. His freedom hung in the balance, on the fifteenth floor, with a man who had made all of his goals attainable only as part of an elaborate scheme that would lead to ruin. It was a face that Tokus had seen before, but it still hurt whenever it smiled.

"Okay," T'Challa said. "I got it." He paused and stepped closer to his brother. "Look, I got your back. Just remember that. I got your back." Slowly, he extended a clenched fist toward Tokus.

"No doubt." Tokus returned and tapped the hand with a clenched fist of his own. T'Challa turned for a door that led to the stairs. Tokus called out to him.

"T'Challa, be careful, yo!"

T'Challa shrugged. He had a small, bamboo stick in one hand; two poison tipped darts in the other. Tokus had seen those little missiles before and he remembered their deadly impact. His brother pushed through the door and was gone. Tokus waited a few minutes before he pushed the button to signal the elevator.

Way Jalon had played him. The very thought of it pissed Tokus off. All his life, he had worked and worked hard with a goal in mind: prosperous freedom. From the abuse of his step-father to his mother leaving him to the drug-dealing nights and tough school days, he had fought each battle and been thrilled with each victory. He had found a new family. A brother, a sister, and even a precious nephew who had put a little color back into the picture of his life. The bad things-the drugs, the fight, Five-O-they had been filed away in a gray area, no longer a part of what counted. The here and now. The living.

But Way Jalon would destroy all that. Way Jalon would count Tokus' life as a mere plaything, a toy to be discarded when the batteries wore out. It was all so obvious now.

Way Jalon had hired him to smuggle Feenin because Tokus had a past history of drug involvement. He would be the perfect victim to a perfect setup, and he would fall forever into the pit of a cage that spoke in steel "clangs" and hollow "snicks." Cells that don't multiply; they just retreat into solitude. Alone forever.

The elevator arrived and Tokus stepped inside. He pushed the button for the fifteenth floor, the home office of Way Jalon Holdings. Tokus knew he was up there. Way Jalon had used him from day one-even before that-and he was waiting there now. It was just too poetic to pass up! He was probably sitting behind his foolish desk in front of that giant glass wall of his with his hands folded, waiting. Master of the game. He didn't know that Tokus had changed the rules.

The elevator doors opened and Tokus stepped out. Down the hallway to the right sat the office of Way Jalon. Tokus walked quietly to the door, opened it and slipped inside. He closed the door halfway, careful to be quiet, walked over to the double doors and pushed past them, leaving the doors open behind him. Way Jalon sat behind his desk drumming his fingers impatiently.

"It's about time," he said. "Come in, Tokus. Come in."

Tokus looked from side to side, surveying the room, as he approached the desk. He was about to speak when he spotted Eva standing off to his left by the wall near the futons. She wore a tight-fitting bodysuit that made Tokus' pulse jump, despite the circumstances. Hard to believe such beauty could be so cruel. She eyed Tokus as if he were a test specimen that had failed.

"Stunning," Tokus stated.

She raised a gloved finger to her lips. Tokus turned to Way Jalon.

"Your jig is up, Way Jalon. You can't get me."

"Tokus! You sound so melodramatic. You know, niggers are known for reacting without rhyme or reason. They just come off the top of their heads, you know, a gut reaction. It really is a detriment. I know for a fact that you aren't one of those people."

Way Jalon motioned toward a chair. "Please, sit."

"I'll stand," Tokus replied, unmoved.

"Sure you will." Way grinned at him. "Okay, let's start at the beginning. One question. Answer any way you like. Who are you? I mean, look around you. It's obvious who I am but in a real sense, exactly who are you?" He looked at Tokus expectantly.

"I'm daddy's little preacher," Tokus spat. "Listen, Way Jalon, spare me the bullshit philosophies, theories and other self-injected stupidity and tell me why you did this to me. And I mean 'me' in particular. I don't care if your grandfather or great-grandfather or your uncle-cousin-nephew's brother, the great Klan Jalon discovered the joys of inbreeding. I just want answers."

"Answers, huh?" Way Jalon stared at Tokus. "The answer to your question is: I hate the Moor. Quite simple, isn't it? I mean history is my basis. This entire country oper-

ates on that one simple concept. It's how I got to be . . . me!
I hate the Moor. Go back, Tokus. Go back in history. You'll
find that . . ."

"Miss me with that shit," Tokus interrupted. "I don't care.
You still haven't answered my question. Let me rephrase.
Why me?"

"Don't interrupt the teacher," Way warned. "I proscribe to
the theory of one of our forefathers. He said, and I quote, 'I
will say in addition to this that there is a physical difference
between the black and white races which I believe will forever forbid the two races living together on terms of social
and political equality.' That is beautiful shit!"

Way Jalon was standing now, his face flushed with conviction. The two men faced each other across the expanse of carpet and animosity. After a moment, Tokus spoke.

"While they do remain together there must be the position of superior and inferior," Tokus recited to a stunned Way
Jalon. "And I am in favor of having the superior position
assigned to the white race."

Tokus paused to look Way in the eye. "Abraham Lincoln.
You found an old racist to sing your theme song, huh?"

"Very good," Way responded, regaining his composure.

"No, very bad. Not only are you outdated . . . you're
deadly. You would turn Feenin loose on this entire city, with
all the other drug problems out there, and point every finger
at me. Because I'm black?"

"No," Way answered. "Not just because you're a spade.
A spade is a spade. Because I hate the Moor. I mean, I have
the right to hate something, don't I? I hate with the heart of

Iago . . . and you're my Othello. I hate with the lust that
cursed you and your kind with the skin on your back. I'd ship
you all back to Africa but you've been around good, white
people so long that you don't want to go. I guess we gave you
dreams."

"You are one sick bitch!" Tokus snapped.

"Well, I have a dream, too," Way yelled. "If I can't send
the niggers back to the jungles, I'll bring the jungles to them."

"Feenin," Tokus stated.

"That's right," Way roared. "Feenin. I'll dope them all!"

"Not me, you won't." Tokus turned for the door.

"Tokus Stone," Way called out. "You don't actually think
that you are just going to walk out that door?"

Eva stepped forward.

"Let me introduce you to Pause. She's a killer. Sometimes
she goes by the name of Eva, but that's only when she
relaxes." Pause reached behind her back and pulled out a star-
shaped disk, its metal twinkled dully in her hand. She went
into a karate stance with the disk held at shoulder height, a
good throwing position, and moved closer to Tokus as Way
narrated.

"I think those are called shurikens. I'm not sure, but I
think they are coated with a deadly poison. She's very good,
too, Tokus. She never misses."

Pause reared her arm back poised to fire the star toward
Tokus when she suddenly yelled out and stumbled back
against the wall. A small dart protruded from her shoulder.
She looked toward the door. T'Challa stood there with the
bamboo reed down by his side, and she threw the shuriken at

him. The disk sliced through the air toward T'Challa, who
dove out of its path but it bit into his calf, imbedding him
with its poison. T'Challa rolled over to the door and looked
up at Pause, who had fallen, weakly, to one knee.

"You have sixty seconds to live," he yelled.

"That's five seconds longer than you have," she screamed
before struggling to her feet. T'Challa rose from the floor.
They stared at each other, determined to watch the other die.
They walked toward each other until they stood face-to-face
in the center of the room.

Tokus saw Way Jalon had gone into his desk drawer. He
covered the distance to the desk in one stride. With the second
step, he launched himself toward Way. The gun swung toward
Tokus while he was in midair and a shot went off. The blast of
the explosion assaulted his ear as the bullet streaked past and
burned into the soft flesh of his shoulder before he crashed into
Way Jalon. Way had been leaning forward and the blow sent
his body into the glass wall with a loud "thwack." Tokus' arm
exploded in pain when he landed on it, and his body trembled
in protest as he lay on the floor. He struggled to his feet, trying
to push the pain down, when he saw that Way Jalon had made
it to one knee, the gun swinging upward.

Pause and T'Challa stood face-to-face, inches apart,
searching for death in each other's eyes. T'Challa felt his
heart begin to race but his eyes showed no hint of its
sequence. Beads of sweat began popping up on his forehead.

"No fear, Undamo."

A voice spoke to T'Challa. His mentor. His savior. The
one who had cut away the Bug in him. He had returned. The

Undamo had taken away his weak, cowardly spirit once before, in a dream of hope and renewal, and replaced it with the honor of a man. The Undamo had imbibed T'Challa with a warrior's pride and that pride, that sense of himself, helped him to stand taller.

Pause was breaking. Her face had turned an angry red. Little tremors rocked her like toy lightning as her body slightly convulsed. She seemed determined. T'Challa looked into her eyes and saw the light of life dimming from them. A flicker caught his attention and T'Challa looked deeper into Pause's eyes. The spark of light began to take shape. It pulsed and moved until the image of the Undamo appeared. Pause was a fighter but she was fighting alone. T'Challa had the Undamo.

Pause suddenly pitched forward into T'Challa's arms in an awkward, deadly embrace. Her arms went around his neck, her lips nearly touching his. She looked into his eyes before she pulled him toward her and their lips touched.

"All I ever wanted," she rasped. "Was a kissss . . ."

She flopped from his arms to the floor.

T'Challa looked down at her lifeless body. His fate would come calling soon. He felt death coming for him. T'Challa's vision was going gray, his brain was going soft and a fire was burning in his ear. He dragged his body over to the futon in the corner of the office and collapsed into the cushions. His hands began to shake and his vision went a shade darker, yet he had to complete his mission. With a trembling hand he reached into his pocket and pulled out the remaining dart. He felt someone walk past him and then a light invaded his gray. With pain-racked fingers, he pushed the dart into the bamboo reed.

Tokus dove as far to his right as his leg muscles would allow and the bullet missed, high and behind him. Tokus rolled into a crouch and sprinted toward the sitting area-the futons and wet bar. Way Jalon squeezed off two more shots, missing the moving target but shattering a few glasses on the bar. Tokus looked up at the huge oak doors and bolted through them. He veered hard to his right, out of the open doorway and crashed into something wooden that sent him sprawling. Electric pain shot up his arm, into his throat and he cried out in anguish.

Way called out to him.

"You're in my room! No one goes in my room! But since you did . . . how do you like it?"

Tokus bit down on his lip to keep from screaming. His shoulder was hot with pain. He fought it down and decided to ignore it.

Way continued ranting. "How do you like my motif?"

Tokus looked around the room for a weapon. He looked for anything of use, preferably something heavy. As his eyes adjusted to the dim light, the odd shapes in the room began to take form.

In the middle of the room was a large, canopied, four-poster bed. It was elegant. A work of art surrounded by filth and madness. The walls were decorated with chains, shackle, long-handled whips and hangman's nooses. Next to the bed in the corner was a mock theater-a balcony with two chairs enclosed behind a wooden rail. Two mannequins, a man and a woman, were seated in each chair facing a stage that stood about six feet away from them. On that stage was a surreal scene that shook Tokus to the core. A pregnant slave girl was suspended in midair from ropes that were tied to each ankle. The other ends of the ropes were tied to a pair of plastic mules who pulled them artificially taut. The slave girl's head was thrown back in agony and the unborn baby's head stuck out between her legs as it was pulled forcefully from the womb.

"It's my Lincoln menagerie," he heard Way announce. "You know it's really ironic. You see, Tokus, I'm out here reloading and I'm coming to get you. You're dead, fucker! Dead!"

Tokus looked around wildly. Directly across from him was another horror scene. An almond-toned man was spread-eagled against the wall with both of his arms pinned helplessly. Long, red streaks of blood ran the length of his bare back.

The light streamed through the open door, and Tokus heard Way Jalon lumbering toward it. Tokus reached up over his head and grabbed a whip. He uncurled the long coil and hefted the handle, his hand testing the grip. The lash of the whip seemed to be at least six feet long and it shone an angry tongue.

"As I told you before," Way's voice was getting closer. "I hate the Moor. And in your heart . . . you hate yourself. But it won't be much longer."

With his free hand, he pushed the door until the doorknob banged against the wall. Satisfied that Tokus wasn't hiding behind it, he reached inside for the light switch on the wall.

He spun into the room gun first. As it swung toward him, Tokus lashed out with the whip. It caught Way Jalon across the face and his finger squeezed the trigger, sending a bullet into the wall just over Tokus' head. Tokus pulled his arm back as the gun clattered to the floor and Way Jalon staggered backwards. His arm went forward and the whip caught Way Jalon across the neck. Way shrieked and dove for the gun lying on the floor. Tokus sent the lash forward again. It struck Way Jalon across the back and he bucked in pain before he turned over with the gun in his hand. He pulled the trigger before Tokus could move, but his aim was off. He set the sights on Tokus' heart, but the whipping affected his aim and the bullet grazed a bloody shoulder instead. Tokus staggered toward the door and fell through the open doorway. He got up and started running toward Way's desk. He had taken three off-balanced strides before Way Jalon appeared in the doorway.

"Why fight it?" Way Jalon was eerily calm. He rubbed the mark that streaked across his face. "You're poison."

He stepped through the door, faltered suddenly and swore. "Ooh, shit!"

A dart protruded from his neck. He pulled it out and growled before he looked down at a dying T'Challa taking his last breath-one that had launched a poison dart into Way Jalon's flesh. Tokus stood behind Way Jalon's desk with blood leaking down his arm. He looked at Way in disgust.

"You have sixty seconds to live."

Way Jalon was stunned.

"Sixty seconds! Sixty . . ."

Way Jalon raised his gun and fired at Tokus, missing and hitting the glass wall. Tokus hit the floor behind the desk. Way Jalon kept shooting. The glass wall didn't shatter; there were holes where the bullets went through and solid cracks reached out in every direction but it held. It wouldn't withstand a barrage of gunshots, but Way Jalon continued pulling the trigger until his mind registered the hollow clicking of metal. Tokus dared a peek over the desk. The fool was digging in his pockets and pulling out bullets to reload! Tokus cursed. He couldn't reach Way in time; his shoulder was a licking flame that flashed up his shoulder and he didn't think he could move at all. But the window! Fifteen floors up!

"What the fuck are you doing, Way?" Tokus cried.

Way shoved a bullet in the chamber and looked at Tokus. Tokus noticed that his face was getting pasty. He had already used up at least thirty seconds. He hoped that Way would fall before he blew out the window behind him. Way's legs began to tremble.

Tears began running down his face.

"I'm going . . ." he faltered. "To kill you." He raised the gun and opened fire. Tokus ducked under the desk as three more bullets blasted the glass behind him. He heard the sounds of Way's pounding footsteps coming directly toward the desk. He rolled to the side-away from his bad arm. Way Jalon came over the top of the desk, landed directly behind it and looked to the left. Tokus was on the right. He launched himself at Way Jalon and smashed him in the face. He knocked Way Jalon solidly into the window wall. The bullet holes screamed in protest and bounced Way back. He staggered forward with the gun raised. Tokus' arm felt paralyzed. He couldn't move it, so he jumped forward and kicked with every ounce of energy he had left. Way Jalon had the gun pointed toward him and as the kick broke his nose and sent him flying, he squeezed the trigger. Tokus never saw the gun, only a flash of metal as Way swung his free arm up. A red flash is all he would remember, dream about sometimes, in the days that followed. His brain didn't register the darkness that followed the blinding flash that careened off his left eye, shrouding it in darkness. Nor would his mind recollect Way Jalon crashing through the glass wall, falling, slowly as his heart attacked him, killing him before he splattered on the ground fifteen stories below. Tokus would only remember a burning haze that darkened half his vision.

He awoke in a hospital bed.

The African warrior from T'Challa's house; the one on the shelf-the Undamo-floated before his eyes. He sat in a field of red, black and green while he whispered one word. "Imande'." Tokus eyes popped open. The first thing he felt . . . was the handcuff on his ankle.

# About the Author

Nane Quartay is a new voice in urban fiction. Feenin is his first foray into what he calls "hard drama." Nane Q currently resides in upstate New York and is at work on his next novel entitled, *The Badness*.

# EXCERPT FROM *THE BADNESS*

# A Badness

Memories of childhood held no joy for Doin. Any happiness that he might find was simply a harbinger of disaster, the yin and yang of dysfunctionality. More than anyone, his dark step-father had colored Doin's life, shaped his development into a hard, distant thing. An entity that couldn't be reached by caring, emotion or compassion. A badness is what it was. A badness that spread through his inner self and separated him from the most basic, human desire; to love someone passionately . . . and to be loved the same in return. Memories of childhood.

Memories. . . .

His stepfather stood in the doorway, watching. His face was etched with regret, all traces of alcohol seemed vacant from his red-rimmed eyes as he stepped halfway through the screen door and stood silently with an outstretched hand. A single tear rolled down his face.

Doin didn't see that drop of sorrow trail down the dark skinned cheek. All Doin saw was the menacing devil of pain.

The maker of scars. The giver of life marks. Doin ran his fingers across his disfiguration, a scar that tore a swath across his face, the mark from the devil who stood before him. The blotted soul who had come for him one fateful day and altered his life forever.

His stepfather kept his demon in a bottle, trapped in the fluid of vodka. It was a thirsty little devil that couldn't be slaked, absorbing mothers and fathers, sister and brothers, dollars and dollars until entire paychecks were consumed. Alcoholics never made enough money.

They never make good providers either so at the tender age of twelve, Doin found himself working on a farm alongside migrant workers, picking apples in order to buy his own clothes. He had managed to save over twenty-five dollars in a savings account for a pair of sneakers that had caught his eye. A few more dollars and they would be on his feet.

Doin walked into his house and found his stepfather in a rage. He had been gambling and had lost all of his drinking money. He angrily summoned Doin to the kitchen.

"Boy!" he thundered and pointed at an opened letter laying on the kitchen table. It was Doin's bank statement.

"You got some money in the bank, nigga," his stepfather commanded.

Doin's heart sank.

"Come on," the stepfather bustled out the front door.

Doin followed him with unformed tears stinging his eyes. They piled into the car and his stepfather raced to the bank trying to beat the closing time.

"I know you don't like this shit, nigga!"

The car roared around the corner onto Warren Street. They had ten minutes left before the doors at the bank were locked. Doin prayed that they wouldn't make it. Maybe a cop would pull them over for speeding.

"How you think I feel when you wanna eat eva' day? I got to go down in my pocket eva' time yo' black ass wanna eat!" They pulled up in front of the bank and screeched to a stop in the handicapped parking space.

His stepfather turned to him. "Now go on! Get up in there, nigga!"

Doin crawled out of the car, his heart aching, and slowly trod into the bank. Shortly, he emerged with a closed-out bank book in one hand, twenty-five dollars in the other. He climbed into the front seat and held the money out to his stepfather, who snatched the cash from his grasp and stomped the gas, making a beeline to the nearest liquor store.

When they pulled up to the glass storefront, his stepfather hopped out and vanished through the front door. Doin waited in the car and watched his stepfather through the store window as he strode up to the counter to pay for his drinks. Doin cursed the devil and wiped away a tear, wishing to God that he had never met this drunk-ass man. Motherfucker.

The front door swung open and his stepfather came bustling out of the package store like he had hit the number. He had a brown bag in each hand. He tossed one carelessly through the open window into the backseat, snatched the door open and eased his considerable bulk behind the wheel. He pulled the other bottle out of the bag in his hand, (Vodka was printed on the label) and twisted it open. He paused to look at Doin.

"From you . . . to me," he cheered and raised the bottle to his lips. He chugged his vodka madly, his big ugly lips sucking and slurping as Doin watched. Huge air bubbles rushed toward the bottom of the bottle as the devil raised the quart to the sky and toasted his demon. When the bottle came down . . . it was empty. Doin stared, open-mouthed, as his stepfather tossed the drained container into the backseat and started the car. It didn't seem possible that a human being could drink that much liquor, that fast.

"That ain't nothin' but water," the devil belched before he wrenched the wheel and pulled away from the curb.

"Count your blessings," his stepfather began singing as the car began to pick up speed. "Count them one by one."

The car squealed around the corner, tires screeching, and Doin knew that the devil had dues to pay.

"Count your blessings," his stepfather sang drunkenly as the car skidded around another corner and went into a spin. Doin screamed and tried to find something to hold onto.

"See what I have done." His stepfather's voice was tight as he battled the wheel and swung onto Second Street. When the wheels caught traction he pressed his foot on the accelerator. The car shot forward with such velocity that they were both thrown back in their seats. They went barreling toward the intersection on Warren Street, the busiest street in the city, and the light facing them was red. . . . but the devil never hesitated.

First Edition

ISBN 0-316-80883-0

*Sports Illustrated 1996 Sports Almanac* was produced by Bishop Books
of New York City.

*Sports Illustrated* Editorial Director for Books: Joe Marshall

Front cover photography credits:
Grant Hill (top left): John Biever
Steve Young (bottom): John Biever
Back cover photography credits:
Jim Brown (top): Neil Leifer
Ben Crenshaw (middle): John Biever
Rebecca Lobo (bottom): *The Hartford Courant*
Title page photography credit: David Liam Kyle

10   9   8   7   6   5   4   3   2   1

COM

Published simultaneously in Canada by
Little, Brown & Company (Canada) Limited

PRINTED IN THE UNITED STATES OF AMERICA

# CONTENTS

# Expanded Contents

In compiling the *Sports Illustrated 1996 Sports Almanac*, the editors would again like to thank Natasha Simon and Linda Wachtel of the Sports Illustrated library for their invaluable assistance. They would also like to extend their gratitude to the media relations offices of the following organizations for their help in providing information and materials relating to their sports: Major League Baseball; the Canadian Football League; the National Football League; the National Collegiate Athletic Association; the National Basketball Association; the National Hockey League; the Association of Tennis Professionals; the World Tennis Association; the U.S. Tennis Association; the U.S. Golf Association; the Ladies Professional Golf Association; the Professional Golfers Association; Thoroughbred Racing Communications, Inc.; the U.S. Trotting Association; the Breeders' Cup; Churchill Downs; the New York Racing Association Inc.; the Maryland Jockey Club; Championship Auto Racing Teams; the National Hot Rod Association; the International Motor Sports Association; the National Association for Stock Car Auto Racing; the Professional Bowlers Association; the Ladies Professional Bowlers Tour; the American Professional Soccer League; the National Professional Soccer League; the *Fédération Internationale De Football* Association; the U.S. Soccer Federation; the U.S. Olympic Committee; USA Track & Field; U.S. Swimming; U.S. Diving; U.S. Skiing; U.S. Skating; the U.S. Chess Federation; U.S. Curling; the Iditarod Trail Committee; the International Game Fish Association; the U.S. Gymnastics Federation; the Lacrosse Foundation; the American Power Boat Association; the Professional Rodeo Cowboys Association; U.S. Rowing; the American Softball Association; the Triathlon Federation USA; the National Archery Association; USA Wrestling; the U.S. Squash Racquets Association; the U.S. Polo Association; ABC Sports and the U.S. Volleyball Association.

The following sources were consulted in gathering information:

**Baseball**  *The Baseball Encyclopedia*, Macmillan Publishing Co., 1990; *Total Baseball*, Warner Books, 1995; *Baseballistics*, St. Martin's Press, 1990; *The Book of Baseball Records*, Seymour Siwoff, publisher, 1991; *The Complete Baseball Record Book*, The Sporting News Publishing Co., 1992; *The Sporting News Baseball Guide*, The Sporting News Publishing Co., 1993; *The Sporting News Baseball Register*, The Sporting News Publishing Co., 1993; *National League Green Book—1994*, The Sporting News Publishing Co., 1993; *American League Red Book—1994*, The Sporting News Publishing Co., 1993; *The Scouting Report: 1995*, Stats, Inc., Harper Perennial, 1995.

**Pro Football**  *The Official 1994 National Football League Record & Fact Book*, The National Football League, 1994; *The Official National Football League Encyclopedia*, New American Library, 1990; *The Sporting News Football Guide*, The Sporting News Publishing Co., 1993; *The Sporting News Football Register*, The Sporting News Publishing Co., 1993; *The 1993 National Football League Record & Fact Book*, Workman Publishing, 1993; *The Football Encyclopedia,* David Neft and Richard Cohen, St. Martin's Press, 1991.

**College Football**  *1994 NCAA Football*, The National Collegiate Athletic Association, 1993.

**Pro Basketball**  *The Official NBA Basketball Encyclopedia*, Villard Books, 1989; *The Sporting News Official 1993–94 NBA Guide*, The Sporting News Publishing Co., 1993.

**College Basketball**  *1994 NCAA Basketball*, The National Collegiate Athletic Association, 1993.

**Hockey** *The National Hockey League Official Guide & Record Book 1994-95*, The National Hockey League, 1994; *The Sporting News Complete Hockey Book*, The Sporting News Publishing Co., 1993; *The Complete Encyclopedia of Hockey*, Visible Ink Press, 1993.

**Tennis** *1993 Official USTA Tennis Yearbook*, H. O. Zimman, Inc., 1993; *IBM/ATP Tour 1995 Player Guide*, Association of Tennis Professionals, 1995; *WTA Official 1995 Media Guide*, Women's Tennis Association, 1995.

**Golf** *PGA Tour Book 1994*, PGA Tour Creative Services, 1994; *LPGA 1994 Player Guide*, LPGA Communications Department, 1994; *Senior PGA Tour Book 1994*, PGA Tour Creative Services, 1994; *USGA Yearbook 1994*, U.S. Golf Association, 1994.

**Boxing** *The Ring 1986–87 Record Book and Boxing Encyclopedia*, The Ring Publishing Corp., 1987. (To subscribe to *The Ring* magazine, write to P.O. Box 768, Rockville Centre, New York 11571-9905; or call (516) 678-7464); *Computer Boxing Update*, Ralph Citro, Inc., 1992; Bob Yalen, boxing statistician at ESPN.

**Horse Racing** *The American Racing Manual 1994*, Daily Racing Form, Inc., 1994; *1994 Directory and Record Book*, The Thoroughbred Racing Association, 1994; *The Trotting and Pacing Guide, 1994*, United States Trotting Association, 1994; *Breeders' Cup 1993 Statistics*, Breeders' Cup Limited, 1993; *NYRA Media Guide 1993*, The New York Racing Association, 1994; *The 120th Kentucky Derby Media Guide, 1994*, Churchill Downs Public Relations Dept., 1994; *The 120th Preakness Press Guide, 1994*, Maryland Jockey Club, 1994; *Harness Racing News*, Harness Racing Communications.

**Motor Sports** *The Official NASCAR Yearbook and Press Guide 1994*, UMI Publications, Inc., 1994; *1994 Indianapolis 500 Media Fact Book*, Indy 500 Publications, 1994; *IMSA 1994 Yearbook*, International Motor Sports Association, 1994; *1994 Winston Drag Racing Series Media Guide*, Sports Marketing Enterprises, 1994.

**Bowling** *1994 Professional Bowlers Association Press, Radio and Television Guide*, Professional Bowlers Association, Inc., 1994; *The Ladies Pro Bowlers Tour 1994 Souvenir Tour Guide*, Ladies Pro Bowlers Tour, 1994.

**Soccer** *Major Soccer League Official Guide 1991–92*, Major Soccer League, Inc., 1991; *Rothmans Football Yearbook 1993–94*, Headline Book Publishing, 1993; *American Professional Soccer League 1992 Media Guide*, APSL Media Relations Department, 1992; The *European Football Yearbook*, Facer Publications Limited, 1988; *Soccer America*, Burling Communications.

**NCAA Sports** *1993–94 National Collegiate Championships*, The National Collegiate Athletic Association, 1994; *1993-94 National Directory of College Athletics*, Collegiate Directories Inc., 1993.

**Olympics** *The Complete Book of the Olympics*, Little, Brown and Co., 1991.

**Track and Field** *American Athletics Annual 1993*, The Athletics Congress/USA, 1993.

**Swimming** *6th World Swimming Championships Media Guide*, The World Swimming Championships Organizing Committee, 1991.

**Skiing** *U.S. Ski Team 1994 Media Guide / USSA Directory*, U.S. Ski Association, 1993; *Ski Racing Annual Competition Guide 1993–94*, Ski Racing International, 1993; *Ski Magazine's Encyclopedia of Skiing*, Harper & Row, 1974; *Caffä Lavazza Ski World Cup Press Kit*, Biorama, 1991.

# Scorecard

Why the Patriots don't win   Why Steve Spurrier doesn't lose

OCTOBER 23, 1995
$2.95 (CAN. $3.95)

**Sports Illustrated**

BULLS
91

JORDAN
23

# AIR & SPACE

Can Michael Jordan tame the NBA's weirdest player?
A report from inside the Bulls' camp

*A summary of Fall 1995 events*

PASCAL RONDEAU/ALLSPORT

**After locking up his second straight F1 title, Schumacher popped off at his rival Hill.**

## AUTO RACING

Michael Schumacher clinched his second straight Formula One championship when he won the Pacific Grand Prix on Oct. 22 in Aida, Japan, but the win did not come without controversy. Schumacher was incensed by the blocking tactics of Damon Hill, with whom he had crashed twice earlier in the season. "He pushed me to the outside, but in doing that he spoiled his race as well," said the German, who at 26 became the youngest man to win back-to-back F1 driving titles. Hostilities continued on the victory podium when Hill refused to shake Schumacher's hand. "This is something between me and Damon," said Schumacher. "We should sort it out ourselves."

## PRO BASKETBALL

The bull staring so menacingly from the back of Dennis Rodman's head was charcoal black, while the rest of his head was a volatile mixture of Halloween pumpkin orange and fiery red. How did you think the flamboyant Rodman was going to tell the world that he had become a Chicago Bull? On Oct. 2 Chicago traded its 7-foot center Will Perdue to the San Antonio Spurs in exchange for Rodman, the 6'8" forward who, depending on what you think of his antics, is a rebounding fool, a just-plain-fool or both. "Why run off to the circus when the circus comes to you?" asked Bull coach Phil Jackson. "We're going to see a lot of unusual behavior in Chicago."

But make no mistake. This is one circus that should do a lot more than just entertain. Rodman, after all, has led the NBA in rebounding by a wide margin each of the last four years, averaging 17.8 per game over that stretch. He was also named the NBA's top defensive player in 1990 and '91. So forgive his new teammates if, in spite of his dabbling in black and red, everything was looking just rosy to them. "He's here because he wants to win," said Michael Jordan. "I expect him to give his heart on the basketball floor, and that's what counts. He's a grown man. We cannot control him or dictate what he should do off the court."

Certainly the addition of Rodman meant that the Bulls would pose a considerable obstacle to the title hopes of both the Houston Rockets, who were aiming to emulate the three-peat success of the 1991–93 Bulls, and the young and talented Orlando Magic. Indeed, Orlando's chances of getting off to a quick start were dampened considerably when center Shaquille O'Neal fractured a bone in the base of his right thumb on Oct. 24. O'Neal, who underwent surgery two days later, was expected to miss at least six weeks of the regular season. Also missing opening day was Chris Webber of the Washington Bullets, who was expected to sit out at least four weeks with a dislocated left shoulder.

In other major trades, the Bullets acquired four-time All-Star guard Mark Price from the

Cleveland Cavaliers in exchange for a No. 1 pick in the 1996 draft, and the Phoenix Suns, shopping for size, traded 6'6" guard Dan Majerle to the Cleveland Cavaliers for 6' 11" forward John Williams.

## BOXING

For years now, boxing has been its own most fearsome opponent. In October the sport absorbed blows heavy enough to stop—or at least slow down—any sport ruled by common sense, decency or law, but that, of course, rarely seems to include the sweet science.

Quite simply, there continue to be far too many reminders of the sport's inherent brutality. On Oct. 15, two days after he was knocked out by Drew Docherty in the 12th round of their fight for the British bantamweight title, James Murray of Scotland was taken off a life-support machine and died. Later that day Filipino flyweight Restituto Espineli died from a brain hemorrhage sustained during a fight against Marlon Carillo near Manila. A week later flyweight Marvin Corpuz died of head injuries sustained in his Oct. 21 bout against Allan Llaneta. Coming as they did in a year that had already borne tragic witness to Gerald McClellan's descent into an 11-day coma in February and

**What, me worry? King spent most of the fall in court, battling mail fraud charges.**

JOHN IACONO

the deaths of super featherweight Jimmy Garcia of Colombia on May 19 and South Korean Lee Tong-choon on Sept. 9, these three deaths again raised questions about the brutal business of boxing.

If boxing doesn't succeed in pummelling itself into oblivion, it may yet manage to be litigated to death. Don King spent much of the fall in a federal court in Manhattan, facing nine counts of mail fraud. The charges stemmed from a fight between Julio César Chávez and Harold Brazier that was scheduled for June 28, 1991, but was canceled when Chávez cut his nose. King, 63, was alleged to have submitted to Lloyds of London a bogus insurance claim for $350,000 in unrefundable training expenses. On Oct. 17 Chávez testified that the contract King submitted to Lloyds was not the one he'd signed and that the first time he'd seen the part of the contract mentioning training expenses was when prosecutors showed it to him in court. Chávez also said he'd only spent $50,000 to $60,000 training for the fight. However, on Oct. 26 Richard Hummers, an accountant who worked for King, testified that King was entitled to the settlement, citing paperwork that he'd submitted to Lloyds in January 1992. If convicted King faced up to five years in prison and a $250,000 fine on each of the nine charges.

## CHESS

The Intel World Chess Championship was held, appropriately enough, high above the heads of ordinary folk, in a soundproof glass cage on the 107th floor of New York City's World Trade Center. Though it was expected to be a one-sided match, with 32-year-old Russian Gary Kasparov the overwhelming favorite to beat Viswanathan Anand, a 25-year-old from India, the best-of-20 series actually looked like a battle—for nine games. Upon winning Game 9 after eight straight draws, Anand said prophetically, "You catch a tiger by the whiskers, next day he's going to be ferocious."

Sure enough, Kasparov came roaring back in the next match. He captured Games 10, 11, 13 and 14. He drew Game 17 on Oct. 9 to secure his fifth title defense since 1985 and claim the winner's purse of $900,000. Chess

**If the view wasn't enough to dizzy him, Anand had to cope with Kasparov's play.**

mavens were left wondering how well Anand, the constitutionally jokey son of a Madras railroad executive, would cope with the intellectual battering he had absorbed.

## COLLEGE FOOTBALL

Along with the most wide-open Heisman race in years, the 1995 season had more than its share of surprises. Who would have guessed that at the beginning of November the University of Miami would have fallen far out of the Top 25—a week earlier *The New York Times*'s computer poll had actually placed the 'Canes 41st, one spot behind Miami of Ohio!—and that Northwestern would be in the Top 10? But for all its surprises, 1995 also had something in common with its 52 predecessors. Nineteen-ninety-five marks Eddie Robinson's 53rd year as football coach at Grambling. To appreciate how long that really is, one need only remember that when Robinson took over the program in 1941, the president of the United States was Franklin Delano Roosevelt. On Oct. 7 Robinson beat the rest of the coaching fraternity to yet another milestone, notching his 400th win in the Tigers' 42–6 drubbing of Mississippi Valley State.

The great surprise of the 1995 season was the success of Northwestern. It was not so long ago that the Wildcats were the unrivaled patsies of the Big Ten, bad enough to have lost 34 straight games from 1979–82. In 1994 Northwestern

failed to win a single Big Ten game and finished the season 2–9. But when November arrived, the Wildcats were tied with Ohio State atop the Big Ten with a 5–0 conference record. One reason for their improvement was Darnell Autry, who had rushed for at least 100 yards every game and was averaging 131 per game.

The Big Ten's other great running back was Ohio State's Eddie George, who through eight games had rushed for 1,100 yards and 15 touchdowns. But in winning their first eight games, the Buckeyes relied not just on George but also on quarterback Bob Hoying, who was leading the nation in passing efficiency.

Indeed, as the season entered its final month, the Buckeyes were only one of four major programs that still boasted perfect records. Florida State, led by another pair of Heisman candidates—tailback Warrick Dunn (9.4 yards per carry) and quarterback Danny Kanell (168 for 230 with 25 TDs)—was 7–0 and ranked first in many polls. The Gators had their own Heisman candidate in quarterback Danny Wuerffel, who had completed 65.2% of his passes and thrown 22 touchdown passes.

There was no shortage of worthy Heisman candidates. Among them were Iowa State's Troy Davis, who led the nation in rushing with 190.8 yards per game; Karim Abdul-Jabbar of UCLA, who was averaging 151.5 rushing yards a game; and Tennessee quarterback Peyton Manning, who had completed 67.8% of his passes for the 7–1 Volunteers.

Still, many were of the opinion that the most valuable player in the college game was Nebraska quarterback Tommie Frazier. Frazier's numbers might not have been as gaudy as some of his rivals', but his performance in key games made him a strong contender, especially if the Huskers end up going undefeated for the regular season. That became more likely on Oct. 28, when Nebraska passed what was probably its final big test, whipping Big Eight rival Colorado 44–21 on the road. The Huskers ran their winning streak to 21 games, best among major colleges. Frazier completed 14 of 23 passes for 241 yards and two touchdowns, and by the end of the game their fans were chanting, perhaps prophetically, *Tommie Heisman, Tommie Heisman, Tommie Heisman.*

AL MESSERSCHMIDT

## PRO FOOTBALL

The fiercest battling in the first half of the 1995 NFL season came not on the playing field, but in boardrooms around the league and in the NFL's head office. Most of it focused on Cowboy owner Jerry Jones, who seemed determined to challenge the way the NFL does business on every possible front, flaunting the concepts of revenue sharing and the salary cap. First Jones defied the league by signing a $25 million deal to sell Pepsi at Texas Stadium when the league has a contract with Coca Cola. Then on Sept. 4 he announced—with a press release headlined COWBOY OWNER BUCKS NFL AGAIN—that he had signed a seven-year, $2.5 million sponsorship deal with Nike. Less than a week later, Jones announced that he had signed cornerback Deion Sanders to a seven-year, $35 million contract, the specific terms of which were creative, to say the least, loading the bulk of the Cowboys' payment to Sanders up front, as a $13 million signing bonus, and paying the bulk of the difference after

1999, the uncapped year of the collective bargaining agreement.

The league struck back quickly. On Sept. 18 it filed a $300 million lawsuit challenging Jones's deals with Pepsi and Nike. That hardly deterred Jones, who went right back out and negotiated a deal with American Express.

The Cowboy players did not seem to be troubled by all the legal maneuvering going on around them. They jumped out to a 7–1 start, tying the Kansas City Chiefs for the best record midway through the season. Cowboy running back Emmitt Smith seemed to be well on his way to threatening John Riggins's record for touchdowns in a season, scoring 14 in the Cowboys' first eight games.

Injuries sidelined an alarming number of the game's top players, quarterbacks especially. San Francisco's Steve Young, the NFL's top-rated passer in each of the last four years, bruised his throwing shoulder in the Niners' 18–17 loss to the Indianapolis Colts on Oct. 15 and was expected to miss at least a month. Also spending time on the DL were Boomer Esiason of the New York Jets and Dan Marino of the Miami Dolphins, both of whom got hurt on Oct. 8. Marino injured his right knee and left hip, underwent surgery on Oct. 9 and missed two games. Esiason sustained a concussion after getting hit by the Buffalo Bills' Bruce Smith and still had not returned as of Oct. 29.

Two of the game's alltime greats set NFL career records. On Oct. 8, in the Miami Dolphins' 27–24 loss to the Colts, Dan Marino completed 19 passes to surpass by 16 Fran Tarkenton's NFL record of 3,686 completions. Three weeks later, Jerry Rice of the 49ers became the NFL career leader in receiving yardage. Though the Niners lost 11–7 to the lowly New Orleans Saints, Rice's 108 yards gave him 14,040 yards, 36 more than James Lofton.

Elsewhere, in October the Carolina Panthers set a record for expansion teams by winning three straight games. After beating the New York Jets 26–15 on Oct. 15—the first win in franchise history—the Panthers went on to defeat New Orleans 20–3 and New England 20–17 in overtime.

## GOLF

In the wake—and boy, is *that* the right word—of the U.S. team's collapse at the Ryder Cup, a number of U.S. players traveled to Europe in hopes of reestablishing the nation's golfing supremacy. "Maybe if I can win this, the Americans will forget for a while that we lost the Ryder Cup," said Lee Janzen, on the eve of the World Match Play Championship, held Oct. 12–15 in Surrey, England. Janzen started beautifully, beating match play champion Katsuyoshi Tomori of Japan 7 and 6 in their scheduled 36-hole match. On the following day, however, Janzen ran into Ernie Els, the man who succeeded him as U.S. Open champion. After dispatching Janzen 4 and 3, Els proceeded to edge Bernhard Langer 1-up in the semis and then to defend his title successfully by beating Steve Elkington 2 and 1 in the final.

Host team Scotland won the Dunhill Cup for the first time in 11 years, beating Zimbabwe 2–1 in the final, which was held Oct. 22 at St. Andrews. To do so, the Scottish team of Colin Montgomerie, Sam Torrance and Andrew Coltart had to offset the sterling play of Nick Price, who shot five straight sub-70 rounds and finished 20-under-par, a St. Andrews record. The U.S. team of Ben Crenshaw, Lee Janzen and Peter Jacobsen finished last in its group, losing to both Canada and Ireland.

The 1995 PGA tour concluded on Oct. 29 with the TOUR Championship at Southern Hills Country Club in Tulsa. For the first time in 15 years, a 72-hole score of even-par was enough to win a PGA tournament. Indeed, on the final day Billy Mayfair shot a three-over-par 73 and still beat Corey Pavin and Steve Elkington by three strokes. "When I was adding up my score and saw it was 73 I thought, 'Boy, you're not supposed to win on this tour shooting 73 on the last day,' " said the 29-year-old Mayfair. His winner's share of $540,000 gave him $1,543,192 for the season, second on the annual money list to Greg Norman, who won $1,654,959.

Norman also finished the season with the lowest scoring average on the tour, 69.06, but was miffed at being locked out of the Vardon Trophy (won by Steve Elkington with 69.62) because he withdrew from the second round of the MCI Heritage Classic.

## ICE HOCKEY

On Oct. 18 a group of investors from Minnesota bought the Winnipeg Jets for $68 million, despite the fact that they had not yet secured a home arena for the team. New owners Steven Gluckstern and Richard Burke hoped to place the team in Minneapolis's Target Center, but insisted that they couldn't do so unless the Center and its principal current residents, the Minnesota Timberwolves, gave them favorable terms.

Pittsburgh Penguin wing Mario Lemieux returned to the ice after a 17-month absence while fighting Hodgkin's disease and back problems. On Oct. 26, in the Penguins' 7–5 defeat of the New York Islanders, Lemieux scored the 500th goal of his career, making him the 20th player to reach that plateau but the second fastest. Lemieux's historic goal came in his 605th NHL game; only Wayne Gretzky reached that plateau more quickly (in 575 games).

**Els won his second consecutive world match play title.**

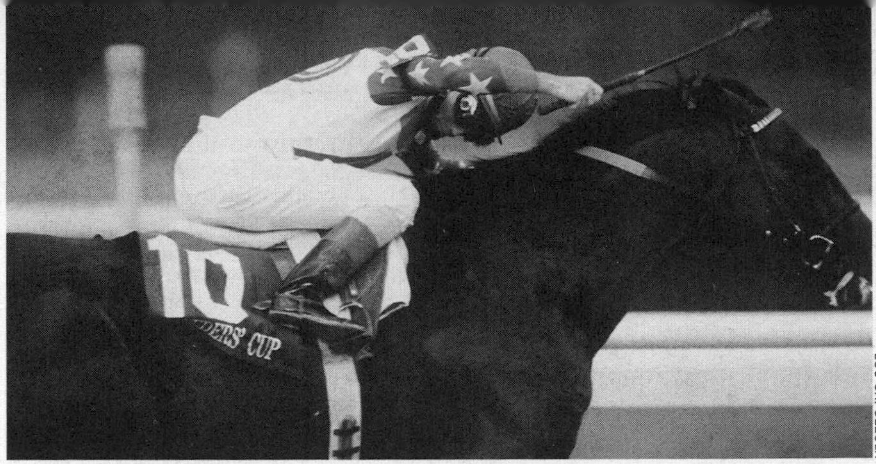


LOU CAPOZZOLA

**Cigar won his 12th straight race at the Breeders' Cup, four short of the record.**

## HORSE RACING

If any questions lingered over just how great a horse Cigar is, they were put to rest once and for all at the 12th running of the Breeders' Cup Classic, held Oct. 28 at New York's Belmont Park. Starting from the No. 10 slot, Cigar, with Jerry Bailey up, bided his time in the race's early stages, running just off the pace. Then, when the field turned for home, he made a strong move and pulled away to score a two-and-a-half length victory over runnerup L'Carriere. Despite running on a Belmont track rated "muddy," Cigar ran the mile-and-a-quarter in 1:59⅖, making him the first horse to break two minutes in the Breeders' Cup Classic.

"We overcame today," said Bailey, who has ridden four of the last five winners of the Classic. "Tenth hole, wet track, delays. We overcame it all."

And Cigar set other records too. With the $1.5 million first prize, he raised his 1995 earnings to $4,819,800—a record for one year—and guaranteed himself Horse of the Year honors. He also became the first colt or stallion since Spectacular Bid in 1980 to go through an entire year undefeated.

It was a remarkable year for a horse whose early career did not produce such lofty expectations. Bred to run on grass, Cigar won his first race on a dirt track in 1993 and then was switched to the grass, where he performed disappointingly for 17 months. Trainer Bill Mott decided to give him one more chance on dirt, at Aqueduct on Oct. 28, 1994. He won by eight lengths and the following month won again at Aqueduct, by seven lengths. The rest, as they say, is history. Though Cigar's win in the Breeders' Cup Classic was his 12th straight, leaving him four shy of Citation's record string of 16 wins from 1948 to '50, his owner, Allen Paulson, was noncommital about his future, offering only that "We'll have to see."

Here are the results of other Breeders' Cup races:

• In the Distaff, Inside Information, with Mike Smith up, beat her stablemate Heavenly Prize by 13½ lengths, easily the largest margin of victory in Breeders' Cup history. Inside Information ran the 1⅛ miles in 1:46.

• Jerry Bailey, atop My Flag, took the 1¹⁄₁₆-mile race for Juvenile Filies in a stakes-record 1:42⅕, edging runnerup Cara Rafaela by half-a-length.

• In the Sprint, Desert Stormer, with Kent Desormeaux in the saddle, held off Mr. Greeley to win by a neck. Starting at 14–1, the filly ran the six furlongs in 1:09 to become just the second field horse to win a Breeders' Cup race.

• European horses swept the Mile, with Ridgewood Pearl, from Ireland, pulling steadily away in the home straight to beat Fastness by two lengths. With John Murtagh up, Ridgewood Pearl ran the mile in 1:43⅗.

• Unbridled's Song, with Mike Smith up, barrelled from off the pace and beat Hennessy by a neck to win the Juvenile. Unbridled's Song ran the 1¹⁄₁₆-mile course in 1:41⅗ to make himself an early favorite for next year's Triple Crown.

DAVID LEAH/ALLSPORT

• In the Turf race, Northern Spur, with Chris McCarron in the saddle, beat Freedom Cry by a neck, finishing the 1½ miles in a slow 2:42.

## TENNIS

With Andre Agassi sidelined for several weeks with a pulled chest muscle, Pete Sampras headed to the Paris Open assured that no matter how he played he would regain the world No. 1 ranking which Andre Agassi had held since wresting it from Sampras on April 10.

The world's top-ranked female player could also have used a little bit of luck. Steffi Graf's father, Peter, had been in jail since early August, suspected of failing to report $35.3 million of her income. Graf herself was questioned as part of an ongoing investigation. Despite the fact that charges had not been filed against her, on Oct. 16 Opel, the German subsidiary of General Motors, announced it would not renew its $1.2 million annual sponsorship deal with her. On Oct. 28 Graf's lawyer said that, after locating some overseas accounts, Graf had deposited $14.3 million with German authorities to cover back taxes she and her father might not have paid.

## TRIATHLON

**Smyers won her first Ironman when Newby-Fraser collapsed near the finish.**

Is there a more punishing route than the 140.6 miles of road and rough water that comprise the course for the Ironman Triathlon in Kailua-Kona, Hawaii? Over the years they've offered athletes an extreme test, separating the men from the boys, the women from the girls. This year they succeeded in temporarily separating the race's most decorated champion from her mind.

Having announced before the race that it would be her last, seven-time women's champion Paula Newby-Fraser was determined to go out with a bang. Setting off at an ambitious pace, she looked the sure winner until, just 500 feet from the finish, she began weaving, waving her arms and crying, "Where's Karen [Smyers, who at the time was her closest pursuer]?" Two hundred feet from the finish Newby-Fraser sat on the curb and wept. Smyers raced past the weeping Newby-Fraser, who sat for 22 minutes before pulling herself together and walking barefoot across the finish line in fourth place. "I thought I was going to die," she said. "I was delusional. I felt like I was going into a seizure." Smyers's winning time was 9:16:46.

For Mark Allen, who had won the Ironman five straight years from 1989 through '93 before choosing not to enter last year's race, the 1995 race marked a return to business as normal. At the end of the bike leg, Allen trailed the leader, Thomas Hellriegel of Germany, by 13 minutes. Allen picked Hellriegel off just two miles from the finish, sweeping past the exhausted German to win his sixth title in 8:20:34.

"A lot of people go too hard on the bike, forgetting they have to run 26.2 miles," said Allen. "There's a finite equation to the amount of energy anybody has."

# Year in Sport

John Biever (top), Richard Mackson

John Biever

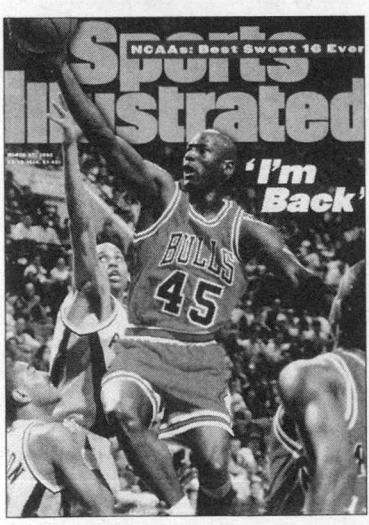

David E. Klutho

Illustration by C.F. Payne

# Hails and Farewells

**In a weird year, full of long-awaited returns and sudden departures, sports fans were lucky just to have games to root for**

## by Alexander Wolff

NINETEEN NINETY-FIVE had no Olympics, no World Cup and very nearly no baseball or hockey. The year was a sort of caesura—in short, shortened; on the whole, humdrum; in essence, a time of interruption and change, marked by events postponed or canceled or otherwise rendered not as we knew them. The grandiose yielded to the novel, the quirky, the black-and-white. If the year were to be recorded on film, Cecil B. DeMille wouldn't get the call to shoot it; Jim Jarmusch would.

Work stoppages bedeviled the majors and the NHL. Pro basketball's big story was its greatest player's transit from retirement to reactivity. Hockey conjurer Mario Lemieux and college basketball maestro Mike Krzyzewski sat the entire year out, albeit not by choice, while one of college football's leading coaches, Bill McCartney of Colorado, chucked it all to devote himself full time to Promise Keepers, the Christian men's group he had founded. Major League Soccer, conceived to exploit the footie-frenzy whipped up by the World Cup of the previous summer, dawdled, thus missing a spring start-up that would

have been welcomed by fans fed up with baseball.

But it was also a year of getting back on the beam, of restoration—of absences ended, as sport welcomed back not only Michael Jordan but also Evander Holyfield, Monica Seles, Mike Tyson and Jerry Tarkanian, plus boxing to Madison Square Garden after an absence of almost three years.

In short, if only to keep up with Deion Sanders (who went from the 49ers to the baseball Giants to the Cowboys), it was a good year for sports fans to turn first to the TRANSACTIONS section of the agate page.

ALTERED: The gender of *America³*, the yacht originally featuring an all-female crew, with the addition of a y-chromosome-carrying tactician midway through the Defender's Series of the America's Cup.

LEFT TO TWIST SLOWLY, SLOWLY: Interim U.S. national soccer coach Steve Sampson, despite guiding the Americans to a U.S. Cup title and into the semifinals of the Copa America. (He was eventually hired permanently.)

HOSED: Steve McNair, the quarterback who put up Heisman-worthy numbers at Alcorn State but placed third in the ballot-

**Seles gathered up her courage and made a brilliant return to tennis.**

ing because voters were loath to honor someone who plays at a Division I-AA school—even if he did set an NCAA record for total offense, racking up more than 500 yards each time out.

FREQUENTLY MISPRONOUNCED: The name of Haile Gebrselassie, the Ethiopian who set world records in the 10,000 meters and the two-mile, and lowered the standard in the 5,000 meters by almost 11 jaw-dropping seconds.

The year wasn't rendered in broad strokes so much as niggling details. A technicality in Hideo Nomo's Japanese contract allowed him to sign with the Los Angeles Dodgers and bring his Tiantesque delivery to Ameri-

can mounds. Olympic negotiators granted NBC a chance to bid preemptively for the Sydney and Salt Lake Games, both of which the Peacock strutted off with for $1.27 billion in rights fees. We thought we knew the rules of the America's Cup, but when it became clear that the existing bylaws weren't going to permit Dennis Conner to sail into the finals on merit, we got to see the rules rewritten to accommodate him and his corporate sponsors. Conner was outchutz-pah-ed only by the Lord of the Olympic Rings, Juan Antonio Samaranch. The president of the International Olympic Committee somehow engineered a rules change that pushed the mandatory retirement age for his position back five years, from 75—the age he happened to be—to 80.

There was a brace of almosts and not

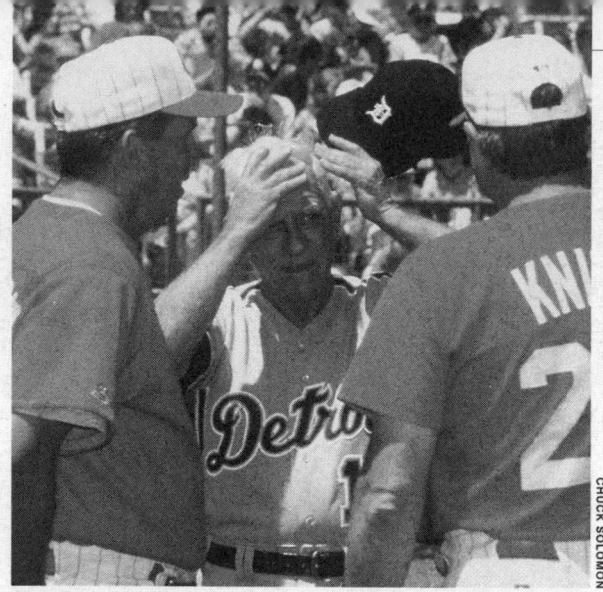

40-year-old golfer named Brad (Dr. Dirt) Bryant, after 18 years and 460 events, finally won a Tour title. The New York Yankees' Don Mattingly suited up for a playoff game for the first time in his 14-year career. And Nebraska coach Tom Osborne's Cornhuskers, who had been to college football's base camp many times during his 22 years in Lincoln, finally reached the summit of a national championship.

quites: Seven-time Ironman Triathlon winner Paula Newby-Fraser had a physical and mental breakdown 500 feet from the finish of this year's event; the California Angels pulled an *el foldo* in the American League West worthy of the '64 Phillies and the '69 Cubs; and Cuba's Ivan Pedroso seemed to have broken Mike Powell's world record in the long jump, only to have the leap disallowed because a factotum in a raincoat had blocked the wind gauge. All the aforementioned were close, but no . . . Cigar, the 5-year-old Horse of the Year who ripped off 11 stakes race wins in a row.

Those absent made news as often as those who cried "here": In 1995 we witnessed an Indy 500 without Team Penske, an entire PGA calendar without Nick Price atop the leader board at the end of a Sunday afternoon, and an America's Cup that ended without *oneAustralia 95*, the Aussie boat that broke in two and sank during the Challenger's Series. Those announcing their retirement included Jud Heathcote, Vreni Schneider, Sparky Anderson and John Kruk, the man who once said, "I'm not an athlete, I'm a baseball player."

And longstanding droughts came to noteworthy ends. The Cleveland Indians won a pennant for the first time in 41 years. A

UCLA's basketball title, which came 20 years after the Bruins won the last of their 10 NCAA crowns, was just one of many harkenings back. In flashes Jordan resurrected his form of 21 months earlier, before he had become a banjo-hitting rightfielder and still played the NBA's big rooms with his gutbucket style; the Baltimore Orioles' Cal Ripken Jr. evoked 1982, when he trotted out to short for the first of those 2,130 consecutive games.

Despite the work stoppages there was a businesslike, get-it-done style pervading much of what happened in sport. By breaking Lou Gehrig's consecutive-game streak Ripken served baseball's desperate need, in the aftermath of a labor dispute soiling parts of two seasons, to showcase someone who worked hard for his money. Steve Young merely led the NFL in passing for the fourth straight season without harvesting any of the accolades accorded his more swashbuckling predecessor, Joe Montana. (The name of the 49er president—Carmen Policy—seemed to get just right the team that easily throttled the San Diego Chargers in the Super Bowl: operatic drama, routinely supplied.)

Others who abided by this workaday spirit included Peter Blake and the New Zealanders who crewed *Black Magic*, the boat that failed to finish first in only one of 43 starts all year; the Kiwis swept all five races from Conner and the U.S. in the America's Cup final. The Virginia men and North Carolina women won NCAA soccer titles for the fourth straight year and the 12th in 13 years, respectively. At Stanford, "the Farm" to undergrads and alums, they seem to raise NCAA titles—the Cardinal won crowns in men's gymnastics, tennis and water polo and women's swimming and volleyball—like so many crops.

Sometimes the demarcation between winning and losing blurred so completely that one could pass for the other. NBA management won when labor won its fight against an effort by dissident players to decertify the union. The acclaimed documentary *Hoop Dreams*, an elegiac chronicle of inner-city life and basketball in Chicago, turned its snubbing for an Oscar into a windfall of sympathetic publicity—attention that allowed it to reach a much wider audience than it might have otherwise. Seles lost the U.S. Open final to Steffi Graf and showed the giddiness of a winner; Graf, the unwitting beneficiary of the unemployed lathe operator who had stabbed Seles 29 months earlier, won that event, and barricaded herself in a bathroom, crying her eyes out, distraught over the jailing of her father by German authorities for alleged tax evasion. The winners of two of the most prestigious events in their respective sports, Pete Sampras at Wimbledon and Ben Crenshaw at the Masters, took dewy-eyed inspiration from mentors ailing (Sampras's coach, Tim Gullikson, who suffered from brain cancer) or dead (Crenshaw's teacher, golf pedagogue and epigrammarian Harvey Penick). Thus the year's incongruous image: winners in tears.

**Sampras had a brilliant season, but suffered with his ailing coach.**

The NFL had to come to terms with the passing from existence of the Los Angeles Rams and the Los Angeles Raiders. Who could have envisioned the league with a team in the Carolinas and none on the West Coast south of Candlestick Park (which, in the spirit of disfigurement marking the year, will henceforth be known as 3Com Park)? The NFL *was* recognizable in that there was the usual Super Bowl blowout of the AFC champion, in this case the San Diego Chargers, by the NFC's best. With the Niners and the Cowboys meeting in the de facto title game two weeks earlier, a call went out for seeding the playoffs, as the NCAA does for its basketball tournament, in anticipation of a truly Super climax. Instead the NFC champs whupped the "junior circuit" for the 11th straight time—

BOB MARTIN

**Boosted by Horry's superb play, the Rockets repeated as NBA champions.**

as if the Super Bowl were nothing more than baseball's Midsummer Classic.

Speaking of baseball: Ringing up dingers in the thin mountain air, the expansion Colorado Rockies made the playoffs in only their third season, which was either (take your pick) an inspirationally meteoric rise or evidence of how watered-down the game had become. Seattle Mariner star Ken Griffey Jr., out from late May to mid-August with a broken wrist, may have assumed the title of Mr. October from Reggie Jackson. In the Mariners' thrilling five-game wild-card win over Jackson's former team, the Yankees, Griffey belted five round-trippers. Ironically it was the wild-card series, that much-maligned new round of play-offs, which turned out to be baseball's best case to woo the fans back.

Penn State's lot was that of the bridesmaid, several times over: The Nittany Lions were unbeaten but uncrowned, while their star tailback, Ki-Jana Carter, and quarterback Kerry Collins were left to congratulate Rashaan Salaam, the Colorado running back who won the Heisman Trophy. In this year of the nondescript, it was the faceless Huskers, known for the doughy, pasty mass of their offensive line, who scored the most satisfying of victories over Miami in the Orange Bowl.

Ed O'Bannon, the UCLA tri-captain with the warrior's knees, showed that a latter-day Bruin team won't always come up short on character in a big game; John Wooden

JOHN W. MCDONOUGH

looked talismanically on as the Bruins beat Arkansas for their first NCAA title since the old coach last unrolled his program. The Husky women of UConn did something with which Wooden is quite familiar, mushing their way from wire to wire without a loss; that they did so in the pale of Madison Avenue's tastemakers, and on the brink of an Olympics in Atlanta, touched off a whoopee over women's basketball that made a media star of their center, Wade Trophy–winner

Rebecca Lobo, and helped bring about a standing women's national team.

After 18 straight seasons in which no team successfully defended a title, the NBA has now crowned nothing but multiple-time wonders since 1986-87. The Houston Rockets seemed to take to heart all the bellyaching about the unsightliness with which they had beaten the New York Knicks in the Finals a year earlier; en route to defending their crown they looked sublime, particularly Robert Horry's feathery outside shooting and Hakeem Olajuwon's dreamy hipwork. Houston beat the San Antonio Spurs, the team with the league's best regular-season record and league MVP David Robinson, and then emphatically swept the Orlando Magic, a team of here-and-now flash and dash, of Shaq and Penny—but still only of the future. Meanwhile Jordan didn't have the most auspicious of comebacks. His shooting stroke came and went, he seemed occasionally out of sync with his teammates, and he famously frittered the ball away at a crucial moment of a playoff game against the Magic. But by laying 55 on the New York Knicks in Madison Square Garden only five games into his comeback, he left an impression of invulnerability.

The New Jersey Devils won the Stanley Cup in the most humdrum way possible—in a sweep and while employing an eye-glazing hockey tactic called the neutral-zone trap. Indeed, to summarize the difference between the sports year '94 and that of '95, one need only contrast the ado made over the New York Rangers' Cup victory with the palpable indifference when that cistern crossed the river. Even apart from the truncated 48-game regular season, things were slightly off form in the NHL. The "wrong" Lemieux set the tone for the playoffs: As Super Mario sat out the season to recover from Hodgkin's disease, Claude, the non-relative whose bruising style is found at the right extreme of the Devils' front line, saved his best hockey for the finals. Purists were alarmed at the ascendancy of brawn over skill, as Jersey's burlier line dominated the defter Detroit Red Wings in the finals, and

huge Philadelphia Flyer Eric Lindros supplanted Los Angeles King Wayne Gretzky as the league's totemic star.

Tyson's "return" was the year's singular sporting travesty. Peter McNeeley, a great white hopeless who had run up a 36–1 record by knocking over a row of opponents supplied by Contadina, promised to wrap the freed former heavyweight champ in "a cocoon of horror." Instead, 89 seconds into the first round, McNeeley's manager, Vinnie Vecchione, barged into the ring, putting a stop to the so-called fight. But there were sweet scientists whose efforts weren't shrouded in infamy. Lightweight Oscar De La Hoya—22 years old, already 19–0 and a self-described "young puppy in a game of big dogs"—proved to be so gifted and precocious that he invited comparisons to Sugar Ray Leonard. In winning the IBF super middleweight title with a pummeling of James Toney, who had been considered, pound-for-pound, the best fighter alive, Roy Jones Jr. appropriated that distinction. Meanwhile Pernell Whitaker distinguished himself as a fistic Renaissance man. By winning the WBA junior middleweight crown, he joined Leonard, Hearns and Duran as the only fighters to have won belts in four different divisions.

How could Thunder Gulch, a horse that had won the Fountain of Youth and the Florida Derby, go off at ridiculously long 25–1 odds when the Kentucky Derby rolled around? Well, it helped that the colt's trainer, D. Wayne Lukas, had also entered Timber Country and Serena's Song at Churchill Downs and talked them up so enthusiastically. By the end of Derby Day, Lukas looked like the guy who had gotten a bet down on every number on the wheel: Gulch, paying the highest price at the Derby in 28 years, outdistanced the field by more than two lengths. After Timber Country won the Preakness, and Gulch hoofed it to the winner's circle at the Belmont, Lukas became the first trainer to win the Triple Crown with different horses.

Like ducktailed greasers hot-rodding the strip, three drivers in their mid-20's auda-

**Indurain took the Tour de France for an unprecedented fifth straight time.**

ciously divvied up the auto racing universe among themselves. Jeff Gordon made NASCAR his own; Michael Schumacher assumed the mantle of the late Ayrton Senna, dominating the Formula One season; and Jacques Villeneuve, the son of racing great Gilles Villeneuve and the winner at Indy, lorded over the CART circuit.

Absent a World Cup, the U.S. national soccer team downed Chile, Argentina and Mexico in the Copa America, the team's most important competition outside the Mundial—and one from which two years earlier the Americans had made a prompt exit. (Alas, the Copa was available only regionally and on Spanish-language cable TV, so the benefit to the game's profile was minimal.) With no Olympics, there was no Kerriganza, no Tanyarama. In figure skating two workmanlike Americans, Todd Eldredge and Nicole Bobek, won the U.S. championships, and they were good citizens both. (What's that? Bobek had been named

in one burglary count of home invasion? Phooey; the charge was dropped.) At the worlds, the unindicted prevailed too: China's Chen Lu among the women, and Canada's Elvis Stojko among the men.

Track and field made do with a staging of the World Championships. "He's not doing anything for [fans of track and field]," grumbled Carl Lewis about Michael Johnson, the charisma-free sprinter with the tightly held emotions, who won three golds, including the 200 and 400 meters—a double never before accomplished at such a level. The reserve implied by the puritan name of British triple jumper Jonathan Edwards, who broke the 60-foot barrier in that event, got just about right the reception afforded track as a spectator sport on the Yank side of the pond.

There was nothing routine about the year to Corey Pavin, for a long time the best golfer never to win a major, who won the U.S. Open; or Mary Pierce, who won her first Grand Slam title, the Australian Open, without losing a set; or Boston Red Sox knuckleballer Tim Wakefield, who had the most losses in the American Association the season before and then fluttered his way to 16 wins in the majors. But much else about the year was routine, numbingly so. Nineteen-year-old Tiger Woods—yawn—won his second straight U.S. Amateur golf title, after bagging three Junior Amateur crowns in a row. Miguel Induráin—ho-hum—won the Tour de France, the 31-year-old Spaniard's fifth straight, a streak unmatched by Anquetil, Merckx, Hinault, LeMond or anyone else. Thomas Muster—so what else is new?—slugged out 35 straight victories on clay, including the final of the French. So it went, too, with Sergei Bubka (who at age 31 won yet another world pole-vault title) and Tony Gwynn (who once more slugged out hits more reliably than anyone in baseball).

The year marked the passing of NFL pioneer Woody Strode; sprinter Wilma Rudolph; boxer Jimmy Garcia, who died from injuries suffered in the ring; and two basketball big men who had somehow slipped into the crevices of obscurity, former Kentucky star Bill Spivey and Kresimir Cosic, the ex-BYU dervish from Croatia. The day after Fabio Casartelli was killed on a perilous descent during the Tour de France, the peloton saluted him by riding in a solemn processional. And the losses of the two most charismatic figures from their respective sports, Juan Manuel Fangio and Mickey Mantle, hit auto racing and baseball hard. Mantle seemed wryly conscious of the twisted world he would

soon be leaving; shortly after undergoing a liver transplant he wondered what his diseased organ might fetch on the memorabilia market.

So it went during this year of comings and goings, of activations and suspensions. With some things once part of the scene no longer there, and other things long gone suddenly restored, the 365 days could have been played out in the bustling ennui of a train station. In the end it really didn't matter so much who won or lost or even how they played the game. In the end, during 1995, what mattered most was that they played the game at all.

JONATHAN DANIEL/ALLSPORT

**The great Gwynn rapped out 197 hits and batted .368.**

compiled by John Bolster

## Baseball

**Nov 1, 1994**—With major league baseball in the third month of its work stoppage, a group including former New York congressman Robert J. Mrazek and ex-Major League Players' Association lawyer Dick Moss calls a news conference in New York City to announce plans for the United Baseball League. The organizers plan to field 10 teams beginning in 1996. If successful, the UBL would be the first league to rival MLB since the Federal League in 1914-15.

**Nov 4**—Free agent pitcher Dwight Gooden, the former ace of the New York Met staff, is suspended for the entire 1995 season for violating his aftercare program and baseball's drug policy.

**Nov 10**—"I did not expect any breakthroughs, and there weren't any." Those are the comments of players' union chief Don Fehr after players and owners meet in Rye Brook, N.Y., with mediator Bill Usery. It is just the fifth meeting between the two sides, and the first with a mediator, since the players struck on Aug. 12.

**Nov 17**—Major league owners set aside their salary cap plan and propose in its stead a graduated luxury tax. The proposal would include taxes of up to 100% when teams exceed a predetermined payroll level. The meetings in Herndon, Va., are adjourned for a week to give the players' union time to study the 102-page proposal.

**Nov 22**—The Houston Astros re-sign first baseman Jeff Bagwell, the Most Valuable Player in the NL in 1994, for seven years and $27.5 million.

**Nov 29**—At the bargaining table in Leesburg, Va., major league players make no counterproposal to the owners luxury tax plan of Nov.17, prompting owners to state that they are prepared to open spring training with replacement players.

**Nov 30**—Mediator Bill Usery convinces the owners to delay the unilateral implementation of a salary cap. The move would have gone hand-in-hand with a declaration of an impasse in negotiations.

**Nov 30**—Reliever Mitch (Wild Thing) Williams signs a one-year, non-guaranteed deal with the California Angels.

**Dec 5**—The owners' chief negotiator Richard Ravitch announces he will resign when his contract expires on Dec. 31.

**Dec 8**—San Francisco Giant outfielder Darryl Strawberry and his agent Eric Goldschmidt are indicted on federal tax evasion charges.

**Dec 9**—The Texas Rangers trade Jose Canseco to the Red Sox for Otis Nixon and prospect Luis Ortiz.

**Dec 14**—After an exchange of counterproposals regarding the owners' graduated taxation plan, talks in Rye Brook, N.Y., between the owners and striking players break down without a settlement.

**Dec 14**—The Chicago White Sox trade 1993 Cy Young Award winner Jack McDowell to the New York Yankees for minor leaguers Keith Heberling, a pitcher, and Lyle Mouton, an outfielder.

**Dec 15**—Major league owners again vote to postpone implementation of the

TOM DiPACE

**McDowell took the hill for New York.**

RICHARD MACKSON

**Nomo fanned 236 National League batters.**

salary cap. They set the deadline for a settlement at Dec. 22.

**Dec 15**—The New York Yankees sign free agent shortstop Tony Fernandez.

**Dec 19**—Negotiations between players and owners resume in Washington, D.C., with the goal of ending the four-month-old work stoppage by the end of the week.

**Dec 21**—Former Chicago White Sox DH Julio Franco signs with the Chiba Lotte Marines of Japan for $7 million over two years. The deal is the most lucrative in Japanese baseball history.

**Dec 22**—Major league owners announce that they will declare an impasse and impose their final salary cap proposal as of midnight, thereby sending the bitter labor dispute to the courtroom.

**Jan 1, 1995**—With the two sides unable to agree on a suitable wage increase as they negotiate a new labor pact, major league owners lock out the umpires.

**Jan 3**—While major league owners begin the task of hiring replacements for striking players, the incoming Congress begins formulating legislation that will repeal baseball's antitrust exemption.

**Jan 4**—Free agent outfielder Shane Mack, who hit .333 for the Minnesota Twins in 1994, signs with the Yomiuri Giants of Japan.

**Jan 9**—Former Philadelphia Phillie third baseman Mike Schmidt is elected to the Hall of Fame. Schmidt, whose 548 home runs place him seventh on the alltime list, received the most votes (444 of 460) ever cast by the Baseball Writers Association of America.

**Jan 18**—Ron Luciano, the former American League umpire known for his flamboyant style, is found dead of self-inflicted carbon monoxide poisoning in his garage in Binghamton, N.Y.

**Jan 26**—President Clinton orders players and owners to resume negotiations and empowers mediator Bill Usery to recommend a solution if appreciable progress is not made by Feb. 6.

**Feb 3**—Fred Feinstein, general counsel of the National Labor Relations Board (NLRB), notifies baseball owners that he plans to issue a complaint of unfair labor practices against them.

**Feb 7**—Major league players firmly reject Bill Usery's six-year plan for labor peace in baseball, and President Clinton fails to bring the two sides any closer during a five-hour meeting at the White House. Clinton will go to Congress with legislation calling for binding arbitration to settle the dispute.

**Feb 7**—The Major League Players' Association files an unfair labor practices charge with the NLRB.

**Feb 13**—The Los Angeles Dodgers sign five-time Japanese All-Star pitcher Hideo Nomo. Nomo becomes the first player ever to move from the Japanese majors to a North American major league team.

**Feb 16**—Spring training camps open with replacement players.

**Mar 1**—With replacement teams squaring off down the road in Tempe, major league owners and players meet in Scottsdale, Ariz., working toward a March 5 deadline for settlement if the season is to begin on time with regular players.

**Mar 5**—Negotiations in Scottsdale, Ariz., break down without a settlement.

**Mar 7**—Richie Ashburn, who patrolled center field for the Philadelphia Phillies from 1948 to 1959, is selected by the Veterans Committee for induction into the Hall of Fame. Ashburn hit .308 for his 15-year career.

**Mar 7**—Leon Day, the 78-year-old former star pitcher in the Negro Leagues, is selected by the Veterans Committee for induction into the Hall of Fame. Day opened the 1946 season with the Newark Eagles by pitching an 18-strikeout no-hitter, fanning future Hall of Famer Roy Campanella three times. Six days after his selection, Day dies.

**Mar 9**—Major League Baseball welcomes, at a price of $130 million apiece, the expansion franchises the Tampa Bay Devil Rays and the

Arizona Diamondbacks. The teams will begin play in 1998.

**Mar 14**—The NLRB announces it will charge major league owners with two counts of unfair labor practices but does not seek an immediate injunction against the owners.

**Mar 21**—With opening day only 12 days away, mediator Bill Usery fails to achieve a settlement after two days of secret meetings in Washington, D.C., with player rep Don Fehr and interim Commissioner Bud Selig.

**Mar 31**—Major league players end their strike, begun Aug. 12, after U.S. District Judge Sonia Sotomayor issues an injunction forcing owners to to return to the rules of the old labor pact. Two days later the owners accept the players' offer to return without an agreement, and it is decided that the 1995 season will be played, beginning April 26, under the previous labor conditions.

**Apr 3**—Bo Jackson, who was a star in both the NFL and Major League Baseball until a hip injury ended his football career in 1991, announces his retirement from baseball.

**Apr 7**—Citing financial difficulty, the Kansas City Royals trade pitcher David Cone to the Toronto Blue Jays for three minor leaguers.

**Apr 10**—Major league umpires, locked out by the owners since Jan. 1, decide to picket selected spring training sites.

**Apr 11**—The New York Mets sign free agent centerfielder Brett Butler, 38, to a one-year, $2 million contract.

**April 18**—Pitcher Jack Morris, 39, announces his retirement. Morris was the MVP of the 1991 World Series.

**April 19**—After 22 seasons with nine different teams, Rich (Goose) Gossage, 43, announces his

retirement. The following day reliever Jeff Reardon retires at the age of 39.

**April 25**—Darryl Strawberry is sentenced to three years probation and ordered to pay $350,000 for federal tax evasion.

**April 25**—Opening Night … Finally! Though the fans boo during pregame introductions, Miami's Joe Robbie Stadium is sold out for the league opener between the Florida Marlins and the Los Angeles Dodgers. The Dodgers' Raul Mondesi launches a 421-foot home run on the game's 11th pitch, and adds another in the seventh inning to pace Los Angeles's 8–7 victory. Labor problems persist, however, as the game is played with replacement umpires while the locked-out regular umps picket the stadium gates.

**April 26**—Opening days around the league, with exceptions in Colorado and Toronto, are significantly under-attended as the fans express their disillusionment after the offseason labor dispute.

**May 1**—Major League Baseball's 120-day lockout of the umpires ends as the two sides strike a five-year deal during nonstop weekend negotiations.

**May 2**—Hideo Nomo, the first Japanese-born major leaguer in 30 years, makes his debut with the Los Angeles Dodgers. He strikes out seven in five innings of work.

**May 2**—Rowdy fan protests break out at several major league stadiums during baseball's first week, with the the most extreme case in Detroit during the Tigers-Indians game. Detroit fans hurl "ugly verbal abuse" as well as bottles, baseballs, beercans and a napkin dispenser at Cleveland players, nearly stopping the game.

**May 7**—The Minnesota Twins and Cleveland Indians play for six hours and 36 minutes, using a combined total of 47 players. Kenny Lofton puts an end to the marathon in the bottom of the 17th with an RBI single that gives the Indians a 10–9 victory.

DAVID LIAM KYLE

**May 8**—Former Cincinnati Red Gus Bell, 66, dies after suffering a heart attack.

**May 25**—Oakland reliever Dennis Eckersley records the 300th save of his career.

**May 26**—Seattle centerfielder Ken Griffey Jr. breaks his left wrist after slamming into the wall while making a catch against the Orioles. The Mariner star will be out of action until August.

**The Boss offered Strawberry a chance to get back on his feet.**

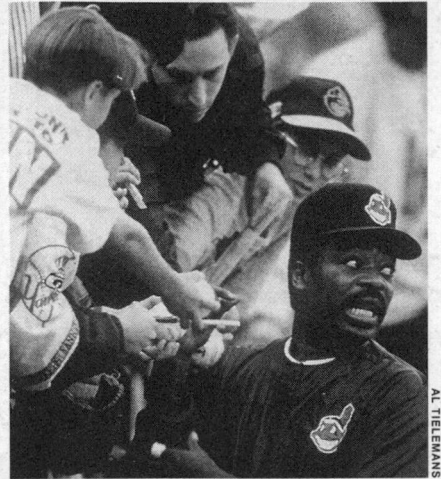

AL TIELEMANS

**Murray wrote his own ticket to Cooperstown.**

**May 30**—Glenn Burke, an outfielder for the Los Angeles Dodgers and the Oakland A's in the late '70s, dies of AIDS in San Leandro, Calif. Burke, 42, was the only major league ballplayer to go public about his homosexuality.

**June 3**—San Francisco Giant slugger Matt Williams fouls a ball off of his foot, breaking a bone and sidelining him for six weeks. At the time of his injury Williams is leading the league in hitting (.381), homers (13) and RBI (35).

**June 3**—Montreal pitcher Pedro Martinez takes a perfect game into the 10th inning before yielding a double to San Diego's Bip Roberts. The Expos win 1–0.

**June 6**—Don Zimmer, 64, retires after 47 years in the game as a player, coach and manager.

**June 8**—Hall of Famer Mickey Mantle undergoes liver transplant surgery in Dallas.

**June 14**—Hideo Nomo strikes out 16 Pirates in an 8–5 Dodger victory, and Giant infielder Mike Benjamin gets six hits against the Cubs to give him 14 over three games, a major league record.

**June 19**—The New York Yankees sign beleaguered outfielder Darryl Strawberry.

**June 25**—Colorado first baseman Andres Galarraga becomes the fourth player in history to homer in three consecutive innings during an 11–3 rout of the Padres.

**June 30**—Cleveland's Eddie Murray becomes the 20th major leaguer to amass 3,000 hits.

**July 11**—With three hits, all of them home runs, the National League wins the 66th All-Star Game, 3–2.

**July 14**—Ramon Martinez of the Dodgers

pitches the first and only no-hitter of the season against Florida.

**July 20**—Hall of Famers Duke Snider and Willie McCovey plead guilty to income tax evasion regarding income derived in autograph signings.

**July 21**—The Cincinnati Reds trade Deion Sanders to San Francisco in an eight-player deal.

**July 23**—Pitcher Dave Stewart, who starred for Oakland and Toronto, announces his retirement.

**July 30**—White Sox DH John Kruk singles in the first inning at Baltimore, then retires from baseball.

**July 31**—In a flurry of activity before the day's trading deadline, the New York Yankees acquire pitcher David Cone from Toronto and trade Danny Tartabull to Oakland for Ruben Sierra; the Colorado Rockies acquire pitcher Bret Saberhagen from the Mets for two minor leaguers; and the Mariners deal pitcher Ron Villone and outfielder Marc Newfield to San Diego for pitcher Andy Benes.

**Aug 3**—The Senate Judiciary Committee votes 9–8 to repeal baseball's antitrust exemption.

**Aug 9**—Doctors at Baylor University Medical Center in Dallas announce that Yankee legend Mickey Mantle has an aggressive form of cancer known as hepatoma. Mantle dies on Aug. 13.

**Sept 4**—Chicago White Sox third baseman Robin Ventura belts two grand slams in a 14–3 rout of the Texas Rangers. He is the eighth player in history to accomplish the feat.

**Sept 5**—Cal Ripken plays in his 2,130th consecutive game, tying Lou Gehrig's ironman record, set in 1939. Ripken homers in the sixth inning; the following day he hits another home run and eclipses Gehrig in an emotional celebration at Baltimore's Camden Yards.

**Sept 8**—The Cleveland Indians clinch the AL Central title, their first division crown since 1954.

**Sept 13**—The Atlanta Braves clinch the NL East, their fourth consecutive division title.

**Sept 19**—Colorado's Andres Galarraga hits his 30th home run, making the Rockies the second team in major league history to have four players hit 30 homers in a season.

**Oct 2**—Randy Johnson pitches a three-hitter with 12 strikeouts as Seattle beats California 9–1 in a one-game playoff to seal the AL West crown and their first trip to the playoffs in 19 years as a franchise.

**Oct 6**—The Indians beat the Red Sox 8–2 to sweep their first-round playoff series.

**Oct 6**—The Cincinnati Reds sweep the Dodgers out of the playoffs with a 10–1 rout in Game 3 of their division series.

**Oct 7**—The Atlanta Braves down Colorado 10–4 to take their first-round series in four games.

**Oct 8**—In the most exciting first-round playoff tilt

the Mariners beat New York 6–5 in 11 innings to take the series three games to two. The Yankees won Game 2 on a home run by Jim Leyritz in the 15th inning.

**Oct 14**—The Braves complete a four-game sweep of Cincinnati in the NLCS with a 6–0 win at Atlanta-Fulton County Stadium. Atlanta's pitching staff compiles a 1.15 ERA for the series, and Mike Devereaux, who has game-winning hits in Games 1 and 4, is named MVP.

**Oct 17**—The Indians defeat the Mariners 4–0 to win the ALCS in six games and advance to the World Series for the first time in 41 years. Orel Hershiser, who won Games 2 and 5 with a 1.29 ERA, is named MVP of the series.

**Oct 28**—The Braves win their first World Series title since 1957 with a 1–0 victory over Cleveland in Game 6 in Atlanta. David Justice hits a sixth-inning homer, and Tom Glavine, who throws eight innings of one-hit ball, is named World Series MVP.

## Boxing

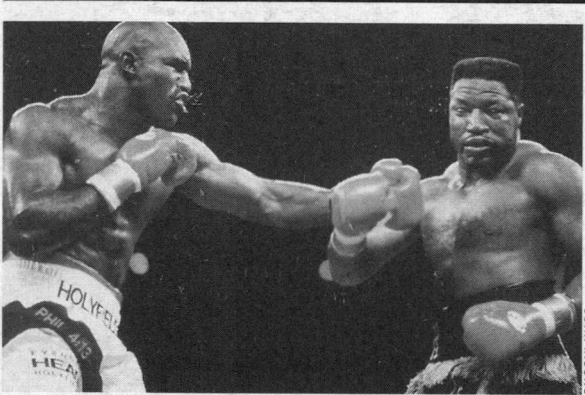

**Holyfield (left) came back with a jarring win over Mercer.**

**Jan 9, 1995**—Carlos Monzon, a former middleweight champion who was convicted in 1988 of murdering his estranged lover, is killed in a car accident outside Buenos Aires.

**Feb 25**—Gerald McClellan collapses and slips into a coma during the 10th round of his super middleweight title fight with Nigel Benn in London. Doctors say the immediate medical care he receives saves his life. He regains consciousness 11 days later.

**Nov 5, 1994**—George Foreman stuns Michael Moorer with a short right in the 10th round of their heavyweight title fight in Las Vegas. The blow knocks Moorer out and makes the 45-year-old Foreman, who last held the title in 1974, the oldest heavyweight champion in history.

**Nov 12**—Terry Norris loses his WBC junior middleweight title in Mexico City after being disqualified in the fourth round for hitting challenger Luis Santana in the neck. On the undercard, Humberto Gonzalez defends his WBC and IBF junior flyweight titles with a hard-fought majority decision over No. 1-contender Michael Carbajal; and Ricardo Lopez retains his WBC strawweight title with an eighth-round TKO of Javier Varguez.

**Nov 16**—Michael Moorer retires. He will un-retire the following spring.

**Nov 18**—Super middleweight Roy Jones Jr. runs his record to 27–0 and stakes his claim to the world "pound for pound" title with an impressive unanimous decision over James Toney in their IBF title bout.

**Nov 23**—Former heavyweight champion Evander Holyfield, who was diagnosed with a heart condition last April, receives medical clearance from the Mayo Clinic to resume his career.

**Mar 25**—Heavyweight Mike Tyson is released from the Indiana Youth Center in Plainfield where he served three years for rape. Five days later he confirms that Don King will be his promoter as he resumes his boxing career.

**Apr 8**—Two segments of the fractured, mediocre heavyweight division are settled in Las Vegas as Oliver McCall narrowly outpoints 45-year-old ex-champ Larry Holmes to retain the WBC title, and former Mike Tyson sparring partner Bruce Seldon stops Tony Tucker in the seventh round to win the WBA belt.

**Apr 8**—For the second time in five months junior middleweight Terry Norris is disqualified from a title fight with Luis Santana. This time he decks Santana seven seconds after the bell sounds to end the third round, and Santana, who had hit the canvas twice in Round 2, is carried out of the ring, still champion.

**Apr 22**—George Foreman narrowly retains his heavyweight title in Las Vegas with a disputed majority decision over little-known Axel Schulz of Germany.

**May 19**—Super featherweight Jimmy Garcia dies in a Las Vegas hospital from injuries he sustained in his May 6 title fight with Gabriel Ruelas.

**May 20**—Evander Holyfield is impressive in his return to the ring, outpointing a tough Ray Mercer over 10 rounds in Atlantic City.

**June 17**—Riddick Bowe floors Jorge Gonzalez in the sixth round of their WBO heavyweight title fight.

**June 25**—Undefeated IBF super middleweight champion Roy Jones Jr. stops Vinny Pazienza in the sixth round of their bout in Atlantic City.

**July 9**—Tracy Patterson, son of former heavyweight champ Floyd Patterson, scores a second-round TKO of Eddie Hopson in Reno for the IBF junior lightweight title.

**Aug 19**—Mike Tyson's much-anticipated return to the ring lends new dimension to the term *travesty*. With over a million pay-per-view customers tuning in at up to $50 a pop, and ringside seats going for $1,500, Tyson floors someone named Peter McNeeley, who sports a questionable 36–1 record, in six seconds. Less than 90 seconds later McNeeley's trainer, Vinnie Vecchione, jumps into the ring, causing the "fight" to end in a disqualification.

# College Basketball

**Nov 8, 1994**—Southern Cal coach George Raveling walks with the help of a cane out of a Los Angeles hospital. He has spent six weeks recuperating from a Sept. 25 automobile accident in which he sustained lung and heart trauma, a broken collarbone and a broken pelvis. One week later he resigns as Southern Cal men's basketball coach in order to focus on his recovery. Former assistant Charlie Parker will take over as head coach.

**Nov 20**—In the women's Hall of Fame Tip-Off Classic in Jackson, Tenn., No. 1-ranked Tennessee downs No. 2 Louisiana Tech 69–62.

**Nov 23**—Washington wins the first preseason Women's National Invitation Tournament, defeating Texas Tech 79–75 in the final at Lubbock, Tex. The defeat ends Texas Tech's 25-game home winning streak.

**Nov 26**—Minnesota guard Voshon Lenard scores 24 points to lead the Gophers to a 79–74 victory over Brigham Young in the final of the men's Great Alaska Shootout.

**Nov 25**—Gary Trent of Ohio scores 33 points and grabs 20 rebounds during the 15th-ranked Bobcats' 84–80 overtime victory against New Mexico St. in the final of the preseason National Invitation Tournament.

**Nov 28**—For just the fourth time in NCAA basketball history a coaching matchup pitting father against son occurs as Hugh Durham leads Georgia to an 87–57 rout of his son Doug Durham's Georgia Southern team.

**Dec 4**—After a ten-year absence the dunk returns to women's basketball when six-foot Charlotte Smith of North Carolina steals a pass early in the Tar Heels 113–58 trouncing of North Carolina A&T, races the length of the court and throws it down one-handed.

**Jan 16, 1995**—Connecticut (13–0) grabs the No. 1 women's ranking by defeating previously unbeaten Tennessee, 77–66, at Storrs, Conn.

**Jan 22**—Duke athletic director Tom Butters announces that coach Mike Krzyzewski, recovering from back surgery and exhaustion, will be out for the rest of the season.

**Floor general Edney specialized in the slash-and-dish.**

# College Basketball (Cont.)

**Feb 7**—Some 150 students take over the court at halftime of the Rutgers-UMass game to protest racially charged comments made by Rutgers University President Francis Lawrence.

**Feb 13**—After key weekend victories, both the Connecticut men's and women's teams are ranked No. 1 in the coaches' polls, an NCAA first.

**Feb 21**—Kansas loses to unranked Oklahoma, 76–73, to become the fourth team in four weeks to drop out of the top spot in the polls.

**Mar 16**—March Madness descends as No. 13-seed Manhattan, whose at-large bid was largely criticized, knocks off No. 4 Oklahoma in the Southeast Regional of the NCAA tournament. In the Midwest, No. 5 Arizona performs its seemingly annual swoon, falling to No. 12 Miami (OH), 71–62.

**Mar 19**—Top seed UCLA survives a scare from Missouri and wins, 75–74, thanks to guard Tyus Edney's coast-to-coast rush for a buzzer-beating layup. Georgetown joins the Bruins in the Sweet 16, and in similar fashion: Hoya forward Don Reid grabs a last-second air ball from guard Allen Iverson and stuffs it through for a 53–51 victory. Four ACC teams reach the Sweet 16, while the Big Ten, with six tourney bids, fails to place one team in the third round.

**Mar 26**—Fourth-seeded Oklahoma State surprises No. 2 Massachusetts, 68–54, to win the East Regional and advance to the Final Four where they join defending champ Arkansas, North Carolina and UCLA. In the women's tournament, unbeaten Connecticut reaches the semis with a 67–63 win over Virginia and will face Stanford (30–2). The other bracket pits Tennessee against Georgia.

**Mar 29**—Virginia Tech defeats Marquette 65–64 in overtime to win the National Invitation Tournament in New York City.

**Apr 2**—Connecticut defeats Tennessee 70–64 to win the women's national championship. The Huskies are the first team from the Northeast ever to win the tournament, and their 35–0 record is the best in Division I history.

**Apr 3**—UCLA defeats Arkansas 89–78 to win the school's first national title in 20 years. Ed O'Bannon scores 30 points and grabs 17 rebounds and is named the Outstanding Player of the Final Four. Bruin freshman Toby Bailey rises to the occasion with nine rebounds and 26 points.

**May 8**—Four days after teammate and fellow sophomore Rasheed Wallace does so, North Carolina's Jerry Stackhouse, a 6'6" forward, announces he will enter the NBA draft in June.

# College Football

**Oct 29, 1994**—Third-ranked Nebraska (9–0) asserts itself as a national title contender with a convincing 24–7 win over No. 2 Colorado in Lincoln. In Eugene, Ore., the surprising Oregon Ducks upend eighth-ranked Arizona 10–9 to create a four-way tie for first in the Pac-10.

**Nov 5**—Despite a 35–29 victory over Indiana—which makes three late, meaningless scores—Penn State (8–0) drops out of the top spot in the polls it shared with Nebraska (10–0), a 45–17 winnner over Kansas.

**Nov 5**—Miami (7–1, No. 3) moves closer to the Big East title and an Orange Bowl bid with a 27–6 pasting of ninth-ranked Syracuse in the Carrier Dome. Sixth-ranked Florida State wins its 23rd consecutive game in the ACC, wrecking Georgia Tech 41–10.

**Nov 8**—Michigan State coach George Perles, who has been accused by a former player of violating NCAA rules and is feeling the pressure of several mediocre seasons, announces he will not return for the 1995-96 season.

**Nov 10**—Wisconsin running back Brent Moss, MVP of the 1994 Rose Bowl, is suspended from the Badger team in the wake of his arrest on a cocaine possession charge.

**Nov 12**—Trailing Illinois 31–21 in the fourth quarter in Champaign, Ill., No. 2 Penn State rallies to a 35–31 victory, preserving its 9–0 record. Third-ranked Alabama also rallies from a 10-point fourth-quarter deficit to remain undefeated, downing No. 20 Mississippi State 29–25 in Starkville, Miss. With the victory the Crimson Tide clinches its third straight trip to the SEC title game.

**Nov 12**—In Lawrence, Kan., Colorado's Heisman Trophy candidate Rashaan Salaam rushes for 232 yards and three TDs in the Buffaloes' 51–26 pounding of Kansas. Salaam regains the national lead in rushing yards with the performance, and his three scores give him 132 points on the year, breaking Byron (Whizzer) White's 57-year-old record for points in a season. Alcorn State's Steve McNair, another Heisman candidate, helps his case by passing for 476 yards and rushing for another 110 in a comeback win over Troy State.

**Nov 17**—Wisonsin running back Brent Moss pleads guilty to cocaine possession in Madison, Wisc., and is fined $250 and sentenced to two years' probation.

**Nov 19**—Oregon defeats Oregon State 17–13 to clinch the Pac-10 title and its first trip to the Rose Bowl since 1958. Many (including SI) had picked the Ducks to finish near the bottom of the conference, but after a 1–2 start the team wins eight of its last nine and heads to Pasadena.

**Nov 19**—In the annual war for bragging rights in the state of Alabama, Alabama (11–0) holds on to a 21–14 victory over Auburn (9-1-1) when the Tigers fall short on fourth-and-three in the closing seconds. Yale defeats Harvard 32–13 in the 111th game between the two schools. Ohio State beats Michigan for the first time in seven years, 22–6. Colorado State rallies to beat Fresno State 44–42 and win its first WAC title since joining the conference in 1968.

**Nov 19**—Rashaan Salaam of Colorado gains 259 yards rushing against Iowa State to raise his season total to 2,055 yards. Only three other backs—Marcus Allen (1981), Mike Rozier ('83) and Barry Sanders ('88)—have broken the 2,000-yard barrier in a season; all three won the Heisman. After the Buffs' 41–20 victory Colorado coach Bill McCartney announces he will resign following the season to spend more time with his family.

**Nov 26**—With quarterback Tommie Frazier back in the lineup for the first time since being sidelined Sept. 24 because of blood clots in his leg, top-ranked Nebraska flattens Oklahoma 13–3 to finish the regular season at 12–0. Penn State running back Ki-Jana Carter makes a strong closing statement for his Heisman Trophy candidacy with a 227-yard, five-TD performance in the Nittany Lions' 59–31 win over Michigan State. Rose Bowl-bound Penn State closes the regular season with a Big Ten title and an 11–0 record—but a No. 2 national ranking.

**Nov 26**—Florida State, down 31–3 in the fourth quarter, scores 28 unanswered points and ties Florida 31–31 before a record 80,210 in Tallahassee. Steve McNair ends his career at Alcorn State with a 63–20 first-round playoff loss to defending I-AA champ Youngstown State. Young's closing line: 52-for-82, 514 yards, 3 TD, 3 INT.

**Nov 28**—Bill Walsh, 63, resigns as head coach at Stanford. Rick Neuheisel is hired to replace Bill McCartney at Colorado.

**Dec 3**—Alabama sees its national title hopes dashed in a 24–23 loss to Florida in the SEC title game. The outcome puts Florida in the Sugar Bowl for a rematch with Florida State and relegates Alabama to the Citrus Bowl against Ohio State.

**Dec 3**—Army defeats Navy 22–20 thanks to Kurt Heiss's 52-yard field goal with six minutes remaining. Navy coach George Chaump, who is 1–4 against the Cadets, is fired the next day.

**Dec 10**—Colorado running back Rashaan Salaam wins the 1994 Heisman Trophy, outpointing Penn State's Ki-Jana Carter 1,743 to 901. In other awards presented during the week Nebraska's Zach Wiegert wins the Outland Trophy as the nation's top interior lineman, Kerry

**Air McNair meant instant 0 for Alcorn State.**

Collins of Penn State wins the Davey O'Brien Memorial Award as the best quarterback in the country, and Illinois linebacker Dana Howard wins the Butkus Award.

**Dec 10**—North Alabama holds off Texas A&M-Kingsville to win the Division II national championship game in Florence, Ala., 16–10. In the Division III title tilt, also known as the Amos Alonzo Stagg Bowl, Albion routs Washington & Jefferson 38–15.

**Dec 17**—Youngstown State defeats Boise State 28–14 to win the Division I-AA national championship, the school's third title in four years.

**Dec 19**—Alcorn State quarterback Steve McNair wins the Walter Payton Award as the top player in Division I-AA. Jim Tressel of Youngstown State is named Division I-AA Coach of the Year.

**Jan 1, 1995**—Trailing Miami 17–9 entering the fourth quarter, Nebraska rallies behind fullback Corey Schlesinger's two fourth-quarter touchdown runs to win 24–17. It is Nebraska's first bowl victory in its past eight tries.

**Jan 2**—Penn State trounces Oregon 38–20 in the Rose Bowl to complete a perfect 12–0 season. Florida State (10-1-1) downs Florida 23–17 in the Sugar Bowl and Colorado (11–1) wins the Fiesta bowl 41–24 over Notre Dame.

**Jan 3**—Both the Associated Press and the *USA Today/*CNN polls rank 13–0 Nebraska No. 1, giving coach Tom Osborne his first national title in 22 years as a head coach. Penn State, which also finished undefeated, at 12–0, is ranked second in both polls, and Colorado is third.

**Jan 3**—Heisman Trophy winner Rashaan Salaam of Colorado decides to forego his final year of NCAA eligibility and enter the NFL draft. Also leaving for the NFL as juniors are Brigham Young quarterback John Walsh and Miami defensive end Warren Sapp.

**Jan 4**—The NCAA releases 1994-95 attendance figures and, for the 21st consecutive year, Michigan tops the list, averaging an alltime record 106,217 fans per game. Penn State is second with an average of 96,289. Attendance for all 568 NCAA teams tops 36 million.

**Jan 11**—Nebraska's Tom Osborne is named Division I-A Coach of the Year by the American Football Coaches Association.

**May 1**—Michigan coach Gary Moeller is suspended indefinitely with pay following a drunken altercation with police and customers in a Southfield, Mich., restaurant on April 28. Moeller was asked to leave the restaurant after he became abusive and disorderly. When he refused, police were called and the coach pushed and punched an officer in the chest. He spent the night in jail.

**May 4**—Gary Moeller resigns as Michigan football coach following his April 28 arrest on disorderly conduct and assault and battery charges. The school names former defensive coordinator Lloyd Carr as interim coach, and begins the search, with the season less than four months away, for a permanent successor. Moeller won three Big Ten titles and compiled a 44-13-3 record in five seasons at Michigan.

**May 16**—The NCAA announces the addition of the Haka Bowl, to be played in Auckland, New Zealand, as early as 1996. The bowl will be played in Auckland's 52,000-seat, Eden Park Stadium and most likely will involve Pac-10 or WAC teams.

**July 18**—The NCAA eligibility committee reduces the suspension of Maryland quarterback Scott Milanovich from eight to four games. Two days later Milanovich, who was suspended for

gambling on college football and college basketball from 1992 to '94, decides to remain at Maryland after considering a jump to the NFL.

**Aug 2**—After finding the Alabama football program guilty of several rules violations, including improper bank loans to a former player, the NCAA Committee on Infractions imposes a three-year probation, a one-year ban from postseason play and a reduction by four of the program's overall scholarship limit.

**Aug 28**—Ohio State and Boston College launch the 1995-96 season in the Kickoff Classic at Giants Stadium in East Rutherford, N.J. The tenth-ranked Buckeyes rout the No. 23 Eagles 38–6. In the Pigskin Classic in Ann Arbor, Mich., Michigan edges Virginia 18–17 with a touchdown on the game's final play.

**Aug 31**—Nebraska opens its defense of the national title in impressive fashion, overwhelming Oklahoma State 64–21 in Stillwater, Okla.

**Sept 2**—The season's first shocker occurs in South Bend, Ind., where unranked Northwestern upsets Notre Dame 17–15. The last time the Wildcats defeated the Irish was in 1962. In Pasadena, Calif., 15th-ranked UCLA trounces No. 9 Miami 31–8.

**Sept 10**—Running back Lawrence Phillips, a Heisman Trophy candidate for second-ranked Nebraska, is suspended from the Husker team following his arrest on misdemeanor assault of a female acquaintance.

**Oct 7**—Fourth-ranked Ohio State travels to State College, Pa., and nips defending Big Ten champ Penn State 28–25. The Buckeyes are 5–0.

**Oct 14**—Iowa gets off to its best start since 1986, going 5–0 with a 22–13 win against Indiana. Top-ranked Florida State, averaging 66 points per game in the ACC, torches Duke 72–13, and No. 2 Nebraska keeps pace, steamrolling Missouri 57–0. Others in the national title picture are Florida (6–0) and Ohio State (7–0).

**Oct 21**—Notre Dame rebounds from two early losses to hand USC its first loss of the season, 38–10 in South Bend. Northwestern improves to 6–1 with a 35–0 blanking of Wisconsin and assures its first winning season since 1971. Kansas streaks to 7–0—its best start since 1968—with a 38–17 win over Oklahoma.

**Nov 27, 1994**—Tom Watson sinks a 15-foot birdie putt on the first playoff hole to win The Skins Game Championship in Palm Desert, Calif. He earns $210,000 over the two-day event; Fred Couples finishes second, earning $170,000.

**Dec 6**—Ernie Els of South Africa, who earned a

rookie-record $684,000 in 1994, is named PGA Tour Rookie of the Year. Two days later Nick Price, who won five tournaments and $1,499,927, is named PGA Player of the Year.

**Jan 22, 1995**—Pat Bradley earns her first LPGA Tour victory since her Hall of Fame-clinching win

**Daly showed his resilience by winning the British Open.**

on Sept. 29,1991, claiming the HealthSouth Inaugural title in Lake Buena Vista, Fla.

**Feb 26**—Corey Pavin becomes the first player since Arnold Palmer in 1966-67 to win back-to-back Nissan Open titles.

**Mar 26**—Nanci Bowen wins the Nabisco Dinah Shore in Rancho Mirage, Calif., shooting a final-round 70 to defeat Susie Redman by one stroke.

**Apr 9**—Tying Ben Hogan for the second-best score in Masters history, Ben Crenshaw shoots a 14-under-par 274 to win at Augusta for the second time in the past 12 years. It is an emotional victory for Crenshaw, who served as a pallbearer at his lifelong friend and mentor Harvey Penick's funeral on the eve of the tournament.

**May 14**—Trailing Britain's Laura Davies by three strokes with seven holes to play, Kelly Robbins rallies to win the LPGA Championship in Wilmington, Del.

**June 18**—Long known as one of the Tour's toughest competitors, Corey Pavin finally wins a major, taking the U.S. Open title at Shinnecock Hills in Southampton, New York. Pavin hits an instant classic of a shot on his approach to the 18th in the final round to secure the victory.

**June 25**—Betsy King shoots a final-round 67 to win the ShopRite Classic at Somers Point, N.J. It is the 30th victory of her career and makes her the 15th player to qualify for the LPGA Hall Of Fame.

**July 2**—Wearing a pink ribbon on his cap in honor of his wife, who is undergoing treatment for breast cancer, Tom Weiskopf shoots a 13-under-par 275 for a stirring victory at the U.S. Senior Open in Bethesda, Md.

**July 16**—Sweden's Annika Sorenstam shoots three consecutive birdies, beginning with the ninth hole, and then holds on for a one-stroke victory over Meg Mallon at the U.S. Open in Colorado Springs.

**July 23**—John Daly wins the British Open at St. Andrews, Scotland, following a four-hole playoff with Costantino Rocca.

**Aug 13**—Six strokes off the pace entering the final round of the PGA Championship in Pacific Palisades, Calif., Australia's Steve Elkington shoots a 64 to tie for the lead, then sinks a 25-foot putt to win on the first hole of a sudden-death playoff with Colin Montgomerie of Scotland.

**Aug 27**—Jenny Lidback gets her first career victory at the du Maurier Ltd. Classic in Pointe Claire, Quebec. Leading Sweden's Liselotte Neumann by one stroke throughout the tournament, Lidback shoots par in the final round to hold on for the win.

**Aug 27**—Tiger Woods wins his second consecutive U.S. Men's Amateur title in Newport, R.I., defeating Buddy Marucci, two-up. In Akron, Ohio, Greg Norman sinks a 66-foot chip shot on the first playoff hole to beat Nick Price and Billy Mayfair for the PGA Tour World Series of Golf title.

**Sept 17**—Shooting a course-record 61 in the final round, Hal Sutton wins for the first time in almost nine years, taking the B.C. Open by one stroke over Jim McGovern.

**Sept 24**—Europe wins seven of the last 10 singles matches to rally from a 10–7 deficit and defeat the U.S. at the Ryder Cup. It is Europe's second victory on U.S soil in the 62-year history of the event.

**Oct 22**—Duffy Waldorf shoots a final round 65 at the Texas Open for the first victory of his nine-year PGA career. The $198,000 he wins in prize money, however, is not enough to qualify him for the Tour Championship. Second place finisher Justin Leonard earns $118,000 to move from 33rd to 24th on the season money list. The top 30 earners qualify for the Tour Championship.

**Oct 22**—Scotland wins its first Dunhill Cup in 11 years, defeating Zimbabwe 2–1 at St. Andrews. Nick Price shoots a record 20-under-par to earn Zimbabwe's point. The U.S. finishes last in its group.

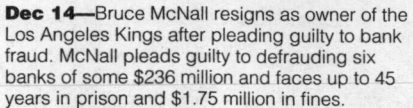

**Nov 3, 1994**—With the NHL lockout reaching its 33rd day the league announces it will cut 10 more games from the upcoming schedule, reducing it to 70 games.

**Nov 15**—Three men are inducted into the Hockey Hall of Fame in Toronto. Defenseman Lionel Conacher, who won Stanley Cup titles with Chicago and Montreal, and Harry Watson, a left wing who won four Stanley Cups with Toronto and one with Detroit, are inducted in the Veterans category, and administrator Brian O'Neill is inducted in the Builders category.

**Nov 17**—After an exchange of proposals between the players' union and NHL owners produces no settlement, the league cuts ten more games from the schedule, reducing the season to 60 games.

**Nov 26**—The players' union decides to take time out to study the proposals that have come out of six marathon negotiating sessions over the past 10 days.

**Dec 6**—With salary arbitration, free agency and a rookie salary cap among the major sticking points, talks in Chicago between players and NHL owners break down without a settlement. Commissioner Gary Bettman considers calling a deadline for canceling the season.

**Dec 8**—The NHL cancels the All-Star Game, scheduled for Jan. 21.

**Dec 14**—Bruce McNall resigns as owner of the Los Angeles Kings after pleading guilty to bank fraud. McNall pleads guilty to defrauding six banks of some $236 million and faces up to 45 years in prison and $1.75 million in fines.

**Dec 29**—NHL commissioner Gary Bettman sets a Jan. 16 deadline for settlement of the labor dispute. Without a settlement before that date, the season will be canceled.

**Jan 11, 1995**—With each side grumbling about concessions made to the other, the NHL owners and players' union sign a new six-year Collective Bargaining Agreement, thereby ending the 103-day lockout. The season, cut from 84 to 48 games, will begin Jan. 20.

**Jan 20**—The NHL season resumes, and if fans have resentment concerning the five-month labor dispute, they do not express it. With few exceptions, large crowds turn out around the league. In Tampa Bay the second-largest crowd in league history (26,387) attends the Lightning's opener against Pittsburgh.

**Jan 26**—Mark Messier signs a two-year deal with the New York Rangers that will pay him roughly $6 million a year, making him the second-highest paid player in the NHL, behind Wayne Gretzky.

**Jan 26**—Five-time All-Star Michel Goulet, a left wing who scored 548 goals during his 15-year career with Quebec and Chicago, announces his retirement.

DAVID E. KLUTHO

**Feb 2**—Mike Keenan earns his 400th career coaching victory in the St Louis Blues' 5–4 defeat of Winnipeg. Keenan reaches the milestone in his 731st game, fourth fastest in NHL history.

**Feb 7**—Pittsburgh Penguin right wing Joe Mullen becomes the first U.S.-born player to score 1,000 career points. He reaches the 1,000-point plateau by assisting on John Cullen's second period goal during the Pens' 7–3 rout of Florida.

**Feb 9**—The Philadelphia Flyers deal right wing Mark Recchi to the Montreal Canadiens in exchange for center John LeClair, left wing Gilbert Dionne and defenseman Eric Desjardins.

**Feb 18**—The Pittsburgh Penguins lose to Hartford 4–2, ending their season-opening unbeaten streak at 13 games, third longest in NHL history.

**Mar 13**—Washington goalie Jim Carey is named NHL player of the week. Called up from the minors on

**Keith Primeau and the Red Wings had the NHL's best record, but no title.**

## Brodeur blanked Boston in three of five games.

Mar. 2, Carey goes 6-0-1, capping the run with a 3–0 shutout of Tampa Bay.

**Mar 16**—Pat LaFontaine returns to action for the first time since tearing his anterior cruciate ligament in Nov. 1993. The Buffalo center scores a goal and assists on another as the Sabres beat the Islanders 6–3.

**Apr 1**—Alexei Zhamnov of the Winnipeg Jets scores five goals in a 7–7 tie with Los Angeles.

**Apr 2**—For the first time in over 20 years the NHL returns to network television in the U.S. with six regional telecasts on the Fox Network.

**Apr 2**—Jim Carey becomes the first player ever to win both the player and rookie of the month awards. Starting every game since being called up from the minors March 2, the Washington goalie goes 12-2-2 with a 1.73 goals against average.

**May 1**—The Buffalo Sabres defeat Montreal 2–0, eliminating the Canadiens from playoff contention and snapping the Habs' streak of 24 straight playoff appearances, third longest in league history.

**May 1**—The defending Stanley Cup champion New York Rangers defeat the Philadelphia Flyers 2–0 to clinch a playoff berth on the last day of their regular season.

**May 3**—The Boston Bruins conclude the 28th straight season in which they have qualified for the playoffs, extending their NHL record.

**May 12**—New Jersey Devil Martin Brodeur becomes just the fifth goalie since 1939 to register three shutouts in a playoff series when he blanks the Bruins 1–0 in Game 3 of their first-round series.

**May 15**—The Vancouver Canucks score two shorthanded goals in an NHL-record 17 seconds during their 6–5 win over the St Louis Blues in Game 5 of the conference quarterfinals.

**May 16**—The New York Rangers, seeded eighth in the Eastern Conference playoffs, knock off top seed Quebec, four games to two. Nine days later the Nordiques are sold to a group in Denver, Colo., and announce they will relocate and play the 1995-96 season as the Colorado Avalanche.

**May 19**—Following a 19-25-4 regular season the San Jose Sharks eliminate the second-seeded Calgary Flames in the Western Conference quarterfinals. Ray Whitney scores the winner at 1:54 of the second overtime. Goalie Wade Flaherty makes 56 saves in the game.

**June 11**—The Detroit Red Wings defeat the Chicago Blackhawks 2–1 in double overtime to win the Western Conference final four games to one and advance to the Stanley Cup for the first time since 1966.

**June 13**—The New Jersey Devils down the

DAMIAN STROHMEYER

Philadelphia Flyers 4–2 to win the Eastern Conference final in six games and make their first trip to the Stanley Cup in the 14-year history of the franchise.

**June 17**—The Stanley Cup final begins, as the New Jersey Devils beat the Detroit Red Wings 2–1. Claude Lemieux scores the deciding goal, his third game-winner of the playoffs.

**June 20**—Trailing Detroit 2–1 in the third period, the Devils score three goals to win the game 4–2 and take a commanding 2–0 lead as the series heads to New Jersey. It is the 10th consecutive road win for the Devils, an NHL playoff record.

**June 20**—Pittsburgh superstar Mario Lemieux, who sat out the 1994-95 season for medical reasons, announces he will return for the 1995-96 season.

**June 24**—The New Jersey Devils beat Detroit 5–2 to complete a stunning four-game sweep to the Stanley Cup championship. New Jersey's Claude Lemieux, who led all playoff scorers with 13 goals, wins the Conn Smythe Trophy as the MVP of the playoffs.

**Sept 11**—Former Montreal Canadien Larry Robinson is elected to the Hockey Hall of Fame.

**Sept 24**—The San Jose Sharks release legendary right wing Sergei Makarov.

**Sept 26**—The Boston Bruins close Boston Garden with an exhibition game against the Montreal Canadiens, the same team they hosted in the Garden's first game in 1928.

**Sept 27**—Detroit defenseman Mark Howe announces his retirement after 22 NHL seasons.

**Oct 17**—After the team struggles to an 0–4 start the Montreal Canadiens announce the firings of General Manager Serge Savard, coach Jacques Demers and assistant GM Andre Boudrias.

**Oct 18**—A group from Minnesota headed by Richard Burke and Steven Gluckstern buys the Winnipeg Jets for $68 million.

# Horse Racing

**Nov 5, 1994**—Trainer D. Wayne Lukas has a banner day at the Breeders' Cup, but his accomplishments—first place finishes by Timber Country and Flanders in the Juvenile and Juvenile Fillies, respectively, and the second place run of Tabasco Cat in the Classic—are tainted by the revelation that Flanders has fractured two small bones in her foreleg during her race.

**Nov 5**—Jockey Mike Smith rides Cherokee Run to victory in the Breeders' Cup Sprint and Tikannen to first place in the Turf for his 63rd and 64th stakes wins of the year, a national record; Ireland's Barathea, one of 27 European horses in the B.C., wins the mile; and One Dreamer, a 47–1 long shot, steals the Distaff.

**Feb 12, 1995**—Holy Bull, the 1994 Horse of the Year, pulls up lame during the Donn Handicap with a tendon injury in his left front leg. The injury ends the colt's racing career and he is shipped to

stand stud at Jonabell Farm for the 1995 season. Cigar goes on to win the Donn.

**Feb 26**—Educated Risk closes out her career by winning the Rampart Handicap at Gulfstream Park. The 5-year-old mare has won 11 of 23 starts and earned $1,163,717; she will be bred to top stallion Danzig.

**Mar 5**—Erstwhile turf specialist Cigar wins the Gulfstream Park Handicap, his fifth consecutive victory since switching to the dirt.

**Mar 11**—Thunder Gulch establishes himself as an early Kentucky Derby favorite with a nose victory over Sauve Prospect in the $500,000 Florida Derby.

**Apr 1**—Serena's Song, another one of D. Wayne Lukas's Derby hopefuls, wins the Jim Beam Stakes. She is the first filly ever to win the race.

**Apr 29**—D. Wayne Lukas announces that the filly Serena's Song will skip the Kentucky Oaks and race in the Kentucky Derby, making her just

**Cigar smoked the competition all year long.**

MANNY MILLAN

the 36th filly to enter the prestigious race. Three fillies have won the Derby.

**May 6**—Thunder Gulch, who went off at 25–1 odds because of lackluster recent performances, wins the 121st running of the Kentucky Derby in the sixth-fastest time ever.

**May 20**—In a reversal of the top three Kentucky Derby finishers, Timber Country overtakes stablemate Thunder Gulch and then Oliver's Twist to win the 120th running of the Preakness Stakes.

**June 10**—Kentucky Derby winner Thunder Gulch wins the Belmont Stakes by two lengths over Star Standard. The win gives trainer D. Wayne Lukas five straight Triple Crown victories and makes him the first trainer ever to sweep the Triple Crown in one year with different horses; the Lukas-trained Timber Country won the Preakness.

**Sept 16**—Cigar wins the Woodward Stakes at Belmont Park for his 10th consecutive victory.

**Sept 21**—Hall of Fame harness driver John Campbell win the third Little Brown Jug of his career.

**Oct 1**—Angel Cordero, 51, makes a triumphant return to the track from a Jan. 7, 1992 accident that left him with multiple injuries. He sets a track record and wins at El Commandante in Puerto Rico.

**Oct 7**—The year's biggest showdown is spoiled when Thunder Gulch fractures his leg in the Gold Cup at Belmont Park. The race was Gulch's first confrontation with his rival for Horse of the Year, Cigar, and would have set up a dramatic rematch at the Breeders' Cup on Oct. 28. Cigar wins the race for his 11th consecutive victory.

# Motor Sports

**Nov 7, 1994**—Damon Hill wins the Japanese Grand Prix to pull within one point of Formula One standings leader Michael Schumacher with one race to go.

**Nov 13**—Michael Schumacher of Germany finishes 19th in the season-ending Australian Grand Prix, one place ahead of archrival Damon Hill with whom he collided during the race. The margin is enough to secure the first Formula One season title of Schumacher's career.

**Nov 14**—Despite finishing 31st in the season-ending Hampton 500 at the Atlanta Motor Speedway, Jeff Burton clinches the NASCAR Rookie of the Year award. The 27-year-old from South Boston, Va., had two top-five and three top-ten finishes during the season.

**Jan 26, 1995**—Former Indy Car driver Mario Andretti receives a shock when IMSA mandates rules changes that will ban his Porsche World Sports Car from competing in the 24 Hours of Daytona. Andretti had hoped to use the Daytona event to prepare for June's 24 Hours of LeMans.

**Feb 5**—Actor Paul Newman, 70, becomes the oldest driver ever to win a professionally sanctioned race when he co-drives—along with Mark Martin, Michael Brockman and Tommy Kendall—the Jack Roush-Ford Mustang to the GTS-1 class title at the 24 Hours of Daytona.

**Feb 19**—Sterling Marlin becomes the first driver to win consecutive Daytona 500s since Cale Yarborough in 1983-84. Dale Earnhardt makes a late charge but finishes second.

**Feb 27**—Jeff Gordon, 23, wins the pole and the race at the Rockingham 500 in North Carolina, taking home $167,600 for his efforts.

**Mar 5**—Jacques Villeneuve wins the first Indy Car event of the season, driving his Renault to victory at Miami.

**Mar 19**—Paul Tracy of Canada wins his second straight Indy Car Australian Grand Prix.

**Mar 26**—Defending Formula One champ Michael Schumacher wins the season-opening Brazilian Grand Prix.

**Apr 9**—Al Unser Jr. wins his sixth Long Beach Grand Prix with an average speed of 91.4 mph.

**May 7**—Dale Earnhardt, who has 64 career NASCAR victories, wins his first on a road course when he slips past Mark Martin with two laps remaining to win the Sonoma 300.

**May 8**—Arie Luyendyk zips off the fastest practice lap in Indy 500 history, rounding the 2.5 mile Brickyard course at an average speed of 234.107 mph.

**May 23**—The McLaren Formula One team fires driver Nigel Mansell less than four months after signing him.

**May 28**—Last year's second place finisher and Rookie of the Year Jacques Villeneuve wins the Indy 500. Villeneuve recovers from a two-lap penalty to regain the lead with four laps to go, then holds on for the win.

**June 25**—Three hours after winning the Portland 200, Indy Car driver Al Unser Jr. is stripped of the victory by the sport's sanctioning body for having less than the two inches of ground clearance beneath his Penske-Mercedes. The win is awarded to second place finisher Jimmy Vasser.

**July 17**—Grand Prix legend Juan Manuel Fangio, 84, dies of pneumonia in Buenos Aires.

**Aug 5**—Seventeen-year NASCAR veteran Dale Earnhardt holds Rusty Wallace to claim the Brickyard 400 title and $565,600.

**Aug 16**—In a day of multimillion-dollar signings by top racers, Formula One champion Michael

Schumacher announces he will leave Benetton-Renault for Ferrari, Indy 500 winner Jacques Villeneuve signs with Williams-Renault to make the jump to Formula One, and Damon Hill resigns with Williams, where he and Villeneuve will be teammates.

**Sept 10**—At the Italian Grand Prix in Monza, archrivals Michael Schumacher of Germany and Britain's Damon Hill nearly come to blows after colliding on the track. Hill is given a suspended one-race ban following the incident, the latest in a series of dust-ups between the two drivers.

**Sep 10**—Jacques Villeneuve finishes 11th at the season-ending Monterey Grand Prix, high enough to clinch his first Indy Car season title in just his second year on the circuit.

**Oct 1**—Wearing a patch over his left eye, Ernie Irvan returns to the track for the Wilkesboro 400 following a 13-month absence due to near-fatal injuries sustained in an August, 1994 crash. He finishes sixth in the race.

**Oct 22**—Michael Schumacher wins the Pacific Grand Prix to clinch his second straight Formula One season title. With two races remaining on the NASCAR circuit, Dale Earnhardt trails series leader Jeff Gordon by 162 points.

## Olympics

**Dec 4, 1994**—The Olympic Council of Asia strips 11 Chinese athletes of medals they won in the Asian Games in Hiroshima, Japan, because they tested positive for a performance-enhancing testosterone derivative. The athletes had won medals in swimming, cycling and the decathlon.

**Dec 14**—In an effort to reclaim its status as a world power in women's basketball, USA Basketball announces that it will form a women's national team one year prior to the Olympics. The team will consist of 10 players, each compensated $50,000 for the year. Though top players can earn salaries of up to $150,000 competing in Europe, many say they will take a pay cut to remain in the U.S. Previously, the Olympic team was selected two or three months prior to the Games.

**Feb 22, 1995**—Four-time Olympic gold medalist Greg Louganis, who disclosed his homosexuality at the 1994 Gay Games, announces that he has AIDS.

**Feb 27**—Speed skater Dan Jansen, who competed in four Olympics and finally won a gold medal in the 1,000 meters at Lillehammer, is named the winner of the 65th annual James E. Sullivan Award as the country's top amateur athlete.

**Mar 18**—Bonnie Blair closes her legendary speed skating career with two gold medal performances in Calgary. She just misses the world record in winning the 500 meters, then wins the 1,000 meters in a U.S.-record 1:18.05.

**June 16**—In a stunning first-ballot victory (54 of 89 votes) in Budapest, Hungary, Salt Lake City is awarded the 2002 Winter Olympics by the International Olympic Committee.

**June 16**—In the fourth and final session of the IOC's Budapest meeting, IOC President Juan Antonio Samaranch, who is soon to turn 75, introduces a petition to raise the organization's mandatory retirement age from 75 to 80. There is some grumbling but after a swift show of hands, the motion passes.

**June 25**—Dick Schultz, 65, is elected as executive director of the United States Olympic Committee. He resigned as executive director of the NCAA in 1993.

**July 19**—Billy Payne, the president of the Atlanta Committee for the Olympic Games, announces that, with one year to go, 80% of the record $1.58 billion budgeted for the 1996 Atlanta Olympics has been raised.

**July 31**—At an international regatta in Savannah, Georgia, intended as a pre-Olympic

JOHN BIEVER

**Blair closed her career—how else?—with a win.**

st event, there are unanimous complaints from the 53 participating countries. The primary grievance concerns the two- to three-hour water tow required to reach the racing courses in Wassaw Sound from the new Olympic marina near Savannah.

**Aug 1**—For the first time since the series began in 1986 the U.S. national baseball team defeats Cuba in a four-game series. The U.S. wins the fourth game 6–5 to complete a surprising sweep, unsettling the notion that Cuba is a lock for the gold in Atlanta.

**Aug 4**—NBC makes a blockbuster deal with the IOC and Olympic organizers to broadcast both the 2000 Summer Games in Sydney, Australia, and the 2002 Winter Games in Salt Lake City, paying $1.27 billion for the unprecedented arrangement.

**Oct 8**—The U.S. women's gymnastic team wins the bronze medal at the World Championships in Sabae, Japan. The U.S. men finish ninth. Both placings qualify the teams for the 1996 Summer Olympics.

**Oct 8**—At its board of directors meeting in Atlanta the United States Olympic Committee approves a budget that eliminates the U.S. Olympic festival and funding for the World University Games. The USOC festival, which cost $11 million dollars to stage in 1994, will be replaced by a smaller, possibly elite-level event beginning in 1999. U.S. Athletes will still be able to participate inthe World University Games, but will do so at the expense of their sport's national governing body.

**Oct 24**—Bruce Arena, 44, who coached the University of Virginia to an unprecedented four consecutive NCAA men's soccer championships, is hired to coach the U.S. Olympic men's soccer team.

## Pro Basketball

**Nov 1, 1994**—The San Antonio Spurs suspend forward Dennis Rodman for the first three games of the season for "conduct detrimental to the club." Rodman was ejected from the previous night's preseason game against Charlotte after picking up his second technical foul. He then threw a bag of ice toward the court.

**Nov 3**—Holdout rookie Glenn Robinson signs the most lucrative first-year contract in NBA history, getting a guaranteed $72 million over 10 years from the Milwaukee Bucks.

**Nov 10**—Los Angeles Laker forward James Worthy, 33, announces his retirement after 12 NBA seasons.

**Nov 17**—Former Michigan teammates Juwan Howard and Chris Webber are reunited as members of the Washington Bullets. Howard, an unsigned rookie, agrees to a 12-year, $41.3 million with the Bullets; and Webber, a holdout free agent unhappy with Golden State, agrees to terms with the Warriors, and they trade him to Washington for Tom Gugliotta and three future first-round draft picks.

**Dec 7**—The Los Angeles Clippers win their first game of the season after 16 straight losses, and avoid tying the NBA's worst-ever start, 0–17 by the 1988 Miami Heat.

**Dec 7**—Dennis Rodman fails to show up for practice following a month-long paid leave of absence, and is suspended again by the Spurs.

**Dec 27**—New York Knick Charles Oakley undergoes surgery for a dislocated toe and will be sidelined for six to eight weeks.

**Jan 4, 1995**—Gary Payton of the Seattle SuperSonics goes 14-for-14 from the field in a 116–84 win over the Cleveland Cavaliers.

**Jan 6**—Atlanta Hawk coach Lenny Wilkens earns career win No. 939 in a victory over the Washington Bullets. With the triumph Wilkens surpasses Red Auerbach as the NBA coach with the most wins.

**Jan 14**—Cleveland guard Mark Price breaks his right wrist in a game against Golden State. The injury will require surgery, shelving Price for six to eight weeks. He is the third Cav to be hit by significant injury this season.

**Jan 26**—Detroit's Grant Hill leads all vote-getters in fan balloting for the NBA All-Star Game. He is the first rookie ever to do so.

**Feb 1**—In a 129–88 rout of the Denver Nuggets Utah Jazz guard John Stockton becomes the NBA's alltime assist leader, surpassing Magic Johnson on his 11th assist of the game, the 9,922nd of his career.

**Feb 2**—Utah loses to the Houston Rockets 121–101, missing a chance to tie the NBA record of 16 consecutive road victories set by the Los Angeles Lakers in 1971-72.

**Feb 6**—The Phoenix Suns lose star forward Danny Manning for the season when he tears his anterior cruciate ligament in practice.

**Feb 7**—Kareem Abdul-Jabbar leads a class of two women and five men elected to the Basketball Hall of Fame. Former USC standout and current Trojan women's coach Cheryl Miller is also elected.

AL TIELEMANS

**Kidd grew up fast in the NBA, sharing Rookie of the Year honors with Hill.**

**May 7**—In Game 1 of the Eastern Conference semifinal, Indiana's Reggie Miller singlehandedly brings the Pacers back from a six-point deficit with 18 seconds left against the Knicks. Miller hits a three-pointer, makes a steal, sinks another trey, grabs a rebound and sinks two free-throws—all inside 1 seconds—to give the Pacers a stunning 107–105 victory. Indiana goes on to win the series in seven games.

**May 10**—Michael Jordan returns to his old No. 23 for Game 2 of the Eastern Conference semifinal against the Magic and scores 38 points as the Bulls even the series with a 104–94 victory.

**May 11**—Kevin Garnett, a 6'11" high school senior from Chicago, announces that he will forego college and enter the NBA draft.

**May 17**—Dallas guard Jason Kidd and Detroit forward Grant Hill are announced as co-Rookies of the Year. The only other such tie in NBA history was between Dave Cowens and Geoff Petrie in 1970-71.

**May 18**—The Orlando Magic defeat Chicago 108–102 at the United Center to clinch the Eastern Conference semifinal in six games. In Los Angeles, San Antonio knocks off the young Laker team 100–88 to take the Western semifinal four games to two.

**May 20**—For the second straight year Houston drops the first two games of the Western Conference semifinal to Phoenix, then comes back to eliminate the Suns in seven games. The Rockets win the tense seventh game at Phoenix, 115–114.

**June 1**—Houston's Hakeem Olajuwon caps a remarkable Western Conference final series with a 39-point, 17-rebound performance in Game 6 against San Antonio. With their 100–95 victory the Rockets eliminate the Spurs, the team with the NBA's best regular-season record, and win a return trip to the NBA Finals.

**June 4**—After losing Game 6 by 27 points, the Orlando Magic trounce the Indiana Pacers 105–81 in Game 7 to win an exciting, back-and-forth Eastern Conference final series.

**June 15**—The Houston Rockets dismiss the Orlando Magic in four games to win their second consecutive NBA title. After a 120–118 overtime victory in Game 1, the Rockets reel off three convincing wins. They take Game 4 113–101, and Hakeem Olajuwon, who averages 32.8 points and 11.5 rebounds for the series, wins the MVP award.

**Feb 12**—Mitch Richmond is named MVP of the All-Star game as he leads the West to a 139–112 win, sinking 10 of his 13 shots from the field.

**Feb 13**—Following a tumultuous stretch of poor play, injuries and feuds with players, Don Nelson resigns as coach and GM of the Warriors.

**Feb 14**—The Portland Trail Blazers trade Clyde Drexler to Houston for Otis Thorpe.

**Mar 7**—Boston's Dominique Wilkins becomes the ninth player in NBA history to score 25,000 career points. He reaches the milestone during a 115–110 loss to the Knicks.

**Mar 19**—Michael Jordan, wearing uniform No. 45 instead of his old 23, makes a dramatic return to the NBA after a 17-month retirement. He shows flashes of his old brilliance but shoots poorly; the Bulls lose 103–96 in overtime.

**Mar 28**—In his fifth game back in the NBA Michael Jordan scores 55 points as the Bulls defeat the Knicks 113–111 in Madison Square Garden.

**Apr 5**—The Hornets and the 76ers combine for 19 points in the second quarter of their game at Charlotte, registering the second-lowest scoring quarter in NBA history.

**Apr 15**—Miami's Glenn Rice scores 56 points in the Heat's 123–117 victory over Orlando.

**May 4**—For the second straight year, the Seattle SuperSonics follow an excellent regular season with a first-round exit from the playoffs, losing to the Lakers in four games.

**June 15**—Pat Riley resigns as coach of the New York Knicks following a dispute over his role in personnel decisions. He has one year remaining on his contract with New York, but after a deal is worked out between the Knicks and Miami, he signs to coach the Heat.

**June 20**—A group of players led by Michael Jordan and Patrick Ewing petitions for decertification of the players' union. They are displeased with the union's negotiations for a new collective bargaining agreement.

**June 28**—At the NBA draft in New York City, Golden State selects Maryland sophomore Joe Smith with the first pick. The LA Clippers take Alabama's Antonio McDyess with the second pick, then trade him to Denver for Rodney Rogers and 15th pick Brent Barry. North Carolina's Jerry Stackhouse goes third to Philadelphia.

**July 1**—With the two sides unable to reach a new collective bargaining agreement the NBA imposes a lockout on its players.

**July 6**—Don Nelson is hired to coach the New York Knicks.

**Sept 12**—The players vote 226–134 to retain the union. Two days later they vote 25–2 in favor of the new collective bargaining agreement.

**Sept 18**—The NBA lifts the 79-day player lockout, clearing the way for the 1995-96 season.

**Sept 27**—The Bullets sign top rookie Rasheed Wallace, and acquire Mark Price from Cleveland in exchange for a 1996 first-round draft pick.

**Oct 2**—The Bulls trade center Will Perdue to the Spurs for controversial rebound specialist Dennis Rodman.

# Pro Football

**Oct 23, 1994**—The San Diego Chargers (6–1) are the last team to fall from the ranks of the unbeaten, losing to Denver 20–15.

**Oct 24**—Dallas Cowboy offensive lineman Erik Williams is injured in a 3 a.m. car accident in Dallas. Williams suffers two torn ligaments in his knee, a broken rib, torn ligaments in his left thumb and facial cuts. He later pleads no contest to a misdemeanor drunken driving charge.

**Nov 2**—The NFL announces that the expansion Jacksonville Jaguars and Carolina Panthers will play in the AFC Central and the NFC West, respectively.

**Nov 6**—With 261 yards in a 22–21 win over the Indianapolis Colts, Miami Dolphin quarterback Dan Marino passes Dan Fouts and moves into second place on the career passing yardage list. Marino has 43,151 career passing yards, second to Fran Tarkenton's 47,003.

**Nov 12**—In a showdown of the NFL's top two teams the San Francisco 49ers beat Dallas 21–14 in Candlestick Park.

**Nov 12**—Drew Bledsoe sets NFL records for completions (45) and attempts (70) while passing for 426 yards in New England's 26–20 overtime victory against Minnesota.

**Nov 24**—With Troy Aikman and Rodney Peete injured, Dallas Cowboy third-string quarterback Jason Garrett, a graduate of Princeton, completes 15 of 26 passes for 311 yards and two touchdowns to lead the Cowboys to 42–31 comeback win over Green Bay.

**Dec 2**—Seattle Seahawk defensive tackle Mike Frier is paralyzed in a car accident on a rain-slickened street near Seahawk headquarters. Frier's teammate running back Chris Warren is also in the car, and breaks two ribs.

PETER READ MILLER

**Humphries passed the Chargers to a 6–0 start.**

**Dec 11**—Jet wide receiver Art Monk breaks Steve Largent's record of 177 straight games with at least one reception when he catches a five-yard toss from Boomer Esiason on the first play of the Jets' 18–7 loss to the Detroit Lions.

**Dec 18**—The New England Patriots win their sixth straight game, downing Buffalo 41–17 and eliminating the Bills, the AFC champion for the past four years, from the playoffs.

DAMIAN STROHMEYER

## Coates led the AFC in receptions with 96.

**Dec 18**—During their victory over the Bills the Patriots become the first team in NFL history to have five receivers with more than 51 catches in a season. Vincent Brisby becomes the fifth Patriot to reach 51 catches when he makes four against Buffalo. The others: AFC leader tight end Ben Coates (93), Michael Timpson (71), Le Roy Thompson (60) and Kevin Turner (52).

**Dec 25**—On the NFL's final weekend the Minnesota Vikings defeat the 49ers 21–14 to clinch the NFC Central title; the New England Patriots win their seventh consecutive game, 13–3 over Chicago, to finish 10–6 and clinch a wild-card berth; and the New York Giants, who will miss the playoffs, score a moral victory, defeating Dallas 15–10. Also, two records are safe as Detroit's Barry Sanders falls short of 2,000 rushing yards, needing 169 yards and gaining only 52 in a 27–20 loss to Miami; and Emmitt Smith (22 season touchdowns, two short of John Riggins's record) sits out with injuries against the Giants.

**Dec 27**—Miami defensive tackle Tim Bowens, considered by many a longshot for the NFL, is named Defensive Rookie of the Year.

**Dec 28**—Green Bay wide receiver Sterling Sharpe, who made 112 catches in 1993, announces he will have surgery to repair damaged vertebrae in his neck. He will require at least eight months to recover.

**Dec 31**—The playoffs begin with the Packers edging Detroit 16–12 in the NFC wild-card. In the AFC Miami knocks Joe Montana and the Chiefs

out with a 27–17 victory. The following day the Browns eliminate New England 30–13 and the Bears rout Minnesota 35–18.

**Jan 5, 1995**—The Jets fire first-year coach Pete Carroll after a 6–10 season and replace him with Rich Kotite, who was 7–9 this year with the Eagles.

**Jan 7**—The Pittsburgh Steelers flatten the Browns 29–9 in the AFC divisional playoffs. The following day the Chargers rally from a 21–6 first-half deficit to nip Miami 22–21.

**Jan 8**—The Dallas Cowboys overwhelm Green Bay 39–9 in the NFC divisional playoffs. The rout follows the 49ers' 44–15 shellacking of Chicago in the previous day's NFC divisional matchup.

**Jan 11**—The Seattle Seahawks sign former University of Miami coach Dennis Erickson to a five-year head coaching contract.

**Jan 15**—San Diego linebacker Dennis Gibson knocks down Steeler Neil O'Donnell's end zone pass to Barry Foster in the waning seconds of the AFC championship game to preserve a 17–13 Charger victory. The surprising Chargers, who again come from behind to win, advance to the Super Bowl for the first time in franchise history.

**Jan 15**—The San Francisco 49ers score three times in the first ten minutes of the NFC championship against Dallas, and go on to lead 31–14 at halftime. They withstand a second-half rally by Dallas and win 38–28 to advance to the Super Bowl.

**Jan 16**—Rams owner Georgia Frontiere announces she will move the team from Los Angeles to her hometown of St. Louis.

**Jan 29**—Former Seattle wide receiver Steve Largent is elected to the Pro Football Hall of Fame. Joining him are former GM Jim Finks, ex-Packer defensive great Henry Jordan, six-time Pro Bowler Lee Roy Selmon, who played for Tampa Bay, and ex-Charger tight end Kellen Winslow.

**Jan 29**—Scoring the fastest touchdown in Super Bowl history, a 44-yard pass from Steve Young to Jerry Rice at 1:24 of the first quarter, the 49ers set the tone for their 49–26 rout of San Diego in Super Bowl XXIX. San Francisco breaks or ties 16 records in the game, and Young, who completes 24 of 36 passes for 325 yards and six touchdowns, wins the MVP award.

**Jan 31**—The Denver Broncos hire former San Francisco offensive coordinator Mike Shanahan as head coach.

**Feb 2**—Ray Rhodes, who was the 49ers' defensive coordinator, signs to coach the Philadelphia Eagles. With Art Shell's firing by the Los Angeles Raiders on the same day, the number of African-American head coaches in the NFL remains two. Shell later signs with Kansas City as offensive line coach.

**Feb 28**—The Green Bay Packers release wide receiver Sterling Sharpe, who recently underwent surgery to repair damaged vertebrae in his neck.

**Mar 8**—Tampa Bay outbids the Jets for the services of free agent wide receiver Alvin Harper, formerly of Dallas. The next day the Buffalo Bills sign free agent linebacker Bryce Paup to a three-year, $7.6 million contract.

**Mar 15**—NFL owners vote down the Rams proposed move to St. Louis. Georgia Frontiere vows to continue her efforts to move the team.

**Mar 27**—Career backup Frank Reich, who played 10 years with the Bills, signs a one-year contract with the expansion Carolina Panthers.

**Apr 2**—Herschel Walker, recently released from the Eagles for refusing a pay cut, signs with the Giants for three years and $4.8 million.

**Apr 9**—The World League of American Football (WLAF), shut down in 1992 for financial reasons, resumes play with six European franchises competing in a 10-week season. Rhein beats Scotland 19–17 in the league opener.

**Apr 12**—After paying roughly $30 million in relocation fees and another $17 million in licensing revenue, Rams owner Georgia Frontiere gets the 23 votes she needs from NFL owners to move her team St. Louis.

**Apr 18**—Joe Montana makes it official: After 16 NFL seasons, 40,551 passing yards and four Super Bowl titles, he is retiring.

**Apr 23**—At the NFL draft in New York City, the Cincinnati Bengals select Penn State running back Ki-Jana Carter with the No. 1 pick. Rounding out the top five are: USC offensive tackle Tony Boselli, to the Jacksonville Jaguars; Alcorn State quarterback Steve McNair to the Houston Oilers; Colorado receiver Michael Westbrook to Washington; and Penn State quarterback Kerry Collins to the Carolina Panthers.

**June 18**—The Frankfurt Galaxy wins World Bowl '95, the championship of the WLAF, defeating the Amsterdam Admirals 26–22 before 23,847 in Amsterdam's Olympic Stadium.

**June 20**—San Diego Charger linebacker David Griggs, 28, is killed in a one-car accident near Fort Lauderdale, Fla.

**June 23**—Al Davis signs a letter of intent to return the Raiders to Oakland. The move is later approved by the NFL and Oakland and Alameda County officials. The Raiders will resume occupancy of the Oakland Coliseum for the 1995 season.

**July 19**—Felicia Moon declines to press charges against her husband, Viking quarterback Warren Moon, after she flees the couple's home in Missouri City, Tex., following an argument in which Moon struck and choked her. The police responded to a 911 call, and term the investigation "still open."

**July 20**—New England quarterback Drew Bledsoe re-signs with the Patriots for seven years and $42 million. The New Orleans Saints cut kicker Morten Andersen with the hope of re-signing him at a lower salary, but the Falcons descend upon the six-time Pro Bowler and sign him to an undisclosed contract.

**Sept 3**—Opening day features nine new coaches, two relocated franchises and two new ones. Mike White leads the once-again Oakland

PATRICK MURPHY-RACEY

**Drafted No. 5, Collins wears No. 12 for Carolina.**

Raiders past the Chargers, 17–7; Rich Brooks guides the used-to-be LA Rams past the Packers 17–14. Tom Coughlin oversees the expansion Jaguars' tough 10–3 loss to Houston and Dom Capers' Carolina Panthers take Atlanta to overtime before succumbing 23–20.

**Sept 4**—Cowboy owner Jerry Jones announces a $2.5 million apparel-licensing deal with Nike that flouts NFL regulations.

**Sept 6**—Seattle Seahawk receiver Brian Blades is charged with manslaughter in the July 5 shooting death of his cousin Charles Blades. He insists the shooting was accidental.

**Sept 10**—The Dallas Cowboys sign free agent defensive back Deion Sanders to a seven-year, $25 million contract.

**Sept 17**—Former Saint kicker Morten Andersen boots four field goals, including the game-winner, in the Falcons 27–24 overtime win against his old team. In Denver, John Elway leads the 35th fourth-quarter comeback of his career, completing a 43-yard touchdown pass to Rod Smith on the game's final play to beat the Redskins 38–31.

**Sept 18**—NFL Properties files a $300 million suit against Dallas owner Jerry Jones alleging that the owner's outside marketing deals "undermine existing NFL Properties' sponsorships and contracts."

**Oct 1**—Quarterback Mark Brunell completes a 15-yard touchdown pass to Desmond Howard with 1:03 left to give the Jacksonville Jaguars their first victory in franchise history, 17–16 over Houston.

**Oct 4**—For the first time in modern league history the NFL fines two officials for blown calls in a game. Gordon Carter and Ben Montgomery are each fined one game's pay for incorrectly ruling that Pittsburgh had 12 men on the field while defending a field goal against Minnesota on Oct 1.

**Oct 8**—Dan Marino surpasses Fran Tarkenton to become the alltime completions leader, but the Dolphins lose to the Colts 27–24, and Marino hurts his right knee, requiring surgery which will shelve him for at least two weeks.

**Oct 15**—The Carolina Panthers get their first win, besting the Jets 26–15. The Colts knock off the 49ers 18–17 and knock Steve Young out of the lineup for four weeks with a shoulder injury. The following night the Denver Broncos defeat the Raiders for just the second time in 13 years, winning 27–0 at Mile High Stadium.

**Nov 16, 1994**—At a news conference in New York City the organizers of Major League Soccer (MLS) announce they will postpone the original start date for the league, moving the launch to April 1996, one year later than originally planned. They also disclose the charter team of financial backers for the league, which includes Kansas City Chief owner Lamar Hunt and Virginia billionaire John Kluge, among others. The league will have a single-entity ownership structure, meaning franchises will belong to MLS, and not to individual owners.

**Nov 19**—U.S. national team striker Eric Wynalda, who plays for VfL Bochum in the German Bundesliga, breaks his leg in a game against VfB Stuttgart and will be out for two months.

**Dec 15**—Tony Meola, who started in goal for the U.S. at the 1990 and '94 World Cups, signs with the Buffalo Blizzard of the indoor National Professional Soccer League.

**Dec 19**—Hristo Stoitchkov of Bulgaria, who co-led the 1994 World Cup in scoring, is named European Footballer of the Year.

**Dec 19**—Timo Liekoski is named director of coaching and player development for the U.S. Soccer Federation (USSF). He will coach the under-23 national team that will compete in the Pan Am Games and the Atlanta Olympics.

**Jan 4, 1995**—Midfielder Tab Ramos, who assisted on the U.S.'s game-winning goal against Colombia in the 1994 World Cup, becomes the first player to sign with Major League Soccer.

**Jan 30**—Brazil's Romario is named World Footballer of the Year.

**Feb 24**—The U.S. women's national team, pointing toward the World Championships in June, opens its 1995 season with a 7–0 thrashing of Denmark.

**Apr 14**—Bora Milutinovic, who coached the U.S national team to the second round of the 1994 World Cup, resigns when the USSF asks him to take on an expanded role that would include becoming the director of player development. Assistant coach Steve Sampson is named interim head coach.

**May 15**—In the search for a successor to Bora Milutinovic the USSF is turned down at the last minute by Carlos Queiroz, who enters negotiations then abruptly re-signs for three years to continue coaching Sporting Lisbon of the Portuguese first division.

**May 24**—New England Patriots owner Robert Kraft joins the roster of MLS investors; he will oversee the franchise using Foxboro Stadium as its home field.

**June 4**—Goalkeeper Jorge Campos of Mexico signs a three-year contract to play with MLS. He will play for the Los Angeles franchise.

**June 11**—U.S. Cup '95 opens in Foxboro, Mass., with the U.S. defeating Nigeria 3–2 before a crowd of 22,578. Cobi Jones scores the game winner in the 67th minute.

**June 15**—At the second FIFA Women's World Championship in Sweden, the defending champion U.S. national team falls to Norway 1–0 in the semifinals.

**June 18**—Claudio Reyna scores a goal and assists on two others as the U.S. blanks Mexico 4–0 before 38,615 in Washington's RFK Stadium. Reyna, 21, was the youngest player on the '94 World Cup roster but didn't play because of an injury.

**June 25**—Defender Alexi Lalas, who is the first U.S. player ever to play in the top Italian league, signs a two-year contract with MLS. He will be on loan to MLS from Padova of Italy.

**June 25**—The U.S. ties Colombia 0–0 at Rutgers Stadium to clinch the 1995 U.S. Cup title.

**July 2**—The U.S. under-23 team defeats Chile 2–1 in a pre-Olympic tuneup at Hartwick College. UCLA star Ante Razov scores both goals.

**July 9**—With interim coach Steve Sampson still at the helm, the U.S. begins play in the Copa America, the world's oldest tournament, defeating Chile 2–1 in Paysandu, Uruguay. Eric Wynalda scores both goals.

**July 11**—Bolivia, which is outshot by a 2–1 margin, defeats the U.S. 1–0 in group play at the Copa America.

**July 14**—Needing at least a tie against heavily-favored Argentina to advance to the second round of the Copa America, the U.S. delivers a shocking 3–0 shutout of the world power. Frank Klopas, Alexi Lalas and Eric Wynalda are the goal scorers in the win that ranks with the best in U.S. soccer history.

**July 17**—The U.S. defeats Mexico on penalty kicks, 4–1, and advances to the semifinals of the Copa America.

**July 20**—World champion Brazil ends the U.S.'s stunning run through the Copa America with a 1–0 victory in the semifinals at Maldonado, Uruguay.

**Aug 2**—Steve Sampson is named permanent coach of the U.S. men's national team.

**Aug 6**—The U.S. women's national team wins U.S. Women's Cup '95, avenging their June loss to Norway with a 2–1 sudden death overtime

**Foes tried everything to stop Harkes and Co. at U.S. Cup '95.**

victory in Washington, D.C. Tammy Pearlman scores the game-winner.

**Aug 6**—Frank Klopas and Roy Lassiter score for the U.S. in a 2–1 victory over Benfica (Portugal) in the consolation game of the Parmalat Cup at Giants Stadium.

**Aug 13**—Bora Milutinovic signs on—for the second time—to coach Mexico's national team. He guided Mexico to the quarterfinals of the 1986 World Cup.

**Sept 26**—Timo Liekoski is dismissed as Olympic (under-23) men's soccer coach.

**Oct 1**—Diego Maradona returns from a 15-month drug suspension to play for Boca Juniors as they defeat South Korea 2–1 in Seoul.

**Oct 10**—Cobi Jones, a midfielder on the U.S. national team, signs with Atletico Rentistas of the Brazilian first division, and is then loaned to Vasco da Gama of Rio de Janiero.

**Oct 12**—The Seattle Sounders win the 1995 A League Cup title with a 2–1 shootout victory over the Atlanta Ruckus at Memorial Stadium in Seattle.

**Oct 16**—MLS announces the signings of 1994 World Cup team members John Harkes, Mike Sorber and Tony Meola, bringing to five the number of World Cup starters committed to the new league.

**Oct 17**—At a news conference in New York City MLS unveils the nicknames and logos of the 10 franchises that will begin play on April 6.

**Oct 19**—Alexi Lalas is named Male Athlete of the Year by the USSF.

**Oct 24**—Bruce Arena, who led the University of Virginia to four consecutive NCAA men's soccer titles, is named to succeed Timo Liekoski as the U.S. Olympic coach.

# Tennis

RON ANGLE

**Pierce's Australian win was her first Slam title.**

**Nov 15, 1994**—Martina Navratilova loses 6–4, 6–2 to Gabriela Sabatini in the first round of the Virginia Slims Championships and closes her career with the defeat.

**Nov 20**—Gabriela Sabatini and Pete Sampras close the season with victories as Sabatini takes the Virginia Slims title, defeating Lindsay Davenport 6–3, 6–2, 6–4, and Sampras wins the ATP Tour World Championship, beating Boris Becker in the final 4–6, 6–3, 7–5, 6–4.

**Dec 20**—Citing recurring back problems, Ivan Lendl retires.

**Jan 24, 1995**—Pete Sampras makes an emotional comeback in the quarterfinals of the Australian Open against Jim Courier. Unsuccessfully fighting back tears prompted by thoughts of his coach, Tim Gullikson, who has had two strokes in the past three months, Sampras battles back to beat Courier 6–7 (4-7), 6–7 (3-7), 6–3, 6–4, 6–3.

**Jan 29**—Andre Agassi wins his second straight Grand Slam title, defeating Pete Sampras 4–6, 6–1, 7–6 (8-6), 6–4 to win the Australian Open.

**Jan 29**—Mary Pierce wins the first Grand Slam title of her career, beating Arantxa Sanchez Vicario 6–3, 6–2 in the final of the Australian Open. She moves to No. 3 in the world with the victory.

**Feb 20**—Steffi Graf defeats Mary Pierce 6–2, 6–2 in the final of the Paris Open to reclaim the No. 1 ranking from Arantxa Sanchez Vicario.

**Mar 26**—In a showdown of the world No. 1 and 2 at the Lipton Championships final, Andre Agassi outduels Pete Sampras 3–6, 6–2, 7–6 (7-3). Steffi Graf wins the women's final for her fourth Lipton title.

**Apr 10**—Andre Agassi, who has beaten Pete Sampras in two of their three matches this year, replaces Sampras as the No. 1 player in the world. Sampras held the top spot for 82 weeks.

**June 10**—Though she has been plagued this season by a bad back, calf problems and the flu, Steffi Graf summons the strength to defeat Arantxa Sanchez Vicario 7–5, 4–6, 6–0 to claim her fourth French Open singles title.

**June 11**—Thomas Muster defeats Michael Chang 7–5, 6–2, 6-4 to take his 35th consecutive match on clay and win the French Open title.

**July 1**—Jeff Tarango, the 80th-ranked player on the tour, quits his third-round match at Wimbledon after accusing chair umpire Bruno Rebeuh of corruption.

**July 3**—Pancho Gonzales dies of cancer at the age of 67.

**July 8**—Steffi Graf wins her sixth Wimbledon singles title, defeating Arantxa Sanchez Vicario in the final, 4–6, 6–1, 7–5.

**July 9**—Pete Sampras defeats Boris Becker 6–7 (5-7), 6–2, 6–4, 6–2 to win his third consecutive Wimbledon title. He dedicates the victory to his coach Tim Gullikson, who is undergoing treatment for brain tumors.

**July 17**—Chris Evert is inducted into the International Tennis Hall of Fame.

**July 23**—Spain beats Germany 3–2 to advance to the finals of the Federation Cup, where they will meet the U.S., a 3–2 winner over France.

**Aug 20**—In her first tournament back since being stabbed by a demented fan in April 1993, Monica Seles blazes the field at the du Maurier Ltd. Open in Montreal. In the final she dispatches Amanda Coetzer 6–0, 6–1 for her 33rd career title.

**Sept 9**—The women's U.S. Open singles final is a storybook matchup of Monica Seles and Steffi Graf, the top two players at the time of the attack on Seles. Graf, whose father is imprisoned in Germany on tax evasion charges, prevails 7–6 (7-5), 0–6, 6–3 for her third Grand Slam title of the year.

**Sept 10**—Pete Sampras becomes the fourth player with three Wimbledon and three U.S. Open titles when he defeats world No. 1 Andre Agassi 6–4, 6–3, 4–6, 7–5 in the final of the U.S. Open.

**Sept 24**—Todd Martin of the U.S. defeats Sweden's Thomas Enqvist 7–5, 7–5, 7–6 (6-2) to preserve a 4–1 team victory and send the U.S. into the Davis Cup finals, where they will meet Russia, a 3–2 winner over Germany.

**Oct 17, 1994**—Greg Welch defeats Dave Scott at the Ironman Triathlon World Championship in Kailua-Kona, Hawaii. Welch completes the 2.5-mile swim, 100-mile bike and 26-mile run in 8 hours, 20 minutes, 27 seconds, four minutes ahead of Scott. Paula Newby-Fraser wins her fourth straight women's title in 9:20:14.

**Nov 6**—German Silva wins the New York City Marathon in 2:11:21. Tecla Loroupe wins the women's race in 2:27:37.

**Nov 6**—Tony Rominger of Switzerland breaks his own world record for the one-hour bicycle ride, covering 34.357 miles, nine-tenths more than he did on his last attempt.

**Nov 12**—Wilma Rudolph, who won three gold medals at the 1960 Olympics in Rome, dies of cancer in Nashville.

**Nov 20**—The North Carolina women's soccer team wraps up its ninth consecutive NCAA title with a 5–0 blanking of Notre Dame. Senior midfielder Tisha Venturini, a three-time All-America, scores two goals as she and nine others in her class leave the school with a 97-1-1 record over four years. It is the Tar Heels 12th championship in the past 13 years.

**Nov 21**—The Iowa State men knock off four-time defending champion Arkansas to win the NCAA cross-country title, while the Villanova women, under new coach John Marshall and without star Carole Zajac, capture their sixth straight.

**Dec 3**—Three-time Tour de France winner Greg LeMond announces his retirement, citing mitochondrial myopathy, a rare muscular disease.

**Dec 4**—Ruben Reina wins the national men's cross-country championship in Portland, Ore. Olga Appell defeats Gwyn Coogan and eight-time champion Lynn Jennings to claim the women's title.

**Dec 5**—The Virginia Cavaliers win an unprecedented fourth consecutive NCAA men's soccer title. Forward A.J Wood scores in the 1–0 championship game victory over Indiana.

**Dec 7**—Chinese swimmer Lu Bin, who set a world record and won four gold medals at the Asian Games, is suspended for two years for failing a drug test.

**Dec 9**—Following the lead of teammate Hilary Lindh, who won at Vail on Dec. 2, U.S. skier

**Street made fresh tracks for the U.S. in the downhill.**

Picabo Street wins World Cup downhill at Lake Louise, Alberta.

**Dec 11**—Ty Murray wins his sixth consecutive and seventh career all-around title at the National Finals Rodeo. Other winners include Marvin Garrett in the bareback, Dan Mortensen in the saddle-bronc, Herbert Theriot in calf roping and Blaine Pederson in steer wrestling.

**Jan 9, 1995**—The NCAA announces it will wait one year before raising academic standards for incoming athletes. Revisions including higher grade point average requirements and higher standardized test scores will be enacted in August 1996.

**Jan 21**—U.S. skier Kyle Rasmussen wins his first World Cup downhill title at Wengen, Switzerland.

**Jan 22**—Picabo Street wins the downhill at Cortina d'Ampezzo, Italy for her second World Cup victory of the season.

**Feb 8**—USA Track and Field announces there will be legalized gambling on races at the Reno Air Games, the second of five indoor track events NBC will televise this year The move is designed to revive flagging interest in the sport in the U.S.

**Feb 10**—Though there is little gambling action at the Reno Air Games, the action on the track is spectacular enough, as Michael Johnson of the U.S. sets a world record (44.97) in the 400 meters and the following day Lance Deal breaks the world record in the 35-pound weight throw with a mark of 81 feet 8½ inches.

**Feb 11**—Todd Eldredge defeats Scott Davis to win the U.S. men's figure skating title in Providence, R.I. With the victory he completes his comeback from a career-threatening back injury he suffered after winning the title 1991. Nicole

CARL YARBROUGH

Bobek upends the favored Michelle Kwan for the women's title.

**Feb 12**—Moses Kiptanui of Kenya breaks his 3,000-meter world record by more than two seconds, running 7:35.15 in Ghent, Belgium. In Karlsruhe, Germany, China's Sun Caiyun vaults 13'6½" to set her fourth pole vault record in 15 days.

**Feb 14**—Allen Johnson sets a world record in the 110-meter hurdles at the Russian winter track and field championships, clocking 13.34 in Moscow.

**Feb 18**—Picabo Street wins her third World CUp downhill of the year, taking the race in Are, Sweden.

**Feb 19**—Alberto Tomba sees his seven-race winning streak in the slalom ended at Furano, Japan when he loses to Austria's Michael Tritscher. Tomba complains that the course is subpar.

**Feb 19**—Linford Christie of Great Britain breaks the world indoor 200-meter record, clocking 20.25. Second-place finisher Frankie Fredericks of Namibia also broke the record.

**Feb 25**—Scott Alexander wins the Pro Bowlers Association National Championship in Toledo, Ohio, defeating Wayne Webb 246–210 in the championship game.

**Mar 4**—Michael Johnson wins his 40th consecutive race at the USA/Mobil Indoor Championships in Atlanta. He runs 44.63 in the 400 meters to break his previous indoor world record of 44.97.

**Mar 9**—Todd Eldredge of the U.S. wins the silver medal at the World Figure Skating Championships in Birmingham, England, narrowly losing to Canada's Elvis Stojko.

**Mar 11**—U.S. skater Nicole Bobek, who has struggled recently with injuries, a weight problem and charges (later dropped) of breaking and entering, wins the bronze medal at the World Championships in Birmingham, England. China's Chen Lu is first and Surya Bonaly of France wins the silver. In the pairs, Todd Sand and Jenni Meno of the U.S. win the bronze.

**Mar 11**—Arkansas wins its 12th consecutive NCAA men's indoor track title, and the LSU women win their third straight. Another astonishing NCAA dynasty, that of the Kenyon women in Division III swimming, is extended to 12 straight national titles.

**Mar 12**—Picabo Street wins her fourth consecutive downhill in Lenzeheide, Switzerland, wrapping up the season title with the victory. She is the first U.S. skier in history to win a season downhill title.

**Mar 14**—Doug Swingley shatters Marin Buser's

1994 record by over 24 hours when he wins the Iditarod Trail Sled Dog Race in 9 days 2 hours 42 minutes and 19 seconds. He receives $52,500 and a pickup truck for winning the 1,100-mile race.

**Mar 15**—Picabo Street closes her astonishing downhill season with her fifth consecutive victory and her sixth of the year with a win in Bormio, Italy. Street and teammate Hilary Lindh have combined to win eight of the nine downhills this season.

**Mar 18**—Janet Evans wins her 45th national title at the indoor National Championships in Minneapolis, taking the 1,500-meter freestyle

**Mar 18**—Kenyon College wins an astonishing 16th consecutive NCAA Division III men's swimming title, with a meet-record 687 points. Second-place finisher Hope scores 259 points. Seven Kenyon swimmers win individual events.

**Mar 18**—The Iowa Hawkeyes clinch their fourth NCAA wrestling title in five years, outpointing second-place Oregon 134–77½. The Hawkeyes' Jeff McGinness wins the 126-pound title but Iowa's Lincoln McIlravy sees his 57-match winning streak stopped by Illinois' Steve Marianetti, who defeats him 13–10 in the 150-pound final.

**Mar 19**—Stanford, led by Jenny Thompson, wins its fourth consecutive NCAA Division I women's swimming title in Texas. The Cardinal rallies to defeat Michigan 497½ to 478½. Thompson wins three events and is a member of two winning relay teams.

**Mar 25**—Michigan wins the NCAA Division I men's swimming title in Indianapolis, with 561 points to Stanford's 475. Michigan's Tom Dolan is the star of the meet, winning the 400-yard IM and the 500- and 1,650-yard freestyles, setting U.S. records in each event.

**Mar 25**—Paul Tergat of Kenya wins the senior men's title at the world cross-country championships in Durham, England. Derartu Tulu of Ethiopia wins the women's title.

**Mar 28**—Olga Kalinovskaya leads Penn State to the NCAA men's and women's fencing title. She wins her third consecutive women's foil title and Penn State finishes with 440 points, 27 better than runner-up St. John's (N.Y.). Sean McClain of Stanford wins the men's foil title.

**Apr 1**—Boston University routs Maine 6–2 to win the NCAA men's hockey title, the school's first since 1978.

**Apr 17**—Uta Pippig wins her second consecutive Boston Marathon in 2:25:11. Cosmas N'Deti repeats as men's winner, finishing in 2:09:22.

**Apr 17**—Skier Vreny Schneider of Switzerland, who has 55 World Cup titles, announces her retirement. Schneider won gold medals in the

**Despite off-ice distractions, Bobek enjoyed a championship season.**

championship game. With the victory, Aulby becomes the first bowler in history to win all four major titles—the PBA, the U.S. Open, the Tournament of Champions and the ABC Masters.

**May 7**—Lance Armstrong of the U.S. defeats defending champion Viatcheslav Ekimov of Russia by 2 minutes to win cycling's 1,130-mile, 12-day Tour DuPont.

**May 18**—Sandy Postma beats Carolyn Dorin 226–187 to win the WIBC Queens bowling tournament.

**May 21**—Maryland defeats Princeton 13–5 to win the NCAA women's Division I lacrosse championship.

**May 29**—Syracuse wins the men's NCAA Division I lacrosse title, defeating host Maryland 13–9 before a crowd of 26,229.

**May 29**—Tanya Harding (no, not the skater) pitches UCLA to a 4–2 victory over Arizona for the NCAA Division I softball title.

**June 3**—Arkansas captures its fourth consecutive team title at the men's NCAA Division I outdoor track and field championships. LSU women win their eighth straight title, the second-longest title reign in NCAA outdoor track and field history.

**June 4**—Cyclist Norm Alvis of the U.S. nips Italy's Maurizio De Pasquale by 55 seconds to win the CoorStates USPRO championships in Philadelphia.

**June 5**—Ethiopia's Haile Gebrselassie sets his third world record of the year, clocking 26:43.53 in the 10,000-meters at Hengelo, Netherlands.

**June 10**—Cal State-Fullerton overwhelms Southern California 11–5 to win its third NCAA Division I baseball title. Titan Mark Kotsay, an outfielder/relief pitcher who hit .563 with three home runs and ten RBIs for the tournament, wins the Most Outstanding Player award.

**June 18**—Michael Johnson wins the 200- and 400-meters at the USA/Mobil track and field championships in Sacramento, a feat unmatched in the 20th century.

**June 20**—Stanford wins the Sears Directors' Cup for all-around excellence in college athletics. The Cardinal won national titles in five sports—women's water polo, men's gymnastics, men's

slalom and giant slalom in the 1988 Olympics and the slalom in 1994 at Lillehammer.

**Apr 22**—Kentucky's Jenny Hansen becomes the most successful female gymnast in NCAA history when she wins four individual titles at the national championships at the University of Georgia, raising her career total to eight. The Utah women win their second consecutive team title, their ninth in the 14-year history of the event. Stanford edges Nebraska 232.4–231.525 for the men's team title. Richard Grace of Nebraska wins the all-around and parallel bar individual titles.

**Apr 22**—Mike Aulby captures bowling's General Tire Tournament of Champions, defeating Bob Spaulding 237–232 in Lake Zurich, Illinois.

**May 6**—At the U.S. National Wrestling Championships in Las Vegas, heavyweight Bruce Baumgartner wins his 16th national title, breaking a U.S. record.

**May 6**—UCLA beats Penn State in the NCAA men's volleyball championship to avenge its loss of the previous year.

**May 6**—Mike Aulby wins the American Bowling Congress Masters Tournament in Reno, Nev., defeating Mark Williams 200–187 in the

tennis, women's volleyball and women's swimming and diving—in 1994-95.

**June 24**—South Africa defeats New Zealand 15–12 in extra time at Johannesburg for the Rugby World Cup title.

**July 12**—Noureddine Morceli of Algeria breaks the world record in the 1,500-meters, clocking 3:27.37 in Nice.

**July 18**—Fabio Casartelli of Italy is killed in a mountain crash during the 15th stage of the Tour de France. He is the third cyclist to die during the race in the Tour's 92-year history.

**July 23**—Spain's Miguel Induráin becomes the only cyclist to win the Tour de France five consecutive times, defeating Alex Zulle of Switzerland by 4 minutes, 35 seconds.

**Aug 4**—Fifteen-year-old Brooke Bennett wins the 1,500-meter freestyle to complete a sweep of the distance free events at the U.S. outdoor championships in Pasadena. She defeats perennial champion Janet Evans in each event. In the men's competition, Tripp Schwenk sets an U.S. record in the 200-meter backstroke with a time of 1:58.33.

**Aug 7**—Mark Davis pulls a total of 47 pounds, 14 ounces of bass out of High Rock Lake in North Carolina to claim the $50,000 first prize at the BASS Masters Classic. Davis also becomes the first fisherman to win the Classic and angler of the year honors in the same season.

**Aug 7**—Triple jumper Jonathan Edwards of Great Britain becomes the first man to break 60' in the event, with a world record leap of 60'¼'' at the world championships in Göteborg, Sweden.

**Aug 11**—Michael Johnson of the U.S. completes an unprecedented double at the world championships in Göteborg, Sweden, when he wins the 200-meter in 19.79. He won the 400-meter on Aug. 9 in 43.39, the second-fastest time in history.

**Aug 11**—Ana Quirot of Cuba completes a miraculous recovery from a 1993 accident that left her with third-degree burns by winning the 800-meters at the world championships in Göteborg, Sweden.

**Aug 12**—The U.S. men's 4x100 freestyle relay team sets an American and world record at the Pan Pacific championships in Atlanta, clocking 3:15.11. The following day, Amy Van Dyken sets the only women's American record of the year in the 50-meter freestyle with a time of 25.03.

**Aug 16**—Moses Kiptanui of Kenya becomes the first man to break eight minutes in the 3,000-meter steeplechase when he runs 7:59.18 in Zurich. At the same meet, Kiptanui loses a record to Ethiopia's Haile Gebrselassie, who

shatters the 5,000-meter world mark by nearly 11 seconds with a time of 12:44.39.

**Aug 18**—Thirteen-year-old Dominique Moceanu becomes the youngest champion in U.S. history after winning the overall title at the U.S. Gymnastics Championships in New Orleans. Dominique Dawes wins the floor exercise and uneven bars.

**Aug 23**—Denis Pankratov of Russia sets his second world record of the year with a 52.32 win in the 100 butterfly at the European championships in Vienna. On June 14 in Canet, France, he set a record in the 200 butterfly, winning in 1:55.22.

**Aug 26**—Taiwan wins its 16th Little League World Series title with a 17–3 drubbing of Spring, Tex., at Williamsport, Pa. The game is called after four innings because of the 10-run mercy rule.

**Sept 6**—Yu Zhoucheng of China wins the men's one-meter springboard at the ninth Diving World Cup in Atlanta. Vera Ilyina of Russia takes the women's title.

**Sept 20**—The U.S. Swimming Board of Directors votes to award $50,000 to swimmers winning gold medals at the 1996 Olympics. Silver and bronze medalists will receive approximately $10,000 and $5,000 each. Relay teams will divide prize money.

**Oct 7**—Thirty-seven-year-old Mark Allen of Boulder, Colo., makes an astounding comeback to win his sixth Ironman Triathlon title in Kailua-Kona, Hawaii. Allen trails 24-year-old Thomas Hellriegel of Germany by 13 minutes entering the marathon stage and makes up the deficit at the 24-mile mark, moving by Hellriegel and never looking back. In the women's race, seven-time winner Paula Newby-Fraser of the U.S. suffers a physical and mental breakdown 500 feet from the finish line and is passed by Karen Smyers of Massachusetts, who wins her first Ironman title in 9:16:46. Newby-Fraser finishes fifth.

**Oct 10**—Cheryl Daniels wins the BPAA Women's U.S. Open at the National Sports Center in Blaine, Minn, defeating Tish Johnson 235–180 in the championship game.

**Oct 10**—Gary Kasparov of Russia retains his world chess championship, defeating India's Viswanathan Anand 10½ to 7½ in New York City's World Trade Center. Kasparov, making his fifth defense since he became the youngest world champion at 22 in 1985, takes home $900,000 to Anand's $450,000.

**Oct 10**—Dominique Moceanu wins the only individual medal for the U.S. in the World Gymnastics Championships in Sabae, Japan, taking the silver medal in the balance beam.

# Baseball

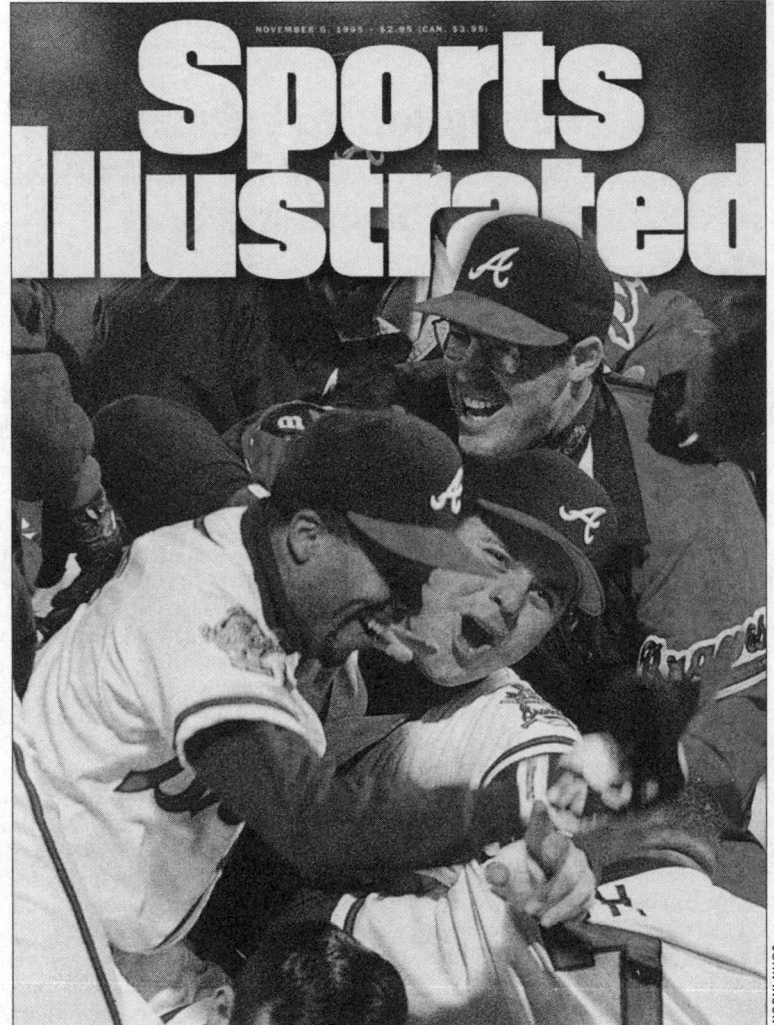

NOVEMBER 6, 1995 • $2.95 (CAN. $3.95)

# Sports Illustrated

JOHN IACONO

# Winners At Last

## A season of redemption for baseball ended in a dramatic victory for perennial Series bridesmaids the Atlanta Braves

### by Tim Kurkjian

WHEN ATLANTA centerfielder Marquis Grissom caught the final out of the 1995 World Series, the strike, the replacement players and the cancelled '94 Series seemed a lifetime away. Finally, after two crushing setbacks in the Series in this decade, the Braves were the world champions. And at least for one night, baseball was back.

It took a staunch union activist, pitcher Tom Glavine, to deliver the first major sports championship to Atlanta with a near-perfect performance in Game 6. Glavine stopped the mighty Cleveland Indians on one hit over eight innings and David Justice's home run in the sixth inning gave the Braves a 1–0 win. Reliever Mark Wohlers got the final three outs, sending a sellout crowd at Atlanta-Fulton County Stadium into a frenzy. "This was a great series for us and great for baseball," Wohlers said, dripping with champagne during the celebration. "I want to play this game until they plant me in the ground."

The '95 Series will be remembered for great pitching, mostly by the spectacular Atlanta staff. The Indians, making their first World Series appearance since 1954, batted only .179 and scored only 19 runs in the six games. In four of the six, they managed six or fewer hits. This was astonishing considering Cleveland had hit .291 with 207 homers in the regular season and their offense was being called the best baseball had seen since Cincinnati's Big Red Machine. But the Indians, who went 100–44 in the strike-shortened season, were no match for the crafty Atlanta hurlers, who made the Cleveland hitters look silly with a barrage of changeups and perfectly-located fastballs.

The game's best pitcher, Atlanta's Greg Maddux, was magnificent in Game 1, firing a two-hitter (both opposite-field singles), walking no one and allowing only four balls out of the infield in a 3–2 win. Both runs were unearned. Cleveland's Orel Hershiser was nearly Maddux's match for six innings, but he walked the first two hitters in the seventh, then took himself out of the game because he had lost the release point on his pitches. Another walk followed a run-scoring ground out and a squeeze bunt gave Maddux a 3–1 lead. It seemed like 30–1.

Glavine started Game 2, and he didn't make many mistakes, either. One came in

Justice's solo shot
proved to be the
difference in Game 6.

until Braves first baseman Fred McGriff homered in the sixth and Ryan Klesko homered in the seventh. The Braves scored three times in the eighth—twice off tiring starter Charles Nagy—to take a 6–5 lead. But the Indians tied it in the last of the eighth on a run-scoring double by Sandy Alomar off Wohlers, who proceeded to end the threat by striking out Omar Vizquel on three pitches and inducing Carlos Baerga to ground out.

That started an epic duel of closers, Wohlers against Cleveland's Jose Mesa. "When's the last time you saw two closers throwing 100 miles an hour each for three innings?" Hershiser asked. Mesa won the duel, but Wohlers didn't get the loss. He was replaced by Alejandro Pena to start the 11th. Baerga drilled a lead-off double. Following an intentional walk to Belle, Murray rifled Pena's first pitch to center field, scoring Baerga for a 7–6 win. "They were fighting for a championship," said Hershiser. "And we were fighting for our lives."

The Braves had more fight in them the next night. Steve Avery, chosen to start so Maddux could get another day's rest, quashed the critics by allowing only three hits in six innings of a 5–2 win. The hitting star was Justice, whose two-run single in the seventh atoned for a mostly disappointing postseason at that point.

With Maddux pitching in Game 5, the Series was supposed to be all but over. But it was obvious early on that this wouldn't be the same kind of dominant performance

the second inning when Eddie Murray drilled a belt-high fastball over the left field fence for a 2–0 lead. It gave Murray a World Series homer in three decades; Yogi Berra and Joe DiMaggio are the only other players who can make that claim. But the Braves tied it off Dennis Martinez in the third, then took a 4–2 lead in the sixth on a two-run homer by catcher Javy Lopez. Glavine and three relievers, the last being Wohlers, held on for a 4–3 victory.

So it was on to Jacobs Field for Game 3. And the first Series game played in Cleveland since 1954 was a classic despite a wind chill temperature at game time of 29°. The Indians came out flying, rocking Atlanta starter John Smoltz for six hits and four runs in 2⅓ innings. The 4–1 lead seemed safe

**Maddux was unhittable in Series Game 1, but mortal in Game 5.**

RICHARD MACKSON

Maddux posted in Game 1. In the first, Cleveland's Albert Belle lined a two-run homer to right for a 2–0 lead. The Braves tied it in the fifth, but the Indians' Jim Thome and Manny Ramirez singled home runs with two out in the sixth for a 4–2 lead. Hershiser allowed one earned run in eight innings of a 5–4 victory, sending the Series back to Atlanta for Game 6 and Glavine's magnificent Series-clinching performance.

"From day one this year, we were on a mission," Glavine said. "We knew that the only thing that would make our season a success would be a World Series title."

Finally, they got it.

The long-suffering Indians fell two wins shy of the ring. They advanced to the World Series by eliminating the darlings of the playoffs, the Mariners, who were making their first postseason trip in their 19-year history. Seattle was 12½ games out of first place in the AL West on Aug. 15, came back to beat the Angels in a one-game playoff, lost the first two games to the Yankees in the Division Series, then swept the next three for the right to play for the pennant.

The Mariners won Game 1 in Seattle behind rookie Bob Wolcott, who was starting only because the rest of the staff was exhausted from overwork. Wolcott pitched seven strong innings in a 3–2 win—the fourth of his major league career. Hershiser threw a gem in Game 2—four hits in eight innings—to spark a 5–2 win for the Indians. The ALCS shifted to Cleveland where Mariner rightfielder Jay Buhner bashed a three-run homer off reliever Eric Plunk in the 11th for a 5–2 victory. Indians fans were worried. Seattle fans repeated their battle cry: Refuse to Lose.

But that was it for the Mariners. Ken Hill and relief help blanked Seattle in Game 4, 7–0, and the Indians took a 3–2 lead back to Seattle with a 3–2 win in Game 5. Even 50,000-plus fans screaming inside the Kingdome couldn't help the M's in Game 6. Randy Johnson, the AL's best pitcher, gave up an unearned run in the fifth, then three more in the eighth—two of them scoring on a passed ball as Cleveland's Kenny Lofton made a daring dash home from second on the play. Dennis Martinez, 40, outdueled Johnson in the 4–0 victory.

The Braves had a much easier time in the NLCS. Their World's Greatest Pitching Staff enjoyed its finest hour against the formidable Reds, holding them to five runs in the four-game sweep (an NLCS record for fewest runs scored in a four-game series). Atlanta's awesome starting pitching staff compiled a 1.29 ERA and the bullpen, a disappointment in previous postseasons, allowed just one run in 11 innings. "I'm numb, I'm dumbfounded," said Cincinnati shortstop Barry Larkin, wondering how a series that was supposed to go seven games could end so quickly. How could this happen? Well, Cincinnati's 3-4 hitters, Ron Gant and Reggie Sanders, went a combined 5 for 32 and Sanders struck out 10 times. In his seven postseason games this year, Sanders struck out 19 times—four more than Tony Gwynn did all year.

Yet the MVP of the NLCS wasn't a pitcher, it was Mike Devereaux, a reserve outfielder who was acquired in late August from the White Sox. In Game 1, Devereaux's

DAVID LIAM KYLE

**At 37, Hershiser showed he can still get them out.**

11th-inning single gave Atlanta a 2–1 win. The Braves also won Game 2 in extra innings, 6–2, on a run-scoring wild pitch by Mark Portugal followed by a three-run homer by catcher Javy Lopez. Another Atlanta catcher, Charlie O'Brien, nailed a three-run homer in Game 3 to give Maddux and the Braves a 5–2 win. They clinched the next night, 6–0, when Devereaux hit a three-run homer in the seventh to support Steve Avery's standout pitching.

The best series of the postseason came in the divisional playoffs, a system widely derided because it allowed a wild-card team into the playoffs for the first time. As it turned out, it was a great idea. The Mariners and the Yankees, the wild-card team, played one of the greatest series in baseball history.

The Bombers won the first two games in New York; the second, a 7–5, 15-inning marathon, was the longest postseason game (five hours and 12 minutes) ever. Only two teams had ever lost the first two games of a five-game series in a non-strike season and come back to win. But the Mariners were heading home to the Kingdome, where they had been invincible down the stretch. They won Game 3, 7–4, behind Johnson. The Mariners fell behind 5–0 after three innings of Game 4 but rallied to win 11–8. DH Edgar Martinez's second homer of the game—a grand slam off John Wetteland in the eighth—gave him seven RBIs, the most ever in a postseason game.

In Game 5, the Yankees took a 4–2 lead into the eighth behind David Cone. But Ken Griffey Jr. crushed his fifth homer of the series—making him the first player to hit that many in a five-game series—to bring the

Mariners within a run at 4–3. It was the 22nd homer in the series, another record in a series of any length. A tiring Cone walked in another run to tie the score. Johnson, working on one day's rest, made his first relief appearance since 1993 and bailed the Mariners out of a jam in the ninth. He struck out the side in the 10th, but Randy Velarde's RBI single gave the Yankees a 5–4 lead in the 11th. New York's Jack McDowell, also working on one day's rest, entered in the 10th inning for the first relief appearance of his major league career. Joey Cora beat out a bunt to start the 11th. Griffey singled. Martinez drilled a double down the leftfield line. Griffey scored from first to win it 6–5. The Kingdome exploded.

"The guys put their careers on the line. One pitch could have blown out their arms," Cone said. "You hear the rap people put on the modern-day player—I, I, I and me, me, me—well, this series was anything but that. If this doesn't do a lot to diminish the greedy ballplayer image, I don't know what will."

The Atlanta-Colorado series couldn't match its AL counterpart, but it was great theater nonetheless. Atlanta won in four games, but the first three games were decided in the final at bat—a first in postseason history. The Braves won the first two in Colorado as rookie third baseman Chipper Jones homered in the ninth to win Game 1, then doubled to start the ninth in Game 2, sparking a four-run rally that gave Atlanta a 7–4 win. The wild-card Rockies, who reached the postseason faster (in their third season) than any expansion team in history, fought back, winning Game 3 in 10 innings, 7–5, after blowing another lead in the ninth. But Brave first baseman Fred McGriff homered twice in Game 4, and Marquis Grissom went 5 for 5 to lead a 10–4 victory.

The other two series ended quickly. The Indians swept the Red Sox, who ran their postseason losing streak to a record 13 games. The series turned in Game 1 when Cleveland backup catcher Tony Pena homered in the 13th inning off Zane Smith for a 5–4 win. The Indians won the next two 4–0 and 8–2. The Reds had an even easier time with the underachieving Dodgers. They trailed for a total of three innings en route to a 7–2, 5–4 and 10–1 sweep.

The terrific play in the divisional series followed a fascinating regular season—especially if you're a fan of lots of hitting and Oriole shortstop Cal Ripken Jr.

On Sept. 6 Ripken became the greatest ironman in major league history when he played in his 2,131st consecutive game, passing the great Lou Gehrig. It was time for celebration not only in Baltimore but also all across baseball, when the banner on the warehouse beyond the rightfield wall at Camden Yards was changed to 2,131 before the bottom of the fifth inning. During a 22-minute stoppage in play—perhaps the most stirring, emotional 22 minutes in baseball history—Ripken made five curtain calls, took off his jersey and hat and presented them to his two young children, and then, after much prodding from his teammates, circled the warning track with a victory lap. He slapped hands with fans, and hugged opposing players and umpires.

"It was like an out-of-body experience," said Ripken. "It's like when your wife has a baby. You're standing there watching and thinking, This can't be happening to me.

This can't be my wife. This can't be my baby. I kept thinking this was happening to someone else. This couldn't be happening to me." For one night, all was right in baseball and America.

Ripken wasn't the only player to enter the record books in 1995. His former teammate from Baltimore, Eddie Murray of the Indians, became the 19th player in history to reach 3,000 hits—guaranteeing him a spot in Cooperstown. The Dodgers' Ramon Martinez pitched the only no-hitter of the season, dominating the Marlins on July 14, 7–0. But the best game of the season was pitched by his little brother. On June 3, Montreal's Pedro Martinez pitched nine perfect innings against the Padres, but the score was tied after nine innings. He gave up a hit to start the 10th and was taken out. Under the new rules of baseball, he won't be credited with a perfect game or a no-hitter.

There were a few other pitching highlights. Maddux, a lock for his fourth straight NL Cy Young Award, went 19–2 with a 1.63 ERA, and became the first pitcher since Walter Johnson (1918–19) to post consecutive seasons with an ERA under 1.80. Maddux struck out 181 and walked 23—the greatest strikeout-to-walk ratio of any pitcher in history with 200 or more innings. Seattle's Johnson was nearly as dominant, going 18–2 and leading the league in ERA (2.48) and strikeouts (294). Baltimore's Mike Mussina won 19 games, preventing Johnson from becoming the first AL pitcher since Hal Newhouser (1945) to finish first in the league in wins, ERA and strikeouts. Mussina was also part of an Oriole staff that tied the AL record (held by the '74 Orioles) with five straight shutouts to end the season. As for ending games, no one topped Cleveland's Jose Mesa, who saved 46.

For starters there was no one more intriguing than Dodger pitcher Hideo Nomo, the second Japanese player ever to play in the major leagues. Nomo, 26, dazzled NL hitters all season but was virtually unhittable in the first half, going 6–1 and starting the All-Star Game in Arlington, Texas, against Seattle's Johnson. Nomo, using a delivery called the Tornado, literally turned his back to the hitter

**Wakefield and his baffling knuckleball produced 16 wins in 1995.**

but his home run–per–at bat ratio wasn't the highest in the league. That belonged to Oakland's Mark McGwire, who hit 39 in 317 at bats—the greatest ratio ever. Belle also was the eighth player in history to amass 100 extra-base hits. San Diego's Tony Gwynn won his sixth batting title (.368) and became the first NL player to hit at least .350 for three consecutive seasons since St. Louis's Ducky Medwick had his third straight in 1937. Seattle's Edgar Martinez won the AL batting title (.356). Bichette led the league in homers (40) and RBIs (128) and was third in hitting (.340)—the last NL player to match those totals in a season was Duke Snider in 1954.

Another disappointing season in Detroit (60–84)

during his windup, then exploded toward the plate with, among other pitches, a demonic forkball. Trailed all season by a huge media contingent from Japan, Nomo tailed off in the second half but finished 13–6 and led the NL in strikeouts (236).

The comeback story of the season was Boston knuckleballer Tim Wakefield. He was perhaps the worst pitcher in Triple A last season, but he appeared from nowhere in late May and carried the Red Sox staff for nearly three months. He was 14–1 and a leading candidate for the AL Cy Young in mid-August, but the magic finally wore off, and he faltered down the stretch to finish 16–8.

The rest of the season belonged to the hitters. Despite the 144-game schedule, 60 players hit 20 homers, 21 hit 30 homers, four hit 40, and Cleveland's Albert Belle hit 50—

forced the resignation of manager Sparky Anderson, who had guided the Tigers since 1979 but hadn't been to the playoffs since 1987. He wasn't the only manager on the move. The White Sox's Gene Lamont was canned on June 2. The Cardinals' Joe Torre was axed two weeks later, but neither team improved much with the changes.

The White Sox were supposed to be a major player in the AL Central race but lost seven of their first eight and were never a factor, finishing 32 games out. But even in a good year Chicago would have been no match for Cleveland. The Indians won 15 of their first 21 to open a four-game lead that wasn't challenged. They set a major league record for the largest lead—30 games.

There was only slightly more suspense in the AL East. Boston, picked by most to finish fourth, took the lead for good on May 13. A

12-game winning streak in early August opened a 10-game lead that made September almost irrelevant. The East's underachiever was Baltimore, which finished 15 games out.

The best race in the AL came in the West. The Angels, picked to finish last in the division, moved into a tie for the lead on July 2, scored 201 runs in that month and opened a 10½-game lead by Aug. 15. But 36 days later they had fallen into a first-place tie with the Mariners. It marked the quickest disappearance in this century of a lead that big. After dropping three games behind Seattle, the Angels won their last five games to force a one-game playoff. But Seattle's Johnson beat them 9–1 on a three-hitter with 12 strikeouts.

The Braves ran away with the NL East title, winning by 21 games. But it didn't come easily, at least not initially. The Phillies set a National League record by not losing two games in a row the first 34 games of the year. But as soon as their sizzling start (37–18) ended, they went nearly a month without winning two in a row. Atlanta took over first on July 5 and never looked back.

The Reds lost their first six games, and eight of their first nine, but won their next six and 22 of their next 27 to take over first place for good on June 5. They won by nine games over the Astros, who were derailed in late July when star first baseman Jeff Bagwell broke his left hand.

The Giants were in contention until star third baseman Matt Williams broke his right foot with a foul ball on June 3 and was lost for almost three months. Without

him the Giants weren't a serious factor, nor were the Padres, other than a brief surge in mid-August. That left the Rockies and the Dodgers to fight it out. L.A. won the division on the second-to-last day of the season. The Rockies came from six runs down against the Giants on the last day of the season to win 10–9 and secure the wild-card.

In the end, baseball was left with one burning question: Was this season exciting enough to bring the fans back? It's a tough question to answer, but if next season has as many home runs, as many postseason thrills and a hero as simply decent as Ripken, America's pastime might have a chance to be just that again.

JOHN IACONO

**McGwire knocked out an amazing 39 home runs in just 317 at bats.**

## Final Standings

### National League

#### EASTERN DIVISION

| Team | Won | Lost | Pct | GB | Home | Away |
|---|---|---|---|---|---|---|
| Atlanta | 90 | 54 | .625 | — | 44-28 | 46-26 |
| New York | 69 | 75 | .479 | 21 | 40-32 | 29-43 |
| Philadelphia | 69 | 75 | .479 | 21 | 35-37 | 34-38 |
| Florida | 67 | 76 | .469 | 22½ | 37-34 | 30-42 |
| Montreal | 66 | 78 | .458 | 24 | 31-41 | 35-37 |

#### CENTRAL DIVISION

| Team | Won | Lost | Pct | GB | Home | Away |
|---|---|---|---|---|---|---|
| Cincinnati | 85 | 59 | .590 | — | 44-28 | 41-31 |
| Houston | 76 | 68 | .528 | 9 | 36-36 | 40-32 |
| Chicago | 73 | 71 | .507 | 12 | 34-38 | 39-33 |
| St. Louis | 62 | 81 | .434 | 22½ | 39-33 | 23-48 |
| Pittsburgh | 58 | 86 | .403 | 27 | 31-41 | 27-45 |

#### WESTERN DIVISION

| Team | Won | Lost | Pct | GB | Home | Away |
|---|---|---|---|---|---|---|
| Los Angeles | 78 | 66 | .542 | — | 39-33 | 39-33 |
| Colorado | 77 | 67 | .535 | 1 | 44-28 | 33-39 |
| San Diego | 70 | 74 | .486 | 8 | 40-32 | 30-38 |
| San Francisco | 67 | 77 | .465 | 11 | 37-35 | 30-42 |

### American League

#### EASTERN DIVISION

| Team | Won | Lost | Pct | GB | Home | Away |
|---|---|---|---|---|---|---|
| Boston | 86 | 58 | .597 | — | 42-30 | 44-28 |
| New York | 79 | 65 | .549 | 7 | 46-26 | 33-39 |
| Baltimore | 71 | 73 | .493 | 15 | 36-36 | 35-37 |
| Detroit | 60 | 84 | .417 | 26 | 35-37 | 25-47 |
| Toronto | 56 | 88 | .389 | 30 | 29-43 | 27-45 |

#### CENTRAL DIVISION

| Team | Won | Lost | Pct | GB | Home | Away |
|---|---|---|---|---|---|---|
| Cleveland | 100 | 44 | .694 | — | 54-18 | 46-26 |
| Kansas City | 70 | 74 | .486 | 30 | 35-37 | 35-37 |
| Chicago | 68 | 76 | .472 | 32 | 38-34 | 30-44 |
| Milwaukee | 65 | 79 | .451 | 35 | 33-39 | 32-40 |
| Minnesota | 56 | 88 | .389 | 44 | 29-43 | 27-45 |

#### WESTERN DIVISION

| Team | Won | Lost | Pct | GB | Home | Away |
|---|---|---|---|---|---|---|
| California | 78 | 66 | .542 | — | 39-33 | 39-33 |
| Seattle | 78 | 66 | .542 | — | 45-27 | 33-39 |
| Texas | 74 | 70 | .514 | 4 | 41-31 | 33-39 |
| Oakland | 67 | 77 | .465 | 11 | 38-34 | 29-43 |

## 1995 Playoffs

### National League Divisional Playoffs

Oct 3 ..............Atlanta 5 at Colorado 4
Oct 4 ..............Atlanta 7 at Colorado 4

Oct 6 ..............Colorado 7 at Atlanta 5 (10 innings)
Oct 7 ..............Colorado 4 at Atlanta 10

(Atlanta won series 3–1.)

Oct 3 ..............Cincinnati 7 at Los Angeles 2
Oct 4 ..............Cincinnati 5 at Los Angeles 4

Oct 6 ..............Los Angeles 1 at Cincinnati 10

(Cincinnati won series 3–0.)

### National League Championship Series

Oct 10 ............Atlanta 2 at Cincinnati 1 (11 innings)
Oct 11 ............Atlanta 6 at Cincinnati 2 (10 innings)

Oct 13 ............Cincinnati 2 at Atlanta 5
Oct 14 ............Cincinnati 0 at Atlanta 6

(Atlanta won series 4–0.)

#### GAME 1

| | | | | | | | | | | | |
|---|---|---|---|---|---|---|---|---|---|---|---|
| Atlanta | 0 0 0 | 0 0 0 | 0 0 1 | 0 1 | —2 |
| Cincinnati | 0 0 0 | 1 0 0 | 0 0 0 | 0 0 | —1 |

**WP**—Wohlers. **LP**—Jackson. **Save**—McMichael. **LOB**—Atlanta 9, Cincinnati 6. **2B**—Cincinnati: Larkin (1), Morris (1), Howard (1). **3B**—Cincinnati: Larkin (1). **CS**—Atlanta: Klesko. **Sac**—Atlanta: Polonia. **GIDP**—Cincinnati: Boone (2), Walton, Santiago, Sanders. **T**—3:18. **A**—40,382.
**Recap:** Tom Glavine and Pete Schourek pitched well, giving up one earned run apiece in 7 and 8⅓ innings, respectively. Trailing 2–1 in the ninth, Atlanta tied it up when Chipper Jones singled, went to third on Fred McGriff's single and scored on David Justice's grounder to second. Atlanta won in the 11th when McGriff walked, took second on Luis Polonia's sacrifice fly and then scored on Mike Devereaux's single.

#### GAME 2

| | | | | | | | | | | | |
|---|---|---|---|---|---|---|---|---|---|---|---|
| Atlanta | 1 0 0 | 1 0 0 | 0 0 0 | 4 | —6 |
| Cincinnati | 0 0 0 | 0 2 0 | 0 0 0 | 0 | —2 |

**WP**—McMichael. **LP**—Portugal.
**E**—Atlanta: Smoltz (1); Cincinnati: Sanders (1). **LOB**—Atlanta 8, Cincinnati 9. **2B**—Atlanta: McGriff (3), Devereaux (1); Cincinnati: Larkin (2). **HR**—Atlanta: Lopez (1). **SB**—Atlanta: Smoltz (1); Cincinnati: Branson (1), Harris (1), Larkin (1), Morris (1). **CS**—Cincinnati: Howard, Sanders. **Sac**—Cincinnati: Branson. **GIDP**—Atlanta: Devereaux (1). **T**—3:26. **A**—44,624.
**Recap:** After Jeff Branson stole home—a NLCS first—in the fifth inning, the game went into extra innings tied 2–2. In the top of the 10th, Mark Lemke singled off reliever Mark Portugal and eventually scored on a wild pitch. Fred McGriff and David Justice scored when Javy Lopez homered down the leftfield line.

## National League Championship Series *(Cont.)*

### GAME 3

| | | | | | | | | | | |
|---|---|---|---|---|---|---|---|---|---|---|
| Cincinnati | 0 0 0 | 0 0 0 | 0 1 1 | —2 |
| Atlanta | 0 0 0 | 0 0 3 | 2 0 x | —5 |

**WP**—Maddux. **LP**—Wells.
**E**—Atlanta: Grissom (1). **LOB**—Cincinnati 9, Atlanta 8. **2B**—Cincinnati: Branson (1); Atlanta: McGriff (4). **HR**—Atlanta: Jones (1), O'Brien (1). **SB**—Atlanta: Jones (1). **CS**—Cincinnati: Larkin. **Sac**—Cincinnati: Howard. **GIDP**—Atlanta: Lemke.
**T**—2:42. **A**—51,424.
**Recap:** Greg Maddux went eight strong innings, giving up just one earned run. Chipper Jones had three hits for the Braves, including a two-run homer in the seventh.

### GAME 4

| | | | | | | | | | | |
|---|---|---|---|---|---|---|---|---|---|---|
| Cincinnati | 0 0 0 | 0 0 0 | 0 0 0 | —0 |
| Atlanta | 0 0 1 | 0 0 0 | 5 0 x | —6 |

**WP**—Avery. **LP**—Schourek.
**E**—Cincinnati: Larkin (1); Atlanta: Belliard (1). **LOB**—Cincinnati 4, Atlanta 11. **2B**—Atlanta: Lopez (1). **3B**—Atlanta: Grissom (1). **HR**—Atlanta: Devereaux (1). **GIDP**—Cincinnati: Duncan, Sanders, Gant; Atlanta: Devereaux. **T**—2:54. **A**—52,067.
**Recap:** In a pitchers' duel, Steve Avery and Pete Schourek each went six innings, Avery giving up no earned runs and only two hits, Schourek just one earned run. In the seventh, Marquis Grissom's triple to left center opened the door for Atlanta to storm ahead. Grissom scored on a passed ball, then Mike Devereaux hit a three-run homer to bury the Reds.

## American League Divisional Playoffs

Oct 2 ...............California 1 at Seattle 9

(Seattle won AL West title)

Oct 3 ...............Boston 4 at Cleveland 5 (13 innings)
Oct 4 ...............Boston 0 at Cleveland 4

Oct 6 ...............Cleveland 8 at Boston 2

(Cleveland won series 3–0.)

Oct 3 ...............Seattle 6 at New York 9
Oct 4 ...............Seattle 5 at New York 7 (15 innings)
Oct 6 ...............New York 4 at Seattle 7

Oct 7 ...............New York 8 at Seattle 11
Oct 8 ...............New York 5 at Seattle 6 (11 innings)

(Seattle won series 3–2.)

## American League Championship Series

Oct 10 ............Cleveland 2 at Seattle 3
Oct 11 ............Cleveland 5 at Seattle 2
Oct 13 ............Seattle 5 at Cleveland 2 (11 innings)

Oct 14 ............Seattle 0 at Cleveland 7
Oct 15 ............Seattle 2 at Cleveland 3
Oct 17 ............Cleveland 4 at Seattle 0

(Cleveland won series 4–2.)

### GAME 1

| | | | | | | | | | | |
|---|---|---|---|---|---|---|---|---|---|---|
| Cleveland | 0 0 1 | 0 0 0 | 1 0 0 | —2 |
| Seattle | 0 2 0 | 0 0 0 | 1 0 x | —3 |

**WP**—Wolcott. **LP**—Martinez.
**E**—Cleveland: Thome (1). **LOB**—Cleveland 12, Seattle 7. **2B**—Cleveland: Sorrento (1); Seattle: Cora (1), Buhner (1), Sojo (1), Griffey (1). **3B**—Cleveland: Lofton (1). **HR**—Cleveland: Belle (1); Seattle: Blowers (1). **CS**—Seattle: Griffey (1). **GIDP**—Cleveland: Sorrento; Seattle: E. Martinez. **T**—3:07. **A**—57,065.
**Recap:** Bob Wolcott, returned to the roster for the postseason, pitched seven strong innings, yielding just two earned runs. Mike Blowers's two-run homer in the second was the single big blow for the Mariners.

### GAME 2

| | | | | | | | | | | |
|---|---|---|---|---|---|---|---|---|---|---|
| Cleveland | 0 0 0 | 0 2 2 | 0 1 0 | —5 |
| Seattle | 0 0 0 | 0 0 1 | 0 0 1 | —2 |

**WP**—Hershiser. **LP**—Belcher.
**E**—Seattle: Sojo (1). **LOB**—Cleveland 10, Seattle 7. **3B**—Cleveland: Alomar (1). **HR**—Cleveland: Ramirez 2 (2); Seattle: Griffey (1), Buhner (1). **SB**—Cleveland: Vizquel (1); Seattle: Coleman (1). **GIDP**—Cleveland: Sorrento, Thome. **T**—3:14. **A**—58,144.
**Recap:** Orel Hershiser gave up just one earned run and Manny Ramirez went 4 for 4 with two homers to power the Indians.

### GAME 3

| | | | | | | | | | | |
|---|---|---|---|---|---|---|---|---|---|---|
| Seattle | 0 1 1 | 0 0 0 | 0 0 0 | 0 3 | —5 |
| Cleveland | 0 0 0 | 1 0 0 | 0 1 0 | 0 0 | —2 |

**WP**—Charlton. **LP**—Tavarez.
**E**—Seattle: Buhner (1); Cleveland: Alomar (1), Espinoza (1). **LOB**—Seattle 5, Cleveland 6. **3B**—Cleveland: Lofton (1). **HR**—Seattle: Buhner 2 (3). **SB**—Seattle: Griffey (1), Cora (1); Cleveland: Lofton (1). **CS**—Cleveland: Perry; Seattle: E. Martinez. **Sac**—Cleveland: Vizquel. **T**—3:18. **A**—43,643.
**Recap:** Cleveland suffered its first extra-inning loss of the year on a three-run homer by Jay Buhner in the top of the 11th. Randy Johnson struck out six in eight innings.

### GAME 4

| | | | | | | | | | | |
|---|---|---|---|---|---|---|---|---|---|---|
| Seattle | 0 0 0 | 0 0 0 | 0 0 0 | —0 |
| Cleveland | 3 1 2 | 0 0 1 | 0 0 x | —7 |

**WP**—Hill. **LP**—Benes.
**E**—Seattle: Wilson (1). **LOB**—Seattle 9, Cleveland 7. **2B**—Seattle: Buhner (2); Cleveland: Vizquel (1). **HR**—Cleveland: Murray (1), Thome (1). **SB**—Seattle: Coleman (2), Griffey (2); Cleveland: Lofton (2), Kirby (1). **Sac**—Cleveland: Lofton. **GIDP**—Cleveland: Sorrento, Kirby. **T**—3:30. **A**—43,686.
**Recap:** Ken Hill was superlative, pitching seven scoreless innings while Andy Benes got shelled, giving up six earned runs in 2⅓ innings.

## American League Championship Series *(Cont.)*

### GAME 5

| | | | | | | | | | | |
|---|---|---|---|---|---|---|---|---|---|---|
| Seattle | 0 | 0 1 | 0 1 0 | 0 0 0 | —2 |
| Cleveland | 1 | 0 0 | 0 0 2 | 0 0 x | —3 |

**WP**—Hershiser (2). **LP**—Bosio. **Save**—Mesa.
**E**—Seattle: T. Martinez (1), Griffey (1); Cleveland: Belle (2), Sorrento (2). **LOB**—Seattle 9, Cleveland 11. **2B**—Seattle: Griffey (2), Diaz (1); Cleveland: Murray (1), Alomar (1). **HR**—Cleveland: Thome (2). **SB**—Seattle: Cora (2), Coleman (3); Cleveland: Vizquel 2 (3), Lofton 2 (4). **Sac**—Seattle: Strange (1); Cleveland: Kirby (1). **GIDP**—Cleveland: Ramirez. **T**—3:37. **A**—43,607.
**Recap:** Orel Hershiser struck out eight to continue his perfect record in the postseason. Eddie Murray doubled to right and scored on Thome's homer in the sixth.

### GAME 6

| | | | | | | | | | | |
|---|---|---|---|---|---|---|---|---|---|---|
| Cleveland | 0 | 0 0 | 0 1 0 | 0 3 0 | —4 |
| Seattle | 0 | 0 0 | 0 0 0 | 0 0 0 | —0 |

**WP**—D. Martinez. **LP**—Johnson.
**E**—Seattle: Cora (1). **LOB**—Cleveland 4, Seattle 6. **2B**—Cleveland: Belle (1), Pena (1); Seattle: Sojo (1). **HR**—Cleveland: Baerga (1). **SB**—Cleveland: Lofton (5); Seattle: Coleman (4), E. Martinez (1). **GIDP**—Seattle: Sojo. **T**—2:54. **A**—58,489.
**Recap:** 40-year-old Dennis Martinez got the first postseason victory of his long career, pitching seven shutout innings to become the oldest pitcher to win an LCS game. AL stolen-base king Kenny Lofton scored from second base on a passed ball in the eighth.

## Composite Box Scores

### National League Championship Series

#### ATLANTA

| BATTING | AB | R | H | HR | RBI | Avg |
|---|---|---|---|---|---|---|
| Polonia | 2 | 0 | 1 | 0 | 1 | .500 |
| Jones | 16 | 3 | 7 | 1 | 3 | .438 |
| McGriff | 16 | 5 | 7 | 0 | 0 | .438 |
| O'Brien | 5 | 1 | 2 | 1 | 3 | .400 |
| Lopez | 14 | 2 | 5 | 1 | 3 | .357 |
| Devereaux | 13 | 2 | 4 | 1 | 5 | .308 |
| Belliard | 11 | 1 | 3 | 0 | 0 | .273 |
| Justice | 11 | 1 | 3 | 0 | 1 | .273 |
| Grissom | 19 | 2 | 5 | 0 | 0 | .263 |
| Lemke | 18 | 2 | 3 | 0 | 1 | .167 |
| 8 others | 24 | 0 | 2 | 0 | 0 | .083 |
| Totals | 149 | 19 | 42 | 4 | 17 | .282 |

| PITCHING | G | IP | H | BB | SO | ERA |
|---|---|---|---|---|---|---|
| Avery | 2 | 6 | 2 | 4 | 6 | 0.00 |
| Pena | 3 | 3 | 2 | 1 | 4 | 0.00 |
| McMichael | 3 | 2⅔ | 0 | 1 | 2 | 0.00 |
| Clontz | 1 | ⅓ | 1 | 0 | 0 | 0.00 |
| Maddux | 1 | 8 | 7 | 2 | 4 | 1.13 |
| Glavine | 1 | 7 | 7 | 2 | 5 | 1.29 |
| Wohlers | 4 | 5 | 2 | 0 | 8 | 1.80 |
| Smoltz | 1 | 7 | 7 | 2 | 2 | 2.57 |
| Totals | 4 | 39 | 28 | 12 | 31 | 1.15 |

#### CINCINNATI

| BATTING | AB | R | H | HR | RBI | Avg |
|---|---|---|---|---|---|---|
| Harris | 2 | 0 | 2 | 0 | 1 | 1.000 |
| Taubensee | 2 | 0 | 1 | 0 | 0 | .500 |
| Wells | 2 | 0 | 1 | 0 | 0 | .500 |
| Larkin | 18 | 1 | 7 | 0 | 0 | .389 |
| Howard | 8 | 0 | 2 | 0 | 1 | .250 |
| Lewis | 4 | 0 | 1 | 0 | 0 | .250 |
| Santiago | 13 | 0 | 3 | 0 | 0 | .231 |
| Boone | 14 | 1 | 3 | 0 | 0 | .214 |
| Gant | 16 | 1 | 3 | 0 | 1 | .188 |
| Morris | 12 | 0 | 2 | 0 | 1 | .167 |
| Sanders | 16 | 2 | 2 | 0 | 0 | .125 |
| Branson | 9 | 2 | 1 | 0 | 0 | .111 |
| 6 others | 18 | 0 | 0 | 0 | 0 | .000 |
| Totals | 134 | 5 | 28 | 0 | 4 | .209 |

| PITCHING | G | IP | H | BB | SO | ERA |
|---|---|---|---|---|---|---|
| Burba | 2 | 3⅓ | 3 | 4 | 0 | 0.00 |
| Brantley | 2 | 2⅔ | 0 | 2 | 1 | 0.00 |
| Carrasco | 1 | 1⅓ | 1 | 0 | 3 | 0.00 |
| Schourek | 2 | 14⅓ | 14 | 3 | 13 | 1.26 |
| Smiley | 1 | 5 | 5 | 0 | 1 | 3.60 |
| Wells | 1 | 6 | 8 | 2 | 3 | 4.50 |
| Jackson | 3 | 2⅓ | 5 | 4 | 1 | 23.14 |
| Hernandez | 1 | ⅔ | 3 | 0 | 0 | 27.00 |
| Portugal | 1 | 1 | 3 | 1 | 0 | 36.00 |
| Totals | 4 | 37 | 42 | 16 | 22 | 4.62 |

## American League Championship Series

| CLEVELAND BATTING | AB | R | H | HR | RBI | Avg |
|---|---|---|---|---|---|---|
| Lofton | 24 | 4 | 11 | 0 | 3 | .458 |
| Baerga | 25 | 3 | 10 | 1 | 4 | .400 |
| Pena | 6 | 1 | 2 | 0 | 0 | .333 |
| Ramirez | 21 | 2 | 6 | 2 | 2 | .286 |
| Alomar | 15 | 0 | 4 | 0 | 1 | .267 |
| Thome | 15 | 2 | 4 | 2 | 5 | .267 |
| Murray | 24 | 2 | 6 | 1 | 3 | .250 |
| Belle | 18 | 1 | 4 | 1 | 1 | .222 |
| Kirby | 5 | 2 | 1 | 0 | 0 | .200 |
| Sorrento | 13 | 2 | 2 | 0 | 0 | .154 |
| Espinoza | 8 | 1 | 1 | 0 | 0 | .125 |
| Vizquel | 23 | 2 | 2 | 0 | 2 | .087 |
| 2 others | 9 | 1 | 0 | 0 | 0 | .000 |
| Totals | 206 | 23 | 53 | 7 | 21 | .257 |

| CLEVELAND PITCHING | G | IP | H | BB | SO | ERA |
|---|---|---|---|---|---|---|
| Hill | 1 | 7 | 5 | 3 | 6 | 0.00 |
| Assenmacher | 3 | 1⅓ | 0 | 1 | 2 | 0.00 |
| Poole | 1 | 1 | 0 | 0 | 2 | 0.00 |
| Nagy | 1 | 8 | 5 | 0 | 6 | 1.12 |
| Hershiser | 2 | 14 | 9 | 3 | 15 | 1.29 |
| D. Martinez | 2 | 13⅓ | 10 | 3 | 7 | 2.03 |
| Mesa | 4 | 4 | 3 | 1 | 1 | 2.25 |
| Tavarez | 4 | 3⅓ | 3 | 1 | 2 | 2.70 |
| Plunk | 3 | 2 | 1 | 3 | 2 | 9.00 |
| Totals | 6 | 55 | 37 | 15 | 46 | 1.64 |

| SEATTLE BATTING | AB | R | H | HR | RBI | Avg |
|---|---|---|---|---|---|---|
| Diaz | 7 | 0 | 3 | 0 | 0 | .429 |
| Griffey Jr. | 21 | 2 | 7 | 1 | 2 | .333 |
| Buhner | 23 | 5 | 7 | 3 | 5 | .304 |
| Sojo | 20 | 2 | 5 | 0 | 1 | .250 |
| Cora | 23 | 2 | 4 | 0 | 0 | .174 |
| Blowers | 18 | 1 | 4 | 1 | 2 | .222 |
| T. Martinez | 22 | 0 | 3 | 0 | 0 | .136 |
| Coleman | 20 | 0 | 2 | 0 | 0 | .100 |
| E. Martinez | 23 | 0 | 2 | 0 | 0 | .087 |
| Wilson | 16 | 0 | 0 | 0 | 0 | .000 |
| Strange | 4 | 0 | 0 | 0 | 0 | .000 |
| 4 others | 4 | 0 | 0 | 0 | 0 | .000 |
| Totals | 201 | 12 | 37 | 5 | 10 | .184 |

| SEATTLE PITCHING | G | IP | H | BB | SO | ERA |
|---|---|---|---|---|---|---|
| Charlton | 3 | 6 | 1 | 1 | 5 | 0.00 |
| Nelson | 3 | 3 | 3 | 5 | 3 | 0.00 |
| Risley | 3 | 2⅔ | 2 | 1 | 2 | 0.00 |
| Johnson | 2 | 15⅓ | 12 | 2 | 13 | 2.35 |
| Ayala | 2 | 3⅔ | 3 | 3 | 3 | 2.45 |
| Wolcott | 1 | 7 | 8 | 5 | 2 | 2.57 |
| Wells | 1 | 3 | 2 | 2 | 2 | 3.00 |
| Bosio | 1 | 5⅓ | 7 | 2 | 3 | 3.38 |
| Belcher | 1 | 5⅔ | 9 | 2 | 1 | 6.35 |
| Benes | 1 | 2⅓ | 6 | 2 | 3 | 23.14 |
| Totals | 6 | 54 | 53 | 25 | 37 | 3.33 |

# 1995 World Series

Oct 21 .............Cleveland 2 at Atlanta 3
Oct 22 .............Cleveland 3 at Atlanta 4
Oct 24 .............Atlanta 6 at Cleveland 7 (11 innings)
Oct 25 .............Atlanta 5 at Cleveland 2
Oct 26 .............Atlanta 4 at Cleveland 5
Oct 28 .............Cleveland 0 at Atlanta 1
(Atlanta won series 4–2.)

### GAME 1

| | | | | | | | | | | |
|---|---|---|---|---|---|---|---|---|---|---|
| Cleveland | 1 0 0 | 0 0 0 | 0 0 1 | —2 |
| Atlanta | 0 1 0 | 0 0 0 | 2 0 x | —3 |

**WP**—Maddux. **LP**—Hershiser.
**E**—Atlanta: Belliard (1), McGriff (1). **LOB**—Cleveland 1, Atlanta 4. **HR**—Atlanta: McGriff (1). **SB**—Cleveland: Lofton (2). **Sac**—Atlanta: Belliard. **T**—2:37. **A**—51,876.
**Recap:** Greg Maddux shut down Cleveland, holding them to their lowest hit total (2) this season. Orel Hershiser suffered his first postseason defeat after seven victories. Kenny Lofton tied a series record, stealing two bases in the first inning.

### GAME 2

| | | | | | | | | | | |
|---|---|---|---|---|---|---|---|---|---|---|
| Cleveland | 0 2 0 | 0 0 0 | 1 0 0 | —3 |
| Atlanta | 0 0 2 | 0 0 2 | 0 0 x | —4 |

**WP**—Glavine. **LP**—Martinez. **Save**—Wohlers.
**E**—Cleveland: Martinez (1), Belle (1); Atlanta: Jones (1), Devereaux (1). **LOB**—Cleveland 9, Atlanta 7. **2B**—Atlanta: Jones (1). **HR**—Cleveland: Murray (1); Atlanta: Lopez (1). **SB**—Cleveland: Lofton 2 (4), Vizquel (1). **Sac**—Atlanta: Jones. **GIDP**—Atlanta: McGriff, Belliard. **T**—3:17. **A**—51,877.
**Recap:** Javy Lopez hit a two-run homer to center in the sixth inning to put the Braves ahead. Mark Wohlers got the save in 1⅓ innings.

### GAME 3

| | | | | | | | | | | |
|---|---|---|---|---|---|---|---|---|---|---|
| Atlanta | 1 0 0 | 0 0 1 | 1 3 0 | 0 0 | —6 |
| Cleveland | 2 0 2 | 0 0 0 | 1 1 0 | 0 1 | —7 |

**WP**—Mesa. **LP**—A. Pena.
**E**—Atlanta: Belliard (2); Cleveland: Baerga (1), Sorrento (1). **LOB**—Atlanta 7, Cleveland 13. **2B**—Atlanta: Grissom (1), Jones (2); Cleveland: Lofton (1), Baerga (1), S. Alomar (1). **3B**—Cleveland: Vizquel (1). **HR**—Atlanta: McGriff (2), Klesko (1); Cleveland: Lofton (5), M. Ramirez (1). **SB**—Atlanta: Polonia (1), McGriff (1); Cleveland: Lofton (5), M. Ramirez (1). **CS**—Atlanta: Grissom (1); Cleveland: Lofton (1). **Sac**—Atlanta: Mordecai. **GIDP**—Atlanta: Grissom, Lopez; Cleveland: M. Ramirez (1). **T**—4:09. **A**—43,584.
**Recap:** Eddie Murray drove in Jose Espinoza with an 11th-inning single to win the game for Cleveland. The Indians had tied the game in the bottom of the eighth when Manny Ramirez scored on Sandy Alomar's double to right. Some controversy followed Cleveland manager Mike Hargrove's decision to stick with starter Charles Nagy until early in the eighth. Kenny Lofton continued his postseason brilliance, going 3 for 3 with three runs scored and raising his series batting average to .417.

## GAME 4

| | | | | | | | | | | |
|---|---|---|---|---|---|---|---|---|---|---|
| Atlanta | 0 | 0 | 0 | 0 | 0 | 1 | 3 | 0 | 1 | —5 |
| Cleveland | 0 | 0 | 0 | 0 | 0 | 1 | 0 | 0 | 1 | —2 |

**WP**—Avery. **LP**—Hill. **Save**—Borbon. **E**—Lemke. **LOB**—Atlanta 12, Cleveland 8. **2B**—Atlanta: Lopez (2), Polonia (1), McGriff (1); Cleveland: Thome (1), Sorrento (1). **HR**—Atlanta: Klesko (2); Cleveland: Belle (1), Ramirez (1). **SB**—Atlanta: Grissom (2). **CS**—Cleveland: Espinoza. **GIDP**—Cleveland: Baerga. **T**—3:14. **A**—43,578.
**Recap:** Steve Avery pitched six strong innings, again virtually shutting down the Cleveland hitters. With the game tied 1–1 in the top of the seventh, the Braves scored three when Marquis Grissom walked then scored on Luis Polonia's double to right center. David Justice's single brought in two runs.

## GAME 5

| | | | | | | | | | | |
|---|---|---|---|---|---|---|---|---|---|---|
| Atlanta | 0 | 0 | 0 | 1 | 1 | 0 | 0 | 0 | 2 | —4 |
| Cleveland | 2 | 0 | 0 | 0 | 0 | 2 | 0 | 1 | x | —5 |

**WP**—Hershiser. **LP**—Maddux. **Save**—Mesa. **E**—Cleveland: Hershiser (1). **LOB**—Atlanta 3, Cleveland 5. **2B**—Atlanta: Jones (3), McGriff (2); Cleveland: Alomar (2), Baerga (2). **HR**—Atlanta: Polonia (1), Klesko (3); Cleveland: Belle (2), Thome (1). **Sac**—Atlanta: O'Brien. **GIDP**—Atlanta: Polonia. **T**—2:33. **A**—43,595.
**Recap:** Greg Maddux lost his aura of invincibility in the first inning when Cleveland's Albert Belle broke out of his slump with a two-run homer to right. The Indians chased Maddux with two more runs in the sixth, and starter Orel Hershiser pitched eight brilliant innings, striking out six and giving up just one earned run.

## GAME 6

| | | | | | | | | | | |
|---|---|---|---|---|---|---|---|---|---|---|
| Cleveland | 0 | 0 | 0 | 0 | 0 | 0 | 0 | 0 | 0 | —0 |
| Atlanta | 0 | 0 | 0 | 0 | 0 | 1 | 0 | 0 | 0 | —1 |

**WP**—Glavine. **LP**—Poole. **Save**—Wohlers (2). **E**—Cleveland: Thome (1). **LOB**—Cleveland 3, Atlanta 11. **2B**—Atlanta: Justice (1). **HR**—Atlanta: Justice (1). **SB**—Cleveland: Lofton (6); Atlanta: Grissom (3). **CS**—Cleveland: Belle (1); Atlanta: Lemke (1). **Sac**—Atlanta: Lemke (1). **GIDP**—Atlanta: Belliard. **T**—3:02. **A**—51,875.
**Recap:** Atlanta starter Tom Glavine pitched eight outstanding innings, striking out eight and giving up just one hit to earn MVP honors for the series. Atlanta's sole run came in the bottom of the sixth when David Justice, who had incurred the wrath of Atlanta fans by criticizing their lack of support early in the series, hit a homer to right off Jim Poole. Mark Wohlers earned his second save of the series to help make the Braves the first team to win titles in three cities—Boston, Milwaukee and their present home, Atlanta.

# 1995 World Series Composite Box Score

## ATLANTA

| BATTING | AB | R | H | HR | RBI | Avg |
|---|---|---|---|---|---|---|
| Smith | 2 | 0 | 1 | 0 | 0 | .500 |
| Grissom | 25 | 3 | 9 | 0 | 1 | .360 |
| Mordecai | 3 | 0 | 1 | 0 | 0 | .333 |
| Klesko | 16 | 4 | 5 | 3 | 4 | .313 |
| Jones | 21 | 3 | 6 | 0 | 1 | .286 |
| Polonia | 14 | 3 | 4 | 1 | 4 | .286 |
| Lemke | 22 | 1 | 6 | 0 | 0 | .273 |
| McGriff | 23 | 5 | 6 | 2 | 3 | .261 |
| Justice | 20 | 3 | 5 | 1 | 5 | .250 |
| Devereaux | 4 | 0 | 1 | 0 | 0 | .250 |
| Lopez | 17 | 1 | 3 | 1 | 3 | .176 |
| Belliard | 16 | 0 | 0 | 0 | 1 | .000 |
| 3 others | 10 | 0 | 0 | 0 | 0 | .000 |
| Totals | 193 | 23 | 47 | 8 | 23 | .244 |

| PITCHING | G | IP | H | BB | SO | ERA |
|---|---|---|---|---|---|---|
| Borbon | 1 | 1 | 0 | 0 | 2 | 0.00 |
| Glavine | 2 | 14 | 4 | 6 | 11 | 1.29 |
| Avery | 1 | 6 | 3 | 5 | 3 | 1.50 |
| Wohlers | 4 | 5 | 4 | 3 | 3 | 1.80 |
| Maddux | 2 | 16 | 9 | 3 | 8 | 2.25 |
| Clontz | 2 | 3⅓ | 2 | 0 | 2 | 2.70 |
| McMichael | 3 | 3⅓ | 3 | 2 | 2 | 2.70 |
| Mercker | 1 | 2 | 1 | 2 | 2 | 4.50 |
| A. Pena | 2 | 1 | 3 | 2 | 0 | 9.00 |
| Smoltz | 1 | 2⅓ | 6 | 2 | 4 | 15.43 |
| Totals | 6 | 54 | 35 | 25 | 37 | 2.67 |

## CLEVELAND

| BATTING | AB | R | H | HR | RBI | Avg |
|---|---|---|---|---|---|---|
| Espinoza | 2 | 1 | 1 | 0 | 0 | .500 |
| Belle | 17 | 4 | 4 | 2 | 4 | .235 |
| Ramirez | 18 | 2 | 4 | 1 | 2 | .222 |
| Thome | 19 | 1 | 4 | 1 | 2 | .211 |
| Lofton | 25 | 6 | 5 | 0 | 0 | .200 |
| Alomar | 15 | 0 | 3 | 0 | 1 | .200 |
| Baerga | 26 | 1 | 5 | 0 | 4 | .192 |
| Sorrento | 11 | 0 | 2 | 0 | 0 | .182 |
| Vizquel | 23 | 3 | 4 | 0 | 1 | .174 |
| T. Pena | 6 | 0 | 1 | 0 | 0 | .167 |
| Murray | 19 | 1 | 2 | 1 | 3 | .105 |
| Perry | 5 | 0 | 0 | 0 | 0 | .000 |
| Martinez | 3 | 0 | 0 | 0 | 0 | .000 |
| 4 others | 6 | 0 | 0 | 0 | 0 | .000 |
| Totals | 195 | 19 | 35 | 5 | 17 | .179 |

| PITCHING | G | IP | H | BB | SO | ERA |
|---|---|---|---|---|---|---|
| Tavarez | 5 | 4⅓ | 3 | 2 | 1 | 0.00 |
| Hershiser | 2 | 14 | 8 | 4 | 13 | 2.57 |
| Embree | 4 | 3⅓ | 2 | 2 | 2 | 2.70 |
| Martinez | 2 | 10⅓ | 12 | 8 | 5 | 3.48 |
| Poole | 2 | 2⅓ | 1 | 0 | 1 | 3.86 |
| Hill | 2 | 6⅓ | 7 | 4 | 1 | 4.26 |
| Mesa | 2 | 4 | 5 | 1 | 4 | 4.50 |
| Nagy | 1 | 7 | 8 | 1 | 4 | 6.43 |
| Assenmacher | 4 | 1⅓ | 1 | 3 | 3 | 6.75 |
| Totals | 6 | 53 | 47 | 25 | 34 | 3.57 |

## National League Batting

### BATTING AVERAGE

| | |
|---|---|
| Gwynn, SD | .368 |
| Piazza, LA | .346 |
| Bichette, Col | .340 |
| Bell, Hou | .334 |
| Grace, Chi | .326 |
| Larkin, Cin | .319 |
| Segui, Mtl | .309 |
| Castilla, Col | .309 |
| Jefferies, Phil | .306 |
| Walker, Col | .306 |
| Sanders, Cin | .306 |

### HITS

| | |
|---|---|
| Bichette, Col | 197 |
| Gwynn, SD | 197 |
| Grace, Chi | 180 |
| Biggio, Hou | 167 |
| Finley, SD | 167 |
| McRae, Chi | 167 |
| Karros, LA | 164 |
| Castilla, Col | 163 |
| Caminiti, SD | 159 |
| Larkin, Cin | 158 |

### DOUBLES

| | |
|---|---|
| Grace, Chi | 51 |
| Bichette, Col | 38 |
| McRae, Chi | 38 |
| Sanders, Cin | 36 |

Three tied with 35.

### TRIPLES

| | |
|---|---|
| Butler, LA | 9 |
| Young, Col | 9 |
| Sanders, SF | 8 |
| Finley, SD | 8 |
| Gonzalez, Chi | 8 |

### HOME RUNS

| | |
|---|---|
| Bichette, Col | 40 |
| Walker, Col | 36 |
| Sosa, Chi | 36 |
| Bonds, SF | 33 |
| Karros, LA | 32 |
| Piazza, LA | 32 |
| Castilla, Col | 32 |
| Galarraga, Col | 31 |
| Gant, Cin | 29 |
| Sanders, Cin | 28 |

### RUNS SCORED

| | |
|---|---|
| Biggio, Hou | 123 |
| Bonds, SF | 109 |
| Finley, SD | 104 |
| Bichette, Col | 103 |
| Larkin, Cin | 98 |
| Grace, Chi | 97 |
| Walker, Col | 96 |
| McRae, Chi | 92 |
| Mondesi, LA | 91 |
| Sanders, Cin | 91 |

### TOTAL BASES

| | |
|---|---|
| Bichette, Col | 359 |
| Walker, Col | 300 |
| Castilla, Col | 297 |
| Karros, LA | 295 |
| Bonds, SF | 292 |

### STOLEN BASES

| | |
|---|---|
| Veras, Fla | 56 |
| Larkin, Cin | 51 |
| DeShields, LA | 39 |
| Sanders, Cin | 36 |
| Young, Col | 35 |
| Finley, SD | 35 |

### RUNS BATTED IN

| | |
|---|---|
| Bichette, Col | 128 |
| Sosa, Chi | 119 |
| Galarraga, Col | 106 |
| Conine, Fla | 105 |
| Karros, LA | 105 |
| Bonds, SF | 104 |
| Walker, Col | 101 |
| Sanders, Cin | 99 |
| Caminiti, SD | 94 |
| Piazza, LA | 93 |

### SLUGGING PERCENTAGE

| | |
|---|---|
| Bichette, Col | .620 |
| Walker, Col | .607 |
| Piazza, LA | .606 |
| Sanders, Cin | .579 |
| Bonds, SF | .577 |

### ON-BASE PERCENTAGE

| | |
|---|---|
| Bonds, SF | .431 |
| Biggio, Hou | .406 |
| Gwynn, SD | .404 |
| Weiss, Col | .403 |
| Piazza, LA | .400 |

### BASES ON BALLS

| | |
|---|---|
| Bonds, SF | 120 |
| Weiss, Col | 98 |
| Biggio, Hou | 80 |
| Veras, Fla | 80 |
| Bagwell, Hou | 79 |

## National League Pitching

### EARNED RUN AVERAGE

| | |
|---|---|
| Maddux, Atl | 1.63 |
| Nomo, LA | 2.54 |
| Ashby, SD | 2.94 |
| Valdes, LA | 3.05 |
| Glavine, Atl | 3.08 |
| Hamilton, SD | 3.08 |
| Smoltz, Atl | 3.18 |
| Castillo, Chi | 3.21 |
| Schourek, Cin | 3.22 |
| Navarro, Chi | 3.28 |

### SAVES

| | |
|---|---|
| Myers, Chi | 38 |
| Henke, StL | 36 |
| Beck, SF | 33 |
| Slocumb, Phil | 32 |
| Worrell, LA | 32 |
| Hoffman, SD | 31 |
| Rojas, Mtl | 30 |
| Franco, NY | 29 |
| Brantley, Cin | 28 |
| Wohlers, Atl | 25 |

### WINS

| | |
|---|---|
| Maddux, Atl | 19 |
| Schourek, Cin | 18 |
| Martinez, LA | 17 |
| Glavine, Atl | 16 |
| Burkett, Fla | 14 |
| Navarro, Chi | 14 |
| Martinez, Mtl | 14 |
| Rapp, Fla | 14 |

Four tied with 13.

### GAMES PITCHED

| | |
|---|---|
| Leskanic, Col | 76 |
| Veres, Hou | 72 |
| Reed, Col | 71 |
| Perez, Fla | 69 |

Three tied with 68.

### INNINGS PITCHED

| | |
|---|---|
| Neagle, Pit | 209⅔ |
| Maddux, Atl | 209⅔ |
| Martinez, LA | 206⅓ |
| Hamilton, SD | 204⅓ |
| Navarro, Chi | 200⅓ |

### STRIKEOUTS

| | |
|---|---|
| Nomo, LA | 236 |
| Smoltz, Atl | 193 |
| Maddux, Atl | 181 |
| Reynolds, Hou | 175 |
| Martinez, Mtl | 174 |
| Fassero, Mtl | 164 |
| Schourek, Cin | 160 |
| Valdes, LA | 150 |
| Neagle, Pit | 150 |
| Ashby, SD | 149 |

### COMPLETE GAMES

| | |
|---|---|
| Maddux, Atl | 10 |
| Leiter, SF | 7 |
| Valdes, LA | 6 |
| Neagle, Pit | 5 |
| Nomo, LA | 5 |

### SHUTOUTS

| | |
|---|---|
| Maddux, Atl | 3 |
| Nomo, LA | 3 |

Ten tied with two.

## American League Batting

### BATTING AVERAGE

| | |
|---|---|
| E. Martinez, Sea | .356 |
| Knoblauch, Minn | .333 |
| Salmon, Cal | .330 |
| Boggs, NY | .324 |
| Murray, Clev | .323 |
| Surhoff, Mil | .320 |
| Davis, Cal | .318 |
| Belle, Clev | .317 |
| Baerga, Clev | .314 |
| Puckett, Minn | .314 |
| Thome, Clev | .314 |

### HITS

| | |
|---|---|
| Johnson, Chi | 186 |
| E. Martinez, Sea | 182 |
| Knoblauch, Minn | 179 |
| Salmon, Cal | 177 |
| Baerga, Clev | 175 |
| Nixon, Tex | 174 |
| Williams, NY | 173 |
| Belle, Clev | 173 |
| Palmeiro, Balt | 172 |
| Puckett, Minn | 169 |

### DOUBLES

| | |
|---|---|
| Belle, Clev | 52 |
| E. Martinez, Sea | 52 |
| Puckett, Minn | 39 |
| Valentin, Bos | 37 |
| T. Martinez, Sea | 35 |

### TRIPLES

| | |
|---|---|
| Lofton, Clev | 13 |
| Johnson, Chi | 12 |
| Anderson, Balt | 10 |
| Williams, NY | 9 |
| Knoblauch, Minn | 8 |

### HOME RUNS

| | |
|---|---|
| Belle, Clev | 50 |
| Buhner, Sea | 40 |
| Thomas, Chi | 40 |
| Vaughn, Bos | 39 |
| McGwire, Oak | 39 |
| Palmeiro, Balt | 39 |
| Gaetti, KC | 35 |
| Salmon, Cal | 34 |
| Edmonds, Cal | 33 |
| Tettleton, Tex | 32 |

### RUNS SCORED

| | |
|---|---|
| Belle, Clev | 121 |
| E. Martinez, Sea | 121 |
| Phillips, Cal | 120 |
| Edmonds, Cal | 119 |
| Salmon, Cal | 111 |
| Anderson, Balt | 108 |
| Valentin, Bos | 108 |
| Knoblauch, Minn | 107 |
| Thomas, Chi | 102 |
| Johnson, Chi | 98 |
| Vaughn, Bos | 98 |

### TOTAL BASES

| | |
|---|---|
| Belle, Clev | 377 |
| Palmeiro, Balt | 323 |
| E. Martinez, Sea | 321 |
| Salmon, Cal | 319 |
| Vaughn, Bos | 316 |

### STOLEN BASES

| | |
|---|---|
| Lofton, Clev | 54 |
| Nixon, Tex | 50 |
| Goodwin, KC | 50 |
| Knoblauch, Minn | 46 |
| Coleman, Sea | 41 |

### RUNS BATTED IN

| | |
|---|---|
| Belle, Clev | 126 |
| Vaughn, Bos | 126 |
| Buhner, Sea | 121 |
| E. Martinez, Sea | 113 |
| Thomas, Chi | 111 |
| T. Martinez, Sea | 111 |
| Edmonds, Cal | 107 |
| Ramirez, Clev | 107 |
| Salmon, Cal | 105 |
| Palmeiro, Bal | 104 |

### SLUGGING PERCENTAGE

| | |
|---|---|
| Belle, Clev | .690 |
| E. Martinez, Sea | .628 |
| Thomas, Chi | .606 |
| Salmon, Cal | .594 |
| Palmeiro, Balt | .583 |

### ON-BASE PERCENTAGE

| | |
|---|---|
| E. Martinez, Sea | .479 |
| Thomas, Chi | .454 |
| Thome, Clev | .438 |
| Davis, Cal | .429 |
| Salmon, Cal | .429 |

### BASES ON BALLS

| | |
|---|---|
| Thomas, Chi | 136 |
| E. Martinez, Sea | 116 |
| Phillips, Cal | 113 |
| Tettleton, Tex | 107 |
| Thome, Clev | 97 |

## American League Pitching

### EARNED RUN AVERAGE

| | |
|---|---|
| Johnson, Sea | 2.48 |
| Wakefield, Bos | 2.95 |
| Martinez, Clev | 3.08 |
| Mussina, Balt | 3.29 |
| Rogers, Tex | 3.38 |
| Cone, NY | 3.57 |
| Brown, Balt | 3.60 |
| Abbott, Cal | 3.70 |
| Gubicza, KC | 3.75 |
| Leiter, Tor | 3.79 |

### SAVES

| | |
|---|---|
| Mesa, Clev | 46 |
| Smith, Cal | 37 |
| Aguilera, Bos | 32 |
| Hernandez, Chi | 32 |
| Montgomery, KC | 31 |
| Wetteland, NY | 31 |
| Eckersley, Oak | 29 |
| Jones, Balt | 22 |
| Fetters, Mil | 22 |
| Russell, Tex | 20 |

### WINS

| | |
|---|---|
| Mussina, Balt | 19 |
| Cone, NY | 18 |
| Johnson, Sea | 18 |
| Rogers, Tex | 17 |
| Hershiser, Clev | 16 |
| Nagy, Clev | 16 |
| Wakefield, Bos | 16 |
| Five tied with 15. | |

### GAMES PITCHED

| | |
|---|---|
| Orosco, Balt | 65 |
| McDowell, Tex | 64 |
| Ayala, Sea | 63 |
| Belinda, Bos | 63 |
| Wickman, NY | 63 |

### INNINGS PITCHED

| | |
|---|---|
| Cone, NY | 229⅓ |
| Mussina, Balt | 221⅔ |
| McDowell, NY | 217⅔ |
| Johnson, Sea | 214¼ |
| Gubicza, KC | 213⅓ |

### STRIKEOUTS

| | |
|---|---|
| Johnson, Sea | 294 |
| Stottlemyre, Oak | 205 |
| Finley, Cal | 195 |
| Cone, NY | 191 |
| Appier, KC | 185 |
| Fernandez, Chi | 159 |
| Mussina, Balt | 158 |
| McDowell, NY | 157 |
| Leiter, Tor | 153 |
| Pavlik, Tex | 149 |

### COMPLETE GAMES

| | |
|---|---|
| McDowell, NY | 8 |
| Erickson, Balt | 7 |
| Mussina, Balt | 7 |
| Cone, NY | 6 |
| Johnson, Sea | 6 |
| Wakefield, Bos | 6 |

### SHUTOUTS

| | |
|---|---|
| Mussina, Balt | 4 |
| Johnson, Sea | 3 |
| Six tied with two. | |

# 1995 Team Statistics

## National League

| TEAM BATTING | BA | AB | R | H | TB | 2B | 3B | HR | RBI | SB | BB | SO |
|---|---|---|---|---|---|---|---|---|---|---|---|---|
| Colorado | .282 | 4994 | 785 | 1406 | 2351 | 259 | 43 | 200 | 749 | 125 | 483 | 942 |
| Houston | .275 | 5096 | 747 | 1402 | 2032 | 259 | 22 | 109 | 695 | 176 | 568 | 990 |
| San Diego | .272 | 4951 | 668 | 1345 | 1968 | 233 | 20 | 116 | 618 | 122 | 446 | 871 |
| Cincinnati | .270 | 4899 | 746 | 1325 | 2155 | 277 | 35 | 161 | 695 | 190 | 518 | 946 |
| New York | .267 | 4958 | 657 | 1323 | 1983 | 217 | 34 | 125 | 616 | 57 | 446 | 994 |
| Chicago | .265 | 4964 | 693 | 1315 | 2134 | 267 | 39 | 158 | 648 | 104 | 440 | 953 |
| Los Angeles | .264 | 4942 | 634 | 1303 | 1976 | 191 | 31 | 140 | 593 | 127 | 468 | 1026 |
| Florida | .262 | 4884 | 673 | 1278 | 1982 | 214 | 29 | 144 | 638 | 131 | 516 | 915 |
| Philadelphia | .262 | 4950 | 614 | 1295 | 1902 | 265 | 30 | 94 | 576 | 70 | 497 | 886 |
| Pittsburgh | .260 | 4936 | 629 | 1281 | 1955 | 245 | 27 | 125 | 587 | 82 | 456 | 969 |
| Montreal | .259 | 4905 | 621 | 1268 | 1935 | 265 | 24 | 118 | 572 | 120 | 400 | 900 |
| San Francisco | .254 | 4975 | 653 | 1257 | 2008 | 229 | 33 | 152 | 611 | 138 | 472 | 1056 |
| Atlanta | .250 | 4814 | 645 | 1202 | 1971 | 211 | 27 | 168 | 618 | 72 | 519 | 933 |
| St Louis | .247 | 4779 | 563 | 1182 | 1788 | 237 | 24 | 107 | 533 | 80 | 436 | 916 |

| TEAM PITCHING | ERA | W | L | Sho | CG | SV | Inn | H | R | ER | BB | SO |
|---|---|---|---|---|---|---|---|---|---|---|---|---|
| Atlanta | 3.44 | 90 | 54 | 12 | 19 | 34 | 1291⅔ | 1184 | 540 | 494 | 436 | 1087 |
| Los Angeles | 3.68 | 78 | 66 | 11 | 17 | 37 | 1295 | 1188 | 609 | 529 | 462 | 1059 |
| New York | 3.88 | 69 | 75 | 9 | 9 | 36 | 1291 | 1296 | 618 | 556 | 401 | 901 |
| Cincinnati | 4.03 | 85 | 59 | 10 | 9 | 38 | 1289⅓ | 1270 | 623 | 578 | 423 | 901 |
| Houston | 4.06 | 76 | 68 | 8 | 6 | 32 | 1320⅓ | 1356 | 674 | 595 | 459 | 1055 |
| Montreal | 4.10 | 66 | 78 | 9 | 7 | 42 | 1282⅔ | 1286 | 638 | 584 | 416 | 950 |
| St Louis | 4.10 | 62 | 81 | 6 | 4 | 38 | 1265⅔ | 1289 | 658 | 576 | 445 | 843 |
| Chicago | 4.12 | 73 | 71 | 13 | 6 | 44 | 1301 | 1312 | 671 | 596 | 519 | 926 |
| San Diego | 4.15 | 70 | 74 | 10 | 6 | 35 | 1284⅔ | 1242 | 672 | 593 | 512 | 1044 |
| Philadelphia | 4.21 | 69 | 75 | 8 | 8 | 41 | 1290⅓ | 1240 | 658 | 603 | 538 | 980 |
| Florida | 4.27 | 67 | 76 | 7 | 12 | 29 | 1286 | 1299 | 673 | 610 | 562 | 994 |
| Pittsburgh | 4.71 | 58 | 86 | 7 | 1 | 29 | 1275⅓ | 1407 | 736 | 668 | 477 | 871 |
| San Francisco | 4.86 | 67 | 77 | 5 | 12 | 34 | 1293⅔ | 1368 | 776 | 699 | 505 | 801 |
| Colorado | 4.97 | 77 | 67 | 1 | 1 | 43 | 1288⅓ | 1443 | 783 | 711 | 512 | 891 |

## American League

| TEAM BATTING | BA | AB | R | H | TB | 2B | 3B | HR | RBI | SB | BB | SO |
|---|---|---|---|---|---|---|---|---|---|---|---|---|
| Cleveland | .291 | 5028 | 840 | 1461 | 2407 | 279 | 23 | 207 | 804 | 132 | 542 | 766 |
| Boston | .280 | 4997 | 791 | 1399 | 2272 | 286 | 31 | 175 | 754 | 99 | 560 | 922 |
| Chicago | .280 | 5060 | 755 | 1417 | 2181 | 252 | 37 | 146 | 712 | 110 | 576 | 767 |
| Minnesota | .279 | 5005 | 703 | 1398 | 2096 | 270 | 34 | 120 | 662 | 105 | 471 | 916 |
| California | .277 | 5020 | 801 | 1390 | 2250 | 252 | 25 | 186 | 761 | 58 | 563 | 890 |
| New York | .276 | 4946 | 749 | 1365 | 2079 | 280 | 34 | 122 | 709 | 50 | 625 | 851 |
| Seattle | .275 | 4991 | 794 | 1375 | 2237 | 276 | 20 | 182 | 767 | 110 | 549 | 872 |
| Milwaukee | .266 | 5000 | 740 | 1329 | 2046 | 249 | 42 | 128 | 699 | 104 | 502 | 800 |
| Texas | .265 | 4913 | 691 | 1304 | 2011 | 247 | 23 | 138 | 648 | 90 | 526 | 877 |
| Oakland | .264 | 4915 | 730 | 1296 | 2067 | 228 | 18 | 169 | 696 | 112 | 565 | 911 |
| Baltimore | .262 | 4837 | 704 | 1267 | 2070 | 230 | 27 | 173 | 669 | 91 | 576 | 805 |
| Kansas City | .260 | 4908 | 631 | 1277 | 1944 | 240 | 35 | 119 | 579 | 121 | 475 | 849 |
| Toronto | .260 | 5036 | 642 | 1309 | 2058 | 275 | 27 | 140 | 613 | 75 | 492 | 906 |
| Detroit | .247 | 4865 | 654 | 1204 | 1966 | 227 | 29 | 159 | 619 | 72 | 549 | 985 |

| TEAM PITCHING | ERA | W | L | Sho | CG | SV | Inn | H | R | ER | BB | SO |
|---|---|---|---|---|---|---|---|---|---|---|---|---|
| Cleveland | 3.84 | 100 | 44 | 10 | 10 | 50 | 1301 | 1261 | 607 | 555 | 445 | 926 |
| Baltimore | 4.32 | 71 | 73 | 10 | 19 | 29 | 1267 | 1165 | 640 | 608 | 523 | 930 |
| Boston | 4.40 | 86 | 58 | 9 | 7 | 39 | 1292⅔ | 1339 | 698 | 632 | 476 | 888 |
| Kansas City | 4.49 | 70 | 74 | 10 | 11 | 37 | 1288 | 1322 | 691 | 642 | 503 | 763 |
| California | 4.42 | 78 | 67 | 9 | 8 | 41 | 1284⅓ | 1309 | 697 | 645 | 486 | 901 |
| Seattle | 4.52 | 79 | 66 | 8 | 10 | 39 | 1289⅓ | 1343 | 708 | 647 | 592 | 1068 |
| New York | 4.55 | 79 | 65 | 5 | 18 | 35 | 1284⅔ | 1284 | 688 | 649 | 535 | 908 |
| Texas | 4.67 | 74 | 70 | 4 | 14 | 34 | 1285 | 1385 | 720 | 667 | 514 | 839 |
| Milwaukee | 4.83 | 65 | 79 | 4 | 7 | 31 | 1286 | 1391 | 747 | 690 | 603 | 699 |
| Chicago | 4.85 | 68 | 76 | 4 | 12 | 36 | 1284⅔ | 1374 | 758 | 693 | 617 | 892 |
| Toronto | 4.90 | 56 | 88 | 8 | 16 | 22 | 1292⅔ | 1336 | 777 | 704 | 654 | 894 |
| Oakland | 4.97 | 67 | 77 | 4 | 8 | 34 | 1273 | 1320 | 761 | 703 | 556 | 890 |
| Detroit | 5.50 | 60 | 84 | 3 | 5 | 38 | 1275 | 1509 | 844 | 779 | 536 | 728 |
| Minnesota | 5.77 | 56 | 88 | 2 | 7 | 27 | 1272⅔ | 1452 | 889 | 816 | 533 | 791 |

# National League Team-by-Team Statistical Leaders

## Atlanta Braves

| BATTING | BA | G | AB | R | H | TB | 2B | 3B | HR | RBI | SB | BB | SO |
|---|---|---|---|---|---|---|---|---|---|---|---|---|---|
| Lopez, Javy | .315 | 100 | 333 | 37 | 105 | 166 | 11 | 4 | 14 | 51 | 0 | 14 | 57 |
| Klesko, Ryan | .310 | 107 | 329 | 48 | 102 | 200 | 25 | 2 | 23 | 70 | 5 | 47 | 72 |
| McGriff, Fred | .280 | 144 | 528 | 85 | 148 | 258 | 27 | 1 | 27 | 93 | 3 | 65 | 99 |
| Mordecai, Mike | .280 | 69 | 75 | 10 | 21 | 36 | 6 | 0 | 3 | 11 | 0 | 9 | 16 |
| Jones, Chipper | .265 | 140 | 524 | 87 | 139 | 236 | 22 | 3 | 23 | 86 | 8 | 73 | 99 |
| Polonia, Luis | .264 | 28 | 53 | 6 | 14 | 21 | 7 | 0 | 0 | 2 | 3 | 3 | 9 |
| Grissom, Marquis | .258 | 139 | 551 | 80 | 142 | 207 | 23 | 3 | 12 | 42 | 29 | 47 | 61 |
| Devereaux, Mike | .255 | 29 | 55 | 7 | 14 | 20 | 3 | 0 | 1 | 8 | 2 | 2 | 11 |
| Lemke, Mark | .253 | 116 | 399 | 42 | 101 | 142 | 16 | 5 | 5 | 38 | 2 | 44 | 40 |
| Justice, David | .253 | 120 | 411 | 73 | 104 | 197 | 17 | 2 | 24 | 78 | 4 | 73 | 68 |
| Smith, Dwight | .252 | 103 | 131 | 16 | 33 | 54 | 8 | 2 | 3 | 21 | 0 | 13 | 35 |
| O'Brien, Charlie | .227 | 67 | 198 | 18 | 45 | 79 | 7 | 0 | 9 | 23 | 0 | 29 | 40 |
| Belliard, Rafael | .222 | 75 | 180 | 12 | 40 | 44 | 2 | 1 | 0 | 7 | 2 | 6 | 28 |
| Blauser, Jeff | .211 | 115 | 431 | 60 | 91 | 147 | 16 | 2 | 12 | 31 | 8 | 57 | 107 |
| Kelly, Mike | .190 | 97 | 137 | 26 | 26 | 43 | 6 | 1 | 3 | 17 | 7 | 11 | 49 |

| PITCHING | ERA | W | L | G | GS | CG | SV | INN | H | R | ER | BB | SO |
|---|---|---|---|---|---|---|---|---|---|---|---|---|---|
| Maddux, Greg | 1.63 | 19 | 2 | 28 | 28 | 10 | 0 | 209⅔ | 147 | 39 | 38 | 23 | 181 |
| Wohlers, Mark | 2.09 | 7 | 3 | 65 | 0 | 0 | 25 | 64⅔ | 51 | 16 | 15 | 24 | 90 |
| Pena, Alejandro | 2.61 | 2 | 0 | 27 | 0 | 0 | 0 | 31 | 22 | 9 | 9 | 7 | 39 |
| McMichael, Greg | 2.79 | 7 | 2 | 67 | 0 | 0 | 2 | 80⅔ | 64 | 27 | 25 | 32 | 74 |
| Glavine, Tom | 3.08 | 16 | 7 | 29 | 29 | 3 | 0 | 198⅔ | 182 | 76 | 68 | 66 | 127 |
| Borbon, Pedro | 3.09 | 2 | 2 | 41 | 0 | 0 | 2 | 32 | 29 | 12 | 11 | 17 | 33 |
| Smoltz, John | 3.18 | 12 | 7 | 29 | 29 | 2 | 0 | 192⅔ | 166 | 76 | 68 | 72 | 193 |
| Clontz, Brad | 3.65 | 8 | 1 | 59 | 0 | 0 | 4 | 69 | 71 | 29 | 28 | 22 | 55 |
| Mercker, Kent | 4.15 | 7 | 8 | 29 | 26 | 0 | 0 | 143 | 140 | 73 | 66 | 61 | 102 |
| Avery, Steve | 4.67 | 7 | 13 | 29 | 29 | 3 | 0 | 173⅓ | 165 | 92 | 90 | 52 | 141 |
| Stanton, Mike | 5.59 | 1 | 1 | 26 | 0 | 0 | 1 | 19⅓ | 31 | 14 | 12 | 6 | 13 |

## Chicago Cubs

| BATTING | BA | G | AB | R | H | TB | 2B | 3B | HR | RBI | SB | BB | SO |
|---|---|---|---|---|---|---|---|---|---|---|---|---|---|
| Haney, Todd | .411 | 25 | 73 | 11 | 30 | 44 | 8 | 0 | 2 | 6 | 0 | 7 | 11 |
| Grace, Mark | .326 | 143 | 552 | 97 | 180 | 285 | 51 | 3 | 16 | 92 | 6 | 65 | 46 |
| Dunston, Shawon | .296 | 127 | 477 | 58 | 141 | 225 | 30 | 6 | 14 | 69 | 10 | 10 | 75 |
| McRae, Brian | .288 | 137 | 580 | 92 | 167 | 255 | 38 | 7 | 12 | 48 | 27 | 47 | 92 |
| Sanchez, Rey | .278 | 114 | 428 | 57 | 119 | 154 | 22 | 2 | 3 | 27 | 6 | 14 | 48 |
| Gonzalez, Luis | .276 | 133 | 471 | 69 | 130 | 214 | 29 | 8 | 13 | 69 | 6 | 57 | 63 |
| Bullett, Scott | .273 | 104 | 150 | 19 | 41 | 69 | 5 | 7 | 3 | 22 | 8 | 12 | 30 |
| Sosa, Sammy | .268 | 144 | 564 | 89 | 151 | 282 | 17 | 3 | 36 | 119 | 34 | 58 | 134 |
| Servais, Scott | .265 | 80 | 264 | 38 | 70 | 131 | 22 | 0 | 13 | 47 | 2 | 32 | 52 |
| Timmons, Ozzie | .263 | 77 | 171 | 30 | 45 | 81 | 10 | 1 | 8 | 28 | 3 | 13 | 32 |
| Zeile, Todd | .246 | 113 | 426 | 50 | 105 | 169 | 22 | 0 | 14 | 52 | 1 | 34 | 76 |
| Hernandez, Jose | .245 | 93 | 245 | 37 | 60 | 118 | 11 | 4 | 13 | 40 | 1 | 13 | 69 |
| Parent, Mark | .234 | 81 | 265 | 30 | 62 | 127 | 11 | 0 | 18 | 38 | 0 | 26 | 69 |
| Johnson, Howard | .195 | 87 | 169 | 26 | 33 | 60 | 4 | 1 | 7 | 22 | 1 | 34 | 46 |
| Buechele, Steve | .189 | 32 | 106 | 10 | 20 | 25 | 2 | 0 | 1 | 9 | 0 | 11 | 19 |

| PITCHING | ERA | W | L | G | GS | CG | SV | INN | H | R | ER | BB | SO |
|---|---|---|---|---|---|---|---|---|---|---|---|---|---|
| Swartzbaugh, Dave | 0.00 | 0 | 0 | 7 | 0 | 0 | 0 | 7⅓ | 5 | 2 | 0 | 3 | 5 |
| Casian, Larry | 1.93 | 1 | 0 | 42 | 0 | 0 | 0 | 23⅓ | 23 | 6 | 5 | 15 | 11 |
| Castillo, Frank | 3.21 | 11 | 10 | 29 | 29 | 2 | 0 | 188 | 179 | 75 | 67 | 52 | 135 |
| Walker, Mike | 3.22 | 1 | 3 | 42 | 0 | 0 | 1 | 44⅔ | 45 | 22 | 16 | 24 | 20 |
| Navarro, Jaime | 3.28 | 14 | 6 | 29 | 29 | 1 | 0 | 200⅓ | 194 | 79 | 73 | 56 | 128 |
| Perez, Mike | 3.66 | 2 | 6 | 68 | 0 | 0 | 2 | 71⅓ | 72 | 30 | 29 | 27 | 49 |
| Young, Anthony | 3.70 | 3 | 4 | 32 | 1 | 0 | 2 | 41⅓ | 47 | 20 | 17 | 14 | 15 |
| Myers, Randy | 3.88 | 1 | 2 | 57 | 0 | 0 | 38 | 55⅔ | 49 | 25 | 24 | 28 | 59 |
| Bullinger, Jim | 4.14 | 12 | 8 | 24 | 24 | 1 | 0 | 150 | 152 | 80 | 69 | 65 | 93 |
| Foster, Kevin | 4.51 | 12 | 11 | 30 | 28 | 0 | 0 | 167⅔ | 149 | 90 | 84 | 65 | 146 |
| Wendell, Turk | 4.92 | 3 | 1 | 43 | 0 | 0 | 0 | 60⅓ | 71 | 35 | 33 | 24 | 50 |
| Trachsel, Steve | 5.15 | 7 | 13 | 30 | 29 | 2 | 0 | 160⅔ | 174 | 104 | 92 | 76 | 117 |
| Nabholz, Chris | 5.40 | 0 | 1 | 34 | 0 | 0 | 0 | 23⅓ | 22 | 15 | 14 | 14 | 21 |
| Rivera, Roberto | 5.40 | 0 | 0 | 7 | 0 | 0 | 0 | 5 | 8 | 3 | 3 | 2 | 2 |
| Edens, Tom | 6.00 | 1 | 0 | 5 | 0 | 0 | 0 | 3 | 6 | 3 | 2 | 3 | 2 |

## National League Team-by-Team Statistical Leaders *(Cont.)*

### Cincinnati Reds

| BATTING | BA | G | AB | R | H | TB | 2B | 3B | HR | RBI | SB | BB | SO |
|---|---|---|---|---|---|---|---|---|---|---|---|---|---|
| Lewis, Mark | .339 | 81 | 171 | 25 | 58 | 82 | 13 | 1 | 3 | 30 | 0 | 21 | 33 |
| Larkin, Barry | .319 | 131 | 496 | 98 | 158 | 244 | 29 | 6 | 15 | 66 | 51 | 61 | 49 |
| Sanders, Reggie | .306 | 133 | 484 | 91 | 148 | 280 | 36 | 6 | 28 | 99 | 36 | 69 | 122 |
| Howard, Thomas | .302 | 113 | 281 | 42 | 85 | 113 | 15 | 2 | 3 | 26 | 17 | 20 | 37 |
| Walton, Jerome | .290 | 102 | 162 | 32 | 47 | 85 | 12 | 1 | 8 | 22 | 10 | 17 | 25 |
| Duncan, Mariano | .287 | 81 | 265 | 36 | 76 | 112 | 14 | 2 | 6 | 36 | 1 | 5 | 62 |
| Santiago, Benito | .286 | 81 | 266 | 40 | 76 | 129 | 20 | 0 | 11 | 44 | 2 | 24 | 48 |
| Taubensee, Eddie | .284 | 80 | 218 | 32 | 62 | 107 | 14 | 2 | 9 | 44 | 2 | 22 | 52 |
| Morris, Hal | .279 | 101 | 359 | 53 | 100 | 162 | 25 | 2 | 11 | 51 | 1 | 29 | 58 |
| Gant, Ron | .276 | 119 | 410 | 79 | 113 | 227 | 19 | 4 | 29 | 88 | 23 | 74 | 108 |
| Anthony, Eric | .269 | 47 | 134 | 19 | 36 | 57 | 6 | 0 | 5 | 23 | 2 | 13 | 30 |
| Boone, Bret | .267 | 138 | 513 | 63 | 137 | 220 | 34 | 2 | 15 | 68 | 5 | 41 | 84 |
| Branson, Jeff | .260 | 122 | 331 | 43 | 86 | 144 | 18 | 2 | 12 | 45 | 2 | 44 | 69 |
| Lewis, Darren | .250 | 132 | 472 | 66 | 118 | 140 | 13 | 3 | 1 | 24 | 32 | 34 | 57 |
| Hunter, Brian | .215 | 40 | 79 | 9 | 17 | 26 | 6 | 0 | 1 | 9 | 2 | 11 | 21 |
| Harris, Lenny | .208 | 101 | 197 | 32 | 41 | 61 | 8 | 3 | 2 | 16 | 10 | 14 | 20 |

| PITCHING | ERA | W | L | G | GS | CG | SV | INN | H | R | ER | BB | SO |
|---|---|---|---|---|---|---|---|---|---|---|---|---|---|
| Jackson, Mike | 2.39 | 6 | 1 | 40 | 0 | 0 | 2 | 49 | 38 | 13 | 13 | 19 | 41 |
| Brantley, Jeff | 2.82 | 3 | 2 | 56 | 0 | 0 | 28 | 70⅓ | 53 | 22 | 22 | 20 | 62 |
| Schourek, Pete | 3.22 | 18 | 7 | 29 | 29 | 2 | 0 | 190⅓ | 158 | 72 | 68 | 45 | 160 |
| Smiley, John | 3.46 | 12 | 5 | 28 | 27 | 1 | 0 | 176⅔ | 173 | 72 | 68 | 39 | 124 |
| Wells, David | 3.59 | 6 | 5 | 11 | 11 | 3 | 0 | 72⅔ | 74 | 34 | 29 | 16 | 50 |
| Pugh, Tim | 3.84 | 6 | 5 | 28 | 12 | 0 | 0 | 98⅓ | 100 | 46 | 42 | 32 | 38 |
| Burba, Dave | 3.97 | 10 | 4 | 52 | 9 | 1 | 0 | 106⅔ | 90 | 50 | 47 | 51 | 96 |
| Portugal, Mark | 4.01 | 11 | 10 | 31 | 31 | 1 | 0 | 181⅔ | 185 | 91 | 81 | 56 | 96 |
| Carrasco, Hector | 4.12 | 2 | 7 | 64 | 0 | 0 | 5 | 87⅓ | 86 | 45 | 40 | 46 | 64 |
| Rijo, Jose | 4.17 | 5 | 4 | 14 | 14 | 0 | 0 | 69 | 76 | 33 | 32 | 22 | 62 |
| Hernandez, Xavier | 4.60 | 7 | 2 | 59 | 0 | 0 | 3 | 90 | 95 | 47 | 46 | 31 | 84 |
| Jarvis, Kevin | 5.70 | 3 | 4 | 19 | 11 | 1 | 0 | 79 | 91 | 56 | 50 | 32 | 33 |

### Colorado Rockies

| BATTING | BA | G | AB | R | H | TB | 2B | 3B | HR | RBI | SB | BB | SO |
|---|---|---|---|---|---|---|---|---|---|---|---|---|---|
| VanderWal, John | .347 | 105 | 101 | 15 | 35 | 60 | 8 | 1 | 5 | 21 | 1 | 16 | 23 |
| Bichette, Dante | .340 | 139 | 579 | 102 | 197 | 359 | 38 | 2 | 40 | 128 | 13 | 22 | 96 |
| Young, Eric | .317 | 120 | 366 | 68 | 116 | 173 | 21 | 9 | 6 | 36 | 35 | 49 | 29 |
| Hubbard, Trenidad | .310 | 24 | 58 | 13 | 18 | 31 | 4 | 0 | 3 | 9 | 2 | 8 | 6 |
| Castilla, Vinny | .309 | 139 | 527 | 82 | 163 | 297 | 34 | 2 | 32 | 90 | 2 | 30 | 87 |
| Walker, Larry | .306 | 131 | 494 | 96 | 151 | 300 | 31 | 5 | 36 | 101 | 16 | 49 | 72 |
| Galarraga, Andres | .280 | 143 | 554 | 89 | 155 | 283 | 29 | 3 | 31 | 106 | 12 | 32 | 146 |
| Kingery, Mike | .269 | 119 | 350 | 66 | 94 | 144 | 18 | 4 | 8 | 37 | 13 | 45 | 40 |
| Bates, Jason | .267 | 116 | 322 | 42 | 86 | 135 | 17 | 4 | 8 | 46 | 3 | 42 | 70 |
| Burks, Ellis | .266 | 103 | 278 | 41 | 74 | 138 | 10 | 6 | 14 | 49 | 7 | 39 | 72 |
| Girardi, Joe | .262 | 125 | 462 | 63 | 121 | 166 | 17 | 2 | 8 | 55 | 3 | 29 | 76 |
| Weiss, Walt | .260 | 137 | 427 | 65 | 111 | 137 | 17 | 3 | 1 | 25 | 15 | 98 | 57 |
| Owens, Jayhawk | .244 | 18 | 45 | 7 | 11 | 25 | 2 | 0 | 4 | 12 | 0 | 2 | 15 |
| Tatum, Jim | .235 | 34 | 34 | 4 | 8 | 11 | 1 | 1 | 0 | 4 | 0 | 1 | 7 |

| PITCHING | ERA | W | L | G | GS | CG | SV | INN | H | R | ER | BB | SO |
|---|---|---|---|---|---|---|---|---|---|---|---|---|---|
| Ruffin, Bruce | 2.12 | 0 | 1 | 37 | 0 | 0 | 11 | 34 | 26 | 8 | 8 | 19 | 23 |
| Reed, Steve | 2.14 | 5 | 2 | 71 | 0 | 0 | 3 | 84 | 61 | 24 | 20 | 21 | 79 |
| Holmes, Darren | 3.24 | 6 | 1 | 68 | 0 | 0 | 14 | 66⅔ | 59 | 26 | 24 | 28 | 61 |
| Leskanic, Curt | 3.40 | 6 | 3 | 76 | 0 | 0 | 10 | 98 | 83 | 38 | 37 | 33 | 107 |
| Saberhagen, Bret | 4.18 | 7 | 6 | 25 | 25 | 3 | 0 | 153 | 165 | 78 | 71 | 33 | 100 |
| Ritz, Kevin | 4.21 | 11 | 11 | 31 | 28 | 0 | 2 | 173⅓ | 171 | 91 | 81 | 65 | 120 |
| Painter, Lance | 4.37 | 3 | 0 | 33 | 1 | 0 | 1 | 45⅓ | 55 | 23 | 22 | 10 | 36 |
| Swift, Bill | 4.94 | 9 | 3 | 19 | 19 | 0 | 0 | 105⅔ | 122 | 62 | 58 | 43 | 68 |
| Rekar, Bryan | 4.98 | 4 | 6 | 15 | 14 | 1 | 0 | 85 | 95 | 51 | 47 | 24 | 60 |
| Bailey, Roger | 4.98 | 7 | 6 | 39 | 6 | 0 | 0 | 81⅓ | 88 | 49 | 45 | 39 | 33 |
| Grahe, Joe | 5.08 | 4 | 3 | 17 | 9 | 0 | 0 | 56⅔ | 69 | 42 | 32 | 27 | 27 |
| Reynoso, Armando | 5.32 | 7 | 7 | 20 | 18 | 0 | 0 | 93 | 116 | 61 | 55 | 36 | 40 |
| Freeman, Marvin | 5.89 | 3 | 7 | 22 | 18 | 0 | 0 | 94⅔ | 122 | 64 | 62 | 41 | 61 |

## National League Team-by-Team Statistical Leaders *(Cont.)*

### Florida Marlins

| BATTING | BA | G | AB | R | H | TB | 2B | 3B | HR | RBI | SB | BB | SO |
|---|---|---|---|---|---|---|---|---|---|---|---|---|---|
| Sheffield, Gary | .324 | 63 | 213 | 46 | 69 | 125 | 8 | 0 | 16 | 46 | 19 | 55 | 45 |
| Conine, Jeff | .302 | 133 | 483 | 72 | 146 | 251 | 26 | 2 | 25 | 105 | 2 | 66 | 94 |
| Pendleton, Terry | .290 | 133 | 513 | 70 | 149 | 225 | 32 | 1 | 14 | 78 | 1 | 38 | 84 |
| Tavarez, Jesus | .289 | 63 | 190 | 31 | 55 | 71 | 6 | 2 | 2 | 13 | 7 | 16 | 27 |
| Morman, Russ | .278 | 34 | 72 | 9 | 20 | 33 | 2 | 1 | 3 | 7 | 0 | 3 | 12 |
| Colbrunn, Greg | .277 | 138 | 528 | 70 | 146 | 239 | 22 | 1 | 23 | 89 | 11 | 22 | 69 |
| Arias, Alex | .269 | 94 | 216 | 22 | 58 | 80 | 9 | 2 | 3 | 26 | 1 | 22 | 20 |
| Veras, Quilvio | .261 | 124 | 440 | 86 | 115 | 164 | 20 | 7 | 5 | 32 | 56 | 80 | 68 |
| Dawson, Andre | .257 | 79 | 226 | 30 | 58 | 98 | 10 | 3 | 8 | 37 | 0 | 9 | 45 |
| Browne, Jerry | .255 | 77 | 184 | 21 | 47 | 54 | 4 | 0 | 1 | 17 | 1 | 25 | 20 |
| Abbott, Kurt | .255 | 120 | 420 | 60 | 107 | 190 | 18 | 7 | 17 | 60 | 4 | 36 | 110 |
| Johnson, Charles | .251 | 97 | 315 | 40 | 79 | 129 | 15 | 1 | 11 | 39 | 0 | 46 | 71 |
| Gregg, Tommy | .237 | 72 | 156 | 20 | 37 | 60 | 5 | 0 | 6 | 20 | 3 | 16 | 33 |
| Carr, Chuck | .227 | 105 | 308 | 54 | 70 | 96 | 20 | 0 | 2 | 20 | 25 | 46 | 49 |
| Decker, Steve | .226 | 51 | 133 | 12 | 30 | 43 | 2 | 1 | 3 | 13 | 1 | 19 | 22 |

| PITCHING | ERA | W | L | G | GS | CG | SV | INN | H | R | ER | BB | SO |
|---|---|---|---|---|---|---|---|---|---|---|---|---|---|
| Nen, Robb | 3.29 | 0 | 7 | 62 | 0 | 0 | 23 | 65⅔ | 62 | 26 | 24 | 23 | 68 |
| Mathews, Terry | 3.38 | 4 | 4 | 57 | 0 | 0 | 3 | 82⅔ | 70 | 32 | 31 | 27 | 72 |
| Rapp, Pat | 3.44 | 14 | 7 | 28 | 28 | 3 | 0 | 167⅓ | 158 | 72 | 64 | 76 | 102 |
| Lewis, Richie | 3.75 | 0 | 1 | 21 | 1 | 0 | 0 | 36 | 30 | 15 | 15 | 15 | 32 |
| Hammond, Chris | 3.80 | 9 | 6 | 25 | 24 | 3 | 0 | 161 | 157 | 73 | 68 | 47 | 126 |
| Veres, Randy | 3.88 | 4 | 4 | 47 | 0 | 0 | 1 | 48⅔ | 46 | 25 | 21 | 22 | 31 |
| Witt, Bobby | 3.90 | 2 | 7 | 19 | 19 | 1 | 0 | 110⅔ | 104 | 52 | 48 | 47 | 95 |
| Burkett, John | 4.30 | 14 | 14 | 30 | 30 | 4 | 0 | 188⅓ | 208 | 95 | 90 | 57 | 126 |
| Gardner, Mark | 4.49 | 5 | 5 | 39 | 11 | 1 | 1 | 102⅓ | 109 | 60 | 51 | 43 | 87 |
| Perez, Yorkis | 5.21 | 2 | 6 | 69 | 0 | 0 | 1 | 46⅔ | 35 | 29 | 27 | 28 | 47 |
| Banks, Willie | 5.66 | 2 | 6 | 25 | 15 | 0 | 0 | 90⅔ | 106 | 71 | 57 | 58 | 62 |
| Weathers, Dave | 5.98 | 4 | 5 | 28 | 15 | 0 | 0 | 90⅓ | 104 | 68 | 60 | 52 | 60 |
| Groom, Buddy | 7.20 | 1 | 2 | 14 | 0 | 0 | 0 | 15 | 26 | 12 | 12 | 6 | 12 |
| Murphy, Rob | 10.95 | 1 | 2 | 14 | 0 | 0 | 0 | 12⅓ | 14 | 16 | 15 | 8 | 7 |
| Garces, Rich | 4.44 | 0 | 2 | 18 | 0 | 0 | 0 | 24⅓ | 25 | 15 | 12 | 11 | 22 |

### Houston Astros

| BATTING | BA | G | AB | R | H | TB | 2B | 3B | HR | RBI | SB | BB | SO |
|---|---|---|---|---|---|---|---|---|---|---|---|---|---|
| Bell, Derek | .334 | 112 | 452 | 63 | 151 | 200 | 21 | 2 | 8 | 86 | 27 | 33 | 71 |
| Cangelosi, John | .318 | 90 | 201 | 46 | 64 | 79 | 5 | 2 | 2 | 18 | 21 | 48 | 42 |
| Magadan, Dave | .313 | 127 | 348 | 44 | 109 | 139 | 24 | 0 | 2 | 51 | 2 | 71 | 56 |
| Hunter, Brian | .302 | 78 | 321 | 52 | 97 | 127 | 14 | 5 | 2 | 28 | 24 | 21 | 52 |
| Biggio, Craig | .302 | 141 | 553 | 123 | 167 | 267 | 30 | 2 | 22 | 77 | 33 | 80 | 85 |
| May, Derrick | .301 | 78 | 206 | 229 | 62 | 103 | 15 | 1 | 8 | 41 | 5 | 19 | 24 |
| Donnels, Chris | .300 | 19 | 30 | 4 | 9 | 9 | 0 | 0 | 0 | 2 | 0 | 3 | 6 |
| Eusebio, Tony | .299 | 113 | 368 | 46 | 110 | 151 | 21 | 1 | 6 | 58 | 0 | 31 | 59 |
| Bagwell, Jeff | .290 | 114 | 448 | 88 | 130 | 222 | 29 | 0 | 21 | 87 | 12 | 79 | 102 |
| Gutierrez, Ricky | .276 | 52 | 156 | 22 | 43 | 49 | 6 | 0 | 0 | 12 | 5 | 10 | 33 |
| Shipley, Craig | .263 | 92 | 232 | 23 | 61 | 80 | 8 | 1 | 3 | 24 | 6 | 8 | 28 |
| Miller, Orlando | .262 | 92 | 324 | 36 | 85 | 122 | 20 | 1 | 5 | 36 | 3 | 22 | 71 |
| Mouton, James | .262 | 104 | 298 | 42 | 78 | 112 | 18 | 2 | 4 | 27 | 25 | 25 | 59 |
| Simms, Mike | .256 | 50 | 121 | 14 | 31 | 62 | 4 | 0 | 9 | 24 | 1 | 13 | 28 |
| Thompson, Milt | .220 | 92 | 132 | 14 | 29 | 44 | 9 | 0 | 2 | 19 | 4 | 14 | 37 |
| Wilkins, Rick | .203 | 65 | 202 | 30 | 41 | 65 | 3 | 0 | 7 | 19 | 0 | 46 | 61 |

| PITCHING | ERA | W | L | G | GS | CG | SV | INN | H | R | ER | BB | SO |
|---|---|---|---|---|---|---|---|---|---|---|---|---|---|
| Veres, Dave | 2.26 | 5 | 1 | 72 | 0 | 0 | 1 | 103⅓ | 89 | 29 | 26 | 30 | 94 |
| Jones, Todd | 3.07 | 6 | 5 | 68 | 0 | 0 | 15 | 99⅔ | 89 | 38 | 34 | 52 | 96 |
| Hartgraves, Dean | 3.22 | 2 | 0 | 40 | 0 | 0 | 0 | 36⅓ | 30 | 14 | 13 | 16 | 24 |
| Tabaka, Jeff | 3.23 | 1 | 0 | 34 | 0 | 0 | 0 | 30⅔ | 27 | 11 | 11 | 17 | 25 |
| Hampton, Mike | 3.35 | 9 | 8 | 24 | 24 | 0 | 0 | 150⅔ | 141 | 73 | 56 | 49 | 115 |
| Reynolds, Shane | 3.47 | 10 | 11 | 30 | 30 | 3 | 0 | 189⅓ | 196 | 87 | 73 | 37 | 175 |
| Brocail, Doug | 4.19 | 6 | 4 | 36 | 7 | 0 | 1 | 77⅓ | 87 | 40 | 36 | 22 | 39 |
| Swindell, Greg | 4.47 | 10 | 9 | 33 | 26 | 1 | 0 | 153 | 180 | 86 | 76 | 39 | 96 |
| Drabek, Doug | 4.77 | 10 | 9 | 31 | 31 | 2 | 0 | 185 | 205 | 104 | 98 | 54 | 143 |
| Dougherty, Jim | 4.92 | 8 | 4 | 56 | 0 | 0 | 0 | 67⅔ | 76 | 37 | 37 | 25 | 49 |
| Kile, Darryl | 4.96 | 4 | 12 | 25 | 21 | 0 | 0 | 127 | 114 | 81 | 70 | 73 | 113 |

## Los Angeles Dodgers

| BATTING | BA | G | AB | R | H | TB | 2B | 3B | HR | RBI | SB | BB | SO |
|---|---|---|---|---|---|---|---|---|---|---|---|---|---|
| Piazza, Mike | .346 | 112 | 434 | 82 | 150 | 263 | 17 | 0 | 32 | 93 | 1 | 39 | 80 |
| Butler, Brett | .300 | 129 | 513 | 78 | 154 | 193 | 18 | 9 | 1 | 38 | 32 | 67 | 51 |
| Karros, Eric | .298 | 143 | 551 | 83 | 164 | 295 | 29 | 3 | 32 | 105 | 4 | 61 | 115 |
| Hansen, Dave | .287 | 100 | 181 | 19 | 52 | 65 | 10 | 0 | 1 | 14 | 0 | 28 | 28 |
| Offerman, Jose | .287 | 119 | 429 | 69 | 123 | 161 | 14 | 6 | 4 | 33 | 2 | 69 | 67 |
| Mondesi, Raul | .285 | 139 | 536 | 91 | 153 | 266 | 23 | 6 | 26 | 88 | 27 | 33 | 96 |
| Fonville, Chad | .278 | 102 | 320 | 43 | 89 | 97 | 6 | 1 | 0 | 16 | 20 | 23 | 42 |
| Kelly, Roberto | .278 | 136 | 504 | 58 | 140 | 188 | 23 | 2 | 7 | 57 | 19 | 22 | 79 |
| Parker, Rick | .276 | 27 | 29 | 3 | 8 | 8 | 0 | 0 | 0 | 4 | 1 | 2 | 4 |
| Wallach, Tim | .266 | 97 | 327 | 24 | 87 | 140 | 22 | 2 | 9 | 38 | 0 | 27 | 69 |
| DeShields, Delino | .256 | 127 | 425 | 66 | 109 | 157 | 18 | 3 | 8 | 37 | 39 | 63 | 83 |
| Ashley, Billy | .237 | 81 | 215 | 17 | 51 | 80 | 5 | 0 | 8 | 27 | 0 | 25 | 88 |
| Hollandsworth, Todd | .233 | 41 | 103 | 16 | 24 | 41 | 2 | 0 | 5 | 13 | 2 | 10 | 29 |
| Gwynn, Chris | .214 | 67 | 84 | 8 | 18 | 28 | 3 | 2 | 1 | 10 | 0 | 6 | 23 |

| PITCHING | ERA | W | L | G | GS | CG | SV | INN | H | R | ER | BB | SO |
|---|---|---|---|---|---|---|---|---|---|---|---|---|---|
| Worrell, Todd | 2.02 | 4 | 1 | 59 | 0 | 0 | 32 | 62⅓ | 50 | 15 | 14 | 19 | 61 |
| Nomo, Hideo | 2.54 | 13 | 6 | 28 | 28 | 4 | 0 | 191⅓ | 124 | 63 | 54 | 78 | 236 |
| Cummings, John | 3.00 | 3 | 1 | 35 | 0 | 0 | 0 | 39 | 38 | 16 | 13 | 10 | 21 |
| Valdes, Ismael | 3.05 | 13 | 11 | 33 | 27 | 6 | 1 | 197⅔ | 168 | 76 | 67 | 51 | 150 |
| Candiotti, Tom | 3.50 | 7 | 14 | 30 | 30 | 1 | 0 | 190½ | 187 | 93 | 74 | 58 | 141 |
| Martinez, Ramon | 3.66 | 17 | 7 | 30 | 30 | 4 | 0 | 206⅓ | 176 | 95 | 84 | 81 | 138 |
| Astacio, Pedro | 4.24 | 7 | 8 | 48 | 11 | 1 | 0 | 104 | 103 | 53 | 49 | 29 | 80 |
| Osuna, Antonio | 4.43 | 2 | 4 | 39 | 0 | 0 | 0 | 44⅔ | 39 | 22 | 22 | 20 | 46 |
| Tapani, Kevin | 5.05 | 4 | 2 | 13 | 11 | 0 | 0 | 57 | 72 | 37 | 32 | 14 | 43 |
| Seanez, Rudy | 6.75 | 1 | 3 | 37 | 0 | 0 | 3 | 34⅔ | 39 | 27 | 26 | 18 | 29 |
| Daal, Omar | 7.20 | 4 | 0 | 28 | 0 | 0 | 0 | 20 | 29 | 19 | 16 | 15 | 11 |

## Montreal Expos

| BATTING | BA | G | AB | R | H | TB | 2B | 3B | HR | RBI | SB | BB | SO |
|---|---|---|---|---|---|---|---|---|---|---|---|---|---|
| Berry, Sean | .318 | 103 | 314 | 38 | 100 | 166 | 22 | 1 | 14 | 55 | 3 | 25 | 53 |
| Segui, David | .309 | 130 | 456 | 68 | 141 | 210 | 25 | 4 | 12 | 68 | 2 | 40 | 47 |
| Santangelo, F.P. | .296 | 35 | 98 | 11 | 29 | 39 | 5 | 1 | 1 | 9 | 1 | 12 | 9 |
| White, Rondell | .295 | 130 | 474 | 87 | 140 | 220 | 33 | 4 | 13 | 57 | 25 | 41 | 87 |
| Cordero, Wilfredo | .286 | 131 | 514 | 64 | 147 | 216 | 35 | 2 | 10 | 49 | 9 | 36 | 88 |
| Fletcher, Scott | .286 | 110 | 350 | 42 | 100 | 156 | 21 | 1 | 11 | 45 | 0 | 32 | 23 |
| Alou, Moises | .273 | 93 | 344 | 48 | 94 | 158 | 22 | 0 | 14 | 58 | 4 | 29 | 56 |
| Silvestri, Dave | .264 | 39 | 72 | 12 | 19 | 31 | 6 | 0 | 2 | 7 | 2 | 9 | 27 |
| Lansing, Mike | .255 | 127 | 467 | 47 | 119 | 183 | 30 | 2 | 10 | 62 | 27 | 28 | 65 |
| Tarasco, Tony | .249 | 126 | 438 | 64 | 109 | 177 | 18 | 4 | 14 | 40 | 24 | 51 | 78 |
| Grudzielanek, Mark | .245 | 78 | 269 | 27 | 66 | 85 | 12 | 2 | 1 | 20 | 8 | 14 | 47 |
| Rodriguez, Henry | .239 | 45 | 138 | 13 | 33 | 45 | 4 | 1 | 2 | 15 | 0 | 11 | 28 |
| Laker, Tim | .234 | 64 | 141 | 17 | 33 | 52 | 8 | 1 | 3 | 20 | 0 | 14 | 38 |
| Andrews, Shane | .214 | 84 | 220 | 27 | 47 | 83 | 10 | 1 | 8 | 31 | 1 | 17 | 68 |
| Treadway, Jeff | .209 | 58 | 67 | 6 | 14 | 18 | 2 | 1 | 0 | 13 | 0 | 5 | 4 |

| PITCHING | ERA | W | L | G | GS | CG | SV | INN | H | R | ER | BB | SO |
|---|---|---|---|---|---|---|---|---|---|---|---|---|---|
| Harris, Greg | 2.61 | 2 | 3 | 45 | 0 | 0 | 0 | 48⅓ | 45 | 18 | 14 | 16 | 47 |
| Henry, Butch | 2.84 | 7 | 9 | 21 | 21 | 1 | 0 | 126⅔ | 133 | 47 | 40 | 28 | 60 |
| Rueter, Kirk | 3.23 | 5 | 3 | 9 | 9 | 1 | 0 | 47⅓ | 38 | 17 | 17 | 9 | 28 |
| Martinez, Pedro | 3.51 | 14 | 10 | 30 | 30 | 2 | 0 | 194¾ | 158 | 79 | 76 | 66 | 174 |
| Perez, Carlos | 3.69 | 10 | 8 | 28 | 23 | 2 | 0 | 141⅓ | 142 | 61 | 58 | 28 | 106 |
| Scott, Tim | 3.98 | 2 | 0 | 62 | 0 | 0 | 2 | 63⅓ | 52 | 30 | 28 | 23 | 57 |
| Rojas, Mel | 4.12 | 1 | 4 | 59 | 0 | 0 | 30 | 67¾ | 69 | 32 | 31 | 29 | 61 |
| Heredia, Gil | 4.31 | 5 | 6 | 40 | 18 | 0 | 1 | 119 | 137 | 60 | 57 | 21 | 74 |
| Fassero, Jeff | 4.33 | 13 | 14 | 30 | 30 | 1 | 0 | 189 | 207 | 102 | 91 | 74 | 164 |
| Shaw, Jeff | 4.62 | 1 | 6 | 50 | 0 | 0 | 3 | 62½ | 58 | 35 | 32 | 26 | 45 |
| Alvarez, Tavo | 6.75 | 1 | 5 | 8 | 8 | 0 | 0 | 37⅓ | 46 | 30 | 28 | 14 | 17 |

## New York Mets

| BATTING | BA | G | AB | R | H | TB | 2B | 3B | HR | RBI | SB | BB | SO |
|---|---|---|---|---|---|---|---|---|---|---|---|---|---|
| Bonilla, Bobby | .325 | 80 | 317 | 49 | 103 | 190 | 25 | 4 | 18 | 53 | 0 | 31 | 48 |
| Bogar, Timothy | .290 | 78 | 145 | 17 | 42 | 52 | 7 | 0 | 1 | 21 | 1 | 9 | 25 |
| Brogna, Rico | .289 | 134 | 495 | 72 | 143 | 240 | 27 | 2 | 22 | 76 | 0 | 39 | 111 |
| Vizcaino, Jose | .287 | 135 | 509 | 66 | 146 | 186 | 21 | 5 | 3 | 56 | 8 | 35 | 76 |
| Orsulak, Joe | .283 | 108 | 290 | 41 | 82 | 108 | 19 | 2 | -1 | 37 | 1 | 19 | 35 |
| Jones, Chris | .280 | 79 | 182 | 33 | 51 | 85 | 6 | 2 | 8 | 31 | 2 | 13 | 45 |
| Hundley, Todd | .280 | 90 | 275 | 39 | 77 | 133 | 11 | 0 | 15 | 51 | 1 | 42 | 64 |
| Alfonzo, Edgar | .278 | 101 | 335 | 26 | 93 | 128 | 13 | 5 | 4 | 41 | 1 | 12 | 37 |
| Kent, Jeff | .278 | 125 | 472 | 65 | 131 | 219 | 22 | 3 | 20 | 65 | 3 | 29 | 89 |
| Everett, Carl | .260 | 79 | 289 | 48 | 75 | 126 | 13 | 1 | 12 | 54 | 2 | 39 | 67 |
| Thompson, Ryan | .251 | 75 | 267 | 39 | 67 | 101 | 13 | 0 | 7 | 31 | 3 | 19 | 77 |
| Buford, Damon | .235 | 44 | 136 | 24 | 32 | 49 | 5 | 0 | 4 | 12 | 7 | 19 | 28 |
| Stinnett, Kelly | .219 | 77 | 196 | 23 | 43 | 65 | 8 | 1 | 4 | 18 | 2 | 29 | 65 |
| Huskey, Butch | .189 | 28 | 90 | 8 | 17 | 27 | 1 | 0 | 3 | 11 | 1 | 10 | 16 |

| PITCHING | ERA | W | L | G | GS | CG | SV | INN | H | R | ER | BB | SO |
|---|---|---|---|---|---|---|---|---|---|---|---|---|---|
| Birkbeck, Mike | 1.63 | 0 | 1 | 4 | 4 | 0 | 0 | 27⅓ | 22 | 5 | 5 | 2 | 14 |
| Byrd, Paul | 2.05 | 2 | 0 | 17 | 0 | 0 | 0 | 22 | 18 | 6 | 5 | 7 | 26 |
| Franco, John | 2.44 | 5 | 3 | 48 | 0 | 0 | 29 | 51⅔ | 48 | 17 | 14 | 17 | 41 |
| Isringhausen, Jason | 2.81 | 9 | 2 | 14 | 14 | 1 | 0 | 93 | 88 | 29 | 29 | 31 | 55 |
| Henry, Doug | 2.96 | 3 | 6 | 51 | 0 | 0 | 4 | 67 | 48 | 23 | 22 | 25 | 62 |
| Minor, Blas | 3.66 | 4 | 2 | 35 | 0 | 0 | 1 | 46⅔ | 44 | 21 | 19 | 13 | 43 |
| Harnisch, Pete | 3.68 | 2 | 8 | 18 | 18 | 0 | 0 | 110 | 11 | 55 | 45 | 24 | 82 |
| DiPoto, Jerry | 3.78 | 4 | 6 | 58 | 0 | 0 | 2 | 78⅔ | 77 | 41 | 33 | 29 | 49 |
| Pulsipher, Bill | 3.98 | 5 | 7 | 17 | 17 | 2 | 0 | 126⅔ | 122 | 58 | 56 | 45 | 81 |
| Jones, Bobby | 4.19 | 10 | 10 | 30 | 30 | 3 | 0 | 195⅔ | 209 | 107 | 91 | 53 | 127 |
| Mlicki, Dave | 4.26 | 9 | 7 | 29 | 25 | 0 | 0 | 160⅔ | 160 | 82 | 76 | 54 | 123 |
| Cornelius, Reid | 5.54 | 3 | 7 | 18 | 10 | 0 | 0 | 66⅔ | 75 | 44 | 41 | 30 | 39 |

## Philadelphia Phillies

| BATTING | BA | G | AB | R | H | TB | 2B | 3B | HR | RBI | SB | BB | SO |
|---|---|---|---|---|---|---|---|---|---|---|---|---|---|
| Longmire, Tony | .356 | 59 | 104 | 21 | 37 | 53 | 7 | 0 | 3 | 19 | 1 | 11 | 19 |
| Gallagher, Dave | .318 | 62 | 157 | 12 | 50 | 65 | 12 | 0 | 1 | 12 | 0 | 16 | 20 |
| Eisenreich, Jim | .316 | 129 | 377 | 46 | 119 | 175 | 22 | 2 | 10 | 55 | 10 | 38 | 44 |
| Jefferies, Gregg | .306 | 114 | 480 | 69 | 147 | 215 | 31 | 2 | 11 | 56 | 9 | 35 | 26 |
| Marsh, Tom | .294 | 43 | 109 | 13 | 32 | 46 | 3 | 1 | 3 | 15 | 0 | 4 | 25 |
| Morandini, Mickey | .283 | 127 | 494 | 65 | 140 | 206 | 34 | 7 | 6 | 49 | 9 | 42 | 80 |
| Hayes, Charlie | .276 | 141 | 529 | 58 | 146 | 215 | 30 | 3 | 11 | 85 | 5 | 50 | 88 |
| Whiten, Mark | .269 | 60 | 212 | 38 | 57 | 102 | 10 | 1 | 11 | 37 | 7 | 31 | 63 |
| Webster, Lenny | .267 | 49 | 150 | 18 | 40 | 61 | 9 | 0 | 4 | 14 | 0 | 16 | 27 |
| Dykstra, Lenny | .264 | 62 | 254 | 37 | 67 | 90 | 15 | 1 | 2 | 18 | 10 | 33 | 28 |
| Varsho, Gary | .252 | 72 | 103 | 7 | 26 | 29 | 1 | 1 | 0 | 11 | 2 | 7 | 17 |
| Daulton, Darren | .249 | 98 | 342 | 44 | 85 | 137 | 19 | 3 | 9 | 55 | 3 | 55 | 52 |
| Van Slyke, Andy | .243 | 63 | 214 | 26 | 52 | 75 | 10 | 2 | 3 | 16 | 7 | 28 | 41 |
| Hollins, Dave | .229 | 65 | 205 | 46 | 47 | 84 | 12 | 2 | 7 | 25 | 1 | 53 | 38 |
| Stocker, Kevin | .218 | 125 | 412 | 42 | 90 | 113 | 14 | 3 | 1 | 32 | 6 | 43 | 75 |

| PITCHING | ERA | W | L | G | GS | CG | SV | INN | H | R | ER | BB | SO |
|---|---|---|---|---|---|---|---|---|---|---|---|---|---|
| Bottalico, Ricky | 2.46 | 5 | 3 | 62 | 0 | 0 | 1 | 87⅓ | 50 | 25 | 24 | 42 | 87 |
| Slocumb, Heathcliff | 2.89 | 5 | 6 | 61 | 0 | 0 | 32 | 65⅓ | 64 | 26 | 21 | 35 | 63 |
| Williams, Mike | 3.29 | 3 | 3 | 33 | 8 | 0 | 0 | 87⅓ | 78 | 37 | 32 | 29 | 57 |
| Fernandez, Sid | 3.34 | 6 | 1 | 11 | 11 | 0 | 0 | 64⅔ | 48 | 25 | 24 | 21 | 79 |
| Schilling, Curt | 3.57 | 7 | 5 | 17 | 17 | 1 | 0 | 116 | 96 | 52 | 46 | 26 | 114 |
| West, David | 3.79 | 3 | 2 | 8 | 8 | 0 | 0 | 38 | 34 | 17 | 16 | 19 | 25 |
| Juden, Jeff | 4.02 | 2 | 4 | 13 | 10 | 1 | 0 | 62⅔ | 53 | 31 | 28 | 31 | 47 |
| Mimbs, Mike | 4.15 | 9 | 7 | 35 | 19 | 2 | 1 | 136⅔ | 127 | 70 | 63 | 75 | 93 |
| Quantrill, Paul | 4.67 | 11 | 12 | 33 | 29 | 0 | 0 | 179⅓ | 212 | 102 | 93 | 44 | 103 |
| Green, Tyler | 5.31 | 8 | 9 | 26 | 25 | 4 | 0 | 140⅔ | 157 | 86 | 83 | 66 | 55 |

## Pittsburgh Pirates

| BATTING | BA | G | AB | R | H | TB | 2B | 3B | HR | RBI | SB | BB | SO |
|---|---|---|---|---|---|---|---|---|---|---|---|---|---|
| Wehner, John | .308 | 52 | 107 | 13 | 33 | 39 | 0 | 3 | 0 | 5 | 3 | 10 | 17 |
| Slaught, Don | .304 | 35 | 112 | 13 | 34 | 40 | 6 | 0 | 0 | 13 | 0 | 9 | 8 |
| Merced, Orlando | .300 | 132 | 487 | 75 | 146 | 228 | 29 | 4 | 15 | 83 | 7 | 52 | 74 |
| Garcia, Carlos | .294 | 104 | 367 | 41 | 108 | 154 | 24 | 2 | 6 | 50 | 8 | 25 | 55 |
| Liriano, Nelson | .286 | 107 | 259 | 29 | 74 | 103 | 12 | 1 | 5 | 38 | 2 | 24 | 34 |
| Martin, Al | .282 | 124 | 439 | 70 | 124 | 194 | 25 | 3 | 13 | 41 | 20 | 44 | 92 |
| Clark, Dave | .281 | 77 | 196 | 30 | 55 | 73 | 6 | 0 | 4 | 24 | 3 | 24 | 38 |
| Brumfield, Jacob | .271 | 116 | 402 | 64 | 109 | 148 | 23 | 2 | 4 | 26 | 22 | 37 | 71 |
| King, Jeff | .265 | 122 | 445 | 61 | 118 | 203 | 27 | 2 | 18 | 87 | 7 | 55 | 63 |
| Bell, Jay | .262 | 138 | 530 | 79 | 139 | 214 | 28 | 4 | 13 | 55 | 2 | 55 | 110 |
| Aude, Rich | .248 | 42 | 109 | 10 | 27 | 41 | 8 | 0 | 2 | 19 | 1 | 6 | 20 |
| Pegues, Steve | .246 | 82 | 171 | 17 | 42 | 68 | 8 | 0 | 6 | 16 | 1 | 4 | 36 |
| Cummings, Midre | .243 | 59 | 152 | 13 | 37 | 52 | 7 | 1 | 2 | 15 | 1 | 13 | 30 |
| Young, Kevin | .232 | 56 | 181 | 13 | 42 | 69 | 9 | 0 | 6 | 22 | 1 | 8 | 53 |
| Encarnacion, Angelo | .226 | 58 | 159 | 18 | 36 | 53 | 7 | 2 | 2 | 10 | 1 | 13 | 28 |
| Johnson, Mark | .208 | 79 | 221 | 32 | 46 | 93 | 6 | 1 | 13 | 28 | 5 | 37 | 66 |

| PITCHING | ERA | W | L | G | GS | CG | SV | INN | H | R | ER | BB | SO |
|---|---|---|---|---|---|---|---|---|---|---|---|---|---|
| Neagle, Denny | 3.43 | 13 | 8 | 31 | 31 | 5 | 0 | 209⅔ | 221 | 91 | 80 | 45 | 150 |
| Plesac, Dan | 3.58 | 4 | 4 | 58 | 0 | 0 | 3 | 60½ | 53 | 26 | 24 | 27 | 57 |
| Christiansen, Jason | 4.15 | 1 | 3 | 63 | 0 | 0 | 0 | 56½ | 49 | 28 | 26 | 34 | 53 |
| Dyer, Mike | 4.34 | 4 | 5 | 55 | 0 | 0 | 0 | 74⅔ | 81 | 40 | 36 | 30 | 53 |
| Ericks, John | 4.58 | 3 | 9 | 19 | 18 | 1 | 0 | 106 | 108 | 59 | 54 | 50 | 80 |
| Miceli, Dan | 4.66 | 4 | 4 | 58 | 0 | 0 | 21 | 58 | 61 | 30 | 30 | 28 | 56 |
| White, Rick | 4.75 | 2 | 3 | 15 | 9 | 0 | 0 | 55 | 66 | 33 | 29 | 18 | 29 |
| Wagner, Paul | 4.80 | 5 | 16 | 33 | 25 | 3 | 1 | 165 | 174 | 96 | 88 | 72 | 120 |
| McCurry, Jeff | 5.02 | 1 | 4 | 55 | 0 | 0 | 1 | 61 | 82 | 38 | 34 | 30 | 27 |
| Loaiza, Esteban | 5.16 | 8 | 9 | 32 | 31 | 1 | 0 | 172⅔ | 205 | 115 | 99 | 55 | 85 |
| Parris, Steve | 5.38 | 6 | 6 | 15 | 15 | 1 | 0 | 82 | 89 | 49 | 49 | 33 | 61 |
| Lieber, Jon | 6.32 | 4 | 7 | 21 | 12 | 0 | 0 | 72⅔ | 103 | 56 | 51 | 14 | 45 |

## St. Louis Cardinals

| BATTING | BA | G | AB | R | H | TB | 2B | 3B | HR | RBI | SB | BB | SO |
|---|---|---|---|---|---|---|---|---|---|---|---|---|---|
| Mabry, John | .307 | 129 | 388 | 35 | 119 | 157 | 21 | 1 | 5 | 41 | 0 | 24 | 45 |
| Gilkey, Bernard | .298 | 121 | 480 | 73 | 143 | 235 | 33 | 4 | 17 | 69 | 12 | 42 | 70 |
| Jordan, Brian | .296 | 131 | 490 | 83 | 145 | 239 | 20 | 4 | 22 | 81 | 24 | 22 | 79 |
| Lankford, Ray | .277 | 132 | 483 | 81 | 134 | 248 | 35 | 2 | 25 | 82 | 24 | 63 | 110 |
| Battle, Allen | .271 | 61 | 118 | 13 | 32 | 37 | 5 | 0 | 0 | 2 | 3 | 15 | 26 |
| Pena, Geronimo | .267 | 32 | 101 | 20 | 27 | 38 | 6 | 1 | 1 | 8 | 3 | 16 | 30 |
| Bell, David | .250 | 39 | 144 | 13 | 36 | 53 | 7 | 2 | 2 | 19 | 1 | 4 | 25 |
| Sheaffer, Danny | .231 | 76 | 208 | 24 | 48 | 75 | 10 | 1 | 5 | 30 | 0 | 23 | 38 |
| Cooper, Scott | .230 | 118 | 374 | 29 | 86 | 117 | 18 | 2 | 3 | 40 | 0 | 49 | 85 |
| Cromer, Tripp | .226 | 105 | 345 | 36 | 78 | 112 | 19 | 0 | 5 | 18 | 0 | 14 | 66 |
| Coles, Darnell | .225 | 63 | 138 | 13 | 31 | 47 | 7 | 0 | 3 | 16 | 0 | 16 | 20 |
| Pagnozzi, Tom | .215 | 62 | 219 | 17 | 47 | 69 | 14 | 1 | 2 | 15 | 0 | 11 | 31 |
| Oquendo, Jose | .209 | 88 | 220 | 31 | 46 | 66 | 8 | 3 | 2 | 17 | 1 | 35 | 21 |
| Smith, Ozzie | .199 | 44 | 156 | 16 | 31 | 38 | 5 | 1 | 0 | 11 | 4 | 17 | 12 |
| Hemond, Scott | .144 | 57 | 118 | 11 | 17 | 27 | 1 | 0 | 3 | 9 | 0 | 12 | 31 |
| Oliva, Jose | .142 | 70 | 183 | 15 | 26 | 52 | 5 | 0 | 7 | 20 | 0 | 12 | 46 |

| PITCHING | ERA | W | L | G | GS | CG | SV | INN | H | R | ER | BB | SO |
|---|---|---|---|---|---|---|---|---|---|---|---|---|---|
| Fossas, Tony | 1.47 | 3 | 0 | 58 | 0 | 0 | 0 | 36⅔ | 28 | 6 | 6 | 10 | 40 |
| Mathews, T.J. | 1.52 | 1 | 1 | 23 | 0 | 0 | 2 | 29⅔ | 21 | 7 | 5 | 11 | 28 |
| Henke, Tom | 1.82 | 1 | 1 | 52 | 0 | 0 | 36 | 54⅓ | 42 | 11 | 11 | 18 | 48 |
| Habyan, John | 2.88 | 3 | 2 | 31 | 0 | 0 | 0 | 40⅔ | 32 | 18 | 13 | 15 | 35 |
| DeLucia, Rich | 3.39 | 8 | 7 | 56 | 1 | 0 | 0 | 82½ | 63 | 38 | 31 | 36 | 76 |
| Morgan, Mike | 3.56 | 7 | 7 | 21 | 21 | 1 | 0 | 131⅓ | 133 | 56 | 52 | 34 | 61 |
| Parrett, Jeff | 3.64 | 4 | 7 | 59 | 0 | 0 | 0 | 76⅔ | 71 | 33 | 31 | 28 | 71 |
| Urbani, Tom | 3.70 | 3 | 5 | 24 | 13 | 0 | 0 | 82⅓ | 99 | 40 | 34 | 21 | 52 |
| Osborne, Donovan | 3.81 | 4 | 6 | 19 | 19 | 0 | 0 | 113⅓ | 112 | 58 | 48 | 34 | 82 |
| Arocha, Rene | 3.99 | 3 | 5 | 41 | 0 | 0 | 0 | 49⅔ | 55 | 24 | 22 | 18 | 25 |
| Petkovsek, Mark | 4.00 | 6 | 6 | 26 | 21 | 1 | 0 | 137½ | 136 | 71 | 61 | 35 | 71 |
| Watson, Allen | 4.96 | 7 | 9 | 21 | 19 | 0 | 0 | 114⅓ | 126 | 68 | 63 | 41 | 49 |
| Hill, Ken | 5.06 | 6 | 7 | 18 | 18 | 0 | 0 | 110⅓ | 125 | 71 | 62 | 45 | 50 |
| Jackson, Danny | 5.90 | 2 | 12 | 19 | 19 | 2 | 0 | 100⅔ | 120 | 82 | 66 | 48 | 52 |

## San Diego Padres

| BATTING | BA | G | AB | R | H | TB | 2B | 3B | HR | RBI | SB | BB | SO |
|---|---|---|---|---|---|---|---|---|---|---|---|---|---|
| Gwynn, Tony | .368 | 135 | 535 | 82 | 197 | 259 | 33 | 1 | 9 | 90 | 17 | 35 | 15 |
| Livingstone, Scott | .337 | 99 | 196 | 26 | 66 | 96 | 15 | 0 | 5 | 32 | 2 | 15 | 22 |
| Roberts, Bip | .304 | 73 | 296 | 40 | 90 | 110 | 14 | 0 | 2 | 25 | 20 | 17 | 36 |
| Caminiti, Ken | .302 | 143 | 526 | 74 | 159 | 270 | 33 | 0 | 26 | 94 | 12 | 69 | 94 |
| Finley, Steve | .297 | 139 | 562 | 104 | 167 | 236 | 23 | 8 | 10 | 44 | 36 | 59 | 62 |
| Ausmus, Brad | .293 | 103 | 328 | 44 | 96 | 135 | 16 | 4 | 5 | 34 | 16 | 31 | 56 |
| Cianfrocco, Archi | .263 | 51 | 118 | 22 | 31 | 53 | 7 | 0 | 5 | 31 | 0 | 11 | 28 |
| Williams, Eddie | .260 | 97 | 296 | 35 | 77 | 126 | 11 | 1 | 12 | 47 | 0 | 23 | 47 |
| Reed, Jody | .256 | 131 | 445 | 58 | 114 | 146 | 18 | 1 | 4 | 40 | 6 | 59 | 38 |
| Plantier, Phil | .255 | 76 | 216 | 33 | 55 | 88 | 6 | 0 | 9 | 34 | 1 | 28 | 48 |
| Johnson, Brian | .251 | 68 | 207 | 20 | 52 | 70 | 9 | 0 | 3 | 29 | 0 | 11 | 39 |
| Petagine, Roberto | .234 | 89 | 124 | 15 | 29 | 46 | 8 | 0 | 3 | 17 | 0 | 26 | 41 |
| Clark, Phil | .216 | 75 | 97 | 12 | 21 | 30 | 3 | 0 | 2 | 7 | 0 | 8 | 18 |
| Cedeno, Andujar | .210 | 120 | 390 | 42 | 82 | 120 | 16 | 2 | 6 | 31 | 5 | 28 | 92 |
| Nieves, Melvin | .205 | 98 | 234 | 32 | 48 | 98 | 6 | 1 | 14 | 38 | 2 | 19 | 88 |

| PITCHING | ERA | W | L | G | GS | CG | SV | INN | H | R | ER | BB | SO |
|---|---|---|---|---|---|---|---|---|---|---|---|---|---|
| Ashby, Andy | 2.94 | 12 | 10 | 31 | 31 | 2 | 0 | 192⅔ | 180 | 79 | 63 | 62 | 150 |
| Florie, Bryce | 3.01 | 2 | 2 | 47 | 0 | 0 | 1 | 68⅔ | 49 | 30 | 23 | 38 | 68 |
| Hamilton, Joey | 3.08 | 6 | 9 | 31 | 30 | 2 | 0 | 204½ | 189 | 89 | 70 | 56 | 123 |
| Bochtler, Doug | 3.57 | 4 | 4 | 34 | 0 | 0 | 1 | 45¼ | 38 | 18 | 18 | 19 | 45 |
| Hoffman, Trevor | 3.88 | 7 | 4 | 55 | 0 | 0 | 31 | 53⅓ | 48 | 25 | 23 | 14 | 52 |
| Benes, Andy | 4.17 | 4 | 7 | 19 | 19 | 1 | 0 | 118⅓ | 121 | 65 | 55 | 45 | 126 |
| Sanders, Scott | 4.30 | 5 | 5 | 17 | 15 | 1 | 0 | 90 | 79 | 46 | 43 | 31 | 88 |
| Blair, Willie | 4.34 | 7 | 5 | 40 | 12 | 0 | 0 | 114 | 112 | 60 | 55 | 45 | 83 |
| Valenzuela, Fernando | 4.98 | 8 | 3 | 29 | 15 | 0 | 0 | 90½ | 101 | 53 | 50 | 34 | 57 |
| Dishman, Glenn | 5.01 | 4 | 8 | 19 | 16 | 0 | 0 | 97 | 104 | 60 | 54 | 34 | 43 |
| Williams, Brian | 6.00 | 3 | 10 | 44 | 6 | 0 | 0 | 72 | 79 | 54 | 48 | 38 | 75 |

## San Francisco Giants

| BATTING | BA | G | AB | R | H | TB | 2B | 3B | HR | RBI | SB | BB | SO |
|---|---|---|---|---|---|---|---|---|---|---|---|---|---|
| Williams, Matt | .336 | 76 | 283 | 53 | 95 | 183 | 17 | 1 | 23 | 65 | 2 | 30 | 58 |
| Carreon, Mark | .301 | 117 | 396 | 53 | 119 | 194 | 24 | 0 | 17 | 65 | 0 | 23 | 37 |
| Bonds, Barry | .294 | 144 | 506 | 109 | 149 | 292 | 30 | 7 | 33 | 104 | 31 | 120 | 83 |
| Sanders, Deion | .268 | 85 | 343 | 48 | 92 | 137 | 11 | 8 | 6 | 28 | 24 | 27 | 60 |
| Scarsone, Steve | .266 | 80 | 233 | 33 | 62 | 111 | 10 | 3 | 11 | 29 | 3 | 18 | 82 |
| Reed, Jeff | .265 | 66 | 113 | 12 | 30 | 32 | 2 | 0 | 0 | 9 | 0 | 20 | 17 |
| Hill, Glenallen | .264 | 132 | 497 | 71 | 131 | 240 | 29 | 4 | 24 | 86 | 25 | 39 | 98 |
| Manwaring, Kirt | .251 | 118 | 379 | 21 | 95 | 126 | 15 | 2 | 4 | 36 | 1 | 27 | 72 |
| Clayton, Royce | .244 | 138 | 509 | 56 | 124 | 174 | 29 | 3 | 5 | 58 | 24 | 38 | 109 |
| Thompson, Robby | .223 | 95 | 336 | 51 | 75 | 114 | 15 | 0 | 8 | 23 | 1 | 42 | 76 |
| Benjamin, Mike | .220 | 68 | 186 | 19 | 41 | 56 | 6 | 0 | 3 | 12 | 11 | 8 | 51 |
| Patterson, John | .205 | 95 | 205 | 27 | 42 | 56 | 5 | 3 | 1 | 14 | 4 | 14 | 41 |
| Phillips, J.R. | .195 | 92 | 231 | 27 | 45 | 81 | 9 | 0 | 9 | 28 | 19 | 1 | 69 |

| PITCHING | ERA | W | L | G | GS | CG | SV | INN | H | R | ER | BB | SO |
|---|---|---|---|---|---|---|---|---|---|---|---|---|---|
| Dewey, Mark | 3.13 | 1 | 0 | 27 | 0 | 0 | 0 | 31⅔ | 30 | 12 | 11 | 17 | 32 |
| Service, Scott | 3.19 | 3 | 1 | 28 | 0 | 0 | 0 | 31 | 18 | 11 | 11 | 20 | 30 |
| Van Landingham, W. | 3.67 | 6 | 3 | 18 | 18 | 1 | 0 | 122⅔ | 124 | 58 | 50 | 40 | 95 |
| Leiter, Mark | 3.82 | 10 | 12 | 30 | 29 | 7 | 0 | 195⅔ | 185 | 91 | 83 | 55 | 129 |
| Wilson, Trevor | 3.92 | 3 | 4 | 17 | 17 | 0 | 0 | 82⅔ | 82 | 42 | 36 | 38 | 38 |
| Barton, Shawn | 4.26 | 4 | 1 | 52 | 0 | 0 | 1 | 44⅓ | 37 | 22 | 21 | 19 | 22 |
| Beck, Rod | 4.45 | 5 | 6 | 60 | 0 | 0 | 33 | 58⅔ | 60 | 31 | 29 | 21 | 42 |
| Brewington, Jamie | 4.54 | 6 | 4 | 13 | 13 | 0 | 0 | 75½ | 68 | 38 | 38 | 45 | 45 |
| Valdez, Sergio | 4.75 | 4 | 5 | 13 | 11 | 1 | 0 | 66½ | 78 | 43 | 35 | 17 | 29 |
| Aquino, Luis | 5.10 | 0 | 3 | 34 | 0 | 0 | 2 | 42½ | 57 | 34 | 24 | 13 | 26 |
| Hook, Chris | 5.50 | 5 | 1 | 45 | 0 | 0 | 0 | 52⅓ | 55 | 33 | 32 | 29 | 40 |
| Mulholland, Terry | 5.80 | 5 | 13 | 29 | 24 | 2 | 0 | 149 | 190 | 112 | 96 | 38 | 65 |
| Bautista, Jose | 6.44 | 3 | 8 | 52 | 6 | 0 | 0 | 100⅔ | 120 | 77 | 72 | 26 | 45 |

## Baltimore Orioles

| BATTING | BA | G | AB | R | H | TB | 2B | 3B | HR | RBI | SB | BB | SO |
|---|---|---|---|---|---|---|---|---|---|---|---|---|---|
| Bonilla, Bobby | .333 | 61 | 237 | 47 | 79 | 129 | 12 | 4 | 10 | 46 | 0 | 23 | 31 |
| Palmeiro, Rafael | .310 | 143 | 554 | 89 | 172 | 323 | 30 | 2 | 39 | 104 | 3 | 62 | 65 |
| Baines, Harold | .299 | 127 | 385 | 60 | 115 | 208 | 19 | 1 | 24 | 63 | 0 | 70 | 45 |
| Goodwin, Curtis | .293 | 87 | 289 | 40 | 76 | 96 | 11 | 3 | 1 | 24 | 22 | 15 | 53 |
| Ripken, Cal, Jr. | .262 | 144 | 550 | 71 | 144 | 232 | 33 | 2 | 17 | 88 | 0 | 52 | 59 |
| Anderson, Brady | .262 | 143 | 554 | 108 | 145 | 246 | 33 | 10 | 16 | 64 | 26 | 87 | 111 |
| Zaun, Greg | .260 | 40 | 104 | 18 | 27 | 41 | 5 | 0 | 3 | 14 | 1 | 16 | 14 |
| Manto, Jeff | .256 | 89 | 254 | 31 | 65 | 125 | 9 | 0 | 17 | 38 | 0 | 24 | 69 |
| Hoiles, Chris | .250 | 114 | 352 | 53 | 88 | 162 | 15 | 1 | 19 | 58 | 1 | 67 | 80 |
| Huson, Jeff | .248 | 66 | 161 | 24 | 40 | 51 | 4 | 2 | 1 | 19 | 5 | 15 | 20 |
| Bass, Kevin | .244 | 111 | 295 | 32 | 72 | 99 | 12 | 0 | 5 | 32 | 8 | 24 | 47 |
| Hammonds, Jeffrey | .242 | 57 | 178 | 18 | 43 | 66 | 9 | 1 | 4 | 23 | 4 | 9 | 30 |
| Barberie, Bret | .241 | 90 | 237 | 32 | 57 | 77 | 14 | 0 | 2 | 25 | 3 | 36 | 50 |
| Gomez, Leo | .236 | 53 | 127 | 16 | 30 | 47 | 5 | 0 | 4 | 12 | 0 | 18 | 23 |
| Alexander, Manny | .236 | 94 | 242 | 35 | 57 | 77 | 9 | 1 | 3 | 23 | 11 | 20 | 3 |
| Smith, Mark | .231 | 37 | 104 | 11 | 24 | 38 | 5 | 0 | 3 | 15 | 3 | 12 | 22 |

| PITCHING | ERA | W | L | G | GS | CG | SV | INN | H | R | ER | BB | SO |
|---|---|---|---|---|---|---|---|---|---|---|---|---|---|
| Haynes, Jimmy | 2.25 | 2 | 1 | 4 | 3 | 0 | 0 | 24 | 11 | 6 | 6 | 12 | 22 |
| Orosco, Jesse | 3.26 | 2 | 4 | 65 | 0 | 0 | 3 | 49⅔ | 28 | 19 | 18 | 27 | 58 |
| Mussina, Mike | 3.29 | 19 | 9 | 32 | 32 | 7 | 0 | 221⅓ | 187 | 86 | 81 | 50 | 158 |
| Clark, Terry | 3.46 | 2 | 5 | 38 | 0 | 0 | 1 | 39 | 40 | 15 | 15 | 15 | 18 |
| Brown, Kevin | 3.60 | 10 | 9 | 26 | 26 | 3 | 0 | 172⅓ | 155 | 73 | 69 | 48 | 117 |
| McDonald, Ben | 4.16 | 3 | 6 | 14 | 13 | 1 | 0 | 80 | 67 | 40 | 37 | 38 | 62 |
| Oquist, Mike | 4.17 | 2 | 1 | 27 | 0 | 0 | 0 | 54 | 51 | 27 | 25 | 41 | 27 |
| Krivda, Rick | 4.54 | 2 | 7 | 13 | 13 | 1 | 0 | 75⅓ | 76 | 40 | 38 | 25 | 53 |
| Erickson, Scott | 4.81 | 13 | 10 | 32 | 31 | 7 | 0 | 196⅓ | 213 | 108 | 105 | 67 | 106 |
| Jones, Doug | 5.01 | 0 | 4 | 52 | 0 | 0 | 22 | 46⅔ | 55 | 30 | 26 | 16 | 42 |
| Moyer, Jamie | 5.21 | 8 | 6 | 27 | 18 | 0 | 0 | 115⅔ | 117 | 70 | 67 | 30 | 65 |
| Rhodes, Arthur | 6.21 | 2 | 5 | 19 | 9 | 0 | 0 | 75⅓ | 68 | 53 | 52 | 48 | 77 |

## Boston Red Sox

| BATTING | BA | G | AB | R | H | TB | 2B | 3B | HR | RBI | SB | BB | SO |
|---|---|---|---|---|---|---|---|---|---|---|---|---|---|
| O'Leary, Troy | .308 | 112 | 399 | 60 | 123 | 196 | 31 | 6 | 10 | 49 | 5 | 29 | 64 |
| Naehring, Tim | .307 | 126 | 433 | 61 | 133 | 194 | 27 | 2 | 10 | 57 | 0 | 77 | 66 |
| Canseco, Jose | .306 | 102 | 396 | 64 | 121 | 220 | 25 | 1 | 24 | 81 | 4 | 42 | 93 |
| Vaughn, Mo | .300 | 140 | 550 | 98 | 165 | 316 | 28 | 3 | 39 | 126 | 11 | 68 | 150 |
| Valentin, John | .298 | 135 | 520 | 108 | 155 | 277 | 37 | 2 | 27 | 102 | 20 | 81 | 67 |
| Greenwell, Mike | .297 | 120 | 481 | 67 | 143 | 221 | 25 | 4 | 15 | 76 | 9 | 38 | 35 |
| Jefferson, Reggie | .289 | 46 | 121 | 21 | 35 | 58 | 8 | 0 | 5 | 26 | 0 | 9 | 24 |
| McGee, Willie | .285 | 67 | 200 | 32 | 57 | 80 | 11 | 3 | 2 | 15 | 5 | 9 | 41 |
| Tinsley, Lee | .284 | 100 | 341 | 61 | 97 | 137 | 17 | 1 | 7 | 41 | 18 | 39 | 74 |
| Alicea, Luis | .270 | 132 | 419 | 64 | 113 | 157 | 20 | 3 | 6 | 44 | 13 | 63 | 61 |
| James, Chris | .268 | 42 | 82 | 0 | 22 | 32 | 4 | 0 | 2 | 8 | 1 | 7 | 14 |
| Stairs, Matt | .261 | 39 | 88 | 8 | 23 | 35 | 7 | 1 | 1 | 17 | 0 | 4 | 14 |
| Donnels, Chris | .253 | 40 | 91 | 13 | 23 | 35 | 2 | 2 | 2 | 11 | 0 | 9 | 18 |
| Haselman, Bill | .243 | 64 | 152 | 22 | 37 | 60 | 6 | 1 | 5 | 23 | 0 | 17 | 30 |
| MacFarlane, Mike | .225 | 115 | 164 | 45 | 82 | 147 | 18 | 1 | 15 | 51 | 2 | 38 | 78 |
| Whiten, Mark | .185 | 32 | 108 | 13 | 20 | 26 | 3 | 0 | 1 | 10 | 1 | 8 | 23 |

| PITCHING | ERA | W | L | G | GS | CG | SV | INN | H | R | ER | BB | SO |
|---|---|---|---|---|---|---|---|---|---|---|---|---|---|
| Aguilera, Rick | 2.60 | 3 | 3 | 52 | 0 | 0 | 32 | 55⅓ | 46 | 16 | 16 | 13 | 52 |
| Wakefield, Tim | 2.95 | 16 | 8 | 27 | 27 | 6 | 0 | 195⅓ | 163 | 76 | 64 | 68 | 119 |
| Sele, Aaron | 3.06 | 3 | 1 | 6 | 6 | 0 | 0 | 32⅓ | 32 | 14 | 11 | 14 | 21 |
| Belinda, Stan | 3.10 | 8 | 1 | 63 | 0 | 0 | 10 | 69⅔ | 51 | 25 | 24 | 28 | 57 |
| Maddux, Mike | 3.61 | 4 | 1 | 36 | 4 | 0 | 1 | 89⅔ | 86 | 40 | 36 | 15 | 65 |
| Cormier, Rheal | 4.07 | 7 | 5 | 48 | 12 | 0 | 0 | 115 | 131 | 60 | 52 | 31 | 69 |
| Clemens, Roger | 4.18 | 10 | 5 | 23 | 3 | 0 | 0 | 140 | 141 | 70 | 65 | 60 | 132 |
| Hanson, Erik | 4.24 | 15 | 5 | 29 | 29 | 1 | 0 | 186⅔ | 187 | 94 | 88 | 59 | 139 |
| Eshelman, Vaughn | 4.85 | 6 | 3 | 23 | 14 | 0 | 0 | 81⅓ | 86 | 47 | 44 | 36 | 41 |
| Ryan, Ken | 4.96 | 0 | 4 | 28 | 0 | 0 | 7 | 32⅔ | 34 | 20 | 18 | 24 | 34 |
| Smith, Zane | 5.61 | 8 | 8 | 24 | 21 | 0 | 0 | 110⅔ | 114 | 78 | 69 | 23 | 47 |

# American League Team-by-Team Statistical Leaders *(Cont.)*

## California Angels

| BATTING | BA | G | AB | R | H | TB | 2B | 3B | HR | RBI | SB | BB | SO |
|---|---|---|---|---|---|---|---|---|---|---|---|---|---|
| Salmon, Tim | .330 | 143 | 537 | 111 | 177 | 319 | 34 | 3 | 34 | 105 | 5 | 91 | 111 |
| Anderson, Garret | .321 | 106 | 374 | 50 | 120 | 189 | 19 | 1 | 16 | 69 | 6 | 19 | 65 |
| Davis, Chili | .318 | 119 | 424 | 81 | 135 | 218 | 23 | 0 | 20 | 86 | 3 | 89 | 79 |
| DiSarcina, Gary | .307 | 99 | 362 | 61 | 111 | 166 | 28 | 6 | 5 | 41 | 7 | 20 | 25 |
| Edmonds, Jim | .290 | 141 | 558 | 120 | 162 | 299 | 30 | 4 | 33 | 107 | 1 | 51 | 130 |
| Snow, J.T. | .289 | 143 | 544 | 80 | 157 | 253 | 22 | 1 | 24 | 102 | 2 | 52 | 91 |
| Aldrete, Mike | .268 | 78 | 149 | 19 | 40 | 60 | 8 | 0 | 4 | 24 | 0 | 19 | 31 |
| Hudler, Rex | .265 | 84 | 223 | 30 | 59 | 93 | 16 | 0 | 6 | 27 | 12 | 10 | 48 |
| Phillips, Tony | .261 | 139 | 525 | 119 | 137 | 241 | 21 | 1 | 27 | 61 | 13 | 113 | 35 |
| Myers, Greg | .260 | 85 | 273 | 35 | 71 | 114 | 12 | 2 | 9 | 38 | 0 | 17 | 49 |
| Fabregas, Jorge | .247 | 73 | 227 | 24 | 56 | 69 | 10 | 0 | 1 | 22 | 0 | 17 | 28 |
| Lind, Jose | .236 | 44 | 140 | 9 | 33 | 38 | 5 | 0 | 0 | 7 | 0 | 6 | 12 |
| Owen, Spike | .229 | 82 | 218 | 17 | 50 | 68 | 9 | 3 | 1 | 28 | 3 | 18 | 22 |
| Easley, Damion | .216 | 114 | 357 | 35 | 77 | 107 | 14 | 2 | 4 | 35 | 5 | 32 | 47 |

| PITCHING | ERA | W | L | G | GS | CG | SV | INN | H | R | ER | BB | SO |
|---|---|---|---|---|---|---|---|---|---|---|---|---|---|
| Percival, Troy | 1.95 | 3 | 2 | 62 | 0 | 0 | 3 | 74 | 37 | 19 | 16 | 26 | 94 |
| Patterson, Bob | 3.04 | 5 | 2 | 62 | 0 | 0 | 0 | 53⅓ | 48 | 18 | 18 | 13 | 41 |
| Smith, Lee | 3.47 | 0 | 5 | 52 | 0 | 0 | 37 | 49⅓ | 42 | 19 | 19 | 25 | 43 |
| Abbott, Jim | 3.70 | 11 | 8 | 30 | 30 | 4 | 0 | 197 | 209 | 93 | 81 | 64 | 86 |
| James, Mike | 3.88 | 3 | 0 | 46 | 0 | 0 | 1 | 55⅔ | 49 | 27 | 24 | 26 | 36 |
| Finley, Chuck | 4.21 | 15 | 12 | 32 | 32 | 2 | 0 | 203 | 192 | 106 | 95 | 93 | 195 |
| Langston, Mark | 4.63 | 15 | 7 | 31 | 31 | 2 | 0 | 200⅓ | 212 | 109 | 103 | 64 | 142 |
| Butcher, Mike | 4.73 | 6 | 1 | 40 | 0 | 0 | 0 | 51⅓ | 49 | 28 | 27 | 31 | 29 |
| Harkey, Mike | 5.44 | 8 | 9 | 26 | 20 | 1 | 0 | 127⅓ | 155 | 78 | 77 | 47 | 56 |
| Boskie, Shawn | 5.64 | 7 | 7 | 20 | 20 | 1 | 0 | 111⅔ | 127 | 73 | 70 | 25 | 51 |
| Anderson, Brian | 5.87 | 6 | 8 | 18 | 17 | 1 | 0 | 99⅔ | 110 | 66 | 65 | 30 | 45 |
| Bielecki, Mike | 5.97 | 4 | 6 | 22 | 11 | 0 | 0 | 75⅓ | 80 | 56 | 50 | 31 | 45 |

## Chicago White Sox

| BATTING | BA | G | AB | R | H | TB | 2B | 3B | HR | RBI | SB | BB | SO |
|---|---|---|---|---|---|---|---|---|---|---|---|---|---|
| Thomas, Frank | .308 | 145 | 493 | 102 | 152 | 299 | 27 | 0 | 40 | 111 | 3 | 136 | 74 |
| Kruk, John | .308 | 45 | 159 | 13 | 49 | 62 | 7 | 0 | 2 | 23 | 0 | 26 | 33 |
| Martinez, Dave | .307 | 119 | 303 | 49 | 93 | 132 | 16 | 4 | 5 | 37 | 8 | 32 | 41 |
| Johnson, Lance | .306 | 142 | 607 | 98 | 186 | 258 | 18 | 12 | 10 | 57 | 40 | 32 | 31 |
| Devereaux, Mike | .306 | 92 | 333 | 48 | 102 | 155 | 21 | 1 | 10 | 55 | 6 | 25 | 51 |
| Mouton, Lyle | .302 | 58 | 179 | 23 | 54 | 85 | 16 | 0 | 5 | 27 | 1 | 19 | 46 |
| Ventura, Robin | .295 | 135 | 492 | 79 | 145 | 245 | 22 | 0 | 26 | 93 | 4 | 75 | 98 |
| Raines, Tim | .285 | 133 | 502 | 81 | 143 | 212 | 25 | 4 | 12 | 67 | 13 | 70 | 52 |
| Martin, Norberto | .269 | 72 | 160 | 17 | 43 | 64 | 7 | 4 | 2 | 17 | 5 | 3 | 25 |
| Grebeck, Craig | .260 | 53 | 154 | 19 | 40 | 55 | 12 | 0 | 1 | 18 | 0 | 21 | 23 |
| Durham, Ray | .257 | 125 | 471 | 68 | 121 | 181 | 27 | 6 | 7 | 51 | 18 | 31 | 83 |
| Sabo, Chris | .254 | 20 | 71 | 10 | 18 | 26 | 5 | 0 | 1 | 8 | 2 | 3 | 12 |
| Guillen, Ozzie | .248 | 122 | 415 | 50 | 103 | 132 | 20 | 3 | 1 | 41 | 6 | 13 | 25 |
| LaValliere, Mike | .245 | 46 | 98 | 7 | 24 | 33 | 6 | 0 | 1 | 19 | 0 | 9 | 15 |
| Karkovice, Ron | .217 | 113 | 323 | 44 | 70 | 125 | 14 | 1 | 13 | 51 | 2 | 39 | 84 |

| PITCHING | ERA | W | L | G | GS | CG | SV | INN | H | R | ER | BB | SO |
|---|---|---|---|---|---|---|---|---|---|---|---|---|---|
| Karchner, Matt | 1.69 | 4 | 2 | 31 | 0 | 0 | 0 | 32 | 33 | 8 | 6 | 12 | 24 |
| Fernandez, Alex | 3.80 | 12 | 8 | 30 | 30 | 5 | 0 | 203⅔ | 200 | 98 | 86 | 65 | 159 |
| Hernandez, Roberto | 3.92 | 3 | 7 | 60 | 0 | 0 | 32 | 59⅔ | 63 | 30 | 26 | 28 | 84 |
| Sirotka, Mike | 4.19 | 1 | 2 | 6 | 6 | 0 | 0 | 34⅓ | 39 | 16 | 16 | 17 | 19 |
| Righetti, Dave | 4.20 | 3 | 2 | 10 | 9 | 0 | 0 | 49⅓ | 65 | 24 | 23 | 18 | 29 |
| Alvarez, Wilson | 4.32 | 8 | 11 | 29 | 29 | 3 | 0 | 175 | 171 | 96 | 84 | 93 | 118 |
| McCaskill, Kirk | 4.89 | 6 | 4 | 55 | 1 | 0 | 2 | 81 | 97 | 50 | 44 | 33 | 50 |
| Keyser, Brian | 4.97 | 5 | 6 | 23 | 10 | 0 | 0 | 92⅓ | 114 | 53 | 51 | 27 | 48 |
| DeLeon, Jose | 5.19 | 5 | 3 | 38 | 0 | 0 | 0 | 67⅔ | 60 | 41 | 39 | 28 | 53 |
| Radinsky, Scott | 5.45 | 2 | 1 | 46 | 0 | 0 | 1 | 38 | 46 | 23 | 23 | 17 | 14 |
| Fortugno, Tim | 5.59 | 1 | 3 | 37 | 0 | 0 | 0 | 38⅔ | 30 | 24 | 24 | 19 | 24 |
| Bere, Jason | 7.19 | 8 | 15 | 27 | 27 | 1 | 0 | 137⅔ | 151 | 120 | 110 | 106 | 110 |

## Cleveland Indians

| BATTING | BA | G | AB | R | H | TB | 2B | 3B | HR | RBI | SB | BB | SO |
|---|---|---|---|---|---|---|---|---|---|---|---|---|---|
| Murray, Eddie | .323 | 113 | 436 | 68 | 141 | 225 | 21 | 0 | 21 | 82 | 5 | 39 | 65 |
| Belle, Albert | .317 | 143 | 546 | 121 | 173 | 377 | 52 | 1 | 50 | 126 | 5 | 73 | 80 |
| Perry, Herb | .315 | 52 | 162 | 23 | 51 | 75 | 13 | 1 | 3 | 23 | 1 | 13 | 28 |
| Baerga, Carlos | .314 | 135 | 557 | 87 | 175 | 252 | 28 | 2 | 15 | 90 | 11 | 35 | 31 |
| Thome, Jim | .314 | 137 | 452 | 92 | 142 | 252 | 29 | 3 | 25 | 73 | 4 | 97 | 113 |
| Lofton, Kenny | .310 | 118 | 481 | 93 | 149 | 218 | 22 | 13 | 7 | 53 | 54 | 40 | 49 |
| Ramirez, Manny | .308 | 137 | 484 | 85 | 149 | 270 | 26 | 1 | 31 | 107 | 6 | 75 | 112 |
| Alomar, Sandy, Jr. | .300 | 66 | 203 | 32 | 61 | 97 | 6 | 0 | 10 | 35 | 3 | 7 | 26 |
| Vizquel, Omar | .266 | 136 | 542 | 87 | 144 | 190 | 28 | 0 | 6 | 56 | 29 | 59 | 59 |
| Pena, Tony | .262 | 91 | 263 | 25 | 69 | 99 | 15 | 0 | 5 | 28 | 1 | 14 | 44 |
| Espinoza, Alvaro | .252 | 66 | 143 | 15 | 36 | 46 | 4 | 0 | 2 | 17 | 0 | 2 | 16 |
| Sorrento, Paul | .235 | 104 | 323 | 50 | 76 | 165 | 14 | 0 | 25 | 79 | 1 | 51 | 71 |
| Kirby, Wayne | .207 | 101 | 188 | 29 | 39 | 56 | 10 | 2 | 1 | 14 | 10 | 13 | 32 |
| Winfield, Dave | .191 | 46 | 115 | 11 | 22 | 33 | 5 | 0 | 2 | 4 | 1 | 14 | 26 |

| PITCHING | ERA | W | L | G | GS | CG | SV | INN | H | R | ER | BB | SO |
|---|---|---|---|---|---|---|---|---|---|---|---|---|---|
| Mesa, Jose | 1.13 | 3 | 0 | 62 | 0 | 0 | 46 | 64 | 49 | 9 | 8 | 17 | 58 |
| Tavarez, Julian | 2.44 | 10 | 2 | 57 | 0 | 0 | 0 | 85 | 76 | 36 | 23 | 21 | 68 |
| Plunk, Eric | 2.67 | 6 | 2 | 56 | 0 | 0 | 2 | 64 | 48 | 19 | 19 | 27 | 71 |
| Assenmacher, Paul | 2.82 | 6 | 2 | 47 | 0 | 0 | 0 | 38⅓ | 32 | 13 | 12 | 12 | 40 |
| Ogea, Chad | 3.05 | 8 | 3 | 20 | 14 | 1 | 0 | 106⅓ | 95 | 38 | 36 | 29 | 57 |
| Martinez, Dennis | 3.08 | 12 | 5 | 28 | 28 | 3 | 0 | 187 | 174 | 71 | 64 | 46 | 99 |
| Poole, Jim | 3.75 | 3 | 3 | 42 | 0 | 0 | 0 | 50⅓ | 40 | 22 | 21 | 17 | 41 |
| Hershiser, Orel | 3.87 | 16 | 6 | 26 | 26 | 1 | 0 | 167⅓ | 151 | 76 | 72 | 51 | 111 |
| Hill, Ken | 3.98 | 4 | 1 | 12 | 11 | 1 | 0 | 74⅔ | 77 | 36 | 33 | 32 | 48 |
| Nagy, Charles | 4.55 | 16 | 6 | 29 | 29 | 2 | 0 | 178 | 194 | 95 | 90 | 61 | 139 |
| Clark, Mark | 5.27 | 9 | 7 | 22 | 21 | 2 | 0 | 124⅔ | 143 | 77 | 73 | 42 | 68 |
| Black, Bud | 6.85 | 4 | 2 | 11 | 10 | 0 | 0 | 47⅓ | 63 | 42 | 36 | 16 | 34 |

## Detroit Tigers

| BATTING | BA | G | AB | R | H | TB | 2B | 3B | HR | RBI | SB | BB | SO |
|---|---|---|---|---|---|---|---|---|---|---|---|---|---|
| Whitaker, Lou | .293 | 84 | 249 | 36 | 73 | 129 | 14 | 0 | 14 | 44 | 4 | 31 | 41 |
| Fryman, Travis | .275 | 144 | 567 | 79 | 156 | 232 | 21 | 5 | 15 | 81 | 4 | 63 | 100 |
| Trammell, Alan | .269 | 74 | 223 | 28 | 60 | 78 | 12 | 0 | 2 | 23 | 3 | 27 | 19 |
| Curtis, Chad | .268 | 144 | 586 | 96 | 157 | 255 | 29 | 3 | 21 | 67 | 27 | 70 | 93 |
| Gibson, Kirk | .260 | 70 | 227 | 37 | 59 | 102 | 12 | 2 | 9 | 35 | 9 | 33 | 61 |
| Stubbs, Franklin | .250 | 62 | 116 | 13 | 29 | 46 | 11 | 0 | 2 | 19 | 0 | 19 | 27 |
| Flaherty, John | .243 | 112 | 354 | 39 | 86 | 143 | 22 | 1 | 11 | 40 | 0 | 18 | 47 |
| Fielder, Cecil | .243 | 136 | 494 | 70 | 120 | 233 | 18 | 1 | 31 | 82 | 0 | 75 | 116 |
| Clark, Tony | .238 | 27 | 101 | 10 | 24 | 40 | 5 | 1 | 3 | 11 | 0 | 8 | 30 |
| Fletcher, Scott | .231 | 67 | 182 | 19 | 42 | 57 | 10 | 1 | 1 | 17 | 1 | 19 | 27 |
| Tingley, Ron | .226 | 54 | 124 | 14 | 28 | 50 | 8 | 1 | 4 | 16 | 0 | 15 | 38 |
| Higginson, Bob | .224 | 131 | 410 | 61 | 92 | 161 | 17 | 5 | 14 | 43 | 6 | 62 | 107 |
| Gomez, Leo | .223 | 123 | 431 | 49 | 96 | 153 | 20 | 2 | 11 | 50 | 4 | 41 | 96 |
| Nevin, Phil | .219 | 29 | 96 | 9 | 21 | 32 | 3 | 1 | 2 | 12 | 0 | 11 | 27 |
| Cuyler, Milt | .205 | 41 | 88 | 15 | 18 | 27 | 1 | 4 | 0 | 5 | 2 | 8 | 16 |
| Bautista, Danny | .203 | 89 | 271 | 28 | 55 | 85 | 9 | 0 | 7 | 27 | 4 | 12 | 68 |

| PITCHING | ERA | W | L | G | GS | CG | SV | INN | H | R | ER | BB | SO |
|---|---|---|---|---|---|---|---|---|---|---|---|---|---|
| Henneman, Mike | 1.53 | 0 | 1 | 29 | 0 | 0 | 18 | 29⅓ | 24 | 5 | 5 | 9 | 24 |
| Wells, David | 3.04 | 10 | 3 | 18 | 18 | 3 | 0 | 130⅓ | 120 | 54 | 44 | 37 | 83 |
| Christopher, Mike | 3.82 | 4 | 0 | 36 | 0 | 0 | 1 | 61⅓ | 71 | 28 | 26 | 14 | 34 |
| Lira, Felipe | 4.31 | 9 | 13 | 37 | 22 | 0 | 1 | 146⅓ | 151 | 74 | 70 | 56 | 89 |
| Doherty, John | 5.10 | 5 | 9 | 48 | 2 | 0 | 6 | 113 | 130 | 66 | 64 | 37 | 46 |
| Bergman, Sean | 5.12 | 7 | 10 | 28 | 28 | 1 | 0 | 135⅓ | 169 | 95 | 77 | 67 | 86 |
| Bohanon, Brian | 5.54 | 1 | 1 | 52 | 10 | 0 | 1 | 105⅔ | 121 | 68 | 65 | 41 | 63 |
| Lima, Jose | 6.11 | 3 | 9 | 15 | 15 | 0 | 0 | 73⅔ | 85 | 52 | 50 | 18 | 37 |
| Boever, Joe | 6.39 | 5 | 7 | 60 | 0 | 0 | 3 | 98⅔ | 128 | 74 | 70 | 44 | 71 |
| Maxcy, Brian | 6.88 | 4 | 5 | 41 | 0 | 0 | 0 | 52⅓ | 61 | 48 | 40 | 31 | 20 |
| Nitkowski, C.J. | 7.09 | 1 | 4 | 11 | 11 | 0 | 0 | 39⅓ | 53 | 32 | 31 | 20 | 13 |
| Groom, Buddy | 7.52 | 1 | 3 | 23 | 4 | 0 | 1 | 40⅔ | 55 | 35 | 34 | 26 | 23 |
| Moore, Mike | 7.53 | 5 | 15 | 25 | 25 | 1 | 0 | 132⅔ | 179 | 118 | 111 | 68 | 64 |

## Kansas City Royals

| BATTING | BA | G | AB | R | H | TB | 2B | 3B | HR | RBI | SB | BB | SO |
|---|---|---|---|---|---|---|---|---|---|---|---|---|---|
| Lockhart, Keith | .321 | 94 | 274 | 41 | 88 | 131 | 19 | 3 | 6 | 33 | 8 | 14 | 21 |
| Joyner, Wally | .310 | 131 | 465 | 69 | 144 | 208 | 28 | 0 | 12 | 83 | 3 | 69 | 65 |
| Goodwin, Tom | .288 | 133 | 480 | 72 | 138 | 172 | 16 | 3 | 4 | 28 | 50 | 38 | 72 |
| Damon, Johnny | .282 | 47 | 188 | 32 | 53 | 83 | 11 | 5 | 3 | 23 | 7 | 12 | 22 |
| Samuel, Juan | .263 | 91 | 205 | 31 | 54 | 102 | 10 | 1 | 12 | 39 | 6 | 29 | 49 |
| Gaetti, Gary | .261 | 137 | 514 | 76 | 134 | 266 | 27 | 0 | 35 | 96 | 3 | 47 | 91 |
| Tucker, Mike | .260 | 62 | 177 | 23 | 46 | 68 | 10 | 0 | 4 | 17 | 2 | 18 | 51 |
| Gagne, Greg | .256 | 120 | 430 | 58 | 110 | 161 | 25 | 4 | 6 | 49 | 3 | 38 | 60 |
| Vitello, Joe | .254 | 53 | 130 | 13 | 33 | 58 | 4 | 0 | 7 | 21 | 0 | 8 | 25 |
| Mayne, Brent | .251 | 110 | 307 | 23 | 77 | 100 | 18 | 1 | 1 | 27 | 0 | 25 | 41 |
| Nunnally, Jon | .244 | 119 | 303 | 51 | 74 | 143 | 15 | 6 | 14 | 42 | 6 | 51 | 86 |
| Howard, David | .243 | 95 | 255 | 23 | 62 | 83 | 13 | 4 | 0 | 19 | 6 | 24 | 41 |
| Caceres, Edgar | .239 | 55 | 117 | 13 | 28 | 41 | 6 | 2 | 1 | 17 | 2 | 8 | 15 |
| Borders, Pat | .231 | 52 | 143 | 14 | 33 | 55 | 8 | 1 | 4 | 13 | 0 | 7 | 22 |

| PITCHING | ERA | W | L | G | GS | CG | SV | INN | H | R | ER | BB | SO |
|---|---|---|---|---|---|---|---|---|---|---|---|---|---|
| Montgomery, Jeff | 3.43 | 2 | 3 | 54 | 0 | 0 | 31 | 65⅔ | 60 | 27 | 25 | 25 | 49 |
| Haney, Chris | 3.56 | 3 | 4 | 16 | 13 | 1 | 0 | 81⅓ | 78 | 35 | 33 | 33 | 31 |
| Gubicza, Mark | 3.75 | 12 | 14 | 33 | 33 | 3 | 0 | 213⅓ | 222 | 97 | 89 | 62 | 81 |
| Appier, Kevin | 3.89 | 15 | 10 | 31 | 31 | 4 | 0 | 201½ | 163 | 90 | 87 | 80 | 185 |
| Olson, Gregg | 4.09 | 3 | 3 | 23 | 0 | 0 | 3 | 33 | 28 | 15 | 15 | 19 | 21 |
| Magnante, Mike | 4.23 | 1 | 1 | 28 | 0 | 0 | 0 | 44⅔ | 45 | 23 | 21 | 16 | 28 |
| Pichardo, Hipolito | 4.36 | 8 | 4 | 44 | 0 | 0 | 1 | 64 | 66 | 34 | 31 | 30 | 43 |
| Gordon, Tom | 4.43 | 12 | 12 | 31 | 31 | 2 | 0 | 189 | 204 | 110 | 93 | 89 | 119 |
| Meacham, Rusty | 4.98 | 4 | 3 | 49 | 0 | 0 | 2 | 59⅔ | 72 | 36 | 33 | 19 | 30 |
| Jacome, Jason | 5.36 | 4 | 6 | 15 | 14 | 1 | 0 | 84 | 101 | 52 | 50 | 21 | 39 |
| Brewer, Billy | 5.56 | 2 | 4 | 48 | 0 | 0 | 0 | 45½ | 54 | 28 | 28 | 20 | 31 |
| Fleming, Dave | 5.96 | 1 | 6 | 25 | 12 | 1 | 0 | 80 | 84 | 61 | 53 | 53 | 40 |

## Milwaukee Brewers

| BATTING | BA | G | AB | R | H | TB | 2B | 3B | HR | RBI | SB | BB | SO |
|---|---|---|---|---|---|---|---|---|---|---|---|---|---|
| Surhoff, B.J. | .320 | 117 | 415 | 72 | 133 | 204 | 26 | 3 | 13 | 73 | 7 | 37 | 43 |
| Jaha, John | .313 | 88 | 316 | 59 | 99 | 183 | 20 | 2 | 20 | 65 | 2 | 36 | 66 |
| Seitzer, Kevin | .311 | 132 | 492 | 56 | 153 | 207 | 33 | 3 | 5 | 69 | 2 | 64 | 57 |
| Nilsson, Dave | .278 | 81 | 263 | 41 | 73 | 123 | 12 | 1 | 12 | 53 | 2 | 24 | 41 |
| Cirillo, Jeff | .277 | 125 | 328 | 57 | 91 | 145 | 19 | 4 | 9 | 39 | 7 | 47 | 42 |
| Oliver, Joe | .273 | 97 | 337 | 43 | 92 | 148 | 20 | 0 | 12 | 51 | 2 | 27 | 66 |
| Hamilton, Darryl | .271 | 112 | 398 | 54 | 108 | 155 | 20 | 6 | 5 | 44 | 11 | 47 | 35 |
| Ward, Turner | .264 | 44 | 129 | 19 | 34 | 51 | 3 | 1 | 4 | 16 | 6 | 14 | 21 |
| Vina, Fernando | .257 | 113 | 288 | 46 | 74 | 104 | 7 | 7 | 3 | 29 | 6 | 22 | 28 |
| Mieske, Matt | .251 | 117 | 267 | 42 | 67 | 118 | 13 | 1 | 12 | 48 | 2 | 27 | 45 |
| Hulse, David | .251 | 119 | 339 | 46 | 85 | 117 | 11 | 6 | 3 | 47 | 15 | 18 | 60 |
| May, Derrick | .248 | 32 | 113 | 15 | 28 | 36 | 3 | 1 | 1 | 9 | 0 | 5 | 18 |
| Matheny, Mike | .247 | 80 | 166 | 13 | 41 | 52 | 9 | 1 | 0 | 21 | 2 | 12 | 28 |
| Vaughn, Greg | .224 | 108 | 392 | 67 | 88 | 160 | 19 | 1 | 17 | 59 | 10 | 55 | 89 |
| Valentin, Jose | .219 | 112 | 338 | 62 | 74 | 136 | 23 | 3 | 11 | 49 | 16 | 37 | 83 |
| Listach, Pat | .219 | 101 | 334 | 35 | 73 | 85 | 8 | 2 | 0 | 25 | 13 | 25 | 61 |

| PITCHING | ERA | W | L | G | GS | CG | SV | INN | H | R | ER | BB | SO |
|---|---|---|---|---|---|---|---|---|---|---|---|---|---|
| Reyes, Al | 2.43 | 1 | 1 | 27 | 0 | 0 | 1 | 33⅓ | 19 | 9 | 9 | 18 | 29 |
| Fetters, Mike | 3.38 | 0 | 3 | 40 | 0 | 0 | 22 | 34⅔ | 40 | 16 | 13 | 20 | 33 |
| Kiefer, Mark | 3.44 | 4 | 1 | 24 | 0 | 0 | 0 | 49⅔ | 37 | 20 | 19 | 27 | 41 |
| Karl, Scott | 4.14 | 6 | 7 | 25 | 18 | 1 | 0 | 124 | 141 | 65 | 57 | 50 | 59 |
| Lloyd, Graeme | 4.50 | 0 | 5 | 33 | 0 | 0 | 4 | 32 | 28 | 16 | 16 | 8 | 13 |
| Bones, Ricky | 4.63 | 10 | 12 | 32 | 31 | 3 | 0 | 200⅓ | 218 | 108 | 103 | 83 | 77 |
| Sparks, Steve | 4.63 | 9 | 11 | 33 | 27 | 3 | 0 | 202 | 210 | 111 | 104 | 86 | 96 |
| McAndrew, Jamie | 4.71 | 2 | 3 | 10 | 4 | 0 | 0 | 36⅓ | 37 | 21 | 19 | 12 | 19 |
| Givens, Brian | 4.95 | 5 | 7 | 19 | 19 | 0 | 0 | 107⅓ | 116 | 71 | 59 | 54 | 73 |
| Miranda, Angel | 5.23 | 4 | 5 | 30 | 10 | 0 | 1 | 74 | 83 | 47 | 43 | 49 | 45 |
| Wegman, Bill | 5.35 | 5 | 7 | 37 | 4 | 0 | 2 | 70⅔ | 89 | 45 | 42 | 21 | 50 |
| Rightnowar, Ron | 5.40 | 2 | 1 | 34 | 0 | 0 | 1 | 36⅔ | 35 | 23 | 22 | 18 | 22 |
| Roberson, Sid | 5.76 | 6 | 4 | 26 | 13 | 0 | 0 | 84⅓ | 102 | 55 | 54 | 37 | 40 |
| Ignasiak, Mike | 5.90 | 4 | 1 | 25 | 0 | 0 | 0 | 39⅔ | 51 | 27 | 26 | 23 | 26 |
| Scanlan, Bob | 6.59 | 4 | 7 | 17 | 14 | 0 | 0 | 83½ | 101 | 66 | 61 | 44 | 29 |

# American League Team-by-Team Statistical Leaders *(Cont.)*

## Minnesota Twins

| BATTING | BA | G | AB | R | H | TB | 2B | 3B | HR | RBI | SB | BB | SO |
|---|---|---|---|---|---|---|---|---|---|---|---|---|---|
| Cole, Alex | .342 | 28 | 79 | 10 | 27 | 37 | 3 | 2 | 1 | 14 | 1 | 8 | 15 |
| Clark, Jerald | .339 | 36 | 109 | 17 | 37 | 60 | 8 | 3 | 3 | 15 | 3 | 2 | 11 |
| Knoblauch, Chuck | .333 | 136 | 538 | 107 | 179 | 262 | 34 | 8 | 11 | 63 | 46 | 78 | 95 |
| Puckett, Kirby | .314 | 137 | 538 | 83 | 169 | 277 | 39 | 0 | 23 | 99 | 3 | 56 | 89 |
| Munoz, Pedro | .301 | 104 | 376 | 45 | 113 | 184 | 17 | 0 | 18 | 58 | 0 | 19 | 86 |
| Reboulet, Jeff | .292 | 87 | 216 | 39 | 63 | 86 | 11 | 0 | 4 | 23 | 1 | 27 | 34 |
| Merullo, Matt | .282 | 76 | 195 | 19 | 55 | 74 | 14 | 1 | 1 | 27 | 0 | 14 | 27 |
| Cordova, Marty | .277 | 137 | 512 | 81 | 142 | 249 | 27 | 4 | 24 | 84 | 20 | 52 | 111 |
| Meares, Pat | .269 | 116 | 390 | 57 | 105 | 168 | 19 | 4 | 12 | 49 | 10 | 15 | 68 |
| Stahoviak, Scott | .266 | 94 | 263 | 28 | 70 | 98 | 19 | 0 | 3 | 23 | 5 | 30 | 61 |
| Hale, Chip | .262 | 69 | 103 | 10 | 27 | 37 | 4 | 0 | 2 | 18 | 0 | 11 | 20 |
| Coomer, Ron | .257 | 37 | 101 | 15 | 26 | 46 | 3 | 1 | 5 | 19 | 0 | 9 | 11 |
| Walbeck, Matt | .257 | 115 | 393 | 40 | 101 | 124 | 18 | 1 | 1 | 44 | 3 | 25 | 71 |
| Leius, Scott | .247 | 117 | 372 | 51 | 92 | 130 | 16 | 5 | 4 | 45 | 2 | 49 | 54 |
| Masteller, Dan | .237 | 71 | 198 | 21 | 47 | 68 | 12 | 0 | 3 | 21 | 1 | 18 | 19 |
| Becker, Rich | .237 | 106 | 392 | 45 | 93 | 116 | 15 | 1 | 2 | 33 | 8 | 34 | 95 |

| PITCHING | ERA | W | L | G | GS | CG | SV | INN | H | R | ER | BB | SO |
|---|---|---|---|---|---|---|---|---|---|---|---|---|---|
| Robertson, Rich | 3.83 | 2 | 0 | 25 | 4 | 1 | 0 | 51⅔ | 48 | 28 | 22 | 31 | 38 |
| Guthrie, Mark | 4.46 | 5 | 3 | 36 | 0 | 0 | 0 | 42⅓ | 47 | 22 | 21 | 16 | 48 |
| Tapani, Kevin | 4.92 | 6 | 11 | 20 | 20 | 3 | 0 | 133⅔ | 155 | 79 | 73 | 34 | 88 |
| Stevens, Dave | 5.07 | 5 | 4 | 56 | 0 | 0 | 10 | 65⅔ | 74 | 40 | 37 | 32 | 47 |
| Guardado, Eddie | 5.12 | 4 | 9 | 51 | 5 | 0 | 2 | 91⅓ | 99 | 54 | 52 | 45 | 71 |
| Radke, Brad | 5.32 | 11 | 14 | 29 | 28 | 2 | 0 | 181 | 195 | 112 | 107 | 47 | 75 |
| Trombley, Mike | 5.62 | 4 | 8 | 20 | 18 | 0 | 0 | 97⅔ | 107 | 68 | 61 | 42 | 68 |
| Rodriguez, Frank | 6.13 | 5 | 8 | 25 | 18 | 0 | 0 | 105⅔ | 114 | 83 | 72 | 57 | 59 |
| Mahomes, Pat | 6.37 | 4 | 10 | 47 | 7 | 0 | 3 | 94⅔ | 100 | 74 | 67 | 47 | 67 |
| Klingenbeck, Scott | 7.12 | 2 | 4 | 24 | 9 | 0 | 0 | 79⅔ | 101 | 65 | 63 | 42 | 42 |
| Parra, Jose | 7.59 | 1 | 5 | 12 | 12 | 0 | 0 | 61⅔ | 83 | 59 | 52 | 22 | 29 |

## New York Yankees

| BATTING | BA | G | AB | R | H | TB | 2B | 3B | HR | RBI | SB | BB | SO |
|---|---|---|---|---|---|---|---|---|---|---|---|---|---|
| Boggs, Wade | .324 | 126 | 460 | 76 | 149 | 194 | 22 | 4 | 5 | 63 | 1 | 74 | 50 |
| Williams, Bernie | .307 | 144 | 563 | 93 | 173 | 274 | 29 | 9 | 18 | 82 | 8 | 75 | 98 |
| O'Neill, Paul | .300 | 127 | 460 | 82 | 138 | 242 | 30 | 4 | 22 | 96 | 1 | 71 | 76 |
| Mattingly, Don | .288 | 128 | 458 | 59 | 132 | 189 | 32 | 2 | 7 | 49 | 0 | 40 | 35 |
| James, Dion | .287 | 85 | 209 | 22 | 60 | 74 | 6 | 1 | 2 | 26 | 4 | 20 | 16 |
| Velarde, Randy | .278 | 111 | 367 | 60 | 102 | 144 | 19 | 1 | 7 | 46 | 5 | 55 | 64 |
| Strawberry, Darryl | .276 | 32 | 87 | 15 | 24 | 39 | 4 | 1 | 3 | 13 | 0 | 10 | 22 |
| Davis, Russ | .276 | 40 | 98 | 14 | 27 | 42 | 5 | 2 | 2 | 12 | 0 | 10 | 26 |
| Leyritz, Jim | .269 | 77 | 264 | 37 | 71 | 104 | 12 | 0 | 7 | 37 | 1 | 37 | 73 |
| Stanley, Mike | .268 | 118 | 399 | 63 | 107 | 192 | 29 | 1 | 18 | 83 | 1 | 57 | 106 |
| Sierra, Ruben | .263 | 126 | 479 | 73 | 126 | 215 | 32 | 0 | 19 | 86 | 5 | 46 | 76 |
| Polonia, Luis | .261 | 67 | 238 | 37 | 62 | 83 | 9 | 3 | 2 | 15 | 10 | 25 | 29 |
| Williams, Gerald | .247 | 100 | 182 | 33 | 45 | 85 | 18 | 2 | 6 | 28 | 4 | 22 | 34 |
| Fernandez, Tony | .245 | 108 | 384 | 57 | 94 | 133 | 20 | 2 | 5 | 45 | 6 | 42 | 40 |
| Kelly, Pat | .237 | 89 | 270 | 32 | 64 | 90 | 12 | 1 | 4 | 29 | 8 | 23 | 65 |

| PITCHING | ERA | W | L | G | GS | CG | SV | INN | H | R | ER | BB | SO |
|---|---|---|---|---|---|---|---|---|---|---|---|---|---|
| Wetteland, John | 2.93 | 1 | 5 | 60 | 0 | 0 | 31 | 61⅓ | 40 | 22 | 20 | 14 | 66 |
| Honeycutt, Rick | 2.96 | 5 | 1 | 52 | 0 | 0 | 2 | 45⅔ | 39 | 16 | 15 | 10 | 21 |
| Cone, David | 3.57 | 18 | 8 | 30 | 30 | 6 | 0 | 229⅓ | 195 | 95 | 91 | 88 | 191 |
| McDowell, Jack | 3.93 | 15 | 10 | 30 | 30 | 8 | 0 | 217⅔ | 211 | 106 | 95 | 78 | 157 |
| Kamieniecki, Scott | 4.01 | 7 | 6 | 17 | 16 | 1 | 0 | 89⅔ | 83 | 43 | 40 | 49 | 43 |
| Wickman, Bob | 4.05 | 2 | 4 | 63 | 1 | 0 | 1 | 80 | 77 | 38 | 36 | 33 | 51 |
| Pettitte, Andy | 4.17 | 12 | 9 | 31 | 26 | 3 | 0 | 175 | 183 | 86 | 81 | 63 | 114 |
| Hitchcock, Sterling | 4.70 | 11 | 10 | 27 | 27 | 4 | 0 | 168⅓ | 155 | 91 | 88 | 68 | 121 |
| MacDonald, Bob | 4.86 | 1 | 1 | 33 | 0 | 0 | 0 | 46⅓ | 50 | 25 | 25 | 22 | 41 |
| Howe, Steve | 4.96 | 6 | 3 | 56 | 0 | 0 | 2 | 49 | 66 | 29 | 27 | 17 | 28 |
| Rivera, Mariano | 5.51 | 5 | 3 | 19 | 10 | 0 | 0 | 67 | 71 | 43 | 41 | 30 | 51 |
| Perez, Melido | 5.58 | 5 | 5 | 13 | 12 | 1 | 0 | 69⅓ | 70 | 46 | 40 | 31 | 44 |
| Key, Jimmy | 5.64 | 1 | 2 | 5 | 5 | 0 | 0 | 30⅓ | 40 | 20 | 19 | 6 | 14 |
| Ausanio, Joe | 5.73 | 2 | 0 | 28 | 0 | 0 | 1 | 37⅔ | 42 | 24 | 24 | 23 | 36 |
| Bankhead, Scott | 6.00 | 1 | 1 | 20 | 1 | 0 | 0 | 39 | 44 | 26 | 26 | 16 | 20 |

## Oakland Athletics

| BATTING | BA | G | AB | R | H | TB | 2B | 3B | HR | RBI | SB | BB | SO |
|---|---|---|---|---|---|---|---|---|---|---|---|---|---|
| Henderson, Rickey | .300 | 112 | 407 | 67 | 122 | 182 | 31 | 1 | 9 | 54 | 32 | 72 | 66 |
| Williams, George | .291 | 29 | 79 | 13 | 23 | 39 | 5 | 1 | 3 | 14 | 0 | 11 | 21 |
| Berroa, Geronimo | .278 | 141 | 546 | 87 | 152 | 246 | 22 | 3 | 22 | 88 | 7 | 63 | 98 |
| Steinbach, Terry | .278 | 114 | 406 | 43 | 113 | 186 | 26 | 1 | 15 | 65 | 1 | 25 | 74 |
| Javier, Stan | .278 | 130 | 442 | 81 | 123 | 171 | 20 | 2 | 8 | 56 | 36 | 49 | 63 |
| McGwire, Mark | .274 | 104 | 317 | 75 | 87 | 217 | 13 | 0 | 39 | 90 | 1 | 88 | 77 |
| Bordick, Mike | .264 | 126 | 428 | 46 | 113 | 150 | 13 | 0 | 8 | 44 | 11 | 35 | 48 |
| Brosius, Scott | .263 | 123 | 388 | 69 | 102 | 176 | 19 | 2 | 17 | 46 | 4 | 41 | 67 |
| Giambi, Jason | .256 | 54 | 176 | 27 | 45 | 70 | 7 | 0 | 6 | 25 | 2 | 28 | 31 |
| Gates, Brent | .254 | 136 | 524 | 60 | 133 | 180 | 24 | 4 | 5 | 56 | 3 | 46 | 84 |
| Herrera, Jose | .243 | 33 | 70 | 9 | 17 | 22 | 1 | 2 | 0 | 2 | 1 | 6 | 11 |
| Tartabull, Danny | .236 | 83 | 280 | 34 | 66 | 106 | 16 | 0 | 8 | 35 | 0 | 43 | 82 |
| Gallego, Mike | .233 | 43 | 120 | 11 | 28 | 28 | 0 | 0 | 0 | 8 | 0 | 9 | 24 |
| Paquette, Craig | .226 | 105 | 283 | 42 | 64 | 118 | 13 | 1 | 13 | 49 | 5 | 12 | 88 |

| PITCHING | ERA | W | L | G | GS | CG | SV | INN | H | R | ER | BB | SO |
|---|---|---|---|---|---|---|---|---|---|---|---|---|---|
| Corsi, Jim | 2.20 | 2 | 4 | 38 | 0 | 0 | 0 | 45 | 31 | 14 | 11 | 26 | 26 |
| Ontiveros, Steve | 4.37 | 9 | 6 | 22 | 22 | 2 | 0 | 129⅔ | 144 | 75 | 63 | 38 | 77 |
| Stottlemyre, Todd | 4.55 | 14 | 7 | 31 | 31 | 2 | 0 | 209⅔ | 228 | 117 | 106 | 80 | 205 |
| Johns, Doug | 4.61 | 5 | 3 | 11 | 9 | 1 | 0 | 54⅔ | 44 | 32 | 28 | 26 | 25 |
| Eckersley, Dennis | 4.83 | 4 | 6 | 52 | 0 | 0 | 29 | 50⅓ | 53 | 29 | 27 | 11 | 40 |
| Van Poppel, Todd | 4.88 | 4 | 8 | 36 | 14 | 1 | 0 | 138½ | 125 | 77 | 75 | 56 | 122 |
| Prieto, Ariel | 4.97 | 2 | 6 | 14 | 9 | 1 | 0 | 58 | 57 | 35 | 32 | 32 | 37 |
| Reyes, Carlos | 5.09 | 4 | 6 | 40 | 1 | 0 | 0 | 69 | 71 | 43 | 39 | 28 | 48 |
| Wojciechowski, Steve | 5.18 | 2 | 3 | 14 | 7 | 0 | 0 | 48⅔ | 51 | 28 | 28 | 28 | 13 |
| Acre, Mark | 5.71 | 1 | 2 | 43 | 0 | 0 | 0 | 52 | 52 | 35 | 33 | 28 | 47 |
| Darling, Ron | 6.23 | 4 | 7 | 21 | 21 | 1 | 0 | 104 | 124 | 79 | 72 | 46 | 69 |
| Stewart, Dave | 6.89 | 3 | 7 | 16 | 16 | 0 | 0 | 81 | 101 | 65 | 62 | 39 | 58 |

## Seattle Mariners

| BATTING | BA | G | AB | R | H | TB | 2B | 3B | HR | RBI | SB | BB | SO |
|---|---|---|---|---|---|---|---|---|---|---|---|---|---|
| Martinez, Edgar | .356 | 145 | 511 | 121 | 182 | 321 | 52 | 0 | 29 | 113 | 4 | 116 | 87 |
| Cora, Joey | .297 | 120 | 427 | 64 | 127 | 159 | 19 | 2 | 3 | 39 | 18 | 37 | 31 |
| Martinez, Tino | .293 | 141 | 519 | 92 | 152 | 286 | 35 | 3 | 31 | 111 | 0 | 62 | 91 |
| Sojo, Luis | .289 | 102 | 339 | 50 | 98 | 141 | 18 | 2 | 7 | 39 | 4 | 23 | 19 |
| Coleman, Vince | .288 | 115 | 455 | 66 | 131 | 181 | 23 | 6 | 5 | 29 | 42 | 37 | 80 |
| Amaral, Rich | .282 | 90 | 238 | 45 | 67 | 91 | 14 | 2 | 2 | 19 | 21 | 21 | 33 |
| Wilson, Dan | .278 | 119 | 399 | 40 | 111 | 166 | 22 | 3 | 9 | 51 | 2 | 33 | 63 |
| Strange, Doug | .271 | 74 | 155 | 19 | 42 | 61 | 9 | 2 | 2 | 21 | 0 | 10 | 25 |
| Buhner, Jay | .262 | 126 | 470 | 86 | 123 | 266 | 23 | 0 | 40 | 121 | 0 | 60 | 120 |
| Newson, Warren | .261 | 84 | 157 | 34 | 41 | 62 | 2 | 2 | 5 | 15 | 2 | 39 | 45 |
| Griffey, Ken, Jr | .258 | 72 | 260 | 52 | 67 | 125 | 7 | 0 | 17 | 42 | 4 | 52 | 53 |
| Blowers, Mike | .257 | 134 | 439 | 59 | 113 | 208 | 24 | 1 | 23 | 96 | 2 | 53 | 128 |
| Diaz, Alex | .248 | 103 | 270 | 44 | 67 | 90 | 14 | 0 | 3 | 27 | 18 | 13 | 27 |
| Bragg, Darren | .234 | 52 | 145 | 20 | 34 | 50 | 5 | 1 | 3 | 12 | 9 | 18 | 37 |
| Rodriguez, Alex | .232 | 48 | 142 | 15 | 33 | 58 | 6 | 2 | 5 | 19 | 4 | 6 | 42 |
| Fermin, Felix | .195 | 73 | 200 | 21 | 39 | 45 | 6 | 0 | 0 | 15 | 2 | 6 | 6 |

| PITCHING | ERA | W | L | G | GS | CG | SV | INN | H | R | ER | BB | SO |
|---|---|---|---|---|---|---|---|---|---|---|---|---|---|
| Charlton, Norm | 1.51 | 2 | 1 | 30 | 0 | 0 | 14 | 47⅔ | 23 | 12 | 8 | 16 | 58 |
| Nelson, Jeff | 2.17 | 7 | 3 | 62 | 0 | 0 | 2 | 78⅔ | 58 | 21 | 19 | 27 | 96 |
| Johnson, Randy | 2.48 | 18 | 2 | 30 | 30 | 6 | 0 | 214⅓ | 159 | 65 | 59 | 65 | 294 |
| Risley, Bill | 3.13 | 2 | 1 | 45 | 0 | 0 | 1 | 60½ | 55 | 21 | 21 | 18 | 65 |
| Wolcott, Bob | 4.42 | 3 | 2 | 7 | 6 | 0 | 0 | 36⅔ | 43 | 18 | 18 | 14 | 19 |
| Ayala, Bobby | 4.44 | 6 | 5 | 63 | 0 | 0 | 19 | 71 | 73 | 42 | 35 | 30 | 77 |
| Belcher, Tim | 4.52 | 10 | 12 | 28 | 28 | 1 | 0 | 179½ | 188 | 101 | 90 | 88 | 96 |
| Bosio, Chris | 4.92 | 10 | 8 | 31 | 31 | 0 | 0 | 170 | 211 | 98 | 93 | 69 | 85 |
| Carmona, Rafael | 5.66 | 2 | 4 | 15 | 3 | 0 | 1 | 47⅔ | 55 | 31 | 30 | 34 | 28 |
| Wells, Bob | 5.75 | 4 | 3 | 30 | 4 | 0 | 0 | 76⅔ | 88 | 51 | 49 | 39 | 38 |
| Benes, Andy | 5.86 | 7 | 2 | 12 | 12 | 0 | 0 | 63 | 72 | 42 | 41 | 33 | 45 |
| Torres, Salomon | 6.00 | 3 | 8 | 16 | 13 | 1 | 0 | 72 | 87 | 53 | 48 | 42 | 45 |

## Texas Rangers

| BATTING | BA | G | AB | R | H | TB | 2B | 3B | HR | RBI | SB | BB | SO |
|---|---|---|---|---|---|---|---|---|---|---|---|---|---|
| Palmer, Dean | .336 | 36 | 119 | 30 | 40 | 73 | 6 | 0 | 9 | 24 | 1 | 21 | 21 |
| Rodriguez, Ivan | .303 | 130 | 492 | 56 | 149 | 221 | 32 | 2 | 12 | 67 | 0 | 16 | 48 |
| Clark, Will | .302 | 123 | 454 | 85 | 137 | 218 | 27 | 3 | 16 | 92 | 0 | 68 | 50 |
| Gonzalez, Juan | .295 | 90 | 352 | 57 | 104 | 209 | 20 | 2 | 27 | 82 | 0 | 17 | 66 |
| Nixon, Otis | .295 | 139 | 589 | 87 | 174 | 199 | 21 | 2 | 0 | 45 | 50 | 58 | 85 |
| Frye, Jeff | .278 | 90 | 313 | 38 | 87 | 118 | 15 | 2 | 4 | 29 | 3 | 24 | 45 |
| Greer, Rusty | .271 | 131 | 417 | 58 | 113 | 177 | 21 | 2 | 13 | 61 | 3 | 55 | 66 |
| Maldonado, Candy | .263 | 74 | 190 | 28 | 50 | 93 | 16 | 0 | 9 | 30 | 1 | 32 | 50 |
| McLemore, Mark | .261 | 129 | 467 | 73 | 122 | 167 | 20 | 5 | 5 | 41 | 21 | 59 | 71 |
| Valle, Dave | .240 | 36 | 75 | 7 | 18 | 21 | 3 | 0 | 0 | 5 | 1 | 6 | 18 |
| Tettleton, Mickey | .238 | 134 | 429 | 76 | 102 | 219 | 19 | 1 | 32 | 78 | 0 | 107 | 110 |
| Pagliarulo, Mike | .232 | 86 | 241 | 27 | 56 | 84 | 16 | 0 | 4 | 27 | 0 | 15 | 49 |
| Ortiz, Luis | .231 | 41 | 108 | 10 | 25 | 37 | 5 | 2 | 1 | 18 | 0 | 6 | 18 |
| Worthington, Craig | .221 | 26 | 68 | 4 | 15 | 25 | 4 | 0 | 2 | 6 | 0 | 7 | 8 |
| Gil, Benji | .219 | 130 | 415 | 36 | 91 | 144 | 20 | 3 | 9 | 46 | 2 | 26 | 147 |

| PITCHING | ERA | W | L | G | GS | CG | SV | INN | H | R | ER | BB | SO |
|---|---|---|---|---|---|---|---|---|---|---|---|---|---|
| Vosberg, Ed | 3.00 | 5 | 5 | 44 | 0 | 0 | 4 | 36 | 32 | 15 | 12 | 16 | 36 |
| Russell, Jeff | 3.03 | 1 | 0 | 37 | 0 | 0 | 20 | 32⅔ | 36 | 12 | 11 | 9 | 21 |
| Rogers, Kenny | 3.38 | 17 | 7 | 31 | 31 | 3 | 0 | 208 | 192 | 87 | 78 | 76 | 140 |
| McDowell, Roger | 4.02 | 7 | 4 | 64 | 0 | 0 | 4 | 85 | 86 | 39 | 38 | 34 | 49 |
| Whiteside, Matt | 4.08 | 5 | 4 | 40 | 0 | 0 | 3 | 53 | 48 | 24 | 24 | 19 | 46 |
| Oliver, Darren | 4.22 | 4 | 2 | 17 | 7 | 0 | 0 | 49 | 47 | 25 | 23 | 32 | 39 |
| Pavlik, Roger | 4.37 | 10 | 10 | 31 | 31 | 2 | 0 | 191⅓ | 174 | 96 | 93 | 90 | 149 |
| Cook, Dennis | 4.53 | 0 | 2 | 46 | 1 | 0 | 2 | 57⅔ | 63 | 32 | 29 | 26 | 53 |
| Witt, Bobby | 4.55 | 3 | 4 | 10 | 10 | 1 | 0 | 61⅔ | 81 | 35 | 31 | 21 | 46 |
| Tewksbury, Bob | 4.58 | 8 | 7 | 21 | 21 | 4 | 0 | 129⅔ | 169 | 75 | 66 | 20 | 53 |
| Gross, Kevin | 5.54 | 9 | 15 | 31 | 30 | 4 | 0 | 183⅔ | 200 | 124 | 113 | 89 | 106 |
| Burrows, Terry | 6.45 | 2 | 2 | 28 | 3 | 0 | 1 | 44⅔ | 60 | 37 | 32 | 19 | 22 |
| Darwin, Danny | 7.45 | 3 | 10 | 20 | 15 | 1 | 0 | 99 | 131 | 87 | 82 | 31 | 58 |

## Toronto Blue Jays

| BATTING | BA | G | AB | R | H | TB | 2B | 3B | HR | RBI | SB | BB | SO |
|---|---|---|---|---|---|---|---|---|---|---|---|---|---|
| Alomar, Roberto | .300 | 130 | 517 | 71 | 155 | 232 | 24 | 7 | 13 | 66 | 30 | 47 | 45 |
| Olerud, John | .291 | 135 | 492 | 72 | 143 | 199 | 32 | 0 | 8 | 54 | 0 | 84 | 54 |
| Green, Shawn | .288 | 121 | 379 | 52 | 109 | 193 | 31 | 4 | 15 | 54 | 1 | 20 | 68 |
| White, Devon | .283 | 101 | 427 | 61 | 121 | 184 | 23 | 5 | 10 | 53 | 11 | 29 | 97 |
| Molitor, Paul | .270 | 130 | 525 | 63 | 142 | 222 | 31 | 2 | 15 | 60 | 12 | 61 | 57 |
| Carter, Joe | .253 | 139 | 558 | 70 | 141 | 239 | 23 | 0 | 25 | 76 | 12 | 37 | 87 |
| Perez, Tomas | .245 | 41 | 98 | 12 | 24 | 32 | 3 | 1 | 1 | 8 | 10 | 7 | 18 |
| Sprague, Ed | .244 | 144 | 521 | 77 | 127 | 212 | 27 | 2 | 18 | 74 | 0 | 58 | 96 |
| Gonzalez, Alex | .243 | 111 | 367 | 51 | 89 | 146 | 19 | 4 | 10 | 42 | 4 | 44 | 114 |
| Martinez, Angel | .241 | 62 | 191 | 12 | 46 | 64 | 12 | 0 | 2 | 25 | 0 | 7 | 45 |
| Cedeno, Domingo | .236 | 51 | 161 | 18 | 38 | 58 | 6 | 1 | 4 | 14 | 0 | 10 | 35 |
| Huff, Mike | .232 | 61 | 138 | 14 | 32 | 46 | 9 | 1 | 1 | 9 | 1 | 22 | 21 |
| Knorr, Randy | .212 | 45 | 132 | 18 | 28 | 45 | 8 | 0 | 3 | 16 | 0 | 11 | 28 |
| Parrish, Lance | .202 | 70 | 178 | 15 | 36 | 57 | 9 | 0 | 4 | 22 | 0 | 15 | 52 |

| PITCHING | ERA | W | L | G | GS | CG | SV | INN | H | R | ER | BB | SO |
|---|---|---|---|---|---|---|---|---|---|---|---|---|---|
| Timlin, Mike | 2.14 | 4 | 3 | 31 | 0 | 0 | 5 | 42 | 38 | 13 | 10 | 17 | 36 |
| Crabtree, Tim | 3.09 | 0 | 2 | 31 | 0 | 0 | 0 | 32 | 30 | 16 | 11 | 13 | 21 |
| Castillo, Tony | 3.22 | 1 | 5 | 55 | 0 | 0 | 13 | 72⅓ | 64 | 27 | 26 | 24 | 38 |
| Leiter, Al | 3.64 | 11 | 11 | 28 | 28 | 2 | 0 | 183 | 162 | 80 | 74 | 108 | 153 |
| Williams, Woody | 3.69 | 1 | 2 | 23 | 3 | 0 | 0 | 53⅔ | 44 | 23 | 22 | 28 | 41 |
| Robinson, Ken | 3.69 | 1 | 2 | 21 | 0 | 0 | 0 | 39 | 25 | 21 | 16 | 22 | 31 |
| Menhart, Paul | 4.92 | 1 | 4 | 21 | 9 | 1 | 0 | 78⅔ | 72 | 49 | 43 | 47 | 50 |
| Hentgen, Pat | 5.11 | 10 | 14 | 30 | 30 | 2 | 0 | 200⅔ | 236 | 129 | 114 | 90 | 135 |
| Hurtado, Edwin | 5.45 | 5 | 2 | 14 | 10 | 1 | 0 | 77⅔ | 81 | 50 | 47 | 40 | 33 |
| Guzman, Juan | 6.32 | 4 | 14 | 24 | 24 | 3 | 0 | 135⅓ | 151 | 101 | 95 | 73 | 94 |
| Carrara, Giovanni | 7.21 | 2 | 4 | 12 | 7 | 1 | 0 | 48⅔ | 64 | 46 | 49 | 25 | 27 |
| Cox, Danny | 7.40 | 1 | 3 | 24 | 0 | 0 | 0 | 45 | 57 | 40 | 37 | 33 | 38 |

# FOR THE RECORD·Year by Year

## The World Series

### Results

| | |
|---|---|
| 1903 ...............Boston (A) 5, Pittsburgh (N) 3 | 1950 ...............New York (A) 4, Philadelphia (N) 0 |
| 1904 ...............No series | 1951 ...............New York (A) 4, New York (N) 2 |
| 1905 ...............New York (N) 4, Philadelphia (A) 1 | 1952 ...............New York (A) 4, Brooklyn (N) 3 |
| 1906 ...............Chicago (A) 4, Chicago (N) 2 | 1953 ...............New York (A) 4, Brooklyn (N) 2 |
| 1907 ...............Chicago (N) 4, Detroit (A) 0; 1 tie | 1954 ...............New York (N) 4, Cleveland (A) 0 |
| 1908 ...............Chicago (N) 4, Detroit (A) 1 | 1955 ...............Brooklyn (N) 4, New York (A) 3 |
| 1909 ...............Pittsburgh (N) 4, Detroit (A) 3 | 1956 ...............New York (A) 4, Brooklyn (N) 3 |
| 1910 ...............Philadelphia (A) 4, Chicago (N) 1 | 1957 ...............Milwaukee (N) 4, New York (A) 3 |
| 1911 ...............Philadelphia (A) 4, New York (N) 2 | 1958 ...............New York (A) 4, Milwaukee (N) 3 |
| 1912 ...............Boston (A) 4, New York (N) 3; 1 tie | 1959 ...............Los Angeles (N) 4, Chicago (A) 2 |
| 1913 ...............Philadelphia (A) 4, New York (N) 1 | 1960 ...............Pittsburgh (N) 4, New York (A) 3 |
| 1914 ...............Boston (N) 4, Philadelphia (A) 0 | 1961 ...............New York (A) 4, Cincinnati (N) 1 |
| 1915 ...............Boston (A) 4, Philadelphia (N) 1 | 1962 ...............New York (A) 4, San Francisco (N) 3 |
| 1916 ...............Boston (A) 4, Brooklyn (N) 1 | 1963 ...............Los Angeles (N) 4, New York (A) 0 |
| 1917 ...............Chicago (A) 4, New York (N) 2 | 1964 ...............St Louis (N) 4, New York (A) 3 |
| 1918 ...............Boston (A) 4, Chicago (N) 2 | 1965 ...............Los Angeles (N) 4, Minnesota (A) 3 |
| 1919 ...............Cincinnati (N) 5, Chicago (A) 3 | 1966 ...............Baltimore (A) 4, Los Angeles (N) 0 |
| 1920 ...............Cleveland (A) 5, Brooklyn (N) 2 | 1967 ...............St Louis (N) 4, Boston (A) 3 |
| 1921 ...............New York (N) 5, New York (A) 3 | 1968 ...............Detroit (A) 4, St Louis (N) 3 |
| 1922 ...............New York (N) 4, New York (A) 0; 1 tie | 1969 ...............New York (N) 4, Baltimore (A) 1 |
| 1923 ...............New York (A) 4, New York (N) 2 | 1970 ...............Baltimore (A) 4, Cincinnati (N) 1 |
| 1924 ...............Washington (A) 4, New York (N) 3 | 1971 ...............Pittsburgh (N) 4, Baltimore (A) 3 |
| 1925 ...............Pittsburgh (N) 4, Washington (A) 3 | 1972 ...............Oakland (A) 4, Cincinnati (N) 3 |
| 1926 ...............St Louis (N) 4, New York (A) 3 | 1973 ...............Oakland (A) 4, New York (N) 3 |
| 1927 ...............New York (A) 4, Pittsburgh (N) 0 | 1974 ...............Oakland (A) 4, Los Angeles (N) 1 |
| 1928 ...............New York (A) 4, St Louis (N) 0 | 1975 ...............Cincinnati (N) 4, Boston (A) 3 |
| 1929 ...............Philadelphia (A) 4, Chicago (N) 1 | 1976 ...............Cincinnati (N) 4, New York (A) 0 |
| 1930 ...............Philadelphia (A) 4, St Louis (N) 2 | 1977 ...............New York (A) 4, Los Angeles (N) 2 |
| 1931 ...............St Louis (N) 4, Philadelphia (A) 3 | 1978 ...............New York (A) 4, Los Angeles (N) 2 |
| 1932 ...............New York (A) 4, Chicago (N) 0 | 1979 ...............Pittsburgh (N) 4, Baltimore (A) 3 |
| 1933 ...............New York (N) 4, Washington (A) 1 | 1980 ...............Philadelphia (N) 4, Kansas City (A) 2 |
| 1934 ...............St Louis (N) 4, Detroit (A) 3 | 1981 ...............Los Angeles (N) 4, New York (A) 2 |
| 1935 ...............Detroit (A) 4, Chicago (N) 2 | 1982 ...............St Louis (N) 4, Milwaukee (A) 3 |
| 1936 ...............New York (A) 4, New York (N) 2 | 1983 ...............Baltimore (A) 4, Philadelphia (N) 1 |
| 1937 ...............New York (A) 4, New York (N) 1 | 1984 ...............Detroit (A) 4, San Diego (N) 1 |
| 1938 ...............New York (A) 4, Chicago (N) 0 | 1985 ...............Kansas City (A) 4, St Louis (N) 3 |
| 1939 ...............New York (A) 4, Cincinnati (N) 0 | 1986 ...............New York (N) 4, Boston (A) 3 |
| 1940 ...............Cincinnati (N) 4, Detroit (A) 3 | 1987 ...............Minnesota (A) 4, St Louis (N) 3 |
| 1941 ...............New York (A) 4, Brooklyn (N) 1 | 1988 ...............Los Angeles (N) 4, Oakland (A) 1 |
| 1942 ...............St Louis (N) 4, New York (A) 1 | 1989 ...............Oakland (A) 4, San Francisco (N) 0 |
| 1943 ...............New York (A) 4, St Louis (N) 1 | 1990 ...............Cincinnati (N) 4, Oakland (A) 0 |
| 1944 ...............St Louis (N) 4, St Louis (A) 2 | 1991 ...............Minnesota (A) 4, Atlanta (N) 3 |
| 1945 ...............Detroit (A) 4, Chicago (N) 3 | 1992 ...............Toronto (A) 4, Atlanta (N) 2 |
| 1946 ...............St Louis (N) 4, Boston (A) 3 | 1993 ...............Toronto (A) 4, Philadelphia (N) 2 |
| 1947 ...............New York (A) 4, Brooklyn (N) 3 | 1994 ...............Series canceled due to players' strike |
| 1948 ...............Cleveland (A) 4, Boston (N) 2 | 1995 ...............Atlanta (N) 4, Cleveland (A) 2 |
| 1949 ...............New York (A) 4, Brooklyn (N) 1 | |

### Reverse Jordan

Perhaps you've heard of the Chicago athlete, accustomed to competition at the highest level of his game, who left the Windy City to try his hand at another sport, one he hadn't played in years. No, we're not referring to that smooth-pated former Bull—we're talking about Cub relief pitcher Randy Myers. Tired of cooling his heels during the baseball strike, Myers decided to kick them up on the basketball court at Clark College, a juco in Vancouver, Wash. Myers, 32, played baseball at Clark in 1981 and '82 but never went out for hoops. He hadn't even played in high school. After enrolling in business courses this winter, Myers showed up for a few workouts and won the 12th spot on the roster. It's a long way from Wrigley Field, but in one respect the 6'1" Myers, who in February was averaging 1.3 points per game for the 14–7 Penguins, should have felt at home. "Randy tends to get in toward the end of the game, when we have things sewn up," says Clark athletic director Roger Daniels.
Yes, but does he get the save?

## Most Valuable Players

| | |
|---|---|
| 1955 | Johnny Podres, Bklyn |
| 1956 | Don Larsen, NY (A) |
| 1957 | Lew Burdette, Mil |
| 1958 | Bob Turley, NY (A) |
| 1959 | Larry Sherry, LA |
| 1960 | Bobby Richardson, NY (A) |
| 1961 | Whitey Ford, NY (A) |
| 1962 | Ralph Terry, NY (A) |
| 1963 | Sandy Koufax, LA |
| 1964 | Bob Gibson, StL |
| 1965 | Sandy Koufax, LA |
| 1966 | Frank Robinson, Balt |
| 1967 | Bob Gibson, StL |
| 1968 | Mickey Lolich, Det |
| 1969 | Donn Clendenon, NY (N) |
| 1970 | Brooks Robinson, Balt |
| 1971 | Roberto Clemente, Pitt |
| 1972 | Gene Tenace, Oak |
| 1973 | Reggie Jackson, Oak |
| 1974 | Rollie Fingers, Oak |
| 1975 | Pete Rose, Cin |
| 1976 | Johnny Bench, Cin |
| 1977 | Reggie Jackson, NY (A) |
| 1978 | Bucky Dent, NY (A) |
| 1979 | Willie Stargell, Pitt |
| 1980 | Mike Schmidt, Phil |
| 1981 | Ron Cey, LA |
| | Pedro Guerrero, LA |
| | Steve Yeager, LA |
| 1982 | Darrell Porter, StL |
| 1983 | Rick Dempsey, Balt |
| 1984 | Alan Trammell, Det |
| 1985 | Bret Saberhagen, KC |
| 1986 | Ray Knight, NY (N) |
| 1987 | Frank Viola, Minn |
| 1988 | Orel Hershiser, LA |
| 1989 | Dave Stewart, Oak |
| 1990 | Jose Rijo, Cin |
| 1991 | Jack Morris, Minn |
| 1992 | Pat Borders, Tor |
| 1993 | Paul Molitor, Tor |
| 1994 | Series canceled due to strike |
| 1995 | Tom Glavine, Atl |

## Career Batting Leaders (Minimum 50 at bats)

### GAMES

| | |
|---|---|
| Yogi Berra | 75 |
| Mickey Mantle | 65 |
| Elston Howard | 54 |
| Hank Bauer | 53 |
| Gil McDougald | 53 |
| Phil Rizzuto | 52 |
| Joe DiMaggio | 51 |
| Frankie Frisch | 50 |
| Pee Wee Reese | 44 |
| Roger Maris | 41 |
| Babe Ruth | 41 |

### AT BATS

| | |
|---|---|
| Yogi Berra | 259 |
| Mickey Mantle | 230 |
| Joe DiMaggio | 199 |
| Frankie Frisch | 197 |
| Gil McDougald | 190 |
| Hank Bauer | 188 |
| Phil Rizzuto | 183 |
| Elston Howard | 171 |
| Pee Wee Reese | 169 |
| Roger Maris | 152 |

### HITS

| | |
|---|---|
| Yogi Berra | 71 |
| Mickey Mantle | 59 |
| Frankie Frisch | 58 |
| Joe DiMaggio | 54 |
| Pee Wee Reese | 46 |
| Hank Bauer | 46 |
| Phil Rizzuto | 45 |
| Gil McDougald | 45 |
| Lou Gehrig | 43 |
| Eddie Collins | 42 |
| Babe Ruth | 42 |
| Elston Howard | 42 |

### BATTING AVERAGE

| | |
|---|---|
| Pepper Martin | .418 |
| Paul Molitor | .418 |
| Lou Brock | .391 |
| Thurman Munson | .373 |
| George Brett | .373 |
| Hank Aaron | .364 |
| Frank Baker | .363 |
| Roberto Clemente | .362 |
| Lou Gehrig | .361 |
| Reggie Jackson | .357 |

### HOME RUNS

| | |
|---|---|
| Mickey Mantle | 18 |
| Babe Ruth | 15 |
| Yogi Berra | 12 |
| Duke Snider | 11 |
| Reggie Jackson | 10 |
| Lou Gehrig | 10 |
| Frank Robinson | 8 |
| Bill Skowron | 8 |
| Joe DiMaggio | 8 |
| Goose Goslin | 7 |
| Hank Bauer | 7 |
| Gil McDougald | 7 |

### RUNS BATTED IN

| | |
|---|---|
| Mickey Mantle | 40 |
| Yogi Berra | 39 |
| Lou Gehrig | 35 |
| Babe Ruth | 33 |
| Joe DiMaggio | 30 |
| Bill Skowron | 29 |
| Duke Snider | 26 |
| Reggie Jackson | 24 |
| Bill Dickey | 24 |
| Hank Bauer | 24 |
| Gil McDougald | 24 |

### RUNS

| | |
|---|---|
| Mickey Mantle | 42 |
| Yogi Berra | 41 |
| Babe Ruth | 37 |
| Lou Gehrig | 30 |
| Joe DiMaggio | 27 |
| Roger Maris | 26 |
| Elston Howard | 25 |
| Gil McDougald | 23 |
| Jackie Robinson | 22 |
| Gene Woodling | 21 |
| Reggie Jackson | 21 |
| Duke Snider | 21 |
| Phil Rizzuto | 21 |
| Hank Bauer | 21 |

### STOLEN BASES

| | |
|---|---|
| Lou Brock | 14 |
| Eddie Collins | 14 |
| Frank Chance | 10 |
| Davey Lopes | 10 |
| Phil Rizzuto | 10 |
| Honus Wagner | 9 |
| Frankie Frisch | 9 |
| Johnny Evers | 8 |
| Pepper Martin | 7 |
| Joe Morgan | 7 |
| Rickey Henderson | 7 |

### TOTAL BASES

| | |
|---|---|
| Mickey Mantle | 123 |
| Yogi Berra | 117 |
| Babe Ruth | 96 |
| Lou Gehrig | 87 |
| Joe DiMaggio | 84 |
| Duke Snider | 79 |
| Hank Bauer | 75 |
| Reggie Jackson | 74 |
| Frankie Frisch | 74 |
| Gil McDougald | 72 |

## Career Batting Leaders *(Cont.)*

| SLUGGING AVERAGE | | STRIKEOUTS | |
|---|---|---|---|
| Reggie Jackson | .755 | Mickey Mantle | 54 |
| Paul Molitor | .636 | Elston Howard | 37 |
| Babe Ruth | .744 | Duke Snider | 33 |
| Lou Gehrig | .731 | Babe Ruth | 30 |
| Al Simmons | .658 | Gil McDougald | 29 |
| Lou Brock | .655 | Bill Skowron | 26 |
| Pepper Martin | .636 | Hank Bauer | 25 |
| Hank Greenberg | .624 | Reggie Jackson | 24 |
| Charlie Keller | .611 | Bob Meusel | 24 |
| Jimmie Foxx | .609 | Frank Robinson | 23 |
| Dave Henderson | .606 | George Kelly | 23 |
| | | Tony Kubek | 23 |
| | | Joe DiMaggio | 23 |

## Career Pitching Leaders (Minimum 25 innings pitched)

| GAMES | | LOSSES | | COMPLETE GAMES | |
|---|---|---|---|---|---|
| Whitey Ford | 22 | Whitey Ford | 8 | Christy Mathewson | 10 |
| Rollie Fingers | 16 | Eddie Plank | 5 | Chief Bender | 9 |
| Allie Reynolds | 15 | Schoolboy Rowe | 5 | Bob Gibson | 8 |
| Bob Turley | 15 | Joe Bush | 5 | Red Ruffing | 7 |
| Clay Carroll | 14 | Rube Marquard | 5 | Whitey Ford | 7 |
| Clem Labine | 13 | Christy Mathewson | 5 | George Mullin | 6 |
| Waite Hoyt | 12 | | | Eddie Plank | 6 |
| Catfish Hunter | 12 | **SAVES** | | Art Nehf | 6 |
| Art Nehf | 12 | | | Waite Hoyt | 6 |
| Paul Derringer | 11 | Rollie Fingers | 6 | | |
| Carl Erskine | 11 | Allie Reynolds | 4 | **STRIKEOUTS** | |
| Rube Marquard | 11 | Johnny Murphy | 4 | | |
| Christy Mathewson | 11 | Roy Face | 3 | Whitey Ford | 94 |
| Vic Raschi | 11 | Herb Pennock | 3 | Bob Gibson | 92 |
| | | Kent Tekulve | 3 | Allie Reynolds | 62 |
| **INNINGS PITCHED** | | Firpo Marberry | 3 | Sandy Koufax | 61 |
| | | Will McEnaney | 3 | Red Ruffing | 61 |
| Whitey Ford | 146 | Todd Worrell | 3 | Chief Bender | 59 |
| Christy Mathewson | 101⅔ | Tug McGraw | 3 | George Earnshaw | 56 |
| Red Ruffing | 85⅔ | | | Waite Hoyt | 49 |
| Chief Bender | 85 | **EARNED RUN AVERAGE** | | Christy Mathewson | 48 |
| Waite Hoyt | 83⅔ | | | Bob Turley | 46 |
| Bob Gibson | 81 | Jack Billingham | .36 | | |
| Art Nehf | 79 | Harry Brecheen | .83 | **BASES ON BALLS** | |
| Allie Reynolds | 77 | Babe Ruth | .87 | | |
| Jim Palmer | 65 | Sherry Smith | .89 | Whitey Ford | 34 |
| Catfish Hunter | 63 | Sandy Koufax | .95 | Allie Reynolds | 32 |
| | | Hippo Vaughn | 1.00 | Art Nehf | 32 |
| **WINS** | | Monte Pearson | 1.01 | Jim Palmer | 31 |
| | | Christy Mathewson | 1.15 | Bob Turley | 29 |
| Whitey Ford | 10 | Babe Adams | 1.29 | Paul Derringer | 27 |
| Bob Gibson | 7 | Eddie Plank | 1.32 | Red Ruffing | 27 |
| Red Ruffing | 7 | | | Don Gullett | 26 |
| Allie Reynolds | 7 | **SHUTOUTS** | | Burleigh Grimes | 26 |
| Lefty Gomez | 6 | | | Vic Raschi | 25 |
| Chief Bender | 6 | Christy Mathewson | 4 | | |
| Waite Hoyt | 6 | Three Finger Brown | 3 | | |
| Jack Coombs | 5 | Whitey Ford | 3 | | |
| Three Finger Brown | 5 | Bill Hallahan | 2 | | |
| Herb Pennock | 5 | Lew Burdette | 2 | | |
| Christy Mathewson | 5 | Bill Dinneen | 2 | | |
| Vic Raschi | 5 | Sandy Koufax | 2 | | |
| Catfish Hunter | 5 | Allie Reynolds | 2 | | |
| | | Art Nehf | 2 | | |
| | | Bob Gibson | 2 | | |

# League Championship Series

## National League

1969 ............... New York (E) 3, Atlanta (W) 0
1970 ............... Cincinnati (W) 3, Pittsburgh (E) 0
1971 ............... Pittsburgh (E) 3, San Francisco (W) 1
1972 ............... Cincinnati (W) 3, Pittsburgh (E) 2
1973 ............... New York (E) 3, Cincinnati (W) 2
1974 ............... Los Angeles (W) 3, Pittsburgh (E) 1
1975 ............... Cincinnati (W) 3, Pittsburgh (E) 0
1976 ............... Cincinnati (W) 3, Philadelphia (E) 0
1977 ............... Los Angeles (W) 3, Philadelphia (E) 1
1978 ............... Los Angeles (W) 3, Philadelphia (E) 1
1979 ............... Pittsburgh (E) 3, Cincinnati (W) 0
1980 ............... Philadelphia (E) 3, Houston (W) 2
1981 ............... Los Angeles (W) 3, Montreal (E) 2
1982 ............... St Louis (E) 3, Atlanta (W) 0
1983 ............... Philadelphia (E) 3, Los Angeles (W) 1
1984 ............... San Diego (W) 3, Chicago (E) 2
1985 ............... St Louis (E) 4, Los Angeles (W) 2
1986 ............... New York (E) 4, Houston (W) 2
1987 ............... St Louis (E) 4, San Francisco (W) 3
1988 ............... Los Angeles (W) 4, New York (E) 3
1989 ............... San Francisco (W) 4, Chicago (E) 1
1990 ............... Cincinnati (W) 4, Pittsburgh (E) 2
1991 ............... Atlanta (W) 4, Pittsburgh (E) 3
1992 ............... Atlanta (W) 4, Pitsburgh (E) 3
1993 ............... Philadelphia (E) 4, Atlanta (W) 2
1994 ............... Playoffs canceled due to players' strike
1995 ............... Atlanta (E) 4, Cincinnati (C) 0

## American League

1969 ............... Baltimore (E) 3, Minnesota (W) 0
1970 ............... Baltimore (E) 3, Minnesota (W) 0
1971 ............... Baltimore (E) 3, Oakland (W) 0
1972 ............... Oakland (W) 3, Detroit (E) 2
1973 ............... Oakland (W) 3, Baltimore (E) 2
1974 ............... Oakland (W) 3, Baltimore (E) 1
1975 ............... Boston (E) 3, Oakland (W) 0
1976 ............... New York (E) 3, Kansas City (W) 2
1977 ............... New York (E) 3, Kansas City (W) 2
1978 ............... New York (E) 3, Kansas City (W) 1
1979 ............... Baltimore (E) 3, California (W) I
1980 ............... Kansas City (W) 3, New York (E) 0
1981 ............... New York (E) 3, Oakland (W) 0
1982 ............... Milwaukee (E) 3, California (W) 2
1983 ............... Baltimore (E) 3, Chicago (W) 1
1984 ............... Detroit (E) 3, Kansas City (W) 0
1985 ............... Kansas City (W) 4, Toronto (E) 3
1986 ............... Boston (E) 4, California (W) 3
1987 ............... Minnesota (W) 4, Detroit (E) 1
1988 ............... Oakland (W) 4, Boston (E) 0
1989 ............... Oakland (W) 4, Toronto (E) 1
1990 ............... Oakland (W) 4, Boston (E) 0
1991 ............... Minnesota (W) 4, Toronto (E) 1
1992 ............... Toronto (E) 4, Oakland (W) 2
1993 ............... Toronto (E) 4, Chicago (W) 2
1994 ............... Playoffs canceled due to players' strike
1995 ............... Cleveland (C) 4, Seattle (W) 2

### NLCS Most Valuable Player

1977 ....... Dusty Baker, LA
1978 ....... Steve Garvey, LA
1979 ....... Willie Stargell, Pitt
1980 ....... Manny Trillo, Phil
1981 ....... Burt Hooton, LA
1982 ....... Darrell Porter, StL
1983 ....... Gary Matthews, Phil

1984 ....... Steve Garvey, SD
1985 ....... Ozzie Smith, StL
1986 ....... Mike Scott, Hou
1987 ....... Jeffrey Leonard, SF
1988 ....... Orel Hershiser, LA
1989 ....... Will Clark, SF

1990 ....... Randy Myers, Cin
            Rob Dibble, Cin
1991 ....... Steve Avery, Atl
1992 ....... John Smoltz, Atl
1993 ....... Curt Schilling, Phil
1994 ....... Playoffs canceled
1995 ....... Mike Devereaux, Atl

### ALCS Most Valuable Player

1980 ....... Frank White, KC
1981 ....... Graig Nettles, NY
1982 ....... Fred Lynn, Calif
1983 ....... Mike Boddicker, Balt
1984 ....... Kirk Gibson, Det
1985 ....... George Brett, KC

1986 ....... Marty Barrett, Bos
1987 ....... Gary Gaetti, Minn
1988 ....... Dennis Eckersley, Oak
1989 ....... Rickey Henderson, Oak
1990 ....... Dave Stewart, Oak
1991 ....... Kirby Puckett, Minn

1992 ....... Roberto Alomar, Tor
1993 ....... Dave Stewart, Tor
1994 ....... Playoffs canceled
1995 ....... Orel Hershiser, Clev

# The All Star Game

## Results

| Date | Winner | Score | Site |
|---|---|---|---|
| 7-6-33 | American | 4-2 | Comiskey Park, Chi |
| 7-10-34 | American | 9-7 | Polo Grounds, NY |
| 7-8-35 | American | 4-1 | Municipal Stadium, Clev |
| 7-7-36 | National | 4-3 | Braves Field, Bos |
| 7-7-37 | American | 8-3 | Griffith Stadium, Wash |
| 7-6-38 | National | 4-1 | Crosley Field, Cin |
| 7-11-39 | American | 3-1 | Yankee Stadium, NY |
| 7-10-40 | National | 4-0 | Sportsman's Park, StL |
| 7-8-41 | American | 7-5 | Briggs Stadium, Det |
| 7-6-42 | American | 3-1 | Polo Grounds, NY |
| 7-13-43 | American | 5-3 | Shibe Park, Phil |
| 7-11-44 | National | 7-1 | Forbes Field, Pitt |
| 1945 | No game due to wartime travel restrictions | | |
| 7-9-46 | American | 12-0 | Fenway Park, Bos |
| 7-8-47 | American | 2-1 | Wrigley Field, Chi |
| 7-13-48 | American | 5-2 | Sportsman's Park, StL |

## Results *(Cont.)*

| Date | Winner | Score | Site |
|------|--------|-------|------|
| 7-12-49 | American | 11-7 | Ebbets Field, Bklyn |
| 7-11-50 | National | 4-3 | Comiskey Park, Chi |
| 7-10-51 | National | 8-3 | Briggs Stadium, Det |
| 7-8-52 | National | 3-2 | Shibe Park, Phil |
| 7-14-53 | National | 5-1 | Crosley Field, Cin |
| 7-13-54 | American | 11-9 | Municipal Stadium, Clev |
| 7-12-55 | National | 6-5 | County Stadium, Mil |
| 7-10-56 | National | 7-3 | Griffith Stadium, Wash |
| 7-9-57 | American | 6-5 | Busch Stadium, StL |
| 7-8-58 | American | 4-3 | Memorial Stadium, Balt |
| 7-7-59 | National | 5-4 | Forbes Field, Pitt |
| 8-3-59 | American | 5-3 | Memorial Coliseum, LA |
| 7-11-60 | National | 5-3 | Municipal Stadium, KC |
| 7-13-60 | National | 6-0 | Yankee Stadium, NY |
| 7-11-61 | National | 5-4 | Candlestick Park, SF |
| 7-31-61 | Tie* | 1-1 | Fenway Park, Bos |
| 7-10-62 | National | 3-1 | D.C. Stadium, Wash |
| 7-30-62 | American | 9-4 | Wrigley Field, Chi |
| 7-9-63 | National | 5-3 | Municipal Stadium, Clev |
| 7-7-64 | National | 7-4 | Shea Stadium, NY |
| 7-13-65 | National | 6-5 | Metropolitan Stadium, Minn |
| 7-12-66 | National | 2-1 | Busch Stadium, StL |
| 7-11-67 | National | 2-1 | Anaheim Stadium, Anaheim |
| 7-9-68 | National | 1-0 | Astrodome, Hou |
| 7-23-69 | National | 9-3 | R.F.K. Memorial Stadium, Wash |
| 7-14-70 | National | 5-4 | Riverfront Stadium, Cin |
| 7-13-71 | American | 6-4 | Tiger Stadium, Det |
| 7-25-72 | National | 4-3 | Atlanta Stadium, Atl |
| 7-24-73 | National | 7-1 | Royals Stadium, KC |
| 7-23-74 | National | 7-2 | Three Rivers Stadium, Pitt |
| 7-15-75 | National | 6-3 | County Stadium, Mil |
| 7-13-76 | National | 7-1 | Veterans Stadium, Phil |
| 7-19-77 | National | 7-5 | Yankee Stadium, NY |
| 7-11-78 | National | 7-3 | Jack Murphy Stadium, SD |
| 7-17-79 | National | 7-6 | Kingdome, Sea |
| 7-8-80 | National | 4-2 | Dodger Stadium, LA |
| 8-9-81 | National | 5-4 | Municipal Stadium, Clev |
| 7-13-82 | National | 4-1 | Olympic Stadium, Mtl |
| 7-6-83 | American | 13-3 | Comiskey Park, Chi |
| 7-10-84 | National | 3-1 | Candlestick Park, SF |
| 7-16-85 | National | 6-1 | Metrodome, Minn |
| 7-15-86 | American | 3-2 | Astrodome, Hou |
| 7-14-87 | National | 2-0 | Oakland Coliseum, Oak |
| 7-12-88 | American | 2-1 | Riverfront Stadium, Cin |
| 7-11-89 | American | 5-3 | Anaheim Stadium, Anaheim |
| 7-10-90 | American | 2-0 | Wrigley Field, Chi |
| 7-9-91 | American | 4-2 | SkyDome, Toronto |
| 7-14-92 | American | 13-6 | Jack Murphy Stadium, SD |
| 7-13-93 | American | 9-3 | Camden Yards, Balt |
| 7-12-94 | National | 8-7 | Three Rivers Stadium, Pitt |
| 7-11-95 | National | 3-2 | The Ballpark in Arlington, TX |

*Game called because of rain after 9 innings.

## Most Valuable Players

|  |  |  |
|------|--------|--------|
| 1962 | Maury Wills, LA | NL |
| | Leon Wagner, LA | AL |
| 1963 | Willie Mays, SF | NL |
| 1964 | Johnny Callison, Phil | NL |
| 1965 | Juan Marichal, SF | NL |
| 1966 | Brooks Robinson, Balt | AL |
| 1967 | Tony Perez, Cin | NL |
| 1968 | Willie Mays, SF | NL |
| 1969 | Willie McCovey, SF | NL |
| 1970 | Carl Yastrzemski, Bos | AL |
| 1971 | Frank Robinson, Balt | AL |
| 1972 | Joe Morgan, Cin | NL |
| 1973 | Bobby Bonds, SF | NL |
| 1974 | Steve Garvey, LA | NL |
| 1975 | Bill Madlock, Chi | NL |
| | Jon Matlack, NY | NL |
| 1976 | George Foster, Cin | NL |
| 1977 | Don Sutton, LA | NL |
| 1978 | Steve Garvey, LA | NL |
| 1979 | Dave Parker, Pitt | NL |
| 1980 | Ken Griffey, Cin | NL |
| 1981 | Gary Carter, Mtl | NL |
| 1982 | Dave Concepcion, Cin | NL |
| 1983 | Fred Lynn, Calif | AL |
| 1984 | Gary Carter, Mtl | NL |
| 1985 | LaMarr Hoyt, SD | NL |

### Most Valuable Players (Cont.)

| | | | | | | |
|---|---|---|---|---|---|---|
| 1986 | Roger Clemens, Bos | AL | | 1991 | Cal Ripken Jr, Balt | AL |
| 1987 | Tim Raines, Mtl | NL | | 1992 | Ken Griffey Jr, Sea | AL |
| 1988 | Terry Steinbach, Oak | AL | | 1993 | Kirby Puckett, Minn | AL |
| 1989 | Bo Jackson, KC | AL | | 1994 | Fred McGriff, Atl | NL |
| 1990 | Julio Franco, Tex | AL | | 1995 | Jeff Conine, Fla | NL |

## The Regular Season

### Most Valuable Players

#### NATIONAL LEAGUE

| Year | Name and Team | Position | Noteworthy |
|---|---|---|---|
| 1911 | Wildfire Schulte, Chi | Outfield | 21 HR†, 121 RBI†, .300 |
| 1912 | *Larry Doyle, NY | Second base | 10 HR, 90 RBI, .330 |
| 1913 | Jake Daubert, Bklyn | First base | 52 RBI, .350† |
| 1914 | *Johnny Evers, Bos | Second base | F.A. .976†, .279 |
| 1915-23 | No selection | | |
| 1924 | Dazzy Vance, Bklyn | Pitcher | 28†-6, 2.16 ERA†, 262 K† |
| 1925 | Rogers Hornsby, StL | Second base, Manager | 39 HR†, 143 RBI†, .403† |
| 1926 | *Bob O'Farrell, StL | Catcher | 7 HR, 68 RBI, .293 |
| 1927 | *Paul Waner, Pitt | Outfield | 237 hits†, 131 RBI†, .380† |
| 1928 | *Jim Bottomley, StL | First base | 31 HR†, 136 RBI†, .325 |
| 1929 | *Rogers Hornsby, Chi | Second base | 39 HR, 149 RBI, 156 runs†, .380 |
| 1930 | No selection | | |
| 1931 | *Frankie Frisch, StL | Second base | 4 HR, 82 RBI, 28 SB†, .311 |
| 1932 | Chuck Klein, Phil | Outfield | 38 HR†, 137 RBI, 226 hits†, .348 |
| 1933 | *Carl Hubbell, NY | Pitcher | 23†-12, 1.66 ERA†, 10 SO† |
| 1934 | *Dizzy Dean, StL | Pitcher | 30†-7, 2.66 ERA, 195 K† |
| 1935 | *Gabby Hartnett, Chi | Catcher | 13 HR, 91 RBI, .344 |
| 1936 | *Carl Hubbell, NY | Pitcher | 26†-6, 2.31 ERA† |
| 1937 | Joe Medwick, StL | Outfield | 31 HR‡, 154 RBI†, 111 runs†, .374† |
| 1938 | Ernie Lombardi, Cin | Catcher | 19 HR, 95 RBI, .342† |
| 1939 | *Bucky Walters, Cin | Pitcher | 27†-11, 2.29 ERA†, 137 K‡ |
| 1940 | *Frank McCormick, Cin | First base | 19 HR, 127 RBI, 191 hits†, .309 |
| 1941 | *Dolph Camilli, Bklyn | First base | 34 HR†, 120 RBI†, .285 |
| 1942 | *Mort Cooper, StL | Pitcher | 22†-7, 1.78 ERA†, 10 SO† |
| 1943 | *Stan Musial, StL | Outfield | 13 HR, 81 RBI, 220 hits†, .357† |
| 1944 | *Marty Marion, StL | Shortstop | F.A. .972†, 63 RBI |
| 1945 | *Phil Cavarretta, Chi | First base | 6 HR, 97 RBI, .355† |
| 1946 | *Stan Musial, StL | First base, Outfield | 103 RBI, 124 runs†, 228 hits†, .365† |
| 1947 | Bob Elliott, Bos | Third base | 22 HR, 113 RBI, .317 |
| 1948 | Stan Musial, StL | Outfield | 39 HR, 131 RBI†, .376† |
| 1949 | *Jackie Robinson, Bklyn | Second base | 16 HR, 124 RBI, 37 SB†, .342† |
| 1950 | *Jim Konstanty, Phil | Pitcher | 16-7, 22 saves†, 2.66 ERA |
| 1951 | Roy Campanella, Bklyn | Catcher | 33 HR, 108 RBI, .325 |
| 1952 | Hank Sauer, Chi | Outfield | 37 HR‡, 121 RBI‡, .270 |
| 1953 | *Roy Campanella, Bklyn | Catcher | 41 HR, 142 RBI†, .312 |
| 1954 | *Willie Mays, NY | Outfield | 41 HR, 110 RBI, 13 3B†, .345† |
| 1955 | *Roy Campanella, Bklyn | Catcher | 32 HR, 107 RBI, .318 |
| 1956 | *Don Newcombe, Bklyn | Pitcher | 27†-7, 3.06 ERA |
| 1957 | *Hank Aaron, Mil | Outfield | 44 HR†, 132 RBI†, .322 |
| 1958 | Ernie Banks, Chi | Shortstop | 47 HR†, 129 RBI†, .313 |
| 1959 | Ernie Banks, Chi | Shortstop | 45 HR, 143 RBI†, .304 |
| 1960 | *Dick Groat, Pitt | Shortstop | 2 HR, 50 RBI, .325† |
| 1961 | *Frank Robinson, Cin | Outfield | 37 HR, 124 RBI, .323 |
| 1962 | Maury Wills, LA | Shortstop | 104 SB†, 208 hits, .299, GG |
| 1963 | *Sandy Koufax, LA | Pitcher | 25‡-5, 1.88 ERA†, 306 K† |
| 1964 | *Ken Boyer, StL | Third Base | 24 HR, 119 RBI†, .295 |
| 1965 | Willie Mays, SF | Outfield | 52 HR†, 112 RBI, .317, GG |
| 1966 | Roberto Clemente, Pitt | Outfield | 29 HR, 119 RBI, 202 hits, .317, GG |
| 1967 | *Orlando Cepeda, StL | First base | 25 HR, 111 RBI†, .325 |
| 1968 | *Bob Gibson, StL | Pitcher | 22-9, 1.12 ERA†, 268 K†, 13 SO†, GG |
| 1969 | Willie McCovey, SF | First base | 45 HR†, 126 RBI†, .320 |
| 1970 | *Johnny Bench, Cin | Catcher | 45 HR†, 148 RBI†, .293, GG |
| 1971 | Joe Torre, StL | Third base | 24 HR, 137 RBI†, .363† |

*Played for pennant or, after 1968, division winner. †Led league. ‡Tied for league lead.

## Most Valuable Players (Cont.)

### NATIONAL LEAGUE (Cont.)

| Year | Name and Team | Position | Noteworthy |
|---|---|---|---|
| 1972 | *Johnny Bench, Cin | Catcher | 40 HR†, 125 RBI†, .270, GG |
| 1973 | *Pete Rose, Cin | Outfield | 5 HR, 64 RBI, .338†, 230 hits† |
| 1974 | *Steve Garvey, LA | First base | 21 HR, 111 RBI, 200 hits, .312, GG |
| 1975 | *Joe Morgan, Cin | Second base | 17 HR, 94 RBI, 67 SB, .327, GG |
| 1976 | *Joe Morgan, Cin | Second base | 27 HR, 111 RBI, 60 SB, .320, GG |
| 1977 | George Foster, Cin | Outfield | 52 HR†, 149 RBI†, .320 |
| 1978 | Dave Parker, Pitt | Outfield | 30 HR, 117 RBI, .334†, GG |
| 1979 | Keith Hernandez, StL | First base | 11 HR, 105 RBI, 210 hits, .344†, GG |
|  | *Willie Stargell, Pitt | First base | 32 HR, 82 RBI, .281 |
| 1980 | *Mike Schmidt, Phil | Third base | 48 HR†, 121 RBI†, .286, GG |
| 1981 | Mike Schmidt, Phil | Third base | 31 HR†, 91 RBI†, 78 runs†, .316, GG |
| 1982 | *Dale Murphy, Atl | Outfield | 36 HR, 109 RBI‡, .281, GG |
| 1983 | Dale Murphy, Atl | Outfield | 36 HR, 121 RBI†, .302, GG |
| 1984 | *Ryne Sandberg, Chi | Second base | 19 HR, 84 RBI, 114 runs†, .314, GG |
| 1985 | *Willie McGee, StL | Outfield | 10 HR, 82 RBI, 18 3B†, .353†, GG |
| 1986 | Mike Schmidt, Phil | Third base | 37 HR†, 119 RBI†, .290, GG |
| 1987 | Andre Dawson, Chi | Outfield | 49 HR†, 137 RBI†, .287, GG |
| 1988 | *Kirk Gibson, LA | Outfield | 25 HR, 76 RBI, 106 runs, .290 |
| 1989 | *Kevin Mitchell, SF | Outfield | 47 HR†, 125 RBI†, .291 |
| 1990 | *Barry Bonds, Pitt | Outfield | 33 HR, 114 RBI, .301 |
| 1991 | *Terry Pendleton, Atl | Third base | 23 HR, 86 RBI, .319† |
| 1992 | Barry Bonds, SF | Outfield | 34 HR, 103 RBI, .311 |
| 1993 | Barry Bonds, SF | Outfield | 46 HR†, 123 RBI†, .336 |
| 1994 | Jeff Bagwell, Hou | First base | 39 HR, 116 RBI†, .368 |

### AMERICAN LEAGUE

| Year | Name and Team | Position | Noteworthy |
|---|---|---|---|
| 1911 | Ty Cobb, Det | Outfield | 8 HR, 144 RBI†, 24 3B†, .420† |
| 1912 | *Tris Speaker, Bos | Outfield | 10 HR‡, 98 RBI, 53 2B†, .383 |
| 1913 | Walter Johnson, Wash | Pitcher | 36†-7, 1.09 ERA†, 11 SO†, 243 K† |
| 1914 | *Eddie Collins, Phil | Second base | 2 HR, 85 RBI, 122 runs†, .344 |
| 1915-21 | No selection |  |  |
| 1922 | George Sisler, StL | First base | 8 HR, 105 RBI, 246 hits†, .420† |
| 1923 | *Babe Ruth, NY | Outfield | 41 HR†, 131 RBI†, .393 |
| 1924 | *Walter Johnson, Wash | Pitcher | 23†-7, 2.72 ERA†, 158 K† |
| 1925 | *Roger Peckinpaugh, Wash | Shortstop | 4 HR, 64 RBI, .294 |
| 1926 | George Burns, Clev | First base | 114 RBI, 216 hits†, 64 2B†, .358 |
| 1927 | *Lou Gehrig, NY | First base | 47 HR, 175 RBI†, 52 2B†, .373 |
| 1928 | Mickey Cochrane, Phil | Catcher | 10 HR, 57 RBI, .293 |
| 1929 | No selection |  |  |
| 1930 | No selection |  |  |
| 1931 | *Lefty Grove, Phil | Pitcher | 31†-4, 2.06 ERA†, 175 K† |
| 1932 | Jimmie Foxx, Phil | First base | 58 HR†, 169 RBI†, 151 runs†, .364 |
| 1933 | Jimmie Foxx, Phil | First base | 48 HR†, 163 RBI†, .356† |
| 1934 | *Mickey Cochrane, Det | Catcher | 2 HR, 76 RBI, .320 |
| 1935 | *Hank Greenberg, Det | First base | 36 HR‡, 170 RBI†, 203 hits, .328 |
| 1936 | *Lou Gehrig, NY | First base | 49 HR†, 152 RBI, 167 runs†, .354 |
| 1937 | Charlie Gehringer, Det | Second base | 14 HR, 96 RBI, 133 runs, .371† |
| 1938 | Jimmie Foxx, Bos | First base | 50 HR, 175 RBI†, .349† |
| 1939 | *Joe DiMaggio, NY | Outfield | 30 HR, 126 RBI, .381† |
| 1940 | *Hank Greenberg, Det | Outfield | 41 HR†, 150 RBI†, 50 2B†, .340 |
| 1941 | *Joe DiMaggio, NY | Outfield | 30 HR, 125 RBI†, .357 |
| 1942 | *Joe Gordon, NY | Second base | 18 HR, 103 RBI, .322 |
| 1943 | *Spud Chandler, NY | Pitcher | 20†-4, 1.64 ERA†, 5 SO‡ |
| 1944 | Hal Newhouser, Det | Pitcher | 29†-9, 2.22 ERA†, 187 K† |
| 1945 | *Hal Newhouser, Det | Pitcher | 25†-9, 1.81 ERA†, 8 SO†, 212 K† |
| 1946 | *Ted Williams, Bos | Outfield | 38 HR, 123 RBI, 142 runs†, .342 |
| 1947 | *Joe DiMaggio, NY | Outfield | 20 HR, 97 RBI, .315 |
| 1948 | *Lou Boudreau, Clev | Shortstop | 18 HR, 106 RBI, .355 |
| 1949 | Ted Williams, Bos | Outfield | 43 HR†, 159 RBI‡, 150 runs†, .343 |
| 1950 | *Phil Rizzuto, NY | Shortstop | 125 runs, 200 hits, .324 |
| 1951 | *Yogi Berra, NY | Catcher | 27 HR, 88 RBI, .294 |
| 1952 | Bobby Shantz, Phil | Pitcher | 24†-7, 2.48 ERA |

*Played for pennant or, after 1968, division winner. †Led league. ‡Tied for league lead.

## Most Valuable Players (Cont.)

### AMERICAN LEAGUE (Cont.)

| Year | Name and Team | Position | Noteworthy |
|------|---------------|----------|------------|
| 1953 | Al Rosen, Clev | Third base | 43 HR†, 145 RBI†, 115 runs†, .336 |
| 1954 | Yogi Berra, NY | Catcher | 22 HR, 125 RBI, .307 |
| 1955 | *Yogi Berra, NY | Catcher | 27 HR, 108 RBI, .272 |
| 1956 | *Mickey Mantle, NY | Outfield | 52 HR†, 130 RBI†, 132 runs†, .353† |
| 1957 | *Mickey Mantle, NY | Outfield | 34 HR, 94 RBI, 121 runs†, .365 |
| 1958 | Jackie Jensen, Bos | Outfield | 35 HR, 122 RBI†, .286 |
| 1959 | *Nellie Fox, Chi | Second base | 2 HR, 70 RBI, .306, GG |
| 1960 | *Roger Maris, NY | Outfield | 39 HR, 112 RBI†, .283, GG |
| 1961 | *Roger Maris, NY | Outfield | 61 HR†, 142 RBI†, .269 |
| 1962 | *Mickey Mantle, NY | Outfield | 30 HR, 89 RBI, .321, GG |
| 1963 | *Elston Howard, NY | Catcher | 28 HR, 85 RBI, .287, GG |
| 1964 | Brooks Robinson, Balt | Third base | 28 HR, 118 RBI†, .317, GG |
| 1965 | *Zoilo Versalles, Minn | Shortstop | 126 runs†, 45 2B‡, 12 3B‡, GG |
| 1966 | *Frank Robinson, Balt | Outfield | 49 HR†, 122 RBI†, 122 runs†, .316† |
| 1967 | *Carl Yastrzemski, Bos | Outfield | 44 HR‡, 121 RBI†, 112 runs†, .326†, GG |
| 1968 | *Denny McLain, Det | Pitcher | 31†-6, 1.96 ERA, 280 K |
| 1969 | *Harmon Killebrew, Minn | Third base, First base | 49 HR†, 140 RBI†, .276 |
| 1970 | *Boog Powell, Balt | First base | 35 HR, 114 RBI, .297 |
| 1971 | *Vida Blue, Oak | Pitcher | 24-8, 1.82 ERA†, 8 SO†, 301 K |
| 1972 | Dick Allen, Chi | First base | 37 HR†, 113 RBI†, .308 |
| 1973 | *Reggie Jackson, Oak | Outfield | 32 HR†, 117 RBI†, 99 runs†, .293 |
| 1974 | Jeff Burroughs, Tex | Outfield | 25 HR, 118 RBI†, .301 |
| 1975 | *Fred Lynn, Bos | Outfield | 21 HR, 105 RBI, 103 runs†, .331, GG |
| 1976 | *Thurman Munson, NY | Catcher | 17 HR, 105 RBI, .302 |
| 1977 | Rod Carew, Minn | First base | 100 RBI, 128 runs†, 239 hits†, .388† |
| 1978 | Jim Rice, Bos | Outfield, designated hitter | 46 HR†, 139 RBI†, 213 hits†, .315 |
| 1979 | *Don Baylor, Calif | Outfield, designated hitter | 36 HR, 139 RBI†, 120 runs†, .296 |
| 1980 | *George Brett, KC | Third base | 24 HR, 118 RBI, .390† |
| 1981 | *Rollie Fingers, Mil | Pitcher | 6-3, 28 saves†, 1.04 ERA |
| 1982 | *Robin Yount, Mil | Shortstop | 29 HR, 114 RBI, 210 hits†, .331, GG |
| 1983 | *Cal Ripken, Balt | Shortstop | 27 HR, 102 RBI, 121 runs†, 211 hits†, .318 |
| 1984 | *Willie Hernandez, Det | Pitcher | 9-3, 32 saves, 1.92 ERA |
| 1985 | Don Mattingly, NY | First base | 35 HR, 145 RBI†, 48 2B†, .324, GG |
| 1986 | *Roger Clemens, Bos | Pitcher | 24†-4, 2.48 ERA†, 238 K |
| 1987 | George Bell, Tor | Outfield | 47 HR, 134 RBI†, .308 |
| 1988 | *Jose Canseco, Oak | Outfield | 42 HR†, 124 RBI†, 40 SB, .307 |
| 1989 | Robin Yount, Mil | Outfield | 21 HR, 103 RBI, 101 runs, .318 |
| 1990 | *Rickey Henderson, Oak | Outfield | 28 HR, 119 runs†, 65 SB†, .325 |
| 1991 | Cal Ripken, Jr, Balt | Shortstop | 34 HR, 114 RBI, .323 |
| 1992 | Dennis Eckersley, Oak | Pitcher | 7-1, 1.91 ERA, 51 saves |
| 1993 | Frank Thomas, Chi | First base | 41 HR, 128 RBI, .317 |
| 1994 | Frank Thomas, Chi | First base | 38 HR, 101 RBI, .353 |

*Played for pennant or, after 1968, division winner. †Led league. ‡Tied for league lead.

Notes: 2B=doubles; 3B=triples; F.A.=fielding average; GG=won Gold Glove, award begun in 1957; K=strikeouts; SO=shutouts; SB=stolen bases.

## Rookies of the Year

| NATIONAL LEAGUE | | AMERICAN LEAGUE | |
|---|---|---|---|
| 1947* | Jackie Robinson, Bklyn (1B) | 1949 | Roy Sievers, StL (OF) |
| 1948* | Alvin Dark, Bos (SS) | 1950 | Walt Dropo, Bos (1B) |
| 1949 | Don Newcombe, Bklyn (P) | 1951 | Gil McDougald, NY (3B) |
| 1950 | Sam Jethroe, Bos (OF) | 1952 | Harry Byrd, Phil (P) |
| 1951 | Willie Mays, NY (OF) | 1953 | Harvey Kuenn, Det (SS) |
| 1952 | Joe Black, Bklyn (P) | 1954 | Bob Grim, NY (P) |
| 1953 | Junior Gilliam, Bklyn (2B) | 1955 | Herb Score, Clev (P) |
| 1954 | Wally Moon, StL (OF) | 1956 | Luis Aparicio, Chi (SS) |
| 1955 | Bill Virdon, StL (OF) | 1957 | Tony Kubek, NY (OF, SS) |
| 1956 | Frank Robinson, Cin (OF) | 1958 | Albie Pearson, Wash (OF) |
| 1957 | Jack Sanford, Phil (P) | 1959 | Bob Allison, Wash (OF) |
| 1958 | Orlando Cepeda, SF (1B) | 1960 | Ron Hansen, Balt (SS) |

*Just one selection for both leagues.

## Rookies of the Year *(Cont.)*

### NATIONAL LEAGUE *(Cont.)*

| | |
|---|---|
| 1959 | Willie McCovey, SF (1B) |
| 1960 | Frank Howard, LA (OF) |
| 1961 | Billy Williams, Chi (OF) |
| 1962 | Ken Hubbs, Chi (2B) |
| 1963 | Pete Rose, Cin (2B) |
| 1964 | Dick Allen, Phil (3B) |
| 1965 | Jim Lefebvre, LA (2B) |
| 1966 | Tommy Helms, Cin (2B) |
| 1967 | Tom Seaver, NY (P) |
| 1968 | Johnny Bench, Cin (C) |
| 1969 | Ted Sizemore, LA (2B) |
| 1970 | Carl Morton, Mont (P) |
| 1971 | Earl Williams, Atl (C) |
| 1972 | Jon Matlack, NY (P) |
| 1973 | Gary Matthews, SF (OF) |
| 1974 | Bake McBride, StL (OF) |
| 1975 | John Montefusco, SF (P) |
| 1976 | Pat Zachry, Cin (P) |
| | Butch Metzger, SD (P) |
| 1977 | Andre Dawson, Mont (OF) |
| 1978 | Bob Horner, Atl (3B) |
| 1979 | Rick Sutcliffe, LA (P) |
| 1980 | Steve Howe, LA (P) |
| 1981 | Fernando Valenzuela, LA (P) |
| 1982 | Steve Sax, LA (2B) |
| 1983 | Darryl Strawberry, NY (OF) |
| 1984 | Dwight Gooden, NY (P) |
| 1985 | Vince Coleman, StL (OF) |
| 1986 | Todd Worrell, StL (P) |
| 1987 | Benito Santiago, SD (C) |
| 1988 | Chris Sabo, Cin (3B) |
| 1989 | Jerome Walton, Chi (OF) |
| 1990 | Dave Justice, Atl (OF) |
| 1991 | Jeff Bagwell, Hou (3B) |
| 1992 | Eric Karros, LA (1B) |
| 1993 | Mike Piazza, LA (C) |
| 1994 | Raul Mondesi, LA (OF) |

### AMERICAN LEAGUE *(Cont.)*

| | |
|---|---|
| 1961 | Don Schwall, Bos (P) |
| 1962 | Tom Tresh, NY (SS) |
| 1963 | Gary Peters, Chi (P) |
| 1964 | Tony Oliva, Minn (OF) |
| 1965 | Curt Blefary, Balt (OF) |
| 1966 | Tommie Agee, Chi (OF) |
| 1967 | Rod Carew, Minn (2B) |
| 1968 | Stan Bahnsen, NY (P) |
| 1969 | Lou Piniella, KC (OF) |
| 1970 | Thurman Munson, NY (C) |
| 1971 | Chris Chambliss, Clev (1B) |
| 1972 | Carlton Fisk, Bos (C) |
| 1973 | Al Bumbry, Balt (OF) |
| 1974 | Mike Hargrove, Tex (1B) |
| 1975 | Fred Lynn, Bos (OF) |
| 1976 | Mark Fidrych, Det (P) |
| 1977 | Eddie Murray, Balt (DH) |
| 1978 | Lou Whitaker, Det (2B) |
| 1979 | Alfredo Griffin, Tor (SS) |
| | John Castino, Minn (3B) |
| 1980 | Joe Charboneau, Clev (OF) |
| 1981 | Dave Righetti, NY (P) |
| 1982 | Cal Ripken, Balt (SS) |
| 1983 | Ron Kittle, Chi (OF) |
| 1984 | Alvin Davis, Sea (1B) |
| 1985 | Ozzie Guillen, Chi (SS) |
| 1986 | Jose Canseco, Oak (OF) |
| 1987 | Mark McGwire, Oak (1B) |
| 1988 | Walt Weiss, Oak (SS) |
| 1989 | Gregg Olson, Balt (P) |
| 1990 | Sandy Alomar Jr, Clev (C) |
| 1991 | Chuck Knoblauch, Minn (2B) |
| 1992 | Pat Listach, Mil (SS) |
| 1993 | Tim Salmon, Calif (OF) |
| 1994 | Bob Hamelin, Minn (DH) |

## Cy Young Award

| Year | W-L | Sv | ERA | Year | W-L | Sv | ERA |
|---|---|---|---|---|---|---|---|
| 1956....*Don Newcombe, Bklyn (NL) | 27-7 | 0 | 3.06 | 1962....Don Drysdale, LA (NL) | 25-9 | 1 | 2.83 |
| 1957....Warren Spahn, Mil (NL) | 21-11 | 3 | 2.69 | 1963....*Sandy Koufax, LA (NL) | 25-5 | 0 | 1.88 |
| 1958....Bob Turley, NY (AL) | 21-7 | 1 | 2.97 | 1964....Dean Chance, LA (AL) | 20-9 | 4 | 1.65 |
| 1959....Early Wynn, Chi (AL) | 22-10 | 0 | 3.17 | 1965....Sandy Koufax, LA (NL) | 26-8 | 2 | 2.04 |
| 1960....Vernon Law, Pitt (NL) | 20-9 | 0 | 3.08 | 1966....Sandy Koufax, LA (NL) | 27-9 | 0 | 1.73 |
| 1961....Whitey Ford, NY (AL) | 25-4 | 0 | 3.21 | | | | |

### NATIONAL LEAGUE

| Year | W-L | Sv | ERA |
|---|---|---|---|
| 1967.....Mike McCormick, SF | 22-10 | 0 | 2.85 |
| 1968.....*Bob Gibson, StL | 22-9 | 0 | 1.12 |
| 1969.....Tom Seaver, NY | 25-7 | 0 | 2.21 |
| 1970.....Bob Gibson, StL | 23-7 | 0 | 3.12 |
| 1971.....Ferguson Jenkins, Chi | 24-13 | 0 | 2.77 |
| 1972.....Steve Carlton, Phil | 27-10 | 0 | 1.97 |
| 1973.....Tom Seaver, NY | 19-10 | 0 | 2.08 |
| 1974.....Mike Marshall, LA | 15-12 | 21 | 2.42 |
| 1975.....Tom Seaver, NY | 22-9 | 0 | 2.38 |
| 1976.....Randy Jones, SD | 22-14 | 0 | 2.74 |
| 1977.....Steve Carlton, Phil | 23-10 | 0 | 2.64 |
| 1978.....Gaylord Perry, SD | 21-6 | 0 | 2.72 |
| 1979.....Bruce Sutter, Chi | 6-6 | 37 | 2.23 |
| 1980.....Steve Carlton, Phil | 24-9 | 0 | 2.34 |

### AMERICAN LEAGUE

| Year | W-L | Sv | ERA |
|---|---|---|---|
| 1967.....Jim Lonborg, Bos | 22-9 | 0 | 3.16 |
| 1968.....*Denny McLain, Det | 31-6 | 0 | 1.96 |
| 1969.....Denny McLain, Det | 24-9 | 0 | 2.80 |
| | Mike Cuellar, Balt | 23-11 | 0 | 2.38 |
| 1970.....Jim Perry, Minn | 24-12 | 0 | 3.03 |
| 1971.....*Vida Blue, Oak | 24-8 | 0 | 1.82 |
| 1972.....Gaylord Perry, Clev | 24-16 | 1 | 1.92 |
| 1973.....Jim Palmer, Balt | 22-9 | 1 | 2.40 |
| 1974.....Catfish Hunter, Oak | 25-12 | 0 | 2.49 |
| 1975.....Jim Palmer, Balt | 23-11 | 1 | 2.09 |
| 1976.....Jim Palmer, Balt | 22-13 | 0 | 2.51 |
| 1977.....Sparky Lyle, NY | 13-5 | 26 | 2.17 |
| 1978.....Ron Guidry, NY | 25-3 | 0 | 1.74 |
| 1979.....Mike Flanagan, Balt | 23-9 | 0 | 3.08 |

## Cy Young Award (Cont.)

| NATIONAL LEAGUE | | | | AMERICAN LEAGUE | | | |
|---|---|---|---|---|---|---|---|
| Year | W-L | Sv | ERA | Year | W-L | Sv | ERA |
| 1981.....Fernando Valenzuela, LA | 13-7 | 0 | 2.48 | 1980.....Steve Stone, Balt | 25-7 | 0 | 3.23 |
| 1982.....Steve Carlton, Phil | 23-11 | 0 | 3.10 | 1981.....*Rollie Fingers, Mil | 6-3 | 28 | 1.04 |
| 1983.....John Denny, Phil | 19-6 | 0 | 2.37 | 1982.....Pete Vuckovich, Mi | 18-6 | 0 | 3.34 |
| 1984.....†Rick Sutcliffe, Chi | 16-1 | 0 | 2.69 | 1983.....LaMarr Hoyt, Chi | 24-10 | 0 | 3.66 |
| 1985.....Dwight Gooden, NY | 24-4 | 0 | 1.53 | 1984.....*Willie Hernandez, Det | 9-3 | 32 | 1.92 |
| 1986.....Mike Scott, Hou | 18-10 | 0 | 2.22 | 1985.....Bret Saberhagen, KC | 20-6 | 0 | 2.87 |
| 1987.....Steve Bedrosian, Phil | 5-3 | 40 | 2.83 | 1986.....*Roger Clemens, Bos | 24-4 | 0 | 2.48 |
| 1988.....Orel Hershiser, LA | 23-8 | 1 | 2.26 | 1987.....Roger Clemens, Bos | 20-9 | 0 | 2.97 |
| 1989.....Mark Davis, SD | 4-3 | 44 | 1.85 | 1988.....Frank Viola, Minn | 24-7 | 0 | 2.64 |
| 1990.....Doug Drabek, Pitt | 22-6 | 0 | 2.76 | 1989.....Bret Saberhagen, KC | 23-6 | 0 | 2.16 |
| 1991.....Tom Glavine, Atl | 20-11 | 0 | 2.55 | 1990.....Bob Welch, Oak | 27-6 | 0 | 2.95 |
| 1992.....Greg Maddux, Chi | 20-11 | 0 | 2.18 | 1991.....Roger Clemens, Bos | 18-10 | 0 | 2.62 |
| 1993.....Greg Maddux, Atl | 20-10 | 0 | 2.36 | 1992.....*Dennis Eckersley, Oak | 7-1 | 51 | 1.91 |
| 1994.....Greg Maddux, Atl | 16-6 | 0 | 1.56 | 1993.....Jack McDowell, Chi | 22-10 | 0 | 3.37 |
| | | | | 1994.....David Cone, KC | 16-4 | 0 | 2.94 |

*Pitchers who won the MVP and Cy Young awards in the same season.

†NL games only. Sutcliffe pitched 15 games with Cleveland before being traded to the Cubs.

## Career Individual Batting

| GAMES | | HOME RUNS | | BATTING AVERAGE | |
|---|---|---|---|---|---|
| Pete Rose | 3562 | Hank Aaron | 755 | Ty Cobb | .366 |
| Carl Yastrzemski | 3308 | Babe Ruth | 714 | Rogers Hornsby | .358 |
| Hank Aaron | 3298 | Willie Mays | 660 | Joe Jackson | .356 |
| Ty Cobb | 3035 | Frank Robinson | 586 | Ed Delahanty | .346 |
| Stan Musial | 3026 | Harmon Killebrew | 573 | Tris Speaker | .345 |
| Willie Mays | 2992 | Reggie Jackson | 563 | Ted Williams | .344 |
| Dave Winfield | 2973 | Mike Schmidt | 548 | Billy Hamilton | .344 |
| Rusty Staub | 2951 | Mickey Mantle | 536 | Dan Brouthers | .342 |
| Brooks Robinson | 2896 | Jimmie Foxx | 534 | Babe Ruth | .342 |
| Robin Yount | 2856 | Ted Williams | 521 | Harry Heilmann | .342 |
| Al Kaline | 2834 | Willie McCovey | 521 | Pete Browning | .341 |
| Eddie Collins | 2826 | Eddie Mathews | 512 | Willie Keeler | .341 |
| Reggie Jackson | 2820 | Ernie Banks | 512 | Bill Terry | .341 |
| Eddie Murray | 2819 | Mel Ott | 511 | George Sisler | .340 |
| Frank Robinson | 2808 | Lou Gehrig | 493 | Lou Gehrig | .340 |
| Honus Wagner | 2792 | Eddie Murray | 479 | Jesse Burkett | .338 |
| Tris Speaker | 2789 | Willie Stargell | 475 | Nap Lajoie | .338 |
| Tony Perez | 2777 | Stan Musial | 475 | Tony Gwynn | .336 |
| Mel Ott | 2730 | Dave Winfield | 465 | Riggs Stephenson | .336 |
| George Brett | 2707 | Carl Yastrzemski | 452 | Wade Boggs | .334 |
| | | | | Al Simmons | .334 |

| AT BATS | | HITS | | RUNS | |
|---|---|---|---|---|---|
| Pete Rose | 14053 | Pete Rose | 4256 | Ty Cobb | 2246 |
| Hank Aaron | 12364 | Ty Cobb | 4189 | Babe Ruth | 2174 |
| Carl Yastrzemski | 11988 | Hank Aaron | 3771 | Hank Aaron | 2174 |
| Ty Cobb | 11434 | Stan Musial | 3630 | Pete Rose | 2165 |
| Robin Yount | 11008 | Tris Speaker | 3514 | Willie Mays | 2062 |
| Dave Winfield | 11003 | Carl Yastrzemski | 3419 | Stan Musial | 1949 |
| Stan Musial | 10972 | Honus Wagner | 3415 | Lou Gehrig | 1888 |
| Willie Mays | 10881 | Eddie Collins | 3312 | Tris Speaker | 1882 |
| Brooks Robinson | 10654 | Willie Mays | 3283 | Mel Ott | 1859 |
| Eddie Murray | 10603 | Nap Lajoie | 3242 | Frank Robinson | 1829 |
| Honus Wagner | 10430 | George Brett | 3154 | Eddie Collins | 1821 |
| George Brett | 10349 | Paul Waner | 3152 | Carl Yastrzemski | 1816 |
| Lou Brock | 10332 | Robin Yount | 3142 | Ted Williams | 1798 |
| Luis Aparicio | 10230 | Dave Winfield | 3110 | Charlie Gehringer | 1774 |
| Tris Speaker | 10195 | Eddie Murray | 3071 | Jimmie Foxx | 1751 |
| Al Kaline | 10116 | Rod Carew | 3053 | Honus Wagner | 1736 |
| Rabbit Maranville | 10078 | Lou Brock | 3023 | Jesse Burkett | 1720 |
| Frank Robinson | 10006 | Al Kaline | 3007 | Cap Anson | 1719 |
| Eddie Collins | 9949 | Roberto Clemente | 3000 | Rickey Henderson | 1719 |
| Andre Dawson | 9869 | Cap Anson | 2995 | Willie Keeler | 1719 |

## Career Individual Batting (Cont.)

### DOUBLES

| | |
|---|---|
| Tris Speaker | 792 |
| Pete Rose | 746 |
| Stan Musial | 725 |
| Ty Cobb | 724 |
| George Brett | 665 |
| Nap Lajoie | 657 |
| Carl Yastrzemski | 646 |
| Honus Wagner | 640 |
| Hank Aaron | 624 |
| Paul Waner | 605 |
| Robin Yount | 583 |
| Charlie Gehringer | 574 |
| Harry Heilmann | 542 |
| Rogers Hornsby | 541 |
| Joe Medwick | 540 |
| Dave Winfield | 540 |
| Al Simmons | 539 |
| Lou Gehrig | 534 |
| Eddie Murray | 532 |
| Al Oliver | 529 |

### TRIPLES

| | |
|---|---|
| Sam Crawford | 309 |
| Ty Cobb | 295 |
| Honus Wagner | 252 |
| Jake Beckley | 243 |
| Roger Connor | 233 |
| Tris Speaker | 222 |
| Fred Clarke | 220 |
| Dan Brouthers | 205 |
| Joe Kelley | 194 |
| Paul Waner | 191 |
| Bid McPhee | 188 |
| Eddie Collins | 186 |
| Ed Delahanty | 185 |
| Sam Rice | 184 |
| Jesse Burkett | 182 |
| Edd Roush | 182 |
| Ed Konetchy | 181 |
| Buck Ewing | 178 |
| Rabbit Maranville | 177 |
| Stan Musial | 177 |

### BASES ON BALLS

| | |
|---|---|
| Babe Ruth | 2056 |
| Ted Williams | 2019 |
| Joe Morgan | 1865 |
| Carl Yastrzemski | 1845 |
| Mickey Mantle | 1733 |
| Mel Ott | 1708 |
| Eddie Yost | 1614 |
| Darrell Evans | 1605 |
| Stan Musial | 1599 |
| Pete Rose | 1566 |
| Harmon Killebrew | 1559 |
| Rickey Henderson | 1550 |
| Lou Gehrig | 1508 |
| Mike Schmidt | 1507 |
| Eddie Collins | 1499 |
| Willie Mays | 1464 |
| Jimmie Foxx | 1452 |
| Eddie Mathews | 1444 |
| Frank Robinson | 1420 |
| Hank Aaron | 1402 |

### RUNS BATTED IN

| | |
|---|---|
| Hank Aaron | 2297 |
| Babe Ruth | 2213 |
| Lou Gehrig | 1995 |
| Stan Musial | 1951 |
| Ty Cobb | 1937 |
| Jimmie Foxx | 1922 |
| Willie Mays | 1903 |
| Cap Anson | 1879 |
| Mel Ott | 1860 |
| Carl Yastrzemski | 1844 |
| Ted Williams | 1839 |
| Dave Winfield | 1833 |
| Al Simmons | 1827 |
| Eddie Murray | 1820 |
| Frank Robinson | 1812 |
| Honus Wagner | 1732 |
| Reggie Jackson | 1702 |
| Tony Perez | 1652 |
| Ernie Banks | 1636 |
| Goose Goslin | 1609 |

### SLUGGING AVERAGE

| | |
|---|---|
| Babe Ruth | .690 |
| Ted Williams | .634 |
| Lou Gehrig | .632 |
| Jimmie Foxx | .609 |
| Hank Greenberg | .605 |
| Joe DiMaggio | .579 |
| Rogers Hornsby | .577 |
| Johnny Mize | .562 |
| Stan Musial | .559 |
| Willie Mays | .557 |
| Mickey Mantle | .557 |
| Hank Aaron | .555 |
| Ralph Kiner | .548 |
| Hack Wilson | .545 |
| Chuck Klein | .543 |
| Barry Bonds | .541 |
| Duke Snider | .540 |
| Frank Robinson | .537 |
| Al Simmons | .535 |
| Fred McGriff | .535 |

### STOLEN BASES

| | |
|---|---|
| Rickey Henderson | 1149 |
| Lou Brock | 938 |
| Billy Hamilton | 912 |
| Ty Cobb | 892 |
| Tim Raines | 777 |
| Eddie Collins | 744 |
| Vince Coleman | 740 |
| Arlie Latham | 739 |
| Max Carey | 738 |
| Honus Wagner | 722 |
| Joe Morgan | 689 |
| Willie Wilson | 668 |
| Tom Brown | 657 |
| Bert Campaneris | 649 |
| George Davis | 616 |
| Dummy Hoy | 594 |
| Maury Wills | 586 |
| George Van Haltren | 583 |
| Hugh Duffy | 574 |
| Ozzie Smith | 573 |

### PINCH HITS

| | |
|---|---|
| Manny Mota | 150 |
| Smoky Burgess | 145 |
| Greg Gross | 143 |
| Jose Morales | 123 |
| Jerry Lynch | 116 |
| Red Lucas | 114 |
| Steve Braun | 113 |
| Terry Crowley | 108 |
| Denny Walling | 108 |
| Gates Brown | 107 |
| Mike Lum | 103 |
| Jim Dwyer | 102 |
| Rusty Staub | 100 |
| Larry Biittner | 95 |
| Vic Davalillo | 95 |
| Jerry Hairston | 94 |
| Dave Philley | 93 |
| Joel Youngblood | 93 |
| Jay Johnstone | 92 |
| Ed Kranepool | 90 |
| Elmer Valo | 90 |

### TOTAL BASES

| | |
|---|---|
| Hank Aaron | 6856 |
| Stan Musial | 6134 |
| Willie Mays | 6066 |
| Ty Cobb | 5854 |
| Babe Ruth | 5793 |
| Pete Rose | 5752 |
| Carl Yastrzemski | 5539 |
| Frank Robinson | 5373 |
| Dave Winfield | 5221 |
| Eddie Murray | 5108 |
| Tris Speaker | 5101 |
| Lou Gehrig | 5060 |
| George Brett | 5044 |
| Mel Ott | 5041 |
| Jimmie Foxx | 4956 |
| Ted Williams | 4884 |
| Honus Wagner | 4862 |
| Al Kaline | 4852 |
| Reggie Jackson | 4834 |
| Andre Dawson | 4763 |

### STRIKEOUTS

| | |
|---|---|
| Reggie Jackson | 2597 |
| Willie Stargell | 1936 |
| Mike Schmidt | 1883 |
| Tony Perez | 1867 |
| Dave Kingman | 1816 |
| Bobby Bonds | 1757 |
| Dale Murphy | 1748 |
| Lou Brock | 1730 |
| Mickey Mantle | 1710 |
| Harmon Killebrew | 1699 |
| Dwight Evans | 1697 |
| Dave Winfield | 1686 |
| Lee May | 1570 |
| Dick Allen | 1556 |
| Willie McCovey | 1550 |
| Dave Parker | 1537 |
| Frank Robinson | 1532 |
| Lance Parrish | 1527 |
| Willie Mays | 1526 |
| Rick Monday | 1513 |

## Career Individual Pitching

### GAMES

| | |
|---|---|
| Hoyt Wilhelm | 1070 |
| Kent Tekulve | 1050 |
| Goose Gossage | 1002 |
| Lindy McDaniel | 987 |
| Rollie Fingers | 944 |
| Lee Smith | 943 |
| Gene Garber | 931 |
| Cy Young | 906 |
| Dennis Eckersley | 901 |
| Sparky Lyle | 899 |
| Jim Kaat | 898 |
| Jeff Reardon | 880 |
| Don McMahon | 874 |
| Phil Niekro | 864 |
| Charlie Hough | 858 |
| Roy Face | 848 |
| Tug McGraw | 824 |
| Jesse Orosco | 819 |
| Nolan Ryan | 807 |
| Walter Johnson | 802 |

### INNINGS PITCHED

| | |
|---|---|
| Cy Young | 7356.2 |
| Pud Galvin | 5941.1 |
| Walter Johnson | 5914.2 |
| Phil Niekro | 5404.1 |
| Nolan Ryan | 5386.0 |
| Gaylord Perry | 5350.1 |
| Don Sutton | 5282.1 |
| Warren Spahn | 5243.2 |
| Steve Carlton | 5217.1 |
| Grover Alexander | 5190.0 |
| Kid Nichols | 5056.1 |
| Tim Keefe | 5047.1 |
| Bert Blyleven | 4970.0 |
| Mickey Welch | 4802.0 |
| Tom Seaver | 4782.2 |
| Christy Mathewson | 4780.2 |
| Tommy John | 4710.1 |
| Robin Roberts | 4688.2 |
| Early Wynn | 4564.0 |
| John Clarkson | 4536.1 |

### WINS

| | |
|---|---|
| Cy Young | 511 |
| Walter Johnson | 417 |
| Grover Alexander | 373 |
| Christy Mathewson | 373 |
| Warren Spahn | 363 |
| Kid Nichols | 361 |
| Pud Galvin | 360 |
| Tim Keefe | 342 |
| Steve Carlton | 329 |
| John Clarkson | 328 |
| Eddie Plank | 326 |
| Nolan Ryan | 324 |
| Don Sutton | 324 |
| Phil Niekro | 318 |
| Gaylord Perry | 314 |
| Tom Seaver | 311 |
| Charley Radbourn | 309 |
| Mickey Welch | 307 |
| Lefty Grove | 300 |
| Early Wynn | 300 |

### LOSSES

| | |
|---|---|
| Cy Young | 316 |
| Pud Galvin | 308 |
| Nolan Ryan | 292 |
| Walter Johnson | 279 |
| Phil Niekro | 274 |
| Gaylord Perry | 265 |
| Don Sutton | 256 |
| Jack Powell | 254 |
| Eppa Rixey | 251 |
| Bert Blyleven | 250 |
| Robin Roberts | 245 |
| Warren Spahn | 245 |
| Steve Carlton | 244 |
| Early Wynn | 244 |
| Jim Kaat | 237 |
| Frank Tanana | 236 |
| Gus Weyhing | 232 |
| Tommy John | 231 |
| Bob Friend | 230 |
| Ted Lyons | 230 |

### WINNING PERCENTAGE

| | |
|---|---|
| Dave Foutz | .690 |
| Whitey Ford | .690 |
| Bob Caruthers | .688 |
| Lefty Grove | .680 |
| Vic Raschi | .667 |
| Larry Corcoran | .665 |
| Christy Mathewson | .665 |
| Sam Leever | .660 |
| Sal Maglie | .657 |
| Sandy Koufax | .655 |
| Johnny Allen | .654 |
| Ron Guidry | .651 |
| Roger Clemens | .650 |
| Lefty Gomez | .649 |
| Dwight Gooden | .649 |
| John Clarkson | .648 |
| Three Finger Brown | .648 |
| Dizzy Dean | .644 |
| Grover Alexander | .642 |
| Jim Palmer | .638 |

### SAVES

| | |
|---|---|
| Lee Smith | 471 |
| Jeff Reardon | 367 |
| Rollie Fingers | 341 |
| Dennis Eckersley | 323 |
| Tom Henke | 311 |
| Goose Gossage | 310 |
| Bruce Sutter | 300 |
| John Franco | 295 |
| Dave Righetti | 252 |
| Dan Quisenberry | 244 |
| Randy Myers | 243 |
| Doug Jones | 239 |
| Sparky Lyle | 238 |
| Hoyt Wilhelm | 227 |
| Gene Garber | 218 |
| Jeff Montgomery | 218 |
| Dave Smith | 216 |
| Rick Aguilera | 211 |
| Bobby Thigpen | 201 |
| Roy Face | 193 |

### EARNED RUN AVERAGE

| | |
|---|---|
| Ed Walsh | 1.82 |
| Addie Joss | 1.89 |
| Three Finger Brown | 2.06 |
| John Ward | 2.10 |
| Christy Mathewson | 2.13 |
| Rube Waddell | 2.16 |
| Walter Johnson | 2.17 |
| Orval Overall | 2.23 |
| Tommy Bond | 2.25 |
| Ed Reulbach | 2.28 |
| Will White | 2.28 |
| Jim Scott | 2.30 |
| Eddie Plank | 2.35 |
| Larry Corcoran | 2.36 |
| Eddie Cicotte | 2.38 |
| Ed Killian | 2.38 |
| George McQuillan | 2.38 |
| Doc White | 2.39 |
| Nap Rucker | 2.42 |
| Terry Larkin | 2.43 |
| Jim McCormick | 2.43 |
| Jeff Tesreau | 2.43 |

### SHUTOUTS

| | |
|---|---|
| Walter Johnson | 110 |
| Grover Alexander | 90 |
| Christy Mathewson | 79 |
| Cy Young | 76 |
| Eddie Plank | 69 |
| Warren Spahn | 63 |
| Nolan Ryan | 61 |
| Tom Seaver | 61 |
| Bert Blyleven | 60 |
| Don Sutton | 58 |
| Pud Galvin | 57 |
| Ed Walsh | 57 |
| Bob Gibson | 56 |
| Three Finger Brown | 55 |
| Steve Carlton | 55 |
| Jim Palmer | 53 |
| Gaylord Perry | 53 |
| Juan Marichal | 52 |
| Rube Waddell | 50 |
| Vic Willis | 50 |

### COMPLETE GAMES

| | |
|---|---|
| Cy Young | 749 |
| Pud Galvin | 639 |
| Tim Keefe | 554 |
| Walter Johnson | 531 |
| Kid Nichols | 531 |
| Mickey Welch | 525 |
| Charley Radbourn | 489 |
| John Clarkson | 485 |
| Tony Mullane | 468 |
| Jim McCormick | 466 |
| Gus Weyhing | 448 |
| Grover Alexander | 437 |
| Christy Mathewson | 434 |
| Jack Powell | 422 |
| Eddie Plank | 410 |
| Will White | 394 |
| Amos Rusie | 392 |
| Vic Willis | 388 |
| Warren Spahn | 382 |
| Jim Whitney | 377 |

## Career Individual Pitching *(Cont.)*

| STRIKEOUTS | | BASES ON BALLS | |
|---|---|---|---|
| Nolan Ryan | 5714 | Nolan Ryan | 2795 |
| Steve Carlton | 4136 | Steve Carlton | 1833 |
| Bert Blyleven | 3701 | Phil Niekro | 1809 |
| Tom Seaver | 3640 | Early Wynn | 1775 |
| Don Sutton | 3574 | Bob Feller | 1764 |
| Gaylord Perry | 3534 | Bobo Newsom | 1732 |
| Walter Johnson | 3509 | Amos Rusie | 1704 |
| Phil Niekro | 3342 | Charlie Hough | 1665 |
| Ferguson Jenkins | 3192 | Gus Weyhing | 1566 |
| Bob Gibson | 3117 | Red Ruffing | 1541 |
| Jim Bunning | 2855 | Bump Hadley | 1442 |
| Mickey Lolich | 2832 | Warren Spahn | 1434 |
| Cy Young | 2803 | Earl Whitehill | 1431 |
| Frank Tanana | 2773 | Tony Mullane | 1408 |
| Warren Spahn | 2583 | Sad Sam Jones | 1396 |
| Bob Feller | 2581 | Jack Morris | 1390 |
| Jerry Koosman | 2556 | Tom Seaver | 1390 |
| Tim Keefe | 2543 | Gaylord Perry | 1379 |
| Christy Mathewson | 2502 | Mike Torrez | 1371 |
| Don Drysdale | 2486 | Walter Johnson | 1363 |

## Individual Batting (Single Season)

| HITS | | TOTAL BASES | | RUNS BATTED IN | |
|---|---|---|---|---|---|
| George Sisler, 1920 | 257 | Babe Ruth, 1921 | 457 | Hack Wilson, 1930 | 190 |
| Lefty O'Doul, 1929 | 254 | Rogers Hornsby, 1922 | 450 | Lou Gehrig, 1931 | 184 |
| Bill Terry, 1930 | 254 | Lou Gehrig, 1927 | 447 | Hank Greenberg, 1937 | 183 |
| Al Simmons, 1925 | 253 | Chuck Klein, 1930 | 445 | Lou Gehrig, 1927 | 175 |
| Rogers Hornsby, 1922 | 250 | Jimmie Foxx, 1932 | 438 | Jimmie Foxx, 1938 | 175 |
| Chuck Klein, 1930 | 250 | Stan Musial, 1948 | 429 | Lou Gehrig, 1930 | 174 |
| Ty Cobb, 1911 | 248 | Hack Wilson, 1930 | 423 | Babe Ruth, 1921 | 171 |
| George Sisler, 1922 | 246 | Chuck Klein, 1932 | 420 | Chuck Klein, 1930 | 170 |
| Heinie Manush, 1928 | 241 | Lou Gehrig, 1930 | 419 | Hank Greenberg, 1935 | 170 |
| Babe Herman, 1930 | 241 | Joe DiMaggio, 1937 | 418 | Jimmie Foxx, 1932 | 169 |

| BATTING AVERAGE | | TRIPLES | | STRIKEOUTS | |
|---|---|---|---|---|---|
| Hugh Duffy, 1894 | .440 | Chief Wilson, 1912 | 36 | Bobby Bonds, 1970 | 189 |
| Tip O'Neill, 1887 | .435 | Dave Orr, 1886 | 31 | Bobby Bonds, 1969 | 187 |
| Ross Barnes, 1876 | .429 | Heinie Reitz, 1894 | 31 | Rob Deer, 1987 | 186 |
| Nap Lajoie, 1901 | .426 | Perry Werden, 1893 | 29 | Pete Incaviglia, 1986 | 185 |
| Willie Keeler, 1897 | .424 | Harry Davis, 1897 | 28 | Cecil Fielder, 1990 | 182 |
| Rogers Hornsby, 1924 | .424 | George Davis, 1893 | 27 | Mike Schmidt, 1975 | 180 |
| George Sisler, 1922 | .420 | Sam Thompson, 1894 | 27 | Rob Deer, 1986 | 179 |
| Ty Cobb, 1911 | .420 | Jimmy Williams, 1899 | 27 | Dave Nicholson, 1963 | 175 |
| Fred Dunlap, 1884 | .412 | John Reilly, 1890 | 26 | Gorman Thomas, 1979 | 175 |
| Ed Delahanty, 1899 | .410 | George Treadway, 1894 | 26 | Jose Canseco, 1986 | 175 |
| | | Joe Jackson, 1912 | 26 | Rob Deer, 1991 | 175 |

| DOUBLES | | | | | |
|---|---|---|---|---|---|
| Earl Webb, 1931 | 67 | Sam Crawford, 1914 | 26 | | |
| George Burns, 1926 | 64 | Kiki Cuyler, 1925 | 26 | | |
| Joe Medwick, 1936 | 64 | | | | |
| Hank Greenberg, 1934 | 63 | **HOME RUNS** | | **RUNS** | |
| Paul Waner, 1932 | 62 | | | Billy Hamilton, 1894 | 192 |
| Charlie Gehringer, 1936 | 60 | Roger Maris, 1961 | 61 | Tom Brown, 1891 | 177 |
| Tris Speaker, 1923 | 59 | Babe Ruth, 1927 | 60 | Babe Ruth, 1921 | 177 |
| Chuck Klein, 1930 | 59 | Babe Ruth, 1921 | 59 | Tip O'Neill, 1887 | 167 |
| Billy Herman, 1936 | 57 | Jimmie Foxx, 1932 | 58 | Lou Gehrig, 1936 | 167 |
| Billy Herman, 1935 | 57 | Hank Greenberg, 1938 | 58 | Billy Hamilton, 1895 | 166 |
| | | Hack Wilson, 1930 | 56 | Willie Keeler, 1894 | 165 |
| | | Babe Ruth, 1920 | 54 | Joe Kelley, 1894 | 165 |
| | | Babe Ruth, 1928 | 54 | Arlie Latham, 1887 | 163 |
| | | Ralph Kiner, 1949 | 54 | Babe Ruth, 1928 | 163 |
| | | Mickey Mantle, 1961 | 54 | Lou Gehrig, 1931 | 163 |

## Individual Batting (Single Season) *(Cont.)*

### STOLEN BASES

Hugh Nicol, 1887 ................138
Rickey Henderson, 1982 .....130
Arlie Latham, 1887 .............129
Lou Brock, 1974 .................118
Charlie Comiskey, 1887.......117
John Ward, 1887 .................111
Billy Hamilton, 1889 .............111
Billy Hamilton, 1891 .............111
Vince Coleman, 1985 ..........110
Arlie Latham, 1888...............109
Vince Coleman, 1987 ..........109

### BASES ON BALLS

Babe Ruth, 1923.................170
Ted Williams, 1947 .............162
Ted Williams, 1949 .............162
Ted Williams, 1946 .............156
Eddie Yost, 1956 ................151
Eddie Joost, 1949................149
Babe Ruth, 1920.................148
Eddie Stanky, 1945.............148
Jimmy Wynn, 1969 .............148
Jimmy Sheckard, 1911.......147

### SLUGGING AVERAGE

Babe Ruth, 1920.................847
Babe Ruth, 1921.................846
Babe Ruth, 1927.................772
Lou Gehrig, 1927.................765
Babe Ruth, 1923.................764
Rogers Hornsby, 1925........756
Jeff Bagwell, 1994...............750
Jimmie Foxx, 1932...............749
Babe Ruth, 1924.................739
Babe Ruth, 1926.................737

## Individual Pitching (Single Season)

### GAMES

Mike Marshall, 1974.............106
Kent Tekulve, 1979................94
Mike Marshall, 1973................92
Kent Tekulve, 1978................91
Wayne Granger, 1969 ..........90
Mike Marshall, 1979................90
Kent Tekulve, 1987................90
Mark Eichhorn, 1987.............89
Wilbur Wood, 1968 ................88
Rob Murphy, 1987 ................87

### WINS

Charley Radbourn, 1884 .......59
John Clarkson, 1885.............53
Guy Hecker, 1884.................52
John Clarkson, 1889.............49
Charley Radbourn, 1883 .......48
Charlie Buffinton, 1884 .........48
Al Spalding, 1876 .................47
John Ward, 1879 .................47
Jim Galvin, 1883 ..................46
Jim Galvin, 1884 ..................46
Matt Kilroy, 1887 .................46

### SAVES

Bobby Thigpen, 1990............57
Randy Myers, 1993................53
Dennis Eckersley, 1992.........51
Dennis Eckersley, 1990.........48
Rod Beck, 1993.....................48
Lee Smith, 1991 ...................47
Lee Smith, 1993 ...................46
Dave Righetti, 1986 ..............46
Bryan Harvey, 1991 ..............46
Jose Mesa, 1995 ..................46
Six tied with 45.

### GAMES STARTED

Will White, 1879 ....................75
Jim Galvin, 1883 ..................75
Jim McCormick, 1880............74
Charley Radbourn, 1884 .......73
Guy Hecker, 1884.................73
Jim Galvin, 1884 ..................72
John Clarkson, 1889.............72
Bill Hutchison, 1892..............71
John Clarkson, 1885.............70
Matt Kilroy, 1887..................69

### LOSSES

John Coleman, 1883.............48
Will White, 1880 ...................42
Larry McKeon, 1884 .............41
George Bradley, 1879 ...........40
Jim McCormick, 1879............40
Henry Porter, 1888...............37
Kid Carsey, 1891..................37
George Cobb, 1892...............37
Stump Weidman, 1886 ..........36
Bill Hutchison, 1892..............36

### EARNED RUN AVERAGE

Tim Keefe, 1880...................0.86
Dutch Leonard, 1914...........0.96
Three Finger Brown, 1906....1.04
Bob Gibson, 1968................1.12
Christy Mathewson, 1909 ...1.14
Walter Johnson, 1913..........1.14
Jack Pfiester, 1907 ..............1.15
Addie Joss, 1908.................1.16
Carl Lundgren, 1907...........1.17
Denny Driscoll, 1882 ..........1.21

### INNINGS PITCHED

Will White, 1878 ................680.0
Charley Radbourn, 1884....678.2
Guy Hecker, 1884..............670.2
Jim McCormick, 1880........657.2
Jim Galvin, 1883 ...............656.1
Jim Galvin, 1884 ...............636.1
Charley Radbourn, 1883....632.1
Bill Hutchison, 1892...........627.0
John Clarkson, 1885..........623.0
Jim Devlin, 1876 ...............622.0

### WINNING PERCENTAGE

Roy Face, 1959...................947
Johnny Allen, 1937 ............938
Greg Maddux, 1995 ...........905
Randy Johnson, 1995.........900
Ron Guidry, 1978................893
Freddie Fitzsimmons, 1940... .889
Lefty Grove, 1931 ..............886
Bob Stanley, 1978 ..............882
Preacher Roe, 1951...........880
Fred Goldsmith, 1880........875
Tom Seaver, 1981..............875

### SHUTOUTS

George Bradley, 1876 ..........16
Grover Alexander, 1916 ........16
Jack Coombs, 1910..............13
Bob Gibson, 1968.................13
Jim Galvin, 1884 ..................12
Ed Morris, 1886 ...................12
Grover Alexander, 1915 ........12
Tommy Bond, 1879 ...............11
Charley Radbourn, 1884 .......11
Dave Foutz, 1886..................11
Christy Mathewson, 1908 ...11
Ed Walsh, 1908....................11
Walter Johnson, 1913............11
Sandy Koufax, 1963 .............11
Dean Chance, 1964...............11

## Individual Pitching (Single Season) (Cont.)

| COMPLETE GAMES | STRIKEOUTS | BASES ON BALLS |
|---|---|---|
| Will White, 1879 ......................75 | Matt Kilroy, 1886..................513 | Amos Rusie, 1890..............289 |
| Charley Radbourn, 1884 .......73 | Toad Ramsey, 1886.............499 | Mark Baldwin, 1889.............274 |
| Jim McCormick, 1880............72 | Hugh Daily, 1884................483 | Amos Rusie, 1892................267 |
| Jim Galvin, 1883 ...................72 | Dupee Shaw, 1884 ..............451 | Amos Rusie, 1891................262 |
| Guy Hecker, 1884..................72 | Charley Radbourn, 1884 .....441 | Mark Baldwin, 1890.............249 |
| Jim Galvin, 1884 ...................71 | Charlie Buffinton, 1884 ......417 | Jack Stivetts, 1891...............232 |
| Tim Keefe, 1883....................68 | Guy Hecker, 1884................385 | Mark Baldwin, 1891.............227 |
| John Clarkson, 1885..............68 | Nolan Ryan, 1973 ...............383 | Phil Knell, 1891 ...................226 |
| John Clarkson, 1889..............68 | Sandy Koufax, 1965 ...........382 | Bob Barr, 1890 ....................219 |
| Bill Hutchison, 1892..............67 | Bill Sweeney, 1884 .............374 | Amos Rusie 1893................218 |

## Manager of the Year

| NATIONAL LEAGUE | AMERICAN LEAGUE |
|---|---|
| 1983 ..................Tommy Lasorda, LA | 1983 ..................Tony La Russa, Chi |
| 1984 ..................Jim Frey, Chi | 1984 ..................Sparky Anderson, Det |
| 1985 ..................Whitey Herzog, StL | 1985 ..................Bobby Cox, Tor |
| 1986 ..................Hal Lanier, Hou | 1986 ..................John McNamara, Bos |
| 1987 ..................Buck Rodgers, Mtl | 1987 ..................Sparky Anderson, Det |
| 1988 ..................Tommy Lasorda, LA | 1988 ..................Tony La Russa, Oak |
| 1989 ..................Don Zimmer, Chi | 1989 ..................Frank Robinson, Balt |
| 1990 ..................Jim Leyland, Pitt | 1990 ..................Jeff Torborg, Chi |
| 1991 ..................Bobby Cox, Atl | 1991 ..................Tom Kelly, Minn |
| 1992 ..................Jim Leyland, Pitt | 1992 ..................Tony La Russa, Oak |
| 1993 ..................Dusty Baker, SF | 1993 ..................Gene Lamont, Chi |
| 1994 ..................Felipe Alou, Mtl | 1994 ..................Buck Showalter, NY |

## Individual Batting (Single Game)

### MOST RUNS

7 .......Guy Hecker, Lou      Aug 15, 1886

### MOST HITS

7 .......Wilbert Robinson, Balt   June 10, 1892
Rennie Stennett, Pitt   Sept 16, 1975

### MOST HOME RUNS

4 .......Bobby Lowe, Bos (N)   May 30, 1894
Ed Delahanty, Phil    July 13, 1896
Lou Gehrig, NY (A)    June 3, 1932
Gil Hodges, Bklyn     Aug 31, 1950
Joe Adcock, Mil (N)    July 31, 1954
Rocky Colavito, Clev   June 10, 1959
Willie Mays, SF       April 30, 1961
Bob Horner, Atl       July 6, 1986
Mark Whiten, StL      Sept 7, 1993

### MOST GRAND SLAMS

2 .......Tony Lazzeri, NY (A)   May 24, 1936
Jim Tabor, Bos (A)     July 4, 1939
Rudy York, Bos (A)     July 27, 1946
Jim Gentile, Balt      May 9, 1961
Tony Cloninger, Atl    July 3, 1966
Jim Northrup, Det      June 24, 1968
Frank Robinson, Balt   June 26, 1970
Robin Ventura, Chi (A)  Sept 4, 1995

### MOST RBI

12 .....Jim Bottomley, StL    Sept 16, 1924
Mark Whiten, StL      Sept 7, 1993

## Individual Batting (Single Inning)

### MOST RUNS

3 .......Tommy Burns, Chi (N)  Sept 6, 1883, 7th inning
Ned Williamson, Chi (N) Sept 6, 1883, 7th inning
Sammy White, Bos (A)  June 18, 1953,
                       7th inning

### MOST HITS

3 .......Tommy Burns, Chi (N)  Sept 6, 1883, 7th inning
Fred Pfeiffer, Chi (N)   Sept 6, 1883, 7th inning
Ned Williamson, Chi (N) Sept 6, 1883, 7th inning
Gene Stephens, Bos (A)  June 18, 1953,
                       7th inning

Note: All single game hitting records for nine-inning game.

### MOST RBI

6 .......Fred Merkle, NY (N)    May 13, 1911 (RBIs not
                       officially adopted until
                       1920)
Bob Johnson, Phil (A)  Aug 29, 1937
Tom McBride, Bos (A)  Aug 4, 1945
Joe Astroth, Phil (A)   Sept 23, 1950
Gil McDougald, NY (A)  May 3, 1951
Sam Mele, Chi (A)     June 10, 1952
Jim Lemon, Wash      Sept 5, 1959
Jim Ray Hart, SF      July 8, 1970
Andre Dawson, Mont   Sept 24, 1985
Dale Murphy, Atl      July 27, 1989
Carlos Quintana, Bos (A) July 30, 1991

## Individual Pitching (Single Game)

### MOST INNINGS PITCHED

26 .....Leon Cadore, Bklyn     May 1, 1920, tie 1-1
         Joe Oeschger, Bos (N) May 1, 1920, tie 1-1

### MOST RUNS ALLOWED

24 .....Al Travers, Det     May 18, 1912 (only major league game)

### MOST HITS ALLOWED

36 .....Jack Wadsworth, Lou  Aug 17, 1894

### MOST STRIKEOUTS

20 .....Roger Clemens, Bos (A) April 29, 1986

### MOST WALKS ALLOWED

16 .....Bill George, NY (N)       May 30, 1887
         George Van Haltren,     June 27, 1887
         Chi (N)
         Henry Gruber, Clev      Apr 19, 1890
         Bruno Haas, Phil (A)    June 2, 1915

### MOST WILD PITCHES

6 .......J.R. Richard, Hou       April 10, 1979
         Phil Niekro, Atl        Aug 14, 1979
         Bill Gullickson, Mtl    April 10, 1982

## Individual Pitching (Single Inning)

### MOST RUNS ALLOWED

13 .....Lefty O'Doul, Bos (A)   July 7, 1923

### MOST WALKS ALLOWED

8 .......Dolly Gray, Wash    Aug 28, 1909

### MOST WILD PITCHES

4 .......Walter Johnson, Wash Sept 21, 1914
         Phil Niekro, Atl       Aug 14, 1979

## Miscellaneous

### LONGEST GAME, BY INNINGS

26 .....Brooklyn 1, Boston 1  May 1, 1920

### LONGEST NINE-INNING GAME, BY TIME

4:18...LA 8, SF 7          Oct 2, 1962

# Baseball Hall of Fame

## Players

| | Position | Career Dates | Year Selected | | Position | Career Dates | Year Selected |
|---|---|---|---|---|---|---|---|
| Hank Aaron | OF | 1954-76 | 1982 | Jack Chesbro | P | 1899-1909 | 1946 |
| Grover Alexander | P | 1911-30 | 1938 | Fred Clarke | OF | 1894-1915 | 1945 |
| Cap Anson | 1B | 1876-97 | 1939 | John Clarkson | P | 1882-94 | 1963 |
| Luis Aparicio | SS | 1956-73 | 1984 | Roberto Clemente | OF | 1955-72 | 1973 |
| Luke Appling | SS | 1930-50 | 1964 | Ty Cobb | OF | 1905-28 | 1936 |
| Richie Ashburn | OF | 1948-62 | 1995 | Mickey Cochrane | C | 1925-37 | 1947 |
| Earl Averill | OF | 1929-41 | 1975 | Eddie Collins | 2B | 1906-30 | 1939 |
| Frank Baker | 3B | 1908-22 | 1955 | Jimmy Collins | 3B | 1895-1908 | 1945 |
| Dave Bancroft | SS | 1915-30 | 1971 | Earle Combs | OF | 1924-35 | 1970 |
| Ernie Banks | SS-1B | 1953-71 | 1977 | Roger Connor | 1B | 1880-97 | 1976 |
| Jake Beckley | 1B | 1888-1907 | 1971 | Stan Coveleski | P | 1912-28 | 1969 |
| Cool Papa Bell* | OF | | 1974 | Sam Crawford | OF | 1899-1917 | 1957 |
| Johnny Bench | C | 1967-83 | 1989 | Joe Cronin | SS | 1926-45 | 1956 |
| Chief Bender | P | 1903-25 | 1953 | Candy Cummings | P | 1872-77 | 1939 |
| Yogi Berra | C | 1946-65 | 1972 | Kiki Cuyler | OF | 1921-38 | 1968 |
| Jim Bottomley | 1B | 1922-37 | 1974 | Ray Dandridge* | 3B | | 1987 |
| Lou Boudreau | SS | 1938-52 | 1970 | Leon Day* | P | | 1995 |
| Roger Bresnahan | C | 1897-1915 | 1945 | Dizzy Dean | P | 1930-47 | 1953 |
| Lou Brock | OF | 1961-79 | 1985 | Ed Delahanty | OF | 1888-1903 | 1945 |
| Dan Brouthers | 1B | 1879-1904 | 1945 | Bill Dickey | C | 1928-46 | 1954 |
| Three Finger Brown | P | 1903-16 | 1949 | Martin Dihigo* | P-OF | | 1977 |
| Jesse Burkett | OF | 1890-1905 | 1946 | Joe DiMaggio | OF | 1936-51 | 1955 |
| Roy Campanella | C | 1948-57 | 1969 | Bobby Doerr | 2B | 1937-51 | 1986 |
| Rod Carew | 1B-2B | 1967-85 | 1991 | Don Drysdale | P | 1956-69 | 1984 |
| Max Carey | OF | 1910-29 | 1961 | Hugh Duffy | OF | 1888-1906 | 1945 |
| Steve Carlton | P | 1965-88 | 1994 | Johnny Evers | 2B | 1902-29 | 1939 |
| Frank Chance | 1B | 1898-1914 | 1946 | Buck Ewing | C | 1880-97 | 1946 |
| Oscar Charleston* | OF | | 1976 | Red Faber | P | 1914-33 | 1964 |

Note: Career dates indicate first and last appearances in the majors.
*Elected on the basis of his career in the Negro leagues.

## Players (Cont.)

| Name | Position | Career Dates | Year Selected |
|---|---|---|---|
| Bob Feller | P | 1936-56 | 1962 |
| Rick Ferrell | C | 1929-47 | 1984 |
| Rollie Fingers | P | 1968-85 | 1992 |
| Elmer Flick | OF | 1898-1910 | 1963 |
| Whitey Ford | P | 1950-67 | 1974 |
| Jimmie Foxx | 1B | 1925-45 | 1951 |
| Frankie Frisch | 2B | 1919-37 | 1947 |
| Pud Galvin | P | 1879-92 | 1965 |
| Lou Gehrig | 1B | 1923-39 | 1939 |
| Charlie Gehringer | 2B | 1924-42 | 1949 |
| Bob Gibson | P | 1959-75 | 1981 |
| Josh Gibson* | C | | 1972 |
| Lefty Gomez | P | 1930-43 | 1972 |
| Goose Goslin | OF | 1921-38 | 1968 |
| Hank Greenberg | 1B | 1930-47 | 1956 |
| Burleigh Grimes | P | 1916-34 | 1964 |
| Lefty Grove | P | 1925-41 | 1947 |
| Chick Hafey | OF | 1924-37 | 1971 |
| Jesse Haines | P | 1918-37 | 1970 |
| Billy Hamilton | OF | 1888-1901 | 1961 |
| Gabby Hartnett | C | 1922-41 | 1955 |
| Harry Heilmann | OF | 1914-32 | 1952 |
| Billy Herman | 2B | 1931-47 | 1975 |
| Harry Hooper | OF | 1909-25 | 1971 |
| Rogers Hornsby | 2B | 1915-37 | 1942 |
| Waite Hoyt | P | 1918-38 | 1969 |
| Carl Hubbell | P | 1928-43 | 1947 |
| Catfish Hunter | P | 1965-79 | 1987 |
| Monte Irvin* | OF | 1949-56 | 1973 |
| Reggie Jackson | OF | 1967-87 | 1993 |
| Travis Jackson | SS | 1922-36 | 1982 |
| Ferguson Jenkins | P | 1965-83 | 1991 |
| Hugh Jennings | SS | 1891-1918 | 1945 |
| Judy Johnson* | 3B | | 1975 |
| Walter Johnson | P | 1907-27 | 1936 |
| Addie Joss | P | 1902-10 | 1978 |
| Al Kaline | OF | 1953-74 | 1980 |
| Tim Keefe | P | 1880-93 | 1964 |
| Willie Keeler | OF | 1892-1910 | 1939 |
| George Kell | 3B | 1943-57 | 1983 |
| Joe Kelley | OF | 1891-1908 | 1971 |
| George Kelly | 1B | 1915-32 | 1973 |
| King Kelly | C | 1878-93 | 1945 |
| Harmon Killebrew | 1B-3B | 1954-75 | 1984 |
| Ralph Kiner | OF | 1946-55 | 1975 |
| Chuck Klein | OF | 1928-44 | 1980 |
| Sandy Koufax | P | 1955-66 | 1972 |
| Nap Lajoie | 2B | 1896-1916 | 1937 |
| Tony Lazzeri | 2B | 1926-39 | 1991 |
| Bob Lemon | P | 1941-58 | 1976 |
| Buck Leonard* | 1B | | 1972 |
| Fred Lindstrom | 3B | 1924-36 | 1976 |
| Pop Lloyd* | SS-1B | | 1977 |
| Ernie Lombardi | C | 1931-47 | 1986 |
| Ted Lyons | P | 1923-46 | 1955 |
| Mickey Mantle | OF | 1951-68 | 1974 |
| Heinie Manush | OF | 1923-39 | 1964 |
| Rabbit Maranville | SS-2B | 1912-35 | 1954 |
| Juan Marichal | P | 1960-75 | 1983 |
| Rube Marquard | P | 1908-25 | 1971 |
| Eddie Mathews | 3B | 1952-68 | 1978 |
| Christy Mathewson | P | 1900-16 | 1936 |
| Willie Mays | OF | 1951-73 | 1979 |
| Tommy McCarthy | OF | 1884-96 | 1946 |
| Willie McCovey | 1B | 1959-80 | 1986 |
| Joe McGinnity | P | 1899-1908 | 1946 |
| Joe Medwick | OF | 1932-48 | 1968 |
| Johnny Mize | 1B | 1936-53 | 1981 |
| Joe Morgan | 2B | 1963-84 | 1990 |
| Stan Musial | OF-1B | 1941-63 | 1969 |
| Hal Newhouser | P | 1939-55 | 1992 |
| Kid Nichols | P | 1890-1906 | 1949 |
| Jim O'Rourke | OF | 1876-1904 | 1945 |
| Mel Ott | OF | 1926-47 | 1951 |
| Satchel Paige* | P | 1948-65 | 1971 |
| Jim Palmer | P | 1965-84 | 1990 |
| Herb Pennock | P | 1912-34 | 1948 |
| Gaylord Perry | P | 1962-83 | 1991 |
| Eddie Plank | P | 1901-17 | 1946 |
| Charley Radbourn | P | 1880-91 | 1939 |
| Pee Wee Reese | SS | 1940-58 | 1984 |
| Sam Rice | OF | 1915-35 | 1963 |
| Eppa Rixey | P | 1912-33 | 1963 |
| Phil Rizzuto | SS | 1941-56 | 1994 |
| Robin Roberts | P | 1948-66 | 1976 |
| Brooks Robinson | 3B | 1955-77 | 1983 |
| Frank Robinson | OF | 1956-76 | 1982 |
| Jackie Robinson | 2B | 1947 56 | 1962 |
| Edd Roush | OF | 1913-31 | 1962 |
| Red Ruffing | P | 1924-47 | 1967 |
| Amos Rusie | P | 1889-1901 | 1977 |
| Babe Ruth | OF | 1914-35 | 1936 |
| Ray Schalk | C | 1912-29 | 1955 |
| Mike Schmidt | 3B | 1972-89 | 1995 |
| Red Schoendienst | 2B | 1945-63 | 1989 |
| Tom Seaver | P | 1967-86 | 1992 |
| Joe Sewell | SS | 1920-33 | 1977 |
| Al Simmons | OF | 1924-44 | 1953 |
| George Sisler | 1B | 1915-30 | 1939 |
| Enos Slaughter | OF | 1938-59 | 1985 |
| Duke Snider | OF | 1947-64 | 1980 |
| Warren Spahn | P | 1942-65 | 1973 |
| Al Spalding | P | 1871-78 | 1939 |
| Tris Speaker | OF | 1907-28 | 1937 |
| Willie Stargell | OF-1B | 1962-82 | 1988 |
| Bill Terry | 1B | 1923-36 | 1954 |
| Sam Thompson | OF | 1885-1906 | 1974 |
| Joe Tinker | SS | 1902-16 | 1946 |
| Pie Traynor | 3B | 1920-37 | 1948 |
| Dazzy Vance | P | 1915-35 | 1955 |
| Arky Vaughan | SS | 1932-48 | 1985 |
| Rube Waddell | P | 1897-1910 | 1946 |
| Honus Wagner | SS | 1897-1917 | 1936 |
| Bobby Wallace | SS | 1894-1918 | 1953 |
| Ed Walsh | P | 1904-17 | 1946 |
| Lloyd Waner | OF | 1927-45 | 1967 |
| Paul Waner | OF | 1926-45 | 1952 |
| John Ward | 2B-P | 1878-94 | 1964 |
| Mickey Welch | P | 1880-92 | 1973 |
| Zach Wheat | OF | 1909-27 | 1959 |
| Hoyt Wilhelm | P | 1952-72 | 1985 |
| Billy Williams | OF | 1959-76 | 1987 |
| Ted Williams | OF | 1939-60 | 1966 |
| Vic Willis | P | 1898-1910 | 1995 |
| Hack Wilson | OF | 1923-34 | 1979 |
| Early Wynn | P | 1939-63 | 1972 |
| Carl Yastrzemski | OF | 1961-83 | 1989 |
| Cy Young | P | 1890-1911 | 1937 |
| Ross Youngs | OF | 1917-26 | 1972 |

## Umpires

| | Year Selected |
|---|---|
| Al Barlick | 1989 |
| Jocko Conlan | 1974 |
| Tom Connolly | 1953 |
| Billy Evans | 1973 |
| Cal Hubbard | 1976 |
| Bill Klem | 1953 |
| Bill McGowan | 1992 |

## Pioneers/Executives

| | Year Selected |
|---|---|
| Ed Barrow (manager-executive) | 1953 |
| Morgan Bulkeley (executive) | 1937 |
| Alexander Cartwright (executive) | 1938 |
| Henry Chadwick (writer-executive) | 1938 |
| Happy Chandler (commissioner) | 1982 |
| Charles Comiskey (manager-executive) | 1939 |
| Rube Foster (player-manager-executive) | 1981 |
| Ford Frick (commissioner-executive) | 1970 |
| Warren Giles (executive) | 1979 |
| Will Harridge (executive) | 1972 |
| William Hulbert (executive) | 1995 |
| Ban Johnson (executive) | 1937 |
| Kenesaw M. Landis (commissioner) | 1944 |
| Larry MacPhail (executive) | 1978 |
| Branch Rickey (manager-executive) | 1967 |
| Al Spalding (player-executive) | 1939 |
| Bill Veeck (owner) | 1991 |
| George Weiss (executive) | 1971 |
| George Wright (player-manager) | 1937 |
| Harry Wright (player-manager-executive) | 1953 |
| Tom Yawkey (executive) | 1980 |

## Managers

| | Years Managed | Year Selected |
|---|---|---|
| Walt Alston | 1954-76 | 1983 |
| Leo Durocher | 1939-73 | 1994 |
| Clark Griffith | 1901-20 | 1946 |
| Bucky Harris | 1924-56 | 1975 |
| Miller Huggins | 1913-29 | 1964 |
| Al Lopez | 1951-69 | 1977 |
| Connie Mack | 1894-1950 | 1937 |
| Joe McCarthy | 1926-50 | 1957 |
| John McGraw | 1899-1932 | 1937 |
| Bill McKechnie | 1915-46 | 1962 |
| Wilbert Robinson | 1902-31 | 1945 |
| Casey Stengel | 1934-65 | 1966 |

## THEY SAID IT

*Ron Davis, former Minnesota Twin reliever who had a knack for giving up late-game homers, on the boos he still hears at appearances in the Twin Cities: "When it's 10 years later and they still hate you, that's what you call charisma."*

# Notable Achievements

## No-Hit Games, 9 Innings or More
### NATIONAL LEAGUE

| Date | | Pitcher and Game | Date | | Pitcher and Game |
|---|---|---|---|---|---|
| 1876 | July 15 | George Bradley, StL vs Hart 2-0 | 1897 | Sep 18 | Cy Young, Clev vs Cin 6-0 |
| 1880 | June 12 | John Richmond, Wor vs Clev 1-0 (perfect game) | 1898 | Apr 22 | Ted Breitenstein, Cin vs Pitt 11-0 |
| | June 17 | Monte Ward, Prov vs Buff 5-0 (perfect game) | | Apr 22 | Jim Hughes, Balt vs Bos 8-0 |
| | | | | July 8 | Frank Donahue, Phil vs Bos 5-0 |
| | Aug 19 | Larry Corcoran, Chi vs Bos 6-0 | | Aug 21 | Walter Thornton, Chi vs Bklyn 2-0 |
| | Aug 20 | Pud Galvin, Buff at Wor 1-0 | 1899 | May 25 | Deacon Phillippe, Lou vs NY 7-0 |
| 1882 | Sep 20 | Larry Corcoran, Chi vs Wor 5-0 | | Aug 7 | Vic Willis, Bos vs Wash 7-1 |
| | Sep 22 | Tim Lovett, Bklyn vs NY 4-0 | 1900 | July 12 | Noodles Hahn, Cin vs Phil 4-0 |
| 1883 | July 25 | Hoss Radbourn, Prov at Clev 8-0 | 1901 | July 15 | Christy Mathewson, NY at StL 5-0 |
| | Sep 13 | Hugh Daily, Clev at Phil 1-0 | 1903 | Sep 18 | Chick Fraser, Phil at Chi 10-0 |
| 1884 | June 27 | Larry Corcoran, Chi vs Prov 6-0 | 1904 | June 11 | Bob Wicker, Chi at NY 1-0 (hit in 10th; won in 12th) |
| | Aug 4 | Pud Galvin, Buff at Det 18-0 | | | |
| 1885 | July 27 | John Clarkson, Chi at Prov 4-0 | 1905 | June 13 | Christy Mathewson, NY at Chi 1-0 |
| | Aug 29 | Charles Ferguson, Phil vs Prov 1-0 | 1906 | May 1 | John Lush, Phil at Bklyn 6-0 |
| 1891 | July 31 | Amos Rusie, NY vs Bklyn 6-0 | | July 20 | Mal Eason, Bklyn at StL 2-0 |
| | June 22 | Tom Lovett, Bklyn vs NY 4-0 | | Aug 1 | Harry McIntire, Bklyn vs Pitt 0-1 (hit in 11th; lost in 13th) |
| 1892 | Aug 6 | Jack Stivetts, Bos vs Bklyn 11-0 | | | |
| | Aug 22 | Alex Sanders, Lou vs Balt 6-2 | 1907 | May 8 | Frank Pfeffer, Bos vs Cin 6-0 |
| | Oct 15 | Bumpus Jones, Cin vs Pitt 7-1 (first major league game) | | Sep 20 | Nick Maddox, Pitt vs Bklyn 2-1 |
| | | | 1908 | July 4 | George Wiltse, NY vs Phil 1-0 (10 innings) |
| 1893 | Aug 16 | Bill Hawke, Balt vs Wash 5-0 | | Sep 5 | Nap Rucker, Bklyn vs Bos 6-0 |

## No-Hit Games, 9 Innings or More *(Cont.)*

### NATIONAL LEAGUE *(Cont.)*

| Date | Pitcher and Game | Date | Pitcher and Game |
|---|---|---|---|
| 1909......Apr 15 | Leon Ames, NY vs Bklyn 0-3 (hit in 10th; lost in 13th) | 1965......Aug 19 | Jim Maloney, Cin at Chi 1-0 (10 innings) |
| 1912......Sep 6 | Jeff Tesreau, NY at Phil 3-0 | Sep 9 | Sandy Koufax, LA vs Chi 1-0 (perfect game) |
| 1914......Sep 9 | George Davis, Bos vs Phil 7-0 | 1967......June 18 | Don Wilson, Hou vs Atl 2-0 |
| 1915......Apr 15 | Rube Marquard, NY vs Bklyn 2-0 | 1968......July 29 | George Culver, Cin at Phil 6-1 |
| Aug 31 | Jimmy Lavender, Chi at NY 2-0 | Sep 17 | Gaylord Perry, SF vs StL 1-0 |
| 1916......June 16 | Tom Hughes, Bos vs Pitt 2-0 | Sep 18 | Ray Washburn, StL at SF 2-0 |
| 1917......May 2 | Jim Vaughn, Chi vs Cin 0-1 (hit in 10th; lost in 10th) | 1969......Apr 17 | Bill Stoneman, Mtl at Phil 7-0 |
| May 2 | Fred Toney, Cin at Chi 1-0 (10 innings) | Apr 30 | Jim Maloney, Cin vs Hou 10-0 |
| 1919......May 11 | Hod Eller, Cin vs StL 6-0 | May 1 | Don Wilson, Hou at Cin 4-0 |
| 1922......May 7 | Jesse Barnes, NY vs Phil 6-0 | Aug 19 | Ken Holtzman, Chi vs Atl 3-0 |
| 1924......July 17 | Jesse Haines, StL vs Bos 5-0 | Sep 20 | Bob Moose, Pitt at NY 4-0 |
| 1925......Sep 13 | Dazzy Vance, Bklyn vs Phil 10-1 | 1970......June 12 | Dock Ellis, Pitt at SD 2-0 |
| 1929......May 8 | Carl Hubbell, NY vs Pitt 11-0 | July 20 | Bill Singer, LA vs Phil 5-0 |
| 1934......Sep 21 | Paul Dean, StL vs Bklyn 3-0 | 1971......June 3 | Ken Holtzman, Chi at Cin 1-0 |
| 1938......June 11 | Johnny Vander Meer, Cin vs Bos 3-0 | June 23 | Rick Wise, Phil at Cin 4-0 |
| June 15 | Johnny Vander Meer, Cin at Bklyn 6-0 | Aug 14 | Bob Gibson, StL at Pitt 11-0 |
| 1940......Apr 30 | Tex Carleton, Bklyn at Cin, 3-0 | 1972......Apr 16 | Burt Hooton, Chi vs Phil 4-0 |
| 1941......Aug 30 | Lon Warneke, StL at Cin 2-0 | Sep 2 | Milt Pappas, Chi vs SD 8-0 |
| 1944......Apr 27 | Jim Tobin, Bos vs Bklyn 2-0 | Oct 2 | Bill Stoneman, Mtl vs NY 7-0 |
| May 15 | Clyde Shoun, Cin vs Bos 1-0 | 1973......Aug 5 | Phil Niekro, Atl vs SD 9-0 |
| 1946......Apr 23 | Ed Head, Bklyn vs Bos 5-0 | 1975......Aug 24 | Ed Halicki, SF vs NY 6-0 |
| 1947......June 18 | Ewell Blackwell, Cin vs Bos 6-0 | 1976......July 9 | Larry Dierker, Hou vs Mtl 6-0 |
| 1948......Sep 9 | Rex Barney, Bklyn at NY 2-0 | Aug 9 | John Candelaria, Pitt vs LA 2-0 |
| 1950......Aug 11 | Vern Bickford, Bos vs Bklyn 7-0 | Sep 29 | John Mtlefusco, SF at Atl 9-0 |
| 1951......May 6 | Cliff Chambers, Pitt at Bos 3-0 | 1978......Apr 16 | Bob Forsch, StL vs Phil 5-0 |
| 1952......June 19 | Carl Erskine, Bklyn vs Chi 5-0 | June 16 | Tom Seaver, Cin vs StL 4-0 |
| 1954......June 12 | Jim Wilson, Mil vs Phil 2-0 | 1979......Apr 7 | Ken Forsch, Hou vs Atl 6-0 |
| 1955......May 12 | Sam Jones, Chi vs Pitt 4-0 | 1980......June 27 | Jerry Reuss, LA at SF 8-0 |
| 1956......May 12 | Carl Erskine, Bklyn vs NY 3-0 | 1981......May 10 | Charlie Lea, Mtl vs SF 4-0 |
| Sep 25 | Sal Maglie, Bklyn vs Phil 5-0 | Sep 26 | Nolan Ryan, Hou vs LA 5-0 |
| 1959......May 26 | Harvey Haddix, Pitt at Mil 0-1 (hit in 13th; lost in 13th) | 1983......Sep 26 | Bob Forsch, StL vs Mtl 3-0 |
| 1960......May 15 | Don Cardwell, Chi vs StL 4-0 | 1986......Sep 25 | Mike Scott, Hou vs SF 2-0 |
| Aug 18 | Lew Burdette, Mil vs Phil 1-0 | 1988......Sep 16 | Tom Browning, Cin vs LA 1-0 (perfect game) |
| Sep 16 | Warren Spahn, Mil vs Phil 4-0 | 1990......June 29 | Fernando Valenzuela, LA vs StL 6-0 |
| 1961......Apr 28 | Warren Spahn, Mil vs SF 1-0 | 1990......Aug 15 | Terry Mulholland, Phil vs SF 6-0 |
| 1962......June 30 | Sandy Koufax, LA vs NY 5-0 | 1991......May 23 | Tommy Greene, Phil at Mtl 2-0 |
| 1963......May 11 | Sandy Koufax, LA vs SF 8-0 | July 26 | Mark Gardner, Mtl at LA 0-1 (hit in 10th, lost in 10th) |
| May 17 | Don Nottebart, Hou vs Phil 4-1 | July 28 | Dennis Martinez, Mtl at LA 2-0 (perfect game) |
| June 15 | Juan Marichal, SF vs Hou 1-0 | Sep 11 | Kent Mercker (6), Mark Wohlers (2), and Alejandro Pena (1), Atl at SD 1-0 |
| 1964......Apr 23 | Ken Johnson, Hou vs Cin 0-1 | 1992......Aug 17 | Kevin Gross, LA vs SF 2-0 |
| June 4 | Sandy Koufax, LA at Phil 3-0 | 1993......Sep 8 | Darryl Kile, Hou vs NY 7-1 |
| June 21 | Jim Bunning, Phil at NY 6-0 (perfect game) | 1994......Apr 8 | Kent Mercker, Atl vs LA 6-0 |
| 1965......June 14 | Jim Maloney, Cin vs NY 0-1 (hit in 11th; lost in 11th) | 1995......June 3 | Pedro Martinez, Mtl vs SD 1-0 (perfect through 9, hit in 10th) |
| | | July 14 | Ramon Martinez, LA vs Fla 7-0 |

Note: Includes the games struck from the record book on September 4, 1991, when baseball's committee on statistical accuracy voted to define no-hitters as games of 9 innings or more that end with a team getting no hits.

### No-Hit Games, 9 Innings or More *(Cont.)*

#### AMERICAN LEAGUE

| Date | Pitcher and Game | Date | Pitcher and Game |
|---|---|---|---|
| 1901......May 9 | Earl Moore, Clev vs Chi 2-4 (hit in 10th; lost in 10th) | 1966......Oct 8 | Don Larsen, NY (A) vs Bklyn (N) 2-0 (World Series) (perfect game) |
| 1902......Sep 20 | Jimmy Callahan, Chi vs Det 3-0 | 1957......Aug 20 | Bob Keegan, Chi vs Wash 6-0 |
| 1904......May 5 | Cy Young, Bos vs Phil 3-0 (perfect game) | 1958......July 20 | Jim Bunning, Det at Bos 3-0 |
| Aug 17 | Jesse Tannehill, Bos at Chi 6-0 | Sep 20 | Hoyt Wilhelm, Balt vs NY 1-0 |
| 1905......July 22 | Weldon Henley, Phil at StL 6-0 | 1962......May 5 | Bo Belinsky, LA vs Balt 2-0 |
| Sep 6 | Frank Smith, Chi at Det 15-0 | June 26 | Earl Wilson, Bos vs LA 2-0 |
| Sep 27 | Bill Dinneen, Bos vs Chi 2-0 | Aug 1 | Bill Monbouquette, Bos at Chi 1-0 |
| 1908......June 30 | Cy Young, Bos at NY 8-0 | Aug 26 | Jack Kralick, Minn vs KC 1-0 |
| Sep 18 | Bob Rhoades, Clev vs Bos 2-1 | 1965......Sep 16 | Dave Morehead, Bos vs Clev 2-0 |
| Sep 20 | Frank Smith, Chi vs Phil 1-0 | 1966......June 10 | Sonny Siebert, Clev vs Wash 2-0 |
| Oct 2 | Addie Joss, Clev vs Chi 1-0 (perfect game) | 1967......Apr 30 | Steve Barber (8⅔) and Stu Miller (⅓), Balt vs Det 1-2 |
| 1910......Apr 20 | Addie Joss, Clev at Chi 1-0 | Aug 25 | Dean Chance, Minn at Clev 2-1 |
| May 12 | Chief Bender, Phil vs Clev 4-0 | Sep 10 | Joel Horlen, Chi vs Det 6-0 |
| Aug 30 | Tom Hughes, NY vs Clev 0-5 (hit in 10th; lost in 11th) | 1968......Apr 27 | Tom Phoebus, Balt vs Bos 6-0 |
| 1911......July 29 | Joe Wood, Bos vs StL 5-0 | May 8 | Catfish Hunter, Oak vs Minn 4-0 (perfect game) |
| Aug 27 | Ed Walsh, Chi vs Bos 5-0 | 1969......Aug 13 | Jim Palmer, Balt vs Oak 8-0 |
| 1912......July 4 | George Mullin, Det vs StL 7-0 | 1970......July 3 | Clyde Wright, Calif vs Oak 4-0 |
| Aug 30 | Earl Hamilton, StL at Det 5-1 | Sep 21 | Vida Blue, Oak vs Minn 6-0 |
| 1914......May 14 | Jim Scott, Chi at Wash 0-1 (hit in 10th; lost in 10th) | 1973......Apr 27 | Steve Busby, KC at Det 3-0 |
| May 31 | Joe Benz, Chi vs Clev 6-1 | May 15 | Nolan Ryan, Calif at KC 3-0 |
| 1916......June 21 | George Foster, Bos vs NY 2-0 | July 15 | Nolan Ryan, Calif at Det 6-0 |
| Aug 26 | Joe Bush, Phil vs Clev 5-0 | July 30 | Jim Bibby, Tex at Oak 6-0 |
| Aug 30 | Dutch Leonard, Bos vs StL 4-0 | 1974......June 19 | Steve Busby, KC at Mil 2-0 |
| 1917......Apr 14 | Ed Cicotte, Chi at StL 11-0 | July 19 | Dick Bosman, Clev vs Oak 4-0 |
| Apr 24 | George Mogridge, NY at Bos 2-1 | Sep 28 | Nolan Ryan, Calif vs Minn 4-0 |
| May 5 | Ernie Koob, StL vs Chi 1-0 | 1975......June 1 | Nolan Ryan, Calif vs Balt 1-0 |
| May 6 | Bob Groom, StL vs Chi 3-0 | Sep 28 | Vida Blue (5), Glenn Abbott and Paul Lindblad (1), Rollie Fingers (2), Oak vs Calif 5-0 |
| June 23 | Ernie Shore, Bos vs Wash 4-0 (perfect game) | 1976......July 28 | John Odom (5) and Francisco Barrios (4), Chi at Oak 2-1 |
| 1918......June 3 | Dutch Leonard, Bos at Det 5-0 | 1977......May 14 | Jim Colborn, KC vs Tex 6-0 |
| 1919......Sep 10 | Ray Caldwell, Clev at NY 3-0 | May 30 | Dennis Eckersley, Clev vs Calif 1-0 |
| 1920......July 1 | Walter Johnson, Wash at Bos 1-0 | Sep 22 | Bert Blyleven, Tex at Calif 6-0 |
| 1922......Apr 30 | Charlie Robertson, Chi at Det 2-0 (perfect game) | 1981......May 15 | Len Barker, Clev vs Tor 3-0 (perfect game) |
| 1923......Sep 4 | Sam Jones, NY at Phil 2-0 | 1983......July 4 | Dave Righetti, NY vs Bos 4-0 |
| Sep 7 | Howard Ehmke, Bos at Phil 4-0 | Sep 29 | Mike Warren, Oak vs Chi 3-0 |
| 1926......Aug 21 | Ted Lyons, Chi at Bos 6-0 | 1984......Apr 7 | Jack Morris, Det at Chi 4-0 |
| 1931......Apr 29 | Wes Ferrell, Clev vs StL 9-0 | Sep 30 | Mike Witt, Calif at Tex 1-0 (perfect game) |
| Aug 8 | Bob Burke, Wash vs Bos 5-0 | 1986......Sep 19 | Joe Cowley, Chi at Calif 7-1 |
| 1934......Sep 18 | Bobo Newsom, StL vs Bos 1-2 (hit in 10th; lost in 10th) | 1987......Apr 15 | Juan Nieves, Mil at Balt 7-0 |
| 1935......Aug 31 | Vern Kennedy, Chi vs Clev 5-0 | 1990......Apr 11 | Mark Langston (7), Mike Witt (2), Calif vs Sea 1-0 |
| 1937......June 1 | Bill Dietrich, Chi vs StL 8-0 | June 2 | Randy Johnson, Sea vs Det 2-0 |
| 1938......Aug 27 | Mtle Pearson, NY vs Clev 13-0 | June 11 | Nolan Ryan, Tex at Oak 5-0 |
| 1940......Apr 16 | Bob Feller, Clev at Chi 1-0 (opening day) | June 29 | Dave Stewart, Oak at Tor 5-0 |
| 1945......Sep 9 | Dick Fowler, Phil vs StL 1-0 | 1990......July 1 | Andy Hawkins, NY at Chi 0-4 (pitched 8 innings of 9-inning game) |
| 1946......Apr 30 | Bob Feller, Clev at NY 1-0 | Sep 2 | Dave Stieb, Tor at Clev 3-0 |
| 1947......July 10 | Don Black, Clev vs Phil 3-0 | 1991......May 1 | Nolan Ryan, Tex vs Tor 3-0 |
| Sep 3 | Bill McCahan, Phil vs Wash 3-0 | July 13 | Bob Milacki (6), Mike Flanagan (1), Mark Williamson (1), and Gregg Olson (1), Balt at Oak 2-0 |
| 1948......June 30 | Bob Lemon, Clev at Det 2-0 | Aug 11 | Wilson Alvarez, Chi at Balt 7-0 |
| 1951......July 1 | Bob Feller, Clev vs Det 2-1 | Aug 26 | Bret Saberhagen, KC vs Chi 7-0 |
| July 12 | Allie Reynolds, NY at Clev 1-0 | 1993......Apr 22 | Chris Bosio, Sea vs Bos 7-0 |
| Sep 28 | Allie Reynolds, NY vs Bos 8-0 | Sep 4 | Jim Abbott, NY vs Clev 4-0 |
| 1952......May 15 | Virgil Trucks, Det vs Wash 1-0 | 1994......Apr 27 | Scott Erickson, Minn vs Mil 6-0 |
| Aug 25 | Virgil Trucks, Det at NY 1-0 | July 28 | Kenny Rogers, Texas vs Calif. 4-0 (perfect game) |
| 1953......May 6 | Bobo Holloman, StL vs Phil 6-0 (first major league start) | | |
| 1956......July 14 | Mel Parnell, Bos vs Chi 4-0 | | |

## Longest Hitting Streaks

| NATIONAL LEAGUE | | | | AMERICAN LEAGUE | | |
|---|---|---|---|---|---|---|
| Player and Team | Year | G | | Player and Team | Year | G |
| Willie Keeler, Balt | 1897 | 44 | | Joe DiMaggio, NY | 1941 | 56 |
| Pete Rose, Cin | 1978 | 44 | | George Sisler, StL | 1922 | 41 |
| Bill Dahlen, Chi | 1894 | 42 | | Ty Cobb, Det | 1911 | 40 |
| Tommy Holmes, Bos | 1945 | 37 | | Paul Molitor, Mil | 1987 | 39 |
| Billy Hamilton, Phil | 1894 | 36 | | Ty Cobb, Det | 1917 | 35 |
| Fred Clarke, Lou | 1895 | 35 | | Ty Cobb, Det | 1912 | 34 |
| Benito Santiago, SD | 1987 | 34 | | George Sisler, StL | 1925 | 34 |
| George Davis, NY | 1893 | 33 | | John Stone, Det | 1930 | 34 |
| Rogers Hornsby, StL | 1922 | 32 | | George McQuinn, StL | 1938 | 34 |
| Ed Delahanty, Phil | 1899 | 31 | | Dom DiMaggio, Bos | 1949 | 34 |
| Willie Davis, LA | 1969 | 31 | | Hal Chase, NY | 1907 | 33 |
| Rico Carty, Atl | 1970 | 31 | | Heinie Manush, Wash | 1933 | 33 |
| | | | | Nap Lajoie, Clev | 1906 | 31 |
| | | | | Sam Rice, Wash | 1924 | 31 |
| | | | | Ken Landreaux, Minn | 1980 | 31 |

## Triple Crown Hitters

| NATIONAL LEAGUE | | | | | AMERICAN LEAGUE | | | | |
|---|---|---|---|---|---|---|---|---|---|
| Player and Team | Year | HR | RBI | BA | Player and Team | Year | HR | RBI | BA |
| Paul Hines, Prov | 1878 | 4 | 50 | .358 | Nap Lajoie, Phil | 1901 | 14 | 125 | .422 |
| Hugh Duffy, Bos | 1894 | 18 | 145 | .438 | Ty Cobb, Det | 1909 | 9 | 115 | .377 |
| Heinie Zimmerman*, Chi | 1912 | 14 | 103 | .372 | Jimmie Foxx, Phil | 1933 | 48 | 163 | .356 |
| Rogers Hornsby, StL | 1922 | 42 | 152 | .401 | Lou Gehrig, NY | 1934 | 49 | 165 | .363 |
| | 1925 | 39 | 143 | .403 | Ted Williams, Bos | 1942 | 36 | 137 | .356 |
| Chuck Klein, Phil | 1933 | 28 | 120 | .368 | | 1947 | 32 | 114 | .343 |
| Joe Medwick, StL | 1937 | 31 | 154 | .374 | Mickey Mantle, NY | 1956 | 52 | 130 | .353 |
| | | | | | Frank Robinson, Balt | 1966 | 49 | 122 | .316 |
| | | | | | Carl Yastrzemski, Bos | 1967 | 44 | 121 | .326 |

*Zimmerman ranked first in RBIs as calculated by Ernie Lanigan, but only third as calculated by Information Concepts Inc.

## Triple Crown Pitchers

| NATIONAL LEAGUE | | | | | AMERICAN LEAGUE | | | | |
|---|---|---|---|---|---|---|---|---|---|
| Player and Team | Year | W | L | SO | ERA | Player and Team | Year | W | L | SO | ERA |
| Tommy Bond, Bos | 1877 | 40 | 17 | 170 | 2.11 | Cy Young, Bos | 1901 | 33 | 10 | 158 | 1.62 |
| Hoss Radbourn, Prov | 1884 | 60 | 12 | 441 | 1.38 | Rube Waddell, Phil | 1905 | 26 | 11 | 287 | 1.48 |
| Tim Keefe, NY | 1888 | 35 | 12 | 333 | 1.74 | Walter Johnson, Wash | 1913 | 36 | 7 | 303 | 1.09 |
| John Clarkson, Bos | 1889 | 49 | 19 | 284 | 2.73 | | 1918 | 23 | 13 | 162 | 1.27 |
| Amos Rusie, NY | 1894 | 36 | 13 | 195 | 2.78 | | 1924 | 23 | 7 | 158 | 2.72 |
| Christy Mathewson, NY | 1905 | 31 | 8 | 206 | 1.27 | Lefty Grove, Phil | 1930 | 28 | 5 | 209 | 2.54 |
| | 1908 | 37 | 11 | 259 | 1.43 | | 1931 | 31 | 4 | 175 | 2.06 |
| Grover Alexander, Phil | 1915 | 31 | 10 | 241 | 1.22 | Lefty Gomez, NY | 1934 | 26 | 5 | 158 | 2.33 |
| | 1916 | 33 | 12 | 167 | 1.55 | | 1937 | 21 | 11 | 194 | 2.33 |
| | 1917 | 30 | 13 | 201 | 1.86 | Hal Newhouser, Det | 1945 | 25 | 9 | 212 | 1.81 |
| Hippo Vaughn, Chi | 1918 | 22 | 10 | 148 | 1.74 | | | | | | |
| Grover Alexander, Chi | 1920 | 27 | 14 | 173 | 1.91 | | | | | | |
| Dazzy Vance, Bklyn | 1924 | 28 | 6 | 262 | 2.16 | | | | | | |
| Bucky Walters, Cin | 1939 | 27 | 11 | 137 | 2.29 | | | | | | |
| Sandy Koufax, LA | 1963 | 25 | 5 | 306 | 1.88 | | | | | | |
| | 1965 | 26 | 8 | 382 | 2.04 | | | | | | |
| | 1966 | 27 | 9 | 317 | 1.73 | | | | | | |
| Steve Carlton, Phil | 1972 | 27 | 10 | 310 | 1.97 | | | | | | |
| Dwight Gooden, NY | 1985 | 24 | 4 | 268 | 1.53 | | | | | | |

## Consecutive Games Played,
## 500 or More Games

| | | | |
|---|---|---|---|
| Cal Ripken Jr. | 2153* | Frank McCormick | 652 |
| Lou Gehrig | 2130 | Sandy Alomar Sr | 648 |
| Everett Scott | 1307 | Eddie Brown | 618 |
| Steve Garvey | 1207 | Roy McMillan | 585 |
| Billy Williams | 1117 | George Pinckney | 577 |
| Joe Sewell | 1103 | Steve Brodie | 574 |
| Stan Musial | 895 | Aaron Ward | 565 |
| Eddie Yost | 829 | Candy LaChance | 540 |
| Gus Suhr | 822 | Buck Freeman | 535 |
| Nellie Fox | 798 | Fred Luderus | 533 |
| Pete Rose | 745 | Clyde Milan | 511 |
| Dale Murphy | 740 | Charlie Gehringer | 511 |
| Richie Ashburn | 730 | Vada Pinson | 508 |
| Ernie Banks | 717 | Tony Cuccinello | 504 |
| Earl Averill | 673 | Charlie Gehringer | 504 |
| Pete Rose | 678 | Omar Moreno | 503 |

*Streak in progress at the end of the 1995 season.

## Unassisted Triple Plays

| Player and Team | Date | Pos | Opp | Opp Batter |
|---|---|---|---|---|
| Neal Ball, Clev | 7-19-09 | SS | Bos | Amby McConnell |
| Bill Wambsganss, Clev | 10-10-20 | 2B | Bklyn | Clarence Mitchell |
| George Burns, Bos | 9-14-23 | 1B | Clev | Frank Brower |
| Ernie Padgett, Bos | 10-6-23 | SS | Phil | Walter Holke |
| Glenn Wright, Pitt | 5-7-25 | SS | StL | Jim Bottomley |
| Jimmy Cooney, Chi | 5-30-27 | SS | Pitt | Paul Waner |
| Johnny Neun, Det | 5-31-27 | 1B | Clev | Homer Summa |
| Ron Hansen, Wash | 7-30-68 | SS | Clev | Joe Azcue |
| Mickey Morandini, Phil | 9-20-92 | 2B | Pitt | Jeff King |
| John Valentin, Bos | 7-15-94 | SS | Minn | Marc Newfield |

# National League

## Pennant Winners

| Year | Team | Manager | W | L | Pct | GA |
|---|---|---|---|---|---|---|
| 1900 | Brooklyn | Ned Hanlon | 82 | 54 | .603 | 4½ |
| 1901 | Pittsburgh | Fred Clarke | 90 | 49 | .647 | 7½ |
| 1902 | Pittsburgh | Fred Clarke | 103 | 36 | .741 | 27½ |
| 1903 | Pittsburgh | Fred Clarke | 91 | 49 | .650 | 6½ |
| 1904 | New York | John McGraw | 106 | 47 | .693 | 13 |
| 1905 | New York | John McGraw | 105 | 48 | .686 | 9 |
| 1906 | Chicago | Frank Chance | 116 | 36 | .763 | 20 |
| 1907 | Chicago | Frank Chance | 107 | 45 | .704 | 17 |
| 1908 | Chicago | Frank Chance | 99 | 55 | .643 | 1 |
| 1909 | Pittsburgh | Fred Clarke | 110 | 42 | .724 | 6½ |
| 1910 | Chicago | Frank Chance | 104 | 50 | .675 | 13 |
| 1911 | New York | John McGraw | 99 | 54 | .647 | 7½ |
| 1912 | New York | John McGraw | 103 | 48 | .682 | 10 |
| 1913 | New York | John McGraw | 101 | 51 | .664 | 12½ |
| 1914 | Boston | George Stallings | 94 | 59 | .614 | 10½ |
| 1915 | Philadelphia | Pat Moran | 90 | 62 | .592 | 7 |
| 1916 | Brooklyn | Wilbert Robinson | 94 | 60 | .610 | 2½ |
| 1917 | New York | John McGraw | 98 | 56 | .636 | 10 |
| 1918 | Chicago | Fred Mitchell | 84 | 45 | .651 | 10½ |
| 1919 | Cincinnati | Pat Moran | 96 | 44 | .686 | 9 |
| 1920 | Brooklyn | Wilbert Robinson | 93 | 61 | .604 | 7 |
| 1921 | New York | John McGraw | 94 | 59 | .614 | 4 |
| 1922 | New York | John McGraw | 93 | 61 | .604 | 7 |
| 1923 | New York | John McGraw | 95 | 58 | .621 | 4½ |
| 1924 | New York | John McGraw | 93 | 60 | .608 | 1½ |

## Pennant Winners (Cont.)

| Year | Team | Manager | W | L | Pct | GA |
|------|------|---------|---|---|-----|-----|
| 1925 | Pittsburgh | Bill McKechnie | 95 | 58 | .621 | 8½ |
| 1926 | St Louis | Rogers Hornsby | 89 | 65 | .578 | 2 |
| 1927 | Pittsburgh | Donie Bush | 94 | 60 | .610 | 1½ |
| 1928 | St Louis | Bill McKechnie | 95 | 59 | .617 | 2 |
| 1929 | Chicago | Joe McCarthy | 98 | 54 | .645 | 10½ |
| 1930 | St Louis | Gabby Street | 92 | 62 | .597 | 2 |
| 1931 | St Louis | Gabby Street | 101 | 53 | .656 | 13 |
| 1932 | Chicago | Charlie Grimm | 90 | 64 | .584 | 4 |
| 1933 | New York | Bill Terry | 91 | 61 | .599 | 5 |
| 1934 | St Louis | Frankie Frisch | 95 | 58 | .621 | 2 |
| 1935 | Chicago | Charlie Grimm | 100 | 54 | .649 | 4 |
| 1936 | New York | Bill Terry | 92 | 62 | .597 | 5 |
| 1937 | New York | Bill Terry | 95 | 57 | .625 | 3 |
| 1938 | Chicago | Gabby Hartnett | 89 | 63 | .586 | 2 |
| 1939 | Cincinnati | Bill McKechnie | 97 | 57 | .630 | 4½ |
| 1940 | Cincinnati | Bill McKechnie | 100 | 53 | .654 | 12 |
| 1941 | Brooklyn | Leo Durocher | 100 | 54 | .649 | 2½ |
| 1942 | St Louis | Billy Southworth | 106 | 48 | .688 | 2 |
| 1943 | St Louis | Billy Southworth | 105 | 49 | .682 | 18 |
| 1944 | St Louis | Billy Southworth | 105 | 49 | .682 | 14½ |
| 1945 | Chicago | Charlie Grimm | 98 | 56 | .636 | 3 |
| 1946 | St Louis* | Eddie Dyer | 98 | 58 | .628 | 2 |
| 1947 | Brooklyn | Burt Shotton | 94 | 60 | .610 | 5 |
| 1948 | Boston | Billy Southworth | 91 | 62 | .595 | 6½ |
| 1949 | Brooklyn | Burt Shotton | 97 | 57 | .630 | 1 |
| 1950 | Philadelphia | Eddie Sawyer | 91 | 63 | .591 | 2 |
| 1951 | New York† | Leo Durocher | 98 | 59 | .624 | 1 |
| 1952 | Brooklyn | Chuck Dressen | 96 | 57 | .627 | 4½ |
| 1953 | Brooklyn | Chuck Dressen | 105 | 49 | .682 | 13 |
| 1954 | New York | Leo Durocher | 97 | 57 | .630 | 5 |
| 1955 | Brooklyn | Walt Alston | 98 | 55 | .641 | 13½ |
| 1956 | Brooklyn | Walt Alston | 93 | 61 | .604 | 1 |
| 1957 | Milwaukee | Fred Haney | 95 | 59 | .617 | 8 |
| 1958 | Milwaukee | Fred Haney | 92 | 62 | .597 | 8 |
| 1959 | Los Angeles‡ | Walt Alston | 88 | 68 | .564 | 2 |
| 1960 | Pittsburgh | Danny Murtaugh | 95 | 59 | .617 | 7 |
| 1961 | Cincinnati | Fred Hutchinson | 93 | 61 | .604 | 4 |
| 1962 | San Francisco# | Al Dark | 103 | 62 | .624 | 1 |
| 1963 | Los Angeles | Walt Alston | 99 | 63 | .611 | 6 |
| 1964 | St Louis | Johnny Keane | 93 | 69 | .574 | 1 |
| 1965 | Los Angeles | Walt Alston | 97 | 65 | .599 | 2 |
| 1966 | Los Angeles | Walt Alston | 95 | 67 | .586 | 1½ |
| 1967 | St Louis | Red Schoendienst | 101 | 60 | .627 | 10½ |
| 1968 | St Louis | Red Schoendienst | 97 | 65 | .599 | 9 |
| 1969 | New York (E)†† | Gil Hodges | 100 | 62 | .617 | 8 |
| 1970 | Cincinnati (W)†† | Sparky Anderson | 102 | 60 | .630 | 14½ |
| 1971 | Pittsburgh (E)†† | Danny Murtaugh | 97 | 65 | .599 | 7 |
| 1972 | Cincinnati (W)†† | Sparky Anderson | 95 | 59 | .617 | 10½ |
| 1973 | New York (E)†† | Yogi Berra | 82 | 79 | .509 | 1½ |
| 1974 | Los Angeles (W)†† | Walt Alston | 102 | 60 | .630 | 4 |
| 1975 | Cincinnati (W)†† | Sparky Anderson | 108 | 54 | .667 | 20 |
| 1976 | Cincinnati (W)†† | Sparky Anderson | 102 | 60 | .630 | 10 |
| 1977 | Los Angeles (W)†† | Tommy Lasorda | 98 | 64 | .605 | 10 |
| 1978 | Los Angeles (W)†† | Tommy Lasorda | 95 | 67 | .586 | 2½ |
| 1979 | Pittsburgh (E)†† | Chuck Tanner | 98 | 64 | .605 | 2 |
| 1980 | Philadelphia (E)†† | Dallas Green | 91 | 71 | .562 | 1 |
| 1981 | Los Angeles (W)†† | Tommy Lasorda | 63 | 47 | .573 | ** |
| 1982 | St Louis (E)†† | Whitey Herzog | 92 | 70 | .568 | 3 |
| 1983 | Philadelphia (E)†† | Pat Corrales/Paul Owens | 90 | 72 | .556 | 6 |
| 1984 | San Diego (W)†† | Dick Williams | 92 | 70 | .568 | 12 |

*Defeated Brooklyn, two games to none, in playoff for pennant. †Defeated Brooklyn, two games to one, in playoff for pennant. ‡Defeated Milwaukee, two games to none, in playoff for pennant. #Defeated Los Angeles, two games to one, in playoff for pennant. ††Won Championship Series **First half 36-21; second half 27-26, in season split by strike; defeated Houston in playoff for Western Division title.

### Pennant Winners (Cont.)

| Year | Team | Manager | W | L | Pct | GA |
|------|------|---------|---|---|-----|-----|
| 1985 | St Louis (E)†† | Whitey Herzog | 101 | 61 | .623 | 3 |
| 1986 | New York (E)†† | Dave Johnson | 108 | 54 | .667 | 21½ |
| 1987 | St Louis (E)†† | Whitey Herzog | 95 | 67 | .586 | 3 |
| 1988 | Los Angeles (W)†† | Tommy Lasorda | 94 | 67 | .584 | 7 |
| 1989 | San Francisco (W)†† | Roger Craig | 92 | 70 | .568 | 3 |
| 1990 | Cincinnati (W)†† | Lou Piniella | 91 | 71 | .562 | 5 |
| 1991 | Atlanta (W)†† | Bobby Cox | 94 | 68 | .580 | 1 |
| 1992 | Atlanta (W)†† | Bobby Cox | 98 | 64 | .605 | 8 |
| 1993 | Philadelphia (E)†† | Jim Fregosi | 97 | 65 | .599 | 3 |
| 1994 | Season ended Aug. 11 due to players' strike | | | | | |
| 1995 | Atlanta (E)†† | Bobby Cox | 90 | 54 | .625 | 21 |

††Won Championship Series

### Leading Batsmen

| Year | Player and Team | BA | Year | Player and Team | BA |
|------|-----------------|-----|------|-----------------|-----|
| 1900 | Honus Wagner, Pitt | .381 | 1930 | Bill Terry, NY | .401 |
| 1901 | Jesse Burkett, StL | .382 | 1931 | Chick Hafey, StL | .349 |
| 1902 | Ginger Beaumtl, Pitt | .357 | 1932 | Lefty O'Doul, Bklyn | .368 |
| 1903 | Honus Wagner, Pitt | .355 | 1933 | Chuck Klein, Phil | .368 |
| 1904 | Honus Wagner, Pitt | .349 | 1934 | Paul Waner, Pitt | .362 |
| 1905 | Cy Seymour, Cin | .377 | 1935 | Arky Vaughan, Pitt | .385 |
| 1906 | Honus Wagner, Pitt | .339 | 1936 | Paul Waner, Pitt | .373 |
| 1907 | Honus Wagner, Pitt | .350 | 1937 | Joe Medwick, StL | .374 |
| 1908 | Honus Wagner, Pitt | .354 | 1938 | Ernie Lombardi, Cin | .342 |
| 1909 | Honus Wagner, Pitt | .339 | 1939 | Johnny Mize, StL | .349 |
| 1910 | Sherry Magee, Phil | .331 | 1940 | Debs Garms, Pitt | .355 |
| 1911 | Honus Wagner, Pitt | .334 | 1941 | Pete Reiser, Bklyn | .343 |
| 1912 | Heinie Zimmerman, Chi | .372 | 1942 | Ernie Lombardi, Bos | .330 |
| 1913 | Jake Daubert, Bklyn | .350 | 1943 | Stan Musial, StL | .357 |
| 1914 | Jake Daubert, Bklyn | .329 | 1944 | Dixie Walker, Bklyn | .357 |
| 1915 | Larry Doyle, NY | .320 | 1945 | Phil Cavarretta, Chi | .355 |
| 1916 | Hal Chase, Cin | .339 | 1946 | Stan Musial, StL | .365 |
| 1917 | Edd Roush, Cin | .341 | 1947 | Harry Walker, StL-Phil | .363 |
| 1918 | Zach Wheat, Bklyn | .335 | 1948 | Stan Musial, StL | .376 |
| 1919 | Edd Roush, Cin | .321 | 1949 | Jackie Robinson, Bklyn | .342 |
| 1920 | Rogers Hornsby, StL | .370 | 1950 | Stan Musial, StL | .346 |
| 1921 | Rogers Hornsby, StL | .397 | 1951 | Stan Musial, StL | .355 |
| 1922 | Rogers Hornsby, StL | .401 | 1952 | Stan Musial, StL | .336 |
| 1923 | Rogers Hornsby, StL | .384 | 1953 | Carl Furillo, Bklyn | .344 |
| 1924 | Rogers Hornsby, StL | .424 | 1954 | Willie Mays, NY | .345 |
| 1925 | Rogers Hornsby, StL | .403 | 1955 | Richie Ashburn, Phil | .338 |
| 1926 | Bubbles Hargrave, Cin | .353 | 1956 | Hank Aaron, Mil | .328 |
| 1927 | Paul Waner, Pitt | .380 | 1957 | Stan Musial, StL | .351 |
| 1928 | Rogers Hornsby, Bos | .387 | 1958 | Richie Ashburn, Phil | .350 |
| 1929 | Lefty O'Doul, Phil | .398 | 1959 | Hank Aaron, Mil | .355 |

## THEY SAID IT

*Kevin Malone, Montreal Expo general manager, on his team's needs during the players' strike: "For 25 years the Expos have been looking for a shortstop who could pick it. Now we're looking for a shortstop who won't picket."*

## Leading Batsmen (Cont.)

| Year | Player and Team | BA | Year | Player and Team | BA |
|---|---|---|---|---|---|
| 1960 | Dick Groat, Pitt | .325 | 1978 | Dave Parker, Pitt | .334 |
| 1961 | Roberto Clemente, Pitt | .351 | 1979 | Keith Hernandez, StL | .344 |
| 1962 | Tommy Davis, LA | .346 | 1980 | Bill Buckner, Chi | .324 |
| 1963 | Tommy Davis, LA | .326 | 1981 | Bill Madlock, Pitt | .341 |
| 1964 | Roberto Clemente, Pitt | .339 | 1982 | Al Oliver, Mtl | .331 |
| 1965 | Roberto Clemente, Pitt | .329 | 1983 | Bill Madlock, Pitt | .323 |
| 1966 | Matty Alou, Pitt | .342 | 1984 | Tony Gwynn, SD | .351 |
| 1967 | Roberto Clemente, Pitt | .357 | 1985 | Willie McGee, StL | .353 |
| 1968 | Pete Rose, Cin | .335 | 1986 | Tim Raines, Mtl | .334 |
| 1969 | Pete Rose, Cin | .348 | 1987 | Tony Gwynn, SD | .370 |
| 1970 | Rico Carty, Atl | .366 | 1988 | Tony Gwynn, SD | .313 |
| 1971 | Joe Torre, StL | .363 | 1989 | Tony Gwynn, SD | .336 |
| 1972 | Billy Williams, Chi | .333 | 1990 | Willie McGee, StL | .335 |
| 1973 | Pete Rose, Cin | .338 | 1991 | Terry Pendleton, Atl | .319 |
| 1974 | Ralph Garr, Atl | .353 | 1992 | Gary Sheffield, SD | .330 |
| 1975 | Bill Madlock, Chi | .354 | 1993 | Andres Galarraga, Col | .370 |
| 1976 | Bill Madlock, Chi | .339 | 1994 | Tony Gwynn, SD | .394 |
| 1977 | Dave Parker, Pitt | .338 | 1995 | Tony Gwynn, SD | .368 |

## Leaders in Runs Scored

| Year | Player and Team | Runs | Year | Player and Team | Runs |
|---|---|---|---|---|---|
| 1900 | Roy Thomas, Phil | 131 | 1938 | Mel Ott, NY | 116 |
| 1901 | Jesse Burkett, StL | 139 | 1939 | Billy Werber, Cin | 115 |
| 1902 | Honus Wagner, Pitt | 105 | 1940 | Arky Vaughan, Pitt | 113 |
| 1903 | Ginger Beaumont, Pitt | 137 | 1941 | Pete Reiser, Bklyn | 117 |
| 1904 | George Browne, NY | 99 | 1942 | Mel Ott, NY | 118 |
| 1905 | Mike Donlin, NY | 124 | 1943 | Arky Vaughan, Bklyn | 112 |
| 1906 | Honus Wagner, Pitt | 103 | 1944 | Bill Nicholson, Chi | 116 |
|  | Frank Chance, Chi | 103 | 1945 | Eddie Stanky, Bklyn | 128 |
| 1907 | Spike Shannon, NY | 104 | 1946 | Stan Musial, StL | 124 |
| 1908 | Fred Tenney, NY | 101 | 1947 | Johnny Mize, NY | 137 |
| 1909 | Tommy Leach, Pitt | 126 | 1948 | Stan Musial, StL | 135 |
| 1910 | Sherry Magee, Phil | 110 | 1949 | Pee Wee Reese, Bklyn | 132 |
| 1911 | Jimmy Sheckard, Chi | 121 | 1950 | Earl Torgeson, Bos | 120 |
| 1912 | Bob Bescher, Cin | 120 | 1951 | Stan Musial, StL | 124 |
| 1913 | Tommy Leach, Chi | 99 |  | Ralph Kiner, Pitt | 124 |
|  | Max Carey, Pitt | 99 | 1952 | Stan Musial, StL | 105 |
| 1914 | George Burns, NY | 100 |  | Solly Hemus, StL | 105 |
| 1915 | Gavvy Cravath, Phil | 89 | 1953 | Duke Snider, Bklyn | 132 |
| 1916 | George Burns, NY | 105 | 1954 | Stan Musial, StL | 120 |
| 1917 | George Burns, NY | 103 |  | Duke Snider, Bklyn | 120 |
| 1918 | Heinie Groh, Cin | 88 | 1955 | Duke Snider, Bklyn | 126 |
| 1919 | George Burns, NY | 86 | 1956 | Frank Robinson, Cin | 122 |
| 1920 | George Burns, NY | 115 | 1957 | Hank Aaron, Mil | 118 |
| 1921 | Rogers Hornsby, StL | 131 | 1958 | Willie Mays, SF | 121 |
| 1922 | Rogers Hornsby, StL | 141 | 1959 | Vada Pinson, Cin | 131 |
| 1923 | Ross Youngs, NY | 121 | 1960 | Bill Bruton, Mil | 112 |
| 1924 | Frankie Frisch, NY | 121 | 1961 | Willie Mays, SF | 129 |
|  | Rogers Hornsby, StL | 121 | 1962 | Frank Robinson, Cin | 134 |
| 1925 | Kiki Cuyler, Pitt | 144 | 1963 | Hank Aaron, Mil | 121 |
| 1926 | Kiki Cuyler, Pitt | 113 | 1964 | Dick Allen, Phil | 125 |
| 1927 | Lloyd Waner, Pitt | 133 | 1965 | Tommy Harper, Cin | 126 |
|  | Rogers Hornsby, NY | 133 | 1966 | Felipe Alou, Atl | 122 |
| 1928 | Paul Waner, Pitt | 142 | 1967 | Hank Aaron, Atl | 113 |
| 1929 | Rogers Hornsby, Chi | 156 |  | Lou Brock, StL | 113 |
| 1930 | Chuck Klein, Phil | 158 | 1968 | Glenn Beckert, Chi | 98 |
| 1931 | Bill Terry, NY | 121 | 1969 | Bobby Bonds, SF | 120 |
|  | Chuck Klein, Phil | 121 |  | Pete Rose, Cin | 120 |
| 1932 | Chuck Klein, Phil | 152 | 1970 | Billy Williams, Chi | 137 |
| 1933 | Pepper Martin, StL | 122 | 1971 | Lou Brock, StL | 126 |
| 1934 | Paul Waner, Pitt | 122 | 1972 | Joe Morgan, Cin | 122 |
| 1935 | Augie Galan, Chi | 133 | 1973 | Bobby Bonds, SF | 131 |
| 1936 | Arky Vaughan, Pitt | 122 | 1974 | Pete Rose, Cin | 110 |
| 1937 | Joe Medwick, StL | 111 | 1975 | Pete Rose, Cin | 112 |

## Leader in Runs Scored *(Cont.)*

| Year | Player and Team | Runs | Year | Player and Team | Runs |
|---|---|---|---|---|---|
| 1976 | Pete Rose, Cin | 130 | 1987 | Tim Raines, Mtl | 123 |
| 1977 | George Foster, Cin | 124 | 1988 | Brett Butler, SF | 109 |
| 1978 | Ivan DeJesus, Chi | 104 | 1989 | Howard Johnson, NY | 104 |
| 1979 | Keith Hernandez, StL | 116 | | Will Clark, SF | 104 |
| 1980 | Keith Hernandez, StL | 111 | | Ryne Sandberg, Chi | 104 |
| 1981 | Mike Schmidt, Phil | 78 | 1990 | Ryne Sandberg, Chi | 116 |
| 1982 | Lonnie Smith, StL | 120 | 1991 | Brett Butler, LA | 112 |
| 1983 | Tim Raines, Mtl | 133 | 1992 | Barry Bonds, Pitt | 109 |
| 1984 | Ryne Sandberg, Chi | 114 | 1993 | Lenny Dykstra, Phil | 143 |
| 1985 | Dale Murphy, Atl | 118 | 1994 | Jeff Bagwell, Hou | 104 |
| 1986 | Von Hayes, Phil | 107 | 1995 | Craig Biggio, Hou | 123 |
| | Tony Gwynn, SD | 107 | | | |

## Leaders in Hits

| Year | Player and Team | Hits | Year | Player and Team | Hits |
|---|---|---|---|---|---|
| 1900 | Willie Keeler, Bklyn | 208 | 1945 | Tommy Holmes, Bos | 224 |
| 1901 | Jesse Burkett, StL | 228 | 1946 | Stan Musial, StL | 228 |
| 1902 | Ginger Beaumont, Pitt | 194 | 1947 | Tommy Holmes, Bos | 191 |
| 1903 | Ginger Beaumont, Pitt | 209 | 1948 | Stan Musial, StL | 230 |
| 1904 | Ginger Beaumont, Pitt | 185 | 1949 | Stan Musial, StL | 207 |
| 1905 | Cy Seymour, Cin | 219 | 1950 | Duke Snider, Bklyn | 199 |
| 1906 | Harry Steinfeldt, Chi | 176 | 1951 | Richie Ashburn, Phil | 221 |
| 1907 | Ginger Beaumont, Bos | 187 | 1952 | Stan Musial, StL | 194 |
| 1908 | Honus Wagner, Pitt | 201 | 1953 | Richie Ashburn, Phil | 205 |
| 1909 | Larry Doyle, NY | 172 | 1954 | Don Mueller, NY | 212 |
| 1910 | Honus Wagner, Pitt | 178 | 1955 | Ted Kluszewski, Cin | 192 |
| | Bobby Byrne, Pitt | 178 | 1956 | Hank Aaron, Mil | 200 |
| 1911 | Doc Miller, Bos | 192 | 1957 | Red Schoendienst, NY-Mil | 200 |
| 1912 | Heinie Zimmerman, Chi | 207 | 1958 | Richie Ashburn, Phil | 215 |
| 1913 | Gavvy Cravath, Phil | 179 | 1959 | Hank Aaron, Mil | 223 |
| 1914 | Sherry Magee, Phil | 171 | 1960 | Willie Mays, SF | 190 |
| 1915 | Larry Doyle, NY | 189 | 1961 | Vada Pinson, Cin | 208 |
| 1916 | Hal Chase, Cin | 184 | 1962 | Tommy Davis, LA | 230 |
| 1917 | Heinie Groh, Cin | 182 | 1963 | Vada Pinson, Cin | 204 |
| 1918 | Charlie Hollocher, Chi | 161 | 1964 | Roberto Clemente, Pitt | 211 |
| 1919 | Ivy Olson, Bklyn | 164 | | Curt Flood, StL | 211 |
| 1920 | Rogers Hornsby, StL | 218 | 1965 | Pete Rose, Cin | 209 |
| 1921 | Rogers Hornsby, StL | 235 | 1966 | Felipe Alou, Atl | 218 |
| 1922 | Rogers Hornsby, StL | 250 | 1967 | Roberto Clemente, Pitt | 209 |
| 1923 | Frankie Frisch, NY | 223 | 1968 | Felipe Alou, Atl | 210 |
| 1924 | Rogers Hornsby, StL | 227 | | Pete Rose, Cin | 210 |
| 1925 | Jim Bottomley, StL | 227 | 1969 | Matty Alou, Pitt | 231 |
| 1926 | Eddie Brown, Bos | 201 | 1970 | Pete Rose, Cin | 205 |
| 1927 | Paul Waner, Pitt | 237 | | Billy Williams, Chi | 205 |
| 1928 | Freddy Lindstrom, NY | 231 | 1971 | Joe Torre, StL | 230 |
| 1929 | Lefty O'Doul, Phil | 254 | 1972 | Pete Rose, Cin | 198 |
| 1930 | Bill Terry, NY | 254 | 1973 | Pete Rose, Cin | 230 |
| 1931 | Lloyd Waner, Pitt | 214 | 1974 | Ralph Garr, Atl | 214 |
| 1932 | Chuck Klein, Phil | 226 | 1975 | Dave Cash, Phil | 213 |
| 1933 | Chuck Klein, Phil | 223 | 1976 | Pete Rose, Cin | 215 |
| 1934 | Paul Waner, Pitt | 217 | 1977 | Dave Parker, Pitt | 215 |
| 1935 | Billy Herman, Chi | 227 | 1978 | Steve Garvey, LA | 202 |
| 1936 | Joe Medwick, StL | 223 | 1979 | Garry Templeton, StL | 211 |
| 1937 | Joe Medwick, StL | 237 | 1980 | Steve Garvey, LA | 200 |
| 1938 | Frank McCormick, Cin | 209 | 1981 | Pete Rose, Phil | 140 |
| 1939 | Frank McCormick, Cin | 209 | 1982 | Al Oliver, Mtl | 204 |
| 1940 | Stan Hack, Chi | 191 | 1983 | Jose Cruz, Hou | 189 |
| | Frank McCormick, Cin | 191 | | Andre Dawson, Mtl | 189 |
| 1941 | Stan Hack, Chi | 186 | 1984 | Tony Gwynn, SD | 213 |
| 1942 | Enos Slaughter, StL | 188 | 1985 | Willie McGee, StL | 216 |
| 1943 | Stan Musial, StL | 220 | 1986 | Tony Gwynn, SD | 211 |
| 1944 | Stan Musial, StL | 197 | 1987 | Tony Gwynn, SD | 218 |
| | Phil Cavarretta, Chi | 197 | 1988 | Andres Galarraga, Mtl | 184 |

## Leaders in Hits (Cont.)

| Year | Player and Team | Hits | Year | Player and Team | Hits |
|------|-----------------|------|------|-----------------|------|
| 1989 | Tony Gwynn, SD | 203 | 1993 | Lenny Dykstra, Phil | 194 |
| 1990 | Brett Butler, SF | 192 | 1994 | Tony Gwynn, SD | 165 |
|      | Lenny Dykstra, Phil | 192 | 1995 | Dante Bichette, Col | 197 |
| 1991 | Terry Pendleton, Atl | 187 |      | Tony Gwynn, SD | 197 |
| 1992 | Terry Pendleton, Atl | 199 |      |                 |      |
|      | Andy Van Slyke, Pitt | 199 |      |                 |      |

## Home Run Leaders

| Year | Player and Team | HR | Year | Player and Team | HR |
|------|-----------------|----|------|-----------------|----|
| 1900 | Herman Long, Bos | 12 | 1947 | Ralph Kiner, Pitt | 51 |
| 1901 | Sam Crawford, Cin | 16 |      | Johnny Mize, NY | 51 |
| 1902 | Tommy Leach, Pitt | 6 | 1948 | Ralph Kiner, Pitt | 40 |
| 1903 | Jimmy Sheckard, Bklyn | 9 |      | Johnny Mize, NY | 40 |
| 1904 | Harry Lumley, Bklyn | 9 | 1949 | Ralph Kiner, Pitt | 54 |
| 1905 | Fred Odwell, Cin | 9 | 1950 | Ralph Kiner, Pitt | 47 |
| 1906 | Tim Jordan, Bklyn | 12 | 1951 | Ralph Kiner, Pitt | 42 |
| 1907 | Dave Brain, Bos | 10 | 1952 | Ralph Kiner, Pitt | 37 |
| 1908 | Tim Jordan, Bklyn | 12 |      | Hank Sauer, Chi | 37 |
| 1909 | Red Murray, NY | 7 | 1953 | Eddie Mathews, Mil | 47 |
| 1910 | Fred Beck, Bos | 10 | 1954 | Ted Kluszewski, Cin | 49 |
|      | Wildfire Schulte, Chi | 10 | 1955 | Willie Mays, NY | 51 |
| 1911 | Wildfire Schulte, Chi | 21 | 1956 | Duke Snider, Bklyn | 43 |
| 1912 | Heinie Zimmerman, Chi | 14 | 1957 | Hank Aaron, Mil | 44 |
| 1913 | Gavvy Cravath, Phil | 19 | 1958 | Ernie Banks, Chi | 47 |
| 1914 | Gavvy Cravath, Phil | 19 | 1959 | Eddie Mathews, Mil | 46 |
| 1915 | Gavvy Cravath, Phil | 24 | 1960 | Ernie Banks, Chi | 41 |
| 1916 | Dave Robertson, NY | 12 | 1961 | Orlando Cepeda, SF | 46 |
|      | Cy Williams, Chi | 12 | 1962 | Willie Mays, SF | 49 |
| 1917 | Dave Robertson, NY | 12 | 1963 | Hank Aaron, Mil | 44 |
|      | Gavvy Cravath, Phil | 12 |      | Willie McCovey, SF | 44 |
| 1918 | Gavvy Cravath, Phil | 8 | 1964 | Willie Mays, SF | 47 |
| 1919 | Gavvy Cravath, Phil | 12 | 1965 | Willie Mays, SF | 52 |
| 1920 | Cy Williams, Phil | 15 | 1966 | Hank Aaron, Atl | 44 |
| 1921 | George Kelly, NY | 23 | 1967 | Hank Aaron, Atl | 39 |
| 1922 | Rogers Hornsby, StL | 42 | 1968 | Willie McCovey, SF | 36 |
| 1923 | Cy Williams, Phil | 41 | 1969 | Willie McCovey, SF | 45 |
| 1924 | Jack Fournier, Bklyn | 27 | 1970 | Johnny Bench, Cin | 45 |
| 1925 | Rogers Hornsby, StL | 39 | 1971 | Willie Stargell, Pitt | 48 |
| 1926 | Hack Wilson, Chi | 21 | 1972 | Johnny Bench, Cin | 40 |
| 1927 | Hack Wilson, Chi | 30 | 1973 | Willie Stargell, Pitt | 44 |
|      | Cy Williams, Phil | 30 | 1974 | Mike Schmidt, Phil | 36 |
| 1928 | Hack Wilson, Chi | 31 | 1975 | Mike Schmidt, Phil | 38 |
|      | Jim Bottomley, StL | 31 | 1976 | Mike Schmidt, Phil | 38 |
| 1929 | Chuck Klein, Phil | 43 | 1977 | George Foster, Cin | 52 |
| 1930 | Hack Wilson, Chi | 56 | 1978 | George Foster, Cin | 40 |
| 1931 | Chuck Klein, Phil | 31 | 1979 | Dave Kingman, Chi | 48 |
| 1932 | Chuck Klein, Phil | 38 | 1980 | Mike Schmidt, Phil | 48 |
|      | Mel Ott, NY | 38 | 1981 | Mike Schmidt, Phil | 31 |
| 1933 | Chuck Klein, Phil | 28 | 1982 | Dave Kingman, NY | 37 |
| 1934 | Ripper Collins, StL | 35 | 1983 | Mike Schmidt, Phil | 40 |
|      | Mel Ott, NY | 35 | 1984 | Dale Murphy, Atl | 36 |
| 1935 | Wally Berger, Bos | 34 |      | Mike Schmidt, Phil | 36 |
| 1936 | Mel Ott, NY | 33 | 1985 | Dale Murphy, Atl | 37 |
| 1937 | Mel Ott, NY | 31 | 1986 | Mike Schmidt, Phil | 37 |
|      | Joe Medwick, StL | 31 | 1987 | Andre Dawson, Chi | 49 |
| 1938 | Mel Ott, NY | 36 | 1988 | Darryl Strawberry, NY | 39 |
| 1939 | Johnny Mize, StL | 28 | 1989 | Kevin Mitchell, SF | 47 |
| 1940 | Johnny Mize, StL | 43 | 1990 | Ryne Sandberg, Chi | 40 |
| 1941 | Dolph Camilli, Bklyn | 34 | 1991 | Howard Johnson, NY | 38 |
| 1942 | Mel Ott, NY | 30 | 1992 | Fred McGriff, SD | 35 |
| 1943 | Bill Nicholson, Chi | 29 | 1993 | Barry Bonds, SF | 46 |
| 1944 | Bill Nicholson, Chi | 33 | 1994 | Matt Williams, SF | 43 |
| 1945 | Tommy Holmes, Bos | 28 | 1995 | Dante Bichette, Col | 40 |
| 1946 | Ralph Kiner, Pitt | 23 |      |                 |    |

## Runs Batted In Leaders

| Year | Player and Team | RBI | Year | Player and Team | RBI |
|------|-----------------|-----|------|-----------------|-----|
| 1900 | Elmer Flick, Phil | 110 | 1948 | Stan Musial, StL | 131 |
| 1901 | Honus Wagner, Pitt | 126 | 1949 | Ralph Kiner, Pitt | 127 |
| 1902 | Honus Wagner, Pitt | 91 | 1950 | Del Ennis, Phil | 126 |
| 1903 | Sam Mertes, NY | 104 | 1951 | Monte Irvin, NY | 121 |
| 1904 | Bill Dahlen, NY | 80 | 1952 | Hank Sauer, Chi | 121 |
| 1905 | Cy Seymour, Cin | 121 | 1953 | Roy Campanella, Bklyn | 142 |
| 1906 | Jim Nealon, Pitt | 83 | 1954 | Ted Kluszewski, Cin | 141 |
|  | Harry Steinfeldt, Chi | 83 | 1955 | Duke Snider, Bklyn | 136 |
| 1907 | Sherry Magee, Phil | 85 | 1956 | Stan Musial, StL | 109 |
| 1908 | Honus Wagner, Pitt | 109 | 1957 | Hank Aaron, Mil | 132 |
| 1909 | Honus Wagner, Pitt | 100 | 1958 | Ernie Banks, Chi | 129 |
| 1910 | Sherry Magee, Phil | 123 | 1959 | Ernie Banks, Chi | 143 |
| 1911 | Wildfire Schulte, Chi | 121 | 1960 | Hank Aaron, Mil | 126 |
| 1912 | Heinie Zimmerman, Chi | 103 | 1961 | Orlando Cepeda, SF | 142 |
| 1913 | Gavvy Cravath, Phil | 128 | 1962 | Tommy Davis, LA | 153 |
| 1914 | Sherry Magee, Phil | 103 | 1963 | Hank Aaron, Mil | 130 |
| 1915 | Gavvy Cravath, Phil | 115 | 1964 | Ken Boyer, StL | 119 |
| 1916 | Heinie Zimmerman, Chi-NY | 83 | 1965 | Deron Johnson, Cin | 130 |
| 1917 | Heinie Zimmerman, NY | 102 | 1966 | Hank Aaron, Atl | 127 |
| 1918 | Sherry Magee, Phil | 76 | 1967 | Orlando Cepeda, StL | 111 |
| 1919 | Hi Myers, Bklyn | 73 | 1968 | Willie McCovey, SF | 105 |
| 1920 | George Kelly, NY | 94 | 1969 | Willie McCovey, SF | 126 |
|  | Rogers Hornsby, StL | 94 | 1970 | Johnny Bench, Cin | 148 |
| 1921 | Rogers Hornsby, StL | 126 | 1971 | Joe Torre, StL | 137 |
| 1922 | Rogers Hornsby, StL | 152 | 1972 | Johnny Bench, Cin | 125 |
| 1923 | Irish Meusel, NY | 125 | 1973 | Willie Stargell, Pitt | 119 |
| 1924 | George Kelly, NY | 136 | 1974 | Johnny Bench, Cin | 129 |
| 1925 | Rogers Hornsby, StL | 143 | 1975 | Greg Luzinski, Phil | 120 |
| 1926 | Jim Bottomley, StL | 120 | 1976 | George Foster, Cin | 121 |
| 1927 | Paul Waner, Pitt | 131 | 1977 | George Foster, Cin | 149 |
| 1928 | Jim Bottomley, StL | 136 | 1978 | George Foster, Cin | 120 |
| 1929 | Hack Wilson, Chi | 159 | 1979 | Dave Winfield, SD | 118 |
| 1930 | Hack Wilson, Chi | 190 | 1980 | Mike Schmidt, Phil | 121 |
| 1931 | Chuck Klein, Phil | 121 | 1981 | Mike Schmidt, Phil | 91 |
| 1932 | Don Hurst, Phil | 143 | 1982 | Dale Murphy, Atl | 109 |
| 1933 | Chuck Klein, Phil | 120 |  | Al Oliver, Mtl | 109 |
| 1934 | Mel Ott, NY | 135 | 1983 | Dale Murphy, Atl | 121 |
| 1935 | Wally Berger, Bos | 130 | 1984 | Gary Carter, Mtl | 106 |
| 1936 | Joe Medwick, StL | 138 |  | Mike Schmidt, Phil | 106 |
| 1937 | Joe Medwick, StL | 154 | 1985 | Dave Parker, Cin | 125 |
| 1938 | Joe Medwick, StL | 122 | 1986 | Mike Schmidt, Phil | 119 |
| 1939 | Frank McCormick, Cin | 128 | 1987 | Andre Dawson, Chi | 137 |
| 1940 | Johnny Mize, StL | 137 | 1988 | Will Clark, SF | 109 |
| 1941 | Dolph Camilli, Bklyn | 120 | 1989 | Kevin Mitchell, SF | 125 |
| 1942 | Johnny Mize, NY | 110 | 1990 | Matt Williams, SF | 122 |
| 1943 | Bill Nicholson, Chi | 128 | 1991 | Howard Johnson, NY | 117 |
| 1944 | Bill Nicholson, Chi | 122 | 1992 | Darren Daulton, Phil | 109 |
| 1945 | Dixie Walker, Bklyn | 124 | 1993 | Barry Bonds, SF | 123 |
| 1946 | Enos Slaughter, StL | 130 | 1994 | Jeff Bagwell, Hou | 116 |
| 1947 | Johnny Mize, NY | 138 | 1995 | Dante Bichette, Col | 128 |

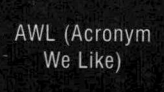

**AWL (Acronym We Like)**

Connoisseurs of the inspired acronym will remember CREEP, the Watergate-era Committee to Re-Elect the President; and COYOTE, the prostitutes' rights organization whose initials stand for Cast Off Your Old Tired Ethics. Well, the baseball strike created at least one by-product for which we are grateful: A group of disaffected fans mustered as the Newly Organized Society to Condemn Artificial Baseball, or NO-SCAB.

## Leading Base Stealers

| Year | Player and Team | SB | Year | Player and Team | SB |
|------|-----------------|-----|------|-----------------|-----|
| 1900 | George Van Haltren, NY | 45 | 1953 | Bill Bruton, Mil | 26 |
|      | Patsy Donovan, StL | 45 | 1954 | Bill Bruton, Mil | 34 |
| 1901 | Honus Wagner, Pitt | 48 | 1955 | Bill Bruton, Mil | 35 |
| 1902 | Honus Wagner, Pitt | 43 | 1956 | Willie Mays, NY | 40 |
| 1903 | Jimmy Sheckard, Bklyn | 67 | 1957 | Willie Mays, NY | 38 |
|      | Frank Chance, Chi | 67 | 1958 | Willie Mays, SF | 31 |
| 1904 | Honus Wagner, Pitt | 53 | 1959 | Willie Mays, SF | 27 |
| 1905 | Billy Maloney, Chi | 59 | 1960 | Maury Wills, LA | 50 |
|      | Art Devlin, NY | 59 | 1961 | Maury Wills, LA | 35 |
| 1906 | Frank Chance, Chi | 57 | 1962 | Maury Wills, LA | 104 |
| 1907 | Honus Wagner, Pitt | 61 | 1963 | Maury Wills, LA | 40 |
| 1908 | Honus Wagner, Pitt | 53 | 1964 | Maury Wills, LA | 53 |
| 1909 | Bob Bescher, Cin | 54 | 1965 | Maury Wills, LA | 94 |
| 1910 | Bob Bescher, Cin | 70 | 1966 | Lou Brock, StL | 74 |
| 1911 | Bob Bescher, Cin | 80 | 1967 | Lou Brock, StL | 52 |
| 1912 | Bob Bescher, Cin | 67 | 1968 | Lou Brock, StL | 62 |
| 1913 | Max Carey, Pitt | 61 | 1969 | Lou Brock, StL | 53 |
| 1914 | George Burns, NY | 62 | 1970 | Bobby Tolan, Cin | 57 |
| 1915 | Max Carey, Pitt | 36 | 1971 | Lou Brock, StL | 64 |
| 1916 | Max Carey, Pitt | 63 | 1972 | Lou Brock, StL | 63 |
| 1917 | Max Carey, Pitt | 46 | 1973 | Lou Brock, StL | 70 |
| 1918 | Max Carey, Pitt | 58 | 1974 | Lou Brock, StL | 118 |
| 1919 | George Burns, NY | 40 | 1975 | Davey Lopes, LA | 77 |
| 1920 | Max Carey, Pitt | 52 | 1976 | Davey Lopes, LA | 63 |
| 1921 | Frankie Frisch, NY | 49 | 1977 | Frank Taveras, Pitt | 70 |
| 1922 | Max Carey, Pitt | 51 | 1978 | Omar Moreno, Pitt | 71 |
| 1923 | Max Carey, Pitt | 51 | 1979 | Omar Moreno, Pitt | 77 |
| 1924 | Max Carey, Pitt | 49 | 1980 | Ron LeFlore, Mtl | 97 |
| 1925 | Max Carey, Pitt | 46 | 1981 | Tim Raines, Mtl | 71 |
| 1926 | Kiki Cuyler, Pitt | 35 | 1982 | Tim Raines, Mtl | 78 |
| 1927 | Frankie Frisch, StL | 48 | 1983 | Tim Raines, Mtl | 90 |
| 1928 | Kiki Cuyler, Chi | 37 | 1984 | Tim Raines, Mtl | 75 |
| 1929 | Kiki Cuyler, Chi | 43 | 1985 | Vince Coleman, StL | 110 |
| 1930 | Kiki Cuyler, Chi | 37 | 1986 | Vince Coleman, StL | 107 |
| 1931 | Frankie Frisch, StL | 28 | 1987 | Vince Coleman, StL | 109 |
| 1932 | Chuck Klein, Phil | 20 | 1988 | Vince Coleman, StL | 81 |
| 1933 | Pepper Martin, StL | 26 | 1989 | Vince Coleman, StL | 65 |
| 1934 | Pepper Martin, StL | 23 | 1990 | Vince Coleman, StL | 77 |
| 1935 | Augie Galan, Chi | 22 | 1991 | Marquis Grissom, Mtl | 76 |
| 1936 | Pepper Martin, StL | 23 | 1992 | Marquis Grissom, Mtl | 78 |
| 1937 | Augie Galan, Chi | 23 | 1993 | Chuck Carr, Flor | 58 |
| 1938 | Stan Hack, Chi | 16 | 1994 | Craig Biggio, Hou | 39 |
| 1939 | Stan Hack, Chi | 17 | 1995 | Quilvio Veras, Fla | 56 |
|      | Lee Handley, Pitt | 17 | | | |
| 1940 | Lonny Frey, Cin | 22 | | | |
| 1941 | Danny Murtaugh, Phil | 18 | | | |
| 1942 | Pete Reiser, Bklyn | 20 | | | |
| 1943 | Arky Vaughan, Bklyn | 20 | | | |
| 1944 | Johnny Barrett, Pitt | 28 | | | |
| 1945 | Red Schoendienst, StL | 26 | | | |
| 1946 | Pete Reiser, Bklyn | 34 | | | |
| 1947 | Jackie Robinson, Bklyn | 29 | | | |
| 1948 | Richie Ashburn, Phil | 32 | | | |
| 1949 | Jackie Robinson, Bklyn | 37 | | | |
| 1950 | Sam Jethroe, Bos | 35 | | | |
| 1951 | Sam Jethroe, Bos | 35 | | | |
| 1952 | Pee Wee Reese, Bklyn | 30 | | | |

## THEY SAID IT

*Steve Blass, Pittsburgh Pirate broadcaster, on Buc replacement player Jimmy Boudreau, who last appeared professionally in 1986: "He should have been better, pitching on 3,195 days' rest."*

## Leading Pitchers—Winning Percentage

| Year | Pitcher and Team | W | L | Pct | Year | Pitcher and Team | W | L | Pct |
|------|-----------------|---|---|-----|------|------------------|---|---|-----|
| 1900 | Jesse Tannehill, Pitt | 20 | 6 | .769 | 1949 | Preacher Roe, Bklyn | 15 | 6 | .714 |
| 1901 | Jack Chesbro, Pitt | 21 | 10 | .677 | 1950 | Sal Maglie, NY | 18 | 4 | .818 |
| 1902 | Jack Chesbro, Pitt | 28 | 6 | .824 | 1951 | Preacher Roe, Bklyn | 22 | 3 | .880 |
| 1903 | Sam Leever, Pitt | 25 | 7 | .781 | 1952 | Hoyt Wilhelm, NY | 15 | 3 | .833 |
| 1904 | Joe McGinnity, NY | 35 | 8 | .814 | 1953 | Carl Erskine, Bklyn | 20 | 6 | .769 |
| 1905 | Sam Leever, Pitt | 20 | 5 | .800 | 1954 | Johnny Antonelli, NY | 21 | 7 | .750 |
| 1906 | Ed Reulbach, Chi | 19 | 4 | .826 | 1955 | Don Newcombe, Bklyn | 20 | 5 | .800 |
| 1907 | Ed Reulbach, Chi | 17 | 4 | .810 | 1956 | Don Newcombe, Bklyn | 27 | 7 | .794 |
| 1908 | Ed Reulbach, Chi | 24 | 7 | .774 | 1957 | Bob Buhl, Mil | 18 | 7 | .720 |
| 1909 | Christy Mathewson, NY | 25 | 6 | .806 | 1958 | Warren Spahn, Mil | 22 | 11 | .667 |
|      | Howie Camnitz, Pitt | 25 | 6 | .806 |      | Lew Burdette, Mil | 20 | 10 | .667 |
| 1910 | King Cole, Chi | 20 | 4 | .833 | 1959 | Roy Face, Pitt | 18 | 1 | .947 |
| 1911 | Rube Marquard, NY | 24 | 7 | .774 | 1960 | Ernie Broglio, StL | 21 | 9 | .700 |
| 1912 | Claude Hendrix, Pitt | 24 | 9 | .727 | 1961 | Johnny Podres, LA | 18 | 5 | .783 |
| 1913 | Bert Humphries, Chi | 16 | 4 | .800 | 1962 | Bob Purkey, Cin | 23 | 5 | .821 |
| 1914 | Bill James, Bos | 26 | 7 | .788 | 1963 | Ron Perranoski, LA | 16 | 3 | .842 |
| 1915 | Grover Alexander, Phil | 31 | 10 | .756 | 1964 | Sandy Koufax, LA | 19 | 5 | .792 |
| 1916 | Tom Hughes, Bos | 16 | 3 | .842 | 1965 | Sandy Koufax, LA | 26 | 8 | .765 |
| 1917 | Ferdie Schupp, NY | 21 | 7 | .750 | 1966 | Juan Marichal, SF | 25 | 6 | .806 |
| 1918 | Claude Hendrix, Chi | 19 | 7 | .731 | 1967 | Dick Hughes, StL | 16 | 6 | .727 |
| 1919 | Dutch Ruether, Cin | 19 | 6 | .760 | 1968 | Steve Blass, Pitt | 18 | 6 | .750 |
| 1920 | Burleigh Grimes, Bklyn | 23 | 11 | .676 | 1969 | Tom Seaver, NY | 25 | 7 | .781 |
| 1921 | Bill Doak, StL | 15 | 6 | .714 | 1970 | Bob Gibson, StL | 23 | 7 | .767 |
| 1922 | Pete Donohue, Cin | 18 | 9 | .667 | 1971 | Don Gullett, Cin | 16 | 6 | .727 |
| 1923 | Dolf Luque, Cin | 27 | 8 | .771 | 1972 | Gary Nolan, Cin | 15 | 5 | .750 |
| 1924 | Emil Yde, Pitt | 16 | 3 | .842 | 1973 | Tommy John, LA | 16 | 7 | .696 |
| 1925 | Bill Sherdel, StL | 15 | 6 | .714 | 1974 | Andy Messersmith, LA | 20 | 6 | .769 |
| 1926 | Ray Kremer, Pitt | 20 | 6 | .769 | 1975 | Don Gullett, Cin | 15 | 4 | .789 |
| 1927 | Larry Benton, Bos-NY | 17 | 7 | .708 | 1976 | Steve Carlton, Phil | 20 | 7 | .741 |
| 1928 | Larry Benton, NY | 25 | 9 | .735 | 1977 | John Candelaria, Pitt | 20 | 5 | .800 |
| 1929 | Charlie Root, Chi | 19 | 6 | .760 | 1978 | Gaylord Perry, SD | 21 | 6 | .778 |
| 1930 | Freddie Fitzsimmons, NY | 19 | 7 | .731 | 1979 | Tom Seaver, Cin | 16 | 6 | .727 |
| 1931 | Paul Derringer, StL | 18 | 8 | .692 | 1980 | Jim Bibby, Pitt | 19 | 6 | .760 |
| 1932 | Lon Warneke, Chi | 22 | 6 | .786 | 1981* | Tom Seaver, Cin | 14 | 2 | .875 |
| 1933 | Ben Cantwell, Bos | 20 | 10 | .667 | 1982 | Phil Niekro, Atl | 17 | 4 | .810 |
| 1934 | Dizzy Dean, StL | 30 | 7 | .811 | 1983 | John Denny, Phil | 19 | 6 | .760 |
| 1935 | Bill Lee, Chi | 20 | 6 | .769 | 1984 | Rick Sutcliffe, Chi | 16 | 1 | .941 |
| 1936 | Carl Hubbell, NY | 26 | 6 | .813 | 1985 | Orel Hershiser, LA | 19 | 3 | .864 |
| 1937 | Carl Hubbell, NY | 22 | 8 | .733 | 1986 | Bob Ojeda, NY | 18 | 5 | .783 |
| 1938 | Bill Lee, Chi | 22 | 9 | .710 | 1987 | Dwight Gooden, NY | 15 | 7 | .682 |
| 1939 | Paul Derringer, Cin | 25 | 7 | .781 | 1988 | David Cone, NY | 20 | 3 | .870 |
| 1940 | Freddie Fitzsimmons, Bklyn | 16 | 2 | .889 | 1989 | Mike Bielecki, Chi | 18 | 7 | .720 |
| 1941 | Elmer Riddle, Cin | 19 | 4 | .826 | 1990 | Doug Drabeck, Pitt | 22 | 6 | .786 |
| 1942 | Larry French, Bklyn | 15 | 4 | .789 | 1991 | John Smiley, Pitt | 20 | 8 | .714 |
| 1943 | Mort Cooper, StL | 21 | 8 | .724 |      | Jose Rijo, Cin | 15 | 6 | .714 |
| 1944 | Ted Wilks, StL | 17 | 4 | .810 | 1992 | Bob Tewksbury, StL | 16 | 5 | .762 |
| 1945 | Harry Brecheen, StL | 15 | 4 | .789 | 1993 | Tom Glavine, Atl | 22 | 6 | .786 |
| 1946 | Murray Dickson, StL | 15 | 6 | .714 | 1994 | Ken Hill, Mtl | 16 | 5 | .762 |
| 1947 | Larry Jansen, NY | 21 | 5 | .808 | 1995 | Greg Maddux, Atl | 19 | 2 | .905 |
| 1948 | Harry Brecheen, StL | 20 | 7 | .741 |      |                  |    |    |      |

*1981 percentages based on 10 or more victories.

Note: Based on 15 or more victories.

| Stale Air Down There | With fresh angles to the story of Michael Jordan's leaving baseball to return to the NBA in short supply, the Chicago media have been hard-pressed to find new variations on old themes. A particularly desperate reporter asked Jordan last April, "Michael, a lot of people have said you don't have your height back. Is that true?" Replied Jordan, "No, I'm still 6'6"." |
|---|---|

## Leading Pitchers—Earned-Run Average

| Year | Player and Team | ERA | Year | Player and Team | ERA |
|---|---|---|---|---|---|
| 1900 | Rube Waddell, Pitt | 2.37 | 1948 | Harry Brecheen, StL | 2.24 |
| 1901 | Jesse Tannehill, Pitt | 2.18 | 1949 | Dave Koslo, NY | 2.50 |
| 1902 | Jack Taylor, Chi | 1.33 | 1950 | Jim Hearn, StL-NY | 2.49 |
| 1903 | Sam Leever, Pitt | 2.06 | 1951 | Chet Nichols, Bos | 2.88 |
| 1904 | Joe McGinnity, NY | 1.61 | 1952 | Hoyt Wilhelm, NY | 2.43 |
| 1905 | Christy Mathewson, NY | 1.27 | 1953 | Warren Spahn, Mil | 2.10 |
| 1906 | Three Finger Brown, Chi | 1.04 | 1954 | Johnny Antonelli, NY | 2.29 |
| 1907 | Jack Pfiester, Chi | 1.15 | 1955 | Bob Friend, Pitt | 2.84 |
| 1908 | Christy Mathewson, NY | 1.43 | 1956 | Lew Burdette, Mil | 2.71 |
| 1909 | Christy Mathewson, NY | 1.14 | 1957 | Johnny Podres, Bklyn | 2.66 |
| 1910 | George McQuillan, Phil | 1.60 | 1958 | Stu Miller, SF | 2.47 |
| 1911 | Christy Mathewson, NY | 1.99 | 1959 | Sam Jones, SF | 2.82 |
| 1912 | Jeff Tesreau, NY | 1.96 | 1960 | Mike McCormick, SF | 2.70 |
| 1913 | Christy Mathewson, NY | 2.06 | 1961 | Warren Spahn, Mil | 3.01 |
| 1914 | Bill Doak, StL | 1.72 | 1962 | Sandy Koufax, LA | 2.54 |
| 1915 | Grover Alexander, Phil | 1.22 | 1963 | Sandy Koufax, LA | 1.88 |
| 1916 | Grover Alexander, Phil | 1.55 | 1964 | Sandy Koufax, LA | 1.74 |
| 1917 | Grover Alexander, Phil | 1.83 | 1965 | Sandy Koufax, LA | 2.04 |
| 1918 | Hippo Vaughn, Chi | 1.74 | 1966 | Sandy Koufax, LA | 1.73 |
| 1919 | Grover Alexander, Chi | 1.72 | 1967 | Phil Niekro, Atl | 1.87 |
| 1920 | Grover Alexander, Chi | 1.91 | 1968 | Bob Gibson, StL | 1.12 |
| 1921 | Bill Doak, StL | 2.58 | 1969 | Juan Marichal, SF | 2.10 |
| 1922 | Rosy Ryan, NY | 3.00 | 1970 | Tom Seaver, NY | 2.81 |
| 1923 | Dolf Luque, Cin | 1.93 | 1971 | Tom Seaver, NY | 1.76 |
| 1924 | Dazzy Vance, Bklyn | 2.16 | 1972 | Steve Carlton, Phil | 1.98 |
| 1925 | Dolf Luque, Cin | 2.63 | 1973 | Tom Seaver, NY | 2.08 |
| 1926 | Ray Kremer, Pitt | 2.61 | 1974 | Buzz Capra, Atl | 2.28 |
| 1927 | Ray Kremer, Pitt | 2.47 | 1975 | Randy Jones, SD | 2.24 |
| 1928 | Dazzy Vance, Bklyn | 2.09 | 1976 | John Denny, StL | 2.52 |
| 1929 | Bill Walker, NY | 3.08 | 1977 | John Candelaria, Pitt | 2.34 |
| 1930 | Dazzy Vance, Bklyn | 2.61 | 1978 | Craig Swan, NY | 2.43 |
| 1931 | Bill Walker, NY | 2.26 | 1979 | J.R. Richard, Hou | 2.71 |
| 1932 | Lon Warneke, Chi | 2.37 | 1980 | Don Sutton, LA | 2.21 |
| 1933 | Carl Hubbell, NY | 1.66 | 1981 | Nolan Ryan, Hou | 1.69 |
| 1934 | Carl Hubbell, NY | 2.30 | 1982 | Steve Rogers, Mtl | 2.40 |
| 1935 | Cy Blanton, Pitt | 2.59 | 1983 | Atlee Hammaker, SF | 2.25 |
| 1936 | Carl Hubbell, NY | 2.31 | 1984 | Alejandro Pena, LA | 2.48 |
| 1937 | Jim Turner, Bos | 2.38 | 1985 | Dwight Gooden, NY | 1.53 |
| 1938 | Bill Lee, Chi | 2.66 | 1986 | Mike Scott, Hou | 2.22 |
| 1939 | Bucky Walters, Cin | 2.29 | 1987 | Nolan Ryan, Hou | 2.76 |
| 1940 | Bucky Walters, Cin | 2.48 | 1988 | Joe Magrane, StL | 2.18 |
| 1941 | Elmer Riddle, Cin | 2.24 | 1989 | Scott Garrelts, SF | 2.28 |
| 1942 | Mort Cooper, StL | 1.77 | 1990 | Danny Darwin, Hou | 2.21 |
| 1943 | Howie Pollet, StL | 1.75 | 1991 | Dennis Martinez, Mtl | 2.39 |
| 1944 | Ed Heusser, Cin | 2.38 | 1992 | Bill Swift, SF | 2.08 |
| 1945 | Hank Borowy, Chi | 2.14 | 1993 | Greg Maddux, Atl | 2.36 |
| 1946 | Howie Pollet, StL | 2.10 | 1994 | Greg Maddux, Atl | 1.56 |
| 1947 | Warren Spahn, Bos | 2.33 | 1995 | Greg Maddux, Atl | 1.63 |

Note: Based on 10 complete games through 1950, then 154 innings until National League expanded in 1962, when it became 162 innings. In strike-shortened 1981, one inning per game required.

## Leading Pitchers—Strikeouts

| Year | Player and Team | SO | Year | Player and Team | SO |
|---|---|---|---|---|---|
| 1900 | Rube Waddell, Pitt | 133 | 1912 | Grover Alexander, Phil | 195 |
| 1901 | Noodles Hahn, Cin | 233 | 1913 | Tom Seaton, Phil | 168 |
| 1902 | Vic Willis, Bos | 226 | 1914 | Grover Alexander, Phil | 214 |
| 1903 | Christy Mathewson, NY | 267 | 1915 | Grover Alexander, Phil | 241 |
| 1904 | Christy Mathewson, NY | 212 | 1916 | Grover Alexander, Phil | 167 |
| 1905 | Christy Mathewson, NY | 206 | 1917 | Grover Alexander, Phil | 200 |
| 1906 | Fred Beebe, Chi-StL | 171 | 1918 | Hippo Vaughn, Chi | 148 |
| 1907 | Christy Mathewson, NY | 178 | 1919 | Hippo Vaughn, Chi | 141 |
| 1908 | Christy Mathewson, NY | 259 | 1920 | Grover Alexander, Chi | 173 |
| 1909 | Orval Overall, Chi | 205 | 1921 | Burleigh Grimes, Bklyn | 136 |
| 1910 | Christy Mathewson, NY | 190 | 1922 | Dazzy Vance, Bklyn | 134 |
| 1911 | Rube Marquard, NY | 237 | 1923 | Dazzy Vance, Bklyn | 197 |

## Leading Pitchers—Strikeouts (Cont.)

| Year | Player and Team | SO | Year | Player and Team | SO |
|------|-----------------|-----|------|-----------------|-----|
| 1924 | Dazzy Vance, Bklyn | 262 | 1959 | Don Drysdale, LA | 242 |
| 1925 | Dazzy Vance, Bklyn | 221 | 1960 | Don Drysdale, LA | 246 |
| 1926 | Dazzy Vance, Bklyn | 140 | 1961 | Sandy Koufax, LA | 269 |
| 1927 | Dazzy Vance, Bklyn | 184 | 1962 | Don Drysdale, LA | 232 |
| 1928 | Dazzy Vance, Bklyn | 200 | 1963 | Sandy Koufax, LA | 306 |
| 1929 | Pat Malone, Chi | 166 | 1964 | Bob Veale, Pitt | 250 |
| 1930 | Bill Hallahan, StL | 177 | 1965 | Sandy Koufax, LA | 382 |
| 1931 | Bill Hallahan, StL | 159 | 1966 | Sandy Koufax, LA | 317 |
| 1932 | Dizzy Dean, StL | 191 | 1967 | Jim Bunning, Phil | 253 |
| 1933 | Dizzy Dean, StL | 199 | 1968 | Bob Gibson, StL | 268 |
| 1934 | Dizzy Dean, StL | 195 | 1969 | Ferguson Jenkins, Chi | 273 |
| 1935 | Dizzy Dean, StL | 182 | 1970 | Tom Seaver, NY | 283 |
| 1936 | Van Lingle Mungo, Bklyn | 238 | 1971 | Tom Seaver, NY | 289 |
| 1937 | Carl Hubbell, NY | 159 | 1972 | Steve Carlton, Phil | 310 |
| 1938 | Clay Bryant, Chi | 135 | 1973 | Tom Seaver, NY | 251 |
| 1939 | Claude Passeau, Phil-Chi | 137 | 1974 | Steve Carlton, Phil | 240 |
|  | Bucky Walters, Cin | 137 | 1975 | Tom Seaver, NY | 243 |
| 1940 | Kirby Higbe, Phil | 137 | 1976 | Tom Seaver, NY | 235 |
| 1941 | Johnny Vander Meer, Cin | 202 | 1977 | Phil Niekro, Atl | 262 |
| 1942 | Johnny Vander Meer, Cin | 186 | 1978 | J.R. Richard, Hou | 303 |
| 1943 | Johnny Vander Meer, Cin | 174 | 1979 | J.R. Richard, Hou | 313 |
| 1944 | Bill Voiselle, NY | 161 | 1980 | Steve Carlton, Phil | 286 |
| 1945 | Preacher Roe, Pitt | 148 | 1981 | Fernando Valenzuela, LA | 180 |
| 1946 | Johnny Schmitz, Chi | 135 | 1982 | Steve Carlton, Phil | 286 |
| 1947 | Ewell Blackwell, Cin | 193 | 1983 | Steve Carlton, Phil | 275 |
| 1948 | Harry Brecheen, StL | 149 | 1984 | Dwight Gooden, NY | 276 |
| 1949 | Warren Spahn, Bos | 151 | 1985 | Dwight Gooden, NY | 268 |
| 1950 | Warren Spahn, Bos | 191 | 1986 | Mike Scott, Hou | 306 |
| 1951 | Warren Spahn, Bos | 164 | 1987 | Nolan Ryan, Hou | 270 |
|  | Don Newcombe, Bklyn | 164 | 1988 | Nolan Ryan, Hou | 228 |
| 1952 | Warren Spahn, Bos | 183 | 1989 | Jose DeLeon, StL | 201 |
| 1953 | Robin Roberts, Phil | 198 | 1990 | David Cone, NY | 233 |
| 1954 | Robin Roberts, Phil | 185 | 1991 | David Cone, NY | 241 |
| 1955 | Sam Jones, Chi | 198 | 1992 | John Smoltz, Atl | 215 |
| 1956 | Sam Jones, Chi | 176 | 1993 | Jose Rijo, Cin | 227 |
| 1957 | Jack Sanford, Phil | 188 | 1994 | Andy Benes, SD | 189 |
| 1958 | Sam Jones, StL | 225 | 1995 | Hideo Nomo, LA | 236 |

## Leading Pitchers—Saves

| Year | Player and Team | SV | Year | Player and Team | SV |
|------|-----------------|-----|------|-----------------|-----|
| 1947 | Hugh Casey, Bklyn | 18 | 1971 | Dave Giusti, Pitt | 30 |
| 1948 | Harry Gumpert, Cin | 17 | 1972 | Clay Carroll, Cin | 37 |
| 1949 | Ted Wilks, StL | 9 | 1973 | Mike Marshall, Mtl | 13 |
| 1950 | Jim Konstanty, Phil | 22 | 1974 | Mike Marshall, LA | 21 |
| 1951 | Ted Wilks, StL, Pitt | 13 | 1975 | Al Hrabosky, StL | 22 |
| 1952 | Al Brazle, StL | 16 |  | Rawly Eastwick, Cin | 22 |
| 1953 | Al Brazle, StL | 18 | 1976 | Rawly Eastwick, Cin | 26 |
| 1954 | Jim Hughes, Bklyn | 24 | 1977 | Rollie Fingers, SD | 35 |
| 1955 | Jack Meyer, Phil | 16 | 1978 | Rollie Fingers, SD | 37 |
| 1956 | Clem Labine, Bklyn | 19 | 1979 | Bruce Sutter, Chi | 37 |
| 1957 | Clem Labine, Bklyn | 17 | 1980 | Bruce Sutter, Chi | 28 |
| 1958 | Roy Face, Pitt | 20 | 1981 | Bruce Sutter, StL | 25 |
| 1959 | Lindy McDaniel, StL | 15 | 1982 | Bruce Sutter, StL | 36 |
|  | Don McMahon, Mil | 15 | 1983 | Lee Smith, Chi | 29 |
| 1960 | Lindy McDaniel, StL | 26 | 1984 | Bruce Sutter, StL | 45 |
| 1961 | Stu Miller, SF | 17 | 1985 | Jeff Reardon, Mtl | 41 |
|  | Roy Face, Pitt | 17 | 1986 | Todd Worrell, StL | 36 |
| 1962 | Roy Face, Pitt | 28 | 1987 | Steve Bedrosian, Phil | 40 |
| 1963 | Lindy McDaniel, Chi | 22 | 1988 | John Franco, Cin | 39 |
| 1964 | Hal Woodeshick, Hou | 23 | 1989 | Mark Davis, SD | 44 |
| 1965 | Ted Abernathy, Chi | 31 | 1990 | John Franco, NY | 33 |
| 1966 | Phil Regan, LA | 21 | 1991 | Lee Smith, StL | 47 |
| 1967 | Ted Abernathy, Cin | 28 | 1992 | Lee Smith, StL | 42 |
| 1968 | Phil Regan, Chi, LA | 25 | 1993 | Randy Myers, Chi | 53 |
| 1969 | Fred Gladding, Hou | 29 | 1994 | John Franco, NY | 30 |
| 1970 | Wayne Granger, Cin | 35 | 1995 | Randy Myers, Chi | 38 |

## Pennant Winners

| Year | Team | Manager | W | L | Pct | GA |
|------|------|---------|---|---|-----|-----|
| 1901 | Chicago | Clark Griffith | 83 | 53 | .610 | 4 |
| 1902 | Philadelphia | Connie Mack | 83 | 53 | .610 | 5 |
| 1903 | Boston | Jimmy Collins | 91 | 47 | .659 | 14½ |
| 1904 | Boston | Jimmy Collins | 95 | 59 | .617 | 1½ |
| 1905 | Philadelphia | Connie Mack | 92 | 56 | .622 | 2 |
| 1906 | Chicago | Fielder Jones | 93 | 58 | .616 | 3 |
| 1907 | Detroit | Hughie Jennings | 92 | 58 | .613 | 1½ |
| 1908 | Detroit | Hughie Jennings | 90 | 63 | .588 | ½ |
| 1909 | Detroit | Hughie Jennings | 98 | 54 | .645 | 3½ |
| 1910 | Philadelphia | Connie Mack | 102 | 48 | .680 | 14½ |
| 1911 | Philadelphia | Connie Mack | 101 | 50 | .669 | 13½ |
| 1912 | Boston | Jake Stahl | 105 | 47 | .691 | 14 |
| 1913 | Philadelphia | Connie Mack | 96 | 57 | .627 | 6½ |
| 1914 | Philadelphia | Connie Mack | 99 | 53 | .651 | 8½ |
| 1915 | Boston | Bill Carrigan | 101 | 50 | .669 | 2½ |
| 1916 | Boston | Bill Carrigan | 91 | 63 | .591 | 2 |
| 1917 | Chicago | Pants Rowland | 100 | 54 | .649 | 9 |
| 1918 | Boston | Ed Barrow | 75 | 51 | .595 | 2½ |
| 1919 | Chicago | Kid Gleason | 88 | 52 | .629 | 3½ |
| 1920 | Cleveland | Tris Speaker | 98 | 56 | .636 | 2 |
| 1921 | New York | Miller Huggins | 98 | 55 | .641 | 4½ |
| 1922 | New York | Miller Huggins | 94 | 60 | .610 | 1 |
| 1923 | New York | Miller Huggins | 98 | 54 | .645 | 16 |
| 1924 | Washington | Bucky Harris | 92 | 62 | .597 | 2 |
| 1925 | Washington | Bucky Harris | 96 | 55 | .636 | 8½ |
| 1926 | New York | Miller Huggins | 91 | 63 | .591 | 3 |
| 1927 | New York | Miller Huggins | 110 | 44 | .714 | 19 |
| 1928 | New York | Miller Huggins | 101 | 53 | .656 | 2½ |
| 1929 | Philadelphia | Connie Mack | 104 | 46 | .693 | 18 |
| 1930 | Philadelphia | Connie Mack | 102 | 52 | .662 | 8 |
| 1931 | Philadelphia | Connie Mack | 107 | 45 | .704 | 13½ |
| 1932 | New York | Joe McCarthy | 107 | 47 | .695 | 13 |
| 1933 | Washington | Joe Cronin | 99 | 53 | .651 | 7 |
| 1934 | Detroit | Mickey Cochrane | 101 | 53 | .656 | 7 |
| 1935 | Detroit | Mickey Cochrane | 93 | 58 | .616 | 3 |
| 1936 | New York | Joe McCarthy | 102 | 51 | .667 | 19½ |
| 1937 | New York | Joe McCarthy | 102 | 52 | .662 | 13 |
| 1938 | New York | Joe McCarthy | 99 | 53 | .651 | 9½ |
| 1939 | New York | Joe McCarthy | 106 | 45 | .702 | 17 |
| 1940 | Detroit | Del Baker | 90 | 64 | .584 | 1 |
| 1941 | New York | Joe McCarthy | 101 | 53 | .656 | 17 |
| 1942 | New York | Joe McCarthy | 103 | 51 | .669 | 9 |
| 1943 | New York | Joe McCarthy | 98 | 56 | .636 | 13½ |
| 1944 | St Louis | Luke Sewell | 89 | 65 | .578 | 1 |
| 1945 | Detroit | Steve O'Neill | 88 | 65 | .575 | 1½ |
| 1946 | Boston | Joe Cronin | 104 | 50 | .675 | 12 |
| 1947 | New York | Bucky Harris | 97 | 57 | .630 | 12 |
| 1948 | Cleveland† | Lou Boudreau | 97 | 58 | .626 | 1 |
| 1949 | New York | Casey Stengel | 97 | 57 | .630 | 1 |
| 1950 | New York | Casey Stengel | 98 | 56 | .636 | 3 |
| 1951 | New York | Casey Stengel | 98 | 56 | .636 | 5 |
| 1952 | New York | Casey Stengel | 95 | 59 | .617 | 2 |
| 1953 | New York | Casey Stengel | 99 | 52 | .656 | 8½ |
| 1954 | Cleveland | Al Lopez | 111 | 43 | .721 | 8 |
| 1955 | New York | Casey Stengel | 96 | 58 | .623 | 3 |
| 1956 | New York | Casey Stengel | 97 | 57 | .630 | 9 |
| 1957 | New York | Casey Stengel | 98 | 56 | .636 | 8 |
| 1958 | New York | Casey Stengel | 92 | 62 | .597 | 10 |
| 1959 | Chicago | Al Lopez | 94 | 60 | .610 | 5 |
| 1960 | New York | Casey Stengel | 97 | 57 | .630 | 8 |
| 1961 | New York | Ralph Houk | 109 | 53 | .673 | 8 |
| 1962 | New York | Ralph Houk | 96 | 66 | .593 | 5 |
| 1963 | New York | Ralph Houk | 104 | 57 | .646 | 10½ |
| 1964 | New York | Yogi Berra | 99 | 63 | .611 | 1 |

## Pennant Winners *(Cont.)*

| Year | Team | Manager | W | L | Pct | GA |
|------|------|---------|---|---|-----|-----|
| 1965 | Minnesota | Sam Mele | 102 | 60 | .630 | 7 |
| 1966 | Baltimore | Hank Bauer | 97 | 63 | .606 | 9 |
| 1967 | Boston | Dick Williams | 92 | 70 | .568 | 1 |
| 1968 | Detroit | Mayo Smith | 103 | 59 | .636 | 12 |
| 1969 | Baltimore (E)‡ | Earl Weaver | 109 | 53 | .673 | 19 |
| 1970 | Baltimore (E)‡ | Earl Weaver | 108 | 54 | .667 | 15 |
| 1971 | Baltimore (E)‡ | Earl Weaver | 101 | 57 | .639 | 12 |
| 1972 | Oakland (W)‡ | Dick Williams | 93 | 62 | .600 | 5½ |
| 1973 | Oakland (W)‡ | Dick Williams | 94 | 68 | .580 | 6 |
| 1974 | Oakland (W)‡ | Al Dark | 90 | 72 | .556 | 5 |
| 1975 | Boston (E)‡ | Darrell Johnson | 95 | 65 | .594 | 4½ |
| 1976 | New York (E)‡ | Billy Martin | 97 | 62 | .610 | 10½ |
| 1977 | New York (E)‡ | Billy Martin | 100 | 62 | .617 | 2½ |
| 1978 | New York (E)†‡ | Billy Martin, Bob Lemon | 100 | 63 | .613 | 1 |
| 1979 | Baltimore (E)‡ | Earl Weaver | 102 | 57 | .642 | 8 |
| 1980 | Kansas City (W)‡ | Jim Frey | 97 | 65 | .599 | 14 |
| 1981 | New York (E)‡ | Gene Michael, Bob Lemon | 59 | 48 | .551 | # |
| 1982 | Milwaukee (E)‡ | Buck Rodgers, Harvey Kuenn | 95 | 67 | .586 | 1 |
| 1983 | Baltimore (E)‡ | Joe Altobelli | 98 | 64 | .605 | 6 |
| 1984 | Detroit (E)‡ | Sparky Anderson | 104 | 58 | .642 | 15 |
| 1985 | Kansas City (W)‡ | Dick Howser | 91 | 71 | .562 | 1 |
| 1986 | Boston (E)‡ | John McNamara | 95 | 66 | .590 | 5½ |
| 1987 | Minnesota (W)‡ | Tom Kelly | 85 | 77 | .525 | 2 |
| 1988 | Oakland (W)‡ | Tony La Russa | 104 | 58 | .642 | 13 |
| 1989 | Oakland (W)‡ | Tony La Russa | 99 | 63 | .611 | 7 |
| 1990 | Oakland (W)‡ | Tony La Russa | 103 | 59 | .636 | 9 |
| 1991 | Minnesota (W)‡ | Tom Kelly | 95 | 67 | .586 | 8 |
| 1992 | Toronto‡ | Cito Gaston | 96 | 66 | .593 | 4 |
| 1993 | Toronto‡ | Cito Gaston | 95 | 67 | .586 | 7 |
| 1994 | Season ended Aug. 11 due to players' strike | | | | | |
| 1995 | Cleveland (C)‡ | Mike Hargrove | 100 | 44 | .694 | 30 |

†Defeated Boston in one-game playoff. ‡Won championship series.
#First half 34-22; second 25-26, in season split by strike; defeated Milwaukee in playoff for Eastern Divison title.

## Leading Batsmen

| Year | Player and Team | BA | Year | Player and Team | BA |
|------|-----------------|-----|------|-----------------|-----|
| 1901 | Nap Lajoie, Phil | .422 | 1925 | Harry Heilmann, Det | .393 |
| 1902 | Ed Delahanty, Wash | .376 | 1926 | Heinie Manush, Det | .378 |
| 1903 | Nap Lajoie, Clev | .355 | 1927 | Harry Heilmann, Det | .398 |
| 1904 | Nap Lajoie, Clev | .381 | 1928 | Goose Goslin, Wash | .379 |
| 1905 | Elmer Flick, Clev | .306 | 1929 | Lew Fonseca, Clev | .369 |
| 1906 | George Stone, StL | .358 | 1930 | Al Simmons, Phil | .381 |
| 1907 | Ty Cobb, Det | .350 | 1931 | Al Simmons, Phil | .390 |
| 1908 | Ty Cobb, Det | .324 | 1932 | Dale Alexander, Det-Bos | .367 |
| 1909 | Ty Cobb, Det | .377 | 1933 | Jimmie Foxx, Phil | .356 |
| 1910 | Nap Lajoie, Clev* | .383 | 1934 | Lou Gehrig, NY | .363 |
| 1911 | Ty Cobb, Det | .420 | 1935 | Buddy Myer, Wash | .349 |
| 1912 | Ty Cobb, Det | .410 | 1936 | Luke Appling, Chi | .388 |
| 1913 | Ty Cobb, Det | .390 | 1937 | Charlie Gehringer, Det | .371 |
| 1914 | Ty Cobb, Det | .368 | 1938 | Jimmie Foxx, Bos | .349 |
| 1915 | Ty Cobb, Det | .369 | 1939 | Joe DiMaggio, NY | .381 |
| 1916 | Tris Speaker, Clev | .386 | 1940 | Joe DiMaggio, NY | .352 |
| 1917 | Ty Cobb, Det | .383 | 1941 | Ted Williams, Bos | .406 |
| 1918 | Ty Cobb, Det | .382 | 1942 | Ted Williams, Bos | .356 |
| 1919 | Ty Cobb, Det | .384 | 1943 | Luke Appling, Chi | .328 |
| 1920 | George Sisler, StL | .407 | 1944 | Lou Boudreau, Clev | .327 |
| 1921 | Harry Heilmann, Det | .394 | 1945 | Snuffy Stirnweiss, NY | .309 |
| 1922 | George Sisler, StL | .420 | 1946 | Mickey Vernon, Wash | .353 |
| 1923 | Harry Heilmann, Det | .403 | 1947 | Ted Williams, Bos | .343 |
| 1924 | Babe Ruth, NY | .378 | 1948 | Ted Williams, Bos | .369 |

## Leading Batsmen (Cont.)

| Year | Player and Team | BA | Year | Player and Team | BA |
|------|-----------------|-----|------|-----------------|-----|
| 1949 | George Kell, Det | .343 | 1973 | Rod Carew, Minn | .350 |
| 1950 | Billy Goodman, Bos | .354 | 1974 | Rod Carew, Minn | .364 |
| 1951 | Ferris Fain, Phil | .344 | 1975 | Rod Carew, Minn | .359 |
| 1952 | Ferris Fain, Phil | .327 | 1976 | George Brett, KC | .333 |
| 1953 | Mickey Vernon, Wash | .337 | 1977 | Rod Carew, Minn | .388 |
| 1954 | Bobby Avila, Clev | .341 | 1978 | Rod Carew, Minn | .333 |
| 1955 | Al Kaline, Det | .340 | 1979 | Fred Lynn, Bos | .333 |
| 1956 | Mickey Mantle, NY | .353 | 1980 | George Brett, KC | .390 |
| 1957 | Ted Williams, Bos | .388 | 1981 | Carney Lansford, Bos | .336 |
| 1958 | Ted Williams, Bos | .328 | 1982 | Willie Wilson, KC | .332 |
| 1959 | Harvey Kuenn, Det | .353 | 1983 | Wade Boggs, Bos | .361 |
| 1960 | Pete Runnels, Bos | .320 | 1984 | Don Mattingly, NY | .343 |
| 1961 | Norm Cash, Det | .361 | 1985 | Wade Boggs, Bos | .368 |
| 1962 | Pete Runnels, Bos | .326 | 1986 | Wade Boggs, Bos | .357 |
| 1963 | Carl Yastrzemski, Bos | .321 | 1987 | Wade Boggs, Bos | .363 |
| 1964 | Tony Oliva, Minn | .323 | 1988 | Wade Boggs, Bos | .366 |
| 1965 | Tony Oliva, Minn | .321 | 1989 | Kirby Puckett, Minn | .339 |
| 1966 | Frank Robinson, Balt | .316 | 1990 | George Brett, KC | .329 |
| 1967 | Carl Yastrzemski, Bos | .326 | 1991 | Julio Franco, Tex | .341 |
| 1968 | Carl Yastrzemski, Bos | .301 | 1992 | Edgar Martinez, Sea | .343 |
| 1969 | Rod Carew, Minn | .332 | 1993 | John Olerud, Tor | .363 |
| 1970 | Alex Johnson, Calif | .329 | 1994 | Paul O'Neill, NY | .359 |
| 1971 | Tony Oliva, Minn | .337 | 1995 | Edgar Martinez, Sea | .356 |
| 1972 | Rod Carew, Minn | .318 | | | |

*League president Ban Johnson declared Ty Cobb batting champion with a .385 average, beating Lajoie's .384. However, subsequent research has led to the revision of Lajoie's average to .383 and Cobb's to .382.

## Leaders in Runs Scored

| Year | Player and Team | Runs | Year | Player and Team | Runs |
|------|-----------------|------|------|-----------------|------|
| 1901 | Nap Lajoie, Phil | 145 | 1936 | Lou Gehrig, NY | 167 |
| 1902 | Dave Fultz, Phil | 110 | 1937 | Joe DiMaggio, NY | 151 |
| 1903 | Patsy Dougherty, Bos | 108 | 1938 | Hank Greenberg, Det | 144 |
| 1904 | Patsy Dougherty, Bos-NY | 113 | 1939 | Red Rolfe, NY | 139 |
| 1905 | Harry Davis, Phil | 92 | 1940 | Ted Williams, Bos | 134 |
| 1906 | Elmer Flick, Clev | 98 | 1941 | Ted Williams, Bos | 135 |
| 1907 | Sam Crawford, Det | 102 | 1942 | Ted Williams, Bos | 141 |
| 1908 | Matty McIntyre, Det | 105 | 1943 | George Case, Wash | 102 |
| 1909 | Ty Cobb, Det | 116 | 1944 | Snuffy Stirnweiss, NY | 125 |
| 1910 | Ty Cobb, Det | 106 | 1945 | Snuffy Stirnweiss, NY | 107 |
| 1911 | Ty Cobb, Det | 147 | 1946 | Ted Williams, Bos | 142 |
| 1912 | Eddie Collins, Phil | 137 | 1947 | Ted Williams, Bos | 125 |
| 1913 | Eddie Collins, Phil | 125 | 1948 | Tommy Henrich, NY | 138 |
| 1914 | Eddie Collins, Phil | 122 | 1949 | Ted Williams, Bos | 150 |
| 1915 | Ty Cobb, Det | 144 | 1950 | Dom DiMaggio, Bos | 131 |
| 1916 | Ty Cobb, Det | 113 | 1951 | Dom DiMaggio, Bos | 113 |
| 1917 | Donie Bush, Det | 112 | 1952 | Larry Doby, Clev | 104 |
| 1918 | Ray Chapman, Clev | 84 | 1953 | Al Rosen, Clev | 115 |
| 1919 | Babe Ruth, Bos | 103 | 1954 | Mickey Mantle, NY | 129 |
| 1920 | Babe Ruth, NY | 158 | 1955 | Al Smith, Clev | 123 |
| 1921 | Babe Ruth, NY | 177 | 1956 | Mickey Mantle, NY | 132 |
| 1922 | George Sisler, StL | 134 | 1957 | Mickey Mantle, NY | 121 |
| 1923 | Babe Ruth, NY | 151 | 1958 | Mickey Mantle, NY | 127 |
| 1924 | Babe Ruth, NY | 143 | 1959 | Eddie Yost, Det | 115 |
| 1925 | Johnny Mostil, Chi | 135 | 1960 | Mickey Mantle, NY | 119 |
| 1926 | Babe Ruth, NY | 139 | 1961 | Mickey Mantle, NY | 132 |
| 1927 | Babe Ruth, NY | 158 | | Roger Maris, NY | 132 |
| 1928 | Babe Ruth, NY | 163 | 1962 | Albie Pearson, LA | 115 |
| 1929 | Charlie Gehringer, Det | 131 | 1963 | Bob Allison, Minn | 99 |
| 1930 | Al Simmons, Phil | 152 | 1964 | Tony Oliva, Minn | 109 |
| 1931 | Lou Gehrig, NY | 163 | 1965 | Zoilo Versalles, Minn | 126 |
| 1932 | Jimmie Foxx, Phil | 151 | 1966 | Frank Robinson, Balt | 122 |
| 1933 | Lou Gehrig, NY | 138 | 1967 | Carl Yastrzemski, Bos | 112 |
| 1934 | Charlie Gehringer, Det | 134 | 1968 | Dick McAuliffe, Det | 95 |
| 1935 | Lou Gehrig, NY | 125 | 1969 | Reggie Jackson, Oak | 123 |

## Leaders in Runs Scored (Cont.)

| Year | Player and Team | Runs | Year | Player and Team | Runs |
|------|-----------------|------|------|-----------------|------|
| 1970 | Carl Yastrzemski, Bos | 125 | 1984 | Dwight Evans, Bos | 121 |
| 1971 | Don Buford, Balt | 99 | 1985 | Rickey Henderson, NY | 146 |
| 1972 | Bobby Murcer, NY | 102 | 1986 | Rickey Henderson, NY | 130 |
| 1973 | Reggie Jackson, Oak | 99 | 1987 | Paul Molitor, Mil | 114 |
| 1974 | Carl Yastrzemski, Bos | 93 | 1988 | Wade Boggs, Bos | 128 |
| 1975 | Fred Lynn, Bos | 103 | 1989 | Rickey Henderson, NY-Oak | 113 |
| 1976 | Roy White, NY | 104 | | Wade Boggs, Bos | 113 |
| 1977 | Rod Carew, Minn | 128 | 1990 | Rickey Henderson, Oak | 119 |
| 1978 | Ron LeFlore, Det | 126 | 1991 | Paul Molitor, Mil | 133 |
| 1979 | Don Baylor, Calif | 120 | 1992 | Tony Phillips, Det | 114 |
| 1980 | Willie Wilson, KC | 133 | 1993 | Rafael Palmeiro, Tex | 124 |
| 1981 | Rickey Henderson, Oak | 89 | 1994 | Frank Thomas, Chi | 106 |
| 1982 | Paul Molitor, Mil | 136 | 1995 | Albert Belle, Clev | 121 |
| 1983 | Cal Ripken, Balt | 121 | | Edgar Martinez, Sea | 121 |

## Leaders in Hits

| Year | Player and Team | Hits | Year | Player and Team | Hits |
|------|-----------------|------|------|-----------------|------|
| 1901 | Nap Lajoie, Phil | 229 | 1943 | Dick Wakefield, Det | 200 |
| 1902 | Piano Legs Hickman, Bos-Clev | 194 | 1944 | Snuffy Stirnweiss, NY | 205 |
| 1903 | Patsy Dougherty, Bos | 195 | 1945 | Snuffy Stirnweiss, NY | 195 |
| 1904 | Nap Lajoie, Clev | 211 | 1946 | Johnny Pesky, Bos | 208 |
| 1905 | George Stone, StL | 187 | 1947 | Johnny Pesky, Bos | 207 |
| 1906 | Nap Lajoie, Clev | 214 | 1948 | Bob Dillinger, StL | 207 |
| 1907 | Ty Cobb, Det | 212 | 1949 | Dale Mitchell, Clev | 203 |
| 1908 | Ty Cobb, Det | 188 | 1950 | George Kell, Det | 218 |
| 1909 | Ty Cobb, Det | 216 | 1951 | George Kell, Det | 191 |
| 1910 | Nap Lajoie, Clev | 227 | 1952 | Nellie Fox, Chi | 192 |
| 1911 | Ty Cobb, Det | 248 | 1953 | Harvey Kuenn, Det | 209 |
| 1912 | Ty Cobb, Det | 227 | 1954 | Nellie Fox, Chi | 201 |
| 1913 | Joe Jackson, Clev | 197 | | Harvey Kuenn, Det | 201 |
| 1914 | Tris Speaker, Bos | 193 | 1955 | Al Kaline, Det | 200 |
| 1915 | Ty Cobb, Det | 208 | 1956 | Harvey Kuenn, Det | 196 |
| 1916 | Tris Speaker, Clev | 211 | 1957 | Nellie Fox, Chi | 196 |
| 1917 | Ty Cobb, Det | 225 | 1958 | Nellie Fox, Chi | 187 |
| 1918 | George Burns, Phil | 178 | 1959 | Harvey Kuenn, Det | 198 |
| 1919 | Ty Cobb, Det | 191 | 1960 | Minnie Minoso, Chi | 184 |
| | Bobby Veach, Det | 191 | 1961 | Norm Cash, Det | 193 |
| 1920 | George Sisler, StL | 257 | 1962 | Bobby Richardson, NY | 209 |
| 1921 | Harry Heilmann, Det | 237 | 1963 | Carl Yastrzemski, Bos | 183 |
| 1922 | George Sisler, StL | 246 | 1964 | Tony Oliva, Minn | 217 |
| 1923 | Charlie Jamieson, Clev | 222 | 1965 | Tony Oliva, Minn | 185 |
| 1924 | Sam Rice, Wash | 216 | 1966 | Tony Oliva, Minn | 191 |
| 1925 | Al Simmons, Phil | 253 | 1967 | Carl Yastrzemski, Bos | 189 |
| 1926 | George Burns, Clev | 216 | 1968 | Bert Campaneris, Oak | 177 |
| | Sam Rice, Wash | 216 | 1969 | Tony Oliva, Minn | 197 |
| 1927 | Earle Combs, NY | 231 | 1970 | Tony Oliva, Minn | 204 |
| 1928 | Heinie Manush, StL | 241 | 1971 | Cesar Tovar, Minn | 204 |
| 1929 | Dale Alexander, Det | 215 | 1972 | Joe Rudi, Oak | 181 |
| | Charlie Gehringer, Det | 215 | 1973 | Rod Carew, Minn | 203 |
| 1930 | Johnny Hodapp, Clev | 225 | 1974 | Rod Carew, Minn | 218 |
| 1931 | Lou Gehrig, NY | 211 | 1975 | George Brett, KC | 195 |
| 1932 | Al Simmons, Phil | 216 | 1976 | George Brett, KC | 215 |
| 1933 | Heinie Manush, Wash | 221 | 1977 | Rod Carew, Minn | 239 |
| 1934 | Charlie Gehringer, Det | 214 | 1978 | Jim Rice, Bos | 213 |
| 1935 | Joe Vosmik, Clev | 216 | 1979 | George Brett, KC | 212 |
| 1936 | Earl Averill, Clev | 232 | 1980 | Willie Wilson, KC | 230 |
| 1937 | Beau Bell, StL | 218 | 1981 | Rickey Henderson, Oak | 135 |
| 1938 | Joe Vosmik, Bos | 201 | 1982 | Robin Yount, Mil | 210 |
| 1939 | Red Rolfe, NY | 213 | 1983 | Cal Ripken, Balt | 211 |
| 1940 | Rip Radcliff, StL | 200 | 1984 | Don Mattingly, NY | 207 |
| | Barney McCosky, Det | 200 | 1985 | Wade Boggs, Bos | 240 |
| | Doc Cramer, Bos | 200 | 1986 | Don Mattingly, NY | 238 |
| 1941 | Cecil Travis, Wash | 218 | 1987 | Kirby Puckett, Minn | 207 |
| 1942 | Johnny Pesky, Bos | 205 | | Kevin Seitzer, KC | 207 |

## Leaders in Hits (Cont.)

| Year | Player and Team | Hits | Year | Player and Team | Hits |
|------|-----------------|------|------|-----------------|------|
| 1988 | Kirby Puckett, Minn | 234 | 1992 | Kirby Puckett, Minn | 210 |
| 1989 | Kirby Puckett, Minn | 215 | 1993 | Paul Molitor, Tor | 211 |
| 1990 | Rafael Palmeiro, Tex | 191 | 1994 | Kenny Lofton, Clev | 160 |
| 1991 | Paul Molitor, Mil | 216 | 1995 | Lance Johnson, Chi | 186 |

## Home Run Leaders

| Year | Player and Team | HR | Year | Player and Team | HR |
|------|-----------------|-----|------|-----------------|-----|
| 1901 | Nap Lajoie, Phil | 13 | 1951 | Gus Zernial, Chi-Phil | 33 |
| 1902 | Socks Seybold, Phil | 16 | 1952 | Larry Doby, Clev | 32 |
| 1903 | Buck Freeman, Bos | 13 | 1953 | Al Rosen, Clev | 43 |
| 1904 | Harry Davis, Phil | 10 | 1954 | Larry Doby, Clev | 32 |
| 1905 | Harry Davis, Phil | 8 | 1955 | Mickey Mantle, NY | 37 |
| 1906 | Harry Davis, Phil | 12 | 1956 | Mickey Mantle, NY | 52 |
| 1907 | Harry Davis, Phil | 8 | 1957 | Roy Sievers, Wash | 42 |
| 1908 | Sam Crawford, Det | 7 | 1958 | Mickey Mantle, NY | 42 |
| 1909 | Ty Cobb, Det | 9 | 1959 | Rocky Colavito, Clev | 42 |
| 1910 | Jake Stahl, Bos | 10 | | Harmon Killebrew, Wash | 42 |
| 1911 | Frank Baker, Phil | 9 | 1960 | Mickey Mantle, NY | 40 |
| 1912 | Frank Baker, Phil | 10 | 1961 | Roger Maris, NY | 61 |
| | Tris Speaker, Bos | 10 | 1962 | Harmon Killebrew, Minn | 48 |
| 1913 | Frank Baker, Phil | 13 | 1963 | Harmon Killebrew, Minn | 45 |
| 1914 | Frank Baker, Phil | 9 | 1964 | Harmon Killebrew, Minn | 49 |
| 1915 | Braggo Roth, Chi-Clev | 7 | 1965 | Tony Conigliaro, Bos | 32 |
| 1916 | Wally Pipp, NY | 12 | 1966 | Frank Robinson, Balt | 49 |
| 1917 | Wally Pipp, NY | 9 | 1967 | Harmon Killebrew, Minn | 44 |
| 1918 | Babe Ruth, Bos | 11 | | Carl Yastrzemski, Bos | 44 |
| | Tilly Walker, Phil | 11 | 1968 | Frank Howard, Wash | 44 |
| 1919 | Babe Ruth, Bos | 29 | 1969 | Harmon Killebrew, Minn | 49 |
| 1920 | Babe Ruth, NY | 54 | 1970 | Frank Howard, Wash | 44 |
| 1921 | Babe Ruth, NY | 59 | 1971 | Bill Melton, Chi | 33 |
| 1922 | Ken Williams, StL | 39 | 1972 | Dick Allen, Chi | 37 |
| 1923 | Babe Ruth, NY | 41 | 1973 | Reggie Jackson, Oak | 32 |
| 1924 | Babe Ruth, NY | 46 | 1974 | Dick Allen, Chi | 32 |
| 1925 | Bob Meusel, NY | 33 | 1975 | Reggie Jackson, Oak | 36 |
| 1926 | Babe Ruth, NY | 47 | | George Scott, Mil | 36 |
| 1927 | Babe Ruth, NY | 60 | 1976 | Graig Nettles, NY | 32 |
| 1928 | Babe Ruth, NY | 54 | 1977 | Jim Rice, Bos | 39 |
| 1929 | Babe Ruth, NY | 46 | 1978 | Jim Rice, Bos | 46 |
| 1930 | Babe Ruth, NY | 49 | 1979 | Gorman Thomas, Mil | 45 |
| 1931 | Babe Ruth, NY | 46 | 1980 | Reggie Jackson, NY | 41 |
| | Lou Gehrig, NY | 46 | | Ben Oglivie, Mil | 41 |
| 1932 | Jimmie Foxx, Phil | 58 | 1981 | Tony Armas, Oak | 22 |
| 1933 | Jimmie Foxx, Phil | 48 | 1981 | Dwight Evans, Bos | 22 |
| 1934 | Lou Gehrig, NY | 49 | | Bobby Grich, Calif | 22 |
| 1935 | Jimmie Foxx, Phil | 36 | | Eddie Murray, Balt | 22 |
| | Hank Greenberg, Det | 36 | 1982 | Reggie Jackson, Calif | 39 |
| 1936 | Lou Gehrig, NY | 49 | | Gorman Thomas, Mil | 39 |
| 1937 | Joe DiMaggio, NY | 46 | 1983 | Jim Rice, Bos | 39 |
| 1938 | Hank Greenberg, Det | 58 | 1984 | Tony Armas, Bos | 43 |
| 1939 | Jimmie Foxx, Bos | 35 | 1985 | Darrell Evans, Det | 40 |
| 1940 | Hank Greenberg, Det | 41 | 1986 | Jesse Barfield, Tor | 40 |
| 1941 | Ted Williams, Bos | 37 | 1987 | Mark McGwire, Oak | 49 |
| 1942 | Ted Williams, Bos | 36 | 1988 | Jose Canseco, Oak | 42 |
| 1943 | Rudy York, Det | 34 | 1989 | Fred McGriff, Tor | 36 |
| 1944 | Nick Etten, NY | 22 | 1990 | Cecil Fielder, Det | 51 |
| 1945 | Vern Stephens, StL | 24 | 1991 | Jose Canseco, Oak | 44 |
| 1946 | Hank Greenberg, Det | 44 | | Cecil Fielder, Det | 44 |
| 1947 | Ted Williams, Bos | 32 | 1992 | Juan Gonzalez, Tex | 43 |
| 1948 | Joe DiMaggio, NY | 39 | 1993 | Juan Gonzalez, Tex | 46 |
| 1949 | Ted Williams, Bos | 43 | 1994 | Ken Griffey Jr, Sea | 40 |
| 1950 | Al Rosen, Clev | 37 | 1995 | Albert Belle, Clev | 50 |

## Runs Batted In Leaders

| Year | Player and Team | RBI | Year | Player and Team | RBI |
|---|---|---|---|---|---|
| 1907 | Ty Cobb, Det | 116 | 1951 | Gus Zernial, Chi-Phil | 129 |
| 1908 | Ty Cobb, Det | 108 | 1952 | Al Rosen, Clev | 105 |
| 1909 | Ty Cobb, Det | 107 | 1953 | Al Rosen, Clev | 145 |
| 1910 | Sam Crawford, Det | 120 | 1954 | Larry Doby, Clev | 126 |
| 1911 | Ty Cobb, Det | 144 | 1955 | Ray Boone, Det | 116 |
| 1912 | Frank Baker, Phil | 133 | | Jackie Jensen, Bos | 116 |
| 1913 | Frank Baker, Phil | 126 | 1956 | Mickey Mantle, NY | 130 |
| 1914 | Sam Crawford, Det | 104 | 1957 | Roy Sievers, Wash | 114 |
| 1915 | Sam Crawford, Det | 112 | 1958 | Jackie Jensen, Bos | 122 |
| | Bobby Veach, Det | 112 | 1959 | Jackie Jensen, Bos | 112 |
| 1916 | Del Pratt, StL | 103 | 1960 | Roger Maris, NY | 112 |
| 1917 | Bobby Veach, Det | 103 | 1961 | Roger Maris, NY | 142 |
| 1918 | Bobby Veach, Det | 78 | 1962 | Harmon Killebrew, Minn | 126 |
| 1919 | Babe Ruth, Bos | 114 | 1963 | Dick Stuart, Bos | 118 |
| 1920 | Babe Ruth, NY | 137 | 1964 | Brooks Robinson, Balt | 118 |
| 1921 | Babe Ruth, NY | 171 | 1965 | Rocky Colavito, Clev | 108 |
| 1922 | Ken Williams, StL | 155 | 1966 | Frank Robinson, Balt | 122 |
| 1923 | Babe Ruth, NY | 131 | 1967 | Carl Yastrzemski, Bos | 121 |
| 1924 | Goose Goslin, Wash | 129 | 1968 | Ken Harrelson, Bos | 109 |
| 1925 | Bob Meusel, NY | 138 | 1969 | Harmon Killebrew, Minn | 140 |
| 1926 | Babe Ruth, NY | 145 | 1970 | Frank Howard, Wash | 126 |
| 1927 | Lou Gehrig, NY | 175 | 1971 | Harmon Killebrew, Minn | 119 |
| 1928 | Babe Ruth, NY | 142 | 1972 | Dick Allen, Chi | 113 |
| | Lou Gehrig, NY | 142 | 1973 | Reggie Jackson, Oak | 117 |
| 1929 | Al Simmons, Phil | 157 | 1974 | Jeff Burroughs, Tex | 118 |
| 1930 | Lou Gehrig, NY | 174 | 1975 | George Scott, Mil | 109 |
| 1931 | Lou Gehrig, NY | 184 | 1976 | Lee May, Balt | 109 |
| 1932 | Jimmie Foxx, Phil | 169 | 1977 | Larry Hisle, Minn | 119 |
| 1933 | Jimmie Foxx, Phil | 163 | 1978 | Jim Rice, Bos | 139 |
| 1934 | Lou Gehrig, NY | 165 | 1979 | Don Baylor, Calif | 139 |
| 1935 | Hank Greenberg, Det | 170 | 1980 | Cecil Cooper, Mil | 122 |
| 1936 | Hal Trosky, Clev | 162 | 1981 | Eddie Murray, Balt | 78 |
| 1937 | Hank Greenberg, Det | 183 | 1982 | Hal McRae, KC | 133 |
| 1938 | Jimmie Foxx, Bos | 175 | 1983 | Cecil Cooper, Mil | 126 |
| 1939 | Ted Williams, Bos | 145 | | Jim Rice, Bos | 126 |
| 1940 | Hank Greenberg, Det | 150 | 1984 | Tony Armas, Bos | 123 |
| 1941 | Joe DiMaggio, NY | 125 | 1985 | Don Mattingly, NY | 145 |
| 1942 | Ted Williams, Bos | 137 | 1986 | Joe Carter, Clev | 121 |
| 1943 | Rudy York, Det | 118 | 1987 | George Bell, Tor | 134 |
| 1944 | Vern Stephens, StL | 109 | 1988 | Jose Canseco, Oak | 124 |
| 1945 | Nick Etten, NY | 111 | 1989 | Ruben Sierra, Tex | 119 |
| 1946 | Hank Greenberg, Det | 127 | 1990 | Cecil Fielder, Det | 132 |
| 1947 | Ted Williams, Bos | 114 | 1991 | Cecil Fielder, Det | 133 |
| 1948 | Joe DiMaggio, NY | 155 | 1992 | Cecil Fielder, Det | 124 |
| 1949 | Ted Williams, Bos | 159 | 1993 | Albert Belle, Clev | 129 |
| | Vern Stephens, Bos | 159 | 1994 | Kirby Puckett, Minn | 112 |
| 1950 | Walt Dropo, Bos | 144 | 1995 | Albert Belle, Clev | 126 |
| | Vern Stephens, Bos | 144 | | Mo Vaughn, Bos | 126 |

Note: Runs Batted In not compiled before 1907; officially adopted in 1920.

## Leading Base Stealers

| Year | Player and Team | SB | Year | Player and Team | SB |
|---|---|---|---|---|---|
| 1901 | Frank Isbell, Chi | 48 | 1911 | Ty Cobb, Det | 83 |
| 1902 | Topsy Hartsel, Phil | 54 | 1912 | Clyde Milan, Wash | 88 |
| 1903 | Harry Bay, Clev | 46 | 1913 | Clyde Milan, Wash | 75 |
| 1904 | Elmer Flick, Clev | 42 | 1914 | Fritz Maisel, NY | 74 |
| | Harry Bay, Clev | 42 | 1915 | Ty Cobb, Det | 96 |
| 1905 | Danny Hoffman, Phil | 46 | 1916 | Ty Cobb, Det | 68 |
| 1906 | Elmer Flick, Clev | 39 | 1917 | Ty Cobb, Det | 55 |
| | John Anderson, Wash | 39 | 1918 | George Sisler, StL | 45 |
| 1907 | Ty Cobb, Det | 49 | 1919 | Eddie Collins, Chi | 33 |
| 1908 | Patsy Dougherty, Chi | 47 | 1920 | Sam Rice, Wash | 63 |
| 1909 | Ty Cobb, Det | 76 | 1921 | George Sisler, StL | 35 |
| 1910 | Eddie Collins, Phil | 81 | 1922 | George Sisler, StL | 51 |

## Leading Base Stealers *(Cont.)*

| Year | Player and Team | SB | Year | Player and Team | SB |
|------|-----------------|-----|------|-----------------|-----|
| 1923 | Eddie Collins, Chi | 49 | 1959 | Luis Aparicio, Chi | 56 |
| 1924 | Eddie Collins, Chi | 42 | 1960 | Luis Aparicio, Chi | 51 |
| 1925 | John Mostil, Chi | 43 | 1961 | Luis Aparicio, Chi | 53 |
| 1926 | John Mostil, Chi | 35 | 1962 | Luis Aparicio, Chi | 31 |
| 1927 | George Sisler, StL | 27 | 1963 | Luis Aparicio, Balt | 40 |
| 1928 | Buddy Myer, Bos | 30 | 1964 | Luis Aparicio, Balt | 57 |
| 1929 | Charlie Gehringer, Det | 27 | 1965 | Bert Campaneris, KC | 51 |
| 1930 | Marty McManus, Det | 23 | 1966 | Bert Campaneris, KC | 52 |
| 1931 | Ben Chapman, NY | 61 | 1967 | Bert Campaneris, KC | 55 |
| 1932 | Ben Chapman, NY | 38 | 1968 | Bert Campaneris, Oak | 62 |
| 1933 | Ben Chapman, NY | 27 | 1969 | Tommy Harper, Sea | 73 |
| 1934 | Bill Werber, Bos | 40 | 1970 | Bert Campaneris, Oak | 42 |
| 1935 | Bill Werber, Bos | 29 | 1971 | Amos Otis, KC | 52 |
| 1936 | Lyn Lary, StL | 37 | 1972 | Bert Campaneris, Oak | 52 |
| 1937 | Bill Werber, Phil | 35 | 1973 | Tommy Harper, Bos | 54 |
|      | Ben Chapman, Wash-Bos | 35 | 1974 | Bill North, Oak | 54 |
| 1938 | Frank Crosetti, NY | 27 | 1975 | Mickey Rivers, Calif | 70 |
| 1939 | George Case, Wash | 51 | 1976 | Bill North, Oak | 75 |
| 1940 | George Case, Wash | 35 | 1977 | Freddie Patek, KC | 53 |
| 1941 | George Case, Wash | 33 | 1978 | Ron LeFlore, Det | 68 |
| 1942 | George Case, Wash | 44 | 1979 | Willie Wilson, KC | 83 |
| 1943 | George Case, Wash | 61 | 1980 | Rickey Henderson, Oak | 100 |
| 1944 | Snuffy Stirnweiss, NY | 55 | 1981 | Rickey Henderson, Oak | 56 |
| 1945 | Snuffy Stirnweiss, NY | 33 | 1982 | Rickey Henderson, Oak | 130 |
| 1946 | George Case, Clev | 28 | 1983 | Rickey Henderson, Oak | 108 |
| 1947 | Bob Dillinger, StL | 34 | 1984 | Rickey Henderson, Oak | 66 |
| 1948 | Bob Dillinger, StL | 28 | 1985 | Rickey Henderson, NY | 80 |
| 1949 | Bob Dillinger, StL | 20 | 1986 | Rickey Henderson, NY | 87 |
| 1950 | Dom DiMaggio, Bos | 15 | 1987 | Harold Reynolds, Sea | 60 |
| 1951 | Minnie Minoso, Clev-Chi | 31 | 1988 | Rickey Henderson, NY | 93 |
| 1952 | Minnie Minoso, Chi | 22 | 1989 | Rickey Henderson, NY-Oak | 77 |
| 1953 | Minnie Minoso, Chi | 25 | 1990 | Rickey Henderson, Oak | 65 |
| 1954 | Jackie Jensen, Bos | 22 | 1991 | Rickey Henderson, Oak | 58 |
| 1955 | Jim Rivera, Chi | 25 | 1992 | Kenny Lofton, Clev | 66 |
| 1956 | Luis Aparicio, Chi | 21 | 1993 | Kenny Lofton, Clev | 70 |
| 1957 | Luis Aparicio, Chi | 28 | 1994 | Kenny Lofton, Clev | 60 |
| 1958 | Luis Aparicio, Chi | 29 | 1995 | Kenny Lofton, Clev | 54 |

## Leading Pitchers—Winning Percentage

| Year | Pitcher and Team | W | L | Pct | Year | Pitcher and Team | W | L | Pct |
|------|------------------|----|----|------|------|------------------|----|----|------|
| 1901 | Clark Griffith, Chi | 24 | 7 | .774 | 1926 | George Uhle, Clev | 27 | 11 | .711 |
| 1902 | Bill Bernhard, Phil-Clev | 18 | 5 | .783 | 1927 | Waite Hoyt, NY | 22 | 7 | .759 |
| 1903 | Earl Moore, Clev | 22 | 7 | .759 | 1928 | General Crowder, StL | 21 | 5 | .808 |
| 1904 | Jack Chesbro, NY | 41 | 12 | .774 | 1929 | Lefty Grove, Phil | 20 | 6 | .769 |
| 1905 | Jess Tannehill, Bos | 22 | 9 | .710 | 1930 | Lefty Grove, Phil | 28 | 5 | .848 |
| 1906 | Eddie Plank, Phil | 19 | 6 | .760 | 1931 | Lefty Grove, Phil | 31 | 4 | .886 |
| 1907 | Wild Bill Donovan, Det | 25 | 4 | .862 | 1932 | Johnny Allen, NY | 17 | 4 | .810 |
| 1908 | Ed Walsh, Chi | 40 | 15 | .727 | 1933 | Lefty Grove, Phil | 24 | 8 | .750 |
| 1909 | George Mullin, Det | 29 | 8 | .784 | 1934 | Lefty Gomez, NY | 26 | 5 | .839 |
| 1910 | Chief Bender, Phil | 23 | 5 | .821 | 1935 | Eldon Auker, Det | 18 | 7 | .720 |
| 1911 | Chief Bender, Phil | 17 | 5 | .773 | 1936 | Monte Pearson, NY | 19 | 7 | .731 |
| 1912 | Smoky Joe Wood, Bos | 34 | 5 | .872 | 1937 | Johnny Allen, Clev | 15 | 1 | .938 |
| 1913 | Walter Johnson, Wash | 36 | 7 | .837 | 1938 | Red Ruffing, NY | 21 | 7 | .750 |
| 1914 | Chief Bender, Phil | 17 | 3 | .850 | 1939 | Lefty Grove, Bos | 15 | 4 | .789 |
| 1915 | Smoky Joe Wood, Bos | 15 | 5 | .750 | 1940 | Schoolboy Rowe, Det | 16 | 3 | .842 |
| 1916 | Eddie Cicotte, Chi | 15 | 7 | .682 | 1941 | Lefty Gomez, NY | 15 | 5 | .750 |
| 1917 | Reb Russell, Chi | 15 | 5 | .750 | 1942 | Ernie Bonham, NY | 21 | 5 | .808 |
| 1918 | Sad Sam Jones, Bos | 16 | 5 | .762 | 1943 | Spud Chandler, NY | 20 | 4 | .833 |
| 1919 | Eddie Cicotte, Chi | 29 | 7 | .806 | 1944 | Tex Hughson, Bos | 18 | 5 | .783 |
| 1920 | Jim Bagby, Clev | 31 | 12 | .721 | 1945 | Hal Newhouser, Det | 25 | 9 | .735 |
| 1921 | Carl Mays, NY | 27 | 9 | .750 | 1946 | Boo Ferriss, Bos | 25 | 6 | .806 |
| 1922 | Joe Bush, NY | 26 | 7 | .788 | 1947 | Allie Reynolds, NY | 19 | 8 | .704 |
| 1923 | Herb Pennock, NY | 19 | 6 | .760 | 1948 | Jack Kramer, Bos | 18 | 5 | .783 |
| 1924 | Walter Johnson, Wash | 23 | 7 | .767 | 1949 | Ellis Kinder, Bos | 23 | 6 | .793 |
| 1925 | Stan Coveleski, Wash | 20 | 5 | .800 | 1950 | Vic Raschi, NY | 21 | 8 | .724 |

## Leading Pitchers—Winning Percentage (Cont.)

| Year | Pitcher and Team | W | L | Pct | Year | Pitcher and Team | W | L | Pct |
|------|------------------|---|---|-----|------|------------------|---|---|-----|
| 1951 | Bob Feller, Clev | 22 | 8 | .733 | 1974 | Mike Cuellar, Balt | 22 | 10 | .688 |
| 1952 | Bobby Shantz, Phil | 24 | 7 | .774 | 1975 | Mike Torrez, Balt | 20 | 9 | .690 |
| 1953 | Ed Lopat, NY | 16 | 4 | .800 | 1976 | Bill Campbell, Minn | 17 | 5 | .773 |
| 1954 | Sandy Consuegra, Chi | 16 | 3 | .842 | 1977 | Paul Splittorff, KC | 16 | 6 | .727 |
| 1955 | Tommy Byrne, NY | 16 | 5 | .762 | 1978 | Ron Guidry, NY | 25 | 3 | .893 |
| 1956 | Whitey Ford, NY | 19 | 6 | .760 | 1979 | Mike Caldwell, Mil | 16 | 6 | .727 |
| 1957 | Dick Donovan, Chi | 16 | 6 | .727 | 1980 | Steve Stone, Balt | 25 | 7 | .781 |
|      | Tom Sturdivant, NY | 16 | 6 | .727 | 1981* | Pete Vuckovich, Mil | 14 | 4 | .778 |
| 1958 | Bob Turley, NY | 21 | 7 | .750 | 1982 | Pete Vuckovich, Mil | 18 | 6 | .750 |
| 1959 | Bob Shaw, Chi | 18 | 6 | .750 |      | Jim Palmer, Balt | 15 | 5 | .750 |
| 1960 | Jim Perry, Clev | 18 | 10 | .643 | 1983 | Richard Dotson, Chi | 22 | 7 | .759 |
| 1961 | Whitey Ford, NY | 25 | 4 | .862 | 1984 | Doyle Alexander, Tor | 17 | 6 | .739 |
| 1962 | Ray Herbert, Chi | 20 | 9 | .690 | 1985 | Ron Guidry, NY | 22 | 6 | .786 |
| 1963 | Whitey Ford, NY | 24 | 7 | .774 | 1986 | Roger Clemens, Bos | 24 | 4 | .857 |
| 1964 | Wally Bunker, Balt | 19 | 5 | .792 | 1987 | Roger Clemens, Bos | 20 | 9 | .690 |
| 1965 | Mudcat Grant, Minn | 21 | 7 | .750 | 1988 | Frank Viola, Minn | 24 | 7 | .774 |
| 1966 | Sonny Siebert, Clev | 16 | 8 | .667 | 1989 | Bret Saberhagen, KC | 23 | 6 | .793 |
| 1967 | Joel Horlen, Chi | 19 | 7 | .731 | 1990 | Bob Welch, Oak | 27 | 6 | .818 |
| 1968 | Denny McLain, Det | 31 | 6 | .838 | 1991 | Scott Erickson, Minn | 20 | 8 | .714 |
| 1969 | Jim Palmer, Balt | 16 | 4 | .800 | 1992 | Mike Mussina, Balt | 18 | 5 | .783 |
| 1970 | Mike Cuellar, Balt | 24 | 8 | .750 | 1993 | Jimmy Key, NY | 18 | 6 | .750 |
| 1971 | Dave McNally, Balt | 21 | 5 | .808 | 1994 | Jimmy Key, NY | 17 | 4 | .810 |
| 1972 | Catfish Hunter, Oak | 21 | 7 | .750 | 1995 | Randy Johnson, Sea | 18 | 2 | .900 |
| 1973 | Catfish Hunter, Oak | 21 | 5 | .808 |      |                  |   |   |      |

*1981 percentages based on 10 or more victories.

Note: Based on 15 or more victories.

## Leading Pitchers—Earned-Run Average

| Year | Player and Team | ERA | Year | Player and Team | ERA |
|------|-----------------|-----|------|-----------------|-----|
| 1913 | Walter Johnson, Wash | 1.14 | 1949 | Mel Parnell, Bos | 2.78 |
| 1914 | Dutch Leonard, Bos | 1.01 | 1950 | Early Wynn, Clev | 3.20 |
| 1915 | Smoky Joe Wood, Bos | 1.49 | 1951 | Saul Rogovin, Det-Chi | 2.78 |
| 1916 | Babe Ruth, Bos | 1.75 | 1952 | Allie Reynolds, NY | 2.07 |
| 1917 | Eddie Cicotte, Chi | 1.53 | 1953 | Ed Lopat, NY | 2.43 |
| 1918 | Walter Johnson, Wash | 1.27 | 1954 | Mike Garcia, Clev | 2.64 |
| 1919 | Walter Johnson, Wash | 1.49 | 1955 | Billy Pierce, Chi | 1.97 |
| 1920 | Bob Shawkey, NY | 2.46 | 1956 | Whitey Ford, NY | 2.47 |
| 1921 | Red Faber, Chi | 2.47 | 1957 | Bobby Shantz, NY | 2.45 |
| 1922 | Red Faber, Chi | 2.80 | 1958 | Whitey Ford, NY | 2.01 |
| 1923 | Stan Coveleski, Clev | 2.76 | 1959 | Hoyt Wilhelm, Balt | 2.19 |
| 1924 | Walter Johnson, Wash | 2.72 | 1960 | Frank Baumann, Chi | 2.68 |
| 1925 | Stan Coveleski, Wash | 2.84 | 1961 | Dick Donovan, Wash | 2.40 |
| 1926 | Lefty Grove, Phil | 2.51 | 1962 | Hank Aguirre, Det | 2.21 |
| 1927 | Wilcy Moore, NY# | 2.28 | 1963 | Gary Peters, Chi | 2.33 |
| 1928 | Garland Braxton, Wash | 2.52 | 1964 | Dean Chance, LA | 1.65 |
| 1929 | Lefty Grove, Phil | 2.81 | 1965 | Sam McDowell, Clev | 2.18 |
| 1930 | Lefty Grove, Phil | 2.54 | 1966 | Gary Peters, Chi | 1.98 |
| 1931 | Lefty Grove, Phil | 2.06 | 1967 | Joe Horlen, Chi | 2.06 |
| 1932 | Lefty Grove, Phil | 2.84 | 1968 | Luis Tiant, Clev | 1.60 |
| 1933 | Monte Pearson, Clev | 2.33 | 1969 | Dick Bosman, Wash | 2.19 |
| 1934 | Lefty Gomez, NY | 2.33 | 1970 | Diego Segui, Oak | 2.56 |
| 1935 | Lefty Grove, Bos | 2.70 | 1971 | Vida Blue, Oak | 1.82 |
| 1936 | Lefty Grove, Bos | 2.81 | 1972 | Luis Tiant, Bos | 1.91 |
| 1937 | Lefty Gomez, NY | 2.33 | 1973 | Jim Palmer, Balt | 2.40 |
| 1938 | Lefty Grove, Bos | 3.07 | 1974 | Catfish Hunter, Oak | 2.49 |
| 1939 | Lefty Grove, Bos | 2.54 | 1975 | Jim Palmer, Balt | 2.09 |
| 1940 | Bob Feller, Clev† | 2.62 | 1976 | Mark Fidrych, Det | 2.34 |
| 1941 | Thornton Lee, Chi | 2.37 | 1977 | Frank Tanana, Calif | 2.54 |
| 1942 | Ted Lyons, Chi | 2.10 | 1978 | Ron Guidry, NY | 1.74 |
| 1943 | Spud Chandler, NY | 1.64 | 1979 | Ron Guidry, NY | 2.78 |
| 1944 | Dizzy Trout, Det | 2.12 | 1980 | Rudy May, NY | 2.47 |
| 1945 | Hal Newhouser, Det | 1.81 | 1981 | Steve McCatty, Oak | 2.32 |
| 1946 | Hal Newhouser, Det | 1.94 | 1982 | Rick Sutcliffe, Clev | 2.96 |
| 1947 | Spud Chandler, NY | 2.46 | 1983 | Rick Honeycutt, Tex | 2.42 |
| 1948 | Gene Bearden, Clev | 2.43 | 1984 | Mike Boddicker, Balt | 2.79 |

## Leading Pitchers—Earned-Run Average (Cont.)

| Year | Player and Team | ERA | Year | Player and Team | ERA |
|------|-----------------|-----|------|-----------------|-----|
| 1985 | Dave Stieb, Tor | 2.48 | 1991 | Roger Clemens, Bos | 2.62 |
| 1986 | Roger Clemens, Bos | 2.48 | 1992 | Roger Clemens, Bos | 2.41 |
| 1987 | Jimmy Key, Tor | 2.76 | 1993 | Kevin Appier, KC | 2.56 |
| 1988 | Allan Anderson, Minn | 2.45 | 1994 | Steve Ontiveros, Oak | 2.65 |
| 1989 | Bret Saberhagen, KC | 2.16 | 1995 | Randy Johnson, Sea | 2.48 |
| 1990 | Roger Clemens, Bos | 1.93 | | | |

Note: Based on 10 complete games through 1950, then, 154 innings until the American League expanded in 1961, when it became 162 innings. In strike-shortened 1981, one inning per game required. Earned runs not tabulated in American League prior to 1913.

#Wilcy Moore pitched only six complete games—he started 12—in 1927, but was recognized as leader because of 213 innings pitched.

†Ernie Bonham, New York, had 1.91 ERA and 10 complete games in 1940, but appeared in only 12 games and 99 innings, and Bob Feller was recognized as leader.

## Leading Pitchers—Strikeouts

| Year | Player and Team | SO | Year | Player and Team | SO |
|------|-----------------|-----|------|-----------------|-----|
| 1901 | Cy Young, Bos | 159 | 1948 | Bob Feller, Clev | 164 |
| 1902 | Rube Waddell, Phil | 210 | 1949 | Virgil Trucks, Det | 153 |
| 1903 | Rube Waddell, Phil | 301 | 1950 | Bob Lemon, Clev | 170 |
| 1904 | Rube Waddell, Phil | 349 | 1951 | Vic Raschi, NY | 164 |
| 1905 | Rube Waddell, Phil | 286 | 1952 | Allie Reynolds, NY | 160 |
| 1906 | Rube Waddell, Phil | 203 | 1953 | Billy Pierce, Chi | 186 |
| 1907 | Rube Waddell, Phil | 226 | 1954 | Bob Turley, Balt | 185 |
| 1908 | Ed Walsh, Chi | 269 | 1955 | Herb Score, Clev | 245 |
| 1909 | Frank Smith, Chi | 177 | 1956 | Herb Score, Clev | 263 |
| 1910 | Walter Johnson, Wash | 313 | 1957 | Early Wynn, Clev | 184 |
| 1911 | Ed Walsh, Chi | 255 | 1958 | Early Wynn, Chi | 179 |
| 1912 | Walter Johnson, Wash | 303 | 1959 | Jim Bunning, Det | 201 |
| 1913 | Walter Johnson, Wash | 243 | 1960 | Jim Bunning, Det | 201 |
| 1914 | Walter Johnson, Wash | 225 | 1961 | Camilo Pascual, Minn | 221 |
| 1915 | Walter Johnson, Wash | 203 | 1962 | Camilo Pascual, Minn | 206 |
| 1916 | Walter Johnson, Wash | 228 | 1963 | Camilo Pascual, Minn | 202 |
| 1917 | Walter Johnson, Wash | 188 | 1964 | Al Downing, NY | 217 |
| 1918 | Walter Johnson, Wash | 162 | 1965 | Sam McDowell, Clev | 325 |
| 1919 | Walter Johnson, Wash | 147 | 1966 | Sam McDowell, Clev | 225 |
| 1920 | Stan Coveleski, Clev | 133 | 1967 | Jim Lonborg, Bos | 246 |
| 1921 | Walter Johnson, Wash | 143 | 1968 | Sam McDowell, Clev | 283 |
| 1922 | Urban Shocker, StL | 149 | 1969 | Sam McDowell, Clev | 279 |
| 1923 | Walter Johnson, Wash | 130 | 1970 | Sam McDowell, Clev | 304 |
| 1924 | Walter Johnson, Wash | 158 | 1971 | Mickey Lolich, Det | 308 |
| 1925 | Lefty Grove, Phil | 116 | 1972 | Nolan Ryan, Calif | 329 |
| 1926 | Lefty Grove, Phil | 194 | 1973 | Nolan Ryan, Calif | 383 |
| 1927 | Lefty Grove, Phil | 174 | 1974 | Nolan Ryan, Calif | 367 |
| 1928 | Lefty Grove, Phil | 183 | 1975 | Frank Tanana, Calif | 269 |
| 1929 | Lefty Grove, Phil | 170 | 1976 | Nolan Ryan, Calif | 327 |
| 1930 | Lefty Grove, Phil | 209 | 1977 | Nolan Ryan, Calif | 341 |
| 1931 | Lefty Grove, Phil | 175 | 1978 | Nolan Ryan, Calif | 260 |
| 1932 | Red Ruffing, NY | 190 | 1979 | Nolan Ryan, Calif | 223 |
| 1933 | Lefty Gomez, NY | 163 | 1980 | Len Barker, Clev | 187 |
| 1934 | Lefty Gomez, NY | 158 | 1981 | Len Barker, Clev | 127 |
| 1935 | Tommy Bridges, Det | 163 | 1982 | Floyd Bannister, Sea | 209 |
| 1936 | Tommy Bridges, Det | 175 | 1983 | Jack Morris, Det | 232 |
| 1937 | Lefty Gomez, NY | 194 | 1984 | Mark Langston, Sea | 204 |
| 1938 | Bob Feller, Clev | 240 | 1985 | Bert Blyleven, Clev-Minn | 206 |
| 1939 | Bob Feller, Clev | 246 | 1986 | Mark Langston, Sea | 245 |
| 1940 | Bob Feller, Clev | 261 | 1987 | Mark Langston, Sea | 262 |
| 1941 | Bob Feller, Clev | 260 | 1988 | Roger Clemens, Bos | 291 |
| 1942 | Bobo Newsom, Wash | 113 | 1989 | Nolan Ryan, Tex | 301 |
| | Tex Hughson, Bos | 113 | 1990 | Nolan Ryan, Tex | 232 |
| 1943 | Allie Reynolds, Clev | 151 | 1991 | Roger Clemens, Bos | 241 |
| 1944 | Hal Newhouser, Det | 187 | 1992 | Randy Johnson, Sea | 241 |
| 1945 | Hal Newhouser, Det | 212 | 1993 | Randy Johnson, Sea | 308 |
| 1946 | Bob Feller, Clev | 348 | 1994 | Randy Johnson, Sea | 204 |
| 1947 | Bob Feller, Clev | 196 | 1995 | Randy Johnson, Sea | 294 |

## Leading Pitchers—Saves

| Year | Player and Team | SV | Year | Player and Team | SV |
|------|-----------------|-----|------|-----------------|-----|
| 1947 | Joe Page, NY | 17 | 1972 | Sparky Lyle, NY | 35 |
| 1948 | Russ Christopher, Clev | 17 | 1973 | John Hiller, Det | 38 |
| 1949 | Joe Page, NY | 29 | 1974 | Terry Forster, Chi | 24 |
| 1950 | Mickey Harris, Wash | 15 | 1975 | Goose Gossage, Chi | 26 |
| 1951 | Ellis Kinder, Bos | 14 | 1976 | Sparky Lyle, NY | 23 |
| 1952 | Harry Dorish, Chi | 11 | 1977 | Bill Campbell, Bos | 31 |
| 1953 | Ellis Kinder, Bos | 27 | 1978 | Goose Gossage, NY | 27 |
| 1954 | Johnny Sain, NY | 22 | 1979 | Mike Marshall, Minn | 32 |
| 1955 | Ray Narleski, Clev | 19 | 1980 | Dan Quisenberry, KC | 33 |
| 1956 | George Zuverink, Bal | 16 | 1981 | Goose Gossage, NY | 33 |
| 1957 | Bob Grim, NY | 19 | 1982 | Rollie Fingers, Mil | 28 |
| 1958 | Ryne Duren, NY | 20 | 1983 | Dan Quisenberry, KC | 35 |
| 1959 | Turk Lown, Chi | 15 | 1984 | Dan Quisenberry, KC | 45 |
| 1960 | Mike Fornieles, Bos | 14 | 1985 | Dan Quisenberry, KC | 37 |
|      | Johnny Klippstein, Clev | 14 | 1986 | Dave Righetti, NY | 46 |
| 1961 | Luis Arroyo, NY | 29 | 1987 | Tom Henke, Tor | 34 |
| 1962 | Dick Radatz, Bos | 24 | 1988 | Dennis Eckersley, Oak | 45 |
| 1963 | Stu Miller, Bal | 27 | 1989 | Jeff Russell, Tex | 38 |
| 1964 | Dick Radatz, Bos | 29 | 1990 | Bobby Thigpen, Chi | 57 |
| 1965 | Ron Kline, Wash | 29 | 1991 | Bryan Harvey, Cal | 46 |
| 1966 | Jack Aker, KC | 32 | 1992 | Dennis Eckersley, Oak | 51 |
| 1967 | Minnie Rojas, Cal | 27 | 1993 | Jeff Montgomery, KC | 45 |
| 1968 | Al Worthington, Minn | 18 |      | Duane Ward, Tor | 45 |
| 1969 | Ron Perranoski, Minn | 31 | 1994 | Lee Smith, Bal | 33 |
| 1970 | Ron Perranoski, Minn | 34 | 1995 | Jose Mesa, Clev | 46 |
| 1971 | Ken Sanders, Mil | 31 |      |                 |     |

# The Commissioners of Baseball

Kenesaw Mountain Landis .......Elected November 12, 1920. Served until his death on November 25, 1944.

Happy Chandler .....................Elected April 24, 1945. Served until July 15, 1951.

Ford Frick ...............................Elected September 20, 1951. Served until November 16, 1965.

William Eckert ..........................Elected November 17, 1965. Served until December 20, 1968.

Bowie Kuhn ...........................Elected February 8, 1969. Served until September 30, 1984.

Peter Ueberroth ......................Elected March 3, 1984. Took office October 1, 1984. Served through March 31, 1989.

A. Bartlett Giamatti .................Elected September 8, 1988. Took office April 1, 1989. Served until his death on September 1, 1989.

Francis Vincent Jr ...................Appointed Acting Commissioner September 2, 1989. Elected Commissioner September 13, 1989. Served through September 7, 1992.

Allan H. (Bud) Selig .................Elected chairman of the executive council and given the powers of interim commissioner on September 9, 1992.

## THEY SAID IT

*Marge Schott, Cincinnati Red owner, when asked if she had plans to do anything "special" for fans returning after the strike: "What do you mean?"*

# Pro Football

FEBRUARY 6, 1995 • $2.95 (CAN. $3.95)

# Sports Illustrated
# Victory!

Super Bowl MVP
Steve Young

PETER READ MILLER

# Shedding the Weight

## With his MVP performance in the Niners' Super Bowl rout of San Diego, Steve Young got a Montana-sized monkey off his back

### by Peter King

WHEN SUPER Bowl XXIX Most Valuable Player Steve Young walked (levitated?) onto the victors' podium in the San Francisco 49er locker room after the Niners' 49–26 dismantling of San Diego in January 1995, the first thing he did was hug the trophy. And hug it. And hug it some more.

The nice guy finished first.

"Aaaaahhhhh," he said. He squeezed and caressed this Vince Lombardi Trophy like a father might hug a son just returned from kidnappers. He put his head down on the sterling-silver football on top of the trophy as though it were a pillow, rocking back and forth. And then, after a while, Young gave the team its postgame speech. Not George Seifert, the coach. Steve Young, the quarterback, gave the team its talking-to after the 49ers won their fifth Super Bowl title, a record.

"There were times this was hard!" he shouted, his voice hoarse from a day of signal-calling and touchdown-celebrating. "But this is the greatest feeling IN THE WORLD!" Then, with the veins sticking out of his neck, he almost blew his vocal cords with: "No one—NO ONE—can ever take this away from us! NO ONE! EVER! It's ours!"

Quite true. The fifth 49er Super Bowl title—the most any NFL franchise has won—established owner Eddie DeBartolo's team as one of the most enduring dynasties in NFL history. It also gave the weight-of-the-world-on-his-shoulders Young, the first man to win four consecutive NFL passing titles, the credit he deserves for being a great player, the credit that so often eluded him as the Man Who Succeeded Joe Montana.

But it gave the 49ers one more thing, as every recent champion in Salary Cap Ball has learned: a very heavy crown. Because after the 49ers begged, borrowed and deferred on the way to their January 1995 Super Bowl win, the rest of 1995 became a struggle akin to their annual Armageddon bowls against the Cowboys. The week after the win over San Diego, both coordinators (Mike Shanahan on offense, Ray Rhodes

**Rice opened the scoring in Super Bowl XXIX with a 44-yard TD reception.**

on defense) left to become head coaches—Shanahan to Denver and Rhodes to Philadelphia. This had nothing to do with the cap, only with the terrific pedigree of 49er coaches. But then free agency stripped the 49ers of one star and a big chunk of their depth. To Philadelphia went prize running back Ricky Watters and backup defensive tackle Rhett Hall. To Denver went backup quarterback Bill Musgrave and wideout Ed McCaffrey. The Jets stole return specialist Dexter Carter, and punter Klaus Wilmsmeyer went to New Orleans. Veteran elements like defensive end Rickey Jackson and cornerback Toi Cook were late re-signees, and defensive end Richard Dent left to test the waters of free agency. And some were predicting that the loss of cornerback Deion Sanders to arch-rival Dallas in September would do more damage to the Niners title chances than all of their off-season depletions combined.

This is the way football works now. It's just business, baby. Perfect example: The 49ers, still snug up against the salary cap, were pursuing one of the better two-way defensive ends in free agency last March, the Jets' Jeff Lageman. In the midst of said pursuit, Dent filed an injury grievance against the club, claiming it cut him while he was still injured, which would be a violation of NFL rules if true. Because the grievance required the 49ers to keep half of Dent's $1.7 million 1995 salary counting against the cap, the 49ers had to drop out of the Lageman stakes. He signed with Jacksonville. "Do you know how well Lageman would have fit in with our team?" a thoroughly disappointed 49er president Carmen Policy said. "We loved him. He'd have been perfect for us."

The cap and its various vagaries were helping the league keep San Francisco fairly close to the pack. Their only free agent of significance, cornerback Marquez Pope, made nary a Dent in their losses. Still, entering the 1995–96 season, the NFL bal-

**San Diego and Humphries were the NFC's 11th straight Super Bowl victims.**

ance of power had changed remarkably little from the previous year. The 49ers and Dallas were a clear one-two, and everyone else was fighting for number three. The 49er-Cowboy fight was the story of the year in the NFL, with only a few sidelights competing for attention on that level: the April move of the Rams to St. Louis, the June return of the Raiders to Oakland (*see sidebar*) and the September openings of expansionists Carolina and Jacksonville. It was so simple to see why the Cowboys and the 49ers dominated. They had great supporting casts, desperado front offices and starry youth. They also had franchise-foundation quarterbacks in Young and Troy Aikman.

Young and Aikman. Aikman and Young. Who's better? Depends on which Sunday you're talking about. It's no myth that a preeminent team needs a preeminent quarterback, and these two guys were the best the NFL had to offer after the 1994 season.

At 28—the age at which many quarterbacks are just beginning a starting career—Aikman has won more Super Bowls (two) than Dan Marino, John Elway, Warren Moon, Jim Kelly and Young combined have won (one) in 56 collective seasons. Aikman's 7–1 playoff record is the best record of any playoff quarterback ever. And he's piloting a team with the talent and the playoff savvy to be a contender for the rest of the century. "From the time he came into the league," says Dallas wide receiver Michael Irvin, "I've always thought, This is the man I want to play with for the rest of my career. He's that special, that great."

What sets Aikman apart is what set Montana apart for so many years. He plays his best when it matters the most. That's a rare trait in any sport and almost always leads to greatness. In his two Super Bowl victories, both against Buffalo, Aikman completed a combined 72% of his passes. That's 10% higher than the already fine completion percentage he has earned for his career. He almost led the Cowboys to a third

**Crying the St. Louis Blues: Frontiere got to move her Rams, but not without a fight.**

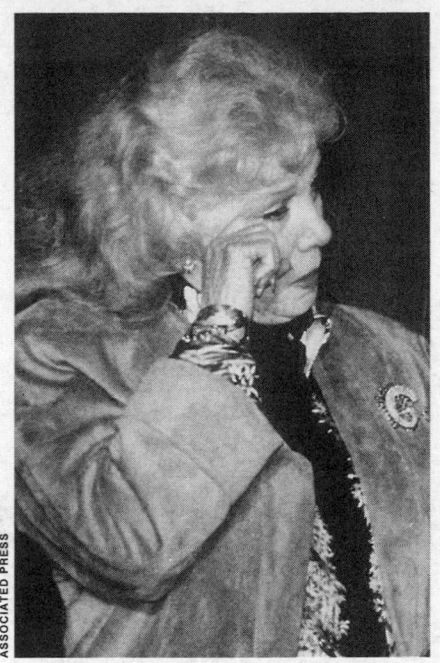

ASSOCIATED PRESS

straight Super Bowl after the 1994 season, rescuing the team from a late-year slump. When the Cowboys were stalled and misfiring entering the playoffs against Green Bay, Aikman took the brunt of the blame, and two nights before the game swore we would see the real Aikman on Sunday. "Troy Aikman ain't dead," he said pointedly. Against the Packers only two of his 30 passes were uncatchable, and the Cowboys hung on to 23 of the throws in a 35–9 rout. "You saw the real Troy Aikman out there today," said coach Barry Switzer. It *was* the real Troy Aikman out there: self-assured, determined, rifle-armed and filled with a quiet bravado.

Young's path to greatness wasn't quite as smooth. The 1994 season was his 11th as a pro. He'd bounced from the United States Football League's Los Angeles Express to the downtrodden Tampa Bay Yucs before landing as Montana's backup with the 49ers in 1987. He spent four years yo-yoing from bench to field, then won the job when Montana was hurt in 1991. And though he won passing championships in each of his four starting seasons, it was never enough ... until that night in January, when he just embarrassed the Chargers. Twenty-four of his 36 passes were complete, for 325 yards, six touchdowns and one MVP trophy. "The weight of the entire world was on his shoulders," said tackle Harris Barton. "Everyone was waiting for Steve to fall apart." In the winners' locker room that night Young said, "It's great to play your best game in the biggest game of your life. I wasn't going to let all the expectations drag me down, even though it was frustrating at times. Harris Barton has come up to me before every game and rubbed my back and said, 'I'm taking the monkey off your back.' Today he said, 'I'm taking it off for the last time.' You know, for a long time I tried to pretend it wasn't there. But I guess it was." The Montana thing, he meant.

After the Super Bowl, in a Miami hotel suite provided by the club, 44 people (mostly Mormons, like Young) stayed until the wee hours. In this small two-room unit were his mom and dad, four siblings and three of their spouses, six relatives, nine BYU buddies led by Bengal punter Lee Johnson, girlfriend Stephanie Weston, 10 Mormon friends, three agents, one reporter, some other hangers-on ... and soon, three members of the Metro Dade Fire Rescue 35 unit. They had to give a dehydrated Young a couple of pints of IV saline solution, right there on the bed. There he received visitors like a bedridden ambassador. "Is this great or what?" he said to no one in particular. "I mean, I haven't thrown six touchdown passes in any game in my life. Then I throw six today in the Super Bowl! Unbelievable." Someone in the crowd said, "Joe who?" "No, don't do that," Young said. "Don't worry about that. That's the past. Let's talk the future."

When Johnson walked into the room, he went to Young's side and kneeled. "Bro!" he said. "It happened! How great is that?"

Young, leaning over on one elbow, said, "I wish every player who ever played in the NFL could feel what I feel right now. It's so incredible after all I've gone through to finally be on the mountaintop looking down."

Alas, only one team and its players can be on that mountaintop. The NFL roadside was littered with news from other contenders and pretenders as 1995 went on. That news:

• Whither the Rams? In March the NFL blocked a move of the Rams from Anaheim to St. Louis, then took $40 million in a ransom-like transfer fee to allow the club to move in April. So the NFL was left with only the peripatetic Raiders in the number two market in the country. And that didn't last long. Owner Al Davis kept making noise about moving to Baltimore or to any other city that would have him, and then in June he hightailed it back to Oakland with his franchise. Just like that, the league's second-biggest market is laid to waste. For now, at least.

• Why Can't the AFC Win the Big One? San Francisco's rout of San Diego made the Super Bowl scoreboard NFC 11, AFC 0 since 1984, which is certainly one of sport's biggest continuing oddities. The NFC leads the interconference series only 290–275, with one tie, from 1984 through the 1994 season, and yet the Super Bowl has been ridiculously lopsided. Why? Try this one on for size: In the 10 Super Bowls previous to the Charger-49er game, the NFC offensive

## Just Move, Baby

In the end, Al Davis took the easy way out. When the calculating Raider owner moved his team back up the California coast from Los Angeles to Oakland 10 weeks before the start of the 1995 season, it wasn't a bold, insightful or brilliant move. It was the only move that, given Davis's Quixotic nature, made sense to him.

The return to home gave Davis:

• A comfort zone. In July, when Davis held his first press conference after the move, *The Oakland Tribune* bannered this headline: WELCOME BACK, MR. DAVIS. Los Angeles was always a sort of show-me city for the Raiders—for any entity, really. The East Bay never seemed to hate the Raiders, even though the franchise had jilted one of the most supportive NFL cities in history by moving south before the 1982 season. In the month after it became apparent that Davis would move the Raiders back, 80,000 calls flooded the Coliseum switchboard looking for ticket applications. Davis and his minions can sit back now and concentrate on football, not football and marketing, which leads us to point number two.

• A reprieve from the realities of the football world. In Los Angeles, Davis would have had to go into business with the folks at Hollywood Park, where a fabulous new stadium with guarantees of hosting two future Super Bowls would have been built for him. He would have had to market his team, selling the Raiders to the business community, making big spenders spend big bucks on luxury boxes and seat-licensing fees. He would have had to win over a town that never bought into the blindly loyal, just-win-baby mentality—until playoff games or

**Davis took his team back to the comfort zone of the Oakland Coliseum.**

**The NFL needs more talented young guns like New England's Bledsoe.**

JOE TRAVER

line outweighed the AFC defensive front seven by an average of 238 pounds. Not so coincidentally, in those 10 games the NFC teams outrushed the AFC teams by a 2-to-1 margin.

• Go, Joe, Go. After months of speculation, Joe Montana finally retired in April, hanging his Superman cape in a closet on 1,100 acres in the Napa Valley, where he hoped to become an amateur vintner. Hard to believe. Montana doesn't stay an amateur at anything for very long. The pro's pro left his mark on the game as, quite arguably, the greatest quarterback in history.

the Cowboys came to town. Instead of spending all the time and energy to get L.A. hot for the Raiders, Davis and the Raiders went back into the womb.

• His best chance to win. "The roar of the Oakland crowd will live with me forever," Davis said. There is little doubt that the Oakland Coliseum will be worth points to the Raiders over the coming seasons. The mausoleum that is the Los Angeles Coliseum never gave the Raiders a true home field edge. In Oakland, Davis estimates the fan frenzy will mean a four- to six-point advantage per Sunday. That's almost impossible to quantify, but all the Raiders know is that they never had the fan edge in Los Angeles. "People in L.A. never understood the importance of the 12th man," said Raider defensive tackle Nolan Harrison. "You don't just show up for playoff games."

The loss of the Raiders left the league embarrassingly without a team in the second-largest TV market. On the day the city of Oakland announced that the Raiders were returning, 18 moving vans left Anaheim for St. Louis with all of the Rams' belongings. It's likely that the league will be without a team in the Los Angeles area.

through the 1996–97 season. But no one at 410 Park Avenue in Manhattan, where the league does business, was crying.

The NFL will probably help entice a struggling team (Tampa Bay, perhaps) to move to Los Angeles in the next year or two by giving a prospective owner a stadium deal he can't refuse. Then, in the next wave of expansion (probably around 1999), Los Angeles will get another team. So long, Raiders and Rams. Hello, Bucs and Llamas—or whatever the expansion team would be called.

The smart move, however, might be to make L.A. a one-team market. Harrison is right. The region doesn't deserve two teams. It barely has the spirit to support one. "What makes you think L.A.'s going to support some team that comes in from another city and isn't as good?" Harrison asked, with reason.

Those are other owners' problems. Davis, 66, did the best thing for his team and his adoptive city for now. For the first time in over a decade he has a region nutso over his team. And for the first time in years he has a legitimate home field advantage. He did take the easy way out, but for this time and this team, it was the only way out.

PRO FOOTBALL    **123**

AL TIELEMANS

Favre of Green Bay, the NFL has no proven great quarterbacks of the future. So concerned is the league that it hired former 49er coach Bill Walsh, the quarterback guru, as its "director of quarterback development" in January 1995. Walsh worked with quarterbacks in the revitalized World League, retooled the delivery of No. 1 Carolina draft pick Kerry Collins and polished other quarterbacks before the draft. The problem is, it's a tougher position than ever, the pass rushers are faster than ever, and the schemes are more complicated than ever. The 1995 rookie crop—a pretty good one, led by Collins, Alcorn State's Steve McNair and USC's Rob Johnson—hopes to reverse the recent trend of mediocre young quarterbacks.

• Retire, Phil, Retire. One of the game's stranger stories was the saga of Phil Simms. In 1994, at 38, he spurned an offer from the Cardinals to come out of retirement in order to stay on the ESPN pro football set. In 1995, at 39, he ditched ESPN for the Cleveland Browns, agreeing to terms (but not signing) to be Vinny Testaverde's back-up for the 1995 season. Few people thought Testaverde would keep Simms on the bench for long, and with Cleveland signing receiving ace Andre Rison in free agency, the Browns looked to be a solid challenger for Super Bowl XXX. Oops. Simms decided to ditch Cleveland to return to TV—only not with ESPN but with NBC, to be a game analyst. ESPN cried foul, saying Simms owed them a second year on a verbal contract agreement. The Browns were stunned. NBC shuffled its announcing teams to find a comfy spot in big games for Simms. "I hate controversy," Simms said. Phil, in early 1995, you patented it.

• The Dearth of Young Quarterbacks. Annual story. Other than 25-and-under kids Drew Bledsoe of New England and Brett

• The Continuing Problem of Affirmative Action. Although about 60% of the league's players are African-Americans, among the league's 30 head coaches, only the Eagles' Ray Rhodes and the Vikings' Dennis Green are black, and none of the general managers or club presidents are. (Jacksonville does have a vice president of football operations, Michael Huygue, who is African-American.) And it's progressively becoming a bigger and bigger mark of shame for the league. Before Rhodes got the job, the 20 previous coaching hires in the NFL had been white. It seems ludicrous that Minnesota defensive coordinator Tony Dungy, who is black, could run the NFL's top-rated defense in 1993 and then go two straight off-seasons without getting a head coaching job. Asked about the pressure of being the only African-American hired as a coach this season, Rhodes said, "I was hired as the best available man for the job. That's what's important to me."

It should be important to the rest of the league too.

# FOR THE RECORD · 1994 – 1995

## 1994 NFL Final Standings

### American Football Conference

#### EASTERN DIVISION

|  | W | L | T | Pct | Pts | OP |
|---|---|---|---|---|---|---|
| Miami | 10 | 6 | 0 | .625 | 389 | 327 |
| †New England | 10 | 6 | 0 | .625 | 351 | 312 |
| Indianapolis | 8 | 8 | 0 | .500 | 307 | 320 |
| Buffalo | 7 | 9 | 0 | .438 | 340 | 356 |
| NY Jets | 6 | 10 | 0 | .375 | 264 | 320 |

#### CENTRAL DIVISION

|  | W | L | T | Pct | Pts | OP |
|---|---|---|---|---|---|---|
| Pittsburgh | 12 | 4 | 0 | .750 | 316 | 234 |
| †Cleveland | 11 | 5 | 0 | .688 | 340 | 204 |
| Cincinnati | 3 | 13 | 0 | .188 | 276 | 406 |
| Houston | 2 | 14 | 0 | .125 | 226 | 352 |

#### WESTERN DIVISION

|  | W | L | T | Pct | Pts | OP |
|---|---|---|---|---|---|---|
| San Diego | 11 | 5 | 0 | .688 | 381 | 306 |
| †Kansas City | 9 | 7 | 0 | .563 | 319 | 298 |
| LA Raiders | 9 | 7 | 0 | .563 | 303 | 327 |
| Denver | 7 | 9 | 0 | .438 | 347 | 396 |
| Seattle | 6 | 10 | 0 | .375 | 287 | 323 |

† Wild-card team.

### National Football Conference

#### EASTERN DIVISION

|  | W | L | T | Pct | Pts | OP |
|---|---|---|---|---|---|---|
| Dallas | 12 | 4 | 0 | .750 | 414 | 248 |
| NY Giants | 9 | 7 | 0 | .563 | 279 | 305 |
| Arizona | 8 | 8 | 0 | .500 | 235 | 267 |
| Philadelphia | 7 | 9 | 0 | .438 | 308 | 308 |
| Washington | 3 | 13 | 0 | .188 | 320 | 412 |

#### CENTRAL DIVISION

|  | W | L | T | Pct | Pts | OP |
|---|---|---|---|---|---|---|
| Minnesota | 10 | 6 | 0 | .625 | 356 | 314 |
| †Green Bay | 9 | 7 | 0 | .563 | 382 | 287 |
| †Detroit | 9 | 7 | 0 | .563 | 357 | 342 |
| †Chicago | 9 | 7 | 0 | .563 | 271 | 307 |
| Tampa Bay | 6 | 10 | 0 | .375 | 251 | 351 |

#### WESTERN DIVISION

|  | W | L | T | Pct | Pts | OP |
|---|---|---|---|---|---|---|
| San Francisco | 13 | 3 | 0 | .813 | 505 | 296 |
| New Orleans | 7 | 9 | 0 | .438 | 348 | 407 |
| Atlanta | 7 | 9 | 0 | .438 | 313 | 389 |
| LA Rams | 4 | 12 | 0 | .250 | 286 | 365 |

## 1995 NFL Playoffs

| AFC FIRST ROUND | AFC DIVISIONAL PLAYOFF | AFC CHAMPIONSHIP | NFC CHAMPIONSHIP | NFC DIVISIONAL PLAYOFF | NFC FIRST ROUND |
|---|---|---|---|---|---|

**SUPER BOWL XXIX**
January 29, 1995

Kansas City 17
Miami 27

Miami 21

San Diego 17

Dallas 28

Green Bay 9

Green Bay 16
Detroit 12

San Diego 22

Dallas 35

SAN FRANCISCO 49
San Diego 26

New England 13
Cleveland 20

Cleveland 9

Pittsburgh 13

San Francisco 38

Chicago 15

Chicago 35
Minnesota 18

Pittsburgh 29

San Francisco 44

# NFL Playoff Box Scores

## AFC Wild-card Games

New England..........0   10   0   3—13
Cleveland..............3    7   7   3—20

Kansas City..........14   3   0   0—17
Miami ....................7   10  10   0—27

### FIRST QUARTER

Cleveland: FG Stover 30, 7:20. Drive: 74 yards, 10 plays.

### SECOND QUARTER

New England: Thompson 13 pass from Bledsoe (Bahr kick), 4:12. Drive: 60 yards, 9 plays.
Cleveland: Carrier 5 pass from Testaverde (Stover kick), 7:57. Drive: 51 yards, 7 plays.
New England: FG Bahr 23, 14:30. Drive: 71 yards, 16 plays.

### THIRD QUARTER

Cleveland: Hoard 10 run (Stover kick), 12:39. Drive: 79 yards, 10 plays.

### FOURTH QUARTER

Cleveland: FG Stover 21, 11:24. Drive: 33 yards, 7 plays.
New England: FG Bahr 33, 13:30. Drive: 63 yards, 14 plays.

A: 77,452; T: 2:57.

### FIRST QUARTER

Kansas City: Walker 1 pass from Montana (Elliott kick), 6:28. Drive: 80 yards, 11 plays.
Miami: Parmalee 1 run (Stoyanovich kick), 12:40. Drive: 72 yards, 10 plays.
Kansas City: Anders 57 pass from Montana (Elliott kick),14:20. Drive: 83 yards, 4 plays.

### SECOND QUARTER

Miami: FG Stoyanovich 40, 2:45. Drive 35 yards, 7 plays.
Kansas City: FG Elliot 21, 8:48. Drive 69 yards, 12 plays.
Miami: R. Williams 1 pass from Marino (Stoyanovich kick), 14:38. Drive: 80 yards, 13 plays.

### THIRD QUARTER

Miami: Fryar 7 pass from Marino (Stoyanovich kick), 3:02. Drive: 64 yards, 6 plays.
Miami: FG Stoyanovich 40, 13:14. Drive: 59 yards, 10 plays.

A: 67,487; T: 2:47.

## NFC Wild-card Games

Detroit....................0   0   3   9—12
Green Bay ..............7   3   3   3—16

Chicago..................0   14   7  14—35
Minnesota ..............3   6   3   6—18

### FIRST QUARTER

Green Bay: Levens 3 run (Jacke kick), 7:24. Drive: 76 yards, 14 plays.

### SECOND QUARTER

Green Bay: FG Jacke 51, 12:04. Drive: 37 yards, 8 plays.

### THIRD QUARTER

Detroit: FG Hanson 38, 9:22. Drive: 41 yards, 5 plays.
Green Bay: FG Jacke 32, 14:49. Drive: 32 yards, 6 plays.

### FOURTH QUARTER

Detroit: Perriman 3 pass from Krieg (Hanson kick), 1:25. Drive: 18 yards, 5 plays.
Green Bay: FG Jacke 28, 9:25. Drive: 40 yards, 8 plays.

A: 58,125; T: 3:07.

### FIRST QUARTER

Minnesota: FG Reveiz 29, 6:59. Drive: minus 6 yards, 4 plays.

### SECOND QUARTER

Chicago: Tillman 1 run (Butler kick), 3:14. Drive: 80 yards, 16 plays.
Chicago: Jennings 9 pass from S. Walsh (Butler kick), 6:57. Drive: 71 yards, 4 plays.
Minnesota: C. Carter 4 pass from Moon (pass failed), 14:41. Drive 47 yards, 6 plays.

### THIRD QUARTER

Chicago: Ra. Harris 29 run (Butler kick), 2:03. Drive 75 yards, 4 plays
Minnesota: FG Reveiz 48, 14:55. Drive: 37 yards, 6 plays.

### FOURTH QUARTER

Chicago: J. Graham 21 pass from S. Walsh (Butler kick), 2:18. Drive 60 yards, 6 plays.
Minnesota: Lee 11 pass from Moon (pass failed), 9:24. Drive: 76 yards, 16 plays.
Chicago: Miniefield 48 fumble return (Butler kick), 11:55.

A: 60,347; T: 3:14.

## AFC Divisional Games

```
Cleveland ...............0    3    0    6— 9     Miami ......................7   14    0    0—21
Pittsburgh .............3   21    3    2—29     San Diego...............0    6    9    7—22
```

### FIRST QUARTER

Pittsburgh: FG Anderson 39, 9:38. Drive: 65 yards, 13 plays.

### SECOND QUARTER

Pittsburgh: Green 2 pass from O'Donnell (Anderson kick), :48. Drive 53 yards, 8 plays.
Pittsburgh: J. Williams 26 run (Anderson kick), 5:57. Drive: 74 yards, 6 plays.
Cleveland: FG Stover 22, 12:23. Drive: 25 yards, 6 plays.
Pittsburgh Thigpen 9 pass from O'Donnell (Anderson kick), 14:44. Drive: 6 yards, 3 plays.

### THIRD QUARTER

Pittsburgh: FG Anderson 40, 12:25. Drive 72 yards, 14 plays.

### FOURTH QUARTER

Cleveland: McCardell 20 pass from Testaverde (pass failed), 9:07. Drive: 73 yards, 3 plays.
Pittsburgh: Safety (Lake sacked Testaverde in end zone), 12:15.

A: 58, 185; T: 2:56.

### FIRST QUARTER

Miami: K. Jackson 8 pass from Marino (Stoyanovich kick), 12:36. Drive 79 yards, 9 plays.

### SECOND QUARTER

San Diego: FG Carney 20, 4:24. Drive 72 yards, 15 plays.
Miami: K. Jackson 9 pass from Marino (Stoyanovich kick), 7:39. Drive 52 yards, 6 plays.
San Diego: FG Carney 21, 12:13. Drive 70 yards, 9 plays.
Miami: M. Williams 16 pass from Marino (Stoyanovich kick), 14:33. Drive 70 yards, 9 plays.

### THIRD QUARTER

San Diego: Safety (R. Davis tackled Parmalee in end zone). 8:06.
San Diego: Means 24 run (Carney kick), 12:18. Drive: 54 yards, 6 plays.

### FOURTH QUARTER

San Diego: Seay 8 pass from Humphries (Carney kick), 14:25. Drive 61 yards, 10 plays.

A: 63,381; T: 3:03.

## NFC Divisional Games

```
Green Bay ..............3    6    0    0— 9     Chicago.................3    0    0   12—15
Dallas...................14   14    0    7—35     San Francisco........7   23    7    7—44
```

### FIRST QUARTER

Dallas: E. Smith 5 run (Boniol kick), 3:53. Drive 51 yards, 7 plays.
Green Bay: FG Jacke 50, 7:28. Drive: 42 yards, 9 plays.
Dallas: Harper 94 pass from Aikman (Boniol kick), 11:20. Drive 94 yards, 1 play.

### SECOND QUARTER

Dallas: B. Thomas 1 run (Boniol kick), 8:15. Drive 80 yards, 7 plays.
Green Bay: Bennett 1 run (pass failed), 10:29. Drive 74 yards, 6 plays.
Dallas: Galbraith 1 pass from Aikman (Boniol kick), 14:49. Drive 48 yards, 12 plays.

### FOURTH QUARTER

Dallas: B. Thomas 2 run (Boniol kick), 3:32. Drive 60 yards, 9 plays.

A:64,745; T: 3:20.

### FIRST QUARTER

Chicago: FG Butler 39, 3:58. Drive: 14 yards, 6 plays.
San Francisco: Floyd 2 run (Brien kick), 11:19. Drive 68 yards, 13 plays.

### SECOND QUARTER

San Francisco: Jones 8 pass from S. Young (kick failed), :44. Drive: 54 yards, 6 plays.
San Francisco: Floyd 4 run (Brien kick), 8:56. Drive: 61 yards, 9 plays.
San Francisco: FG Brien 36, 12:15. Drive: 14 yards, 8 plays.
San Francisco: S. Young 6 run (Brien kick), 13:43. Drive: 32 yards, 5 plays.

### THIRD QUARTER

San Francisco: Floyd 1 run (Brien kick), 8:01. Drive: 70 yards, 9 plays.

### FOURTH QUARTER

Chicago: Flanigan 2 pass from Kramer (pass failed), :49. Drive: 71 yards, 10 plays.
San Francisco: Walker 1 run (Brien kick), 3:09. Drive: 37 yards, 4 plays.
Chicago: Tillman 1 run (pass failed), 9:16. Drive 70 yards, 16 plays.

A:64,644; T: 3:03.

## AFC Championship

| | | | |
|---|---|---|---|
| San Diego...............0 | 3 | 7 | 7—17 |
| Pittsburgh .............7 | 3 | 3 | 0—13 |

### FIRST QUARTER

Pittsburgh: Williams 16 pass from O'Donnell (Anderson kick), 7:32. Drive 67 yards, 13 plays.

### SECOND QUARTER

San Diego: FG Carney 20, 11:19. Drive 77 yards, 6 plays.
Pittsburgh: FG Anderson 39, 14:51. Drive 51 yards, 12 plays.

### THIRD QUARTER

Pittsburgh: FG Anderson 23, 4:23. Drive 50 yards, 9 plays.
San Diego: Pupunu 43 pass from Humphries (Carney kick), 6:57. Drive 64 yards, 5 plays.

### FOURTH QUARTER

San Diego: Martin 43 pass from Humphries (Carney kick), 9:47. Drive 80 yards, 8 plays.

A: 61,545; T: 2:54.

## NFC Championship

| | | | |
|---|---|---|---|
| Dallas ....................7 | 7 | 7 | 7—28 |
| San Francisco......21 | 10 | 7 | 0—38 |

### FIRST QUARTER

San Francisco: Davis 44 int. return (Brien kick), 1:02.
San Francisco: Watters 29 pass from S. Young (Brien kick), 4:19. Drive: 39 yards, 5 plays.
San Francisco: Floyd 1 run (Brien kick), 7:27. Drive 35 yards, 7 plays.
Dallas: Irvin 44 pass from Aikman (Boniol kick), 12:46. Drive: 62 yards, 8 plays.

### SECOND QUARTER

San Francisco: FG Brien 34, 9:06. Drive: 64 yards, 11 plays.
Dallas: E. Smith 4 run (Boniol kick), 3:12. Drive: 63 yards, 8 plays.
San Francisco: Rice 28 pass from S. Young (Brien kick), 14:52. Drive: 39 yards, 3 plays.

### THIRD QUARTER

Dallas: E. Smith 1 run (Boniol kick), 3:12. Drive: 25 yards, 7 plays.
San Francisco: S. Young 3 run (Brien kick), 8:21. Drive: 70 yards, 10 plays.

### FOURTH QUARTER

Dallas: Irvin 10 pass from Aikman (Boniol kick), 6:31. Drive: 89 yards, 14 plays.

A: 69,125; T: 3:26.

# Super Bowl Box Score

| | | | |
|---|---|---|---|
| San Diego...............7 | 3 | 8 | 8—26 |
| San Francisco......14 | 14 | 14 | 7—49 |

### FIRST QUARTER

San Francisco: Rice 44 pass from Young (Brien kick), 1:24. Drive: 3 plays, 59 yards. Key play: SD Miller 15-yard face mask penalty on opening kickoff. San Francisco 7-0.
San Francisco: Watters 51 pass from Young (Brien kick), 4:55. Drive: 4 plays, 79 yards. Key play: Young 21-yard run on 3rd-and-3 to SF 49. San Francisco 14-0.
San Diego: Means 1 run (Carney kick), 12:16. Drive: 13 plays, 78 yards. Key plays: Humphries 17-yard pass to Harmon on 3rd-and-4 to SF 43; Harmon 10-yard run on 3rd-and-1 to SF 24; Pass interference on Sanders in end zone gives SD a 1st-and-goal at the 1. San Francisco 14-7.

### SECOND QUARTER

San Francisco: Floyd 5 pass from Young (Brien kick), 1:58. Drive: 9 plays, 69 yards. Key plays: Young 19-yard pass to Rice to SF 49; Young 15-yard run to SD 15; San Francisco 21-7.
San Francisco: Watters 8 pass from Young (Brien kick), 1:58. Drive: 9 plays, 69 yards. Key plays: Young 19-yard pass to Rice to SF 49; Young 15-yard run to SD 15. San Francisco 21-7.
San Francisco: Watters 8 pass from Young (Brien kick), 10:16. Drive: 9 plays, 49 yards. Key plays: Young 11-yard pass to Rice to SD 27; Young 8-yard pass to Rice to SD 15. San Francisco 28-7.

San Diego: FG Carney 31, 13:16. Drive: 8 plays, 62 yards. Key plays: Humphries 17-yard pass to Seay to SD 44; Jefferson 10-yard run on reverse to SF 46; Humphries 33-yard pass to Bieniemy to SF 13. San Francisco 28-10.

### THIRD QUARTER

San Francisco: Watters 9 run (Brien kick), 5:25. Drive: 7 plays, 62 yards. Key plays: Young 21-yard pass to Rice on 3rd-and-17 to SD 32; Young 16-yard pass to Taylor to San Diego 16. San Francisco 35-10.
San Francisco: Rice 15 pass from Young (Brien kick), 11:42. Drive 10 plays, 67 yards. Key plays: 22-yard pass interference on Gordon on 3rd-and-14 to SD 38; Young 13-yard run to SD 12. San Francisco 42-10.
San Diego: Coleman 98 kickoff return (Humphries pass to Seay), 11:59. San Francisco 42-18.

### FOURTH QUARTER

San Francisco: Rice 7 pass from Young (Brien kick), 1:11. Drive: 6 plays, 32 yards. Key plays: Watters 13-yard run on 3rd-and-2 to San Diego 11. San Francisco 49-18.
San Diego: Martin 30 pass from Humphries (Humphries pass to Pupunu), 12:35. Drive: 8 plays, 67 yards. Key plays: Humphries 12-yard pass to Martin to SF 43; Humphries 22-yard pass to Seay to SF 30. San Francisco 49-26.

A: 74,107; T: 3:36.

## Team Statistics

| | S.D. | S.F. |
|---|---|---|
| FIRST DOWNS | 20 | 28 |
| Rushing | 5 | 10 |
| Passing | 14 | 17 |
| Penalty | 1 | 1 |
| THIRD DOWN EFF | 6-16 | 7-13 |
| FOURTH DOWN EFF | 0-4 | 0-0 |
| TOTAL NET YARDS | 354 | 449 |
| Total plays | 76 | 73 |
| Avg gain | 4.7 | 6.2 |
| NET YARDS RUSHING | 67 | 133 |
| Rushes | 19 | 32 |
| Avg per rush | 3.5 | 4.2 |
| NET YARDS PASSING | 287 | 316 |
| Completed-Att | 27-55 | 25-38 |
| Yards per pass | 5.0 | 7.7 |
| Sacked-yards lost | 2-18 | 3-15 |
| Had intercepted | 3 | 0 |
| PUNTS-Avg | 4-48.8 | 5-39.8 |
| TOTAL RETURN YARDS | 243 | 76 |
| Punt returns | 3-1 | 2-12 |
| Kickoff returns | 8-242 | 4-48 |
| Interceptions | 0-0 | 3-16 |
| PENALTIES-Yds | 6-63 | 3-18 |
| FUMBLES-Lost | 1-0 | 2-0 |
| TIME OF POSSESSION | 28:29 | 31:31 |

## Passing

### SAN DIEGO

| | Comp | Att | Yds | Int | TD |
|---|---|---|---|---|---|
| Humphries | 24 | 49 | 275 | 2 | 0 |
| Gilbert | 3 | 6 | 30 | 1 | 0 |

### SAN FRANCISCO

| | Comp | Att | Yds | Int | TD |
|---|---|---|---|---|---|
| S. Young | 24 | 36 | 325 | 0 | 6 |

## Rushing

### SAN DIEGO

| | No. | Yds | Lg | TD |
|---|---|---|---|---|
| Means | 13 | 33 | 11 | 1 |
| Harmon | 2 | 10 | 10 | 0 |
| Jefferson | 1 | 10 | 10 | 0 |
| Gilbert | 1 | 8 | 8 | 0 |
| Bieniemy | 1 | 3 | 3 | 0 |
| Humphries | 1 | 3 | 3 | 0 |

### SAN FRANCISCO

| | No. | Yds | Lg | TD |
|---|---|---|---|---|
| S. Young | 5 | 49 | 21 | 0 |
| Watters | 15 | 47 | 13 | 1 |
| Floyd | 9 | 32 | 6 | 0 |
| Rice | 1 | 10 | 10 | 0 |
| Carter | 2 | -5 | 1 | 0 |

## Receiving

### SAN DIEGO

| | No. | Yds | Lg | TD |
|---|---|---|---|---|
| Harmon | 8 | 68 | 20 | 0 |
| Seay | 7 | 75 | 22 | 0 |
| Pupunu | 4 | 48 | 23 | 0 |
| Martin | 3 | 59 | 30 | 1 |
| Jefferson | 2 | 15 | 9 | 0 |
| Bieniemy | 1 | 33 | 33 | 0 |
| Means | 1 | 4 | 4 | 0 |
| D. Young | 1 | 3 | 3 | 0 |

### SAN FRANCISCO

| | No. | Yds | Lg | TD |
|---|---|---|---|---|
| Rice | 10 | 149 | 44 | 3 |
| J. Taylor | 4 | 43 | 16 | 0 |
| Floyd | 4 | 26 | 9 | 1 |
| Watters | 3 | 61 | 51 | 2 |
| Jones | 2 | 41 | 33 | 0 |
| Popson | 1 | 6 | 6 | 0 |
| McCaffrey | 1 | 5 | 5 | 0 |

## Defense

### SAN DIEGO

| | Tck | Ast | Int | Sack |
|---|---|---|---|---|
| Gibson | 9 | 2 | 0 | 0 |
| J. Seau | 9 | 2 | 0 | 1 |
| Gordon | 5 | 0 | 0 | 0 |
| Mims | 5 | 0 | 0 | 0 |
| Griggs | 3 | 2 | 0 | 0 |
| Carrington | 4 | 0 | 0 | 0 |
| D. Harper | 3 | 0 | 0 | 0 |
| Johnson | 2 | 0 | 0 | 2 |
| Lee | 2 | 0 | 0 | 0 |
| Richard | 1 | 1 | 0 | 0 |
| Clark | 1 | 0 | 0 | 0 |
| R. Davis | 1 | 0 | 0 | 0 |
| O'Neal | 1 | 0 | 0 | 0 |
| Vanhorse | 1 | 0 | 0 | 0 |

### SAN FRANCISCO

| | Tck | Ast | Int | Sack |
|---|---|---|---|---|
| McDonald | 8 | 1 | 0 | 0 |
| Norton | 5 | 2 | 0 | 0 |
| Davis | 6 | 0 | 1 | 0 |
| Drakeford | 4 | 0 | 0 | 0 |
| D. Brown | 3 | 1 | 0 | .5 |
| Plummer | 2 | 2 | 0 | 0 |
| Sanders | 2 | 2 | 1 | 0 |
| Young | 3 | 0 | 0 | 0 |
| Cook | 2 | 1 | 1 | 0 |
| Jackson | 2 | 0 | 0 | 0 |
| Stubblefield | 2 | 0 | 0 | 1 |
| D. Hall | 1 | 1 | 0 | 0 |
| Hanks | 1 | 1 | 0 | 0 |
| Harris | 1 | 1 | 0 | .5 |
| Mann | 1 | 0 | 0 | 0 |
| Woodall | 0 | 1 | 0 | 0 |

# 1994 Associated Press All-NFL Team

## OFFENSE

| | |
|---|---|
| Jerry Rice, San Francisco | Wide Receiver |
| Cris Carter, Minnesota | Wide Receiver |
| Ben Coates, New England | Tight End |
| William Roaf, New Orleans | Tackle |
| Richmond Webb, Miami | Tackle |
| Nate Newton, Dallas | Guard |
| Randall McDaniel, Minnesota | Guard |
| Dermontti Dawson, Pittsburgh | Center |
| Steve Young, San Francisco | Quarterback |
| Barry Sanders, Detroit | Running Back |
| Emmitt Smith, Dallas | Running Back |

## DEFENSE

| | |
|---|---|
| Charles Haley, Dallas | Defensive End |
| Bruce Smith, Buffalo | Defensive End |
| Cortez Kennedy, Seattle | Defensive Tackle |
| John Randle, Minnesota | Nose Tackle |
| Greg Lloyd, Pittsburgh | Outside Linebacker |
| Kevin Greene, Pittsburgh | Outside Linebacker |
| Junior Seau, San Diego | Inside Linebacker |
| Rod Woodson, Pittsburgh | Cornerback |
| Deion Sanders, San Francisco | Cornerback |
| Eric Turner, Cleveland | Safety |
| Darren Woodson, Dallas | Safety |

## SPECIALISTS

| | |
|---|---|
| John Carney, San Diego | Kicker |
| Reggie Roby, Washington | Punter |
| Mel Gray, Detroit | Kick Returner |

# 1994 AFC Team-by-Team Results

| BUFFALO BILLS (7-9) | | | CINCINNATI BENGALS (3-13) | | | CLEVELAND BROWNS (11-5) | |
|---:|---|---:|---:|---|---:|---:|---|---:|
| 3 | N.Y. JETS | 23 | 20 | CLEVELAND | 28 | 28 | at Cincinnati | 20 |
| 38 | at New England | 35 | 10 | at San Diego | 27 | 10 | PITTSBURGH | 17 |
| 15 | at Houston | 7 | 28 | NEW ENGLAND | 31 | 32 | ARIZONA | 0 |
| 27 | DENVER | 20 | 13 | at Houston | 20 | 21 | at Indianapolis | 14 |
| 13 | at Chicago | 20 | 7 | MIAMI | 23 | 27 | N.Y. JETS | 7 |
| 21 | MIAMI | 11 | | OPEN DATE | | | OPEN DATE | |
| 17 | INDIANAPOLIS | 27 | 10 | at Pittsburgh | 14 | 11 | at Houston | 8 |
| | OPEN DATE | | 13 | at Cleveland | 37 | 37 | CINCINNATI | 13 |
| 44 | KANSAS CITY | 10 | 20 | DALLAS | 23 | 14 | at Denver | 26 |
| 17 | at N.Y. Jets | 22 | 20 | at Seattle | 17 | 13 | NEW ENGLAND | 6 |
| 10 | at Pittsburgh | 23 | 34 | HOUSTON | 31 | 26 | at Philadelphia | 7 |
| 29 | GREEN BAY | 20 | 13 | INDIANAPOLIS | 17 | 13 | at Kansas City | 20 |
| 21 | at Detroit | 35 | 13 | at Denver | 15 | 34 | HOUSTON | 10 |
| 42 | at Miami | 31 | 15 | PITTSBURGH | 38 | 13 | N.Y. GIANTS | 16 |
| 17 | MINNESOTA | 21 | 20 | at N.Y. Giants | 27 | 19 | at Dallas | 14 |
| 17 | NEW ENGLAND | 41 | 7 | at Arizona | 28 | 7 | at Pittsburgh | 17 |
| 9 | at Indianapolis | 10 | 33 | PHILADELPHIA | 30 | 35 | SEATTLE | 9 |
| 329 | | 242 | 276 | | 406 | 340 | | 204 |

## DENVER BRONCOS (7-9)

| | | |
|---|---|---|
| 34 | SAN DIEGO | 37 |
| 22 | at N.Y. Jets | 25 |
| 16 | L.A. RAIDERS | 48 |
| 20 | at Buffalo | 27 |
| | OPEN DATE | |
| 16 | at Seattle | 9 |
| 28 | KANSAS CITY | 31 |
| 20 | at San Diego | 15 |
| 26 | CLEVELAND | 14 |
| 21 | at L.A. Rams | 27 |
| 17 | SEATTLE | 10 |
| 32 | ATLANTA | 28 |
| 15 | CINCINNATI | 13 |
| 20 | at Kansas City | 17(OT) |
| 13 | at L.A. Raiders | 23 |
| 19 | at San Francisco | 42 |
| 28 | NEW ORLEANS | 30 |
| 347 | | 396 |

## HOUSTON OILERS (2-14)

| | | |
|---|---|---|
| 21 | at Indianapolis | 45 |
| 17 | at Dallas | 20 |
| 7 | BUFFALO | 15 |
| 20 | CINCINNATI | 13 |
| 14 | at Pittsburgh | 30 |
| | OPEN DATE | |
| 8 | CLEVELAND | 11 |
| 6 | at Philadelphia | 21 |
| 14 | at L.A. Raiders | 17 |
| 9 | PITTSBURGH | 12 |
| 31 | at Cincinnati | 34 |
| 10 | N.Y. GIANTS | 13 |
| 10 | at Cleveland | 34 |
| 12 | ARIZONA | 30 |
| 14 | SEATTLE | 16 |
| 9 | at Kansas City | 31 |
| 24 | N.Y. JETS | 10 |
| 226 | | 352 |

## INDIANAPOLIS COLTS (8-8)

| | | |
|---|---|---|
| 45 | HOUSTON | 21 |
| 10 | at Tampa Bay | 24 |
| 21 | at Pittsburgh | 31 |
| 14 | CLEVELAND | 21 |
| 17 | SEATTLE | 15 |
| 6 | at N.Y. Jets | 16 |
| 27 | at Buffalo | 17 |
| 27 | WASHINGTON | 41 |
| 28 | N.Y. JETS | 25 |
| 21 | at Miami | 22 |
| | OPEN DATE | |
| 17 | at Cincinnati | 13 |
| 10 | NEW ENGLAND | 12 |
| 31 | at Seattle | 19 |
| 13 | at New England | 28 |
| 10 | MIAMI | 6 |
| 10 | BUFFALO | 9 |
| 307 | | 320 |

## KANSAS CITY CHIEFS (9-7)

| | | |
|---|---|---|
| 30 | at New Orleans | 17 |
| 24 | SAN FRANCISCO | 17 |
| 30 | at Atlanta | 10 |
| 0 | L.A. RAMS | 16 |
| | OPEN DATE | |
| 6 | at San Diego | 20 |
| 31 | at Denver | 28 |
| 38 | SEATTLE | 23 |
| 10 | at Buffalo | 44 |
| 13 | L.A. RAIDERS | 3 |
| 13 | SAN DIEGO | 14 |
| 20 | CLEVELAND | 13 |
| 9 | at Seattle | 10 |
| 17 | DENVER | 20(OT) |
| 28 | at Miami | 45 |
| 31 | HOUSTON | 9 |
| 19 | at L.A. Raiders | 9 |
| 319 | | 298 |

## LOS ANGELES RAIDERS (9-7)

| | | |
|---|---|---|
| 14 | at San Francisco | 44 |
| 9 | SEATTLE | 38 |
| 48 | at Denver | 16 |
| 24 | SAN DIEGO | 26 |
| | OPEN DATE | |
| 21 | at New England | 17 |
| 17 | at Miami | 20(OT) |
| 30 | ATLANTA | 17 |
| 17 | HOUSTON | 14 |
| 3 | at Kansas City | 13 |
| 20 | at L.A. Rams | 17 |
| 24 | NEW ORLEANS | 19 |
| 3 | PITTSBURGH | 21 |
| 24 | at San Diego | 17 |
| 23 | DENVER | 13 |
| 17 | at Seattle | 16 |
| 9 | KANSAS CITY | 19 |
| 306 | | 326 |

## MIAMI DOLPHINS (10-6)

| | | |
|---|---|---|
| 39 | New England | 35 |
| 24 | vs. Green Bay | 14 |
| 28 | N.Y. JETS | 14 |
| 35 | at Minnesota | 38 |
| 23 | at Cincinnati | 7 |
| 11 | at Buffalo | 21 |
| 20 | L.A. RAIDERS | 17(OT) |
| | OPEN DATE | |
| 23 | at New England | 3 |
| 22 | INDIANAPOLIS | 21 |
| 14 | CHICAGO | 17 |
| 13 | at Pittsburgh | 16(OT) |
| 28 | at N.Y. Jets | 24 |
| 31 | BUFFALO | 42 |
| 45 | KANSAS CITY | 28 |
| 6 | at Indianapolis | 10 |
| 27 | DETROIT | 20 |
| 389 | | 327 |

## NEW ENGLAND PATRIOTS (10-6)

| | | |
|---|---|---|
| 35 | at Miami | 39 |
| 35 | BUFFALO | 38 |
| 31 | at Cincinnati | 28 |
| 23 | at Detroit | 17 |
| 17 | GREEN BAY | 16 |
| 17 | L.A. RAIDERS | 21 |
| 17 | at N.Y. Jets | 24 |
| | OPEN DATE | |
| 3 | MIAMI | 23 |
| 6 | at Cleveland | 13 |
| 26 | MINNESOTA | 20 |
| 23 | SAN DIEGO | 17 |
| 12 | at Indianapolis | 10 |
| 24 | N.Y. JETS | 13 |
| 28 | INDIANAPOLIS | 13 |
| 41 | at Buffalo | 17 |
| 13 | at Chicago | 3 |
| 351 | | 312 |

## NEW YORK JETS (6-10)

| | | |
|---|---|---|
| 23 | at Buffalo | 3 |
| 25 | DENVER | 22 |
| 14 | at Miami | 28 |
| 7 | CHICAGO | 19 |
| 7 | at Cleveland | 27 |
| 16 | INDIANAPOLIS | 6 |
| 24 | NEW ENGLAND | 17 |
| | OPEN DATE | |
| 25 | at Indianapolis | 28 |
| 22 | BUFFALO | 17 |
| 10 | at Green Bay | 17 |
| 31 | at Minnesota | 21 |
| 24 | MIAMI | 28 |
| 13 | at New England | 24 |
| 7 | DETROIT | 18 |
| 6 | SAN DIEGO | 21 |
| 10 | at Houston | 24 |
| 264 | | 320 |

## PITTSBURGH STEELERS (12-4)

| | | |
|---|---|---|
| 9 | DALLAS | 26 |
| 17 | at Cleveland | 10 |
| 31 | INDIANAPOLIS | 21 |
| 13 | at Seattle | 30 |
| 30 | HOUSTON | 14 |
| | OPEN DATE | |
| 14 | CINCINNATI | 10 |
| 10 | at N.Y. Giants | 6 |
| 17 | at Arizona | 20 |
| 12 | at Houston | 9 |
| 23 | BUFFALO | 10 |
| 16 | MIAMI | 13(OT) |
| 21 | at L.A. Raiders | 3 |
| 38 | at Cincinnati | 15 |
| 14 | PHILADELPHIA | 3 |
| 17 | CLEVELAND | 7 |
| 34 | at San Diego | 37 |
| 316 | | 234 |

## SAN DIEGO CHARGERS (11-5)

| | | |
|---|---|---|
| 37 | at Denver | 34 |
| 27 | CINCINNATI | 10 |
| 24 | at Seattle | 10 |
| 26 | at L.A. Raiders | 24 |
| | OPEN DATE | |
| 20 | KANSAS CITY | 6 |
| 36 | at New Orleans | 22 |
| 15 | DENVER | 20 |
| 35 | SEATTLE | 15 |
| 9 | at Atlanta | 10 |
| 14 | at Kansas City | 13 |
| 17 | at New England | 23 |
| 31 | L.A. RAMS | 17 |
| 17 | L.A. RAIDERS | 24 |
| 15 | SAN FRANCISCO | 38 |
| 21 | at N.Y. Jets | 6 |
| 37 | PITTSBURGH | 34 |
| **381** | | **306** |

## SEATTLE SEAHAWKS (6-10)

| | | |
|---|---|---|
| 28 | at Washington | 7 |
| 38 | at L.A. Raiders | 9 |
| 10 | SAN DIEGO | 24 |
| 30 | PITTSBURGH | 13 |
| 15 | at Indianapolis | 17 |
| 9 | DENVER | 16 |
| | OPEN DATE | |
| 23 | at Kansas City | 38 |
| 15 | at San Diego | 35 |
| 17 | CINCINNATI | 20 |
| 10 | at Denver | 17 |
| 22 | TAMPA BAY | 21 |
| 10 | KANSAS CITY | 9 |
| 19 | INDIANAPOLIS | 31 |
| 16 | at Houston | 14 |
| 16 | L.A. RAIDERS | 17 |
| 9 | at Cleveland | 35 |
| **287** | | **323** |

# 1994 NFC Team-by-Team Results

## ARIZONA (8-8)

| | | |
|---|---|---|
| 12 | at L.A. Rams | 14 |
| 17 | N.Y. GIANTS | 20 |
| 0 | at Cleveland | 32 |
| | OPEN DATE | |
| 17 | MINNESOTA | 7 |
| 3 | at Dallas | 38 |
| 19 | at Washington | 16(OT) |
| 21 | DALLAS | 28 |
| 20 | PITTSBURGH | 17(OT) |
| 7 | at Philadelphia | 17 |
| 10 | at N.Y. Giants | 9 |
| 12 | PHILADELPHIA | 6 |
| 16 | CHICAGO | 19(OT) |
| 30 | at Houston | 12 |
| 17 | WASHINGTON | 15 |
| 28 | CINCINNATI | 7 |
| 6 | at Atlanta | 10 |
| **235** | | **267** |

## ATLANTA FALCONS (7-9)

| | | |
|---|---|---|
| 28 | at Detroit | 31 |
| 31 | L.A. RAMS | 13 |
| 10 | KANSAS CITY | 30 |
| 27 | at Washington | 20 |
| 8 | at L.A. Rams | 5 |
| 34 | TAMPA BAY | 13 |
| 3 | SAN FRANCISCO | 42 |
| 17 | at L.A. Raiders | 30 |
| | OPEN DATE | |
| 10 | SAN DIEGO | 9 |
| 32 | at New Orleans | 33 |
| 28 | at Denver | 32 |
| 28 | PHILADELPHIA | 21 |
| 14 | at San Francisco | 50 |
| 20 | NEW ORLEANS | 29 |
| 17 | vs. Green Bay | 21 |
| 10 | ARIZONA | 6 |
| **313** | | **389** |

## CHICAGO BEARS (9-7)

| | | |
|---|---|---|
| 21 | TAMPA BAY | 9 |
| 22 | at Philadelphia | 30 |
| 14 | MINNESOTA | 42 |
| 19 | N.Y. JETS | 7 |
| 20 | BUFFALO | 13 |
| 17 | NEW ORLEANS | 7 |
| | OPEN DATE | |
| 16 | at Detroit | 21 |
| 6 | GREEN BAY | 33 |
| 20 | at Tampa Bay | 6 |
| 17 | at Miami | 14 |
| 20 | DETROIT | 10 |
| 19 | at Arizona | 16(OT) |
| 27 | at Minnesota | 33(OT) |
| 3 | at Green Bay | 40 |
| 27 | L.A. RAMS | 13 |
| 3 | NEW ENGLAND | 13 |
| **271** | | **307** |

## DALLAS COWBOYS (12-4)

| | | |
|---|---|---|
| 26 | at Pittsburgh | 9 |
| 20 | HOUSTON | 17 |
| 17 | DETROIT | 20 |
| | OPEN DATE | |
| 34 | at Washington | 7 |
| 38 | ARIZONA | 3 |
| 24 | PHILADELPHIA | 13 |
| 28 | at Arizona | 21 |
| 23 | at Cincinnati | 20 |
| 38 | N.Y. GIANTS | 10 |
| 14 | at San Francisco | 21 |
| 31 | WASHINGTON | 7 |
| 42 | GREEN BAY | 31 |
| 31 | at Philadelphia | 19 |
| 14 | CLEVELAND | 19 |
| 24 | at New Orleans | 16 |
| 10 | at N.Y. Giants | 15 |
| **414** | | **248** |

## DETROIT LIONS (9-7)

| | | |
|---|---|---|
| 31 | ATLANTA | 28 |
| 3 | at Minnesota | 10 |
| 20 | at Dallas | 17 |
| 17 | NEW ENGLAND | 23 |
| 14 | at Tampa Bay | 24 |
| 21 | SAN FRANCISCO | 27 |
| | OPEN DATE | |
| 21 | CHICAGO | 16 |
| 28 | at N.Y. Giants | 25 |
| 30 | vs. Green Bay | 38 |
| 14 | TAMPA BAY | 9 |
| 10 | at Chicago | 20 |
| 35 | BUFFALO | 21 |
| 34 | GREEN BAY | 31 |
| 18 | at N.Y. Jets | 17 |
| 41 | MINNESOTA | 19 |
| 20 | at Miami | 27 |
| **357** | | **342** |

## GREEN BAY PACKERS (9-7)

| | | |
|---|---|---|
| 16 | MINNESOTA | 10 |
| 14 | MIAMI | 24 |
| 7 | at Philadelphia | 13 |
| 30 | TAMPA BAY | 3 |
| 16 | at New England | 17 |
| 24 | L.A. RAMS | 17 |
| | OPEN DATE | |
| 10 | at Minnesota | 13(OT) |
| 38 | at Chicago | 6 |
| 33 | DETROIT | 30 |
| 17 | N.Y. JETS | 10 |
| 20 | at Buffalo | 29 |
| 31 | at Dallas | 42 |
| 31 | at Detroit | 34 |
| 40 | CHICAGO | 3 |
| 21 | ATLANTA | 17 |
| 34 | at Tampa Bay | 19 |
| **382** | | **287** |

### LOS ANGELES RAMS (4-12)

| | | |
|---|---|---|
| 14 | ARIZONA | 12 |
| 13 | at Atlanta | 31 |
| 19 | SAN FRANCISCO | 34 |
| 16 | at Kansas City | 0 |
| 5 | ATLANTA | 8 |
| 17 | at Green Bay | 24 |
| 17 | N.Y. GIANTS | 10 |
| 34 | at New Orleans | 37 |
| | OPEN DATE | |
| 27 | DENVER | 21 |
| 17 | L.A. RAIDERS | 20 |
| 27 | at San Francisco | 31 |
| 17 | at San Diego | 31 |
| 15 | NEW ORLEANS | 31 |
| 14 | at Tampa Bay | 24 |
| 13 | at Chicago | 27 |
| 21 | WASHINGTON | 24 |
| 286 | | 365 |

### MINNESOTA VIKINGS (10-6)

| | | |
|---|---|---|
| 10 | at Green Bay | 16 |
| 10 | DETROIT | 3 |
| 42 | at Chicago | 14 |
| 38 | MIAMI | 35 |
| 7 | at Arizona | 17 |
| 27 | at N.Y. Giants | 10 |
| | OPEN DATE | |
| 13 | GREEN BAY | 10(OT) |
| 36 | at Tampa Bay | 13 |
| 21 | NEW ORLEANS | 20 |
| 20 | at New England | 26 |
| 21 | N.Y. JETS | 31 |
| 17 | TAMPA BAY | 20 |
| 33 | CHICAGO | 27(OT) |
| 21 | at Buffalo | 17 |
| 19 | at Detroit | 41 |
| 21 | SAN FRANCISCO | 14 |
| 356 | | 314 |

### NEW ORLEANS SAINTS (7-9)

| | | |
|---|---|---|
| 17 | KANSAS CITY | 30 |
| 24 | WASHINGTON | 38 |
| 9 | at Tampa Bay | 7 |
| 13 | at San Francisco | 24 |
| 27 | N.Y. GIANTS | 22 |
| 7 | at Chicago | 17 |
| 22 | SAN DIEGO | 36 |
| 37 | L.A. RAMS | 34 |
| | OPEN DATE | |
| 20 | at Minnesota | 21 |
| 33 | ATLANTA | 32 |
| 19 | at L.A. Raiders | 24 |
| 14 | SAN FRANCISCO | 35 |
| 31 | at L.A. Rams | 15 |
| 29 | at Atlanta | 20 |
| 16 | DALLAS | 24 |
| 30 | at Denver | 28 |
| 348 | | 407 |

### NEW YORK GIANTS (9-7)

| | | |
|---|---|---|
| 28 | PHILADELPHIA | 23 |
| 20 | at Arizona | 17 |
| 31 | WASHINGTON | 23 |
| | OPEN DATE | |
| 22 | at New Orleans | 27 |
| 10 | MINNESOTA | 27 |
| 10 | at L.A. Rams | 17 |
| 6 | PITTSBURGH | 10 |
| 25 | DETROIT | 28 |
| 10 | at Dallas | 38 |
| 9 | ARIZONA | 10 |
| 13 | at Houston | 10 |
| 21 | at Washington | 19 |
| 16 | at Cleveland | 13 |
| 27 | CINCINNATI | 20 |
| 16 | at Philadelphia | 13 |
| 15 | DALLAS | 10 |
| 279 | | 305 |

### PHILADELPHIA EAGLES (7-9)

| | | |
|---|---|---|
| 23 | at N.Y. Giants | 28 |
| 30 | CHICAGO | 22 |
| 13 | GREEN BAY | 7 |
| | OPEN DATE | |
| 40 | at San Francisco | 8 |
| 21 | WASHINGTON | 17 |
| 13 | at Dallas | 24 |
| 21 | HOUSTON | 6 |
| 31 | at Washington | 29 |
| 17 | ARIZONA | 7 |
| 7 | CLEVELAND | 26 |
| 6 | at Arizona | 12 |
| 21 | at Atlanta | 28 |
| 19 | DALLAS | 31 |
| 3 | at Pittsburgh | 14 |
| 13 | N.Y. GIANTS | 16 |
| 30 | at Cincinnati | 33 |
| 308 | | 308 |

### SAN FRANCISCO 49ERS (13-3)

| | | |
|---|---|---|
| 44 | L.A. RAIDERS | 14 |
| 17 | at Kansas City | 24 |
| 34 | at L.A. Rams | 19 |
| 24 | NEW ORLEANS | 13 |
| 8 | PHILADELPHIA | 40 |
| 27 | at Detroit | 21 |
| 42 | at Atlanta | 3 |
| 41 | TAMPA BAY | 16 |
| | OPEN DATE | |
| 37 | at Washington | 22 |
| 21 | DALLAS | 14 |
| 31 | L.A. RAMS | 27 |
| 35 | at New Orleans | 14 |
| 50 | ATLANTA | 14 |
| 3 | at San Diego | 15 |
| 42 | DENVER | 19 |
| 14 | at Minnesota | 21 |
| 505 | | 296 |

### TAMPA BAY BUCCANEERS (6-10)

| | | |
|---|---|---|
| 9 | at Chicago | 21 |
| 24 | INDIANAPOLIS | 10 |
| 7 | NEW ORLEANS | 9 |
| 3 | at Green Bay | 30 |
| 24 | DETROIT | 14 |
| 13 | at Atlanta | 34 |
| | OPEN DATE | |
| 16 | at San Francisco | 41 |
| 13 | MINNESOTA | 36 |
| 6 | CHICAGO | 20 |
| 9 | at Detroit | 14 |
| 21 | at Seattle | 22 |
| 20 | at Minnesota | 17(OT) |
| 26 | WASHINGTON | 21 |
| 24 | L.A. RAMS | 14 |
| 17 | at Washington | 14 |
| 19 | GREEN BAY | 34 |
| 382 | | 287 |

### WASHINGTON REDSKINS (3-13)

| | | |
|---|---|---|
| 7 | SEATTLE | 28 |
| 38 | at New Orleans | 24 |
| 23 | at N.Y. Giants | 31 |
| 20 | ATLANTA | 27 |
| 7 | DALLAS | 34 |
| 17 | at Philadelphia | 21 |
| 16 | ARIZONA | 19(OT) |
| 41 | at Indianapolis | 27 |
| 29 | PHILADELPHIA | 31 |
| 22 | SAN FRANCISCO | 37 |
| | OPEN DATE | |
| 7 | at Dallas | 31 |
| 19 | N.Y. GIANTS | 21 |
| 21 | at Tampa Bay | 26 |
| 15 | at Arizona | 17 |
| 14 | TAMPA BAY | 17 |
| 24 | at L.A. Rams | 21 |
| 320 | | 412 |

## American Football Conference
### Scoring

| TOUCHDOWNS | TD | Rush | Rec | Ret | Pts | KICKING | PAT | FG | Lg | Pts |
|---|---|---|---|---|---|---|---|---|---|---|
| Faulk, Ind | 12 | 11 | 1 | 0 | 72 | Carney, SD | 33/33 | 34/38 | 50 | 135 |
| Means, SD | 12 | 12 | 0 | 0 | 72 | Elam, Den | 29/29 | 30/37 | 54 | 119 |
| C. Warren, Sea | 11 | 9 | 2 | 0 | 68 | Bahr, NE | 36/36 | 27/34 | 48 | 117 |
| Pickens, Cin | 11 | 0 | 11 | 0 | 66 | Christie, Buf | 38/38 | 24/28 | 52 | 110 |
| Brown, Rai | 9 | 0 | 9 | 0 | 54 | Stover, Cle | 32/32 | 26/28 | 45 | 110 |
| Hoard, Cle | 9 | 5 | 4 | 0 | 54 | Pelfrey, Cin | 24/25 | 28/33 | 54 | 108 |
| L. Russell, Den | 9 | 9 | 0 | 0 | 54 | Stoyanovich, Mia | 35/35 | 24/31 | 50 | 107 |
| T. Thomas, Buf | 9 | 7 | 2 | 0 | 54 | Elliott, KC | 30/30 | 25/30 | 49 | 105 |
| Butts, NE | 8 | 8 | 0 | 0 | 48 | Anderson, Pitt | 32/32 | 24/29 | 50 | 104 |
| Reed, Buf | 8 | 0 | 8 | 0 | 48 | Jaeger, Rai | 31/31 | 22/28 | 51 | 97 |

### Passing

| | Att | Comp | Pct Comp | Yds | Avg Gain | TD | Pct TD | Int | Pct Int | Lg | Rating Pts |
|---|---|---|---|---|---|---|---|---|---|---|---|
| Marino, Mia | 615 | 385 | 62.6 | 4453 | 7.24 | 30 | 4.9 | 17 | 2.8 | t64 | 89.2 |
| Elway, Den | 494 | 307 | 62.1 | 3490 | 7.06 | 16 | 3.2 | 10 | 2.0 | 63 | 85.7 |
| Kelly, Buf | 448 | 285 | 63.6 | 3114 | 6.95 | 22 | 4.9 | 17 | 3.8 | t83 | 84.6 |
| Montana, KC | 493 | 299 | 60.6 | 3283 | 6.66 | 16 | 3.2 | 9 | 1.8 | t57 | 83.6 |
| Humphries, SD | 453 | 264 | 58.3 | 3209 | 7.08 | 17 | 3.8 | 12 | 2.6 | t99 | 81.6 |
| Hostetler, Rai | 454 | 263 | 57.9 | 3334 | 7.34 | 20 | 4.4 | 16 | 3.5 | t77 | 81.0 |
| O'Donnell, Pitt | 370 | 212 | 57.3 | 2443 | 6.60 | 13 | 3.5 | 9 | 2.4 | t60 | 78.9 |
| Esiason, NYJ | 440 | 255 | 58.0 | 2782 | 6.32 | 17 | 3.9 | 13 | 3.0 | 69 | 77.3 |
| Blake, Cin | 306 | 156 | 51.0 | 2154 | 7.04 | 14 | 4.6 | 9 | 2.9 | 76 | 76.9 |
| Bledsoe, NE | 691 | 400 | 57.9 | 4555 | 6.59 | 25 | 3.6 | 27 | 3.9 | t62 | 73.6 |

### Pass Receiving

| RECEPTIONS | No. | Yds | Avg | Lg | TD | YARDS | Yds | No. | Avg | Lg | TD |
|---|---|---|---|---|---|---|---|---|---|---|---|
| Coates, NE | 96 | 1174 | 12.2 | t62 | 7 | Brown, Rai | 1309 | 89 | 14.7 | t77 | 9 |
| Reed, Buf | 90 | 1303 | 14.5 | t83 | 8 | Reed, Buf | 1303 | 90 | 14.5 | t83 | 8 |
| Brown, Rai | 89 | 1309 | 14.7 | t77 | 9 | Fryar, Mia | 1270 | 73 | 17.4 | t54 | 7 |
| Sharpe, Den | 87 | 1010 | 11.6 | 44 | 4 | Coates, NE | 1174 | 96 | 12.2 | t62 | 7 |
| Blades, Sea | 81 | 1086 | 13.4 | 45 | 4 | Pickens, Cin | 1127 | 71 | 15.9 | t70 | 11 |
| Moore, NYJ | 78 | 1010 | 12.9 | t41 | 3 | Miller, Den | 1107 | 60 | 18.5 | 76 | 5 |
| Milburn, Den | 77 | 549 | 7.1 | 33 | 3 | Blades, Sea | 1086 | 81 | 13.4 | 45 | 4 |
| Timpson, NE | 74 | 941 | 12.7 | 37 | 3 | Moore, NYJ | 1010 | 78 | 12.9 | t41 | 6 |
| Fryar, Mia | 73 | 1270 | 17.4 | t54 | 7 | Sharpe, Den | 1010 | 87 | 11.6 | 44 | 4 |
| Pickens, Cin | 71 | 1127 | 15.9 | t70 | 11 | Timpson, NE | 941 | 74 | 12.7 | 37 | 3 |

### Rushing

| | Att | Yds | Avg | Lg | TD | Total Yards from Scrimmage | Total | Rush | Rec |
|---|---|---|---|---|---|---|---|---|---|
| C. Warren, Sea | 333 | 1545 | 4.6 | 41 | 9 | C. Warren, Sea | 1868 | 1545 | 323 |
| Means, SD | 343 | 1350 | 3.9 | 25 | 12 | Faulk, Ind | 1804 | 1282 | 522 |
| Faulk, Ind | 314 | 1282 | 4.1 | 52 | 11 | Means, SD | 1585 | 1350 | 235 |
| T. Thomas, Buf | 287 | 1093 | 3.8 | 29 | 7 | T. Thomas, Buf | 1442 | 1093 | 349 |
| H. Williams, Rai | 282 | 983 | 3.5 | 28 | 4 | Reed, Buf | 1390 | 87 | 1303 |
| J. Johnson, NYJ | 240 | 931 | 3.9 | 90 | 3 | H. Williams, Rai | 1374 | 983 | 391 |
| Hoard, Cle | 209 | 890 | 4.3 | 39 | 5 | Hoard, Cle | 1335 | 890 | 445 |
| Parmalee, Mia | 216 | 868 | 4.0 | t47 | 6 | Brown, Rai | 1309 | 0 | 1309 |
| Foster, Pitt | 216 | 851 | 3.9 | t29 | 5 | Fryar, Mia | 1270 | 0 | 1270 |
| Morris, Pitt | 198 | 836 | 4.2 | 20 | 7 | J. Johnson, NYJ | 1234 | 931 | 303 |

### Interceptions

| | No. | Yds | Lg | TD |
|---|---|---|---|---|
| Turner, Cle | 9 | 199 | t93 | 1 |
| Buchanan, Ind | 8 | 221 | t90 | 3 |
| McDaniel, Rai | 7 | 103 | 35 | 2 |
| Hurst, NE | 7 | 68 | 24 | 0 |
| Perry, Pitt | 7 | 112 | 42 | 0 |

Four tied with 5

### Sacks

| | |
|---|---|
| Greene, Pitt | 14.0 |
| O'Neal, SD | 12.5 |
| N. Smith, KC | 11.5 |
| Mims, SD | 11.0 |
| Thomas, KC | 11.0 |
| B. Smith, Buf | 10.0 |
| Burnett, Cle | 10.0 |
| Lloyd, Pitt | 10.0 |

## American Football Conference (*Cont.*)

### Punting

| | No. | Yds | Avg | Net Avg | TB | In 20 | Lg | Blk | Ret | Ret Yds |
|---|---|---|---|---|---|---|---|---|---|---|
| Gossett, Rai | 77 | 3377 | 43.9 | 35.2 | 15 | 19 | 65 | 0 | 38 | 366 |
| L. Johnson, Cin | 79 | 3461 | 43.8 | 35.3 | 9 | 19 | 64 | 1 | 43 | 459 |
| Rouen, Den | 76 | 3258 | 42.9 | 37.1 | 8 | 23 | 59 | 0 | 39 | 275 |
| Tuten, Sea | 91 | 3905 | 42.9 | 36.7 | 7 | 23 | 64 | 0 | 43 | 426 |
| Camarillo, Hou | 96 | 4115 | 42.9 | 36.4 | 9 | 34 | 58 | 0 | 50 | 438 |

### Punt Returns

| | No. | Yds | Avg | Lg | TD |
|---|---|---|---|---|---|
| Gordon, SD | 36 | 475 | 13.2 | t90 | 2 |
| Brown, Rai | 40 | 487 | 12.2 | 48 | 0 |
| Sawyer, Cin | 26 | 307 | 11.8 | t82 | 1 |
| Burris, Buff | 32 | 332 | 10.4 | 57 | 0 |
| Metcalf, Cle | 35 | 348 | 9.9 | t92 | 2 |

### Kickoff Returns

| | No. | Yds | Avg | Lg | TD |
|---|---|---|---|---|---|
| Baldwin, Cle | 28 | 753 | 26.9 | t85 | 1 |
| Coleman, SD | 49 | 1293 | 26.4 | t90 | 2 |
| By'Not'e, Den | 24 | 545 | 22.7 | 41 | 0 |
| Dickerson, KC | 21 | 472 | 22.5 | 62 | 0 |
| Humphrey, Ind | 35 | 783 | 22.4 | t95 | 1 |

## National Football Conference

### Scoring

| TOUCHDOWNS | TD | Rush | Rec | Ret | Pts | KICKING | PAT | FG | Lg | Pts |
|---|---|---|---|---|---|---|---|---|---|---|
| E. Smith, Dall | 22 | 21 | 1 | 0 | 132 | Reveiz, Minn | 30/30 | 34/39 | 51 | 132 |
| Sharpe, GB | 18 | 0 | 18 | 0 | 108 | Andersen, NO | 32/32 | 28/29 | 48 | 116 |
| Rice, SF | 15 | 2 | 13 | 0 | 92 | Boniol, Dall | 48/48 | 22/29 | 47 | 114 |
| Mathis, Atl | 11 | 0 | 11 | 0 | 70 | Brien, SF | 60/62 | 15/20 | 48 | 105 |
| H. Moore, Det | 11 | 0 | 11 | 0 | 66 | Jacke, GB | 41/43 | 19/26 | 50 | 98 |
| Watters, SF | 11 | 6 | 5 | 0 | 66 | Murray, Phil | 33/33 | 21/25 | 42 | 96 |
| Jones, SF | 9 | 0 | 9 | 0 | 56 | N. Johnson, Atl | 32/32 | 21/25 | 50 | 95 |
| Bennett, GB | 9 | 5 | 4 | 0 | 54 | Hanson, Det | 39/40 | 18/27 | 49 | 93 |
| Allen, Minn | 8 | 8 | 0 | 0 | 50 | Lohmiller, Wash | 30/32 | 20/28 | 54 | 90 |
| Rison, Atl | 8 | 0 | 8 | 0 | 50 | Husted, TB | 20/20 | 23/35 | 53 | 89 |

### Passing

| | Att | Comp | Pct Comp | Yds | Avg Gain | TD | Pct TD | Int | Pct Int | Lg | Rating Pts |
|---|---|---|---|---|---|---|---|---|---|---|---|
| S. Young, SF | 461 | 324 | 70.3 | 3969 | 8.61 | 35 | 7.6 | 10 | 2.2 | t69 | 112.8 |
| Favre, GB | 582 | 363 | 62.4 | 3882 | 6.67 | 33 | 5.7 | 14 | 2.4 | 49 | 90.7 |
| Everett, NO | 540 | 346 | 64.1 | 3855 | 7.14 | 22 | 4.1 | 18 | 3.3 | t78 | 84.9 |
| Aikman, Dall | 361 | 233 | 64.5 | 2676 | 7.41 | 13 | 3.6 | 12 | 3.3 | 90 | 84.9 |
| J. George, Atl | 524 | 322 | 61.5 | 3734 | 7.13 | 23 | 4.4 | 18 | 3.4 | t85 | 83.3 |
| Erickson, TB | 399 | 225 | 56.4 | 2919 | 7.32 | 16 | 4.0 | 10 | 2.5 | t71 | 82.5 |
| Moon, Minn | 601 | 371 | 61.7 | 4264 | 7.09 | 18 | 3.0 | 19 | 3.2 | t65 | 79.9 |
| Walsh, Chi | 343 | 208 | 60.6 | 2078 | 6.06 | 10 | 2.9 | 8 | 2.3 | 50 | 77.9 |
| Cunningham, Phil | 490 | 265 | 54.1 | 3229 | 6.59 | 16 | 3.3 | 13 | 2.7 | 93 | 74.4 |
| Miller, Rams | 317 | 173 | 54.6 | 2104 | 6.64 | 16 | 5.0 | 14 | 4.4 | 54 | 73.6 |

### Pass Receiving

| RECEPTIONS | No. | Yds | Avg | Lg | TD | YARDS | Yds | No. | Avg | Lg | TD |
|---|---|---|---|---|---|---|---|---|---|---|---|
| Carter, Minn | 122 | 1256 | 10.3 | t65 | 7 | Rice, SF | 1499 | 112 | 13.4 | t69 | 13 |
| Rice, SF | 112 | 1499 | 13.4 | t69 | 13 | Ellard, Wash | 1397 | 74 | 18.9 | t73 | 6 |
| Mathis, Atl | 111 | 1342 | 12.1 | 81 | 11 | Mathis, Atl | 1342 | 111 | 12.1 | 81 | 11 |
| Sharpe, GB | 94 | 1119 | 11.9 | 49 | 18 | Carter, Minn | 1256 | 122 | 10.3 | t65 | 7 |
| Reed, Minn | 85 | 1175 | 13.8 | 59 | 4 | Irvin, Dall | 1241 | 79 | 15.7 | t65 | 6 |
| Early, NO | 82 | 894 | 10.9 | 33 | 4 | Reed, Minn | 1175 | 85 | 13.8 | 59 | 4 |
| Rison, Atl | 81 | 1088 | 13.4 | t69 | 8 | H. Moore, Det | 1173 | 72 | 16.3 | t51 | 11 |
| Irvin, Dall | 79 | 1241 | 15.7 | t65 | 6 | Barnett, Phil | 1127 | 78 | 14.4 | 54 | 5 |
| Barnett, Phil | 78 | 1127 | 14.4 | 54 | 5 | Sharpe, GB | 1119 | 94 | 11.9 | 49 | 18 |
| Bennett, GB | 78 | 546 | 7.0 | 40 | 4 | Rison, Atl | 1088 | 81 | 13.4 | t69 | 8 |

## National Football Conference (Cont.)

### Rushing

| | Att | Yds | Avg | Lg | TD |
|---|---|---|---|---|---|
| Sanders, Det | 331 | 1883 | 5.7 | 85 | 7 |
| E. Smith, Dall | 368 | 1484 | 4.0 | 46 | 21 |
| Hampton, NYG | 327 | 1075 | 3.3 | t27 | 6 |
| Allen, Minn | 255 | 1031 | 4.0 | 45 | 8 |
| Bettis, Rams | 319 | 1025 | 3.2 | 19 | 3 |
| Rhett, TB | 284 | 1011 | 3.6 | 27 | 7 |
| Tillman, Chi | 275 | 899 | 3.3 | t25 | 7 |
| Watters, SF | 239 | 877 | 3.7 | 23 | 6 |
| R. Moore, Ariz | 232 | 780 | 3.4 | 24 | 4 |
| Heyward, Atl | 183 | 779 | 4.3 | 17 | 7 |

### Total Yards from Scrimmage

| | Total | Rush | Rec |
|---|---|---|---|
| Sanders, Det | 2166 | 1883 | 283 |
| E. Smith, Dall | 1825 | 1484 | 341 |
| Watters, SF | 1596 | 877 | 719 |
| Rice, SF | 1592 | 93 | 1499 |
| Ellard, Wash | 1392 | -5 | 1397 |
| Mathis, Atl | 1342 | 0 | 1342 |
| Bettis, Rams | 1318 | 1025 | 293 |
| Carter, Minn | 1256 | 0 | 1256 |
| Irvin, Dall | 1241 | 0 | 1241 |
| Allen, Minn | 1179 | 1031 | 148 |

### Interceptions

| | No. | Yds | Lg | TD |
|---|---|---|---|---|
| A. Williams, Ariz | 9 | 89 | 43 | 0 |
| Hanks, SF | 7 | 93 | 38 | 0 |
| Sanders, SF | 6 | 303 | t93 | 3 |
| G. Jackson, Phil | 6 | 86 | t55 | 1 |

Six tied with 5

### Sacks

| | |
|---|---|
| Harvey, Wash | 13.5 |
| Randle, Minn | 13.5 |
| Haley, Dall | 12.5 |
| C. Smith, Atl | 11.0 |
| Conner, NO | 10.5 |
| Jones, GB | 10.5 |
| Fuller, Phil | 10.5 |
| Martin, NO | 10.0 |

### Punting

| | No. | Yds | Avg | Net Avg | TB | In 20 | Lg | Blk | Ret | Ret Yds |
|---|---|---|---|---|---|---|---|---|---|---|
| Landeta, Rams | 78 | 3494 | 44.8 | 34.3 | 9 | 23 | 62 | 0 | 47 | 637 |
| Roby, Wash | 82 | 3639 | 44.4 | 36.1 | 12 | 21 | 65 | 0 | 45 | 441 |
| Montgomery, Det | 63 | 2782 | 44.2 | 34.2 | 8 | 19 | 64 | 1 | 36 | 431 |
| Barnhardt, NO | 67 | 2920 | 43.6 | 33.5 | 9 | 14 | 57 | 0 | 40 | 495 |
| Saxon, Minn | 77 | 3301 | 42.9 | 36.2 | 5 | 28 | 67 | 0 | 44 | 410 |

### Punt Returns

| | No. | Yds | Avg | Lg | TD |
|---|---|---|---|---|---|
| Mitchell, Wash | 32 | 452 | 14.1 | t78 | 2 |
| Meggett, NYG | 26 | 323 | 12.4 | t68 | 2 |
| Gray, Det | 21 | 233 | 11.1 | 24 | 0 |
| Turner, TB | 21 | 218 | 10.4 | t80 | 1 |
| Sydner, Phil | 40 | 381 | 9.5 | 49 | 0 |

### Kickoff Returns

| | No. | Yds | Avg | Lg | TD |
|---|---|---|---|---|---|
| Gray, Det | 45 | 1276 | 28.4 | t102 | 3 |
| Walker, Phil | 21 | 581 | 27.7 | t94 | 1 |
| K. Williams, Dall | 43 | 1148 | 26.7 | t87 | 1 |
| Mitchell, Wash | 58 | 1478 | 25.5 | 86 | 0 |
| Lewis, Chi | 35 | 874 | 25.0 | 55 | 0 |

## Preseason Sack

The comments that Denver Bronco quarterback John Elway made before his team's final preseason game against the Arizona Cardinals last August—"I could care less.... This game means absolutely nothing, just like this whole preseason"—sting the ears of fans who shell out as much as 45 bucks to sit in the stands for these games. Still, Elway was voicing an opinion that was heard more and more around the league in past weeks.

The notion that four or five preseason games are necessary to prepare a team for the season is absurd. Further, it's a pity that fans pay top dollar for games that are often little more than controlled scrimmages. Before one preseason game the opposing coaches got together and decided they would blitz only four players in order to protect the quarterbacks. Says one coach, "That kind of thing happens in the preseason all the time."

When it comes to preseason football games, it's obviously caveat emptor.

## AFC Total Offense

| | Total Yds | Yds Rush | Yds Pass | Time of Poss | Avg Pts/Game |
|---|---|---|---|---|---|
| Miami | 6078 | 1658 | 4420 | 31:46 | 24.3 |
| Kansas City | 5962 | 1732 | 3960 | 30:55 | 19.9 |
| New England | 5776 | 1332 | 4444 | 32:08 | 21.9 |
| Denver | 5487 | 1470 | 4017 | 30:58 | 21.7 |
| Buffalo | 5244 | 1831 | 3413 | 29:21 | 21.3 |
| San Diego | 5220 | 1852 | 3368 | 30.19 | 23.8 |
| Pittsburgh | 5138 | 2180 | 2958 | 31:58 | 19.8 |
| Cleveland | 4832 | 1657 | 3175 | 28:44 | 21.3 |
| Cincinnati | 4792 | 1556 | 3236 | 27:11 | 17.2 |
| L.A. Raiders | 4779 | 1512 | 3267 | 29:30 | 19.1 |
| N.Y. Jets | 4703 | 1566 | 3137 | 29:54 | 16.5 |
| Seattle | 4652 | 2084 | 2568 | 28:35 | 17.9 |
| Houston | 4481 | 1682 | 2799 | 29:06 | 14.1 |
| Indianapolis | 4413 | 2060 | 2353 | 28:39 | 19.2 |

## AFC Total Defense

| | Opp Total Yds | Opp Yds Rush | Opp Yds Pass | Avg PA/Game |
|---|---|---|---|---|
| Pittsburgh | 4326 | 1452 | 2874 | 14.6 |
| Cleveland | 4826 | 1669 | 3157 | 12.8 |
| Houston | 4915 | 2120 | 2795 | 22.0 |
| L.A. Raiders | 4943 | 1543 | 3400 | 20.4 |
| Kansas City | 5000 | 1734 | 3266 | 18.6 |
| San Diego | 5056 | 1404 | 3652 | 19.1 |
| Cincinnati | 5154 | 1906 | 3248 | 25.4 |
| Buffalo | 5175 | 1515 | 3660 | 15.1 |
| New England | 5207 | 1760 | 3447 | 19.5 |
| Miami | 5224 | 1430 | 3794 | 20.4 |
| Indianapolis | 5325 | 1646 | 3679 | 20.0 |
| N.Y. Jets | 5338 | 1809 | 3529 | 20.0 |
| Seattle | 5349 | 1952 | 3397 | 20.2 |
| Denver | 5907 | 1752 | 4155 | 14.8 |

## NFC Total Offense

| | Total Yds | Yds Rush | Yds Pass | Time of Poss | Avg Pts/Game |
|---|---|---|---|---|---|
| San Francisco | 6060 | 1897 | 4163 | 31:38 | 31.6 |
| Minnesota | 5848 | 1524 | 4324 | 32:06 | 22.2 |
| Atlanta | 5361 | 1249 | 4112 | 29.10 | 19.6 |
| Dallas | 5321 | 1953 | 3368 | 31:35 | 25.9 |
| Green Bay | 5316 | 1543 | 3773 | 30:56 | 23.9 |
| New Orleans | 5182 | 1336 | 3846 | 29:04 | 21.8 |
| Philadelphia | 5125 | 1761 | 3364 | 30:47 | 19.3 |
| Detroit | 5002 | 2080 | 2922 | 26:06 | 22.3 |
| Washington | 4793 | 1415 | 3378 | 26:55 | 20.0 |
| Tampa Bay | 4754 | 1489 | 3265 | 29:55 | 23.9 |
| L.A. Rams | 4747 | 1389 | 3358 | 27:59 | 17.9 |
| Chicago | 4679 | 1588 | 3091 | 31:37 | 16.9 |
| Arizona | 4607 | 1560 | 3047 | 32:37 | 14.7 |
| N.Y. Giants | 4316 | 1754 | 2562 | 30:28 | 17.4 |

## NFC Total Defense

| | Opp Total Yds | Opp Yds Rush | Opp Yds Pass | Avg PA/Game |
|---|---|---|---|---|
| Dallas | 4313 | 1561 | 2752 | 15.5 |
| Arizona | 4453 | 1370 | 3038 | 16.7 |
| Philadelphia | 4710 | 1616 | 3094 | 19.3 |
| Minnesota | 4742 | 1090 | 3652 | 19.6 |
| Green Bay | 4764 | 1363 | 3401 | 17.9 |
| San Francisco | 4839 | 1338 | 3501 | 18.5 |
| N.Y. Giants | 4950 | 1728 | 3222 | 19.1 |
| Chicago | 5009 | 1922 | 3087 | 19.2 |
| L.A. Rams | 5170 | 1781 | 3389 | 22.8 |
| Tampa Bay | 5336 | 1964 | 3372 | 17.9 |
| Detroit | 5405 | 1859 | 3546 | 21.4 |
| New Orleans | 5569 | 1758 | 3811 | 25.4 |
| Washington | 5609 | 1975 | 3634 | 25.8 |
| Atlanta | 5829 | 1693 | 4136 | 24.3 |

## Takeaways/Giveaways

### AFC

| | Takeaways Int | Takeaways Fum | Takeaways Total | Giveaways Int | Giveaways Fum | Giveaways Total | Net Diff |
|---|---|---|---|---|---|---|---|
| Pittsburgh | 17 | 14 | 31 | 9 | 8 | 17 | 14 |
| Kansas City | 12 | 26 | 38 | 14 | 12 | 26 | 12 |
| N.Y. Jets | 17 | 21 | 38 | 18 | 10 | 28 | 10 |
| San Diego | 17 | 15 | 32 | 14 | 9 | 23 | 9 |
| New England | 22 | 18 | 40 | 27 | 11 | 38 | 2 |
| Seattle | 19 | 11 | 30 | 9 | 19 | 28 | 2 |
| Miami | 23 | 9 | 32 | 18 | 14 | 32 | 0 |
| Indianapolis | 18 | 10 | 28 | 14 | 17 | 31 | -3 |
| Cleveland | 18 | 13 | 31 | 21 | 14 | 35 | -4 |
| Denver | 12 | 14 | 26 | 13 | 18 | 31 | -5 |
| L.A. Raiders | 12 | 13 | 25 | 16 | 14 | 30 | -5 |
| Buffalo | 16 | 12 | 28 | 21 | 13 | 34 | -6 |
| Houston | 14 | 12 | 26 | 17 | 25 | 42 | -16 |
| Cincinnati | 10 | 8 | 18 | 19 | 22 | 41 | -23 |

### NFC

| | Takeaways Int | Takeaways Fum | Takeaways Total | Giveaways Int | Giveaways Fum | Giveaways Total | Net Diff |
|---|---|---|---|---|---|---|---|
| San Francisco | 23 | 12 | 35 | 11 | 13 | 24 | 11 |
| Green Bay | 21 | 12 | 33 | 14 | 8 | 22 | 11 |
| Philadelphia | 21 | 14 | 35 | 14 | 12 | 26 | 9 |
| N.Y. Giants | 16 | 16 | 32 | 18 | 7 | 25 | 7 |
| Arizona | 23 | 13 | 36 | 19 | 10 | 29 | 7 |
| Dallas | 22 | 9 | 31 | 14 | 10 | 24 | 7 |
| Minnesota | 18 | 16 | 34 | 20 | 14 | 34 | 0 |
| New Orleans | 17 | 14 | 31 | 18 | 14 | 32 | -1 |
| Detroit | 12 | 11 | 23 | 14 | 10 | 24 | -1 |
| Tampa Bay | 9 | 12 | 21 | 16 | 7 | 23 | -2 |
| Atlanta | 22 | 11 | 33 | 25 | 11 | 36 | -3 |
| Chicago | 12 | 10 | 22 | 16 | 10 | 26 | -4 |
| L.A. Rams | 14 | 6 | 20 | 18 | 13 | 31 | -11 |
| Washington | 17 | 6 | 23 | 27 | 13 | 40 | -17 |

## THEY SAID IT

*Bum Philllips, ex-NFL coach, on how he's spending his retirement: "I ain't doing a damn thing, and I don't start until noon."*

## Conference Rankings

### American Football Conference

| | Total | Rush | Pass | Total | Rush | Pass |
|---|---|---|---|---|---|---|
| | **Offense** | | | **Defense** | | |
| Buffalo | 5 | 5 | 5 | 8 | 4 | 11 |
| Cincinnati | 9 | 11 | 8 | 7 | 12 | 4 |
| Cleveland | 8 | 9 | 9 | 2 | 7 | 3 |
| Denver | 4 | 13 | 3 | 14 | 9 | 14 |
| Houston | 13 | 7 | 12 | 3 | 14 | 1 |
| Indianapolis | 14 | 3 | 14 | 11 | 6 | 12 |
| Kansas City | 3 | 6 | 4 | 5 | 8 | 5 |
| L.A. Raiders | 10 | 12 | 7 | 4 | 5 | 7 |
| Miami | 1 | 8 | 2 | 10 | 2 | 13 |
| New England | 2 | 14 | 1 | 9 | 10 | 8 |
| N.Y. Jets | 11 | 10 | 10 | 12 | 11 | 9 |
| Pittsburgh | 7 | 1 | 11 | 1 | 3 | 2 |
| San Diego | 6 | 4 | 6 | 6 | 1 | 10 |
| Seattle | 12 | 2 | 13 | 13 | 13 | 6 |

### National Football Conference

| | Total | Rush | Pass | Total | Rush | Pass |
|---|---|---|---|---|---|---|
| | **Offense** | | | **Defense** | | |
| Arizona | 13 | 7 | 12 | 2 | 4 | 2 |
| Atlanta | 3 | 14 | 3 | 14 | 7 | 14 |
| Chicago | 12 | 6 | 11 | 8 | 12 | 3 |
| Dallas | 4 | 2 | 7 | 1 | 5 | 1 |
| Detroit | 8 | 1 | 13 | 11 | 11 | 10 |
| Green Bay | 5 | 8 | 5 | 5 | 3 | 8 |
| L.A. Rams | 11 | 12 | 9 | 9 | 10 | 7 |
| Minnesota | 2 | 9 | 1 | 4 | 1 | 12 |
| New Orleans | 6 | 13 | 4 | 12 | 9 | 13 |
| N.Y. Giants | 14 | 5 | 14 | 7 | 8 | 5 |
| Philadelphia | 7 | 4 | 8 | 3 | 6 | 4 |
| San Francisco | 1 | 3 | 2 | 6 | 2 | 9 |
| Tampa Bay | 10 | 10 | 10 | 10 | 13 | 6 |
| Washington | 9 | 11 | 6 | 13 | 14 | 11 |

# 1994 AFC Team-by-Team Statistical Leaders

## Buffalo Bills

| SCORING | Rush | Rec | Ret | PAT | FG | S | Pts |
|---|---|---|---|---|---|---|---|
| | | **TD** | | | | | |
| Christie | 0 | 0 | 0 | 38/38 | 24/28 | 0 | 110 |
| T. Thomas | 7 | 2 | 0 | 0/0 | 0/0 | 0 | 54 |
| Reed | 0 | 8 | 0 | 0/0 | 0/0 | 0 | 48 |
| Metzelaars | 0 | 5 | 0 | 0/0 | 0/0 | 0 | 30 |
| Beebe | 0 | 4 | 0 | 0/0 | 0/0 | 0 | 24 |

| RUSHING | No. | Yds | Avg | Lg | TD |
|---|---|---|---|---|---|
| T. Thomas | 287 | 1093 | 3.8 | 29 | 7 |
| K. Davis | 91 | 381 | 4.2 | 60 | 2 |
| Gardner | 41 | 135 | 3.3 | 13 | 4 |

| PASSING | Att | Comp | Pct Comp | Yds | Avg Gain | TD | Int | Rating Pts |
|---|---|---|---|---|---|---|---|---|
| Kelly | 448 | 285 | 63.6 | 3114 | 6.95 | 22 | 17 | 84.6 |
| Reich | 93 | 56 | 60.2 | 568 | 6.11 | 1 | 4 | 63.4 |

| RECEIVING | No. | Yds | Avg | Lg | TD |
|---|---|---|---|---|---|
| Reed | 90 | 1303 | 14.5 | t83 | 8 |
| T. Thomas | 50 | 349 | 7.0 | 28 | 2 |
| Metzelaars | 49 | 428 | 8.7 | t35 | 5 |
| Bi. Brooks | 42 | 482 | 11.5 | 32 | 2 |
| Beebe | 40 | 527 | 13.2 | t72 | 4 |
| Copeland | 21 | 255 | 12.1 | 35 | 1 |
| K. Davis | 18 | 82 | 4.6 | 12 | 0 |

**INTERCEPTIONS:** Darby, 4

| PUNTING | No. | Yds | Avg | Net Avg | TB | In 20 | Lg | Blk |
|---|---|---|---|---|---|---|---|---|
| Mohr | 67 | 2799 | 41.8 | 36.0 | 3 | 13 | 71 | 0 |

**SACKS:** Smith, 10

## Cincinnati Bengals

| SCORING | Rush | Rec | Ret | PAT | FG | S | Pts |
|---|---|---|---|---|---|---|---|
| | | **TD** | | | | | |
| Pelfrey | 0 | 0 | 0 | 24/25 | 28/33 | 0 | 108 |
| Pickens | 0 | 11 | 0 | 0/0 | 0/0 | 0 | 66 |
| Scott | 0 | 5 | 0 | 0/0 | 0/0 | 0 | 30 |
| Broussard | 2 | 0 | 0 | 0/0 | 0/0 | 0 | 14 |

Two tied with 12 pts.

| RUSHING | No. | Yds | Avg | Lg | TD |
|---|---|---|---|---|---|
| Fenner | 141 | 468 | 3.3 | 21 | 1 |
| Broussard | 94 | 403 | 4.3 | t37 | 2 |
| Green | 76 | 223 | 2.9 | 22 | 1 |
| Blake | 37 | 204 | 5.5 | 16 | 1 |

| PASSING | Att | Comp | Pct Comp | Yds | Avg Gain | TD | Int | Rating Pts |
|---|---|---|---|---|---|---|---|---|
| Blake | 306 | 156 | 51.0 | 2154 | 7.04 | 14 | 9 | 76.9 |
| Klinger | 231 | 131 | 56.7 | 1327 | 5.74 | 6 | 9 | 65.7 |

| RECEIVING | No. | Yds | Avg | Lg | TD |
|---|---|---|---|---|---|
| Pickens | 71 | 1127 | 15.9 | t70 | 11 |
| Scott | 46 | 866 | 18.8 | 76 | 5 |
| To. McGee | 40 | 492 | 12.3 | 54 | 1 |
| Fenner | 36 | 276 | 7.7 | 29 | 1 |
| Broussard | 34 | 218 | 6.4 | 25 | 0 |

**INTERCEPTIONS:** Oliver, 3

| PUNTING | No. | Yds | Avg | Net Avg | TB | In 20 | Lg | Blk |
|---|---|---|---|---|---|---|---|---|
| L. Johnson | 79 | 3461 | 43.8 | 35.3 | 9 | 19 | 64 | 1 |

**SACKS:** A. Williams, 9.5

## Cleveland Browns

### SCORING

| | Rush | Rec | Ret | PAT | FG | S | Pts |
|---|---|---|---|---|---|---|---|
| Stover | 0 | 0 | 0 | 32/32 | 26/28 | 0 | 110 |
| Hoard | 5 | 4 | 0 | 0/0 | 0/0 | 0 | 54 |
| Metcalf | 2 | 3 | 0 | 0/0 | 0/0 | 0 | 42 |
| Carrier | 1 | 5 | 0 | 0/0 | 0/0 | 0 | 36 |
| Alexander | 0 | 2 | 0 | 0/0 | 0/0 | 0 | 14 |

Three tied with 12 pts.

### RUSHING

| | No. | Yds | Avg | Lg | TD |
|---|---|---|---|---|---|
| Hoard | 209 | 890 | 4.3 | 39 | 5 |
| Metcalf | 93 | 329 | 3.5 | t37 | 2 |
| Byner | 75 | 219 | 2.9 | 15 | 2 |

### PASSING

| | Att | Comp | Pct Comp | Yds | Avg Gain | TD | Int | Rating Pts |
|---|---|---|---|---|---|---|---|---|
| Testaverde | 377 | 207 | 54.9 | 2575 | 6.83 | 16 | 18 | 70.6 |
| Rypien | 127 | 59 | 46.5 | 694 | 5.46 | 4 | 3 | 64.2 |

### RECEIVING

| | No. | Yds | Avg | Lg | TD |
|---|---|---|---|---|---|
| Alexander | 48 | 828 | 17.3 | t81 | 2 |
| Motcalf | 47 | 436 | 9.3 | t57 | 3 |
| Hoard | 45 | 445 | 9.9 | t65 | 4 |
| Carrier | 29 | 452 | 15.6 | 43 | 5 |

**INTERCEPTIONS:** Turner, 9

### PUNTING

| | No. | Yds | Avg | Net Avg | TB | In 20 | Lg | Blk |
|---|---|---|---|---|---|---|---|---|
| Tupa | 80 | 3211 | 65 | 35.4 | 8 | 27 | 65 | 0 |

**SACKS:** Burnett, 10

## Houston Oilers

### SCORING

| | Rush | Rec | Ret | PAT | FG | S | Pts |
|---|---|---|---|---|---|---|---|
| Del Greco | 0 | 0 | 0 | 18/18 | 16/20 | 0 | 66 |
| Jeffires | 0 | 6 | 0 | 0/0 | 0/0 | 0 | 42 |
| G. Brown | 4 | 1 | 0 | 0/0 | 0/0 | 0 | 30 |
| White | 3 | 1 | 0 | 0/0 | 0/0 | 0 | 24 |

Three tied with 12.

### RUSHING

| | No. | Yds | Avg | Lg | TD |
|---|---|---|---|---|---|
| White | 191 | 757 | 4.0 | 33 | 3 |
| G. Brown | 169 | 648 | 3.8 | 18 | 4 |
| Richardson | 30 | 217 | 7.2 | 18 | 1 |

### PASSING

| | Att | Comp | Pct Comp | Yds | Avg Gain | TD | Int | Rating Pts |
|---|---|---|---|---|---|---|---|---|
| Tolliver | 240 | 121 | 50.4 | 1287 | 5.36 | 7 | 12 | 62.6 |
| Richardson | 181 | 94 | 51.9 | 1202 | 6.64 | 6 | 6 | 70.3 |
| Carlson | 132 | 59 | 44.7 | 727 | 5.51 | 1 | 4 | 52.2 |

### RECEIVING

| | No. | Yds | Avg | Lg | TD |
|---|---|---|---|---|---|
| Slaughter | 68 | 846 | 12.4 | 57 | 2 |
| Jeffires | 68 | 783 | 11.5 | 50 | 6 |
| Givins | 36 | 521 | 14.5 | t76 | 1 |
| White | 21 | 188 | 9.0 | 41 | 1 |
| Coleman | 20 | 298 | 14.9 | 81 | 1 |
| G. Brown | 18 | 194 | 10.8 | 24 | 1 |

**INTERCEPTIONS:** D. Lewis, 5

### PUNTING

| | No. | Yds | Avg | Net Avg | TB | In 20 | Lg | Blk |
|---|---|---|---|---|---|---|---|---|
| Camarillo | 96 | 4115 | 42.9 | 36.4 | 9 | 34 | 58 | 0 |

**SACKS:** Lathon, 8.5

## Denver Broncos

### SCORING

| | Rush | Rec | Ret | PAT | FG | S | Pts |
|---|---|---|---|---|---|---|---|
| Elam | 0 | 0 | 0 | 29/29 | 30/37 | 0 | 119 |
| L. Russell | 9 | 0 | 0 | 0/0 | 0/0 | 0 | 54 |
| Miller | 0 | 5 | 0 | 0/0 | 0/0 | 0 | 32 |
| Sharpe | 0 | 4 | 0 | 0/0 | 0/0 | 0 | 28 |

Two tied with 24.

### RUSHING

| | No. | Yds | Avg | Lg | TD |
|---|---|---|---|---|---|
| L. Russell | 190 | 620 | 3.3 | t22 | 9 |
| Elway | 58 | 235 | 4.1 | 22 | 4 |
| Milburn | 58 | 201 | 3.5 | 20 | 1 |
| Clark | 56 | 168 | 3.0 | 12 | 3 |

### PASSING

| | Att | Comp | Pct Comp | Yds | Avg Gain | TD | Int | Rating Pts |
|---|---|---|---|---|---|---|---|---|
| Elway | 494 | 307 | 62.1 | 3490 | 7.06 | 16 | 10 | 85.7 |
| Millen | 131 | 81 | 61.8 | 893 | 6.82 | 2 | 3 | 77.6 |

### RECEIVING

| | No. | Yds | Avg | Lg | TD |
|---|---|---|---|---|---|
| Sharpe | 87 | 1010 | 11.6 | 44 | 4 |
| Milburn | 77 | 549 | 7.1 | 33 | 3 |
| Miller | 60 | 1107 | 18.5 | 76 | 5 |
| L. Russell | 38 | 227 | 6.0 | 19 | 0 |
| Tillman | 28 | 455 | 16.3 | 63 | 1 |

**INTERCEPTIONS:** Jones, Hillard and Crockett, 2

### PUNTING

| | No. | Yds | Avg | Net Avg | TB | In 20 | Lg | Blk |
|---|---|---|---|---|---|---|---|---|
| Rouen | 76 | 3258 | 42.9 | 37.1 | 8 | 23 | 59 | 0 |

**SACKS:** Fletcher, 7

## Indianapolis Colts

### SCORING

| | Rush | Rec | Ret | PAT | FG | S | Pts |
|---|---|---|---|---|---|---|---|
| Biasucci | 0 | 0 | 0 | 37/37 | 16/24 | 0 | 85 |
| Faulk | 11 | 1 | 0 | 0/0 | 0/0 | 0 | 72 |
| Turner | 0 | 6 | 0 | 0/0 | 0/0 | 0 | 36 |

Two tied with 18.

### RUSHING

| | No. | Yds | Avg | Lg | TD |
|---|---|---|---|---|---|
| Faulk | 314 | 1282 | 4.1 | 52 | 11 |
| Potts | 77 | 336 | 4.4 | 52 | 1 |

### PASSING

| | Att | Comp | Pct Comp | Yds | Avg Gain | TD | Int | Rating Pts |
|---|---|---|---|---|---|---|---|---|
| Harbaugh | 202 | 125 | 61.9 | 1440 | 7.13 | 9 | 6 | 85.8 |
| Majkowski | 152 | 84 | 55.3 | 1010 | 6.64 | 6 | 7 | 69.8 |

### RECEIVING

| | No. | Yds | Avg | Lg | TD |
|---|---|---|---|---|---|
| Turner | 52 | 593 | 11.4 | 28 | 6 |
| Faulk | 52 | 522 | 10.0 | t85 | 1 |
| Dawkins | 51 | 742 | 14.5 | 49 | 5 |
| Potts | 26 | 251 | 9.7 | 30 | 1 |
| Cash | 16 | 190 | 11.9 | 24 | 1 |
| Jackson | 8 | 97 | 12.1 | 22 | 1 |
| Warren | 3 | 47 | 15.7 | 29 | 0 |

**INTERCEPTIONS:** Buchanan, 8

### PUNTING

| | No. | Yds | Avg | Net Avg | TB | In 20 | Lg | Blk |
|---|---|---|---|---|---|---|---|---|
| Stark | 73 | 3092 | 42.4 | 34.1 | 10 | 22 | 60 | 1 |

**SACKS:** Bennett, 9

## Kansas City Chiefs

| SCORING | TD Rush | Rec | Ret | PAT | FG | S | Pts |
|---|---|---|---|---|---|---|---|
| Elliot | 0 | 0 | 0 | 30/30 | 25/30 | 0 | 105 |
| Allen | 7 | 0 | 0 | 0/0 | 0/0 | 0 | 44 |
| W. Davis | 0 | 5 | 0 | 0/0 | 0/0 | 0 | 32 |
| Vaughn | 1 | 1 | 2 | 0/0 | 0/0 | 0 | 26 |

| RUSHING | No. | Yds | Avg | Lg | TD |
|---|---|---|---|---|---|
| Allen | 189 | 709 | 3.8 | t36 | 7 |
| Hill | 141 | 574 | 4.1 | 20 | 1 |
| Anders | 62 | 231 | 3.7 | 19 | 2 |

| PASSING | Att | Comp | Pct Comp | Yds | Avg Gain | TD | Int | Rating Pts |
|---|---|---|---|---|---|---|---|---|
| Montana | 493 | 299 | 60.6 | 3283 | 6.66 | 16 | 9 | 83.6 |
| Bono | 117 | 66 | 56.4 | 796 | 6.80 | 4 | 4 | 74.6 |

| RECEIVING | No. | Yds | Avg | Lg | TD |
|---|---|---|---|---|---|
| Anders | 67 | 525 | 7.8 | 30 | 1 |
| W. Davis | 51 | 822 | 16.1 | t62 | 5 |
| Birden | 48 | 637 | 13.3 | 44 | 4 |
| Allen | 42 | 349 | 8.3 | 38 | 0 |
| Dawson | 37 | 537 | 14.5 | 50 | 2 |
| D. Walker | 36 | 382 | 10.6 | t57 | 2 |

**INTERCEPTIONS:** Mincy, 3

| PUNTING | No. | Yds | Avg | Net Avg | TB | In 20 | Lg | Blk |
|---|---|---|---|---|---|---|---|---|
| Aguiar | 85 | 3582 | 42.1 | 34.5 | 7 | 15 | 61 | 0 |

**SACKS:** Smith, 11.5

## Los Angeles Raiders

| SCORING | TD Rush | Rec | Ret | PAT | FG | S | Pts |
|---|---|---|---|---|---|---|---|
| Jaeger | 0 | 0 | 0 | 31/31 | 22/28 | 0 | 97 |
| Brown | 0 | 9 | 0 | 0/0 | 0/0 | 0 | 54 |
| H. Williams | 4 | 3 | 0 | 0/0 | 0/0 | 0 | 44 |
| Ismail | 0 | 5 | 0 | 0/0 | 0/0 | 0 | 30 |
| McDaniel | 0 | 0 | 3 | 0/0 | 0/0 | 0 | 18 |

Three tied with 12 pts.

| RUSHING | No. | Yds | Avg | Lg | TD |
|---|---|---|---|---|---|
| H. Williams | 282 | 983 | 3.5 | 28 | 4 |
| Hostetler | 46 | 159 | 3.5 | 14 | 2 |
| Rathman | 28 | 118 | 4.2 | 14 | 0 |

| PASSING | Att | Comp | Pct Comp | Yds | Avg Gain | TD | Int | Rating Pts |
|---|---|---|---|---|---|---|---|---|
| Hostetler | 454 | 263 | 57.9 | 3334 | 7.34 | 20 | 16 | 81.0 |
| Evans | 33 | 18 | 54.5 | 222 | 6.73 | 2 | 0 | 95.8 |

| RECEIVING | No. | Yds | Avg | Lg | TD |
|---|---|---|---|---|---|
| Brown | 89 | 1309 | 14.7 | t77 | 9 |
| H. Williams | 47 | 391 | 8.3 | t27 | 3 |
| Ismail | 34 | 513 | 15.1 | 42 | 5 |
| Glover | 33 | 371 | 11.2 | t27 | 2 |
| Rathman | 26 | 194 | 7.5 | 18 | 0 |

**INTERCEPTIONS:** McDaniel, 7

| PUNTING | No. | Yds | Avg | Net Avg | TB | In 20 | Lg | Blk |
|---|---|---|---|---|---|---|---|---|
| Gossett | 77 | 3377 | 43.9 | 35.2 | 15 | 19 | 65 | 0 |

**SACKS:** McGlockton, 9.5

## Miami Dolphins

| SCORING | TD Rush | Rec | Ret | PAT | FG | S | Pts |
|---|---|---|---|---|---|---|---|
| Stoyanovich | 0 | 0 | 0 | 35/35 | 24/31 | 0 | 107 |
| Fryar | 0 | 7 | 0 | 0/0 | 0/0 | 0 | 46 |
| Parmalee | 6 | 1 | 0 | 0/0 | 0/0 | 0 | 44 |
| K. Jackson | 0 | 7 | 0 | 0/0 | 0/0 | 0 | 44 |
| Byars | 2 | 5 | 0 | 0/0 | 0/0 | 0 | 42 |
| Ingram | 0 | 6 | 0 | 0/0 | 0/0 | 0 | 36 |

| RUSHING | No. | Yds | Avg | Lg | TD |
|---|---|---|---|---|---|
| Parmalee | 216 | 868 | 4.0 | t47 | 6 |
| Spikes | 70 | 312 | 4.5 | 40 | 2 |
| Kirby | 60 | 233 | 3.9 | 30 | 2 |

| PASSING | Att | Comp | Pct Comp | Yds | Avg Gain | TD | Int | Rating Pts |
|---|---|---|---|---|---|---|---|---|
| Marino | 615 | 385 | 62.6 | 4453 | 7.24 | 30 | 17 | 89.2 |

| RECEIVING | No. | Yds | Avg | Lg | TD |
|---|---|---|---|---|---|
| Fryar | 73 | 1270 | 17.4 | t54 | 7 |
| K. Jackson | 59 | 673 | 11.4 | 35 | 7 |
| Byars | 49 | 418 | 8.5 | 34 | 5 |
| Ingram | 44 | 506 | 11.5 | t64 | 6 |
| McDuffie | 37 | 488 | 13.2 | 30 | 3 |
| Parmalee | 34 | 249 | 7.3 | 22 | 1 |

**INTERCEPTIONS:** Vincent, 5

| PUNTING | No. | Yds | Avg | Net Avg | TB | In 20 | Lg | Blk |
|---|---|---|---|---|---|---|---|---|
| Arnold | 46 | 1810 | 39.3 | 33.5 | 4 | 14 | 53 | 0 |
| Kidd | 14 | 602 | 43.0 | 29.1 | 3 | 2 | 58 | 0 |

**SACKS:** Cross, 9.5

## New England Patriots

| SCORING | TD Rush | Rec | Ret | PAT | FG | S | Pts |
|---|---|---|---|---|---|---|---|
| Bahr | 0 | 0 | 0 | 36/36 | 27/34 | 0 | 117 |
| Butts | 8 | 0 | 0 | 0/0 | 0/0 | 0 | 48 |
| Coates | 0 | 7 | 0 | 0/0 | 0/0 | 0 | 42 |
| Thompson | 2 | 5 | 0 | 0/0 | 0/0 | 0 | 42 |
| Brisby | 0 | 5 | 0 | 0/0 | 0/0 | 0 | 30 |

| RUSHING | No. | Yds | Avg | Lg | TD |
|---|---|---|---|---|---|
| Butts | 243 | 703 | 2.9 | 26 | 8 |
| Thompson | 102 | 312 | 3.1 | 13 | 2 |
| Turner | 36 | 111 | 3.1 | 13 | 1 |

| PASSING | Att | Comp | Pct Comp | Yds | Avg Gain | TD | Int | Rating Pts |
|---|---|---|---|---|---|---|---|---|
| Bledsoe | 691 | 400 | 57.9 | 4555 | 6.59 | 25 | 27 | 73.6 |

| RECEIVING | No. | Yds | Avg | Lg | TD |
|---|---|---|---|---|---|
| Coates | 96 | 1174 | 12.2 | t62 | 7 |
| Timpson | 74 | 941 | 12.7 | 37 | 3 |
| Thompson | 65 | 465 | 7.2 | t27 | 5 |
| Brisby | 58 | 904 | 15.6 | 43 | 5 |
| Turner | 52 | 471 | 9.1 | 32 | 2 |
| Crittenden | 28 | 379 | 13.5 | 32 | 3 |

**INTERCEPTIONS:** Hurst, 7

| PUNTING | No. | Yds | Avg | Net Avg | TB | In 20 | Lg | Blk |
|---|---|---|---|---|---|---|---|---|
| O'Neill | 69 | 2841 | 41.2 | 35.7 | 6 | 25 | 67 | 0 |

**SACKS:** Slade, 9.5

## New York Jets

| SCORING | TD Rush | Rec | Ret | PAT | FG | S | Pts |
|---|---|---|---|---|---|---|---|
| Lowery | 0 | 0 | 0 | 26/27 | 20/23 | 0 | 86 |
| Moore | 0 | 6 | 0 | 0/0 | 0/0 | 0 | 40 |
| J. Johnson | 3 | 2 | 0 | 0/0 | 0/0 | 0 | 30 |
| B. Baxter | 4 | 0 | 0 | 0/0 | 0/0 | 0 | 24 |
| Mitchell | 0 | 4 | 0 | 0/0 | 0/0 | 0 | 24 |
| Monk | 0 | 3 | 0 | 0/0 | 0/0 | 0 | 18 |

| RUSHING | No. | Yds | Avg | Lg | TD |
|---|---|---|---|---|---|
| J. Johnson | 240 | 931 | 3.9 | 90 | 3 |
| R. Anderson | 43 | 207 | 4.8 | 55 | 1 |
| B. Baxter | 60 | 170 | 2.8 | 13 | 4 |

| PASSING | Att | Comp | Pct Comp | Yds | Avg Gain | TD | Int | Rating Pts |
|---|---|---|---|---|---|---|---|---|
| Esiason | 440 | 255 | 58.0 | 2782 | 6.32 | 17 | 13 | 77.3 |
| Trudeau | 91 | 50 | 54.9 | 496 | 5.45 | 1 | 4 | 55.9 |

| RECEIVING | No. | Yds | Avg | Lg | TD |
|---|---|---|---|---|---|
| Moore | 78 | 1010 | 12.9 | t41 | 6 |
| Mitchell | 58 | 749 | 12.9 | 55 | 4 |
| Monk | 46 | 581 | 12.6 | 69 | 3 |
| J. Johnson | 42 | 303 | 7.2 | 24 | 2 |
| R. Anderson | 25 | 212 | 8.5 | t27 | 1 |

**INTERCEPTIONS:** Turner and Hasty, 5

| PUNTING | No. | Yds | Avg | Net Avg | TB | In 20 | Lg | Blk |
|---|---|---|---|---|---|---|---|---|
| Hansen | 84 | 3534 | 42.1 | 36.1 | 12 | 25 | 64 | 0 |

**SACKS:** Lageman, 6.5

## Pittsburgh Steelers

| SCORING | TD Rush | Rec | Ret | PAT | FG | S | Pts |
|---|---|---|---|---|---|---|---|
| Anderson | 0 | 0 | 0 | 32/32 | 24/29 | 0 | 104 |
| Morris | 7 | 0 | 0 | 0/0 | 0/0 | 0 | 42 |
| Foster | 5 | 0 | 0 | 0/0 | 0/0 | 0 | 30 |
| Thigpen | 0 | 4 | 0 | 0/0 | 0/0 | 0 | 24 |
| Green | 0 | 4 | 0 | 0/0 | 0/0 | 0 | 24 |

| RUSHING | No. | Yds | Avg | Lg | TD |
|---|---|---|---|---|---|
| Foster | 216 | 851 | 3.9 | t29 | 5 |
| Morris | 198 | 836 | 4.2 | 20 | 7 |
| J. Williams | 68 | 317 | 4.7 | 23 | 1 |

| PASSING | Att | Comp | Pct Comp | Yds | Avg Gain | TD | Int | Rating Pts |
|---|---|---|---|---|---|---|---|---|
| O'Donnell | 370 | 212 | 57.3 | 2443 | 6.60 | 13 | 9 | 78.9 |
| Tomczak | 93 | 54 | 58.1 | 804 | 8.65 | 4 | 0 | 100.8 |

| RECEIVING | No. | Yds | Avg | Lg | TD |
|---|---|---|---|---|---|
| J. Williams | 51 | 378 | 7.4 | 23 | 2 |
| Green | 46 | 618 | 13.4 | 46 | 4 |
| Johnson | 38 | 577 | 15.2 | t84 | 3 |
| Thigpen | 36 | 546 | 15.2 | t60 | 4 |
| Morris | 22 | 204 | 9.3 | 49 | 0 |
| Hastings | 20 | 281 | 14.1 | 46 | 2 |
| Foster | 20 | 124 | 6.2 | 27 | 0 |

**INTERCEPTIONS:** Perry, 7

| PUNTING | No. | Yds | Avg | Net Avg | TB | In 20 | Lg | Blk |
|---|---|---|---|---|---|---|---|---|
| Royals | 97 | 3849 | 39.7 | 35.7 | 6 | 35 | 64 | 0 |

**SACKS:** Greene, 14

## San Diego Chargers

| SCORING | TD Rush | Rec | Ret | PAT | FG | S | Pts |
|---|---|---|---|---|---|---|---|
| Carney | 0 | 0 | 0 | 33/33 | 34/38 | 0 | 135 |
| Means | 12 | 0 | 0 | 0/0 | 0/0 | 0 | 72 |
| Martin | 0 | 7 | 0 | 0/0 | 0/0 | 0 | 42 |
| Seay | 0 | 6 | 0 | 0/0 | 0/0 | 0 | 36 |
| Jefferson | 0 | 3 | 0 | 0/0 | 0/0 | 0 | 18 |
| Harmon | 1 | 1 | 0 | 0/0 | 0/0 | 0 | 12 |

| RUSHING | No. | Yds | Avg | Lg | TD |
|---|---|---|---|---|---|
| Means | 343 | 1350 | 3.9 | 25 | 12 |
| Bieniemy | 73 | 295 | 4.0 | 36 | 0 |

| PASSING | Att | Comp | Pct Comp | Yds | Avg Gain | TD | Int | Rating Pts |
|---|---|---|---|---|---|---|---|---|
| Humphries | 453 | 264 | 58.3 | 3209 | 7.08 | 17 | 12 | 81.6 |
| Gilbert | 67 | 41 | 61.2 | 410 | 6.12 | 3 | 1 | 87.3 |

| RECEIVING | No. | Yds | Avg | Lg | TD |
|---|---|---|---|---|---|
| Seay | 58 | 645 | 11.1 | t49 | 6 |
| Harmon | 58 | 615 | 10.6 | 35 | 1 |
| Martin | 50 | 885 | 17.7 | t99 | 7 |
| Jefferson | 43 | 627 | 14.6 | t52 | 3 |
| Means | 39 | 235 | 6.0 | 22 | 0 |
| Pupunu | 21 | 214 | 10.2 | 25 | 2 |

**INTERCEPTIONS:** Richard and Gordon, 4

| PUNTING | No. | Yds | Avg | Net Avg | TB | In 20 | Lg | Blk |
|---|---|---|---|---|---|---|---|---|
| Wagner | 65 | 2702 | 41.6 | 35.3 | 3 | 20 | 59 | 0 |

**SACKS:** O'Neal, 12.5

## Seattle Seahawks

| SCORING | TD Rush | Rec | Ret | PAT | FG | S | Pts |
|---|---|---|---|---|---|---|---|
| Kasay | 0 | 0 | 0 | 25/26 | 20/24 | 0 | 85 |
| C. Warren | 9 | 2 | 0 | 0/0 | 0/0 | 0 | 68 |
| Blades | 0 | 4 | 0 | 0/0 | 0/0 | 0 | 26 |
| S. Smith | 2 | 1 | 0 | 0/0 | 0/0 | 0 | 18 |

| RUSHING | No. | Yds | Avg | Lg | TD |
|---|---|---|---|---|---|
| C. Warren | 333 | 1545 | 4.6 | 41 | 9 |
| Mirer | 34 | 153 | 4.5 | 14 | 0 |
| Strong | 27 | 114 | 4.2 | 14 | 2 |

| PASSING | Att | Comp | Pct Comp | Yds | Avg Gain | TD | Int | Rating Pts |
|---|---|---|---|---|---|---|---|---|
| Mirer | 381 | 195 | 51.2 | 2151 | 5.65 | 11 | 7 | 70.2 |
| McGwire | 105 | 51 | 48.6 | 578 | 5.50 | 1 | 2 | 60.7 |

| RECEIVING | No. | Yds | Avg | Lg | TD |
|---|---|---|---|---|---|
| Blades | 81 | 1086 | 13.4 | 45 | 4 |
| Martin | 56 | 681 | 12.2 | 32 | 1 |
| C. Warren | 41 | 323 | 7.9 | 51 | 2 |
| Green | 30 | 208 | 6.9 | 20 | 1 |
| S. Smith | 11 | 142 | 12.9 | 25 | 1 |
| Johnson | 10 | 91 | 9.1 | 17 | 0 |

**INTERCEPTIONS:** Four tied with 3.

| PUNTING | No. | Yds | Avg | Net Avg | TB | In 20 | Lg | Blk |
|---|---|---|---|---|---|---|---|---|
| Tuten | 91 | 3905 | 42.9 | 36.7 | 7 | 33 | 64 | 0 |

**SACKS:** Sinclair, 4.5

## Arizona Cardinals

| SCORING | Rush | TD Rec | Ret | PAT | FG | S | Pts |
|---|---|---|---|---|---|---|---|
| Davis | 0 | 0 | 0 | 17/17 | 20/26 | 0 | 77 |
| Centers | 5 | 2 | 0 | 0/0 | 0/0 | 0 | 42 |
| R. Moore | 4 | 1 | 0 | 0/0 | 0/0 | 0 | 32 |
| Proehl | 0 | 5 | 0 | 0/0 | 0/0 | 0 | 30 |
| Five tied with 6 | | | | | | | |

| RUSHING | No. | Yds | Avg | Lg | TD |
|---|---|---|---|---|---|
| R. Moore | 232 | 780 | 3.4 | 24 | 4 |
| Centers | 115 | 336 | 2.9 | 17 | 5 |
| Hearst | 37 | 169 | 4.6 | 36 | 1 |

| PASSING | Att | Comp | Pct Comp | Yds | Avg Gain | TD | Int | Rating Pts |
|---|---|---|---|---|---|---|---|---|
| Beuerlein | 255 | 130 | 51.0 | 1545 | 6.06 | 5 | 9 | 61.6 |
| Schroeder | 238 | 133 | 55.9 | 1510 | 6.34 | 4 | 7 | 68.4 |
| McMahon | 43 | 23 | 53.5 | 219 | 5.09 | 1 | 3 | 46.6 |

| RECEIVING | No. | Yds | Avg | Lg | TD |
|---|---|---|---|---|---|
| Centers | 77 | 647 | 8.4 | 36 | 2 |
| Proehl | 51 | 651 | 12.8 | 63 | 5 |
| Clark | 50 | 771 | 15.4 | 45 | 1 |
| R. Hill | 38 | 544 | 14.3 | 51 | 0 |
| Ware | 17 | 171 | 10.1 | 33 | 1 |

**INTERCEPTIONS:** A. Williams, 9

| PUNTING | No. | Yds | Avg | Net Avg | TB | In 20 | Lg | Blk |
|---|---|---|---|---|---|---|---|---|
| Feagles | 98 | 3997 | 40.8 | 36.0 | 10 | 33 | 54 | 0 |

**SACKS:** Swann, 7.5

## Atlanta Falcons

| SCORING | Rush | TD Rec | Ret | PAT | FG | S | Pts |
|---|---|---|---|---|---|---|---|
| N. Johnson | 0 | 0 | 0 | 32/32 | 21/25 | 0 | 95 |
| Mathis | 0 | 11 | 0 | 0/0 | 0/0 | 0 | 70 |
| Rison | 0 | 8 | 0 | 0/0 | 0/0 | 0 | 50 |
| Heyward | 7 | 1 | 0 | 0/0 | 0/0 | 0 | 48 |
| Emanuel | 0 | 4 | 0 | 0/0 | 0/0 | 0 | 24 |

| RUSHING | No. | Yds | Avg | Lg | TD |
|---|---|---|---|---|---|
| Heyward | 183 | 779 | 4.3 | 17 | 7 |
| Pegram | 103 | 358 | 3.5 | 25 | 1 |

| PASSING | Att | Comp | Pct Comp | Yds | Avg Gain | TD | Int | Rating Pts |
|---|---|---|---|---|---|---|---|---|
| J. George | 524 | 322 | 61.5 | 3734 | 7.13 | 23 | 18 | 83.3 |
| Hebert | 103 | 52 | 50.5 | 610 | 5.92 | 2 | 6 | 51.0 |

| RECEIVING | No. | Yds | Avg | Lg | TD |
|---|---|---|---|---|---|
| Mathis | 111 | 1342 | 12.1 | 81 | 11 |
| Rison | 81 | 1088 | 13.4 | t69 | 8 |
| Sanders | 67 | 599 | 8.9 | 28 | 1 |
| Emanuel | 46 | 649 | 14.1 | t85 | 4 |
| Heyward | 32 | 335 | 10.5 | 34 | 1 |
| Pegram | 16 | 99 | 6.2 | 28 | 0 |

**INTERCEPTIONS:** D. Johnson, 5

| PUNTING | No. | Yds | Avg | Net Avg | TB | In 20 | Lg | Blk |
|---|---|---|---|---|---|---|---|---|
| Alexander | 71 | 2836 | 39.9 | 34.8 | 6 | 12 | 61 | 0 |

**SACKS:** C. Smith, 11

## Chicago Bears

| SCORING | Rush | TD Rec | Ret | PAT | FG | S | Pts |
|---|---|---|---|---|---|---|---|
| Butler | 0 | 0 | 0 | 24/24 | 21/29 | 0 | 87 |
| Tillman | 7 | 0 | 0 | 0/0 | 0/0 | 0 | 42 |
| Graham | 0 | 4 | 1 | 0/0 | 0/0 | 0 | 32 |
| Gedney | 0 | 3 | 0 | 0/0 | 0/0 | 0 | 18 |
| Jennings | 0 | 3 | 0 | 0/0 | 0/0 | 0 | 18 |

| RUSHING | No. | Yds | Avg | Lg | TD |
|---|---|---|---|---|---|
| Tillman | 275 | 899 | 3.3 | t25 | 7 |
| Harris | 123 | 464 | 3.8 | 13 | 1 |
| Green | 25 | 122 | 4.9 | 14 | 0 |

| PASSING | Att | Comp | Pct Comp | Yds | Avg Gain | TD | Int | Rating Pts |
|---|---|---|---|---|---|---|---|---|
| Walsh | 343 | 208 | 60.6 | 2078 | 6.06 | 10 | 8 | 77.9 |
| Kramer | 158 | 99 | 62.7 | 1129 | 7.15 | 8 | 8 | 79.9 |

| RECEIVING | No. | Yds | Avg | Lg | TD |
|---|---|---|---|---|---|
| Graham | 68 | 944 | 13.9 | t76 | 4 |
| Conway | 39 | 546 | 14.0 | t85 | 2 |
| Harris | 39 | 236 | 6.1 | 18 | 0 |
| Tillman | 27 | 222 | 8.2 | 39 | 0 |
| Waddle | 25 | 244 | 9.8 | 22 | 1 |
| Green | 24 | 199 | 8.3 | t39 | 2 |
| Cook | 21 | 212 | 10.1 | 34 | 1 |

**INTERCEPTIONS:** Woolford, 5

| PUNTING | No. | Yds | Avg | Net Avg | TB | In 20 | Lg | Blk |
|---|---|---|---|---|---|---|---|---|
| Gardocki | 76 | 2871 | 37.8 | 32.4 | 9 | 23 | 57 | 0 |

**SACKS:** Armstrong, 7.5

## Dallas Cowboys

| SCORING | Rush | TD Rec | Ret | PAT | FG | S | Pts |
|---|---|---|---|---|---|---|---|
| E. Smith | 21 | 1 | 0 | 0/0 | 0/0 | 0 | 132 |
| Boniol | 0 | 0 | 0 | 48/48 | 22/29 | 0 | 114 |
| Harper | 0 | 8 | 0 | 0/0 | 0/0 | 0 | 48 |
| Irvin | 0 | 6 | 0 | 0/0 | 0/0 | 0 | 36 |
| Johnston | 2 | 2 | 0 | 0/0 | 0/0 | 0 | 24 |

| RUSHING | No. | Yds | Avg | Lg | TD |
|---|---|---|---|---|---|
| E. Smith | 368 | 1484 | 4.0 | 46 | 21 |
| Coleman | 64 | 180 | 2.8 | 13 | 1 |
| Johnston | 40 | 138 | 3.5 | t9 | 2 |

| PASSING | Att | Comp | Pct Comp | Yds | Avg Gain | TD | Int | Rating Pts |
|---|---|---|---|---|---|---|---|---|
| Aikman | 361 | 233 | 64.5 | 2676 | 7.41 | 13 | 12 | 84.9 |
| Peete | 56 | 33 | 58.9 | 470 | 8.39 | 4 | 1 | 102.5 |
| Garrett | 31 | 16 | 51.6 | 315 | 10.16 | 2 | 1 | 95.5 |

| RECEIVING | No. | Yds | Avg | Lg | TD |
|---|---|---|---|---|---|
| Irvin | 79 | 1241 | 15.7 | t65 | 6 |
| E. Smith | 50 | 341 | 6.8 | 68 | 1 |
| Novacek | 47 | 475 | 10.1 | 27 | 2 |
| Johnston | 44 | 325 | 7.4 | 24 | 2 |
| Harper | 33 | 821 | 24.9 | 90 | 8 |
| K. Williams | 13 | 181 | 13.9 | 29 | 0 |

**INTERCEPTIONS:** Woodson and Washington, 5

| PUNTING | No. | Yds | Avg | Net Avg | TB | In 20 | Lg | Blk |
|---|---|---|---|---|---|---|---|---|
| Jett | 70 | 2935 | 41.9 | 35.4 | 4 | 26 | 58 | 0 |

**SACKS:** Haley, 12.5

## Detroit Lions

| SCORING | Rush | Rec | Ret | PAT | FG | S | Pts |
|---|---|---|---|---|---|---|---|
| | | | TD | | | | |
| Hanson | 0 | 0 | 0 | 39/40 | 18/27 | 0 | 93 |
| H. Moore | 0 | 11 | 0 | 0/0 | 0/0 | 0 | 66 |
| Sanders | 7 | 1 | 0 | 0/0 | 0/0 | 0 | 48 |
| Perriman | 0 | 4 | 0 | 0/0 | 0/0 | 0 | 28 |
| D. Moore | 4 | 0 | 0 | 0/0 | 0/0 | 0 | 24 |

| RUSHING | No. | Yds | Avg | Lg | TD |
|---|---|---|---|---|---|
| Sanders | 331 | 1883 | 5.7 | 85 | 7 |
| Perriman | 9 | 86 | 9.6 | 25 | 0 |

| PASSING | Att | Comp | Pct Comp | Yds | Avg Gain | TD | Int | Rating Pts |
|---|---|---|---|---|---|---|---|---|
| Mitchell | 246 | 119 | 48.4 | 1456 | 5.92 | 10 | 11 | 62.0 |
| Krieg | 212 | 131 | 61.8 | 1629 | 7.68 | 14 | 3 | 101.7 |

| RECEIVING | No. | Yds | Avg | Lg | TD |
|---|---|---|---|---|---|
| H. Moore | 72 | 1173 | 16.3 | t51 | 11 |
| Perriman | 56 | 761 | 13.6 | 39 | 4 |
| Sanders | 44 | 283 | 6.4 | 22 | 1 |
| Matthews | 29 | 359 | 12.4 | 33 | 3 |
| Holman | 17 | 163 | 9.6 | 18 | 0 |
| Hall | 10 | 106 | 10.6 | 18 | 0 |

**INTERCEPTIONS:** Massey, 4

| PUNTING | No. | Yds | Avg | Net Avg | TB | In 20 | Lg | Blk |
|---|---|---|---|---|---|---|---|---|
| M'gomery | 63 | 2782 | 44.2 | 34.2 | 8 | 19 | 64 | 1 |

**SACKS:** Thomas, 7

## Los Angeles Rams

| SCORING | Rush | Rec | Ret | PAT | FG | S | Pts |
|---|---|---|---|---|---|---|---|
| | | | TD | | | | |
| Zendejas | 0 | 0 | 0 | 28/28 | 18/23 | 0 | 82 |
| Drayton | 0 | 6 | 0 | 0/0 | 0/0 | 0 | 36 |
| Anderson | 0 | 5 | 0 | 0/0 | 0/0 | 0 | 30 |
| Bettis | 3 | 1 | 0 | 0/0 | 0/0 | 0 | 28 |
| Kinchen | 1 | 3 | 0 | 0/0 | 0/0 | 0 | 24 |

| RUSHING | No. | Yds | Avg | Lg | TD |
|---|---|---|---|---|---|
| Bettis | 319 | 1025 | 3.2 | 19 | 3 |
| Miller | 20 | 100 | 5.0 | 16 | 0 |

| PASSING | Att | Comp | Pct Comp | Yds | Avg Gain | TD | Int | Rating Pts |
|---|---|---|---|---|---|---|---|---|
| Miller | 317 | 173 | 54.6 | 2104 | 6.64 | 16 | 14 | 73.6 |
| Chandler | 176 | 108 | 61.4 | 1352 | 7.68 | 7 | 2 | 93.8 |

| RECEIVING | No. | Yds | Avg | Lg | TD |
|---|---|---|---|---|---|
| J. Bailey | 58 | 516 | 8.9 | 28 | 0 |
| Anderson | 46 | 945 | 20.5 | t72 | 5 |
| Hester | 45 | 644 | 14.3 | 41 | 3 |
| Drayton | 32 | 276 | 8.6 | t22 | 6 |
| Bettis | 31 | 293 | 9.5 | 34 | 1 |
| Kinchen | 23 | 352 | 15.3 | 43 | 3 |
| Bruce | 21 | 272 | 13.0 | t34 | 3 |

**INTERCEPTIONS:** Pope and Henley, 3

| PUNTING | No. | Yds | Avg | Net Avg | TB | In 20 | Lg | Blk |
|---|---|---|---|---|---|---|---|---|
| Landeta | 78 | 3494 | 44.8 | 34.3 | 9 | 23 | 62 | 0 |

**SACKS:** Young, 6.5

## Green Bay Packers

| SCORING | Rush | Rec | Ret | PAT | FG | S | Pts |
|---|---|---|---|---|---|---|---|
| | | | TD | | | | |
| Jacke | 0 | 0 | 0 | 41/43 | 19/26 | 0 | 98 |
| Sharpe | 0 | 18 | 0 | 0/0 | 0/0 | 0 | 108 |
| Bennett | 5 | 4 | 0 | 0/0 | 0/0 | 0 | 54 |
| Brooks | 0 | 4 | 2 | 0/0 | 0/0 | 0 | 36 |

Two tied with 24

| RUSHING | No. | Yds | Avg | Lg | TD |
|---|---|---|---|---|---|
| Bennett | 178 | 623 | 3.5 | t39 | 5 |
| Cobb | 153 | 579 | 3.8 | 30 | 3 |
| Favre | 42 | 202 | 4.8 | t36 | 2 |

| PASSING | Att | Comp | Pct Comp | Yds | Avg Gain | TD | Int | Rating Pts |
|---|---|---|---|---|---|---|---|---|
| Favre | 582 | 363 | 62.4 | 3882 | 6.67 | 33 | 14 | 90.7 |
| Brunell | 27 | 12 | 44.4 | 95 | 3.52 | 0 | 0 | 53.8 |

| RECEIVING | No. | Yds | Avg | Lg | TD |
|---|---|---|---|---|---|
| Sharpe | 94 | 1119 | 11.9 | 49 | 18 |
| Bennett | 78 | 546 | 7.0 | 40 | 4 |
| Brooks | 58 | 648 | 11.2 | 35 | 4 |
| Cobb | 35 | 299 | 8.5 | t37 | 1 |
| West | 31 | 377 | 12.2 | 26 | 2 |
| Morgan | 28 | 397 | 14.2 | t47 | 4 |

**INTERCEPTIONS:** Buckley, 5

| PUNTING | No. | Yds | Avg | Net Avg | TB | In 20 | Lg | Blk |
|---|---|---|---|---|---|---|---|---|
| Hentrich | 81 | 3351 | 41.4 | 35.5 | 10 | 24 | 70 | 0 |

**SACKS:** Jones, 10.5

## Minnesota Vikings

| SCORING | Rush | Rec | Ret | PAT | FG | S | Pts |
|---|---|---|---|---|---|---|---|
| | | | TD | | | | |
| Reveiz | 0 | 0 | 0 | 30/30 | 34/39 | 0 | 132 |
| Allen | 8 | 0 | 0 | 0/0 | 0/0 | 0 | 50 |
| Carter | 0 | 7 | 0 | 0/0 | 0/0 | 0 | 46 |
| Ismail | 0 | 5 | 0 | 0/0 | 0/0 | 0 | 30 |
| Reed | 0 | 4 | 0 | 0/0 | 0/0 | 0 | 24 |

| RUSHING | No. | Yds | Avg | Lg | TD |
|---|---|---|---|---|---|
| Allen | 255 | 1031 | 4.0 | 45 | 8 |
| Graham | 64 | 207 | 3.2 | 11 | 2 |
| R. Smith | 31 | 106 | 3.4 | t14 | 1 |

| PASSING | Att | Comp | Pct Comp | Yds | Avg Gain | TD | Int | Rating Pts |
|---|---|---|---|---|---|---|---|---|
| Moon | 601 | 371 | 61.7 | 4264 | 7.09 | 18 | 19 | 79.9 |
| Johnson | 37 | 22 | 59.5 | 150 | 4.05 | 0 | 0 | 68.5 |
| Salisbury | 34 | 16 | 47.1 | 156 | 4.59 | 0 | 1 | 48.2 |

| RECEIVING | No. | Yds | Avg | Lg | TD |
|---|---|---|---|---|---|
| Carter | 122 | 1256 | 10.3 | t65 | 7 |
| Reed | 85 | 1175 | 13.8 | 59 | 4 |
| Ismail | 45 | 696 | 15.5 | t65 | 5 |
| Lee | 45 | 368 | 8.2 | 35 | 2 |
| A. Jordan | 35 | 336 | 9.6 | 25 | 0 |
| Cooper | 32 | 363 | 11.3 | 34 | 0 |
| Allen | 17 | 148 | 8.7 | 31 | 0 |

**INTERCEPTIONS:** Parker and Glenn, 4

| PUNTING | No. | Yds | Avg | Net Avg | TB | In 20 | Lg | Blk |
|---|---|---|---|---|---|---|---|---|
| Saxon | 77 | 3301 | 42.9 | 36.2 | 5 | 28 | 67 | 0 |

**SACKS:** Randle, 13.5

## New Orleans Saints

### SCORING

| | Rush | Rec | Ret | PAT | FG | S | Pts |
|---|---|---|---|---|---|---|---|
| Andersen | 0 | 0 | 0 | 32/32 | 28/39 | 0 | 116 |
| Bates | 6 | 0 | 0 | 0/0 | 0/0 | 0 | 36 |
| Small | 0 | 5 | 0 | 0/0 | 0/0 | 0 | 32 |
| Haynes | 0 | 5 | 0 | 0/0 | 0/0 | 0 | 30 |
| Walls | 0 | 4 | 0 | 0/0 | 0/0 | 0 | 26 |

### RUSHING

| | No. | Yds | Avg | Lg | TD |
|---|---|---|---|---|---|
| Bates | 151 | 579 | 3.8 | 40 | 6 |
| Brown | 146 | 489 | 3.3 | 16 | 3 |

### PASSING

| | Att | Comp | Pct Comp | Yds | Avg Gain | TD | Int | Rating Pts |
|---|---|---|---|---|---|---|---|---|
| Everett | 540 | 346 | 64.1 | 3855 | 7.14 | 22 | 18 | 84.9 |
| W. Wilson | 28 | 20 | 71.4 | 172 | 6.14 | 0 | 0 | 87.2 |

### RECEIVING

| | No. | Yds | Avg | Lg | TD |
|---|---|---|---|---|---|
| Early | 82 | 894 | 10.9 | 33 | 4 |
| Haynes | 77 | 985 | 12.8 | t78 | 5 |
| Small | 49 | 719 | 14.7 | t75 | 5 |
| Brown | 44 | 428 | 9.7 | 37 | 1 |
| Smith | 41 | 330 | 8.0 | 19 | 3 |
| Walls | 38 | 406 | 10.7 | 31 | 4 |
| Ned | 13 | 86 | 6.6 | 19 | 0 |

**INTERCEPTIONS:** Spencer, 5

### PUNTING

| | No. | Yds | Avg | Net Avg | TB | In 20 | Lg | Blk |
|---|---|---|---|---|---|---|---|---|
| Barnhardt | 67 | 2920 | 43.6 | 33.5 | 9 | 14 | 57 | 0 |

**SACKS:** Conner, 10.5

## Philadelphia Eagles

### SCORING

| | Rush | Rec | Ret | PAT | FG | S | Pts |
|---|---|---|---|---|---|---|---|
| Murray | 0 | 0 | 0 | 33/33 | 21/25 | 0 | 96 |
| Walker | 5 | 2 | 1 | 0/0 | 0/0 | 0 | 48 |
| Barnett | 0 | 5 | 0 | 0/0 | 0/0 | 0 | 30 |

Five tied with 18

### RUSHING

| | No. | Yds | Avg | Lg | TD |
|---|---|---|---|---|---|
| Walker | 113 | 528 | 4.7 | t91 | 5 |
| Garner | 109 | 399 | 3.7 | t28 | 3 |
| Hebron | 82 | 325 | 4.0 | 19 | 2 |
| Cunningham | 65 | 288 | 4.4 | 22 | 3 |

### PASSING

| | Att | Comp | Pct Comp | Yds | Avg Gain | TD | Int | Rating Pts |
|---|---|---|---|---|---|---|---|---|
| Cunn'ham | 490 | 265 | 54.1 | 3229 | 6.59 | 16 | 13 | 74.4 |
| Brister | 76 | 51 | 67.1 | 507 | 6.67 | 2 | 1 | 89.1 |

### RECEIVING

| | No. | Yds | Avg | Lg | TD |
|---|---|---|---|---|---|
| Barnett | 78 | 1127 | 14.4 | 54 | 5 |
| C. Williams | 58 | 813 | 14.0 | 53 | 3 |
| Walker | 50 | 500 | 10.0 | 93 | 2 |
| Joseph | 43 | 344 | 8.0 | t35 | 2 |
| M. Johnson | 21 | 204 | 9.7 | 22 | 2 |
| Bailey | 20 | 311 | 15.6 | 61 | 1 |
| Hebron | 18 | 137 | 7.6 | 29 | 0 |
| Bavaro | 17 | 215 | 12.6 | t27 | 3 |

**INTERCEPTIONS:** G. Jackson, 6

### PUNTING

| | No. | Yds | Avg | Net Avg | TB | In 20 | Lg | Blk |
|---|---|---|---|---|---|---|---|---|
| Barker | 66 | 2696 | 40.8 | 36.3 | 7 | 20 | 67 | 0 |
| Berger | 25 | 951 | 38.0 | 31.3 | 2 | 8 | 57 | 0 |

**SACKS:** Fuller, 10.5

## New York Giants

### SCORING

| | Rush | Rec | Ret | PAT | FG | S | Pts |
|---|---|---|---|---|---|---|---|
| Treadwell | 0 | 0 | 0 | 22/23 | 11/17 | 0 | 55 |
| Hampton | 6 | 0 | 0 | 0/0 | 0/0 | 0 | 38 |
| Meggett | 4 | 0 | 2 | 0/0 | 0/0 | 0 | 36 |
| Sherrrard | 0 | 6 | 0 | 0/0 | 0/0 | 0 | 36 |
| Pierce | 0 | 4 | 0 | 0/0 | 0/0 | 0 | 24 |
| Cross | 0 | 4 | 0 | 0/0 | 0/0 | 0 | 24 |

### RUSHING

| | No. | Yds | Avg | Lg | TD |
|---|---|---|---|---|---|
| Hampton | 327 | 1075 | 3.3 | t27 | 6 |
| Meggett | 91 | 298 | 3.3 | t26 | 4 |
| Da. Brown | 60 | 196 | 3.3 | 21 | 2 |

### PASSING

| | Att | Comp | Pct Comp | Yds | Av Gain | TD | Int | Rating Pts |
|---|---|---|---|---|---|---|---|---|
| Da. Brown | 350 | 201 | 57.4 | 2536 | 7.25 | 12 | 16 | 72.5 |
| Graham | 53 | 24 | 45.3 | 295 | 5.57 | 3 | 2 | 66.5 |

### RECEIVING

| | No. | Yds | Avg | Lg | TD |
|---|---|---|---|---|---|
| Sherrard | 53 | 825 | 15.6 | 56 | 6 |
| Calloway | 43 | 666 | 15.5 | t51 | 2 |
| Meggett | 32 | 293 | 9.2 | 34 | 0 |
| Cross | 31 | 364 | 11.7 | 40 | 4 |
| Pierce | 20 | 214 | 10.7 | 29 | 4 |
| Marshall | 16 | 219 | 13.7 | 34 | 0 |
| Hampton | 14 | 103 | 7.4 | 17 | 0 |

**INTERCEPTIONS:** Booty and Sparks, 3

### PUNTING

| | No. | Yds | Avg | Net Avg | TB | In 20 | Lg | Blk |
|---|---|---|---|---|---|---|---|---|
| Horan | 85 | 3521 | 41.4 | 35.3 | 7 | 25 | 63 | 2 |

**SACKS:** Hamilton, 6.5

## San Francisco 49ers

### SCORING

| | Rush | Rec | Ret | PAT | FG | S | Pts |
|---|---|---|---|---|---|---|---|
| Brien | 0 | 0 | 0 | 60/62 | 15/20 | 0 | 105 |
| Rice | 2 | 13 | 0 | 0/0 | 0/0 | 0 | 92 |
| Watters | 6 | 5 | 0 | 0/0 | 0/0 | 0 | 66 |
| Jones | 0 | 9 | 0 | 0/0 | 0/0 | 0 | 56 |
| S. Young | 7 | 0 | 0 | 0/0 | 0/0 | 0 | 42 |
| Floyd | 6 | 0 | 0 | 0/0 | 0/0 | 0 | 36 |
| Taylor | 0 | 5 | 0 | 0/0 | 0/0 | 0 | 30 |
| Sanders | 0 | 0 | 3 | 0/0 | 0/0 | 0 | 18 |

### RUSHING

| | No. | Yds | Avg | Lg | TD |
|---|---|---|---|---|---|
| Watters | 239 | 877 | 3.7 | 23 | 6 |
| Floyd | 87 | 305 | 3.5 | 26 | 6 |
| S. Young | 58 | 293 | 5.1 | 27 | 7 |

### PASSING

| | Att | Comp | Pct Comp | Yds | Avg Gain | TD | Int | Rating Pts |
|---|---|---|---|---|---|---|---|---|
| S.Young | 461 | 324 | 70.3 | 3969 | 8.61 | 35 | 10 | 112.8 |
| Grbac | 50 | 35 | 70.0 | 393 | 7.86 | 2 | 1 | 98.2 |

### RECEIVING

| | No. | Yds | Avg | Lg | TD |
|---|---|---|---|---|---|
| Rice | 112 | 1499 | 13.4 | t69 | 13 |
| Watters | 66 | 719 | 10.9 | t65 | 5 |
| Jones | 49 | 670 | 13.7 | t69 | 9 |
| Taylor | 41 | 531 | 13.0 | 35 | 5 |
| Singleton | 21 | 294 | 14.0 | t43 | 2 |

**INTERCEPTIONS:** Hanks, 7

### PUNTING

| | No. | Yds | Avg | Net Avg | TB | In 20 | Lg | Blk |
|---|---|---|---|---|---|---|---|---|
| Wil'meyer | 54 | 2235 | 41.4 | 35.8 | 3 | 18 | 60 | 0 |

**SACKS:** Stubblefield, 8.5

## Tampa Bay Buccaneers

| SCORING | Rush | Rec | Ret | PAT | FG | S | Pts |
|---|---|---|---|---|---|---|---|
| Husted ................ | 0 | 0 | 0 | 20/20 | 23/35 | 0 | 89 |
| Rhett.................... | 7 | 0 | 0 | 0/0 | 0/0 | 0 | 44 |
| C. Wilson............. | 0 | 6 | 0 | 0/0 | 0/0 | 0 | 36 |
| Hawkins .............. | 0 | 5 | 0 | 0/0 | 0/0 | 0 | 30 |
| J. Harris.............. | 0 | 3 | 0 | 0/0 | 0/0 | 0 | 20 |

| RUSHING | No. | Yds | Avg | Lg | TD |
|---|---|---|---|---|---|
| Rhett...................... | 284 | 1011 | 3.6 | 27 | 7 |
| Workman .................. | 79 | 291 | 3.7 | 18 | 0 |

| PASSING | Att | Comp | Pct Comp | Yds | Avg Gain | TD | Int | Rating Pts |
|---|---|---|---|---|---|---|---|---|
| Erickson ....... | 399 | 225 | 56.4 | 2919 | 7.32 | 16 | 10 | 82.5 |
| Dilfer.............. | 82 | 38 | 46.3 | 433 | 5.28 | 1 | 6 | 36.3 |

| RECEIVING | No. | Yds | Avg | Lg | TD |
|---|---|---|---|---|---|
| Dawsey .................... | 46 | 673 | 14.6 | 46 | 1 |
| Hawkins................... | 37 | 438 | 11.8 | 32 | 5 |
| C. Wilson ................. | 31 | 652 | 21.0 | t71 | 6 |
| McDowell ................. | 29 | 193 | 6.7 | 19 | 1 |
| J. Harris.................... | 26 | 337 | 13.0 | t48 | 3 |
| Armstrong ............... | 22 | 265 | 12.0 | 29 | 1 |
| Rhett........................ | 22 | 119 | 5.4 | 12 | 0 |

**INTERCEPTIONS:** King, 3

| PUNTING | No. | Yds | Avg | Net Avg | TB | In 20 | Lg | Blk |
|---|---|---|---|---|---|---|---|---|
| Stryzinski.. | 72 | 2800 | 38.9 | 35.9 | 6 | 20 | 53 | 0 |

**SACKS:** Culpepper, 4

## Washington Redskins

| SCORING | Rush | Rec | Ret | PAT | FG | S | Pts |
|---|---|---|---|---|---|---|---|
| Lohmiller .............. | 0 | 0 | 0 | 30/32 | 20/28 | 0 | 90 |
| Ellard.................... | 0 | 6 | 0 | 0/0 | 0/0 | 0 | 36 |
| Howard ................ | 0 | 5 | 0 | 0/0 | 0/0 | 0 | 32 |
| Jenkins................. | 0 | 4 | 0 | 0/0 | 0/0 | 0 | 24 |
| Ervins ................... | 3 | 1 | 0 | 0/0 | 0/0 | 0 | 24 |

| RUSHING | No. | Yds | Avg | Lg | TD |
|---|---|---|---|---|---|
| Ervins...................... | 185 | 650 | 3.5 | 49 | 3 |
| Mitchell ...................... | 78 | 311 | 4.0 | 33 | 0 |
| Brooks ...................... | 100 | 297 | 3.0 | 15 | 2 |

| PASSING | Att | Comp | Pct Comp | Yds | Avg Gain | TD | Int | Rating Pts |
|---|---|---|---|---|---|---|---|---|
| Shuler ...... | 265 | 120 | 45.3 | 1658 | 6.26 | 10 | 12 | 59.6 |
| Friesz....... | 180 | 105 | 58.3 | 1266 | 7.03 | 10 | 9 | 77.7 |
| Frerotte.... | 100 | 46 | 46.0 | 600 | 6.00 | 5 | 5 | 61.3 |

| RECEIVING | No. | Yds | Avg | Lg | TD |
|---|---|---|---|---|---|
| Ellard ...................... | 74 | 1397 | 18.9 | t73 | 6 |
| Ervins ...................... | 51 | 293 | 5.7 | 21 | 1 |
| Howard.................... | 40 | 727 | 18.2 | t81 | 5 |
| Mitchell.................... | 26 | 236 | 9.1 | t46 | 1 |
| Winans .................... | 19 | 344 | 18.1 | 51 | 2 |

**INTERCEPTIONS:** A. Collins, 4

| PUNTING | No. | Yds | Avg | Net Avg | TB | In 20 | Lg | Blk |
|---|---|---|---|---|---|---|---|---|
| Roby ........... | 82 | 3639 | 44.4 | 36.1 | 12 | 21 | 65 | 0 |

**SACKS:** Harvey, 13.5

### Tipping the Cap

After being dumped by the New York Giants last summer, quarterback Phil Simms said, "I'd still be a Giant if the salary cap didn't exist." Who could argue? NFL commissioner Paul Tagliabue, for one. He said,"It wasn't only the effect of the cap on the Giants that produced the Phil Simms retirement."

It's true that New York couldn't be sure that the 38-year-old Simms would make it through another 16-game season.But it's just as certain he would be calling signals for the Giants if the owners and players' union had not agreed on the cap, which this season mandates that each team spend no more than $34.6 million on its player payroll. Last year Simms threw for 3,000 yards and led New York to 12 wins. Now two unproven quarterbacks have taken his place, and he's an ESPN commentator.

Having heard Tagliabue repeatedly say that, even with the cap, teams will be able to keep the players they want, Simms finally vented his feelings. "He should be tested for drugs," he told *The New York Times*. "I was not let go because of the salary cap? That's one of the stupidest things I've ever heard."

It's time for Tagliabue and the players' union to admit that the cap can cripple teams—the Giants, for example, have lost seven starters since last season because of caponomics—and to say it will take a couple of years for everyone to adjust to the new NFL. To deny the cap's impact in the waiving of players like Simms and 1993 AFC reception leader Reggie Langhorne (by the Indianapolis Colts) is, to quote Simms again, "absurd."

First two rounds of the 60th annual NFL Draft held April 22-23 in New York City.

## First Round

| | Team | Selection | Position |
|---|---|---|---|
| 1. | Cincinnati | Ki-Jana Carter, Penn St | RB |
| 2. | Jacksonville | Tony Boselli, USC | OT |
| 3. | Houston | Steve McNair, Alcorn St | QB |
| 4. | Washington | Michael Westbrook, Col | WR |
| 5. | Carolina | Kerry Collins, Penn St | QB |
| 6. | St Louis | Kevin Carter, Florida | DE |
| 7. | Philadelphia | Mike Mamula, Boston College | DE |
| 8. | Seattle | Joey Galloway, Ohio St | WR |
| 9. | NY Jets | Kyle Brady, Penn St | TE |
| 10. | San Francisco | J.J. Stokes, UCLA | WR |
| 11. | Minnesota | Derrick Alexander, Florida St | DE |
| 12. | Tampa Bay | Warren Sapp, Miami (FL) | DT |
| 13. | New Orleans | Mark Fields, Wash St | LB |
| 14. | Buffalo | Reuben Brown, Pitt | G |
| 15. | Indianapolis | Ellis Johnson, Florida | DT |
| 16. | NY Jets | Hugh Douglas, Central State (OH) | DE |
| 17. | NY Giants | Tyrone Wheatley, Michigan | RB |
| 18. | Los Angeles | Napoleon Kaufman, Washington | RB |
| 19. | Jacksonville | James Stewart, Tenn | RB |
| 20. | Detroit | Luther Elliss, Utah | DE |
| 21. | Chicago | Rashaan Salaam, Col | RB |
| 22. | Carolina | Tyrone Poole, Fort Valley St | CB |
| 23. | New England | Ty Law, Michigan | CB |
| 24. | Minnesota | Korey Stringer, Ohio St | OT |
| 25. | Miami | Billy Milner, Houston | OT |
| 26. | Atlanta | Devin Bush, Florida St | SS |
| 27. | Pittsburgh | Mark Bruener, Washington | TE |
| 28. | Tampa Bay | Derrick Brooks, Florida St | LB |
| 29. | Carolina | Blake Brockermeyer, Texas | OT |
| 30. | Cleveland | Craig Powell, Ohio St | LB |
| 31. | Kansas City | Trezelle Jenkins, Mich | OT |
| 32. | Green Bay | Craig Newsome, Arizona St | CB |

## Second Round

| | Team | Selection | Position |
|---|---|---|---|
| 33. | NY Jets | Matt O'Dwyer, Northwestern | G |
| 34. | San Diego | Terrance Shaw, Stephen F. Austin | DB |
| 35. | Houston | Anthony Cook, S Carolina St | DT |
| 36. | Carolina | Shawn King, NE Louisiana | DE |
| 37. | Washington | Cory Raymer, Wisconsin | C |
| 38. | St. Louis | Zach Wiegert, Nebraska | OT |
| 39. | Seattle | Christian Fauria, Colorado | TE |
| 40. | Jacksonville | Brian DeMarco, Mich St | OT |
| 41. | Atlanta | Ronald Davis, Tennessee | DB |
| 42. | Minnesota | Orlando Thomas, SW Louisiana | DB |
| 43. | Tampa Bay | Melvin Johnson, Kentucky | DB |
| 44. | New Orleans | Ray Zellars, Notre Dame | RB |
| 45. | Buffalo | Todd Collins, Michigan | QB |
| 46. | Dallas | Sherman Williams, Alabama | RB |
| 47. | Arizona | Frank Sanders, Auburn | WR |
| 48. | Indianapolis | Ken Dilger, Illinois | TE |
| 49. | Los Angeles | Barret Robbins, TCU | C |
| 50. | Philadelphia | Bobby Taylor, Notre Dame | DB |
| 51. | San Diego | Terrell Fletcher, Wisconsin | RB |
| 52. | Chicago | Patrick Riley, Miami (FL) | DT |
| 53. | Miami | Andrew Greene, Indiana | G |
| 54. | NY Giants | Scott Gragg, Montana | OT |
| 55. | Minnesota | Corey Fuller, Florida St | DB |
| 56. | Chicago | Todd Sauerbrun, W Va | P |
| 57. | New England | Ted Johnson, Colorado | LB |
| 58. | Philadelphia | Barrett Brooks, Kansas St | OT |
| 59. | Dallas | Kendall Watkins, Mississippi St | TE |
| 60. | Pittsburgh | Kordell Stewart, Colorado | QB |
| 61. | San Diego | Jimmy Oliver, TCU | WR |
| 62. | St. Louis | Jesse James, Miss St | G |
| 63. | Dallas | Shane Hannah, Michigan St | G |
| 64. | Jacksonville | Bryan Schwartz, Augustana (SD) | LB |

## Keeping the Books

If you take his answering machine seriously, John Pease, who was hired on January 12 as defensive line coach of the expansion Jacksonville Jaguars of the NFL, took more than hard feelings with him when he left his former employers, the New Orleans Saints, who fired him late in December 1994. The recorded greeting on his home phone now offers callers copies of Saint playbooks.

### Second Half Standings

| | W | L | T | Pct | Pts/ Tm | Pts/ Opp |
|---|---|---|---|---|---|---|
| Amsterdam | 4 | 1 | 0 | .800 | 137 | 107 |
| Frankfurt | 4 | 1 | 0 | .800 | 164 | 105 |
| Barcelona | 2 | 3 | 0 | .400 | 123 | 145 |
| London | 2 | 3 | 0 | .400 | 84 | 102 |
| Rhein | 2 | 3 | 0 | .400 | 134 | 157 |
| Scotland | 1 | 4 | 0 | .200 | 99 | 125 |

### Final Standings

| | W | L | T | Pct | Pts/ Tm | Pts/ Opp |
|---|---|---|---|---|---|---|
| Amsterdam* | 9 | 1 | 0 | .800 | 246 | 152 |
| Frankfurt* | 6 | 4 | 0 | .600 | 279 | 202 |
| Barcelona | 5 | 5 | 0 | .500 | 237 | 247 |
| London | 4 | 6 | 0 | .400 | 174 | 220 |
| Rhein | 4 | 6 | 0 | .400 | 221 | 279 |
| Scotland | 2 | 8 | 0 | .200 | 153 | 210 |

*Clinched World Bowl '95 berth.

### 1995 World Bowl

June 17, 1995 in Amsterdam, Holland

| | | | | |
|---|---|---|---|---|
| Frankfurt | 0 | 6 | 14 | 6—26 |
| Amsterdam | 0 | 7 | 0 | 15—22 |

#### SECOND QUARTER

Amsterdam: E. Jones 5 pass from Furrer (Belden kick), 13:44
Frankfurt: Olive 11 pass from Justin (Kleinman kick failed), 14:10

#### THIRD QUARTER

Frankfurt: Olive 4 pass from Justin (Kleinman kick), 7:26
Frankfurt: Bellamy 31 pass from Justin (Kleinmann kick), 11:08

#### FOURTH QUARTER

Frankfurt: Bolton 30 run (Kleinmann kick failed), 4:37
Amsterdam: Wright 1 run (Belden kick), 5:06
Amsterdam: Wright 9 pass from Furrer (Beach pass from Furrer), 14:28

A: 23,847.

## WLAF Individual Leaders

### PASSING

| | Att | Comp | Pct Comp | Yds | Avg Gain | TD | Pct TD | Int | Pct Int | Lg | Rating Pts |
|---|---|---|---|---|---|---|---|---|---|---|---|
| P. Justin, Frankfurt | 279 | 172 | 61.6 | 2394 | 8.58 | 17 | 6.1 | 12 | 4.3 | 64 | 91.6 |
| J. Martin, Amsterdam | 219 | 126 | 57.5 | 1433 | 6.54 | 11 | 5.0 | 6 | 2.7 | t68 | 82.6 |
| B. Johnson, London | 328 | 194 | 59.1 | 2227 | 6.79 | 13 | 4.0 | 14 | 4.3 | t58 | 75.1 |
| G. Torretta, Rhein | 144 | 81 | 56.3 | 940 | 6.53 | 5 | 3.5 | 6 | 4.2 | t49 | 70.4 |
| J. Walker, Barcelona | 288 | 146 | 50.7 | 1874 | 6.51 | 7 | 2.4 | 7 | 2.4 | t71 | 69.4 |

### RECEIVING

| RECEPTIONS | No. | Yds | Avg | Lg | TD | YARDS | Yds | No. | Avg | Lg | TD |
|---|---|---|---|---|---|---|---|---|---|---|---|
| B. Olive, Frankfurt | 57 | 899 | 15.8 | 64 | 2 | B. Olive, Frankfurt | 899 | 57 | 15.8 | 64 | 2 |
| T. Davis, Barcelona | 56 | 855 | 15.3 | t69 | 6 | T. Davis, Barcelona | 855 | 56 | 15.3 | t69 | 6 |
| M. Bailey, Frankfurt | 46 | 654 | 14.2 | t59 | 7 | A. Allen, London | 781 | 38 | 20.6 | t58 | 4 |
| M. Titley, London | 45 | 457 | 10.2 | 45 | 3 | M. Bailey, Frankfurt | 654 | 46 | 14.2 | t59 | 7 |
| A. DeGraffenreid, Scot | 44 | 624 | 14.2 | t65 | 4 | A. DeGraffenreid, Scot | 624 | 44 | 14.2 | t65 | 4 |

### RUSHING

| | Att | Yds | Avg | Lg | TD |
|---|---|---|---|---|---|
| S. Stacy, Scotland | 214 | 785 | 3.7 | 48 | 5 |
| T. Brooks, London | 172 | 480 | 2.8 | 30 | 5 |
| R. Dawkins, Amster. | 132 | 479 | 3.6 | t38 | 3 |
| N. Bolton, Frankfurt | 106 | 420 | 4.0 | 42 | 3 |
| R. Blake, Barcelona | 98 | 398 | 4.1 | t29 | 2 |

### Other Statistical Leaders

| | | |
|---|---|---|
| Points (TDs) | M. Bellamy, Frankfurt | 48 |
| Points (Kicking) | S. Szeredy, Barcelona | 85 |
| Yards from Scrimmage | S. Stacy, Scotland | 1109 |
| Interceptions | C. Hall, Frankfurt | 8 |
| Sacks | M. Showell, Amsterdam | 8.5 |
| Punting Avg. | D. Alcorn, Frankfurt | 40.6 |
| Punt Return Avg. | T.C. Wright, Amsterdam | 13.4 |
| Kickoff Return Avg. | A. DeGraffenreid, Scot | 23.3 |

# 1994 Canadian Football League

## EASTERN DIVISION

| | W | L | T | Pts | Pct | PF | PA |
|---|---|---|---|---|---|---|---|
| Winnipeg | 13 | 5 | 0 | 26 | .722 | 651 | 572 |
| Baltimore | 12 | 6 | 0 | 24 | .687 | 561 | 431 |
| Toronto | 7 | 11 | 0 | 14 | .389 | 504 | 578 |
| Ottawa | 4 | 14 | 0 | 8 | .222 | 480 | 647 |
| Hamilton | 4 | 14 | 0 | 8 | .222 | 436 | 582 |
| Shreveport | 3 | 15 | 0 | 6 | .167 | 330 | 661 |

## WESTERN DIVISION

| | W | L | T | Pts | Pct | PF | PA |
|---|---|---|---|---|---|---|---|
| Calgary | 15 | 3 | 0 | 30 | .833 | 686 | 356 |
| Edmonton | 13 | 5 | 0 | 26 | .722 | 518 | 401 |
| B.C. | 11 | 6 | 1 | 23 | .647 | 604 | 456 |
| Saskatchewan | 11 | 7 | 0 | 22 | .611 | 512 | 454 |
| Sacramento | 9 | 8 | 1 | 19 | .529 | 438 | 436 |
| Las Vegas | 5 | 13 | 0 | 10 | .278 | 447 | 622 |

## Regular Season Statistical Leaders

| | | |
|---|---|---|
| Points (TDs) | Pitts, Calgary | 126 |
| Points (Kicking) | Westwood, Winnipeg | 213 |
| Yards (Rushing) | Pringle, Baltimore | 1972 |
| Yards (Passing) | Flutie, Calgary | 5728 |
| Yards (Receiving) | Pitts, Calgary | 2036 |
| Receptions | Pitts, Calgary | 126 |

## 1994 Playoff Results

### DIVISION SEMIFINALS

Eastern: Toronto 15, BALTIMORE 34
Ottawa 16, WINNIPEG 26
Western: British Columbia 24, EDMONTON 23
Saskatchewan 3, CALGARY 36

### DIVISION FINALS

Eastern: Baltimore 14, WINNIPEG 12
Western: British Columbia 37, CALGARY 36

## 1994 Grey Cup Championship

Nov. 27, 1994, at Vancouver

| | | | | |
|---|---|---|---|---|
| Baltimore CFL'ers | 0 | 17 | 3 | 3—23 |
| British Columbia Lions | 3 | 7 | 10 | 6—26 |

A: 55,097

---

## No Gain

Over the past three years the NFL, some 60% of whose players are black, ran its string of white head-coaching hires to 20. During the streak the Dallas Cowboys signed Barry Switzer, who had no pro experience and had not lifted a clipboard for nearly six years; the New York Jets chose Richie Kotite who was fresh from leading the Philadelphia Eagles to seven straight losses; and the Carolina Panthers preferred Don Capers, a soft-spoken, teaching-oriented, white defensive coordinator who turned the Pittsburgh Steeler defense into the second best in the league in 1994, to Tony Dungy, a soft-spoken, teaching-oriented black defensive coordinator who turned the Minnesota Vikings into the *best* in the league in 1993.

It was encouraging to see the Eagles hire an African-American, San Francisco 49er defensive coordinator Ray Rhodes, in early February.

But Rhodes's hiring came the same day that the Los Angeles Raiders fired Art Shell, which left the league with the same number of black head coaches—two—as 37 months ago. Rhodes was the only black interviewee for the current vacancy in St. Louis, even though Dungy, Washington Redskin receivers coach Terry Robiskie and Buffalo Bill assistant head coach Elijah Pitts are qualified candidates.

"We're concerned about this," says NFL commissioner Paul Tagliabue, who lobbied behind the scenes on Rhodes behalf. The pool of high-profile black assistants *is* small, but that's not an excuse, only another symptom of the problem. It may be time for Tagliabue to browbeat his owners into reserving more spots on all staffs for black assistants. Otherwise, the NFL risks not joining the 20th century until that century is over.

# FOR THE RECORD · Year by Year

## The Super Bowl

### Results

| Date | Winner (Share) | Loser (Share) | Score | Site (Attendance) |
|---|---|---|---|---|
| I .............. 1-15-67 | Green Bay ($15,000) | Kansas City ($7,500) | 35-10 | Los Angeles (61,946) |
| II .............. 1-14-68 | Green Bay ($15,000) | Oakland ($7,500) | 33-14 | Miami (75,546) |
| III .............. 1-12-69 | NY Jets ($15,000) | Baltimore ($7,500) | 16-7 | Miami (75,389) |
| IV .............. 1-11-70 | Kansas City ($15,000) | Minnesota ($7,500) | 23-7 | New Orleans (80,562) |
| V .............. 1-17-71 | Baltimore ($15,000) | Dallas ($7,500) | 16-13 | Miami (79,204) |
| VI .............. 1-16-72 | Dallas ($15,000) | Miami ($7,500) | 24-3 | New Orleans (81,023) |
| VII .............. 1-14-73 | Miami ($15,000) | Washington ($7,500) | 14-7 | Los Angeles (90,182) |
| VIII .......... 1-13-74 | Miami ($15,000) | Minnesota ($7,500) | 24-7 | Houston (71,882) |
| IX .............. 1-12-75 | Pittsburgh ($15,000) | Minnesota ($7,500) | 16-6 | New Orleans (80,997) |
| X .............. 1-18-76 | Pittsburgh ($15,000) | Dallas ($7,500) | 21-17 | Miami (80,187) |
| XI .............. 1-9-77 | Oakland ($15,000) | Minnesota ($7,500) | 32-14 | Pasadena (103,438) |
| XII .............. 1-15-78 | Dallas ($18,000) | Denver ($9,000) | 27-10 | New Orleans (75,583) |
| XIII .......... 1-21-79 | Pittsburgh ($18,000) | Dallas ($9,000) | 35-31 | Miami (79,484) |
| XIV .......... 1-20-80 | Pittsburgh ($18,000) | Los Angeles ($9,000) | 31-19 | Pasadena (103,985) |
| XV .............. 1-25-81 | Oakland ($18,000) | Philadelphia ($9,000) | 27-10 | New Orleans (76,135) |
| XVI .......... 1-24-82 | San Francisco ($18,000) | Cincinnati ($9,000) | 26-21 | Pontiac (81,270) |
| XVII .......... 1-30-83 | Washington ($36,000) | Miami ($18,000) | 27-17 | Pasadena (103,667) |
| XVIII .......... 1-22-84 | LA Raiders ($36,000) | Washington ($18,000) | 38-9 | Tampa (72,920) |
| XIX .......... 1-20-85 | San Francisco ($36,000) | Miami ($18,000) | 38-16 | Stanford (84,059) |
| XX .............. 1-26-86 | Chicago ($36,000) | New England ($18,000) | 46-10 | New Orleans (73,818) |
| XXI .......... 1-25-87 | NY Giants ($36,000) | Denver ($18,000) | 39-20 | Pasadena (101,063) |
| XXII .......... 1-31-88 | Washington ($36,000) | Denver ($18,000) | 42-10 | San Diego (73,302) |
| XXIII .......... 1-22-89 | San Francisco ($36,000) | Cincinnati ($18,000) | 20-16 | Miami (75,129) |
| XXIV .......... 1-28-90 | San Francisco ($36,000) | Denver ($18,000) | 55-10 | New Orleans (72,919) |
| XXV .......... 1-27-91 | NY Giants ($36,000) | Buffalo ($18,000) | 20-19 | Tampa (73,813) |
| XXVI .......... 1-26-92 | Washington ($36,000) | Buffalo ($18,000) | 37-24 | Minneapolis (63,130) |
| XXVII .......... 1-31-93 | Dallas ($36,000) | Buffalo ($18,000) | 52-17 | Pasadena (98,374) |
| XXVIII .......... 1-30-94 | Dallas ($38,000) | Buffalo ($23,500) | 30-13 | Atlanta (72,817) |
| XXIX .......... 1-29-95 | San Francisco ($42,000) | San Diego ($26,000) | 49-26 | Miami (74,107) |

### Most Valuable Players

| | | Position |
|---|---|---|
| I .................. | Bart Starr, GB | QB |
| II .................. | Bart Starr, GB | QB |
| III .................. | Joe Namath, NY Jets | QB |
| IV .................. | Len Dawson, KC | QB |
| V .................. | Chuck Howley, Dall | LB |
| VI .................. | Roger Staubach, Dall | QB |
| VII .................. | Jake Scott, Mia | S |
| VIII .................. | Larry Csonka, Mia | RB |
| IX .................. | Franco Harris, Pitt | RB |
| X .................. | Lynn Swann, Pitt | WR |
| XI .................. | Fred Biletnikoff, Oak | WR |
| XII .................. | Randy White, Dall | DT |
| | Harvey Martin, Dall | DE |
| XIII .................. | Terry Bradshaw, Pitt | QB |
| XIV .................. | Terry Bradshaw, Pitt | QB |
| XV .................. | Jim Plunkett, Oak | QB |
| XVI .................. | Joe Montana, SF | QB |
| XVII .................. | John Riggins, Wash | RB |
| XVIII .................. | Marcus Allen, LA Raiders | RB |
| XIX .................. | Joe Montana, SF | QB |
| XX .................. | Richard Dent, Chi | DE |
| XXI .................. | Phil Simms, NY Giants | QB |
| XXII .................. | Doug Williams, Wash | QB |
| XXIII .................. | Jerry Rice, SF | WR |
| XXIV .................. | Joe Montana, SF | QB |
| XXV .................. | Ottis Anderson, NY Giants | RB |
| XXVI .................. | Mark Rypien, Washington | QB |
| XXVII .................. | Troy Aikman, Dallas | QB |
| XXVIII .................. | Emmitt Smith, Dallas | RB |
| XXIX .................. | Steve Young, SF | QB |

### Composite Standings

| | W | L | Pct | Pts | Opp Pts |
|---|---|---|---|---|---|
| San Francisco 49ers ...... | 5 | 0 | 1.000 | 188 | 89 |
| Pittsburgh Steelers ........ | 4 | 0 | 1.000 | 103 | 73 |
| Green Bay Packers ........ | 2 | 0 | 1.000 | 68 | 24 |
| N.Y. Giants .................. | 2 | 0 | 1.000 | 59 | 39 |
| Chicago Bears .............. | 1 | 0 | 1.000 | 46 | 10 |
| N.Y. Jets ...................... | 1 | 0 | 1.000 | 16 | 7 |
| Oakland/LA Raiders ...... | 3 | 1 | .750 | 111 | 66 |
| Washington Redskins ...... | 3 | 2 | .600 | 122 | 103 |
| Dallas Cowboys ............ | 4 | 3 | .571 | 194 | 115 |
| Baltimore Colts .............. | 1 | 1 | .500 | 23 | 29 |
| Kansas City Chiefs ........ | 1 | 1 | .500 | 33 | 42 |
| Miami Dolphins .............. | 2 | 3 | .400 | 74 | 103 |
| L.A. Rams .................... | 0 | 1 | .000 | 19 | 31 |
| New England Patriots ...... | 0 | 1 | .000 | 10 | 46 |
| Philadelphia Eagles ...... | 0 | 1 | .000 | 10 | 27 |
| San Diego Chargers ...... | 0 | 1 | .000 | 26 | 49 |
| Cincinnati Bengals ........ | 0 | 2 | .000 | 37 | 46 |
| Buffalo Bills .................. | 0 | 4 | .000 | 73 | 139 |
| Denver Broncos ............ | 0 | 4 | .000 | 50 | 163 |
| Minnesota Vikings .......... | 0 | 4 | .000 | 34 | 95 |

## Career Leaders
### Passing

| | GP | Att | Comp | Pct Comp | Yds | Avg Gain | TD | Pct TD | Int | Pct Int | Lg | Rating Pts |
|---|---|---|---|---|---|---|---|---|---|---|---|---|
| Joe Montana, SF | 4 | 122 | 83 | 68.0 | 1142 | 9.36 | 11 | 9.0 | 0 | 0.0 | 44 | 127.8 |
| Jim Plunkett, Raiders | 2 | 46 | 29 | 63.0 | 433 | 9.41 | 4 | 8.7 | 0 | 0.0 | t80 | 122.8 |
| Troy Aikman, Dall | 2 | 57 | 41 | 71.9 | 480 | 8.42 | 4 | 7.0 | 1 | 1.8 | t56 | 113.2 |
| Terry Bradshaw, Pitt | 4 | 84 | 49 | 58.3 | 932 | 11.10 | 9 | 10.7 | 4 | 4.8 | t75 | 112.8 |
| Bart Starr, GB | 2 | 47 | 29 | 61.7 | 452 | 9.62 | 3 | 6.4 | 1 | 2.1 | t62 | 106.0 |
| Roger Staubach, Dall | 4 | 98 | 61 | 62.2 | 734 | 7.49 | 8 | 8.2 | 4 | 4.1 | t45 | 95.4 |
| Len Dawson, KC | 2 | 44 | 28 | 63.6 | 353 | 8.02 | 2 | 4.5 | 2 | 4.5 | t46 | 84.8 |
| Bob Griese, Mia | 3 | 41 | 26 | 63.4 | 295 | 7.20 | 1 | 2.4 | 2 | 4.9 | t28 | 72.7 |
| Dan Marino, Mia | 1 | 50 | 29 | 58.0 | 318 | 6.36 | 1 | 2.0 | 2 | 4.0 | 30 | 66.9 |
| Jim Kelly, Buff | 4 | 145 | 81 | 55.9 | 829 | 5.72 | 2 | 1.4 | 7 | 4.8 | 61 | 57.2 |
| Joe Theismann, Wash | 2 | 58 | 31 | 53.4 | 386 | 6.66 | 2 | 3.4 | 4 | 6.9 | 60 | 57.1 |

Note: Minimum 40 attempts.

### Rushing

| | GP | Yds | Att | Avg | Lg | TD |
|---|---|---|---|---|---|---|
| Franco Harris, Pitt | 4 | 354 | 101 | 3.5 | 25 | 4 |
| Larry Csonka, Mia | 3 | 297 | 57 | 5.2 | 9 | 2 |
| Emmitt Smith, Dall | 2 | 240 | 52 | 4.6 | 38 | 3 |
| John Riggins, Wash | 2 | 230 | 64 | 3.6 | 43 | 2 |
| Timmy Smith, Wash | 1 | 204 | 22 | 9.3 | 58 | 2 |
| Thurman Thomas, Buff | 4 | 204 | 52 | 3.9 | 31 | 4 |
| Roger Craig, SF | 3 | 198 | 52 | 3.8 | 18 | 2 |
| Marcus Allen, LA Raiders | 1 | 191 | 20 | 9.6 | t74 | 2 |
| Tony Dorsett, Dall | 2 | 162 | 31 | 5.2 | 29 | 1 |
| Mark van Eeghen, Oak | 2 | 148 | 36 | 4.1 | 11 | 0 |

### Receiving

| | GP | No. | Yds | Avg | Lg | TD |
|---|---|---|---|---|---|---|
| Jerry Rice, SF | 3 | 28 | 512 | 18.3 | t44 | 7 |
| Andre Reed, Buff | 4 | 27 | 323 | 11.9 | 40 | 0 |
| Roger Craig, SF | 3 | 20 | 212 | 10.6 | 40 | 2 |
| Thurman Thomas, Buff | 4 | 20 | 144 | 7.2 | 24 | 0 |
| Lynn Swann, Pitt | 4 | 16 | 364 | 22.8 | t64 | 3 |
| Chuck Foreman, Minn | 3 | 15 | 139 | 9.3 | 26 | 0 |
| Cliff Branch, Raiders | 3 | 14 | 181 | 12.9 | 50 | 3 |
| Preston Pearson, Balt-Pitt-Dall | 5 | 12 | 105 | 8.8 | 14 | 0 |
| Don Beebe, Buff | 3 | 12 | 171 | 14.3 | 43 | 2 |
| Tom Novacek, Dall | 2 | 12 | 128 | 10.6 | 23 | 1 |
| Kenneth Davis, Buff | 4 | 12 | 72 | 6.0 | 19 | 0 |

## Single-Game Leaders

### Scoring

| | Pts |
|---|---|
| Roger Craig: XIX, San Francisco vs Miami (1 R, 2 P) | 18 |
| Jerry Rice: XXIV, San Francisco vs Denver (3 P); XXIX SF vs San Diego (3 P) | 18 |
| Ricky Watters: XXIX, San Francisco vs San Diego (1 R, 2 P) | 18 |

### Touchdown Passes

| | No. |
|---|---|
| Steve Young: XXIX, San Francisco vs San Diego | 6 |
| Joe Montana: XXIV, San Francisco vs Denver | 5 |
| Terry Bradshaw: XIII, Pittsburgh vs Dallas | 4 |
| Doug Williams: XXII, Washington vs Denver | 4 |
| Troy Aikman: XXVII, Dallas vs Buffalo | 4 |

Four tied with 3

### Rushing Yards

| | Yds |
|---|---|
| Timmy Smith: XXII, Washington vs Denver | 204 |
| Marcus Allen: XVIII, LA Raiders vs Washington | 191 |
| John Riggins: XVII, Washington vs Miami | 166 |
| Franco Harris: IX, Pittsburgh vs Minnesota | 158 |
| Larry Csonka: VIII, Miami vs Minnesota | 145 |
| Clarence Davis: XI, Oakland vs Minnesota | 137 |
| Thurman Thomas: XXV, Buffalo vs NY Giants | 135 |
| Emmitt Smith: XXVIII, Dallas vs Buffalo | 132 |

### Receiving Yards

| | Yds |
|---|---|
| Jerry Rice: XXIII, San Francisco vs Cincinnati | 215 |
| Ricky Sanders: XXII, Washington vs Denver | 193 |
| Lynn Swann: X, Pittsburgh vs Dallas | 161 |
| Andre Reed: XXVII, Buffalo vs Dallas | 152 |
| Jerry Rice: XXIX, San Francisco vs San Diego | 149 |
| Jerry Rice: XXIV, San Francisco vs Denver | 148 |
| Max McGee: I, Green Bay vs Kansas City | 138 |
| George Sauer: III, NY Jets vs Baltimore | 133 |

### Receptions

| | No. |
|---|---|
| Dan Ross: XVI, Cincinnati vs San Francisco | 11 |
| Jerry Rice: XXIII, San Francisco vs Cincinnati | 11 |
| Tony Nathan: XIX, Miami vs San Francisco | 10 |
| Jerry Rice: XXIX, San Francisco vs San Diego | 10 |
| Ricky Sanders: XXII, Washington vs Denver | 9 |

Five tied with 8

### Passing Yards

| | Yds |
|---|---|
| Joe Montana: XXIII, San Francisco vs Cincinnati | 357 |
| Doug Williams: XXII, Washington vs Denver | 340 |
| Joe Montana: XIX, San Francisco vs Miami | 331 |
| Steve Young: XXIX, San Francisco vs San Diego | 325 |
| Terry Bradshaw: XIII, Pittsburgh vs Dallas | 318 |
| Dan Marino: XIX, Miami vs San Francisco | 318 |
| Terry Bradshaw: XIV, Pittsburgh vs LA Rams | 309 |
| John Elway: XXI, Denver vs NY Giants | 304 |

# NFL Playoff History

**1933**
NFL championship  Chicago Bears 23, NY Giants 21

**1934**
NFL championship  NY Giants 30, Chicago Bears 13

**1935**
NFL championship  Detroit 26, NY Giants 7

**1936**
NFL championship  Green Bay 21, Boston 6

**1937**
NFL championship  Washington 28,
Chicago Bears 21

**1938**
NFL championship  NY Giants 23, Green Bay 17

**1939**
NFL championship  Green Bay 27, NY Giants 0

**1940**
NFL championship  Chicago Bears 73, Washington 0

**1941**
W. div. playoff  Chicago Bears 33, Green Bay 14
NFL championship  Chicago Bears 37, NY Giants 9

**1942**
NFL championship  Washington 14, Chicago Bears 6

**1943**
E. div. playoff  Washington 28, NY Giants 0
NFL championship  Chicago Bears 41,
Washington 21

**1944**
NFL championship  Green Bay 14, NY Giants 7

**1945**
NFL championship  Cleveland 15, Washington 14

**1946**
NFL championship  Chicago Bears 24, NY Giants 14

**1947**
E. div. playoff  Philadelphia 21, Pittsburgh 0
NFL championship  Chicago Cardinals 28,
Philadelphia 21

**1948**
NFL championship  Philadelphia 7,
Chicago Cardinals 0

**1949**
NFL championship  Philadelphia 14, Los Angeles 0

**1950**
Am. Conf. playoff  Cleveland 8, NY Giants 3
Nat. Conf. playoff  Los Angeles 24,
Chicago Bears 14
NFL championship  Cleveland 30, Los Angeles 28

**1951**
NFL championship  Los Angeles 24, Cleveland 17

**1952**
Nat. Conf. playoff  Detroit 31, Los Angeles 21
NFL championship  Detroit 17, Cleveland 7

**1953**
NFL championship  Detroit 17, Cleveland 16

**1954**
NFL championship  Cleveland 56, Detroit 10

**1955**
NFL championship  Cleveland 38, Los Angeles 14

**1956**
NFL championship  NY Giants 47, Chicago Bears 7

**1957**
W. Conf. playoff  Detroit 31, San Francisco 27
NFL championship  Detroit 59, Cleveland 14

**1958**
E. Conf. playoff  NY Giants 10, Cleveland 0
NFL championship  Baltimore 23, NY Giants 17

**1959**
NFL championship  Baltimore 31, NY Giants 16

**1960**
NFL championship  Philadelphia 17, Green Bay 13
AFL championship  Houston 24, LA Chargers 16

**1961**
NFL championship  Green Bay 37, NY Giants 0
AFL championship  Houston 10, San Diego 3

**1962**
NFL championship  Green Bay 16, NY Giants 7
AFL championship  Dallas Texans 20, Houston 17

**1963**
NFL championship  Chicago 14, NY Giants 10
AFL E. div. playoff  Boston 26, Buffalo 8
AFL championship  San Diego 51, Boston 10

**1964**
NFL championship  Cleveland 27, Baltimore 0
AFL championship  Buffalo 20, San Diego 7

**1965**
NFL W. Conf.  Green Bay 13, Baltimore 10
playoff
NFL championship  Green Bay 23, Cleveland 12
AFL championship  Buffalo 23, San Diego 0

**1966**
NFL championship  Green Bay 34, Dallas 27
AFL championship  Kansas City 31, Buffalo 7

**1967**
NFL E. Conf.  Dallas 52, Cleveland 14
championship
NFL W. Conf.  Green Bay 28, Los Angeles 7
championship
NFL championship  Green Bay 21, Dallas 17
AFL championship  Oakland 40, Houston 7

## 1968

| | |
|---|---|
| NFL E. Conf. championship | Cleveland 31, Dallas 20 |
| NFL W. Conf. championship | Baltimore 24, Minnesota 14 |
| NFL championship | Baltimore 34, Cleveland 0 |
| AFL W. div. playoff | Oakland 41, Kansas City 6 |
| AFL championship | NY Jets 27, Oakland 23 |

## 1969

| | |
|---|---|
| NFL E. Conf. championship | Cleveland 38, Dallas 14 |
| NFL W. Conf. championship | Minnesota 23, Los Angeles 20 |
| NFL championship | Minnesota 27, Cleveland 7 |
| AFL div. playoffs | Kansas City 13, NY Jets 6 |
| | Oakland 56, Houston 7 |
| AFL championship | Kansas City 17, Oakland 7 |

## 1970

| | |
|---|---|
| AFC div. playoffs | Baltimore 17, Cincinnati 0 |
| | Oakland 21, Miami 14 |
| AFC championship | Baltimore 27, Oakland 17 |
| NFC div. playoffs | Dallas 5, Detroit 0 |
| | San Francisco 17, Minnesota 14 |
| NFC championship | Dallas 17, San Francisco 10 |

## 1971

| | |
|---|---|
| AFC div. playoffs | Miami 27, Kansas City 24 |
| | Baltimore 20, Cleveland 3 |
| AFC championship | Miami 21, Baltimore 0 |
| NFC div. playoffs | Dallas 20, Minnesota 12 |
| | San Francisco 24, Washington 20 |
| NFC championship | Dallas 14, San Francisco 3 |

## 1972

| | |
|---|---|
| AFC div. playoffs | Pittsburgh 13, Oakland 7 |
| | Miami 20, Cleveland 14 |
| AFC championship | Miami 21, Pittsburgh 17 |
| NFC div. playoffs | Dallas 30, San Francisco 28 |
| | Washington 16, Green Bay 3 |
| NFC championship | Washington 26, Dallas 3 |

## 1973

| | |
|---|---|
| AFC div. playoffs | Oakland 33, Pittsburgh 14 |
| | Miami 34, Cincinnati 16 |
| AFC championship | Miami 27, Oakland 10 |
| NFC div. playoffs | Minnesota 27, Washington 20 |
| | Dallas 27, Los Angeles 16 |
| NFC championship | Minnesota 27, Dallas 10 |

## 1974

| | |
|---|---|
| AFC div. playoffs | Oakland 28, Miami 26 |
| | Pittsburgh 32, Buffalo 14 |
| AFC championship | Pittsburgh 24, Oakland 13 |
| NFC div. playoffs | Minnesota 30, St Louis 14 |
| | Los Angeles 19, Washington 10 |
| NFC championship | Minnesota 14, Los Angeles 10 |

## 1975

| | |
|---|---|
| AFC div. playoffs | Pittsburgh 28, Baltimore 10 |
| | Oakland 31, Cincinnati 28 |
| AFC championship | Pittsburgh 16, Oakland 10 |
| NFC div. playoffs | Los Angeles 35, St Louis 23 |
| | Dallas 17, Minnesota 14 |
| NFC championship | Dallas 37, Los Angeles 7 |

## 1976

| | |
|---|---|
| AFC div. playoffs | Oakland 24, New England 21 |
| | Pittsburgh 40, Baltimore 14 |
| AFC championship | Oakland 24, Pittsburgh 7 |
| NFC div. playoffs | Minnesota 35, Washington 20 |
| | Los Angeles 14, Dallas 12 |
| NFC championship | Minnesota 24, Los Angeles 13 |

## 1977

| | |
|---|---|
| AFC div. playoffs | Denver 34, Pittsburgh 21 |
| | Oakland 37, Baltimore 31 |
| AFC championship | Denver 20, Oakland 17 |
| NFC div. playoffs | Dallas 37, Chicago 7 |
| | Minnesota 14, Los Angeles 7 |
| NFC championship | Dallas 23, Minnesota 6 |

## 1978

| | |
|---|---|
| AFC 1st-rd. playoff | Houston 17, Miami 9 |
| AFC div. playoffs | Houston 31, New England 14 |
| | Pittsburgh 33, Denver 10 |
| AFC championship | Pittsburgh 34, Houston 5 |
| NFC 1st-rd. playoff | Atlanta 14, Philadelphia 13 |
| NFC div. playoffs | Dallas 27, Atlanta 20 |
| | Los Angeles 34, Minnesota 10 |
| NFC championship | Dallas 28, Los Angeles 0 |

## 1979

| | |
|---|---|
| AFC 1st-rd. playoff | Houston 13, Denver 7 |
| AFC div. playoffs | Houston 17, San Diego 14 |
| | Pittsburgh 34, Miami 14 |
| AFC championship | Pittsburgh 27, Houston 13 |
| NFC 1st-rd. playoff | Philadelphia 27, Chicago 17 |
| NFC div. playoffs | Tampa Bay 24, Philadelphia 17 |
| | Los Angeles 21, Dallas 19 |
| NFC championship | Los Angeles 9, Tampa Bay 0 |

## 1980

| | |
|---|---|
| AFC 1st-rd. playoff | Oakland 27, Houston 7 |
| AFC div. playoffs | San Diego 20, Buffalo 14 |
| | Oakland 14, Cleveland 12 |
| AFC championship | Oakland 34, San Diego 27 |
| NFC 1st-rd. playoff | Dallas 34, Los Angeles 13 |
| NFC div. playoffs | Philadelphia 31, Minnesota 16 |
| | Dallas 30, Atlanta 27 |
| NFC championship | Philadelphia 20, Dallas 7 |

## 1981

| | |
|---|---|
| AFC 1st-rd. playoff | Buffalo 31, NY Jets 27 |
| AFC div. playoffs | San Diego 41, Miami 38 |
| | Cincinnati 28, Buffalo 21 |
| AFC championship | Cincinnati 27, San Diego 7 |
| NFC 1st-rd. playoff | NY Giants 27, Philadelphia 21 |
| NFC div. playoffs | Dallas 38, Tampa Bay 0 |
| | San Francisco 38, NY Giants 24 |
| NFC championship | San Francisco 28, Dallas 27 |

## 1982

| | |
|---|---|
| AFC 1st-rd. playoffs | Miami 28, New England 13 |
| | LA Raiders 27, Cleveland 10 |
| | NY Jets 44, Cincinnati 17 |
| | San Diego 31, Pittsburgh 28 |
| AFC div. playoffs | NY Jets 17, LA Raiders 14 |
| | Miami 34, San Diego 13 |
| AFC championship | Miami 14, NY Jets 0 |
| NFC 1st-rd. playoffs | Washington 31, Detroit 7 |
| | Green Bay 41, St Louis 16 |
| | Minnesota 30, Atlanta 24 |

**1982 *(Cont.)***

| | |
|---|---|
| NFC 1st-rd. *(cont.)* | Dallas 30, Tampa Bay 17 |
| NFCdiv. playoffs | Washington 21, Minnesota 7 |
| | Dallas 37, Green Bay 26 |
| NFC championship | Washington 31, Dallas 17 |

**1983**

| | |
|---|---|
| AFC 1st-rd. playoff | Seattle 31, Denver 7 |
| AFC div. playoffs | Seattle 27, Miami 20 |
| | LA Raiders 38, Pittsburgh 10 |
| AFC championship | LA Raiders 30, Seattle 14 |
| NFC 1st-rd. playoff | LA Rams 24, Dallas 17 |
| NFC div. playoffs | San Francisco 24, Detroit 23 |
| | Washington 51, LA Rams 7 |
| NFC championship | Washington 24, San Francisco 21 |

**1984**

| | |
|---|---|
| AFC 1st-rd. playoff | Seattle 13, LA Raiders 7 |
| AFC div. playoffs | Miami 31, Seattle 10 |
| | Pittsburgh 24, Denver 17 |
| AFC championship | Miami 45, Pittsburgh 28 |
| NFC 1st-rd. playoff | NY Giants 16, LA Rams 13 |
| NFC div. playoffs | San Francisco 21, NY Giants 10 |
| | Chicago 23, Washington 19 |
| NFC championship | San Francisco 23, Chicago 0 |

**1985**

| | |
|---|---|
| AFC 1st-rd. playoff | New England 26, NY Jets 14 |
| AFC div. playoffs | Miami 24, Cleveland 21 |
| | New England 27, LA Raiders 20 |
| AFC championship | New England 31, Miami 14 |
| NFC 1st-rd. playoff | NY Giants 17, San Francisco 3 |
| NFC div. playoffs | LA Rams 20, Dallas 0 |
| | Chicago 21, NY Giants 0 |
| NFC championship | Chicago 24, LA Rams 0 |

**1986**

| | |
|---|---|
| AFC 1st-rd. playoff | NY Jets 35, Kansas City 15 |
| AFC div. playoffs | Cleveland 23, NY Jets 20 |
| | Denver 22, New England 17 |
| AFC championship | Denver 23, Cleveland 20 |
| NFC 1st-rd. playoff | Washington 19, LA Rams 7 |
| NFC div playoffs | Washington 27, Chicago 13 |
| | NY Giants 49, San Francisco 3 |
| NFC championship | NY Giants 17, Washington 0 |

**1987**

| | |
|---|---|
| AFC div. playoffs | Cleveland 38, Indianapolis 21 |
| | Denver 34, Houston 10 |
| AFC championship | Denver 38, Cleveland 33 |
| NFC 1st-rd. playoff | Minnesota 44, New Orleans 10 |
| NFC div playoffs | Minnesota 36, San Francisco 24 |
| | Washington 21, Chicago 17 |
| NFC championship | Washington 17, Minnesota 10 |

**1988**

| | |
|---|---|
| AFC 1st-rd. playoff | Houston 24, Cleveland 23 |
| AFC div. playoffs | Cincinnati 21, Seattle 13 |
| | Buffalo 17, Houston 10 |
| AFC championship | Cincinnati 21, Buffalo 10 |
| NFC 1st-rd. playoff | Minnesota 28, LA Rams 17 |
| NFC div. playoffs | Chicago 20, Philadelphia 12 |
| | San Francisco 34, Minnesota 9 |
| NFC championship | San Francisco 28, Chicago 3 |

**1989**

| | |
|---|---|
| AFC 1st-rd. playoff | Pittsburgh 26, Houston 23 |
| AFC div. playoffs | Cleveland 34, Buffalo 30 |

**1989 *(Cont.)***

| | |
|---|---|
| AFC div. playoffs *(cont.)* | Denver 24, Pittsburgh 23 |
| AFC championship | Denver 37, Cleveland 21 |
| NFC 1st-rd. playoff | LA Rams 21, Philadelphia 7 |
| NFC div. playoffs | LA Rams 19, NY Giants 13 |
| | San Francisco 41, Minnesota 13 |
| NFC championship | San Francisco 30, LA Rams 3 |

**1990**

| | |
|---|---|
| AFC 1st-rd. playoffs | Miami 17, Kansas City 16 |
| | Cincinnati 41, Houston 14 |
| AFC div. playoffs | Buffalo 44, Miami 34 |
| | LA Raiders 20, Cincinnati 10 |
| AFC championship | Buffalo 51, LA Raiders 3 |
| NFC 1st-rd. playoffs | Chicago 16, New Orleans 6 |
| | Washington 20, Philadelphia 6 |
| NFC div. playoffs | NY Giants 31, Chicago 3 |
| | San Francisco 28, Washington 10 |
| NFC championship | NY Giants 15, San Francisco 13 |

**1991**

| | |
|---|---|
| AFC 1st-rd. playoffs | Houston 17, NY Jets 10 |
| | Kansas City 10, LA Raiders 6 |
| AFC div. playoffs | Denver 26, Houston 24 |
| | Buffalo 37, Kansas City 14 |
| AFC championship | Buffalo 10, Denver 7 |
| NFC 1st-rd. playoffs | Atlanta 27, New Orleans 20 |
| | Dallas 17, Chicago 13 |
| NFC div. playoffs | Washington 24, Atlanta 7 |
| | Detroit 38, Dallas 6 |
| NFC championship | Washington 41, Detroit 10 |

**1992**

| | |
|---|---|
| AFC 1st-rd. playoffs | San Diego 17, Kansas City 0 |
| | Buffalo 41, Houston 38 (OT) |
| AFC div. playoffs | Buffalo 24, Pittsburgh 3 |
| | Miami 31, San Diego 0 |
| AFC championship | Buffalo 29, Miami 10 |
| NFC 1st-rd. playoffs | Washington 24, Minnesota 7 |
| | Philadelphia 36, New Orleans 20 |
| NFC div. playoffs | San Francisco 20, Washington 13 |
| | Dallas 34, Philadelphia 10 |
| NFC championship | Dallas 30, San Francisco 20 |

**1993**

| | |
|---|---|
| AFC 1st-rd. playoffs | LA Raiders 42, Denver 24 |
| | Kansas City 27. Pittsburgh 24 (OT) |
| AFC div. playoffs | Buffalo 29, LA Raiders 23 |
| | Kansas City 28, Houston 20 |
| AFC championship | Buffalo 30, Kansas City 13 |
| NFC 1st-rd. playoffs | NY Giants 17, Minnesota 10 |
| | Green Bay 28, Detroit 24 |
| NFC div. playoffs | San Francisco 44, NY Giants 3 |
| | Dallas 27, Green Bay 17 |
| NFC championship | Dallas 38, San Francisco 21 |

**1994**

| | |
|---|---|
| AFC 1st-rd. playoffs | Miami 27, Kansas City 17 |
| | Cleveland 20, New England 13 |
| AFC div. playoffs | San Diego 22, Miami 21 |
| | Pittsburgh 29, Cleveland 9 |
| AFC championship | San Diego 17, Pittsburgh 13 |
| NFC 1st-rd. playoffs | Green Bay 16, Detroit 12 |
| | Chicago 35, Minnesota 18 |
| NFC div. playoffs | Dallas 35, Green Bay 9 |
| | San Francisco 44, Chicago 15 |
| NFC championship | San Francisco 38, Dallas 28 |

## Career Leaders

### Scoring

| | Yrs | TD | FG | PAT | Pts |
|---|---|---|---|---|---|
| George Blanda | 26 | 9 | 335 | 943 | 2002 |
| Jan Stenerud | 19 | 0 | 373 | 580 | 1699 |
| †Nick Lowery | 16 | 0 | 349 | 512 | 1559 |
| Pat Leahy | 18 | 0 | 304 | 558 | 1470 |
| Jim Turner | 16 | 1 | 304 | 521 | 1439 |
| Mark Moseley | 16 | 0 | 300 | 482 | 1382 |
| Jim Bakken | 17 | 0 | 282 | 534 | 1380 |
| Fred Cox | 15 | 0 | 282 | 519 | 1365 |
| †Eddie Murray | 17 | 0 | 298 | 465 | 1359 |
| Lou Groza | 17 | 1 | 234 | 641 | 1349 |
| †Gary Anderson | 13 | 0 | 309 | 416 | 1343 |
| †Matt Bahr | 17 | 0 | 277 | 495 | 1326 |
| †Morten Andersen | 13 | 0 | 302 | 412 | 1318 |
| Jim Breech | 14 | 0 | 243 | 517 | 1246 |
| Chris Bahr | 14 | 0 | 241 | 490 | 1213 |
| †Norm Johnson | 13 | 0 | 243 | 476 | 1205 |
| Gino Cappelletti | 11 | 42 | 176 | 350 | 1130 |
| Ray Wersching | 15 | 0 | 222 | 456 | 1122 |
| Don Cockroft | 13 | 0 | 216 | 432 | 1080 |
| Garo Yepremian | 14 | 0 | 210 | 444 | 1074 |

Cappelletti's total includes four two-point conversions.

### Rushing

| | Yrs | Att | Yds | Avg | Lg | TD |
|---|---|---|---|---|---|---|
| Walter Payton | 13 | 3,838 | 16,726 | 4.4 | 76 | 110 |
| Eric Dickerson | 13 | 2,996 | 13,259 | 4.4 | 85 | 90 |
| Tony Dorsett | 12 | 2,936 | 12,739 | 4.3 | 99 | 77 |
| Jim Brown | 9 | 2,359 | 12,312 | 5.2 | 80 | 106 |
| Franco Harris | 13 | 2,949 | 12,120 | 4.1 | 75 | 91 |
| John Riggins | 14 | 2,916 | 11,352 | 3.9 | 66 | 104 |
| O.J. Simpson | 11 | 2,404 | 11,236 | 4.7 | 94 | 61 |
| Ottis Anderson | 16 | 2,562 | 10,273 | 4.0 | 76 | 81 |
| †Marcus Allen | 13 | 2,485 | 10,018 | 4.0 | 61 | 98 |
| Earl Campbell | 8 | 2,187 | 9,407 | 4.3 | 81 | 74 |
| †Thurman Thomas | 7 | 2,018 | 8,724 | 4.3 | 80 | 48 |
| †Barry Sanders | 6 | 1,763 | 8,672 | 4.9 | 85 | 62 |
| Jim Taylor | 10 | 1,941 | 8,597 | 4.4 | 84 | 83 |
| Joe Perry | 14 | 1,737 | 8,378 | 4.8 | 78 | 53 |
| Roger Craig | 11 | 1,991 | 8,189 | 4.1 | 71 | 56 |
| Gerald Riggs | 10 | 1,989 | 8,188 | 4.2 | 58 | 69 |
| Larry Csonka | 11 | 1,891 | 8,081 | 4.3 | 54 | 64 |
| Freeman McNeil | 12 | 1,798 | 8,074 | 4.5 | 69 | 38 |
| †Herschel Walker | 11 | 1,907 | 7,996 | 4.2 | 91 | 59 |
| James Brooks | 12 | 1,685 | 7,962 | 4.7 | 65 | 49 |

## Touchdowns

| | Yrs | Rush | Pass Rec | Ret | Total TD |
|---|---|---|---|---|---|
| †Jerry Rice | 10 | 8 | 131 | 0 | 139 |
| Jim Brown | 9 | 106 | 20 | 0 | 126 |
| Walter Payton | 13 | 110 | 15 | 0 | 125 |
| †Marcus Allen | 13 | 98 | 21 | 1 | 120 |
| John Riggins | 14 | 104 | 12 | 0 | 116 |
| Lenny Moore | 12 | 63 | 48 | 2 | 113 |
| Don Hutson | 11 | 3 | 99 | 3 | 105 |
| Steve Largent | 14 | 1 | 100 | 0 | 101 |
| Franco Harris | 13 | 91 | 9 | 0 | 100 |
| Eric Dickerson | 13 | 90 | 6 | 0 | 96 |

| | Yrs | Rush | Pass Rec | Ret | Total TD |
|---|---|---|---|---|---|
| Jim Taylor | 10 | 83 | 10 | 0 | 93 |
| Tony Dorsett | 12 | 77 | 13 | 1 | 91 |
| Bobby Mitchell | 11 | 18 | 65 | 8 | 91 |
| Leroy Kelly | 10 | 74 | 13 | 3 | 90 |
| Charley Taylor | 13 | 11 | 79 | 0 | 90 |
| Don Maynard | 15 | 0 | 88 | 0 | 88 |
| Lance Alworth | 11 | 2 | 85 | 0 | 87 |
| Paul Warfield | 13 | 1 | 85 | 0 | 86 |
| Ottis Anderson | 13 | 81 | 5 | 0 | 86 |
| Tommy McDonald | 12 | 0 | 84 | 1 | 85 |
| Mark Clayton | 11 | 0 | 85 | 0 | 85 |

## Longest Plays

| RUSHING | Opponent | Year | Yds |
|---|---|---|---|
| Tony Dorsett, Dall | Minn | 1983 | 99 |
| Andy Uram, GB | Chi Cards | 1939 | 97 |
| Bob Gage, Pitt | Chi | 1949 | 97 |
| Jim Spitival, Balt | GB | 1950 | 96 |
| Bob Hoernschemeyer, Det | NY Yanks | 1950 | 96 |

| PASSING | Opponent | Year | Yds |
|---|---|---|---|
| Frank Filchock to Andy Farkas, Washington | Pitt | 1939 | 99 |
| George Izo to Bobby Mitchell, Washington | Cle | 1963 | 99 |
| Karl Sweetan to Pat Studstill, Detroit | Balt | 1966 | 99 |
| Sonny Jurgensen to Gerry Allen, Washington | Chi | 1968 | 99 |
| Jim Plunkett to Cliff Branch, LA Raiders | Wash | 1983 | 99 |
| Ron Jaworski to Mike Quick, Philadelphia | Atl | 1985 | 99 |

| FIELD GOALS | Opponent | Year | Yds |
|---|---|---|---|
| Tom Dempsey, NO | Det | 1970 | 63 |
| Steve Cox, Cle | Cin | 1984 | 60 |
| Morten Andersen, NO | Chi | 1991 | 60 |

| PUNTS | Opponent | Year | Yds |
|---|---|---|---|
| Steve O'Neal, NY Jets | Den | 1969 | 98 |
| Joe Lintzenich, Chi | NY Giants | 1931 | 94 |
| Shawn McCarthy, NE | Buff | 1991 | 93 |
| Randall Cunningham, Phi | NY Giants | 1989 | 91 |

### THEY SAID IT

*Buddy Ryan, Arizona Cardinal coach, on the salary options he gave wide receiver Gary Clark: "It's either a 30% cut or a 100% cut."*

† Active player

## Career Leaders (Cont.)

### Combined Yards Gained

| | Yrs | Total | Rush | Rec | Int Ret | Punt Ret | Kickoff Ret | Fum Ret |
|---|---|---|---|---|---|---|---|---|
| Walter Payton | 13 | 21,803 | 16,726 | 4,538 | 0 | 0 | 539 | 0 |
| Tony Dorsett | 12 | 16,326 | 12,739 | 3,554 | 0 | 0 | 0 | 33 |
| Jim Brown | 9 | 15,459 | 12,312 | 2,499 | 0 | 0 | 648 | 0 |
| Eric Dickerson | 13 | 15,396 | 13,259 | 2,137 | 0 | 0 | 0 | 15 |
| †Marcus Allen | 13 | 14,863 | 10,018 | 4,845 | 0 | 0 | 0 | 0 |
| James Brooks | 12 | 14,644 | 7,962 | 3,621 | 0 | 565 | 2,762 | 0 |
| Franco Harris | 13 | 14,622 | 12,120 | 2,287 | 0 | 0 | 233 | -18 |
| O.J. Simpson | 11 | 14,368 | 11,236 | 2,142 | 0 | 0 | 990 | 0 |
| James Lofton | 16 | 14,234 | 246 | 13,988 | 0 | 0 | 0 | 27 |
| Bobby Mitchell | 11 | 14,078 | 2,735 | 7,954 | 0 | 699 | 2,690 | 0 |
| †Jerry Rice | 10 | 13,986 | 711 | 13,275 | 0 | 0 | 0 | 0 |
| John Riggins | 14 | 13,435 | 11,352 | 2,090 | 0 | 0 | 0 | -7 |
| Steve Largent | 14 | 13,396 | 83 | 13,089 | 0 | 68 | 156 | 0 |
| Ottis Anderson | 14 | 13,364 | 10,273 | 3,062 | 0 | 0 | 0 | 29 |
| Greg Pruitt | 12 | 13,262 | 5,672 | 3,069 | 0 | 2,007 | 2,514 | 0 |
| Roger Craig | 11 | 13,100 | 8,189 | 4,911 | 0 | 0 | 0 | 0 |
| †Art Monk | 15 | 12,939 | 332 | 12,607 | 0 | 0 | 0 | 0 |
| Ollie Matson | 14 | 12,884 | 5,173 | 3,285 | 51 | 595 | 3,746 | 34 |
| Tim Brown | 10 | 12,684 | 3,862 | 3,399 | 0 | 639 | 4,781 | 3 |
| Lenny Moore | 12 | 12,451 | 5,174 | 6,039 | 0 | 56 | 1,180 | 2 |

### *Passing

| | Yrs | Att | Comp | Pct Comp | Yds | Avg Gain | TD | Pct TD | Int | Pct Int | Rating Pts |
|---|---|---|---|---|---|---|---|---|---|---|---|
| †Steve Young | 10 | 2,429 | 1,546 | 63.7 | 19,869 | 8.18 | 140 | 5.8 | 68 | 2.8 | 96.9 |
| Joe Montana | 15 | 5,391 | 3,409 | 63.2 | 40,551 | 7.52 | 273 | 5.1 | 139 | 2.6 | 92.3 |
| †Dan Marino | 12 | 6,049 | 3,604 | 59.6 | 45,173 | 7.47 | 328 | 5.4 | 185 | 3.1 | 88.0 |
| †Jim Kelly | 9 | 3,942 | 2,397 | 60.8 | 29,527 | 7.49 | 201 | 5.1 | 143 | 3.6 | 86.0 |
| Roger Staubach | 11 | 2,958 | 1,685 | 57.0 | 22,700 | 7.67 | 153 | 5.2 | 109 | 3.7 | 83.4 |
| †Dave Krieg | 15 | 4,390 | 2,562 | 58.4 | 32,114 | 7.32 | 231 | 5.3 | 166 | 3.8 | 83.1 |
| Neil Lomax | 8 | 3,153 | 1,817 | 57.6 | 22,771 | 7.22 | 136 | 4.3 | 90 | 2.9 | 82.7 |
| Sonny Jurgensen | 18 | 4,262 | 2,433 | 57.1 | 32,224 | 7.56 | 255 | 6.0 | 189 | 4.4 | 82.6 |
| Len Dawson | 19 | 3,741 | 2,136 | 57.1 | 28,711 | 7.67 | 239 | 6.4 | 183 | 4.9 | 82.6 |
| †Bernie Kosar | 10 | 3,225 | 1,896 | 58.8 | 22,394 | 6.94 | 120 | 3.7 | 82 | 2.5 | 81.9 |
| Ken Anderson | 16 | 4,475 | 2,654 | 59.3 | 32,838 | 7.34 | 197 | 4.4 | 160 | 3.6 | 81.9 |
| †Brett Favre | 4 | 1,580 | 983 | 62.2 | 10,412 | 6.59 | 70 | 4.4 | 53 | 3.4 | 81.9 |
| Danny White | 13 | 2,950 | 1,761 | 59.7 | 21,959 | 7.44 | 155 | 5.3 | 132 | 4.5 | 81.7 |
| †Troy Aikman | 6 | 2,281 | 1,424 | 62.4 | 16,303 | 7.15 | 82 | 3.6 | 78 | 3.4 | 81.7 |
| †Boomer Esiason | 11 | 4,291 | 2,440 | 56.9 | 31,874 | 7.43 | 207 | 4.8 | 153 | 3.6 | 81.5 |
| Ken O'Brien | 10 | 3,602 | 2,110 | 58.6 | 25,094 | 6.97 | 128 | 3.6 | 98 | 2.7 | 80.7 |
| †Warren Moon | 11 | 5,147 | 3,003 | 58.4 | 37,949 | 7.37 | 214 | 4.2 | 185 | 3.6 | 80.5 |
| Bart Starr | 16 | 3,149 | 1,808 | 57.4 | 24,718 | 7.85 | 152 | 4.8 | 138 | 4.4 | 80.5 |
| Fran Tarkenton | 18 | 6,467 | 3,686 | 57.0 | 47,003 | 7.27 | 342 | 5.3 | 266 | 4.1 | 80.4 |
| Dan Fouts | 15 | 5,604 | 3,297 | 58.8 | 43,040 | 7.68 | 254 | 4.5 | 242 | 4.3 | 80.2 |

*1,500 or more attempts. The passing ratings are based on performance standards established for completion percentage, interception percentage, touchdown percentage, and average gain. Passers are allocated points according to how their marks compare with those standards.

### Receiving

| | Yrs | No. | Yds | Avg | Lg | TD | | Yrs | No. | Yds | Avg | Lg | TD |
|---|---|---|---|---|---|---|---|---|---|---|---|---|---|
| †Art Monk | 15 | 934 | 12,607 | 13.5 | 79 | 68 | Drew Hill | 14 | 634 | 9,831 | 15.5 | 81 | 60 |
| †Jerry Rice | 10 | 820 | 13,275 | 16.2 | 96 | 131 | Don Maynard | 15 | 633 | 11,834 | 18.7 | 87 | 88 |
| Steve Largent | 14 | 819 | 13,089 | 16.0 | 74 | 100 | Raymond Berry | 13 | 631 | 9,275 | 14.7 | 70 | 68 |
| James Lofton | 16 | 763 | 13,988 | 18.3 | 80 | 75 | †Sterling Sharpe | 7 | 595 | 8,134 | 13.7 | 76 | 65 |
| Charlie Joiner | 18 | 750 | 12,146 | 16.2 | 87 | 65 | Harold Carmichael | 14 | 590 | 8,985 | 15.2 | 85 | 79 |
| †Andre Reed | 10 | 676 | 9,536 | 14.1 | 83 | 66 | Fred Biletnikoff | 14 | 589 | 8,974 | 15.2 | 82 | 76 |
| †Henry Ellard | 12 | 667 | 11,158 | 16.7 | 81 | 54 | Mark Clayton | 11 | 582 | 8,974 | 15.4 | 78 | 85 |
| †Gary Clark | 10 | 662 | 10,331 | 15.6 | 84 | 63 | Harold Jackson | 16 | 579 | 10,372 | 17.9 | 79 | 76 |
| Ozzie Newsome | 13 | 662 | 7,980 | 12.1 | 74 | 47 | Lionel Taylor | 10 | 567 | 7,195 | 12.7 | 80 | 45 |
| Charley Taylor | 13 | 649 | 9,110 | 14.0 | 88 | 79 | Roger Craig | 11 | 566 | 4,911 | 8.7 | 73 | 17 |

† Active player

## Career Leaders *(Cont.)*

### Interceptions

| | Yrs | No. | Yds | Avg | Lg | TD |
|---|---|---|---|---|---|---|
| Paul Krause | 16 | 81 | 1185 | 14.6 | 81 | 3 |
| Emlen Tunnell | 14 | 79 | 1282 | 16.2 | 55 | 4 |
| Dick (Night Train) Lane | 14 | 68 | 1207 | 17.8 | 80 | 5 |
| Ken Riley | 15 | 65 | 596 | 9.2 | 66 | 5 |
| †Ronnie Lott | 14 | 63 | 730 | 11.3 | 83 | 5 |

### Punting

| | Yrs | No. | Yds | Avg | Lg | Blk |
|---|---|---|---|---|---|---|
| Sammy Baugh | 16 | 338 | 15,245 | 45.1 | 85 | 9 |
| Tommy Davis | 11 | 511 | 22,833 | 44.7 | 82 | 2 |
| Yale Lary | 11 | 503 | 22,279 | 44.3 | 74 | 4 |
| †Rohn Stark | 13 | 985 | 43,152 | 43.8 | 72 | 7 |
| Horace Gillom | 7 | 385 | 16,872 | 43.8 | 80 | 5 |

†Active player

### Punt Returns

| | Yrs | No. | Yds | Avg | Lg | TD |
|---|---|---|---|---|---|---|
| George McAfee | 8 | 112 | 1431 | 12.8 | 74 | 2 |
| Jack Christiansen | 8 | 85 | 1084 | 12.8 | 89 | 8 |
| Claude Gibson | 5 | 110 | 1381 | 12.6 | 85 | 3 |
| Bill Dudley | 9 | 124 | 1515 | 12.2 | 96 | 3 |
| Rick Upchurch | 9 | 248 | 3008 | 12.1 | 92 | 8 |

### Kickoff Returns

| | Yrs | No. | Yds | Avg | Lg | TD |
|---|---|---|---|---|---|---|
| Gale Sayers | 7 | 91 | 2781 | 30.6 | 103 | 6 |
| Lynn Chandnois | 7 | 92 | 2720 | 29.6 | 93 | 3 |
| Abe Woodson | 9 | 193 | 5538 | 28.7 | 105 | 5 |
| Claude (Buddy) Young | 6 | 90 | 2514 | 27.9 | 104 | 2 |
| Travis Williams | 5 | 102 | 2801 | 27.5 | 105 | 6 |

## Single-Season Leaders

### Scoring

#### POINTS

| | Year | TD | PAT | FG | Pts |
|---|---|---|---|---|---|
| Paul Hornung, GB | 1960 | 15 | 41 | 15 | 176 |
| Mark Moseley, Wash | 1983 | 0 | 62 | 33 | 161 |
| Gino Cappelletti, Bos | 1964 | 7 | 38 | 25 | 155 |
| Chip Lohmiller, Wash | 1991 | 0 | 56 | 31 | 149 |
| Gino Cappelletti, Bos | 1961 | 8 | 48 | 17 | 147 |
| Paul Hornung, GB | 1961 | 10 | 41 | 15 | 146 |
| Jim Turner, NY Jets | 1968 | 0 | 43 | 34 | 145 |
| John Riggins, Wash | 1983 | 24 | 0 | 0 | 144 |
| Kevin Butler, Chi | 1985 | 0 | 51 | 31 | 144 |
| Tony Franklin, NE | 1986 | 0 | 44 | 32 | 140 |

Note: Cappelletti's 1964 total includes a two-point conversion.

#### TOUCHDOWNS

| | Year | Rush | Rec | Ret | Total |
|---|---|---|---|---|---|
| John Riggins, Wash | 1983 | 24 | 0 | 0 | 24 |
| O.J. Simpson, Buff | 1975 | 16 | 7 | 0 | 23 |
| Jerry Rice, SF | 1987 | 1 | 22 | 0 | 23 |
| Gale Sayers, Chi | 1965 | 14 | 6 | 2 | 22 |
| Emmitt Smith, Dall | 1994 | 21 | 1 | 0 | 22 |

#### FIELD GOALS

| | Year | Att | No. |
|---|---|---|---|
| Jeff Jaeger, LA Raiders | 1993 | 44 | 35 |
| Ali Haji-Sheikh, NY Giants | 1983 | 42 | 35 |
| Jim Turner, NY Jets | 1968 | 46 | 34 |
| Jason Hanson, Det | 1993 | 43 | 34 |
| John Carney, SD | 1994 | 38 | 34 |
| Fuad Reveiz, Minn | 1994 | 39 | 34 |

### Rushing

#### YARDS GAINED

| | Year | Att | Yds | Avg |
|---|---|---|---|---|
| Eric Dickerson, LA Rams | 1984 | 379 | 2105 | 5.6 |
| O.J. Simpson, Buff | 1973 | 332 | 2003 | 6.0 |
| Earl Campbell, Hou | 1980 | 373 | 1934 | 5.2 |
| Jim Brown, Clev | 1963 | 291 | 1883 | 6.4 |
| Barry Sanders, Det | 1994 | 331 | 1883 | 5.7 |
| Walter Payton, Chi | 1977 | 339 | 1852 | 5.5 |
| Eric Dickerson, LA Rams | 1986 | 404 | 1821 | 4.5 |
| O.J. Simpson, Buff | 1975 | 329 | 1817 | 5.5 |
| Eric Dickerson, LA Rams | 1983 | 390 | 1808 | 4.6 |
| Marcus Allen, LA Raiders | 1985 | 390 | 1759 | 4.6 |
| Gerald Riggs, Atl | 1985 | 397 | 1719 | 4.3 |
| Emmitt Smith, Dall | 1992 | 373 | 1713 | 4.6 |

#### AVERAGE GAIN

| | Year | Avg |
|---|---|---|
| Beattie Feathers, Chi | 1934 | 8.44 |
| Randall Cunningham, Phil | 1990 | 7.98 |
| Bobby Douglass, Chi | 1972 | 6.87 |

#### TOUCHDOWNS

| | Year | No. |
|---|---|---|
| John Riggins, Wash | 1983 | 24 |
| Emmitt Smith, Dall | 1994 | 22 |
| Joe Morris, NY Giants | 1985 | 21 |
| Jim Taylor, GB | 1962 | 19 |
| Earl Campbell, Hou | 1979 | 19 |
| Chuck Muncie, SD | 1981 | 19 |
| Emmitt Smith, Dall | 1992 | 18 |

## Single-Season Leaders (*Cont.*)

### Passing

**YARDS GAINED**

| | Year | Att | Comp | Pct | Yds |
|---|---|---|---|---|---|
| Dan Marino, Mia | 1984 | 564 | 362 | 64.2 | 5084 |
| Dan Fouts, SD | 1981 | 609 | 360 | 59.1 | 4802 |
| Dan Marino, Mia | 1986 | 623 | 378 | 60.7 | 4746 |
| Dan Fouts, SD | 1980 | 589 | 348 | 59.1 | 4715 |
| Warren Moon, Hou | 1991 | 655 | 404 | 61.7 | 4690 |
| Warren Moon, Hou | 1990 | 584 | 362 | 62.0 | 4689 |
| Neil Lomax, StL | 1984 | 560 | 345 | 61.6 | 4614 |
| Drew Bledsoe, NE | 1994 | 691 | 400 | 57.9 | 4555 |
| Lynn Dickey, GB | 1983 | 484 | 289 | 59.7 | 4458 |
| Dan Marino, Mia | 1994 | 615 | 385 | 62.6 | 4453 |
| Dan Marino, Mia | 1988 | 606 | 354 | 58.4 | 4434 |
| Bill Kenney, KC | 1983 | 603 | 346 | 57.4 | 4348 |

**PASS RATING**

| | Year | Rat. |
|---|---|---|
| Steve Young, SF | 1994 | 112.8 |
| Joe Montana, SF | 1989 | 112.4 |
| Milt Plum, Clev | 1960 | 110.4 |
| Sammy Baugh, Wash | 1945 | 109.9 |
| Dan Marino, Mia | 1984 | 108.9 |

**TOUCHDOWNS**

| | Year | No. |
|---|---|---|
| Dan Marino, Mia | 1984 | 48 |
| Dan Marino, Mia | 1986 | 44 |
| George Blanda, Hou | 1961 | 36 |
| Y. A. Tittle, NY Giants | 1963 | 36 |
| Steve Young, SF | 1994 | 35 |

### Receiving

**RECEPTIONS**

| | Year | No. | Yds |
|---|---|---|---|
| Cris Carter, Minn | 1994 | 122 | 1256 |
| Sterling Sharpe, GB | 1993 | 112 | 1274 |
| Jerry Rice, SF | 1994 | 112 | 1499 |
| Terance Mathis, Atl | 1994 | 111 | 1342 |
| Sterling Sharpe, GB | 1992 | 108 | 1461 |
| Art Monk, Wash | 1984 | 106 | 1372 |
| Charley Hennigan, Hou | 1964 | 101 | 1546 |
| Lionel Taylor, Den | 1961 | 100 | 1176 |
| Jerry Rice, SF | 1990 | 100 | 1502 |
| Haywood Jeffires, Hou | 1991 | 100 | 1181 |
| Jerry Rice, SF | 1993 | 98 | 1503 |
| Ben Coates, NE | 1994 | 96 | 1174 |
| Todd Christensen, Rai | 1986 | 95 | 1153 |

**YARDS GAINED**

| | Year | Yds |
|---|---|---|
| Charley Hennigan, Hou | 1961 | 1746 |
| Lance Alworth, SD | 1965 | 1602 |
| Jerry Rice, SF | 1986 | 1570 |
| Roy Green, StL | 1984 | 1555 |

**TOUCHDOWNS**

| | Year | No. |
|---|---|---|
| Jerry Rice, SF | 1987 | 22 |
| Mark Clayton, Mia | 1984 | 18 |
| Sterling Sharpe, GB | 1994 | 18 |
| Don Hutson, GB | 1942 | 17 |
| Elroy (Crazylegs) Hirsch, LA Rams | 1951 | 17 |
| Bill Groman, Hou | 1961 | 17 |
| Jerry Rice, SF | 1989 | 17 |

### All-Purpose Yards

| | Year | Run | Rec | Ret | Total |
|---|---|---|---|---|---|
| Lionel James, SD | 1985 | 516 | 1027 | 992 | 2535 |
| Terry Metcalf, StL | 1975 | 816 | 378 | 1268 | 2462 |
| Mack Herron, NE | 1974 | 824 | 474 | 1146 | 2444 |
| Gale Sayers, Chi | 1966 | 1231 | 447 | 762 | 2440 |
| Timmy Brown, Phil | 1963 | 841 | 487 | 1100 | 2428 |
| Tim Brown, Rai | 1988 | 50 | 725 | 1542 | 2317 |
| Marcus Allen, Rai | 1985 | 1759 | 555 | −6 | 2308 |
| Timmy Brown, Phil | 1962 | 545 | 849 | 912 | 2306 |
| Gale Sayers, Chi | 1965 | 867 | 507 | 898 | 2272 |
| Eric Dickerson, LA Rams | 1984 | 2105 | 139 | 15 | 2259 |
| O.J. Simpson, Buff | 1975 | 1817 | 426 | 0 | 2243 |

### Punting

| | Year | No. | Yds | Avg |
|---|---|---|---|---|
| Sammy Baugh, Wash | 1940 | 35 | 1799 | 51.4 |
| Yale Lary, Det | 1963 | 35 | 1713 | 48.9 |
| Sammy Baugh, Wash | 1941 | 30 | 1462 | 48.7 |
| Yale Lary, Det | 1961 | 52 | 2516 | 48.4 |
| Sammy Baugh, Wash | 1942 | 37 | 1783 | 48.2 |

### Sacks

| | Year | No. |
|---|---|---|
| Mark Gastineau, NY Jets | 1984 | 22 |
| Reggie White, Phil | 1987 | 21 |
| Chris Doleman, Minn | 1989 | 21 |
| Lawrence Taylor, NY Giants | 1986 | 20.5 |

### Interceptions

| | Year | No. |
|---|---|---|
| Dick (Night Train) Lane, LA Rams | 1952 | 14 |
| Dan Sandifer, Wash | 1948 | 13 |
| Spec Sanders, NY Yanks | 1950 | 13 |
| Lester Hayes, Oak | 1980 | 13 |

### Kickoff Returns

| | Year | Avg |
|---|---|---|
| Travis Williams, GB | 1967 | 41.1 |
| Gale Sayers, Chi | 1967 | 37.7 |
| Ollie Matson, Chi Cardinals | 1958 | 35.5 |
| Jim Duncan, Balt | 1970 | 35.4 |
| Lynn Chandnois, Pitt | 1952 | 35.2 |

### Punt Returns

| | Year | Avg |
|---|---|---|
| Herb Rich, Balt | 1950 | 23.0 |
| Jack Christiansen, Det | 1952 | 21.5 |
| Dick Christy, NY Titans | 1961 | 21.3 |
| Bob Hayes, Dall | 1968 | 20.8 |

## Single-Game Leaders
### Scoring

#### POINTS

| | Date | Pts |
|---|---|---|
| Ernie Nevers, Cards vs Bears | 11-28-29 | 40 |
| Dub Jones, Clev vs Chi Bears | 11-25-51 | 36 |
| Gale Sayers, Chi Bears vs SF | 12-12-65 | 36 |
| Paul Hornung, GB vs Balt | 10-8-61 | 33 |

On Thanksgiving Day, 1929, Nevers scored all the Cardinals' points on six rushing TDs and four PATs. The Cards defeated Red Grange and the Bears, 40-6. Jones and Sayers each rushed for four touchdowns and scored two more on returns in their teams' victories. Hornung scored four touchdowns and kicked 6 PATs and a field goal in a 45-7 win over the Colts.

#### FIELD GOALS

| | Date | No. |
|---|---|---|
| Jim Bakken, StL vs Pitt | 9-24-67 | 7 |
| Rich Karlis, Minn vs LA Rams | 11-5-89 | 7 |

Eight players tied with 6 FGs each.

Bakken was 7 for 9, Karlis 7 for 7.

#### TOUCHDOWNS

| | Date | No. |
|---|---|---|
| Ernie Nevers, Cards vs Bears | 11-28-29 | 6 |
| Dub Jones, Clev vs Chi Bears | 11-25-51 | 6 |
| Gale Sayers, Chi vs SF | 12-12-65 | 6 |
| Bob Shaw, Chi Cards vs Balt | 10-2-50 | 5 |
| Jim Brown, Clev vs Balt | 11-1-59 | 5 |
| Abner Haynes, Dall Texans vs Oak | 11-26-61 | 5 |
| Billy Cannon, Hous vs NY Titans | 12-10-61 | 5 |
| Cookie Gilchrist, Buff vs NY Jets | 12-8-63 | 5 |
| Paul Hornung, GB vs Balt | 12-12-65 | 5 |
| Kellen Winslow, SD vs Oak | 11-22-81 | 5 |
| Jerry Rice, SF vs Atl | 10-14-90 | 5 |

### Rushing

#### YARDS GAINED

| | Date | Yds |
|---|---|---|
| Walter Payton, Chi vs Minn | 11-20-77 | 275 |
| O.J. Simpson, Buff vs Det | 11-25-76 | 273 |
| O.J. Simpson, Buff vs NE | 9-16-73 | 250 |
| Willie Ellison, LA Rams vs NO | 12-5-71 | 247 |
| Cookie Gilchrist, Buff vs NY Jets | 12-8-63 | 243 |

#### CARRIES

| | Date | No. |
|---|---|---|
| Jamie Morris, Wash vs Cin | 12-17-88 | 45 |
| Butch Woolfolk, NY Giants vs Phil | 11-20-83 | 43 |
| James Wilder, TB vs GB | 9-30-84 | 43 |
| James Wilder, TB vs Pitt | 10-30-83 | 42 |
| Franco Harris, Pitt vs Cin | 10-17-76 | 41 |
| Gerald Riggs, Atl vs LA Rams | 11-17-85 | 41 |

#### TOUCHDOWNS

| | Date | No. |
|---|---|---|
| Ernie Nevers, Cards vs Bears | 11-28-29 | 6 |
| Jim Brown, Clev vs Balt | 11-1-59 | 5 |
| Cookie Gilchrist, Buff vs NY Jets | 12-8-63 | 5 |

### Passing

#### YARDS GAINED

| | Date | Yds |
|---|---|---|
| Norm Van Brocklin, LA vs NY Yanks | 9-28-51 | 554 |
| Warren Moon, Hou vs KC | 12-16-90 | 527 |
| Dan Marino, Mia vs NY Jets | 10-23-88 | 521 |
| Phil Simms, NY Giants vs Cin | 10-13-85 | 513 |
| Vince Ferragamo, LA Rams vs Chi | 12-26-82 | 509 |
| Y. A. Tittle, NY Giants vs Wash | 10-28-62 | 505 |

#### COMPLETIONS

| | Date | No. |
|---|---|---|
| Drew Bledsoe, NE vs Minn | 11-13-94 | 45 |
| Richard Todd, NY Jets vs SF | 9-21-80 | 42 |
| Warren Moon, Hou vs Dall | 11-10-91 | 41 |
| Ken Anderson, Cin vs SD | 12-20-82 | 40 |
| Phil Simms, NY Giants vs Cin | 10-13-85 | 40 |
| Dan Marino, Mia vs Buff | 11-16-86 | 39 |

Two tied with 38

#### TOUCHDOWNS

| | Date | No. |
|---|---|---|
| Sid Luckman, Chi Bears vs NY Giants | 11-14-43 | 7 |
| Adrian Burk, Phil vs Wash | 10-17-54 | 7 |
| George Blanda, Hou vs NY Titans | 11-19-61 | 7 |
| Y. A. Tittle, NY Giants vs Wash | 10-28-62 | 7 |
| Joe Kapp, Minn vs Balt | 9-28-69 | 7 |

## THEY SAID IT

*Buffalo Bill linebacker Cornelius Bennett, after a loss to New England ended the Bills' playoff hopes and their AFC dynasty: "It hurts ... looking across the field and seeing someone else celebrate the way we used to."*

### Single-Game Leaders *(Cont.)*
#### Receiving

**YARDS GAINED**

| | Date | Yds |
|---|---|---|
| Flipper Anderson, LA Rams vs NO | 11-26-89 | 336 |
| Stephone Paige, KC vs SD | 12-22-85 | 309 |
| Jim Benton, Clev vs Det | 11-22-45 | 303 |
| Cloyce Box, Det vs Balt | 12-3-50 | 302 |
| John Taylor, SF vs LA Rams | 12-11-89 | 286 |

**TOUCHDOWNS**

| | Date | No. |
|---|---|---|
| Bob Shaw, Chi Cards vs Balt | 10-2-50 | 5 |
| Kellen Winslow, SD vs Oak | 11-22-81 | 5 |
| Jerry Rice, SF vs Atl | 10-14-90 | 5 |

**RECEPTIONS**

| | Date | No. |
|---|---|---|
| Tom Fears, LA Rams vs GB | 12-3-50 | 18 |
| Clark Gaines, NY Jets vs SF | 9-21-80 | 17 |
| Sonny Randle, StL vs NY Giants | 11-4-62 | 16 |
| Jerry Rice, SF vs LA Rams | 11-20-94 | 16 |
| Rickey Young, Minn vs NE | 12-16-79 | 15 |
| William Andrews, Atl vs Pitt | 11-15-81 | 15 |
| Andre Reed Buff vs GB | 11-20-94 | 15 |

### All-Purpose Yards

| | Date | Yds |
|---|---|---|
| Billy Cannon, Hou vs NY Titans | 12-10-61 | 373 |
| Lionel James, SD vs LA Raiders | 11-10-85 | 345 |
| Timmy Brown, Phil vs StL | 12-16-62 | 341 |
| Gale Sayers, Chi vs Minn | 12-18-66 | 339 |
| Gale Sayers, Chi vs SF | 12-12-65 | 336 |

## Annual NFL Individual Statistical Leaders

### Rushing

| Year | Player, Team | Att. | Yards | Avg. | TD | Year | Player, Team | Att. | Yards | Avg. | TD |
|---|---|---|---|---|---|---|---|---|---|---|---|
| 1932 | Cliff Battles, Bos | 148 | 576 | 3.9 | 3 | 1961 | Jim Brown, Clev, NFL | 305 | 1408 | 4.6 | 8 |
| 1933 | Jim Musick, Bos | 173 | 809 | 4.7 | 5 | | Billy Cannon, Hou, AFL | 200 | 948 | 4.7 | 6 |
| 1934 | Beattie Feathers, Chicago Bears | 101 | 1004 | 9.9 | 8 | 1962 | Jim Taylor, GB, NFL | 272 | 1474 | 5.4 | 19 |
| 1935 | Doug Russell, Chicago Cards | 140 | 499 | 3.6 | 0 | | Cookie Gilchrist, Buff, AFL | 214 | 1096 | 5.1 | 13 |
| 1936 | Alphonse Leemans, NY | 206 | 830 | 4.0 | 2 | 1963 | Jim Brown, Clev, NFL | 291 | 1863 | 6.4 | 12 |
| 1937 | Cliff Battles, Wash | 216 | 874 | 4.0 | 5 | | Clem Daniels, Oak, AFL | 215 | 1099 | 5.1 | 3 |
| 1938 | Byron White, Pitt | 152 | 567 | 3.7 | 4 | 1964 | Jim Brown, Clev, NFL | 280 | 1446 | 5.2 | 7 |
| 1939 | Bill Osmanski, Chi | 121 | 699 | 5.8 | 7 | | Cookie Gilchrist, Buff, AFL | 230 | 981 | 4.3 | 6 |
| 1940 | Byron White, Det | 146 | 514 | 3.5 | 5 | 1965 | Jim Brown, Clev, NFL | 289 | 1544 | 5.3 | 17 |
| 1941 | Clarence Manders, Bklyn | 111 | 486 | 4.4 | 5 | | Paul Lowe, SD, AFL | 222 | 1121 | 5.0 | 7 |
| 1942 | Bill Dudley, Pitt | 162 | 696 | 4.3 | 5 | 1966 | Jim Nance, Bos, AFL | 299 | 1458 | 4.9 | 11 |
| 1943 | Bill Paschal, NY | 147 | 572 | 3.9 | 10 | | Gale Sayers, Chi, NFL | 229 | 1231 | 5.4 | 8 |
| 1944 | Bill Paschal, NY | 196 | 737 | 3.8 | 9 | 1967 | Jim Nance, Bos, AFL | 269 | 1216 | 4.5 | 7 |
| 1945 | Steve Van Buren, Phil | 143 | 832 | 5.8 | 15 | | Leroy Kelly, Clev, NFL | 235 | 1205 | 5.1 | 11 |
| 1946 | Bill Dudley, Pitt | 146 | 604 | 4.1 | 3 | 1968 | Leroy Kelly, Clev, NFL | 248 | 1239 | 5.0 | 16 |
| 1947 | Steve Van Buren, Phil | 217 | 1008 | 4.6 | 13 | | Paul Robinson, Cinn, AFL | 238 | 1023 | 4.3 | 8 |
| 1948 | Steve Van Buren, Phil | 201 | 945 | 4.7 | 10 | 1969 | Gale Sayers, Chi, NFL | 236 | 1032 | 4.4 | 8 |
| 1949 | Steve Van Buren, Phil | 263 | 1146 | 4.4 | 11 | | Dickie Post, SD, AFL | 182 | 873 | 4.8 | 6 |
| 1950 | Marion Motley, Clev | 140 | 810 | 5.8 | 3 | 1970 | Larry Brown, Wash, NFC | 237 | 1125 | 4.7 | 5 |
| 1951 | Eddie Price, NY | 271 | 971 | 3.6 | 7 | | Floyd Little, Den, AFC | 209 | 901 | 4.3 | 3 |
| 1952 | Dan Towler, LA | 156 | 894 | 5.7 | 10 | 1971 | Floyd Little, Den, AFC | 284 | 1133 | 4.0 | 6 |
| 1953 | Joe Perry, SF | 192 | 1018 | 5.3 | 10 | | John Brockington, GB, NFC | 216 | 1105 | 5.1 | 4 |
| 1954 | Joe Perry, SF | 173 | 1049 | 6.1 | 8 | 1972 | O.J. Simpson, Buff, AFC | 292 | 1251 | 4.3 | 6 |
| 1955 | Alan Ameche, Balt | 213 | 961 | 4.5 | 9 | | Larry Brown, Wash, NFC | 285 | 1216 | 4.3 | 8 |
| 1956 | Rick Casares, Chicago Bears | 234 | 1126 | 4.8 | 12 | 1973 | O.J. Simpson, Buff, AFC | 332 | 2003 | 6.0 | 12 |
| 1957 | Jim Brown, Clev | 202 | 942 | 4.7 | 9 | | John Brockington, GB, NFC | 265 | 1144 | 4.3 | 3 |
| 1958 | Jim Brown, Clev | 257 | 1527 | 5.9 | 17 | | | | | | |
| 1959 | Jim Brown, Clev | 290 | 1329 | 4.6 | 14 | | | | | | |
| 1960 | Jim Brown, Clev, NFL | 215 | 1257 | 5.8 | 9 | | | | | | |
| | Abner Haynes, Dall Texans, AFL | 156 | 875 | 5.6 | 9 | | | | | | |

## Rushing *(Cont.)*

| Year | Player, Team | Att. | Yards | Avg. | TD |
|---|---|---|---|---|---|
| 1974 | Otis Armstrong, Den, AFC | 263 | 1407 | 5.3 | 9 |
| | Lawrence McCutcheon, LA Rams, NFC | 236 | 1109 | 4.7 | 3 |
| 1975 | O.J. Simpson, Buff, AFC | 329 | 1817 | 5.5 | 16 |
| | Jim Otis, StL, NFC | 269 | 1076 | 4.0 | 5 |
| 1976 | O.J. Simpson, Buff, AFC | 290 | 1503 | 5.2 | 8 |
| | Walter Payton, Chi, NFC | 311 | 1390 | 4.5 | 13 |
| 1977 | Walter Payton, Chi, NFC | 339 | 1852 | 5.5 | 14 |
| | Mark van Eeghen, Oak, AFC | 324 | 1273 | 3.9 | 7 |
| 1978 | Earl Campbell, Hou, AFC | 302 | 1450 | 4.8 | 13 |
| | Walter Payton, Chi, NFC | 333 | 1395 | 4.2 | 11 |
| 1979 | Earl Campbell, Hou, AFC | 368 | 1697 | 4.6 | 19 |
| | Walter Payton, Chi, NFC | 369 | 1610 | 4.4 | 14 |
| 1980 | Earl Campbell, Hou, AFC | 373 | 1934 | 5.2 | 13 |
| | Walter Payton, Chi, NFC | 317 | 1460 | 4.6 | 6 |
| 1981 | George Rogers, NO, NFC | 378 | 1674 | 4.4 | 13 |
| | Earl Campbell, Hou, AFC | 361 | 1376 | 3.8 | 10 |
| 1982 | Freeman McNeil, NY Jets, AFC | 151 | 786 | 5.2 | 6 |
| | Tony Dorsett, Dall, NFC | 177 | 745 | 4.2 | 5 |
| 1983 | Eric Dickerson, LA Rams, NFC | 390 | 1808 | 4.6 | 18 |
| | Curt Warner, Sea, AFC | 335 | 1449 | 4.3 | 13 |
| 1984 | Eric Dickerson, LA Rams, NFC | 379 | 2105 | 5.6 | 14 |
| | Earnest Jackson, SD, AFC | 296 | 1179 | 4.0 | 8 |
| 1985 | Marcus Allen, LA Raiders, AFC | 380 | 1759 | 4.6 | 11 |
| | Gerald Riggs, Atl, NFC | 397 | 1719 | 4.3 | 10 |
| 1986 | Eric Dickerson, LA Rams, NFC | 404 | 1821 | 4.5 | 11 |
| | Curt Warner, Sea, AFC | 319 | 1481 | 4.6 | 13 |
| 1987 | Charles White, LA Rams, NFC | 324 | 1374 | 4.2 | 11 |
| | Eric Dickerson, Ind, AFC | 223 | 1011 | 4.5 | 5 |
| 1988 | Eric Dickerson, Ind, AFC | 388 | 1659 | 4.3 | 14 |
| | Herschel Walker, Dall, NFC | 361 | 1514 | 4.2 | 5 |
| 1989 | Christian Okoye, KC, AFC | 370 | 1480 | 4.0 | 12 |
| | Barry Sanders, Det, NFC | 280 | 1470 | 5.3 | 14 |
| 1990 | Barry Sanders, Det, NFC | 255 | 1304 | 5.1 | 13 |
| | Thurman Thomas, Buff, AFC | 271 | 1297 | 4.8 | 11 |
| 1991 | Emmitt Smith, Dall, NFC | 365 | 1563 | 4.3 | 12 |
| | Thurman Thomas, Buff, AFC | 288 | 1407 | 4.9 | 7 |
| 1992 | Emmitt Smith, Dall, NFC | 373 | 1713 | 4.6 | 18 |
| | Barry Foster, Pitt, AFC | 390 | 1690 | 4.3 | 11 |
| 1993 | Emmitt Smith, Dall, NFC | 283 | 1486 | 5.3 | 9 |
| | Thurman Thomas, Buff, AFC | 355 | 1315 | 3.7 | 6 |
| 1994 | Barry Sanders, Det, NFC | 331 | 1883 | 5.7 | 7 |
| | Chris Warren, Sea, AFC | 333 | 1545 | 4.6 | 9 |

## Passing

| Year | Player, Team | Att. | Comp. | Yards | TD | Int |
|---|---|---|---|---|---|---|
| 1932 | Arnie Herber, GB | 101 | 37 | 639 | 9 | 9 |
| 1933 | Harry Newman, NY | 136 | 53 | 973 | 11 | 17 |
| 1934 | Arnie Herber, GB | 115 | 42 | 799 | 8 | 12 |
| 1935 | Ed Danowski, NY | 113 | 57 | 794 | 10 | 9 |
| 1936 | Arnie Herber, GB | 173 | 77 | 1239 | 11 | 13 |
| 1937 | Sammy Baugh, Wash | 171 | 81 | 1127 | 8 | 14 |
| 1938 | Ed Danowski, NY | 129 | 70 | 848 | 7 | 8 |
| 1939 | Parker Hall, Clev | 208 | 106 | 1227 | 9 | 13 |
| 1940 | Sammy Baugh, Wash | 177 | 111 | 1367 | 12 | 10 |
| 1941 | Cecil Isbell, GB | 206 | 117 | 1479 | 15 | 11 |
| 1942 | Cecil Isbell, GB | 268 | 146 | 2021 | 24 | 14 |
| 1943 | Sammy Baugh, Wash | 239 | 133 | 1754 | 23 | 19 |
| 1944 | Frank Filchock, Wash | 147 | 84 | 1139 | 13 | 9 |
| 1945 | Sammy Baugh, Wash | 182 | 128 | 1669 | 11 | 4 |
| | Sid Luckman, Chi | 217 | 117 | 1725 | 14 | 10 |
| 1946 | Bob Waterfield, LA | 251 | 127 | 1747 | 18 | 17 |
| 1947 | Sammy Baugh, Wash | 354 | 210 | 2938 | 25 | 15 |
| 1948 | Tommy Thompson, Phi | 246 | 141 | 1965 | 25 | 11 |
| 1949 | Sammy Baugh, Wash | 255 | 145 | 1903 | 18 | 14 |
| 1950 | Norm Van Brocklin, LA | 233 | 127 | 2061 | 18 | 14 |
| 1951 | Bob Waterfield, LA | 176 | 88 | 1566 | 13 | 10 |
| 1952 | Norm Van Brocklin, LA | 205 | 113 | 1736 | 14 | 17 |
| 1953 | Otto Graham, Clev | 258 | 167 | 2722 | 11 | 9 |
| 1954 | Norm Van Brocklin, LA | 260 | 139 | 2637 | 13 | 21 |
| 1955 | Otto Graham, Clev | 185 | 98 | 1721 | 15 | 8 |
| 1956 | Ed Brown, Chi | 168 | 96 | 1667 | 11 | 12 |
| 1957 | Tommy O'Connell, Clev. | 110 | 63 | 1229 | 9 | 8 |
| 1958 | Eddie LeBaron, Wash | 145 | 79 | 1365 | 11 | 10 |
| 1959 | Charlie Conerly, NY | 194 | 113 | 1706 | 14 | 4 |
| 1960 | Milt Plum, Clev, NFL | 250 | 151 | 2297 | 21 | 5 |
| | Jack Kemp, LA, AFL | 406 | 211 | 3018 | 20 | 25 |
| 1961 | George Blanda, Hou, AFL | 362 | 187 | 3330 | 36 | 22 |
| | Milt Plum, Clev, NFL | 302 | 177 | 2416 | 18 | 10 |
| 1962 | Len Dawson, Dall, AFL | 310 | 189 | 2759 | 29 | 17 |
| | Bart Starr, GB, NFL | 285 | 178 | 2438 | 12 | 9 |
| 1963 | Y.A. Tittle, NY, NFL | 367 | 221 | 3145 | 36 | 14 |
| | Tobin Rote, SD, AFL | 286 | 170 | 2510 | 20 | 17 |
| 1964 | Len Dawson, KC, AFL | 354 | 199 | 2879 | 30 | 18 |
| | Bart Starr, GB, NFL | 272 | 163 | 2144 | 15 | 4 |
| 1965 | Rudy Bukich, Chi, NFL | 312 | 176 | 2641 | 20 | 9 |
| | John Hadl, SD, AFL | 348 | 174 | 2798 | 20 | 21 |
| 1966 | Bart Starr, GB, NFL | 251 | 156 | 2257 | 14 | 3 |
| | Len Dawson, KC, AFL | 284 | 159 | 2527 | 26 | 10 |
| 1967 | Sonny Jurgensen, Wash, NFL | 508 | 288 | 3747 | 31 | 16 |
| | Daryle Lamonica, Oakland, AFL | 425 | 220 | 3228 | 30 | 20 |
| 1968 | Len Dawson, KC, AFL | 224 | 131 | 2109 | 17 | 9 |
| | Earl Morrall, Balt, NFL | 317 | 182 | 2909 | 26 | 17 |
| 1969 | Sonny Jurgensen, Wash, NFL | 442 | 274 | 3102 | 22 | 15 |
| | Greg Cook, Cin, AFL | 197 | 106 | 1854 | 15 | 11 |
| 1970 | John Brodie, SF, NFC | 378 | 223 | 2941 | 24 | 10 |
| | Daryle Lamonica, Oak, AFC | 356 | 179 | 2516 | 22 | 15 |

## Passing *(Cont.)*

| Year | Player, Team | Att. | Comp | Yards | TD | Int |
|------|-------------|------|------|-------|-----|-----|
| 1971 | Roger Staubach, Dall, NFC | 211 | 126 | 1882 | 15 | 4 |
|      | Bob Griese, Mia, AFC | 263 | 145 | 2089 | 19 | 9 |
| 1972 | Norm Snead, NY, NFC | 325 | 196 | 2307 | 17 | 12 |
|      | Earl Morrall, Mia, AFC | 150 | 83 | 1360 | 11 | 7 |
| 1973 | Roger Staubach, Dall, NFC | 286 | 179 | 2428 | 23 | 15 |
|      | Ken Stabler, Oak, AFC | 260 | 163 | 1997 | 14 | 10 |
| 1974 | Ken Anderson, Cin, AFC | 328 | 213 | 2667 | 18 | 10 |
|      | Sonny Jurgensen, Wash, NFC | 167 | 107 | 1185 | 11 | 5 |
| 1975 | Ken Anderson, Cin, AFC | 377 | 228 | 3169 | 21 | 11 |
|      | Fran Tarkenton, Minn, NFC | 425 | 273 | 2994 | 25 | 13 |
| 1976 | Ken Stabler, Oak, AFC | 291 | 194 | 2737 | 27 | 17 |
|      | James Harris, LA, NFC | 158 | 91 | 1460 | 8 | 6 |
| 1977 | Bob Griese, Mia, AFC | 307 | 180 | 2252 | 22 | 13 |
|      | Roger Staubach, Dall, NFC | 361 | 210 | 2620 | 18 | 9 |
| 1978 | Roger Staubach, Dall, NFC | 413 | 231 | 3190 | 25 | 16 |
|      | Terry Bradshaw, Pitt, AFC | 368 | 207 | 2915 | 28 | 20 |
| 1979 | Roger Staubach, Dall, NFC | 461 | 267 | 3586 | 27 | 11 |
|      | Dan Fouts, SD, AFC | 530 | 332 | 4082 | 24 | 24 |
| 1980 | Brian Sipe, Clev, AFC | 554 | 337 | 4132 | 30 | 14 |
|      | Ron Jaworski, Phi, NFC | 451 | 257 | 3529 | 27 | 12 |
| 1981 | Ken Anderson, Cin, AFC | 479 | 300 | 3754 | 29 | 10 |
|      | Joe Montana, SF, NFC | 488 | 311 | 3565 | 19 | 12 |
| 1982 | Ken Anderson, Cin, AFC | 309 | 218 | 2495 | 12 | 9 |
|      | Joe Theismann, Wash, NFC | 252 | 161 | 2033 | 13 | 9 |
| 1983 | Steve Bartkowski, Atl, NFC | 432 | 274 | 3167 | 22 | 5 |
|      | Dan Marino, Mia AFC | 296 | 173 | 2210 | 20 | 6 |
| 1984 | Dan Marino, Mia, AFC | 564 | 362 | 5084 | 48 | 17 |
|      | Joe Montana, SF, NFC | 432 | 279 | 3630 | 28 | 10 |
| 1985 | Ken O'Brien, NY, AFC | 488 | 297 | 3888 | 25 | 8 |
|      | Joe Montana, SF, NFC | 494 | 303 | 3653 | 27 | 13 |
| 1986 | Tommy Kramer, Minn, NFC | 372 | 208 | 3000 | 24 | 10 |
|      | Dan Marino, Mia, AFC | 623 | 378 | 4746 | 44 | 23 |
| 1987 | Joe Montana, SF, NFC | 398 | 266 | 3054 | 31 | 13 |
|      | Bernie Kosar, Clev, AFC | 389 | 241 | 3033 | 22 | 9 |
| 1988 | Boomer Esiason, Cin, AFC | 388 | 223 | 3572 | 28 | 14 |
|      | Wade Wilson, Minn, NFC | 332 | 204 | 2746 | 15 | 9 |
| 1989 | Joe Montana, SF, NFC | 386 | 271 | 3521 | 26 | 8 |
|      | Boomer Esiason, Cin, AFC | 455 | 258 | 3525 | 28 | 11 |
| 1990 | Jim Kelly, Buffalo, AFC | 346 | 219 | 2829 | 24 | 9 |
|      | Phil Simms, NY, NFC | 311 | 184 | 2284 | 15 | 4 |
| 1991 | Steve Young, SF, NFC | 279 | 180 | 2517 | 17 | 8 |
|      | Jim Kelly, Buff, AFC | 474 | 304 | 3844 | 33 | 17 |
| 1992 | Steve Young, SF, NFC | 402 | 268 | 3465 | 25 | 7 |
|      | Warren Moon, Hou AFC | 346 | 224 | 2521 | 18 | 12 |
| 1993 | Steve Young, SF, NFC | 462 | 314 | 4023 | 29 | 16 |
|      | John Elway, Den, AFC | 551 | 348 | 4030 | 25 | 10 |
| 1994 | Steve Young, SF, NFC | 461 | 324 | 3969 | 35 | 10 |
|      | Dan Marino, Mia, AFC | 615 | 385 | 4453 | 30 | 17 |

## Pass Receiving

| Year | Player, Team | No. | Yds | Avg | TD |
|------|-------------|-----|-----|-----|-----|
| 1932 | Ray Flaherty, NY | 21 | 350 | 16.7 | 3 |
| 1933 | John Kelly, Brooklyn | 22 | 246 | 11.2 | 3 |
| 1934 | Joe Carter, Phil | 16 | 238 | 14.9 | 4 |
|      | Morris Badgro, NY | 16 | 206 | 12.9 | 1 |
| 1935 | Tod Goodwin, NY | 26 | 432 | 16.6 | 4 |
| 1936 | Don Hutson, GB | 34 | 536 | 15.8 | 8 |
| 1937 | Don Hutson, GB | 41 | 552 | 13.5 | 7 |
| 1938 | Gaynell Tinsley, Chi Cards | 41 | 516 | 12.6 | 1 |
| 1939 | Don Hutson, GB | 34 | 846 | 24.9 | 6 |
| 1940 | Don Looney, Phil | 58 | 707 | 12.2 | 4 |
| 1941 | Don Hutson, GB | 58 | 738 | 12.7 | 10 |
| 1942 | Don Hutson, GB | 74 | 1211 | 16.4 | 17 |
| 1943 | Don Hutson, GB | 47 | 776 | 16.5 | 11 |
| 1944 | Don Hutson, GB | 58 | 866 | 14.9 | 9 |
| 1945 | Don Hutson, GB | 47 | 834 | 17.7 | 9 |
| 1946 | Jim Benton, LA | 63 | 981 | 15.6 | 6 |
| 1947 | Jim Keane, Chi | 64 | 910 | 14.2 | 10 |
| 1948 | Tom Fears, LA | 51 | 698 | 13.7 | 4 |
| 1949 | Tom Fears, LA | 77 | 1013 | 13.2 | 9 |
| 1950 | Tom Fears, LA | 84 | 1116 | 13.3 | 7 |
| 1951 | Elroy Hirsch, LA | 66 | 1495 | 22.7 | 17 |
| 1952 | Mac Speedie, Clev | 62 | 911 | 14.7 | 5 |
| 1953 | Pete Pihos, Phil | 63 | 1049 | 16.7 | 10 |
| 1954 | Pete Pihos, Phil | 60 | 872 | 14.5 | 10 |
|      | Billy Wilson, SF | 60 | 830 | 13.8 | 5 |
| 1955 | Pete Pihos, Phil | 62 | 864 | 13.9 | 7 |
| 1956 | Billy Wilson, SF | 60 | 889 | 14.8 | 5 |
| 1957 | Billy Wilson, SF | 52 | 757 | 14.6 | 6 |
| 1958 | Raymond Berry, Balt | 56 | 794 | 14.2 | 9 |
|      | Pete Retzlaff, Phil | 56 | 766 | 13.7 | 2 |
| 1959 | Raymond Berry, Balt | 66 | 959 | 14.5 | 14 |
| 1960 | Lionel Taylor, Den, AFL | 92 | 1235 | 13.4 | 12 |
|      | Raymond Berry, Baltimore, NFL | 74 | 1298 | 17.5 | 10 |
| 1961 | Lionel Taylor, Den, AFL | 100 | 1176 | 11.8 | 4 |
|      | Jim Phillips, LA, NFL | 78 | 1092 | 14.0 | 5 |
| 1962 | Lionel Taylor, Den, AFL | 77 | 908 | 11.8 | 4 |
|      | Bobby Mitchell, Wash, NFL | 72 | 1384 | 19.2 | 11 |
| 1963 | Lionel Taylor, Den, AFL | 78 | 1101 | 14.1 | 10 |
|      | Bobby Joe Conrad, St. Louis, NFL | 73 | 967 | 13.2 | 10 |
| 1964 | Charley Hennigan, Houston, AFL | 101 | 1546 | 15.3 | 8 |
|      | Johnny Morris, Chi, NFL | 93 | 1200 | 12.9 | 10 |
| 1965 | Lionel Taylor, Den, AFL | 85 | 1131 | 13.3 | 6 |
|      | Dave Parks, SF, NFL | 80 | 1344 | 16.8 | 12 |
| 1966 | Lance Alworth, SD, AFL | 73 | 1383 | 18.9 | 13 |
|      | Charley Taylor, Wash, NFL | 72 | 1119 | 15.5 | 12 |
| 1967 | George Sauer, NY, AFL | 75 | 1189 | 15.9 | 6 |
|      | Charley Taylor, Wash, NFL | 70 | 990 | 14.1 | 9 |

## Pass Receiving *(Cont.)*

| Year | Player, Team | No. | Yds | Avg | TD |
|---|---|---|---|---|---|
| 1968 | Clifton McNeil, SF, NFL | 71 | 994 | 14.0 | 7 |
| | Lance Alworth, SD, AFL | 68 | 1312 | 19.3 | 10 |
| 1969 | Dan Abramowicz, NO, NFL | 73 | 1015 | 13.9 | 7 |
| | Lance Alworth, SD, AFL | 64 | 1003 | 15.7 | 4 |
| 1970 | Dick Gordon, Chi, NFC | 71 | 1026 | 14.5 | 13 |
| | Marlin Briscoe, Buff, AFC | 57 | 1036 | 18.2 | 8 |
| 1971 | Fred Biletnikoff, Oak, AFC | 61 | 929 | 15.2 | 9 |
| | Bob Tucker, NY, NFC | 59 | 791 | 13.4 | 4 |
| 1972 | Harold Jackson, Phi, NFC | 62 | 1048 | 16.9 | 4 |
| | Fred Biletnikoff, Oak, AFC | 58 | 802 | 13.8 | 7 |
| 1973 | Harold Carmichael, Phi, NFC | 67 | 1116 | 16.7 | 9 |
| | Fred Willis, Hou, AFC | 57 | 371 | 6.5 | 1 |
| 1974 | Lydell Mitchell, Balt, AFC | 72 | 544 | 7.6 | 2 |
| | Charles Young, Phi, NFC | 63 | 696 | 11.0 | 3 |
| 1975 | Chuck Foreman, Minn, NFC | 73 | 691 | 9.5 | 9 |
| | Reggie Rucker, Clev, AFC | 60 | 770 | 12.8 | 3 |
| | Lydell Mitchell, Balt, AFC | 60 | 544 | 9.1 | 4 |
| 1976 | MacArthur Lane, KC, AFC | 66 | 686 | 10.4 | 1 |
| | Drew Pearson, Dall, NFC | 58 | 806 | 13.9 | 6 |
| 1977 | Lydell Mitchell, Balt, AFC | 71 | 620 | 8.7 | 4 |
| | Ahmad Rashad, Minn, NFC | 51 | 681 | 13.4 | 2 |
| 1978 | Rickey Young, Minn, NFC | 88 | 704 | 8.0 | 5 |
| | Steve Largent, Sea, AFC | 71 | 1168 | 16.5 | 8 |
| 1979 | Joe Washington, Balt, AFC | 82 | 750 | 9.1 | 3 |
| | Ahmad Rashad, Minn, NFC | 80 | 1156 | 14.5 | 9 |
| 1980 | Kellen Winslow, SD, AFC | 89 | 1290 | 14.5 | 9 |
| | Earl Cooper, SF, NFC | 83 | 567 | 6.8 | 4 |
| 1981 | Kellen Winslow, SD, AFC | 88 | 1075 | 12.2 | 10 |
| | Dwight Clark, SF, NFC | 85 | 1105 | 13.0 | 4 |
| 1982 | Dwight Clark, SF, NFC | 60 | 913 | 15.2 | 5 |
| | Kellen Winslow, SD, AFC | 54 | 721 | 13.4 | 6 |
| 1983 | Todd Christensen, Los Angeles, AFC | 92 | 1247 | 13.6 | 12 |
| | Roy Green, StL, NFC | 78 | 1227 | 15.7 | 14 |
| | Charlie Brown, Wash, NFC | 78 | 1225 | 15.7 | 8 |
| | Earnest Gray, NY, NFC | 78 | 1139 | 14.6 | 5 |
| 1984 | Art Monk, Wash, NFC | 106 | 1372 | 12.9 | 7 |
| | Ozzie Newsome, Clev, AFC | 89 | 1001 | 11.2 | 5 |
| 1985 | Roger Craig, SF, NFC | 92 | 1016 | 11.0 | 6 |
| | Lionel James, SD, AFC | 86 | 1027 | 11.9 | 6 |
| 1986 | Todd Christensen, Los Angeles, AFC | 95 | 1153 | 12.1 | 8 |
| | Jerry Rice, SF, NFC | 86 | 1570 | 18.3 | 15 |
| 1987 | J.T. Smith, StL, NFC | 91 | 1117 | 12.3 | 8 |
| | Al Toon, NY, AFC | 68 | 976 | 14.4 | 5 |
| 1988 | Al Toon, NY, AFC | 93 | 1067 | 11.5 | 5 |
| | Henry Ellard, LA Rams, NFC | 86 | 1414 | 16.4 | 10 |
| 1989 | Sterling Sharpe, GB, NFC | 90 | 1423 | 15.8 | 12 |
| | Andre Reed, Buff, AFC | 88 | 1312 | 14.9 | 9 |
| 1990 | Jerry Rice, SF, NFC | 100 | 1502 | 15.0 | 13 |
| | Haywood Jeffires, Houston, AFC | 74 | 1048 | 14.2 | 8 |
| | Drew Hill, Hou, AFC | 74 | 1019 | 13.8 | 5 |
| 1991 | Haywood Jeffires, Hou, AFC | 100 | 1181 | 11.8 | 7 |
| | Michael Irvin, Dall, NFC | 93 | 1523 | 16.4 | 8 |
| 1992 | Sterling Sharpe, GB, NFC | 108 | 1461 | 13.5 | 13 |
| | Haywood Jeffires, Hou, AFC | 90 | 913 | 10.1 | 9 |
| 1993 | Sterling Sharpe, GB, NFC | 112 | 1274 | 11.4 | 11 |
| | Reggie Langhorne, Ind, AFC | 85 | 1038 | 12.2 | 3 |
| 1994 | Cris Carter, Minn, NFC | 122 | 1256 | 10.3 | 7 |
| | Ben Coates, NE, AFC | 96 | 1174 | 12.2 | 7 |

## Scoring

| Year | Player, Team | TD | FG | PAT | TP |
|---|---|---|---|---|---|
| 1932 | Earl Clark, Portsmouth | 6 | 3 | 10 | 55 |
| 1933 | Ken Strong, NY | 6 | 5 | 13 | 64 |
| | Glenn Presnell, Ports | 6 | 6 | 10 | 64 |
| 1934 | Jack Manders, Chi | 3 | 10 | 31 | 79 |
| 1935 | Earl Clark, Det | 6 | 1 | 16 | 55 |
| 1936 | Earl Clark, Det | 7 | 4 | 19 | 73 |
| 1937 | Jack Manders, Chi | 5 | 18 | 15 | 69 |
| 1938 | Clarke Hinkle, GB | 7 | 3 | 7 | 58 |
| 1939 | Andy Farkas, Wash | 11 | 0 | 2 | 68 |
| 1940 | Don Hutson, GB | 7 | 0 | 15 | 57 |
| 1941 | Don Hutson, GB | 12 | 1 | 20 | 95 |
| 1942 | Don Hutson, GB | 17 | 1 | 33 | 138 |
| 1943 | Don Hutson, GB | 12 | 3 | 36 | 117 |
| 1944 | Don Hutson, GB | 9 | 0 | 31 | 85 |
| 1945 | Steve Van Buren, Phil | 18 | 0 | 2 | 110 |
| 1946 | Ted Fritsch, GB | 10 | 9 | 13 | 100 |
| 1947 | Pat Harder, Chicago Cards | 7 | 7 | 39 | 102 |
| 1948 | Pat Harder, Chicago Cards | 6 | 7 | 53 | 110 |
| 1949 | Pat Harder, Chicago Cards | 8 | 3 | 45 | 102 |
| | Gene Roberts, NY | 17 | 0 | 0 | 102 |
| 1950 | Doak Walker, Det | 11 | 8 | 38 | 128 |
| 1951 | Elroy Hirsch, LA | 17 | 0 | 0 | 102 |
| 1952 | Gordy Soltau, SF | 7 | 6 | 34 | 94 |
| 1953 | Gordy Soltau, SF | 6 | 10 | 48 | 114 |
| 1954 | Bobby Walston, Phil | 11 | 4 | 36 | 114 |
| 1955 | Doak Walker, Det | 7 | 9 | 27 | 96 |
| 1956 | Bobby Layne, Det | 5 | 12 | 33 | 99 |
| 1957 | Sam Baker, Wash | 1 | 14 | 29 | 77 |
| | Lou Groza, Clev | 0 | 15 | 32 | 77 |
| 1958 | Jim Brown, Clev | 18 | 0 | 0 | 108 |
| 1959 | Paul Hornung, GB | 7 | 7 | 31 | 94 |
| 1960 | Paul Hornung, GB, NFL | 15 | 15 | 41 | 176 |
| | Gene Mingo, Den, AFL | 6 | 18 | 33 | 123 |
| 1961 | Gino Cappelletti, Bos, AFL | 8 | 17 | 48 | 147 |
| | Paul Hornung, GB, NFL | 10 | 15 | 41 | 146 |
| 1962 | Gene Mingo, Den, AFL | 4 | 27 | 32 | 137 |
| | Jim Taylor, GB, NFL | 19 | 0 | 0 | 114 |
| 1963 | Gino Cappelletti, Bos, AFL | 2 | 22 | 35 | 113 |
| | Don Chandler, NY, NFL | 0 | 18 | 52 | 106 |
| 1964 | Gino Cappelletti, Bos, AFL | 7 | 25 | 36 | 155 |
| | Lenny Moore, Balt, NFL | 20 | 0 | 0 | 120 |
| 1965 | Gale Sayers, Chi, NFL | 22 | 0 | 0 | 132 |
| | Gino Cappelletti, Bos, AFL | 9 | 17 | 27 | 132 |
| 1966 | Gino Cappelletti, Bos, AFL | 6 | 16 | 35 | 119 |
| | Bruce Gossett, LA, NFL | 0 | 28 | 29 | 113 |
| 1967 | Jim Bakken, StL, NFL | 0 | 27 | 36 | 117 |
| | George Blanda, Oak, AFL | 0 | 20 | 56 | 116 |
| 1968 | Jim Turner, NY, AFL | 0 | 34 | 43 | 145 |
| | Leroy Kelly, Clev, NFL | 20 | 0 | 0 | 120 |

## Scoring *(Cont.)*

| Year | Player, Team | TD | FG | PAT | TP | Year | Player, Team | TD | FG | PAT | TP |
|---|---|---|---|---|---|---|---|---|---|---|---|
| 1969 | Jim Turner, NY, AFL | 0 | 32 | 33 | 129 | 1982 | Marcus Allen, LA, AFC | 14 | 0 | 0 | 84 |
| | Fred Cox, Minn, NFL | 0 | 26 | 43 | 121 | | Wendell Tyler, LA, NFC | 13 | 0 | 0 | 78 |
| 1970 | Fred Cox, Minn, NFC | 0 | 30 | 35 | 125 | 1983 | Mark Moseley, Wash, NFC | 0 | 33 | 62 | 161 |
| | Jan Stenerud, KC, AFC | 0 | 30 | 26 | 116 | | Gary Anderson, Pitt, AFC | 0 | 27 | 38 | 119 |
| 1971 | Garo Yepremian, Mia, AFC | 0 | 28 | 33 | 117 | 1984 | Ray Wersching, SF, NFC | 0 | 25 | 56 | 131 |
| | Curt Knight, Wash, NFC | 0 | 29 | 27 | 114 | | Gary Anderson, Pitt, AFC | 0 | 24 | 45 | 117 |
| 1972 | Chester Marcol, GB, NFC | 0 | 33 | 29 | 128 | 1985 | Kevin Butler, Chi, NFC | 0 | 31 | 51 | 144 |
| | Bobby Howfield, NY AFC | 0 | 27 | 40 | 121 | | Gary Anderson, Pitt, AFC | 0 | 33 | 40 | 139 |
| 1973 | David Ray, LA, NFC | 0 | 30 | 40 | 130 | 1986 | Tony Franklin, NE, AFC | 0 | 32 | 44 | 140 |
| | Roy Gerela, Pitt, AFC | 0 | 29 | 36 | 123 | | Kevin Butler, Chi, NFC | 0 | 28 | 36 | 120 |
| 1974 | Chester Marcol, GB, NFC | 0 | 25 | 19 | 94 | 1987 | Jerry Rice, SF, NFC | 23 | 0 | 0 | 138 |
| | Roy Gerela, Pitt, AFC | 0 | 20 | 33 | 93 | | Jim Breech, Cin, AFC | 0 | 24 | 25 | 97 |
| 1975 | O.J. Simpson, Buff, AFC | 23 | 0 | 0 | 138 | 1988 | Scott Norwood, Buff, AFC | 0 | 32 | 33 | 129 |
| | Chuck Foreman, Minn, NFC | 22 | 0 | 0 | 132 | | Mike Cofer, SF, NFC | 0 | 27 | 40 | 121 |
| 1976 | Toni Linhart, Balt, AFC | 0 | 20 | 49 | 109 | 1989 | Mike Cofer, SF, NFC | 0 | 29 | 49 | 136 |
| | Mark Moseley, Wash, NFC | 0 | 22 | 31 | 97 | | David Treadwell, Den, AFC | 0 | 27 | 39 | 120 |
| 1977 | Errol Mann, Oak, AFC | 0 | 20 | 39 | 99 | 1990 | Nick Lowery, KC, AFC | 0 | 34 | 37 | 139 |
| | Walter Payton, Chi, NFC | 16 | 0 | 0 | 96 | | Chip Lohmiller, Wash, NFC | 0 | 30 | 41 | 131 |
| 1978 | Frank Corral, LA, NFC | 0 | 29 | 31 | 118 | 1991 | Chip Lohmiller, Wash, NFC | 0 | 31 | 56 | 149 |
| | Pat Leahy, NY, AFC | 0 | 22 | 41 | 107 | | Pete Stoyanovich, Mia, AFC | 0 | 31 | 28 | 121 |
| 1979 | John Smith, NE, AFC | 0 | 23 | 46 | 115 | 1992 | Pete Stoyanovich, Mia, AFC | 0 | 30 | 34 | 124 |
| | Mark Moseley, Wash, NFC | 0 | 25 | 39 | 114 | | Morten Anderson, NO, NFC | 0 | 29 | 33 | 120 |
| 1980 | John Smith, NE, AFC | 0 | 26 | 51 | 129 | | Chip Lohmiller, Wash, NFC | 0 | 30 | 30 | 120 |
| | Ed Murray, Det, NFC | 0 | 27 | 35 | 116 | 1993 | Jeff Jaeger, Rai, AFC | 0 | 35 | 27 | 132 |
| 1981 | Ed Murray, Det, NFC | 0 | 25 | 46 | 121 | | Jason Hanson, Det, NFC | 0 | 34 | 28 | 130 |
| | Rafael Septien, Dall, NFC | 0 | 27 | 40 | 121 | 1994 | John Carney, SD, AFC | 0 | 34 | 33 | 135 |
| | Jim Breech, Cin, AFC | 0 | 22 | 49 | 115 | | Fuad Reveiz, Minn, NFC | 0 | 34 | 30 | 132 |
| | Nick Lowery, KC, AFC | 0 | 26 | 37 | 115 | | Emmitt Smith, Dall, NFC | 22 | 0 | 0 | 132 |

## Pro Bowl Alltime Results

| Date | Result | Date | Result | Date | Result |
|---|---|---|---|---|---|
| 1-15-39 | NY Giants 13, Pro All-Stars 10 | 1-7-62 | AFL West 47, East 27 | 1-20-74 | AFC 15, NFC 13 |
| 1-14-40 | Green Bay 16, NFL All-Stars 7 | 1-14-62 | NFL West 31, East 30 | 1-20-75 | NFC 17, AFC 10 |
| 12-29-40 | Chi Bears 28, NFL All-Stars 14 | 1-13-63 | AFL West 21, East 14 | 1-26-76 | NFC 23, AFC 20 |
| 1-4-42 | Chi Bears 35, NFL All-Stars 24 | 1-13-63 | NFL East 30, West 20 | 1-17-77 | AFC 24, NFC 14 |
| 12-27-42 | NFL All-Stars 17, Washington 14 | 1-12-64 | NFL West 31, East 17 | 1-23-78 | NFC 14, AFC 13 |
| 1-14-51 | A Conf 28, N Conf 27 | 1-19-64 | AFL West 27, East 24 | 1-29-79 | NFC 13, AFC 7 |
| 1-12-52 | N Conf 30, A Conf 13 | 1-10-65 | NFL West 34, East 14 | 1-27-80 | NFC 37, AFC 27 |
| 1-10-53 | N Conf 27, A Conf 7 | 1-16-65 | AFL West 38, East 14 | 2-1-81 | NFC 21, AFC 7 |
| 1-17-54 | East 20, West 9 | 1-15-66 | AFL All-Stars 30, Buffalo 19 | 1-31-82 | AFC 16, NFC 13 |
| 1-16-55 | West 26, East 19 | 1-15-66 | NFL East 36, West 7 | 2-6-83 | NFC 20, AFC 19 |
| 1-15-56 | East 31, West 30 | 1-21-67 | AFL East 30, West 23 | 1-29-84 | NFC 45, AFC 3 |
| 1-13-57 | West 19, East 10 | 1-22-67 | NFL East 20, West 10 | 1-27-85 | AFC 22, NFC 14 |
| 1-12-58 | West 26, East 7 | 1-21-68 | AFL East 25, West 24 | 2-2-86 | NFC 28, AFC 24 |
| 1-11-59 | East 28, West 21 | 1-21-68 | NFL West 38, East 20 | 2-1-87 | AFC 10, NFC 6 |
| 1-17-60 | West 38, East 21 | 1-19-69 | AFL West 38, East 25 | 2-7-88 | AFC 15, NFC 6 |
| 1-15-61 | West 35, East 31 | 1-19-69 | NFL West 10, East 7 | 1-29-89 | NFC 34, AFC 3 |
| | | 1-17-70 | AFL West 26, East 3 | 2-4-90 | NFC 27, AFC 21 |
| | | 1-18-70 | NFL West 16, East 13 | 2-3-91 | AFC 23, NFC 21 |
| | | 1-24-71 | NFC 27, AFC 6 | 2-2-92 | NFC 21, AFC 15 |
| | | 1-23-72 | AFC 26, NFC 13 | 2-7-93 | AFC 23, NFC 20 |
| | | 1-21-73 | AFC 33, NFC 28 | 2-6-94 | NFC 17, AFC 3 |
| | | | | 2-5-95 | AFC 41, NFC 13 |

# Chicago All-Star Game Results

| Date | Result (Attendance) |
|------|---------------------|
| 8-31-34 | Chi Bears 0, All-Stars 0 (79,432) |
| 8-29-35 | Chi Bears 5, All-Stars 0 (77,450) |
| 9-3-36 | All-Stars 7, Detroit 7 (76,000) |
| 9-1-37 | All-Stars 6, Green Bay 0 (84,560) |
| 8-31-38 | All-Stars 28, Washington 16 (74,250) |
| 8-30-39 | NY Giants 9, All-Stars 0 (81,456) |
| 8-29-40 | Green Bay 45, All-Stars 28 (84,567) |
| 8-28-41 | Chi Bears 37, All-Stars 13 (98,203) |
| 8-28-42 | Chi Bears 21, All-Stars 0 (101,100) |
| 8-25-43 | All-Stars 27, Washington 7 (48,471) |
| 8-30-44 | Chi Bears 24, All-Stars 21 (48,769) |
| 8-30-45 | Green Bay 19, All-Stars 7 (92,753) |
| 8-23-46 | All-Stars 16, Los Angeles 0 (97,380) |
| 8-22-47 | All-Stars 16, Chi Bears 0 (105,840) |
| 8-20-48 | Chi Cardinals 28, All-Stars 0 (101,220) |
| 8-12-49 | Philadelphia 38, All-Stars 0 (93,780) |
| 8-11-50 | All-Stars 17, Philadelphia 7 (88,885) |
| 8-17-51 | Cleveland 33, All-Stars 0 (92,180) |
| 8-15-52 | Los Angeles 10, All-Stars 7 (88,316) |
| 8-14-53 | Detroit 24, All-Stars 10 (93,818) |
| 8-13-54 | Detroit 31, All-Stars 6 (93,470) |
| 8-12-55 | All-Stars 30, Cleveland 27 (75,000) |
| 8-10-56 | Cleveland 26, All-Stars 0 (75,000) |
| 8-9-57 | NY Giants 22, All-Stars 12 (75,000) |
| 8-15-58 | All-Stars 35, Detroit 19 (70,000) |
| 8-14-59 | Baltimore 29, All-Stars 0 (70,000) |
| 8-12-60 | Baltimore 32, All-Stars 7 (70,000) |
| 8-4-61 | Philadelphia 28, All-Stars 14 (66,000) |
| 8-3-62 | Green Bay 42, All-Stars 20 (65,000) |
| 8-2-63 | All-Stars 20, Green Bay 17 (65,000) |
| 8-7-64 | Chicago 28, All-Stars 17 (65,000) |
| 8-6-65 | Cleveland 24, All-Stars 16 (68,000) |
| 8-5-66 | Green Bay 38, All-Stars 0 (72,000) |
| 8-4-67 | Green Bay 27, All-Stars 0 (70,934) |
| 8-2-68 | Green Bay 34, All-Stars 17 (69,917) |
| 8-1-69 | NY Jets 26, All-Stars 24 (74,208) |
| 7-31-70 | Kansas City 24, All-Stars 3 (69,940) |
| 7-30-71 | Baltimore 24, All-Stars 17 (52,289) |
| 7-28-72 | Dallas 20, All-Stars 7 (54,162) |
| 7-27-73 | Miami 14, All-Stars 3 (54,103) |
| 1974 | No game |
| 8-1-75 | Pittsburgh 21, All-Stars 14 (54,103) |
| 7-23-76 | Pittsburgh 24, All-Stars 0 (52,895) |

# Alltime Winningest NFL Coaches

## Most Career Wins

| Coach | Yrs | Teams | Regular Season | | | | Career | | | |
|-------|-----|-------|----|----|----|-----|----|----|----|-----|
| | | | W | L | T | Pct | W | L | T | Pct |
| †Don Shula | 32 | Colts, Dolphins | 319 | 149 | 6 | .679 | 338 | 165 | 6 | .670 |
| George Halas | 40 | Bears | 319 | 148 | 31 | .672 | 324 | 151 | 31 | .671 |
| Tom Landry | 29 | Cowboys | 250 | 162 | 6 | .605 | 270 | 178 | 6 | .601 |
| Curly Lambeau | 33 | Packers, Cardinals, Redskins | 226 | 132 | 22 | .623 | 229 | 134 | 22 | .623 |
| Chuck Noll | 23 | Steelers | 193 | 148 | 1 | .566 | 209 | 156 | 1 | .572 |
| Chuck Knox | 21 | Rams, Bills, Seahawks | 186 | 147 | 1 | .558 | 193 | 158 | 1 | .550 |
| Paul Brown | 21 | Browns, Bengals | 166 | 100 | 6 | .621 | 170 | 108 | 6 | .609 |
| Bud Grant | 18 | Vikings | 158 | 96 | 5 | .620 | 168 | 108 | 5 | .607 |
| Steve Owen | 23 | Giants | 151 | 100 | 17 | .595 | 153 | 108 | 17 | .582 |
| Joe Gibbs | 12 | Redskins | 124 | 60 | 0 | .674 | 140 | 65 | 0 | .683 |
| †Dan Reeves | 14 | Broncos, Giants | 130 | 85 | 1 | .604 | 137 | 91 | 1 | .600 |
| Hank Stram | 17 | Chiefs, Saints | 131 | 97 | 10 | .571 | 136 | 100 | 10 | .573 |
| Weeb Ewbank | 20 | Colts, Jets | 130 | 129 | 7 | .502 | 134 | 130 | 7 | .507 |
| †Marv Levy | 14 | Chiefs, Bills | 117 | 90 | 0 | .565 | 127 | 96 | 0 | .570 |
| Sid Gillman | 18 | Rams, Chargers, Oilers | 122 | 99 | 7 | .550 | 123 | 104 | 7 | .541 |
| George Allen | 12 | Rams, Redskins | 116 | 47 | 5 | .705 | 118 | 54 | 5 | .681 |
| Don Coryell | 14 | Cardinals, Chargers | 111 | 83 | 1 | .572 | 114 | 89 | 1 | .561 |
| John Madden | 10 | Raiders | 103 | 32 | 7 | .750 | 112 | 39 | 7 | .731 |
| Mike Ditka | 11 | Bears | 106 | 62 | 0 | .631 | 112 | 68 | 0 | .622 |
| †M. Schottenheimer | 11 | Browns, Chiefs | 103 | 63 | 1 | .620 | 108 | 72 | 1 | .600 |

## Top Winning Percentages

| | W | L | T | Pct | | W | L | T | Pct |
|---|---|---|---|-----|---|---|---|---|-----|
| Vince Lombardi | 105 | 35 | 6 | .740 | †Don Shula | 338 | 165 | 6 | .670 |
| John Madden | 112 | 39 | 7 | .731 | Curly Lambeau | 229 | 134 | 22 | .623 |
| Joe Gibbs | 140 | 65 | 0 | .683 | Mike Ditka | 112 | 68 | 0 | .622 |
| George Allen | 118 | 54 | 5 | .681 | Bill Walsh | 102 | 63 | 1 | .617 |
| George Halas | 324 | 151 | 31 | .671 | Paul Brown | 170 | 108 | 6 | .609 |

Note: Minimum 100 victories

†Active coach

# Alltime Number-One Draft Choices

| Year | Team | Selection | Position |
|------|------|-----------|----------|
| 1936 | Philadelphia | Jay Berwanger, Chicago | HB |
| 1937 | Philadelphia | Sam Francis, Nebraska | FB |
| 1938 | Cleveland | Corbett Davis, Indiana | FB |
| 1939 | Chicago Cardinals | Ki Aldrich, Texas Christian | C |
| 1940 | Chicago Cardinals | George Cafego, Tennessee | HB |
| 1941 | Chicago Bears | Tom Harmon, Michigan | HB |
| 1942 | Pittsburgh | Bill Dudley, Virginia | HB |
| 1943 | Detroit | Frank Sinkwich, Georgia | HB |
| 1944 | Boston | Angelo Bertelli, Notre Dame | QB |
| 1945 | Chicago Cardinals | Charley Trippi, Georgia | HB |
| 1946 | Boston | Frank Dancewicz, Notre Dame | QB |
| 1947 | Chicago Bears | Bob Fenimore, Oklahoma A&M | HB |
| 1948 | Washington | Harry Gilmer, Alabama | QB |
| 1949 | Philadelphia | Chuck Bednarik, Pennsylvania | C |
| 1950 | Detroit | Leon Hart, Notre Dame | E |
| 1951 | New York Giants | Kyle Rote, Southern Methodist | HB |
| 1952 | Los Angeles | Bill Wade, Vanderbilt | QB |
| 1953 | San Francisco | Harry Babcock, Georgia | E |
| 1954 | Cleveland | Bobby Garrett, Stanford | QB |
| 1955 | Baltimore | George Shaw, Oregon | QB |
| 1956 | Pittsburgh | Gary Glick, Colorado A&M | DB |
| 1957 | Green Bay | Paul Hornung, Notre Dame | HB |
| 1958 | Chicago Cardinals | King Hill, Rice | QB |
| 1959 | Green Bay | Randy Duncan, Iowa | QB |
| 1960 | Los Angeles | Billy Cannon, Louisiana St | RB |
| 1961 | Minnesota | Tommy Mason, Tulane | RB |
|      | Buffalo (AFL) | Ken Rice, Auburn | G |
| 1968 | Minnesota | Ron Yary, Southern California | T |
| 1969 | Buffalo (AFL) | O.J. Simpson, Southern California | RB |
| 1970 | Pittsburgh | Terry Bradshaw, Louisiana Tech | QB |
| 1971 | New England | Jim Plunkett, Stanford | QB |
| 1972 | Buffalo | Walt Patulski, Notre Dame | DE |
| 1973 | Houston | John Matuszak, Tampa | DE |
| 1974 | Dallas | Ed Jones, Tennessee St | DE |
| 1975 | Atlanta | Steve Bartkowski, California | QB |
| 1976 | Tampa Bay | Lee Roy Selmon, Oklahoma | DE |
| 1977 | Tampa Bay | Ricky Bell, Southern California | RB |
| 1978 | Houston | Earl Campbell, Texas | RB |
| 1979 | Buffalo | Tom Cousineau, Ohio St | LB |
| 1980 | Detroit | Billy Sims, Oklahoma | RB |
| 1981 | New Orleans | George Rogers, South Carolina | RB |
| 1982 | New England | Kenneth Sims, Texas | DT |
| 1983 | Baltimore | John Elway, Stanford | QB |
| 1984 | New England | Irving Fryar, Nebraska | WR |
| 1985 | Buffalo | Bruce Smith, Virginia Tech | DE |
| 1986 | Tampa Bay | Bo Jackson, Auburn | RB |
| 1987 | Tampa Bay | Vinny Testaverde, Miami (FL) | QB |
| 1988 | Atlanta | Aundray Bruce, Auburn | LB |
| 1989 | Dallas | Troy Aikman, UCLA | QB |
| 1990 | Indianapolis | Jeff George, Illinois | QB |
| 1991 | Dallas | Russell Maryland, Miami (FL) | DT |
| 1992 | Indianapolis | Steve Emtman, Washington | DT |
| 1993 | New England | Drew Bledsoe, Washington St | QB |
| 1994 | Cincinnati | Dan Wilkinson, Ohio St | DT |
| 1995 | Cincinnati | Ki-Jana Carter, Penn St | RB |

From 1947 through 1958, the first selection in the draft was a bonus pick, awarded to the winner of a random draw. That club, in turn, forfeited its last-round draft choice. The winner of the bonus choice was eliminated from future draws. The system was abolished after 1958, by which time all clubs had received a bonus choice.

# Members of the Pro Football Hall of Fame

Herb Adderley
Lance Alworth
Doug Atkins
Morris "Red" Badgro
Lem Barney
Cliff Battles
Sammy Baugh
Chuck Bednarik
Bert Bell
Bobby Bell
Raymond Berry
Charles W. Bidwill, Sr.
Fred Biletnikoff
George Blanda
Mel Blount
Terry Bradshaw
Jim Brown
Paul Brown
Roosevelt Brown
Willie Brown
Buck Buchanan
Dick Butkus
Earl Campbell
Tony Canadeo
Joe Carr
Guy Chamberlin
Jack Christiansen
Earl "Dutch" Clark
George Connor
Jimmy Conzelman
Larry Csonka
Al Davis
Willie Davis
Len Dawson
Mike Ditka
Art Donovan
Tony Dorsett
John "Paddy" Driscoll
Bill Dudley
Glen "Turk" Edwards
Weeb Ewbank
Tom Fears
Jim Finks
Ray Flaherty
Len Ford
Dan Fortmann
Dan Fouts
Frank Gatski
Bill George
Frank Gifford
Sid Gillman
Otto Graham
Harold "Red" Grange
Bud Grant
Joe Greene
Forrest Gregg
Bob Griese
Lou Groza
Joe Guyon
George Halas

Jack Ham
John Hannah
Franco Harris
Ed Healey
Mel Hein
Ted Hendricks
Wilbur "Pete" Henry
Arnie Herber
Bill Hewitt
Clarke Hinkle
Elroy "Crazylegs" Hirsch
Paul Hornung
Ken Houston
Cal Hubbard
Sam Huff
Lamar Hunt
Don Hutson
Jimmy Johnson
John Henry Johnson
David "Deacon" Jones
Stan Jones
Henry Jordan
Sonny Jurgensen
Leroy Kelly
Walt Kiesling
Frank "Bruiser" Kinard
Earl "Curly" Lambeau
Jack Lambert
Tom Landry
Dick "Night Train" Lane
Jim Langer
Willie Lanier
Steve Largent
Yale Lary
Dante Lavelli
Bobby Layne
Alphonse "Tuffy" Leemans
Bob Lilly
Larry Little
Vince Lombardi
Sid Luckman
Roy "Link" Lyman
John Mackey
Tim Mara
Gino Marchetti
George Preston Marshall
Ollie Matson
Don Maynard
George McAfee
Mike McCormack
Hugh McElhenny
Johnny "Blood" McNally
Mike Michalske
Wayne Millner
Bobby Mitchell
Ron Mix
Lenny Moore
Marion Motley
George Musso
Bronko Nagurski

Joe Namath
Earle "Greasy" Neale
Ernie Nevers
Ray Nitschke
Chuck Noll
Leo Nomellini
Merlin Olsen
Jim Otto
Steve Owen
Alan Page
Clarence "Ace" Parker
Jim Parker
Walter Payton
Joe Perry
Pete Pihos
Hugh "Shorty" Ray
Dan Reeves
John Riggins
Jim Ringo
Andy Robustelli
Art Rooney
Pete Rozelle
Bob St. Clair
Gale Sayers
Joe Schmidt
Tex Schramm
Lee Roy Selmon
Art Shell
O. J. Simpson
Jackie Smith
Bart Starr
Roger Staubach
Ernie Stautner
Jan Stenerud
Ken Strong
Joe Stydahar
Fran Tarkenton
Charley Taylor
Jim Taylor
Jim Thorpe
Y. A. Tittle
George Trafton
Charley Trippi
Emlen Tunnell
Clyde "Bulldog" Turner
Johnny Unitas
Gene Upshaw
Norm Van Brocklin
Steve Van Buren
Doak Walker
Bill Walsh
Paul Warfield
Bob Waterfield
Arnie Weinmeister
Randy White
Bill Willis
Larry Wilson
Kellen Winslow
Alex Wojciechowicz
Willie Wood

# Champions of Other Leagues

## Canadian Football League Grey Cup

| Year | Results | Site | Attendance |
|---|---|---|---|
| 1909 | U of Toronto 26, Parkdale 6 | Toronto | 3,807 |
| 1910 | U of Toronto 16, Hamilton Tigers 7 | Hamilton | 12,000 |
| 1911 | U of Toronto 14, Toronto 7 | Toronto | 13,687 |
| 1912 | Hamilton Alerts 11, Toronto 4 | Hamilton | 5,337 |
| 1913 | Hamilton Tigers 44, Parkdale 2 | Hamilton | 2,100 |
| 1914 | Toronto 14, U of Toronto 2 | Toronto | 10,500 |
| 1915 | Hamilton Tigers 13, Toronto RAA 7 | Toronto | 2,808 |
| 1916-19 | No game | | |
| 1920 | U of Toronto 16, Toronto 3 | Toronto | 10,088 |
| 1921 | Toronto 23, Edmonton 0 | Toronto | 9,558 |
| 1922 | Queen's U 13, Edmonton 1 | Kingston | 4,700 |
| 1923 | Queen's U 54, Regina 0 | Toronto | 8,629 |
| 1924 | Queen's U 11, Balmy Beach 3 | Toronto | 5,978 |
| 1925 | Ottawa Senators 24, Winnipeg 1 | Ottawa | 6,900 |
| 1926 | Ottawa Senators 10, Toronto U 7 | Toronto | 8,276 |
| 1927 | Balmy Beach 9, Hamilton Tigers 6 | Toronto | 13,676 |
| 1928 | Hamilton Tigers 30, Regina 0 | Hamilton | 4,767 |
| 1929 | Hamilton Tigers 14, Regina 3 | Hamilton | 1,906 |
| 1930 | Balmy Beach 11, Regina 6 | Toronto | 3,914 |
| 1931 | Montreal AAA 22, Regina 0 | Montreal | 5,112 |
| 1932 | Hamilton Tigers 25, Regina 6 | Hamilton | 4,806 |
| 1933 | Toronto 4, Sarnia 3 | Sarnia | 2,751 |
| 1934 | Sarnia 20, Regina 12 | Toronto | 8,900 |
| 1935 | Winnipeg 18, Hamilton Tigers 12 | Hamilton | 6,405 |
| 1936 | Sarnia 26, Ottawa RR 20 | Toronto | 5,883 |
| 1937 | Toronto 4, Winnipeg 3 | Toronto | 11,522 |
| 1938 | Toronto 30, Winnipeg 7 | Toronto | 18,778 |
| 1939 | Winnipeg 8, Ottawa 7 | Ottawa | 11,738 |
| 1940 | Ottawa 12, Balmy Beach 5 | Ottawa | 1,700 |
| 1940 | Ottawa 8, Balmy Beach 2 | Toronto | 4,998 |
| 1941 | Winnipeg 18, Ottawa 16 | Toronto | 19,065 |
| 1942 | Toronto RCAF 8, Winnipeg RCAF 5 | Toronto | 12,455 |
| 1943 | Hamilton F Wild 23, Winnipeg RCAF 14 | Toronto | 16,423 |
| 1944 | Montreal St H-D Navy 7, Hamilton F Wild 6 | Hamilton | 3,871 |
| 1945 | Toronto 35, Winnipeg 0 | Toronto | 18,660 |
| 1946 | Toronto 28, Winnipeg 6 | Toronto | 18,960 |
| 1947 | Toronto 10, Winnipeg 9 | Toronto | 18,885 |
| 1948 | Calgary 12, Ottawa 7 | Toronto | 20,013 |
| 1949 | Montreal Als 28, Calgary 15 | Toronto | 20,087 |
| 1950 | Toronto 13, Winnipeg 0 | Toronto | 27,101 |
| 1951 | Ottawa 21, Saskatchewan 14 | Toronto | 27,341 |
| 1952 | Toronto 21, Edmonton 11 | Toronto | 27,391 |
| 1953 | Hamilton Ticats 12, Winnipeg 6 | Toronto | 27,313 |
| 1954 | Edmonton 26, Montreal 25 | Toronto | 27,321 |
| 1955 | Edmonton 34, Montreal 19 | Vancouver | 39,417 |
| 1956 | Edmonton 50, Montreal 27 | Toronto | 27,425 |
| 1957 | Hamilton 32, Winnipeg 7 | Toronto | 27,051 |
| 1958 | Winnipeg 35, Hamilton 28 | Vancouver | 36,567 |
| 1959 | Winnipeg 21, Hamilton 7 | Toronto | 33,133 |
| 1960 | Ottawa 16, Edmonton 6 | Vancouver | 38,102 |
| 1961 | Winnipeg 21, Hamilton 14 | Toronto | 32,651 |
| 1962 | Winnipeg 28, Hamilton 27 | Toronto | 32,655 |
| 1963 | Hamilton 21, British Columbia 10 | Vancouver | 36,545 |
| 1964 | British Columbia 34, Hamilton 24 | Toronto | 32,655 |
| 1965 | Hamilton 22, Winnipeg 16 | Toronto | 32,655 |
| 1966 | Saskatchewan 29, Ottawa 14 | Vancouver | 36,553 |
| 1967 | Hamilton 24, Saskatchewan 1 | Ottawa | 31,358 |
| 1968 | Ottawa 24, Calgary 21 | Toronto | 32,655 |
| 1969 | Ottawa 29, Saskatchewan 11 | Montreal | 33,172 |
| 1970 | Montreal 23, Toronto 10 | Toronto | 32,669 |
| 1971 | Calgary 14, Toronto 11 | Vancouver | 34,484 |
| 1972 | Hamilton 13, Saskatchewan 10 | Hamilton | 33,993 |
| 1973 | Ottawa 22, Edmonton 18 | Toronto | 36,653 |
| 1974 | Montreal 20, Edmonton 7 | Vancouver | 34,450 |
| 1975 | Edmonton 9, Montreal 8 | Calgary | 32,454 |

## Canadian Football League Grey Cup *(Cont.)*

| Year | Results | Site | Attendance |
|------|---------|------|-----------|
| 1976 | Ottawa 23, Saskatchewan 20 | Toronto | 53,467 |
| 1977 | Montreal 41, Edmonton 6 | Montreal | 68,318 |
| 1978 | Edmonton 20, Montreal 13 | Toronto | 54,695 |
| 1979 | Edmonton 17, Montreal 9 | Montreal | 65,113 |
| 1980 | Edmonton 48, Hamilton 10 | Toronto | 54,661 |
| 1981 | Edmonton 26, Ottawa 23 | Montreal | 52,478 |
| 1982 | Edmonton 32, Toronto 16 | Toronto | 54,741 |
| 1983 | Toronto 18, British Columbia 17 | Vancouver | 59,345 |
| 1984 | Winnipeg 47, Hamilton 17 | Edmonton | 60,081 |
| 1985 | British Columbia 37, Hamilton 24 | Montreal | 56,723 |
| 1986 | Hamilton 39, Edmonton 15 | Vancouver | 59,621 |
| 1987 | Edmonton 38, Toronto 36 | Vancouver | 59,478 |
| 1988 | Winnipeg 22, British Columbia 21 | Ottawa | 50,604 |
| 1989 | Saskatchewan 43, Hamilton 40 | Toronto | 54,088 |
| 1990 | Winnipeg 50, Edmonton 11 | Vancouver | 46,968 |
| 1991 | Toronto 36, Calgary 21 | Winnipeg | 51,985 |
| 1992 | Calgary 24, Winnipeg 10 | Toronto | 45,863 |
| 1993 | Edmonton 33, Winnipeg 23 | Calgary | 50,035 |
| 1994 | British Columbia 26, Baltimore 23 | Vancouver | 55,097 |

In 1909, Earl Grey, the Governor-General of Canada, donated a trophy for the Rugby Football Championship of Canada. The trophy, which subsequently became known as the Grey Cup, was originally open only to teams registered with the Canada Rugby Union. Since 1954, it has been awarded to the winner of the Canadian Football League's championship game.

### AMERICAN FOOTBALL LEAGUE I

| Year | Champion | Record |
|------|----------|--------|
| 1926 | Philadelphia Quakers | 7-2 |

### AMERICAN FOOTBALL LEAGUE II

| Year | Champion | Record |
|------|----------|--------|
| 1936 | Boston Shamrocks | 8-3 |
| 1937 | LA Bulldogs | 8-0 |

### AMERICAN FOOTBALL LEAGUE III

| Year | Champion | Record |
|------|----------|--------|
| 1940 | Columbus Bullies | 8-1-1 |
| 1941 | Columbus Bullies | 5-1-2 |

### WORLD LEAGUE OF AMERICAN FOOTBALL

| Year | Champion | Record |
|------|----------|--------|
| 1992 | Sacramento | 8-2-0 |
| 1995 | Frankfurt | 6-4-0 |

### ALL-AMERICAN FOOTBALL CONFERENCE

| Year | Championship Game |
|------|-------------------|
| 1946 | Cleveland 14, NY Yankees 9 |
| 1947 | Cleveland 14, NY Yankees 3 |
| 1948 | Cleveland 49, Buffalo 7 |
| 1949 | Cleveland 21, San Francisco 7 |

### WORLD FOOTBALL LEAGUE

| Year | World Bowl Championship |
|------|-------------------------|
| 1974 | Birmingham 22, Florida 21 |
| 1975 | Disbanded midseason |

### UNITED STATES FOOTBALL LEAGUE

| Year | Championship Game |
|------|-------------------|
| 1983 | Michigan 24, Philadelphia 22, at Denver |
| 1984 | Philadelphia 23, Arizona 3, at Tampa |
| 1985 | Baltimore 28, Oakland 24, at East Rutherford |

## Taglia-Boo

The mahogany-walled auditorium of New York City's 92nd Street Y is usually a forum for poetry readings and cultural symposia. But last December the commissioners of the three major league sports that still *have* commissioners got together to adress the state of their respective games. The NBA's David Stern, the NHL's Gary Bettman and the NFL's Paul Tagliabue took turns responding to questions from journalist David Halberstam, and their anwers were predictably guarded and equivocal on the subject of labor relations. More troubling—and less explicable—was Tagliabue's cavalier response to a query about head injuries in football. Calling the matter "a pack journalism issue," he waved away concern, saying that the NFL has "one concussion every three or four games." After a few more calculations, Tagliabue pronounced a figure of 2.5 concussions for every 22,000 players engaged." His response echoes for Halberstam, who won a Pulitzer Prize for his war coverage in Souteast Asia. "I feel like I'm back in Vietnam hearing McNamara give statistics," he said.

Tagliabue's numbers still mean about four concussions a week. The last player to become a statistic was Boomer Esiason, whom Junior Seau knocked senseless during the New York Jets' 21–6 loss to the San Diego Chargers in late '94. Tagliabue's head has been spared this season's spate of bruising hits; on this issue he ought to be making better use of it.

# Coll●ge Footb●ll

**How Sweet It Is!**

*Tom Osborne celebrates Nebraska's national championship*

ROBERT ROGERS

# Unfinished Business

## The Nebraska Cornhuskers considered themselves the best team in the land in 1993; in '94 they proved it

### by Tim Layden

NEBRASKA COACH Tom Osborne was carried from the floor of the Orange Bowl on the shoulders of his players on New Year's night. Surely it was a light load, as Osborne was unburdened of more than two decades of waiting. It was never intended that the national championship of college football become a Lifetime Achievement Award, although in recent years it has come to coaches and programs with long histories of success (Washington's Don James in 1991 and Florida State's Bobby Bowden in 1993), but without the imprimatur of a title. None have waited more patiently than Osborne or lingered as close to greatness as Nebraska.

Their chase ended with a 24–17 victory over Miami, the final step in a 13–0 season, in a stadium where some of the Cornhuskers' most exasperating scenes have been played. Junior quarterback Tommie Frazier, who hadn't played since a blood clot was found in his right leg more than three months earlier, led the Cornhuskers on two fourth-quarter touchdown drives

that overhauled the Hurricanes and made meaningless unbeaten No. 2 Penn State's Rose Bowl victory the following day.

In 1994, college football gave us a season of frozen images and of teams and players falling just short. The snapshot of Osborne, whisked from the field by his players, is the one exception—a finished product.

Beginning in the heat of summer, Nebraska promised to complete the job that it had started in 1993, when the Cornhuskers were beaten 18–16 in the Orange Bowl by Florida State. "Unfinished Business" was the theme of their season. They practiced every day with 1:16 on the scoreboard clock, because with that much time remaining, they had gone ahead of Florida State, only to lose on a field goal with 21 seconds left. "We played well enough to win that game last year," Osborne said.

Nebraska left nothing unfinished in '94. Other teams and players rose high and often came up agonizingly short:
• Penn State, which for the fourth time in coach Joe Paterno's sublime 28-year reign

AL TIELEMANS

**Frazier engineered two fourth-quarter TD drives in the Orange Bowl.**

as king of the Nittany Lions went undefeated and failed to win the national championship. The Lions featured an offense that crunched numbers like a CD-ROM drive (an average of 47.8 points a game in the regular season) and won the Big Ten in their second year of membership. Tailback Ki-Jana Carter and quarterback Kerry Collins both finished in the top five in voting for the Heisman Trophy, and wideout Bobby Engram and tight end Kyle Brady were both first team All-Americas. Southern California coach John Robinson's Trojans lost at Penn State 38-14 in September, and when Robinson considered the possibility of a Rose Bowl rematch with the Lions, he said, "If it's us, we're not going."

But after reaching No. 1 with a 31–24 victory over Michigan in Ann Arbor on Oct. 15, the Nittany Lions lost control of their destiny in a puzzling two-week drop. On Oct. 29, Penn State annihilated a decent Ohio State team 63–14, yet dropped out of first place in the Associated Press media poll. "We dropped?" said Penn State linebacker Willie Smith on the day the poll was announced. "What do they want us to do to these teams?" The reason for the fall? Nebraska's dominating 24–7 win over Colorado on the same day, moving the Cornhuskers into No. 1.

A week later Penn State beat Indiana by the artificially close score of 35–29. The Nittany Lions led 35–14 with 1:49 to play. The Hoosiers subsequently scored twice against Penn State reserves, including a Hail Mary pass on the last play of the game, and the result was that Penn State dropped to No. 2 in the *CNN/USA Today* coaches' poll. "That was ridiculous," said Paterno. "That game was never in doubt. Never. We had a bunch of kids in at the end who hadn't even *practiced*." (It also was ironic, since it was the coaches who in previous poll controversies had derided media for placing too much emphasis on margins of victory.)

In the end it didn't matter in the least that Penn State finished its regular season without a loss or that the Lions beat Oregon in the Rose Bowl 38–20. Their hopes of winning the national championship came to an end as they sat in their rooms at the Hotel Inter-Continental, watching the Orange Bowl. When Nebraska fullback Cory Schlesinger scored the winning touchdown, Penn State defensive back Brian

**Carter was runner-up in the Heisman voting but No. 1 in the draft.**

Miller said, "I heard a big crash next door. I guess some guys were throwing things around." They knew it was over.

• Colorado quarterback Kordell Stewart and receiver Michael Westbrook provided the single most electric moment of the season: the Catch on Oct. 24 at Michigan Stadium. On that splendid Midwestern afternoon Michigan rode the momentum of a victory over Notre Dame two weeks earlier and led Colorado 26–14 with 3:52 to play.

The Buffaloes drove 72 yards and made it 26–21 on Rashaan Salaam's one-yard run with 2:16 left. A Michigan punt pinned Colorado to its 15-yard line with 15 seconds left and no timeouts. Stewart threw 21 yards over the middle to Westbrook and then slammed the ball into the ground to stop the clock with six seconds left and 64 yards of grass in front of him. Stewart dropped back into a deep pocket, bought time against Michigan's inexplicable three-man

AL TIELEMANS

rush and then threw a tight spiral into the twilight. "I just heaved it out there," said Stewart. Six players—three from each team—converged as the ball reached the goal line. Colorado's Blake Anderson, the son of NFL Hall of Fame defensive back Dick Anderson, a Colorado alumnus, batted the ball with his right hand, keeping it alive. Westbrook, a senior who was raised on the west side of Detroit, not 20 miles from the Michigan campus, soared in from the sideline and plucked the ball off the back of Michigan defender Ty Law's jersey, cradling it against his chest as he fell to the ground. Two officials simultaneously signaled touchdown, making Colorado a 27–26 winner. Most in the crowd of more than 106,000 fell instantly silent. "That was some sound, all of a sudden," said Colorado safety Steve Rosga.

And some play. It was the most remarkable single moment in a college football game since Doug Flutie's bomb to Gerard Phelan gave Boston College a 47–45 victory over Miami, 10 years earlier.

It also might have forewarned that Colorado was destined to win its second national championship in five years (the first was in 1990). But on the last Saturday of October, five weeks after the Catch, came the Rout. Nebraska steamrollered the Buffaloes. Colorado went on to finish 11–1, but there was more to the Buffalo season.

On Nov. 19, just after his team had beaten Iowa State, Colorado coach Bill McCartney shocked the school by announcing his resignation. He was replaced nine days later by 33-year-old assistant coach Rick Neuheisel, who beat out three other more tenured staff members for the job. And finally, on Dec. 9, Salaam, who rushed for a school-record 2,000 yards, became the first Colorado player to win the Heisman Trophy.

•Steve McNair of Alcorn State was the most spectacular player in the nation throughout the season, yet could finish no better than third in the Heisman voting. McNair eclipsed Ty Detmer's career total offensive output and finished with 16,823

yards. He averaged more than 500 yards a game in his senior season; he was a smart, skilled passer and a dangerous scrambler. Yet his season-long excellence was tainted by incessant debate over his Heisman worthiness, focusing on the fact that he played only in Division I-AA. All of this became moot when McNair was selected in the first round of the NFL draft by the Houston Oilers and was projected to have a long and prosperous career.

•Michigan running back Tyrone Wheatley was projected after the 1993 season to be one of the top picks in the NFL draft—if he chose to skip his senior year. But Wheatley returned ... and injured his right shoulder on the first day of full-contact practice. He returned in the third game of the season and rushed for 1,144 yards but also became the poster child for athletes who choose to risk injury by staying in school an extra year. When Penn State's Carter was mulling his draft decision (he ultimately left early and was the No. 1 player picked), he said, "I don't know if Wheatley's stock dropped at all, but something like that makes you think hard." Sadly, Carter's words proved to be prophetic. He ended up tearing his anterior cruciate ligament in the preseason with the Cincinnati Bengals and missed what would have been his rookie year in the NFL.

•Florida State, in pursuit of a second consecutive national title, became only the latest major program tainted by scandal. A *Sports Illustrated* investigation showed that six members of the Seminoles' '93 championship team received cash payments and took part in an in-season buying binge at a Tallahassee sporting goods store, all sponsored by a sports agent. Playing under NCAA scrutiny, the Seminoles nonetheless went 10-1-1, losing only to Miami at the Orange Bowl and rallying from a 31–3 deficit to tie Florida 31–31 in the last game of the regular season.

•Oregon, which hadn't played in the Rose Bowl since 1958, was picked in some quarters (SI was one) to finish last in the Pac-10. But under veteran coach Rich Brooks (who has since left to coach the St. Louis Rams),

JOHN BIEVER

**Can Air McNair fly in the NFL? The Oilers think so; they took the agile QB with the third pick.**

Alabama in Birmingham. In '95 they rejoin the bowl eligibles. The Crimson Tide threatened to repeat its silent national championship assault of 1992 but lost to Florida in the SEC title game. That loss only served to fortify what critics of the game have always suspected: An 11-game regular-season schedule is tough enough; forcing SEC teams to play a title game will make it nearly impossible for the conference to win a national title.

•Notre Dame had no such worries. Amid preseason predictions of greatness for the team and first-year quarterback Ron Powlus, the Fighting Irish stammered to a 6-5-1 record, including back-to-back midseason losses to Boston College and Brigham Young. "I can give you a million excuses, but no reasons," coach Lou Holtz said. "Some seasons things just don't fit."

In their own way, Nebraskans could sympathize with Holtz. The Cornhuskers' drought between national championships had lasted 23 years, broken down into small moments of agony, impatience and frustration. Nebraska won consecutive titles in 1970 and '71 under legendary coach Bob Devaney and in the process built itself into a national power of the highest magnitude. It seemed only reasonable to expect that more titles would be brought home to Lincoln and that someday Nebraska would fill trophy cases not just with the busts of famous offensive linemen and running backs but also with championship booty. When Devaney retired in 1973, Osborne replaced him. He won 81.1% of his games in 21 years but lost enough of the most important ones to leave

the Ducks emerged from a wild conference race with a 7–1 league record (9–3 overall) and earned the right to play Penn State in the Rose Bowl. Even there, the Ducks hung together, playing the mighty Lions to a 14–14 stalemate deep into the third quarter.

•In the Southeastern Conference, Auburn continued its remarkable, probation-strapped run under 38-year-old coach Terry Bowden, Bobby's son. The Tigers, who went 11–0 in '93, their first year of probation, won their first nine games before tying Georgia and losing the annual Iron Bowl to

Nebraska always somewhere beneath No. 1 on the second day in January.

In 1975 Nebraska was 10–0 and ranked No. 2 in the country when they lost 35–10 to Oklahoma. The Sooners went on to win the national championship. In '79 the Cornhuskers were 10–0 and ranked No. 3 before losing to Oklahoma and Houston to finish the season. In '81 they lost to national champion Clemson in the Orange Bowl. And from 1987 to '93 Nebraska lost seven consecutive bowl games, carving out a reputation as cornfed bullies who could annually drill Oklahoma State but never win a truly big game.

Their combination of excellence and futility reached comic proportions in the latter half of the '80s. In the 10 years from 1984 through 1993, Nebraska won 98 games, a ridiculous average of nearly 10 wins a season. But the Cornhuskers also lost eight of 10 bowl games, including those seven in a row, beginning with a 31–28 Fiesta Bowl loss to Florida State on Jan. 1, 1988.

The Orange Bowl held its own particular demons. It was there that Osborne's 1983 team—the Mike Rozier–Irving Fryar–Turner Gill outfit that some people called the best college team ever assembled—was expected to beat upstart Miami for its 13th win in an unbeaten season and win that first title. Instead Miami and quarterback Bernie Kosar beat the Cornhuskers 31–30 to win its first national championship. Nebraska scored with 48 seconds to play and could have kicked an extra point to tie the game, and still probably have been voted No. 1, but Osborne elected to play for the victory. Gill's pass was batted away in the end zone by Miami defensive back Ken Calhoun.

Nebraska returned to the Orange Bowl again after the 1988 season and again lost to Miami. It was after that loss that the Huskers vowed to expand their recruiting, to chase the type of speed that dominated sunbelt rosters. "But then we had to go out and get the personnel," said Nebraska defensive coordinator Charlie McBride, "which wasn't something that happened overnight." And while the Huskers retooled, they lost more bowl games, including the Orange after the '91 and '92 seasons. That they came so close to Florida State after '93 was a shock to some.

To the Cornhuskers it was a sign that they were ready. "We were the best team last year," said offensive tackle Zach Wiegert, the anchor of a brilliant and powerful offensive line. "We're back to win the national championship."

The season began as if it would be a waltz, with a 31–0 pasting of West Virginia in the Kickoff Classic in New Jersey. Texas Tech fell on a Thursday night in Lubbock, Texas, and in what was supposed to be Nebraska's first test of the season, the Huskers waxed UCLA 49–21 in Lincoln. But the following Saturday, in a laughable 70–21 victory over Pacific, Frazier played only sparingly, and the next day, Sept. 25, doctors discovered a blood clot behind and slightly above his right knee. It was expected that Frazier's absence would be brief, but tests on Oct. 4 showed that the clot had re-formed, and it was suddenly likely that Frazier—the catalyst, one of the players who set the Cornhuskers apart from previous Nebraska teams—would not play again in '94.

But somehow Nebraska rolled on. Brook Berringer, a tall junior from Goodland, Kans., replaced Frazier and suffered a collapsed lung in his first game and a recollapse in his second. Osborne put his faith in that offensive line and in sophomore running back Lawrence Phillips, who ran for 1,722 yards, a Big Eight sophomore class record. The offense was altered and sometimes improvised. Matt Turman, a 165-pound walk-on quarterback from Wahoo, Neb., played the entire second half of a 32–3 victory over Oklahoma State. Berringer and Turman were asked to throw only 11 passes in a 17–3 win over a good Kansas State team. "Coach thought they might be susceptible to smashmouth football," said Turman after that game. Nebraska football, in other words. It began to look as if Nebraska, not Colorado, was blessed by the Midwestern football gods.

Florida State and finished at 10–1. And while Frazier started and wrestled with his timing, Miami took a 17–9 lead early in the fourth quarter. Berringer, back in the game, threw an interception in the end zone, and Miami players ran off the field in celebration. "We were pretty much saying, 'Ball game,'" said Hurricane defensive tackle Warren Sapp.

But before the lights were turned out on another Nebraska season, Frazier was re-inserted into the game. Twice he drove the Cornhuskers to touchdowns. Frazier led and created; the offensive line pounded weary and outweighed Miami. Frazier was named the MVP of the game; Osborne was freed from the weight of past failures. Yet he remained in character to the end. "I know everybody wants me to say, 'Gee, everything's different,'" Osborne said. "But I feel about the same as after any game we won."

Two mornings later the Cornhuskers were summarily voted into their title. And there was a bonus to consider. Beginning with the 1995 season, bowl matchups will be determined by a new alliance, with the No. 1 and No. 2 available teams (all those except the winners of the Big Ten and the Pac-10, who will continue to play in the Rose Bowl) playing in one of three bowls: the Fiesta, Sugar or Orange. After the '95 season it will be the Fiesta Bowl, after '96 the Sugar and after '97 the Orange. All conference tie-ins are eliminated, meaning that the Big Eight champion no longer goes to the Orange Bowl.

And the Orange Bowl game itself is moving north to Joe Robbie Stadium for the 1997 edition. So for Nebraska the exorcism is complete, the picture finished. Win the title, beat Miami, close the stadium. And ride off the field, as light as dust.

They rolled through the rest of the season, pounding Colorado to dash the Buffs' hopes. They beat back stubborn Oklahoma and its lame duck coach, Gary Gibbs, 13–3, and wrapped up a spot in the ... gulp ... Orange Bowl. "We're like the Buffalo Bills," said offensive guard Rob Zatechka. "We're back. Live with it."

A quarterback discussion dominated the week leading up to the game. Frazier was taken off anticoagulants in late December and would dress for the game. But would he start? The other principal topic was Nebraska's past Orange Bowl failures. Miami had struggled occasionally during the regular season, losing its 58-game Orange Bowl winning streak to Washington on Sept. 24., but still the Hurricanes beat

## Final Polls

### Associated Press

| | Record | Pts | Head Coach | SI Preseason Rank |
|---|---|---|---|---|
| 1............................Nebraska (51½) | 13-0-0 | 1539½ | Tom Osborne | 3 |
| 2............................Penn State (10½) | 12-0-0 | 1497½ | Joe Paterno | 6 |
| 3............................Colorado | 11-1-0 | 1410 | Bill McCartney | 2 |
| 4............................Florida St | 10-1-1 | 1320 | Bobby Bowden | 10 |
| 5............................Alabama | 12-1-0 | 1312 | Gene Stallings | 16 |
| 6............................Miami (FL) | 10-2-0 | 1249 | Dennis Erickson | 7 |
| 7............................Florida | 10-2-1 | 1153 | Steve Spurrier | 8 |
| 8............................Texas A&M | 10-0-1 | 1117 | R.C. Slocum | 22 |
| 9............................Auburn | 9-1-1 | 1110 | Terry Bowden | 18 |
| 10..........................Utah | 10-2-0 | 955 | Ron McBride | 20 |
| 11..........................Oregon | 9-4-0 | 810 | Rich Brooks | 74 |
| 12..........................Michigan | 8-4-0 | 732 | Gary Moeller | 4 |
| 13..........................Southern Cal | 8-3-1 | 691 | John Robinson | 14 |
| 14..........................Ohio St | 9-4-0 | 672 | John Cooper | 29 |
| 15..........................Virginia | 9-3-0 | 648 | George Welsh | 36 |
| 16..........................Colorado St | 10-2-0 | 630 | Sonny Lubick | 32 |
| 17..........................N Carolina St | 9-3-0 | 511 | Mike O'Cain | 40 |
| 18..........................Brigham Young | 10-3-0 | 500 | LaVell Edwards | 26 |
| 19..........................Kansas St | 9-3-0 | 496 | Bill Snyder | 30 |
| 20..........................Arizona | 8-4-0 | 364 | Dick Tomey | 1 |
| 21..........................Washington St | 8-4-0 | 344 | Mike Price | 63 |
| 22..........................Tennessee | 8-4-0 | 303 | Phillip Fulmer | 9 |
| 23..........................Boston College | 7-4-1 | 236 | Dan Henning | 19 |
| 24..........................Mississippi St | 8-4-0 | 160 | Jackie Sherrill | 37 |
| 25..........................Texas | 8-4-0 | 90 | John Mackovic | 24 |

Note: As voted by panel of 60 sportswriters and broadcasters following bowl games (1st-place votes in parentheses).

### USA Today/CNN

| | Pts | Prev Rank | | Pts | Prev Rank |
|---|---|---|---|---|---|
| 1 ..............Nebraska (54) | 1542 | 1 | 14 .............Colorado St | 681 | 10 |
| 2 ..............Penn St (8) | 1496 | 2 | 15 .............Southern Cal | 670 | 22 |
| 3 ..............Colorado | 1382 | 5 | 16 .............Kansas St | 661 | 8 |
| 4 ..............Alabama | 1344 | 6 | 17 .............N Carolina St | 626 | 20 |
| 5 ..............Florida St | 1329 | 7 | 18 .............Tennessee | 520 | 24 |
| 6 ..............Miami (FL) | 1229 | 3 | 19 .............Washington St | 449 | 23 |
| 7 ..............Florida | 1186 | 4 | 20 .............Arizona | 405 | 13 |
| 8 ..............Utah | 1029 | 12 | 21 .............N Carolina | 313 | 14 |
| 9 ..............Ohio St | 842 | 11 | 22 .............Boston College | 304 | 25 |
| 10 ............Brigham Young | 832 | 19 | 23 .............Texas | 244 | — |
| 11 ............Oregon | 831 | 9 | 24 .............Virginia Tech | 189 | 15 |
| 12 ............Michigan | 787 | 18 | 25 .............Mississippi St | 158 | 17 |
| 13 ............Virginia | 765 | 16 | | | |

Note: As voted by panel of 60 Division I-A head coaches; 25 points for 1st, 24 for 2nd, etc. (1st-place votes in parentheses).

## Bowls and Playoffs

### NCAA Division I-A Bowl Results

| Date | Bowl | Result | Payout/Team ($) | Attendance |
|---|---|---|---|---|
| 12-15-94..............Las Vegas | | UNLV 52, Central Michigan 24 | 247,688 | 17,562 |
| 12-25-94..............Aloha | | Boston College 12, Kansas St 7 | 750,000 | 44,862 |
| 12-28-94..............Independence | | Virginia 20, Texas Christian 10 | 750,000 | 27,242 |
| 12-29-94..............Copper | | Brigham Young 30, Oklahoma 6 | 750,000 | 45,122 |
| 12-29-94..............Freedom | | Utah 16, Arizona 13 | 750,000 | 27,477 |
| 12-30-94..............Holiday | | Michigan 24, Colorado St 14 | 1.7 million | 59,453 |
| 12-30-94..............Sun | | Texas 35, N Carolina 31 | 1.1 million | 50,612 |

## NCAA Division I-A Bowl Results

| Date | Bowl | Result | Payout/Team ($) | Attendance |
|---|---|---|---|---|
| 12-30-94 | Gator | Tennessee 45, Virginia Tech 23 | 3 million | 62,200 |
| 12-31-94 | Liberty | Illinois 30, East Carolina 0 | 776,000 | 33,280 |
| 12-31-94 | Alamo | Washington State 10, Baylor 3 | 750,000 | 44,106 |
| 1-1-95 | Orange | Nebraska 24, Miami (FL) 17 | 4.6 million | 81,753 |
| 1-1-95 | Peach | N Carolina State 28, Miss State 24 | 1.131 million | 64,902 |
| 1-2-95 | Cotton | Southern Cal 55, Texas Tech 14 | 3 million | 70,218 |
| 1-2-95 | Fiesta | Colorado 41, Notre Dame 24 | 3 million | 73,968 |
| 1-2-95 | Sugar | Florida State 23, Florida 17 | 4.45 million | 76,224 |
| 1-2-95 | Hall of Fame | Wisconsin 34, Duke 20 | 1 million | 61,384 |
| 1-2-95 | Florida Citrus | Alabama 24, Ohio State 17 | 2.5 million | 71,195 |
| 1-2-95 | Carquest | South Carolina 24, West Virginia 21 | 1 million | 50,833 |
| 1-2-95 | Rose | Penn St 38, Oregon 20 | 6.7 million | 102,247 |

## NCAA Division I-AA Championship Boxscore

| | | | | |
|---|---|---|---|---|
| Youngstown St | 0 | 14 | 7 | 7—28 |
| Boise St | 7 | 0 | 0 | 7—14 |

**FIRST QUARTER**
BSU: Matyshock 5 pass from Hilde (Erickson kick), 2:46.

**SECOND QUARTER**
YSU: Brungard 2 run (Massaro kick), 9:43.
YSU: Brungard 38 run (Massaro kick), 0:35.

**THIRD QUARTER**
YSU: Zwisler 5 pass from Brungard (Massaro kick), 3:02

**FOURTH QUARTER**
YSU: Patton 55 run (Massaro kick), 7:15
BSU: Matyshock 6 pass from Hilde (Erickson kick), 4:19

| | YSU | BSU |
|---|---|---|
| First downs | 20 | 13 |
| Rushing yardage | 263 | 59 |
| Passing yardage | 159 | 166 |
| Return yardage | 18 | 58 |
| Passes (comp-att-int) | 9-19-2 | 17-31-2 |
| Punts (no.-avg) | 6-37.0 | 6-38.8 |
| Fumbles (no.-lost) | 1-0 | 3-0 |
| Penalties (no.-yards) | 3-40 | 4-40 |

Att: 27,674

## Small College Championship Summaries

### NCAA DIVISION II

**First round:** Ferris St 43, West Chester 40; Indiana (PA) 35, Grand Valley St 27; Texas A&M-Kingsville 43, Western St 7; Portland St 29, Angelo St 0; N Dakota St 18, Pittsburg St 12 (3 OT); North Dakota 18, NE Missouri St 6; North Alabama 17, Carson-Newman 13; Valdosta St 14, Albany St (GA) 7
**Quarterfinals:** Indiana (PA) 21, Ferris St 17; Texas A&M-Kingsville 21, Portland St 16; North Dakota 14, N Dakota St 7; North Alabama 27, Valdosta St 24 (2 OT).
**Semifinals:** Texas A&M-Kingsville 46, Indiana (PA) 20; North Alabama 35, North Dakota 7.

**Championship:** 12-10-94 Florence, AL

| | | | | |
|---|---|---|---|---|
| Texas A&M-Kingsville | 0 | 3 | 7 | 0—10 |
| North Alabama | 7 | 9 | 0 | 0—16 |

### NCAA DIVISION III

**First round:** Mount Union 28, Allegheny 19; Albion 28, Augustana (IL) 21; Wartburg 22, Central (IA) 21; St John's (MN) 51, La Verne 12; Widener 14, Dickinson 0; Wash&Jeff. 28, Trinity (TX) 0; Plymouth St 19, Merchant Marine 18; Ithaca 10, Buffalo St 7 (2 OT).
**Quarterfinals:** Albion 34, Mt Union 33; St John's (MN) 42, Wartburg 14; Wash&Jeff. 37, Widener 21; Ithaca 22, Plymouth St 7.
**Semifinals:** Albion 19, St John's (MN) 16; Wash&Jeff 23, Ithaca 19.

**Championship:** 12-10-93 Salem, VA

| | | | | |
|---|---|---|---|---|
| Albion | 7 | 17 | 7 | 7—38 |
| Washington&Jefferson | 7 | 0 | 0 | 8—15 |

### NAIA DIVISION I PLAYOFFS

**First Round:** Arkansas-Pine Bluff 21, Central St (OH)14; Northeastern St (OK) 14, Moorhead St (MN) 7; Western Montana 48, Glenville St (WV) 38; Langston (OK) 56, Arkansas Tech 42.
**Semifinals:** Arkansas-Pine Bluff 60, Western Montana 53 (OT); Northeastern St (OK) 3, Langston (OK) 0.

**Championship:** 12-10-94 Pine Bluff, AR

| | | | | |
|---|---|---|---|---|
| Northeastern St (OK) | 0 | 3 | 3 | 7—13 |
| Arkansas-Pine Bluff | 3 | 7 | 0 | 2—12 |

### NAIA DIVISION II PLAYOFFS

**First round:** Western Washington 21, Linfield (OR) 2; Pacific Lutheran (WA) 34, Midland Lutheran (NE) 14; Westminster (PA) 41, Findlay (OH) 30; Tiffin (OH) 41, Eureka (IL) 14; Hardin-Simmons (TX) 49, Missouri Valley 21; Minot St (ND) 20, Sioux Falls (SD) 13; Lambuth (TN) 48, Evangel (MO) 19; Northwestern (IA) 38, Trinity (IL) 20.
**Quarterfinals:** Lambuth (TN) 57, Hardin-Simmons (TX) 54; Westminster (PA) 42, Tiffin (OH) 14; Northwestern (IA) 28, Minot St (ND) 26; Pacific Lutheran (WA) 25, Western Washington 20.
**Semifinals:** Pacific Lutheran (WA) 28, Northwestern (IA) 7; Westminster (PA) 46, Lambuth (TN) 6.

**Championship:** 12-17-94 Portand, OR

| | | | | |
|---|---|---|---|---|
| Westminster (PA) | 7 | 7 | 7 | 6—27 |
| Pacific Lutheran (WA) | 0 | 7 | 0 | 0—7 |

# Awards

## Heisman Memorial Trophy

| Player/School | Class | Pos | 1st | 2nd | 3rd | Total |
|---|---|---|---|---|---|---|
| Rashaan Salaam, Colorado ..........Jr | | RB | 400 | 229 | 85 | 1,743 |
| Ki-Jana Carter, Penn St................Jr | | RB | 115 | 205 | 146 | 901 |
| Steve McNair, Alcorn St ................Sr | | QB | 111 | 85 | 152 | 655 |
| Kerry Collins, Penn St....................Sr | | QB | 101 | 117 | 102 | 639 |
| Jay Barker, Alabama......................Sr | | QB | 36 | 58 | 71 | 295 |
| Warren Sapp, Miami (FL) ...............Jr | | DT | 17 | 37 | 67 | 192 |
| Eric Zeier, Georgia .......................Sr | | QB | 7 | 15 | 32 | 83 |
| Lawrence Phillips, Nebraska..........So | | RB | 1 | 8 | 21 | 40 |
| Napoleon Kaufman, Washington ...Sr | | RB | 3 | 3 | 12 | 27 |
| Zach Wiegert, Nebraska ...............Sr | | OT | 1 | 7 | 10 | 27 |

Note: Former Heisman winners and the media vote, with ballots allowing for 3 names (3 points for 1st, 2 for 2nd, 1 for 3rd).

## Offensive Players of the Year

Maxwell Award (Player)..............................Kerry Collins, Penn St, QB
Walter Camp Player of the Year (Back) .....Rashaan Salaam, Colorado, RB
Davey O'Brien Award (QB) ........................Kerry Collins, Penn St, QB
Doak Walker Award (RB) ...........................Rashaan Salaam, Colorado, RB

## Other Awards

Vince Lombardi/Rotary Award (Lineman) ..Waren Sapp, Miami (FL), DT
Outland Trophy (Interior lineman) ..............Zach Wiegert, Nebraska, OG
Butkus Award (Linebacker).......................Dana Howard, Illinois, LB
Jim Thorpe Award (Defensive back)..........Chris Hudson, Colorado, DB
Sporting News Player of the Year .............Rashaan Salaam, Colorado, RB
Walter Payton Award (Div I-AA Player) ......Steve McNair, Alcorn St, QB
Harlon Hill Trophy (Div II Player) ...............Chris Hatcher, Valdosta St, QB

## Coaches' Awards

Walter Camp Award ...................................Joe Paterno, Penn St
Eddie Robinson Award (Div I-AA)..............Jim Tressel, Youngstown St
Bobby Dodd Award ...................................Fred Goldsmith, Duke
Bear Bryant Award ....................................Rich Brooks, Oregon

### AFCA COACHES OF THE YEAR

Division I-A ................................................Tom Osborne, Nebraska
Division I-AA..............................................Jim Tressel, Youngstown St
Division II and NAIA Division I....................Bobby Wallace, North Alabama
Division III and NAIA Division II..................Pete Schmidt, Albion

## Football Writers Association of America All-America Team

### OFFENSE

Jack Jackson, Florida, Jr ...................Wide receiver
Frank Sanders, Auburn, Sr.................Wide receiver
Pete Mitchell, Boston College, Sr........Tight end
Clay Shiver, Florida St, Jr ...................OL
Tony Boselli, Southern Caifornia, Sr....OL
Blake Brockermeyer, Texas, Jr ...........OL
Brenden Stai, Nebraska, Sr..................OL
Zach Wiegert, Nebraska, Sr................OL
Kerry Collins, Penn St, Sr ...................Quarterback
Ki-Jana Carter, Penn St, Jr..................Running back
Rashaan Salaam, Colorado, Jr ..........Running back
Steve McLaughlin, Arizona, Sr.............PK
Leeland McElroy, Texas A&M, So.......Kick returner

### DEFENSE

Luther Elliss, Utah, Sr........................DL
Warren Sapp, Miami (FL), Jr ...............DL
Derrick Alexander, Florida St, Jr .........DL
Tedy Bruschi, Arizona, Jr ....................DL
Derrick Brooks, Florida St, Sr ..............Linebacker
Dana Howard, Illinois, Sr....................Linebacker
Ed Stewart, Nebraska, Sr ...................Linebacker
Chris Hudson, Colorado, Sr ...............Defensive back
Greg Myers, Colorado St, Jr ..............Defensive back
Herman O'Berry, Oregon, Sr..............Defensive back
Chris Shelling, Auburn, Sr ..................Defensive back
Todd Sauerbrun, West Virginia, Sr......Punter

## Division I-A

### ATLANTIC COAST CONFERENCE

| | Conference | | | Full Season | | | |
|---|---|---|---|---|---|---|---|
| | W | L | T | W | L | T | Pct |
| Florida St | 8 | 0 | 0 | 10 | 1 | 1 | .875 |
| N Carolina St | 6 | 2 | 0 | 9 | 3 | 0 | .750 |
| Virginia | 5 | 3 | 0 | 9 | 3 | 0 | .750 |
| Duke | 5 | 3 | 0 | 8 | 4 | 0 | .667 |
| N Carolina | 5 | 3 | 0 | 8 | 4 | 0 | .667 |
| Clemson | 4 | 4 | 0 | 5 | 6 | 0 | .455 |
| Maryland | 2 | 6 | 0 | 4 | 7 | 0 | .364 |
| Wake Forest | 1 | 7 | 0 | 3 | 8 | 0 | .273 |
| Georgia Tech | 0 | 8 | 0 | 1 | 10 | 0 | .091 |

### BIG EAST CONFERENCE

| | Conference | | | Full Season | | | |
|---|---|---|---|---|---|---|---|
| | W | L | T | W | L | T | Pct |
| Miami (FL) | 7 | 0 | 0 | 10 | 2 | 0 | .833 |
| Virginia Tech | 5 | 2 | 0 | 8 | 4 | 0 | .667 |
| Syracuse | 4 | 3 | 0 | 7 | 4 | 0 | .636 |
| W Virginia | 4 | 3 | 0 | 7 | 6 | 0 | .539 |
| Boston College | 3 | 3 | 1 | 7 | 4 | 1 | .625 |
| Rutgers | 2 | 4 | 1 | 5 | 5 | 1 | .500 |
| Pittsburgh | 2 | 5 | 0 | 3 | 8 | 0 | .273 |
| Temple | 0 | 7 | 0 | 2 | 9 | 0 | .182 |

### BIG EIGHT CONFERENCE

| | Conference | | | Full Season | | | |
|---|---|---|---|---|---|---|---|
| | W | L | T | W | L | T | Pct |
| Nebraska | 7 | 0 | 0 | 13 | 0 | 0 | 1.000 |
| Colorado | 6 | 1 | 0 | 11 | 1 | 0 | .917 |
| Kansas St | 5 | 2 | 0 | 9 | 3 | 0 | .750 |
| Oklahoma | 4 | 3 | 0 | 6 | 6 | 0 | .500 |
| Kansas | 3 | 4 | 0 | 6 | 5 | 0 | .545 |
| Missouri | 2 | 5 | 0 | 3 | 8 | 1 | .292 |
| Oklahoma St | 0 | 6 | 1 | 3 | 7 | 1 | .318 |
| Iowa St | 0 | 6 | 1 | 0 | 10 | 1 | .045 |

### BIG TEN CONFERENCE

| | Conference | | | Full Season | | | |
|---|---|---|---|---|---|---|---|
| | W | L | T | W | L | T | Pct |
| Penn St | 8 | 0 | 0 | 12 | 0 | 0 | 1.000 |
| Ohio St | 6 | 2 | 0 | 9 | 4 | 0 | .692 |
| Michigan | 5 | 3 | 0 | 8 | 4 | 0 | .667 |
| Wisconsin | 4 | 3 | 1 | 7 | 4 | 1 | .625 |
| Illinois | 4 | 4 | 0 | 7 | 5 | 0 | .583 |
| Michigan St | 4 | 4 | 0 | 5 | 6 | 0 | .455 |
| Iowa | 3 | 4 | 1 | 5 | 5 | 1 | .500 |
| Indiana | 3 | 5 | 0 | 6 | 5 | 0 | .545 |
| Purdue | 2 | 4 | 2 | 4 | 5 | 2 | .455 |
| Northwestern | 2 | 6 | 0 | 3 | 7 | 0 | .300 |
| Minnesota | 1 | 7 | 0 | 3 | 8 | 0 | .273 |

### BIG WEST CONFERENCE

| | Conference | | | Full Season | | | |
|---|---|---|---|---|---|---|---|
| | W | L | T | W | L | T | Pct |
| Nevada | 5 | 1 | 0 | 9 | 2 | 0 | .818 |
| UNLV | 5 | 1 | 0 | 7 | 5 | 0 | .583 |
| SW Louisiana | 5 | 1 | 0 | 6 | 5 | 0 | .545 |
| Pacific | 4 | 2 | 0 | 6 | 5 | 0 | .545 |
| N Illinois | 3 | 3 | 0 | 4 | 7 | 0 | .364 |
| San Jose St | 3 | 3 | 0 | 3 | 8 | 0 | .273 |
| New Mexico St | 2 | 4 | 0 | 3 | 8 | 0 | .273 |
| Utah St | 2 | 4 | 0 | 3 | 8 | 0 | .273 |
| La Tech | 1 | 5 | 0 | 3 | 8 | 0 | .273 |
| Arkansas St | 0 | 6 | 0 | 1 | 10 | 0 | .091 |

## Division I-A *(Cont.)*

### MID-AMERICAN CONFERENCE

| | Conference | | | Full Season | | | |
|---|---|---|---|---|---|---|---|
| | W | L | T | W | L | T | Pct |
| Cent Michigan | 8 | 1 | 0 | 9 | 3 | 0 | .750 |
| Bowling Green | 7 | 1 | 0 | 9 | 2 | 0 | .818 |
| W Michigan | 5 | 3 | 0 | 7 | 4 | 0 | .636 |
| Miami (OH) | 5 | 3 | 0 | 5 | 5 | 1 | .500 |
| Ball St | 5 | 3 | 1 | 5 | 5 | 1 | .500 |
| Toledo | 4 | 3 | 1 | 6 | 4 | 1 | .590 |
| E Michigan | 5 | 4 | 0 | 5 | 6 | 0 | .455 |
| Kent | 2 | 7 | 0 | 2 | 9 | 0 | .181 |
| Akron | 1 | 8 | 0 | 1 | 10 | 0 | .091 |
| Ohio U | 0 | 9 | 0 | 0 | 11 | 0 | .000 |

### PACIFIC-10 CONFERENCE

| | Conference | | | Full Season | | | |
|---|---|---|---|---|---|---|---|
| | W | L | T | W | L | T | Pct |
| Oregon | 7 | 1 | 0 | 9 | 4 | 0 | .692 |
| Southern Cal | 6 | 2 | 0 | 8 | 3 | 1 | .708 |
| Arizona | 6 | 2 | 0 | 8 | 4 | 0 | .667 |
| Washington St | 5 | 3 | 0 | 8 | 4 | 0 | .667 |
| Washington | 4 | 4 | 0 | 7 | 4 | 0 | .636 |
| UCLA | 3 | 5 | 0 | 5 | 6 | 0 | .455 |
| California | 3 | 5 | 0 | 4 | 7 | 0 | .364 |
| Oregon St | 2 | 6 | 0 | 4 | 7 | 0 | .364 |
| Stanford | 2 | 6 | 0 | 3 | 7 | 1 | .318 |
| Arizona St | 2 | 6 | 0 | 3 | 8 | 0 | .273 |

### SOUTHEASTERN CONFERENCE

| | Conference | | | Full Season* | | | |
|---|---|---|---|---|---|---|---|
| **EAST** | W | L | T | W | L | T | Pct |
| Florida | 8 | 1 | 0 | 10 | 2 | 1 | .808 |
| Tennessee | 5 | 3 | 0 | 8 | 4 | 0 | .667 |
| S Carolina | 4 | 4 | 0 | 7 | 5 | 0 | .583 |
| Georgia | 3 | 4 | 1 | 6 | 4 | 1 | .590 |
| Vanderbilt | 2 | 6 | 0 | 5 | 6 | 0 | .455 |
| Kentucky | 0 | 8 | 0 | 1 | 10 | 0 | .091 |
| **WEST** | | | | | | | |
| Alabama | 8 | 1 | 0 | 12 | 1 | 0 | .923 |
| Auburn | 6 | 1 | 1 | 9 | 1 | 1 | .818 |
| Mississippi St | 5 | 3 | 0 | 8 | 4 | 0 | .667 |
| Louisiana St | 3 | 5 | 0 | 4 | 7 | 0 | .364 |
| Arkansas | 2 | 6 | 0 | 4 | 7 | 0 | .364 |
| Mississippi | 2 | 6 | 0 | 4 | 7 | 0 | .364 |

*Full season record includes SEC Championship Game in which Florida defeated Alabama, 24–23, on Dec 3. Auburn was ineligible for postseason play in 1994 due to NCAA probation.

### SOUTHWEST ATHLETIC CONFERENCE

| | Conference | | | Full Season | | | |
|---|---|---|---|---|---|---|---|
| | W | L | T | W | L | T | Pct |
| Texas A&M | 6 | 0 | 1 | 10 | 0 | 1 | .955 |
| Texas | 4 | 3 | 0 | 8 | 4 | 0 | .667 |
| Baylor | 4 | 3 | 0 | 7 | 5 | 0 | .583 |
| TCU | 4 | 3 | 0 | 7 | 5 | 0 | .583 |
| Texas Tech | 4 | 3 | 0 | 6 | 6 | 0 | .500 |
| Rice | 4 | 3 | 0 | 5 | 6 | 0 | .454 |
| Houston | 1 | 6 | 0 | 1 | 10 | 0 | .091 |
| SMU | 0 | 6 | 1 | 1 | 9 | 1 | .136 |

## Division I-A (Cont.)

### WESTERN ATHLETIC CONFERENCE

| | Conference | | | Full Season | | | |
|---|---|---|---|---|---|---|---|
| | W | L | T | W | L | T | Pct |
| Colorado St | 7 | 1 | 0 | 10 | 2 | 0 | .833 |
| Utah | 6 | 2 | 0 | 10 | 2 | 0 | .833 |
| BYU | 6 | 2 | 0 | 10 | 3 | 0 | .769 |
| Air Force | 6 | 2 | 0 | 8 | 4 | 0 | .667 |
| Wyoming | 4 | 4 | 0 | 6 | 6 | 0 | .500 |
| New Mexico | 4 | 4 | 0 | 5 | 7 | 0 | .417 |
| Fresno St | 3 | 4 | 1 | 5 | 7 | 1 | .423 |
| San Diego St | 2 | 6 | 0 | 4 | 7 | 0 | .364 |
| UTEP | 1 | 6 | 1 | 3 | 7 | 1 | .318 |
| Hawaii | 0 | 8 | 0 | 3 | 8 | 1 | .292 |

### INDEPENDENTS

| | Full Season | | | |
|---|---|---|---|---|
| | W | L | T | Pct |
| E Carolina | 7 | 5 | 0 | .583 |
| Notre Dame | 6 | 5 | 1 | .542 |
| Louisville | 6 | 5 | 0 | .545 |
| Memphis | 6 | 5 | 0 | .545 |
| S Mississippi | 6 | 5 | 0 | .545 |
| Army | 4 | 7 | 0 | .364 |
| Navy | 3 | 8 | 0 | .273 |
| NE Louisiana | 3 | 8 | 0 | .273 |
| Tulsa | 3 | 8 | 0 | .273 |
| Cincinnati | 2 | 8 | 1 | .227 |
| Tulane | 1 | 10 | 0 | .091 |

## Division I-AA

### BIG SKY CONFERENCE

| | Conference | | | Full Season | | | |
|---|---|---|---|---|---|---|---|
| | W | L | T | W | L | T | Pct |
| Boise St | 6 | 1 | 0 | 13 | 2 | 0 | .867 |
| Montana | 5 | 2 | 0 | 11 | 3 | 0 | .786 |
| Idaho | 5 | 2 | 0 | 9 | 3 | 0 | .750 |
| N Arizona | 4 | 3 | 0 | 7 | 4 | 0 | .636 |
| Idaho St | 4 | 3 | 0 | 6 | 5 | 0 | .546 |
| Weber St | 2 | 5 | 0 | 5 | 6 | 0 | .455 |
| E Washington | 2 | 5 | 0 | 4 | 7 | 0 | .364 |
| Montana St | 0 | 7 | 0 | 3 | 8 | 0 | .273 |

### GATEWAY COLLEGIATE ATHLETIC CONFERENCE

| | Conference | | | Full Season | | | |
|---|---|---|---|---|---|---|---|
| | W | L | T | W | L | T | Pct |
| N Iowa | 6 | 0 | 0 | 8 | 4 | 0 | .667 |
| W Illinois | 4 | 2 | 0 | 8 | 3 | 0 | .727 |
| E Illinois | 4 | 2 | 0 | 6 | 5 | 0 | .546 |
| Illinois St | 3 | 3 | 0 | 5 | 5 | 1 | .500 |
| Indiana St | 2 | 4 | 0 | 5 | 6 | 0 | .455 |
| SW Missouri St | 2 | 4 | 0 | 4 | 7 | 0 | .364 |
| S Illinois | 0 | 6 | 0 | 1 | 10 | 0 | .091 |

## Division I-AA (Cont.)

### IVY GROUP

| | Conference | | | Full Season | | | |
|---|---|---|---|---|---|---|---|
| | W | L | T | W | L | T | Pct |
| Penn | 7 | 0 | 0 | 9 | 0 | 0 | 1.000 |
| Brown | 4 | 3 | 0 | 7 | 3 | 0 | .700 |
| Princeton | 4 | 3 | 0 | 7 | 3 | 0 | .700 |
| Cornell | 3 | 4 | 0 | 6 | 4 | 0 | .600 |
| Columbia | 3 | 4 | 0 | 5 | 4 | 1 | .550 |
| Yale | 3 | 4 | 0 | 5 | 5 | 0 | .500 |
| Dartmouth | 2 | 5 | 0 | 4 | 6 | 0 | .400 |
| Harvard | 2 | 5 | 0 | 4 | 6 | 0 | .400 |

### MID-EASTERN ATHLETIC CONFERENCE

| | Conference | | | Full Season | | | |
|---|---|---|---|---|---|---|---|
| | W | L | T | W | L | T | Pct |
| S Carolina St | 6 | 0 | 0 | 10 | 2 | 0 | .833 |
| Delaware St | 4 | 2 | 0 | 7 | 4 | 0 | .636 |
| N Carolina A&T | 3 | 3 | 0 | 6 | 5 | 0 | .545 |
| Bethune-Cookman | 3 | 3 | 0 | 5 | 6 | 0 | .455 |
| Florida A&M | 2 | 4 | 0 | 6 | 5 | 0 | .546 |
| Morgan St | 2 | 4 | 0 | 3 | 8 | 0 | .273 |
| Howard | 1 | 5 | 0 | 4 | 7 | 0 | .364 |

### OHIO VALLEY CONFERENCE

| | Conference | | | Full Season | | | |
|---|---|---|---|---|---|---|---|
| | W | L | T | W | L | T | Pct |
| Eastern Kentucky | 8 | 0 | 0 | 10 | 3 | 0 | .769 |
| Middle Tennessee St | 7 | 1 | 0 | 8 | 3 | 1 | .708 |
| SE Missouri | 5 | 3 | 0 | 7 | 5 | 0 | .583 |
| Murray St | 4 | 4 | 0 | 5 | 6 | 0 | .455 |
| Tennessee St | 4 | 4 | 0 | 5 | 6 | 0 | .455 |
| Tenn-Martin | 3 | 5 | 0 | 6 | 5 | 0 | .545 |
| Tennessee Tech | 3 | 5 | 0 | 5 | 6 | 0 | .455 |
| Austin Peay | 2 | 6 | 0 | 3 | 8 | 0 | .273 |
| Morehead | 0 | 8 | 0 | 0 | 11 | 0 | .000 |

### PATRIOT LEAGUE

| | Conference | | | Full Season | | | |
|---|---|---|---|---|---|---|---|
| | W | L | T | W | L | T | Pct |
| Lafayette | 5 | 0 | 0 | 5 | 6 | 0 | .455 |
| Lehigh | 3 | 2 | 0 | 5 | 5 | 1 | .500 |
| Holy Cross | 3 | 2 | 0 | 3 | 8 | 0 | .273 |
| Bucknell | 2 | 3 | 0 | 5 | 6 | 0 | .455 |
| Colgate | 2 | 3 | 0 | 3 | 8 | 0 | .273 |
| Fordham | 0 | 5 | 0 | 0 | 11 | 0 | .000 |

### SOUTHERN CONFERENCE

| | Conference | | | Full Season | | | |
|---|---|---|---|---|---|---|---|
| | W | L | T | W | L | T | Pct |
| Marshall | 7 | 1 | 0 | 12 | 2 | 0 | .857 |
| Appalachian St | 6 | 2 | 0 | 9 | 4 | 0 | .692 |
| Georgia Southern | 5 | 3 | 0 | 6 | 5 | 0 | .545 |
| W Carolina | 5 | 3 | 0 | 6 | 5 | 0 | .545 |
| Citadel | 4 | 4 | 0 | 6 | 5 | 0 | .545 |
| E Tennessee St | 4 | 4 | 0 | 6 | 5 | 0 | .545 |
| Furman | 2 | 6 | 0 | 3 | 8 | 0 | .273 |
| TN-Chattanooga | 2 | 6 | 0 | 3 | 8 | 0 | .273 |
| Virginia Military | 1 | 7 | 0 | 1 | 10 | 0 | .091 |

## Division I-AA *(Cont.)*

### SOUTHLAND CONFERENCE

| | Conference | | | Full Season | | | |
|---|---|---|---|---|---|---|---|
| | W | L | T | W | L | T | Pct |
| North Texas | 5 | 0 | 1 | 7 | 4 | 1 | .625 |
| McNeese St | 5 | 1 | 0 | 10 | 3 | 0 | .769 |
| SF Austin St | 4 | 1 | 1 | 6 | 3 | 2 | .636 |
| Northwestern (LA) | 3 | 3 | 0 | 5 | 6 | 0 | .455 |
| Sam Houston St | 1 | 5 | 0 | 6 | 5 | 0 | .545 |
| Nicholls St | 1 | 5 | 0 | 5 | 6 | 0 | .455 |
| SW Texas St | 1 | 5 | 0 | 4 | 7 | 0 | .364 |

### SOUTHWESTERN ATHLETIC CONFERENCE

| | Conference | | | Full Season | | | |
|---|---|---|---|---|---|---|---|
| | W | L | T | W | L | T | Pct |
| Grambling | 6 | 1 | 0 | 9 | 3 | 0 | .750 |
| Alcorn St | 6 | 1 | 0 | 8 | 3 | 1 | .708 |
| Southern | 5 | 2 | 0 | 6 | 5 | 0 | .545 |
| Jackson St | 4 | 3 | 0 | 7 | 4 | 0 | .636 |
| Alabama St | 3 | 4 | 0 | 6 | 5 | 0 | .545 |
| Texas Southern | 2 | 5 | 0 | 4 | 7 | 0 | .364 |
| Mississippi Valley | 2 | 5 | 0 | 3 | 7 | 0 | .300 |
| Prairie View A&M | 0 | 7 | 0 | 0 | 11 | 0 | .000 |

### YANKEE CONFERENCE

| | Conference | | | Full Season | | | |
|---|---|---|---|---|---|---|---|
| | W | L | T | W | L | T | Pct |
| **MID-ATLANTIC** | | | | | | | |
| James Madison | 6 | 2 | 0 | 10 | 3 | 0 | .769 |
| William & Mary | 6 | 2 | 0 | 8 | 3 | 0 | .727 |
| Delaware | 5 | 3 | 0 | 7 | 3 | 1 | .682 |
| Villanova | 2 | 6 | 0 | 5 | 6 | 0 | .455 |
| Northeastern | 2 | 6 | 0 | 2 | 9 | 0 | .182 |
| Richmond | 1 | 7 | 0 | 3 | 8 | 0 | .273 |
| **NEW ENGLAND** | | | | | | | |
| New Hampshire | 8 | 0 | 0 | 10 | 2 | 0 | .833 |
| Boston University | 6 | 2 | 0 | 9 | 3 | 0 | .750 |
| Massachusetts | 4 | 4 | 0 | 5 | 6 | 0 | .455 |
| Connecticut | 4 | 4 | 0 | 4 | 7 | 0 | .364 |
| Maine | 2 | 6 | 0 | 3 | 8 | 0 | .273 |
| Rhode Island | 2 | 6 | 0 | 2 | 9 | 0 | .182 |

### INDEPENDENTS

| | Full Season | | |
|---|---|---|---|
| | W | L | T | Pct |
| Youngstown St | 14 | 0 | 1 | .967 |
| Hofstra | 8 | 1 | 1 | .850 |
| Robert Morris | 7 | 1 | 1 | .833 |
| Towson St | 8 | 2 | 0 | .800 |
| Monmouth (NJ) | 7 | 2 | 0 | .778 |
| St. Mary's (CA) | 7 | 3 | 0 | .700 |
| Troy St | 8 | 4 | 0 | .667 |
| Alabama-Birmingham | 7 | 4 | 0 | .636 |
| Central Florida | 7 | 4 | 0 | .636 |
| Wagner | 6 | 5 | 0 | .545 |
| Liberty | 5 | 6 | 0 | .455 |
| W Kentucky | 5 | 6 | 0 | .455 |
| Samford | 4 | 6 | 1 | .409 |
| Central Connecticut | 4 | 6 | 0 | .400 |
| Davidson | 3 | 7 | 0 | .300 |
| Buffalo | 3 | 8 | 0 | .273 |
| St. Francis (PA) | 2 | 7 | 1 | .250 |
| Charleston Southern | 0 | 11 | 0 | .000 |

### Division I-A

#### SCORING

| | Class | GP | TD | XP | FG | Pts | Pts/Game |
|---|---|---|---|---|---|---|---|
| Rashaan Salaam, Colorado | Jr | 11 | 24 | 0 | 0 | 144 | 13.09 |
| Ki-Jana Carter, Penn St | Jr | 11 | 23 | 0 | 0 | 138 | 12.55 |
| Brian Pruitt, Central Michigan | Sr | 11 | 22 | 0 | 0 | 132 | 12.00 |
| Brian Leaver, Bowling Green | Sr | 11 | 0 | 42 | 21 | 105 | 9.55 |
| Judd Davis, Florida | Sr | 12 | 0 | 65 | 14 | 107 | 8.92 |
| Rodney Thomas, Texas A&M | Sr | 11 | 16 | 0 | 0 | 96 | 8.73 |
| Tyrone Wheatley, Michigan | Sr | 9 | 13 | 0 | 0 | 78 | 8.67 |
| Remy Hamilton, Michigan | So | 11 | 0 | 23 | 24 | 95 | 8.64 |
| Steve McLaughlin, Arizona | Sr | 11 | 0 | 26 | 23 | 95 | 8.64 |
| Brett Conway, Penn St | So | 11 | 0 | 62 | 10 | 92 | 8.36 |

#### FIELD GOALS

| | Class | GP | FGA | FG | Pct | FG/Game |
|---|---|---|---|---|---|---|
| Remy Hamilton, Michigan | So | 11 | 29 | 24 | .828 | 2.18 |
| Steve McLaughlin, Arizona | Sr | 11 | 29 | 23 | .793 | 2.09 |
| Brian Leaver, Bowling Green | Sr | 11 | 24 | 21 | .875 | 1.91 |
| Nick Garritano, UNLV | Sr | 11 | 26 | 21 | .808 | 1.91 |
| Ryan Williams, Virginia Tech | Sr | 10 | 21 | 17 | .810 | 1.70 |
| Mike Chalberg, Minnesota | Jr | 10 | 23 | 17 | .739 | 1.70 |
| John Wales, Washington | So | 11 | 25 | 18 | .720 | 1.64 |

#### TOTAL OFFENSE

| | | | Rushing | | Passing | | Total Offense | | | |
|---|---|---|---|---|---|---|---|---|---|---|
| | Class | GP | Car | Net | Att | Yds | Yds | Yds/Play | TDR* | Yds/Game |
| Mike Maxwell, Nevada | Jr | 11 | 30 | -39 | 447 | 3537 | 3498 | 7.33 | 32 | 318.00 |
| Eric Zeier, Georgia | Sr | 11 | 21 | 61 | 433 | 3396 | 3457 | 7.61 | 25 | 314.27 |
| Stoney Case, New Mexico | Sr | 12 | 140 | 532 | 409 | 3117 | 3649 | 6.65 | 33 | 304.08 |
| Steve Stenstrom, Stanford | Sr | 9 | 65 | -108 | 333 | 2822 | 2714 | 6.82 | 19 | 301.56 |
| John Walsh, Brigham Young | Jr | 12 | 77 | -239 | 463 | 3712 | 3473 | 6.43 | 29 | 289.42 |
| Mike McCoy, Utah | Sr | 11 | 75 | 69 | 381 | 3035 | 3104 | 6.81 | 29 | 282.18 |
| Craig Whelihan, Pacific (CA) | Sr | 9 | 24 | -12 | 326 | 2318 | 2306 | 6.59 | 18 | 256.22 |
| Marcus Crandell, E Carolina | So | 11 | 71 | 96 | 401 | 2687 | 2783 | 5.90 | 22 | 253.00 |
| Anthoney Hill, Colorado St | Sr | 11 | 93 | 163 | 290 | 2552 | 2715 | 7.09 | 21 | 246.82 |
| Kordell Stewart, Colorado | Sr | 11 | 122 | 639 | 237 | 2071 | 2710 | 7.55 | 17 | 246.36 |

*Touchdowns responsible for.

#### RUSHING

| | Class | GP | Car | Yds | Avg | TD | Yds/Game |
|---|---|---|---|---|---|---|---|
| Rashaan Salaam, Colorado | Jr | 11 | 298 | 2055 | 6.9 | 24 | 186.82 |
| Brian Pruitt, Central Michigan | Sr | 11 | 292 | 1890 | 6.5 | 20 | 171.82 |
| Lawrence Phillips, Nebraska | So | 12 | 286 | 1722 | 6.0 | 16 | 143.50 |
| Ki-Jana Carter, Penn St | Jr | 11 | 198 | 1539 | 7.8 | 23 | 139.91 |
| Andre Davis, Texas Christian | Jr | 11 | 260 | 1494 | 5.7 | 7 | 135.82 |
| Alex Smith, Indiana | Fr | 11 | 265 | 1475 | 5.6 | 10 | 134.09 |
| Chris Darkins, Minnesota | Jr | 11 | 277 | 1443 | 5.2 | 11 | 131.18 |
| Napoleon Kaufman, Washington | Sr | 11 | 255 | 1390 | 5.5 | 9 | 126.36 |
| Billy West, Pittsburgh | So | 11 | 252 | 1358 | 5.4 | 6 | 123.45 |
| Ryan Christopherson, Wyoming | Sr | 12 | 300 | 1455 | 4.8 | 10 | 121.25 |

**Signing Off?**

Down South, when the February college football signing date rolls around, recruiting and rumors go together like grits and gravy. Recently word reached *The Atlanta Journal-Constitution* that Chauncey McGee, a six-foot, 180-pound defensive back at Atlanta's Westlake High, had committed suicide. The paper quickly dispatched a correspondent to check out the report. "Chauncey didn't commit suicide," word came back. "Chauncey committed to Mississippi State."

## Division I-A *(Cont.)*

### PASSING EFFICIENCY

| | Class | GP | Att | Comp | Pct Comp | Yds | Yds/Att | TD | Int | Rating Pts |
|---|---|---|---|---|---|---|---|---|---|---|
| Kerry Collins, Penn St. | Sr | 11 | 264 | 176 | 66.67 | 2679 | 10.15 | 21 | 7 | 172.9 |
| Terry Dean, Florida | Jr | 10 | 180 | 109 | 60.56 | 1492 | 8.29 | 20 | 10 | 155.7 |
| Jay Barker, Alabama | Sr | 12 | 226 | 139 | 61.50 | 1996 | 8.83 | 14 | 5 | 151.7 |
| Danny Wuerffel, Florida | So | 12 | 212 | 132 | 62.26 | 1754 | 8.27 | 18 | 9 | 151.3 |
| Rob Johnson, Southern Cal | Sr | 9 | 255 | 170 | 66.67 | 2210 | 8.67 | 12 | 6 | 150.3 |
| Mike McCoy, Utah | Sr | 11 | 381 | 247 | 64.83 | 3035 | 7.97 | 28 | 11 | 150.2 |
| Max Knake, Texas Christian | Jr | 11 | 316 | 184 | 58.23 | 2624 | 8.30 | 24 | 7 | 148.6 |
| Steve Stenstrom, Stanford | Sr | 9 | 333 | 217 | 65.17 | 2822 | 8.47 | 16 | 6 | 148.6 |
| Todd Collins, Michigan | Sr | 11 | 264 | 172 | 65.15 | 2356 | 8.92 | 11 | 7 | 148.6 |
| Ryan Henry, Bowling Green | So | 11 | 293 | 174 | 59.39 | 2368 | 8.08 | 25 | 11 | 147.9 |
| Kordell Stewart, Colorado | Sr | 11 | 237 | 147 | 62.03 | 2071 | 8.74 | 10 | 3 | 146.8 |
| John Gustin, Wyoming | Sr | 12 | 306 | 181 | 59.15 | 2757 | 9.01 | 17 | 13 | 144.7 |

Note: Minimum 15 attempts per game.

### RECEPTIONS PER GAME

| | Class | GP | No. | Yds | TD | R/Game |
|---|---|---|---|---|---|---|
| Alex Van Dyke, Nevada | Jr | 11 | 98 | 1246 | 10 | 8.91 |
| Randy Gatewood, UNLV | Sr | 11 | 88 | 1203 | 6 | 8.00 |
| Mick Rossley, Southern Methodist | Sr | 11 | 83 | 857 | 4 | 7.55 |
| Geroy Simon, Maryland | So | 11 | 77 | 891 | 5 | 7.00 |
| Wes Caswell, Tulsa | So | 11 | 74 | 893 | 3 | 6.73 |

### RECEIVING YARDS PER GAME

| | Class | GP | No. | Yds | TD | Yds/Game |
|---|---|---|---|---|---|---|
| Marcus Harris, Wyoming | So | 12 | 71 | 1431 | 11 | 119.25 |
| Keyshawn Johnson, Southern Cal | Jr | 10 | 58 | 1140 | 6 | 114.00 |
| Alex Van Dyke, Nevada | Jr | 11 | 98 | 1246 | 10 | 113.27 |
| Kevin Jordan, UCLA | Jr | 11 | 73 | 1228 | 7 | 111.64 |
| Randy Gatewood, UNLV | Sr | 11 | 88 | 1203 | 6 | 109.36 |

### ALL-PURPOSE RUNNERS

| | Class | GP | Rush | Rec | PR | KOR | Yds | Yds/Game |
|---|---|---|---|---|---|---|---|---|
| Rashaan Salaam, Colorado | Jr | 11 | 2055 | 294 | 0 | 0 | 2349 | 213.55 |
| Brian Pruitt, Central Michigan | Sr | 11 | 1890 | 69 | 0 | 330 | 2289 | 208.09 |
| Andre Davis, Texas Christian | Jr | 11 | 1494 | 522 | 0 | 0 | 2016 | 183.27 |
| Napoleon Kaufman, Washington | Sr | 11 | 1390 | 199 | 8 | 229 | 1826 | 166.00 |
| Ki-Jana Carter, Penn St. | Jr | 11 | 1539 | 123 | 0 | 81 | 1743 | 158.45 |

### INTERCEPTIONS

| | Class | GP | No. | Yds | TD | Int/Game |
|---|---|---|---|---|---|---|
| Aaron Beasley, West Virginia | Jr | 12 | 10 | 133 | 2 | .83 |
| Brian Robinson, Auburn | Jr | 11 | 8 | 140 | 1 | .73 |
| Ronde Barber, Virginia | Fr | 11 | 8 | 56 | 0 | .73 |
| Demetrice Martin, Michigan St. | Jr | 11 | 7 | 41 | 0 | .64 |

### PUNTING

| | Class | No. | Avg |
|---|---|---|---|
| Todd Sauerbrun, West Virginia | Sr | 72 | 48.42 |
| Jason Bender, Georgia Tech | Sr | 55 | 45.51 |
| Brad Maynard, Ball St. | Jr | 59 | 45.49 |

Note: Minimum of 3.6 per game.

### PUNT RETURNS

| | Class | No. | Yds | TD | Avg |
|---|---|---|---|---|---|
| Steve Clay, E Michigan | Jr | 14 | 278 | 1 | 19.86 |
| Nilo Silvan, Tennessee | Jr | 15 | 272 | 0 | 18.13 |
| Ray Peterson, San Diego St. | Jr | 12 | 190 | 2 | 15.83 |
| Kevin Alexander, Utah St. | Jr | 14 | 199 | 1 | 14.21 |
| Eddie Kennison, LSU | So | 36 | 439 | 1 | 12.19 |

Note: Minimum 1.2 per game.

## Division I-A (Cont.)

### KICKOFF RETURNS

| | Class | No. | Yds | TD | Avg |
|---|---|---|---|---|---|
| Eric Moulds, Mississippi St | Jr | 13 | 426 | 0 | 32.77 |
| David Dunn, Fresno St | Sr | 35 | 1013 | 0 | 28.94 |
| Marcus Wall, N Carolina | Jr | 27 | 743 | 1 | 27.52 |
| Parrish Foster, New Mexico St | Sr | 14 | 385 | 0 | 27.50 |
| Derrick Mason, Michigan St | So | 36 | 966 | 1 | 26.83 |
| Joey Galloway, Ohio St | Sr | 15 | 401 | 1 | 26.73 |

Note: Minimum of 1.2 per game.

## Division I-A Single-Game Highs

### RUSHING AND PASSING

Rushing and passing plays: 77—Stoney Case,
New Mexico, Sep 10 (vs Texas Christian).
Rushing and passing yards: 494—Eric Zeier,
Georgia, Sep 3 (vs S Carolina).
Rushing plays: 44—Jason Cooper, Louisiana Tech,
Oct 8 (vs UNLV).
Net rushing yards: 356—Brian Pruitt, Central
Michigan, Nov 5 (vs Toledo).
Passes attempted: 62—Stoney Case, New Mexico,
Sep 10 (vs Texas Christian).
Passes completed: 40—Danny Kanell, Florida St,
Nov 26 (vs Florida).
Passing yards: 485—Eric Zeier,
Georgia, Sep 3 (vs S Carolina).

### RECEIVING AND RETURNS

Passes caught: 23—Randy Gatewood, UNLV,
Sep 17 (vs Idaho).
Receiving yards: 363—Randy Gatewood, UNLV,
Sep 17 (vs Idaho).
Punt return yards: 194—Ryan Roskelly, Memphis,
Sep 10 (vs Tulsa).
Kickoff return yards: 186—Derrick Mason, Michigan St
Nov 26 (vs Penn St).

## Division I-AA

### SCORING

| | Class | GP | TD | XP | FG | Pts | Pts/Game |
|---|---|---|---|---|---|---|---|
| Michael Hicks, S Carolina St | Jr | 11 | 22 | 0 | 0 | 132 | 12.00 |
| Arnold Mickens, Butler | Jr | 10 | 18 | 0 | 0 | 108 | 10.80 |
| Brian McCarty, Towson St | Sr | 10 | 17 | 0 | 0 | 102 | 10.20 |
| Chris Parker, Marshall | Jr | 11 | 18 | 2 | 0 | 110 | 10.00 |
| Wayne Chrebet, Hofstra | Sr | 10 | 16 | 2 | 0 | 98 | 9.80 |

### FIELD GOALS

| | Class | GP | FGA | FG | Pct | FG/Game |
|---|---|---|---|---|---|---|
| Andy Glockner, Pennsylvania | Sr | 9 | 20 | 14 | .700 | 1.56 |
| Matt Waller, Northern Iowa | So | 11 | 26 | 17 | .654 | 1.55 |
| Jim Richter, Furman | Jr | 11 | 19 | 16 | .842 | 1.45 |
| Bob Warden, Brown | Sr | 10 | 16 | 14 | .875 | 1.40 |
| John Coursey, James Madison | So | 11 | 23 | 15 | .652 | 1.36 |

## Division I-AA (Cont.)

### TOTAL OFFENSE

| | Class | GP | Rushing | | | | Passing | | Total Offense | | | |
| --- | --- | --- | --- | --- | --- | --- | --- | --- | --- | --- | --- | --- |
| | | | Car | Gain | Loss | Net | Att | Yds | Yds | Yds/Play | TDR* | Yds/Game |
| Steve McNair, Alcorn St.......Sr | | 11 | 119 | 1128 | 192 | 936 | 530 | 4863 | 5799 | 8.94 | 53 | 527.18 |
| Dave Dickenson, Montana...Jr | | 9 | 95 | 361 | 306 | 55 | 336 | 3053 | 3108 | 7.21 | 27 | 345.33 |
| Jeff Lewis, N Arizona ..........Jr | | 11 | 108 | 338 | 306 | 32 | 450 | 3355 | 3387 | 6.07 | 32 | 307.91 |
| Mitch Maher, North Texas...Sr | | 10 | 79 | 321 | 146 | 175 | 319 | 2840 | 3015 | 7.58 | 31 | 301.50 |
| Robert Dougherty, BU ........Sr | | 11 | 90 | 350 | 258 | 92 | 387 | 3173 | 3265 | 6.84 | 29 | 296.82 |

*Touchdowns responsible for.

### RUSHING

| | Class | GP | Car | Yds | Avg | TD | Yds/Game |
| --- | --- | --- | --- | --- | --- | --- | --- |
| Arnold Mickens, Butler.............................Jr | | 10 | 409 | 2255 | 5.5 | 18 | 225.50 |
| Tim Hall, Robert Morris ..............................Jr | | 9 | 154 | 1336 | 8.7 | 11 | 148.44 |
| Don Wilkerson, SW Texas St ....................Sr | | 11 | 302 | 1569 | 5.2 | 9 | 142.64 |
| Thomas Haskins, Virginia Military ............So | | 11 | 258 | 1509 | 5.8 | 11 | 137.18 |
| Rene Ingoglia, Massachusetts...................Jr | | 11 | 258 | 1505 | 5.8 | 14 | 136.82 |

### PASSING EFFICIENCY

| | Class | GP | Att | Comp | Pct Comp | Yds | Yds/Att | TD | Int | Rating Pts |
| --- | --- | --- | --- | --- | --- | --- | --- | --- | --- | --- |
| Dave Dickenson, Montana ..........Jr | | 9 | 336 | 229 | 68.15 | 3053 | 9.09 | 24 | 6 | 164.5 |
| Todd Donnan, Marshall ...............Sr | | 11 | 288 | 182 | 63.19 | 2403 | 8.34 | 28 | 8 | 159.8 |
| Brian Brennan, Idaho ..................Fr | | 10 | 200 | 116 | 58.00 | 1766 | 8.83 | 18 | 4 | 157.9 |
| Mitch Maher, North Texas ...........Sr | | 10 | 319 | 202 | 63.32 | 2840 | 8.90 | 25 | 12 | 156.4 |
| Steve McNair, Alcorn St ..............Sr | | 11 | 530 | 304 | 57.36 | 4863 | 9.18 | 44 | 17 | 155.4 |

Note: Minimum 15 attempts per game.

### RECEPTIONS PER GAME

| | Class | GP | No. | Yds | TD | R/Game |
| --- | --- | --- | --- | --- | --- | --- |
| Jeff Johnson, E Tenn St.......................Sr | | 9 | 73 | 857 | 8 | 8.11 |
| Ray Marshall, St. Peter's......................Sr | | 9 | 69 | 797 | 4 | 7.67 |
| Derrick Ingram, Alabama-Birmingham..Sr | | 11 | 83 | 1457 | 13 | 7.55 |
| Heston Sutman, Central Conn St...........Sr | | 10 | 70 | 1018 | 7 | 7.00 |
| Tim McNair, Alcorn St............................Sr | | 11 | 74 | 1230 | 13 | 6.73 |

### RECEIVING YARDS PER GAME

| | Class | GP | No. | Yds | TD | Yds/Game |
| --- | --- | --- | --- | --- | --- | --- |
| Mark Orlando, Towson St.....................Sr | | 9 | 55 | 1223 | 12 | 135.89 |
| Derrick Ingram, Alabama-Birmingham..Sr | | 11 | 83 | 1457 | 13 | 132.45 |
| Wayne Chrebet, Hofstra .......................Sr | | 10 | 57 | 1200 | 16 | 120.00 |
| Reggie Barlow, Alabama St ..................Jr | | 11 | 58 | 1267 | 12 | 115.18 |
| Tim McNair, Alcorn St............................Sr | | 11 | 74 | 1230 | 13 | 111.82 |

### ALL-PURPOSE RUNNERS

| | Class | GP | Rush | Rec | PR | KOR | Yds* | Yds/Game |
| --- | --- | --- | --- | --- | --- | --- | --- | --- |
| Arnold Mickens, Butler......................Jr | | 10 | 2250 | 7 | 0 | 0 | 2262 | 226.20 |
| Anthony Jordan, Samford .................Sr | | 11 | 924 | 400 | 169 | 767 | 2260 | 205.45 |
| Tim Hall, Robert Morris......................Jr | | 9 | 1336 | 460 | 0 | 0 | 1796 | 199.56 |
| Don Wilkerson, SW Texas St.............Sr | | 11 | 1569 | 131 | 21 | 327 | 2048 | 186.18 |
| Ozzie Young, Valparaiso...................Jr | | 9 | 606 | 426 | 96 | 533 | 1661 | 184.56 |

*Includes interceptions return yards

### INTERCEPTIONS

| | Class | GP | No. | Yds | TD | Int/Game |
| --- | --- | --- | --- | --- | --- | --- |
| Joseph Vaughn, Cal St-Northridge .......Sr | | 10 | 9 | 265 | 4 | .90 |
| Brian Clark, Hofstra ...............................Jr | | 10 | 9 | 56 | 0 | .90 |
| Chris Hanson, Cornell ...........................Sr | | 10 | 8 | 83 | 0 | .80 |
| Jason Wilson, St Francis (PA) ..............Sr | | 10 | 8 | 52 | 1 | .80 |
| Shayne Snider, Valparaiso ...................Sr | | 10 | 8 | 49 | 0 | .80 |

Three tied at .70 Int/Game.

## Division I-AA *(Cont.)*

### PUNTING

| | Class | No. | Avg |
|---|---|---|---|
| Scott Holmes, Samford | Jr | 49 | 42.84 |
| Brian Desselles, Nicholls St | Sr | 54 | 42.76 |
| Ross Schulte, W Illinois | Sr | 43 | 42.26 |
| Kevin O'Leary, N Arizona | Jr | 44 | 42.02 |

Note: Minimum 3.6 per game.

## Division II

### SCORING

| | Class | GP | TD | XP | FG | Pts | Pts/Game |
|---|---|---|---|---|---|---|---|
| Leonard Davis, Lenoir-Rhyne | Sr | 9 | 19 | 0 | 0 | 114 | 12.7 |
| LaMonte Coleman, Slippery Rock | Sr | 10 | 21 | 0 | 0 | 126 | 12.6 |
| Bobby Felix, W New Mexico | Jr | 8 | 16 | 4 | 0 | 100 | 12.5 |
| Dave Ludy, Winona St | Sr | 11 | 22 | 4 | 0 | 136 | 12.4 |
| Darick Holmes, Portland St | Sr | 10 | 19 | 0 | 0 | 114 | 11.4 |

### FIELD GOALS

| | Class | GP | FGA | FG | Pct | FG/Game |
|---|---|---|---|---|---|---|
| Matt Seagraves, E Stroudsburg | So | 10 | 26 | 15 | 57.7 | 1.50 |
| Ryan Anderson, N Colorado | Jr | 11 | 23 | 14 | 60.9 | 1.27 |
| Scott Doyle, Chadron St | Jr | 11 | 19 | 14 | 73.7 | 1.27 |
| Matt Hemenway, St Cloud St | Fr | 10 | 20 | 12 | 60.0 | 1.20 |
| Eric Myers, W Virginia Wesleyan | So | 10 | 17 | 12 | 70.6 | 1.20 |
| Mike Foster, Mesa St | So | 10 | 16 | 12 | 75.0 | 1.20 |

### TOTAL OFFENSE

| | Class | GP | Yds | Yds/Game |
|---|---|---|---|---|
| Grady Benton, W Texas A&M | Jr | 9 | 3699 | 411.0 |
| Alfred Montez, W New Mexico | Jr | 6 | 2130 | 355.0 |
| Kevin Vickers, Tarleton St | Sr | 10 | 3232 | 323.2 |
| Chris Hatcher, Valdosta St | Sr | 11 | 3512 | 319.3 |
| Aaron Sparrow, Norfolk St | Jr | 10 | 3152 | 315.2 |

### RUSHING

| | Class | GP | Car | Yds | TD | Yds/Game |
|---|---|---|---|---|---|---|
| Leonard Davis, Lenoir-Rhyne | Sr | 9 | 216 | 1559 | 19 | 173.2 |
| Larry Jackson, Edinboro | Sr | 10 | 274 | 1660 | 15 | 166.0 |
| Richard Huntley, Winston-Salem | Jr | 11 | 251 | 1815 | 18 | 165.0 |
| Joe Aska, Central Oklahoma | Sr | 10 | 278 | 1629 | 15 | 162.9 |
| Fred Lane, Lane | Fr | 11 | 280 | 1779 | 14 | 161.7 |

### PASSING EFFICIENCY

| | Class | GP | Att | Comp | Yds | Pct Comp | TD | Int | Rating Pts |
|---|---|---|---|---|---|---|---|---|---|
| Chris Hatcher, Valdosta St | Sr | 11 | 430 | 321 | 3591 | 74.6 | 50 | 9 | 179.0 |
| Robb Stamey, Lenoir-Rhyne | Sr | 10 | 197 | 106 | 1986 | 53.8 | 18 | 3 | 165.6 |
| Sultan Cooper, Albany St (GA) | Jr | 11 | 190 | 114 | 1539 | 60.0 | 22 | 4 | 162.0 |
| Alfred Montez, W New Mexico | Jr | 6 | 231 | 133 | 2182 | 57.5 | 18 | 7 | 156.6 |
| Aaron Sparrow, Norfolk St | Jr | 10 | 361 | 216 | 3212 | 59.8 | 31 | 14 | 155.2 |

Note: Minimum 15 attempts per game.

### RECEPTIONS PER GAME

| | Class | GP | No. | Yds | TD | Rec/Game |
|---|---|---|---|---|---|---|
| Chris George, Glenville St | Sr | 10 | 113 | 1339 | 15 | 11.3 |
| Brad Bailey, W Texas A&M | Sr | 11 | 119 | 1552 | 16 | 10.8 |
| Keylie Martin, N Mex Highlands | Jr | 10 | 87 | 911 | 10 | 8.7 |
| Greg Hopkins, Slippery Rock | Sr | 10 | 83 | 1283 | 12 | 8.3 |
| Jerry Garrett, Wayne St (Neb.) | Sr | 10 | 83 | 879 | 9 | 8.3 |
| Byron Chamberlin, Wayne St (Neb.) | Sr | 10 | 83 | 926 | 7 | 8.3 |

## Division II *(Cont.)*

### RECEIVING YARDS PER GAME

| | Class | GP | No. | Yds | TD | Yds/Game |
|---|---|---|---|---|---|---|
| James Roe, Norfolk St | Jr | 10 | 77 | 1454 | 17 | 145.4 |
| Brad Bailey, W Texas A&M | Sr | 11 | 119 | 1552 | 16 | 141.1 |
| Chris George, Glenville St | Sr | 10 | 113 | 1339 | 15 | 133.9 |
| Greg Hopkins, Slippery Rock | Sr | 10 | 83 | 1283 | 12 | 128.3 |
| Brian Penecale, West Chester | Jr | 11 | 77 | 1283 | 18 | 116.6 |

### INTERCEPTIONS

| | Class | GP | No. | Yds | Int/ Game |
|---|---|---|---|---|---|
| Keith Hawkins, Humboldt St | Sr | 10 | 11 | 159 | 1.1 |
| Elton Rhoades, Central Okla | Sr | 10 | 11 | 126 | 1.1 |
| Scott Elwer, Hillsdale | Jr | 11 | 10 | 136 | .9 |
| Tyrone Andrews, Miles | Jr | 9 | 8 | 111 | .9 |

Three tied with .8 Int/Game

### PUNTING

| | Class | No. | Avg |
|---|---|---|---|
| Pat Hogelin, CO-Mines | Sr | 48 | 45.1 |
| Adam Vinatieri, S Dakota St | Sr | 57 | 43.5 |
| Bob Koning, NM Highlands | Sr | 54 | 43.0 |
| Phil Schmitten, Fort Lewis | So | 58 | 42.9 |
| John McGhee, Indiana (PA) | Jr | 42 | 42.1 |

Note: Minimum 3.6 per game.

## Division III

### SCORING

| | Class | GP | TD | XP | FG | Pts | Pts/Game |
|---|---|---|---|---|---|---|---|
| Carey Bender, Coe | Sr | 10 | 32 | 2 | 0 | 194 | 19.4 |
| Rob Marchitello, Maine-Maritime | Jr | 9 | 25 | 4 | 0 | 154 | 17.1 |
| Steve Harris, Carroll (WI) | Sr | 9 | 20 | 2 | 0 | 122 | 13.6 |
| Matt Taylor, Catholic | So | 10 | 22 | 2 | 0 | 134 | 13.4 |
| Mark Kacmarynski, Central (IA) | Jr | 10 | 21 | 2 | 0 | 128 | 12.8 |

### FIELD GOALS

| | Class | GP | FGA | FG | Pct | FG/Game |
|---|---|---|---|---|---|---|
| Chris Kondik, Baldwin-Wallace | Fr | 10 | 17 | 13 | 76.5 | 1.30 |
| Dennis Unger, Albright | Fr | 9 | 19 | 11 | 57.9 | 1.22 |
| Jason Goldberg, John Carroll | So | 10 | 16 | 12 | 75.0 | 1.20 |
| Mike LaCroix, Alfred | So | 9 | 16 | 10 | 62.5 | 1.11 |
| Evan Hjerpe, Center | Jr | 10 | 13 | 11 | 84.6 | 1.10 |
| Brian Anthony, Cortland St | So | 10 | 16 | 11 | 68.8 | 1.10 |

### TOTAL OFFENSE

| | Class | GP | Yds | Yds/Game |
|---|---|---|---|---|
| Terry Peebles, Hanover | Jr | 10 | 3441 | 344.1 |
| Eric Noble, Wilmington (OH) | Jr | 9 | 3072 | 341.3 |
| John Shipp, Claremont-M-S | Sr | 9 | 2871 | 319.0 |
| Mark Novara, Lakeland | Fr | 9 | 2576 | 286.2 |
| Darrin Fox, Bluffton | So | 9 | 2551 | 283.4 |

### RUSHING

| | Class | GP | Car | Yds | TD | Yds/Game |
|---|---|---|---|---|---|---|
| Carey Bender, Coe | Sr | 10 | 295 | 2243 | 29 | 224.3 |
| Kelvin Gladney, Millsaps | Sr | 10 | 307 | 1882 | 19 | 188.2 |
| Mark Kacmarynski, Central (IA) | Jr | 10 | 236 | 1741 | 21 | 174.1 |
| Spencer Johnson, WI-Whitewater | Sr | 10 | 290 | 1697 | 18 | 169.7 |
| Rob Marchitello, Maine-Maritime | Jr | 9 | 298 | 1457 | 25 | 161.9 |

### PASSING EFFICIENCY

| | Class | GP | Att | Comp | Yds | Pct Comp | TD | Int | Rating Pts |
|---|---|---|---|---|---|---|---|---|---|
| Mike Simpson, Eureka | So | 10 | 158 | 116 | 1988 | 73.4 | 25 | 5 | 225.0 |
| Kurt Ramler, St John's (MN) | So | 9 | 154 | 93 | 1560 | 60.3 | 22 | 4 | 187.4 |
| Paul Bell, Allegheny | Sr | 10 | 215 | 142 | 2137 | 66.0 | 17 | 2 | 173.8 |
| Chris Adams, Gettysburg | Sr | 10 | 211 | 139 | 1977 | 65.8 | 19 | 2 | 172.4 |
| Kyle Klein, Albion | So | 9 | 146 | 87 | 1488 | 59.5 | 13 | 4 | 169.0 |

Note: Minimum 15 attempts per game

## Division III (Cont.)

### RECEPTIONS PER GAME

| | Class | GP | No. | Yds | TD | C/Game |
|---|---|---|---|---|---|---|
| Jason Tincher, Wilmington (OH)...Sr | | 9 | 85 | 1298 | 9 | 9.4 |
| Steve Wilkerson, Catholic.............Sr | | 10 | 90 | 1457 | 13 | 9.0 |
| Ryan Ditze, Albright.....................Jr | | 10 | 82 | 1023 | 5 | 8.2 |
| Mike Cook, Claremont-M-S.........So | | 9 | 70 | 1014 | 12 | 7.8 |
| Ryan Davis, St Thomas (MN)........Jr | | 10 | 75 | 1164 | 9 | 7.5 |

### RECEIVING YARDS PER GAME

| | Class | GP | No. | Yds | TD | Yds/Game |
|---|---|---|---|---|---|---|
| Steve Wilkerson, Catholic.............Sr | | 10 | 90 | 1457 | 13 | 145.7 |
| Jason Tincher, Wilmington (OH)...Sr | | 9 | 85 | 1298 | 9 | 144.2 |
| D.R. Moreland, Menlo...................Sr | | 9 | 66 | 1179 | 6 | 131.0 |
| Ryan Davis, St Thomas (MN)........Jr | | 10 | 75 | 1164 | 9 | 116.4 |
| Mike Cook, Claremont-M-S.........So | | 9 | 70 | 1014 | 12 | 112.7 |

### INTERCEPTIONS

| | Class | GP | No. | Yds | Int/Game |
|---|---|---|---|---|---|
| Antonio Moore, Widener ............So | | 10 | 13 | 116 | 1.3 |
| Greg Schramm, Trinity (CT).......Sr | | 8 | 8 | 66 | 1.0 |
| Ron Contreras, Salve Regina ....So | | 8 | 8 | 88 | 1.0 |
| Brian Fitzpatrick, Wooster St ....Sr | | 10 | 9 | 223 | .9 |
| Adam Smith, Heidelberg ...........Sr | | 10 | 9 | 194 | .9 |
| Chad Zollman, Kalamazoo ........Jr | | 9 | 8 | 137 | .9 |
| Heath Allard, Cornell College ....Jr | | 9 | 8 | 80 | .9 |
| Mike Benson, Redlands.............So | | 9 | 8 | 52 | .9 |

### PUNTING

| | Class | No. | Avg |
|---|---|---|---|
| Ryan Haley, John Carroll ...................Sr | | 54 | 42.8 |
| Tomek Mikler, Redlands.....................Jr | | 45 | 41.6 |
| Kevin Feighery, Merchant Marine......Sr | | 36 | 40.1 |
| Bryan Weber, WI-Platteville ...............Jr | | 39 | 39.8 |
| Matt Carlson, North Central...............Jr | | 38 | 39.2 |

Note: Minimum 3.6 per game

# 1994 NCAA Division I-A Team Leaders

## Offense

### SCORING

| | GP | Pts | Avg |
|---|---|---|---|
| Penn St...................11 | | 526 | 47.8 |
| Florida ....................12 | | 521 | 43.4 |
| Nevada...................11 | | 414 | 37.6 |
| Utah.......................11 | | 410 | 37.3 |
| Florida St................11 | | 405 | 36.8 |
| Nebraska................12 | | 435 | 36.3 |
| Colorado.................11 | | 398 | 36.2 |
| Bowling Green.........11 | | 391 | 35.5 |
| Colorado St.............11 | | 386 | 35.1 |
| Central Michigan ....11 | | 376 | 34.2 |

### RUSHING

| | GP | Car | Yds | Avg | TD | Yds/Game |
|---|---|---|---|---|---|---|
| Nebraska................12 | | 687 | 4080 | 5.9 | 44 | 340.0 |
| Air Force................12 | | 720 | 3657 | 5.1 | 36 | 304.8 |
| Colorado ................11 | | 517 | 3206 | 6.2 | 40 | 291.5 |
| Central Michigan.....11 | | 571 | 3132 | 5.5 | 37 | 284.7 |
| Oregon St...............11 | | 640 | 3072 | 4.8 | 24 | 279.3 |
| Penn St..................11 | | 450 | 2760 | 6.1 | 45 | 250.9 |
| Army......................11 | | 619 | 2738 | 4.4 | 22 | 248.9 |
| Kansas ..................11 | | 558 | 2718 | 4.9 | 31 | 247.1 |
| Toledo ...................11 | | 509 | 2667 | 5.2 | 28 | 242.5 |
| Wisconsin...............11 | | 497 | 2649 | 5.3 | 23 | 240.8 |

### TOTAL OFFENSE

| | GP | Plays | Yds | Avg | TD* | Yds/Game |
|---|---|---|---|---|---|---|
| Penn St ....................................11 | | 749 | 5722 | 7.6 | 68 | 520.18 |
| Nevada .....................................11 | | 901 | 5581 | 6.2 | 55 | 507.36 |
| Colorado....................................11 | | 773 | 5448 | 7.0 | 52 | 495.27 |
| Florida St ..................................11 | | 853 | 5314 | 6.2 | 52 | 483.09 |
| Nebraska ..................................12 | | 897 | 5734 | 6.4 | 59 | 477.83 |
| New Mexico...............................12 | | 937 | 5664 | 6.0 | 51 | 472.00 |
| Georgia.....................................11 | | 754 | 5135 | 6.8 | 41 | 466.82 |
| Florida ......................................12 | | 851 | 5553 | 6.5 | 62 | 462.75 |
| Brigham Young...........................12 | | 955 | 5489 | 5.7 | 45 | 457.42 |
| Wyoming....................................12 | | 929 | 5468 | 5.9 | 38 | 455.67 |

*Defensive and special teams TDs not included.

## PASSING

| | G | Att | Comp | Yds | Pct Comp | Yds/Att | TD | Int | Yds/Game |
|---|---|---|---|---|---|---|---|---|---|
| Georgia | 11 | 462 | 276 | 3721 | 59.7 | 8.1 | 25 | 14 | 338.3 |
| Nevada | 11 | 463 | 279 | 3625 | 60.3 | 7.8 | 29 | 16 | 329.5 |
| Brigham Young | 12 | 475 | 287 | 3755 | 60.4 | 7.9 | 29 | 14 | 312.9 |
| Florida | 12 | 435 | 267 | 3740 | 61.4 | 8.6 | 43 | 21 | 311.7 |
| Stanford | 11 | 422 | 255 | 3358 | 60.4 | 8.0 | 18 | 12 | 305.3 |
| San Diego St | 11 | 410 | 257 | 3244 | 62.7 | 7.9 | 27 | 16 | 294.9 |
| Florida St | 11 | 441 | 264 | 3234 | 59.9 | 7.3 | 21 | 18 | 294.0 |
| Wyoming | 12 | 409 | 225 | 3367 | 55.0 | 8.2 | 21 | 19 | 280.6 |
| Utah | 11 | 387 | 249 | 3061 | 64.3 | 7.9 | 28 | 11 | 278.3 |
| Maryland | 11 | 428 | 291 | 3037 | 68.0 | 7.1 | 23 | 13 | 276.1 |

## Single-Game Highs

Points scored: 73—Florida, Sep 10 (vs Kentucky).
Net rushing yards: 564—Indiana, Sep 17 (vs Kentucky).
Passing yards: 635—UNLV, Sep 17 (vs Idaho).
Total yards: 731—Florida St, Sep 10 (vs Maryland).
Fewest total yards allowed: 46—Illinois, Sep 10 (vs Missouri).
Passes attempted: 62—New Mexico, Sep 10 (vs Texas Christian).
Passes completed: 40—Florida St, Nov 26 (vs Florida).

## Defense

### SCORING

| | GP | Pts | Avg |
|---|---|---|---|
| Miami (FL) | 11 | 119 | 10.8 |
| Nebraska | 12 | 145 | 12.1 |
| Washington St | 11 | 133 | 12.1 |
| Texas A&M | 11 | 147 | 13.4 |
| Kansas St | 11 | 156 | 14.2 |
| Illinois | 11 | 156 | 14.2 |
| Alabama | 12 | 173 | 14.4 |
| Memphis | 11 | 159 | 14.5 |
| Boston College | 11 | 162 | 14.7 |
| Ohio St | 12 | 187 | 15.6 |

### TOTAL DEFENSE

| | GP | Plays | Yds | Avg | Yds/Game |
|---|---|---|---|---|---|
| Miami (FL) | 11 | 702 | 2430 | 3.5 | 220.9 |
| Washington St | 11 | 732 | 2519 | 3.4 | 229.0 |
| Memphis | 11 | 729 | 2774 | 3.8 | 252.2 |
| Nebraska | 12 | 765 | 3106 | 4.1 | 258.8 |
| Texas A&M | 11 | 758 | 2920 | 3.9 | 265.5 |
| Boston College | 11 | 697 | 2927 | 4.2 | 266.1 |
| Florida St | 11 | 754 | 2937 | 3.9 | 267.0 |
| W Michigan | 11 | 726 | 3047 | 4.2 | 277.0 |
| Illinois | 11 | 700 | 3138 | 4.5 | 285.3 |
| Arizona | 11 | 688 | 3140 | 4.6 | 285.5 |

### RUSHING

| | GP | Car | Yds | Avg | TD | Yds/Game |
|---|---|---|---|---|---|---|
| Virginia | 11 | 323 | 700 | 2.2 | 9 | 63.6 |
| Arizona | 11 | 369 | 715 | 1.9 | 6 | 65.0 |
| Washington St | 11 | 418 | 812 | 1.9 | 4 | 73.8 |
| Nebraska | 12 | 401 | 951 | 2.4 | 8 | 79.3 |
| Florida | 12 | 387 | 1015 | 2.6 | 9 | 84.6 |
| Texas A&M | 11 | 440 | 1016 | 2.3 | 11 | 92.4 |
| Miami (FL) | 11 | 409 | 1065 | 2.6 | 4 | 96.8 |
| Florida St | 11 | 378 | 1077 | 2.8 | 6 | 97.9 |
| Utah | 11 | 410 | 1163 | 2.8 | 11 | 105.7 |
| Memphis | 11 | 419 | 1172 | 2.8 | 8 | 106.5 |

### TURNOVER MARGIN

| | | Turnovers Gained | | | Turnovers Lost | | | Margin/ |
|---|---|---|---|---|---|---|---|---|
| | GP | Fum | Int | Total | Fum | Int | Total | Game |
| Clemson | 11 | 13 | 16 | 29 | 2 | 10 | 12 | 1.55 |
| Duke | 11 | 12 | 17 | 29 | 4 | 9 | 13 | 1.45 |
| Auburn | 11 | 11 | 22 | 33 | 11 | 7 | 18 | 1.36 |
| Mississippi | 11 | 13 | 19 | 32 | 13 | 6 | 19 | 1.18 |
| SMU | 11 | 20 | 9 | 29 | 6 | 10 | 16 | 1.18 |
| Kansas St | 11 | 12 | 12 | 24 | 5 | 6 | 11 | 1.18 |
| Penn St | 11 | 12 | 11 | 23 | 4 | 7 | 11 | 1.09 |

## PASSING EFFICIENCY

| | GP | Att | Comp | Yds | Pct Comp | Yds/Att | TD | Pct TD | Int | Pct Int | Rating Pts |
|---|---|---|---|---|---|---|---|---|---|---|---|
| Miami (FL) | 11 | 293 | 143 | 1365 | 48.8 | 4.7 | 5 | 1.7 | 18 | 6.1 | 81.3 |
| SW Louisiana | 11 | 309 | 135 | 1626 | 43.7 | 5.3 | 10 | 3.2 | 19 | 6.2 | 86.3 |
| Texas Tech | 11 | 283 | 122 | 1623 | 43.1 | 5.7 | 8 | 2.8 | 17 | 6.0 | 88.6 |
| Florida St | 11 | 376 | 180 | 1860 | 47.9 | 5.0 | 13 | 3.5 | 15 | 4.0 | 92.9 |
| Washington St | 11 | 314 | 140 | 1707 | 44.6 | 5.4 | 9 | 2.9 | 10 | 3.2 | 93.3 |
| Mississippi | 11 | 300 | 134 | 1708 | 44.7 | 5.7 | 13 | 4.3 | 19 | 6.3 | 94.1 |
| Kansas St | 11 | 279 | 130 | 1596 | 46.6 | 5.7 | 7 | 2.5 | 12 | 4.3 | 94.3 |
| Virginia Tech | 11 | 354 | 168 | 1945 | 47.5 | 5.5 | 10 | 2.8 | 15 | 4.2 | 94.5 |
| Memphis | 11 | 310 | 162 | 1602 | 52.3 | 5.2 | 7 | 2.3 | 13 | 4.2 | 94.7 |
| Nebraska | 12 | 364 | 172 | 2155 | 47.3 | 5.9 | 10 | 2.8 | 17 | 4.7 | 96.7 |

# FOR THE RECORD·Year by Year

## National Champions

| Year | Champion | Record | Bowl Game | Head Coach |
|------|----------|--------|-----------|------------|
| 1883 | Yale | 8-0-0 | No bowl | Ray Tompkins (Captain) |
| 1884 | Yale | 9-0-0 | No bowl | Eugene L. Richards (Captain) |
| 1885 | Princeton | 9-0-0 | No bowl | Charles DeCamp (Captain) |
| 1886 | Yale | 9-0-1 | No bowl | Robert N. Corwin (Captain) |
| 1887 | Yale | 9-0-0 | No bowl | Harry W. Beecher (Captain) |
| 1888 | Yale | 13-0-0 | No bowl | Walter Camp |
| 1889 | Princeton | 10-0-0 | No bowl | Edgar Poe (Captain) |
| 1890 | Harvard | 11-0-0 | No bowl | George A. Stewart/George C. Adams |
| 1891 | Yale | 13-0-0 | No bowl | Walter Camp |
| 1892 | Yale | 13-0-0 | No bowl | Walter Camp |
| 1893 | Princeton | 11-0-0 | No bowl | Tom Trenchard (Captain) |
| 1894 | Yale | 16-0-0 | No bowl | William C. Rhodes |
| 1895 | Pennsylvania | 14-0-0 | No bowl | George Woodruff |
| 1896 | Princeton | 10-0-1 | No bowl | Garrett Cochran |
| 1897 | Pennsylvania | 15-0-0 | No bowl | George Woodruff |
| 1898 | Harvard | 11-0-0 | No bowl | W. Cameron Forbes |
| 1899 | Harvard | 10-0-1 | No bowl | Benjamin H. Dibblee |
| 1900 | Yale | 12-0-0 | No bowl | Malcolm McBride |
| 1901 | Michigan | 11-0-0 | Won Rose | Fielding Yost |
| 1902 | Michigan | 11-0-0 | No bowl | Fielding Yost |
| 1903 | Princeton | 11-0-0 | No bowl | Art Hillebrand |
| 1904 | Pennsylvania | 12-0-0 | No bowl | Carl Williams |
| 1905 | Chicago | 11-0-0 | No bowl | Amos Alonzo Stagg |
| 1906 | Princeton | 9-0-1 | No bowl | Bill Roper |
| 1907 | Yale | 9-0-1 | No bowl | Bill Knox |
| 1908 | Pennsylvania | 11-0-1 | No bowl | Sol Metzger |
| 1909 | Yale | 10-0-0 | No bowl | Howard Jones |
| 1910 | Harvard | 8-0-1 | No bowl | Percy Houghton |
| 1911 | Princeton | 8-0-2 | No bowl | Bill Roper |
| 1912 | Harvard | 9-0-0 | No bowl | Percy Houghton |
| 1913 | Harvard | 9-0-0 | No bowl | Percy Houghton |
| 1914 | Army | 9-0-0 | No bowl | Charley Daly |
| 1915 | Cornell | 9-0-0 | No bowl | Al Sharpe |
| 1916 | Pittsburgh | 8-0-0 | No bowl | Pop Warner |
| 1917 | Georgia Tech | 9-0-0 | No bowl | John Heisman |
| 1918 | Pittsburgh | 4-1-0 | No bowl | Pop Warner |
| 1919 | Harvard | 9-0-1 | Won Rose | Bob Fisher |
| 1920 | California | 9-0-0 | Won Rose | Andy Smith |
| 1921 | Cornell | 8-0-0 | No bowl | Gil Dobie |
| 1922 | Cornell | 8-0-0 | No bowl | Gil Dobie |
| 1923 | Illinois | 8-0-0 | No bowl | Bob Zuppke |
| 1924 | Notre Dame | 10-0-0 | Won Rose | Knute Rockne |
| 1925 | Alabama (H) | 10-0-0 | Won Rose | Wallace Wade |
| | Dartmouth (D) | 8-0-0 | No bowl | Jesse Hawley |
| 1926 | Alabama (H) | 9-0-1 | Tied Rose | Wallace Wade |
| | Stanford (D)(H) | 10-0-1 | Tied Rose | Pop Warner |
| 1927 | Illinois | 7-0-1 | No bowl | Bob Zuppke |
| 1928 | Georgia Tech (H) | 10-0-0 | Won Rose | Bill Alexander |
| | Southern Cal (D) | 9-0-1 | No bowl | Howard Jones |
| 1929 | Notre Dame | 9-0-0 | No bowl | Knute Rockne |
| 1930 | Notre Dame | 10-0-0 | No bowl | Knute Rockne |
| 1931 | Southern Cal | 10-1-0 | Won Rose | Howard Jones |
| 1932 | Southern Cal (H) | 10-0-0 | Won Rose | Howard Jones |
| | Michigan (D) | 8-0-0 | No bowl | Harry Kipke |
| 1933 | Michigan | 7-0-1 | No bowl | Harry Kipke |
| 1934 | Minnesota | 8-0-0 | No bowl | Bernie Bierman |
| 1935 | Minnesota (H) | 8-0-0 | No bowl | Bernie Bierman |
| | Southern Meth (D) | 12-1-0 | Lost Rose | Matty Bell |
| 1936 | Minnesota | 7-1-0 | No bowl | Bernie Bierman |
| 1937 | Pittsburgh | 9-0-1 | No bowl | Jock Sutherland |
| 1938 | Texas Christian (AP) | 11-0-0 | Won Sugar | Dutch Meyer |
| | Notre Dame (D) | 8-1-0 | No bowl | Elmer Layden |
| 1939 | Southern Cal (D) | 8-0-2 | Won Rose | Howard Jones |
| | Texas A&M (AP) | 11-0-0 | Won Sugar | Homer Norton |

| Year | Champion | Record | Bowl Game | Head Coach |
|---|---|---|---|---|
| 1940 | Minnesota | 8-0-0 | No bowl | Bernie Bierman |
| 1941 | Minnesota | 8-0-0 | No bowl | Bernie Bierman |
| 1942 | Ohio St | 9-1-0 | No bowl | Paul Brown |
| 1943 | Notre Dame | 9-1-0 | No bowl | Frank Leahy |
| 1944 | Army | 9-0-0 | No bowl | Red Blaik |
| 1945 | Army | 9-0-0 | No bowl | Red Blaik |
| 1946 | Notre Dame | 8-0-1 | No bowl | Frank Leahy |
| 1947 | Notre Dame | 9-0-0 | No bowl | Frank Leahy |
| | Michigan* | 10-0-0 | Won Rose | Fritz Crisler |
| 1948 | Michigan | 9-0-0 | No bowl | Bennie Oosterbaan |
| 1949 | Notre Dame | 10-0-0 | No bowl | Frank Leahy |
| 1950 | Oklahoma | 10-1-0 | Lost Sugar | Bud Wilkinson |
| 1951 | Tennessee | 10-1-0 | Lost Sugar | Bob Neyland |
| 1952 | Michigan St | 9-0-0 | No bowl | Biggie Munn |
| 1953 | Maryland | 10-1-0 | Lost Orange | Jim Tatum |
| 1954 | Ohio St | 10-0-0 | Won Rose | Woody Hayes |
| | UCLA (UP) | 9-0-0 | No bowl | Red Sanders |
| 1955 | Oklahoma | 11-0-0 | Won Orange | Bud Wilkinson |
| 1956 | Oklahoma | 10-0-0 | No bowl | Bud Wilkinson |
| 1957 | Auburn | 10-0-0 | No bowl | Shug Jordan |
| | Ohio St (UP) | 9-1-0 | Won Rose | Woody Hayes |
| 1958 | Louisiana St | 11-0-0 | Won Sugar | Paul Dietzel |
| 1959 | Syracuse | 11-0-0 | Won Cotton | Ben Schwartzwalder |
| 1960 | Minnesota | 8-2-0 | Lost Rose | Murray Warmath |
| 1961 | Alabama | 11-0-0 | Won Sugar | Bear Bryant |
| 1962 | Southern Cal | 11-0-0 | Won Rose | John McKay |
| 1963 | Texas | 11-0-0 | Won Cotton | Darrell Royal |
| 1964 | Alabama | 10-1-0 | Lost Orange | Bear Bryant |
| 1965 | Alabama | 9-1-1 | Won Orange | Bear Bryant |
| | Michigan St (UPI) | 10-1-0 | Lost Rose | Duffy Daugherty |
| 1966 | Notre Dame | 9-0-1 | No bowl | Ara Parseghian |
| 1967 | Southern Cal | 10-1-0 | Won Rose | John McKay |
| 1968 | Ohio St | 10-0-0 | Won Rose | Woody Hayes |
| 1969 | Texas | 11-0-0 | Won Cotton | Darrell Royal |
| 1970 | Nebraska | 11-0-1 | Won Orange | Bob Devaney |
| | Texas (UPI) | 10-1-0 | Lost Cotton | Darrell Royal |
| 1971 | Nebraska | 13-0-0 | Won Orange | Bob Devaney |
| 1972 | Southern Cal | 12-0-0 | Won Rose | John McKay |
| 1973 | Notre Dame | 11-0-0 | Won Sugar | Ara Parseghian |
| | Alabama (UPI) | 11-1-0 | Lost Sugar | Bear Bryant |
| 1974 | Oklahoma | 11-0-0 | No bowl | Barry Switzer |
| | Southern Cal (UPI) | 10-1-1 | Won Rose | John McKay |
| 1975 | Oklahoma | 11-1-0 | Won Orange | Barry Switzer |
| 1976 | Pittsburgh | 12-0-0 | Won Sugar | Johnny Majors |
| 1977 | Notre Dame | 11-1-0 | Won Cotton | Dan Devine |
| 1978 | Alabama | 11-1-0 | Won Sugar | Bear Bryant |
| | Southern Cal (UPI) | 12-1-0 | Won Rose | John Robinson |
| 1979 | Alabama | 12-0-0 | Won Sugar | Bear Bryant |
| 1980 | Georgia | 12-0-0 | Won Sugar | Vince Dooley |
| 1981 | Clemson | 12-0-0 | Won Orange | Danny Ford |
| 1982 | Penn St | 11-1-0 | Won Sugar | Joe Paterno |
| 1983 | Miami (FL) | 11-1-0 | Won Orange | Howard Schnellenberger |
| 1984 | Brigham Young | 13-0-0 | Won Holiday | LaVell Edwards |
| 1985 | Oklahoma | 11-1-0 | Won Orange | Barry Switzer |
| 1986 | Penn St | 12-0-0 | Won Fiesta | Joe Paterno |
| 1987 | Miami (FL) | 12-0-0 | Won Orange | Jimmy Johnson |
| 1988 | Notre Dame | 12-0-0 | Won Fiesta | Lou Holtz |
| 1989 | Miami (FL) | 11-1-0 | Won Sugar | Dennis Erickson |
| 1990 | Colorado | 11-1-1 | Won Orange | Bill McCartney |
| | Georgia Tech (UPI) | 11-0-1 | Won Citrus | Bobby Ross |
| 1991 | Miami (FL) | 12-0-0 | Won Orange | Dennis Erickson |
| | Washington (CNN) | 12-0-0 | Won Rose | Don James |
| 1992 | Alabama | 13-0-0 | Won Sugar | Gene Stallings |
| 1993 | Florida St | 12-1-0 | Won Orange | Bobby Bowden |
| 1994 | Nebraska | 13-0-0 | Won Orange | Tom Osborne |

*The AP, which had voted Notre Dame No. 1, took a second vote, giving the national title to Michigan after its 49-0 win over Southern Cal in the Rose Bowl.

Note: Selectors: Helms Athletic Foundation (H) 1883-1935, The Dickinson System (D) 1924-40, The Associated Press (AP) 1936-present, United Press International (UPI) 1958-90, and USA Today/CNN (CNN) 1991-present.

# Results of Major Bowl Games

## Rose Bowl

| | |
|---|---|
| 1-1-2 | Michigan 49, Stanford 0 |
| 1-1-16 | Washington St 14, Brown 0 |
| 1-1-17 | Oregon 14, Pennsylvania 0 |
| 1-1-18 | Mare Island 19, Camp Lewis 7 |
| 1-1-19 | Great Lakes 17, Mare Island 0 |
| 1-1-20 | Harvard 7, Oregon 6 |
| 1-1-21 | California 28, Ohio St 0 |
| 1-2-22 | Washington & Jefferson 0, California 0 |
| 1-1-23 | Southern Cal 14, Penn St 3 |
| 1-1-24 | Navy 14, Washington 14 |
| 1-1-25 | Notre Dame 27, Stanford 10 |
| 1-1-26 | Alabama 20, Washington 19 |
| 1-1-27 | Alabama 7, Stanford 7 |
| 1-2-28 | Stanford 7, Pittsburgh 6 |
| 1-1-29 | Georgia Tech 8, California 7 |
| 1-1-30 | Southern Cal 47, Pittsburgh 14 |
| 1-1-31 | Alabama 24, Washington St 0 |
| 1-1-32 | Southern Cal 21, Tulane 12 |
| 1-2-33 | Southern Cal 35, Pittsburgh 0 |
| 1-1-34 | Columbia 7, Stanford 0 |
| 1-1-35 | Alabama 29, Stanford 13 |
| 1-1-36 | Stanford 7, Southern Meth 0 |
| 1-1-37 | Pittsburgh 21, Washington 0 |
| 1-1-38 | California 13, Alabama 0 |
| 1-2-39 | Southern Cal 7, Duke 3 |
| 1-1-40 | Southern Cal 14, Tennessee 0 |
| 1-1-41 | Stanford 21, Nebraska 13 |
| 1-1-42 | Oregon St 20, Duke 16 |
| 1-1-43 | Georgia 9, UCLA 0 |
| 1-1-44 | Southern Cal 29, Washington 0 |
| 1-1-45 | Southern Cal 25, Tennessee 0 |
| 1-1-46 | Alabama 34, Southern Cal 14 |
| 1-1-47 | Illinois 45, UCLA 14 |
| 1-1-48 | Michigan 49, Southern Cal 0 |
| 1-1-49 | Northwestern 20, California 14 |
| 1-2-50 | Ohio St 17, California 14 |
| 1-1-51 | Michigan 14, California 6 |
| 1-1-52 | Illinois 40, Stanford 7 |
| 1-1-53 | Southern Cal 7, Wisconsin 0 |
| 1-1-54 | Michigan St 28, UCLA 20 |
| 1-1-55 | Ohio St 20, Southern Cal 7 |
| 1-2-56 | Michigan St 17, UCLA 14 |
| 1-1-57 | Iowa 35, Oregon St 19 |
| 1-1-58 | Ohio St 10, Oregon 7 |
| 1-1-59 | Iowa 38, California 12 |
| 1-1-60 | Washington 44, Wisconsin 8 |
| 1-2-61 | Washington 17, Minnesota 7 |
| 1-1-62 | Minnesota 21, UCLA 3 |
| 1-1-63 | Southern Cal 42, Wisconsin 37 |
| 1-1-64 | Illinois 17, Washington 7 |
| 1-1-65 | Michigan 34, Oregon St 7 |
| 1-1-66 | UCLA 14, Michigan St 12 |
| 1-2-67 | Purdue 14, Southern Cal 13 |
| 1-1-68 | Southern Cal 14, Indiana 3 |
| 1-1-69 | Ohio St 27, Southern Cal 16 |
| 1-1-70 | Southern Cal 10, Michigan 3 |
| 1-1-71 | Stanford 27, Ohio St 17 |
| 1-1-72 | Stanford 13, Michigan 12 |
| 1-1-73 | Southern Cal 42, Ohio St 17 |
| 1-1-74 | Ohio St 42, Southern Cal 21 |
| 1-1-75 | Southern Cal 18, Ohio St 17 |
| 1-1-76 | UCLA 23, Ohio St 10 |
| 1-1-77 | Southern Cal 14, Michigan 6 |
| 1-2-78 | Washington 27, Michigan 20 |
| 1-1-79 | Southern Cal 17, Michigan 10 |
| 1-1-80 | Southern Cal 17, Ohio St 16 |
| 1-1-81 | Michigan 23, Washington 6 |
| 1-1-82 | Washington 28, Iowa 0 |
| 1-1-83 | UCLA 24, Michigan 14 |
| 1-2-84 | UCLA 45, Illinois 9 |
| 1-1-85 | Southern Cal 20, Ohio St 17 |
| 1-1-86 | UCLA 45, Iowa 28 |
| 1-1-87 | Arizona St 22, Michigan 15 |
| 1-1-88 | Michigan St 20, Southern Cal 17 |
| 1-2-89 | Michigan 22, Southern Cal 14 |
| 1-1-90 | Southern Cal 17, Michigan 10 |
| 1-1-91 | Washington 46, Iowa 34 |
| 1-1-92 | Washington 34, Michigan 14 |
| 1-1-93 | Michigan 38, Washington 31 |
| 1-1-94 | Wisconsin 21, UCLA 16 |
| 1-2-95 | Penn St 38, Oregon 20 |

City: Pasadena.

Stadium: Rose Bowl.

Capacity: 104,091.

Automatic Berths: Pacific-10 champ vs Big 10 champ (since 1947).

Playing Sites: Tournament Park (1902, 1916-22), Rose Bowl (1923-41, since 1943), Duke Stadium, Durham, NC (1942).

## Orange Bowl

| | |
|---|---|
| 1-1-35 | Bucknell 26, Miami (FL) 0 |
| 1-1-36 | Catholic 20, Mississippi 19 |
| 1-1-37 | Duquesne 13, Mississippi St 12 |
| 1-1-38 | Auburn 6, Michigan St 0 |
| 1-2-39 | Tennessee 17, Oklahoma 0 |
| 1-1-40 | Georgia Tech 21, Missouri 7 |
| 1-1-41 | Mississippi St 14, Georgetown 7 |
| 1-1-42 | Georgia 40, Texas Christian 26 |
| 1-1-43 | Alabama 37, Boston College 21 |
| 1-1-44 | Louisiana St 19, Texas A&M 14 |
| 1-1-45 | Tulsa 26, Georgia Tech 12 |
| 1-1-46 | Miami (FL) 13, Holy Cross 6 |
| 1-1-47 | Rice 8, Tennessee 0 |
| 1-1-48 | Georgia Tech 20, Kansas 14 |
| 1-1-49 | Texas 41, Georgia 28 |
| 1-2-50 | Santa Clara 21, Kentucky 13 |
| 1-1-51 | Clemson 15, Miami (FL) 14 |
| 1-1-52 | Georgia Tech 17, Baylor 14 |
| 1-1-53 | Alabama 61, Syracuse 6 |
| 1-1-54 | Oklahoma 7, Maryland 0 |
| 1-1-55 | Duke 34, Nebraska 7 |
| 1-2-56 | Oklahoma 20, Maryland 6 |
| 1-1-57 | Colorado 27, Clemson 21 |
| 1-1-58 | Oklahoma 48, Duke 21 |
| 1-1-59 | Oklahoma 21, Syracuse 6 |
| 1-1-60 | Georgia 14, Missouri 0 |
| 1-2-61 | Missouri 21, Navy 14 |
| 1-1-62 | Louisiana St 25, Colorado 7 |
| 1-1-63 | Alabama 17, Oklahoma 0 |
| 1-1-64 | Nebraska 13, Auburn 7 |
| 1-1-65 | Texas 21, Alabama 17 |
| 1-1-66 | Alabama 39, Nebraska 28 |
| 1-2-67 | Florida 27, Georgia Tech 12 |
| 1-1-68 | Oklahoma 26, Tennessee 24 |
| 1-1-69 | Penn St 15, Kansas 14 |
| 1-1-70 | Penn St 10, Missouri 3 |
| 1-1-71 | Nebraska 17, Louisiana St 12 |
| 1-1-72 | Nebraska 38, Alabama 6 |
| 1-1-73 | Nebraska 40, Notre Dame 6 |
| 1-1-74 | Penn St 16, Louisiana St 9 |
| 1-1-75 | Notre Dame 13, Alabama 11 |
| 1-1-76 | Oklahoma 14, Michigan 6 |
| 1-1-77 | Ohio St 27, Colorado 10 |

### Orange Bowl *(Cont.)*

1-2-78 ..............Arkansas 31, Oklahoma 6
1-1-79 ..............Oklahoma 31, Nebraska 24
1-1-80 ..............Oklahoma 24, Florida St 7
1-1-81 ..............Oklahoma 18, Florida St 17
1-1-82 ..............Clemson 22, Nebraska 15
1-1-83 ..............Nebraska 21, Louisiana St 20
1-2-84 ..............Miami (FL) 31, Nebraska 30
1-1-85 ..............Washington 28, Oklahoma 17
1-1-86 ..............Oklahoma 25, Penn St 10
1-1-87 ..............Oklahoma 42, Arkansas 8
1-1-88 ..............Miami (FL) 20, Oklahoma 14
1-2-89 ..............Miami (FL) 23, Nebraska 3
1-1-90 ..............Notre Dame 41, Colorado 6
1-1-91 ..............Colorado 10, Notre Dame 9
1-1-92 ..............Miami (FL) 22, Nebraska 0
1-1-93 ..............Florida State 27, Nebraska 14
1-1-94 ..............Florida State 18, Nebraska 16
1-1-95 ..............Nebraska 24, Miami (FL) 17
City: Miami.
Stadium: Orange Bowl.
Capacity: 75,500.
Automatic Berths: Big 8 champ (1954-64, since 1976).

### Sugar Bowl

1-1-35 ..............Tulane 20, Temple 14
1-1-36 ..............Texas Christian 3, Louisiana St 2
1-1-37 ..............Santa Clara 21, Louisiana St 14
1-1-38 ..............Santa Clara 6, Louisiana St 0
1-2-39 ..............Texas Christian 15, Carnegie Tech 7
1-1-40 ..............Texas A&M 14, Tulane 13
1-1-41 ..............Boston Col 19, Tennessee 13
1-1-42 ..............Fordham 2, Missouri 0
1-1-43 ..............Tennessee 14, Tulsa 7
1-1-44 ..............Georgia Tech 20, Tulsa 18
1-1-45 ..............Duke 29, Alabama 26
1-1-46 ..............Oklahoma St 33, St Mary's (CA) 13
1-1-47 ..............Georgia 20, N Carolina 10
1-1-48 ..............Texas 27, Alabama 7
1-1-49 ..............Oklahoma 14, N Carolina 6
1-2-50 ..............Oklahoma 35, Louisiana St 0
1-1-51 ..............Kentucky 13, Oklahoma 7
1-1-52 ..............Maryland 28, Tennessee 13
1-1-53 ..............Georgia Tech 24, Mississippi 7
1-1-54 ..............Georgia Tech 42, W Virginia 19
1-1-55 ..............Navy 21, Mississippi 0
1-2-56 ..............Georgia Tech 7, Pittsburgh 0
1-1-57 ..............Baylor 13, Tennessee 7
1-1-58 ..............Mississippi 39, Texas 7
1-1-59 ..............Louisiana St 7, Clemson 0
1-1-60 ..............Mississippi 21, Louisiana St 0
1-2-61 ..............Mississippi 14, Rice 6
1-1-62 ..............Alabama 10, Arkansas 3
1-1-63 ..............Mississippi 17, Arkansas 13
1-1-64 ..............Alabama 12, Mississippi 7
1-1-65 ..............Louisiana St 13, Syracuse 10
1-1-66 ..............Missouri 20, Florida 18
1-2-67 ..............Alabama 34, Nebraska 7
1-1-68 ..............Louisiana St 20, Wyoming 13
1-1-69 ..............Arkansas 16, Georgia 2
1-1-70 ..............Mississippi 27, Arkansas 22
1-1-71 ..............Tennessee 34, Air Force 13
1-1-72 ..............Oklahoma 40, Auburn 22
12-31-72 .........Oklahoma 14, Penn St 0
12-31-73 .........Notre Dame 24, Alabama 23
12-31-74 .........Nebraska 13, Florida 10
12-31-75 .........Alabama 13, Penn St 6

### Sugar Bowl *(Cont.)*

1-1-77 ..............Pittsburgh 27, Georgia 3
1-2-78 ..............Alabama 35, Ohio St 6
1-1-79 ..............Alabama 14, Penn St 7
1-1-80 ..............Alabama 24, Arkansas 9
1-1-81 ..............Georgia 17, Notre Dame 10
1-1-82 ..............Pittsburgh 24, Georgia 20
1-1-83 ..............Penn St 27, Georgia 23
1-2-84 ..............Auburn 9, Michigan 7
1-1-85 ..............Nebraska 28, Louisiana St 10
1-1-86 ..............Tennessee 35, Miami (FL) 7
1-1-87 ..............Nebraska 30, Louisiana St 15
1-1-88 ..............Syracuse 16, Auburn 16
1-2-89 ..............Florida St 13, Auburn 7
1-1-90 ..............Miami (FL) 33, Alabama 25
1-1-91 ..............Tennessee 23, Virginia 22
1-1-92 ..............Notre Dame 39, Florida 28
1-1-93 ..............Alabama 34, Miami (FL) 13
1-1-94 ..............Florida 41, West Virginia 7
1-2-95 ..............Florida St 23, Florida 17
City: New Orleans.
Stadium: Louisiana Superdome.
Capacity: 69,548.
Automatic Berths: Southeastern champ (since 1977).
Playing Sites: Tulane Stadium (1935-74), Superdome (1974)

### Cotton Bowl

1-1-37 ..............Texas Christian 16, Marquette 6
1-1-38 ..............Rice 28, Colorado 14
1-2-39 ..............St. Mary's (CA) 20, Texas Tech 13
1-1-40 ..............Clemson 6, Boston Col 3
1-1-41 ..............Texas A&M 13, Fordham 12
1-1-42 ..............Alabama 29, Texas A&M 21
1-1-43 ..............Texas 14, Georgia Tech 7
1-1-44 ..............Texas 7, Randolph Field 7
1-1-45 ..............Oklahoma St 34, Texas Christian 0
1-1-46 ..............Texas 40, Missouri 27
1-1-47 ..............Arkansas 0, Louisiana St 0
1-1-48 ..............Southern Meth 13, Penn St 13
1-1-49 ..............Southern Meth 21, Oregon 13
1-2-50 ..............Rice 27, N Carolina 13
1-1-51 ..............Tennessee 20, Texas 14
1-1-52 ..............Kentucky 20, Texas Christian 7
1-1-53 ..............Texas 16, Tennessee 0
1-1-54 ..............Rice 28, Alabama 6
1-1-55 ..............Georgia Tech 14, Arkansas 6
1-2-56 ..............Mississippi 14, Texas Christian 13
1-1-57 ..............Texas Christian 28, Syracuse 27
1-1-58 ..............Navy 20, Rice 7
1-1-59 ..............Texas Christian 0, Air Force 0
1-1-60 ..............Syracuse 23, Texas 14
1-2-61 ..............Duke 7, Arkansas 6
1-1-62 ..............Texas 12, Mississippi 7
1-1-63 ..............Louisiana St 13, Texas 0
1-1-64 ..............Texas 28, Navy 6
1-1-65 ..............Arkansas 10, Nebraska 7
1-1-66 ..............Louisiana St 14, Arkansas 7
12-31-66 .........Georgia 24, Southern Meth 9
1-1-68 ..............Texas A&M 20, Alabama 16
1-1-69 ..............Texas 36, Tennessee 13
1-1-70 ..............Texas 21, Notre Dame 17
1-1-71 ..............Notre Dame 24, Texas 11
1-1-72 ..............Penn St 30, Texas 6
1-1-73 ..............Texas 17, Alabama 13
1-1-74 ..............Nebraska 19, Texas 3
1-1-75 ..............Penn St 41, Baylor 20

## Cotton Bowl *(Cont.)*

1-1-76 ..............Arkansas 31, Georgia 10
1-1-77 ..............Houston 30, Maryland 21
1-2-78 ..............Notre Dame 38, Texas 10
1-1-79 ..............Notre Dame 35, Houston 34
1-1-80 ..............Houston 17, Nebraska 14
1-1-81 ..............Alabama 30, Baylor 2
1-1-82 ..............Texas 14, Alabama 12
1-1-83 ..............Southern Meth 7, Pittsburgh 3
1-2-84 ..............Georgia 10, Texas 9
1-1-85 ..............Boston Col 45, Houston 28
1-1-86 ..............Texas A&M 36, Auburn 16
1-1-87 ..............Ohio St 28, Texas A&M 12
1-1-88 ..............Texas A&M 35, Notre Dame 10
1-2-89 ..............UCLA 17, Arkansas 3
1-1-90 ..............Tennessee 31, Arkansas 27
1-1-91 ..............Miami (FL) 46, Texas 3
1-1-92 ..............Florida St 10, Texas A&M 2
1-1-93 ..............Notre Dame 28, Texas A&M 3
1-1-94 ..............Notre Dame 24, Texas A&M 21
1-2-95 ..............Southern Cal 55, Texas Tech 14
City: Dallas.
Stadium: Cotton Bowl.
Capacity: 72,032.
Automatic Berths: Southwest champ (since 1942).
Playing Sites: Fair Park Stadium (1937), Cotton Bowl (since 1938).

## Sun Bowl

1-1-36 ..............Hardin-Simmons 14, New Mexico St 14
1-1-37 ..............Hardin-Simmons 34, UTEP 6
1-1-38 ..............W Virginia 7, Texas Tech 6
1-2-39 ..............Utah 26, New Mexico 0
1-1-40 ..............Catholic 0, Arizona St 0
1-1-41 ..............Case Reserve 26, Arizona St 13
1-1-42 ..............Tulsa 6, Texas Tech 0
1-1-43 ..............2nd Air Force 13, Hardin-Simmons 7
1-1-44 ..............Southwestern (TX) 7, New Mexico 0
1-1-45 ..............Southwestern (TX) 35, New Mexico 0
1-1-46 ..............New Mexico 34, Denver 24
1-1-47 ..............Cincinnati 18, Virginia Tech 6
1-1-48 ..............Miami (OH) 13, Texas Tech 12
1-1-49 ..............W Virginia 21, UTEP 12
1-2-50 ..............UTEP 33, Georgetown 20
1-1-51 ..............West Texas St 14, Cincinnati 13
1-1-52 ..............Texas Tech 25, Pacific 14
1-1-53 ..............Pacific 26, Southern Miss 7
1-1-54 ..............UTEP 37, Southern Miss 14
1-1-55 ..............UTEP 47, Florida St 20
1-2-56 ..............Wyoming 21, Texas Tech 14
1-1-57 ..............George Washington 13, UTEP 0
1-1-58 ..............Louisville 34, Drake 20
12-31-58 ..........Wyoming 14, Hardin-Simmons 6
12-31-59 ..........New Mexico St 28, N Texas 8
12-31-60 ..........New Mexico St 20, Utah St 13
12-30-61 ..........Villanova 17, Wichita St 9
12-31-62 ..........W Texas St 15, Ohio 14
12-31-63 ..........Oregon 21, Southern Meth 14
12-26-64 ..........Georgia 7, Texas Tech 0
12-31-65 ..........UTEP 13, Texas Christian 12
12-24-66 ..........Wyoming 28, Florida St 20
12-30-67 ..........UTEP 14, Mississippi 7
12-28-68 ..........Auburn 34, Arizona 10
12-20-69 ..........Nebraska 45, Georgia 6
12-19-70 ..........Georgia Tech 17, Texas Tech 9
12-18-71 ..........Louisiana St 33, Iowa St 15
12-30-72 ..........N Carolina 32, Texas Tech 28

## Sun Bowl *(Cont.)*

12-29-73 ..........Missouri 34, Auburn 17
12-28-74 ..........Mississippi St 26, N Carolina 24
12-26-75 ..........Pittsburgh 33, Kansas 19
1-2-77 ..............Texas A&M 37, Florida 14
12-31-77 ..........Stanford 24, Louisiana St 14
12-23-78 ..........Texas 42, Maryland 0
12-22-79 ..........Washington 14, Texas 7
12-27-80 ..........Nebraska 31, Mississippi St 17
12-26-81 ..........Oklahoma 40, Houston 14
12-25-82 ..........N Carolina 26, Texas 10
12-24-83 ..........Alabama 28, Southern Meth 7
12-22-84 ..........Maryland 28, Tennessee 27
12-28-85 ..........Georgia 13, Arizona 13
12-25-86 ..........Alabama 28, Washington 6
12-25-87 ..........Oklahoma St 35, W Virginia 33
12-24-88 ..........Alabama 29, Army 28
12-30-89 ..........Pittsburgh 31, Texas A&M 28
12-31-90 ..........Michigan St 17, Southern Cal 16
12-31-91 ..........UCLA 6, Illinois 3
12-31-92 ..........Baylor 20, Arizona 15
12-24-93 ..........Oklahoma 41, Texas Tech 10
12-30-94 ..........Texas 35, N Carolina 31
City: El Paso.
Stadium: Sun Bowl.
Capacity: 52,000.
Automatic Berths: None.
Name Changes: Sun Bowl (1936-86; 94-), John Hancock Sun Bowl (1987-88), John Hancock Bowl (1989-93).
Playing Sites: Kidd Field (1936-62), Sun Bowl (since 1963).

## Gator Bowl

1-1-46 ..............Wake Forest 26, S Carolina 14
1-1-47 ..............Oklahoma 34, N Carolina St 13
1-1-48 ..............Maryland 20, Georgia 20
1-1-49 ..............Clemson 24, Missouri 23
1-2-50 ..............Maryland 20, Missouri 7
1-1-51 ..............Wyoming 20, Washington & Lee 7
1-1-52 ..............Miami (FL) 14, Clemson 0
1-1-53 ..............Florida 14, Tulsa 13
1-1-54 ..............Texas Tech 35, Auburn 13
12-31-54 ..........Auburn 33, Baylor 13
12-31-55 ..........Vanderbilt 25, Auburn 13
12-29-56 ..........Georgia Tech 21, Pittsburgh 14
12-28-57 ..........Tennessee 3, Texas A&M 0
12-27-58 ..........Mississippi 7, Florida 3
1-2-60 ..............Arkansas 14, Georgia Tech 7
12-31-60 ..........Florida 13, Baylor 12
12-30-61 ..........Penn St 30, Georgia Tech 15
12-29-62 ..........Florida 17, Penn St 7
12-28-63 ..........N Carolina 35, Air Force 0
1-2-65 ..............Florida St 36, Oklahoma 19
12-31-65 ..........Georgia Tech 31, Texas Tech 21
12-31-66 ..........Tennessee 18, Syracuse 12
12-30-67 ..........Penn St 17, Florida St 17
12-28-68 ..........Missouri 35, Alabama 10
12-27-69 ..........Florida 14, Tennessee 13
1-2-71 ..............Auburn 35, Mississippi 28
12-31-71 ..........Georgia 7, N Carolina 3
12-30-72 ..........Auburn 24, Colorado 3
12-29-73 ..........Texas Tech 28, Tennessee 19
12-30-74 ..........Auburn 27, Texas 3
12-29-75 ..........Maryland 13, Florida 0
12-27-76 ..........Notre Dame 20, Penn St 9
12-30-77 ..........Pittsburgh 34, Clemson 3
12-29-78 ..........Clemson 17, Ohio St 15
12-28-79 ..........N Carolina 17, Michigan 15

### Gator Bowl *(Cont.)*

12-29-80 .........Pittsburgh 37, S Carolina 9
12-28-81 .........N Carolina 31, Arkansas 27
12-30-82 .........Florida St 31, W Virginia 12
12-30-83 .........Florida 14, Iowa 6
12-28-84 .........Oklahoma St 21, S Carolina 14
12-30-85 .........Florida St 34, Oklahoma St 23
12-27-86 .........Clemson 27, Stanford 21
12-31-87 .........Louisiana St 30, S Carolina 13
1-1-89 ............Georgia 34, Michigan St 27
12-30-89 .........Clemson 27, W Virginia 7
1-1-91 ............Michigan 35, Mississippi 3
12-29-91 .........Oklahoma 48, Virginia 14
12-31-92 .........Florida 27, N Carolina St 10
12-31-93 .........Alabama 24, North Carolina 10
12-30-94 .........Tennessee 45, Virginia Tech 23
City: Jacksonville, FL.
Stadium: Gator Bowl.
Capacity: 82,000. Automatic Berths: None.

### Florida Citrus Bowl

1-1-47 ............Catawba 31, Maryville (TN) 6
1-1-48 ............Catawba 7, Marshall 0
1-1-49 ............Murray St 21, Sul Ross St 21
1-2-50 ............St Vincent 7, Emory & Henry 6
1-1-51 ............Morris Harvey 35, Emory & Henry 14
1-1-52 ............Stetson 35, Arkansas St 20
1-1-53 ............E Texas St 33, Tennessee Tech 0
1-1-54 ............E Texas St 7, Arkansas St 7
1-1-55 ............NE-Omaha 7, Eastern Kentucky 6
1-2-56 ............Juniata 6, Missouri Valley 6
1-1-57 ............W Texas St 20, Southern Miss 13
1-1-58 ............E Texas St 10, Southern Miss 9
12-27-58 .........E Texas St 26, Missouri Valley 7
1-1-60 ............Middle Tennessee St 21, Presbyterian 12
12-30-60 .........Citadel 27, Tennessee Tech 0
12-29-61 .........Lamar 21, Middle Tennessee St 14
12-22-62 .........Houston 49, Miami (OH) 21
12-28-63 .........Western Kentucky 27, Coast Guard 0
12-12-64 .........E Carolina 14, Massachusetts 13
12-11-65 .........E Carolina 31, Maine 0
12-10-66 .........Morgan St 14, West Chester 6
12-16-67 .........TN-Martin 25, West Chester 8
12-27-68 .........Richmond 49, Ohio 42
12-26-69 .........Toledo 56, Davidson 33
12-28-70 .........Toledo 40, William & Mary 12
12-28-71 .........Toledo 28, Richmond 3
12-29-72 .........Tampa 21, Kent St 18
12-22-73 .........Miami (OH) 16, Florida 7
12-21-74 .........Miami (OH) 21, Georgia 10
12-20-75 .........Miami (OH) 20, S Carolina 7
12-18-76 .........Oklahoma St 49, Brigham Young 21
12-23-77 .........Florida St 40, Texas Tech 17
12-23-78 .........N Carolina St 30, Pittsburgh 17
12-22-79 .........Louisiana St 34, Wake Forest 10
12-20-80 .........Florida 35, Maryland 20
12-19-81 .........Missouri 19, Southern Miss 17
12-18-82 .........Auburn 33, Boston Col 26
12-17-83 .........Tennessee 30, Maryland 23
12-22-84 .........Georgia 17, Florida St 17
12-28-85 .........Ohio St 10, Brigham Young 7
1-1-87 ............Auburn 16, Southern Cal 7
1-1-88 ............Clemson 35, Penn St 10
1-2-89 ............Clemson 13, Oklahoma 6
1-1-90 ............Illinois 31, Virginia 21
1-1-91 ............Georgia Tech 45, Nebraska 21
1-1-92 ............California 37, Clemson 13

### Florida Citrus Bowl *(Cont.)*

1-1-93 ............Georgia 21, Ohio State 14
1-1-94 ............Penn State 31, Tennessee 13
1-2-95 ............Alabama 24, Ohio St 17
City: Orlando, FL.
Stadium: Florida Citrus Bowl-Orlando.
Capacity: 52,300. Automatic Berths: None.
Name Change: Tangerine Bowl (1947-82), Florida Citrus Bowl (since 1983).
Playing Sites: Tangerine Bowl (1947-72, 1974-82); Florida Field, Gainesville (1973); Orlando Stadium (1983-85); Florida Citrus Bowl- Orlando (since 1986). Tangerine Bowl, Orlando Stadium and Florida Citrus Bowl-Orlando are identical site.

### Liberty Bowl

12-19-59 .........Penn St 7, Alabama 0
12-17-60 .........Penn St 41, Oregon 12
12-16-61 .........Syracuse 15, Miami (FL) 14
12-15-62 .........Oregon St 6, Villanova 0
12-21-63 .........Mississippi St 16, N Carolina St
12-19-64 .........Utah 32, W Virginia 6
12-18-65 .........Mississippi 13, Auburn 7
12-10-66 .........Miami (FL) 14, Virginia Tech 7
12-16-67 .........N Carolina St 14, Georgia 7
12-14-68 .........Mississippi 34, Virginia Tech 17
12-13-69 .........Colorado 47, Alabama 33
12-12-70 .........Tulane 17, Colorado 3
12-20-71 .........Tennessee 14, Arkansas 13
12-18-72 .........Georgia Tech 31, Iowa St 30
12-17-73 .........N Carolina St 31, Kansas 18
12-16-74 .........Tennessee 7, Maryland 3
12-22-75 .........Southern Cal 20, Texas A&M 0
12-20-76 .........Alabama 36, UCLA 6
12-19-77 .........Nebraska 21, N Carolina 17
12-23-78 .........Missouri 20, Louisiana St 15
12-22-79 .........Penn St 9, Tulane 6
12-27-80 .........Purdue 28, Missouri 25
12-30-81 .........Ohio St 31, Navy 28
12-29-82 .........Alabama 21, Illinois 15
12-29-83 .........Notre Dame 19, Boston Col 18
12-27-84 .........Auburn 21, Arkansas 15
12-27-85 .........Baylor 21, Louisiana St 7
12-29-86 .........Tennessee 21, Minnesota 14
12-29-87 .........Georgia 20, Arkansas 17
12-28-88 .........Indiana 34, S Carolina 10
12-28-89 .........Mississippi 42, Air Force 29
12-27-90 .........Air Force 23, Ohio St 11
12-31-91 .........Air Force 38, Mississippi St 15
12-31-92 .........Mississippi 13, Air Force 0
12-28-93 .........Louisville 18, Michigan St 7
12-31-94 .........Illinois 30, E Carolina 0
City: Memphis (since 1965).
Stadium: Liberty Bowl Memorial Stadium.
Capacity: 63,000.
Automatic Berths: 1989-92, winner of Commander-in-Chief's Trophy (Air Force, Army, Navy).
Playing Sites: Philadelphia (Municipal Stadium, 1959-63), Atlantic City (Convention Center, 1964), Memphis.

### Peach Bowl

12-30-68 .........Louisiana St 31, Florida St 27
12-30-69 .........W Virginia 14, S Carolina 3
12-30-70 .........Arizona St 48, N Carolina 26
12-30-71 .........Mississippi 41, Georgia Tech 18
12-29-72 .........N Carolina St 49, W Virginia 13

## Peach Bowl *(Cont.)*

12-28-73 .........Georgia 17, Maryland 16
12-28-74 .........Vanderbilt 6, Texas Tech 6
12-31-75 .........W Virginia 13, N Carolina St 10
12-31-76 .........Kentucky 21, N Carolina 0
12-31-77 .........N Carolina St 24, Iowa St 14
12-25-78 .........Purdue 41, Georgia Tech 21
12-31-79 .........Baylor 24, Clemson 18
1-2-81 ..............Miami (FL) 20, Virginia Tech 10
12-31-81 .........W Virginia 26, Florida 6
12-31-82 .........Iowa 28, Tennessee 22
12-30-83 .........Florida St 28, N Carolina 3
12-31-84 .........Virginia 27, Purdue 24
12-31-85 .........Army 31, Illinois 29
12-31-86 .........Virginia Tech 25, N Carolina St 24
1-2-88 ..............Tennessee 27, Indiana 22
12-31-88 .........N Carolina St 28, Iowa 23
12-30-89 .........Syracuse 19, Georgia 18
12-29-90 .........Auburn 27, Indiana 23
1-1-92 ..............E Carolina 37, N Carolina St 34
1-2-93 ..............North Carolina 21, Miss. St 17
12-31-93 .........Clemson 14, Kentucky 13
1-1-95 ..............N Carolina St 28, Mississippi St 24

City: Atlanta.
Stadium: Atlanta Fulton County Stadium.
Capacity: 59,800.
Automatic Berths: None.
Playing Sites: Grant Field (1968-70), Atlanta Stadium (since 1971).

## Fiesta Bowl

12-27-71 .........Arizona St 45, Florida St 38
12-23-72 .........Arizona St 49, Missouri 35
12-21-73 .........Arizona St 28, Pittsburgh 7
12-28-74 .........Oklahoma St 16, Brigham Young 6
12-26-75 .........Arizona St 17, Nebraska 14
12-25-76 .........Oklahoma 41, Wyoming 7
12-25-77 .........Penn St 42, Arizona St 30
12-25-78 .........Arkansas 10, UCLA 10
12-25-79 .........Pittsburgh 16, Arizona 10
12-26-80 .........Penn St 31, Ohio St 19
1-1-82 ..............Penn St 26, Southern Cal 10
1-1-83 ..............Arizona St 32, Oklahoma 21
1-2-84 ..............Ohio St 28, Pittsburgh 23
1-1-85 ..............UCLA 39, Miami (FL) 37
1-1-86 ..............Michigan 27, Nebraska 23
1-2-87 ..............Penn St 14, Miami (FL) 10
1-1-88 ..............Florida St 31, Nebraska 28
1-2-89 ..............Notre Dame 34, W Virginia 21
1-1-90 ..............Florida St 41, Nebraska 17
1-1-91 ..............Louisville 34, Alabama 7
1-1-92 ..............Penn St 42, Tennessee 17
1-1-93 ..............Syracuse 26, Colorado 22
1-1-94 ..............Arizona 29, Miami (FL) 0
1-2-95 ..............Colorado 41, Notre Dame 24

City: Tempe, AZ.
Stadium: Sun Devil Stadium.
Capacity: 74,000.
Automatic Berths: None.

## Independence Bowl

12-13-76 .........McNeese St 20, Tulsa 16
12-17-77 .........Louisiana Tech 24, Louisville 14
12-16-78 .........E Carolina 35, Louisiana Tech 13
12-15-79 .........Syracuse 31, McNeese St 7

## Independence Bowl *(Cont.)*

12-13-80 .........Southern Miss 16, McNeese St 14
12-12-81 .........Texas A&M 33, Oklahoma St 16
12-11-82 .........Wisconsin 14, Kansas St 3
12-10-83 .........Air Force 9, Mississippi 3
12-15-84 .........Air Force 23, Virginia Tech 7
12-21-85 .........Minnesota 20, Clemson 13
12-20-86 .........Mississippi 20, Texas Tech 17
12-19-87 .........Washington 24, Tulane 12
12-23-88 .........Southern Miss 38, UTEP 18
12-16-89 .........Oregon 27, Tulsa 24
12-15-90 .........Louisiana State 34, Maryland 34
12-29-91 .........Georgia 24, Arkansas 15
12-31-92 .........Wake Forest 39, Oregon 35
12-31-93 .........Virginia Tech 45, Indiana 20
12-28-94 .........Virginia 20, Texas Christian 10

City: Shreveport, LA.
Stadium: Independence Stadium.
Capacity: 50,560.
Automatic Berths: None.

## All-American Bowl (Discontinued)

12-22-77 .........Maryland 17, Minnesota 7
12-20-78 .........Texas A&M 28, Iowa St 12
12-29-79 .........Missouri 24, S Carolina 14
12-27-80 .........Arkansas 34, Tulane 15
12-31-81 .........Mississippi St 10, Kansas 0
12-31-82 .........Air Force 36, Vanderbilt 28
12-22-83 .........W Virginia 20, Kentucky 16
12-29-84 .........Kentucky 20, Wisconsin 19
12-31-85 .........Georgia Tech 17, Michigan St 14
12-31-86 .........Florida St 27, Indiana 13
12-22-87 .........Virginia 22, Brigham Young 16
12-29-88 .........Florida 14, Illinois 10
12-28-89 .........Texas Tech 49, Duke 21
12-28-90 .........N Carolina St 31, S Mississippi 27

City: Birmingham, AL.
Stadium: Legion Field.
Capacity: 75,808.
Automatic Berths: None.
Name Change: Hall of Fame Classic (1977-84), All-American Bowl (1985-90).

## Holiday Bowl

12-22-78 .........Navy 23, Brigham Young 16
12-21-79 .........Indiana 38, Brigham Young 37
12-19-80 .........Brigham Young 46, SMU 45
12-18-81 .........Brigham Young 38, Washington St 36
12-17-82 .........Ohio St 47, Brigham Young 17
12-23-83 .........Brigham Young 21, Missouri 17
12-21-84 .........Brigham Young 24, Michigan 17
12-22-85 .........Arkansas 18, Arizona St 17
12-30-86 .........Iowa 39, San Diego St 38
12-30-87 .........Iowa 20, Wyoming 19
12-30-88 .........Oklahoma St 62, Wyoming 14
12-29-89 .........Penn St 50, Brigham Young 39
12-29-90 .........Texas A&M 65, Brigham Young 14
12-30-91 .........Iowa 13, Brigham Young 13
12-30-92 .........Hawaii 27, Illinois 17
12-30-93 .........Ohio St 28, Brigham Young 21
12-30-94 .........Michigan 24, Colorado St 14

City: San Diego.
Stadium: Jack Murphy Stadium.
Capacity: 60,750.
Automatic Berths: Western Athletic champ (except 1985).

## Las Vegas Bowl

12-19-81..........Toledo 27, San Jose St 25
12-18-82..........Fresno St 29, Bowling Green 28
12-17-83..........Northern Illinois 20, Cal St-Fullerton 13
12-15-84..........NV-Las Vegas 13*
12-14-85..........Fresno St 51, Bowling Green 7
12-13-86..........San Jose St 37, Miami (OH) 7
12-12-87..........Eastern Michigan 30, San Jose St 27
12-10-88..........Fresno St 35, Western Michigan 30
12-9-89............Fresno St 27, Ball St 6
12-8-90............San Jose St 48, Central Michigan 24
12-14-91..........Bowling Green 28, Fresno St 21
12-18-92..........Bowling Green 35, Nevada 34
12-17-93..........Utah St 42, Ball St 33
12-15-94..........UNLV 52, Central Michigan 24
* Toledo won later by forfeit.
City: Fresno, CA.
Stadium: Bulldog Stadium. Capacity: 30,000.
Automatic Berths: Mid-American and Big West champs.
Name change: California Bowl (1981-91).

## Aloha Bowl

12-25-82..........Washington 21, Maryland 20
12-26-83..........Penn St 13, Washington 10
12-29-84..........Southern Meth 27, Notre Dame 20
12-28-85..........Alabama 24, Southern Cal 3
12-27-86..........Arizona 30, N Carolina 21
12-25-87..........UCLA 20, Florida 16
12-25-88..........Washington St 24, Houston 22
12-25-89..........Michigan St 33, Hawaii 13
12-25-90..........Syracuse 28, Arizona 0
12-25-91..........Georgia Tech 18, Stanford 17
12-25-92..........Kansas 23, Brigham Young 20
12-25-93..........Colorado 41, Fresno St 30
12-25-94..........Boston College 12, Kansas St 7
City: Honolulu.
Stadium: Aloha Stadium.
Capacity: 50,000.
Automatic Berths: None.

## Freedom Bowl

12-16-84..........Iowa 55, Texas 17
12-30-85..........Washington 20, Colorado 17
12-30-86..........UCLA 31, Brigham Young 10
12-30-87..........Arizona St 33, Air Force 28
12-29-88..........Brigham Young 20, Colorado 17
12-30-89..........Washington 34, Florida 7
12-29-90..........Colorado St 32, Oregon 31
12-30-91..........Tulsa 28, San Diego St 17
12-29-92..........Fresno St 24, Southern Cal 7
12-30-93..........Southern Cal 28, Utah 21
12-29-94..........Utah 16, Arizona 13
City: Anaheim.
Stadium: Anaheim Stadium.
Capacity: 70,500.
Automatic Berths: None.

## Hall of Fame Bowl

12-23-86..........Boston College 27, Georgia 24
1-2-88..............Michigan 28, Alabama 24
1-2-89..............Syracuse 23, Louisiana St 10
1-1-90..............Auburn 31, Ohio St 14
1-1-91..............Clemson 30, Illinois 0
1-1-92..............Syracuse 24, Ohio St 17

## Hall of Fame Bowl *(Cont.)*

1-1-93..............Tennessee 38, Boston College 23
1-1-94..............Michigan 42, N Carolina St 7
1-2-95..............Wisconsin 34, Duke 20
City: Tampa.
Stadium: Tampa Stadium.
Capacity: 74,315.
Automatic Berths: None.

## Copper Bowl

12-31-89..........Arizona 17, N Carolina St 10
12-31-90..........California 17, Wyoming 15
12-31-91..........Indiana 24, Baylor 0
12-29-92..........Washington St 31, Utah 28
12-29-93..........Kansas St 52, Wyoming 17
12-29-94..........Brigham Young 31, Oklahoma 6
City: Tucson.
Stadium: Arizona Stadium.
Capacity: 57,000.
Automatic Berths: None.

## Carquest Bowl

12-28-90..........Florida St 24, Penn St 17
12-28-91..........Alabama 30, Colorado 25
1-1-93..............Stanford 24, Penn St 3
1-1-94..............Boston College 31, Virginia 13
1-2-95..............S Carolina 24, W Virginia 21
City: Miami.
Stadium: Joe Robbie.
Capacity: 75,000.    Automatic Berths: None
Name Change: Blockbuster Bowl (1990-93).

## Bluebonnet Bowl (Discontinued)

12-19-59..........Clemson 23, Texas Christian 7
12-17-60..........Texas 3, Alabama 3
12-16-61..........Kansas 33, Rice 7
12-22-62..........Missouri 14, Georgia Tech 10
12-21-63..........Baylor 14, LSU 7
12-19-64..........Tulsa 14, Mississippi 7
12-18-65..........Tennessee 27, Tulsa 6
12-17-66..........Texas 19, Mississippi 0
12-23-67..........Colorado 31, Miami (FL) 21
12-31-68..........Southern Meth 28, Oklahoma 27
12-31-69..........Houston 36, Auburn 7
12-31-70..........Alabama 24, Oklahoma 24
12-31-71..........Colorado 29, Houston 17
12-30-72..........Tennessee 24, LSU 17
12-29-73..........Houston 47, Tulane 7
12-23-74..........N Carolina St 31, Houston 31
12-27-75..........Texas 38, Colorado 21
12-31-76..........Nebraska 27, Texas Tech 24
12-31-77..........Southern Cal 47, Texas A&M 28
12-31-78..........Stanford 25, Georgia 22
12-31-79..........Purdue 27, Tennessee 22
12-31-80..........N Carolina 16, Texas 7
12-31-81..........Michigan 33, UCLA 14
12-31-82..........Arkansas 28, Florida 24
12-31-83..........Oklahoma St 24, Baylor 14
12-31-84..........W Virginia 31, Texas Christian 14
12-31-85..........Air Force 24, Texas 16
12-31-86..........Baylor 21, Colorado 9
12-31-87..........Texas 32, Pittsburgh 27
City: Houston. Name change: Astro-Bluebonnet Bowl ('68-'76).
Playing sites: Rice Stadium (1959-67; 1985-86),
Astrodome (1968-84, 1987).

## Division I-AA

| Year | Winner | Runner-Up | Score |
|------|--------|-----------|-------|
| 1978 | Florida A&M | Massachusetts | 35-28 |
| 1979 | Eastern Kentucky | Lehigh | 30-7 |
| 1980 | Boise St | Eastern Kentucky | 31-29 |
| 1981 | Idaho St | Eastern Kentucky | 34-23 |
| 1982 | Eastern Kentucky | Delaware | 17-14 |
| 1983 | Southern Illinois | Western Carolina | 43-7 |
| 1984 | Montana St | Louisiana Tech | 19-6 |
| 1985 | Georgia Southern | Furman | 44-42 |
| 1986 | Georgia Southern | Arkansas St | 48-21 |
| 1987 | NE Louisiana | Marshall | 43-42 |
| 1988 | Furman | Georgia Southern | 17-12 |
| 1989 | Georgia Southern | SF Austin St | 37-34 |
| 1990 | Georgia Southern | NV-Reno | 36-13 |
| 1991 | Youngstown St | Marshall | 25-17 |
| 1992 | Marshall | Youngstown St | 31-28 |
| 1993 | Youngstown St | Marshall | 17-5 |
| 1994 | Youngstown St | Boise St | 28-14 |

## Division II

| Year | Winner | Runner-Up | Score |
|------|--------|-----------|-------|
| 1973 | Louisiana Tech | Western Kentucky | 34-0 |
| 1974 | Central Michigan | Delaware | 54-14 |
| 1975 | Northern Michigan | Western Kentucky | 16-14 |
| 1976 | Montana St | Akron | 24-13 |
| 1977 | Lehigh | Jacksonville St | 33-0 |
| 1978 | Eastern Illinois | Delaware | 10-9 |
| 1979 | Delaware | Youngstown St | 38-21 |
| 1980 | Cal Poly SLO | Eastern Illinois | 21-13 |
| 1981 | SW Texas St | N Dakota St | 42-13 |
| 1982 | SW Texas St | UC-Davis | 34-9 |
| 1983 | N Dakota St | Central St (OH) | 41-21 |
| 1984 | Troy St | N Dakota St | 18-17 |
| 1985 | N Dakota St | N Alabama | 35-7 |
| 1986 | N Dakota St | S Dakota | 27-7 |
| 1987 | Troy St | Portland St | 31-17 |
| 1988 | N Dakota St | Portland St | 35-21 |
| 1989 | Mississippi Col | Jacksonville St | 3-0 |
| 1990 | N Dakota St | Indiana (PA) | 51-11 |
| 1991 | Pittsburg St | Jacksonville St | 23-6 |
| 1992 | Jacksonville St | Pittsburg St | 17-13 |
| 1993 | N Alabama | Indiana (PA) | 41-34 |
| 1994 | N Alabama | Texas A&M-Kingsville | 16-10 |

## Division III

| Year | Winner | Runner-Up | Score |
|------|--------|-----------|-------|
| 1973 | Wittenberg | Juniata | 41-0 |
| 1974 | Central (IA) | Ithaca | 10-8 |
| 1975 | Wittenberg | Ithaca | 28-0 |
| 1976 | St John's (MN) | Towson St | 31-28 |
| 1977 | Widener | Wabash | 39-36 |
| 1978 | Baldwin-Wallace | Wittenberg | 24-10 |
| 1979 | Ithaca | Wittenberg | 14-10 |
| 1980 | Dayton | Ithaca | 63-0 |
| 1981 | Widener | Dayton | 17-10 |
| 1982 | W Georgia | Augustana (IL) | 14-0 |
| 1983 | Augustana (IL) | Union (NY) | 21-17 |
| 1984 | Augustana (IL) | Central (IA) | 21-12 |
| 1985 | Augustana (IL) | Ithaca | 20-7 |
| 1986 | Augustana (IL) | Salisbury St | 31-3 |
| 1987 | Wagner | Dayton | 19-3 |
| 1988 | Ithaca | Central (IA) | 39-24 |
| 1989 | Dayton | Union (NY) | 17-7 |
| 1990 | Allegheny | Lycoming | 21-14 (OT) |
| 1991 | Ithaca | Dayton | 34-20 |
| 1992 | Wisconsin-LaCrosse | Washington & Jefferson | 16-12 |
| 1993 | Mount Union | Rowan | 34-24 |
| 1994 | Albion | Washington & Jefferson | 38-15 |

# NAIA Divisional Championships

## Division I

| Year | Winner | Runner-Up | Score |
|------|--------|-----------|-------|
| 1956 | St Joseph's (IN) /Montana St | | 0-0 |
| 1957 | Kansas St-Pittsburg | Hillsdale (MI) | 27-26 |
| 1958 | Northeastern Oklahoma | Northern Arizona | 19-13 |
| 1959 | Texas A&I | Lenoir-Rhyne (NC) | 20-7 |
| 1960 | Lenoir-Rhyne | Humboldt St (CA) | 15-14 |
| 1961 | Kansas St-Pittsburg | Linfield (OR) | 12-7 |
| 1962 | Central St (OK) | Lenoir-Rhyne (NC) | 28-13 |
| 1963 | St John's (MN) | Prairie View (TX) | 33-27 |
| 1964 | Concordia-Moorhead/Sam Houston | | 7-7 |
| 1965 | St John's (MN) | Linfield (OR) | 33-0 |
| 1966 | Waynesburg (PA) | WI-Whitewater | 42-21 |
| 1967 | Fairmont St (WV) | Eastern Washington | 28-21 |
| 1968 | Troy St (MI) | Texas A&I | 43-35 |
| 1969 | Texas A&I | Concordia-Moorhead | 32-7 |
| 1970 | Texas A&I | Wofford (SC) | 48-7 |
| 1971 | Livingston (AL) | Arkansas Tech | 14-12 |
| 1972 | E Texas St | Carson-Newman | 21-18 |
| 1973 | Abilene Christian | Elon (NC) | 42-14 |
| 1974 | Texas A&I | Henderson St (AR) | 34-23 |
| 1975 | Texas A&I | Salem (WV) | 37-0 |
| 1976 | Texas A&I | Central Arkansas | 26-0 |
| 1977 | Abilene Christian | Southwestern Oklahoma | 24-7 |
| 1978 | Angelo St | Elon (NC) | 34-14 |
| 1979 | Texas A&I | Central St (OK) | 20-14 |
| 1980 | Elon (NC) | Northeastern Oklahoma | 17-10 |
| 1981 | Elon (NC) | Pittsburg St | 3-0 |
| 1982 | Central St (OK) | Mesa (CO) | 14-11 |
| 1983 | Carson-Newman (TN) | Mesa (CO) | 36-28 |
| 1984 | Carson-Newman (TN) Central Arkansas | | 19-19 |
| 1985 | Central Arkansas/ Hillsdale (MI) | | 10-10 |
| 1986 | Carson-Newman (TN) | Cameron (OK) | 17-0 |
| 1987 | Cameron (OK) | Carson-Newman (TN) | 30-2 |
| 1988 | Carson-Newman (TN) | Adams St (CO) | 56-21 |
| 1989 | Carson-Newman (TN) | Emporia St (KS) | 34-20 |
| 1990 | Central St (OH) | Mesa St (CO) | 38-16 |
| 1991 | Central Arkansas | Central St (OH) | 19-16 |
| 1992 | Central St (OH) | Gardner-Webb (NC) | 19-16 |
| 1993 | East Central (OK) | Glenville St (WV) | 49-35 |
| 1994 | Northeastern St (OK) | Arkansas-Pine Bluff | 13-12 |

## Division II

| Year | Winner | Runner-Up | Score |
|------|--------|-----------|-------|
| 1970 | Westminster (PA) | Anderson (IN) | 21-16 |
| 1971 | California Lutheran | Westminster (PA) | 30-14 |
| 1972 | Missouri Southern | Northwestern (IA) | 21-14 |
| 1973 | Northwestern (IA) | Glenville St (WV) | 10-3 |
| 1974 | Texas Lutheran | Missouri Valley | 42-0 |
| 1975 | Texas Lutheran | California Lutheran | 34-8 |
| 1976 | Westminster (PA) | Redlands (CA) | 20-13 |
| 1977 | Westminster (PA) | California Lutheran | 17-9 |
| 1978 | Concordia-Moorhead | Findlay (OH) | 7-0 |
| 1979 | Findlay (OH) | Northwestern (IA) | 51-6 |
| 1980 | Pacific Lutheran | Wilmington | 38-10 |
| 1981 | Austin Coll./ Conc.-Moorhead | | 24-24 |
| 1982 | Linfield (OR) | William Jewell (MO) | 33-15 |
| 1983 | Northwestern (IA) | Pacific Lutheran | 25-21 |
| 1984 | Linfield (OR) | Northwestern (IA) | 33-22 |
| 1985 | WI-La Crosse | Pacific Lutheran | 24-7 |
| 1986 | Linfield (OR) | Baker (KS) | 17-0 |
| 1987 | Pacific Lutheran | WI-Stevens Point* | 16-16 |
| 1988 | Westminster (PA) | WI-La Crosse | 21-14 |
| 1989 | Westminster (PA) | WI-La Crosse | 51-30 |
| 1990 | Peru St (NEB) | Westminster (PA) | 17-7 |
| 1991 | Georgetown (KY) | Pacific Lutheran | 28-20 |
| 1992 | Findlay (OH) | Linfield (OR) | 26-13 |
| 1993 | Pacific Lutheran (WA) | Westminster (PA) | 50-20 |
| 1994 | Westminster (PA) | Pacific Lutheran (WA) | 27-7 |

*Forfeited 1987 season due to use of an ineligible player.

# Awards

## Heisman Memorial Trophy

Awarded to the best college player by the Downtown Athletic Club of New York City. The trophy is named after John W. Heisman, who coached Georgia Tech to the national championship in 1917 and later served as DAC athletic director.

| Year | Winner, College, Position<br>Winner's Season Statistics | Runner-up, College |
|------|------------------------------------------------|--------------------|
| 1935 | **Jay Berwanger, Chicago, HB**<br>Rush: 119 Yds: 577 TD: 6 | Monk Meyer, Army |
| 1936 | **Larry Kelley, Yale, E**<br>Rec: 17 Yds: 372 TD: 6 | Sam Francis, Nebraska |
| 1937 | **Clint Frank, Yale, HB**<br>Rush: 157 Yds: 667 TD: 11 | Byron White, Colorado |
| 1938 | **†Davey O'Brien, Texas Christian, QB**<br>Att/Comp: 194/110 Yds: 1733 TD: 19 | Marshall Goldberg, Pittsburgh |
| 1939 | **Nile Kinnick, Iowa, HB**<br>Rush: 106 Yds: 374 TD: 5 | Tom Harmon, Michigan |
| 1940 | **Tom Harmon, Michigan, HB**<br>Rush: 191 Yds: 852 TD: 16 | John Kimbrough, Texas A&M |
| 1941 | **†Bruce Smith, Minnesota, HB**<br>Rush: 98 Yds: 480 TD: 6 | Angelo Bertelli, Notre Dame |
| 1942 | **Frank Sinkwich, Georgia, HB**<br>Att/Comp: 166/84 Yds: 1392 TD: 10 | Paul Governali, Columbia |
| 1943 | **Angelo Bertelli, Notre Dame, QB**<br>Att/Comp: 36/25 Yds: 511 TD: 10 | Bob Odell, Pennsylvania |
| 1944 | **Les Horvath, Ohio State, QB**<br>Rush: 163 Yds: 924 TD: 12 | Glenn Davis, Army |
| 1945 | ***†Doc Blanchard, Army, FB**<br>Rush: 101 Yds: 718 TD: 13 | Glenn Davis, Army |
| 1946 | **Glenn Davis, Army, HB**<br>Rush: 123 Yds: 712 TD: 7 | Charley Trippi, Georgia |
| 1947 | **†John Lujack, Notre Dame, QB**<br>Att/Comp: 109/61 Yds: 777 TD: 9 | Bob Chappius, Michigan |
| 1948 | ***Doak Walker, Southern Methodist, HB**<br>Rush: 108 Yds: 532 TD: 8 | Charlie Justice, N Carolina |
| 1949 | **†Leon Hart, Notre Dame, E**<br>Rec: 19 Yds: 257 TD: 5 | Charlie Justice, N Carolina |
| 1950 | ***Vic Janowicz, Ohio St, HB**<br>Att/Comp: 77/32 Yds: 561 TD: 12 | Kyle Rote, Southern Methodist |
| 1951 | **Dick Kazmaier, Princeton, HB**<br>Rush: 149 Yds: 861 TD: 9 | Hank Lauricella, Tennessee |
| 1952 | **Billy Vessels, Oklahoma, HB**<br>Rush: 167 Yds: 1072 TD: 17 | Jack Scarbath, Maryland |
| 1953 | **John Lattner, Notre Dame, HB**<br>Rush: 134 Yds: 651 TD: 6 | Paul Giel, Minnesota |
| 1954 | **Alan Ameche, Wisconsin, FB**<br>Rush: 146 Yds: 641 TD: 9 | Kurt Burris, Oklahoma |
| 1955 | **Howard Cassady, Ohio St, HB**<br>Rush: 161 Yds: 958 TD: 15 | Jim Swink, Texas Christian |
| 1956 | **Paul Hornung, Notre Dame, QB**<br>Att/Comp: 111/59 Yds: 917 TD: 3 | Johnny Majors, Tennessee |
| 1957 | **John David Crow, Texas A&M, HB**<br>Rush: 129 Yds: 562 TD: 10 | Alex Karras, Iowa |
| 1958 | **Pete Dawkins, Army, HB**<br>Rush: 78 Yds: 428 TD: 6 | Randy Duncan, Iowa |
| 1959 | **Billy Cannon, Louisiana St, HB**<br>Rush: 139 Yds: 598 TD: 6 | Rich Lucas, Penn St |
| 1960 | **Joe Bellino, Navy, HB**<br>Rush: 168 Yds: 834 TD: 18 | Tom Brown, Minnesota |
| 1961 | **Ernie Davis, Syracuse, HB**<br>Rush: 150 Yds: 823 TD: 15 | Bob Ferguson, Ohio St |
| 1962 | **Terry Baker, Oregon St, QB**<br>Att/Comp: 203/112 Yds: 1738 TD: 15 | Jerry Stovall, Louisiana St |
| 1963 | ***Roger Staubach, Navy, QB**<br>Att/Comp: 161/107 Yds: 1474 TD: 7 | Billy Lothridge, Georgia Tech |
| 1964 | **John Huarte, Notre Dame, QB**<br>Att/Comp: 205/114 Yds: 2062 TD: 16 | Jerry Rhome, Tulsa |

## Heisman Memorial Trophy (Cont.)

| Year | Winner, College, Position<br>Winner's Season Statistics | Runner-up, College |
|------|------------------------------------------|---------------------|
| 1965 | **Mike Garrett, Southern Cal, HB**<br>Rush: 267 Yds: 1440 TD: 16 | Howard Twilley, Tulsa |
| 1966 | **Steve Spurrier, Florida, QB**<br>Att/Comp: 291/179 Yds: 2012 TD: 16 | Bob Griese, Purdue |
| 1967 | **Gary Beban, UCLA, QB**<br>Att/Comp: 156/87 Yds: 1359 TD: 8 | O.J. Simpson, Southern Cal |
| 1968 | **O.J. Simpson, Southern Cal, HB**<br>Rush: 383 Yds: 1880 TD: 23 | Leroy Keyes, Purdue |
| 1969 | **Steve Owens, Oklahoma, FB**<br>Rush: 358 Yds: 1523 TD: 23 | Mike Phipps, Purdue |
| 1970 | **Jim Plunkett, Stanford, QB**<br>Att/Comp: 358/191 Yds: 2715 TD: 18 | Joe Theismann, Notre Dame |
| 1971 | **Pat Sullivan, Auburn, QB**<br>Att/Comp: 281/162 Yds: 2012 TD: 20 | Ed Marinaro, Cornell |
| 1972 | **Johnny Rodgers, Nebraska, FL**<br>Rec: 55 Yds: 942 TD: 17 | Greg Pruitt, Oklahoma |
| 1973 | **John Cappelletti, Penn St, HB**<br>Rush: 286 Yds: 1522 TD: 17 | John Hicks, Ohio St |
| 1974 | ***Archie Griffin, Ohio St, HB**<br>Rush: 256 Yds: 1695 TD: 12 | Anthony Davis, Southern Cal |
| 1975 | **Archie Griffin, Ohio St, HB**<br>Rush: 262 Yds: 1450 TD: 4 | Chuck Muncie, California |
| 1976 | **†Tony Dorsett, Pittsburgh, HB**<br>Rush: 370 Yds: 2150 TD: 23 | Ricky Bell, Southern Cal |
| 1977 | **Earl Campbell, Texas, FB**<br>Rush: 267 Yds: 1744 TD: 19 | Terry Miller, Oklahoma St |
| 1978 | ***Billy Sims, Oklahoma, HB**<br>Rush: 231 Yds: 1762 TD: 20 | Chuck Fusina, Penn St |
| 1979 | **Charles White, Southern Cal, HB**<br>Rush: 332 Yds: 1803 TD: 19 | Billy Sims, Oklahoma |
| 1980 | **George Rogers, S Carolina, HB**<br>Rush: 324 Yds: 1894 TD: 14 | Hugh Green, Pittsburgh |
| 1981 | **Marcus Allen, Southern Cal, HB**<br>Rush: 433 Yds: 2427 TD: 23 | Herschel Walker, Georgia |
| 1982 | ***Herschel Walker, Georgia, HB**<br>Rush: 335 Yds: 1752 TD: 17 | John Elway, Stanford |
| 1983 | **Mike Rozier, Nebraska, HB**<br>Rush: 275 Yds: 2148 TD: 29 | Steve Young, Brigham Young |
| 1984 | **Doug Flutie, Boston College, QB**<br>Att/Comp: 396/233 Yds: 3454 TD: 27 | Keith Byars, Ohio St |
| 1985 | **Bo Jackson, Auburn, HB**<br>Rush: 278 Yds: 1786 TD: 17 | Chuck Long, Iowa |
| 1986 | **Vinny Testaverde, Miami (FL), QB**<br>Att/Comp: 276/175 Yds: 2557 TD: 26 | Paul Palmer, Temple |
| 1987 | **Tim Brown, Notre Dame, WR**<br>Rec: 39 Yds: 846 TD: 7 | Don McPherson, Syracuse |
| 1988 | ***Barry Sanders, Oklahoma St, RB**<br>Rush: 344 Yds: 2628 TD: 39 | Rodney Peete, Southern Cal |
| 1989 | ***Andre Ware, Houston, QB**<br>Att/Comp: 578/365 Yds: 4699 TD: 46 | Anthony Thompson, Indiana |
| 1990 | ***Ty Detmer, Brigham Young, QB**<br>Att/Comp: 562/361 Yds: 5188 TD: 41 | Raghib Ismail, Notre Dame |
| 1991 | ***Desmond Howard, Michigan, WR**<br>Rec: 61 Yds: 950 TD: 23 | Casey Weldon, Florida St |
| 1992 | **Gino Torretta, Miami (FL), QB**<br>Att/Comp: 402/228 Yds: 3060 TD: 19 | Marshall Faulk, San Diego St |
| 1993 | **†Charlie Ward, Florida St, QB**<br>Att/Comp: 380/264 Yds: 3032 TD: 27 | Heath Shuler, Tennessee |
| 1994 | **Rashaan Salaam, Colorado, RB**<br>Rush: 298 Yds: 2055 TD: 24 | Ki-Jana Carter, Penn St |

*Juniors (all others seniors). †Winners who played for national championship teams the same year.

Note: Former Heisman winners and national media cast votes, with ballots allowing for three names (3 points for first, 2 for second and 1 for third).

### Jim Thorpe Award

Given to the best defensive back of the year, the award is presented by the Jim Thorpe Athletic Club of Oklahoma City.

| Year | Player, College | Year | Player, College |
|---|---|---|---|
| 1986 | Thomas Everett, Baylor | 1990 | Darryl Lewis, Arizona |
| 1987 | Bennie Blades, Miami (FL) | 1991 | Terrell Buckley, Florida St |
| | Rickey Dixon, Oklahoma | 1992 | Deon Figures, Colorado |
| 1988 | Deion Sanders, Florida St | 1993 | Antonio Langham, Alabama |
| 1989 | Mark Carrier, Southern Cal | 1994 | Chris Hudson, Colorado |

### Outland Trophy

Given to the outstanding interior lineman, selected by the Football Writers Association of America.

| Year | Player, College, Position | Year | Player, College, Position |
|---|---|---|---|
| 1946 | George Connor, Notre Dame, T | 1971 | Larry Jacobson, Nebraska, DT |
| 1947 | Joe Steffy, Army, G | 1972 | Rich Glover, Nebraska, MG |
| 1948 | Bill Fischer, Notre Dame, G | 1973 | John Hicks, Ohio St, OT |
| 1949 | Ed Bagdon, Michigan St, G | 1974 | Randy White, Maryland, DE |
| 1950 | Bob Gain, Kentucky, T | 1975 | Lee Roy Selmon, Oklahoma, DT |
| 1951 | Jim Weatherall, Oklahoma, T | 1976 | *Ross Browner, Notre Dame, DE |
| 1952 | Dick Modzelewski, Maryland, T | 1977 | Brad Shearer, Texas, DT |
| 1953 | J. D. Roberts, Oklahoma, G | 1978 | Greg Roberts, Oklahoma, G |
| 1954 | Bill Brooks, Arkansas, G | 1979 | Jim Ritcher, N Carolina St, C |
| 1955 | Calvin Jones, Iowa, G | 1980 | Mark May, Pittsburgh, OT |
| 1956 | Jim Parker, Ohio St, G | 1981 | *Dave Rimington, Nebraska, C |
| 1957 | Alex Karras, Iowa, T | 1982 | Dave Rimington, Nebraska, C |
| 1958 | Zeke Smith, Auburn, G | 1983 | Dean Steinkuhler, Nebraska, G |
| 1959 | Mike McGee, Duke, T | 1984 | Bruce Smith, Virginia Tech, DT |
| 1960 | Tom Brown, Minnesota, G | 1985 | Mike Ruth, Boston Col, NG |
| 1961 | Merlin Olsen, Utah St, T | 1986 | Jason Buck, Brigham Young, DT |
| 1962 | Bobby Bell, Minnesota, T | 1987 | Chad Hennings, Air Force, DT |
| 1963 | Scott Appleton, Texas, T | 1988 | Tracy Rocker, Auburn, DT |
| 1964 | Steve DeLong, Tennessee, T | 1989 | Mohammed Elewonibi, Brigham Young, G |
| 1965 | Tommy Nobis, Texas, G | 1990 | Russell Maryland, Miami (FL), DT |
| 1966 | Loyd Phillips, Arkansas, T | 1991 | *Steve Emtman, Washington, DT |
| 1967 | Ron Yary, Southern Cal, T | 1992 | Will Shields, Nebraska, G |
| 1968 | Bill Stanfill, Georgia, T | 1993 | Rob Waldrop, Arizona, NG |
| 1969 | Mike Reid, Penn St, DT | 1994 | Zach Wiegert, Nebraska, G |
| 1970 | Jim Stillwagon, Ohio St, MG | | |

*Juniors (all others seniors).

### Vince Lombardi/Rotary Award

Given to the outstanding college lineman of the year, the award is sponsored by the Rotary Club of Houston.

| Year | Player, College, Position | Year | Player, College, Position |
|---|---|---|---|
| 1970 | Jim Stillwagon, Ohio St, MG | 1982 | Dave Rimington, Nebraska, C |
| 1971 | Walt Patulski, Notre Dame, DE | 1983 | Dean Steinkuhler, Nebraska, G |
| 1972 | Rich Glover, Nebraska, MG | 1984 | Tony Degrate, Texas, DT |
| 1973 | John Hicks, Ohio St, OT | 1985 | Tony Casillas, Oklahoma, NG |
| 1974 | Randy White, Maryland, DT | 1986 | Cornelius Bennett, Alabama, LB |
| 1975 | Lee Roy Selmon, Oklahoma, DT | 1987 | Chris Spielman, Ohio St, LB |
| 1976 | Wilson Whitley, Houston, DT | 1988 | Tracy Rocker, Auburn, DT |
| 1977 | Ross Browner, Notre Dame, DE | 1989 | Percy Snow, Michigan St, LB |
| 1978 | Bruce Clark, Penn St, DT | 1990 | Chris Zorich, Notre Dame, NG |
| 1979 | Brad Budde, Southern Cal, G | 1991 | Steve Emtman, Washington, DT |
| 1980 | Hugh Green, Pittsburgh, DE | 1992 | Marvin Jones, Florida St, LB |
| 1981 | Kenneth Sims, Texas, DT | 1993 | Aaron Taylor, Notre Dame, OT |
| | | 1994 | Warren Sapp, Miami (FL), DT |

### Butkus Award

Given to the top collegiate linebacker, the award was established by the Downtown Athletic Club of Orlando and named for college hall of famer Dick Butkus of Illinois.

| Year | Player, College | Year | Player, College |
|---|---|---|---|
| 1985 | Brian Bosworth, Oklahoma | 1990 | Alfred Williams, Colorado |
| 1986 | Brian Bosworth, Oklahoma | 1991 | Erick Anderson, Michigan |
| 1987 | Paul McGowan, Florida St | 1992 | Marvin Jones, Florida St |
| 1988 | Derrick Thomas, Alabama | 1993 | Trev Alberts, Nebraska |
| 1989 | Percy Snow, Michigan St | 1994 | Dana Howard, Illinois |

### Davey O'Brien National Quarterback Award

Given to the No. 1 quarterback in the nation by the Davey O'Brien Educational and Charitable Trust of Fort Worth. Named for Texas Christian Hall of Fame quarterback Davey O'Brien (1936-38).

| Year | Player, College |
|------|------|
| 1981 | Jim McMahon, Brigham Young |
| 1982 | Todd Blackledge, Penn St |
| 1983 | Steve Young, Brigham Young |
| 1984 | Doug Flutie, Boston College |
| 1985 | Chuck Long, Iowa |
| 1986 | Vinny Testaverde, Miami (FL) |
| 1987 | Don McPherson, Syracuse |
| 1988 | Troy Aikman, UCLA |
| 1989 | Andre Ware, Houston |
| 1990 | Ty Detmer, Brigham Young |
| 1991 | Ty Detmer, Brigham Young |
| 1992 | Gino Torretta, Miami (FL) |
| 1993 | Charlie Ward, Florida St |
| 1994 | Kerry Collins, Penn St |

Note: Originally known as the Davey O'Brien Memorial Trophy, honoring the outstanding football player in the Southwest as follows: 1977—Earl Campbell, Texas, RB; 1978—Billy Sims, Oklahoma, RB; 1979—Mike Singletary, Baylor, LB; 1980—Mike Singletary, Baylor, LB.

### Maxwell Award

Given to the nation's outstanding college football player by the Maxwell Football Club of Philadelphia.

| Year | Player, College, Position |
|------|------|
| 1937 | Clint Frank, Yale, HB |
| 1938 | Davey O'Brien, Texas Christian, QB |
| 1939 | Nile Kinnick, Iowa, HB |
| 1940 | Tom Harmon, Michigan, HB |
| 1941 | Bill Dudley, Virginia, HB |
| 1942 | Paul Governali, Columbia, QB |
| 1943 | Bob Odell, Pennsylvania, HB |
| 1944 | Glenn Davis, Army, HB |
| 1945 | Doc Blanchard, Army, FB |
| 1946 | Charley Trippi, Georgia, HB |
| 1947 | Doak Walker, Southern Meth, HB |
| 1948 | Chuck Bednarik, Pennsylvania, C |
| 1949 | Leon Hart, Notre Dame, E |
| 1950 | Reds Bagnell, Pennsylvania, HB |
| 1951 | Dick Kazmaier, Princeton, HB |
| 1952 | John Lattner, Notre Dame, HB |
| 1953 | John Lattner, Notre Dame, HB |
| 1954 | Ron Beagle, Navy, E |
| 1955 | Howard Cassady, Ohio St, HB |
| 1956 | Tommy McDonald, Oklahoma, HB |
| 1957 | Bob Reifsnyder, Navy, T |
| 1958 | Pete Dawkins, Army, HB |
| 1959 | Rich Lucas, Penn St, QB |
| 1960 | Joe Bellino, Navy, HB |
| 1961 | Bob Ferguson, Ohio St, FB |
| 1962 | Terry Baker, Oregon St, QB |
| 1963 | Roger Staubach, Navy, QB |
| 1964 | Glenn Ressler, Penn St, C |
| 1965 | Tommy Nobis, Texas, LB |
| 1966 | Jim Lynch, Notre Dame, LB |
| 1967 | Gary Beban, UCLA, QB |
| 1968 | O.J. Simpson, Southern Cal, RB |
| 1969 | Mike Reid, Penn St, DT |
| 1970 | Jim Plunkett, Stanford, QB |
| 1971 | Ed Marinaro, Cornell, RB |
| 1972 | Brad Van Pelt, Michigan St, DB |
| 1973 | John Cappelletti, Penn St, RB |
| 1974 | Steve Joachim, Temple, QB |
| 1975 | Archie Griffin, Ohio St, RB |
| 1976 | Tony Dorsett, Pittsburgh, RB |
| 1977 | Ross Browner, Notre Dame, DE |
| 1978 | Chuck Fusina, Penn St, QB |
| 1979 | Charles White, Southern Cal, RB |
| 1980 | Hugh Green, Pittsburgh, DE |
| 1981 | Marcus Allen, Southern Cal, RB |
| 1982 | Herschel Walker, Georgia, RB |
| 1983 | Mike Rozier, Nebraska, RB |
| 1984 | Doug Flutie, Boston College, QB |
| 1985 | Chuck Long, Iowa, QB |
| 1986 | Vinny Testaverde, Miami (FL), QB |
| 1987 | Don McPherson, Syracuse, QB |
| 1988 | Barry Sanders, Oklahoma St, RB |
| 1989 | Anthony Thompson, Indiana, RB |
| 1990 | Ty Detmer, Brigham Young, QB |
| 1991 | Desmond Howard, Michigan, WR |
| 1992 | Gino Torretta, Miami (FL), QB |
| 1993 | Charlie Ward, Florida St, QB |
| 1994 | Kerry Collins, Penn St, QB |

### Walter Payton Player of the Year Award

Given to the top Division I-AA football player, the award is sponsored by Sports Network and voted on by Division I-AA sports information directors.

| Year | Player, College, Position |
|------|------|
| 1987 | Kenny Gamble, Colgate, RB |
| 1988 | Dave Meggett, Towson St, RB |
| 1989 | John Friesz, Idaho, QB |
| 1990 | Walter Dean, Grambling, RB |
| 1991 | Jamie Martin, Weber St, QB |
| 1992 | Michael Payton, Marshall, QB |
| 1993 | Doug Nussmeier, Idaho, QB |
| 1994 | Steve McNair, Alcorn St, QB |

### The Harlon Hill Trophy

Given to the outstanding NCAA Division II college football player, the award is sponsored by the National Harlon Hill Awards Committee, Florence, AL.

| Year | Player, College, Position |
|------|------|
| 1986 | Jeff Bentrim, N Dakota St, QB |
| 1987 | Johnny Bailey, Texas A&I, RB |
| 1988 | Johnny Bailey, Texas A&I, RB |
| 1989 | Johnny Bailey, Texas A&I, RB |
| 1990 | Chris Simdorn, N Dakota St, QB |
| 1991 | Ronnie West, Pittsburg St, WR |
| 1992 | Ronald Moore, Pittsburg St, RB |
| 1993 | Roger Graham, New Haven, RB |
| 1994 | Chris Hatcher, Valdosta St, QB |

## Career

### SCORING

**Most Points Scored:** 423 — Roman Anderson, Houston, 1988-91
**Most Points Scored per Game:** 12.1 — Marshall Faulk, San Diego St, 1991-93
**Most Touchdowns Scored:** 65 — Anthony Thompson, Indiana, 1986-89
**Most Touchdowns Scored per Game:** 2.0 — Marshall Faulk, San Diego St, 1991-93
**Most Touchdowns Scored, Rushing:** 64 — Anthony Thompson, Indiana, 1986-89
**Most Touchdowns Scored, Passing**: 121 — Ty Detmer, Brigham Young, 1988-91
**Most Touchdowns Scored, Receiving:** 43 — Aaron Turner, Pacific, 1989-92
**Most Touchdowns Scored, Interception Returns:** 5 — Ken Thomas, San Jose St, 1979-82; Jackie Walker, Tennessee, 1969-71
**Most Touchdowns Scored, Punt Returns:** 7 — Johnny Rodgers, Nebraska, 1970-72; Jack Mitchell, Oklahoma, 1946-48
**Most Touchdowns Scored, Kickoff Returns:** 6 — Anthony Davis, Southern Cal, 1972-74

### TOTAL OFFENSE

**Most Plays:** 1795 — Ty Detmer, Brigham Young, 1988-91
**Most Plays per Game:** 48.5 — Doug Gaynor, Long Beach St, 1984-85
**Most Yards Gained:** 14,665 — Ty Detmer, Brigham Young, 1988-91 (15,031 passing, -366 rushing)
**Most Yards Gained per Game:** 320.9 — Chris Vargas, Nevada, 1992-93
**Most 300+ Yard Games:** 33 —Ty Detmer, Brigham Young, 1988-91

### RUSHING

**Most Rushes:** 1215 — Steve Bartalo, Colorado St, 1983-86 (4813 yds)
**Most Rushes per Game:** 34.0 — Ed Marinaro, Cornell, 1969-71
**Most Yards Gained:** 6082 — Tony Dorsett, Pittsburgh, 1973-76
**Most Yards Gained per Game:** 174.6 — Ed Marinaro, Cornell, 1969-71
**Most 100+ Yard Games:** 33 — Tony Dorsett, Pittsburgh, 1973-76; Archie Griffin, Ohio St, 1972-75
**Most 200+ Yard Games:** 11 — Marcus Allen, Southern Cal, 1978-81

### SPECIAL TEAMS

**Highest Punt Return Average:** 23.6 — Jack Mitchell, Oklahoma, 1946-48
**Highest Kickoff Return Average:** 36.2 — Forrest Hall, San Francisco, 1946-47
**Highest Average Yards per Punt:** 46.3 — Todd Sauerbrun, West Virginia, 1991-94

### PASSING

**Highest Passing Efficiency Rating:** 162.7 — Ty Detmer, Brigham Young, 1988-91 (1530 attempts, 958 completions, 65 interceptions, 15,031 yards, 121 TD passes)
**Most Passes Attempted:** 1,530 — Ty Detmer, Brigham Young, 1988-91
**Most Passes Attempted per Game:** 39.6 — Mike Perez, San Jose St, 1986-87
**Most Passes Completed:** 958 — Ty Detmer, Brigham Young, 1988-91
**Most Passes Completed per Game:** 25.9 — Doug Gaynor, Long Beach St, 1984-85
**Highest Completion Percentage:** 65.2 — Steve Young, Brigham Young, 1981-83
**Most Yards Gained:** 15,031 — Ty Detmer, Brigham Young, 1988-91
**Most Yards Gained per Game:** 326.7 — Ty Detmer, Brigham Young, 1988-91

### RECEIVING

**Most Passes Caught:** 266 — Aaron Turner, Pacific, 1989-92
**Most Passes Caught per Game:** 10.5 — Emmanuel Hazard, Houston, 1989-90
**Most Yards Gained:** 4,357— Ryan Yarborough, Wyoming, 1990-93
**Most Yards Gained per Game:** 128.6 — Howard Twilley, Tulsa, 1963-65
**Highest Average Gain per Reception:** 25.7 — Wesley Walker, California, 1973-75

### ALL-PURPOSE RUNNING

**Most Plays:** 1347 — Steve Bartalo, Colorado St, 1983-86 (1215 rushes, 132 receptions)
**Most Yards Gained**: 7172 — Napoleon McCallum, Navy, 1981-85 (4179 rushing, 796 receiving, 858 punt returns, 1339 kickoff returns)
**Most Yards Gained per Game:** 237.8 — Ryan Benjamin, Pacific, 1990-92
**Highest Average Gain per Play:** 17.4 — Anthony Carter, Michigan, 1979-82.

### INTERCEPTIONS

**Most Passes Intercepted:** 29 — Al Brosky, Illinois, 1950-52
**Most Passes Intercepted per Game:** 1.1 — Al Brosky, Illinois, 1950-52
**Most Yards on Interception Returns**: 501 — Terrell Buckley, Florida St, 1989-91
**Highest Average Gain per Interception:** 26.5 — Tom Pridemore, W Virginia, 1975-77

## Single Season

### SCORING
**Most Points Scored:** 234 — Barry Sanders, Oklahoma St, 1988
**Most Points Scored per Game:** 21.27 — Barry Sanders, Oklahoma St, 1988
**Most Touchdowns Scored:** 39 — Barry Sanders, Oklahoma St, 1988
**Most Touchdowns Scored, Rushing:** 37 — Barry Sanders, Oklahoma St, 1988
**Most Touchdowns Scored, Passing:** 54 — David Klingler, Houston, 1990
**Most Touchdowns Scored, Receiving:** 22 — Emmanuel Hazard, Houston, 1989
**Most Touchdowns Scored, Interception Returns:** 3 — by many players
**Most Touchdowns Scored, Punt Returns:** 4 — James Henry, Southern Miss, 1987; Golden Richards, Brigham Young, 1971; Cliff Branch , Colorado, 1971
**Most Touchdowns Scored, Kickoff Returns:** 3 — Leland McElroy, Texas A&M, 1993; Terance Mathis, New Mexico, 1989; Willie Gault, Tennessee, 1980; Anthony Davis, Southern Cal, 1974; Stan Brown, Purdue, 1970; Forrest Hall, San Francisco, 1946

### TOTAL OFFENSE
**Most Plays:** 704 — David Klingler, Houston, 1990
**Most Yards Gained:** 5221 — David Klingler, Houston, 1990
**Most Yards Gained per Game:** 474.6 — David Klingler, Houston, 1990
**Most 300+ Yard Games:** 12 — Ty Detmer, Brigham Young, 1990

### RUSHING
**Most Rushes:** 403 — Marcus Allen, Southern Cal, 1981
**Most Rushes per Game:** 39.6 — Ed Marinaro, Cornell, 1971
**Most Yards Gained:** 2628 — Barry Sanders, Oklahoma St, 1988
**Most Yards Gained per Game:** 238.9 — Barry Sanders, Oklahoma St, 1988
**Most 100+ Yard Games:** 11 — By nine players, most recently Barry Sanders, Oklahoma St, 1988

---

---

### PASSING
**Highest Passing Efficiency Rating:** 176.9 — Jim McMahon, Brigham Young, 1980 (445 attempts, 284 completions, 18 interceptions, 4571 yards, 47 TD passes)
**Most Passes Attempted:** 643 — David Klingler, Houston, 1990
**Most Passes Attempted per Game:** 58.5 — David Klingler, Houston, 1990
**Most Passes Completed:** 374 — David Klingler, Houston, 1990
**Most Passes Completed per Game:** 34.0 — David Klingler, Houston, 1990
**Highest Completion Percentage:** 71.3 — Steve Young, Brigham Young, 1983
**Most Yards Gained:** (12 games) 5188 — Ty Detmer, Brigham Young, 1990; (11 games) 5140 — David Klingler, Houston, 1990
**Most Yards Gained per Game:** 467.3 — David Klingler, Houston, 1990

### RECEIVING
**Most Passes Caught:** 142 — Emmanuel Hazard, Houston, 1989
**Most Passes Caught per Game:** 13.4 — Howard Twilley, Tulsa, 1965
**Most Yards Gained:** 1779 — Howard Twilley, Tulsa, 1965
**Most Yards Gained per Game:** 177.9 — Howard Twilley, Tulsa, 1965
**Highest Average Gain per Reception:** 27.9 — Elmo Wright, Houston, 1968 (min. 30 receptions)

### ALL-PURPOSE RUNNING
**Most Plays:** 432 — Marcus Allen, Southern Cal, 1981
**Most Yards Gained:** 3250 — Barry Sanders, Oklahoma St, 1988
**Most Yards Gained per Game:** 295.5 — Barry Sanders, Oklahoma St, 1988
**Highest Average Gain per Play:** 18.5 — Henry Bailey, UNLV, 1992

### INTERCEPTIONS
**Most Passes Intercepted:** 14 — Al Worley, Washington, 1968
**Most Yards on Interception Returns:** 302 — Charles Phillips, Southern Cal, 1974
**Highest Average Gain per Interception:** 50.6 — Norm Thompson, Utah, 1969

### SPECIAL TEAMS
**Highest Punt Return Average:** 25.9 — Bill Blackstock, Tennessee, 1951
**Highest Kickoff Return Average:** 38.2 — Forrest Hall, San Francisco, 1946
**Highest Average Yards per Punt:** 49.8 — Reggie Roby, Iowa, 1981

## Single Game

### SCORING

**Most Points Scored:** 48 — Howard Griffith, Illinois, 1990 (vs Southern Illinois)

**Most Field Goals:** 7 — Dale Klein, Nebraska, 1985 (vs Missouri); Mike Prindle, Western Michigan, 1984 (vs Marshall)

**Most Extra Points (Kick):** 13 — Derek Mahoney, Fresno St, 1991 (vs New Mexico); 13 — Terry Leiweke, Houston, 1968 (vs Tulsa)

**Most Extra Points (2-Pts):** 6 — Jim Pilot, New Mexico St, 1961 (vs Hardin-Simmons)

### TOTAL OFFENSE

**Most Yards Gained:** 732 — David Klingler, Houston, 1990 (vs Arizona St)

### RUSHING

**Most Yards Gained:** 396 — Tony Sands, Kansas, 1991 (vs Missouri)

### RUSHING *(Cont.)*

**Most Touchdowns Rushed:** 8 — Howard Griffith, Illinois, 1990 (vs Southern Illinois)

### PASSING

**Most Passes Completed:** 48 — David Klingler, Houston, 1990 (vs Southern Methodist)

**Most Yards Gained:** 716 — David Klingler, Houston, 1990 (vs Arizona St)

**Most Touchdowns Passed:** 11 — David Klingler, Houston, 1990 [vs Eastern Washington (I-AA)]

### RECEIVING

**Most Passes Caught:** 23 — Randy Gatewood, UNLV, 1994 (vs Idaho)

**Most Yards Gained:** 363 — Randy Gatewood, UNLV, 1994 (vs Idaho)

**Most Touchdown Catches:** 6 — Tim Delaney, San Diego St, 1969 (vs New Mexico St)

# NCAA Division I-AA Individual Records

## Career

### SCORING

**Most Points Scored:** 385 — Marty Zendejas, NV-Reno, 1984-87

**Most Touchdowns Scored:** 61 — Sherriden May, Idaho, 1992-94

**Most Touchdowns Scored, Rushing:** 55 — Kenny Gamble, Colgate, 1984-87

**Most Touchdowns Scored, Passing:** 139 — Willie Totten, Mississippi Valley, 1982-85

**Most Touchdowns Scored, Receiving:** 50 — Jerry Rice, Mississippi Valley, 1981-84

### PASSING

**Highest Passing Efficiency Rating:** 170.8 — Shawn Knight, William & Mary, 1991-94

**Most Passes Attempted:** 1,680 — Steve McNair, Alcorn St, 1991-94

**Most Passes Completed:** 938 — Neil Lomax, Portland St, 1977-80

**Most Passes Completed per Game:** 23.8 — Stan Greene, Boston U, 1989-90

**Highest Completion Percentage:** 66.9 — Jason Garrett, Princeton, 1987-88

### PASSING *(CONT.)*

**Most Yards Gained:** 14,496 — Steve McNair, Alcorn St, 1991-94

**Most Yards Gained per Game:** 345.1 — Steve McNair, Alcorn St, 1991-94

### RUSHING

**Most Rushes:** 1,027 — Erik Marsh, Lafayette, 1991-94

**Most Rushes per Game:** 24.5 — Keith Elias, Princeton, 1991-93

**Most Yards Gained:** 5,333 — Frank Hawkins, NV-Reno, 1977-80

**Most Yards Gained per Game:** 124.3 — Kenny Gamble, Colgate, 1984-87

### RECEIVING

**Most Passes Caught:** 301 — Jerry Rice, Mississippi Valley, 1981-84

**Most Yards Gained:** 4,693 — Jerry Rice, Mississippi Valley, 1981-84

**Most Yards Gained per Game:** 114.5 — Jerry Rice, Mississippi Valley, 1981-84

**Highest Average Gain per Reception:** 24.3 — John Taylor, Delaware St, 1982-85

## Single Season

### SCORING

**Most Points Scored:** 170 — Geoff Mitchell, Weber St, 1991

**Most Touchdowns Scored:** 28 — Geoff Mitchell, Weber St, 1991

**Most Touchdowns Scored, Rushing:** 24 — Geoff Mitchell, Weber St, 1991

**Most Touchdowns Scored, Passing:** 56 — Willie Totten, Mississippi Valley, 1984

**Most Touchdowns Scored, Receiving:** 27 — Jerry Rice, Mississippi Valley, 1984

### PASSING

**Highest Passing Efficiency Rating:** 204.6 — Shawn Knight, William & Mary, 1993

### PASSING *(CONT.)*

**Most Passes Attempted:** 530 — Steve McNair, Alcorn St, 1994

**Most Passes Completed:** 324 — Willie Totten, Mississippi Valley, 1984

**Most Passes Completed per Game:** 32.4 — Willie Totten, Mississippi Valley, 1984

**Highest Completion Percentage:** 68.2 — Jason Garrett, Princeton, 1988; Dave Dickenson, Montana, 1994

**Most Yards Gained:** 4,863 — Steve McNair, Alcorn St, 1994

**Most Yards Gained per Game:** 455.7 — Willie Totten, Mississippi Valley, 1984

## Single Season (Cont.)

### RUSHING

**Most Rushes:** 409 — Arnold Mickens, Butler, 1994
**Most Rushes per Game:** 40.9 — Arnold Mickens, Butler, 1994
**Most Yards Gained:** 2255 — Arnold Mickens, Butler, 1994
**Most Yards Gained per Game:** 225.5 — Arnold Mickens, Butler, 1994

### RECEIVING

**Most Passes Caught:** 115 — Brian Forster, Rhode Island, 1985
**Most Yards Gained:** 1,682 — Jerry Rice, Mississippi Valley, 1984
**Most Yards Gained per Game:** 168.2 — Jerry Rice, Mississippi Valley, 1984
**Highest Average Gain per Reception:** 26.3 — Brian Allen, Idaho, 1983 (min. 30 receptions)

## Single Game

### SCORING

**Most Points Scored:** 36 — By five players. Most recently Erwin Matthews, Richmond, 1987 (vs Massachusetts)
**Most Field Goals:** 8 — Goran Lingmerth, Northern Arizona, 1986 (vs Idaho)

### PASSING

**Most Passes Completed:** 47 — Jamie Martin, Weber St, 1991 (vs Idaho St)
**Most Yards Gained:** 649 — Steve McNair, Alcorn St, 1994 (vs Southern-BR)
**Most Touchdowns Passed:** 9 — Willie Totten, Mississippi Valley, 1984 (vs Kentucky St)

### RUSHING

**Most Yards Gained:** 364 — Tony Vinson, Towson St, 1993 (vs Bucknell)
**Most Touchdowns Rushed:** 6 — Gene Lake, Delaware St, 1984 (vs. Howard); Gill Fenerty, Holy Cross, 1983 (vs Columbia); Henry Odom, S Carolina St, 1980 (vs Morgan St)

### RECEIVING

**Most Passes Caught:** 24 — Jerry Rice, Mississippi Valley 1983 (vs Southern-BR)
**Most Yards Gained:** 370 — Michael Lerch, Princeton, 1991 (vs Brown)
**Most Touchdown Catches:** 5 — Rennie Benn, Lehigh, 1985 [vs Indiana (PA)]; Jerry Rice, Mississippi Valley, 1984 (vs Prairie View and vs Kentucky St)

# NCAA Division II Individual Records

## Career

### SCORING

**Most Points Scored:** 464 — Walter Payton, Jackson St, 1971-74
**Most Touchdowns Scored:** 72 — Shawn Graves, Wofford, 1989-92
**Most Touchdowns Scored, Rushing:** 72 — Shawn Graves, Wofford, 1989-92
**Most Touchdowns Scored, Passing:** 93 — Doug Williams, Grambling, 1974-77
**Most Touchdowns Scored, Receiving:** 49 — Bruce Cerone, Yankton/Emporia St, 1966-69

### PASSING

**Highest Passing Efficiency Rating:** 164.0 — Chris Petersen, UC-Davis, 1985-86
**Most Passes Attempted:** 1,442 — Earl Harvey, N Carolina Central, 1985-88
**Most Passes Completed:** 748 — Rob Tomlinson, Cal-St Chico, 1988-91
**Most Passes Completed per Game:** 25.0 — Tim Von Dulm, Portland St, 1969-70
**Highest Completion Percentage:** 69.6 — Chris Peterson, UC-Davis, 1985-86
**Most Yards Gained:** 10,621 — Earl Harvey, N Carolina Central, 1985-88
**Most Yards Gained per Game:** 298.4 — Tim Von Dulm, Portland St, 1969-70

### RUSHING

**Most Rushes:** 1,072 — Bernie Peeters, Luther, 1968-71
**Most Rushes per Game:** 29.8 — Bernie Peeters, Luther, 1968-71
**Most Yards Gained:** 6,320 — Johnny Bailey, Texas A&I*, 1986-89
**Most Yards Gained per Game:** 162.1 — Johnny Bailey, Texas A&I*, 1986-89

### RECEIVING

**Most Passes Caught:** 253 — Chris Myers, Kenyon, 1967-70
**Most Yards Gained:** 4,354 — Bruce Cerone, Yankton/Emporia St, 1966-69
**Most Yards Gained per Game:** 137.3 — Ed Bell, Idaho St, 1968-69
**Highest Average Gain per Reception:** 22.8 — Tyrone Johnson, Western St (CO), 1990-93

*Became Texas A&M-Kingsville in 1993

## Single Season

### SCORING
**Most Points Scored:** 178 — Terry Metcalf, Long Beach St, 1971
**Most Touchdowns Scored:** 29 — Terry Metcalf, Long Beach St, 1971
**Most Touchdowns Scored, Rushing:** 28 — Terry Metcalf, Long Beach St, 1971
**Most Touchdowns Scored, Passing:** 50 — Chris Hatcher, Valdosta St, 1994
**Most Touchdowns Scored, Receiving:** 20 — Ed Bell, Idaho St, 1969

### PASSING
**Highest Passing Efficiency Rating:** 210.1 — Boyd Crawford, College of Idaho, 1953
**Most Passes Attempted:** 515 — Todd Mayfield, W Texas St, 1986
**Most Passes Completed:** 334 — Chris Hatcher, Valdosta St, 1993
**Most Passes Completed per Game:** 30.4 — Chris Hatcher, Valdosta St, 1993
**Highest Completion Percentage:** 74.6 — Chris Hatcher, Valdosta St, 1994
**Most Yards Gained:** 3,757 — Perry Klein, LIU-CW Post, 1993
**Most Yards Gained per Game:** 393.4 — Grady Benton, W Texas A&M, 1994

### RUSHING
**Most Rushes:** 385 — Joe Gough, Wayne St (MI), 1994
**Most Rushes per Game:** 38.6 — Mark Perkins, Hobart, 1968
**Most Yards Gained:** 2,011 — Johnny Bailey, Texas A&I, 1986
**Most Yards Gained per Game:** 182.8 — Johnny Bailey, Texas A&I, 1986

### RECEIVING
**Most Passes Caught:** 119 — Brad Bailey, W Texas A&M, 1994
**Most Yards Gained:** 1,876 — Chris George, Glenville St, 1993
**Most Yards Gained per Game:** 187.6 — Chris George, Glenville St, 1993
**Highest Average Gain per Reception:** 32.5 — Tyrone Johnson, Western St, 1991 (min. 30 receptions)

## Single Game

### SCORING
**Most Points Scored:** 48 — Paul Zaeske, N Park, 1968 (vs N Central); Junior Wolf, Panhandle St, 1958 [vs St Mary (KS)]
**Most Field Goals:** 6 — Steve Huff, Central Missouri St, 1985 (vs SE Missouri St)

### PASSING
**Most Passes Completed:** 45 — Chris Hatcher, Valdosta St, 1993 (vs W Georgia; vs Miss. College)
**Most Yards Gained:** 614 — Alfred Montez, W New Mexico, 1994 (vs W Texas A&M); Perry Klein, 1993 (vs Salisbury St)
**Most Touchdowns Passed:** 10 — Bruce Swanson, N Park, 1968 (vs N Central)

### RUSHING
**Most Yards Gained:** 382 — Kelly Ellis, Northern Iowa, 1979 (vs Western Illinois)
**Most Touchdowns Rushed:** 8 — Junior Wolf, Panhandle St, 1958 [vs St Mary (KS)]

### RECEIVING
**Most Passes Caught:** 23 — Chris George, Glenville St, 1994 (vs W VA Wesleyan); Barry Wagner, Alabama A&M, 1989 (vs Clark Atlanta)
**Most Yards Gained:** 370 — Barry Wagner, Alabama A&M, 1989 (vs Clark Atlanta)
**Most Touchdown Catches:** 8 — Paul Zaeske, N Park, 1968 (vs N Central)

## NCAA Division III Individual Records

## Career

### SCORING
**Most Points Scored:** 474 — Joe Dudek, Plymouth St, 1982-85
**Most Touchdowns Scored:** 79 — Joe Dudek, Plymouth St, 1982-85
**Most Touchdowns Scored, Rushing:** 76 — Joe Dudek, Plymouth St, 1982-85
**Most Touchdowns Scored, Passing:** 115 — Jim Ballard, Wilmington (OH)1990, Mt Union (OH) 91-93
**Most Touchdowns Scored, Receiving:** 55 — Chris Bisaillon, Illinois Wesleyan, 1989-92

### RUSHING
**Most Rushes:** 1,152 — Anthony Russo, St John's (NY), 1990-93
**Most Rushes per Game:** 32.7 — Chris Sizemore, Bridgewater (VA), 1972-74
**Most Yards Gained:** 5,834 — Anthony Russo, St John's (NY), 1990-93
**Most Yards Gained per Game:** 154.8 — Kirk Matthieu, Maine-Maritime, 1989-93

## Career (Cont.)

### PASSING

**Highest Passing Efficiency Rating:** 159.5 — Jim Ballard, Wilmington (OH)1990, Mt Union (OH) 91-93
**Most Passes Attempted:** 1,696 — Kirk Baumgartner, WI-Stevens Point, 1986-89
**Most Passes Completed:** 883 — Kirk Baumgartner, WI-Stevens Point, 1986-89
**Most Passes Completed per Game:** 24.9 — Keith Bishop, Illinois Wesleyan, 1981; Wheaton (IL), 1983-85
**Highest Completion Percentage:** 62.2 — Brian Moore, Baldwin-Wallace, 1981-84
**Most Yards Gained:** 13,028 — Kirk Baumgartner, WI-Stevens Point, 1986-89
**Most Yards Gained per Game:** 317.8 — Kirk Baumgartner, WI-Stevens Point, 1986-89

### RECEIVING

**Most Passes Caught:** 287 — Matt Newton, Principia (IL), 1990-93
**Most Yards Gained:** 3,846 — Dale Amos, Franklin & Marshall, 1986-89
**Most Yards Gained per Game:** 110.5 — Matt Newton, Principia (IL), 1990-93
**Highest Average Gain per Reception:** 20.0 — Marty Redlawsk, Concordia (IL), 1984-87

## Single Season

### SCORING

**Most Points Scored:** 194 — Carey Bender, Coe, 1994
**Most Points Scored per Game:** 19.4 — Carey Bender, Coe, 1994
**Most Touchdowns Scored:** 32 — Carey Bender, Coe, 1994
**Most Touchdowns Scored, Rushing:** 29 — Carey Bender, Coe, 1994
**Most Touchdowns Scored, Passing:** 39 — Kirk Baumgartner, WI-Stevens Point, 1989
**Most Touchdowns Scored, Receiving:** 20 — John Aromando, Trenton St, 1983

### RUSHING

**Most Rushes:** 380 — Mike Birosak, Dickinson, 1989
**Most Rushes per Game:** 38.0 — Mike Birosak, Dickinson, 1989
**Most Yards Gained:** 2,243 — Carey Bender, Coe, 1994
**Most Yards Gained per Game:** 224.3 — Carey Bender, Coe, 1994

### PASSING

**Highest Passing Efficiency Rating:** 225.0 — Mike Simpson, Eureka, 1994
**Most Passes Attempted:** 527 — Kirk Baumgartner, WI-Stevens Point, 1988
**Most Passes Completed:** 276 — Kirk Baumgartner, WI-Stevens Point, 1988
**Most Passes Completed per Game:** 29.1 — Keith Bishop, Illinois Wesleyan, 1985
**Highest Completion Percentage:** 73.4 — Mike Simpson, Eureka, 1994
**Most Yards Gained:** 3,828 — Kirk Baumgartner, WI-Stevens Point, 1988
**Most Yards Gained per Game:** 369.2 — Kirk Baumgartner, WI-Stevens Point, 1989

### RECEIVING

**Most Passes Caught:** 106 — Theo Blanco, WI-Stevens Point, 1987
**Most Yards Gained:** 1,693 — Sean Munroe, Mass-Boston, 1992
**Most Yards Gained per Game:** 188.1 — Sean Munroe, Mass-Boston 1992
**Highest Average Gain per Reception:** 26.9 — Marty Redlawsk, Concordia (IL), 1985

## Single Game

### SCORING

**Most Field Goals:** 6 — Jim Hever, Rhodes, 1984 (vs Millsaps)

### PASSING

**Most Passes Completed:** 50 — Tim Lynch, Hofstra, 1991 (vs Fordham)
**Most Yards Gained:** 602 — Tom Stallings, St Thomas (MN), 1993 (vs Bethel)
**Most Touchdowns Passed:** 8 — Steve Austin, Mass-Boston, 1992 (vs Framingham St); Kirk Baumgartner, WI-Stevens Point, 1989 (vs WI-Superior)

### RUSHING

**Most Yards Gained:** 417 — Corey Bender, Coe, 1993 (vs Grinnell)
**Most Touchdowns Rushed:** 6 — Eric Leiser, Eureka, 1991, (vs Concordia); Rob Sinclair, Simpson, 1990 (vs Upper Iowa)

### RECEIVING

**Most Passes Caught:** 23 — Sean Munroe, Mass-Boston, 1992 (vs Mass-Maritime)
**Most Yards Gained:** 332 — Sean Munroe, Mass-Boston, 1992 (vs Mass-Maritime)
**Most Touchdown Catches:** 5 — By 10 players. Most Recent: Sean Munroe, Mass-Boston, 1992 (vs Framingham St)

## Career

### Scoring

**POINTS (KICKERS)**

| | Years | Pts |
|---|---|---|
| Roman Anderson, Houston | 1988-91 | 423 |
| Carlos Huerta, Miami (FL) | 1988-91 | 397 |
| Jason Elam, Hawaii | 1988-92 | 395 |
| Derek Schmidt, Florida St | 1984-87 | 393 |
| Luis Zendejas, Arizona St | 1981-84 | 368 |

**POINTS (NON-KICKERS)**

| | Years | Pts |
|---|---|---|
| Anthony Thompson, Indiana | 1986-89 | 394 |
| Marshall Faulk, San Diego St | 1991-93 | 376 |
| Tony Dorsett, Pittsburgh | 1973-76 | 356 |
| Glenn Davis, Army | 1943-46 | 354 |
| Art Luppino, Arizona | 1953-56 | 337 |

**POINTS PER GAME (NON-KICKERS)**

| | Years | Pts/Game |
|---|---|---|
| Marshall Faulk, San Diego St | 1991-93 | 12.1 |
| Bob Gaiters, New Mexico St | 1959-60 | 11.9 |
| Ed Marinaro, Cornell | 1969-71 | 11.8 |
| Bill Burnett, Arkansas | 1968-70 | 11.3 |
| Steve Owens, Oklahoma | 1967-69 | 11.2 |

### Total Offense

**YARDS GAINED**

| | Years | Yds |
|---|---|---|
| Ty Detmer, Brigham Young | 1988-91 | 14,665 |
| Doug Flutie, Boston Col | 1981-84 | 11,317 |
| Alex Van Pelt, Pittsburgh | 1989-92 | 10,814 |
| Todd Santos, San Diego St | 1984-87 | 10,513 |
| Kevin Sweeney, Fresno St | 1982-86 | 10,252 |

**YARDS PER GAME**

| | Years | Yds/Game |
|---|---|---|
| Chris Vargas, Nevada | 1992-93 | 320.9 |
| Ty Detmer, Brigham Young | 1988-91 | 318.8 |
| Mike Perez, San Jose St | 1986-87 | 309.1 |
| Doug Gaynor, Long Beach St | 1984-85 | 305.0 |
| Tony Eason, Illinois | 1981-82 | 299.5 |

### Rushing

**YARDS GAINED**

| | Years | Yds |
|---|---|---|
| Tony Dorsett, Pittsburgh | 1973-76 | 6,082 |
| Charles White, Southern Cal | 1976-79 | 5,598 |
| Herschel Walker, Georgia | 1980-82 | 5,259 |
| Archie Griffin, Ohio St | 1972-75 | 5,177 |
| Darren Lewis, Texas A&M | 1987-90 | 5,012 |

**YARDS PER GAME**

| | Years | Yds/Game |
|---|---|---|
| Ed Marinaro, Cornell | 1969-71 | 174.6 |
| O. J. Simpson, Southern Cal | 1967-68 | 164.4 |
| Herschel Walker, Georgia | 1980-82 | 159.4 |
| LeShon Johnson, N Illionis | 1992-93 | 150.6 |
| Marshall Faulk, San Diego St | 1991-93 | 148.0 |

**TOUCHDOWNS RUSHING**

| | Years | TD |
|---|---|---|
| Anthony Thompson, Indiana | 1986-89 | 64 |
| Marshall Faulk, San Diego St | 1991-93 | 57 |
| Steve Owens, Oklahoma | 1967-69 | 56 |
| Tony Dorsett, Pittsburgh | 1973-76 | 55 |
| Ed Marinaro, Cornell | 1969-71 | 50 |

### Passing

**PASSING EFFICIENCY**

| | Years | Rating |
|---|---|---|
| Ty Detmer, Brigham Young | 1988-91 | 162.7 |
| Jim McMahon, Brigham Young | 1977-78, 80-81 | 156.9 |
| Steve Young, Brigham Young | 1982, 84-86 | 149.8 |
| Robbie Bosco, Brigham Young | 1981-83 | 149.4 |
| Chuck Long, Iowa | 1981-85 | 148.9 |

Note: Minimum 500 completions.

**YARDS GAINED**

| | Years | Yds |
|---|---|---|
| Ty Detmer, Brigham Young | 1988-91 | 15,031 |
| Todd Santos, San Diego St | 1984-87 | 11,425 |
| Alex Van Pelt, Pittsburgh | 1989-92 | 10,913 |
| Kevin Sweeney, Fresno St | 1982-86 | 10,623 |
| Doug Flutie, Boston Col | 1981-84 | 10,579 |

Note: Minimum 500 completions.

**COMPLETIONS**

| | Years | Comp |
|---|---|---|
| Ty Detmer, Brigham Young | 1988-91 | 958 |
| Todd Santos, San Diego St | 1984-87 | 910 |
| Brian McClure, Bowling Green | 1982-85 | 900 |
| Eric Wilhelm, Oregon St | 1989-92 | 870 |
| Alex Van Pelt, Pittsburgh | 1989-92 | 845 |

Note: Minimum 500 completions.

**TOUCHDOWNS PASSING**

| | Years | TD |
|---|---|---|
| Ty Detmer, Brigham Young | 1988-91 | 121 |
| David Klingler, Houston | 1988-91 | 92 |
| Troy Kopp, Pacific | 1989-92 | 87 |
| Jim McMahon, Brigham Young | 1977-78,80-81 | 84 |
| Joe Adams, Tennessee St | 1977-80 | 81 |

### Receiving

**CATCHES**

| | Years | No. |
|---|---|---|
| Aaron Turner, Pacific | 1989-92 | 266 |
| Terance Mathis, New Mexico | 1985-87, 89 | 263 |
| Mark Templeton, Long Beach St | 1983-86 | 262 |
| Howard Twilley, Tulsa | 1963-65 | 261 |
| David Williams, Illinois | 1983-85 | 245 |

**CATCHES PER GAME**

| | Years | No./Game |
|---|---|---|
| Emmanuel Hazard, Houston | 1989-90 | 10.5 |
| Howard Twilley, Tulsa | 1963-65 | 10.0 |
| Jason Phillips, Houston | 1987-88 | 9.4 |
| Bryan Reeves Nevada | 1991-93 | 7.6 |

Two tied with 7.4 rec. per game

**YARDS GAINED**

| | Years | Yds |
|---|---|---|
| Ryan Yarborough | 1990-93 | 4,357 |
| Aaron Turner, Pacific | 1989-92 | 4,345 |
| Terance Mathis, New Mexico | 1985-87,89 | 4,254 |
| Marc Zeno, Tulane | 1984-87 | 3,725 |
| Ron Sellers, Florida St | 1966-68 | 3,598 |

**TOUCHDOWN CATCHES**

| | Years | TD |
|---|---|---|
| Aaron Turner, Pacific | 1989-92 | 43 |
| Ryan Yarborough, Wyoming | 1990-93 | 42 |
| Clarkston Hines, Duke | 1986-89 | 38 |
| Terance Mathis, New Mexico | 1985-87,89 | 36 |
| Elmo Wright, Houston | 1968-70 | 34 |

## Career (Cont.)

### All-Purpose Running

| YARDS GAINED | Years | Yds |
|---|---|---|
| Napoleon McCallum, Navy | 1981-85 | 7172 |
| Darrin Nelson, Stanford | 1977-78,80-81 | 6885 |
| Terance Mathis, New Mexico | 1985-87,89 | 6691 |
| Tony Dorsett, Pittsburgh | 1973-76 | 6615 |
| Paul Palmer, Temple | 1983-86 | 6609 |

| YARDS PER GAME | Years | Yds/Game |
|---|---|---|
| Ryan Benjamin, Pacific, | 1990-92 | 237.8 |
| Sheldon Canley, San Jose St | 1988-90 | 205.8 |
| Howard Stevens, Louisville | 1971-72 | 193.7 |
| O.J. Simpson, Southern Cal | 1967-68 | 192.9 |
| Ed Marinaro, Cornell | 1969-71 | 183.0 |

### Interceptions

| PLAYER/SCHOOL | Years | Int |
|---|---|---|
| Al Brosky, Illinois | 1950-52 | 29 |
| John Provost, Holy Cross | 1972-74 | 27 |
| Martin Bayless, Bowling Green | 1980-83 | 27 |
| Tom Curtis, Michigan | 1967-69 | 25 |
| Tony Thurman, Boston Col | 1981-84 | 25 |
| Tracy Saul, Texas Tech | 1989-92 | 25 |

### Punting Average

| PLAYER/SCHOOL | Years | Avg |
|---|---|---|
| Todd Sauerbrun, W Virginia | 1991-94 | 46.3 |
| Reggie Roby, Iowa | 1979-82 | 45.6 |
| Greg Montgomery, Michigan St | 1985-87 | 45.4 |
| Tom Tupa, Ohio St | 1984-87 | 45.2 |
| Barry Helton, Colorado | 1984-87 | 44.9 |

Note: At least 150 punts kicked.

### Punt Return Average

| PLAYER/SCHOOL | Years | Avg |
|---|---|---|
| Jack Mitchell, Oklahoma | 1946-48 | 23.6 |
| Gene Gibson, Cincinnati | 1949-50 | 20.5 |
| Eddie Macon, Pacific | 1949-51 | 18.9 |
| Jackie Robinson, UCLA | 1939-40 | 18.8 |
| Mike Fuller, Auburn | 1972-74 | 17.7 |
| Bobby Dillon, Texas | 1949-51 | 17.7 |

Note: At least 1.2 punt returns per game.

### Kickoff Return Average

| PLAYER/SCHOOL | Years | Avg |
|---|---|---|
| Forrest Hall, San Francisco | 1946-47 | 36.2 |
| Anthony Davis, Southern Cal | 1972-74 | 35.1 |
| Overton Curtis, Utah St | 1957-58 | 31.0 |
| Fred Montgomery, New Mexico St | 1991-92 | 30.5 |
| Altie Taylor, Utah St | 1966-68 | 29.3 |

Note: At least 1.2 kickoff returns per game.

### Mr. O'Leary's Cow

Rarely is heard a discouraging word these days from coaches about juniors who come out for the NFL draft. Rarely, but not never. "I'll be seeing you Sundays if I go to an NFL game," Georgia Tech assistant George O'Leary told Elliott Fortune, the Yellow Jacket defensive tackle who threw his name into the 1995 draft last spring. "Same as you, I'll be buying a ticket."

With his decision the 276-pound Fortune is severely testing his surname. Last season he started only four games. Still, he might have expected at least some moral support from his coach. Instead, O'Leary says, "I wish him well in his pursuit of impossibility. I told him. 'You've done some dumb things, but this is the dumbest.'"

## Single Season

### Scoring

| POINTS | Year | Pts |
|---|---|---|
| Barry Sanders, Oklahoma St | 1988 | 234 |
| Mike Rozier, Nebraska | 1983 | 174 |
| Lydell Mitchell, Penn St | 1971 | 174 |
| Art Luppino, Arizona | 1954 | 166 |
| Bobby Reynolds, Nebraska | 1950 | 157 |

| FIELD GOALS | Year | FG |
|---|---|---|
| John Lee, UCLA | 1984 | 29 |
| Paul Woodside, W Virginia | 1982 | 28 |
| Luis Zendejas, Arizona St | 1983 | 28 |
| Fuad Reveiz, Tennessee | 1982 | 27 |

Note: Three tied with 25 each.

### All-Purpose Running

| YARDS GAINED | Year | Yds |
|---|---|---|
| Barry Sanders, Oklahoma St | 1988 | 3250 |
| Ryan Benjamin, Pacific | 1991 | 2995 |
| Mike Pringle, Fullerton St | 1989 | 2690 |
| Paul Palmer, Temple | 1986 | 2633 |
| Ryan Benjamin, Pacific | 1992 | 2597 |

### All-Purpose Running (Cont.)

| YARDS PER GAME | Years | Yds/Game |
|---|---|---|
| Barry Sanders, Oklahoma St | 1988 | 295.5 |
| Ryan Benjamin, Pacific | 1991 | 249.6 |
| Byron (Whizzer) White, Colorado | 1937 | 246.3 |
| Mike Pringle, Fullerton St | 1989 | 244.6 |
| Paul Palmer, Temple | 1986 | 239.4 |

### Total Offense

| YARDS GAINED | Year | Yds |
|---|---|---|
| David Klingler, Houston | 1990 | 5221 |
| Ty Detmer, Brigham Young | 1990 | 5022 |
| Andre Ware, Houston | 1989 | 4661 |
| Jim McMahon, Brigham Young | 1980 | 4627 |
| Ty Detmer, Brigham Young | 1989 | 4433 |

| YARDS PER GAME | Year | Yds/Game |
|---|---|---|
| David Klingler, Houston | 1990 | 474.6 |
| Andre Ware, Houston | 1989 | 423.7 |
| Ty Detmer, Brigham Young | 1990 | 418.5 |
| Steve Young, Brigham Young | 1983 | 395.1 |
| Chris Vargas, Nevada | 1993 | 393.8 |

## Single Season *(Cont.)*

### Rushing

**YARDS GAINED**

| | Year | Yds |
|---|---|---|
| Barry Sanders, Oklahoma St | 1988 | 2628 |
| Marcus Allen, Southern Cal | 1981 | 2342 |
| Mike Rozier, Nebraska | 1983 | 2148 |
| Rashaan Salaam, Colorado | 1994 | 2055 |
| LeShon Johnson, N Illinois | 1993 | 1976 |

**YARDS PER GAME**

| | Year | Yds/Game |
|---|---|---|
| Barry Sanders, Oklahoma St | 1988 | 238.9 |
| Marcus Allen, Southern Cal | 1981 | 212.9 |
| Ed Marinaro, Cornell | 1971 | 209.0 |
| Rashaan Salaam, Colorado | 1994 | 186.8 |
| Charles White, Southern Cal | 1979 | 180.3 |

**TOUCHDOWNS RUSHING**

| | Year | TD |
|---|---|---|
| Barry Sanders, Oklahoma St | 1988 | 37 |
| Mike Rozier, Nebraska | 1983 | 29 |
| Ed Marinaro, Cornell | 1971 | 24 |
| Anthony Thompson, Indiana | 1988 | 24 |
| Anthony Thompson, Indiana | 1989 | 24 |
| Rashaan Salaam, Colorado | 1994 | 24 |

### Passing

**PASSING EFFICIENCY**

| | Year | Rating |
|---|---|---|
| Jim McMahon, Brigham Young | 1980 | 176.9 |
| Ty Detmer, Brigham Young | 1989 | 175.6 |
| Trent Dilfer, Fresno St | 1993 | 173.1 |
| Kerry Collins, Penn St | 1994 | 172.9 |
| Jerry Rhome, Tulsa | 1964 | 172.6 |

### Passing *(Cont.)*

**YARDS GAINED**

| | Year | Yds |
|---|---|---|
| Ty Detmer, Brigham Young | 1990 | 5188 |
| David Klingler, Houston | 1990 | 5140 |
| Andre Ware, Houston | 1989 | 4699 |
| Jim McMahon, Brigham Young | 1980 | 4571 |
| Ty Detmer, Brigham Young | 1989 | 4560 |

**COMPLETIONS**

| | Year | Att | Comp |
|---|---|---|---|
| David Klingler, Houston | 1990 | 643 | 374 |
| Andre Ware, Houston | 1989 | 578 | 365 |
| Ty Detmer, Brigham Young | 1990 | 562 | 361 |
| Robbie Bosco, Brigham Young | 1985 | 511 | 338 |
| Chris Vargas, Nevada | 1993 | 490 | 331 |

**TOUCHDOWNS PASSING**

| | Year | TD |
|---|---|---|
| David Klingler, Houston | 1990 | 54 |
| Jim McMahon, Brigham Young | 1980 | 47 |
| Andre Ware, Houston | 1989 | 46 |
| Ty Detmer, Brigham Young | 1990 | 41 |
| Dennis Shaw, San Diego St | 1969 | 39 |

### Receiving

**CATCHES**

| | Year | GP | No. |
|---|---|---|---|
| Emmanuel Hazard, Houston | 1989 | 11 | 142 |
| Howard Twilley, Tulsa | 1965 | 10 | 134 |
| Jason Phillips, Houston | 1988 | 11 | 108 |
| Fred Gilbert, Houston | 1991 | 11 | 106 |
| Chris Penn, Tulsa | 1993 | 11 | 105 |

**CATCHES PER GAME**

| | Year | No. | No./Game |
|---|---|---|---|
| Howard Twilley, Tulsa | 1965 | 134 | 13.4 |
| Emmanuel Hazard, Houston | 1989 | 142 | 12.9 |
| Jason Phillips, Houston | 1988 | 108 | 9.8 |
| Chris Penn, Tulsa | 1993 | 105 | 9.6 |
| Fred Gilbert, Houston | 1991 | 106 | 9.6 |
| Jerry Hendren, Idaho | 1969 | 95 | 9.5 |
| Howard Twilley, Tulsa | 1964 | 95 | 9.5 |

**YARDS GAINED**

| | Year | Yds |
|---|---|---|
| Howard Twilley, Tulsa | 1965 | 1779 |
| Emmanuel Hazard, Houston | 1989 | 1689 |
| Aaron Turner, Pacific | 1991 | 1604 |
| Chris Penn, Tulsa | 1993 | 1578 |
| Chuck Hughes, UTEP* | 1965 | 1519 |

*UTEP was Texas Western in 1965.

**TOUCHDOWN CATCHES**

| | Year | TD |
|---|---|---|
| Emmanuel Hazard, Houston | 1989 | 22 |
| Desmond Howard, Michigan | 1991 | 19 |
| Aaron Turner, Pacific | 1991 | 18 |
| Dennis Smith, Utah | 1989 | 18 |
| Tom Reynolds, San Diego St | 1969 | 18 |

## Single Game

### Scoring

**POINTS**

| | Opponent | Year | Pts |
|---|---|---|---|
| Howard Griffith, Illinois | Southern Illinois | 1990 | 48 |
| Marshall Faulk, San Diego St | Pacific | 1991 | 44 |
| Jim Brown, Syracuse | Colgate | 1956 | 43 |
| Showboat Boykin, Mississippi | Mississippi St | 1951 | 42 |
| Fred Wendt, UTEP* | New Mexico St | 1948 | 42 |
| Dick Bass, Pacific | San Diego St | 1958 | 38 |

*UTEP was Texas Mines in 1948.

**FIELD GOALS**

| | Opponent | Year | FG |
|---|---|---|---|
| Dale Klein, Nebraska | Missouri | 1985 | 7 |
| Mike Prindle, Western Michigan | Marshall | 1984 | 7 |

Note: Klein's distances were 32-22-43-44-29-43-43.
Prindle's distances were 32-44-42-23-48-41-27.

## Single Game *(Cont.)*

### Total Offense

| YARDS GAINED | Opponent | Year | Yds |
|---|---|---|---|
| David Klingler, Houston | Arizona St | 1990 | 732 |
| Matt Vogler, Texas Christian | Houston | 1990 | 696 |
| David Klingler, Houston | Texas Christian | 1990 | 625 |
| Scott Mitchell, Utah | Air Force | 1988 | 625 |
| Jimmy Klingler, Houston | Rice | 1992 | 612 |

### Passing

| YARDS GAINED | Opponent | Year | Yds |
|---|---|---|---|
| David Klingler, Houston | Arizona St | 1990 | 716 |
| Matt Vogler, Texas Christian | Houston | 1990 | 690 |
| Scott Mitchell, Utah | Air Force | 1988 | 631 |
| Jeremy Leach, New Mexico | Utah | 1989 | 622 |
| Dave Wilson, Illinois | Ohio St | 1980 | 621 |

| COMPLETIONS | Opponent | Year | Comp |
|---|---|---|---|
| David Klingler, Houston | Southern Methodist | 1990 | 48 |
| Jimmy Klingler, Houston | Rice | 1992 | 46 |
| Sandy Schwab, Northwestern | Michigan | 1982 | 45 |
| Chuck Hartlieb, Iowa | Indiana | 1988 | 44 |
| Jim McMahon, Brigham Young | Colorado St | 1981 | 44 |

| TOUCHDOWNS PASSING | Opponent | Year | TD |
|---|---|---|---|
| David Klingler, Houston | E. Wash | 1990 | 11 |

Note: Klingler's TD passes were 5-48-29-7-3-7-40-10-7-8-51.

### Rushing

| YARDS GAINED | Opponent | Year | Yds |
|---|---|---|---|
| Tony Sands, Kansas | Missouri | 1991 | 396 |
| Marshall Faulk, San Diego St | Pacific | 1991 | 386 |
| Anthony Thompson, Indiana | Wisconsin | 1989 | 377 |
| Mike Pringle, California St-Fullerton | New Mexico St | 1989 | 357 |
| Rueben Mayes, Washington St | Oregon | 1984 | 357 |

| TOUCHDOWNS RUSHING | Opponent | Year | TD |
|---|---|---|---|
| Howard Griffith, Illinois | Southern Illinois | 1990 | 8 |

Note: Griffith's TD runs were 5-51-7-41-5-18-5-3.

### Receiving

| CATCHES | Opponent | Year | No. |
|---|---|---|---|
| Randy Gatewood, UNLV | Idaho | 1994 | 23 |
| Jay Miller, Brigham Young | New Mexico | 1973 | 22 |
| Rick Eber, Tulsa | Idaho St | 1967 | 20 |
| Emmanuel Hazard, Hou | Texas Christian | 1989 | 19 |
| Emmanuel Hazard, Hou | Texas | 1989 | 19 |
| Ron Fair, Arizona St | Washington St | 1989 | 19 |
| Howard Twilley, Tulsa | Colorado St | 1965 | 19 |

| YARDS GAINED | Opponent | Year | Yds |
|---|---|---|---|
| Randy Gatewood, UNLV | Idaho | 1994 | 363 |
| Chuck Hughes, UTEP* | N Texas St | 1965 | 349 |
| Rick Eber, Tulsa | Idaho St | 1967 | 322 |
| Harry Wood, Tulsa | Idaho St | 1967 | 318 |
| Jeff Evans, New Mexico St | Southern Illinois | 1978 | 316 |

*UTEP was Texas Western in 1965.

| TOUCHDOWN CATCHES | Opponent | Year | TD |
|---|---|---|---|
| Tim Delaney, San Diego St | New Mexico St | 1969 | 6 |

Note: Delaney's TD catches were 2-22-34-31-30-9.

## Longest Plays (since 1941)

### Rushing

| RUSHING | Opponent | Year | Yds |
|---|---|---|---|
| Gale Sayers, Kansas | Nebraska | 1963 | 99 |
| Max Anderson, Arizona St | Wyoming | 1967 | 99 |
| Ralph Thompson, W Texas St | Wichita St | 1970 | 99 |
| Kelsey Finch, Tennessee | Florida | 1977 | 99 |

### Passing

| PASSING | Opponent | Year | Yds |
|---|---|---|---|
| Fred Owens to Jack Ford, Portland | St Mary's (CA) | 1947 | 99 |
| Bo Burris to Warren McVea, Houston | Washington St | 1966 | 99 |
| Colin Clapton to Eddie Jenkins, Holy Cross | Boston U | 1970 | 99 |
| Terry Peel to Robert Ford, Houston | Syracuse | 1970 | 99 |
| Terry Peel to Robert Ford, Houston | San Diego St | 1972 | 99 |
| Cris Collinsworth to Derrick Gaffney, Florida | Rice | 1977 | 99 |
| Scott Ankrom to James Maness, Texas Christian | Rice | 1984 | 99 |
| Gino Toretta to Horace Copeland, Miami | Arkansas | 1991 | 99 |

### Field Goals

| FIELD GOALS | Opponent | Year | Yds |
|---|---|---|---|
| Steve Little, Arkansas | Texas | 1977 | 67 |
| Russell Erxleben, Texas | Rice | 1977 | 67 |
| Joe Williams, Wichita St | Southern Illinois | 1978 | 67 |
| Tony Franklin, Texas A&M | Baylor | 1976 | 65 |
| Tony Franklin, Texas A&M | Baylor | 1976 | 64 |
| Russell Erxleben, Texas | Oklahoma | 1977 | 64 |

### Punts

| PUNTS | Opponent | Year | Yds |
|---|---|---|---|
| Pat Brady, Nevada* | Loyola (CA) | 1950 | 99 |
| George O'Brien, Wisconsin | Iowa | 1952 | 96 |
| John Hadl, Kansas | Oklahoma | 1959 | 94 |
| Carl Knox, Texas Christian | Oklahoma St | 1947 | 94 |
| Preston Johnson, SMU | Pittsburgh | 1940 | 94 |

*Note: Nevada was Nevada-Reno in 1950.

### DIVISION I-A WINNINGEST TEAMS
#### Alltime Winning Percentage

| | Yrs | W | L | T | Pct | GP | Bowl Record |
|---|---|---|---|---|---|---|---|
| Notre Dame | 106 | 729 | 216 | 42 | .760 | 987 | 12-7-0 |
| Michigan | 115 | 747 | 246 | 36 | .743 | 1,029 | 13-13-0 |
| Alabama | 100 | 703 | 238 | 44 | .736 | 985 | 27-17-3 |
| Oklahoma | 100 | 665 | 246 | 52 | .718 | 963 | 20-11-1 |
| Texas | 102 | 695 | 277 | 32 | .708 | 1,004 | 17-16-2 |
| Southern Cal | 102 | 638 | 256 | 53 | .702 | 947 | 24-13-0 |
| Ohio St | 105 | 668 | 269 | 53 | .702 | 990 | 13-14-0 |
| Nebraska | 105 | 686 | 290 | 40 | .695 | 1,016 | 15-18-0 |
| Penn St | 108 | 686 | 291 | 41 | .694 | 1,018 | 19-10-2 |
| Tennessee | 98 | 644 | 280 | 53 | .686 | 977 | 19-16-0 |
| Central Michigan | 94 | 489 | 258 | 36 | .648 | 783 | 3-2-0 |
| Florida St | 48 | 325 | 177 | 17 | .643 | 519 | 15-7-2 |
| Washington | 105 | 569 | 314 | 49 | .637 | 932 | 12-8-1 |
| Army | 105 | 592 | 336 | 50 | .632 | 976 | 2-1-0 |
| Miami (OH) | 106 | 551 | 313 | 43 | .631 | 907 | 5-2-0 |
| Georgia | 101 | 595 | 337 | 54 | .631 | 986 | 15-13-3 |
| Louisiana St | 101 | 577 | 332 | 46 | .628 | 955 | 11-16-1 |
| Arizona St | 82 | 447 | 263 | 24 | .625 | 734 | 9-5-1 |
| Auburn | 102 | 567 | 336 | 47 | .622 | 950 | 12-9-2 |
| Colorado | 105 | 568 | 349 | 36 | .615 | 953 | 7-12-0 |
| Miami (FL) | 68 | 421 | 262 | 19 | .613 | 702 | 10-11-0 |
| Bowling Green | 76 | 398 | 245 | 52 | .610 | 695 | 2-3-0 |
| Michigan St | 98 | 526 | 334 | 43 | .606 | 903 | 5-6-0 |
| UCLA | 76 | 442 | 286 | 37 | .602 | 765 | 10-8-1 |
| Minnesota | 111 | 558 | 367 | 43 | .599 | 968 | 2-3-0 |

Note: Includes bowl games.

#### Alltime Victories

| | | | |
|---|---|---|---|
| Michigan | 747 | Georgia | 595 | Minnesota | 558 |
| Notre Dame | 729 | Army | 592 | N Carolina | 556 |
| Alabama | 703 | Syracuse | 590 | Georgia Tech | 556 |
| Texas | 695 | Louisiana St | 577 | Arkansas | 554 |
| Penn St | 686 | Pittsburgh | 569 | Miami (OH) | 551 |
| Nebraska | 686 | Washington | 569 | Navy | 549 |
| Ohio St | 668 | Colorado | 568 | Rutgers | 535 |
| Oklahoma | 665 | Auburn | 567 | California | 533 |
| Tennessee | 644 | W Virginia | 564 | Clemson | 530 |
| Southern Cal | 638 | Texas A&M | 559 | Michigan St | 526 |

### NUMBER ONE VS NUMBER TWO

The number 1 and number 2 teams, according to the Associated Press Poll, have met 29 times, including 10 bowl games, since the poll's inception in 1936. The number 1 teams have a 17-10-2 record in these matchups. Notre Dame (4-3-2) has played in 9 of the games.

| Date | Results | Stadium |
|---|---|---|
| 10-9-43 | No. 1 Notre Dame 35, No. 2 Michigan 12 | Michigan (Ann Arbor) |
| 11-20-43 | No. 1 Notre Dame 14, No. 2 Iowa Pre-Flight 13 | Notre Dame (South Bend) |
| 12-2-44 | No. 1 Army 23, No. 2 Navy 7 | Municipal (Baltimore) |
| 11-10-45 | No. 1 Army 48, No. 2 Notre Dame 0 | Yankee (New York) |
| 12-1-45 | No. 1 Army 32, No. 2 Navy 13 | Municipal (Philadelphia) |
| 11-9-46 | No. 1 Army 0, No. 2 Notre Dame 0 | Yankee (New York) |
| 1-1-63 | No. 1 Southern Cal 42, No. 2 Wisconsin 37 (Rose Bowl) | Rose Bowl (Pasadena) |
| 10-12-63 | No. 2 Texas 28, No. 1 Oklahoma 7 | Cotton Bowl (Dallas) |
| 1-1-64 | No. 1 Texas 28, No. 2 Navy 6 (Cotton Bowl) | Cotton Bowl (Dallas) |
| 11-19-66 | No. 1 Notre Dame 10, No. 2 Michigan St 10 | Spartan (East Lansing) |
| 9-28-68 | No. 1 Purdue 37, No. 2 Notre Dame 22 | Notre Dame (South Bend) |
| 1-1-69 | No. 1 Ohio St 27, No. 2 Southern Cal 16 (Rose Bowl) | Rose Bowl (Pasadena) |
| 12-6-69 | No. 1 Texas 15, No. 2 Arkansas 14 | Razorback (Fayetteville) |
| 11-25-71 | No. 1 Nebraska 35, No. 2 Oklahoma 31 | Owen Field (Norman) |
| 1-1-72 | No. 1 Nebraska 38, No. 2 Alabama 6 (Orange Bowl) | Orange Bowl (Miami) |

### NUMBER ONE VS NUMBER TWO *(Cont.)*

| Date | Results | Stadium |
|------|---------|---------|
| 1-1-79 | No. 2 Alabama 14, No. 1 Penn St 7 (Sugar Bowl) | Sugar Bowl (New Orleans) |
| 9-26-81 | No. 1 Southern Cal 28, No. 2 Oklahoma 24 | Coliseum (Los Angeles) |
| 1-1-83 | No. 2 Penn St 27, No. 1 Georgia 23 (Sugar Bowl) | Sugar Bowl (New Orleans) |
| 10-19-85 | No. 1 Iowa 12, No. 2 Michigan 10 | Kinnick (Iowa City) |
| 9-27-86 | No. 2 Miami (FL) 28, No. 1 Oklahoma 16 | Orange Bowl (Miami) |
| 1-2-87 | No. 2 Penn St 14, No. 1 Miami (FL) 10 (Fiesta Bowl) | Fiesta Bowl (Tempe) |
| 11-21-87 | No. 2 Oklahoma 17, No. 1 Nebraska 7 | Memorial (Lincoln) |
| 1-1-88 | No. 2 Miami (FL) 20, No. 1 Oklahoma 14 (Orange Bowl) | Orange Bowl (Miami) |
| 11-26-88 | No. 1 Notre Dame 27, No. 2 Southern Cal 10 | Coliseum (Los Angeles) |
| 9-16-89 | No. 1 Notre Dame 24, No. 2 Michigan 19 | Michigan (Ann Arbor) |
| 11-16-91 | No. 2 Miami (FL) 17, No. 1 Florida St 16 | Campbell (Tallahassee) |
| 1-1-93 | No. 2 Alabama 34, No. 1 Miami (FL) 13 | Superdome (New Orleans) |
| 11-13-93 | No. 2 Notre Dame 31, No. 1 Florida St 24 | Notre Dame (South Bend) |
| 1-1-94 | No. 1 Florida St 18, No. 2 Nebraska 16 (Orange Bowl) | Orange Bowl (Miami) |

### Longest Winning Streaks

| Wins | Team | Yrs | Ended by | Score |
|------|------|-----|----------|-------|
| 47 | Oklahoma | 1953-57 | Notre Dame | 7-0 |
| 39 | Washington | 1908-14 | Oregon St | 0-0 |
| 37 | Yale | 1890-93 | Princeton | 6-0 |
| 37 | Yale | 1887-89 | Princeton | 10-0 |
| 35 | Toledo | 1969-71 | Tampa | 21-0 |
| 34 | Pennsylvania | 1894-96 | Lafayette | 6-4 |
| 31 | Oklahoma | 1948-50 | Kentucky | 13-7 |
| 31 | Pittsburgh | 1914-18 | Cleveland Naval Reserve | 10-9 |
| 31 | Pennsylvania | 1896-98 | Harvard | 10-0 |
| 30 | Texas | 1968-70 | Notre Dame | 24-11 |
| 29 | Michigan | 1901-03 | Minnesota | 6-6 |
| 29 | Miami (FL) | 1990-93 | Alabama | 34-13 |

### Longest Unbeaten Streaks

| No. | W | T | Team | Yrs | Ended by | Score |
|-----|---|---|------|-----|----------|-------|
| 63 | 59 | 4 | Washington | 1907-17 | California | 27-0 |
| 56 | 55 | 1 | Michigan | 1901-05 | Chicago | 2-0 |
| 50 | 46 | 4 | California | 1920-25 | Olympic Club | 15-0 |
| 48 | 47 | 1 | Oklahoma | 1953-57 | Notre Dame | 7-0 |
| 48 | 47 | 1 | Yale | 1885-89 | Princeton | 10-0 |
| 47 | 42 | 5 | Yale | 1879-85 | Princeton | 6-5 |
| 44 | 42 | 2 | Yale | 1894-96 | Princeton | 24-6 |
| 42 | 39 | 3 | Yale | 1904-08 | Harvard | 4-0 |
| 39 | 37 | 2 | Notre Dame | 1946-50 | Purdue | 28-14 |
| 37 | 36 | 1 | Oklahoma | 1972-75 | Kansas | 23-3 |
| 37 | 37 | 0 | Yale | 1890-93 | Princeton | 6-0 |
| 35 | 35 | 0 | Toledo | 1969-71 | Tampa | 21-0 |
| 35 | 34 | 1 | Minnesota | 1903-05 | Wisconsin | 16-12 |
| 34 | 33 | 1 | Nebraska | 1912-16 | Kansas | 7-3 |
| 34 | 34 | 0 | Pennsylvania | 1894-96 | Lafayette | 6-4 |
| 34 | 32 | 2 | Princeton | 1884-87 | Harvard | 12-0 |
| 34 | 29 | 5 | Princeton | 1877-82 | Harvard | 1-0 |
| 33 | 30 | 3 | Tennessee | 1926-30 | Alabama | 18-6 |
| 33 | 31 | 2 | Georgia Tech | 1914-18 | Pittsburgh | 32-0 |
| 33 | 30 | 3 | Harvard | 1911-15 | Cornell | 10-0 |
| 32 | 31 | 1 | Nebraska | 1969-71 | UCLA | 20-17 |
| 32 | 30 | 2 | Army | 1944-47 | Columbia | 21-20 |
| 32 | 31 | 1 | Harvard | 1898-1900 | Yale | 28-0 |
| 31 | 30 | 1 | Penn St | 1967-70 | Colorado | 41-13 |
| 31 | 30 | 1 | San Diego St | 1967-70 | Long Beach St | 27-11 |
| 31 | 29 | 2 | Georgia Tech | 1950-53 | Notre Dame | 27-14 |
| 31 | 30 | 1 | Alabama | 1991-93 | Louisiana St | 17-13 |
| 31 | 31 | 0 | Oklahoma | 1948-50 | Kentucky | 13-7 |
| 31 | 31 | 0 | Pittsburgh | 1919-22 | Cleveland Naval | 10-9 |
| 31 | 31 | 0 | Pennsylvania | 1896-98 | Harvard | 10-0 |

Note: Includes bowl games.

### Longest Losing Streaks

| L | | Seasons | Ended Against | Score |
|---|---|---|---|---|
| 44 | Columbia | 1983-88 | Princeton | 16-14 |
| 34 | Northwestern | 1979-82 | Northern Illinois | 31-6 |
| 28 | Virginia | 1958-61 | William & Mary | 21-6 |
| 28 | Kansas St | 1945-48 | Arkansas St | 37-6 |
| 27 | Eastern Michigan | 1980-82 | Kent St | 9-7 |

### Longest Series

| GP | Opponents (Series Leader Listed First) | Record | First Game | GP | Opponents (Series Leader Listed First) | Record | First Game |
|---|---|---|---|---|---|---|---|
| 104 | Minnesota-Wisconsin | 57-39-8 | 1890 | 95 | Navy-Army | 44-44-7 | 1890 |
| 103 | Missouri-Kansas | 48-46-9 | 1891 | 92 | Penn St-Pittsburgh† | 47-41-4 | 1893 |
| 101 | Nebraska-Kansas | 77-21-3 | 1892 | 92 | Louisiana St-Tulane* | 63-22-7 | 1893 |
| 101 | Texas Christian-Baylor | 47-47-7 | 1899 | 92 | Clemson-S Carolina | 54-34-4 | 1896 |
| 101 | Texas-Texas A&M | 64-32-5 | 1894 | 92 | Kansas-Kansas St | 61-26-5 | 1902 |
| 99 | N Carolina-Virginia | 54-41-4 | 1892 | 92 | Oklahoma-Kansas | 62-24-6 | 1903 |
| 99 | Miami (OH)-Cincinnati | 53-39-7 | 1888 | 92 | Utah-Utah St | 61-27-4 | 1892 |
| 98 | Auburn-Georgia | 46-44-8 | 1892 | 91 | Michigan-Ohio St | 51-34-6 | 1897 |
| 98 | Oregon-Oregon St | 48-40-10 | 1894 | 91 | Mississippi-Miss St | 52-33-6 | 1901 |
| 97 | Purdue-Indiana | 58-33-6 | 1891 | 90 | Auburn-Georgia Tech# | 47-39-4 | 1892 |
| 97 | Stanford-California | 47-39-11 | 1892 | | | | |

†Have not met since 1992; *Disputed series record. Tulane claims 23-61-7 record. #Have not met since 1989

## NCAA Coaches' Records

### ALLTIME WINNINGEST DIVISION I-A COACHES
### By Percentage

| Coach (Alma mater) | Colleges Coached | Yrs | W | L | T | Pct |
|---|---|---|---|---|---|---|
| Knute Rockne (Notre Dame '14)† | Notre Dame 1918-30 | 13 | 105 | 12 | 5 | .881 |
| Frank W. Leahy (Notre Dame '31)† | Boston Col 1939-40; Notre Dame 1941-43, 1946-53 | 13 | 107 | 13 | 9 | .864 |
| George W. Woodruff (Yale '89)† | Pennsylvania 1892-01; Illinois 1903; Carlisle 1905 | 12 | 142 | 25 | 2 | .846 |
| Barry Switzer (Arkansas '60) | Oklahoma 1973-88 | 16 | 157 | 29 | 4 | .837 |
| Percy D. Haughton (Harvard '99)† | Cornell 1899-1900; Harvard 1908-16; Columbia 1923-24 | 13 | 96 | 17 | 6 | .832 |
| Bob Neyland (Army '16)† | Tennessee 1926-34, 1936-40, 1946-52 | 21 | 173 | 31 | 12 | .829 |
| Fielding (Hurry Up) Yost (Lafayette '97)† | Ohio Wesleyan 1897; Nebraska 1898; Kansas 1899; Stanford 1900; Michigan 1901-23, 1925-26 | 29 | 196 | 36 | 12 | .828 |
| Bud Wilkinson (Minnesota '37)† | Oklahoma 1947-63 | 17 | 145 | 29 | 4 | .826 |
| Tom Osborne (Hastings '59)* | Nebraska 1973-present | 22 | 219 | 47 | 3 | .820 |
| Jock Sutherland (Pittsburgh '18)† | Lafayette 1919-23; Pittsburgh 1924-38 | 20 | 144 | 28 | 14 | .812 |
| Bob Devaney (Alma, MI '39)† | Wyoming 1957-61; Nebraska 1962-72 | 16 | 136 | 30 | 7 | .806 |
| Frank W. Thomas (Notre Dame '23)† | Chattanooga 1925-28; Alabama 1931-42, 1944-46 | 19 | 141 | 33 | 9 | .795 |
| Joe Paterno (Brown '50)* | Penn St 1966-present | 29 | 269 | 69 | 3 | .793 |
| Henry L. Williams (Yale '91)† | Army 1891; Minnesota 1900-21 | 23 | 141 | 34 | 12 | .786 |
| Gil Dobie (Minnesota '02)† | N Dakota St 1906-07; Washington 1908-16; Navy 1917-19; Cornell 1920-35; Boston Col 1936-38 | 33 | 180 | 45 | 15 | .781 |
| Paul W. (Bear) Bryant (Alabama '36)† | Maryland 1945; Kentucky 1946-53; Texas A&M 1954-57; Alabama 1958-82 | 38 | 323 | 85 | 17 | .780 |

*Active coach. †Hall of Fame member.

Note: Minimum 10 years as head coach at Division I institutions; record at 4-year colleges only; bowl games included; ties computed as half won, half lost.

## ALLTIME WINNINGEST DIVISION I-A COACHES (Cont.)
### By Victories

| | Yrs | W | L | T | Pct | | Yrs | W | L | T | Pct |
|---|---|---|---|---|---|---|---|---|---|---|---|
| Paul (Bear) Bryant | 38 | 323 | 85 | 17 | .780 | Jess Neely | 40 | 207 | 176 | 19 | .539 |
| Glenn (Pop) Warner | 44 | 319 | 106 | 32 | .733 | *LaVell Edwards | 23 | 207 | 76 | 3 | .729 |
| Amos Alonzo Stagg | 57 | 314 | 199 | 35 | .605 | *Hayden Fry | 33 | 205 | 157 | 10 | .563 |
| *Joe Paterno | 29 | 269 | 69 | 3 | .793 | Warren Woodson | 31 | 203 | 95 | 14 | .673 |
| *Bobby Bowden | 29 | 249 | 79 | 4 | .756 | Vince Dooley | 25 | 201 | 77 | 10 | .715 |
| Woody Hayes | 33 | 238 | 72 | 10 | .759 | Eddie Anderson | 39 | 201 | 128 | 15 | .606 |
| Bo Schembechler | 27 | 234 | 65 | 8 | .775 | Lou Holtz | 25 | 199 | 89 | 7 | .686 |
| *Tom Osborne | 22 | 219 | 47 | 3 | .820 | Dana Bible | 33 | 198 | 72 | 23 | .715 |

### Most Bowl Victories

| | W | L | T | | W | L | T |
|---|---|---|---|---|---|---|---|
| *Joe Paterno | 16 | 8 | 1 | *Terry Donahue | 8 | 3 | 1 |
| Paul (Bear) Bryant | 15 | 12 | 2 | Barry Switzer | 8 | 5 | 0 |
| *Bobby Bowden | 14 | 3 | 1 | Darrell Royal | 8 | 7 | 1 |
| Jim Wacker | 13 | 2 | 0 | Vince Dooley | 8 | 10 | 2 |
| Don James | 10 | 5 | 0 | Bob Devaney | 7 | 3 | 0 |
| *Lou Holtz | 10 | 7 | 2 | Dan Devine | 7 | 3 | 0 |
| John Vaught | 10 | 8 | 0 | Earle Bruce | 7 | 5 | 0 |
| Bobby Dodd | 9 | 4 | 0 | Charlie McClendon | 7 | 6 | 0 |
| *Johnny Majors | 9 | 7 | 0 | *Active coach. | | | |
| *Tom Osborne | 9 | 13 | 0 | | | | |

### WINNINGEST ACTIVE DIVISION I-A COACHES
#### By Percentage

| Coach, College | Yrs | W | L | T | Pct# | Bowls | | |
|---|---|---|---|---|---|---|---|---|
| | | | | | | W | L | T |
| R.C. Slocum, Texas A&M | 6 | 59 | 12 | 2 | .822 | 1 | 4 | 0 |
| Tom Osborne, Nebraska | 22 | 219 | 47 | 3 | .820 | 9 | 13 | 0 |
| Joe Paterno, Penn St | 29 | 269 | 69 | 3 | .793 | 16 | 8 | 1 |
| John Robinson, Southern Cal | 9 | 83 | 22 | 3 | .782 | 6 | 1 | 0 |
| Bobby Bowden, Florida St | 29 | 249 | 79 | 4 | .756 | 14 | 3 | 1 |
| Steve Spurrier, Florida | 8 | 69 | 25 | 2 | .729 | 2 | 3 | 0 |
| LaVell Edwards, Brigham Young | 23 | 207 | 76 | 3 | .729 | 6 | 12 | 1 |
| Danny Ford, Arkansas | 14 | 105 | 41 | 5 | .712 | 6 | 2 | 0 |
| Lou Holtz, Notre Dame | 25 | 199 | 89 | 7 | .686 | 10 | 7 | 2 |
| Terry Donahue, UCLA | 19 | 144 | 69 | 8 | .670 | 8 | 3 | 1 |

#Bowl games included. Ties computed as half win, half loss.
Note: Minimum 5 years as Division I-A head coach; record at 4-year colleges only.

### Happy Valley Trails

After 33 college underclassmen renounced their remaining eligibility in mid-January to enter April's NFL draft, we were struck by how a hide-bound attitude, long prevalent in college football, has diminished over the past decade. Remember when Bernie Kosar left Miami in 1985 with two years of eligibility remaining? Though Kosar had already earned his degree, doing so in 3.27 style, and delivered a national championship to Coral Gables, he was labeled an ingrate by the Miami faithful, and the school declined to retire his number. A year and a half later the Hurricanes' Vinny Testaverde, who indentured himself for four seasons, had his jersey retired—even though he didn't graduate or win a national title.

Contrast those reactions with the way Penn State handled the news that Ki-Jana Carter, who intends to graduate with this year's class, will pass up his senior season. Fans, students, local sportswriters and coach Joe Paterno have all wished Carter the best. It has taken a while, but the college football world seems finally to have gotten the message: You go to college to get your degree. After that it's O.K. to get on with your life, whether or not that life includes the NFL.

### WINNINGEST ACTIVE DIVISION I-A COACHES (Cont.)
#### By Victories

| | | | |
|---|---|---|---|
| Joe Paterno, Penn St | 269 | Don Nehlen, W Virginia | 163 |
| Bobby Bowden, Florida St | 249 | Bill Mallory, Indiana | 162 |
| Tom Osborne, Nebraska | 219 | Al Molde, W Michigan | 159 |
| LaVell Edwards, Brigham Young | 207 | Jim Wacker, Minnesota | 153 |
| Hayden Fry, Iowa | 205 | Terry Donahue, UCLA | 144 |
| Lou Holtz, Notre Dame | 199 | George Welsh, Virginia | 144 |
| Jim Sweeney, Fresno St | 191 | John Cooper, Ohio St | 135 |
| Johnny Majors, Tennessee, Pitt | 179 | | |

### WINNINGEST ACTIVE DIVISION I-AA COACHES
#### By Percentage

| Coach, College | Yrs | W | L | T | Pct* |
|---|---|---|---|---|---|
| Terry Allen, N Iowa | 6 | 55 | 19 | 0 | .743 |
| Jim Donnan, Marshall | 5 | 52 | 18 | 0 | .743 |
| Roy Kidd, Eastern Kentucky | 31 | 257 | 91 | 8 | .733 |
| Eddie Robinson, Grambling | 52 | 397 | 143 | 15 | .729 |
| Jim Tressel, Youngstown St | 9 | 84 | 33 | 2 | .714 |
| Tubby Raymond, Delaware | 29 | 239 | 95 | 3 | .714 |
| Tim Stowers, Georgia Southern | 5 | 42 | 19 | 0 | .689 |
| Steve Tosches, Princeton | 8 | 53 | 26 | 1 | .669 |
| Bobby Keasler, McNeese St | 5 | 40 | 20 | 2 | .661 |
| Bill Hayes, N Carolina A&T | 19 | 137 | 71 | 2 | .657 |

*Playoff games included.
Note: Minimum 5 years as a Division I-A and/or Division I-AA head coach; record at 4-year colleges only.

#### By Victories

| | | | |
|---|---|---|---|
| Eddie Robinson, Grambling | 397 | Bill Bowes, New Hampshire | 152 |
| Roy Kidd, Eastern Kentucky | 257 | Willie Jeffries, S Carolina St | 142 |
| Tubby Raymond, Delaware | 239 | Don Read, Montana | 141 |
| Carmen Cozza, Yale | 174 | Bill Hayes, N Carolina A&T | 137 |
| Ron Randleman, Sam Houston St | 161 | James Donnelly, Middle Tennessee St | 132 |

### WINNINGEST ACTIVE DIVISION II COACHES
#### By Percentage

| Coach, College | Yrs | W | L | T | Pct* |
|---|---|---|---|---|---|
| Chuck Broyles, Pittsburg St | 5 | 57 | 7 | 1 | .885 |
| Rocky Hager, N Dakota St | 8 | 75 | 18 | 1 | .803 |
| Ken Sparks, Carson-Newman | 15 | 140 | 37 | 2 | .788 |
| Peter Yetten, Bentley | 7 | 49 | 13 | 1 | .786 |
| Ron Taylor, Quincy | 6 | 43 | 15 | 2 | .733 |
| Bob Cortese, Fort Hays St | 15 | 119 | 43 | 4 | .729 |
| Danny Hale, Bloomsburg | 7 | 53 | 22 | 0 | .707 |
| Frank Cignetti, Indiana (PA) | 13 | 109 | 45 | 1 | .706 |
| Dick Lowry, Hillsdale | 21 | 159 | 66 | 3 | .704 |
| Hal Mumme, Valdosta St | 6 | 48 | 20 | 1 | .703 |

*Ties computed as half win, half loss. Playoff games included.
Note: Minimum 5 years as a college head coach; record at 4-year colleges only.

#### By Victories

| | | | |
|---|---|---|---|
| Jim Malosky, MN-Duluth | 235 | Bud Elliott, E New Mexico St | 143 |
| Gene Carpenter, Millersville | 175 | Ken Sparks, Carson-Newman | 140 |
| Ron Harms, Texas A&M-Kingsville* | 175 | Claire Boroff, Kearney St | 140 |
| Dick Lowry, Hillsdale | 159 | Dennis Douds, E Stroudsburg | 129 |
| Willard Bailey, Virginia Union | 158 | Bob Cortese, Fort Hays St | 119 |
| Douglas Porter, Fort Valley St | 146 | *Formerly Texas A&I | |

## WINNINGEST ACTIVE DIVISION III COACHES
### By Percentage

| Coach, College | Yrs | W | L | T | Pct* |
|---|---|---|---|---|---|
| Ken O'Keefe, Allegheny | 5 | 51 | 6 | 1 | .888 |
| Bob Reade, Augustana (IL) | 16 | 146 | 23 | 1 | .862 |
| Dick Farley, Williams | 8 | 53 | 9 | 2 | .844 |
| Larry Kehres, Mt Union | 9 | 84 | 15 | 3 | .838 |
| Ron Schipper, Central (IA) | 34 | 270 | 63 | 3 | .808 |
| John Luckhardt, Wash&Jeff | 13 | 108 | 27 | 2 | .796 |
| Bob Packard, Baldwin-Wallace | 14 | 111 | 29 | 2 | .789 |
| Roger Harring, WI-LaCrosse | 26 | 218 | 62 | 7 | .772 |
| Pete Schmidt, Albion | 12 | 87 | 25 | 4 | .767 |
| John Gagliardi, St John's (MN) | 46 | 317 | 98 | 10 | .758 |

*Ties computed as half win, half loss. Playoff games included.

Note: Minimum 5 years as a college head coach; record at 4-year colleges only.

### By Victories

| | | | |
|---|---|---|---|
| John Gagliardi, St John's (MN) | 317 | Frank Girardi, Lycoming | 161 |
| Ron Schipper, Central (IA) | 270 | Don Miller, Trinity (CT) | 154 |
| Roger Harring, WI-LaCrosse | 218 | Joe McDaniel, Centre | 150 |
| Bill Manlove, Delaware Valley | 189 | Bob Reade, Augustana (IL) | 146 |
| Jim Christopherson, Concordia-M'head | 181 | Peter Mazzaferro, Bridgewater (MA) | 145 |

# NAIA Coaches' Records

## WINNINGEST ACTIVE NAIA COACHES
### By Percentage

| Coach, College | Yrs | W | L | T | Pct* |
|---|---|---|---|---|---|
| Ted Kessinger, Bethany (KS) | 19 | 154 | 36 | 1 | .809 |
| Frosty Westering, Pacific Lutheran (WA) | 29 | 235 | 73 | 6 | .758 |
| Hank Biesiot, Dickinson State, (ND) | 19 | 117 | 42 | 1 | .734 |
| Dick Strahm, Findlay (OH) | 21 | 142 | 57 | 3 | .710 |
| Dick Lowry, Hillsdale (MI) | 20 | 159 | 66 | 3 | .704 |
| Bob Petrino, Carroll (MT) | 24 | 147 | 63 | 1 | .699 |
| Brian Byers, Friends (KS) | 7 | 48 | 25 | 0 | .658 |
| Jimmie Keeling, Hardin-Simmons (TX) | 5 | 36 | 19 | 0 | .655 |
| Rob Smith, Western Washington | 6 | 36 | 20 | 1 | .640 |
| Morris Sloan, Southeastern Oklahoma | 6 | 36 | 20 | 3 | .636 |

*Playoff games included.

Note: Minimum five years as a collegiate head coach and includes record against four-year institutions only.

### By Victories

| | | | |
|---|---|---|---|
| Frosty Westering, Pacific Lutheran (WA) | 235 | Dick Strahm, Findlay (OH) | 142 |
| Buddy Benson, Ouachita Baptist (AR) | 160 | Bill Ramseyer, Clinch Valley (VA) | 131 |
| Dick Lowry, Hillsdale (MI) | 159 | Hank Biesiot, Dickinson State (ND) | 117 |
| Ted Kessinger, Bethany (KS) | 154 | Tom Dowling, Cumberland (KY) | 104 |
| Bob Petrino, Carroll (MT) | 147 | Bob Brush, Georgetown (KY) | 104 |

# Pro Basketball

JUNE 19, 1995·$2.95 (CAN. $3.95)

## Sports Illustrated

## RED HOT

Clyde Drexler lifts the Houston Rockets toward their second straight NBA title

JOHN W. MCDONOUGH

# Recurring Dream

## Hakeem Olajuwon put together an awesome postseason and led the Rockets to an improbable second straight NBA title

### by Phil Taylor

IT WAS a time machine of a season. One moment we were years into the future, watching tomorrow's team, the Orlando Magic, dominate the NBA as if its time had already come. The next second we had taken a step back into the league's recent, glorious past, as Michael Jordan laid down his bat and glove and made a thrilling return to the Chicago Bulls, at times soaring and slashing as if he had never left, a memory come back to life.

But in the end the Houston Rockets brought us back to the present and made us realize that they are the team of the moment. The Rockets meandered through the 1994–95 regular season largely unnoticed as flashier teams and players took turns grabbing the public's attention. But the spotlight finally came back to Houston, and when it did, it found the Rockets hugging the championship trophy for the second consecutive year after finishing a four-game sweep of Orlando.

Indeed, the season ended much as it had the year before, with Houston center Hakeem (The Dream) Olajuwon, the 7-foot

package of grace and class from Nigeria, carrying the Rockets to the title and earning another Finals MVP award. But this time Olajuwon surpassed even his own lofty standards. The Rockets, who entered the playoffs with only the sixth-best record in the Western Conference, became champions again largely because Olajuwon would not let them lose. The Dream produced a playoff performance for the ages, one of the greatest series of individual efforts any sport has seen in years.

Olajuwon averaged 33 points and 10.3 rebounds in the playoffs, including 16 games of more than 30 points and five of more than 40, but numbers cannot do him justice. With his feints and spins and pump fakes, he not only outplayed opponents, he embarrassed them. Even David Robinson, the San Antonio Spurs' All-Star center, was victimized by the Dream. The Spurs had finished with the best record in the regular season, Robinson had been named the league MVP, and San Antonio had won five of the six games against Houston in the regular season, but it quickly became clear that none of that mat-

**Olajuwon's performance in the conference final was one for the ages.**

tered because this was Olajuwon's series. He so thoroughly humiliated Robinson that the San Antonio center looked lost. "I've never felt this way before," Robinson said after the Rockets had won the series in six games. "The strange thing is, I actually thought I played him pretty well."

It wasn't that Robinson played poorly, it was that Olajuwon was magnificent. "The series he played against San Antonio is going to be legendary," Houston coach Rudy Tomjanovich said. "People will be talking about that series and how he played for many, many years to come."

But despite Olajuwon's brilliance, the Rockets' championship will be associated just as much with his close friend guard Clyde Drexler. College teammates at the University of Houston, Drexler and Olajuwon were members of the 1983 Phi Slama Jama squad that fell to North Carolina State in one of the greatest championship game upsets in history. Drexler, a Houston native, had gone on to a stellar pro career with the Portland Trail Blazers, but unlike Olajuwon, he had never been able to complete the climb to a championship. The two had often talked over the years about how wonderful it would be to play together again, but neither thought it would ever be anything more than a fantasy until the Rockets traded forward Otis Thorpe to Portland in February for Drexler and forward Tracy Murray.

DAVID E. KLUTHO

championship, his desire for a title was evident with every length-of-the-court rush he took in the Finals, racing headlong for the basket as if the championship ring were waiting there. "It's as sweet as I thought it would be," he said when it was over. "I don't know if I can describe the feeling." He didn't have to.

Jordan is quite familiar with that championship feeling. He led the Bulls to three straight titles before retiring in 1993 and taking up baseball. But discouraged by the labor problems in baseball and by his .202 batting average with the Double A Birmingham Barons, Jordan abruptly decided to return to the NBA in March, in time for the Bulls' last 17 regular-season games and the playoffs. After weeks of speculation and rumors, Jordan made his return official by issuing a two-word statement, "I'm back."

His return—wearing number 45 instead of his old number 23—sent a buzz of excitement through the league. At 32, could he simply pick up where he left off, in midair? Could he transform the Bulls from a mediocre team to a championship contender almost overnight? Some nights, the answer to both questions seemed to be yes. Although his jump shot betrayed him in the early going, as in his 7-for-28 shooting performance in his first game back, against Indiana, Jordan was his old spectacular self amazingly often. He beat the Atlanta Hawks with a buzzer-beating jumper in his first week back, then "dropped a double-nickel on the Knicks," as film director Spike Lee put it, devastating New York with an incendiary 55-point performance that ended with a brilliant pass to teammate Bill

The Houston front office was heavily criticized for the trade, even by some of the Rocket players. By giving up Thorpe the Rockets had created a rebounding hole that they appeared unable to fill. "Nothing against Clyde, but this is a hard one to figure out," forward Mario Elie said the day after the trade was announced. "I don't know how we're going to replace O.T."

But Drexler eventually won his teammates over by providing badly needed offense, especially during a 15-day stretch in March and April when Olajuwon was sidelined by anemia. In addition to offense, Drexler brought hunger to Houston. If there was any complacency among the Rockets after their first championship, bringing in a 32-year-old star who had never won a title was the perfect antidote. Although Drexler is a master of the plain vanilla quote, even when talking about his passion for winning a

**Shaq was a force, leading the Magic all the way to the Finals.**

Wennington for a dunk that won the game for Chicago.

But it eventually became clear that not even the great Jordan could come back and dominate the league as if he had never left. Age, rust and lack of familiarity with his teammates combined to keep him from leading the Bulls back to the championship. In the eagerly anticipated and over-hyped Eastern Conference semifinals against Orlando—the battle of Air Jordan vs. Shaq—Jordan made misplays in Games 1 and 6 that cost the Bulls dearly, and the Magic dispatched Chicago in six games.

In retrospect it's clear that anyone who expected Jordan to turn back the clock to the Bulls' championship years was asking too much. Jordan was competing not so much against other NBA teams as against our memory of him, which had become distorted during his absence. We remembered only the hang time and the wagging tongue and the championships, and so the mistakes caught us by surprise. In the end even Jordan gave in to the temptation to try to step back in time. After Game 1 against Orlando, in which Magic guard Nick Anderson stole the ball from him in the final minutes to help Orlando to a come-from-behind win, Jordan came out for Game 2 in number 23, despite the fact that the Bulls had retired it in an emotional ceremony before the season. The switch came as a complete surprise to even Jordan's teammates and especially to the officials in the NBA office, who fined the Bulls for the unapproved switch.

Jordan wore 23 for the rest of the playoffs, but that couldn't stop the Magic. After Orlando eliminated the Bulls, Jordan sat at his locker for more than an hour, analyzing his return for reporters. "I probably expected too much of myself," he said. "I saw a league where only Houston had any real championship experience, and I thought there was a chance for me to come in and maybe help this team steal a title. But my teammates and I never really got to know each other as well as you have to if you're going to win a championship. It didn't work out as well as I planned, but I have no regrets about doing it this way. I'm glad I came back." Basketball fans around the world no doubt felt the same way.

Jordan's return made O'Neal the second-most-famous player in the league, but it didn't keep Shaq from winning his first scoring title, with 29.3 points per game. O'Neal and the Magic looked close to invincible for most of the season, maintaining the league's best record for much of the year before stumbling during the last month of the regular season. O'Neal was still busy with endorsements and other off-the-court

MANNY MILLAN

riors, which in turn led to Nelson's resignation three months later. Nelson, however, wasn't unemployed for long. In July he was named the new coach of the Knicks.

Other players missed practices and shootarounds without permission, including New Jersey Net forward Derrick Coleman, Golden State guard Latrell Sprewell, Minnesota Timberwolf guard Isaiah Rider, and the poster child for misbehavior, San Antonio Spur forward Dennis Rodman. Seattle forward Vincent Askew refused coach George Karl's order to enter a game (although he later acknowledged his mistake and apologized for it), but the single most ridiculous act of defiance was perpetrated by New Jersey's Chris Morris. The Nets' forward took the floor for a practice shootaround one morning in December with his shoelaces undone. Then he refused coach Butch Beard's order to tie them. His explanation: "I wasn't planning on doing much running."

Fortunately for the NBA, Grant Hill came along just in time to remind everyone that not all of the league's young players were immature and spoiled. Hill, the first-round draft choice of the Detroit Pistons, was a model of humility and grace as well as a smooth and explosive forward. Fans loved him as much for his off-the-court personality as for his on-the-court excellence, and they showed it by making him the leading vote-getter in the All-Star Game balloting. It was the first time a rookie had ever earned the most All-Star votes, but Hill had to share the Rookie of the Year award with Dallas Maverick guard Jason Kidd, a passing and defensive marvel whose suspect outside shot improved dramatically by season's end.

activities, but he silenced many of those who criticized him for not working hard enough to improve his basketball skills by unveiling a variety of new offensive moves.

In fact, the 23-year-old Shaq set an example for behavior both on and off the court that several of the other young players in the league would have done well to follow. Players rebelled against their coaches during the 1994–95 season as never before, and the lack of respect for authority was especially apparent in, but not limited to, some of the league's young stars. The confrontation between Golden State coach Don Nelson and his star forward, second-year player Chris Webber, set the tone for the season. Unhappy with what he considered overly harsh treatment by Nelson, Webber held out at the start of the year and basically forced the Warrior management to choose between him and Nelson. The Warriors ended up losing both men. Golden State traded Webber to the Washington Bullets in November, which led to a malaise among the other War-

It was an excellent year for rookies. The Milwaukee Bucks' Glenn Robinson, the top overall pick of the draft, was such an offensive threat that teams quickly began double-teaming him on a regular basis, a rare kind of honor for a rookie. After an early-season holdout, Robinson led the

Bucks in scoring, with 21.9 points per game. Washington's Juwan Howard progressed even faster than even the Bullets expected, and a pair of rookie forwards, Brian Grant and Michael Smith, helped transform the previously hapless Sacramento Kings into a competitive club that missed the playoffs by only one game.

But although the action on the floor was as exciting as ever, the league continued to suffer blemishes in other areas. *The Wall Street Journal* delivered a serious blow with a story in March that suggested that the death of Boston Celtic star Reggie Lewis two years earlier was not simply the tragic case of a player succumbing to a heart abnormality. *The Journal* alleged that Lewis was a cocaine user and that the drug might have been a contributing factor in his death. The story also raised several other issues, the most serious of which were that the Celtics may have allowed financial and public-relations concerns to take precedence over Lewis's medical care; that the supposedly enlightened NBA drug policy helped prevent an accurate assessment of Lewis's condition; and that his wife, Donna Harris Lewis, intimidated the state of Massachusetts into officially declaring a phony cause of death.

The Celtics and Harris Lewis angrily denied the article's allegations, and though some questions remained unanswered about Lewis's death, it didn't stop the Celtics from staging an emotional ceremony retiring his number a few weeks after the publication of the article. Whatever the circumstances surrounding his death, it was clear that a great many Celtic fans chose to remember his life and career fondly.

Again, the games came to the rescue. The allegations about Lewis arose at almost exactly the same time that word of Jordan's comeback plans became public. San Antonio fans went wild over the Spurs' brilliant 62–20 regular season, highlighted by Robinson's MVP award and the relentless rebounding—and rotating hair colors—of

**Miller smoked the Knicks for eight points in 18 seconds in the semis.**

JOHN W. MCDONOUGH

and made two foul shots all in that 18 second span to give the Pacers a 107–105 victory. The stunned Knicks never really recovered from that game, losing the series in seven to the Pacers.

Miller's Game 1 heroics began the final chapter in New York coach Pat Riley's tenure with the Knicks. Three weeks after the Knicks' elimination, Riley resigned, unhappy with Knick management's refusal to give him greater front-office control of the club. Riley and Knick president Dave Checketts parted bitterly, and the Knicks filed tampering charges against the Miami Heat when it became clear that Riley was interested in taking over as the Heat's coach. Miami and New York finally reached a settlement, with the Heat giving the Knicks a first-round draft pick and $1 million in exchange for the Knicks dropping their tampering charge and releasing Riley from the final year of his contract. Several days later Riley signed a lucrative deal with the Heat that made him coach—at a reported $3 million per year—and part owner of the team.

Riley's move was one of the few transactions in the two months following the NBA Finals, because the league imposed a lockout of the players on July 1, having reached an impasse in negotiations with the NBA Players Association for a new collective bargaining agreement. The issue quickly became even more complicated than most labor disputes in sports, with a large segment of the players, led by Jordan and Knick center Patrick Ewing, pushing for decertification of the NBAPA.

However, as the summer came to a close and the opening of training camps loomed, the players voted by a landslide margin to both retain the union and ratify the new collective bargaining agreement, thereby ending the 79-day lockout.

No doubt the fans will have forgotten the entire dispute by the time they see Jordan soar to the hoop in November, and therein lies a lesson for all pro sports.

Rodman. But Rodman's individualism finally became a problem in the playoffs when he was benched for a game because he took his shoes off and blatantly ignored coach Bob Hill in a timeout during the Spurs' series against the Los Angeles Lakers. That was just the beginning, as Rodman made a spectacle of himself during the playoffs and proved a distraction to the Spurs, who finally fell to Houston in the conference finals.

But if the Spurs had a disappointing playoff performance, others, like Olajuwon and Indiana Pacer guard Reggie Miller, had superb ones. The highlight of Miller's postseason effort—and perhaps the single best individual performance of the playoffs—was his last-second devastation of the Knicks. With New York leading by six points with 18 seconds left, it appeared that the Knicks had the victory in Game 1 of their semifinal series wrapped up. But Miller hit a three-pointer, made a steal, hit another three-pointer, grabbed a rebound

# FOR THE RECORD·1994–1995

## NBA Final Standings

### Eastern Conference

**ATLANTIC DIVISION**

| Team | W | L | Pct | GB |
|---|---|---|---|---|
| Orlando | 57 | 25 | .695 | — |
| New York | 55 | 27 | .671 | 2 |
| Boston | 35 | 47 | .427 | 22 |
| Miami | 32 | 50 | .390 | 25 |
| New Jersey | 30 | 52 | .366 | 27 |
| Philadelphia | 24 | 58 | .293 | 33 |
| Washington | 21 | 61 | .256 | 36 |

**CENTRAL DIVISION**

| Team | W | L | Pct | GB |
|---|---|---|---|---|
| Indiana | 52 | 30 | .634 | — |
| Charlotte | 50 | 32 | .610 | 2 |
| Chicago | 47 | 35 | .573 | 5 |
| Cleveland | 43 | 39 | .524 | 9 |
| Atlanta | 42 | 40 | .512 | 10 |
| Milwaukee | 34 | 48 | .415 | 17 |
| Detroit | 28 | 54 | .341 | 24 |

### Western Conference

**MIDWEST DIVISION**

| Team | W | L | Pct | GB |
|---|---|---|---|---|
| San Antonio | 62 | 20 | .756 | — |
| Utah | 60 | 22 | .732 | 2 |
| Houston | 47 | 35 | .573 | 15 |
| Denver | 41 | 41 | .500 | 21 |
| Dallas | 36 | 46 | .439 | 26 |
| Minnesota | 21 | 61 | .256 | 41 |

**PACIFIC DIVISION**

| Team | W | L | Pct | GB |
|---|---|---|---|---|
| Phoenix | 59 | 23 | .720 | — |
| Seattle | 57 | 25 | .695 | 2 |
| LA Lakers | 48 | 34 | .585 | 11 |
| Portland | 44 | 38 | .537 | 15 |
| Sacramento | 39 | 43 | .476 | 20 |
| Golden State | 26 | 56 | .317 | 33 |
| LA Clippers | 17 | 65 | .207 | 42 |

## 1995 NBA Playoffs

**EASTERN CONFERENCE**

1st ROUND · SEMIFINALS · FINALS

Orlando
Boston
Charlotte
Chicago
New York
Cleveland
Indiana
Atlanta

Orlando (3-1)
Chicago (3-1)
New York (3-1)
Indiana (3-0)

Orlando (4-2)
Orlando (4-3)
Indiana (4-3)

**NBA FINALS**

HOUSTON (4-0)

**WESTERN CONFERENCE**

FINALS · SEMIFINALS · 1st ROUND

San Antonio (3-0)
Phoenix (3-0)
Houston (3-2)
LA Lakers (3-1)

San Antonio (4-2)
Houston (4-2)
Houston (4-3)

San Antonio
Denver
Phoenix
Portland
Utah
Houston
Seattle
LA Lakers

# 1995 NBA Playoff Results

## Eastern Conference First Round

| | | | | |
|---|---|---|---|---|
| Apr 27 | Atlanta | 82 | at Indiana | 90 |
| Apr 29 | Atlanta | 97 | at Indiana | 105 |
| May 2 | Indiana | 105 | at Atlanta | 89 |

Indiana won series 3–0.

| | | | | |
|---|---|---|---|---|
| Apr 28 | Boston | 77 | at Orlando | 124 |
| Apr 30 | Boston | 99 | at Orlando | 92 |
| May 3 | Orlando | 82 | at Boston | 77 |
| May 5 | Orlando | 95 | at Boston | 92 |

Orlando won series 3–1.

| | | | | |
|---|---|---|---|---|
| Apr 27 | Cleveland | 79 | at New York | 103 |
| Apr 29 | Cleveland | 90 | at New York | 84 |
| May 1 | New York | 83 | at Cleveland | 81 |
| May 4 | New York | 93 | at Cleveland | 80 |

New York won series 3–1.

| | | | | |
|---|---|---|---|---|
| Apr 28 | Chicago | 108 | at Charlotte | 100* |
| Apr 30 | Chicago | 89 | at Charlotte | 106 |
| May 2 | Charlotte | 80 | at Chicago | 103 |
| May 4 | Charlotte | 84 | at Chicago | 85 |

Chicago won series 3–1.

## Western Conference First Round

| | | | | |
|---|---|---|---|---|
| Apr 28 | Denver | 88 | at San Antonio | 104 |
| Apr 30 | Denver | 96 | at San Antonio | 122 |
| May 2 | San Antonio | 99 | at Denver | 95 |

San Antonio won series 3–0.

| | | | | |
|---|---|---|---|---|
| Apr 28 | Portland | 102 | at Phoenix | 129 |
| Apr 30 | Portland | 94 | at Phoenix | 103 |
| May 2 | Phoenix | 117 | at Portland | 109 |

Phoenix won series 3–0.

| | | | | |
|---|---|---|---|---|
| Apr 27 | Houston | 100 | at Utah | 102 |
| Apr 29 | Houston | 140 | at Utah | 126 |
| May 3 | Utah | 95 | at Houston | 82 |
| May 5 | Utah | 106 | at Houston | 123 |
| May 7 | Houston | 95 | at Utah | 91 |

Houston won series 3–2.

| | | | | |
|---|---|---|---|---|
| Apr 27 | LA Lakers | 71 | at Seattle | 96 |
| Apr 29 | LA Lakers | 84 | at Seattle | 82 |
| May 1 | Seattle | 101 | at LA Lakers | 105 |
| May 4 | Seattle | 110 | at LA Lakers | 114 |

LA Lakers won series 3–1.

## Eastern Conference Semifinals

| | | | | |
|---|---|---|---|---|
| May 7 | Indiana | 107 | at New York | 105 |
| May 9 | Indiana | 77 | at New York | 96 |
| May 11 | New York | 95 | at Indiana | 97* |
| May 13 | New York | 84 | at Indiana | 98 |
| May 17 | Indiana | 95 | at New York | 96 |
| May 19 | New York | 92 | at Indiana | 82 |
| May 21 | Indiana | 97 | at New York | 95 |

Indiana won series 4–3.

| | | | | |
|---|---|---|---|---|
| May 7 | Chicago | 91 | at Orlando | 94 |
| May 10 | Chicago | 104 | at Orlando | 94 |
| May 12 | Orlando | 110 | at Chicago | 101 |
| May 14 | Orlando | 95 | at Chicago | 106 |
| May 16 | Chicago | 95 | at Orlando | 103 |
| May 18 | Orlando | 108 | at Chicago | 102 |

Orlando won series 4–2.

## Western Conference Semifinals

| | | | | |
|---|---|---|---|---|
| May 6 | LA Lakers | 94 | at San Antonio | 110 |
| May 8 | LA Lakers | 90 | at San Antonio | 97* |
| May 12 | San Antonio | 85 | at LA Lakers | 92 |
| May 14 | San Antonio | 80 | at LA Lakers | 71 |
| May 16 | LA Lakers | 98 | at San Antonio | 96* |
| May 18 | San Antonio | 100 | at LA Lakers | 88 |

San Antonio won series 4–2.

| | | | | |
|---|---|---|---|---|
| May 9 | Houston | 108 | at Phoenix | 130 |
| May 11 | Houston | 94 | at Phoenix | 118 |
| May 13 | Phoenix | 85 | at Houston | 118 |
| May 14 | Phoenix | 114 | at Houston | 110 |
| May 16 | Houston | 103 | at Phoenix | 97* |
| May 18 | Phoenix | 103 | at Houston | 116 |
| May 20 | Houston | 115 | at Phoenix | 114 |

Houston won series 4–3.

## Eastern Conference Finals

| | | | | |
|---|---|---|---|---|
| May 23 | Indiana | 101 | at Orlando | 105 |
| May 25 | Indiana | 114 | at Orlando | 119 |
| May 27 | Orlando | 100 | at Indiana | 105 |
| May 29 | Orlando | 93 | at Indiana | 94 |
| May 31 | Indiana | 106 | at Orlando | 108 |
| June 2 | Orlando | 96 | at Indiana | 123 |
| June 4 | Indiana | 81 | at Orlando | 105 |

Orlando won series 4–3.

## Western Conference Finals

| | | | | |
|---|---|---|---|---|
| May 22 | Houston | 94 | at San Antonio | 93 |
| May 24 | Houston | 106 | at San Antonio | 96 |
| May 26 | San Antonio | 107 | at Houston | 102 |
| May 28 | San Antonio | 103 | at Houston | 81 |
| May 30 | Houston | 111 | at San Antonio | 90 |
| June 1 | San Antonio | 95 | at Houston | 100 |

Houston won series 4–2.

## Finals

| | | | | |
|---|---|---|---|---|
| June 7 | Houston | 120 | at Orlando | 118* |
| June 9 | Houston | 117 | at Orlando | 106 |
| June 11 | Orlando | 103 | at Houston | 106 |
| June 15 | Orlando | 101 | at Houston | 113 |

Houston won series 4–0.

* Overtime game.

# NBA Finals Composite Box Score

## HOUSTON ROCKETS

| Player | GP | Field Goals | | 3-Pt FG | | Free Throws | | Rebounds | | A | Stl | TO | BS | Avg | Hi |
|---|---|---|---|---|---|---|---|---|---|---|---|---|---|---|---|
| | | FGM | Pct | FGM | FGA | FTM | Pct | Off | Total | | | | | | |
| Olajuwon | 4 | 56 | 48.3 | 1 | 1 | 18 | 69.2 | 11 | 46 | 22 | 8 | 11 | 8 | 32.8 | 35 |
| Drexler | 4 | 27 | 45.0 | 2 | 13 | 30 | 78.9 | 13 | 38 | 27 | 4 | 6 | 1 | 21.5 | 25 |
| Horry | 4 | 23 | 43.4 | 11 | 29 | 14 | 66.7 | 9 | 40 | 15 | 12 | 5 | 9 | 17.8 | 21 |
| Elie | 4 | 24 | 64.9 | 8 | 14 | 9 | 90.0 | 4 | 17 | 13 | 8 | 7 | 0 | 16.3 | 22 |
| Cassell | 4 | 15 | 42.9 | 7 | 15 | 20 | 83.3 | 1 | 7 | 12 | 7 | 6 | 0 | 12 | 31 |
| Smith | 4 | 11 | 37.9 | 8 | 19 | 0 | — | 2 | 7 | 16 | 1 | 2 | 0 | 7.5 | 23 |
| Brown | 4 | 5 | 45.4 | 0 | 1 | 2 | 100.0 | 3 | 11 | 0 | 0 | 1 | 2 | 3.0 | 8 |
| Jones | 4 | 1 | 50.0 | 0 | 0 | 2 | 100.0 | 1 | 7 | 0 | 0 | 1 | 0 | 1.0 | 2 |
| Chilcutt | 3 | 0 | — | 0 | 0 | 0 | — | 0 | 0 | 0 | 0 | 0 | 0 | 0.0 | 0 |
| Total | 4 | 162 | 47.2 | 37 | 92 | 95 | 77.2 | 44 | 173 | 105 | 40 | 39 | 20 | 114.0 | 120 |

## ORLANDO MAGIC

| Player | GP | Field Goals | | 3-Pt FG | | Free Throws | | Rebounds | | A | Stl | TO | BS | Avg | Hi |
|---|---|---|---|---|---|---|---|---|---|---|---|---|---|---|---|
| | | FGM | Pct | FGM | FGA | FTM | Pct | Off | Total | | | | | | |
| O'Neal | 4 | 44 | 59.5 | 0 | 0 | 24 | 57.1 | 11 | 50 | 25 | 1 | 21 | 10 | 28.0 | 33 |
| Hardaway | 4 | 35 | 50.0 | 11 | 24 | 21 | 91.3 | 6 | 19 | 32 | 5 | 14 | 3 | 25.5 | 32 |
| Grant | 4 | 25 | 53.2 | 0 | 0 | 4 | 80.0 | 19 | 48 | 6 | 2 | 6 | 2 | 13.5 | 18 |
| Shaw | 4 | 20 | 42.5 | 10 | 28 | 0 | — | 4 | 13 | 13 | 2 | 8 | 1 | 12.5 | 17 |
| Anderson | 4 | 18 | 36.0 | 10 | 31 | 3 | 30.0 | 6 | 34 | 17 | 7 | 5 | 2 | 12.3 | 26 |
| Scott | 4 | 13 | 30.9 | 7 | 27 | 9 | 100.0 | 2 | 14 | 9 | 4 | 7 | 1 | 10.5 | 14 |
| Bowie | 4 | 6 | 60.0 | 1 | 2 | 0 | — | 0 | 2 | 6 | 0 | 2 | 1 | 3.3 | 5 |
| Turner | 4 | 2 | 20.0 | 2 | 6 | 0 | — | 0 | 4 | 2 | 0 | 1 | 0 | 1.5 | 3 |
| Royal | 1 | 0 | — | 0 | 0 | 0 | — | 0 | 0 | 0 | 0 | 0 | 0 | 0.0 | 0 |
| Total | 4 | 163 | 46.6 | 41 | 118 | 61 | 68.5 | 48 | 184 | 110 | 21 | 64 | 20 | 107.0 | 118 |

# NBA Finals Box Scores

## Game 1

### HOUSTON 120

| HOUSTON | Min | FG M-A | FT M-A | Reb O-T | A | PF | S | TO | TP |
|---|---|---|---|---|---|---|---|---|---|
| Horry | 47 | 7-18 | 1-2 | 0-8 | 3 | 4 | 3 | 0 | 19 |
| Elie | 39 | 7-11 | 3-4 | 2-5 | 4 | 2 | 3 | 4 | 18 |
| Olajuwon | 48 | 13-26 | 5-7 | 1-6 | 7 | 5 | 2 | 3 | 31 |
| Drexler | 48 | 7-19 | 8-8 | 4-11 | 7 | 3 | 1 | 1 | 23 |
| Smith | 42 | 8-13 | 0-0 | 0-3 | 9 | 3 | 0 | 1 | 23 |
| Cassell | 11 | 1-3 | 1-2 | 0-1 | 1 | 2 | 0 | 2 | 4 |
| Brown | 14 | 1-5 | 0-0 | 2-5 | 0 | 0 | 0 | 0 | 2 |
| Jones | 15 | 0-1 | 0-0 | 0-2 | 0 | 2 | 0 | 0 | 0 |
| Chilcutt | 1 | 0-0 | 0-0 | 0-0 | 0 | 0 | 0 | 0 | 0 |
| Totals | 265 | 44-96 | 18-23 | 9-41 | 31 | 21 | 9 | 11 | 120 |

Percentages: FG—.458, FT—.783. 3-pt goals: 14-32, .438 (Horry 4-10, Elie 1-2, Drexler 1-6, Smith 7-11, Cassell 1-2, C. Brown 0-1). Team rebounds: 10. Blocked shots: 10 (Horry 5, Olajuwon 4, Drexler).

### ORLANDO 118

| ORLANDO | Min | FG M-A | FT M-A | Reb O-T | A | PF | S | TO | TP |
|---|---|---|---|---|---|---|---|---|---|
| Scott | 38 | 3-10 | 3-3 | 0-4 | 5 | 4 | 1 | 1 | 11 |
| Grant | 47 | 7-15 | 1-1 | 7-16 | 2 | 2 | 0 | 1 | 15 |
| O'Neal | 44 | 10-16 | 6-9 | 3-16 | 9 | 5 | 0 | 7 | 26 |
| Anderson | 45 | 11-25 | 3-3 | 2-4 | 5 | 3 | 2 | 3 | 26 |
| Hardaway | 50 | 9-18 | 0-4 | 3-11 | 5 | 0 | 3 | 2 | 22 |
| Turner | 14 | 1-4 | 0-0 | 0-1 | 1 | 1 | 0 | 1 | 3 |
| Shaw | 22 | 5-12 | 0-0 | 1-5 | 4 | 4 | 1 | 2 | 11 |
| Bowie | 4 | 2-3 | 0-0 | 0-0 | 1 | 3 | 0 | 1 | 4 |
| Royal | 1 | 0-0 | 0-0 | 0-0 | 0 | 0 | 0 | 0 | 0 |
| Totals | 265 | 48-103 | 13-20 | 16-57 | 32 | 22 | 7 | 18 | 118 |

Percentages: FG—.466, FT—.650. 3-pt goals: 9-30, .300 (Scott 2-7, Anderson 1-6, Hardaway 4-10, Turner 1-2, Shaw 1-5). Team rebounds: 11. Blocked shots: 6 (O'Neal 3, Grant, Hardaway, Anderson). A: 16,610. Officials: J. Crawford, Bavetta, Javie.

# THEY SAID IT

*Gary Payton, the Seattle SuperSonics' $2.7 million-a-year guard, on the most recent NBA collective bargaining proposal: "People would have to cut their lifestyle, and they'd live like penny-pinchers."*

# NBA Finals Box Scores (Cont.)

## Game 2

### HOUSTON 117

| HOUSTON | Min | FG M-A | FT M-A | Reb O-T | A | PF | S | TO | TP |
|---|---|---|---|---|---|---|---|---|---|
| Elie | 41 | 2-6 | 4-4 | 2-7 | 4 | 2 | 1 | 0 | 8 |
| Horry | 48 | 2-10 | 2-2 | 2-10 | 3 | 7 | 1 | 1 | 11 |
| Olajuwon | 42 | 14-30 | 6-9 | 3-11 | 2 | 5 | 1 | 3 | 34 |
| Drexler | 32 | 7-10 | 9-12 | 1-5 | 5 | 4 | 7 | 1 | 23 |
| Smith | 19 | 0-2 | 0-0 | 0-0 | 1 | 1 | 0 | 1 | 0 |
| Brown | 12 | 4-5 | 0-0 | 1-2 | 0 | 1 | 0 | 1 | 8 |
| Jones | 15 | 0-0 | 2-2 | 0-2 | 0 | 5 | 0 | 0 | 2 |
| Cassell | 30 | 8-12 | 11-12 | 0-1 | 3 | 4 | 3 | 2 | 34 |
| Chilcutt | 1 | 0-0 | 0-0 | 0-0 | 0 | 0 | 0 | 0 | 0 |
| Totals | 240 | 39-75 | 34-41 | 9-38 | 18 | 23 | 13 | 9 | 117 |

Percentages: FG—.520, FT—.829. 3-pt goals: 5-14,
.357 (Elie 0-2, Horry 1-5, Smith 0-1, Cassell 4-6). Team
rebounds: 6. Blocked shots: 7 (Olajuwon 4, Horry 2,
Brown).

### ORLANDO 106

| ORLANDO | Min | FG M-A | FT M-A | Reb O-T | A | PF | S | TO | TP |
|---|---|---|---|---|---|---|---|---|---|
| Scott | 35 | 3-10 | 1-1 | 1-3 | 1 | 2 | 0 | 1 | 9 |
| Grant | 40 | 4-7 | 2-2 | 5-10 | 1 | 5 | 0 | 0 | 10 |
| O'Neal | 45 | 12-22 | 9-14 | 3-12 | 7 | 5 | 0 | 4 | 33 |
| Hardaway | 44 | 12-21 | 4-5 | 2-5 | 8 | 3 | 0 | 5 | 32 |
| Anderson | 43 | 4-13 | 2-4 | 1-6 | 5 | 2 | 2 | 2 | 11 |
| Shaw | 19 | 3-8 | 0-0 | 2-3 | 2 | 3 | 1 | 2 | 8 |
| Turner | 11 | 1-4 | 0-0 | 0-1 | 0 | 4 | 0 | 0 | 3 |
| Bowie | 3 | 0-0 | 0-0 | 0-1 | 0 | 2 | 0 | 1 | 0 |
| Totals | 240 | 39-85 | 18-26 | 14-41 | 24 | 26 | 3 | 15 | 106 |

Percentages: FG—.459, FT—.692. 3-pt goals: 10-26,
.385 (Scott 2-7, Hardaway 4-6, Anderson 1-5, Shaw
2-5, Turner 1-3). Team rebounds: 12. Blocked shots:
1 (Anderson).
A: 16,610. Officials: E. T. Rush, Hollins, D. Crawford.

## Game 3

### ORLANDO 103

| ORLANDO | Min | FG M-A | FT M-A | Reb O-T | A | PF | S | TO | TP |
|---|---|---|---|---|---|---|---|---|---|
| Grant | 40 | 9-13 | 0-0 | 3-10 | 1 | 3 | 1 | 3 | 18 |
| Scott | 39 | 2-11 | 3-3 | 1-6 | 0 | 5 | 1 | 1 | 8 |
| O'Neal | 45 | 11-17 | 6-11 | 2-10 | 6 | 3 | 1 | 4 | 28 |
| Anderson | 37 | 4-14 | 0-0 | 0-10 | 3 | 3 | 0 | 0 | 12 |
| Hardaway | 44 | 4-10 | 10-11 | 1-4 | 14 | 4 | 1 | 3 | 19 |
| Shaw | 20 | 6-12 | 0-0 | 0-1 | 3 | 3 | 0 | 1 | 14 |
| Turner | 11 | 0-1 | 0-0 | 0-0 | 1 | 1 | 0 | 0 | 0 |
| Bowie | 7 | 2-3 | 0-0 | 0-0 | 2 | 1 | 0 | 0 | 4 |
| Totals | 240 | 38-81 | 19-25 | 7-14 | 30 | 23 | 4 | 12 | 103 |

Percentages: FG—.469, FT—.760. 3-pt goals: 8-31,
.258 (Scott 1-9, Anderson 4-12, Hardaway 1-4, Shaw
2-5, Turner 0-1). Team rebounds: 7. Blocked shots: 6
(O'Neal 3, Hardaway 2, Grant).

### HOUSTON 106

| HOUSTON | Min | FG M-A | FT M-A | Reb O-T | A | PF | S | TO | TP |
|---|---|---|---|---|---|---|---|---|---|
| Elie | 38 | 6-9 | 2-2 | 0-2 | 3 | 2 | 0 | 1 | 17 |
| Horry | 46 | 6-11 | 6-8 | 2-9 | 4 | 2 | 0 | 2 | 20 |
| Olajuwon | 45 | 14-30 | 3-5 | 4-14 | 7 | 4 | 2 | 0 | 31 |
| Drexler | 41 | 9-18 | 6-10 | 5-13 | 7 | 4 | 0 | 2 | 25 |
| Smith | 22 | 1-7 | 0-0 | 0-2 | 3 | 2 | 1 | 0 | 2 |
| Jones | 12 | 0-0 | 0-0 | 0-0 | 0 | 4 | 0 | 1 | 0 |
| Cassell | 26 | 3-9 | 2-3 | 0-4 | 4 | 2 | 3 | 2 | 9 |
| Chilcutt | 1 | 0-0 | 0-0 | 0-0 | 0 | 0 | 0 | 0 | 0 |
| Brown | 9 | 0-0 | 2-2 | 0-4 | 0 | 1 | 0 | 0 | 2 |
| Totals | 240 | 39-84 | 21-30 | 11-46 | 28 | 21 | 7 | 10 | 106 |

Percentages: FG—.464, FT—.700. 3-pt goals: 7-19,
.368 (Elie 3-4, Horry 2-5, Drexler 1-3, Smith 0-4, Cassell
1-3). Team rebounds: 9. Blocked shots: 2 (Horry 2).
A: 16,611. Officials: Evans, Mathis, Salvatore.

## Game 4

### ORLANDO 101

| ORLANDO | Min | FG M-A | FT M-A | Reb O-T | A | PF | S | TO | TP |
|---|---|---|---|---|---|---|---|---|---|
| Grant | 41 | 5-12 | 1-2 | 4-12 | 2 | 3 | 1 | 2 | 11 |
| Scott | 38 | 5-11 | 2-2 | 0-1 | 3 | 1 | 2 | 4 | 14 |
| O'Neal | 46 | 11-9 | 3-8 | 3-12 | 3 | 5 | 0 | 6 | 25 |
| Anderson | 31 | 1-5 | 1-2 | 2-7 | 4 | 4 | 3 | 0 | 4 |
| Hardaway | 42 | 8-14 | 4-4 | 1-6 | 5 | 5 | 1 | 4 | 25 |
| Shaw | 23 | 6-15 | 0-0 | 1-4 | 4 | 5 | 0 | 3 | 17 |
| Turner | 7 | 0-1 | 0-0 | 0-2 | 0 | 0 | 0 | 0 | 0 |
| Bowie | 12 | 2-4 | 0-0 | 0-1 | 3 | 3 | 0 | 0 | 5 |
| Totals | 240 | 38-81 | 11-18 | 11-45 | 24 | 26 | 7 | 19 | 101 |

Percentages: FG—.469, FT—.611. 3-pt goals: 4-31,
.452 (Scott 2-6, Anderson 1-4, Hardaway 5-8, Shaw
5-11, Bowie 1-2). Team rebounds: 6. Blocked shots:
7 (O'Neal 4, Scott, Shaw, Bowie).

### HOUSTON 113

| HOUSTON | Min | FG M-A | FT M-A | Reb O-T | A | PF | S | TO | TP |
|---|---|---|---|---|---|---|---|---|---|
| Elie | 43 | 9-11 | 0-0 | 0-3 | 2 | 3 | 4 | 2 | 22 |
| Horry | 46 | 6-14 | 5-9 | 5-13 | 5 | 2 | 1 | 2 | 21 |
| Olajuwon | 44 | 15-30 | 4-5 | 3-15 | 6 | 4 | 3 | 4 | 35 |
| Drexler | 41 | 4-13 | 7-8 | 3-9 | 8 | 3 | 2 | 3 | 15 |
| Smith | 22 | 2-7 | 0-0 | 2-2 | 3 | 1 | 0 | 0 | 5 |
| Cassell | 26 | 4-8 | 6-7 | 1-3 | 4 | 1 | 1 | 0 | 13 |
| Brown | 3 | 0-1 | 0-0 | 0-0 | 0 | 0 | 0 | 1 | 2 |
| Jones | 15 | 1-1 | 0-0 | 1-3 | 0 | 4 | 0 | 0 | 2 |
| Totals | 240 | 40-88 | 22-29 | 15-48 | 28 | 18 | 11 | 11 | 113 |

Percentages: FG—.455, FT—.759. 3-pt goals: 11-27,
.407 (Elie 4-6, Horry 4-9, Olajuwon 1-1, Drexler 0-4,
Smith 1-3, Cassell 1-4). Team rebounds: 6. Blocked
shots: 1 (Brown).
A: 16,611. Officials: J. Crawford, Kersey, Oakes.

# NBA Awards

## All-NBA Teams

| FIRST TEAM | SECOND TEAM | THIRD TEAM |
|---|---|---|
| G John Stockton, Utah | Mitch Richmond, Sacramento | Clyde Drexler, Houston |
| G Anfernee Hardaway, Orlando | Gary Payton, Seattle | Reggie Miller, Indiana |
| C David Robinson, San Antonio | Shaquille O'Neal, Orlando | Hakeem Olajuwon, Houston |
| F Karl Malone, Utah | Charles Barkley, Phoenix | Dennis Rodman, San Antonio |
| F Scottie Pippen, Chicago | Shawn Kemp, Seattle | Detlef Schrempf, Seattle |

## Master Lock NBA All-Defensive Teams

| FIRST TEAM | SECOND TEAM |
|---|---|
| G Gary Payton, Seattle | John Stockton, Utah |
| G Mookie Blaylock, Atlanta | Nate McMillan, Seattle |
| C David Robinson, San Antonio | Dikembe Mutombo, Denver |
| F Scottie Pippen, Chicago | Horace Grant, Orlando |
| F Dennis Rodman, San Antonio | Derrick McKey, Indiana |

## All-Rookie Teams
### (Chosen Without Regard to Position)

| FIRST TEAM | SECOND TEAM |
|---|---|
| Jason Kidd, Dallas | Juwan Howard, Washington |
| Grant Hill, Detroit | Eric Montross, Boston |
| Glenn Robinson, Milwaukee | Wesley Person, Phoenix |
| Eddie Jones, LA Lakers | Jalen Rose, Denver |
| Brian Grant, Sacramento | Donyell Marshall, Golden State |
| | Sharone Wright, Philadelphia |

## Dressing Down

At first glance Houston Rocket center Hakeem Olajuwon's signing of a new sneaker deal may not seem like big news. But in a significant break from the established practice of superstar athletes, Olajuwon's shoe contract isn't with Nike, Reebok or any of the other "top-end" manufacturers that produce the $100-and-up, bells-and-whistles models that young people hanker for. The NBA's reigning MVP has instead agreed to a deal with Spalding under which he will endorse a line of shoes retailing for no more than $60 a pair and available in discount stores like Wal-Mart, Payless and Target, where Americans buy close to half of the 400 million pairs of athletic shoes sold in the U.S. each year.

Olajuwon, who for the Rockets' seven games leading up to the All-Star break wore the prototype of a model scheduled to reach the stores in the fall, signed the contract in part because he's alarmed at the values he sometimes sees youngsters espouse. "A lot of kids just go with the name brand," he says. "They bother their parents for "$150 shoes." A cheaper shoe needn't impair performance, he believes—and he demonstrated that in those seven games, shooting 56.8% while in Spaldings, compared with his season average of 49.7%. Of course, Hakeem would still be the Dream even in Birkenstocks. It's nonetheless refreshing when a star athlete has the ability to see the big picture.

# NBA Individual Leaders

## Scoring

| | GP | Pts | Avg |
|---|---|---|---|
| Shaquille O'Neal, Orl | 79 | 2315 | 29.3 |
| Hakeem Olajuwon, Hou | 72 | 2005 | 27.9 |
| David Robinson, SA | 81 | 2238 | 27.6 |
| Karl Malone, Utah | 82 | 2187 | 26.7 |
| Jimmy Jackson, Dal | 51 | 1309 | 25.7 |
| Jamal Mashburn, Dal | 80 | 1926 | 24.1 |
| Patrick Ewing, NY | 79 | 1886 | 23.9 |
| Charles Barkley, Phoe | 68 | 1561 | 23.0 |
| Mitch Richmond, Sac | 82 | 1867 | 22.8 |
| Glenn Rice, Mia | 82 | 1831 | 22.3 |

## Assists

| | GP | Assists | Avg |
|---|---|---|---|
| John Stockton, Utah | 82 | 1011 | 12.3 |
| Kenny Anderson, NJ | 72 | 680 | 9.4 |
| Tim Hardaway, GS | 62 | 578 | 9.3 |
| Rod Strickland, Por | 64 | 562 | 8.8 |
| Tyrone Bogues, Char | 78 | 675 | 8.7 |
| Nick Van Exel, LA Lakers | 80 | 660 | 8.3 |
| Avery Johnson, SA | 82 | 670 | 8.2 |
| Pooh Richardson, LA Clippers | 80 | 632 | 7.9 |
| Mookie Blaylock, Atl | 80 | 616 | 7.7 |
| Jason Kidd, Dal | 79 | 607 | 7.7 |

## Free-Throw Percentage

| | FTA | FTM | Pct |
|---|---|---|---|
| Spud Webb, Sac | 242 | 226 | 93.4 |
| Mark Price, Clev | 162 | 148 | 91.4 |
| Dana Barros, Phi | 386 | 347 | 89.9 |
| Reggie Milller, Ind | 427 | 383 | 89.7 |
| Tyrone Bogues, Char | 180 | 160 | 88.9 |
| Scott Skiles, Was | 202 | 179 | 88.6 |
| Mahmoud Abdul-Rauf, Den | 156 | 138 | 88.5 |
| B.J. Armstrong, Chi | 233 | 206 | 88.4 |
| Jeff Hornacek, Utah | 322 | 284 | 88.2 |
| Keith Jennings, GS | 153 | 134 | 87.6 |

## Steals

| | GP | Steals | Avg |
|---|---|---|---|
| Scottie Pippen, Chi | 79 | 232 | 2.94 |
| Mookie Blaylock, Atl | 80 | 200 | 2.50 |
| Gary Payton, Sea | 82 | 204 | 2.49 |
| John Stockton, Utah | 82 | 194 | 2.37 |
| Nate McMillan, Sea | 80 | 165 | 2.06 |
| Eddie Jones, LA Lakers | 64 | 131 | 2.05 |
| Rod Strickland, Por | 64 | 123 | 1.92 |
| Jason Kidd, Dal | 79 | 151 | 1.91 |
| Elliot Perry, Pho | 82 | 155 | 1.89 |
| Hakeem Olajuwon, Hou | 72 | 133 | 1.85 |

## Rebounds

| | GP | Reb | Avg |
|---|---|---|---|
| Dennis Rodman, SA | 49 | 823 | 16.8 |
| Dikembe Mutombo, Den | 82 | 1029 | 12.6 |
| Shaquille O'Neal, Orl | 79 | 901 | 11.4 |
| Charles Barkley, Pho | 68 | 756 | 11.1 |
| Patrick Ewing, NY | 79 | 867 | 11.0 |
| Tyrone Hill, Cle | 70 | 765 | 10.9 |
| Kevin Willis, Mia | 67 | 732 | 10.9 |
| Shawn Kemp, Sea | 82 | 893 | 10.9 |
| David Robinson, SA | 81 | 872 | 10.8 |
| Hakeem Olajuwon, Hou | 72 | 775 | 10.8 |

## Field-Goal Percentage

| | FGA | FGM | Pct |
|---|---|---|---|
| Chris Gatling, GS | 512 | 324 | 63.3 |
| Shaquille O'Neal, Orl | 1594 | 930 | 58.3 |
| Horace Grant, Orl | 707 | 401 | 56.7 |
| Otis Thorpe, Por | 681 | 385 | 56.5 |
| Dale Davis, Ind | 576 | 324 | 56.3 |
| Gheorghe Muresan, Was | 541 | 303 | 56.0 |
| Dikembe Mutombo, Den | 628 | 349 | 55.6 |
| Danny Manning, Pho | 622 | 340 | 54.7 |
| Shawn Kemp, Sea | 1000 | 545 | 54.5 |
| Olden Polynice, Sea | 691 | 376 | 54.4 |

## Three-Point Field-Goal Percentage

| | FGA | FGM | Pct |
|---|---|---|---|
| Steve Kerr, Chi | 170 | 89 | 52.4 |
| Detlef Schrempf, Sea | 181 | 93 | 51.4 |
| Dana Barros, Phi | 426 | 197 | 46.2 |
| Hubert Davis, NY | 288 | 131 | 45.5 |
| John Stockton, Utah | 227 | 102 | 44.9 |
| Hersey Hawkins, Char | 298 | 131 | 44.0 |
| Wesley Person, Pho | 266 | 116 | 43.6 |
| Kenny Smith, Hou | 331 | 142 | 42.9 |
| Dell Curry, Char | 361 | 154 | 42.7 |
| B.J. Armstrong, Chi | 253 | 108 | 42.7 |

## Blocked Shots

| | GP | BS | Avg |
|---|---|---|---|
| Dikembe Mutombo, Den | 82 | 321 | 3.91 |
| Hakeem Olajuwon, Hou | 72 | 242 | 3.36 |
| Shawn Bradley, Phi | 82 | 274 | 3.34 |
| David Robinson, SA | 81 | 262 | 3.23 |
| Alonzo Mourning, Char | 77 | 225 | 2.92 |
| Shaquille O'Neal, Orl | 79 | 192 | 2.43 |
| Vlade Divac, LA Lakers | 80 | 174 | 2.18 |
| Patrick Ewing, NY | 79 | 159 | 2.01 |
| Bo Outlaw, LA Clippers | 81 | 151 | 1.86 |
| Oliver Miller, Det | 64 | 116 | 1.81 |

# NBA Team Statistics

## Offense

| Team | Field Goals FGM | Pct | 3-Pt Field Goals 3FGM | Pct | Free Throws FTM | Pct | Rebounds Off | Total | A | Stl | Scoring Avg |
|------|-----|-----|------|-----|-----|-----|-----|-------|---|-----|-----|
| Orlando | 3460 | 50.2 | 523 | 37.0 | 1648 | 66.9 | 1149 | 3606 | 2281 | 672 | 110.9 |
| Phoenix | 3356 | 48.2 | 584 | 36.9 | 1777 | 75.6 | 1027 | 3430 | 2198 | 687 | 110.6 |
| Seattle | 3310 | 49.1 | 491 | 37.6 | 1944 | 75.8 | 1068 | 3405 | 2115 | 917 | 110.4 |
| San Antonio | 3236 | 48.4 | 434 | 37.5 | 1836 | 73.8 | 1029 | 3690 | 1919 | 656 | 106.6 |
| Utah | 3243 | 51.2 | 301 | 37.6 | 1939 | 78.1 | 874 | 3286 | 2256 | 758 | 106.4 |
| Golden State | 3217 | 46.8 | 546 | 34.1 | 1687 | 70.4 | 1101 | 3472 | 2017 | 649 | 105.7 |
| LA Lakers | 3284 | 46.3 | 525 | 35.2 | 1523 | 73.5 | 1126 | 3442 | 2078 | 750 | 105.1 |
| Houston | 3159 | 48.0 | 646 | 36.8 | 1527 | 74.9 | 880 | 3320 | 2060 | 721 | 103.5 |
| Dallas | 3227 | 44.0 | 386 | 32.2 | 1622 | 73.4 | 1514 | 3947 | 1941 | 579 | 103.2 |
| Portland | 3217 | 45.1 | 462 | 36.5 | 1555 | 69.7 | 1352 | 3795 | 1846 | 668 | 103.1 |
| Boston | 3179 | 46.4 | 362 | 36.8 | 1708 | 75.3 | 1156 | 3476 | 1783 | 612 | 102.8 |
| Chicago | 3191 | 47.6 | 443 | 37.3 | 1500 | 72.6 | 1106 | 3400 | 1970 | 797 | 101.5 |
| Denver | 3098 | 47.9 | 413 | 35.6 | 1700 | 73.8 | 1040 | 3442 | 1836 | 660 | 101.3 |
| Miami | 3144 | 46.7 | 436 | 36.9 | 1569 | 73.6 | 1092 | 3364 | 1779 | 662 | 101.1 |
| Charlotte | 3051 | 47.4 | 560 | 39.7 | 1587 | 77.7 | 832 | 3227 | 2072 | 620 | 100.6 |
| Washington | 3176 | 46.0 | 433 | 34.3 | 1457 | 72.4 | 1044 | 3263 | 1749 | 648 | 100.5 |
| Milwaukee | 3022 | 45.9 | 494 | 36.6 | 1608 | 71.2 | 1063 | 3250 | 1737 | 674 | 99.3 |
| Indiana | 2983 | 47.7 | 374 | 38.0 | 1796 | 75.1 | 1051 | 3341 | 1877 | 703 | 99.2 |
| Sacramento | 3025 | 46.8 | 359 | 34.6 | 1647 | 71.1 | 1073 | 3398 | 1824 | 650 | 98.2 |
| New York | 2985 | 46.7 | 532 | 36.8 | 1552 | 73.4 | 929 | 3402 | 2055 | 591 | 98.2 |
| Detroit | 3060 | 46.1 | 494 | 35.4 | 1439 | 74.1 | 958 | 3162 | 1872 | 705 | 98.2 |
| New Jersey | 2939 | 43.6 | 414 | 31.9 | 1750 | 75.9 | 1213 | 3782 | 1884 | 544 | 98.1 |
| LA Clippers | 3060 | 44.4 | 331 | 31.5 | 1476 | 71.0 | 1064 | 3140 | 1805 | 787 | 96.7 |
| Atlanta | 2986 | 44.7 | 539 | 34.1 | 1410 | 72.4 | 1104 | 3376 | 1757 | 738 | 96.6 |
| Philadelphia | 2949 | 44.8 | 355 | 37.9 | 1567 | 73.7 | 1105 | 3335 | 1556 | 643 | 95.4 |
| Minnesota | 2792 | 44.9 | 318 | 31.3 | 1824 | 77.5 | 883 | 2973 | 1780 | 609 | 94.2 |
| Cleveland | 2756 | 44.1 | 398 | 38.5 | 1507 | 76.0 | 1045 | 3282 | 1672 | 630 | 90.5 |

## Defense (Opponent's Statistics)

| Team | Field Goals FGM | Pct | 3-Pt Field Goals 3FGM | Pct | Free Throws FTM | Pct | Rebounds Off | Total | Stl | Scoring Avg | Diff |
|------|-----|-----|------|-----|-----|-----|-----|-------|-----|-----|-----|
| Cleveland | 2803 | 46.1 | 396 | 35.7 | 1364 | 75.7 | 851 | 3097 | 556 | 89.8 | +0.6 |
| New York | 2800 | 43.7 | 397 | 34.1 | 1802 | 73.6 | 1021 | 3338 | 639 | 95.1 | +3.1 |
| Atlanta | 3001 | 46.3 | 420 | 34.7 | 1394 | 72.6 | 1051 | 3442 | 608 | 95.3 | +1.3 |
| Indiana | 2921 | 45.6 | 475 | 36.4 | 1516 | 72.6 | 1048 | 3204 | 691 | 95.5 | +3.7 |
| Chicago | 2923 | 45.7 | 401 | 34.9 | 1682 | 73.8 | 1068 | 3320 | 687 | 96.7 | +4.8 |
| Charlotte | 3088 | 45.4 | 429 | 33.3 | 1375 | 74.0 | 1102 | 3467 | 535 | 97.3 | +3.3 |
| Utah | 2845 | 45.3 | 546 | 38.2 | 1835 | 74.1 | 917 | 3042 | 648 | 98.4 | +8.0 |
| Sacramento | 2964 | 45.3 | 377 | 30.4 | 1833 | 74.1 | 1145 | 3413 | 756 | 99.2 | -1.0 |
| Portland | 2951 | 45.6 | 442 | 37.2 | 1794 | 75.4 | 883 | 3178 | 638 | 99.2 | +3.8 |
| Philadelphia | 3100 | 46.5 | 467 | 36.3 | 1569 | 76.3 | 1143 | 3460 | 712 | 100.4 | -5.1 |
| Denver | 3050 | 45.6 | 419 | 34.7 | 1721 | 75.0 | 1021 | 3228 | 640 | 100.5 | +0.8 |
| San Antonio | 3168 | 45.4 | 426 | 34.1 | 1491 | 71.4 | 1017 | 3320 | 633 | 100.6 | +6.0 |
| New Jersey | 3182 | 46.1 | 440 | 37.4 | 1495 | 72.1 | 1056 | 3491 | 733 | 101.2 | -3.1 |
| Houston | 3202 | 45.3 | 506 | 37.6 | 1407 | 75.1 | 1165 | 3551 | 744 | 101.4 | +2.1 |
| Seattle | 3008 | 45.3 | 520 | 34.3 | 1848 | 73.5 | 1064 | 3271 | 652 | 102.2 | +8.2 |
| Miami | 3092 | 47.1 | 511 | 36.1 | 1732 | 74.0 | 1039 | 3391 | 656 | 102.8 | -1.6 |
| Minnesota | 3088 | 47.4 | 468 | 37.7 | 1820 | 73.1 | 1169 | 3474 | 703 | 103.2 | -9.0 |
| Milwaukee | 3248 | 49.3 | 491 | 39.5 | 1517 | 72.9 | 1014 | 3351 | 770 | 103.7 | -4.4 |
| Orlando | 3242 | 45.7 | 468 | 37.8 | 1560 | 74.1 | 1136 | 3362 | 700 | 103.8 | +7.1 |
| Boston | 3303 | 48.4 | 375 | 35.8 | 1601 | 72.0 | 1064 | 3399 | 653 | 104.7 | -1.9 |
| LA Lakers | 3299 | 46.8 | 456 | 35.2 | 1580 | 70.8 | 1283 | 3757 | 644 | 105.3 | -0.2 |
| Detroit | 3120 | 47.6 | 448 | 36.3 | 1936 | 72.2 | 1147 | 3579 | 693 | 105.5 | -7.3 |
| LA Clippers | 3207 | 49.6 | 388 | 37.0 | 1876 | 75.0 | 1083 | 3619 | 693 | 105.8 | -9.2 |
| Dallas | 3407 | 48.8 | 432 | 36.6 | 1454 | 73.4 | 1053 | 3432 | 722 | 106.1 | -2.9 |
| Washington | 3246 | 48.0 | 438 | 38.3 | 1771 | 76.5 | 1107 | 3628 | 701 | 106.1 | -5.6 |
| Phoenix | 3320 | 47.7 | 525 | 34.0 | 1590 | 74.4 | 1038 | 3469 | 658 | 106.8 | +3.9 |
| Golden State | 3527 | 48.8 | 492 | 35.5 | 1565 | 72.0 | 1196 | 3723 | 865 | 111.1 | -5.4 |

## Atlanta Hawks

| Player | GP | Min | Field Goals | | 3-Pt FG | | Free Throws | | Rebounds | | A | Stl | TO | BS | Avg |
|--------|----|----|----|----|----|----|----|----|----|----|----|----|----|----|----|
| | | | FGM | Pct | FGA | FGM | FTM | Pct | Off | Total | | | | | |
| Blaylock | 80 | 3,069 | 509 | 42.5 | 555 | 199 | 156 | 72.9 | 117 | 393 | 616 | 200 | 242 | 26 | 17.2 |
| Smith | 80 | 2,665 | 428 | 42.6 | 416 | 137 | 312 | 84.1 | 104 | 276 | 274 | 62 | 155 | 33 | 16.3 |
| Augmon | 76 | 2,362 | 397 | 45.3 | 26 | 7 | 252 | 72.8 | 157 | 368 | 197 | 100 | 152 | 47 | 13.9 |
| Norman | 74 | 1,879 | 388 | 45.3 | 285 | 98 | 64 | 45.7 | 103 | 362 | 94 | 34 | 96 | 20 | 12.7 |
| Long | 81 | 2,641 | 342 | 47.8 | 31 | 11 | 244 | 75.1 | 191 | 606 | 131 | 109 | 155 | 34 | 11.6 |
| Ehlo | 49 | 1,166 | 191 | 45.3 | 134 | 51 | 44 | 62.0 | 55 | 147 | 113 | 46 | 73 | 6 | 9.7 |
| Lang | 82 | 2,340 | 320 | 47.3 | 3 | 2 | 152 | 80.9 | 154 | 456 | 72 | 45 | 108 | 144 | 9.7 |
| Corbin | 81 | 1,389 | 205 | 44.2 | 56 | 14 | 78 | 68.4 | 98 | 262 | 67 | 55 | 74 | 16 | 6.2 |
| Anderson | 51 | 622 | 57 | 54.8 | 0 | 0 | 34 | 47.9 | 62 | 188 | 17 | 23 | 32 | 32 | 2.9 |
| Koncak | 62 | 945 | 77 | 41.2 | 36 | 12 | 13 | 54.2 | 23 | 184 | 52 | 36 | 20 | 46 | 2.9 |
| Whatley | 27 | 292 | 24 | 45.3 | 8 | 2 | 20 | 62.5 | 9 | 30 | 54 | 19 | 19 | 0 | 2.6 |
| Les | 24 | 188 | 11 | 28.9 | 23 | 5 | 23 | 85.2 | 6 | 26 | 44 | 4 | 21 | 0 | 2.1 |
| Edwards | 38 | 212 | 22 | 45.8 | 1 | 0 | 23 | 71.9 | 19 | 48 | 13 | 5 | 22 | 4 | 1.8 |
| **Hawks** | 82 | 19,855 | 2,986 | 44.7 | 1,580 | 539 | 1,410 | 72.4 | 1,104 | 3,376 | 1,757 | 738 | 1,221 | 412 | 96.6 |
| **Opponents** | 82 | 19,855 | 3,001 | 46.3 | 1,212 | 420 | 1,394 | 72.6 | 1,051 | 3,442 | 1,733 | 608 | 1,359 | 320 | 95.3 |

## Boston Celtics

| Player | GP | Min | Field Goals | | 3-Pt FG | | Free Throws | | Rebounds | | A | Stl | TO | BS | Avg |
|--------|----|----|----|----|----|----|----|----|----|----|----|----|----|----|----|
| | | | FGM | Pct | FGA | FGM | FTM | Pct | Off | Total | | | | | |
| Wilkins | 77 | 2,423 | 496 | 42.4 | 289 | 112 | 266 | 78.2 | 157 | 401 | 166 | 61 | 173 | 14 | 17.8 |
| Radja | 66 | 2,147 | 450 | 49.0 | 1 | 0 | 233 | 75.9 | 149 | 573 | 111 | 60 | 159 | 86 | 17.2 |
| Brown | 79 | 2,792 | 437 | 44.7 | 327 | 126 | 236 | 85.2 | 63 | 249 | 301 | 110 | 146 | 49 | 15.6 |
| Douglas | 65 | 2,048 | 365 | 47.5 | 82 | 20 | 204 | 68.9 | 48 | 170 | 446 | 80 | 162 | 2 | 14.7 |
| Montross | 78 | 2,315 | 307 | 53.4 | 1 | 0 | 167 | 63.5 | 196 | 566 | 36 | 29 | 112 | 61 | 10.0 |
| Fox | 53 | 1,039 | 169 | 48.1 | 75 | 31 | 95 | 77.2 | 61 | 155 | 139 | 52 | 78 | 19 | 8.8 |
| McDaniel | 68 | 1,430 | 246 | 45.1 | 21 | 6 | 89 | 71.2 | 94 | 300 | 108 | 30 | 89 | 20 | 8.6 |
| Wesley | 51 | 1,380 | 128 | 40.9 | 119 | 51 | 71 | 75.5 | 31 | 117 | 266 | 82 | 87 | 9 | 7.4 |
| Ellison | 55 | 1,083 | 152 | 50.7 | 2 | 0 | 71 | 71.7 | 124 | 309 | 34 | 22 | 76 | 54 | 6.8 |
| Strong | 70 | 1,344 | 149 | 45.3 | 7 | 2 | 141 | 82.0 | 136 | 375 | 44 | 24 | 79 | 13 | 6.3 |
| Minor | 63 | 945 | 155 | 51.5 | 12 | 2 | 65 | 83.3 | 49 | 137 | 66 | 32 | 44 | 16 | 6.0 |
| Dawson | 2 | 13 | 3 | 37.5 | 3 | 1 | 1 | 100.0 | 0 | 3 | 1 | 0 | 2 | 0 | 4.0 |
| Earl | 30 | 206 | 26 | 38.2 | 0 | 0 | 14 | 48.3 | 19 | 45 | 2 | 6 | 14 | 8 | 2.2 |
| Humphries | 18 | 201 | 8 | 23.5 | 4 | 2 | 2 | 50.0 | 4 | 13 | 19 | 9 | 17 | 0 | 1.1 |
| **Celtics** | 82 | 19,805 | 3,179 | 46.4 | 984 | 362 | 1,708 | 75.3 | 1,156 | 3,476 | 1,783 | 612 | 1,305 | 361 | 102.8 |
| **Opponents** | 82 | 19,805 | 3,303 | 48.4 | 1,047 | 375 | 1,601 | 72.0 | 1,064 | 3,399 | 1,999 | 653 | 1,232 | 454 | 104.7 |

## Charlotte Hornets

| Player | GP | Min | Field Goals | | 3-Pt FG | | Free Throws | | Rebounds | | A | Stl | TO | BS | Avg |
|--------|----|----|----|----|----|----|----|----|----|----|----|----|----|----|----|
| | | | FGM | Pct | FGA | FGM | FTM | Pct | Off | Total | | | | | |
| Mourning | 77 | 2,941 | 571 | 51.9 | 34 | 11 | 490 | 76.1 | 200 | 761 | 111 | 49 | 241 | 225 | 21.3 |
| Johnson | 81 | 3,234 | 585 | 48.0 | 210 | 81 | 274 | 77.4 | 190 | 585 | 369 | 78 | 207 | 28 | 18.8 |
| Hawkins | 82 | 2,731 | 390 | 48.2 | 298 | 131 | 261 | 86.7 | 60 | 314 | 262 | 122 | 150 | 18 | 14.3 |
| Curry | 69 | 1,718 | 343 | 44.1 | 361 | 154 | 95 | 85.6 | 41 | 168 | 113 | 55 | 98 | 18 | 13.6 |
| Burrell | 65 | 2,014 | 277 | 46.7 | 235 | 96 | 100 | 69.4 | 96 | 368 | 161 | 75 | 85 | 40 | 11.5 |
| Bogues | 78 | 2,629 | 348 | 47.7 | 30 | 6 | 160 | 88.9 | 51 | 257 | 675 | 103 | 132 | 0 | 11.1 |
| Adams | 29 | 443 | 67 | 45.3 | 81 | 29 | 25 | 83.3 | 6 | 29 | 95 | 23 | 26 | 1 | 6.5 |
| Gattison | 21 | 409 | 47 | 47.0 | 1 | 0 | 31 | 60.8 | 21 | 75 | 17 | 7 | 22 | 15 | 6.0 |
| Sutton | 53 | 690 | 94 | 40.9 | 115 | 43 | 32 | 71.1 | 8 | 56 | 91 | 33 | 51 | 2 | 5.0 |
| Parish | 81 | 1,352 | 159 | 42.7 | 0 | 0 | 71 | 70.3 | 93 | 350 | 44 | 27 | 66 | 36 | 4.8 |
| Bennett | 3 | 46 | 6 | 46.2 | 9 | 2 | 0 | — | 0 | 2 | 4 | 0 | 3 | 0 | 4.7 |
| Hancock | 46 | 424 | 68 | 56.2 | 3 | 1 | 16 | 41.0 | 14 | 53 | 30 | 19 | 30 | 4 | 3.3 |
| Wingate | 52 | 515 | 50 | 41.0 | 22 | 4 | 18 | 75.0 | 11 | 60 | 56 | 19 | 27 | 6 | 2.3 |
| Wolf | 63 | 583 | 38 | 46.9 | 6 | 2 | 12 | 75.0 | 34 | 129 | 37 | 9 | 22 | 6 | 1.4 |
| **Hornets** | 82 | 19,805 | 3,051 | 47.4 | 1,409 | 560 | 1,587 | 77.7 | 832 | 3,227 | 2,072 | 620 | 1,224 | 399 | 100.6 |
| **Opponents** | 82 | 19,805 | 3,088 | 45.4 | 1,289 | 429 | 1,375 | 74.0 | 1,102 | 3,467 | 1,898 | 535 | 1,216 | 368 | 97.3 |

## Chicago Bulls

| Player | GP | Min | Field Goals | | 3-Pt FG | | Free Throws | | Rebounds | | A | Stl | TO | BS | Avg |
|--------|----|-----|-----|-----|-----|-----|-----|-----|-----|-------|---|-----|----|----|-----|
| | | | FGM | Pct | FGA | FGM | FTM | Pct | Off | Total | | | | | |
| Jordan | 17 | 668 | 166 | 41.1 | 32 | 16 | 109 | 80.1 | 25 | 117 | 90 | 30 | 35 | 13 | 26.9 |
| Pippen | 79 | 3,014 | 634 | 48.0 | 316 | 109 | 315 | 71.6 | 175 | 639 | 409 | 232 | 271 | 89 | 21.4 |
| Kukoc | 81 | 2,584 | 487 | 50.4 | 198 | 62 | 235 | 74.8 | 155 | 440 | 372 | 102 | 165 | 16 | 15.7 |
| Armstrong | 82 | 2,577 | 418 | 46.8 | 253 | 108 | 206 | 88.4 | 25 | 186 | 244 | 84 | 103 | 8 | 14.0 |
| Kerr | 82 | 1,839 | 261 | 52.7 | 170 | 89 | 63 | 77.8 | 20 | 119 | 151 | 44 | 48 | 3 | 8.2 |
| Perdue | 78 | 1,592 | 254 | 55.3 | 1 | 0 | 113 | 58.2 | 211 | 522 | 90 | 26 | 116 | 56 | 8.0 |
| Harper | 77 | 1,536 | 209 | 42.6 | 110 | 31 | 81 | 61.8 | 51 | 180 | 157 | 97 | 100 | 27 | 6.9 |
| Longley | 55 | 1,001 | 135 | 44.7 | 2 | 0 | 88 | 82.2 | 82 | 263 | 73 | 24 | 86 | 45 | 6.5 |
| Wennington | 73 | 956 | 156 | 49.2 | 4 | 0 | 51 | 81.0 | 64 | 190 | 40 | 22 | 39 | 17 | 5.0 |
| Myers | 71 | 1,270 | 119 | 41.5 | 39 | 10 | 70 | 61.4 | 57 | 139 | 148 | 58 | 88 | 15 | 4.5 |
| Krystkowiak | 19 | 287 | 28 | 38.9 | 0 | 0 | 27 | 90.0 | 19 | 59 | 26 | 9 | 25 | 2 | 4.4 |
| Buechler | 57 | 605 | 90 | 49.2 | 48 | 15 | 22 | 56.4 | 36 | 98 | 50 | 24 | 30 | 12 | 3.8 |
| Blount | 68 | 889 | 100 | 47.6 | 2 | 0 | 38 | 56.7 | 107 | 240 | 60 | 26 | 59 | 33 | 3.5 |
| Simpkins | 59 | 586 | 78 | 42.4 | 0 | 0 | 50 | 69.4 | 60 | 151 | 37 | 10 | 45 | 7 | 3.5 |
| **Bulls** | **82** | **19,830** | **3,191** | **47.6** | **1,187** | **443** | **1,500** | **72.6** | **1,106** | **3,400** | **1,970** | **797** | **1,297** | **352** | **101.5** |
| **Opponents** | **82** | **19,830** | **2,923** | **45.7** | **1,150** | **401** | **1,682** | **73.8** | **1,068** | **3,320** | **1,713** | **687** | **1,485** | **369** | **96.7** |

## Cleveland Cavaliers

| Player | GP | Min | Field Goals | | 3-Pt FG | | Free Throws | | Rebounds | | A | Stl | TO | BS | Avg |
|--------|----|-----|-----|-----|-----|-----|-----|-----|-----|-------|---|-----|----|----|-----|
| | | | FGM | Pct | FGA | FGM | FTM | Pct | Off | Total | | | | | |
| Price | 48 | 1,375 | 253 | 41.3 | 253 | 103 | 148 | 91.4 | 25 | 112 | 335 | 35 | 142 | 4 | 15.8 |
| Hill | 70 | 2,397 | 350 | 50.4 | 1 | 0 | 263 | 66.2 | 269 | 765 | 55 | 55 | 151 | 41 | 13.8 |
| Brandon | 67 | 1,961 | 341 | 44.8 | 121 | 48 | 159 | 85.5 | 35 | 186 | 363 | 107 | 144 | 14 | 13.3 |
| Williams | 74 | 2,641 | 366 | 45.0 | 5 | 1 | 196 | 68.5 | 173 | 507 | 192 | 83 | 149 | 101 | 12.6 |
| Mills | 80 | 2,814 | 359 | 42.0 | 240 | 94 | 174 | 81.7 | 99 | 366 | 154 | 59 | 120 | 35 | 12.3 |
| Phillis | 80 | 2,500 | 338 | 41.4 | 55 | 19 | 183 | 77.9 | 90 | 265 | 180 | 115 | 113 | 25 | 11.0 |
| Ferry | 82 | 1,290 | 223 | 44.6 | 233 | 94 | 74 | 88.1 | 30 | 143 | 96 | 27 | 59 | 22 | 7.5 |
| Campbell | 78 | 1,128 | 161 | 41.1 | 42 | 15 | 132 | 83.0 | 60 | 153 | 69 | 32 | 65 | 8 | 6.0 |
| Cage | 82 | 2,040 | 177 | 52.1 | 2 | 0 | 53 | 60.2 | 203 | 564 | 56 | 61 | 56 | 67 | 5.0 |
| Battle | 28 | 280 | 43 | 37.7 | 31 | 11 | 19 | 73.1 | 3 | 11 | 37 | 8 | 17 | 1 | 4.1 |
| Roberts | 21 | 223 | 28 | 38.9 | 11 | 4 | 20 | 76.9 | 13 | 34 | 8 | 6 | 7 | 3 | 3.8 |
| Colter | 57 | 752 | 67 | 39.6 | 35 | 8 | 54 | 76.1 | 13 | 59 | 101 | 30 | 36 | 6 | 3.4 |
| Dreiling | 58 | 483 | 42 | 41.2 | 0 | 0 | 26 | 63.4 | 32 | 116 | 22 | 6 | 25 | 22 | 1.9 |
| **Cavs** | **82** | **19,930** | **2,756** | **44.1** | **1,033** | **398** | **1,507** | **76.0** | **1,045** | **3,282** | **1,672** | **630** | **1,176** | **349** | **90.5** |
| **Opponents** | **82** | **19,930** | **2,803** | **46.1** | **1,108** | **396** | **1,364** | **75.7** | **851** | **3,097** | **1,812** | **556** | **1,213** | **433** | **89.8** |

## Dallas Mavericks

| Player | GP | Min | Field Goals | | 3-Pt FG | | Free Throws | | Rebounds | | A | Stl | TO | BS | Avg |
|--------|----|-----|-----|-----|-----|-----|-----|-----|-----|-------|---|-----|----|----|-----|
| | | | FGM | Pct | FGA | FGM | FTM | Pct | Off | Total | | | | | |
| Jackson | 51 | 1,962 | 484 | 47.2 | 110 | 35 | 306 | 80.5 | 120 | 260 | 191 | 28 | 160 | 12 | 25.7 |
| Mashburn | 80 | 2,980 | 683 | 43.6 | 344 | 113 | 447 | 73.9 | 116 | 331 | 298 | 82 | 235 | 8 | 24.1 |
| Tarpley | 55 | 1,354 | 292 | 47.9 | 18 | 5 | 102 | 83.6 | 142 | 449 | 58 | 45 | 109 | 55 | 12.6 |
| Kidd | 79 | 2,668 | 330 | 38.5 | 257 | 70 | 192 | 69.8 | 152 | 430 | 607 | 151 | 250 | 24 | 11.7 |
| Jones | 80 | 2,385 | 372 | 44.3 | 12 | 1 | 80 | 64.5 | 329 | 844 | 163 | 35 | 124 | 27 | 10.3 |
| McCloud | 42 | 802 | 144 | 43.9 | 89 | 34 | 80 | 83.3 | 82 | 147 | 53 | 23 | 40 | 9 | 9.6 |
| Harris | 79 | 1,695 | 280 | 45.9 | 142 | 55 | 136 | 80.0 | 85 | 220 | 132 | 58 | 77 | 14 | 9.5 |
| Brooks | 59 | 808 | 126 | 45.8 | 69 | 25 | 64 | 81.0 | 14 | 66 | 116 | 34 | 47 | 4 | 5.8 |
| Smith | 63 | 826 | 131 | 41.7 | 12 | 1 | 57 | 76.0 | 43 | 144 | 44 | 29 | 37 | 26 | 5.1 |
| Durnas | 58 | 613 | 96 | 38.4 | 73 | 22 | 50 | 64.9 | 32 | 62 | 57 | 13 | 50 | 4 | 4.6 |
| Williams | 82 | 2,383 | 145 | 47.7 | 0 | 0 | 38 | 37.6 | 291 | 690 | 124 | 52 | 105 | 148 | 4.0 |
| Hodge | 54 | 633 | 83 | 40.7 | 14 | 4 | 39 | 76.5 | 40 | 122 | 41 | 10 | 39 | 14 | 3.9 |
| Davis | 46 | 580 | 49 | 43.3 | 2 | 0 | 42 | 63.6 | 63 | 156 | 10 | 6 | 30 | 3 | 3.0 |
| **Mavericks** | **82** | **19,930** | **3,227** | **44.0** | **1,200** | **386** | **1,622** | **73.4** | **1,514** | **3,947** | **1,941** | **579** | **1,345** | **348** | **103.2** |
| **Opponents** | **82** | **19,930** | **3,407** | **48.8** | **1,181** | **432** | **1,454** | **73.4** | **1,053** | **3,432** | **1,991** | **722** | **1,250** | **502** | **106.1** |

## Denver Nuggets

| Player | GP | Min | FGM | Pct | FGA | FGM | FTM | Pct | Off | Total | A | Stl | TO | BS | Avg |
|---|---|---|---|---|---|---|---|---|---|---|---|---|---|---|---|
| | | | Field Goals | | 3-Pt FG | | Free Throws | | Rebounds | | | | | | |
| Abdul-Rauf | 73 | 2,082 | 472 | 47.0 | 215 | 83 | 138 | 88.5 | 32 | 137 | 263 | 77 | 119 | 9 | 16.0 |
| R. Williams | 74 | 2,198 | 388 | 45.9 | 266 | 85 | 132 | 75.9 | 94 | 329 | 231 | 114 | 124 | 67 | 13.4 |
| Rogers | 80 | 2,142 | 375 | 48.8 | 148 | 50 | 179 | 65.1 | 132 | 385 | 161 | 95 | 173 | 46 | 12.2 |
| Pack | 42 | 1,144 | 170 | 43.0 | 72 | 30 | 137 | 78.3 | 19 | 113 | 290 | 61 | 134 | 6 | 12.1 |
| Mutombo | 82 | 3,100 | 349 | 55.6 | 0 | 0 | 248 | 65.4 | 319 | 1029 | 113 | 40 | 192 | 321 | 11.5 |
| D. Ellis | 81 | 1,996 | 351 | 45.3 | 263 | 106 | 110 | 86.6 | 56 | 222 | 57 | 37 | 81 | 9 | 11.3 |
| Stith | 81 | 2,329 | 312 | 47.2 | 68 | 20 | 267 | 82.4 | 95 | 268 | 153 | 91 | 110 | 18 | 11.2 |
| Rose | 81 | 1,798 | 227 | 45.4 | 114 | 36 | 173 | 73.9 | 57 | 217 | 389 | 65 | 160 | 22 | 8.2 |
| B. Williams | 63 | 1,261 | 196 | 58.9 | 0 | 0 | 106 | 65.4 | 98 | 298 | 53 | 38 | 114 | 43 | 7.9 |
| Hammonds | 70 | 956 | 139 | 53.5 | 1 | 0 | 132 | 74.6 | 55 | 222 | 36 | 11 | 56 | 14 | 5.9 |
| Slater | 25 | 236 | 40 | 49.4 | 0 | 0 | 40 | 72.7 | 21 | 57 | 12 | 7 | 26 | 3 | 4.8 |
| L. Ellis | 6 | 58 | 9 | 36.0 | 0 | 0 | 6 | 100.0 | 7 | 17 | 4 | 1 | 5 | 5 | 4.0 |
| Levingston | 57 | 469 | 55 | 42.3 | 1 | 0 | 19 | 42.2 | 49 | 124 | 27 | 13 | 21 | 20 | 2.3 |
| Grant | 14 | 151 | 10 | 30.3 | 7 | 2 | 9 | 75.0 | 2 | 9 | 43 | 6 | 14 | 2 | 2.2 |
| Randall | 8 | 39 | 3 | 30.0 | 1 | 0 | 9 | — | 4 | 12 | 1 | 0 | 1 | 0 | 0.8 |
| **Nuggets** | **82** | **19,980** | **3,098** | **47.9** | **1,160** | **413** | **1,700** | **73.8** | **1,040** | **3,442** | **1,836** | **660** | **1,381** | **585** | **101.3** |
| **Opponents** | **82** | **19,980** | **3,050** | **45.6** | **1,208** | **419** | **1,721** | **75.0** | **1,021** | **3,228** | **1,784** | **640** | **1,167** | **460** | **100.5** |

## Detroit Pistons

| Player | GP | Min | FGM | Pct | FGA | FGM | FTM | Pct | Off | Total | A | Stl | TO | BS | Avg |
|---|---|---|---|---|---|---|---|---|---|---|---|---|---|---|---|
| | | | Field Goals | | 3-Pt FG | | Free Throws | | Rebounds | | | | | | |
| Hill | 70 | 2,678 | 508 | 47.7 | 27 | 4 | 374 | 73.2 | 125 | 445 | 353 | 124 | 202 | 62 | 19.9 |
| Dumars | 67 | 2,544 | 417 | 43.0 | 338 | 103 | 277 | 80.5 | 47 | 158 | 368 | 72 | 219 | 7 | 18.1 |
| Mills | 72 | 2,514 | 417 | 44.7 | 285 | 109 | 175 | 79.9 | 124 | 558 | 160 | 68 | 144 | 33 | 15.5 |
| Houston | 76 | 1,996 | 398 | 46.3 | 373 | 158 | 147 | 86.0 | 29 | 167 | 164 | 61 | 113 | 14 | 14.5 |
| Miller | 64 | 1,558 | 232 | 55.5 | 13 | 3 | 78 | 62.9 | 162 | 475 | 93 | 60 | 115 | 116 | 8.5 |
| Addison | 79 | 1,776 | 279 | 47.6 | 83 | 24 | 74 | 74.7 | 67 | 242 | 109 | 53 | 76 | 25 | 8.3 |
| Hunter | 42 | 944 | 119 | 37.4 | 108 | 36 | 40 | 72.7 | 24 | 75 | 159 | 51 | 79 | 7 | 7.5 |
| West | 67 | 1,543 | 217 | 55.6 | 0 | 0 | 66 | 47.8 | 160 | 408 | 18 | 27 | 85 | 102 | 7.5 |
| Macon | 55 | 721 | 101 | 38.1 | 62 | 20 | 54 | 79.4 | 29 | 76 | 63 | 67 | 41 | 1 | 5.0 |
| Knight | 47 | 708 | 85 | 39.7 | 28 | 11 | 18 | 72.0 | 21 | 61 | 127 | 21 | 49 | 5 | 4.2 |
| Leckner | 57 | 623 | 87 | 52.7 | 2 | 0 | 51 | 70.8 | 47 | 174 | 14 | 15 | 39 | 15 | 3.9 |
| Curley | 53 | 595 | 58 | 43.3 | 0 | 0 | 27 | 75.0 | 54 | 124 | 25 | 21 | 25 | 21 | 2.7 |
| Newbill | 34 | 331 | 16 | 35.6 | 0 | 0 | 8 | 36.4 | 40 | 81 | 17 | 11 | 12 | 11 | 1.2 |
| **Pistons** | **82** | **19,730** | **3,060** | **46.1** | **1,396** | **494** | **1,439** | **74.1** | **958** | **3,162** | **1,872** | **705** | **1,318** | **420** | **98.2** |
| **Opponents** | **82** | **19,730** | **3,120** | **47.6** | **1,235** | **448** | **1,963** | **72.2** | **1,147** | **3,579** | **2,013** | **693** | **1,286** | **439** | **105.5** |

## Golden State Warriors

| Player | GP | Min | FGM | Pct | FGA | FGM | FTM | Pct | Off | Total | A | Stl | TO | BS | Avg |
|---|---|---|---|---|---|---|---|---|---|---|---|---|---|---|---|
| | | | Field Goals | | 3-Pt FG | | Free Throws | | Rebounds | | | | | | |
| Sprewell | 69 | 2,771 | 490 | 41.8 | 326 | 90 | 350 | 78.1 | 58 | 256 | 279 | 112 | 230 | 46 | 20.6 |
| Hardaway | 62 | 2,321 | 430 | 42.7 | 444 | 168 | 219 | 76.0 | 46 | 190 | 578 | 88 | 214 | 12 | 20.1 |
| Mullin | 25 | 890 | 170 | 48.9 | 93 | 42 | 94 | 87.9 | 25 | 115 | 125 | 38 | 93 | 19 | 19.0 |
| Gatling | 58 | 1,470 | 324 | 63.3 | 1 | 0 | 148 | 59.2 | 144 | 443 | 51 | 39 | 117 | 52 | 13.7 |
| Marshall | 72 | 2,066 | 345 | 39.4 | 243 | 69 | 147 | 66.2 | 137 | 405 | 105 | 45 | 115 | 88 | 12.6 |
| Pierce | 27 | 673 | 111 | 43.7 | 70 | 23 | 93 | 87.7 | 12 | 64 | 40 | 22 | 24 | 2 | 12.5 |
| Seikaly | 36 | 1,035 | 162 | 51.6 | 0 | 0 | 111 | 69.4 | 77 | 266 | 45 | 20 | 104 | 37 | 12.1 |
| Alexander | 50 | 1,237 | 230 | 51.5 | 25 | 6 | 36 | 60.0 | 87 | 291 | 60 | 28 | 76 | 29 | 10.0 |
| Rogers | 49 | 1,017 | 180 | 52.9 | 14 | 2 | 76 | 52.1 | 108 | 278 | 37 | 22 | 84 | 52 | 8.9 |
| Jennings | 80 | 1,722 | 190 | 44.7 | 204 | 75 | 134 | 87.6 | 26 | 148 | 373 | 95 | 120 | 2 | 7.4 |
| Lorthridge | 37 | 672 | 106 | 47.5 | 14 | 3 | 57 | 64.8 | 24 | 71 | 101 | 28 | 57 | 1 | 7.4 |
| Legler | 24 | 371 | 60 | 52.2 | 50 | 26 | 30 | 88.2 | 12 | 40 | 27 | 12 | 20 | 1 | 7.3 |
| Rozier | 66 | 1,494 | 189 | 48.5 | 7 | 2 | 68 | 44.7 | 200 | 486 | 45 | 35 | 89 | 39 | 6.8 |
| Wood | 78 | 1,336 | 153 | 46.9 | 91 | 31 | 91 | 77.8 | 83 | 241 | 65 | 28 | 53 | 13 | 5.5 |
| Morton | 41 | 395 | 50 | 38.8 | 25 | 9 | 58 | 68.2 | 21 | 58 | 18 | 11 | 27 | 15 | 4.1 |
| **Warriors** | **82** | **19,905** | **3,217** | **46.8** | **1,602** | **546** | **1,687** | **70.4** | **1,101** | **3,472** | **2,017** | **649** | **1,497** | **391** | **105.7** |
| **Opponents** | **82** | **19,905** | **3,527** | **48.8** | **1,384** | **492** | **1,565** | **72.0** | **1,196** | **3,723** | **2,345** | **865** | **1,326** | **412** | **111.1** |

## Houston Rockets

| Player | GP | Min | FGM | Pct | FGA | FGM | FTM | Pct | Off | Total | A | Stl | TO | BS | Avg |
|---|---|---|---|---|---|---|---|---|---|---|---|---|---|---|---|
| | | | Field Goals | | 3-Pt FG | | Free Throws | | Rebounds | | | | | | |
| Olajuwon | 72 | 2,853 | 798 | 51.7 | 16 | 3 | 406 | 75.6 | 172 | 775 | 255 | 133 | 237 | 242 | 27.8 |
| Drexler | 76 | 2,728 | 571 | 46.1 | 480 | 147 | 364 | 82.4 | 152 | 480 | 362 | 136 | 186 | 45 | 21.8 |
| Maxwell | 64 | 2,038 | 306 | 39.4 | 441 | 143 | 99 | 68.8 | 18 | 164 | 274 | 75 | 137 | 13 | 13.3 |
| Smith | 81 | 2,030 | 287 | 48.4 | 331 | 142 | 126 | 85.1 | 27 | 155 | 323 | 71 | 123 | 10 | 10.4 |
| Horry | 64 | 2,074 | 240 | 44.7 | 227 | 86 | 86 | 76.1 | 81 | 324 | 216 | 94 | 122 | 76 | 10.2 |
| Cassell | 82 | 1,882 | 253 | 42.7 | 191 | 63 | 214 | 84.3 | 38 | 211 | 405 | 94 | 167 | 14 | 9.5 |
| Elie | 81 | 1,896 | 243 | 49.9 | 201 | 80 | 144 | 84.2 | 50 | 196 | 189 | 65 | 104 | 12 | 8.8 |
| Herrera | 61 | 1,331 | 171 | 52.3 | 2 | 0 | 73 | 62.4 | 98 | 278 | 44 | 40 | 71 | 38 | 6.8 |
| Brown | 41 | 814 | 105 | 60.3 | 3 | 1 | 38 | 61.3 | 64 | 189 | 30 | 11 | 29 | 14 | 6.1 |
| Chilcutt | 68 | 1,347 | 146 | 44.5 | 86 | 35 | 31 | 73.8 | 106 | 317 | 66 | 25 | 61 | 43 | 5.3 |
| Murray | 54 | 516 | 95 | 40.8 | 86 | 35 | 33 | 78.6 | 20 | 59 | 19 | 14 | 35 | 4 | 4.8 |
| Breaux | 42 | 340 | 45 | 37.2 | 25 | 6 | 32 | 65.3 | 16 | 34 | 15 | 11 | 16 | 4 | 3.0 |
| Tabak | 37 | 182 | 24 | 45.3 | 1 | 0 | 27 | 61.4 | 23 | 57 | 4 | 2 | 18 | 7 | 2.0 |
| **Rockets** | **82** | **19,730** | **3,159** | **48.0** | **1,757** | **646** | **1,527** | **74.9** | **880** | **3,320** | **2,060** | **721** | **1,322** | **514** | **103.5** |
| **Opponents** | **82** | **19,730** | **3,202** | **45.3** | **1,345** | **506** | **1,407** | **75.1** | **1,165** | **3,551** | **1,940** | **744** | **1,274** | **365** | **101.4** |

## Indiana Pacers

| Player | GP | Min | FGM | Pct | FGA | FGM | FTM | Pct | Off | Total | A | Stl | TO | BS | Avg |
|---|---|---|---|---|---|---|---|---|---|---|---|---|---|---|---|
| | | | Field Goals | | 3-Pt FG | | Free Throws | | Rebounds | | | | | | |
| Miller | 81 | 2,665 | 505 | 46.2 | 470 | 195 | 383 | 89.7 | 30 | 210 | 242 | 98 | 151 | 16 | 19.6 |
| Smits | 78 | 2,381 | 558 | 52.6 | 2 | 0 | 284 | 75.3 | 192 | 601 | 111 | 40 | 189 | 79 | 17.9 |
| McKey | 81 | 2,805 | 411 | 49.3 | 89 | 32 | 221 | 74.4 | 125 | 394 | 276 | 125 | 168 | 49 | 13.3 |
| D. Davis | 74 | 2,346 | 324 | 56.3 | 1 | 0 | 138 | 53.3 | 259 | 696 | 58 | 72 | 124 | 116 | 10.6 |
| Scott | 80 | 1,528 | 265 | 45.5 | 203 | 79 | 193 | 85.0 | 18 | 151 | 108 | 61 | 119 | 13 | 10.0 |
| A. Davis | 44 | 1,030 | 109 | 44.5 | 0 | 0 | 117 | 67.2 | 105 | 280 | 25 | 19 | 64 | 29 | 7.6 |
| Jackson | 82 | 2,402 | 239 | 42.2 | 87 | 27 | 119 | 77.8 | 73 | 306 | 616 | 105 | 210 | 16 | 7.6 |
| Mitchell | 81 | 1,377 | 201 | 48.7 | 10 | 1 | 126 | 72.4 | 95 | 243 | 61 | 43 | 54 | 20 | 6.5 |
| Fleming | 55 | 686 | 93 | 49.5 | 7 | 0 | 65 | 72.2 | 20 | 88 | 109 | 27 | 43 | 1 | 4.6 |
| Workman | 69 | 1,028 | 101 | 37.5 | 98 | 35 | 55 | 74.3 | 21 | 111 | 194 | 59 | 73 | 5 | 4.2 |
| Ferrell | 56 | 607 | 83 | 48.0 | 6 | 1 | 64 | 75.3 | 50 | 88 | 31 | 26 | 43 | 6 | 4.1 |
| Thompson | 38 | 453 | 49 | 41.5 | 0 | 0 | 14 | 87.5 | 28 | 89 | 18 | 18 | 33 | 10 | 2.9 |
| Kite | 11 | 77 | 3 | 17.6 | 0 | 0 | 2 | 20.0 | 12 | 22 | 1 | 0 | 6 | 0 | 0.7 |
| **Pacers** | **82** | **19,780** | **2,983** | **47.7** | **985** | **374** | **1,796** | **75.1** | **1,051** | **3,341** | **1,877** | **703** | **1,340** | **363** | **99.2** |
| **Opponents** | **82** | **19,780** | **2,921** | **45.6** | **1,304** | **475** | **1,516** | **72.6** | **1,048** | **3,204** | **1,804** | **691** | **1,370** | **416** | **95.5** |

## Los Angeles Clippers

| Player | GP | Min | FGM | Pct | FGA | FGM | FTM | Pct | Off | Total | A | Stl | TO | BS | Avg |
|---|---|---|---|---|---|---|---|---|---|---|---|---|---|---|---|
| | | | Field Goals | | 3-Pt FG | | Free Throws | | Rebounds | | | | | | |
| Vaught | 80 | 2,966 | 609 | 51.4 | 33 | 7 | 176 | 71.0 | 261 | 772 | 139 | 104 | 166 | 29 | 17.5 |
| Murray | 81 | 2,556 | 439 | 40.2 | 218 | 65 | 199 | 75.4 | 132 | 354 | 133 | 72 | 163 | 55 | 14.1 |
| Sealy | 60 | 1,604 | 291 | 43.5 | 73 | 22 | 174 | 78.0 | 77 | 214 | 107 | 72 | 83 | 25 | 13.0 |
| Richardson | 80 | 2,664 | 353 | 39.4 | 244 | 87 | 81 | 64.8 | 38 | 261 | 632 | 129 | 171 | 12 | 10.9 |
| Dehere | 80 | 1,774 | 279 | 40.7 | 163 | 48 | 229 | 78.4 | 35 | 152 | 225 | 45 | 157 | 7 | 10.4 |
| Massenburg | 80 | 2,127 | 282 | 46.9 | 3 | 0 | 177 | 75.3 | 160 | 455 | 67 | 48 | 118 | 58 | 9.3 |
| Piatkowski | 81 | 1,208 | 201 | 44.1 | 198 | 74 | 90 | 78.3 | 63 | 133 | 77 | 37 | 63 | 15 | 7.0 |
| Spencer | 19 | 368 | 52 | 44.1 | 1 | 0 | 28 | 56.0 | 11 | 65 | 25 | 14 | 48 | 23 | 6.9 |
| Grant | 33 | 470 | 78 | 47.0 | 16 | 4 | 45 | 81.8 | 8 | 35 | 93 | 29 | 44 | 3 | 6.2 |
| Smith | 29 | 319 | 63 | 47.0 | 8 | 1 | 26 | 86.7 | 13 | 56 | 20 | 6 | 18 | 2 | 5.3 |
| Outlaw | 81 | 1,655 | 170 | 52.3 | 5 | 0 | 82 | 44.1 | 121 | 313 | 84 | 90 | 78 | 151 | 5.2 |
| Riley | 40 | 434 | 65 | 44.8 | 1 | 0 | 47 | 73.4 | 45 | 112 | 11 | 17 | 31 | 35 | 4.4 |
| Ellis | 69 | 656 | 91 | 48.1 | 13 | 1 | 69 | 59.0 | 56 | 88 | 40 | 67 | 49 | 12 | 3.7 |
| Woods | 62 | 495 | 37 | 31.6 | 74 | 22 | 28 | 73.7 | 10 | 44 | 134 | 41 | 55 | 0 | 2.0 |
| **Clippers** | **82** | **19,880** | **3,060** | **44.4** | **1,051** | **331** | **1,476** | **71.0** | **1,064** | **3,140** | **1,805** | **787** | **1,334** | **435** | **96.7** |
| **Opponents** | **82** | **19,880** | **3,207** | **49.6** | **1,049** | **388** | **1,876** | **75.0** | **1,083** | **3,619** | **1,917** | **693** | **1,506** | **459** | **105.8** |

## Los Angeles Lakers

| Player | GP | Min | Field Goals | | 3-Pt FG | | Free Throws | | Rebounds | | A | Stl | TO | BS | Avg |
|---|---|---|---|---|---|---|---|---|---|---|---|---|---|---|---|
| | | | FGM | Pct | FGA | FGM | FTM | Pct | Off | Total | | | | | |
| Ceballos | 58 | 2,029 | 497 | 50.9 | 146 | 58 | 209 | 71.6 | 169 | 464 | 105 | 60 | 143 | 19 | 21.7 |
| Van Exel | 80 | 2,944 | 465 | 42.0 | 511 | 183 | 235 | 78.3 | 27 | 223 | 660 | 97 | 220 | 6 | 16.9 |
| Divac | 80 | 2,807 | 485 | 50.7 | 53 | 10 | 297 | 77.7 | 261 | 829 | 329 | 109 | 205 | 174 | 16.0 |
| Jones | 64 | 1,981 | 342 | 46.0 | 246 | 91 | 122 | 72.2 | 79 | 249 | 128 | 131 | 75 | 41 | 14.0 |
| Campell | 73 | 2,076 | 360 | 45.9 | 1 | 0 | 193 | 66.6 | 168 | 445 | 92 | 69 | 98 | 132 | 12.5 |
| Peeler | 73 | 1,559 | 285 | 43.2 | 216 | 84 | 102 | 79.7 | 62 | 168 | 122 | 52 | 82 | 13 | 10.4 |
| Threatt | 59 | 1,384 | 217 | 49.7 | 95 | 36 | 88 | 79.3 | 21 | 124 | 248 | 54 | 70 | 12 | 9.5 |
| Lynch | 56 | 953 | 138 | 46.8 | 21 | 3 | 62 | 72.1 | 75 | 184 | 62 | 51 | 73 | 10 | 6.1 |
| Smith | 61 | 1,024 | 132 | 42.7 | 91 | 32 | 44 | 69.8 | 43 | 107 | 102 | 46 | 50 | 7 | 5.6 |
| Bowie | 67 | 1,225 | 118 | 44.2 | 11 | 2 | 68 | 76.4 | 72 | 288 | 118 | 21 | 91 | 80 | 4.6 |
| Miller | 46 | 527 | 70 | 53.0 | 5 | 2 | 47 | 61.8 | 67 | 152 | 35 | 20 | 38 | 7 | 4.1 |
| Keys | 6 | 83 | 9 | 34.6 | 9 | 0 | 2 | 100.0 | 6 | 17 | 2 | 1 | 2 | 2 | 3.3 |
| Harvey | 59 | 572 | 77 | 43.8 | 1 | 1 | 24 | 53.3 | 39 | 102 | 23 | 15 | 25 | 41 | 3.0 |
| Rambis | 26 | 195 | 18 | 51.4 | 0 | 0 | 8 | 66.7 | 10 | 34 | 16 | 3 | 8 | 9 | 1.7 |
| **Lakers** | **82** | **19,905** | **3,284** | **46.3** | **1,492** | **525** | **1,523** | **73.5** | **1,126** | **3,442** | **2,078** | **750** | **1,243** | **563** | **105.1** |
| **Opponents** | **82** | **19,905** | **3,299** | **46.8** | **1,294** | **456** | **1,580** | **70.8** | **1,283** | **3,757** | **2,203** | **644** | **1,390** | **489** | **105.3** |

## Miami Heat

| Player | GP | Min | Field Goals | | 3-Pt FG | | Free Throws | | Rebounds | | A | Stl | TO | BS | Avg |
|---|---|---|---|---|---|---|---|---|---|---|---|---|---|---|---|
| | | | FGM | Pct | FGA | FGM | FTM | Pct | Off | Total | | | | | |
| Rice | 82 | 3,014 | 667 | 47.5 | 451 | 185 | 312 | 85.5 | 99 | 378 | 192 | 112 | 153 | 14 | 22.3 |
| Willis | 67 | 2,390 | 473 | 46.6 | 15 | 3 | 205 | 69.0 | 227 | 732 | 86 | 60 | 162 | 36 | 17.2 |
| Owens | 70 | 2,296 | 403 | 49.1 | 22 | 2 | 194 | 62.0 | 203 | 502 | 246 | 80 | 204 | 30 | 14.3 |
| Coles | 68 | 2,207 | 261 | 43.0 | 76 | 16 | 141 | 81.0 | 46 | 191 | 416 | 99 | 156 | 13 | 10.0 |
| Reeves | 67 | 1,462 | 206 | 44.3 | 171 | 67 | 140 | 71.4 | 52 | 186 | 288 | 77 | 132 | 10 | 9.2 |
| Geiger | 74 | 1,712 | 260 | 53.6 | 10 | 4 | 93 | 65.0 | 146 | 413 | 55 | 41 | 113 | 51 | 8.3 |
| Gamble | 77 | 1,223 | 220 | 48.9 | 98 | 39 | 87 | 78.4 | 29 | 122 | 119 | 52 | 49 | 10 | 7.4 |
| Eackles | 54 | 898 | 143 | 43.9 | 41 | 18 | 91 | 72.2 | 33 | 95 | 72 | 19 | 53 | 2 | 7.3 |
| Miner | 45 | 871 | 123 | 40.3 | 49 | 14 | 69 | 72.6 | 38 | 117 | 69 | 15 | 77 | 6 | 7.3 |
| Salley | 75 | 1,955 | 197 | 49.9 | 0 | 0 | 153 | 73.9 | 110 | 336 | 123 | 47 | 97 | 85 | 7.3 |
| Askins | 50 | 854 | 81 | 39.1 | 78 | 21 | 46 | 80.7 | 86 | 198 | 39 | 35 | 25 | 17 | 4.6 |
| Lohaus | 61 | 730 | 97 | 42.0 | 155 | 63 | 10 | 66.7 | 28 | 102 | 43 | 20 | 29 | 25 | 4.4 |
| Pritchard | 19 | 194 | 13 | 40.6 | 8 | 2 | 16 | 76.2 | 0 | 12 | 34 | 2 | 12 | 1 | 2.3 |
| **Heat** | **82** | **19,805** | **3,144** | **46.7** | **1,182** | **436** | **1,569** | **73.6** | **1,092** | **3,364** | **1,779** | **662** | **1,291** | **298** | **101.1** |
| **Opponents** | **82** | **19,805** | **3,092** | **47.1** | **1,417** | **511** | **1,732** | **74.0** | **1,036** | **3,391** | **1,860** | **656** | **1,332** | **385** | **102.8** |

## Milwaukee Bucks

| Player | GP | Min | Field Goals | | 3-Pt FG | | Free Throws | | Rebounds | | A | Stl | TO | BS | Avg |
|---|---|---|---|---|---|---|---|---|---|---|---|---|---|---|---|
| | | | FGM | Pct | FGA | FGM | FTM | Pct | Off | Total | | | | | |
| Robinson | 80 | 2,958 | 636 | 45.1 | 268 | 86 | 397 | 79.6 | 169 | 513 | 197 | 115 | 313 | 22 | 21.9 |
| Baker | 82 | 3,361 | 594 | 48.3 | 24 | 7 | 256 | 59.3 | 289 | 846 | 296 | 86 | 221 | 116 | 17.7 |
| Day | 82 | 2,717 | 445 | 42.4 | 418 | 163 | 257 | 75.4 | 95 | 322 | 134 | 104 | 157 | 63 | 16.0 |
| Murdock | 75 | 2,158 | 338 | 41.5 | 240 | 90 | 211 | 79.0 | 48 | 214 | 482 | 113 | 194 | 12 | 13.0 |
| Conlon | 82 | 2,064 | 344 | 53.2 | 29 | 8 | 119 | 61.3 | 160 | 426 | 110 | 42 | 123 | 18 | 9.9 |
| Newman | 82 | 1,896 | 226 | 46.3 | 128 | 45 | 137 | 80.1 | 72 | 173 | 91 | 69 | 86 | 13 | 7.7 |
| Mayberry | 82 | 1,744 | 172 | 42.2 | 177 | 72 | 58 | 69.9 | 21 | 82 | 276 | 51 | 106 | 4 | 5.8 |
| Mobley | 46 | 587 | 78 | 59.1 | 2 | 2 | 22 | 48.9 | 55 | 153 | 21 | 8 | 24 | 27 | 3.9 |
| Barry | 52 | 602 | 57 | 42.5 | 48 | 16 | 61 | 76.3 | 15 | 49 | 85 | 30 | 41 | 4 | 3.7 |
| Lister | 60 | 776 | 66 | 49.3 | 1 | 0 | 35 | 50.0 | 67 | 236 | 12 | 16 | 38 | 57 | 2.8 |
| Pinckney | 62 | 835 | 48 | 49.5 | 0 | 0 | 44 | 71.0 | 65 | 211 | 21 | 34 | 26 | 17 | 2.3 |
| George | 3 | 8 | 1 | 33.3 | 1 | 0 | 2 | 100 | 1 | 1 | 0 | 0 | 2 | 0 | 1.3 |
| **Bucks** | **82** | **19,855** | **3,022** | **45.9** | **1,349** | **494** | **1,608** | **71.2** | **1,063** | **3,250** | **1,737** | **674** | **1,393** | **359** | **99.3** |
| **Opponents** | **82** | **19,855** | **3,248** | **49.3** | **1,242** | **491** | **1,517** | **72.9** | **1,014** | **3,351** | **2,103** | **770** | **1,359** | **407** | **103.7** |

## Minnesota Timberwolves

| Player | GP | Min | FGM | Pct | FGA | FGM | FTM | Pct | Off | Total | A | Stl | TO | BS | Avg |
|---|---|---|---|---|---|---|---|---|---|---|---|---|---|---|---|
| | | | Field Goals | | 3-Pt FG | | Free Throws | | Rebounds | | | | | | |
| Rider | 75 | 2,645 | 558 | 44.7 | 396 | 139 | 277 | 81.7 | 90 | 249 | 245 | 69 | 232 | 23 | 20.4 |
| Laettner | 81 | 2,770 | 450 | 48.9 | 40 | 13 | 409 | 81.8 | 164 | 613 | 234 | 101 | 225 | 87 | 16.3 |
| West | 71 | 2,328 | 351 | 46.1 | 61 | 11 | 206 | 83.7 | 60 | 227 | 185 | 65 | 126 | 24 | 12.9 |
| Gugliotta | 77 | 2,568 | 371 | 44.3 | 186 | 60 | 174 | 69.0 | 165 | 572 | 279 | 132 | 189 | 62 | 12.7 |
| Rooks | 80 | 2,405 | 289 | 47.0 | 5 | 0 | 290 | 76.1 | 165 | 486 | 97 | 29 | 142 | 71 | 10.9 |
| Martin | 34 | 803 | 95 | 40.8 | 38 | 7 | 57 | 87.7 | 14 | 64 | 133 | 34 | 62 | 0 | 7.5 |
| Garland | 73 | 1,931 | 170 | 41.5 | 75 | 19 | 89 | 79.5 | 48 | 168 | 318 | 71 | 105 | 13 | 6.1 |
| Williams | 1 | 28 | 1 | 25.0 | 0 | 0 | 4 | 80.0 | 0 | 1 | 3 | 2 | 3 | 0 | 6.0 |
| King | 50 | 792 | 99 | 46.7 | 1 | 0 | 68 | 66.7 | 54 | 165 | 26 | 24 | 64 | 20 | 5.3 |
| Durham | 59 | 852 | 117 | 49.4 | 26 | 5 | 63 | 65.6 | 37 | 94 | 53 | 36 | 45 | 32 | 5.1 |
| Smith | 64 | 1,073 | 116 | 43.0 | 108 | 47 | 41 | 65.1 | 14 | 73 | 146 | 32 | 50 | 22 | 5.0 |
| Foster | 78 | 1,144 | 150 | 47.2 | 23 | 7 | 78 | 70.3 | 85 | 259 | 39 | 15 | 71 | 28 | 4.9 |
| Shackleford | 21 | 239 | 39 | 60.0 | 0 | 0 | 16 | 80.0 | 16 | 67 | 8 | 8 | 8 | 6 | 4.5 |
| Guibert | 17 | 167 | 16 | 34.0 | 4 | 0 | 13 | 68.4 | 16 | 45 | 10 | 8 | 12 | 1 | 2.6 |
| T'wolves | 82 | 19,780 | 2,792 | 44.9 | 1,016 | 318 | 1,824 | 77.5 | 883 | 2,973 | 1,780 | 609 | 1,400 | 402 | 94.2 |
| Opponents | 82 | 19,780 | 3,088 | 47.4 | 1,243 | 468 | 1,820 | 73.1 | 1,169 | 3,474 | 2,069 | 703 | 1,323 | 512 | 103.2 |

## New Jersey Nets

| Player | GP | Min | FGM | Pct | FGA | FGM | FTM | Pct | Off | Total | A | Stl | TO | BS | Avg |
|---|---|---|---|---|---|---|---|---|---|---|---|---|---|---|---|
| | | | Field Goals | | 3-Pt FG | | Free Throws | | Rebounds | | | | | | |
| Coleman | 56 | 2,103 | 371 | 42.4 | 120 | 28 | 376 | 76.7 | 167 | 591 | 187 | 35 | 172 | 94 | 20.5 |
| Anderson | 72 | 2,689 | 411 | 39.9 | 294 | 97 | 348 | 84.1 | 73 | 250 | 680 | 103 | 225 | 14 | 17.6 |
| Gilliam | 82 | 2,472 | 455 | 50.3 | 2 | 0 | 302 | 77.0 | 192 | 613 | 99 | 67 | 152 | 89 | 14.8 |
| Edwards | 14 | 466 | 69 | 44.8 | 45 | 18 | 40 | 95.2 | 10 | 37 | 27 | 19 | 35 | 5 | 14.0 |
| Morris | 71 | 2,131 | 351 | 41.0 | 317 | 106 | 142 | 72.8 | 181 | 402 | 147 | 86 | 117 | 51 | 13.4 |
| Benjamin | 61 | 1,598 | 271 | 51.0 | 0 | 0 | 133 | 76.0 | 94 | 440 | 38 | 23 | 125 | 64 | 11.1 |
| Brown | 80 | 2,466 | 254 | 44.6 | 24 | 4 | 139 | 67.1 | 178 | 487 | 135 | 69 | 80 | 135 | 8.1 |
| Walters | 80 | 1,435 | 206 | 43.9 | 196 | 71 | 40 | 76.9 | 18 | 93 | 121 | 37 | 71 | 16 | 6.5 |
| Childs | 53 | 1,021 | 106 | 38.0 | 125 | 41 | 55 | 75.3 | 14 | 69 | 219 | 42 | 76 | 3 | 5.8 |
| Williams | 75 | 982 | 149 | 46.1 | 5 | 0 | 65 | 53.3 | 179 | 425 | 35 | 26 | 59 | 33 | 4.8 |
| Higgins | 57 | 735 | 105 | 38.5 | 78 | 23 | 35 | 87.5 | 25 | 77 | 29 | 10 | 35 | 9 | 4.7 |
| Floyd | 48 | 831 | 71 | 33.5 | 88 | 25 | 30 | 69.8 | 8 | 54 | 126 | 13 | 51 | 6 | 4.1 |
| Mahorn | 58 | 630 | 79 | 52.3 | 3 | 1 | 39 | 79.6 | 45 | 162 | 26 | 11 | 34 | 12 | 3.4 |
| Schintzius | 43 | 318 | 41 | 38.0 | 0 | 0 | 6 | 54.5 | 29 | 81 | 15 | 3 | 17 | 17 | 2.0 |
| Dare | 1 | 3 | 0 | 00.0 | 0 | 0 | 0 | — | 0 | 1 | 0 | 0 | 1 | 0 | 0.0 |
| Nets | 82 | 19,880 | 2,939 | 43.6 | 1,297 | 414 | 1,750 | 75.9 | 1,213 | 3,782 | 1,884 | 544 | 1,300 | 548 | 98.1 |
| Opponents | 82 | 19,880 | 3,182 | 46.1 | 1,176 | 440 | 1,495 | 72.1 | 1,056 | 3,491 | 1,826 | 733 | 1,104 | 440 | 101.2 |

## New York Knickerbockers

| Player | GP | Min | FGM | Pct | FGA | FGM | FTM | Pct | Off | Total | A | Stl | TO | BS | Avg |
|---|---|---|---|---|---|---|---|---|---|---|---|---|---|---|---|
| | | | Field Goals | | 3-Pt FG | | Free Throws | | Rebounds | | | | | | |
| Ewing | 79 | 2,920 | 730 | 50.3 | 21 | 6 | 420 | 75.0 | 157 | 867 | 212 | 68 | 256 | 159 | 23.9 |
| Starks | 80 | 2,725 | 419 | 39.5 | 611 | 217 | 168 | 73.7 | 34 | 219 | 411 | 92 | 160 | 4 | 15.3 |
| Smith | 76 | 2,150 | 352 | 47.1 | 31 | 7 | 255 | 79.2 | 144 | 324 | 120 | 49 | 147 | 10 | 12.7 |
| Harper | 80 | 2,716 | 337 | 44.6 | 292 | 106 | 139 | 72.4 | 31 | 194 | 458 | 79 | 151 | 10 | 11.5 |
| Oakley | 50 | 1,567 | 192 | 48.9 | 12 | 3 | 119 | 79.3 | 155 | 445 | 126 | 60 | 103 | 7 | 10.1 |
| Davis | 82 | 1,697 | 296 | 48.0 | 288 | 131 | 97 | 80.8 | 30 | 110 | 150 | 35 | 87 | 11 | 10.0 |
| Mason | 77 | 2,496 | 287 | 56.6 | 1 | 0 | 191 | 64.1 | 182 | 650 | 240 | 69 | 123 | 21 | 9.9 |
| Anthony | 61 | 943 | 128 | 43.7 | 155 | 56 | 60 | 78.9 | 7 | 64 | 160 | 50 | 57 | 7 | 6.1 |
| Bonner | 58 | 1,126 | 88 | 45.6 | 5 | 1 | 44 | 65.7 | 113 | 262 | 80 | 48 | 79 | 23 | 3.8 |
| M. Williams | 41 | 503 | 60 | 45.1 | 8 | 0 | 17 | 44.7 | 42 | 98 | 49 | 20 | 41 | 4 | 3.3 |
| H. Williams | 56 | 743 | 82 | 45.6 | 0 | 0 | 23 | 62.2 | 23 | 132 | 27 | 13 | 40 | 45 | 3.3 |
| Ward | 10 | 44 | 14 | 21.1 | 10 | 1 | 7 | 70.0 | 1 | 6 | 4 | 2 | 8 | 0 | 1.6 |
| Christie | 12 | 79 | 5 | 22.7 | 7 | 1 | 4 | 80.0 | 3 | 13 | 8 | 2 | 13 | 1 | 1.3 |
| Knicks | 82 | 19,780 | 2,985 | 46.7 | 1,446 | 532 | 1,552 | 73.4 | 929 | 3,402 | 2,055 | 591 | 1,305 | 387 | 98.2 |
| Opponents | 82 | 19,780 | 2,800 | 43.7 | 1,165 | 397 | 1,802 | 73.6 | 1,021 | 3,338 | 1,584 | 639 | 1,264 | 324 | 95.1 |

### Orlando Magic

| Player | GP | Min | FGM | Pct | FGA | FGM | FTM | Pct | Off | Total | A | Stl | TO | BS | Avg |
|---|---|---|---|---|---|---|---|---|---|---|---|---|---|---|---|
| | | | Field Goals | | 3-Pt FG | | Free Throws | | Rebounds | | | | | | |
| O'Neal | 79 | 2,923 | 930 | 58.3 | 5 | 0 | 455 | 53.3 | 328 | 901 | 214 | 73 | 204 | 192 | 29.3 |
| Hardaway | 77 | 2,901 | 585 | 51.2 | 249 | 87 | 356 | 76.9 | 139 | 336 | 551 | 130 | 258 | 26 | 20.9 |
| Anderson | 76 | 2,588 | 439 | 47.6 | 431 | 179 | 143 | 70.4 | 85 | 335 | 314 | 125 | 141 | 22 | 15.8 |
| Scott | 62 | 1,499 | 283 | 43.9 | 352 | 150 | 86 | 75.4 | 25 | 146 | 131 | 45 | 57 | 14 | 12.9 |
| Grant | 74 | 2,693 | 401 | 56.7 | 8 | 0 | 146 | 69.2 | 223 | 715 | 173 | 76 | 85 | 88 | 12.8 |
| Royal | 70 | 1,841 | 206 | 47.5 | 4 | 0 | 223 | 74.6 | 83 | 279 | 198 | 45 | 125 | 16 | 9.1 |
| Shaw | 78 | 1,836 | 192 | 38.9 | 184 | 48 | 70 | 73.7 | 52 | 241 | 406 | 73 | 184 | 18 | 6.4 |
| Bowie | 77 | 1,261 | 177 | 48.0 | 40 | 12 | 61 | 83.6 | 54 | 139 | 159 | 47 | 86 | 21 | 5.5 |
| Turner | 49 | 576 | 73 | 41.0 | 75 | 27 | 26 | 89.7 | 23 | 97 | 38 | 12 | 22 | 3 | 4.1 |
| Hammink | 1 | 7 | 1 | 33.3 | 0 | 0 | 2 | 100.0 | 0 | 2 | 1 | 0 | 0 | 0 | 4.0 |
| Avent | 71 | 1066 | 105 | 43.0 | 0 | 0 | 48 | 64.0 | 97 | 293 | 41 | 28 | 53 | 50 | 3.6 |
| Armstrong | 3 | 8 | 3 | 37.5 | 6 | 2 | 2 | 100.0 | 1 | 1 | 3 | 1 | 1 | 0 | 3.3 |
| Thompson | 38 | 246 | 45 | 39.5 | 58 | 18 | 8 | 66.7 | 7 | 23 | 43 | 10 | 27 | 2 | 3.1 |
| Rollins | 51 | 478 | 20 | 47.6 | 0 | 0 | 21 | 67.7 | 31 | 95 | 9 | 7 | 23 | 36 | 1.2 |
| **Magic** | **82** | **19,930** | **3,460** | **50.2** | **1,412** | **523** | **1,648** | **66.9** | **1,149** | **3,606** | **2,281** | **672** | **1,297** | **488** | **110.9** |
| **Opponents** | **82** | **19,930** | **3,242** | **45.7** | **1,239** | **468** | **1,560** | **74.1** | **1,136** | **3,362** | **1,986** | **700** | **1,234** | **367** | **103.8** |

### Philadelphia 76ers

| Player | GP | Min | FGM | Pct | FGA | FGM | FTM | Pct | Off | Total | A | Stl | TO | BS | Avg |
|---|---|---|---|---|---|---|---|---|---|---|---|---|---|---|---|
| | | | Field Goals | | 3-Pt FG | | Free Throws | | Rebounds | | | | | | |
| Barros | 82 | 3,318 | 571 | 49.0 | 425 | 197 | 347 | 89.9 | 27 | 242 | 619 | 149 | 242 | 4 | 20.6 |
| Malone | 19 | 660 | 144 | 50.7 | 28 | 11 | 51 | 86.4 | 11 | 29 | 29 | 15 | 29 | 0 | 18.4 |
| Weatherspoon | 76 | 2,991 | 543 | 43.9 | 21 | 4 | 283 | 75.1 | 144 | 191 | 215 | 115 | 191 | 67 | 18.1 |
| Burton | 53 | 1,564 | 243 | 40.1 | 275 | 106 | 220 | 82.4 | 49 | 122 | 96 | 32 | 122 | 19 | 15.3 |
| Wright | 79 | 2,044 | 361 | 46.5 | 8 | 0 | 182 | 64.5 | 191 | 151 | 48 | 37 | 151 | 104 | 11.4 |
| Bradley | 82 | 2,365 | 315 | 45.5 | 3 | 0 | 148 | 63.8 | 243 | 142 | 53 | 54 | 142 | 274 | 9.5 |
| Grayer | 47 | 1,098 | 163 | 42.8 | 15 | 5 | 58 | 69.9 | 58 | 56 | 74 | 27 | 56 | 4 | 8.3 |
| Williams | 77 | 1,781 | 206 | 47.5 | 7 | 0 | 79 | 73.8 | 173 | 84 | 59 | 71 | 84 | 40 | 6.4 |
| Graham | 50 | 775 | 95 | 42.6 | 28 | 6 | 55 | 75.3 | 19 | 48 | 66 | 29 | 48 | 6 | 5.0 |
| Gaines | 11 | 280 | 24 | 47.1 | 15 | 2 | 5 | 45.5 | 1 | 14 | 33 | 8 | 14 | 1 | 5.0 |
| Alston | 64 | 1,032 | 120 | 46.5 | 4 | 0 | 59 | 49.2 | 98 | 53 | 33 | 39 | 53 | 35 | 4.7 |
| Harmon | 10 | 158 | 21 | 39.6 | 1 | 1 | 3 | 50.0 | 9 | 7 | 12 | 9 | 7 | 0 | 4.6 |
| Tyler | 55 | 809 | 72 | 38.1 | 51 | 16 | 35 | 70.0 | 13 | 97 | 174 | 36 | 97 | 2 | 3.5 |
| Perry | 42 | 446 | 27 | 34.6 | 14 | 0 | 22 | 55.0 | 38 | 21 | 12 | 10 | 21 | 15 | 1.8 |
| **76ers** | **82** | **19,805** | **2,949** | **44.8** | **936** | **355** | **1,567** | **73.7** | **1,105** | **3,335** | **1,566** | **643** | **1,355** | **576** | **95.4** |
| **Opponents** | **82** | **19,805** | **3,100** | **46.5** | **1,287** | **467** | **1,569** | **76.3** | **1,143** | **3,406** | **1,992** | **712** | **1,299** | **422** | **100.4** |

### Phoenix Suns

| Player | GP | Min | FGM | Pct | FGA | FGM | FTM | Pct | Off | Total | A | Stl | TO | BS | Avg |
|---|---|---|---|---|---|---|---|---|---|---|---|---|---|---|---|
| | | | Field Goals | | 3-Pt FG | | Free Throws | | Rebounds | | | | | | |
| Barkley | 68 | 2,382 | 554 | 48.6 | 219 | 74 | 379 | 74.8 | 203 | 756 | 276 | 110 | 150 | 45 | 23.0 |
| Manning | 46 | 1,510 | 340 | 54.7 | 21 | 6 | 136 | 67.3 | 97 | 276 | 154 | 41 | 121 | 57 | 17.9 |
| Majerle | 82 | 3,091 | 438 | 42.5 | 548 | 199 | 206 | 73.0 | 104 | 375 | 340 | 96 | 105 | 38 | 15.6 |
| Johnson | 47 | 1,352 | 246 | 47.0 | 26 | 4 | 234 | 81.0 | 32 | 115 | 360 | 47 | 105 | 18 | 15.5 |
| Green | 82 | 2,687 | 311 | 50.4 | 127 | 43 | 251 | 73.2 | 194 | 669 | 127 | 55 | 114 | 31 | 11.2 |
| Person | 78 | 1,800 | 309 | 48.4 | 266 | 116 | 80 | 79.2 | 67 | 201 | 105 | 48 | 79 | 24 | 10.4 |
| Tisdale | 65 | 1,276 | 278 | 48.4 | 0 | 0 | 94 | 77.0 | 83 | 247 | 45 | 29 | 64 | 27 | 10.0 |
| Perry | 82 | 1,977 | 306 | 52.0 | 60 | 25 | 158 | 81.0 | 51 | 151 | 394 | 156 | 163 | 4 | 9.7 |
| Ainge | 74 | 1,374 | 194 | 46.0 | 214 | 78 | 105 | 80.8 | 25 | 109 | 210 | 46 | 79 | 7 | 7.7 |
| Dumas | 15 | 167 | 37 | 50.7 | 1 | 0 | 8 | 50.0 | 18 | 29 | 7 | 10 | 9 | 2 | 5.5 |
| Ruffin | 49 | 319 | 84 | 42.6 | 99 | 38 | 27 | 71.1 | 8 | 23 | 48 | 14 | 47 | 2 | 4.8 |
| Schayes | 69 | 823 | 126 | 50.8 | 1 | 1 | 50 | 72.5 | 57 | 208 | 89 | 20 | 64 | 37 | 4.4 |
| Kleine | 75 | 968 | 119 | 44.9 | 2 | 0 | 42 | 85.7 | 82 | 259 | 39 | 14 | 35 | 18 | 3.7 |
| Lang | 12 | 53 | 4 | 40.0 | 0 | 0 | 3 | 75.0 | 3 | 4 | 1 | 0 | 5 | 2 | 0.9 |
| **Suns** | **82** | **19,830** | **3,356** | **48.2** | **1,584** | **584** | **1,777** | **75.6** | **1,027** | **3,430** | **2,198** | **687** | **1,167** | **312** | **110.6** |
| **Opponents** | **82** | **19,830** | **3,320** | **47.7** | **1,544** | **525** | **1,590** | **74.4** | **1,038** | **3,469** | **2,149** | **658** | **1,285** | **391** | **106.8** |

### Portland Trail Blazers

| Player | GP | Min | Field Goals FGM | Pct | 3-Pt FG FGA | FGM | Free Throws FTM | Pct | Rebounds Off | Total | A | Stl | TO | BS | Avg |
|---|---|---|---|---|---|---|---|---|---|---|---|---|---|---|---|
| C. Robinson | 75 | 2,725 | 597 | 45.2 | 383 | 142 | 265 | 69.4 | 152 | 423 | 198 | 79 | 158 | 82 | 21.3 |
| Strickland | 64 | 2,267 | 441 | 46.6 | 123 | 46 | 283 | 74.5 | 73 | 317 | 562 | 123 | 209 | 9 | 18.9 |
| Thorpe | 70 | 2,096 | 385 | 56.5 | 7 | 0 | 167 | 59.4 | 202 | 558 | 112 | 41 | 132 | 28 | 13.4 |
| Williams | 82 | 2,422 | 309 | 51.2 | 2 | 1 | 138 | 67.3 | 251 | 669 | 78 | 67 | 119 | 69 | 9.2 |
| J. Robinson | 71 | 1,539 | 255 | 40.9 | 223 | 76 | 65 | 59.1 | 42 | 132 | 180 | 48 | 127 | 13 | 9.2 |
| Grant | 75 | 1,771 | 286 | 46.1 | 26 | 8 | 103 | 70.5 | 103 | 284 | 82 | 56 | 62 | 53 | 9.1 |
| Porter | 35 | 770 | 105 | 39.3 | 114 | 44 | 58 | 70.7 | 18 | 81 | 133 | 30 | 58 | 2 | 8.9 |
| Kersey | 63 | 1,143 | 203 | 41.5 | 27 | 7 | 95 | 76.6 | 93 | 256 | 82 | 52 | 64 | 35 | 8.1 |
| McKie | 45 | 827 | 116 | 44.4 | 28 | 11 | 50 | 68.5 | 35 | 129 | 89 | 36 | 39 | 16 | 6.5 |
| Dudley | 82 | 2,245 | 181 | 40.6 | 1 | 0 | 85 | 46.4 | 325 | 764 | 34 | 43 | 81 | 126 | 5.5 |
| Bryant | 49 | 658 | 101 | 52.6 | 2 | 1 | 41 | 65.1 | 55 | 161 | 28 | 19 | 39 | 16 | 5.0 |
| Henson | 37 | 380 | 37 | 43.0 | 52 | 23 | 22 | 88.0 | 3 | 26 | 85 | 9 | 30 | 0 | 3.2 |
| Edwards | 28 | 266 | 32 | 38.6 | 0 | 0 | 11 | 64.7 | 10 | 43 | 8 | 5 | 14 | 8 | 2.7 |
| **Trail Blazers** | 82 | 19,705 | 3,217 | 45.1 | 1,266 | 462 | 1,555 | 69.7 | 1,352 | 3,795 | 1,846 | 668 | 1,212 | 467 | 103.1 |
| **Opponents** | 82 | 19,705 | 2,951 | 45.6 | 1,189 | 442 | 1,794 | 75.4 | 883 | 3,178 | 1,789 | 638 | 1,302 | 405 | 99.2 |

### Sacramento Kings

| Player | GP | Min | Field Goals FGM | Pct | 3-Pt FG FGA | FGM | Free Throws FTM | Pct | Rebounds Off | Total | A | Stl | TO | BS | Avg |
|---|---|---|---|---|---|---|---|---|---|---|---|---|---|---|---|
| Richmond | 82 | 3,172 | 668 | 44.6 | 424 | 156 | 375 | 84.3 | 69 | 234 | 311 | 91 | 234 | 29 | 22.8 |
| Williams | 77 | 2,739 | 445 | 44.6 | 296 | 103 | 266 | 73.1 | 100 | 243 | 316 | 123 | 243 | 63 | 16.4 |
| Grant | 80 | 2,289 | 413 | 51.1 | 4 | 1 | 231 | 63.6 | 207 | 163 | 99 | 49 | 163 | 116 | 13.2 |
| Webb | 76 | 2,458 | 302 | 43.8 | 145 | 48 | 266 | 93.4 | 29 | 185 | 468 | 75 | 185 | 8 | 11.6 |
| Polynice | 81 | 2,534 | 376 | 54.4 | 1 | 1 | 231 | 63.9 | 277 | 113 | 62 | 48 | 113 | 52 | 10.8 |
| M. Smith | 82 | 1,736 | 220 | 54.2 | 2 | 0 | 226 | 48.5 | 174 | 106 | 67 | 61 | 106 | 49 | 6.9 |
| Simmons | 58 | 1,064 | 131 | 42.0 | 16 | 6 | 124 | 70.2 | 61 | 70 | 89 | 28 | 70 | 23 | 5.6 |
| Brown | 67 | 1,086 | 124 | 43.2 | 47 | 14 | 127 | 67.1 | 24 | 78 | 133 | 99 | 78 | 19 | 4.7 |
| Hurley | 68 | 1,105 | 103 | 36.3 | 76 | 21 | 59 | 76.3 | 14 | 110 | 226 | 29 | 110 | 0 | 4.2 |
| Causwell | 58 | 820 | 76 | 51.7 | 1 | 0 | 55 | 58.2 | 57 | 33 | 15 | 14 | 33 | 80 | 3.6 |
| Turner | 30 | 149 | 23 | 40.4 | 5 | 2 | 58 | 57.1 | 17 | 12 | 7 | 8 | 12 | 1 | 2.3 |
| Lee | 22 | 75 | 9 | 36.0 | 18 | 7 | 57 | 85.7 | 0 | 5 | 5 | 6 | 5 | 3 | 2.0 |
| Phelps | 3 | 5 | 0 | 00.0 | 1 | 0 | 20 | 00.0 | 0 | 0 | 1 | 0 | 0 | 0 | 0.0 |
| **Kings** | 82 | 19,855 | 3,025 | 46.8 | 1,037 | 359 | 1,647 | 71.1 | 1,073 | 3,398 | 1,824 | 650 | 1,449 | 457 | 98.2 |
| **Opponents** | 82 | 19,855 | 2,964 | 45.3 | 1,240 | 377 | 1,833 | 74.1 | 1,145 | 3,413 | 1,820 | 756 | 1,348 | 515 | 99.2 |

### San Antonio Spurs

| Player | GP | Min | Field Goals FGM | Pct | 3-Pt FG FGA | FGM | Free Throws FTM | Pct | Rebounds Off | Total | A | Stl | TO | BS | Avg |
|---|---|---|---|---|---|---|---|---|---|---|---|---|---|---|---|
| Robinson | 81 | 3,074 | 788 | 53.0 | 20 | 6 | 656 | 77.4 | 234 | 877 | 236 | 134 | 233 | 262 | 27.6 |
| Elliott | 81 | 2,858 | 502 | 46.8 | 333 | 136 | 326 | 80.7 | 63 | 287 | 206 | 78 | 151 | 38 | 18.1 |
| Johnson | 82 | 3,011 | 448 | 51.9 | 22 | 3 | 202 | 68.5 | 49 | 208 | 670 | 114 | 207 | 13 | 13.4 |
| Del Negro | 75 | 2,360 | 372 | 48.6 | 162 | 66 | 128 | 79.0 | 28 | 192 | 226 | 61 | 56 | 14 | 12.5 |
| Person | 81 | 2,033 | 317 | 42.3 | 445 | 172 | 66 | 64.7 | 49 | 258 | 106 | 45 | 102 | 12 | 10.8 |
| Rodman | 49 | 1,568 | 137 | 57.1 | 2 | 0 | 75 | 67.6 | 274 | 823 | 97 | 31 | 98 | 23 | 7.1 |
| Reid | 81 | 1,566 | 201 | 50.8 | 2 | 1 | 160 | 68.7 | 120 | 393 | 55 | 60 | 113 | 32 | 7.0 |
| Cummings | 76 | 1,273 | 224 | 48.3 | 0 | 0 | 72 | 58.5 | 138 | 378 | 59 | 36 | 95 | 19 | 6.8 |
| Rivers | 63 | 989 | 108 | 35.8 | 127 | 45 | 60 | 73.2 | 15 | 109 | 162 | 65 | 60 | 21 | 5.1 |
| Anderson | 38 | 556 | 76 | 46.9 | 19 | 3 | 30 | 73.2 | 15 | 55 | 52 | 26 | 38 | 10 | 4.9 |
| Malone | 17 | 149 | 13 | 37.1 | 2 | 1 | 22 | 68.8 | 20 | 46 | 6 | 2 | 11 | 3 | 2.9 |
| Haley | 31 | 117 | 26 | 42.6 | 1 | 0 | 21 | 65.5 | 8 | 27 | 2 | 3 | 13 | 5 | 2.4 |
| Nwosu | 23 | 84 | 9 | 32.1 | 0 | 0 | 13 | 76.5 | 11 | 24 | 3 | 0 | 9 | 3 | 1.3 |
| **Spurs** | 82 | 19,855 | 3,236 | 48.4 | 1,158 | 434 | 1,836 | 73.8 | 1,029 | 3,690 | 1,919 | 656 | 1,246 | 456 | 106.6 |
| **Opponents** | 82 | 19,855 | 3,168 | 45.4 | 1,251 | 426 | 1,491 | 71.4 | 1,017 | 3,320 | 1,878 | 633 | 1,182 | 408 | 100.6 |

### Seattle SuperSonics

| Player | GP | Min | Field Goals | | 3-Pt FG | | Free Throws | | Rebounds | | A | Stl | TO | BS | Avg |
|---|---|---|---|---|---|---|---|---|---|---|---|---|---|---|---|
| | | | FGM | Pct | FGA | FGM | FTM | Pct | Off | Total | | | | | |
| Payton | 82 | 3,015 | 685 | 50.9 | 232 | 70 | 249 | 71.6 | 108 | 281 | 583 | 204 | 201 | 13 | 20.6 |
| Schrempf | 82 | 2,886 | 521 | 52.3 | 181 | 93 | 437 | 83.9 | 135 | 508 | 310 | 93 | 176 | 35 | 19.2 |
| Kemp | 82 | 2,679 | 545 | 54.7 | 7 | 2 | 438 | 74.9 | 318 | 893 | 149 | 102 | 259 | 122 | 18.7 |
| Gill | 73 | 2,125 | 392 | 45.7 | 171 | 63 | 155 | 74.2 | 99 | 290 | 192 | 117 | 138 | 28 | 13.7 |
| Perkins | 82 | 2,356 | 346 | 46.6 | 343 | 136 | 215 | 79.9 | 96 | 398 | 135 | 72 | 77 | 45 | 12.7 |
| Askew | 71 | 1,721 | 248 | 49.2 | 94 | 31 | 176 | 73.9 | 65 | 181 | 176 | 49 | 85 | 13 | 9.9 |
| Marciulionis | 66 | 1,194 | 216 | 47.3 | 87 | 35 | 145 | 73.2 | 17 | 68 | 110 | 72 | 98 | 3 | 9.3 |
| McMillan | 80 | 2,070 | 166 | 41.8 | 155 | 53 | 34 | 58.6 | 65 | 302 | 421 | 165 | 126 | 53 | 5.2 |
| Houston | 39 | 258 | 49 | 45.8 | 22 | 6 | 28 | 73.7 | 20 | 55 | 6 | 13 | 20 | 5 | 3.4 |
| Johnson | 64 | 907 | 85 | 44.3 | 1 | 0 | 29 | 63.0 | 101 | 289 | 16 | 17 | 54 | 67 | 3.1 |
| Cartwright | 29 | 430 | 27 | 39.1 | 0 | 0 | 15 | 62.5 | 25 | 87 | 10 | 6 | 18 | 3 | 2.4 |
| Wingfield | 20 | 81 | 18 | 35.3 | 12 | 2 | 8 | 80.0 | 11 | 30 | 3 | 5 | 8 | 3 | 2.3 |
| Scheffler | 18 | 102 | 12 | 52.2 | 0 | 0 | 15 | 83.3 | 8 | 23 | 4 | 2 | 3 | 2 | 2.2 |
| King | 2 | 6 | 0 | 00.0 | 0 | 0 | 0 | 00.0 | 0 | 0 | 0 | 0 | 0 | 0 | 0.0 |
| SuperSonics | 82 | 19,830 | 3,310 | 49.1 | 1,305 | 491 | 1,944 | 75.8 | 1,068 | 3,405 | 2,115 | 917 | 1,295 | 392 | 110.4 |
| Opponents | 82 | 19,830 | 3,008 | 45.3 | 1,514 | 520 | 1,848 | 73.5 | 1,064 | 3,271 | 1,849 | 652 | 1,485 | 493 | 102.2 |

### Utah Jazz

| Player | GP | Min | Field Goals | | 3-Pt FG | | Free Throws | | Rebounds | | A | Stl | TO | BS | Avg |
|---|---|---|---|---|---|---|---|---|---|---|---|---|---|---|---|
| | | | FGM | Pct | FGA | FGM | FTM | Pct | Off | Total | | | | | |
| Malone | 82 | 3,126 | 830 | 53.6 | 41 | 11 | 516 | 74.2 | 156 | 871 | 285 | 129 | 236 | 85 | 26.7 |
| Hornacek | 81 | 2,696 | 482 | 51.4 | 219 | 89 | 284 | 88.2 | 53 | 210 | 347 | 129 | 145 | 17 | 16.5 |
| Stockton | 82 | 2,867 | 429 | 54.2 | 227 | 102 | 246 | 80.4 | 57 | 251 | 1011 | 194 | 267 | 22 | 14.7 |
| Benoit | 71 | 1,841 | 285 | 48.6 | 115 | 38 | 132 | 84.1 | 96 | 368 | 58 | 45 | 75 | 47 | 10.4 |
| Carr | 78 | 1,677 | 290 | 53.1 | 4 | 1 | 165 | 82.1 | 81 | 265 | 67 | 24 | 87 | 68 | 9.6 |
| Spenser | 34 | 905 | 105 | 48.8 | 0 | 0 | 107 | 79.3 | 90 | 260 | 17 | 12 | 68 | 32 | 9.3 |
| Edwards | 67 | 1,112 | 181 | 46.1 | 75 | 22 | 75 | 83.3 | 50 | 130 | 77 | 43 | 81 | 16 | 6.9 |
| Chambers | 81 | 1,240 | 195 | 45.7 | 24 | 4 | 109 | 80.7 | 66 | 213 | 73 | 25 | 52 | 30 | 6.2 |
| Keefe | 75 | 1,270 | 172 | 57.7 | 0 | 0 | 117 | 67.6 | 135 | 327 | 30 | 36 | 62 | 25 | 6.1 |
| Russell | 63 | 860 | 104 | 43.7 | 44 | 13 | 62 | 66.7 | 44 | 141 | 34 | 48 | 42 | 11 | 4.5 |
| Crotty | 80 | 1,019 | 93 | 40.3 | 36 | 11 | 98 | 81.0 | 27 | 97 | 205 | 39 | 70 | 6 | 3.7 |
| Watson | 60 | 673 | 76 | 50.0 | 19 | 5 | 38 | 67.9 | 16 | 74 | 59 | 35 | 51 | 11 | 3.3 |
| Donaldson | 43 | 613 | 44 | 59.5 | 0 | 0 | 22 | 71.0 | 19 | 107 | 14 | 6 | 22 | 28 | 2.6 |
| Jazz | 82 | 19,780 | 3,243 | 51.2 | 801 | 301 | 1,939 | 78.1 | 874 | 3,286 | 2,256 | 758 | 1,289 | 392 | 106.4 |
| Opponents | 82 | 19,780 | 2,845 | 45.3 | 1,431 | 546 | 1,835 | 74.1 | 917 | 3,042 | 1,713 | 648 | 1,353 | 429 | 98.4 |

### Washington Bullets

| Player | GP | Min | Field Goals | | 3-Pt FG | | Free Throws | | Rebounds | | A | Stl | TO | BS | Avg |
|---|---|---|---|---|---|---|---|---|---|---|---|---|---|---|---|
| | | | FGM | Pct | FGA | FGM | FTM | Pct | Off | Total | | | | | |
| Webber | 54 | 2,067 | 464 | 49.5 | 145 | 40 | 117 | 50.2 | 200 | 518 | 256 | 83 | 167 | 85 | 20.1 |
| Howard | 65 | 2,348 | 455 | 48.9 | 7 | 0 | 194 | 66.4 | 184 | 545 | 165 | 52 | 166 | 15 | 17.0 |
| Cheaney | 78 | 2,651 | 512 | 45.3 | 283 | 96 | 173 | 81.2 | 105 | 321 | 177 | 80 | 151 | 21 | 16.6 |
| Chapman | 45 | 1,468 | 254 | 39.7 | 274 | 86 | 137 | 86.2 | 23 | 113 | 128 | 67 | 62 | 15 | 16.2 |
| Skiles | 62 | 2,077 | 265 | 45.5 | 228 | 96 | 179 | 88.6 | 26 | 159 | 452 | 70 | 172 | 6 | 13.0 |
| MacLean | 39 | 1,052 | 158 | 43.8 | 40 | 10 | 104 | 76.5 | 46 | 165 | 51 | 15 | 44 | 3 | 11.0 |
| Muresan | 73 | 1,720 | 303 | 56.0 | 0 | 0 | 124 | 70.9 | 179 | 488 | 38 | 48 | 115 | 127 | 10.0 |
| Butler | 76 | 1,554 | 214 | 42.1 | 141 | 46 | 123 | 66.5 | 43 | 170 | 91 | 61 | 106 | 10 | 7.9 |
| Duckworth | 40 | 818 | 118 | 44.2 | 10 | 2 | 45 | 64.3 | 65 | 195 | 20 | 21 | 59 | 24 | 7.1 |
| Overton | 82 | 1,704 | 207 | 41.6 | 125 | 53 | 109 | 87.2 | 26 | 143 | 246 | 53 | 104 | 2 | 7.0 |
| Tucker | 62 | 982 | 96 | 45.7 | 1 | 0 | 51 | 61.4 | 44 | 170 | 68 | 46 | 56 | 11 | 3.9 |
| Stewart | 40 | 346 | 41 | 46.1 | 2 | 0 | 20 | 66.7 | 28 | 67 | 18 | 16 | 16 | 9 | 2.6 |
| Walker | 24 | 266 | 18 | 42.9 | 0 | 0 | 21 | 75.0 | 19 | 47 | 7 | 5 | 15 | 5 | 2.4 |
| McIlvaine | 55 | 534 | 34 | 47.9 | 0 | 0 | 28 | 68.3 | 40 | 105 | 10 | 10 | 19 | 60 | 1.7 |
| Bullets | 82 | 19,855 | 3,176 | 46.0 | 1,264 | 433 | 1,457 | 72.4 | 1,044 | 3,263 | 1,749 | 648 | 1,301 | 404 | 100.5 |
| Opponents | 82 | 19,855 | 3,246 | 48.0 | 1,145 | 438 | 1,771 | 76.5 | 1,107 | 3,628 | 1,959 | 701 | 1,359 | 446 | 106.1 |

# 1995 NBA Draft

## First Round

1. Joe Smith, Golden State
2. Antonio McDyess, LA Clippers (to Den)
3. Jerry Stackhouse, Philadelphia
4. Rasheed Wallace, Washington
5. Kevin Garnett, Minnesota
6. Bryant Reeves, Vancouver
7. Damon Stoudamire, Toronto
8. Shawn Respert, Portland (to Milwaukee)
9. Ed O'Bannon, New Jersey
10. Kurt Thomas, Miami
11. Gary Trent, Milwaukee (to Portland)
12. Cherokee Parks, Dallas
13. Corliss Williamson, Sacramento
14. Eric Williams, Boston
15. Brent Barry, Denver (to LA Clippers)
16. Alan Henderson, Atlanta
17. Bob Sura, Cleveland
18. Theo Ratliff, Detroit
19. Randolph Childress, Detroit
20. Jason Caffey, Chicago
21. Michael Finley, Phoenix
22. George Zidek, Charlotte
23. Travis Best, Indiana
24. Loren Meyer, Dallas
25. David Vaughn, Orlando
26. Sherell Ford, Seattle
27. Mario Bennett, Phoenix
28. Greg Ostertag, Utah
29. Cory Alexander, San Antonio

## Second Round

30. Lou Roe, Detroit
31. Dragan Tarlac, Chicago
32. Terrence Rencher, Washington
33. Junior Burrough, Boston
34. Andrew DeClercq, Golden State
35. Jimmy King, Toronto
36. Lawrence Moten, Vancouver
37. Frankie King, LA Lakers
38. Rashard Griffith, Milwaukee
39. Donny Marshall, Cleveland
40. Dwayne Whitfield, Golden State
41. Erik Meek, Houston
42. Donnie Boyce, Atlanta
43. Eric Snow, Milwuukee
44. Anthony Pelle, Denver
45. Troy Brown, Atlanta
46. George Banks, Miami
47. Tyus Edney, Sacramento
48. Mark Davis, Minnesota
49. Jerome Allen, Minnesota
50. Martin Lewis, Golden State
51. Dejan Bodiroga, Sacramento
52. Fred Holberg, Indiana
53. Constantin Popa, LA Clippers
54. Zydrunas Ilgauskas, Seattle
55. Michael McDonald, Golden State
56. Chris Carr, Phoenix
57. Cuonzo Martin, Atlanta
58. Don Reid, Detroit

## THEY SAID IT

*Bryant Reeves, senior Oklahoma State center, when asked if his strong performance during the NCAAs might have bolstered his status in the NBA draft: "What happens to me next year will happen to me no matter what happens."*

### Clothes Call

The usual protocol for players on NBA injured lists is simple: You show up in mufti for home games and sit on the bench. But what happens if two disabled players wear almost exactly the same thing—as Derrick Coleman and Sean Higgins did for the New Jersey Nets' game against the Charlotte Hornets at the Meadowlands Arena last week? Each came in black courduroy slacks and a $400 Coogi multicolored sweater that appeared to have been designed at a state fair spin-art booth. "They looked like twins," said New Jersey coach Butch Beard.

Did either say to the other, "Well, one of us is going to have to go home and change"? Uh, no. Coleman and Higgins holed up in the locker room and watched the game on TV—vanity particularly surprising from Coleman, who earlier this season offered Beard a blank check for the fines he would incur for his flouting of the Nets' dress code on road trips.

## NBA Champions

| Season | Winner | Series | Runner-Up | Winning Coach |
|---|---|---|---|---|
| 1946-47 | Philadelphia | 4–1 | Chicago | Eddie Gottlieb |
| 1947-48 | Baltimore | 4–2 | Philadelphia | Buddy Jeannette |
| 1948-49 | Minneapolis | 4–2 | Washington | John Kundla |
| 1949-50 | Minneapolis | 4–2 | Syracuse | John Kundla |
| 1950-51 | Rochester | 4–3 | New York | Les Harrison |
| 1951-52 | Minneapolis | 4–3 | New York | John Kundla |
| 1952-53 | Minneapolis | 4–1 | New York | John Kundla |
| 1953-54 | Minneapolis | 4–3 | Syracuse | John Kundla |
| 1954-55 | Syracuse | 4–3 | Ft Wayne | Al Cervi |
| 1955-56 | Philadelphia | 4–1 | Ft Wayne | George Senesky |
| 1956-57 | Boston | 4–3 | St Louis | Red Auerbach |
| 1957-58 | St Louis | 4–2 | Boston | Alex Hannum |
| 1958-59 | Boston | 4–0 | Minneapolis | Red Auerbach |
| 1959-60 | Boston | 1–3 | St Louis | Red Auerbach |
| 1960-61 | Boston | 4–1 | St Louis | Red Auerbach |
| 1961-62 | Boston | 4–3 | LA Lakers | Red Auerbach |
| 1962-63 | Boston | 4–2 | LA Lakers | Red Auerbach |
| 1963-64 | Boston | 4–1 | San Francisco | Red Auerbach |
| 1964-65 | Boston | 4–1 | LA Lakers | Red Auerbach |
| 1965-66 | Boston | 4–3 | LA Lakers | Red Auerbach |
| 1966-67 | Philadelphia | 4–2 | San Francisco | Alex Hannum |
| 1967-68 | Boston | 4–2 | LA Lakers | Bill Russell |
| 1968-69 | Boston | 4–3 | LA Lakers | Bill Russell |
| 1969-70 | New York | 4–3 | LA Lakers | Red Holzman |
| 1970-71 | Milwaukee | 4–0 | Baltimore | Larry Costello |
| 1971-72 | LA Lakers | 4–1 | New York | Bill Sharman |
| 1972-73 | New York | 4–1 | LA Lakers | Red Holzman |
| 1973-74 | Boston | 4–3 | Milwaukee | Tommy Heinsohn |
| 1974-75 | Golden State | 4–0 | Washington | Al Attles |
| 1975-76 | Boston | 4–2 | Phoenix | Tommy Heinsohn |
| 1976-77 | Portland | 4–2 | Philadelphia | Jack Ramsay |
| 1977-78 | Washington | 4–3 | Seattle | Dick Motta |
| 1978-79 | Seattle | 4–1 | Washington | Lenny Wilkens |
| 1979-80 | LA Lakers | 4–2 | Philadelphia | Paul Westhead |
| 1980-81 | Boston | 4–2 | Houston | Bill Fitch |
| 1981-82 | LA Lakers | 4–2 | Philadelphia | Pat Riley |
| 1982-83 | Philadelphia | 4–0 | LA Lakers | Billy Cunningham |
| 1983-84 | Boston | 4–3 | LA Lakers | K.C. Jones |
| 1984-85 | LA Lakers | 4–2 | Boston | Pat Riley |
| 1985-86 | Boston | 4–2 | Houston | K.C. Jones |
| 1986-87 | LA Lakers | 4–2 | Boston | Pat Riley |
| 1987-88 | LA Lakers | 4–3 | Detroit | Pat Riley |
| 1988-89 | Detroit | 4–0 | LA Lakers | Chuck Daly |
| 1989-90 | Detroit | 4–1 | Portland | Chuck Daly |
| 1990-91 | Chicago | 4–1 | LA Lakers | Phil Jackson |
| 1991-92 | Chicago | 4–2 | Portland | Phil Jackson |
| 1992-93 | Chicago | 4–2 | Phoenix | Phil Jackson |
| 1993-94 | Houston | 4–3 | New York | Rudy Tomjanovich |
| 1994-95 | Houston | 4–0 | Orlando | Rudy Tomjanovich |

## NBA Finals Most Valuable Player

| | | | |
|---|---|---|---|
| 1969 | Jerry West, LA | 1983 | Moses Malone, Phil |
| 1970 | Willis Reed, NY | 1984 | Larry Bird, Bos |
| 1971 | Kareem Abdul-Jabbar, Mil | 1985 | Kareem Abdul-Jabbar, LA Lakers |
| 1972 | Wilt Chamberlain, LA | 1986 | Larry Bird, Bos |
| 1973 | Willis Reed, NY | 1987 | Magic Johnson, LA Lakers |
| 1974 | John Havlicek, Bos | 1988 | James Worthy, LA Lakers |
| 1975 | Rick Barry, GS | 1989 | Joe Dumars, Det |
| 1976 | JoJo White, Bos | 1990 | Isiah Thomas, Det |
| 1977 | Bill Walton, Port | 1991 | Michael Jordan, Chi |
| 1978 | Wes Unseld, Wash | 1992 | Michael Jordan, Chi |
| 1979 | Dennis Johnson, Sea | 1993 | Michael Jordan, Chi |
| 1980 | Magic Johnson, LA | 1994 | Hakeem Olajuwon, Hou |
| 1981 | Cedric Maxwell, Bos | 1995 | Hakeem Olajuwon, Hou |
| 1982 | Magic Johnson, LA | | |

## NBA Most Valuable Player: Maurice Podoloff Trophy

| Season | Player, Team | GP | Field Goals FGM | Pct | 3-Pt FG FGM | Pct | Free Throws FTM | Pct | Rebounds Off | Total | A | Stl | BS | Avg |
|--------|--------------|----|-----|-----|-----|-----|-----|-----|-----|-------|---|-----|-----|-----|
| 1955-56 | Bob Pettit, StL | 72 | 646 | 42.9 | – | – | 557 | 73.6 | – | 1,164 | 189 | – | – | 25.7 |
| 1956-57 | Bob Cousy, Bos | 64 | 478 | 37.8 | – | – | 363 | 82.1 | – | 309 | 478 | – | – | 20.6 |
| 1957-58 | Bill Russell, Bos | 69 | 456 | 44.2 | – | – | 230 | 51.9 | – | 1,564 | 202 | – | – | 16.6 |
| 1958-59 | Bob Pettit, StL | 72 | 719 | 43.8 | – | – | 667 | 75.9 | – | 1,182 | 221 | – | – | 29.2 |
| 1959-60 | Wilt Chamberlain, Phil | 72 | 1,065 | 46.1 | – | – | 577 | 58.2 | – | 1,941 | 168 | – | – | 37.6 |
| 1960-61 | Bill Russell, Bos | 78 | 532 | 42.6 | – | – | 258 | 55.0 | – | 1,868 | 264 | – | – | 16.9 |
| 1961-62 | Bill Russell, Bos | 76 | 575 | 45.7 | – | – | 286 | 59.5 | – | 1,891 | 341 | – | – | 18.9 |
| 1962-63 | Bill Russell, Bos | 78 | 511 | 43.2 | – | – | 287 | 55.5 | – | 1,843 | 348 | – | – | 16.8 |
| 1963-64 | Oscar Robertson, Cin | 79 | 840 | 48.3 | – | – | 800 | 85.3 | – | 783 | 868 | – | – | 31.4 |
| 1964-65 | Bill Russell, Bos | 78 | 429 | 43.8 | – | – | 244 | 57.3 | – | 1,878 | 410 | – | – | 14.1 |
| 1965-66 | Wilt Chamberlain, Phil | 79 | 1,074 | 54.0 | – | – | 501 | 51.3 | – | 1,943 | 414 | – | – | 33.5 |
| 1966-67 | Wilt Chamberlain, Phil | 81 | 785 | 68.3 | – | – | 386 | 44.1 | – | 1,957 | 630 | – | – | 24.1 |
| 1967-68 | Wilt Chamberlain, Phil | 82 | 819 | 59.5 | – | – | 354 | 38.0 | – | 1,952 | 702 | – | – | 24.3 |
| 1968-69 | Wes Unseld, Balt | 82 | 427 | 47.6 | – | – | 277 | 60.5 | – | 1,491 | 213 | – | – | 13.8 |
| 1969-70 | Willis Reed, NY | 81 | 702 | 50.7 | – | – | 351 | 75.6 | – | 1,126 | 161 | – | – | 21.7 |
| 1970-71 | Kareem Abdul-Jabbar, Mil | 82 | 1,063 | 57.7 | – | – | 470 | 69.0 | – | 1,311 | 272 | – | – | 31.7 |
| 1971-72 | Kareem Abdul-Jabbar, Mil | 81 | 1,159 | 57.4 | – | – | 504 | 68.9 | – | 1,346 | 370 | – | – | 34.8 |
| 1972-73 | Dave Cowens, Bos | 82 | 740 | 45.2 | – | – | 204 | 77.9 | – | 1,329 | 333 | – | – | 20.5 |
| 1973-74 | Kareem Abdul-Jabbar, Mil | 81 | 948 | 53.9 | – | – | 295 | 70.2 | 287 | 1,178 | 386 | 112 | 283 | 27.0 |
| 1974-75 | Bob McAdoo, Buff | 82 | 1,095 | 51.2 | – | – | 641 | 80.5 | 307 | 1,155 | 179 | 92 | 174 | 34.5 |
| 1975-76 | Kareem Abdul-Jabbar, LA | 82 | 914 | 52.9 | – | – | 447 | 70.3 | 272 | 1,383 | 413 | 119 | 338 | 37.7 |
| 1976-77 | Kareem Abdul-Jabbar, LA | 82 | 888 | 57.9 | – | – | 376 | 70.1 | 266 | 1,090 | 319 | 101 | 261 | 26.2 |
| 1977-78 | Bill Walton, Port | 58 | 460 | 52.2 | – | – | 177 | 72.0 | 118 | 766 | 291 | 60 | 146 | 18.9 |
| 1978-79 | Moses Malone, Hou | 82 | 716 | 54.0 | – | – | 599 | 73.9 | 587 | 1,444 | 147 | 79 | 119 | 24.8 |
| 1979-80 | Kareem Abdul-Jabbar, LA | 82 | 835 | 60.4 | 0 | 00.0 | 364 | 76.5 | 190 | 886 | 371 | 81 | 280 | 24.8 |
| 1980-81 | Julius Erving, Phil | 82 | 794 | 52.1 | 4 | 22.2 | 422 | 78.7 | 244 | 657 | 364 | 173 | 147 | 24.6 |
| 1981-82 | Moses Malone, Hou | 81 | 945 | 51.9 | 0 | 00.0 | 630 | 76.2 | 558 | 1,188 | 142 | 76 | 125 | 31.1 |
| 1982-83 | Moses Malone, Phil | 78 | 654 | 50.1 | 0 | 00.0 | 600 | 76.1 | 445 | 1,194 | 101 | 89 | 157 | 24.5 |
| 1983-84 | Larry Bird, Bos | 79 | 758 | 49.2 | 18 | 24.7 | 374 | 88.8 | 181 | 796 | 520 | 144 | 69 | 24.2 |
| 1984-85 | Larry Bird, Bos | 80 | 918 | 52.2 | 56 | 42.7 | 403 | 88.2 | 164 | 842 | 531 | 129 | 98 | 28.7 |
| 1985-86 | Larry Bird, Bos | 82 | 796 | 49.6 | 82 | 42.3 | 441 | 89.6 | 190 | 805 | 557 | 166 | 51 | 25.8 |
| 1986-87 | Magic Johnson, LA Lakers | 80 | 683 | 52.2 | 8 | 20.5 | 535 | 84.8 | 122 | 504 | 977 | 138 | 36 | 23.9 |
| 1987-88 | Michael Jordan, Chi | 82 | 1,069 | 53.5 | 7 | 13.2 | 723 | 84.1 | 139 | 449 | 485 | 259 | 131 | 35.0 |
| 1988-89 | Magic Johnson, LA Lakers | 77 | 579 | 50.9 | 59 | 31.4 | 513 | 91.1 | 111 | 607 | 988 | 138 | 22 | 22.5 |
| 1989-90 | Magic Johnson, LA Lakers | 79 | 546 | 48.0 | 106 | 38.4 | 567 | 89.0 | 128 | 522 | 907 | 132 | 34 | 22.3 |
| 1990-91 | Michael Jordan, Chi | 82 | 990 | 53.9 | 29 | 31.2 | 571 | 85.1 | 118 | 492 | 453 | 223 | 83 | 31.5 |
| 1991-92 | Michael Jordan, Chi | 80 | 943 | 51.9 | 27 | 27.0 | 491 | 83.2 | 91 | 511 | 489 | 182 | 75 | 30.1 |
| 1992-93 | Charles Barkley, Phoe | 76 | 716 | 52.0 | 67 | 30.5 | 445 | 76.5 | 237 | 928 | 385 | 119 | 74 | 25.6 |
| 1993-94 | Hakeem Olajuwon, Hou | 80 | 894 | 52.8 | 8 | 42.1 | 388 | 71.6 | 229 | 955 | 287 | 128 | 297 | 27.3 |
| 1994-95 | David Robinson, SA | 81 | 788 | 53.0 | 6 | 30.0 | 656 | 77.4 | 234 | 877 | 236 | 134 | 262 | 27.6 |

## Coach of the Year: Arnold "Red" Auerbach Trophy

| | | | |
|---|---|---|---|
| 1962-63 | Harry Gallatin, StL | 1979-80 | Bill Fitch, Bos |
| 1963-64 | Alex Hannum, SF | 1980-81 | Jack McKinney, Ind |
| 1964-65 | Red Auerbach, Bos | 1981-82 | Gene Shue, Wash |
| 1965-66 | Dolph Schayes, Phil | 1982-83 | Don Nelson, Mil |
| 1966-67 | Johnny Kerr, Chi | 1983-84 | Frank Layden, Utah |
| 1967-68 | Richie Guerin, StL | 1984-85 | Don Nelson, Mil |
| 1968-69 | Gene Shue, Balt | 1985-86 | Mike Fratello, Atl |
| 1969-70 | Red Holzman, NY | 1986-87 | Mike Schuler, Port |
| 1970-71 | Dick Motta, Chi | 1987-88 | Doug Moe, Den |
| 1971-72 | Bill Sharman, LA | 1988-89 | Cotton Fitzsimmons, Phoe |
| 1972-73 | Tom Heinsohn, Bos | 1989-90 | Pat Riley, LA Lakers |
| 1973-74 | Ray Scott, Det | 1990-91 | Don Chaney, Hou |
| 1974-75 | Phil Johnson, KC-Oma | 1991-92 | Don Nelson, GS |
| 1975-76 | Bill Fitch, Clev | 1992-93 | Pat Riley, NY |
| 1976-77 | Tom Nissalke, Hou | 1993-94 | Lenny Wilkens, Atl |
| 1977-78 | Hubie Brown, Atl | 1994-95 | Del Harris, LA Lakers |
| 1978-79 | Cotton Fitzsimmons, KC | | |

Note: Award named after Auerbach in 1986.

## NBA Rookie of the Year: Eddie Gottlieb Trophy

| | | |
|---|---|---|
| 1952-53...Don Meineke, FW | 1967-68...Earl Monroe, Balt | 1981-82...Buck Williams, NJ |
| 1953-54...Ray Felix, Balt | 1968-69...Wes Unseld, Balt | 1982-83...Terry Cummings, SD |
| 1954-55...Bob Pettit, Mil | 1969-70...K. Abdul-Jabbar, Mil | 1983-84...Ralph Sampson, Hou |
| 1955-56...Maurice Stokes, Roch | 1970-71...Dave Cowens, Bos | 1984-85...Michael Jordan, Chi |
| 1956-57...Tom Heinsohn, Bos | Geoff Petrie, Port | 1985-86...Patrick Ewing, NY |
| 1957-58...Woody Sauldsberry, Phil | 1971-72...Sidney Wicks, Port | 1986-87...Chuck Person, Ind |
| 1958-59...Elgin Baylor, Minn | 1972-73...Bob McAdoo, Buff | 1987-88...Mark Jackson, NY |
| 1959-60...Wilt Chamberlain, Phil | 1973-74...Ernie DiGregorio, Buff | 1988-89...Mitch Richmond, GS |
| 1960-61...Oscar Robertson, Cin | 1974-75...Keith Wilkes, GS | 1989-90...David Robinson, SA |
| 1961-62...Walt Bellamy, Chi | 1975-76...Alvan Adams, Phoe | 1990-91...Derrick Coleman, NJ |
| 1962-63...Terry Dischinger, Chi | 1976-77...Adrian Dantley, Buff | 1991-92...Larry Johnson, Char |
| 1963-64...Jerry Lucas, Cin | 1977-78...Walter Davis, Phoe | 1992-93...Shaquille O'Neal, Orl |
| 1964-65...Willis Reed, NY | 1978-79...Phil Ford, KC | 1993-94...Chris Webber, GS |
| 1965-66...Rick Barry, SF | 1979-80...Larry Bird, Bos | 1994-95...Jason Kidd, Dal |
| 1966-67...Dave Bing, Det | 1980-81...Darrell Griffith, Utah | Grant Hill, Det |

## NBA Defensive Player of the Year

| | |
|---|---|
| 1982-83 | Sidney Moncrief, Mil |
| 1983-84 | Sidney Moncrief, Mil |
| 1984-85 | Mark Eaton, Utah |
| 1985-86 | Alvin Robertson, SA |
| 1986-87 | Michael Cooper, LA Lakers |
| 1987-88 | Michael Jordan, Chi |
| 1988-89 | Mark Eaton, Utah |
| 1989-90 | Dennis Rodman, Det |
| 1990-91 | Dennis Rodman, Det |
| 1991-92 | David Robinson, SA |
| 1992-93 | Hakeem Olajuwon, Hou |
| 1993-94 | Hakeem Olajuwon, Hou |
| 1994-95 | Dikembe Mutombo, Den |

## NBA Sixth Man Award

| | |
|---|---|
| 1982-83 | Bobby Jones, Phil |
| 1983-84 | Kevin McHale, Bos |
| 1984-85 | Kevin McHale, Bos |
| 1985-86 | Bill Walton, Bos |
| 1986-87 | Ricky Pierce, Mil |
| 1987-88 | Roy Tarpley, Dall |
| 1988-89 | Eddie Johnson, Phoe |
| 1989-90 | Ricky Pierce, Mil |
| 1990-91 | Detlef Schrempf, Ind |
| 1991-92 | Detlef Schrempf, Ind |
| 1992-93 | Cliff Robinson, Port |
| 1993-94 | Dell Curry, Char |
| 1994-95 | Anthony Mason, NY |

## J. Walter Kennedy Citizenship Award

| | |
|---|---|
| 1974-75 | Wes Unseld, Wash |
| 1975-76 | Slick Watts, Sea |
| 1976-77 | Dave Bing, Wash |
| 1977-78 | Bob Lanier, Det |
| 1978-79 | Calvin Murphy, Hou |
| 1979-80 | Austin Carr, Clev |
| 1980-81 | Mike Glenn, NY |
| 1981-82 | Kent Benson, Det |
| 1982-83 | Julius Erving, Phil |
| 1983-84 | Frank Layden, Utah |
| 1984-85 | Dan Issel, Den |
| 1985-86 | Michael Cooper, LA Lakers |
| | Rory Sparrow, NY |
| 1986-87 | Isiah Thomas, Det |
| 1987-88 | Alex English, Den |
| 1988-89 | Thurl Bailey, Utah |

## Kennedy Citizenship Award (Cont.)

| | |
|---|---|
| 1989-90 | Glenn Rivers, Atl |
| 1990-91 | Kevin Johnson, Phoe |
| 1991-92 | Magic Johnson, LA Lakers |
| 1992-93 | Terry Porter, Port |
| 1993-94 | Joe Dumars, Det |
| 1994-95 | Joe O'Toole, Atl |

## NBA Most Improved Player

| | |
|---|---|
| 1985-86 | Alvin Robertson, SA |
| 1986-87 | Dale Ellis, Sea |
| 1987-88 | Kevin Duckworth, Port |
| 1988-89 | Kevin Johnson, Phoe |
| 1989-90 | Rony Seikaly, Mia |
| 1990-91 | Scott Skiles, Orl |
| 1991-92 | Pervis Ellison, Wash |
| 1992-93 | Chris Jackson, Den |
| 1993-94 | Don MacLean, Wash |
| 1994-95 | Dana Barros, Phil |

## NBA Executive of the Year

| | |
|---|---|
| 1972-73 | Joe Axelson, KC-Oma |
| 1973-74 | Eddie Donovan, Buff |
| 1974-75 | Dick Vertlieb, GS |
| 1975-76 | Jerry Colangelo, Phoe |
| 1976-77 | Ray Patterson, Hou |
| 1977-78 | Angelo Drossos, SA |
| 1978-79 | Bob Ferry, Wash |
| 1979-80 | Red Auerbach, Bos |
| 1980-81 | Jerry Colangelo, Phoe |
| 1981-82 | Bob Ferry, Wash |
| 1982-83 | Zollie Volchok, Sea |
| 1983-84 | Frank Layden, Utah |
| 1984-85 | Vince Boryla, Den |
| 1985-86 | Stan Kasten, Atl |
| 1986-87 | Stan Kasten, Atl |
| 1987-88 | Jerry Krause, Chi |
| 1988-89 | Jerry Colangelo, Phoe |
| 1989-90 | Bob Bass, SA |
| 1990-91 | Bucky Buckwalter, Port |
| 1991-92 | Wayne Embry, Cle |
| 1992-93 | Jerry Colangelo, Phoe |
| 1993-94 | Bob Whitsitt, Seattle |
| 1994-95 | Jerry West, LA Lakers |

Selected by *The Sporting News*.

# NBA All-Time Individual Leaders

## Scoring

### MOST POINTS, LIFETIME

| | |
|---|---|
| Kareem Abdul-Jabbar | 38,387 |
| Wilt Chamberlain | 31,419 |
| Moses Malone | 27,409 |
| Elvin Hayes | 27,313 |
| Oscar Robertson | 26,710 |
| John Havlicek | 26,395 |
| Alex English | 25,613 |
| Dominique Wilkins | 25,389 |
| Jerry West | 25,192 |
| Adrian Dantley | 23,177 |

### MOST POINTS, SEASON

| | | |
|---|---|---|
| Wilt Chamberlain, Phil | 4,029 | 1961-62 |
| Wilt Chamberlain, SF | 3,586 | 1962-63 |
| Michael Jordan, Chi | 3,041 | 1986-87 |
| Wilt Chamberlain, Phil | 3,033 | 1960-61 |
| Wilt Chamberlain, SF | 2,948 | 1963-64 |
| Michael Jordan, Chi | 2,868 | 1986-87 |
| Bob McAdoo, Buff | 2,831 | 1974-75 |
| Rick Barry, SF | 2,775 | 1966-67 |
| Michael Jordan, Chi | 2,753 | 1989-90 |
| Elgin Baylor, LA | 2,719 | 1962-63 |

### HIGHEST SCORING AVERAGE, CAREER

| | | |
|---|---|---|
| Michael Jordan | 32.2 | 684 games |
| Wilt Chamberlain | 30.1 | 1,045 games |
| Elgin Baylor | 27.4 | 846 games |
| Jerry West | 27.0 | 932 games |
| Bob Pettit | 26.4 | 792 games |
| George Gervin | 26.2 | 791 games |
| Karl Malone | 26.0 | 816 games |
| Dominique Wilkins | 25.8 | 984 games |
| David Robinson | 25.7 | 475 games |
| Oscar Robertson | 25.7 | 1,040 games |

## Field Goal Percentage

Highest Field Goal Percentage, Career: .599—Artis Gilmore

Highest Field Goal Percentage, Season: .727—Wilt Chamberlain, LA Lakers, 1972-73 (426/586)

## Free Throw Percentage

### HIGHEST FREE THROW PERCENTAGE, CAREER

| | |
|---|---|
| Mark Price | .906 |
| Rick Barry | .900 |
| Calvin Murphy | .892 |
| Scott Skiles | .890 |
| Larry Bird | .886 |

Note: Minimum 1200 free throws made.

### HIGHEST FREE THROW PERCENTAGE, SEASON

| | | |
|---|---|---|
| Calvin Murphy, Hou | .958 | 1980-81 |
| Mahmoud Abdul-Rauf | .956 | 1993-94 |
| Mark Price, Clev | .948 | 1992-93 |
| Mark Price, Clev | .947 | 1991-92 |
| Rick Barry, Hou | .946 | 1978-79 |

### HIGHEST SCORING AVERAGE, SEASON

| | | |
|---|---|---|
| Wilt Chamberlain, Phil | 50.4 | 1961-62 |
| Wilt Chamberlain, SF | 44.8 | 1962-63 |
| Wilt Chamberlain, Phil | 38.4 | 1960-61 |
| Wilt Chamberlain, Phil | 37.6 | 1959-60 |
| Michael Jordan, Chi | 37.1 | 1986-87 |
| Wilt Chamberlain, SF | 36.9 | 1963-64 |
| Rick Barry, SF | 35.6 | 1966-67 |
| Michael Jordan, Chi | 35.0 | 1987-88 |
| Elgin Baylor, LA | 34.8 | 1960-61 |

Note: Minimum 70 games.

### MOST POINTS, GAME

| | Player, Team | Opp | Date |
|---|---|---|---|
| 100 | Wilt Chamberlain, Phi | NY | 3/2/62 |
| 78 | Wilt Chamberlain, Phi | LA | 12/8/61 |
| 73 | Wilt Chamberlain, Phi | Chi | 1/13/62 |
| 73 | Wilt Chamberlain, SF | NY | 11/16/62 |
| 73 | David Thompson, Den | Det | 4/9/78 |
| 72 | Wilt Chamberlain, SF | LA | 11/3/62 |
| 71 | David Robinson, SA | LAC | 4/24/94 |
| 71 | Elgin Baylor, LA | NY | 11/15/60 |
| 70 | Wilt Chamberlain, SF | Syr | 3/10/63 |
| 69 | Michael Jordan, Chi | Cle | 3/28/90 |

## THEY SAID IT

*Brian Williams, Denver Nugget forward, on how the fractious atmosphere surrounding his team could be improved: "We all need to join hands and sing 'Kumbaya.' "*

## Three-Point Field Goal Percentage*

Most Three-Point Field Goals, Career: Dale Ellis—1,119

Highest Three-Point Field Goal Percentage, Career: Steve Kerr—.467

Most Three-Point Field Goals, Season: John Starks, NY—217, 1994-95

Highest Three-Point Field Goal Percentage, Season: Steve Kerr, Chi—.524, 1994-95

Most Three-Point Field Goals, Game: 10—Brian Shaw, Miami vs Milwaukee, 4/8/93; Joe Dumars, Detroit vs Minnesota, 11/8/94

*First Year of Shot: 1979-80.

## Steals

Most Steals, Career: 2,310—Maurice Cheeks

Most Steals, Season: 301—Alvin Robertson, San Antonio, 1985-86

Most Steals, Game: 11—Larry Kenon, San Antonio vs Kansas City, 12/26/76

## Rebounds

### MOST REBOUNDS, CAREER

| | |
|---|---|
| Wilt Chamberlain | 23,924 |
| Bill Russell | 21,620 |
| Kareem Abdul-Jabbar | 17,440 |
| Elvin Hayes | 16,279 |
| Moses Malone | 16,212 |
| Nate Thurmond | 14,464 |
| Robert Parish | 14,323 |
| Walt Bellamy | 14,241 |
| Wes Unseld | 13,769 |
| Jerry Lucas | 12,942 |

### MOST REBOUNDS, SEASON

| | | |
|---|---|---|
| Wilt Chamberlain, Phil | 2,149 | 1960-61 |
| Wilt Chamberlain, Phil | 2,052 | 1961-62 |
| Wilt Chamberlain, Phil | 1,957 | 1966-67 |
| Wilt Chamberlain, Phil | 1,952 | 1967-68 |
| Wilt Chamberlain, SF | 1,946 | 1962-63 |
| Wilt Chamberlain, Phil | 1,943 | 1965-66 |
| Wilt Chamberlain, Phil | 1,941 | 1959-60 |
| Bill Russell, Bos | 1,930 | 1963-64 |
| Bill Russell, Bos | 1,878 | 1964-65 |
| Bill Russell, Bos | 1,868 | 1960-61 |

### MOST REBOUNDS, GAME

| | Player, Team | Opp | Date |
|---|---|---|---|
| 55 | Wilt Chamberlain, Phi | Bos | 11/24/60 |
| 51 | Bill Russell, Bos | Syr | 2/5/60 |
| 49 | Bill Russell, Bos | Phi | 11/16/57 |
| 49 | Bill Russell, Bos | Det | 3/11/65 |
| 45 | Wilt Chamberlain, Phil | Syr | 2/6/60 |
| 45 | Wilt Chamberlain, Phil | LA | 1/21/61 |

## Assists

### MOST ASSISTS, CAREER

| | |
|---|---|
| John Stockton | 10,394 |
| Magic Johnson | 9,921 |
| Oscar Robertson | 9,887 |
| Isiah Thomas | 9,061 |
| Maurice Cheeks | 7,392 |

### MOST ASSISTS, SEASON

| | | |
|---|---|---|
| John Stockton, Utah | 1,164 | 1990-91 |
| John Stockton, Utah | 1,134 | 1989-90 |
| John Stockton, Utah | 1,128 | 1987-88 |
| John Stockton, Utah | 1,126 | 1991-92 |
| Isiah Thomas, Det | 1,123 | 1984-85 |

**MOST ASSISTS, GAME:** 30—Scott Skiles, Orlando vs Denver, 12/30/90

## Blocked Shots

### MOST BLOCKED SHOTS, CAREER

| | |
|---|---|
| Kareem Abdul-Jabbar | 3,189 |
| Mark Eaton | 3,064 |
| Hakeem Olajuwon | 2,983 |
| Wayne (Tree) Rollins | 2,542 |

### MOST BLOCKED SHOTS, SEASON

| | | |
|---|---|---|
| Mark Eaton, Utah | 456 | 1984-85 |
| Manute Bol, Wash | 397 | 1985-86 |
| Elmore Smith, LA | 393 | 1973-74 |

**MOST BLOCKED SHOTS, GAME:** 17—Elmore Smith, LA Lakers vs Portland, 10/28/73

# NBA Season Leaders

## Scoring

| | | |
|---|---|---|
| 1946-47 | Joe Fulks, Phil | 1389 |
| 1947-48 | Max Zaslofsky, Chi | 1007 |
| 1948-49 | George Mikan, Minn | 1698 |
| 1949-50 | George Mikan, Minn | 1865 |
| 1950-51 | George Mikan, Minn | 1932 |
| 1951-52 | Paul Arizin, Phil | 1674 |
| 1952-53 | Neil Johnston, Phil | 1564 |
| 1953-54 | Neil Johnston, Phil | 1759 |
| 1954-55 | Neil Johnston, Phil | 1631 |
| 1955-56 | Bob Pettit, StL | 1849 |
| 1956-57 | Paul Arizin, Phil | 1817 |
| 1957-58 | George Yardley, Det | 2001 |
| 1958-59 | Bob Pettit, StL | 2105 |
| 1959-60 | Wilt Chamberlain, Phil | 2707 |
| 1960-61 | Wilt Chamberlain, Phil | 3033 |
| 1961-62 | Wilt Chamberlain, Phil | 4029 |
| 1962-63 | Wilt Chamberlain, SF | 3586 |
| 1963-64 | Wilt Chamberlain, SF | 2948 |
| 1964-65 | Wilt Chamberlain, SF-Phil | 2534 |
| 1965-66 | Wilt Chamberlain, Phil | 2649 |
| 1966-67 | Rick Barry, SF | 2775 |
| 1967-68 | Dave Bing, Det | 2142 |
| 1968-69 | Elvin Hayes, SD | 2327 |
| 1969-70 | Jerry West, LA | *31.2 |
| 1970-71 | Kareem Abdul-Jabbar, Mil | 31.7 |
| 1971-72 | Kareem Abdul-Jabbar, Mil | 34.8 |
| 1972-73 | Nate Archibald, KC-Oma | 34.0 |
| 1973-74 | Bob McAdoo, Buff | 30.6 |
| 1974-75 | Bob McAdoo, Buff | 34.5 |
| 1975-76 | Bob McAdoo, Buff | 31.1 |
| 1976-77 | Pete Maravich, NO | 31.1 |
| 1977-78 | George Gervin, SA | 27.2 |
| 1978-79 | George Gervin, SA | 29.6 |
| 1979-80 | George Gervin, SA | 33.1 |
| 1980-81 | Adrian Dantley, Utah | 30.7 |
| 1981-82 | George Gervin, SA | 32.3 |
| 1982-83 | Alex English, Den | 28.4 |
| 1983-84 | Adrian Dantley, Utah | 30.6 |
| 1984-85 | Bernard King, NY | 32.9 |
| 1985-86 | Dominique Wilkins, Atl | 30.3 |
| 1986-87 | Michael Jordan, Chi | 37.1 |
| 1987-88 | Michael Jordan, Chi | 35.0 |
| 1988-89 | Michael Jordan, Chi | 32.5 |
| 1989-90 | Michael Jordan, Chi | 33.6 |
| 1990-91 | Michael Jordan, Chi | 31.5 |
| 1991-92 | Michael Jordan, Chi | 30.1 |
| 1992-93 | Michael Jordan, Chi | 32.6 |
| 1993-94 | David Robinson, SA | 29.8 |
| 1994-95 | Shaquille O'Neal, Orl | 29.3 |

*Based on per game average since 1969-70.

## Rebounding

| | | |
|---|---|---|
| 1950-51 | Dolph Schayes, Syr | 1080 |
| 1951-52 | Larry Foust, FW | 880 |
| | Mel Hutchins, Mil | 880 |
| 1952-53 | George Mikan, Minn | 1007 |
| 1953-54 | Harry Gallatin, NY | 1098 |
| 1954-55 | Neil Johnston, Phil | 1085 |
| 1955-56 | Bob Pettit, StL | 1164 |
| 1956-57 | Maurice Stokes, Roch | 1256 |
| 1957-58 | Bill Russell, Bos | 1564 |
| 1958-59 | Bill Russell, Bos | 1612 |
| 1959-60 | Wilt Chamberlain, Phil | 1941 |
| 1960-61 | Wilt Chamberlain, Phil | 2149 |
| 1961-62 | Wilt Chamberlain, Phil | 2052 |
| 1962-63 | Wilt Chamberlain, SF | 1946 |
| 1963-64 | Bill Russell, Bos | 1930 |
| 1964-65 | Bill Russell, Bos | 1878 |
| 1965-66 | Wilt Chamberlain, Phil | 1943 |
| 1966-67 | Wilt Chamberlain, Phil | 1957 |
| 1967-68 | Wilt Chamberlain, Phil | 1952 |
| 1968-69 | Wilt Chamberlain, LA | 1712 |
| 1969-70 | Elvin Hayes, SD | *16.9 |
| 1970-71 | Wilt Chamberlain, LA | 18.2 |
| 1971-72 | Wilt Chamberlain, LA | 19.2 |
| 1972-73 | Wilt Chamberlain, LA | 18.6 |
| 1973-74 | Elvin Hayes, Capital | 18.1 |
| 1974-75 | Wes Unseld, Wash | 14.8 |
| 1975-76 | Kareem Abdul-Jabbar, LA | 16.9 |
| 1976-77 | Bill Walton, Port | 14.4 |
| 1977-78 | Len Robinson, NO | 15.7 |
| 1978-79 | Moses Malone, Hou | 17.6 |
| 1979-80 | Swen Nater, SD | 15.0 |
| 1980-81 | Moses Malone, Hou | 14.8 |
| 1981-82 | Moses Malone, Hou | 14.7 |
| 1982-83 | Moses Malone, Phil | 15.3 |
| 1983-84 | Moses Malone, Phil | 13.4 |
| 1984-85 | Moses Malone, Phil | 13.1 |
| 1985-86 | Bill Laimbeer, Det | 13.1 |
| 1986-87 | Charles Barkley, Phil | 14.6 |
| 1987-88 | Michael Cage, LA Clippers | 13.0 |
| 1988-89 | Hakeem Olajuwon, Hou | 13.5 |
| 1989-90 | Hakeem Olajuwon, Hou | 14.0 |
| 1990-91 | David Robinson, SA | 13.0 |
| 1991-92 | Dennis Rodman, Detroit | 18.7 |
| 1992-93 | Dennis Rodman, Detroit | 18.3 |
| 1993-94 | Dennis Rodman, San Antonio | 17.3 |
| 1994-95 | Dennis Rodman, San Antonio | 16.8 |

*Based on per game average since 1969-70.

## Assists

| | | |
|---|---|---|
| 1946-47 | Ernie Calverly, Prov | 202 |
| 1947-48 | Howie Dallmar, Phil | 120 |
| 1948-49 | Bob Davies, Roch | 321 |
| 1949-50 | Dick McGuire, NY | 386 |
| 1950-51 | Andy Phillip, Phil | 414 |
| 1951-52 | Andy Phillip, Phil | 539 |
| 1952-53 | Bob Cousy, Bos | 547 |
| 1953-54 | Bob Cousy, Bos | 578 |
| 1954-55 | Bob Cousy, Bos | 557 |
| 1955-56 | Bob Cousy, Bos | 642 |
| 1956-57 | Bob Cousy, Bos | 478 |
| 1957-58 | Bob Cousy, Bos | 463 |
| 1958-59 | Bob Cousy, Bos | 557 |
| 1959-60 | Bob Cousy, Bos | 715 |
| 1960-61 | Oscar Robertson, Cin | 690 |
| 1961-62 | Oscar Robertson, Cin | 899 |
| 1962-63 | Guy Rodgers, SF | 825 |
| 1963-64 | Oscar Robertson, Cin | 868 |
| 1964-65 | Oscar Robertson, Cin | 861 |
| 1965-66 | Oscar Robertson, Cin | 847 |
| 1966-67 | Guy Rodgers, Chi | 908 |
| 1967-68 | Wilt Chamberlain, Phil | 702 |
| 1968-69 | Oscar Robertson, Cin | 772 |
| 1969-70 | Len Wilkens, Sea | *9.1 |
| 1970-71 | Norm Van Lier, Cin | 10.1 |
| 1971-72 | Jerry West, LA | 9.7 |
| 1972-73 | Nate Archibald, KC-Oma | 11.4 |
| 1973-74 | Ernie DiGregorio, Buff | 8.2 |
| 1974-75 | Kevin Porter, Wash | 8.0 |
| 1975-76 | Don Watts, Sea | 8.1 |
| 1976-77 | Don Buse, Ind | 8.5 |
| 1977-78 | Kevin Porter, NJ-Det | 10.2 |
| 1978-79 | Kevin Porter, Det | 13.4 |
| 1979-80 | Micheal Richardson, NY | 10.1 |
| 1980-81 | Kevin Porter, Wash | 9.1 |
| 1981-82 | Johnny Moore, SA | 9.6 |
| 1982-83 | Magic Johnson, LA | 10.5 |
| 1983-84 | Magic Johnson, LA | 13.1 |
| 1984-85 | Isiah Thomas, Det | 13.9 |
| 1985-86 | Magic Johnson, LA Lakers | 12.6 |
| 1986-87 | Magic Johnson, LA Lakers | 12.2 |
| 1987-88 | John Stockton, Utah | 13.8 |
| 1988-89 | John Stockton, Utah | 13.6 |
| 1989-90 | John Stockton, Utah | 14.5 |
| 1990-91 | John Stockton, Utah | 14.2 |
| 1991-92 | John Stockton, Utah | 13.7 |
| 1992-93 | John Stockton, Utah | 12.0 |
| 1993-94 | John Stockton, Utah | 12.6 |
| 1994-95 | John Stockton, Utah | 12.3 |

*Based on per game average since 1969-70.

## Field Goal Percentage

| | | |
|---|---|---|
| 1946-47 | Bob Feerick, Wash | 40.1 |
| 1947-48 | Bob Feerick, Wash | 34.0 |
| 1948-49 | Arnie Risen, Roch | 42.3 |
| 1949-50 | Alex Groza, Ind | 47.8 |
| 1950-51 | Alex Groza, Ind | 47.0 |
| 1951-52 | Paul Arizin, Phil | 44.8 |
| 1952-53 | Neil Johnston, Phil | 45.2 |
| 1953-54 | Ed Macauley, Bos | 48.6 |
| 1954-55 | Larry Foust, FW | 48.7 |
| 1955-56 | Neil Johnston, Phil | 45.7 |
| 1956-57 | Neil Johnston, Phil | 44.7 |
| 1957-58 | Jack Twyman, Cin | 45.2 |
| 1958-59 | Ken Sears, NY | 49.0 |
| 1959-60 | Ken Sears, NY | 47.7 |
| 1960-61 | Wilt Chamberlain, Phil | 50.9 |
| 1961-62 | Walt Bellamy, Chi | 51.9 |
| 1962-63 | Wilt Chamberlain, SF | 52.8 |
| 1963-64 | Jerry Lucas, Cin | 52.7 |
| 1964-65 | Wilt Chamberlain, SF-Phil | 51.0 |
| 1965-66 | Wilt Chamberlain, Phil | 54.0 |
| 1966-67 | Wilt Chamberlain, Phil | 68.3 |
| 1967-68 | Wilt Chamberlain, Phil | 59.5 |

## Field Goal Percentage (Cont.)

| | | |
|---|---|---|
| 1968-69 | Wilt Chamberlain, LA | 58.3 |
| 1969-70 | Johnny Green, Cin | 55.9 |
| 1970-71 | Johnny Green, Cin | 58.7 |
| 1971-72 | Wilt Chamberlain, LA | 64.9 |
| 1972-73 | Wilt Chamberlain, LA | 72.7 |
| 1973-74 | Bob McAdoo, Buff | 54.7 |
| 1974-75 | Don Nelson, Bos | 53.9 |
| 1975-76 | Wes Unseld, Wash | 56.1 |
| 1976-77 | Kareem Abdul-Jabbar, LA | 57.9 |
| 1977-78 | Bobby Jones, Den | 57.8 |
| 1978-79 | Cedric Maxwell, Bos | 58.4 |
| 1979-80 | Cedric Maxwell, Bos | 60.9 |
| 1980-81 | Artis Gilmore, Chi | 67.0 |
| 1981-82 | Artis Gilmore, Chi | 65.2 |
| 1982-83 | Artis Gilmore, SA | 62.6 |
| 1983-84 | Artis Gilmore, SA | 63.1 |
| 1984-85 | James Donaldson, LA Clippers | 63.7 |
| 1985-86 | Steve Johnson, SA | 63.2 |
| 1986-87 | Kevin McHale, Bos | 60.4 |
| 1987-88 | Kevin McHale, Bos | 60.4 |
| 1988-89 | Dennis Rodman, Det | 59.5 |
| 1989-90 | Mark West, Phoe | 62.5 |
| 1990-91 | Buck Williams, Port | 60.2 |
| 1991-92 | Buck Williams, Port | 60.4 |
| 1992-93 | Cedric Ceballos, Phoe | 57.6 |
| 1993-94 | Shaquille O'Neal, Orl | 59.9 |
| 1994-95 | Chris Gatling, GS | 63.3 |

## Free Throw Percentage

| | | |
|---|---|---|
| 1946-47 | Fred Scolari, Wash | 81.1 |
| 1947-48 | Bob Feerick, Wash | 78.8 |
| 1948-49 | Bob Feerick, Wash | 85.9 |
| 1949-50 | Max Zaslofsky, Chi | 84.3 |
| 1950-51 | Joe Fulks, Phil | 85.5 |
| 1951-52 | Bob Wanzer, Roch | 90.4 |
| 1952-53 | Bill Sharman, Bos | 85.0 |
| 1953-54 | Bill Sharman, Bos | 84.4 |
| 1954-55 | Bill Sharman, Bos | 89.7 |
| 1955-56 | Bill Sharman, Bos | 86.7 |
| 1956-57 | Bill Sharman, Bos | 90.5 |
| 1957-58 | Dolph Schayes, Syr | 90.4 |
| 1958-59 | Bill Sharman, Bos | 93.2 |
| 1959-60 | Dolph Schayes, Syr | 89.2 |
| 1960-61 | Bill Sharman, Bos | 92.1 |
| 1961-62 | Dolph Schayes, Syr | 89.6 |
| 1962-63 | Larry Costello, Syr | 88.1 |
| 1963-64 | Oscar Robertson, Cin | 85.3 |
| 1964-65 | Larry Costello, Phil | 87.7 |
| 1965-66 | Larry Siegfried, Bos | 88.1 |
| 1966-67 | Adrian Smith, Cin | 90.3 |
| 1967-68 | Oscar Robertson, Cin | 87.3 |
| 1968-69 | Larry Siegfried, Bos | 86.4 |
| 1969-70 | Flynn Robinson, Mil | 89.8 |
| 1970-71 | Chet Walker, Chi | 85.9 |
| 1971-72 | Jack Marin, Balt | 89.4 |
| 1972-73 | Rick Barry, GS | 90.2 |
| 1973-74 | Ernie DiGregorio, Buff | 90.2 |
| 1974-75 | Rick Barry, GS | 90.4 |
| 1975-76 | Rick Barry, GS | 92.3 |
| 1976-77 | Ernie DiGregorio, Buff | 94.5 |
| 1977-78 | Rick Barry, GS | 92.4 |
| 1978-79 | Rick Barry, Hou | 94.7 |
| 1979-80 | Rick Barry, Hou | 93.5 |
| 1980-81 | Calvin Murphy, Hou | 95.8 |
| 1981-82 | Kyle Macy, Phoe | 89.9 |
| 1982-83 | Calvin Murphy, Hou | 92.0 |
| 1983-84 | Larry Bird, Bos | 88.8 |
| 1984-85 | Kyle Macy, Phoe | 90.7 |
| 1985-86 | Larry Bird, Bos | 89.6 |
| 1986-87 | Larry Bird, Bos | 91.0 |
| 1987-88 | Jack Sikma, Mil | 92.2 |
| 1988-89 | Magic Johnson, LA Lakers | 91.1 |
| 1989-90 | Larry Bird, Bos | 93.0 |
| 1990-91 | Reggie Miller, Ind | 91.8 |
| 1991-92 | Mark Price, Clev | 94.7 |
| 1992-93 | Mark Price, Clev | 94.8 |
| 1993-94 | Mahmoud Abdul-Rauf, Den | 95.6 |
| 1994-95 | Spud Webb, Sac | 93.4 |

## Three-Point Field Goal Percentage

| | | |
|---|---|---|
| 1979-80 | Fred Brown, Sea | 44.3 |
| 1980-81 | Brian Taylor, SD | 38.3 |
| 1981-82 | Campy Russell, NY | 43.9 |
| 1982-83 | Mike Dunleavy, SA | 34.5 |
| 1983-84 | Darrell Griffith, Utah | 36.1 |
| 1984-85 | Byron Scott, LA Lakers | 43.3 |
| 1985-86 | Craig Hodges, Mil | 45.1 |
| 1986-87 | Kiki Vandeweghe, Por | 48.1 |
| 1987-88 | Craig Hodges, Mil-Phoe | 49.1 |
| 1988-89 | Jon Sundvold, Mia | 52.2 |
| 1989-90 | Steve Kerr, Clev | 50.7 |
| 1990-91 | Jim Les, Sac | 46.1 |
| 1991-92 | Dana Barros, Sea | 44.6 |
| 1992-93 | B.J. Armstrong, Chi | 45.3 |
| 1993-94 | Tracy Murray, Por | 45.9 |
| 1994-95 | Steve Kerr, Chi | 52.4 |

## Steals

| | | |
|---|---|---|
| 1973-74 | Larry Steele, Por | 2.68 |
| 1974-75 | Rick Barry, GS | 2.85 |
| 1975-76 | Don Watts, Sea | 3.18 |
| 1976-77 | Don Buse, Ind | 3.47 |
| 1977-78 | Ron Lee, Phoe | 2.74 |
| 1978-79 | M. L. Carr, Det | 2.46 |
| 1979-80 | Micheal Richardson, NY | 3.23 |
| 1980-81 | Magic Johnson, LA | 3.43 |
| 1981-82 | Magic Johnson, LA | 2.67 |
| 1982-83 | Micheal Richardson, GS-NJ | 2.84 |
| 1983-84 | Rickey Green, Utah | 2.65 |
| 1984-85 | Micheal Richardson, NJ | 2.96 |
| 1985-86 | Alvin Robertson, SA | 3.67 |
| 1986-87 | Alvin Robertson, SA | 3.21 |
| 1987-88 | Michael Jordan, Chi | 3.16 |
| 1988-89 | John Stockton, Utah | 3.21 |
| 1989-90 | Michael Jordan, Chi | 2.77 |
| 1990-91 | Alvin Robertson, Mil | 3.04 |
| 1991-92 | John Stockton, Utah | 2.98 |
| 1992-93 | Michael Jordan, Chi | 2.83 |
| 1993-94 | Nate McMillan, Sea | 2.96 |
| 1994-95 | Scottie Pippen, Chi | 2.94 |

## Blocked Shots

| | | | | | |
|---|---|---|---|---|---|
| 1973-74 | Elmore Smith, LA | 4.85 | 1984-85 | Mark Eaton, Utah | 5.56 |
| 1974-75 | Kareem Abdul-Jabbar, Mil | 3.26 | 1985-86 | Manute Bol, Wash | 4.96 |
| 1975-76 | Kareem Abdul-Jabbar, LA | 4.12 | 1986-87 | Mark Eaton, Utah | 4.06 |
| 1976-77 | Bill Walton, Port | 3.25 | 1987-88 | Mark Eaton, Utah | 3.71 |
| 1977-78 | George Johnson, NJ | 3.38 | 1988-89 | Manute Bol, GS | 4.31 |
| 1978-79 | Kareem Abdul-Jabbar, LA | 3.95 | 1989-90 | Hakeem Olajuwon, Hou | 4.59 |
| 1979-80 | Kareem Abdul-Jabbar, LA | 3.41 | 1990-91 | Hakeem Olajuwon, Hou | 3.95 |
| 1980-81 | George Johnson, SA | 3.39 | 1991-92 | David Robinson, SA | 4.49 |
| 1981-82 | George Johnson, SA | 3.12 | 1992-93 | Hakeem Olajuwon, Hou | 4.17 |
| 1982-83 | Wayne Rollins, Atl | 4.29 | 1993-94 | Dikembe Mutombo, Den | 4.10 |
| 1983-84 | Mark Eaton, Utah | 4.28 | 1994-95 | Dikembe Mutombo, Den | 3.91 |

# NBA All-Star Game Results

| Year | Result | Site | Winning Coach | Most Valuable Player |
|---|---|---|---|---|
| 1951 | East 111, West 94 | Boston | Joe Lapchick | Ed Macauley, Bos |
| 1952 | East 108, West 91 | Boston | Al Cervi | Paul Arizin, Phil |
| 1953 | West 79, East 75 | Ft Wayne | John Kundla | George Mikan, Minn |
| 1954 | East 98, West 93 (OT) | New York | Joe Lapchick | Bob Cousy, Bos |
| 1955 | East 100, West 91 | New York | Al Cervi | Bill Sharman, Bos |
| 1956 | West 108, East 94 | Rochester | Charley Eckman | Bob Pettit, StL |
| 1957 | East 109, West 97 | Boston | Red Auerbach | Bob Cousy, Bos |
| 1958 | East 130, West 118 | St Louis | Red Auerbach | Bob Pettit, StL |
| 1959 | West 124, East 108 | Detroit | Ed Macauley | Bob Pettit, StL |
| | | | | Elgin Baylor, Minn |
| 1960 | East 125, West 115 | Philadelphia | Red Auerbach | Wilt Chamberlain, Phil |
| 1961 | West 153, East 131 | Syracuse | Paul Seymour | Oscar Robertson, Cin |
| 1962 | West 150, East 130 | St Louis | Fred Schaus | Bob Pettit, StL |
| 1963 | East 115, West 108 | Los Angeles | Red Auerbach | Bill Russell, Bos |
| 1964 | East 111, West 107 | Boston | Red Auerbach | Oscar Robertson, Cin |
| 1965 | East 124, West 123 | St Louis | Red Auerbach | Jerry Lucas, Cin |
| 1966 | East 137, West 94 | Cincinnati | Red Auerbach | Adrian Smith, Cin |
| 1967 | West 135, East 120 | San Francisco | Fred Schaus | Rick Barry, SF |
| 1968 | East 144, West 124 | New York | Alex Hannum | Hal Greer, Phil |
| 1969 | East 123, West 112 | Baltimore | Gene Shue | Oscar Robertson, Cin |
| 1970 | East 142, West 135 | Philadelphia | Red Holzman | Willis Reed, NY |
| 1971 | West 108, East 107 | San Diego | Larry Costello | Lenny Wilkens, Sea |
| 1972 | West 112, East 110 | Los Angeles | Bill Sharman | Jerry West, LA |
| 1973 | East 104, West 84 | Chicago | Tom Heinsohn | Dave Cowens, Bos |
| 1974 | West 134, East 123 | Seattle | Larry Costello | Bob Lanier, Det |
| 1975 | East 108, West 102 | Phoenix | K. C. Jones | Walt Frazier, NY |
| 1976 | East 123, West 109 | Philadelphia | Tom Heinsohn | Dave Bing, Wash |
| 1977 | West 125, East 124 | Milwaukee | Larry Brown | Julius Erving, Phil |
| 1978 | East 133, West 125 | Atlanta | Billy Cunningham | Randy Smith, Buff |
| 1979 | West 134, East 129 | Detroit | Lenny Wilkens | David Thompson, Den |
| 1980 | East 144, West 135 (OT) | Washington | Billy Cunningham | George Gervin, SA |
| 1981 | East 123, West 120 | Cleveland | Billy Cunningham | Nate Archibald, Bos |
| 1982 | East 120, West 118 | New Jersey | Bill Fitch | Larry Bird, Bos |
| 1983 | East 132, West 123 | Los Angeles | Billy Cunningham | Julius Erving, Phil |
| 1984 | East 154, West 145 (OT) | Denver | K. C. Jones | Isiah Thomas, Det |
| 1985 | West 140, East 129 | Indiana | Pat Riley | Ralph Sampson, Hou |
| 1986 | East 139, West 132 | Dallas | K. C. Jones | Isiah Thomas, Det |
| 1987 | West 154, East 149 (OT) | Seattle | Pat Riley | Tom Chambers, Sea |
| 1988 | East 138, West 133 | Chicago | Mike Fratello | Michael Jordan, Chi |
| 1989 | West 143, East 134 | Houston | Pat Riley | Karl Malone, Utah |
| 1990 | East 130, West 113 | Miami | Chuck Daly | Magic Johnson, LA Lakers |
| 1991 | East 116, West 114 | Charlotte | Chris Ford | Charles Barkley, Phil |
| 1992 | West 153, East 113 | Orlando | Don Nelson | Magic Johnson, LA Lakers |
| 1993 | West 135, East 132 | Salt Lake City | Paul Westphal | Karl Malone, Utah |
| | | | | John Stockton, Utah |
| 1994 | East 127, West 118 | Minneapolis | Lenny Wilkens | Scottie Pippen, Chi |
| 1995 | West 139, East 112 | Phoenix | Paul Westphal | Mitch Richmond, Sac |

# Members of the Basketball Hall of Fame

## Contributors

Senda Abbott (1984)
Forest C. "Phog" Allen (1959)
Clair F. Bee (1967)
Walter A. Brown (1965)
John W. Bunn (1964)
Bob Douglas (1971)
Al Duer (1981)
Clifford Fagan (1983)
Harry A. Fisher (1973)
Larry Fleisher (1991)
Edward Gottlieb (1971)
Luther H. Gulick (1959)
Lester Harrison (1979)
Ferenc Hepp (1980)
Edward J. Hickox (1959)

Paul D. "Tony" Hinkle (1965)
Ned Irish (1964)
R. William Jones (1964)
J. Walter Kennedy (1980)
Emil S. Liston (1974)
John B. McLendon (1978)
Bill Mokray (1965)
Ralph Morgan (1959)
Frank Morgenweck (1962)
James Naismith (1959)
Peter F. Newell (1978)
John J. O'Brien (1961)
Larry O'Brien (1991)
Harold G. Olsen (1959)
Maurice Podoloff (1973)

H.V. Porter (1960)
William A. Reid (1963)
Elmer Ripley (1972)
Lynn W. St. John (1962)
Abe Saperstein (1970)
Arthur A. Schabinger (1961)
Amos Alonzo Stagg (1959)
Boris Stankovic (1991)
Edward Steitz (1983)
Chuck Taylor (1968)
Oswald Tower (1959)
Arthur L. Trester (1961)
Clifford Wells (1971)
Lou Wilke (1982)

## Players

Kareem Abdul-Jabbar (1995)
Nate "Tiny" Archibald (1991)
Paul J. Arizin (1977)
Thomas B. Barlow (1980)
Rick Barry (1986)
Elgin Baylor (1976)
John Beckman (1972)
Walt Bellamy (1993)
Sergei Belov (1992)
Dave Bing (1989)
Carol Blazejowski (1994)
Bennie Borgmann (1961)
Bill Bradley (1982)
Joseph Brennan (1974)
Al Cervi (1984)
Wilt Chamberlain (1978)
Charles "Tarzan" Cooper (1976)
Bob Cousy (1970)
Dave Cowens (1991)
Billy Cunningham (1985)
Bob Davies (1969)
Forrest S. DeBernardi (1961)
Dave DeBusschere (1982)
H. G. "Dutch" Dehnert (1968)
Anne Donovan (1995)
Paul Endacott (1971)
Julius Erving (1993)
Harold "Bud" Foster (1964)
Walter "Clyde" Frazier (1986)
Max "Marty" Friedman (1971)
Joe Fulks (1977)
Lauren "Laddie" Gale (1976)
Harry "the Horse" Gallatin (1991)
William Gates (1988)

Tom Gola (1975)
Hal Greer (1981)
Robert "Ace" Gruenig (1963)
Clifford O. Hagan (1977)
Victor Hanson (1960)
John Havlicek (1983)
Connie Hawkins (1992)
Elvin Hayes (1989)
Tom Heinsohn (1985)
Nat Holman (1964)
Robert J. Houbregs (1986)
Chuck Hyatt (1959)
Dan Issel (1993)
Harry (Buddy) Jeannette (1994)
William C. Johnson (1976)
D. Neil Johnston (1989)
K. C. Jones (1988)
Sam Jones (1983)
Edward "Moose" Krause (1975)
Bob Kurland (1961)
Joe Lapchick (1966)
Clyde Lovellette (1987)
Jerry Lucas (1979)
Angelo "Hank" Luisetti (1959)
C. Edward Macauley (1960)
Peter P. Maravich (1986)
Slater Martin (1981)
Branch McCracken (1960)
Jack McCracken (1962)
Bobby McDermott (1987)
Dick McGuire (1993)
Ann Meyers (1993)
George L. Mikan (1959)
Vern Mikkelsen (1995)

Cheryl Miller (1995)
Earl Monroe (1989)
Calvin Murphy (1993)
Charles "Stretch" Murphy (1960)
H. O. "Pat" Page (1962)
Bob Pettit (1970)
Andy Phillip (1961)
Jim Pollard (1977)
Frank Ramsey (1981)
Willis Reed (1981)
Oscar Robertson (1979)
John S. Roosma (1961)
Bill Russell (1974)
John "Honey" Russell (1964)
Adolph Schayes (1972)
Ernest J. Schmidt (1973)
John J. Schommer (1959)
Barney Sedran (1962)
Uljana Semjonova (1993)
Bill Sharman (1975)
Christian Steinmetz (1961)
Lusia Harris Stewart (1992)
John A. "Cat" Thompson (1962)
Nate Thurmond (1984)
Jack Twyman (1982)
Wes Unseld (1987)
Robert "Fuzzy" Vandivier (1974)
Edward A. Wachter (1961)
Bill Walton (1993)
Robert F. Wanzer (1986)
Jerry West (1979)
Nera White (1992)
Lenny Wilkens (1988)
John R. Wooden (1960)

## Coaches

Harold Anderson (1984)
Red Auerbach (1968)
Sam Barry (1978)
Ernest A. Blood (1960)
Howard G. Cann (1967)
H. Clifford Carlson (1959)
Lou Carnesecca (1992)
Ben Carnevale (1969)
Everett Case (1981)
Denny Crum (1994)
Chuck Daly (1994)
Everett S. Dean (1966)

Edgar A. Diddle (1971)
Bruce Drake (1972)
Clarence Gaines (1981)
Jack Gardner (1983)
Amory T. "Slats" Gill (1967)
Aleksandr Gomelsky (1995)
Marv Harshman (1984)
Edgar S. Hickey (1978)
Howard A. Hobson (1965)
Red Holzman (1985)
Hank Iba (1968)
Alvin F. "Doggie" Julian (1967)

Frank W. Keaney (1960)
George E. Keogan (1961)
Bob Knight (1991)
John Kundla (1995)
Ward L. Lambert (1960)
Harry Litwack (1975)
Kenneth D. Loeffler (1964)
A. C. "Dutch" Lonborg (1972)
Arad A. McCutchan (1980)
Al McGuire (1992)
Frank McGuire (1976)
Walter E. Meanwell (1959)

Note: Year of election in parentheses.

### Coaches *(Cont.)*

Raymond J. Meyer (1978)
Ralph Miller (1987)
Jack Ramsay (1992)
Cesare Rubini (1994)
Adolph F. Rupp (1968)

Leonard D. Sachs (1961)
Everett F. Shelton (1979)
Dean Smith (1982)
Fred R. Taylor (1985)

Bertha Teague (1984)
Margaret Wade (1984)
Stanley H. Watts (1985)
John R. Wooden (1972)

### Referees

James E. Enright (1978)
George T. Hepbron (1960)
George Hoyt (1961)
Matthew P. Kennedy (1959)
Lloyd Leith (1982)
Zigmund J. Mihalik (1985)
John P. Nucatola (1977)
Ernest C. Quigley (1961)
J. Dallas Shirley (1979)
Earl Strom (1995)
David Tobey (1961)
David H. Walsh (1961)

### Teams

Buffalo Germans (1961)
First Team (1959)
Original Celtics (1959)
Renaissance (1963)

Note: Year of election in parentheses.

## ABA Champions

| Year | Champion | Series | Loser | Winning Coach |
|------|----------|--------|-------|---------------|
| 1968 | Pittsburgh Pipers | 4–2 | New Orleans Bucs | Vince Cazetta |
| 1969 | Oakland Oaks | 4–1 | Indiana Pacers | Alex Hannum |
| 1970 | Indiana Pacers | 4–2 | Los Angeles Stars | Bob Leonard |
| 1971 | Utah Stars | 4–3 | Kentucky Colonels | Bill Sharman |
| 1972 | Indiana Pacers | 4–2 | New York Nets | Bob Leonard |
| 1973 | Indiana Pacers | 4–3 | Kentucky Colonels | Bob Leonard |
| 1974 | New York Nets | 4–1 | Utah Stars | Kevin Loughery |
| 1975 | Kentucky Colonels | 4–1 | Indiana Pacers | Hubie Brown |
| 1976 | New York Nets | 4–2 | Denver Nuggets | Kevin Loughery |

## ABA Postseason Awards

### Most Valuable Player

| | |
|---|---|
| 1967-68 | Connie Hawkins, Pitt |
| 1968-69 | Mel Daniels, Ind |
| 1969-70 | Spencer Haywood, Den |
| 1970-71 | Mel Daniels, Ind |
| 1971-72 | Artis Gilmore, Ken |
| 1972-73 | Billy Cunningham, Car |
| 1973-74 | Julius Erving, NY |
| 1974-75 | Julius Erving, NY |
| | George McGinnis, Ind |
| 1975-76 | Julius Erving, NY |

### Coach of the Year

| | |
|---|---|
| 1967-68 | Vince Cazetta, Pitt |
| 1968-69 | Alex Hannum, Oak |
| 1969-70 | Bill Sharman, LA |
| | Joe Belmont, Den |
| 1970-71 | Al Bianchi, Vir |
| 1971-72 | Tom Nissalke, Dall |
| 1972-73 | Larry Brown, Car |
| 1973-74 | Babe McCarthy, Ken |
| | Joe Mullaney, Utah |
| 1974-75 | Larry Brown, Den |
| 1975-76 | Larry Brown, Den |

### Rookie of the Year

| | |
|---|---|
| 1967-68 | Mel Daniels, Minn |
| 1968-69 | Warren Armstrong, Oak |
| 1969-70 | Spencer Haywood, Den |
| 1970-71 | Charlie Scott, Vir |
| | Dan Issel, Ken |
| 1971-72 | Artis Gilmore, Ken |
| 1972-73 | Brian Taylor, NY |
| 1973-74 | Swen Nater, SA |
| 1974-75 | Marvin Barnes, SL |
| 1975-76 | David Thompson, Den |

## THEY SAID IT

*Craig Kilborn, ESPN anchor, on notoriously porous Washington Bullet forward Don MacLean, who got into a brawl while defending a girlfriend: "That's the first person he's defended this year."*

## ABA Season Leaders

### Scoring

| | GP | Pts | Avg |
|---|---|---|---|
| 1967-68...Connie Hawkins, Pitt | 70 | 1875 | 26.8 |
| 1968-69...Rick Barry, Oak | 35 | 1190 | 34.0 |
| 1969-70...Spencer Haywood, Den | 84 | 2519 | 30.0 |
| 1970-71...Dan Issel, Ken | 83 | 2480 | 29.4 |
| 1971-72...Charlie Scott, Vir | 73 | 2524 | 34.6 |
| 1972-73...Julius Erving, Vir | 71 | 2268 | 31.9 |
| 1973-74...Julius Erving, NY | 84 | 2299 | 27.4 |
| 1974-75...George McGinnis, Ind | 79 | 2353 | 29.8 |
| 1975-76...Julius Erving, NY | 84 | 2462 | 29.3 |

### Rebounds

| | |
|---|---|
| 1967-68 .................Mel Daniels, Minn | 15.6 |
| 1968-69 .................Mel Daniels, Ind | 16.5 |
| 1969-70 ...............Spencer Haywood, Den | 19.5 |
| 1970-71 .................Mel Daniels, Ind | 18.0 |
| 1971-72 ...............Artis Gilmore, Ken | 17.8 |
| 1972-73 ...............Artis Gilmore, Ken | 17.5 |
| 1973-74 ...............Artis Gilmore, Ken | 18.3 |
| 1974-75 ...............Swen Nater, SA | 16.4 |
| 1975-76 ...............Artis Gilmore, Ken | 15.5 |

### Assists

| | |
|---|---|
| 1967-68 .................Larry Brown, NO | 6.5 |
| 1968-69 .................Larry Brown, Oak | 7.1 |
| 1969-70 .................Larry Brown, Wash | 7.1 |
| 1970-71 .................Bill Melchionni, NY | 8.3 |
| 1971-72 .................Bill Melchionni, NY | 8.4 |
| 1972-73 .................Bill Melchionni, NY | 7.5 |
| 1973-74 .................Al Smith, Den | 8.2 |
| 1974-75 .................Mack Calvin, Den | 7.7 |
| 1975-76 .................Don Buse, Ind | 8.2 |

### Steals

| | |
|---|---|
| 1973-74 .................Ted McClain, Car | 2.98 |
| 1974-75 .................Brian Taylor, NY | 2.80 |
| 1975-76 .................Don Buse, Ind | 4.12 |

### Blocked Shots

| | |
|---|---|
| 1973-74 ...............Caldwell Jones, SD | 4.00 |
| 1974-75 ...............Caldwell Jones, SD | 3.24 |
| 1975-76 ...............Billy Paultz, SA | 3.05 |

## World Championship of Basketball

| Year | Winner | Runner-Up | Score | Site |
|---|---|---|---|---|
| 1950 ..........................Argentina | United States | † | Rio de Janeiro |
| 1954 ..........................United States | Brazil | † | Rio de Janeiro |
| 1959 ..........................Brazil | United States | † | Santiago, Chile |
| 1963 ..........................Brazil | Yugoslavia | † | Rio de Janeiro |
| 1967 ..........................Soviet Union | Yugoslavia | † | Montevideo, Uruguay |
| 1970 ..........................Yugoslavia | Brazil | † | Ljubljana, Yugoslavia |
| 1974 ..........................Soviet Union | Yugoslavia | † | San Juan |
| 1978 ..........................Yugoslavia | Soviet Union | 82-81 OT | Manila |
| 1982 ..........................Soviet Union | United States | 95-94 | Cali, Colombia |
| 1986 ..........................United States | Soviet Union | 87-85 | Madrid |
| 1990 ..........................Yugoslavia | Soviet Union | 92-75 | Buenos Aires |
| 1994* ..........................United States | Russia | 137-91 | Toronto |

*U.S. professionals began competing in 1994.
†Result determined by overall record in final round of competition.

## THEY SAID IT

*Brother Ray Page, teacher at St. Anthony High School in Jersey City, on alumnus and Sacramento King guard Bobby Hurley: "He once asked me if Beirut was named after that famous baseball player who hit home runs."*

# College Basketball

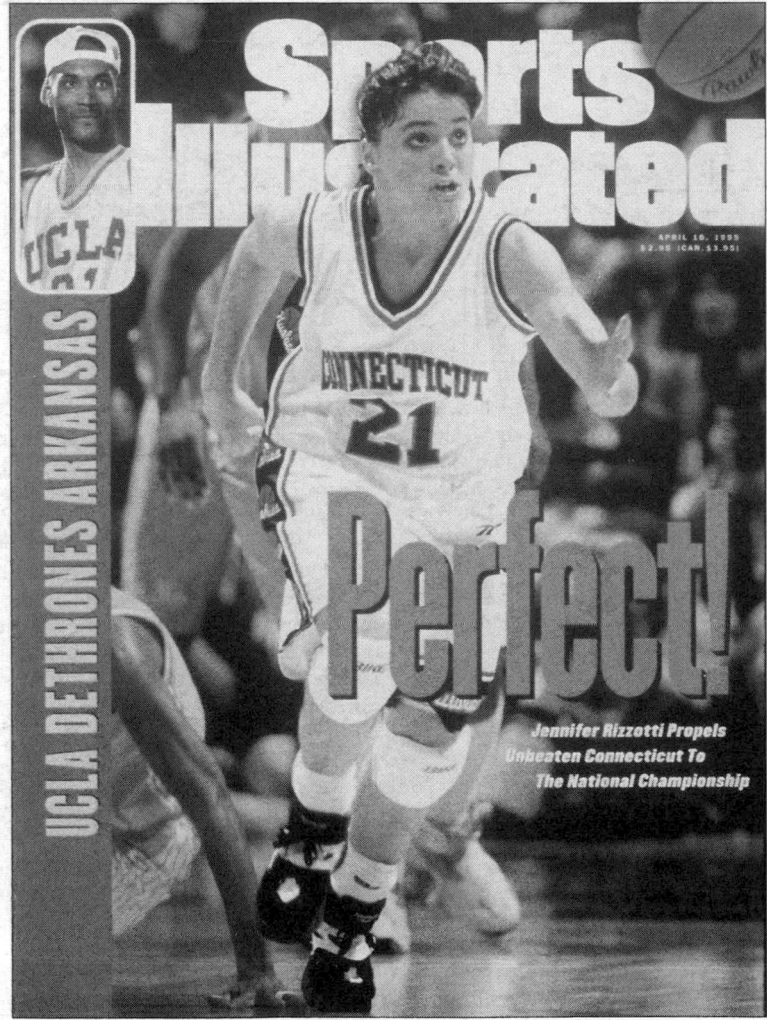

Sports Illustrated

APRIL 10, 1995
$2.95 (CAN. $3.95)

UCLA

CONNECTICUT
21

Perfect!

Jennifer Rizzotti Propels
Unbeaten Connecticut To
The National Championship

UCLA DETHRONES ARKANSAS

JOHN BIEVER (INSET), DAVID E. KLUTHO

# History Made, and Repeated

## An unpredictable season ended with the first NCAA title for the women of UConn and a record 11th for the men of UCLA

### by Jack McCallum

WHY PLAY? Why test the stress level of all those excitable coaches, spend all that money on cross-country travel and expose all those helpless eardrums to relentless attacks of Vitale-ism? Just hand the NCAA championship trophy to defending champion Arkansas and schedule Nolan Richardson and the boys for another Rose Garden summit with the Chief Hog on Pennsylvania Avenue.

That is only a slight exaggeration of the preseason prognoses centering around the near certainty that Arkansas, a talented and tenacious squad that wore the presidential stamp of approval on its big snout, would repeat as the 1995 college basketball king.

Oh, when will the experts learn? Chalk picks in this sport went out with Johnny Wooden and hightop Converse, and, aside from Duke's back-to-backer in 1991 and '92, so did repeat champions. Yet almost everyone looked at the Hogs' roster, intact from the 1994 championship season, and wondered how they could lose. That included the Hogs themselves. "Bring that pressure on," said Richardson in the preseason. "We love it. We want it."

But something was, if not exactly rotten, then a little out of kilter in Fayetteville. Corliss Williamson came back slightly overweight and still not fully healed from a broken wrist suffered in the 1994 championship game against Duke. Shooting guard and title-game hero Scotty Thurman had lost some of the consistency on his shot and, perhaps, a little of his competitive edge. Ditto for point guard and spiritual leader Corey Beck, who had preseason arthroscopic knee surgery. With Williamson, Thurman and off-the-bench flinger Alex Dillard all looking to the hoop, it was sometimes hard for big men Dwight Stewart, Darnell Robinson and Lee Wilson to find their shots in the offense. Richardson's work with the Black Coaches Association and other organizations admittedly distracted him sometimes from the task at hand.

But most of all, there were simply too

**With Camby (21) ruling the paint, UMass dominated the early going.**

JOHN BIEVER

many great teams in the land to guarantee Arkansas a smooth road to No. 1. And the Razorbacks ran into one of them right away. On the day after Thanksgiving, at the Tipoff Classic in Springfield, Mass., the Hogs were thoroughly humiliated by the University of Massachusetts 104–80. Williamson, in particular, seemed to shrink in stature right before our eyes as Minutemen power forward Lou Roe went over, around and through him for 34 points and 13 rebounds. Yes, the college season that promised to be a second Hog toast began as a Hog roast.

But UMass was no fluke ... and no one was more eager to tell you that than UMass. On Oct. 19, four days after preseason practice began, *The Boston Globe* had reported that seven of UMass's 13 scholarship players were either on academic probation or "academic warning." The Minutemen felt violated by the report and others that followed. Armed with righteous indignation, a formidable frontcourt of Roe and center Marcus Camby and plenty of depth, UMass set out to *make a statement*, a slight variation on the we-don't-get-no-respect theme that had been played to perfection last year by Richardson and Arkansas. And no one was better at righteous indignation than Minutemen coach John Calipari. Hardly a sentence could be written about the 36-year-old Calipari without conjuring up the name of the young genius from whom he seemed cloned—Kentucky's Rick Pitino. See, there was one right there.

Inevitably UMass's high profile went down when its Atlantic-10 season began. The Minutemen did lose three games in the conference (one to Temple and two to George Washington), but even hard core fans had trouble *naming* the league's 10 teams much less caring about them. Still, the college season's biggest off-the-court story occurred in the Atlantic-10. A statement made by Rutgers president Francis Lawrence was construed as racist by a segment of the student body, which protested by taking over the court at halftime of the Rutgers-UMass game on Feb. 7. It was, then, an off-the-court story that became an on-the-court story. The suspended game was replayed on March 3 with UMass winning 77–62.

UMass also shared early-season

**Lobo lifted the Huskies to an undefeated season and the national title.**

DAVID E. KLUTHO

attention, as well as a turn at No. 1, with not-so-friendly neighbor Connecticut, which is located in Storrs, just 50 miles from UMass's Amherst campus. Husky coach Jim Calhoun may have ducked a nonconference showdown with the Minutemen over the years, but on the court UConn wasn't afraid of anyone. Their tone of toughness was set by point guard Kevin Ollie, who hails from inner-city Los Angeles, and smooth swingman Ray Allen, who for the first two months of the season played as well as anyone in the college game.

But UConn didn't only feel tweaked by the attention given UMass. Right on its own campus another phenomenon was building—Lobo Fever. Game after game, week after week, the UConn women's team, led by All-America Rebecca Lobo, dismantled everyone in its path. Sure, the Big East was not a strong women's conference, but when it came time for the Husky women to step up and play then-No. 1 Tennessee from the powerful Southeast Conference, Lobo & Co. responded with a 77–66 victory. The win on Jan. 16 at Storrs was as big a regular-season game as the women's sport had ever seen, and there were few doubts that a UConn-Tennessee rematch in the NCAA final on April 2 would, if it happened, be a major moment for the women's game.

Despite its success in recent years, the UConn men were not the consensus favorite to win the Big East title—Syracuse and Georgetown were mentioned as frequently. And the most watched players in the conference were not Ollie and Allen

but newcomers Allen Iverson of Georgetown and Felipe Lopez of St. John's. Iverson was so good so fast that conservative Hoya coach John Thompson all but turned his offense over to the gifted young point guard, sometimes with spectacular results, sometimes with disastrous ones. As for Lopez, the burden of carrying a team on his back seemed overwhelming at times, and the question of whether or not he will live up to his advance billing has not yet been answered.

The ACC certainly lived up to its advance billing as the deepest and best conference in the country. On the first night of intraconference play, in fact, one of the league's worst, North Carolina State, beat one of the ACC's best, North Carolina. That did not indicate a trend, however. While State struggled after that initial upset, the Tar Heels, led by super sophs Jerry Stackhouse and Rasheed Wallace, quickly played their way into the nation's elite. Moreover, they did it with a brand of up-and-down basketball that seemed to go against the nature of coach Dean Smith. Observers wondered, though, how far the run-and-gun Heels would go with only a six-deep rotation. They got their answer in the NCAA tournament—pretty far.

The most refreshing story in the ACC was the continued renaissance of Maryland. The sad days of recruiting violations and NCAA probation that followed the cocaine-induced death of Len Bias were all but erased by the firebrand coaching of Gary Williams and the graceful, no-nonsense play of center Joe Smith. Other perennials that made the ACC tough were Virginia, which flourished in surprising fashion after star guard Cory Alexander went down with a broken ankle, Wake Forest (with a one-two punch of guard Randolph Childress and center Tim Duncan), Georgia Tech and Florida State.

Wait a minute—an ACC roundup without Duke? That's right. Blue Devil coach Mike Krzyzewski, by any standard the most successful college coach of the last decade, began the season with a protective brace and instructions to take it easy following off-season back surgery. He didn't do it. By Jan. 4 Krzyzewski was off the bench and at home, and the Blue Devils were en route to their worst season ever—a 13–18 record that didn't get them within sniffing distance of even the NIT. But Coach K will be back for the 1995–96 season, and, armed with a lot of young talent, so will the Devils.

The SEC was the only other conference that could rightfully challenge the ACC for No. 1, not just because of Arkansas and archrival Kentucky, but also because of Mississippi State, Alabama and Florida. Two of the nation's better unknown players emerged from the SEC, too—State's Erick Dampier and Alabama's Antonio McDyess, a pair of quiet, no-frills inside bangers. Arguably the best regular-season game of the year was Arkansas's nationally televised 94–92 win over visiting Kentucky on Jan. 29, achieved when Mr. Clutch, Thurman, hit a three-pointer with 11 seconds left.

As the season wore on, the Big Eight had something to say about toughness, too. The Kansas Jayhawks were the No. 1 team in the country in late February, yet they had to struggle to stay ahead of: Oklahoma, which was led by two-sport star Ryan Minor, a pro pitching prospect; Iowa State, which was led by homegrown jump shooter Fred Hoiberg, a player so popular in Ames that he is known as the Mayor; Oklahoma State, which was led by one of the most successful "projects" in NCAA history, Bryant (Big Country) Reeves; and Missouri, whose tenacious playing style raised ire around the league. And out in the West, even the much criticized Pac-10 made some noise. Arizona State flexed unexpected muscle early by winning the Maui Invitational, and, at times, Stanford, Cal, Washington State and Oregon all made a run at perennial powers Arizona and UCLA.

But, really, could the pack in the Pac-10 be taken seriously? All right, maybe Arizona. The Wildcats boasted both a superstar (point guard extraordinaire and player of the year candidate Damon Stoudamire) and a track record, having been the only Pac-10 team to make the Final Four in the past 15 years. (They did it twice—last year and in 1988.) The best talent in the conference belonged to UCLA but so did the best chance for failure. "We know what people think about us," senior leader Ed O'Bannon said during the season. What people thought about the Bruins was that they were an underachieving band of choke artists, as they had been the year before when, after a 21–7 regular season, they were rudely nudged from the NCAA tournament field by Tulsa, 112–102.

But there was something different about this UCLA team, something, to borrow an

**Richardson exhorted Arkansas all the way back to the championship game.**

expression from La-La Land, a little gnarly. Yes, Ed and his brother Charles could play above the rim, and point guard Tyus Edney was a blur with the ball, probably only a step slower than the Bruins' alltime burner, "Rocket" Rod Foster, a member of the last Bruin team (1980) to play for the NCAA title. But they did the tough things, too, the blue-collar battling that had never been associated with either the Pac-10 or the Bruins.

In seasons past, perhaps, the Bruins might've been battling UNLV for supremacy in the West. But Jerry Tarkanian is gone and so, it seems, is the Runnin' Rebels' good fortune. They had little of it during the 1994–95 season. Head coach Tim Grgurich, a former Tark assistant who was widely considered the only man who could restore the past magic, ended up being hospitalized for exhaustion and left the job after seven games. UNLV finished in the middle of the Big West Conference with no sign that its winning number would be coming up anytime soon.

A more subtle, yet more widespread flameout, occurred in the Big Ten, a conference in which only two teams played up to their potential—Michigan State and Purdue. Yes, Indiana flexed its muscle from time to time, particularly in an 80–61 dismantling of Kansas on Dec. 17, and Minnesota, Illinois and underachieving Michigan weren't bad. But the conference simply did not deserve the six NCAA bids received on Selection Sunday, not when teams like Georgia Tech from the ACC and George Washington from the Atlantic-10 (conquerors of both Syracuse and UMass) were left out.

Otherwise, though, the selection committee did a reasonable job. The No. 1 seeds were Wake Forest in the East, Kentucky in the Southeast, Kansas in the Midwest and UCLA in the West. All were considered legitimate title contenders, as were all four No. 2's—Arkansas (Midwest), North Carolina (Southeast), UConn (West) and UMass (East). None of that, of course, would prevent at least one "nonfavorite" from coming out of nowhere to make the Final Four. It turned out to be the team with the big, country-boy center and the collective twang—Oklahoma State.

But much went on before the Cowboys bulled their way to Seattle along with UCLA, Arkansas and North Carolina. Arizona's Stoudamire was held to six of 18 shooting from the field in a shocking 71–62 first-round loss to Miami of Ohio in the Midwest. Indiana coach Bobby Knight went ballistic on an unassuming NCAA official after a 65–60 loss to Missouri in the West. The college game said goodbye to its most congenial curmudgeon, Jud Heathcote, when his Michigan State Spartans lost to Weber State 79–72 in the Southeast. And in that regional's final, North Carolina's Smith bested Kentucky's Pitino in a battle of superstar coaches and superstar programs.

If there was an unfortunate loser in the tournament it had to be Syracuse. With its Midwest second-rounder all but won, Lawrence Moten's call of a fourth timeout with 4.3 seconds left resulted in a technical foul and an eventual 96–94 loss in overtime. And if there was a lucky winner it had to be Arkansas, which was the beneficiary not only of Moten's timeout gaffe but also of a one-point first-round victory over Texas Southern and an overtime edging of Memphis in the Sweet 16. Did all those great escapes mean they were primed to fall or destined to prevail?

"Winning an NCAA championship is all about knowing how to win the close ones," Richardson said before the Hogs packed their bags for Seattle. "And no one knows about that more than us."

If Oklahoma State felt intimidated by its role as Final Four underdog, then Reeves didn't show it. On Friday afternoon, 24 hours before the semifinal against UCLA, Country unleashed a powerful dunk during shootaround that tore down a basket at the Kingdome. "I guess he's trying to send a message to all of us," said North Carolina's Wallace. But the real messenger was UCLA's Edney, nicknamed (ironically) Scary Boy, who scored 21 points, collected

JOHN BIEVER

**Making Jordanesque moves to the hoop, Bruin freshman Bailey scored 26 points in the title game.**

his wrist, Williamson and Thurman played video games with family and friends at their hotel, and a record number of TV viewers for a women's game tuned into the Connecticut-Tennessee final in Minneapolis to see if storybook unbeaten seasons still happen. "The other teams here are playing for a national championship," UConn coach Geno Auriemma said before the title game. "We're playing for a piece of history." And they got it. The Huskies beat the Lady Vols 70–64 to finish with a 35–0 record and the school's first NCAA hoops title.

History was a big part of the men's final, too. Legendary Bruin coach John Wooden, who won 10 titles in 12 years in Westwood, slipped into the Kingdome minutes before the game to silently cheer on the Bruins and particularly Harrick, to whom he was extremely close. UCLA's play against Arkansas, however, was distinctly contemporary. Edney's wrist kept him out for all but the first few minutes, but his replacement, sophomore Cameron Dollar, slipped and slithered through seams in the Arkansas defense to create plays. Freshman Toby Bailey was a West Coast miniversion of—don't laugh—Michael Jordan, making countless athletic plays for which Arkansas had no counter. And the high-wire act of the O'Bannons, combined with the old-fashioned power of pivotman George Zidek, contained Williamson, who was held to 12 points. All this produced a decisive 89–78 victory and the Bruins' first title since 1975, when Wooden last patrolled the sidelines with his rolled-up program.

UCLA's final season record was 31–2, which put the combined mark of the two national champions at a remarkable 66–2. But, listen, just don't expect repeat performances next year—it won't happen.

five assists and turned in most of the big plays in a 74–61 victory over the Cowboys that was much closer than it sounds. Unbeknownst to most Bruin fans, however, Edney had severely sprained his right wrist during a first-half fall and spent part of Saturday night getting it wrapped in a temporary cast. Had Carolina been able to keep a wrap on its patience, it just might have prevailed in the other semifinal against Arkansas. But the cumulative effects of Hog pressure unnerved the Tar Heels down the stretch, and Arkansas stormed into its second straight NCAA final, a remarkable achievement itself, with a 75–68 victory.

On the off day between the semis and the Monday night final, UCLA coach Jim Harrick accompanied Ed O'Bannon to the Kingdome while the UCLA senior received a player of the year award, Edney nursed

## NCAA Championship Game Box Score

### Arkansas 78

| ARKANSAS | Min | FG M-A | FT M-A | Reb O-T | A | PF | TP |
|---|---|---|---|---|---|---|---|
| Thurman | 32 | 2-9 | 0-0 | 0-3 | 1 | 2 | 5 |
| Williamson | 33 | 3-16 | 6-10 | 2-4 | 6 | 1 | 12 |
| Martin | 6 | 1-2 | 0-0 | 1-3 | 1 | 2 | 3 |
| McDaniel | 35 | 5-10 | 3-4 | 1-3 | 1 | 5 | 16 |
| Beck | 25 | 4-6 | 1-2 | 2-3 | 2 | 3 | 11 |
| Stewart | 22 | 5-10 | 1-2 | 2-5 | 0 | 4 | 12 |
| Dillard | 15 | 2-4 | 0-0 | 1-2 | 1 | 1 | 6 |
| Robinson | 10 | 2-3 | 0-0 | 0-2 | 0 | 3 | 4 |
| Rimac | 12 | 1-1 | 0-0 | 1-2 | 3 | 0 | 2 |
| Wilson | 7 | 3-4 | 1-2 | 0-0 | 0 | 1 | 7 |
| Williams | 1 | 0-0 | 0-0 | 0-0 | 0 | 0 | 0 |
| Totals | 200 | 28-65 | 12-20 | 10-27 | 15 | 22 | 78 |

Percentages: FG—.431, FT—.600. 3-pt goals: 10-28, .357 (Thurman 1-7, Martin 1-2, McDaniel 3-7, Beck 2-3, Stewart 1-5, Dillard 2-3, Robinson 0-1). Team rebounds: 4. Blocked shots: 4 (Robinson 2, Beck, Wilson). Turnovers: 18 (Williamson 3, Beck 2, Dillard 2, Martin 2, Rimac 2, Robinson 2, Stewart 2, Thurman 2, McDaniel). Steals: 15 (Williamson 4, McDaniel 4, Beck 3, Rimac 2, Martin, Thurman).

### UCLA 89

| UCLA | Min | FG M-A | FT M-A | Reb O-T | A | PF | TP |
|---|---|---|---|---|---|---|---|
| E. O'Bannon | 40 | 10-21 | 9-11 | 6-17 | 3 | 2 | 30 |
| C. O'Bannon | 36 | 4-10 | 3-4 | 4-9 | 6 | 1 | 11 |
| Zidek | 29 | 5-8 | 4-7 | 4-6 | 0 | 4 | 14 |
| Bailey | 39 | 12-20 | 1-2 | 4-9 | 3 | 3 | 26 |
| Edney | 3 | 0-0 | 0-0 | 0-0 | 0 | 0 | 0 |
| Dollar | 36 | 1-4 | 4-5 | 0-3 | 8 | 4 | 6 |
| Henderson | 17 | 1-5 | 0-0 | 1-2 | 1 | 1 | 2 |
| Totals | 200 | 33-68 | 21-29 | 19-46 | 21 | 15 | 89 |

Percentages: FG—.485, FT—.724. 3-pt goals: 2-7, .286 (E. O'Bannon 1-4, Bailey 1-2, Dollar 0-1). Team rebounds: 4. Blocked shots: 4 (C. O'Bannon 2, Dollar, Henderson). Turnovers: 20 (E. O'Bannon 5, Bailey 3, C. O'Bannon 3, Dollar 3, Henderson 3, Zidek 2, Edney). Steals: 11 (Dollar 4, E. O'Bannon 3, Bailey 2, C. O'Bannon 2).
Halftime: UCLA 40, Arkansas 39. A: 38,540. Officials: Valentine, Cahill, Burr.

## Final AP Top 25

Poll taken before NCAA Tournament.

| | | |
|---|---|---|
| 1. UCLA | 25–2 | |
| 2. Kentucky | 25–4 | |
| 3. Wake Forest | 24–5 | |
| 4. North Carolina | 24–5 | |
| 5. Kansas | 23–5 | |
| 6. Arkansas | 27–6 | |
| 7. Massachusetts | 26–4 | |
| 8. Connecticut | 25–4 | |
| 9. Villanova | 25–7 | |
| 10. Maryland | 24–7 | |
| 11. Michigan St | 22–5 | |
| 12. Purdue | 24–6 | |
| 13. Virginia | 22–8 | |
| 14. Oklahoma St | 23–9 | |
| 15. Arizona | 23–7 | |
| 16. Arizona St | 22–8 | |
| 17. Oklahoma | 23–8 | |
| 18. Mississippi St | 20–7 | |
| 19. Utah | 27–5 | |
| 20. Alabama | 22–9 | |
| 21. Western Kentucky | 26–3 | |
| 22. Georgetown | 19–9 | |
| 23. Missouri | 19–8 | |
| 24. Iowa St | 22–10 | |
| 25. Syracuse | 19–9 | |

## National Invitation Tournament Scores

**First round:** Penn St 62, Miami (FL) 56; Nebraska 69, Georgia 61; Iowa 96, DePaul 87; Ohio 83, George Washington 71; Marquette 68, Auburn 61; St Bonaventure 75, Southern Miss 70; Coppin St 75, St Joseph 68 (OT); South Florida 74, St John's (NY) 67; Providence 72, Charleston 54; Virginia Tech 62, Clemson 54; New Mexico St 97, Colorado 83; UTEP 90, Montana 60; Bradley 86, Eastern Michigan 85 (2OT); Canisius 83, Seton Hall 71; Illinois St 93, Utah St 87; Washington St 94, Texas Tech 82.
**Second round:** Penn St 65, Nebraska 59; Iowa 66, Ohio 62; Marquette 70, St Bonaventure 61; South Florida 75, Coppin St 59; Virginia Tech 91, Providence 78; New Mexico St 92, UTEP 89; Canisius 55, Bradley 53; Washington St 83, Illinois St 80 (OT).
**Third round:** Penn St 67, Iowa 64; Marquette 57, South Florida 50 (OT); Virginia Tech 64, New Mexico St 61; Canisius 89, Washington St 80.
**Semifinals:** Marquette 87, Penn St 79; Virginia Tech 71, Canisius 59.
**Championship:** Virginia Tech 65, Marquette 64 (OT).
**Consolation game:** Penn St 66, Canisius 62.

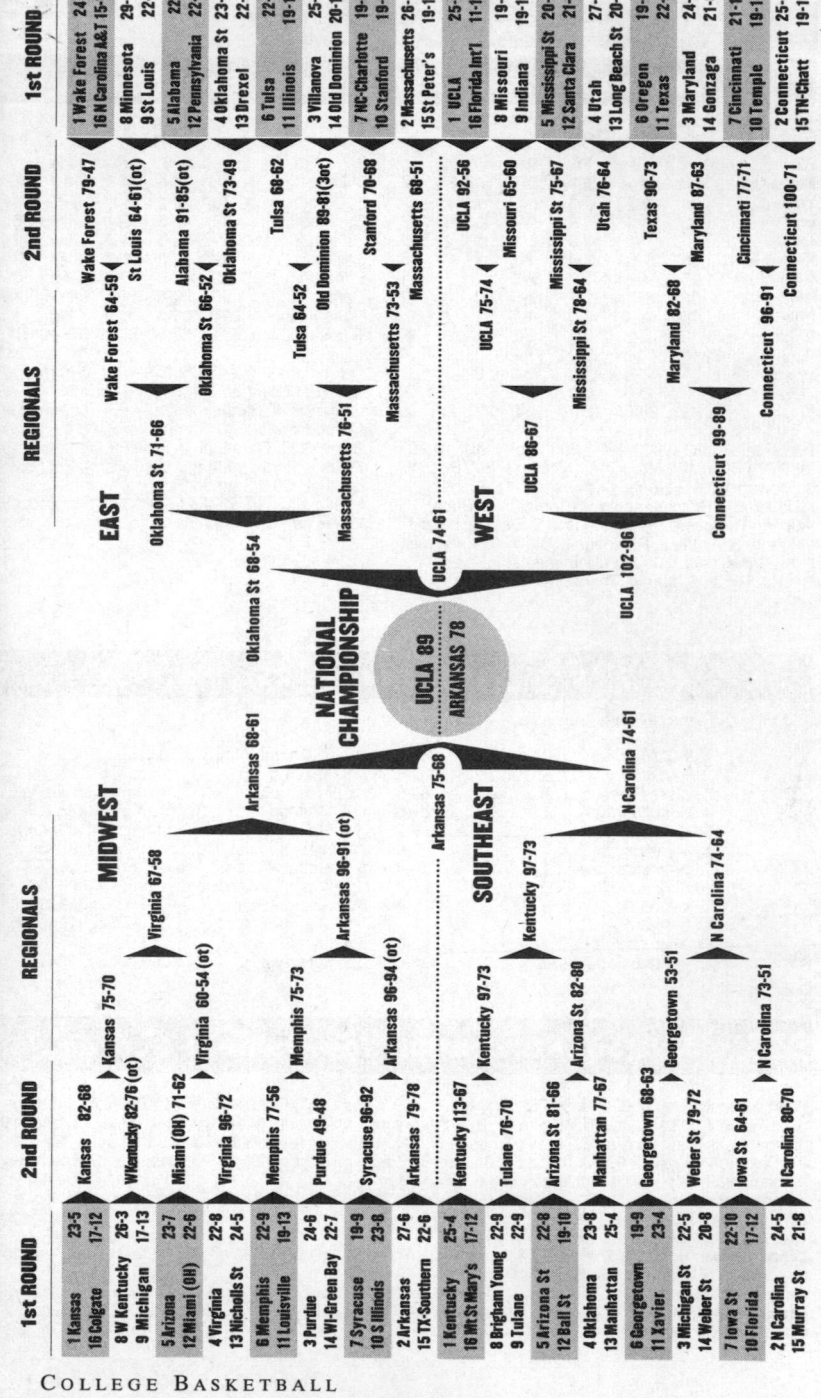

# 1995 NCAA Basketball Men's Division I Tournament

## EAST

### 1st ROUND
| | |
|---|---|
| 1 Kansas | 24-5 |
| 16 Colgate | 17-12 |
| 8 W Kentucky | 26-3 |
| 9 Michigan | 17-13 |
| 5 Arizona | 23-7 |
| 12 Miami (OH) | 22-6 |
| 4 Virginia | 22-8 |
| 13 Nicholls St | 24-5 |
| 6 Memphis | 22-9 |
| 11 Louisville | 19-13 |
| 3 Purdue | 24-6 |
| 14 WI-Green Bay | 22-7 |
| 7 Syracuse | 19-9 |
| 10 S Illinois | 23-8 |
| 2 Arkansas | 27-6 |
| 15 TX-Southern | 22-6 |

### 2nd ROUND
- Kansas 82-68
- W Kentucky 82-76 (ot)
- Miami (OH) 71-62
- Virginia 96-72
- Memphis 77-56
- Purdue 49-48
- Syracuse 96-92
- Arkansas 79-78

### REGIONALS
- Kansas 75-70
- Virginia 60-54 (ot)
- Memphis 75-73
- Arkansas 96-94 (ot)

- Virginia 67-58
- Arkansas 96-91 (ot)

### MIDWEST
- Arkansas 68-61

## SOUTHEAST

### 2nd ROUND
- Kentucky 113-67
- Tulane 76-70
- Arizona St 81-66
- Manhattan 77-67
- Georgetown 68-63
- Weber St 79-72
- Iowa St 64-61
- N Carolina 80-70

### 1st ROUND
| | |
|---|---|
| 1 Kentucky | 25-4 |
| 16 Mt St Mary's | 17-12 |
| 8 Brigham Young | 22-9 |
| 9 Tulane | 22-9 |
| 5 Arizona St | 22-8 |
| 12 Ball St | 19-10 |
| 4 Oklahoma | 23-8 |
| 13 Manhattan | 25-4 |
| 6 Georgetown | 19-9 |
| 11 Xavier | 23-4 |
| 3 Michigan St | 22-5 |
| 14 Weber St | 20-8 |
| 7 Iowa St | 22-10 |
| 10 Florida | 17-12 |
| 2 N Carolina | 24-5 |
| 15 Murray St | 21-8 |

### REGIONALS
- Kentucky 97-73
- Arizona St 82-80
- Georgetown 53-51
- N Carolina 73-51

- Kentucky 97-73
- N Carolina 74-64

### SOUTHEAST
- N Carolina 74-61

## 1st ROUND (right side)
| | |
|---|---|
| 1 Wake Forest | 24-5 |
| 16 N Carolina A&T | 15-14 |
| 8 Minnesota | 29-11 |
| 9 St Louis | 22-7 |
| 5 Alabama | 22-9 |
| 12 Pennsylvania | 22-5 |
| 4 Oklahoma St | 23-9 |
| 13 Drexel | 22-7 |
| 6 Tulsa | 22-7 |
| 11 Illinois | 19-11 |
| 3 Villanova | 25-7 |
| 14 Old Dominion | 20-11 |
| 10 NC-Charlotte | 19-8 |
| 10 Stanford | 19-8 |
| 2 Massachusetts | 26-4 |
| 15 St Peter's | 19-10 |

## 2nd ROUND (right side)
- Wake Forest 79-47
- St Louis 64-61(ot)
- Alabama 91-85(ot)
- Oklahoma St 73-49
- Tulsa 68-62
- Old Dominion 89-81(3ot)
- Stanford 70-68
- Massachusetts 68-51

## REGIONALS (right side EAST)
- Wake Forest 64-59
- Oklahoma St 66-52
- Tulsa 64-52
- Massachusetts 73-53

- Oklahoma St 71-66
- Massachusetts 76-51

### EAST
- Oklahoma St 68-54

## WEST

### 2nd ROUND
- UCLA 92-56
- Missouri 65-60
- Mississippi St 75-67
- Utah 76-64
- Texas 90-73
- Maryland 82-68
- Cincinnati 77-71
- Connecticut 100-71

### 1st ROUND
| | |
|---|---|
| 1 UCLA | 25-2 |
| 16 Florida Int'l | 11-18 |
| 8 Missouri | 19-8 |
| 9 Indiana | 19-11 |
| 5 Mississippi St | 20-7 |
| 12 Santa Clara | 21-6 |
| 4 Utah | 27-5 |
| 13 Long Beach St | 20-9 |
| 6 Oregon | 19-8 |
| 11 Texas | 22-6 |
| 3 Maryland | 24-7 |
| 14 Gonzaga | 21-8 |
| 7 Cincinnati | 21-11 |
| 10 Temple | 19-10 |
| 2 Connecticut | 25-4 |
| 15 TN-Chatt | 19-10 |

### REGIONALS
- UCLA 75-74
- Mississippi St 78-64
- Maryland 87-63
- Connecticut 96-91

- UCLA 86-67
- Connecticut 99-89

### WEST
- UCLA 102-96

## NATIONAL CHAMPIONSHIP
- Arkansas 75-68
- UCLA 74-61

### UCLA 89
### ARKANSAS 78

268    COLLEGE BASKETBALL

## Assoc. of Mid-Continent

| | Conference | | | All Games | | |
|---|---|---|---|---|---|---|
| | W | L | Pct | W | L | Pct |
| Valparaiso*† | 14 | 4 | .778 | 20 | 8 | .714 |
| Western Illinois | 13 | 5 | .722 | 20 | 8 | .714 |
| Buffalo | 12 | 6 | .667 | 18 | 10 | .643 |
| Youngstown St | 10 | 8 | .556 | 18 | 10 | .643 |
| Eastern Illinois | 10 | 8 | .556 | 16 | 3 | .842 |
| Troy St | 10 | 8 | .556 | 11 | 16 | .407 |
| MO-Kansas City | 7 | 11 | .389 | 7 | 19 | .269 |
| Central Conn | 6 | 12 | .333 | 8 | 18 | .308 |
| Chicago St | 6 | 12 | .333 | 6 | 20 | .231 |
| NE Illinois | 2 | 16 | .111 | 4 | 22 | .154 |

## Atlantic Coast

| | Conference | | | All Games | | |
|---|---|---|---|---|---|---|
| | W | L | Pct | W | L | Pct |
| Wake Forest*† | 12 | 4 | .750 | 26 | 6 | .813 |
| North Carolina | 12 | 4 | .750 | 27 | 6 | .818 |
| Maryland | 12 | 4 | .750 | 26 | 8 | .765 |
| Virginia | 12 | 4 | .750 | 25 | 9 | .735 |
| Georgia Tech | 8 | 8 | .500 | 18 | 12 | .600 |
| Clemson | 5 | 11 | .313 | 15 | 13 | .535 |
| Florida St | 5 | 11 | .313 | 12 | 15 | .444 |
| N Carolina St | 4 | 12 | .250 | 12 | 15 | .444 |
| Duke | 2 | 14 | .125 | 13 | 18 | .419 |

## Atlantic 10

| | Conference | | | All Games | | |
|---|---|---|---|---|---|---|
| | W | L | Pct | W | L | Pct |
| Massachusetts*† | 13 | 3 | .813 | 29 | 5 | .853 |
| Temple | 10 | 6 | .625 | 19 | 11 | .633 |
| Geo Washington | 10 | 6 | .625 | 18 | 14 | .563 |
| St Joseph's | 9 | 7 | .563 | 17 | 12 | .586 |
| St Bonaventure | 9 | 7 | .563 | 18 | 13 | .581 |
| West Virginia | 7 | 9 | .438 | 13 | 13 | .500 |
| Rutgers | 7 | 9 | .438 | 13 | 15 | .464 |
| Dusquesne | 5 | 11 | .313 | 10 | 18 | .357 |
| Rhode Island | 2 | 14 | .125 | 7 | 20 | .259 |

## Big East

| | Conference | | | All Games | | |
|---|---|---|---|---|---|---|
| | W | L | Pct | W | L | Pct |
| Connecticut* | 16 | 2 | .889 | 28 | 5 | .848 |
| Villlanova† | 14 | 4 | .777 | 25 | 8 | .758 |
| Syracuse | 12 | 6 | .667 | 20 | 10 | .667 |
| Georgetown | 11 | 7 | .611 | 21 | 10 | .677 |
| Miami (FL) | 9 | 9 | .500 | 15 | 13 | .536 |
| Providence | 7 | 11 | .389 | 17 | 13 | .566 |
| Seton Hall | 7 | 11 | .389 | 16 | 14 | .533 |
| St John's | 7 | 11 | .389 | 14 | 14 | .500 |
| Pittsburgh | 5 | 13 | .277 | 10 | 18 | .357 |
| Boston College | 2 | 16 | .111 | 9 | 19 | .321 |

## Big Eight

| | Conference | | | All Games | | |
|---|---|---|---|---|---|---|
| | W | L | Pct | W | L | Pct |
| Kansas* | 11 | 3 | .786 | 25 | 6 | .806 |
| Oklahoma St† | 10 | 4 | .714 | 27 | 10 | .729 |
| Oklahoma | 9 | 5 | .642 | 23 | 9 | .718 |
| Missouri | 8 | 6 | .571 | 20 | 9 | .689 |
| Iowa St | 6 | 8 | .428 | 23 | 11 | .676 |
| Colorado | 5 | 9 | .357 | 15 | 13 | .535 |
| Nebraska | 4 | 10 | .285 | 18 | 14 | .562 |
| Kansas St | 3 | 11 | .214 | 12 | 15 | .444 |

## Big Sky

| | Conference | | | All Games | | |
|---|---|---|---|---|---|---|
| | W | L | Pct | W | L | Pct |
| Weber St*† | 11 | 3 | .785 | 21 | 9 | .700 |
| Montana | 11 | 3 | .785 | 21 | 9 | .700 |
| Montana St | 8 | 6 | .571 | 21 | 8 | .724 |
| Idaho St | 7 | 7 | .500 | 18 | 10 | .642 |
| Boise St | 7 | 7 | .500 | 17 | 10 | .629 |
| Idaho | 6 | 8 | .428 | 12 | 15 | .444 |
| Northern Arizona | 4 | 10 | .285 | 8 | 18 | .307 |
| Eastern Washington | 2 | 12 | .142 | 6 | 20 | .230 |

## Big South

| | Conference | | | All Games | | |
|---|---|---|---|---|---|---|
| | W | L | Pct | W | L | Pct |
| NC-Greensboro* | 14 | 2 | .875 | 23 | 6 | .793 |
| Charleston So† | 12 | 4 | .750 | 19 | 10 | .655 |
| MD-Balt. County | 10 | 6 | .625 | 13 | 14 | .481 |
| Radford | 9 | 7 | .562 | 16 | 12 | .571 |
| Liberty | 7 | 9 | .437 | 12 | 16 | .428 |
| NC-Asheville | 7 | 9 | .437 | 11 | 16 | .407 |
| Towson St | 6 | 10 | .375 | 12 | 15 | .444 |
| Winthrop | 4 | 12 | .250 | 7 | 20 | .259 |
| Coastal Carolina | 3 | 13 | .187 | 6 | 20 | .230 |

## Big Ten

| | Conference | | | All Games | | |
|---|---|---|---|---|---|---|
| | W | L | Pct | W | L | Pct |
| Purdue | 15 | 3 | .833 | 25 | 7 | .781 |
| Michigan St | 14 | 4 | .777 | 22 | 6 | .785 |
| Michigan | 11 | 7 | .611 | 17 | 14 | .548 |
| Indiana | 11 | 7 | .611 | 19 | 12 | .612 |
| Illinois | 10 | 8 | .556 | 19 | 12 | .612 |
| Minnesota | 10 | 8 | .556 | 19 | 12 | .612 |
| Iowa | 9 | 9 | .500 | 21 | 11 | .656 |
| Penn St | 9 | 9 | .500 | 20 | 11 | .645 |
| Wisconsin | 7 | 11 | .388 | 13 | 14 | .481 |
| Ohio St | 2 | 16 | .111 | 6 | 22 | .214 |
| Northwestern | 1 | 17 | .055 | 5 | 22 | .185 |

*Conf. champ; †Conf. tourney winner.

## Big West

| | Conference | | | All Games | | |
|---|---|---|---|---|---|---|
| | W | L | Pct | W | L | Pct |
| Utah St* | 14 | 4 | .777 | 21 | 8 | .724 |
| New Mexico St | 13 | 5 | .722 | 25 | 10 | .714 |
| Long Beach St† | 13 | 5 | .722 | 20 | 10 | .667 |
| Nevada | 12 | 6 | .667 | 18 | 10 | .642 |
| Pacific | 9 | 9 | .500 | 14 | 13 | .518 |
| UC-Santa Barbara | 8 | 10 | .444 | 13 | 14 | .928 |
| UNLV | 7 | 11 | .388 | 12 | 16 | .428 |
| UC-Irvine | 6 | 12 | .333 | 13 | 16 | .448 |
| Cal St Fullerton | 5 | 13 | .277 | 7 | 20 | .259 |
| San Jose St | 3 | 15 | .166 | 4 | 23 | .148 |

## Colonial Athletic Association

| | Conference | | | All Games | | |
|---|---|---|---|---|---|---|
| | W | L | Pct | W | L | Pct |
| Old Dominion*† | 12 | 2 | .857 | 21 | 12 | .636 |
| NC-Wilmington | 10 | 4 | .714 | 16 | 11 | .592 |
| James Madison | 9 | 5 | .642 | 16 | 13 | .551 |
| E Carolina | 7 | 7 | .500 | 18 | 11 | .620 |
| American | 7 | 7 | .500 | 9 | 19 | .321 |
| William & Mary | 6 | 8 | .428 | 8 | 19 | .296 |
| Richmond | 3 | 11 | .214 | 8 | 20 | .285 |
| George Mason | 2 | 12 | .142 | 7 | 20 | .259 |

## Great Midwest

| | Conference | | | All Games | | |
|---|---|---|---|---|---|---|
| | W | L | Pct | W | L | Pct |
| Memphis* | 9 | 3 | .750 | 25 | 10 | .714 |
| St Louis | 8 | 4 | .667 | 23 | 8 | .741 |
| Cincinnati† | 7 | 5 | .583 | 22 | 12 | .647 |
| Marquette | 7 | 5 | .583 | 20 | 12 | .625 |
| DePaul | 6 | 6 | .500 | 18 | 11 | .642 |
| AL-Birmingham | 5 | 7 | .416 | 14 | 16 | .466 |
| Dayton | 0 | 12 | .000 | 7 | 20 | .259 |

## Ivy League

| | Conference | | | All Games | | |
|---|---|---|---|---|---|---|
| | W | L | Pct | W | L | Pct |
| Pennsylvania* | 14 | 0 | 1.000 | 22 | 6 | .785 |
| Princeton | 10 | 4 | .714 | 16 | 10 | .615 |
| Dartmouth | 10 | 4 | .714 | 13 | 13 | .500 |
| Brown | 8 | 6 | .571 | 13 | 13 | .500 |
| Yale | 5 | 9 | .357 | 9 | 17 | .346 |
| Cornell | 4 | 10 | .285 | 9 | 17 | .346 |
| Harvard | 4 | 10 | .285 | 6 | 20 | .230 |
| Columbia | 1 | 13 | .071 | 4 | 22 | .153 |

## Metro

| | Conference | | | All Games | | |
|---|---|---|---|---|---|---|
| | W | L | Pct | W | L | Pct |
| NC-Charlotte* | 8 | 4 | .667 | 19 | 9 | .678 |
| Tulane | 7 | 5 | .583 | 23 | 10 | .696 |
| Louisville† | 7 | 5 | .583 | 19 | 14 | .575 |
| Virginia Tech | 6 | 6 | .500 | 24 | 10 | .705 |
| S Mississippi | 6 | 6 | .500 | 17 | 12 | .586 |
| S Florida | 5 | 7 | .416 | 18 | 12 | .600 |
| VCU | 3 | 9 | .250 | 16 | 14 | .533 |

## Metro Atlantic

| | Conference | | | All Games | | |
|---|---|---|---|---|---|---|
| | W | L | Pct | W | L | Pct |
| Manhattan* | 12 | 2 | .857 | 26 | 5 | .838 |
| St Peter's† | 10 | 4 | .714 | 19 | 11 | .633 |
| Canisius | 10 | 4 | .714 | 21 | 13 | .617 |
| Fairfield | 6 | 8 | .428 | 13 | 15 | .464 |
| Iona | 6 | 8 | .428 | 10 | 17 | .370 |
| Loyola (MD) | 5 | 9 | .357 | 9 | 18 | .333 |
| Siena | 5 | 9 | .357 | 8 | 19 | .296 |
| Niagara | 2 | 12 | .142 | 5 | 25 | .166 |

## Mid-American

| | Conference | | | All Games | | |
|---|---|---|---|---|---|---|
| | W | L | Pct | W | L | Pct |
| Miami (OH)* | 16 | 2 | .888 | 23 | 7 | .766 |
| Ohio University | 13 | 5 | .722 | 24 | 10 | .705 |
| E Michigan | 12 | 6 | .667 | 20 | 10 | .667 |
| Ball St† | 11 | 7 | .611 | 19 | 11 | .633 |
| Bowling Green | 10 | 8 | .556 | 16 | 11 | .593 |
| Toledo | 10 | 8 | .556 | 16 | 11 | .593 |
| W Michigan | 9 | 9 | .500 | 14 | 13 | .518 |
| Kent | 5 | 13 | .277 | 8 | 19 | .296 |
| Akron | 4 | 14 | .222 | 8 | 18 | .307 |
| Central Michigan | 0 | 18 | .000 | 3 | 23 | .130 |

## Mid-Eastern Athletic

| | Conference | | | All Games | | |
|---|---|---|---|---|---|---|
| | W | L | Pct | W | L | Pct |
| Coppin St* | 15 | 1 | .937 | 21 | 10 | .677 |
| S Carolina St | 11 | 5 | .687 | 15 | 13 | .535 |
| N Carolina A&T† | 10 | 6 | .625 | 15 | 15 | .500 |
| MD-Eastern Shore | 9 | 7 | .562 | 13 | 14 | .481 |
| Bethune-Cookman | 9 | 7 | .562 | 12 | 16 | .428 |
| Howard | 8 | 8 | .500 | 9 | 18 | .333 |
| Morgan St | 5 | 11 | .312 | 5 | 22 | .185 |
| Delaware St | 3 | 13 | .187 | 7 | 21 | .250 |
| Florida A&M | 2 | 14 | .125 | 5 | 22 | .185 |

## Midwestern Collegiate

| | Conference | | | All Games | | |
|---|---|---|---|---|---|---|
| | W | L | Pct | W | L | Pct |
| Xavier (OH)* | 14 | 0 | 1.000 | 23 | 5 | .821 |
| WI-Green Bay† | 11 | 4 | .733 | 22 | 8 | .733 |
| Illinois-Chicago | 11 | 4 | .733 | 18 | 9 | .666 |
| Detroit | 9 | 5 | .642 | 13 | 15 | .464 |
| Butler | 8 | 7 | .533 | 15 | 12 | .555 |
| La Salle | 7 | 7 | .500 | 13 | 14 | .481 |
| N Illinois | 7 | 8 | .466 | 19 | 10 | .655 |
| Wright St | 6 | 8 | .428 | 13 | 17 | .433 |
| Cleveland St | 3 | 11 | .214 | 10 | 17 | .370 |
| Loyola (IL) | 2 | 13 | .133 | 5 | 22 | .074 |
| WI-Milwaukee | 2 | 13 | .133 | 3 | 24 | .111 |

*Conf. champ; †Conf. tourney winner.

## Missouri Valley

| | Conference | | | All Games | | |
|---|---|---|---|---|---|---|
| | W | L | Pct | W | L | Pct |
| Tulsa* | 15 | 3 | .833 | 24 | 8 | .750 |
| S Illinois† | 13 | 5 | .722 | 23 | 9 | .719 |
| Illinois St | 13 | 5 | .722 | 20 | 13 | .606 |
| Bradley | 12 | 6 | .667 | 20 | 10 | .667 |
| Evansville | 11 | 7 | .611 | 18 | 9 | .667 |
| SW Missouri St | 9 | 9 | .500 | 16 | 11 | .593 |
| Drake | 9 | 9 | .500 | 12 | 15 | .444 |
| Wichita St | 6 | 12 | .333 | 13 | 14 | .482 |
| N Iowa | 4 | 14 | .222 | 8 | 20 | .400 |
| Creighton | 4 | 14 | .222 | 7 | 19 | .269 |
| Indiana St | 3 | 15 | .167 | 7 | 19 | .269 |

## North Atlantic

| | Conference | | | All Games | | |
|---|---|---|---|---|---|---|
| | W | L | Pct | W | L | Pct |
| Drexel*† | 12 | 4 | .750 | 22 | 8 | .733 |
| New Hampshire | 11 | 5 | .688 | 19 | 9 | .678 |
| Northeastern | 10 | 6 | .625 | 18 | 11 | .620 |
| Vermont | 7 | 9 | .438 | 14 | 13 | .518 |
| Boston U | 7 | 9 | .438 | 15 | 16 | .483 |
| Delaware | 7 | 9 | .438 | 12 | 15 | .444 |
| Hartford | 7 | 9 | .438 | 11 | 16 | .407 |
| Maine | 6 | 10 | .375 | 11 | 16 | .407 |
| Hofstra | 5 | 11 | .313 | 10 | 18 | .357 |

## Northeast

| | Conference | | | All Games | | |
|---|---|---|---|---|---|---|
| | W | L | Pct | W | L | Pct |
| Rider* | 13 | 5 | .722 | 18 | 11 | .620 |
| Marist | 12 | 6 | .667 | 17 | 11 | .607 |
| Mt St Mary's† | 12 | 6 | .667 | 17 | 13 | .566 |
| FDU-Teaneck | 11 | 7 | .611 | 16 | 12 | .571 |
| Monmouth (NJ) | 11 | 7 | .611 | 13 | 14 | .481 |
| Wagner | 9 | 9 | .500 | 10 | 17 | .370 |
| LIU-Brooklyn | 8 | 10 | .444 | 11 | 17 | .392 |
| St Francis (PA) | 7 | 11 | .388 | 12 | 16 | .428 |
| St Francis (NY) | 5 | 13 | .277 | 9 | 18 | .333 |
| Robert Morris | 2 | 16 | .111 | 4 | 23 | .148 |

## Ohio Valley

| | Conference | | | All Games | | |
|---|---|---|---|---|---|---|
| | W | L | Pct | W | L | Pct |
| Tennessee St* | 11 | 5 | .687 | 17 | 10 | .629 |
| Murray St†† | 11 | 5 | .687 | 21 | 9 | .700 |
| Morehead St | 10 | 6 | .625 | 15 | 12 | .555 |
| Tennessee Tech | 9 | 7 | .562 | 13 | 14 | .481 |
| Austin Peay | 8 | 8 | .500 | 13 | 16 | .448 |
| SE Missouri | 7 | 9 | .438 | 13 | 14 | .481 |
| E Kentucky | 6 | 10 | .375 | 9 | 19 | .321 |
| Middle Tenn St | 5 | 11 | .312 | 12 | 15 | .444 |
| TN-Martin | 5 | 11 | .312 | 7 | 20 | .259 |

## Pacific-10

| | Conference | | | All Games | | |
|---|---|---|---|---|---|---|
| | W | L | Pct | W | L | Pct |
| UCLA* | 16 | 2 | .888 | 31 | 2 | .939 |
| Arizona | 13 | 5 | .722 | 23 | 8 | .741 |
| Arizona St | 12 | 6 | .667 | 24 | 9 | .727 |
| Oregon | 11 | 7 | .611 | 19 | 9 | .678 |
| Stanford | 10 | 8 | .556 | 20 | 9 | .689 |
| Washington St | 10 | 8 | .556 | 18 | 12 | .600 |
| Oregon St | 6 | 12 | .333 | 9 | 18 | .333 |
| California | 5 | 13 | .277 | 13 | 14 | .481 |
| Washington | 5 | 13 | .277 | 9 | 18 | .333 |
| Southern Cal | 2 | 16 | .111 | 7 | 21 | .250 |

## Patriot

| | Conference | | | All Games | | |
|---|---|---|---|---|---|---|
| | W | L | Pct | W | L | Pct |
| Colgate*† | 11 | 3 | .785 | 17 | 13 | .566 |
| Bucknell | 11 | 3 | .785 | 13 | 14 | .481 |
| Navy | 10 | 4 | .714 | 20 | 9 | .689 |
| Holy Cross | 9 | 5 | .643 | 15 | 12 | .555 |
| Fordham | 6 | 8 | .428 | 11 | 17 | .392 |
| Lehigh | 5 | 9 | .357 | 11 | 16 | .407 |
| Army | 4 | 10 | .286 | 12 | 16 | .428 |
| Lafayette | 0 | 14 | .000 | 2 | 25 | .074 |

## Southeastern

### EAST

| | Conference | | | All Games | | |
|---|---|---|---|---|---|---|
| | W | L | Pct | W | L | Pct |
| Kentucky*† | 14 | 2 | .875 | 28 | 5 | .875 |
| Georgia | 9 | 7 | .562 | 18 | 10 | .642 |
| Florida | 8 | 8 | .500 | 17 | 13 | .566 |
| Vanderbilt | 6 | 10 | .375 | 13 | 15 | .464 |
| S Carolina | 5 | 11 | .454 | 10 | 17 | .370 |
| Tennessee | 4 | 12 | .250 | 11 | 16 | .407 |

### WEST

| | Conference | | | All Games | | |
|---|---|---|---|---|---|---|
| | W | L | Pct | W | L | Pct |
| Arkansas | 12 | 4 | .750 | 32 | 7 | .820 |
| Mississippi St | 12 | 4 | .750 | 22 | 8 | .733 |
| Alabama | 10 | 6 | .625 | 23 | 10 | .696 |
| Auburn | 7 | 9 | .437 | 16 | 13 | .551 |
| LSU | 6 | 10 | .375 | 12 | 15 | .444 |
| Mississippi | 3 | 13 | .187 | 8 | 19 | .296 |

*Conf. champ; †Conf. tourney winner.

## Southern

### NORTH

| | Conference | | | All Games | | |
|---|---|---|---|---|---|---|
| | W | L | Pct | W | L | Pct |
| Marshall | 10 | 4 | .714 | 18 | 9 | .666 |
| E Tennessee St | 9 | 5 | .642 | 14 | 14 | .500 |
| Davidson | 7 | 7 | .500 | 14 | 13 | .518 |
| VMI | 6 | 8 | .428 | 10 | 17 | .370 |
| Appalachian St | 4 | 10 | .285 | 9 | 20 | .333 |

### SOUTH

| | Conference | | | All Games | | |
|---|---|---|---|---|---|---|
| | W | L | Pct | W | L | Pct |
| TN-Chattanooga*† | 11 | 3 | .785 | 19 | 11 | .633 |
| W Carolina | 8 | 6 | .571 | 14 | 14 | .500 |
| The Citadel | 6 | 8 | .428 | 11 | 16 | .407 |
| Furman | 6 | 8 | .428 | 10 | 17 | .370 |
| Georgia Southern | 3 | 11 | .214 | 8 | 20 | .285 |

## Southland

| | Conference | | | All Games | | |
|---|---|---|---|---|---|---|
| | W | L | Pct | W | L | Pct |
| Nicholls St*† | 17 | 1 | .944 | 24 | 6 | .800 |
| TX-San Antonio | 11 | 7 | .611 | 15 | 13 | .535 |
| NE Louisiana | 11 | 7 | .611 | 14 | 18 | .437 |
| N Texas St | 9 | 9 | .500 | 14 | 13 | .518 |
| Stephen Austin | 9 | 9 | .500 | 14 | 13 | .518 |
| NW Louisana | 8 | 10 | .444 | 13 | 14 | .481 |
| SW Texas St | 7 | 11 | .388 | 12 | 14 | .461 |
| McNeese St | 7 | 11 | .388 | 11 | 16 | .407 |
| TX-Arlington | 7 | 11 | .388 | 10 | 17 | .370 |
| Sam Houston St | 4 | 14 | .222 | 7 | 19 | .269 |

## Southwest

| | Conference | | | All Games | | |
|---|---|---|---|---|---|---|
| | W | L | Pct | W | L | Pct |
| Texas*† | 11 | 3 | .785 | 23 | 7 | .766 |
| Texas Tech | 11 | 3 | .785 | 20 | 10 | .666 |
| TCU | 8 | 6 | .571 | 16 | 11 | .592 |
| Rice | 8 | 6 | .571 | 15 | 13 | .535 |
| Texas A&M | 7 | 7 | .500 | 14 | 16 | .466 |
| Houston | 5 | 9 | .357 | 9 | 19 | .321 |
| Baylor | 3 | 11 | .214 | 9 | 19 | .321 |
| SMU | 3 | 11 | .214 | 7 | 20 | .259 |

## Southwestern Athletic

| | Conference | | | All Games | | |
|---|---|---|---|---|---|---|
| | W | L | Pct | W | L | Pct |
| Texas Southern*† | 12 | 2 | .857 | 22 | 7 | .758 |
| Miss Valley St | 10 | 4 | .714 | 17 | 10 | .629 |
| Alabama St | 8 | 6 | .571 | 10 | 15 | .400 |
| Southern-BR | 7 | 7 | .500 | 13 | 13 | .500 |
| Jackson St | 7 | 7 | .500 | 12 | 19 | .444 |
| Grambling St | 5 | 9 | .357 | 11 | 17 | .392 |
| Alcorn St | 4 | 10 | .285 | 7 | 19 | .250 |
| Prairie View | 3 | 11 | .214 | 5 | 21 | .192 |

*Conf. champ; †Conf. tourney winner.

## Sun Belt

| | Conference | | | All Games | | |
|---|---|---|---|---|---|---|
| | W | L | Pct | W | L | Pct |
| W Kentucky*† | 17 | 1 | .944 | 27 | 4 | .870 |
| New Orleans | 13 | 5 | .722 | 20 | 11 | .645 |
| Jacksonville | 12 | 6 | .667 | 18 | 9 | .667 |
| TX-Pan American | 10 | 8 | .555 | 14 | 14 | .500 |
| AR-Little Rock | 9 | 9 | .500 | 17 | 12 | .586 |
| Louisiana Tech | 9 | 9 | .500 | 14 | 13 | .518 |
| South Alabama | 7 | 11 | .388 | 9 | 18 | .333 |
| Lamar | 6 | 12 | .333 | 11 | 16 | .407 |
| SW Louisiana | 4 | 14 | .222 | 7 | 22 | .241 |
| Arkansas St | 3 | 15 | .166 | 8 | 20 | .285 |

## Trans-America

| | Conference | | | All Games | | |
|---|---|---|---|---|---|---|
| | W | L | Pct | W | L | Pct |
| Coll of Charleston* | 15 | 1 | .937 | 23 | 6 | .793 |
| Samford | 11 | 5 | .687 | 16 | 11 | .592 |
| Stetson | 11 | 5 | .687 | 16 | 11 | .592 |
| Mercer | 8 | 8 | .500 | 15 | 14 | .517 |
| SE Louisiana | 7 | 9 | .437 | 12 | 16 | .428 |
| Central Florida | 7 | 9 | .437 | 11 | 16 | .407 |
| Centenary | 7 | 9 | .437 | 10 | 17 | .370 |
| Georgia St | 6 | 10 | .375 | 11 | 17 | .392 |
| Florida Int'l† | 4 | 12 | .250 | 11 | 19 | .366 |
| Campbell | 4 | 12 | .250 | 8 | 18 | .307 |
| Florida Atlantic | 0 | 0 | .000 | 9 | 18 | .333 |

## West Coast

| | Conference | | | All Games | | |
|---|---|---|---|---|---|---|
| | W | L | Pct | W | L | Pct |
| Santa Clara* | 12 | 2 | .857 | 21 | 7 | .750 |
| Portland | 10 | 4 | .714 | 21 | 8 | .724 |
| St Mary's | 10 | 4 | .714 | 18 | 10 | .642 |
| Gonzaga† | 7 | 7 | .500 | 21 | 9 | .700 |
| San Diego | 5 | 9 | .357 | 11 | 16 | .407 |
| Loyola Marymount | 4 | 10 | .285 | 13 | 15 | .464 |
| San Francisco | 4 | 10 | .285 | 10 | 19 | .344 |
| Pepperdine | 4 | 10 | .285 | 8 | 19 | .296 |

## Western Athletic

| | Conference | | | All Games | | |
|---|---|---|---|---|---|---|
| | W | L | Pct | W | L | Pct |
| Utah*† | 15 | 3 | .833 | 28 | 6 | .823 |
| BYU | 13 | 5 | .722 | 22 | 10 | .687 |
| UTEP | 13 | 5 | .722 | 20 | 10 | .666 |
| New Mexico | 9 | 9 | .500 | 15 | 15 | .500 |
| Wyoming | 9 | 9 | .500 | 13 | 15 | .464 |
| Hawaii | 8 | 10 | .444 | 16 | 13 | .551 |
| Colorado St | 7 | 11 | .388 | 17 | 14 | .548 |
| Fresno St | 7 | 11 | .388 | 13 | 15 | .464 |
| San Diego St | 5 | 13 | .277 | 11 | 17 | .392 |
| Air Force | 4 | 14 | .222 | 8 | 20 | .285 |

## Independents

| | W | L | Pct |
|---|---|---|---|
| Notre Dame | 15 | 12 | .555 |
| Oral Roberts | 10 | 17 | .370 |

## Scoring

| | | | Field Goals | | | 3-Pt FG | | Free Throws | | | | | |
|---|---|---|---|---|---|---|---|---|---|---|---|---|---|
| | Class | GP | FGA | FG | Pct | FGA | FG | FTA | FT | Pct | Reb | Pts | Avg |
| Kurt Thomas, Texas Christian | Sr | 27 | 526 | 288 | 54.8 | 12 | 3 | 283 | 202 | 71.4 | 393 | 781 | 28.9 |
| Frankie King, Western Carolina | Sr | 28 | 520 | 249 | 47.9 | 134 | 52 | 232 | 193 | 83.2 | 204 | 743 | 26.5 |
| Kenny Sykes, Grambling | Sr | 26 | 571 | 245 | 42.9 | 220 | 82 | 146 | 112 | 76.7 | 107 | 684 | 26.3 |
| Sherell Ford, IL-Chicago | Sr | 27 | 562 | 265 | 47.2 | 113 | 47 | 170 | 130 | 76.5 | 283 | 707 | 26.2 |
| Tim Roberts, Southern-BR | Jr | 26 | 570 | 233 | 40.9 | 313 | 108 | 145 | 106 | 73.1 | 123 | 680 | 26.2 |
| Kareem Townes, La Salle | Sr | 27 | 553 | 242 | 43.8 | 284 | 103 | 139 | 112 | 80.6 | 88 | 699 | 25.9 |
| Joe Griffin, LIU-Brooklyn | Sr | 28 | 548 | 271 | 49.5 | 31 | 11 | 256 | 170 | 66.4 | 229 | 723 | 25.8 |
| Shawn Respert, Michigan St | Sr | 28 | 484 | 229 | 47.3 | 251 | 119 | 160 | 139 | 86.9 | 111 | 716 | 25.6 |
| Rob Feaster, Holy Cross | Sr | 27 | 503 | 225 | 44.7 | 168 | 55 | 226 | 167 | 73.9 | 186 | 672 | 24.9 |
| Shannon Smith, WI-Milwaukee | Jr | 27 | 505 | 199 | 39.4 | 157 | 51 | 268 | 212 | 79.1 | 148 | 661 | 24.5 |
| Mark Lueking, Army | Jr | 28 | 498 | 204 | 41.0 | 243 | 98 | 202 | 176 | 87.1 | 65 | 682 | 24.4 |
| Otis Jones, Air Force | Sr | 28 | 495 | 213 | 43.0 | 210 | 71 | 228 | 173 | 75.9 | 130 | 670 | 23.9 |
| Ryan Minor, Oklahoma | Jr | 32 | 535 | 260 | 48.6 | 176 | 69 | 203 | 167 | 82.3 | 269 | 756 | 23.6 |
| Alan Henderson, Indiana | Sr | 31 | 476 | 284 | 59.7 | 10 | 2 | 251 | 159 | 63.3 | 302 | 729 | 23.5 |
| Ronnie Henderson, LSU | So | 27 | 511 | 219 | 42.9 | 212 | 68 | 169 | 124 | 73.4 | 142 | 630 | 23.3 |
| Scott Drapeau, New Hampshire | Sr | 28 | 456 | 241 | 52.9 | 65 | 21 | 205 | 145 | 70.7 | 273 | 648 | 23.1 |
| Tucker Neale, Colgate | Sr | 30 | 509 | 229 | 45.0 | 224 | 84 | 195 | 150 | 76.9 | 138 | 692 | 23.1 |
| Gary Trent, Ohio | Jr | 33 | 556 | 293 | 52.7 | 35 | 8 | 254 | 163 | 64.2 | 423 | 757 | 22.9 |
| Joe Wilbert, Texas A&M | Sr | 30 | 473 | 253 | 53.5 | 14 | 4 | 245 | 177 | 72.2 | 226 | 687 | 22.9 |
| Damon Stoudamire, Arizona | Sr | 30 | 466 | 222 | 47.6 | 241 | 112 | 155 | 128 | 82.6 | 128 | 684 | 22.8 |
| Marcus Brown, Murray St | Jr | 30 | 429 | 219 | 51.0 | 119 | 44 | 211 | 189 | 89.6 | 147 | 671 | 22.4 |
| Matt Alosa, New Hampshire | Jr | 28 | 476 | 197 | 41.4 | 234 | 87 | 168 | 142 | 84.5 | 106 | 623 | 22.3 |
| Danya Abrams, Boston College | So | 28 | 418 | 215 | 51.4 | 8 | 0 | 264 | 190 | 72.0 | 254 | 620 | 22.1 |
| Petey Sessoms, Old Dominion | Sr | 33 | 495 | 213 | 43.0 | 242 | 89 | 259 | 215 | 83.0 | 276 | 730 | 22.1 |
| Chris Carr, Southern Illinois | Jr | 32 | 521 | 250 | 46.0 | 101 | 40 | 214 | 165 | 77.1 | 232 | 705 | 22.0 |
| Aundre Branch, Baylor | Sr | 28 | 506 | 213 | 42.1 | 278 | 104 | 104 | 78 | 75.0 | 127 | 608 | 21.7 |
| Louis Rowe, James Madison | Sr | 29 | 453 | 241 | 53.2 | 92 | 33 | 148 | 114 | 77.0 | 164 | 629 | 21.7 |
| Reggie Jackson, Nicholls St | Sr | 30 | 433 | 251 | 58.0 | 4 | 0 | 228 | 147 | 64.5 | 325 | 649 | 21.6 |
| Gerard King, Nicholls St | Sr | 28 | 423 | 238 | 56.3 | 1 | 1 | 182 | 128 | 70.3 | 218 | 605 | 21.6 |
| Bryant Reeves, Oklahoma St | Sr | 37 | 493 | 289 | 58.6 | 5 | 0 | 310 | 219 | 70.6 | 350 | 797 | 21.5 |

### REBOUNDS

| | Class | GP | Reb | Avg |
|---|---|---|---|---|
| Kurt Thomas, Texas Christian | Sr | 27 | 393 | 14.6 |
| Malik Rose, Drexel | Jr | 30 | 404 | 13.5 |
| Gary Trent, Ohio | Jr | 33 | 423 | 12.8 |
| Dan Callahan, Northeastern | Sr | 29 | 364 | 12.6 |
| Tim Duncan, Wake Forest | So | 32 | 401 | 12.5 |
| Adonal Foyle, Colgate | Fr | 30 | 371 | 12.4 |
| Tunji Awojobi, Boston University | So | 31 | 378 | 12.2 |
| Kareem Carpenter, E Michigan | Sr | 29 | 343 | 11.8 |
| Marcus Mann, Mississippi Valley | Jr | 27 | 317 | 11.7 |
| Chris Ensminger, Valparaiso | Jr | 28 | 315 | 11.3 |

### ASSISTS

| | Class | GP | A | Avg |
|---|---|---|---|---|
| Nelson Haggerty, Baylor | Sr | 28 | 284 | 10.1 |
| Curtis McCants, George Mason | So | 27 | 251 | 9.3 |
| Raimonds Miglinieks, UC-Irvine | Jr | 29 | 245 | 8.4 |
| Eric Snow, Michigan St | Sr | 28 | 217 | 7.8 |
| Jacque Vaughn, Kansas | So | 31 | 238 | 7.7 |
| Anthony Foster, South Alabama | Sr | 27 | 203 | 7.5 |
| Tony Miller, Marquette | Sr | 33 | 248 | 7.5 |
| Hassan Sanders, Southern-BR | Jr | 24 | 179 | 7.5 |
| Ray Washington, Nicholls St | Sr | 29 | 213 | 7.3 |
| Damon Stoudamire, Arizona | Sr | 30 | 220 | 7.3 |
| Eathan O'Bryant, Nevada | Sr | 29 | 211 | 7.3 |
| Marcell Capers, Arizona St | Sr | 33 | 233 | 7.1 |

### 3-POINT FIELD GOALS MADE PER GAME

| | Class | GP | FG | Avg |
|---|---|---|---|---|
| Mitch Taylor, Southern-BR | Jr | 25 | 109 | 4.4 |
| Shawn Respert, Michigan St | Sr | 28 | 119 | 4.3 |
| Tim Roberts, Southern-BR | Jr | 26 | 108 | 4.2 |
| Randy Rutherford, Oklahoma St | Sr | 37 | 146 | 3.9 |
| Kareem Townes, La Salle | Sr | 27 | 103 | 3.8 |
| Lazelle Durden, Cincinnati | Sr | 34 | 127 | 3.7 |
| Damon Stoudamire, Arizona | Sr | 30 | 112 | 3.7 |
| Aundre Branch, Baylor | Sr | 28 | 104 | 3.7 |
| Noy Castillo, Citadel | So | 27 | 96 | 3.6 |
| Chris Kingsbury, Iowa | So | 33 | 117 | 3.5 |
| Adam Jacobsen, Pacific (CA) | So | 27 | 95 | 3.5 |

### 3-POINT FIELD GOAL PERCENTAGE

| | Class | GP | FGA | FG | Pct |
|---|---|---|---|---|---|
| Brian Jackson, Evansville | Jr | 27 | 95 | 53 | 55.8 |
| Scott Kegler, Pennsylvania | Sr | 28 | 114 | 58 | 50.9 |
| Chris Westlake, WI-Green Bay | Sr | 30 | 174 | 87 | 50.0 |
| Dante Calabria, N Carolina | Jr | 33 | 133 | 66 | 49.6 |
| Malik Hightower, Marshall | Jr | 27 | 95 | 46 | 48.4 |
| Jeremy Lake, Montana | Sr | 30 | 157 | 76 | 48.4 |
| Dion Cross, Stanford | Jr | 29 | 171 | 82 | 48.0 |
| Shawn Respert, Michigan St | Sr | 28 | 251 | 119 | 47.4 |
| Daryl Christopher, Southern Utah | Jr | 27 | 112 | 53 | 47.3 |
| Rob Wooster, St. Francis (PA) | Jr | 28 | 174 | 82 | 47.1 |

Note: Minimum 1.5 made per game.

## STEALS

| | Class | GP | S | Avg |
|---|---|---|---|---|
| Roderick Anderson, Texas | Sr | 30 | 101 | 3.4 |
| Greg Black, TX-Pan American | Sr | 28 | 94 | 3.4 |
| Nate Langley, George Mason | So | 26 | 87 | 3.3 |
| Ray Washington, Nicholls St | Sr | 29 | 88 | 3.0 |
| Clarence Ceasar, LSU | Sr | 22 | 66 | 3.0 |
| Allen Iverson, Georgetown | Fr | 30 | 89 | 3.0 |
| Shandue McNeill, St Bonaventure | So | 31 | 90 | 2.9 |
| Dominick Young, Fresno St | So | 28 | 81 | 2.9 |
| Erick Strickland, Nebraska | Jr | 31 | 89 | 2.9 |
| Gerald Walker, San Francisco | Jr | 28 | 80 | 2.9 |

## BLOCKED SHOTS

| | Class | GP | BS | Avg |
|---|---|---|---|---|
| Keith Closs, Central Conn St | Fr | 26 | 139 | 5.3 |
| Theo Ratcliff, Wyoming | Sr | 28 | 144 | 5.1 |
| Adonal Foyle, Colgate | Fr | 30 | 147 | 4.9 |
| Pascal Fleury, MD-Baltimore County | Sr | 27 | 124 | 4.6 |
| Lorenzo Coleman, Tennessee Tech | So | 27 | 122 | 4.5 |
| Tim Duncan, Wake Forest | So | 32 | 145 | 4.2 |
| Brian Gilpin, Dartmouth | So | 26 | 92 | 3.5 |
| Mario Bennett, Arizona St | Jr | 33 | 115 | 3.5 |
| Peter Aluma, Liberty | So | 28 | 97 | 3.5 |

Four tied with 3.4.

## FIELD GOAL PERCENTAGE

| | Class | GP | FGA | FG | Pct |
|---|---|---|---|---|---|
| Shane Kline-Ruminski, Bowl Gr | Sr | 26 | 265 | 181 | 68.3 |
| George Spain, Davidson | Sr | 27 | 210 | 141 | 67.1 |
| Rasheed Wallace, N Carolina | So | 34 | 364 | 238 | 65.4 |
| Erick Dampier, Mississippi St | So | 30 | 239 | 153 | 64.0 |
| Alexander Koul, Geo Wash | Fr | 32 | 253 | 160 | 63.2 |
| Joe McNaull, Long Beach St | Sr | 30 | 248 | 156 | 62.9 |
| Mark Hendrickson, Wash St | Jr | 30 | 292 | 183 | 62.7 |
| Darnell McCulloch, Fresno St | So | 28 | 244 | 152 | 62.3 |
| Lorenzo Coleman, Tenn Tech | So | 27 | 270 | 168 | 62.2 |
| Chuckie Robinson, E Carolina | So | 29 | 293 | 181 | 61.8 |

Note: Minimum 5 made per game.

## FREE-THROW PERCENTAGE

| | Class | GP | FTA | FT | Pct |
|---|---|---|---|---|---|
| Greg Bibb, Tennessee Tech | Jr | 27 | 117 | 106 | 90.6 |
| Scott Hartzell, NC-Greensboro | Jr | 29 | 108 | 97 | 89.8 |
| Marcus Brown, Murray St | Jr | 30 | 211 | 189 | 89.6 |
| Keith Cornett, TX-Arlington | Jr | 27 | 79 | 70 | 88.6 |
| Arlando Johnson, E Kentucky | Sr | 28 | 139 | 123 | 88.5 |
| Danny Basile, Marist | Jr | 28 | 84 | 74 | 88.1 |
| Steve Nash, Santa Clara | Jr | 27 | 174 | 153 | 87.9 |
| John Rillie, Gonzaga | Sr | 30 | 99 | 87 | 87.9 |
| Lance Barker, Valparaiso | Sr | 28 | 82 | 72 | 87.8 |
| Michael Heary, Navy | Fr | 28 | 105 | 120 | 87.5 |

Note: Minimum 2.5 made per game.

## Single-Game Highs

### POINTS

56 .............Tim Roberts, Southern-BR, Dec 12 (vs Faith Baptist)
52 .............Jareem Townes, La Salle, Feb 4 (vs Loyola [IL])
50 .............Kenny Sykes, Grambling, Jan 8 (vs Southern BR)

### REBOUNDS

27 .............Kareem Carpenter, Eastern Mich, Feb 8 (vs Western Michigan)
26 .............Kareem Carpenter, Eastern Mich, Jan 14 (vs Central Michigan)

### ASSISTS

20 .............Ray Washington, Nicholls St, Jan 28 (vs McNeese St)

### 3-POINT FIELD GOALS

12 .............Mitch Taylor, Southern-BR, Dec 1 (vs LA Christian)
11 .............Randy Rutherford, Oklahoma St, Mar 5 (vs Kansas)

### FREE THROWS

21 .............Steve Nash, Santa Clara, Jan 7 (vs St Mary's [CA])
19 .............Malik Rose, Drexel, Feb 5 (vs Hofstra)
19 .............Sidney Goodman, Coppin St, Feb 18 (vs N Carolina A&T)

## Single-Game Highs (Cont.)

### STEALS

11 ............Tyus Edney, UCLA, Dec 22 (vs George Mason)
10 ............Brandon Born, TN-Chatt, Nov 26 (vs SC-Aiken)
10 ............Mario Miller, Bethune-Cookman, Dec 3 (vs Warner Southern)
10 ............Tick Rogers, Louisville, Dec 5 (vs Western Carolina)

### BLOCKED SHOTS

13 ............Keith Closs, Central Conn St, Dec 21 (vs St Francis [PA])
12 ............Kurt Thomas, Texas Christian, Feb 25 (vs Texas A&M)
Three tied with 11.

# NCAA Men's Division I Team Leaders

### SCORING OFFENSE

| | GP | W | L | Pts | Avg | | GP | W | L | Pts | Avg |
|---|---|---|---|---|---|---|---|---|---|---|---|
| Texas Christian | 27 | 16 | 11 | 2529 | 93.7 | Nicholls St | 30 | 24 | 6 | 2709 | 90.3 |
| Southern-BR | 26 | 13 | 13 | 2425 | 93.3 | Texas Tech | 30 | 20 | 10 | 2664 | 88.8 |
| Texas | 30 | 23 | 7 | 2787 | 92.9 | Stephen F. Austin | 28 | 14 | 14 | 2461 | 87.9 |
| George Mason | 27 | 7 | 20 | 2499 | 92.6 | Arkansas | 39 | 32 | 7 | 3416 | 87.6 |
| Troy St | 27 | 11 | 16 | 2468 | 91.4 | UCLA | 33 | 31 | 2 | 2889 | 87.5 |

### SCORING DEFENSE

| | GP | W | L | Pts | Avg | | GP | W | L | Pts | Avg |
|---|---|---|---|---|---|---|---|---|---|---|---|
| Princeton | 26 | 16 | 10 | 1501 | 57.7 | Clemson | 28 | 15 | 13 | 1749 | 62.5 |
| WI-Green Bay | 30 | 22 | 8 | 1767 | 58.9 | St Louis | 31 | 23 | 8 | 1940 | 62.6 |
| Temple | 30 | 19 | 11 | 1792 | 59.7 | Charleston (SC) | 29 | 23 | 6 | 1819 | 62.7 |
| Miami (OH) | 30 | 23 | 7 | 1827 | 60.9 | Wake Forest | 32 | 26 | 6 | 2011 | 62.8 |
| Manhattan | 31 | 26 | 5 | 1929 | 62.2 | TX-Pan American | 28 | 14 | 14 | 1769 | 63.2 |

### SCORING MARGIN

| | Off | Def | Mar | | Off | Def | Mar |
|---|---|---|---|---|---|---|---|
| Kentucky | 87.4 | 69.0 | 18.4 | Evansville | 77.0 | 63.7 | 13.3 |
| Massachusetts | 80.9 | 65.7 | 15.1 | St Louis | 75.8 | 62.6 | 13.2 |
| Pennsylvania | 82.2 | 67.5 | 15.1 | Manhattan | 75.3 | 62.2 | 13.0 |
| UCLA | 87.5 | 73.9 | 13.7 | Kansas | 83.0 | 70.0 | 13.0 |
| Montana St | 84.2 | 70.8 | 13.4 | Oklahoma St | 77.3 | 64.3 | 12.9 |

### FIELD GOAL PERCENTAGE

| | FGA | FG | Pct | | FGA | FG | Pct |
|---|---|---|---|---|---|---|---|
| Washington St | 1743 | 902 | 51.7 | Utah St | 1650 | 831 | 50.4 |
| UCLA | 2102 | 1079 | 51.3 | Oklahoma St | 2025 | 1016 | 50.2 |
| North Carolina | 2055 | 1044 | 50.8 | Michigan St | 1664 | 829 | 49.8 |
| Montana St | 1832 | 930 | 50.8 | Maryland | 2080 | 1035 | 49.8 |
| Bowling Green | 1427 | 721 | 50.5 | Evansville | 1457 | 723 | 49.6 |

## FIELD GOAL PERCENTAGE DEFENSE

| | FGA | FG | Pct | | FGA | FG | Pct |
|---|---|---|---|---|---|---|---|
| Alabama | 2048 | 771 | 37.6 | Massachusetts | 2072 | 799 | 38.6 |
| Kansas | 2032 | 768 | 37.8 | Temple | 1623 | 628 | 38.7 |
| Marquette | 1957 | 747 | 38.2 | Wake Forest | 1898 | 736 | 38.8 |
| Mississippi St | 1821 | 698 | 38.3 | Virginia | 2058 | 803 | 39.0 |
| Manhattan | 1747 | 670 | 38.4 | Charleston (SC) | 1634 | 639 | 39.1 |

## FREE-THROW PERCENTAGE

| | FTA | FT | Pct | | FTA | FT | Pct |
|---|---|---|---|---|---|---|---|
| Brigham Young | 798 | 617 | 77.3 | Coppin St | 633 | 476 | 75.2 |
| Murray St | 719 | 553 | 76.9 | Towson St | 503 | 377 | 75.0 |
| Wake Forest | 622 | 475 | 76.4 | Oklahoma | 755 | 564 | 74.7 |
| Samford | 622 | 472 | 75.9 | Morehead St | 572 | 427 | 74.7 |
| Iowa St | 610 | 806 | 75.7 | Connecticut | 746 | 556 | 74.5 |
| | | | | NC-Charlotte | 626 | 466 | 74.4 |

## 3-POINT FIELD GOALS MADE PER GAME

| | GP | FG | Avg | | GP | FG | Avg |
|---|---|---|---|---|---|---|---|
| Troy St | 27 | 287 | 10.6 | Southern-BR | 26 | 361 | 9.3 |
| Samford | 27 | 279 | 10.3 | St Louis | 31 | 284 | 9.2 |
| Vermont | 27 | 268 | 9.9 | VMI | 27 | 247 | 9.1 |
| Baylor | 28 | 265 | 9.5 | Stephen F. Austin | 28 | 248 | 8.9 |
| Marshall | 27 | 253 | 9.4 | Pennsylvania | 28 | 247 | 8.8 |
| Arkansas | 39 | 361 | 9.3 | | | | |

## 3-POINT FIELD GOAL PERCENTAGE

| | GP | FGA | FG | Pct | | GP | FGA | FG | Pct |
|---|---|---|---|---|---|---|---|---|---|
| Southern Utah | 28 | 571 | 244 | 42.7 | Michigan St | 28 | 387 | 158 | 40.8 |
| Evansville | 27 | 424 | 181 | 42.7 | Pennsylvania | 28 | 387 | 158 | 40.8 |
| WI-Green Bay | 30 | 451 | 188 | 41.7 | Gonzaga | 30 | 573 | 232 | 40.5 |
| Arizona | 31 | 593 | 245 | 41.3 | Southern Illinois | 32 | 645 | 257 | 39.8 |
| N Carolina | 34 | 648 | 266 | 41.0 | Ohio St | 28 | 404 | 160 | 39.6 |
| Note: Minimum 3.0 made per game. | | | | | Valparaiso | 28 | 528 | 209 | 39.6 |
| | | | | | Samford | 27 | 705 | 279 | 39.6 |

# NCAA Women's Championship Game Box Score

## Connecticut 70

| Connecticut | Min | FG M-A | FT M-A | Reb O-T | A | PF | TP |
|---|---|---|---|---|---|---|---|
| Elliot | 39 | 5-7 | 3-4 | 2-7 | 3 | 3 | 13 |
| Lobo | 28 | 5-10 | 7-8 | 2-8 | 2 | 4 | 17 |
| Wolters | 31 | 4-9 | 2-4 | 1-3 | 0 | 4 | 10 |
| Rizzotti | 32 | 6-8 | 2-2 | 0-3 | 3 | 3 | 15 |
| Webber | 17 | 0-1 | 0-0 | 1-1 | 2 | 1 | 0 |
| Sales | 33 | 4-12 | 1-4 | 2-6 | 3 | 3 | 10 |
| Berube | 20 | 1-6 | 3-5 | 2-3 | 2 | 0 | 5 |
| Totals | 200 | 25-53 | 18-27 | 10-31 | 15 | 18 | 70 |

Percentages: FG—.472, FT—.667. 3-pt goals: 2-10, .200 (Lobo 0-2, Rizzotti 1-2, Webber 0-1, Sales 1-4, Berube 0-1). Team rebounds: 12. Blocked shots: 4 (Lobo 2, Wolters 2). Turnovers: 16 (Elliot 5, Rizzotti 4, Berube 3, Lobo 2, Sales, Wolters). Steals: 7 (Rizzotti 3, Sales 3, Elliot).

## Tennessee 64

| Tennessee | Min | FG M-A | FT M-A | Reb O-T | A | PF | TP |
|---|---|---|---|---|---|---|---|
| McCray | 31 | 3-12 | 1-2 | 3-5 | 4 | 2 | 7 |
| Thompson | 10 | 1-1 | 2-2 | 3-3 | 1 | 2 | 4 |
| D. Johnson | 33 | 3-11 | 3-3 | 3-10 | 0 | 2 | 9 |
| Marciniak | 30 | 3-11 | 1-3 | 0-0 | 5 | 3 | 8 |
| Davis | 31 | 5-12 | 0-1 | 3-5 | 1 | 4 | 11 |
| Ward | 16 | 2-5 | 2-2 | 1-2 | 1 | 3 | 6 |
| T. Johnson | 21 | 3-7 | 1-1 | 2-5 | 1 | 3 | 7 |
| M. Johnson | 13 | 2-3 | 0-0 | 0-3 | 1 | 2 | 5 |
| Milligan | 10 | 1-3 | 2-2 | 0-0 | 2 | 0 | 4 |
| Conklin | 5 | 1-1 | 0-0 | 1-1 | 0 | 1 | 3 |
| Totals | 200 | 24-66 | 12-16 | 16-34 | 16 | 22 | 64 |

Percentages: FG—.364, FT—.750. 3-pt goals: 4-14, .286 (McCray 0-1, Marciniak 1-6, Davis 1-4, M. Johnson 1-2, Conklin1-1). Team rebounds: 3. Blocked shots: 1 (T. Johnson). Turnovers: 14 (Marciniak 3, McCray 3, Conklin 2, T. Johnson 2, D. Johnson, Davis, Milligan, Thompson). Steals: 6 (D. Johnson 2, Marciniak 2, Davis, McCray).

Halftime: Tennessee 38, Connecticut 32.
A: 18,038. Officials: Kantner, Shepherd.

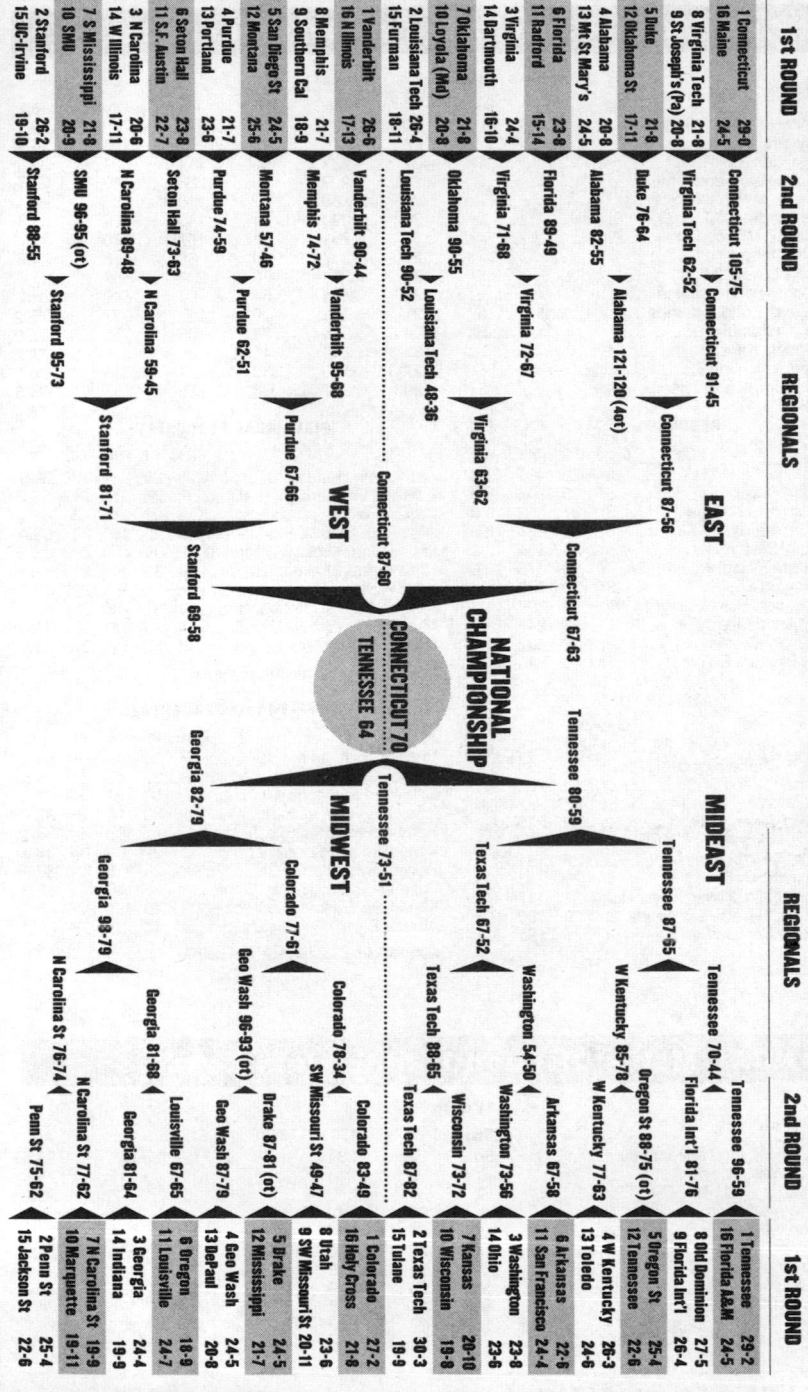

# 1995 NCAA Basketball Women's Division I Tournament

## EAST

| 1st ROUND | 2nd ROUND | REGIONALS |
|---|---|---|
| 1 Connecticut 29-0 | | |
| 16 Maine 24-5 | Connecticut 105-75 | |
| 8 Virginia Tech 21-8 | | Connecticut 91-45 |
| 9 St.Joseph's (Pa) 20-8 | Virginia Tech 62-52 | |
| 5 Duke 21-9 | | |
| 12 Oklahoma St 17-11 | Duke 76-64 | |
| 4 Alabama 20-8 | | Alabama 82-55 |
| 13 Mt St Mary's 24-5 | Alabama 82-55 | |
| 3 Virginia 24-4 | | |
| 14 Radford 16-10 | Virginia 71-68 | |
| 6 Florida 23-8 | | Florida 89-49 |
| 11 Radford 15-14 | Florida 89-49 | |
| 7 Oklahoma 21-8 | | |
| 10 Loyola (Md) 20-8 | Oklahoma 90-55 | |
| 2 Louisiana Tech 26-4 | | Louisiana Tech 90-52 |
| 15 Furman 18-11 | Louisiana Tech 90-52 | |

## WEST

| 1st ROUND | 2nd ROUND | REGIONALS |
|---|---|---|
| 1 Vanderbilt 26-6 | | |
| 16 N Illinois 17-13 | Vanderbilt 90-44 | |
| 8 Memphis 21-7 | | Vanderbilt 95-68 |
| 9 Southern Cal 18-9 | Memphis 74-72 | |
| 5 San Diego St 24-5 | | |
| 12 Montana 25-6 | Montana 57-46 | |
| 4 Purdue 21-7 | | Purdue 62-51 |
| 13 Portland 23-6 | Purdue 74-59 | |
| 6 Seton Hall 23-8 | | |
| 11 S.F. Austin 22-7 | Seton Hall 73-63 | |
| 3 N Carolina 20-6 | | N Carolina 59-45 |
| 14 W Illinois 17-11 | N Carolina 89-48 | |
| 7 S Mississippi 21-8 | | |
| 10 SMU 20-9 | SMU 96-95 (ot) | |
| 2 Stanford 26-2 | | Stanford 88-55 |
| 15 UC-Irvine 19-10 | Stanford 88-55 | |

## REGIONALS — MIDEAST

| REGIONALS | 2nd ROUND | 1st ROUND |
|---|---|---|
| | | 1 Tennessee 29-2 |
| | Tennessee 96-59 | 16 Florida A&M 24-5 |
| Tennessee 70-44 | | 8 Old Dominion 27-5 |
| | Florida Int'l 81-76 | 9 Florida Int'l 26-4 |
| | | 5 Oregon St 25-4 |
| | Oregon St 88-75 (ot) | 12 Tennessee 22-6 |
| W Kentucky 85-78 | | 4 W Kentucky 26-3 |
| | W Kentucky 77-83 | 13 Toledo 24-6 |
| | | 3 Washington 23-8 |
| | Washington 73-56 | 14 Ohio 23-6 |
| Washington 54-50 | | 6 Arkansas 22-6 |
| | Arkansas 67-58 | 11 San Francisco 22-6 |

## MIDWEST

| REGIONALS | 2nd ROUND | 1st ROUND |
|---|---|---|
| | | 7 Kansas 20-10 |
| | Wisconsin 73-72 | 10 Wisconsin 19-8 |
| Texas Tech 89-85 | | 2 Texas Tech 30-3 |
| | Texas Tech 87-82 | 15 Tulane 19-9 |
| | | 1 Colorado 27-2 |
| | Colorado 83-49 | 16 Holy Cross 21-8 |
| Colorado 78-34 | | 8 Utah 23-6 |
| | SW Missouri St 49-47 | 9 SW Missouri St 20-11 |
| | | 5 Drake 24-5 |
| | Drake 87-81 (ot) | 12 Mississippi 21-7 |
| Geo Wash 96-93 (ot) | | 4 Geo Wash 24-5 |
| | Geo Wash 87-79 | 13 DePaul 20-8 |
| | | 6 Oregon 18-9 |
| | Louisville 67-65 | 11 Louisville 24-7 |
| Georgia 81-68 | | 3 Georgia 24-4 |
| | Georgia 81-64 | 14 Indiana 19-9 |
| | | 7 N Carolina St 19-9 |
| | N Carolina St 77-62 | 10 Marquette 19-11 |
| N Carolina St 76-74 | | 2 Penn St 25-4 |
| | Penn St 75-62 | 15 Jackson St 22-6 |

### WEST (regional finals)

Connecticut 87-56

Connecticut 87-60

Stanford 69-58

Connecticut 67-63

### MIDEAST

Tennessee 87-65

Tennessee 80-59

Texas Tech 67-52

Tennessee 73-51

### MIDWEST

Georgia 82-79

Georgia 93-79

Colorado 77-61

## NATIONAL CHAMPIONSHIP

### CONNECTICUT 70
### TENNESSEE 64

# NCAA Women's Division I Individual Leaders

## SCORING

| | Class | GP | TFG | 3FG | FT | Pts | Avg |
|---|---|---|---|---|---|---|---|
| Koko Lahanas, Cal St-Fullerton | Jr | 29 | 329 | 0 | 120 | 778 | 26.8 |
| Latasha Byears, DePaul | Jr | 28 | 316 | 11 | 97 | 740 | 26.4 |
| Cornelia Gayden, LSU | Sr | 27 | 239 | 105 | 114 | 697 | 25.8 |
| Kim Mays, Eastern Kentucky | Sr | 28 | 229 | 35 | 226 | 719 | 25.7 |
| Anita Maxwell, New Mexico St | Jr | 29 | 288 | 2 | 160 | 738 | 25.4 |
| DeShawne Blocker, E Tennessee St | Sr | 30 | 290 | 1 | 149 | 730 | 24.3 |
| Gray Harris, SE Missouri St | Jr | 26 | 231 | 1 | 167 | 630 | 24.2 |
| Korie Hlede, Duquesne | Fr | 26 | 257 | 34 | 80 | 628 | 24.2 |
| Patty Stoffey, Loyola (MD) | Sr | 29 | 244 | 0 | 209 | 697 | 24.0 |
| Shannon Johnson, S Carolina | Jr | 27 | 214 | 64 | 154 | 646 | 23.9 |
| Melissa Gower, Long Beach St | Sr | 27 | 235 | 0 | 167 | 637 | 23.6 |
| Sha Hopson, Grambling | Sr | 28 | 238 | 73 | 106 | 655 | 23.4 |
| Angela Aycock, Kansas | Sr | 31 | 240 | 41 | 195 | 716 | 23.1 |
| Amy Burnett, Wyoming | Sr | 27 | 195 | 30 | 194 | 614 | 22.7 |
| Carolyn Aldridge, Tennessee St | Sr | 29 | 217 | 98 | 125 | 657 | 22.7 |

## REBOUNDS

| | Class | GP | Reb | Avg |
|---|---|---|---|---|
| Tera Sheriff, Jackson St | Sr | 29 | 401 | 13.8 |
| Rene Doctor, Coppin St | Sr | 25 | 344 | 13.8 |
| Melissa Gower, Long Beach St | Sr | 27 | 352 | 13.0 |
| Oberon Pitterson, W Illinois | Sr | 28 | 354 | 12.6 |
| Dana Wynne, Seton Hall | So | 33 | 415 | 12.6 |
| Joskeen Garner, Northwestern St | Jr | 30 | 376 | 12.6 |
| Niamh Darcy, VCU | Sr | 30 | 363 | 12.1 |
| Scherrie Jackson, Beth.-Cookman | So | 25 | 298 | 11.9 |
| Stephanie Minor, Murray St | So | 21 | 245 | 11.7 |
| Carrie Coffman, Bradley | Sr | 26 | 302 | 11.6 |
| DeShawne Blocker, E Tenn St | Sr | 30 | 345 | 11.5 |

## ASSISTS

| | Class | GP | A | Avg |
|---|---|---|---|---|
| Andrea Nagy, Florida Int'l | Sr | 32 | 315 | 9.8 |
| Dayna Smith, Rhode Island | Jr | 27 | 239 | 8.9 |
| Tina Nicholson, Penn St | Jr | 31 | 250 | 8.1 |
| Tabitha Truesdale, Texas Tech | Sr | 37 | 281 | 7.6 |
| Tiffany Martin, Georgia Tech | So | 30 | 220 | 7.3 |
| Lori Goerlitz, Marquette | Sr | 31 | 222 | 7.2 |
| Dani Maziur, New Orleans | Jr | 27 | 191 | 7.1 |
| Boky Vidic, Oregon St | Jr | 29 | 203 | 7.0 |
| Gretchen Hollifield, Wake Forest | Jr | 21 | 147 | 7.0 |
| Gwynn Hobbs, Nevada-Las Vegas | Sr | 26 | 180 | 6.9 |
| Heather Fiore, Canisius | So | 27 | 185 | 6.9 |

## FIELD GOAL PERCENTAGE

| | Class | GP | FGA | FG | Pct |
|---|---|---|---|---|---|
| Alisha Hill, Howard | Fr | 28 | 281 | 194 | 69.0 |
| LeFreda Deckard, N Texas | Fr | 27 | 217 | 147 | 67.7 |
| Kristen Ferrucci, Davidson | Jr | 27 | 216 | 139 | 64.4 |
| Albena Branzova, Florida Int'l | Sr | 32 | 459 | 291 | 63.4 |
| DeShawne Blocker, E Tenn St | Sr | 30 | 459 | 290 | 63.2 |
| Kristi Kinne, Drake | Sr | 31 | 344 | 217 | 63.1 |
| Kara Wolters, Connecticut | So | 33 | 354 | 222 | 62.7 |
| Katryna Gaither, Notre Dame | So | 31 | 406 | 252 | 62.1 |
| Myndee Larsen, S Utah | Jr | 26 | 271 | 167 | 61.6 |
| Dana Johnson, Tennessee | Sr | 37 | 349 | 215 | 61.6 |

Note: Minimum 5 made per game.

## FREE-THROW PERCENTAGE

| | Class | GP | FTA | FT | Pct |
|---|---|---|---|---|---|
| Christy Smith, Arkansas | Fr | 30 | 149 | 134 | 89.9 |
| Shelley Sheetz, Colorado | Sr | 33 | 115 | 103 | 89.6 |
| Julie Krommenhoek, Utah | Fr | 30 | 89 | 78 | 87.6 |
| Lisa Gerton, NC-Charlotte | Jr | 20 | 96 | 84 | 87.5 |
| Heather Prater, Middle Tenn St | Jr | 28 | 105 | 91 | 86.7 |
| Kerry Giroux, Rhode Island | Jr | 27 | 89 | 77 | 86.5 |
| Sally Crowe, Oregon | So | 26 | 118 | 102 | 86.4 |
| Suzanne Ressa, Santa Clara | Jr | 28 | 146 | 126 | 86.3 |
| Kim Mays, Eastern Kentucky | Sr | 28 | 264 | 226 | 85.6 |
| Albena Branzova, Florida Int'l | Sr | 32 | 95 | 81 | 85.3 |

Note: Minimum 2.5 made per game.

# NCAA Men's Division II Individual Leaders

## SCORING

| | Class | GP | TFG | 3FG | FT | Pts | Avg |
|---|---|---|---|---|---|---|---|
| Carlos Knox, IU/PU-Indianapolis | So | 29 | 284 | 39 | 218 | 825 | 28.4 |
| Eric Bovaird, West Liberty St | Sr | 26 | 215 | 92 | 193 | 715 | 27.5 |
| Dennis Edwards, Fort Hayes St | Sr | 30 | 340 | 0 | 126 | 806 | 26.9 |
| Tyrone Mason, Edinboro | Jr | 26 | 242 | 83 | 124 | 691 | 26.6 |
| Brett Beeson, Moorhead St | Jr | 27 | 246 | 34 | 189 | 715 | 26.5 |
| Tyrone Latimer, Central Missouri St | Sr | 32 | 300 | 55 | 177 | 832 | 26.0 |
| Shawn Hadley, W Georgia | Sr | 19 | 158 | 64 | 98 | 478 | 25.2 |
| Hassan Robinson, Springfield | Sr | 26 | 239 | 67 | 105 | 650 | 25.0 |
| Joel McDonald, St Cloud St | Sr | 27 | 195 | 100 | 180 | 670 | 24.8 |
| Jason Kaiser, AK-Anchorage | Sr | 27 | 259 | 59 | 91 | 668 | 24.7 |

## REBOUNDS

| | Class | GP | Reb | Avg |
|---|---|---|---|---|
| Lorenzo Poole, Albany St (GA) | Sr | 26 | 417 | 16.0 |
| Garth Joseph, St Rose | Fr | 31 | 396 | 12.8 |
| Rob Layton, Emporia St | Jr | 25 | 300 | 12.0 |
| Kevin Lee, Shippensburg | So | 26 | 307 | 11.8 |
| Larry Steimer, Molloy | Fr | 24 | 278 | 11.6 |
| Joe Banks, NM Highlands | Sr | 27 | 309 | 11.4 |
| Jonathan Maddox, Tuskegee | Sr | 27 | 299 | 11.1 |
| Dalon Bynum, AK-Fairbanks | Sr | 27 | 296 | 11.0 |
| J.D. Asselta, Bentley | Jr | 27 | 296 | 11.0 |
| Steve Ryan, Northwood | Sr | 26 | 284 | 10.9 |

## ASSISTS

| | Class | GP | A | Avg |
|---|---|---|---|---|
| Ernest Jenkins, NM Highlands | Sr | 27 | 291 | 10.8 |
| Brent Schremp, Slippery Rock | Sr | 25 | 259 | 10.4 |
| Rob Paternostro, New Hamp Coll | Sr | 33 | 309 | 9.4 |
| Craig Lottie, Alabama A&M | Jr | 32 | 287 | 9.0 |
| Marcus Talbert, CO Christian | Sr | 27 | 230 | 8.5 |
| Cal Butler, Morris Brown | Jr | 26 | 216 | 8.3 |
| Jordan Canfield, Washburn | Jr | 30 | 242 | 8.1 |
| Candice Pickens, California (PA) | Jr | 29 | 228 | 7.9 |
| Trent McHenry, Tuskegee | Jr | 27 | 209 | 7.7 |
| Deon Moyd, AK-Fairbanks | Sr | 27 | 208 | 7.7 |
| Willis Cheaney, Kentucky Wesleyan | Sr | 29 | 214 | 7.4 |

## FIELD GOAL PERCENTAGE

| | Class | GP | FGA | FG | Pct |
|---|---|---|---|---|---|
| John Pruett, SIU-Edwardsville | Fr | 26 | 193 | 138 | 71.5 |
| Chris Morris, Alderson-Broaddus | Jr | 28 | 326 | 231 | 70.9 |
| Garth Joseph, St Rose | Fr | 31 | 271 | 184 | 67.9 |
| Al Lindsey, Henderson St | Jr | 23 | 198 | 133 | 67.2 |
| DeWayne Ansley, Queens (NC) | Jr | 26 | 228 | 153 | 67.1 |
| DeRon Rutledge, TX A&M-King | Jr | 28 | 377 | 252 | 66.8 |
| Anthony Russell, W Florida | Fr | 28 | 226 | 150 | 66.4 |
| Yogi Leo, Queens (NC) | Jr | 27 | 217 | 144 | 66.4 |
| Jason Burkholder, Oakland | Jr | 29 | 266 | 176 | 66.2 |
| Dennis Edwards, Fort Hays St | Sr | 30 | 514 | 340 | 66.1 |

Note: Minimum 5 made per game.

## FREE-THROW PERCENTAGE

| | Class | GP | FTA | FT | Pct |
|---|---|---|---|---|---|
| Jim Borodawka, Mass-Lowell | So | 27 | 80 | 74 | 92.5 |
| Marcus Albert, MO-St Louis | Sr | 27 | 93 | 101 | 92.1 |
| Travis Tuttle, North Dakota | So | 28 | 99 | 108 | 91.7 |
| Mike Lake, Hillsdale | Sr | 29 | 143 | 129 | 90.2 |
| Lance Luitjens, Northern St | Jr | 33 | 172 | 155 | 90.1 |
| Jake Biddle, Francis Marion | Fr | 26 | 97 | 87 | 89.7 |
| Thaddeus Breckenridge, Concord | Jr | 31 | 199 | 178 | 89.4 |
| Michael Shue, Lock Haven | So | 26 | 136 | 121 | 89.0 |
| Mike Ellzy, Bloomsburg | So | 27 | 118 | 104 | 88.1 |
| Jason Holmes, SIU-Edwardsville | So | 26 | 132 | 116 | 87.9 |

Note: Minimum 2.5 made per game.

# NCAA Women's Division II Individual Leaders

## SCORING

| | Class | GP | TFG | 3FG | FT | Pts | Avg |
|---|---|---|---|---|---|---|---|
| Shander Gary, Lynn | Sr | 20 | 235 | 0 | 149 | 619 | 31.0 |
| Nicole Collins, Angelo St | Sr | 25 | 231 | 80 | 98 | 640 | 25.6 |
| Jennifer Clarkson, Abilene Christian | Jr | 28 | 255 | 2 | 182 | 694 | 24.8 |
| Rachel Matakas, Central Missouri St | Jr | 27 | 264 | 12 | 124 | 664 | 24.6 |
| LeAnn Freeland, Southern Indiana | So | 27 | 265 | 2 | 126 | 658 | 24.4 |
| Attala Young, Erskine | Sr | 27 | 236 | 1 | 163 | 636 | 23.6 |
| Debra Williams, Lincoln (MO) | Jr | 26 | 249 | 0 | 104 | 602 | 23.2 |
| Michelle Doonan, Stonehill | Sr | 33 | 265 | 68 | 160 | 758 | 23.0 |
| Libby Corry, Wofford | Sr | 24 | 205 | 20 | 119 | 549 | 22.9 |
| Marqueetta Randolph, Virginia Union | So | 26 | 240 | 2 | 105 | 587 | 22.6 |

## REBOUNDS

| | Class | GP | Reb | Avg |
|---|---|---|---|---|
| Robin Scott, Lees-McRae | Sr | 19 | 309 | 16.3 |
| Kisha Conway, Francis Marion | Jr | 26 | 366 | 14.1 |
| Rachel Matakas, Central Missouri St | Jr | 27 | 374 | 13.9 |
| Sharon Yarbrough, W Georgia | Sr | 27 | 367 | 13.6 |
| Carrolyn Burke, Queens (NY) | Jr | 23 | 312 | 13.6 |
| Krista Kandere, St Rose | Fr | 31 | 412 | 13.3 |
| Monique Pierce, St Augustine's | So | 28 | 356 | 12.7 |
| Christine DeSaine, West Va Tech | Sr | 24 | 301 | 12.5 |
| Christine Hollins, Fayetteville St | Jr | 29 | 359 | 12.4 |
| Marchelle Bonner, Henderson St | Jr | 26 | 321 | 12.3 |

## ASSISTS

| | Class | GP | A | Avg |
|---|---|---|---|---|
| Lorraine Lynch, District of Columbia | Jr | 26 | 246 | 9.5 |
| Cynthia Thomas, Wingate | Sr | 31 | 289 | 9.3 |
| Joanna Bernabei, West Liberty St | So | 30 | 278 | 9.3 |
| Carla Bronson, Mankato St | Jr | 27 | 248 | 9.2 |
| Ursula Jackson, Alderson-Broaddus | Jr | 22 | 195 | 8.9 |
| Lisa Rice, Norfolk St | Sr | 30 | 264 | 8.8 |
| Stephanie Hall, Charleston (WV) | Jr | 26 | 226 | 8.7 |
| Hayley Lystlund, Augusta | Jr | 28 | 229 | 8.2 |
| Barbara Hester, Columbus | Jr | 28 | 228 | 8.1 |
| Theresa Perry, Delta St | Sr | 30 | 234 | 7.8 |

## NCAA Women's Division II Individual Leaders *(Cont.)*

### FIELD GOAL PERCENTAGE

| | Class | GP | FGA | FG | Pct |
|---|---|---|---|---|---|
| Tarra Blackwell, Fla Southern | Fr | 32 | 361 | 239 | 66.2 |
| Angela Watson, Central Arkansas | Jr | 26 | 297 | 195 | 65.7 |
| Jennifer Clarson, Abilene Christian | Jr | 28 | 392 | 255 | 65.1 |
| Danielle Box, SW Baptist | Jr | 25 | 220 | 142 | 64.5 |
| Kim Davis, Mississippi College | Fr | 27 | 308 | 197 | 64.0 |
| LeAnn Freeland, S Indiana | So | 27 | 420 | 265 | 63.1 |
| Elizabeth Davies, Bryant | Jr | 27 | 301 | 186 | 61.8 |
| Kim Trudel, Stonehill | So | 33 | 223 | 361 | 61.8 |
| Paulita Murrell, W Texas A&M | Jr | 30 | 269 | 166 | 61.7 |
| Krista Kandere, St Rose | Fr | 31 | 342 | 207 | 60.5 |

Two tied with 60.1.

Note: Minimum 5 made per game.

### FREE-THROW PERCENTAGE

| | Class | GP | FTA | FT | Pct |
|---|---|---|---|---|---|
| Darlene Hildebrand, Philadelphia Textile | Sr | 31 | 230 | 210 | 91.3 |
| Janelle Needham, Kutztown | So | 20 | 58 | 51 | 87.9 |
| Melissa Graham, Indianapolis | Sr | 28 | 132 | 115 | 87.1 |
| Elizabeth Davies, Bryant | Jr | 27 | 204 | 172 | 84.3 |
| Julie Plahn, MN-Morris | So | 28 | 127 | 107 | 84.3 |
| Julie Jensen, Northern St | Sr | 28 | 151 | 127 | 84.1 |
| Trina Pinner, Texas Woman's | Fr | 21 | 75 | 63 | 84.0 |
| Melissa Swain, E Stroudsburg | Jr | 30 | 91 | 76 | 83.5 |
| Kathleen Shippee, St Anselm | Sr | 31 | 115 | 96 | 83.5 |
| Heather Lopes, Bryant | Jr | 27 | 94 | 78 | 83.0 |

Note: Minimum 2.5 made per game.

## NCAA Men's Division III Individual Leaders

### SCORING

| | Class | GP | TFG | 3FG | FT | Pts | Avg |
|---|---|---|---|---|---|---|---|
| Steve Diekman, Grinnell | Sr | 20 | 223 | 137 | 162 | 745 | 37.3 |
| David Otte, Simpson | Sr | 26 | 284 | 0 | 229 | 797 | 30.7 |
| Ed Brands, Grinnell | Jr | 20 | 196 | 129 | 88 | 609 | 30.5 |
| Lance Castle, Monmouth (IL) | Sr | 23 | 230 | 71 | 127 | 658 | 28.6 |
| Rick Hughes, Thomas More | Jr | 24 | 257 | 1 | 143 | 658 | 27.4 |
| Billy Collins, Nichols | Sr | 21 | 189 | 87 | 104 | 569 | 27.1 |
| Phil Dixon, Shenandoah | Jr | 25 | 230 | 90 | 127 | 677 | 27.1 |
| Kyle Jefferson, Salisbury St | Sr | 25 | 231 | 20 | 194 | 676 | 27.0 |
| Will Flowers, Aurora | Sr | 25 | 228 | 43 | 166 | 665 | 26.6 |
| Alex Marsh, Gwynedd-Mercy | Sr | 24 | 255 | 13 | 104 | 627 | 26.1 |

### REBOUNDS

| | Class | GP | Reb | Avg |
|---|---|---|---|---|
| Scott Suhr, Milwaukee Engr | Sr | 25 | 349 | 14.0 |
| Sean McGee, Baruch | So | 23 | 318 | 13.8 |
| Kevin Braaten, Baldwin-Wallace | So | 28 | 373 | 13.3 |
| Antoine Harden, Eastern | Jr | 23 | 298 | 13.0 |
| Andrew South, New Jersey Tech | Sr | 27 | 335 | 12.4 |
| Jason Hayes, Marietta | So | 24 | 295 | 12.3 |
| Mark Harris, Coast Guard | Jr | 27 | 326 | 12.1 |
| Joe Mrozienski, Hamilton | Jr | 27 | 320 | 11.9 |
| Eric Fisher, Delaware Valley | Sr | 25 | 293 | 11.7 |
| Larry Jones, Lehman | So | 27 | 302 | 11.2 |

### ASSISTS

| | Class | GP | A | Avg |
|---|---|---|---|---|
| Joe Marcotte, New Jersey Tech | Sr | 30 | 292 | 9.7 |
| Phil Dixon, Shenandoah | Jr | 25 | 226 | 9.0 |
| Andre Bolton, Christopher Newport | Jr | 28 | 243 | 8.7 |
| David Genovese, Mt St Vincent | Sr | 27 | 234 | 8.7 |
| Troy McKelvin, Trinity (CT) | Jr | 29 | 226 | 7.8 |
| Greg Small, Gwynedd-Mercy | Jr | 24 | 186 | 7.8 |
| Adam Dzierzynski, Chapman | So | 25 | 188 | 7.5 |
| Kevin Alexander, Emory & Henry | Jr | 26 | 192 | 7.4 |
| Sammy Briggs, Catholic | So | 26 | 189 | 7.3 |
| Chad Hutson, Illinois Wesleyan | Sr | 28 | 198 | 7.1 |

### FIELD GOAL PERCENTAGE

| | Class | GP | FGA | FG | Pct |
|---|---|---|---|---|---|
| Justin Wilkins, Neb Wesleyan | Sr | 28 | 237 | 163 | 68.8 |
| David Otte, Simpson | Sr | 26 | 416 | 284 | 68.3 |
| Alida Ellerbee, New Jersey Tech | So | 30 | 280 | 185 | 66.1 |
| Dan Rush, Bridgewater (VA) | Sr | 25 | 379 | 250 | 66.0 |
| Jamie Yount, Bluffton | Sr | 26 | 298 | 195 | 65.4 |
| Brad Keenan, Concordia-M'head | Sr | 25 | 225 | 146 | 64.9 |
| Brent Nerat, WI-Oshkosh | Jr | 23 | 217 | 138 | 63.6 |
| Scott Launiger, Gust. Adolphus | Jr | 24 | 314 | 199 | 63.4 |
| Neal Richards, Mount Union | So | 26 | 242 | 153 | 63.2 |
| Rick Hughes, Thomas More | Jr | 24 | 407 | 257 | 63.1 |

Note: Minimum 5 made per game.

### FREE-THROW PERCENTAGE

| | Class | GP | FTA | FT | Pct |
|---|---|---|---|---|---|
| Matt Freesemann, Wartburg | Sr | 24 | 138 | 128 | 92.8 |
| Ryan Billet, Elizabethtown | So | 24 | 79 | 71 | 89.9 |
| Mike Guth, Franklin | Sr | 24 | 116 | 104 | 89.7 |
| Jordan Barnhorst, Macalester | Fr | 22 | 65 | 58 | 89.2 |
| Travis Crozier, Elizabethtown | Sr | 24 | 74 | 66 | 89.2 |
| Darin Pint, Coe | Sr | 23 | 109 | 97 | 89.0 |
| Kurt Axe, Randolph-Macon | Jr | 24 | 99 | 88 | 88.9 |
| Bernie Rogers, Ursinus | Jr | 24 | 99 | 88 | 88.9 |
| Mark Specht, Neb Wesleyan | Jr | 27 | 128 | 113 | 88.3 |
| Matt George, Colby-Sawyer | Fr | 28 | 140 | 123 | 87.9 |

Note: Minimum 2.5 made per game.

# NCAA Women's Division III Individual Leaders

## SCORING

| | Class | GP | TFG | 3FG | FT | Pts | Avg |
|---|---|---|---|---|---|---|---|
| Emilie Hanson, Central (IA) | Sr | 25 | 277 | 11 | 128 | 693 | 27.7 |
| Leslee Rogers, La Verne | Jr | 25 | 224 | 88 | 98 | 634 | 25.4 |
| Peggie Sweeney, Pine Manor | Jr | 25 | 203 | 20 | 208 | 634 | 25.4 |
| Rita Hurtgen, WI-River Falls | So | 26 | 225 | 0 | 199 | 649 | 25.0 |
| Katie Smith, Geneseo St | Sr | 29 | 294 | 11 | 110 | 709 | 24.4 |
| Denise Murray, Gwynedd-Mercy | Jr | 23 | 199 | 0 | 144 | 542 | 23.6 |
| Ellen Cosgrove, Ursinus | Sr | 26 | 229 | 57 | 87 | 602 | 23.2 |
| Danielle Potter, Rockford | Sr | 25 | 203 | 28 | 140 | 574 | 23.0 |
| Rebecca Morris, Wentworth Inst | So | 20 | 148 | 10 | 153 | 459 | 23.0 |
| Jennifer Nish, Scranton | So | 26 | 238 | 3 | 117 | 596 | 22.9 |

## REBOUNDS

| | Class | GP | Reb | Avg |
|---|---|---|---|---|
| Sybil Smith, Baruch | Sr | 22 | 523 | *23.8 |
| Jennifer White, Neumann | Jr | 24 | 421 | 17.5 |
| Denise Murray, Gwynedd-Mercy | Jr | 23 | 354 | 15.4 |
| Leslie Ferguson, Redlands | Sr | 25 | 362 | 14.5 |
| Glossary Smith, Ferrum | So | 27 | 374 | 13.9 |
| Carolyn McGuire, Manchester | Sr | 24 | 328 | 13.7 |
| Sue Burtoft, Bridgewater (MA) | Sr | 23 | 313 | 13.6 |
| Allison Palmer, Wesleyan (CT) | Sr | 23 | 310 | 13.5 |
| Koren Miller, Haverford | Sr | 24 | 321 | 13.4 |
| Erin Preseau, Utica | Jr | 21 | 276 | 13.1 |

## FIELD GOAL PERCENTAGE

| | Class | GP | FGA | FG | Pct |
|---|---|---|---|---|---|
| Kari Tufte, Luther | Jr | 26 | 320 | 210 | 65.6 |
| Tina Kampa, St Benedict | Sr | 29 | 254 | 165 | 65.0 |
| Steph Sprenger, Lakeland | Jr | 25 | 233 | 145 | 62.2 |
| Rita Hurtgen, WI-River Falls | So | 26 | 362 | 225 | 62.2 |
| Natalie DeMichei, WI-Oshkosh | Sr | 31 | 293 | 181 | 61.8 |
| Lanett Stephan, Franklin | Jr | 26 | 272 | 164 | 60.3 |
| Arlene Meinholz, WI-Eau Claire | Sr | 29 | 370 | 221 | 59.7 |
| Alisa Haase, Lawrence | Jr | 21 | 203 | 120 | 59.1 |
| Mindy Bagatelos, Claremont-M-S | So | 27 | 248 | 146 | 58.9 |
| Jody Prete, Upper Iowa | Sr | 24 | 220 | 129 | 58.6 |

Note: Minimum 5 made per game.

## ASSISTS

| | Class | GP | A | Avg |
|---|---|---|---|---|
| Chris Webb, NC Wesleyan | Jr | 26 | 204 | 7.8 |
| Stephanie Teter, Mary Washington | Jr | 24 | 180 | 7.5 |
| Shelly Anderson, Oglethorpe | Sr | 23 | 168 | 7.3 |
| Megan Dillon, Cabrini | So | 26 | 184 | 7.1 |
| Cathy Finney, Marymount (VA) | Sr | 28 | 194 | 6.9 |
| Ivette Correa, Salem St | Jr | 32 | 219 | 6.8 |
| Colleen Mewes, Carthage | So | 25 | 171 | 6.8 |
| Kim Wilson, York (NY) | Jr | 19 | 119 | 6.3 |
| Emili McCluer, Defiance | So | 27 | 169 | 6.3 |
| Stephanie Rom, Binghamton | Fr | 27 | 168 | 6.2 |

*Division III record.

## FREE-THROW PERCENTAGE

| | Class | GP | FTA | FT | Pct |
|---|---|---|---|---|---|
| Kari Tufte, Luther | Jr | 26 | 127 | 112 | 88.2 |
| Jasmine Obhrai, Bowdoin | Fr | 25 | 86 | 75 | 87.2 |
| Tina Sharp, Eureka | Jr | 24 | 91 | 79 | 86.8 |
| Felicia Lofton, Millsaps | Sr | 26 | 98 | 85 | 86.7 |
| Angie Sapp, Illinois College | So | 24 | 87 | 75 | 86.2 |
| Sarah Bay, Wellesley | Jr | 23 | 99 | 84 | 84.8 |
| Stephanie Duncan, Methodist | Sr | 23 | 77 | 65 | 84.4 |
| Shelly Brown, Trenton St | Jr | 24 | 120 | 101 | 84.2 |
| Cindy Pearson, Bridgewater (VA) | Jr | 25 | 93 | 78 | 83.9 |
| Kim Coia, W New England | Sr | 25 | 85 | 71 | 83.5 |

Note: Minimum 2.5 made per game.

## One-Armed Guard

During an AAU game in Washington, D.C. last summer, 18-year-old Doug Dormu knocked down five straight three-pointers against a bunch of guys two years his senior. As Doug peeled back on defense following his fifth trey, he could hear the opposing coach melting down: That boy has one arm. What's wrong with you guys?

That was one of the few times in recent years that Doug, a senior guard at Washington's Theodore Roosevelt High, has been conscious of his handicap on the court. Born with nerve damage in his left shoulder that kept his left arm from fully developing, he still has feeling in his left hand. So when as an eight-year-old he first taught himself to play basketball, he cradled the ball between his left elbow and right hand and shot from that position.

At the end of last week Doug was averaging 17 points in D.C.'s rarefied public league.

Earlier this season he scored 40 points against Eastern High. Doug, who also played fullback on the Roosevelt football team this season, believes he can do anything any other guard can do—and some things others can't, like dunk. "When Doug first came here, of course, I had some reservations about what his limitations might be," says Roosevelt coach Maurice Butler. "But we have a lot of guys on this team that can't use their left hand. And they have two hands."

Though he'll likely enroll at a junior college next fall, Doug's dream is to play at a Division I school. "I like to surprise people," he says. "Most people know me now, but there was a time I'd warm up before a game and be messing around, dribbling the ball off my feet, throwing up bricks, and guys were dying to take me. Pretty soon the same guys were saying, 'Let's stay away from the guy with the arm. He's got game!'"

## NCAA Division I Men's Championship Results

### NCAA Final Four Results

| Year | Winner | Score | Runner-up | Third Place | Fourth Place | Winning Coach |
|------|--------|-------|-----------|-------------|--------------|---------------|
| 1939 | Oregon | 46-33 | Ohio St | *Oklahoma | *Villanova | Howard Hobson |
| 1940 | Indiana | 60-42 | Kansas | *Duquesne | *Southern Cal | Branch McCracken |
| 1941 | Wisconsin | 39-34 | Washington St | *Pittsburgh | *Arkansas | Harold Foster |
| 1942 | Stanford | 53-38 | Dartmouth | *Colorado | *Kentucky | Everett Dean |
| 1943 | Wyoming | 46-34 | Georgetown | *Texas | *DePaul | Everett Shelton |
| 1944 | Utah | 42-40 (OT) | Dartmouth | *Iowa St | *Ohio St | Vadal Peterson |
| 1945 | Oklahoma St | 49-45 | NYU | *Arkansas | *Ohio St | Hank Iba |
| 1946 | Oklahoma St | 43-40 | N Carolina | Ohio St | California | Hank Iba |
| 1947 | Holy Cross | 58-47 | Oklahoma | Texas | CCNY | Alvin Julian |
| 1948 | Kentucky | 58-42 | Baylor | Holy Cross | Kansas St | Adolph Rupp |
| 1949 | Kentucky | 46-36 | Oklahoma St | Illinois | Oregon St | Adolph Rupp |
| 1950 | CCNY | 71-68 | Bradley | N Carolina St | Baylor | Nat Holman |
| 1951 | Kentucky | 68-58 | Kansas St | Illinois | Oklahoma St | Adolph Rupp |
| 1952 | Kansas | 80-63 | St John's (NY) | Illinois | Santa Clara | Forrest Allen |
| 1953 | Indiana | 69-68 | Kansas | Washington | Louisiana St | Branch McCracken |
| 1954 | La Salle | 92-76 | Bradley | Penn St | Southern Cal | Kenneth Loeffler |
| 1955 | San Francisco | 77-63 | La Salle | Colorado | Iowa | Phil Woolpert |
| 1956 | San Francisco | 83-71 | Iowa | Temple | Southern Meth | Phil Woolpert |
| 1957 | N Carolina | 54-53† | Kansas | San Francisco | Michigan St | Frank McGuire |
| 1958 | Kentucky | 84-72 | Seattle | Temple | Kansas St | Adolph Rupp |
| 1959 | California | 71-70 | W Virginia | Cincinnati | Louisville | Pete Newell |
| 1960 | Ohio St | 75-55 | California | Cincinnati | NYU | Fred Taylor |
| 1961 | Cincinnati | 70-65 (OT) | Ohio St | Vacated‡ | Utah | Edwin Jucker |
| 1962 | Cincinnati | 71-59 | Ohio St | Wake Forest | UCLA | Edwin Jucker |
| 1963 | Loyola (IL) | 60-58 (OT) | Cincinnati | Duke | Oregon St | George Ireland |
| 1964 | UCLA | 98-83 | Duke | Michigan | Kansas St | John Wooden |
| 1965 | UCLA | 91-80 | Michigan | Princeton | Wichita St | John Wooden |
| 1966 | UTEP | 72-65 | Kentucky | Duke | Utah | Don Haskins |
| 1967 | UCLA | 79-64 | Dayton | Houston | N Carolina | John Wooden |
| 1968 | UCLA | 78-55 | N Carolina | Ohio St | Houston | John Wooden |
| 1969 | UCLA | 92-72 | Purdue | Drake | N Carolina | John Wooden |
| 1970 | UCLA | 80-69 | Jacksonville | New Mexico St | St Bonaventure | John Wooden |
| 1971 | UCLA | 68-62 | Vacated‡ | Vacated‡ | Kansas | John Wooden |
| 1972 | UCLA | 81-76 | Florida St | N Carolina | Louisville | John Wooden |
| 1973 | UCLA | 87-66 | Memphis St | Indiana | Providence | John Wooden |
| 1974 | N Carolina St | 76-64 | Marquette | UCLA | Kansas | Norm Sloan |
| 1975 | UCLA | 92-85 | Kentucky | Louisville | Syracuse | John Wooden |
| 1976 | Indiana | 86-68 | Michigan | UCLA | Rutgers | Bob Knight |
| 1977 | Marquette | 67-59 | N Carolina | NV-Las Vegas | NC-Charlotte | Al McGuire |
| 1978 | Kentucky | 94-88 | Duke | Arkansas | Notre Dame | Joe Hall |
| 1979 | Michigan St | 75-64 | Indiana St | DePaul | Penn | Jud Heathcote |
| 1980 | Louisville | 59-54 | Vacated‡ | Purdue | Iowa | Denny Crum |
| 1981 | Indiana | 63-50 | N Carolina | Virginia | Louisiana St | Bob Knight |
| 1982 | N Carolina | 63-62 | Georgetown | *Houston | *Louisville | Dean Smith |
| 1983 | N Carolina St | 54-52 | Houston | *Georgia | *Louisville | Jim Valvano |
| 1984 | Georgetown | 84-75 | Houston | *Kentucky | *Virginia | John Thompson |
| 1985 | Villanova | 66-64 | Georgetown | *St John's (NY) | Vacated‡ | Rollie Massimino |
| 1986 | Louisville | 72-69 | Duke | *Kansas | *Louisiana St | Denny Crum |
| 1987 | Indiana | 74-73 | Syracuse | *NV-Las Vegas | *Providence | Bob Knight |
| 1988 | Kansas | 83-79 | Oklahoma | *Arizona | *Duke | Larry Brown |
| 1989 | Michigan | 80-79 (OT) | Seton Hall | *Duke | *Illinois | Steve Fisher |
| 1990 | UNLV | 103-73 | Duke | *Arkansas | *Georgia Tech | Jerry Tarkanian |
| 1991 | Duke | 72-65 | Kansas | *UNLV | *N Carolina | Mike Krzyzewski |
| 1992 | Duke | 71-51 | Michigan | *Cincinnati | *Indiana | Mike Krzyzewski |
| 1993 | N Carolina | 77-71 | Michigan | *Kansas | *Kentucky | Dean Smith |
| 1994 | Arkansas | 76-72 | Duke | *Arizona | *Florida | Nolan Richardson |
| 1995 | UCLA | 89-78 | Arkansas | *N Carolina | *Oklahoma St | Jim Harrick |

*Tied for third place.

†Three overtimes.

‡Student-athletes representing St Joseph's (PA) in 1961, Villanova in 1971 (runner-up), Western Kentucky in 1971 (third), UCLA (1980) and Memphis State (1985) were declared ineligible subsequent to the tournament. Under NCAA rules, the teams' and ineligible student-athletes' records were deleted, and the teams' places in the standings were vacated.

## NCAA Final Four MVPs

| Year | Winner, School | GP | Field Goals | | 3-Pt FG | | Free Throws | | Reb | A | Stl | BS | Avg |
|------|----------------|----|-----|------|-----|-----|-----|-------|-----|---|-----|----|-----|
| | | | FGM | Pct | FGA | FGM | FTM | Pct | | | | | |
| 1939 | ....None selected | | | | | | | | | | | | |
| 1940 | ....Marv Huffman, Indiana | 2 | 7 | — | — | — | 4 | — | — | — | — | — | 9.0 |
| 1941 | ....John Kotz, Wisconsin | 2 | 8 | — | — | — | 6 | — | — | — | — | — | 11.0 |
| 1942 | ....Howard Dallmar, Stanford | 2 | 8 | — | — | — | 4 | 66.7 | — | — | — | — | 10.0 |
| 1943 | ....Ken Sailors, Wyoming | 2 | 10 | — | — | — | 8 | 72.7 | — | — | — | — | 14.0 |
| 1944 | ....Arnie Ferrin, Utah | 2 | 11 | — | — | — | 6 | — | — | — | — | — | 14.0 |
| 1945 | ....Bob Kurland, Oklahoma St | 2 | 16 | — | — | — | 5 | — | — | — | — | — | 18.5 |
| 1946 | ....Bob Kurland, Oklahoma St | 2 | 21 | — | — | — | 10 | 66.7 | — | — | — | — | 26.0 |
| 1947 | ....George Kaftan, Holy Cross | 2 | 18 | — | — | — | 12 | 70.6 | — | — | — | — | 24.0 |
| 1948 | ....Alex Groza, Kentucky | 2 | 16 | — | — | — | 5 | — | — | — | — | — | 18.5 |
| 1949 | ....Alex Groza, Kentucky | 2 | 19 | — | — | — | 14 | — | — | — | — | — | 26.0 |
| 1950 | ....Irwin Dambrot, CCNY | 2 | 12 | 42.9 | — | — | 4 | 50.0 | — | — | — | — | 14.0 |
| 1951 | ....None selected | | | | | | | | | | | | |
| 1952 | ....Clyde Lovellette, Kansas | 2 | 24 | — | — | — | 18 | — | — | — | — | — | 33.0 |
| 1953 | ....*B.H. Horn, Kansas | 2 | 17 | — | — | — | 17 | — | — | — | — | — | 25.5 |
| 1954 | ....Tom Gola, La Salle | 2 | 12 | — | — | — | 14 | — | — | — | — | — | 19.0 |
| 1955 | ....Bill Russell, San Francisco | 2 | 19 | — | — | — | 9 | — | — | — | — | — | 23.5 |
| 1956 | ....*Hal Lear, Temple | 2 | 32 | — | — | — | 16 | — | — | — | — | — | 40.0 |
| 1957 | ....*Wilt Chamberlain, Kansas | 2 | 18 | 51.4 | — | — | 19 | 70.4 | 25 | — | — | — | 32.5 |
| 1958 | ....*Elgin Baylor, Seattle | 2 | 18 | 34.0 | — | — | 12 | 75.0 | 41 | — | — | — | 24.0 |
| 1959 | ....*Jerry West, West Virginia | 2 | 22 | 66.7 | — | — | 22 | 68.8 | 25 | — | — | — | 33.0 |
| 1960 | ....Jerry Lucas, Ohio State | 2 | 16 | 66.7 | — | — | 3 | 100.0 | 23 | — | — | — | 17.5 |
| 1961 | ....*Jerry Lucas, Ohio State | 2 | 20 | 71.4 | — | — | 16 | 94.1 | 25 | — | — | — | 28.0 |
| 1962 | ....Paul Hogue, Cincinnati | 2 | 23 | 63.9 | — | — | 12 | 63.2 | 38 | — | — | — | 29.0 |
| 1963 | ....Art Heyman, Duke | 2 | 18 | 41.0 | — | — | 15 | 68.2 | 19 | — | — | — | 25.5 |
| 1964 | ....Walt Hazzard, UCLA | 2 | 11 | 55.0 | — | — | 8 | 66.7 | 10 | — | — | — | 15.0 |
| 1965 | ....*Bill Bradley, Princeton | 2 | 34 | 63.0 | — | — | 19 | 95.0 | 24 | — | — | — | 43.5 |
| 1966 | ....*Jerry Chambers, Utah | 2 | 25 | 53.2 | — | — | 20 | 83.3 | 35 | — | — | — | 35.0 |
| 1967 | ....Lew Alcindor, UCLA | 2 | 14 | 60.9 | — | — | 11 | 45.8 | 38 | — | — | — | 19.5 |
| 1968 | ....Lew Alcindor, UCLA | 2 | 22 | 62.9 | — | — | 9 | 90.0 | 34 | — | — | — | 26.5 |
| 1969 | ....Lew Alcindor, UCLA | 2 | 23 | 67.7 | — | — | 16 | 64.0 | 41 | — | — | — | 31.0 |
| 1970 | ....Sidney Wicks, UCLA | 2 | 15 | 71.4 | — | — | 9 | 60.0 | 34 | — | — | — | 19.5 |
| 1971 | ....*Howard Porter, Villanova | 2 | 20 | 48.8 | — | — | 7 | 77.8 | 24 | — | — | — | 23.5 |
| 1972 | ...Bill Walton, UCLA | 2 | 20 | 69.0 | — | — | 17 | 73.9 | 41 | — | — | — | 28.5 |
| 1973 | ....Bill Walton, UCLA | 2 | 28 | 82.4 | — | — | 2 | 40.0 | 30 | — | — | — | 29.0 |
| 1974 | ....David Thompson, NC State | 2 | 19 | 51.4 | — | — | 11 | 78.6 | 17 | — | — | — | 24.5 |
| 1975 | ....Richard Washington, UCLA | 2 | 23 | 54.8 | — | — | 8 | 72.7 | 20 | — | — | — | 27.0 |
| 1976 | ....Kent Benson, Indiana | 2 | 17 | 50.0 | — | — | 7 | 63.6 | 18 | — | — | — | 20.5 |
| 1977 | ....Butch Lee, Marquette | 2 | 11 | 34.4 | — | — | 8 | 100.0 | 6 | 2 | 1 | 1 | 15.0 |
| 1978 | ....Jack Givens, Kentucky | 2 | 28 | 65.1 | — | — | 8 | 66.7 | 17 | 4 | 1 | 3 | 32.0 |
| 1979 | ....Earvin Johnson, Michigan St | 2 | 17 | 68.0 | — | — | 19 | 86.4 | 17 | 3 | 0 | 2 | 26.5 |
| 1980 | ....Darrell Griffith, Louisville | 2 | 23 | 62.2 | — | — | 11 | 68.8 | 7 | 15 | 0 | 2 | 28.5 |
| 1981 | ....Isiah Thomas, Indiana | 2 | 14 | 56.0 | — | — | 9 | 81.8 | 4 | 9 | 3 | 4 | 18.5 |
| 1982 | ....James Worthy, N Carolina | 2 | 20 | 74.1 | — | — | 2 | 28.6 | 8 | 9 | 0 | 4 | 21.0 |
| 1983 | ....*Akeem Olajuwon, Houston | 2 | 16 | 55.2 | — | — | 9 | 64.3 | 40 | 3 | 2 | 5 | 20.5 |
| 1984 | ....Patrick Ewing, Georgetown | 2 | 8 | 57.1 | — | — | 2 | 100.0 | 18 | 1 | 15 | 1 | 9.0 |
| 1985 | ....Ed Pinckney, Villanova | 2 | 8 | 57.1 | — | — | 12 | 75.0 | 15 | 6 | 3 | 0 | 14.0 |
| 1986 | ....Pervis Ellison, Louisville | 2 | 15 | 60.0 | — | — | 6 | 75.0 | 24 | 2 | 3 | 1 | 18.0 |
| 1987 | ....Keith Smart, Indiana | 2 | 14 | 63.6 | 1 | 0 | 7 | 77.8 | 7 | 7 | 0 | 2 | 17.5 |
| 1988 | ... Danny Manning, Kansas | 2 | 25 | 55.6 | 1 | 0 | 6 | 66.7 | 17 | 4 | 8 | 9 | 28.0 |
| 1989 | ....Glenn Rice, Michigan | 2 | 24 | 49.0 | 16 | 7 | 4 | 100.0 | 16 | 1 | 0 | 3 | 29.5 |
| 1990 | ....Anderson Hunt, UNLV | 2 | 19 | 61.3 | 16 | 9 | 2 | 50.0 | 4 | 9 | 1 | 1 | 24.5 |
| 1991 | ....Christian Laettner, Duke | 2 | 12 | 54.5 | 1 | 1 | 21 | 91.3 | 17 | 2 | 1 | 2 | 23.0 |
| 1992 | ....Bobby Hurley, Duke | 2 | 10 | 41.7 | 12 | 7 | 8 | 80.0 | 3 | 11 | 0 | 3 | 17.5 |
| 1993 | ....Donald Williams, N Carolina | 2 | 15 | 65.2 | 14 | 10 | 10 | 100.0 | 4 | 2 | 2 | 0 | 25.0 |
| 1994 | ....Corliss Williamson, Arkansas | 2 | 21 | 50.0 | 0 | 0 | 10 | 71.4 | 21 | 8 | 4 | 3 | 26.0 |
| 1995 | ....Ed O'Bannon, UCLA | 2 | 16 | 45.7 | 8 | 3 | 10 | 76.9 | 25 | 3 | 7 | 1 | 22.5 |

*Not a member of the championship-winning team.

## Best NCAA Tournament Single-Game Scoring Performances

| Player and Team | Year | Round | FG | 3FG | FT | TP |
|---|---|---|---|---|---|---|
| Austin Carr, Notre Dame vs Ohio | 1970 | 1st | 25 | — | 11 | 61 |
| Bill Bradley, Princeton vs Wichita St. | 1965 | C* | 22 | — | 14 | 58 |
| Oscar Robertson, Cincinnati vs Arkansas | 1958 | C | 21 | — | 14 | 56 |
| Austin Carr, Notre Dame vs Kentucky | 1970 | 2nd | 22 | — | 8 | 52 |
| Austin Carr, Notre Dame vs Texas Christian | 1971 | 1st | 20 | — | 12 | 52 |
| David Robinson, Navy vs Michigan | 1987 | 1st | 22 | 0 | 6 | 50 |
| Elvin Hayes, Houston vs Loyola (IL) | 1968 | 1st | 20 | — | 9 | 49 |
| Hal Lear, Temple vs Southern Meth | 1956 | C* | 17 | — | 14 | 48 |
| Austin Carr, Notre Dame vs Houston | 1971 | C | 17 | — | 13 | 47 |
| Dave Corzine, DePaul vs Louisville | 1978 | 2nd | 18 | — | 10 | 46 |
| Bob Houbregs, Washington vs Seattle | 1953 | 2nd | 20 | — | 5 | 45 |
| Austin Carr, Notre Dame vs Iowa | 1970 | C | 21 | — | 3 | 45 |
| Bo Kimble, Loyola Marymount vs New Mexico St | 1990 | 1st | 17 | 5 | 6 | 45 |

C regional third place; C* third-place game.

## NIT Championship Results

| Year | Winner | Score | Runner-up | Year | Winner | Score | Runner-up |
|---|---|---|---|---|---|---|---|
| 1938 | Temple | 60-36 | Colorado | 1967 | Southern Illinois | 71-56 | Marquette |
| 1939 | Long Island U | 44-32 | Loyola (IL) | 1968 | Dayton | 61-48 | Kansas |
| 1940 | Colorado | 51-40 | Duquesne | 1969 | Temple | 89-76 | Boston College |
| 1941 | Long Island U | 56-42 | Ohio U | 1970 | Marquette | 65-53 | St John's (NY) |
| 1942 | W Virginia | 47-45 | W Kentucky | 1971 | N Carolina | 84-66 | Georgia Tech |
| 1943 | St John's (NY) | 48-27 | Toledo | 1972 | Maryland | 100-69 | Niagara |
| 1944 | St John's (NY) | 47-39 | DePaul | 1973 | Virginia Tech | 92-91 (OT) | Notre Dame |
| 1945 | DePaul | 71-54 | Bowling Green | 1974 | Purdue | 97-81 | Utah |
| 1946 | Kentucky | 46-45 | Rhode Island | 1975 | Princeton | 80-69 | Providence |
| 1947 | Utah | 49-45 | Kentucky | 1976 | Kentucky | 71-67 | NC-Charlotte |
| 1948 | St Louis | 65-52 | NYU | 1977 | St Bonaventure | 94-91 | Houston |
| 1949 | San Francisco | 48-47 | Loyola (IL) | 1978 | Texas | 101-93 | N Carolina St |
| 1950 | CCNY | 69-61 | Bradley | 1979 | Indiana | 53-52 | Purdue |
| 1951 | BYU | 62-43 | Dayton | 1980 | Virginia | 58-55 | Minnesota |
| 1952 | La Salle | 75-64 | Dayton | 1981 | Tulsa | 86-84 (OT) | Syracuse |
| 1953 | Seton Hall | 58-46 | St John's (NY) | 1982 | Bradley | 67-58 | Purdue |
| 1954 | Holy Cross | 71-62 | Duquesne | 1983 | Fresno St | 69-60 | DePaul |
| 1955 | Duquesne | 70-58 | Dayton | 1984 | Michigan | 83-63 | Notre Dame |
| 1956 | Louisville | 93-80 | Dayton | 1985 | UCLA | 65-62 | Indiana |
| 1957 | Bradley | 84-83 | Memphis St | 1986 | Ohio St | 73-63 | Wyoming |
| 1958 | Xavier (OH) | 78-74 (OT) | Dayton | 1987 | Southern Miss | 84-80 | La Salle |
| 1959 | St John's (NY) | 76-71 (OT) | Bradley | 1988 | Connecticut | 72-67 | Ohio St |
| 1960 | Bradley | 88-72 | Providence | 1989 | St John's (NY) | 73-65 | St Louis |
| 1961 | Providence | 62-59 | St Louis | 1990 | Vanderbilt | 74-72 | St Louis |
| 1962 | Dayton | 73-67 | St John's (NY) | 1991 | Stanford | 78-72 | Oklahoma |
| 1963 | Providence | 81-66 | Canisius | 1992 | Virginia | 81-76 | Notre Dame |
| 1964 | Bradley | 86-54 | New Mexico | 1993 | Minnesota | 62-61 | Georgetown |
| 1965 | St John's (NY) | 55-51 | Villanova | 1994 | Villanova | 80-73 | Vanderbilt |
| 1966 | BYU | 97-84 | NYU | 1995 | Virginia Tech | 65-64 (OT) | Marquette |

# NCAA Division I Men's Season Leaders

## Scoring Average

| Year | Player and Team | Ht | Class | GP | FG | 3FG | FT | Pts | Avg |
|---|---|---|---|---|---|---|---|---|---|
| 1948 | Murray Wier, Iowa | 5-9 | Sr | 19 | 152 | — | 95 | 399 | 21.0 |
| 1949 | Tony Lavelli, Yale | 6-3 | Sr | 30 | 228 | — | 215 | 671 | 22.4 |
| 1950 | Paul Arizin, Villanova | 6-3 | Sr | 29 | 260 | — | 215 | 735 | 25.3 |
| 1951 | Bill Mlkvy, Temple | 6-4 | Sr | 25 | 303 | — | 125 | 731 | 29.2 |
| 1952 | Clyde Lovellette, Kansas | 6-9 | Sr | 28 | 315 | — | 165 | 795 | 28.4 |
| 1953 | Frank Selvy, Furman | 6-3 | Jr | 25 | 272 | — | 194 | 738 | 29.5 |
| 1954 | Frank Selvy, Furman | 6-3 | Sr | 29 | 427 | — | 355 | 1209 | 41.7 |
| 1955 | Darrell Floyd, Furman | 6-1 | Jr | 25 | 344 | — | 209 | 897 | 35.9 |
| 1956 | Darrell Floyd, Furman | 6-1 | Sr | 28 | 339 | — | 268 | 946 | 33.8 |
| 1957 | Grady Wallace, S Carolina | 6-4 | Sr | 29 | 336 | — | 234 | 906 | 31.2 |
| 1958 | Oscar Robertson, Cincinnati | 6-5 | So | 28 | 352 | — | 280 | 984 | 35.1 |

## Scoring Average (Cont.)

| Year | Player and Team | Ht | Class | GP | FG | 3FG | FT | Pts | Avg |
|------|-----------------|-----|-------|-----|-----|------|-----|------|------|
| 1959 | Oscar Robertson, Cincinnati | 6-5 | Jr | 30 | 331 | — | 316 | 978 | 32.6 |
| 1960 | Oscar Robertson, Cincinnati | 6-5 | Sr | 30 | 369 | — | 273 | 1011 | 33.7 |
| 1961 | Frank Burgess, Gonzaga | 6-1 | Sr | 26 | 304 | — | 234 | 842 | 32.4 |
| 1962 | Billy McGill, Utah | 6-9 | Sr | 26 | 394 | — | 221 | 1009 | 38.8 |
| 1963 | Nick Werkman, Seton Hall | 6-3 | Jr | 22 | 221 | — | 208 | 650 | 29.5 |
| 1964 | Howard Komives, Bowling Green | 6-1 | Sr | 23 | 292 | — | 260 | 844 | 36.7 |
| 1965 | Rick Barry, Miami (FL) | 6-7 | Sr | 26 | 340 | — | 293 | 973 | 37.4 |
| 1966 | Dave Schellhase, Purdue | 6-4 | Sr | 24 | 284 | — | 213 | 781 | 32.5 |
| 1967 | Jim Walker, Providence | 6-3 | Sr | 28 | 323 | — | 205 | 851 | 30.4 |
| 1968 | Pete Maravich, Louisiana St | 6-5 | So | 26 | 432 | — | 274 | 1138 | 43.8 |
| 1969 | Pete Maravich, Louisiana St | 6-5 | Jr | 26 | 433 | — | 282 | 1148 | 44.2 |
| 1970 | Pete Maravich, Louisiana St | 6-5 | Sr | 31 | 522 | — | 337 | 1381 | 44.5 |
| 1971 | Johnny Neumann, Mississippi | 6-6 | So | 23 | 366 | — | 191 | 923 | 40.1 |
| 1972 | Dwight Lamar, Southwestern Louisiana | 6-1 | Jr | 29 | 429 | — | 196 | 1054 | 36.3 |
| 1973 | William Averitt, Pepperdine | 6-1 | Sr | 25 | 352 | — | 144 | 848 | 33.9 |
| 1974 | Larry Fogle, Canisius | 6-5 | So | 25 | 326 | — | 183 | 835 | 33.4 |
| 1975 | Bob McCurdy, Richmond | 6-7 | Sr | 26 | 321 | — | 213 | 855 | 32.9 |
| 1976 | Marshall Rodgers, TX-Pan American | 6-2 | Sr | 25 | 361 | — | 197 | 919 | 36.8 |
| 1977 | Freeman Williams, Portland St | 6-4 | Jr | 26 | 417 | — | 176 | 1010 | 38.8 |
| 1978 | Freeman Williams, Portland St | 6-4 | Sr | 27 | 410 | — | 149 | 969 | 35.9 |
| 1979 | Lawrence Butler, Idaho St | 6-3 | Sr | 27 | 310 | — | 192 | 812 | 30.1 |
| 1980 | Tony Murphy, Southern-BR | 6-3 | Sr | 29 | 377 | — | 178 | 932 | 32.1 |
| 1981 | Zam Fredrick, S Carolina | 6-2 | Sr | 27 | 300 | — | 181 | 781 | 28.9 |
| 1982 | Harry Kelly, Texas Southern | 6-7 | Jr | 29 | 336 | — | 190 | 862 | 29.7 |
| 1983 | Harry Kelly, Texas Southern | 6-7 | Sr | 29 | 333 | — | 169 | 835 | 28.8 |
| 1984 | Joe Jakubick, Akron | 6-5 | Sr | 27 | 304 | — | 206 | 814 | 30.1 |
| 1985 | Xavier McDaniel, Wichita St | 6-8 | Sr | 31 | 351 | — | 142 | 844 | 27.2 |
| 1986 | Terrance Bailey, Wagner | 6-2 | Jr | 29 | 321 | — | 212 | 854 | 29.4 |
| 1987 | Kevin Houston, Army | 5-11 | Sr | 29 | 311 | 63 | 268 | 953 | 32.9 |
| 1988 | Hersey Hawkins, Bradley | 6-3 | Sr | 31 | 377 | 87 | 284 | 1125 | 36.3 |
| 1989 | Hank Gathers, Loyola Marymount | 6-7 | Jr | 31 | 419 | 0 | 177 | 1015 | 32.7 |
| 1990 | Bo Kimble, Loyola Marymount | 6-5 | Sr | 32 | 404 | 92 | 231 | 1131 | 35.3 |
| 1991 | Kevin Bradshaw, U.S. Int'l | 6-6 | Sr | 28 | 358 | 60 | 278 | 1054 | 37.6 |
| 1992 | Brett Roberts, Morehead St | 6-8 | Sr | 29 | 278 | 66 | 193 | 815 | 28.1 |
| 1993 | Greg Guy, TX-Pan American | 6-1 | Jr | 19 | 189 | 67 | 111 | 556 | 29.3 |
| 1994 | Glenn Robinson, Purdue | 6-8 | Jr | 34 | 368 | 79 | 215 | 1030 | 30.3 |
| 1995 | Kurt Thomas, Texas Christian | 6-9 | Sr | 27 | 288 | 3 | 202 | 781 | 28.9 |

## Rebounds

| Year | Player and Team | Ht | Class | GP | Reb | Avg |
|------|-----------------|-----|-------|-----|------|------|
| 1951 | Ernie Beck, Pennsylvania | 6-4 | So | 27 | 556 | 20.6 |
| 1952 | Bill Hannon, Army | 6-3 | So | 17 | 355 | 20.9 |
| 1953 | Ed Conlin, Fordham | 6-5 | So | 26 | 612 | 23.5 |
| 1954 | Art Quimby, Connecticut | 6-5 | Jr | 26 | 588 | 22.6 |
| 1955 | Charlie Slack, Marshall | 6-5 | Jr | 21 | 538 | 25.6 |
| 1956 | Joe Holup, George Washington | 6-6 | Sr | 26 | 604 | †.256 |
| 1957 | Elgin Baylor, Seattle | 6-6 | Jr | 25 | 508 | †.235 |
| 1958 | Alex Ellis, Niagara | 6-5 | Sr | 25 | 536 | †.262 |
| 1959 | Leroy Wright, Pacific | 6-8 | Jr | 26 | 652 | †.238 |
| 1960 | Leroy Wright, Pacific | 6-8 | Sr | 17 | 380 | †.234 |
| 1961 | Jerry Lucas, Ohio St | 6-8 | Jr | 27 | 470 | †.198 |
| 1962 | Jerry Lucas, Ohio St | 6-8 | Sr | 28 | 499 | †.211 |
| 1963 | Paul Silas, Creighton | 6-7 | Sr | 27 | 557 | 20.6 |
| 1964 | Bob Pelkington, Xavier (OH) | 6-7 | Sr | 26 | 567 | 21.8 |
| 1965 | Toby Kimball, Connecticut | 6-8 | Sr | 23 | 483 | 21.0 |
| 1966 | Jim Ware, Oklahoma City | 6-8 | Sr | 29 | 607 | 20.9 |
| 1967 | Dick Cunningham, Murray St | 6-10 | Jr | 22 | 479 | 21.8 |
| 1968 | Neal Walk, Florida | 6-10 | Jr | 25 | 494 | 19.8 |
| 1969 | Spencer Haywood, Detroit | 6-8 | So | 22 | 472 | 21.5 |
| 1970 | Artis Gilmore, Jacksonville | 7-2 | Jr | 28 | 621 | 22.2 |
| 1971 | Artis Gilmore, Jacksonville | 7-2 | Sr | 26 | 603 | 23.2 |
| 1972 | Kermit Washington, American | 6-8 | Jr | 23 | 455 | 19.8 |
| 1973 | Kermit Washington, American | 6-8 | Sr | 22 | 439 | 20.0 |
| 1974 | Marvin Barnes, Providence | 6-9 | Sr | 32 | 597 | 18.7 |
| 1975 | John Irving, Hofstra | 6-9 | So | 21 | 323 | 15.4 |

## Rebounds *(Cont.)*

| Year | Player and Team | Ht | Class | GP | Reb | Avg |
|------|-----------------|-----|-------|-----|-----|-----|
| 1976 | Sam Pellom, Buffalo | 6-8 | So | 26 | 420 | 16.2 |
| 1977 | Glenn Mosley, Seton Hall | 6-8 | Sr | 29 | 473 | 16.3 |
| 1978 | Ken Williams, N Texas St | 6-7 | Sr | 28 | 411 | 14.7 |
| 1979 | Monti Davis, Tennessee St | 6-7 | Jr | 26 | 421 | 16.2 |
| 1980 | Larry Smith, Alcorn St | 6-8 | Sr | 26 | 392 | 15.1 |
| 1981 | Darryl Watson, Miss Valley | 6-7 | Sr | 27 | 379 | 14.0 |
| 1982 | LaSalle Thompson, Texas | 6-10 | Jr | 27 | 365 | 13.5 |
| 1983 | Xavier McDaniel, Wichita St | 6-7 | So | 28 | 403 | 14.4 |
| 1984 | Akeem Olajuwon, Houston | 7-0 | Jr | 37 | 500 | 13.5 |
| 1985 | Xavier McDaniel, Wichita St | 6-8 | Sr | 31 | 460 | 14.8 |
| 1986 | David Robinson, Navy | 6-11 | Jr | 35 | 455 | 13.0 |
| 1987 | Jerome Lane, Pittsburgh | 6-6 | So | 33 | 444 | 13.5 |
| 1988 | Kenny Miller, Loyola (IL) | 6-9 | Fr | 29 | 395 | 13.6 |
| 1989 | Hank Gathers, Loyola (CA) | 6-7 | Jr | 31 | 426 | 13.7 |
| 1990 | Anthony Bonner, St Louis | 6-8 | Sr | 33 | 456 | 13.8 |
| 1991 | Shaquille O'Neal, Louisiana St | 7-1 | So | 28 | 411 | 14.7 |
| 1992 | Popeye Jones, Murray St | 6-8 | Sr | 30 | 431 | 14.4 |
| 1993 | Warren Kidd, Middle Tenn St | 6-9 | Sr | 26 | 386 | 14.8 |
| 1994 | Jerome Lambert, Baylor | 6-8 | Jr | 24 | 355 | 14.8 |
| 1995 | Kurt Thomas, Texas Christian | 6-9 | Sr | 27 | 393 | 14.6 |

†From 1956-1962, title was based on highest individual recoveries out of total by both teams in all games.

## Assists

| Year | Player and Team | Class | GP | A | Avg |
|------|-----------------|-------|-----|-----|-----|
| 1984 | Craig Lathen, IL-Chicago | Jr | 29 | 274 | 9.45 |
| 1985 | Rob Weingard, Hofstra | Sr | 24 | 228 | 9.50 |
| 1986 | Mark Jackson, St John's (NY) | Jr | 36 | 328 | 9.11 |
| 1987 | Avery Johnson, Southern-BR | Jr | 31 | 333 | 10.74 |
| 1988 | Avery Johnson, Southern-BR | Sr | 30 | 399 | 13.30 |
| 1989 | Glenn Williams, Holy Cross | Sr | 28 | 278 | 9.93 |
| 1990 | Todd Lehmann, Drexel | Sr | 28 | 260 | 9.29 |
| 1991 | Chris Corchiani, N Carolina St | Sr | 31 | 299 | 9.65 |
| 1992 | Van Usher, Tennessee Tech | Sr | 29 | 254 | 8.76 |
| 1993 | Sam Crawford, New Mex St | Sr | 34 | 310 | 9.12 |
| 1994 | Jason Kidd, California | So | 30 | 272 | 9.06 |
| 1995 | Nelson Haggerty, Baylor | Sr | 28 | 284 | 10.1 |

## Blocked Shots

| Year | Player and Team | Class | GP | BS | Avg |
|------|-----------------|-------|-----|-----|-----|
| 1986 | David Robinson, Navy | Jr | 35 | 207 | 5.91 |
| 1987 | David Robinson, Navy | Sr | 32 | 144 | 4.50 |
| 1988 | Rodney Blake, St Joseph's (PA) | Sr | 29 | 116 | 4.00 |
| 1989 | Alonzo Mourning, Georgetown | Fr | 34 | 169 | 4.97 |
| 1990 | Kenny Green, Rhode Island | Sr | 26 | 124 | 4.77 |
| 1991 | Shawn Bradley, Brigham Young | Fr | 34 | 177 | 5.21 |
| 1992 | Shaquille O'Neal, Louisiana St | Jr | 30 | 157 | 5.23 |
| 1993 | Theo Ratliff, Wyoming | Jr | 28 | 124 | 4.43 |
| 1994 | Grady Livingston, Howard | Jr | 26 | 115 | 4.42 |
| 1995 | Keith Closs, Central Conn St | Fr | 26 | 139 | 5.35 |

## Steals

| Year | Player and Team | Class | GP | S | Avg |
|------|-----------------|-------|-----|-----|-----|
| 1986 | Darron Brittman, Chicago St | Sr | 28 | 139 | 4.96 |
| 1987 | Tony Fairley, Charleston Sou | Sr | 28 | 114 | 4.07 |
| 1988 | Aldwin Ware, Florida A&M | Sr | 29 | 142 | 4.90 |
| 1989 | Kenny Robertson, Cleveland St | Jr | 28 | 111 | 3.96 |
| 1990 | Ronn McMahon, E Washington | Sr | 29 | 130 | 4.48 |
| 1991 | Van Usher, Tennessee Tech | Jr | 28 | 104 | 3.71 |
| 1992 | Victor Snipes, NE Illinois | So | 25 | 86 | 3.44 |
| 1993 | Jason Kidd, California | Fr | 29 | 110 | 3.80 |
| 1994 | Shawn Griggs, SW Louisiana | Sr | 30 | 120 | 4.00 |
| 1995 | Roderick Anderson, Texas | Sr | 30 | 101 | 3.37 |

## Single-Game Records

### SCORING HIGHS VS DIVISION I OPPONENT

| Pts | Player and Team vs Opponent | Date |
|---|---|---|
| 72 | Kevin Bradshaw, U.S. Int'l vs Loyola Marymount | 1-5-91 |
| 69 | Pete Maravich, Louisiana St vs Alabama | 2-7-70 |
| 68 | Calvin Murphy, Niagara vs Syracuse | 12-7-68 |
| 66 | Jay Handlan, Washington & Lee vs Furman | 2-17-51 |
| 66 | Pete Maravich, Louisiana St vs Tulane | 2-10-69 |
| 66 | Anthony Roberts, Oral Roberts vs N Carolina A&T | 2-19-77 |
| 65 | Anthony Roberts, Oral Roberts vs Oregon | 3-9-77 |
| 65 | Scott Haffner, Evansville vs Dayton | 2-18-89 |
| 64 | Pete Maravich, Louisiana St vs Kentucky | 2-21-70 |
| 63 | Johnny Neumann, Mississippi vs Louisiana St | 1-30-71 |
| 63 | Hersey Hawkins, Bradley vs Detroit | 2-22-88 |

### SCORING HIGHS VS NON-DIVISION I OPPONENT

| Pts | Player and Team vs Opponent | Date |
|---|---|---|
| 100 | Frank Selvy, Furman vs Newberry | 2-13-54 |
| 85 | Paul Arizin, Villanova vs Philadelphia NAMC | 2-12-49 |
| 81 | Freeman Williams, Portland St vs Rocky Mountain | 2-3-78 |
| 73 | Bill Mlkvy, Temple vs Wilkes | 3-3-51 |
| 71 | Freeman Williams, Portland St vs Southern Oregon | 2-9-77 |

### REBOUNDING HIGHS BEFORE 1973

| Reb | Player and Team vs Opponent | Date |
|---|---|---|
| 51 | Bill Chambers, William & Mary vs Virginia | 2-14-53 |
| 43 | Charlie Slack, Marshall vs Morris Harvey | 1-12-54 |
| 42 | Tom Heinsohn, Holy Cross vs Boston College | 3-1-55 |
| 40 | Art Quimby, Connecticut vs Boston U | 1-11-55 |
| 39 | Maurice Stokes, St Francis (PA) vs John Carroll | 1-28-55 |
| 39 | Dave DeBusschere, Detroit vs Central Michigan | 1-30-60 |
| 39 | Keith Swagerty, Pacific vs UC-Santa Barbara | 3-5-65 |

### REBOUNDING HIGHS SINCE 1973

| Reb | Player and Team vs Opponent | Date |
|---|---|---|
| 34 | David Vaughn, Oral Roberts vs Brandeis | 1-8-73 |
| 33 | Robert Parish, Centenary vs Southern Miss | 1-22-73 |
| 32 | Jervaughn Scales, Southern-BR vs Grambling | 2-7-94 |
| 32 | Durand Macklin, Louisiana St vs Tulane | 11-26-76 |
| 31 | Jim Bradley, Northern Illinois vs WI-Milwaukee | 2-19-73 |
| 31 | Calvin Natt, Northeast Louisiana vs Georgia Southern | 12-29-76 |

### ASSISTS

| A | Player and Team vs Opponent | Date |
|---|---|---|
| 22 | Tony Fairley, Baptist vs Armstrong St | 2-9-87 |
| 22 | Avery Johnson, Southern-BR vs Texas Southern | 1-25-88 |
| 22 | Sherman Douglas, Syracuse vs Providence | 1-28-89 |
| 21 | Mark Wade, NV-Las Vegas vs Navy | 12-29-86 |
| 21 | Kelvin Scarborough, New Mexico vs Hawaii | 2-13-87 |
| 21 | Anthony Manuel, Bradley vs UC-Irvine | 12-19-87 |
| 21 | Avery Johnson, Southern-BR vs Alabama St | 1-16-88 |

### STEALS

| S | Player and Team vs Opponent | Date |
|---|---|---|
| 13 | Mookie Blaylock, Oklahoma vs Centenary | 12-12-87 |
| 13 | Mookie Blaylock, Oklahoma vs Loyola Marymount | 12-17-88 |
| 12 | Kenny Robertson, Cleveland St vs Wagner | 12-3-88 |
| 12 | Terry Evans, Oklahoma vs Florida A&M | 1-27-93 |
| 11 | Darron Brittman, Chicago St vs McKendree | 2-24-86 |
| 11 | Darron Brittman, Chicago St vs St Xavier | 2-8-86 |
| 11 | Marty Johnson, Towson St vs Bucknell | 2-17-88 |
| 11 | Aldwin Ware, Florida A&M vs Tuskegee | 2-24-88 |
| 11 | Mark Macon, Temple vs Notre Dame | 1-29-89 |
| 11 | Carl Thomas, E Michigan vs Chicago St | 2-20-91 |
| 11 | Ron Arnold, St Francis (NY) vs Mt St Mary's (MD) | 2-4-93 |
| 11 | Tyus Edney, UCLA vs George Mason | 12-22-94 |

## Single-Game Records (Cont.)

### BLOCKED SHOTS

| BS | Player and Team vs Opponent | Date |
|----|------------------------------|------|
| 14 | David Robinson, Navy vs NC-Wilmington | 1-4-86 |
| 14 | Shawn Bradley, Brigham Young vs E Kentucky | 12-7-90 |
| 13 | Kevin Roberson, Vermont vs New Hampshire | 1-9-92 |
| 13 | Jim McIlvaine, Marquette vs Northeastern (IL) | 12-9-92 |
| 13 | Keith Closs, Central Conn St vs St. Francis (PA) | 12-21-94 |
| 12 | David Robinson, Navy vs James Madison | 1-9-86 |
| 12 | Derrick Lewis, Maryland vs James Madison | 1-28-87 |
| 12 | Rodney Blake, St Joseph's (PA) vs Cleveland St | 12-2-87 |
| 12 | Walter Palmer, Dartmouth vs Harvard | 1-9-88 |
| 12 | Alan Ogg, AL-Birmingham vs Florida A&M | 12-16-88 |
| 12 | Dikembe Mutombo, Georgetown vs St John's (NY) | 1-23-89 |
| 12 | Shaquille O'Neal, Louisiana St vs Loyola Marymount | 2-3-90 |
| 12 | Cedric Lewis, Maryland vs S Florida | 1-19-91 |
| 12 | Ervin Johnson, New Orleans vs Texas A&M | 12-29-92 |
| 12 | Kurt Thomas, Texas Christian vs Texas A&M | 2-25-95 |

## Season Records

### POINTS

| Player and Team | Year | GP | FG | 3FG | FT | Pts |
|-----------------|------|----|----|-----|----|----|
| Pete Maravich, Louisiana St | 1970 | 31 | 522 | — | 337 | 1381 |
| Elvin Hayes, Houston | 1968 | 33 | 519 | — | 176 | 1214 |
| Frank Selvy, Furman | 1954 | 29 | 427 | — | 355 | 1209 |
| Pete Maravich, Louisiana St | 1969 | 26 | 433 | — | 282 | 1148 |
| Pete Maravich, Louisiana St | 1968 | 26 | 432 | — | 274 | 1138 |
| Bo Kimble, Loyola Marymount | 1990 | 32 | 404 | 92 | 231 | 1131 |
| Hersey Hawkins, Bradley | 1988 | 31 | 377 | 87 | 284 | 1125 |
| Austin Carr, Notre Dame | 1970 | 29 | 444 | — | 218 | 1106 |
| Austin Carr, Notre Dame | 1971 | 29 | 430 | — | 241 | 1101 |
| Otis Birdsong, Houston | 1977 | 36 | 452 | — | 186 | 1090 |

### SCORING AVERAGE

| Player and Team | Year | GP | FG | FT | Pts | Avg |
|-----------------|------|----|----|----|----|-----|
| Pete Maravich, Louisiana St | 1970 | 31 | 522 | 337 | 1381 | 44.5 |
| Pete Maravich, Louisiana St | 1969 | 26 | 433 | 282 | 1148 | 44.2 |
| Pete Maravich, Louisiana St | 1968 | 26 | 432 | 274 | 1138 | 43.8 |
| Frank Selvy, Furman | 1954 | 29 | 427 | 355 | 1209 | 41.7 |
| Johnny Neumann, Mississippi | 1971 | 23 | 366 | 191 | 923 | 40.1 |
| Freeman Williams, Portland St | 1977 | 26 | 417 | 176 | 1010 | 38.8 |
| Billy McGill, Utah | 1962 | 26 | 394 | 221 | 1009 | 38.8 |
| Calvin Murphy, Niagara | 1968 | 24 | 337 | 242 | 916 | 38.2 |
| Austin Carr, Notre Dame | 1970 | 29 | 444 | 218 | 1106 | 38.1 |
| Austin Carr, Notre Dame | 1971 | 29 | 430 | 241 | 1101 | 38.0 |
| Kevin Bradshaw, U.S. Int'l | 1991 | 28 | 358 | 278 | 1054 | 37.6 |

### REBOUNDS

| Player and Team | Year | GP | Reb | Player and Team | Year | GP | Reb |
|-----------------|------|----|-----|-----------------|------|----|-----|
| Walt Dukes, Seton Hall | 1953 | 33 | 734 | Artis Gilmore, Jacksonville | 1970 | 28 | 621 |
| Leroy Wright, Pacific | 1959 | 26 | 652 | Tom Gola, La Salle | 1955 | 31 | 618 |
| Tom Gola, La Salle | 1954 | 30 | 652 | Ed Conlin, Fordham | 1953 | 26 | 612 |
| Charlie Tyra, Louisville | 1956 | 29 | 645 | Art Quimby, Connecticut | 1955 | 25 | 611 |
| Paul Silas, Creighton | 1964 | 29 | 631 | Bill Russell, San Francisco | 1956 | 29 | 609 |
| Elvin Hayes, Houston | 1968 | 33 | 624 | Jim Ware, Oklahoma City | 1966 | 29 | 607 |

### REBOUND AVERAGE BEFORE 1973

| Player and Team | Year | GP | Reb | Avg |
|-----------------|------|----|-----|-----|
| Charlie Slack, Marshall | 1955 | 21 | 538 | 25.6 |
| Leroy Wright, Pacific | 1959 | 26 | 652 | 25.1 |
| Art Quimby, Connecticut | 1955 | 25 | 611 | 24.4 |
| Charlie Slack, Marshall | 1956 | 22 | 520 | 23.6 |
| Ed Conlin, Fordham | 1953 | 26 | 612 | 23.5 |

## Season Records *(Cont.)*

### REBOUND AVERAGE SINCE 1973

| Player and Team | Year | GP | Reb | Avg |
|---|---|---|---|---|
| Kermit Washington, American | 1973 | 22 | 439 | 20.0 |
| Marvin Barnes, Providence | 1973 | 30 | 571 | 19.0 |
| Marvin Barnes, Providence | 1974 | 32 | 597 | 18.7 |
| Pete Padgett, NV-Reno | 1973 | 26 | 462 | 17.8 |
| Jim Bradley, Northern Illinois | 1973 | 24 | 426 | 17.8 |

### ASSISTS

| Player and Team | Year | GP | A | Player and Team | Year | GP | A |
|---|---|---|---|---|---|---|---|
| Mark Wade, UNLV | 1987 | 38 | 406 | Sherman Douglas, Syracuse | 1989 | 38 | 326 |
| Avery Johnson, Southern-BR | 1988 | 30 | 399 | Sam Crawford, N Mex St | 1993 | 34 | 310 |
| Anthony Manuel, Bradley | 1988 | 31 | 373 | Greg Anthony, UNLV | 1991 | 35 | 310 |
| Avery Johnson, Southern-BR | 1987 | 31 | 333 | Reid Gettys, Houston | 1984 | 37 | 309 |
| Mark Jackson, St John's (NY) | 1986 | 32 | 328 | Carl Golston, Loyola (IL) | 1985 | 33 | 305 |

### ASSIST AVERAGE

| Player and Team | Year | GP | A | Avg | Player and Team | Year | GP | A | Avg |
|---|---|---|---|---|---|---|---|---|---|
| Avery Johnson, Southern-BR | 1988 | 30 | 399 | 13.3 | Chris Corchiani, N Carolina St | 1991 | 31 | 299 | 9.6 |
| Anthony Manuel, Bradley | 1988 | 31 | 373 | 12.0 | Tony Fairley, Baptist | 1987 | 28 | 270 | 9.6 |
| Avery Johnson, Southern-BR | 1987 | 31 | 333 | 10.7 | Tyrone Bogues, Wake Forest | 1987 | 29 | 276 | 9.5 |
| Mark Wade, NV-Las Vegas | 1987 | 38 | 406 | 10.7 | Craig Neal, Georgia Tech | 1988 | 32 | 303 | 9.5 |
| Nelson Haggerty, Baylor | 1995 | 28 | 284 | 10.1 | Ron Weingard, Hofstra | 1985 | 24 | 228 | 9.5 |
| Glenn Williams, Holy Cross | 1989 | 28 | 278 | 9.9 | | | | | |

### FIELD-GOAL PERCENTAGE

| Player and Team | Year | GP | FG | FGA | Pct |
|---|---|---|---|---|---|
| Steve Johnson, Oregon St | 1981 | 28 | 235 | 315 | 74.6 |
| Dwayne Davis, Florida | 1989 | 33 | 179 | 248 | 72.2 |
| Keith Walker, Utica | 1985 | 27 | 154 | 216 | 71.3 |
| Steve Johnson, Oregon St | 1980 | 30 | 211 | 297 | 71.0 |
| Oliver Miller, Arkansas | 1991 | 38 | 254 | 361 | 70.4 |
| Alan Williams, Princeton | 1987 | 25 | 163 | 232 | 70.3 |
| Mark McNamara, California | 1982 | 27 | 231 | 329 | 70.2 |
| Warren Kidd, Middle Tennessee St | 1991 | 30 | 173 | 247 | 70.0 |
| Pete Freeman, Akron | 1991 | 28 | 175 | 250 | 70.0 |
| Joe Senser, West Chester | 1977 | 25 | 130 | 186 | 69.9 |
| Lee Campbell, SW Missouri St | 1990 | 29 | 192 | 275 | 69.8 |
| Stephen Scheffler, Purdue | 1990 | 30 | 173 | 248 | 69.8 |

Based on qualifiers for annual championship.

### FREE-THROW PERCENTAGE

| Player and Team | Year | GP | FT | FTA | Pct |
|---|---|---|---|---|---|
| Craig Collins, Penn St | 1985 | 27 | 94 | 98 | 95.9 |
| Rod Foster, UCLA | 1982 | 27 | 95 | 100 | 95.0 |
| Danny Basile, Marist | 1994 | 27 | 84 | 89 | 94.4 |
| Carlos Gibson, Marshall | 1978 | 28 | 84 | 89 | 94.4 |
| Jim Barton, Dartmouth | 1986 | 26 | 65 | 69 | 94.2 |
| Jack Moore, Nebraska | 1982 | 27 | 123 | 131 | 93.9 |
| Dandrea Evans, Troy St | 1994 | 27 | 72 | 77 | 93.5 |
| Rob Robbins, New Mexico | 1990 | 34 | 101 | 108 | 93.5 |
| Tommy Boyer, Arkansas | 1962 | 23 | 125 | 134 | 93.3 |
| Damon Goodwin, Dayton | 1986 | 30 | 95 | 102 | 93.1 |
| Brian Magid, George Washington | 1980 | 26 | 79 | 85 | 92.9 |
| Mike Joseph, Bucknell | 1990 | 29 | 144 | 155 | 92.9 |

Based on qualifiers for annual championship.

## Season Records *(Cont.)*

### THREE-POINT FIELD-GOAL PERCENTAGE

| Player and Team | Year | GP | 3FG | 3FGA | Pct |
|---|---|---|---|---|---|
| Glenn Tropf, Holy Cross | 1988 | 29 | 52 | 82 | 63.4 |
| Sean Wightman, Western Michigan | 1992 | 30 | 48 | 76 | 63.2 |
| Keith Jennings, E Tennessee St | 1991 | 33 | 84 | 142 | 59.2 |
| Dave Calloway, Monmouth (NJ) | 1989 | 28 | 48 | 82 | 58.5 |
| Steve Kerr, Arizona | 1988 | 38 | 114 | 199 | 57.3 |
| Reginald Jones, Prairie View | 1987 | 28 | 64 | 112 | 57.1 |
| Joel Tribelhorn, Colorado St | 1989 | 33 | 76 | 135 | 56.3 |
| Mike Joseph, Bucknell | 1988 | 28 | 65 | 116 | 56.0 |
| Brian Jackson, Evansville | 1995 | 27 | 53 | 95 | 55.8 |
| Christian Laettner, Duke | 1992 | 35 | 54 | 97 | 55.7 |
| Reginald Jones, Prairie View | 1988 | 27 | 85 | 155 | 54.8 |

Based on qualifiers for annual championship.

### STEALS

| Player and Team | Year | GP | S |
|---|---|---|---|
| Mookie Blaylock, Oklahoma | 1988 | 39 | 150 |
| Aldwin Ware, Florida A&M | 1988 | 29 | 142 |
| Darron Brittman, Chicago St | 1986 | 28 | 139 |
| Nadav Henefeld, Connecticut | 1990 | 37 | 138 |
| Mookie Blaylock, Oklahoma | 1989 | 35 | 131 |

### BLOCKED SHOTS

| Player and Team | Year | GP | BS |
|---|---|---|---|
| David Robinson, Navy | 1986 | 35 | 207 |
| Shawn Bradley, BYU | 1991 | 34 | 177 |
| Alonzo Mourning, Georgetown | 1989 | 34 | 169 |
| Alonzo Mourning, Georgetown | 1992 | 32 | 160 |
| Shaquille O'Neal, Louisiana St | 1992 | 30 | 157 |

### STEAL AVERAGE

| Player and Team | Year | GP | S | Avg |
|---|---|---|---|---|
| Darron Brittman, Chicago St | 1986 | 28 | 139 | 4.96 |
| Aldwin Ware, Florida A&M | 1988 | 29 | 142 | 4.90 |
| Ronn McMahon, E Washington | 1990 | 29 | 130 | 4.48 |
| Jim Paguaga, St Francis (NY) | 1986 | 28 | 120 | 4.29 |
| Marty Johnson, Towson St | 1988 | 30 | 124 | 4.13 |

### BLOCKED SHOT AVERAGE

| Player and Team | Year | GP | BS | Avg |
|---|---|---|---|---|
| David Robinson, Navy | 1986 | 35 | 207 | 5.91 |
| Keith Closs, Central Conn St | 1995 | 26 | 139 | 5.34 |
| Shaquille O'Neal, Louisiana St | 1992 | 30 | 157 | 5.23 |
| Shawn Bradley, BYU | 1991 | 34 | 177 | 5.21 |
| Theo Ratliff, Wyoming | 1995 | 28 | 144 | 5.14 |

## Career Records

### POINTS

| Player and Team | Ht | Final Year | GP | FG | 3FG* | FT | Pts |
|---|---|---|---|---|---|---|---|
| Pete Maravich, Louisiana St | 6-5 | 1970 | 83 | 1387 | — | 893 | 3667 |
| Freeman Williams, Portland St | 6-4 | 1978 | 106 | 1369 | — | 511 | 3249 |
| Lionel Simmons, La Salle | 6-7 | 1990 | 131 | 1244 | 56 | 673 | 3217 |
| Alphonso Ford, Mississippi Valley | 6-2 | 1993 | 109 | 1121 | 333 | 590 | 3165 |
| Harry Kelly, Texas Southern | 6-7 | 1983 | 110 | 1234 | — | 598 | 3066 |
| Hersey Hawkins, Bradley | 6-3 | 1988 | 125 | 1100 | 118 | 690 | 3008 |
| Oscar Robertson, Cincinnati | 6-5 | 1960 | 88 | 1052 | — | 869 | 2973 |
| Danny Manning, Kansas | 6-10 | 1988 | 147 | 1216 | 10 | 509 | 2951 |
| Alfredrick Hughes, Loyola (IL) | 6-5 | 1985 | 120 | 1226 | — | 462 | 2914 |
| Elvin Hayes, Houston | 6-8 | 1968 | 93 | 1215 | — | 454 | 2884 |
| Larry Bird, Indiana St | 6-9 | 1979 | 94 | 1154 | — | 542 | 2850 |
| Otis Birdsong, Houston | 6-4 | 1977 | 116 | 1176 | — | 480 | 2832 |
| Kevin Bradshaw, Bethune-Cookman, U.S. Int'l | 6-6 | 1991 | 111 | 1027 | 132 | 618 | 2804 |
| Allan Houston, Tennessee | 6-6 | 1993 | 128 | 902 | 346 | 651 | 2801 |
| Hank Gathers, Southern Cal, Loyola Marymount | 6-7 | 1990 | 117 | 1127 | 0 | 469 | 2723 |
| Reggie Lewis, Northeastern | 6-7 | 1987 | 122 | 1043 | 30 (1) | 592 | 2708 |
| Daren Queenan, Lehigh | 6-5 | 1988 | 118 | 1024 | 29 | 626 | 2703 |
| Byron Larkin, Xavier (OH) | 6-3 | 1988 | 121 | 1022 | 51 | 601 | 2696 |
| David Robinson, Navy | 7-1 | 1987 | 127 | 1032 | 1 | 604 | 2669 |
| Wayman Tisdale, Oklahoma | 6-9 | 1985 | 104 | 1077 | — | 507 | 2661 |

*Listed is the number of three-pointers scored since it became the national rule in 1987; the number in the parentheses is number scored prior to 1987—these counted as three points in the game but counted as two-pointers in the national rankings. The three-pointers in the parentheses are not included in total points.

## Career Records *(Cont.)*

### SCORING AVERAGE

| Player and Team | Final Year | GP | FG | FT | Pts | Avg |
|---|---|---|---|---|---|---|
| Pete Maravich, Louisiana St | 1968 | 83 | 1387 | 893 | 3667 | 44.2 |
| Austin Carr, Notre Dame | 1971 | 74 | 1017 | 526 | 2560 | 34.6 |
| Oscar Robertson, Cincinnati | 1960 | 88 | 1052 | 869 | 2973 | 33.8 |
| Calvin Murphy, Niagara | 1970 | 77 | 947 | 654 | 2548 | 33.1 |
| Dwight Lamar, Southwestern Louisiana | 1973 | 57 | 768 | 326 | 1862 | 32.7 |
| Frank Selvy, Furman | 1954 | 78 | 922 | 694 | 2538 | 32.5 |
| Rick Mount, Purdue | 1970 | 72 | 910 | 503 | 2323 | 32.3 |
| Darrell Floyd, Furman | 1956 | 71 | 868 | 545 | 2281 | 32.1 |
| Nick Werkman, Seton Hall | 1964 | 71 | 812 | 649 | 2273 | 32.0 |
| Willie Humes, Idaho St | 1971 | 48 | 565 | 380 | 1510 | 31.5 |
| William Averitt, Pepperdine | 1973 | 49 | 615 | 311 | 1541 | 31.4 |
| Elgin Baylor, Coll of Idaho, Seattle | 1958 | 80 | 956 | 588 | 2500 | 31.3 |
| Elvin Hayes, Houston | 1968 | 93 | 1215 | 454 | 2884 | 31.0 |
| Freeman Williams, Portland St | 1978 | 106 | 1369 | 511 | 3249 | 30.7 |
| Larry Bird, Indiana St | 1979 | 94 | 1154 | 542 | 2850 | 30.3 |

### REBOUNDS BEFORE 1973

| Player and Team | Final Year | GP | Reb |
|---|---|---|---|
| Tom Gola, La Salle | 1955 | 118 | 2201 |
| Joe Holup, George Washington | 1956 | 104 | 2030 |
| Charlie Slack, Marshall | 1956 | 88 | 1916 |
| Ed Conlin, Fordham | 1955 | 102 | 1884 |
| Dickie Hemric, Wake Forest | 1955 | 104 | 1802 |

### REBOUNDS FOR CAREERS BEGINNING IN 1973 OR AFTER*

| Player and Team | Final Year | GP | Reb |
|---|---|---|---|
| Derrick Coleman, Syracuse | 1990 | 143 | 1537 |
| Ralph Sampson, Virginia | 1983 | 132 | 1511 |
| Pete Padgett, NV-Reno | 1976 | 104 | 1464 |
| Lionel Simmons, La Salle | 1990 | 131 | 1429 |
| Anthony Bonner, St Louis | 1990 | 133 | 1424 |

### ASSISTS

| Player and Team | Final Year | GP | A |
|---|---|---|---|
| Bobby Hurley, Duke | 1993 | 140 | 1076 |
| Chris Corchiani, N Carolina St | 1991 | 124 | 1038 |
| Keith Jennings, E Tennessee St | 1991 | 127 | 983 |
| Sherman Douglas, Syracuse | 1989 | 138 | 960 |
| Tony Miller, Marquette | 1995 | 123 | 956 |

### FIELD-GOAL PERCENTAGE

| Player and Team | Final Year | FG | FGA | Pct |
|---|---|---|---|---|
| Ricky Nedd, Appalachian St | 1994 | 412 | 597 | 69.0 |
| Stephen Scheffler, Purdue | 1990 | 408 | 596 | 68.5 |
| Steve Johnson, Oregon St | 1981 | 828 | 1222 | 67.8 |
| Murray Brown, Florida St | 1980 | 566 | 847 | 66.8 |
| Lee Campbell, SW Missouri St | 1990 | 411 | 618 | 66.6 |

Note: Minimum 400 field goals.

### FREE-THROW PERCENTAGE

| Player and Team | Final Year | FT | FTA | Pct |
|---|---|---|---|---|
| Greg Starrick, Kentucky, Southern Illinois | 1972 | 341 | 375 | 90.9 |
| Jack Moore, Nebraska | 1982 | 446 | 495 | 90.1 |
| Steve Henson, Kansas St | 1990 | 361 | 401 | 90.0 |
| Steve Alford, Indiana | 1987 | 535 | 596 | 89.8 |
| Bob Lloyd, Rutgers | 1967 | 543 | 605 | 89.8 |

Note: Minimum 300 free throws.
*Freshmen became eligible for varsity play in 1973

## Career Records *(Cont.)*

### THREE-POINT FIELD GOALS MADE

| Player and Team | Final Year | GP | 3FG |
|---|---|---|---|
| Doug Day, Radford | 1993 | 117 | 401 |
| Ronnie Schmitz, MO-Kansas City | 1993 | 112 | 378 |
| Mark Alberts, Akron | 1993 | 103 | 375 |
| Jeff Fryer, Loyola Marymount | 1990 | 112 | 363 |
| Dennis Scott, Georgia Tech | 1990 | 99 | 351 |

### THREE-POINT FIELD-GOAL PERCENTAGE

| Player and Team | Final Year | 3FG | 3FGA | Pct |
|---|---|---|---|---|
| Tony Bennett, WI-Green Bay | 1992 | 290 | 584 | 49.7 |
| Keith Jennings, E Tennessee St | 1991 | 223 | 452 | 49.3 |
| Kirk Manns, Michigan St | 1990 | 212 | 446 | 47.5 |
| Tim Locum, Wisconsin | 1991 | 227 | 481 | 47.2 |
| David Olson, Eastern Illinois | 1992 | 262 | 562 | 46.6 |

Note: Minimum 200 3-point field goals.

### STEALS

| Player and Team | Final Year | GP | S |
|---|---|---|---|
| Eric Murdock, Providence | 1991 | 117 | 376 |
| Michael Anderson, Drexel | 1988 | 115 | 341 |
| Kenny Robertson, New Mexico, Clev St | 1990 | 119 | 341 |
| Keith Jennings, E Tennessee St | 1991 | 127 | 334 |
| Greg Anthony, Portland, UNLV | 1991 | 138 | 329 |

### BLOCKED SHOTS

| Player and Team | Final Year | GP | BS |
|---|---|---|---|
| Alonzo Mourning, Georgetown | 1992 | 120 | 453 |
| Theo Ratliff, Wyoming | 1995 | 111 | 425 |
| Rodney Blake, St Joseph's (PA) | 1988 | 116 | 419 |
| Shaquille O'Neal, Louisiana St | 1992 | 90 | 412 |
| Kevin Roberson, Vermont | 1992 | 112 | 409 |

# NCAA Division I Team Leaders

## Division I Team Alltime Wins

| Team | First Year | Yrs | W | L | T |
|---|---|---|---|---|---|
| N Carolina | 1911 | 85 | 1626 | 577 | 0 |
| Kentucky | 1903 | 92 | 1615 | 518 | 1 |
| Kansas | 1899 | 97 | 1567 | 703 | 0 |
| St John's (NY) | 1908 | 88 | 1508 | 666 | 0 |
| Duke | 1906 | 90 | 1474 | 727 | 0 |
| Temple | 1895 | 99 | 1435 | 780 | 0 |
| Oregon St | 1902 | 94 | 1430 | 927 | 0 |
| Pennsylvania | 1902 | 94 | 1408 | 796 | 0 |
| Syracuse | 1901 | 94 | 1403 | 661 | 0 |
| Notre Dame | 1898 | 90 | 1389 | 730 | 1 |
| Indiana | 1901 | 95 | 1369 | 732 | 0 |
| UCLA | 1920 | 76 | 1351 | 588 | 0 |
| Washington | 1896 | 93 | 1332 | 861 | 0 |
| Western Kentucky | 1915 | 76 | 1331 | 621 | 0 |
| Princeton | 1901 | 95 | 1313 | 830 | 0 |

Note: Years in Division I only.

## Division I Alltime Winning Percentage

| Team | First Year | Yrs | W | L | T | Pct |
|---|---|---|---|---|---|---|
| Kentucky | 1903 | 92 | 1616 | 518 | 1 | .757 |
| NV-Las Vegas | 1959 | 37 | 779 | 268 | 0 | .744 |
| N Carolina | 1911 | 85 | 1626 | 577 | 0 | .738 |
| UCLA | 1920 | 76 | 1351 | 588 | 0 | .697 |
| St John's (NY) | 1908 | 88 | 1508 | 666 | 0 | .694 |
| Kansas | 1899 | 97 | 1567 | 703 | 0 | .690 |
| Western Kentucky | 1915 | 76 | 1331 | 621 | 0 | .682 |
| Syracuse | 1901 | 94 | 1403 | 661 | 0 | .680 |
| Duke | 1906 | 90 | 1474 | 727 | 0 | .670 |
| DePaul | 1924 | 72 | 1166 | 582 | 0 | .667 |

Note: Minimum of 20 years in Division I.

# NCAA Division I Men's Winning Streaks

## Longest—Full Season

| Team | Games | Years | Ended by |
|------|-------|-------|----------|
| UCLA | 88 | 1971-74 | Notre Dame (71-70) |
| San Francisco | 60 | 1955-57 | Illinois (62-33) |
| UCLA | 47 | 1966-68 | Houston (71-69) |
| UNLV | 45 | 1990-91 | Duke (79-77) |
| Texas | 44 | 1913-17 | Rice (24-18) |
| Seton Hall | 43 | 1939-41 | LIU-Brooklyn (49-26) |
| LIU-Brooklyn | 43 | 1935-37 | Stanford (45-31) |
| UCLA | 41 | 1968-69 | Southern Cal (46-44) |
| Marquette | 39 | 1970-71 | Ohio St (60-59) |
| Cincinnati | 37 | 1962-63 | Wichita St (65-64) |
| N Carolina | 37 | 1957-58 | W Virginia (75-64) |

## Longest—Home Court

| Team | Games | Years |
|------|-------|-------|
| Kentucky | 129 | 1943-55 |
| St Bonaventure | 99 | 1948-61 |
| UCLA | 98 | 1970-76 |
| Cincinnati | 86 | 1957-64 |
| Marquette | 81 | 1967-73 |
| Arizona | 81 | 1945-51 |
| Lamar | 80 | 1978-84 |
| Long Beach St | 75 | 1968-74 |
| NV-Las Vegas | 72 | 1974-78 |
| Arizona | 71 | 1987-92 |
| Cincinnati | 68 | 1972-78 |

## Longest—Regular Season

| Team | Games | Years | Ended by |
|------|-------|-------|----------|
| UCLA | 76 | 1971-74 | Notre Dame (71-70) |
| Indiana | 57 | 1975-77 | Toledo (59-57) |
| Marquette | 56 | 1970-72 | Detroit (70-49) |
| Kentucky | 54 | 1952-55 | George Tech (59-58) |
| San Francisco | 51 | 1955-57 | Illinois (62-33) |
| Pennsylvania | 48 | 1970-72 | Temple (57-52) |
| Ohio St | 47 | 1960-62 | Wisconsin (86-67) |
| Texas | 44 | 1913-17 | Rice (24-18) |
| UCLA | 43 | 1966-68 | Houston (71-69) |
| LIU-Brooklyn | 43 | 1935-37 | Stanford (45-31) |
| Seton Hall | 42 | 1939-41 | LIU-Brooklyn (49-26) |

# NCAA Division I Winningest Men's Coaches

## Active Coaches

### WINS

| Coach and Team | W |
|----------------|---|
| Dean Smith, N Carolina | 830 |
| James Phelan, Mt St Mary's (MD) | 737 |
| Don Haskins, UTEP | 665 |
| Norm Stewart, Missouri | 660 |
| Bob Knight, Indiana | 659 |
| Lefty Driesell, James Madison | 657 |
| Lou Henson, Illinois | 645 |
| Gene Bartow, AL-Birmingham | 631 |
| Jerry Tarkanian, Fresno St | 625 |
| Denny Crum, Louisville | 565 |

Note: Minimum 5 years as a Division I head coach; includes record at 4-year colleges only.

### WINNING PERCENTAGE

| Coach and Team | Yrs | W | L | Pct |
|----------------|-----|---|---|-----|
| Jerry Tarkanian, Fresno St | 24 | 625 | 122 | .837 |
| Roy Williams, Kansas | 7 | 184 | 51 | .783 |
| Dean Smith, N Carolina | 34 | 830 | 236 | .779 |
| Nolan Richardson, Arkansas | 15 | 371 | 119 | .757 |
| Jim Boeheim, Syracuse | 19 | 454 | 150 | .752 |
| John Chaney, Temple | 23 | 520 | 175 | .748 |
| Larry Hunter, Ohio | 19 | 414 | 145 | .741 |
| Bob Knight, Indiana | 30 | 659 | 235 | .737 |
| Denny Crum, Louisville | 24 | 565 | 212 | .727 |
| Eddie Sutton, Oklahoma St | 25 | 553 | 209 | .726 |

Note: Minimum 5 years as a Division I head coach; includes record at 4-year colleges only.

## Alltime Winningest Division I Men's Coaches

### WINS

| Coach (Team) | W |
|--------------|---|
| Adolph Rupp (Kentucky) | 876 |
| Dean Smith (N Carolina) | 830 |
| Hank Iba (NW Missouri St, Colorado, Oklahoma St) | 767 |
| Ed Diddle (Western Kentucky) | 759 |
| Phog Allen (Baker, Kansas, Haskell, Central Missouri St, Kansas) | 746 |
| Ray Meyer (DePaul) | 724 |
| Don Haskins (UTEP) | 665 |
| John Wooden (Indiana St, UCLA) | 664 |
| Norm Stewart (Missouri) | 660 |
| Bob Knight (Army, Indiana) | 659 |
| Lefty Driesell (Davidson, Maryland, James Madison) | 657 |
| Ralph Miller (Wichita St, Iowa, Oregon St) | 657 |
| Marv Harshman (Pacific Lutheran, Washington St, Washington) | 654 |
| Lou Henson (Hardin-Simmons, New Mexico St, Illinois) | 645 |
| Gene Bartow (C MO St, Valparaiso, Memphis St, Illinois, UCLA, UAB) | 631 |

Note: Minimum 10 head coaching seasons in Division I.

# NCAA Division I Winningest Men's Coaches (Cont.)

## WINNING PERCENTAGE

| Coach (Team) | Yrs | W | L | Pct |
|---|---|---|---|---|
| Jerry Tarkanian (Long Beach St 69-73, UNLV 74-92, Fresno St 95-) | 24 | 625 | 122 | .837 |
| Clair Bee (Rider 29-31, LIU-Brooklyn 32-45, 46-51) | 21 | 412 | 87 | .826 |
| Adolph Rupp (Kentucky 31-72) | 41 | 876 | 190 | .822 |
| John Wooden (Indiana St 47-48, UCLA 49-75) | 29 | 664 | 162 | .804 |
| Dean Smith (N Carolina 62-) | 34 | 830 | 236 | .779 |
| Harry Fisher (Columbia 07-16, Army 22-23, 25) | 13 | 147 | 44 | .770 |
| Frank Keaney (Rhode Island 21-48) | 27 | 387 | 117 | .768 |
| George Keogan (St Louis 16, Allegheny 19, Valparaiso 20-21, Notre Dame 24-43) | 24 | 385 | 117 | .767 |
| Jack Ramsay (St Joseph's [PA] 56-66) | 11 | 231 | 71 | .765 |
| Vic Bubas (Duke 60-69) | 10 | 213 | 67 | .761 |
| Nolan Richardson (Tulsa 81-85, Arkansas 86-) | 15 | 371 | 119 | .757 |
| Jim Boeheim (Syracuse 77-) | 19 | 454 | 150 | .752 |
| John Chaney (Cheyney 73-82, Temple 83-) | 23 | 520 | 175 | .748 |
| Charles "Chick" Davies (Duquesne 25-43, 47-48) | 21 | 314 | 106 | .748 |
| Ray Mears (Wittenberg 57-62, Tennessee 63-77) | 21 | 399 | 135 | .747 |
| Phog Allen (Baker 06-08, Kansas 08-09, Haskell 09, Cent MO St 13-19, Kansas 20-56) | 48 | 746 | 264 | .739 |
| Al McGuire (Belmont Abbey 58-64, Marquette 65-77) | 20 | 405 | 143 | .739 |
| Everett Chase (N Carolina St 47-64) | 18 | 376 | 133 | .739 |
| Bob Knight (Army 66-71, Indiana 72-) | 30 | 659 | 235 | .737 |
| Walter Meanwell (Wisconsin 12-17, 21-34; Missouri 18, 20) | 22 | 280 | 101 | .735 |

Note: Minimum 10 head coaching seasons in Division I.

# NCAA Division I Women's Championship Results

| Year | Winner | Score | Runner-up | Winning Coach |
|---|---|---|---|---|
| 1982 | Louisiana Tech | 76–62 | Cheyney | Sonja Hogg |
| 1983 | Southern Cal | 69–67 | Louisiana Tech | Linda Sharp |
| 1984 | Southern Cal | 72–61 | Tennessee | Linda Sharp |
| 1985 | Old Dominion | 70–65 | Georgia | Marianne Stanley |
| 1986 | Texas | 97–81 | Southern Cal | Jody Conradt |
| 1987 | Tennessee | 67–44 | Louisiana Tech | Pat Summitt |
| 1988 | Louisiana Tech | 56–54 | Auburn | Leon Barmore |
| 1989 | Tennessee | 76–60 | Auburn | Pat Summitt |
| 1990 | Stanford | 88–81 | Auburn | Tara VanDerveer |
| 1991 | Tennessee | 70–67 (OT) | Virginia | Pat Summitt |
| 1992 | Stanford | 78–62 | Western Kentucky | Tara VanDerveer |
| 1993 | Texas Tech | 84–82 | Ohio State | Marsha Sharp |
| 1994 | N Carolina | 60–59 | Louisiana Tech | Sylvia Hatchell |
| 1995 | Connecticut | 70–64 | Tennessee | Geno Auriemma |

# NCAA Division I Women's Alltime Individual Leaders

## Single-Game Records

### SCORING HIGHS

| Pts | Player and Team vs Opponent | Year |
|---|---|---|
| 60 | Cindy Brown, Long Beach St vs San Jose St | 1987 |
| 58 | Kim Perrot, SW Louisiana vs SE Louisiana | 1990 |
| 58 | Lorri Bauman, Drake vs SW Missouri St | 1984 |
| 55 | Patricia Hoskins, Mississippi Valley vs Southern-BR | 1989 |
| 55 | Patricia Hoskins, Mississippi Valley vs Alabama St | 1989 |
| 54 | Anjinea Hopson, Grambling vs Jackson St | 1994 |
| 54 | Mary Lowry, Baylor vs Texas | 1994 |
| 54 | Wanda Ford, Drake vs SW Missouri St | 1986 |
| 53 | Felisha Edwards, NE Louisiana vs Southern Mississippi | 1991 |
| 53 | Chris Starr, NV-Reno vs Cal St-Sacramento | 1983 |
| 53 | Sheryl Swoopes, Texas Tech vs Texas | 1993 |

### REBOUNDING HIGHS

| Reb | Player and Team vs Opponent | Year |
|---|---|---|
| 40 | Deborah Temple, Delta St vs AL-Birmingham | 1983 |
| 37 | Rosina Pearson, Bethune-Cookman vs Florida Memorial | 1985 |
| 33 | Maureen Formico, Pepperdine vs Loyola (CA) | 1985 |

## REBOUNDING HIGHS *(Cont.)*

| Reb | Player and Team vs Opponent | Year |
|---|---|---|
| 31 | Darlene Beale, Howard vs S Carolina St | 1987 |
| 30 | Cindy Bonforte, Wagner vs Queens (NY) | 1983 |
| 30 | Kayone Hankins, New Orleans vs. Nicholls St | 1994 |
| 29 | Gail Norris, Alabama St vs Texas Southern | 1992 |
| 29 | Joy Kellogg, Oklahoma City vs Oklahoma Christian | 1984 |
| 29 | Joy Kellogg, Oklahoma City vs UTEP | 1984 |

Six tied with 28.

## ASSISTS

| A | Player and Team vs Opponent | Year |
|---|---|---|
| 23 | Michelle Burden, Kent St vs Ball St | 1991 |
| 22 | Shawn Monday, Tennessee Tech vs Morehead St | 1988 |
| 22 | Veronica Pettry, Loyola (IL) vs Detroit | 1989 |
| 22 | Tine Freil, Pacific vs Wichita St | 1991 |
| 21 | Tine Freil, Pacific vs Fresno St | 1992 |
| 21 | Amy Bauer, Wisconsin vs Detroit | 1989 |
| 21 | Neacole Hall, Alabama St vs Southern-BR | 1989 |
| 20 | Anja Bordt, St Mary's (CA) vs Loyola (CA) | 1991 |
| 20 | Gaynor O'Donnell, E Carolina vs NC-Asheville | 1992 |
| 20 | Ira Fuquay, Alcorn St vs Grambling | 1993 |

# Season Records

## POINTS

| Player and Team | Year | GP | FG | 3FG | FT | Pts |
|---|---|---|---|---|---|---|
| Cindy Brown, Long Beach St | 1987 | 35 | 362 | — | 250 | 974 |
| Genia Miller, Cal St-Fullerton | 1991 | 33 | 376 | 0 | 217 | 969 |
| Sheryl Swoopes, Texas Tech | 1993 | 34 | 356 | 32 | 211 | 955 |
| Andrea Congreaves, Mercer | 1992 | 28 | 353 | 77 | 142 | 925 |
| Wanda Ford, Drake | 1986 | 30 | 390 | — | 139 | 919 |
| Barbara Kennedy, Clemson | 1982 | 31 | 392 | — | 124 | 908 |
| Patricia Hoskins, Mississippi Valley | 1989 | 27 | 345 | 13 | 205 | 908 |
| LaTaunya Pollard, Long Beach St | 1983 | 31 | 376 | — | 155 | 907 |
| Tina Hutchinson, San Diego St | 1984 | 30 | 383 | — | 132 | 898 |
| Jan Jensen, Drake | 1991 | 30 | 358 | 6 | 166 | 888 |

## SEASON SCORING AVERAGE

| Player and Team | Year | GP | FG | 3FG | FT | Pts | Avg |
|---|---|---|---|---|---|---|---|
| Patricia Hoskins, Mississippi Valley | 1989 | 27 | 345 | 13 | 205 | 908 | 33.6 |
| Andrea Congreaves, Mercer | 1992 | 28 | 353 | 77 | 142 | 925 | 33.0 |
| Deborah Temple, Delta St | 1984 | 28 | 373 | — | 127 | 873 | 31.2 |
| Andrea Congreaves, Mercer | 1993 | 26 | 302 | 51 | 150 | 805 | 31.0 |
| Wanda Ford, Drake | 1986 | 30 | 390 | — | 139 | 919 | 30.6 |
| Anucha Browne, Northwestern | 1985 | 28 | 341 | — | 173 | 855 | 30.5 |
| LeChandra LeDay, Grambling | 1988 | 28 | 334 | 36 | 146 | 850 | 30.4 |
| Kim Perrot, Southwestern Louisiana | 1990 | 28 | 308 | 95 | 128 | 839 | 30.0 |
| Tina Hutchinson, San Diego St | 1984 | 30 | 383 | — | 132 | 898 | 29.9 |
| Jan Jensen, Drake | 1991 | 30 | 358 | 6 | 166 | 888 | 29.6 |
| Genia Miller, Cal St-Fullerton | 1991 | 33 | 376 | 0 | 217 | 969 | 29.4 |
| Barbara Kennedy, Clemson | 1982 | 31 | 392 | — | 124 | 908 | 29.3 |
| LaTaunya Pollard, Long Beach St | 1983 | 31 | 376 | — | 155 | 907 | 29.3 |
| Lisa McMullen, Alabama St | 1991 | 28 | 285 | 126 | 119 | 815 | 29.1 |
| Tresa Spaulding, BYU | 1987 | 28 | 347 | — | 116 | 810 | 28.9 |
| Hope Linthicum, Central Conn St | 1987 | 23 | 282 | — | 101 | 665 | 28.9 |

## Season Records (Cont.)

### REBOUNDS

| Player and Team | Year | GP | Reb | Player and Team | Year | GP | Reb |
|---|---|---|---|---|---|---|---|
| Wanda Ford, Drake | 1985 | 30 | 534 | Rosina Pearson, Beth-Cookman | 1985 | 26 | 480 |
| Wanda Ford, Drake | 1986 | 30 | 506 | Patricia Hoskins, Miss Valley | 1987 | 28 | 476 |
| Anne Donovan, Old Dominion | 1983 | 35 | 504 | Cheryl Miller, Southern Cal | 1985 | 30 | 474 |
| Darlene Jones, Miss Valley | 1983 | 31 | 487 | Darlene Beale, Howard | 1987 | 29 | 459 |
| Melanie Simpson, Okla City | 1982 | 37 | 481 | Olivia Bradley, W Virginia | 1985 | 30 | 458 |

### REBOUND AVERAGE

| Player and Team | Year | GP | Reb | Avg |
|---|---|---|---|---|
| Rosina Pearson, Bethune-Cookman | 1985 | 26 | 480 | 18.5 |
| Wanda Ford, Drake | 1985 | 30 | 534 | 17.8 |
| Katie Beck, E Tennessee St | 1988 | 25 | 441 | 17.6 |
| DeShawne Blocker, E Tenn St | 1994 | 26 | 450 | 17.3 |
| Patricia Hoskins, Mississippi Valley | 1987 | 28 | 476 | 17.0 |
| Wanda Ford, Drake | 1986 | 30 | 506 | 16.9 |
| Patricia Hoskins, Mississippi Valley | 1989 | 27 | 440 | 16.3 |
| Joy Kellogg, Oklahoma City | 1984 | 23 | 373 | 16.2 |
| Deborah Mitchell, Mississippi Coll | 1983 | 28 | 447 | 16.0 |

### FIELD-GOAL PERCENTAGE

| Player and Team | Year | GP | FG | FGA | Pct |
|---|---|---|---|---|---|
| Renay Adams, Tennessee Tech | 1991 | 30 | 185 | 258 | 71.7 |
| Regina Days, Georgia Southern | 1986 | 27 | 234 | 332 | 70.5 |
| Kim Wood, WI-Green Bay | 1994 | 27 | 188 | 271 | 69.4 |
| Kelly Lyons, Old Dominion | 1990 | 31 | 308 | 444 | 69.4 |
| Alisha Hill, Howard | 1995 | 28 | 194 | 281 | 69.0 |
| Trina Roberts, Georgia Southern | 1982 | 31 | 189 | 277 | 68.2 |
| Lidiya Varbanova, Boise St | 1991 | 22 | 128 | 188 | 68.1 |
| LaFreda Deckard, North Texas | 1995 | 27 | 147 | 217 | 67.7 |
| Sharon McDowell, NC-Wilmington | 1987 | 28 | 170 | 251 | 67.7 |
| Lidiya Varbanova, Boise St | 1992 | 29 | 228 | 338 | 67.5 |
| Mary Raese, Idaho | 1986 | 31 | 254 | 380 | 66.8 |
| Lydia Sawney, Tennessee Tech | 1983 | 27 | 167 | 250 | 66.8 |

Based on qualifiers for annual championship.

### FREE-THROW PERCENTAGE

| Player and Team | Year | GP | FT | FTA | Pct |
|---|---|---|---|---|---|
| Ginny Doyle, Richmond | 1992 | 29 | 96 | 101 | 95.0 |
| Linda Cyborski, Delaware | 1991 | 29 | 74 | 79 | 93.7 |
| Jennifer Howard, N Carolina St | 1994 | 27 | 118 | 127 | 92.9 |
| Keely Feeman, Cincinnati | 1986 | 30 | 76 | 82 | 92.7 |
| Amy Slowikowski, Kent St | 1989 | 27 | 112 | 121 | 92.6 |
| Lea Ann Parsley, Marshall | 1990 | 28 | 96 | 104 | 92.3 |
| Chris Starr, NV-Reno | 1986 | 25 | 119 | 129 | 92.2 |
| DeAnn Craft, Central Florida | 1987 | 24 | 94 | 102 | 92.2 |
| Tracey Sneed, La Salle | 1988 | 30 | 151 | 165 | 91.5 |

Based on qualifiers for annual championship.

## THEY SAID IT

*Geno Auriemma, Connecticut
women's basketball coach, to his
33–0 Huskies prior to the Final Four:
"The other teams here are playing for
a national championship. We're
playing for a piece of history."*

## Career Records

### POINTS

| Player and Team | Yrs | GP | Pts |
|---|---|---|---|
| Patricia Hoskins, Mississippi Valley | 1985-89 | 110 | 3122 |
| Lorri Bauman, Drake | 1981-84 | 120 | 3115 |
| Cheryl Miller, Southern Cal | 1983-86 | 128 | 3018 |
| Valorie Whiteside, Appalachian St | 1984-88 | 116 | 2944 |
| Joyce Walker, Louisiana St | 1981-84 | 117 | 2906 |
| Sandra Hodge, New Orleans | 1981-84 | 107 | 2860 |
| Andrea Congreaves, Mercer | 1989-93 | 108 | 2796 |
| Karen Pelphrey, Marshall | 1983-86 | 114 | 2746 |
| Cindy Brown, Long Beach St | 1983-87 | 128 | 2696 |
| Carolyn Thompson, Texas Tech | 1981-84 | 121 | 2655 |
| Sue Wicks, Rutgers | 1984-88 | 125 | 2655 |

### SCORING AVERAGE

| Player and Team | Yrs | GP | FG | 3FG | FT | Pts | Avg |
|---|---|---|---|---|---|---|---|
| Patricia Hoskins, Mississippi Valley | 1985-89 | 110 | 1196 | 24 | 706 | 3122 | 28.4 |
| Sandra Hodge, New Orleans | 1981-84 | 107 | 1194 | — | 472 | 2860 | 26.7 |
| Lorri Bauman, Drake | 1981-84 | 120 | 1104 | — | 907 | 3115 | 26.0 |
| Andrea Congreaves, Mercer | 1989-93 | 108 | 1107 | 153 | 429 | 2796 | 25.9 |
| Valorie Whiteside, Appalachian St | 1984-88 | 116 | 1153 | 0 | 638 | 2944 | 25.4 |
| Joyce Walker, Louisiana St | 1981-84 | 117 | 1259 | — | 388 | 2906 | 24.8 |
| Tarcha Hollis, Grambling | 1988-91 | 85 | 904 | 3 | 247 | 2058 | 24.2 |
| Karen Pelphrey, Marshall | 1983-86 | 114 | 1175 | — | 396 | 2746 | 24.1 |
| Erma Jones, Bethune-Cookman | 1982-84 | 87 | 961 | — | 173 | 2095 | 24.1 |
| Cheryl Miller, Southern Cal | 1983-86 | 128 | 1159 | — | 700 | 3018 | 23.6 |
| Chris Starr, Nevada-Reno | 1983-86 | 101 | 881 | — | 594 | 2356 | 23.3 |

# NCAA Division II Men's Championship Results

| Year | Winner | Score | Runner-up | Third Place | Fourth Place |
|---|---|---|---|---|---|
| 1957 | Wheaton (IL) | 89-65 | Kentucky Wesleyan | Mount St Mary's (MD) | Cal St-Los Angeles |
| 1958 | S Dakota | 75-53 | St Michael's | Evansville | Wheaton (IL) |
| 1959 | Evansville | 83-67 | SW Missouri St | N Carolina A&T | Cal St-Los Angeles |
| 1960 | Evansville | 90-69 | Chapman | Kentucky Wesleyan | Cornell College |
| 1961 | Wittenberg | 42-38 | SE Missouri St | S Dakota St | Mount St Mary's (MD) |
| 1962 | Mount St Mary's (MD) | 58-57 (OT) | Cal St-Sacramento | Southern Illinois | Nebraska Wesleyan |
| 1963 | S Dakota St | 44-42 | Wittenberg | Oglethorpe | Southern Illinois |
| 1964 | Evansville | 72-59 | Akron | N Carolina A&T | Northern Iowa |
| 1965 | Evansville | 85-82 (OT) | Southern Illinois | N Dakota | St Michael's |
| 1966 | Kentucky Wesleyan | 54-51 | Southern Illinois | Akron | N Dakota |
| 1967 | Winston-Salem | 77-74 | SW Missouri St | Kentucky Wesleyan | Illinois St |
| 1968 | Kentucky Wesleyan | 63-52 | Indiana St | Trinity (TX) | Ashland |
| 1969 | Kentucky Wesleyan | 75-71 | SW Missouri St | †Vacated | Ashland |
| 1970 | Philadelphia Textile | 76-65 | Tennessee St | UC-Riverside | Buffalo St |
| 1971 | Evansville | 97-82 | Old Dominion | †Vacated | Kentucky Wesleyan |
| 1972 | Roanoke | 84-72 | Akron | Tennessee St | Eastern Mich |
| 1973 | Kentucky Wesleyan | 78-76 (OT) | Tennessee St | Assumption | Brockport St |
| 1974 | Morgan St | 67-52 | SW Missouri St | Assumption | New Orleans |
| 1975 | Old Dominion | 76-74 | New Orleans | Assumption | TN-Chattanooga |
| 1976 | Puget Sound | 83-74 | TN-Chattanooga | Eastern Illinois | Old Dominion |
| 1977 | TN-Chattanooga | 71-62 | Randolph-Macon | N Alabama | Sacred Heart |
| 1978 | Cheyney | 47-40 | WI-Green Bay | Eastern Illinois | Central Florida |
| 1979 | N Alabama | 64-50 | WI-Green Bay | Cheyney | Bridgeport |
| 1980 | Virginia Union | 80-74 | New York Tech | Florida Southern | N Alabama |
| 1981 | Florida Southern | 73-68 | Mount St Mary's (MD) | Cal Poly-SLO | WI-Green Bay |
| 1982 | District of Columbia | 73-63 | Florida Southern | Kentucky Wesleyan | Cal St-Bakersfield |
| 1983 | Wright St | 92-73 | District of Columbia | *Cal St-Bakersfield | *Morningside |
| 1984 | Central Missouri St | 81-77 | St Augustine's | *Kentucky Wesleyan | *N Alabama |
| 1985 | Jacksonville St | 74-73 | S Dakota St | *Kentucky Wesleyan | *Mount St Mary's (MD) |
| 1986 | Sacred Heart | 93-87 | SE Missouri St | *Cheyney | *Florida Southern |
| 1987 | Kentucky Wesleyan | 92-74 | Gannon | *Delta St | *Eastern Montana |

| Year | Winner | Score | Runner-up | Third Place | Fourth Place |
|------|--------|-------|-----------|-------------|--------------|
| 1988 | Lowell | 75-72 | AK-Anchorage | Florida Southern | Troy St |
| 1989 | N Carolina Central | 73-46 | SE Missouri St | UC-Riverside | Jacksonville St |
| 1990 | Kentucky Wesleyan | 93-79 | Cal St-Bakersfield | N Dakota | Morehouse |
| 1991 | N Alabama | 79-72 | Bridgeport (CT) | *Cal St-Bakersfield | *Virginia Union |
| 1992 | Virginia Union | 100-75 | Bridgeport (CT) | *Cal St-Bakersfield | *California (PA) |
| 1993 | Cal St-Bakersfield | 85-72 | Troy St (AL) | *New Hampshire Coll | *Wayne St (MI) |
| 1994 | Cal St-Bakersfield | 92-86 | Southern Indiana | *New Hampshire Coll | *Washburn |
| 1995 | Southern Indiana | 71-63 | UC-Riverside | *Norfolk St | *Indiana (PA) |

*Indicates tied for third. †Student-athletes representing American International in 1969 and Southwestern Louisiana in 1971 were declared ineligible subsequent to the tournament. Under NCAA rules, the teams' and ineligible student-athletes' records were deleted, and the teams' places in the final standings were vacated.

# NCAA Division II Men's Alltime Individual Leaders

### SINGLE-GAME SCORING HIGHS

| Pts | Player and Team vs Opponent | Date |
|-----|------------------------------|------|
| 113 | Bevo Francis, Rio Grande vs Hillsdale | 1954 |
| 84 | Bevo Francis, Rio Grande vs Alliance | 1954 |
| 82 | Bevo Francis, Rio Grande vs Bluffton | 1954 |
| 80 | Paul Crissman, Southern Cal Col vs Pacific Christian | 1966 |
| 77 | William English, Winston-Salem vs Fayetteville St | 1968 |

## Season Records

### SCORING AVERAGE

| Player and Team | Year | GP | FG | FT | Pts | Avg |
|-----------------|------|----|----|----|-----|-----|
| Bevo Francis, Rio Grande | 1954 | 27 | 444 | 367 | 1255 | 46.5 |
| Earl Glass, Mississippi Industrial | 1963 | 19 | 322 | 171 | 815 | 42.9 |
| Earl Monroe, Winston-Salem | 1967 | 32 | 509 | 311 | 1329 | 41.5 |
| John Rinka, Kenyon | 1970 | 23 | 354 | 234 | 942 | 41.0 |
| Willie Shaw, Lane | 1964 | 18 | 303 | 121 | 727 | 40.4 |

### REBOUND AVERAGE

| Player and Team | Year | GP | Reb | Avg |
|-----------------|------|----|-----|-----|
| Tom Hart, Middlebury | 1956 | 21 | 620 | 29.5 |
| Tom Hart, Middlebury | 1955 | 22 | 649 | 29.5 |
| Frank Stronczek, American Int'l | 1966 | 26 | 717 | 27.6 |
| R.C. Owens, College of Idaho | 1954 | 25 | 677 | 27.1 |
| Maurice Stokes, St Francis (PA) | 1954 | 26 | 689 | 26.5 |

### ASSISTS

| Player and Team | Year | GP | A |
|-----------------|------|----|----|
| Steve Ray, Bridgeport | 1989 | 32 | 400 |
| Steve Ray, Bridgeport | 1990 | 33 | 385 |
| Tony Smith, Pfeiffer | 1992 | 35 | 349 |
| Jim Ferrer, Bentley | 1989 | 31 | 309 |
| Brian Gregory, Oakland | 1989 | 28 | 300 |

### ASSIST AVERAGE

| Player and Team | Year | GP | A | Avg |
|-----------------|------|----|----|-----|
| Steve Ray, Bridgeport | 1989 | 32 | 400 | 12.5 |
| Steve Ray, Bridgeport | 1990 | 33 | 385 | 11.7 |
| Demetri Beekman, Assumption | 1993 | 23 | 264 | 11.5 |
| Ernest Jenkins, NM Highlands | 1995 | 27 | 291 | 10.8 |
| Brian Gregory, Oakland | 1989 | 28 | 300 | 10.7 |

### FIELD-GOAL PERCENTAGE

| Player and Team | Year | Pct |
|-----------------|------|-----|
| Todd Linder, Tampa | 1987 | 75.2 |
| Maurice Stafford, N Alabama | 1984 | 75.0 |
| Matthew Cornegay, Tuskegee | 1982 | 74.8 |
| Brian Moten, W Georgia | 1992 | 73.4 |
| Ed Phillips, Alabama A&M | 1968 | 73.3 |

### FREE-THROW PERCENTAGE

| Player and Team | Year | Pct |
|-----------------|------|-----|
| Billy Newton, Morgan St | 1976 | 94.4 |
| Kent Andrews, McNeese St | 1968 | 94.4 |
| Mike Sanders, Northern Colorado | 1987 | 94.3 |
| Jay Harrie, E Montana | 1994 | 93.5 |
| Joe Cullen, Hartwick | 1969 | 93.2 |

## Career Records

### POINTS

| Player and Team | Yrs | Pts |
|---|---|---|
| Travis Grant, Kentucky St | 1969-72 | 4045 |
| Bob Hopkins, Grambling | 1953-56 | 3759 |
| Tony Smith, Pfeiffer | 1989-92 | 3350 |
| Earnest Lee, Clark Atlanta | 1984-87 | 3298 |
| Joe Miller, Alderson-Broaddus | 1954-57 | 3294 |

### CAREER SCORING AVERAGE

| Player and Team | Yrs | GP | Pts | Avg |
|---|---|---|---|---|
| Travis Grant, Kentucky St | 1969-72 | 121 | 4045 | 33.4 |
| John Rinka, Kenyon | 1967-70 | 99 | 3251 | 32.8 |
| Florindo Vieira, Quinnipiac | 1954-57 | 69 | 2263 | 32.8 |
| Willie Shaw, Lane | 1961-64 | 76 | 2379 | 31.3 |
| Mike Davis, Virginia Union | 1966-69 | 89 | 2758 | 31.0 |

### REBOUND AVERAGE

| Player and Team | Yrs | GP | Reb | Avg |
|---|---|---|---|---|
| Tom Hart, Middlebury | 1953, 55-56 | 63 | 1738 | 27.6 |
| Maurice Stokes, St Francis (PA) | 1953-55 | 72 | 1812 | 25.2 |
| Frank Stronczek, American Int'l | 1965-67 | 62 | 1549 | 25.0 |
| Bill Thieben, Hofstra | 1954-56 | 76 | 1837 | 24.2 |
| Hank Brown, Lowell Tech | 1965-67 | 49 | 1129 | 23.0 |

### ASSISTS

| Player and Team | Yrs | A |
|---|---|---|
| Demetri Beekman, Assumption | 1990-93 | 1044 |
| Rob Paternostro, New Hamp Coll | 1992-95 | 919 |
| Gallagher Driscoll, St Rose | 1989-92 | 878 |
| Tony Smith, Pfeiffer | 1989-92 | 828 |
| Steve Ray, Bridgeport | 1989-90 | 785 |

### ASSIST AVERAGE

| Player and Team | Yrs | GP | A | Avg |
|---|---|---|---|---|
| Steve Ray, Bridgeport | 1989-90 | 65 | 785 | 12.1 |
| Demetri Beekman, Assumption | 1990-93 | 119 | 1044 | 8.8 |
| Ernest Jenkins, NM Highlands | 1992-95 | 84 | 699 | 8.3 |
| Mark Benson, Texas A&I | 1989-91 | 86 | 674 | 7.8 |
| Pat Madden, Jacksonville St | 1989-91 | 88 | 688 | 7.8 |

Note: Minimum 550 Assists.

### FIELD-GOAL PERCENTAGE

| Player and Team | Yrs | Pct |
|---|---|---|
| Todd Linder, Tampa | 1984-87 | 70.8 |
| Tom Schurfranz, Bellarmine | 1989-92 | 70.2 |
| Chad Scott, California (PA) | 1991-94 | 70.0 |
| Ed Phillips, Alabama, A&M | 1968-71 | 68.9 |
| Ulysses Hackett, SC-Spartanburg | 1990-92 | 67.9 |

Note: Minimum 400 FGM.

### FREE-THROW PERCENTAGE

| Player and Team | Yrs | Pct |
|---|---|---|
| Kent Andrews, McNeese St | 1967-69 | 91.6 |
| Jon Hagen, Mankato St | 1963-65 | 90.0 |
| Dave Reynolds, Davis & Elkins | 1986-89 | 89.3 |
| Terry Gill, New Orleans | 1972-74 | 88.2 |
| Tony Budzik, Mansfield | 1989-92 | 88.2 |

Note: Minimum 250 FTM.

# NCAA Division III Men's Championship Results

| Year | Winner | Score | Runner-up | Third Place | Fourth Place |
|---|---|---|---|---|---|
| 1975 | LeMoyne-Owen | 57-54 | Glassboro St | Augustana (IL) | Brockport St |
| 1976 | Scranton | 60-57 | Wittenberg | Augustana (IL) | Plattsburgh St |
| 1977 | Wittenberg | 79-66 | Oneonta St | Scranton | Hamline |
| 1978 | North Park | 69-57 | Widener | Albion | Stony Brook |
| 1979 | North Park | 66-62 | Potsdam St | Franklin & Marshall | Centre |
| 1980 | North Park | 83-76 | Upsala | Wittenberg | Longwood |
| 1981 | Potsdam St | 67-65 (OT) | Augustana (IL) | Ursinus | Otterbein |
| 1982 | Wabash | 83-62 | Potsdam St | Brooklyn | Cal St-Stanislaus |
| 1983 | Scranton | 64-63 | Wittenberg | Roanoke | WI-Whitewater |
| 1984 | WI-Whitewater | 103-86 | Clark (MA) | DePauw | Upsala |
| 1985 | North Park | 72-71 | Potsdam St | Nebraska Wesleyan | Widener |
| 1986 | Potsdam St | 76-73 | LeMoyne-Owen | Nebraska Wesleyan | Jersey City St |
| 1987 | North Park | 106-100 | Clark (MA) | Wittenberg | Stockton St |
| 1988 | Ohio Wesleyan | 92-70 | Scranton | Nebraska Wesleyan | Hartwick |
| 1989 | WI-Whitewater | 94-86 | Trenton St | Southern Maine | Centre |
| 1990 | Rochester | 43-42 | DePauw | Washington (MD) | Calvin |
| 1991 | WI-Platteville | 81-74 | Franklin & Marshall | Otterbein | Ramapo (NJ) |
| 1992 | Calvin | 62-49 | Rochester | WI-Platteville | Jersey City St |
| 1993 | Ohio Northern | 71-68 | Augustana | Mass-Dartmouth | Rowan |
| 1994 | Lebanon Valley Coll | 66-59 (OT) | New York University | Wittenberg | St Thomas (MN) |
| 1995 | WI-Platteville | 69-55 | Manchester | Rowan | Trinity (CT) |

# NCAA Division III Men's Alltime Individual Leaders

## SINGLE-GAME SCORING HIGHS

| Pts | Player and Team vs Opponent | Year |
|---|---|---|
| 69 | Steve Diekmann, Grinnell vs Simpson | 1995 |
| 63 | Joe DeRoche, Thomas vs St Joseph's (ME) | 1988 |
| 62 | Shannon Lilly, Bishop vs Southwest Assembly of God | 1983 |
| 61 | Steve Honderd, Calvin vs Kalamazoo | 1993 |
| 61 | Dana Wilson, Husson vs Ricker | 1974 |

## Season Records

### SCORING AVERAGE

| Player and Team | Year | GP | FG | FT | Pts | Avg |
|---|---|---|---|---|---|---|
| Steve Diekmann, Grinnell | 1995 | 20 | 223 | 162 | 745 | 37.3 |
| Rickey Sutton, Lyndon St | 1976 | 14 | 207 | 93 | 507 | 36.2 |
| Shannon Lilly, Bishop | 1983 | 26 | 345 | 218 | 908 | 34.9 |
| Dana Wilson, Husson | 1974 | 20 | 288 | 122 | 698 | 34.9 |
| Rickey Sutton, Lyndon St | 1977 | 16 | 223 | 112 | 558 | 34.9 |

### REBOUND AVERAGE

| Player and Team | Year | GP | Reb | Avg |
|---|---|---|---|---|
| Joe Manley, Bowie St | 1976 | 29 | 579 | 20.0 |
| Fred Petty, New Hampshire College | 1974 | 22 | 436 | 19.8 |
| Larry Williams, Pratt | 1977 | 24 | 457 | 19.0 |
| Charles Greer, Thomas | 1977 | 17 | 318 | 18.7 |
| Larry Parker, Plattsburgh St | 1975 | 23 | 430 | 18.7 |

### ASSISTS

| Player and Team | Year | GP | A |
|---|---|---|---|
| Robert James, Kean | 1989 | 29 | 391 |
| Ricky Spicer, WI-Whitewater | 1989 | 31 | 295 |
| Joe Marcotte, New Jersey Tech | 1995 | 30 | 292 |
| Ron Torgalski, Hamilton | 1989 | 26 | 275 |
| Albert Kirchner, Mt St Vincent | 1990 | 24 | 267 |

### ASSIST AVERAGE

| Player and Team | Year | GP | A | Avg |
|---|---|---|---|---|
| Robert James, Kean | 1989 | 29 | 391 | 13.5 |
| Albert Kirchner, Mt St Vincent | 1990 | 24 | 267 | 11.1 |
| Ron Torgalski, Hamilton | 1989 | 26 | 275 | 10.6 |
| Louis Adams, Rust | 1989 | 22 | 227 | 10.3 |
| Eric Johnson, Coe | 1991 | 24 | 238 | 9.9 |

### FIELD-GOAL PERCENTAGE

| Player and Team | Year | Pct |
|---|---|---|
| Travis Weiss, St John's (MN) | 1994 | 76.6 |
| Pete Metzelaars, Wabash | 1982 | 75.3 |
| Tony Rychlec, Mass Maritime | 1981 | 74.9 |
| Tony Rychlec, Mass Maritime | 1982 | 73.1 |
| Russ Newnan, Menlo | 1991 | 73.0 |

### FREE-THROW PERCENTAGE

| Player and Team | Year | Pct |
|---|---|---|
| Andy Enfield, Johns Hopkins | 1991 | 95.3 |
| Yudi Teichman, Yeshiva | 1989 | 95.2 |
| Chris Carideo, Widener | 1992 | 95.2 |
| Mike Scheib, Susquehanna | 1977 | 94.1 |
| Jason Prevenost, Middlebury | 1994 | 93.8 |

## Career Records

### POINTS

| Player and Team | Yrs | Pts |
|---|---|---|
| Andre Foreman, Salisbury St | 1989-92 | 2940 |
| Lamont Strothers, Chris Newport | 1988-91 | 2709 |
| Matt Hancock, Colby | 1987-90 | 2678 |
| Scott Fitch, Geneseo St | 1990-94 | 2634 |
| Greg Grant, Trenton St | 1987-89 | 2611 |

### CAREER SCORING AVERAGE

| Player and Team | Yrs | GP | Avg |
|---|---|---|---|
| Dwain Govan, Bishop | 1974-75 | 55 | 32.8 |
| Dave Russell, Shepherd | 1974-75 | 60 | 30.6 |
| Rickey Sutton, Lyndon St | 1976-79 | 80 | 29.7 |
| John Atkins, Knoxville | 1976-78 | 70 | 28.7 |
| Jeff deLaveaga, Cal Lutheran | 1989-92 | 80 | 28.1 |

### REBOUND AVERAGE

| Player and Team | Yrs | GP | Reb | Avg |
|---|---|---|---|---|
| Larry Parker, Plattsburgh St | 1975-78 | 85 | 1482 | 17.4 |
| Charles Greer, Thomas | 1975-77 | 58 | 926 | 16.0 |
| Willie Parr, LeMoyne-Owen | 1974-76 | 76 | 1182 | 15.6 |
| Michael Smith, Hamilton | 1989-92 | 107 | 1632 | 15.2 |
| Dave Kufeld, Yeshiva | 1977-80 | 81 | 1222 | 15.1 |

### ASSIST AVERAGE

| Player and Team | Yrs | Avg |
|---|---|---|
| Steve Artis, Chris. Newport | 1990-93 | 8.1 |
| David Genovese, Mt St Vincent | 1992-95 | 7.5 |
| Kevin Root, Eureka | 1989-91 | 7.1 |
| Dennis Jacobi, Bowdoin | 1989-92 | 7.1 |
| Eric Johnson, Coe | 1989-92 | 7.1 |
| Pat Skerry, Tufts | 1989-92 | 6.6 |

# Hockey

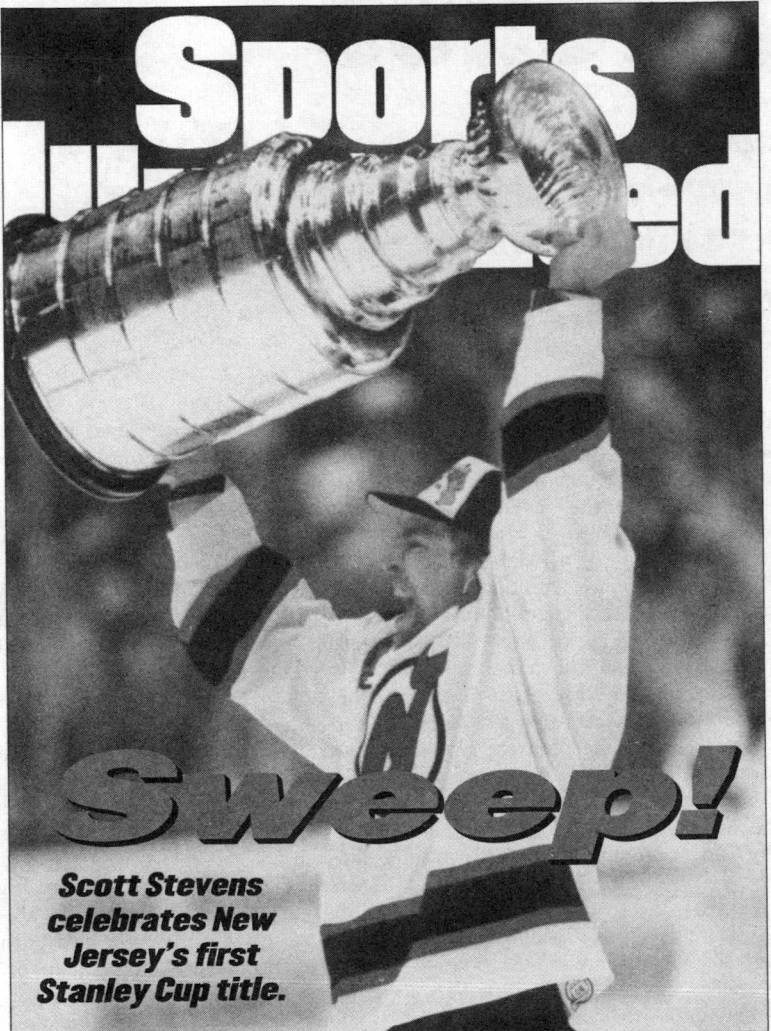

Sweep!

Scott Stevens celebrates New Jersey's first Stanley Cup title.

LOU CAPOZZOLA

# A Devilish Defense

## Employing the confounding—some say boring—neutral-zone trap, the New Jersey Devils won their first Stanley Cup

### by Michael Farber

THE MOST aggravating of National Hockey League seasons belonged to the swamp-dwellin', trap-playin', low-payin' New Jersey Devils, the best, and most aggravating, team in hockey.

The season began with a 103-day lockout and featured more interference than Bill Clinton gets from the Republican Congress. High-flying action was choked by the neutral-zone trap, and the game's top line was the Maginot Line. The playoff picture threatened to degenerate into a full-scale game of franchise roulette and the playoffs themselves failed to offer a single seven-game series after the first round. In view of all this, there was no more appropriate Stanley Cup champion than the little-loved Devils.

The Devils, the third franchise in the New York area in terms of history and, until recently, fan support, are an iron-on patch on the fabric of New Jersey life—a team that seems to be from the state but not of the state. These Rand-McNallys of the rink began life in 1974 as the Kansas City

Scouts, transmogrified two seasons later into the Colorado Rockies (a team so egregiously pathetic it gave an entire mountain range a bad name), skedaddled to the Meadowlands in 1982 and, as they neared their crowning moment, seemed headed to the hockey hotbed of Nashville. (A new lease agreed upon after the playoffs by owner John McMullen and the New Jersey Sports and Exposition Authority averted the move.) As rumors about an imminent departure swirled during the final against Detroit, the nonplussed Devils rallied behind brilliant sophomore goaltender Martin Brodeur, defenseman Scott Stevens and rightwinger Claude Lemieux to sweep the Red Wings.

If the NHL was going to have an anti-season, there was no worthier playoff MVP than the game's ultimate anti-hero, Lemieux. The playoffs always have brought out the overachiever in Lemieux, once named the most hated player in hockey. He scored two overtime winners in his rookie season with the 1986 Montreal Canadiens,

and the player who personifies chalk squealing on a blackboard has been as much Mr. May as Mr. Mayhem ever since. Lemieux, who ranks 30th in career playoff goals with 52, wound up putting the con back in Conn Smythe by scoring 13 playoff goals in 20 games (including three winners) and checking mercilessly after a somnambulant regular season in which he scored six goals in 45 games, had a protracted contract dispute and was nearly traded.

Just two of Lemieux's goals came in the finals, but it hardly mattered because 17 different Devils contributed points in the four games. Their depth was as overwhelming as their selflessness. While the Devils lack the copious talent that might brand them as a dynasty, they do have a blueprint for success—size and speed—in a league where hooking, holding and interference are commonplace. The Devils, whose forwards were a half inch taller and nine pounds heavier than the preternaturally skilled Red Wings, dominated a team that had lost just twice in three playoff rounds. Because they did not

**The scrappy Lemieux (22) elevated his game for the playoffs, scoring 13 goals, including three game-winners.**

see Detroit during the season—the truncated 48-game schedule had no interconference play—the Devils were apprehensive about facing Team Octopus. At least for the first 10 minutes of Game 1. "We heard how good they were," said Devil center Bob Carpenter, one of 11 U.S.-born players on the team, a strikingly high number in a league which takes just 18% of its players from the lower 48. "But in those 10 minutes, we found out we could play with them, we could check them."

"I thought our guys deserved a little more [respect] from their opponents," New Jersey coach Jacques Lemaire said. "That's the one reason our guys were aggressive on the ice. They showed up every game mad. They wanted to win because they got no credit. It's great to see a bunch of guys play together and score more than the guys with talent."

Lemaire is a hockey purist, a coach who

lives for the 60 minutes but none of the other, if you will pardon the expression, trappings of big-time hockey. If it were up to him, Lemaire probably would coach in a hermetically sealed laboratory, which, until recently, was an apt description of the Meadowlands. Lemaire installed the trap, hockey's latest four-letter word. Of course Lemaire didn't invent this forechecking system, which forces the opposing puck carrier to the boards and then floods center ice with defenders who cut off passing lanes. "Montreal trapped for 23 Cups," Calgary Flame coach Pierre Pagé said. But unlike the 17 other teams that employed the trap in 1995, the Devils played it with an uncommon verve, using their defense to create offense. If the Devil trap seemed dull, at its best it was no more boring than the Chicago Bear 46 defense of the mid-1980s. Still

styles make hockey matches as surely as they make fights, and some officials were concerned that games between trapping teams would take the NHL to the yawn of a new era, death for a league in which 65% of revenues are generated at the gate. Pagé predicted the proliferation of the trap would follow a Devil victory, but early indications are the trap has reached a plateau. Trapmeister Roger Neilson, whose upstart Florida Panthers missed the playoffs by one point their first two years by utilizing the most cautious, stultifying forecheck in the NHL, was fired after the season.

The Red Wings, who have not won the Cup since 1955, were the Devils' antithesis, the rare team capable of playing firewagon hockey in the year when swamp hockey was the rage. But even Detroit tightened up considerably from its old devil-may-care

## Game On, for Now

In the year of labor pains for North American sports, the game that once had the coziest relationship between owners and players was not immune to a work stoppage.

The kid gloves were dropped early in the 103-day National Hockey League lockout when Chicago Blackhawk defenseman Chris Chelios said he wouldn't be surprised if someone tried to hurt Commissioner Gary Bettman, a suggestion that usually comes from those serving a few years in medium-security facilities rather than two minutes in penalty boxes. Bettman brushed off the implied threat, and, of course, hockey survived the craziness, too. The season, which finally began on Jan. 20, was pared to 48 games, and the playoffs ran until June 24—Game 7 of the Stanley Cup final was scheduled for June 30— but hockey's natural rhythms returned for the 1995–96 season. Although either side can reopen it after the 1997–98 season, the six-year contract proved that a) players don't necessarily have to win a

labor dispute, and b) the gestation period for a collective bargaining agreement in hockey is shorter than in baseball.

The battlegrounds of the baseball strike and the hockey lockout were similar: the salary cap and its more subtle sibling, the luxury tax. As they wrestled with their own profligacy and mushrooming salaries—the St. Louis Blues' payroll shot up from $3.5 million in 1989–90 to $23 million in 1995—owners viewed a salary cap or luxury tax as a fail safe system that would control labor costs. But the National Hockey League Players Association carved a line in the ice, insisting it would abide neither. The association stood steadfast on the cap/tax, except in the case of rookies, but it yielded so much in the areas of free agency and arbitration that its victory was Pyrrhic.

The toll:
•Elimination of restricted free agency for players with less than three years experience;

style with a system known as the left wing lock. A forward, usually a leftwinger, would hang back near the attacking blue line, playing almost like a third defenseman, to prevent the odd-man breaks that had made the Wings first-round playoff victims the previous two springs. Coach Scott Bowman did an extraordinary job selling a new style to a veteran team, getting the Wings to rein in some of their offensive instincts and prodding roving defenseman Paul Coffey to take care of his own end first. Detroit had the best regular-season record with 70 points, and Coffey, who last won the Norris Trophy in 1986, was voted the league's best defenseman; the stretch of nine years between major awards is the third longest in NHL history.

Detroit disposed of Dallas in five games in the first round

and then whipped San Jose 6–0, 6–2, 6–2, 6–2 in what reads in agate type like a bad tennis match. The Red Wings eliminated Chicago in the Western Conference final in a Hobbesian series: nasty, brutish and short (five games). Despite the efficiency with which the Red Wings barged into the final, they were banged up against New Jersey, especially at center. Steve Yzerman needed arthroscopic surgery on his knee after the San Jose series. Sergei Fedorov suffered a separated shoulder in Game 3 against Chicago and returned for Game 5 only after prodding by teammate Slava Fetisov. But the biggest Wing loss might have been Keith Primeau, who injured his oblique muscles in his side in the opener against

DAMIAN STROHMEYER

**In his second year at the helm Bettman negotiated some very rough waters.**

• A rookie salary cap of $850,000, the death knell for mind-boggling inflationary deals like the five-year, $12.25 million contract No. 1 draft pick Alexandre Daigle signed with Ottawa in 1993;

• No salary arbitration for the first five years; owners can walk away from three arbitration awards in a two-year period;

• Mandatory two-way contracts (a player takes a salary cut if he is sent to the minors);

• Players now can become unrestricted free agents at 32, but with lower entry-level pay and reduced possibilities for arbitration, veterans' salaries are expected to rise more slowly. Since 1989 the average salary has exploded from $232,000 to $733,000 last season.

The players ratified the deal on Jan. 13—Friday the 13th, naturally. At a press conference Bettman and Bob Goodenow, the players' association executive director, donned black hats emblazoned with GAME ON, a slogan borrowed from the movie *Wayne's World*. "Sure," Goodenow said, "concessions were made, but the game's in a position to go forward." Party on, Bob. Party on, Gary.

New Jersey. The 6'5½", 215-pounder had been the dominant player in the grinding series against Chicago, a breakout five games for Primeau that established him as a player to watch.

As size assumes a premium place in the pantheon of NHL attributes for the first time since the Broad Street Bullies era, it is fitting that the biggest of the big boys is in Philadelphia. Eric Lindros is maybe an inch shorter than Primeau, but he is as thick as a sequoia and as artful a passer as any behemoth ever to play the game. After two injury-marred seasons—greatness postponed—Lindros became the NHL's poster

**Talented, tenacious and telegenic: Lindros emerged as the superstar to carry the NHL into the 21st century.**

boy in 1995, a star capable of carrying the league on his hopelessly broad shoulders for the next decade. He is the package: mean, tough, smart, telegenic, well-spoken. And English is his first language, a fact not lost on a league that has had to count on Europeans for its flair the past few seasons. The NHL remains a league of teams and not of players, but in terms of its marketing for the rest of the decade, NHL might as well stand for Now Here's Lindros. "The best player in the world," Buffalo general manager John Muckler raved. Flyer teammate Shawn Antoski said, "There's no one else out there capable of scoring 50 goals and using you as a speed bump." Lindros, who tied Pittsburgh's Jaromir Jagr with 70 points but lost the scoring title because Jagr had 32 goals to his 29, won the first of what figures to be a string of Hart Trophies. Lindros was flanked on the Legion of Doom by Mikael Renberg (6'1", 218) and John Leclair (6'2", 219). Leclair came in February from Montreal with Eric Desjardins, who was the Flyers' best defenseman, as part of a package for rightwinger Mark Recchi, a no-brainer as Most Lopsided Trade of the Year. Managing director Serge Savard now must rebuild the Canadiens, who failed to make the playoffs for the first time in a quarter of a century. Savard has practice; with one trade he rebuilt the Flyers.

The Flyers breezed into the Stanley Cup semifinals by brushing aside the New York Rangers in four games. The Rangers' Stanley Cup jinx now stands at one year. After ending a 54-year Cup drought the previous spring, the Rangers were a shadow of their dynamic and committed championship team. Indeed, New York was fortunate to even make the playoffs, slipping into the final spot in the Eastern Conference with 47 points. Goalie Mike Richter and defenseman Brian Leetch slipped, and many of New York's gritty players, including Esa Tikkanen, were exiled and replaced by able but inconsistent will-o'-the-wisps such as Petr Nedved. Only Mark Messier seemed to soldier on under Colin Campbell, who did not have the presence of former coach Mike Keenan.

Of course, few do. After winning the Cup Keenan lammed it to St. Louis, where, as coach and general manager, he began stockpiling veterans with Stanley Cup rings. Keenan and the Blues' deep pockets—the payroll reached $23 million last season—were supposed to produce immediate fireworks if not a Stanley Cup. Alas, the Blues were a dud. Not only did St. Louis lose to Vancouver in the first round, but there were also only a few of the contretemps surrounding a Keenan team that always provide dubious entertainment value. Keenan got along famously with his best scorer, Brett Hull, but clashed with Brendan Shanahan, a star power forward, and Curtis Joseph, a past playoff hero. They were traded during a wild summer in St. Louis as the Blues signed free agents Grant Fuhr, Dale Hawerchuk and Geoff Courtnall and acquired, among others, Shayne Corson and Chris Pronger. Keenan was on the prowl for "Mike kind of guys." The Blues finished with a creditable 61 points in 1995 and should be better in 1996, although the pregame introductions will be for the players' benefit as much as the fans'. This franchise takes some getting used to.

Hockey fans also will have to get used to the idea that Wayne Gretzky is mortal. Considering that the Great One owns every NHL career scoring record, this might be difficult. But Gretzky, who turned 34 last January, averaged (just!) one point per game in 1995, an estimable figure for almost anyone except a legend who entered the season averaging 2.185 points per game. Stuck on a mediocre Los Angeles King team with muddled ownership, Gretzky's genius came in flashes instead of in the floodlights. Perhaps the return of scoring rival Mario Lemieux to Pittsburgh in 1996—Lemieux skipped 1995 because of a bad back—and new coach Larry Robinson will lift Gretzky.

One team on the rise in 1995 was the Quebec Nordiques. They went from 300 feet above sea level to a mile high, moving to Denver when Marcel Aubut's ownership group sold them to COMSAT for $75 million after the season. The inevitable dividends of the Nordiques' ineptitude—since 1986 they drafted lower than 10th just once—finally paid off under rookie coach Marc Crawford, the Coach of the Year. The quicksilver Nordiques won the Eastern Conference with 65 points before losing to the Rangers in the first round. As the Denver Avalanche, the artists formerly known

**Quebec fans will miss Rookie of the Year Forsberg and the rest of the Nordiques, who are bound for Denver.**

as the Nordiques have a nucleus that should make it the most exciting team of the late 1990s. Peter Forsberg, who had been called the best player not in the league, had a brilliant first NHL season, beating out Washington goalie Jim Carey, a March call-up, and Anaheim left wing Paul Kariya as Rookie of the Year.

The defection of the Nordiques and a last-minute and perhaps temporary reprieve for the seemingly Minneapolis-bound Winnipeg Jets sent a chill through the Great White North. Canada, victimized by its weak dollar (relative to the U.S. buck) and the smaller economy of scale, sensed that it was losing its game to the Americans. Attendance problems in many Canadian cities were attributed to lingering resentment over the lockout. Commissioner Gary Bettman said Canada will always be an important part of the NHL, and the league has vowed to tackle the discrepancies between currencies and a growing gap between haves and have-nots. But pessimists, including Hall of Famer Guy Lafleur, have predicted that of the seven remaining Canadian franchises, only Toronto and Montreal will still be in the NHL in 10 years. Woe, Canada.

## NHL Final Team Standings

### Western Conference

#### CENTRAL DIVISION

| | GP | W | L | T | GF | GA | Pts |
|---|---|---|---|---|---|---|---|
| Detroit | 48 | 33 | 11 | 4 | 180 | 117 | 70 |
| St Louis | 48 | 28 | 15 | 5 | 178 | 135 | 61 |
| Chicago | 48 | 24 | 19 | 5 | 156 | 115 | 53 |
| Toronto | 48 | 21 | 19 | 8 | 135 | 146 | 50 |
| Dallas | 48 | 17 | 23 | 8 | 136 | 135 | 42 |
| Winnipeg | 48 | 16 | 25 | 7 | 157 | 177 | 39 |

#### PACIFIC DIVISION

| | GP | W | L | T | GF | GA | Pts |
|---|---|---|---|---|---|---|---|
| Calgary | 48 | 24 | 17 | 7 | 163 | 135 | 55 |
| Vancouver | 48 | 18 | 18 | 12 | 153 | 148 | 48 |
| San Jose | 48 | 19 | 25 | 4 | 129 | 161 | 42 |
| Los Angeles | 48 | 16 | 23 | 9 | 142 | 174 | 41 |
| Edmonton | 48 | 17 | 27 | 4 | 136 | 183 | 38 |
| Anaheim | 48 | 16 | 27 | 5 | 125 | 164 | 37 |

### Eastern Conference

#### NORTHEAST DIVISION

| | GP | W | L | T | GF | GA | Pts |
|---|---|---|---|---|---|---|---|
| Quebec | 48 | 30 | 13 | 5 | 185 | 134 | 65 |
| Pittsburgh | 48 | 29 | 16 | 3 | 181 | 158 | 61 |
| Boston | 48 | 27 | 18 | 3 | 150 | 127 | 57 |
| Buffalo | 48 | 22 | 19 | 7 | 130 | 119 | 51 |
| Hartford | 48 | 19 | 24 | 5 | 127 | 141 | 43 |
| Montreal | 48 | 18 | 23 | 7 | 125 | 148 | 43 |
| Ottawa | 48 | 9 | 34 | 5 | 117 | 174 | 23 |

#### ATLANTIC DIVISION

| | GP | W | L | T | GF | GA | Pts |
|---|---|---|---|---|---|---|---|
| Philadelphia | 48 | 28 | 16 | 4 | 150 | 132 | 60 |
| New Jersey | 48 | 22 | 18 | 8 | 136 | 121 | 52 |
| Washington | 48 | 22 | 18 | 8 | 136 | 120 | 52 |
| NY Rangers | 48 | 22 | 23 | 3 | 139 | 134 | 47 |
| Florida | 48 | 20 | 22 | 6 | 115 | 127 | 46 |
| Tampa Bay | 48 | 17 | 28 | 3 | 120 | 144 | 37 |
| NY Islanders | 48 | 15 | 28 | 5 | 126 | 158 | 35 |

## 1995 Stanley Cup Playoffs

EASTERN CONFERENCE — QUARTERFINALS · SEMI-FINALS · CONFERENCE FINAL

WESTERN CONFERENCE — CONFERENCE FINAL · SEMI-FINALS · QUARTERFINALS

**STANLEY CUP**

**New Jersey (4-0)**

Eastern Conference:
- NY Rangers
- Quebec → NY Rangers (4-2)
- Buffalo
- Philadelphia → Philadelphia (4-1) → Philadelphia (4-0)
- Washington
- Pittsburgh → Pittsburgh (4-3) → New Jersey (4-2)
- New Jersey
- Boston → New Jersey (4-1) → New Jersey (4-1)

Western Conference:
- Dallas
- Detroit → Detroit (4-1) → Detroit (4-0)
- San Jose
- Calgary → San Jose (4-3) → Detroit (4-1)
- Vancouver
- St Louis → Vancouver (4-3) → Chicago (4-0)
- Toronto
- Chicago → Chicago (4-0)

## Stanley Cup Playoff Results

### Conference Quarterfinals

#### EASTERN CONFERENCE

| | | | | | | | |
|---|---|---|---|---|---|---|---|
| May 6 | NY Rangers | 4 | at Quebec | 5 | | | |
| May 8 | NY Rangers | 8 | at Quebec | 3 | | | |
| May 10 | Quebec | 3 | at NY Rangers | 4 | | | |
| May 12 | Quebec | 2 | at NY Rangers | 3* | | | |
| May 14 | NY Rangers | 2 | at Quebec | 4 | | | |
| May 16 | Quebec | 2 | at NY Rangers | 4 | | | |

NY Rangers won series 4-2.

| | | | | | |
|---|---|---|---|---|---|
| May 7 | Buffalo | 3 | at Philadelphia | 4* |
| May 8 | Buffalo | 1 | at Philadelphia | 3 |
| May 10 | Philadelphia | 1 | at Buffalo | 3 |
| May 12 | Philadelphia | 4 | at Buffalo | 2 |
| May 14 | Buffalo | 4 | at Philadelphia | 6 |

Philadelphia won series 4-1.

## Conference Quarterfinals *(Cont.)*

### EASTERN CONFERENCE *(Cont.)*

| | | | | | | | | |
|---|---|---|---|---|---|---|---|---|
| May 6 | Washington | 5 | at Pittsburgh | 4 | May 7 | New Jersey | 5 | at Boston | 0 |
| May 8 | Washington | 3 | at Pittsburgh | 5 | May 8 | New Jersey | 3 | at Boston | 0 |
| May 10 | Pittsburgh | 2 | at Washington | 6 | May 10 | Boston | 3 | at New Jersey | 2 |
| May 12 | Pittsburgh | 2 | at Washington | 6 | May 12 | Boston | 0 | at New Jersey | 1* |
| May 14 | Washington | 5 | at Pittsburgh | 6* | May 14 | New Jersey | 3 | at Boston | 2 |
| May 16 | Pittsburgh | 7 | at Washington | 1 | | New Jersey won series 4-1. | | | |
| May 18 | Washington | 0 | at Pittsburgh | 3 | | | | | |
| | Pittsburgh won series 4-3. | | | | | | | | |

### WESTERN CONFERENCE

| | | | | | | | | |
|---|---|---|---|---|---|---|---|---|
| May 7 | Dallas | 3 | at Detroit | 4 | May 7 | San Jose | 5 | at Calgary | 4 |
| May 9 | Dallas | 1 | at Detroit | 4 | May 9 | San Jose | 5 | at Calgary | 4* |
| May 11 | Detroit | 5 | at Dallas | 1 | May 11 | Calgary | 9 | at San Jose | 2 |
| May 14 | Detroit | 1 | at Dallas | 4 | May 13 | Calgary | 6 | at San Jose | 4 |
| May 15 | Dallas | 1 | at Detroit | 3 | May 15 | San Jose | 0 | at Calgary | 5 |
| | Detroit won series 4-1. | | | | May 17 | Calgary | 3 | at San Jose | 5 |
| | | | | | May 19 | San Jose | 5 | at Calgary | 4† |
| | | | | | | San Jose won series 4-3. | | | |

| | | | | | | | | |
|---|---|---|---|---|---|---|---|---|
| May 7 | Vancouver | 1 | at St Louis | 2 | May 7 | Toronto | 5 | at Chicago | 3 |
| May 9 | Vancouver | 5 | at St Louis | 3 | May 9 | Toronto | 3 | at Chicago | 0 |
| May 11 | St Louis | 1 | at Vancouver | 6 | May 11 | Chicago | 3 | at Toronto | 2 |
| May 13 | St Louis | 5 | at Vancouver | 2 | May 13 | Chicago | 3 | at Toronto | 1 |
| May 15 | Vancouver | 6 | at St Louis | 5* | May 15 | Toronto | 2 | at Chicago | 4 |
| May 17 | St Louis | 8 | at Vancouver | 2 | May 17 | Chicago | 4 | at Toronto | 5* |
| May 19 | Vancouver | 5 | at St Louis | 3 | May 19 | Toronto | 2 | at Chicago | 5 |
| | Vancouver won series 4-3. | | | | | Chicago won series 4-3. | | | |

## Conference Semifinals

### WESTERN CONFERENCE

| | | | | | | | | |
|---|---|---|---|---|---|---|---|---|
| May 21 | San Jose | 0 | at Detroit | 6 | May 21 | NY Rangers | 4 | at Philadelphia | 5* |
| May 23 | San Jose | 2 | at Detroit | 6 | May 22 | NY Rangers | 3 | at Philadelphia | 4* |
| May 25 | Detroit | 6 | at San Jose | 2 | May 24 | Philadelphia | 5 | at NY Rangers | 2 |
| May 27 | Detroit | 6 | at San Jose | 2 | May 26 | Philadelphia | 4 | at NY Rangers | 1 |
| | Detroit won series 4-0. | | | | | Philadelphia won series 4-0. | | | |

### EASTERN CONFERENCE

| | | | | | | | | |
|---|---|---|---|---|---|---|---|---|
| May 21 | Vancouver | 1 | at Chicago | 2* | May 20 | New Jersey | 2 | at Pittsburgh | 3 |
| May 23 | Vancouver | 0 | at Chicago | 2 | May 22 | New Jersey | 4 | at Pittsburgh | 2 |
| May 25 | Chicago | 3 | at Vancouver | 2* | May 24 | Pittsburgh | 1 | at New Jersey | 5 |
| May 27 | Chicago | 4 | at Vancouver | 3* | May 26 | Pittsburgh | 1 | at New Jersey | 2* |
| | Chicago won series 4-0. | | | | May 28 | New Jersey | 4 | at Pittsburgh | 1 |
| | | | | | | New Jersey won series 4-1. | | | |

## Western Final

| | | | | |
|---|---|---|---|---|
| June 1 | Chicago | 1 | at Detroit | 2* |
| June 4 | Chicago | 2 | at Detroit | 3 |
| June 6 | Detroit | 4 | at Chicago | 3† |
| June 8 | Detroit | 2 | at Chicago | 5 |
| June 11 | Chicago | 1 | at Detroit | 2† |
| | Detroit won series 4-1. | | | |

## Eastern Final

| | | | | |
|---|---|---|---|---|
| June 3 | New Jersey | 4 | at Philadelphia | 1 |
| June 5 | New Jersey | 5 | at Philadelphia | 2 |
| June 7 | Philadelphia | 3 | at New Jersey | 2* |
| June 10 | Philadelphia | 4 | at New Jersey | 2 |
| June 11 | New Jersey | 3 | at Philadelphia | 2 |
| June 13 | Philadelphia | 2 | at New Jersey | 4 |
| | New Jersey won series 4-2. | | | |

## Stanley Cup Championship

| | | | | |
|---|---|---|---|---|
| June 17 | New Jersey | 2 | at Detroit | 1 |
| June 20 | New Jersey | 4 | at Detroit | 2 |
| June 22 | Detroit | 2 | at New Jersey | 5 |
| June 24 | Detroit | 2 | at New Jersey | 5 |
| | New Jersey won series 4-0. | | | |

*Overtime game. †Double overtime game.

## Game 1

| | | | |
|---|---|---|---|
| New Jersey | 0 | 1 | 1—2 |
| Detroit | 0 | 1 | 0—1 |

### FIRST PERIOD
Scoring: None. Penalties: Guerin, NJ (holding), 6:47; Konstantinov, Det (holding stick), 11:05.

### SECOND PERIOD
Scoring: 1, NJ, Richer 5 (power play) (Albelin, Broten), 9:41. 2, Det, Ciccarelli 9 (power play) (Lidstrom, Coffey), 13:03. Penalties: Draper, Det (roughing), 9:35; Holik, NJ (high-sticking), 11:37; Lemieux, NJ (hooking),

13:41; Daneyko, NJ (roughing), 15:44; Ciccarelli, Det (roughing), 15:44.

### THIRD PERIOD
Scoring: 3, NJ, Lemieux 12 (MacLean, Chorske), 3:17. Penalty: Brown, Det (tripping), 4:48.

Shots on goal: NJ—9-10-9—28. Det—7-5-5—17. Power-play opportunities: NJ 1-of-3; Det 1-of-3. Goalies: NJ, Brodeur (17 shots, 16 saves). Det, Vernon (28 shots, 26 saves). A: 19,875. Referee: McCreary. Linesmen: Murphy, Collins.

## Game 2

| | | | |
|---|---|---|---|
| New Jersey | 0 | 1 | 3—4 |
| Detroit | 0 | 1 | 1—2 |

### FIRST PERIOD
Scoring: None. Penalties: Stevens, NJ (roughing), :37; Ciccarelli, Det (slashing), 5:57; McCarty, Det (roughing), 8:49; Broten, NJ (high-sticking), 9:27.

### SECOND PERIOD
Scoring: 1, Det, Kozlov 9 (power play) (Ciccarelli, Fedorov), 7:17. 2, NJ, MacLean 5 (Niedermayer, Broten), 9:40. Penalties: Brodeur, NJ, served by Rolston (delay of game), 6:56; Guerin, NJ (slashing), 8:58; McCarty, Det (slashing), 8:58; Errey, Det (charging), 16:01; Dowd, NJ (interference), 18:30.

### THIRD PERIOD
Scoring: 3, Det, Fedorov 5 (Brown, Fetisov), 1:36. 4, NJ Niedermayer 4 (Dowd), 9:47. 5, NJ, Dowd 2 (Chambers, Albelin), 18:36. 6, NJ, Richer 6 (empty net) (Niedermayer), 19:39. Penalties: Holik, NJ (boarding), 4:58.

Shots on goal: NJ—3-9-11—23. Det—7-6-5—18. Power-play opportunities: NJ 0-of 3; Det 1-of-5. Goalies: NJ, Brodeur (18 shots, 16 saves). Det, Vernon (22 shots, 19 saves). A: 19,875. Referee: Gregson. Linesmen: Scapinello, Bonney.

## Game 3

| | | | |
|---|---|---|---|
| Detroit | 0 | 0 | 2—2 |
| New Jersey | 2 | 2 | 1—5 |

### FIRST PERIOD
Scoring: 1, NJ, Driver 1 (power play) (Broten, MacLean), 10:30. 2, NJ, Lemieux 13 (Carpenter, Stevens), 16:52. Penalties: Lemieux, NJ (roughing), 1:09; Primeau, Det (slashing), 1:09; Konstantinov, Det (holding stick), 8:56; Holik, NJ (tripping), 10:58; Guerin, NJ (unsportsmanlike conduct), 16:38; Lapointe, Det (unsportsmanlike conduct), 16:38.

### SECOND PERIOD
Scoring: 3, NJ, Broten 5 (Stevens, MacLean), 6:59. 4, NJ, McKay 8 (Holik, Driver), 8:20. Penalties: Broten, NJ (holding stick), 11:01; Primeau, Det (tripping), 16:03; Carpenter, NJ (cross checking), 19:47.

### THIRD PERIOD
Scoring: 5, NJ, Holik 4 (power play) (Guerin, Richer), 8:14. 6, Det, Fedorov 6 (power play) (Fetisov, Brown),

16:57. 7, Det, Yzerman 4 (power play) (Sheppard, Lidstrom), 18:27. Penalties: Albelin, NJ (high sticking), 2:30; Konstantinov, Det (high sticking), 4:25; Draper, Det (high sticking), 5:17; Primeau, Det (cross checking), 6:31; Holik, NJ (cross checking), 8:44; Richer, NJ (hooking), 12:28; Taylor, Det (roughing), 15:37; Lapointe, Det (double roughing minor), 15:37; Ciccarelli, Det (roughing), 15:37; Guerin, NJ (boarding, roughing), 15:37; Brylin, NJ (high sticking, roughing), 15:37; Zelepukin, NJ (double roughing minor), 15:37.

Shots on goal: Det—7-5-12—24. NJ—15-8-8—31. Power-play opportunities: Det 2-of-8; NJ 2-of-5. Goalies: Det, Vernon (20 shots, 16 saves), Osgood (8:20 of 2nd period; 11 shots, 10 saves). NJ, Brodeur (24 shots, 22 saves). A: 19,040. Referee: Fraser. Linesmen: Collins, Murphy.

## Game 4

| | | | |
|---|---|---|---|
| Detroit | 2 | 0 | 0—2 |
| New Jersey | 2 | 1 | 2—5 |

### FIRST PERIOD
Scoring: 1, NJ, Broten 6 (Richer, Chorske), 1:08. 2, Det, Fedorov 7 (Lapointe, Fetisov), 2:03. 3, Det, Coffey 6 (shorthanded) (Brown, Fedorov), 13:01. 4, NJ, Chambers 3 (Driver, MacLean), 17:45. Penalties: Errey, Det (hooking), 11:03; Daneyko, NJ (roughing), 13:36; Primeau, Det (goalie interference), 15:36.

### SECOND PERIOD
Scoring: 5, NJ, Broten 7 (Niedermayer, Guerin), 7:56. Penalties: Daneyko, NJ (slashing), :30; Lapointe, Det (roughing), 10:09; Stevens, NJ (roughing), 10:09; Guerin, NJ (interference), 12:40; Konstantinov, Det (hooking), 19:12.

### THIRD PERIOD
Scoring: 6, NJ, Brylin 1 (Rolston, Guerin), 7:46. 7, NJ, Chambers 4 (Brylin, Guerin), 12:32. Penalty: Grimson, Det (roughing), 10:24.

Shots on goal: Det—8-7-1—16. NJ—8-8-10—26. Power-play opportunities: Det 0-of-3; NJ 0-of-4. Goalies: Det, Vernon (26 shots, 21 saves). NJ, Brodeur (16 shots, 14 saves). A: 19,040. Referee: McCreary. Linesmen: Bonney, Scapinello.

# Individual Playoff Leaders

## Scoring

### POINTS

| Player and Team | GP | G | A | Pts | +/− | PM | Player and Team | GP | G | A | Pts | +/− | PM |
|---|---|---|---|---|---|---|---|---|---|---|---|---|---|
| Sergei Fedorov, Det | 17 | 7 | 17 | 24 | 13 | 6 | Vyacheslav Kozlov, Det | 18 | 9 | 7 | 16 | 12 | 10 |
| Stephane Richer, NJ | 19 | 6 | 15 | 21 | 9 | 2 | Nicklas Lidstrom, Det | 18 | 4 | 12 | 16 | 4 | 8 |
| Neal Broten, NJ | 20 | 7 | 12 | 19 | 13 | 6 | Jaromir Jagr, Pitt | 12 | 10 | 5 | 15 | 3 | 6 |
| Ron Francis, Pitt | 12 | 6 | 13 | 19 | 3 | 4 | Rod Brind'amour, Phil | 15 | 6 | 9 | 15 | 5 | 8 |
| Denis Savard, Chi | 16 | 7 | 11 | 18 | 12 | 10 | Eric Lindros, Phil | 12 | 4 | 11 | 15 | 7 | 18 |
| Paul Coffey, Det | 18 | 6 | 12 | 18 | 4 | 10 | Larry Murphy, Pitt | 12 | 2 | 13 | 15 | 3 | 0 |
| John MacLean, NJ | 20 | 5 | 13 | 18 | 8 | 14 | Theoren Fleury, Cgy | 7 | 7 | 7 | 14 | 8 | 2 |
| Claude Lemieux, NJ | 20 | 13 | 3 | 16 | 12 | 20 | Brian Leetch, NYR | 10 | 6 | 8 | 14 | −1 | 8 |

### GOALS

| Player and Team | GP | G |
|---|---|---|
| Claude Lemieux, NJ | 20 | 13 |
| Jaromir Jagr, Pitt | 12 | 10 |
| Dino Ciccarelli, Det | 16 | 9 |
| Joe Murphy, Chi | 16 | 9 |
| Vyacheslav Koslov, Det | 18 | 9 |

### GAME WINNING GOALS

| Player and Team | GP | GW |
|---|---|---|
| Vyacheslav Koslov, Det | 18 | 4 |
| Neal Broten, NJ | 20 | 4 |
| Chris Chelios, Chi | 16 | 3 |
| Joe Murphy, Chi | 16 | 3 |
| Claude Lemieux, NJ | 20 | 3 |

### ASSISTS

| Player and Team | GP | A |
|---|---|---|
| Sergei Fedorov, Det | 17 | 17 |
| Stephane Richer, NJ | 19 | 15 |
| Ron Francis, Pitt | 12 | 13 |
| Larry Murphy, Pitt | 12 | 13 |
| John MacLean, NJ | 20 | 13 |

### POWER PLAY GOALS

| Player and Team | GP | PP |
|---|---|---|
| Dino Ciccarelli, Det | 16 | 6 |
| Mike Rathje, SJ | 11 | 5 |

10 tied with 3.

### SHORT HANDED GOALS

| Player and Team | GP | SH |
|---|---|---|
| Russ Courtnall, Van | 11 | 2 |
| Pavel Bure, Van | 11 | 2 |

25 tied with one.

### PLUS/MINUS

| Player and Team | GP | +/− |
|---|---|---|
| Doug Brown, Det | 18 | 14 |
| Eric Desjardins, Phil | 15 | 13 |
| Bruce Driver, NJ | 17 | 13 |
| Sergei Fedorov, Det | 17 | 13 |
| Neal Broten, NJ | 20 | 13 |

## Goaltending (Minimum 420 minutes)

### GOALS AGAINST AVERAGE

| Player and Team | GP | Mins | GA | Avg |
|---|---|---|---|---|
| Martin Brodeur, NJ | 20 | 1222 | 34 | 1.67 |
| Ed Belfour, Chi | 16 | 1014 | 37 | 2.19 |
| Mike Vernon, Det | 18 | 1063 | 41 | 2.31 |
| Ron Hextall, Phil | 15 | 897 | 42 | 2.81 |
| Felix Potvin, Tor | 7 | 424 | 20 | 2.83 |

### SAVE PERCENTAGE

| Player and Team | GP | Mins | GA | SA | Pct | W | L |
|---|---|---|---|---|---|---|---|
| Martin Brodeur, NJ | 20 | 1222 | 34 | 463 | .927 | 16 | 4 |
| Ed Belfour, Chi | 16 | 1014 | 37 | 479 | .923 | 9 | 7 |
| Felix Potvin, Tor | 7 | 424 | 20 | 253 | .920 | 3 | 4 |
| Ken Wregget, Pitt | 11 | 661 | 33 | 349 | .905 | 5 | 6 |
| Ron Hextall, Phil | 15 | 897 | 42 | 437 | .904 | 10 | 5 |

## Expunsion Teams

There's a late-night parlor game that sports fans play in which one fan names a place and another comes up with the punniest possible nickname for a franchise based there. A team in Norman, Okla., for instance, would be called the Conquest; one in Augusta, Maine, would be the Wind. If you were a commissioner of a loopy sports league, you would want to expand to Alaska, so you could add the Nome Chomskys and the Juneau Whats, while an International Division would include the Havana Good Times, the Kenya Believeits, the Crimea Rivers and the Nice Guys, who would always finish last.

One perennial favorite in this fanciful league—the Macon Whoopees—actually existed in the old Southern Hockey League for a few months before folding during the 1973-1974 season. Last spring came word that those icemen of euphemism will be back. On May 2, 1995, the Macon City Council approved the request of two businessmen, who are reviving the Whoopees, to play in that Georgia city's coliseum as part of a reconsituted SHL. Look for the Whoopees to begin play in the '96–'97 season. No word yet on whether Bob Eubanks wil do play-by-play.

## NHL Awards

| Award | Player and Team |
|---|---|
| Hart Trophy (MVP) | Eric Lindros, Phil |
| Calder Trophy (top rookie) | Peter Forsberg, Que |
| Vezina Trophy (top goaltender) | Dominik Hasek, Buff |
| Norris Trophy (top defenseman) | Paul Coffey, Det |
| Lady Byng Trophy (for gentlemanly play) | Ron Francis, Pitt |

| Award | Player and Team |
|---|---|
| Selke Trophy (top defensive forward) | Ron Francis, Pitt |
| Adams Award (top coach) | Marc Crawford, Que |
| Jennings Trophy (goaltender on club allowing fewest goals) | Ed Belfour, Chi |
| Conn Smythe Trophy (playoff MVP) | Claude Lemieux, NJ |

## NHL Individual Leaders

### Scoring

#### POINTS

| Player and Team | GP | G | A | Pts | +/– | PM |
|---|---|---|---|---|---|---|
| Jaromir Jagr, Pitt | 48 | 32 | 38 | 70 | 23 | 37 |
| Eric Lindros, Phil | 46 | 29 | 41 | 70 | 27 | 60 |
| Alexei Zhamnov, Winn | 48 | 30 | 35 | 65 | 5 | 20 |
| Joe Sakic, Que | 47 | 19 | 43 | 62 | 7 | 30 |
| Ron Francis, Pitt | 44 | 11 | 48 | 59 | 30 | 18 |
| Theoren Fleury, Cgy | 47 | 29 | 29 | 58 | 6 | 112 |
| Paul Coffey, Det | 45 | 14 | 44 | 58 | 18 | 72 |
| Mikael Renberg, Phil | 47 | 26 | 31 | 57 | 20 | 20 |
| John Leclair, Mtl-Phil | 46 | 26 | 28 | 54 | 20 | 30 |
| Mark Messier, NYR | 46 | 14 | 39 | 53 | 8 | 40 |
| Adam Oates, Bos | 48 | 12 | 41 | 53 | -11 | 8 |
| Bernie Nicholls, Chi | 48 | 22 | 29 | 51 | 4 | 32 |
| Keith Tkachuk, Winn | 48 | 22 | 29 | 51 | -4 | 152 |

Four tied with 50.

#### GOALS

| Player and Team | GP | G |
|---|---|---|
| Peter Bondra, Wash | 47 | 34 |
| Jaromir Jagr, Pitt | 48 | 32 |
| Ray Sheppard, Det | 43 | 30 |
| Owen Nolan, Que | 46 | 30 |
| Alexei Zhamnov, Win | 48 | 30 |

#### GAME WINNING GOALS

| Player and Team | GP | GW |
|---|---|---|
| Owen Nolan, Que | 46 | 8 |
| Donald Audette, Buff | 46 | 7 |
| John Leclair, Mtl-Phil | 46 | 7 |
| Jaromir Jagr, Pitt | 48 | 7 |
| Brendan Shanahan, StL | 45 | 6 |
| Brett Hull, StL | 48 | 6 |

#### ASSISTS

| Player and Team | GP | A |
|---|---|---|
| Ron Francis, Pitt | 44 | 48 |
| Paul Coffey, Det | 45 | 44 |
| Joe Sakic, Que | 47 | 43 |
| Eric Lindros, Phil | 46 | 41 |
| Adam Oates, Bos | 48 | 41 |

#### POWER PLAY GOALS

| Player and Team | GP | PP |
|---|---|---|
| Cam Neely, Bos | 42 | 16 |
| Donald Audette, Buff | 46 | 13 |
| Owen Nolan, Que | 46 | 13 |
| Alex Mogilny, Buff | 44 | 12 |
| Peter Bondra, Wash | 47 | 12 |

#### SHORT HANDED GOALS

| Player and Team | GP | SHG |
|---|---|---|
| Peter Bondra, Wash | 47 | 6 |
| Wayne Presley, Buff | 46 | 5 |

Eight tied with three.

#### PLUS/MINUS

| Player and Team | GP | +/– |
|---|---|---|
| Ron Francis, Pitt | 44 | 30 |
| Curtis Leschyshyn, Que | 44 | 29 |
| Steve Duchesne, StL | 47 | 29 |
| Eric Lindros, Phil | 46 | 27 |
| Jaromir Jagr, Pitt | 48 | 23 |

### Goaltending
### (Minimum 13 games)

#### GOALS AGAINST AVERAGE

| Player and Team | GP | Mins | GA | Avg |
|---|---|---|---|---|
| Dominik Hasek, Buff | 41 | 2416 | 85 | 2.11 |
| Rick Tabaracci, Wsh-Cgy | 13 | 596 | 21 | 2.11 |
| *Jim Carey, Wash | 28 | 1604 | 57 | 2.13 |
| Chris Osgood, Det | 19 | 1087 | 41 | 2.26 |
| Ed Belfour, Chi | 42 | 2450 | 93 | 2.28 |

#### WINS

| Player and Team | GP | Mins | W | L | T |
|---|---|---|---|---|---|
| Ken Wregget, Pitt | 38 | 2208 | 25 | 9 | 2 |
| Ed Belfour, Chi | 42 | 2450 | 22 | 15 | 3 |
| Trevor Kidd, Cgy | 43 | 2463 | 22 | 14 | 6 |
| Curtis Joseph, StL | 36 | 1914 | 20 | 10 | 1 |

Four tied with 19.

#### SAVE PERCENTAGE

| Player and Team | GP | GA | SA | Pct | W | L | T |
|---|---|---|---|---|---|---|---|
| Dominik Hasek, Buff | 41 | 85 | 1221 | .930 | 19 | 14 | 7 |
| Chris Osgood, Det | 19 | 41 | 496 | .917 | 14 | 5 | 0 |
| Jocelyn Thibault, Que | 18 | 35 | 423 | .917 | 12 | 2 | 2 |
| Andy Moog, Dall | 31 | 72 | 846 | .915 | 10 | 12 | 7 |
| *Damian Rhodes, Tor | 13 | 34 | 404 | .915 | 6 | 6 | 1 |
| J. Vanbiesbrouck, Fla | 37 | 86 | 1000 | .914 | 14 | 15 | 4 |

Three tied at .913.

#### SHUTOUTS

| Player and Team | GP | Mins | SO | W | L | T |
|---|---|---|---|---|---|---|
| Dominik Hasek, Buff | 41 | 2416 | 5 | 19 | 14 | 7 |
| Ed Belfour, Chi | 42 | 2450 | 5 | 22 | 15 | 3 |
| *Jim Carey, Wash | 28 | 1604 | 4 | 18 | 6 | 3 |
| *Blaine Lacher, Bos | 35 | 1965 | 4 | 19 | 11 | 2 |
| Arturs Irbe, SJ | 38 | 2043 | 4 | 14 | 19 | 3 |
| J. Vanbiesbrouck, Fla | 37 | 2087 | 4 | 14 | 15 | 4 |

* Rookie.

# NHL Team-by-Team Statistical Leaders

## Anaheim Mighty Ducks

### SCORING

| Player | GP | G | A | Pts | +/– | PM |
|---|---|---|---|---|---|---|
| *Paul Kariya, L | 47 | 18 | 21 | 39 | -17 | 4 |
| Shaun Van Allen, C | 45 | 8 | 21 | 29 | -4 | 32 |
| Stephan Lebeau, C | 38 | 8 | 16 | 24 | 6 | 12 |
| Todd Krygier, L | 35 | 11 | 11 | 22 | 1 | 10 |
| Peter Douris, R | 46 | 10 | 11 | 21 | 4 | 12 |
| Patrik Carnback, R | 41 | 6 | 15 | 21 | -8 | 32 |
| Bobby Dollas, D | 45 | 7 | 13 | 20 | -3 | 12 |
| Bob Corkum, C | 44 | 10 | 9 | 19 | -7 | 25 |
| Joe Sacco, R | 41 | 10 | 8 | 18 | -8 | 23 |
| *Steve Rucchin, C | 43 | 6 | 11 | 17 | 7 | 23 |
| Mike Sillinger, R | 28 | 4 | 11 | 15 | 4 | 8 |
| *Oleg Tverdovsky, D | 36 | 3 | 9 | 12 | -6 | 14 |
| *Valeri Karpov, L | 30 | 4 | 7 | 11 | -4 | 6 |
| *Jason York, D | 25 | 1 | 10 | 11 | 4 | 14 |
| *Milos Holan, D | 25 | 2 | 8 | 10 | 4 | 14 |
| Garry Valk, L | 36 | 3 | 6 | 9 | -4 | 34 |
| Tom Kurvers, D | 22 | 4 | 3 | 7 | -13 | 6 |
| Randy Ladouceur, D | 44 | 2 | 4 | 6 | 2 | 36 |
| Dave Karpa, D | 28 | 1 | 5 | 6 | -1 | 91 |
| *John Lilley, C | 9 | 2 | 2 | 4 | 2 | 5 |
| David Williams, D | 21 | 2 | 2 | 4 | -5 | 24 |
| *Denny Lambert, L | 13 | 1 | 3 | 4 | 3 | 4 |
| Robert Dirk, D | 38 | 1 | 3 | 4 | -3 | 56 |

### GOALTENDING

| Player | GP | Mins | Avg | W | L | T | SO |
|---|---|---|---|---|---|---|---|
| Guy Hebert | 39 | 2092 | 3.13 | 12 | 20 | 4 | 2 |
| Mikhail Shtalenkov | 18 | 810 | 3.63 | 4 | 7 | 1 | 0 |
| Team total | 48 | 2913 | 3.38 | 16 | 27 | 5 | 2 |

*Rookie.

## Boston Bruins

### SCORING

| Player | GP | G | A | Pts | +/– | PM |
|---|---|---|---|---|---|---|
| Adam Oates, C | 48 | 12 | 41 | 53 | -11 | 8 |
| Ray Bourque, D | 46 | 12 | 31 | 43 | 3 | 20 |
| Cam Neely, R | 42 | 27 | 14 | 41 | 7 | 72 |
| Bryan Smolinski, C | 44 | 18 | 13 | 31 | -3 | 31 |
| *Mariusz Czerkawski, R | 47 | 12 | 14 | 26 | 4 | 31 |
| Mats Naslund, L | 34 | 8 | 14 | 22 | -4 | 4 |
| Don Sweeney, D | 47 | 3 | 19 | 22 | 6 | 24 |
| Ted Donato, C | 47 | 10 | 10 | 20 | 3 | 10 |
| Jozef Stumpel, R | 44 | 5 | 13 | 18 | 4 | 8 |
| Steve Heinze, R | 36 | 7 | 9 | 16 | 0 | 23 |
| Alexei Kasatonov, D | 44 | 2 | 14 | 16 | -2 | 33 |
| Brent Hughes, L | 44 | 6 | 6 | 12 | 6 | 139 |
| Stephen Leach, R | 35 | 5 | 6 | 11 | -3 | 68 |
| *Jon Rohloff, D | 34 | 3 | 8 | 11 | 1 | 39 |
| Dave Reid, L | 38 | 5 | 5 | 10 | 8 | 10 |
| *Sandy Moger, R | 18 | 2 | 6 | 8 | -1 | 6 |
| Glen Murray, R | 35 | 5 | 2 | 7 | -11 | 46 |
| David Shaw, D | 44 | 3 | 4 | 7 | -9 | 36 |
| Jamie Huscroft, D | 34 | 0 | 6 | 6 | -3 | 103 |
| *John Gruden, D | 38 | 0 | 6 | 6 | 3 | 22 |
| *Fred Knipscheer, L | 16 | 3 | 1 | 4 | 1 | 2 |
| Mikko Makela, R | 11 | 1 | 2 | 3 | 0 | 0 |

### GOALTENDING

| Player | GP | Mins | Avg | W | L | T | SO |
|---|---|---|---|---|---|---|---|
| *Blaine Lacher | 35 | 1965 | 2.41 | 19 | 11 | 2 | 4 |
| Vincent Riendeau | 11 | 565 | 2.87 | 3 | 6 | 1 | 0 |
| †Craig Billington | 8 | 373 | 3.06 | 5 | 1 | 0 | 0 |
| Team total | 48 | 2911 | 2.62 | 27 | 18 | 3 | 4 |

†Played 9 games with Ottawa.

---

## Child of Kings

When she was two years old and had been attending Los Angeles King games for less than a year, Jenna Belcher admonished her mother: "Sit down. I can't see the power play." Now, four years later, Jenna is an experienced television analyst. Filling in on Prime Sports network's pre-game show on April 12, Jenna, 6, appeared at ease, flashing made-for-TV dimples that disappeared only when she assessed the Kings' grim playoff prospects. Later that day Jenna joined the L.A. media in its ritual of tormenting coach Barry Melrose. "He's traded all the good players," she said of Melrose, who was fired nine days later.

Jenna's angelic blue eyes and drape of blonde hair belie an uncommon fearlessness. While attending one game, she rose to her full stature (4' 4") to challenge a fan who had been heckling goalie Kelly Hrudey. "Leave Kelly alone," she said. "He hurt his knee, and he can't get low."

## Buffalo Sabres

### SCORING

| Player | GP | G | A | Pts | +/- | PM |
|---|---|---|---|---|---|---|
| Alexander Mogilny, R....44 | | 19 | 28 | 47 | 0 | 36 |
| Donald Audette, R...........46 | | 24 | 13 | 37 | -3 | 27 |
| Garry Galley, D ..............47 | | 3 | 29 | 32 | 4 | 30 |
| Pat LaFontaine, C...........22 | | 12 | 15 | 27 | 2 | 4 |
| Yuri Khmylev, L .............48 | | 8 | 17 | 25 | 8 | 14 |
| Derek Plante, C ..............47 | | 3 | 19 | 22 | -4 | 12 |
| Doug Bodger, D............44 | | 3 | 17 | 20 | -3 | 47 |
| Wayne Presley, R .........46 | | 14 | 5 | 19 | 5 | 41 |
| Dale Hawerchuk, C .......23 | | 5 | 11 | 16 | -2 | 2 |
| Dave Hannan, C.............42 | | 4 | 12 | 16 | 3 | 32 |
| Alexei Zhitnik, D ............32 | | 4 | 10 | 14 | -6 | 61 |
| Jason Dawe, L ...............42 | | 7 | 4 | 11 | -6 | 19 |
| Craig Simpson, L ...........24 | | 4 | 7 | 11 | -5 | 26 |
| Richard Smehlik, D .......39 | | 4 | 7 | 11 | 5 | 46 |
| Bob Sweeney, C ............45 | | 5 | 4 | 9 | -6 | 18 |
| Scott Pearson, L............42 | | 3 | 5 | 8 | -14 | 74 |
| Charlie Huddy, D ..........41 | | 2 | 5 | 7 | -7 | 42 |
| Brad May, L..................33 | | 3 | 3 | 6 | 5 | 87 |
| Craig Muni, D ................40 | | 0 | 6 | 6 | -4 | 36 |
| *Mark Astley, D .............14 | | 2 | 1 | 3 | -2 | 12 |
| Doug Houda, D ..............28 | | 1 | 2 | 3 | 1 | 68 |
| *Brian Holzinger, C ........4 | | 0 | 3 | 3 | 2 | 0 |
| Rob Ray, L ....................46 | | 0 | 3 | 3 | -4 | 173 |

### GOALTENDING

| Player | GP | Mins | Avg | W | L | T | SO |
|---|---|---|---|---|---|---|---|
| Dominik Hasek .....41 | | 2416 | 2.11 | 19 | 14 | 7 | 5 |
| †Robb Stauber ......6 | | 317 | 3.79 | 2 | 3 | 0 | 0 |
| Grant Fuhr ..............3 | | 180 | 4.00 | 1 | 2 | 0 | 0 |
| Team total............48 | | 2920 | 2.45 | 22 | 19 | 7 | 5 |

†Played 1 game with Los Angeles.

## Calgary Flames

### SCORING

| Player | GP | G | A | Pts | +/- | PM |
|---|---|---|---|---|---|---|
| Theoren Fleury, R..........47 | | 29 | 29 | 58 | 6 | 112 |
| Joe Nieuwendyk, C........46 | | 21 | 29 | 50 | 11 | 33 |
| Phil Housley, D..............43 | | 8 | 35 | 43 | 17 | 18 |
| Robert Reichel, C..........48 | | 18 | 17 | 35 | -2 | 28 |
| Zarley Zalapski, D.........48 | | 4 | 24 | 28 | 9 | 46 |
| Steve Chiasson, D.........45 | | 2 | 23 | 25 | 10 | 39 |
| German Titov, C............40 | | 12 | 12 | 24 | 6 | 16 |
| Joel Otto, C ...................47 | | 8 | 13 | 21 | 8 | 130 |
| Wes Walz, C..................39 | | 6 | 12 | 18 | 7 | 11 |
| Paul Kruse, L.................45 | | 11 | 5 | 16 | 13 | 141 |
| Sheldon Kennedy, R ......30 | | 7 | 8 | 15 | 5 | 45 |
| Ronnie Stern, R .............39 | | 9 | 4 | 13 | 4 | 163 |
| Kevin Dahl, D ................34 | | 4 | 8 | 12 | 8 | 38 |
| Kelly Kisio, C .................12 | | 7 | 4 | 11 | 2 | 6 |
| Mike Sullivan, C.............38 | | 4 | 7 | 11 | -2 | 14 |
| Nikolai Borschevsky, R...27 | | 0 | 10 | 10 | 10 | 0 |
| James Patrick, D............43 | | 0 | 10 | 10 | -3 | 14 |
| Sandy McCarthy, R.........37 | | 5 | 3 | 8 | 1 | 101 |
| Leonard Esau, D............15 | | 0 | 6 | 6 | -10 | 15 |
| Dan Keczmer, D.............28 | | 2 | 3 | 5 | 7 | 10 |
| Alan May, L ...................34 | | 2 | 3 | 5 | 3 | 119 |
| Frank Musil, D ...............35 | | 0 | 5 | 5 | 6 | 61 |
| Gary Roberts, L...............8 | | 2 | 2 | 4 | 1 | 43 |
| *Vesa Viitakoski, L.........10 | | 1 | 2 | 3 | -1 | 6 |

### GOALTENDING

| Player | GP | Mins | Avg | W | L | T | SO |
|---|---|---|---|---|---|---|---|
| *Jason Muzzatti ......1 | | 10 | .00 | 0 | 0 | 0 | 0 |
| †Rick Tabaracci .....5 | | 202 | 1.49 | 2 | 0 | 1 | 0 |
| Trevor Kidd............43 | | 2463 | 2.61 | 22 | 14 | 6 | 3 |
| *Andrei Trefilov......6 | | 236 | 4.07 | 0 | 3 | 0 | 0 |
| Team total............48 | | 2922 | 2.77 | 24 | 17 | 7 | 3 |

†Played 8 games with Washington.

## Chicago Blackhawks

### SCORING

| Player | GP | G | A | Pts | +/- | PM |
|---|---|---|---|---|---|---|
| Bernie Nicholls, C .........48 | | 22 | 29 | 51 | 4 | 32 |
| Joe Murphy, R...............40 | | 23 | 18 | 41 | 7 | 89 |
| Chris Chelios, D ............48 | | 5 | 33 | 38 | 17 | 72 |
| Gary Suter, D .................48 | | 10 | 27 | 37 | 14 | 42 |
| Tony Amonte, R.............48 | | 15 | 20 | 35 | 7 | 41 |
| Jeremy Roenick, C.........33 | | 10 | 24 | 34 | 5 | 14 |
| Patrick Poulin, L ............45 | | 15 | 15 | 39 | 13 | 53 |
| Denis Savard, C............43 | | 10 | 15 | 25 | -3 | 18 |
| *Sergei Krivokrasov, R...41 | | 12 | 7 | 19 | 9 | 33 |
| Jeff Shantz, C................45 | | 6 | 12 | 18 | 11 | 33 |
| Brent Sutter, C..............47 | | 7 | 8 | 15 | 6 | 51 |
| Dirk Graham, R .............40 | | 4 | 9 | 13 | 2 | 42 |
| Eric Weinrich, D.............48 | | 3 | 10 | 13 | 1 | 33 |
| Steve Smith, D...............48 | | 1 | 12 | 13 | 6 | 128 |
| Murray Craven, L ..........16 | | 4 | 3 | 7 | 2 | 2 |
| Brent Grieve, L ..............24 | | 1 | 5 | 6 | 2 | 23 |
| Jim Cummins, R.............37 | | 4 | 1 | 5 | -6 | 158 |
| Gerald Diduck, D ..........35 | | 2 | 3 | 5 | -5 | 63 |
| Cam Russell, D .............33 | | 1 | 3 | 4 | 4 | 88 |
| Greg Smyth, D ..............22 | | 0 | 3 | 3 | 2 | 33 |
| Ed Belfour, G.................42 | | 0 | 3 | 3 | 0 | 11 |

### GOALTENDING

| Player | GP | Mins | Avg | W | L | T | SO |
|---|---|---|---|---|---|---|---|
| Ed Belfour.............42 | | 2450 | 2.28 | 22 | 15 | 3 | 5 |
| Jeff Hackett ............7 | | 328 | 2.38 | 1 | 3 | 2 | 0 |
| Jim Waite ................2 | | 119 | 2.52 | 1 | 1 | 0 | 0 |
| Team total............48 | | 2909 | 2.37 | 24 | 19 | 5 | 5 |

*Rookie.

## Dallas Stars

### SCORING

| Player | GP | G | A | Pts | +/– | PM |
|---|---|---|---|---|---|---|
| Dave Gagner, C | 48 | 14 | 28 | 42 | 2 | 42 |
| Mike Modano, C | 30 | 12 | 17 | 29 | 7 | 8 |
| Kevin Hatcher, D | 47 | 10 | 19 | 29 | -4 | 66 |
| Mike Donnelly, L | 44 | 12 | 15 | 27 | -4 | 33 |
| Corey Millen, C | 45 | 5 | 18 | 23 | 6 | 36 |
| Trent Klatt, R | 47 | 12 | 10 | 22 | -2 | 26 |
| Greg Adams, L | 43 | 8 | 13 | 21 | -3 | 16 |
| *Todd Harvey, C | 40 | 11 | 9 | 20 | -3 | 67 |
| *Mike Kennedy, L | 44 | 6 | 12 | 18 | 4 | 33 |
| Grant Ledyard, D | 38 | 5 | 13 | 18 | 6 | 20 |
| Paul Broten, R | 47 | 7 | 9 | 16 | -7 | 36 |
| Derian Hatcher, D | 43 | 5 | 11 | 16 | 3 | 105 |
| Dean Evason, C | 47 | 8 | 7 | 15 | 3 | 48 |
| Brent Gilchrist, C | 32 | 9 | 4 | 13 | -3 | 16 |
| Paul Cavallini, D | 44 | 1 | 11 | 12 | 8 | 28 |
| Peter Zezel, C | 30 | 6 | 5 | 11 | -6 | 19 |
| Craig Ludwig, D | 47 | 2 | 7 | 9 | -6 | 61 |
| Doug Zmolek, D | 42 | 0 | 5 | 5 | -6 | 67 |
| Shane Churla, R | 27 | 1 | 3 | 4 | 0 | 186 |
| *Jarkko Varvio, R | 5 | 1 | 1 | 2 | 1 | 0 |
| Richard Matvichuk, D | 14 | 0 | 2 | 2 | -7 | 14 |

### GOALTENDING

| Player | GP | Mins | Avg | W | L | T | SO |
|---|---|---|---|---|---|---|---|
| Andy Moog | 31 | 1770 | 2.44 | 10 | 12 | 7 | 2 |
| *E. Fernandez | 1 | 59 | 3.05 | 0 | 1 | 0 | 0 |
| Darcy Wakaluk | 15 | 754 | 3.18 | 4 | 8 | 0 | 2 |
| *Mike Torchia | 6 | 327 | 3.30 | 3 | 2 | 1 | 0 |
| Team total | 48 | 2925 | 2.77 | 17 | 23 | 8 | 4 |

## Detroit Red Wings

### SCORING

| Player | GP | G | A | Pts | +/– | PM |
|---|---|---|---|---|---|---|
| Paul Coffey, D | 45 | 14 | 44 | 58 | 18 | 72 |
| Sergei Fedorov, C | 42 | 20 | 30 | 50 | 6 | 24 |
| Dino Ciccarelli, R | 42 | 16 | 27 | 43 | 12 | 39 |
| Keith Primeau, L | 45 | 15 | 27 | 42 | 17 | 99 |
| Ray Sheppard, R | 43 | 30 | 10 | 40 | 11 | 17 |
| Steve Yzerman, C | 47 | 12 | 26 | 38 | 6 | 40 |
| Vyacheslav Kozlov, C | 46 | 13 | 20 | 33 | 12 | 45 |
| Nicklas Lidstrom, D | 43 | 10 | 16 | 26 | 15 | 6 |
| Doug Brown, R | 45 | 9 | 12 | 21 | 14 | 16 |
| Bob Errey, L | 43 | 8 | 13 | 21 | 13 | 58 |
| Viacheslav Fetisov, D | 18 | 3 | 12 | 15 | 1 | 2 |
| Shawn Burr, L | 42 | 6 | 8 | 14 | 13 | 60 |
| Vlad. Konstantinov, D | 47 | 3 | 11 | 14 | 10 | 101 |
| Darren McCarty, R | 31 | 5 | 8 | 13 | 5 | 88 |
| Martin Lapointe, R | 39 | 4 | 6 | 10 | 1 | 73 |
| Greg Johnson, C | 22 | 3 | 5 | 8 | 1 | 14 |
| Kris Draper, C | 36 | 2 | 6 | 8 | 1 | 22 |
| Bob Rouse, D | 48 | 1 | 7 | 8 | 14 | 36 |
| Mark Howe, D | 18 | 1 | 5 | 6 | -3 | 10 |
| Mike Krushelnyski, C | 20 | 2 | 3 | 5 | 3 | 6 |
| *Tim Taylor, C | 22 | 0 | 4 | 4 | 3 | 16 |
| Terry Carkner, D | 20 | 1 | 2 | 3 | 7 | 21 |
| Mike Ramsey, D | 33 | 1 | 2 | 3 | 11 | 23 |

### GOALTENDING

| Player | GP | Mins | Avg | W | L | T | S |
|---|---|---|---|---|---|---|---|
| Chris Osgood | 19 | 1087 | 2.26 | 14 | 5 | 0 | 1 |
| Mike Vernon | 30 | 1807 | 2.52 | 19 | 6 | 4 | 1 |
| Team total | 48 | 2900 | 2.42 | 33 | 11 | 4 | 2 |

## Edmonton Oilers

### SCORING

| Player | GP | G | A | Pts | +/– | PM |
|---|---|---|---|---|---|---|
| Doug Weight, C | 48 | 7 | 33 | 40 | -17 | 69 |
| Jason Arnott, C | 42 | 15 | 22 | 37 | -14 | 128 |
| Shayne Corson, L | 48 | 12 | 24 | 36 | -17 | 86 |
| *David Oliver, R | 44 | 16 | 14 | 30 | -11 | 20 |
| *Todd Marchant, C | 45 | 13 | 14 | 28 | -3 | 32 |
| Kelly Buchberger, L | 48 | 7 | 17 | 24 | 0 | 82 |
| Scott Thornton, C | 47 | 10 | 12 | 22 | -4 | 89 |
| Igor Kravchuk, D | 36 | 7 | 11 | 18 | -15 | 29 |
| Mike Stapleton, C | 46 | 6 | 11 | 17 | -12 | 21 |
| Luke Richardson, D | 46 | 3 | 10 | 13 | -6 | 40 |
| Jiri Slegr, D | 31 | 2 | 10 | 12 | -5 | 46 |
| Kirk Maltby, R | 47 | 8 | 3 | 11 | -11 | 49 |
| Dean Kennedy, D | 40 | 2 | 8 | 10 | 2 | 25 |
| Fredrik Olausson, D | 33 | 0 | 10 | 10 | -4 | 20 |
| Boris Mironov, D | 29 | 1 | 7 | 8 | -9 | 40 |
| Ken Sutton, D | 24 | 4 | 3 | 7 | -3 | 42 |
| *Peter White, C | 9 | 2 | 4 | 6 | 1 | 0 |
| Bryan Marchment, D | 40 | 1 | 5 | 6 | -11 | 184 |
| Zdeno Ciger, L | 5 | 2 | 2 | 4 | -1 | 0 |
| Iain Fraser, C | 13 | 3 | 0 | 3 | 0 | 0 |
| Louie Debrusk, L | 34 | 2 | 0 | 2 | -4 | 93 |
| Gordon Mark, D | 18 | 0 | 2 | 2 | -9 | 35 |
| Bill Ranford, G | 40 | 0 | 2 | 2 | 0 | 2 |

### GOALTENDING

| Player | GP | Mins | Avg | W | L | T | SO |
|---|---|---|---|---|---|---|---|
| Bill Ranford | 40 | 2203 | 3.62 | 15 | 20 | 3 | 2 |
| *Fred Brathwaite | 14 | 601 | 3.99 | 2 | 5 | 1 | 0 |
| *Joaquin Gage | 2 | 99 | 4.24 | 0 | 2 | 0 | 0 |
| Team total | 48 | 2912 | 3.77 | 17 | 27 | 4 | 2 |

\* Rookie.

## Florida Panthers

### SCORING

| Player | GP | G | A | Pts | +/– | PM |
|---|---|---|---|---|---|---|
| Jesse Belanger, C | 47 | 15 | 14 | 29 | -5 | 18 |
| Stu Barnes, C | 41 | 10 | 19 | 29 | 7 | 8 |
| Scott Mellanby, R | 48 | 13 | 12 | 25 | -16 | 90 |
| Gord Murphy, D | 46 | 6 | 16 | 22 | -14 | 24 |
| Dave Lowry, L | 45 | 10 | 10 | 20 | -3 | 25 |
| Jody Hull, R | 46 | 11 | 8 | 19 | -1 | 8 |
| Bill Lindsay, L | 48 | 10 | 9 | 19 | 1 | 46 |
| Tom Fitzgerald, R | 48 | 3 | 13 | 16 | -3 | 31 |
| Brian Skrudland, C | 48 | 5 | 9 | 14 | 0 | 88 |
| Johan Garpenlov, L | 40 | 4 | 10 | 14 | 1 | 2 |
| Mike Hough, L | 48 | 6 | 7 | 13 | 1 | 38 |
| Jason Woolley, D | 34 | 4 | 9 | 13 | -1 | 18 |
| Gaetan Duchesne, L | 46 | 3 | 9 | 12 | -3 | 16 |
| Rob Niedermayer, C | 48 | 4 | 6 | 10 | -13 | 36 |
| Bob Kudelski, R | 26 | 6 | 3 | 9 | 2 | 2 |
| Brian Benning, D | 24 | 1 | 7 | 8 | -6 | 18 |
| Magnus Svensson, D | 19 | 2 | 5 | 7 | 5 | 10 |
| Andrei Lomakin, L | 31 | 1 | 6 | 7 | -5 | 6 |
| Paul Laus, D | 37 | 0 | 7 | 7 | 12 | 138 |

### GOALTENDING

| Player | GP | Mins | Avg | W | L | T | SO |
|---|---|---|---|---|---|---|---|
| J. Vanbiesbrouck | 37 | 2087 | 2.47 | 14 | 15 | 4 | 4 |
| Mark Fitzpatrick | 15 | 819 | 2.64 | 6 | 7 | 2 | 2 |
| Team total | 48 | 2916 | 2.61 | 20 | 22 | 6 | 6 |

## Hartford Whalers

### SCORING

| Player | GP | G | A | Pts | +/– | PM |
|---|---|---|---|---|---|---|
| Andrew Cassels, C | 46 | 7 | 30 | 37 | -3 | 18 |
| Darren Turcotte, C | 47 | 18 | 35 | 1 | | 22 |
| Geoff Sanderson, C | 46 | 18 | 14 | 32 | -10 | 24 |
| Steven Rice, R | 40 | 11 | 10 | 21 | 2 | 61 |
| Paul Ranheim, L | 47 | 6 | 14 | 20 | -3 | 10 |
| Frantisek Kucera, D | 48 | 3 | 17 | 20 | 3 | 30 |
| Jimmy Carson, C | 38 | 9 | 10 | 19 | 5 | 29 |
| Robert Kron, C | 38 | 10 | 8 | 18 | -3 | 10 |
| *Andrei Nikolishin, R | 39 | 8 | 10 | 18 | 7 | 10 |
| Adam Burt, D | 46 | 7 | 11 | 18 | 0 | 65 |
| Glen Wesley, D | 48 | 2 | 14 | 16 | -6 | 50 |
| Chris Pronger, D | 43 | 5 | 9 | 14 | -12 | 54 |
| Jocelyn Lemieux, L | 41 | 6 | 5 | 11 | -7 | 32 |
| Ted Drury, C | 34 | 3 | 6 | 9 | -3 | 21 |
| Mark Janssens, C | 46 | 2 | 5 | 7 | -8 | 93 |
| Brian Glynn, D | 43 | 1 | 6 | 7 | -2 | 32 |
| *Kevin Smyth, L | 16 | 1 | 5 | 6 | -3 | 13 |
| Igor Chibirev, C | 8 | 3 | 1 | 4 | 1 | 0 |
| Kelly Chase, R | 28 | 0 | 4 | 4 | 0 | 141 |
| Glen Featherstone, D | 19 | 2 | 1 | 3 | -7 | 50 |
| Jim Storm, L | 6 | 0 | 3 | 3 | 2 | 0 |
| *Scott Daniels, L | 12 | 0 | 2 | 2 | 1 | 55 |

### GOALTENDING

| Player | GP | Mins | Avg | W | L | T | SO |
|---|---|---|---|---|---|---|---|
| Sean Burke | 42 | 2418 | 2.68 | 17 | 19 | 4 | 0 |
| Jeff Reese | 11 | 477 | 3.27 | 2 | 5 | 1 | 0 |
| Team total | 48 | 2914 | 2.90 | 19 | 24 | 5 | 0 |

*Rookie.

## Los Angeles Kings

### SCORING

| Player | GP | G | A | Pts | +/– | PM |
|---|---|---|---|---|---|---|
| Wayne Gretzky, C | 48 | 11 | 37 | 48 | -20 | 6 |
| Rick Tocchet, R | 36 | 18 | 17 | 35 | -8 | 70 |
| Dan Quinn, C | 44 | 14 | 17 | 31 | -3 | 32 |
| Jari Kurri, L | 38 | 10 | 19 | 29 | -17 | 24 |
| Tony Granato, L | 33 | 13 | 11 | 24 | 9 | 68 |
| Darryl Sydor, D | 48 | 4 | 19 | 23 | -2 | 36 |
| Marty McSorley, D | 41 | 3 | 18 | 21 | -14 | 83 |
| John Druce, R | 43 | 15 | 5 | 20 | -3 | 20 |
| Randy Burridge, L | 40 | 4 | 15 | 19 | -4 | 10 |
| Michel Petit, D | 40 | 5 | 12 | 18 | 4 | 84 |
| *Eric Lacroix, L | 45 | 9 | 7 | 16 | 2 | 54 |
| Pat Conacher, L | 48 | 7 | 9 | 16 | -9 | 12 |
| Robert Lang, C | 36 | 4 | 8 | 12 | -7 | 4 |
| Rob Blake, D | 24 | 4 | 7 | 11 | -16 | 38 |
| Kevin Todd, C | 33 | 3 | 8 | 11 | -5 | 12 |
| Gary Shuchuk, C | 22 | 3 | 6 | 9 | -2 | 6 |
| *Chris Snell, D | 32 | 2 | 7 | 9 | -7 | 22 |
| Rob Cowie, D | 32 | 2 | 7 | 9 | -6 | 20 |
| *Yanic Perreault, C | 26 | 2 | 5 | 7 | 3 | 20 |
| Philippe Boucher, D | 15 | 2 | 4 | 6 | 3 | 4 |
| *Kevin Brown, R | 23 | 2 | 3 | 5 | -7 | 18 |
| Troy Crowder, R | 29 | 1 | 2 | 3 | 0 | 99 |

### GOALTENDING

| Player | GP | Mins | Avg | W | L | T | SO |
|---|---|---|---|---|---|---|---|
| *Pauli Jaks | 1 | 40 | 3.00 | 0 | 0 | 0 | 0 |
| Kelly Hrudey | 35 | 1894 | 3.14 | 14 | 13 | 5 | 0 |
| *Jamie Storr | 5 | 263 | 3.88 | 1 | 3 | 1 | 0 |
| †Grant Fuhr | 14 | 698 | 4.04 | 1 | 7 | 3 | 0 |
| Robb Stauber | 1 | 16 | 7.50 | 0 | 0 | 0 | 0 |
| Team total | 48 | 2925 | 3.57 | 16 | 23 | 9 | 0 |

†Played 3 games with Buffalo.

## Montreal Canadiens

### SCORING

| Player | GP | G | A | Pts | +/– | PM |
|---|---|---|---|---|---|---|
| Mark Recchi, R | 49 | 16 | 32 | 48 | -9 | 28 |
| Pierre Turgeon, C | 49 | 24 | 23 | 47 | 0 | 14 |
| Vincent Damphousse, L | 48 | 10 | 30 | 40 | 15 | 42 |
| Benoit Brunet, L | 45 | 7 | 18 | 25 | 7 | 16 |
| Vladimir Malakhov, D | 40 | 4 | 17 | 21 | -3 | 46 |
| Mike Keane, R | 48 | 10 | 10 | 20 | 5 | 15 |
| *Brian Savage, C | 37 | 12 | 7 | 19 | 5 | 27 |
| Brian Bellows, L | 41 | 8 | 8 | 16 | -7 | 8 |
| Patrice Brisebois, D | 35 | 4 | 8 | 12 | -2 | 26 |
| Yves Racine, D | 47 | 4 | 7 | 11 | -1 | 42 |
| Lyle Odelein, D | 48 | 3 | 7 | 10 | -13 | 152 |
| J. J. Daigneault, D | 45 | 3 | 5 | 8 | 2 | 40 |
| *Turner Stevenson, R | 41 | 6 | 1 | 7 | 0 | 86 |
| Bryan Fogarty, D | 21 | 5 | 2 | 7 | -3 | 34 |
| Oleg Petrov, R | 12 | 2 | 3 | 5 | -7 | 4 |
| Ed Ronan, R | 30 | 1 | 4 | 5 | -7 | 12 |
| Peter Popovic, D | 33 | 0 | 5 | 5 | -10 | 8 |
| *Valeri Bure, R | 24 | 3 | 1 | 4 | -1 | 6 |
| Mark Lamb, C | 47 | 1 | 2 | 3 | -12 | 20 |
| *Donald Brashear, L | 20 | 1 | 1 | 2 | -5 | 63 |

### GOALTENDING

| Player | GP | Mins | Avg | W | L | T | SO |
|---|---|---|---|---|---|---|---|
| Patrick Roy | 43 | 2566 | 2.97 | 17 | 20 | 6 | 1 |
| Ron Tugnutt | 7 | 346 | 3.12 | 1 | 3 | 1 | 0 |
| Team total | 48 | 2921 | 3.04 | 18 | 23 | 7 | 1 |

## New Jersey Devils

### SCORING

| Player | GP | G | A | Pts | +/- | PM |
|---|---|---|---|---|---|---|
| Stephane Richer, R | 45 | 23 | 16 | 39 | 8 | 10 |
| Neal Broten, C | 47 | 8 | 24 | 32 | 1 | 24 |
| John MacLean, R | 46 | 17 | 12 | 29 | 13 | 32 |
| Bill Guerin, R | 48 | 12 | 13 | 25 | 6 | 72 |
| Scott Stevens, D | 48 | 2 | 20 | 22 | 4 | 56 |
| Shawn Chambers, D | 45 | 4 | 17 | 21 | 2 | 12 |
| Bobby Holik, L | 48 | 10 | 10 | 20 | 9 | 18 |
| Claude Lemieux, R | 45 | 6 | 13 | 19 | 2 | 86 |
| Scott Niedermayer, D | 48 | 4 | 15 | 19 | 19 | 18 |
| Tom Chorske, L | 42 | 10 | 8 | 18 | -4 | 16 |
| *Brian Rolston, C | 40 | 7 | 11 | 18 | 5 | 17 |
| Bob Carpenter, L | 41 | 5 | 11 | 16 | -1 | 19 |
| Bruce Driver, D | 41 | 4 | 12 | 16 | -1 | 18 |
| Tommy Albelin, D | 48 | 5 | 10 | 15 | 9 | 20 |
| *Sergei Brylin, C | 26 | 6 | 8 | 14 | 12 | 8 |
| Randy McKay, R | 33 | 5 | 7 | 12 | 10 | 44 |
| Mike Peluso, L | 46 | 2 | 9 | 11 | 5 | 167 |
| Danton Cole, R | 38 | 4 | 5 | 9 | -1 | 14 |
| Jim Dowd, C | 10 | 1 | 4 | 5 | -5 | 0 |
| Valeri Zelepukin, L | 4 | 1 | 2 | 3 | 3 | 6 |
| Ken Daneyko, D | 25 | 1 | 2 | 3 | 4 | 54 |
| *Chris McAlpine, D | 24 | 0 | 3 | 3 | 4 | 17 |

### GOALTENDING

| Player | GP | Mins | Avg | W | L | T | SO |
|---|---|---|---|---|---|---|---|
| Martin Brodeur | 40 | 2184 | 2.45 | 19 | 11 | 6 | 3 |
| Chris Terreri | 15 | 734 | 2.53 | 3 | 7 | 2 | 0 |
| Team total | 48 | 2926 | 2.48 | 22 | 18 | 8 | 3 |

## New York Islanders

### SCORING

| Player | GP | G | A | Pts | +/- | PM |
|---|---|---|---|---|---|---|
| Ray Ferraro, C | 47 | 22 | 21 | 43 | 1 | 30 |
| Mathieu Schneider, D | 43 | 8 | 21 | 29 | -8 | 79 |
| Kirk Muller, L | 45 | 11 | 16 | 27 | -18 | 47 |
| Patrick Flatley, R | 45 | 7 | 20 | 27 | 9 | 12 |
| Steve Thomas, L | 47 | 11 | 15 | 26 | -14 | 60 |
| Derek King, L | 43 | 10 | 16 | 26 | -5 | 41 |
| *Zigmund Palffy, L | 33 | 10 | 7 | 17 | 3 | 6 |
| Marty McInnis, C | 41 | 9 | 7 | 16 | -1 | 8 |
| Scott Lachance, D | 26 | 6 | 7 | 13 | 2 | 26 |
| Travis Green, C | 42 | 5 | 7 | 12 | -10 | 25 |
| Dennis Vaske, D | 41 | 1 | 11 | 12 | 3 | 53 |
| Bob Beers, D | 22 | 2 | 7 | 9 | -8 | 6 |
| Brent Severyn, D | 28 | 2 | 4 | 6 | -2 | 71 |
| Brad Dalgarno, R | 22 | 3 | 2 | 5 | -8 | 14 |
| *Chris Marinucci, C | 12 | 1 | 4 | 5 | -1 | 2 |
| Ron Sutter, C | 27 | 1 | 4 | 5 | -8 | 21 |
| *Brett Lindros, R | 33 | 1 | 3 | 4 | -8 | 100 |
| Chris Luongo, D | 47 | 1 | 3 | 4 | -2 | 36 |
| Paul Stanton, D | 18 | 0 | 4 | 4 | -6 | 9 |
| *Chris Taylor, C | 10 | 0 | 3 | 3 | 1 | 2 |

### GOALTENDING

| Player | GP | Mins | Avg | W | L | T | SO |
|---|---|---|---|---|---|---|---|
| *Tommy Salo | 6 | 358 | 3.02 | 1 | 5 | 0 | 0 |
| T. Soderstrom | 26 | 1350 | 3.11 | 8 | 12 | 3 | 1 |
| *Jamie McLennan | 21 | 1185 | 3.39 | 6 | 11 | 2 | 0 |
| Team total | 48 | 2909 | 3.26 | 15 | 28 | 5 | 1 |

* Rookie.

## New York Rangers

### SCORING

| Player | GP | G | A | Pts | +/- | PM |
|---|---|---|---|---|---|---|
| Mark Messier, C | 46 | 14 | 39 | 53 | 8 | 40 |
| Brian Leetch, D | 48 | 9 | 32 | 41 | 0 | 18 |
| Sergei Zubov, D | 38 | 10 | 26 | 36 | -2 | 18 |
| Pat Verbeek, R | 48 | 17 | 16 | 33 | -2 | 71 |
| Adam Graves, C | 47 | 17 | 14 | 31 | 9 | 51 |
| Steve Larmer, R | 47 | 14 | 15 | 29 | 8 | 16 |
| Alexei Kovalev, R | 48 | 13 | 15 | 28 | -6 | 30 |
| Brian Noonan, R | 45 | 14 | 13 | 27 | -3 | 26 |
| Petr Nedved, C | 46 | 11 | 12 | 23 | -1 | 26 |
| Sergei Nemchinov, C | 47 | 7 | 6 | 13 | -6 | 16 |
| A. Karpovtsev, D | 47 | 4 | 8 | 12 | -4 | 30 |
| Troy Loney, L | 30 | 5 | 4 | 9 | -2 | 23 |
| Jay Wells, D | 43 | 2 | 7 | 9 | 0 | 36 |
| Nathan Lafayette, C | 39 | 4 | 4 | 8 | 3 | 2 |
| Stephane Matteau, L | 41 | 3 | 5 | 8 | -8 | 25 |
| Kevin Lowe, D | 44 | 1 | 7 | 8 | -2 | 58 |
| Mark Osborne, L | 37 | 1 | 3 | 4 | -2 | 19 |
| Nick Kypreos, L | 40 | 1 | 3 | 4 | 0 | 93 |
| Jeff Beukeboom, D | 44 | 11 | 3 | 4 | 3 | 70 |
| Joey Kocur, R | 48 | 1 | 2 | 3 | -4 | 71 |
| *Mattias Norstrom, D | 9 | 0 | 3 | 3 | 2 | 2 |

### GOALTENDING

| Player | GP | Mins | Avg | W | L | T | SO |
|---|---|---|---|---|---|---|---|
| Glenn Healy | 17 | 888 | 2.36 | 8 | 6 | 1 | 1 |
| Mike Richter | 35 | 1993 | 2.92 | 14 | 17 | 2 | 2 |
| Team total | 48 | 2895 | 2.78 | 22 | 23 | 3 | 3 |

## Ottawa Senators

### SCORING

| Player | GP | G | A | Pts | +/- | PM |
|---|---|---|---|---|---|---|
| Alexei Yashin, C | 47 | 21 | 23 | 44 | -20 | 20 |
| Alexandre Daigle, C | 47 | 16 | 21 | 37 | -22 | 14 |
| Sylvain Turgeon, L | 33 | 11 | 8 | 19 | -1 | 29 |
| Martin Straka, R | 37 | 5 | 13 | 18 | -1 | 16 |
| *Steve Larouche, C | 18 | 8 | 7 | 15 | -5 | 6 |
| Sean Hill, D | 45 | 1 | 14 | 15 | -11 | 30 |
| Rob Gaudreau, C | 36 | 5 | 9 | 14 | -16 | 8 |
| Michel Picard, L | 24 | 5 | 8 | 13 | -1 | 14 |
| Scott Levins, C | 24 | 5 | 6 | 11 | 4 | 51 |
| Dave McIlwain, C | 43 | 5 | 6 | 11 | -26 | 22 |
| *Radek Bonk, C | 42 | 3 | 8 | 11 | -5 | 28 |
| Randy Cunneyworth, L | 48 | 5 | 5 | 10 | -19 | 68 |
| Pat Elynuik, R | 41 | 3 | 7 | 10 | -11 | 51 |
| Troy Mallette, L | 23 | 3 | 5 | 8 | 6 | 35 |
| Chris Dahlquist, D | 46 | 1 | 7 | 8 | -30 | 36 |
| *Pavol Demitra, R | 16 | 4 | 3 | 7 | -4 | 0 |
| Phil Bourque, L | 38 | 4 | 37 | 7 | -17 | 20 |
| Kerry Huffman, D | 37 | 2 | 4 | 6 | -17 | 46 |
| David Archibald, C | 14 | 2 | 2 | 4 | -7 | 19 |
| *Stanislav Neckar, D | 48 | 1 | 3 | 4 | -20 | 37 |
| Dennis Vial, D | 27 | 0 | 4 | 4 | 0 | 65 |
| Evgeny Davydov, R | 3 | 1 | 2 | 3 | 2 | 0 |

### GOALTENDING

| Player | GP | Mins | Avg | W | L | T | SO |
|---|---|---|---|---|---|---|---|
| *Mike Bales | 1 | 3 | .00 | 0 | 0 | 0 | 0 |
| Don Beaupre | 38 | 2161 | 3.36 | 8 | 25 | 3 | 1 |
| Darrin Madeley | 5 | 255 | 3.53 | 1 | 3 | 0 | 0 |
| Craig Billington | 9 | 472 | 4.07 | 0 | 6 | 2 | 0 |
| Team total | 48 | 2913 | 3.58 | 9 | 34 | 5 | 1 |

## Philadelphia Flyers

### SCORING

| Player | GP | G | A | Pts | +/- | PM |
|---|---|---|---|---|---|---|
| Eric Lindros, C | 46 | 29 | 41 | 70 | 27 | 60 |
| Mikael Renburg, L | 47 | 26 | 31 | 57 | 20 | 20 |
| John Leclair, C | 46 | 26 | 28 | 54 | 20 | 30 |
| Rod Brind'amour, C | 48 | 12 | 27 | 39 | -4 | 33 |
| Eric Desjardins, D | 43 | 5 | 24 | 29 | 12 | 14 |
| Dimitri Yushkevich, D | 40 | 5 | 9 | 14 | -4 | 47 |
| Kevin Dineen, R | 40 | 8 | 5 | 13 | -1 | 39 |
| *Chris Therien, D | 48 | 3 | 10 | 13 | 8 | 38 |
| Brent Fedyk, R | 30 | 8 | 4 | 12 | -2 | 14 |
| Craig MacTavish, C | 45 | 3 | 9 | 12 | 2 | 23 |
| Anatoli Semenov, C | 41 | 4 | 6 | 10 | -12 | 10 |
| Shjon Podein, C | 44 | 3 | 7 | 10 | -2 | 33 |
| Kevin Haller, D | 36 | 2 | 7 | 9 | 16 | 48 |
| Gilbert Dionne, L | 26 | 0 | 9 | 9 | -4 | 4 |
| Karl Dykhuis, D | 33 | 2 | 6 | 8 | 7 | 37 |
| Petr Svoboda, D | 37 | 0 | 8 | 8 | -5 | 70 |
| *Patrick Juhlin, L | 42 | 4 | 3 | 7 | -13 | 6 |
| Rob Dimaio, C | 36 | 3 | 1 | 4 | 8 | 53 |
| Dave Brown, R | 28 | 1 | 2 | 3 | -1 | 53 |
| Jim Montgomery, C | 13 | 1 | 1 | 2 | -4 | 8 |

### GOALTENDING

| Player | GP | Mins | Avg | W | L | T | SO |
|---|---|---|---|---|---|---|---|
| Dominic Roussel | 19 | 1075 | 2.34 | 11 | 7 | 0 | 1 |
| Ron Hextall | 31 | 1824 | 2.89 | 17 | 9 | 4 | 1 |
| Team total | 48 | 2906 | 2.73 | 28 | 16 | 4 | 2 |

## Pittsburgh Penguins

### SCORING

| Player | GP | G | A | Pts | +/- | PM |
|---|---|---|---|---|---|---|
| Jaromir Jagr, R | 48 | 32 | 38 | 70 | 23 | 37 |
| Ron Francis, C | 44 | 11 | 48 | 59 | 30 | 18 |
| Tomas Sandstrom, R | 47 | 21 | 23 | 44 | 1 | 42 |
| Luc Robitaille, L | 46 | 23 | 19 | 42 | 10 | 37 |
| Larry Murphy, D | 48 | 13 | 25 | 38 | 12 | 18 |
| Joe Mullen, R | 45 | 16 | 21 | 37 | 15 | 6 |
| John Cullen, C | 46 | 13 | 24 | 37 | -4 | 66 |
| Kevin Stevens, L | 27 | 15 | 12 | 27 | 0 | 51 |
| Shawn McEachern, C | 44 | 13 | 13 | 26 | 4 | 22 |
| Norm Maciver, D | 41 | 4 | 16 | 20 | -2 | 16 |
| Troy Murray, C | 46 | 4 | 12 | 16 | -2 | 39 |
| Ulf Samuelsson, D | 44 | 1 | 15 | 16 | 11 | 113 |
| Chris Joseph, D | 33 | 5 | 10 | 15 | 3 | 46 |
| *Len Barrie, C | 48 | 3 | 11 | 14 | -4 | 66 |
| Mike Hudson, C | 40 | 2 | 9 | 11 | -1 | 34 |
| Kjell Samuelsson, D | 41 | 1 | 6 | 7 | 8 | 54 |
| Greg Hawgood, D | 21 | 1 | 4 | 5 | 2 | 25 |
| Markus Naslund, R | 14 | 2 | 2 | 4 | 0 | 2 |
| *Greg Andrusak, D | 7 | 0 | 4 | 4 | -1 | 6 |
| Jim McKenzie, L | 39 | 2 | 1 | 3 | -7 | 63 |

### GOALTENDING

| Player | GP | Mins | Avg | W | L | T | SO |
|---|---|---|---|---|---|---|---|
| *P. De Rouville | 1 | 60 | 3.00 | 1 | 0 | 0 | 0 |
| Ken Wregget | 38 | 2208 | 3.21 | 25 | 9 | 2 | 0 |
| Wendell Young | 10 | 497 | 3.26 | 3 | 6 | 0 | 0 |
| Tom Barrasso | 2 | 125 | 3.84 | 0 | 1 | 1 | 0 |
| Team total | 48 | 2901 | 3.27 | 29 | 16 | 3 | 0 |

## Quebec Nordiques

### SCORING

| Player | GP | G | A | Pts | +/- | PM |
|---|---|---|---|---|---|---|
| Joe Sakic, C | 47 | 19 | 43 | 62 | 7 | 30 |
| *Peter Forsberg, C | 47 | 15 | 35 | 50 | 17 | 16 |
| Owen Nolan, R | 46 | 30 | 19 | 49 | 21 | 46 |
| Scott Young, R | 48 | 18 | 21 | 39 | 9 | 14 |
| Mike Ricci, C | 48 | 15 | 21 | 36 | 5 | 40 |
| Wendel Clark, L | 37 | 12 | 18 | 30 | -1 | 45 |
| Valeri Kamensky, L | 40 | 10 | 20 | 30 | 3 | 22 |
| Bob Bassen, C | 47 | 12 | 15 | 27 | 14 | 33 |
| Andrei Kovalenko, R | 45 | 14 | 10 | 24 | -4 | 31 |
| Uwe Krupp, D | 44 | 6 | 17 | 23 | 14 | 20 |
| *Adam Deadmarsh, R | 48 | 9 | 8 | 17 | 16 | 56 |
| Curtis Leschyshyn, D | 44 | 2 | 13 | 15 | 29 | 20 |
| Sylvain Lefebvre, D | 48 | 2 | 11 | 13 | 13 | 17 |
| Claude Lapointe, C | 29 | 4 | 8 | 12 | 5 | 41 |
| Chris Simon, L | 29 | 3 | 9 | 12 | 14 | 106 |
| Martin Rucinsky, L | 20 | 3 | 6 | 9 | 5 | 14 |
| Craig Wolanin, D | 40 | 3 | 6 | 9 | 12 | 40 |
| Adam Foote, D | 35 | 0 | 7 | 7 | 17 | 52 |
| Bill Huard, L | 33 | 3 | 3 | 6 | 0 | 77 |
| Paul MacDermid, R | 14 | 3 | 1 | 4 | 3 | 22 |
| *Dwayne Norris, R | 13 | 1 | 2 | 3 | 1 | 2 |
| Alexei Gusarov, D | 14 | 1 | 2 | 3 | -1 | 6 |
| *Rene Corbet, L | 8 | 0 | 3 | 3 | 3 | 2 |
| *Aaron Miller, D | 9 | 0 | 3 | 3 | 2 | 6 |
| *Janne Laukkanen, D | 11 | 0 | 3 | 3 | 3 | 4 |
| Stephane Fiset, G | 32 | 0 | 3 | 3 | 0 | 2 |
| Steven Finn, D | 40 | 0 | 3 | 3 | 1 | 64 |

### GOALTENDING

| Player | GP | Mins | Avg | W | L | T | SO |
|---|---|---|---|---|---|---|---|
| Jocelyn Thibault | 18 | 898 | 2.34 | 12 | 2 | 2 | 1 |
| Stephane Fiset | 32 | 1879 | 2.78 | 17 | 10 | 3 | 2 |
| *Garth Snow | 2 | 119 | 5.55 | 1 | 1 | 0 | 0 |
| Team total | 48 | 2908 | 2.76 | 30 | 13 | 5 | 3 |

* Rookie.

## St Louis Blues

### SCORING

| Player | GP | G | A | Pts | +/- | PM |
|---|---|---|---|---|---|---|
| Brett Hull, R | 48 | 29 | 21 | 50 | 13 | 10 |
| Brendan Shanahan, L | 45 | 20 | 21 | 40 | 7 | 136 |
| Steve Duchesne, D | 47 | 12 | 26 | 38 | 29 | 36 |
| Esa Tikkanen, L | 43 | 12 | 23 | 35 | 13 | 22 |
| Adam Creighton, C | 48 | 14 | 20 | 34 | 17 | 74 |
| Jeff Norton, D | 48 | 3 | 27 | 30 | 22 | 72 |
| Al MacInnis, D | 32 | 8 | 20 | 28 | 19 | 43 |
| *Ian Laperriere, C | 37 | 13 | 14 | 27 | 12 | 85 |
| Glenn Anderson, R | 36 | 12 | 14 | 26 | 9 | 37 |
| Greg Gilbert, L | 46 | 11 | 14 | 25 | 22 | 11 |
| Todd Elik, C | 35 | 9 | 14 | 23 | 8 | 22 |
| Bill Houlder, D | 41 | 5 | 13 | 18 | 16 | 20 |
| *Denis Chasse, R | 47 | 7 | 9 | 16 | 12 | 133 |
| Guy Carbonneau, C | 42 | 5 | 11 | 16 | 11 | 16 |
| *Patrice Tardif, C | 27 | 3 | 10 | 13 | 4 | 29 |
| *David Roberts, L | 19 | 6 | 5 | 11 | 2 | 10 |
| Vitali Karamnov, L | 26 | 3 | 7 | 10 | 7 | 14 |
| Doug Lidster, D | 37 | 2 | 7 | 9 | 9 | 12 |
| *Craig Johnson, L | 15 | 3 | 3 | 6 | 4 | 6 |
| Rick Zombo, D | 23 | 1 | 4 | 5 | 7 | 24 |
| Basil McRae, L | 21 | 0 | 5 | 5 | 4 | 72 |
| Murray Baron, D | 39 | 0 | 5 | 5 | 9 | 93 |
| Tony Twist, L | 28 | 3 | 0 | 3 | 0 | 89 |
| Donald Dufresne, D | 22 | 0 | 3 | 3 | 2 | 10 |
| Peter Stastny, C | 6 | 1 | 1 | 2 | 1 | 0 |

### GOALTENDING

| Player | GP | Mins | Avg | W | L | T | SO |
|---|---|---|---|---|---|---|---|
| Jon Casey | 19 | 872 | 2.75 | 7 | 5 | 4 | 0 |
| Curtis Joseph | 36 | 1914 | 2.79 | 20 | 10 | 1 | 1 |
| *Geoff Sarjeant | 4 | 120 | 3.00 | 1 | 0 | 0 | 0 |
| Team total | 48 | 2912 | 2.78 | 28 | 15 | 5 | 1 |

## San Jose Sharks

### SCORING

| Player | GP | G | A | Pts | +/- | PM |
|---|---|---|---|---|---|---|
| Ulf Dahlen, R | 46 | 11 | 23 | 34 | -2 | 11 |
| Craig Janney, C | 35 | 7 | 20 | 27 | -1 | 10 |
| *Jeff Friesen, L | 48 | 15 | 10 | 25 | -8 | 14 |
| Ray Whitney, C | 39 | 13 | 12 | 25 | -7 | 14 |
| Sandis Ozolinsh, D | 48 | 9 | 16 | 25 | -6 | 30 |
| Sergei Makarov, R | 43 | 10 | 14 | 24 | -4 | 40 |
| Igor Larionov, C | 33 | 4 | 20 | 24 | -3 | 14 |
| Kevin Miller, R | 36 | 8 | 12 | 20 | 4 | 13 |
| Pat Falloon, R | 46 | 12 | 7 | 19 | -4 | 25 |
| Tom Pederson, D | 47 | 5 | 11 | 16 | -14 | 31 |
| Chris Tancill, C | 26 | 3 | 11 | 14 | 1 | 10 |
| Jamie Baker, C | 43 | 7 | 4 | 11 | -7 | 22 |
| Mike Rathje, D | 42 | 2 | 7 | 9 | -1 | 29 |
| *Andrei Nazarov, R | 26 | 3 | 5 | 8 | -1 | 94 |
| Jeff Odgers, R | 48 | 4 | 3 | 7 | -8 | 117 |
| Jim Kyte, D | 18 | 2 | 5 | 7 | -7 | 33 |
| Jay More, D | 45 | 0 | 6 | 6 | 7 | 71 |
| Ilya Byakin, D | 13 | 0 | 5 | 5 | -9 | 14 |
| *Michal Sykora, D | 16 | 0 | 4 | 4 | 6 | 10 |

### GOALTENDING

| Player | GP | Mins | Avg | W | L | T | SO |
|---|---|---|---|---|---|---|---|
| Wade Flaherty | 18 | 852 | 3.10 | 5 | 6 | 1 | 1 |
| Arturs Irbe | 38 | 2043 | 3.26 | 14 | 19 | 3 | 4 |
| Team total | 48 | 2904 | 3.33 | 19 | 25 | 4 | 5 |

## Tampa Bay Lightning

### SCORING

| Player | GP | G | A | Pts | +/- | PM |
|---|---|---|---|---|---|---|
| Brian Bradley, C | 46 | 13 | 27 | 40 | -6 | 42 |
| Paul Ysebaert, L | 44 | 12 | 16 | 28 | 3 | 18 |
| Chris Gratton, C | 46 | 7 | 20 | 27 | -2 | 89 |
| Petr Klima, R | 47 | 13 | 13 | 26 | -13 | 26 |
| John Tucker, R | 46 | 12 | 13 | 25 | -10 | 14 |
| Roman Hamrlik, D | 48 | 12 | 11 | 23 | -18 | 86 |
| Alexander Semak, C | 41 | 7 | 11 | 18 | -7 | 25 |
| *Alexander Selivanov, R | 43 | 10 | 6 | 16 | -2 | 14 |
| Rob Zamuner, L | 43 | 9 | 6 | 15 | -3 | 24 |
| Marc Bureau, C | 48 | 2 | 12 | 14 | -8 | 30 |
| Mikael Andersson, L | 36 | 4 | 7 | 11 | -3 | 4 |
| Enrico Ciccone, D | 41 | 2 | 4 | 6 | 3 | 225 |
| Mark Bergevin, D | 44 | 2 | 4 | 6 | -6 | 51 |
| *Cory Cross, D | 43 | 1 | 5 | 6 | -6 | 41 |
| Bob Halkidis, D | 31 | 1 | 4 | 5 | -10 | 46 |
| *Jason Wiemer, L | 36 | 1 | 4 | 5 | -2 | 44 |
| *Eric Charron, D | 45 | 1 | 4 | 5 | 1 | 26 |
| Adrien Plavsic, D | 18 | 2 | 2 | 4 | 8 | 8 |
| *Brantt Myhres, R | 15 | 2 | 0 | 2 | -2 | 81 |
| Rudy Poeschek, D | 25 | 1 | 1 | 2 | 0 | 92 |
| *Ben Hankinson, R | 26 | 0 | 2 | 2 | -5 | 13 |

### GOALTENDING

| Player | GP | Mins | Avg | W | L | T | SO |
|---|---|---|---|---|---|---|---|
| Daren Puppa | 36 | 2013 | 2.68 | 14 | 19 | 2 | 1 |
| J.C. Bergeron | 17 | 883 | 3.33 | 3 | 9 | 1 | 1 |
| Team total | 48 | 2906 | 2.97 | 17 | 28 | 3 | 2 |

* Rookie.

## Toronto Maple Leafs

### SCORING

| Player | GP | G | A | Pts | +/- | PM |
|---|---|---|---|---|---|---|
| Mats Sundin, C | 47 | 23 | 24 | 47 | -5 | 14 |
| Dave Andreychuk, L | 48 | 22 | 16 | 38 | -7 | 34 |
| Mike Ridley, C | 48 | 10 | 27 | 37 | 1 | 14 |
| Doug Gilmour, C | 44 | 10 | 23 | 33 | -5 | 26 |
| Todd Gill, D | 47 | 7 | 25 | 32 | -8 | 64 |
| Randy Wood, L | 48 | 13 | 11 | 24 | 7 | 34 |
| Mike Gartner, R | 38 | 12 | 8 | 20 | 0 | 6 |
| Dmitri Mironov, D | 33 | 5 | 12 | 17 | 6 | 28 |
| Benoit Hogue, C | 45 | 9 | 7 | 16 | 0 | 34 |
| Dave Ellett, D | 33 | 5 | 10 | 15 | -6 | 26 |
| Paul Dipietro, C | 34 | 5 | 6 | 11 | 9 | 10 |
| Mike Craig, R | 37 | 5 | 5 | 10 | -21 | 12 |
| Jamie Macoun, D | 46 | 2 | 8 | 10 | -6 | 75 |
| Tie Domi, R | 40 | 4 | 5 | 9 | -5 | 159 |
| *Kenny Jonsson, D | 39 | 2 | 7 | 9 | -8 | 16 |
| Garth Butcher, D | 45 | 1 | 7 | 8 | -5 | 59 |
| Warren Rychel, L | 33 | 1 | 6 | 7 | -4 | 120 |
| Bill Berg, L | 32 | 5 | 1 | 6 | -11 | 26 |
| Grant Jennings, D | 35 | 0 | 6 | 6 | -4 | 43 |
| Terry Yake, R | 19 | 3 | 2 | 5 | 1 | 2 |
| Dixon Ward, R | 22 | 0 | 3 | 3 | -4 | 31 |
| Rich Sutter, R | 37 | 0 | 3 | 3 | -6 | 38 |

### GOALTENDING

| Player | GP | Mins | Avg | W | L | T | SO |
|---|---|---|---|---|---|---|---|
| *Damian Rhodes | 13 | 760 | 2.68 | 6 | 6 | 1 | 0 |
| Felix Potvin | 36 | 2144 | 2.91 | 15 | 13 | 7 | 0 |
| Team total | 48 | 2920 | 3.00 | 21 | 19 | 8 | 0 |

## Vancouver Canucks

### SCORING

| Player | GP | G | A | Pts | +/- | PM |
|---|---|---|---|---|---|---|
| Pavel Bure, L | 44 | 20 | 23 | 43 | -8 | 47 |
| Trevor Linden, C | 48 | 18 | 22 | 40 | -5 | 40 |
| Russ Courtnall, R | 45 | 11 | 24 | 35 | 2 | 17 |
| Geoff Courtnall, L | 45 | 16 | 18 | 34 | 2 | 81 |
| Josef Beranek, C | 51 | 13 | 18 | 31 | -7 | 30 |
| Jeff Brown, D | 33 | 8 | 23 | 31 | -2 | 16 |
| Sergio Momesso, L | 48 | 10 | 15 | 25 | -2 | 65 |
| Cliff Ronning, C | 41 | 6 | 19 | 25 | -4 | 27 |
| Martin Gelinas, L | 46 | 13 | 10 | 23 | 8 | 36 |
| *Roman Oksiuta, R | 38 | 16 | 4 | 20 | -12 | 10 |
| Christian Ruuttu, C | 45 | 7 | 11 | 18 | 14 | 29 |
| Jyrki Lumme, D | 36 | 5 | 12 | 17 | 4 | 26 |
| Dave Babych, D | 40 | 3 | 11 | 14 | -13 | 18 |
| Bret Hedican, D | 45 | 2 | 11 | 13 | -3 | 34 |
| *Mike Peca, C | 33 | 6 | 6 | 12 | -6 | 30 |
| Gino Odjick, L | 23 | 4 | 5 | 9 | -3 | 109 |
| Dana Murzyn, D | 40 | 0 | 8 | 8 | 14 | 129 |
| Tim Hunter, R | 34 | 3 | 2 | 5 | 1 | 120 |
| John McIntyre, C | 28 | 0 | 4 | 4 | -3 | 37 |
| *Jassen Cullimore, D | 34 | 1 | 2 | 3 | -2 | 39 |
| *Y. Namestnikov, D | 16 | 0 | 3 | 3 | 2 | 4 |

### GOALTENDING

| Player | GP | Mins | Avg | W | L | T | SO |
|---|---|---|---|---|---|---|---|
| Kirk McLean | 40 | 2374 | 2.75 | 18 | 12 | 10 | 1 |
| Kay Whitmore | 11 | 558 | 3.98 | 0 | 6 | 2 | 0 |
| Team total | 48 | 2942 | 3.02 | 18 | 18 | 12 | 1 |

## Washington Capitals

### SCORING

| Player | GP | G | A | Pts | +/- | PM |
|---|---|---|---|---|---|---|
| Peter Bondra, R | 47 | 34 | 9 | 43 | 9 | 24 |
| Joe Juneau, C | 44 | 5 | 38 | 43 | -1 | 8 |
| Michal Pivonka, C | 46 | 10 | 23 | 33 | 3 | 50 |
| Calle Johansson, D | 46 | 5 | 26 | 31 | -6 | 35 |
| Dimitri Khristich, L | 48 | 12 | 14 | 26 | 0 | 41 |
| Steve Konowalchuk, C | 46 | 11 | 14 | 25 | 7 | 44 |
| Kelly Miller, L | 48 | 10 | 13 | 23 | 5 | 6 |
| Dale Hunter, C | 45 | 8 | 15 | 23 | -4 | 101 |
| Keith Jones, R | 40 | 14 | 6 | 20 | -2 | 65 |
| Sylvain Cote, D | 47 | 5 | 14 | 19 | 2 | 53 |
| Jim Johnson, D | 47 | 0 | 13 | 13 | 6 | 43 |
| Mark Tinordi, D | 42 | 3 | 9 | 12 | -5 | 71 |
| Dave Poulin, C | 29 | 4 | 5 | 9 | 2 | 10 |
| Mike Eagles, C | 40 | 3 | 4 | 7 | -11 | 48 |
| *Sergei Gonchar, D | 31 | 2 | 5 | 7 | 4 | 22 |
| Joe Reekie, D | 48 | 1 | 6 | 7 | 10 | 97 |
| Craig Berube, L | 43 | 2 | 4 | 6 | -5 | 173 |
| Rob Pearson, R | 32 | 0 | 6 | 6 | -6 | 96 |
| Igor Ulanov, D | 22 | 1 | 4 | 5 | 1 | 29 |
| *Ken Klee, D | 23 | 3 | 1 | 4 | 2 | 41 |
| Pat Peake, C | 18 | 0 | 4 | 4 | -6 | 12 |
| *Martin Gendron, R | 8 | 2 | 1 | 3 | 3 | 2 |
| *Jason Allison, C | 12 | 2 | 1 | 3 | -3 | 6 |
| John Slaney, D | 16 | 0 | 3 | 3 | -3 | 6 |

### GOALTENDING

| Player | GP | Mins | Avg | W | L | T | SO |
|---|---|---|---|---|---|---|---|
| *Jim Carey | 28 | 1604 | 2.13 | 18 | 6 | 3 | 4 |
| Rick Tabaracci | 8 | 394 | 2.44 | 1 | 3 | 2 | 0 |
| *Olaf Kolzig | 14 | 724 | 2.49 | 2 | 8 | 2 | 0 |
| *Bryan Dafoe | 4 | 187 | 3.53 | 1 | 1 | 1 | 0 |
| Team total | 48 | 2922 | 2.46 | 22 | 18 | 8 | 4 |

* Rookie.

## Winnipeg Jets

### SCORING

| Player | GP | G | A | Pts | +/– | PM |
|---|---|---|---|---|---|---|
| Alexei Zhamnov, C | 48 | 30 | 35 | 65 | 5 | 20 |
| Keith Tkachuk, L | 48 | 22 | 29 | 51 | -4 | 152 |
| Teemu Selanne, R | 45 | 22 | 26 | 48 | 1 | 2 |
| Nelson Emerson, R | 48 | 14 | 23 | 37 | -12 | 26 |
| Igor Korolev, R | 45 | 8 | 22 | 30 | 1 | 10 |
| Dallas Drake, C | 43 | 8 | 18 | 26 | -6 | 30 |
| Stephane Quintal, D | 43 | 6 | 17 | 23 | 0 | 78 |
| Teppo Numminen, D | 42 | 5 | 16 | 21 | 12 | 16 |
| Mike Eastwood, C | 49 | 8 | 11 | 19 | -9 | 36 |
| Dave Manson, D | 44 | 3 | 15 | 18 | -20 | 139 |
| Thomas Steen, C | 31 | 5 | 10 | 15 | -13 | 14 |
| Darryl Shannon, D | 40 | 5 | 9 | 14 | 1 | 48 |
| Ed Olczyk, C | 33 | 4 | 9 | 13 | -1 | 12 |
| Randy Gilhen, C | 44 | 5 | 6 | 11 | -17 | 52 |
| Darrin Shannon, L | 19 | 5 | 3 | 8 | -6 | 14 |
| Kris King, L | 48 | 4 | 2 | 6 | 0 | 85 |
| Neil Wilkinson, D | 40 | 1 | 4 | 5 | -26 | 75 |
| *Michal Grosek, L | 24 | 2 | 2 | 4 | -3 | 21 |
| Greg Brown, D | 9 | 0 | 3 | 3 | 1 | 17 |
| Rob Murray, C | 10 | 0 | 2 | 2 | 1 | 2 |
| Oleg Mikulchik, D | 25 | 0 | 2 | 2 | 10 | 12 |

### GOALTENDING

| Player | GP | Mins | Avg | W | L | T | SO |
|---|---|---|---|---|---|---|---|
| *N. Khabibulin | 26 | 1339 | 3.41 | 8 | 9 | 4 | 0 |
| Tim Cheveldae | 30 | 1571 | 3.70 | 8 | 16 | 3 | 0 |
| Team total | 48 | 2923 | 3.63 | 16 | 25 | 7 | 0 |

* Rookie.

# 1995 NHL Draft

## First Round

The opening round of the 1995 NHL draft was held in Edmonton on July 8.

| | Team | Selection | Position |
|---|---|---|---|
| 1 | Ottawa | Bryan Berard, Detroit | D |
| 2 | NY Islanders | Wade Redden, Brandon | D |
| 3 | Los Angeles | Aki-Petteri Berg, Kiekko | D |
| 4 | Anaheim | Chad Kilger, Kingston | C |
| 5 | Tampa Bay | Daymond Langkow, Tri-City | C |
| 6 | Edmonton | Steve Kelly, Prince Albert | C |
| 7 | Winnipeg | Shane Doan, Kamloops | R |
| 8 | Montreal | Terry Ryan, Tri-City | L |
| 9 | Boston | Kyle McLaren, Tacoma | D |
| 10 | Florida | Radek Dvorak, Budjovice | C |
| 11 | Dallas | Jarome Iginla, Kamloops | R |
| 12 | San Jose | Teemu Riihijarvi, Espoo Jr. | L |
| 13 | Buffalo | Jay McKee, Niagara Falls | D |
| 14 | Hartford | J. S. Giguere, Halifax | G |
| 15 | Toronto | Jeff Ware, Oshawa | D |
| 16 | Buffalo | Martin Biron, Beauport | G |
| 17 | Washington | Brad Church, Prince Albert | L |
| 18 | New Jersey | Petr Sykora, Detroit | C |
| 19 | Chicago | Dimitri Nabokov, Krylja Sovetov | C |
| 20 | Calgary | Denis Gauthier, Drummondville | D |
| 21 | Boston | Sean Brown, Belleville | D |
| 22 | Philadelphia | Brian Boucher, Tri-City | G |
| 23 | Washington | Mikka Elomo, Kiekko Jr. | L |
| 24 | Pittsburgh | Alexei Morozov, Krylja Sovetov | R |
| 25 | Colorado | Marc Denis, Chicoutimi | G |
| 26 | Detroit | M. Kuznetsov, Dynamo Moscow | D |

**Spamdemonium**

The folks in the front office of the Minnesota Moose of the International Hockey League have fashioned a new recipe: Spam on ice. Between periods at the Saint Paul Civic Center, the Spamboni, a Zamboni painted like a giant can of Spam, resurfaces the rink. Hormel Foods, the Minnesota-based company that produces the hamlike food product, bought the ad rights to the Zamboni for the season, and the success of its advertising vehicle has spawned everything from Spamburger giveaways to the frightening notion of Spam as training-table fare. "Our players are required to eat at least 100 pounds of Spam per season," says Moose vice president of business operations Ron Minegar. "It's why we have the best-conditioned team in the league. I'm joking, of course."

## The Stanley Cup

Awarded annually to the team that wins the NHL's best-of-seven final-round playoffs. The Stanley Cup is the oldest trophy competed for by professional athletes in North America. It was donated in 1893 by Frederick Arthur, Lord Stanley of Preston.

### Results

#### WINNERS PRIOR TO FORMATION OF NHL IN 1917

| | |
|---|---|
| 1892-93 | Montreal A.A.A. |
| 1893-94 | Montreal A.A.A. |
| 1894-95 | Montreal Victorias |
| 1895-96 | Winnipeg Victorias (Feb) |
| 1895-96 | Montreal Victorias (Dec) |
| 1896-97 | Montreal Victorias |
| 1897-98 | Montreal Victorias |
| 1898-99 | Montreal Victorias (Feb) |
| 1898-99 | Montreal Shamrocks (Mar) |
| 1899-1900 | Montreal Shamrocks |
| 1900-01 | Winnipeg Victorias |
| 1901-02 | Winnipeg Victorias (Jan) |
| 1901-02 | Montreal A.A.A. (Mar) |
| 1902-03 | Montreal A.A.A. (Feb) |
| 1902-03 | Ottawa Silver Seven (Mar) |
| 1903-04 | Ottawa Silver Seven |
| 1904-05 | Ottawa Silver Seven |
| 1905-06 | Ottawa Silver Seven (Feb) |
| 1905-06 | Montreal Wanderers (Mar) |
| 1906-07 | Kenora Thistles (Jan) |
| 1906-07 | Montreal Wanderers (Mar) |
| 1907-08 | Montreal Wanderers |
| 1908-09 | Ottawa Senators |
| 1909-10 | Montreal Wanderers |
| 1910-11 | Ottawa Senators |
| 1911-12 | Quebec Bulldogs |
| 1912-13 | Quebec Bulldogs |
| 1913-14 | Toronto Blueshirts |
| 1914-15 | Vancouver Millionaires |
| 1915-16 | Montreal Canadiens |
| 1916-17 | Seattle Metropolitans |

#### NHL WINNERS AND FINALISTS

| Season | Champion | Finalist | GP in Final |
|---|---|---|---|
| 1917-18 | Toronto Arenas | Vancouver Millionaires | 5 |
| 1918-19 | No decision* | No decision* | |
| 1919-20 | Ottawa Senators | Seattle Metropolitans | 5 |
| 1920-21 | Ottawa Senators | Vancouver Millionaires | 5 |
| 1921-22 | Toronto St Pats | Vancouver Millionaires | 5 |
| 1922-23 | Ottawa Senators | Vancouver Millionaires, Edmonton | 3, 2 |
| 1923-24 | Montreal Canadiens | Vancouver Millionaires, Calgary | 2, 2 |
| 1924-25 | Victoria Cougars | Montreal Canadiens | 4 |
| 1925-26 | Montreal Maroons | Victoria Cougars | 4 |
| 1926-27 | Ottawa Senators | Boston Bruins | 4 |
| 1927-28 | New York Rangers | Montreal Maroons | 5 |
| 1928-29 | Boston Bruins | New York Rangers | 2 |
| 1929-30 | Montreal Canadiens | Boston Bruins | 2 |
| 1930-31 | Montreal Canadiens | Chicago Blackhawks | 5 |
| 1931-32 | Toronto Maple Leafs | New York Rangers | 3 |
| 1932-33 | New York Rangers | Toronto Maple Leafs | 4 |
| 1933-34 | Chicago Blackhawks | Detroit Red Wings | 4 |
| 1934-35 | Montreal Maroons | Toronto Maple Leafs | 3 |
| 1935-36 | Detroit Red Wings | Toronto Maple Leafs | 4 |
| 1936-37 | Detroit Red Wings | New York Rangers | 5 |
| 1937-38 | Chicago Blackhawks | Toronto Maple Leafs | 4 |
| 1938-39 | Boston Bruins | Toronto Maple Leafs | 5 |
| 1939-40 | New York Rangers | Toronto Maple Leafs | 6 |
| 1940-41 | Boston Bruins | Detroit Red Wings | 4 |
| 1941-42 | Toronto Maple Leafs | Detroit Red Wings | 7 |
| 1942-43 | Detroit Red Wings | Boston Bruins | 4 |
| 1943-44 | Montreal Canadiens | Chicago Blackhawks | 4 |
| 1944-45 | Toronto Maple Leafs | Detroit Red Wings | 7 |
| 1945-46 | Montreal Canadiens | Boston Bruins | 5 |
| 1946-47 | Toronto Maple Leafs | Montreal Canadiens | 6 |
| 1947-48 | Toronto Maple Leafs | Detroit Red Wings | 4 |
| 1948-49 | Toronto Maple Leafs | Detroit Red Wings | 4 |
| 1949-50 | Detroit Red Wings | New York Rangers | 7 |
| 1950-51 | Toronto Maple Leafs | Montreal Canadiens | 5 |
| 1951-52 | Detroit Red Wings | Montreal Canadiens | 4 |
| 1952-53 | Montreal Canadiens | Boston Bruins | 5 |
| 1953-54 | Detroit Red Wings | Montreal Canadiens | 7 |

## NHL WINNERS AND FINALISTS (Cont.)

| | | |
|---|---|---|
| 1954-55 | Detroit Red Wings | Montreal Canadiens | 7 |
| 1955-56 | Montreal Canadiens | Detroit Red Wings | 5 |
| 1956-57 | Montreal Canadiens | Boston Bruins | 5 |
| 1957-58 | Montreal Canadiens | Boston Bruins | 6 |
| 1958-59 | Montreal Canadiens | Toronto Maple Leafs | 5 |
| 1959-60 | Montreal Canadiens | Toronto Maple Leafs | 4 |
| 1960-61 | Chicago Blackhawks | Detroit Red Wings | 6 |
| 1961-62 | Toronto Maple Leafs | Chicago Blackhawks | 6 |
| 1962-63 | Toronto Maple Leafs | Detroit Red Wings | 5 |
| 1963-64 | Toronto Maple Leafs | Detroit Red Wings | 7 |
| 1964-65 | Montreal Canadiens | Chicago Blackhawks | 7 |
| 1965-66 | Montreal Canadiens | Detroit Red Wings | 6 |
| 1966-67 | Toronto Maple Leafs | Montreal Canadiens | 6 |
| 1967-68 | Montreal Canadiens | St Louis Blues | 4 |
| 1968-69 | Montreal Canadiens | St Louis Blues | 4 |
| 1969-70 | Boston Bruins | St Louis Blues | 4 |
| 1970-71 | Montreal Canadiens | Chicago Blackhawks | 7 |
| 1971-72 | Boston Bruins | New York Rangers | 6 |
| 1972-73 | Montreal Canadiens | Chicago Blackhawks | 6 |
| 1973-74 | Philadelphia Flyers | Boston Bruins | 6 |
| 1974-75 | Philadelphia Flyers | Buffalo Sabres | 6 |
| 1975-76 | Montreal Canadiens | Philadelphia Flyers | 4 |
| 1976-77 | Montreal Canadiens | Boston Bruins | 6 |
| 1977-78 | Montreal Canadiens | Boston Bruins | 6 |
| 1978-79 | Montreal Canadiens | New York Rangers | 5 |
| 1979-80 | New York Islanders | Philadelphia Flyers | 6 |
| 1980-81 | New York Islanders | Minnesota North Stars | 5 |
| 1981-82 | New York Islanders | Vancouver Canucks | 4 |
| 1982-83 | New York Islanders | Edmonton Oilers | 4 |
| 1983-84 | Edmonton Oilers | New York Islanders | 5 |
| 1984-85 | Edmonton Oilers | Philadelphia Flyers | 5 |
| 1985-86 | Montreal Canadiens | Calgary Flames | 6 |
| 1986-87 | Edmonton Oilers | Philadelphia Flyers | 7 |
| 1987-88 | Edmonton Oilers | Boston Bruins | 4 |
| 1988-89 | Calgary Flames | Montreal Canadiens | 6 |
| 1989-90 | Edmonton Oilers | Boston Bruins | 5 |
| 1990-91 | Pittsburgh Penguins | Minnesota North Stars | 6 |
| 1991-92 | Pittsburgh Penguins | Chicago Blackhawks | 4 |
| 1992-93 | Montreal Canadiens | Los Angeles Kings | 5 |
| 1993-94 | New York Rangers | Vancouver Canucks | 7 |
| 1994-95 | New Jersey Devils | Detroit Red Wings | 4 |

*In 1919 the Montreal Canadiens traveled to meet Seattle, the PCHL champions. After 5 games had been played—the teams were tied at 2 wins and 1 tie—the series was called off by the local Department of Health because of the influenza epidemic and the death of Canadian defenseman Joe Hall from influenza.

## Conn Smythe Trophy

Awarded to the Most Valuable Player of the Stanley Cup playoffs, as selected by the Professional Hockey Writers Association. The trophy is named after the former coach, general manager, president and owner of the Toronto Maple Leafs.

| | | | |
|---|---|---|---|
| 1965 | Jean Beliveau, Mtl | 1981 | Butch Goring, NYI |
| 1966 | Roger Crozier, Det | 1982 | Mike Bossy, NYI |
| 1967 | Dave Keon, Tor | 1983 | Bill Smith, NYI |
| 1968 | Glenn Hall, StL | 1984 | Mark Messier, Edm |
| 1969 | Serge Savard, Mtl | 1985 | Wayne Gretzky, Edm |
| 1970 | Bobby Orr, Bos | 1986 | Patrick Roy, Mtl |
| 1971 | Ken Dryden, Mtl | 1987 | Ron Hextall, Phil |
| 1972 | Bobby Orr, Bos | 1988 | Wayne Gretzky, Edm |
| 1973 | Yvan Cournoyer, Mtl | 1989 | Al MacInnis, Cgy |
| 1974 | Bernie Parent, Phil | 1990 | Bill Ranford, Edm |
| 1975 | Bernie Parent, Phil | 1991 | Mario Lemieux, Pitt |
| 1976 | Reggie Leach, Phil | 1992 | Mario Lemieux, Pitt |
| 1977 | Guy Lafleur, Mtl | 1993 | Patrick Roy, Mtl |
| 1978 | Larry Robinson, Mtl | 1994 | Brian Leetch, NYR |
| 1979 | Bob Gainey, Mtl | 1995 | Claude Lemieux, NJ |
| 1980 | Bryan Trottier, NYI | | |

## Alltime Stanley Cup Playoff Leaders

### Points

| | Yrs | GP | G | A | Pts | | Yrs | GP | G | A | Pts |
|---|---|---|---|---|---|---|---|---|---|---|---|
| *Wayne Gretzky, Edm, LA | 14 | 180 | 110 | 236 | 346 | *Doug Gilmour, StL, Cgy, Tor | 11 | 132 | 48 | 104 | 152 |
| *Mark Messier, Edm, NYR | 15 | 210 | 102 | 170 | 272 | Stan Mikita, Chi | 18 | 155 | 59 | 91 | 150 |
| *Jari Kurri, Edm, LA | 12 | 174 | 102 | 120 | 222 | Brian Propp, Phil, Bos, Minn | 13 | 160 | 64 | 84 | 148 |
| *Glenn Anderson, four teams | 14 | 214 | 92 | 117 | 209 | Larry Robinson, Mtl, LA | 20 | 227 | 28 | 116 | 144 |
| Bryan Trottier, NYI, Pitt | 17 | 221 | 71 | 113 | 184 | Jacques Lemaire, Mtl | 11 | 145 | 61 | 78 | 139 |
| Jean Beliveau, Mtl | 17 | 162 | 79 | 97 | 176 | *Ray Bourque, Bos | 16 | 157 | 33 | 106 | 139 |
| *Paul Coffey,Edm,Pitt,LA,Det | 13 | 155 | 53 | 119 | 172 | Phil Esposito, Chi, Bos, NYR | 15 | 130 | 61 | 76 | 137 |
| *Denis Savard, Chi, Mtl | 14 | 153 | 65 | 105 | 170 | Guy Lafleur, Mtl, NYR | 14 | 128 | 58 | 76 | 134 |
| Denis Potvin, NYI | 14 | 185 | 56 | 108 | 164 | Steve Larmer, Chi, NYR | 13 | 140 | 56 | 75 | 131 |
| Mike Bossy, NYI | 10 | 129 | 85 | 75 | 160 | Bobby Hull, Chi, Hart | 14 | 119 | 62 | 67 | 129 |
| Gordie Howe, Det, Hart | 20 | 157 | 68 | 92 | 160 | Henri Richard, Mtl | 18 | 180 | 49 | 80 | 129 |
| Bobby Smith, Minn, Mtl | 13 | 184 | 64 | 96 | 160 | | | | | | |

*Active player.

### Goals

| | Yrs | GP | G | | | Yrs | GP | A |
|---|---|---|---|---|---|---|---|---|
| *Wayne Gretzky, Edm, LA | 14 | 180 | 110 | *Wayne Gretzky, Edm, LA | 15 | 180 | 236 | |
| *Jari Kurri, Edm, LA | 12 | 174 | 102 | *Mark Messier, Edm, NYR | 15 | 210 | 170 | |
| *Mark Messier, Edm, NYR | 15 | 210 | 102 | *Jari Kurri, Edm, LA | 12 | 174 | 120 | |
| *Glenn Anderson, four teams | 14 | 214 | 92 | *Paul Coffey, Edm, Pitt, LA, Det | 13 | 155 | 119 | |
| Mike Bossy, NYI | 10 | 129 | 85 | *Glenn Anderson, four teams | 14 | 214 | 117 | |
| Maurice Richard, Mtl | 15 | 133 | 82 | Larry Robinson, Mtl, LA | 20 | 227 | 116 | |
| Jean Beliveau, Mtl | 17 | 162 | 79 | Bryan Trottier, NYI, Pitt | 17 | 221 | 113 | |
| Bryan Trottier, NYI, Pitt | 17 | 221 | 71 | Denis Potvin, NYI | 14 | 185 | 108 | |
| Gordie Howe, Det, Hart | 20 | 157 | 68 | *Ray Bourque, Bos | 16 | 157 | 106 | |
| Yvan Cournoyer, Mtl | 12 | 147 | 64 | *Denis Savard, Chi, Mtl | 14 | 153 | 105 | |
| Brian Propp, Phil, Bos, Minn | 13 | 160 | 64 | *Doug Gilmour, StL, Cgy, Tor | 11 | 132 | 104 | |
| Bobby Smith, Minn, Mtl | 13 | 184 | 64 | | | | | |

### Assists (heading)

*Active player.

### Goaltending

| WINS | W | L | Pct | SHUTOUTS | GP | W | SO |
|---|---|---|---|---|---|---|---|
| Billy Smith, LA, NYI | 88 | 36 | .710 | Clint Benedict, Ott, Mtl M | 48 | 25 | 15 |
| Ken Dryden, Mtl | 80 | 32 | .714 | Jacques Plante, five teams | 112 | 71 | 14 |
| *Grant Fuhr, Edm, Tor, Buff, LA | 77 | 36 | .681 | Turk Broda, Tor | 101 | 58 | 13 |
| Jacques Plante, five teams | 71 | 37 | .657 | Terry Sawchuk, five teams | 106 | 54 | 12 |
| *Patrick Roy, Mtl | 70 | 42 | .625 | Ken Dryden, Mtl | 112 | 80 | 10 |
| *Andy Moog, Edm, Bos, Dall | 61 | 48 | .560 | | | | |
| Turk Broda, Tor | 58 | 42 | .580 | | | | |
| *Mike Vernon, Cgy, Det | 55 | 39 | .585 | GOALS AGAINST AVG | | | Avg |
| Terry Sawchuk, five teams | 54 | 48 | .529 | George Hainsworth, Mtl, Tor | | | 1.93 |
| Glenn Hall, Det, Chi, StL | 49 | 65 | .429 | Turk Broda, Tor | | | 1.98 |
| | | | | Jacques Plante, five teams | | | 2.17 |
| | | | | Ken Dryden, Mtl | | | 2.40 |
| | | | | Bernie Parent, Bos, Tor, Phil | | | 2.43 |

*Active player.

Note: At least 50 games played.

## Alltime Stanley Cup Standings

| TEAM | W | L | Pct | TEAM | W | L | Pct |
|---|---|---|---|---|---|---|---|
| Montreal | 374 | 235 | .614 | Pittsburgh | 74 | 63 | .540 |
| Boston | 227 | 238 | .488 | Calgary | 69 | 83 | .454 |
| Toronto | 200 | 217 | .480 | Buffalo | 62 | 81 | .434 |
| Detroit | 180 | 188 | .489 | Los Angeles | 55 | 87 | .387 |
| Chicago | 179 | 206 | .465 | Vancouver | 52 | 66 | .441 |
| NY Rangers | 169 | 183 | .480 | Washington | 50 | 60 | .454 |
| NY Islanders | 128 | 90 | .587 | New Jersey | 47 | 40 | .540 |
| Philadelphia | 126 | 112 | .529 | Quebec | 35 | 45 | .437 |
| Edmonton | 120 | 60 | .667 | Hartford | 18 | 31 | .367 |
| St Louis | 96 | 121 | .442 | Winnipeg | 17 | 39 | .304 |
| Dallas* | 86 | 94 | .478 | San Jose | 11 | 18 | .379 |

*Minnesota North Stars 1967-93. Note: Teams ranked by playoff victories.

## Stanley Cup Coaching Records

| Coach | Team | Yrs | Series | Series W | L | Games G | W | L | T | Cups | Pct |
|---|---|---|---|---|---|---|---|---|---|---|---|
| Toe Blake................... | Mtl | 13 | 23 | 18 | 5 | 119 | 82 | 37 | 0 | 8 | .689 |
| Glen Sather................. | Edm | 11 | 30 | 23 | 7 | *142 | 97 | 45 | 0 | 4 | .683 |
| †Jacques Lemaire....... | Mtl, NJ | 4 | 13 | 10 | 3 | 67 | 42 | 25 | 0 | 1 | .627 |
| †Scott Bowman .......... | Five teams | 21 | 44 | 29 | 15 | 244 | 152 | 92 | 0 | 6 | .622 |
| Hap Day ...................... | Tor | 9 | 14 | 10 | 4 | 80 | 49 | 31 | 0 | 5 | .613 |
| Al Arbour .................... | StL, NYI | 16 | 42 | 30 | 12 | 209 | 123 | 86 | 0 | 4 | .589 |
| †Mike Keenan.............. | Phil, Chi, NYR, StL | 10 | 26 | 17 | 9 | 147 | 84 | 63 | 0 | 1 | .571 |
| Fred Shero................. | Phil, NYR | 8 | 21 | 15 | 6 | 108 | 61 | 47 | 0 | 2 | .565 |
| Jacques Demers ......... | Que, StL, Det, Mtl | 8 | 19 | 12 | 7 | 98 | 55 | 43 | 0 | 1 | .561 |
| Lester Patrick............. | NYR | 12 | 24 | 14 | 10 | 65 | 31 | 26 | 8 | 2 | .538 |

*Does not include suspended game, May 24, 1988.
Note: Coaches ranked by winning percentage. Minimum: 65 games. †Active coach.

## The 10 Longest Overtime Games

| Date | Scorer | OT | Results | Series | Series Winner |
|---|---|---|---|---|---|
| 3-24-36 .................... | Mud Bruneteau | 116:30 | Det 1 vs Mtl M 0 | SF | Det |
| 4-3-33 ...................... | Ken Doraty | 104:46 | Tor 1 vs Bos 0 | SF | Tor |
| 3-23-43 .................... | Jack McLean | 70:18 | Tor 3 vs Det 2 | SF | Det |
| 3-28-30 .................... | Gus Rivers | 68:52 | Mtl 2 vs NYR 1 | SF | Mtl |
| 4-18-87 .................... | Pat LaFontaine | 68:47 | NYI 3 vs Wash 2 | DSF | NYI |
| 4-27-94 .................... | Dave Hannan | 65:43 | Buff 1 vs NJ 0 | CQF | NJ |
| 3-27-51 .................... | Maurice Richard | 61:09 | Mtl 3 vs Det 2 | SF | Mtl |
| 3-27-38 .................... | Lorne Carr | 60:40 | NYA 3 vs NYR 2 | QF | NYA |
| 3-26-32 .................... | Fred Cook | 59:32 | NYR 4 vs Mtl 3 | SF | NYR |
| 3-21-39 .................... | Mel Hill | 59:25 | Bos 2 vs NYR 1 | SF | Bos |

# NHL Awards

## Hart Memorial Trophy

Awarded annually "to the player adjudged to be the most valuable to his team." The original trophy was donated by Dr. David A. Hart, father of Cecil Hart, former manager-coach of the Montreal Canadiens. In the decade of the 1980s Wayne Gretzky won the award nine of 10 times.

| | Winner | Key Statistics | Runner-Up |
|---|---|---|---|
| 1924 | Frank Nighbor, Ott | 10 goals, 3 assists in 20 games | Sprague Cleghorn, Mtl |
| 1925 | Billy Burch, Ham | 20 goals, 4 assists in 27 games | Howie Morenz, Mtl |
| 1926 | Nels Stewart, Mtl M | 42 points in 36 games | Sprague Cleghorn, Mtl |
| 1927 | Herb Gardiner, Mtl | 12 points in 44 games as defenseman | Bill Cook, NYR |
| 1928 | Howie Morenz, Mtl | 33 goals, 18 assists | Roy Worters, Pitt |
| 1929 | Roy Worters, NYA | 1.21 goals against, 13 shutouts | Ace Bailey, Tor |
| 1930 | Nels Stewart, Mtl M | 39 goals, 16 assists | Lionel Hitchman, Bos |
| 1931 | Howie Morenz, Mtl | 28 goals, 23 assists | Eddie Shore, Bos |
| 1932 | Howie Morenz, Mtl | 24 goals, 25 assists | Ching Johnson, NYR |
| 1933 | Eddie Shore, Bos | 27 assists in 48 games as defenseman | Bill Cook, NYR |
| 1934 | Aurel Joliat, Mtl | 27 points | Lionel Conacher, Chi |
| 1935 | Eddie Shore, Bos | 26 assists in 48 games as defenseman | Charlie Conacher, Tor |
| 1936 | Eddie Shore, Bos | 16 assists in 46 games as defenseman | Hooley Smith, Mtl M |
| 1937 | Babe Siebert, Mtl | 28 points | Lionel Conacher, Mtl M |
| 1938 | Eddie Shore, Bos | 17 points in 47 games as defenseman | Paul Thompson, Chi |
| 1939 | Toe Blake, Mtl | led NHL in points (47) | Syl Apps, Tor |
| 1940 | Ebbie Goodfellow, Det | 28 points | Syl Apps, Tor |
| 1941 | Bill Cowley, Bos | led NHL in assists (45) and points (62) | Dit Clapper, Bos |
| 1942 | Tom Anderson, Bos | 41 points | Syl Apps, Tor |
| 1943 | Bill Cowley, Bos | led NHL in assists (45) | Doug Bentley, Chi |
| 1944 | Babe Pratt, Tor | 57 points in 50 games | Bill Cowley, Bos |
| 1945 | Elmer Lach, Mtl | led NHL in assists (54) and points (80) | Maurice Richard, Mtl |
| 1946 | Max Bentley, Chi | 61 points in 47 games | Gaye Stewart, Tor |
| 1947 | Maurice Richard, Mtl | led NHL in goals (45); 26 assists | Milt Schmidt, Bos |
| 1948 | Buddy O'Connor, NYR | 60 points in 60 games | Frank Brimsek, Bos |
| 1949 | Sid Abel, Det | 28 goals, 26 assists | Bill Durnan, Mtl |

## Hart Memorial Trophy (Cont.)

| Year | Winner | Key Statistics | Runner-Up |
|------|--------|----------------|-----------|
| 1950 | Charlie Rayner, NYR | 6 shutouts | Ted Kennedy, Tor |
| 1951 | Milt Schmidt, Bos | 61 points in 62 games | Maurice Richard, Mtl |
| 1952 | Gordie Howe, Det | led NHL in goals (47) and points (86) | Elmer Lach, Mtl |
| 1953 | Gordie Howe, Det | led NHL in goals (49) and points (95) | Al Rollins, Chi |
| 1954 | Al Rollins, Chi | 5 shutouts | Red Kelly, Det |
| 1955 | Ted Kennedy, Tor | 52 points | Harry Lumley, Tor |
| 1956 | Jean Beliveau, Mtl | led NHL in goals (47) and points (88) | Tod Sloan, Tor |
| 1957 | Gordie Howe, Det | led NHL in goals (44) and points (89) | Jean Beliveau, Mtl |
| 1959 | Andy Bathgate, NYR | 74 points in 70 games | Gordie Howe, Det |
| 1960 | Gordie Howe, Det | 45 assists, 73 points | Bobby Hull, Chi |
| 1961 | Bernie Geoffrion, Mtl | 50 goals, 95 points | Johnny Bower, Tor |
| 1962 | Jacques Plante, Mtl | 42 wins, 2.37 goals against | Doug Harvey, NYR |
| 1963 | Gordie Howe, Det | 47 assists, 73 points | Stan Mikita, Chi |
| 1964 | Jean Beliveau, Mtl | 50 assists, 78 points | Bobby Hull, Chi |
| 1965 | Bobby Hull, Chi | 39 goals, 32 assists | Norm Ullman, Det |
| 1966 | Bobby Hull, Chi | led NHL in goals (54) and points (97) | Jean Beliveau, Mtl |
| 1967 | Stan Mikita, Chi | led NHL in assists (62) and points (97) | Ed Giacomin, NYR |
| 1968 | Stan Mikita, Chi | 40 goals, 47 assists | Jean Beliveau, Mtl |
| 1969 | Phil Esposito, Bos | led NHL in assists (77) and points (126) | Jean Beliveau, Mtl |
| 1970 | Bobby Orr, Bos | led NHL in assists (87) and points (120) | Tony Esposito, Chi |
| 1971 | Bobby Orr, Bos | 102 assists, 139 points | Tony Esposito, Chi |
| 1972 | Bobby Orr, Bos | 80 assists, 117 points | Ken Dryden, Mtl |
| 1973 | Bobby Clarke, Phil | 67 assists, 104 points | Phil Esposito, Bos |
| 1974 | Phil Esposito, Bos | led NHL in goals (68) and points (145) | Bernie Parent, Phil |
| 1975 | Bobby Clarke, Phil | 89 assists, 116 points | Rogatien Vachon, LA |
| 1976 | Bobby Clarke, Phil | 89 assists, 119 points | Denis Potvin, NYI |
| 1977 | Guy Lafleur, Mtl | led NHL in assists (80) and points (136) | Bobby Clarke, Phil |
| 1978 | Guy Lafleur, Mtl | led NHL in goals (60) and points (132) | Bryan Trottier, NYI |
| 1979 | Bryan Trottier, NYI | led NHL in assists (87) and points (134) | Guy Lafleur, Mtl |
| 1980 | Wayne Gretzky, Edm | 51 goals, 86 assists | Marcel Dionne, LA |
| 1981 | Wayne Gretzky, Edm | led NHL in assists (109) and points (164) | Mike Liut, StL |
| 1982 | Wayne Gretzky, Edm | NHL-record 92 goals and 212 points | Bryan Trottier, NYI |
| 1983 | Wayne Gretzky, Edm | led NHL in goals (71) and points (196) | Pete Peeters, Bos |
| 1984 | Wayne Gretzky, Edm | led NHL in goals (87) and points (205) | Rod Langway, Wash |
| 1985 | Wayne Gretzky, Edm | led NHL in goals (73) and points (208) | Dale Hawerchuk, Winn |
| 1986 | Wayne Gretzky, Edm | NHL-record 163 assists and 215 points | Mario Lemieux, Pitt |
| 1987 | Wayne Gretzky, Edm | led NHL in assists (121) and points (183) | Ray Bourque, Bos |
| 1988 | Mario Lemieux, Pitt | led NHL in goals (70) and points (168) | Grant Fuhr, Edm |
| 1989 | Wayne Gretzky, LA | 114 assists, 168 points | Mario Lemieux, Pitt |
| 1990 | Mark Messier, Edm | 84 assists, 129 points | Ray Bourque, Bos |
| 1991 | Brett Hull, StL | led NHL in goals (86); 131 points | Wayne Gretzky, LA |
| 1992 | Mark Messier, NYR | 72 assists, 107 points | Patrick Roy, Mtl |
| 1993 | Mario Lemieux, Pitt | 69 goals, 91 assists in 60 games | Doug Gilmour, Tor |
| 1994 | Sergei Fedorov, Det | 56 goals, 64 assists | Dominik Hasek, Buff |
| 1995 | Eric Lindros, Phil | 29 goals, 41 assists in 46 games | Jaromir Jagr, Pitt |

## Art Ross Trophy

Awarded annually "to the player who leads the league in scoring points at the end of the regular season." The trophy was presented to the NHL in 1947 by Arthur Howie Ross, former manager-coach of the Boston Bruins. The tie-breakers, in order, are as follows: (1) player with most goals, (2) player with fewer games played, (3) player scoring first goal of the season. Bobby Orr is the only defenseman in NHL history to win this trophy, and he won it twice (1970 and 1975).

| Year | Winner | Pts | Year | Winner | Pts |
|------|--------|-----|------|--------|-----|
| 1919 | Newsy Lalonde, Mtl | 44 | 1927 | Bill Cook, NYR | 42 |
| 1920 | Joe Malone, Que | 30 | 1928 | Howie Morenz, Mtl | 37 |
| 1921 | Newsy Lalonde, Mtl | 48 | 1929 | Ace Bailey, Tor | 51 |
| 1922 | Punch Broadbent, Ott | 41 | 1930 | Cooney Weiland, Bos | 32 |
| 1923 | Babe Dye, Tor | 46 | 1931 | Howie Morenz, Mtl | 73 |
| 1924 | Cy Denneny, Ott | 37 | 1932 | Harvey Jackson, Tor | 51 |
| 1925 | Babe Dye, Tor | 23 | 1933 | Bill Cook, NYR | 53 |
| 1926 | Nels Stewart, Mtl M | 44 | 1934 | Charlie Conacher, Tor | 50 |

## Art Ross Trophy (Cont.)

| Year | Winner | Pts | | Year | Winner | Pts |
|------|--------|-----|---|------|--------|-----|
| 1935 | Charlie Conacher, Tor | 57 | | 1966 | Bobby Hull, Chi | 97 |
| 1936 | Sweeney Schriner, NYA | 45 | | 1967 | Stan Mikita, Chi | 97 |
| 1937 | Sweeney Schriner, NYA | 46 | | 1968 | Stan Mikita, Chi | 87 |
| 1938 | Gordie Drillon, Tor | 52 | | 1969 | Phil Esposito, Bos | 126 |
| 1939 | Toe Blake, Mtl | 47 | | 1970 | Bobby Orr, Bos | 120 |
| 1940 | Milt Schmidt, Bos | 52 | | 1971 | Phil Esposito, Bos | 152 |
| 1941 | Bill Cowley, Bos | 62 | | 1972 | Phil Esposito, Bos | 133 |
| 1942 | Bryan Hextall, NYR | 56 | | 1973 | Phil Esposito, Bos | 130 |
| 1943 | Doug Bentley, Chi | 73 | | 1974 | Phil Esposito, Bos | 145 |
| 1944 | Herb Cain, Bos | 82 | | 1975 | Bobby Orr, Bos | 135 |
| 1945 | Elmer Lach, Mtl | 80 | | 1976 | Guy Lafleur, Mtl | 125 |
| 1946 | Max Bentley, Chi | 61 | | 1977 | Guy Lafleur, Mtl | 136 |
| 1947 | *Max Bentley, Chi | 72 | | 1978 | Guy Lafleur, Mtl | 132 |
| 1948 | Elmer Lach, Mtl | 61 | | 1979 | Bryan Trottier, NYI | 134 |
| 1949 | Roy Conacher, Chi | 68 | | 1980 | Marcel Dionne, LA | 137 |
| 1950 | Ted Lindsay, Det | 78 | | 1981 | Wayne Gretzky, Edm | 164 |
| 1951 | Gordie Howe, Det | 86 | | 1982 | Wayne Gretzky, Edm | 212 |
| 1952 | Gordie Howe, Det | 86 | | 1983 | Wayne Gretzky, Edm | 196 |
| 1953 | Gordie Howe, Det | 95 | | 1984 | Wayne Gretzky, Edm | 205 |
| 1954 | Gordie Howe, Det | 81 | | 1985 | Wayne Gretzky, Edm | 208 |
| 1955 | Bernie Geoffrion, Mtl | 75 | | 1986 | Wayne Gretzky, Edm | 215 |
| 1956 | Jean Beliveau, Mtl | 88 | | 1987 | Wayne Gretzky, Edm | 183 |
| 1957 | Gordie Howe, Det | 89 | | 1988 | Mario Lemieux, Pitt | 168 |
| 1958 | Dickie Moore, Mtl | 84 | | 1989 | Mario Lemieux, Pitt | 199 |
| 1959 | Dickie Moore, Mtl | 96 | | 1990 | Wayne Gretzky, LA | 142 |
| 1960 | Bobby Hull, Chi | 81 | | 1991 | Wayne Gretzky, LA | 163 |
| 1961 | Bernie Geoffrion, Mtl | 95 | | 1992 | Mario Lemieux, Pitt | 131 |
| 1962 | Bobby Hull, Chi | 84 | | 1993 | Mario Lemieux, Pitt | 160 |
| 1963 | Gordie Howe, Det | 86 | | 1994 | Wayne Gretzky, LA | 130 |
| 1964 | Stan Mikita, Chi | 89 | | 1995 | Jaromir Jagr, Pitt | 70 |
| 1965 | Stan Mikita, Chi | 87 | | | | |

Note: Listing includes scoring leaders prior to inception of Art Ross Trophy in 1947-48.

## Lady Byng Memorial Trophy

Awarded annually "to the player adjudged to have exhibited the best type of sportsmanship and gentlemanly conduct combined with a high standard of playing ability." Lady Byng, who first presented the trophy in 1925, was the wife of Canada's Governor-General. She donated a second trophy in 1936 after the first was given permanently to Frank Boucher of the New York Rangers, who won it seven times in eight seasons. Stan Mikita, one of the league's most penalized players during his early years in the NHL, won the trophy twice late in his career (1967 and 1968).

| Year | Winner | Year | Winner | Year | Winner |
|------|--------|------|--------|------|--------|
| 1925 | Frank Nighbor, Ott | 1949 | Bill Quackenbush, Det | 1973 | Gilbert Perreault, Buff |
| 1926 | Frank Nighbor, Ott | 1950 | Edgar Laprade, NYR | 1974 | John Bucyk, Bos |
| 1927 | Billy Burch, NYA | 1951 | Red Kelly, Det | 1975 | Marcel Dionne, Det |
| 1928 | Frank Boucher, NYR | 1952 | Sid Smith, Tor | 1976 | Jean Ratelle, NYR-Bos |
| 1929 | Frank Boucher, NYR | 1953 | Red Kelly, Det | 1977 | Marcel Dionne, LA |
| 1930 | Frank Boucher, NYR | 1954 | Red Kelly, Det | 1978 | Butch Goring, LA |
| 1931 | Frank Boucher, NYR | 1955 | Sid Smith, Tor | 1979 | Bob MacMillan, Atl |
| 1932 | Joe Primeau, Tor | 1956 | Earl Reibel, Det | 1980 | Wayne Gretzky, Edm |
| 1933 | Frank Boucher, NYR | 1957 | Andy Hebenton, NYR | 1981 | Rick Kehoe, Pitt |
| 1934 | Frank Boucher, NYR | 1958 | Camille Henry, NYR | 1982 | Rick Middleton, Bos |
| 1935 | Frank Boucher, NYR | 1959 | Alex Delvecchio, Det | 1983 | Mike Bossy, NYI |
| 1936 | Doc Romnes, Chi | 1960 | Don McKenney, Bos | 1984 | Mike Bossy, NYI |
| 1937 | Marty Barry, Det | 1961 | Red Kelly, Det | 1985 | Jari Kurri, Edm |
| 1938 | Gordie Drillon, Tor | 1962 | Dave Keon, Tor | 1986 | Mike Bossy, NYI |
| 1939 | Clint Smith, NYR | 1963 | Dave Keon, Tor | 1987 | Joe Mullen, Cgy |
| 1940 | Bobby Bauer, Bos | 1964 | Ken Wharram, Chi | 1988 | Mats Naslund, Mtl |
| 1941 | Bobby Bauer, Bos | 1965 | Bobby Hull, Chi | 1989 | Joe Mullen, Cgy |
| 1942 | Syl Apps, Tor | 1966 | Alex Delvecchio, Det | 1990 | Brett Hull, StL |
| 1943 | Max Bentley, Chi | 1967 | Stan Mikita, Chi | 1991 | Wayne Gretzky, LA |
| 1944 | Clint Smith, Chi | 1968 | Stan Mikita, Chi | 1992 | Wayne Gretzky, LA |
| 1945 | Billy Mosienko, Chi | 1969 | Alex Delvecchio, Det | 1993 | Pierre Turgeon, NYI |
| 1946 | Toe Blake, Mtl | 1970 | Phil Goyette, StL | 1994 | Wayne Gretzky, LA |
| 1947 | Bobby Bauer, Bos | 1971 | John Bucyk, Bos | 1995 | Ron Francis, Pitt |
| 1948 | Buddy O'Connor, NYR | 1972 | Jean Ratelle, NYR | | |

## James Norris Memorial Trophy

Awarded annually "to the defense player who demonstrates throughout the season the greatest all-around ability in the position." James Norris was the former owner-president of the Detroit Red Wings. Bobby Orr holds the record for most consecutive times winning the award (eight, 1968-1975).

| | | |
|---|---|---|
| 1954 ......Red Kelly, Det | 1968 ......Bobby Orr, Bos | 1982 ......Doug Wilson, Chi |
| 1955 ......Doug Harvey, Mtl | 1969 ......Bobby Orr, Bos | 1983 ......Rod Langway, Wash |
| 1956 ......Doug Harvey, Mtl | 1970 ......Bobby Orr, Bos | 1984 ......Rod Langway, Wash |
| 1957 ......Doug Harvey, Mtl | 1971 ......Bobby Orr, Bos | 1985 ......Paul Coffey, Edm |
| 1958 ......Doug Harvey, Mtl | 1972 ......Bobby Orr, Bos | 1986 ......Paul Coffey, Edm |
| 1959 ......Tom Johnson, Mtl | 1973 ......Bobby Orr, Bos | 1987 ......Ray Bourque, Bos |
| 1960 ......Doug Harvey, Mtl | 1974 ......Bobby Orr, Bos | 1988 ......Ray Bourque, Bos |
| 1961 ......Doug Harvey, Mtl | 1975 ......Bobby Orr, Bos | 1989 ......Chris Chelios, Mtl |
| 1962 ......Doug Harvey, NYR | 1976 ......Denis Potvin, NYI | 1990 ......Ray Bourque, Bos |
| 1963 ......Pierre Pilote, Chi | 1977 ......Larry Robinson, Mtl | 1991 ......Ray Bourque, Bos |
| 1964 ......Pierre Pilote, Chi | 1978 ......Denis Potvin, NYI | 1992 ......Brian Leetch, NYR |
| 1965 ......Pierre Pilote, Chi | 1979 ......Denis Potvin, NYI | 1993 ......Chris Chelios, Chi |
| 1966 ......Jacques Laperriere, Mtl | 1980 ......Larry Robinson, Mtl | 1994 ......Ray Bourque, Bos |
| 1967 ......Harry Howell, NYR | 1981 ......Randy Carlyle, Pitt | 1995 ......Paul Coffey, Det |

## Calder Memorial Trophy

Awarded annually "to the player selected as the most proficient in his first year of competition in the National Hockey League." Frank Calder was a former NHL president. Sergei Makarov, who won the award in 1989-1990, was the oldest recipient of the trophy, at 31. Players are no longer eligible for the award if they are 26 or older as of September 15th of the season in question.

| | | |
|---|---|---|
| 1933 ......Carl Voss, Det | 1954 ......Camille Henry, NYR | 1975 ......Eric Vail, Atl |
| 1934 ......Russ Blinko, Mtl M | 1955 ......Ed Litzenberger, Chi | 1976 ......Bryan Trottier, NYI |
| 1935 ......Dave Schriner, NYA | 1956 ......Glenn Hall, Det | 1977 ......Willi Plett, Atl |
| 1936 ......Mike Karakas, Chi | 1957 ......Larry Regan, Bos | 1978 ......Mike Bossy, NYI |
| 1937 ......Syl Apps, Tor | 1958 ......Frank Mahovlich, Tor | 1979 ......Bobby Smith, Minn |
| 1938 ......Cully Dahlstrom, Chi | 1959 ......Ralph Backstrom, Mtl | 1980 ......Ray Bourque, Bos |
| 1939 ......Frank Brimsek, Bos | 1960 ......Bill Hay, Chi | 1981 ......Peter Stastny, Que |
| 1940 ......Kilby MacDonald, NYR | 1961 ......Dave Keon, Tor | 1982 ......Dale Hawerchuk, Winn |
| 1941 ......Johnny Quilty, Mtl | 1962 ......Bobby Rousseau, Mtl | 1983 ......Steve Larmer, Chi |
| 1942 ......Grant Warwick, NYR | 1963 ......Kent Douglas, Tor | 1984 ......Tom Barrasso, Buff |
| 1943 ......Gaye Stewart, Tor | 1964 ......Jacques Laperriere, Mtl | 1985 ......Mario Lemieux, Pitt |
| 1944 ......Gus Bodnar, Tor | 1965 ......Roger Crozier, Det | 1986 ......Gary Suter, Cgy |
| 1945 ......Frank McCool, Tor | 1966 ......Brit Selby, Tor | 1987 ......Luc Robitaille, LA |
| 1946 ......Edgar Laprade, NYR | 1967 ......Bobby Orr, Bos | 1988 ......Joe Nieuwendyk, Cgy |
| 1947 ......Howie Meeker, Tor | 1968 ......Derek Sanderson, Bos | 1989 ......Brian Leetch, NYR |
| 1948 ......Jim McFadden, Det | 1969 ......Danny Grant, Minn | 1990 ......Sergei Makarov, Cgy |
| 1949 ......Pentti Lund, NYR | 1970 ......Tony Esposito, Chi | 1991 ......Ed Belfour, Chi |
| 1950 ......Jack Gelineau, Bos | 1971 ......Gilbert Perreault, Buff | 1992 ......Pavel Bure, Van |
| 1951 ......Terry Sawchuk, Det | 1972 ......Ken Dryden, Mtl | 1993 ......Teemu Selanne, Winn |
| 1952 ......Bernie Geoffrion, Mtl | 1973 ......Steve Vickers, NYR | 1994 ......Martin Brodeur, NJ |
| 1953 ......Gump Worsley, NYR | 1974 ......Denis Potvin, NYI | 1995 ......Peter Forsberg, Que |

## Vezina Trophy

Awarded annually "to the goalkeeper adjudged to be the best at his position." The trophy is named after Georges Vezina, an outstanding goalie for the Montreal Canadiens who collapsed during a game on November 28, 1925, and died a few months later of tuberculosis. The general managers of the 21 NHL teams vote on the award.

| | | |
|---|---|---|
| 1927 ......George Hainsworth, Mtl | 1940 ......Dave Kerr, NYR | 1953 ......Terry Sawchuk, Det |
| 1928 ......George Hainsworth, Mtl | 1941 ......Turk Broda, Tor | 1954 ......Harry Lumley, Tor |
| 1929 ......George Hainsworth, Mtl | 1942 ......Frank Brimsek, Bos | 1955 ......Terry Sawchuk, Det |
| 1930 ......Tiny Thompson, Bos | 1943 ......Johnny Mowers, Det | 1956 ......Jacques Plante, Mtl |
| 1931 ......Roy Worters, NYA | 1944 ......Bill Durnan, Mtl | 1957 ......Jacques Plante, Mtl |
| 1932 ......Charlie Gardiner, Chi | 1945 ......Bill Durnan, Mtl | 1958 ......Jacques Plante, Mtl |
| 1933 ......Tiny Thompson, Bos | 1946 ......Bill Durnan, Mtl | 1959 ......Jacques Plante, Mtl |
| 1934 ......Charlie Gardiner, Chi | 1947 ......Bill Durnan, Mtl | 1960 ......Jacques Plante, Mtl |
| 1935 ......Lorne Chabot, Chi | 1948 ......Turk Broda, Tor | 1961 ......Johnny Bower, Tor |
| 1936 ......Tiny Thompson, Bos | 1949 ......Bill Durnan, Mtl | 1962 ......Jacques Plante, Mtl |
| 1937 ......Normie Smith, Det | 1950 ......Bill Durnan, Mtl | 1963 ......Glenn Hall, Chi |
| 1938 ......Tiny Thompson, Bos | 1951 ......Al Rollins, Tor | 1964 ......Charlie Hodge, Mtl |
| 1939 ......Frank Brimsek, Bos | 1952 ......Terry Sawchuk, Det | |

## Vezina Trophy (Cont.)

| | | |
|---|---|---|
| 1965 ........Terry Sawchuk, Tor | 1975 .......Bernie Parent, Phil | 1985 ........Pelle Lindbergh, Phil |
| Johnny Bower, Tor | 1976 .......Ken Dryden, Mtl | 1986 ........John Vanbiesbrouck, |
| 1966 ........Gump Worsley, Mtl | 1977 .......Ken Dryden, Mtl | NYR |
| Charlie Hodge, Mtl | Michel Larocque, Mtl | 1987 ........Ron Hextall, Phil |
| 1967 ........Glenn Hall, Chi | 1978 .......Ken Dryden, Mtl | 1988 ........Grant Fuhr, Edm |
| Rogie Vachon, Mtl | Michel Larocque, Mtl | 1989 ........Patrick Roy, Mtl |
| 1969 ........Jacques Plante, StL | 1979 .......Ken Dryden, Mtl | 1990 ........Patrick Roy, Mtl |
| Glenn Hall, StL | Michel Larocque, Mtl | 1991 ........Ed Belfour, Chi |
| 1970 ........Tony Esposito, Chi | 1980 ........Bob Sauve, Buff | 1992 ........Patrick Roy, Mtl |
| 1971 ........Ed Giacomin, NYR | Don Edwards, Buff | 1993 ........Ed Belfour, Chi |
| Gilles Villemure, NYR | 1981 ........Richard Sevigny, Mtl | 1994 ........Dominik Hasek, Buff |
| 1972 ........Tony Esposito, Chi | Denis Herron, Mtl | 1995 ........Dominik Hasek, Buff |
| Gary Smith, Chi | Michel Larocque, Mtl | |
| 1973 ........Ken Dryden, Mtl | 1982 .......Bill Smith, NYI | |
| 1974 ........Bernie Parent, Phil | 1983 .......Pete Peeters, Bos | |
| Tony Esposito, Chi | 1984 .......Tom Barrasso, Buff | |

## Selke Trophy

Awarded annually "to the forward who best excels in the defensive aspects of the game." The trophy is named after Frank J. Selke, the architect of the Montreal Canadians dynasty that won five consecutive Stanley Cups in the late '50s. The winner is selected by a vote of the Professional Hockey Writers Association.

| | | |
|---|---|---|
| 1978........Bob Gainey, Mtl | 1984........Doug Jarvis, Wash | 1990........Rick Meagher, StL |
| 1979........Bob Gainey, Mtl | 1985........Craig Ramsay, Buff | 1991........Dirk Graham, Chi |
| 1980........Bob Gainey, Mtl | 1986........Troy Murray, Chi | 1992........Guy Carbonneau, Mtl |
| 1981........Bob Gainey, Mtl | 1987........Dave Poulin, Phil | 1993........Doug Gilmour, Tor |
| 1982........Steve Kasper, Bos | 1988........Guy Carbonneau, Mtl | 1994........Sergei Fedorov, Det |
| 1983........Bobby Clarke, Phil | 1989........Guy Carbonneau, Mtl | 1995........Ron Francis, Pitt |

## Adams Award

Awarded annually "to the NHL coach adjudged to have contributed the most to his team's success." The trophy is named in honor of Jack Adams, longtime coach and general manager of the Detroit Red Wings. The winner is selected by a vote of the National Hockey League Broadcasters' Association.

| | | |
|---|---|---|
| 1974 .....Fred Shero, Phil | 1982 .....Tom Watt, Winn | 1990 .....Bob Murdoch, Winn |
| 1975 .....Bob Pulford, LA | 1983 ....Orval Tessier, Chi | 1991 .....Brian Sutter, StL |
| 1976 .....Don Cherry, Bos | 1984 .....Bryan Murray, Wash | 1992 .....Pat Quinn, Van |
| 1977 .....Scott Bowman, Mtl | 1985 .....Mike Keenan, Phil | 1993 .....Pat Burns, Tor |
| 1978 .....Bobby Kromm, Det | 1986 .....Glen Sather, Edm | 1994 .....Jacques Lemaire, NJ |
| 1979 .....Al Arbour, NYI | 1987 .....Jacques Demers, Det | 1995 .....Marc Crawford, Que |
| 1980 .....Pat Quinn, Phil | 1988 .....Jacques Demers, Det | |
| 1981 .....Red Berenson, StL | 1989 .....Pat Burns, Mtl | |

## Help, Can't Stop

It looks as if we've opened a Texarkana Worms with our item about the soon-to-be real-life Macon (Ga.) Whoopees of the Southern Hockey League and other groan-inducing expunsion teams (see page 312). Reader Michael McConnell of Fort Worth writes to nominate the Worms—along with the Altoona Fish, the Schenectady Dots, the Tucumcari Okies, the Olympia Zadoras, the Helena Handbaskets and a pair of potential farm clubs for the Minnesota Twins, the Bemidji Whiz and the Mankato Kaelins. Another correspondent, James P. Finnegan of Chappaqua, N.Y., evinces a more international bent. He suggests the Ankara Ways, the Sofia Lorens, the Bonn Vivants, the Riga Mortis, the Manila Folders, the Taiwan Ons and the New Delhi Catessans.

Dangerously, McConnell's flights of fancy extend beyond sports franchises. He suggests that someone open a racetrack in Alabama and call it Eufaula Downs.

# Career Records

## Alltime Point Leaders

| | Player | Yrs | GP | G | A | Pts | Pts/game |
|---|---|---|---|---|---|---|---|
| 1. | *Wayne Gretzky, Edm, LA | 16 | 1173 | 814 | 1692 | 2506 | 2.136 |
| 2. | Gordie Howe, Det, Hart | 26 | 1767 | 801 | 1049 | 1850 | 1.047 |
| 3. | Marcel Dionne, Det, LA, NYR | 18 | 1348 | 731 | 1040 | 1771 | 1.314 |
| 4. | Phil Esposito, Chi, Bos, NYR | 18 | 1282 | 717 | 873 | 1590 | 1.240 |
| 5. | Stan Mikita, Chi | 22 | 1394 | 541 | 926 | 1467 | 1.052 |
| 6. | Bryan Trottier, NYI, Pitt | 18 | 1279 | 524 | 901 | 1425 | 1.114 |
| 7. | John Bucyk, Det, Bos | 23 | 1540 | 556 | 813 | 1369 | .889 |
| 8. | *Mark Messier, Edm, NYR | 16 | 1127 | 492 | 877 | 1369 | 1.215 |
| 9. | Guy Lafleur, Mtl, NYR, Que | 17 | 1126 | 560 | 793 | 1353 | 1.201 |
| 10. | *Paul Coffey, Edm, Pitt, LA, Det | 15 | 1078 | 358 | 978 | 1336 | 1.240 |
| 11. | Gilbert Perreault, Buff | 17 | 1191 | 512 | 814 | 1326 | 1.113 |
| 12. | *Dale Hawerchuk, Winn, Buff | 14 | 1055 | 489 | 825 | 1314 | 1.246 |
| 13. | *Jari Kurri, Edm, LA | 14 | 1028 | 565 | 731 | 1296 | 1.261 |
| 14. | Alex Delvecchio, Det | 24 | 1549 | 456 | 825 | 1281 | .827 |
| 15. | Jean Ratelle, NYR, Bos | 21 | 1281 | 491 | 776 | 1267 | .989 |

*Active player.

## Alltime Goal-Scoring Leaders

| | Player | Yrs | GP | G | G/game |
|---|---|---|---|---|---|
| 1. | *Wayne Gretzky, Edm, LA | 16 | 1173 | 814 | .693 |
| 2. | Gordie Howe, Det, Hart | 26 | 1767 | 801 | .453 |
| 3. | Marcel Dionne, Det, LA, NYR | 18 | 1348 | 731 | .542 |
| 4. | Phil Esposito, Chi, Bos, NYR | 18 | 1282 | 717 | .559 |
| 5. | *Mike Gartner, Wash, Minn, NYR, Tor | 16 | 1208 | 629 | .521 |
| 6. | Bobby Hull, Chi, Winn, Hart | 16 | 1063 | 610 | .574 |
| 7. | Mike Bossy, NYI | 10 | 752 | 573 | .762 |
| 8. | *Jari Kurri, Edm, LA | 14 | 1028 | 565 | .550 |
| 9. | Guy Lafleur, Mtl, NYR, Que | 17 | 1126 | 560 | .497 |
| 10. | John Bucyk, Det, Bos | 23 | 1540 | 556 | .361 |

*Active player.

## Alltime Assist Leaders

| | Player | Yrs | GP | A | A/game |
|---|---|---|---|---|---|
| 1. | *Wayne Gretzky, Edm, LA | 16 | 1173 | 1692 | 1.443 |
| 2. | Gordie Howe, Det, Hart | 26 | 1767 | 1049 | .594 |
| 3. | Marcel Dionne, Det, LA, NYR | 18 | 1348 | 1040 | .772 |
| 4. | *Paul Coffey, Edm, Pitt, LA, Det | 15 | 1078 | 978 | .907 |
| 5. | Stan Mikita, Chi | 22 | 1394 | 926 | .664 |
| 6. | *Ray Bourque, Bos | 16 | 1146 | 908 | .792 |
| 7. | Bryan Trottier, NYI, Pitt | 18 | 1279 | 901 | .705 |
| 8. | *Mark Messier, Edm, NYR | 16 | 1127 | 877 | .778 |
| 9. | Phil Esposito, Chi, Bos, NYR | 18 | 1282 | 873 | .681 |
| 10. | Bobby Clarke, Phil | 15 | 1144 | 852 | .745 |

*Active player.

## Alltime Penalty Minutes Leaders

| | Player | Yrs | GP | PIM | Min/game |
|---|---|---|---|---|---|
| 1. | Dave Williams, Tor, Van, Det, LA, Hart | 13 | 962 | 3966 | 4.12 |
| 2. | *Dale Hunter, Que, Wash | 15 | 1099 | 3104 | 2.82 |
| 3. | Chris Nilan, Mtl, NYR, Bos | 13 | 688 | 3043 | 4.42 |
| 4. | *Tim Hunter, Cgy, Que, Van | 14 | 709 | 2889 | 4.08 |
| 5. | *Marty McSorley, Edm, LA | 12 | 707 | 2723 | 3.85 |
| 6. | Willi Plett, Atl, Cgy, Minn, Bos | 12 | 834 | 2572 | 3.08 |
| 7. | *Basil McRae, Que, Tor, Det, Minn, StL | 14 | 550 | 2405 | 4.37 |
| 8. | Dave Schultz, Phil, LA, Pitt, Buff | 9 | 535 | 2294 | 4.29 |
| 9. | *Jay Wells, LA, Phil, Buff, NYR | 16 | 1001 | 2279 | 2.28 |
| 10. | Laurie Boschman, Tor, Edm, Winn, NJ, Ott | 14 | 1009 | 2265 | 2.24 |

*Active player.

## Goaltending Records

### ALLTIME WIN LEADERS

| Goaltender | W | L | T | Pct |
|---|---|---|---|---|
| Terry Sawchuk, five teams | 435 | 337 | 188 | .551 |
| Jacques Plante, five teams | 434 | 246 | 137 | .615 |
| Tony Esposito, Mtl, Chi | 423 | 307 | 151 | .566 |
| Glenn Hall, Det, Chi, StL | 407 | 327 | 165 | .544 |
| Rogie Vachon, Mtl, LA, Det, Bos | 355 | 291 | 115 | .542 |
| Gump Worsley, NYR, Mtl, Minn | 335 | 353 | 150 | .489 |
| Harry Lumley, five teams | 332 | 324 | 143 | .505 |
| *Andy Moog, Edm, Bos, Dall | 313 | 160 | 71 | .641 |
| Billy Smith, LA, NYI | 305 | 233 | 105 | .556 |
| Turk Broda, Tor | 302 | 224 | 101 | .562 |

*Active player.

### ACTIVE GOALTENDING LEADERS

| Goaltender | W | L | T | Pct |
|---|---|---|---|---|
| Andy Moog, Edm, Bos | 313 | 160 | 71 | .641 |
| Mike Vernon, Cgy, Det | 267 | 161 | 55 | .610 |
| Patrick Roy, Mtl | 277 | 166 | 65 | .609 |
| Ed Belfour, Chi | 168 | 106 | 40 | .599 |
| Grant Fuhr, Edm, Tor, Buff, LA | 290 | 195 | 71 | .585 |
| Tom Barrasso, Buff, Pitt | 266 | 197 | 61 | .566 |
| Ron Hextall, Phil, Que, NYI | 203 | 161 | 46 | .551 |
| Tim Cheveldae, Det, Winn | 141 | 117 | 34 | .541 |
| Kelly Hrudey, NYI, LA | 244 | 210 | 71 | .532 |
| Daren Puppa, Buff, Tor, TB | 138 | 122 | 36 | .527 |

Note: Ranked by winning percentage; minimum 250 games played.

### ALLTIME SHUTOUT LEADERS

| Goaltender | Team | Yrs | GP | SO |
|---|---|---|---|---|
| Terry Sawchuk | Det, Bos, Tor, LA, NYR | 21 | 971 | 103 |
| George Hainsworth | Mtl, Tor | 11 | 464 | 94 |
| Glenn Hall | Det, Chi, StL | 18 | 906 | 84 |
| Jacques Plante | Mtl, NYR, StL, Tor, Bos | 18 | 837 | 82 |
| Tiny Thompson | Bos, Det | 12 | 553 | 81 |
| Alex Connell | Ott, Det, NYA, Mtl M | 12 | 417 | 81 |
| Tony Esposito | Mtl, Chi | 16 | 886 | 76 |
| Lorne Chabot | NYR, Tor, Mtl, Chi, Mtl M, NYA | 11 | 411 | 73 |
| Harry Lumley | Det, NYR, Chi, Tor, Bos | 16 | 804 | 71 |
| Roy Worters | Pitt Pir, NYA, *Mtl | 12 | 484 | 66 |

*Played 1 game for Canadiens in 1929-30, not a shutout.

## Coaching Records

| Coach | Team | Seasons | W | L | T | Pct* |
|---|---|---|---|---|---|---|
| Scott Bowman | five teams | 1967– | 913 | 421 | 234 | .657 |
| Toe Blake | Mtl | 1955-68 | 500 | 255 | 159 | .634 |
| Glen Sather | Edm | 1979-89, 93-94 | 464 | 268 | 110 | .616 |
| Fred Shero | Phil, NYR | 1971-81 | 390 | 225 | 119 | .612 |
| Tommy Ivan | Det, Chi | 1947-54, 56-58 | 302 | 196 | 112 | .587 |
| Emile Francis | NYR, StL | 1965-77, 81-83 | 393 | 273 | 112 | .577 |
| Bryan Murray | Wash, Det | 1981-93 | 467 | 337 | 112 | .571 |
| Billy Reay | Tor, Chi | 1957-59, 63-77 | 542 | 385 | 175 | .571 |
| Al Arbour | StL, NYI | 1970-86, 88-94 | 781 | 577 | 248 | .564 |
| Dick Irvin | Chi, Tor, Mtl | 1930-56 | 690 | 521 | 226 | .559 |

*Percentage arrived at by dividing possible points into actual points.
Note: Minimum 600 regular-season games. Ranked by percentage.

# Single-Season Records

## Points per Game

| Player | Season | GP | Pts | Avg | Player | Season | GP | Pts | Avg |
|---|---|---|---|---|---|---|---|---|---|
| Wayne Gretzky, Edm | 1985-86 | 80 | 215 | 2.69 | Wayne Gretzky, LA | 1990-91 | 78 | 163 | 2.08 |
| Mario Lemieux, Pitt | 1992-93 | 60 | 160 | 2.66 | Mario Lemieux, Pitt | 1989-90 | 59 | 123 | 2.08 |
| Wayne Gretzky, Edm | 1981-82 | 80 | 212 | 2.65 | Wayne Gretzky, Edm | 1980-81 | 80 | 164 | 2.05 |
| Mario Lemieux, Pitt | 1988-89 | 76 | 199 | 2.62 | Bill Cowley, Bos | 1943-44 | 36 | 71 | 1.97 |
| Wayne Gretzky, Edm | 1984-85 | 80 | 208 | 2.60 | Phil Esposito, Bos | 1970-71 | 78 | 152 | 1.95 |
| Wayne Gretzky, Edm | 1982-83 | 80 | 196 | 2.45 | Wayne Gretzky, LA | 1989-90 | 73 | 142 | 1.95 |
| Wayne Gretzky, Edm | 1987-88 | 64 | 149 | 2.33 | Steve Yzerman, Det | 1988-89 | 80 | 155 | 1.94 |
| Wayne Gretzky, Edm | 1986-87 | 79 | 183 | 2.32 | Bernie Nicholls, LA | 1988-89 | 79 | 150 | 1.90 |
| Mario Lemieux, Pitt | 1987-88 | 77 | 168 | 2.18 | Phil Esposito, Bos | 1973-74 | 78 | 145 | 1.86 |
| Wayne Gretzky, LA | 1988-89 | 78 | 168 | 2.15 | | | | | |

## Goals per Game

| Player | Season | GP | G | Avg |
|---|---|---|---|---|
| Joe Malone, Mtl | 1917-18 | 20 | 44 | 2.20 |
| Cy Denneny, Ott | 1917-18 | 22 | 36 | 1.64 |
| Newsy Lalonde, Mtl | 1917-18 | 14 | 23 | 1.64 |
| Joe Malone, Que | 1919-20 | 24 | 39 | 1.63 |
| Newsy Lalonde, Mtl | 1919-20 | 23 | 36 | 1.57 |
| Joe Malone, Ham | 1920-21 | 20 | 30 | 1.50 |
| Babe Dye, Ham-Tor | 1920-21 | 24 | 35 | 1.46 |
| Cy Denneny, Ott | 1920-21 | 24 | 34 | 1.42 |
| Reg Noble, Tor | 1917-18 | 20 | 28 | 1.40 |
| Newsy Lalonde, Mtl | 1920-21 | 24 | 33 | 1.38 |

Note: Minimum 20 goals in one season.

## Assists per Game

| Player | Season | GP | A | Avg |
|---|---|---|---|---|
| Wayne Gretzky, Edm | 1985-86 | 80 | 163 | 2.04 |
| Wayne Gretzky, Edm | 1987-88 | 64 | 109 | 1.70 |
| Wayne Gretzky, Edm | 1984-85 | 80 | 135 | 1.69 |
| Wayne Gretzky, Edm | 1983-84 | 74 | 118 | 1.59 |
| Wayne Gretzky, Edm | 1982-83 | 80 | 125 | 1.56 |
| Wayne Gretzky, LA | 1990-91 | 78 | 122 | 1.56 |
| Wayne Gretzky, Edm | 1986-87 | 79 | 121 | 1.53 |
| Mario Lemieux, Pitt | 1992-93 | 60 | 91 | 1.52 |
| Wayne Gretzky, Edm | 1981-82 | 80 | 120 | 1.50 |
| Mario Lemieux, Pitt | 1988-89 | 76 | 114 | 1.50 |
| Adam Oates, StL | 1990-91 | 60 | 90 | 1.50 |

## Shutout Leaders

| | Season | SO | Length of Schedule |
|---|---|---|---|
| George Hainsworth, Mtl | 1928-29 | 22 | 44 |
| Alex Connell, Ott | 1925-26 | 15 | 36 |
| Alex Connell, Ott | 1927-28 | 15 | 44 |
| Hal Winkler, Bos | 1927-28 | 15 | 44 |
| Tony Esposito, Chi | 1969-70 | 15 | 76 |
| George Hainsworth, Mtl | 1926-27 | 14 | 44 |
| Clint Benedict, Mtl M | 1926-27 | 13 | 44 |
| Alex Connell, Ott | 1926-27 | 13 | 44 |
| George Hainsworth, Mtl | 1927-28 | 13 | 44 |
| Roy Worters, NYA | 1927-28 | 13 | 44 |
| John Roach, NYR | 1928-29 | 13 | 44 |
| Roy Worters, NYA | 1928-29 | 13 | 44 |
| Harry Lumley, Tor | 1953-54 | 13 | 70 |
| Tiny Thompson, Bos | 1928-29 | 12 | 44 |
| Lorne Chabot, Tor | 1928-29 | 12 | 44 |
| Chuck Gardiner, Chi | 1930-31 | 12 | 44 |
| Terry Sawchuk, Det | 1951-52 | 12 | 70 |
| Terry Sawchuk, Det | 1953-54 | 12 | 70 |
| Terry Sawchuk, Det | 1954-55 | 12 | 70 |
| Glenn Hall, Det | 1955-56 | 12 | 70 |

| | Season | SO | Length of Schedule |
|---|---|---|---|
| Bernie Parent, Phil | 1973-74 | 12 | 78 |
| Bernie Parent, Phil | 1974-75 | 12 | 80 |
| Lorne Chabot, NYR | 1927-28 | 11 | 44 |
| Harry Holmes, Det | 1927-28 | 11 | 44 |
| Clint Benedict, Mtl M | 1928-29 | 11 | 44 |
| Joe Miller, Pitt Pirates | 1928-29 | 11 | 44 |
| Tiny Thompson, Bos | 1932-33 | 11 | 48 |
| Terry Sawchuk, Det | 1950-51 | 11 | 70 |
| Lorne Chabot, NYR | 1926-27 | 10 | 44 |
| Roy Worters, Pitt Pirates | 1927-28 | 10 | 44 |
| Clarence Dolson, Det | 1928-29 | 10 | 44 |
| John Roach, Det | 1932-33 | 10 | 48 |
| Chuck Gardiner, Chi | 1933-34 | 10 | 48 |
| Tiny Thompson, Bos | 1935-36 | 10 | 48 |
| Frank Brimsek, Bos | 1938-39 | 10 | 48 |
| Bill Durnan, Mtl | 1948-49 | 10 | 60 |
| Gerry McNeil, Mtl | 1952-53 | 10 | 70 |
| Harry Lumley, Tor | 1952-53 | 10 | 70 |
| Tony Esposito, Chi | 1973-74 | 10 | 78 |
| Ken Dryden, Mtl | 1976-77 | 10 | 80 |

# Single-Game Records

## Goals

| | Date | G |
|---|---|---|
| Joe Malone, Que vs Tor | 1-31-20 | 7 |
| Newsy Lalonde, Mtl vs Tor | 1-10-20 | 6 |
| Joe Malone, Que vs Ott | 3-10-20 | 6 |
| Corb Denneny, Tor vs Ham | 1-26-21 | 6 |
| Cy Denneny, Ott vs Ham | 3-7-21 | 6 |
| Syd Howe, Det vs NYR | 2-3-44 | 6 |
| Red Berenson, StL vs Phil | 11-7-68 | 6 |
| Darryl Sittler, Tor vs Bos | 2-7-76 | 6 |

## Assists

| | Date | A |
|---|---|---|
| Billy Taylor, Det vs Chi | 3-16-47 | 7 |
| Wayne Gretzky, Edm vs Wash | 2-15-80 | 7 |
| Wayne Gretzky, Edm vs Chi | 12-11-85 | 7 |
| Wayne Gretzky, Edm vs Que | 2-14-86 | 7 |

Note: 19 tied with 6.

## Points

| | Date | G | A | Pts |
|---|---|---|---|---|
| Darryl Sittler, Tor vs Bos | 2-7-76 | 6 | 4 | 10 |
| Maurice Richard, Mtl vs Det | 12-28-44 | 5 | 3 | 8 |
| Bert Olmstead, Mtl vs Chi | 1-9-54 | 4 | 4 | 8 |
| Tom Bladon, Phil vs Clev | 12-11-77 | 4 | 4 | 8 |
| Bryan Trottier, NYI vs NYR | 12-23-78 | 5 | 3 | 8 |
| Peter Stastny, Que vs Wash | 2-22-81 | 4 | 4 | 8 |
| Anton Stastny, Que vs Wash | 2-22-81 | 3 | 5 | 8 |
| Wayne Gretzky, Edm vs NJ | 11-19-83 | 3 | 5 | 8 |
| Wayne Gretzky, Edm vs Minn | 1-4-84 | 4 | 4 | 8 |
| Paul Coffey, Edm vs Det | 3-14-86 | 2 | 6 | 8 |
| Mario Lemieux, Pitt vs StL | 10-15-88 | 2 | 6 | 8 |
| Bernie Nicholls, LA vs Tor | 12-1-88 | 2 | 6 | 8 |
| Mario Lemieux, Pitt vs NJ | 12-31-88 | 5 | 3 | 8 |

# NHL Season Leaders

## Points

| Season | Player and Club | Pts | Season | Player and Club | Pts |
|--------|-----------------|-----|--------|-----------------|-----|
| 1917-18 | Joe Malone, Mtl | 44* | 1957-58 | Dickie Moore, Mtl | 84 |
| 1918-19 | Newsy Lalonde, Mtl | 30 | 1958-59 | Dickie Moore, Mtl | 96 |
| 1919-20 | Joe Malone, Que | 48 | 1959-60 | Bobby Hull, Chi | 81 |
| 1920-21 | Newsy Lalonde, Mtl | 41 | 1960-61 | Bernie Geoffrion, Mtl | 95 |
| 1921-22 | Punch Broadbent, Ott | 46 | 1961-62 | Andy Bathgate, NY | 84 |
| 1922-23 | Babe Dye, Tor | 37 | | Bobby Hull, Chi | 84 |
| 1923-24 | Cy Denneny, Ott | 23 | 1962-63 | Gordie Howe, Det | 86 |
| 1924-25 | Babe Dye, Tor | 44 | 1963-64 | Stan Mikita, Chi | 89 |
| 1925-26 | Nels Stewart, Mtl M | 42 | 1964-65 | Stan Mikita, Chi | 87 |
| 1926-27 | Bill Cook, NY | 37 | 1965-66 | Bobby Hull, Chi | 97 |
| 1927-28 | Howie Morenz, Mtl | 51 | 1966-67 | Stan Mikita, Chi | 97 |
| 1928-29 | Ace Bailey, Tor | 32 | 1967-68 | Stan Mikita, Chi | 87 |
| 1929-30 | Cooney Weiland, Bos | 73 | 1968-69 | Phil Esposito, Bos | 126 |
| 1930-31 | Howie Morenz, Mtl | 51 | 1969-70 | Bobby Orr, Bos | 120 |
| 1931-32 | Harvey Jackson, Tor | 53 | 1970-71 | Phil Esposito, Bos | 152 |
| 1932-33 | Bill Cook, NY | 50 | 1971-72 | Phil Esposito, Bos | 133 |
| 1933-34 | Charlie Conacher, Tor | 52 | 1972-73 | Phil Esposito, Bos | 130 |
| 1934-35 | Charlie Conacher, Tor | 57 | 1973-74 | Phil Esposito, Bos | 145 |
| 1935-36 | Sweeney Schriner, NYA | 45 | 1974-75 | Bobby Orr, Bos | 135 |
| 1936-37 | Sweeney Schriner, NYA | 46 | 1975-76 | Guy Lafleur, Mtl | 125 |
| 1937-38 | Gord Drillon, Tor | 52 | 1976-77 | Guy Lafleur, Mtl | 136 |
| 1938-39 | Hector Blake, Mtl | 47 | 1977-78 | Guy Lafleur, Mtl | 132 |
| 1939-40 | Milt Schmidt, Bos | 52 | 1978-79 | Bryan Trottier, NYI | 134 |
| 1940-41 | Bill Cowley, Bos | 62 | 1979-80 | Marcel Dionne, LA | 137 |
| 1941-42 | Bryan Hextall, NY | 54 | | Wayne Gretzky, Edm | 137 |
| 1942-43 | Doug Bentley, Chi | 73 | 1980-81 | Wayne Gretzky, Edm | 164 |
| 1943-44 | Herb Cain, Bos | 82 | 1981-82 | Wayne Gretzky, Edm | 212 |
| 1944-45 | Elmer Lach, Mtl | 80 | 1982-83 | Wayne Gretzky, Edm | 196 |
| 1945-46 | Max Bentley, Chi | 61 | 1983-84 | Wayne Gretzky, Edm | 205 |
| 1946-47 | Max Bentley, Chi | 72 | 1984-85 | Wayne Gretzky, Edm | 208 |
| 1947-48 | Elmer Lach, Mtl | 61 | 1985-86 | Wayne Gretzky, Edm | 215 |
| 1948-49 | Roy Conacher, Chi | 68 | 1986-87 | Wayne Gretzky, Edm | 183 |
| 1949-50 | Ted Lindsay, Det | 78 | 1987-88 | Mario Lemieux, Pitt | 168 |
| 1950-51 | Gordie Howe, Det | 86 | 1988-89 | Mario Lemieux, Pitt | 199 |
| 1951-52 | Gordie Howe, Det | 86 | 1989-90 | Wayne Gretzky, LA | 142 |
| 1952-53 | Gordie Howe, Det | 95 | 1990-91 | Wayne Gretzky, LA | 163 |
| 1953-54 | Gordie Howe, Det | 81 | 1991-92 | Mario Lemieux, Pitt | 131 |
| 1954-55 | Bernie Geoffrion, Mtl | 75 | 1992-93 | Mario Lemieux, Pitt | 160 |
| 1955-56 | Jean Beliveau, Mtl | 88 | 1993-94 | Wayne Gretzky, LA | 130 |
| 1956-57 | Gordie Howe, Det | 89 | 1994-95 | Jaromir Jagr, Pitt | 70 |

## Goals

| Season | Player and Club | Pts | Season | Player and Club | Pts |
|--------|-----------------|-----|--------|-----------------|-----|
| 1917-18 | Joe Malone, Mtl | 44 | 1936-37 | Larry Aurie, Det | 23 |
| 1918-19 | Odie Cleghorn, Mtl | 23 | | Nels Stewart, Bos-NYA | 23 |
| 1919-20 | Joe Malone, Que | 39 | 1937-38 | Gord Drill, Tor | 26 |
| 1920-21 | Babe Dye, Ham-Tor | 35 | 1938-39 | Roy Conacher, Bos | 26 |
| 1921-22 | Punch Broadbent, Ott | 32 | 1939-40 | Bryan Hextall, NY | 24 |
| 1922-23 | Babe Dye, Tor | 26 | 1940-41 | Bryan Hextall, NY | 26 |
| 1923-24 | Cy Denneny, Ott | 22 | 1941-42 | Lynn Patrick, NY | 32 |
| 1924-25 | Babe Dye, Tor | 38 | 1942-43 | Doug Bentley, Chi | 43 |
| 1925-26 | Nels Stewart, Mtl | 34 | 1943-44 | Doug Bentley, Chi | 38 |
| 1926-27 | Bill Cook, NY | 33 | 1944-45 | Maurice Richard, Mtl | 50 |
| 1927-28 | Howie Morenz, Mtl | 33 | 1945-46 | Gaye Stewart, Tor | 37 |
| 1928-29 | Ace Bailey, Tor | 22 | 1946-47 | Maurice Richard, Mtl | 50 |
| 1929-30 | Cooney Weiland, Bos | 43 | 1947-48 | Ted Lindsay, Det | 33 |
| 1930-31 | Bill Cook, NY | 30 | 1948-49 | Sid Abel, Det | 28 |
| 1931-32 | Charlie Conacher, Tor | 34 | 1949-50 | Maurice Richard, Mtl | 43 |
| | Bill Cook, NY | 34 | 1950-51 | Gordie Howe, Det | 43 |
| 1932-33 | Bill Cook, NY | 28 | 1951-52 | Gordie Howe, Det | 47 |
| 1933-34 | Charlie Conacher, Tor | 32 | 1952-53 | Gordie Howe, Det | 49 |
| 1934-35 | Charlie Conacher, Tor | 36 | 1953-54 | Maurice Richard, Mtl | 37 |
| 1935-36 | Charlie Conacher, Tor | 23 | 1954-55 | Bernie Geoffrion, Mtl | 38 |
| | Bill Thoms, Tor | 23 | | Maurice Richard, Mtl | 38 |
| | | | 1955-56 | Jean Beliveau, Mtl | 47 |
| | | | 1956-57 | Gordie Howe, Det | 44 |

## Goals (Cont.)

| Season | Player and Club | G |
|---|---|---|
| 1957-58 | Dickie Moore, Mtl | 36 |
| 1958-59 | Jean Beliveau, Mtl | 45 |
| 1959-60 | Bobby Hull, Chi | 39 |
| | Bronco Horvath, Bos | 39 |
| 1960-61 | Bernie Geoffrion, Mtl | 50 |
| 1961-62 | Bobby Hull, Chi | 50 |
| 1962-63 | Gordie Howe, Det | 38 |
| 1963-64 | Bobby Hull, Chi | 43 |
| 1964-65 | Norm Ullman, Det | 42 |
| 1965-66 | Bobby Hull, Chi | 54 |
| 1966-67 | Bobby Hull, Chi | 52 |
| 1967-68 | Bobby Hull, Chi | 44 |
| 1968-69 | Bobby Hull, Chi | 58 |
| 1969-70 | Phil Esposito, Bos | 43 |
| 1970-71 | Phil Esposito, Bos | 76 |
| 1971-72 | Phil Esposito, Bos | 66 |
| 1972-73 | Phil Esposito, Bos | 55 |
| 1973-74 | Phil Esposito, Bos | 68 |
| 1974-75 | Phil Esposito, Bos | 61 |
| 1975-76 | Guy Lafleur, Mtl | 56 |
| 1976-77 | Steve Shutt, Mtl | 60 |

| Season | Player and Club | G |
|---|---|---|
| 1977-78 | Guy Lafleur, Mtl | 60 |
| 1978-79 | Mike Bossy, NYI | 69 |
| 1979-80 | Charlie Simmer, LA | 56 |
| | Blaine Stoughton, Hart | 56 |
| 1980-81 | Mike Bossy, NYI | 68 |
| 1981-82 | Wayne Gretzky, Edm | 92 |
| 1982-83 | Wayne Gretzky, Edm | 71 |
| 1983-84 | Wayne Gretzky, Edm | 87 |
| 1984-85 | Wayne Gretzky, Edm | 73 |
| 1985-86 | Jari Kurri, Edm | 68 |
| 1986-87 | Wayne Gretzky, Edm | 62 |
| 1987-88 | Mario Lemieux, Pitt | 70 |
| 1988-89 | Mario Lemieux, Pitt | 85 |
| 1989-90 | Brett Hull, StL | 72 |
| 1990-91 | Brett Hull, StL | 78 |
| 1991-92 | Brett Hull, StL | 70 |
| 1992-93 | Alexander Mogilny, Buff | 76 |
| | Teemu Selanne, Winn | 76 |
| 1993-94 | Pavel Bure, Van | 60 |
| 1994-95 | Peter Bondra, Wash | 34 |

## Assists

| Season | Player and Club | A |
|---|---|---|
| 1917-18 | statistic not kept | |
| 1918-19 | Newsy Lalonde, Mtl | 9 |
| 1919-20 | Corbett Denneny, Tor | 12 |
| 1920-21 | Louis Berlinquette, Mtl | 9 |
| 1921-22 | Punch Broadbench, Ott | 14 |
| 1922-23 | Babe Dye, Tor | 11 |
| 1923-24 | Billy Boucher, Mtl | 6 |
| 1924-25 | Cy Denneny, Ott | 15 |
| 1925-26 | Cy Denneny, Ott | 12 |
| 1926-27 | Dick Irvin, Chi | 18 |
| 1927-28 | Howie Morenz, Mtl | 18 |
| 1928-29 | Frank Boucher, NY | 16 |
| 1929-30 | Frank Boucher, NY | 36 |
| 1930-31 | Joe Primeau, Tor | 36 |
| 1931-32 | Joe Primeau, Tor | 37 |
| 1932-33 | Frank Boucher, NY | 28 |
| 1933-34 | Joe Primeau, Tor | 32 |
| 1934-35 | Art Chapman, NYA | 28 |
| 1935-36 | Art Chapman, NYA | 28 |
| 1936-37 | Syl Apps, Tor | 29 |
| 1937-38 | Syl Apps, Tor | 29 |
| 1938-39 | Bill Cowley, Bos | 34 |
| 1939-40 | Milt Schmidt, Bos | 30 |
| 1940-41 | Bill Cowley, Bos | 45 |
| 1941-42 | Phil Watson, NY | 37 |
| 1942-43 | Bill Cowley, Bos | 45 |
| 1943-44 | Clint Smith, Chi | 49 |
| 1944-45 | Elmer Lach, Mtl | 54 |
| 1945-46 | Elmer Lach, Mtl | 34 |
| 1946-47 | Billy Taylor, Det | 46 |
| 1947-48 | Doug Bentley, Chi | 37 |
| 1948-49 | Doug Bentley, Chi | 43 |
| 1949-50 | Ted Lindsay, Det | 55 |
| 1950-51 | Gordie Howe, Det | 43 |
| | Ted Kennedy, Tor | 43 |
| 1951-52 | Elmer Lach, Mtl | 50 |
| 1952-53 | Gordie Howe, Det | 46 |
| 1953-54 | Gordie Howe, Det | 48 |
| 1954-55 | Bert Olmstead, Mtl | 48 |
| 1955-56 | Bert Olmstead, Mtl | 56 |
| 1956-57 | Ted Lindsay, Det | 55 |
| 1957-58 | Henri Richard, Mtl | 52 |

| Season | Player and Club | A |
|---|---|---|
| 1958-59 | Dickie Moore, Mtl | 55 |
| 1959-60 | Bobby Hull, Chi | 42 |
| 1960-61 | Jean Beliveau, Mtl | 58 |
| 1961-62 | Andy Bathgate, NY | 56 |
| 1962-63 | Henri Richard, Mtl | 50 |
| 1963-64 | Andy Bathgate, NY-Tor | 58 |
| 1964-65 | Stan Mikita, Chi | 59 |
| 1965-66 | Stan Mikita, Chi | 48 |
| | Bobby Rousseau, Mtl | 48 |
| | Jean Beliveau, Mtl | 48 |
| 1966-67 | Stan Mikita, Chi | 62 |
| 1967-68 | Phil Esposito, Bos | 49 |
| 1968-69 | Phil Esposito, Bos | 77 |
| 1969-70 | Bobby Orr, Bos | 87 |
| 1970-71 | Bobby Orr, Bos | 102 |
| 1971-72 | Bobby Orr, Bos | 80 |
| 1972-73 | Phil Esposito, Bos | 75 |
| 1973-74 | Bobby Orr, Bos | 89 |
| 1974-75 | Bobby Clarke, Phil | 89 |
| | Bobby Orr, Bos | 89 |
| 1975-76 | Bobby Clarke, Phil | 89 |
| 1976-77 | Guy Lafleur, Mtl | 80 |
| 1977-78 | Bryan Trottier, NYI | 77 |
| 1978-79 | Bryan Trottier, NYI | 87 |
| 1979-80 | Wayne Gretzky, Edm | 86 |
| 1980-81 | Wayne Gretzky, Edm | 109 |
| 1981-82 | Wayne Gretzky, Edm | 120 |
| 1982-83 | Wayne Gretzky, Edm | 125 |
| 1983-84 | Wayne Gretzky, Edm | 118 |
| 1984-85 | Wayne Gretzky, Edm | 135 |
| 1985-86 | Wayne Gretzky, Edm | 163 |
| 1986-87 | Wayne Gretzky, Edm | 121 |
| 1987-88 | Wayne Gretzky, Edm | 109 |
| 1988-89 | Wayne Gretzky, LA | 114 |
| | Mario Lemieux, Pitt | 114 |
| 1989-90 | Wayne Gretzky, LA | 102 |
| 1990-91 | Wayne Gretzky, LA | 122 |
| 1991-92 | Wayne Gretzky, LA | 90 |
| 1992-93 | Adam Oates, Bos | 97 |
| 1993-94 | Wayne Gretzky, LA | 92 |
| 1994-95 | Ron Francis, Pitt | 48 |

## Goals Against Average

| Season | Goaltender and Club | GP | Min | GA | SO | Avg |
|--------|---------------------|-----|------|-----|-----|------|
| 1917-18 | Georges Vezina, Mtl | 21 | 1282 | 84 | 1 | 3.93 |
| 1918-19 | Clint Benedict, Ott | 18 | 1113 | 53 | 2 | 2.86 |
| 1919-20 | Clint Benedict, Ott | 24 | 1444 | 64 | 5 | 2.66 |
| 1920-21 | Clint Benedict, Ott | 24 | 1457 | 75 | 2 | 3.09 |
| 1921-22 | Clint Benedict, Ott | 24 | 1508 | 84 | 2 | 3.34 |
| 1922-23 | Clint Benedict, Ott | 24 | 1478 | 54 | 4 | 2.19 |
| 1923-24 | Georges Vezina, Mtl | 24 | 1459 | 48 | 3 | 1.97 |
| 1924-25 | Georges Vezina, Mtl | 30 | 1860 | 56 | 5 | 1.81 |
| 1925-26 | Alex Connell, Ott | 36 | 2251 | 42 | 15 | 1.12 |
| 1926-27 | Clint Benedict, Mtl M | 43 | 2748 | 65 | 13 | 1.42 |
| 1927-28 | George Hainsworth, Mtl | 44 | 2730 | 48 | 13 | 1.05 |
| 1928-29 | George Hainsworth, Mtl | 44 | 2800 | 43 | 22 | 0.92 |
| 1929-30 | Tiny Thompson, Bos | 44 | 2680 | 98 | 3 | 2.19 |
| 1930-31 | Roy Worters, NYA | 44 | 2760 | 74 | 8 | 1.61 |
| 1931-32 | Chuck Gardiner, Chi | 48 | 2989 | 92 | 4 | 1.85 |
| 1932-33 | Tiny Thompson, Bos | 48 | 3000 | 88 | 11 | 1.76 |
| 1933-34 | Wilf Cude, Det-Mtl | 30 | 1920 | 47 | 5 | 1.47 |
| 1934-35 | Lorne Chabot, Chi | 48 | 2940 | 88 | 8 | 1.80 |
| 1935-36 | Tiny Thompson, Bos | 48 | 2930 | 82 | 10 | 1.68 |
| 1936-37 | Normie Smith, Det | 48 | 2980 | 102 | 6 | 2.05 |
| 1937-38 | Tiny Thompson, Bos | 48 | 2970 | 89 | 7 | 1.80 |
| 1938-39 | Frank Brimsek, Bos | 43 | 2610 | 68 | 10 | 1.56 |
| 1939-40 | Dave Kerr, NYR | 48 | 3000 | 77 | 8 | 1.54 |
| 1940-41 | Turk Broda, Tor | 48 | 2970 | 99 | 5 | 2.00 |
| 1941-42 | Frank Brimsek, Bos | 47 | 2930 | 115 | 3 | 2.35 |
| 1942-43 | Johnny Mowers, Det | 50 | 3010 | 124 | 6 | 2.47 |
| 1943-44 | Bill Durnan, Mtl | 50 | 3000 | 109 | 2 | 2.18 |
| 1944-45 | Bill Durnan, Mtl | 50 | 3000 | 121 | 1 | 2.42 |
| 1945-46 | Bill Durnan, Mtl | 40 | 2400 | 104 | 4 | 2.60 |
| 1946-47 | Bill Durnan, Mtl | 60 | 3600 | 138 | 4 | 2.30 |
| 1947-48 | Turk Broda, Tor | 60 | 3600 | 143 | 5 | 2.38 |
| 1948-49 | Bill Durnan, Mtl | 60 | 3600 | 126 | 10 | 2.10 |
| 1949-50 | Bill Durnan, Mtl | 64 | 3840 | 141 | 8 | 2.20 |
| 1950-51 | Al Rollins, Tor | 40 | 2367 | 70 | 5 | 1.77 |
| 1951-52 | Terry Sawchuk, Det | 70 | 4200 | 133 | 12 | 1.90 |
| 1952-53 | Terry Sawchuk, Det | 63 | 3780 | 120 | 9 | 1.90 |
| 1953-54 | Harry Lumley, Tor | 69 | 4140 | 128 | 13 | 1.86 |
| 1954-55 | Harry Lumley, Tor | 69 | 4140 | 134 | 8 | 1.94 |
| | Terry Sawchuk, Det | 68 | 4060 | 132 | 12 | 1.94 |
| 1955-56 | Jacques Plante, Mtl | 64 | 3840 | 119 | 7 | 1.86 |
| 1956-57 | Jacques Plante, Mtl | 61 | 3660 | 123 | 9 | 2.02 |
| 1957-58 | Jacques Plante, Mtl | 57 | 3386 | 119 | 9 | 2.11 |
| 1958-59 | Jacques Plante, Mtl | 67 | 4000 | 144 | 9 | 2.16 |
| 1959-60 | Jacques Plante, Mtl | 69 | 4140 | 175 | 3 | 2.54 |
| 1960-61 | Johnny Bower, Tor | 58 | 3480 | 145 | 2 | 2.50 |
| 1961-62 | Jacques Plante, Mtl | 70 | 4200 | 166 | 4 | 2.37 |
| 1962-63 | Jacques Plante, Mtl | 56 | 3320 | 138 | 5 | 2.49 |
| 1963-64 | Johnny Bower, Tor | 51 | 3009 | 106 | 5 | 2.11 |
| 1964-65 | Johnny Bower, Tor | 34 | 2040 | 81 | 3 | 2.38 |
| 1965-66 | Johnny Bower, Tor | 35 | 1998 | 75 | 3 | 2.25 |
| 1966-67 | Glenn Hall, Chi | 32 | 1664 | 66 | 2 | 2.38 |
| 1967-68 | Gump Worsley, Mtl | 40 | 2213 | 73 | 6 | 1.98 |
| 1968-69 | Jacques Plante, StL | 37 | 2139 | 70 | 5 | 1.96 |
| 1969-70 | Ernie Wakely, StL | 30 | 1651 | 58 | 4 | 2.11 |
| 1970-71 | Jacques Plante, Tor | 40 | 2329 | 73 | 4 | 1.88 |
| 1971-72 | Tony Esposito, Chi | 48 | 2780 | 82 | 9 | 1.77 |
| 1972-73 | Ken Dryden, Mtl | 54 | 3165 | 119 | 6 | 2.26 |
| 1973-74 | Bernie Parent, Phil | 73 | 4314 | 136 | 12 | 1.89 |
| 1974-75 | Bernie Parent, Phil | 68 | 4041 | 137 | 12 | 2.03 |
| 1975-76 | Ken Dryden, Mtl | 62 | 3580 | 121 | 8 | 2.03 |
| 1976-77 | Michael Larocque, Mtl | 26 | 1525 | 53 | 4 | 2.09 |
| 1977-78 | Ken Dryden, Mtl | 52 | 3071 | 105 | 5 | 2.05 |
| 1978-79 | Ken Dryden, Mtl | 47 | 2814 | 108 | 5 | 2.30 |
| 1979-80 | Bob Sauve, Buff | 32 | 1880 | 74 | 4 | 2.36 |
| 1980-81 | Richard Sevigny, Mtl | 33 | 1777 | 71 | 2 | 2.40 |
| 1981-82 | Denis Herron, Mtl | 27 | 1547 | 68 | 3 | 2.64 |

## Goals Against Average (Cont.)

| Season | Goaltender and Club | GP | Min | GA | SO | Avg |
|---|---|---|---|---|---|---|
| 1982-83 | Pete Peeters, Bos | 62 | 3611 | 142 | 8 | 2.36 |
| 1983-84 | Pat Riggin, Wash | 41 | 2299 | 102 | 4 | 2.66 |
| 1984-85 | Tom Barrasso, Buff | 54 | 3248 | 144 | 5 | 2.66 |
| 1985-86 | Bob Froese, Phil | 51 | 2728 | 116 | 5 | 2.55 |
| 1986-87 | Brian Hayward, Mtl | 37 | 2178 | 102 | 1 | 2.81 |
| 1987-88 | Pete Peeters, Wash | 35 | 1896 | 88 | 2 | 2.78 |
| 1988-89 | Patrick Roy, Mtl | 48 | 2744 | 113 | 4 | 2.47 |
| 1989-90 | Patrick Roy, Mtl | 54 | 3173 | 134 | 3 | 2.53 |
| | Mike Liut, Hart-Wash | 37 | 2161 | 91 | 4 | 2.53 |
| 1990-91 | Ed Belfour, Chi | 74 | 4127 | 170 | 4 | 2.47 |
| 1991-92 | Patrick Roy, Mtl | 67 | 3935 | 155 | 5 | 2.36 |
| 1992-93 | *Felix Potvin, Tor | 48 | 2781 | 116 | 2 | 2.50 |
| 1993-94 | Dominik Hasek, Buff | 58 | 3358 | 109 | 7 | 1.95 |
| 1994-95 | Dominik Hasek, Buff | 41 | 2416 | 85 | 5 | 2.11 |

*Rookie.

## Penalty Minutes

| Season | Player and Club | GP | PIM | Season | Player and Club | GP | PIM |
|---|---|---|---|---|---|---|---|
| 1918-19 | Joe Hall, Mtl | 17 | 85 | 1957-58 | Lou Fontinato, NYR | 70 | 152 |
| 1919-20 | Cully Wilson, Tor | 23 | 79 | 1958-59 | Ted Lindsay, Chi | 70 | 184 |
| 1920-21 | Bert Corbeau, Mtl | 24 | 86 | 1959-60 | Carl Brewer, Tor | 67 | 150 |
| 1921-22 | S Cleghorn, Mtl | 24 | 63 | 1960-61 | Pierre Pilote, Chi | 70 | 165 |
| 1922-23 | Billy Boucher, Mtl | 24 | 52 | 1961-62 | Lou Fontinato, Mtl | 54 | 167 |
| 1923-24 | Bert Corbeau, Tor | 24 | 55 | 1962-63 | Howie Young, Det | 64 | 273 |
| 1924-25 | Billy Boucher, Mtl | 30 | 92 | 1963-64 | Vic Hadfield, NYR | 69 | 151 |
| 1925-26 | Bert Corbeau, Tor | 36 | 121 | 1964-65 | Carl Brewer, Tor | 70 | 177 |
| 1926-27 | Nels Stewart, Mtl M | 44 | 133 | 1965-66 | R Fleming, Bos-NYR | 69 | 166 |
| 1927-28 | Eddie Shore, Bos | 44 | 165 | 1966-67 | John Ferguson, Mtl | 67 | 177 |
| 1928-29 | Red Dutton, Mtl M | 44 | 139 | 1967-68 | Barclay Plager, StL | 49 | 153 |
| 1929-30 | Joe Lamb, Ott | 44 | 119 | 1968-69 | F Kennedy, Phil-Tor | 77 | 219 |
| 1930-31 | Harvey Rockburn, Det | 42 | 118 | 1969-70 | Keith Magnuson, Chi | 76 | 213 |
| 1931-32 | Red Dutton, NYA | 47 | 107 | 1970-71 | Keith Magnuson, Chi | 76 | 291 |
| 1932-33 | Red Horner, Tor | 48 | 144 | 1971-72 | Brian Watson, Pitt | 75 | 212 |
| 1933-34 | Red Horner, Tor | 42 | 126 | 1972-73 | Dave Schultz, Phil | 76 | 259 |
| 1934-35 | Red Horner, Tor | 46 | 125 | 1973-74 | Dave Schultz, Phil | 73 | 348 |
| 1935-36 | Red Horner, Tor | 43 | 167 | 1974-75 | Dave Schultz, Phil | 76 | 472 |
| 1936-37 | Red Horner, Tor | 48 | 124 | 1975-76 | S Durbano, Pitt-KC | 69 | 370 |
| 1937-38 | Red Horner, Tor | 47 | 82 | 1976-77 | Dave Williams, Tor | 77 | 338 |
| 1938-39 | Red Horner, Tor | 48 | 85 | 1977-78 | Dave Schultz, LA-Pitt | 74 | 405 |
| 1939-40 | Red Horner, Tor | 30 | 87 | 1978-79 | Dave Williams, Tor | 77 | 298 |
| 1940-41 | Jimmy Orlando, Det | 48 | 99 | 1979-80 | Jimmy Mann, Winn | 72 | 287 |
| 1941-42 | Jimmy Orlando, Det | 48 | 81 | 1980-81 | Dave Williams, Van | 77 | 343 |
| 1942-43 | Jimmy Orlando, Det | 40 | 89 | 1981-82 | Paul Baxter, Pitt | 76 | 409 |
| 1943-44 | Mike McMahon, Mtl | 42 | 98 | 1982-83 | Randy Holt, Wash | 70 | 275 |
| 1944-45 | Pat Egan, Bos | 48 | 86 | 1983-84 | Chris Nilan, Mtl | 76 | 338 |
| 1945-46 | Jack Stewart, Det | 47 | 73 | 1984-85 | Chris Nilan, Mtl | 77 | 358 |
| 1946-47 | Gus Mortson, Tor | 60 | 133 | 1985-86 | Joey Kocur, Det | 59 | 377 |
| 1947-48 | Bill Barilko, Tor | 57 | 147 | 1986-87 | Tim Hunter, Cgy | 73 | 361 |
| 1948-49 | Bill Ezinicki, Tor | 52 | 145 | 1987-88 | Bob Probert, Det | 74 | 398 |
| 1949-50 | Bill Ezinicki, Tor | 67 | 144 | 1988-89 | Tim Hunter, Cgy | 75 | 375 |
| 1950-51 | Gus Mortson, Tor | 60 | 142 | 1989-90 | Basil McRae, Minn | 66 | 351 |
| 1951-52 | Gus Kyle, Bos | 69 | 127 | 1990-91 | Bob Ray, Buff | 66 | 350 |
| 1952-53 | Maurice Richard, Mtl | 70 | 112 | 1991-92 | Mike Peluso, Chi | 63 | 408 |
| 1953-54 | Gus Mortson, Chi | 68 | 132 | 1992-93 | Marty McSorley, LA | 81 | 399 |
| 1954-55 | Fern Flaman, Bos | 70 | 150 | 1993-94 | Tie Domi, Winn | 81 | 347 |
| 1955-56 | Lou Fontinato, NYR | 70 | 202 | 1994-95 | Enrico Ciccone, TB | 41 | 225 |
| 1956-57 | Gus Mortson, Chi | 70 | 147 | | | | |

# NHL All-Star Game

First played in 1947, this game was scheduled before the start of the regular season and used to match the defending Stanley Cup champions against a squad made up of league All-Stars from other teams. In 1966 the games were moved to mid season, although there was no game that year. The format changed to a conference versus conference showdown in 1969.

## Results

| Year | Site | Score | MVP | Attendance |
|------|------|-------|-----|-----------:|
| 1947 | Toronto | All-Stars 4, Toronto 3 | None named | 14,169 |
| 1948 | Chicago | All-Stars 3, Toronto 1 | None named | 12,794 |
| 1949 | Toronto | All-Stars 3, Toronto 1 | None named | 13,541 |
| 1950 | Detroit | Detroit 7, All-Stars 1 | None named | 9,166 |
| 1951 | Toronto | 1st team 2, 2nd team 2 | None named | 11,469 |
| 1952 | Detroit | 1st team 1, 2nd team 1 | None named | 10,680 |
| 1953 | Montreal | All-Stars 3, Montreal 1 | None named | 14,153 |
| 1954 | Detroit | All-Stars 2, Detroit 2 | None named | 10,689 |
| 1955 | Detroit | Detroit 3, All-Stars 1 | None named | 10,111 |
| 1956 | Montreal | All-Stars 1, Montreal 1 | None named | 13,095 |
| 1957 | Montreal | All-Stars 5, Montreal 3 | None named | 13,003 |
| 1958 | Montreal | Montreal 6, All-Stars 3 | None named | 13,989 |
| 1959 | Montreal | Montreal 6, All-Stars 1 | None named | 13,818 |
| 1960 | Montreal | All-Stars 2, Montreal 1 | None named | 13,949 |
| 1961 | Chicago | All-Stars 3, Chicago 1 | None named | 14,534 |
| 1962 | Toronto | Toronto 4, All-Stars 1 | Eddie Shack, Tor | 14,236 |
| 1963 | Toronto | All-Stars 3, Toronto 3 | Frank Mahovlich, Tor | 14,034 |
| 1964 | Toronto | All-Stars 3, Toronto 2 | Jean Beliveau, Mtl | 14,232 |
| 1965 | Montreal | All-Stars 5, Montreal 2 | Gordie Howe, Det | 13,529 |
| 1967 | Montreal | Montreal 3, All-Stars 0 | Henri Richard, Mtl | 14,284 |
| 1968 | Toronto | Toronto 4, All-Stars 3 | Bruce Gamble, Tor | 15,753 |
| 1969 | Montreal | East 3, West 3 | Frank Mahovlich, Det | 16,260 |
| 1970 | St Louis | East 4, West 1 | Bobby Hull, Chi | 16,587 |
| 1971 | Boston | West 2, East 1 | Bobby Hull, Chi | 14,790 |
| 1972 | Minnesota | East 3, West 2 | Bobby Orr, Bos | 15,423 |
| 1973 | NY Rangers | East 5, West 4 | Greg Polis, Pitt | 16,986 |
| 1974 | Chicago | West 6, East 4 | Garry Unger, StL | 16,426 |
| 1975 | Montreal | Wales 7, Campbell 1 | Syl Apps Jr, Pitt | 16,080 |
| 1976 | Philadelphia | Wales 7, Campbell 5 | Pete Mahovlich, Mtl | 16,436 |
| 1977 | Vancouver | Wales 4, Campbell 3 | Rick Martin, Buff | 15,607 |
| 1978 | Buffalo | Wales 3, Campbell 2 (OT) | Billy Smith, NYI | 16,433 |
| 1980 | Detroit | Wales 6, Campbell 3 | Reg Leach, Phil | 21,002 |
| 1981 | Los Angeles | Campbell 4, Wales 1 | Mike Liut, StL | 15,761 |
| 1982 | Washington | Wales 4, Campbell 2 | Mike Bossy, NYI | 18,130 |
| 1983 | NY Islanders | Campbell 9, Wales 3 | Wayne Gretzky, Edm | 15,230 |
| 1984 | NJ Devils | Wales 7, Campbell 6 | Don Maloney, NYR | 18,939 |
| 1985 | Calgary | Wales 6, Campbell 4 | Mario Lemieux, Pitt | 16,825 |
| 1986 | Hartford | Wales 4, Campbell 3 (OT) | Grant Fuhr, Edm | 15,100 |
| 1988 | St Louis | Wales 6, Campbell 5 (OT) | Mario Lemieux, Pitt | 17,878 |
| 1989 | Edmonton | Campbell 9, Wales 5 | Wayne Gretzky, LA | 17,503 |
| 1990 | Pittsburgh | Wales 12, Campbell 7 | Mario Lemieux, Pitt | 16,236 |
| 1991 | Chicago | Campbell 11, Wales 5 | Vince Damphousse, Tor | 18,472 |
| 1992 | Philadelphia | Campbell 10, Wales 6 | Brett Hull, StL | 17,380 |
| 1993 | Montreal | Wales 16, Campbell 6 | Mike Gartner, NYR | 17,137 |
| 1994 | NY Rangers | East 9, West 8 | Mike Richter, NYR | 18,200 |

Note: The Challenge Cup, a series between the NHL All-Stars and the Soviet Union, was played instead of the All-Star Game in 1979. Eight years later, Rendez-Vous '87, a two-game series matching the Soviet Union and the NHL All-Stars, replaced the All-Star Game. The 1995 NHL All-Star game was cancelled due to a labor dispute.

# Hockey Hall of Fame

Located in Toronto, the Hockey Hall of Fame was officially opened on August 26, 1961. The current president is Ian "Scotty" Morrison, a former NHL referee. There are, at present, 281 members of the Hockey Hall of Fame—192 players, 77 "Builders," and 12 on-ice officials. To be eligible, player and referee/linesman candidates should have been out of the game for three years, but the Hall's Board of Directors can make exceptions.

## Players

Sid Abel (1969)
Jack Adams (1959)
Charles "Syl" Apps (1961)
George Armstrong (1975)
Irvine "Ace" Bailey (1975)
Donald H. "Dan" Bain (1945)
Hobey Baker (1945)
Bill Barber (1990)
Marty Barry (1965)
Andy Bathgate (1978)
Jean Beliveau (1972)
Clint Benedict (1965)
Douglas Bentley (1964)
Max Bentley (1966)
Hector "Toe" Blake (1966)
Leo Boivin (1986)
Dickie Boon (1952)
Mike Bossy (1991)
Emile "Butch" Bouchard (1966)
Frank Boucher (1958)
George "Buck" Boucher (1960)
Johnny Bower (1976)
Russell Bowie (1945)
Frank Brimsek (1966)
Harry L. "Punch" Broadbent (1962)
Walter "Turk" Broda (1967)
John Bucyk (1981)
Billy Burch (1974)
Harry Cameron (1962)
Gerry Cheevers (1985)
Francis "King" Clancy (1958)
Aubrey "Dit" Clapper (1947)
Bobby Clarke (1987)
Sprague Cleghorn (1958)
Neil Colville (1967)
Charlie Conacher (1961)
Lionel Conacher (1994)
Alex Connell (1958)
Bill Cook (1952)
Arthur Coulter (1974)
Yvan Cournoyer (1982)
Bill Cowley (1968)
Samuel "Rusty" Crawford (1962)
Jack Darragh (1962)
Allan M. "Scotty" Davidson (1950)
Clarence "Hap" Day (1961)
Alex Delvecchio (1977)
Cy Denneny (1959)
Marcel Dionne (1992)
Gordie Drillon (1975)
Charles Drinkwater (1950)
Ken Dryden (1983)
Woody Dumart (1992)

Thomas Dunderdale (1974)
Bill Durnan (1964)
Mervyn A. "Red" Dutton (1958)
Cecil "Babe" Dye (1970)
Phil Esposito (1984)
Tony Esposito (1988)
Arthur F. Farrell (1965)
Ferdinand "Fern" Flaman (1990)
Frank Foyston (1958)
Frank Frederickson (1958)
Bill Gadsby (1970)
Bob Gainey (1992)
Chuck Gardiner (1945)
Herb Gardiner (1958)
Jimmy Gardner (1962)
Bernie "Boom Boom" Geoffrion (1972)
Eddie Gerard (1945)
Ed Giacomin (1987)
Rod Gilbert (1982)
Hamilton "Billy" Gilmour (1962)
Frank "Moose" Goheen (1952)
Ebenezer R. "Ebbie" Goodfellow (1963)
Mike Grant (1950)
Wilfred "Shorty" Green (1962)
Si Griffis (1950)
George Hainsworth (1961)
Glenn Hall (1975)
Joe Hall (1961)
Doug Harvey (1973)
George Hay (1958)
William "Riley" Hern (1962)
Bryan Hextall (1969)
Harry "Hap" Holmes (1972)
Tom Hooper (1962)
George "Red" Horner (1965)
Miles "Tim" Horton (1977)
Gordie Howe (1972)
Syd Howe (1965)
Harry Howell (1979)
Bobby Hull (1983)
John "Bouse" Hutton (1962)
Harry M. Hyland (1962)
James "Dick" Irvin (1958)
Harvey "Busher" Jackson (1971)
Ernest "Moose" Johnson (1952)
Ivan "Ching" Johnson (1958)
Tom Johnson (1970)
Aurel Joliat (1947)
Gordon "Duke" Keats (1958)
Leonard "Red" Kelly (1969)
Ted "Teeder" Kennedy (1966)
Dave Keon (1986)

Elmer Lach (1966)
Guy Lafleur (1988)
Edouard "Newsy" Lalonde (1950)
Jacques Laperriere (1987)
Guy LaPointe (1993)
Edgar Laprade (1993)
Jean "Jack" Laviolette (1962)
Hugh Lehman (1958)
Jacques Lemaire (1984)
Percy LeSueur (1961)
Herbert A. Lewis (1989)
Ted Lindsay (1966)
Harry Lumley (1980)
Lanny McDonald (1992)
Frank McGee (1945)
Billy McGimsie (1962)
George McNamara (1958)
Duncan "Mickey" MacKay (1952)
Frank Mahovlich (1981)
Joe Malone (1950)
Sylvio Mantha (1960)
Jack Marshall (1965)
Fred G. "Steamer" Maxwell (1962)
Stan Mikita (1983)
Dicky Moore (1974)
Patrick "Paddy" Moran (1958)
Howie Morenz (1945)
Billy Mosienko (1965)
Frank Nighbor (1947)
Reg Noble (1962)
Herbert "Buddy" O'Connor (1988)
Harry Oliver (1967)
Bert Olmstead (1985)
Bobby Orr (1979)
Bernie Parent (1984)
Brad Park (1988)
Lester Patrick (1947)
Lynn Patrick (1980)
Gilbert Perreault (1990)
Tommy Phillips (1945)
Pierre Pilote (1975)
Didier "Pit" Pitre (1962)
Jacques Plante (1978)
Denis Potvin (1991)
Walter "Babe" Pratt (1966)
Joe Primeau (1963)
Marcel Pronovost (1978)
Bob Pulford (1991)
Harvey Pulford (1945)
Hubert "Bill" Quackenbush (1976)

## Players *(Cont.)*

Frank Rankin (1961)
Jean Ratelle (1985)
Claude "Chuck" Rayner (1973)
Kenneth Reardon (1966)
Henri Richard (1979)
Maurice "Rocket" Richard
　(1961)
George Richardson (1950)
Gordon Roberts (1971)
Art Ross (1945)
Blair Russel (1965)
Ernest Russell (1965)
Jack Ruttan (1962)
Serge Savard (1986)
Terry Sawchuk (1971)
Fred Scanlan (1965)
Milt Schmidt (1961)
Dave "Sweeney" Schriner
　(1962)
Earl Seibert (1963)
Oliver Seibert (1961)
Eddie Shore (1947)
Steve Shutt (1993)
Albert C. "Babe" Siebert (1964)
Harold "Bullet Joe" Simpson
　(1962)
Daryl Sittler (1989)
Alfred E. Smith (1962)
Billy Smith (1993)
Clint Smith (1991)
Reginald "Hooley" Smith (1972)
Thomas Smith (1973)
Allan Stanley (1981)
Russell "Barney" Stanley
　(1962)
John "Black Jack" Stewart
　(1964)
Nels Stewart (1962)
Bruce Stuart (1961)
Hod Stuart (1945)
Frederic "Cyclone" (O.B.E.)
　Taylor (1947)
Cecil R. "Tiny" Thompson
　(1959)
Vladislav Tretiak (1989)
Harry J. Trihey (1950)
Norm Ullman (1982)
Georges Vezina (1945)
Jack Walker (1960)
Marty Walsh (1962)
Harry Watson (1994)
Harry E. Watson (1962)
Ralph "Cooney" Weiland (1971)
Harry Westwick (1962)
Fred Whitcroft (1962)
Gordon "Phat" Wilson (1962)
Lorne "Gump" Worsley (1980)
Roy Worters (1969)

## Builders

Charles Adams (1960)
Weston W. Adams (1972)
Thomas "Frank" Ahearn (1962)
John "Bunny" Ahearne (1977)
Montagu Allan (C.V.O.) (1945)
Keith Allen (1992)
Harold Ballard (1977)
David Bauer (1989)
John Bickell (1978)
Scott Bowman (1991)
George V. Brown (1961)
Walter A. Brown (1962)
Frank Buckland (1975)
Jack Butterfield (1980)
Frank Calder (1947)
Angus D. Campbell (1964)
Clarence Campbell (1966)
Joe Cattarinich (1977)
Joseph "Leo" Dandurand
　(1963)
Francis Dilio (1964)
George S. Dudley (1958)
James A. Dunn (1968)
Alan Eagleson (1989)
Emile Francis (1982)
Jack Gibson (1976)
Tommy Gorman (1963)
Frank Griffiths (1993)
William Hanley (1986)
Charles Hay (1974)
James C. Hendy (1968)
Foster Hewitt (1965)
William Hewitt (1947)
Fred J. Hume (1962)
George "Punch" Imlach (1984)
Tommy Ivan (1974)
William M. Jennings (1975)
Bob Johnson (1992)
Gordon W. Juckes (1979)
John Kilpatrick (1960)
Seymour Knox III (1993)
George Leader (1969)
Robert LeBel (1970)
Thomas F. Lockhart (1965)
Paul Loicq (1961)
Frederic McLaughlin (1963)
John Mariucci (1985)
Frank Mathers (1992)
John "Jake" Milford (1984)
Hartland Molson (1973)
Francis Nelson (1947)
Bruce A. Norris (1969)
James Norris, Sr. (1958)
James D. Norris (1962)
William M. Northey (1947)
John O'Brien (1962)
Brian O'Neill (1994)
Fred Page (1993)
Frank Patrick (1958)
Allan W. Pickard (1958)
Rudy Pilous (1985)
Norman "Bud" Poile (1990)

## Builders *(Cont.)*

Samuel Pollock (1978)
Donat Raymond (1958)
John Robertson (1947)
Claude C. Robinson (1947)
Philip D. Ross (1976)
Frank J. Selke (1960)
Harry Sinden (1983)
Frank D. Smith (1962)
Conn Smythe (1958)
Edward M. Snider (1988)
Lord Stanley of Preston
　(G.C.B.) (1945)
James T. Sutherland (1947)
Anatoli V. Tarasov (1974)
Lloyd Turner (1958)
William Tutt (1978)
Carl Potter Voss (1974)
Fred C. Waghorn (1961)
Arthur Wirtz (1971)
Bill Wirtz (1976)
John A. Ziegler, Jr. (1987)

## Referees/Linesmen

Neil Armstrong (1991)
John Ashley (1981)
William L. Chadwick (1964)
John D'Amico (1993)
Chaucer Elliott (1961)
George Hayes (1988)
Robert W. Hewitson (1963)
Fred J. "Mickey" Ion (1961)
Matt Pavelich (1987)
Mike Rodden (1962)
J. Cooper Smeaton (1961)
Roy "Red" Storey (1967)
Frank Udvari (1973)

Note: Year of election to the Hall
of Fame is in parentheses after
the member's name.

# Tennis

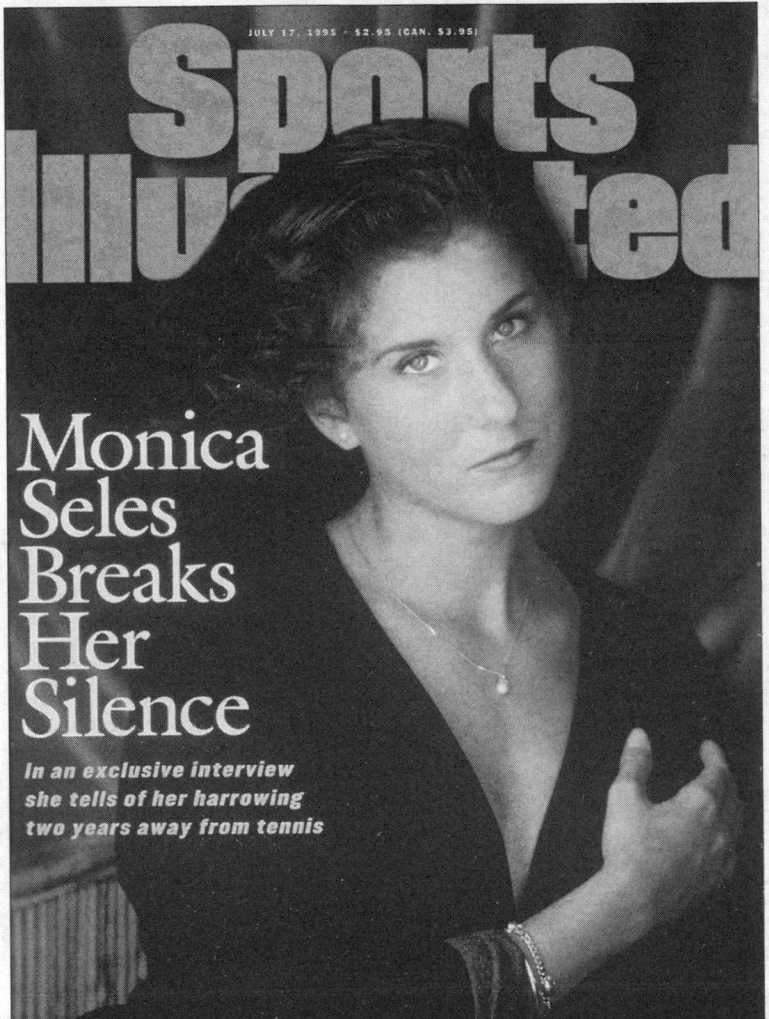

JULY 17, 1995 · $2.95 (CAN. $3.95)

## Sports Illustrated

## Monica Seles Breaks Her Silence

*In an exclusive interview she tells of her harrowing two years away from tennis*

GREGORY HEISLER

# Eyes On The Prize

## The game's top players had outstanding seasons despite a plethora of off-court distractions

## by Sally Jenkins

IT WAS a year of comebacks and heartaches. Everyone won, and everyone cried. Twenty-eight months after she was stabbed by a German fanatic, Monica Seles made an emotional and triumphant return to the game she once dominated. Pained by a chronic back ailment and beset by family scandal, Steffi Graf tearfully clung to the No. 1 ranking through it all. Silencing critics who said he would never be a true champion, Andre Agassi became the top-ranked men's player. And Pete Sampras endured personal tragedy to stake a claim as the most accomplished player of his generation.

It all began with Agassi's haircut. He appeared at the Australian Open for the first Grand Slam event of the season shorn of the flowing peroxided mane that had been his signature. Judging by his cropped head and scaled-down entourage, Agassi meant business. (He had gotten the new do from a fashionable hairdresser while lounging in the kitchen of girlfriend Brooke Shields's New York City apartment over the Christmas break, after fortifying

himself with champagne.) Australians labeled him the Pirate King and the Black Prince, for the bandana he sported. However, not all of Agassi's fans were charmed by the new image. While his older constituency wholeheartedly approved, the teenybopper set was furious. "An oldy, baldy codger" is how one Australian adolescent described him.

Agassi didn't care. The reason for the redesign of his head was twofold: First, it was time to admit that his hairline was receding. Second, he wanted a tough new image emblematic of his newfound professional commitment. "To be honest, I think it was long overdue," he said. Agassi thus served notice that he would finally blend consistency and dedication with his talent. The time that he used to put into his hair now went into his tennis. "It used to take about 27 minutes a day, now it takes six and half," he said.

Agassi was determined to make the Australian a convincing follow-up to the U.S. Open title with which he had closed out 1994. With a chance to win two Grand

**Unveiling a new attitude as well as a new look, Agassi pirated the Australian title.**

Slam events in a row for the first time in his career, he kept an uncharacteristically low profile, cooking banana pancakes for himself in his rented home and getting his game face on by watching slasher and action movies: Freddy Krueger films, *Die Harder* and *The Exorcist*. "I've come to terms with myself and with my tennis," he said. "It used to be I thought I had to live up to something, to validate what I did on the TV commercials. Now everything has its rightful place." The result of his focus: He swept into the final at Flinders Park without losing so much as a set. He then defeated 4–6, 6–1, 7–6 (8–6), 6–4 an emotionally spent Sampras, who had a far more dramatic path to the final.

On the women's side, Graf sat out the Australian in an effort to rest her aching back. Suffering from a painful bone spur in her spine, Graf wondered if she would be able to play again at all. Such thoughts also went through the mind of Seles, who struggled with depression and was only beginning to contemplate a return. The Australian thus belonged to Mary Pierce, the expressive 20-year-old with blinding hair and roundhouse strokes. Pierce claimed the first Grand Slam title of her career, finally arriving as a champion, without the loss of a set or more than six games in any match, including the final. She overwhelmed second-ranked Arantxa Sanchez Vicario 6–3, 6–2. "Everybody said, 'Mary can play, but can she play well all the time?'" Pierce said. "This was important for me."

But ultimately the Australian would be remembered less for its victors than for a tragic event off the court. Sampras's coach and good friend, Tim Gullikson, was hospi-talized in midtournament after collapsing with what was later diagnosed as brain cancer. Sampras spent much of his time at Gullikson's side. When Sampras asked a local specialist for a worst-case scenario, he was told Gullikson might have only six months to live. Devastated, Sampras carried on. Twice he rallied from two sets down to win matches, including a quarterfinal meeting with Jim Courier that ranked among the most stirring on-court confrontations ever. Fatigued and agonizing over Gullikson, Sampras stood in the middle of the court during the fifth set and sobbed openly. "I started thinking about Tim, and it just broke my heart," he said.

RUSS ADAMS

Sampras will never again be mistaken for a casual or passionless player, two labels with which he had been stuck in his exceedingly shy youth. In fact he is a deeply feeling young man. Sampras tried to compose himself on a changeover but had to bury his head in a towel, shoulders heaving. When he took the court again, Sampras leaned on his racket, still crying uncontrollably. Courier, on the far side of the net, could not tell what was going on. "You O.K., Pete?" he asked. "We can come back and finish this tomorrow." Sampras straightened up and stopped weeping. And served an ace. He went on to one of the defining victories of his career: 6–7 (4–7), 6–7 (3–7), 6–3, 6–4, 6–3.

Sampras was clearly exhausted physically and emotionally against Agassi as he surrendered the title. Disappointment would be the hallmark of Sampras's first half of the year. He played without complaint through a sprained ankle, a first-round loss at the French Open and the loss of his No. 1 ranking to Agassi.

The French Open was a tale of persistence and renewal for Thomas Muster of Austria. Muster was 21 and a rising star in 1989 when he was hit by a car in the parking lot at a tournament in Miami, severing the ligaments in his left knee. It was not certain that Muster would ever walk normally again, much less play. But Muster was practicing again within six months, albeit from a specially designed wheelchair. When he left Paris this year he was a career-high No. 3 and on a remarkable winning streak, although he still could not completely extend his left leg. By defeating Michael Chang in the final in straight sets, he ran his clay court record for '95 to 35–0.

The French also marked the return of Graf, whose fitness was a moment-to-moment affair, but who dispatched Sanchez Vicario 7–5, 4–6, 6–0, for one of the most surprising titles of her career. Two weeks prior to the tournament, Graf wasn't even sure she could play—because of the bone spur. "I didn't expect to be in the finals, or win it," Graf said. She was so taken aback that when she accepted a microphone to speak to the stadium crowd she said, "The only thing I can say is, *Mon chapeau est bien*," drawing a burst of laughter from spectators.

The profiles in courage continued at Wimbledon, where Sampras resurfaced to win his first Grand Slam title in a year and accomplish his historical "ThreePete"; he's only the third man since World War I to win three consecutive titles at the All England Club. Sampras's victory lent some decorum to an otherwise weird and controversial tournament, which seemed to go sun silly in the 100° temperatures: Three players were defaulted, including Jeff Tarango, who was fined and suspended for accusing an umpire of corruption.

Sampras's unexpected opponent in the final was the renewed Boris Becker. On the 10th anniversary of his first Wimbledon title, won at the age of 17, the now 27-year-old Becker celebrated by reaching his first Grand Slam final since 1991. He was the oldest finalist since 31-year-old Jimmy Connors in 1984. The age factor was barely perceptible but told in the end.

Becker played a semifinal against Agassi that was reminiscent of his old bullying style, when it seemed that he could turn a match around by simply imposing his will. Trailing a set and two service breaks to Agassi, Becker, making thunderous shots, turned the match around and won 2–6, 7–6, 6–4, 7–6. Agassi was reduced to a little chap in funny clothes as he was able to take only a single point in each of the tiebreakers.

But Becker could not follow that upset with another. Heavy-legged against Sampras the following day, he was unable to cope with the defending champion's 125 mph serve, while committing 15 double faults of his own. Sampras struck 68 winners to just seven unforced errors, and when Becker tried to match that marvelous level of play, he seemed to be reaching for something no longer there. In defeat (6–7, 6–2, 6–4, 6–2) Becker was forced to concede that Sampras had displaced him once and for all as the

RUSS ADAMS

preeminent grass court player in the world. "This used to be my court; now it's his," said Becker.

The normally reticent Sampras tore off his shirt and flung it into the crowd, following that with a cup of water. Sampras then dedicated the victory to Gullikson. The ankle injury, the loss of his ranking, the loss at the French, all paled in comparison to the illness of his best friend. "This is the most emotional one, just because of the way the year has been," Sampras said later, lounging in the basement of the stadium court. "There is no better feeling than waking up after one of these. If I ever get to sleep."

For Graf, too, Wimbledon represented yet another long hard pull. Her sixth title at the All England Club may have been her hardest won. Yet another injury, this one to her wrist, caused her to fly home to Germany for treatment four days before the tournament began. She played pumped full of anti-inflammatories to quell the constant ache in her back. However, she went on to defeat the most durable player around, and her ever-present foil, Sanchez Vicario. In what was arguably one of the best women's matches ever played on Centre Court, Graf prevailed 4–6, 6–1, 7–5. The turning point was the 11th game of the final set, a 32-point, 13-deuce affair that broke the Spaniard's serve and spirit.

There was one last crescendo: the U.S. Open. A dramatic buildup began long before the field arrived in New York. Seles finally stepped on the court again, in an exhibition against Martina Navratilova at Caesars Palace in Atlantic City, her first public match since the horrific stabbing that sidelined her. (Seles was knifed in the back by an unemployed German lathe operator, Günther Parche, during a tournament in Hamburg in 1993. Parche said his aim was to return the No. 1 ranking to his heroine, Graf.)

In a hilariously campy but convincing exhibition complete with Caesars, Cleopatras and centurions, Seles defeated Navratilova with blockbuster strokes. She then entered the Canadian Open in Toronto, her first official event in 2½ years. Seles devoured the field there like mere appetizers, tearing through the draw without the loss of a set. She was back, make no mis-

JOHN IACONO

**No one welcomed the return of Seles (right) more than Graf, her biggest rival.**

take about it. Seles had won seven of eight Grand Slam titles before the knifing, and it is clear she intends to compile more.

Meanwhile, off-court events once again marred the game. Graf's father, Peter, who served as her financial manager, was jailed in Germany on tax-evasion charges. Graf herself was also the target of investigators, who claimed Peter had failed to pay taxes on millions of dollars of unreported income. Peter was denied bond, and Steffi was prohibited from communicating with him.

In New York, Graf and Seles admitted to roiling nerves and emotions throughout. Nevertheless they each got to the final without losing a set. Their pairing made for the most intriguing story of the year: Each was saddled with emotional baggage concerning Seles's long absence, and Graf carried the additional burden of her father's legal troubles. Both said that they never expected to reach the final. Under the circumstances, Graf's 7–6, 0–6, 6–4 victory was surely the crowning achievement of her career. It was also her 18th career Grand Slam singles title, tying her with

Chris Evert and Navratilova for third on the alltime list. "This has been the biggest win I have ever achieved," said Graf. "There is nothing that even comes close to this one." But Seles could take a moral victory from it as well: Though she was perhaps not yet match-tough, her long battle to recuperate mentally and physically was over. She was back.

The men's side was resolved in equally fitting and satisfying fashion. Agassi and Sampras met in the final with a private gentleman's agreement that whoever won should be considered the player of the year. The victor was Sampras in four sets, 6–4, 6–3, 4–6, 7–5. Agassi would continue to hold the No. 1 ranking mathematically, but the look on his face told the real story. Afterward he remarked that he would give back all of his smaller victories for that one trophy. Sampras had collected his third Open and seventh Grand Slam title at the tender age of 24. That tied him with John McEnroe and left him one shy of Connors.

As Sampras sat in his chair at courtside, he wept one last time. Then he looked into a TV camera and dedicated another trophy to Gullikson. "This is for you, Timmy," he said. "Thanks for your help, buddy. Wish you were here."

# FOR THE RECORD·1994–1995

## 1995 Grand Slam Champions

## Australian Open

### Men's Singles

| | Winner | Finalist | Score |
|---|---|---|---|
| Quarterfinals | Pete Sampras (1) | Jim Courier (9) | 6-7, 6-7, 6-3, 6-4, 6-3 |
| | Michael Chang (5) | Andrei Medvedev (13) | 7-6 (9-7), 7-5, 6-3 |
| | Aaron Krickstein | Jacco Eltingh | 7-6 (7-3), 6-4, 5-7, 6-4 |
| | Andre Agassi (2) | Yevgeny Kafelnikov (10) | 6-2, 7-5, 6-0 |
| Semifinals | Pete Sampras | Michael Chang | 6-7 (6-8), 6-3, 6-4, 6-4 |
| | Andre Agassi | Aaron Krickstein | 6-4, 6-4, 3-0 ret. |
| Final | Andre Agassi | Pete Sampras | 4-6, 6-1,7-6 (8-6), 6-4 |

### Women's Singles

| | Winner | Finalist | Score |
|---|---|---|---|
| Quarterfinals | Mary Pierce (4) | Natasha Zvereva (8) | 6-1, 6-4 |
| | Conchita Martinez (2) | Lindsay Davenport (6) | 6-3, 4-6, 6-3 |
| | Arantxa Sanchez Vicario (1) | Naoka Sawamatsu | 6-1, 6-3 |
| | Marianne Werdel Witmeyer | Angelica Gavaldon | 6-1, 6-2 |
| Semifinals | Mary Pierce | Conchita Martinez | 6-3, 6-1 |
| | Arantxa Sanchez Vicario | Marianne Werdel Witmeyer | 6-4, 6-1 |
| Final | Mary Pierce | Arantxa Sanchez Vicario | 6-3, 6-2 |

### Doubles

| | Winner | Finalist | Score |
|---|---|---|---|
| Men's Final | Jared Palmer/ Richey Reneberg (13) | Mark Knowles/ Daniel Nestor | 6-3, 3-6, 6-3, 6-2 |
| Women's Final | Jana Novtona/ Arantxa Sanchez Vicario (2) | Gigi Fernandez/ Natalia Zvereva (1) | 6-3, 6-7 (3-7), 6-4 |
| Mixed Final | Rick Leach/ Natasha Zvereva | Cyril Suk/ Gigi Fernandez (5) | 7-6 (7-4), 6-7 (3-7), 6-4 |

## French Open

### Men's Singles

| | Winner | Finalist | Score |
|---|---|---|---|
| Quarterfinals | Yevgeny Kafelnikov (9) | Andre Agassi (1) | 6-4, 6-3, 7-5 |
| | Thomas Muster (5) | Alberto Costa | 6-2, 3-6, 6-7 (6-8), 7-5, 6-2 |
| | Michael Chang (6) | Adrian Voinea | 7-5, 6-0, 6-1 |
| | Sergi Bruguera (7) | Renzo Furlan | 6-2, 7-5, 6-2 |
| Semifinals | Thomas Muster | Yevgeny Kafelnikov | 6-4, 6-0, 6-4 |
| | Michael Chang | Sergi Bruguera | 6-4, 7-6 (7-5), 7-6 (7-0) |
| Final | Thomas Muster | Michael Chang | 7-5, 6-2, 6-4 |

### Women's Singles

| | Winner | Finalist | Score |
|---|---|---|---|
| Quarterfinals | Steffi Graf (2) | Gabriela Sabatini (8) | 6-1, 6-0 |
| | Conchita Martinez (4) | Virginia Ruano-Pascual | 6-0, 6-4 |
| | Arantxa Sanchez-Vicario (1) | Chanda Rubin | 6-3, 6-1 |
| | Kimiko Date (9) | Iva Majoli (12) | 7-5, 6-1 |
| Semifinals | Steffi Graf | Conchita Martinez | 6-3, 6-7(5-7), 6-3 |
| | Arantxa Sanchez Vicario | Kimiko Date | 7-5, 6-3 |
| Final | Steffi Graf | Arantxa Sanchez Vicario | 7-5, 4-6, 6-0 |

Note: Seedings in parentheses.

## French Open (Cont.)

### Doubles

| | Winner | Finalist | Score |
|---|---|---|---|
| **Men's Final** | Jacco Eltingh/ ........................Paul Haarhuis (2) | Nicklas Kulti/ Magnus Larsson | 6-7 (3-7), 6-4, 6-1 |
| **Women's Final** | Gigi Fernandez/ .....................Natasha Zvereva (2) | Arantxa Sanchez Vicario/ Jana Novotna (1) | 6-7 (8-6), 6-4, 7-5 |
| **Mixed Final** | Larisa Neiland/ ......................Mark Woodforde (1) | Jill Hetherington/ John-Laffnie de Jager | 7-6 (12-10), 7-6 (7-4) |

## Wimbledon

### Men's Singles

| | Winner | Finalist | Score |
|---|---|---|---|
| **Quarterfinals** | Pete Sampras (2) ..................Shuzo Matsuoka | | 6-7 (5-7), 6-3, 6-4, 6-2 |
| | Goran Ivanisevic (4)...............Yevgeny Kafelnikov (6) | | 7-5, 7-6 (13-11), 6-3 |
| | Boris Becker (3) .....................Cedric Pioline | | 6-3, 6-1, 6-7 (6-8), 6-7 (10-12), 9-7 |
| **Semifinals** | Andre Agassi (1).....................Jacco Eltingh | | 6-2, 6-3, 6-4 |
| | Boris Becker...........................Andre Agassi | | 2-6, 7-6 (7-1), 6-4, 7-6 (7-1) |
| | Pete Sampras.........................Goran Ivanisevic | | 7-6 (9-7), 4-6, 6-3, 4-6, 6-3 |
| **Final** | Pete Sampras.........................Boris Becker | | 6-7 (5-7), 6-2, 6-4, 6-2 |

### Women's Singles

| | Winner | Finalist | Score |
|---|---|---|---|
| **Quarterfinals** | Steffi Graf (1)..........................Mary Joe Fernandez (13) | | 6-3, 6-0 |
| | Jana Novotna (4).....................Kimiko Date (6) | | 6-2, 6-3 |
| | Arantxa Sanchez Vicario (2) ...Brenda Schultz-McCarthy (15) | | 6-4, 7-6 (7-4) |
| **Semifinals** | Conchita Martinez (3)..............Gabriela Sabatini (8) | | 7-5, 7-6 (7-5) |
| | Steffi Graf ..............................Jana Novotna | | 5-7, 6-4, 6-2 |
| **Final** | Arantxa Sanchez Vicario.........Conchita Martinez | | 6-3, 6-7 (5-7), 6-1 |
| | Steffi Graf ..............................Arantxa Sanchez Vicario | | 4-6, 6-1, 7-5 |

### Doubles

| | Winner | Finalist | Score |
|---|---|---|---|
| **Men's Final** | Todd Woodbridge/..................Mark Woodforde (1) | Rickey Leach/ Scott Melville | 7-5, 7-6 (10-8), 7-6 (7-5) |
| **Women's Final** | Arantxa Sanchez Vicario/........Jana Novotna (2) | Gigi Fernandez/ Natasha Zvereva (1) | 5-7, 7-5, 6-4 |
| **Mixed Final** | Jonathan Stark/ ......................Martina Navratilova (3) | Cyril Suk/ Gigi Fernandez (4) | 6-4, 6-4 |

## U.S. Open

### Men's Singles

| | Winner | Finalist | Score |
|---|---|---|---|
| **Quarterfinals** | Andre Agassi (1).....................Petr Korda | | 6-4, 6-2, 1-6, 7-5 |
| | Boris Becker (4) .....................Patrick McEnroe | | 6-4, 7-6 (7-2), 6-7 (3-7), 7-6 (8-6) |
| | Jim Courier (14).......................Michael Chang (5) | | 7-6 (7-5), 7-6 (7-3), 7-5 |
| **Semifinals** | Pete Sampras (2) ...................Byron Black | | 7-6 (7-3), 6-4, 6-0 |
| | Andre Agassi .........................Boris Becker | | 7-6 (7-4), 7-6 (7-2), 4-6, 6-4 |
| **Final** | Pete Sampras.........................Jim Courier | | 7-4, 4-6, 6-4, 7-5 |
| | Pete Sampras.........................Andre Agassi | | 6-4, 6-3, 4-6, 7-5 |

Note: Seedings in parentheses.

## U.S. Open *(Cont.)*

### Women's Singles

| | Winner | Finalist | Score |
|---|---|---|---|
| **Quarterfinals** | Steffi Graf (1) | Amy Frazier | 6-2, 6-3 |
| | Gabriela Sabatini (9) | Mary Joe Fernandez (14) | 6-1, 6-3 |
| | Monica Seles (2) | Jana Novotna (5) | 7-6 (7-5), 6-2 |
| | Conchita Martinez (4) | Brenda Schultz-McCarthy (16) | 3-6, 7-6 (7-3), 6-2 |
| **Semifinals** | Steffi Graf | Gabriela Sabatini | 6-4, 7-6 (7-5) |
| | Monica Seles | Conchita Martinez | 6-2, 6-2 |
| **Final** | Steffi Graf | Monica Seles | 7-6 (8-6), 0-6, 6-3 |

### Doubles

| | Winner | Finalist | Score |
|---|---|---|---|
| **Men's Final** | Todd Woodbridge/ | Alex O'Brien/ | 6-3, 6-3 |
| | Mark Woodforde (2) | Sandon Stolle (15) | |
| **Women's Final** | Gigi Fernandez/ | Brenda Schultz-McCarthy/ | 7-5, 6-3 |
| | Natasha Zvereva (2) | Rennae Stubbs (6) | |
| **Mixed Final** | Meredith McGrath/ | Gigi Fernandez/ | 6-4, 6-4 |
| | Matt Lucena | Cyril Suk (3) | |

Note: Seedings in parentheses.

## Major Tournament Results

### Men's Tour (Late 1994)

| Date | Tournament | Site | Winner | Finalist | Score |
|---|---|---|---|---|---|
| Sept 26-Oct 2 | Swiss Indoors | Basel | Wayne Ferreira | Patrick McEnroe | 6-6, 6-2, 7-6 (9-7), 6-3 |
| Oct 3-9 | Australian Indoor | Sydney | Richard Krajicek | Boris Becker | 7-6 (7-5), 7-6 (9-7), 2-6, 6-3 |
| Oct 10-16 | Seiko Super Tennis | Tokyo | Goran Ivanisevic | Michael Chang | 6-4, 6-4 |
| Oct 17-23 | Grand Prix de Tennis | Lyon | Marc Rosset | Jim Courier | 6-4, 7-6 (7-2) |
| Oct 24-30 | Stockholm Open | Stockholm | Boris Becker | Goran Ivanisevic | 4-6, 6-4, 6-3, 7-6 (7-4) |
| Oct 31- Nov 6 | Open de Paris | Paris | Andre Agassi | Marc Rosset | 6-3, 6-3, 4-6, 7-5 |
| Nov 7-13 | European Comm Champ | Antwerp | Pete Sampras | Magnus Larsson | 7-6 (7-5), 6-4 |
| Nov 15-22 | ATP Tour World Champ | Frankfurt | Pete Sampras | Boris Becker | 4-6, 6-3, 7-5, 6-4 |

### Men's Tour (through September 17, 1995)

| Date | Tournament | Site | Winner | Finalist | Score |
|---|---|---|---|---|---|
| Jan 16-29 | Australian Open | Melbourne | Andre Agassi | Pete Sampras | 4-6, 6-1, 7-6 (8-6), 6-4 |
| Feb 6-12 | Dubai Tennis Open | Dubai, United Arab Emirates | Wayne Ferreira | Andrea Gaudenzi | 3-6, 7-6 (7-3), 6-4 |
| Feb 13-19 | Milan Open | Milan | Yevgeny Kafelnikov | Boris Becker | 7-5, 5-7, 7-6 (8-6) |
| Feb 20-26 | Eurocard Open | Stuttgart | Richard Krajicek | Michael Stich | 7-6 (7-4), 6-3 6-7 (6-8), 1-6, 6-3 |
| Feb 27-Mar 5 | Newsweek Champions Cup | Indian Wells, CA | Pete Sampras | Andre Agassi | 7-5, 6-3, 7-5 |
| Mar 16-26 | Lipton Intl Players Championships | Key Biscayne | Andre Agassi | Pete Sampras | 3-6, 6-2, 7-6 (7-3) |
| Apr 10-16 | Japan Open Tennis Championship | Tokyo | Jim Courier | Andre Agassi | 6-3, 6-4 |
| Apr 24-30 | Volvo Monte Carlo Open | Monte Carlo | Thomas Muster | Boris Becker | 4-6, 5-7, 6-1, 7-6 (8-6), 6-0 |
| May 8-14 | Panasonic German Open | Hamburg | Andrei Medvedev | Goran Ivanisevic | 6-3, 6-2, 6-1 |
| May15-21 | Mercedes Italian Open | Rome | Thomas Muster | Sergi Bruguera | 3-6, 7-6 (7-5), 6-2, 6-3 |
| May 29-Jun 11 | French Open | Paris | Thomas Muster | Michael Chang | 7-5, 6-2, 6-4 |

## Men's Tour (through September 17) *(Cont.)*

| Date | Tournament | Site | Winner | Finalist | Score |
|---|---|---|---|---|---|
| Jun 26-July 9 | Wimbledon Championships | Wimbledon | Pete Sampras | Boris Becker | 6-7 (5-7), 6-2, 6-4, 6-2 |
| July 17-23 | Mercedes Cup | Stuttgart | Thomas Muster | Jan Apell | 6-2, 6-2 |
| July 24-30 | The du Maurier Ltd. Open | Montreal | Andre Agassi | Pete Sampras | 3-6, 6-2, 6-3 |
| Aug 7-13 | Thriftway ATP Championship | Cincinnati | Andre Agassi | Michael Chang | 7-5, 6-2 |
| Aug 14-20 | RCA/US Men's Hardcourt Championships | Indianapolis | Thomas Enqvist | Bernd Carbacher | 6-4, 6-3 |
| Aug 14-20 | Volvo Intl Tennis Tournament | New Haven | Andre Agassi | Richard Krajicek | 3-6, 7-6 (7-2), 6-3 |
| Aug 28-Sept 10 | US Open | New York | Pete Sampras | Andre Agassi | 6-4, 6-3, 6-4, 7-5 |
| Sept 11-17 | Romanian Open | Bucharest | Thomas Muster | Gilbert Schaller | 6-3, 6-4 |

## Women's Tour (Late 1994)

| Date | Tournament | Site | Winner | Finalist | Score |
|---|---|---|---|---|---|
| Sept 20-25 | Nichirei International Ladies Championships | Tokyo | Arantxa Sanchez Vicario | Amy Frazier | 6-1, 6-2 |
| Sept 26-Oct 2 | International Damen Grand Prix | Leipzig | Jana Novotna | Mary Pierce | 7-5, 6-1 |
| Oct 3-9 | European Indoors | Zurich | Magdalena Maleeva | Natasha Zvereva | 7-5, 3-6, 6-4 |
| Oct 10-16 | Porsche Tennis Grand Prix | Filderstadt, Germany | Anke Huber | Mary Pierce | 6-4, 6-2 |
| Oct 18-23 | Brighton International | Brighton, England | Jana Novotna | Helena Sukova | 6-7 (4-7), 6-3, 6-4 |
| Oct 24-30 | Nokia Grand Prix | Essen, Germany | Jana Novotna | Iva Majoli | 6-2, 6-4 |
| Oct 31-Nov 6 | Bank of the West Classic | Oakland, CA | Arantxa Sanchez Vicario | Martina Navratilova | 1-6, 7-6 (7-5), 7-6 (7-5) |
| Nov 7-13 | Virginia Slims of Philadelphia | Philadelphia | Anke Huber | Mary Pierce | 6-0, 6-7 (4-7), 7-5 |
| Nov 14-20 | Virginia Slims Championships | New York | Gabriela Sabatini | Lindsay Davenport | 6-3, 6-2, 6-4 |

## Women's Tour (through September 10, 1995)

| Date | Tournament | Site | Winner | Finalist | Score |
|---|---|---|---|---|---|
| Jan 9-15 | Peters International | Sydney | Gabriela Sabatini | Lindsay Davenport | 6-3, 6-4 |
| Jan 16-29 | Australian Open | Melbourne | Mary Pierce | Arantxa Sanchez Vicario | 6-3, 6-2 |
| Jan 31-Feb 5 | Toray Pan Pacific Open | Tokyo | Kimiko Date | Lindsay Davenport | 6-1, 6-2 |
| Feb 6-12 | Ameritech Cup | Chicago | Magdalena Maleeva | Lisa Raymond | 7-5, 7-6 (7-2) |
| Feb 14-19 | Open Gaz de France | Paris | Steffi Graf | Mary Pierce | 6-2, 6-2 |
| Feb 27-Mar 5 | State Farm Evert Cup | Indian Wells, CA | Mary Joe Fernandez | Natasha Zvereva | 6-4, 6-3 |
| Mar 6-12 | Delray Beach Winter Championships | Delray Beach, FL | Steffi Graf | Conchita Martinez | 6-2, 6-4 |
| Mar 17-26 | The Lipton Championships | Key Biscayne, FL | Steffi Graf | Kimiko Date | 6-1, 6-4 |
| Mar 27-Apr 2 | Family Circle Magazine Cup | Hilton Head Island, SC | Conchita Martinez | Magdalena Maleeva | 6-1, 6-1 |
| Apr 3-9 | Bausch & Lomb Championships | Amelia Island, FL | Conchita Martinez | Gabriela Sabatini | 6-1, 6-4 |
| Apr 10-18 | Houston Women's Tennis Championships | Houston | Steffi Graf | Asa Carlsson | 6-1, 6-1 |
| Apr 24-30 | International Championships of Spain | Barcelona | Arantxa Sanchez Vicario | Iva Majoli | 5-7, 6-0, 6-2 |
| May 1-7 | Citizen Cup | Hamburg | Conchita Martinez | Martina Hingis | 6-1, 6-0 |

## Women's Tour *(Cont.)*

| Date | Tournament | Site | Winner | Finalist | Score |
|------|-----------|------|--------|----------|-------|
| May 8-14 ........Italian Open | | Rome | Conchita Martinez | Arantxa Sanchez Vicario | 6-3, 6-1 |
| May 15-21 .......German Open | | Berlin | Arantxa Sanchez Vicario | Magdalena Maleeva | 6-4, 6-1 |
| May 29-Jun 11 .French Open | | Paris | Steffi Graf | Arantxa Sanchez Vicario | 7-5, 4-6, 6-0 |
| June 19-25 ......Direct Line International Tennis Championships | | Eastbourne, England | Nathalie Tauziat | Chanda Rubin | 3-6, 6-0, 7-5 |
| Jun 26-Jul 9.....Wimbledon Championships | | Wimbledon | Steffi Graf | Arantxa Sanchez Vicario | 4-6, 6-1, 7-5 |
| July 31-Aug 6 ..Toshiba Tennis Classic | | San Diego | Conchita Martinez | Lisa Raymond | 6-2, 6-0 |
| Aug 7-13 .........Acura Classic | | Manhattan Beach | Conchita Martinez | Chanda Rubin | 4-6, 6-1, 6-3 |
| Aug 14-21 .......Du Maurier Ltd. Open | | Montreal | Monica Seles | Amanda Coetzer | 6-0, 6-1 |
| Aug 28-Sept 10.US Open | | New York | Steffi Graf | Monica Seles | 7-6 (8-6), 0-6, 6-3 |

## 1994 Singles Leaders

### Men

| Rank | Player | Tournament Wins | Match Record | Earnings ($) |
|------|--------|------|--------|--------------|
| 1 .......Pete Sampras | | 10 | 74-11 | 3,607,812 |
| 2. ......Andre Agassi | | 5 | 51-13 | 1,941,667 |
| 3. ......Boris Becker | | 4 | 48-16 | 2,029,756 |
| 4 .......Sergi Bruguera | | 3 | 65–24 | 3,031,874 |
| 5 .......Goran Ivanisevic | | 2 | 63-26 | 2,060,278 |
| 6. ......Michael Chang | | 6 | 65-20 | 1,789,495 |
| 7. .....Stefan Edberg | | 3 | 60-25 | 2,489,161 |
| 8. .....Alberto Berasategui | | 7 | 65-25 | 939,651 |
| 9. ......Michael Stich | | 3 | 60-24 | 2,033,623 |
| 10. ....Todd Martin | | 2 | 51-19 | 888,324 |
| 11. ....Yevgeny Kafelnikov | | 3 | 67-28 | 1,011,563 |
| 12. ....Wayne Ferreira | | 5 | 69-25 | 1,063,341 |
| 13. ....Jim Courier | | 0 | 47-19 | 1,921,584 |
| 14. ....Marc Rosset | | 2 | 49-26 | 768,004 |
| 15. ....Andre Medvedev | | 2 | 34-17 | 1,211,134 |
| 16 ....Thomas Muster | | 3 | 58-24 | 654,829 |
| 17. ....Richard Krajicek | | 3 | 33-14 | 555,116 |
| 18. ....Petr Korda | | 0 | 38-22 | 612,012 |
| 19. ....Magnus Larsson | | 2 | 35-22 | 639,105 |
| 20. ....Jason Stoltenberg | | 1 | 38-25 | 498,842 |

Note: Compiled by the Association of Tennis Professionals (ATP).

### Women

| Rank | Player | Tournament Wins | Match Record | Earnings ($) |
|------|--------|------|--------|--------------|
| 1. ......Steffi Graf | | 7 | 58-6 | 1,481,670 |
| 2. ......Arantxa Sanchez Vicario | | 8 | 74-9 | 2,563,675 |
| 3. ......Conchita Martinez | | 4 | 55-15 | 1,503,540 |
| 4. ......Jana Novotna | | 3 | 43-11 | 576,049 |
| 5. ......Mary Pierce | | 1 | 45-18 | 741,761 |
| 6. ......Lindsay Davenport | | 2 | 48-15 | 476,032 |
| 7. ......Gabriela Sabatini | | 1 | 42-17 | 807,612 |
| 8. ......Martina Navratilova | | 1 | 33-14 | 746,468 |
| 9. ......Kimiko Date | | 2 | 33-14 | 369,404 |
| 10. ....Natasha Zvereva | | 1 | 30-12 | 399,372 |
| 11. ....Magdalena Maleeva | | 2 | 33-12 | 311,723 |
| 12. ....Anke Huber | | 3 | 41-17 | 436,321 |
| 13. ....Iva Majoli | | 0 | 39-19 | 297,098 |
| 14. ....Mary Joe Fernandez | | 1 | 25-10 | 147,998 |
| 15. ....Brenda Schultz | | 1 | 49-23 | 290,337 |
| 16. ...Amy Frazier | | 1 | 28-15 | 219,381 |
| 17. ....Lori McNeil | | 1 | 26-15 | 233,701 |
| 18. ....Amanda Coetzer | | 1 | 38-19 | 292,404 |
| 19. ....Sabine Hack | | 1 | 35-18 | 279,396 |
| 20. ....Ines Gorrochategui | | 0 | 23-10 | 125,429 |

Note: Compiled by the Women's Tennis Association (WTA).

## 1994 Davis Cup
### FINALS

Sweden d. Russia 4-1 at Moscow
Stefan Edberg (Swe) d. Alexander Volkov (Rus) 6-4, 6-2, 6-7, 0-6, 8-6
Magnus Larsson (Swe) d. Yevgeny Kafelnikov (Rus) 6-0, 6-2, 3-6, 2-6, 6-3
Jan Apell/Jonas Bjorkman (Swe) d. Yevgeny Kafelnikov/Andrei Olhovskiy (Rus) 6-7, 6-2, 6-3, 1-6, 8-6
Yevgeny Kafelnikov (Rus) d. Stefan Edberg (Swe) 4-6, 6-4, 6-0
Magnus Larsson (Swe) d. Alexander Volkov (Rus) 7-6, 6-4

## 1995 Davis Cup World Group

### FIRST ROUND

United States d. France 4-1
Italy d. Czech Republic 4-1
Sweden d. Denmark 3-2
Austria d. Spain 4-1
South Africa d. Australia 3-2
Russia d. Belgium 4-1
Netherlands d. Switzerland 4-1
Germany d. Croatia 4-1

### QUARTER FINAL ROUND

United States d. Italy 5-0
Sweden d. Austria 5-0
Russia d. South Africa 4-1
Germany d. Netherlands 4-1

### SEMIFINALS

United States d. Sweden 4-1
Pete Sampras (U.S.) d. Thomas Enqvist (Swe) 6-3, 6-4, 3-6, 6-3
Andre Agassi (U.S.) d. Mats Wilander (Swe) 7-6 (7-5), 6-2, 6-2
Jonas Bjorkman/Stefan Edberg (Swe) d. Todd Martin/Jonathan Stark (U.S.) 6-3, 6-4, 6-4
Todd Martin (U.S.) d. Thomas Enqvist (Swe) 7-5, 7-5, 7-6 (7-2)
Pete Sampras (U.S.) d. Mats Wilander (Swe) 2-6, 7-6 (7-4), 6-3

Russia d. Germany 3-2
Boris Becker (Ger) d. Andrei Chesnokov (Rus) 6-7 (7-4), 6-3, 7-6 (7-3), 7-5
Michael Stich (Ger) d. Yevgeny Kafelnikov (Rus) 6-1, 4-6, 6-3, 6-4
Yevgeny Kafelnikov/Andrei Olhovskiy (Rus) d. Boris Becker/Michael Stich (Ger) 7-6 (7-3), 6-4, 2-6, 6-7 (5-7), 7-5
Yevgeny Kafelnikov (Rus) d. Bernd Karbacher (Ger) 6-1, 7-6 (7-5), 6-2
Andrei Chesnokov (Rus) d. Michael Stich (Ger) 6-4, 1-6, 1-6, 6-3, 14-12

FINAL: Russia versus United States to be held Dec 1-3 in Moscow.

## 1995 Federation Cup

### FIRST ROUND

Spain d. Bulgaria 3-2
Germany d. Japan 4-1
France d. South Africa 3-2
United States d. Austria 5-0

### SEMIFINALS

Spain d. Germany 3-2
Conchita Martinez (Spain) d. Anke Huber (Ger) 6-2, 2-6, 6-0
Sabine Hack (Ger) d. Arantxa Sanchez Vicario (Spain) 6-4, 6-2
Arantxa Sanchez Vicario (Spain) d. Anke Huber (Ger) 6-3, 1-6, 6-2
Conchita Martines (Spain) d. Sabine Hack (Ger) 6-0, 6-0
Anke Huber/Claudia Porwick (Ger) d. Virginia Ruano Pascual/ Maria Antonia Sanchez Lorenzo (Spain) 6-2, 6-2

United States d. France 3–2
Mary Pierce (Fra) d. Mary Joe Fernandez (U.S.) 7-6 (7-1), 6-3
Lindsay Davenport (U.S.) d. Julie Halard (Fra) 7-6 (7-0), 7-5
Lindsay Davenport (U.S.) d. Mary Pierce (Fra) 6-3, 4-6, 6-0
Julie Halard (Fra) d. Mary Joe Fernandez (U.S.) 1-6, 7-5, 6-1
Lindsay Davenport/Gigi Fernandez (U.S.) d. Julie Halard/Nathalie Tauziat (Fra) 6-1, 7-6 (7-2)

FINAL: Spain versus United States to be held Nov 25-26 in Spain.

## Grand Slam Tournaments

### MEN
### Australian Championships

| Year | Winner | Finalist | Score |
|------|--------|----------|-------|
| 1905 | Rodney Heath | A. H. Curtis | 4-6, 6-3, 6-4, 6-4 |
| 1906 | Tony Wilding | H. A. Parker | 6-0, 6-4, 6-4 |
| 1907 | Horace M. Rice | H. A. Parker | 6-3, 6-4, 6-4 |
| 1908 | Fred Alexander | A. W. Dunlop | 3-6, 3-6, 6-0, 6-2, 6-3 |
| 1909 | Tony Wilding | E. F. Parker | 6-1, 7-5, 6-2 |
| 1910 | Rodney Heath | Horace M. Rice | 6-4, 6-3, 6-2 |
| 1911 | Norman Brookes | Horace M. Rice | 6-1, 6-2, 6-3 |
| 1912 | J. Cecil Parke | A. E. Beamish | 3-6, 6-3, 1-6, 6-1, 7-5 |
| 1913 | E. F. Parker | H. A. Parker | 2-6, 6-1, 6-2, 6-3 |
| 1914 | Pat O'Hara Wood | G. L. Patterson | 6-4, 6-3, 5-7, 6-1 |
| 1915 | Francis G. Lowe | Horace M. Rice | 4-6, 6-1, 6-1, 6-4 |
| 1916-18 | No tournament | | |
| 1919 | A. R. F. Kingscote | E. O. Pockley | 6-4, 6-0, 6-3 |
| 1920 | Pat O'Hara Wood | Ron Thomas | 6-3, 4-6, 6-8, 6-1, 6-3 |
| 1921 | Rhys H. Gemmell | A. Hedeman | 7-5, 6-1, 6-4 |
| 1922 | Pat O'Hara Wood | Gerald Patterson | 6-0, 3-6, 3-6, 6-3, 6-2 |
| 1923 | Pat O'Hara Wood | C. B. St John | 6-1, 6-1, 6-3 |
| 1924 | James Anderson | R. E. Schlesinger | 6-3, 6-4, 3-6, 5-7, 6-3 |
| 1925 | James Anderson | Gerald Patterson | 11-9, 2-6, 6-2, 6-3 |
| 1926 | John Hawkes | J. Willard | 6-1, 6-3, 6-1 |
| 1927 | Gerald Patterson | John Hawkes | 3-6, 6-4, 3-6, 18-16, 6-3 |
| 1928 | Jean Borotra | R. O. Cummings | 6-4, 6-1, 4-6, 5-7, 6-3 |
| 1929 | John C. Gregory | R. E. Schlesinger | 6-2, 6-2, 5-7, 7-5 |
| 1930 | Gar Moon | Harry C. Hopman | 6-3, 6-1, 6-3 |
| 1931 | Jack Crawford | Harry C. Hopman | 6-4, 6-2, 2-6, 6-1 |
| 1932 | Jack Crawford | Harry C. Hopman | 4-6, 6-3, 3-6, 6-3, 6-1 |
| 1933 | Jack Crawford | Keith Gledhill | 2-6, 7-5, 6-3, 6-2 |
| 1934 | Fred Perry | Jack Crawford | 6-3, 7-5, 6-1 |
| 1935 | Jack Crawford | Fred Perry | 2-6, 6-4, 6-4, 6-4 |
| 1936 | Adrian Quist | Jack Crawford | 6-2, 6-3, 4-6, 3-6, 9-7 |
| 1937 | Vivian B. McGrath | John Bromwich | 6-3, 1-6, 6-0, 2-6, 6-1 |
| 1938 | Don Budge | John Bromwich | 6-4, 6-2, 6-1 |
| 1939 | John Bromwich | Adrian Quist | 6-4, 6-1, 6-3 |
| 1940 | Adrian Quist | Jack Crawford | 6-3, 6-1, 6-2 |
| 1941-45 | No tournament | | |
| 1946 | John Bromwich | Dinny Pails | 5-7, 6-3, 7-5, 3-6, 6-2 |
| 1947 | Dinny Pails | John Bromwich | 4 6, 6 4, 3-6, 7-5, 8-6 |
| 1948 | Adrian Quist | John Bromwich | 6-4, 3-6, 6-3, 2-6, 6-3 |
| 1949 | Frank Sedgman | Ken McGregor | 6-3, 6-3, 6-2 |
| 1950 | Frank Sedgman | Ken McGregor | 6-3, 6-4, 4-6, 6-1 |
| 1951 | Richard Savitt | Ken McGregor | 6-3, 2-6, 6-3, 6-1 |
| 1952 | Ken McGregor | Frank Sedgman | 7-5, 12-10, 2-6, 6-2 |
| 1953 | Ken Rosewall | Mervyn Rose | 6-0, 6-3, 6-4 |
| 1954 | Mervyn Rose | Rex Hartwig | 6-2, 0-6, 6-4, 6-2 |
| 1955 | Ken Rosewall | Lew Hoad | 9-7, 6-4, 6-4 |
| 1956 | Lew Hoad | Ken Rosewall | 6-4, 3-6, 6-4, 7-5 |
| 1957 | Ashley Cooper | Neale Fraser | 6-3, 9-11, 6-4, 6-2 |
| 1958 | Ashley Cooper | Mal Anderson | 7-5, 6-3, 6-4 |
| 1959 | Alex Olmedo | Neale Fraser | 6-1, 6-2, 3-6, 6-3 |
| 1960 | Rod Laver | Neale Fraser | 5-7, 3-6, 6-3, 8-6, 8-6 |
| 1961 | Roy Emerson | Rod Laver | 1-6, 6-3, 7-5, 6-4 |
| 1962 | Rod Laver | Roy Emerson | 8-6, 0-6, 6-4, 6-4 |
| 1963 | Roy Emerson | Ken Fletcher | 6-3, 6-3, 6-1 |
| 1964 | Roy Emerson | Fred Stolle | 6-3, 6-4, 6-2 |
| 1965 | Roy Emerson | Fred Stolle | 7-9, 2-6, 6-4, 7-5, 6-1 |
| 1966 | Roy Emerson | Arthur Ashe | 6-4, 6-8, 6-2, 6-3 |
| 1967 | Roy Emerson | Arthur Ashe | 6-4, 6-1, 6-1 |
| 1968 | Bill Bowrey | Juan Gisbert | 7-5, 2-6, 9-7, 6-4 |
| 1969* | Rod Laver | Andres Gimeno | 6-3, 6-4, 7-5 |
| 1970 | Arthur Ashe | Dick Crealy | 6-4, 9-7, 6-2 |
| 1971 | Ken Rosewall | Arthur Ashe | 6-1, 7-5, 6-3 |

## Australian Championships (Cont.)

| Year | Winner | Finalist | Score |
|------|--------|----------|-------|
| 1972 | Ken Rosewall | Mal Anderson | 7-6, 6-3, 7-5 |
| 1973 | John Newcombe | Onny Parun | 6-3, 6-7, 7-5, 6-1 |
| 1974 | Jimmy Connors | Phil Dent | 7-6, 6-4, 4-6, 6-3 |
| 1975 | John Newcombe | Jimmy Connors | 7-5, 3-6, 6-4, 7-5 |
| 1976 | Mark Edmondson | John Newcombe | 6-7, 6-3, 7-6, 6-1 |
| 1977 (Jan) | Roscoe Tanner | Guillermo Vilas | 6-3, 6-3, 6-3 |
| 1977 (Dec) | Vitas Gerulaitis | John Lloyd | 6-3, 7-6, 5-7, 3-6, 6-2 |
| 1978 | Guillermo Vilas | John Marks | 6-4, 6-4, 3-6, 6-3 |
| 1979 | Guillermo Vilas | John Sadri | 7-6, 6-3, 6-2 |
| 1980 | Brian Teacher | Kim Warwick | 7-5, 7-6, 6-3 |
| 1981 | Johan Kriek | Steve Denton | 6-2, 7-6, 6-7, 6-4 |
| 1982 | Johan Kriek | Steve Denton | 6-3, 6-3, 6-2 |
| 1983 | Mats Wilander | Ivan Lendl | 6-1, 6-4, 6-4 |
| 1984 | Mats Wilander | Kevin Curren | 6-7, 6-4, 7-6, 6-2 |
| 1985 (Dec) | Stefan Edberg | Mats Wilander | 6-4, 6-3, 6-3 |
| 1987 (Jan) | Stefan Edberg | Pat Cash | 6-3, 6-4, 3-6, 5-7, 6-3 |
| 1988 | Mats Wilander | Pat Cash | 6-3, 6-7, 3-6, 6-1, 8-6 |
| 1989 | Ivan Lendl | Miloslav Mecir | 6-2, 6-2, 6-2 |
| 1990 | Ivan Lendl | Stefan Edberg | 4-6, 7-6, 5-2 ret |
| 1991 | Boris Becker | Ivan Lendl | 1-6, 6-4, 6-4, 6-4 |
| 1992 | Jim Courier | Stefan Edberg | 6-3, 3-6, 6-4, 6-2 |
| 1993 | Jim Courier | Stefan Edberg | 6-2, 6-1, 2-6, 7-5 |
| 1994 | Pete Sampras | Todd Martin | 7-6 (7-4), 6-4, 6-4 |
| 1995 | Andre Agassi | Pete Sampras | 4-6, 6-1, 7-6 (8-6), 6-4 |

*Became Open (amateur and professional) in 1969.

## French Championships

| Year | Winner | Finalist | Score |
|------|--------|----------|-------|
| 1925† | Rene Lacoste | Jean Borotra | 7-5, 6-1, 6-4 |
| 1926 | Henri Cochet | Rene Lacoste | 6-2, 6-4, 6-3 |
| 1927 | Rene Lacoste | Bill Tilden | 6-4, 4-6, 5-7, 6-3, 11-9 |
| 1928 | Henri Cochet | Rene Lacoste | 5-7, 6-3, 6-1, 6-3 |
| 1929 | Rene Lacoste | Jean Borotra | 6-3, 2-6, 6-0, 2-6, 8-6 |
| 1930 | Henri Cochet | Bill Tilden | 3-6, 8-6, 6-3, 6-1 |
| 1931 | Jean Borotra | Claude Boussus | 2-6, 6-4, 7-5, 6-4 |
| 1932 | Henri Cochet | Giorgio de Stefani | 6-0, 6-4, 4-6, 6-3 |
| 1933 | Jack Crawford | Henri Cochet | 8-6, 6-1, 6-3 |
| 1934 | Gottfried von Cramm | Jack Crawford | 6-4, 7-9, 3-6, 7-5, 6-3 |
| 1935 | Fred Perry | Gottfried von Cramm | 6-3, 3-6, 6-1, 6-3 |
| 1936 | Gottfried von Cramm | Fred Perry | 6-0, 2-6, 6-2, 2-6, 6-0 |
| 1937 | Henner Henkel | Henry Austin | 6-1, 6-4, 6-3 |
| 1938 | Don Budge | Roderick Menzel | 6-3, 6-2, 6-4 |
| 1939 | Don McNeill | Bobby Riggs | 7-5, 6-0, 6-3 |
| 1940 | No tournament | | |
| 1941‡ | Bernard Destremau | n/a | n/a |
| 1942‡ | Bernard Destremau | n/a | n/a |
| 1943‡ | Yvon Petra | n/a | n/a |
| 1944‡ | Yvon Petra | n/a | n/a |
| 1945‡ | Yvon Petra | Bernard Destremau | 7-5, 6-4, 6-2 |
| 1946 | Marcel Bernard | Jaroslav Drobny | 3-6, 2-6, 6-1, 6-4, 6-3 |
| 1947 | Joseph Asboth | Eric Sturgess | 8-6, 7-5, 6-4 |
| 1948 | Frank Parker | Jaroslav Drobny | 6-4, 7-5, 5-7, 8-6 |
| 1949 | Frank Parker | Budge Patty | 6-3, 1-6, 6-1, 6-4 |
| 1950 | Budge Patty | Jaroslav Drobny | 6-1, 6-2, 3-6, 5-7, 7-5 |
| 1951 | Jaroslav Drobny | Eric Sturgess | 6-3, 6-3, 6-3 |
| 1952 | Jaroslav Drobny | Frank Sedgman | 6-2, 6-0, 3-6, 6-4 |
| 1953 | Ken Rosewall | Vic Seixas | 6-3, 6-4, 1-6, 6-2 |
| 1954 | Tony Trabert | Arthur Larsen | 6-4, 7-5, 6-1 |
| 1955 | Tony Trabert | Sven Davidson | 2-6, 6-1, 6-4, 6-2 |
| 1956 | Lew Hoad | Sven Davidson | 6-4, 8-6, 6-3 |
| 1957 | Sven Davidson | Herbie Flam | 6-3, 6-4, 6-4 |
| 1958 | Mervyn Rose | Luis Ayala | 6-3, 6-4, 6-4 |
| 1959 | Nicola Pietrangeli | Ian Vermaak | 3-6, 6-3, 6-4, 6-1 |
| 1960 | Nicola Pietrangeli | Luis Ayala | 3-6, 6-3, 6-4, 4-6, 6-3 |
| 1961 | Manuel Santana | Nicola Pietrangeli | 4-6, 6-1, 3-6, 6-0, 6-2 |

## French Championships (Cont.)

| Year | Winner | Finalist | Score |
|------|--------|----------|-------|
| 1962 | Rod Laver | Roy Emerson | 3-6, 2-6, 6-3, 9-7, 6-2 |
| 1963 | Roy Emerson | Pierre Darmon | 3-6, 6-1, 6-4, 6-4 |
| 1964 | Manuel Santana | Nicola Pietrangeli | 6-3, 6-1, 4-6, 7-5 |
| 1965 | Fred Stolle | Tony Roche | 3-6, 6-0, 6-2, 6-3 |
| 1966 | Tony Roche | Istvan Gulyas | 6-1, 6-4, 7-5 |
| 1967 | Roy Emerson | Tony Roche | 6-1, 6-4, 2-6, 6-2 |
| 1968* | Ken Rosewall | Rod Laver | 6-3, 6-1, 2-6, 6-2 |
| 1969 | Rod Laver | Ken Rosewall | 6-4, 6-3, 6-4 |
| 1970 | Jan Kodes | Zeljko Franulovic | 6-2, 6-4, 6-0 |
| 1971 | Jan Kodes | Ilie Nastase | 8-6, 6-2, 2-6, 7-5 |
| 1972 | Andres Gimeno | Patrick Proisy | 4-6, 6-3, 6-1, 6-1 |
| 1973 | Ilie Nastase | Nikki Pilic | 6-3, 6-3, 6-0 |
| 1974 | Bjorn Borg | Manuel Orantes | 6-7, 6-0, 6-1, 6-1 |
| 1975 | Bjorn Borg | Guillermo Vilas | 6-2, 6-3, 6-4 |
| 1976 | Adriano Panatta | Harold Solomon | 6-1, 6-4, 4-6, 7-6 |
| 1977 | Guillermo Vilas | Brian Gottfried | 6-0, 6-3, 6-0 |
| 1978 | Bjorn Borg | Guillermo Vilas | 6-1, 6-1, 6-3 |
| 1979 | Bjorn Borg | Victor Pecci | 6-3, 6-1, 6-7, 6-4 |
| 1980 | Bjorn Borg | Vitas Gerulaitis | 6-4, 6-1, 6-2 |
| 1981 | Bjorn Borg | Ivan Lendl | 6-1, 4-6, 6-2, 3-6, 6-1 |
| 1982 | Mats Wilander | Guillermo Vilas | 1-6, 7-6, 6-0, 6-4 |
| 1983 | Yannick Noah | Mats Wilander | 6-2, 7-5, 7-6 |
| 1984 | Ivan Lendl | John McEnroe | 3-6, 2-6, 6-4, 7-5, 7-5 |
| 1985 | Mats Wilander | Ivan Lendl | 3-6, 6-4, 6-2, 6-2 |
| 1986 | Ivan Lendl | Mikael Pernfors | 6-3, 6-2, 6-4 |
| 1987 | Ivan Lendl | Mats Wilander | 7-5, 6-2, 3-6, 7-6 |
| 1988 | Mats Wilander | Henri Leconte | 7-5, 6-2, 6-1 |
| 1989 | Michael Chang | Stefan Edberg | 6-1, 3-6, 4-6, 6-4, 6-2 |
| 1990 | Andres Gomez | Andre Agassi | 6-3, 2-6, 6-4, 6-4 |
| 1991 | Jim Courier | Andre Agassi | 3-6, 6-4, 2-6, 6-1, 6-4 |
| 1992 | Jim Courier | Petr Korda | 7-5, 6-2, 6-1 |
| 1993 | Sergi Bruguera | Jim Courier | 6-4, 2-6, 6-2, 3-6, 6-3 |
| 1994 | Sergi Bruguera | Alberto Berasategui | 6-3, 7-5, 2-6, 6-1 |
| 1995 | Thomas Muster | Michael Chang | 7-5, 6-2, 6-4 |

†1925 was the first year that entries were accepted from all countries.
‡From 1941 to 1945 the event was called Tournoi de France and was closed to all foreigners.
*Became Open (amateur and professional) in 1968 but closed to contract professionals in 1972.

## Wimbledon Championships

| Year | Winner | Finalist | Score |
|------|--------|----------|-------|
| 1877 | Spencer W. Gore | William C. Marshall | 6-1, 6-2, 6-4 |
| 1878 | P. Frank Hadow | Spencer W. Gore | 7-5, 6-1, 9-7 |
| 1879 | John T. Hartley | V. St Leger Gould | 6-2, 6-4, 6-2 |
| 1880 | John T. Hartley | Herbert F. Lawford | 6-0, 6-2, 2-6, 6-3 |
| 1881 | William Renshaw | John T. Hartley | 6-0, 6-2, 6-1 |
| 1882 | William Renshaw | Ernest Renshaw | 6-1, 2-6, 4-6, 6-2, 6-2 |
| 1883 | William Renshaw | Ernest Renshaw | 2-6, 6-3, 6-3, 4-6, 6-3 |
| 1884 | William Renshaw | Herbert F. Lawford | 6-0, 6-4, 9-7 |
| 1885 | William Renshaw | Herbert F. Lawford | 7-5, 6-2, 4-6, 7-5 |
| 1886 | William Renshaw | Herbert F. Lawford | 6-0, 5-7, 6-3, 6-4 |
| 1887 | Herbert F. Lawford | Ernest Renshaw | 1-6, 6-3, 3-6, 6-4, 6-4 |
| 1888 | Ernest Renshaw | Herbert F. Lawford | 6-3, 7-5, 6-0 |
| 1889 | William Renshaw | Ernest Renshaw | 6-4, 6-1, 3-6, 6-0 |
| 1890 | William J. Hamilton | William Renshaw | 6-8, 6-2, 3-6, 6-1, 6-1 |
| 1891 | Wilfred Baddeley | Joshua Pim | 6-4, 1-6, 7-5, 6-0 |
| 1892 | Wilfred Baddeley | Joshua Pim | 4-6, 6-3, 6-3, 6-2 |
| 1893 | Joshua Pim | Wilfred Baddeley | 3-6, 6-1, 6-3, 6-2 |
| 1894 | Joshua Pim | Wilfred Baddeley | 10-8, 6-2, 8-6 |
| 1895 | Wilfred Baddeley | Wilberforce V. Eaves | 4-6, 2-6, 8-6, 6-2, 6-3 |
| 1896 | Harold S. Mahoney | Wilfred Baddeley | 6-2, 6-8, 5-7, 8-6, 6-3 |
| 1897 | Reggie F. Doherty | Harold S. Mahoney | 6-4, 6-4, 6-3 |
| 1898 | Reggie F. Doherty | H. Laurie Doherty | 6-3, 6-3, 2-6, 5-7, 6-1 |
| 1899 | Reggie F. Doherty | Arthur W. Gore | 1-6, 4-6, 6-2, 6-3, 6-3 |
| 1900 | Reggie F. Doherty | Sidney H. Smith | 6-8, 6-3, 6-1, 6-2 |

## Wimbledon Championship *(Cont.)*

| Year | Winner | Finalist | Score |
|------|--------|----------|-------|
| 1901 | Arthur W. Gore | Reggie F. Doherty | 4-6, 7-5, 6-4, 6-4 |
| 1902 | H. Laurie Doherty | Arthur W. Gore | 6-4, 6-3, 3-6, 6-0 |
| 1903 | H. Laurie Doherty | Frank L. Riseley | 7-5, 6-3, 6-0 |
| 1904 | H. Laurie Doherty | Frank L. Riseley | 6-1, 7-5, 8-6 |
| 1905 | H. Laurie Doherty | Norman E. Brookes | 8-6, 6-2, 6-4 |
| 1906 | H. Laurie Doherty | Frank L. Riseley | 6-4, 4-6, 6-2, 6-3 |
| 1907 | Norman E. Brookes | Arthur W. Gore | 6-4, 6-2, 6-2 |
| 1908 | Arthur W. Gore | H. Roper Barrett | 6-3, 6-2, 4-6, 3-6, 6-4 |
| 1909 | Arthur W. Gore | M. J. G. Ritchie | 6-8, 1-6, 6-2, 6-2, 6-2 |
| 1910 | Anthony F. Wilding | Arthur W. Gore | 6-4, 7-5, 4-6, 6-2 |
| 1911 | Anthony F. Wilding | H. Roper Barrett | 6-4, 4-6, 2-6, 6-2 ret |
| 1912 | Anthony F. Wilding | Arthur W. Gore | 6-4, 6-4, 4-6, 6-4 |
| 1913 | Anthony F. Wilding | Maurice E. McLoughlin | 8-6, 6-3, 10-8 |
| 1914 | Norman E. Brookes | Anthony F. Wilding | 6-4, 6-4, 7-5 |
| 1915-18 | No tournament | | |
| 1919 | Gerald L. Patterson | Norman E. Brookes | 6-3, 7-5, 6-2 |
| 1920 | Bill Tilden | Gerald L. Patterson | 2-6, 6-3, 6-2, 6-4 |
| 1921 | Bill Tilden | Brian I. C. Norton | 4-6, 2-6, 6-1, 6-0, 7-5 |
| 1922 | Gerald L. Patterson | Randolph Lycett | 6-3, 6-4, 6-2 |
| 1923 | Bill Johnston | Francis T. Hunter | 6-0, 6-3, 6-1 |
| 1924 | Jean Borotra | Rene Lacoste | 6-1, 3-6, 6-1, 3-6, 6-4 |
| 1925 | Rene Lacoste | Jean Borotra | 6-3, 6-3, 4-6, 8-6 |
| 1926 | Jean Borotra | Howard Kinsey | 8-6, 6-1, 6-3 |
| 1927 | Henri Cochet | Jean Borotra | 4-6, 4-6, 6-3, 6-4, 7-5 |
| 1928 | Rene Lacoste | Henri Cochet | 6-1, 4-6, 6-4, 6-2 |
| 1929 | Henri Cochet | Jean Borotra | 6-4, 6-3, 6-4 |
| 1930 | Bill Tilden | Wilmer Allison | 6-3, 9-7, 6-4 |
| 1931 | Sidney B. Wood Jr | Francis X. Shields | walkover |
| 1932 | Ellsworth Vines | Henry Austin | 6-4, 6-2, 6-0 |
| 1933 | Jack Crawford | Ellsworth Vines | 4-6, 11-9, 6-2, 2-6, 6-4 |
| 1934 | Fred Perry | Jack Crawford | 6-3, 6-0, 7-5 |
| 1935 | Fred Perry | Gottfried von Cramm | 6-2, 6-4, 6-4 |
| 1936 | Fred Perry | Gottfried von Cramm | 6-1, 6-1, 6-0 |
| 1937 | Don Budge | Gottfried von Cramm | 6-3, 6-4, 6-2 |
| 1938 | Don Budge | Henry Austin | 6-1, 6-0, 6-3 |
| 1939 | Bobby Riggs | Elwood Cooke | 2-6, 8-6, 3-6, 6-3, 6-2 |
| 1940-45 | No tournament | | |
| 1946 | Yvon Petra | Geoff E. Brown | 6-2, 6-4, 7-9, 5-7, 6-4 |
| 1947 | Jack Kramer | Tom P. Brown | 6-1, 6-3, 6-2 |
| 1948 | Bob Falkenburg | John Bromwich | 7-5, 0-6, 6-2, 3-6, 7-5 |
| 1949 | Ted Schroeder | Jaroslav Drobny | 3-6, 6-0, 6-3, 4-6, 6-4 |
| 1950 | Budge Patty | Frank Sedgman | 6-1, 8-10, 6-2, 6-3 |
| 1951 | Dick Savitt | Ken McGregor | 6-4, 6-4, 6-4 |
| 1952 | Frank Sedgman | Jaroslav Drobny | 4-6, 6-3, 6-2, 6-3 |
| 1953 | Vic Seixas | Kurt Nielsen | 9-7, 6-3, 6-4 |
| 1954 | Jaroslav Drobny | Ken Rosewall | 13-11, 4-6, 6-2, 9-7 |
| 1955 | Tony Trabert | Kurt Nielsen | 6-3, 7-5, 6-1 |
| 1956 | Lew Hoad | Ken Rosewall | 6-2, 4-6, 7-5, 6-4 |
| 1957 | Lew Hoad | Ashley Cooper | 6-2, 6-1, 6-2 |
| 1958 | Ashley Cooper | Neale Fraser | 3-6, 6-3, 6-4, 13-11 |
| 1959 | Alex Olmedo | Rod Laver | 6-4, 6-3, 6-4 |
| 1960 | Neale Fraser | Rod Laver | 6-4, 3-6, 9-7, 7-5 |
| 1961 | Rod Laver | Chuck McKinley | 6-3, 6-1, 6-4 |
| 1962 | Rod Laver | Martin Mulligan | 6-2, 6-2, 6-1 |
| 1963 | Chuck McKinley | Fred Stolle | 9-7, 6-1, 6-4 |
| 1964 | Roy Emerson | Fred Stolle | 6-4, 12-10, 4-6, 6-3 |
| 1965 | Roy Emerson | Fred Stolle | 6-2, 6-4, 6-4 |
| 1966 | Manuel Santana | Dennis Ralston | 6-4, 11-9, 6-4 |
| 1967 | John Newcombe | Wilhelm Bungert | 6-3, 6-1, 6-1 |
| 1968* | Rod Laver | Tony Roche | 6-3, 6-4, 6-2 |
| 1969 | Rod Laver | John Newcombe | 6-4, 5-7, 6-4, 6-4 |
| 1970 | John Newcombe | Ken Rosewall | 5-7, 6-3, 6-2, 3-6, 6-1 |
| 1971 | John Newcombe | Stan Smith | 6-3, 5-7, 2-6, 6-4, 6-4 |
| 1972 | Stan Smith | Ilie Nastase | 4-6, 6-3, 6-3, 4-6, 7-5 |
| 1973 | Jan Kodes | Alex Metreveli | 6-1, 9-8, 6-3 |
| 1974 | Jimmy Connors | Ken Rosewall | 6-1, 6-1, 6-4 |

## Wimbledon Championships *(Cont.)*

| Year | Winner | Finalist | Score |
|------|--------|----------|-------|
| 1975 | Arthur Ashe | Jimmy Connors | 6-1, 6-1, 5-7, 6-4 |
| 1976 | Bjorn Borg | Ilie Nastase | 6-4, 6-2, 9-7 |
| 1977 | Bjorn Borg | Jimmy Connors | 3-6, 6-2, 6-1, 5-7, 6-4 |
| 1978 | Bjorn Borg | Jimmy Connors | 6-2, 6-2, 6-3 |
| 1979 | Bjorn Borg | Roscoe Tanner | 6-7, 6-1, 3-6, 6-3, 6-4 |
| 1980 | Bjorn Borg | John McEnroe | 1-6, 7-5, 6-3, 6-7, 8-6 |
| 1981 | John McEnroe | Bjorn Borg | 4-6, 7-6, 7-6, 6-4 |
| 1982 | Jimmy Connors | John McEnroe | 3-6, 6-3, 6-7, 7-6, 6-4 |
| 1983 | John McEnroe | Chris Lewis | 6-2, 6-2, 6-2 |
| 1984 | John McEnroe | Jimmy Connors | 6-1, 6-1, 6-2 |
| 1985 | Boris Becker | Kevin Curren | 6-3, 6-7, 7-6, 6-4 |
| 1986 | Boris Becker | Ivan Lendl | 6-4, 6-3, 7-5 |
| 1987 | Pat Cash | Ivan Lendl | 7-6, 6-2, 7-5 |
| 1988 | Stefan Edberg | Boris Becker | 4-6, 7-6, 6-4, 6-2 |
| 1989 | Boris Becker | Stefan Edberg | 6-0, 7-6, 6-4 |
| 1990 | Stefan Edberg | Boris Becker | 6-2, 6-2, 3-6, 3-6, 6-4 |
| 1991 | Michael Stich | Boris Becker | 6-4, 7-6, 6-4 |
| 1992 | Andre Agassi | Goran Ivanisevic | 6-7, 6-4, 6-4, 1-6, 6-4 |
| 1993 | Pete Sampras | Jim Courier | 7-6 (7-3), 7-6 (8-6), 3-6, 6-3 |
| 1994 | Pete Sampras | Goran Ivanisevic | 7-6 (7-2), 7-6 (7-5), 6-0 |
| 1995 | Pete Sampras | Boris Becker | 6-7 (5-7), 6-2, 6-4, 6-2 |

*Became Open (amateur and professional) in 1968 but closed to contract professionals in 1972.
Note: Prior to 1922 the tournament was run on a challenge-round system. The previous year's winner "stood out" of an All Comers event, which produced a challenger to play him for the title.

## United States Championships

| Year | Winner | Finalist | Score |
|------|--------|----------|-------|
| 1881 | Richard D. Sears | W. E. Glyn | 6-0, 6-3, 6-2 |
| 1882 | Richard D. Sears | C. M. Clark | 6-1, 6-4, 6-0 |
| 1883 | Richard D. Sears | James Dwight | 6-2, 6-0, 9-7 |
| 1884 | Richard D. Sears | H. A. Taylor | 6-0, 1-6, 6-0, 6-2 |
| 1885 | Richard D. Sears | G. M. Brinley | 6-3, 4-6, 6-0, 6-3 |
| 1886 | Richard D. Sears | R. L. Beeckman | 4-6, 6-1, 6-3, 6-4 |
| 1887 | Richard D. Sears | H. W. Slocum Jr | 6-1, 6-3, 6-2 |
| 1888‡ | H. W. Slocum Jr | H. A. Taylor | 6-4, 6-1, 6-0 |
| 1889 | H. W. Slocum Jr | Q. A. Shaw | 6-3, 6-1, 4-6, 6-2 |
| 1890 | Oliver S. Campbell | H. W. Slocum Jr | 6-2, 4-6, 6-3, 6-1 |
| 1891 | Oliver S. Campbell | Clarence Hobart | 2-6, 7-5, 7-9, 6-1, 6-2 |
| 1892 | Oliver S. Campbell | Frederick H. Hovey | 7-5, 3-6, 6-3, 7-5 |
| 1893‡ | Robert D. Wrenn | Frederick H. Hovey | 6-4, 3-6, 6-4, 6-4 |
| 1894 | Robert D. Wrenn | M. F. Goodbody | 6-8, 6-1, 6-4, 6-4 |
| 1895 | Frederick H. Hovey | Robert D. Wrenn | 6-3, 6-2, 6-4 |
| 1896 | Robert D. Wrenn | Frederick H. Hovey | 7-5, 3-6, 6-0, 1-6, 6-1 |
| 1897 | Robert D. Wrenn | Wilberforce V. Eaves | 4-6, 8-6, 6-3, 2-6, 6-2 |
| 1898‡ | Malcolm D. Whitman | Dwight F. Davis | 3-6, 6-2, 6-2, 6-1 |
| 1899 | Malcolm D. Whitman | J. Parmly Paret | 6-1, 6-2, 3-6, 7-5 |
| 1900 | Malcolm D. Whitman | William A. Larned | 6-4, 1-6, 6-2, 6-2 |
| 1901‡ | William A. Larned | Beals C. Wright | 6-2, 6-8, 6-4, 6-4 |
| 1902 | William A. Larned | Reggie F. Doherty | 4-6, 6-2, 6-4, 8-6 |
| 1903 | H. Laurie Doherty | William A. Larned | 6-0, 6-3, 10-8 |
| 1904‡ | Holcombe Ward | William J. Clothier | 10-8, 6-4, 9-7 |
| 1905 | Beals C. Wright | Holcombe Ward | 6-2, 6-1, 11-9 |
| 1906 | William J. Clothier | Beals C. Wright | 6-3, 6-0, 6-4 |
| 1907‡ | William A. Larned | Robert LeRoy | 6-2, 6-2, 6-4 |
| 1908 | William A. Larned | Beals C. Wright | 6-1, 6-2, 8-6 |
| 1909 | William A. Larned | William J. Clothier | 6-1, 6-2, 5-7, 1-6, 6-1 |
| 1910 | William A. Larned | Thomas C. Bundy | 6-1, 5-7, 6-0, 6-8, 6-1 |
| 1911 | William A. Larned | Maurice E. McLoughlin | 6-4, 6-4, 6-2 |
| 1912† | Maurice E. McLoughlin | Bill Johnson | 3-6, 2-6, 6-2, 6-4, 6-2 |
| 1913 | Maurice E. McLoughlin | Richard N. Williams | 6-4, 5-7, 6-3, 6-1 |
| 1914 | Richard N. Williams | Maurice E. McLoughlin | 6-3, 8-6, 10-8 |
| 1915 | Bill Johnston | Maurice E. McLoughlin | 1-6, 6-0, 7-5, 10-8 |
| 1916 | Richard N. Williams | Bill Johnston | 4-6, 6-4, 0-6, 6-2, 6-4 |
| 1917# | R. L. Murray | N. W. Niles | 5-7, 8-6, 6-3, 6-3 |

## United States Championships *(Cont.)*

| Year | Winner | Finalist | Score |
|------|--------|----------|-------|
| 1918 | R. L. Murray | Bill Tilden | 6-3, 6-1, 7-5 |
| 1919 | Bill Johnston | Bill Tilden | 6-4, 6-4, 6-3 |
| 1920 | Bill Tilden | Bill Johnston | 6-1, 1-6, 7-5, 5-7, 6-3 |
| 1921 | Bill Tilden | Wallace F. Johnson | 6-1, 6-3, 6-1 |
| 1922 | Bill Tilden | Bill Johnston | 4-6, 3-6, 6-2, 6-3, 6-4 |
| 1923 | Bill Tilden | Bill Johnston | 6-4, 6-1, 6-4 |
| 1924 | Bill Tilden | Bill Johnston | 6-1, 9-7, 6-2 |
| 1925 | Bill Tilden | Bill Johnston | 4-6, 11-9, 6-3, 4-6, 6-3 |
| 1926 | Rene Lacoste | Jean Borotra | 6-4, 6-0, 6-4 |
| 1927 | Rene Lacoste | Bill Tilden | 11-9, 6-3, 11-9 |
| 1928 | Henri Cochet | Francis T. Hunter | 4-6, 6-4, 3-6, 7-5, 6-3 |
| 1929 | Bill Tilden | Francis T. Hunter | 3-6, 6-3, 4-6, 6-2, 6-4 |
| 1930 | John H. Doeg | Francis X. Shields | 10-8, 1-6, 6-4, 16-14 |
| 1931 | Ellsworth Vines | George M. Lott Jr | 7-9, 6-3, 9-7, 7-5 |
| 1932 | Ellsworth Vines | Henri Cochet | 6-4, 6-4, 6-4 |
| 1933 | Fred Perry | Jack Crawford | 6-3, 11-13, 4-6, 6-0, 6-1 |
| 1934 | Fred Perry | Wilmer L. Allison | 6-4, 6-3, 1-6, 8-6 |
| 1935 | Wilmer L. Allison | Sidney B. Wood Jr | 6-2, 6-2, 6-3 |
| 1936 | Fred Perry | Don Budge | 2-6, 6-2, 8-6, 1-6, 10-8 |
| 1937 | Don Budge | Gottfried von Cramm | 6-1, 7-9, 6-1, 3-6, 6-1 |
| 1938 | Don Budge | Gene Mako | 6-3, 6-8, 6-2, 6-1 |
| 1939 | Bobby Riggs | Welby van Horn | 6-4, 6-2, 6-4 |
| 1940 | Don McNeill | Bobby Riggs | 4-6, 6-8, 6-3, 6-3, 7-5 |
| 1941 | Bobby Riggs | Francis Kovacs II | 5-7, 6-1, 6-3, 6-3 |
| 1942 | Ted Schroeder | Frank Parker | 8-6, 7-5, 3-6, 4-6, 6-2 |
| 1943 | Joseph R. Hunt | Jack Kramer | 6-3, 6-8, 10-8, 6-0 |
| 1944 | Frank Parker | William F. Talbert | 6-4, 3-6, 6-3, 6-3 |
| 1945 | Frank Parker | William F. Talbert | 14-12, 6-1, 6-2 |
| 1946 | Jack Kramer | Tom P. Brown | 9-7, 6-3, 6-0 |
| 1947 | Jack Kramer | Frank Parker | 4-6, 2-6, 6-1, 6-0, 6-3 |
| 1948 | Pancho Gonzales | Eric W. Sturgess | 6-2, 6-3, 14-12 |
| 1949 | Pancho Gonzales | Ted Schroeder | 16-18, 2-6, 6-1, 6-2, 6-4 |
| 1950 | Arthur Larsen | Herbie Flam | 6-3, 4-6, 5-7, 6-4, 6-3 |
| 1951 | Frank Sedgman | Vic Seixas | 6-4, 6-1, 6-1 |
| 1952 | Frank Sedgman | Gardnar Mulloy | 6-1, 6-2, 6-3 |
| 1953 | Tony Trabert | Vic Seixas | 6-3, 6-2, 6-3 |
| 1954 | Vic Seixas | Rex Hartwig | 3-6, 6-2, 6-4, 6-4 |
| 1955 | Tony Trabert | Ken Rosewall | 9-7, 6-3, 6-3 |
| 1956 | Ken Rosewall | Lew Hoad | 4-6, 6-2, 6-3, 6-3 |
| 1957 | Mal Anderson | Ashley J. Cooper | 10-8, 7-5, 6-4 |
| 1958 | Ashley J. Cooper | Mal Anderson | 6-2, 3-6, 4-6, 10-8, 8-6 |
| 1959 | Neale Fraser | Alex Olmedo | 6-3, 5-7, 6-2, 6-4 |
| 1960 | Neale Fraser | Rod Laver | 6-4, 6-4, 9-7 |
| 1961 | Roy Emerson | Rod Laver | 7-5, 6-3, 6-2 |
| 1962 | Rod Laver | Roy Emerson | 6-2, 6-4, 5-7, 6-4 |
| 1963 | Rafael Osuna | Frank Froehling III | 7-5, 6-4, 6-2 |
| 1964 | Roy Emerson | Fred Stolle | 6-4, 6-2, 6-4 |
| 1965 | Manuel Santana | Cliff Drysdale | 6-2, 7-9, 7-5, 6-1 |
| 1966 | Fred Stolle | John Newcombe | 4-6, 12-10, 6-3, 6-4 |
| 1967 | John Newcombe | Clark Graebner | 6-4, 6-4, 8-6 |
| 1968** | Arthur Ashe | Bob Lutz | 4-6, 6-3, 8-10, 6-0, 6-4 |
| 1968* | Arthur Ashe | Tom Okker | 14-12, 5-7, 6-3, 3-6, 6-3 |
| 1969** | Stan Smith | Bob Lutz | 9-7, 6-3, 6-1 |
| 1969* | Rod Laver | Tony Roche | 7-9, 6-1, 6-3, 6-2 |
| 1970 | Ken Rosewall | Tony Roche | 2-6, 6-4, 7-6, 6-3 |
| 1971 | Stan Smith | Jan Kodes | 3-6, 6-3, 6-2, 7-6 |
| 1972 | Ilie Nastase | Arthur Ashe | 3-6, 6-3, 6-7, 6-4, 6-3 |
| 1973 | John Newcombe | Jan Kodes | 6-4, 1-6, 4-6, 6-2, 6-3 |
| 1974 | Jimmy Connors | Ken Rosewall | 6-1, 6-0, 6-1 |
| 1975 | Manuel Orantes | Jimmy Connors | 6-4, 6-3, 6-3 |
| 1976 | Jimmy Connors | Bjorn Borg | 6-4, 3-6, 7-6, 6-4 |
| 1977 | Guillermo Vilas | Jimmy Connors | 2-6, 6-3, 7-6, 6-0 |
| 1978 | Jimmy Connors | Bjorn Borg | 6-4, 6-2, 6-2 |
| 1979 | John McEnroe | Vitas Gerulaitis | 7-5, 6-3, 6-3 |
| 1980 | John McEnroe | Bjorn Borg | 7-6, 6-1, 6-7, 5-7, 6-4 |
| 1981 | John McEnroe | Bjorn Borg | 4-6, 6-2, 6-4, 6-3 |

## United States Championships *(Cont.)*

| Year | Winner | Finalist | Score |
|------|--------|----------|-------|
| 1982 | Jimmy Connors | Ivan Lendl | 6-3, 6-2, 4-6, 6-4 |
| 1983 | Jimmy Connors | Ivan Lendl | 6-3, 6-7, 7-5, 6-0 |
| 1984 | John McEnroe | Ivan Lendl | 6-3, 6-4, 6-1 |
| 1985 | Ivan Lendl | John McEnroe | 7-6, 6-3, 6-4 |
| 1986 | Ivan Lendl | Miloslav Mecir | 6-4, 6-2, 6-0 |
| 1987 | Ivan Lendl | Mats Wilander | 6-7, 6-0, 7-6, 6-4 |
| 1988 | Mats Wilander | Ivan Lendl | 6-4, 4-6, 6-3, 5-7, 6-4 |
| 1989 | Boris Becker | Ivan Lendl | 7-6, 1-6, 6-3, 7-6 |
| 1990 | Pete Sampras | Andre Agassi | 6-4, 6-3, 6-2 |
| 1991 | Stefan Edberg | Jim Courier | 6-2, 6-4, 6-0 |
| 1992 | Stefan Edberg | Pete Sampras | 3-6, 6-4, 7-6, 6-2 |
| 1993 | Pete Sampras | Cédric Pioline | 6-4, 6-4, 6-3 |
| 1994 | Andre Agassi | Michael Stich | 6-1, 7-6 (7-5), 7-5 |
| 1995 | Pete Sampras | Andre Agassi | 6-4, 6-3, 4-6, 7-5 |

*Became Open (amateur and professional) in 1968; †Challenge round abolished; ‡No challenge round played. #National Patriotic Tournament; **Amateur event held.

## WOMEN

## Australian Championships

| Year | Winner | Finalist | Score |
|------|--------|----------|-------|
| 1922 | Margaret Molesworth | Esna Boyd | 6-3, 10-8 |
| 1923 | Margaret Molesworth | Esna Boyd | 6-1, 7-5 |
| 1924 | Sylvia Lance | Esna Boyd | 6-3, 3-6, 6-4 |
| 1925 | Daphne Akhurst | Esna Boyd | 1-6, 8-6, 6-4 |
| 1926 | Daphne Akhurst | Esna Boyd | 6-1, 6-3 |
| 1927 | Esna Boyd | Sylvia Harper | 5-7, 6-1, 6-2 |
| 1928 | Daphne Akhurst | Esna Boyd | 7-5, 6-2 |
| 1929 | Daphne Akhurst | Louise Bickerton | 6-1, 5-7, 6-2 |
| 1930 | Daphne Akhurst | Sylvia Harper | 10-8, 2-6, 7-5 |
| 1931 | Coral Buttsworth | Margorie Crawford | 1-6, 6-3, 6-4 |
| 1932 | Coral Buttsworth | Kathrine Le Messurier | 9-7, 6-4 |
| 1933 | Joan Hartigan | Coral Buttsworth | 6-4, 6-3 |
| 1934 | Joan Hartigan | Margaret Molesworth | 6-1, 6-4 |
| 1935 | Dorothy Round | Nancye Wynne Bolton | 1-6, 6-1, 6-3 |
| 1936 | Joan Hartigan | Nancye Wynne Bolton | 6-4, 6-4 |
| 1937 | Nancye Wynne Bolton | Emily Westacott | 6-3, 5-7, 6-4 |
| 1938 | Dorothy Bundy | D. Stevenson | 6-3, 6-2 |
| 1939 | Emily Westacott | Nell Hopman | 6-1, 6-2 |
| 1940 | Nancye Wynne Bolton | Thelma Coyne | 5-7, 6-4, 6-0 |
| 1941-45 | No tournament | | |
| 1946 | Nancye Wynne Bolton | Joyce Fitch | 6-4, 6-4 |
| 1947 | Nancye Wynne Bolton | Nell Hopman | 6-3, 6-2 |
| 1948 | Nancye Wynne Bolton | Marie Toomey | 6-3, 6-1 |
| 1949 | Doris Hart | Nancye Wynne Bolton | 6-3, 6-4 |
| 1950 | Louise Brough | Doris Hart | 6-4, 3-6, 6-4 |
| 1951 | Nancye Wynne Bolton | Thelma Long | 6-1, 7-5 |
| 1952 | Thelma Long | H. Angwin | 6-2, 6-3 |
| 1953 | Maureen Connolly | Julia Sampson | 6-3, 6-2 |
| 1954 | Thelma Long | J. Staley | 6-3, 6-4 |
| 1955 | Beryl Penrose | Thelma Long | 6-4, 6-3 |
| 1956 | Mary Carter | Thelma Long | 3-6, 6-2, 9-7 |
| 1957 | Shirley Fry | Althea Gibson | 6-3, 6-4 |
| 1958 | Angela Mortimer | Lorraine Coghlan | 6-3, 6-4 |
| 1959 | Mary Carter-Reitano | Renee Schuurman | 6-2, 6-3 |
| 1960 | Margaret Smith | Jan Lehane | 7-5, 6-2 |
| 1961 | Margaret Smith | Jan Lehane | 6-1, 6-4 |
| 1962 | Margaret Smith | Jan Lehane | 6-0, 6-2 |
| 1963 | Margaret Smith | Jan Lehane | 6-2, 6-2 |
| 1964 | Margaret Smith | Lesley Turner | 6-3, 6-2 |
| 1965 | Margaret Smith | Maria Bueno | 5-7, 6-4, 5-2 ret |
| 1966 | Margaret Smith | Nancy Richey | Default |
| 1967 | Nancy Richey | Lesley Turner | 6-1, 6-4 |
| 1968 | Billie Jean King | Margaret Smith | 6-1, 6-2 |

## Australian Championships *(Cont.)*

| Year | Winner | Finalist | Score |
|------|--------|----------|-------|
| 1969* | Margaret Smith Court | Billie Jean King | 6-4, 6-1 |
| 1970 | Margaret Smith Court | Kerry Melville Reid | 6-3, 6-1 |
| 1971 | Margaret Smith Court | Evonne Goolagong | 2-6, 7-6, 7-5 |
| 1972 | Virginia Wade | Evonne Goolagong | 6-4, 6-4 |
| 1973 | Margaret Smith Court | Evonne Goolagong | 6-4, 7-5 |
| 1974 | Evonne Goolagong | Chris Evert | 7-6, 4-6, 6-0 |
| 1975 | Evonne Goolagong | Martina Navratilova | 6-3, 6-2 |
| 1976 | Evonne Goolagong Cawley | Renata Tomanova | 6-2, 6-2 |
| 1977 (Jan) | Kerry Melville Reid | Dianne Balestrat | 7-5, 6-2 |
| 1977 (Dec) | Evonne Goolagong Cawley | Helen Gourlay | 6-3, 6-0 |
| 1978 | Chris O'Neil | Betsy Nagelsen | 6-3, 7-6 |
| 1979 | Barbara Jordan | Sharon Walsh | 6-3, 6-3 |
| 1980 | Hana Mandlikova | Wendy Turnbull | 6-0, 7-5 |
| 1981 | Martina Navratilova | Chris Evert Lloyd | 6-7, 6-4, 7-5 |
| 1982 | Chris Evert Lloyd | Martina Navratilova | 6-3, 2-6, 6-3 |
| 1983 | Martina Navratilova | Kathy Jordan | 6-2, 7-6 |
| 1984 | Chris Evert Lloyd | Helena Sukova | 6-7, 6-1, 6-3 |
| 1985 (Dec) | Martina Navratilova | Chris Evert Lloyd | 6-2, 4-6, 6-2 |
| 1987 (Jan) | Hana Mandlikova | Martina Navratilova | 7-5, 7-6 |
| 1988 | Steffi Graf | Chris Evert | 6-1, 7-6 |
| 1989 | Steffi Graf | Helena Sukova | 6-4, 6-4 |
| 1990 | Steffi Graf | Mary Joe Fernandez | 6-3, 6-4 |
| 1991 | Monica Seles | Jana Novotna | 5-7, 6-3, 6-1 |
| 1992 | Monica Seles | Mary Joe Fernandez | 6-2, 6-3 |
| 1993 | Monica Seles | Steffi Graf | 4-6, 6-3, 6-2 |
| 1994 | Steffi Graf | Arantxa Sanchez Vicario | 6-0, 6-2 |
| 1995 | Mary Pierce | Arantxa Sanchez Vicario | 6-3, 6-2 |

*Became Open (amateur and professional) in 1969.

## French Championships

| Year | Winner | Finalist | Score |
|------|--------|----------|-------|
| 1925† | Suzanne Lenglen | Kathleen McKane | 6-1, 6-2 |
| 1926 | Suzanne Lenglen | Mary K. Browne | 6-1, 6-0 |
| 1927 | Kea Bouman | Irene Peacock | 6-2, 6-4 |
| 1928 | Helen Wills | Eileen Bennett | 6-1, 6-2 |
| 1929 | Helen Wills | Simone Mathieu | 6-3, 6-4 |
| 1930 | Helen Wills Moody | Helen Jacobs | 6-2, 6-1 |
| 1931 | Cilly Aussem | Betty Nuthall | 8-6, 6-1 |
| 1932 | Helen Wills Moody | Simone Mathieu | 7-5, 6-1 |
| 1933 | Margaret Scriven | Simone Mathieu | 6-2, 4-6, 6-4 |
| 1934 | Margaret Scriven | Helen Jacobs | 7-5, 4-6, 6-1 |
| 1935 | Hilde Sperling | Simone Mathieu | 6-2, 6-1 |
| 1936 | Hilde Sperling | Simone Mathieu | 6-3, 6-4 |
| 1937 | Hilde Sperling | Simone Mathieu | 6-2, 6-4 |
| 1938 | Simone Mathieu | Nelly Landry | 6-0, 6-3 |
| 1939 | Simone Mathieu | Jadwiga Jedrzejowska | 6-3, 8-6 |
| 1940-45 | No tournament | | |
| 1946 | Margaret Osborne | Pauline Betz | 1-6, 8-6, 7-5 |
| 1947 | Patricia Todd | Doris Hart | 6-3, 3-6, 6-4 |
| 1948 | Nelly Landry | Shirley Fry | 6-2, 0-6, 6-0 |
| 1949 | Margaret Osborne duPont | Nelly Adamson | 7-5, 6-2 |
| 1950 | Doris Hart | Patricia Todd | 6-4, 4-6, 6-2 |
| 1951 | Shirley Fry | Doris Hart | 6-3, 3-6, 6-3 |
| 1952 | Doris Hart | Shirley Fry | 6-4, 6-4 |
| 1953 | Maureen Connolly | Doris Hart | 6-2, 6-4 |
| 1954 | Maureen Connolly | Ginette Bucaille | 6-4, 6-1 |
| 1955 | Angela Mortimer | Dorothy Knode | 2-6, 7-5, 10-8 |
| 1956 | Althea Gibson | Angela Mortimer | 6-0, 12-10 |
| 1957 | Shirley Bloomer | Dorothy Knode | 6-1, 6-3 |
| 1958 | Zsuzsi Kormoczi | Shirley Bloomer | 6-4, 1-6, 6-2 |
| 1959 | Christine Truman | Zsuzsi Kormoczi | 6-4, 7-5 |
| 1960 | Darlene Hard | Yola Ramirez | 6-3, 6-4 |
| 1961 | Ann Haydon | Yola Ramirez | 6-2, 6-1 |
| 1962 | Margaret Smith | Lesley Turner | 6-3, 3-6, 7-5 |

### French Championships (Cont.)

| Year | Winner | Finalist | Score |
|------|--------|----------|-------|
| 1963 | Lesley Turner | Ann Haydon Jones | 2-6, 6-3, 7-5 |
| 1964 | Margaret Smith | Maria Bueno | 5-7, 6-1, 6-2 |
| 1965 | Lesley Turner | Margaret Smith | 6-3, 6-4 |
| 1966 | Ann Jones | Nancy Richey | 6-3, 6-1 |
| 1967 | Francoise Durr | Lesley Turner | 4-6, 6-3, 6-4 |
| 1968* | Nancy Richey | Ann Jones | 5-7, 6-4, 6-1 |
| 1969 | Margaret Smith Court | Ann Jones | 6-1, 4-6, 6-3 |
| 1970 | Margaret Smith Court | Helga Niessen | 6-2, 6-4 |
| 1971 | Evonne Goolagong | Helen Gourlay | 6-3, 7-5 |
| 1972 | Billie Jean King | Evonne Goolagong | 6-3, 6-3 |
| 1973 | Margaret Smith Court | Chris Evert | 6-7, 7-6, 6-4 |
| 1974 | Chris Evert | Olga Morozova | 6-1, 6-2 |
| 1975 | Chris Evert | Martina Navratilova | 2-6, 6-2, 6-1 |
| 1976 | Sue Barker | Renata Tomanova | 6-2, 0-6, 6-2 |
| 1977 | Mima Jausovec | Florenza Mihai | 6-2, 6-7, 6-1 |
| 1978 | Virginia Ruzici | Mima Jausovec | 6-2, 6-2 |
| 1979 | Chris Evert Lloyd | Wendy Turnbull | 6-2, 6-0 |
| 1980 | Chris Evert Lloyd | Virginia Ruzici | 6-0, 6-3 |
| 1981 | Hana Mandlikova | Sylvia Hanika | 6-2, 6-4 |
| 1982 | Martina Navratilova | Andrea Jaeger | 7-6, 6-1 |
| 1983 | Chris Evert Lloyd | Mima Jausovec | 6-1, 6-2 |
| 1984 | Martina Navratilova | Chris Evert Lloyd | 6-3, 6-1 |
| 1985 | Chris Evert Lloyd | Martina Navratilova | 6-3, 6-7, 7-5 |
| 1986 | Chris Evert Lloyd | Martina Navratilova | 2-6, 6-3, 6-3 |
| 1987 | Steffi Graf | Martina Navratilova | 6-4, 4-6, 8-6 |
| 1988 | Steffi Graf | Natalia Zvereva | 6-0, 6-0 |
| 1989 | Arantxa Sanchez Vicario | Steffi Graf | 7-6, 3-6, 7-5 |
| 1990 | Monica Seles | Steffi Graf | 7-6, 6-4 |
| 1991 | Monica Seles | Arantxa Sanchez Vicario | 6-3, 6-4 |
| 1992 | Monica Seles | Steffi Graf | 6-2, 3-6, 10-8 |
| 1993 | Steffi Graf | Mary Joe Fernandez | 4-6, 6-2, 6-4 |
| 1994 | Arantxa Sanchez Vicario | Mary Pierce | 6-4, 6-4 |
| 1995 | Steffi Graf | Arantxa Sanchez Vicario | 7-5, 4-6, 6-0 |

*Became Open (amateur and professional) in 1968 but closed to contract professionals in 1972.

†1925 was the first year that entries were accepted from all countries.

### Wimbledon Championships

| Year | Winner | Finalist | Score |
|------|--------|----------|-------|
| 1884 | Maud Watson | Lilian Watson | 6-8, 6-3, 6-3 |
| 1885 | Maud Watson | Blanche Bingley | 6-1, 7-5 |
| 1886 | Blanche Bingley | Maud Watson | 6-3, 6-3 |
| 1887 | Charlotte Dod | Blanche Bingley | 6-2, 6-0 |
| 1888 | Charlotte Dod | Blanche Bingley Hillyard | 6-3, 6-3 |
| 1889 | Blanche Bingley Hillyard | | |
| 1890 | Lena Rice | | |
| 1891 | Charlotte Dod | | |
| 1892 | Charlotte Dod | Blanche Bingley Hillyard | 6-1, 6-1 |
| 1893 | Charlotte Dod | Blanche Bingley Hillyard | 6-8, 6-1, 6-4 |
| 1894 | Blanche Bingley Hillyard | | |
| 1895 | Charlotte Cooper | | |
| 1896 | Charlotte Cooper | Mrs. W. H. Pickering | 6-2, 6-3 |
| 1897 | Blanche Bingley Hillyard | Charlotte Cooper | 5-7, 7-5, 6-2 |
| 1898 | Charlotte Cooper | | |
| 1899 | Blanche Bingley Hillyard | Charlotte Cooper | 6-2, 6-3 |
| 1900 | Blanche Bingley Hillyard | Charlotte Cooper | 4-6, 6-4, 6-4 |
| 1901 | Charlotte Cooper Sterry | Blanche Bingley Hillyard | 6-2, 6-2 |
| 1902 | Muriel Robb | Charlotte Cooper Sterry | 7-5, 6-1 |
| 1903 | Dorothea Douglass | | |
| 1904 | Dorothea Douglass | Charlotte Cooper Sterry | 6-0, 6-3 |
| 1905 | May Sutton | Dorothea Douglass | 6-3, 6-4 |
| 1906 | Dorothea Douglass | May Sutton | 6-3, 9-7 |
| 1907 | May Sutton | Dorothea Douglass Lambert Chambers | 6-1, 6-4 |
| 1908 | Charlotte Cooper Sterry | | |

## Wimbledon Championships (Cont.)

| Year | Winner | Finalist | Score |
|------|--------|----------|-------|
| 1909 | Dora Boothby | | |
| 1910 | Dorothea Douglass Lambert Chambers | Dora Boothby | 6-2, 6-2 |
| 1911 | Dorothea Douglass Lambert Chambers | Dora Boothby | 6-0, 6-0 |
| 1912 | Ethel Larcombe | | |
| 1913 | Dorothea Douglass Lambert Chambers | | |
| 1914 | Dorothea Douglass Lambert Chambers | Ethel Larcombe | 7-5, 6-4 |
| 1915-18 | No tournament | | |
| 1919 | Suzanne Lenglen | Dorothea Douglass Lambert Chambers | 10-8, 4-6, 9-7 |
| 1920 | Suzanne Lenglen | Dorothea Douglass Lambert Chambers | 6-3, 6-0 |
| 1921 | Suzanne Lenglen | Elizabeth Ryan | 6-2, 6-0 |
| 1922 | Suzanne Lenglen | Molla Mallory | 6-2, 6-0 |
| 1923 | Suzanne Lenglen | Kathleen McKane | 6-2, 6-2 |
| 1924 | Kathleen McKane | Helen Wills | 4-6, 6-4, 6-2 |
| 1925 | Suzanne Lenglen | Joan Fry | 6-2, 6-0 |
| 1926 | Kathleen McKane Godfree | Lili de Alvarez | 6-2, 4-6, 6-3 |
| 1927 | Helen Wills | Lili de Alvarez | 6-2, 6-4 |
| 1928 | Helen Wills | Lili de Alvarez | 6-2, 6-3 |
| 1929 | Helen Wills | Helen Jacobs | 6-1, 6-2 |
| 1930 | Helen Wills Moody | Elizabeth Ryan | 6-2, 6-2 |
| 1931 | Cilly Aussem | Hilde Kranwinkel | 7-5, 7-5 |
| 1932 | Helen Wills Moody | Helen Jacobs | 6-3, 6-1 |
| 1933 | Helen Wills Moody | Dorothy Round | 6-4, 6-8, 6-3 |
| 1934 | Dorothy Round | Helen Jacobs | 6-2, 5-7, 6-3 |
| 1935 | Helen Wills Moody | Helen Jacobs | 6-3, 3-6, 7-5 |
| 1936 | Helen Jacobs | Hilde Kranwinkel Sperling | 6-2, 4-6, 7-5 |
| 1937 | Dorothy Round | Jadwiga Jedrzejowska | 6-2, 2-6, 7-5 |
| 1938 | Helen Wills Moody | Helen Jacobs | 6-4, 6-0 |
| 1939 | Alice Marble | Kay Stammers | 6-2, 6-0 |
| 1940-45 | No tournament | | |
| 1946 | Pauline Betz | Louise Brough | 6-2, 6-4 |
| 1947 | Margaret Osborne | Doris Hart | 6-2, 6-4 |
| 1948 | Louise Brough | Doris Hart | 6-3, 8-6 |
| 1949 | Louise Brough | Margaret Osborne duPont | 10-8, 1-6, 10-8 |
| 1950 | Louise Brough | Margaret Osborne duPont | 6-1, 3-6, 6-1 |
| 1951 | Doris Hart | Shirley Fry | 6-1, 6-0 |
| 1952 | Maureen Connolly | Louise Brough | 6-4, 6-3 |
| 1953 | Maureen Connolly | Doris Hart | 8-6, 7-5 |
| 1954 | Maureen Connolly | Louise Brough | 6-2, 7-5 |
| 1955 | Louise Brough | Beverly Fleitz | 7-5, 8-6 |
| 1956 | Shirley Fry | Angela Buxton | 6-3, 6-1 |
| 1957 | Althea Gibson | Darlene Hard | 6-3, 6-2 |
| 1958 | Althea Gibson | Angela Mortimer | 8-6, 6-2 |
| 1959 | Maria Bueno | Darlene Hard | 6-4, 6-3 |
| 1960 | Maria Bueno | Sandra Reynolds | 8-6, 6-0 |
| 1961 | Angela Mortimer | Christine Truman | 4-6, 6-4, 7-5 |
| 1962 | Karen Hantze Susman | Vera Sukova | 6-4, 6-4 |
| 1963 | Margaret Smith | Billie Jean Moffitt | 6-3, 6-4 |
| 1964 | Maria Bueno | Margaret Smith | 6-4, 7-9, 6-3 |
| 1965 | Margaret Smith | Maria Bueno | 6-4, 7-5 |
| 1966 | Billie Jean King | Maria Bueno | 6-3, 3-6, 6-1 |
| 1967 | Billie Jean King | Ann Haydon Jones | 6-3, 6-4 |
| 1968* | Billie Jean King | Judy Tegart | 9-7, 7-5 |
| 1969 | Ann Haydon Jones | Billie Jean King | 3-6, 6-3, 6-2 |
| 1970 | Margaret Smith Court | Billie Jean King | 14-12, 11-9 |
| 1971 | Evonne Goolagong | Margaret Smith Court | 6-4, 6-1 |
| 1972 | Billie Jean King | Evonne Goolagong | 6-3, 6-3 |
| 1973 | Billie Jean King | Chris Evert | 6-0, 7-5 |
| 1974 | Chris Evert | Olga Morozova | 6-0, 6-4 |
| 1975 | Billie Jean King | Evonne Goolagong Cawley | 6-0, 6-1 |
| 1976 | Chris Evert | Evonne Goolagong Cawley | 6-3, 4-6, 8-6 |

## Wimbledon Championships *(Cont.)*

| Year | Winner | Finalist | Score |
|------|--------|----------|-------|
| 1977 | Virginia Wade | Betty Stove | 4-6, 6-3, 6-1 |
| 1978 | Martina Navratilova | Chris Evert | 2-6, 6-4, 7-5 |
| 1979 | Martina Navratilova | Chris Evert Lloyd | 6-4, 6-4 |
| 1980 | Evonne Goolagong Cawley | Chris Evert Lloyd | 6-1, 7-6 |
| 1981 | Chris Evert Lloyd | Hana Mandlikova | 6-2, 6-2 |
| 1982 | Martina Navratilova | Chris Evert Lloyd | 6-1, 3-6, 6-2 |
| 1983 | Martina Navratilova | Andrea Jaeger | 6-0, 6-3 |
| 1984 | Martina Navratilova | Chris Evert Lloyd | 7-6, 6-2 |
| 1985 | Martina Navratilova | Chris Evert Lloyd | 4-6, 6-3, 6-2 |
| 1986 | Martina Navratilova | Hana Mandlikova | 7-6, 6-3 |
| 1987 | Martina Navratilova | Steffi Graf | 7-5, 6-3 |
| 1988 | Steffi Graf | Martina Navratilova | 5-7, 6-2, 6-1 |
| 1989 | Steffi Graf | Martina Navratilova | 6-2, 6-7, 6-1 |
| 1990 | Martina Navratilova | Zina Garrison | 6-4, 6-1 |
| 1991 | Steffi Graf | Gabriela Sabatini | 6-4, 3-6, 8-6 |
| 1992 | Steffi Graf | Monica Seles | 6-2, 6-1 |
| 1993 | Steffi Graf | Jana Novotna | 7-6 (8-6), 1-6, 6-4 |
| 1994 | Conchita Martinez | Martina Navratilova | 6-4, 3-6, 6-3 |
| 1995 | Steffi Graf | Arantxa Sanchez Vicario | 4-6, 6-1, 7-5 |

\*Became Open (amateur and professional) in 1968 but closed to contract professionals in 1972.

Note: Prior to 1922 the tournament was run on a challenge round system. The previous year's winner "stood out" of an All Comers event, which produced a challenger to play her for the title.

## United States Championships

| Year | Winner | Finalist | Score |
|------|--------|----------|-------|
| 1887 | Ellen Hansell | Laura Knight | 6-1, 6-0 |
| 1888 | Bertha L. Townsend | Ellen Hansell | 6-3, 6-5 |
| 1889 | Bertha L. Townsend | Louise Voorhes | 7-5, 6-2 |
| 1890 | Ellen C. Roosevelt | Bertha L. Townsend | 6-2, 6-2 |
| 1891 | Mabel Cahill | Ellen C. Roosevelt | 6-4, 6-1, 4-6, 6-3 |
| 1892 | Mabel Cahill | Elisabeth Moore | 5-7, 6-3, 6-4, 4-6, 6-2 |
| 1893 | Aline Terry | Alice Schultze | 6-1, 6-3 |
| 1894 | Helen Hellwig | Aline Terry | 7-5, 3-6, 6-0, 3-6, 6-3 |
| 1895 | Juliette Atkinson | Helen Hellwig | 6-4, 6-2, 6-1 |
| 1896 | Elisabeth Moore | Juliette Atkinson | 6-4, 4-6, 6-2, 6-2 |
| 1897 | Juliette Atkinson | Elisabeth Moore | 6-3, 6-3, 4-6, 3-6, 6-3 |
| 1898 | Juliette Atkinson | Marion Jones | 6-3, 5-7, 6-4, 2-6, 7-5 |
| 1899 | Marion Jones | Maud Banks | 6-1, 6-1, 7-5 |
| 1900 | Myrtle McAteer | Edith Parker | 6-2, 6-2, 6-0 |
| 1901 | Elisabeth Moore | Myrtle McAteer | 6-4, 3-6, 7-5, 2-6, 6-2 |
| 1902** | Marion Jones | Elisabeth Moore | 6-1, 1-0 retired |
| 1903 | Elisabeth Moore | Marion Jones | 7-5, 8-6 |
| 1904 | May Sutton | Elisabeth Moore | 6-1, 6-2 |
| 1905 | Elisabeth Moore | Helen Homans | 6-4, 5-7, 6-1 |
| 1906 | Helen Homans | Maud Barger-Wallach | 6-4, 6-3 |
| 1907 | Evelyn Sears | Carrie Neely | 6-3, 6-2 |
| 1908 | Maud Barger-Wallach | Evelyn Sears | 6-3, 1-6, 6-3 |
| 1909 | Hazel Hotchkiss | Maud Barger-Wallach | 6-0, 6-1 |
| 1910 | Hazel Hotchkiss | Louise Hammond | 6-4, 6-2 |
| 1911 | Hazel Hotchkiss | Florence Sutton | 8-10, 6-1, 9-7 |
| 1912† | Mary K. Browne | Eleanora Sears | 6-4, 6-2 |
| 1913 | Mary K. Browne | Dorothy Green | 6-2, 7-5 |
| 1914 | Mary K. Browne | Marie Wagner | 6-2, 1-6, 6-1 |
| 1915 | Molla Bjurstedt | Hazel Hotchkiss Wightman | 4-6, 6-2, 6-0 |
| 1916 | Molla Bjurstedt | Louise Hammond Raymond | 6-0, 6-1 |
| 1917‡ | Molla Bjurstedt | Marion Vanderhoef | 4-6, 6-0, 6-2 |
| 1918 | Molla Bjurstedt | Eleanor Goss | 6-4, 6-3 |
| 1919 | Hazel Hotchkiss Wightman | Marion Zinderstein | 6-1, 6-2 |
| 1920 | Molla Bjurstedt Mallory | Marion Zinderstein | 6-3, 6-1 |
| 1921 | Molla Bjurstedt Mallory | Mary K. Browne | 4-6, 6-4, 6-2 |
| 1922 | Molla Bjurstedt Mallory | Helen Wills | 6-3, 6-1 |
| 1923 | Helen Wills | Molla Bjurstedt Mallory | 6-2, 6-1 |
| 1924 | Helen Wills | Molla Bjurstedt Mallory | 6-1, 6-3 |
| 1925 | Helen Wills | Kathleen McKane | 3-6, 6-0, 6-2 |

## United States Championship (Cont.)

| Year | Winner | Finalist | Score |
|------|--------|----------|-------|
| 1926 | Molla Bjurstedt Mallory | Elizabeth Ryan | 4-6, 6-4, 9-7 |
| 1927 | Helen Wills | Betty Nuthall | 6-1, 6-4 |
| 1928 | Helen Wills | Helen Jacobs | 6-2, 6-1 |
| 1929 | Helen Wills | Phoebe Holcroft Watson | 6-4, 6-2 |
| 1930 | Betty Nuthall | Anna McCune Harper | 6-1, 6-4 |
| 1931 | Helen Wills Moody | Eileen Whitingstall | 6-4, 6-1 |
| 1932 | Helen Jacobs | Carolin Babcock | 6-2, 6-2 |
| 1933 | Helen Jacobs | Helen Wills Moody | 8-6, 3-6, 3-0 retired |
| 1934 | Helen Jacobs | Sarah Palfrey | 6-1, 6-4 |
| 1935 | Helen Jacobs | Sarah Palfrey Fabyan | 6-2, 6-4 |
| 1936 | Alice Marble | Helen Jacobs | 4-6, 6-3, 6-2 |
| 1937 | Anita Lizane | Jadwiga Jedrzejowska | 6-4, 6-2 |
| 1938 | Alice Marble | Nancye Wynne | 6-0, 6-3 |
| 1939 | Alice Marble | Helen Jacobs | 6-0, 8-10, 6-4 |
| 1940 | Alice Marble | Helen Jacobs | 6-2, 6-3 |
| 1941 | Sarah Palfrey Cooke | Pauline Betz | 7-5, 6-2 |
| 1942 | Pauline Betz | Louise Brough | 4-6, 6-1, 6-4 |
| 1943 | Pauline Betz | Louise Brough | 6-3, 5-7, 6-3 |
| 1944 | Pauline Betz | Margaret Osborne | 6-3, 8-6 |
| 1945 | Sarah Palfrey Cooke | Pauline Betz | 3-6, 8-6, 6-4 |
| 1946 | Pauline Betz | Patricia Canning | 11-9, 6-3 |
| 1947 | Louise Brough | Margaret Osborne | 8-6, 4-6, 6-1 |
| 1948 | Margaret Osborne duPont | Louise Brough | 4-6, 6-4, 15-13 |
| 1949 | Margaret Osborne duPont | Doris Hart | 6-4, 6-1 |
| 1950 | Margaret Osborne duPont | Doris Hart | 6-4, 6-3 |
| 1951 | Maureen Connolly | Shirley Fry | 6-3, 1-6, 6-4 |
| 1952 | Maureen Connolly | Doris Hart | 6-3, 7-5 |
| 1953 | Maureen Connolly | Doris Hart | 6-2, 6-4 |
| 1954 | Doris Hart | Louise Brough | 6-8, 6-1, 8-6 |
| 1955 | Doris Hart | Patricia Ward | 6-4, 6-2 |
| 1956 | Shirley Fry | Althea Gibson | 6-3, 6-4 |
| 1957 | Althea Gibson | Louise Brough | 6-3, 6-2 |
| 1958 | Althea Gibson | Darlene Hard | 3-6, 6-1, 6-2 |
| 1959 | Maria Bueno | Christine Truman | 6-1, 6-4 |
| 1960 | Darlene Hard | Maria Bueno | 6-4, 10-12, 6-4 |
| 1961 | Darlene Hard | Ann Haydon | 6-3, 6-4 |
| 1962 | Margaret Smith | Darlene Hard | 9-7, 6-4 |
| 1963 | Maria Bueno | Margaret Smith | 7-5, 6-4 |
| 1964 | Maria Bueno | Carole Graebner | 6-1, 6-0 |
| 1965 | Margaret Smith | Billie Jean Moffitt | 8-6, 7-5 |
| 1966 | Maria Bueno | Nancy Richey | 6-3, 6-1 |
| 1967 | Billie Jean King | Ann Haydon Jones | 11-9, 6-4 |
| 1968* | Virginia Wade | Billie Jean King | 6-4, 6-4 |
| 1968# | Margaret Smith Court | Maria Bueno | 6-2, 6-2 |
| 1969* | Margaret Smith Court | Nancy Richey | 6-2, 6-2 |
| 1969# | Margaret Smith Court | Virginia Wade | 4-6, 6-3, 6-0 |
| 1970 | Margaret Smith Court | Rosie Casals | 6-2, 2-6, 6-1 |
| 1971 | Billie Jean King | Rosie Casals | 6-4, 7-6 |
| 1972 | Billie Jean King | Kerry Melville | 6-3, 7-5 |
| 1973 | Margaret Smith Court | Evonne Goolagong | 7-6, 5-7, 6-2 |
| 1974 | Billie Jean King | Evonne Goolagong | 3-6, 6-3, 7-5 |
| 1975 | Chris Evert | Evonne Goolagong Cawley | 5-7, 6-4, 6-2 |
| 1976 | Chris Evert | Evonne Goolagong Cawley | 6-3, 6-0 |
| 1977 | Chris Evert | Wendy Turnbull | 7-6, 6-2 |
| 1978 | Chris Evert | Pam Shriver | 7-6, 6-4 |
| 1979 | Tracy Austin | Chris Evert Lloyd | 6-4, 6-3 |
| 1980 | Chris Evert Lloyd | Hana Mandlikova | 5-7, 6-1, 6-1 |
| 1981 | Tracy Austin | Martina Navratilova | 1-6, 7-6, 7-6 |
| 1982 | Chris Evert Lloyd | Hana Mandlikova | 6-3, 6-1 |
| 1983 | Martina Navratilova | Chris Evert Lloyd | 6-1, 6-3 |
| 1984 | Martina Navratilova | Chris Evert Lloyd | 4-6, 6-4, 6-4 |
| 1985 | Hana Mandlikova | Martina Navratilova | 7-6, 1-6, 7-6 |
| 1986 | Martina Navratilova | Helena Sukova | 6-3, 6-2 |
| 1987 | Martina Navratilova | Steffi Graf | 7-6, 6-1 |
| 1988 | Steffi Graf | Gabriela Sabatini | 6-3, 3-6, 6-1 |
| 1989 | Steffi Graf | Martina Navratilova | 3-6, 6-4, 6-2 |

### United States Championship *(Cont.)*

| Year | Winner | Finalist | Score |
|---|---|---|---|
| 1990 | Gabriela Sabatini | Steffi Graf | 6-2, 7-6 |
| 1991 | Monica Seles | Martina Navratilova | 7-6, 6-1 |
| 1992 | Monica Seles | Arantxa Sanchez Vicario | 6-3, 6-2 |
| 1993 | Steffi Graf | Helena Sukova | 6-3, 6-3 |
| 1994 | Arantxa Sanchez Vicario | Steffi Graf | 1-6, 7-6 (7-3), 6-4 |
| 1995 | Steffi Graf | Monica Seles | 7-6 (8-6), 0-6, 6-3 |

*Became Open (amateur and professional) in 1968; †Challenge round abolished.
‡National Patriotic Tournament; #Amateur event held; **Five-set final abolished.

## Grand Slams

### Singles

Don Budge, 1938
Maureen Connolly, 1953
Rod Laver, 1962, 1969
Margaret Smith Court, 1970
Steffi Graf, 1988

### Doubles

Frank Sedgman and Ken McGregor, 1951
Martina Navratilova and Pam Shriver, 1984
Maria Bueno and two partners: Christine Truman
    (Australian), Darlene Hard (French, Wimbledon
    and U.S. Championships), 1960

### Mixed Doubles

Margaret Smith and Ken Fletcher, 1963
Owen Davidson and two partners: Lesley Turner
    (Australian), Billie Jean King (French, Wimbledon
    and U.S. Championships), 1967

## The Alltime Grand Slam Champions

### MEN

| Player | Aus. S-D-M | French S-D-M | Wim. S-D-M | U.S. S-D-M | Total |
|---|---|---|---|---|---|
| Roy Emerson | 6-3-0 | 2-6-0 | 2-3-0 | 2-4-0 | 28 |
| John Newcombe | 2-5-0 | 0-3-0 | 3-6-0 | 2-3-1 | 25 |
| Frank Sedgman | 2-2-2 | 0-2-2 | 1-3-2 | 2-2-2 | 22 |
| Bill Tilden | * | 0-0-1 | 3-1-0 | 7-5-4 | 21 |
| Rod Laver | 3-4-0 | 2-1-1 | 4-1-2 | 2-0-0 | 20 |
| John Bromwich | 2-8-1 | 0-0-0 | 0-2-2 | 0-3-1 | 19 |
| Jean Borotra | 1-1-1 | 1-5-2 | 2-3-1 | 0-0-1 | 18 |
| Fred Stolle | 0-3-1 | 1-2-0 | 0-2-3 | 1-3-2 | 18 |
| Ken Rosewall | 4-3-0 | 2-2-0 | 0-2-0 | 2-2-1 | 18 |
| Neale Fraser | 0-3-1 | 0-3-0 | 1-2-0 | 2-3-3 | 18 |
| Adrian Quist | 3-10-0 | 0-1-0 | 0-2-0 | 0-1-0 | 17 |
| John McEnroe | 0-0-0 | 0-0-1 | 3-4-0 | 4-5-0 | 17 |
| Jack Crawford | 4-4-3 | 1-1-1 | 1-1-1 | 0-0-0 | 17 |

### WOMEN

| Player | Aus. S-D-M | French S-D-M | Wim. S-D-M | U.S. S-D-M | Total |
|---|---|---|---|---|---|
| Margaret Court | 11-8-2 | 5-4-4 | 3-2-5 | 7-7-8 | 66 |
| Martina Navratilova | 3-8-0 | 2-7-2 | 9-7-3 | 4-9-2 | 56 |
| Billie Jean King | 1-0-1 | 1-1-2 | 6-10-4 | 4-5-4 | 39 |
| Margaret duPont | * | 2-3-0 | 1-5-1 | 3-13-9 | 37 |
| Louise Brough | 1-1-0 | 0-3-0 | 4-5-4 | 1-12-4 | 35 |
| Doris Hart | 1-1-2 | 2-5-3 | 1-4-5 | 2-4-5 | 35 |
| Helen Wills Moody | * | 4-2-0 | 8-3-1 | 7-4-2 | 31 |
| Elizabeth Ryan | * | 0-4-0 | 0-12-7 | 0-1-2 | 26 |
| Suzanne Lenglen | * | 6-2-2 | 6-6-3 | 0-0-0 | 25 |
| Pam Shriver | 0-7-0 | 0-4-1 | 0-5-0 | 0-5-0 | 22 |
| Chris Evert | 2-0-0 | 7-2-0 | 3-1-0 | 6-0-0 | 21 |
| Darlene Hard | * | 1-3-2 | 0-4-3 | 2-6-0 | 21 |
| Steffi Graf | 4-0-0 | 4-0-0 | 6-1-0 | 4-0-0 | 19 |
| Maria Bueno | 0-1-0 | 0-1-1 | 3-5-0 | 4-4-0 | 19 |
| Thelma Coyne Long | 2-12-4 | 0-0-1 | 0-0-0 | 0-0-0 | 19 |

*Did not compete.

## Davis Cup

Started in 1900 as the International Lawn Tennis Challenge Trophy by America's Dwight Davis, the runner-up in the 1898 U.S. Championships. A Davis Cup meeting between two countries is known as a tie and is a three-day event consisting of two singles matches, followed by one doubles match and then two more singles matches. The United States boasts the greatest number of wins (30), followed by Australia (20).

| Year | Winner | Finalist | Site | Score |
|---|---|---|---|---|
| 1900 | United States | Great Britain | Boston | 3-0 |
| 1901 | No tournament | | | |
| 1902 | United States | Great Britain | New York | 3-2 |
| 1903 | Great Britain | United States | Boston | 4-1 |
| 1904 | Great Britain | Belgium | Wimbledon | 5-0 |
| 1905 | Great Britain | United States | Wimbledon | 5-0 |
| 1906 | Great Britain | United States | Wimbledon | 5-0 |
| 1907 | Australasia | Great Britain | Wimbledon | 3-2 |
| 1908 | Australasia | United States | Melbourne | 3-2 |
| 1909 | Australasia | United States | Sydney | 5-0 |
| 1910 | No tournament | | | |
| 1911 | Australasia | United States | Christchurch, NZ | 5-0 |
| 1912 | Great Britain | Australasia | Melbourne | 3-2 |
| 1913 | United States | Great Britain | Wimbledon | 3-2 |
| 1914 | Australasia | United States | New York | 3-2 |
| 1915-18 | No tournament | | | |
| 1919 | Australasia | Great Britain | Sydney | 4-1 |
| 1920 | United States | Australasia | Auckland, NZ | 5-0 |
| 1921 | United States | Japan | New York | 5-0 |
| 1922 | United States | Australasia | New York | 4-1 |
| 1923 | United States | Australasia | New York | 4-1 |
| 1924 | United States | Australia | Philadelphia | 5-0 |
| 1925 | United States | France | Philadelphia | 5-0 |
| 1926 | United States | France | Philadelphia | 4-1 |
| 1927 | France | United States | Philadelphia | 3-2 |
| 1928 | France | United States | Paris | 4-1 |
| 1929 | France | United States | Paris | 3-2 |
| 1930 | France | United States | Paris | 4-1 |
| 1931 | France | Great Britain | Paris | 3-2 |
| 1932 | France | United States | Paris | 3-2 |
| 1933 | Great Britain | France | Paris | 3-2 |
| 1934 | Great Britain | United States | Wimbledon | 4-1 |
| 1935 | Great Britain | United States | Wimbledon | 5-0 |
| 1936 | Great Britain | Australia | Wimbledon | 3-2 |
| 1937 | United States | Great Britain | Wimbledon | 4-1 |
| 1938 | United States | Australia | Philadelphia | 3-2 |
| 1939 | Australia | United States | Philadelphia | 3-2 |
| 1940-45 | No tournament | | | |
| 1946 | United States | Australia | Melbourne | 5-0 |
| 1947 | United States | Australia | New York | 4-1 |
| 1948 | United States | Australia | New York | 5-0 |
| 1949 | United States | Australia | New York | 4-1 |
| 1950 | Australia | United States | New York | 4-1 |
| 1951 | Australia | United States | Sydney | 3-2 |
| 1952 | Australia | United States | Adelaide | 4-1 |
| 1953 | Australia | United States | Melbourne | 3-2 |
| 1954 | United States | Australia | Sydney | 3-2 |
| 1955 | Australia | United States | New York | 5-0 |
| 1956 | Australia | United States | Adelaide | 5-0 |
| 1957 | Australia | United States | Melbourne | 3-2 |
| 1958 | United States | Australia | Brisbane | 3-2 |
| 1959 | Australia | United States | New York | 3-2 |
| 1960 | Australia | Italy | Sydney | 4-1 |
| 1961 | Australia | Italy | Melbourne | 5-0 |
| 1962 | Australia | Mexico | Brisbane | 5-0 |
| 1963 | United States | Australia | Adelaide | 3-2 |
| 1964 | Australia | United States | Cleveland | 3-2 |
| 1965 | Australia | Spain | Sydney | 4-1 |
| 1966 | Australia | India | Melbourne | 4-1 |
| 1967 | Australia | Spain | Brisbane | 4-1 |
| 1968 | United States | Australia | Adelaide | 4-1 |
| 1969 | United States | Romania | Cleveland | 5-0 |

## Davis Cup *(Cont.)*

| Year | Winner | Finalist | Site | Score |
|------|--------|----------|------|-------|
| 1970 | United States | West Germany | Cleveland | 5-0 |
| 1971 | United States | Romania | Charlotte, NC | 3-2 |
| 1972 | United States | Romania | Bucharest | 3-2 |
| 1973 | Australia | United States | Cleveland | 5-0 |
| 1974 | South Africa | India | * | walkover |
| 1975 | Sweden | Czechoslovakia | Stockholm | 3-2 |
| 1976 | Italy | Chile | Santiago | 4-1 |
| 1977 | Australia | Italy | Sydney | 3-1 |
| 1978 | United States | Great Britain | Palm Springs | 4-1 |
| 1979 | United States | Italy | San Francisco | 5-0 |
| 1980 | Czechoslovakia | Italy | Prague | 4-1 |
| 1981 | United States | Argentina | Cincinnati | 3-1 |
| 1982 | United States | France | Grenoble | 4-1 |
| 1983 | Australia | Sweden | Melbourne | 3-2 |
| 1984 | Sweden | United States | Gothenburg | 4-1 |
| 1985 | Sweden | West Germany | Munich | 3-2 |
| 1986 | Australia | Sweden | Melbourne | 3-2 |
| 1987 | Sweden | India | Gothenburg | 5-0 |
| 1988 | West Germany | Sweden | Gothenburg | 4-1 |
| 1989 | West Germany | Sweden | Stuttgart | 3-2 |
| 1990 | United States | Australia | St Petersburg | 3-2 |
| 1991 | France | United States | Lyon | 3-1 |
| 1992 | United States | Switzerland | Fort Worth, TX | 3-1 |
| 1993 | Germany | Australia | Dusseldorf | 4-1 |
| 1994 | Sweden | Russia | Moscow | 4-1 |

*India refused to play the final in protest over South Africa's governmental policy of apartheid.
Note: Prior to 1972 the challenge-round system was in effect, with the previous year's winner "standing out" of the competition until the finals. A straight 16-nation tournament has been held since 1981.

## Federation Cup

The women's equivalent of the Davis Cup, this competition was started in 1963 by the International Lawn Tennis Federation (now the ITF). Unlike the Davis Cup, though, all entrants gather at one site at one time for a tournament that is concluded within one week. Matches consist of two singles and one doubles. The United States boasts the greatest number of wins (14), followed by Australia (7).

| Year | Winner | Finalist | Site | Score |
|------|--------|----------|------|-------|
| 1963 | United States | Australia | London | 2-1 |
| 1964 | Australia | United States | Philadelphia | 2-1 |
| 1965 | Australia | United States | Melbourne | 2-1 |
| 1966 | United States | West Germany | Turin | 3-0 |
| 1967 | United States | Great Britain | West Berlin | 2-0 |
| 1968 | Australia | Netherlands | Paris | 3-0 |
| 1969 | United States | Australia | Athens | 2-1 |
| 1970 | Australia | Great Britain | Freiburg | 3-0 |
| 1971 | Australia | Great Britain | Perth | 3-0 |
| 1972 | South Africa | Great Britain | Johannesburg | 2-1 |
| 1973 | Australia | South Africa | Bad Homburg | 3-0 |
| 1974 | Australia | United States | Naples | 2-1 |
| 1975 | Czechoslovakia | Australia | Aix-en-Provence | 3-0 |
| 1976 | United States | Australia | Philadelphia | 2-1 |
| 1977 | United States | Australia | Eastbourne | 2-1 |
| 1978 | United States | Australia | Melbourne | 2-1 |
| 1979 | United States | Australia | Madrid | 3-0 |
| 1980 | United States | Australia | West Berlin | 3-0 |
| 1981 | United States | Great Britain | Nagoya | 3-0 |
| 1982 | United States | West Germany | Santa Clara | 3-0 |
| 1983 | Czechoslovakia | West Germany | Zurich | 2-1 |
| 1984 | Czechoslovakia | Australia | Sao Paulo | 2-1 |
| 1985 | Czechoslovakia | United States | Tokyo | 2-1 |
| 1986 | United States | Czechoslovakia | Prague | 3-0 |
| 1987 | West Germany | United States | Vancouver | 2-1 |
| 1988 | Czechoslovakia | USSR | Melbourne | 2-1 |
| 1989 | United States | Spain | Tokyo | 3-0 |
| 1990 | United States | USSR | Atlanta | 2-1 |
| 1991 | Spain | United States | Nottingham | 2-1 |

## Federation Cup *(Cont.)*

| Year | Winner | Finalist | Site | Score |
|------|--------|----------|------|-------|
| 1992 | Germany | Spain | Frankfurt | 2-1 |
| 1993 | Spain | Australia | Frankfurt | 3-0 |
| 1994 | Spain | United States | Frankfurt | 3-0 |

# Rankings

## ATP Computer Year-End Top 10

**1973**

Ilie Nastase
John Newcombe
Jimmy Connors
Tom Okker
Stan Smith
Ken Rosewall
Manuel Orantes
Rod Laver
Jan Kodes
Arthur Ashe

**1974**

Jimmy Connors
John Newcombe
Bjorn Borg
Rod Laver
Guillermo Vilas
Tom Okker
Arthur Ashe
Ken Rosewall
Stan Smith
Ilie Nastase

**1975**

Jimmy Connors
Guillermo Vilas
Bjorn Borg
Arthur Ashe
Manuel Orantes
Ken Rosewall
Ilie Nastase
John Alexander
Roscoe Tanner
Rod Laver

**1976**

Jimmy Connors
Bjorn Borg
Ilie Nastase
Manuel Orantes
Raul Ramirez
Guillermo Vilas
Adriano Panatta
Harold Solomon
Eddie Dibbs
Brian Gottfried

**1977**

Jimmy Connors
Guillermo Vilas
Bjorn Borg
Vitas Gerulaitis
Brian Gottfried
Eddie Dibbs
Manuel Orantes
Raul Ramirez
Ilie Nastase
Dick Stockton

**1978**

Jimmy Connors
Bjorn Borg
Guillermo Vilas
John McEnroe
Vitas Gerulaitis
Eddie Dibbs
Brian Gottfried
Raul Ramirez
Harold Solomon
Corrado Barazzutti

**1979**

Bjorn Borg
Jimmy Connors
John McEnroe
Vitas Gerulaitis
Roscoe Tanner
Guillermo Vilas
Arthur Ashe
Harold Solomon
Jose Higueras
Eddie Dibbs

**1980**

Bjorn Borg
John McEnroe
Jimmy Connors
Gene Mayer
Guillermo Vilas
Ivan Lendl
Harold Solomon
Jose-Luis Clerc
Vitas Gerulaitis
Eliot Teltscher

**1981**

John McEnroe
Ivan Lendl
Jimmy Connors
Bjorn Borg
Jose-Luis Clerc
Guillermo Vilas
Gene Mayer
Eliot Teltscher
Vitas Gerulaitis
Peter McNamara

**1982**

John McEnroe
Jimmy Connors
Ivan Lendl
Guillermo Vilas
Vitas Gerulaitis
Jose-Luis Clerc
Mats Wilander
Gene Mayer
Yannick Noah
Peter McNamara

**1983**

John McEnroe
Ivan Lendl
Jimmy Connors
Mats Wilander
Yannick Noah
Jimmy Arias
Jose Higueras
Jose-Luis Clerc
Kevin Curren
Gene Mayer

**1984**

John McEnroe
Jimmy Connors
Ivan Lendl
Mats Wilander
Andres Gomez
Anders Jarryd
Henrik Sundstrom
Pat Cash
Eliot Teltscher
Yannick Noah

## ATP Computer Year-End Top 10 (Cont.)

### 1985

Ivan Lendl
John McEnroe
Mats Wilander
Jimmy Connors
Stefan Edberg
Boris Becker
Yannick Noah
Anders Jarryd
Miloslav Mecir
Kevin Curren

### 1986

Ivan Lendl
Boris Becker
Mats Wilander
Yannick Noah
Stefan Edberg
Henri Leconte
Joakim Nystrom
Jimmy Connors
Miloslav Mecir
Andres Gomez

### 1987

Ivan Lendl
Stefan Edberg
Mats Wilander
Jimmy Connors
Boris Becker
Miloslav Mecir
Pat Cash
Yannick Noah
Tim Mayotte
John McEnroe

### 1988

Mats Wilander
Ivan Lendl
Andre Agassi
Boris Becker
Stefan Edberg
Kent Carlsson
Jimmy Connors
Jakob Hlasek
Henri Leconte
Tim Mayotte

### 1989

Ivan Lendl
Boris Becker
Stefan Edberg
John McEnroe
Michael Chang
Brad Gilbert
Andre Agassi
Aaron Krickstein
Alberto Mancini
Jay Berger

### 1990

Stefan Edberg
Boris Becker
Ivan Lendl
Andre Agassi
Pete Sampras
Andres Gomez
Thomas Muster
Emilio Sanchez
Goran Ivanisevic
Brad Gilbert

### 1991

Stefan Edberg
Jim Courier
Boris Becker
Michael Stich
Ivan Lendl
Pete Sampras
Guy Forget
Karel Novacek
Petr Korda
Andre Agassi

### 1992

Jim Courier
Stefan Edberg
Pete Sampras
Goran Ivanisevic
Boris Becker
Michael Chang
Petr Korda
Ivan Lendl
Andre Agassi
Richard Krajicek

### 1993

Pete Sampras
Michael Stich
Jim Courier
Sergi Bruguera
Stefan Edberg
Andrei Medvedev
Goran Ivanisevic
Michael Chang
Thomas Muster
Cedric Pioline

### 1994

Pete Sampras
Andre Agassi
Boris Becker
Sergi Bruguera
Goran Ivanisevic
Michael Chang
Stefan Edberg
Alberto Berasategui
Michael Stich
Todd Martin

## WTA Computer Year-End Top 10

### 1973

Margaret Smith Court
Billie Jean King
Evonne Goolagong
Chris Evert
Rosie Casals
Virginia Wade
Kerry Reid
Nancy Gunter
Julie Heldman
Helga Masthoff

### 1974

Billie Jean King
Evonne Goolagong
Chris Evert
Virginia Wade
Julie Heldman
Rosie Casals
Kerry Reid
Olga Morozova
Lesley Hunt
Francoise Durr

### 1975

Chris Evert
Billie Jean King
Evonne Goolagong Cawley
Martina Navratilova
Virginia Wade
Margaret Smith Court
Olga Morozova
Nancy Gunter
Francoise Durr
Rosie Casals

## WTA Computer Year-End Top 10 *(Cont.)*

### 1976

Chris Evert
Evonne Goolagong Cawley
Virginia Wade
Martina Navratilova
Sue Barker
Betty Stove
Dianne Balestrat
Mima Jausovec
Rosie Casals
Francoise Durr

### 1977

Chris Evert
Billie Jean King
Martina Navratilova
Virginia Wade
Sue Barker
Rosie Casals
Betty Stove
Dianne Balestrat
Wendy Turnbull
Kerry Reid

### 1978

Martina Navratilova
Chris Evert
Evonne Goolagong Cawley
Virginia Wade
Billie Jean King
Tracy Austin
Wendy Turnbull
Kerry Reid
Betty Stove
Dianne Balestrat

### 1979

Martina Navratilova
Chris Evert Lloyd
Tracy Austin
Evonne Goolagong Cawley
Billie Jean King
Dianne Balestrat
Wendy Turnbull
Virginia Wade
Kerry Reid
Sue Barker

### 1980

Chris Evert Lloyd
Tracy Austin
Martina Navratilova
Hana Mandlikova
Evonne Goolagong Cawley
Billie Jean King
Andrea Jaeger
Wendy Turnbull
Pam Shriver
Greer Stevens

### 1981

Chris Evert Lloyd
Tracy Austin
Martina Navratilova
Andrea Jaeger
Hana Mandlikova
Sylvia Hanika
Pam Shriver
Wendy Turnbull
Bettina Bunge
Barbara Potter

### 1982

Martina Navratilova
Chris Evert Lloyd
Andrea Jaeger
Tracy Austin
Wendy Turnbull
Pam Shriver
Hana Mandlikova
Barbara Potter
Bettina Bunge
Sylvia Hanika

### 1983

Martina Navratilova
Chris Evert Lloyd
Andrea Jaeger
Pam Shriver
Sylvia Hanika
Jo Durie
Bettina Bunge
Wendy Turnbull
Tracy Austin
Zina Garrison

### 1984

Martina Navratilova
Chris Evert Lloyd
Hana Mandlikova
Pam Shriver
Wendy Turnbull
Manuela Maleeva
Helena Sukova
Claudia Kohde-Kilsch
Zina Garrison
Kathy Jordan

### 1985

Martina Navratilova
Chris Evert Lloyd
Hana Mandlikova
Pam Shriver
Claudia Kohde-Kilsch
Steffi Graf
Manuela Maleeva
Zina Garrison
Helena Sukova
Bonnie Gadusek

### 1986

Martina Navratilova
Chris Evert Lloyd
Steffi Graf
Hana Mandlikova
Helena Sukova
Pam Shriver
Claudia Kohde-Kilsch
Manuela Maleeva
Kathy Rinaldi
Gabriela Sabatini

### 1987

Steffi Graf
Martina Navratilova
Chris Evert
Pam Shriver
Hana Mandlikova
Gabriela Sabatini
Helena Sukova
Manuela Maleeva
Zina Garrison
Claudia Kohde-Kilsch

### 1988

Steffi Graf
Martina Navratilova
Chris Evert
Gabriela Sabatini
Pam Shriver
Manuela Maleeva-Fragniere
Natalia Zvereva
Helena Sukova
Zina Garrison
Barbara Potter

### 1989

Steffi Graf
Martina Navratilova
Gabriela Sabatini
Zina Garrison
Arantxa Sanchez Vicario
Monica Seles
Conchita Martinez
Helena Sukova
Manuela Maleeva-Fragniere
*Chris Evert

### 1990

Steffi Graf
Monica Seles
Martina Navratilova
Mary Joe Fernandez
Gabriela Sabatini
Katerina Maleeva
Arantxa Sanchez Vicario
Jennifer Capriati
Manuela Maleeva-Fragniere
Zina Garrison

*When Chris Evert announced her retirement at the 1989 United States Open, she was ranked 4 in the world. That was her last official series tournament.

## WTA Computer Year-End Top 10 *(Cont.)*

**1991**

Monica Seles
Steffi Graf
Gabriela Sabatini
Martina Navratilova
Arantxa Sanchez Vicario
Jennifer Capriati
Jana Novotna
Mary Joe Fernandez
Conchita Martinez
Manuela Maleeva-Fragniere

**1992**

Monica Seles
Steffi Graf
Gabriela Sabatini
Arantxa Sanchez Vicario
Martina Navratilova

**1992** *(Cont.)*

Mary Joe Fernandez
Jennifer Capriati
Conchita Martinez
Manuela Maleeva-Fragniere
Jana Novotna

**1993**

Steffi Graf
Arantxa Sanchez Vicario
Martina Navratilova
Conchita Martinez
Gabriela Sabatini
Jana Novotna
Mary Joe Fernandez
Monica Seles
Jennifer Capriati
Anke Huber

**1994**

Steffi Graf
Arantxa Sanchez Vicario
Conchita Martinez
Jana Novotna
Mary Pierce
Lindsay Davenport
Gabriela Sabatini
Martina Navratilova
Kimiko Date
Natasha Zvereva

# Prize Money

### Top 25 Men's Career Prize Money Leaders

| | Earnings ($) |
|---|---|
| Ivan Lendl | 21,262,417 |
| Stefan Edberg | 19,454,364 |
| Pete Sampras | 18,165,028 |
| Boris Becker | 16,908,195 |
| John McEnroe | 12,539,622 |
| Michael Stich | 11,396,054 |
| Jim Courier | 11,259,456 |
| Andre Agassi | 10,580,446 |
| Michael Chang | 10,144,480 |
| Goran Ivanisevic | 8,905,815 |
| Jimmy Connors | 8,637,490 |
| Mats Wilander | 7,882,555 |
| Sergi Bruguera | 7,813,785 |
| Petr Korda | 6,666,315 |
| Thomas Muster | 5,797,718 |
| Brad Gilbert | 5,507,195 |
| Anders Jarryd | 5,294,669 |
| Emilio Sanchez | 5,112,671 |
| Guy Forget | 4,956,640 |
| Guillermo Vilas | 4,923,882 |
| David Wheaton | 4,693,789 |
| Jakob Hlasek | 4,544,512 |
| Andres Gomez | 4,384,725 |
| Mark Woodforde | 3,999,722 |
| Wayne Ferreira | 3,991,873 |

Note: From arrival of Open tennis in 1968 through October 9, 1995.

### Top 25 Women's Career Prize Money Leaders

| | Earnings ($) |
|---|---|
| Martina Navratilova | 20,337,902 |
| Steffi Graf | 16,530,040 |
| Arantxa Sanchez Vicario | 9,644,272 |
| Chris Evert | 8,896,195 |
| Gabriela Sabatini | 8,462,930 |
| Monica Seles | 7,805,991 |
| Helena Sukova | 5,447,678 |
| Pam Shriver | 5,363,285 |
| Conchita Martinez | 5,142,625 |
| Jana Novotna | 5,085,938 |
| Natasha Zvereva | 4,754,158 |
| Zina Garrison Jackson | 4,453,976 |
| Gigi Fernandez | 3,781,075 |
| Mary Joe Fernandez | 3,410,655 |
| Hana Mandlikova | 3,340,959 |
| Manuela Maleeva-Fragniere | 3,244,811 |
| Lori McNeil | 2,876,281 |
| Wendy Turnbull | 2,769,024 |
| Larisa Neiland | 2,768,276 |
| Claudia Kohde-Kilsch | 2,226,664 |
| Katerina Maleeva | 2,194,260 |
| Nathalie Tauziat | 2,108,099 |
| Mary Pierce | 2,096,510 |
| Tracy Austin | 1,992,380 |
| Billie Jean King | 1,966,487 |

Note: From arrival of Open tennis in 1968 through October 9, 1995.

## Dutch Treat

After an ATP tour event in Stuttgart in July, 19-year-old Marcelo Rios of Chile wanted nothing more than to board an airliner back to his homeland. But Rios, a lefty who climbed 55 places in the rankings in 1995, missed his flight to Santiago. Stuck on the Continent, he did his ponytail and earring proud by schlepping to Amsterdam. There he took a qualifier's berth in the $500,000 Netherlands International, played his way into the tournament's main draw with two victories and then won five straight matches, including the final over Jan Siemerink of Holland, 6-4, 7-5, 6-4. All of which made Rios, the first qualifier to win any event on the circuit since 1993, king of the ATP detour.

## Men's Career Leaders—Tournaments Won

The top tournament-winning men from the institution of Open tennis in 1968 through October 9, 1995.

| | W |
|---|---|
| Jimmy Connors | 109 |
| Ivan Lendl | 94 |
| John McEnroe | 77 |
| Bjorn Borg | 62 |
| Guillermo Vilas | 62 |
| Ilie Nastase | 57 |
| Rod Laver | 47 |
| Boris Becker | 43 |
| Stefan Edberg | 41 |
| Stan Smith | 39 |

| | W |
|---|---|
| Pete Sampras | 35 |
| Thomas Muster | 34 |
| Arthur Ashe | 33 |
| Mats Wilander | 33 |
| John Newcombe | 32 |
| Manuel Orantes | 32 |
| Ken Rosewall | 32 |
| Andre Agassi | 31 |
| Tom Okker | 31 |
| Vitas Gerulaitis | 27 |

## Women's Career Leaders—Tournaments Won

The top tournament-winning women from the institution of Open tennis in 1968 through October 9, 1995.

| | W |
|---|---|
| Martina Navratilova | 167 |
| Chris Evert | 157 |
| Steffi Graf | 93 |
| Evonne Goolagong Cawley | 88 |
| Margaret Court | 79 |
| Billie Jean King | 67 |
| Virginia Wade | 55 |
| Helga Masthoff | 37 |
| Monica Seles | 33 |
| Olga Morozova | 31 |

| | W |
|---|---|
| Conchita Martinez | 29 |
| Tracy Austin | 29 |
| Hana Mandlikova | 27 |
| Gabriela Sabatini | 27 |
| Nancy Richey | 25 |
| Arantxa Sanchez Vicario | 22 |
| Kerry Melville Reid | 22 |
| Sue Barker | 21 |
| Pam Shriver | 21 |
| Julie Heldman | 20 |

## Men's ATP Tour—World Championship

| Year | Player |
|---|---|
| 1970 | Stan Smith |
| 1971 | Ilie Nastase |
| 1972 | Ilie Nastase |
| 1973 | Ilie Nastase |
| 1974 | Guillermo Vilas |
| 1975 | Ilie Nastase |
| 1976 | Manuel Orantes |
| 1977 | Not held |
| 1978 | Jimmy Connors |
| 1979 | John McEnroe |
| 1980 | Bjorn Borg |
| 1981 | Bjorn Borg |

| Year | Player |
|---|---|
| 1982 | Ivan Lendl |
| 1983 | Ivan Lendl |
| 1984 | John McEnroe |
| 1985 | John McEnroe |
| 1986 | Ivan Lendl |
| 1986 | Ivan Lendl |
| 1987 | Ivan Lendl |
| 1988 | Boris Becker |
| 1989 | Stefan Edberg |
| 1990 | Andre Agassi |
| 1991 | Pete Sampras |
| 1992 | Boris Becker |
| 1993 | Michael Stich |
| 1994 | Pete Sampras |

Note: Event held twice in 1986.

# THEY SAID IT

*Goran Ivanisevic, the screwy, seventh-ranked tennis player from Croatia, on why he would never see a sports psychologist: "You lie on a couch, they take your money, and you walk out more bananas than when you walk in."*

## Annual ATP/WTA Champions *(Cont.)*

### Women—Virginia Slims Championship

| Year | Player | Year | Player |
|------|--------|------|--------|
| 1972 | Chris Evert | 1984 | Martina Navratilova |
| 1973 | Chris Evert | 1985 | Martina Navratilova |
| 1974 | Evonne Goolagong | 1986 | Martina Navratilova |
| 1975 | Chris Evert | 1986 | Martina Navratilova |
| 1976 | Evonne Goolagong | 1987 | Steffi Graf |
| 1977 | Chris Evert | 1988 | Gabriela Sabatini |
| 1978 | Martina Navratilova | 1989 | Steffi Graf |
| 1979 | Martina Navratilova | 1990 | Monica Seles |
| 1980 | Tracy Austin | 1991 | Monica Seles |
| 1981 | Martina Navratilova | 1992 | Monica Seles |
| 1982 | Sylvia Hanika | 1993 | Steffi Graf |
| 1983 | Martina Navratilova | 1994 | Gabriela Sabatini |

Note: Virginia Slims Championship held twice in 1986.

## The Tarango Fandango

*Senior writer Sally Jenkins reported from Wimbledon on tennis's new fun couple:*

It was the ugliest display in the history of ugly Americans at Wimbledon. What was Jeff Tarango's point when he walked off during his third-round match at the All-England Club? Either Tarango had uncovered a nasty bit of corruption in tennis (extremely unlikely) or he was pitching a Grand Slam tantrum (much more likely). A third possibility was that Tarango is "absolutely barking," as one Wimbledon official described him.

Whether Tarango acted out of conviction, meanness or lunacy doesn't really matter. And his penalty—some $15,000 in fines—was not stiff enough. There was no justification for the behavior of Tarango and his wife, Benedicte Carriere, who verbally (he) and physically (she) attacked chair umpire Bruno Rebeuh after Tarango defaulted his match against Alex Mronz over a disputed call.

The rantings of the couple recalled the worst excesses of Jim Pierce, the belligerent father of Mary Pierce, who was banned from the women's tour for erratic behavior that included attacking a spectator at the French Open. If it's good enough for Jim, it's good enough for Benedicte, who slapped Rebeuh after the match, an outrage for which Tarango refused to apologize. "Women are emotional," he said.

So, it seems, are men. In his post-tantrum press conference, Tarango, who is 26 and ranked 80th on the tour, accused Rebeuh of throwing matches to his favorite players. It was not the first time Tarango had made that serious charge, even though Rebeuh is, in fact, one of the most respected chair umpires. Anyway, claiming that a chair umpire, whose role during a match is more peacekeeper and scorekeeper than anything else, can determine the outcome of a match is rather like claiming that a third base ump can throw a baseball game.

There is much to suggest that Tarango is either spoiled, attention-hungry or a few sandwiches shy of a picnic basket. As an undergraduate at Stanford, he once dumped doubles partner David Wheaton out of a golf cart by careening wildly down a steep hill. In Tokyo in 1994 he dropped his shorts on the court during a match with Michael Chang. At the Lipton Championships in Key Biscayne, Fla., in March 1995, he slugged a ball in frustration, striking a ball girl.

It was telling that no players came to Tarango's defense after the incident at Wimbledon. Andre Agassi seemed to express the prevailing mood among his peers when he said Tarango deserves whatever he gets. Tarango has achieved the attention he apparently craves—so has his wife—but could never earn with his tennis. He still has not moved beyond the third round of a Grand Slam event. He has had his 15 minutes of fame. Now give him the hook.

# International Tennis Hall of Fame

Pauline Betz Addie (1965)
George T. Adee (1964)
Fred B. Alexander (1961)
Wilmer L. Allison (1963)
Manuel Alonso (1977)
Arthur Ashe (1985)
Juliette Atkinson (1974)
Tracy Austin (1992)
Lawrence A. Baker (1975)
Maud Barger-Wallach (1958)
Angela Mortimer Barrett (1993)
Karl Behr (1969)
Mallory Molla Bjurstedt (1958)
Bjorn Borg (1987)
Jean Borotra (1976)
Maureen Connolly Brinker(1968)
John Bromwich (1984)
Norman Everard Brookes (1977)
Mary K. Browne (1957)
Jacques Brugnon (1976)
J. Donald Budge (1964)
Maria E. Bueno (1978)
May Sutton Bundy (1956)
Mabel E. Cahill (1976)
Oliver S. Campbell (1955)
Malcom Chace (1961)
Dorothea Douglass Lambert
Chambers (1981)
Philippe Chatrier (1992)
Louise Brough Clapp (1967)
Clarence Clark (1983)
Joseph S. Clark (1955)
William J. Clothier (1956)
Henri Cochet (1976)
Bud Collins (1994)
Ashley Cooper (1991)
Margaret Smith Court (1979)
Gottfried von Cramm (1977)
John H. Crawford (1979)
Joseph F. Cullman III (1990)
Allison Danzig (1968)
Sarah Palfrey Danzig (1963)
Dwight F. Davis (1956)
Charlotte Dod (1983)
John H. Doeg (1962)
Laurie Doherty (1980)
Reggie Doherty (1980)
Jaroslav Drobny (1983)
Margaret Osborne duPont
(1967)
James Dwight (1955)
Roy Emerson (1982)
Pierre Etchebaster (1978)
Chris Evert (1995)
Robert Falkenburg (1974)
Neale Fraser (1984)
Charles S. Garland (1969)
Althea Gibson (1971)

Kathleen McKane Godfree
(1978)
Richard A. Gonzales (1968)
Evonne Goolagong Cawley
(1988)
Bryan M. Grant Jr (1972)
David Gray (1985)
Clarence Griffin (1970)
King Gustaf V of Sweden
(1980)
Harold H. Hackett (1961)
Ellen Forde Hansell (1965)
Darlene R. Hard (1973)
Doris J. Hart (1969)
Gladys M. Heldman (1979)
W. E. "Slew" Hester Jr (1981)
Bob Hewitt (1992)
Lew Hoad (1980)
Harry Hopman (1978)
Fred Hovey (1974)
Joseph R. Hunt (1966)
Lamar Hunt (1993)
Francis T. Hunter (1961)
Shirley Fry Irvin (1970)
Helen Hull Jacobs (1962)
William Johnston (1958)
Ann Haydon Jones (1985)
Perry Jones (1970)
Billie Jean King (1987)
Jan Kodes (1990)
John A. Kramer (1968)
Rene Lacoste (1976)
Al Laney (1979)
William A. Larned (1956)
Arthur D. Larsen (1969)
Rod G. Laver (1981)
Suzanne Lenglen (1978)
Dorothy Round Little (1986)
George M. Lott Jr (1964)
Gene Mako (1973)
Hana Mandlikova (1994)
Alice Marble (1964)
Alastair B. Martin (1973)
William McChesney Martin (1982)
Chuck McKinley (1986)
Maurice McLoughlin (1957)
Frew McMillan (1992)
W. Donald McNeill (1965)
Elisabeth H. Moore (1971)
Gardnar Mulloy (1972)
R. Lindley Murray (1958)
Julian S. Myrick (1963)
Ilie Nastase (1991)
John D. Newcombe (1986)
Arthur C. Nielsen Sr (1971)
Betty Nuthall (1977)
Alex Olmedo (1987)
Rafael Osuna (1979)

Mary Ewing Outerbridge (1981)
Frank A. Parker (1966)
Gerald Patterson (1989)
Budge Patty (1977)
Theodore R. Pell (1967)
Fred Perry (1975)
Tom Pettitt (1982)
Nicola Pietrangeli (1986)
Adrian Quist (1984)
Dennis Ralston (1987)
Ernest Renshaw (1983)
Willie Renshaw (1983)
Vincent Richards (1961)
Robert L. Riggs (1967)
Helen Wills Moody Roark
(1959)
Anthony D. Roche (1986)
Ellen C. Roosevelt (1975)
Ken Rosewall (1980)
Elizabeth Ryan (1972)
Manuel Santana (1984)
Richard Savitt (1976)
Frederick R. Schroeder (1966)
Eleonora Sears (1968)
Richard D. Sears (1955)
Frank Sedgman (1979)
Pancho Sogura (1984)
Vic Seixas Jr (1971)
Francis X. Shields (1964)
Henry W. Slocum Jr (1955)
Stan Smith (1987)
Fred Stolle (1985)
William F. Talbert (1967)
Bill Tilden (1959)
Lance Tingay (1982)
Ted Tinling (1986)
Bertha Townsend Toulmin
(1974)
Tony Trabert (1970)
James H. Van Alen (1965)
John Van Ryn (1963)
Guillermo Vilas (1991)
Ellsworth Vines (1962)
Virginia Wade (1989)
Marie Wagner (1969)
Holcombe Ward (1956)
Watson Washburn (1965)
Malcolm D. Whitman (1955)
Hazel Hotchkiss Wightman
(1957)
Anthony Wilding (1978)
Richard Norris Williams II
(1957)
Sidney B. Wood (1964)
Robert D. Wrenn (1955)
Beals C. Wright (1956)

Note: Years in parentheses are dates of induction.

# Golf

JULY 31, 1995 · $2.95 (CAN. $3.95)

Sports Illustrated

## LONG SHOT

Against all odds, John Daly powers his way to a dramatic British Open victory

JACQUELINE DUVOISIN

# Pleasant Surprises

## Expect the unexpected was the motto in a storybook season that produced a host of happy endings
## by Jaime Diaz

GOLF BEING as unpredictable as a California jury, there were plenty of surprises in 1995. The U.S. lost the Ryder Cup on home turf, Nick Price didn't win a single tournament after two years in which he won ten, and Greg Norman started beating people with the kind of you've-got-to-be-kidding shots that used to beat him.

But it was the particularly nice surprises at the biggest moments that made 1995 special. More than anything else it was a year of beautiful, improbable, perfect marriages of people and places.

Specifically the couplings of Ben Crenshaw and Augusta, Corey Pavin and Shinnecock Hills, John Daly and St. Andrews and Tiger Woods and Newport all possessed a lasting poetry. Respectively they gave us the most sentimental Masters ever, a centennial U.S. Open in which the game's most inventive shotmaker was given the perfect canvas to paint a masterpiece, a British Open in which the game's longest hitter was validated as much more in the cradle of golf, and a U.S. Amateur on a historic site that proved another giant step toward stardom for the greatest teenager ever to play.

All four of the winners were Americans, which represented the best collective performance by U.S. players in the major championships in this decade. Only Steve Elkington of Australia prevented a clean sweep when he won the PGA Championship at Riviera.

Outside the majors, however, 1995 was a great year for golfers from the rest of the world. That other Australian, Norman, was the dominating force on the PGA Tour, winning three times and leading the money list despite playing in only 15 official events. In each of his victories—Memorial, Hartford and the World Series of Golf—Norman holed a shot from off the green either late in the final nine or in sudden death to ice the win. Annika Sorenstam of Sweden won the U.S. Women's Open at the Broadmoor in Colorado Springs. Meanwhile, in team events, it was the U.S. that got swept. Besides the upset at the Ryder Cup, Americans were also beaten in the Walker and Curtis Cups, marking the first time teams from this country have ever lost all three of the biennial matches in one year.

The most romantic episode belonged to Crenshaw at the 59th Masters. At the age of 43, Crenshaw came to Augusta a much beloved but waning force. Of his 18 official career victories, it seemed a given that his crowning glory would always be his triumph in the 1984 Masters, where he had overcome his own emotional attachment to golf history to win on the course of his idol, Bobby Jones. Crenshaw is one of the most mercurial of golfers; his four victories in the 1990s proved that he could be formidable when on his game. But he has rarely been on, particularly in the major championships. More and more the abiding passion in Crenshaw's life seemed to be building golf courses rather than playing them.

But the magic Crenshaw caught at the Masters will take a place in the annals he loves. The Sunday before the first round, his lifelong teacher, Harvey Penick, died at the age of 90 after a long illness. Since giving a six-year-old Crenshaw his first lesson at the Austin Country Club, Penick had remained his counselor and touchstone, and Crenshaw was grief stricken at the loss.

Somehow the occasion also filled him with the resolve and control. He had seen Penick for the last time a week before his death, when the old teacher had a look at his putting grip and sent him on his way with a gentle admonition: "Just trust yourself." By the time Crenshaw returned to

**Norman won three of the 15 events he entered and topped the earnings list.**

Augusta after he and Tom Kite served as pallbearers at Penick's funeral on Wednesday, Crenshaw said, "It was kind of like I felt this hand on my shoulder, guiding me along." Said Crenshaw's wife, Julie, "There was a calmness to him all week that I have never seen before."

The final piece was put in place by Crenshaw's Augusta caddie, Carl Jackson, who on the practice tee on Tuesday quietly said, "Put the ball a little bit back in your stance, Ben." Instantly Crenshaw started hitting the ball solid and straight. "I've never had a confidence transformation like that in my life," he would say later.

Crenshaw played steadily for three rounds, tying Brian Henninger for the 54-hole lead at 10-under-par 206. On Sunday he was tied with Norman and Davis Love III, who were several groups ahead. But when Love bogeyed the 16th and Norman the 17th Crenshaw's putting, perhaps the best the game has ever seen, took over. He sank a 15-footer for birdie on the 13th, a five-footer for another on the 16th after a spectacular six-iron, and finally "an absolute perfect putt" on a left-to-right 13-footer at the 17th to take a two-stroke lead.

Crenshaw needed the cushion, because his composure started to crumble under

BOB MARTIN

Major, and it was starting to bug him. After surviving some scratchy play to salvage an opening two-over-par 72, he dug in and took what Shinnecock offered, which was precious few birdies. But after starting the final round three strokes behind Norman (that name again) and Tom Lehman, Pavin vaulted into contention with a birdie on the hellacious par-4 9th, got into a four-way tie with another at the 12th and took the lead for the first time by holing a eight-footer for a birdie on the 15th. Behind him Lehman, Norman and Bob Tway were limping home, but Pavin only led by one when he stepped up to the 450-yard 18th. He got his drive into the fairway and then came through with his epic approach.

"The ball was blocking out the flagstick, and I thought, Oh, man, that thing might go in," said Pavin, who along with joining the major-championship club at the age of 35 cemented his position as golf's toughest competitor. "It was probably the best shot I've hit under pressure."

Pavin's closing 68 gave him a total of even par 280, two better than Norman, who finished with a 73 that included, once again, a bogey on the 71st hole. It was Norman's seventh second-place finish in a major, six of which came after he led after three rounds.

"No, it never haunts me," he said. "I put myself in there with a chance to win more times than anybody else."

Perhaps, but what then of John Daly, a player who is almost never in there, and has now won the same number of majors—two—as Norman? Daly went to St. Andrews, and in perhaps the most surprising result in a major championship since, well, since Daly won the 1991 PGA, took home the claret jug in the 124th British Open.

The incongruity was this. The world's oldest championship, particularly when it is at St. Andrews, stands for subtlety, shot-making, keeping the ball close to the

the gathering emotion. In the end he had an 18-incher for a bogey to win, and when it went in, Crenshaw "let it all go" and collapsed into the most enduring pose of 1995. As Crenshaw wept, with his hands on his knees, unable to right himself, Jackson solemnly patted his charge on the back while repeating the words, "It's all right."

A profoundly moved Crenshaw was still in a daze an hour later. "I believe in fate," he said in his characteristically slow cadence. "I don't know how it happened. I don't." Pressed to hazard a guess, Crenshaw put a bow on the fairy tale. "I had the 15th club in my bag," he said, "and it was Harvey."

At the U.S. Open, Pavin only carried 14 clubs, but one of them was a four-wood. And with it he hit the shot of the year, a low draw from 228 yards on the 72nd hole, against a strong left-to-right wind, that stopped five feet from the cup.

As it turned out, Pavin didn't need the putt, which he missed, but his approach was a symbol of the grit and skill with which he tamed Shinnecock.

Coming into the Open, Pavin was carrying the label Best Player Never to Have Won a

ground, patience, discipline, judgment and character. Coming into the championship, Daly stood for Grip It and Rip It, impossibly high iron shots, rehabilitation clinics, parking lot fights, unsigned scorecards, fast food and bad hair. British bookmakers made him 66–1 to win.

"It's unbelievable," said Daly after defeating Costantino Rocca of Italy in a four-hole playoff. It is a standard answer to many questions, but this time he was right.

Actually Daly came to St. Andrews with both a preference for the Old Course and a plan. "I can't explain it, but there is just something about this course that I love," said Daly, who had fond memories of St. Andrews from the 1993 Dunhill Cup. It was a week in which Daly felt free from the mood swings and withdrawal symptoms he said had committed him to sobriety in late 1992. His mantra for the week was "Stay patient, and stay out of bunkers." His caddie, Greg Rita, also saw something special after Daly's opening 67 tied him for the first-round lead. "John can lose interest, but when he is focused, he is tough. In the hunt, he is focused."

Daly stayed in the hunt throughout, although howling winds sent him to a 73 on Saturday that put him four strokes off the 54-hole pace. But on Sunday, Daly showed that he is talented enough to adapt to any conditions and that while he may have a troubled head, he is driven by a stout heart.

That was never more true than after Daly lost a three-stroke lead with three holes to go by bogeying the 16th and 17th holes. He finished with a par on the 18th, and seemed to be the winner after Rocca chunked his short pitch to the home hole and saw his ball roll sickeningly into the Valley of Sin. Simply trying to two-putt the remaining 60 feet, Rocca made the most improbable shot of the year by holing out for a tying birdie. As the Auld Grey Toon went nuts, Rocca fell facedown on the ground, and Daly's mouth nearly dropped the same distance.

To his everlasting credit Daly regrouped and overwhelmed Rocca in the playoff, smashing his drives down the center and on the second playoff hole making a 30-footer for a birdie that put him up by two. When Rocca took three to get out of the Road Bunker on the next hole, while Daly parred, the final hole became a formality.

"I've come through an awful lot the past few years," said Daly. "I know one thing. There's no way I would be here today, holding this trophy, if I was still drinking."

The 19-year-old Woods may not have Daly's baggage, but he also impressed with his maturity and mastery at the Newport Country Club, a classic, links-style course that was the site of the first U.S. Amateur, in 1895. Woods, who had won three straight U.S. Junior Amateur crowns, took his second consecutive Amateur by defeating 43-year-old George (Buddy) Marucci of Berwyn, Pa., 2 up in the final. Once again, Woods demonstrated his flair for the dramatic. On the final hole, with Marucci within 20 feet for a birdie putt that could have sent the match into extra holes, Woods hit a controlled eight-iron from 140 yards to within two feet of the hole. It was just the kind of geared-down shot Woods has been working on with his teacher, Butch Harmon, and the fact that he had the confidence to try it and the skill to pull it off in the pressure-packed situation is just more evidence that the young man is the real deal.

The U.S. team could have used a tiger in its tank on the final day of the Ryder Cup at Oak Hill in Rochester, N.Y. This was the year that looked like a walkover for America, with the Europeans missing José María Olazábal, and the games of stalwarts like Seve Ballesteros, Ian Woosnam and even Nick Faldo in various stages of disrepair. Moreover, captain Lanny Wadkins had ordered that Oak Hill be set up like a U.S. Open, all the better to thwart the Europeans. The projected blowout seemed on target when, punctuated by Pavin's winning chip-in for birdie on the 18th hole of Saturday's final best-ball match, the U.S. took a 9–7 lead into the singles.

Only twice since 1957 had an American team been outscored in the Ryder Cup sin-

gles, so Sunday figured to be a pleasant formality for Wadkins's team. Instead, it turned into the most dramatic comeback—and most bitter defeat—in Ryder Cup history.

After going up 10–7 and needing only four more points in the remaining 11 matches to retain the cup, the Americans stalled. Five of the remaining matches went to the 18th hole, and the best the U.S. could do was get a half point in one of them. In the others, Peter Jacobsen, Brad Faxon, Curtis Strange and Jay Haas all lost one up.

Strange's match against Faldo was pivotal. The 40-year-old Virginian, who had been the most controversial of Wadkins's two wild-card picks because he is winless since the 1989 U.S. Open, stood one up on the 16th hole. He ended up losing when he missed a seven-foot putt on the final hole and Faldo holed from four feet.

The U.S. had a final chance to retain the Cup if Haas could salvage a tie with Philip Walton of Ireland, but after winning the 16th and 17th holes to get to one down on the 18th hole, Haas pulled his drive into the trees. When both men bogeyed, the cup that the U.S. had regained in 1991 was back in European hands by a score of 14½ to 13½. Just when it appeared that the golden days of the Ryder Cup might be over, the 1997 edition, to be played in Spain, promises to have more buildup than any since the 1991 War by the Shore at Kiawah Island.

## Woods established himself as among the greatest amateurs ever.

The main dramas should not obscure some notable achievements. On the Senior tour, some of the game's greatest names added to their vitae. Lee Trevino, coming back from a serious neck injury at 55, recorded his 25th career Senior victory, passing Miller Barber as the alltime leader in wins. Jack Nicklaus, also 55, won another Senior major, the Tradition, and was second in two events. Gary Player won at Lexington two months before his 60th birthday, and Arnold Palmer, who played in his final British Open, shot his age for the first time, during the third round of the Northwest Classic on Sept. 10, the day he turned 66.

It was an eventful year for women's golf, with LPGA commissioner Charlie Mechem stepping down after five years at the helm to make way for Jim Ritts. On the golf course, Betsy King finally made the LPGA Hall of Fame with her 30th win at the ShopRite LPGA Classic, leaving Amy Alcott and Beth Daniel on the bubble. Along with Open winner Sorenstam, the other bona fide young star on the tour, Kelly Robbins, won the McDonald's LPGA Championship, while the other two women's majors, the Nabisco Dinah Shore and the du Maurier Classic, were taken by surprise winners Nanci Bowen and Jenny Lidback.

On the amateur scene, 18-year-old Kelli Kuehne followed her victory in last year's U.S. Girls' Junior Amateur by winning the U.S. Women's Amateur at the Country Club in Brookline, Mass.

As the year came to a close, the Golf Channel, the first 24-hour network devoted solely to golf, was gaining a foothold in the cable universe. Meanwhile, the PGA Tour breathed a sigh when the Federal Trade Commission abruptly dropped its five-year investigation of the Tour for possible unreasonable restraint of competition. Considering that Tour commissioner Tim Finchem saw the investigation as a threat to the existence of the Tour, it was one more nice surprise in a year of particularly nice surprises.

# FOR THE RECORD·1994–1995

## The Masters

**Augusta National GC; Augusta, GA**
**(par 72; 6,925 yds) April 6-9**

| Player | Score | Earnings ($) |
|---|---|---|
| Ben Crenshaw | 70-67-69-68—274 | 396,000 |
| Davis Love III | 69-69-71-66—275 | 237,600 |
| Greg Norman | 73-68-68-68—277 | 127,600 |
| Jay Haas | 71-64-72-70—277 | 127,600 |
| David Frost | 66-71-71-71—279 | 83,600 |
| Steve Elkington | 73-67-67-72—279 | 83,600 |
| Phil Mickelson | 66-71-70-73—280 | 70,950 |
| Scott Hoch | 69-67-71-73—280 | 70,950 |
| Curtis Strange | 72-71-65-73—281 | 63,800 |
| Fred Couples | 71-69-67-75—282 | 57,200 |
| Brian Henninger | 70-68-68-76—282 | 57,200 |
| Kenny Perry | 73-70-71-69—283 | 48,400 |
| Lee Janzen | 69-69-74-71—283 | 48,400 |
| José María Olazábal | 66-74-72-72—284 | 39,600 |
| Tom Watson | 73-70-69-72—284 | 39,600 |
| Hale Irwin | 69-72-71-72—284 | 39,600 |
| Ian Woosnam | 69-72-71-73—285 | 28,786 |
| Raymond Floyd | 71-70-70-74—285 | 28,786 |
| Brad Faxon | 76-69-69-71—285 | 28,786 |
| Paul Azinger | 70-72-73-70—285 | 28,786 |
| Colin Montgomerie | 71-69-76-69—285 | 28,786 |
| Corey Pavin | 67-71-72-75—285 | 28,786 |
| John Huston | 70-66-72-77—285 | 28,786 |

## U.S. Open

**Shinnecock Hills GC; Southampton, N.Y.**
**(par 70; 6,944 yds) June 15-18**

| Player | Score | Earnings ($) |
|---|---|---|
| Corey Pavin | 72-69-71-68—280 | 350,000 |
| Greg Norman | 68-67-74-73—282 | 207,000 |
| Tom Lehman | 70-72-67-74—283 | 131,974 |
| Davis Love III | 72-68-73-71—284 | 66,634 |
| Phil Mickelson | 68-70-72-74—284 | 66,634 |
| Bill Glasson | 69-70-76-69—284 | 66,634 |
| Jay Haas | 70-73-72-69—284 | 66,634 |
| Neal Lancaster | 70-72-77-65—284 | 66,634 |
| Jeff Maggert | 69-72-77-66—284 | 66,634 |
| Frank Nobilo | 72-72-70-71—285 | 44,184 |
| Vijay Singh | 70-71-72-72—285 | 44,184 |
| Bob Tway | 69-69-72-75—285 | 44,184 |
| Nick Price | 66-73-73-74—286 | 30,934 |
| Steve Stricker | 71-70-71-74—286 | 30,934 |
| Mark McCumber | 70-71-77-68—286 | 30,934 |
| Duffy Waldorf | 72-70-75-69—286 | 30,934 |
| Brad Bryant | 71-75-70-70—286 | 30,934 |
| Jeff Sluman | 72-69-74-71—286 | 30,934 |
| Lee Janzen | 70-72-72-72—286 | 30,934 |
| Mark Roe | 71-69-74-72—286 | 30,934 |

## British Open

**Royal & Ancient; St Andrews, Scotland**
**(par 72; 6,933 yds) July 20-23**

| Player | Score | Earnings ($) |
|---|---|---|
| John Daly* | 67-71-73-71—282 | 200,000 |
| Costantino Rocca | 69-70-70-73—282 | 160,000 |
| Michael Campbell | 71-71-65-76—283 | 105,065 |
| Steven Bottomley | 70-72-72-69—283 | 105,065 |
| Mark Brooks | 70-69-73-71—283 | 105,065 |
| Vijay Singh | 68-72-73-71—284 | 64,800 |
| Steve Elkington | 72-69-69-74—284 | 64,000 |
| Corey Pavin | 69-70-72-74—285 | 53,333 |
| Bob Estes | 72-70-71-72—285 | 53,333 |
| Mark James | 72-75-68-70—285 | 53,333 |
| Payne Stewart | 72-68-75-71—286 | 41,600 |
| Ernie Els | 71-68-72-75—286 | 41,600 |
| Sam Torrance | 71-70-71-74—286 | 41,600 |
| Brett Ogle | 73-69-71-73—286 | 41,600 |
| Greg Norman | 71-74-72-70—287 | 29,120 |
| Ben Crenshaw | 67-72-76-72—287 | 29,120 |
| Brad Faxon | 71-67-75-74—287 | 29,120 |
| Robert Allenby | 71-74-71-71—287 | 29,120 |
| Per-Ulrick Johansson | 69-78-68-72—287 | 29,120 |
| David Duval | 71-75-70-72—288 | 21,600 |
| Peter Mitchell | 73-74-71-70—288 | 21,600 |
| Andrew Coltart | 70-74-71-73—288 | 21,600 |
| Barry Lane | 72-73-68-75—288 | 21,600 |

* won four-hole playoff

## PGA Championship

**Riviera CC; Pacific Palisades, CA**
**(par 71; 6,956 yds) August 10-13**

| Player | Score | Earnings ($) |
|---|---|---|
| Steve Elkington* | 68-67-68-64—267 | 360,000 |
| Colin Montgomerie | 68-67-67-65—267 | 216,000 |
| Ernie Els | 66-65-66-72—269 | 116,000 |
| Jeff Maggert | 66-69-65-69—269 | 116,000 |
| Brad Faxon | 70-67-71-63—271 | 80,000 |
| Mark O'Meara | 64-67-69-73—273 | 68,500 |
| Rob Estes | 69-68-68-68—273 | 68,500 |
| Craig Stadler | 71 66-66-71—274 | 50,000 |
| Steve Lowery | 69-68-68-69—274 | 50,000 |
| Justin Leonard | 68-66-70-70—274 | 50,000 |
| Jay Haas | 69-71-64-70—274 | 50,000 |
| Jeff Sluman | 69-67-68-70—274 | 50,000 |
| Payne Stewart | 69-70-69-67—275 | 33,750 |
| Kirk Triplett | 71-69-68-67—275 | 33,750 |
| Jim Furyk | 68-70-69-68—275 | 33,750 |
| Miguel Jimenez | 69-69-67-70—275 | 33,750 |
| Curtis Strange | 72-68-68-68—276 | 26,000 |
| Michael Campbell | 71-65-71-69—276 | 26,000 |
| Costantino Rocca | 70-69-68-69—276 | 26,000 |
| Jesper Parnevik | 69-69-70-69—277 | 21,000 |
| Greg Norman | 66-69-70-72—277 | 21,000 |
| Duffy Waldorf | 69-69-67-72—277 | 21,000 |

* won on first playoff hole

## Late 1994 PGA Tour Events

| Tournament | Final Round | Winner | Score/ Under Par | Earnings ($) |
|---|---|---|---|---|
| Kapalua International | Nov 6 | Fred Couples | 279/–13 | 180,000 |
| World Cup of Golf | Nov 13 | Fred Couples/Davis Love III | 536/–40 | 150,000 each |
| JC Penney Classic | Dec 4 | M. Figueras-Dotti/Brad Bryant**** | 262/–22 | 150,000 each |

## 1995 PGA Tour Events

| Tournament | Final Round | Winner | Score/ Under Par | Earnings ($) |
|---|---|---|---|---|
| Mercedes Championships | Jan 8 | Steve Elkington** | 278/–10 | 180,000 |
| Hawaiian Open | Jan 15 | John Morse | 269/–19 | 216,000 |
| Northern Telecom Open | Jan 23 | Phil Mickelson | 269/–18 | 225,000 |
| Phoenix Open | Jan 29 | Vijay Singh | 269/–15 | 234,000 |
| AT&T Pebble Beach National Pro-Am | Feb 5 | Peter Jacobsen | 271/–17 | 252,000 |
| Buick Invitational | Feb 12 | Peter Jacobsen | 269/–19 | 216,000 |
| Bob Hope Classic | Feb 19 | Kenny Perry | 335/–25 | 216,000 |
| Los Angeles Open | Feb 26 | Corey Pavin | 268/–16 | 216,000 |
| Doral Open | Mar 5 | Nick Faldo | 273/–15 | 270,000 |
| Honda Classic | Mar 12 | Mark O'Meara | 275/–9 | 216,000 |
| Nestle Invitational | Mar 19 | Loren Roberts | 272/–16 | 216,000 |
| The Players Championship | Mar 26 | Lee Janzen | 283/–5 | 540,000 |
| Freeport-McMoran Classic | Apr 2 | Davis Love III** | 274/–14 | 216,000 |
| The Masters | Apr 9 | Ben Crenshaw | 274/–14 | 396,000 |
| MCI Classic | Apr 16 | Bob Tway ** | 275/–9 | 234,000 |
| Greater Greensboro Open | Apr 23 | Jim Gallagher Jr | 274/–14 | 270,000 |
| Houston Open | Apr 30 | Payne Stewart* | 276/–12 | 252,000 |
| BellSouth Classic | May 7 | Mark Calcavecchia | 271/–17 | 234,000 |
| Byron Nelson Classic | May 14 | Ernie Els | 263/–17 | 234,000 |
| Buick Classic | May 21 | Vijay Singh***** | 278/–6 | 216,000 |
| Colonial Invitation | May 28 | Tom Lehman | 271/–9 | 252,000 |
| The Memorial | June 4 | Greg Norman | 269/–19 | 306,000 |
| Kemper Open | June 11 | Lee Janzen * | 272/–12 | 252,000 |
| U.S. Open | June 18 | Corey Pavin | 280/even | 350,000 |
| Greater Hartford Open | June 25 | Greg Norman | 267/–13 | 216,000 |
| St. Jude Classic | July 2 | Jim Gallagher Jr | 267/–17 | 225,000 |
| Western Open | July 9 | Billy Mayfair | 279/–9 | 360,000 |
| Anheuser-Busch Classic | July 16 | Ted Tryba | 272/–12 | 198,200 |
| British Open | July 23 | John Daly@ | 282/–6 | 200,000 |
| Deposit Guaranty Classic | July 23 | Ed Dougherty | 282/–16 | 126,000 |
| Ideon Classic | July 30 | Fred Funk | 268/–16 | 180,000 |
| Buick Open | Aug 6 | Woody Austin** | 270/–18 | 216,000 |
| PGA Championship | Aug 13 | Steve Elkington* | 267/–17 | 360,000 |
| The International | Aug 20 | Lee Janzen | +34 ‡ | 270,000 |
| World Series of Golf | Aug 27 | Greg Norman* | 278/–2 | 360,000 |
| Greater Milwaukee Open | Sept 3 | Scott Hoch | 269/–15 | 180,000 |
| Canadian Open | Sept 10 | Mark O'Meara | 274/–14 | 234,000 |
| B.C. Open | Sept 17 | Hal Sutton | 269/–15 | 180,000 |
| Quad City Open # | Sept 24 | D.A. Weibring | 197/–13 | 180,000 |
| Buick Challenge | Oct 1 | Fred Funk | 272/–16 | 180,000 |
| Disney World Classic # | Oct 8 | Brad Bryant | 198/–18 | 216,000 |
| Las Vegas Invitational | Oct 15 | Jim Furyk | 331/–28 | 270,000 |
| Texas Open | Oct 22 | Duffy Waldorf | 268/–20 | 198,000 |
| TOUR Championship | Oct 28 | Billy Mayfair | 280/even | 540,000 |

*Won on 1st playoff hole. **Won on 2nd playoff hole. ****Won on 4th playoff hole. *****Won on 5th playoff hole.
@ Won four-hole playoff. ‡Revised Stableford scoring.
#Tournament shortened by rain.

# Women's Majors

## Nabisco Dinah Shore

**Mission Hills CC; Rancho Mirage, CA**
**(par 72; 6,460 yds) March 23-26**

| Player | Score | Earnings ($) |
|---|---|---|
| Nanci Bowen | 69-75-71-70—285 | 127,500 |
| Susie Redman | 75-70-70-71—286 | 79,129 |
| Brandie Burton | 76-71-71-69—287 | 42,237 |
| Sherri Turner | 72-74-71-70—287 | 42,237 |
| Laura Davies | 75-69-70-73—287 | 42,237 |
| Nancy Lopez | 74-71-68-74—287 | 42,237 |
| Colleen Walker | 74-73-69-72—288 | 23,738 |
| Tammie Green | 71-70-70-77—288 | 23,738 |
| Dawn Coe-Jones | 71-75-71-72—289 | 20,103 |
| Caroline Pierce | 77-71-73-69—290 | 17,964 |
| Betsy King | 77-75-71-68—291 | 14,200 |
| Dottie Mochrie | 78-73-70-70—291 | 14,200 |
| Barb Mucha | 74-74-72-71—291 | 14,200 |
| Sandra Palmer | 72-73-74-72—291 | 14,200 |
| Debbie Massey | 71-75-72-73—291 | 14,200 |
| Alicia Dibos | 77-74-75-66—292 | 10,056 |
| Sherri Steinhauer | 78-74-72-68—292 | 10,056 |
| Alison Nicholas | 75-74-73-70—292 | 10,056 |
| Pat Bradley | 74-75-71-72—292 | 10,056 |
| Juli Inkster | 76-70-73-73—292 | 10,056 |
| Terry-Jo Myers | 77-68-73-74—292 | 10,056 |
| Michelle Estill | 72-72-74-74—292 | 10,056 |
| Meg Mallon | 74-72-71-75—292 | 10,056 |

## LPGA Championship

**DuPont Country Club; Wilmington, DE**
**(par 71; 6,386 yds) May 11-14**

| Player | Score | Earnings ($) |
|---|---|---|
| Kelly Robbins | 66-68-72-68—274 | 180,000 |
| Laura Davies | 68-68-69-70—275 | 111,711 |
| Julie Larsen | 71-68-69-71—280 | 65,416 |
| Marianne Morris | 67-71-70-72—280 | 65,416 |
| Patty Sheehan | 67-68-72-73—280 | 65,416 |
| Barb Thomas | 70-66-73-72—281 | 38,947 |
| Dottie Mochrie | 67-70-71-73—281 | 38,947 |
| Pat Bradley | 71-70-70-71—282 | 29,890 |
| Tammie Green | 69-72-70-71—282 | 29,890 |
| Annika Sorenstam | 71-71-72-69—283 | 25,362 |
| Kristi Albers | 71-71-72-70—284 | 20,681 |
| Dale Eggeling | 72-72-68-72—284 | 20,681 |
| Joan Pitcock | 75-66-71-72—284 | 20,681 |
| Betsy King | 69-71-72-72—284 | 20,681 |
| Lisa Kiggens | 70-70-75-70—285 | 16,504 |
| Meg Mallon | 70-72-71-72—285 | 16,504 |
| Barb Mucha | 71-69-71-74—285 | 16,504 |
| Beth Daniel | 71-73-72-70—286 | 13,080 |
| Nancy Scranton | 71-75-69-71—286 | 13,080 |
| Susie Redman | 73-71-71-71—286 | 13,080 |
| Lori Garbacz | 71-71-72-72—286 | 13,080 |
| Kris Tschetter | 73-69-71-73—286 | 13,080 |
| Nancy Lopez | 73-71-68-74—286 | 13,080 |
| Colleen Walker | 70-70-72-74—286 | 13,080 |
| Alison Finney | 71-68-70-77—286 | 13,080 |

## U.S. Women's Open

**Broadmoor GC, Colorado Springs, CO**
**(par 70; 6,398 yds) July 13-16**

| Player | Score | Earnings ($) |
|---|---|---|
| Annika Sorenstam | 67-71-72-68—278 | 175,000 |
| Meg Mallon | 70-69-66-74—279 | 103,500 |
| Betsy King | 72-69-72-67—280 | 56,238 |
| Pat Bradley | 67-71-72-70—280 | 56,238 |
| Leta Lindley | 70-68-74-69—281 | 35,285 |
| Rosie Jones | 69-70-70-72—281 | 35,285 |
| Tammie Green | 68-70-75-69—282 | 28,009 |
| Dawn Coe-Jones | 68-70-74-70—282 | 28,009 |
| Julie Larsen | 68-71-68-75—282 | 28,009 |
| Marianne Morris | 73-73-70-67—283 | 22,190 |
| Patty Sheehan | 70-73-71-69—283 | 22,190 |
| Val Skinner | 68-72-72-71—283 | 22,190 |
| Dottie Mochrie | 73-70-69-72—284 | 18,007 |
| Kris Tschetter | 68-74-69-73—284 | 18,007 |
| Kelly Robbins | 74-68-68-74—284 | 18,007 |
| Chris Johnson | 71-70-74-70—285 | 14,454 |
| Jill Briles-Hinton | 66-72-74-73—285 | 14,454 |
| Tania Abitol | 67-72-72-74—285 | 14,454 |
| Dale Eggeling | 70-68-73-74—285 | 14,454 |
| Michele Redman | 70-75-71-70—286 | 12,449 |
| Liselotte Neumann | 70-71-75-71—287 | 11,154 |
| Ayako Okamoto | 70-73-71-73—287 | 11,154 |
| Alice Ritzman | 75-69-69-74—287 | 11,154 |

## du Maurier Ltd. Classic

**Beaconsfield GC; Pointe-Claire, Quebec**
**(par 72; 6,261 yds) August 24-27**

| Player | Score | Earnings ($) |
|---|---|---|
| Jenny Lidback | 71-69-68-72—280 | 150,000 |
| Liselotte Neumann | 71-66-72-72—281 | 93,093 |
| Juli Inkster | 72-71-70-70—283 | 67,933 |
| Tammie Green | 75-71-68-70—284 | 52,837 |
| Betsy King | 76-70-67-72—285 | 38,998 |
| Jane Geddes | 71-73-69-72—285 | 38,998 |
| Michelle Estill | 73-77-69-67—286 | 27,928 |
| L. Rinker-Graham | 71-71-70-74—286 | 27,928 |
| Helen Alfredsson | 76-70-70-71—287 | 21,314 |
| D. Ammaccapane | 76-71-68-72—287 | 21,314 |
| Hollis Stacy | 73-73-69-72—287 | 21,314 |
| Dottie Mochrie | 74-73-72-69—288 | 16,136 |
| Meg Mallon | 73-72-73-70—288 | 16,136 |
| Val Skinner | 74-72-71-71—288 | 16,136 |
| Kris Tschetter | 75-70-71-72—288 | 16,136 |
| Rosie Jones | 79-70-73-67—289 | 13,369 |
| Joan Pitcock | 76-70-69-74—289 | 13,369 |
| Emilee Klein | 79-71-69-71—290 | 11,859 |
| Cindy Schreyer | 73-74-72-71—290 | 11,859 |
| H. Kobayashi | 76-70-72-72—290 | 11,859 |
| Dana Dormann | 74-72-72-72—290 | 11,859 |
| Cindy Rarick | 73-72-75-71—291 | 10,180 |
| Tracy Kerdyk | 76-72-71-72—291 | 10,180 |
| Patty Jordan | 72-72-74-73—291 | 10,180 |

# Women's Tour Results

## Late 1994 LPGA Tour Events

| Tournament | Final Round | Winner | Score/ Under Par | Earnings ($) |
|---|---|---|---|---|
| JC Penney Classic | Dec 4 | M. Figueras-Dotti/Brad Bryant**** | 262/-22 | 150,000 each |

## 1995 LPGA Tour Events

| Tournament | Final Round | Winner | Score/ Under Par | Earnings ($) |
|---|---|---|---|---|
| Tournament of Champions | Jan 15 | Dawn Coe-Jones | 281/-7 | 115,000 |
| HEALTHSOUTH Inaugural | Jan 22 | Pat Bradley | 211/-5 | 67,500 |
| Hawaiian Ladies Open | Feb 18 | Barb Thomas | 204/-12 | 82,500 |
| Ping/Welch's Championship | Mar 12 | Dottie Mochrie | 278/-10 | 67,500 |
| Standard Register/Ping | Mar 19 | Laura Davies | 280/-12 | 105,000 |
| Nabisco Dinah Shore | Mar 26 | Nanci Bowen | 285/-3 | 127,500 |
| Pinewild Women's Championship | Apr 16 | Rosie Jones * | 211/-5 | 97,500 |
| Chick-fil-A Charity Championship | Apr 23 | Laura Davies | 201/-15 | 75,000 |
| Spring Championship | Apr 30 | Val Skinner | 273/-15 | 180,000 |
| Sara Lee Classic | May 7 | Michelle McGann | 202/-14 | 78,750 |
| McDonald's LPGA Championship | May 14 | Kelly Robbins | 274/-10 | 180,000 |
| The Star Bank LPGA Classic | May 21 | Chris Johnson | 210/-6 | 75,000 |
| LPGA Corning Classic | May 28 | Alison Nicholas | 275/-13 | 82,500 |
| Oldsmobile Classic | June 4 | Dale Eggeling | 274/-14 | 90,000 |
| Edina Realty Classic | June 11 | Julie Larsen | 205/-11 | 75,000 |
| Rochester International | June 18 | Patty Sheehan | 278/-10 | 82,500 |
| ShopRite LPGA Classic | June 25 | Betsy King | 204/-9 | 97,500 |
| Youngstown-Warren LPGA Classic | July 2 | Michelle McGann *** | 205/-11 | 82,500 |
| Jamie Farr Toledo Classic | July 9 | Kathryn Marshall | 205/-8 | 75,000 |
| U.S. Women's Open | July 16 | Annika Sorenstam | 278/-2 | 175,000 |
| JAL Big Apple Classic | July 23 | Tracy Kerdyk | 273/-11 | 105,000 |
| Friendly's Classic | July 30 | Becky Iverson | 276/-12 | 75,000 |
| McCall's LPGA Classic | Aug 6 | Dottie Mochrie | 204/-12 | 75,000 |
| PING Welch's Championship | Aug 14 | Beth Daniel | 271/-17 | 67,500 |
| Weetabix Women's British Open | Aug 20 | Karrie Webb | 278/-14 | 92,400 |
| du Maurier Ltd. Classic | Aug 27 | Jenny Lidback | 280/-8 | 150,000 |
| LPGA Rail Classic | Sept 4 | Mary Beth Zimmerman ** | 206/-10 | 82,500 |
| Ping-AT&T LPGA Golf Championship | Sept 10 | Alison Nicholas | 207/-9 | 75,000 |
| Safeco Classic | Sept 17 | Patty Sheehan | 274/-14 | 75,000 |
| Heartland Classic | Sept 24 | Annika Sorenstam | 278/-10 | 78,750 |
| Fieldcrest Cannon Classic | Oct 1 | Gail Graham | 273/-15 | 75,000 |
| World Championship of Women's Golf | Oct 15 | Annika Sorenstam* | 282/-6 | 117,500 |

* Won on first hole of playoff. ** Won on second playoff hole. *** Won on third playoff hole.

# Senior Men's Tour Results

## Late 1994 Senior Tour Events

| Tournament | Final Round | Winner | Score/ Under Par | Earnings ($) |
|---|---|---|---|---|
| Maui Kaanapali Classic | Oct 30 | Bob Murphy | 197/-16 | 82,500 |
| Senior TOUR Championship | Nov 13 | Ray Floyd***** | 273/-15 | 240,000 |

## 1995 Senior Tour Events

| Tournament | Final Round | Winner | Score/ Under Par | Earnings ($) |
|---|---|---|---|---|
| Senior Tournament of Champions | Jan 15 | Jim Colbert*** | 209/-7 | 148,000 |
| Royal Caribbean Classic | Feb 5 | J.C. Snead* | 209/-4 | 127,500 |
| IntelliNet Challenge # | Feb 12 | Bob Murphy | 137/-7 | 90,000 |
| GTE Suncoast Classic | Feb 19 | Dave Stockton | 204/-9 | 112,500 |
| FHP Healthcare Classic | Mar 5 | Bruce Devlin | 130/-10 | 112,500 |
| The Dominion Seniors | Mar 12 | Jim Albus | 205/-11 | 97,500 |

## 1995 Senior Tour Events *(Cont.)*

| Tournament | Final Round | Winner | Score/Under Par | Earnings ($) |
|---|---|---|---|---|
| Toshiba Senior Classic | Mar 19 | George Archer | 199/–11 | 120,000 |
| The Tradition | Apr 2 | Jack Nicklaus*** | 276/–12 | 150,000 |
| PGA Seniors' Championship | Apr 16 | Ray Floyd | 277/–11 | 180,000 |
| Las Vegas Senior Classic | Apr 30 | Jim Colbert | 205/–11 | 150,000 |
| Paine Webber Invitational | May 7 | Bob Murphy | 203/–13 | 120,000 |
| Cadillac NFL Classic | May 14 | George Archer | 205/–11 | 142,500 |
| Bell Atlantic Classic | May 21 | Jim Colbert | 207/–3 | 135,000 |
| Quicksilver Classic | May 28 | Dave Stockton | 208/–8 | 165,000 |
| Bruno's Memorial Classic | June 4 | Graham Marsh | 201/–15 | 157,500 |
| BellSouth Senior Classic | June 11 | Jim Dent | 203/–13 | 165,000 |
| Dallas Reunion Pro Am | June 18 | Tom Wargo | 197/–13 | 82,500 |
| Nationwide Championship | June 25 | Bob Murphy | 203/–13 | 180,000 |
| U.S. Senior Open | July 2 | Tom Weiskopf | 275/–13 | 175,000 |
| Kroger Classic | July 9 | Mike Hill | 196/–17 | 135,000 |
| Ford Senior Players Championship | July 16 | J.C. Snead | 272/–16 | 225,000 |
| First of America Classic | July 23 | Jimmy Powell | 201/–15 | 105,000 |
| Ameritech Senior Open | July 30 | Hale Irwin | 195/–21 | 127,500 |
| VFW Senior Championship | Aug 6 | Bob Murphy | 195/–15 | 135,000 |
| Burnet Senior Classic | Aug 13 | Raymond Floyd | 201/–15 | 165,000 |
| Northville Long Island | Aug 20 | Lee Trevino | 202/–14 | 120,000 |
| Bank of Boston Senior Golf Classic | Aug 27 | Isao Aoki | 204/–12 | 120,000 |
| Franklin Quest Championship | Sept 3 | Tony Jacklin | 206/–10 | 90,000 |
| GTE Northwest Classic | Sept 10 | Walt Morgan | 203/–13 | 90,000 |
| Brickyard Crossing Championship | Sept 17 | Simon Hobday | 204/–12 | 112,500 |
| Bank One Classic | Sept 24 | Gary Player | 211/–5 | 90,000 |
| Vantage Championship | Oct 1 | Hale Irwin | 199/–17 | 225,000 |
| The Transamerica | Oct 8 | Lee Trevino | 201/–15 | 97,500 |
| Raley's Senior Gold Rush | Oct 15 | Don Bies | 205/–11 | 105,000 |
| Ralph's Senior Classic | Oct 22 | John Bland | 201/–12 | 120,000 |
| Kaanapali Classic | Oct 29 | Bob Charles*** | 204/–9 | 90,000 |

*Won on 1st playoff hole. *** Won on 3rd playoff hole. ***** Won on fifth playoff hole. # Tournament shortened by rain.

# Amateur Results

| Tournament | Final Round | Winner | Score | Runner-Up |
|---|---|---|---|---|
| Women's Amateur Public Links | June 25 | Jo Jo Robertson | 2 & 1 | Betsy Dramboar |
| Men's Amateur Public Links | July 22 | Chris Wollman | 4 & 3 | Bill Camping |
| Junior Amateur | July 29 | D. Scott Hailes | 1-up | James Driscoll |
| Girls' Junior | Aug 5 | Marcy Newton | 4 & 3 | Andrea Cordova |
| Women's Amateur | Aug 12 | Kelli Kuehne | 4 & 3 | Anne-Marie Knight |
| Men's Amateur | Aug 27 | Tiger Woods | 2 up | Buddy Marucci |
| Women's Mid-Amateur | Sept 23 | Ellen Port | 3 & 1 | Brenda Corrie-Kuehn |
| Men's Mid-Amateur | Sept 21 | Jerry Courville | 1-up | Warren Sye |
| Senior Women | Sept 15 | Jean Smith | 228 (+9) | Marlene Streit |
| Senior Men | Oct 2 | James Stahl Jr | 2 & 1 | Rennie Law |

# International Results

| Tournament | Final Round | Winner | Score | Runner-Up |
|---|---|---|---|---|
| Walker Cup | Sept 10 | GB/Ireland | 14–10 | United States |
| Ryder Cup | Sept 24 | Europe | 14½–13½ | United States |

## PGA Tour Final 1995 Money Leaders

| Name | Events | Best Finish | Scoring Average | Money ($) |
|---|---|---|---|---|
| Greg Norman | 16 | 1 (3) | 69.06 | 1,654,959 |
| Billy Mayfair | 28 | 1 (2) | 70.29 | 1,543,192 |
| Lee Janzen | 28 | 1 (3) | 70.58 | 1,378,966 |
| Corey Pavin | 22 | 1 (2) | 70.04 | 1,340,079 |
| Steve Elkington | 21 | 1 (2) | 69.59 | 1,254,352 |
| Davis Love III | 24 | 1 | 70.09 | 1,111,999 |
| Peter Jacobsen | 25 | 1 (2) | 70.03 | 1,075,057 |
| Jim Gallagher Jr | 27 | 1 (2) | 70.37 | 1,057,241 |
| Vijay Singh | 22 | 1 (2) | 69.92 | 1,018,713 |
| Mark O'Meara | 27 | 1 (2) | 70.25 | 914,129 |

## LPGA Tour Final 1994 Money Leaders

| Name | Events | Best Finish | Scoring Average | Money ($) |
|---|---|---|---|---|
| Laura Davies | 22 | 1 (3) | 70.91 | 687,201 |
| Beth Daniel | 25 | 1 (4) | 71.90 | 659,426 |
| Liselotte Neumann | 21 | 1 (3) | 71.46 | 505,701 |
| Dottie Mochrie | 27 | 1 | 70.98 | 472,728 |
| Donna Andrews | 23 | 1 (3) | 71.18 | 429,015 |
| Tammie Green | 24 | 1 | 72.09 | 418,969 |
| Sherri Steinhauer | 27 | 1 | 71.60 | 413,398 |
| Kelly Robbins | 25 | 1 | 71.74 | 396,778 |
| Betsy King | 27 | 2 (2) | 71.52 | 390,239 |
| Meg Mallon | 27 | 2 | 71.43 | 353,385 |

## Senior Tour Final 1994 Money Leaders

| Name | Events | Best Finish | Scoring Average | Money ($) |
|---|---|---|---|---|
| Dave Stockton | 32 | 1 (3) | 69.41 | 1,402,519 |
| Ray Floyd | 20 | 1 (4) | 69.08 | 1,382,762 |
| Jim Albus | 35 | 1 (2) | 69.85 | 1,237,128 |
| Lee Trevino | 23 | 1 (6) | 69.55 | 1,202,369 |
| Jim Colbert | 33 | 1 (2) | 70.15 | 1,012,115 |
| Tom Wargo | 36 | 1 | 69.88 | 1,005,344 |
| Jim Dent | 30 | 1 | 70.12 | 950,891 |
| Bob Murphy | 30 | 1 (2) | 70.15 | 855,862 |
| Larry Gilbert | 31 | 1 (2) | 70.44 | 848,544 |
| George Archer | 30 | 1 | 69.96 | 717,578 |

## Messing Links

At age 100 the Van Cortlandt Park golf course in the Bronx is the oldest public course in the country, but its most challenging feature has only recently been added. The 203-yard par-3 17th hole now confronts Gotham's golfers with a 20,000-cubic-yard stretch of garbage alongside the fairway. The junk hazard, made up mostly of construction debris illegally dumped by contractors over the past year, has altered the soil chemistry around the hole, killing off 96 trees. American Golf Corp., which runs Van Cortlandt, called the dumping "an error on the part of one of our middle managers" and has promised to restore the "integrity" of the hole. Then again, American Golf also runs the Pelham/Split Rock Golf Course elsewhere in the Bronx. That's where detectives from the city's auto crimes division recently unearthed a 1988 Honda buried near Pelham's 14th hole.

Who says you can't find a parking place in New York?

## Men's Golf

# THE MAJOR TOURNAMENTS
## The Masters

| Year | Winner | Score | Runner-Up |
|------|--------|-------|-----------|
| 1934 | Horton Smith | 284 | Craig Wood |
| 1935 | Gene Sarazen* (144) | 282 | Craig Wood (149) (only 36-hole playoff) |
| 1936 | Horton Smith | 285 | Harry Cooper |
| 1937 | Byron Nelson | 283 | Ralph Guldahl |
| 1938 | Henry Picard | 285 | Ralph Guldahl, Harry Cooper |
| 1939 | Ralph Guldahl | 279 | Sam Snead |
| 1940 | Jimmy Demaret | 280 | Lloyd Mangrum |
| 1941 | Craig Wood | 280 | Byron Nelson |
| 1942 | Byron Nelson* (69) | 280 | Ben Hogan (70) |
| 1943-45 | No tournament | | |
| 1946 | Herman Keiser | 282 | Ben Hogan |
| 1947 | Jimmy Demaret | 281 | Byron Nelson, Frank Stranahan |
| 1948 | Claude Harmon | 279 | Cary Middlecoff |
| 1949 | Sam Snead | 282 | Johnny Bulla, Lloyd Mangrum |
| 1950 | Jimmy Demaret | 283 | Jim Ferrier |
| 1951 | Ben Hogan | 280 | Skee Riegel |
| 1952 | Sam Snead | 286 | Jack Burke, Jr |
| 1953 | Ben Hogan | 274 | Ed Oliver, Jr |
| 1954 | Sam Snead* (70) | 289 | Ben Hogan (71) |
| 1955 | Cary Middlecoff | 279 | Ben Hogan |
| 1956 | Jack Burke, Jr | 289 | Ken Venturi |
| 1957 | Doug Ford | 282 | Sam Snead |
| 1958 | Arnold Palmer | 284 | Doug Ford, Fred Hawkins |
| 1959 | Art Wall, Jr | 284 | Cary Middlecoff |
| 1960 | Arnold Palmer | 282 | Ken Venturi |
| 1961 | Gary Player | 280 | Charles R. Coe, Arnold Palmer |
| 1962 | Arnold Palmer* (68) | 280 | Gary Player (71), Dow Finsterwald (77) |
| 1963 | Jack Nicklaus | 286 | Tony Lema |
| 1964 | Arnold Palmer | 276 | Dave Marr, Jack Nicklaus |
| 1965 | Jack Nicklaus | 271 | Arnold Palmer, Gary Player |
| 1966 | Jack Nicklaus* (70) | 288 | Tommy Jacobs (72), Gay Brewer, Jr (78) |
| 1967 | Gay Brewer, Jr | 280 | Bobby Nichols |
| 1968 | Bob Goalby | 277 | Roberto DeVicenzo |
| 1969 | George Archer | 281 | Billy Casper, George Knudson, Tom Weiskopf |
| 1970 | Billy Casper* (69) | 279 | Gene Littler (74) |
| 1971 | Charles Coody | 279 | Johnny Miller, Jack Nicklaus |
| 1972 | Jack Nicklaus | 286 | Bruce Crampton, Bobby Mitchell, Tom Weiskopf |
| 1973 | Tommy Aaron | 283 | J. C. Snead |
| 1974 | Gary Player | 278 | Tom Weiskopf, Dave Stockton |
| 1975 | Jack Nicklaus | 276 | Johnny Miller, Tom Weiskopf |
| 1976 | Ray Floyd | 271 | Ben Crenshaw |
| 1977 | Tom Watson | 276 | Jack Nicklaus |
| 1978 | Gary Player | 277 | Hubert Green, Rod Funseth, Tom Watson |
| 1979† | Fuzzy Zoeller* (4-3) | 280 | Ed Sneed (4-4), Tom Watson (4-4) |
| 1980 | Seve Ballesteros | 275 | Gibby Gilbert, Jack Newton |
| 1981 | Tom Watson | 280 | Johnny Miller, Jack Nicklaus |
| 1982 | Craig Stadler* (4) | 284 | Dan Pohl (5) |
| 1983 | Seve Ballesteros | 280 | Ben Crenshaw, Tom Kite |
| 1984 | Ben Crenshaw | 277 | Tom Watson |
| 1985 | Bernhard Langer | 282 | Curtis Strange, Seve Ballesteros, Ray Floyd |
| 1986 | Jack Nicklaus | 279 | Greg Norman, Tom Kite |
| 1987 | Larry Mize* (4-3) | 285 | Seve Ballesteros (5), Greg Norman (4-4) |
| 1988 | Sandy Lyle | 281 | Mark Calcavecchia |
| 1989 | Nick Faldo* (5-3) | 283 | Scott Hoch (5-4) |
| 1990 | Nick Faldo* (4-4) | 278 | Ray Floyd (4-x) |
| 1991 | Ian Woosnam | 277 | José María Olázabal |
| 1992 | Fred Couples | 275 | Ray Floyd |
| 1993 | Bernhard Langer | 277 | Chip Beck |
| 1994 | José María Olázabal | 279 | Tom Lehman |
| 1995 | Ben Crenshaw | 274 | Davis Love III |

*Winner in playoff. Playoff scores are in parentheses. †Playoff cut from 18 holes to sudden death.
Note: Played at Augusta National Golf Club, Augusta, GA.

## United States Open Championship

| Year | Winner | Score | Runner-Up | Site |
|---|---|---|---|---|
| 1895........Horace Rawlins | | †173 | Willie Dunn | Newport GC, Newport, RI |
| 1896........James Foulis | | †152 | Horace Rawlins | Shinnecock Hills GC, Southampton, NY |
| 1897........Joe Lloyd | | †162 | Willie Anderson | Chicago GC, Wheaton, IL |
| 1898........Fred Herd | | 328 | Alex Smith | Myopia Hunt Club, Hamilton, MA |
| 1899........Willie Smith | | 315 | George Low | Baltimore CC, Baltimore |
| | | | Val Fitzjohn | |
| | | | W. H. Way | |
| 1900........Harry Vardon | | 313 | John H. Taylor | Chicago GC, Wheaton, IL |
| 1901........Willie Anderson* (85) | | 331 | Alex Smith (86) | Myopia Hunt Club, Hamilton, MA |
| 1902........Laurie Auchterlonie | | 307 | Stewart Gardner | Garden City GC, Garden City, NY |
| 1903........Willie Anderson* (82) | | 307 | David Brown (84) | Baltusrol GC, Springfield, NJ |
| 1904........Willie Anderson | | 303 | Gil Nicholls | Glen View Club, Golf, IL |
| 1905........Willie Anderson | | 314 | Alex Smith | Myopia Hunt Club, Hamilton, MA |
| 1906........Alex Smith | | 295 | Willie Smith | Onwentsia Club, Lake Forest, IL |
| 1907........Alex Ross | | 302 | Gil Nicholls | Philadelphia Cricket Club, Chestnut Hill, PA |
| 1908........Fred McLeod* (77) | | 322 | Willie Smith (83) | Myopia Hunt Club, Hamilton, MA |
| 1909........George Sargent | | 290 | Tom McNamara | Englewood GC, Englewood, NJ |
| 1910........Alex Smith* (71) | | 298 | John McDermott (75) | Philadelphia Cricket Club, Chestnut Hill, PA |
| | | | Macdonald Smith (77) | |
| 1911........John McDermott* (80) | | 307 | Mike Brady (82) | Chicago GC, Wheaton, IL |
| | | | George Simpson (85) | |
| 1912........John McDermott | | 294 | Tom McNamara | CC of Buffalo, Buffalo |
| 1913........Francis Ouimet* (72) | | 304 | Harry Vardon (77) | The Country Club, Brookline, MA |
| | | | Edward Ray (78) | |
| 1914........Walter Hagen | | 290 | Chick Evans | Midlothian CC, Blue Island, IL |
| 1915........Jerry Travers | | 297 | Tom McNamara | Baltusrol GC, Springfield, NJ |
| 1916........Chick Evans | | 286 | Jock Hutchison | Minikahda Club, Minneapolis |
| 1917-18 ..No tournament | | | | |
| 1919........Walter Hagen* (77) | | 301 | Mike Brady (78) | Brae Burn CC, West Newton, MA |
| 1920........Edward Ray | | 295 | Harry Vardon | Inverness CC, Toledo |
| | | | Jack Burke | |
| | | | Leo Diegel | |
| | | | Jock Hutchison | |
| 1921........Jim Barnes | | 289 | Walter Hagen | Columbia CC, Chevy Chase, MD |
| | | | Fred McLeod | |
| 1922........Gene Sarazen | | 288 | John L. Black | Skokie CC, Glencoe, IL |
| | | | Bobby Jones | |
| 1923........Bobby Jones* (76) | | 296 | Bobby Cruickshank (78) | Inwood CC, Inwood, NY |
| 1924........Cyril Walker | | 297 | Bobby Jones | Oakland Hills CC, Birmingham, MI |
| 1925........W. MacFarlane* (75-72) | | 291 | Bobby Jones (75-73) | Worcester CC, Worcester, MA |
| 1926........Bobby Jones | | 293 | Joe Turnesa | Scioto CC, Columbus, OH |
| 1927........Tommy Armour* (76) | | 301 | Harry Cooper (79) | Oakmont CC, Oakmont, PA |
| 1928........Johnny Farrell* (143) | | 294 | Bobby Jones (144) | Olympia Fields CC, Matteson, IL |
| 1929........Bobby Jones* (141) | | 294 | Al Espinosa (164) | Winged Foot GC, Mamaroneck, NY |
| 1930........Bobby Jones | | 287 | Macdonald Smith | Interlachen CC, Hopkins, MN |
| 1931........Billy Burke* (149-148) | | 292 | George Von Elm | Inverness Club, Toledo |
| | | | (149-149) | |
| 1932........Gene Sarazen | | 286 | Phil Perkins | Fresh Meadows CC, Flushing, NY |
| | | | Bobby Cruickshank | |
| 1933........Johnny Goodman | | 287 | Ralph Guldahl | North Shore CC, Glenview, IL |
| 1934........Olin Dutra | | 293 | Gene Srazen | Merion Cricket Club, Ardmore, PA |
| 1935........Sam Parks, Jr | | 299 | Jimmy Thompson | Oakmont CC, Oakmont, PA |
| 1936........Tony Manero | | 282 | Harry Cooper | Baltusrol GC (Upper Course), Springfield, NJ |
| 1937........Ralph Guldahl | | 281 | Sam Snead | Oakland Hills CC, Birmingham, MI |
| 1938........Ralph Guldahl | | 284 | Dick Metz | Cherry Hills CC, Denver, CO |
| 1939........Byron Nelson* (68-70) | | 284 | Craig Wood (68-73) | Philadelphia CC, Philadelphia |
| | | | Denny Shute (76) | |
| 1940........Lawson Little* (70) | | 287 | Gene Sarazen (73) | Canterbury GC, Cleveland |
| 1941........Craig Wood | | 284 | Denny Shute | Colonial Club, Fort Worth |
| 1942-45 ..No tournament | | | | |
| 1946........Lloyd Mangrum* (72-72) | | 284 | Vic Ghezzi (72-73) | Canterbury GC, Cleveland |
| | | | Byron Nelson (72-73) | |
| 1947........Lew Worsham* (69) | | 282 | Sam Snead (70) | St Louis CC, Clayton, MO |
| 1948........Ben Hogan | | 276 | Jimmy Demaret | Riviera CC, Los Angeles |
| 1949........Cary Middlecoff | | 286 | Sam Snead | Medinah CC, Medinah, IL |
| | | | Clayton Heafner | |

## United States Open Championship (Cont.)

| Year | Winner | Score | Runner-Up | Site |
|------|--------|-------|-----------|------|
| 1950........ | Ben Hogan* (69) | 287 | Lloyd Mangrum (73) | Merion GC, Ardmore, PA |
| | | | George Fazio (75) | |
| 1951........ | Ben Hogan | 287 | Clayton Heafner | Oakland Hills CC, Birmingham, MI |
| 1952........ | Julius Boros | 281 | Ed Oliver | Northwood CC, Dallas |
| 1953........ | Ben Hogan | 283 | Sam Snead | Oakmont CC, Oakmont, PA |
| 1954........ | Ed Furgol | 284 | Gene Littler | Baltusrol GC (Lower Course), Springfield, NJ |
| 1955........ | Jack Fleck* (69) | 287 | Ben Hogan (72) | Olympic Club (Lake Course), San Francisco |
| 1956........ | Cary Middlecoff | 281 | Ben Hogan | Oak Hill CC, Rochester, NY |
| | | | Julius Boros | |
| 1957........ | Dick Mayer* (72) | 282 | Cary Middlecoff (79) | Inverness Club, Toledo |
| 1958........ | Tommy Bolt | 283 | Gary Player | Southern Hills CC, Tulsa |
| 1959........ | Billy Casper | 282 | Bob Rosburg | Winged Foot GC, Mamaroneck, NY |
| 1960........ | Arnold Palmer | 280 | Jack Nicklaus | Cherry Hills CC, Denver |
| 1961........ | Gene Littler | 281 | Bob Goalby | Oakland Hills CC, Birmingham, MI |
| | | | Doug Sanders | |
| 1962........ | Jack Nicklaus* (71) | 283 | Arnold Palmer (74) | Oakmont CC, Oakmont, PA |
| 1963........ | Julius Boros* (70) | 293 | Jacky Cupit (73) | The Country Club, Brookline, MA |
| | | | Arnold Palmer (76) | |
| 1964........ | Ken Venturi | 278 | Tommy Jacobs | Congressional CC, Washington, DC |
| 1965........ | Gary Player* (71) | 282 | Kel Nagle (74) | Bellerive CC, St Louis |
| 1966........ | Billy Casper* (69) | 278 | Arnold Palmer (73) | Olympic Club (Lake Course), San Francisco |
| 1967........ | Jack Nicklaus | 275 | Arnold Palmer | Baltusrol GC (Lower Course), Springfield, NJ |
| 1968........ | Lee Trevino | 275 | Jack Nicklaus | Oak Hill CC, Rochester, NY |
| 1969........ | Orville Moody | 281 | Deane Beman | Champions GC (Cypress Creek Course), |
| | | | Al Geiberger | Houston |
| | | | Bob Rosburg | |
| 1970........ | Tony Jacklin | 281 | Dave Hill | Hazeltine GC, Chaska, MN |
| 1971........ | Lee Trevino* (68) | 280 | Jack Nicklaus (71) | Merion GC (East Course), Ardmore, PA |
| 1972........ | Jack Nicklaus | 290 | Bruce Crampton | Pebble Beach GL, Pebble Beach, CA |
| 1973........ | Johnny Miller | 279 | John Schlee | Oakmont CC, Oakmont, PA |
| 1974........ | Hale Irwin | 287 | Forrest Fezler | Winged Foot GC, Mamaroneck, NY |
| 1975........ | Lou Graham* (71) | 287 | John Mahaffey (73) | Medinah CC, Medinah, IL |
| 1976........ | Jerry Pate | 277 | Tom Weiskopf | Atlanta Athletic Club, Duluth, GA |
| | | | Al Geiberger | |
| 1977........ | Hubert Green | 278 | Lou Graham | Southern Hills CC, Tulsa |
| 1978........ | Andy North | 285 | Dave Stockton | Cherry Hills CC, Denver |
| | | | J. C. Snead | |
| 1979........ | Hale Irwin | 284 | Gary Player | Inverness Club, Toledo |
| | | | Jerry Pate | |
| 1980........ | Jack Nicklaus | 272 | Isao Aoki | Baltusrol GC (Lower Course), Springfield, NJ |
| 1981........ | David Graham | 273 | George Burns | Merion GC, Ardmore, PA |
| | | | Bill Rogers | |
| 1982........ | Tom Watson | 282 | Jack Nicklaus | Pebble Beach GL, Pebble Beach, CA |
| 1983........ | Larry Nelson | 280 | Tom Watson | Oakmont CC, Oakmont, PA |
| 1984........ | Fuzzy Zoeller* (67) | 276 | Greg Norman (75) | Winged Foot GC, Mamaroneck, NY |
| 1985........ | Andy North | 279 | Dave Barr | Oakland Hills CC, Birmingham, MI |
| | | | T. C. Chen | |
| | | | Denis Watson | |
| 1986........ | Ray Floyd | 279 | Lanny Wadkins | Shinnecock Hills GC, Southampton, NY |
| | | | Chip Beck | |
| 1987........ | Scott Simpson | 277 | Tom Watson | Olympic Club (Lake Course), San Francisco |
| 1988........ | Curtis Strange* (71) | 278 | Nick Faldo (75) | The Country Club, Brookline, MA |
| 1989........ | Curtis Strange | 278 | Chip Beck | Oak Hill CC, Rochester, NY |
| | | | Mark McCumber | |
| | | | Ian Woosnam | |
| 1990........ | Hale Irwin* (74) (3) | 280 | Mike Donald (74) (4) | Medinah CC, Medinah, IL |
| 1991........ | Payne Stewart (75) | 282 | Scott Simpson (77) | Hazeltine GC, Chaska, MN |
| 1992........ | Tom Kite | 285 | Jeff Sluman | Pebble Beach GL, Pebble Beach, CA |
| 1993........ | Lee Janzen | 272 | Payne Stewart | Baltusrol GC, Springfield, NJ |
| 1994........ | Ernie Els* | 279 | Loren Roberts | Oakmont CC, Oakmont, PA |
| | | | Colin Montgomerie | |
| 1995........ | Corey Pavin | 280 | Greg Norman | Shinnecock Hills GC, Southampton, NY |

*Winner in playoff. Playoff scores are in parentheses. The 1990 playoff went to one hole of sudden death after an 18-hole playoff. In the 1994 playoff, Montgomerie was eliminated after 18 playoff holes, and Els beat Roberts on the 20th.
†Before 1898, 36 holes. From 1898 on, 72 holes.

# Men's Golf (Cont.)

## British Open

| Year | Winner | Score | Runner-Up | Site |
|---|---|---|---|---|
| 1860† | ........Willie Park | 174 | Tom Morris, Sr | Prestwick, Scotland |
| 1861‡ | ........Tom Morris, Sr | 163 | Willie Park | Prestwick, Scotland |
| 1862 | ..........Tom Morris, Sr | 163 | Willie Park | Prestwick, Scotland |
| 1863 | ..........Willie Park | 168 | Tom Morris, Sr | Prestwick, Scotland |
| 1864 | ..........Tom Morris, Sr | 160 | Andrew Strath | Prestwick, Scotland |
| 1865 | ..........Andrew Strath | 162 | Willie Park | Prestwick, Scotland |
| 1866 | ..........Willie Park | 169 | David Park | Prestwick, Scotland |
| 1867 | ..........Tom Morris, Sr | 170 | Willie Park | Prestwick, Scotland |
| 1868 | ..........Tom Morris, Jr | 154 | Tom Morris, Sr | Prestwick, Scotland |
| 1869 | ..........Tom Morris, Jr | 157 | Tom Morris, Sr | Prestwick, Scotland |
| 1870 | ..........Tom Morris, Jr | 149 | David Strath | Prestwick, Scotland |
|  |  |  | Bob Kirk |  |
| 1871 | ..........No tournament |  |  |  |
| 1872 | ..........Tom Morris, Jr | 166 | David Strath | Prestwick, Scotland |
| 1873 | ..........Tom Kidd | 179 | Jamie Anderson | St Andrews, Scotland |
| 1874 | ..........Mungo Park | 159 | No record | Musselburgh, Scotland |
| 1875 | ..........Willie Park | 166 | Bob Martin | Prestwick, Scotland |
| 1876 | ..........Bob Martin# | 176 | David Strath | St Andrews, Scotland |
| 1877 | ..........Jamie Anderson | 160 | Bob Pringle | Musselburgh, Scotland |
| 1878 | ..........Jamie Anderson | 157 | Robert Kirk | Prestwick, Scotland |
| 1879 | ..........Jamie Anderson | 169 | Andrew Kirkaldy | St Andrews, Scotland |
|  |  |  | James Allan |  |
| 1880 | ..........Robert Ferguson | 162 | No record | Musselburgh, Scotland |
| 1881 | ..........Robert Ferguson | 170 | Jamie Anderson | Prestwick, Scotland |
| 1882 | ..........Robert Ferguson | 171 | Willie Fernie | St Andrews, Scotland |
| 1883 | ..........Willie Fernie* | 159 | Robert Ferguson | Musselburgh, Scotland |
| 1884 | ..........Jack Simpson | 160 | Douglas Rolland | Prestwick, Scotland |
|  |  |  | Willie Fernie |  |
| 1885 | ..........Bob Martin | 171 | Archie Simpson | St Andrews, Scotland |
| 1886 | ..........David Brown | 157 | Willie Campbell | Musselburgh, Scotland |
| 1887 | ..........Willie Park, Jr | 161 | Bob Martin | Prestwick, Scotland |
| 1888 | ..........Jack Burns | 171 | Bernard Sayers | St Andrews, Scotland |
|  |  |  | David Anderson |  |
| 1889 | ..........Willie Park, Jr* (158) | 155 | Andrew Kirkaldy (163) | Musselburgh, Scotland |
| 1890 | ..........John Ball | 164 | Willie Fernie | Prestwick, Scotland |
| 1891 | ..........Hugh Kirkaldy | 166 | Andrew Kirkaldy | St Andrews, Scotland |
|  |  |  | Willie Fernie |  |
| 1892 | ..........Harold Hilton | **305 | John Ball | Muirfield, Scotland |
|  |  |  | Hugh Kirkaldy |  |
| 1893 | ..........William Auchterlonie | 322 | John E. Laidlay | Prestwick, Scotland |
| 1894 | ..........John H. Taylor | 326 | Douglas Rolland | Royal St George's, England |
| 1895 | ..........John H. Taylor | 322 | Alexander Herd | St Andrews, Scotland |
| 1896 | ..........Harry Vardon* (157) | 316 | John H. Taylor (161) | Muirfield, Scotland |
| 1897 | ..........Harold Hilton | 314 | James Braid | Hoylake, England |
| 1898 | ..........Harry Vardon | 307 | Willie Park, Jr | Prestwick, Scotland |
| 1899 | ..........Harry Vardon | 310 | Jack White | Royal St George's, England |
| 1900 | ..........John H. Taylor | 309 | Harry Vardon | St Andrews, Scotland |
| 1901 | ..........James Braid | 309 | Harry Vardon | Muirfield, Scotland |
| 1902 | ..........Alexander Herd | 307 | Harry Vardon | Hoylake, England |
| 1903 | ..........Harry Vardon | 300 | Tom Vardon | Prestwick, Scotland |
| 1904 | ..........Jack White | 296 | John H. Taylor | Royal St George's, England |
| 1905 | ..........James Braid | 318 | John H. Taylor | St Andrews, Scotland |
|  |  |  | Rolland Jones |  |
| 1906 | ..........James Braid | 300 | John H. Taylor | Muirfield, Scotland |
| 1907 | ..........Arnaud Massy | 312 | John H. Taylor | Hoylake, England |
| 1908 | ..........James Braid | 291 | Tom Ball | Prestwick, Scotland |
| 1909 | ..........John H. Taylor | 295 | James Braid | Deal, England |
|  |  |  | Tom Ball |  |
| 1910 | ..........James Braid | 299 | Alexander Herd | St Andrews, Scotland |
| 1911 | ..........Harry Vardon | 303 | Arnaud Massy | Royal St George's, England |
| 1912 | ..........Ted Ray | 295 | Harry Vardon | Muirfield, Scotland |
| 1913 | ..........John H. Taylor | 304 | Ted Ray | Hoylake, England |
| 1914 | ..........Harry Vardon | 306 | John H. Taylor | Prestwick, Scotland |
| 1915-19 | ......No tournament |  |  |  |
| 1920 | ..........George Duncan | 303 | Alexander Herd | Deal, England |
| 1921 | ..........Jock Hutchison* (150) | 296 | Roger Wethered (159) | St Andrews, Scotland |

## British Open (Cont.)

| Year | Winner | Score | Runner-Up | Site |
|------|--------|-------|-----------|------|
| 1922 | Walter Hagen | 300 | George Duncan Jim Barnes | Royal St George's, England |
| 1923 | Arthur G. Havers | 295 | Walter Hagen | Troon, Scotland |
| 1924 | Walter Hagen | 301 | Ernest Whitcombe | Hoylake, England |
| 1925 | Jim Barnes | 300 | Archie Compston Ted Ray | Prestwick, Scotland |
| 1926 | Bobby Jones | 291 | Al Watrous | Royal Lytham and St Annes GC, St Anne's-on-the-Sea, England |
| 1927 | Bobby Jones | 285 | Aubrey Boomer | St Andrews, Scotland |
| 1928 | Walter Hagen | 292 | Gene Sarazen | Royal St George's, England |
| 1929 | Walter Hagen | 292 | Johnny Farrell | Muirfield, Scotland |
| 1930 | Bobby Jones | 291 | Macdonald Smith Leo Diegel | Hoylake, England |
| 1931 | Tommy Armour | 296 | Jose Jurado | Carnoustie, Scotland |
| 1932 | Gene Sarazen | 283 | Macdonald Smith | Prince's, England |
| 1933 | Denny Shute* (149) | 292 | Craig Wood (154) | St Andrews, Scotland |
| 1934 | Henry Cotton | 283 | Sidney F. Brews | Royal St George's, England |
| 1935 | Alfred Perry | 283 | Alfred Padgham | Muirfield, Scotland |
| 1936 | Alfred Padgham | 287 | James Adams | Hoylake, England |
| 1937 | Henry Cotton | 290 | Reginald A. Whitcombe | Carnoustie, Scotland |
| 1938 | Reginald A. Whitcombe | 295 | James Adams | Royal St George's, England |
| 1939 | Richard Burton | 290 | Johnny Bulla | St Andrews, Scotland |
| 1940-45 | No tournament | | | |
| 1946 | Sam Snead | 290 | Bobby Locke Johnny Bulla | St Andrews, Scotland |
| 1947 | Fred Daly | 293 | Reginald W. Horne Frank Stranahan | Hoylake, England |
| 1948 | Henry Cotton | 294 | Fred Daly | Muirfield, Scotland |
| 1949 | Bobby Locke* (135) | 283 | Harry Bradshaw (147) | Royal St George's, England |
| 1950 | Bobby Locke | 279 | Roberto DeVicenzo | Troon, Scotland |
| 1951 | Max Faulkner | 285 | Tony Cerda | Portrush, Ireland |
| 1952 | Bobby Locke | 287 | Peter Thomson | Royal Lytham, England |
| 1953 | Ben Hogan | 282 | Frank Stranahan Dai Rees Peter Thomson Tony Cerda | Carnoustie, Scotland |
| 1954 | Peter Thomson | 283 | Sidney S. Scott Dai Rees Bobby Locke | Royal Birkdale, England |
| 1955 | Peter Thomson | 281 | John Fallon | St Andrews, Scotland |
| 1956 | Peter Thomson | 286 | Flory Van Donck | Hoylake, England |
| 1957 | Bobby Locke | 279 | Peter Thomson | St Andrews, Scotland |
| 1958 | Peter Thomson* (139) | 278 | Dave Thomas (143) | Royal Lytham, England |
| 1959 | Gary Player | 284 | Fred Bullock Flory Van Donck | Muirfield, Scotland |
| 1960 | Kel Nagle | 278 | Arnold Palmer | St Andrews, Scotland |
| 1961 | Arnold Palmer | 284 | Dai Rees | Royal Birkdale, England |
| 1962 | Arnold Palmer | 276 | Kel Nagle | Troon, Scotland |
| 1963 | Bob Charles* (140) | 277 | Phil Rodgers (148) | Royal Lytham, England |
| 1964 | Tony Lema | 279 | Jack Nicklaus | St Andrews, Scotland |
| 1965 | Peter Thomson | 285 | Brian Huggett Christy O'Connor | Southport, England |
| 1966 | Jack Nicklaus | 282 | Doug Sanders Dave Thomas | Muirfield, Scotland |
| 1967 | Robert DeVicenzo | 278 | Jack Nicklaus | Hoylake, England |
| 1968 | Gary Player | 289 | Jack Nicklaus Bob Charles | Carnoustie, Scotland |
| 1969 | Tony Jacklin | 280 | Bob Charles | Royal Lytham, England |
| 1970 | Jack Nicklaus* (72) | 283 | Doug Sanders (73) | St Andrews, Scotland |
| 1971 | Lee Trevino | 278 | Lu Liang Huan | Royal Birkdale, England |
| 1972 | Lee Trevino | 278 | Jack Nicklaus | Muirfield, Scotland |
| 1973 | Tom Weiskopf | 276 | Johnny Miller | Troon, Scotland |
| 1974 | Gary Player | 282 | Peter Oosterhuis | Royal Lytham, England |
| 1975 | Tom Watson* (71) | 279 | Jack Newton (72) | Carnoustie, Scotland |
| 1976 | Johnny Miller | 279 | Jack Nicklaus Seve Ballesteros | Royal Birkdale, England |

## British Open (Cont.)

| Year | Winner | Score | Runner-Up | Site |
|---|---|---|---|---|
| 1977 | Tom Watson | 268 | Jack Nicklaus | Turnberry, Scotland |
| 1978 | Jack Nicklaus | 281 | Ben Crenshaw | St Andrews, Scotland |
| | | | Tom Kite | |
| | | | Ray Floyd | |
| | | | Simon Owen | |
| 1979 | Seve Ballesteros | 283 | Ben Crenshaw | Royal Lytham, England |
| | | | Jack Nicklaus | |
| 1980 | Tom Watson | 271 | Lee Trevino | Muirfield, Scotland |
| 1981 | Bill Rogers | 276 | Bernhard Langer | Royal St George's, England |
| 1982 | Tom Watson | 284 | Nick Price | Royal Troon, Scotland |
| | | | Peter Oosterhuis | |
| 1983 | Tom Watson | 275 | Andy Bean | Royal Birkdale, England |
| 1984 | Seve Ballesteros | 276 | Tom Watson | St Andrews, Scotland |
| | | | Bernhard Langer | |
| 1985 | Sandy Lyle | 282 | Payne Stewart | Royal St George's, England |
| 1986 | Greg Norman | 280 | Gordon Brand | Turnberry, Scotland |
| 1987 | Nick Faldo | 279 | Paul Azinger | Muirfield, Scotland |
| | | | Rodger Davis | |
| 1988 | Seve Ballesteros | 273 | Nick Price | Royal Lytham, England |
| 1989†† | Mark Calcavecchia* | 275 | Wayne Grady (4-4-4-4) | Royal Troon, Scotland |
| | (4-3-3-3) | | Greg Norman (3-3-4-x) | |
| 1990 | Nick Faldo | 270 | Payne Stewart | St Andrews, Scotland |
| | | | Mark McNulty | |
| 1991 | Ian Baker-Finch | 272 | Mike Harwood | Royal Birkdale, England |
| 1992 | Nick Faldo | 272 | John Cook | Muirfield, Scotland |
| 1993 | Greg Norman | 267 | Nick Faldo | Royal St George's, England |
| 1994 | Nick Price | 268 | Jesper Parnevik | Turnberry, Scotland |
| 1995 | John Daly* (4-3-4-4) | 282 | C. Rocca (5-4-7-3) | St Andrews, Scotland |

*Winner in playoff. Playoff scores are in parentheses. †The first event was open only to professional golfers.
‡The second annual open was open to amateurs and pros. #Tied, but refused playoff.
**Championship extended from 36 to 72 holes. ††Playoff cut from 18 holes to 4 holes.

## PGA Championship

| Year | Winner | Score | Runner-Up | Site |
|---|---|---|---|---|
| 1916 | Jim Barnes | 1 up | Jock Hutchison | Siwanoy CC, Bronxville, NY |
| 1917-18 | No tournament | | | |
| 1919 | Jim Barnes | 6 & 5 | Fred McLeod | Engineers CC, Roslyn, NY |
| 1920 | Jock Hutchison | 1 up | J. Douglas Edgar | Flossmoor CC, Flossmoor, IL |
| 1921 | Walter Hagen | 3 & 2 | Jim Barnes | Inwood CC, Far Rockaway, NY |
| 1922 | Gene Sarazen | 4 & 3 | Emmet French | Oakmont CC, Oakmont, PA |
| 1923 | Gene Sarazen | 1 up 38 holes | Walter Hagen | Pelham CC, Pelham, NY |
| 1924 | Walter Hagen | 2 up | Jim Barnes | French Lick CC, French Lick, IN |
| 1925 | Walter Hagen | 6 & 5 | William Mehlhorn | Olympia Fields CC, Olympia Fields, IL |
| 1926 | Walter Hagen | 5 & 3 | Leo Diegel | Salisbury GC, Westbury, NY |
| 1927 | Walter Hagen | 1 up | Joe Turnesa | Cedar Crest CC, Dallas |
| 1928 | Leo Diegel | 6 & 5 | Al Espinosa | Five Farms CC, Baltimore |
| 1929 | Leo Diegel | 6 & 4 | Johnny Farrell | Hillcrest CC, Los Angeles |
| 1930 | Tommy Armour | 1 up | Gene Sarazen | Fresh Meadow CC, Flushing, NY |
| 1931 | Tom Creavy | 2 & 1 | Denny Shute | Wannamoisett CC, Rumford, RI |
| 1932 | Olin Dutra | 4 & 3 | Frank Walsh | Keller GC, St Paul |
| 1933 | Gene Sarazen | 5 & 4 | Willie Goggin | Blue Mound CC, Milwaukee |
| 1934 | Paul Runyan | 1 up | Craig Wood | Park CC, Williamsville, NY |
| 1935 | Johnny Revolta | 5 & 4 38 holes | Tommy Armour | Twin Hills CC, Oklahoma City |
| 1936 | Denny Shute | 3 & 2 | Jimmy Thomson | Pinehurst CC, Pinehurst, NC |
| 1937 | Denny Shute | 1 up 37 holes | Harold McSpaden | Pittsburgh FC, Aspinwall, PA |
| 1938 | Paul Runyan | 8 & 7 | Sam Snead | Shawnee CC, Shawnee-on-Delaware, PA |
| 1939 | Henry Picard | 1 up 37 holes | Byron Nelson | Pomonok CC, Flushing, NY |
| 1940 | Byron Nelson | 1 up | Sam Snead | Hershey CC, Hershey, PA |
| 1941 | Vic Ghezzi | 1 up 38 holes | Byron Nelson | Cherry Hills CC, Denver |
| 1942 | Sam Snead | 2 & 1 | Jim Turnesa | Seaview CC, Atlantic City |

## PGA Championship (Cont.)

| Year | Winner | Score | Runner-Up | Site |
|------|--------|-------|-----------|------|
| 1943 | No tournament | | | |
| 1944 | Bob Hamilton | 1 up | Byron Nelson | Manito G & CC, Spokane, WA |
| 1945 | Byron Nelson | 4 & 3 | Sam Byrd | Morraine CC, Dayton |
| 1946 | Ben Hogan | 6 & 4 | Ed Oliver | Portland GC, Portland, OR |
| 1947 | Jim Ferrier | 2 & 1 | Chick Harbert | Plum Hollow CC, Detroit |
| 1948 | Ben Hogan | 7 & 6 | Mike Turnesa | Norwood Hills CC, St Louis |
| 1949 | Sam Snead | 3 & 2 | Johnny Palmer | Hermitage CC, Richmond |
| 1950 | Chandler Harper | 4 & 3 | Henry Williams, Jr | Scioto CC, Columbus, OH |
| 1951 | Sam Snead | 7 & 6 | Walter Burkemo | Oakmont CC, Oakmont, PA |
| 1952 | Jim Turnesa | 1 up | Chick Harbert | Big Spring CC, Louisville |
| 1953 | Walter Burkemo | 2 & 1 | Felice Torza | Birmingham CC, Birmingham, MI |
| 1954 | Chick Harbert | 4 & 3 | Walter Burkemo | Keller GC, St Paul |
| 1955 | Doug Ford | 4 & 3 | Cary Middlecoff | Meadowbrook CC, Detroit |
| 1956 | Jack Burke | 3 & 2 | Ted Kroll | Blue Hill CC, Boston |
| 1957 | Lionel Hebert | 2 & 1 | Dow Finsterwald | Miami Valley CC, Dayton |
| 1958 | Dow Finsterwald | 276 | Billy Casper | Llanerch CC, Havertown, PA |
| 1959 | Bob Rosburg | 277 | Jerry Barber | Minneapolis GC, St Louis Park, MN |
| | | | Doug Sanders | |
| 1960 | Jay Hebert | 281 | Jim Ferrier | Firestone CC, Akron |
| 1961 | Jerry Barber* (67) | 277 | Don January (68) | Olympia Fields CC, Olympia Fields, IL |
| 1962 | Gary Player | 278 | Bob Goalby | Aronimink GC, Newton Square, PA |
| 1963 | Jack Nicklaus | 279 | Dave Ragan, Jr | Dallas Athletic Club, Dallas |
| 1964 | Bobby Nichols | 271 | Jack Nicklaus | Columbus CC, Columbus, OH |
| | | | Arnold Palmer | |
| 1965 | Dave Marr | 280 | Billy Casper | Laurel Valley CC, Ligonier, PA |
| | | | Jack Nicklaus | |
| 1966 | Al Geiberger | 280 | Dudley Wysong | Firestone CC, Akron |
| 1967 | Don January* (69) | 281 | Don Massengale (71) | Columbine CC, Littleton, CO |
| 1968 | Julius Boros | 281 | Bob Charles | Pecan Valley CC, San Antonio |
| | | | Arnold Palmer | |
| 1969 | Ray Floyd | 276 | Gary Player | NCR CC, Dayton |
| 1970 | Dave Stockton | 279 | Arnold Palmer | Southern Hills CC, Tulsa |
| | | | Bob Murphy | |
| 1971 | Jack Nicklaus | 281 | Billy Casper | PGA Natl GC, Palm Beach Gardens, FL |
| 1972 | Gary Player | 281 | Tommy Aaron | Oakland Hills CC, Birmingham, MI |
| | | | Jim Jamieson | |
| 1973 | Jack Nicklaus | 277 | Bruce Crampton | Canterbury GC, Cleveland |
| 1974 | Lee Trevino | 276 | Jack Nicklaus | Tanglewood GC, Winston-Salem, NC |
| 1975 | Jack Nicklaus | 276 | Bruce Crampton | Firestone CC, Akron |
| 1976 | Dave Stockton | 281 | Ray Floyd | Congressional CC, Bethesda, MD |
| | | | Don January | |
| 1977† | Lanny Wadkins* (4-4-4) | 282 | Gene Littler (4-4-5) | Pebble Beach GL, Pebble Beach, CA |
| 1978 | John Mahaffey* (4-3) | 276 | Jerry Pate (4-4) | Oakmont CC, Oakmont, PA |
| | | | Tom Watson (4-5) | |
| 1979 | David Graham* (4-4-2) | 272 | Ben Crenshaw (4-4-4) | Oakland Hills CC, Birmingham, MI |
| 1980 | Jack Nicklaus | 274 | Andy Bean | Oak Hill CC, Rochester, NY |
| 1981 | Larry Nelson | 273 | Fuzzy Zoeller | Atlanta Athletic Club, Duluth, GA |
| 1982 | Raymond Floyd | 272 | Lanny Wadkins | Southern Hills CC, Tulsa |
| 1983 | Hal Sutton | 274 | Jack Nicklaus | Riviera CC, Pacific Palisades, CA |
| 1984 | Lee Trevino | 273 | Gary Player | Shoal Creek, Birmingham, AL |
| | | | Lanny Wadkins | |
| 1985 | Hubert Green | 278 | Lee Trevino | Cherry Hills CC, Denver |
| 1986 | Bob Tway | 276 | Greg Norman | Inverness CC, Toledo |
| 1987 | Larry Nelson* (4) | 287 | Lanny Wadkins (5) | PGA Natl GC, Palm Beach Gardens, FL |
| 1988 | Jeff Sluman | 272 | Paul Azinger | Oak Tree GC, Edmond, OK |
| 1989 | Payne Stewart | 276 | Mike Reid | Kemper Lakes GC, Hawthorn Woods, IL |
| 1990 | Wayne Grady | 282 | Fred Couples | Shoal Creek, Birmingham, AL |
| 1991 | John Daly | 276 | Bruce Lietzke | Crooked Stick GC, Carmel, IN |
| 1992 | Nick Price | 278 | Jim Gallagher Jr | Bellerive CC, St. Louis |
| 1993 | Paul Azinger* (4-4) | 272 | Greg Norman (4-5) | Inverness CC, Toldeo, OH |
| 1994 | Nick Price | 269 | Corey Pavin | Southern Hills CC, Tulsa, OK |
| 1995 | Steve Elkington* (3) | 267 | Colin Montgomerie (4) | Riviera CC, Pacific Palisades, CA |

*Winner in playoff. Playoff scores are in parentheses.

†Playoff changed from 18 holes to sudden death.

# THE PGA TOUR
## Season Money Leaders

| Year | Player | Earnings ($) | | Year | Player | Earnings ($) |
|---|---|---|---|---|---|---|
| 1934 | Paul Runyan | 6,767.00 | | 1966 | Billy Casper | 121,944.92 |
| 1935 | Johnny Revolta | 9,543.00 | | 1967 | Jack Nicklaus | 188,998.08 |
| 1936 | Horton Smith | 7,682.00 | | 1968 | Billy Casper | 205,168.67 |
| 1937 | Harry Cooper | 14,138.69 | | 1969 | Frank Beard | 164,707.11 |
| 1938 | Sam Snead | 19,534.49 | | 1970 | Lee Trevino | 157,037.63 |
| 1939 | Henry Picard | 10,303.00 | | 1971 | Jack Nicklaus | 244,490.50 |
| 1940 | Ben Hogan | 10,655.00 | | 1972 | Jack Nicklaus | 320,542.26 |
| 1941 | Ben Hogan | 18,358.00 | | 1973 | Jack Nicklaus | 308,362.10 |
| 1942 | Ben Hogan | 13,143.00 | | 1974 | Johnny Miller | 353,021.59 |
| 1943 | No statistics compiled | | | 1975 | Jack Nicklaus | 298,149.17 |
| 1944 | Byron Nelson (war bonds) | 37,967.69 | | 1976 | Jack Nicklaus | 266,438.57 |
| 1945 | Byron Nelson (war bonds) | 63,335.66 | | 1977 | Tom Watson | 310,653.16 |
| 1946 | Ben Hogan | 42,556.16 | | 1978 | Tom Watson | 362,428.93 |
| 1947 | Jimmy Demaret | 27,936.83 | | 1979 | Tom Watson | 462,636.00 |
| 1948 | Ben Hogan | 32,112.00 | | 1980 | Tom Watson | 530,808.33 |
| 1949 | Sam Snead | 31,593.83 | | 1981 | Tom Kite | 375,698.84 |
| 1950 | Sam Snead | 35,758.83 | | 1982 | Craig Stadler | 446,462.00 |
| 1951 | Lloyd Mangrum | 26,088.83 | | 1983 | Hal Sutton | 426,668.00 |
| 1952 | Julius Boros | 37,032.97 | | 1984 | Tom Watson | 476,260.00 |
| 1953 | Lew Worsham | 34,002.00 | | 1985 | Curtis Strange | 542,321.00 |
| 1954 | Bob Toski | 65,819.81 | | 1986 | Greg Norman | 653,296.00 |
| 1955 | Julius Boros | 63,121.55 | | 1987 | Curtis Strange | 925,941.00 |
| 1956 | Ted Kroll | 72,835.83 | | 1988 | Curtis Strange | 1,147,644.00 |
| 1957 | Dick Mayer | 65,835.00 | | 1989 | Tom Kite | 1,395,278.00 |
| 1958 | Arnold Palmer | 42,607.50 | | 1990 | Greg Norman | 1,165,477.00 |
| 1959 | Art Wall | 53,167.60 | | 1991 | Corey Pavin | 979,430.00 |
| 1960 | Arnold Palmer | 75,262.85 | | 1992 | Fred Couples | 1,344,188.00 |
| 1961 | Gary Player | 64,540.45 | | 1993 | Nick Price | 1,478,557.00 |
| 1962 | Arnold Palmer | 81,448.33 | | 1994 | Nick Price | 1,499,927.00 |
| 1963 | Arnold Palmer | 128,230.00 | | 1995 | Greg Norman | 1,654,959.00 |
| 1964 | Jack Nicklaus | 113,284.50 | | | | |
| 1965 | Jack Nicklaus | 140,752.14 | | | | |

Note: Total money listed from 1968 through 1974. Official money listed from 1975 on.

## Career Money Leaders‡

| | Player | Earnings ($) | | Player | Earnings ($) | | Player | Earnings ($) |
|---|---|---|---|---|---|---|---|---|
| 1. | Greg Norman | 9,592,829 | 18. | Davis Love III | 5,623,890 | 35. | Lee Janzen | 3,910,397 |
| 2. | Tom Kite | 9,337,998 | 19. | Scott Hoch | 5,465,898 | 36. | Jeff Sluman | 3,860,431 |
| 3. | Payne Stewart | 7,389,479 | 20. | David Frost | 5,458,172 | 37. | John Mahaffey | 3,828,008 |
| 4. | Nick Price | 7,338,119 | 21. | Jack Nicklaus | 5,440,357 | 38. | Bob Tway | 3,815,540 |
| 5. | Fred Couples | 7,188,408 | 22. | Jay Haas | 5,426,821 | 39. | Loren Roberts | 3,809,733 |
| 6. | Corey Pavin | 7,175,523 | 23. | Ray Floyd | 5,194,044 | 40. | Steve Pate | 3,661,591 |
| 7. | Tom Watson | 7,072,113 | 24. | Gil Morgan | 4,991,433 | 41. | David Edwards | 3,646,2?? |
| 8. | Paul Azinger | 6,957,324 | 25. | Fuzzy Zoeller | 4,918,771 | 42. | D.A. Weibring | 3,6?? |
| 9. | Ben Crenshaw | 6,845,235 | 26. | Mark McCumber | 4,799,702 | 43. | Joey Sindelar | 3,5?? |
| 10. | Curtis Strange | 6,791,618 | 27. | Scott Simpson | 4,768,955 | 44. | Brad Faxon | 3,537,?? |
| 11. | Mark O'Meara | 6,126,466 | 28. | Larry Mize | 4,584,287 | 45. | Lee Trevino | 3,478,4?? |
| 12. | Lanny Wadkins | 6,028,855 | 29. | Jim Gallagher, Jr | 4,583,940 | 46. | John Huston | 3,408,0?? |
| 13. | Craig Stadler | 6,008,753 | 30. | Peter Jacobsen | 4,547,564 | 47. | Billy Mayfair | 3,397,6.. |
| 14. | Mark Calcavecchia | 5,866,716 | 31. | Steve Elkington | 4,525,487 | 48. | Tim Simpson | 3,351,47? |
| 15. | Hale Irwin | 5,845,024 | 32. | Hal Sutton | 4,486,587 | 49. | Ken Green | 3,347,802 |
| 16. | Chip Beck | 5,755,844 | 33. | John Cook | 4,461,954 | 50. | Larry Nelson | 3,313,938 |
| 17. | Bruce Lietzke | 5,710,262 | 34. | Wayne Levi | 4,237,387 | | | |

## Top Single-Season Earnings‡

| Player | Earnings ($) | Year | | Player | Earnings ($) | Year |
|---|---|---|---|---|---|---|
| Greg Norman | 1,654,959 | 1995 | | Lee Janzen | 1,378,966 | 1995 |
| Billy Mayfair | 1,543,192 | 1995 | | Greg Norman | 1,359,653 | 1993 |
| Nick Price | 1,499,927 | 1994 | | Fred Couples | 1,344,188 | 1992 |
| Nick Price | 1,478,557 | 1993 | | Corey Pavin | 1,340,079 | 1995 |
| Paul Azinger | 1,458,456 | 1993 | | Greg Norman | 1,330,307 | 1994 |
| Tom Kite | 1,395,278 | 1989 | | Steve Elkington | 1,254,352 | 1995 |

‡Through 10/31/95.

Ken Daneyko (top) and the New Jersey Devils upended the Detroit Red Wings in the Stanley Cup.

**Steffi Graf won three majors in '95, including a dramatic win over Monica Seles in the U.S. Open.**

DAVID WALBERG

JOHN BIEVER

Eric Alford and Nebraska were indeed No. 1 after trouncing Colorado 24–7 in October

**Justice Smith ran for 147 yards as Boston College easily defeated Notre Dame 30–11.**

Jerry Rice snared this TD pass from Steve Young to put the Niners up 31–14 in the NFC title game.

PETER READ MILLER

Natrone Means ran for 1,350 yards to power the San Diego Chargers to their first Super Bowl.

Clyde Drexler's arrival ignited the Rockets in their quest for a second straight NBA title.

Orlando's Shaquille O'Neal (top) and Houston's Hakeem Olajuwon clashed in the NBA Finals.

**The midair artistry of Jerry Stackhouse was critical to North Carolina's success all season long.**

**UCLA's Toby Bailey helped the Bruins leap over UConn and into their first Final Four in 19 years.**

Talkin Man charged to victory in the Wood in April, but faded to 12th in the Derby in May.

BOB MARTIN

Ben Crenshaw's victory in the Masters was one of the year's most emotional moments

**Dashing Double: Michael Johnson won the 200 (above) and the 400 at the world championships.**

Eric Wynalda's sterling play produced three goals for the United States in the Copa America.

In a season of fan disillusionment, Dodger rookie Hideo Nomo was a breath of fresh air.

**Cal Ripken took an unforgettable victory lap after breaking Lou Gehrig's iron-man record.**

## Most Career Wins‡

| | Wins | | Wins | | Wins |
|---|---|---|---|---|---|
| Sam Snead | 81 | Billy Casper | 51 | Horton Smith | 32 |
| Jack Nicklaus | 70 | Walter Hagen | 40 | Tom Watson | 32 |
| Ben Hogan | 63 | Cary Middlecoff | 40 | Harry Cooper | 31 |
| Arnold Palmer | 60 | Gene Sarazen | 38 | Jimmy Demaret | 31 |
| Byron Nelson | 52 | Lloyd Mangrum | 36 | Leo Diegel | 30 |

‡Statistics through 10/31/95.

## Year by Year Statistical Leaders

### SCORING AVERAGE

| 1980 | Lee Trevino | 69.73 |
|---|---|---|
| 1981 | Tom Kite | 69.80 |
| 1982 | Tom Kite | 70.21 |
| 1983 | Raymond Floyd | 70.61 |
| 1984 | Calvin Peete | 70.56 |
| 1985 | Don Pooley | 70.36 |
| 1986 | Scott Hoch | 70.08 |
| 1987 | David Frost | 70.09 |
| 1988 | Greg Norman | 69.38 |
| 1989 | Payne Stewart | 69.485† |
| 1990 | Greg Norman | 69.10 |
| 1991 | Fred Couples | 69.59 |
| 1992 | Fred Couples | 69.38 |
| 1993 | Greg Norman | 68.90 |
| 1994 | Greg Norman | 68.81 |
| 1995 | Greg Norman | 69.06 |

Note: Scoring average per round, with adjustments made at each round for the field's course scoring average.

### DRIVING DISTANCE

| | | Yds |
|---|---|---|
| 1980 | Dan Pohl | 274.3 |
| 1981 | Dan Pohl | 280.1 |
| 1982 | Bill Calfee | 275.3 |
| 1983 | John McComish | 277.4 |
| 1984 | Bill Glasson | 276.5 |
| 1985 | Andy Bean | 278.2 |
| 1986 | Davis Love III | 285.7 |
| 1987 | John McComish | 283.9 |
| 1988 | Steve Thomas | 284.6 |
| 1989 | Ed I lumenik | 280.9 |
| 1990 | Tom Purtzer | 279.6 |
| 1991 | John Daly | 288.9 |
| 1992 | John Daly | 283.4 |
| 1993 | John Daly | 288.9 |
| 1994 | Davis Love III | 283.8 |
| 1995 | John Daly | 289.0 |

Note: Average computed by charting distance of two tee shots on a predetermined par-four or par-five hole (one on front nine, one on back nine).

### DRIVING ACCURACY

| 1980 | Mike Reid | 79.5 |
|---|---|---|
| 1981 | Calvin Peete | 81.9 |
| 1982 | Calvin Peete | 84.6 |
| 1983 | Calvin Peete | 81.3 |
| 1984 | Calvin Peete | 77.5 |
| 1985 | Calvin Peete | 80.6 |
| 1986 | Calvin Peete | 81.7 |
| 1987 | Calvin Peete | 83.0 |
| 1988 | Calvin Peete | 82.5 |
| 1989 | Calvin Peete | 82.6 |
| 1990 | Calvin Peete | 83.7 |

### DRIVING ACCURACY *(Cont.)*

| 1991 | Hale Irwin | 78.3 |
|---|---|---|
| 1992 | Doug Tewell | 82.3 |
| 1993 | Doug Tewell | 82.5 |
| 1994 | David Edwards | 81.6 |
| 1995 | Fred Funk | 81.3 |

Note: Percentage of fairways hit on number of par-four and par-five holes played; par-three holes excluded.

### GREENS IN REGULATION

| 1980 | Jack Nicklaus | 72.1 |
|---|---|---|
| 1981 | Calvin Peete | 73.1 |
| 1982 | Calvin Peete | 72.4 |
| 1983 | Calvin Peete | 71.4 |
| 1984 | Andy Bean | 72.1 |
| 1985 | John Mahaffey | 71.9 |
| 1986 | John Mahaffey | 72.0 |
| 1987 | Gil Morgan | 73.3 |
| 1988 | John Adams | 73.9 |
| 1989 | Bruce Lietzke | 72.6 |
| 1990 | Doug Tewell | 70.9 |
| 1991 | Bruce Lietzke | 73.3 |
| 1992 | Tim Simpson | 74.0 |
| 1993 | Fuzzy Zoeller | 73.6 |
| 1994 | Bill Glasson | 73.0 |
| 1995 | Lenny Clements | 72.3 |

Note: Average of greens reached in regulation out of total holes played; hole is considered hit in regulation if any part of the ball rests on the putting surface in two shots less than the hole's-five hit in two shots is one green in regulation.

### PUTTING

| 1980 | Jerry Pate | 28.81 |
|---|---|---|
| 1981 | Alan Tapie | 28.70 |
| 1982 | Ben Crenshaw | 28.65 |
| 1983 | Morris Hatalsky | 27.96 |
| 1984 | Gary McCord | 28.57 |
| 1985 | Craig Stadler | 28.627† |
| 1986 | Greg Norman | 1.736 |
| 1987 | Ben Crenshaw | 1.743 |
| 1988 | Don Pooley | 1.729 |
| 1989 | Steve Jones | 1.734 |
| 1990 | Larry Rinker | 1.7467† |
| 1991 | Jay Don Blake | 1.7326† |
| 1992 | Mark O'Meara | 1.731 |
| 1993 | David Frost | 1.739 |
| 1994 | Loren Roberts | 1.737 |
| 1995 | Jim Furyk | 1.708 |

Note: Average number of putts taken on greens reached in regulation; prior to 1986, based on average number of putts per 18 holes.

### ALL-AROUND

| 1987 | Dan Pohl | 170 |
|---|---|---|
| 1988 | Payne Stewart | 170 |
| 1989 | Paul Azinger | 250 |
| 1990 | Paul Azinger | 162 |
| 1991 | Scott Hoch | 283 |
| 1992 | Fred Couples | 256 |
| 1993 | Gil Morgan | 252 |
| 1994 | Bob Estes | 227 |
| 1995 | Justin Leonard | 323 |

Note: Addition of the places of standing from the other nine statistical categories; the player with the number closest to zero leads.

### SAND SAVES

| 1980 | Bob Eastwood | 65.4 |
|---|---|---|
| 1981 | Tom Watson | 60.1 |
| 1982 | Isao Aoki | 60.2 |
| 1983 | Isao Aoki | 62.3 |
| 1984 | Peter Oosterhuis | 64.7 |
| 1985 | Tom Purtzer | 60.8 |
| 1986 | Paul Azinger | 63.8 |
| 1987 | Paul Azinger | 63.2 |
| 1988 | Greg Powers | 63.5 |
| 1989 | Mike Sullivan | 66.0 |
| 1990 | Paul Azinger | 67.2 |
| 1991 | Ben Crenshaw | 64.9 |
| 1992 | Mitch Adcock | 66.9 |
| 1993 | Ken Green | 64.4 |
| 1994 | Corey Pavin | 65.4 |
| 1995 | Billy Mayfair | 68.6 |

Note: Percentage of up-and-down efforts from greenside sand traps only; fairway bunkers excluded.

### PAR BREAKERS

| 1980 | Tom Watson | .213 |
|---|---|---|
| 1981 | Bruce Lietzke | .225 |
| 1982 | Tom Kite | .2154† |
| 1983 | Tom Watson | .211 |
| 1984 | Craig Stadler | .220 |
| 1985 | Craig Stadler | .218 |
| 1986 | Greg Norman | .248 |
| 1987 | Mark Calcavecchia | .221 |
| 1988 | Ken Green | .236 |
| 1989 | Greg Norman | .224 |
| 1990 | Greg Norman | .219 |

Note: Average based on total birdies and eagles scored out of total holes played. Discontinued as an official category after 1990.

† Number had to be carried to extra decimal place to determine winner.

## Year by Year Statistical Leaders (Cont.)

| EAGLES | | | BIRDIES | | |
|---|---|---|---|---|---|
| 1980 | Dave Eichelberger | 16 | 1980 | Andy Bean | 388 |
| 1981 | Bruce Lietzke | 12 | 1981 | Vance Heafner | 388 |
| 1982 | Tom Weiskopf | 10 | 1982 | Andy Bean | 392 |
| | J. C. Snead | 10 | 1983 | Hal Sutton | 399 |
| | Andy Bean | 10 | 1984 | Mark O'Meara | 419 |
| 1983 | Chip Beck | 15 | 1985 | Joey Sindelar | 411 |
| 1984 | Gary Hallberg | 15 | 1986 | Joey Sindelar | 415 |
| 1985 | Larry Rinker | 14 | 1987 | Dan Forsman | 409 |
| 1986 | Joey Sindelar | 16 | 1988 | Dan Forsman | 465 |
| 1987 | Phil Blackmar | 20 | 1989 | Ted Schulz | 415 |
| 1988 | Ken Green | 21 | 1990 | Mike Donald | 401 |
| 1989 | Lon Hinkle | 14 | 1991 | Scott Hoch | 446 |
| | Duffy Waldorf | 14 | 1992 | Jeff Sluman | 417 |
| 1990 | Paul Azinger | 14 | 1993 | John Huston | 426 |
| 1991 | Andy Bean | 15 | 1994 | Brad Bryant | 397 |
| 1992 | Dan Forsman | 18 | 1995 | Steve Lowery | 410 |
| 1993 | Davis Love III | 15 | | | |
| 1994 | Davis Love III | 18 | Note: Total of birdies scored. | | |
| 1995 | Kelly Gibson | 16 | | | |

Note: Total of eagles scored.

## PGA Player of the Year Award

| | | |
|---|---|---|
| 1948 | Ben Hogan | |
| 1949 | Sam Snead | |
| 1950 | Ben Hogan | |
| 1951 | Ben Hogan | |
| 1952 | Julius Boros | |
| 1953 | Ben Hogan | |
| 1954 | Ed Furgol | |
| 1955 | Doug Ford | |
| 1956 | Jack Burke | |
| 1957 | Dick Mayer | |
| 1958 | Dow Finsterwald | |
| 1959 | Art Wall | |
| 1960 | Arnold Palmer | |
| 1961 | Jerry Barber | |
| 1962 | Arnold Palmer | |
| 1963 | Julius Boros | |
| 1964 | Ken Venturi | |
| 1965 | Dave Marr | |
| 1966 | Billy Casper | |
| 1967 | Jack Nicklaus | |
| 1968 | Not awarded | |
| 1969 | Orville Moody | |
| 1970 | Billy Casper | |
| 1971 | Lee Trevino | |
| 1972 | Jack Nicklaus | |
| 1973 | Jack Nicklaus | |
| 1974 | Johnny Miller | |
| 1975 | Jack Nicklaus | |
| 1976 | Jack Nicklaus | |
| 1977 | Tom Watson | |
| 1978 | Tom Watson | |
| 1979 | Tom Watson | |
| 1980 | Tom Watson | |
| 1981 | Bill Rogers | |
| 1982 | Tom Watson | |
| 1983 | Hal Sutton | |
| 1984 | Tom Watson | |
| 1985 | Lanny Wadkins | |
| 1986 | Bob Tway | |
| 1987 | Paul Azinger | |
| 1988 | Curtis Strange | |
| 1989 | Tom Kite | |
| 1990 | Wayne Levi | |
| 1991 | Fred Couples | |
| 1992 | Fred Couples | |
| 1993 | Nick Price | |
| 1994 | Nick Price | |
| 1995 | Greg Norman | |

## Vardon Trophy: Scoring Average

| Year | Winner | Avg | Year | Winner | Avg | Year | Winner | Avg |
|---|---|---|---|---|---|---|---|---|
| 1937 | Harry Cooper | *500 | 1960 | Billy Casper | 69.95 | 1979 | Tom Watson | 70.27 |
| 1938 | Sam Snead | 520 | 1961 | Arnold Palmer | 69.85 | 1980 | Lee Trevino | 69.73 |
| 1939 | Byron Nelson | 473 | 1962 | Arnold Palmer | 70.27 | 1981 | Tom Kite | 69.80 |
| 1940 | Ben Hogan | 423 | 1963 | Billy Casper | 70.58 | 1982 | Tom Kite | 70.21 |
| 1941 | Ben Hogan | 494 | 1964 | Arnold Palmer | 70.01 | 1983 | Raymond Floyd | 70.61 |
| 1942-46 | No award | | 1965 | Billy Casper | 70.85 | 1984 | Calvin Peete | 70.56 |
| 1947 | Jimmy Demaret | 69.90 | 1966 | Billy Casper | 70.27 | 1985 | Don Pooley | 70.36 |
| 1948 | Ben Hogan | 69.30 | 1967 | Arnold Palmer | 70.18 | 1986 | Scott Hoch | 70.08 |
| 1949 | Sam Snead | 69.37 | 1968 | Billy Casper | 69.82 | 1987 | Don Pohl | 70.25 |
| 1950 | Sam Snead | 69.23 | 1969 | Dave Hill | 70.34 | 1988 | Chip Beck | 69.46 |
| 1951 | Lloyd Mangrum | 70.05 | 1970 | Lee Trevino | 70.64 | 1989 | Greg Norman | 69.49 |
| 1952 | Jack Burke | 70.54 | 1971 | Lee Trevino | 70.27 | 1990 | Greg Norman | 69.10 |
| 1953 | Lloyd Mangrum | 70.22 | 1972 | Lee Trevino | 70.89 | 1991 | Fred Couples | 69.59 |
| 1954 | E. J. Harrison | 70.41 | 1973 | Bruce Crampton | 70.57 | 1992 | Fred Couples | 69.38 |
| 1955 | Sam Snead | 69.86 | 1974 | Lee Trevino | 70.53 | 1993 | Nick Price | 69.11 |
| 1956 | Cary Middlecoff | 70.35 | 1975 | Bruce Crampton | 70.51 | 1994 | Greg Norman | 68.81 |
| 1957 | Dow Finsterwald | 70.30 | 1976 | Don January | 70.56 | 1995 | Steve Elkington | 69.62 |
| 1958 | Bob Rosburg | 70.11 | 1977 | Tom Watson | 70.32 | | | |
| 1959 | Art Wall | 70.35 | 1978 | Tom Watson | 70.16 | | | |

*Point system used, 1937-41.

Note: As of 1988, based on minimum of 60 rounds per year.

## Alltime PGA Tour Records*

### Scoring

#### 90 HOLES

**325**—(67-67-64-65-62) by Tom Kite, at four courses, La Quinta, CA, in winning the 1993 Bob Hope Classic (35 under par).

#### 72 HOLES

**257**—(60-68-64-65) by Mike Souchak, at Brackenridge Park GC, San Antonio, to win 1955 Texas Open (27 under par).

#### 54 HOLES

##### Opening rounds

**191**—(66-64-61) by Gay Brewer, at Pensacola CC, Pensacola, FL, in winning the 1967 Pensacola Open.

##### Consecutive rounds

**189**—(63-63-63) by Chandler Harper in the last three rounds to win the 1954 Texas Open at Brackenridge Park GC, San Antonio.

#### 36 HOLES

##### Opening rounds

**126**—(64-62) by Tommy Bolt, at Cavalier Yacht & CC, Virginia Beach, VA, in 1954 Virginia Beach Open.

**126**—(64-62) by Paul Azinger, at Oak Hills CC, San Antonio, in 1989 Texas Open.

##### Consecutive rounds

**125**—(64-61) by Gay Brewer in the middle rounds of the 1967 Pensacola Open, which he won, at Pensacola CC, Pensacola, FL.

**125**—(63-62) by Ron Streck in the last two rounds to win the 1978 Texas Open at Oak Hills CC, San Antonio.

**125**—(62-63) by Blaine McCallister in the middle two rounds in winning the 1988 Hardee's Golf Classic at Oakwood CC, Coal Valley, IL.

#### 18 HOLES

**59**—by Al Geiberger, at Colonial Country Club, Memphis, in second round in winning 1977 Memphis Classic.

**59**—by Chip Beck, at Sunrise Golf Club, Las Vegas, in third round of the 1991 Las Vegas Invitational.

#### 9 HOLES

**27**—by Mike Souchak, at Brackenridge Park GC, San Antonio, on par-35 second nine of first round in 1955 Texas Open.

**27**—by Andy North at En-Joie GC, Endicott, NY, on par-34 second nine of first round in 1975 BC Open.

#### MOST CONSECUTIVE ROUNDS UNDER 70

**19**—Byron Nelson in 1945.

#### MOST BIRDIES IN A ROW

**8**—Bob Goalby at Pasadena GC, St Petersburg, FL, during fourth round in winning the 1961 St Petersburg Open.

**8**—Fuzzy Zoeller, at Oakwood CC, Coal Valley, IL, during first round of 1976 Quad Cities Open.

**8**—Dewey Arnette, Warwick Hills GC, Grand Blanc, MI, during first round of the 1987 Buick Open.

### Scoring (Cont.)

#### MOST BIRDIES IN A ROW TO WIN

**5**—Jack Nicklaus to win 1978 Jackie Gleason Inverrary Classic (last 5 holes).

### Wins

#### MOST CONSECUTIVE YEARS WINNING AT LEAST ONE TOURNAMENT

**17**—Jack Nicklaus, 1962-78.
**17**—Arnold Palmer, 1955-71.
**16**—Billy Casper, 1956-71.

#### MOST CONSECUTIVE WINS

**11**—Byron Nelson, from Miami Four Ball, March 8-11, 1945, through Canadian Open, August 2-4, 1945.

#### MOST WINS IN A SINGLE EVENT

**8**—Sam Snead, Greater Greensboro Open, 1938, 1946, 1949, 1950, 1955, 1956, 1960, and 1965.

#### MOST CONSECUTIVE WINS IN A SINGLE EVENT

**4**—Walter Hagen, PGA Championships, 1924-27.

#### MOST WINS IN A CALENDAR YEAR

**18**—Byron Nelson, 1945

#### MOST YEARS BETWEEN WINS

**12**—Howard Twitty, 1980–93.

#### MOST YEARS FROM FIRST WIN TO LAST

**29**—Sam Snead, 1936-65.
**29**—Ray Floyd, 1963-92.

#### YOUNGEST WINNERS

John McDermott, 19 years and 10 months, 1911 US Open.

#### OLDEST WINNER

Sam Snead, 52 years and 10 months, 1965 Greater Greensboro Open.

#### WIDEST WINNING MARGIN: STROKES

**16**—Bobby Locke, 1948 Chicago Victory National Championship.

### Putting

#### FEWEST PUTTS, ONE ROUND

**18**—Andy North, at Kingsmill GC, in second round of 1990 Anheuser Busch Golf Classic.

**18**—Kenny Knox, at Harbour Town GL, in first round of 1989 MCI Heritage Classic.

**18**—Mike McGee, at Colonial CC, in first round of 1987 Federal Express St Jude Classic.

**18**—Sam Trahan, at Whitemarsh Valley CC, in final round of 1979 IVB Philadelphia Golf Classic.

**18**—Jim McGovern, at TPC at Southwind, in second round of 1992 Federal Express St. Jude Classic.

#### FEWEST PUTTS, FOUR ROUNDS

**93**—Kenny Knox, in 1989 MCI Heritage Classic at Harbour Town GL.

*Through 10/31/95.

# THE MAJOR TOURNAMENTS
## LPGA Championship

| Year | Winner | Score | Runner-Up | Site |
|---|---|---|---|---|
| 1955 | Beverly Hanson† (4 and 3) | 220 | Louise Suggs | Orchard Ridge CC, Ft Wayne, IN |
| 1956 | Marlene Hagge* (5) | 291 | Patty Berg (6) | Forest Lake CC, Detroit |
| 1957 | Louise Suggs | 285 | Wiffi Smith | Churchill Valley CC, Pittsburgh |
| 1958 | Mickey Wright | 288 | Fay Crocker | Churchill Valley CC, Pittsburgh |
| 1959 | Betsy Rawls | 288 | Patty Berg | Sheraton Hotel CC, French Lick, IN |
| 1960 | Mickey Wright | 292 | Louise Suggs | Sheraton Hotel CC, French Lick, IN |
| 1961 | Mickey Wright | 287 | Louise Suggs | Stardust CC, Las Vegas |
| 1962 | Judy Kimball | 282 | Shirley Spork | Stardust CC, Las Vegas |
| 1963 | Mickey Wright | 294 | Mary Lena Faulk Mary Mills Louise Suggs | Stardust CC, Las Vegas |
| 1964 | Mary Mills | 278 | Mickey Wright | Stardust CC, Las Vegas |
| 1965 | Sandra Haynie | 279 | Clifford A. Creed | Stardust CC, Las Vegas |
| 1966 | Gloria Ehret | 282 | Mickey Wright | Stardust CC, Las Vegas |
| 1967 | Kathy Whitworth | 284 | Shirley Englehorn | Pleasant Valley CC, Sutton, MA |
| 1968 | Sandra Post* (68) | 294 | Kathy Whitworth (75) | Pleasant Valley CC, Sutton, MA |
| 1969 | Betsy Rawls | 293 | Susie Berning Carol Mann | Concord GC, Kiameshia Lake, NY |
| 1970 | Shirley Englehorn* (74) | 285 | Kathy Whitworth (78) | Pleasant Valley CC, Sutton, MA |
| 1971 | Kathy Whitworth | 288 | Kathy Ahern | Pleasant Valley CC, Sutton, MA |
| 1972 | Kathy Ahern | 293 | Jane Blalock | Pleasant Valley CC, Sutton, MA |
| 1973 | Mary Mills | 288 | Betty Burfeindt | Pleasant Valley CC, Sutton, MA |
| 1974 | Sandra Haynie | 288 | JoAnne Carner | Pleasant Valley CC, Sutton, MA |
| 1975 | Kathy Whitworth | 288 | Sandra Haynie | Pine Ridge GC, Baltimore |
| 1976 | Betty Burfeindt | 287 | Judy Rankin | Pine Ridge GC, Baltimore |
| 1977 | Chako Higuchi | 279 | Pat Bradley Sandra Post Judy Rankin | Bay Tree Golf Plantation, N. Myrtle Beach, SC |
| 1978 | Nancy Lopez | 275 | Amy Alcott | Jack Nicklaus GC, Kings Island, OH |
| 1979 | Donna Caponi | 279 | Jerilyn Britz | Jack Nicklaus GC, Kings Island, OH |
| 1980 | Sally Little | 285 | Jane Blalock | Jack Nicklaus GC, Kings Island, OH |
| 1981 | Donna Caponi | 280 | Jerilyn Britz Pat Meyers | Jack Nicklaus GC, Kings Island, OH |
| 1982 | Jan Stephenson | 279 | JoAnne Carner | Jack Nicklaus GC, Kings Island, OH |
| 1983 | Patty Sheehan | 279 | Sandra Haynie | Jack Nicklaus GC, Kings Island, OH |
| 1984 | Patty Sheehan | 272 | Beth Daniel Pat Bradley | Jack Nicklaus GC, Kings Island, OH |
| 1985 | Nancy Lopez | 273 | Alice Miller | Jack Nicklaus GC, Kings Island, OH |
| 1986 | Pat Bradley | 277 | Patty Sheehan | Jack Nicklaus GC, Kings Island, OH |
| 1987 | Jane Geddes | 275 | Betsy King | Jack Nicklaus GC, Kings Island, OH |
| 1988 | Sherri Turner | 281 | Amy Alcott | Jack Nicklaus GC, Kings Island, OH |
| 1989 | Nancy Lopez | 274 | Ayako Okamoto | Jack Nicklaus GC, Kings Island, OH |
| 1990 | Beth Daniel | 280 | Rosie Jones | Bethesda CC, Bethesda, MD |
| 1991 | Meg Mallon | 274 | Pat Bradley Ayako Okamoto | Bethesda CC, Bethesda, MD |
| 1992 | Betsy King | 267 | Karen Noble | Bethesda CC, Bethesda, MD |
| 1993 | Patty Sheehan | 275 | Lauri Merten | Bethesda CC, Bethesda, MD |
| 1994 | Laura Davies | 279 | Alice Ritzman | DuPont CC, Wilmington, DE |
| 1995 | Kelly Robbins | 274 | Laura Davies | DuPont CC, Wilmington, DE |

*Won in playoff. Playoff scores are in parentheses. 1956 was sudden death; 1968 and 1970 were 18-hole playoffs.
†Won match play final.

## U.S. Women's Open

| Year | Winner | Score | Runner-Up | Site |
|---|---|---|---|---|
| 1946 | Patty Berg | 5 & 4 | Betty Jameson | Spokane CC, Spokane, WA |
| 1947 | Betty Jameson | 295 | Sally Sessions Polly Riley | Starmount Forest CC, Greensboro, NC |
| 1948 | Babe Zaharias | 300 | Betty Hicks | Atlantic City CC, Northfield, NJ |
| 1949 | Louise Suggs | 291 | Babe Zaharias | Prince George's G & CC, Landover, MD |
| 1950 | Babe Zaharias | 291 | Betsy Rawls | Rolling Hills CC, Wichita, KS |
| 1951 | Betsy Rawls | 293 | Louise Suggs | Druid Hills GC, Atlanta |

## U.S. Women's Open (Cont.)

| Year | Winner | Score | Runner-Up | Site |
|------|--------|-------|-----------|------|
| 1952 | Louise Suggs | 284 | Marlene Bauer<br>Betty Jameson | Bala GC, Philadelphia |
| 1953 | Betsy Rawls* (71) | 302 | Jackie Pung (77) | CC of Rochester, Rochester, NY |
| 1954 | Babe Zaharias | 291 | Betty Hicks | Salem CC, Peabody, MA |
| 1955 | Fay Crocker | 299 | Mary Lena Faulk<br>Louise Suggs | Wichita CC, Wichita, KS |
| 1956 | Kathy Cornelius* (75) | 302 | Barbara McIntire (82) | Northland CC, Duluth, MN |
| 1957 | Betsy Rawls | 299 | Patty Berg | Winged Foot GC, Mamaroneck, NY |
| 1958 | Mickey Wright | 290 | Louise Suggs | Forest Lake CC, Detroit |
| 1959 | Mickey Wright | 287 | Louise Suggs | Churchill Valley CC, Pittsburgh |
| 1960 | Betsy Rawls | 292 | Joyce Ziske | Worcester CC, Worcester, MA |
| 1961 | Mickey Wright | 293 | Betsy Rawls | Baltusrol GC (Lower Course), Springfield, NJ |
| 1962 | Murle Breer | 301 | Jo Ann Prentice<br>Ruth Jessen | Dunes GC, Myrtle Beach, SC |
| 1963 | Mary Mills | 289 | Sandra Haynie<br>Louise Suggs | Kenwood CC, Cincinnati |
| 1964 | Mickey Wright* (70) | 290 | Ruth Jessen (72) | San Diego CC, Chula Vista, CA |
| 1965 | Carol Mann | 290 | Kathy Cornelius | Atlantic City CC, Northfield, NJ |
| 1966 | Sandra Spuzich | 297 | Carol Mann | Hazeltine Natl GC, Chaska, MN |
| 1967 | Catherine LaCoste | 294 | Susie Berning<br>Beth Stone | Hot Springs GC (Cascades Course), Hot Springs, VA |
| 1968 | Susie Berning | 289 | Mickey Wright | Moslem Springs GC, Fleetwood, PA |
| 1969 | Donna Caponi | 294 | Peggy Wilson | Scenic Hills CC, Pensacola, FL |
| 1970 | Donna Caponi | 287 | Sandra Haynie<br>Sandra Spuzich | Muskogee CC, Muskogee, OK |
| 1971 | JoAnne Carner | 288 | Kathy Whitworth | Kahkwa CC, Erie, PA |
| 1972 | Susie Berning | 299 | Kathy Ahern<br>Pam Barnett<br>Judy Rankin | Winged Foot GC, Mamaroneck, NY |
| 1973 | Susie Berning | 290 | Gloria Ehret<br>Shelley Hamlin | CC of Rochester, Rochester, NY |
| 1974 | Sandra Haynie | 295 | Carol Mann<br>Beth Stone | La Grange CC, La Grange, IL |
| 1975 | Sandra Palmer | 295 | JoAnne Carner<br>Sandra Post<br>Nancy Lopez | Atlantic City CC, Northfield, NJ |
| 1976 | JoAnne Carner* (76) | 292 | Sandra Palmer (78) | Rolling Green CC, Springfield, PA |
| 1977 | Hollis Stacy | 292 | Nancy Lopez | Hazeltine Natl GC, Chaska, MN |
| 1978 | Hollis Stacy | 289 | JoAnne Carner<br>Sally Little | CC of Indianapolis, Indianapolis |
| 1979 | Jerilyn Britz | 284 | Debbie Massey<br>Sandra Palmer | Brooklawn CC, Fairfield, CT |
| 1980 | Amy Alcott | 280 | Hollis Stacy | Richland CC, Nashville |
| 1981 | Pat Bradley | 279 | Beth Daniel | La Grange CC, La Grange, IL |
| 1982 | Janet Anderson | 283 | Beth Daniel<br>Sandra Haynie<br>Donna White<br>JoAnne Carner | Del Paso CC, Sacramento |
| 1983 | Jan Stephenson | 290 | JoAnne Carner<br>Patty Sheehan | Cedar Ridge CC, Tulsa |
| 1984 | Hollis Stacy | 290 | Rosie Jones | Salem CC, Peabody, MA |
| 1985 | Kathy Baker | 280 | Judy Dickinson | Baltusrol GC (Upper Course), Springfield, NJ |
| 1986 | Jane Geddes* (71) | 287 | Sally Little (73) | NCR GC, Dayton |
| 1987 | Laura Davies* (71) | 285 | Ayako Okamoto (73)<br>JoAnne Carner (74) | Plainfield CC, Plainfield, NJ |
| 1988 | Liselotte Neumann | 277 | Patty Sheehan | Baltimore CC, Baltimore |
| 1989 | Betsy King | 278 | Nancy Lopez | Indianwood G & CC, Lake Orion, MI |
| 1990 | Betsy King | 284 | Patty Sheehan | Atlanta Athletic Club, Duluth, GA |
| 1991 | Meg Mallon | 283 | Pat Bradley | Colonial Club, Fort Worth |
| 1992 | Patty Sheehan* (72) | 280 | Juli Inkster | Oakmont CC, Oakmont, PA |
| 1993 | Lauri Merten | 280 | Donna Andrew<br>Helen Alfredsson | Crooked Stick, Carmel, IN |
| 1994 | Patty Sheehan | 277 | Tammie Green | Indianwood G & CC, Lake Orion, MI |
| 1995 | Annika Sorenstam | 278 | Meg Mallon | The Broadmoor GC, Colorado Springs, CO |

*Winner in playoff. 18-hole playoff scores are in parentheses.

## Dinah Shore

| Year | Winner | Score | Runner-Up |
|------|--------|-------|-----------|
| 1972 | Jane Blalock | 213 | Carol Mann, Judy Rankin |
| 1973 | Mickey Wright | 284 | Joyce Kazmierski |
| 1974 | Jo Ann Prentice* | 289 | Jane Blalock, Sandra Haynie |
| 1975 | Sandra Palmer | 283 | Kathy McMullen |
| 1976 | Judy Rankin | 285 | Betty Burfeindt |
| 1977 | Kathy Whitworth | 289 | JoAnne Carner, Sally Little |
| 1978 | Sandra Post* | 283 | Penny Pulz |
| 1979 | Sandra Post | 276 | Nancy Lopez |
| 1980 | Donna Caponi | 275 | Amy Alcott |
| 1981 | Nancy Lopez | 277 | Carolyn Hill |
| 1982 | Sally Little | 278 | Hollis Stacy, Sandra Haynie |
| 1983 | Amy Alcott | 282 | Beth Daniel, Kathy Whitworth |
| 1984 | Juli Inkster* | 280 | Pat Bradley |
| 1985 | Alice Miller | 275 | Jan Stephenson |
| 1986 | Pat Bradley | 280 | Val Skinner |
| 1987 | Betsy King* | 283 | Patty Sheehan |
| 1988 | Amy Alcott | 274 | Colleen Walker |
| 1989 | Juli Inkster | 279 | Tammie Green, JoAnne Carner |
| 1990 | Betsy King | 283 | Kathy Postlewait, Shirley Furlong |
| 1991 | Amy Alcott | 273 | Dottie Mochrie |
| 1992 | Dottie Mochrie* | 279 | Juli Inkster |
| 1993 | Helen Alfredsson | 284 | Amy Benz, Tina Barrett, Betsy King |
| 1994 | Donna Andrews | 276 | Laura Davies |
| 1995 | Nanci Bowen | 285 | Susie Redman |

*Winner in sudden-death playoff.

Note: Designated fourth major in 1983.

Played at Mission Hills CC, Rancho Mirage, CA.

## du Maurier Classic

| Year | Winner | Score | Runner-Up | Site |
|------|--------|-------|-----------|------|
| 1973 | Jocelyne Bourassa* | 214 | Sandra Haynie Judy Rankin | Montreal GC, Montreal |
| 1974 | Carole Jo Callison | 208 | JoAnne Carner | Candiac GC, Montreal |
| 1975 | JoAnne Carner* | 214 | Carol Mann | St George's CC, Toronto |
| 1976 | Donna Caponi* | 212 | Judy Rankin | Cedar Brae G & CC, Toronto |
| 1977 | Judy Rankin | 214 | Pat Meyers Sandra Palmer | Lachute G & CC, Montreal |
| 1978 | JoAnne Carner | 278 | Hollis Stacy | St George's CC, Toronto |
| 1979 | Amy Alcott | 285 | Nancy Lopez | Richelieu Valley CC, Montreal |
| 1980 | Pat Bradley | 277 | JoAnne Carner | St George's CC, Toronto |
| 1981 | Jan Stephenson | 278 | Nancy Lopez Pat Bradley | Summerlea CC, Dorion, Quebec |
| 1982 | Sandra Haynie | 280 | Beth Daniel | St George's CC, Toronto |
| 1983 | Hollis Stacy | 277 | JoAnne Carner Alice Miller | Beaconsfield GC, Montreal |
| 1984 | Juli Inkster | 279 | Ayako Okamoto | St George's G & CC, Toronto |
| 1985 | Pat Bradley | 278 | Jane Geddes | Beaconsfield CC, Montreal |
| 1986 | Pat Bradley* | 276 | Ayako Okamoto | Board of Trade CC, Toronto |
| 1987 | Jody Rosenthal | 272 | Ayako Okamoto | Islesmere GC, Laval, Quebec |
| 1988 | Sally Little | 279 | Laura Davies | Vancouver GC, Coquitlam, British Columbia |
| 1989 | Tammie Green | 279 | Pat Bradley Betsy King | Beaconsfield GC, Montreal |
| 1990 | Cathy Johnston | 276 | Patty Sheehan | Westmount G & CC, Kitchener, Ontario |
| 1991 | Nancy Scranton | 279 | Debbie Massey | Vancouver GC, Coquitlam, British Columbia |
| 1992 | Sherri Steinhauer | 277 | Judy Dickinson | St. Charles CC, Winnipeg, Manitoba |
| 1993 | Brandie Burton | 277 | Betsy King | London Hunt and CC, London, Ontario |
| 1994 | Martha Nause | 279 | Michelle McGann | Ottawa Hunt and GC, Ottawa, Ont. |
| 1995 | Jenny Lidback | 280 | Liselotte Neumann | Beaconsfield GC, Pointe-Claire, Quebec |

*Winner in sudden-death playoff.

Note: Designated third major in 1979.

# THE LPGA TOUR

## Season Money Leaders

| | | Earnings ($) |
|---|---|---|
| 1950 | Babe Zaharias | 14,800 |
| 1951 | Babe Zaharias | 15,087 |
| 1952 | Betsy Rawls | 14,505 |
| 1953 | Louise Suggs | 19,816 |
| 1954 | Patty Berg | 16,011 |
| 1955 | Patty Berg | 16,492 |
| 1956 | Marlene Hagge | 20,235 |
| 1957 | Patty Berg | 16,272 |
| 1958 | Beverly Hanson | 12,639 |
| 1959 | Betsy Rawls | 26,774 |
| 1960 | Louise Suggs | 16,892 |
| 1961 | Mickey Wright | 22,236 |
| 1962 | Mickey Wright | 21,641 |
| 1963 | Mickey Wright | 31,269 |
| 1964 | Mickey Wright | 29,800 |
| 1965 | Kathy Whitworth | 28,658 |
| 1966 | Kathy Whitworth | 33,517 |
| 1967 | Kathy Whitworth | 32,937 |
| 1968 | Kathy Whitworth | 48,379 |
| 1969 | Carol Mann | 49,152 |
| 1970 | Kathy Whitworth | 30,235 |
| 1971 | Kathy Whitworth | 41,181 |
| 1972 | Kathy Whitworth | 65,063 |

| | | Earnings ($) |
|---|---|---|
| 1973 | Kathy Whitworth | 82,864 |
| 1974 | JoAnne Carner | 87,094 |
| 1975 | Sandra Palmer | 76,374 |
| 1976 | Judy Rankin | 150,734 |
| 1977 | Judy Rankin | 122,890 |
| 1978 | Nancy Lopez | 189,814 |
| 1979 | Nancy Lopez | 197,489 |
| 1980 | Beth Daniel | 231,000 |
| 1981 | Beth Daniel | 206,998 |
| 1982 | JoAnne Carner | 310,400 |
| 1983 | JoAnne Carner | 291,404 |
| 1984 | Betsy King | 266,771 |
| 1985 | Nancy Lopez | 416,472 |
| 1986 | Pat Bradley | 492,021 |
| 1987 | Ayako Okamoto | 466,034 |
| 1988 | Sherri Turner | 350,851 |
| 1989 | Betsy King | 654,132 |
| 1990 | Beth Daniel | 863,578 |
| 1991 | Pat Bradley | 763,118 |
| 1992 | Dottie Mochrie | 693,335 |
| 1993 | Betsy King | 595,992 |
| 1994 | Laura Davies | 687,201 |

## Career Money Leaders*

| | Earnings ($) |
|---|---|
| 1. Betsy King | 4,892,873.50 |
| 2. Pat Bradley | 4,772,115.03 |
| 3. Beth Daniel | 4,492,091.80 |
| 4. Patty Sheehan | 4,455,399.01 |
| 5. Nancy Lopez | 4,064,802.83 |
| 6. Amy Aloctt | 3,064,889.14 |
| 7. JoAnne Carner | 2,840,071.63 |
| 8. Ayako Okamoto | 2,715,678.85 |
| 9. Dottie Mochrie | 2,574,716.00 |
| 10. Jan Stephenson | 2,275,075.00 |

| | Earnings ($) |
|---|---|
| 11. Jane Geddes | 2,269,254.30 |
| 12. Rosie Jones | 2,193,048.97 |
| 13. Juli Inkster | 2,070,418.23 |
| 14. Hollis Stacy | 2,005,087.99 |
| 15. Colleen Walker | 1,991,323.71 |
| 16. Judy Dickinson | 1,990,807.92 |
| 17. Meg Mallon | 1,862,059.00 |
| 18. Kathy Whitworth | 1,726,597.01 |
| 19. Tammie Green | 1,715,863.00 |
| 20. Laura Davies | 1,685,657.00 |

| | Earnings ($) |
|---|---|
| 21. Deb Richard | 1,674,690.00 |
| 22. Sally Little | 1,648,210.80 |
| 23. D. Ammaccapane | 1,631,836.00 |
| 24. Chris Johnson | 1,553,666.50 |
| 25. Dawn Coe-Jones | 1,529,175.57 |
| 26. Sherri Steinhauer | 1,468,046.00 |
| 27. Donna Caponi | 1,387,919.73 |
| 28. Kathy Postlewait | 1,381,510.27 |
| 29. L. Neumann | 1,364,478.00 |
| 30. Alice Ritzman | 1,362,909.32 |

*Through 12/31/94.

## LPGA Player of the Year

| 1966 | Kathy Whitworth |
|---|---|
| 1967 | Kathy Whitworth |
| 1968 | Kathy Whitworth |
| 1969 | Kathy Whitworth |
| 1970 | Sandra Haynie |
| 1971 | Kathy Whitworth |
| 1972 | Kathy Whitworth |
| 1973 | Kathy Whitworth |
| 1974 | JoAnne Carner |
| 1975 | Sandra Palmer |
| 1976 | Judy Rankin |
| 1977 | Judy Rankin |
| 1978 | Nancy Lopez |
| 1979 | Nancy Lopez |
| 1980 | Beth Daniel |

| 1981 | JoAnne Carner |
|---|---|
| 1982 | JoAnne Carner |
| 1983 | Patty Sheehan |
| 1984 | Betsy King |
| 1985 | Nancy Lopez |
| 1986 | Pat Bradley |
| 1987 | Ayako Okamoto |
| 1988 | Nancy Lopez |
| 1989 | Betsy King |
| 1990 | Beth Daniel |
| 1991 | Pat Bradley |
| 1992 | Dottie Mochrie |
| 1993 | Betsy King |
| 1994 | Beth Daniel |

## Vare Trophy: Best Scoring Average

| | | Avg | | | Avg | | | Avg |
|---|---|---|---|---|---|---|---|---|
| 1953 | Patty Berg | 75.00 | 1967 | Kathy Whitworth | 72.74 | 1981 | JoAnne Carner | 71.75 |
| 1954 | Babe Zaharias | 75.48 | 1968 | Carol Mann | 72.04 | 1982 | JoAnne Carner | 71.49 |
| 1955 | Patty Berg | 74.47 | 1969 | Kathy Whitworth | 72.38 | 1983 | JoAnne Carner | 71.41 |
| 1956 | Patty Berg | 74.57 | 1970 | Kathy Whitworth | 72.26 | 1984 | Patty Sheehan | 71.40 |
| 1957 | Louise Suggs | 74.64 | 1971 | Kathy Whitworth | 72.88 | 1985 | Nancy Lopez | 70.73 |
| 1958 | Beverly Hanson | 74.92 | 1972 | Kathy Whitworth | 72.38 | 1986 | Pat Bradley | 71.10 |
| 1959 | Betsy Rawls | 74.03 | 1973 | Judy Rankin | 73.08 | 1987 | Betsy King | 71.14 |
| 1960 | Mickey Wright | 73.25 | 1974 | JoAnne Carner | 72.87 | 1988 | Colleen Walker | 71.26 |
| 1961 | Mickey Wright | 73.55 | 1975 | JoAnne Carner | 72.40 | 1989 | Beth Daniel | 70.38 |
| 1962 | Mickey Wright | 73.67 | 1976 | Judy Rankin | 72.25 | 1990 | Beth Daniel | 70.54 |
| 1963 | Mickey Wright | 72.81 | 1977 | Judy Rankin | 72.16 | 1991 | Pat Bradley | 70.76 |
| 1964 | Mickey Wright | 72.46 | 1978 | Nancy Lopez | 71.76 | 1992 | Dottie Mochrie | 70.80 |
| 1965 | Kathy Whitworth | 72.61 | 1979 | Nancy Lopez | 71.20 | 1993 | Nancy Lopez | 70.83 |
| 1966 | Kathy Whitworth | 72.60 | 1980 | Amy Alcott | 71.51 | 1994 | Beth Daniel | 70.90 |

## Most Career Wins*

| | Wins | | Wins | | Wins |
|---|---|---|---|---|---|
| Kathy Whitworth | 88 | JoAnne Carner | 42 | Pat Bradley | 30 |
| Mickey Wright | 82 | Sandra Haynie | 42 | Amy Alcott | 29 |
| Patty Berg | 57 | Carol Mann | 38 | Jane Blalock | 29 |
| Betsy Rawls | 55 | Patty Sheehan | 32 | Betsy King | 29 |
| Louise Suggs | 50 | Babe Zaharias | 31 | Judy Rankin | 26 |
| Nancy Lopez | 47 | Beth Daniel | 31 | | |

*Through 12/31/94.

## Alltime LPGA Tour Records*

### Scoring

#### 72 HOLES

**268**—(66-67-69-66) by Nancy Lopez to win at the Willow Creek GC, High Point, NC, in the 1985 Henredon Classic (20 under par).

**268**—(67-63-70-68) by Beth Daniel to win at the Walnut Hills CC, E. Lansing, MI, in the 1994 Oldsmobile Classic (20 under par).

#### 54 HOLES

**197**—(67-65-65) by Pat Bradley to win at the Rail GC, Springfield, Ill., in the 1991 Rail Charity Golf Classic (19 under par).

#### 36 HOLES

**129**—(64-65) by Judy Dickinson at Pasadena Yacht & CC, St Petersburg, in the 1985 S&H Golf Classic (15 under par).

#### 18 HOLES

**62**—by Mickey Wright at Hogan Park GC, Midland, TX, in the first round in winning the 1964 Tall City Open (9 under par).

**62**—by Vicki Fergon at Almaden G & CC, San Jose, CA, in the second round of the 1984 San Jose Classic (11 under par).

**62**—by Laura Davies at the Rail Golf Club, Springfield, Ill., in the first round of the 1991 Rail Charity Golf Classic (10 under par).

**62**—by Hollis Stacy at Meridian Valley Country Club, Seattle, WA, in the second round of the 1992 Safeco Classic (10 under par).

#### 9 HOLES

**28**—by Mary Beth Zimmerman at Rail GC, 1984 Rail Charity Golf Classic, Springfield, IL (par 36). Zimmerman shot 64.

**28**—by Pat Bradley at Green Gables CC, Denver,

### Scoring *(Cont.)*

#### 9 HOLES *(Cont.)*

1984 Columbia Savings Classic (par 35). Bradley shot 65.

**28**—by Muffin Spencer-Devlin at Knollwood CC, Elmsford, NY, in winning the 1985 MasterCard International Pro-Am (par 35). Spencer-Devlin shot 64.

**28**—by Peggy Kirsch at Squaw Creek CC, Vienna, OH, in the 1991 Phar-Mor (par 35).

#### MOST CONSECUTIVE ROUNDS UNDER 70

**9**—Beth Daniel, in 1990.

#### MOST BIRDIES IN A ROW

**8**—Mary Beth Zimmerman at Rail GC in Springfield, IL, in the second round of the 1984 Rail Charity Classic. Zimmerman shot 64 (8 under par).

### Wins

#### MOST CONSECUTIVE WINS IN SCHEDULED EVENTS

**4**—Mickey Wright, in 1962.
**4**—Mickey Wright, in 1963.
**4**—Kathy Whitworth, in 1969.

#### MOST CONSECUTIVE WINS IN ENTERED TOURNAMENTS

**5**—Nancy Lopez, in 1987.

#### MOST WINS IN A CALENDAR YEAR

**13**—Mickey Wright, in 1963.

#### WIDEST WINNING MARGIN, STROKES

**14**—Louise Suggs, 1949 US Women's Open.
**14**—Cindy Mackey, 1986 MasterCard Int'l Pro-Am.

*Through 12/31/94.

# Senior Golf

## U.S. Senior Open

| Year | Winner | Score | Runner-Up | Site |
|------|--------|-------|-----------|------|
| 1980 | Roberto DeVicenzo | 285 | William C. Campbell | Winged Foot GC, Mamaroneck, NY |
| 1981 | Arnold Palmer* (70) | 289 | Bob Stone (74) | Oakland Hills CC, Birmingham, MI |
| | | | Billy Casper (77) | |
| 1982 | Miller Barber | 282 | Gene Littler | Portland GC, Portland, OR |
| | | | Dan Sikes, Jr | |
| 1983 | Billy Casper* (75) (3) | 288 | Rod Funseth (75) (4) | Hazeltine GC, Chaska, MN |
| 1984 | Miller Barber | 286 | Arnold Palmer | Oak Hill CC, Rochester, NY |
| 1985 | Miller Barber | 285 | Roberto DeVicenzo | Edgewood Tahoe GC, Stateline, NV |
| 1986 | Dale Douglass | 279 | Gary Player | Scioto CC, Columbus, OH |
| 1987 | Gary Player | 270 | Doug Sanders | Brooklawn CC, Fairfield, CT |
| 1988 | Gary Player* (68) | 288 | Bob Charles (70) | Medinah CC, Medinah, IL |
| 1989 | Orville Moody | 279 | Frank Beard | Laurel Valley GC, Ligonier, PA |
| 1990 | Lee Trevino | 275 | Jack Nicklaus | Ridgewood CC, Paramus, NJ |
| 1991 | Jack Nicklaus (65) | 282 | Chi Chi Rodriguez (69) | Oakland Hills CC, Birmingham, MI |
| 1992 | Larry Laoretti | 275 | Jim Colbert | Saucon Valley CC, Bethlehem, PA |
| 1993 | Jack Nicklaus | 278 | Tom Weiskopf | Cherry Hills CC, Englewood, CO |
| 1994 | Simon Hobday | 274 | Jim Albus | Pinehurst Resort & CC, Pinehurst, NC |
| 1995 | Tom Weiskopf | 275 | Jack Nicklaus | Congressional CC, Bethesda, MD |

*Winner in playoff. Playoff scores are in parentheses. The 1983 playoff went to one hole of sudden death after an 18-hole playoff.

# SENIOR TOUR

## Season Money Leaders*

| Year | Leader | Earnings ($) | Year | Leader | Earnings ($) |
|------|--------|-------------|------|--------|-------------|
| 1980 | Don January | 44,100 | 1988 | Bob Charles | 533,929 |
| 1981 | Miller Barber | 83,136 | 1989 | Bob Charles | 725,887 |
| 1982 | Miller Barber | 106,890 | 1990 | Lee Trevino | 1,190,518 |
| 1983 | Don January | 237,571 | 1991 | Mike Hill | 1,065,657 |
| 1984 | Don January | 328,597 | 1992 | Lee Trevino | 1,027,000 |
| 1985 | Peter Thomson | 386,724 | 1993 | Dave Stockton | 1,175,944 |
| 1986 | Bruce Crampton | 454,299 | 1994 | Dave Stockton | 1,402,519 |
| 1987 | Chi Chi Rodriguez | 509,145 | | | |

## Career Money Leaders*

| # | Player | Earnings ($) | # | Player | Earnings ($) |
|---|--------|-------------|---|--------|-------------|
| 1. | Bob Charles | 5,201,105 | 17. | Charles Coody | 2,692,028 |
| 2. | Chi Chi Rodriguez | 5,110,722 | 18. | Jim Albus | 2,585,543 |
| 3. | Lee Trevino | 5,108,902 | 19. | Ray Floyd | 2,532,920 |
| 4. | Mike Hill | 4,554,599 | 20. | Walter Zembriski | 2,374,070 |
| 5. | George Archer | 4,352,085 | 21. | Rocky Thompson | 2,295,704 |
| 6 | Dale Douglass | 4,113,377 | 22. | Jim Ferree | 2,126,146 |
| 7. | Jim Dent | 3,618,605 | 23. | Dave Hill | 2,067,259 |
| 8. | Bruce Crampton | 3,604,534 | 24. | Simon Hobday | 2,056,175 |
| 9. | Jim Colbert | 3,498,521 | 25. | Gene Littler | 2,044,991 |
| 10. | Gary Player | 3,466,026 | 26. | Gibby Gilbert | 2,009,702 |
| 11. | Miller Barber | 3,393,652 | 27. | Don Bies | 1,901,353 |
| 12. | Dave Stockton | 3,247,885 | 28. | Jimmy Powell | 1,822,473 |
| 13. | Al Geiberger | 3,101,060 | 29. | J.C. Snead | 1,805,843 |
| 14. | Orville Moody | 3,057,323 | 30. | Bobby Nichols | 1,637,662 |
| 15. | Harold Henning | 2,942,073 | | | |
| 16. | Don January | 2,827,192 | | *Through 12/31/94. | |

## Most Career Wins*

| Player | Wins | Player | Wins |
|--------|------|--------|------|
| Miller Barber | 24 | Gary Player | 17 |
| Lee Trevino | 24 | Mike Hill | 15 |
| Chi Chi Rodriguez | 22 | Mike Hill | 16 |
| Don January | 22 | George Archer | 15 |
| Bob Charles | 21 | Orville Moody | 11 |
| Bruce Crampton | 19 | Peter Thompson | 11 |

* Through 12/31/94.

# MAJOR MEN'S AMATEUR CHAMPIONSHIPS

## U.S. Amateur

| Year | Winner | Score | Runner-Up | Site |
|------|--------|-------|-----------|------|
| 1895 | Charles B. Macdonald | 12 & 11 | Charles E. Sands | Newport GC, Newport, RI |
| 1896 | H. J. Whigham | 8 & 7 | J.G Thorp | Shinnecock Hills GC, Southampton, NY |
| 1897 | H. J. Whigham | 8 & 6 | W. Rossiter Betts | Chicago GC, Wheaton, IL |
| 1898 | Findlay S. Douglas | 5 & 3 | Walter B. Smith | Morris County GC, Morristown, NJ |
| 1899 | H. M. Harriman | 3 & 2 | Findlay S. Douglas | Onwentsia Club, Lake Forest, IL |
| 1900 | Walter Travis | 2 up | Findlay S. Douglas | Garden City GC, Garden City, NY |
| 1901 | Walter Travis | 5 & 4 | Walter E. Egan | CC of Atlantic City, NJ |
| 1902 | Louis N. James | 4 & 2 | Eben M. Byers | Glen View Club, Golf, Ill. |
| 1903 | Walter Travis | 5 & 4 | Eben M. Byers | Nassau CC, Glen Cove, NY |
| 1904 | H. Chandler Egan | 8 & 6 | Fred Herreshoff | Baltusrol GC, Springfield, NJ |
| 1905 | H. Chandler Egan | 6 & 5 | D.E. Sawyer | Chicago GC, Wheaton, IL |
| 1906 | Eben M. Byers | 2 up | George S. Lyon | Englewood GC, Englewood, NJ |
| 1907 | Jerry Travers | 6 & 5 | Archibald Graham | Euclid Club, Cleveland, OH |
| 1908 | Jerry Travers | 8 & 7 | Max H. Behr | Garden City GC, Garden City, NY |
| 1909 | Robert A. Gardner | 4 & 3 | H. Chandler Egan | Chicago GC, Wheaton, IL |
| 1910 | William C. Fownes, Jr | 4 & 3 | Warren K. Wood | The Country Club, Brookline, MA |
| 1911 | Harold Hilton | 1 up | Fred Herreshoff | The Apawamis Club, Rye, NY |
| 1912 | Jerry Travers | 7 & 6 | Charles Evans, Jr. | Chicago GC, Wheaton, IL |
| 1913 | Jerry Travers | 5 & 4 | John G. Anderson | Garden City GC, Garden City, NY |
| 1914 | Francis Ouimet | 6 & 5 | Jerry Travers | Ekwanok CC, Manchester, VT |
| 1915 | Robert A. Gardner | 5 & 4 | John G. Anderson | CC of Detroit, Grosse Pt. Farms, MI |
| 1916 | Chick Evans | 4 & 3 | Robert A. Gardner | Merion Cricket Club, Haverford, PA |
| 1917-18 | No tournament | | | |
| 1919 | S. Davidson Herron | 5 & 4 | Bobby Jones | Oakmont CC, Oakmont, PA |
| 1920 | Chick Evans | 7 & 6 | Francis Ouimet | Engineers' CC, Roslyn, NY |
| 1921 | Jesse P. Guilford | 7 & 6 | Robert A. Gardner | St. Louis CC, Clayton, MO |
| 1922 | Jess W. Sweetser | 3 & 2 | Chick Evans | The Country Club, Brookline, MA |
| 1923 | Max R. Marston | 1 up | Jess W. Sweetser | Flossmoor CC, Flossmoor, IL |
| 1924 | Bobby Jones | 9 & 8 | George Von Elm | Merion Cricket Club, Ardmore, PA |
| 1925 | Bobby Jones | 8 & 7 | Watts Gunn | Oakmont CC, Oakmont, PA |
| 1926 | George Von Elm | 2 & 1 | Bobby Jones | Baltusrol GC, Springfield, NJ |
| 1927 | Bobby Jones | 8 & 7 | Chick Evans | Minikahda Club, Minneapolis |
| 1928 | Bobby Jones | 10 & 9 | T. Phillip Perkins | Brae Burn CC, West Newton, MA |
| 1929 | Harrison R. Johnston | 4 & 3 | Dr. O.F. Willing | Del Monte G & CC, Pebble Beach, CA |
| 1930 | Bobby Jones | 8 & 7 | Eugene V. Homans | Merion Cricket Club, Ardmore, PA |
| 1931 | Francis Ouimet | 6 & 5 | Jack Westland | Beverly CC, Chicago, IL |
| 1932 | C. Ross Somerville | 2 & 1 | John Goodman | Baltimore CC, Timonium, MD |
| 1933 | George T. Dunlap, Jr | 6 & 5 | Max R. Marston | Kenwood CC, Cincinnati, OH |
| 1934 | Lawson Little | 8 & 7 | David Goldman | The Country Club, Brookline, MA |
| 1935 | Lawson Little | 4 & 2 | Walter Emery | The Country Club, Cleveland, OH |
| 1936 | John W. Fischer | 1 up | Jack McLean | Garden City GC, Garden City, NY |
| 1937 | John Goodman | 2 up | Raymond E. Billows | Alderwood CC, Portland, OR |
| 1938 | William P. Turnesa | 8 & 7 | B. Patrick Abbott | Oakmont CC, Oakmont, PA |
| 1939 | Marvin H. Ward | 7 & 5 | Raymond E. Billows | North Shore CC, Glenview, IL |
| 1940 | Richard D. Chapman | 11 & 9 | W. McCullough, Jr | Winged Foot GC, Mamaroneck, NY |
| 1941 | Marvin H. Ward | 4 & 3 | B. Patrick Abbott | Omaha Field Club, Omaha, NE |
| 1942-45 | No tournament | | | |
| 1946 | Ted Bishop | 1 up | Smiley L. Quick | Baltusrol GC, Springfield, NJ |
| 1947 | Skee Riegel | 2 & 1 | John W. Dawson | Del Monte G & CC, Pebble Beach, CA |
| 1948 | William P. Turnesa | 2 & 1 | Raymond E. Billows | Memphis CC, Memphis, TN |
| 1949 | Charles R. Coe | 11 & 10 | Rufus King | Oak Hill CC, Rochester, NY |
| 1950 | Sam Urzetta | 1 up | Frank Stranahan | Minneapolis GC, Minneapolis, MN |
| 1951 | Billy Maxwell | 4 & 3 | Joseph F. Gagliardi | Saucon Valley CC, Bethlehem, PA |
| 1952 | Jack Westland | 3 & 2 | Al Mengert | Seattle GC, Seattle, WA |
| 1953 | Gene Littler | 1 up | Dale Morey | Oklahoma City G & CC, Oklahoma City |
| 1954 | Arnold Palmer | 1 up | Robert Sweeny | CC of Detroit, Grosse Pt. Farms, MI |
| 1955 | E. Harvie Ward, Jr | 9 & 8 | Wm. Hyndman III | CC of Virginia, Richmond, VA |
| 1956 | E. Harvie Ward, Jr | 5 & 4 | Charles Kocsis | Knollwood Club, Lake Forest, IL |
| 1957 | Hillman Robbins, Jr | 5 & 4 | Dr. Frank M. Taylor | The Country Club, Brookline, MA |
| 1958 | Charles R. Coe | 5 & 4 | Tommy Aaron | Olympic Club, San Francisco, CA |
| 1959 | Jack Nicklaus | 1 up | Charles R. Coe | Broadmoor GC, Colorado Springs, CO |
| 1960 | Deane Beman | 6 & 4 | Robert W. Gardner | St. Louis CC, Clayton, MO |
| 1961 | Jack Nicklaus | 8 & 6 | H. Dudley Wysong | Pebble Beach GL, Pebble Beach, CA |

## U.S. Amateur (Cont.)

| Year | Winner | Score | Runner-Up | Site |
|------|--------|-------|-----------|------|
| 1962 | Labron E. Harris, Jr | 1 up | Downing Gray | Pinehurst CC, Pinehurst, NC |
| 1963 | Deane Beman | 2 & 1 | Richard H. Sikes | Wakonda Club, Des Moines, IA |
| 1964 | William C. Campbell | 1 up | Edgar M. Tutwiler | Canterbury GC, Cleveland, OH |
| 1965 | Robert J. Murphy, Jr | 291 | Robert B. Dickson | Southern Hills, CC, Tulsa, OK |
| 1966 | Gary Cowan | 285-75 | Deane Beman | Merion GC, Ardmore, PA |
| 1967 | Robert B. Dickson | 285 | Marvin Giles III | Broadmoor GC, Colorado Springs, CO |
| 1968 | Bruce Fleisher | 284 | Marvin Giles III | Scioto CC, Columbus, OH |
| 1969 | Steven N. Melnyk | 286 | Marvin Giles III | Oakmont CC, Oakmont, PA |
| 1970 | Lanny Wadkins | 279 | Tom Kite | Waverley CC, Portland, OR |
| 1971 | Gary Cowan | 280 | Eddie Pearce | Wilmington CC, Wilmington DE |
| 1972 | Marvin Giles, III | 285 | two tied | Charlotte CC, Charlotte, NC |
| 1973 | Craig Stadler | 6 & 5 | David Strawn | Inverness Club, Toledo, OH |
| 1974 | Jerry Pate | 2 & 1 | John P. Grace | Ridgewood CC, Ridgewood, NJ |
| 1975 | Fred Ridley | 2 up | Keith Fergus | CC of Virginia, Richmond, VA |
| 1976 | Bill Sander | 8 & 6 | C. Parker Moore, Jr | Bel Air CC, Los Angeles, CA |
| 1977 | John Fought | 9 & 8 | Doug Fischesser | Aronimink GC, Newton Square, PA |
| 1978 | John Cook | 5 & 4 | Scott Hoch | Plainfield CC, Plainfield, NJ |
| 1979 | Mark O'Meara | 8 & 7 | John Cook | Canterbury GC, Cleveland, OH |
| 1980 | Hal Sutton | 9 & 8 | Bob Lewis | CC of North Carolina, Pinehurst, NC |
| 1981 | Nathaniel Crosby | 1 up | Brian Lindley | Olympic Club, San Francisco, CA |
| 1982 | Jay Sigel | 8 & 7 | David Tolley | The Country Club, Brookline, MA |
| 1983 | Jay Sigel | 8 & 7 | Chris Perry | North Shore CC, Glenviedw IL |
| 1984 | Scott Verplank | 4 & 3 | Sam Randolph | Oak Tree GC, Edmond, OK |
| 1985 | Sam Randolph | 1 up | Peter Persons | Montclair GC, West Orange, NJ |
| 1986 | Buddy Alexander | 5 & 3 | Chris Kite | Shoal Creek, Shoal Creek AL |
| 1987 | Bill Mayfair | 4 & 3 | Eric Rebmann | Jupiter Hills Club, Jupiter, FL |
| 1988 | Eric Meeks | 7 & 6 | Danny Yates | Va. Hot Springs G & CC, VA |
| 1989 | Chris Patton | 3 & 1 | Danny Green | Merion GC, Ardmore, PA |
| 1990 | Phil Mickelson | 5 & 4 | Manny Zerman | Cherry Hills CC, Englewood, CO |
| 1991 | Mitch Voges | 7 & 6 | Manny Zerman | The Honors Course, Ooltewah, TN |
| 1992 | Justin Leonard | 8 & 7 | Tom Scherrer | Muirfield Village GC, Dublin, OH |
| 1993 | John Harris | 5 & 3 | Danny Ellis | Champions GC, Houston, TX |
| 1994 | Tiger Woods | 2 up | Trip Kuehne | TPC-Sawgrass, Ponte Vedre, FL |
| 1995 | Tiger Woods | 2 up | Buddy Marucci | Newport Country Club, Newport, RI |

Note: All stroke play from 1965 to 1972.

## U.S. Junior Amateur

| | | | | | |
|------|--------|------|--------|------|--------|
| 1948 | Dean Lind | 1964 | Johnny Miller | 1980 | Eric Johnson |
| 1949 | Gay Brewer | 1965 | James Masserio | 1981 | Scott Erickson |
| 1950 | Mason Rudolph | 1966 | Gary Sanders | 1982 | Rich Marik |
| 1951 | Tommy Jacobs | 1967 | John Crooks | 1983 | Tim Straub |
| 1952 | Don Bisplinghoff | 1968 | Eddie Pearce | 1984 | Doug Martin |
| 1953 | Rex Baxter | 1969 | Aly Trompas | 1985 | Charles Rymer |
| 1954 | Foster Bradley | 1970 | Gary Koch | 1986 | Brian Montgomery |
| 1955 | William Dunn | 1971 | Mike Brannan | 1987 | Brett Quigley |
| 1956 | Harlan Stevenson | 1972 | Bob Byman | 1988 | Jason Widener |
| 1957 | Larry Beck | 1973 | Jack Renner | 1989 | David Duval |
| 1958 | Buddy Baker | 1974 | David Nevatt | 1990 | Mathew Todd |
| 1959 | Larry Lee | 1975 | Brett Mullin | 1991 | Tiger Woods |
| 1960 | Bill Tindall | 1976 | Madden Hatcher, III | 1992 | Tiger Woods |
| 1961 | Charles McDowell | 1977 | Willie Wood, Jr | 1993 | Tiger Woods |
| 1962 | Jim Wiechers | 1978 | Don Hurter | 1994 | Terry Noe |
| 1963 | Gregg McHatton | 1979 | Jack Larkin | 1995 | D. Scott Hailes |

Note: Event is for amateur golfers younger than 18 years of age.

## Mid-Amateur Championship

| | | | | | |
|------|--------|------|--------|------|--------|
| 1981 | Jim Holtgrieve | 1986 | Bill Loeffler | 1991 | Jim Stuart |
| 1982 | William Hoffer | 1987 | Jay Sigel | 1992 | Danny Yates |
| 1983 | Jay Sigel | 1988 | David Eger | 1993 | Jeff Thomas |
| 1984 | Mike Podolak | 1989 | James Taylor | 1994 | Tim Jackson |
| 1985 | Jay Sigel | 1990 | Jim Stuart | 1995 | Jerry Courville Jr |

Note: Event is for amateur golfers at least 25 years of age.

## British Amateur

| | | | | | |
|---|---|---|---|---|---|
| 1887 | H. G. Hutchinson | 1925 | R. Harris | 1964 | C. Clark |
| 1888 | John Ball | 1926 | Jess Sweetser | 1965 | M. Bonallack |
| 1889 | J.E. Laidlay | 1927 | Dr. W. Tweddell | 1966 | C.R. Cole |
| 1890 | John Ball | 1928 | T.P. Perkins | 1967 | R. Dickson |
| 1891 | J.E. Laidlay | 1929 | C.J.H. Tolley | 1968 | M. Bonallack |
| 1892 | John Ball | 1930 | Robert T. Jones, Jr. | 1969 | M. Bonallack |
| 1893 | Peter Anderson | 1931 | E. Martin Smith | 1970 | M. Bonallack |
| 1894 | John Ball | 1932 | J. DeForest | 1971 | Steve Melnyk |
| 1895 | L.M.B. Melville | 1933 | M. Scott | 1972 | Trevor Homer |
| 1896 | F.G. Tait | 1934 | W. Lawson Little | 1973 | R. Siderowf |
| 1897 | A.J.T. Allan | 1935 | W. Lawson Little | 1974 | Trevor Homer |
| 1898 | F.G. Tait | 1936 | H. Thomson | 1975 | M. Giles |
| 1899 | John Ball | 1937 | R. Sweeney, Jr. | 1976 | R. Siderowf |
| 1900 | H.H. Hilton | 1938 | C.R. Yates | 1977 | P. McEvoy |
| 1901 | H.H. Hilton | 1939 | A.T. Kyle | 1978 | P. McEvoy |
| 1902 | C. Hutchings | 1940-45 | not held | 1979 | J. Sigel |
| 1903 | R. Maxwell | 1946 | J. Bruen | 1980 | D. Evans |
| 1904 | W.J. Travis | 1947 | Willie D. Turnesa | 1981 | P. Ploujoux |
| 1905 | A.G. Barry | 1948 | Frank R. Stranahan | 1982 | M. Thompson |
| 1906 | James Robb | 1949 | S.M. McReady | 1983 | A. Parkin |
| 1907 | John Ball | 1950 | Frank R. Stranahan | 1984 | J.M. Olazabal |
| 1908 | E.A. Lassen | 1951 | Richard D. Chapman | 1985 | G. McGimpsey |
| 1909 | R. Maxwell | 1952 | E.H. Ward | 1986 | D. Curry |
| 1910 | John Ball | 1953 | J.B. Carr | 1987 | P. Mayo |
| 1911 | H.H. Hilton | 1954 | D.W. Bachli | 1988 | C. Hardin |
| 1912 | John Ball | 1955 | J.W. Conrad | 1989 | S. Dodd |
| 1913 | H.H. Hilton | 1956 | J.C. Beharrel | 1990 | R. Muntz |
| 1914 | J.L.C. Jenkins | 1957 | R. Reid Jack | 1991 | G. Wolstenholme |
| 1915-19 | not held | 1958 | J.B. Carr | 1992 | S. Dundas |
| 1920 | C.J.H. Tolley | 1959 | Deane Beman | 1993 | I. Pyman |
| 1921 | W.I. Hunter | 1960 | J.B. Carr | 1994 | L. James |
| 1922 | E.W.E. Holderness | 1961 | M. Bonallack | 1995 | G. Sherry |
| 1923 | R.H. Wethered | 1962 | R. Davies | | |
| 1924 | E.W.E. Holderness | 1963 | M. Lunt | | |

## Amateur Public Links

| | | | | | |
|---|---|---|---|---|---|
| 1922 | Edmund R. Held | 1948 | Michael R. Ferentz | 1972 | Bob Allard |
| 1923 | Richard J. Walsh | 1949 | Kenneth J. Towns | 1973 | Stan Stopa |
| 1924 | Joseph Coble | 1950 | Stanley Bielat | 1974 | Charles Barenaba |
| 1925 | Raymond J. McAuliffe | 1951 | Dave Stanley | 1975 | Randy Barenaba |
| 1926 | Lester Bolstad | 1952 | Omer L. Bogan | 1976 | Eddie Mudd |
| 1927 | Carl F. Kauffmann | 1953 | Ted Richards, Jr. | 1977 | Jerry Vidovic |
| 1928 | Carl F. Kauffmann | 1954 | Gene Andrews | 1978 | Dean Prince |
| 1929 | Carl F. Kauffmann | 1955 | Sam D. Kocsis | 1979 | Dennis Walsh |
| 1930 | Robert E. Wingate | 1956 | James H. Buxbaum | 1980 | Jodie Mudd |
| 1931 | Charles Ferrera | 1957 | Don Essig III | 1981 | Jodie Mudd |
| 1932 | R.L. Miller | 1958 | Daniel D. Sikes, Jr. | 1982 | Billy Tuten |
| 1933 | Charles Ferrera | 1959 | William A. Wright | 1983 | Billy Tuten |
| 1934 | David A. Mitchell | 1960 | Verne Callison | 1984 | Bill Malley |
| 1935 | Frank Strafaci | 1961 | Richard H. Sikes | 1985 | Jim Sorenson |
| 1936 | B. Patrick Abbott | 1962 | Richard H. Sikes | 1986 | Bill Mayfair |
| 1937 | Bruce N. McCormick | 1963 | Robert Lunn | 1987 | Kevin Johnson |
| 1938 | Al Leach | 1964 | William McDonald | 1988 | Ralph Howe, III |
| 1939 | Andrew Szwedko | 1965 | Arne Dokka | 1989 | Tim Hobby |
| 1940 | Robert C. Clark | 1966 | Lamont Kaser | 1990 | Michael Combs |
| 1941 | William M. Welch, Jr. | 1967 | Verne Callison | 1991 | David Berganio, Jr. |
| 1942-45 | not held | 1968 | Gene Towry | 1992 | Warren Schulte |
| 1946 | Smiley L. Quick | 1969 | John M. Jackson, Jr. | 1993 | David Berganio, Jr. |
| 1947 | Wilfred Crossley | 1970 | Robert Risch | 1994 | Guy Yamamoto |
| | | 1971 | Fred Haney | 1995 | Chris Wollmann |

## U.S. Senior Golf

| | | |
|---|---|---|
| 1955 ...........J. Wood Platt | 1969 ...........Curtis Person, Sr | 1983 ...........William Hyndman, III |
| 1956 ...........Frederick J. Wright | 1970 ...........Gene Andrews | 1984 ...........Bob Rawlins |
| 1957 ...........J. Clark Espie | 1971 ...........Tom Draper | 1985 ...........Lewis W. Oehmig |
| 1958 ...........Thomas C. Robbins | 1972 ...........Lewis W. Oehmig | 1986 ...........Bo Williams |
| 1959 ...........J. Clark Espie | 1973 ...........William Hyndman, III | 1987 ...........John Richardson |
| 1960 ...........Michael Cestone | 1974 ...........Dale Morey | 1988 ...........Clarence Moore |
| 1961 ...........Dexter H. Daniels | 1975 ...........William F. Colm | 1989 ...........Bo Williams |
| 1962 ...........Merrill L. Carlsmith | 1976 ...........Lewis W. Oehmig | 1990 ...........Jackie Cummings |
| 1963 ...........Merrill L. Carlsmith | 1977 ...........Dale Morey | 1991 ...........Bill Bosshard |
| 1964 ...........William D. Higgins | 1978 ...........K. K. Compton | 1992 ...........Clarence Moore |
| 1965 ...........Robert B. Kiersky | 1979 ...........William C. Campbell | 1993 ...........Joe Ungvary |
| 1966 ...........Dexter H. Daniels | 1980 ...........William C. Campbell | 1994 ...........O. Gordon Brewer |
| 1967 ...........Ray Palmer | 1981 ...........Ed Updegraff | 1995 ...........James Stahl Jr |
| 1968 ...........Curtis Person, Sr | 1982 ...........Alton Duhon | |

Event is for golfers at least 55 years of age.

# MAJOR WOMEN'S AMATEUR CHAMPIONSHIPS

## U.S. Women's Amateur

| Year | Winner | Score | Runner-Up | Site |
|---|---|---|---|---|
| 1895 ...........Mrs. Charles S. Brown | | 132 | Nellie Sargent | Meadow Brook Club, Hempstead, NY |
| 1896 ...........Beatrix Hoyt | | 2 & 1 | Mrs. Arthur Turnure | Morris Couty GC, Morristown, NJ |
| 1897 ...........Beatrix Hoyt | | 5 & 4 | Nellie Sargent | Essex County Club, Manchester, MA |
| 1898 ...........Beatrix Hoyt | | 5 &3 | Maude Wetmore | Ardsley Club, Ardsley-on-Hudson, NY |
| 1899 ...........Ruth Underhill | | 2 & 1 | Margaret Fox | Philadelphia CC, Philadelphia, PA |
| 1900 ...........Frances C. Griscom | | 6 & 5 | Margaret Curtis | Shinnecock Hills GC, Shinnecock Hills, NY |
| 1901 ...........Genevieve Hecker | | 5 & 3 | Lucy Herron | Baltusrol GC, Springfield, NJ |
| 1902 ...........Genevieve Hecker | | 4 & 3 | Louisa A. Wells | The Country Club, Brookline, MA |
| 1903 ...........Bessie Anthony | | 7 & 6 | J. Anna Carpenter | Chicago GC, Wheaton, IL |
| 1904 ...........Georgianna M. Bishop | | 5 & 3 | Mrs. E.F. Sanford | Merion Cricket Club, Haverford, PA |
| 1905 ...........Pauline Mackay | | 1 up | Margaret Curtis | Morris County GC, Convent, NJ |
| 1906 ...........Harriot S. Curtis | | 2 & 1 | Mary B. Adams | Brae Burn CC, West Newton, MA |
| 1907 ...........Margaret Curtis | | 7 & 6 | Harriot S. Curtis | Midlothian CC, Blue Island, IL |
| 1908 ...........Katherine C. Harley | | 6 & 5 | Mrs. T.H. Polhemus | Chevy Chase Club, Chevy Chase, MD |
| 1909 ...........Dorothy I. Campbell | | 3 & 2 | Nonna Barlow | Merion Cricket Club, Haverford, PA |
| 1910 ...........Dorothy I. Campbell | | 2 & 1 | Mrs. G.M. Martin | Homewood CC, Flossmoor, IL |
| 1911 ...........Margaret Curtis | | 5 & 3 | Lillian B. Hyde | Baltusrol GC, Springfield, NJ |
| 1912 ...........Margaret Curtis | | 3 & 2 | Nonna Barlow | Essex County Club, Manchester, MA |
| 1913 ...........Gladys Ravenscroft | | 2 up | Marion Hollins | Wilmington CC, Wilmington, DE |
| 1914 ...........Katherine Harley | | 1 up | Elaine V. Rosenthal | Nassau CC, Glen Cove, NY |
| 1915 ...........Florence Vanderbeck | | 3 & 2 | Margaret Gavin | Onwentsia Club, Lake Forest, IL |
| 1916 ...........Alexa Stirling | | 2 & 1 | Mildred Caverly | Belmont Springs CC, Waverley, MA |
| 1917-18 ......No tournament | | | | |
| 1919...........Alexa Stirling | | 6 & 5 | Margaret Gavin | Shawnee CC, Shawnee-on Delaware, PA |
| 1920 ...........Alexa Stirling | | 5 & 4 | Dorothy Campbell | Mayfield CC, Cleveland, OH |
| 1921 ...........Marion Hollins | | 5 & 4 | Alexa Stirling | Hollywood GC, Deal, NJ |
| 1922 ...........Glenna Collett | | 5 & 4 | Margaret Gavin | Greenbriar GC, White Sulphur Springs, WV |
| 1923 ...........Edith Cummings | | 3 & 2 | Alexa Stirling | Westchester-Biltmore CC, Rye, NY |
| 1924 ...........Dorothy Campbell | | 7 & 6 | Mary K. Browne | Rhode Island CC, Nyatt, RI |
| 1925 ...........Glenna Collett | | 9 & 8 | Alexa Stirling | St. Louis CC, Clayton, MO |
| 1926 ...........Helen Stetson | | 3 & 1 | Elizabeth Goss | Merion Cricket Club, Ardmore, PA |
| 1927 ...........Miiriam Burns Horn | | 5 & 4 | Maureen Orcutt | Cherry Valley Club, Garden City, NY |
| 1928 ...........Glenna Collett | | 13 & 12 | Virginia Van Wie | Va. Hot Springs G & TC, Hot Springs, VA |
| 1929 ...........Glenna Collett | | 4 & 3 | Leona Pressler | Oakland Hills CC, Birmingham, MI |
| 1930 ...........Glenna Collett | | 6 & 5 | Virginia Van Wie | Los Angeles CC, Beverly Hills, CA |
| 1931 ...........Helen Hicks | | 2 & 1 | Glenna Collet Vare | CC of Buffalo, Williamsville, NY |
| 1932 ...........Virginia Van Wie | | 10 & 8 | Glenna Collet Vare | Salem CC, Peabody, MA |
| 1933 ...........Virginia Van Wie | | 4 & 3 | Helen Hicks | Exmoor CC, Highland Park, IL |
| 1934 ...........Virginia Van Wie | | 2 & 1 | Dorothy Traung | Whitemarsh Valley CC, Chestnut Hill, PA |
| 1935 ...........Glenna Collett Vare | | 3 & 2 | Patty Berg | Interlachen CC, Hopkins, MN |
| 1936 ...........Pamela Barton | | 4 & 3 | Maureen Orcutt | Canoe Brook CC, Summit, NJ |
| 1937 ...........Estelle Lawson | | 7 & 6 | Patty Berg | Memphis CC, Memphis, TN |
| 1938 ...........Patty Berg | | 6 & 5 | Estelle Lawson | Westmoreland CC, Wilmette, IL |
| 1939 ...........Betty Jameson | | 3 & 2 | Dorothy Kirby | Wee Burn Club, Darien, CT |

## U.S. Women's Amateur *(Cont.)*

| Year | Winner | Score | Runner-Up | Site |
|------|--------|-------|-----------|------|
| 1940 | Betty Jameson | 6 & 5 | Jane S. Cothran | Del Monte G & CC, Pebble Beach, CA |
| 1941 | Elizabeth Hicks | 5 & 3 | Helen Sigel | The Country Club, Brookline, MA |
| 1942-45 | No tournament | | | |
| 1946 | Babe Zaharias | 11 & 9 | Clara Sherman | Southern Hills CC, Tulsa, OK |
| 1947 | Louise Suggs | 2 up | Dorothy Kirby | Franklin Hills CC, Franklin, MI |
| 1948 | Grace S. Lenczyk | 4 & 3 | Helen Sigel | Del Monte G & CC, Pebble Beach, CA |
| 1949 | Dorothy Porter | 3 & 2 | Dorothy Kielty | Merion GC, Ardmore, PA |
| 1950 | Beverly Hanson | 6 & 4 | Mae Murray | Atlanta AC, Atlanta, GA |
| 1951 | Dorothy Kirby | 2 & 1 | Claire Doran | Town & CC, St. Paul, MN |
| 1952 | Jacqueline Pung | 2 & 1 | Shirley McFedters | Waverley CC, Portland, OR |
| 1953 | Mary Lena Faulk | 3 & 2 | Polly Riley | Rhode Island CC, West Barrington, RI |
| 1954 | Barbara Romack | 4 & 2 | Miickey Wright | Allegheny CC, Sewickley, PA |
| 1955 | Patricia A. Lesser | 7 & 6 | Jane Nelson | Myers Park CC, Charlotte, NC |
| 1956 | Marlene Stewart | 2 & 1 | JoAnne Gunderson | Meridian Hills CC, Indianapolis, IN |
| 1957 | JoAnne Gunderson | 8 & 6 | Ann Casey Johnstone | Del Paso CC, Sacramento, CA |
| 1958 | Anne Quast | 3 & 2 | Barbara Romack | Wee Burn CC, Darien, CT |
| 1959 | Barbara McIntire | 4 & 3 | Joanne Goodwin | Congressional CC, Washington, D.C. |
| 1960 | JoAnne Gunderson | 6 & 5 | Jean Ashley | Tulsa CC, Tulsa, OK |
| 1961 | Anne Quast Sander | 14 & 13 | Phyllis Preuss | Tacoma G & CC, Tacoma, WA |
| 1962 | JoAnne Gunderson | 9 & 8 | Anne Baker | CC of Rochester, Rochester, NY |
| 1963 | Anne Quast Sander | 2 & 1 | Peggy Conley | Taconic GC, Williamstown, MA |
| 1964 | Barbara McIntire | 3 & 2 | JoAnne Gunderson | Prairie Dunes CC, Hutchinson, KS |
| 1965 | Jean Ashley | 5 & 4 | Anne Quast Sander | Lakewood CC, Denver, CO |
| 1966 | JoAnne Gunderson | 1 up | Marlene Stewart Streit | Sewickley Heights GC, Sewickley, PA |
| 1967 | Mary Lou Dill | 5 & 4 | Jean Ashley | Annandale GC, Pasadena, CA |
| 1968 | JoAnne Gunderson Carner | 5 & 4 | Anne Quast Sander | Birmingham CC, Birmingham, MI |
| 1969 | Catherine Lacoste | 3 & 2 | Shelley Hamling | Las Colinas CC, Irving, TX |
| 1970 | Martha Wilkinson | 3 & 2 | Cynthia Hall | Wee Burn CC, Darien, CT |
| 1971 | Laura Baugh | 1 up | Beth Barry | Atlanta CC, Atlanta, GA |
| 1972 | Mary Budke | 5 & 4 | Cynthia Hill | St. Louis CC, St. Louis, MO |
| 1973 | Carol Semple | 1 up | Anne Quast Sander | Montclair GC, Montclair, NJ |
| 1974 | Cynthia Hill | 5 & 4 | Carol Semple | Broadmoor GC, Seattle, WA |
| 1975 | Beth Daniel | 3 & 2 | Donna Horton | Brae Burn CC, West Newton, MA |
| 1976 | Donna Horton | 2 & 1 | Marianne Bretton | Del Paso CC, Sacramento, CA |
| 1977 | Beth Daniel | 3 & 1 | Cathy Sherk | Cincinnati CC, Cincinnati, OH |
| 1978 | Cathy Sherk | 4 & 3 | Judith Oliver | Sunnybrook GC, Plymouth Meeting, PA |
| 1979 | Carolyn Hill | 7 & 6 | Patty Sheehan | Memphis CC, Memphis, TN |
| 1980 | Juli Inkster | 2 up | Patti Rizzo | Prairie Dunes CC, Hutchinson, KS |
| 1981 | Juli Inkster | 1 up | Lindy Goggin | Waverley CC, Portland, OR |
| 1982 | Juli Inkster | 4 & 3 | Cathy Hanlon | Broadmoor GC, Colorado Springs, CO |
| 1983 | Joanne Pacillo | 2 & 1 | Sally Quinlan | Canoe Brook CC, Summit, NJ |
| 1984 | Deb Richard | 1 up | Kimberly Williams | Broadmoor GC, Seattle, WA |
| 1985 | Michiko Hattori | 5 & 4 | Cheryl Stacy | Fox Chapel CC, Pittsburgh, PA |
| 1986 | Kay Cockerill | 9 & 7 | Kathleen McCarthy | Pasatiempo GC, Santa Cruz, CA |
| 1987 | Kay Cockerill | 3 & 2 | Tracy Kerdyk | Rhode Island CC, Barrington, RI |
| 1988 | Pearl Sinn | 6 & 5 | Karen Noble | Minikahda Club, Miinneapolis, MN |
| 1989 | Vicki Goetze | 4 & 3 | Brandie Burton | Pinehurst CC (No. 2), Pinehurst, NC |
| 1990 | Pat Hurst | 37 holes | Stephanie Davis | Canoe Brook CC, Summit, NJ |
| 1991 | Amy Fruhwirth | 5 & 4 | Heidi Voorhees | Prairie Dunes CC, Hutchinson, KN |
| 1992 | Vicki Goetz | 1-up | Annika Sorensteam | Kemper Lakes GC, Hawthorne Hills, IL |
| 1993 | Jill McGill | 1-up | Sarah Ingram | San Diego CC, Chula Vista, CA |
| 1994 | Wendy Ward | 2 & 1 | Jill McGill | The Homestead, Hot Springs, WV |
| 1995 | Kelli Kuehne | 4 & 3 | Anne-Marie Knight | The Country Club, Brookline, MA |

## Girls' Junior Championship

| | | |
|---|---|---|
| 1949 ..........Marlene Bauer | 1966 ..........Claudia Mayhew | 1983 ..........Kim Saiki |
| 1950 ..........Patricia Lesser | 1967 ..........Elizabeth Story | 1984 ..........Cathy Mockett |
| 1951 ..........Arlene Brooks | 1968 ..........Peggy Harmon | 1985 ..........Dana Lofland |
| 1952 ..........Mickey Wright | 1969 ..........Hollis Stacy | 1986 ..........Pat Hurst |
| 1953 ..........Millie Meyerson | 1970 ..........Hollis Stacy | 1987 ..........Michelle McGann |
| 1954 ..........Margaret Smith | 1971 ..........Hollis Stacy | 1988 ..........Jamille Jose |
| 1955 ..........Carole Jo Kabler | 1972 ..........Nancy Lopez | 1989 ..........Brandie Burton |
| 1956 ..........JoAnne Gunderson | 1973 ..........Amy Alcott | 1990 ..........Sandrine Mendiburu |
| 1957 ..........Judy Eller | 1974 ..........Nancy Lopez | 1991 ..........Emilee Klein |
| 1958 ..........Judy Eller | 1975 ..........Dayna Benson | 1992 ..........Jamie Koizumi |
| 1959 ..........Judy Rand | 1976 ..........Pilar Dorado | 1993 ..........Kellee Booth |
| 1960 ..........Carol Sorenson | 1977 ..........Althea Tome | 1962 ..........Maureen Orcutt |
| 1961 ..........Mary Lowell | 1978 ..........Lori Castillo | 1963 ..........Sis Choate |
| 1962 ..........Mary Lou Daniel | 1979 ..........Penny Hammel | 1994 ..........Kelli Kuehne |
| 1963 ..........Janis Ferraris | 1980 ..........Laurie Rinker | 1995 ..........Marcy Newton |
| 1964 ..........Peggy Conley | 1981 ..........Kay Cornelius | |
| 1965 ..........Gail Sykes | 1982 ..........Heather Farr | |

## Women's British Amateur

| | | |
|---|---|---|
| 1893 ..............Lady Margaret Scott | 1927 ..............Miss Thion de la | 1961 ..............M. Spearman |
| 1894 ..............Lady Margaret Scott |    Chaume | 1962 ..............M. Spearman |
| 1895 ..............Lady Margaret Scott | 1928 ..............Miss N. Le Blan | 1963 ..............B. Varangot |
| 1896 ..............Miss Pascoe | 1929 ..............Miss J. Wethered | 1964 ..............C. Sorenson |
| 1897 ..............Miss E.C. Orr | 1930 ..............Miss D. Fishwick | 1965 ..............B. Varangot |
| 1898 ..............Miss L. Thomson | 1931 ..............Miss E. Wilson | 1966 ..............E. Chadwick |
| 1899 ..............Miss M. Hezlet | 1932 ..............Miss E. Wilson | 1967 ..............E. Chadwick |
| 1900 ..............Miss Adair | 1933 ..............Miss E. Wilson | 1968 ..............B. Varangot |
| 1901 ..............Miss Graham | 1934 ..............Mrs. A.M. Holm | 1975 ..............C. Lacoste |
| 1902 ..............Miss M. Hezlet | 1935 ..............Miss W. Morgan | 1976 ..............D. Oxley |
| 1903 ..............Miss Adair | 1936 ..............Miss P. Barton | 1977 ..............A. Uzielli |
| 1904 ..............Miss L. Dod | 1937 ..............Miss J. Anderson | 1978 ..............E. Kennedy |
| 1905 ..............Miss B. Thompson | 1938 ..............Mrs. A.M. Holm | 1979 ..............M. Madill |
| 1906 ..............Mrs. Kennon | 1939 ..............Miss P. Barton | 1980 ..............A. Quast |
| 1907 ..............Miss M. Hezlet | 1940–45 .......not held | 1981 ..............I.C. Robertson |
| 1908 ..............Miss M. Titterton | 1946 ..............G.W. Hetherington | 1982 ..............K. Douglas |
| 1909 ..............Miss D. Campbell | 1947 ..............B. Zaharias | 1983 ..............J. Thornhill |
| 1910 ..............Miss Grant Suttie | 1948 ..............L. Suggs | 1984 ..............J. Rosenthal |
| 1911 ..............Miss D. Campbell | 1949 ..............F. Stephens | 1985 ..............L. Beman |
| 1912 ..............Miss G. Ravenscroft | 1950 ..............Vicomtesse de Saint | 1986 ..............M. McGuire |
| 1913 ..............Miss M. Dodd |    Sauveur | 1987 ..............J. Collingham |
| 1914 ..............Miss C. Leitch | 1951 ..............P.J. MacCann | 1988 ..............J. Furby |
| 1915–19 .......not held | 1952 ..............M. Paterson | 1989 ..............H. Dobson |
| 1920 ..............Miss C. Leitch | 1953 ..............M. Stewart | 1990 ..............J. Hall |
| 1921 ..............Miss C. Leitch | 1954 ..............F. Stephens | 1991 ..............V. Michaud |
| 1922 ..............Miss J. Wethered | 1955 ..............J. Valentine | 1992 ..............P. Pedersen |
| 1923 ..............Miss D. Chambers | 1956 ..............M. Smith | 1993 ..............Catriona Lambert |
| 1924 ..............Miss J. Wethered | 1957 ..............P. Garvey | 1994 ..............Emma Duggleby |
| 1925 ..............Miss J. Wethered | 1958 ..............J. Valentine | 1995 ..............Julie Hall |
| 1926 ..............Miss C. Leitch | 1959 ..............E. Price | |
| | 1960 ..............B. McIntyre | |

## Women's Amateur Public Links

| | | |
|---|---|---|
| 1977 ..............Kelly Fuiks | 1984 ..............Heather Farr | 1990 ..............Cathy Mockett |
| 1978 ..............Kelly Fuiks | 1985 ..............Danielle | 1991 ..............Tracy Hanson |
| 1979 ..............Lori Castillo |    Ammaccapane | 1992 ..............Amy Fruhwirth |
| 1980 ..............Lori Castillo | 1986 ..............Cindy Schreyer | 1993 ..............Connie Masterson |
| 1981 ..............Mary Enright | 1987 ..............Tracy Kerdyk | 1994 ..............Jill McGill |
| 1982 ..............Nancy Taylor | 1988 ..............Pearl Sinn | 1995 ..............Jo Jo Robertson |
| 1983 ..............Kelli Antolock | 1989 ..............Pearl Sinn | |

# Amateur Golf (Cont.)

## U.S. Senior Women's Amateur

| | | |
|---|---|---|
| 1964 ..........Loma Smith | 1975 ..........Alberta Bower | 1986 ..........Connie Guthrie |
| 1965 ..........Loma Smith | 1976 ..........Cecile H. Maclaurin | 1987 ..........Anne Sander |
| 1966 ..........Maureen Orcutt | 1977 ..........Dorothy Porter | 1988 ..........Lois Hodge |
| 1967 ..........Marge Mason | 1978 ..........Alice Dye | 1989 ..........Anne Sander |
| 1968 ..........Carolyn Cudone | 1979 ..........Alice Dye | 1990 ..........Anne Sander |
| 1969 ..........Carolyn Cudone | 1980 ..........Dorothy Porter | 1991 ..........Phyllis Preuss |
| 1970 ..........Carolyn Cudone | 1981 ..........Dorothy Porter | 1992 ..........Rosemary Thompson |
| 1971 ..........Carolyn Cudone | 1982 ..........Edean Ihlanfeldt | 1993 ..........Anne Sander |
| 1972 ..........Carolyn Cudone | 1983 ..........Dorothy Porter | 1994 ..........Marlene Streit |
| 1973 ..........Gwen Hibbs | 1984 ..........Constance Guthrie | 1995 ..........Jean Smith |
| 1974 ..........Justine Cushing | 1985 ..........Marlene Streit | |

## Women's Mid-Amateur Championship

1987 .................................................Cindy Scholefield
1988 .................................................Martha Lang
1989 .................................................Robin Weiss
1990 .................................................Carol Semple Thompson
1991 .................................................Sarah LeBrun Ingram
1992 .................................................Marion Mamey-McInerney
1993 .................................................Sarah Ingram
1994 .................................................Sarah Ingram
1995 .................................................Ellen Port

# International Golf

## Ryder Cup Matches

| Year | Results | Site |
|---|---|---|
| 1927 ..............United States 9½, Great Britain 2½ | | Worcester CC, Worcester, MA |
| 1929 ..............Great Britain 7, United States 5 | | Moortown GC, Leeds, England |
| 1931 ..............United States 9, Great Britain 3 | | Scioto CC, Columbus, OH |
| 1933 ..............Great Britain 6½, United States 5½ | | Southport and Ainsdale Courses, Southport, England |
| 1935 ..............United States 9, Great Britain 3 | | Ridgewood CC, Ridgewood, NJ |
| 1937 ..............United States 8, Great Britain 4 | | Southport and Ainsdale Courses, Southport, England |
| 1939-1945 .....No tournament | | |
| 1947 ..............United States 11, Great Britain 1 | | Portland GC, Portland, OR |
| 1949 ..............United States 7, Great Britain 5 | | Ganton GC, Scarborough, England |
| 1951 ..............United States 9½, Great Britain 2½ | | Pinehurst CC, Pinehurst, NC |
| 1953 ..............United States 6½, Great Britain 5½ | | Wentworth Club, Surrey, England |
| 1955 ..............United States 8, Great Britain 4 | | Thunderbird Ranch & CC, Palm Springs, CA |
| 1957 ..............Great Britain 7½, United States 4½ | | Lindrick GC, Yorkshire, England |
| 1959 ..............United States 8½, Great Britain 3½ | | Eldorado CC, Palm Desert, CA |
| 1961 ..............United States 14½, Great Britain 9½ | | Royal Lytham & St Anne's GC, St Anne's-on-the-Sea, England |
| 1963 ..............United States 23, Great Britain 9 | | East Lake CC, Atlanta |
| 1965 ..............United States 19½, Great Britain 12½ | | Royal Birkdale GC, Southport, England |
| 1967 ..............United States 23½, Great Britain 8½ | | Champions GC, Houston |
| 1969 ..............United States 16, Great Britain 16 | | Royal Birkdale GC, Southport, England |
| 1971 ..............United States 18½, Great Britain 13½ | | Old Warson CC, St Louis |
| 1973 ..............United States 19, Great Britain 13 | | Hon Co of Edinburgh Golfers, Muirfield, Scotland |
| 1975 ..............United States 21, Great Britain 11 | | Laurel Valley GC, Ligonier, PA |
| 1977 ..............United States 12½, Great Britain 7½ | | Royal Lytham & St Anne's GC, St Anne's-on-the-Sea, England |
| 1979 ..............United States 17, Europe 11 | | Greenbrier, White Sulphur Springs, WV |
| 1981 ..............United States 18½, Europe 9½ | | Walton Heath GC, Surrey, England |
| 1983 ..............United States 14½, Europe 13½ | | PGA National GC, Palm Beach Gardens, FL |
| 1985 ..............Europe 16½, United States 11½ | | Belfry GC, Sutton Coldfield, England |
| 1987 ..............Europe 15, United States 13 | | Muirfield GC, Dublin, OH |
| 1989 ..............Europe 14, United States 14 | | Belfry GC, Sutton Coldfield, England |
| 1991 ..............United States 14½, Europe 13½ | | Ocean Course, Kiawah Island, SC |
| 1993 ..............United States 15, Europe 13 | | Belfry GC, Sutton Coldfield, England |
| 1995 ..............Europe 14½, United States 13½ | | Oak Hill CC, Rochester, NY |

Team matches held every odd year between US professionals and those of Great Britain/Europe (since 1979, prior to which was US vs GB). Team members selected on basis of finishes in PGA and European tour events.

## Walker Cup Matches

| Year | Results | Site |
|------|---------|------|
| 1922 | United States 8, Great Britain 4 | Nat. Golf Links of America, Southampton, NY |
| 1923 | United States 6, Great Britain 5 | St. Andrews, Scotland |
| 1924 | United States 9, Great Britain 3 | Garden City GC, Garden City, NY |
| 1926 | United States 6, Great Britain 5 | St. Andrews, Scotland |
| 1928 | United States 11, Great Britain 1 | Chicago GC, Wheaton, IL |
| 1930 | United States 10, Great Britain 2 | Royal St. George GC, Sandwich, England |
| 1932 | United States 8, Great Britain 1 | The Country Club, Brookline, MA |
| 1934 | United States 9, Great Britain 2 | St. Andrews, Scotland |
| 1936 | United States 9, Great Britain 0 | Pine Valley GC, Clementon, NJ |
| 1938 | Great Britain 7, United States 4 | St. Andrews, Scotland |
| 1940-46 | No tournament | |
| 1947 | United States 8, Great Britain 4 | St. Andrews, Scotland |
| 1949 | United States 10, Great Britain 2 | Winged Foot GC, Mamaroneck, NY |
| 1951 | United States 6, Great Britain 3 | Birkdale GC, Southport, England |
| 1953 | United States 9, Great Britain 3 | The Kittansett Club, Marion, MA |
| 1955 | United States 10, Great Britain 2 | St. Andrews, Scotland |
| 1957 | United States 8, Great Britain 3 | Minikahda Club, Minneapolis, MN |
| 1959 | United States 9, Great Britain 3 | Muirfield, Scotland |
| 1961 | United States 11, Great Britain 1 | Seattle GC, Seattle, WA |
| 1963 | United States 12, Great Britain 8 | Ailsa Course, Turnberry, Scotland |
| 1965 | Great Britain 11, United States 11 | Baltimore CC, Five Farms, Baltimore, MD |
| 1967 | United States 13, Great Britain 7 | Royal St. George's GC, Sandwich, England |
| 1969 | United States 10, Great Britain 8 | Milwaukee CC, Milwaukee, WI |
| 1971 | Great Britain 13, United States 11 | St. Andrews, Scotland |
| 1973 | United States 14, Great Britain 10 | The Country Club, Brookline, MA |
| 1975 | United States 15½, Great Britain 8½ | St. Andrews, Scotland |
| 1977 | United States 16, Great Britain 8 | Shinnecock Hills GC, Southampton, NY |
| 1979 | United States 15½, Great Britain 8½ | Muirfield, Scotland |
| 1981 | United States 15, Great Britain 9 | Cypress Point Club, Pebble Beach, CA |
| 1983 | United States 13½, Great Britain 10½ | Royal Liverpool GC, Hoylake, England |
| 1985 | United States 13, Great Britain 11 | Pine Valley GC, Pine Valley, NJ |
| 1987 | United States 16½, Great Britain 7½ | Sunningdale GC, Berkshire, England |
| 1989 | Great Britain 12½, United States 11½ | Peachtree Golf Club, Atlanta, GA |
| 1991 | United States 14, Great Britain 10 | Portmarnock GC, Dublin, Ireland |
| 1993 | United States 19, Great Britain 5 | Interlachen CC, Edina, MN |
| 1995 | Great Britain/Ireland 14, United States 10 | Royal Porthcawl, Porthcawl, Wales |

Men's amateur team competition every other year between United States and Great Britain. US team members selected by USGA.

## Curtis Cup Matches

| Year | Results | Site |
|------|---------|------|
| 1932 | United States 5½, British Isles 3½ | Wentworth GC, Wentworth, England |
| 1934 | United States 6½, British Isles 2½ | Chevy Chase Club, Chevy Chase, MD |
| 1936 | United States 4½, British Isles 4½ | King's Course, Gleneagles, Scotland |
| 1938 | United States 5½, British Isles 3½ | Essex CC, Manchester, MA |
| 1940-46 | No tournament | |
| 1948 | United States 6½, British Isles 2½ | Birkdale GC, Southport, England |
| 1950 | United States 7½, British Isles 1½ | CC of Buffalo, Williamsville, NY |
| 1952 | British Isles 5, United States 4 | Muirfield, Scotland |
| 1954 | United States 6, British Isles 3 | Merion GC, Ardmore, PA |
| 1956 | British Isles 5, United States 4 | Prince's GC, Sandwich Bay, England |
| 1958 | British Isles 4½, United States 4½ | Brae Burn CC, West Newton, Mass. |
| 1960 | United States 6½, British Isles 2½ | Lindrick GC, Worksop, England |
| 1962 | United States 8, British Isles 1 | Broadmoor CG, Colorado Springs,CO |
| 1964 | United States 10½, British Isles 7½ | Royal Porthcawl GC, Porthcawl, South Wales |
| 1966 | United States 13, British Isles 5 | Va. Hot Springs G & TC, Hot Springs, VA |
| 1968 | United States 10½, British Isles 7½ | Royal County Down GC, Newcastle, N. Ire. |
| 1970 | United States 11½, British Isles 6½ | Brae Burn CC, West Newton, MA |
| 1972 | United States 10, British Isles 8 | Western Gailes, Ayrshire, Scotland |
| 1974 | United States 13, British Isles 5 | San Francisco GC, San Francisco, CA |
| 1976 | United States 11½, British Isles 6½ | Royal Lytham & St. Annes GC, England |

## Curtis Cup Matches (Cont.)

| Year | Results | Site |
|------|---------|------|
| 1978 | United States 12, British Isles 6 | Apawamis Club, Rye, NY |
| 1980 | United States 13, British Isles 5 | St. Pierre G & CC, Chepstow, Wales |
| 1982 | United States 14½, British Isles 3½ | Denver CC, Denver, CO |
| 1984 | United States 9½, British Isles 8½ | Muirfield, Scotland |
| 1986 | British Isles 13, United States 5 | Prairie Dunes CC, Hutchinson, KS |
| 1988 | British Isles 11, United States 7 | Royal St. George's GC, Sandwich, England |
| 1990 | United States 14, British Isles 4 | Somerset Hills CC, Bernardsville, NJ |
| 1992 | Great Britain/Ireland 10, United States 8 | Royal Liverpool GC, Hoylake, England |
| 1994 | Great Britain/Ireland 9, United States 9 | The Honors Course, Ooltewah, TN |

Women's amateur team competition every other year between the United States and Great Britain. US team members selected by USGA.

### Fin de Siècle Shot

More than 38,000 holes in one are recorded annually in the U.S. Many of them are sunk by such worm burners as Brad Hockmeyer, a 44-year-old broadcasting executive who registered his first-ever hole in one last month at the Taos (N. Mex.) Country Club. What made Hockmeyer's ace notable was that it occurred on the 100th anniversary of what was, according to at least one account, the first hole in one in American history. The duffer who drained that shot? The late Otto Hockmeyer, Brad's great-grandfather.

While the significance of his feat was not lost on him, Brad had a more pressing concern. "I talked to somebody who once got a hole in one and had to spend $800 buying the club drinks," says Hockmeyer, referring to the traditional post-ace ritual. Otto's great-grandson was lucky: Taos C.C. has yet to construct a 19th hole.

# Boxing

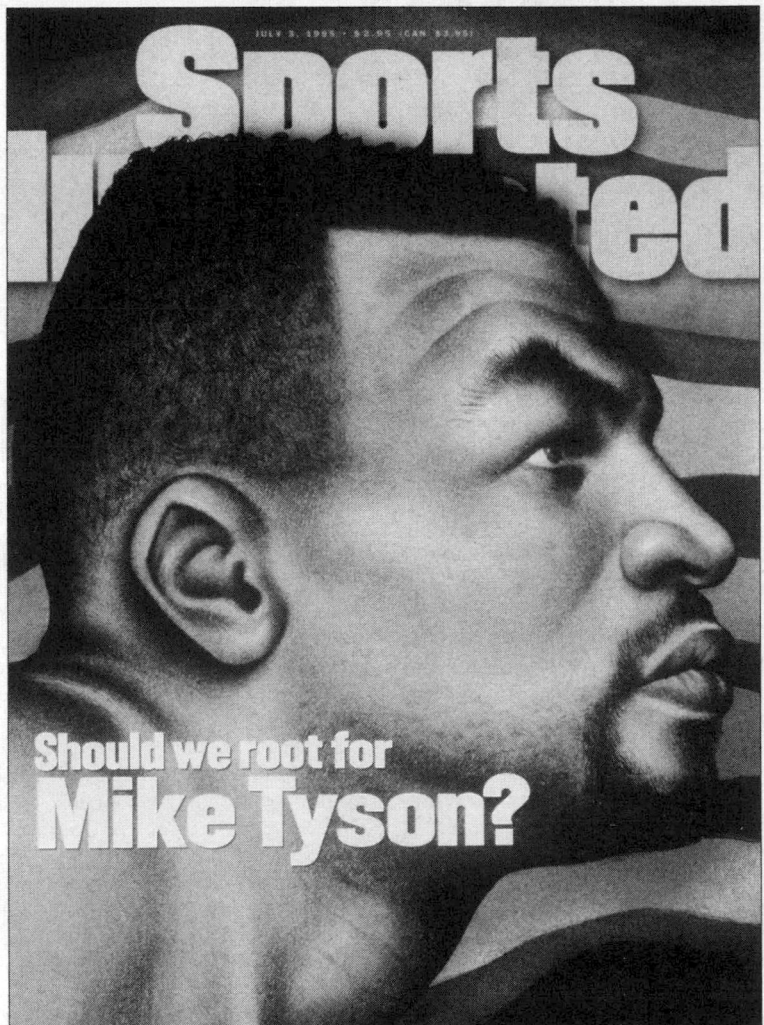

JULY 3, 1995 • $2.95 (CAN $3.95)

## Sports Illustrated

Should we root for
Mike Tyson?

ILLUSTRATION BY ANITA KUNZ

# Return of a Heavy

## When Mike Tyson walked out of an Indiana prison in March, no one knew precisely how to handicap his boxing future

## by Richard Hoffer

A MAN walked out of prison in the Indiana dawn last March, ducked into a black limousine and led a covey of helicopters, a fleet of rental cars, an armada of mini-cammed minivans down a two-lane road to a ... mosque. It was one of the most improbable left turns in all of sports history. Mike Tyson, boxing's most electrifying performer until his rape conviction and three-year prison term, had made prayer the first order of business upon freedom. And nobody could know what it signified. Wearing a white *kufi* cap, he knelt quietly on the soft carpet, met with religious leaders, took counsel from a similarly converted Muhammad Ali and then disappeared. Into retirement? Training? A life of good works? It was impossible to say.

But it was important to know. The game had been in a deepening state of confusion ever since he left. To be sure, he precipitated some of that confusion, losing the heavyweight titles he had so spectacularly unified to Buster Douglas in 1990. But the turnover of titles after that became almost comical (not to mention—talk about comedy—the

invention of three more governing bodies, bringing the number of potential champions to six). In the hapless parade of pretenders, some had not the skill to retain a title and some had not the sense. The period is memorable for big George Foreman, at 45, winning one of the titles from Michael Moorer (with one punch) and for young Riddick Bowe actually discarding one of his in a garbage can (from which it was more or less retrieved by Lennox Lewis, who immediately lost it to Oliver McCall, who handed off to Frank Bruno—you get the idea).

So here was Mike Tyson, only 29 at his release, able but perhaps not willing to resuscitate boxing. His longtime promoter Don King had gotten control of two extremely mediocre heavyweight champions by the time Tyson was sprung (the third mediocre champion would come into his fold a little later), thus preparing the stage for the fighter's return to title-unifying glory. All Tyson had to do was give a nod.

Well, he finally nodded. After a monumental spending spree—new cars for friends, fabulous threads for himself, and a

new compound in Las Vegas—he re-upped with King, aligned himself with two boyhood friends as managers and signed a six-fight deal with the MGM Grand and Showtime's pay-per-view arm for a minimum of $35 million. Then he got down to training. Although he worked secretly and allowed no more than passing glimpses of his growing bulk, boxing was nevertheless relieved. Tyson had made his intentions plain. He was back.

He returned just in time. Not only had the heavyweight division grown ridiculous, with 45-year-old Larry Holmes nearly outpointing McCall in a title fight and Foreman abandoning all his titles rather than suffer a rematch with the redoubtable Axel Schulz, but the rest of boxing suffered as well. Although there were memorable performances—super middleweight champion Roy Jones Jr. solidified his "pound-for-pound" title (won in 1994's methodical destruction of James Toney) with an impressive dismantling of Vinny Pazienza in June—there was far more despair than delight in 1995.

Shortly before Tyson's release from

**His look was tough, but Tyson's first fight revealed little about his skills.**

prison, former middleweight champion Gerald McClellan traveled to London in grim pursuit of Nigel Benn's WBC super middleweight title. McClellan, who often compared himself to his three pit bulls, was a vicious fighter accustomed to quick knockouts. He'd had eight first-round knockouts in his last 10 fights, including his last three title defenses. He was a violent caricature of a boxer, the kind of character much celebrated in the ring. And indeed McClellan knocked Benn clean out of the ring in the first round of their fight. Getting the better of Benn for much of the fight, he floored him again in the eighth round. Benn came back each time, in a fight that observers recalled as ragged yet memorable. By the time the 10th round began, McClellan was ahead on two of the three judges' cards.

Then as the 10th progressed, McClellan seemed strangely weak. He took a solid right from Benn, went down on a knee for a seven count, then resumed action. But 20 seconds later, after a no-account uppercut from Benn, he again took a knee. The announcers wondered at this strange surrender. McClellan rose, stepped back to his corner and, sliding into a coma before everyone's eyes, slumped to the canvas.

Nothing could arrest his descent. Ringside medical care was immediate, and it was agreed that there was nothing more that could have been done. This, of course, rallied boxing's critics all the more. They pointed out that there was no further reform to be made. There was nothing that could have saved McClellan except the sport's abolition. Boxing had done this.

McClellan came out of his coma and, though badly damaged, is undergoing rehabilitation at home in Detroit. Not so fortunate was Jimmy Garcia, a light hitter of slim credentials who traveled from Colombia to take an undercard payday in Las Vegas last May. Although Garcia was challenging Gabriel Ruelas for the WBC super-featherweight title, the night's attraction was Oscar De La Hoya, the Golden Boy from Los Angeles, the country's only gold medal winner from the 1992 Olympics, all teeth and charisma and flashing left hooks.

De La Hoya, 22, was becoming a promotional engine. Although he is cheeky and given to arrogant dismissals of his opponents ("an ordinary fighter" is how he handicapped rival Rafael Ruelas, Gabe's brother), he has the looks, the wit and the enormous skills to be a superstar. Sports agent Leigh Steinberg, who ordinarily represents NFL quarterbacks, was trailing De La Hoya the week of the fight, putting together endorsement deals for him. That's how big he was becoming.

Love him or hate him, the fighter delivers. He stopped Ruelas in the second round to add the IBF lightweight belt to the WBO belt he already owned. The ease with which he did so, in only his 18th fight, promised many more belts to come.

Unfortunately De La Hoya's little stop on the way to greatness will be better remembered as the night that Jimmy Garcia absorbed a fatal beating. Gabriel Ruelas, in the undercard, battered his challenger relentlessly, until Garcia, attended in his corner by family, slumped unconscious to the canvas after the fight was stopped in the 11th round. Garcia may not have ever belonged in the same ring with Ruelas, but he certainly didn't belong there in the later rounds, when it became obvious he couldn't possibly win. Now, he couldn't possibly live. He died from his injuries two weeks later.

This was disheartening stuff, and there wasn't much going on elsewhere to balance it. The heavyweights awaiting Tyson's return were a largely dispiriting bunch, their only redeeming quality being their guaranteed safety in the ring. It was unlikely that one of these heavyweights would ever hurt another.

It might have been enough to know that the middle-aged Foreman had knocked out Moorer to win the WBA and IBF titles in late 1994. Foreman was a popular performer, but he did not shape up as the future of boxing. That was evident when he engaged little-known Schulz last April in Las Vegas. It was supposed to be a walkthrough, a warmup for a mega-payday down the road with Tyson. But Schulz, confounding Foreman by actually moving in the ring (about which Foreman would complain bitterly, as if opponents were contractually obligated to remain as still as the heavy bag), nearly outpointed the champion. In fact, the decision given to Foreman was so unpopular that the IBF immediately called for a rematch, preferably in Schulz's homeland of Germany. Foreman, who came out of the fight with a welt on his brow the size of a bratwurst, politely declined and let his titles lapse. Schulz and Frans Botha were later paired for the vacant IBF championship, a fight to be promoted by King. The world did not hold its breath.

King's other heavyweights were similarly uninspiring. In April, McCall, a former Tyson sparring partner, had all he could handle in the aged Holmes, a fighter the Las Vegas commission had been shocked to learn had made his last fight there

**The brash De La Hoya, an easy winner over Ruelas, has looks and skills to match.**

wearing contact lenses. By normal athletic standards, Holmes ought to require a cane as well. Even so, the closeness of that match did not augur well for McCall's continued reign. At year's end he lost his title in London to perennial also-ran Bruno.

The WBA title, which King also controlled and which was decided on the McCall-Holmes undercard, did not look much more permanent. Contender Bruce Seldon, despite his marvelous physique, was more famous for a jail term, a fondness for nightlife and back-to-back KO losses to McCall and Bowe. Going into his fight with veteran Tony Tucker for the other title vacated by Foreman, Seldon presented himself as newly dedicated, reformed and eager. Any one of those qualities was refreshing in this division. As it happened, Seldon was a bit luckier than Tucker, stopping him on cuts to win the title.

Now that King controlled the three major titles, all the other heavyweights were on the outside looking in. Bowe, by consensus the most talented of them, had been made WBO champion, but nobody took that very seriously. He has been on-again off-again since Evander Holyfield decisioned him in their 1993 rematch, but he was truly impressive in his summer bout with MGM house fighter Jorge Gonzalez, the Cuban madman. Bowe destroyed him. This set up a third meeting with Holyfield, scheduled for November. Holyfield, who has come back from what he says was an incorrectly diagnosed heart condition, set up that match by beating a tough Ray Mercer.

Nonetheless, everything seemed a kind of orchestrated prelude to Tyson's return, as if only he could restore excitement to boxing. Largely forgotten was the fact that it had been four years since Tyson had fought at all, in a lackluster bout with Razor Ruddock, and perhaps 10 since he had fought with the brilliance he is celebrated for. Veteran trainer Emmanuel Steward would not abide comparisons to Muhammad Ali, who came back from his three-year political exile to become a greater fighter than he had ever been. "Ali's style permitted longevity," Steward said. "Tyson, his kind don't have long careers." Indeed, the history has been that fast, furious, aggressive fighters like Tyson flame out, a la Joe Frazier. Indeed, Tyson may have flamed out before he ever went in.

Still, the reality was that Tyson didn't have to be as good as he had been. Or very good at all. His undeniable charisma—the shocking ring violence complicated by his recklessness outside it—would be riveting enough to satisfy this crowd. The reality, for the moment,

WILL HART

**Forget about his 36–1 record: McNeeley went down fast in his fight with Tyson.**

was that Tyson didn't even need an opponent.

For Tyson's first fight back, King scrounged up a fellow named Peter McNeeley, whose ring record of 36–1 with 30 KOs promised Tyson some danger. But closer inspection of McNeeley's record, which included fights with a large number of winless stiffs, seemed to promise him and the promoter scorn instead. The MGM was pricing ringside seats at $1,500, and Showtime was pricing the pay-per-view show as high as $50. To be sure, this wasn't being promoted as a McNeeley fight, but wasn't this a bit rich just to watch a Tyson workout, one that might not even require a sweat? "First punch knocks this guy out," said rival promoter Bob Arum.

Tyson's handlers limited his prefight media exposure and generally encouraged an atmosphere of mystery about their fighter. This was shrewd as it turned out. The curiosity factor, really, was all this fight had going for it. Could Tyson still hit? Could he take a punch? Would he return to the style, the peek-a-boo defense, that made him so frightening in the 1980s?

The MGM was full for the August fight, and more than one million viewers coughed up the pay-per-view dough, making it a bonanza for Team Tyson (the fighter got at least $25 million, perhaps $40 million). But the fight itself was so terrible—it answered none of the important questions about his comeback—that Team Tyson had to scramble to fend off a backlash. Tyson, in the so-called fight, was hardly sharp, though he floored McNeeley twice in the first round. But whatever fireworks display he planned was shelved when McNeeley's manager, Vinnie Vecchione, jumped into the ring 89 seconds into the first round to save his fighter and disqualify him. Everybody agreed that McNeeley was not going to last, but they also agreed that Vecchione's stoppage was premature. The fans were robbed of the only thing the promoters dared promise, a Tyson knockout.

So what began in mystery—Tyson leaving prison for morning prayer—ended in mystery. Tyson was back, that much was obvious, but it couldn't be known for how long. Apparently King was going to nurse him along—one more setup, against Buster Mathis Jr., was scheduled for November—until he could grab the titles, one by one, from Seldon, Bruno and the Botha-Schulz winner. It would be difficult, under these circumstances, for Tyson to fail to unify the division. Given that, it still remained for him to restore some excitement to boxing, and who knows if and when he can do that? One wonders, after this extended drought, if it's even possible.

# FOR THE RECORD·1994–1995

## Current Champions

| Division | Weight Limit | WBC Champion | WBA Champion | IBF Champion |
|---|---|---|---|---|
| Heavyweight | None | Frank Bruno | Bruce Seldon | vacant |
| Cruiserweight | 190 | Marcelo Dominguez | Nate Miller | Alfred Cole |
| Light heavyweight | 175 | Fabrice Tiozzo | Virgil Hill | Henry Maske |
| Super middleweight | 168 | Nigel Benn | Frank Liles | Roy Jones |
| Middleweight | 160 | Quincy Taylor | Jorge Castro | Bernard Hopkins |
| Junior middleweight | 154 | Terry Norris | Carl Daniels | Paul Vaden |
| Welterweight | 147 | Pernell Whitaker | Ike Quartey | Felix Trinidad |
| Junior welterweight | 140 | Julio César Chávez | Frankie Randall | Konstantin Tszyu |
| Lightweight | 135 | Miguel Gonzalez | Orzubek Nazarov | Phillip Holiday |
| Junior lightweight | 130 | Gabriel Ruelas | vacant | Tracy Patterson |
| Featherweight | 126 | Manuel Medina | Eloy Rojas | Tom Johnson |
| Junior featherweight | 122 | Hector Acero Sanchez | Antonio Cermeno | Vuyani Bungu |
| Bantamweight | 118 | Wayne McCullough | Veeraphol Sahaprom | Mbulelo Botile |
| Junior bantamweight | 115 | Hiroshi Kawashima | Alimi Goitia | Carlos Salazar |
| Flyweight | 112 | Yuri Arbachakov | Saen Sow Ploenchit | Danny Romero |
| Junior flyweight | 108 | Saman Sorjaturong | Choi Hi-Yong | Saman Sorjaturong |
| Strawweight | 105 | Ricardo Lopez | Chana Porpaoin | Ratanaapol Sow Voraphin |

Note: WBC = World Boxing Council; WBA = World Boxing Association; IBF = International Boxing Federation

## Championship and Major Fights of 1994 and 1995

Abbreviations: WBC=World Boxing Council; WBA= World Boxing Association; IBF=International Boxing Federation; KO=knockout; TKO=technical knockout; Dec=decision; Split=split decision; Disq=disqualification.

### Heavyweight

| Date | Winner | Loser | Result | Title | Site |
|---|---|---|---|---|---|
| Nov 4 | George Foreman | Michael Moorer | KO 10 | IBF, WBA | Las Vegas |
| Mar 11 | Riddick Bowe | Herbie Hide | KO 6 | WBO | Las Vegas |
| Apr 22 | George Foreman | Axel Schulz | Dec 12 | IBF | Las Vegas |
| Aug 19 | Bruce Seldon | Joe Hipp | TKO 10 | WBA | Las Vegas |
| Sept 2 | Frank Bruno | Oliver McCall | Dec 12 | WBC | London |

### Cruiserweight

| Date | Winner | Loser | Result | Title | Site |
|---|---|---|---|---|---|
| Nov 12 | Orlin Norris | James Heath | KO 2 | WBA | Mexico City |
| Dec 3 | Anaclet Wamba | Marcelo Dominguez | Dec 12 | WBC | Salta, Argentina |
| Mar 18 | Orlin Norris | Adolpho Washington | Dec 12 | WBA | Worcester, MA |
| June 24 | Alfred Cole | Uriah Grant | Dec 12 | IBF | Atlantic City, NJ |
| July 23 | Nate Miller | Orlin Morris | KO 8 | WBA | London |
| Sept 2 | Marcelo Dominguez | Reynaldo Gimenez | TKO 12 | WBC | Gualeguaychu, Arg. |

### Light Heavyweight

| Date | Winner | Loser | Result | Title | Site |
|---|---|---|---|---|---|
| Oct 8 | Henry Maske | Iran Barkley | TKO 9 | IBF | Halle, Germany |
| Feb 25 | Mike McCallum | Carl Jones | TKO 7 | WBC | London |
| Apr 1 | Virgil Hill | Crawford Ashley | Dec 12 | WBA | Stateline, NV |
| May 27 | Henry Maske | Graciano Rocchigiani | Dec 12 | IBF | Dortmund, Germany |
| June 16 | Fabrice Tiozzo | Mike McCallum | Dec 12 | WBC | Lyon, France |
| Sept 2 | Virgil Hill | Drake Thadzi | Dec 12 | WBA | London |

### Super Middleweight

| Date | Winner | Loser | Result | Title | Site |
|---|---|---|---|---|---|
| Dec 17 | Frank Liles | Michael Nunn | Dec 12 | WBA | Quito, Ecuador |
| Feb 25 | Nigel Benn | Gerald McClellan | KO 10 | WBC | London |
| Mar 18 | Roy Jones | Antoino Byrd | TKO 1 | IBF | Pensacola, FL |
| May 27 | Frank Liles | Frederic Seillier | TKO 6 | WBA | Fort Lauderdale, FL |
| June 24 | Roy Jones | Vinny Pazienza | TKO 6 | IBF | Atlantic City, NJ |
| Sept 2 | Nigel Benn | Danny Perez | KO 7 | WBC | London |
| Sept 30 | Roy Jones | Tony Thornton | TKO 3 | IBF | Pensacola, FL |

## Middleweight

| Date | Winner | Loser | Result | Title | Site |
|------|--------|-------|--------|-------|------|
| Nov 5 | Jorge Castro | Alex Ramos | KO 2 | WBA | Caleta Olivia, Argentina |
| Dec 10 | Jorge Castro | John David Jackson | TKO 9 | WBA | Monterrey, Mexico |
| Mar 17 | Julian Jackson | Agostino Cardamone | TKO 2 | WBC | Worcester, MA |
| Apr 29 | Bernard Hopkins | Segundo Mercado | TKO 7 | IBF | Landover, MD |
| May 27 | Jorge Castro | Anthony Andrews | TKO 12 | WBA | Fort Lauderdale, FL |
| Aug 19 | Quincy Taylor | Julian Jackson | TKO 6 | WBC | Las Vegas |

## Junior Middleweight (Super Welterweight)

| Date | Winner | Loser | Result | Title | Site |
|------|--------|-------|--------|-------|------|
| Nov 11 | Julio César Vasquez | Tony Marshall | Dec 12 | WBA | Tucuman, Argentina |
| Nov 12 | Luis Santana | Terry Norris | Disq 5 | WBC | Mexico City |
| Mar 4 | Pernell Whitaker | Julio César Vasquez | Dec 12 | WBA | Atlantic City, NJ |
| Apr 8 | Luis Santana | Terry Norris | Disq 3 | WBC | Las Vegas |
| Apr 29 | Vincent Pettway | Simon Brown | KO 6 | IBF | Landover, MD |
| June 16 | Carl Daniels | Julio César Vasquez | Dec 12 | WBA | Lyon, France |
| Aug 12 | Paul Vaden | Vincent Pettway | TKO 12 | IBF | Las Vegas |
| Aug 19 | Terry Norris | Luis Santana | TKO 2 | WBC | Las Vegas |

## Welterweight

| Date | Winner | Loser | Result | Title | Site |
|------|--------|-------|--------|-------|------|
| Oct 1 | Pernell Whitaker | Buddy McGirt | Dec 12 | WBC | Norfolk, VA |
| Dec 10 | Felix Trinidad | Oba Carr | TKO 8 | IBF | Monterrey, Mexico |
| Mar 4 | Ike Quartey | Park Jung-Oh | TKO 4 | WBA | Atlantic City, NJ |
| Apr 8 | Felix Trinidad | Roger Turner | TKO 2 | IBF | Las Vegas |
| Aug 23 | Ike Quartey | Andrew Murray | TKO 4 | WBA | Rocheville, France |
| Aug 26 | Pernell Whitaker | Gary Jacobs | Dec 12 | WBC | Atlantic City |

## Junior Welterweight (Super Lightweight)

| Date | Winner | Loser | Result | Title | Site |
|------|--------|-------|--------|-------|------|
| Dec 10 | Julio César Chávez | Tony Lopez | TKO 10 | WBC | Monterrey, Mexico |
| Dec 10 | Frankie Randall | Rodney Moore | TKO 7 | WBA | Monterrey, Mexico |
| Jan 28 | Konstantin Tszyu | Jake Rodriguez | TKO 6 | IBF | Las Vegas |
| Apr 8 | Julio César Chávez | Giovanni Parisi | Dec 12 | WBC | Las Vegas |
| June 16 | Frankie Randall | Jose Barboza | Split 12 | WBA | Lyon, France |
| June 25 | Kostya Tszyu | Roger Mayweather | Dec 12 | IBF | Newcastle, Australia |
| Sept 16 | Julio César Chávez | David Kamau | Dec 12 | WBC | Las Vegas |

## Lightweight

| Date | Winner | Loser | Result | Title | Site |
|------|--------|-------|--------|-------|------|
| Nov 18 | Oscar De La Hoya | Carl Griffith | TKO 3 | WBO | Las Vegas |
| Dec 10 | Orzubek Nazarov | Joey Gamache | TKO 2 | WBA | Portland, ME |
| Dec 10 | Oscar De La Hoya | John Avila | TKO 9 | WBO | Los Angeles |
| Dec 13 | Miguel Angel Gonzalez | Calvin Grove | TKO 5 | WBC | Albuquerque, NM |
| Jan 28 | Rafael Ruelas | Billy Schwer | TKO 8 | IBF | Las Vegas |
| Feb 18 | Oscar De La Hoya | Juan Molina | Dec 12 | WBO | Las Vegas |
| Apr 25 | Miguel Angel Gonzalez | Ricardo Silva | Dec 12 | WBC | South Padre Island, TX |
| May 6 | Oscar De La Hoya | Rafael Ruelas | TKO 2 | WBO/IBF | Las Vegas |
| May 15 | Orzubek Nazarov | Won Park | KO 2 | WBA | Tokyo |
| June 2 | Miguel Angel Gonzalez | Marty Jakubowski | Dec 12 | WBC | Mashantucket, CT |
| Aug 19 | Miguel Angel Gonzalez | Lamar Murphy | Dec 12 | WBC | Las Vegas |
| Aug 19 | Phillip Holiday | Miguel Julio | TKO 10 | IBF | Sun City, South Africa |
| Sept 9 | Oscar De La Hoya | Genaro Hernandez | TKO 6 | WBO | Las Vegas |

# Championship and Major Fights of 1994 and 1995 *(Cont.)*

## Junior Lightweight (Super Featherweight)

| Date | Winner | Loser | Result | Title | Site |
|------|--------|-------|--------|-------|------|
| Nov 12 | Genaro Hernandez | Jimmy Garcia | Dec 12 | WBA | Mexico City |
| Nov 26 | Juan Molina | Wilson Rodriguez | KO 10 | IBF | Bayamon, Puerto Rico |
| Jan 28 | Gabriel Ruelas | Fred Libertore | TKO 2 | WBC | Las Vegas |
| Apr 22 | Eddie Hopson | Moises Pedroza | KO 7 | IBF | Atlantic City, NJ |
| May 6 | Gabriel Ruelas | Jimmy Garcia | TKO 11 | WBC | Las Vegas |
| July 9 | Tracy Patterson | Eddie Hopson | TKO 2 | IBF | Reno, Nevada |

## Featherweight

| Date | Winner | Loser | Result | Title | Site |
|------|--------|-------|--------|-------|------|
| Oct 22 | Tom Johnson | Francisco Segura | Dec 12 | IBF | Atlantic City, NJ |
| Dec 3 | Eloy Rojas | Luis Mendoza | Dec 12 | WBA | Bogota, Columbia |
| Jan 7 | Alejandro Gonzalez | Kevin Kelley | TKO 10 | WBC | San Antonio, TX |
| Jan 28 | Tom Johnson | Manuel Medina | Dec 12 | IBF | Atlantic City, NJ |
| Mar 31 | Alejandro Gonzalez | Louie Espinoza | Dec 12 | WBC | Anaheim, CA |
| May 27 | Eloy Rojas | Park Yong-Kyun | Split 12 | WBA | Kwangju, South Korea |
| June 2 | Alejandro Gonzalez | Tony Green | TKO 9 | WBC | Mashantucket, CT |
| May 28 | Tom Johnson | Eddie Croft | Dec 12 | IBF | South Padre Island, TX |
| Aug 13 | Eloy Rojas | Nobutoshi Hiranaka | Dec 12 | WBA | Tagawa City, Japan |
| Sept 23 | Manuel Medina | Alejandro Gonzalez | Split 12 | WBC | Sacramento, CA |

## Junior Featherweight (Super Bantamweight)

| Date | Winner | Loser | Result | Title | Site |
|------|--------|-------|--------|-------|------|
| Oct 13 | Wilfredo Vasquez | Juan Polo Perez | Dec 12 | WBA | Levallois-Perret, France |
| Nov 19 | Vuyani Bungu | Felix Camacho | Dec 12 | IBF | Hammanskraal, S.A. |
| Jan 7 | Wilfredo Vasquez | Orlando Canizales | Split 12 | WBA | San Antonio, TX |
| Mar 4 | Vuyani Bungu | Mohammed Nurhuda | Dec 12 | IBF | Hammanskraal, S.A. |
| Mar 11 | Hector Acero-Sanchez | Julio Gervacio | Dec 12 | WBC | Atlantic City, NJ |
| Apr 29 | Vuyani Bungu | Victor Llerena | Dec 12 | IBF | Johannesburg, S.A. |
| May 13 | Antonio Cermeno | Wilfredo Vasquez | Dec 12 | WBA | Bayamon, Puerto Rico |
| Jun 2 | Hector Acero-Sanchez | Daniel Zaragoza | Maj draw | WBC | Mashantucket, CT |
| Sept 26 | Vuyani Bungu | Laureano Ramirez | Dec 12 | IBF | Hammanskraal, S.A. |

## Bantamweight

| Date | Winner | Loser | Result | Title | Site |
|------|--------|-------|--------|-------|------|
| Oct 15 | Orlando Canizales | Sergio Reyes | Dec 12 | IBF | Laredo, TX |
| Nov 20 | Daorung Chuvatana | Koh In-Sik | TKO 5 | WBA | Chiang Rai, Thailand |
| Dec 4 | Yasuei Yakushiji | Joichiro Tatsuyoshi | Dec 12 | WBC | Nagoya, Japan |
| Jan 21 | Harold Mestre | Juvenal Berrio | TKO 8 | IBF | Cartagena, Columbia |
| Apr 29 | Mbulelo Botile | Harold Mestre | TKO 2 | IBF | Johannesburg, S.A. |
| May 27 | Daorung Chuvatana | Lakhin CP Gym | Split draw | WBA | Nakhon Si Thammarat, Thailand |
| July 4 | Mbulelo Botile | Sammy Stewart | Dec 12 | IBF | Hammanskraal, S.A. |
| July 30 | Wayne McCullough | Yasuei Yakusiji | Split 12 | WBC | Nagoya, Japan |
| Sept 17 | Veeraphol Sahaprom | Daorung MP-Petroleum | Split 12 | WBA | Bangkok, Thailand |

## Junior Bantamweight (Super Flyweight)

| Date | Winner | Loser | Result | Title | Site |
|------|--------|-------|--------|-------|------|
| Dec 17 | Harold Grey | Vincenzo Belcastro | Split 12 | IBF | Cagliari, Italy |
| Jan 18 | Hiroshi Kawashima | Jose Luis Bueno | Dec 12 | WBC | Yokohama, Japan |
| Feb 25 | Lee Hyung-Chul | Tomonori Tamura | TKO 12 | WBA | Pusan, South Korea |
| Mar 18 | Harold Grey | Orlando Tobon | Dec 12 | IBF | Cartagena, Columbia |
| May 24 | Hiroshi Kawashima | Lee Seung-Koo | Dec 12 | WBC | Yokohama, Japan |
| June 24 | Harold Grey | Julio Cesar Borboa | Split 12 | IBF | Cartagena, Columbia |
| July 22 | Alimi Goitia | Lee Hyung-Chul | KO 4 | WBA | Seoul, South Korea |
| Oct 6 | Carlos Salazar | Harold Grey | Split 12 | WBC | Mar del Plata, Arg. |

## Flyweight

| Date | Winner | Loser | Result | Title | Site |
|------|--------|-------|--------|-------|------|
| Sep 25 | Saen Sow Ploenchit | Kim Yong-Kang | Dec 12 | WBA | Kanchanaburi, Thailand |
| Dec 25 | Saen Sow Ploenchit | Danny Nunez | TKO 11 | WBA | Rayong, Thailand |
| Jan 30 | Yuri Arbachakov | Oscar Arciniega | Dec 12 | WBC | Sapporo, Japan |
| Feb 18 | Francisco Tejedor | Jose Luis Zepeda | TKO 6 | IBF | Cartagena, Colombia |
| Apr 22 | Danny Romero | Francisco Tejedor | Dec 12 | IBF | Las Vegas |
| May 7 | Saen Sow Ploenchit | Evangelio Perez | Dec 12 | WBA | Hat Yai, Thailand |
| July 29 | Danny Romero | Miguel Martinez | KO 6 | IBF | San Antonio, TX |
| Sept 25 | Yuri Arbachakov | Chatchai Elite-Gym | Dec 12 | WBC | Tokyo |

## Junior Flyweight

| Date | Winner | Loser | Result | Title | Site |
|------|--------|-------|--------|-------|------|
| Oct 9 | Leo Gamez | P. Sithbangprachan | TKO 6 | WBA | Bangkok, Thailand |
| Nov 12 | Humberto Gonzalez | Michael Carbajal | Dec 12 | WBC/IBF | Mexico City |
| Feb 4 | Choi Hi-Yong | Leo Gamez | Dec 12 | WBA | Ulsan, South Korea |
| Mar 31 | Humberto Gonzalez | Jesus Zuniga | KO 5 | WBC/IBF | Anaheim, CA |
| July 15 | Saman Sor Jaturong | Humberto Gonzalez | KO 7 | WBC/IBF | Inglewood, CA |
| Sept 5 | Choi Hi-Yong | Keiji Yamaguchi | Split 12 | WBA | Osaka, Japan |

## Strawweight (Mini Flyweight)

| Date | Winner | Loser | Result | Title | Site |
|------|--------|-------|--------|-------|------|
| Nov 5 | Chana Porpaoin | Manuel Herrera | Split 12 | WBA | Hat Yai, Thailand |
| Nov 12 | Ratanapal Sow Voraphin | Carlos Rodriguez | TKO 3 | IBF | Khon Kaen, Thailand |
| Nov 12 | Ricardo Lopez | Javier Varguez | TKO 8 | WBC | Mexico City |
| Dec 10 | Ricardo Lopez | Yamil Caraballo | TKO 1 | WBC | Monterrey, Mexico |
| Jan 28 | Chana Porpaoin | Kim Jin-Ho | Dec 12 | WBA | Bangkok, Thailand |
| Feb 25 | Ratanapal Sow Voraphin | Jerry Pahayahay | TKO 3 | IBF | Bangkok, Thailand |
| Apr 1 | Ricardo Lopez | Andy Tabanas | TKO 12 | WBC | Stateline, NV |
| May 20 | Ratanapal Sow Voraphin | Oscar Flores | TKO 2 | IBF | Chiang Mai, Thailand |
| Aug 6 | Chana Popaoin | Ernesto Rubillar Jr | KO 6 | WBA | Bangkok, Thailand |

### Harlem Shuffle

Reaction to the announced homecoming celebration for New York City native Mike Tyson has sent the former heavyweight champ's supporters reeling as if they'd been hit by a Buster Douglas left. The local *Amsterdam News* reported in June that a "gala festival" for Tyson, featuring a parade and a musical tribute, had been planned for June 20 in Harlem. Event organizer Sylvester Leaks boasted that the celebration would "surpass anything ever accorded any sports figure in New York or the entire nation."

The counterpunching began almost immediately. The idea of feting a recently released rapist was condemned by columnists, Mayor Rudolph Giuliani and a civic group that billed itself as the Committee for Rational African Americans Against the Parade (CRAAAP). Even the usually staid *New York Times* ran the tabloidlike headline on its op-ed page: WELCOME HOME, CONVICTED MOLESTER.

Gala backers, most notably New York congressman Charles Rangel, backed off. Even the normally mouthy Al Sharpton, another of the event's organizers, found himself against the ropes. In the end the occasion was scaled back to a couple of press conferences. That such a celebration was even proposed reflects Tyson's enduring appeal. But it's one thing to allow him to put his past behind him, quite another to extend a hero's welcome suggesting the civic credo Be Like Mike.

## World Champions

Sanctioning bodies include the National Boxing Association (NBA), the New York State Athletic Commission (NY), the World Boxing Association (WBA), the World Boxing Council (WBC), and the International Boxing Federation (IBF).

### Heavyweights
### (Weight: Unlimited)

| Champion | Reign | Champion | Reign | Champion | Reign |
|---|---|---|---|---|---|
| John L. Sullivan | 1885-92 | Ingemar Johansson | 1959-60 | Pinklon Thomas* WBC | 1984-86 |
| James J. Corbett | 1892-97 | Floyd Patterson | 1960-62 | Greg Page* WBA | 1984-85 |
| Bob Fitzsimmons | 1897-99 | Sonny Liston | 1962-64 | Michael Spinks | 1985-87 |
| James J. Jeffries | 1899-1905† | Muhammad Ali | 1964-70 | Tim Witherspoon* WBA | 1986 |
| Marvin Hart | 1905-06 | Ernie Terrell* WBA | 1965-67 | Trevor Berbick* WBC | 1986 |
| Tommy Burns | 1906-08 | Joe Frazier* NY | 1968-70 | Mike Tyson* WBC | 1986-87 |
| Jack Johnson | 1908-15 | Jimmy Ellis* WBA | 1968-70 | James Bonecrusher | |
| Jess Willard | 1915-19 | Joe Frazier | 1970-73 | Smith* WBA | 1986-87 |
| Jack Dempsey | 1919-26 | George Foreman | 1973-74 | Tony Tucker* IBF | 1987 |
| Gene Tunney | 1926-28 | Muhammad Ali | 1974-78 | Mike Tyson | 1987-90 |
| Max Schmeling | 1930-32 | Leon Spinks | 1978 | Buster Douglas | 1990 |
| Jack Sharkey | 1932-33 | Ken Norton* WBC | 1978 | Evander Holyfield | 1990-92 |
| Primo Carnera | 1933-34 | Larry Holmes* WBC | 1978-80 | Lennox Lewis* WBC | 1993-95 |
| Max Baer | 1934-35 | Muhammad Ali | 1978-79† | Riddick Bowe | 1992-93 |
| James J. Braddock | 1935-37 | John Tate* WBA | 1979-80 | Evander Holyfield | 1993-94 |
| Joe Louis | 1937-49† | Mike Weaver* WBA | 1980-82 | Michael Moorer | 1994 |
| Ezzard Charles | 1949-51 | Larry Holmes | 1980-85 | George Foreman | 1994-95 |
| Jersey Joe Walcott | 1951-52 | Michael Dokes* WBA | 1982-83 | Frank Bruno* WBC | 1995- |
| Rocky Marciano | 1952-56† | Gerrie Coetzee* WBA | 1983-84 | Bruce Seldon* WBA | 1995- |
| Floyd Patterson | 1956-59 | Tim Witherspoon* WBC | 1984 | | |

### Cruiserweights
### (Weight Limit: 190 pounds)

| Champion | Reign | Champion | Reign | Champion | Reign |
|---|---|---|---|---|---|
| Marvin Camel* WBC | 1980 | Evander Holyfield * WBA | 1986-88 | Massimiliano | |
| Carlos De Leon* WBC | 1980-82 | Ricky Parkey* IBF | 1986-87 | Duran* WBC | 1990-91 |
| Ossie Ocasio* WBA | 1982-84 | Evander Holyfield | | Bobby Czyz*† WBA | 1991-92 |
| S.T. Gordon* WBC | 1982-83 | * WBA/IBF | 1987-88 | Anaclet Wamba* WBC | 1991-95 |
| Carlos De Leon* WBC | 1983-85 | Evander Holyfield | | James Pritchard* IBF | 1991 |
| Marvin Camel* IBF | 1983-84 | WBA/IBF/WBC | 1988† | James Warring* IBF | 1991-92 |
| Lee Roy Murphy* IBF | 1984-86 | Toufik Belbouli* WBA | 1989 | Alfred Cole* IBF | 1992- |
| Piet Crous* WBA | 1984-85 | Robert Daniels* WBA | 1989-91 | Orlin Norris* WBA | 1993-95 |
| Alfonso Ratliff* WBC | 1985 | Carlos De Leon* WBC | 1989-90 | Nate Miller* WBA | 1995- |
| Dwight Braxton* WBA | 1985-86 | Glenn McCrory* IBF | 1989-90 | Marcello | |
| Bernard Benton* WBC | 1985-86 | Jeff Lampkin* IBF | 1990 | Dominguez* WBC | 1995- |
| Carlos De Leon* WBC | 1986-88 | | | | |

Note: Division called Junior Heavyweights by the WBA.

### Light Heavyweights
### (Weight Limit: 175 pounds)

| Champion | Reign | Champion | Reign | Champion | Reign |
|---|---|---|---|---|---|
| Jack Root | 1903 | George Nichols* NBA | 1932 | Dick Tiger | 1966-68 |
| George Gardner | 1903 | Bob Godwin* NBA | 1933 | Bob Foster | 1968-74† |
| Bob Fitzsimmons | 1903-05 | Bob Olin | 1934-35 | Vicente Rondon* WBA | 1971-72 |
| Philadelphia Jack | | John Henry Lewis | 1935-38 | John Conteh* WBC | 1974-77 |
| O'Brien | 1905-12† | Melio Bettina | 1939 | Victor Galindez* WBA | 1974-78 |
| Jack Dillon | 1914-16 | Billy Conn | 1939-40† | Miguel A. Cuello* WBC | 1977-78 |
| Battling Levinsky | 1916-20 | Anton Christoforidis | 1941 | Mate Parlov* WBC | 1978 |
| Georges Carpentier | 1920-22 | Gus Lesnevich | 1941-48 | Mike Rossman* WBA | 1978-79 |
| Battling Siki | 1922-23 | Freddie Mills | 1948-50 | Marvin Johnson* WBC | 1978-79 |
| Mike McTigue | 1923-25 | Joey Maxim | 1950-52 | Matthew Saad | |
| Paul Berlenbach | 1925-26 | Archie Moore | 1952-62† | Muhammad* WBC | 1979-81 |
| Jack Delaney | 1926-27† | Harold Johnson* NBA | 1961 | Marvin Johnson* WBA | 1979-80 |
| Jimmy Slattery* NBA | 1927 | Harold Johnson | 1962-63 | Eddie Mustapha | |
| Tommy Loughran | 1927-29 | Willie Pastrano | 1963-65 | Muhammad* WBA | 1980-81 |
| Maxie Rosenbloom | 1930-34 | Jose Torres | 1965-66 | Michael Spinks* WBA | 1981-83 |

*Champion not generally recognized.  †Champion retired or relinquished title.

## Light Heavyweights *(Cont.)*

| Champion | Reign |
|---|---|
| Dwight Muhammad Qawi* WBC | 1981-83 |
| Michael Spinks* | 1983-85† |
| J. B. Williamson* WBC | 1985-86 |
| Slobodan Kacar* IBF | 1985-86 |
| Marvin Johnson* WBA | 1986-87 |
| Dennis Andries* WBC | 1986-87 |
| Bobby Czyz* IBF | 1986-87 |
| Leslie Stewart* WBA | 1987 |

| Champion | Reign |
|---|---|
| Virgil Hill* WBA | 1987 |
| Prince Charles Williams* IBF | 1987- |
| Thomas Hearns* WBC | 1987† |
| Donny Lalonde* WBC | 1987-88 |
| Sugar Ray Leonard* WBC | 1988 |
| Dennis Andries* WBC | 1989 |
| Jeff Harding* WBC | 1989-90 |
| Dennis Andries* WBC | 1990-91 |

| Champion | Reign |
|---|---|
| Thomas Hearns* WBA | 1991-92 |
| Jeff Harding* WBC | 1991-94 |
| Iran Barkley* WBA | 1992 |
| Virgil Hill* WBA | 1992- |
| Henry Maske* IBF | 1993- |
| Mike McCallum* WBC | 1994-95 |
| Fabrice Tiozzo* WBC | 1995- |

## Super Middleweights
## (Weight Limit: 168 pounds)

| Champion | Reign |
|---|---|
| Murray Sutherland* IBF | 1984 |
| Chong-Pal Park* IBF | 1984-87 |
| Chong-Pal Park* WBA | 1987-88 |
| G. Rocchigiani* IBF | 1988-89 |
| F. Obelmejias* WBA | 1988-89 |
| Sugar Ray Leonard* WBC | 1988-90† |

| Champion | Reign |
|---|---|
| In-Chul Baek* WBA | 1989-90 |
| Lindell Holmes* IBF | 1990-91 |
| C. Tiozzo* WBA | 1990-91 |
| Mauro Galvano* WBC | 1990- |
| Victor Cordova* WBA | 1991 |
| Darrin Van Horn* IBF | 1991-92 |
| Iran Barkley *WBA | 1992 |

| Champion | Reign |
|---|---|
| Nigel Benn* WBC | 1992- |
| James Toney* IBF | 1992-94 |
| Michael Nunn* WBA | 1992-94 |
| Steve Little* WBA | 1994 |
| Frank Liles* WBA | 1994- |
| Roy Jones* IBF | 1994- |

## Middleweights
## (Weight Limit: 160 pounds)

| Champion | Reign |
|---|---|
| Jack Dempsey | 1884-91 |
| Bob Fitzsimmons | 1891-97 |
| Kid McCoy | 1897-98 |
| Tommy Ryan | 1898-1907 |
| Stanley Ketchel | 1908 |
| Billy Papke | 1908 |
| Stanley Ketchel | 1908-10 |
| Frank Klaus | 1913 |
| George Chip | 1913-14 |
| Al McCoy | 1914-17 |
| Mike O'Dowd | 1917-20 |
| Johnny Wilson | 1920-23 |
| Harry Greb | 1923-26 |
| Tiger Flowers | 1926 |
| Mickey Walker | 1926-31† |
| Gorilla Jones | 1931-32 |
| Marcel Thil | 1932-37 |
| Fred Apostoli | 1937-39 |
| Al Hostak* NBA | 1938 |
| Solly Krieger* NBA | 1938-39 |
| Al Hostak* NBA | 1939-40 |
| Ceferino Garcia | 1939-40 |
| Ken Overlin | 1940-41 |
| Tony Zale* NBA | 1940-41 |
| Billy Soose | 1941 |

| Champion | Reign |
|---|---|
| Tony Zale | 1941-47 |
| Rocky Graziano | 1947-48 |
| Tony Zale | 1948 |
| Marcel Cerdan | 1948-49 |
| Jake La Motta | 1949-51 |
| Sugar Ray Robinson | 1951 |
| Randy Turpin | 1951 |
| Sugar Ray Robinson | 1951-52 |
| Bobo Olson | 1953-55 |
| Sugar Ray Robinson | 1955-57 |
| Gene Fullmer | 1957 |
| Sugar Ray Robinson | 1957 |
| Carmen Basilio | 1957-58 |
| Sugar Ray Robinson | 1958-60 |
| Gene Fullmer* NBA | 1959-62 |
| Paul Pender | 1960-61 |
| Terry Downes | 1961-62 |
| Paul Pender | 1962-63 |
| Dick Tiger* WBA | 1962-63 |
| Dick Tiger | 1963 |
| Joey Giardello | 1963-65 |
| Dick Tiger | 1965-66 |
| Emile Griffith | 1966-67 |
| Nino Benvenuti | 1967 |
| Emile Griffith | 1967-68 |

| Champion | Reign |
|---|---|
| Nino Benvenuti | 1968-70 |
| Carlos Monzon | 1970-77† |
| Rodrigo Valdez* WBC | 1974-76 |
| Rodrigo Valdez | 1977-78 |
| Hugo Corro | 1978-79 |
| Vito Antuofermo | 1979-80 |
| Alan Minter | 1980 |
| Marvin Hagler | 1980-87 |
| Sugar Ray Leonard | 1987 |
| Frank Tate* IBF | 1987-88 |
| Sumbu Kalambay* WBA | 1987-89 |
| Thomas Hearns* WBC | 1987-88 |
| Iran Barkley* WBC | 1988-89 |
| Michael Nunn* IBF | 1988-91 |
| Roberto Duran* WBC | 1989-90 |
| Mike McCallum* WBA | 1989-91 |
| Julian Jackson* WBC | 1990- |
| James Toney* IBF | 1991- |
| Reggie Johnson* WBA | 1992-94 |
| Roy Jones*† IBF | 1993-95 |
| G. McClellan*† WBC | 1993-95 |
| Jorge Castro* WBA | 1994- |
| Jullian Jackson*WBC | 1995 |
| Quincy Taylor* WBC | 1995- |
| Bernard Hopkins* IBF | 1995- |

## Junior Middleweights
## (Weight Limit: 154 pounds)

| Champion | Reign |
|---|---|
| Emile Griffith (EBU) | 1962-63 |
| Dennis Moyer | 1962-63 |
| Ralph Dupas | 1963 |
| Sandro Mazzinghi | 1963-65 |
| Nino Benvenuti | 1965-66 |
| Ki-Soo Kim | 1966-68 |
| Sandro Mazzinghi | 1968 |
| Freddie Little | 1969-70 |
| Carmelo Bossi | 1970-71 |
| Koichi Wajima | 1971-74 |
| Oscar Albarado | 1974-75 |

| Champion | Reign |
|---|---|
| Koichi Wajima | 1975 |
| Miguel de Oliveira* WBC | 1975-76 |
| Jae-Do Yuh | 1975-76 |
| Elisha Obed* WBC | 1975-76 |
| Koichi Wajima | 1976 |
| Jose Duran | 1976 |
| Eckhard Dagge* WBC | 1976-77 |
| Miguel Angel Castellini | 1976-77 |
| Eddie Gazo | 1977-78 |
| Rocky Mattioli* WBC | 1977-79 |
| Masashi Kudo | 1978-79 |

| Champion | Reign |
|---|---|
| Maurice Hope* WBC | 1979-81 |
| Ayub Kalule | 1979-81 |
| Wilfred Benitez* WBC | 1981-82 |
| Sugar Ray Leonard | 1981-82 |
| Tadashi Mihara* WBA | 1981-82 |
| Davey Moore* WBA | 1982-83 |
| Thomas Hearns* WBC | 1982-84 |
| Roberto Duran* WBA | 1983-84 |
| Mark Medal* IBF | 1984 |
| Thomas Hearns | 1984-86 |
| Mike McCallum* WBA | 1984-87 |

*Champion not generally recognized.  †Champion retired or relinquished title.

### Junior Middleweights (Cont.)

| Champion | Reign | Champion | Reign | Champion | Reign |
|----------|-------|----------|-------|----------|-------|
| Carlos Santos* IBF | 1984-86 | Robert Hines* IBF | 1988-89 | Julio C. Vasquez* WBA | 1992-95 |
| Buster Drayton* IBF | 1986-87 | Darrin Van Horn* IBF | 1989 | Simon Brown* WBC | 1994 |
| Duane Thomas* WBC | 1986-87 | Rene Jacquot* WBC | 1989 | Terry Norris *WBC | 1994 |
| Matthew Hilton* IBF | 1987-88 | John Mugabi* WBC | 1989-90 | Vincent Pettway* IBF | 1994-95 |
| Lupe Aquino* WBC | 1987 | Gianfranco Rosi* IBF | 1989-94 | Paul Vaden* IBF | 1995- |
| Gianfranco Rosi* WBC | 1987-88 | Terry Norris* WBC | 1990-94 | Carl Daniels* WBA | 1995- |
| Julian Jackson* WBA | 1987-90 | Gilbert Dele* WBA | 1991 | | |
| Donald Curry* WBC | 1988-89 | Vinny Pazienza* WBA | 1991-92 | | |

Note: Division called Super Welterweight by the WBC.

### Welterweights
### (Weight Limit: 147 pounds)

| Champion | Reign | Champion | Reign | Champion | Reign |
|----------|-------|----------|-------|----------|-------|
| Paddy Duffy | 1888-90 | Young Corbett III | 1933 | John H. Stracey | 1975-76 |
| Mysterious Billy Smith | 1892-94 | Jimmy McLarnin | 1933-34 | Carlos Palomino | 1976-79 |
| Tommy Ryan | 1894-98 | Barney Ross | 1934 | Pipino Cuevas* WBA | 1976-80 |
| Mysterious Billy Smith | 1898-1900 | Jimmy McLarnin | 1934-35 | Wilfredo Benitez | 1979 |
| Rube Ferns | 1900 | Barney Ross | 1935-38 | Sugar Ray Leonard | 1979-80 |
| Matty Matthews | 1900-01 | Henry Armstrong | 1938-40 | Roberto Duran | 1980 |
| Rube Ferns | 1901 | Fritzie Zivic | 1940-41 | Thomas Hearns* WBA | 1980-81 |
| Joe Walcott | 1901-04 | Red Cochrane | 1941-46 | Sugar Ray Leonard | 1980-82 |
| The Dixie Kid | 1904-05 | Marty Servo | 1946 | Donald Curry* WBA | 1983-85 |
| Honey Mellody | 1906-07 | Sugar Ray Robinson | 1946-51† | Milton McCrory* WBC | 1983-85 |
| Twin Sullivan | 1907-08 | Johnny Bratton | 1951 | Donald Curry | 1985-86 |
| Jimmy Gardner | 1908 | Kid Gavilan | 1951-54 | Lloyd Honeyghan | 1986-87 |
| Jimmy Clabby | 1910-11 | Johnny Saxton | 1954-55 | Jorge Vaca WBC | 1987-88 |
| Waldemar Holberg | 1914 | Tony DeMarco | 1955 | Lloyd Honeyghan WBC | 1988-89 |
| Tom McCormick | 1914 | Carmen Basilio | 1955-56 | Mark Breland* WBA | 1987 |
| Matt Wells | 1914-15 | Johnny Saxton | 1956 | Marlon Starling* WBC | 1987-88 |
| Mike Glover | 1915 | Carmen Basilio | 1956-57 | Tomas Molinares* WBA | 1988-89 |
| Jack Britton | 1915 | Virgil Akins | 1958 | Simon Brown* IBF | 1988-91 |
| Ted "Kid" Lewis | 1915-16 | Don Jordan | 1958-60 | Mark Breland* WBA | 1989-90 |
| Jack Britton | 1916-17 | Kid Paret | 1960-61 | Marlon Starling* WBC | 1989-90 |
| Ted "Kid" Lewis | 1917-19 | Emile Griffith | 1961 | Aaron Davis* WBA | 1990-91 |
| Jack Britton | 1919-22 | Kid Paret | 1961-62 | Maurice Blocker* WBC | 1990-91 |
| Mickey Walker | 1922-26 | Emile Griffith | 1962-63 | Meldrick Taylor* WBA | 1991-1992 |
| Pete Latzo | 1926-27 | Luis Rodriguez | 1963 | Simon Brown* WBC | 1991 |
| Joe Dundee | 1927-29 | Emile Griffith | 1963-66 | Buddy McGirt* WBC | 1991-1993 |
| Jackie Fields | 1929-30 | Curtis Cokes | 1966-69 | Felix Trinidad* IBF | 1992- |
| Young Jack Thompson | 1930 | Jose Napoles | 1969-70 | Pernell Whitaker WBC | 1993- |
| Tommy Freeman | 1930-31 | Billy Backus | 1970-71 | Crisanto Espana* WBA | 1992-94 |
| Young Jack Thompson | 1931 | Jose Napoles | 1971-75 | Ike Quartey* WBA | 1994- |
| Lou Brouillard | 1931-32 | Hedgemon Lewis* NY | 1972-73 | | |
| Jackie Fields | 1932-33 | Angel Espada* WBA | 1975-76 | | |

### Junior Welterweight
### (Weight Limit: 140 pounds)

| Champion | Reign | Champion | Reign | Champion | Reign |
|----------|-------|----------|-------|----------|-------|
| Pinkey Mitchell | 1922-25 | Eddie Perkins | 1963-65 | Saoul Mamby* WBC | 1980-82 |
| Red Herring | 1925 | Carlos Hernandez | 1965-66 | Aaron Pryor* WBA | 1980-83 |
| Mushy Callahan | 1926-30 | Sandro Lopopolo | 1966-67 | Leroy Haley* WBC | 1982-83 |
| Jack (Kid) Berg | 1930-31 | Paul Fujii | 1967-68 | Aaron Pryor* IBF | 1983-85 |
| Tony Canzoneri | 1931-32 | Nicolino Loche | 1968-72 | Bruce Curry* WBC | 1983-84 |
| Johnny Jadick | 1932-33 | Pedro Adigue* WBC | 1968-70 | Johnny Bumphus* WBA | 1984 |
| Sammy Fuller* | 1932-33 | Bruno Arcari* WBC | 1970-74 | Bill Costello* WBC | 1984- |
| Battling Shaw | 1933 | Alfonso Frazer | 1972 | Gene Hatcher* WBA | 1984-85 |
| Tony Canzoneri | 1933 | Antonio Cervantes | 1972-76 | Ubaldo Sacco* WBA | 1985-86 |
| Barney Ross | 1933-35 | Perico Fernandez* WBC | 1974-75 | Lonnie Smith* WBC | 1985-86 |
| Tippy Larkin | 1946 | S. Muangsurin* WBC | 1975-76 | Patrizio Oliva* WBA | 1986-87 |
| Carlos Ortiz | 1959-60 | Wilfred Benitez | 1976-79 | Gary Hinton* IBF | 1986 |
| Duilio Loi | 1960-62 | M. Velasquez* WBC | 1976 | Rene Arredondo* WBC | 1986 |
| Eddie Perkins | 1962 | S. Muangsurin* WBC | 1976-78 | Tsuyoshi Hamada* WBC | 1986-87 |
| Duilio Loi | 1962-63 | A. Cervantes* WBA | 1977-80 | Joe Louis Manley* IBF | 1986-87 |
| Roberto Cruz* WBA | 1963 | Sang-Hyun Kim* WBC | 1978-80 | Terry Marsh* IBF | 1987 |

*Champion not generally recognized. †Champion retired or relinquished title.

## Junior Welterweights *(Cont.)*

| Champion | Reign |
|---|---|
| J. M. Coggi* WBA | 1987-90 |
| Rene Arredondo* WBC | 1987 |
| R. Mayweather* WBC | 1987-89 |
| James McGirt* IBF | 1988 |
| Meldrick Taylor* IBF | 1988-90 |
| Julio César Chávez* WBC | 1989-94 |
| Julio César Chávez* IBF | 1990-91 |

| Champion | Reign |
|---|---|
| Loreto Garza* WBA | 1990-91 |
| Juan Coggi* WBA | 1991 |
| Edwin Rosario* WBA | 1991-92 |
| Rafael Pineda* IBF | 1991-92 |
| Akinobu Hiranaka* WBA | 1992 |
| Pernell Whitaker*† IBF | 1992-93 |
| Charles Murray* IBF | 1993-94 |

| Champion | Reign |
|---|---|
| Jake Rodriguez* IBF | 1994-95 |
| Juan Coggi* WBA | 1993-94 |
| Frankie Randall* WBC | 1994- |
| Frankie Randall* WBA | 1994- |
| Julio César Chávez WBC | 1994- |
| Kostantin Tszyu* IBF | 1995- |

## Lightweights
### (Weight Limit: 135 pounds)

| Champion | Reign |
|---|---|
| Jack McAuliffe | 1886-94 |
| Kid Lavigne | 1896-99 |
| Frank Erne | 1899-1902 |
| Joe Gans | 1902-04 |
| Jimmy Britt | 1904-05 |
| Battling Nelson | 1905-06 |
| Joe Gans | 1906-08 |
| Battling Nelson | 1908-10 |
| Ad Wolgast | 1910-12 |
| Willie Ritchie | 1912-14 |
| Freddie Welsh | 1915-17 |
| Benny Leonard | 1917-25† |
| Jimmy Goodrich | 1925 |
| Rocky Kansas | 1925-26 |
| Sammy Mandell | 1926-30 |
| Al Singer | 1930 |
| Tony Canzoneri† | 1930-33 |
| Barney Ross | 1933-35† |
| Tony Canzoneri | 1935-36 |
| Lou Ambers | 1936-38 |
| Henry Armstrong | 1938-39 |
| Lou Ambers | 1939-40 |
| Sammy Angott* NBA | 1940-41 |
| Lew Jenkins | 1940-41 |
| Sammy Angott* | 1941-42† |
| Beau Jack* NY | 1942-43 |
| Bob Montgomery* NY | 1943 |
| Sammy Angott* NBA | 1943-44 |
| Beau Jack* NY | 1943-44 |
| Bob Montgomery* NY | 1944-47 |

| Champion | Reign |
|---|---|
| Juan Zurita* NBA | 1944-45 |
| Ike Williams | 1947-51 |
| James Carter | 1951-52 |
| Lauro Salas | 1952 |
| James Carter | 1952-54 |
| Paddy DeMarco | 1954 |
| James Carter | 1954-55 |
| Wallace Smith | 1955-56 |
| Joe Brown | 1956-62 |
| Carlos Ortiz | 1962-65 |
| Ismael Laguna | 1965 |
| Carlos Ortiz | 1965-68 |
| Carlos Teo Cruz | 1968-69 |
| Mando Ramos | 1969-70 |
| Ismael Laguna | 1970 |
| Ken Buchanan | 1970-72 |
| Roberto Duran | 1972-79† |
| Chango Carmona* WBC | 1972 |
| Rodolfo Gonzalez* WBC | 1972-74 |
| Ishimatsu Suzuki* WBC | 1974-76 |
| Estaban DeJesus* WBC | 1976-78 |
| Jim Watt* WBC | 1979-81 |
| Ernesto Espana* WBA | 1979-80 |
| Hilmer Kenty* WBA | 1980-81 |
| Sean O'Grady* WBA | 1981 |
| Claude Noel* WBA | 1981 |
| Alexis Arguello* WBC | 1981-82 |
| Arturo Frias* WBA | 1981-82 |
| Ray Mancini* WBA | 1982-84 |
| Alexis Arguello | 1982-83 |

| Champion | Reign |
|---|---|
| Edwin Rosario* WBC | 1983-84 |
| Choo Choo Brown* IBF | 1984 |
| L. Bramble* WBA | 1984-86 |
| Jose Luis Ramirez* WBC | 1984-85 |
| Harry Arroyo* IBF | 1984-85 |
| Jimmy Paul* IBF | 1985-86 |
| Hector Camacho* WBC | 1985-86 |
| Greg Haugen* IBF | 1986-87 |
| Edwin Rosario* WBA | 1986-87 |
| Julio César Chávez* WBC | 1987-88 |
| Jose Luis Ramirez* WBC | 1987-88 |
| Julio César Chávez | 1988-89 |
| Vinny Pazienza* IBF | 1987-88 |
| Greg Haugen* IBF | 1988-89 |
| P. Whitaker* WBC, IBF | 1989-90 |
| Edwin Rosario* WBA | 1989-90 |
| | 1991-92 |
| Juan Nazario* WBA | 1990 |
| P. Whitaker* WBA, WBC | 1990-92 |
| Pernell Whitaker* IBF | 1991-92 |
| Julio César Chávez* IBF | 1990-91 |
| Julio César Chávez* WBC | 1990-92 |
| Miguel Gonzalez* WBC | 1992- |
| Joey Gamache* WBA | 1992-93 |
| Dingaan Thobela* WBA | 1993 |
| Fred Pendleton* IBF | 1993-94 |
| Orzubek Nazarov* WBA | 1994- |
| Rafael Ruelas* IBF | 1994-95 |
| Phillip Holiday* IBF | 1995- |

## Junior Lightweights
### (Weight Limit: 130 pounds)

| Champion | Reign |
|---|---|
| Johnny Dundee | 1921-23 |
| Jack Bernstein | 1923 |
| Johnny Dundee | 1923-24 |
| Steve (Kid) Sullivan | 1924-25 |
| Mike Ballerino | 1925 |
| Tod Morgan | 1925-29 |
| Benny Bass | 1929-31 |
| Kid Chocolate | 1931-33 |
| Frankie Klick | 1933-34 |
| Sandy Saddler | 1949-50 |
| Harold Gomes | 1959-60 |
| Gabriel (Flash) Elorde | 1960-67 |
| Yoshiaki Numata | 1967 |
| Hiroshi Kobayashi | 1967-71 |
| Rene Barrientos* WBC | 1969-70 |
| Yoshiaki Numata* WBC | 1970-71 |
| Alfredo Marcano | 1971-72 |
| R. Arredondo* WBC | 1971-74 |
| Ben Villaflor | 1972-73 |

| Champion | Reign |
|---|---|
| Kuniaki Shibata | 1973 |
| Ben Villaflor | 1973-76 |
| Kuniaki Shibata* WBC | 1974-75 |
| Alfredo Escalera* WBC | 1975-78 |
| Samuel Serrano | 1976-80 |
| Alexis Arguello* WBC | 1978-80 |
| Yasutsune Uehara | 1980-81 |
| Rafael Limon* WBC | 1980-81 |
| C. Boza-Edwards* WBC | 1981 |
| Samuel Serrano | 1981-83 |
| R. Navarrete* WBC | 1981-82 |
| Rafael Limon* WBC | 1982 |
| Bobby Chacon* WBC | 1982-83 |
| Roger Mayweather* WBC | 1983-84 |
| Hector Camacho* WBC | 1983-84 |
| Rocky Lockridge | 1984-85 |
| Hwan-Kil Yuh* IBF | 1984-85 |
| Julio César Chávez* WBC | 1984-87 |
| Lester Ellis* IBF | 1985- |

| Champion | Reign |
|---|---|
| Wilfredo Gomez | 1985-86 |
| Barry Michael* IBF | 1985-87 |
| Alfredo Layne* WBA | 1986 |
| Brian Mitchell* WBA | 1986-91 |
| Rocky Lockridge* IBF | 1987-88 |
| Azumah Nelson* WBC | 1988-94 |
| Tony Lopez* IBF | 1988-89 |
| Juan Molina* IBF | 1989-90 |
| Tony Lopez* IBF | 1990-91 |
| Joey Gamache, WBA | 1991 |
| Brian Mitchell* IBF | 1991 |
| Genaro Hernandez* WBA | 1991-95 |
| James Leija* WBC | 1994 |
| Juan Molina* IBF | 1991-95 |
| Gabriel Ruelas* WBC | 1994- |
| Eddie Hopson* IBF | 1995 |
| Tracy Patterson* IBF | 1995- |

*Champion not generally recognized. †Champion retired or relinquished title.

## Featherweights
### (Weight Limit: 126 pounds)

| Champion | Reign |
|---|---|
| Torpedo Billy Murphy | 1890 |
| Young Griffo | 1890-92 |
| George Dixon | 1892-97 |
| Solly Smith | 1897-98 |
| Dave Sullivan | 1898 |
| George Dixon | 1898-1900 |
| Terry McGovern | 1900-01 |
| Young Corbett II | 1901-04 |
| Jimmy Britt | 1904 |
| Tommy Sullivan | 1904-05 |
| Abe Attell | 1906-12 |
| Johnny Kilbane | 1912-23 |
| Eugene Criqui | 1923 |
| Johnny Dundee | 1923-24 |
| "Kid" Kaplan | 1925-26 |
| Benny Bass | 1927-28 |
| Tony Canzoneri | 1928 |
| Andre Routis | 1928-29 |
| Battling Battalino | 1929-32 |
| Tommy Paul* NBA | 1932-33 |
| Kid Chocolate* NY | 1932-33 |
| Freddie Miller* NBA | 1933-36 |
| Mike Beloise* NY | 1936-37 |
| Petey Sarron* NBA | 1936-37 |
| Maurice Holtzer | 1937-38 |
| Henry Armstrong | 1937-38 |
| Joey Archibald* NY | 1938-39 |
| Leo Rodak* NBA | 1938-39 |
| Joey Archibald | 1939-40 |
| Petey Scalzo* NBA | 1940-41 |

| Champion | Reign |
|---|---|
| Harry Jeffra | 1940-41 |
| Joey Archibald | 1941 |
| Richie Lamos* NBA | 1941 |
| Chalky Wright | 1941-42 |
| Jackie Wilson* NBA | 1941-43 |
| Willie Pep | 1942-48 |
| Jackie Callura* NBA | 1943 |
| Phil Terranova* NBA | 1943-44 |
| Sal Bartolo* NBA | 1944-46 |
| Sandy Saddler | 1948-49 |
| Willie Pep | 1949-50 |
| Sandy Saddler | 1950-57† |
| Kid Bassey | 1957-59 |
| Davey Moore | 1959-63 |
| Sugar Ramos | 1963-64 |
| Vicente Saldivar | 1964-67† |
| Paul Rojas* WBA | 1968 |
| Jose Legra* WBC | 1968-69 |
| Shozo Saijyo* WBA | 1968-71 |
| J. Famechon* WBC | 1969-70 |
| Vicente Saldivar WBC | 1970 |
| Kuniaki Shibata WBC | 1970-72 |
| Antonio Gomez* WBA | 1971-72 |
| C. Sanchez WBC | 1972 |
| Ernesto Marcel* WBA | 1972-74 |
| Jose Legra WBC | 1972-73 |
| Eder Jofre WBC | 1973-74 |
| Ruben Olivares* WBA | 1974 |
| Bobby Chacon* WBC | 1974-75 |
| Alexis Arguello WBA | 1974-76 |

| Champion | Reign |
|---|---|
| Ruben Olivares* WBC | 1975 |
| Poison Kotey* WBC | 1975-76 |
| Danny Lopez WBC | 1976-80 |
| Rafael Ortega* WBA | 1977 |
| Cecilio Lastra* WBA | 1977-78 |
| Eusebio Pedroza* WBA | 1978-85 |
| S. Sanchez WBC | 1980-82 |
| Juan LaPorte* WBC | 1982-84 |
| Wilfredo Gomez* WBC | 1984 |
| Min-Keun Oh* IBF | 1984-85 |
| Azumah Nelson* WBC | 1984-88 |
| Barry McGuigan* WBA | 1985-86 |
| Ki Young Chung* IBF | 1985-86 |
| Steve Cruz* WBA | 1986-87 |
| Antonio Rivera* IBF | 1986-88 |
| A. Esparragoza* WBA | 1987-91 |
| Calvin Grove* IBF | 1988 |
| Jorge Paez* IBF | 1988-91 |
| Jeff Fenech* WBC | 1988-90† |
| Marcos Villasana* WBC | 1990-91 |
| Paul Hodkinson* WBC | 1991- |
| Troy Dorsey* IBF | 1991 |
| Manuel Medina* IBF | 1991- |
| Yung Kyun Park* WBA | 1991-93 |
| Gregorio Vargas* WBC | 1993 |
| Tom Johnson* IBF | 1993- |
| Eloy Rojas* WBA | 1993- |
| Kevin Kelley* WBC | 1993-95 |
| A. Gonzalez* WBC | 1995 |
| Manuel Medina* WBC | 1995- |

## Junior Featherweights
### (Weight Limit: 122 pounds)

| Champion | Reign |
|---|---|
| Jack (Kid) Wolfe* | 1922-23 |
| Carl Duane* | 1923-24 |
| Rigoberto Riasco* WBC | 1976 |
| Royal Kobayashi* WBC | 1976 |
| Dong-Kyun Yum* WBC | 1976-77 |
| Wilfredo Gomez* WBC | 1977-83 |
| Soo-Hwan Hong* WBA | 1977-78 |
| Ricardo Cardona* WBA | 1978-80 |
| Leo Randolph* WBA | 1980 |
| Sergio Palma* WBA | 1980-82 |
| Leonardo Cruz* WBA | 1982-84 |
| Jaime Garza* WBC | 1983 |
| Bobby Berna* IBF | 1983-84 |
| Loris Stecca* WBA | 1984 |
| Seung-Il Suh* IBF | 1984-85 |

| Champion | Reign |
|---|---|
| Victor Callejas* WBA | 1984-86 |
| Juan (Kid) Meza* WBC | 1984-85 |
| Ji-Won Kim* IBF | 1985-86 |
| Lupe Pintor* WBC | 1985-86 |
| Samart Payakaroon* WBC | 1986-87 |
| Seung-Hoon Lee* IBF | 1987-88 |
| Louie Espinoza* WBA | 1987 |
| Jeff Fenech* WBC | 1987 |
| Julio Gervacio* WBA | 1987-88 |
| Daniel Zaragoza* WBC | 1988-90 |
| Jose Sanabria* IBF | 1988-89 |
| Bernardo Pinango* WBA | 1988 |
| Juan Jose Estrada* WBA | 1988-89 |

| Champion | Reign |
|---|---|
| Fabrice Benichou* IBF | 1989-90 |
| Jesus Salud* WBA | 1989-90 |
| Welcome Ncita* IBF | 1990- |
| Paul Banke* WBC | 1990 |
| Luis Mendoza* WBA | 1990-91 |
| Rual Perez* WBA | 1992- |
| Pedro Decima* WBC | 1990-91 |
| Kiyoshi Hatanaka* WBC | 1991 |
| Daniel Zaragoza* WBC | 1991-92 |
| Tracy Patterson* WBC | 1992-94 |
| Kennedy McKinney* IBF | 1993-94 |
| Wilfredo Vasquez* WBA | 1992-95 |
| Vuyani Bungu* IBF | 1994- |
| H. Acero Sanchez* WBC | 1994- |
| Antonio Cermeno* WBA | 1995- |

Note: Division called Super Bantamweight by the WBC.

## Bantamweights
### (Weight Limit: 118 pounds)

| Champion | Reign |
|---|---|
| Spider Kelly | 1887 |
| Hughey Boyle | 1887-88 |
| Spider Kelly | 1889 |
| Chappie Moran | 1889-90 |
| George Dixon | 1890-91 |
| Pedlar Palmer* | 1895-99 |
| Terry McGovern | 1899-1900 |
| Harry Harris | 1901-2 |

| Champion | Reign |
|---|---|
| Harry Forbes | 1902-3 |
| Frankie Neil | 1903-4 |
| Joe Bowker | 1904-5 |
| Jimmy Walsh | 1905-6 |
| Owen Moran | 1907-8 |
| Monte Attell* | 1909-10 |
| Frankie Conley | 1910-11 |
| Johnny Coulon | 1911-14 |
| Kid Williams | 1914-17 |

| Champion | Reign |
|---|---|
| Kewpie Ertle* | 1915 |
| Pete Herman | 1917-20 |
| Joe Lynch | 1920-21 |
| Pete Herman | 1921 |
| Johnny Buff | 1921-22 |
| Joe Lynch | 1922-24 |
| Abe Goldstein | 1924 |
| Cannonball Martin | 1924-25 |
| Phil Rosenberg | 1925-27 |

*Champion not generally recognized.  †Champion retired or relinquished title.

## Bantamweights (Cont.)

| Champion | Reign |
|---|---|
| Bud Taylor NBA | 1927-28 |
| Bushy Graham* NY | 1928-29 |
| Panama Al Brown | 1929-35 |
| Sixto Escobar* NBA | 1934-35 |
| Baltazar Sangchilli | 1935-36 |
| Lou Salica* NBA | 1935 |
| Sixto Escobar* NBA | 1935-36 |
| Tony Marino | 1936 |
| Sixto Escobar | 1936-37 |
| Harry Jeffra | 1937-38† |
| Sixto Escobar | 1938-39 |
| Georgie Pace NBA | 1939-40 |
| Lou Salica | 1940-42 |
| Manuel Ortiz | 1942-47 |
| Harold Dade | 1947 |
| Manuel Ortiz | 1947-50 |
| Vic Toweel | 1950-52 |
| Jimmy Carruthers | 1952-54† |
| Robert Cohen | 1954-56 |
| Paul Macias* NBA | 1955-57 |
| Mario D'Agata | 1956-57 |
| Alphonse Halimi | 1957-59 |
| Joe Becerra | 1959-60† |
| Eder Jofre | 1961-65 |

| Champion | Reign |
|---|---|
| Fighting Harada | 1965-68 |
| Lionel Rose | 1968-69 |
| Ruben Olivares | 1969-70 |
| Chucho Castillo | 1970-71 |
| Ruben Olivares | 1971-72 |
| Rafael Herrera | 1972 |
| Enrique Pinder | 1972-73 |
| Romeo Anaya | 1973 |
| Rafael Herrera* WBC | 1973-74 |
| Soo-Hwan Hong | 1974-75 |
| Rodolfo Martinez* WBC | 1974-76 |
| Alfonso Zamora | 1975-77 |
| Carlos Zarate* WBC | 1976-79 |
| Jorge Lujan | 1977-80 |
| Lupe Pintor* WBC | 1979-83 |
| Julian Solis | 1980 |
| Jeff Chandler | 1980-84 |
| Albert Davila* WBC | 1983-85 |
| Richard Sandoval | 1984-86 |
| Satoshi Shingaki* IBF | 1984-85 |
| Jeff Fenech* IBF | 1985 |
| Daniel Zaragoza* WBC | 1985 |
| Miguel Lora* WBC | 1985-88 |
| Gaby Canizales | 1986 |

| Champion | Reign |
|---|---|
| Bernardo Pinango | 1986-87 |
| W. Vasquez* WBA | 1987-88 |
| Kevin Seabrooks* IBF | 1987-88 |
| Kaokor Galaxy* WBA | 1988 |
| Moon Sung-Kil* WBA | 1988-89 |
| Kaokor Galaxy* WBA | 1989 |
| Raul Perez* WBC | 1988-91 |
| O. Canizales* IBF | 1988-95 |
| Luisito Espinosa* WBA | 1989-91 |
| Israel Contreras* WBA | 1991-92 |
| Eddie Cook* WBA | 1992-93 |
| Greg Richardson* WBC | 1991 |
| J. Tatsuyoshi, WBC | 1991-92 |
| Victor Rabanales* WBC | 1992-93 |
| Jung-Il Byun* WBC | 1993 |
| Jorge Julio WBA | 1993 |
| Yasuei Yakushiji* WBC | 1993-95 |
| Junior Jones WBA | 1994 |
| John M. Johnson* WBA | 1994 |
| D. Chuvatana*WBA | 1994-95 |
| V. Sahaprom* WBA | 1995- |
| W. McCullough* WBC | 1995- |
| Harold Mestre* IBF | 1995 |
| Mbulelo Botile* IBF | 1995- |

## Junior Bantamweights
## (Weight Limit: 115 pounds)

| Champion | Reign |
|---|---|
| Rafael Orono* WBC | 1980-81 |
| Chul-Ho Kim* WBC | 1981-82 |
| Gustavo Ballas* WBA | 1981 |
| Rafael Pedroza* WBA | 1981-82 |
| Jiro Watanabe* WBA | 1982-84 |
| Rafael Orono* WBC | 1982-83 |
| Payao Poontarat* WBC | 1983-84 |
| Joo-Do Chun* IBF | 1983-85 |
| Jiro Watanabe | 1984-86 |
| Kaosai Galaxy* WBA | 1984 |
| Ellyas Pical* IBF | 1985-86 |

| Champion | Reign |
|---|---|
| Cesar Polanco* IBF | 1986 |
| Gilberto Roman* WBC | 1986-87 |
| Ellyas Pical* IBF | 1986 |
| Santos Laciar* WBC | 1987 |
| Tae-Il Chang* IBF | 1987 |
| Sugar Rojas* WBC | 1987-88 |
| Ellyas Pical* IBF | 1987-89 |
| Giberto Roman* WBC | 1988-89 |
| Juan Polo Perez* IBF | 1989-90 |
| Nana Konadu* WBC | 1989-90 |
| Sung-Kil Moon* WBC | 1990-93 |

| Champion | Reign |
|---|---|
| Robert Quiroga* IBF | 1990-93 |
| Julio Borboa* IBF | 1993-94 |
| Katsuya Onizuka* WBA | 1993-94 |
| Lee Hyung-Chul* WBA | 1994-95 |
| Jose Luis Bueno* WBC | 1993-94 |
| Hiroshi Kawashima*WBC | 1994- |
| Harold Grey* IBF | 1994-95 |
| Alimi Goitia* WBA | 1995- |
| Carlos Salazar* IBF | 1995- |

Note: Division called Super Flyweight by the WBC.

## Flyweights
## (Weight Limit: 112 pounds)

| Champion | Reign |
|---|---|
| Sid Smith | 1913 |
| Bill Ladbury | 1913-14 |
| Percy Jones | 1914 |
| Joe Symonds | 1914-16 |
| Jimmy Wilde | 1916-23 |
| Pancho Villa | 1923-25 |
| Fidel LaBarba | 1925-27† |
| Frenchy Belanger NBA | 1927-28 |
| Izzy Schwartz NY | 1927-29 |
| Frankie Genaro NBA | 1928-29 |
| Spider Pladner NBA | 1929 |
| Frankie Genaro NBA | 1929-31 |
| Midget Wolgast* NY | 1930-35 |
| Young Perez NBA | 1931-32 |
| Jackie Brown NBA | 1932-35 |
| Benny Lynch | 1935-38 |
| Small Montana* NY | 1935-37 |
| Peter Kane | 1938-43 |
| Little Dado* NY | 1938-40 |
| Jackie Paterson | 1943-48 |

| Champion | Reign |
|---|---|
| Rinty Monaghan | 1948-50 |
| Terry Allen | 1950 |
| Dado Marino | 1950-52 |
| Yoshio Shirai | 1953-54 |
| Pascual Perez | 1954-60 |
| Pone Kingpetch | 1960-62 |
| Masahiko Harada | 1962-63 |
| Pone Kingpetch | 1963 |
| Hiroyuki Ebihara | 1963-64 |
| Pone Kingpetch | 1964-65 |
| Salvatore Burrini | 1965-66 |
| H. Accavallo* WBA | 1966-68 |
| Walter McGowan | 1966 |
| Chartchai Chionoi | 1966-69 |
| Efren Torres | 1969-70 |
| Hiroyuki Ebihara* WBA | 1969 |
| B. Villacampo* WBA | 1969-70 |
| Chartchai Chionoi | 1970 |
| B. Chartvanchai* WBA | 1970 |
| Masao Ohba* WBA | 1970-73 |

| Champion | Reign |
|---|---|
| Erbito Salavarria | 1970-73 |
| B. Gonzalez* WBA | 1972 |
| V. Borkorsor* WBC | 1972-73 |
| Venice Borkorsor | 1973 |
| Chartchai Chionoi* WBA | 1973-74 |
| B. Gonzalez* WBA | 1973-74 |
| Shoji Oguma* WBC | 1974-75 |
| S. Hanagata* WBA | 1974-75 |
| Miguel Canto* WBC | 1975-79 |
| Erbito Salavarria* WBA | 1975-76 |
| Alfonso Lopez* WBA | 1976 |
| G. Espadas* WBA | 1976-78 |
| B. Gonzalez* WBA | 1978-79 |
| Chan-Hee Park* WBC | 1979-80 |
| Luis Ibarra* WBA | 1979-80 |
| Tae-Shik Kim* WBA | 1980 |
| Shoji Oguma* WBC | 1980-81 |
| Peter Mathebula* WBA | 1980-81 |
| Santos Laciar* WBA | 1981 |
| Antonio Avelar* WBC | 1981-82 |

*Champion not generally recognized. †Champion retired or relinquished title.

## Flyweights (Cont.)

| Champion | Reign | Champion | Reign | Champion | Reign |
|---|---|---|---|---|---|
| Luis Ibarra* WBA | 1981 | Chong-Kwan | | Yul-Woo Lee* WBA | 1990 |
| Juan Herrera* WBA | 1981-82 | Chung* IBF | 1985-86 | L. Tamakuma* WBA | 1990-91 |
| P. Cardona* WBC | 1982 | Bi-Won Chung* IBF | 1986 | M. Kittikasem* WBC | 1991-92 |
| Santos Laciar* WBA | 1982-85 | Hi-Sup Shin* IBF | 1986-87 | Yuri Arbachakov* WBC | 1992- |
| Freddie Castillo* WBC | 1982 | Dodie Penalosa* IBF | 1987 | Yong Kang Kim* WBA | 1991-92 |
| E. Mercedes* WBA | 1982-83 | Fidel Bassa* WBA | 1987-89 | Rodolfo Blanco* IBF | 1992-93 |
| Charlie Magri* WBC | 1983 | Choi-Chang Ho* IBF | 1987-88 | P. Sithbangprachan* IBF | 1993-95 |
| Frank Cedeno* WBC | 1983-84 | Rolando Bohol* IBF | 1988 | David Griman* WBA | 1992-94 |
| Soon-Chun Kwon* IBF | 1983-85 | Yong-Kang Kim* WBC | 1988-89 | S. S. Ploenchit* WBA | 1994- |
| Koji Kobayashi* WBC | 1984 | Duke McKenzie* IBF | 1988-89 | Francisco Tejedor* IBF | 1995 |
| Gabriel Bernal* WBC | 1984 | Sot Chitalada* WBC | 1989-91 | Danny Romero* IBF | 1995- |
| Sot Chitalada* WBC | 1984-88 | Dave McAuley* IBF | 1989-92 | | |
| Hilario Zapate* WBA | 1985-87 | Jesus Rojas* WBA | 1989-90 | | |

## Junior Flyweights
### (Weight Limit: 108 pounds)

| Champion | Reign | Champion | Reign | Champion | Reign |
|---|---|---|---|---|---|
| Franco Udella* WBC | 1975 | Tadashi Tomori* WBC | 1982 | Humberto | |
| Jaime Rios* WBA | 1975-76 | Hilario Zapata* WBC | 1982-83 | Gonzalez* WBC | 1989-90 |
| Luis Estaba* WBC | 1975-78 | Jung-Koo Chang* WBC | 1983-88 | Michael Carbajal* IBF | 1990-94 |
| Juan Guzman* WBA | 1976 | Lupe Madera* WBA | 1983-84 | R. Pascua* WBC | 1990 |
| Yoko Gushiken* WBA | 1976-81 | Dodie Penalosa* IBF | 1983-86 | M. C. Castro* WBC | 1991 |
| Freddy Castillo* WBC | 1978 | Francisco Quiroz* WBA | 1984-85 | H. Gonzalez* WBC | 1991-93 |
| Netrnoi Vorasingh* WBC | 1978 | Joey Olivo* WBA | 1985 | Hirokia Ioka* WBA | 1991-92 |
| Sung-Jun Kim* WBC | 1978-80 | Myung-Woo Yuh* WBA | 1985-91 | Michael Carbajal, WBC | 1993-94 |
| Shigeo Nakajima* WBC | 1980 | Jum-Hwan Choi* IBF | 1986-88 | Myung-Woo Yuh* WBA | 1993 |
| Hilario Zapata* WBC | 1980-82 | Tacy Macalos* IBF | 1988-89 | Leo Gamez* WBA | 1993-95 |
| Pedro Flores* WBA | 1981 | German Torres* WBC | 1988-89 | H. Gonzalez* WBC, IBF | 1994-95 |
| Hwan-Jin Kim* WBA | 1981 | Yul-Woo Lee* WBC | 1989 | Choi Hi-Yong* WBA | 1995- |
| Katsuo Tokashiki* WBA | 1981-83 | Muangchai | | S. Sorjaturong* WBC, IBF | 1995- |
| Amado Urzua* WBC | 1982 | Kittikasem* IBF | 1989-90 | | |

Note: Division called Light Flyweight by the WBC.

## Strawweights
### (Weight Limit: 105 pounds)

| Champion | Reign | Champion | Reign | Champion | Reign |
|---|---|---|---|---|---|
| Franco Udella* WBC | 1975 | Katsuo Tokashiki* WBA | 1981-83 | German Torres* WBC | 1988-89 |
| Jaime Rios* WBA | 1975-76 | Amado Urzua* WBC | 1982 | Yul-Woo Lee* WBC | 1989 |
| Luis Estaba* WBC | 1975-78 | Tadashi Tomori* WBC | 1982 | M. Kittikasem* IBF | 1989-90 |
| Juan Guzman* WBA | 1976 | Hilario Zapata* WBC | 1982-83 | H. Gonzalez* WBC | 1989-90 |
| Yoko Gushiken* WBA | 1976-81 | Jung-Koo Chang* WBC | 1983-88 | Michael Carbajal* IBF | 1990 |
| Freddy Castillo* WBC | 1978 | Lupe Madera* WBA | 1983-84 | Rolando Pascua* WBC | 1990 |
| Netrnoi Vorasingh* WBC | 1978 | Dodie Penalosa* IBF | 1983-86 | M. C. Castro* WBC | 1991 |
| Sung-Jun Kim* WBC | 1978-80 | Francisco Quiroz* WBA | 1984-85 | Ricardo Lopez* WBC | 1990- |
| Shigeo Nakajima* WBC | 1980 | Joey Olivo* WBA | 1985 | R. Voraphin* IBF | 1992- |
| Hilario Zapata* WBC | 1980-82 | Myung-Woo Yuh* WBA | 1985-93 | Chana Porpaoin* WBA | 1993- |
| Pedro Flores* WBA | 1981 | Jum-Hwan Choi* IBF | 1986-88 | | |
| Hwan-Jin Kim* WBA | 1981 | Tacy Macalos* IBF | 1988-89 | | |

*Champion not generally recognized.

# Alltime Career Leaders

## Total Bouts

| Name | Years Active | Bouts | Name | Years Active | Bouts |
|---|---|---|---|---|---|
| Len Wickwar | 1928-47 | 463 | Maxie Rosenbloom | 1923-39 | 299 |
| Jack Britton | 1905-30 | 350 | Harry Greb | 1913-26 | 298 |
| Johnny Dundee | 1910-32 | 333 | Young Stribling | 1921-33 | 286 |
| Billy Bird | 1920-48 | 318 | Battling Levinsky | 1910-29 | 282 |
| George Marsden | 1928-46 | 311 | Ted (Kid) Lewis | 1909-29 | 279 |

Note: Based on records in The Ring Record Book and Boxing Encyclopedia.

### Most Knockouts

| Name | Years Active | KOs | Name | Years Active | KOs |
|------|--------------|-----|------|--------------|-----|
| Archie Moore | 1936-63 | 130 | Sandy Saddler | 1944-56 | 103 |
| Young Stribling | 1921-33 | 126 | Sam Langford | 1902-26 | 102 |
| Billy Bird | 1920-48 | 125 | Henry Armstrong | 1931-45 | 100 |
| George Odwell | 1930-45 | 114 | Jimmy Wilde | 1911-23 | 98 |
| Sugar Ray Robinson | 1940-65 | 110 | Len Wickware | 1928-47 | 93 |

Note: Based on records in *The Ring Record Book* and *Boxing Encyclopedia*.

## World Heavyweight Championship Fights

| Date | Winner | Wgt | Loser | Wgt | Result | Site |
|------|--------|-----|-------|-----|--------|------|
| Sept 7, 1892 | James J. Corbett* | 178 | John L. Sullivan | 212 | KO 21 | New Orleans |
| Jan 25, 1894 | James J. Corbett | 184 | Charley Mitchell | 158 | KO 3 | Jacksonville, FL |
| Mar 17, 1897 | Bob Fitzsimmons* | 167 | James J. Corbett | 183 | KO 14 | Carson City, NV |
| June 9, 1899 | James J. Jeffries* | 206 | Bob Fitzsimmons | 167 | KO 11 | Coney Island, NY |
| Nov 3, 1899 | James J. Jeffries | 215 | Tom Sharkey | 183 | Ref 25 | Coney Island, NY |
| Apr 6, 1900 | James J. Jeffries | n/a | Jack Finnegan | n/a | KO 1 | Detroit |
| May 11, 1900 | James J. Jeffries | 218 | James J. Corbett | 188 | KO 23 | Coney Island, NY |
| Nov 15, 1901 | James J. Jeffries | 211 | Gus Ruhlin | 194 | TKO 6 | San Francisco |
| July 25, 1902 | James J. Jeffries | 219 | Bob Fitzsimmons | 172 | KO 8 | San Francisco |
| Aug 14, 1903 | James J. Jeffries | 220 | James J. Corbett | 190 | KO 10 | San Francisco |
| Aug 25, 1904 | James J. Jeffries | 219 | Jack Munroe | 186 | TKO 2 | San Francisco |
| July 3, 1905 | Marvin Hart* | 190 | Jack Root | 171 | KO 12 | Reno |
| Feb 23, 1906 | Tommy Burns* | 180 | Marvin Hart | 188 | Ref 20 | Los Angeles |
| Oct 2, 1906 | Tommy Burns | n/a | Jim Flynn | n/a | KO 15 | Los Angeles |
| Nov 28, 1906 | Tommy Burns | 172 | Jack O'Brien | 163½ | Draw 20 | Los Angeles |
| May 8, 1907 | Tommy Burns | 180 | Jack O'Brien | 167 | Ref 20 | Los Angeles |
| Jul 4, 1907 | Tommy Burns | 181 | Bill Squires | 180 | KO 1 | Colma, CA |
| Dec 2, 1907 | Tommy Burns | 177 | Gunner Moir | 204 | KO 10 | London |
| Feb 10, 1908 | Tommy Burns | n/a | Jack Palmer | n/a | KO 4 | London |
| Mar 17, 1908 | Tommy Burns | n/a | Jem Roche | n/a | KO 1 | Dublin |
| Apr 18, 1908 | Tommy Burns | n/a | Jewey Smith | n/a | KO 5 | Paris |
| June 13, 1908 | Tommy Burns | 184 | Bill Squires | 183 | KO 8 | Paris |
| Aug 24, 1908 | Tommy Burns | 181 | Bill Squires | 184 | KO 13 | Sydney |
| Sept 2, 1908 | Tommy Burns | 183 | Bill Lang | 187 | KO 6 | Melbourne |
| Dec 26, 1908 | Jack Johnson* | 192 | Tommy Burns | 168 | TKO 14 | Sydney |
| Mar 10, 1909 | Jack Johnson | n/a | Victor McLaglen | n/a | ND 6 | Vancouver |
| May 19, 1909 | Jack Johnson | 205 | Jack O'Brien | 161 | ND 6 | Philadelphia |
| June 30, 1909 | Jack Johnson | 207 | Tony Ross | 214 | ND 6 | Pittsburgh |
| Sept 9, 1909 | Jack Johnson | 209 | Al Kaufman | 191 | ND 10 | San Francisco |
| Oct 16, 1909 | Jack Johnson | 205½ | Stanley Ketchel | 170¼ | KO 12 | Colma, CA |
| July 4, 1910 | Jack Johnson | 208 | James J. Jeffries | 227 | KO 15 | Reno |
| July 4, 1912 | Jack Johnson | 195½ | Jim Flynn | 175 | TKO 9 | Las Vegas |
| Dec 19, 1913 | Jack Johnson | n/a | Jim Johnson | n/a | Draw 10 | Paris |
| June 27, 1914 | Jack Johnson | 221 | Frank Moran | 203 | Ref 20 | Paris |
| Apr 5, 1915 | Jess Willard* | 230 | Jack Johnson | 205½ | KO 26 | Havana |
| Mar 25, 1916 | Jess Willard | 225 | Frank Moran | 203 | ND 10 | New York City |
| July 4, 1919 | Jack Dempsey* | 187 | Jess Willard | 245 | TKO 4 | Toledo, OH |
| Sept 6, 1920 | Jack Dempsey | 185 | Billy Miske | 187 | KO 3 | Benton Harbor, MI |
| Dec 14, 1920 | Jack Dempsey | 188¼ | Bill Brennan | 197 | KO 12 | New York City |
| July 2, 1921 | Jack Dempsey | 188 | Georges Carpentier | 172 | KO 4 | Jersey City |
| July 4, 1923 | Jack Dempsey | 188 | Tommy Givvons | 175½ | Ref 15 | Shelby, MT |
| Sept 14, 1923 | Jack Dempsey | 192½ | Luis Firpo | 216½ | KO 2 | New York City |
| Sept 23, 1926 | Gene Tunney* | 189½ | Jack Dempsey | 190 | UD 10 | Philadelphia |
| Sept 22, 1927 | Gene Tunney | 189½ | Jack Dempsey | 192½ | UD 10 | Chicago |
| July 26, 1928 | Gene Tunney | 192 | Tom Heeney | 203½ | TKO 11 | New York City |
| June 12, 1930 | Max Schmeling* | 188 | Jack Sharkey | 197 | Foul 4 | New York City |
| July 3, 1931 | Max Schmeling | 189 | Young Stribling | 186½ | TKO 15 | Cleveland |
| June 21, 1932 | Jack Sharkey* | 205 | Max Schmeling | 188 | Split 15 | Long Island City |
| June 29, 1933 | Primo Carnera* | 260½ | Jack Sharkey | 201 | KO 6 | Long Island City |
| Oct 22, 1933 | Primo Carnera | 259½ | Paulino Uzcudun | 229¼ | UD 15 | Rome |
| Mar 1, 1934 | Primo Carnera | 270 | Tommy Loughran | 184 | UD 15 | Miami |
| June 14, 1934 | Max Baer* | 209½ | Primo Carnera | 263¼ | TKO 11 | Long Island City |
| June 13, 1935 | James J. Braddock* | 193¾ | Max Baer | 209½ | UD 15 | Long Island City |
| June 22, 1937 | Joe Louis | 197¼ | James J. Braddock | 197 | KO 8 | Chicago |
| Aug 30, 1937 | Joe Louis | 197 | Tommy Farr | 204¼ | UD 15 | New York City |
| Feb 23, 1938 | Joe Louis | 200 | Nathan Mann | 193½ | KO 3 | New York City |

## World Heavyweight Championship Fights (*Cont.*)

| Date | Winner | Wgt | Loser | Wgt | Result | Site |
|---|---|---|---|---|---|---|
| Apr 1, 1938 | Joe Louis | 202½ | Harry Thomas | 196 | KO 5 | Chicago |
| June 22, 1938 | Joe Louis | 198¾ | Max Schmeling | 193 | KO 1 | New York City |
| Jan 25, 1939 | Joe Louis | 200¼ | John Henry Lewis | 180¾ | KO 1 | New York City |
| Apr 17, 1939 | Joe Louis | 201¼ | Jack Roper | 204¾ | KO 1 | Los Angeles |
| June 28, 1939 | Joe Louis | 200¾ | Tony Galento | 233¾ | TKO 4 | New York City |
| Sept 20, 1939 | Joe Louis | 200 | Bob Pastor | 183 | KO 11 | Detroit |
| Feb 9, 1940 | Joe Louis | 203 | Arturo Godoy | 202 | Split 15 | New York City |
| Mar 29, 1940 | Joe Louis | 201½ | Johnny Paychek | 187½ | KO 2 | New York City |
| June 20, 1940 | Joe Louis | 199 | Arturo Godoy | 201¼ | TKO 8 | New York City |
| Dec 16, 1940 | Joe Louis | 202¼ | Al McCoy | 180¾ | TKO 6 | Boston |
| Jan 31, 1941 | Joe Louis | 202½ | Red Burman | 188 | KO 5 | New York City |
| Feb 17, 1941 | Joe Louis | 203½ | Gus Dorazio | 193½ | KO 2 | Philadelphia |
| Mar 21, 1941 | Joe Louis | 202 | Abe Simon | 254½ | TKO 13 | Detroit |
| Apr 8, 1941 | Joe Louis | 203½ | Tony Musto | 199½ | TKO 9 | St Louis |
| May 23, 1941 | Joe Louis | 201½ | Buddy Baer | 237½ | Disq 7 | Washington, DC |
| June 18, 1941 | Joe Louis | 199½ | Billy Conn | 174 | KO 13 | New York City |
| Sept 29, 1941 | Joe Louis | 202¼ | Lou Nova | 202½ | TKO 6 | New York City |
| Jan 9, 1942 | Joe Louis | 206¾ | Buddy Baer | 250 | KO 1 | New York City |
| Mar 27, 1942 | Joe Louis | 207½ | Abe Simon | 255½ | KO 6 | New York City |
| June 9, 1946 | Joe Louis | 207 | Billy Conn | 187 | KO 8 | New York City |
| Sept 18, 1946 | Joe Louis | 211 | Tami Mauriello | 198½ | KO 1 | New York City |
| Dec 5, 1947 | Joe Louis | 211½ | Jersey Joe Walcott | 194½ | Split 15 | New York City |
| June 25, 1948 | Joe Louis | 213½ | Jersey Joe Walcott | 194¾ | KO 11 | New York City |
| June 22, 1949 | Ezzard Charles* | 181¾ | Jersey Joe Walcott | 195½ | UD 15 | Chicago |
| Aug 10, 1949 | Ezzard Charles | 180 | Gus Lesnevich | 182 | TKO 8 | New York City |
| Oct 14, 1949 | Ezzard Charles | 182 | Pat Valentino | 188½ | KO 8 | San Francisco |
| Aug 15, 1950 | Ezzard Charles | 183¼ | Freddie Beshore | 184½ | TKO 14 | Buffalo |
| Sept 27, 1950 | Ezzard Charles | 184½ | Joe Louis | 218 | UD 15 | New York City |
| Dec 5, 1950 | Ezzard Charles | 185 | Nick Barone | 178½ | KO 11 | Cincinnati |
| Jan 12, 1951 | Ezzard Charles | 185 | Lee Oma | 193 | TKO 10 | New York City |
| Mar 7, 1951 | Ezzard Charles | 186 | Jersey Joe Walcott | 193 | UD 15 | Detroit |
| May 30, 1951 | Ezzard Charles | 182 | Joey Maxim | 181½ | UD 15 | Chicago |
| July 18, 1951 | Jersey Joe Walcott* | 194 | Ezzard Charles | 182 | KO 7 | Pittsburgh |
| June 5, 1952 | Jersey Joe Walcott | 196 | Ezzard Charles | 191½ | UD 15 | Philadelphia |
| Sept 23, 1952 | Rocky Marciano* | 184 | Jersey Joe Walcott | 196 | KO 13 | Philadelphia |
| May 15, 1953 | Rocky Marciano | 184½ | Jersey Joe Walcott | 197¾ | KO 1 | Chicago |
| Sept 24, 1953 | Rocky Marciano | 185 | Roland LaStarza | 184¾ | TKO 11 | New York City |
| June 17, 1954 | Rocky Marciano | 187½ | Ezzard Charles | 185½ | UD 15 | New York City |
| Sept 17, 1954 | Rocky Marciano | 187 | Ezzard Charles | 192½ | KO 8 | New York City |
| May 16, 1955 | Rocky Marciano | 189 | Don Cockell | 205 | TKO 9 | San Francisco |
| Sept 21, 1955 | Rocky Marciano | 188¼ | Archie Moore | 188 | KO 9 | New York City |
| Nov 30, 1956 | Floyd Patterson* | 182¼ | Archie Moore | 187¾ | KO 5 | Chicago |
| July 29, 1957 | Floyd Patterson | 184 | Tommy Jackson | 192½ | TKO 10 | New York City |
| Aug 22, 1957 | Floyd Patterson | 187¼ | Pete Rademacher | 202 | KO 6 | Seattle |
| Aug 18, 1958 | Floyd Patterson | 184½ | Roy Harris | 194 | TKO 13 | Los Angeles |
| May 1, 1959 | Floyd Patterson | 182½ | Brian London | 206 | KO 11 | Indianapolis |
| June 26, 1959 | Ingemar Johansson* | 196 | Floyd Patterson | 182 | TKO 3 | New York City |
| June 20, 1960 | Floyd Patterson* | 190 | Ingemar Johansson | 194¾ | KO 5 | New York City |
| Mar 13, 1961 | Floyd Patterson | 194¾ | Ingemar Johansson | 206½ | KO 6 | Miami Beach |
| Dec 4, 1961 | Floyd Patterson | 188½ | Tom McNeeley | 197 | KO 4 | Toronto |
| Sept 25, 1962 | Sonny Liston* | 214 | Floyd Patterson | 189 | KO 1 | Chicago |
| July 22, 1963 | Sonny Liston | 215 | Floyd Patterson | 194½ | KO 1 | Las Vegas |
| Feb 25, 1964 | Cassius Clay | 210½ | Sonny Liston | 218 | TKO 7 | Miami Beach |
| Mar 5, 1965 | Ernie Terrell WBA* | 199 | Eddie Machen | 192 | UD 15 | Chicago |
| May 25, 1965 | Muhammad Ali | 206 | Sonny Liston | 215¼ | KO 1 | Lewiston, ME |
| Nov 1, 1965 | Ernie Terrell WBA* | 206 | George Chuvalo | 209 | UD 15 | Toronto |
| Nov 22, 1965 | Muhammad Ali | 210 | Floyd Patterson | 196¾ | TKO 12 | Las Vegas |
| Mar 29, 1966 | Muhammad Ali | 214½ | George Chuvalo | 216 | UD 15 | Toronto |
| May 21, 1966 | Muhammad Ali | 201½ | Henry Cooper | 188 | TKO 6 | London |
| June 28, 1966 | Ernie Terrell WBA* | 209½ | Doug Jones | 187½ | UD 15 | Houston |
| Aug 6, 1966 | Muhammad Ali | 209½ | Brian London | 201½ | KO 3 | London |
| Sept 10, 1966 | Muhammad Ali | 203½ | Karl Mildenberger | 194¼ | TKO 12 | Frankfurt |
| Nov 14, 1966 | Muhammad Ali | 212¾ | Cleveland Williams | 210½ | TKO 3 | Houston |
| Feb 6, 1967 | Muhammad Ali | 212¼ | Ernie Terrell WBA | 212½ | UD 15 | Houston |
| Mar 22, 1967 | Muhammad Ali | 211½ | Zora Folley | 202½ | KO 7 | New York City |
| Mar 4, 1968 | Joe Frazier* | 204½ | Buster Mathis | 243½ | TKO 11 | New York City |
| Apr 27, 1968 | Jimmy Ellis* | 197 | Jerry Quarry | 195 | Maj 15 | Oakland |
| June 24, 1968 | Joe Frazier NY* | 203½ | Manuel Ramos | 208 | TKO 2 | New York City |

## World Heavyweight Championship Fights *(Cont.)*

| Date | Winner | Wgt | Loser | Wgt | Result | Site |
|---|---|---|---|---|---|---|
| Aug 14, 1968 | Jimmy Ellis WBA* | 198 | Floyd Patterson | 188 | Ref 15 | Stockholm |
| Dec 10, 1968 | Joe Frazier NY* | 203 | Oscar Bonavena | 207 | UD 15 | Philadelphia |
| Apr 22, 1969 | Joe Frazier NY* | 204½ | Dave Zyglewicz | 190½ | KO 1 | Houston |
| June 23, 1969 | Joe Frazier NY* | 203½ | Jerry Quarry | 198½ | TKO 8 | New York City |
| Feb 16, 1970 | Joe Frazier NY* | 205 | Jimmy Ellis WBA | 201 | TKO 5 | New York City |
| Nov 18, 1970 | Joe Frazier* | 209 | Bob Foster | 188 | KO 2 | Detroit |
| Mar 8, 1971 | Joe Frazier* | 205½ | Muhammad Ali | 215 | UD 15 | New York City |
| Jan 15, 1972 | Joe Frazier | 215½ | Terry Daniels | 195 | TKO 4 | New Orleans |
| May 26, 1972 | Joe Frazier | 217½ | Ron Stander | 218 | TKO 5 | Omaha |
| Jan 22, 1973 | George Foreman* | 217½ | Joe Frazier | 214 | TKO 2 | Kingston, Jam. |
| Sept 1, 1973 | George Foreman | 219½ | Jose Roman | 196½ | KO 1 | Tokyo |
| Mar 26, 1974 | George Foreman | 224¼ | Ken Norton | 212¼ | TKO 2 | Caracas |
| Oct 30, 1974 | Muhammad Ali* | 216-½ | George Foreman | 220 | KO 8 | Kinshasa, Zaire |
| Mar 24, 1975 | Muhammad Ali | 223½ | Chuck Wepner | 225 | TKO 15 | Cleveland |
| May 16, 1975 | Muhammad Ali | 224½ | Ron Lyle | 219 | TKO 11 | Las Vegas |
| July 1, 1975 | Muhammad Ali | 224½ | Joe Bugner | 230 | UD 15 | Kuala Lumpur, Malaysia |
| Oct 1, 1975 | Muhammad Ali | 224½ | Joe Frazier | 215 | TKO 15 | Manila |
| Feb 20, 1976 | Muhammad Ali | 226 | Jean Pierre Coopman | 206 | KO 5 | San Juan |
| Apr 30, 1976 | Muhammad Ali | 230 | Jimmy Young | 209 | UD 15 | Landover, MD |
| May 24, 1976 | Muhammad Ali | 230 | Richard Dunn | 206½ | TKO 5 | Munich |
| Sept 28, 1976 | Muhammad Ali | 221 | Ken Norton | 217½ | UD 15 | New York City |
| May 16, 1977 | Muhammad Ali | 221¼ | Alfredo Evangelista | 209¼ | UD 15 | Landover, MD |
| Sept 29, 1977 | Muhammad Ali | 225 | Earnie Shavers | 211¼ | UD 15 | New York City |
| Feb 15, 1978 | Leon Spinks* | 197¼ | Muhammad Ali | 224¼ | Split 15 | Las Vegas |
| June 9, 1978 | Larry Holmes* | 209 | Ken Norton WBC | 220 | Split 15 | Las Vegas |
| Sept 15, 1978 | Muhammad Ali* | 221 | Leon Spinks | 201 | UD 15 | New Orleans |
| Nov 10, 1978 | Larry Holmes WBC* | 214 | Alfredo Evangelista | 208¼ | KO 7 | Las Vegas |
| Mar 23, 1979 | Larry Holmes WBC* | 214 | Osvaldo Ocasio | 207 | TKO 7 | Las Vegas |
| June 22, 1979 | Larry Holmes WBC* | 215 | Mike Weaver | 202 | TKO 12 | New York City |
| Sept 28, 1979 | Larry Holmes WBC* | 210 | Earnie Shavers | 211 | TKO 11 | Las Vegas |
| Oct 20, 1979 | John Tate* | 240 | Gerrie Coetzee | 222 | UD 15 | Pretoria |
| Feb 3, 1980 | Larry Holmes WBC* | 213½ | Lorenzo Zanon | 215 | TKO 6 | Las Vegas |
| Mar 31, 1980 | Mike Weaver* | 232 | John Tate WBA | 232 | KO 15 | Knoxville |
| Mar 31, 1980 | Larry Holmes WBC* | 211 | Leroy Jones | 254½ | TKO 8 | Las Vegas |
| July 7, 1980 | Larry Holmes WBC* | 214¼ | Scott LeDoux | 226 | TKO 7 | Minneapolis |
| Oct 2, 1980 | Larry Holmes WBC* | 211¼ | Muhammad Ali | 217½ | TKO 11 | Las Vegas |
| Oct 25, 1980 | Mike Weaver WBA* | 210 | Gerrie Coetzee | 226½ | KO 13 | Sun City |
| Apr 11, 1981 | Larry Holmes | 215 | Trevor Berbick | 215½ | UD 15 | Las Vegas |
| June 12, 1981 | Larry Holmes | 212¼ | Leon Spinks | 200¼ | TKO 3 | Detroit |
| Oct 3, 1981 | Mike Weaver WBA* | 215 | James Quick Tillis | 209 | UD 15 | Rosemont, IL |
| Nov 6, 1981 | Larry Holmes | 213¼ | Renaldo Snipes | 215¾ | TKO 11 | Pittsburgh |
| June 11, 1982 | Larry Holmes | 212½ | Gerry Cooney | 225½ | TKO 13 | Las Vegas |
| Nov 26, 1982 | Larry Holmes | 217½ | Tex Cobb | 234¼ | UD 15 | Houston |
| Dec 10, 1982 | Michael Dokes* | 216 | Mike Weaver WBA | 209¾ | TKO 1 | Las Vegas |
| Mar 27, 1983 | Larry Holmes | 221 | Lucien Rodriguez | 209 | UD 12 | Scranton |
| May 20, 1983 | Michael Dokes WBA* | 223 | Mike Weaver | 218½ | Draw 15 | Las Vegas |
| May 20, 1983 | Larry Holmes | 213 | Tim Witherspoon | 219½ | Split 12 | Las Vegas |
| Sept 10, 1983 | Larry Holmes | 223 | Scott Frank | 211¼ | TKO 5 | Atlantic City |
| Sept 23, 1983 | Gerrie Coetzee* | 215 | Michael Dokes WBA | 217 | KO 10 | Richfield, OH |
| Nov 25, 1983 | Larry Holmes | 219 | Marvis Frazier | 200 | TKO 1 | Las Vegas |
| Mar 9, 1984 | Tim Witherspoon | 220¼ | Greg Page | 239½ | Maj 12 | Las Vegas |
| Aug 31, 1984 | Pinklon Thomas* | 216 | Tim Witherspoon WBC | 217 | Maj 12 | Las Vegas |
| Nov 9, 1984 | Larry Holmes IBF | 221½ | James Smith | 227 | TKO 12 | Las Vegas |
| Dec 1, 1984 | Greg Page* | 236½ | Gerrie Coetzee WBA | 218 | KO 8 | Sun City |
| Mar 15, 1985 | Larry Holmes | 223½ | David Bey | 233¼ | TKO 10 | Las Vegas |
| Apr 29, 1985 | Tony Tubbs* | 229 | Greg Page WBA | 239½ | UD 15 | Buffalo |
| May 20, 1985 | Larry Holmes | 224¼ | Carl Williams | 215 | UD 15 | Las Vegas |
| June 15, 1985 | Pinklon Thomas* | 220¼ | Mike Weaver | 221¼ | KO 8 | Las Vegas |
| Sept 21, 1985 | Michael Spinks* | 200 | Larry Holmes IBF | 221½ | UD 15 | Las Vegas |
| Jan 17, 1986 | Tim Witherspoon | 227 | Tony Tubbs WBA | 229 | Maj 15 | Atlanta |
| Mar 22, 1986 | Trevor Berbick* | 218½ | Pinklon Thomas WBC | 222¾ | UD 15 | Las Vegas |
| Apr 19, 1986 | Michael Spinks | 205 | Larry Holmes | 223 | Split 15 | Las Vegas |
| July 19, 1986 | Tim Witherspoon* | 234¾ | Frank Bruno | 228 | TKO 11 | Wembley, Eng. |
| Sept 6, 1986 | Michael Spinks | 201 | Steffen Tangstad | 214¾ | TKO 4 | Las Vegas |
| Nov 22, 1986 | Mike Tyson* | 221¼ | Trevor Berbick WBC | 218½ | TKO 2 | Las Vegas |
| Dec 12, 1986 | James Smith* | 228½ | Tim Witherspoon WBA | 233½ | TKO 1 | New York City |
| Mar 7, 1987 | Mike Tyson WBC* | 219 | James Smith WBA | 233 | UD 12 | Las Vegas |

| Date | Winner | Wgt | Loser | Wgt | Result | Site |
|---|---|---|---|---|---|---|
| May 30, 1987 | Mike Tyson* | 218¾ | Pinklon Thomas | 217¾ | TKO 6 | Las Vegas |
| May 30, 1987 | Tony Tucker | 222¼ | Buster Douglas | 227¼ | TKO 10 | Las Vegas |
| June 15, 1987 | Michael Spinks | 208¾ | Gerry Cooney | 238 | TKO 5 | Atlantic City |
| Aug 1, 1987 | Mike Tyson* | 221 | Tony Tucker IBF | 221 | UD 12 | Las Vegas |
| Oct 16, 1987 | Mike Tyson* | 216 | Tyrell Biggs | 228¾ | TKO 7 | Atlantic City |
| Jan 22, 1988 | Mike Tyson* | 215¾ | Larry Holmes | 225¾ | TKO 4 | Atlantic City |
| Mar 20, 1988 | Mike Tyson* | 216¼ | Tony Tubbs | 238¼ | KO 2 | Tokyo |
| June 27, 1988 | Mike Tyson* | 218¼ | Michael Spinks | 212¼ | KO 1 | Atlantic City |
| Feb 25, 1989 | Mike Tyson | 218 | Frank Bruno | 228 | TKO 5 | Las Vegas |
| July 21, 1989 | Mike Tyson | 219¼ | Carl Williams | 218 | TKO 1 | Atlantic City |
| Feb 10, 1990 | Buster Douglas* | 231½ | Mike Tyson | 220½ | KO 10 | Tokyo |
| Oct 25, 1990 | Evander Holyfield | 208 | Buster Douglas | 246 | KO 3 | Las Vegas |
| Apr 19, 1991 | Evander Holyfield | 212 | George Foreman | 257 | UD 12 | Atlantic City |
| Nov 23, 1991 | Evander Holyfield | 210 | Bert Cooper | 215 | TKO 7 | Atlanta |
| June 19, 1992 | Evander Holyfield | 210 | Larry Holmes | 233 | UD 12 | Las Vegas |
| Nov 13, 1992 | Riddick Bowe | 235 | Evander Holyfield | 205 | UD 12 | Las Vegas |
| Feb 6, 1993 | Riddick Bowe | 243 | Michael Dokes | 244 | KO 1 | New York City |
| May 8, 1993 | Lennox Lewis | 235 | Tony Tucker | 235 | UD 12 | Las Vegas |
| May 22, 1993 | Riddick Bowe | 244 | Jesse Ferguson | 224 | KO 2 | Washington, DC |
| Oct 2, 1993 | Lennox Lewis | 229 | Frank Bruno | 233 | KO 7 | London |
| Nov 6, 1993 | Evander Holyfield | 217 | Riddick Bowe | 246 | Split 12 | Las Vegas |
| Apr 22, 1994 | Michael Moorer | 214 | Evander Holyfield | 214 | Split 12 | Las Vegas |
| May 6, 1994 | Lennox Lewis | 235 | Phil Jackson | 218 | TKO 8 | Atlantic City |
| Nov 6, 1994 | George Foreman | 250 | Michael Moorer | 222 | KO 10 | Las Vegas |
| Mar 11, 1995 | Riddick Bowe | 241 | Herbie Hide | 214 | KO 6 | Las Vegas |
| Apr 8, 1995 | Oliver McCall | 231 | Larry Holmes | 236 | UD 12 | Las Vegas |
| Apr 8, 1995 | Bruce Seldon | 236 | Tony Tucker | 243 | TKO 7 | Las Vegas |
| Apr 22, 1995 | George Foreman | 256 | Axel Schulz | 221 | Split 12 | Las Vegas |
| Jun 17, 1995 | Riddick Bowe | 243 | Jorge Luis Gonzalez | 237 | KO 6 | Las Vegas |
| Aug 19, 1995 | Bruce Seldon | 234 | Joe Hipp | 233 | TKO 10 | Las Vegas |
| Sept 2, 1995 | Frank Bruno | 247¾ | Oliver McCall | 234¾ | UD 12 | London |

*Champion not generally recognized.

KO=knockout; TKO=technical knockout; UD=unanimous decision; Split=split decision; Ref=referee's decision; Disq=disqualification; ND=no decision.

# Ring Magazine Fighter and Fight of the Year

| Year | Fighter | Year | Fighter | Year | Fighter |
|---|---|---|---|---|---|
| 1928 | Gene Tunney | 1935 | Barney Ross | 1941 | Joe Louis |
| 1929 | Tommy Loughran | 1936 | Joe Louis | 1942 | Ray Robinson |
| 1930 | Max Schmeling | 1937 | Henry Armstrong | 1943 | Fred Apostoli |
| 1932 | Jack Sharkey | 1938 | Joe Louis | 1944 | Beau Jack |
| 1933 | No award | 1939 | Joe Louis | | |
| 1934 | T. Canzoneri/B. Ross | 1940 | Billy Conn | | |

Note: No fight of the year named until 1945

| Year | Fighter | Fight | Winner | Site |
|---|---|---|---|---|
| 1945 | Willie Pep | Rocky Graziano-Cochrane | Rocky Graziano | New York City |
| 1946 | Tony Zale | Tony Zale-Rocky Graziano | Tony Zale | New York City |
| 1947 | Gus Lesnevich | Rocky Graziano-Tony Zale | Rocky Graziano | Chicago |
| 1948 | Ike Williams | Marcel Cerdan-Tony Zale | Marcel Cerdan | Jersey City |
| 1949 | Ezzard Charles | Willie Pep-Sandy Saddler | Willie Pep | New York City |
| 1950 | Ezzard Charles | Jake LaMotta-Laurent Dauthuille | Jake LaMotta | Detroit |
| 1951 | Ray Robinson | Jersey Joe Walcott-Ezzard Charles | Jersey Joe Walcott | Pittsburgh |
| 1952 | Rocky Marciano | Rocky Marciano-Jersey Joe Walcott | Rocky Marciano | Philadelphia |
| 1953 | Carl Olson | Rocky Marciano-Roland LaStarza | Rocky Marciano | New York City |
| 1954 | Rocky Marciano | Rocky Marciano-Ezzard Charles | Rocky Marciano | New York City |
| 1955 | Rocky Marciano | Carmen Basilio-Tony DeMarco | Carmen Basilio | Boston |
| 1956 | Floyd Patterson | Carmen Basilio-Johnny Saxton | Carmen Basilio | Syracuse |
| 1957 | Carmen Basilio | Carmen Basilio-Ray Robinson | Carmen Basilio | New York City |
| 1958 | Ingemar Johansson | Ray Robinson-Carmen Basilio | Ray Robinson | Chicago |
| 1959 | Ingemar Johansson | Gene Fullmer-Carmen Basilio | Gene Fullmer | San Francisco |
| 1960 | Floyd Patterson | Floyd Patterson-Ingemar Johansson | Floyd Patterson | New York City |
| 1961 | Joe Brown | Joe Brown-Dave Charnley | Joe Brown | London |
| 1962 | Dick Tiger | Joey Giardello-Henry Hank | Joey Giardello | Philadelphia |
| 1963 | Cassius Clay | Cassius Clay-Doug Jones | Cassius Clay | New York City |
| 1964 | Emile Griffith | Cassius Clay-Sonny Liston | Cassius Clay | Miami Beach |

| Year | Fighter | Fight | Winner | Site |
|------|---------|-------|--------|------|
| 1965 | Dick Tiger | Floyd Patterson-George Chuvalo | Floyd Patterson | New York City |
| 1966 | No award | Jose Torres-Eddie Cotton | Jose Torres | Las Vegas |
| 1967 | Joe Frazier | Nino Benvenuti-Emile Griffith | Nino Benvenuti | New York City |
| 1968 | Nino Benvenuti | Dick Tiger-Frank DePaula | Dick Tiger | New York City |
| 1969 | Jose Napoles | Joe Frazier-Jerry Quarry | Joe Frazier | New York City |
| 1970 | Joe Frazier | Carlos Monzon-Nino Benvenuti | Carlos Monzon | Rome |
| 1971 | Joe Frazier | Joe Frazier-Muhammed Ali | Joe Frazier | New York City |
| 1972 | Muhammed Ali Carlos Monzon | Bob Foster-Chris Finnegan | Bob Foster | London |
| 1973 | George Foreman | George Foreman-Joe Frazier | George Foreman | Kingston, Jam. |
| 1974 | Muhammed Ali | Muhammed Ali-George Foreman | Muhammed Ali | Kinshasa |
| 1975 | Muhammed Ali | Muhammed Ali-Joe Frazier | Muhammed Ali | Manila |
| 1976 | George Foreman | George Foreman-Ron Lyle | George Foreman | Las Vegas |
| 1977 | Carlos Zarate | Joe Young-George Foreman | Joe Young | San Juan |
| 1978 | Muhammed Ali | Leon Spinks-Muhammed Ali | Leon Spinks | La Vegas |
| 1979 | Ray Leonard | Danny Lopez-Tony Ayala | Danny Lopez | San Antonio |
| 1980 | Thomas Hearns | Saad Muhammed-Danny Lopez | Saad Muhammed | McAfee, NJ |
| 1981 | Ray Leonard Salvador Sanchez | Ray Leonard-Tonny Hearns | Ray Leonard | Las Vegas |
| 1982 | Larry Holmes | Bobby Chacon-Rafael Limon | Bobby Chacon | Sacramento |
| 1983 | Marvin Hagler | Bobby Chacon-Cornelius Boza-Edwards | Bobby Chacon | Las Vegas |
| 1984 | Thomas Hearns | Jose Luis Ramirez-Edwin Rosario | Jose Luis Ramirez | San Juan |
| 1985 | Donald Curry Marvin Hagler | Marvin Hagler-Tommy Hearns | Marvin Hagler | Las Vegas |
| 1986 | Mike Tyson | Stevie Cruz-Barry McGuigan | Stevie Cruz | Las Vegas |
| 1987 | Evander Holyfield | Ray Leonard-Marvin Hagler | Ray Leonard | Las Vegas |
| 1988 | Mike Tyson | Tony Lopez-Rocky Lockridge | Tony Lopez | Inglewood, CA |
| 1989 | Pernell Whitaker | Roberto Duran-Iran Barkley | Roberto Duran | Atlantic City |
| 1990 | Julio César Chávez | Julio César Chávez-Meldrick Taylor | Julio César Chávez | Las Vegas |
| 1991 | James Toney | Robert Quiroga-Kid Akeem Anifowoshe | Robert Quiroga | San Antonio |
| 1992 | Riddick Bowe | Riddick Bowe-Evander Holyfield | Riddick Bowe | Las Vegas |
| 1993 | Michael Carbajal | Michael Carbajal-Humberto Gonzalez | Michael Carbajal | Las Vegas |
| 1994 | Roy Jones | Jorge Castro-John David Jackson | Jorge Castro | Monterrey, Mex. |

## U.S. Olympic Gold Medalists

### LIGHT FLYWEIGHT
| | |
|---|---|
| 1984 | Paul Gonzales |

### FLYWEIGHT
| | |
|---|---|
| 1904 | George Finnegan |
| 1920 | Frank Di Gennara |
| 1024 | Fidel LaBarba |
| 1952 | Nathan Brooks |
| 1976 | Leo Randolph |
| 1984 | Steve McCrory |

### BANTAMWEIGHT
| | |
|---|---|
| 1904 | Oliver Kirk |
| 1988 | Kennedy McKinney |

### FEATHERWEIGHT
| | |
|---|---|
| 1904 | Oliver Kirk |
| 1924 | John Fields |
| 1984 | Meldrick Taylor |

### LIGHTWEIGHT
| | |
|---|---|
| 1904 | Harry Spanger |
| 1920 | Samuel Mosberg |
| 1968 | Ronald W. Harris |

### LIGHTWEIGHT (Cont.)
| | |
|---|---|
| 1976 | Howard Davis |
| 1984 | Pernell Whitaker |
| 1992 | Oscar De La Hoya |

### LIGHT WELTERWEIGHT
| | |
|---|---|
| 1952 | Charles Adkins |
| 1972 | Ray Seales |
| 1976 | Ray Leonard |
| 1984 | Jerry Page |

### WELTERWEIGHT
| | |
|---|---|
| 1904 | Albert Young |
| 1932 | Edward Flynn |
| 1960 | Wilbert McClure |
| 1984 | Mark Breland |
| 1984 | Frank Tate |

### MIDDLEWEIGHT
| | |
|---|---|
| 1904 | Charles Mayer |
| 1932 | Carmen Bath |
| 1952 | Floyd Patterson |
| 1960 | Edward Crook |
| 1976 | Michael Spinks |

### LIGHT HEAVYWEIGHT
| | |
|---|---|
| 1920 | Eddie Eagan |
| 1952 | Norvel Lee |
| 1956 | James Boyd |
| 1960 | Cassius Clay |
| 1976 | Leon Spinks |
| 1988 | Andrew Maynard |

### HEAVYWEIGHT
| | |
|---|---|
| 1984 | Henry Tillman |
| 1988 | Ray Mercer |

### SUPER HEAVYWEIGHT
| | |
|---|---|
| 1904 | Samuel Berger |
| 1952 | H. Edward Sanders |
| 1956 | T. Peter Rademacher |
| 1964 | Joe Frazier |
| 1968 | George Foreman |
| 1984 | Tyrell Biggs |

# Horse Racing

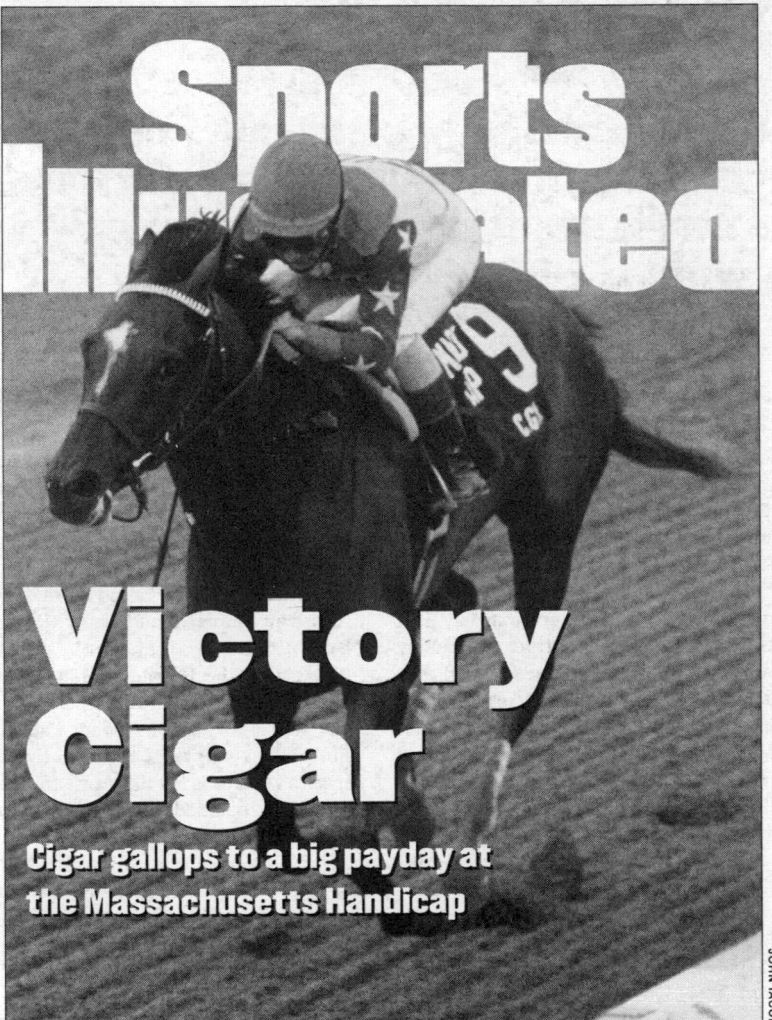

**Sports Illustrated**

## Victory Cigar

Cigar gallops to a big payday at
the Massachusetts Handicap

JOHN IACONO

# D. Wayne's Delights

## D. Wayne Lukas had a number of fine horses in his stable, but Thunder Gulch and Timber Country brought him the Triple Crown

### by William F. Reed

AT YEAR'S end it was as if everyone in thoroughbred racing had been packed into a drawing room for after-dinner drinks and conversation. As usual, a large crowd was gathered around trainer D. Wayne Lukas, hearing about how he had become the first trainer to win the Triple Crown with different horses. Or about how he had brought along Serena's Song, the marvelous filly. But it was impossible to concentrate completely on the garrulous Lukas because of all that Cigar smoke coming from the corner where trainer Bill Mott and owner Allen Paulson were toasting the remarkable 5-year-old who had inspired the year's most popular headline: CIGAR SMOKES FIELD.

The wonderful thing about the final tableau was the number of surprises it contained. At the beginning, the year was supposed to be dominated by Holy Bull, the 1994 Horse of the Year as a 3-year-old. Sadly, the Bull pulled up in the Don Handicap on Feb. 11 with what turned out to be a career-ending leg injury, opening the way for Cigar, an erstwhile turf specialist, to win his fourth consecutive race since being switched to the dirt. Nevertheless, Cigar hardly seemed dominating enough to make anyone think he could win the $500,000 bonus offered by Boston's Suffolk Downs to any horse that swept the Gulfstream Park Handicap, Oaklawn Handicap, Pimlico Special and Massachusetts Handicap.

"After the race in Florida," said Suffolk executive vice president Louis J. Raffeto Jr., "I didn't think Cigar would go to Hot Springs [for the Oaklawn Handicap], and even if he did, I didn't think he was a legitimate route horse." But owner Paulson and trainer Mott surprised Raffeto by sending Cigar to Arkansas for the April 15 race. The classy field included Concern, winner of the 1994 Breeders Cup Classic; Best Pal, then the richest horse in training; and Silver Goblin, who had won eight consecutive races. Despite being banged around in the first turn and inadvertently hit on the nose by a rival jockey's whip while turning for home, Cigar came from off the pace to win by 2½ lengths in what Oaklawn president Charles Cella called "the most impressive race ever put together at Oaklawn Park."

While these developments were unfolding in the handicap division, the Kentucky Derby field was being shaped by the major prep races in New York, Florida, Arkansas, California and Kentucky. Many experts were excited about the likes of Afternoon Deelites, a reputed supercolt owned by songwriter Burt Bacharach, and Talkin Man, an impressive winner of the Wood Memorial in New York. But the trainer who seemed to be holding the strongest hand was Lukas, who had ended a long slump in 1994 by winning the Preakness and the Belmont Stakes with Tabasco Cat.

As the Kentucky Derby approached, Lukas daily issued rave reviews about Timber Country, the 2-year-old champion of 1994, and Serena's Song, an easy winner in the Jim Beam Stakes. He also had a third contender, Thunder Gulch, who had nipped Suave Prospect at the wire in both the Fountain of Youth and the Florida Derby but then had dropped out of sight after finishing a poor fourth in the Blue Grass Stakes.

In the Derby, however, Thunder Gulch and jockey Gary Stevens charged out of the

**Thunder Gulch was just an also-ran until he ran away with the Derby.**

19-horse pack to take the lead in the stretch, then withstood the late charges of Tejano Run, who finished second, and Timber Country, who was flying at the end after finally breaking free of the pack. Incredibly, Thunder Gulch had gone off at odds of almost 25–1, meaning that he paid $51 for a $2 win bet, the highest price since Proud Clarion paid $62.20 in 1967.

Thunder Gulch's owner, Michael Tabor, a resident of Monte Carlo who owns a string of betting shops in Great Britain, had paid $450,000 for the colt the previous fall. The same man who had found the colt for Tabor, Irish veterinarian Demi O'Byrne, also hooked him up with Lukas. Yet the media, instead of giving Lukas credit for developing Thunder Gulch, mainly chastized him for not giving the colt equal billing with Timber Country and Serena's Song. Unfazed, Lukas said he had never slighted Thunder Gulch, then greeted the media the morning after the Derby wearing

**Timber Country (far left) made a late charge to win the Preakness.**

a Timber Country cap—a statement more pointed than anything he said.

The week after the Derby the spotlight swung to Pimlico in Baltimore and back to Cigar. Ted Dipple, a Boston-area insurance executive who had underwritten a policy against the $500,000 bonus through Lloyd's of London, realized going into the Pimlico Special that Cigar might indeed be good enough to sweep the four races. So on May 13, the day Cigar went after the third leg of the bonus, Dipple attempted to recoup some of his potential loss by plunging $5,000 on Cigar at Pimlico and another £2,500 (about $4,000) with the William Hill bookmaking establishment in London. "I wanted to bet £25,000, but they [Hill] would only take 2,500," said Dipple. The problem was, Cigar went off at odds of only 2–5. Cigar again lit up the field, this time going wire-to-wire.

Shortly after Cigar moved out of Pimlico, the 3-year-olds moved in. Asked about Timber Country's Derby finish, Lukas blamed jockey Pat Day's inability to extricate the colt from traffic in time to make a serious run. But Lukas refused to dump Day after the Derby when some members of the Timber Country camp argued that Day's laid-back riding style didn't fit the colt's laid-back personality.

On the Monday before the Preakness, Day worked Timber Country at Churchill Downs with strict orders from Lukas to "startle him if you can." The idea was to sharpen the colt, get him to run more aggressively—something to snap his 0-for-4 record in 1995. When the workout was over, the :59⅗ clocking didn't impress Lukas and Day nearly as much as the way the colt came off the track. "He went jiggedy-jog, just tugging on the bridle," Day said. "He hadn't done that all spring."

That same day Lukas made an announcement about Serena's Song that caused almost as much of a stir in the racing world as his decision three weeks earlier to run her against colts in the Derby: He was shipping her to Baltimore along with Timber Country and Thunder Gulch so she could run against fillies in the Black-Eyed Susan the day before the Preakness.

By the time the Lukas horses were checked into the Pimlico stakes barn on Wednesday afternoon, Serena was the subject of another debate, again inspired by Lukas's decision. In the Derby she had been pressured into setting a suicidal pace that cost her any chance of victory. Mercifully, when it had become obvious that Serena's Song was out of gas, jockey Corey Nakatani had wrapped up on her. So, observers wondered, didn't she need a long rest? Wasn't running her back in the Black-Eyed Susan putting her at risk of a career-ending injury? As he waited for the Black-Eyed Susan to begin, Lukas knew the vultures were circling. "You don't think my head's on the chopping block, do you?" he said. To his relief, Serena's Song responded with a nine-length victory.

But there was still the main business of the week, the second leg of racing's Triple Crown. After the fifth race on Saturday, Lukas visited the Pimlico jockeys' quarters to see Day and Stevens. The trainer devoted most of his attention to Day, reminding him to "be a pilot, not a passenger." And Day, long one of the nation's top riders, understood what was at stake. "My contract lasts only as long as the end of the race," he said.

Moments before the race Day tapped Timber Country with his whip in the post parade "to let him know it was time for business," and he whacked him on the left side as soon as the starting gate sprang open. The result was as desired: Timber Country was never worse than sixth in the 11-horse field and made a powerful move in the stretch to take the lead inside the 16th pole. Timber Country and Day vindicated Lukas's faith by taking a half-length victory over Oliver's Twist. Thunder Gulch, whose game run proved his Derby win was no fluke, was third by a neck. So now the Belmont Stakes shaped up as the rubber match between the two Lukas-trained colts. "We'll get them ready," Lukas said, "then let the horses decide it."

While racing fans were awaiting the Belmont, officials at Suffolk Downs were sweating out whether Cigar would go for the bonus in the Mass 'Cap on Saturday, June 3. Even $500,000 is virtually inconsequential to Paulson, who had made a fortune in the aerospace business, and if Suffolk racing secretary John H. Morrissey assigned too much weight to Cigar—he had carried 120 at Oaklawn and 122 at Pimlico—Paulson wouldn't have hesitated to skip Boston en route to preparing a fresh Cigar for the world's richest race, the $3 million Breeders Cup Classic on Oct. 28 at Belmont Park. But when Morrissey assigned Cigar 124 pounds—the track wasn't going to smoke Cigar out—Paulson and Mott decided to bring their star to New England.

The trainers of the other top handicap horses felt that 124 was too light for Cigar, and they expressed their displeasure by keeping their runners elsewhere, leaving the Mass 'Cap with a weak field that grew even weaker when three horses, all based in New York, were scratched on race day. Naturally, insurance man Dipple had mixed feelings. On the one hand, he wished that Cigar had drawn tougher competition and more weight. On the other, however, the bonus had achieved the desired goal. "We wanted to bring the best handicap horses to Boston," Dipple said, "but we sort of overcooked the stew."

On the Friday before the race Paulson and his entourage were the guests of honor on a Boston harbor cruise sponsored by the track. Sitting on the top deck with Mott, Paulson talked about his unlikely star. A nonsmoker, Paulson named Cigar after a pilot's checkpoint in the Gulf of Mexico between Miami and New Orleans. The only time he had ever tried a cigar, Paulson said, was when he was in the Air Force during World War II. "It made me sort of dizzy, as I recall," Paulson said. Which, of course, is how he had come to feel about Cigar in the wake of the amazing transformation that began on Oct. 28, 1994, when Cigar won his debut on the dirt by eight lengths at Aqueduct. "We did it as sort of an experiment," Mott said. "We were desperate, because he hadn't run well on the grass."

On Mass 'Cap day, Suffolk passed out expensive Macanudo cigars to the first 2,000 customers who wanted them. But Dipple and his associates declined the free stogies,

PETER READ MILLER

**Lukas followed a banner season in 1994 with a historic one in '95.**

having brought their own Cuban-made cigars obtained through Great Britain. "We're hoping the horse doesn't like cigar smoke," Dipple quipped, "because all our employees will be along the rail, blowing cigar smoke as he comes down the stretch."

This time Dipple, resigned to the inevitable, didn't bet in England because of Cigar's unenticing 1–5 odds, the lowest price ever on a Mass 'Cap favorite. The crowd of 12,238 was rewarded with a superstar performance. Down the stretch, jockey Jerry Bailey gathered in his reins, showed Cigar his whip, and hit him twice righthanded, just to make sure his mount kept his wire on his business. At the wire the coasting Cigar was an easy winner. "I wouldn't even say that he's at the top of his game right now," Mott said. "Maybe we reached that a race or two ago, and he's just holding his own now." Added Paulson, "This guy's different."

So, as it turned out, was Thunder Gulch.

At about 5 p.m. on June 9, less than an hour after he had won the prestigious Mother Goose Stakes with Serena's Song, Lukas called the Belmont press box to announce that Timber Country would be scratched from the Belmont Stakes because of fever. Although he might have gambled that the colt's temperature would go down by Saturday morning, Lukas opted to treat him immediately with an anti-inflammatory drug. That meant he had to scratch the colt from the Belmont, because horses taking such medication were not then allowed to race in New York. "There's no sense in crying about it," Lukas said. "We've got to start thinking about getting the other one ready to run."

The other one. That had been Thunder Gulch's plight all spring. But in the Belmont, he became the One. At the top of the stretch, Thunder Gulch hooked the pace-setting Star Standard, ridden by Julie Krone. As Krone kept pushing her colt with a furious lefthanded whip, Thunder Gulch drew clear at the 16th pole and hung on for the victory that made Lukas the first trainer to sweep the Triple Crown in the same year with different horses. He also became the first to win five consecutive Triple Crown races. Said Nick Zito, the trainer of Star Standard, "What he's done is tremendous, unbelievable. I guess I'll have to go get Pegasus to beat him."

Unfortunately for the sophisticated crowds who always patronize the prestigious late-summer meeting at Saratoga Springs, N.Y., both Cigar and Serena's Song stayed in the barn, resting up for the fall campaign. But Lukas brought in Thunder Gulch for the Travers Stakes on Aug. 19. Two days before that race, when Thunder Gulch should have been getting the attention that escaped him during the Triple Crown, Lukas announced that Timber Country had been retired to stud because of a torn tendon suffered in a workout. Poor Thunder Gulch. Even at that late date, Timber Country stole his thunder.

But then Thunder Gulch won the Travers so easily that even his detractors had to admit that they had been underrating him. "He's a pretty good horse," said Lukas, tongue in cheek. A couple of unlikely heroes, Thunder Gulch and Cigar, along with Serena's Song, saved 1995 and made it special. It was too bad that Holy Bull wasn't represented in the drawing room, but who knows? Maybe he would have found all that Lukas chatter as suffocating as the Cigar smoke.

# FOR THE RECORD·1994–1995

## THOROUGHBRED RACING

## The Triple Crown

### 121st Kentucky Derby

May 6, 1995. Grade I, 3-year-olds; 8th race, Churchill Downs, Louisville. All 126 lbs.* Distance: 1¼ miles. Stakes value: $957,400; Winner: $707,400; Second: $145,000; Third: $70,000; Fourth: $35,000. Track: Fast. Off: 5:33 p.m. Winner: Thunder Gulch (Ch c by Gulch-Line of Thunder by Storm Bird); Times: 0:22⅘, 0:45⅘, 1:10⅕, 1:35⅗, 2:01⅕. Won: Driving. Breeder: Peter M. Brant.

| Horse | Finish-PP | Margin | Jockey/Owner |
|---|---|---|---|
| Thunder Gulch | 1-16 | 2¼ | Gary Stevens/ Michael Tabor |
| Tejano Run | 2-14 | head | Jerry Bailey/ Roy Monroe |
| Timber Country | 3-15 | ¾ | Pat Day/ Overbrook Farm, Gainesway Stable and Robert and Beverly Lewis |
| Jumron | 4-10 | head | Goncalino Almeida/ Charles Dunn |
| Mecke | 5-18 | ½ | Robbie Davis/ James Lewis Jr |
| Eltish | 6-7 | 3 | Eddie Delahoussaye/ Juddmonte Farms |
| Knockadoon | 7-2 | neck | Chris McCarron/ William Warren Jr |
| Afternoon Deelites | 8-12 | neck | Kent Desormeaux/ Burt Bacharach |
| Citadeed | 9-19 | ¾ | Eddie Maple/ Ivan Allen |
| In Character | 10-9 | ½ | Chris Antley/ Vince Baker, Dave Farr & Bruce Jackson |
| Suave Prospect | 11-6 | ½ | Julie Krone/ William Condren and Michael Sherman |
| Talkin Man | 12-11 | ½ | Mike Smith/ Kinghaven Farms, Helen Stollery and Peter Wall |
| Dazzling Falls | 13-1 | neck | Garrett Gomez/ Chateau Ridge Farm |
| Ski Captain | 14-17 | 1½ | Yutake Take/ Shadai Racehorse Company Ltd. |
| Jambalaya Jazz | 15-5 | neck | Craig Perret/ John Oxley |
| Serena's Song | 16-13 | 1½ | Corey Nakatani/ Robert and Beverly Lewis |
| Pyramid Peak | 17-3 | 6 | Herb McCauley/ John Oxley |
| Lake George | 18-8 | 21 | Shane Sellers/ Bedford Stable and Stonehenge Stable |
| Wild Syn | 19-4 | — | Randy Romero/ Jurgen Arnemann |

*Except for Serena's Song, a filly, 121 lbs.

### 120th Preakness Stakes

May 20, 1995. Grade I, 3-year-olds; 10th race, Pimlico Race Course, Baltimore. All 126 lbs. Distance: 1³⁄₁₆ miles; Stakes value: $687,400; Winner: $446,810; Second: $137,480; Third: $68,740; Fourth: $34,370. Track: Fast. Off: 5:33 p.m. Winner: Timber Country (Ch C Woodman-Fall Aspen by Pretense); Times: 0:23⅕, 0:47⅕, 1:10⅗, 1:35⅗, 1:54⅗. Won: Driving. Breeder: Lowquest Ltd.

| Horse | Finish-PP | Margin | Jockey/Owner |
|---|---|---|---|
| Timber Country | 1-7 | ½ | Pat Day/ Overbrook Farm, Gainesway Stable and R.& B. Lewis |
| Oliver's Twist | 2-10 | neck | Alberto Delgado/ Charles Oliver |
| Thunder Gulch | 3-11 | 4 | Gary Stevens/ Michael Tabor |
| Star Standard | 4-8 | ½ | Chris McCarron/ William Condren and Joseph Cornacchia |
| Mecke | 5-9 | neck | Robbie Davis/ James Lewis Jr |
| Talkin Man | 6-4 | 5¾ | Mike Smith/ Kinghaven Farms, Helen Stollery and Peter Wall |
| Our Gatsby | 7-2 | neck | Kent Desormeaux/ Charles Heider |
| Mystery Storm | 8-3 | 9 | Craig Perret/ David Beard |
| Tejano Run | 9-5 | 2¾ | Jerry Bailey/ Roy Monroe |
| Pana Brass | 10-6 | 17 | Eddie Maple/ Robert Perez |
| Itron | 11-1 | — | Ricky Frazier/ David Albert |

### 127th Belmont Stakes

June 10, 1995. Grade I, 3-year-olds; 9th race, Belmont Park, Elmont, NY. All 126 lbs. Distance: 1½ miles. Stakes purse: $692,400; Winner: $415,440; Second: $138,480; Third: $76,164; Fourth: $41,544. Track: Fast. Off: 5:33 p.m. Winner: Thunder Gulch (Ch c, 3, by Gulch-Line of Thunder by Storm Bird); Times: 0:24⅗, 0:50⅕, 1:15⅕, 1:40, 2:05⅗, 2:32. Won: Driving. Breeder: Peter M. Brant.

| Horse | Finish-PP | Margin | Jockey/Owner |
|---|---|---|---|
| Thunder Gulch | 1-10 | 2 | Gary Stevens/ Michael Tabor |
| Star Standard | 2-11 | 3½ | Julie Krone/ William Condren and Joseph Cornacchia |
| Citadeed | 3-1 | 1½ | Eddie Maple/ Ivan Allen |
| Knockadoon | 4-9 | 4½ | Chris McCarron/ William Warren Jr |
| Pana Brass | 5-3 | 5 | Wigberto Ramos/ Robert Perez |
| Off'n'Away | 6-2 | 1 | Mike Smith/ Moyglare Stud |
| Ave's Flag | 7-5 | 4 | John Velazquez/ David McNulty and Josef Omland |
| Composer | 8-6 | 7½ | Jerry Bailey/ Henryk de Kwiatkowski |
| Colonial Secretary | 9-8 | 3 | Jose Santos/ Buckland Farm |
| Is Sveikatas | 10-4 | 6½ | Jorge Chavez/ Clarke Whitaker and Alfred Duncan |
| Wild Syn | 11-7 | — | Randy Romero/ Jurgen Arnemann |

# Major Stakes Races

## Late 1994

| Date | Race | Track | Distance | Winner | Jockey/Trainer | Purse ($) |
|------|------|-------|----------|--------|----------------|-----------|
| Sep 17 ....The Woodward | Belmont Park | 1⅛ miles | Holy Bull | Mike Smith/ Jimmy Croll | 500,000 |
| Sep 17 ....Man O'War | Belmont Park | 1⅜ miles | Royal Mountain Inn | Julie Krone/ B. Tagg | 400,000 |
| Sep 18 ....Molson Export Million | Woodbine | 1⅛ miles | Dramatic Gold | Corey Nakatani/ D. Hofmans | 1,000,000 |
| Oct 1.......Super Derby XV | Louisiana Downs | 1¼ miles | Soul of the Matter | Kent Desormeaux/ Richard Mandella | 750,000 |
| Oct 2.......Prix De L'Arc De Triomphe | Longchamp | 1½ miles | Carnegie | T. Jarnet/ Andre Fabre | 1,146,208 |
| Oct 8.......Jockey Club Gold Cup | Belmont Park | 1¼ miles | Colonial Affair | Jose Santos/ F. Schulhofer | 750,000 |
| Oct 8.......Turf Classic Invitational | Belmont Park | 1½ miles | Tikkanen | Cash Asmussen/ J. Pease | 500,000 |
| Oct 8.......Moet Champagne | Belmont Park | 1⅟₁₆ miles | Timber Country | Pat Day/ D. Wayne Lukas | 500,000 |
| Oct 8.......Frizette Stakes | Belmont Park | 1⅟₁₆ miles | Flanders | Pat Day/ D. Wayne Lukas | 250,000 |
| Oct 8.......Beldame Stakes | Belmont Park | 1⅛ miles | Heavenly Prize | Pat Day/ Claude McGaughey | 250,000 |
| Oct 15.....Washington D.C. Int'l. | Laurel | 1¼ miles | Paradise Creek | Pat Day/ William Mott | 600,000 |
| Nov 5 ......Breeders' Cup Sprint | Churchill Downs | 6 furlongs | Cherokee Run | Mike Smith/ F. Alexander | 1,000,000 |
| Nov 5 ......Breeders' Cup Juvenile Fillies | Churchill Downs | 1⅟₁₆ miles | Flanders | Pat Day/ D. Wayne Lukas | 1,000,000 |
| Nov 5 ......Breeders' Cup Distaff | Churchill Downs | 1⅛ miles | One Dreamer | Gary Stevens/ T. Proctor | 1,000,000 |
| Nov 5 ......Breeders' Cup Mile | Churchill Downs | 1 mile | Barathea | Frankie Dettori/ L. Cumani | 1,000,000 |
| Nov 5 ......Breeders' Cup Juvenile | Churchill Downs | 1⅟₁₆ miles | Timber Country | Pat Day/ D. Wayne Lukas | 1,000,000 |
| Nov 5 ......Breeders' Cup Turf | Churchill Downs | 1½ miles | Tikkanen | Mike Smith/ J. Pease | 2,000,000 |
| Nov 5 ......Breeders' Cup Classic | Churchill Downs | 1¼ miles | Concern | Jerry Bailey/ Richard Small | 3,000,000 |
| Nov 6 ......Yellow Ribbon Invitational | Oak Tree | 1¼ miles | Aube Indienne | Kent Desormeaux/ C. Whittingham | 400,000 |
| Nov 26 ....NYRA Mile | Aqueduct | 1 mile | Cigar | Jerry Bailey/ William Mott | 250,000 |
| Nov 27 ....Japan Cup | Tokyo | 1½ miles | Marvelous Crown | Katsumi Minai/ Osawa | 3,475,345 |
| Nov 27 ....Matriarch Stakes | Hollywood Park | 1⅛ miles | Exchange | Laffit Pincay, Jr/ B. Spawr | 400,000 |

## 1995 (Through September 30)

| Date | Race | Track | Distance | Winner | Jockey/Trainer | Purse ($) |
|------|------|-------|----------|--------|----------------|-----------|
| Feb 5 ......Charles H. Strub Stakes | Santa Anita | 1¼ miles | Dare and Go | Alex Solis/ Richard Mandella | 500,000 |
| Feb 11 ....Don Handicap | Gulfstream Park | 1⅛ miles | Cigar | Jerry Bailey/ William Mott | 300,000 |
| Feb 12 ....San Antonio Handicap | Santa Anita | 1⅛ miles | Best Pal | Chris McCarron/ Richard Mandella | 250,000 |
| Feb 18 ....Fountain of Youth Stakes | Gulfstream Park | 1⅟₁₆ miles | Thunder Gulch | Mike Smith/ D. Wayne Lukas | 200,000 |
| Feb 20 ....San Luis Obispo Handicap | Santa Anita | 1½ miles | Square Cut | Chris Antley/ J. Devereux | 220,000 |
| Feb 26 ....Santa Margarita Handicap | Santa Anita | 1⅛ miles | Queens Court Queen | Corey Nakatani/ Ron McAnally | 300,000 |
| Mar 5 ......Gulfstream Park Handicap | Gulfstream Park | 1¼ miles | Cigar | Jerry Bailey/ William Mott | 500,000 |
| Mar 11 ....Santa Anita Handicap | Santa Anita | 1¼ miles | Urgent Request | Gary Stevens/ S. Aitken | 1,000,000 |
| Mar 11 ....Florida Derby | Gulfstream Park | 1⅛ miles | Thunder Gulch | Jerry Bailey/ D. Wayne Lukas | 500,000 |

## 1995 (Through September 30) (Cont.)

| Date | Race | Track | Distance | Winner | Jockey/Trainer | Purse ($) |
|------|------|-------|----------|--------|----------------|-----------|
| Mar 12 | Santa Anita Oaks | Santa Anita | 1 1/16 miles | Serena's Song | Corey Nakatani/ D. Wayne Lukas | 200,000 |
| Mar 16 | Pan American Handicap | Gulfstream Park | 1 1/2 miles | Awad | Eddie Maple/ D. Donk | 300,000 |
| Mar 19 | Louisiana Derby | Fair Grounds | 1 1/16 miles | Petionville | Chris Antley/ R. Bradshaw | 350,000 |
| Mar 25 | Gotham Stakes | Aqueduct | 1 mile | Talkin Man | Mike Smith/ Roger Attfield | 250,000 |
| Mar 26 | San Luis Rey Stakes | Santa Anita | 1 1/2 miles | Sandpit | Cory Nakatani/ Richard Mandella | 250,000 |
| Apr 1 | Jim Beam Stakes | Turfway Park | 1 1/8 miles | Serena's Song | Corey Nakatani/ D. Wayne Lukas | 600,000 |
| Apr 8 | Santa Anita Derby | Santa Anita | 1 1/8 miles | Larry the Legend | Gary Stevens/ C. Lewis | 700,000 |
| Apr 8 | Remington Park Derby | Remington Park | 1 1/8 miles | Dazzling Falls | Garrett Gomez/ C.Turco | 300,000 |
| Apr 15 | The Wood Memorial | Aqueduct | 1 1/8 miles | Talkin Man | Shane Sellers/ Roger Attfield | 500,000 |
| Apr 15 | The Oaklawn Handicap | Oaklawn Park | 1 1/8 miles | Cigar | Jerry Bailey/ William Mott | 750,000 |
| Apr 15 | The Blue Grass | Keeneland | 1 1/8 miles | Wild Syn | Randy Romero/ T. Arnemann | 500,000 |
| Apr 21 | Apple Blossom Handicap | Oaklawn Park | 1 1/16 miles | Heavenly Prize | Pat Day/ Claude McGaughey | 500,000 |
| Apr 22 | Arkansas Derby | Oaklawn Park | 1 1/8 miles | Dazzling Falls | Garrett Gomez/ D. Turco | 500,000 |
| Apr 23 | San Juan Capistrano | Santa Anita | 1 3/4 miles | Red Bishop | Mike Smith/ Saeed Bin Suroor | 400,000 |
| Apr 23 | Ashland Stakes | Keeneland | 1 1/16 miles | Urbane | Eddie Delahoussaye/B. Mayberry | 334,650 |
| May 5 | Kentucky Oaks | Churchill Downs | 1 1/8 miles | Gal in a Ruckus | Herb McCauley/ J. Ward, Jr | 300,000 |
| May 6 | Kentucky Derby | Churchill Downs | 1 1/4 miles | Thunder Gulch | Gary Stevens/ D. Wayne Lukas | 957,400 |
| May 13 | Illinois Derby | Sportsman's Park | 1 1/8 miles | Peaks and Valley | Julie Krone/ J. Day | 500,000 |
| May 13 | Pimlico Special | Pimlico | 1 3/16 miles | Cigar | Jerry Bailey/ William Mott | 600,000 |
| May 20 | The Preakness Stakes | Pimlico | 1 3/16 miles | Timber Country | Pat Day/ D. Wayne Lukas | 687,400 |
| May 29 | Hollywood Turf Handicap | Hollywood Park | 1 1/4 miles | Earl of Barking | G. Almeida/ R. Cross | 500,000 |
| May 29 | Metropolitan Handicap | Belmont Park | 1 mile | You and I | Jorge Chavez/ R. Frankel | 500,000 |
| June 3 | Massachusetts Handicap | Suffolk Downs | 1 1/8 miles | Cigar | Jerry Bailey/ William Mott | 750,000 |
| June 10 | Belmont Stakes | Belmont Park | 1 1/2 miles | Thunder Gulch | Gary Stevens/ D. Wayne Lukas | 692,400 |
| June 11 | Californian Stakes | Hollywood Park | 1 1/8 miles | Concern | Mike Smith/ Richard Small | 273,400 |
| June 25 | Caesars International Handicap | Atlantic City | 1 3/16 miles | Sandpit | Corey Nakatani/ Richard Mandella | 500,000 |
| July 2 | Budweiser Irish Derby | The Curragh | 1 1/2 miles | Winged Love | O. Peslier/ Andre Fabre | 925,683 |
| July 2 | Hollywood Gold Cup Handicap | Hollywood Park | 1 1/4 miles | Cigar | Jerry Bailey/ William Mott | 1,000,000 |
| July 4 | Suburban Handicap | Belmont Park | 1 1/4 miles | Key Contender | Jerry Bailey/ J. Martin | 350,000 |
| July 8 | Coaching Club American Oaks | Belmont Park | 1 1/4 miles | Golden Bri | Jose Santos/ J. Kimmel | 250,000 |
| July 9 | Queen's Plate | Woodbine | 1 1/4 miles | Regal Discovery | T. Kabel/ Roger Attfield | 400,000 |
| July 15 | Frank J. DeFranics Memorial Dash Stakes | Laurel | 6 furlongs | Lite the Fuse | Julie Krone/ R. Dutrow | 300,000 |
| July 22 | Caesars Palace Turf Handicap | Hollywood Park | 1 1/2 miles | Sandpit | Corey Nakatani/ Richard Mandella | 250,000 |

### 1995 (Through September 30) *(Cont.)*

| Date | Race | Track | Distance | Winner | Jockey/Trainer | Purse ($) |
|------|------|-------|----------|--------|----------------|-----------|
| July 23 ....American Derby | | Arlington Park | 1³⁄₁₆ miles | Gold and Steel | A. T. Gryder/ J. Rouget | 300,000 |
| July 23 ....Swaps Stakes | | Hollywood Park | 1⅛ miles | Thunder Gulch | Gary Stevens/ D. Wayne Lukas | 300,000 |
| July 23 ....Vanity Handicap | | Hollywood Park | 1⅛ miles | Private Persuasion | Gary Stevens/ D. Hendricks | 300,000 |
| July 29 ....Sword Dancer Invitational Handicap | | Saratoga | 1½ miles | Kiri's Clown | Mike Luzzi/ P. Johnson | 250,000 |
| July 30 ....Haskell Invitational Handicap | | Monmouth Park | 1⅛ miles | Serena's Song | Gary Stevens/ D. Wayne Lukas | 500,000 |
| Aug 5 ......Whitney Handicap | | Saratoga | 1⅛ miles | Unaccounted For | Pat Day/ F. Schulhofer | 350,000 |
| Aug 5 ......Ramona Handicap | | Del Mar | 1⅛ miles | Possibly Perfect | Corey Nakatani/ Robert Frankel | 300,000 |
| Aug 6 ......Eddie Rad Handicap | | Del Mar | 1⅛ miles | Fastness | Gary Stevens/ J. Sahadi | 300,000 |
| Aug 13 ....Pacific Classic Stakes | | Del Mar | 1¼ miles | Tinners Way | Eddie Delahoussaye/Robert Frankel | 1,000,000 |
| Aug 19 ...Travers Stakes | | Saratoga | 1¼ miles | Thunder Gulch | Gary Stevens/ D. Wayne Lukas | 750,000 |
| Aug 26 ...Beverly D. Stakes | | Arlington Park | 1³⁄₁₆ miles | Possible Perfect | Cory Nakatani/ Robert Frankel | 500,000 |
| Aug 27 ...Arlington Million | | Arlington Park | 1¼ miles | Awad | Eddie Maple/ D. Donk | 1,000,000 |
| Sep 3 .....Gazelle Handicap | | Belmont Park | 1⅛ miles | Serena's Song | Gary Stevens/ D. Wayne Lukas | 150,000 |
| Sep 16 ...Man O'War | | Belmont Park | 1⅜ miles | Millkom | Gary Stevens/ J. C. Rouget | 400,000 |
| Sep 16 ...Woodward Stakes | | Belmont Park | 1⅛ miles | Cigar | Jerry Bailey/ William Mott | 500,000 |
| Sep 17 ...Molson Export Million | | Woodbine | 1⅛ miles | Peaks and Valleys | Julie Krone/ J. Day | 1,000,000 |
| Sep 23 ...Kentucky Cup Classic | | Turfway Park | 1⅛ miles | Thunder Gulch | Gary Stevens/ D. Wayne Lukas | 400,000 |
| Sep 30 ...Isle of Capri Super Derby | | Louisiana Downs | 1¼ miles | Mecke | Jerry Bailey/ E. Tortora | 750,000 |

## 1994 Statistical Leaders

### Horses

| Horse | Starts | 1st | 2nd | 3rd | Purses ($) | Horse | Starts | 1st | 2nd | 3rd | Purses ($) |
|-------|--------|-----|-----|-----|-----------|-------|--------|-----|-----|-----|-----------|
| Paradise Creek......11 | | 8 | 2 | 1 | 2,610,187 | Dramatic Gold .......10 | | 4 | 2 | 2 | 1,294,850 |
| Concern................14 | | 3 | 5 | 6 | 2,541,670 | Go for Gin ............11 | | 2 | 4 | 1 | 1,178,596 |
| Tabasco Cat..........12 | | 5 | 3 | 1 | 2,164,334 | Devil His Due.........12 | | 3 | 6 | 1 | 1,142,000 |
| Holy Bull ...............10 | | 8 | 0 | 0 | 2,095,000 | Cherokee Run .........9 | | 3 | 3 | 3 | 943,690 |
| Tikkanen ................9 | | 3 | 1 | 2 | 1,508,344 | Timber Country........7 | | 4 | 0 | 2 | 927,025 |

### Jockeys

| Jockey | Mounts | 1st | 2nd | 3rd | Purses ($) | Win Pct | $ Pct* |
|--------|--------|-----|-----|-----|-----------|---------|--------|
| Mike Smith | 1,484 | 317 | 250 | 196 | 15,979,820 | .21 | .51 |
| Pat Day | 1,147 | 316 | 194 | 168 | 14,543,715 | .27 | .59 |
| Gary Stevens | 1,402 | 258 | 221 | 236 | 12,651,291 | .18 | .51 |
| Jerry Bailey | 1,221 | 255 | 189 | 167 | 11,515,912 | .21 | .50 |
| Kent Desormeaux | 1,163 | 251 | 188 | 176 | 11,275,077 | .22 | .53 |
| Chris McCarron | 870 | 156 | 142 | 117 | 10,921,495 | .18 | .48 |
| Corey Nakatani | 1,015 | 194 | 165 | 152 | 9,676,658 | .19 | .50 |
| Eddie Delahoussaye | 1,012 | 184 | 156 | 166 | 8,609,179 | .18 | .50 |
| Jose Santos | 1,249 | 208 | 176 | 189 | 8,329,940 | .17 | .46 |
| Alex Solis | 1,372 | 222 | 197 | 188 | 7,685,647 | .16 | .44 |

*Percentage in the Money (1st, 2nd, and 3rd).

## Trainers

| Trainer | Starts | 1st | 2nd | 3rd | Purses ($) | Win Pct | $ Pct* |
|---|---|---|---|---|---|---|---|
| D. Wayne Lukas.......693 | | 147 | 88 | 103 | 9,247,457 | .21 | .49 |
| William Mott .............575 | | 137 | 89 | 91 | 7,043,317 | .24 | .55 |
| Richard Mandella ....350 | | 68 | 53 | 67 | 4,984,977 | .19 | .54 |
| H. Allen Jerkens.......454 | | 111 | 69 | 75 | 4,940,476 | .24 | .56 |
| Ron McAnally...........461 | | 80 | 71 | 59 | 4,736,496 | .17 | .45 |
| Robert Frankel .........280 | | 52 | 42 | 41 | 4,692,793 | .19 | .48 |
| Shug McGaughey....258 | | 80 | 46 | 41 | 4,453,376 | .31 | .65 |
| Richard Small ..........268 | | 49 | 42 | 51 | 4,273,199 | .18 | .53 |
| Gary Jones ..............301 | | 66 | 47 | 41 | 4,160,037 | .22 | .51 |
| Scotty Schulhofer.....411 | | 74 | 61 | 59 | 3,753,869 | .18 | .47 |

*Percentage in the Money (1st, 2nd, and 3rd).

## Owners

| Owner | Starts | 1st | 2nd | 3rd | Purses ($) |
|---|---|---|---|---|---|
| John Franks | 1,080 | 193 | 156 | 132 | 4,518,088 |
| Juddmonte Farms | 170 | 34 | 26 | 24 | 4,323,395 |
| Golden Eagle Farm | 513 | 94 | 74 | 78 | 4,087,680 |
| Robert E. Meyerhoff | 192 | 41 | 33 | 41 | 3,978,752 |
| Frank H. Stronach | 417 | 88 | 70 | 46 | 3,745,412 |
| Allen E. Paulson | 445 | 79 | 63 | 44 | 3,195,070 |
| Augustin Stables | 287 | 67 | 40 | 45 | 2,822,196 |
| Overbrook/Reynolds | 30 | 11 | 6 | 3 | 2,257,035 |
| Warren A. Croll, Jr | 38 | 11 | 3 | 4 | 2,135,445 |
| Dogwood Stable | 377 | 45 | 69 | 49 | 2,110,005 |

Note: 1994 statistical leaders courtesy of *Daily Racing Form*.

# HARNESS RACING

## Major Stakes Races (late 1994)

| Date | Race | Location | Winner | Driver/Trainer | Purse ($) |
|---|---|---|---|---|---|
| Oct 7 | Kentucky Futurity | The Red Mile | Bullville Victory | John Campbell/ Per Eriksson | 162,700 |
| Oct 15 | BC Three and up Mare Trot | Freehold Raceway | Armbro Keepsake | Stig Johansson/ Stig Johansson | 250,000 |
| Oct 15 | BC Three and up Horse/Gelding Trot | Freehold Raceway | Pine Chip | John Campbell/ Charles Sylvester | 300,000 |
| Oct 15 | BC Three and up Mare Pace | Freehold Raceway | Shady Daisy | Michel Lachance/ Louis Bauslaugh | 250,000 |
| Oct 15 | BC Three and up Horse/Gelding Pace | Freehold Raceway | Village Jiffy | Paul MacDonell/ William Wellwood | 334,000 |
| Oct 21 | BC Three-year-old Filly Trot | Garden State Park | Imageofa Clear Day | Bill O'Donnell/ Doug McIntosh | 325,000 |
| Oct 21 | BC Three-year-old Filly Pace | Garden State Park | Hardie Hanover | Tim Twaddle/ John Burns | 325,000 |
| Oct 21 | BC Three-year-old Colt/Gelding Pace | Garden State Park | Incredible Abe | Italo Tamborrino/ Chuck Sylvester | 400,000 |
| Oct 21 | BC Three-year-old Colt/Gelding Pace | Garden State Park | Magical Mike | Michel Lachance/ Tom Haughton | 400,000 |
| Oct 28 | BC Two-year-old Filly Trot | Woodbine | Lookout Victory | John Patterson, Jr/ Per Eriksson | 334,000 |
| Oct 28 | BC Two-year-old Colt/Gelding Trot | Woodbine | Eager Seelster | Teddy Jacobs/ Teddy Jacobs | 384,500 |
| Oct 28 | BC Two-year-old Filly Pace | Woodbine | Yankee Cashmere | Peter Wrenn/ Brett Bittle | 501,400 |
| Oct 28 | BC Two-year-old Colt/Gelding Pace | Woodbine | Jenna's Beach Boy | Bill Fahy/Joe Holloway | 670,000 |
| Nov 19 | Governor's Cup | Garden State Park | CA Connection | Joe Anderson/ Kevin Thomas | 616,400 |

# Major Stakes Races (Cont.)

## 1995 (Through September 22)

| Date | Race | Location | Winner | Driver/Trainer | Purse ($) |
|---|---|---|---|---|---|
| June 24 | North America Cup | Woodbine | David's Pass | John Campbell/ Brett Pelling | 1,000,000 |
| July 1 | Messenger Stakes | Ladbroke at The Meadows | David's Pass | John Campbell/ Brett Pelling | 328,825 |
| July 8 | Yonkers Trot | Yonkers | CR Kay Suzie | Rod Allen/Carl Allen | 276,564 |
| July 15 | Meadowlands Pace | Meadowlands | David's Pass | John Campbell/ Brett Pelling | 1,000,000 |
| Aug 1 | Peter Haughton Memorial | Meadowlands | Dancer's Victory | John Campbell/ Stanley Dancer | 400,000 |
| Aug 2 | Merrie Annabelle Final | Meadowlands | Missie Will Do It | Bill O'Donnell/ John Brennan | 300,500 |
| Aug 5 | Hambletonian | Meadowlands | Tagliabue | John Campbell/ Jim Campbell | 1,200,000 |
| Aug 5 | Hambletonian Oaks | Meadowlands | Lookout Victory | John Patterson, Jr/ Per Eriksson | 375,500 |
| Aug 12 | Sweetheart | Meadowlands | On Her Way | Cat Manzi/Jim Brittingham | 571,100 |
| Aug 12 | Woodrow Wilson | Meadowlands | A Stud Named Sue | George Brennan, Jr/Liz Quesnal | 585,500 |
| Aug 12 | Adios Final | Ladbroke at The Meadows | David's Pass | John Campbell/ Brett Pelling | 441,282 |
| Aug 26 | Cane Pace | Yonkers | Mattgilla Gorilla | David Ingraham/ William Andrews | 384,375 |
| Sep 2 | World Trotting Derby | Du Quoin | CR Kay Suzie | Rod Allen/Carl Allen | 585,000 |
| Sep 20 | BC Three and up Mare Trot | Delaware | CR Kay Suzie | Rod Allen/Carl Allen | 300,000 |
| Sep 21 | BC Three and up Horse/Gelding Trot | Delaware | Panifesto | Luc Ouellette/Bill Robinson | 300,000 |
| Sep 21 | Little Brown Jug | Delaware | Nick's Fantasy | John Campbell/ Caroline Lyon | 543,670 |
| Sep 22 | BC Three and up Mare Pace | Northfield Park | Ellamony | Mike Saftic/ Stephen Doyle | 250,000 |
| Sep 22 | BC Three and up Horse/Gelding Pace | Northfield Park | Thatll Be Me | Roger Mayotte/ Robert Young | 300,000 |

# Major Races

## The Hambletonian

| Horse | Driver | PP | ¼ | ½ | ¾ | Stretch | Finish |
|---|---|---|---|---|---|---|---|
| Tagliabue | John Campbell | 1 | 3 | 1 | 1 | 1-5 | 1-2¼ |
| Abundance | William Fahy | 2 | 4 | 5 | 5 | 3-6½ | 2-2¼ |
| Giant Hit | John Patterson, Jr | 3 | 1 | 2 | 2 | 2-5 | 3-2¼ |
| Earthquake | Berndt Lindstedt | 4 | 5 | 8 | 7 | 4-9¼ | 4-4 |
| Climbing Bud | Malvern Burroughs | 10 | 8 | 7 | 8 | 5-10¾ | 5-5¾ |
| Deliberate Speed | Per Henriksen | 8 | 2 | 3 | 3 | 6-14¾ | 6-15¾ |
| Super Star Ranger | Jack Moiseyev | 9 | 6 | 4 | 6 | 7-19¾ | 7-23 |
| Trustworthy | William O'Donnell | 7 | 9 | 9 | 9 | 8-dis | 8-dis |
| Uma | Cat Manzi | 5 | 7 | 6 | 4 | 9-dis | 9-dis |
| King Pine | Michel Lachance | 6 | 10 | 10 | 10 | 10-dis | 10-dis |

Time: :28, :56.1, 1:24.4, 1:54.4; Fast

### The Little Brown Jug

| Horse | Driver | PP | ¼ | ½ | ¾ | Stretch | Finish |
|---|---|---|---|---|---|---|---|
| Nick's Fantasy | John Campbell | 1 | 3 | 3 | 2 | 1-4 | 1-4 |
| Village Connection | Paul MacDonell | 3 | 2 | 2 | 3 | 2-4 | 2-4 |
| Lisryan | Luc Oulette | 9 | 4 | 4 | 5 | 4-5¼ | 3-4¼ |
| Hensell Hanover | Mike Saftic | 6 | 7 | 5 | 4 | 5-6¼ | 4-8 |
| Powerful Structure | David Miller | 2 | 1 | 1 | 1 | 3-4¼ | 5-8½ |
| Pan It's Cold | B. D. Allen | 5 | 6 | 8 | 8 | 7-7¾ | 6-9¼ |
| Fun Time Go Getter | Ken Holliday | 4 | 5 | 7 | 6 | 6-6¾ | 7-11 |
| Viking Commander | G. M. Haston | 8 | 9 | 6 | 7 | 8-10¼ | 8-13 |
| Wild Dancer | S. O. Noble III | 7 | 8 | 9 | 9 | 9-10¾ | 9-14 |

Time: :26.4, :55.4, 1:23.3, 1:51.2; Fast

## 1994 Statistical Leaders

### 1994 Leading Moneywinners by Age, Sex and Gait

| Division | Horse | Starts | 1st | 2nd | 3rd | Earnings ($) |
|---|---|---|---|---|---|---|
| 2-Year-Old Pacing Colts | Dontgetinmyway | 16 | 6 | 6 | 1 | 610,018 |
| 2-Year-Old Pacing Fillies | Efishnc | 16 | 7 | 4 | 1 | 503,789 |
| 3-Year-Old Pacing Colts | Cam's Card Shark | 18 | 15 | 2 | 0 | 2,264,714 |
| 3-Year-Old Pacing Fillies | Electric Slide | 21 | 13 | 2 | 2 | 659,007 |
| Aged Pacing Horses | Village Jiffy | 28 | 8 | 6 | 5 | 578,585 |
| Aged Pacing Mares | Shady Daisy | 32 | 7 | 9 | 5 | 288,235 |
| 2-Year-Old Trotting Colts | Donerail | 15 | 13 | 0 | 1 | 636,925 |
| 2-Year-Old Trotting Fillies | CR Kay Suzie | 9 | 7 | 0 | 0 | 450,596 |
| 3-Year-Old Trotting Colts | Victory Dream | 17 | 9 | 4 | 1 | 992,662 |
| 3-Year-Old Trotting Fillies | Imageofa Clear Day | 22 | 11 | 7 | 1 | 383,578 |
| Aged Trotting Horses | SJ's Photo | 23 | 9 | 5 | 3 | 379,659 |
| Aged Trotting Mares | Lifetime Dream | 18 | 5 | 2 | 4 | 140,791 |

### Drivers

| Driver | Earnings ($) | Driver | Earnings ($) |
|---|---|---|---|
| John Campbell | 9,834,139 | Cat Manzi | 4,569,712 |
| Jack Moiseyev | 7,108,020 | Dave Magee | 4,358,819 |
| Michel Lachance | 6,255,284 | Steve Condren | 3,460,635 |
| Ron Waples | 4,913,926 | Luc Oulette | 3,301,289 |
| Doug Brown | 4,701,237 | Bill Faby | 3,141,330 |

**Dumb Luck**

Just seconds before post time for the sixth race at Laurel Park on Feb. 20, a track patron placed a $72 bet with a pari-mutuel clerk—only to have it canceled when the clerk inadvertently punched out a ticket worth $738 that the bettor didn't want to pay for. Unable to correct his error in time, the clerk, under track rules, had to assume the obligation for the ticket, a triple box combination that included a 40-1 nag named Nun Bee Wiser.

Nun Bee Luckier is more like it. When Nun Bee Wiser won the race, and the other horses in the triple finished second and third, the once beleaguered clerk found himself with a ticket worth $22,238.40. "After winning he quietly went back to his window and worked through the rest of his shift," says Mary Zambreny, an assistant pari-mutuel manager at Laurel. "I guess he figured he could afford any future mistakes."

# FOR THE RECORD · Year by Year

## THOROUGHBRED RACING

### Kentucky Derby

Run at Churchill Downs, Louisville, KY, on the first Saturday in May.

| Year | Winner (Margin) | Jockey | Second | Third | Time |
|---|---|---|---|---|---|
| 1875 | Aristides (1) | Oliver Lewis | Volcano | Verdigris | 2:37¾ |
| 1876 | Vagrant (2) | Bobby Swim | Creedmoor | Harry Hill | 2:38¼ |
| 1877 | Baden-Baden (2) | William Walker | Leonard | King William | 2:38 |
| 1878 | Day Star (2) | Jimmie Carter | Himyar | Leveler | 2:37¼ |
| 1879 | Lord Murphy (1) | Charlie Shauer | Falsetto | Strathmore | 2:37 |
| 1880 | Fonso (1) | George Lewis | Kimball | Bancroft | 2:37½ |
| 1881 | Hindoo (4) | Jimmy McLaughin | Lelex | Alfambra | 2:40 |
| 1882 | Apollo (½) | Babe Hurd | Runnymede | Bengal | 2:40¼ |
| 1883 | Leonatus (3) | Billy Donohue | Drake Carter | Lord Raglan | 2:43 |
| 1884 | Buchanan (2) | Isaac Murphy | Loftin | Audrain | 2:40¼ |
| 1885 | Joe Cotton (Neck) | Erskine Henderson | Bersan | Ten Booker | 2:37¼ |
| 1886 | Ben Ali (½) | Paul Duffy | Blue Wing | Free Knight | 2:36½ |
| 1887 | Montrose (2) | Isaac Lewis | Jim Gore | Jacobin | 2:39¼ |
| 1888 | MacBeth II (1) | George Covington | Gallifet | White | 2:38¼ |
| 1889 | Spokane (Nose) | Thomas Kiley | Proctor Knott | Once Again | 2:34½ |
| 1890 | Riley (2) | Isaac Murphy | Bill Letcher | Robespierre | 2:45 |
| 1891 | Kingman (1) | Isaac Murphy | Balgowan | High Tariff | 2:52¼ |
| 1892 | Azra (Nose) | Alonzo Clayton | Huron | Phil Dwyer | 2:41½ |
| 1893 | Lookout (5) | Eddie Kunze | Plutus | Boundless | 2:39¼ |
| 1894 | Chant (2) | Frank Goodale | Pearl Song | Sigurd | 2:41 |
| 1895 | Halma (3) | Soup Perkins | Basso | Laureate | 2:37½ |
| 1896 | Ben Brush (Nose) | Willie Simms | Ben Eder | Semper Ego | 2:07¼ |
| 1897 | Typhoon II (Head) | Buttons Garner | Ornament | Dr. Catlett | 2:12½ |
| 1898 | Plaudit (Neck) | Willie Simms | Lieber Karl | Isabey | 2:09 |
| 1899 | Manuel (2) | Fred Taral | Corsini | Mazo | 2:12 |
| 1900 | Lieut. Gibson (4) | Jimmy Boland | Florizar | Thrive | 2:06¼ |
| 1901 | His Eminence (2) | Jimmy Winkfield | Sannazarro | Driscoll | 2:07¾ |
| 1902 | Alan-a-Dale (Nose) | Jimmy Winkfield | Inventor | The Rival | 2:08¾ |
| 1903 | Judge Himes (¾) | Hal Booker | Early | Bourbon | 2:09 |
| 1904 | Elwood (½) | Frankie Prior | Ed Tierney | Brancas | 2:08½ |
| 1905 | Agile (3) | Jack Martin | Ram's Horn | Layson | 2:10¾ |
| 1906 | Sir Huon (2) | Roscoe Troxler | Lady Navarre | James Reddick | 2:08⅕ |
| 1907 | Pink Star (2) | Andy Minder | Zal | Ovelando | 2:12⅗ |
| 1908 | Stone Street (1) | Arthur Pickens | Sir Cleges | Dunvegan | 2:15⅕ |
| 1909 | Wintergreen (4) | Vincent Powers | Miami | Dr. Barkley | 2:08⅕ |
| 1910 | Donau (½) | Fred Herbert | Joe Morris | Fighting Bob | 2:06⅖ |
| 1911 | Meridian (¾) | George Archibald | Governor Gray | Colston | 2:05 |
| 1912 | Worth (Neck) | Carroll H. Schilling | Duval | Flamma | 2:09⅖ |
| 1913 | Donerail (½) | Roscoe Goose | Ten Point | Gowell | 2:04⅘ |
| 1914 | Old Rosebud (8) | John McCabe | Hodge | Bronzewing | 2:03⅖ |
| 1915 | Regret (2) | Joe Notter | Pebbles | Sharpshooter | 2:05⅖ |
| 1916 | George Smith (Neck) | Johnny Loftus | Star Hawk | Franklin | 2:04 |
| 1917 | Omar Khayyam (2) | Charles Borel | Ticket | Midway | 2:04⅗ |
| 1918 | Exterminator (1) | William Knapp | Escoba | Viva America | 2:10⅘ |
| 1919 | Sir Barton (5) | Johnny Loftus | Billy Kelly | Under Fire | 2:09⅘ |
| 1920 | Paul Jones (Head) | Ted Rice | Upset | On Watch | 2:09 |
| 1921 | Behave Yourself (Head) | Charles Thompson | Black Servant | Prudery | 2:04⅕ |
| 1922 | Morvich (½) | Albert Johnson | Bet Mosie | John Finn | 2:04⅗ |
| 1923 | Zev (1½) | Earl Sande | Martingale | Vigil | 2:05⅖ |
| 1924 | Black Gold (½) | John Mooney | Chilhowee | Beau Butler | 2:05⅕ |
| 1925 | Flying Ebony (1½) | Earl Sande | Captain Hal | Son of John | 2:07⅗ |
| 1926 | Bubbling Over (5) | Albert Johnson | Bagenbaggage | Rock Man | 2:03⅘ |
| 1927 | Whiskery (Head) | Linus McAtee | Osmond | Jock | 2:06 |
| 1928 | Reigh Count (3) | Chick Lang | Misstep | Toro | 2:10⅖ |
| 1929 | Clyde Van Dusen (2) | Linus McAtee | Naishapur | Panchio | 2:10⅘ |
| 1930 | Gallant Fox (2) | Earl Sande | Gallant Knight | Ned O. | 2:07⅗ |
| 1931 | Twenty Grand (4) | Charles Kurtsinger | Sweep All | Mate | 2:01⅘ |
| 1932 | Burgoo King (5) | Eugene James | Economic | Stepenfetchit | 2:05⅕ |
| 1933 | Brokers Tip (Nose) | Don Meade | Head Play | Charley O. | 2:06⅘ |

## Kentucky Derby *(Cont.)*

| Year | Winner (Margin) | Jockey | Second | Third | Time |
|---|---|---|---|---|---|
| 1934 | Cavalcade (2½) | Mack Garner | Discovery | Agrarian | 2:04 |
| 1935 | Omaha (1½) | Willie Saunders | Roman Soldier | Whiskolo | 2:05 |
| 1936 | Bold Venture (Head) | Ira Hanford | Brevity | Indian Broom | 2:03⅗ |
| 1937 | War Admiral (1¾) | Charles Kurtsinger | Pompoon | Reaping Reward | 2:03⅕ |
| 1938 | Lawrin (1) | Eddie Arcaro | Dauber | Can't Wait | 2:04⅘ |
| 1939 | Johnstown (8) | James Stout | Challedon | Heather Broom | 2:03⅖ |
| 1940 | Gallahadion (1½) | Carroll Bierman | Bimelech | Dit | 2:05 |
| 1941 | Whirlaway (8) | Eddie Arcaro | Staretor | Market Wise | 2:01⅖ |
| 1942 | Shut Out (2½) | Wayne Wright | Alsab | Valdina Orphan | 2:04⅖ |
| 1943 | Count Fleet (3) | John Longden | Blue Swords | Slide Rule | 2:04 |
| 1944 | Pensive (4½) | Conn McCreary | Broadcloth | Stir Up | 2:04⅕ |
| 1945 | Hoop Jr. (6) | Eddie Arcaro | Pot o' Luck | Darby Dieppe | 2:07 |
| 1946 | Assault (8) | Warren Mehrtens | Spy Song | Hampden | 2:06⅗ |
| 1947 | Jet Pilot (Head) | Eric Guerin | Phalanx | Faultless | 2:06⅘ |
| 1948 | Citation (3½) | Eddie Arcaro | Coaltown | My Request | 2:05⅖ |
| 1949 | Ponder (3) | Steve Brooks | Capot | Palestinian | 2:04⅕ |
| 1950 | Middleground (1¼) | William Boland | Hill Prince | Mr. Trouble | 2:01⅗ |
| 1951 | Count Turf (4) | Conn McCreary | Royal Mustang | Ruhe | 2:02⅗ |
| 1952 | Hill Gail (2) | Eddie Arcaro | Sub Fleet | Blue Man | 2:01⅗ |
| 1953 | Dark Star (Head) | Hank Moreno | Native Dancer | Invigorator | 2:02 |
| 1954 | Determine (1½) | Ray York | Hasty Road | Hasseyampa | 2:03 |
| 1955 | Swaps (1½) | Bill Shoemaker | Nashua | Summer Tan | 2:01⅘ |
| 1956 | Needles (¾) | Dave Erb | Fabius | Come On Red | 2:03⅖ |
| 1957 | Iron Liege (Nose) | Bill Hartack | Gallant Man | Round Table | 2:02⅕ |
| 1958 | Tim Tam (½) | Ismael Valenzuela | Lincoln Road | Noureddin | 2:05 |
| 1959 | Tomy Lee (Nose) | Bill Shoemaker | Sword Dancer | First Landing | 2:02⅕ |
| 1960 | Venetian Way (3½) | Bill Hartack | Bally Ache | Victoria Park | 2:02⅖ |
| 1961 | Carry Back (¾) | John Sellers | Crozier | Bass Clef | 2:04 |
| 1962 | Decidedly (2¼) | Bill Hartack | Roman Line | Ridan | 2:00⅖ |
| 1963 | Chateaugay (1¼) | Braulio Baeza | Never Bend | Candy Spots | 2:01⅘ |
| 1964 | Northern Dancer (Neck) | Bill Hartack | Hill Rise | The Scoundrel | 2:00 |
| 1965 | Lucky Debonair (Neck) | Bill Shoemaker | Dapper Dan | Tom Rolfe | 2:01⅕ |
| 1966 | Kauai King (½) | Don Brumfield | Advocator | Blue Skyer | 2:02 |
| 1967 | Proud Clarion (1) | Bobby Ussery | Barbs Delight | Damascus | 2:00⅗ |
| 1968 | Forward Pass (Disq.) | Ismael Valenzuela | Francie's Hat | T.V. Commercial | 2:02⅕ |
| 1969 | Majestic Prince (Neck) | Bill Hartack | Arts and Letters | Dike | 2:01⅘ |
| 1970 | Dust Commander (5) | Mike Manganello | My Dad George | High Echelon | 2:03⅖ |
| 1971 | Canonero II (3¾) | Gustavo Avila | Jim French | Bold Reason | 2:03⅕ |
| 1972 | Riva Ridge (3¼) | Ron Turcotte | No Le Hace | Hold Your Peace | 2:01⅘ |
| 1973 | Secretariat (2½) | Ron Turcotte | Sham | Our Native | 1:59⅖ |
| 1974 | Cannonade (2¼) | Angel Cordero Jr | Hudson County | Agitate | 2:04 |
| 1975 | Foolish Pleasure (1¾) | Jacinto Vasquez | Avatar | Diabolo | 2:02 |
| 1976 | Bold Forbes (1) | Angel Cordero Jr | Honest Pleasure | Elocutionist | 2:01⅗ |
| 1977 | Seattle Slew (1¾) | Jean Cruguet | Run Dusty Run | Sanhedrin | 2:02⅕ |
| 1978 | Affirmed (1½) | Steve Cauthen | Alydar | Believe It | 2:01⅕ |
| 1979 | Spectacular Bid (2¾) | Ronald J. Franklin | General Assembly | Golden Act | 2:02⅖ |
| 1980 | Genuine Risk (1) | Jacinto Vasquez | Rumbo | Jaklin Klugman | 2:02 |
| 1981 | Pleasant Colony (¾) | Jorge Velasquez | Woodchopper | Partez | 2:02 |
| 1982 | Gato Del Sol (2½) | Eddie Delahoussaye | Laser Light | Reinvested | 2:02⅕ |
| 1983 | Sunny's Halo (2) | Eddie Delahoussaye | Desert Wine | Caveat | 2:02⅕ |
| 1984 | Swale (3¼) | Laffit Pincay Jr | Coax Me Chad | At the Threshold | 2:02⅖ |
| 1985 | Spend A Buck (5) | Angel Cordero Jr | Stephan's Odyssey | Chief's Crown | 2:00⅕ |
| 1986 | Ferdinand (2¼) | Bill Shoemaker | Bold Arrangement | Broad Brush | 2:02⅘ |
| 1987 | Alysheba (¾) | Chris McCarron | Bet Twice | Avies Copy | 2:03⅖ |
| 1988 | Winning Colors (Neck) | Gary Stevens | Forty Niner | Risen Star | 2:02⅕ |
| 1989 | Sunday Silence (2½) | Pat Valenzuela | Easy Goer | Awe Inspiring | 2:05 |
| 1990 | Unbridled (3½) | Craig Perret | Summer Squall | Pleasant Tap | 2:02 |
| 1991 | Strike the Gold (1¾) | Chris Antley | Best Pal | Mane Minister | 2:03 |
| 1992 | Lil E. Tee (1) | Pat Day | Casual Lies | Dance Floor | 2:03 |
| 1993 | Sea Hero (2½) | Jerry Bailey | Prairie Bayou | Wild Gale | 2:02⅖ |
| 1994 | Go for Gin (2½) | Chris McCarron | Strodes Creek | Blumin Affair | 2:03⅗ |
| 1995 | Thunder Gulch (2¼) | Gary Stevens | Tejano Run | Timber Country | 2:01⅕ |

Note: Distance: 1½ miles (1875-95), 1¼ miles (1896-present).

# Preakness

Run at Pimlico Race Course, Baltimore, Md., two weeks after the Kentucky Derby.

| Year | Winner (Margin) | Jockey | Second | Third | Time |
|---|---|---|---|---|---|
| 1873 | Survivor (10) | G. Barbee | John Boulger | Artist | 2:43 |
| 1874 | Culpepper (¾) | W. Donohue | King Amadeus | Scratch | 2:56½ |
| 1875 | Tom Ochiltree (2) | L. Hughes | Viator | Bay Final | 2:43½ |
| 1876 | Shirley (4) | G. Barbee | Rappahannock | Algerine | 2:44¾ |
| 1877 | Cloverbrook (4) | C. Holloway | Bombast | Lucifer | 2:45½ |
| 1878 | Duke of Magenta (6) | C. Holloway | Bayard | Albert | 2:41¾ |
| 1879 | Harold (3) | L. Hughes | Jericho | Rochester | 2:40½ |
| 1880 | Grenada (¾) | L. Hughes | Oden | Emily F. | 2:40½ |
| 1881 | Saunterer (½) | T. Costello | Compensation | Baltic | 2:40½ |
| 1882 | Vanguard (Neck) | T. Costello | Heck | Col Watson | 2:44½ |
| 1883 | Jacobus (4) | G. Barbee | Parnell | | 2:42½ |
| 1884 | Knight of Ellerslie (2) | S. Fisher | Welcher | | 2:39½ |
| 1885 | Tecumseh (2) | Jim McLaughlin | Wickham | John C. | 2:49 |
| 1886 | The Bard (3) | S. Fisher | Eurus | Elkwood | 2:45 |
| 1887 | Dunboyne (1) | W. Donohue | Mahoney | Raymond | 2:39½ |
| 1888 | Refund (3) | F. Littlefield | Judge Murray | Glendale | 2:49 |
| 1889 | Buddhist (8) | W. Anderson | Japhet | | 2:17½ |
| 1890* | Montague (3) | W. Martin | Philosophy | Barrister | 2:36¾ |
| 1894 | Assignee (3) | Fred Taral | Potentate | Ed Kearney | 1:49¼ |
| 1895 | Belmar (1) | Fred Taral | April Fool | Sue Kittie | 1:50½ |
| 1896 | Margrave (1) | H. Griffin | Hamilton II | Intermission | 1:51 |
| 1897 | Paul Kauvar (1½) | C. Thorpe | Elkins | On Deck | 1:51¼ |
| 1898 | Sly Fox (2) | C. W. Simms | The Huguenot | Nuto | 1:49⅗ |
| 1899 | Half Time (1) | R. Clawson | Filigrane | Lackland | 1:47 |
| 1900 | Hindus (Head) | H. Spencer | Sarmation | Ten Candles | 1:48⅖ |
| 1901 | The Parader (2) | F. Landry | Sadie S. | Dr. Barlow | 1:47⅕ |
| 1902 | Old England (Nose) | L. Jackson | Major Daingerfield | Namtor | 1:45⅘ |
| 1903 | Flocarline (½) | W. Gannon | Mackey Dwyer | Rightful | 1:44⅘ |
| 1904 | Bryn Mawr (1) | E. Hildebrand | Wotan | Dolly Spanker | 1:44⅕ |
| 1905 | Cairngorm (Head) | W. Davis | Kiamesha | Coy Maid | 1:45⅘ |
| 1906 | Whimsical (4) | Walter Miller | Content | Larabie | 1:45 |
| 1907 | Don Enrique (1) | G. Mountain | Ethon | Zambesi | 1:45⅖ |
| 1908 | Royal Tourist (4) | E. Dugan | Live Wire | Robert Cooper | 1:46⅖ |
| 1909 | Effendi (1) | Willie Doyle | Fashion Plate | Hilltop | 1:39⅘ |
| 1910 | Layminster (½) | R. Estep | Dalhousie | Sager | 1:40⅗ |
| 1911 | Watervale (1) | E. Dugan | Zeus | The Nigger | 1:51 |
| 1912 | Colonel Holloway (5) | C. Turner | Bwana Tumbo | Tipsand | 1:56⅗ |
| 1913 | Buskin (Neck) | J. Butwell | Kleburne | Barnegat | 1:53⅖ |
| 1914 | Holiday (¾) | A. Schuttinger | Brave Cunarder | Defendum | 1:53⅘ |
| 1915 | Rhine Maiden (1½) | Douglas Hoffman | Half Rock | Runes | 1:58 |
| 1916 | Damrosch (1½) | Linus McAtee | Greenwood | Achievement | 1:54⅘ |
| 1917 | Kalitan (2) | E. Haynes | Al M. Dick | Kentucky Boy | 1:54⅖ |
| 1918 | War Cloud (¾) | Johnny Loftus | Sunny Slope | Lanius | 1:53⅗ |
| 1918 | Jack Hare, Jr (2) | C. Peak | The Porter | Kate Bright | 1:53⅖ |
| 1919 | Sir Barton (4) | Johnny Loftus | Eternal | Sweep On | 1:53 |
| 1920 | Man o' War (1½) | Clarence Kummer | Upset | Wildair | 1:51⅗ |
| 1921 | Broomspun (¾) | F. Coltiletti | Polly Ann | Jeg | 1:54⅕ |
| 1922 | Pillory (Head) | L. Morris | Hea | June Grass | 1:51⅗ |
| 1923 | Vigil (1¼) | B. Marinelli | General Thatcher | Rialto | 1:53⅗ |
| 1924 | Nellie Morse (1½) | J. Merimee | Transmute | Mad Play | 1:57⅕ |
| 1925 | Coventry (4) | Clarence Kummer | Backbone | Almadel | 1:59 |
| 1926 | Display (Head) | J. Maiben | Blondin | Mars | 1:59⅘ |
| 1927 | Bostonian (½) | A. Abel | Sir Harry | Whiskery | 2:01⅗ |
| 1928 | Victorian (Nose) | Sonny Workman | Toro | Solace | 2:00⅕ |
| 1929 | Dr. Freeland (1) | Louis Schaefer | Minotaur | African | 2:01⅗ |
| 1930 | Gallant Fox (¾) | Earl Sande | Crack Brigade | Snowflake | 2:00⅗ |
| 1931 | Mate (1½) | G. Ellis | Twenty Grand | Ladder | 1:59 |
| 1932 | Burgoo King (Head) | E. James | Tick On | Boatswain | 1:59⅘ |
| 1933 | Head Play (4) | Charles Kurtsinger | Ladysman | Utopian | 2:02 |
| 1934 | High Quest (Nose) | R. Jones | Cavalcade | Discovery | 1:58⅕ |
| 1935 | Omaha (6) | Willie Saunders | Firethorn | Psychic Bid | 1:58⅖ |
| 1936 | Bold Venture (Nose) | George Woolf | Granville | Jean Bart | 1:59 |
| 1937 | War Admiral (Head) | Charles Kurtsinger | Pompoon | Flying Scot | 1:58⅖ |
| 1938 | Dauber (7) | M. Peters | Cravat | Menow | 1:59⅘ |

## Preakness (Cont.)

| Year | Winner (Margin) | Jockey | Second | Third | Time |
|---|---|---|---|---|---|
| 1939 | Challedon (1¼) | George Seabo | Gilded Knight | Volitant | 1:59⅘ |
| 1940 | Bimelech (3) | F. A. Smith | Mioland | Gallahadion | 1:58⅗ |
| 1941 | Whirlaway (5½) | Eddie Arcaro | King Cole | Our Boots | 1:58⅘ |
| 1942 | Alsab (1) | B. James | Requested Sun Again | (dead heat for second) | 1:57 |
| 1943 | Count Fleet (8) | Johnny Longden | Blue Swords | Vincentive | 1:57⅖ |
| 1944 | Pensive (¾) | Conn McCreary | Platter | Stir Up | 1:59⅕ |
| 1945 | Polynesian (2½) | W. D. Wright | Hoop Jr | Darby Dieppe | 1:58⅘ |
| 1946 | Assault (Neck) | Warren Mehrtens | Lord Boswell | Hampden | 2:01⅖ |
| 1947 | Faultless (1¼) | Doug Dodson | On Trust | Phalanx | 1:59 |
| 1948 | Citation (5½) | Eddie Arcaro | Vulcan's Forge | Boyard | 2:02⅖ |
| 1949 | Capot (Head) | Ted Atkinson | Palestinian | Noble Impulse | 1:56 |
| 1950 | Hill Prince (5) | Eddie Arcaro | Middleground | Dooley | 1:59⅕ |
| 1951 | Bold (7) | Eddie Arcaro | Counterpoint | Alerted | 1:56⅖ |
| 1952 | Blue Man (3½) | Conn McCreary | Jampol | One Count | 1:57⅖ |
| 1953 | Native Dancer (Neck) | Eric Guerin | Jamie K. | Royal Bay Gem | 1:57⅘ |
| 1954 | Hasty Road (Neck) | Johnny Adams | Correlation | Hasseyampa | 1:57⅖ |
| 1955 | Nashua (1) | Eddie Arcaro | Saratoga | Traffic Judge | 1:54⅗ |
| 1956 | Fabius (¾) | Bill Hartack | Needles | No Regrets | 1:58⅖ |
| 1957 | Bold Ruler (2) | Eddie Arcaro | Iron Liege | Inside Tract | 1:56⅕ |
| 1958 | Tim Tam (1½) | I. Valenzuela | Lincoln Road | Gone Fishin' | 1:57⅕ |
| 1959 | Royal Orbit (4) | William Harmatz | Sword Dancer | Dunce | 1:57 |
| 1960 | Bally Ache (4) | Bobby Ussery | Victoria Park | Celtic Ash | 1:57⅗ |
| 1961 | Carry Back (¾) | Johnny Sellers | Globemaster | Crozier | 1:57⅗ |
| 1962 | Greek Money (Nose) | John Rotz | Ridan | Roman Line | 1:56⅕ |
| 1963 | Candy Spots (3½) | Bill Shoemaker | Chateaugay | Never Bend | 1:56⅕ |
| 1964 | Northern Dancer (2¼) | Bill Hartack | The Scoundrel | Hill Rise | 1:56⅘ |
| 1965 | Tom Rolfe (Neck) | Ron Turcotte | Dapper Dan | Hail to All | 1:56⅕ |
| 1966 | Kauai King (1¾) | Don Brumfield | Stupendous | Amberoid | 1:55⅖ |
| 1967 | Damascus (2¼) | Bill Shoemaker | In Reality | Proud Clarion | 1:55⅕ |
| 1968 | Forward Pass (6) | I. Valenzuela | Out of the Way | Nodouble | 1:56⅘ |
| 1969 | Majestic Prince (Head) | Bill Hartack | Arts and Letters | Jay Ray | 1:55⅗ |
| 1970 | Personality (Neck) | Eddie Belmonte | My Dad George | Silent Screen | 1:56⅕ |
| 1971 | Canonero II (1½) | Gustavo Avila | Eastern Fleet | Jim French | 1:54 |
| 1972 | Bee Bee Bee (1¼) | Eldon Nelson | No Le Hace | Key to the Mint | 1:55⅗ |
| 1973 | Secretariat (2½) | Ron Turcotte | Sham | Our Native | 1:54⅖ |
| 1974 | Little Current (7) | Miguel Rivera | Neapolitan Way | Cannonade | 1:54⅗ |
| 1975 | Master Derby (1) | Darrel McHargue | Foolish Pleasure | Diabolo | 1:56⅖ |
| 1976 | Elocutionist (3) | John Lively | Play the Red | Bold Forbes | 1:55 |
| 1977 | Seattle Slew (1½) | Jean Cruguet | Iron Constitution | Run Dusty Run | 1:54⅖ |
| 1978 | Affirmed (Neck) | Steve Cauthen | Alydar | Believe It | 1:54⅖ |
| 1979 | Spectacular Bid (5½) | Ron Franklin | Golden Act | Screen King | 1:54⅕ |
| 1980 | Codex (4¾) | Angel Cordero Jr | Genuine Risk | Colonel Moran | 1:54⅕ |
| 1981 | Pleasant Colony (1) | Jorge Velasquez | Bold Ego | Paristo | 1:54⅗ |
| 1982 | Aloma's Ruler (½) | Jack Kaenel | Linkage | Cut Away | 1:55⅖ |
| 1983 | Deputed Testamony (2¾) | Donald Miller Jr | Desert Wine | High Honors | 1:55⅖ |
| 1984 | Gate Dancer (1½) | Angel Cordero Jr | Play On | Fight Over | 1:53⅗ |
| 1985 | Tank's Prospect (Head) | Pat Day | Chief's Crown | Eternal Prince | 1:53⅖ |
| 1986 | Snow Chief (4) | Alex Solis | Ferdinand | Broad Brush | 1:54⅘ |
| 1987 | Alysheba (½) | Chris McCarron | Bet Twice | Cryptoclearance | 1:55⅘ |
| 1988 | Risen Star (1¼) | E. Delahoussaye | Brian's Time | Winning Colors | 1:56⅕ |
| 1989 | Sunday Silence (Nose) | Pat Valenzuela | Easy Goer | Rock Point | 1:53⅘ |
| 1990 | Summer Squall (2¼) | Pat Day | Unbridled | Mister Frisky | 1:53⅗ |
| 1991 | Hansel (Head) | Jerry Bailey | Corporate Report | Mane Minister | 1:54 |
| 1992 | Pine Bluff (¾) | Chris McCarron | Alydeed | Casual Lies | 1:55⅗ |
| 1993 | Prairie Bayou (½) | Mike Smith | Cherokee Run | El Bakan | 1:56⅗ |
| 1994 | Tabasco Cat (¾) | Pat Day | Go For Gin | Concern | 1:56⅖ |
| 1995 | Timber Country (½) | Pat Day | Oliver's Twist | Thunder Gulch | 1:54⅖ |

*Preakness was not run 1891-1893. In 1918, it was run in two divisions.

Note: Distance: 1½ miles (1873-88), 1¼ miles (1889), 1½ miles (1890), 1 1/16 miles (1894-1900), 1 mile and 70 yards (1901-1907), 1 1/16 miles (1908), 1 mile (1909-10), 1⅛ miles (1911-24), 1 3/16 miles (1925-present).

# Belmont

Run at Belmont Park, Elmont, NY, three weeks after the Preakness Stakes. Held previously at two locations in the Bronx, NY: Jerome Park (1867—1889) and Morris Park (1890—1904).

| Year | Winner (Margin) | Jockey | Second | Third | Time |
|---|---|---|---|---|---|
| 1867 | Ruthless (Head) | J. Gilpatrick | De Courcy | Rivoli | 3:05 |
| 1868 | General Duke (2) | R. Swim | Northumberland | Fannie Ludlow | 3:02 |
| 1869 | Fenian (Unknown) | C. Miller | Glenelg | Invercauld | 3:04¼ |
| 1870 | Kingfisher (½) | E. Brown | Foster | Midday | 2:59½ |
| 1871 | Harry Bassett (3) | W. Miller | Stockwood | By-the-Sea | 2:56 |
| 1872 | Joe Daniels (¾) | James Rowe | Meteor | Shylock | 2:58¼ |
| 1873 | Springbok (4) | James Rowe | Count d'Orsay | Strachino | 3:01¾ |
| 1874 | Saxon (Neck) | G. Barbee | Grinstead | Aaron Pennington | 2:39½ |
| 1875 | Calvin (2) | R. Swim | Aristides | Milner | 2:40¼ |
| 1876 | Algerine (Head) | W. Donahue | Fiddlestick | Barricade | 2:40½ |
| 1877 | Cloverbrook (1) | C. Holloway | Loiterer | Baden-Baden | 2:46 |
| 1878 | Duke of Magenta (2) | L. Hughes | Bramble | Sparta | 2:43½ |
| 1879 | Spendthrift (5) | S. Evans | Monitor | Jericho | 2:42¾ |
| 1880 | Grenada (½) | L. Hughes | Ferncliffe | Turenne | 2:47 |
| 1881 | Saunterer (Neck) | T. Costello | Eole | Baltic | 2:47 |
| 1882 | Forester (5) | James McLaughlin | Babcock | Wyoming | 2:43 |
| 1883 | George Kinney (2) | James McLaughlin | Trombone | Renegade | 2:42½ |
| 1884 | Panique (½) | James McLaughlin | Knight of Ellerslie | Himalaya | 2:42 |
| 1885 | Tyrant (3½) | Paul Duffy | St Augustine | Tecumseh | 2:43 |
| 1886 | Inspector B (1) | James McLaughlin | The Bard | Linden | 2:41 |
| 1887 | Hanover (28-32) | James McLaughlin | Oneko | | 2:43½ |
| 1888 | Sir Dixon (12) | James McLaughlin | Prince Royal | | 2:40¼ |
| 1889 | Eric (Head) | W. Hayward | Diable | Zephyrus | 2:47 |
| 1890 | Burlington (1) | S. Barnes | Devotee | Padishah | 2:07¾ |
| 1891 | Foxford (Neck) | E. Garrison | Montana | Laurestan | 2:08¾ |
| 1892 | Patron (Unknown) | W. Hayward | Shellbark | | 2:17 |
| 1893 | Comanche (Head)(21) | Willie Simms | Dr. Rice | Rainbow | 1:53¼ |
| 1894 | Henry of Navarre (2-4) | Willie Simms | Prig | Assignee | 1:56½ |
| 1895 | Belmar (Head) | Fred Taral | Counter Tenor | Nanki Pooh | 2:11½ |
| 1896 | Hastings (Neck) | H. Griffin | Handspring | Hamilton II | 2:24½ |
| 1897 | Scottish Chieftain (1) | J. Scherrer | On Deck | Octagon | 2:23¼ |
| 1898 | Bowling Brook (8) | P. Littlefield | Previous | Hamburg | 2:32 |
| 1899 | Jean Bereaud (Head) | R. R. Clawson | Half Time | Glengar | 2:23 |
| 1900 | Ildrim (Head) | N. Turner | Petrucio | Missionary | 2:21½ |
| 1901 | Commando (½) | H. Spencer | The Parader | All Green | 2:21 |
| 1902 | Masterman (2) | John Bullmann | Ranald | King Hanover | 2:22½ |
| 1903 | Africander (2) | John Bullmann | Whorler | Red Knight | 2:23⅕ |
| 1904 | Delhi (3½) | George Odom | Graziallo | Rapid Water | 2:06⅗ |
| 1905 | Tanya (1/2) | E. Hildebrand | Blandy | Hot Shot | 2:08 |
| 1906 | Burgomaster (4) | L. Lyne | The Quail | Accountant | 2:20 |
| 1907 | Peter Pan (1) | G. Mountain | Superman | Frank Gill | Unknown |
| 1908 | Colin (Head) | Joe Notter | Fair Play | King James | Unknown |
| 1909 | Joe Madden (8) | E. Dugan | Wise Mason | Donald MacDonald | 2:21⅗ |
| 1910* | Sweep (6) | J. Butwell | Duke of Ormonde | | 2:22 |
| 1913 | Prince Eugene (½) | Roscoe Troxler | Rock View | Flying Fairy | 2:18 |
| 1914 | Luke McLuke (8) | M. Buxton | Gainer | Charlestonian | 2:20 |
| 1915 | The Finn (4) | G. Byrne | Half Rock | Pebbles | 2:18⅖ |
| 1916 | Friar Rock (3) | E. Haynes | Spur | Churchill | 2:22 |
| 1917 | Hourless (10) | J. Butwell | Skeptic | Wonderful | 2:17⅘ |
| 1918 | Johren (2) | Frank Robinson | War Cloud | Cum Sah | 2:20⅖ |
| 1919 | Sir Barton (5) | Johnny Loftus | Sweep On | Natural Bridge | 2:17⅖ |
| 1920 | Man o' War (20) | Clarence Kummer | Donnacona | | 2:14⅕ |
| 1921 | Grey Lag (3) | Earl Sande | Sporting Blood | Leonardo II | 2:16⅘ |
| 1922 | Pillory (2) | C. H. Miller | Snob II | Hea | 2:18⅘ |
| 1923 | Zev (1½) | Earl Sande | Chickvale | Rialto | 2:19 |
| 1924 | Mad Play (2) | Earl Sande | Mr. Mutt | Modest | 2:18⅘ |
| 1925 | American Flag (8) | Albert Johnson | Dangerous | Swope | 2:16⅘ |
| 1926 | Crusader (1) | Albert Johnson | Espino | Haste | 2:32⅕ |
| 1927 | Chance Shot (1½) | Earl Sande | Bois de Rose | Flambino | 2:32⅖ |
| 1928 | Vito (3) | Clarence Kummer | Genie | Diavolo | 2:33⅕ |

## Belmont (Cont.)

| Year | Winner (Margin) | Jockey | Second | Third | Time |
|---|---|---|---|---|---|
| 1929 | Blue Larkspur (¾) | Mack Garner | African | Jack High | 2:32⅘ |
| 1930 | Gallant Fox (3) | Earl Sande | Whichone | Questionnaire | 2:31⅗ |
| 1931 | Twenty Grand (10) | Charles Kurtsinger | Sun Meadow | Jamestown | 2:29⅗ |
| 1932 | Faireno (1½) | T. Malley | Osculator | Flag Pole | 2:32⅘ |
| 1933 | Hurryoff (1½) | Mack Garner | Nimbus | Union | 2:32⅗ |
| 1934 | Peace Chance (6) | W. D. Wright | High Quest | Good Goods | 2:29⅕ |
| 1935 | Omaha (1½) | Willie Saunders | Firethorn | Rosemont | 2:30⅗ |
| 1936 | Granville (Nose) | James Stout | Mr. Bones | Hollyrood | 2:30 |
| 1937 | War Admiral (3) | Charles Kurtsinger | Sceneshifter | Vamoose | 2:28⅗ |
| 1938 | Pasteurized (Neck) | James Stout | Dauber | Cravat | 2:29⅖ |
| 1939 | Johnstown (5) | James Stout | Belay | Gilded Knight | 2:29⅗ |
| 1940 | Bimelech (¾) | F. A. Smith | Your Chance | Andy K | 2:29⅗ |
| 1941 | Whirlaway (2½) | Eddie Arcaro | Robert Morris | Yankee Chance | 2:31 |
| 1942 | Shut Out (2) | Eddie Arcaro | Alsab | Lochinvar | 2:29⅕ |
| 1943 | Count Fleet (25) | Johnny Longden | Fairy Manhurst | Deseronto | 2:28⅕ |
| 1944 | Bounding Home (½) | G. L. Smith | Pensive | Bull Dandy | 2:32⅕ |
| 1945 | Pavot (5) | Eddie Arcaro | Wildlife | Jeep | 2:30⅕ |
| 1946 | Assault (3) | Warren Mehrtens | Natchez | Cable | 2:30⅘ |
| 1947 | Phalanx (5) | R. Donoso | Tide Rips | Tailspin | 2:29⅖ |
| 1948 | Citation (8) | Eddie Arcaro | Better Self | Escadru | 2:28⅕ |
| 1949 | Capot (½) | Ted Atkinson | Ponder | Palestinian | 2:30⅕ |
| 1950 | Middleground (1) | William Boland | Lights Up | Mr. Trouble | 2:28⅗ |
| 1951 | Counterpoint (4) | D. Gorman | Battlefield | Battle Morn | 2:29 |
| 1952 | One Count (2½) | Eddie Arcaro | Blue Man | Armageddon | 2:30⅕ |
| 1953 | Native Dancer (Neck) | Eric Guerin | Jamie K. | Royal Bay Gem | 2:38⅗ |
| 1954 | High Gun (Neck) | Eric Guerin | Fisherman | Limelight | 2:30⅘ |
| 1955 | Nashua (9) | Eddie Arcaro | Blazing Count | Portersville | 2:29 |
| 1956 | Needles (Neck) | David Erb | Career Boy | Fabius | 2:29⅘ |
| 1957 | Gallant Man (8) | Bill Shoemaker | Inside Tract | Bold Ruler | 2:26⅗ |
| 1958 | Cavan (6) | Pete Anderson | Tim Tam | Flamingo | 2:30⅕ |
| 1959 | Sword Dancer (¾) | Bill Shoemaker | Bagdad | Royal Orbit | 2:28⅖ |
| 1960 | Celtic Ash (5½) | Bill Hartack | Venetian Way | Disperse | 2:29⅗ |
| 1961 | Sherluck (2¼) | Braulio Baeza | Globemaster | Guadalcanal | 2:29⅕ |
| 1962 | Jaipur (Nose) | Bill Shoemaker | Admiral's Voyage | Crimson Satan | 2:28⅘ |
| 1963 | Chateaugay (2½) | Braulio Baeza | Candy Spots | Choker | 2:30⅕ |
| 1964 | Quadrangle (2) | Manuel Ycaza | Roman Brother | Northern Dancer | 2:28⅖ |
| 1965 | Hail to All (Neck) | John Sellers | Tom Rolfe | First Family | 2:28⅖ |
| 1966 | Amberold (2½) | William Boland | Buffle | Advocator | 2:29⅗ |
| 1967 | Damascus (2½) | Bill Shoemaker | Cool Reception | Gentleman James | 2:28⅘ |
| 1968 | Stage Door Johnny (1¼) | Hellodoro Gustines | Forward Pass | Call Me Prince | 2:27⅕ |
| 1969 | Arts and Letters (5½) | Braulio Baeza | Majestic Prince | Dike | 2:28⅘ |
| 1970 | High Echelon (¾) | John L. Rotz | Needles N Pins | Naskra | 2:34 |
| 1971 | Pass Catcher (¾) | Walter Blum | Jim French | Bold Reason | 2:30⅖ |
| 1972 | Riva Ridge (7) | Ron Turcotte | Ruritania | Cloudy Dawn | 2:28 |
| 1973 | Secretariat (31) | Ron Turcotte | Twice a Prince | My Gallant | 2:24 |
| 1974 | Little Current (7) | Miguel A. Rivera | Jolly Johu | Cannonade | 2:29⅕ |
| 1975 | Avatar (Neck) | Bill Shoemaker | Foolish Pleasure | Master Derby | 2:28⅕ |
| 1976 | Bold Forbes (Neck) | Angel Cordero Jr | McKenzie Bridge | Great Contractor | 2:29 |
| 1977 | Seattle Slew (4) | Jean Cruguet | Run Dusty Run | Sanhedrin | 2:29⅗ |
| 1978 | Affirmed (Head) | Steve Cauthen | Alydar | Darby Creek Road | 2:26⅘ |
| 1979 | Coastal (3¼) | Ruben Hernandez | Golden Act | Spectacular Bid | 2:28⅗ |
| 1980 | Temperence Hill (2) | Eddie Maple | Genuine Risk | Rockhill Native | 2:29⅘ |
| 1981 | Summing (Neck) | George Martens | Highland Blade | Pleasant Colony | 2:29 |
| 1982 | Conquistador Cielo (14½) | Laffit Pincay, Jr | Gato Del Sol | Illuminate | 2:28⅕ |
| 1983 | Caveat (3½) | Laffit Pincay Jr | Slew o'Gold | Barberstown | 2:27⅘ |
| 1984 | Swale (4) | Laffit Pincay Jr | Pine Circle | Morning Bob | 2:27⅕ |
| 1985 | Creme Fraiche (½) | Eddie Maple | Stephan's Odyssey | Chief's Crown | 2:27 |
| 1986 | Danzig Connection (1¼) | Chris McCarron | Johns Treasure | Ferdinand | 2:29⅘ |

## Belmont (Cont.)

| Year | Winner (Margin) | Jockey | Second | Third | Time |
|---|---|---|---|---|---|
| 1987 | Bet Twice (14) | Craig Perret | Cryptoclearance | Gulch | 2:28⅕ |
| 1988 | Risen Star (14¾) | Eddie Delahoussaye | Kingpost | Brian's Time | 2:26⅖ |
| 1989 | Easy Goer (8) | Pat Day | Sunday Silence | Le Voyageur | 2:26 |
| 1990 | Go and Go (8¼) | Michael Kinane | Thirty Six Red | Baron de Vaux | 2:27⅕ |
| 1991 | Hansel (Head) | Jerry Bailey | Strike the Gold | Mane Minister | 2:28 |
| 1992 | A.P. Indy (¾) | Eddie Delahoussaye | My Memoirs | Pine Bluff | 2:26 |
| 1993 | Colonial Affair (2¼) | Julie Krone | Kissin Kris | Wild Gale | 2:29⅘ |
| 1994 | Tabasco Cat (2) | Pat Day | Go For Gin | Strodes Creek | 2:26⅘ |
| 1995 | Thunder Gulch (2) | Gary Stevens | Star Standard | Citadeed | 2:32 |

*Race not held in 1911-1912.

Note: Distance: 1 mile 5 furlongs (1867-89), 1¼ miles (1890-1905), 1⅜ miles (1906-25), 1½ miles (1926-present).

## Triple Crown Winners

| Year | Horse | Jockey | Owner | Trainer |
|---|---|---|---|---|
| 1919 | Sir Barton | John Loftus | J. K. L. Ross | H. G. Bedwell |
| 1930 | Gallant Fox | Earle Sande | Belair Stud | James Fitzsimmons |
| 1935 | Omaha | William Saunders | Belair Stud | James Fitzsimmons |
| 1937 | War Admiral | Charles Kurtsinger | Samuel D. Riddle | George Conway |
| 1941 | Whirlaway | Eddie Arcaro | Calumet Farm | Ben Jones |
| 1943 | Count Fleet | John Longden | Mrs J. D. Hertz | Don Cameron |
| 1946 | Assault | Warren Mehrtens | King Ranch | Max Hirsch |
| 1948 | Citation | Eddie Arcaro | Calumet Farm | Jimmy Jones |
| 1973 | Secretariat | Ron Turcotte | Meadow Stable | Lucien Laurin |
| 1977 | Seattle Slew | Jean Cruguet | Karen L. Taylor | William H. Turner Jr |
| 1978 | Affirmed | Steve Cauthen | Harbor View Farm | Laz Barrera |

### Goodbye to the Bull

When Holy Bull suffered a career-ending leg injury during last February's $300,000 Donn Handicap at Gulfstream Park, thoroughbred racing lost more than just another good horse. With the sport battling for survival among the growing sprawl of casinos, lotteries and other forms of legalized gambling, Holy Bull, one of those rare horses who, like Secretariat, stir the public's imagination, was the hero that racing needed.

Why was there such acclaim and affection for a horse who finished 12th in the 1994 Kentucky Derby and didn't even compete in the other two Triple Crown races or the Breeders' Cup? To begin with, the Bull *was* good. In 1994, as a 3-year-old, he won eight of his 10 starts, twice beating the country's best older horses, which was enough to earn him Horse of the Year honors. Beyond that, fans loved his catchy name, his gray color and his front-running style. Whenever the Bull was running, everyone knew the script: Catch him if you can.

Something bad caught Holy Bull in the Donn. Dueling with eventual winner Cigar for the lead at the ⅝ pole, Holy Bull seemed to be running easily. But at that point a tendon in his left foreleg gave way. Said Jerry Bailey, who was riding Cigar a length ahead, "I heard a pop, and then I heard [the Bull's jockey] Mike Smith yell, 'Oh, no.'" Then I lost him as he pulled up his horse." Holy Bull came to a halt near the half-mile pole, where Smith dismounted and soothed him until the equine ambulance arrived.

For the racing world, sadness over the injury was tempered by the knowledge that Holy Bull is expected to recover enough to stand stud at Jonabell Farm in Lexington. Despite the Bull's lackluster pedigree, Jim Bell of Jonabell reports that there has already been keen interest in him as a stallion. Still, whatever his success at stud, the Bull is unlikely to sire a horse with his panache.

## Horse of the Year

| Year | Horse | Owner | Trainer | Breeder |
|------|-------|-------|---------|---------|
| 1936 | Granville | Belair Stud | James Fitzsimmons | Belair Stud |
| 1937 | War Admiral | Samuel D. Riddle | George Conway | Mrs. Samuel D. Riddle |
| 1938 | Seabiscuit | Charles S. Howard | Tom Smith | Wheatley Stable |
| 1939 | Challedon | William L. Brann | Louis J. Schaefer | Branncastle Farm |
| 1940 | Challedon | William L. Brann | Louis J. Schaefer | Branncastle Farm |
| 1941 | Whirlaway | Calumet Farm | Ben Jones | Calumet Farm |
| 1942 | Whirlaway | Calumet Farm | Ben Jones | Calumet Farm |
| 1943 | Count Fleet | Mrs. John D. Hertz | Don Cameron | Mrs. John D. Hertz |
| 1944 | Twilight Tear | Calumet Farm | Ben Jones | Calumet Farm |
| 1945 | Busher | Louis B. Mayer | George Odom | Idle Hour Stock Farm |
| 1946 | Assault | King Ranch | Max Hirsch | King Ranch |
| 1947 | Armed | Calumet Farm | Jimmy Jones | Calumet Farm |
| 1948 | Citation | Calumet Farm | Jimmy Jones | Calumet Farm |
| 1949 | Capot | Greentree Stable | John M. Gaver Sr | Greentree Stable |
| 1950 | Hill Prince | C. T. Chenery | Casey Hayes | C. T. Chenery |
| 1951 | Counterpoint | C. V. Whitney | Syl Veitch | C. V. Whitney |
| 1952 | One Count | Mrs. W. M. Jeffords | O. White | W. M. Jeffords |
| 1953 | Tom Fool | Greentree Stable | John M. Gaver Sr | D. A. Headley |
| 1954 | Native Dancer | A. G. Vanderbilt | Bill Winfrey | A. G. Vanderbilt |
| 1955 | Nashua | Belair Stud | James Fitzsimmons | Belair Stud |
| 1956 | Swaps | Ellsworth-Galbreath | Mesh Tenney | R. Ellsworth |
| 1957 | Bold Ruler | Wheatley Stable | James Fitzsimmons | Wheatley Stable |
| 1958 | Round Table | Kerr Stables | Willy Molter | Claiborne Farm |
| 1959 | Sword Dancer | Brookmeade Stable | Elliott Burch | Brookmeade Stable |
| 1960 | Kelso | Bohemia Stable | C. Hanford | Mrs. R. C. duPont |
| 1961 | Kelso | Bohemia Stable | C. Hanford | Mrs. R. C. duPont |
| 1962 | Kelso | Bohemia Stable | C. Hanford | Mrs. R. C. duPont |
| 1963 | Kelso | Bohemia Stable | C. Hanford | Mrs. R. C. duPont |
| 1964 | Kelso | Bohemia Stable | C. Hanford | Mrs. R. C. duPont |
| 1965 | Roman Brother | Harbor View Stable | Burley Parke | Ocala Stud |
| 1966 | Buckpasser | Ogden Phipps | Eddie Neloy | Ogden Phipps |
| 1967 | Damascus | Mrs. E. W. Bancroft | Frank Y. Whiteley Jr | Mrs. E. W. Bancroft |
| 1968 | Dr. Fager | Tartan Stable | John A. Nerud | Tartan Farms |
| 1969 | Arts and Letters | Rokeby Stable | Elliott Burch | Paul Mellon |
| 1970 | Fort Marcy | Rokeby Stable | Elliott Burch | Paul Mellon |
| 1971 | Ack Ack | E. E. Fogelson | Charlie Whittingham | H. F. Guggenheim |
| 1972 | Secretariat | Meadow Stable | Lucien Laurin | Meadow Stud |
| 1973 | Secretariat | Meadow Stable | Lucien Laurin | Meadow Stud |
| 1974 | Forego | Lazy F Ranch | Sherrill W. Ward | Lazy F Ranch |
| 1975 | Forego | Lazy F Ranch | Sherrill W. Ward | Lazy F Ranch |
| 1976 | Forego | Lazy F Ranch | Frank Y. Whiteley Jr | Lazy F Ranch |
| 1977 | Seattle Slew | Karen L. Taylor | Billy Turner Jr | B. S. Castleman |
| 1978 | Affirmed | Harbor View Farm | Laz Barrera | Harbor View Farm |
| 1979 | Affirmed | Harbor View Farm | Laz Barrera | Harbor View Farm |
| 1980 | Spectacular Bid | Hawksworth Farm | Bud Delp | Mmes. Gilmore and Jason |
| 1981 | John Henry | Dotsam Stable | Ron McAnally and Lefty Nickerson | Golden Chance Farm |
| 1982 | Conquistador Cielo | H. de Kwiatkowski | Woody Stephens | L. E. Landoli |
| 1983 | All Along | Daniel Wildenstein | P. L. Biancone | Dayton |
| 1984 | John Henry | Dotsam Stable | Ron McAnally | Golden Chance Farm |
| 1985 | Spend a Buck | Hunter Farm | Cam Gambolati | Irish Hill Farm & R. W. Harper |
| 1986 | Lady's Secret | Mr. & Mrs. Eugene Klein | D. Wayne Lukas | R. H. Spreen |
| 1987 | Ferdinand | Mrs. H. B. Keck | Charlie Whittingham | H. B. Keck |
| 1988 | Alysheba | D. & P. Scharbauer | Jack Van Berg | Preston Madden |
| 1989 | Sunday Silence | Gaillard, Hancock, & Whittingham | Charlie Whittingham | Oak Cliff Thoroughbreds |

## Horse of the Year (Cont.)

| Year | Horse | Owner | Trainer | Breeder |
|---|---|---|---|---|
| 1990 | Criminal Type | Calumet Farm | D. Wayne Lukas | Calumet Farm |
| 1991 | Black Tie Affair | Jeffrey Sullivan | Ernie Poulos | Stephen D. Peskoff |
| 1992 | A.P. Indy | Tomonori Tsurumaki | Neil Drysdale | W.S. Farish & W.S. Kilroy |
| 1993 | Kotashaan | La Presle Farm | Richard Mandella | La Presle Farm |
| 1994 | Holy Bull | Jimmy Croll | Jimmy Croll | Pelican Stable |

Note: From 1936 to 1970, the *Daily Racing Form* annually selected a "Horse of the Year." In 1971 the *Daily Racing Form*, with the Thoroughbred Racing Association and the National Turf Writers Association, jointly created the Eclipse Awards.

## Eclipse Award Winners

### 2-YEAR-OLD COLT

| 1971 | Riva Ridge |
| 1972 | Secretariat |
| 1973 | Protagonist |
| 1974 | Foolish Pleasure |
| 1975 | Honest Pleasure |
| 1976 | Seattle Slew |
| 1977 | Affirmed |
| 1978 | Spectacular Bid |
| 1979 | Rockhill Native |
| 1980 | Lord Avie |
| 1981 | Deputy Minister |
| 1982 | Roving Boy |
| 1983 | Devil's Bag |
| 1984 | Chief's Crown |
| 1985 | Tasso |
| 1986 | Capote |
| 1987 | Forty Niner |
| 1988 | Easy Goer |
| 1989 | Rhythm |
| 1990 | Fly So Free |
| 1991 | Arazi |
| 1992 | Gilded Time |
| 1993 | Dehere |
| 1994 | Timber Country |

### 2-YEAR-OLD FILLY

| 1971 | Numbered Account |
| 1972 | La Prevoyante |
| 1973 | Talking Picture |
| 1974 | Ruffian |
| 1975 | Dearly Precious |
| 1976 | Sensational |
| 1977 | Lakeville Miss |
| 1978 | Candy Eclair |
|  | It's in the Air |
| 1979 | Smart Angle |
| 1980 | Heavenly Cause |
| 1981 | Before Dawn |
| 1982 | Landaluce |
| 1983 | Althea |
| 1984 | Outstandingly |
| 1985 | Family Style |
| 1986 | Brave Raj |
| 1987 | Epitome |
| 1988 | Open Mind |
| 1989 | Go for Wand |
| 1990 | Meadow Star |
| 1991 | Pleasant Stage |
| 1992 | Eliza |
| 1993 | Phone Chatter |
| 1994 | Flanders |

### 3-YEAR-OLD COLT

| 1971 | Canonero II |
| 1972 | Key to the Mint |
| 1973 | Secretariat |
| 1974 | Little Currant |
| 1975 | Wajima |
| 1976 | Bold Forbes |
| 1977 | Seattle Slew |
| 1978 | Affirmed |
| 1979 | Spectacular Bid |
| 1980 | Temperence Hill |
| 1981 | Pleasant Colony |
| 1982 | Conquistador Cielo |
| 1983 | Slew o' Gold |
| 1984 | Swale |
| 1985 | Spend A Buck |
| 1986 | Snow Chief |
| 1987 | Alysheba |
| 1988 | Risen Star |
| 1989 | Sunday Silence |
| 1990 | Unbridled |
| 1991 | Hansel |
| 1992 | A.P. Indy |
| 1993 | Prairie Bayou |
| 1994 | Holy Bull |

### 3-YEAR-OLD FILLY

| 1971 | Turkish Trousers |
| 1972 | Susan's Girl |
| 1973 | Desert Vixen |
| 1974 | Chris Evert |
| 1975 | Ruffian |
| 1976 | Revidere |
| 1977 | Our Mims |
| 1978 | Tempest Queen |
| 1979 | Davona Dale |
| 1980 | Genuine Risk |
| 1981 | Wayward Lass |
| 1982 | Christmas Past |
| 1983 | Heartlight No. One |
| 1984 | Life's Magic |
| 1985 | Mom's Command |
| 1986 | Tiffany Lass |
| 1987 | Sacahuista |
| 1988 | Winning Colors |
| 1989 | Open Mind |
| 1990 | Go for Wand |
| 1991 | Dance Smartly |
| 1992 | Saratoga Dew |
| 1993 | Hollywood Wildcat |
| 1994 | Heavenly Prize |

### OLDER COLT, HORSE OR GELDING

| 1971 | Ack Ack (5) |
| 1972 | Autobiography (4) |
| 1973 | Riva Ridge (4) |
| 1974 | Forego (4) |
| 1975 | Forego (5) |
| 1976 | Forego (6) |
| 1977 | Forego (7) |
| 1978 | Seattle Slew (4) |
| 1979 | Affirmed (4) |
| 1980 | Spectacular Bid (4) |
| 1981 | John Henry (6) |
| 1982 | Lemhi Gold (4) |
| 1983 | Bates Motel (4) |
| 1984 | Slew o'Gold (4) |
| 1985 | Vanlandingham (4) |
| 1986 | Turkoman (4) |
| 1987 | Ferdinand (4) |
| 1988 | Alysheba (4) |
| 1989 | Blushing John (4) |
| 1990 | Criminal Type (5) |
| 1991 | Black Tie Affair (5) |
| 1992 | Pleasant Tap (5) |
| 1993 | Bertrando (4) |
| 1994 | The Wicked North (5) |

### OLDER FILLY OR MARE

| 1971 | Shuvee (5) |
| 1972 | Typecast (6) |
| 1973 | Susan's Girl (4) |
| 1974 | Desert Vixen (4) |
| 1975 | Susan's Girl (6) |
| 1976 | Proud Delta (4) |
| 1977 | Cascapedia (4) |
| 1978 | Late Bloomer (4) |
| 1979 | Waya (5) |
| 1980 | Glorious Song (4) |
| 1981 | Relaxing (5) |
| 1982 | Track Robbery (6) |
| 1983 | Ambassador of Luck (4) |
| 1984 | Princess Rooney (4) |
| 1985 | Life's Magic (4) |
| 1986 | Lady's Secret (4) |
| 1987 | North Sider (5) |
| 1988 | Personal Ensign (4) |
| 1989 | Bayakoa (5) |
| 1990 | Bayakoa (6) |
| 1991 | Queena (5) |
| 1992 | Paseana (5) |
| 1993 | Paseana (6) |
| 1994 | Sky Beauty (4) |

## Eclipse Awards (Cont.)

### CHAMPION TURF HORSE

1971.....Run the Gantlet (3)
1972.....Cougar II (6)
1973.....Secretariat (3)
1974.....Dahlia (4)
1975.....Snow Knight (4)
1976.....Youth (3)
1977.....Johnny D (3)
1978.....Mac Diarmida (3)

### CHAMPION MALE TURF HORSE

1979.....Bowl Game (5)
1980.....John Henry (5)
1981.....John Henry (6)
1982.....Perrault (5)
1983.....John Henry (8)
1984.....John Henry (9)
1985.....Cozzene (4)
1986.....Manila (3)
1987.....Theatrical (5)
1988.....Sunshine Forever (3)
1989.....Steinlen (6)
1990.....Itsallgreektome (3)
1991.....Tight Spot (4)
1992.....Sky Classic (5)
1993.....Kotashaan (5)
1994.....Paradise Creek (5)

### CHAMPION FEMALE TURF HORSE

1979.....Trillion (5)
1980.....Just a Game II (4)
1981.....De La Rose (3)
1982.....April Run (4)
1983.....All Along (4)
1984.....Royal Heroine (4)
1985.....Pebbles (4)
1986.....Estrapade (6)
1987.....Miesque (3)
1988.....Miesque (4)
1989.....Brown Bess (7)
1990.....Laugh and Be Merry (5)
1991.....Miss Alleged (4)
1992.....Flawlessly (4)
1993.....Flawlessly (5)
1994.....Hatoof (5)

### STEEPLECHASE OR HURDLE HORSE

1971.....Shadow Brook (7)
1972.....Soothsayer (5)
1973.....Athenian Idol (5)
1974.....Gran Kan (8)
1975.....Life's Illusion (4)
1976.....Straight & True (6)
1977.....Cafe Prince (7)
1978.....Cafe Prince (8)
1979.....Martie's Anger (4)
1980.....Zaccio (4)
1981.....Zaccio (5)
1982.....Zaccio (6)
1983.....Flatterer (4)
1984.....Flatterer (5)
1985.....Flatterer (6)

### STEEPLECHASE OR HURDLE HORSE (Cont.)

1986.....Flatterer (7)
1987.....Inlander (6)
1988.....Jimmy Lorenzo (6)
1989.....Highland Bud (4)
1990.....Morley Street (7)
1991.....Morley Street (8)
1992.....Lonesome Glory (4)
1993.....Lonesome Glory (5)
1994.....Warm Spell (6)

### SPRINTER

1971.....Ack Ack (5)
1972.....Chou Croute (4)
1973.....Shecky Greene (3)
1974.....Forego (4)
1975.....Gallant Bob (3)
1976.....My Juliet (4)
1977.....What a Summer (4)
1978.....Dr. Patches (4)
J. O. Tobin (4)
1979.....Star de Naskra (4)
1980.....Plugged Nickel (3)
1981.....Guilty Conscience (5)
1982.....Gold Beauty (3)
1983.....Chinook Pass (4)
1984.....Eillo (4)
1985.....Precisionist (4)
1986.....Smile (4)
1987.....Groovy (4)
1988.....Gulch (4)
1989.....Safely Kept (3)
1990.....Housebuster (3)
1991.....Housebuster (4)
1992.....Rubiano (5)
1993.....Cardmania (7)
1994.....Cherokee Run (4)

### OUTSTANDING OWNER

1971.....Mr. & Mrs. E. E. Fogleson
1974.....Dan Lasater
1975.....Dan Lasater
1976.....Dan Lasater
1977.....Maxwell Gluck
1978.....Harbor View Farm
1979.....Harbor View Farm
1980.....Mr. & Mrs. Bertram Firestone
1981.....Dotsam Stable
1982.....Viola Sommer
1983.....John Franks
1984.....John Franks
1985.....Mr. & Mrs. Eugene Klein
1986.....Mr. & Mrs. Eugene Klein
1987.....Mr. & Mrs. Eugene Klein
1988.....Ogden Phipps
1989.....Ogden Phipps
1990.....Frances Genter
1991.....Sam-Son Farm
1992.....Juddmonte Farms
1993.....John Franks
1994.....John Franks

### OUTSTANDING TRAINER

1971.....Charlie Whittingham
1972.....Lucien Laurin
1973.....H. Allen Jerkens
1974.....Sherrill Ward
1975.....Steve DiMauro
1976.....Lazaro Barrera
1977.....Lazaro Barrera
1978.....Lazaro Barrera
1979.....Lazaro Barrera
1980.....Bud Delp
1981.....Ron McAnally
1982.....Charlie Whittingham
1983.....Woody Stephens
1984.....Jack Van Berg
1985.....D. Wayne Lukas
1986.....D. Wayne Lukas
1987.....D. Wayne Lukas
1988.....Claude R. McGaughey III
1989.....Charlie Whittingham
1990.....Carl Nafzger
1991.....Ron McAnally
1992.....Ron McAnally
1993.....Bobby Frankel
1994.....D. Wayne Lukas

### OUTSTANDING JOCKEY

1971.....Laffit Pincay Jr
1972.....Braulio Baeza
1973.....Laffit Pincay Jr
1974.....Laffit Pincay Jr
1975.....Braulio Baeza
1976.....Sandy Hawley
1977.....Steve Cauthen
1978.....Darrel McHargue
1979.....Laffit Pincay Jr
1980.....Chris McCarron
1981.....Bill Shoemaker
1982.....Angel Cordero Jr
1983.....Angel Cordero Jr
1984.....Pat Day
1985.....Laffit Pincay Jr
1986.....Pat Day
1987.....Pat Day
1988.....Jose Santos
1989.....Kent Desormeaux
1990.....Craig Perret
1991.....Pat Day
1992.....Kent Desormeaux
1993.....Mike Smith
1994.....Mike Smith

### OUTSTANDING APPRENTICE JOCKEY

1971.....Gene St. Leon
1972.....Thomas Wallis
1973.....Steve Valdez
1974.....Chris McCarron
1975.....Jimmy Edwards
1976.....George Martens
1977.....Steve Cauthen
1978.....Ron Franklin
1979.....Cash Asmussen

Note: Number in parentheses is horse's age.

# Awards (Cont.)

## Eclipse Awards (Cont.)

### OUTSTANDING APPRENTICE JOCKEY *(Cont.)*

1980.....Frank Lovato Jr
1981.....Richard Migliore
1982.....Alberto Delgado
1983.....Declan Murphy
1984.....Wesley Ward
1985.....Art Madrid Jr
1986.....Allen Stacy
1987.....Kent Desormeaux
1988.....Steve Capanas
1989.....Michael Luzzi
1990.....Mark Johnston
1991.....Mickey Walls
1992.....Jesus A. Bracho
1993.....Juan Umana
1994.....Dale Beckner

### OUTSTANDING BREEDER

1974.....John W. Galbreath
1975.....Fred W. Hooper
1976.....Nelson Bunker Hunt
1977.....Edward Plunket Taylor
1978.....Harbor View Farm

### OUTSTANDING BREEDER *(Cont.)*

1979.....Claiborne Farm
1980.....Mrs. Henry D. Paxson
1981.....Golden Chance Farm
1982.....Fred W. Hooper
1983.....Edward Plunket Taylor
1984.....Claiborne Farm
1985.....Nelson Bunker Hunt
1986.....Paul Mellon
1987.....Nelson Bunker Hunt
1988.....Ogden Phipps
1989.....North Ridge Farm
1990.....Calumet Farm
1991.....John and Betty Mabee
1992.....William S. Farish III
1993.....Allen Paulson
1994.....William T. Young

### AWARD OF MERIT

1976.....Jack J. Dreyfus
1977.....Steve Cauthen
1978.....Ogden Phipps
1979.....Frank E. Kilroe
1980.....John D. Schapiro

### AWARD OF MERIT *(Cont.)*

1981.....Bill Shoemaker
1984.....John Gaines
1985.....Keene Daingerfield
1986.....Herman Cohen
1987.....J. B. Faulconer
1988.....John Forsythe
1989.....Michael P. Sandler
1991.....Fred W. Hooper
1994.....Alfred G. Vanderbilt

### SPECIAL AWARD

1971.....Robert J. Kleberg
1974.....Charles Hatton
1976.....Bill Shoemaker
1980.....John T. Landry
Pierre E. Bellocq (Peb)
1984.....C. V. Whitney
1985.....Arlington Park
1987.....Anheuser-Busch
1988.....Edward J. DeBartolo Sr
1989.....Richard Duchossois
1994.....John Longden
Edward Arcaro

Note: Special Award and Award of Merit not presented annually. For long-term and/or outstanding service to the industry.

# Breeders' Cup

Location: Hollywood Park (CA) 1984, 1987; Aqueduct Racetrack (NY) 1985; Santa Anita Park (CA) 1986, 1993; Churchill Downs (KY) 1988, 1991, 1995; Gulfstream Park (FL) 1989, 1992; Belmont Park (NY) 1990.

## Juveniles

| Year | Winner (Margin) | Jockey | Second | Third | Time |
|---|---|---|---|---|---|
| 1984 | Chief's Crown (¾) | Don MacBeth | Tank's Prospect | Spend a Buck | 1:36⅕ |
| 1985 | Tasso (Nose) | Laffit Pincay Jr | Storm Cat | Scat Dancer | 1:36⅕ |
| 1986 | Capote (1¼) | Laffit Pincay Jr | Qualify | Alysheba | 1:43⅘ |
| 1987 | Success Express (1¾) | Jose Santos | Regal Classic | Tejano | 1:35⅕ |
| 1988 | Is It True (1¼) | Laffit Pincay Jr | Easy Goer | Tagel | 1:46⅗ |
| 1989 | Rhythm (2) | Craig Perret | Grand Canyon | Slavic | 1:43⅗ |
| 1990 | Fly So Free (3) | Jose Santos | Take Me Out | Lost Mountain | 1:43⅖ |
| 1991 | Arazi (4¾) | Pat Valenzuela | Bertrando | Snappy Landing | 1:44⅗ |
| 1992 | Gilded Time (¾) | Chris McCarron | It'sali'lknownfact | River Special | 1:43⅖ |
| 1993 | Brocco (5) | Gary Stevens | Blumin Affair | Tabasco Cat | 1:42⅘ |
| 1994 | Timber Country (½) | Pat Day | Eltish | Tejano Run | 1:44⅖ |

Note: One mile (1984–85, 87); 1¹⁄₁₆ miles (1986 and since 1988).

## Juvenile Fillies

| Year | Winner (Margin) | Jockey | Second | Third | Time |
|---|---|---|---|---|---|
| 1984 | Outstandingly* | Walter Guerra | Dusty Heart | Fine Spirit | 1:37⅘ |
| 1985 | Twilight Ridge (1) | Jorge Velasquez | Family Style | Steal a Kiss | 1:35⅘ |
| 1986 | Brave Raj (5½) | Pat Valenzuela | Tappiano | Saros Brig | 1:43⅕ |
| 1987 | Epitome (Nose) | Pat Day | Jeanne Jones | Dream Team | 1:36⅖ |
| 1988 | Open Mind (1¾) | Angel Cordero Jr | Darby Shuffle | Lea Lucinda | 1:46⅗ |
| 1989 | Go for Wand (2¾) | Randy Romero | Sweet Roberta | Stella Madrid | 1:44⅕ |
| 1990 | Meadow Star (5) | Jose Santos | Private Treasure | Dance Smartly | 1:44 |
| 1991 | Pleasant Stage (Neck) | Eddie Delahoussaye | La Spia | Cadillac Women | 1:46⅖ |
| 1992 | Eliza (1½) | Pat Valenzuela | Educated Risk | Boots 'n Jackie | 1:42⅘ |
| 1993 | Phone Chatter (Head) | Laffit Pincay | Sardula | Heavenly Prize | 1:43 |
| 1994 | Flanders (Head) | Pat Day | Serena's Song | Stormy Blues | 1:45⅕ |

*In 1984, winner Fran's Valentine was disqualified for interference in the stretch and placed 10th.
Note: One mile (1984–85, 87); 1¹⁄₁₆ miles (1986 and since 1988).

# Breeders' Cup (*Cont.*)

## Sprint

| Year | Winner (Margin) | Jockey | Second | Third | Time |
|---|---|---|---|---|---|
| 1984 | Eillo (Nose) | Craig Perret | Commemorate | Fighting Fit | 1:10⅕ |
| 1985 | Precisionist (¾) | Chris McCarron | Smile | Mt. Livermore | 1:08⅖ |
| 1986 | Smile (1¼) | Jacinto Vasquez | Pine Tree Lane | Bedside Promise | 1:08⅖ |
| 1987 | Very Subtle (4) | Pat Valenzuela | Groovy | Exclusive Enough | 1:08⅘ |
| 1988 | Gulch (¾) | Angel Cordero Jr | Play the King | Afleet | 1:10⅖ |
| 1989 | Dancing Spree (Neck) | Angel Cordero Jr | Safely Kept | Dispersal | 1:09 |
| 1990 | Safely Kept (Neck) | Craig Perret | Dayjur | Black Tie Affair | 1:09⅗ |
| 1991 | Sheikh Albadou (Neck) | Pat Eddery | Pleasant Tap | Robyn Dancer | 1:09⅕ |
| 1992 | Thirty Slews (Neck) | Eddie Delahoussaye | Meafara | Rubiano | 1:08⅕ |
| 1993 | Cardmania (Neck) | Eddie Delahoussaye | Meafara | Gilded Time | 1:08⅗ |
| 1994 | Cherokee Run (Head) | Mike Smith | Soviet Problem | Cardmania | 1:09⅖ |

Note: Six furlongs (since 1984).

## Mile

| Year | Winner (Margin) | Jockey | Second | Third | Time |
|---|---|---|---|---|---|
| 1984 | Royal Heroine (1½) | Fernando Toro | Star Choice | Cozzene | 1:32⅗ |
| 1985 | Cozzene (2¼) | Walter Guerra | Al Mamoon* | Shadeed | 1:35 |
| 1986 | Last Tycoon (Head) | Yves St-Martin | Palace Music | Fred Astaire | 1:35⅕ |
| 1987 | Miesque (3½) | Freddie Head | Show Dancer | Sonic Lady | 1:32⅘ |
| 1988 | Miesque (4) | Freddie Head | Steinlen | Simply Majestic | 1:38⅗ |
| 1989 | Steinlen (¾) | Jose Santos | Sabona | Most Welcome | 1:37⅕ |
| 1990 | Royal Academy (Neck) | Lester Piggott | Itsallgreektome | Priolo | 1:35⅕ |
| 1991 | Opening Verse (2¼) | Pat Valenzuela | Val de Bois | Star of Cozzene | 1:37⅖ |
| 1992 | Lure (3) | Mike Smith | Paradise Creek | Brief Truce | 1:32⅘ |
| 1993 | Lure (2¼) | Mike Smith | Ski Paradise | Fourstars Allstar | 1:33⅖ |
| 1994 | Barathea (Head) | Frankie Dettori | Johann Quatz | Unfinished Symph | 1:34⅖ |

*2nd place finisher Palace Music was disqualified for interference and placed 9th.

## Distaff

| Year | Winner (Margin) | Jockey | Second | Third | Time |
|---|---|---|---|---|---|
| 1984 | Princess Rooney (7) | Eddie Delahoussaye | Life's Magic | Adored | 2:02⅖ |
| 1985 | Life's Magic (6¼) | Angel Cordero Jr | Lady's Secret | Dontstop Themusic | 2:02 |
| 1986 | Lady's Secret (2½) | Pat Day | Fran's Valentine | Outstandingly | 2:01⅕ |
| 1987 | Sacahuista (2¼) | Randy Romero | Clabber Girl | Oueee Bebe | 2:02⅘ |
| 1988 | Personal Ensign (Nose) | Randy Romero | Winning Colors | Goodbye Halo | 1:52 |
| 1989 | Bayakoa (1½) | Laffit Pincay Jr | Gorgeous | Open Mind | 1:47⅖ |
| 1990 | Bayakoa (6¾) | Laffit Pincay Jr | Colonial Waters | Valay Maid | 1:49⅕ |
| 1991 | Dance Smarty (½) | Pat Day | Versailles Treaty | Brought to Mind | 1:50⅘ |
| 1992 | Paseana (4) | Chris McCarron | Versailles Treaty | Magical Maiden | 1:48 |
| 1993 | Hollywood Wildcat (Nose) | Eddie Delahoussaye | Paseana | Re Toss | 1:48⅕ |
| 1994 | One Dreamer (Neck) | Gary Stevens | Heavenly Prize | Miss Dominique | 1:50⅗ |

Note: 1¼ miles (1984-87); 1⅛ miles (since 1988).

## Turf

| Year | Winner (Margin) | Jockey | Second | Third | Time |
|---|---|---|---|---|---|
| 1984 | Lashkari (Neck) | Yves St-Martin | All Along | Raami | 2:25⅕ |
| 1985 | Pebbles (Neck) | Pat Eddery | Strawberry Rd II | Mourjane | 2:27 |
| 1986 | Manila (Neck) | Jose Santos | Theatrical | Estrapade | 2:25⅖ |
| 1987 | Theatrical (½) | Pat Day | Trempolino | Village Star II | 2:24⅖ |
| 1988 | Great Communicator (½) | Ray Sibille | Sunshine Forever | Indian Skimmer | 2:35⅕ |
| 1989 | Prized (Head) | Eddie Delahoussaye | Sierra Roberta | Star Lift | 2:28 |
| 1990 | In the Wings (½) | Gary Stevens | With Approval | El Senor | 2:29⅗ |
| 1991 | Miss Alleged (2) | Eric Legrix | Itsallgreektome | Quest for Fame | 2:30⅘ |
| 1992 | Fraise (Nose) | Pat Valenzuela | Sky Classic | Quest For Fame | 2:24 |
| 1993 | Kotashaan (½) | Kent Desormeaux | Bien Bien | Luazar | 2:25 |
| 1994 | Tikkanen (1½) | Mike Smith | Hatoof | Paradise Creek | 2:26⅖ |

Note: 1½ miles.

## Classic

| Year | Winner (Margin) | Jockey | Second | Third | Time |
|---|---|---|---|---|---|
| 1984 | Wild Again (Head) | Pat Day | Slew o' Gold* | Gate Dancer | 2:03⅖ |
| 1985 | Proud Truth (Head) | Jorge Velasquez | Gate Dancer | Turkoman | 2:00⅘ |
| 1986 | Skywalker (1¼) | Laffit Pincay Jr | Turkoman | Precisionist | 2:00⅖ |

## Breeders' Cup (*Cont.*)

### Classic (*Cont.*)

| Year | Winner (Margin) | Jockey | Second | Third | Time |
|---|---|---|---|---|---|
| 1987 | Ferdinand (Nose) | Bill Shoemaker | Alysheba | Judge Angelucci | 2:01⅖ |
| 1988 | Alysheba (Nose) | Chris McCarron | Seeking the Gold | Waquoit | 2:04⅘ |
| 1989 | Sunday Silence (½) | Chris McCarron | Easy Goer | Blushing John | 2:00⅕ |
| 1990 | Unbridled (1) | Pat Day | Ibn Bey | Thirty Six Red | 2:02⅕ |
| 1991 | Black Tie Affair (1¼) | Jerry Bailey | Twilight Agenda | Unbridled | 2:02⅘ |
| 1992 | A.P. Indy (2) | Eddie Delahoussaye | Pleasant Tap | Jolypha | 2:00⅕ |
| 1993 | Arcangues (2) | Jerry Bailey | Bertrando | Kissin Kris | 2:00⅘ |
| 1994 | Concern (Neck) | Jerry Bailey | Tabasco Cat | Dramatic Gold | 2:02⅖ |

*2nd place finisher Gate Dancer was disqualified for interference and placed 3rd.
Note: 1¼ miles.

## England's Triple Crown Winners

England's Triple Crown consists of the Two Thousand Guineas, held at Newmarket; the Epsom Derby, held at Epsom Downs; and the St. Leger Stakes, held at Doncaster.

| Year | Horse | Owner |
|---|---|---|
| 1853 | West Australian | Mr. Bowes |
| 1865 | Gladiateur | F. DeLagrange |
| 1866 | Lord Lyon | R. Sutton |
| 1886 | *Ormonde | Duke of Westminster |
| 1891 | Common | †F. Johnstone |
| 1893 | Isinglass | H. McCalmont |
| 1897 | Galtee More | J. Gubbins |
| 1899 | Flying Fox | Duke of Westminster |
| 1900 | Diamond Jubilee | Prince of Wales |
| 1903 | *Rock Sand | J. Miller |
| 1915 | Pommern | S. Joel |
| 1917 | Gay Crusader | Mr. Fairie |
| 1918 | Gainsborough | Lady James Douglas |
| 1935 | *Bahram | Aga Khan |
| 1970 | ‡Nijinsky II | C. W. Engelhard |

*Imported into United States. †Raced in name of Lord Alington in Two Thousand Guineas. ‡Canadian-bred.

## Annual Leaders

### Horse—Money Won

| Year | Horse | Age | Starts | 1st | 2nd | 3rd | Winnings ($) |
|---|---|---|---|---|---|---|---|
| 1919 | Sir Barton | 3 | 13 | 8 | 3 | 2 | 88,250 |
| 1920 | Man o'War | 3 | 11 | 11 | 0 | 0 | 166,140 |
| 1921 | Morvich | 2 | 11 | 11 | 0 | 0 | 115,234 |
| 1922 | Pillory | 3 | 7 | 4 | 1 | 1 | 95,654 |
| 1923 | Zev | 3 | 14 | 12 | 1 | 0 | 272,008 |
| 1924 | Sarzen | 3 | 12 | 8 | 1 | 1 | 95,640 |
| 1925 | Pompey | 2 | 10 | 7 | 2 | 0 | 121,630 |
| 1926 | Crusader | 3 | 15 | 9 | 4 | 0 | 166,033 |
| 1927 | Anita Peabody | 2 | 7 | 6 | 0 | 1 | 111,905 |
| 1928 | High Strung | 2 | 6 | 5 | 0 | 0 | 153,590 |
| 1929 | Blue Larkspur | 3 | 6 | 4 | 1 | 0 | 153,450 |
| 1930 | Gallant Fox | 3 | 10 | 9 | 1 | 0 | 308,275 |
| 1931 | Gallant Flight | 2 | 7 | 7 | 0 | 0 | 219,000 |
| 1932 | Gusto | 3 | 16 | 4 | 3 | 2 | 145,940 |
| 1933 | Singing Wood | 2 | 9 | 3 | 2 | 2 | 88,050 |
| 1934 | Cavalcade | 3 | 7 | 6 | 1 | 0 | 111,235 |
| 1935 | Omaha | 3 | 9 | 6 | 1 | 2 | 142,255 |
| 1936 | Granville | 3 | 11 | 7 | 3 | 0 | 110,295 |
| 1937 | Seabiscuit | 4 | 15 | 11 | 2 | 2 | 168,580 |
| 1938 | Stagehand | 3 | 15 | 8 | 2 | 3 | 189,710 |
| 1939 | Challedon | 3 | 15 | 9 | 2 | 3 | 184,535 |
| 1940 | Bimelech | 3 | 7 | 4 | 2 | 1 | 110,005 |
| 1941 | Whirlaway | 3 | 20 | 13 | 5 | 2 | 272,386 |
| 1942 | Shut Out | 3 | 12 | 8 | 2 | 0 | 238,872 |
| 1943 | Count Fleet | 3 | 6 | 6 | 0 | 0 | 174,055 |
| 1944 | Pavot | 2 | 8 | 8 | 0 | 0 | 179,040 |
| 1945 | Busher | 3 | 13 | 10 | 2 | 1 | 273,735 |
| 1946 | Assault | 3 | 15 | 8 | 2 | 3 | 424,195 |
| 1947 | Armed | 6 | 17 | 11 | 4 | 1 | 376,325 |
| 1948 | Citation | 3 | 20 | 19 | 1 | 0 | 709,470 |

Note: Annual leaders on pages 460-465 courtesy of *The American Racing Manual*, a publication of Daily Racing Form, Inc.

## Horse—Money Won (Cont.)

| Year | Horse | Age | Starts | 1st | 2nd | 3rd | Winnings ($) |
|------|-------|-----|--------|-----|-----|-----|--------------|
| 1949 | Ponder | 3 | 21 | 9 | 5 | 2 | 321,825 |
| 1950 | Noor | 5 | 12 | 7 | 4 | 1 | 346,940 |
| 1951 | Counterpoint | 3 | 15 | 7 | 2 | 1 | 250,525 |
| 1952 | Crafty Admiral | 4 | 16 | 9 | 4 | 1 | 277,225 |
| 1953 | Native Dancer | 3 | 10 | 9 | 1 | 0 | 513,425 |
| 1954 | Determine | 3 | 15 | 10 | 3 | 2 | 328,700 |
| 1955 | Nashua | 3 | 12 | 10 | 1 | 1 | 752,550 |
| 1956 | Needles | 3 | 8 | 4 | 2 | 0 | 440,850 |
| 1957 | Round Table | 3 | 22 | 15 | 1 | 3 | 600,383 |
| 1958 | Round Table | 4 | 20 | 14 | 4 | 0 | 662,780 |
| 1959 | Sword Dancer | 3 | 13 | 8 | 4 | 0 | 537,004 |
| 1960 | Bally Ache | 3 | 15 | 10 | 3 | 1 | 445,045 |
| 1961 | Carry Back | 3 | 16 | 9 | 1 | 3 | 565,349 |
| 1962 | Never Bend | 2 | 10 | 7 | 1 | 2 | 402,969 |
| 1963 | Candy Spots | 3 | 12 | 7 | 2 | 1 | 604,481 |
| 1964 | Gun Bow | 4 | 16 | 8 | 4 | 2 | 580,100 |
| 1965 | Buckpasser | 2 | 11 | 9 | 1 | 0 | 568,096 |
| 1966 | Buckpasser | 3 | 14 | 13 | 1 | 0 | 669,078 |
| 1967 | Damascus | 3 | 16 | 12 | 3 | 1 | 817,941 |
| 1968 | Forward Pass | 3 | 13 | 7 | 2 | 0 | 546,674 |
| 1969 | Arts and Letters | 3 | 14 | 8 | 5 | 1 | 555,604 |
| 1970 | Personality | 3 | 18 | 8 | 2 | 1 | 444,049 |
| 1971 | Riva Ridge | 2 | 9 | 7 | 0 | 0 | 503,263 |
| 1972 | Droll Role | 4 | 19 | 7 | 3 | 4 | 471,633 |
| 1973 | Secretariat | 3 | 12 | 9 | 2 | 1 | 860,404 |
| 1974 | Chris Evert | 3 | 8 | 5 | 1 | 2 | 551,063 |
| 1975 | Foolish Pleasure | 3 | 11 | 5 | 4 | 1 | 716,278 |
| 1976 | Forego | 6 | 8 | 6 | 1 | 1 | 401,701 |
| 1977 | Seattle Slew | 3 | 7 | 6 | 0 | 1 | 641,370 |
| 1978 | Affirmed | 3 | 11 | 8 | 2 | 0 | 901,541 |
| 1979 | Spectacular Bid | 3 | 12 | 10 | 1 | 1 | 1,279,334 |
| 1980 | Temperence Hill | 3 | 17 | 8 | 3 | 1 | 1,130,452 |
| 1981 | John Henry | 6 | 10 | 8 | 0 | 0 | 1,798,030 |
| 1982 | Perrault | 5 | 8 | 4 | 1 | 2 | 1,197,400 |
| 1983 | All Along | 4 | 7 | 4 | 1 | 1 | 2,138,963 |
| 1984 | Slew o'Gold | 4 | 6 | 5 | 1 | 0 | 2,627,944 |
| 1985 | Spend A Buck | 3 | 7 | 5 | 1 | 1 | 3,552,704 |
| 1986 | Snow Chief | 3 | 9 | 6 | 1 | 1 | 1,875,200 |
| 1987 | Alysheba | 3 | 10 | 3 | 3 | 1 | 2,511,156 |
| 1988 | Alysheba | 4 | 9 | 7 | 1 | 0 | 3,808,600 |
| 1989 | Sunday Silence | 3 | 9 | 7 | 2 | 0 | 4,578,454 |
| 1990 | Unbridled | 3 | 11 | 4 | 3 | 2 | 3,718,149 |
| 1991 | Dance Smartly | 3 | 8 | 8 | 0 | 0 | 2,876,821 |
| 1992 | A.P. Indy | 3 | 7 | 5 | 0 | 1 | 2,622,560 |
| 1993 | Kotashaan | 3 | 10 | 6 | 3 | 0 | 2,619,014 |
| 1994 | Paradise Creek | 5 | 11 | 8 | 2 | 1 | 2,610,187 |

## Trainer—Money Won

| Year | Trainer | Wins | Winnings ($) | Year | Trainer | Wins | Winnings ($) |
|------|---------|------|--------------|------|---------|------|--------------|
| 1908 | James Rowe, Sr | 50 | 284,335 | 1925 | G. R. Tompkins | 30 | 199,245 |
| 1909 | Sam Hildreth | 73 | 123,942 | 1926 | Scott P. Harlan | 21 | 205,681 |
| 1910 | Sam Hildreth | 84 | 148,010 | 1927 | W. H. Bringloe | 63 | 216,563 |
| 1911 | Sam Hildreth | 67 | 49,418 | 1928 | John F. Schorr | 65 | 258,425 |
| 1912 | John F. Schorr | 63 | 58,110 | 1929 | James Rowe, Jr | 25 | 314,881 |
| 1913 | James Rowe, Sr | 18 | 45,936 | 1930 | Sunny Jim Fitzsimmons | 47 | 397,355 |
| 1914 | R. C. Benson | 45 | 59,315 | 1931 | Big Jim Healey | 33 | 297,300 |
| 1915 | James Rowe, Sr | 19 | 75,596 | 1932 | Sunny Jim Fitzsimmons | 68 | 266,650 |
| 1916 | Sam Hildreth | 39 | 70,950 | 1933 | Humming Bob Smith | 53 | 135,720 |
| 1917 | Sam Hildreth | 23 | 61,698 | 1934 | Humming Bob Smith | 43 | 249,938 |
| 1918 | H. Guy Bedwell | 53 | 80,296 | 1935 | Bud Stotler | 87 | 303,005 |
| 1919 | H. Guy Bedwell | 63 | 208,728 | 1936 | Sunny Jim Fitzsimmons | 42 | 193,415 |
| 1920 | L. Feustal | 22 | 186,087 | 1937 | Robert McGarvey | 46 | 209,925 |
| 1921 | Sam Hildreth | 85 | 262,768 | 1938 | Earl Sande | 15 | 226,495 |
| 1922 | Sam Hildreth | 74 | 247,014 | 1939 | Sunny Jim Fitzsimmons | 45 | 266,205 |
| 1923 | Sam Hildreth | 75 | 392,124 | 1940 | Silent Tom Smith | 14 | 269,200 |
| 1924 | Sam Hildreth | 77 | 255,608 | 1941 | Plain Ben Jones | 70 | 475,318 |

## Trainer—Money Won (Cont.)

| Year | Trainer | Wins | Winnings ($) | Year | Trainer | Wins | Winnings ($) |
|---|---|---|---|---|---|---|---|
| 1942 | John M. Gaver Sr | 48 | 406,547 | 1969 | Elliott Burch | 26 | 1,067,936 |
| 1943 | Plain Ben Jones | 73 | 267,915 | 1970 | Charlie Whittingham | 82 | 1,302,354 |
| 1944 | Plain Ben Jones | 60 | 601,660 | 1971 | Charlie Whittingham | 77 | 1,737,115 |
| 1945 | Silent Tom Smith | 52 | 510,655 | 1972 | Charlie Whittingham | 79 | 1,734,020 |
| 1946 | Hirsch Jacobs | 99 | 560,077 | 1973 | Charlie Whittingham | 85 | 1,865,385 |
| 1947 | Jimmy Jones | 85 | 1,334,805 | 1974 | Pancho Martin | 166 | 2,408,419 |
| 1948 | Jimmy Jones | 81 | 1,118,670 | 1975 | Charlie Whittingham | 93 | 2,437,244 |
| 1949 | Jimmy Jones | 76 | 978,587 | 1976 | Jack Van Berg | 496 | 2,976,196 |
| 1950 | Preston Burch | 96 | 637,754 | 1977 | Laz Barrera | 127 | 2,715,848 |
| 1951 | John M. Gaver Sr | 42 | 616,392 | 1978 | Laz Barrera | 100 | 3,307,164 |
| 1952 | Plain Ben Jones | 29 | 662,137 | 1979 | Laz Barrera | 98 | 3,608,517 |
| 1953 | Harry Trotsek | 54 | 1,028,873 | 1980 | Laz Barrera | 99 | 2,969,151 |
| 1954 | Willie Molter | 136 | 1,107,860 | 1981 | Charlie Whittingham | 74 | 3,993,302 |
| 1955 | Sunny Jim Fitzsimmons | 66 | 1,270,055 | 1982 | Charlie Whittingham | 63 | 4,587,457 |
| 1956 | Willie Molter | 142 | 1,227,402 | 1983 | D. Wayne Lukas | 78 | 4,267,261 |
| 1957 | Jimmy Jones | 70 | 1,150,910 | 1984 | D. Wayne Lukas | 131 | 5,835,921 |
| 1958 | Willie Molter | 69 | 1,116,544 | 1985 | D. Wayne Lukas | 218 | 11,155,188 |
| 1959 | Willie Molter | 71 | 847,290 | 1986 | D. Wayne Lukas | 259 | 12,345,180 |
| 1960 | Hirsch Jacobs | 97 | 748,349 | 1987 | D. Wayne Lukas | 343 | 17,502,110 |
| 1961 | Jimmy Jones | 62 | 759,856 | 1988 | D. Wayne Lukas | 318 | 17,842,358 |
| 1962 | Mesh Tenney | 58 | 1,099,474 | 1989 | D. Wayne Lukas | 305 | 16,103,998 |
| 1963 | Mesh Tenney | 40 | 860,703 | 1990 | D. Wayne Lukas | 267 | 14,508,871 |
| 1964 | Bill Winfrey | 61 | 1,350,534 | 1991 | D. Wayne Lukas | 289 | 15,942,223 |
| 1965 | Hirsch Jacobs | 91 | 1,331,628 | 1992 | D. Wayne Lukas | 230 | 9,806,436 |
| 1966 | Eddie Neloy | 93 | 2,456,250 | 1993 | Robert Frankel | 79 | 8,883,252 |
| 1967 | Eddie Neloy | 72 | 1,776,089 | 1994 | D. Wayne Lukas | 147 | 9,247,457 |
| 1968 | Eddie Neloy | 52 | 1,233,101 | | | | |

## Jockey—Money Won

| Year | Jockey | Mts | 1st | 2nd | 3rd | Pct | Winnings ($) |
|---|---|---|---|---|---|---|---|
| 1919 | John Loftus | 177 | 65 | 36 | 24 | .37 | 252,707 |
| 1920 | Clarence Kummer | 353 | 87 | 79 | 48 | .25 | 292,376 |
| 1921 | Earl Sande | 340 | 112 | 69 | 59 | .33 | 263,043 |
| 1922 | Albert Johnson | 297 | 43 | 57 | 40 | .14 | 345,054 |
| 1923 | Earl Sande | 430 | 122 | 89 | 79 | .28 | 569,394 |
| 1924 | Ivan Parke | 844 | 205 | 175 | 121 | .24 | 290,395 |
| 1925 | Laverne Fator | 315 | 81 | 54 | 44 | .26 | 305,775 |
| 1926 | Laverne Fator | 511 | 143 | 90 | 86 | .28 | 361,435 |
| 1927 | Earl Sande | 179 | 49 | 33 | 19 | .27 | 277,877 |
| 1928 | Pony McAtee | 235 | 55 | 43 | 25 | .23 | 301,295 |
| 1929 | Mack Garner | 274 | 57 | 39 | 33 | .21 | 314,975 |
| 1930 | Sonny Workman | 571 | 152 | 88 | 79 | .27 | 420,438 |
| 1931 | Charles Kurtsinger | 519 | 93 | 82 | 79 | .18 | 392,095 |
| 1932 | Sonny Workman | 378 | 87 | 48 | 55 | .23 | 385,070 |
| 1933 | Robert Jones | 471 | 63 | 57 | 70 | .13 | 226,285 |
| 1934 | Wayne D. Wright | 919 | 174 | 154 | 114 | .19 | 287,185 |
| 1935 | Silvio Coucci | 749 | 141 | 125 | 103 | .19 | 319,760 |
| 1936 | Wayne D. Wright | 670 | 100 | 102 | 73 | .15 | 264,000 |
| 1937 | Charles Kurtsinger | 765 | 120 | 94 | 106 | .16 | 384,202 |
| 1938 | Nick Wall | 658 | 97 | 94 | 82 | .15 | 385,161 |
| 1939 | Basil James | 904 | 191 | 165 | 105 | .21 | 353,333 |
| 1940 | Eddie Arcaro | 783 | 132 | 143 | 112 | .17 | 343,661 |
| 1941 | Don Meade | 1164 | 210 | 185 | 158 | .18 | 398,627 |
| 1942 | Eddie Arcaro | 687 | 123 | 97 | 89 | .18 | 481,949 |
| 1943 | John Longden | 871 | 173 | 140 | 121 | .20 | 573,276 |
| 1944 | Ted Atkinson | 1539 | 287 | 231 | 213 | .19 | 899,101 |
| 1945 | John Longden | 778 | 180 | 112 | 100 | .23 | 981,977 |
| 1946 | Ted Atkinson | 1377 | 233 | 213 | 173 | .17 | 1,036,825 |
| 1947 | Douglas Dodson | 646 | 141 | 100 | 75 | .22 | 1,429,949 |
| 1948 | Eddie Arcaro | 726 | 188 | 108 | 98 | .26 | 1,686,230 |
| 1949 | Steve Brooks | 906 | 209 | 172 | 110 | .23 | 1,316,817 |
| 1950 | Eddie Arcaro | 888 | 195 | 153 | 144 | .22 | 1,410,160 |
| 1951 | Bill Shoemaker | 1161 | 257 | 197 | 161 | .22 | 1,329,890 |
| 1952 | Eddie Arcaro | 807 | 188 | 122 | 109 | .23 | 1,859,591 |
| 1953 | Bill Shoemaker | 1683 | 485 | 302 | 210 | .29 | 1,784,187 |
| 1954 | Bill Shoemaker | 1251 | 380 | 221 | 142 | .30 | 1,876,760 |

### Jockey—Money Won (Cont.)

| Year | Jockey | Mts | 1st | 2nd | 3rd | Pct | Winnings ($) |
|------|--------|-----|-----|-----|-----|-----|--------------|
| 1955 | Eddie Arcaro | 820 | 158 | 126 | 108 | .19 | 1,864,796 |
| 1956 | Bill Hartack | 1387 | 347 | 252 | 184 | .25 | 2,343,955 |
| 1957 | Bill Hartack | 1238 | 341 | 208 | 178 | .28 | 3,060,501 |
| 1958 | Bill Shoemaker | 1133 | 300 | 185 | 137 | .26 | 2,961,693 |
| 1959 | Bill Shoemaker | 1285 | 347 | 230 | 159 | .27 | 2,843,133 |
| 1960 | Bill Shoemaker | 1227 | 274 | 196 | 158 | .22 | 2,123,961 |
| 1961 | Bill Shoemaker | 1256 | 304 | 186 | 175 | .24 | 2,690,819 |
| 1962 | Bill Shoemaker | 1126 | 311 | 156 | 128 | .28 | 2,916,844 |
| 1963 | Bill Shoemaker | 1203 | 271 | 193 | 137 | .22 | 2,526,925 |
| 1964 | Bill Shoemaker | 1056 | 246 | 147 | 133 | .23 | 2,649,553 |
| 1965 | Braulio Baeza | 1245 | 270 | 200 | 201 | .22 | 2,582,702 |
| 1966 | Braulio Baeza | 1341 | 298 | 222 | 190 | .22 | 2,951,022 |
| 1967 | Braulio Baeza | 1064 | 256 | 184 | 127 | .24 | 3,088,888 |
| 1968 | Braulio Baeza | 1089 | 201 | 184 | 145 | .18 | 2,835,108 |
| 1969 | Jorge Velasquez | 1442 | 258 | 230 | 204 | .18 | 2,542,315 |
| 1970 | Laffit Pincay Jr | 1328 | 269 | 208 | 187 | .20 | 2,626,526 |
| 1971 | Laffit Pincay Jr | 1627 | 380 | 288 | 214 | .23 | 3,784,377 |
| 1972 | Laffit Pincay Jr | 1388 | 289 | 215 | 205 | .21 | 3,225,827 |
| 1973 | Laffit Pincay Jr | 1444 | 350 | 254 | 209 | .24 | 4,093,492 |
| 1974 | Laffit Pincay Jr | 1278 | 341 | 227 | 180 | .27 | 4,251,060 |
| 1975 | Braulio Baeza | 1190 | 196 | 208 | 180 | .16 | 3,674,398 |
| 1976 | Angel Cordero Jr | 1534 | 274 | 273 | 235 | .18 | 4,709,500 |
| 1977 | Steve Cauthen | 2075 | 487 | 345 | 304 | .23 | 6,151,750 |
| 1978 | Darrol McHargue | 1762 | 375 | 294 | 263 | .21 | 6,188,353 |
| 1979 | Laffit Pincay Jr | 1708 | 420 | 302 | 261 | .25 | 8,183,535 |
| 1980 | Chris McCarron | 1964 | 405 | 318 | 282 | .20 | 7,666,100 |
| 1981 | Chris McCarron | 1494 | 326 | 251 | 207 | .22 | 8,397,604 |
| 1982 | Angel Cordero Jr | 1838 | 397 | 338 | 227 | .22 | 9,702,520 |
| 1983 | Angel Cordero Jr | 1792 | 362 | 296 | 237 | .20 | 10,116,807 |
| 1984 | Chris McCarron | 1565 | 356 | 276 | 218 | .23 | 12,038,213 |
| 1985 | Laffit Pincay Jr | 1409 | 289 | 246 | 183 | .21 | 13,415,049 |
| 1986 | Jose Santos | 1636 | 329 | 237 | 222 | .20 | 11,329,297 |
| 1987 | Jose Santos | 1639 | 305 | 268 | 208 | .19 | 12,407,355 |
| 1988 | Jose Santos | 1867 | 370 | 287 | 265 | .20 | 14,877,298 |
| 1989 | Jose Santos | 1459 | 285 | 238 | 220 | .20 | 13,847,003 |
| 1990 | Gary Stevens | 1504 | 283 | 245 | 202 | .19 | 13,881,198 |
| 1991 | Chris McCarron | 1440 | 265 | 228 | 206 | .18 | 14,441,083 |
| 1992 | Kent Desormeaux | 1568 | 361 | 260 | 208 | .23 | 14,193,006 |
| 1993 | Mike Smith | 1,510 | 343 | 235 | 214 | .23 | 14,008,148 |
| 1994 | Mike Smith | 1,484 | 317 | 250 | 196 | .21 | 15,979,820 |

### Jockey—Races Won

| Year | Jockey | Mts | 1st | 2nd | 3rd | Pct |
|------|--------|-----|-----|-----|-----|-----|
| 1895 | J. Perkins | 762 | 192 | 177 | 129 | .25 |
| 1896 | J. Scherrer | 1093 | 271 | 227 | 172 | .24 |
| 1897 | H. Martin | 803 | 173 | 152 | 116 | .21 |
| 1898 | T. Burns | 973 | 277 | 213 | 149 | .28 |
| 1899 | T. Burns | 1064 | 273 | 173 | 266 | .26 |
| 1900 | C. Mitchell | 874 | 195 | 140 | 139 | .23 |
| 1901 | W. O'Connor | 1047 | 253 | 221 | 192 | .24 |
| 1902 | J. Ranch | 1069 | 276 | 205 | 181 | .26 |
| 1903 | G.C. Fuller | 918 | 229 | 152 | 122 | .25 |
| 1904 | E. Hildebrand | 1169 | 297 | 230 | 171 | .25 |
| 1905 | D. Nicol | 861 | 221 | 143 | 136 | .26 |
| 1906 | W. Miller | 1384 | 388 | 300 | 199 | .28 |
| 1907 | W. Miller | 1194 | 334 | 226 | 170 | .28 |
| 1908 | V. Powers | 1260 | 324 | 204 | 185 | .26 |
| 1909 | V. Powers | 704 | 173 | 121 | 114 | .25 |
| 1910 | G. Garner | 947 | 200 | 188 | 153 | .20 |
| 1911 | T. Koerner | 813 | 162 | 133 | 112 | .20 |
| 1912 | P. Hill | 967 | 168 | 141 | 129 | .17 |
| 1913 | M. Buxton | 887 | 146 | 131 | 136 | .16 |
| 1914 | J. McTaggart | 787 | 157 | 132 | 106 | .20 |
| 1915 | M. Garner | 775 | 151 | 118 | 90 | .19 |
| 1916 | F. Robinson | 791 | 178 | 131 | 124 | .23 |

## Jockey—Races Won *(Cont.)*

| Year | Jockey | Mts | 1st | 2nd | 3rd | Pct |
|------|--------|-----|-----|-----|-----|-----|
| 1917 | W. Crump | 803 | 151 | 140 | 101 | .19 |
| 1918 | F. Robinson | 864 | 185 | 140 | 108 | .21 |
| 1919 | C. Robinson | 896 | 190 | 140 | 126 | .21 |
| 1920 | J. Butwell | 721 | 152 | 129 | 139 | .21 |
| 1921 | C. Lang | 696 | 135 | 110 | 105 | .19 |
| 1922 | M. Fator | 859 | 188 | 153 | 116 | .22 |
| 1923 | I. Parke | 718 | 173 | 105 | 95 | .24 |
| 1924 | I. Parke | 844 | 205 | 175 | 121 | .24 |
| 1925 | A. Mortensen | 987 | 187 | 145 | 138 | .19 |
| 1926 | R. Jones | 1172 | 190 | 163 | 152 | .16 |
| 1927 | L. Hardy | 1130 | 207 | 192 | 151 | .18 |
| 1928 | J. Inzelone | 1052 | 155 | 152 | 135 | .15 |
| 1929 | M. Knight | 871 | 149 | 132 | 133 | .17 |
| 1930 | H.R. Riley | 861 | 177 | 145 | 123 | .21 |
| 1931 | H. Roble | 1174 | 173 | 173 | 155 | .15 |
| 1932 | J. Gilbert | 1050 | 212 | 144 | 160 | .20 |
| 1933 | J. Westrope | 1224 | 301 | 235 | 166 | .25 |
| 1934 | M. Peters | 1045 | 221 | 179 | 147 | .21 |
| 1935 | C. Stevenson | 1099 | 206 | 169 | 146 | .19 |
| 1936 | B. James | 1106 | 245 | 195 | 161 | .22 |
| 1937 | J. Adams | 1265 | 260 | 186 | 177 | .21 |
| 1938 | J. Longden | 1150 | 236 | 168 | 171 | .21 |
| 1939 | D. Meade | 1284 | 255 | 221 | 180 | .20 |
| 1940 | E. Dew | 1377 | 287 | 201 | 180 | .21 |
| 1941 | D. Meade | 1164 | 210 | 185 | 158 | .18 |
| 1942 | J. Adams | 1120 | 245 | 185 | 150 | .22 |
| 1943 | J. Adams | 1069 | 228 | 159 | 171 | .21 |
| 1944 | T. Atkinson | 1539 | 287 | 231 | 213 | .19 |
| 1945 | J.D. Jessop | 1085 | 290 | 182 | 168 | .27 |
| 1946 | T. Atkinson | 1377 | 233 | 213 | 173 | .17 |
| 1947 | J. Longden | 1327 | 316 | 250 | 195 | .24 |
| 1948 | J. Longden | 1197 | 319 | 233 | 161 | .27 |
| 1949 | G. Glisson | 1347 | 270 | 217 | 181 | .20 |
| 1950 | W. Shoemaker | 1640 | 388 | 266 | 230 | .24 |
| 1951 | C. Burr | 1319 | 310 | 232 | 192 | .24 |
| 1952 | A. DeSpirito | 1482 | 390 | 247 | 212 | .26 |
| 1953 | W. Shoemaker | 1683 | 485 | 302 | 210 | .29 |
| 1954 | W. Shoemaker | 1251 | 380 | 221 | 142 | .30 |
| 1955 | W. Hartack | 1702 | 417 | 298 | 215 | .25 |
| 1956 | W. Hartack | 1387 | 347 | 252 | 184 | .25 |
| 1957 | W. Hartack | 1238 | 341 | 208 | 178 | .28 |
| 1958 | W. Shoemaker | 1133 | 300 | 185 | 137 | .26 |
| 1959 | W. Shoemaker | 1285 | 347 | 230 | 159 | .27 |
| 1960 | W. Hartack | 1402 | 307 | 247 | 190 | .22 |
| 1961 | J. Sellers | 1394 | 328 | 212 | 227 | .24 |
| 1962 | R. Ferraro | 1755 | 352 | 252 | 226 | .20 |
| 1963 | W. Blum | 1704 | 360 | 286 | 215 | .21 |
| 1964 | W. Blum | 1577 | 324 | 274 | 170 | .21 |
| 1965 | J. Davidson | 1582 | 319 | 228 | 190 | .20 |
| 1966 | A. Gomez | 996 | 318 | 173 | 142 | .32 |
| 1967 | J. Velasquez | 1939 | 438 | 315 | 270 | .23 |
| 1968 | A. Cordero Jr. | 1662 | 345 | 278 | 219 | .21 |
| 1969 | L. Snyder | 1645 | 352 | 290 | 243 | .21 |
| 1970 | S. Hawley | 1908 | 452 | 313 | 265 | .24 |
| 1971 | L Pincay Jr. | 1627 | 380 | 288 | 214 | .23 |
| 1972 | S. Hawley | 1381 | 367 | 269 | 200 | .27 |
| 1973 | S. Hawley | 1925 | 515 | 336 | 292 | .27 |
| 1974 | C.J. McCarron | 2199 | 546 | 392 | 297 | .25 |
| 1975 | C.J. McCarron | 2194 | 458 | 389 | 305 | .21 |
| 1976 | S. Hawley | 1637 | 413 | 245 | 201 | .25 |
| 1977 | S. Cauthen | 2075 | 487 | 345 | 304 | .23 |
| 1978 | E. Delahoussaye | 1666 | 384 | 285 | 238 | .23 |
| 1979 | D. Gall | 2146 | 479 | 396 | 326 | .22 |
| 1980 | C.J. McCarron | 1964 | 405 | 318 | 282 | .20 |
| 1981 | D. Gall | 1917 | 376 | 305 | 297 | .20 |
| 1982 | P. Day | 1870 | 399 | 326 | 255 | .21 |

### Jockey—Races Won *(Cont.)*

| Year | Jockey | Mts | 1st | 2nd | 3rd | Pct |
|------|--------|-----|-----|-----|-----|-----|
| 1983 | P. Day | 1725 | 454 | 321 | 251 | .26 |
| 1984 | P. Day | 1694 | 399 | 296 | 259 | .24 |
| 1985 | C.W. Antley | 2335 | 469 | 371 | 288 | .20 |
| 1986 | P. Day | 1417 | 429 | 246 | 202 | .30 |
| 1987 | K. Desormeaux | 2207 | 450 | 370 | 294 | .28 |
| 1988 | K. Desormeaux | 1897 | 474 | 295 | 276 | .25 |
| 1989 | K. Desormeaux | 2312 | 598 | 385 | 309 | .25 |
| 1990 | P. Day | 1421 | 364 | 265 | 222 | .26 |
| 1991 | P. Day | 1405 | 430 | 256 | 213 | .31 |
| 1992 | R.A. Baze | 1691 | 433 | 296 | 237 | .25 |
| 1993 | R.A. Baze | 1579 | 410 | 297 | 225 | .26 |
| 1994 | Mike Smith | 1484 | 317 | 250 | 196 | .21 |

## Leading Jockeys—Career Records Through 1994

| Jockey | Years Riding | Mts | 1st | 2nd | 3rd | Win Pct | Winnings ($) |
|--------|-------------|-----|-----|-----|-----|---------|--------------|
| Shoemaker, W. (1990) | 42 | 40,350 | 8,833 | 6,136 | 4,987 | .219 | 123,375,524 |
| Pincay, L. Jr. | 29 | 39,902 | 8,213 | 6,550 | 5,514 | .206 | 183,910,301 |
| Cordero, A. Jr. | 31 | 38,646 | 7,057 | 6,136 | 5,359 | .183 | 164,526,217 |
| Velasquez, J. | 32 | 39,557 | 6,682 | 6,030 | 5,613 | 169 | 123,252,413 |
| Gall, D. | 38 | 37,859 | 6,611 | 5,794 | 5,457 | .176 | 20,837,406 |
| Snyder, L | 35 | 35,681 | 6,388 | 5,030 | 3,440 | .179 | 47,207,289 |
| Gambardella, C. | 39 | 39,018 | 6,349 | 5,953 | 5,353 | .163 | 29,389,041 |
| Day, P. | 22 | 28,591 | 6,308 | 4,833 | 3,975 | .221 | 149,339,825 |
| Hawley, S. | 28 | 29,972 | 6,205 | 4,607 | 3,941 | .207 | 81,883,408 |
| McCarron, C. J. | 20 | 28,967 | 6,074 | 4,794 | 3,964 | .210 | 177,686,550 |
| Longden, J. (1966) | 40 | 32,413 | 6,032 | 4,914 | 4,273 | .186 | 24,665,800 |
| E. Fires | 30 | 38,421 | 5,678 | 4,804 | 4,593 | .148 | 86,450,725 |
| Delahoussaye, E. J. | 25 | 32,656 | 5,375 | 4,710 | 4,523 | .165 | 138,120,927 |
| Vasquez, J. | 35 | 36,436 | 5,153 | 4,630 | 4,421 | .141 | 78,464,935 |
| Arcaro E. (1961) | 31 | 24,092 | 4,779 | 3,807 | 3,302 | .198 | 30,039,543 |
| Baze, R. A. | 21 | 25,774 | 4,749 | 3,994 | 3,564 | .184 | 63,733,355 |
| Brumfield, D. (1989) | 37 | 33,223 | 4,573 | 4,076 | 3,758 | .138 | 43,567,861 |
| Brooks, S. (1975) | 34 | 30,330 | 4,451 | 4,219 | 3,658 | .147 | 18,239,817 |
| Blum, W. (1975) | 22 | 28,673 | 4,382 | 3,913 | 3,350 | .153 | 26,497,189 |
| Hartack, W. (1974) | 22 | 21,535 | 4,272 | 3,370 | 2,871 | .198 | 26,466,758 |
| Maple, E. | 27 | 32,063 | 4,227 | 4,278 | 4,103 | .132 | 97,382,914 |
| Gomez, A. (1980) | 34 | 17,028 | 4,081 | 2,947 | 2,405 | .240 | 11,777,297 |
| Dittfach, H. (1989) | 33 | 33,905 | 4,000 | 4,092 | 6,113 | .118 | 13,506,052 |
| Perret, C. | 28 | 23,847 | 3,946 | 3,450 | 3,165 | .165 | 84,805,894 |
| Grove, P. | 22 | 26,278 | 3,907 | 3,664 | 3,491 | .149 | 15,720,989 |

Note: Records include available statistics for races ridden in foreign countries. Figures in parentheses after jockey's name indicate last year in which he rode.

Leading jockeys courtesy of *The American Racing Manual*, a publication of Daily Racing Form, Inc.

## National Museum of Racing Hall of Fame

### HORSES

Ack Ack (1986, 1966)
Affectionately (1989, 1960)
Affirmed (1980, 1975)
All Along (1990, 1979)
Alsab (1976, 1939)
Alydar (1989, 1975)
American Eclipse (1970, 1814)
Armed (1963, 1941)
Artful (1956, 1902)
Arts and Letters (1993, 1966)
Assault (1964, 1943)
Battleship (1969, 1927)
Bed o'Roses (1976, 1947)
Beldame (1956, 1901)

Ben Brush (1955, 1893)
Bewitch (1977, 1945)
Bimelech (1990, 1937)
Black Gold (1989, 1921)
Black Helen (1991, 1932)
Blue Larkspur (1957, 1926)
Bold Ruler (1973, 1954)
Bon Nouvel (1976, 1960)
Boston (1955, 1833)
Broomstick (1956, 1901)
Buckpasser (1970, 1963)
Busher (1964, 1942)
Bushranger (1967, 1930)
Cafe Prince (1985, 1970)

Carry Back (1975, 1958)
Challedon (1977, 1936)
Chris Evert (1988, 1971)
Cicada (1967, 1959)
Citation (1959, 1945)
Coaltown (1983, 1945)
Colin (1956, 1905)
Commando (1956, 1898)
Count Fleet (1961, 1940)
Crusader (1994, 1923)
Dahlia (1981, 1970)
Damascus (1974, 1964)
Dark Mirage (1974, 1965)
Davona Dale (1985, 1976)

## HORSES (Cont.)

Desert Vixen (1979, 1970)
Devil Diver (1980, 1939)
Discovery (1969, 1931)
Domino (1955, 1891)
Dr. Fager (1971, 1964)
Eight Thirty (1993, 1936)
Elkridge (1966, 1938)
Emperor of Norfolk (1988, 1885)
Equipoise (1957, 1928)
Exterminator (1957, 1915)
Fairmount (1985, 1921)
Fair Play (1956, 1905)
Fashion (1980, 1837)
Firenze (1981, 1884)
Flatterer (1993, 1979)
Foolish Pleasure (1994, 1972)
Forego (1979, 1970)
Gallant Bloom (1977, 1966)
Gallant Fox (1957, 1927)
Gallant Man (1987, 1954)
Gallorette (1962, 1942)
Gamely (1980, 1964)
Genuine Risk (1986, 1977)
Good and Plenty (1956, 1900)
Grey Lag (1957, 1918)
Hamburg (1986, 1895)
Hanover (1955, 1884)
Henry of Navarre (1985, 1891)
Hill Prince (1991, 1947)
Hindoo (1955, 1878)
Imp (1965, 1894)
Jay Trump (1971, 1957)
John Henry (1990, 1975)

Johnstown (1992, 1982)
Jolly Roger (1965, 1922)
Kelso (1967, 1957)
Kentucky (1983, 1861)
Kingston (1955, 1884)
Lady's Secret (1992, 1982)
La Prevoyante (1994, 1970)
L'Escargot (1977, 1963)
Lexington (1955, 1850)
Longfellow (1971, 1867)
Luke Blackburn (1956, 1877)
Majestic Prince (1988, 1966)
Man o'War (1957, 1917)
Miss Woodford (1967, 1880)
Myrtlewood (1979, 1932)
Nashua (1965, 1952)
Native Dancer (1963, 1950)
Native Diver (1978, 1959)
Neji (1966, 1950)
Northern Dancer (1976, 1961)
Oedipus (1978, 1946)
Old Rosebud (1968, 1911)
Omaha (1965, 1932)
Pan Zareta (1972, 1910)
Parole (1984, 1879)
Peter Pan (1956, 1904)
Princess Doreen (1982, 1921)
Princess Rooney (1991, 1980)
Real Delight (1987, 1949)
Regret (1957, 1912)
Reigh Count (1978, 1925)
Roamer (1981, 1911)
Roseben (1956, 1901)

Round Table (1972, 1954)
Ruffian (1976, 1972)
Ruthless (1975, 1864)
Salvator (1955, 1886)
Sarazen (1957, 1921)
Seabiscuit (1958, 1933)
Searching (1978, 1952)
Seattle Slew (1981, 1974)
Secretariat (1974, 1970)
Shuvee (1975, 1966)
Silver Spoon (1978, 1956)
Sir Archy (1955, 1805)
Sir Barton (1957, 1916)
Slew o' Gold (1992, 1980)
Spectacular Bid (1982, 1976)
Stymie (1975, 1941)
Susan's Girl (1976, 1969)
Swaps (1966, 1952)
Sword Dancer (1977, 1956)
Sysonby (1956, 1902)
Ta Wee (1993, 1967)
Ten Broeck (1982, 1872)
Tim Tam (1985, 1955)
Tom Fool (1960, 1949)
Top Flight (1966, 1929)
Tosmah (1984, 1961)
Twenty Grand (1957, 1928)
Twilight Tear (1963, 1941)
Two Lea (1982, 1946)
War Admiral (1958, 1934)
Whirlaway (1959, 1938)
Whisk Broom II (1979, 1907)
Zev (1983, 1920)

Note: Years of election and foaling in parentheses.

# HARNESS RACING

## Major Races

### Hambletonian

| Year | Winner | Driver | Year | Winner | Driver |
|------|--------|--------|------|--------|--------|
| 1926 | Guy McKinney | Nat Ray | 1949 | Miss Tilly | Fred Egan |
| 1927 | Iosola's Worthy | Marvin Childs | 1950 | Lusty Song | Del Miller |
| 1928 | Spenser | W. H. Leese | 1951 | Mainliner | Guy Crippen |
| 1929 | Walter Dear | Walter Cox | 1952 | Sharp Note | Bion Shively |
| 1930 | Hanover's Bertha | Tom Berry | 1953 | Helicopter | Harry Harvey |
| 1931 | Calumet Butler | R. D. McMahon | 1954 | Newport Dream | Del Cameron |
| 1932 | The Marchioness | William Caton | 1955 | Scott Frost | Joe O'Brien |
| 1933 | Mary Reynolds | Ben White | 1956 | The Intruder | Ned Bower |
| 1934 | Lord Jim | Doc Parshall | 1957 | Hickory Smoke | J. Simpson Sr |
| 1935 | Greyhound | Sep Palin | 1958 | Emily's Pride | Flave Nipe |
| 1936 | Rosalind | Ben White | 1959 | Diller Hanover | Frank Ervin |
| 1937 | Shirley Hanover | Henry Thomas | 1960 | Blaze Hanover | Joe O'Brien |
| 1938 | McLin Hanover | Henry Thomas | 1961 | Harlan Dean | James Arthur |
| 1939 | Peter Astra | Doc Parshall | 1962 | A. C.'s Viking | Sanders Russell |
| 1940 | Spencer Scott | Fred Egan | 1963 | Speedy Scot | Ralph Baldwin |
| 1941 | Bill Gallon | Lee Smith | 1964 | Ayres | J. Simpson, Sr |
| 1942 | The Ambassador | Ben White | 1965 | Egyptian Candor | Del Cameron |
| 1943 | Volo Song | Ben White | 1966 | Kerry Way | Frank Ervin |
| 1944 | Yankee Maid | Henry Thomas | 1967 | Speedy Streak | Del Cameron |
| 1945 | Titan Hanover | H. Pownall Sr | 1968 | Nevele Pride | Stanley Dancer |
| 1946 | Chestertown | Thomas Berry | 1969 | Lindy's Pride | H. Beissinger |
| 1947 | Hoot Mon | Sep Palin | 1970 | Timothy T. | J. Simpson, Jr |
| 1948 | Demon Hanover | Harrison Hoyt | 1971 | Speedy Crown | H. Beissinger |

### Hambletonian (Cont.)

| Year | Winner | Driver | Year | Winner | Driver |
|---|---|---|---|---|---|
| 1972 | Super Bowl | Stanley Dancer | 1985 | Prakas | Bill O'Donnell |
| 1973 | Flirth | Ralph Baldwin | 1986 | Nuclear Kosmos | Ulf Thoresen |
| 1974 | Christopher T. | Bill Haughton | 1987 | Mack Lobell | John Campbell |
| 1975 | Bonefish | Stanley Dancer | 1988 | Armbro Goal | John Campbell |
| 1976 | Steve Lobell | Bill Haughton | 1989 | Park Avenue Joe* | Ron Waples |
| 1977 | Green Speed | Bill Haughton | | Probe* | Bill Fahy |
| 1978 | Speedy Somolli | H. Beissinger | 1990 | Harmonious | John Campbell |
| 1979 | Legend Hanover | George Sholty | 1991 | Giant Victory | Jack Moiseyev |
| 1980 | Burgomeister | Bill Haughton | 1992 | Alf Palema | Mickey McNichol |
| 1981 | Shiaway St. Pat | Ray Remmen | 1993 | American Winner | Ron Pierce |
| 1982 | Speed Bowl | Tom Haughton | 1994 | Victory Dream | Michel Lachance |
| 1983 | Duenna | Stanley Dancer | 1995 | Tagliabue | John Campbell |
| 1984 | Historic Freight | Ben Webster | | | |

*Park Avenue Joe and Probe dead-heated for win. Park Avenue Joe finished first in the summary 2-1-1 to Probe's 1-9-1 finish.
Note: Run at 1 mile since 1947.

### Little Brown Jug

| Year | Winner | Driver | Year | Winner | Driver |
|---|---|---|---|---|---|
| 1946 | Ensign Hanover | Wayne Smart | 1971 | Nansemond | Herve Filion |
| 1947 | Forbes Chief | Del Cameron | 1972 | Strike Out | Keith Waples |
| 1948 | Knight Dream | Frank Safford | 1973 | Melvin's Woe | Joe O'Brien |
| 1949 | Good Time | Frank Ervin | 1974 | Armbro Omaha | Bill Haughton |
| 1950 | Dudley Hanover | Del Miller | 1975 | Seatrain | Ben Webster |
| 1951 | Tar Heel | Del Cameron | 1976 | Keystone Ore | Stanley Dancer |
| 1952 | Meadow Rice | Wayne Smart | 1977 | Governor Skipper | John Chapman |
| 1953 | Keystoner | Frank Ervin | 1978 | Happy Escort | William Popfinger |
| 1954 | Adios Harry | Morris MacDonald | 1979 | Hot Hitter | Herve Filion |
| 1955 | Quick Chief | Bill Haughton | 1980 | Niatross | Clint Galbraith |
| 1956 | Noble Adios | John Simpson Sr | 1981 | Fan Hanover | Glen Garnsey |
| 1957 | Torpid | John Simpso Sr | 1982 | Merger | John Campbell |
| 1958 | Shadow Wave | Joe O'Brien | 1983 | Ralph Hanover | Ron Waples |
| 1959 | Adios Butler | Clint Hodgins | 1984 | Colt Fortysix | Chris Boring |
| 1960 | Bullet Hanover | John Simpson Sr | 1985 | Nihilator | Bill O'Donnell |
| 1961 | Henry T. Adios | Stanley Dancer | 1986 | Barberry Spur | Bill O'Donnell |
| 1962 | Lehigh Hanover | Stanley Dancer | 1987 | Jaguar Spur | Dick Stillings |
| 1963 | Overtrick | John Patterson | 1988 | B. J. Scoot | Michel Lachance |
| 1964 | Vicar Hanover | Bill Haughton | 1989 | Goalie Jeff | Michel Lachance |
| 1965 | Bret Hanover | Frank Ervin | 1990 | Beach Towel | Ray Remmen |
| 1966 | Romeo Hanover | George Sholty | 1991 | Precious Bunny | Jack Moiseye |
| 1967 | Best of All | James Hackett | 1992 | Fake Left | Ron Waples |
| 1968 | Rum Customer | Bill Haughton | 1993 | Life Sign | John Campbell |
| 1969 | Laverne Hanover | Bill Haughton | 1994 | Magical Mike | Michel Lachance |
| 1970 | Most Happy Fella | Stanley Dancer | 1995 | Nick's Fantasy | John Campbell |

### Breeders' Crown

| | 1984 | | | 1985 | |
|---|---|---|---|---|---|
| Div | Winner | Driver | Div | Winner | Driver |
| 2PC | Dragon's Lair | Jeff Mallet | 2PC | Robust Hanover | John Campbell |
| 2PF | Amneris | John Campbell | 2PF | Caressable | Herve Filion |
| 3PC | Troublemaker | Bill O'Donnell | 3PC | Nihilator | Bill O'Donnell |
| 3PF | Naughty But Nice | Tommy Haughton | 3PF | Stienam | Buddy Gilmour |
| 2TC | Workaholic | Berndt Lindstedt | 2TC | Express Ride | John Campbell |
| 2TF | Conifer | George Sholty | 2TF | JEF's Spice | Mickey McNichol |
| 3TC | Baltic Speed | Jan Nordin | 3TC | Prakas | John Campbell |
| 3TF | Fancy Crown | Bill O'Donnell | 3TF | Armbro Devona | Bill O'Donnell |
| | | | AP | Division Street | Michel Lachance |
| | | | AT | Sandy Bowl | John Campbell |

Note: 2=Two-year-old; T=Trotter; C=Colt; 3=Three-year-old; P=Pacer; F=Filly; A=Aged; H=Horse; M=Mare.

## Breeders' Crown (Cont.)

### 1986

| Div | Winner | Driver |
|---|---|---|
| 2PC | Sunset Warrior | Bill Gale |
| 2PF | Halcyon | Ray Remmen |
| 3PC | Masquerade | Richard Silverman |
| 3PF | Glow Softly | Ron Waples |
| 2TC | Mack Lobell | John Campbell |
| 2TF | Super Flora | Ron Waples |
| 3TC | Sugarcane Hanover | Ron Waples |
| 3TF | JEF's Spice | Bill O'Donnell |
| APM | Samshu Bluegrass | Michel Lachance |
| ATM | Grades Singing | Herve Filion |
| APH | Forrest Skipper | Lucien Fontaine |
| ATH | Nearly Perfect | Mickey McNichol |

### 1987

| Div | Winner | Driver |
|---|---|---|
| 2PC | Camtastic | Bill O'Donnell |
| 2PF | Leah Almahurst | Bill Fahy |
| 3PC | Call For Rain | Clint Galbraith |
| 3PF | Pacific | Tom Harmer |
| 2TC | Defiant One | Howard Beissinger |
| 2TF | Nan's Catch | Berndt Lindstedt |
| 3TC | Mack Lobell | John Campbell |
| 3TF | Armbro Fling | George Sholty |
| APM | Follow My Star | John Campbell |
| ATM | Grades Singing | Olle Goop |
| APH | Armbro Emerson | Walter Whelan |
| ATH | Sugarcane Hanover | Ron Waples |

### 1988

| Div | Winner | Driver |
|---|---|---|
| 2PC | Kentucky Spur | Dick Stillings |
| 2PF | Central Park West | John Campbell |
| 3PC | Camtastic | Bill O'Donnell |
| 3PF | Sweet Reflection | Bill O'Donnell |
| 2TC | Valley Victory | Bill O'Donnell |
| 2TF | Peace Corps | John Campbell |
| 3TC | Firm Tribute | Mark O'Mara |
| 3TF | Nalda Hanover | Mickey McNichol |
| APM | Anniecrombie | Dave Magee |
| ATM | Armbro Flori | Larry Walker |
| APH | Call For Rain | Clint Galbraith |
| ATH | Mack Lobell | John Campbell |

### 1989

| Div | Winner | Driver |
|---|---|---|
| 2PC | Till We Meet Again | Mickey McNichol |
| 2PF | Town Pro | Doug Brown |
| 3PC | Goalie Jeff | Michel Lachance |
| 3PF | Cheery Hello | John Campbell |
| 2TC | Royal Troubador | Carl Allen |
| 2TF | Delphi's Lobell | Ron Waples |
| 3TC | Esquire Spur | Dick Stillings |
| 3TF | Pace Corps | John Campbell |
| APM | Armbro Feather | John Kopas |
| ATM | Grades Singing | Olle Goop |
| APH | Matt's Scooter | Michel Lachance |
| ATH | Delray Lobell | John Campbell |

### 1990

| Div | Winner | Driver |
|---|---|---|
| 2PC | Artsplace | John Campbell |
| 2PF | Miss Easy | John Campbell |
| 3PC | Beach Towel | Ray Remmen |
| 3PF | Town Pro | Doug Brown |
| 2TC | Crysta's Best | Dick Richardson Jr |
| 2TF | Jean Bi | Jan Nordin |
| 3TC | Embassy Lobell | Michel Lachance |
| 3TF | Me Maggie | Berndt Lindstedt |
| APM | Caesar's Jackpot | Bill Fahy |
| ATM | Peace Corps | Stig Johansson |
| APH | Bay's Fella | Paul MacDonell |
| ATH | No Sex Please | Ron Waples |

### 1991

| Div | Winner | Driver |
|---|---|---|
| 2PC | Digger Almahurst | Doug Brown |
| 2PF | Hazleton Kay | John Campbell |
| 3PC | Three Wizzards | Bill Gale |
| 3PF | Miss Easy | John Campbell |
| 2TC | King Conch | Bill Gale |
| 2TF | Armbro Keepsake | John Campbell |
| 3TC | Giant Victory | Ron Pierce |
| 3TF | Twelve Speed | Ron Waples |
| APM | Delinquent Account | Bill O'Donnell |
| ATM | Me Maggie | Berndt Lindstedt |
| APH | Camluck | Michel Lachance |
| ATH | Billyjojimbob | Paul MacDonell |

### 1992

| Div | Winner | Driver |
|---|---|---|
| 2PC | Village Jiffy | Ron Waples |
| 2PF | Immortality | John Campbell |
| 3PC | Kingsbridge | Roger Mayotte |
| 3PF | So Fresh | John Campbell |
| 2TC | Giant Chill | John Patterson, Jr |
| 2TF | Winky's Goal | Cat Manzi |
| 3TC | Baltic Striker | Michel Lachance |
| 3TF | Imperfection | Michel Lachance |
| APM | Shady Daisy | Ron Pierce |
| ATM | Peace Corps | Torbjorn Jansson |
| APH | Artsplace | John Campbell |
| ATH | No Sex Please | Ron Waples |

### 1993

| Div | Winner | Driver |
|---|---|---|
| 2PC | Expensive Scooter | Jack Moiseyev |
| 2PF | Electric Scooter | Mike LaChance |
| 3PC | Life Sign | John Campbell |
| 3PF | Immortality | John Campbell |
| 2TC | Westgate Crown | John Campbell |
| 2TF | Gleam | Jimmy Takter |
| 3TC | Pine Chip | John Campbell |
| 3TF | Expressway Hanover | Per Henriksen |
| APM | Swing Back | Kelly Sheppard |
| ATM | Lifetime Dream | Paul MacDonnell |
| APH | Staying Together | Bill O'Donnell |
| ATH | Earl | Chris Christoforou Jr |

Note: 2=Two-year-old; T=Trotter; C=Colt; 3=Three-year-old; P=Pacer; F=Filly; A=Aged; H=Horse; M=Mare.

## Breeders' Crown (Cont.)

### 1994

| Div | Winner | Driver |
|---|---|---|
| 2PC | Jenna's Beach Boy | Bill Fahy |
| 2PF | Yankee Cashmere | Peter Wrenn |
| 3PC | Magical Mike | Michel Lachance |
| 3PF | Hardie Hanover | Tim Twaddle |
| 2TC | Eager Seelster | Teddy Jacobs |
| 2TF | Lookout Victory | John Patterson |

### 1994 (Cont.)

| Div | Winner | Driver |
|---|---|---|
| 3TC | Incredible Abe | Italo Tamborrino |
| 3TF | Imageofa Clear Day | Bill O'Donnell |
| APM | Shady Daisy | Michel Lachance |
| ATM | Armbro Keepsake | Stig Johansson |
| APH | Village Jiffy | Paul MacDonell |
| ATH | Pine Chip | John Campbell |

Note: 2=Two-year-old; T=Trotter; C=Colt; 3=Three-year-old; P=Pacer; F=Filly; A=Aged; H=Horse; M=Mare.

# Triple Crown Winners

## Trotting

Trotting's Triple Crown consists of the Hambletonian (first run in 1926), the Kentucky Futurity (first run in 1893), and the Yonkers Trot (known as the Yonkers Futurity when it began in 1955).

| Year | Horse | Owner | Breeder | Trainer & Driver |
|---|---|---|---|---|
| 1955 | Scott Frost | S.A. Camp Farms | Est of W. N. Reynolds | Joe O'Brien |
| 1963 | Speedy Scot | Castleton Farms | Castleton Farms | Ralph Baldwin |
| 1964 | Ayres | Charlotte Sheppard | Charlotte Sheppard | John Simpson Sr |
| 1968 | Nevele Pride | Nevele Acres & Lou Resnick | Mr & Mrs E. C. Quin | Stanley Dancer |
| 1969 | Lindy's Pride | Lindy Farm | Hanover Shoe Farms | Howard Beissinger |
| 1972 | Super Bowl | Rachel Dancer & Rose Hild Breeding Farm | Stoner Creek Stud | Stanley Dancer |

## Pacing

Pacing's Triple Crown consists of the Cane Pace (called the Cane Futurity when it began in 1955), the Little Brown Jug (first run in 1946), and the Messenger Stake (first run in 1956).

| Year | Horse | Owner | Breeder | Trainer/Driver |
|---|---|---|---|---|
| 1959 | Adios Butler | Paige West & Angelo Pellillo | R. C. Carpenter | Paige West/Clint Hodgins |
| 1965 | Bret Hanover | Richard Downing | Hanover Shoe Farms | Frank Ervin |
| 1966 | Romeo Hanover | Lucky Star Stables & Morton Finder | Hanover Shoe Farms | Jerry Silverman/ William Meyer (Cane) & George Sholty (Jug & Messenger) |
| 1968 | Rum Customer | Kennilworth Farms & L. C. Mancuso | Mr. & Mrs. R. C. Larkin | Bill Haughton |
| 1970 | Most Happy Fella | Egyptian Acres Stable | Stoner Creek Stud | Stanley Dancer |
| 1980 | Niatross | Niagara Acres, C. Galbraith & Niatross Stables | Niagara Acres | Clint Galbraith |
| 1983 | Ralph Hanover | Waples Stable, Pointsetta Stable, Grant's Direct Stable & P. J. Baugh | Hanover Shoe Farms | Stew Firlotte/Ron Waples |

# Awards

## Horse of the Year

| Year | Horse | Gait | Owner | Year | Horse | Gait | Owner |
|---|---|---|---|---|---|---|---|
| 1947 | Victory Song | T | Castleton Farm | 1956 | Scott Frost | T | S. A. Camp Farms |
| 1948 | Rodney | T | R. H. Johnston | 1957 | Torpid | P | Sherwood Farm |
| 1949 | Good Time | P | William Cane | 1958 | Emily's Pride | T | Walnut Hall and Castleton Farms |
| 1950 | Proximity | T | Ralph and Gordon Verhurst | 1959 | Bye Bye Byrd | P | Mr. and Mrs. Rex Larkin |
| 1951 | Pronto Don | T | Hayes Fair Acres Stable | 1960 | Adios Butler | P | Adios Butler Syndicate |
| 1952 | Good Time | P | William Cane | 1961 | Adios Butler | P | Adios Butler Syndicate |
| 1953 | Hi Lo's Forbes | P | Mr. and Mrs. Earl Wagner | 1962 | Su Mac Lad | T | I. W. Berkemeyer |
| 1954 | Stenographer | T | Max Hempt | 1963 | Speedy Scot | T | Castleton Farm |
| 1955 | Scott Frost | T | S. A. Camp Farms | 1964 | Bret Hanover | P | Richard Downing |

## Horse of the Year (Cont.)

| Year | Horse | Gait | Owner | Year | Horse | Gait | Owner |
|------|-------|------|-------|------|-------|------|-------|
| 1965 | Bret Hanover | P | Richard Downing | 1981 | Fan Hanover | P | Dr. J. Glen Brown |
| 1966 | Bret Hanover | P | Richard Downing | 1982 | Cam Fella | P | Norm Clements, Norm Faulkner |
| 1967 | Nevele Pride | T | Nevele Acres | | | | |
| 1968 | Nevele Pride | T | Nevele Acres, Louis Resnick | 1983 | Cam Fella | P | JEF's Standardbred, Norm Clements, Norm Faulkner |
| 1969 | Nevele Pride | T | Nevele Acres, Louis Resnick | 1984 | Fancy Crown | T | Fancy Crown Stable |
| 1970 | Fresh Yankee | T | Duncan MacDonald | 1985 | Nihilator | P | Wall Street-Nihilator Syndicate |
| 1971 | Albatross | P | Albatross Stable | | | | |
| 1972 | Albatross | P | Amicable Stable | 1986 | Forrest Skipper | P | Forrest L. Bartlett |
| 1973 | Sir Dalrae | P | A La Carte Racing Stable | | | | |
| 1974 | Delmonica Hanover | T | Delvin Miller, W. Arnold Hanger | 1987 | Mack Lobell | T | One More Time Stable and Fair Wind Farm |
| 1975 | Savoir | T | Allwood Stable | 1988 | Mack Lobell | T | John Erik Magnusson |
| 1976 | Keystone Ore | P | Mr. and Mrs. Stanley Dancer, Rose Hild Farms, Robert Jones | 1989 | Matt's Scooter | P | Gordon and Illa Rumpel, Charles Jurasvinski |
| | | | | 1990 | Beach Towel | P | Uptown Stables |
| 1977 | Green Speed | T | Beverly Lloyds | 1991 | Precious Bunny | P | R. Peter Heffering |
| 1978 | Abercrombie | P | Shirley Mitchell, L. Keith Bulen | 1992 | Artsplace | P | George Segal |
| 1979 | Niatross | P | Niagara Acres, Clint Galbraith | 1993 | Staying Together | P | Robert Hamather |
| 1980 | Niatross | P | Niatross Syndicate, Niagara Acres, Clint Galbraith | 1994 | Cam's Card Shark | P | Jeffrey S. Snyder |

Note: Balloting is conducted by the U.S Trotting Association and U.S. Harness Writers Association.

## Leading Drivers—Money Won

| Year | Driver | Winnings ($) | Year | Driver | Winnings ($) |
|------|--------|--------------|------|--------|--------------|
| 1946 | Thomas Berry | 121,933 | 1971 | Herve Filion | 1,915,945 |
| 1947 | H. C. Fitzpatrick | 133,675 | 1972 | Herve Filion | 2,473,265 |
| 1948 | Ralph Baldwin | 153,222 | 1973 | Herve Filion | 2,233,303 |
| 1949 | Clint Hodgins | 184,108 | 1974 | Herve Filion | 3,474,315 |
| 1950 | Del Miller | 306,813 | 1975 | Carmine Abbatiello | 2,275,093 |
| 1951 | John Simpson Sr | 333,316 | 1976 | Herve Filion | 2,278,634 |
| 1952 | Bill Haughton | 311,728 | 1977 | Herve Filion | 2,551,058 |
| 1953 | Bill Haughton | 374,527 | 1978 | Carmine Abbatiello | 3,344,457 |
| 1954 | Bill Haughton | 415,577 | 1979 | John Campbell | 3,308,984 |
| 1955 | Bill Haughton | 599,455 | 1980 | John Campbell | 3,732,306 |
| 1956 | Bill Haughton | 572,945 | 1981 | Bill O'Donnell | 4,065,608 |
| 1957 | Bill Haughton | 586,950 | 1982 | Bill O'Donnell | 5,755,067 |
| 1958 | Bill Haughton | 816,659 | 1983 | John Campbell | 6,104,082 |
| 1959 | Bill Haughton | 771,435 | 1984 | Bill O'Donnell | 9,059,184 |
| 1960 | Del Miller | 567,282 | 1985 | Bill O'Donnell | 10,207,372 |
| 1961 | Stanley Dancer | 674,723 | 1986 | John Campbell | 9,515,055 |
| 1962 | Stanley Dancer | 760,343 | 1987 | John Campbell | 10,186,495 |
| 1963 | Bill Haughton | 790,086 | 1988 | John Campbell | 11,148,565 |
| 1964 | Stanley Dancer | 1,051,538 | 1989 | John Campbell | 9,738,450 |
| 1965 | Bill Haughton | 889,943 | 1990 | John Campbell | 11,620,878 |
| 1966 | Stanley Dancer | 1,218,403 | 1991 | Jack Moiseyev | 9,568,468 |
| 1967 | Bill Haughton | 1,305,773 | 1992 | John Campbell | 8,202,108 |
| 1968 | Bill Haughton | 1,654,463 | 1993 | John Campbell | 9,926,482 |
| 1969 | Del Insko | 1,635,463 | 1994 | John Campbell | 9,834,139 |
| 1970 | Herve Filion | 1,647,837 | | | |

# Motor Sports

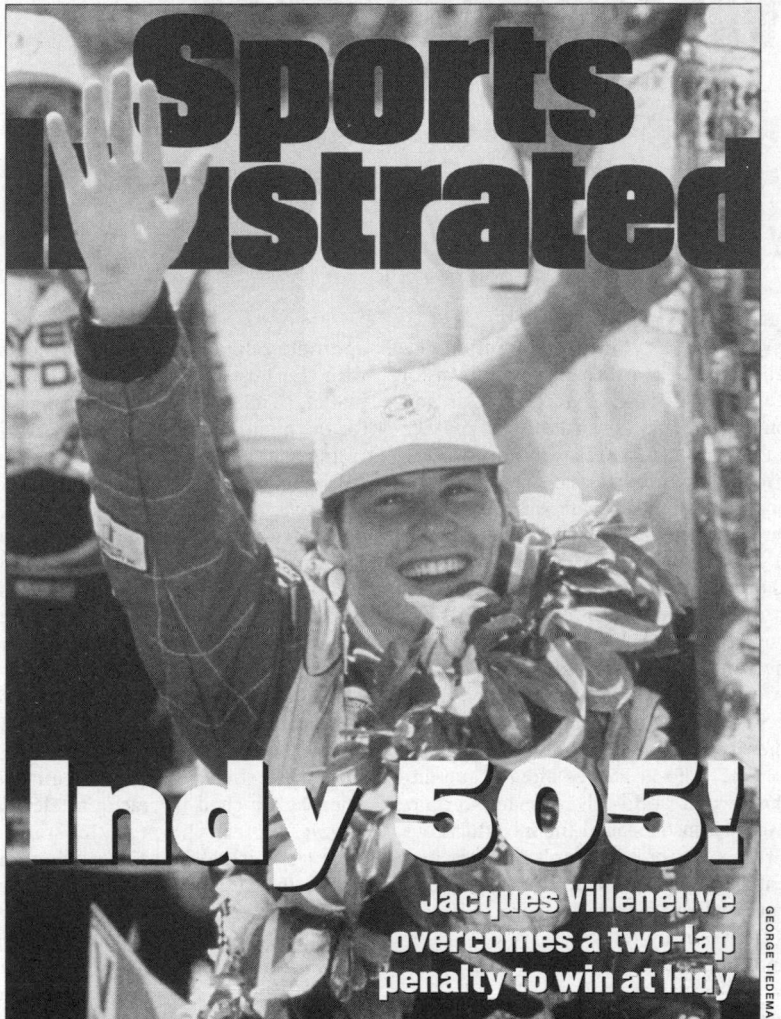

**Sports Illustrated**

**Indy 505!**

Jacques Villeneuve
overcomes a two-lap
penalty to win at Indy

GEORGE TIEDEMANN

# Youth Movement

## Showing no respect for their elders, three young stars drove into the spotlight in '95
## by Ed Hinton

NEVER HAD youth commanded the limelights of the world's big three forms of motor racing—NASCAR, Indy Car and Formula One—as consistently as in 1995. With veteran stars obscured across the board, and the prodigies so savvy and sure, the only remaining debate was over which of three youngsters was the hottest property in all of auto racing.

There was Jeff Gordon of NASCAR, who didn't even turn 24 until halfway through the season in which he emerged as something stock car racing fans hadn't known before—a bona fide darling in an otherwise rough-cut, hard-bitten realm.

There was Michael Schumacher of Formula One, who at 26 was already gunning for his second world driving championship, and in midseason signed the most lucrative contract ever for one man's services at a steering wheel for a single season—at least $24 million, and perhaps as high as $30 million, from Ferrari, for 1996.

And then there was Jacques Villeneuve, who at 24 won the Indianapolis 500, then breezed to the CART Indy Car season championship, then signed to jump to Formula One in 1996—not for the customary

apprenticeship with a marginal team, but with the best racing organization on the planet, Williams Grand Prix Engineering, for the highest rookie-season salary in auto racing history, $6 million.

Depending on the criteria for "hotness," as sports agents call lucrative charisma nowadays, a case could be made for each of the three as the hottest driver in the world.

But it was Villeneuve who soared farthest, fastest. He is the son of the late Gilles Villeneuve, the Quebecois Formula One star who was killed in a crash in 1982, when Jacques was 11. Jacques was born in Quebec, raised in Monaco and schooled in Switzerland—and therefore wasn't even sure what the Indy 500 was until 1992, when he watched the race on television in Japan. Yet in his rookie season he appeared virtually out of nowhere at the end of the 1994 Indy 500 to finish second and hint powerfully at what was to come.

Suddenly, during the week leading up to the 1995 running of the 500, Villeneuve found himself the consensus favorite among most observers. During time trials the 1993 and '94 winners of the race, Penske teammates Emerson Fittipaldi and

**Fox survived his terrifying wreck in the opening seconds at Indy.**

Al Unser Jr., had been bewildered to find their 1995 Penske-Mercedes cars unaccountably, and incurably, ill-engineered for the old 2.5-mile Indianapolis Motor Speedway oval and had failed to make the field at all. With a dark horse, Scott Brayton, on the pole with a suspect stock-block engine in his car, young Villeneuve, with his reputation for smooth, patient driving, was elevated to prerace favorite.

Villeneuve delivered, despite the severest penalty any Indy winner has ever had to overcome, two laps, a judgment levied against him by United States Auto Club officials on the 39th of the race's 200 laps, for failing to fall in behind the pace car during a caution period. By running conservatively to get better fuel mileage, Villeneuve was able to stay out on the track while leaders pitted during ensuing caution periods and made up his two laps. Then, near the end of the race, retributive justice set up Villeneuve for the win. With 10 laps to go, another Canadian driver, Scott Goodyear of Toronto, who appeared to be

in command of the race at that point, passed the pace car a split-second before the final caution period ended and was himself penalized, leaving Villeneuve in the lead for keeps.

Goodyear and his car owner, Steve Horne, protested vehemently but to no avail. The official ruling stood, and public sentiment for them was hard to muster, especially after they'd lost to Villeneuve, who himself had been victim of a penalty whose harshness was suspect. After all, as Villeneuve's team owner, Barry Green, pointed out jubilantly in the moments after the checkered flag, "We've just won the first Indianapolis 505!"

The race had been marred from the opening seconds by an incident darker by far than the driver penalties. Just after the green flag signaled the start of the race, the car of Stan Fox, a veteran of midget and sprint car racing whose custom was to move up to Indy Cars annually just for the 500, veered suddenly and inexplicably to the right, making contact with Eddie Cheever's car before slamming horrifically into the retaining wall between Turns 1 and 2 of the track. Fox suffered severe head

**Gordon and his wife Brooke shared the winner's circle at the Bristol 500.**

injuries, and lay in critical condition at Indianapolis's Methodist Hospital as the race concluded. But in the ensuing weeks, Fox began an amazing recovery, and in July left the hospital able to walk and talk, though months of rehabilitation remained ahead for him.

The Indy 500 win, coupled with a victory in the CART Indy Car season-opening Miami Grand Prix, put Villeneuve firmly in the points lead for the season championship, and he never faltered from first place. While veterans such as Unser, Fittipaldi and Michael Andretti struggled through sporadic seasons, Villeneuve's only real challenge for the championship came from another young driver, 26-year-old Robby Gordon (no relation to Jeff Gordon), and even that challenge was snuffed in July. During practice for the Marlboro 500 at Michigan International Speedway, Gordon crashed due to a suspension failure and was knocked unconscious. Though he wasn't seriously injured, Indy Car rules require any driver who has suffered unconsciousness to wait seven days before racing again. Gordon missed the Michigan race and therefore scored no points that week-

end, leaving Villeneuve in clear command of the championship standings.

Dominant as Villeneuve was, there were rumblings even as he won the Indy 500 that he might not return to defend that victory—that his heart lay in his father's old realm, Formula One, and that the youngster had the superb skills to match his ambitions. But not since Mario Andretti in the 1970s had a driver with an Indy Car background landed a truly competitive ride in Formula One (Michael Andretti had failed miserably in F/1 in 1993, with a McLaren team that wasn't nearly up to its usual competitiveness). During the summer of '95, two major F/1 team bosses, Flavio Briatore of Benetton and Ron Dennis of McLaren, said publicly that they weren't interested in young Villeneuve. So it was expected that if Villeneuve went to F/1 in '96, he would have to settle for at least one "learning year" with a lesser team, a non-winner.

Surprisingly, it was the two hardest taskmasters for a driver to please in all of Formula One, team owner Frank Williams and his chief engineer, Patrick Head, who gave Villeneuve a chance with their Didcot, England–based operation. Villeneuve tested a Williams car for them and wowed them, and they signed him to replace David Coulthard of Scotland and pair with Damon Hill, son of the late two-time world champion Graham Hill, on the Williams team.

And so in 1996, a North American–born driver will have a realistic chance to win Formula One races for the first time since, well, Gilles Villeneuve in the early '80s.

Jeff Gordon was the youngest of the young stars, and was clearly up against the oldest, savviest, toughest competition of the three. Headed down the stretch of the 31-race NASCAR Winston Cup schedule—the most grueling in major motor sports—Gordon, in his third year of competition in stock car racing's top series, led the season point standings, with three vastly more experienced drivers on his tail: Sterling Marlin (age 38, in his 20th year of Winston

**Earnhardt (3) couldn't keep Marlin at bay in the Daytona 500.**

Cup competition), Mark Martin (36, in his 15th year) and seven-time Winston Cup champion Dale Earnhardt (44, in his 21st year). And three more older drivers, brothers Bobby and Terry Labonte, 31 and 38, respectively, and Dale Jarrett, 38, though not factors in the points race, combined to dominate late summer in outright wins and slow Gordon's bid to run away in the season standings.

The NASCAR season began as a premature celebration of what was expected to be an Earnhardt cakewalk to a third straight championship and a record eighth career Winston Cup, breaking his tie with the legendary Richard Petty for career season titles.

Even Earnhardt's traditional heartbreak in the season-opener seemed to be a good omen for him. Marlin won his second straight Daytona 500 and Earnhardt finished second, failing for the 17th straight year to win NASCAR's most-prestigious race. That seemed to project a repetition of Earnhardt's usual course of recent years: Lose the Daytona 500 by a nose, win the Winston Cup by a mile.

But Gordon began a post-Daytona blitz,

winning three of the season's first six races. Though Gordon didn't get his fourth win until the season's midway point, the Pepsi 400 at Daytona in July, he was by then bearing down on the lead in the point standings by virtue of consistently high finishes in races he didn't win outright. Meanwhile Earnhardt, through the shank of the season, finished out of the top 20 a whopping seven times, his most inconsistent stretch in three years.

And so nearly all season, the polite, darkly handsome Gordon, widespread favorite of new-breed NASCAR fans, overshadowed the hard-nosed Earnhardt as the leading figure of America's most popular racing series. Winston Cup attendance, after several years in the three-million-plus per season range, had jumped to 4.9 million in 1994 and was expected to top five million in '95, by the season finale on Nov. 12 at Atlanta Motor Speedway. Though there were several factors behind the big increases the past two seasons—including the addition of the Brickyard 400 at Indianapolis Motor Speedway, with its more than 300,000 seats, to the '94 and '95 Winston Cup schedules—Gordon clearly appealed to an influx of younger, female NASCAR fans. But Gordon lacked one basic measure of the hottest driver, a bid-

ding war for his services, because he was in the third year of a five-year contract with his team owner, Rick Hendrick.

Schumacher, peerless in the global fishbowl of Formula One since the death of three-time world champion Ayrton Senna in May 1994, overcame more vulnerability to distraction than his NASCAR and Indy Car counterparts in '95. In the final year of his contract with Benetton, the young German kept his focus on driving despite the monumental auction swirling around him—his manager, Willi Weber, had stipulated that the bidding for '96 *open* at $20 million a year, which in itself would have been a near-record salary—and despite recurring controversy between the Benetton team and the Federation Internationale de l'Automobile, F/1's governing body.

The FIA initially stripped Schumacher of 10 world championship points earned for winning the season-opening Grand Prix of Brazil on March 26, because the gasoline in his Benetton didn't match the chromatographic "fingerprint" of the fuel designated by the team to the FIA before the season. At first Schumacher appeared headed for a season exasperatingly similar to 1994, in which he'd become the youngest driver ever to win the world championship despite FIA sanctions that banned him from two races and stripped him of points earned in two others that year. But the '95 season set-

tled down to a level playing field for him on April 13, when an FIA appeals tribunal restored his points from Brazil after finding that the fuel mix-up was not advantageous and was simply the result of a shipping mistake by Benetton's fuel supplier, Elf.

Perhaps Schumacher's greatest distraction of '95 was personal. In what quickly turned into a two-man contest for the world championship, Schumacher missed midseason opportunities to put away his increasingly bitter rival, 32-year-old Damon Hill. The rivalry reached a crescendo in July at the British Grand Prix, when Schumacher, leading, was aggressively trying to block Hill, and Hill was struggling to pass in a corner, and they wrecked each other. Next, at the German Grand Prix, Hill fell out early and Schumacher won, increasing his points lead to a borderline-insurmountable 21. Still, he couldn't break the championship chase open. At the next Grand Prix, in Hungary, it was Hill who won and Schumacher who fell out early, and Hill was back to within 11 points. Then in Belgium, Schumacher and Hill finished one-two in the rain, leaving Schumacher 15 points ahead but still not cakewalking to the championship of a season that would end Nov. 12 with the Grand Prix of Australia in Adelaide.

Hot as Schumacher was in sheer money terms, and cool as Gordon remained through a sizzling summer against the best quality and quantity of competition in all the world's motor racing, it was Villeneuve who won the world's biggest race, then dominated his series more relentlessly and took the largest leap to a bigger challenge at season's end. And so, of the three, Jacques Villeneuve emerged as the hottest of the hot.

# FOR THE RECORD·1994–1995

## CART Racing

### Indianapolis 500

Results of the 79th running of the Indianapolis 500 and 6th round of the 1995 Indy Car season. Held Sunday, May 28, at the 2.5-mile Indianapolis Motor Speedway in Speedway, IN.

Distance, 500 miles; starters, 33; time of race, 3:15:18; average speed, 153.616 mph; margin of victory, 2.5 seconds; caution flags, 9 for 58 laps; lead changes, 23 among 10 drivers.

#### TOP 10 FINISHERS

| Pos | Driver (start pos.) | Car | Qual. Speed | Laps | Status |
|---|---|---|---|---|---|
| 1 | Jacques Villeneuve (5) | Reynard-Ford | 228.397 | 200 | running |
| 2 | *Christian Fittipaldi (27) | Reynard-Ford | 226.387 | 200 | running |
| 3 | Bobby Rahal (21) | Lola-Mercedes | 227.086 | 200 | running |
| 4 | *Eliseo Salazar (24) | Lola-Ford | 225.028 | 200 | running |
| 5 | Robby Gordon (7) | Reynard-Ford | 227.531 | 200 | running |
| 6 | Mauricio Gugelmin (6) | Reynard-Ford | 227.935 | 200 | running |
| 7 | Arie Luyendyk (2) | Lola-Menard | 231.036 | 200 | running |
| 8 | Teo Fabi (15) | Reynard-Ford | 225.918 | 199 | running |
| 9 | Danny Sullivan (18) | Reynard-Ford | 225.507 | 199 | running |
| 10 | Hiro Matsushita (10) | Reynard-Ford | 226.872 | 199 | running |

### 1995 Indy Car Results

| Date | Track/Distance | Winner (start pos.) | Car | Avg Speed |
|---|---|---|---|---|
| Mar 5 | Miami Grand Prix | Jacques Villeneuve (8) | Reynard-Ford | 82.801 |
| Mar 19 | IndyCar Australia | Paul Tracy (9) | Lola-Ford | 92.335 |
| Apr 2 | Phoenix 200 | Robby Gordon (9) | Reynard-Ford | 133.980 |
| Apr 9 | Long Beach Grand Prix | Al Unser Jr (4) | Penske-Mercedes | 91.442 |
| Apr 23 | Nazareth Grand Prix | Emerson Fittipaldi (4) | Penske-Mercedes | 131.305 |
| May 28 | Indianapolis 500 | Jacques Villeneuve (5) | Reynard-Ford | 153.616 |
| June 4 | Milwaukee 200 | Paul Tracy (7) | Lola-Ford | 137.304 |
| June 11 | Detroit Grand Prix | Robby Gordon (1) | Reynard-Ford | 83.499 |
| June 25 | Portland 200 | Al Unser Jr (3) | Penske-Mercedes | 103.933 |
| July 9 | Elkhart Lake 200 | Jacques Villeneuve (1) | Reynard-Ford | 103.901 |
| July 16 | Indy Toronto | Michael Andretti (6) | Lola-Ford | 94.787 |
| July 23 | Cleveland Grand Prix | Jacques Villeneuve (2) | Reynard-Ford | 130.113 |
| July 30 | Michigan 500 | Scott Pruett (12) | Lola-Ford | 159.676 |
| Aug 13 | Mid-Ohio 200 | Al Unser Jr (8) | Penske-Mercedes | 107.110 |
| Aug 20 | New England 200 | *Andre Ribeiro (1) | Reynard-Honda | 134.203 |
| Sep 3 | Indy Vancouver | Al Unser Jr (9) | Penske-Mercedes | 95.571 |
| Sep 10 | Monterey Grand Prix | *Gil de Ferran (3) | Reynard-Mercedes | 98.493 |

*Rookie. Note: Distances are in miles.

### Championship Standings

| Driver | Starts | Wins | Pts |
|---|---|---|---|
| Jacques Villeneuve | 17 | 4 | 172 |
| Al Unser Jr | 16 | 4 | 161 |
| Bobby Rahal | 17 | 0 | 128 |
| Michael Andretti | 17 | 1 | 123 |
| Robby Gordon | 16 | 2 | 121 |
| Paul Tracy | 17 | 2 | 115 |
| Scott Pruett | 17 | 1 | 112 |
| Jimmy Vasser | 17 | 0 | 92 |
| Teo Fabi | 17 | 0 | 83 |
| Mauricio Gugelmin | 17 | 0 | 80 |

# NASCAR Racing

## Daytona 500

Results of the opening round of the 1995 Winston Cup series. Held Sunday, February 19, at the 2.5-mile high-banked Daytona International Speedway.

Distance, 500 miles; starters, 42; time of race, 3:31:42; average speed, 141.710 mph; margin of victory, .61 second; caution flags, 10 for 41 laps; lead changes, 12 among 7 drivers.

### TOP 10 FINISHERS

| Pos | Driver (start pos.) | Car | Laps | Winnings ($) |
|---|---|---|---|---|
| 1 | Sterling Marlin (3) | Chevrolet | 200 | 300,460 |
| 2 | Dale Earnhardt (2) | Chevrolet | 200 | 212,250 |
| 3 | Mark Martin (6) | Ford | 200 | 153,700 |
| 4 | Ted Musgrave (12) | Ford | 200 | 111,200 |
| 5 | Dale Jarrett (1) | Ford | 200 | 119,855 |
| 6 | Michael Waltrip (15) | Pontiac | 200 | 86,205 |
| 7 | Steve Grissom (35) | Chevrolet | 200 | 72,065 |
| 8 | Terry Labonte (11) | Chevrolet | 200 | 78,940 |
| 9 | Ken Schrader (9) | Chevrolet | 200 | 70,140 |
| 10 | Morgan Shepherd (30) | Ford | 200 | 66,690 |

## Late 1994 NASCAR Results

| Date | Track/Distance | Winner (start pos.) | Car | Avg Speed | Winnings ($) |
|---|---|---|---|---|---|
| Oct 23 | Rockingham 500 | Dale Earnhardt (20) | Chevrolet | 126.408 | 60,600 |
| Oct 30 | Phoenix 500K | Terry Labonte (19) | Chevrolet | 107.463 | 67,885 |
| Nov 13 | Atlanta 500 | Mark Martin (5) | Ford | 148.982 | 104,200 |

Note: Distances are in miles unless followed by * (laps) or K (kilometers).

## 1995 NASCAR Results (through October 1)

| Date | Track/Distance | Winner (start pos.) | Car | Avg Speed | Winnings ($) |
|---|---|---|---|---|---|
| Feb 19 | Daytona 500 | Sterling Marlin (3) | Chevrolet | 141.710 | 300,460 |
| Feb 26 | Rockingham 500 | Jeff Gordon (1) | Chevrolet | 125.305 | 167,600 |
| Mar 5 | Richmond 400* | Terry Labonte (24) | Chevrolet | 106.425 | 82,950 |
| Mar 12 | Atlanta 500 | Jeff Gordon (3) | Chevrolet | 150.115 | 104,950 |
| Mar 26 | Darlington 400 | Sterling Marlin (5) | Chevrolet | 111.392 | 86,185 |
| Apr 2 | Bristol 500* | Jeff Gordon (2) | Chevrolet | 92.011 | 67,645 |
| Apr 9 | N Wilkesboro 400* | Dale Earnhardt (5) | Chevrolet | 102.424 | 77,400 |
| Apr 23 | Martinsville 500* | Rusty Wallace (15) | Ford | 72.145 | 61,945 |
| Apr 30 | Talladega 500 | Mark Martin (3) | Ford | 178.902 | 98,565 |
| May 7 | Sonoma 300K | Dale Earnhardt (4) | Chevrolet | 70.681 | 74,860 |
| May 28 | World 600 | Bobby Labonte (2) | Chevrolet | 151.952 | 163,850 |
| June 4 | Dover Downs 500 | Kyle Petty (37) | Pontiac | 119.880 | 77,655 |
| June 11 | Pocono 500 | Terry Labonte (27) | Chevrolet | 137.720 | 71,175 |
| June 18 | Michigan 400 | Bobby Labonte (19) | Chevrolet | 134.141 | 84,080 |
| July 1 | Daytona 400 | Jeff Gordon (3) | Chevrolet | 166.976 | 96,580 |
| July 9 | New Hampshire 300* | Jeff Gordon (21) | Chevrolet | 107.029 | 160,300 |
| July 16 | Pocono 500 | Dale Jarrett (15) | Ford | 134.038 | 72,970 |
| July 23 | Talladega 500 | Sterling Martin (1) | Chevrolet | 173.188 | 219,425 |
| Aug 5 | Indianapolis 400 | Dale Earnhardt (13) | Chevrolet | 155.206 | 565,600 |
| Aug 13 | Watkins Glen 90* | Mark Martin (1) | Ford | 103.030 | 95,290 |
| Aug 20 | Michigan 400 | Bobby Labonte (1) | Chevrolet | 157.739 | 97,445 |
| Aug 26 | Bristol 500* | Terry Labonte (2) | Chevrolet | 81.979 | 66,940 |
| Sept 3 | Southern 500 | Jeff Gordon (5) | Chevrolet | 121.231 | 70,630 |
| Sept 9 | Richmond 400 | Rusty Wallace (7) | Ford | 104.459 | 64,515 |
| Sept 17 | Dover 500 | Jeff Gordon (2) | Chevrolet | 124.740 | 74,655 |
| Sept 24 | Martinsville 500* | Dale Earnhardt (2) | Chevrolet | 73.963 | 78,150 |
| Oct 1 | N Wilkesboro 400* | Mark Martin (2) | Ford | 102.998 | 71,590 |

Note: Distances are in miles unless followed by * (laps) or K (kilometers).

## NASCAR Racing *(Cont.)*

### 1994 Winston Cup Standings

| Driver | Car | Starts | Wins | Pts |
|---|---|---|---|---|
| Dale Earnhardt | Chevy | 31 | 4 | 4694 |
| Mark Martin | Ford | 31 | 2 | 4250 |
| Rusty Wallace | Ford | 31 | 8 | 4207 |
| Ken Schrader | Chevy | 31 | — | 4060 |
| Ricky Rudd | Ford | 31 | 1 | 4050 |
| Morgan Shepherd | Ford | 31 | — | 4029 |
| Terry Labonte | Chevy | 31 | 3 | 3876 |
| Jeff Gordon | Chevy | 31 | 2 | 3776 |
| Darrell Waltrip | Chevy | 31 | — | 3688 |
| Bill Elliott | Ford | 31 | 1 | 3617 |

### 1994 Winston Cup Driver Winnings

| Driver | Winnings ($) |
|---|---|
| Dale Earnhardt | 3,400,733 |
| Rusty Wallace | 1,959,072 |
| Jeff Gordon | 1,799,523 |
| Mark Martin | 1,678,906 |
| Ernie Irvan | 1,311,522 |
| Geoff Bodine | 1,287,626 |
| Ken Schrader | 1,211,062 |
| Terry Labonte | 1,150,921 |
| Sterling Marlin | 1,140,683 |
| Morgan Shepherd | 1,119,038 |

## Formula One/Grand Prix Racing

### 1995 Formula One Results (through October 1)

| Date | Grand Prix | Winner | Car | Avg Speed |
|---|---|---|---|---|
| Mar 26 | Brazil | Michael Schumacher | Benetton-Renault | 114.06 |
| Apr 9 | Argentina | Damon Hill | Williams-Renault | 115.672 |
| April 30 | San Marino | Damon Hill | Williams-Renault | 113.701 |
| May 14 | Spain | Michael Schumacher | Benetton-Renault | 121.392 |
| May 28 | Monaco | Michael Schumacher | Benetton-Renault | 85.52 |
| June 11 | Canada | Jean Alesi | Ferrari | 106.747 |
| July 2 | France | Michael Schumacher | Benetton-Renault | 115.806 |
| July 16 | Great Britain | Johnny Herbert | Benetton-Renault | 121.595 |
| July 30 | Germany | Michael Schumacher | Benetton-Renault | 133.272 |
| Aug 13 | Hungary | Damon Hill | Williams-Renault | 107.047 |
| Aug 27 | Belgium | Michael Schumacher | Benetton-Renault | 118.878 |
| Sept 10 | Italy | Johnny Herbert | Benetton-Renault | 146.134 |
| Sept 24 | Portugal | David Coulthard | Williams-Renault | 113.949 |
| Oct 1 | Europe | Michael Schumacher | Benetton-Renault | 109.908 |

### 1994 World Championship Standings

Drivers compete in Grand Prix races for the title of World Driving Champion. Below are the top 10 results from the 1994 season. Points are awarded for places 1-6 as follows: 10-6-4-3-2-1.

| Driver, Country | Starts | Wins | Car | Pts |
|---|---|---|---|---|
| Michael Schumacher, Germany | 16 | 8 | Benetton-Ford | 92 |
| Damon Hill, Great Britain | 16 | 6 | Williams-Renault | 91 |
| Gerhard Berger, Austria | 16 | 1 | Ferrari | 41 |
| Mika Hakkinen, Finland | 16 | 0 | McLaren-Mercedes | 26 |
| Jean Alesi, France | 16 | 0 | Ferrari | 24 |
| Ruebens Barrichello, Brazil | 16 | 0 | Jordan-Peugeot | 19 |
| Martin Brundle, Great Britain | 16 | 0 | Ligier-Mugen Honda | 16 |
| David Coulthard, Great Britain | 16 | 0 | Williams-Renault | 14 |
| Nigel Mansell, Great Britain | 16 | 1 | Williams-Renault | 13 |
| Jos Verstappen, Netherlands | 16 | 0 | Lotus-Ford | 10 |

# IMSA Racing

## The 24 Hours of Daytona

Held at the Daytona International Speedway on February 4-5, 1995, the 24 Hours of Daytona annually serves as the opening round for the International Motor Sports Association sports car season.

| Place | Drivers | Car | Distance |
|---|---|---|---|
| 1 | Jeremy Dale, Fredrik Ekblom, Jay Cochran | Olds Spice BDG02 | 685 laps (101.342 mph) |
| 2 | Massimo Sigala, Fabrizio Barbazza, Gianfranco Brancatelli, Elton Julian | Ferrari 333SP | 645 laps |
| 3 | Jim Downing, Butch Hamlet, Tim McAdam, Jim Pace | Mazda Kudzu | 637 laps |
| 4 | Lee Payne, Brian Williams, David Loring, John Mirro | Olds Denau | 512 (Engine) |
| 5 | Chuck Cottrell, Chuck Goldsborough, Ted Anderson Mike Holt, Elias Chocron, Leigh Miller | Buick Kudzu | 480 laps |

Note: World Sports Cars.

## 1995 World Sports Car Championship Results (through October 1)

| Date | Race | Winner(s) | Car (Class) |
|---|---|---|---|
| Feb 4-5 | 24 Hours of Daytona | Jeremy Dale/Fredrik Ekblom/Jay Cochran | Oldsmobile BDG02 |
| Mar 18 | 12 Hours of Sebring | Andy Evans/Fermin Velez/Eric Van De Poele | Ferrari 333SP |
| Apr 30 | Atlanta GP | James Weaver | Ford R&S MK-3 |
| May 21 | Halifax GP | Mauro Baldi/Fermin Velez | Ferrari 333SP |
| May 29 | Lime Rock GP | Wayne Taylor | Ferrari 333SP |
| June 24 | Glen Continental | James Weaver/Butch Leitzinger | Ford R&S MK-3 |
| July 16 | California GP | James Weaver | Ford R&S MK-3 |
| Aug 13 | Mosport 500 | James Weaver/Andy Wallace | Ford R&S MK-3 |
| Sept 10 | Texas World GP | Wayne Taylor | Ferrari 333SP |
| Sept 30 | WSC Championships* | Fermin Velez | Ferrari 333SP |

*The World Sports Car Championships are for World Sports Cars and GTS-1 Cars.

## 1995 Supreme GT Series Results (through October 1)

| Date | Race | Winner(s) | Car (Class) |
|---|---|---|---|
| Feb 4-5 | 24 Hours of Daytona | Paul Newman/Michael Brockman/Tommy Kendall/Mark Martin | Ford Mustang |
| Mar 18 | 12 Hours of Sebring | Steve Millen/Johnny O'Connell/John Morton | Nissan 300ZX |
| Apr 30 | Atlanta GP | Irv Hoerr | Oldsmobile |
| May 21 | Halifax | Johnny O'Connell | Nissan 300ZX |
| May 29 | Lime Rock GP | Darin Brassfield | Oldsmobile |
| June 24 | Glen Continental | Irv Hoerr | Oldsmobile |
| July 16 | California GP | Johnny O'Connell | Nissan 300ZX |
| Aug 13 | Mosport 500 | Charles Morgan/Rob Morgan | Oldsmobile |
| Sept 10 | Texas World GP | Irv Hoerr | Oldsmobile |

Note: GTS-1 cars.

## 1995 World Sports Car Championship Standings (through October 1)

| Driver | Pts |
|---|---|
| Fermin Velez | 235 |
| James Weaver | 224 |
| Mauro Baldi | 220 |
| Jim Pace | 208 |
| Wayne Taylor | 203 |
| Butch Leitzinger | 157 |
| Roger Mandeville | 137 |
| Henry Camferdam | 137 |
| Gianpiero Moretti | 118 |
| Leigh Miller | 111 |

# FIA World Sports Car Racing

## The 24 Hours of LeMans

Held at LeMans, France, on June 17-18, 1995, the 24 Hours of LeMans is the most prestigious event in the FIA World Sports Car Championship.

| Place | Drivers | Car | Distance |
|---|---|---|---|
| 1 | Yannick Dalmas, J.J. Lehto, Masanori Sekiya | McLaren F1 GTR | 2518.652 |
| 2 | B. Wollek, M. Andretti, E. Helary | Courage C34 | 2512.776 |

### The 24 Hours of LeMans (Cont.)

| Place | Drivers | Car | Distance |
|---|---|---|---|
| 3 | A.Wallace, J. Bell, D. Bell | McLaren F1 GTR | 2502.897 |
| 4 | R. Bellm, M. Sala, M. Blundell | McLaren F1 GTR | 2463.403 |
| 5 | F. Giroix, O. Grouillard, J. Deletraz | McLaren F1 GTR | 2456.877 |
| 6 | R. Stuck, T. Boutsen, C. Bouchut | Kremer K8 | 2446.368 |
| 7 | Y. Yerada, JJ Downing, F. Freon | Mazda DG-3 | 2388.680 |
| 8 | K. Takahashi, K. Tsuchiya, A. Iida | Honda NSX GT | 2326.861 |
| 9 | J. Unser, F. Jelinsky, E. Bertaggia | Callaway GT2 | 2305.956 |
| 10 | H. Fukuyama, M. Kondo, S. Kasuya | Nismo GT-R LM | 2295.141 |

## Drag Racing

### National Hot Rod Association
### 1995 Results (through September 17)

#### TOP FUEL

| Date | Race, Site | Winner | Time | Speed |
|---|---|---|---|---|
| Feb 5 | Winternationals, Pomona, CA | Eddie Hill | 4.859 | 299.50 |
| Feb 19 | ATSCO Nationals, Phoenix | Larry Dixon | 4.821 | 300.00 |
| Mar 5 | Slick 50 Nationals, Houston | Mike Dunn | 4.857 | 296.34 |
| Mar 19 | Gatornationals, Gainesville, FL | Larry Dixon | 4.734 | 302.72 |
| Apr 9 | Winston Invitational, Rockingham, NC | Scott Kalitta | 4.886 | 288.46 |
| Apr 23 | Fram Nationals, Atlanta | Cory McClenathan | 4.806 | 298.90 |
| May 7 | Mid-South Nationals, Memphis | Cory McClenathan | 4.810 | 307.48 |
| May 23 | Mopar Nationals, Englishtown, NJ | Larry Dixon | 4.991 | 281.77 |
| June 4 | Virginia Nationals, Richmond | Cory McClenathan | 4.962 | 293.82 |
| June 11 | Springnationals, Columbus, OH | Scott Kalitta | 4.772 | 305.18 |
| July 2 | Western Auto Nationals, Topeka, KS | Scott Kalitta | 4.820 | 295.27 |
| July 23 | Mile-High Nationals, Denver | Scott Kalitta | 4.813 | 298.30 |
| July 30 | Autolite Nationals, Sonoma, CA | Mike Dunn | 5.107 | 276.83 |
| Aug 6 | Northwest Nationals, Seattle | Ron Capps | 4.930 | 295.76 |
| Aug 20 | Champion Auto Nationals, Brainerd, MN | Mike Dunn | 4.952 | 291.63 |
| Sept 4 | U.S. Nationals, Indianapolis | Larry Dixon | 4.931 | 293.25 |
| Sept 17 | Keystone Nationals, Reading, PA | Scott Kalitta | 4.801 | 298.90 |

#### FUNNY CAR

| Date | Race, Site | Winner | Time | Speed |
|---|---|---|---|---|
| Feb 5 | Winternationals, Pomona, CA | Cruz Pedregon | 5.304 | 278.72 |
| Feb 19 | ATSCO Nationals, Phoenix | John Force | 5.057 | 298.30 |
| Mar 5 | Slick 50 Nationals, Houston | Al Hofmann | 5.207 | 293.15 |
| Mar 19 | Gatornationals, Gainesville, FL | John Force | 5.347 | 263.00 |
| Apr 9 | Winston Invitational, Rockingham, NC | John Force | 5.235 | 283.64 |
| Apr 23 | Fram Nationals, Atlanta | John Force | 5.174 | 297.22 |
| May 7 | Mid-South Nationals, Memphis | Gary Clapshaw | 5.339 | 286.89 |
| May 23 | Mopar Nationals, Englishtown, NJ | Cruz Pedregon | 5.246 | 294.31 |
| June 4 | Virginia Nationals, Richmond | John Force | 5.193 | 270.59 |
| June 11 | Springnationals, Columbus, OH | Al Hofmann | 5.125 | 299.90 |
| July 2 | Western Auto Nationals, Topeka, KS | Cruz Pedregon | 5.912 | 273.39 |
| July 23 | Mile-High Nationals, Denver | John Force | 5.258 | 291.16 |
| July 30 | Autolite Nationals, Sonoma, CA | Al Hofmann | 5.107 | 276.83 |
| Aug 6 | Northwest Nationals, Seattle | Al Hofmann | 5.200 | 285.80 |
| Aug 20 | Champion Auto Nationals, Brainerd, MN | John Force | 5.284 | 291.92 |
| Sept 4 | U.S. Nationals, Indianapolis | Cruz Pedregon | 5.075 | 304.67 |
| Sept 17 | Keystone Nationals, Reading, PA | Chuck Etchells | 6.121 | 264.31 |

## National Hot Rod Association *(Cont.)*

### PRO STOCK

| Date | Race, Site | Winner | Time | Speed |
|------|-----------|--------|------|-------|
| Feb 5 | Winternationals, Pomona, CA | Darrell Alderman | 7.054 | 196.03 |
| Feb 19 | ATSCO Nationals, Phoenix | Darrell Alderman | 7.073 | 194.46 |
| Mar 5 | Slick 50 Nationals, Houston | Scott Geoffrion | 7.062 | 196.03 |
| Mar 19 | Gatornationals, Gainesville, FL | Darrell Alderman | 7.031 | 196.29 |
| Apr 9 | Winston Invitational, Rockingham, NC | Darrell Alderman | 7.037 | 196.93 |
| Apr 23 | Fram Nationals, Atlanta | Mark Osborne | 7.141 | 194.17 |
| May 7 | Mid-South Nationals, Memphis | Mark Pawuk | 7.195 | 192.80 |
| May 23 | Mopar Nationals, Englishtown, NJ | Bob Glidden | 7.117 | 194.42 |
| June 4 | Virginia Nationals, Richmond | Warren Johnson | 7.062 | 196.03 |
| June 11 | Springnationals, Columbus, OH | Steve Schmidt | 7.125 | 193.21 |
| July 2 | Western Auto Nationals, Topeka, KS | Warren Johnson | 7.069 | 194.46 |
| July 23 | Mile-High Nationals, Denver | Kurt Johnson | 7.491 | 183.29 |
| July 30 | Autolite Nationals, Sonoma, CA | Jim Yates | 7.143 | 193.79 |
| Aug 6 | Northwest Nationals, Seattle | Warren Johnson | 7.022 | 197.23 |
| Aug 20 | Champion Auto Nationals, Brainerd, MN | Warren Johnson | 7.202 | 193.05 |
| Sept 4 | U.S. Nationals, Indianapolis | Warren Johnson | 7.059 | 197.02 |
| Sept 17 | Keystone Nationals, Reading, PA | Warren Johnson | 7.060 | 195.43 |

## 1994 Standings

### TOP FUEL

| Driver | Wins | Pts |
|--------|------|-----|
| Scott Kalitta | 5 | 13,600 |
| Don Prudhomme | 3 | 12,090 |
| Cory McClenathan | 2 | 10,924 |
| Connie Kalitta | 3 | 10,582 |
| Joe Amato | 1 | 10,244 |
| Kenny Bernstein | 1 | 9,646 |
| Mike Dunn | — | 8,638 |
| Pat Austin | 1 | 8,588 |
| Tommy Johnson Jr | 1 | 8,414 |
| Shelly Anderson | 1 | 7,936 |

### FUNNY CAR

| Driver | Wins | Pts |
|--------|------|-----|
| John Force | 10 | 16,776 |
| Cruz Pedregon | 3 | 12,512 |
| Al Hofmann | 1 | 11,496 |
| Chuck Etchells | — | 10,852 |
| K. C. Spurlock | 1 | 9,388 |

### FUNNY CAR *(Cont.)*

| Driver | Wins | Pts |
|--------|------|-----|
| Gordie Bonin | 2 | 8,302 |
| Jim Epler | — | 7,922 |
| Dean Skuza | — | 7,832 |
| Gary Bolger | — | 7,824 |
| Kenji Okazaki | — | 7,570 |

### PRO STOCK

| Driver | Wins | Pts |
|--------|------|-----|
| Darrell Alderman | 5 | 16,034 |
| Scott Geoffrion | 6 | 15,252 |
| Warren Johnson | 4 | 13,918 |
| Jim Yates | 1 | 11,382 |
| Kurt Johnson | — | 10,450 |
| Larry Morgan | 1 | 8,866 |
| Steve Schmidt | 1 | 8,340 |
| Mark Pawuk | — | 7,908 |
| Mark Osborne | — | 7,450 |
| Bob Glidden | — | 6,600 |

# FOR THE RECORD · Year by Year

## CART Racing

### Indianapolis 500

First held in 1911, the Indy 500—200 laps of the 2.5-mile Indianapolis Motor Speedway Track (called the Brickyard in honor of its original pavement)—has grown to become the most famous auto race in the world. Held on Memorial Day weekend, it annually draws the largest crowd of any sporting event in the world.

| Year | Winner (Start Position) | Car | Avg MPH | Pole Winner | MPH |
|------|------------------------|-----|---------|-------------|-----|
| 1911 | Ray Harroun (28) | Marmon Wasp | 74.590 | Lewis Strang | Awarded pole |
| 1912 | Joe Dawson (7) | National | 78.720 | Gil Anderson | Drew pole |
| 1913 | Jules Goux (7) | Peugeot | 75.930 | Caleb Bragg | Drew pole |
| 1914 | Rene Thomas (15) | Delage | 82.470 | Jean Chassagne | Drew pole |
| 1915 | Ralph DePalma (2) | Mercedes | 89.840 | Howard Wilcox | 98.90 |
| 1916 | Dario Resta (4) | Peugeot | 84.000 | John Aitken | 96.69 |
| 1917-18 | No race | | | | |
| 1919 | Howard Wilcox (2) | Peugeot | 88.050 | Rene Thomas | 104.78 |
| 1920 | Gaston Chevrolet (6) | Monroe | 88.620 | Ralph DePalma | 99.15 |
| 1921 | Tommy Milton (20) | Frontenac | 89.620 | Ralph DePalma | 100.75 |
| 1922 | Jimmy Murphy (1) | Murphy Special | 94.480 | Jimmy Murphy | 100.50 |
| 1923 | Tommy Milton (1) | H.C.S. Special | 90.950 | Tommy Milton | 108.17 |
| 1924 | L. L. Corum<br>Joe Boyer (21) | Duesenberg Special | 98.230 | Jimmy Murphy | 108.037 |
| 1925 | Peter DePaolo (2) | Duesenberg Special | 101.130 | Leon Duray | 113.196 |
| 1926 | Frank Lockhart (20) | Miller Special | 95.904 | Earl Cooper | 111.735 |
| 1927 | George Souders (22) | Duesenberg | 97.545 | Frank Lockhart | 120.100 |
| 1928 | Louis Meyer (13) | Miller Special | 99.482 | Leon Duray | 122.391 |
| 1929 | Ray Keech (6) | Simplex Piston Ring Special | 97.585 | Cliff Woodbury | 120.599 |
| 1930 | Billy Arnold (1) | Miller Hartz Special | 100.448 | Billy Arnold | 113.268 |
| 1931 | Louis Schneider (13) | Bowes Seal-Fast Special | 96.629 | Russ Snowberger | 112.796 |
| 1932 | Fred Frame (27) | Miller Hartz Special | 104.144 | Lou Moore | 117.363 |
| 1933 | Louis Meyer (6) | Tydol Special | 104.162 | Bill Cummings | 118.524 |
| 1934 | Bill Cummings (10) | Boyle Products Special | 104.863 | Kelly Petillo | 119.329 |
| 1935 | Kelly Petillo (22) | Gilmore Speedway Special | 106.240 | Rex Mays | 120.736 |
| 1936 | Louis Meyer (28) | Ring-Free Special | 109.069 | Rex Mays | 119.664 |
| 1937 | Wilbur Shaw (2) | Shaw-Gilmore Special | 113.580 | Bill Cummings | 123.343 |
| 1938 | Floyd Roberts (1) | Burd Piston Ring Special | 117.200 | Floyd Roberts | 125.681 |
| 1939 | Wilbur Shaw (3) | Boyle Special | 115.035 | Jimmy Snyder | 130.138 |
| 1940 | Wilbur Shaw (2) | Boyle Special | 114.277 | Rex Mays | 127.850 |
| 1941 | Floyd Davis<br>Mauri Rose (17) | Noc-Out Hose Clamp Special | 115.117 | Mauri Rose | 128.691 |
| 1942-45 | No race | | | | |
| 1946 | George Robson (15) | Thorne Engineering Special | 114.820 | Cliff Bergere | 126.471 |
| 1947 | Mauri Rose (3) | Blue Crown Spark Plug Special | 116.338 | Ted Horn | 126.564 |
| 1948 | Mauri Rose (3) | Blue Crown Spark Plug Special | 119.814 | Rex Mays | 130.577 |
| 1949 | Bill Holland (4) | Blue Crown Spark Plug Special | 121.327 | Duke Nalon | 132.939 |
| 1950 | Johnnie Parsons (5) | Wynn's Friction Proofing | 124.002 | Walt Faulkner | 134.343 |
| 1951 | Lee Wallard (2) | Belanger Special | 126.244 | Duke Nalon | 136.498 |
| 1952 | Troy Ruttman (7) | Agajanian Special | 128.922 | Fred Agabashian | 138.010 |
| 1953 | Bill Vukovich (1) | Fuel Injection Special | 128.740 | Bill Vukovich | 138.392 |
| 1954 | Bill Vukovich (19) | Fuel Injection Special | 130.840 | Jack McGrath | 141.033 |
| 1955 | Bob Sweikert (14) | John Zink Special | 128.209 | Jerry Hoyt | 140.045 |
| 1956 | Pat Flaherty (1) | John Zink Special | 128.490 | Pat Flaherty | 145.596 |
| 1957 | Sam Hanks (13) | Belond Exhaust Special | 135.601 | Pat O'Connor | 143.948 |
| 1958 | Jim Bryan (7) | Belond AP Parts Special | 133.791 | Dick Rathmann | 145.974 |
| 1959 | Rodger Ward (6) | Leader Card 500 Roadster | 135.857 | Johnny Thomson | 145.908 |
| 1960 | Jim Rathmann (2) | Ken-Paul Special | 138.767 | Eddie Sachs | 146.592 |
| 1961 | A. J. Foyt (7) | Bowes Seal-Fast Special | 139.130 | Eddie Sachs | 147.481 |
| 1962 | Rodger Ward (2) | Leader Card 500 Roadster | 140.293 | Parnelli Jones | 150.370 |
| 1963 | Parnelli Jones (1) | Agajanian-Willard Special | 143.137 | Parnelli Jones | 151.153 |
| 1964 | A. J. Foyt (5) | Sheraton-Thompson Special | 147.350 | Jim Clark | 158.828 |
| 1965 | Jim Clark (2) | Lotus Ford | 150.686 | A. J. Foyt | 161.233 |
| 1966 | Graham Hill (15) | American Red Ball Special | 144.317 | Mario Andretti | 165.899 |
| 1967 | A. J. Foyt (4) | Sheraton-Thompson Special | 151.207 | Mario Andretti | 168.982 |
| 1968 | Bobby Unser (3) | Rislone Special | 152.882 | Joe Leonard | 171.559 |
| 1969 | Mario Andretti (2) | STP Oil Treatment Special | 156.867 | A. J. Foyt | 170.568 |
| 1970 | Al Unser (1) | Johnny Lightning 500 Special | 155.749 | Al Unser | 170.221 |

### Indianapolis 500 (Cont.)

| Year | Winner (Start Position) | Car | Avg MPH | Pole Winner | MPH |
|------|------------------------|-----|---------|-------------|-----|
| 1971 | Al Unser (5) | Johnny Lightning Special | 157.735 | Peter Revson | 178.696 |
| 1972 | Mark Donohue (3) | Sunoco McLaren | 162.962 | Bobby Unser | 195.940 |
| 1973 | Gordon Johncock (11) | STP Double Oil Filters | 159.036 | Johnny Rutherford | 198.413 |
| 1974 | Johnny Rutherford (25) | McLaren | 158.589 | A. J. Foyt | 191.632 |
| 1975 | Bobby Unser (3) | Jorgensen Eagle | 149.213 | A. J. Foyt | 193.976 |
| 1976 | Johnny Rutherford (1) | Hy-Gain McLaren/Goodyear | 148.725 | Johnny Rutherford | 188.957 |
| 1977 | A. J. Foyt (4) | Gilmore Racing Team | 161.331 | Tom Sneva | 198.884 |
| 1978 | Al Unser (5) | FNCTC Chaparral Lola | 161.361 | Tom Sneva | 202.156 |
| 1979 | Rick Mears (1) | The Gould Charge | 158.899 | Rick Mears | 193.736 |
| 1980 | Johnny Rutherford (1) | Pennzoil Chaparral | 142.862 | Johnny Rutherford | 192.256 |
| 1981 | Bobby Unser (1) | Norton Spirit Penske PC-9B | 139.084 | Bobby Unser | 200.546 |
| 1982 | Gordon Johncock (5) | STP Oil Treatment | 162.026 | Rick Mears | 207.004 |
| 1983 | Tom Sneva (4) | Texaco Star | 162.117 | Teo Fabi | 207.395 |
| 1984 | Rick Mears (3) | Pennzoil Z-7 | 163.612 | Tom Sneva | 210.029 |
| 1985 | Danny Sullivan (8) | Miller American Special | 152.982 | Pancho Carter | 212.583 |
| 1986 | Bobby Rahal (4) | Budweiser/Truesports/March | 170.722 | Rick Mears | 216.828 |
| 1987 | Al Unser (20) | Cummins Holset Turbo | 162.175 | Mario Andretti | 215.390 |
| 1988 | Rick Mears (1) | Penske-Chevrolet | 144.809 | Rick Mears | 219.198 |
| 1989 | Emerson Fittipaldi (3) | Penske-Chevrolet | 167.581 | Rick Mears | 223.885 |
| 1990 | Arie Luyendyk (3) | Domino's Pizza Chevrolet | 185.981* | Emerson Fittipaldi | 225.301† |
| 1991 | Rick Mears (1) | Penske-Chevrolet | 176.457 | Rick Mears | 224.113 |
| 1992 | Al Unser Jr (12) | G92-Chevrolet | 134.477 | Roberto Guerrero | 232.482 |
| 1993 | Emerson Fittipaldi (9) | Penske-Chevrolet | 157.207 | Arie Luyendyk | 223.967 |
| 1994 | Al Unser Jr. (1) | Penske-Mercedes | 160.872 | Al Unser Jr. | 228.011 |
| 1995 | Jacques Villeneuve (5) | Reynard-Ford | 153.616 | Scott Brayton | 231.616 |

*Track record, winning time. †Track record, qualifying time.

### Indianapolis 500 Rookie of the Year Award

| | | |
|---|---|---|
| 1952 | Art Cross | 1968 | Billy Vukovich | 1984 | Michael Andretti |

1952 .............Art Cross
1953 .............Jimmy Daywalt
1954 .............Larry Crockett
1955 .............Al Herman
1956 .............Bob Veith
1957 .............Don Edmunds
1958 .............George Amick
1959 .............Bobby Grim
1960 .............Jim Hurtubise
1961 .............Parnelli Jones*
              Bobby Marshman
1962 .............Jimmy McElreath
1963 .............Jim Clark*
1964 .............Johnny White
1965 .............Mario Andretti*
1966 .............Jackie Stewart
1967 .............Denis Hulme

1968 .............Billy Vukovich
1969 .............Mark Donohue*
1970 .............Donnie Allison
1971 .............Denny Zimmerman
1972 .............Mike Hiss
1973 .............Graham McRae
1974 .............Pancho Carter
1975 .............Bill Puterbaugh
1976 .............Vern Schuppan
1977 .............Jerry Sneva
1978 .............Rick Mears*
              Larry Rice
1979 .............Howdy Holmes
1980 .............Tim Richmond
1981 .............Josele Garza
1982 .............Jim Hickman
1983 .............Teo Fabi

1984 .............Michael Andretti
              Roberto Guerrero
1985 .............Arie Luyendyk
1986 .............Randy Lanier
1987 .............Fabrizio Barbazza
1988 .............Billy Vukovich III
1989 .............Bernard Jourdain
              Scott Pruett
1990 .............Eddie Cheever
1991 .............Jeff Andretti
1992 .............Lyn St. James
1993 .............Nigel Mansell
1994 .............Jacques Villeneuve*
1995 .............Gil de Ferran

*Future winner of Indy 500.

### Indy Car Champions

From 1909 to 1955, this championship was awarded by the American Automobile Association (AAA), and from 1956 to 1979 by United States Auto Club (USAC). Since 1979, Championship Auto Racing Teams (CART) has conducted the championship.

1909 .............George Robertson
1910 .............Ray Harroun
1911 .............Ralph Mulford
1912 .............Ralph DePalma
1913 .............Earl Cooper
1914 .............Ralph DePalma
1915 .............Earl Cooper
1916 .............Dario Resta
1917 .............Earl Cooper
1918 .............Ralph Mulford
1919 .............Howard Wilcox
1920 .............Tommy Milton
1921 .............Tommy Milton
1922 .............Jimmy Murphy
1923 .............Eddie Hearne
1924 .............Jimmy Murphy

1925 .............Peter DePaolo
1926 .............Harry Hartz
1927 .............Peter DePaolo
1928 .............Louis Meyer
1929 .............Louis Meyer
1930 .............Billy Arnold
1931 .............Louis Schneider
1932 .............Bob Carey
1933 .............Louis Meyer
1934 .............Bill Cummings
1935 .............Kelly Petillo
1936 .............Mauri Rose
1937 .............Wilbur Shaw
1938 .............Floyd Roberts
1939 .............Wilbur Shaw
1940 .............Rex Mays

1941 .............Rex Mays
1942-45 ........No racing
1946 .............Ted Horn
1947 .............Ted Horn
1948 .............Ted Horn
1949 .............Johnnie Parsons
1950 .............Henry Banks
1951 .............Tony Bettenhausen
1952 .............Chuck Stevenson
1953 .............Sam Hanks
1954 .............Jimmy Bryan
1955 .............Bob Sweikert
1956 .............Jimmy Bryan
1957 .............Jimmy Bryan
1958 .............Tony Bettenhausen
1959 .............Rodger Ward

## Indy Car Champions (Cont.)

| | | |
|---|---|---|
| 1960 ............A. J. Foyt | 1973 ............Roger McCluskey | 1985 ............Al Unser |
| 1961 ............A. J. Foyt | 1974 ............Bobby Unser | 1986 ............Bobby Rahal |
| 1962 ............Rodger Ward | 1975 ............A. J. Foyt | 1987 ............Bobby Rahal |
| 1963 ............A. J. Foyt | 1976 ............Gordon Johncock | 1988 ............Danny Sullivan |
| 1964 ............A. J. Foyt | 1977 ............Tom Sneva | 1989 ............Emerson Fittipaldi |
| 1965 ............Mario Andretti | 1978 ............Tom Sneva | 1990 ............Al Unser Jr |
| 1966 ............Mario Andretti | 1979 ............A. J. Foyt | 1991 ............Michael Andretti |
| 1967 ............A. J. Foyt | 1979 ............Rick Mears | 1992 ............Bobby Rahal |
| 1968 ............Bobby Unser | 1980 ............Johnny Rutherford | 1993 ............Nigel Mansell |
| 1969 ............Mario Andretti | 1981 ............Rick Mears | 1994 ............Al Unser Jr. |
| 1970 ............Al Unser | 1982 ............Rick Mears | 1995 ............Jacques Villeneuve |
| 1971 ............Joe Leonard | 1983 ............Al Unser | |
| 1972 ............Joe Leonard | 1984 ............Mario Andretti | |

### Alltime Indy Car Leaders

| WINS | | WINNINGS ($) | | POLE POSITIONS | |
|---|---|---|---|---|---|
| A. J. Foyt | 67 | *Al Unser Jr | 15,240,093 | Mario Andretti | 67 |
| Mario Andretti | 52 | *Bobby Rahal | 14,044,508 | A. J. Foyt | 53 |
| Al Unser | 39 | *Emerson Fittipaldi | 12,937,375 | Bobby Unser | 49 |
| Bobby Unser | 35 | *Michael Andretti | 11,917,869 | Rick Mears | 38 |
| *Al Unser Jr | 31 | Mario Andretti | 11,279,654 | *Michael Andretti | 30 |
| *Michael Andretti | 30 | Rick Mears | 11,050,807 | Al Unser | 27 |
| Rick Mears | 29 | Danny Sullivan | 8,254,673 | Johnny Rutherford | 23 |
| Johnny Rutherford | 27 | *Arie Luyendyk | 7,092,188 | Gordon Johncock | 20 |
| Rodger Ward | 26 | Al Unser | 6,740,843 | Rex Mays | 19 |
| Gordon Johncock | 25 | *Raul Boesel | 5,544,137 | *Danny Sullivan | 19 |
| *Bobby Rahal | 24 | A. J. Foyt | 5,357,589 | *Bobby Rahal | 18 |
| Ralph DePalma | 24 | *Scott Brayton | 4,807,214 | *Emerson Fittipaldi | 17 |
| Tommy Milton | 23 | *Teo Fabi | 4,573,131 | Tony Bettenhausen | 14 |
| Tony Bettenhausen | 22 | Tom Sneva | 4,392,993 | Don Branson | 14 |
| *Emerson Fittipaldi | 22 | *Roberto Guerrero | 4,275,163 | Tom Sneva | 14 |
| Earl Cooper | 20 | Johnny Rutherford | 4,209,232 | Parnelli Jones | 12 |
| Jimmy Murphy | 19 | *Scott Goodyear | 4,133,201 | Danny Ongais | 11 |
| Jimmy Bryan | 19 | *Jaques Villeneuve | 3,748,982 | Rodger Ward | 11 |
| Ralph Mulford | 17 | *Paul Tracy | 3,584,020 | | |
| *Danny Sullivan | 17 | Gordon Johncock | 3,431,414 | Four tied with 10. | |

*Active driver.

Note: Leaders through September 11, 1995.

# NASCAR Racing

## Stock Car Racing's Major Events

Winston offers a $1 million bonus to any driver to win 3 of NASCAR's top 4 events in the same season. These races are the richest (Daytona 500), the fastest (Talladega 500), the longest (World 600 at Charlotte) and the oldest (Southern 500 at Darlington). These events form the backbone of NASCAR racing. Only 3 drivers, LeeRoy Yarbrough (1969), David Pearson (1976) and Bill Elliott (1985), have scored the 3-track hat trick.

### Daytona 500

| Year | Winner | Car | Avg MPH | Pole Winner | MPH |
|---|---|---|---|---|---|
| 1959 | Lee Petty | Oldsmobile | 135.520 | Cotton Owens | 143.198 |
| 1960 | Junior Johnson | Chevrolet | 124.740 | Fireball Roberts | 151.556 |
| 1961 | Marvin Panch | Pontiac | 149.601 | Fireball Roberts | 155.709 |
| 1962 | Fireball Roberts | Pontiac | 152.529 | Fireball Roberts | 156.995 |
| 1963 | Tiny Lund | Ford | 151.566 | Johnny Rutherford | 165.183 |
| 1964 | Richard Petty | Plymouth | 154.345 | Paul Goldsmith | 174.910 |
| 1965 | Fred Lorenzen | Ford | 141.539 | Darel Dieringer | 171.151 |
| 1966 | Richard Petty | Plymouth | 160.627 | Richard Petty | 175.165 |
| 1967 | Mario Andretti | Ford | 149.926 | Curtis Turner | 180.831 |
| 1968 | Cale Yarborough | Mercury | 143.251 | Cale Yarborough | 189.222 |
| 1969 | LeeRoy Yarbrough | Ford | 157.950 | David Pearson | 190.029 |
| 1970 | Pete Hamilton | Plymouth | 149.601 | Cale Yarborough | 194.015 |
| 1971 | Richard Petty | Plymouth | 144.462 | A. J. Foyt | 182.744 |
| 1972 | A. J. Foyt | Mercury | 161.550 | Bobby Isaac | 186.632 |

## Daytona 500 *(Cont.)*

| Year | Winner | Car | Avg MPH | Pole Winner | MPH |
|------|--------|-----|---------|-------------|-----|
| 1973 | Richard Petty | Dodge | 157.205 | Buddy Baker | 185.662 |
| 1974 | Richard Petty | Dodge | 140.894 | David Pearson | 185.017 |
| 1975 | Benny Parsons | Chevrolet | 153.649 | Donnie Allison | 185.827 |
| 1976 | David Pearson | Mercury | 152.181 | A. J. Foyt | 185.943 |
| 1977 | Cale Yarborough | Chevrolet | 153.218 | Donnie Allison | 188.048 |
| 1978 | Bobby Allison | Ford | 159.730 | Cale Yarborough | 187.536 |
| 1979 | Richard Petty | Oldsmobile | 143.977 | Buddy Baker | 196.049 |
| 1980 | Buddy Baker | Oldsmobile | 177.602* | A. J. Foyt | 195.020 |
| 1981 | Richard Petty | Buick | 169.651 | Bobby Allison | 194.624 |
| 1982 | Bobby Allison | Buick | 153.991 | Benny Parsons | 196.317 |
| 1983 | Cale Yarborough | Pontiac | 155.979 | Ricky Rudd | 198.864 |
| 1984 | Cale Yarborough | Chevrolet | 150.994 | Cale Yarborough | 201.848 |
| 1985 | Bill Elliott | Ford | 172.265 | Bill Elliott | 205.114 |
| 1986 | Geoff Bodine | Chevrolet | 148.124 | Bill Elliott | 205.039 |
| 1987 | Bill Elliott | Ford | 176.263 | Bill Elliott | 210.364† |
| 1988 | Bobby Allison | Buick | 137.531 | Ken Schrader | 193.823 |
| 1989 | Darrell Waltrip | Chevrolet | 148.466 | Ken Schrader | 196.996 |
| 1990 | Derrike Cope | Chevrolet | 165.761 | Ken Schrader | 196.515 |
| 1991 | Earnie Irvan | Chevrolet | 148.148 | Davey Allison | 195.955 |
| 1992 | Davey Allison | Ford | 160.256 | Sterling Marlin | 192.213 |
| 1993 | Dale Jarrett | Chevrolet | 154.972 | Kyle Petty | 189.426 |
| 1994 | Sterling Marlin | Chevrolet | 156.931 | Loy Allen Jr. | 190.158 |
| 1995 | Sterling Marlin | Chevrolet | 141.710 | Dale Jarrett | 193.498 |

*Track record, winning time. †Track record, qualifying time. Note: The Daytona 500, held annually in February, now opens the NASCAR season with 200 laps around the high-banked Daytona, FL, superspeedway.

## World 600

| Year | Winner | Car | Avg MPH | Pole Winner |
|------|--------|-----|---------|-------------|
| 1960 | Joe Lee Johnson | Chevrolet | 107.752 | J.L. Johnson |
| 1961 | David Pearson | Pontiac | 111.634 | Richard Petty |
| 1962 | Nelson Stacy | Ford | 125.552 | Fireball Roberts |
| 1963 | Fred Lorenzen | Ford | 132.418 | Junior Johnson |
| 1964 | Jim Paschal | Plymouth | 125.772 | Junior Johnson |
| 1965 | Fred Lorenzen | Ford | 121.772 | Fred Lorenzon |
| 1966 | Marvin Panch | Plymouth | 135.042 | Paul Goldsmith |
| 1967 | Jim Paschal | Plymouth | 135.832 | Cale Yarborough |
| 1968 | Buddy Baker | Dodge | 104.207 | Donnie Allison |
| 1969 | Lee Yarbrough | Mercury | 134.631 | Donnie Allison |
| 1970 | Donnie Allison | Ford | 129.680 | Bobby Isaac |
| 1971 | Bobby Allison | Mercury | 140.442 | Charlie Glotzbach |
| 1972 | Buddy Baker | Dodge | 142.255 | Bobby Allison |
| 1973 | Buddy Baker | Dodge | 134.890 | Buddy Baker |
| 1974 | David Pearson | Mercury | 135.720 | David Pearson |
| 1975 | Richard Petty | Dodge | 145.327 | David Pearson |
| 1976 | David Pearson | Mercury | 137.352 | David Pearson |
| 1977 | Richard Petty | Dodge | 137.636 | David Pearson |
| 1978 | Darrell Waltrip | Chevrolet | 138.355 | David Pearson |
| 1979 | Darrell Waltrip | Chevrolet | 136.674 | Neil Bonnet |
| 1980 | Benny Parsons | Chevrolet | 119.265 | Cale Yarborough |
| 1981 | Bobby Allison | Buick | 129.326 | Neil Bonnet |
| 1982 | Neil Bonnett | Ford | 130.508 | David Pearson |
| 1983 | Neil Bonnett | Chevrolet | 140.406 | Buddy Baker |
| 1984 | Bobby Allison | Buick | 129.233 | Harry Gant |
| 1985 | Darrell Waltrip | Chevrolet | 141.807 | Bill Elliott |
| 1986 | Dale Earnhardt | Chevrolet | 140.406 | Geoff Bodine |
| 1987 | Kyle Petty | Ford | 131.483 | Bill Elliott |
| 1988 | Darrell Waltrip | Chevrolet | 124.460 | Davey Allison |
| 1989 | Darrell Waltrip | Chevrolet | 144.077 | Alan Kulwicki |
| 1990 | Rusty Wallace | Pontiac | 137.650 | Ken Schrader |
| 1991 | Davey Allison | Ford | 138.951 | Mark Martin |
| 1992 | Dale Earnhardt | Chevrolet | 132.980 | Bill Elliott |
| 1993 | Dale Earnhardt | Chevrolet | 145.504 | Ken Schrader |
| 1994 | Jeff Gordon | Chevrolet | 139.445 | Jeff Gordon |
| 1995 | Bobby Labonte | Chevrolet | 151.952 | Jeff Gordon |

Note: Held at the 1.5-mile Charlotte, NC, Motor Speedway on Memorial Day weekend.

## Talladega 500

| Year | Winner | Car | Avg MPH | Pole Winner | MPH |
|------|--------|-----|---------|-------------|-----|
| 1969 | Richard Brickhouse | Dodge | 153.778 | Charlie Glotzbach | 199.466 |
| 1970 | Pete Hamilton | Plymouth | 158.517 | Bobby Isaac | 186.834 |
| 1971 | Bobby Allison | Mercury | 145.945 | Davey Allison | 187.323 |
| 1972 | James Hylton | Mercury | 148.728 | Bobby Isaac | 190.677 |
| 1973 | Dick Brooks | Plymouth | 145.454 | Bobby Allison | 187.064 |
| 1974 | Richard Petty | Dodge | 148.637 | David Pearson | 184.926 |
| 1975 | Buddy Baker | Ford | 130.892 | Dave Marcis | 191.340 |
| 1976 | Dave Marcis | Dodge | 157.547 | Dave Marcis | 190.651 |
| 1977 | Davey Allison | Chevrolet | 162.524 | Benny Parsons | 192.682 |
| 1978 | Lennie Pond | Olds | 174.700 | Cale Yarborough | 192.917 |
| 1979 | Darrell Waltrip | Olds | 161.229 | Neil Bonnet | 193.600 |
| 1980 | Neil Bonnet | Mercury | 166.894 | Buddy Baker | 198.545 |
| 1981 | Ron Bouchard | Buick | 156.737 | Harry Gant | 195.897 |
| 1982 | Darrell Waltrip | Buick | 168.157 | Geoff Bodine | 199.400 |
| 1983 | Dale Earnhardt | Ford | 170.611 | Cale Yarborough | 201.744 |
| 1984 | Dale Earnhardt | Chevrolet | 155.485 | Cale Yarborough | 202.474 |
| 1985 | Cale Yarborough | Ford | 148.772 | Bill Elliott | 207.578 |
| 1986 | Bobby Hillin | Buick | 151.552 | Bill Elliott | 209.005 |
| 1987 | Bill Elliott | Ford | 171.293 | Bill Elliott | 203.827 |
| 1988 | Ken Schrader | Chevrolet | 154.505 | Darrell Waltrip | 196.274 |
| 1989 | Terry Labonte | Ford | 157.354 | Mark Martin | 194.800 |
| 1990 | Dale Earnhardt | Chevrolet | 174.430 | Dale Earnhardt | 192.513 |
| 1991 | Harry Gant | Olds | 165.620 | Sterling Marlin | 192.085 |
| 1992 | Ernie Irvan | Chevrolet | 176.309 | Sterling Marlin | 190.586 |
| 1993 | Dale Earnhardt | Chevrolet | 153.858 | Bill Elliott | 192.397 |
| 1994 | Jimmy Spencer | Ford | 163.217 | Dale Earnhardt | 193.470 |
| 1995 | Sterling Marlin | Chevrolet | 173.188 | Sterling Marlin | 194.212 |

Note: Held at the 2.66-mile high-banked Talladega, AL, Superspeedway on the last weekend in July.

## Southern 500

| Year | Winner | Car | Avg MPH | Pole Winner |
|------|--------|-----|---------|-------------|
| 1950 | Johnny Mantz | Plymouth | 76.260 | Wally Campbell |
| 1951 | Herb Thomas | Hudson | 76.900 | Marshall Teague |
| 1952 | Fonty Flock | Olds | 74.510 | Dick Rathman |
| 1953 | Buck Baker | Olds | 92.780 | Fonty Flock |
| 1954 | Herb Thomas | Hudson | 94.930 | Buck Baker |
| 1955 | Herb Thomas | Chevrolet | 92.281 | Tim Flock |
| 1956 | Curtis Turner | Ford | 95.067 | Buck Baker |
| 1957 | Speedy Thompson | Chevrolet | 100.100 | Paul Goldsmith |
| 1958 | Fireball Roberts | Chevrolet | 102.590 | Fireball Roberts |
| 1959 | Jim Reed | Chevrolet | 111.836 | Fireball Roberts |
| 1960 | Buck Baker | Pontiac | 105.901 | Cotton Owens |
| 1961 | Nelson Stacy | Ford | 117.880 | Fireball Roberts |
| 1962 | Larry Frank | Ford | 117.965 | Fireball Roberts |
| 1963 | Fireball Roberts | Ford | 129.784 | Fireball Roberts |
| 1964 | Buck Baker | Dodge | 117.757 | Richard Petty |
| 1965 | Ned Jarrett | Ford | 115.924 | Junior Johnson |
| 1966 | Darel Dieringer | Mercury | 114.830 | Lee Yarborough |
| 1967 | Richard Petty | Plymouth | 131.933 | David Pearson |
| 1968 | Cale Yarborough | Mercury | 126.132 | Charlie Glotzbach |
| 1969 | Lee Yarbrough | Ford | 105.612 | Cale Yarborough |
| 1970 | Buddy Baker | Dodge | 128.817 | David Pearson |
| 1971 | Bobby Allison | Mercury | 131.398 | Bobby Allison |
| 1972 | Bobby Allison | Chevrolet | 128.124 | David Pearson |
| 1973 | Cale Yarborough | Chevrolet | 134.033 | David Pearson |
| 1974 | Cale Yarborough | Chevrolet | 111.075 | Richard Petty |
| 1975 | Bobby Allison | Matador | 116.825 | David Pearson |
| 1976 | David Pearson | Mercury | 120.534 | David Pearson |
| 1977 | David Pearson | Mercury | 106.797 | Darrell Waltrip |
| 1978 | Cale Yarborough | Olds | 116.828 | David Pearson |
| 1979 | David Pearson | Chevrolet | 126.259 | Bobby Allison |
| 1980 | Terry Labonte | Chevrolet | 115.210 | Darrell Waltrip |
| 1981 | Neil Bonnett | Ford | 126.410 | Harry Gant |
| 1982 | Cale Yarborough | Buick | 126.703 | David Pearson |
| 1983 | Bobby Allison | Buick | 123.343 | Neil Bonnett |

## Southern 500 (Cont.)

| Year | Winner | Car | Avg MPH | Pole Winner |
|------|--------|-----|---------|-------------|
| 1984 | Harry Gant | Chevrolet | 128.270 | Harry Gant |
| 1985 | Bill Elliott | Ford | 121.254 | Bill Elliott |
| 1986 | Tim Richmond | Chevrolet | 121.068 | Tim Richmond |
| 1987 | Dale Earnhardt | Chevrolet | 115.520 | Davey Allison |
| 1988 | Bill Elliott | Ford | 128.297 | Bill Elliott |
| 1989 | Dale Earnhardt | Chevrolet | 135.462 | Alan Kulwicki |
| 1990 | Dale Earnhardt | Chevrolet | 123.141 | Dale Earnhardt |
| 1991 | Harry Gant | Olds | 133.508 | Davey Allison |
| 1992 | Darrell Waltrip | Chevrolet | 129.114 | Sterling Marlin |
| 1993 | Mark Martin | Ford | 137.932 | Ken Schrader |
| 1994 | Bill Elliott | Ford | 127.915 | Geoff Bodine |
| 1995 | Jeff Gordon | Chevrolet | 121.231 | John Andretti |

Note: Held at the 1.366-mile Darlington, SC, International Raceway on Labor Day weekend.

## Winston Cup NASCAR Champions

| Year | Driver | Car | Wins | Poles | Winnings ($) |
|------|--------|-----|------|-------|--------------|
| 1949 | Red Byron | Oldsmobile | 2 | 0 | 5,800 |
| 1950 | Bill Rexford | Oldsmobile | 1 | 0 | 6,175 |
| 1951 | Herb Thomas | Hudson | 7 | 4 | 18,200 |
| 1952 | Tim Flock | Hudson | 8 | 4 | 20,210 |
| 1953 | Herb Thomas | Hudson | 11 | 10 | 27,300 |
| 1954 | Lee Petty | Dodge | 7 | 3 | 26,706 |
| 1955 | Tim Flock | Chrysler | 18 | 19 | 33,750 |
| 1956 | Buck Baker | Chrysler | 14 | 12 | 29,790 |
| 1957 | Buck Baker | Chevrolet | 10 | 5 | 24,712 |
| 1958 | Lee Petty | Olds | 7 | 4 | 20,600 |
| 1959 | Lee Petty | Plymouth | 10 | 2 | 45,570 |
| 1960 | Rex White | Chevrolet | 6 | 3 | 45,260 |
| 1961 | Ned Jarrett | Chevrolet | 1 | 4 | 27,285 |
| 1962 | Joe Weatherly | Pontiac | 9 | 6 | 56,110 |
| 1963 | Joe Weatherly | Mercury | 3 | 6 | 58,110 |
| 1964 | Richard Petty | Plymouth | 9 | 8 | 98,810 |
| 1965 | Ned Jarrett | Ford | 13 | 9 | 77,966 |
| 1966 | David Pearson | Dodge | 14 | 7 | 59,205 |
| 1967 | Richard Petty | Plymouth | 27 | 18 | 130,275 |
| 1968 | David Pearson | Ford | 16 | 12 | 118,824 |
| 1969 | David Pearson | Ford | 11 | 14 | 183,700 |
| 1970 | Bobby Isaac | Dodge | 11 | 13 | 121,470 |
| 1971 | Richard Petty | Plymouth | 21 | 9 | 309,225 |
| 1972 | Richard Petty | Plymouth | 8 | 3 | 227,015 |
| 1973 | Benny Parsons | Chevrolet | 1 | 0 | 114,345 |
| 1974 | Richard Petty | Dodge | 10 | 7 | 299,175 |
| 1975 | Richard Petty | Dodge | 13 | 3 | 378,865 |
| 1976 | Cale Yarborough | Chevrolet | 9 | 2 | 387,173 |
| 1977 | Cale Yarborough | Chevrolet | 9 | 3 | 477,499 |
| 1978 | Cale Yarborough | Oldsmobile | 10 | 8 | 530,751 |
| 1979 | Richard Petty | Chevrolet | 5 | 1 | 531,292 |
| 1980 | Dale Earnhardt | Chevrolet | 5 | 0 | 588,926 |
| 1981 | Darrell Waltrip | Buick | 12 | 11 | 693,342 |
| 1982 | Darrell Waltrip | Buick | 12 | 7 | 873,118 |
| 1983 | Bobby Allison | Buick | 6 | 0 | 828,355 |
| 1984 | Terry Labonte | Chevrolet | 2 | 2 | 713,010 |
| 1985 | Darrell Waltrip | Chevrolet | 3 | 4 | 1,318,735 |
| 1986 | Dale Earnhardt | Chevrolet | 5 | 1 | 1,783,880 |
| 1987 | Dale Earnhardt | Chevrolet | 11 | 1 | 2,099,243 |
| 1988 | Bill Elliott | Ford | 6 | 6 | 1,574,639 |
| 1989 | Rusty Wallace | Pontiac | 6 | 4 | 2,247,950 |
| 1990 | Dale Earnhardt | Chevrolet | 9 | 4 | 3,083,056 |
| 1991 | Dale Earnhardt | Chevrolet | 4 | 0 | 2,396,685 |
| 1992 | Alan Kulwicki | Ford | 2 | 6 | 2,322,561 |
| 1993 | Dale Earnhardt | Chevrolet | 6 | 2 | 3,353,789 |
| 1994 | Dale Earnhardt | Chevrolet | 4 | 2 | 3,400,733 |

# NASCAR Racing (Cont.)

## Alltime NASCAR Leaders

| WINS | | WINNINGS ($) | | POLE POSITIONS | |
|---|---|---|---|---|---|
| Richard Petty | 200 | Dale Earnhardt* | 24,754,799 | Richard Petty | 127 |
| David Pearson | 105 | Bill Elliott* | 15,229,173 | David Pearson | 113 |
| Bobby Allison | 84 | Darrell Waltrip* | 14,258,959 | Cale Yarborough | 70 |
| Darrell Waltrip* | 84 | Rusty Wallace* | 12,245,778 | Darrell Waltrip* | 58 |
| Cale Yarborough | 83 | Terry Labonte* | 9,990,201 | Bobby Allison | 57 |
| Dale Earnhardt* | 66 | Ricky Rudd* | 9,567,960 | Bobby Isaac | 51 |
| Lee Petty | 54 | Mark Martin* | 9,375,069 | Bill Elliott* | 48 |
| Ned Jarrett | 50 | Geoff Bodine* | 9,178,233 | Junior Johnson | 47 |
| Junior Johnson | 50 | Harry Gant | 8,438,094 | Buck Baker | 44 |
| Herb Thomas | 49 | Richard Petty | 7,757,964 | Buddy Baker | 40 |
| Buck Baker | 46 | Ken Schrader* | 7,533,412 | Geoff Bodine* | 40 |
| Rusty Wallace* | 41 | Bobby Allison | 7,102,233 | Herb Thomas | 38 |
| Tim Flock | 40 | Kyle Petty* | 7,085,574 | Tim Flock | 37 |
| Bill Elliott* | 40 | Sterling Marlin* | 6,607,840 | Fireball Roberts | 37 |
| Bobby Isaac | 37 | Morgan Shepherd* | 6,466,832 | Ned Jarrett | 36 |
| Fireball Roberts | 32 | Davey Allison | 6,210,589 | Rex White | 36 |

*Active drivers.

Note: NASCAR Leaders through September 17, 1995.

# Formula One/Grand Prix Racing

## World Driving Champions

| Year | Winner | Car | Year | Winner | Car |
|---|---|---|---|---|---|
| 1950 | Guiseppe Farina, Italy | Alfa Romeo | 1969 | Jackie Stewart, Scotland | Matra-Ford |
| 1951 | Juan-Manuel Fangio, Argentina | Alfa Romeo | 1970 | Jochen Rindt, Austria* | Lotus-Ford |
| 1952 | Alberto Ascari, Italy | Ferrari | 1971 | Jackie Stewart, Scotland | Tyrell-Ford |
| 1953 | Alberto Ascari, Italy | Ferrari | 1972 | Emerson Fittipaldi, Brazil | Lotus-Ford |
| 1954 | Juan-Manuel Fangio, Argentina | Maserati/ Mercedes | 1973 | Jackie Stewart, Scotland | Tyrell-Ford |
| | | | 1974 | Emerson Fittipaldi, Brazil | McLaren-Ford |
| 1955 | Juan-Manuel Fangio, Argentina | Mercedes | 1975 | Niki Lauda, Austria | Ferrari |
| | | | 1976 | James Hunt, England | McLaren-Ford |
| 1956 | Juan-Manuel Fangio, Argentina | Ferrari | 1977 | Niki Lauda, Austria | Ferrari |
| | | | 1978 | Mario Andretti, U.S. | Lotus-Ford |
| 1957 | Juan-Manuel Fangio, Argentina | Maserati | 1979 | Jody Scheckter, S Africa | Ferrari |
| | | | 1980 | Alan Jones, Australia | Williams-Ford |
| 1958 | Mike Hawthorne, England | Ferrari | 1981 | Nelson Piquet, Brazil | Brabham-Ford |
| 1959 | Jack Brabham, Australia | Cooper-Climax | 1982 | Keke Rosberg, Finland | Williams-Ford |
| 1960 | Jack Brabham, Australia | Cooper-Climax | 1983 | Nelson Piquet, Brazil | Brabham-BMW |
| 1961 | Phil Hill, United States | Ferrari | 1984 | Niki Lauda, Austria | McLaren-Porsche |
| 1962 | Graham Hill, England | BRM | 1985 | Alain Prost, France | McLaren-Porsche |
| 1963 | Jim Clark, Scotland | Lotus-Climax | 1986 | Alain Prost, France | McLaren-Porsche |
| 1964 | John Surtees, England | Ferrari | 1987 | Nelson Piquet, Brazil | Williams-Honda |
| 1965 | Jim Clark, Scotland | Lotus-Climax | 1988 | Ayrton Senna, Brazil | McLaren-Honda |
| 1966 | Jack Brabham, Australia | Brabham-Climax | 1989 | Alain Prost, France | McLaren-Honda |
| 1967 | Denis Hulme, New Zealand | Brabham-Repco | 1990 | Ayrton Senna, Brazil | McLaren-Honda |
| | | | 1991 | Ayrton Senna, Brazil | McLaren-Honda |
| 1968 | Graham Hill, England | Lotus-Ford | 1992 | Nigel Mansell, Britain | Williams-Renault |
| | | | 1993 | Alain Prost, France | Williams-Renault |
| | | | 1994 | Michael Schumacher, Germ | Benetton-Ford |

*The championship was awarded after Rindt was killed in practice for the Italian Grand Prix.

## Alltime Grand Prix Winners

| Driver | Wins | Driver | Wins |
|---|---|---|---|
| Alain Prost, France | 51 | Juan-Manuel Fangio, Argentina | 24 |
| Ayrton Senna, Brazil | 41 | Nelson Piquet, Brazil | 20 |
| Jackie Stewart, Scotland | 27 | Stirling Moss, England | 16 |
| Nigel Mansell, England* | 29 | Michael Schumacher, Germany* | 17 |
| Jim Clark, Scotland | 25 | Jack Brabham, Australia | 14 |
| Niki Lauda, Austria | 25 | Graham Hill, England | 14 |
| | | Emerson Fittipaldi, Brazil* | 14 |

*Active driver. Note: Grand Prix Winners through October 1, 1995.

## Alltime Grand Prix Pole Winners

| Driver | Poles | Driver | Poles |
|---|---|---|---|
| Ayrton Senna, Brazil | 65 | Mario Andretti, United States | 18 |
| Alain Prost, France | 41 | Jackie Stewart, Scotland | 17 |
| Jim Clark, Scotland | 33 | Stirling Moss, England | 16 |
| Juan-Manuel Fangio, Argentina | 28 | Alberto Ascari, Italy | 14 |
| Niki Lauda, Austria | 24 | Ronnie Peterson, Sweden | 14 |
| Nelson Piquet, Brazil | 24 | James Hunt, England | 14 |

Note: Pole Winners through 1994 season.

# IMSA Racing

## The 24 Hours of Daytona

| Year | Winner | Car | Avg Speed | Distance |
|---|---|---|---|---|
| 1962 | Dan Gurney | Lotus 19-Class SP11 | 104.101 mph | 3 hrs (312.42 mi) |
| 1963 | Pedro Rodriguez | Ferrari-Class 12 | 102.074 mph | 3 hrs (308.61 mi) |
| 1964 | Pedro Rodriguez/Phil Hill | Ferrari 250 LM | 98.230 mph | 2,000 km |
| 1965 | Ken Miles/Lloyd Ruby | Ford | 99.944 mph | 2,000 km |
| 1966 | Ken Miles/Lloyd Ruby | Ford Mark II | 108.020 mph | 24 hrs (2,570.63 mi) |
| 1967 | Lorenzo Bandini/Chris Amon | Ferrari 330 P4 | 105.688 mph | 24 hrs (2,537.46 mi) |
| 1968 | Vic Elford/Jochen Neerpasch | Porsche 907 | 106.697 mph | 24 hrs (2,565.69 mi) |
| 1969 | Mark Donohue/Chuck Parsons | Chevy Lola | 99.268 mph | 24 hrs (2,383.75 mi) |
| 1970 | Pedro Rodriguez/Leo Kinnunen | Porsche 917 | 114.866 mph | 24 hrs (2,758.44 mi) |
| 1971 | Pedro Rodriguez/Jackie Oliver | Porsche 917K | 109.203 mph | 24 hrs (2,621.28 mi) |
| 1972* | Mario Andretti/Jacky Ickx | Ferrari 312/P | 122.573 mph | 6 hrs (738.24 mi) |
| 1973 | Peter Gregg/Hurley Haywood | Porsche Carrera | 106.225 mph | 24 hrs (2,552.7 mi) |
| 1974 | (No race) | | | |
| 1975 | Peter Gregg/Hurley Haywood | Porsche Carrera | 108.531 mph | 24 hrs (2,606.04 mi) |
| 1976† | Peter Gregg/Brian Redman/ John Fitzpatrick | BMW CSL | 104.040 mph | 24 hrs (2,092.8 mi) |
| 1977 | John Graves/Hurley Haywood/ Dave Helmick | Porsche Carrera | 108.801 mph | 24 hrs (2,615 mi) |
| 1978 | Rolf Stommelen/ Antoine Hezemans/Peter Gregg | Porsche Turbo | 108.743 mph | 24 hrs (2,611.2 mi) |
| 1979 | Ted Field/Danny Ongais/ Hurley Haywood | Porsche Turbo | 109.249 mph | 24 hrs (2,626.56 mi) |
| 1980 | Volkert Meri/Rolf Stommelen/ Reinhold Joest | Porsche Turbo | 114.303 mph | 24 hrs |
| 1981 | Bob Garretson/Bobby Rahal/ Brian Redman | Porsche Turbo | 113.153 mph | 24 hrs |
| 1982 | John Paul, Jr/John Paul, Sr/ Rolf Stommelen | Porsche Turbo | 114.794 mph | 24 hrs |
| 1983 | Preston Henn/Bob Wollek/ Claude Ballot-Lena/A. J. Foyt | Porsche Turbo | 98.781 mph | 24 hrs |
| 1984 | Sarel van der Merwe/ Graham Duxbury/Tony Martin | Porsche March | 103.119 mph | 24 hrs (2,476.8 mi) |
| 1985 | A. J. Foyt/Bob Wollek/ Al Unser, Sr/Thierry Boutsen | Porsche 962 | 104.162 mph | 24 hrs (2,502.68 mi) |
| 1986 | Al Holbert/Derek Bell/Al Unser Jr | Porsche 962 | 105.484 mph | 24 hrs (2,534.72 mi) |
| 1987 | Chip Robinson/Derek Bell/ Al Holbert/Al Unser Jr | Porsche 962 | 111.599 mph | 24 hrs (2,680.68 mi) |
| 1988 | Martin Brundle/John Nielsen/ Raul Boesel | Jaguar XJR-9 | 107.943 mph | 24 hrs (2,591.68 mi) |
| 1989 | John Andretti/Derek Bell/ Bob Wollek | Porsche 962 | 92.009 mph | 24 hrs (2,210.76 mi) |
| 1990 | Davy Jones/Jan Lammers/ Andy Wallace | Jaguar XJR-12 | 112.857 mph | 24 hrs (2,709.16 mi) |
| 1991 | Hurley Haywood/John Winter/ Frank Jelinski/Henri Pescarolo/ Bob Wollek | Porsche 962C | 106.633 mph | 24 hrs (2,559.64 mi) |
| 1992 | Massahiro Hasemi/ Kazuoyshi Hoshino/Toshio Suzuki/Anders Olofsson | Nissan R91CP | 112.987 | 24 hrs (2,712.72 mi) |
| 1993 | P.J. Jones/Mark Dismore/ Rocky Moran | Toyota Eagle MK III | 103.537 | 24 hrs (2,484.88 mi) |
| 1994 | Paul Gentilozzi/ Scott Pruett/ Butch Leitzinger/ Steve Millen | Nissan 300 ZX | 104.80 | 24 hrs (2693.67) |

## The 24 Hours of Daytona (Cont.)

| Year | Winner | Car | Avg Speed | Distance |
|------|--------|-----|-----------|----------|
| 1995 | Jeremy Dale/ Fredrik Ekblom/ Jay Cochran | Oldsmoblie BDG02 | 101.342 mph | 685 laps |

*Race shortened due to fuel crisis.

†Course lengthened from 3.81 miles to 3.84 miles.

### World Champions

| Year | Winner | Car | Year | Winner | Car |
|------|--------|-----|------|--------|-----|
| 1971 | Peter Gregg/ Hurley Haywood | Porsche 914 | 1982 | John Paul Jr | Chevy Lola |
| | | | 1983 | Al Holbert | Chevy March |
| 1972 | Hurley Haywood | Porsche 911 | 1984 | Randy Lanier | Chevy March |
| 1973 | Peter Gregg | Porsche Carrera | 1985 | Al Holbert | Porsche 962 |
| 1974 | Peter Gregg | Porsche Carrera | 1986 | Al Holbert | Porsche 962 |
| 1975 | Peter Gregg | Porsche Carrera | 1987 | Chip Robinson | Porsche 962 |
| 1976 | Al Holbert | Chevy Monza | 1988 | Geoff Brabham | Nissan GTP |
| 1977 | Al Holbert | Chevy Monza | 1989 | Geoff Brabham | Nissan GTP |
| 1978 | Peter Gregg | Porsche 935 | 1990 | Geoff Brabham | Nissan GTP |
| 1979 | Peter Gregg | Porsche 935 | 1991 | Geoff Brabham | Nissan NPT |
| 1980 | John Fitzpatrick | Porsche 935 | 1992 | Juan Fangio II | Toyota EGL MKIII |
| 1981 | Brian Redman | Chevy Lola | 1993 | Juan Fangio II | Toyota EGL MKIII |
| | | | 1994 | Wayne Taylor | Mazda Kudzu |

### Alltime IMSA Leaders

**WINS**

| | |
|---|---|
| Al Holbert | 49 |
| Peter Gregg | 41 |
| Hurley Haywood | 28 |
| Irv Hoerr | 28 |
| Geoff Brabham | 26 |
| Gene Felton | 25 |
| Parker Johnstone | 25 |
| Jim Downing | 23 |
| Don Devendorf | 22 |
| Tommy Riggins | 22 |
| Jack Baldwin | 21 |
| Bob Earl | 21 |
| Juan Fangio II | 21 |

**FASTEST QUALIFIERS**

| | |
|---|---|
| Peter Gregg | 37 |
| Al Holbert | 27 |
| Geoff Brabham | 26 |
| John Paul Jr. | 19 |
| John Fitzpatrick | 12 |
| Sarel Van der Merwe | 11 |
| Chip Robinson | 11 |
| Davy Jones | 10 |
| Danny Ongais | 10 |
| David Hobbs | 9 |
| Klaus Ludwig | 9 |
| John Greenwood | 8 |
| Hans Stuck | 8 |
| Bill Whittington | 7 |

Note: Leaders through 1994 season.

# FIA World Sports Car Racing

## The 24 Hours of LeMans

| Year | Winning Drivers | Car |
|------|-----------------|-----|
| 1923 | André Lagache/René Léonard | Chenard & Walker |
| 1924 | John Duff/Francis Clement | Bentley 3-litre |
| 1925 | Gérard de Courcelles/André Rossignol | La Lorraine |
| 1926 | Robert Bloch/André Rossignol | La Lorraine |
| 1927 | J. Dudley Benjafield/Sammy Davis | Bentley 3-litre |
| 1928 | Woolf Barnato/Bernard Rubin | Bentley 4½ |
| 1929 | Woolf Barnato/Sir Henry Birkin | Bentley Speed Six |
| 1930 | Woolf Barnato/Glen Kidston | Bentley Speed Six |
| 1931 | Earl Howe/Sir Henry Birkin | Alfa Romeo 8C-2300 sc |
| 1932 | Raymond Sommer/Luigi Chinetti | Alfa Romeo 8C-2300 sc |
| 1933 | Raymond Sommer/Tazio Nuvolari | Alfa Romeo 8C-2300 sc |
| 1934 | Luigi Chinetti/Philippe Etancelin | Alfa Romeo 8C-2300 sc |

## The 24 Hours of LeMans *(Cont.)*

| Year | Winning Drivers | Car |
|------|----------------|-----|
| 1935 | John Hindmarsh/Louis Fontés | Lagonda M45R |
| 1936 | Race cancelled | |
| 1937 | Jean-Pierre Wimille/Robert Benoist | Bugatti 57G sc |
| 1938 | Eugene Chaboud/Jean Tremoulet | Delahaye 135M |
| 1939 | Jean-Pierre Wimille/Pierre Veyron | Bugatti 57G sc |
| 1940-48 | Races cancelled | |
| 1949 | Luigi Chinetti/Lord Selsdon | Ferrari 166MM |
| 1950 | Louis Rosier/Jean-Louis Rosier | Talbot-Lago |
| 1951 | Peter Walker/Peter Whitehead | Jaguar C |
| 1952 | Hermann Lang/Fritz Reiss | Mercedes-Benz 300 SL |
| 1953 | Tony Rolt/Duncan Hamilton | Jaguar C |
| 1954 | Froilan Gonzales/Maurice Trintignant | Ferrari 375 |
| 1955 | Mike Hawthorn/Ivor Bueb | Jaguar D |
| 1956 | Ron Flockhart/Ninian Sanderson | Jaguar D |
| 1957 | Ron Flockhart/Ivor Buab | Jaguar D |
| 1958 | Olivier Gendebien/Phil Hill | Ferrari 250 TR58 |
| 1959 | Carroll Shelby/Roy Salvadori | Aston Martin DBR1 |
| 1960 | Olivier Gendebien/Paul Fräre | Ferrari 250 TR59/60 |
| 1961 | Olivier Gendebien/Phil Hill | Ferrari 250 TR61 |
| 1962 | Olivier Gendebien/Phil Hill | Ferrari 250P |
| 1963 | Lodovico Scarfiotti/Lorenzo Bandini | Ferrari 250P |
| 1964 | Jean Guichel/Nino Vaccarella | Ferrari 275P |
| 1965 | Jochen Rindt/Masten Gregory | Ferrari 250LM |
| 1966 | Chris Amon/Bruce McLaren | Ford Mk2 |
| 1967 | Dan Gurney/A. J. Foyt | Ford Mk4 |
| 1968 | Pedro Rodriguez/Lucien Bianchi | Ford GT40 |
| 1969 | Jacky Ickx/Jackie Oliver | Ford GT40 |
| 1970 | Hans Herrmann/Richard Attwood | Porsche 917 |
| 1971 | Helmut Marko/Gijs van Lennep | Porsche 917 |
| 1972 | Henri Pescarolo/Graham Hill | Matra-Simca MS670 |
| 1973 | Henri Pescarolo/Gérard Larrousse | Matra-Simca MS670B |
| 1974 | Henri Pescarolo/Gérard Larrousse | Matra-Simca MS670B |
| 1975 | Jacky Ickx/Derek Bell | Mirage-Ford MB |
| 1976 | Jacky Ickx/Gijs van Lennep | Porsche 936 |
| 1977 | Jacky Ickx/Jurgen Barth/Hurley Haywood | Porsche 936 |
| 1978 | Jean-Pierre Jaussaud/Didier Pironi | Renault-Alpine A442 |
| 1979 | Klaus Ludwig/Bill Whttington/Don Whittington | Porsche 935 |
| 1980 | Jean-Pierre Jaussaud/Jean Rondeau | Rondeau-Ford M379B |
| 1981 | Jacky Ickx/Derek Bell | Porsche 936-81 |
| 1982 | Jacky Ickx/Derek Bell | Porsche 956 |
| 1983 | Vern Schuppan/Hurley Haywood/Al Holbert | Porsche 956-83 |
| 1984 | Klaus Ludwig/Henri Pescarolo | Porsche 956B |
| 1985 | Klaus Ludwig/Paolo Barilla/John Winter | Porsche 956B |
| 1986 | Derek Bell/Hans-Joachim Stuck/Al Holbert | Porsche 962C |
| 1987 | Derek Bell/Hans-Joachim Stuck/Al Holbert | Porsche 962C |
| 1988 | Jan Lammers/Johnny Dumfries/Andy Wallace | Jaguar XJR9LM |
| 1989 | Jochen Mass/Manuel Reuter/Stanley Dickens | Sauber-Mercedes C9-88 |
| 1990 | John Nielsen/Price Cobb/Martin Brundle | TWR Jaguar XJR-12 |
| 1991 | Volker Weidler/Johnny Herbert/Bertrand Gachof | Mazda 787B |
| 1992 | Derek Warwick/Yannick Dalmas/Mark Blundell | Peugeot 905B |
| 1993 | Geoff Brabham/Christophe Bouchut/Eric Helary | Peugeot 905 |
| 1994 | Yannick Dalmas/Hurley Haywood/Mauro Baldi | Porsche 962 |
| 1995 | Yannick Dalmas/J.J. Lehto/Masanori Sekiya | McLaren F1 GTR |

## Top Fuel

### ELAPSED TIME

| | | |
|---|---|---|
| 9.00.....................Jack Chrisman | Feb 18, 1961 | Pomona, CA |
| 8.97.....................Jack Chrisman | May 20, 1961 | Empona, VA |
| 7.96.....................Bobby Vodnick | May 16, 1964 | Bayview, MD |
| 6.97.....................Don Johnson | May 7, 1967 | Carlsbad, CA |
| 5.97.....................Mike Snively | Nov 17, 1972 | Ontario, CA |
| 5.78.....................Don Garlits | Nov 18, 1973 | Ontario, CA |
| 5.698...................Gary Beck | Oct 10, 1975 | Ontario, CA |
| 5.573...................Gary Beck | Oct 18, 1981 | Irvine, CA |
| 5.484...................Gary Beck | Sept 6, 1982 | Clermont, IN |
| 5.391...................Gary Beck | Oct 1, 1983 | Fremont, CA |
| 5.280...................Darrell Gwynn | Sept 25, 1986 | Ennis, TX |
| 5.176...................Darrell Gwynn | April 4, 1987 | Ennis, TX |
| 5.090...................Joe Amato | Oct 1, 1987 | Ennis, TX |
| 4.990...................Eddie Hill | April 9, 1988 | Ennis, TX |
| 4.881...................Gary Ormsby | Sept 28, 1990 | Topeka, KS |
| 4.799...................Cory McClenathan | Sept 19, 1992 | Mohnton, PA |
| 4.762...................Cory McClenathan | Oct 3, 1993 | Topeka, KS |
| 4.690...................Michael Brotherton | May 20, 1994 | Englishtown, NJ |

### SPEED

| | | |
|---|---|---|
| 180.36.................Connie Kalitta | Sept 3, 1962 | Indianapolis |
| 190.26.................Don Garlits | Sept 21, 1963 | East Haddam, CT |
| 201.34.................Don Garlits | Aug 1, 1964 | Great Meadows, NJ |
| 211.26.................Donny Milani | May 15, 1965 | Sacramento, CA |
| 223.32.................Don Cook | Apr 24, 1965 | Fremont, CA |
| 230.17.................James Warren | Apr 10, 1967 | Fresno, CA |
| 243.24.................Don Garlits | March 18, 1973 | Gainesville, FL |
| 250.69.................Don Garlits | Oct 11, 1975 | Ontario, CA |
| 260.11.................Joe Amato | March 18, 1984 | Gainesville, FL |
| 272.56.................Don Garlits | March 23, 1986 | Gainesville, FL |
| 282.13.................Joe Amato | Sept 5, 1987 | Clermont, IN |
| 291.54.................Connie Kalitta | Feb 11, 1989 | Pomona, CA |
| 301.70.................Kenny Bernstein | March 20, 1992 | Gainesville, FL |
| 311.86.................Kenny Bernstein | Oct 30, 1994 | Pomona, CA |

## Funny Car

### ELAPSED TIME

| | | |
|---|---|---|
| 6.92.....................Leroy Goldstein | Sept 3, 1970 | Clermont, IN |
| 5.987...................Don Prudhomme | Oct 12, 1975 | Ontario, CA |
| 5.868...................Raymond Beadle | July 16, 1981 | Englishtown, NJ |
| 5.799...................Tom Anderson | Sept 3, 1982 | Clermont, IN |
| 5.637...................Don Prudhomme | Sept 4, 1982 | Clermont, IN |
| 5.588...................Rick Johnson | Feb 3, 1985 | Pomona, CA |
| 5.425...................Kenny Bernstein | Sept 26, 1986 | Ennis, TX |
| 5.397...................Kenny Bernstein | April 5, 1987 | Ennis, TX |
| 5.255...................Ed McCulloch | April 17, 1988 | Ennis, TX |
| 5.193...................Don Prudhomme | March 2, 1989 | Baytown, TX |
| 5.077...................Cruz Pedregon | Sept 20, 1992 | Mohnton, PA |
| 4.987...................Chuck Etcholis | Oct 2, 1993 | Topeka, KA |

### SPEED

| | | |
|---|---|---|
| 200.44.................Gene Snow | August, 1968 | Houston, TX |
| 250.00.................Don Prudhomme | May 23, 1982 | Baton Rouge, LA |
| 260.11.................Kenny Bernstein | March 18, 1984 | Gainesville, FL |
| 271.41.................Kenny Bernstein | Aug 30, 1986 | Indianapolis |
| 280.72.................Mike Dunn | Oct 2, 1987 | Ennis, TX |
| 290.13.................Jim White | Oct 11, 1991 | Ennis TX |
| 291.82.................Jim White | Oct 25, 1991 | Pomona, CA |
| 300.40.................Jim Epler | Oct 3, 1993 | Topeka, KS |

## Pro Stock

### ELAPSED TIME

| | | | |
|---|---|---|---|
| 7.778 | Lee Shepherd | March 12, 1982 | Gainesville, FL |
| 7.655 | Lee Shepherd | Oct 1, 1982 | Fremont, CA |
| 7.557 | Bob Glidden | Feb 2, 1985 | Pomona, CA |
| 7.497 | Bob Glidden | Sep 13, 1985 | Maple Grove, PA |
| 7.377 | Bob Glidden | Aug 28, 1986 | Clermont, IN |
| 7.294 | Frank Sanchez | Oct 7, 1988 | Baytown, TX |
| 7.184 | Darrell Alderman | Oct 12, 1990 | Ennis, TX |
| 7.099 | Scott Geoffrion | Sep 19, 1992 | Mohnton, PA |
| 6.988 | Kurt Johnson | May 20, 1994 | Englishtown, NJ |

### SPEED

| | | | |
|---|---|---|---|
| 181.08 | Warren Johnson | Oct 1, 1982 | Fremont, CA |
| 190.07 | Warren Johnson | Aug 29, 1986 | Clermont, IN |
| 191.32 | Bob Glidden | Sep 4, 1987 | Clermont, IN |
| 192.18 | Warren Johnson | Oct 13, 1990 | Ennis, TX |
| 193.21 | Bob Glidden | July 28, 1991 | Sonoma, CA |
| 194.51 | Warren Johnson | July 31, 1992 | Sonoma, CA |
| 195.99 | Warren Johnson | May 21, 1993 | Englishtown, NJ |
| 196.24 | Warren Johnson | Mar 19, 1993 | Gainesville, FL |
| 197.15 | Warren Johnson | Apr 23, 1994 | Commerce, GA |

## Alltime Drag Racing Leaders

### NATIONAL EVENT WINS

| | |
|---|---|
| Bob Glidden | 84 |
| Don Prudhomme | 49 |
| Warren Johnson | 47 |
| Kenny Bernstein | 42 |
| John Force | 42 |
| Don Garlits | 35 |
| Joe Amato | 34 |
| David Schultz | 34 |
| Lee Shepherd | 26 |
| Terry Vance | 24 |

### BEST WON-LOST RECORD (WINNING PCT)

| | |
|---|---|
| David Schultz | 205-44 (.823) |
| John Myers | 158-37 (.810) |
| Bob Glidden | 768-187 (.804) |
| Darrell Alderman | 171-56 (.753) |
| John Force | 370-156 (70.3) |
| Warren Johnson | 416-180 (.698) |
| James Bernard | 68-30 (.694) |
| Joe Amato | 356-160 (.690) |
| Cruz Pedregon | 109-53 (.673) |
| Kenny Bernstein | 366-181 (.669) |

Note: Drag Racing Leaders through 1994 season.

## THEY SAID IT

*Scott Pruett, Indy Car driver, who counts among his sponsors Firestone tires: "It's been a very good year. Excuse me, it's been a very fine year."*

# Bowling

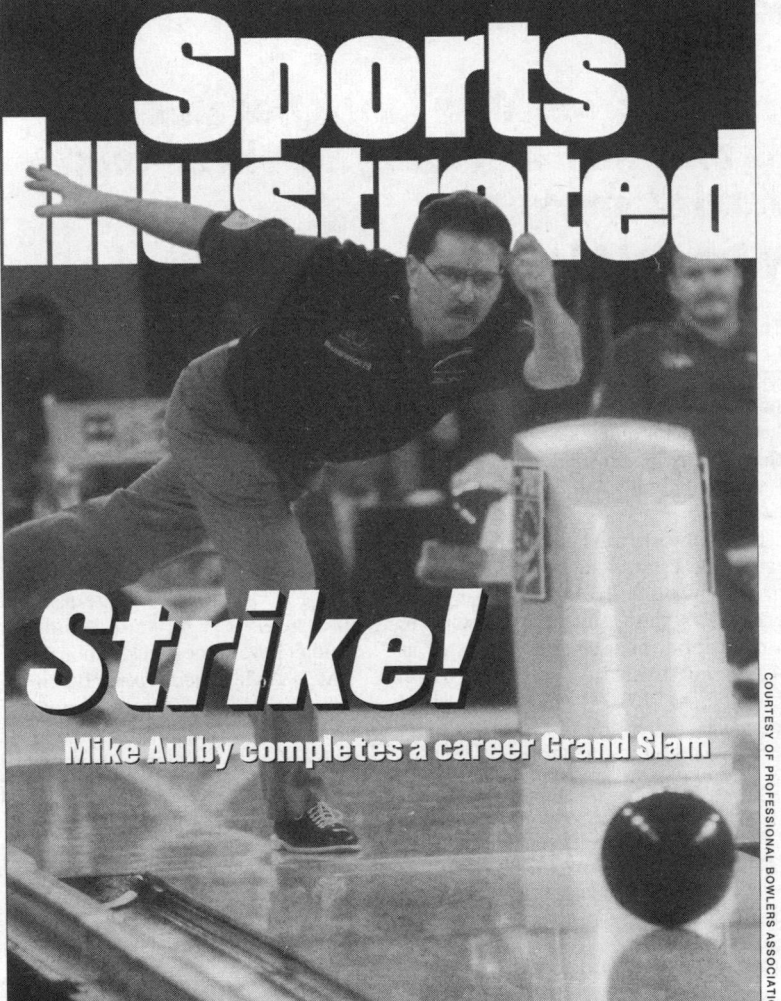

## Sports Illustrated

## Strike!

**Mike Aulby completes a career Grand Slam**

# Aulby Darned

## A rejuvenated Mike Aulby became the only man in history to win all four Grand Slam events

## by Franz Lidz

LATE LAST summer the Agriculture Department ruled that if you can bowl with a grocery store chicken, it's not fresh. Henceforth, chickens frozen solid enough to double as bowling balls will be labeled "hard chilled."

Lack of network cash had a similar chilling effect on the Professional Bowlers Association. The tour, the PBA's showcase and a weekend TV fixture since the Eisenhower administration, headed for the gutter as ABC-TV cut back its rights fees from $3.52 million to $700,000, and the number of tournaments it aired from 24 to 14. "Ratings aren't a problem," said Dennis Lewin of ABC, which has televised the tour for the last 33 years. "Revenues are." Unable to find title sponsors for two of its 15 winter events, the PBA had to scale back events and offer smaller purses. And since entry fees kept getting higher, many bowlers reduced their schedules or retired.

In Bowling's Year of the Frozen Chicken, it was turkeys that resurrected Mike Aulby's career. In the 1980s Aulby was voted Bowler of the Decade. In the early '90s he was remembered mostly for having mowed down rows of beer mugs, family-sized bottles of ketchup and pitchers of strawberry Kool-Aid on David Letterman's show.

Aulby entered 1995 on the heels of a disheartening '94—a year in which his father died, he won a meager $32,303, and he failed to win a single tournament. "I gladly kissed 1994 goodbye at one minute past midnight on January 1," he said. "And that day couldn't have come quickly enough."

At 16 Aulby made *Ripley's Believe It or Not* for racking up six 300's in six months. At 34 the most lethal lefthander since Earl Anthony achieved an even more astounding feat by becoming the first kegler ever to complete bowling's Grand Slam.

The Aulby or Nothing Show hit the road in February at the Peoria Open, where he set a PBA record by averaging 251.3 for 42 games of qualifying and match play, only to fizzle in the final. The next week in Toledo he finished third behind Wayne Webb and the victorious Scott Alexander at the PBA National Championship, an event Aulby had won in 1979 and '85. In early April he barely missed the

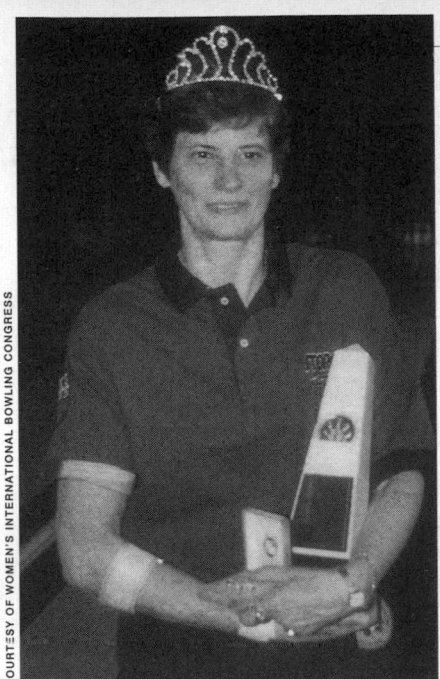

COURTESY OF WOMEN'S INTERNATIONAL BOWLING CONGRESS

edge of elimination. Needing 28 points on his final three shots, Aulby got a turkey. The rest was just giblets: easy wins over Larry Laub, Pat Healey, Kelly Coffman and Ryan Shafer put him in the winner's bracket finals against Mark Williams, the only other unbeaten player. Though Williams triumphed 697-609, Aulby creamed Shafer 711-598 in the stepladder finals to become the No. 2 qualifier. That was all Aulby needed. Williams didn't survive a fourth-frame washout and chalked up a 187. Aulby's 200 made him the first bowler in history to have all four major titles—the PBA, the U.S. Open, the Tournament of Champions and the ABC Masters—on his resumé.

Bowling historians take note: Linda Wallace became the first ABC female member to compete at the Masters since its inception in 1951. Not everyone was bowled over by Wallace's participation, however. When she tried to enter the squad room, a male official snapped, "You can't come in here. Only bowlers are allowed."

"I am bowling," said Wallace, who had qualified by winning the 1994 Arizona Masters.

"There are no women bowling in this."

"I am," said Wallace and handed him a sheet that listed her starting time. She finished 540th in a field of 608. "It's a once in a lifetime thing," Wallace said. "I can't be unhappy no matter how I bowled."

One winner who was the tiniest bit unhappy was Sandy Postma, the 48-year-old grandmother who came out of nowhere to win the Women's International Bowling Congress Queens title in Tucson. A part-timer who took up the sport at 29 to keep busy while her two kids were in school, she had been winless in an 11-year pro career. Postma lost track of the score in the 10th frame and quietly asked Queens officials if she had won. Missing at the victory party was Postma's husband, Richard, who couldn't get off work. Asked to name the worst part of being alone, she said, "I had no one to hug."

championship round of the U.S. Open, finishing a respectable sixth. The Open crown, which Aulby last wore in 1989, was snared by Dave Husted, the '82 champion.

Two weeks later Aulby stormed into the title game of the Brunswick Tournament of Champions in Palatin, Ill. The event's top qualifier, Bob Spaulding, led most of the contest. But he left a 7–10 split in his ninth frame before striking out in the 10th. "How did I feel after I struck out?" sputtered Spaulding. "I felt like I'd lost." Aulby needed a double and four pins to win. He got a double and eight to become only the fourth triple crown winner in the PBA's 36-year history. "There are great bowlers in this game and greater bowlers," observed tour veteran Parker Bohn III. "If you don't consider Mike Aulby one of the greatest bowlers who ever lived after this victory, you don't know much about the sport."

Aulby showed why some think he is the Greatest two weeks later in Reno at the American Bowling Congress Masters, a tournament he won in 1989. In his opening match with Sam Ventura, he tottered on the

## The Majors

### MEN

### Chevrolet PBA National Championship
#### CHAMPIONSHIP ROUND

| Bowler | Games | Total | Earnings ($) |
|---|---|---|---|
| Scott Alexander | 1 | 246 | 35,000 |
| Wayne Webb | 4 | 948 | 18,000 |
| Mike Aulby | 1 | 215 | 10,000 |
| Don Genalo | 1 | 215 | 8,000 |
| Jason Couch | 1 | 225 | 6,500 |

**Playoff Results:** Webb def. Couch, 235-225; Webb def. Genalo, 248-215; Webb def. Aulby, 255-215; Alexander def. Webb, 246-210.

Held at Ducat's Imperial Lanes, Toledo, OH, Feb 19-25, 1995.

### BPAA United States Open
#### CHAMPIONSHIP ROUND

| Bowler | Games | Total | Earnings ($) |
|---|---|---|---|
| Dave Husted | 1 | 266 | 46,000 |
| Paul Koehler | 2 | 523 | 24,000 |
| Steve Hoskins | 3 | 743 | 14,000 |
| Parker Bohn III | 1 | 216 | 10,500 |
| Dave D'Entremont | 1 | 212 | 8,500 |

**Playoff Results:** Hoskins def. D'Entremont, 231-212; Hoskins def. Bohn, 256-216; Koehler def. Hoskins, 278-256; Husted def. Koehler, 266-245.

Held at Bowl One, Troy, MI, April 2-8, 1995.

### Brunswick World Tournament of Champions
#### CHAMPIONSHIP ROUND

| Bowler | Games | Total | Earnings ($) |
|---|---|---|---|
| Mike Aulby | 2 | 502 | 60,000 |
| Bob Spaulding | 1 | 232 | 33,000 |
| Pat Healey | 2 | 408 | 24,000 |
| Dennis Horan | 2 | 490 | 18,000 |
| Parker Bohn III | 1 | 243 | 12,000 |

**Playoff Results:** Horan def. Bohn, 265-243; Healey def. Horan, 231-225; Aulby def. Healey, 265-177; Aulby def. Spaulding, 237-232.

Held at Brunswick Deer Park Lanes, Lake Zurich, IL, April 18-22, 1995.

### ABC Masters Tournament
#### CHAMPIONSHIP ROUND

| Bowler | Games | Total | Earnings ($) |
|---|---|---|---|
| Mike Aulby | 2 | 422 | 50,600 |
| Mark Williams | 1 | 187 | 26,600 |
| Ryan Shafer | 2 | 360 | 20,600 |
| Bob Benoit | 2 | 352 | 15,600 |
| Larry Laub | 1 | 186 | 10,800 |

**Playoff Results:** Benoit def. Laub, 195–186; Shafer def. Benoit, 190–157; Aulby def. Shafer, 222–170; Aulby def. Williams, 200–187.

Held at National Bowling Stadium, Reno, NV, May 2–6, 1995.

## WOMEN

### Sam's Town Invitational

#### CHAMPIONSHIP ROUND

| Bowler | Games | Total | Earnings ($) |
|---|---|---|---|
| Tish Johnson...............................1 | | 178 | 18,000 |
| Carol Gianotti............................2 | | 388 | 9,000 |
| Tammy Turner...........................3 | | 681 | 4,700 |
| Dede Davidson.........................1 | | 177 | 4,300 |
| Jackie Sellers.............................1 | | 188 | 3,800 |

**Playoff Results:** Turner def. Sellers, 214-188; Turner def. Davidson, 277-177; Gianotti def. Turner, 216-290; Johnson def. Gianotti, 178-172.

Held at Sam's Town Bowling Center, Las Vegas, NV, Nov 12-19, 1994.

### WIBC Queens

#### CHAMPIONSHIP ROUND

| Bowler | Games | Total | Earnings ($) |
|---|---|---|---|
| Sandra Postma .........................2 | | 467 | 12,525 |
| Carolyn Dorin............................1 | | 187 | 7,450 |
| Kim Canady...............................2 | | 469 | 4,650 |
| Cathy Dorin...............................2 | | 424 | 3,450 |
| Tish Johnson.............................1 | | 192 | 2,600 |

**Playoff Results:** Cathy Dorin def. Johnson, 244-192; Canady def. Cathy Dorin, 239-180; Postma def. Canady, 241-230; Postma def. Carolyn Dorin, 226-187.

Held at Golden Pins Lanes, Tucson, AZ, May 14-18, 1995.

### BPAA United States Open

#### CHAMPIONSHIP ROUND

| Bowler | Games | Total | Earnings ($) |
|---|---|---|---|
| Cheryl Daniels ..........................2 | | 458 | 18,000 |
| Tish Johnson.............................1 | | 180 | 9,000 |
| Diana Teeters ...........................3 | | 694 | 7,000 |
| Wendy Macpherson-Papanos...1 | | 183 | 5,000 |
| Sandra Jo Shiery ......................1 | | 212 | 4,000 |

**Playoff Results:** Teeters def. Shiery 247-212; Teeters def. Macpherson-Papanos 225-183; Daniels def. Teeters 223-222; Daniels def. Johnson 235-180.

Championship round held at National Sports Center, Blaine, MN, Oct 6, 1995.

## In a Dark Alley

It was a kegler ritual not seen since the dark ages of Fred Flinstone. On the evening of April 12, 1995, 150 men crouched around lane 17 of Marcel's Pinarama Bowl in Oswego, N.Y., many of them holding lighters and flashhlights. In the middle of this muddle stood Matt Berlin, a 30-year-old sanitation worker and Wednesday-night bowler in the local Elks league. An hour earlier he had been one strike shy of a perfect game. Then the power went out. "Not only was it pitch black, but there were no sounds," says Berlin. "Normally you hear the hum of the machines and the smack of pins being knocked down, but there was nothing."

With his friends showing the way, Berlin stared into the half-light and threw a strike. The next minute he found himself at the bottom of a jubilant pile; the next morning, at the bottom of the front page of *The Palladium Times*. "From now on," he says, "I'm just going to look down at the fourth dot and pretend it's dark around me."

# PBA Tour Results

## 1994 Fall Tour

| Date | Event | Winner | Earnings ($) | Runner-Up |
|------|-------|--------|--------------|-----------|
| Sep 30-Oct 5 | AMF Dick Weber Classic | John Mazza | 60,000 | Parker Bohn III |
| Oct 8-12 | Touring Players Championship | Walter Ray Williams Jr | 16,000 | Butch Soper |
| Oct 15-19 | Greater Detroit Open | Bryan Goebel | 14,000 | Eric Forkel |
| Oct 22-26 | Rochester Open | Norm Duke | 16,000 | Doug Kent |
| Oct 29-Nov 2 | Great Lakes PBA Classic | Dave Ferraro | 16,000 | Norm Duke |
| Nov 3-9 | Brunswick Memorial World Open | Erik Forkel | 45,492 | David Ozio |

## 1995 Winter Tour

| Date | Event | Winner | Earnings ($) | Runner-Up |
|------|-------|--------|--------------|-----------|
| Jan 10-14 | AC-Delco Classic | Jess Stayrook | 45,000 | Bob Learn Jr |
| Jan 17-21 | Hilton Hotels Classic | Justin Hromek | 35,000 | Mike Scroggins |
| Jan 22-28 | Showboat Invitational | Dave Husted | 37,000 | Ricky Ward |
| Jan 31-Feb 4 | Quaker State 250 | Bob Spaulding | 48,000 | Kelly Coffman |
| Feb 7-11 | Choice Hotels Classic | Dave D'Entremont | 45,000 | Tommy Evans |
| Feb 14-18 | Greater Peoria Open | Dave D'Entremont | 20,000 | Mike Aulby |
| Feb 19-25 | Chevrolet PBA National Championship | Scott Alexander | 35,000 | Wayne Webb |
| Feb 28-Mar 4 | Greater Baltimore Open | David Traber | 18,000 | Eric Forkel |
| Mar 7-11 | Brunswick Johnny Petraglia Open | John Gant | 34,000 | Ken McNeely |
| Mar 14-18 | Bud Light Championship | Jess Stayrook | 37,000 | Philip Ringener |
| Mar 21-25 | Tums Classic | Jack Jurek | 25,000 | David Traber |
| Mar 28-Apr 1 | Splitfire Spark Plug Open | Danny Wiseman | 39,000 | Steve Jaros |
| Apr 2-8 | BPAA U.S. Open | Dave Husted | 46,000 | Paul Koehler |
| Apr 11-15 | IOF Foresters Open | Mike Roth | 45,000 | Walter Ray Williams, Jr |
| Apr 18-22 | Brunswick World Tournament of Champions | Mike Aulby | 60,000 | Bob Spaulding |

## 1995 Summer Tour

| Date | Event | Winner | Earnings ($) | Runner-Up |
|------|-------|--------|--------------|-----------|
| July 7-11 | Northwest Classic | John Handegard | 18,000 | Mark Williams |
| July 14-18 | Oregon Open | Norm Duke | 18,000 | Justin Hromek |
| July 21-25 | Tucson Open | Bryan Goebel | 16,000 | Bob Belmont |
| July 28-Aug 1 | Columbia 300 Open | Parker Bohn III | 19,000 | Jason Couch |
| Aug 4-8 | Ebonite Kentucky Classic | Randy Pedersen | 19,000 | Mark Williams |
| Aug 11-15 | Cleveland Open | Norm Duke | 16,000 | Bob Learn Jr |
| Aug 18-22 | Bowlers Journal Classic | Jason Couch | 18,500 | Dave D'Entremont |

## 1994 Senior Fall Tour

| Date | Event | Winner | Earnings ($) | Runner-Up |
|------|-------|--------|--------------|-----------|
| Sep 15-20 | Naples Senior Open | Barry Gurney | 10,000 | Richard Beattie |
| Sep 22-27 | St Petersburg/Clearwater Senior Open | Gary Dickinson | 15,000 | Bobby Knipple |
| Oct 1-5 | Palm Beach Senior Classic | Larry Laub | 8,000 | Barry Gurney |

# PBA Tour Results *(Cont.)*

## 1995 Senior Tour (through Aug 29)

| Date | Event | Winner | Earnings ($) | Runner-Up |
|------|-------|--------|--------------|-----------|
| Jan 7-11 | Tri-Cities PBA Senior Classic | Tommy Evans | 7,500 | Dave Soutar |
| Jan 14-18 | Northwest PBA Senior Classic | Tommy Evans | 7,500 | John Handegard |
| June 3-8 | Greater Providence Senior Open | Gary Dickinson | 8,000 | Allie Clarke |
| June 25-30 | ABC Senior Masters | Dave Davis | 38,000 | John Handegard |
| July 2-6 | Twin Falls PBA Senior Open | Hobo Boothe | 6,500 | Bobby Knipple |
| July 30-Aug 3 | Rocky Mountain Senior Open | Barry Gurney | 10,000 | Avery LeBlanc |
| Aug 7-12 | Showboat Senior Invitational | Denny Torgerson | 20,000 | Gene Stus |
| Aug 17-21 | Hoosier PBA Senior Classic | Dan Roche | 8,000 | Les Zikes |
| Aug 23-29 | Jackson PBA Senior Championship | John Handegard | 16,000 | Avery LeBlanc |

# LPBT Tour Results

## 1994 Fall Tour

| Date | Event | Winner | Earnings ($) | Runner-Up |
|------|-------|--------|--------------|-----------|
| Sep 29-Oct 6 | BPAA US Open | Aleta Sill | 18,000 | Anne Marie Duggan |
| Oct 8-13 | Hammer Midwest Open | Kim Canady | 13,500 | Marianne DiRupo |
| Oct 16-20 | Brunswick Three Rivers Open | Kim Straub | 13,500 | Nikki Gianulas |
| Oct 22-27 | Columbia 300 Delaware Open | Aleta Sill | 13,500 | Tish Johnson |
| Oct 29-Nov 3 | Hammer Eastern Open | Carol Gianotti | 13,500 | Anne Marie Duggan |
| Nov 6-10 | South Bend Open | Sandra Jo Shiery | 9,000 | Carol Gianotti |
| Nov 12-19 | Sam's Town Invitational | Tish Johnson | 18,000 | Carol Gianotti |

## 1995 Winter Tour

| Date | Event | Winner | Earnings ($) | Runner-Up |
|------|-------|--------|--------------|-----------|
| Feb 5-9 | Texas Border Shoot-Out | Aleta Sill | 10,800 | Tish Johnson |
| Feb 12-16 | South Texas Open | Sandra Jo Shiery | 10,800 | Rachel Perez |
| Feb 19-23 | Claremore Classic | Kim Canady | 10,800 | Michelle Mullen |
| Feb 26-Mar 2 | Alexandria Louisiana Open | Tish Johnson | 10,800 | Anne Marie Duggan |
| Mar 5-9 | New Orleans Classic | Robin Romeo | 10,800 | Carolyn Dorin |
| Mar 12-16 | AMF XS Challenge | Anne Marie Duggan | 12,600 | Carolyn Dorin |

## 1995 Spring Tour

| Date | Event | Winner | Earnings ($) | Runner-Up |
|------|-------|--------|--------------|-----------|
| May 6-10 | California Classic | Robin Romeo | 10,800 | Cheryl Daniels |
| May 14-18 | WIBC Queens Tournament | Sandra Postma | 12,525 | Carolyn Dorin |
| May 21-25 | Omaha Lancers Open | Wendy Macpherson | 13,500 | Kim Straub |

## 1995 Summer Tour

| Date | Event | Winner | Earnings ($) | Runner-Up |
|------|-------|--------|--------------|-----------|
| July 9-13 | Quantum Technologies Old Dominion Open | Lisa Wagner | 13,500 | Carol Norman |
| July 16-20 | Rocket City Challenge | Tammy Turner | 10,800 | Michelle Mullen |
| July 24-28 | Sam's Town Tunica Classic | Tish Johnson | 10,800 | Sandra Jo Shiery |

# 1994 Tour Leaders

## PBA

### MONEY LEADERS

| Name | Titles | Tournaments | Earnings ($) |
|---|---|---|---|
| Norm Duke | 5 | 21 | 273,753 |
| Walter Ray Williams Jr | 2 | 28 | 189,745 |
| Bryan Goebel | 4 | 30 | 173,922 |
| Eric Forkel | 1 | 23 | 138,639 |
| John Mazza | 2 | 23 | 129,500 |

### AVERAGE

| Name | Games | Pinfall | Average |
|---|---|---|---|
| Norm Duke | 808 | 180,050 | 222.83 |
| Walter Ray Williams Jr | 1062 | 236,397 | 222.59 |
| Amleto Monacelli | 760 | 167,669 | 220.61 |
| Parker Bohn III | 896 | 196,414 | 219.21 |
| Bryan Goebel | 988 | 216,474 | 219.10 |

## Seniors

### MONEY LEADERS

| Name | Titles | Tournaments | Earnings ($) |
|---|---|---|---|
| Gary Dickinson | 1 | 13 | 54,095 |
| Delano Boothe | 1 | 13 | 48,048 |
| John Handegard | 2 | 12 | 46,980 |
| Tommy Evans | 1 | 13 | 42,033 |
| Rich Moores | 0 | 12 | 38,567 |

### AVERAGE

| Name | Games | Pinfall | Average |
|---|---|---|---|
| John Handegard | 459 | 101,956 | 222.12 |
| Dave Davis | 376 | 83,172 | 221.20 |
| Gene Stus | 511 | 112,985 | 221.10 |
| Larry Laub | 344 | 75,866 | 220.54 |
| Gary Dickinson | 451 | 99,325 | 220.23 |

## LPBT

### MONEY LEADERS

| Name | Titles | Tournaments | Earnings ($) |
|---|---|---|---|
| Aleta Sill | 4 | 21 | 126,325 |
| Anne Marie Duggan | 3 | 22 | 124,722 |
| Tish Johnson | 1 | 21 | 82,756 |
| Marianne DiRupo | 1 | 21 | 72,369 |
| Carol Gianotti | 1 | 20 | 68,039 |

### AVERAGE

| Name | Games | Pinfall | Average |
|---|---|---|---|
| Anne Marie Duggan | 762 | 162,667 | 213.47 |
| Dana Miller-Mackie | 480 | 101,132 | 210.69 |
| Tish Johnson | 806 | 169,736 | 210.59 |
| Marianne DiRupo | 661 | 139,046 | 210.36 |
| Kim Couture | 716 | 150,415 | 210.08 |

## Men's Majors

### BPAA United States Open

| Year | Winner | Score | Runner-Up | Site |
|------|--------|-------|-----------|------|
| 1942 | John Crimmins | 265.09-262.33 | Joe Norris | Chicago |
| 1943 | Connie Schwoegler | not available | Frank Benkovic | Chicago |
| 1944 | Ned Day | 315.21-298.21 | Paul Krumske | Chicago |
| 1945 | Buddy Bomar | 304.46-296.16 | Joe Wilman | Chicago |
| 1946 | Joe Wilman | 310.27-305.37 | Therman Gibson | Chicago |
| 1947 | Andy Varipapa | 314.16-308.04 | Allie Brandt | Chicago |
| 1948 | Andy Varipapa | 309.23-309.06 | Joe Wilman | Chicago |
| 1949 | Connie Schwoegler | 312.31-307.27 | Andy Varipapa | Chicago |
| 1950 | Junie McMahon | 318.37-307.17 | Ralph Smith | Chicago |
| 1951 | Dick Hoover | 305.29-304.07 | Lee Jouglard | Chicago |
| 1952 | Junie McMahon | 309.29-305.41 | Bill Lillard | Chicago |
| 1953 | Don Carter | 304.17-297.36 | Ed Lubanski | Chicago |
| 1954 | Don Carter | 308.02-307.25 | Bill Lillard | Chicago |
| 1955 | Steve Nagy | 307.17-303.34 | Ed Lubanski | Chicago |
| 1956 | Bill Lillard | 304.30-304.22 | Joe Wilman | Chicago |
| 1957 | Don Carter | 308.49-305.45 | Dick Weber | Chicago |
| 1958 | Don Carter | 311.03-308.09 | Buzz Fazio | Minneapolis |
| 1959 | Billy Welu | 311.48-310.26 | Ray Bluth | Buffalo |
| 1960 | Harry Smith | 312.24-308.12 | Bob Chase | Omaha |
| 1961 | Bill Tucker | 318.49-309.11 | Dick Weber | San Bernardino, CA |
| 1962 | Dick Weber | 299.34-297.38 | Roy Lown | Miami Beach |
| 1963 | Dick Weber | 642-591 | Billy Welu | Kansas City, MO |
| 1964 | Bob Strampe | 714-616 | Tommy Tuttle | Dallas |
| 1965 | Dick Weber | 608-586 | Jim St. John | Philadelphia |
| 1966 | Dick Weber | 684-681 | Nelson Burton Jr | Lansing, MI |
| 1967 | Les Schissler | 613-610 | Pete Tountas | St. Ann, MO |
| 1968 | Jim Stefanich | 12,401-12,104 | Billy Hardwick | Garden City, NY |
| 1969 | Billy Hardwick | 12,585-11,463 | Dick Weber | Miami |
| 1970 | Bobby Cooper | 12,936-12,307 | Billy Hardwick | Northbrook, IL |
| 1971 | Mike Limongello | 397 (2 games) | Teata Semiz | St. Paul, MN |
| 1972 | Don Johnson | 233 (1 game) | George Pappas | New York City |
| 1973 | Mike McGrath | 712 (3 games) | Earl Anthony | New York City |
| 1974 | Larry Laub | 749 (3 games) | Dave Davis | New York City |
| 1975 | Steve Neff | 279 (1 game) | Paul Colwell | Grand Prairie, TX |
| 1976 | Paul Moser | 226 (1 game) | Jim Frazier | Grand Prairie, TX |
| 1977 | Johnny Petraglia | 279 (1 game) | Bill Spigner | Greensboro, NC |
| 1978 | Nelson Burton Jr | 873 (4 games) | Jeff Mattingly | Greensboro, NC |
| 1979 | Joe Berardi | 445 (2 games) | Earl Anthony | Windsor Locks, CT |
| 1980 | Steve Martin | 930 (4 games) | Earl Anthony | Windsor Locks, CT |
| 1981 | Marshall Holman | 684 (3 games) | Mark Roth | Houston |
| 1982 | Dave Husted | 1011 (4 games) | Gil Sliker | Houston |
| 1983 | Gary Dickinson | 214 (1 game) | Steve Neff | Oak Lawn, IL |
| 1984 | Mark Roth | 244 (1 game) | Guppy Troup | Oak Hill, IL |
| 1985 | Marshall Holman | 233 (1 game) | Wayne Webb | Venice, FL |
| 1986 | Steve Cook | 467 (2 games) | Frank Ellenburg | Venice, FL |
| 1987 | Del Ballard Jr | 525 (2 games) | Pete Weber | Tacoma, WA |
| 1988 | Pete Weber | 929 (4 games) | Marshall Holman | Atlantic City, NJ |
| 1989 | Mike Aulby | 429 (2 games) | Jim Pencak | Edmond, OK |
| 1990 | Ron Palombi Jr | 269 (1 game) | Amleto Monacelli | Indianapolis |
| 1991 | Pete Weber | 956 (4 games) | Mark Thayer | Indianapolis |
| 1992 | Robert Lawrence | 667 (3 games) | Scott Devers | Canandaigua, NY |
| 1993 | Del Ballard Jr | 505 (2 games) | Walter Ray Williams Jr | Canandaigua, NY |
| 1994 | Justin Hromek | 267 (1 game) | Parker Bohn III | Troy, MI |
| 1995 | Dave Husted | 266 (1 game) | Paul Koehler | Troy, MI |

Note: From 1942 to 1970, the tournament was called the BPAA All-Star. Peterson scoring was used from 1942 through 1962. Under this system, the winner of an individual match game gets one point, plus one point for each 50 pins knocked down. From 1963 through 1967, a three-game championship was held between the two top qualifiers. From 1968 through 1970 total pinfall determined the winner. From 1971 to the present, five qualifiers compete for the championship.

## PBA National Championship

| Year | Winner | Score | Runner-Up | Site |
|---|---|---|---|---|
| 1960 | Don Carter | 6512 (30 games) | Ronnie Gaudern | Memphis |
| 1961 | Dave Soutar | 5792 (27 games) | Morrie Oppenheim | Cleveland |
| 1962 | Carmen Salvino | 5369 (25 games) | Don Carter | Philadelphia |
| 1963 | Billy Hardwick | 13,541 (61 games) | Ray Bluth | Long Island, NY |
| 1964 | Bob Strampe | 13,979 (61 games) | Ray Bluth | Long Island, NY |
| 1965 | Dave Davis | 13,895 (61 games) | Jerry McCoy | Detroit |
| 1966 | Wayne Zahn | 14,006 (61 games) | Nelson Burton Jr | Long Island, NY |
| 1967 | Dave Davis | 421 (2 games) | Pete Tountas | New York City |
| 1968 | Wayne Zahn | 14,182 (60 games) | Nelson Burton Jr | New York City |
| 1969 | Mike McGrath | 13,670 (60 games) | Bill Allen | Garden City, NY |
| 1970 | Mike McGrath | 660 (3 games) | Dave Davis | Garden City, NY |
| 1971 | Mike Limongello | 911 (4 games) | Dave Davis | Paramus, NJ |
| 1972 | Johnny Guenther | 12,986 (56 games) | Dick Ritger | Rochester, NY |
| 1973 | Earl Anthony | 212 (1 game) | Sam Flanagan | Oklahoma City |
| 1974 | Earl Anthony | 218 (1 game) | Mark Roth | Downey, CA |
| 1975 | Earl Anthony | 245 (1 game) | Jim Frazier | Downey, CA |
| 1976 | Paul Colwell | 191 (1 game) | Dave Davis | Seattle |
| 1977 | Tommy Hudson | 206 (1 game) | Jay Robinson | Seattle |
| 1978 | Warren Nelson | 453 (2 games) | Joseph Groskind | Reno |
| 1979 | Mike Aulby | 727 (3 games) | Earl Anthony | Las Vegas |
| 1980 | Johnny Petraglia | 235 (1 game) | Gary Dickinson | Sterling Heights, MI |
| 1981 | Earl Anthony | 242 (1 game) | Ernie Schlegel | Toledo, OH |
| 1982 | Earl Anthony | 233 (1 game) | Charlie Tapp | Toledo, OH |
| 1983 | Earl Anthony | 210 (1 game) | Mike Durbin | Toledo, OH |
| 1984 | Bob Chamberlain | 961 (4 games) | Dan Eberl | Toledo, OH |
| 1985 | Mike Aulby | 476 (2 games) | Steve Cook | Toledo, OH |
| 1986 | Tom Crites | 190 (1 game) | Mike Aulby | Toledo, OH |
| 1987 | Randy Pedersen | 759 (3 games) | Amleto Monacelli | Toledo, OH |
| 1988 | Brian Voss | 246 (1 game) | Todd Thompson | Toledo, OH |
| 1989 | Pete Weber | 221 (1 game) | Dave Ferraro | Toledo, OH |
| 1990 | Jim Pencak | 900 (4 games) | Chris Warren | Toledo, OH |
| 1991 | Mike Miller | 450 (2 games) | Norm Duke | Toledo, OH |
| 1992 | Eric Forkel | 833 (4 games) | Bob Vespi | Toledo, OH |
| 1993 | Ron Palombi Jr | 237 (1 game) | Eugene McCune | Toledo, OH |
| 1994 | David Traber | 196 (1 game) | Dale Traber | Toledo, OH |
| 1995 | Scott Alexander | 246 (1 game) | Wayne Webb | Toledo, OH |

Note: Totals from 1963-66, 1968-69 and 1972 include bonus pins.

## Tournament of Champions

| Year | Winner | Score | Runner-Up | Site |
|---|---|---|---|---|
| 1965 | Billy Hardwick | 484 (2 games) | Dick Weber | Akron, OH |
| 1966 | Wayne Zahn | 595 (3 games) | Dick Weber | Akron, OH |
| 1967 | Jim Stefanich | 227 (1 game) | Don Johnson | Akron, OH |
| 1968 | Dave Davis | 213 (1 game) | Don Johnson | Akron, OH |
| 1969 | Jim Godman | 266 (1 game) | Jim Stefanich | Akron, OH |
| 1970 | Don Johnson | 299 (1 game) | Dick Ritger | Akron, OH |
| 1971 | Johnny Petraglia | 245 (1 game) | Don Johnson | Akron, OH |
| 1972 | Mike Durbin | 775 (3 games) | Tim Harahan | Akron, OH |
| 1973 | Jim Godman | 451 (2 games) | Barry Asher | Akron, OH |
| 1974 | Earl Anthony | 679 (3 games) | Johnny Petraglia | Akron, OH |
| 1975 | Dave Davis | 448 (2 games) | Barry Asher | Akron, OH |
| 1976 | Marshall Holman | 441 (2 games) | Billy Hardwick | Akron, OH |
| 1977 | Mike Berlin | 434 (2 games) | Mike Durbin | Akron, OH |
| 1978 | Earl Anthony | 237 (1 game) | Teata Semiz | Akron, OH |
| 1979 | George Pappas | 224 (1 game) | Dick Ritger | Akron, OH |
| 1980 | Wayne Webb | 750 (3 games) | Gary Dickinson | Akron, OH |
| 1981 | Steve Cook | 287 (1 game) | Pete Couture | Akron, OH |
| 1982 | Mike Durbin | 448 (2 games) | Steve Cook | Akron, OH |
| 1983 | Joe Berardi | 865 (4 games) | Henry Gonzalez | Akron, OH |
| 1984 | Mike Durbin | 950 (4 games) | Mike Aulby | Akron, OH |
| 1985 | Mark Williams | 616 (3 games) | Bob Handley | Akron, OH |
| 1986 | Marshall Holman | 233 (1 game) | Mark Baker | Akron, OH |
| 1987 | Pete Weber | 928 (4 games) | Jim Murtishaw | Akron, OH |
| 1988 | Mark Williams | 237 (1 game) | Tony Westlake | Fairlawn, OH |

## Tournament of Champions *(Cont.)*

| Year | Winner | Score | Runner-Up | Site |
|------|--------|-------|-----------|------|
| 1989 | Del Ballard Jr | 490 (2 games) | Walter Ray Williams Jr | Fairlawn, OH |
| 1990 | Dave Ferraro | 226 (1 game) | Tony Westlake | Fairlawn, OH |
| 1991 | David Ozio | 476 (2 games) | Amleto Monacelli | Fairlawn, OH |
| 1992 | Marc McDowell | 471 (2 games) | Don Genalo | Fairlawn, OH |
| 1993 | George Branham III | 227 (1 game) | Parker Bohn III | Fairlawn, OH |
| 1994 | Norm Duke | 422 (2 games) | Eric Forkel | Fairlawn, OH |
| 1995 | Mike Aulby | 502 (2 games) | Bob Spaulding | Lake Zurich, IL |

## ABC Masters Tournament

| Year | Winner | Scoring Avg | Runner-Up | Site |
|------|--------|-------------|-----------|------|
| 1951 | Lee Jouglard | 201.8 | Joe Wilman | St. Paul, MN |
| 1952 | Willard Taylor | 200.32 | Andy Varipapa | Milwaukee |
| 1953 | Rudy Habetler | 200.13 | Ed Brosius | Chicago |
| 1954 | Eugene Elkins | 205.19 | W. Taylor | Seattle |
| 1955 | Buzz Fazio | 204.13 | Joe Kristof | Ft. Wayne, IN |
| 1956 | Dick Hoover | 209.9 | Ray Bluth | Rochester, NY |
| 1957 | Dick Hoover | 216.39 | Bill Lillard | Ft. Worth, TX |
| 1958 | Tom Hennessy | 209.15 | Lou Frantz | Syracuse, NY |
| 1959 | Ray Bluth | 214.26 | Billy Golembiewski | St. Louis, MO |
| 1960 | Billy Golembiewski | 206.13 | Steve Nagy | Toledo, OH |
| 1961 | Don Carter | 211.18 | Dick Hoover | Detroit |
| 1962 | Billy Golembiewski | 223.12 | Ron Winger | Des Moines, IA |
| 1963 | Harry Smith | 219.3 | Bobby Meadows | Buffalo |
| 1964 | Billy Welu | 227 | Harry Smith | Oakland, CA |
| 1965 | Billy Welu | 202.12 | Don Ellis | St. Paul, MN |
| 1966 | Bob Strampe | 219.80 | Al Thompson | Rochester, NY |
| 1967 | Lou Scalia | 216.9 | Bill Johnson | Miami Beach |
| 1968 | Pete Tountas | 220.15 | Buzz Fazio | Cincinnati |
| 1969 | Jim Chestney | 223.2 | Barry Asher | Madison, WI |
| 1970 | Don Glover | 215.10 | Bob Strampe | Knoxville, TN |
| 1971 | Jim Godman | 229.8 | Don Johnson | Detroit |
| 1972 | Bill Beach | 220.27 | Jim Godman | Long Beach, CA |
| 1973 | Dave Soutar | 218.61 | Dick Ritger | Syracuse, NY |
| 1974 | Paul Colwell | 234.17 | Steve Neff | Indianapolis |
| 1975 | Eddie Ressler | 213.51 | Sam Flanagan | Dayton, OH |
| 1976 | Nelson Burton Jr | 220.79 | Steve Carson | Oklahoma City |
| 1977 | Earl Anthony | 218.21 | Jim Godman | Reno |
| 1978 | Frank Ellenburg | 200.61 | Earl Anthony | St. Louis |
| 1979 | Doug Myers | 202.9 | Bill Spigner | Tampa, FL |
| 1980 | Neil Burton | 206.69 | Mark Roth | Louisville |
| 1981 | Randy Lightfoot | 218.3 | Skip Tucker | Memphis |
| 1982 | Joe Berardi | 207.12 | Ted Hannahs | Baltimore |
| 1983 | Mike Lastowski | 212.65 | Pete Weber | Niagara Falls, NY |
| 1984 | Earl Anthony | 212.5 | Gil Sliker | Reno |
| 1985 | Steve Wunderlich | 210.4 | Tommy Kress | Tulsa, OK |
| 1986 | Mark Fahy | 206.5 | Del Ballard Jr | Las Vegas |
| 1987 | Rick Steelsmith | 210.7 | Brad Snell | Niagara Falls, NY |
| 1988 | Del Ballard Jr | 219.1 | Keith Smith | Jacksonville, FL |
| 1989 | Mike Aulby | 218.5 | Mike Edwards | Wichita |
| 1990 | Chris Warren | 231.6 | David Ozio | Reno |
| 1991 | Doug Kent | 226.8 | George Branham III | Toledo, OH |
| 1992 | Ken Johnson | 230.0 | Dave D'Entremont | Corpus Christi, TX |
| 1993 | Norm Duke | 245.68 | Patrick Allen | Tulsa, OK |
| 1994 | Steve Fehr | 213.09 | Steve Anderson | Greenacres, FL |
| 1995 | Mike Aulby | 230.7 | Mark Williams | Reno |

## BPAA United States Open

| Year | Winner | Score | Runner-Up | Site |
|------|--------|-------|-----------|------|
| 1949 | Marion Ladewig | 113.26-104.26 | Catherine Burling | Chicago |
| 1950 | Marion Ladewig | 151.46-146.06 | Stephanie Balogh | Chicago |
| 1951 | Marion Ladewig | 159.17-148.03 | Sylvia Wene | Chicago |
| 1952 | Marion Ladewig | 154.39-142.05 | Shirley Garms | Chicago |
| 1953 | Not held | | | |
| 1954 | Marion Ladewig | 148.29-143.01 | Sylvia Wene | Chicago |
| 1955 | Sylvia Wene | 142.30-141.11 | Sylvia Fanta | Chicago |
| 1955 | Anita Cantaline | 144.40-144.13 | Doris Porter | Chicago |
| 1956 | Marion Ladewig | 150.16-145.41 | Marge Merrick | Chicago |
| 1957 | Not held | | | |
| 1958 | Merle Matthews | 145.09-143.14 | Marion Ladewig | Minneapolis |
| 1959 | Marion Ladewig | 149.33-143.00 | Donna Zimmerman | Buffalo |
| 1960 | Sylvia Wene | 144.14-143.26 | Marion Ladewig | Omaha |
| 1961 | Phyllis Notaro | 144.13-143.12 | Hope Riccilli | San Bernardino, CA |
| 1962 | Shirley Garms | 138.44-135.49 | Joy Abel | Miami Beach |
| 1963 | Marion Ladewig | 586-578 | Bobbie Shaler | Kansas City, MO |
| 1964 | LaVerne Carter | 683-609 | Evelyn Teal | Dallas |
| 1965 | Ann Slattery | 597-550 | Sandy Hooper | Philadelphia |
| 1966 | Joy Abel | 593-538 | Bette Rockwell | Lansing, MI |
| 1967 | Gloria Bouvia | 578-516 | Shirley Garms | St. Ann, MO |
| 1968 | Dotty Fothergill | 9,000-8,187 | Doris Coburn | Garden City, NY |
| 1969 | Dotty Fothergill | 8,284-8,258 | Kayoka Suda | Miami |
| 1970 | Mary Baker | 8,730-8,465 | Judy Cook | Northbrook, IL |
| 1971 | Paula Carter | 5,660-5,650 | June Llewellyn | Kansas City, MO |
| 1972 | Lorrie Nichols | 5,272-5,189 | Mary Baker | Denver |
| 1973 | Millie Martorella | 5,553-5,294 | Patty Costello | Garden City, NY |
| 1974 | Patty Costello | 219-216 | Betty Morris | Irving, TX |
| 1975 | Paula Carter | 6,500-6,352 | Lorrie Nichols | Toledo, OH |
| 1976 | Patty Costello | 11,341-11,281 | Betty Morris | Tulsa, OK |
| 1977 | Betty Morris | 10,511-10,358 | Virginia Norton | Milwaukee |
| 1978 | Donna Adamek | 236-202 | Vesma Grinfelds | Miami |
| 1979 | Diana Silva | 11,775-11,718 | Bev Ortner | Phoenix |
| 1980 | Pat Costello | 223-199 | Shinobu Saitoh | Rockford, IL |
| 1981 | Donna Adamek | 201-190 | Nikki Gianulias | Rockford, IL |
| 1982 | Shinobu Saitoh | 12,184-12,028 | Robin Romeo | Hendersonville, TN |
| 1983 | Dana Miller-Mackie | 247-200 | Aleta Sill | St. Louis |
| 1984 | Karen Ellingsworth | 236-217 | Lorrie Nichols | St. Louis |
| 1985 | Pat Mercatani | 214-178 | Nikki Gianulias | Topeka, KS |
| 1986 | Wendy Macpherson | 265-179 | Lisa Wagner | Topeka, KS |
| 1987 | Carol Norman | 206-179 | Cindy Coburn | Mentor, OH |
| 1988 | Lisa Wagner | 226-218 | Lorrie Nichols | Winston-Salem, NC |
| 1989 | Robin Romeo | 187-163 | Michelle Mullen | Addison, IL |
| 1990 | Dana Miller-Mackie | 190-189 | Tish Johnson | Dearborn Heights, MI |
| 1991 | Anne Marie Duggan | 196-185 | Leanne Barrette | Fountain Valley, CA |
| 1992 | Tish Johnson | 216-213 | Aleta Sill | Fountain Valley, CA |
| 1993 | Dede Davidson | 213-194 | Dana Miller-Mackie | Garland, TX |
| 1994 | Aleta Sill | 229-170 | Anne Marie Duggan | Wichita |
| 1995 | Cheryl Daniels | 235-180 | Tish Johnson | Blaine, MN |

Note: From 1942 to 1970, the tournament was called the BPAA All-Star. Peterson scoring was used from 1949 through 1962. Under this system, the winner of an individual match game gets one point, plus one point for each 50 pins knocked down. From 1963 through 1967, a three-game championship was held between the two top qualifiers. From 1968 through 1973, 1975-77, 1979 and 1982, total pinfall determined the winner. In the other years, five qualifiers competed in a playoff for the championship, with the final match listed above.

## WIBC Queens

| Year | Winner | Score | Runner-Up | Site |
|------|--------|-------|-----------|------|
| 1961 | Janet Harman | 794-776 | Eula Touchette | Fort Wayne, IN |
| 1962 | Dorothy Wilkinson | 799-794 | Marion Ladewig | Phoenix, AZ |
| 1963 | Irene Monterosso | 852-803 | Georgette DeRosa | Memphis, TN |
| 1964 | D. D. Jacobson | 740-682 | Shirley Garms | Minneapolis, MN |
| 1965 | Betty Kuczynski | 772-739 | LaVerne Carter | Portland, OR |
| 1966 | Judy Lee | 771-742 | Nancy Peterson | New Orleans, LA |
| 1967 | Millie Ignizio | 840-809 | Phyllis Massey | Rochester, NY |
| 1968 | Phyllis Massey | 884-853 | Marian Spencer | San Antonio, TX |
| 1969 | Ann Feigel | 832-765 | Millie Ignizio | San Diego, CA |
| 1970 | Millie Ignizio | 807-797 | Joan Holm | Tulsa, OK |
| 1971 | Millie Ignizio | 809-778 | Katherine Brown | Atlanta, GA |
| 1972 | Dotty Fothergill | 890-841 | Maureen Harris | Kansas City, MO |
| 1973 | Dotty Fothergill | 804-791 | Judy Soutar | Las Vegas, NV |
| 1974 | Judy Soutar | 939-705 | Betty Morris | Houston, TX |
| 1975 | Cindy Powell | 758-674 | Patty Costello | Indianapolis, IN |
| 1976 | Pam Buckner | 214-178 | Shirley Sjostrom | Denver, CO |
| 1977 | Dana Stewart | 175-167 | Vesma Grinfelds | Milwaukee, WI |
| 1978 | Loa Boxberger | 197-176 | Cora Fiebig | Miami, FL |
| 1979 | Donna Adamek | 216-181 | Shinobu Saitoh | Tucson, AZ |
| 1980 | Donna Adamek | 213-165 | Cheryl Robinson | Seattle, WA |
| 1981 | Katsuko Sugimoto | 166-158 | Virginia Norton | Baltimore, MD |
| 1982 | Katsuko Sugimoto | 160-137 | Nikki Gianulias | St. Louis, MO |
| 1983 | Aleta Sill | 214-188 | Dana Miller-Mackie | Las Vegas, NV |
| 1984 | Kazue Inahashi | 248-222 | Aleta Sill | Niagara Falls, NY |
| 1985 | Aleta Sill | 279-192 | Linda Graham | Toledo, OH |
| 1986 | Cora Fiebig | 223-177 | Barbara Thorberg | Orange County, CA |
| 1987 | Cathy Alameida | 850-817 | Lorrie Nichols | Hartford, CT |
| 1988 | Wendy Macpherson | 213-199 | Leanne Barrette | Reno/Carson City, NV |
| 1989 | Carol Gianotti | 207-177 | Sandra Jo Shiery | Bismarck-Mandan, ND |
| 1990 | Patty Ann | 207-173 | Vesma Grinfelds | Tampa, FL |
| 1991 | Dede Davidson | 231-159 | Jeanne Maiden | Cedar Rapids, IA |
| 1992 | Cindy Coburn-Carroll | 184-170 | Dana Miller-Mackie | Lansing, MI |
| 1993 | Jan Schmidt | 201-163 | Pat Costello | Baton Rouge, LA |
| 1994 | Anne Marie Duggan | 224-177 | Wendy Macpherson-Papanos | Salt Lake City, UT |
| 1995 | Sandra Postma | 226-187 | Carolyn Dorin | Tucson, AZ |

## Sam's Town Invitational

| Year | Winner | Score | Runner-Up | Site |
|------|--------|-------|-----------|------|
| 1984 | Aleta Sill | 238 (1 game) | Cheryl Daniels | Las Vegas, NV |
| 1985 | Patty Costello | 236 (1 game) | Robin Romeo | Las Vegas, NV |
| 1986 | Aleta Sill | 238 (1 game) | Dina Wheeler | Las Vegas, NV |
| 1987 | Debbie Bennett | 880 (4 games) | Lorrie Nichols | Las Vegas, NV |
| 1988 | Donna Adamek | 634 (3 games) | Robin Romeo | Las Vegas, NV |
| 1989 | Tish Johnson | 210 (1 game) | Dede Davidson | Las Vegas, NV |
| 1990 | Wendy Macpherson | 900 (4 games) | Jeanne Maiden | Las Vegas, NV |
| 1991 | Lorrie Nichols | 469 (2 games) | Dana Miller-Mackie | Las Vegas, NV |
| 1992 | Tish Johnson | 279 (1 game) | Robin Romeo | Las Vegas, NV |
| 1993 | Robin Romeo | 194 (1 game) | Tammy Turner | Las Vegas, NV |
| 1994 | Tish Johnson | 178 (1 game) | Carol Gianotti | Las Vegas, NV |

## PWBA Championships

| | | | |
|---|---|---|---|
| 1960 | Marion Ladewig | 1971 | Patty Costello |
| 1961 | Shirley Garms | 1972 | Patty Costello |
| 1962 | Stephanie Balogh | 1973 | Betty Morris |
| 1963 | Janet Harman | 1974 | Pat Costello |
| 1964 | Betty Kuczynski | 1975 | Pam Buckner |
| 1965 | Helen Duval | 1976 | Patty Costello |
| 1966 | Joy Abel | 1977 | Vesma Grinfelds |
| 1967 | Betty Mivalez | 1978 | Toni Gillard |
| 1968 | Dotty Fothergill | 1979 | Cindy Coburn |
| 1969 | Dotty Fothergill | 1980 | Donna Adamek |
| 1970 | Bobbe North | | |

# Men's Awards

## BWAA Bowler of the Year

| | | |
|---|---|---|
| 1942 ........Johnny Crimmins | 1961 ........Dick Weber | 1978 ........Mark Roth |
| 1943 ........Ned Day | 1962 ........Don Carter | 1979 ........Mark Roth |
| 1944 ........Ned Day | 1963 ........Dick Weber, | 1980 ........Wayne Webb |
| 1945 ........Buddy Bomar | ..............Billy Hardwick (PBA)* | 1981 ........Earl Anthony |
| 1946 ........Joe Wilman | 1964 ........Billy Hardwick, | 1982 ........Earl Anthony |
| 1947 ........Buddy Bomar | ..............Bob Strampe (PBA)* | 1983 ........Earl Anthony |
| 1948 ........Andy Varipapa | 1965 ........Dick Weber | 1984 ........Mark Roth |
| 1949 ........Connie Schwoegler | 1966 ........Wayne Zahn | 1985 ........Mike Aulby |
| 1950 ........Junie McMahon | 1967 ........Dave Davis | 1986 ........Walter Ray Williams Jr |
| 1951 ........Lee Jouglard | 1968 ........Jim Stefanich | 1987 ........Marshall Holman |
| 1952 ........Steve Nagy | 1969 ........Billy Hardwick | 1988 ........Brian Voss |
| 1953 ........Don Carter | 1970 ........Nelson Burton Jr | 1989 ........Mike Aulby, |
| 1954 ........Don Carter | 1971 ........Don Johnson | ..............Amleto Monacelli (PBA)* |
| 1955 ........Steve Nagy | 1972 ........Don Johnson | 1990 ........Amleto Monacelli |
| 1956 ........Bill Lillard | 1973 ........Don McCune | 1991 ........David Ozio |
| 1957 ........Don Carter | 1974 ........Earl Anthony | 1992 ........Dave Ferraro |
| 1958 ........Don Carter | 1975 ........Earl Anthony | 1993 ........Walter Ray Williams Jr |
| 1959 ........Ed Lubanski | 1976 ........Earl Anthony | 1994 ........Norm Duke |
| 1960 ........Don Carter | 1977 ........Mark Roth | |

*The PBA began selecting a player of the year in 1963. Its selection has been the same as the BWAA's in all but three years.

# Women's Awards

## BWAA Bowler of the Year

| | | |
|---|---|---|
| 1948 ........Val Mikiel | 1965 ........Betty Kuczynski | 1982 ........Nikki Gianulias |
| 1949 ........Val Mikiel | 1966 ........Joy Abel | 1983 ........Lisa Wagner |
| 1950 ........Marion Ladewig | 1967 ........Millie Martorella | 1984 ........Aleta Sill |
| 1951 ........Marion Ladewig | 1968 ........Dotty Fothergill | 1985 ........Aleta Sill, |
| 1952 ........Marion Ladewig | 1969 ........Dotty Fothergill | ..............Patty Costello (LPBT)* |
| 1953 ........Marion Ladewig | 1970 ........Mary Baker | 1986 ........Lisa Wagner, |
| 1954 ........Marion Ladewig | 1971 ........Paula Sperber Carter | ..............Jeanne Madden (LPBT)* |
| 1955 ........Marion Ladewig | 1972 ........Patty Costello | 1987 ........Betty Morris |
| 1956 ........Sylvia Martin | 1973 ........Judy Soutar | 1988 ........Lisa Wagner |
| 1957 ........Anita Cantaline | 1974 ........Betty Morris | 1989 ........Robin Romeo |
| 1958 ........Marion Ladewig | 1975 ........Judy Soutar | 1990 ........Tish Johnson, |
| 1959 ........Marion Ladewig | 1976 ........Patty Costello | ..............Leanne Barrette (LPBT)* |
| 1960 ........Sylvia Martin | 1977 ........Betty Morris | 1991 ........Leanne Barrette |
| 1961 ........Shirley Garms | 1978 ........Donna Adamek | 1992 ........Tish Johnson |
| 1962 ........Shirley Garms | 1979 ........Donna Adamek | 1993 ........Lisa Wagner |
| 1963 ........Marion Ladewig | 1980 ........Donna Adamek | 1994 ........Anne Marie Duggan |
| 1964 ........LaVerne Carter | 1981 ........Donna Adamek | |

*The LPBT began selecting a player of the year in 1983. Its selection has been the same as the BWAA's in all but three years.

# Career Leaders

## Earnings

| MEN | | WOMEN | |
|---|---|---|---|
| Pete Weber | $1,734,330 | Aleta Sill | $656,931 |
| Marshall Holman | $1,652,924 | Tish Johnson | $585,605 |
| Mike Aulby | $1,625,022 | Lisa Wagner | $575,442 |
| Walter Ray Williams Jr | $1,510,504 | Robin Romeo | $512,539 |
| Mark Roth | $1,484,948 | Nikki Gianulias | $477,557 |

## Titles

| MEN | | WOMEN | |
|---|---|---|---|
| Earl Anthony | 41 | Lisa Wagner | 28 |
| Mark Roth | 34 | Patty Costello | 25 |
| Don Johnson | 26 | Aleta Sill | 23 |
| Dick Weber | 26 | Donna Adamek | 19 |
| Mike Aulby | 23 | Tish Johnson | 19 |

# Soccer

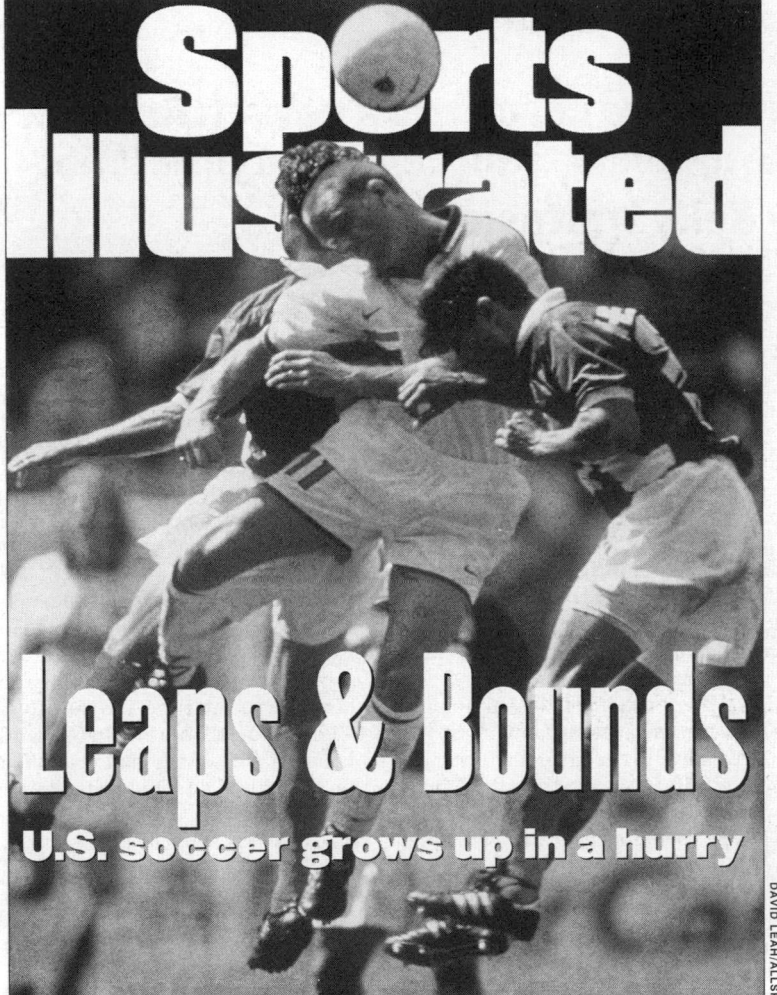

**Sports Illustrated**

**Leaps & Bounds**

U.S. soccer grows up in a hurry

DAVID LEAH/ALLSPORT

# Breaking New Ground

## With a new coach and a new attitude, the U.S. national team came of age in 1995

### by Kelly Whiteside

To STATE it simply and without hyperbole, July 1995 was the most magical month in U.S. soccer history. In Uruguay, from July 5 to July 23, 10 teams from South America, as well as guests Mexico and the U.S., competed in the oldest international tournament in soccer, the biennial Copa America. Though it was winter in the Southern Hemisphere, and the temperature was frigid at times, the U.S. men's national soccer team was hot. To South Americans, La Copa is as important as the World Cup. And for the North Americans in red, white and blue, La Copa runneth over in the summer of 1995.

Before the tournament began nobody expected very much from the U.S. as the team's record versus its first-round foes was a desultory 0-10-5. At such events the Americans have always been polite, yet dull guests, usually long-gone from the party before the fun really starts. At the previous tournament in 1993, the U.S. did not make it beyond the first round, blowing a three-goal lead in its last match against Venezuela.

"This Copa America is an opportunity for us to get more respect in the world," proclaimed U.S. forward Eric Wynalda before La Copa kicked off.

Respect? In Uruguay, U.S. interim coach Steve Sampson was called "Simpson" by local reporters. It was an unintentional slip, but a telling one: Even Homer Simpson was better known in South America than Sampson and his team.

However, the U.S.'s stunning run in Paysandu, Uruguay, soon changed all that. In the U.S.'s opening game, Wynalda scored two first-half goals, and the U.S. defeated Chile 2–1. The win marked the first time the American squad had beaten Chile and the first time it had defeated a South American team on South American soil in 65 years.

Three days later the U.S. lost to Bolivia 1–0 but played so well that even Diego Maradona, still serving the 15-month suspension he received after testing positive for five banned substances at the '94 World Cup, remarked, "It's very emotional to me to see the U.S. playing soccer at a very high level. The country we thought had only baseball, basketball and American football, now has very good soccer. They play clean, classy soccer. And, let's be honest, they didn't deserve to lose." (It should be noted that the Argentine star, who isn't known for always being clean or classy, was on his best behavior in

**Wynalda got the U.S. off on the right foot at the Copa America.**

1995. He did not fire any pellet guns at reporters, though he still faces a possible four-year-prison term for the 1994 incident. His worst transgression was merely pelting a linesman with a water bottle while coaching a game. But don't expect 1996 to be as tame: Maradona's suspension expired Sept. 30, and he rejoined his old club, the Boca Juniors of Buenos Aires.)

Three days after the Bolivia game, the upstart Yanks beat one of the best teams in the world, Argentina, 3–0, for the first time in the 65-year head-to-head series. Since Paysandu is near the Argentine border, the U.S. defeated the gauchos practically on their home *tierra*, in front of a crowd of 18,000. "This has to rate as one of the biggest wins in U.S. soccer history," said the coach who hereafter should be called Homeric Sampson.

Indeed, the victory belongs on the U.S.'s short list of equally earth-shattering soccer events, joining the 1950 World Cup upset of England, the 1993 U.S. Cup win against England and the 1994 World Cup shocker over Colombia.

For Argentina—a two-time World Cup winner and the two-time defending Copa America champion—the game was to be a warmup for the quarterfinals, as they had already clinched a berth in the next round. Clearly Argentina coach Daniel Passarella had underestimated the Americans: Passarella rested nine of his 11 regulars at the start, then, with the game slipping away, brought on several of his top players for the second half. One local Uruguayan newspaper called the U.S.'s win over Argentina a triumph of humility over arrogance, a win by the *yanquis simpaticos* that marked the beginning of the end of "our brothers of the River Plate."

The apocalypse began in the 21st minute when U.S. midfielder Frank Klopas buried an 18-yard shot low into the right corner for the first goal. In the 32nd minute U.S. midfielder Cobi Jones beat a defender down the right wing and crossed a ball to teammate Alexi Lalas at the near post. Lalas flicked the ball under keeper Carlos Bossio for the second score. In the 59th minute forward Joe-Max Moore fed Wynalda, who scored his third goal of the tournament, a sliding effort into an open net.

With the victory the U.S. won its group and the right to meet Mexico in the quarterfinals. After the teams played 90 minutes without a goal, the U.S. beat Mexico on penalty kicks, 4–1, and advanced to the semifinals of the Copa America. "The world respects us now," said Lalas following the game. Lalas, he of the flaming red hair, flowing goatee and flamboyant personality, quickly became a fan favorite. "For a kid from Detroit who never dreamed of playing professional soccer, it means a lot that people know who I am in a place called Paysandu," he said.

The day before the semifinals, the Copa

Kids from America were the big story in the local newspapers. A poll indicated that 16% of Uruguayans thought the U.S. could win the title, and a demographic survey revealed that the Yanks were particularly popular among the 14-to-34-year-old age group.

Meanwhile, back in the States, Prime Deportiva, a Spanish-language cable service available only regionally, was the sole station to carry the games. The quarterfinal package could be ordered for $19.95, interpreter not included. Somehow the U.S. Soccer Federation missed a historic opportunity to capitalize on its team's success yet again (see MLS further down) and failed to make the national-team games from Uruguay widely available on TV.

Playing in the semifinals of a major international tournament for the first time since the 1930 World Cup, the Americans faced the world's best team, Brazil, in Maldonado, and lost a hard-fought game 1–0. "We have closed the gap between the United States and Brazil," Sampson said. "We went forward and played attacking soccer where a year ago [in the second round of the World Cup, also a 1–0 loss for the U.S.] we were defending most of the game, hoping to get to penalty kicks."

The Americans had come far: Not so long ago the team kept close company with weaklings like Iceland and Moldova; now the U.S. was samba dancing with the likes of Brazil. And so it really didn't matter that the U.S. lost its third-place game against Colombia 4–1. (Uruguay beat Brazil 5–3 on penalty kicks after a 1–1 tie in regulation for the championship title.) Though there is no gold, silver or bronze medal for fourth place, the U.S. gained something even more valuable than championship hardware: respect. In terms of prestige, only the World Cup and the European Championships are bigger than the Copa America.

"Getting to the semifinals this time after not doing anything two years ago was a major success for U.S. soccer. We can walk away from this with our heads up very high," said U.S. midfielder John Harkes.

So how to explain the U.S. team's magical

AL. TIELEMANS

**Sampson won his way into the job as head coach of the national team.**

run? Experience. Last season 18 of the team's 22 players were on professional clubs, mostly Latin American or European first- or second-division teams. As a point of comparison, consider that only two players on the 1990 World Cup roster had played abroad professionally.

The players also say that Sampson—and the attacking style of play he has implemented—deserves a double dose of credit. Not only was Sampson under pressure to win games, but the interim coach was also under pressure to win his job.

On April 14 the U.S. Soccer Federation announced that head coach Bora Milutinovic had "stepped down." Instead of giving Milutinovic a new contract as national team coach, the federation offered him a position that added several layers of responsibility, including overseeing the development of U.S. coaches and national team players in all age groups.

"I told them, to do this job I don't have time," the 51-year-old Milutinovic said. "There are so many [international] competitions. It's impossible." Unable to reach an agreement, the federation fired Milutinovic, and by default, 38-year-old assistant Sampson was named interim coach.

The handling of the whole affair was as

sloppy as Milutinovic's caught-in-a-typhoon hairdo. When Sampson took over, he was told to keep the seat warm until a coach with international experience was hired. The federation offered the position to two big-name coaches, Carlos Queiroz, a longtime manager in Portugal, and ex-Brazilian national coach Carlos Alberto Parreira. Both turned the job down.

Before the team's dazzling play in the Copa America, Sampson began proving that he was the right person for the job. In June the national team won the U.S. Cup title, beating 1994 African champion Nigeria, trouncing Mexico by four goals and holding Colombia to a scoreless tie in the finale.

But after the U.S. Cup, federation president Alan Rothenberg could only offer this feeble endorsement: "[Sampson's hiring] is probably inevitable, but I don't know if it's imminent," he said. On Aug. 2, following the team's stirring play in Uruguay, the word *interim* was officially removed from Sampson's title.

Meanwhile, in August, the U.S. women's national team hosted its own party, the four-team U.S. Women's Cup. In a match held at RFK Stadium in Washington, D.C., between the two best teams in the world, the U.S. beat Norway 2–1 in sudden-death overtime for the championship title.

Just two minutes into overtime, two substitutes connected for the game-winner. Jen Grubb, a high school senior who also kicks for her football team in Hoffmann Estates, Ill., sent a long ball near the top of the Norway box to U.S. forward Tammy Pearman, who was making her first national team appearance. Pearman, who has incomparable speed, nodded the ball past charging keeper Bente Nordby and scored into an open net. The win was watched by a record crowd of 7,083, including First Soccer Fan Chelsea Clinton, who mugged with several of her heroes on the field after the game.

The victory avenged a tough loss to Norway at the Women's World Cup in June. The U.S. had won the inaugural Women's World Cup in 1991 in China and entered the 1995 tournament, hosted by Sweden, as favorites. But they ran into 1991 world runner-up Norway in the semifinal game, were outplayed and lost 1–0. Norway went on to beat Germany 2–0 in the championship game in Stockholm.

Said U.S. coach Tony DiCicco after beating Norway in August, "They dethroned us. They took something away that we can never regain fully. But it worked to motivate us for this game, and I'm hoping it motivates us through the Olympics." (Women's soccer will debut at the 1996 Olympics.)

In addition to the men's wonderful Copa America performance and the women's climb back to the top of international soccer, 1995 should also be remembered for what did not happen.

Major League Soccer, a first-rank pro soccer league, was supposed to kick off in the spring of 1995. The extra time it took MLS chairman Rothenberg to collect roughly $75 million in start-up capital pushed the league's debut to April 1996.

Through the end of August, MLS had signed top U.S. national team players like Lalas and midfielder Tab Ramos, as well as international stars like Jorge Campos and Hugo Sanchez, both of Mexico, but six months away from the start of the season, the league's 10 teams did not have nicknames or logos or head coaches, and few fans knew anything about the league, causing some wags to call MLS the "Mythical Soccer League."

And because the start of the league was postponed for a year, MLS missed its chance to take advantage of the wave of excitement created by the 1994 World Cup. When Ramos returned in June from Mexico, where he plays for the first-division club Tigres, he remarked, "Being at home these last couple of weeks, it seems like soccer has disappeared again."

Indeed, from the World Cup until June, U.S. soccer did manage to perform a nifty disappearing act. But little did Ramos know what was to come later that summer. Who could have imagined that the men's national team would pull such victories out of thin air during the magical month of July?

## World Cup 1994

### Group Standings

#### GROUP A

| Country | GP | W | L | T | G | GA | Pts |
|---|---|---|---|---|---|---|---|
| †Romania | 3 | 2 | 1 | 0 | 5 | 5 | 6 |
| †Switzerland | 3 | 1 | 1 | 1 | 5 | 4 | 4 |
| †United States | 3 | 1 | 1 | 1 | 3 | 3 | 4 |
| Colombia | 3 | 1 | 2 | 0 | 4 | 5 | 3 |

#### GROUP B

| Country | GP | W | L | T | G | GA | Pts |
|---|---|---|---|---|---|---|---|
| †Brazil | 3 | 2 | 0 | 1 | 6 | 1 | 7 |
| †Sweden | 3 | 1 | 0 | 2 | 6 | 4 | 5 |
| Russia | 3 | 1 | 2 | 0 | 7 | 6 | 3 |
| Cameroon | 3 | 0 | 2 | 1 | 3 | 11 | 1 |

#### GROUP C

| Country | GP | W | L | T | G | GA | Pts |
|---|---|---|---|---|---|---|---|
| †Germany | 3 | 2 | 0 | 1 | 5 | 3 | 7 |
| †Spain | 3 | 1 | 0 | 2 | 6 | 4 | 5 |
| S Korea | 3 | 0 | 1 | 2 | 4 | 5 | 2 |
| Bolivia | 3 | 0 | 2 | 1 | 1 | 4 | 1 |

#### GROUP D

| Country | GP | W | L | T | G | GA | Pts |
|---|---|---|---|---|---|---|---|
| †Nigeria | 3 | 2 | 1 | 0 | 6 | 2 | 6 |
| †Bulgaria | 3 | 2 | 1 | 0 | 6 | 3 | 6 |
| †Argentina | 3 | 2 | 1 | 0 | 6 | 3 | 6 |
| Greece | 3 | 0 | 3 | 0 | 0 | 8 | 0 |

#### GROUP E

| Country | GP | W | L | T | G | GA | Pts |
|---|---|---|---|---|---|---|---|
| †Mexico | 3 | 1 | 1 | 1 | 3 | 3 | 4 |
| †Ireland | 3 | 1 | 1 | 1 | 2 | 2 | 4 |
| †Italy | 3 | 1 | 1 | 1 | 2 | 2 | 4 |
| Norway | 3 | 1 | 1 | 1 | 1 | 1 | 4 |

#### GROUP F

| Country | GP | W | L | T | G | GA | Pts |
|---|---|---|---|---|---|---|---|
| †N'lands | 3 | 2 | 1 | 0 | 4 | 3 | 6 |
| †S. Arabia | 3 | 2 | 1 | 0 | 4 | 3 | 6 |
| †Belgium | 3 | 2 | 1 | 0 | 2 | 1 | 6 |
| Morocco | 3 | 0 | 3 | 0 | 2 | 5 | 0 |

†Advanced to second round.

Note: In the first round, teams are awarded three points for a victory, one for a tie. The top two in each group, plus the four third place teams with the best records, advance to the round of 16.

### First Round Group Scores

**GROUP A**
U.S. 2, Colombia 1
U.S. 1, Switzerland 1
Romania 1, U.S. 0
Romania 3, Colombia 1
Switzerland 4, Romania 1
Colombia 2, Switzerland 0

**GROUP B**
Cameroon 2, Sweden 2
Brazil 2, Russia 0
Brazil 3, Cameroon 0

**GROUP B (Cont.)**
Sweden 3, Russia 1
Russia 6, Cameroon 1
Brazil 1, Sweden 1

**GROUP C**
Germany 1, Bolivia 0
Spain 2, South Korea 2
Germany 1, Spain 1
South Korea 0, Bolivia 0
Germany 3, South Korea 2
Spain 3, Bolivia 1

**GROUP D**
Argentina 4, Greece 0
Nigeria 3, Bulgaria 0
Argentina 2, Nigeria 1
Bulgaria 4, Greece 0
Nigeria 2, Greece 0
Bulgaria 2, Argentina 0

**GROUP E**
Ireland 1, Italy 0
Norway 1 Mexico 0
Italy 1, Norway 0

**GROUP E (Cont.)**
Mexico 2, Ireland 1
Ireland 0, Norway 0
Italy 1, Mexico 1

**GROUP F**
Belgium 1, Morocco 0
Netherlands 2, S. Arabia 1
Belgium 1, Netherlands 0
Saudi Arabia 2, Morocco 1
Netherlands 2, Morocco 1
Saudi Arabia 1, Belgium 0

### World Cup Tournament

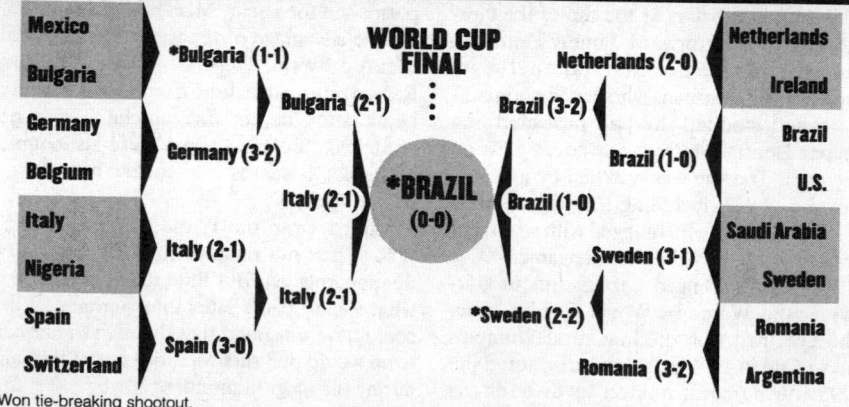

Mexico
Bulgaria
Germany
Belgium
Italy
Nigeria
Spain
Switzerland

*Bulgaria (1-1)
Germany (3-2)
Italy (2-1)
Italy (2-1)
Spain (3-0)

Bulgaria (2-1)
Italy (2-1)

**WORLD CUP FINAL**

*BRAZIL (0-0)

Netherlands (2-0)
Brazil (3-2)

Brazil (1-0)
Brazil (1-0)

Sweden (3-1)
*Sweden (2-2)
Romania (3-2)

Netherlands
Ireland
Brazil
U.S.
Saudi Arabia
Sweden
Romania
Argentina

*Won tie-breaking shootout.

## U.S. Men's National Team 1995 Results

| Date | Opponent | Site | Result | U.S. Goals |
|------|----------|------|--------|------------|
| March 25 | Uruguay | Dallas | 2-2 T# | Kerr, Stewart |
| April 22 | Belgium | Brussels, Belgium | 0-1 L | none |
| May 28 | Costa Rica | Tampa | 1-2 L | Caligiuri |
| June 11 | Nigeria* | Boston | 3-2 W | Harkes, Balboa, Jones |
| June 18 | Mexico* | Washington, D.C. | 4-0 W | Wegerle, Dooley, Harkes, Reyna |
| June 25 | Colombia* | Piscataway, NJ | 0-0 T | none |
| July 8 | Chile† | Paysandu, Uruguay | 2-1 W | Wynalda (2) |
| July 11 | Bolivia† | Paysandu, Uruguay | 0-1 L | none |
| July 14 | Argentina† | Paysandu, Uruguay | 3-0 W | Klopas, Lalas, Wynalda |
| July 17 | Mexico† | Paysandu, Uruguay | 0-0(4-1) W | none |
| July 20 | Brazil† | Maldonado, Uruguay | 0-1 L | none |
| July 22 | Colombia† | Maldonado, Uruguay | 1-4 L | Moore |
| Aug 4 | Parma (Italy) | East Rutherford, NJ | 1-2 L | Lapper |
| Aug 6 | Benfica (Portugal) | East Rutherford, NJ | 2-1 W | Klopas, Lassiter |
| Aug 16 | Sweden | Norrkoping, Sweden | 0-1 L | none |

#Game suspended due to storm; 83 minutes played.

*U.S. Cup '95    †Copa America

## U.S. Women's National Team 1995 Results

| Date | Opponent | Site | Result | U.S. Goals |
|------|----------|------|--------|------------|
| Feb 24 | Denmark | Winter Park, FL | 7-0 W | Akers (3), Hamm (2), Lilly, Roberts |
| Mar 14 | Finland | Faro, Portugal | 2-0 W | Lilly, Hamm |
| Mar 16 | Portugal | Portimao, Portugal | 3-0 W | Milbrett, Gabarra, Lilly |
| Mar 17 | Denmark | Lagos, Portugal | 0-2 L | none |
| Mar 19 | Norway | Quarteira, Portugal | 3-3 (2-4) L | Akers, Gabarra, Lilly |
| April 11 | Italy | Poissy, France | 3-0 W | Akers, Venturini, Gabarra |
| April 12 | Canada | St Maur, France | 5-0 W | Hamm (3), Akers, Milbrett |
| April 15 | France | Strasbourg, France | 3-0 W | Gabarra, Lilly, Hamm |
| April 28 | Finland | Decatur, Georgia | 2-0 W | Akers, Venturini |
| April 30 | Finland | Davidson, NC | 6-0 W | Lilly, Akers, own goal, Neaton, Foudy, Hamm |
| May 12 | Brazil | Tacoma, WA | 3-0 W | Hamm (2), Venturini |
| May 14 | Brazil | Portland, OR | 4-1 W | Akers (2), Gabarra, Milbrett |
| May 19 | Canada | Dallas, TX | 9-1 W | Akers, (2), Hamm (2), Gabarra (2), Lilly (2), Milbrett |
| May 22 | Canada | Edmonton, Canada | 2-1 W | Milbrett, Neaton |
| June 6 | China* | Gavle, Sweden | 3-3 T | Venturini, Milbrett, Hamm |
| June 8 | Denmark* | Gavle, Sweden | 2-0 W | Lilly, Milbrett |
| June 10 | Australia* | Helsingborg, Sweden | 4-1 W | Foudy, Fawcett, Overbeck, Keller |
| June 13 | Japan* | Gavle, Sweden | 4-0 W | Lilly (2), Milbrett, Venturini |
| June 15 | Norway* | Vasteras, Sweden | 0-1 L | none |
| June 17 | China* | Gavle, Sweden | 2-0 W | Venturini, Hamm |
| July 30 | Taipei† | New Britain, CT | 9-0 W | Venturini (3), Hamm (2), Akers (2) Overbeck (2) |
| Aug 3 | Australia† | New Brunswick, NJ | 4-2 W | Hamm (2), Akers, Lilly |
| Aug 6 | Norway† | Washington, D.C. | 2-1 W | Hamm, Pearman |

*FIFA Women's World Championship. †U.S. Women's Cup '95.

### Time on their side

In 1995 the Ontario Lottery Corporation added British soccer to its Pro-Line lottery. Some might frown on what would appear to be government-sponsored gambling, but as the old saying goes, it ain't gambling if you know the outcome.

The scene: Feathers Pub in Toronto. The date: Jan. 2, 1995. A British soccer fan, seeking help in doping out his picks, places a call from the pub to his brother in Manchester, England. The brother proceeds to tick off not only the winners of the matches but the scores as well. Why, asks the Toronto brother, was he so sure? "Because," replies the Manchester brother, "those games ended 40 minutes ago." It seems that the day after New Year's was a holiday in Great Britain, and several matches were played in the afternoon rather than the evening, a wrinkle lottery officials failed to account for in setting the cutoff time for submitting picks. Anyone who caught on had 90 minutes to get in it and win it.

The Toronto brother tipped six of his pals to the scam, and they reportedly took home $12,000 apiece.

Looking for another sure thing? Bet that before its next lottery someone at Pro-Line checks a schedule.

# Club Competition

## 1994 Toyota Cup Final

Competition between winners of European Cup and Libertadores Cup.

### TOKYO: DEC 1, 1994

Velez Sarsfield (Arg.) ......0   2 —2
A.C. Milan (Italy) .............0   0 —0

Goals: Trotta, PK, (50), Asad (57).

Att: 55,860

**Velez Sarsfield:** Chilavert, Trotta, Cardozo, Almandoz, Gomez, Sotomayor, Bassedas, Basualdo, Asad, Pompei, Flores
**A.C. Milan:** Rossi, Tassotti, Maldini, Albertini, Costacurta, Baresi, Donadoni, Desailly,Boban, Savicevic (Simone, 60), Massaro (Panucci, 86).

## European Cup

League champions of the countries belonging to UEFA (Union of European Football Associations).

### VIENNA: MAY 24, 1995

Ajax (Netherlands) ..........0   1 —1
A.C. Milan (Italy) .............0   0 —0

Goal: Kluivert (85).

Att: 49,730.

**Ajax:** Van Der Sar, Reiziger, Blind, Rijkaard, F. De Boer, Seedorf (Kanu, 53), Finidi, Davids, R. De Boer, Litmanen (Kluivert, 69), Overmars.
**A.C. Milan:** Rossi, Panucci, Maldini, Albertini, Costacurta, Baresi, Donadoni, Desailly, Massaro (Eranio, 90), Boban (Lentini, 86), Simone.

## European Cup-Winners' Cup

Cup winners of countries belonging to UEFA.

### PARIS: MAY 10, 1995

Real Zaragoza(Spain)....0   1  1—2
Arsenal (England) ..........0   1  0—1

Goals: Esnaider (68), Nayim (120), Hartson (75).

Att: 42,424

**Real Zaragoza:** Cedrun, Belsue, Aguado, Caceres, Solana, Poyet, Aragon, Nayim, Pardeza, Esnaider, Higuera (Garcia Sanjuan, 67, Gelli, 114).
**Arsenal:** Seaman, Dixon, Linighan, Adams, Winterburn (Morrow, 47), Keown (Hillier, 46), Schwarz, Parlour, Merson, Wright, Hartson.

## UEFA Cup

Competition between teams other than league champions and cup-winners from UEFA.

### (SECOND LEG) MILAN: MAY 17, 1995

Parma (Italy) ....................0   1 —1
Juventus (Italy) .............1   0 —1

Goals: Vialli (33), D. Baggio (53) (aggregate: Parma, 2–1).

Att: 80,750

**Parma:** Bucci, Benarrivo (Mussi 46), Di Chiara (Castellini, 80), Minotti, Susic, Cuoto, Fiore, D. Baggio, Crippa, Zola, Asprilla.
**Juventus:** Peruzzi, Ferrara, Jarni, Torricelli, Porrini Paulo Sousa, Di Livio (Carrera, 81), Marocchi (Del Piero, 74), Vialli, R. Baggio, Ravanelli.

## Libertadores Cup

Competition between champion clubs and runners-up of 10 South American National Associations.

### (SECOND LEG) MEDELLIN: AUG. 30, 1995

Gremio (Brazil) .................0   1 —1
Atl. Nacional (Colombia)...1   0 —1

Goals: Aristizabal (12), Dinho, PK (86) (aggregate: Gremio, 4–2).

Att: 52,000

**Gremio:** Danrlei, Arce, Rivarola, Adilson, Roger, Dinho, Carlos Miguel, Goiano, Arildson, Nunes (Alexandre, 64), Jardel (Nildo, 83).
**Atl. Nacional:** Higulta, Santa (Herrera, 57), Marulanda, Foranda, Mosquera (Pabon , 83), Serna, Arango, Gutierrez, Garcia, Aristizabal, Angel.

### El Boss

Jesús Gil is the Steinbrennerian chairman of Atletico Madrid, one of Spain's biggest soccer clubs, but that's only one of the hats he wears. Gil is also mayor of Marbella, a city on the Costa del Sol, in which capacity he has begun performing marriages. Some 1,500 couples have applied to get hitched at Marbella's town hall, apparently untroubled that Gil has put asunder 17 coaches during the eight years he has run the club.

## National Club Champions—Europe

| Country | League Champion | Cup Winner |
| --- | --- | --- |
| Albania | Tirana | Teuta |
| Armenia | Shirak Gyumri | Ararat Yerevan |
| Austria | Casino Salzburg | Rapid Vienna |
| Azerbaijan | TBC | TBC |
| Belarus | Minsk Dynamo | TBC |
| Belgium | Anderlecht | Club Brugge |
| Bulgaria | Levski | Lok. Sofia |
| Croatia | Hajduk Split | Croatia Zagreb |
| Cyprus | Anorthosis | Apoel |
| Czech Republic | Sparta Prague | Spartak Hradec Kralove |
| Denmark | Aab Aalborg | FC Copenhagen |
| England | Blackburn Rovers | Everton |
| Estonia | Lantana | Trans Narva |
| Faroe Isles | GI | KI |
| Finland | TVP Tampere | HJK Helsinki |
| France | Nantes | Paris St Germain |

### National Club Champions—Europe (Cont.)

| Country | League Champion | Cup Winner |
|---|---|---|
| Georgia | Tibilisi Dynamo | Batumi |
| Germany | Borussia Dortmund | Borussia Monchengladbach |
| Greece | Panathinaikos | AEK Athens |
| Holland | Ajax | Feyenoord |
| Hungary | Ferencvaros | VAC Samsung |
| Iceland | IA Akranes | KR Reykjavik |
| Ireland | Dundalk | Derry City |
| Israel | Maccabi Tel Aviv | Maccabi Haifa |
| Italy | Juventus | Parma |
| Latvia | Skonto Riga | TBC |
| Liechtenstein | FC Vaduz | FC Vaduz |
| Lithuania | Inkaras | Zhalgiris Vilnius |
| Luxembourg | Jeunesse Esch | Grevenmacher |
| Macedonia | Vardar Skopje | Sileks |
| Malta | Hibernian | Valletta |
| Moldova | Zimbru | Tiligul |
| Northern Ireland | Crusaders | Linfield |
| Norway | Rosenborg | Molde |
| Poland | Legia Warsaw | GKS Katowice |
| Portugal | FC Porto | Sporting Lisbon |
| Romania | Steaua Bucharest | Petrolul Ploiesti |
| Russia | Moscow Spartak | Moscow Dynamo |
| Scotland | Rangers | Celtic |
| Slovakia | Slovan Bratislava | Inter Bratislava |
| Slovenia | Olympia | Mura Sobota |
| Spain | Real Madrid | Real Zaragoza |
| Sweden | IFK Gothenburg | Halmstad |
| Switzerland | Grasshopper | Sion |
| Turkey | Besiktas | Trabzonspor |
| Ukraine | Kiev Dynamo | Shakhtyor Donetsk |
| Wales | Bangor City | Wrexham |
| Yugoslavia | Red Star Belgrade | Obilic |

## National Professional Soccer League

### 1994–95 Final Standings

| American | W | L | Pct | GB | PF | PA | National | W | L | Pct | GB | PF | PA |
|---|---|---|---|---|---|---|---|---|---|---|---|---|---|
| Cleveland | 30 | 10 | .750 | — | 742 | 524 | St Louis | 30 | 10 | .750 | — | 711 | 465 |
| Harrisburg | 23 | 17 | .575 | 7.0 | 594 | 526 | Kansas City | 29 | 11 | .725 | 1.0 | 641 | 460 |
| Baltimore | 23 | 17 | .575 | 7.0 | 615 | 572 | Milwaukee | 23 | 17 | .575 | 7.0 | 535 | 459 |
| Buffalo | 20 | 20 | .500 | 10.0 | 579 | 552 | Detroit | 18 | 22 | .450 | 12.0 | 508 | 546 |
| Dayton | 15 | 25 | .375 | 15.0 | 548 | 671 | Wichita | 17 | 23 | .425 | 13.0 | 480 | 583 |
| Canton | 6 | 34 | .150 | 24.0 | 443 | 752 | Chicago | 6 | 34 | .150 | 24.0 | 420 | 706 |

### 1995 Playoff Results

#### HARRISBURG VS CLEVELAND

| Date | Results | Attendance |
|---|---|---|
| Apr 7 | Harrisburg 17 vs Cleveland 7 | 4,206 |
| Apr 10 | Cleveland 18 vs Harrisburg 24 | 5,050 |
| Apr 12 | Cleveland 12 vs Harrisburg 16 | 6,511 |

(Harrisburg wins series 3–0)

#### ST LOUIS VS KANSAS CITY

| Date | Results | Attendance |
|---|---|---|
| Apr 6 | St Louis 40 vs Kansas City 22 | 5,166 |
| Apr 7 | Kansas City 22 vs St Louis 18 | 4,391 |
| Apr 9 | Kansas City 6 vs St Louis 21 | 3,803 |
| Apr 14 | St Louis 11 vs Kansas City 12 | 9,269 |
| Apr 15 | St Louis 25 vs Kansas City 14 | 6,376 |

(St Louis wins series 3–2)

#### CHAMPIONSHIP SERIES

| Date | Results | Attendance |
|---|---|---|
| Apr 20 | St Louis 19 vs Harrisburg 9 | 5,878 |
| Apr 22 | St Louis 18 vs Harrisburg 8 | 12,206 |
| Apr 23 | Harrisburg 7 vs St Louis 12 | 6,578 |
| Apr 25 | Harrisburg 11 vs St Louis 14 | 4,013 |

(St Louis wins series 4–0)

# National Professional Soccer League (Cont.)

## Statistical Leaders

### SCORING

| Rank | Player | 3PG | 2PG | 1PG | Assists | Points |
|------|--------|-----|-----|-----|---------|--------|
| 1 | Hector Marinaro, Clev | 11 | 81 | 7 | 53 | 255 |
| 2 | Zoran Karic, Clev | 8 | 51 | 19 | 96 | 241 |
| 3 | Mark Moser, StL | 6 | 68 | 15 | 26 | 195 |
| 4 | Dennis Brose, Day | 8 | 62 | 16 | 27 | 191 |
| 5 | Goran Kunjak, KC | 3 | 54 | 12 | 52 | 181 |

### THREE-POINT GOALS

| Player | Team | Games | 3PG |
|--------|------|-------|-----|
| 1 Michael King | Mil | 40 | 12 |
| 2 Hector Marinaro | Clev | 32 | 11 |
| 2 Sean Bowers | Det | 40 | 11 |
| 3 Joe Reiniger | StL | 34 | 10 |
| 4 Zoran Karic | Clev | 31 | 8 |

Three tied with 6.

### ASSISTS

| Player | Team | Games | Assists |
|--------|------|-------|---------|
| 1 Zoran Karic | Clev | 31 | 96 |
| 2 Wes Wade | KC | 40 | 71 |
| 3 Pato Margetic | Det | 37 | 62 |
| 4 Franklin McIntosh | Balt | 27 | 59 |
| 5 Hector Marinaro | Clev | 32 | 53 |

### GOALKEEPING LEADERS (Minimum 1410 minutes)

| Player | Team | GP | Min | Shots | Svs | GA | PAA | W | L |
|--------|------|-----|-----|-------|-----|-----|-----|---|---|
| 1 Victor Nogueira | Mil | 35 | 1917:21 | 586 | 422 | 164 | 10.30 | 20 | 14 |
| 2 Warren Westcoat | KC | 29 | 1619:48 | 574 | 425 | 149 | 10.45 | 19 | 7 |
| 3 Jamie Swanner | StL | 35 | 1961:11 | 825 | 626 | 199 | 11.63 | 25 | 8 |
| 4 Scoop Stanisic | Harr | 25 | 1487:45 | 525 | 367 | 158 | 12.62 | 15 | 8 |
| 5 Bryan Finnerty | Det | 36 | 2029:32 | 730 | 500 | 230 | 12.86 | 17 | 18 |

# American Professional Soccer League*

## 1994 Final Standings

| | W | L | GF | GA | Pts | Home | Road |
|---|---|---|----|----|-----|------|------|
| Seattle Sounders | 14 | 6 | 38 | 16 | 121 | 9-1 | 5-5 |
| Los Angeles Salsa | 12 | 8 | 36 | 22 | 106 | 7-3 | 5-5 |
| Montreal Impact | 12 | 8 | 27 | 18 | 93 | 7-3 | 5-5 |
| Colorado Foxes | 12 | 8 | 26 | 26 | 92 | 8-2 | 4-6 |
| Fort Lauderdale Strikers | 8 | 12 | 23 | 33 | 72 | 4-6 | 4-6 |
| Vancouver Eighty-Sixers | 7 | 13 | 25 | 41 | 65 | 5-5 | 2-8 |
| Toronto Rockets | 5 | 15 | 14 | 33 | 44 | 4-6 | 1-9 |

Point system—six points for each victory in regulation or overtime; four points for a Shootout win; two points for a Shootout loss; one bonus point for each goal in regulation up to a maximun of three (regardless of whether team wins or loses).

**Playoff Results:** Four teams—Seattle, Los Angeles, Montreal, and Colorado—qualified for the playoffs. Colorado defeated Seattle 2–1, Montreal defeated Los Angeles 2–1, in the Semis; Montreal defeated Colorado 1–0 in the finals for the APSL championship.

### SCORING LEADERS

| | |
|---|---|
| Paul Wright, Los Angeles | 27 |
| Paulinho, Los Angeles | 27 |
| Chance Fry, Seattle | 26 |
| Jason Dunn, Seattle | 23 |
| Jean Harbor, Montreal | 20 |

### ASSISTS LEADERS

| | |
|---|---|
| Shawn Medved, Seattle | 11 |
| Dale Mitchell, Vancouver | 9 |
| Jason Farrell, Seattle | 7 |
| Paulinho, Los Angeles | 5 |

Ten tied with 4.

### GOALS LEADERS

| | |
|---|---|
| Paul Wright, Los Angeles | 12 |
| Paulinho, Los Angeles | 11 |
| Chance Fry, Seattle | 11 |
| Jason Dunn, Seattle | 10 |
| Jean Harbor, Montreal | 8 |

### GOALS-AGAINST-AVERAGE LEADERS

| | |
|---|---|
| Marcus Hahnemann, Seattle | 0.57 |
| Mike Littman, Los Angeles | 0.76 |
| Pat Harrington, Montreal | 0.95 |
| Mario Jimenez, Los Angeles | 1.05 |
| Mark Dodd, Colorado | 1.10 |

*Known as the A-League since 1995.

## The World Cup

### Results

| Year | Champion | Score | Runner-Up | Winning Coach |
|------|----------|-------|-----------|---------------|
| 1930 | Uruguay | 4-2 | Argentina | Alberto Supicci |
| 1934 | Italy | 2-1 | Czechoslovakia | Vittorio Pozzo |
| 1938 | Italy | 4-2 | Hungary | Vittorio Pozzo |
| 1950 | Uruguay | 2-1 | Brazil | Juan Lopez |
| 1954 | West Germany | 3-2 | Hungary | Sepp Herberger |
| 1958 | Brazil | 5-2 | Sweden | Vicente Feola |
| 1962 | Brazil | 3-1 | Czechoslovakia | Aymore Moreira |
| 1966 | England | 4-2 | West Germany | Alf Ramsey |
| 1970 | Brazil | 4-1 | Italy | Mario Zagalo |
| 1974 | West Germany | 2-1 | Netherlands | Helmut Schoen |
| 1978 | Argentina | 3-1 | Netherlands | César Menotti |
| 1982 | Italy | 3-1 | West Germany | Enzo Bearzot |
| 1986 | Argentina | 3-2 | West Germany | Carlos Bilardo |
| 1990 | West Germany | 1-0 | Argentina | Franz Beckenbauer |
| 1994 | Brazil | 0-0 (3-2) | Italy | Carlos Alberto Parreira |

### Alltime World Cup Participation

Of the 58 nations which have taken part in the World Cup, only Brazil has competed in each of the 15 tournaments held to date. West Germany or an undivided Germany (1934, '38 and '94) have played in 14 World Cups.

| | Matches | W | T | L | Goals For | Goals Against | | Matches | W | T | L | Goals For | Goals Against |
|---|--------|---|---|---|-----------|---------------|---|--------|---|---|---|-----------|---------------|
| Brazil | 73 | 49 | 13 | 11 | 159 | 68 | East Germany | 6 | 2 | 2 | 2 | 5 | 5 |
| *Germany | 73 | 42 | 16 | 15 | 154 | 97 | Costa Rica | 4 | 2 | 0 | 2 | 4 | 6 |
| Italy | 61 | 35 | 14 | 12 | 97 | 59 | Saudi Arabia | 4 | 2 | 0 | 2 | 5 | 6 |
| Argentina | 52 | 26 | 9 | 17 | 90 | 65 | Colombia | 10 | 2 | 2 | 6 | 13 | 20 |
| England | 41 | 18 | 12 | 11 | 55 | 38 | Algeria | 6 | 2 | 1 | 3 | 6 | 10 |
| †Russia | 34 | 16 | 6 | 12 | 60 | 40 | Wales | 5 | 1 | 3 | 1 | 4 | 4 |
| Uruguay | 37 | 15 | 8 | 14 | 61 | 52 | Morocco | 7 | 1 | 3 | 3 | 5 | 8 |
| France | 34 | 15 | 5 | 14 | 71 | 56 | Republic of Ireland | 9 | 1 | 5 | 3 | 4 | 7 |
| Yugoslavia | 33 | 15 | 5 | 13 | 55 | 42 | Tunisia | 3 | 1 | 1 | 1 | 3 | 2 |
| Hungary | 32 | 15 | 3 | 14 | 87 | 57 | North Korea | 4 | 1 | 1 | 2 | 5 | 9 |
| Spain | 37 | 15 | 9 | 13 | 53 | 44 | Cuba | 3 | 1 | 1 | 1 | 5 | 12 |
| Poland | 25 | 13 | 5 | 7 | 39 | 29 | Turkey | 3 | 1 | 0 | 2 | 10 | 11 |
| Sweden | 37 | 13 | 7 | 17 | 62 | 60 | Norway | 4 | 1 | 1 | 2 | 2 | 3 |
| Austria | 26 | 12 | 2 | 12 | 40 | 43 | Israel | 3 | 1 | 0 | 2 | 1 | 3 |
| Czechoslovakia | 30 | 11 | 5 | 14 | 44 | 45 | Honduras | 3 | 0 | 2 | 1 | 2 | 3 |
| Netherlands | 25 | 11 | 6 | 8 | 43 | 29 | Egypt | 4 | 0 | 2 | 2 | 3 | 6 |
| Belgium | 29 | 9 | 4 | 16 | 37 | 53 | Kuwait | 3 | 0 | 1 | 2 | 2 | 6 |
| Mexico | 33 | 7 | 8 | 18 | 31 | 68 | Australia | 3 | 0 | 1 | 2 | 0 | 5 |
| Chile | 21 | 7 | 3 | 11 | 26 | 32 | Iran | 3 | 0 | 1 | 2 | 2 | 8 |
| Portugal | 9 | 6 | 0 | 3 | 19 | 12 | South Korea | 11 | 0 | 3 | 8 | 9 | 34 |
| Romania | 17 | 6 | 4 | 7 | 26 | 29 | Dutch East Indies | 1 | 0 | 0 | 1 | 0 | 6 |
| Switzerland | 22 | 6 | 3 | 13 | 33 | 51 | Iraq | 3 | 0 | 0 | 3 | 1 | 4 |
| United States | 14 | 4 | 1 | 9 | 17 | 33 | Canada | 3 | 0 | 0 | 3 | 0 | 5 |
| Scotland | 20 | 4 | 6 | 10 | 23 | 35 | United Arab Emirates | 3 | 0 | 0 | 3 | 2 | 11 |
| Peru | 15 | 4 | 3 | 8 | 19 | 31 | New Zealand | 3 | 0 | 0 | 3 | 2 | 12 |
| Bulgaria | 22 | 3 | 7 | 12 | 21 | 42 | Haiti | 3 | 0 | 0 | 3 | 2 | 14 |
| Northern Ireland | 13 | 3 | 5 | 5 | 13 | 23 | Zaire | 3 | 0 | 0 | 3 | 0 | 14 |
| Paraguay | 11 | 3 | 4 | 4 | 16 | 25 | Bolivia | 6 | 0 | 1 | 5 | 1 | 20 |
| Cameroon | 11 | 3 | 4 | 4 | 11 | 21 | El Salvador | 6 | 0 | 0 | 6 | 1 | 22 |
| Denmark | 4 | 3 | 0 | 1 | 10 | 6 | Greece | 3 | 0 | 0 | 3 | 0 | 8 |
| Nigeria | 4 | 2 | 0 | 2 | 7 | 4 | | | | | | | |

*Includes West Germany 1950-90. †Includes USSR 1930-1990.
Note: Matches decided by penalty kicks are shown as drawn games.

## World Cup Final Box Scores

### URUGUAY 1930

| Uruguay...........1 | 3 —4 |
|---|---|
| Argentina........2 | 0 —2 |

**FIRST HALF**

Scoring: 1, Uruguay, Dorado (12); 2, Argentina, Peucelle (20); 3, Argentina, Stabile (37).

**SECOND HALF**

Scoring: 4, Uruguay, Cea (57); 5, Uruguay, Iriarte (68); 6, Uruguay, Castro (89).

**Argentina:** Botosso, Della Toree, Paternoster, Evaristo, J., Monti, Suarez, Peucelle, Varallo, Stabile, Ferreira, Evaristo, M.

**Uruguay:** Ballesteros, Nasazzi, Mascheroni, Andrade, Fernandez, Gestido, Dorado, Scarone, Castro, Cea, Iriarte.

Referee: Langenus (Belgium).

### ITALY 1934

| Italy..................0 | 1 | 1—2 |
|---|---|---|
| Czechoslovakia ..0 | 1 | 0—1 |

**SECOND HALF**

Scoring: 1, Czech., Puc (70); 2, Italy, Orsi (80).

**OVERTIME**

Scoring: 3, Italy, Schiavio (95).

**Italy:** Combi, Monzeglio, Allemandi, Ferraris Monti, Monti, Bertolini, Guaita, Meazza, Schiavio, Ferrari, Orsi.

**Czechoslovakia:** Planicka, Zenisek, Ctyroky, Kostalek, Cambal, Cambal, Krcil, Junek, Svoboda, Sobotka, Nejedly, Puc.

Referee: Eklind (Sweden).

### FRANCE 1938

| Italy..................3 | 1 —4 |
|---|---|
| Hungary ...........1 | 1 —2 |

**FIRST HALF**

Scoring: 1, Italy, Colaussi (5); 2, Hungary, Titkos (7); 3, Italy, Piola (16); 4, Italy, Piola (35).

**SECOND HALF**

Scoring: 5, Hungary, Sarosi (70); 6, Italy, Colaussi (82).

**Italy:** Olivieri, Foni, Rava, Serantoni, Andreolo, Locatelli, Biavati, Meazza, Piola, Ferrari, Colaussi.

**Hungary:** Szabo; Polger, Biro, Szalay, Szucs, Lazar, Sas, Vincze, Sarosi, Zsengeller, Titkos.

Referee: Capdeville (France).

### BRAZIL 1950

| Uruguay ...........0 | 2 —2 |
|---|---|
| Brazil................0 | 1 —1 |

**SECOND HALF**

Scoring: 1, Brazil, Friaca (47); 2, Uruguay, Schiaffino (66); 3, Uruguay, Ghiggia (79).

**Uruguay:** Maspoli, Gonzales, Tejera, Gambretta, Varela, Andrade, Ghiggia, Perez, Miguez, Schiffiano, Moran

**Brazil:** Barbosa, Augusto, Juvenal, Bauer, Banilo, Bigode, Friaca, Zizinho, Ademir, Jair, Chico.

Referee: Reader (England).

### SWITZERLAND 1954

| W Germany ......2 | 1 —3 |
|---|---|
| Hungary ...........2 | 0 —2 |

**FIRST HALF**

Scoring: 1, Hungary, Puskas (6); 2, Hungary, Czibor (8); 3, W Germ, Morlock (10); 4, W Germ, Rahn (18).

**SECOND HALF**

Scoring: 5, W Germ, Rahn (84).

**West Germany:** Turek; Posipal, Kohlmeyer, Eckel, Liebrich, Mai, Rahn, Morlock, Walter, O., Walter, F., Schaefer.

**Hungary:** Grosics; Buzansky, Lantos, Bozsik, Lorant, Zakarias, Czibor, Kocsis, Hidegkuti, Puskas, Toth.

Referee: Ling (England).

### SWEDEN 1958

| Brazil.................2 | 3 —5 |
|---|---|
| Sweden.............1 | 1 —2 |

**FIRST HALF**

Scoring:1, Sweden, Liedholm (3); 2, Brazil, Vava (9); 3, Brazil, Vava (32).

**SECOND HALF**

Scoring: 4, Brazil, Pelé (55); 5, Brazil, Zagalo (68); 6, Sweden Simonsson (80); 7, Brazil, Pelé (90).

**Brazil:** Glymar, Santos, D., Santos, N., Zito, Bellini, Orlando, Garrincha, Didi, Vava, Pelé, Zagalo.

**Sweden:** Svensson, Bergmark, Axbom, Boerjesson, Gustavsson, Parling, Hamrin, Gren, Simonsson, Liedholm, Skoglund.

Referee: Guigue (France).

### CHILE 1962

| Brazil.............................1 | 2 —3 |
|---|---|
| Czechoslovakia ...........1 | 0 —1 |

**FIRST HALF**

Scoring: 1, Czech, Masopust (15); 2, Brazil, Amarildo (17).

**SECOND HALF**

Scoring: 3, Brazil, Zito (68); 4, Brazil, Vava (77).

**Brazil:** Glymar; Santos, D., Santos, N., Zito, Mauro, Zozimo, Garrincha, Didi, Vava, Amarildo, Zagalo.

**Czechoslovakia:** Schroiff, Tichy, Novak, Pluskal, Popluhar, Masopust, Pospichal, Scherer, Kvasnak, Kadraba, Jelinek.

Referee: Latychev (USSR).

## World Cup Final Box Scores *(Cont.)*

### ENGLAND 1966

| England | ..........1 | 1 | 2—4 |
|---|---|---|---|
| W. Germany | ........1 | 1 | 0—2 |

**FIRST HALF**

Scoring: 1, Germany, Haller (12); 2, England, Hurst, (18).

**SECOND HALF**

Scoring: 3, England, Peters (78); 4, Germany, Weber (90).

**OVERTIME**

Scoring: 5, England, Hurst (101); 6, England, Hurst (120).

**England:** Banks, Cohen, Wilson, Stiles, Charlton, J., Moore, Ball, Hurst, Hunt, Charlton, R., Peters.

**W. Germany:** Tilkowski, Hottges, Schmellinger, Beckenbauer, Schulz, Weber, Held, Haller, Seeler, Overath, Emmerich.

Referee: Dienst (Switzerland).

### W. GERMANY 1974

| W. Germany | .....2 | 0 —2 |
|---|---|---|
| Netherlands | .....1 | 0 —1 |

**FIRST HALF**

Scoring: 1, The Netherlands, Neeskens, PK, (1); 2, W. Germany, Breitner, PK, (26); 3, W. Germany, Muller, (44).

**W. Germany:** Maier, Vogts, Beckenbauer, Schwarzenbeck, Breitner, Hoeness, Bonhof, Overath, Grabowski, Muller, Holzenbein.

**The Netherlands:** Jongbloed, Suurbier, Rijsbergen (de Jong), Haan, Krol, Jansen, Neeskens, van Hanagem, Cruyff, Rensenbrink (van der Kerkhof).

Referee: Taylor (England).

### ITALY 1982

| Italy | ..................0 | 3 —3 |
|---|---|---|
| W. Germany | .....0 | 1 —1 |

**SECOND HALF**

Scoring: 1, Italy, Rossi (57); 2, Italy, Tardelli (68); 3, Italy, Altobelli (81); 4, Germany, Breitner (83).

**Italy:** Zoff, Bergomi, Scirea, Collovati, Cabrini, Oriali, Gentile, Tardelli, Conti, Rossi, Graziani (Altobelli, Causio).

**W. Germany:** Schumacher, Kaltz, Stielike, Foerster, K., Foerster, B., Dremmler (Hrubesch), Breitner, Briegel, Rummenigge (Mueller), Fishcher (Littbrarski).

Referee: Coelho (Brazil).

### MEXICO 1970

| Brazil | ................1 | 3 —4 |
|---|---|---|
| Italy | ..................1 | 0 —1 |

**FIRST HALF**

Scoring: 1, Brazil, Pelé (18); 2, Italy, Boninsegna (32).

**SECOND HALF**

Scoring: 3, Brazil, Gerson (65); 4, Brazil, Jairzinho (70); 5, Brazil, Alberto (86).

**Brazil:** Feliz, Alberto, Brito, Wilson, Piazza, Everaldo, Clodoaldo, Gerson, Jairzinho, Tostao, Pelé, Rivelino.

**Italy:** Albertosi, Burgnich, Cera, Rosato, Facchetti, Bertini (Juliano), Mazzola, De Sisti, Domenghini, Boninsegna (Rivera), Riva.

Referee: Glockner (E. Germany).

### ARGENTINA 1978

| Argentina | .........1 | 0 | 2—3 |
|---|---|---|---|
| Netherlands | .....0 | 1 | 0—1 |

**FIRST HALF**

Scoring: 1, Argentina, Kempes (38).

**SECOND HALF**

Scoring: 2, The Netherlands, Nanninga (81).

**OVERTIME**

Scoring: 3, Arg., Kempes (104); 4, Arg., Bertoni (114).

**Argentina:** Fillol, Olguin, Galvan, Passarella, Tarantini, Ardiles (Larrosa), Gallego, Kempes, Bertoni, Luque, Ortiz (Houseman).

**The Netherlands:** Jongbloed, Jansen (Suurbier), Krol, Brandts, Poortvliet, Neeskens, Haan, van der Kerkhoff, W., van der Kerkhoff, R., Rep (Nanninga), Rensenbrink.

Referee: Gonella (Italy).

### MEXICO 1986

| Argentina | .........1 | 2 —3 |
|---|---|---|
| W. Germany | .....0 | 2 —2 |

**FIRST HALF**

Scoring: 1, Argentina, Brown (22).

**SECOND HALF**

Scoring: 2, Arg., Valdano (55); 3, W. Germ., Rummenigge (73); 4, W. Germ., Voller (81); 5, Arg., Burruchaga (83).

**Argentina:** Pumpido, Brown, Cuciuffo, Ruggeri, Olarticoecha, Bastista, Giusti, Burruchaga (90, Trobbiani), Enrique, Maradona, Valdona.

**W. Germany:** Schumacher, Jakobs, Forster, Eder, Brehme, Matthaus, Berthold, Magath (62 Hoeness), Briegel, Rummenigge, Allofs (46 Voller).

Referee: Filho (Brazil).

## World Cup Final Box Scores *(Cont.)*

| ITALY 1990 | | |
|---|---|---|
| W Germany.........0 | 1——1 | |
| Argentina ..............0 | 0——0 | |

**SECOND HALF**

Scoring: 1, W. Germany, Brehme, PK, (84).

**W. Germany:** Illgner, Brehme, Kohler, Augenthaler, Buchwald, Berthold (Reuter), Littbarski, Haessler, Mattaeus, Voeller, Klinsmann.

**Argentina:** Goychoechea, Lorenzo, Serrizuela, Sensini, Ruggeri (Monzon), Simon, Basualdo, Burruchag (Calderon), Maradona, Troglio, Dezottir.

Referee: Coelho (Brazil).

| UNITED STATES 1994 | | | |
|---|---|---|---|
| Italy...................0 | 0 | 0——0 | |
| Brazil ..................0 | 0 | 0——0 | |

Scoring: None. Shootout goals: Italy—2: Albertini, Evani; Brazil—3: Romario, Branco, Dunga.

**Italy:** Pagliuca, Benarrivo, Maldini, Baresi, Mussi (Apolloni 35), Albertini, D. Baggio (Evani 95), Berti, Donadoni, Baggio, Massaro,

**Brazil:** Taffarel, Jorginho (Cafu 21), Branco, Aldair, Santos, Silva, Dunga, Zinho (Viola 106), Mazinho, Bebeto, Romario

Referee: Sandor Puhl (Hungary).

## Alltime Leaders

### GOALS

| Player, Nation | Tournaments | Goals | Player, Nation | Tournaments | Goals |
|---|---|---|---|---|---|
| Gerd Muller, West Germany | 1970, '74 | 14 | Ademir, Brazil | 1950 | 9 |
| Just Fontaine, France | 1958 | 13 | Eusebio, Portugal | 1966 | 9 |
| Pelé, Brazil | 1958, '62, '66, '70 | 12 | Jairzinho, Brazil | 1970, '74 | 9 |
| Sandor Kocsis, Hungary | 1954 | 11 | Paolo Rossi, Italy | 1982, '86 | 9 |
| Teofilo Cubillas, Peru | 1970, '78 | 10 | Karl-Heinz Rummenigge, | | |
| Gregorz Lato, Poland | 1974, '78, '82 | 10 | W. Germany | 1978, '82, '86 | 9 |
| Helmut Rahn, West Germany | 1954, '58 | 10 | Uwe Seeler, West Germany | 1958, '62, '66, '70 | 9 |
| Gary Lineker, England | 1986, '90 | 10 | Vava, Brazil | 1958, '62 | 9 |

### LEADING SCORER, CUP BY CUP

| Year | Player/Nation | Goals | Year | Player/Nation | Goals |
|---|---|---|---|---|---|
| 1930 | Guillermo Stabile, Argentina | 8 | 1962 | Leonel Sanchez, Chile | 4 |
| 1934 | Oldrich Nejedly, Czechoslovakia | 5 | | Vava, Brazil | |
| 1938 | Leonidas da Silva, Brazil | 8 | 1966 | Eusebio Ferreira, Portugal | 9 |
| 1950 | Ademir de Menenzes, Brazil | 9 | 1970 | Gerd Mueller, West Germany | 10 |
| 1954 | Sandor Kocsis, Hungary | 11 | 1974 | Gregorz Lato, Poland | 7 |
| 1958 | Just Fontaine, France | 13 | 1978 | Mario Kempes, Argentina | 6 |
| 1962 | Florian Albert, Hungary | 4 | 1982 | Paolo Rossi, Italy | 6 |
| | Valentin Ivanov, USSR | | 1986 | Gary Lineker, England | 6 |
| | Garrincha, Brazil | | 1990 | Salvatore Schillaci, Italy | 6 |
| | Drazan Jerkovic, Yugoslavia | | 1994 | Hristo Stoitchkov, Bulgaria | 6 |
| | | | | Oleg Salenko, Russia | |

## Most Goals, Individual, One Game

| Goals | Player, Nation | Score | Date |
|---|---|---|---|
| 5 | Oleg Salenko, Russia | Russia-Cameroon, 6-1 | 6-28-94 |
| 4 | Leonidas, Brazil | Brazil-Poland, 6-5 | 6-5-38 |
| 4 | Ernest Willimowski, Poland | Brazil-Poland, 6-5 | 6-5-38 |
| 4 | Gustav Wetterstrîm, Sweden | Sweden-Cuba, 8-0 | 6-12-38 |
| 4 | Juan Alberto Schiaffino, Uruguay | Uruguay-Bolivia, 8-0 | 7-2-50 |
| 4 | Ademir, Brazil | Brazil-Sweden, 7-1 | 7-9-50 |
| 4 | Sandor Kocsis, Hungary | Hungary-West Germany, 8-3 | 6-20-54 |
| 4 | Just Fontaine, France | France-West Germany, 6-3 | 6-28-58 |
| 4 | Eusebio, Portugal | Portugal-No. Korea, 5-3 | 7-23-66 |
| 4 | Emilio Butragueño, Spain | Spain-Denmark, 5-1 | 6-18-86 |

Note: 30 players have scored 31 World Cup hat tricks. Gerd Muller of West Germany is the only man to have two World Cup hat tricks, both in 1970. The last hat tricks were 6-23-90, Tomas Skuhravy (Czech) vs. Costa Rica and Michel (Spain) vs. So. Korea, 6-17-90.

## Attendance and Goal Scoring, Year by Year

| Year | Site | No. of Games | Goals | Goals/Game | Attendance | Avg Att |
|---|---|---|---|---|---|---|
| 1930 | Uruguay | 18 | 70 | 3.89 | 434,500 | 24,139 |
| 1934 | Italy | 17 | 70 | 4.12 | 395,000 | 23,235 |
| 1938 | France | 18 | 84 | 4.67 | 483,000 | 26,833 |
| 1950 | Brazil | 22 | 88 | 4.00 | 1,337,000 | 60,773 |
| 1954 | Switzerland | 26 | 140 | 5.38 | 943,000 | 36,269 |
| 1958 | Sweden | 35 | 126 | 3.60 | 868,000 | 24,800 |
| 1962 | Chile | 32 | 89 | 2.78 | 776,000 | 24,250 |
| 1966 | England | 32 | 89 | 2.78 | 1,614,677 | 50,459 |
| 1970 | Mexico | 32 | 95 | 2.97 | 1,673,975 | 52,312 |
| 1974 | West Germany | 38 | 97 | 2.55 | 1,774,022 | 46,685 |
| 1978 | Argentina | 38 | 102 | 2.68 | 1,610,215 | 42,374 |
| 1982 | Spain | 52 | 146 | 2.80 | 1,856,277 | 35,698 |
| 1986 | Mexico | 52 | 132 | 2.54 | 2,441,731 | 46,956 |
| 1990 | Italy | 52 | 115 | 2.21 | 2,514,443 | 48,354 |
| 1994 | United States | 52 | 140 | 2.69 | 3,567,415 | 68,604 |
| Totals | | 516 | 1583 | 3.07 | 22,289,255 | 43,196 |

## The United States in the World Cup

### URUGUAY 1930: FINAL COMPETITION

| Date | Opponent | Result | Scoring |
|---|---|---|---|
| 7-13-30 | Belgium | 3-0 W | US: McGhee 2, Patenaude |
| 7-17-30 | Paraguay | 3-0 W | US: Patenaude 2, Florie |
| 7-26-30 | Argentina | 1-6 L | ARG: Monti 2, Scopelli 2, Stabile 2 US: Brown. |

### ITALY 1934: FINAL COMPETITION

| Date | Opponent | Result | Scoring |
|---|---|---|---|
| 5-27-34 | Italy | 1-7 L | US: Donelli ITA: Schiavio 3, Orsi 2, Meazza, Ferrari |

### BRAZIL 1950: FINAL COMPETITION

| Date | Opponent | Result | Scoring |
|---|---|---|---|
| 6-25-50 | Spain | 1-3 L | US: Pariani SPN: Igoa, Basora, Zarra |
| 6-29-50 | England | 1-0 W | US: Gaetjens. |
| 7-2-50 | Chile | 2-5 L | US: Wallace, Maca CHL: Robledo, Cremaschi 3, Prieto |

### ITALY 1990: FINAL COMPETITION

| Date | Opponent | Result | Scoring |
|---|---|---|---|
| 6-10-90 | Czechoslovakia | 1-5 L | US: Caligiuri Czech: Skuhravy 2, Hasek, Bilek, Luhovy |
| 6-14-90 | Italy | 0-1 L | Italy: Giannini |
| 6-19-90 | Austria | 1-2 L | US: Murray Austria: Rodax, Ogris |

### UNITED STATES 1994: FINAL COMPETITION

| Date | Opponent | Result | Scoring |
|---|---|---|---|
| 6-18-94 | Switzerland | 1-1 T | US: Wynalda Sui: Bregy |
| 6-22-94 | Colombia | 2-1 W | US: Escobar (own goal), Stewart Colombia: Valencia |
| 6-26-94 | Romania | 1-0 L | Romania: Petrescu |
| 7-4-94 | Brazil | 1-0 L | Brazil: Bebeto |

# International Competition

## European Championship

Official name: the European Football Championship. Held every four years since 1960.

| Year | Champion | Score | Runner-up | Year | Champion | Score | Runner-up |
|---|---|---|---|---|---|---|---|
| 1960 | USSR | 2-1 | Yugoslavia | 1980 | West Germany | 2-1 | Belgium |
| 1964 | Spain | 2-1 | USSR | 1984 | France | 2-0 | Spain |
| 1968 | Italy | 2-0 | Yugoslavia | 1988 | Holland | 2-0 | USSR |
| 1972 | West Germany | 3-0 | USSR | 1992 | Denmark | 2-0 | Germany |
| 1976 | Czechoslovakia* | 2-2 | West Germany | | | | |

*Won on penalty kicks.

## Under-20 World Championship

| Year | Host | Champion | Runner-Up |
|------|------|----------|-----------|
| 1977 | Tunisia | USSR | Mexico |
| 1979 | Japan | Argentina | USSR |
| 1981 | Australia | W. Germany | Qatar |
| 1983 | Mexico | Brazil | Argentina |
| 1985 | USSR | Brazil | Spain |
| 1987 | Chile | Yugoslavia | W. Germany |
| 1989 | Saudi Arabia | Portugal | Nigeria |
| 1991 | Portugal | Portugal | Brazil |
| 1993 | Australia | Brazil | Ghana |
| 1995 | Qatar | Argentina | Brazil |

## Under-17 World Championship

| 1985 | Nigeria |
|------|---------|
| 1987 | USSR |
| 1989 | Saudi Arabia |
| 1991 | Ghana |

## Under-17 *(Cont.)*

| 1993 | Nigeria |
|------|---------|
| 1995 | Ghana |

## Pan American Games

| 1951 | Argentina |
|------|-----------|
| 1955 | Argentina |
| 1959 | Argentina |
| 1963 | Brazil |
| 1967 | Mexico |
| 1971 | Argentina |
| 1975 | Brazil-Mexico (tie) |
| 1979 | Brazil |
| 1983 | Uruguay |
| 1987 | Brazil |
| 1991 | United States |
| 1995 | Argentina |

## South American Championship (Copa America)

| Year | Champion | Host | Year | Champion | Host |
|------|----------|------|------|----------|------|
| 1916 | Uruguay | Argentina | 1947 | Argentina | Ecuador |
| 1917 | Uruguay | Uruguay | 1949 | Brazil | Brazil |
| 1919 | Brazil | Brazil | 1953 | Paraguay | Peru |
| 1920 | Uruguay | Chile | 1955 | Argentina | Chile |
| 1921 | Argentina | Argentina | 1956 | Uruguay | Uruguay |
| 1922 | Brazil | Brazil | 1957 | Argentina | Peru |
| 1923 | Uruguay | Uruguay | 1958 | Argentina | Argentina |
| 1924 | Uruguay | Uruguay | 1959 | Uruguay | Ecuador |
| 1925 | Argentina | Argentina | 1963 | Bolivia | Bolivia |
| 1926 | Uruguay | Chile | 1967 | Uruguay | Uruguay |
| 1927 | Argentina | Peru | 1975 | Peru | Various sites |
| 1929 | Argentina | Argentina | 1979 | Paraguay | Various sites |
| 1935 | Uruguay | Peru | 1983 | Uruguay | Various sites |
| 1937 | Argentina | Argentina | 1987 | Uruguay | Argentina |
| 1939 | Peru | Peru | 1989 | Brazil | Brazil |
| 1941 | Argentina | Chile | 1990 | Brazil | Argentina |
| 1942 | Uruguay | Uruguay | 1991 | Argentina | Chile |
| 1945 | Argentina | Chile | 1993 | Argentina | Ecuador |
| 1946 | Argentina | Argentina | 1995 | Uruguay | Uruguay |

# Awards

## European Footballer of the Year

| Year | Player | Team | Year | Player | Team |
|------|--------|------|------|--------|------|
| 1956 | Stanley Matthews | Blackpool | 1973 | Johan Cruyff | Barcelona |
| 1957 | Alfredo Di Stefano | Real Madrid | 1974 | Johan Cruyff | Barcelona |
| 1958 | Raymond Kopa | Real Madrid | 1975 | Oleg Blokhin | Dynamo Kiev |
| 1959 | Alfredo Di Stefano | Real Madrid | 1976 | Franz Beckenbauer | Bayern Munich |
| 1960 | Luis Suarez | Barcelona | 1977 | Allan Simonsen | Borussia Moenchengladbach |
| 1961 | Omar Sivori | Juventus | | | |
| 1962 | Josef Masopust | Dukla Prague | 1978 | Kevin Keegan | SV Hamburg |
| 1963 | Lev Yashin | Moscow Dynamo | 1979 | Kevin Keegan | SV Hamburg |
| 1964 | Denis Law | Manchester United | 1980 | Karl-Heinz Rummenigge | Bayern Munich |
| 1965 | Eusebio | Benfica | | | |
| 1966 | Bobby Charlton | Manchester United | 1981 | Karl-Heinz Rummenigge | Bayern Munich |
| 1967 | Florian Albert | Ferencvaros | | | |
| 1968 | George Best | Manchester United | 1982 | Paolo Rossi | Juventus |
| 1969 | Gianni Rivera | AC Milan | 1983 | Michel Platini | Juventus |
| 1970 | Gerd Mueller | Bayern Munich | 1984 | Michel Platini | Juventus |
| 1971 | Johan Cruyff | Ajax | 1985 | Michel Platini | Juventus |
| 1972 | Franz Beckenbauer | Bayern Munich | 1986 | Igor Belanov | Dynamo Kiev |
| | | | 1987 | Ruud Gullit | AC Milan |

## European Footballer of the Year (Cont.)

| | | |
|---|---|---|
| 1988 .....Marco Van Basten | AC Milan | |
| 1989 .....Marco Van Basten | AC Milan | |
| 1990 .....Lothar Matthaeus | Inter Milan | |
| 1991 .....Jean-Pierre Papin | Olympique Marseille | |

| | |
|---|---|
| 1992 .....Marco Van Basten | AC Milan |
| 1993 .....Roberto Baggio | Juventus |
| 1994 .....Hristo Stoichkov | Barcelona |

## African Footballer of the Year

| Year | Player | Team | Year | Player | Team |
|---|---|---|---|---|---|
| 1970 | Salif Keita | Mali | 1983 | Mahmoud Al-Khatib | Egypt |
| 1971 | Ibrahim Sunday | Ghana | 1984 | ThÇophile Abega | Cameroon |
| 1972 | Chérif Souleyman | Guinea | 1985 | Mohamed Timoumi | Morocco |
| 1973 | Tshimimu Bwanga | Zaire | 1986 | Badou Zaki | Morocco |
| 1974 | Paul Moukila | Congo | 1987 | Rabah Madjer | Algeria |
| 1975 | Ahmed Faras | Morocco | 1988 | Kalusha Bwalya | Zambia |
| 1976 | Roger Milla | Cameroon | 1989 | George Weah | Liberia |
| 1977 | Dhiab Tarak | Tunisia | 1990 | Roger Milla | Cameroon |
| 1978 | Abdul Razak | Ghana | 1991 | Abedi Pele | Ghana |
| 1979 | Thomas Nkono | Cameroon | 1992 | Abedi Pele | Ghana |
| 1980 | Jean Manga Onguene | Cameroon | 1993 | Rashidi Yekini | Nigeria |
| 1981 | Lakhdar Belloumi | Algeria | 1994 | George Weah | Liberia |
| 1982 | Thomas Nkono | Cameroon | | | |

Selected by *France Football*.

## South American Player of the Year

| Year | Player | Team | Year | Player | Team |
|---|---|---|---|---|---|
| 1971 | Tostao | Cruzeiro | 1983 | Socrates | Corinthians |
| 1972 | Teofilo Cubillas | Alianza Lima | 1984 | Enzo Francescoli | River Plate |
| 1973 | Pelé | Santos | 1985 | Julio Cesar Romero | Fluminense |
| 1974 | Elias Figueroa | Internacional | 1986 | Antonio Alzamendi | River Plate |
| 1975 | Elias Figueroa | Internacional | 1987 | Carlos Valderrama | Deportivo Cali |
| 1976 | Elias Figueroa | Internacional | 1988 | Ruben Paz | Racing Buenos Aires |
| 1977 | Zico | Flamengo | 1989 | Bebeto | Vasco da Gama |
| 1978 | Mario Kempes | Valencia | 1990 | Raul Amarilla | Olimpia |
| 1979 | Diego Maradona | Argentinos Juniors | 1991 | Oscar Ruggeri | Velez Sarsfield |
| 1980 | Diego Maradona | Boca Juniors | 1992 | Rai | Sao Paulo |
| 1981 | Zico | Flamengo | 1993 | Carlos Valderrama | Junior Barranquilla |
| 1982 | Zico | Flamengo | 1994 | Cafu | Sao Paulo |

Selected by Uruguayan magazine *El Pais*.

# Club Competition

## Toyota Cup

Competition between winners of European Champion Clubs' Cup and Libertadores Cup.

| | | |
|---|---|---|
| 1960...Real Madrid, Spain | 1972...Ajax, Holland | 1984...Independiente, Argentina |
| 1961...Penarol, Uruguay | 1973...Independiente, Argentina | 1985...Juventus, Italy |
| 1962...Santos, Brazil | 1974...Atletico de Madrid, Spain | 1986...River Plate, Argentina |
| 1963...Santos, Brazil | 1975...No tournament | 1987...Porto, Portugal |
| 1964...Inter, Italy | 1976...Bayern Munich | 1988...Nacional, Uruguay |
| 1965...Inter, Italy | 1977...Boca Juniors, Argentina | 1989...Milan, Italy |
| 1966...Penarol, Uruguay | 1978...No tournament | 1990...Milan, Italy |
| 1967...Racing Club, Argentina | 1979...Olimpia, Paraguay | 1991...Red Star Belgrade, Yugoslavia |
| 1968...Estudiantes, Argentina | 1980...Nacional, Uruguay | |
| 1969...Milan, Italy | 1981...Flamengo, Brazil | 1992...Sao Paulo, Brazil |
| 1970...Feyenoord, Netherlands | 1982...Penarol, Uruguay | 1993...Sao Paulo, Brazil |
| 1971...Nacional, Uruguay | 1983...Gremio, Brazil | 1994...Velez Sarsfield, Argentina |

Note: Until 1968 a best-of-three-games format decided the winner. After that a two-game/total-goal format was used until Toyota became the sponsor in 1980, moved the game to Tokyo, and switched the format to a one game championship. The European Cup runner-up substituted for the winner in 1971, 1973, 1974, and 1979.

## European Cup

| | | |
|---|---|---|
| 1956...Real Madrid, Spain | 1961...Benfica, Portugal | 1966...Real Madrid, Spain |
| 1957...Real Madrid, Spain | 1962...Benfica, Portugal | 1967...Celtic, Scotland |
| 1958...Real Madrid, Spain | 1963...A.C. Milan, Italy | 1968...Manchester United, England |
| 1959...Real Madrid, Spain | 1964...Inter-Milan, Italy | |
| 1960...Real Madrid, Spain | 1965...Inter-Milan, Italy | 1969...A.C. Milan, Italy |

### European Cup *(Cont.)*

1970...Feyenoord, Netherlands
1971...Ajax Amsterdam,
Netherlands
1972...Ajax Amsterdam,
Netherlands
1973...Ajax Amsterdam,
Netherlands
1974...Bayern Munich,
West Germany
1975...Bayern Munich,
West Germany
1976...Bayern Munich,
West Germany

1977...Liverpool, England
1978...Liverpool, England
1979...Nottingham Forest,
England
1980...Nottingham Forest,
England
1981...Liverpool, England
1982...Aston Villa, England
1983...SV Hamburg,
West Germany
1984...Liverpool, England
1985...Juventus, Italy

1986...Steaua Bucharest,
Romania
1987...Porto, Portugal
1988...P.S.V. Eindhoven,
Netherlands
1989...A.C. Milan, Italy
1990...A.C. Milan, Italy
1991...Red Star Belgrade, Yugoslav.
1992...Barcelona, Spain
1993...Olympique Marseille, France
1994...A.C. Milan, Italy
1995...Ajax Amsterdam,
Netherlands

Note: On four occasions the European Cup winner has refused to play in the Intercontinental Cup (now Toyota Cup) and has been replaced by the runner-up: Panathinaikos (Greece) in 1971, Juventus (Italy) in 1973, Atletico Madrid (Spain) in 1974, and Malmo (Sweden) in 1979.

### Libertadores Cup

Competition between champion clubs and runners-up of 10 South American National Associations.

1960...Penarol, Uruguay
1961...Penarol, Uruguay
1962...Santos, Brazil
1963...Santos, Brazil
1964...Independiente, Argentina
1965...Independiente, Argentina
1966...Penarol, Uruguay
1967...Racing Club, Argentina
1968...Estudiantes, Argentina
1969...Estudiantes, Argentina
1970...Estudiantes, Argentina
1971...Nacional, Uruguay
1972...Independiente, Argentina

1973...Independiente, Argentina
1974...Independiente, Argentina
1975...Independiente, Argentina
1976...Cruzeiro, Brazil
1977...Boca Juniors, Argentina
1978...Boca Juniors, Argentina
1979...Olimpia, Paraguay
1980...Nacional, Uruguay
1981...Flamengo, Brazil
1982...Penarol, Uruguay
1983...Gremio, Brazil
1984...Independiente, Argentina

1985...Argentinos Juniors,
Argentina
1986...River Plate, Argentina
1987...Penarol, Uruguay
1988...Nacional, Uruguay
1989...Atletico Nacional,
Colombia
1990...Olimpia, Paraguay
1991...Colo Colo, Chile
1992...Sao Paulo, Brazil
1993...Sao Paulo, Brazil
1994...Velez Sarsfield, Argentina
1995...Gremio, Brazil

### UEFA Cup

Competition between teams other than league champions and cup winners from the Union of European Football Associations.

1958...Barcelona, Spain
1959...No tournament
1960...Barcelona, Spain
1961...AS Roma, Italy
1962...Valencia, Spain
1963...Valencia, Spain
1964...Real Zaragoza, Spain
1965...Ferencvaros, Hungary
1966...Barcelona, Spain
1967...Dynamo Zagreb,
Yugoslavia
1968...Leeds United, England
1969...Newcastle United, England
1970...Arsenal, England
1971...Leeds United, England

1972...Tottenham Hotspur,
England
1973...Liverpool, England
1974...Feyenoord, Netherlands
1975...Borussia Monchengladbach,
West Germany
1976...Liverpool, England
1977...Juventus, Italy
1978...P.S.V. Eindhoven,
Netherlands
1979...Borussia Monchengladbach,
West Germany
1980...Eintracht Frankfurt,
West Germany
1981...Ipswich Town, England
1982...I.F.K. Gothenburg, Sweden

1983...Anderlecht, Belgium
1984...Tottenham Hotspur,
England
1985...Real Madrid, Spain
1986...Real Madrid, Spain
1987...I.F.K. Gothenburg, Sweden
1988...Bayer Leverkusen,
West Germany
1989...Naples, Italy
1990...Juventus, Italy
1991...Inter-Milan, Italy
1992...Torino, Italy
1993...Juventus, Italy
1994...Internazionale, Italy
1995...Parma, Italy

### European Cup-Winners' Cup

Competition between cup winners of countries belonging to UEFA.

1961...A.C. Fiorentina, Italy
1962...Atletico Madrid, Spain
1963...Tottenham Hotspur,
England
1964...Sporting Lisbon, Portugal
1965...West Ham United, England
1966...Borussia Dortmund,
West Germany
1967...Bayern Munich,
West Germany

1968...A.C. Milan, Italy
1969...Slovan Bratislava,
Czechoslovakia
1970...Manchester City, England
1971...Chelsea, England
1972...Glasgow Rangers,
Scotland
1973...A.C. Milan, Italy
1974...Magdeburg, East Germany
1975...Dynamo Kiev, USSR

1976...Anderlecht, Belgium
1977...S.V. Hamburg,
West Germany
1978...Anderlecht, Belgium
1979...Barcelona, Spain
1980...Valencia, Spain
1981...Dynamo Tbilisi, USSR
1982...Barcelona, Spain
1983...Aberdeen, Scotland
1984...Juventus, Italy

### European Cup-Winners' Cup (Cont.)

1985...Everton, England
1986...Dynamo Kiev, USSR
1987...Ajax Amsterdam,
          Netherlands

1988...Mechelen, Belgium
1989...Barcelona, Spain
1990...Sampdoria, Italy
1991...Manchester United, England

1992...Werder Bremen, Germany
1993...Parma, Italy
1994...Arsenal, England
1995...Real Zaragoza, Spain

# Major Soccer League

## Results

Called the Major Indoor Soccer League from 1979–90. Folded in 1992.

| | Champion | Series | Runner-Up | Championship Series Most Valuable Player |
|---|---|---|---|---|
| 1979 | NY Arrows | 2-0 | Philadelphia | Shep Messing, NY |
| 1980 | NY Arrows | 7-4 | Houston | Steve Zungul, NY |
| 1981 | NY Arrows | 6-5 | St Louis | Steve Zungul, NY |
| 1982 | NY Arrows | 3-2 | St Louis | Steve Zungul, NY |
| 1983 | San Diego | 3-2 | Baltimore | Juli Veee, SD |
| 1984 | Baltimore | 4-1 | St Louis | Scott Manning, Balt |
| 1985 | San Diego | 4-1 | Baltimore | Steve Zungul, SD |
| 1986 | San Diego | 4-3 | Minnesota | Brian Quinn, SD |
| 1987 | Dallas | 4-3 | Tacoma | Tatu, Dall |
| 1988 | San Diego | 4-0 | Cleveland | Hugo Perez, SD |
| 1989 | San Diego | 4-3 | Baltimore | Victor Nogueira, SD |
| 1990 | San Diego | 4-2 | Baltimore | Brian Quinn, SD |
| 1991 | San Diego | 4-? | Cleveland | Ben Collins, SD |
| 1992 | San Diego | 4-2 | Dallas | Thomas Usiyan, SD |

Championship format: 1979, best-of-three-games series; 1980-81, one-game championship; 1982-83, best-of-five-games series; 1984 to present, best-of-seven-games series.

## Statistical Leaders

### SCORING

| Year | Player/Team | Points |
|---|---|---|
| 1978-79 | Fred Grgurev, Phil | 74 |
| 1979-80 | Steve Zungul, NY | 136 |
| 1980-81 | Steve Zungul, NY | 152 |
| 1981-82 | Steve Zungul, NY | 163 |
| 1982-83 | Steve Zungul, NY | 122 |
| 1983-84 | Stan Stamenkovic, Balt | 97 |
| 1984-85 | Steve Zungul, SD | 136 |
| 1985-86 | Steve Zungul, Tac | 115 |
| 1986-87 | Tatu, Dall | 111 |
| 1987-88 | Erik Rasmussen, Wich | 112 |
| 1988-89 | Preci, Tac | 104 |
| 1989-90 | Tatu, Dall | 113 |
| 1990-91 | Tatu, Dall | 144 |
| 1991-92 | Zoran Karic, Clev | 102 |

### GOALS

| Year | Player/Team | Goals |
|---|---|---|
| 1978-79 | Fred Grgurev, Phil | 46 |
| 1979-80 | Steve Zungul, NY | 90 |
| 1980-81 | Steve Zungul, NY | 108 |
| 1981-82 | Steve Zungul, NY/GB | 103 |
| 1982-83 | Steve Zungul, NY/GB | 75 |
| 1983-84 | Mark Liveric, NY | 58 |
| 1984-85 | Steve Zungul, SD | 68 |
| 1985-86 | Erik Rasmussen, Wich | 67 |
| 1986-87 | Tatu, Dall | 73 |
| 1987-88 | Hector Marinaro, Minn | 58 |
| 1988-89 | Preki, Tac | 51 |
| 1989-90 | Tatu, Dall | 64 |
| 1990-91 | Tatu, Dall | 78 |
| 1991-92 | Hector Marinaro, Clev | 53 |

### ASSISTS

| Year | Player/Team | Assists |
|---|---|---|
| 1978-79 | Fred Grgurev, Phil | 28 |
| 1979-80 | Steve Zungul, NY | 46 |
| 1980-81 | Jorgen Kristensen, Wich | 52 |
| 1981-82 | Steve Zungul, NY | 60 |
| 1982-83 | Stan Stamenkovic, Mem | 65 |
| 1983-84 | Stan Stamenkovic, Balt | 63 |
| 1984-85 | Steve Zungul, SD | 68 |
| 1985-86 | Steve Zungul, Tac | 60 |
| 1986-87 | Kai Haaskivi, Clev | 55 |
| 1987-88 | Preki, Tac | 58 |
| 1988-89 | Preki, Tac | 53 |
| 1989-90 | Jan Goossens, KC | 55 |
| 1990-91 | Tatu, Dall | 66 |
| 1991-92 | Zoran Karic, Clev | 63 |

### TOP GOALKEEPERS

| Year | Player/Team | Goals Agst Avg |
|---|---|---|
| 1978-79 | Paul Hammond, Hous | 4.16 |
| 1979-80 | Sepp Gantenhammer, Hous | 4.42 |
| 1980-81 | Enzo DiPede, Chi | 4.06 |
| 1981-82 | Slobo Liijevski, StL | 3.85* |
| 1982-83 | Zoltan Toth, NY | 4.01 |
| 1983-84 | Slobo Liijevski, StL | 3.67 |
| 1984-85 | Scott Manning, Balt | 3.89 |
| 1985-86 | Keith Van Eron, Balt | 3.66 |
| 1986-87 | Tino Lettieri, Minn | 3.38 |
| 1987-88 | Zoltan Toth, SD | 2.94 |
| 1988-89 | Victor Nogueira, SD | 2.86 |
| 1989-90 | Joe Papaleo, Dall | 3.34 |
| 1990-91 | Victor Nogueira, SD | 4.37 |
| 1991-92 | Victor Nogueira, SD | 4.60 |

# North American Soccer League

Formed in 1968 by the merger of the National Professional Soccer League and the USA League, both of which had begun operations a year earlier. The NPSL's lone champion was the Oakland Clippers. The USA League, which brought entire teams in from Europe, was won in 1967 by the LA Wolves, who were the English League's Wolverhampton Wanderers.

| Year | Champion | Score | Runner-Up | Regular Season MVP |
|------|----------|-------|-----------|--------------------|
| 1968 | Atlanta | 0-0, 3-0 | San Diego | John Kowalik, Chi |
| 1969 | Kansas City | No game | Atlanta | Cirilio Fernandez, KC |
| 1970 | Rochester | 3-0,1-3 | Washington | Carlos Metidieri, Roch |
| 1971 | Dallas | 1-2, 4-1, 2-0 | Atlanta | Carlos Metidieri, Roch |
| 1972 | NY | 2-1 | St Louis | Randy Horton, NY |
| 1973 | Philadelphia | 2-0 | Dallas | Warren Archibald, Mia |
| 1974 | Los Angeles | 4-3* | Miami | Peter Silvester, Balt |
| 1975 | Tampa Bay | 2-0 | Portland | Steve David, Miami |
| 1976 | Toronto | 3-0 | Minnesota | Pelé, NY |
| 1977 | NY | 2-1 | Seattle | Franz Beckenbauer, NY |
| 1978 | NY | 3-1 | Tampa Bay | Mike Flanagan, NE |
| 1979 | Vancouver | 2-1 | Tampa Bay | Johan Cruyff, LA |
| 1980 | NY | 3-0 | Ft Lauderdale | Roger Davies, Sea |
| 1981 | Chicago | 1-0* | NY | Giorgio Chinaglia, NY |
| 1982 | NY | 1-0 | Seattle | Peter Ward, Sea |
| 1983 | Tulsa | 2-0 | Toronto | Roberto Cabanas, NY |
| 1984 | Chicago | 2-1, 3-2 | Toronto | Steve Zungul, SJ |

*Shootout.

Championship Format: 1968 & 1970: Two games/total goals. 1971 & 1984: Best-of-three game series. 1972-1983: One game championship. Title in 1969 went to the regular season champion.

## Statistical Leaders
### SCORING

| Year | Player/Team | Pts | Year | Player/Team | Pts |
|------|-------------|-----|------|-------------|-----|
| 1968 | John Kowalik, Chi | 69 | 1977 | Steven David, LA | 58 |
| 1969 | Kaiser Motaung, Atl | 36 | 1978 | Giorgio Chinaglia, NY | 79 |
| 1970 | Kirk Apostolidis, Dall | 35 | 1979 | Oscar Fabbiani, Tampa Bay | 58 |
| 1971 | Carlos Metidieri, Roch | 46 | 1980 | Giorgio Chinaglia, NY | 77 |
| 1972 | Randy Horton, NY | 22 | 1981 | Giorgio Chinaglia, NY | 74 |
| 1973 | Kyle Rote, Dall | 30 | 1982 | Giorgio Chinaglia, NY | 55 |
| 1974 | Paul Child, San Jose | 36 | 1983 | Roberto Cabanas, NY | 66 |
| 1975 | Steven David, Miami | 52 | 1984 | Slavisa Zungul, Golden Bay | 50 |
| 1976 | Giorgio Chinaglia, NY | 49 | | | |

# American Professional Soccer League

| Year | Champion | Score | Runner-Up | Regular Season MVP |
|------|----------|-------|-----------|--------------------|
| 1991 | San Francisco | 1-3, 2-0 (1-0 on penalty kicks) | Albany | Jean Harbor, MD |
| 1992 | Colorado | 1-0 | Tampa Bay | Taifour Diane, CO |
| 1993 | Colorado | 3-1 (OT) | Los Angeles | Taifour Diane, CO |
| 1994 | Montreal | 1-0 | Colorado | Paulinho, LA |

# NCAA Sports

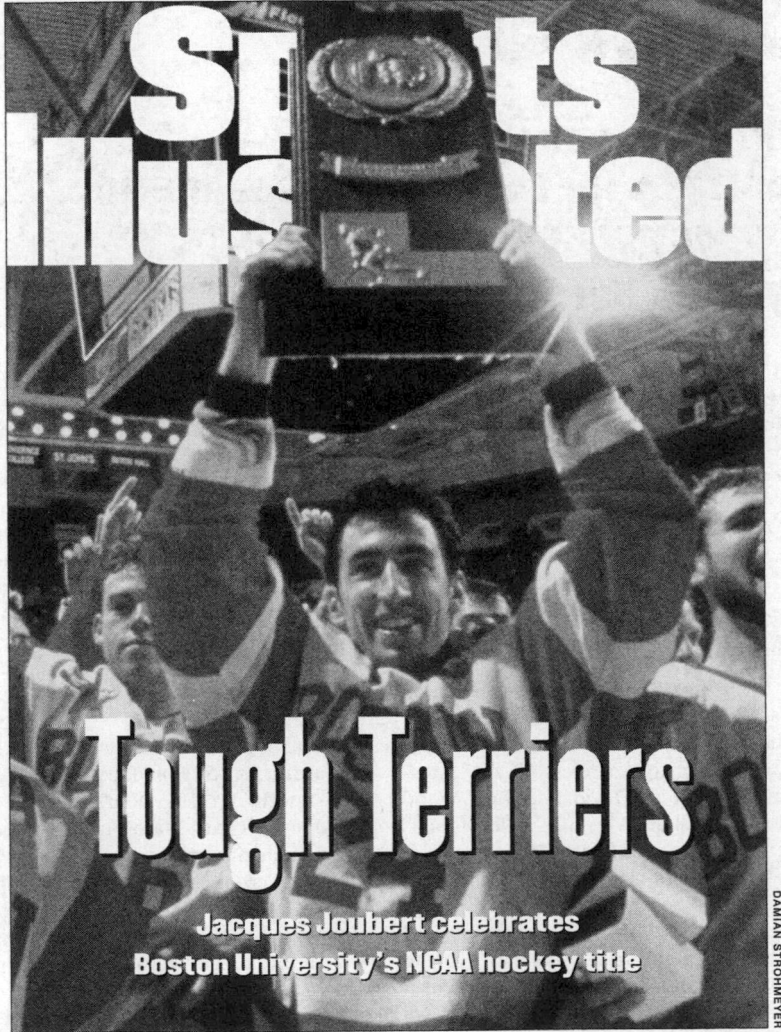

**Tough Terriers**

Jacques Joubert celebrates
Boston University's NCAA hockey title

DAMIAN STROHMEYER

# Shining Stars

## The leading men seized the spotlight for the NCAA champions in soccer, hockey, and baseball

## by Hank Hersch

*YOU GOTTA dance with the gal you brung.* That bit of wisdom—along with the need to both smell the roses and wait for the fat lady to sing—is cited regularly during NCAA tournaments, when contenders are urged to continue relying on their best players. All too often, however, those stalwarts cede the limelight to unlikelier heroes. In 1994–95, they didn't.

MEN'S SOCCER
The cross came into the penalty box low and hot from Virginia defender Brandon Pollard, striking senior forward A.J. Wood in the right shoulder and the neck. In the 21st minute of the scoreless NCAA championship game in Davidson, N.C., Wood settled the ball quickly onto his left foot as Indiana goalkeeper Scott Coufal charged out of the net to challenge. This was what the tireless Wood lived for, these glimmering moments when all his running and bumping and acting a "nuisance" to the opposition created an eyeblink of opportunity to score. An opportunity to finish.

Indeed, an opportunity to finish in his final match what Wood had spoken about before even starting his first. Shortly after he had arrived in Charlottesville from Rockville, Md., in September 1991, Wood let some of his fellow freshmen on the Virginia soccer team know exactly what their mission was. While walking to dinner he rattled on about their winning four national titles in the next four years. And as the seasons passed, Wood's pie-in-the-sky fantasy seemed increasingly prophetic. Entering their Dec. 11 showdown with Indiana, the Cavaliers under coach Bruce Arena had won an unprecedented three straight NCAA tournaments.

Wood and the three other seniors remaining from that freshman class of '91—midfielder Tain Nix, defender Clint Peay and forward Nate Friends—had left their 12 championship rings back in Charlottesville, symbolically demonstrating that these Cavs could not rely on their past glory to fulfill their four-ordained fate. But a far more integral talisman of their previous conquests was missing, too, in onetime classmate Claudio Reyna, a magical midfielder who had skipped his senior season to play for the U.S. World Cup team and

**Wood hit net, delivering the Cavaliers their fourth straight title.**

professionally in Germany. Deftly dictating the tempo, Reyna had been named the MVP of the two previous tournaments.

What's more, after defeating Rutgers 2–1 in the semis, Virginia found itself in an unusual position in the '94 finals: under-dog. The Hoosiers entered with the top ranking in the country and the top mid-fielder, Todd Yeagley, whose father, Jerry, was the Indiana coach. Nonetheless, the Cavs' No. 4 ranking, their lack of jewelry and Reyna's absence couldn't convince Yeagley père that Virginia's depth and experience made them anything but the favorites. "I call this tournament the Bruce Arena Classic," he said. "He's here so much, the team should rent a condo."

"We're like locals here," Wood said of Davidson, host of the Final Four since 1992. "We've outlasted some restaurants. The place we always go to eat is a steak-house now. Last year it was an Italian place. The year before, a sandwich shop."

Besides a fourth ring, only one achieve-ment was missing from the 6'2" 180-pound Wood's college career: to score in a final match. *Soccer America*'s 1994 Player of the Year, Wood would finish as the second-leading scorer in Virginia history, with 56 goals, and his record-setting 23 goals and 56 points in 1994 paced the school's most prolific attack ever. But in his first three title games, Wood had failed to finish with any of his shots on goal. In the '92 final alone, Wood worked his way for eight chances—some of them almost point-blank—and whiffed on them all.

But when Pollard's cross arrived early in the game last December, Wood didn't rush. When Coufal committed, Wood used the outside of his foot to slip the ball into the left side of the net. Thanks to the Cavs' aggressive tackling in the midfield and to midfielder Billy Walsh's deflection of an eight-yard blast steaming straight for the net late in the first half—"Lucky, I guess," Walsh said—Arena and Co. made Wood's score stand up in a tense and hard-fought 1–0 victory.

The goal gave Wood a record 13 over his NCAA tournament career, and clinched an

**O'Sullivan forged a brilliant effort from the fires of adversity.**

unshatterable record for titles in a career by Virginia's fab four seniors. "That's the first goal I've scored in four finals, so I was very happy," Wood said afterward. "I just wanted to produce today in the clutch."

MEN'S HOCKEY

His first goal gave Boston University a 2–0 cushion in the NCAA final, a chip-in of linemate Steve Thornton's missile from the left side. His second came on the power play, a rebound after Maine goalie Blair Allison had blocked defenseman Rich Brennan's slap shot from the left point. That put the Terriers up 5–2 late in the third. Sophomore left wing Chris O'Sullivan punctuated both his goals by skating into the corner, dropping to his knees and, cradling the blade of his stick under his

armpit, pumping imaginary bullets into Allison and the rest of the Black Bears. "That's been going on all year," O'Sullivan would say after BU's 6–2 victory on April 1. "It's just emotion after I score."

While the stick shtick was on the tacky side, if anyone was entitled to a little latitude for passion's sake, it was the 19-year-old O'Sullivan. The eighth of 11 children, Chris suffered through the death of both his parents before he could lace up his skates at BU. John O'Sullivan, a Boston Edison employee, died of lymphatic cancer in May 1990, 17 months before Ann's brain cancer was diagnosed. She watched from a wheelchair as Chris helped Catholic Memorial to the state title in April 1992; three months later she was dead.

Eight O'Sullivan siblings ranging in age from 14 to 30 were at Providence Civic Center to see their brother score three times in dispatching first Minnesota in the semis, then archrival Maine in the title game. Peter, 25, was attending junior college in California, while Stephanie, 23, had gone West as well. The Eastern College Athletic Conference hockey player of the year and a forward on four Providence College NCAA championship teams, she was in San Jose to practice with the U.S. women's national team.

Along with his brothers and sisters, John and Ann were there for Chris in spirit. "Not a game goes by, whether in the locker room or on the ice, that I don't think about them," Chris said. "That gets me going. I'd love to look up and see them in the stands, but they were taken away from us, and we have to live with that and deal with it."

O'Sullivan has been tested by more than the deaths in his family, as the seven-inch scar down the back of his neck attests. As a freshman at BU, he slid headfirst into the boards in a game at Providence and broke a vertebra in his neck. During a six-hour operation, doctors used a bone from his hip to fuse two vertebrae together. After sitting out 1992–93 as a medical redshirt, he came back the following season to play 32 games as a defenseman, the position he had played almost exclusively in high school.

But a shortage of wingers forced Terrier coach Jack Parker to move O'Sullivan to the Red Line with sophomore right wing Mike Grier and Thornton, a senior center. "He had no choice," Parker said. "He has great hands, and he's a terrific puckhandler. Unbelievable. He hangs onto the puck as well as anybody. And he's pretty poised. He doesn't rush anything."

Firepower had been at a premium in BU's Final Four appearances the previous two seasons; they were eliminated in a pair of games by an aggregate score of 15–2. But against the Black Bears, the Terriers were especially effective when it mattered most, killing seven of eight power plays against them while converting on three man–advantages of their own. Maine could muster a mere 23 shots. And for the first time since 1972, BU accomplished a cham-

pionship hat trick, winning the Beanpot, the Hockey East and the NCAA titles.

With his two goals, Nos. 22 and 23 of the season, O'Sullivan wound up as the Terriers' leading scorer, with 56 points. He was also named the tournament's Most Valuable Player. It was an award he shared with John and Ann. "They were great parents," he said. "They instilled values in us. I know they're proud of me."

BASEBALL

After his club had pounded its way to the championship of the College World Series in Omaha, Cal State–Fullerton coach Augie Garrido noted that sophomore centerfielder Mark Kotsay had regularly imperiled the denizens of Henry Doorly Zoo, located down Rosenblatt Stadium's rightfield line. "We decided to protect one of the treasures here," Garrido said. "We put hard hats on the monkeys and the gorillas."

Not even an animal act could have upstaged Kotsay, who did a star turn last June worthy of Fullerton alum Kevin Costner. The climax to his record-breaking, week long run came before a record crowd of 22,027 in the CWS finale, when No. 1 Fullerton drilled USC 11–5. On his first swing, the 6-foot, 180-pound Kotsay smacked a three-run shot that cleared a revolving sign 400 feet away in right centerfield. On his next one he cleared the rightfield fence with a man on to cap a four-run second and put the Titans up to stay, 7–3.

His 5 RBIs set a record for the championship game, but Kotsay didn't stop there. He made a lunging, backhanded catch in right-center and then pitched the final 1⅔ innings without surrendering a run. Not that USC hadn't seen previews of Kotsay's heroics. On Feb. 21, he had driven in four runs, made a sliding grab in right-center and gotten the final out for a save in a 10–9 victory. "About Kotsay, what can you say?" Trojan coach Mike Gillespie asked in Omaha. "He's the messiah. He's unbelievable."

The son of an L.A. motorcycle cop, Kotsay went undrafted out of Santa Fe High in

*Cal St.–Fullerton knocked off USC then mobbed all-around hero Kotsay.*

Santa Fe Springs, Calif., and received only a partial scholarship to Fullerton. "All my life, it's either been my size or my speed," says Kotsay, who runs the 60 in 6.9 seconds. "When I'm in a game and the adrenaline's flowing, I can move pretty fast. When I run a 60, the stopwatches should be able to motivate me, but they don't."

Pride is another matter. "He's our hardest-working player in practice," Garrido says. "No matter how much he does, he still has an overachiever's mentality."

As a freshman Kotsay paid immediate dividends for Garrido, batting .372 for the season and .462 with 8 RBIs in the CWS. In 1995 he became the Titans' stopper as well, warming up his arm in the outfield before trotting in to the mound. In 29 innings he gave up one run while racking up 11 saves and a 2–1 record. At the plate he hit .422, belted 21 homers, drove in 90 runs and struck out only 15 times as Fullerton finished with its best mark ever, 57–9.

While Kotsay received some player of the year honors, he lost on a few ballots to Tennessee pitcher-first baseman Todd Helton. In their two head-to-head meetings at the CWS, Kotsay led the Titans to 11–0 and an 11–1 victories over Helton and the Volunteers. After one win Garrido was asked if there was anything Kotsay hadn't done for his team lately. "Well, he didn't drive the bus over here," Garrido said. "And he didn't pick up the dugout after the game."

By tournament's end Kotsay had hit .563 and slugged 1.250 to raise his career averages to .517 and 1.103, both CWS records.

"I knew the national championship was on the line," Kotsay said. "I just wanted to come in here and be a leader."

## NCAA Team Champions

### Fall 1994

### Cross-Country

#### MEN

| | Champion | Runner-Up |
|---|---|---|
| Division I: | Iowa St | Colorado |
| Division II: | Adams St | Western St |
| Division III: | Williams | N Central |

#### WOMEN

| | Champion | Runner-Up |
|---|---|---|
| Division I: | Villanova | Michigan |
| Division II: | Adams St | Western St |
| Division III: | Cortland St | Calvin |

### Field Hockey

#### WOMEN

| | Champion | Runner-Up |
|---|---|---|
| Division I: | James Madison | N Carolina |
| Division II | Lock Haven | Bloomsburg |
| Division III: | Cortland St | Trenton St |

### Football

#### MEN

| | Champion | Runner-Up |
|---|---|---|
| Division I-A: | Nebraska | Penn St |
| Division I-AA: | Youngstown St | Boise St |
| Division II: | N Alabama | Texas A&M Kingsville |
| Division III: | Albion | Washington & Jefferson |

### Soccer

#### MEN

| | Champion | Runner-Up |
|---|---|---|
| Division I: | Virginia | Indiana |
| Division II: | Tampa | Oakland (MI) |
| Division III: | Bethany (W Va) | Johns Hopkins |

#### WOMEN

| | Champion | Runner-Up |
|---|---|---|
| Division I: | N Carolina | Notre Dame |
| Division II: | Franklin Pierce | Regis (CO) |
| Division III: | Trenton St | UC-San Diego |

### Volleyball

#### WOMEN

| | Champion | Runner-Up |
|---|---|---|
| Division I: | Stanford | UCLA |
| Division II: | Northern Michigan | Cal St-Bakersfield |
| Division III: | Washington (MO) | WI-Oshkosh |

### Water Polo

#### MEN

| Champion | Runner-Up |
|---|---|
| Stanford | Southern Cal |

## Winter 1994-1995

### Basketball

#### MEN

| | Champion | Runner-Up |
|---|---|---|
| Division I: | UCLA | Arkansas |
| Division II: | Southern Indiana | UC-Riverside |
| Division III: | WI-Platteville | Manchester |

#### WOMEN

| | Champion | Runner-Up |
|---|---|---|
| Division I: | Connecticut | Tennessee |
| Division II: | N Dakota St | Portland St |
| Division III: | Capital (OH) | WI-Oshkosh |

### Fencing

| Champion | Runner-Up |
|---|---|
| Penn St | St John's (NY) |

### Gymnastics

#### MEN

| Champion | Runner-Up |
|---|---|
| Stanford | Nebraska |

#### WOMEN

| | |
|---|---|
| Utah | Alabama/ Michigan |

### Ice Hockey

#### MEN

| | Champion | Runner-Up |
|---|---|---|
| Division I: | Boston University | Maine |
| Division II: | Bemidji St | Mercyhurst |
| Division III: | Middlebury | Fredonia St |

### Rifle

| Champion | Runner-Up |
|---|---|
| West Virginia | Air Force |

### Skiing

| Champion | Runner-Up |
|---|---|
| Colorado | Utah |

### Swimming and Diving

#### MEN

| | Champion | Runner-Up |
|---|---|---|
| Division I: | Michigan | Stanford |
| Division II: | Oakland (MI) | Cal St-Bakersfield |
| Division III: | Kenyon | Hope |

#### WOMEN

| | Champion | Runner-Up |
|---|---|---|
| Division I: | Stanford | Michigan |
| Division II: | Air Force | Oakland (MI) |
| Division III: | Kenyon | Williams |

### Wrestling

#### MEN

| | Champion | Runner-Up |
|---|---|---|
| Division I: | Iowa | Oregon |
| Division II: | Central Oklahoma | NE-Omaha |
| Division III: | Augsburg | Trenton St |

## Winter 1994-1995 (Cont.)

### Indoor Track

#### MEN

| | Champion | Runner-Up |
|---|---|---|
| Division I: | Arkansas | George Mason |
| | | Tennessee |
| Division II: | St Augustine's | Abilene Christian |
| Division III: | Lincoln (PA) | Albany (NY) |

#### WOMEN

| | Champion | Runner-Up |
|---|---|---|
| Division I: | Louisiana St | UCLA |
| Division II: | Abilene Christian | Adams St |
| Division III: | WI-Oshkosh | Cortland St |

## Spring 1995

### Baseball

| | Champion | Runner-Up |
|---|---|---|
| Division I: | Cal St-Fullerton | Southern Cal |
| Division II: | Florida Southern | Georgia College |
| Division III: | La Verne | Methodist |

### Golf

#### MEN

| | Champion | Runner-Up |
|---|---|---|
| Division I: | Oklahoma St | Stanford |
| Division II: | Florida Southern | SC-Aiken |
| Division III: | Methodist | Otterbein |

#### WOMEN

| Champion | Runner-Up |
|---|---|
| Arizona St | San Jose St |

### Lacrosse

#### MEN

| | Champion | Runner-Up |
|---|---|---|
| Division I: | Syracuse | Maryland |
| Division II: | Adelphi | Springfield |
| Division III: | Salisbury St | Nazareth |

#### WOMEN

| | Champion | Runner-Up |
|---|---|---|
| Division I: | Maryland | Princeton |
| Division III: | Trenton St | William Smith |

### Softball

| | Champion | Runner-Up |
|---|---|---|
| Division I: | UCLA | Arizona |
| Division II: | Kennesaw St | Bloomsburg |
| Division III: | Chapman | Trenton St |

### Tennis

#### MEN

| | Champion | Runner-Up |
|---|---|---|
| Division I: | Stanford | Mississippi |
| Division II: | Lander (SC) | N Florida |
| Division III: | UC-Santa Cruz | Washington (MD) |

#### WOMEN

| | Champion | Runner-Up |
|---|---|---|
| Division I: | Texas | Florida |
| Division II: | Armstrong St | Grand Canyon |
| Division III: | Kenyon | UC-San Diego |

## Spring 1995 (Cont.)

### Outdoor Track

#### MEN

| | Champion | Runner-Up |
|---|---|---|
| Division I: | Arkansas | UCLA |
| Division II: | St Augustine's | Abilene Christian |
| Division III: | Lincoln (PA) | Williams |

#### WOMEN

| | Champion | Runner-Up |
|---|---|---|
| Division I: | Louisiana St | UCLA |
| Division II: | Abilene Christian | Cal St-Los Angeles |
| Division III: | WI-Oshkosh | St Thomas (MN) |

### Volleyball

#### MEN

| Champion | Runner-Up |
|---|---|
| UCLA | Penn St |

# NCAA Division I Individual Champions

## Fall 1994

### Cross-Country

#### MEN

| Champion | Runner-Up |
|---|---|
| Martin Keino, Arizona | Adam Goucher, Colorado |

#### WOMEN

| Champion | Runner-Up |
|---|---|
| Jennifer Rhines, Villanova | Amy Rudolph, Providence |

## Winter 1994-1995

### Fencing

#### MEN

| | Champion | Runner-Up |
|---|---|---|
| Sabre | Paul Palestis, NYU | Bill Lester, Notre Dame |
| Foil | Sean McClain, Stanford | Brian Moroney, St John's (NY) |
| Épée | Mike Gattner, Lawrence | Keith Lichten, MIT |

#### WOMEN

| | Champion | Runner-Up |
|---|---|---|
| Foil | Olga Kalinovskaya, Penn St | Maria Panyi, Notre Dame |
| Épée | Tina Loven, St John's (NY) | Heidi Chang, Wellesley |

### Gymnastics

#### MEN

| | Champion | Runner-Up |
|---|---|---|
| All-around | Richard Grace, Nebraska | Darren Elg, Brigham Young |
| Vault | Ian Bachrach, Stanford | Sebronzik Wright, William & Mary |
| Parallel bars | Richard Grace, Nebraska | Blaz Puljic, New Mexico |
| Horizontal bar | Rick Kieffer, Nebraska | Blaz Puljic, New Mexico |
| Floor exercise | Jay Thornton, Iowa | Josh Stein, Stanford |
| Pommel horse | Drew Durbin, Ohio St | Jeremiah Landry, Illinois |
| Rings | Dave Frank, Temple | Brian Fox, California |
| | | Blaine Wilson, Ohio St |

#### WOMEN

| | Champion | Runner-Up |
|---|---|---|
| All-around | Jenny Hansen, Kentucky | Agina Simpkins, Georgia |
| Balance beam | Jenny Hansen, Kentucky | Kristen Guise, Florida |
| | | Stella Umeh, UCLA |

## Gymnastics (Cont.)

### WOMEN (Cont.)

| | Champion | Runner-Up |
|---|---|---|
| Uneven bars | Beth Wymer, Michigan | Lori Strong, Georgia |
| Floor exercise | Jenny Hansen, Kentucky | Leah Brown, Georgia |
| | Stella Umeh, UCLA | Aimee Trepanier, Utah |
| | Leslie Angeles, Georgia | |
| Vault | Jenny Hansen, Kentucky | Leah Brown, Georgia |

## Skiing

### MEN

| | Champion | Runner-Up |
|---|---|---|
| Slalom | Scott Wither, Colorado | Hayden Barile, New Hampshire |
| Giant slalom | Bryan Sax, Colorado | Erik Roland, Denver |
| Freestyle cross country | Havard Solbaken, Utah | Alse Slettemoen, Utah |
| Classical cross country | Thomas Weman, Utah | Aki Partanen, Vermont |

### WOMEN

| | Champion | Runner-Up |
|---|---|---|
| Slalom | Narcisa Sehovic, Denver | Christl Hager, Utah |
| Giant slalom | Christl Hager, Utah | Suzie Easterly, New Hampshire |
| Freestyle cross country | Heidi Selenes, Utah | Amy Crawford, Western St |
| Classical cross country | Heidi Selenes, Utah | Gina Marie Legueri, Western St |

## Wrestling

| | Champion | Runner-Up |
|---|---|---|
| 118 lb | Kelvin Jackson, Michigan St | Eric Ivins, Oklahoma |
| 126 lb | Jeff McGinness, Iowa | Sanshiro Abe, Penn St |
| 134 lb | T.J. Jaworsky, N Carolina | Babak Mohammadi, Oregon St |
| 142 lb | John Hughes, Penn St | Gerry Abas, Fresno St |
| 150 lb | Steve Marianetti, Illinois | Lincoln McIlravy, Iowa |
| 158 lb | Ernest Benion, Illinois | Dan Wirnsberger, Michigan St |
| 167 lb | Markus Mollica, Arizona St | Mark Branch, Oklahoma St |
| 177 lb | Les Gutches, Oregon St | Mitch Clark, Ohio St |
| 190 lb | J.J. McGrew, Oklahoma St | Joel Sharratt, Iowa |
| Heavyweight | Tolly Thompson, Nebraska | Justin Greenlee, Northern Iowa |

## Swimming and Diving

### MEN

| | Champion | Time | Runner-Up | Time |
|---|---|---|---|---|
| 50-yard freestyle | Gustavo Borges, Michigan | 19.68 | Scott Claypool, Stanford | 19.78 |
| 100-yard freestyle | Gustavo Borges, Michigan | 42.85 | Lars Frolander, SMU | 43.16 |
| 200-yard freestyle | Gustavo Borges, Michigan | 1:34.61 | Ugur Taner, California | 1:35.02 |
| 500-yard freestyle | Tom Dolan, Michigan | 4:08.75* | Chad Carvin, Arizona | 4:12.36 |
| 1650-yard freestyle | Tom Dolan, Michigan | 14:29.31* | Chad Carvin, Arizona | 14:38.32 |
| 100-yard backstroke | Brian Retterer, Stanford | 45.43* | Kurt Jachimowski, Auburn | 47.35 |
| 200-yard backstroke | Brian Retterer, Stanford | 1:40.61 | Royce Sharp, Michigan | 1:43.03 |
| 100-yard breaststroke | Kurt Grote, Stanford | 53.21 | Jeremy Linn, Tennessee | 53.25 |
| 200-yard breaststroke | Kurt Grote, Stanford | 1:55.02 | Nate Thomson, Louisiana St | 1:56.45 |
| 100-yard butterfly | Lars Frolander, SMU | 46.18* | Matt Beck, Texas | 47.20 |
| 200-yard butterfly | Ugur Taner, California | 1:44.39 | Mike Merrell, Southern Cal | 1:44.58 |
| 200-yard IM | Kurt Jachimowski, Auburn | 1:45.11 | Jason Lancaster, Michigan | 1:45.63 |
| 400-yard IM | Tom Dolan, Michigan | 3:38.18* | Chad Carvin, Arizona | 3:43.55 |

| | Champion | Pts | Runner-Up | Pts |
|---|---|---|---|---|
| 1-meter diving† | Pat Bogart, Minnesota | 593.60 | Kevin McMahon, Louisiana St | 581.20 |
| 3-meter diving† | Evan Stewart, Tennessee | 655.40 | Pat Bogart, Minnesota | 649.45 |
| Platform† | Tyce Routson, Miami (FL) | 785.70 | Bryan Gillooly, Miami (FL) | 771.75 |

*Meet record. †Scoring based on 22 dives.

### WOMEN

| | Champion | Time | Runner-Up | Time |
|---|---|---|---|---|
| 50-yard freestyle | Ashley Tappin, Arizona | 22.34 | Claudia Franco, Stanford | 22.72 |
| 100-yard freestyle | Jenny Thompson, Stanford | 48.38 | Ashley Tappin, Arizona | 48.81 |
| 200-yard freestyle | Ashley Tappin, Arizona | 1:45.23 | Kari Haag, N Carolina | 1:46.28 |

## Swimming and Diving *(Cont.)*
### WOMEN *(Cont.)*

| | Champion | Time | | Runner-Up | Time |
|---|---|---|---|---|---|
| 500-yard freestyle | Mimosa McNerney, Florida | 4:41.86 | | Nikki Dryden, Florida | 4:42.10 |
| 1650-yard freestyle | Mimosa McNerney, Florida | 15:59.71 | | Sandra Cam, SMU | 16:09.19 |
| 100-yard backstroke | Alecia Humphrey, Michigan | 54.10 | | Jessica Tong, Stanford | 54.83 |
| 200-yard backstroke | Alecia Humphrey, Michigan | 1:54.68 | | Anna Simcic, California | 1:56.24 |
| 100-yard breaststroke | Beata Kaszuba, Arizona St | 59.71* | | Penelope Heyns, Nebraska | 1:00.41 |
| 200-yard breaststroke | Beata Kaszuba, Arizona St | 2:09.71* | | Rachel Gustin, Michigan | 2:10.37 |
| 100-yard butterfly | Jenny Thompson, Stanford | 52.77 | | Stacy Potter, Alabama | 53.08 |
| 200-yard butterfly | Berit Puggaard, SMU | 1:57.86 | | Barbara Franco, Florida | 1:58.06 |
| 200-yard IM | Jenny Thompson, Stanford | 1:57.63 | | Allison Wagner, Florida | 1:57.71 |
| 400-yard IM | Allison Wagner, Florida | 4:09.04 | | Kristine Quance, Southern Cal | 4:10.53 |

| | Champion | Pts | | Runner-Up | Pts |
|---|---|---|---|---|---|
| 1-meter diving# | Cheril Santini, SMU | 454.00 | | Karen Dalton, Ohio St | 453.75 |
| 3-meter diving† | Tracy Bonner, Tennessee | 580.20 | | Cheril Santini, SMU | 566.55 |
| Platform† | Eileen Richetelli, Stanford | 630.10 | | Tina Johnson, Kentucky | 615.10 |

*Meet record.  #Scoring based on 20 dives.  †Scoring based on 22 dives.

## Indoor Track
### MEN

| | Champion | Mark | | Runner-Up | Mark |
|---|---|---|---|---|---|
| 55-meter dash | Tim Harden, Kentucky | 6.12 | | Donovan Powell, Texas Christian | 6.19 |
| 55-meter hurdles | Philip Riley, Florida St | 7.10 | | Reggie Torian, Wisconsin | 7.13 |
| 200-meter dash | Dave Dopek, DePaul | 20.78 | | Derrick Thompson, Arkansas | 20.86 |
| 400-meter dash | Deon Minor, Baylor | 46.00 | | Greg Haughton, George Mason | 46.01 |
| 800-meter run | Michael Williams, Manhattan | 1:48.12 | | Bryan Woodward, Georgetown | 1:49.22 |
| Mile run | Kevin Sullivan, Michigan | 3:55.33* | | Graham Hood, Arkansas | 3:55.72 |
| 3000-meter run | Jason Bunston, Arkansas | 8:06.81 | | Richie Boulet, California | 8:06.92 |
| 5000-meter run | Mark Carroll, Providence | 13:55.15 | | Godfrey Siamusiye, Arkansas | 13:58.99 |
| High jump | Petar Malesev, Nebraska | 7 ft 4¼ in | | Ray Doakes, Arkansas | 7 ft 4¼ in |
| Long jump | Kareem Streete-Thompson, Rice | 26 ft 4¼ in | | Darius Pemberton, Tennessee | 25 ft 5¼ in |
| Triple jump | Hrvoje Verzi, Georgia | 54 ft 4½ in | | Lenards Ozolinish, California | 54 ft 2½ in |
| Shot put | John Godina, UCLA | 66 ft 11¼ in | | Mark Parlin, UCLA | 62 ft 3¾ in |
| Pole vault | Tim Mack, Tennessee | 18 ft 4½ in | | Daren McDonough, Illinois | 18 ft ½ in |
| 35-pound wt throw | Alex Papadimitriou, UTEP | 71 ft 5¼ in | | Brian Murer, SMU | 69 ft 10¾ in |

### WOMEN

| | Champion | | | Runner-Up | |
|---|---|---|---|---|---|
| 55-meter dash | Melinda Sergent, UTEP | 6.73 | | Sevatheda Fynes, Eastern Mich | 6.72 |
| 55-meter hurdles | Gillian Russell, Miami (FL) | 7.49 | | Latasha Colander, N Carolina | 7.57 |
| 200-meter dash | Merlene Frazer, Texas | 23.14 | | Sue Walton, Tennessee | 23.23 |
| 400-meter dash | Youlanda Warren, Louisiana St | 52.39 | | Ebony Robinson, Florida | 52.71 |
| 800-meter run | Amy Wickus, Wisconsin | 2:04.86 | | Jennifer Buckley, Kent | 2:05.02 |
| Mile run | Trine Pilskog, Arkansas | 4:39.19 | | Becki Wells, Alabama | 4:40.07 |
| 3000-meter run | Sarah Schwald, Arkansas | 9:19.90 | | Christine Stief, Boston U | 9:20.69 |
| 5000-meter run | Jennifer Rhines, Villanova | 15:41.12* | | Margie McMahon, Providence | 16:50.55 |
| High jump | Amy Acuff, UCLA | 6 ft 5½ in* | | Gwen Wentland, Kansas St | 6 ft 3¼ in |
| Long jump | Diane Guthrie-Gresham, GMU | 21 ft 8¼ in | | Nicole Devonish, Texas | 21 ft ¾ in |
| Triple jump | Najuma Fletcher, Pittsburgh | 44 ft 2¾ in | | Icolyn Kelly, Georgia | 43 ft 9 in |
| Shot put | Dawn Dumble, UCLA | 57 ft 8½ in | | Paulette Mitchell, Nebraska | 55 ft 5in |

*Meet record.

## Rifle

| | Champion | Pts | | Runner-Up | Pts |
|---|---|---|---|---|---|
| Smallbore | Oleg Seleznev, AK-Fairbanks | 1177 | | Trevor Gathman, West Virginia | 1170 |
| Air rifle | Benji Belden, Murray St | 390 | | Erik Anderson, Kentucky | 390 |

## Spring 1995

### Golf

#### MEN

| Champion | Score | Runner-Up | Score |
|----------|-------|-----------|-------|
| Chip Spratlin, Auburn | 283 | Ted Purdy, Arizona | 284 |
| | | Chris Tidland, Oklahoma St | 284 |

#### WOMEN

| Champion | Score | Runner-Up | Score |
|----------|-------|-----------|-------|
| Kristel Mourgue d'Algue, Arizona St | 283 | Vibeke Stensrud, San Jose St | 285 |
| | | Wendy Ward, Arizona St | 285 |

### Outdoor Track

#### MEN

| | Champion | Mark | Runner-Up | Mark |
|---|----------|------|-----------|------|
| 100-meter dash | Tim Harden, Kentucky | 10.05 | Donovan Powell, Texas Christian | 10.07 |
| 200-meter dash | Ato Bolden, UCLA | 20.24 | Dave Dopeck, DePaul | 20.31 |
| 400-meter dash | Greg Haughton, George Mason | 44.62 | Marlon Ramsey, Baylor | 44.74 |
| 800-meter run | Brandon Rock, Arkansas | 1:46.37 | Shaun Benefield, Georgia | 1:47.13 |
| 1,500-meter run | Kevin Sullivan, Michigan | 3:37.57 | Paul McMullen, Eastern Mich | 3:38.74 |
| 3,000-met. steeplech. | Jim Svenoy, UTEP | 8:21.48 | Dmitry Drozdov, Iowa St | 8:35.51 |
| 5,000-meter run | Martin Keino, Arizona | 14:36.78 | Mark Carroll, Providence | 14:37.08 |
| 10,000-meter run | Godfrey Siamusiye, Arkansas | 28:59.60 | Kamiel Maase, Texas | 29:08.52 |
| 110-meter hurdles | Duane Ross, Clemson | 13.32 | Larry Wade, Texas A&M | 13.41 |
| 400-meter hurdles | Ken Harnden, N Carolina | 48.72 | Octavius Terry, Georgia Tech | 49.25 |
| High jump | Ray Doakes, Arkansas | 7 ft 4½ in | Ed Broxterman, Kansas St | 7 ft 4½ in |
| Pole vault | Lawrence Johnson, Tennessee | 18 ft 8¼ in | Chris Pallakis, Washington St | 18 ft ½ in |
| Long jump | Kareem Streete-Thompson, Rice | 27 ft 2in | Andrew Owusu, Alabama | 26 ft 3¾ in |
| Triple jump | Ndabe Mdhlongwa, SW LA | 55 ft 4¾ in | Jerome Romain, Arkansas | 55 ft 2 in |
| Shot put | John Godina, UCLA | 72 ft 2¼ in* | Brent Noon, Georgia | 68 ft 9¾ in |
| Discus throw | John Godina, UCLA | 202 ft 4 in | Andy Bloom, Wake Forest | 191 ft 8 in |
| Hammer throw | Balazs Kiss, Southern Cal | 261 ft 3 in* | Alex Papadimitriou, UTEP | 241 ft 9 in |
| Javelin throw | Greg Johnson, UCLA | 244 ft 3in | Nils Fearnley, Southern Cal | 238 ft 8 in |
| Decathlon | Mario Sategna, Louisiana St | 8172 | Chad Smith, Tennessee | 7992 |

#### WOMEN

| | Champion | Mark | Runner-Up | Mark |
|---|----------|------|-----------|------|
| 100-meter dash | D'Andre Hill, Louisiana St | 11.11 | Sevatheda Fynes, Eastern Mich | 11.12 |
| 200-meter dash | Sevatheda Fynes, Eastern Mich | 22.63 | Merlene Frazer, Texas | 22.77 |
| 400-meter dash | Nicole Green, Kansas St | 52.01 | Charlene Maulseed, Louisiana St | 52.03 |
| 800-meter run | Inez Turner, SW Texas St | 2:00.27 | Tosha Woodward, Villanova | 2:02.51 |
| 1,500-meter run | Amy Wickus, Wisconsin | 4:14.53 | Amy Rudolph, Providence | 4:15.73 |
| 3,000-meter run | Kathy Butler, Wisconsin | 9:09.02 | Joline Staeheli, Georgetown | 9:11.62 |
| 5,000-meter run | Jen Rhines, Villanova | 15:56.18 | Marie McMahon, Providence | 16:15.06 |
| 10,000-meter run | Katie Swords, SMU | 34:28.46 | Rachel Sauder, Auburn | 34:53.91 |
| 100-meter hurdles | Gillian Russell, Miami (FL) | 12.99 | Anjanette Kirkland, Texas A&M | 13.09 |
| 400-meter hurdles | Tonya Williams, Illinois | 55.17 | Lade Akinremi, Arizona St | 55.44 |
| High jump | Amy Acuff, UCLA | 6 ft 5 in* | Najuma Fletcher, Pittsburgh | 6 ft 2¾ in |
| | | | Gwen Wentland, Kansas St | 6 ft 2¾ in |
| Long jump | Pat Itanyi, W Virginia | 22 ft 1 in | Diane Guthrie-Gresham, GMU | 22 ft ¼ in |
| Triple jump | Nicola Martial, Nebraska | 45 ft 1 in | Icolyn Kelly, Georgia | 44 ft 8¼ in |
| Shot put | Valeyta Althouse, UCLA | 59 ft 11 ¾ in* | Dawn Dumble, UCLA | 56 ft 5¾ in |
| Discus throw | Dawn Dumble, UCLA | 187 ft 2 in | Melinda Wirtz, Kent | 186 ft 1 in |
| Javelin throw | Valerie Tulloch, Rice | 192 ft 1 in | Heather Berlin, Minnesota | 183 ft 2 in |
| Heptathlon | Diane Guthrie-Gresham, GMU | 6527* | Ali McKnight, Nevada | 5832 |

*Meet record. w=wind-aided.

### Tennis

#### MEN

| | Champion | Score | Runner-Up |
|---|----------|-------|-----------|
| Singles | Sargis Sargsian, Arizona St | (3-6, 6-3, 6-4) | Brett Hansen, Southern Cal |
| Doubles | Mahesh Bhupathi & Ali Hamadeh, Mississippi | (7-6 (2), 6-2) | Chad Clark & Trey Phillips, Texas |

#### WOMEN

| | Champion | Score | Runner-Up |
|---|----------|-------|-----------|
| Singles | Keri Phebus, UCLA | (6-2, 6-3) | Kelly Pace, Texas |
| Doubles | Keri Phebus & Susie Starrett, UCLA | (6-3, 6-3) | Cristina Moros & Kelly Pace, Texas |

# FOR THE RECORD · Year by Year

## CHAMPIONSHIP RESULTS

### Baseball

#### DIVISION I

| Year | Champion | Coach | Score | Runner-Up | Most Outstanding Player |
|------|----------|-------|-------|-----------|-------------------------|
| 1947 | California* | Clint Evans | 8-7 | Yale | No award |
| 1948 | Southern Cal | Sam Barry | 9-2 | Yale | No award |
| 1949 | Texas* | Bibb Falk | 10-3 | Wake Forest | Charles Teague, Wake Forest, 2B |
| 1950 | Texas | Bibb Falk | 3-0 | Washington St | Ray VanCleef, Rutgers, CF |
| 1951 | Oklahoma* | Jack Baer | 3-2 | Tennnessee | Sidney Hatfield, Tennessee, P-1B |
| 1952 | Holy Cross | Jack Barry | 8-4 | Missouri | James O'Neill, Holy Cross, P |
| 1953 | Michigan | Ray Fisher | 7-5 | Texas | J. L. Smith, Texas, P |
| 1954 | Missouri | John "Hi" Simmons | 4-1 | Rollins | Tom Yewcic, Michigan St, C |
| 1955 | Wake Forest | Taylor Sanford | 7-6 | Western Michigan | Tom Borland, Oklahoma St, P |
| 1956 | Minnesota | Dick Siebert | 12-1 | Arizona | Jerry Thomas, Minnesota, P |
| 1957 | California* | George Wolfman | 1-0 | Penn St | Cal Emery, Penn St, P-1B |
| 1958 | Southern Cal | Rod Dedeaux | 8-7† | Missouri | Bill Thom, Southern Cal, P |
| 1959 | Oklahoma St | Toby Greene | 5-3 | Arizona | Jim Dobson, Oklahoma St, 3B |
| 1960 | Minnesota | Dick Siebert | 2-1‡ | Southern Cal | John Erickson, Minnesota, 2B |
| 1961 | Southern Cal* | Rod Dedeaux | 1-0 | Oklahoma St | Littleton Fowler, Oklahoma St, P |
| 1962 | Michigan | Don Lund | 5-4 | Santa Clara | Bob Garibaldi, Santa Clara, P |
| 1963 | Southern Cal | Rod Dedeaux | 5-2 | Arizona | Bud Hollowell, Southern Cal, C |
| 1964 | Minnesota | Dick Siebert | 5-1 | Missouri | Joe Ferris, Maine, P |
| 1965 | Arizona St | Bobby Winkles | 2-1# | Ohio St | Sal Bando, Arizona St, 3B |
| 1966 | Ohio St | Marty Karow | 8-2 | Oklahoma St | Steve Arlin, Ohio St, P |
| 1967 | Arizona St | Bobby Winkles | 11-2 | Houston | Ron Davini, Arizona St, C |
| 1968 | Southern Cal* | Rod Dedeaux | 4-3 | Southern Illinois | Bill Seinsoth, Southern Cal, 1B |
| 1969 | Arizona St | Bobby Winkles | 10-1 | Tulsa | John Dolinsek, Arizona St, LF |
| 1970 | Southern Cal | Rod Dedeaux | 2-1 | Florida St | Gene Ammann, Florida St, P |
| 1971 | Southern Cal | Rod Dedeaux | 7-2 | Southern Illinois | Jerry Tabb, Tulsa, 1B |
| 1972 | Southern Cal | Rod Dedeaux | 1-0 | Arizona St | Russ McQueen, Southern Cal, P |
| 1973 | Southern Cal* | Rod Dedeaux | 4-3 | Arizona St | Dave Winfield, Minnesota, P-OF |
| 1974 | Southern Cal | Rod Dedeaux | 7-3 | Miami (FL) | George Milke, Southern Cal, P |
| 1975 | Texas | Cliff Gustafson | 5-1 | S Carolina | Mickey Reichenbach, Texas, 1B |
| 1976 | Arizona | Jerry Kindall | 7-1 | Eastern Michigan | Steve Powers, Arizona, P-DH |
| 1977 | Arizona St | Jim Brock | 2-1 | S Carolina | Bob Horner, Arizona St, 3B |
| 1978 | Southern Cal* | Rod Dedeaux | 10-3 | Arizona St | Rod Boxberger, Southern Cal, P |
| 1979 | Cal St-Fullerton | Augie Garrido | 2-1 | Arkansas | Tony Hudson, Cal St-Fullerton, P |
| 1980 | Arizona | Jerry Kindall | 5-3 | Hawaii | Terry Francona, Arizona, LF |
| 1981 | Arizona St | Jim Brock | 7-4 | Oklahoma St | Stan Holmes, Arizona St, LF |
| 1982 | Miami (FL)* | Ron Fraser | 9-3 | Wichita St | Dan Smith, Miami (FL), P |
| 1983 | Texas* | Cliff Gustafson | 4-3 | Alabama | Calvin Schiraldi, Texas, P |
| 1984 | Cal St-Fullerton | Augie Garrido | 3-1 | Texas | John Fishel, Cal St-Fullerton, LF |
| 1985 | Miami (FL) | Ron Fraser | 10-6 | Texas | Greg Ellena, Miami (FL), DH |
| 1986 | Arizona | Jerry Kindall | 10-2 | Florida St | Mike Senne, Arizona, LF |
| 1987 | Stanford | Mark Marquess | 9-5 | Oklahoma St | Paul Carey, Stanford, RF |
| 1988 | Stanford | Mark Marquess | 9-4 | Arizona St | Lee Plemel, Stanford, P |
| 1989 | Wichita St | Gene Stephenson | 5-3 | Texas | Greg Brummett, Wichita St, P |
| 1990 | Georgia | Steve Webber | 2-1 | Oklahoma St | Mike Rebhan, Georgia, P |
| 1991 | Louisiana St | Skip Bertman | 6-3 | Wichita St | Gary Hymel, Louisiana St, C |
| 1992 | Pepperdine | Andy Lopez | 3-2 | Cal St-Fullerton | Phil Nevin, Cal St-Fullerton, 3B |
| 1993 | Louisiana St | Skip Bertman | 8-0 | Wichita St | Todd Walker, Louisiana St, 2B |
| 1994 | Oklahoma | Larry Cochell | 13-5 | Georgia Tech | Chip Glass, Oklahoma, CF |
| 1995 | Cal St-Fullerton* | Augie Garrido | 11-5 | Southern Cal | Mark Kotsay, Cal St-Fullerton, CF-P |

*Undefeated teams in College World Series play. †12 innings. ‡10 innings. #15 innings.

#### DIVISION II

| Year | Champion | Year | Champion | Year | Champion | Year | Champion |
|------|----------|------|----------|------|----------|------|----------|
| 1968 | Chapman* | 1975 | Florida Southern | 1982 | UC-Riverside* | 1989 | Cal Poly-SLO |
| 1969 | Illinois St* | 1976 | Cal Poly-Pomona | 1983 | Cal Poly-Pomona* | 1990 | Jacksonville St |
| 1970 | Cal St-Northridge | 1977 | UC-Riverside | 1984 | Cal St-Northridge | 1991 | Jacksonville St |
| 1971 | Florida Southern | 1978 | Florida Southern | 1985 | Florida Southern* | 1992 | Tampa* |
| 1972 | Florida Southern | 1979 | Valdosta St | 1986 | Troy St | 1993 | Tampa |
| 1973 | UC-Irvine* | 1980 | Cal Poly-Pomona* | 1987 | Troy St* | 1994 | Central Missouri St |
| 1974 | UC-Irvine | 1981 | Florida Southern* | 1988 | Florida Southern* | 1995 | Florida Southern* |

*Undefeated teams.

## DIVISION III

| Year | Champion | Year | Champion | Year | Champion |
|------|----------|------|----------|------|----------|
| 1976 | Cal St-Stanislaus | 1983 | Marietta | 1990 | Eastern Connecticut St |
| 1977 | Cal St-Stanislaus | 1984 | Ramapo | 1991 | Southern Maine |
| 1978 | Glassboro St | 1985 | WI-Oshkosh | 1992 | William Patterson |
| 1979 | Glassboro St | 1986 | Marietta | 1993 | Montclair St |
| 1980 | Ithaca | 1987 | Montclair St | 1994 | WI-Oshkosh |
| 1981 | Marietta | 1988 | Ithaca | 1995 | La Verne |
| 1982 | Eastern Connecticut St | 1989 | NC Wesleyan | | |

# Cross-Country

## Men

### DIVISION I

| Year | Champion | Coach | Pts | Runner-Up | Pts | Individual Champion | Time |
|------|----------|-------|-----|-----------|-----|---------------------|------|
| 1938 | Indiana | Earle Hayes | 51 | Notre Dame | 61 | Greg Rice, Notre Dame | 20:12.9 |
| 1939 | Michigan St | Lauren Brown | 54 | Wisconsin | 57 | Walter Mehl, Wisconsin | 20:30.9 |
| 1940 | Indiana | Earle Hayes | 65 | Eastern Michigan | 68 | Gilbert Dodds, Ashland | 20:30.2 |
| 1941 | Rhode Island | Fred Tootell | 83 | Penn St | 110 | Fred Wilt, Indiana | 20:30.1 |
| 1942 | Indiana | Earle Hayes | 57 | | | Oliver Hunter, Notre Dame | 20:18.0 |
| | Penn St | Charles Werner | 57 | | | | |
| 1943 | No meet | | | | | | |
| 1944 | Drake | Bill Easton | 25 | Notre Dame | 64 | Fred Feiler, Drake | 21:04.2 |
| 1945 | Drake | Bill Easton | 50 | Notre Dame | 65 | Fred Feiler, Drake | 21:14.2 |
| 1946 | Drake | Bill Easton | 42 | NYU | 98 | Quentin Brelsford, Ohio Wesleyan | 20:22.9 |
| 1947 | Penn St | Charles Werner | 60 | Syracuse | 72 | Jack Milne, N Carolina | 20:41.1 |
| 1948 | Michigan St | Karl Schlademan | 41 | Wisconsin | 69 | Robert Black, Rhode Island | 19:52.3 |
| 1949 | Michigan St | Karl Schlademan | 59 | Syracuse | 81 | Robert Black, Rhode Island | 20:25.7 |
| 1950 | Penn St | Charles Werner | 53 | Michigan St | 55 | Herb Semper Jr, Kansas | 20:31.7 |
| 1951 | Syracuse | Robert Grieve | 80 | Kansas | 118 | Herb Semper Jr, Kansas | 20:09.5 |
| 1952 | Michigan St | Karl Schlademan | 65 | Indiana | 68 | Charles Capozzoli, Georgetown | 19:36.7 |
| 1953 | Kansas | Bill Easton | 70 | Indiana | 82 | Wes Santee, Kansas | 19:43.5 |
| 1954 | Oklahoma St | Ralph Higgins | 61 | Syracuse | 118 | Allen Frame, Kansas | 19:54.2 |
| 1955 | Michigan St | Karl Schlademan | 46 | Kansas | 68 | Charles Jones, Iowa | 19:57.4 |
| 1956 | Michigan St | Karl Schlademan | 28 | Kansas | 88 | Walter McNew, Texas | 19:55.7 |
| 1957 | Notre Dame | Alex Wilson | 121 | Michigan St | 127 | Max Truex, Southern Cal | 19:12.3 |
| 1958 | Michigan St | Francis Dittrich | 79 | Western Michigan | 104 | Crawford Kennedy, Michigan State | 20:07.1 |
| 1959 | Michigan St | Francis Dittrich | 44 | Houston | 120 | Al Lawrence, Houston | 20:35.7 |
| 1960 | Houston | John Morriss | 54 | Michigan St | 80 | Al Lawrence, Houston | 19:28.2 |
| 1961 | Oregon St | Sam Bell | 68 | San Jose St | 82 | Dale Story, Oregon St | 19:46.6 |
| 1962 | San Jose St | Dean Miller | 58 | Villanova | 69 | Tom O'Hara, Loyola (IL) | 19:20.3 |
| 1963 | San Jose St | Dean Miller | 53 | Oregon | 68 | Victor Zwolak, Villanova | 19:35.0 |
| 1964 | Western Michigan | George Dales | 86 | Oregon | 116 | Elmore Banton, Ohio | 20:07.5 |
| 1965 | Western Michigan | George Dales | 81 | Northwestern | 114 | John Lawson, Kansas | 29:24.0 |
| 1966 | Villanova | James Elliott | 79 | Kansas St | 155 | Gerry Lindgren, Washington St | 29:01.4 |
| 1967 | Villanova | James Elliott | 91 | Air Force | 96 | Gerry Lindgren, Washington St | 30:45.6 |
| 1968 | Villanova | James Elliott | 78 | Stanford | 100 | Michael Ryan, Air Force | 29:16.8 |
| 1969 | UTEP | Wayne Vandenburg | 74 | Villanova | 88 | Gerry Lindgren, Washington St | 28:59.2 |
| 1970 | Villanova | James Elliott | 85 | Oregon | 86 | Steve Prefontaine, Oregon | 28:00.2 |
| 1971 | Oregon | Bill Dellinger | 83 | Washington St | 122 | Steve Prefontaine, Oregon | 29:14.0 |
| 1972 | Tennessee | Stan Huntsman | 134 | E Tennessee St | 148 | Neil Cusack, E Tennessee St | 28:23.0 |
| 1973 | Oregon | Bill Dellinger | 89 | UTEP | 157 | Steve Prefontaine, Oregon | 28:14.0 |
| 1974 | Oregon | Bill Dellinger | 77 | Western Kentucky | 110 | Nick Rose, Western Kentucky | 29:22.0 |
| 1975 | UTEP | Ted Banks | 88 | Washington St | 92 | Craig Virgin, Illinois | 28:23.3 |
| 1976 | UTEP | Ted Banks | 62 | Oregon | 117 | Henry Rono, Washington St | 28:06.6 |

## Men (Cont.)

### DIVISION I (Cont.)

| Year | Champion | Coach | Pts | Runner-Up | Pts | Individual Champion | Time |
|------|----------|-------|-----|-----------|-----|---------------------|------|
| 1977 | Oregon | Bill Dellinger | 100 | UTEP | 105 | Henry Rono, Washington St | 28:33.5 |
| 1978 | UTEP | Ted Banks | 56 | Oregon | 72 | Alberto Salazar, Oregon | 29:29.7 |
| 1979 | UTEP | Ted Banks | 86 | Oregon | 93 | Henry Rono, Washington St | 28:19.6 |
| 1980 | UTEP | Ted Banks | 58 | Arkansas | 152 | Suleiman Nyambui, UTEP | 29:04.0 |
| 1981 | UTEP | Ted Banks | 17 | Providence | 109 | Mathews Motshwarateu, UTEP | 28:45.6 |
| 1982 | Wisconsin | Dan McClimon | 59 | Providence | 138 | Mark Scrutton, Colorado | 30:12.6 |
| 1983 | Vacated | | | Wisconsin | 164 | Zakarie Barie, UTEP | 29:20.0 |
| 1984 | Arkansas | John McDonnell | 101 | Arizona | 111 | Ed Eyestone, Brigham Young | 29:28.8 |
| 1985 | Wisconsin | Martin Smith | 67 | Arkansas | 104 | Timothy Hacker, Wisconsin | 29:17.88 |
| 1986 | Arkansas | John McDonnell | 69 | Dartmouth | 141 | Aaron Ramirez, Arizona | 30:27.53 |
| 1987 | Arkansas | John McDonnell | 87 | Dartmouth | 119 | Joe Falcon, Arkansas | 29:14.97 |
| 1988 | Wisconsin | Martin Smith | 105 | Northern Arizona | 160 | Robert Kennedy, Indiana | 29:20.0 |
| 1989 | Iowa St | Bill Bergan | 54 | Oregon | 72 | John Nuttall, Iowa St | 29:30.55 |
| 1990 | Arkansas | John McDonnell | 68 | Iowa St | 96 | Jonah Koech, Iowa St | 29:05.0 |
| 1991 | Arkansas | John McDonnell | 52 | Iowa St | 114 | Sean Dollman, Western Ky | 30:17.1 |
| 1992 | Arkansas | John McDonnell | 46 | Wisconsin | 87 | Bob Kennedy, Indiana | 30:15.3 |
| 1993 | Arkansas | John McDonnell | 31 | Brigham Young | 153 | Josephat Kapkory, Wash St | 29:32.4 |
| 1994 | Iowa St | Bill Bergan | 65 | Colorado | 88 | Martin Keino, Arizona | 30:08.7 |

### DIVISION II

| Year | Champion | Year | Champion | Year | Champion |
|------|----------|------|----------|------|----------|
| 1958 | Northern Illinois | 1971 | Cal St-Fullerton | 1984 | SE Missouri St |
| 1959 | S Dakota St | 1972 | N Dakota St | 1985 | S Dakota St |
| 1960 | Central St (OH) | 1973 | S Dakota St | 1986 | Edinboro |
| 1961 | Southern Illinois | 1974 | SW Missouri St | 1987 | Edinboro |
| 1962 | Central St (OH) | 1975 | UC-Irvine | 1988 | Edinboro/ Mankato St |
| 1963 | Emporia St | 1976 | UC-Irvine | 1989 | S Dakota St |
| 1964 | Kentucky St | 1977 | Eastern Illinois | 1990 | Edinboro |
| 1965 | San Diego St | 1978 | Cal Poly-SLO | 1991 | MA-Lowell |
| 1966 | San Diego St | 1979 | Cal Poly-SLO | 1992 | Adams St |
| 1967 | San Diego St | 1980 | Humboldt St | 1993 | Adams St |
| 1968 | Eastern Illinois | 1981 | Millersville | 1994 | Adams St |
| 1969 | Eastern Illinois | 1982 | Eastern Washington | | |
| 1970 | Eastern Michigan | 1983 | Cal Poly-Pomona | | |

### DIVISION III

| Year | Champion | Year | Champion | Year | Champion |
|------|----------|------|----------|------|----------|
| 1973 | Ashland | 1981 | North Central | 1989 | WI-Oshkosh |
| 1974 | Mount Union | 1982 | North Central | 1990 | WI-Oshkosh |
| 1975 | North Central | 1983 | Brandeis | 1991 | Rochester |
| 1976 | North Central | 1984 | St Thomas (MN) | 1992 | North Central |
| 1977 | Occidental | 1985 | Luther | 1993 | North Central |
| 1978 | North Central | 1986 | St Thomas (MN) | 1994 | Williams |
| 1979 | North Central | 1987 | North Central | | |
| 1980 | Carleton | 1988 | WI-Oshkosh | | |

## Women

### DIVISION I

| Year | Champion | Coach | Pts | Runner-Up | Pts | Individual Champion | Time |
|------|----------|-------|-----|-----------|-----|---------------------|------|
| 1981 | Virginia | John Vasvary | 36 | Oregon | 83 | Betty Springs, N Carolina St | 16:19.0 |
| 1982 | Virginia | Martin Smith | 48 | Stanford | 91 | Lesley Welch, Virginia | 16:39.7 |
| 1983 | Oregon | Tom Heinonen | 95 | Stanford | 98 | Betty Springs, N Carolina St | 16:30.7 |
| 1984 | Wisconsin | Peter Tegen | 63 | Stanford | 89 | Cathy Branta, Wisconsin | 16:15.6 |
| 1985 | Wisconsin | Peter Tegen | 58 | Iowa St | 98 | Suzie Tuffey, N Carolina St | 16:22.5 |
| 1986 | Texas | Terry Crawford | 62 | Wisconsin | 64 | Angela Chalmers, N Arizona | 16:55.49 |
| 1987 | Oregon | Tom Heinonen | 97 | N Carolina St | 99 | Kimberly Betz, Indiana | 16:10.85 |
| 1988 | Kentucky | Don Weber | 75 | Oregon | 128 | Michelle Dekkers, Indiana | 16:30.0 |
| 1989 | Villanova | Marty Stern | 99 | Kentucky | 168 | Vicki Huber, Villanova | 15:59.86 |
| 1990 | Villanova | Marty Stern | 82 | Providence | 172 | Sonia O'Sullivan, Villanova | 16:06.0 |
| 1991 | Villanova | Marty Stern | 85 | Arkansas | 168 | Sonia O'Sullivan, Villanova | 16:30.3 |
| 1992 | Villanova | Marty Stern | 123 | Arkansas | 130 | Carole Zajac, Villanova | 17:01.9 |
| 1993 | Villanova | Marty Stern | 66 | Arkansas | 71 | Carole Zajac, Villanova | 16:40.3 |
| 1994 | Villanova | John Marshall | 75 | Michigan | 108 | Jennifer Rhines, Villanova | 16:31.2 |

## Women (Cont.)

### DIVISION II

| Year | Champion | Year | Champion | Year | Champion |
|------|----------|------|----------|------|----------|
| 1981 | S Dakota St | 1986 | Cal Poly-SLO | 1991 | Cal Poly-SLO |
| 1982 | Cal Poly-SLO | 1987 | Cal Poly-SLO | 1992 | Adams St |
| 1983 | Cal Poly-SLO | 1988 | Cal Poly-SLO | 1993 | Adams St |
| 1984 | Cal Poly-SLO | 1989 | Cal Poly-SLO | 1994 | Adams St |
| 1985 | Cal Poly-SLO | 1990 | Cal Poly-SLO | | |

### DIVISION III

| Year | Champion | Year | Champion | Year | Champion |
|------|----------|------|----------|------|----------|
| 1981 | Central (IA) | 1986 | St Thomas (MN) | 1990 | Cortland St |
| 1982 | St Thomas (MN) | 1987 | St Thomas (MN) | 1991 | WI-Oshkosh |
| 1983 | WI-La Crosse | | WI-Oshkosh | 1992 | Cortland St |
| 1984 | St Thomas (MN) | 1988 | WI-Oshkosh | 1993 | Cortland St |
| 1985 | Franklin & Marshall | 1989 | Cortland St | 1994 | Cortland St |

# Fencing

## Men

### TEAM CHAMPIONS

| Year | Champion | Coach | Pts | Runner-Up | Pts |
|------|----------|-------|-----|-----------|-----|
| 1941 | Northwestern | Henry Zettleman | 28½ | Illinois | 27 |
| 1942 | Ohio St | Frank Riebel | 34 | St John's (NY) | 33½ |
| 1943-1946 | No tournament | | | | |
| 1947 | NYU | Martinez Castello | 72 | Chicago | 50½ |
| 1948 | CCNY | James Montague | 30 | Navy | 28 |
| 1949 | Army | Servando Velarde | 63 | | |
| | Rutgers | Donald Cetrulo | 63 | | |
| 1950 | Navy | Joseph Fiems | 67½ | NYU | 66½ |
| | | | | Rutgers | 66½ |
| 1951 | Columbia | Servando Velarde | 69 | Pennsylvania | 64 |
| 1952 | Columbia | Servando Velarde | 71 | NYU | 69 |
| 1953 | Pennsylvania | Lajos Csiszar | 94 | Navy | 86 |
| 1954 | Columbia | Irving DeKoff | 61 | | |
| | NYU | Hugo Castello | 61 | | |
| 1955 | Columbia | Irving DeKoff | 62 | Cornell | 57 |
| 1956 | Illinois | Maxwell Garret | 90 | Columbia | 88 |
| 1957 | NYU | Hugo Castello | 65 | Columbia | 64 |
| 1958 | Illinois | Maxwell Garret | 47 | Columbia | 43 |
| 1959 | Navy | Andre Deladrier | 72 | NYU | 65 |
| 1960 | NYU | Hugo Castello | 65 | Navy | 57 |
| 1961 | NYU | Hugo Castello | 79 | Princeton | 68 |
| 1962 | Navy | Andre Deladrier | 76 | NYU | 74 |
| 1963 | Columbia | Irving DeKoff | 55 | Navy | 50 |
| 1964 | Princeton | Stan Sieja | 81 | NYU | 79 |
| 1965 | Columbia | Irving DeKoff | 76 | NYU | 74 |
| 1966 | NYU | Hugo Castello | 5-0 | Army | 5-2 |
| 1967 | NYU | Hugo Castello | 72 | Pennsylvania | 64 |
| 1968 | Columbia | Louis Bankuti | 92 | NYU | 87 |
| 1969 | Pennsylvania | Lajos Csiszar | 54 | Harvard | 43 |
| 1970 | NYU | Hugo Castello | 71 | Columbia | 63 |
| 1971 | NYU | Hugo Castello | 68 | | |
| | Columbia | Louis Bankuti | 68 | | |
| 1972 | Detroit | Richard Perry | 73 | NYU | 70 |
| 1973 | NYU | Hugo Castello | 76 | Pennsylvania | 71 |
| 1974 | NYU | Hugo Castello | 92 | Wayne St (MI) | 87 |
| 1975 | Wayne St (MI) | Istvan Danosi | 89 | Cornell | 83 |
| 1976 | NYU | Herbert Cohen | 79 | Wayne St (MI) | 77 |
| 1977 | Notre Dame | Michael DeCicco | 114* | NYU | 114 |
| 1978 | Notre Dame | Michael DeCicco | 121 | Pennsylvania | 110 |
| 1979 | Wayne St (MI) | Istvan Danosi | 119 | Notre Dame | 108 |
| 1980 | Wayne St (MI) | Istvan Danosi | 111 | Pennsylvania | 106 |
| | | | | MIT | 106 |
| 1981 | Pennsylvania | Dave Micahnik | 113 | Wayne St (MI) | 111 |

## Men (Cont.)
### TEAM CHAMPIONS (Cont.)

| Year | Champion | Coach | Pts | Runner-Up | Pts |
|------|----------|-------|-----|-----------|-----|
| 1982 | Wayne St (MI) | Istvan Danosi | 85 | Clemson | 77 |
| 1983 | Wayne St (MI) | Aladar Kogler | 86 | Notre Dame | 80 |
| 1984 | Wayne St (MI) | Gil Pezza | 69 | Penn St | 50 |
| 1985 | Wayne St (MI) | Gil Pezza | 141 | Notre Dame | 140 |
| 1986 | Notre Dame | Michael DeCicco | 151 | Columbia | 141 |
| 1987 | Columbia | George Kolombatovich | 86 | Pennsylvania | 78 |
| 1988 | Columbia | George Kolombatovich Aladar Kogler | 90 | Notre Dame | 83 |
| 1989 | Columbia | George Kolombatovich Aladar Kogler | 88 | Penn St | 85 |
| 1990 | Penn St | Emmanuil Kaidanov | 36 | Columbia-Barnard | 35 |
| 1991 | Penn St | Emmanuil Kaidanov | 4700 | Columbia-Barnard | 4200 |
| 1992 | Columbia-Barnard | George Kolumbatovich Aladar Kogler | 4150 | Penn St | 3646 |
| 1993 | Columbia-Barnard | George Kolumbatovich Aladar Kogler | 4525 | Penn St | 4500 |
| 1994 | Notre Dame | Michael DeCicco | 4350 | Penn St | 4075 |
| 1995 | Penn St | Emmanuil Kaidanov | 440 | St John's (NY) | 413 |

*Tie broken by a fence-off. Note: Beginning in 1990, men's and women's combined teams competed for the national championship.

### INDIVIDUAL CHAMPIONS

| | Foil | Sabre | Épée |
|------|------|-------|------|
| 1941 | Edward McNamara, Northwestern | William Meyer, Dartmouth | G. H. Boland, Illinois |
| 1942 | Byron Kreiger, Wayne St (MI) | Andre Deladrier, St John's (NY) | Ben Burtt, Ohio St |
| 1947 | Abraham Balk, NYU | Oscar Parsons, Temple | Abraham Balk, NYU |
| 1948 | Albert Axelrod, CCNY | James Day, Navy | William Bryan, Navy |
| 1949 | Ralph Tedeschi, Rutgers | Alex Treves, Rutgers | Richard C. Bowman, Army |
| 1950 | Robert Nielsen, Columbia | Alex Treves, Rutgers | Thomas Stuart, Navy |
| 1951 | Robert Nielsen, Columbia | Chamberless Johnston, Princeton | Daniel Chafetz, Columbia |
| 1952 | Harold Goldsmith, CCNY | Frank Zimolzak, Navy | James Wallner, NYU |
| 1953 | Ed Nober, Brooklyn | Robert Parmacek, Pennsylvania | Jack Tori, Pennsylvania |
| 1954 | Robert Goldman, Pennsylvania | Steve Sobel, Columbia | Henry Kolowrat, Princeton |
| 1955 | Herman Velasco, Illinois | Barry Pariser, Columbia | Donald Tadrawski, Notre Dame |
| 1956 | Ralph DeMarco, Columbia | Gerald Kaufman, Columbia | Kinmont Hoitsma, Princeton |
| 1957 | Bruce Davis, Wayne St (MI) | Bernie Balaban, NYU | James Margolis, Columbia |
| 1958 | Bruce Davis, Wayne St (MI) | Art Schankin, Illinois | Roland Wommack, Navy |
| 1959 | Joe Paletta, Navy | Al Morales, Navy | Roland Wommack, Navy |
| 1960 | Gene Glazer, NYU | Mike Desaro, NYU | Gil Eisner, NYU |
| 1961 | Herbert Cohen, NYU | Israel Colon, NYU | Jerry Halpern, NYU |
| 1962 | Herbert Cohen, NYU | Barton Nisonson, Columbia | Thane Hawkins, Navy |
| 1963 | Jay Lustig, Columbia | Bela Szentivanyi, Wayne St (MI) | Larry Crum, Navy |
| 1964 | Bill Hicks, Princeton | Craig Bell, Illinois | Paul Pesthy, Rutgers |
| 1965 | Joe Nalven, Columbia | Howard Goodman, NYU | Paul Pesthy, Rutgers |
| 1966 | Al Davis, NYU | Paul Apostol, NYU | Bernhardt Hermann, Iowa |
| 1967 | Mike Gaylor, NYU | Todd Makler, Pennsylvania | George Masin, NYU |
| 1968 | Gerard Esponda, San Francisco | Todd Makler, Pennsylvania | Don Sieja, Cornell |
| 1969 | Anthony Kestler, Columbia | Norman Braslow, Pennsylvania | James Wetzler, Pennsylvania |
| 1970 | Walter Krause, NYU | Bruce Soriano, Columbia | John Nadas, Case Reserve |
| 1971 | Tyrone Simmons, Detroit | Bruce Soriano, Columbia | George Szunyogh, NYU |
| 1972 | Tyrone Simmons, Detroit | Bruce Soriano, Columbia | Ernesto Fernandez, Pennsylvania |
| 1973 | Brooke Makler, Pennsylvania | Peter Westbrock, NYU | Risto Hurme, NYU |
| 1974 | Greg Benko, Wayne St (MI) | Steve Danosi, Wayne St (MI) | Risto Hurme, NYU |
| 1975 | Greg Benko, Wayne St (MI) | Yuri Rabinovich, Wayne St (MI) | Risto Hurme, NYU |
| 1976 | Greg Benko, Wayne St (MI) | Brian Smith, Columbia | Randy Eggleton, Pennsylvania |
| 1977 | Pat Gerard, Notre Dame | Mike Sullivan, Notre Dame | Hans Wieselgren, NYU |
| 1978 | Ernest Simon, Wayne St (MI) | Mike Sullivan, Notre Dame | Bjorne Vaggo, Notre Dame |
| 1979 | Andrew Bonk, Notre Dame | Yuri Rabinovich, Wayne St (MI) | Carlos Songini, Cleveland St |
| 1980 | Ernest Simon, Wayne St (MI) | Paul Friedberg, Pennsylvania | Gil Pezza, Wayne St (MI) |

### Men (Cont.)

#### INDIVIDUAL CHAMPIONS (Cont.)

| Foil | Sabre | Épée |
|---|---|---|
| 1981....Ernest Simon, Wayne St (MI) | Paul Friedberg, Pennsylvania | Gil Pezza, Wayne St (MI) |
| 1982....Alexander Flom, George Mason | Neil Hick, Wayne St (MI) | Peter Schifrin, San Jose St |
| 1983....Demetrios Valsamis, NYU | John Friedberg, North Carolina | Ola Harstrom, Notre Dame |
| 1984....Charles Higgs-Coulthard, Notre Dame | Michael Lofton, NYU | Ettore Bianchi, Wayne St (MI) |
| 1985....Stephan Chauvel, Wayne St (MI) | Michael Lofton, NYU | Ettore Bianchi, Wayne St (MI) |
| 1986....Adam Feldman, Penn St | Michael Lofton, NYU | Chris O'Loughlin, Pennsylvania |
| 1987....William Mindel, Columbia | Michael Lofton, NYU | James O'Neill, Harvard |
| 1988....Marc Kent, Columbia | Robert Cottingham, Columbia | Jon Normile, Columbia |
| 1989....Edward Mufel, Penn St | Peter Cox, Penn St | Jon Normile, Columbia |
| 1990....Nick Bravin, Stanford | David Mandell, Columbia | Jubba Beshin, Notre Dame |
| 1991....Ben Atkins, Columbia | Vitali Nazlimov, Penn St | Marc Oshima, Columbia |
| 1992....Nick Bravin, Stanford | Tom Strzalkowski, Penn St | Harald Bauder, Wayne St |
| 1993....Nick Bravin, Stanford | Tom Strzalkowski, Penn St | Ben Atkins, Columbia |
| 1994....Kwame van Leeuwen, Harvard | Tom Strzalkowski, Penn St | Harald Winkman, Princeton |
| 1995....Sean McClain, Stanford | Paul Palestis, NYU | Mike Gattner, Lawrence |

### Women

#### TEAM CHAMPIONS

| Year | Champion | Coach | Rec | Runner-Up | Rec |
|---|---|---|---|---|---|
| 1982 | Wayne St (MI) | Istvan Danosi | 7-0 | San Jose St | 6-1 |
| 1983 | Penn St | Beth Alphin | 5-0 | Wayne St (MI) | 3-2 |
| 1984 | Yale | Henry Harutunian | 3-0 | Penn St | 2-1 |
| 1985 | Yale | Henry Harutunian | 3-0 | Pennsylvania | 2-1 |
| 1986 | Pennsylvania | David Micahnik | 3-0 | Notre Dame | 2-1 |
| 1987 | Notre Dame | Yves Auriol | 3-0 | Temple | 2-1 |
| 1988 | Wayne St (MI) | Gil Pezza | 3-0 | Notre Dame | 2-1 |
| 1989 | Wayne St (MI) | Gil Pezza | 3-0 | Columbia-Barnard | 2-1 |

Note: Beginning in 1990, men's and women's combined teams competed for the national championship.

#### INDIVIDUAL CHAMPIONS

| Foil | Epée |
|---|---|
| 1982................Joy Ellingson, San Jose St | 1995................Tina Loven, St John's (NY) |
| 1983................Jana Angelakis, Penn St | Note: The women's epée competition was added in 1995. |
| 1984................Mary Jane O'Neill, Pennsylvania | |
| 1985................Caitlin Bilodeaux, Columbia-Barnard | |
| 1986................Molly Sullivan, Notre Dame | |
| 1987................Caitlin Bilodeaux, Columbia-Barnard | |
| 1988................Molly Sullivan, Notre Dame | |
| 1989................Yasemin Topcu, Wayne St (MI) | |
| 1990................Tzu Moy, Columbia-Barnard | |
| 1991................Heidi Piper, Notre Dame | |
| 1992................Olga Cheryak, Penn St | |
| 1993................Olga Kalinovskaya, Penn St | |
| 1994................Olga Kalinovskaya, Penn St | |
| 1995................Olga Kalinovskaya, Penn St | |

## Field Hockey

### DIVISION I

| Year | Champion | Coach | Score | Runner-Up |
|---|---|---|---|---|
| 1981 | Connecticut | Diane Wright | 4-1 | Massachusetts |
| 1982 | Old Dominion | Beth Anders | 3-2 | Connecticut |
| 1983 | Old Dominion | Beth Anders | 3-1 (3 OT) | Connecticut |
| 1984 | Old Dominion | Beth Anders | 5-1 | Iowa |
| 1985 | Connecticut | Diane Wright | 3-2 | Old Dominion |
| 1986 | Iowa | Judith Davidson | 2-1 (2 OT) | New Hampshire |
| 1987 | Maryland | Sue Tyler | 2-1 (OT) | N Carolina |
| 1988 | Old Dominion | Beth Anders | 2-1 | Iowa |
| 1989 | N Carolina | Karen Shelton | 2-1 (3 OT)* | Old Dominion |
| 1990 | Old Dominion | Beth Anders | 5-0 | N Carolina |
| 1991 | Old Dominion | Beth Anders | 2-0 | N Carolina |

## DIVISION I (Cont.)

| Year | Champion | Coach | Score | Runner-Up |
|------|----------|-------|-------|-----------|
| 1992 ....................Old Dominion | | Beth Anders | 4-0 | Iowa |
| 1993 .....................Maryland | | Missy Meharg | 2-1 (3 OT)* | N Carolina |
| 1994 .....................James Madison | | Christy Morgan | 2-1 (3 OT)* | N Carolina |

*Penalty strokes.

## DIVISION II (DISCONTINUED, THEN RENEWED)

| Year | Champion | Coach | Score | Runner-Up |
|------|----------|-------|-------|-----------|
| 1981 ....................Pfeiffer | | Ellen Briggs | 5-3 | Bentley |
| 1982 ....................Lock Haven | | Sharon E. Taylor | 4-1 | Bloomsburg |
| 1983 ....................Bloomsburg | | Jan Hutchinson | 1-0 | Lock Haven |
| 1992 ....................Lock Haven | | Sharon E. Taylor | 3-1 | Bloomsburg |
| 1993 ....................Bloomsburg | | Jan Hutchison | 2-1 (2 OT) | Lock Haven |
| 1994 ....................Lock Haven | | Sharon E. Taylor | 2-1 | Bloomsburg |

### DIVISION III

| Year | Champion | Year | Champion | Year | Champion |
|------|----------|------|----------|------|----------|
| 1981 .......Trenton St | | 1986 .......Salisbury St | | 1991 .......Trenton St | |
| 1982 .......Ithaca | | 1987 .......Bloomsburg | | 1992 .......William Smith | |
| 1983 .......Trenton St | | 1988 .......Trenton St | | 1993 .......Cortland St | |
| 1984 .......Bloomsburg | | 1989 .......Lock Haven | | 1994 .......Cortland St | |
| 1985 .......Trenton St | | 1990 .......Trenton St | | | |

# Golf

## Men

### DIVISION I
### Results, 1897-1938

| Year | Champion | Site | Individual Champion |
|------|----------|------|---------------------|
| 1897 ..................Yale | Ardsley Casino | Louis Bayard Jr, Princeton |
| 1898 ..................Harvard (spring) | | John Reid Jr, Yale |
| 1898 ..................Yale (fall) | | James Curtis, Harvard |
| 1899 ..................Harvard | | Percy Pyne, Princeton |
| 1900 ..................No tournament | | |
| 1901 ..................Harvard | Atlantic City | H. Lindsley, Harvard |
| 1902 ..................Yale (spring) | Garden City | Charles Hitchcock Jr, Yale |
| 1902 ..................Harvard (fall) | Morris County | Chandler Egan, Harvard |
| 1903 ..................Harvard | Garden City | F. O. Reinhart, Princeton |
| 1904 ..................Harvard | Myopia | A. L. White, Harvard |
| 1905 ..................Yale | Garden City | Robert Abbott, Yale |
| 1906 ..................Yale | Garden City | W. E. Clow Jr, Yale |
| 1907 ..................Yale | Nassau | Ellis Knowles, Yale |
| 1908 ..................Yale | Brae Burn | H. H. Wilder, Harvard |
| 1909 ..................Yale | Apawamis | Albert Seckel, Princeton |
| 1910 ..................Yale | Essex County | Robert Hunter, Yale |
| 1911 ..................Yale | Baltusrol | George Stanley, Yale |
| 1912 ..................Yale | Ekwanok | F. C. Davison, Harvard |
| 1913 ..................Yale | Huntingdon Valley | Nathaniel Wheeler, Yale |
| 1914 ..................Princeton | Garden City | Edward Allis, Harvard |
| 1915 ..................Yale | Greenwich | Francis Blossom, Yale |
| 1916 ..................Princeton | Oakmont | J. W. Hubbell, Harvard |
| 1917-18 .............No tournament | | |
| 1919 ..................Princeton | Merion | A. L. Walker Jr, Columbia |
| 1920 ..................Princeton | Nassau | Jess Sweetster, Yale |
| 1921 ..................Dartmouth | Greenwich | Simpson Dean, Princeton |
| 1922 ..................Princeton | Garden City | Pollack Boyd, Dartmouth |
| 1923 ..................Princeton | Siwanoy | Dexter Cummings, Yale |
| 1924 ..................Yale | Greenwich | Dexter Cummings, Yale |
| 1925 ..................Yale | Montclair | Fred Lamprecht, Tulane |
| 1926 ..................Yale | Merion | Fred Lamprecht, Tulane |
| 1927 ..................Princeton | Garden City | Watts Gunn, Georgia Tech |
| 1928 ..................Princeton | Apawamis | Maurice McCarthy, Georgetown |
| 1929 ..................Princeton | Hollywood | Tom Aycock, Yale |
| 1930 ..................Princeton | Oakmont | G. T. Dunlap Jr, Princeton |

## Men (Cont.)
### DIVISION I (Cont.)
### Results, 1897-1938 (Cont.)

| Year | Champion | Site | Individual Champion |
|---|---|---|---|
| 1931 | Yale | Olympia Fields | G. T. Dunlap Jr, Princeton |
| 1932 | Yale | Hot Springs | J. W. Fischer, Michigan |
| 1933 | Yale | Buffalo | Walter Emery, Oklahoma |
| 1934 | Michigan | Cleveland | Charles Yates, Georgia Tech |
| 1935 | Michigan | Congressional | Ed White, Texas |
| 1936 | Yale | North Shore | Charles Kocsis, Michigan |
| 1937 | Princeton | Oakmont | Fred Haas Jr, Louisiana St |
| 1938 | Stanford | Louisville | John Burke, Georgetown |

### Results, 1939-1995

| Year | Champion | Coach | Score | Runner-Up | Score | Host or Site | Individual Champion |
|---|---|---|---|---|---|---|---|
| 1939 | Stanford | Eddie Twiggs | 612 | Northwestern | 614 | Wakonda | Vincent D'Antoni, Tulane |
| | | | | Princeton | 614 | | |
| 1940 | Princeton | Walter Bourne | 601 | | | Ekwanok | Dixon Brooke, Virginia |
| | Louisiana St | Mike Donahue | 601 | | | | |
| 1941 | Stanford | Eddie Twiggs | 580 | Louisiana St | 599 | Ohio St | Earl Stewart, Louisiana St |
| 1942 | Louisiana St | Mike Donahue | 590 | | | Notre Dame | Frank Tatum Jr |
| | Stanford | Eddie Twiggs | 590 | | | | |
| 1943 | Yale | William Neale Jr | 614 | Michigan | 618 | Olympia Fields | Wallace Ulrich, Carleton |
| 1944 | Notre Dame | George Holderith | 311 | Minnesota | 312 | Inverness | Louis Lick, Minnesota |
| 1945 | Ohio St | Robert Kepler | 602 | Northwestern | 621 | Ohio St | John Lorms, Ohio St |
| 1946 | Stanford | Eddie Twiggs | 619 | Michigan | 624 | Princeton | George Hamer, Georgia |
| 1947 | Louisiana St | T. P. Heard | 606 | Duke | 614 | Michigan | Dave Barclay, Michigan |
| 1948 | San Jose St | Wilbur Hubbard | 579 | Louisiana St | 588 | Stanford | Bob Harris, San Jose St |
| 1949 | N Texas | Fred Cobb | 590 | Purdue | 600 | Iowa St | Harvie Ward, N Carolina |
| | | | | Texas | 600 | | |
| 1950 | N Texas | Fred Cobb | 573 | Purdue | 577 | New Mexico | Fred Wampler, Purdue |
| 1951 | N Texas | Fred Cobb | 588 | Ohio St | 589 | Ohio St | Tom Nieporte, Ohio St |
| 1952 | N Texas | Fred Cobb | 587 | Michigan | 593 | Purdue | Jim Vickers, Oklahoma |
| 1953 | Stanford | Charles Finger | 578 | N Carolina | 580 | Broadmoor | Earl Moeller, Oklahoma St |
| 1954 | Southern Meth | Graham Ross | 572 | N Texas | 573 | Houston, Rice | Hillman Robbins, Memphis St |
| 1955 | Louisiana St | Mike Barbato | 574 | N Texas | 583 | Tennessee | Joe Campbell, Purdue |
| 1956 | Houston | Dave Williams | 601 | N Texas | 602 | Ohio St | Rick Jones, Ohio St |
| | | | | Purdue | 602 | | |
| 1957 | Houston | Dave Williams | 602 | Stanford | 603 | Broadmoor | Rex Baxter Jr, Houston |
| 1958 | Houston | Dave Williams | 570 | Oklahoma St | 582 | Williams | Phil Rodgers, Houston |
| 1959 | Houston | Dave Williams | 561 | Purdue | 571 | Oregon | Dick Crawford, Houston |
| 1960 | Houston | Dave Williams | 603 | Purdue | 607 | Broadmoor | Dick Crawford, Houston |
| | | | | Oklahoma St | 607 | | |
| 1961 | Purdue | Sam Voinoff | 584 | Arizona St | 595 | Lafayette | Jack Nicklaus, Ohio St |
| 1962 | Houston | Dave Williams | 588 | Oklahoma St | 598 | Duke | Kermit Zarley, Houston |
| 1963 | Oklahoma St | Labron Harris | 581 | Houston | 582 | Wichita St | R. H. Sikes, Ark. |
| 1964 | Houston | Dave Williams | 580 | Oklahoma St | 587 | Broadmoor | Terry Small, San Jose St |
| 1965 | Houston | Dave Williams | 577 | Cal St-LA | 587 | Tennessee | Marty Fleckman, Houston |

## Men (Cont.)

### DIVISION I (Cont.)

## Results, 1939-1995 (Cont.)

| Year | Champion | Coach | Score | Runner-Up | Score | Host or Site | Individual Champion |
|------|----------|-------|-------|-----------|-------|--------------|---------------------|
| 1966 | Houston | Dave Williams | 582 | San Jose St | 586 | Stanford | Bob Murphy, Florida |
| 1967 | Houston | Dave Williams | 585 | Florida | 588 | Shawnee, PA | Hale Irwin, Colorado |
| 1968 | Florida | Buster Bishop | 1154 | Houston | 1156 | New Mexico St | Grier Jones, Oklahoma St |
| 1969 | Houston | Dave Williams | 1223 | Wake Forest | 1232 | Broadmoor | Bob Clark, Cal St-LA |
| 1970 | Houston | Dave Williams | 1172 | Wake Forest | 1182 | Ohio St | John Mahaffey, Houston |
| 1971 | Texas | George Hannon | 1144 | Houston | 1151 | Arizona | Ben Crenshaw, Texas |
| 1972 | Texas | George Hannon | 1146 | Houston | 1159 | Cape Coral | Ben Crenshaw, Texas Tom Kite, Texas |
| 1973 | Florida | Buster Bishop | 1149 | Oklahoma St | 1159 | Oklahoma St | Ben Crenshaw, Texas |
| 1974 | Wake Forest | Jess Haddock | 1158 | Florida | 1160 | San Diego St | Curtis Strange, Wake Forest |
| 1975 | Wake Forest | Jess Haddock | 1156 | Oklahoma St | 1189 | Ohio St | Jay Haas, Wake Forest |
| 1976 | Oklahoma St | Mike Holder | 1166 | Brigham Young | 1173 | New Mexico | Scott Simpson, Southern Cal |
| 1977 | Houston | Dave Williams | 1197 | Oklahoma St | 1205 | Colgate | Scott Simpson, Southern Cal |
| 1978 | Oklahoma St | Mike Holder | 1140 | Georgia | 1157 | Oregon | David Edwards, Oklahoma St |
| 1979 | Ohio St | James Brown | 1189 | Oklahoma St | 1191 | Wake Forest | Gary Hallberg, Wake Forest |
| 1980 | Oklahoma St | Mike Holder | 1173 | Brigham Young | 1177 | Ohio St | Jay Don Blake, Utah St |
| 1981 | Brigham Young | Karl Tucker | 1161 | Oral Roberts | 1163 | Stanford | Ron Commans, Southern Cal |
| 1982 | Houston | Dave Williams | 1141 | Oklahoma St | 1151 | Pinehurst | Billy Ray Brown, Houston |
| 1983 | Oklahoma St | Mike Holder | 1161 | Texas | 1168 | Fresno St | Jim Carter, Arizona St |
| 1984 | Houston | Dave Williams | 1145 | Oklahoma St | 1146 | Houston | John Inman, N Carolina |
| 1985 | Houston | Dave Williams | 1172 | Oklahoma St | 1175 | Florida | Clark Burroughs, Ohio St |
| 1986 | Wake Forest | Jess Haddock | 1156 | Oklahoma St | 1160 | Wake Forest | Scott Verplank, Oklahoma St |
| 1987 | Oklahoma St | Mike Holder | 1160 | Wake Forest | 1176 | Ohio St | Brian Watts, Oklahoma St |
| 1988 | UCLA | Eddie Merrins | 1176 | UTEP Oklahoma Oklahoma St | 1179 1179 1179 | Southern Cal | E. J. Pfister, Oklahoma St |
| 1989 | Oklahoma | Gregg Grost | 1139 | Texas | 1158 | Oklahoma Oklahoma St | Phil Mickelson, Arizona St |
| 1990 | Arizona St | Steve Loy | 1155 | Florida | 1157 | Florida | Phil Mickelson, Arizona St |
| 1991 | Oklahoma St | Mike Holder | 1161 | N Carolina | 1168 | San Jose St | Warren Schutte, UNLV |
| 1992 | Arizona | Rick LaRose | 1129 | Arizona St | 1136 | New Mexico | Phil Mickelson, Arizona St |
| 1993 | Florida | Buddy Alexander | 1145 | Georgia Tech | 1146 | Kentucky | Todd Demsey, Arizona St |

## Men (Cont.)

### DIVISION I (Cont.)
### Results, 1939-1995 (Cont.)

| Year | Champion | Coach | Score | Runner-Up | Score | Host or Site | Individual Champion |
|---|---|---|---|---|---|---|---|
| 1994 ....Stanford | Wally Goodwin | 1129 | | Texas | 1133 | McKinney, TX | Justin Leonard, Texas |
| 1995 ....Oklahoma St* | Mike Holder | 1156 | | Stanford | 1156 | Ohio St | Chip Spratlin, Auburn |

*Won sudden death playoff. Notes: Match play, 1897-1964; par-70 tournaments held in 1969, 1973 and 1989; par-71 tournaments held in 1968, 1981 and 1988; all other championships par-72 tournaments. Scores are based on 4 rounds instead of 2 after 1967.

### DIVISION II

| Year | Champion | Year | Champion | Year | Champion |
|---|---|---|---|---|---|
| 1963 .........SW Missouri St | | 1974 .........Cal St-Northridge | | 1985 .........Florida Southern | |
| 1964 .........Southern Illinois | | 1975 .........UC-Irvine | | 1986 .........Florida Southern | |
| 1965 .........Middle Tennessee St | | 1976 .........Troy St | | 1987 .........Tampa | |
| 1966 .........Cal St-Chico | | 1977 .........Troy St | | 1988 .........Tampa | |
| 1967 .........Lamar | | 1978 .........Columbus | | 1989 .........Columbus | |
| 1968 .........Lamar | | 1979 .........UC-Davis | | 1990 .........Florida Southern | |
| 1969 .........Cal St-Northridge | | 1980 .........Columbus | | 1991 .........Florida Southern | |
| 1970 .........Rollins | | 1981 .........Florida Southern | | 1992 .........Columbus | |
| 1971 .........New Orleans | | 1982 .........Florida Southern | | 1993 .........Abilene Christian | |
| 1972 .........New Orleans | | 1983 .........SW Texas St | | 1994 .........Columbus | |
| 1973 .........Cal St-Northridge | | 1984 .........Troy St | | 1995 .........Florida Southern | |

### DIVISION III

| Year | Champion | Year | Champion | Year | Champion |
|---|---|---|---|---|---|
| 1975 .........Wooster | | 1982 .........Rampano | | 1989 .........Cal St-Stanislaus | |
| 1976 .........Cal St-Stanislaus | | 1983 .........Allegheny | | 1990 .........Methodist (NC) | |
| 1977 .........Cal St-Stanislaus | | 1984 .........Cal St-Stanislaus | | 1991 .........Methodist (NC) | |
| 1978 .........Cal St-Stanislaus | | 1985 .........Cal St-Stanislaus | | 1992 .........Methodist (NC) | |
| 1979 .........Cal St-Stanislaus | | 1986 .........Cal St-Stanislaus | | 1993 .........UC-San Diego | |
| 1980 .........Cal St-Stanislaus | | 1987 .........Cal St-Stanislaus | | 1994 .........UC-San Diego | |
| 1981 .........Cal St-Stanislaus | | 1988 .........Cal St-Stanislaus | | 1995 .........Methodist | |

Note: All championships par-72 except for 1986 and 1988, which were par-71; fourth round of 1975 championships canceled as a result of bad weather, first round of 1988 championships canceled as a result of rain.

## Women

| Year | Champion | Coach | Score | Runner-Up | Score | Individual Champion |
|---|---|---|---|---|---|---|
| 1982 .....Tulsa | Dale McNamara | 1191 | Texas Christian | 1227 | Kathy Baker, Tulsa |
| 1983 .....Texas Christian | Fred Warren | 1193 | Tulsa | 1196 | Penny Hammel, Miami (FL) |
| 1984 .....Miami (FL) | Lela Cannon | 1214 | Arizona St | 1221 | Cindy Schreyer, Georgia |
| 1985 .....Florida | Mimi Ryan | 1218 | Tulsa | 1233 | Danielle Ammaccapane, Arizona St |
| 1986 .....Florida | Mimi Ryan | 1180 | Miami (FL) | 1188 | Page Dunlap, Florida |
| 1987 .....San Jose St | Mark Gale | 1187 | Furman | 1188 | Caroline Keggi, New Mexico |
| 1988 .....Tulsa | Dale McNamara | 1175 | Georgia | 1182 | Melissa McNamara, Tulsa |
| | | | | Arizona | 1182 | |
| 1989 .....San Jose St | Mark Gale | 1208 | Tulsa | 1209 | Pat Hurst, San Jose St |
| 1990 .....Arizona St | Linda Vollstedt | 1206 | UCLA | 1222 | Susan Slaughter, Arizona |
| 1991 .....UCLA* | Jackie Steinmann | 1197 | San Jose St | 1197 | Annika Sorenstam, Arizona |
| 1992 .....San Jose St | Mark Gale | 1171 | Arizona | 1175 | Vicki Goetze, Georgia |
| 1993 .....Arizona St | Linda Vollstedt | 1187 | Texas | 1189 | Charlotta Sorenstam, Texas |
| 1994 .....Arizona St | Linda Vollstedt | 1189 | Southern Cal | 1205 | Emilee Klein, Arizona St |
| 1995 .....Arizona St | Linda Vollstedt | 1155 | San Jose St | 1181 | Kristel Mourgue d'Algue, Arizona St |

*Won sudden death playoff. Note: Par-74 tournaments held in 1983 and 1988; par-72 tournament held in 1990; all other championships par-73 tournaments.

# Gymnastics

## Men
## Team Champions

| Year | Champion | Coach | Pts | Runner-Up | Pts |
|------|----------|-------|-----|-----------|-----|
| 1938 | Chicago | Dan Hoffer | 22 | Illinois | 18 |
| 1939 | Illinois | Hartley Price | 21 | Army | 17 |
| 1940 | Illinois | Hartley Price | 20 | Navy | 17 |
| 1941 | Illinois | Hartley Price | 68.5 | Minnesota | 52.5 |
| 1942 | Illinois | Hartley Price | 39 | Penn St | 30 |
| 1943-47 | No tournament | | | | |
| 1948 | Penn St | Gene Wettstone | 55 | Temple | 34.5 |
| 1949 | Temple | Max Younger | 28 | Minnesota | 18 |
| 1950 | Illinois | Charley Pond | 26 | Temple | 25 |
| 1951 | Florida St | Hartley Price | 26 | Illinois | 23.5 |
| | | | | Southern Cal | 23.5 |
| 1952 | Florida St | Hartley Price | 89.5 | Southern Cal | 75 |
| 1953 | Penn St | Gene Wettstone | 91.5 | Illinois | 68 |
| 1954 | Penn St | Gene Wettstone | 137 | Illinois | 68 |
| 1955 | Illinois | Charley Pond | 82 | Penn St | 69 |
| 1956 | Illinois | Charley Pond | 123.5 | Penn St | 67.5 |
| 1957 | Penn St | Gene Wettstone | 88.5 | Illinois | 80 |
| 1958 | Michigan St | George Szypula | 79 | | |
| | Illinois | Charley Pond | 79 | | |
| 1959 | Penn St | Gene Wettstone | 152 | Illinois | 87.5 |
| 1960 | Penn St | Gene Wettstone | 112.5 | Southern Cal | 65.5 |
| 1961 | Penn St | Gene Wettstone | 88.5 | Southern Illinois | 80.5 |
| 1962 | Southern Cal | Jack Beckner | 95.5 | Southern Illinois | 75 |
| 1963 | Michigan | Newton Loken | 129 | Southern Illinois | 73 |
| 1964 | Southern Illinois | Bill Meade | 84.5 | Southern Cal | 69.5 |
| 1965 | Penn St | Gene Wettstone | 68.5 | Washington | 51.5 |
| 1966 | Southern Illinois | Bill Meade | 187.200 | California | 185.100 |
| 1967 | Southern Illinois | Bill Meade | 189.550 | Michigan | 187.400 |
| 1968 | California | Hal Frey | 188.250 | Southern Illinois | 188.150 |
| 1969 | Iowa | Mike Jacobson | 161.175 | Penn St | 160.450 |
| | Michigan* | Newton Loken | | Colorado St | |
| 1970 | Michigan | Newton Loken | 164.150 | Iowa St | 164.050 |
| | | | | New Mexico St | |
| 1971 | Iowa St | Ed Gagnier | 319.075 | Southern Illinois | 316.650 |
| 1972 | Southern Illinois | Bill Meade | 315.925 | Iowa St | 312.325 |
| 1973 | Iowa St | Ed Gagnier | 325.150 | Penn St | 323.025 |
| 1974 | Iowa St | Ed Gagnier | 326.100 | Arizona St | 322.050 |
| 1975 | California | Hal Frey | 437.325 | Louisiana St | 433.700 |
| 1976 | Penn St | Gene Wettstone | 432.075 | Louisiana St | 425.125 |
| 1977 | Indiana St | Roger Counsil | 434.475 | | |
| | Oklahoma | Paul Ziert | 434.475 | | |
| 1978 | Oklahoma | Paul Ziert | 439.350 | Arizona St | 437.075 |
| 1979 | Nebraska | Francis Allen | 448.275 | Oklahoma | 446.625 |
| 1980 | Nebraska | Francis Allen | 563.300 | Iowa St | 557.650 |
| 1981 | Nebraska | Francis Allen | 284.600 | Oklahoma | 281.950 |
| 1982 | Nebraska | Francis Allen | 285.500 | UCLA | 281.050 |
| 1983 | Nebraska | Francis Allen | 287.800 | UCLA | 283.900 |
| 1984 | UCLA | Art Shurlock | 287.300 | Penn St | 281.250 |
| 1985 | Ohio St | Michael Willson | 285.350 | Nebraska | 284.550 |
| 1986 | Arizona St | Don Robinson | 283.900 | Nebraska | 283.600 |
| 1987 | UCLA | Art Shurlock | 285.300 | Nebraska | 284.750 |
| 1988 | Nebraska | Francis Allen | 288.150 | Illinois | 287.150 |
| 1989 | Illinois | Yoshi Hayasaki | 283.400 | Nebraska | 282.300 |
| 1990 | Nebraska | Francis Allen | 287.400 | Minnesota | 287.300 |
| 1991 | Oklahoma | Greg Buwick | 288.025 | Penn St | 285.500 |
| 1992 | Stanford | Sadao Hamada | 289.575 | Nebraska | 288.950 |
| 1993 | Stanford | Sadao Hamada | 276.500 | Nebraska | 275.500 |
| 1994 | Nebraska | Francis Allen | 288.250 | Stanford | 285.925 |
| 1995 | Stanford | Sadao Hamada | 232.400 | Nebraska | 231.525 |

*Trampoline.

## Men (Cont.)
## Individual Champions

### ALL-AROUND

1938 .....Joe Giallombardo, Illinois
1939 .....Joe Giallombardo, Illinois
1940 .....Joe Giallombardo, Illinois
Paul Fina, Illinois
1941 .....Courtney Shanken, Chicago
1942 .....Newt Loken, Minnesota
1948 .....Ray Sorenson, Penn St
1949 .....Joe Kotys, Kent
1950 .....Joe Kotys, Kent
1951 .....Bill Roetzheim, Florida St
1952 .....Jack Beckner, Southern Cal
1953 .....Jean Cronstedt, Penn St
1954 .....Jean Cronstedt, Penn St
1955 .....Karl Schwenzfeier, Penn St
1956 .....Don Tonry, Illlinois
1957 .....Armando Vega, Penn St
1958 .....Abie Grossfeld, Illinois
1959 .....Armando Vega, Penn St
1960 .....Jay Werner, Penn St
1961 .....Gregor Weiss, Penn St
1962 .....Robert Lynn, Southern Cal
1963 .....Gil Larose, Michigan
1964 .....Ron Barak, Southern Cal
1965 .....Mike Jacobson, Penn St
1966 .....Steve Cohen, Penn St
1967 .....Steve Cohen, Penn St
1968 .....Makoto Sakamoto, USC
1969 .....Mauno Nissinen, Wash
1970 .....Yoshi Hayasaki, Wash
1971 .....Yoshi Hayasaki, Wash
1972 .....Steve Hug, Stanford
1973 .....Steve Hug, Stanford
Marshall Avener, Penn St.
1974 .....Steve Hug, Stanford
1975 .....Wayne Young, BYU
1976    Peter Kormann, Southern
Conn St
1977 .....Kurt Thomas, Indiana St
1978 .....Bart Conner, Oklahoma
1979 .....Kurt Thomas, Indiana St
1980 .....Jim Hartung, Nebraska
1981 .....Jim Hartung, Nebraska
1982 .....Peter Vidmar, UCLA
1983 .....Peter Vidmar, UCLA
1984 .....Mitch Gaylord, UCLA
1985 .....Wes Suter, Nebraska
1986 .....Jon Louis, Stanford
1987 .....Tom Schlesinger, Nebraska
1988 .....Vacated†
1989 .....Patrick Kirsey, Nebraska
1990 .....Mike Racanelli, Ohio St
1991 .....John Roethlisberger, Minn
1992 .....John Roethlisberger, Minn
1993 .....John Roethlisberger, Minn
1994 .....Dennis Harrison, Nebraska
1995 .....Richard Grace, Nebraska

### HORIZONTAL BAR

1938 .....Bob Sears, Army
1939 .....Adam Walters, Temple
1940 .....Norm Boardman, Temple
1941 .....Newt Loken, Minnesota
1942 .....Norm Boardman, Temple
1948 .....Joe Calvetti, Illinois

1949 .....Bob Stout, Temple
1950 .....Joe Kotys, Kent
1951 .....Bill Roetzheim, Florida St
1952 .....Charles Simms, USC
1953 .....Hal Lewis, Navy
1954 .....Jean Cronstedt, Penn St
1955 .....Carlton Rintz, Michigan St
1956 .....Ronnie Amster, Florida St
1957 .....Abie Grossfeld, Illinois
1958 .....Abie Grossfeld, Illinois
1959 .....Stanley Tarshis, Mich St
1960 .....Stanley Tarshis, Mich St
1961 .....Bruno Klaus, Southern Ill
1962 .....Robert Lynn, USC
1963 .....Gil Larose, Michigan
1964 .....Ron Barak, USC
1965 .....Jim Curzi, Michigan St
Mike Jacobsen, Penn St
1966 .....Rusty Rock, Cal St-
Northridge
1967 .....Rich Grigsby, Cal St-
Northridge
1968 .....Makoto Sakamoto, USC
1969 .....Bob Manna, New Mexico
1970 .....Yoshi Hayasaki, Wash
1971 .....Brent Simmons, Iowa St
1972 .....Tom Lindner, Souhern Ill
1973 .....Jon Aitken, New Mexico
1974 .....Rick Banley, Indiana St
1975 .....Rich Larsen, Iowa St
1976 .....Tom Beach, California
1977 .....John Hart, UCLA
1978 .....Mel Cooley, Washington
1979 .....Kurt Thomas, Indiana St
1980 .....Philip Cahoy, Nebraska
1981 .....Philip Cahoy, Nebraska
1982 .....Peter Vidmar, UCLA
1983 .....Scott Johnson, Nebraska
1984 .....Charles Lakes, Illinois
1985 .....Dan Hayden, Arizona St
Wes Suter, Nebraska
1986 .....Dan Hayden, Arizona St
1987 .....David Moriel, UCLA
1988 .....Vacated†
1989 .....Vacated†
1990 .....Chris Waller, UCLA
1991 .....Luis Lopez, New Mexico
1992 .....Jair Lynch, Stanford
1993 .....Steve McCain, UCLA
1994 .....Jim Foody, UCLA
1995 .....Rick Kieffer, Nebraska

### PARALLEL BARS

1938 .....Erwin Beyer, Chicago
1939 .....Bob Sears, Army
1940 .....Bob Hanning, Minnesota
1941 .....Caton Cobb, Illinois
1942 .....Hal Zimmerman, Penn St
1948 .....Ray Sorenson, Penn St
1949 .....Joe Kotys, Kent
Mel Stout, Michigan St
1950 .....Joe Kotys, Kent
1951 .....Jack Beckner, USC
1952 .....Jack Beckner, USC
1953 .....Jean Cronstedt, Penn St
1954 .....Jean Cronstedt, Penn St

1955 .....Carlton Rintz, Michigan St
1956 .....Armando Vega, Penn St
1957 .....Armando Vega, Penn St
1958 .....Tad Muzyczko, Mich St
1959 .....Armando Vega, Penn St
1960 .....Robert Lynn, Southern Cal
1961 .....Fred Tijerina, Southern Ill
Jeff Cardinalli, Springfield
1962 .....Robert Lynn, Southern Cal
1963 .....Arno Lascari, Michigan
1964 .....Ron Barak, Southern Cal
1965 .....Jim Curzi, Michigan St
1966 .....Jim Curzi, Michigan St
1967 .....Makoto Sakamoto, USC
1968 .....Makoto Sakamoto, USC
1969 .....Ron Rapper, Michigan
1970 .....Ron Rapper, Michigan
1971 .....Brent Simmons, Iowa St
Tom Dunn, Penn St
1972 .....Dennis Mazur, Iowa St
1973 .....Steve Hug, Stanford
1974 .....Steve Hug, Stanford
1975 .....Yoichi Tomita, Long
Beach St
1976 .....Gene Whelan, Penn St
1977 .....Kurt Thomas, Indiana St
1978 .....John Corritore, Michigan
1979 .....Kurt Thomas, Indiana St
1980 .....Philip Cahoy, Nebraska
1981 .....Philip Cahoy, Nebraska
Peter Vidmar, UCLA
Jim Hartung, Nebraska
1982 .....Jim Hartung, Nebraska
1983 .....Scott Johnson, Nebraska
1984 .....Tim Daggett, UCLA
1985 .....Dan Hayden, Arizona St
Noah Riskin, Ohio St
Seth Riskin, Ohio St
1986 .....Dan Hayden, Arizona St
1987 .....Kevin Davis, Nebraska
Tom Schlesinger, Nebraska
1988 .....Kevin Davis, Nebraska
1989 .....Vacated†
1990 .....Patrick Kirksey, Nebraska
1991 .....Scott Keswick, UCLA
John Roethlisberger, Minn
1992 .....Dom Minicucci, Temple
1993 .....Jair Lynch, Stanford
1994 .....Richard Grace, Nebraska
1995 .....Richard Grace, Nebraska

### VAULT

1938 .....Erwin Beyer, Chicago
1939 .....Marv Forman, Illinois
1940 .....Earl Shanken, Chicago
1941 .....Earl Shanken, Chicago
1942 .....Earl Shanken, Chicago
1948 .....Jim Peterson, Minnesota
1962 .....Bruno Klaus, Southern Ill
1963 .....Gil Larose, Michigan
1964 .....Sidney Oglesby, Syracuse
1965 .....Dan Millman, California
1966 .....Frank Schmitz, S Illinois
1967 .....Paul Mayer, S Illinois
1968 .....Bruce Colter, Cal St-Los
Angeles

## Men *(Cont.)*
### Individual Champions *(Cont.)*

| | | |
|---|---|---|
| 1969.....Dan Bowles, California | 1969.....Keith McCanless, Iowa | 1978.....Curt Austin, Iowa St |
|      Jack McCarthy, Illinois | 1970.....Russ Hoffman, Iowa St | 1979.....Mike Wilson, Oklahoma |
| 1970.....Doug Boger, Arizona |      John Russo, Wisconsin |      Bart Conner, Oklahoma |
| 1971.....Pat Mahoney, Cal St- | 1971.....Russ Hoffman, Iowa St | 1980.....Steve Elliott, Nebraska |
|      Northridge | 1972.....Russ Hoffman, Iowa St | 1981.....James Yuhashi, Oregon |
| 1972.....Gary Morava, Southern Ill | 1973.....Ed Slezak, Indiana St | 1982.....Steve Elliott, Nebraska |
| 1973.....John Crosby, S Conn St | 1974.....Ted Marcy, Stanford | 1983.....Scott Johnson, Nebraska |
| 1974.....Greg Goodhue, Oklahoma | 1975.....Ted Marcy, Stanford |      David Branch, Arizona St |
| 1975.....Tom Beach, California | 1976.....Ted Marcy, Stanford |      Donnie Hinton, Arizona St |
| 1976.....Sam Shaw, Cal St- | 1977.....Chuck Walter, New Mexico | 1984.....Kevin Ekburg, Northern Ill |
|      Fullerton | 1978.....Mike Burke, Northern Ill | 1985.....Wes Suter, Nebraska |
| 1977.....Steve Wejmar, Wash | 1979.....Mike Burke, Northern Ill | 1986.....Jerry Burrell, Arizona St |
| 1978......Ron Galimore, Louisiana St | 1980.....David Stoldt, Illinois |      Brian Ginsberg, UCLA |
| 1979.....Leslie Moore, Oklahoma | 1981.....Mark Bergman, California | 1987.....Chad Fox, New Mexico |
| 1980.....Ron Galimore, Iowa St |      Steve Jennings, New Mexico | 1988.....Chris Wyatt, Temple |
| 1981.....Ron Galimore, Iowa St | 1982.....Peter Vidmar, UCLA | 1989.....Jody Newman, Arizona St |
| 1982.....Randall Wickstrom, Cal |      Steve Jennings, New Mexico | 1990.....Mike Racanelli, Ohio St |
|      Steve Elliott, Nebraska | 1983.....Doug Kieso, Northern Ill | 1991.....Brad Hayashi, UCLA |
| 1983.....Chris Riegel, Nebraska | 1984.....Tim Daggett, UCLA | 1992.....Brian Winkler, Michigan |
|      Mark Oates, Oklahoma | 1985.....Tony Pineda, UCLA | 1993.....Richard Grace, Nebraska |
| 1984.....Chris Riegel, Nebraska | 1986.....Curtis Holdsworth, UCLA | 1994.....Mark Booth, Stanford |
| 1985.....Derrick Cornelius, | 1987.....Li Xiao Ping, Cal St- | 1995.....Jay Thornton, Iowa |
|      Cortland St |      Fullerton | **RINGS** |
| 1986.....Chad Fox, New Mexico | 1988.....Vacated† | 1959.....Armando Vega, Penn St |
| 1987.....Chad Fox, New Mexico |      Mark Sohn, Penn St | 1960.....Sam Garcia, Southern Cal |
| 1988.....Chad Fox, New Mexico | 1989.....Mark Sohn, Penn St | 1961.....Fred Orlofsky, Southern Ill |
| 1989.....Chad Fox, New Mexico |      Chris Waller, UCLA | 1962.....Dale Cooper, Michigan St |
| 1990.....Brad Hayashi, UCLA | 1990.....Mark Sohn, Penn St | 1963.....Dale Cooper, Michigan St |
| 1991.....Adam Carton, Penn St | 1991.....Mark Sohn, Penn St | 1964.....Chris Evans, Arizona St |
| 1992.....Jason Hebert, Syracuse | 1992.....Che Bowers, Nebraska | 1965.....Glenn Gailis, Iowa |
| 1993.....Steve Wiegel, N Mexico | 1993.....John Roethlisberger, Minn | 1966.....Ed Gunny, Michigan St |
| 1994.....Steve McCain, UCLA | 1994.....Jason Bertram, California | 1967.....Josh Robison, California |
| 1995.....Ian Bachrach, Stanford | 1995.....Drew Durbin, Ohio St | 1968.....Pat Arnold, Arizona |
| **POMMEL HORSE** | **FLOOR EXERCISE** | 1969.....Paul Vexler, Penn St |
| 1938.....Erwin Beyer, Chicago | 1941.....Lou Fina, Illinois |      Ward Maythaler, Iowa St |
| 1939.....Erwin Beyer, Chicago | 1953.....Bob Sullivan, Illinois | 1970.....Dave Seal, Indiana St |
| 1940.....Harry Koehnemann, Illinois | 1954.....Jean Cronstedt, Penn St | 1971.....Charles Ropiequet, S Illinois |
| 1941.....Caton Cobb, Illinois | 1955.....Don Faber, UCLA | 1972.....Dave Seal, Indiana St |
| 1942.....Caton Cobb, Illinois | 1956.....Jamile Ashmore, Florida St | 1973.....Bob Mahorney, Indiana St |
| 1948.....Steve Greene, Penn St | 1957.....Norman Marks, Cal St- | 1974.....Keith Heaver, Iowa St |
| 1949.....Joe Berenato, Temple |      Los Angeles | 1975.....Keith Heaver, Iowa St |
| 1950.....Gene Rabbitt, Syracuse | 1958.....Abie Grossfeld, Illinois | 1976.....Doug Wood, Iowa St |
| 1951.....Joe Kotys, Kent | 1959.....Don Tonry, Illinois | 1977.....Doug Wood, Iowa St |
| 1952.....Frank Bare, Illinois | 1960.....Ray Hadley, Illinois | 1978.....Scott McEldowney, Oregon |
| 1953.....Carlton Rintz, Michigan St | 1961.....Robert Lynn, Southern Cal | 1979.....Kirk Mango, Northern Ill |
| 1954.....Robert Lawrence, Penn St | 1962.....Robert Lynn, Southern Cal | 1980.....Jim Hartung, Nebraska |
| 1955.....Carlton Rintz, Michigan St | 1963.....Tom Seward, Penn St | 1981.....Jim Hartung, Nebraska |
| 1956.....James Brown, Cal St- |      Mike Henderson, Michigan | 1982.....Jim Hartung, Nebraska |
|      Los Angeles | 1964.....Rusty Mitchell, S Illinois | 1983.....Alex Schwartz, UCLA |
| 1957.....John Davis, Illinois | 1965.....Frank Schmitz, S Illinois | 1984.....Tim Daggett, UCLA |
| 1958.....Bill Buck, Iowa | 1966.....Frank Schmitz, S Illinois | 1985.....Mark Diab, Iowa St |
| 1959.....Art Shurlock, California | 1967.....Dave Jacobs, Michigan | 1986.....Mark Diab, Iowa St |
| 1960.....James Fairchild, California | 1968.....Toby Towson, Michigan St | 1987.....Paul O'Neill, Houst Baptist |
| 1961.....James Fairchild, California | 1969.....Toby Towson, Michigan St | 1988.....Paul O'Neill, New Mexico |
| 1962.....Mike Aufrecht, Illinois | 1970.....Tom Proulx, Colorado St | 1989.....Vacated† |
| 1963.....Russ Mills, Yale | 1971.....Stormy Eaton, New Mexico |      Paul O'Neill, New Mexico |
| 1964.....Russ Mills, Yale | 1972.....Odessa Lovin, Oklahoma | 1990.....Wayne Cowden, Penn St |
| 1965.....Bob Elsinger, Springfield | 1973.....Odessa Lovin, Oklahoma | 1991.....Adam Carton, Penn St |
| 1966.....Gary Hoskins, Cal St- | 1974.....Doug Fitzjarrell, Iowa St | 1992.....Scott Keswick, UCLA |
|      Los Angeles | 1975.....Kent Brown, Arizona St | 1993.....Chris LaMorte, N Mexico |
| 1967.....Keith McCanless, Iowa | 1976.....Bob Robbins, Colorado St | 1994.....Chris LaMorte, N Mexico |
| 1968.....Jack Ryan, Colorado | 1977......Ron Galimore, Louisiana St | 1995.....Dave Frank, Temple |

† Championships won by Miguel Rubio (All Around, 1988; Horizontal Bar, 1988-89) and Alfonso Rodriguez (Pommel Horse, 1988; Rings, 1989; Parallel Bars, 1989) were vacated by action of the NCAA Committee on Infractions.

## Men *(Cont.)*

### DIVISION II (DISCONTINUED)

| Year | Champion | Coach | Pts | Runner-Up | Pts |
|------|----------|-------|-----|-----------|-----|
| 1968 | Cal St-Northridge | Bill Vincent | 179.400 | Springfield | 178.050 |
| 1969 | Cal St-Northridge | Bill Vincent | 151.800 | Southern Connecticut St | 145.075 |
| 1970 | Northwestern Louisiana | Armando Vega | 160.250 | Southern Connecticut St | 159.300 |
| 1971 | Cal St-Fullerton | Dick Wolfe | 158.150 | Springfield | 156.987 |
| 1972 | Cal St-Fullerton | Dick Wolfe | 160.550 | Southern Connecticut St | 153.050 |
| 1973 | Southern Connecticut St | Abe Grossfeld | 160.750 | Cal St-Northridge | 158.700 |
| 1974 | Cal St-Fullerton | Dick Wolfe | 309.800 | Southern Connecticut St | 309.400 |
| 1975 | Southern Connecticut St | Abe Grossfeld | 411.650 | IL-Chicago | 398.800 |
| 1976 | Southern Connecticut St | Abe Grossfeld | 419.200 | IL-Chicago | 388.850 |
| 1977 | Springfield | Frank Wolcott | 395.950 | Cal St-Northridge | 381.250 |
| 1978 | IL-Chicago | C. Johnson/A. Gentile | 406.850 | Cal St-Northridge | 400.400 |
| 1979 | IL-Chicago | Clarence Johnson | 418.550 | WI-Oshkosh | 385.650 |
| 1980 | WI-Oshkosh | Ken Allen | 260.550 | Cal St-Chico | 256.050 |
| 1981 | WI-Oshkosh | Ken Allen | 209.500 | Springfield | 201.550 |
| 1982 | WI-Oshkosh | Ken Allen | 216.050 | East Stroudsburg | 211.200 |
| 1983 | East Stroudsburg | Bruno Klaus | 258.650 | WI-Oshkosh | 257.850 |
| 1984 | East Stroudsburg | Bruno Klaus | 270.800 | Cortland St | 246.350 |

## Women
## Team Champions

| Year | Champion | Coach | Pts | Runner-Up | Pts |
|------|----------|-------|-----|-----------|-----|
| 1982 | Utah | Greg Marsden | 148.60 | Cal St-Fullerton | 144.10 |
| 1983 | Utah | Greg Marsden | 184.65 | Arizona St | 183.30 |
| 1984 | Utah | Greg Marsden | 186.05 | UCLA | 185.55 |
| 1985 | Utah | Greg Marsden | 188.35 | Arizona St | 186.60 |
| 1986 | Utah | Greg Marsden | 186.95 | Arizona St | 186.70 |
| 1987 | Georgia | Suzanne Yoculan | 187.90 | Utah | 187.55 |
| 1988 | Alabama | Sarah Patterson | 190.05 | Utah | 189.50 |
| 1989 | Georgia | Suzanne Yoculan | 192.65 | UCLA | 192.60 |
| 1990 | Utah | Greg Marsden | 194.900 | Alabama | 194.575 |
| 1991 | Alabama | Sarah Patterson | 195.125 | Utah | 194.375 |
| 1992 | Utah | Greg Marsden | 195.650 | Georgia | 194.600 |
| 1993 | Georgia | Suzanne Yoculan | 198.000 | Alabama | 196.825 |
| 1994 | Utah | Greg Marsden | 196.400 | Alabama | 196.350 |
| 1995 | Utah | Greg Marsden | 196.650 | Alabama | 196.425 |
|      |      |      |      | Michigan | 196.425 |

## Individual Champions

### ALL-AROUND

1982 ..... Sue Stednitz, Utah
1983 ..... Megan McCunniff, Utah
1984 ..... Megan McCunniff-Marsden, Utah
1985 ..... Penney Hauschild, Alabama
1986 ..... Penney Hauschild, Alabama
Jackie Brummer, Arizona St
1987 ..... Kelly Garrison-Steves, Oklahoma
1988 ..... Kelly Garrison-Steves, Oklahoma
1989 ..... Corrinne Wright, Georgia
1990 ..... Dee Dee Foster, Alabama
1991 ..... Hope Spivey, Georgia
1992 ..... Missy Marlowe, Utah
1993 ..... Jenny Hansen, Kentucky
1994 ..... Jenny Hansen, Kentucky
1995 ..... Jenny Hansen, Kentucky

### VAULT

1982 ..... Elaine Alfano, Utah
1983 ..... Elaine Alfano, Utah
1984 ..... Megan Marsden, Utah
1985 ..... Elaine Alfano, Utah
1986 ..... Kim Neal, Arizona St
Pam Loree, Penn St

1987 ..... Yumi Mordre, Washington
1988 ..... Jill Andrews, UCLA
1989 ..... Kim Hamilton, UCLA
1990 ..... Michele Bryant, Nebraska
1991 ..... Anna Basaldva, Arizona
1992 ..... Tammy Marshall, Massachusetts
Heather Stepp, Georgia
Kristein Kenoyer, Utah
1993 ..... Heather Stepp, Georgia
1994 ..... Jenny Hansen, Kentucky
1995 ..... Jenny Hansen, Kentucky

### BALANCE BEAM

1982 ..... Sue Stednitz, Utah
1983 ..... Julie Goewey, Cal St-Fullerton
1984 ..... Heidi Anderson, Oregon St
1985 ..... Lisa Zeis, Arizona St
1986 ..... Jackie Brummer, Arizona St
1987 ..... Yumi Mordre, Washington
1988 ..... Kelly Garrison-Steves, Oklahoma
1989 ..... Jill Andrews, UCLA
Joy Selig, Oregon St

1990 ..... Joy Selig, Oregon St
1991 ..... Missy Marlowe, Utah
1992 ..... Missy Marlowe, Utah
Dana Dobransky, Alabama
1993 ..... Dana Dobransky, Alabama
1994 ..... Jenny Hansen, Kentucky
1995 ..... Jenny Hansen, Kentucky

### FLOOR EXERCISE

1982 ..... Mary Ayotte-Law, Oregon St
1983 ..... Kim Neal, Arizona St
1984 ..... Maria Anz, Florida
1985 ..... Lisa Mitzel, Utah
1986 ..... Lisa Zeis, Arizona St
Penney Hauschild, Alabama
1987 ..... Kim Hamilton, UCLA
1988 ..... Kim Hamilton, UCLA
1989 ..... Corrinne Wright, Georgia
Kim Hamilton, UCLA
1990 ..... Joy Selig, Oregon St
1991 ..... Hope Spivey, Georgia
1992 ..... Missy Marlowe, Utah
1993 ..... Heather Stepp, Georgia
Tammy Marshall, UMass
Amy Durham, Oregon St

## Women *(Cont.)*
### Individual Champions *(Cont.)*

1994 .....Hope Spivey-Sheeley,
　　　　Georgia
1995 .....Jenny Hansen, Kentucky
　　　　Stella Umeh, UCLA
　　　　Leslie Angeles, Georgia

**UNEVEN BARS**

1982 .....Lisa Shirk, Pittsburgh
1983 .....Jeri Cameron, Arizona St
1984 .....Jackie Brummer,
　　　　Arizona St

1985 .....Penney Hauschild,
　　　　Alabama
1986 .....Lucy Wener, Georgia
1987 .....Lucy Wener, Georgia
1988 .....Kelly Garrison-Steves,
　　　　Oklahoma
1989 .....Lucy Wener, Georgia
1990 .....Marie Roethlisberger,
　　　　Minnesota
1991 .....Kelly Macy, Georgia

1992 .....Missy Marlowe, Utah
1993 .....Agina Simpkins, Georgia
　　　　Beth Wymer, Michigan
1994 .....Sandy Woolsey, Utah
　　　　Beth Wymer, Michigan
　　　　Lori Strong, Georgia
1995 .....Beth Wymer, Michigan

### DIVISION II *(DISCONTINUED)*

| Year | Champion | Coach | Pts | Runner-Up | Pts |
|------|----------|-------|-----|-----------|-----|
| 1982 | Cal St-Northridge | Donna Stuart | 138.10 | Jacksonville St | 134.05 |
| 1983 | Denver | Dan Garcia | 174.80 | Cal St-Northridge | 174.35 |
| 1984 | Jacksonville St | Robert Dillard | 173.40 | SE Missouri St | 171.45 |
| 1985 | Jacksonville St | Robert Dillard | 176.85 | SE Missouri St | 173.95 |
| 1986 | Seattle Pacific | Laurel Tindall | 175.80 | Jacksonville St | 175.15 |

# Ice Hockey

## DIVISION I

| Year | Champion | Coach | Score | Runner-Up | Most Outstanding Player |
|------|----------|-------|-------|-----------|-------------------------|
| 1948 | Michigan | Vic Heyliger | 8-4 | Dartmouth | Joe Riley, Dartmouth, F |
| 1949 | Boston Col | John Kelley | 4-3 | Dartmouth | Dick Desmond, Dartmouth, G |
| 1950 | Colorado Col | Cheddy Thompson | 13-4 | Boston U | Ralph Bevins, Boston U, G |
| 1951 | Michigan | Vic Heyliger | 7-1 | Brown | Ed Whiston, Brown, G |
| 1952 | Michigan | Vic Heyliger | 4-1 | Colorado Col | Kenneth Kinsley, Colorado Col, G |
| 1953 | Michigan | Vic Heyliger | 7-3 | Minnesota | John Matchefts, Michigan, F |
| 1954 | Rensselaer | Ned Harkness | 5-4 (OT) | Minnesota | Abbie Moore, Rensselaer, F |
| 1955 | Michigan | Vic Heyliger | 5-3 | Colorado Col | Philip Hilton, Colorado Col, D |
| 1956 | Michigan | Vic Heyliger | 7-5 | Michigan Tech | Lorne Howes, Michigan, G |
| 1957 | Colorado Col | Thomas Bedecki | 13-6 | Michigan | Bob McCusker, Colorado Col, F |
| 1958 | Denver | Murray Armstrong | 6-2 | N Dakota | Murray Massier, Denver, F |
| 1959 | N Dakota | Bob May | 4-3 (OT) | Michigan St | Reg Morelli, N Dakota, F |
| 1960 | Denver | Murray Armstrong | 5-3 | Michigan Tech | Bob Marquis, Boston U, F |
| 1961 | Denver | Murray Armstrong | 12-2 | St Lawrence | Barry Urbanski, Boston U, G |
| 1962 | Michigan Tech | John MacInnes | 7-1 | Clarkson | Louis Angotti, Michigan Tech, F |
| 1963 | N Dakota | Barney Thorndycraft | 6-5 | Denver | Al McLean, N Dakota, F |
| 1964 | Michigan | Allen Renfrew | 6-3 | Denver | Bob Gray, Michigan, G |
| 1965 | Michigan Tech | John MacInnes | 8-2 | Boston Col | Gary Milroy, Michigan Tech, F |
| 1966 | Michigan St | Amo Bessone | 6-1 | Clarkson | Gaye Cooley, Michigan St, G |
| 1967 | Cornell | Ned Harkness | 4-1 | Boston U | Walt Stanowski, Cornell, D |
| 1968 | Denver | Murray Armstrong | 4-0 | N Dakota | Gerry Powers, Denver, G |
| 1969 | Denver | Murray Armstrong | 4-3 | Cornell | Keith Magnuson, Denver, D |
| 1970 | Cornell | Ned Harkness | 6-4 | Clarkson | Daniel Lodboa, Cornell, D |
| 1971 | Boston U | Jack Kelley | 4-2 | Minnesota | Dan Brady, Boston U, G |
| 1972 | Boston U | Jack Kelley | 4-0 | Cornell | Tim Regan, Boston U, G |
| 1973 | Wisconsin | Bob Johnson | 4-2 | Vacated | Dean Talafous, Wisconsin, F |
| 1974 | Minnesota | Herb Brooks | 4-2 | Michigan Tech | Brad Shelstad, Minnesota, G |
| 1975 | Michigan Tech | John MacInnes | 6-1 | Minnesota | Jim Warden, Michigan Tech, G |
| 1976 | Minnesota | Herb Brooks | 6-4 | Michigan Tech | Tom Vanelli, Minnesota, F |
| 1977 | Wisconsin | Bob Johnson | 6-5 (OT) | Michigan | Julian Baretta, Wisconsin, G |
| 1978 | Boston U | Jack Parker | 5-3 | Boston Col | Jack O'Callahan, Boston U, D |
| 1979 | Minnesota | Herb Brooks | 4-3 | N Dakota | Steve Janaszak, Minnesota, G |
| 1980 | N Dakota | John Gasparini | 5-2 | Northern Michigan | Doug Smail, N Dakota, F |
| 1981 | Wisconsin | Bob Johnson | 6-3 | Minnesota | Marc Behrend, Wisconsin, G |
| 1982 | N Dakota | John Gasparini | 5-2 | Wisconsin | Phil Sykes, N Dakota, F |
| 1983 | Wisconsin | Jeff Sauer | 6-2 | Harvard | Marc Behrend, Wisconsin, G |
| 1984 | Bowling Green | Jerry York | 5-4 (OT) | MN-Duluth | Gary Kruzich, Bowling Green, G |
| 1985 | Rensselaer | Mike Addesa | 2-1 | Providence | Chris Terreri, Providence, G |
| 1986 | Michigan St | Ron Mason | 6-5 | Harvard | Mike Donnelly, Michigan St, F |
| 1987 | N Dakota | John Gasparini | 5-3 | Michigan St | Tony Hrkac, N Dakota, F |

# Ice Hockey (Cont.)

## DIVISION I (Cont.)

| Year | Champion | Coach | Score | Runner-Up | Most Outstanding Player |
|------|----------|-------|-------|-----------|-------------------------|
| 1988 | Lake Superior St | Frank Anzalone | 4-3 (OT) | St Lawrence | Bruce Hoffort, Lake Superior St, G |
| 1989 | Harvard | Bill Cleary | 4-3 (OT) | Minnesota | Ted Donato, Harvard, F |
| 1990 | Wisconsin | Jeff Sauer | 7-3 | Colgate | Chris Tancill, Wisconsin, F |
| 1991 | N Michigan | Rick Comley | 8-7 (3OT) | Boston U | Scott Beattie, N Michigan, F |
| 1992 | Lake Superior St | Jeff Jackson | 4-2 | Wisconsin | Paul Constantin, Lake Superior St, F |
| 1993 | Maine | Shawn Walsh | 5-4 | Lake Superior St | Jim Montgomery, Maine, F |
| 1994 | Lake Superior St | Jeff Jackson | 9-1 | Boston U | Sean Tallaire, Lake Superior St, F |
| 1995 | Boston U | Jack Parker | 6-2 | Maine | Chris O'Sullivan, Boston U, F |

## DIVISION II (DISCONTINUED, THEN RENEWED)

| Year | Champion | Coach | Score | Runner-Up |
|------|----------|-------|-------|-----------|
| 1978 | Merrimack | Thom Lawler | 12-2 | Lake Forest |
| 1979 | Lowell | Bill Riley Jr | 6-4 | Mankato St |
| 1980 | Mankato St | Don Brose | 5-2 | Elmira |
| 1981 | Lowell | Bill Riley Jr | 5-4 | Plattsburgh St |
| 1982 | Lowell | Bill Riley Jr | 6-1 | Plattsburgh St |
| 1983 | Rochester Inst | Brian Mason | 4-2 | Bemidji St |
| 1984 | Bemidji St | R.H. (Bob) Peters | 14-4* | Merrimack |
| 1993 | Bemidji St | R.H. (Bob) Peters | 15-6* | Mercyhurst |
| 1994 | Bemidji St | R.H. (Bob) Peters | 7-6* | AL-Huntsville |
| 1995 | Bemidji St | R.H. (Bob) Peters | 11-6* | Mercyhurst |

*Two-game, total-goal series.

## DIVISION III

| Year | Champion | Coach | Score | Runner-Up |
|------|----------|-------|-------|-----------|
| 1984 | Babson | Bob Riley | 8-0 | Union (NY) |
| 1985 | Rochester Inst | Bruce Delventhal | 5-1 | Bemidji St |
| 1986 | Bemidji St | R.H. (Bob) Peters | 8-5 | Vacated |
| 1987 | Vacated | | | Oswego St |
| 1988 | WI-River Falls | Rick Kozuback | 7-1, 3-5, 3-0 | Elmira |
| 1989 | WI-Stevens Point | Mark Mazzoleni | 3-3, 3-2 | Rochester Inst |
| 1990 | WI-Stevens Point | Mark Mazzoleni | 10-1, 3-6, 1-0 | Plattsburgh St |
| 1991 | WI-Stevens Point | Mark Mazzoleni | 6-2 | Mankato St |
| 1992 | Plattsburgh St | Bob Emery | 7-3 | WI-Stevens Point |
| 1993 | WI-Stevens Point | Joe Baldarotta | 4-3 | WI-River Falls |
| 1994 | WI-River Falls | Dean Talafous | 6-4 | WI-Superior |
| 1995 | Middlebury | Bill Beany | 1-0 | Fredonia St |

# Lacrosse

## Men

### DIVISION I

| Year | Champion | Coach | Score | Runner-Up |
|------|----------|-------|-------|-----------|
| 1971 | Cornell | Richie Moran | 12-6 | Maryland |
| 1972 | Virginia | Glenn Thiel | 13-12 | Johns Hopkins |
| 1973 | Maryland | Bud Beardmore | 10-9 (2 OT) | Johns Hopkins |
| 1974 | Johns Hopkins | Bob Scott | 17-12 | Maryland |
| 1975 | Maryland | Bud Beardmore | 20-13 | Navy |
| 1976 | Cornell | Richie Moran | 16-13 (OT) | Maryland |
| 1977 | Cornell | Richie Moran | 16-8 | Johns Hopkins |
| 1978 | Johns Hopkins | Henry Ciccarone | 13-8 | Cornell |
| 1979 | Johns Hopkins | Henry Ciccarone | 15-9 | Maryland |
| 1980 | Johns Hopkins | Henry Ciccarone | 9-8 (2 OT) | Virginia |
| 1981 | N Carolina | Willie Scroggs | 14-13 | Johns Hopkins |
| 1982 | N Carolina | Willie Scroggs | 7-5 | Johns Hopkins |
| 1983 | Syracuse | Roy Simmons Jr | 17-16 | Johns Hopkins |
| 1984 | Johns Hopkins | Don Zimmerman | 13-10 | Syracuse |
| 1985 | Johns Hopkins | Don Zimmerman | 11-4 | Syracuse |
| 1986 | N Carolina | Willie Scroggs | 10-9 (OT) | Virginia |
| 1987 | Johns Hopkins | Don Zimmerman | 11-10 | Cornell |
| 1988 | Syracuse | Roy Simmons Jr | 13-8 | Cornell |
| 1989 | Syracuse | Roy Simmons Jr | 13-12 | Johns Hopkins |
| 1990 | Syracuse | Roy Simmons Jr | 21-9 | Loyola (MD) |
| 1991 | N Carolina | Dave Klarmann | 18-13 | Towson St |

## Men (Cont.)

### DIVISION I (Cont.)

| Year | Champion | Coach | Score | Runner-Up |
|------|----------|-------|-------|-----------|
| 1992 | Princeton | Bill Tierney | 10-9 | Syracuse |
| 1993 | Syracuse | Roy Simmons Jr | 13-12 | N Carolina |
| 1994 | Princeton | Bill Tierney | 9-8 (OT) | Virginia |
| 1995 | Syracuse | Roy Simmons Jr | 13-9 | Maryland |

### DIVISION II (DISCONTINUED, THEN RENEWED)

| Year | Champion | Coach | Score | Runner-Up |
|------|----------|-------|-------|-----------|
| 1974 | Towson St | Carl Runk | 18-17 (OT) | Hobart |
| 1975 | Cortland St | Chuck Winters | 12-11 | Hobart |
| 1976 | Hobart | Jerry Schmidt | 18-9 | Adelphi |
| 1977 | Hobart | Jerry Schmidt | 23-13 | Washington (MD) |
| 1978 | Roanoke | Paul Griffin | 14-13 | Hobart |
| 1979 | Adelphi | Paul Doherty | 17-12 | MD-Baltimore County |
| 1980 | MD-Baltimore County | Dick Watts | 23-14 | Adelphi |
| 1981 | Adelphi | Paul Doherty | 17-14 | Loyola (MD) |
| 1993 | Adelphi | Kevin Sheehan | 11-7 | LIU-C.W. Post |
| 1994 | Springfield | Keith Bugbee | 15-12 | New York Tech |
| 1995 | Adelphi | Sandy Kapatos | 12-10 | Springfield |

### DIVISION III

| Year | Champion | Coach | Score | Runner-Up |
|------|----------|-------|-------|-----------|
| 1980 | Hobart | Dave Urick | 11-8 | Cortland St |
| 1981 | Hobart | Dave Urick | 10-8 | Cortland St |
| 1982 | Hobart | Dave Urick | 9-8 (OT) | Washington (MD) |
| 1983 | Hobart | Dave Urick | 13-9 | Roanoke |
| 1984 | Hobart | Dave Urick | 12-5 | Washington (MD) |
| 1985 | Hobart | Dave Urick | 15-8 | Washington (MD) |
| 1986 | Hobart | Dave Urick | 13-10 | Washington (MD) |
| 1987 | Hobart | Dave Urick | 9-5 | Ohio Wesleyan |
| 1988 | Hobart | Dave Urick | 18-9 | Ohio Wesleyan |
| 1989 | Hobart | Dave Urick | 11-8 | Ohio Wesleyan |
| 1990 | Hobart | B.J. O'Hara | 18-6 | Washington (MD) |
| 1991 | Hobart | B.J. O'Hara | 12-11 | Salisbury St |
| 1992 | Nazareth (NY) | Scott Nelson | 13-12 | Hobart |
| 1993 | Hobart | B.J. O'Hara | 16-10 | Ohio Wesleyan |
| 1994 | Salisbury St | Jim Berkman | 15-9 | Hobart |
| 1995 | Salisbury St | Jim Berkman | 22-13 | Nazareth |

## Women

### DIVISION I

| Year | Champion | Coach | Score | Runner-Up |
|------|----------|-------|-------|-----------|
| 1982 | Massachusetts | Pamela Hixon | 9-6 | Trenton St |
| 1983 | Delaware | Janet Smith | 10-7 | Temple |
| 1984 | Temple | Tina Sloan Green | 6-4 | Maryland |
| 1985 | New Hampshire | Marisa Didio | 6-5 | Maryland |
| 1986 | Maryland | Sue Tyler | 11-10 | Penn St |
| 1987 | Penn St | Susan Scheetz | 7-6 | Temple |
| 1988 | Temple | Tina Sloan Green | 15-7 | Penn St |
| 1989 | Penn St | Susan Scheetz | 7-6 | Harvard |
| 1990 | Harvard | Carole Kleinfelder | 8-7 | Maryland |
| 1991 | Virginia | Jane Miller | 8-6 | Maryland |
| 1992 | Maryland | Cindy Timchal | 11-10 | Harvard |
| 1993 | Virginia | Jane Miller | 8-6 (OT) | Princeton |
| 1994 | Princeton | Chris Sailer | 10-7 | Virginia |
| 1995 | Maryland | Cindy Timchal | 13-5 | Princeton |

### DIVISION III

| Year | Champion | Score | Runner-Up | Year | Champion | Score | Runner-Up |
|------|----------|-------|-----------|------|----------|-------|-----------|
| 1985 | Trenton St | 7-4 | Ursinus | 1991 | Trenton St | 7-6 | Ursinus |
| 1986 | Ursinus | 12-10 | Trenton St | 1992 | Trenton St | 5-3 | William Smith |
| 1987 | Trenton St | 8-7 (OT) | Ursinus | 1993 | Trenton St | 10-9 | William Smith |
| 1988 | Trenton St | 14-11 | William Smith | 1994 | Trenton St | 29-11 | William Smith |
| 1989 | Ursinus | 8-6 | Trenton St | 1995 | Trenton St | 14-13 | William Smith |
| 1990 | Ursinus | 7-6 | St Lawrence | | | | |

# Rifle

## Men's and Women's Combined

| Year | Champion | Coach | Score | Runner-Up | Score | Air Rifle | Smallbore |
|------|----------|-------|-------|-----------|-------|-----------|-----------|
| | | | | | | **Individual Champions** | |
| 1980 | Tennessee Tech | James Newkirk | 6201 | W Virginia | 6150 | Rod Fitz-Randolph, Tennessee Tech | Rod Fitz-Randolph, Tennessee Tech |
| 1981 | Tennessee Tech | James Newkirk | 6139 | W Virginia | 6136 | John Rost, W Virginia | Kurt Fitz-Randolph, Tennessee Tech |
| 1982 | Tennessee Tech | James Newkirk | 6138 | W Virginia | 6136 | John Rost, W Virginia | Kurt Fitz-Randolph, Tennessee Tech |
| 1983 | W Virginia | Edward Etzel | 6166 | Tennessee Tech | 6148 | Ray Slonena, Tennessee Tech | David Johnson, W Virginia |
| 1984 | W Virginia | Edward Etzel | 6206 | East Tennessee St | 6142 | Pat Spurgin, Murray St | Bob Broughton, W Virginia |
| 1985 | Murray St | Elvis Green | 6150 | W Virginia | 6149 | Christian Heller, W Virginia | Pat Spurgin, Murray St |
| 1986 | W Virginia | Edward Etzel | 6229 | Murray St | 6163 | Marianne Wallace, Murray St | Mike Anti, W Virginia |
| 1987 | Murray St | Elvis Green | 6205 | W Virginia | 6203 | Rob Harbison, TN-Martin | Web Wright, W Virginia |
| 1988 | W Virginia | Greg Perrine | 6192 | Murray St | 6183 | Deena Wigger, Murray St | Web Wright, W Virginia |
| 1989 | W Virginia | Edward Etzel | 6234 | S Florida | 6180 | Michelle Scarborough, S Florida | Deb Sinclair, AK-Fairbanks |
| 1990 | W Virginia | Marsha Beasley | 6205 | Navy | 6101 | Gary Hardy, W Virginia | Michelle Scarborough, S Florida |
| 1991 | W Virginia | Marsha Beasley | 6171 | Alaska-Fairbanks | 6110 | Ann Pfiffner, W Virginia | Soma Dutta, UTEP |
| 1991 | W Virginia | Marsha Beasley | 6171 | Alaska-Fairbanks | 6110 | Ann Pfiffner, W Virginia | Soma Dutta, UTEP |
| 1992 | W Virginia | Marsha Beasley | 6214 | Alaska-Fairbanks | 6166 | Ann Pfiffner, W Virginia | Tim Manges, W Virginia |
| 1993 | W Virginia | Marsha Beasley | 6179 | Alaska-Fairbanks | 6169 | Trevor Gathman, W Virginia | Eric Uptagrafft, W Virginia |
| 1994 | AK-Fairbanks | Randy Pitney | 6194 | W Virginia | 6187 | Nancy Napolski, Kentucky | Cory Brunetti, AK-Fairbanks |
| 1995 | W Virginia | Marsha Beasley | 6241 | Air Force | 6187 | Benji Belden, Murray St | Oleg Selezner, AK-Fairbanks |

# Skiing

## Men's and Women's Combined

| Year | Champion | Coach | Pts | Runner-Up | Pts | Host or Site |
|------|----------|-------|-----|-----------|-----|--------------|
| 1954 | Denver | Willy Schaeffler | 384.0 | Seattle | 349.6 | NV-Reno |
| 1955 | Denver | Willy Schaeffler | 567.05 | Dartmouth | 558.935 | Norwich |
| 1956 | Denver | Willy Schaeffler | 582.01 | Dartmouth | 541.77 | Winter Park |
| 1957 | Denver | Willy Schaeffler | 577.95 | Colorado | 545.29 | Ogden Snow Basin |
| 1958 | Dartmouth | Al Merrill | 561.2 | Denver | 550.6 | Dartmouth |
| 1959 | Colorado | Bob Beattie | 549.4 | Denver | 543.6 | Winter Park |
| 1960 | Colorado | Bob Beattie | 571.4 | Denver | 568.6 | Bridger Bowl |
| 1961 | Denver | Willy Schaeffler | 376.19 | Middlebury | 366.94 | Middlebury |
| 1962 | Denver | Willy Schaeffler | 390.08 | Colorado | 374.30 | Squaw Valley |
| 1963 | Denver | Willy Schaeffler | 384.6 | Colorado | 381.6 | Solitude |
| 1964 | Denver | Willy Schaeffler | 370.2 | Dartmouth | 368.8 | Franconia Notch |
| 1965 | Denver | Willy Schaeffler | 380.5 | Utah | 378.4 | Crystal Mountain |
| 1966 | Denver | Willy Schaeffler | 381.02 | Western Colorado | 365.92 | Crested Butte |
| 1967 | Denver | Willy Schaeffler | 376.7 | Wyoming | 375.9 | Sugarloaf Mountain |
| 1968 | Wyoming | John Cress | 383.9 | Denver | 376.2 | Mount Werner |
| 1969 | Denver | Willy Schaeffler | 388.6 | Dartmouth | 372.0 | Mount Werner |
| 1970 | Denver | Willy Schaeffler | 386.6 | Dartmouth | 378.8 | Cannon Mountain |
| 1971 | Denver | Peder Pytte | 394.7 | Colorado | 373.1 | Terry Peak |
| 1972 | Colorado | Bill Marolt | 385.3 | Denver | 380.1 | Winter Park |
| 1973 | Colorado | Bill Marolt | 381.89 | Wyoming | 377.83 | Middlebury |
| 1974 | Colorado | Bill Marolt | 176 | Wyoming | 162 | Jackson Hole |
| 1975 | Colorado | Bill Marolt | 183 | Vermont | 115 | Fort Lewis |
| 1976 | Colorado | Bill Marolt | 112 | | | Bates |
| | Dartmouth | Jim Page | 112 | | | |

# Skiing *(Cont.)*

| Year | Champion | Coach | Pts | Runner-Up | Pts | Host or Site |
|------|----------|-------|-----|-----------|-----|--------------|
| 1977 | Colorado | Bill Marolt | 179 | Wyoming | 154.5 | Winter Park |
| 1978 | Colorado | Bill Marolt | 152.5 | Wyoming | 121.5 | Cannon Mountain |
| 1979 | Colorado | Tim Hinderman | 153 | Utah | 130 | Steamboat Springs |
| 1980 | Vermont | Chip LaCasse | 171 | Utah | 151 | Lake Placid and Stowe |
| 1981 | Utah | Pat Miller | 183 | Vermont | 172 | Park City |
| 1982 | Colorado | Tim Hinderman | 461 | Vermont | 436.5 | Lake Placid |
| 1983 | Utah | Pat Miller | 696 | Vermont | 650 | Bozeman |
| 1984 | Utah | Pat Miller | 750.5 | Vermont | 684 | New Hampshire |
| 1985 | Wyoming | Tim Ameel | 764 | Utah | 744 | Bozeman |
| 1986 | Utah | Pat Miller | 612 | Vermont | 602 | Vermont |
| 1987 | Utah | Pat Miller | 710 | Vermont | 627 | Anchorage |
| 1988 | Utah | Pat Miller | 651 | Vermont | 614 | Middlebury |
| 1989 | Vermont | Chip LaCasse | 672 | Utah | 668 | Jackson Hole |
| 1990 | Vermont | Chip LaCasse | 671 | Utah | 571 | Vermont |
| 1991 | Colorado | Richard Rokos | 713 | Vermont | 682 | Park City |
| 1992 | Vermont | Chip LaCasse | 693.5 | New Mexico | 642.5 | New Hampshire |
| 1993 | Utah | Pat Miller | 783 | Vermont | 700.5 | Steamboat Springs |
| 1994 | Vermont | Chip LaCasse | 688 | Utah | 667 | Sugarloaf, ME |
| 1995 | Colorado | Richard Rokos | 720.5 | Utah | 711 | New Hampshire |

# Soccer

## Men

### DIVISION I

| Year | Champion | Coach | Score | Runner-Up |
|------|----------|-------|-------|-----------|
| 1959 | St Louis | Bob Guelker | 5-2 | Bridgeport |
| 1960 | St Louis | Bob Guelker | 3-2 | Maryland |
| 1961 | West Chester | Mel Lorback | 2-0 | St Louis |
| 1962 | St Louis | Bob Guelker | 4-3 | Maryland |
| 1963 | St Louis | Bob Guelker | 3-0 | Navy |
| 1964 | Navy | F. H. Warner | 1-0 | Michigan St |
| 1965 | St Louis | Bob Guelker | 1-0 | Michigan St |
| 1966 | San Francisco | Steve Negoesco | 5-2 | LIU-Brooklyn |
| 1967 | Michigan St | Gene Kenney | 0-0 | Game called |
|      | St Louis | Harry Keough | | due to inclement weather |
| 1968 | Maryland | Doyle Royal | 2-2 (2 OT) | |
|      | Michigan St | Gene Kenney | | |
| 1969 | St Louis | Harry Keough | 4-0 | San Francisco |
| 1970 | St Louis | Harry Keough | 1-0 | UCLA |
| 1971 | Vacated | | 3-2 | St Louis |
| 1972 | St Louis | Harry Keough | 4-2 | UCLA |
| 1973 | St Louis | Harry Keough | 2-1 (OT) | UCLA |
| 1974 | Howard | Lincoln Phillips | 2-1 (4 OT) | St Louis |
| 1975 | San Francisco | Steve Negoesco | 4-0 | SIU-Edwardsville |
| 1976 | San Francisco | Steve Negoesco | 1-0 | Indiana |
| 1977 | Hartwick | Jim Lennox | 2-1 | San Francisco |
| 1978 | Vacated | | 2-0 | Indiana |
| 1979 | SIU-Edwardsville | Bob Guelker | 3-2 | Clemson |
| 1980 | San Francisco | Steve Negoesco | 4-3 (OT) | Indiana |
| 1981 | Connecticut | Joe Morrone | 2-1 (OT) | Alabama A&M |
| 1982 | Indiana | Jerry Yeagley | 2-1 (8 OT) | Duke |
| 1983 | Indiana | Jerry Yeagley | 1-0 (2 OT) | Columbia |
| 1984 | Clemson | I. M. Ibrahim | 2-1 | Indiana |
| 1985 | UCLA | Sigi Schmid | 1-0 (8 OT) | American |
| 1986 | Duke | John Rennie | 1-0 | Akron |
| 1987 | Clemson | I. M. Ibrahim | 2-0 | San Diego St |
| 1988 | Indiana | Jerry Yeagley | 1-0 | Howard |
| 1989 | Santa Clara | Steve Sampson | 1-1 (2 OT) | |
|      | Virginia | Bruce Arena | | |
| 1990 | UCLA | Sigi Schmid | 1-0 (OT) | Rutgers |
| 1991 | Virginia | Bruce Arena | 0-0* | Santa Clara |
| 1992 | Virginia | Bruce Arena | 2-0 | San Diego |

*Under a rule passed in 1991, the NCAA determined that when a score is tied after regulation and overtime, and the championship is determined by penalty kicks, the official score will be 0-0.

## Men (Cont.)

### DIVISION I (Cont.)

| Year | Champion | Coach | Score | Runner-Up |
|------|----------|-------|-------|-----------|
| 1993 | Virginia | Bruce Arena | 2-0 | S Carolina |
| 1994 | Virginia | Bruce Arena | 1-0 | Indiana |

### DIVISION II

| Year | Champion | Year | Champion | Year | Champion |
|------|----------|------|----------|------|----------|
| 1972 | SIU-Edwardsville | 1980 | Lock Haven | 1988 | Florida Tech |
| 1973 | MO-St Louis | 1981 | Tampa | 1989 | New Hampshire Col |
| 1974 | Adelphi | 1982 | Florida Intl | 1990 | Southern Connecticut St |
| 1975 | Baltimore | 1983 | Seattle Pacific | 1991 | Florida Tech |
| 1976 | Loyola (MD) | 1984 | Florida Intl | 1992 | Southern Connecticut St |
| 1977 | Alabama A&M | 1985 | Seattle Pacific | 1993 | Seattle Pacific |
| 1978 | Seattle Pacific | 1986 | Seattle Pacific | 1994 | Tampa |
| 1979 | Alabama A&M | 1987 | Southern Connecticut St | | |

### DIVISION III

| Year | Champion | Year | Champion | Year | Champion |
|------|----------|------|----------|------|----------|
| 1974 | Brockport St | 1981 | Glassboro St | 1988 | UC-San Diego |
| 1975 | Babson | 1982 | NC-Greensboro | 1989 | Elizabethtown |
| 1976 | Brandeis | 1983 | NC-Greensboro | 1990 | Glassboro St |
| 1977 | Lock Haven | 1984 | Wheaton (IL) | 1991 | UC-San Diego |
| 1978 | Lock Haven | 1985 | NC-Greensboro | 1992 | Kean |
| 1979 | Babson | 1986 | NC-Greensboro | 1993 | UC-San Diego |
| 1980 | Babson | 1987 | NC Greensboro | 1994 | Bethany (WV) |

## Women

### DIVISION I

| Year | Champion | Coach | Score | Runner-Up |
|------|----------|-------|-------|-----------|
| 1982 | N Carolina | Anson Dorrance | 2-0 | Central Florida |
| 1983 | N Carolina | Anson Dorrance | 4-0 | George Mason |
| 1984 | N Carolina | Anson Dorrance | 2-0 | Connecticut |
| 1985 | George Mason | Hank Leung | 2-0 | N Carolina |
| 1986 | N Carolina | Anson Dorrance | 2-0 | Colorado Col |
| 1987 | N Carolina | Anson Dorrance | 1-0 | Massachusetts |
| 1988 | N Carolina | Anson Dorrance | 4-1 | N Carolina St |
| 1989 | N Carolina | Anson Dorrance | 2-0 | Colorado Col |
| 1990 | N Carolina | Anson Dorrance | 6-0 | Connecticut |
| 1991 | N Carolina | Anson Dorrance | 3-1 | Wisconsin |
| 1992 | N Carolina | Anson Dorrance | 9-1 | Duke |
| 1993 | N Carolina | Anson Dorrance | 6-0 | George Mason |
| 1994 | N Carolina | Anson Dorrance | 5-0 | Notre Dame |

### DIVISION II

| Year | Champion |
|------|----------|
| 1988 | Cal St-Hayward |
| 1989 | Barry |
| 1990 | Sonoma St |
| 1991 | Cal St-Dominguez Hills |
| 1992 | Barry |
| 1993 | Barry |
| 1994 | Franklin Pierce |

### DIVISION III

| Year | Champion |
|------|----------|
| 1986 | Rochester |
| 1987 | Rochester |
| 1988 | William Smith |
| 1989 | UC-San Diego |
| 1990 | Ithaca |
| 1991 | Ithaca |
| 1992 | Cortland St |
| 1993 | Trenton St |
| 1994 | Trenton St |

# Softball

### DIVISION I

| Year | Champion | Coach | Score | Runner-Up |
|------|----------|-------|-------|-----------|
| 1982 | UCLA* | Sharron Backus | 2-0† | Fresno St |
| 1983 | Texas A&M | Bob Brock | 2-0‡ | Cal St-Fullerton |
| 1984 | UCLA | Sharron Backus | 1-0# | Texas A&M |
| 1985 | UCLA | Sharron Backus | 2-1** | Nebraska |
| 1986 | Cal St-Fullerton* | Judi Garman | 3-0 | Texas A&M |

## DIVISION I (Cont.)

| Year | Champion | Coach | Score | Runner-Up |
|------|----------|-------|-------|-----------|
| 1987 | Texas A&M | Bob Brock | 4-1 | UCLA |
| 1988 | UCLA | Sharron Backus | 3-0 | Fresno St |
| 1989 | UCLA* | Sharron Backus | 1-0 | Fresno St |
| 1990 | UCLA | Sharron Backus | 2-0 | Fresno St |
| 1991 | Arizona | Mike Candrea | 5-1 | UCLA |
| 1992 | UCLA* | Sharron Backus | 2-0 | Arizona |
| 1993 | Arizona | Mike Candrea | 1-0 | UCLA |
| 1994 | Arizona | Mike Candrea | 4-0 | Cal St-Northridge |
| 1995 | UCLA* | Sharron Backus/ Sue Enquist | 4-2 | Arizona |

*Undefeated teams in final series. †8 innings. ‡12 innings. #13 innings. **9 innings.

## DIVISION II

| Year | Champion | Year | Champion | Year | Champion |
|------|----------|------|----------|------|----------|
| 1982 | Sam Houston St | 1987 | Cal St-Northridge | 1992 | Missouri Southern |
| 1983 | Cal St-Northridge | 1988 | Cal St-Bakersfield | 1993 | Florida Southern |
| 1984 | Cal St-Northridge | 1989 | Cal St-Bakersfield | 1994 | Merrimack |
| 1985 | Cal St-Northridge | 1990 | Cal St-Bakersfield | 1995 | Kennesaw St |
| 1986 | SF Austin St | 1991 | Augustana (SD) | | |

## DIVISION III

| Year | Champion | Year | Champion | Year | Champion |
|------|----------|------|----------|------|----------|
| 1982 | Sam Houston St | 1986 | Eastern Connecticut St | 1991 | Central (IA) |
| 1982 | Eastern Connecticut St* | 1987 | Trenton St* | 1992 | Trenton St |
| 1983 | Trenton St | 1988 | Central (IA) | 1993 | Central (IA) |
| 1984 | Buena Vista* | 1989 | Trenton St* | 1994 | Trenton St |
| 1985 | Eastern Connecticut St | 1990 | Eastern Connecticut St | 1995 | Chapman |

*Undefeated teams in final series.

# Swimming and Diving

## Men

### DIVISION I

| Year | Champion | Coach | Pts | Runner-Up | Pts |
|------|----------|-------|-----|-----------|-----|
| 1937 | Michigan | Matt Mann | 75 | Ohio St | 39 |
| 1938 | Michigan | Matt Mann | 46 | Ohio St | 45 |
| 1939 | Michigan | Matt Mann | 65 | Ohio St | 58 |
| 1940 | Michigan | Matt Mann | 45 | Yale | 42 |
| 1941 | Michigan | Matt Mann | 61 | Yale | 58 |
| 1942 | Yale | Robert J. H. Kiphuth | 71 | Michigan | 39 |
| 1943 | Ohio St | Mike Peppe | 81 | Michigan | 47 |
| 1944 | Yale | Robert J. H. Kiphuth | 39 | Michigan | 38 |
| 1945 | Ohio St | Mike Peppe | 56 | Michigan | 48 |
| 1946 | Ohio St | Mike Peppe | 61 | Michigan | 37 |
| 1947 | Ohio St | Mike Peppe | 66 | Michigan | 39 |
| 1948 | Michigan | Matt Mann | 44 | Ohio St | 41 |
| 1949 | Ohio St | Mike Peppe | 49 | Iowa | 35 |
| 1950 | Ohio St | Mike Peppe | 64 | Yale | 43 |
| 1951 | Yale | Robert J. H. Kiphuth | 81 | Michigan St | 60 |
| 1952 | Ohio St | Mike Peppe | 94 | Yale | 81 |
| 1953 | Yale | Robert J. H. Kiphuth | 96½ | Ohio St | 73½ |
| 1954 | Ohio St | Mike Peppe | 94 | Michigan | 67 |
| 1955 | Ohio St | Mike Peppe | 90 | Yale | 51 |
| | | | | Michigan | 51 |
| 1956 | Ohio St | Mike Peppe | 68 | Yale | 54 |
| 1957 | Michigan | Gus Stager | 69 | Yale | 61 |
| 1958 | Michigan | Gus Stager | 72 | Yale | 63 |
| 1959 | Michigan | Gus Stager | 137½ | Ohio St | 44 |
| 1960 | Southern Cal | Peter Daland | 87 | Michigan | 73 |
| 1961 | Michigan | Gus Stager | 85 | Southern Cal | 62 |
| 1962 | Ohio St | Mike Peppe | 92 | Southern Cal | 46 |
| 1963 | Southern Cal | Peter Daland | 81 | Yale | 77 |
| 1964 | Southern Cal | Peter Daland | 96 | Indiana | 91 |
| 1965 | Southern Cal | Peter Daland | 285 | Indiana | 278½ |
| 1966 | Southern Cal | Peter Daland | 302 | Indiana | 286 |

## Men *(Cont.)*

### DIVISION I *(Cont.)*

| Year | Champion | Coach | Pts | Runner-Up | Pts |
|------|----------|-------|-----|-----------|-----|
| 1967 | Stanford | Jim Gaughran | 275 | Southern Cal | 260 |
| 1968 | Indiana | James Counsilman | 346 | Yale | 253 |
| 1969 | Indiana | James Counsilman | 427 | Southern Cal | 306 |
| 1970 | Indiana | James Counsilman | 332 | Southern Cal | 235 |
| 1971 | Indiana | James Counsilman | 351 | Southern Cal | 260 |
| 1972 | Indiana | James Counsilman | 390 | Southern Cal | 371 |
| 1973 | Indiana | James Counsilman | 358 | Tennessee | 294 |
| 1974 | Southern Cal | Peter Daland | 339 | Indiana | 338 |
| 1975 | Southern Cal | Peter Daland | 344 | Indiana | 274 |
| 1976 | Southern Cal | Peter Daland | 398 | Tennessee | 237 |
| 1977 | Southern Cal | Peter Daland | 385 | Alabama | 204 |
| 1978 | Tennessee | Ray Bussard | 307 | Auburn | 185 |
| 1979 | California | Nort Thornton | 287 | Southern Cal | 227 |
| 1980 | California | Nort Thornton | 234 | Texas | 220 |
| 1981 | Texas | Eddie Reese | 259 | UCLA | 189 |
| 1982 | UCLA | Ron Ballatore | 219 | Texas | 210 |
| 1983 | Florida | Randy Reese | 238 | Southern Meth | 227 |
| 1984 | Florida | Randy Reese | 287½ | Texas | 277 |
| 1985 | Stanford | Skip Kenney | 403½ | Florida | 302 |
| 1986 | Stanford | Skip Kenney | 404 | California | 335 |
| 1987 | Stanford | Skip Kenney | 374 | Southern Cal | 296 |
| 1988 | Texas | Eddie Reese | 424 | Southern Cal | 369½ |
| 1989 | Texas | Eddie Reese | 475 | Stanford | 396 |
| 1990 | Texas | Eddie Reese | 506 | Southern Cal | 423 |
| 1991 | Texas | Eddie Reese | 476 | Stanford | 420 |
| 1992 | Stanford | Skip Kenney | 632 | Texas | 356 |
| 1993 | Stanford | Skip Kenney | 520½ | Michigan | 396 |
| 1994 | Stanford | Skip Kenney | 566½ | Texas | 445 |
| 1995 | Michigan | Jon Urbanchek | 561 | Stanford | 475 |

### DIVISION II

| Year | Champion | Year | Champion | Year | Champion |
|------|----------|------|----------|------|----------|
| 1963 | SW Missouri St | 1974 | Cal St-Chico | 1985 | Cal St-Northridge |
| 1964 | Bucknell | 1975 | Cal St-Northridge | 1986 | Cal St-Bakersfield |
| 1965 | San Diego St | 1976 | Cal St-Chico | 1987 | Cal St-Bakersfield |
| 1966 | San Diego St | 1977 | Cal St-Northridge | 1988 | Cal St-Bakersfield |
| 1967 | UC-Santa Barbara | 1978 | Cal St-Northridge | 1989 | Cal St-Bakersfield |
| 1968 | Long Beach St | 1979 | Cal St-Northridge | 1990 | Cal St-Bakersfield |
| 1969 | UC-Irvine | 1980 | Oakland (MI) | 1991 | Cal St-Bakersfield |
| 1970 | UC-Irvine | 1981 | Cal St-Northridge | 1992 | Cal St-Bakersfield |
| 1971 | UC-Irvine | 1982 | Cal St-Northridge | 1993 | Cal St-Bakersfield |
| 1972 | Eastern Michigan | 1983 | Cal St-Northridge | 1994 | Oakland (MI) |
| 1973 | Cal St-Chico | 1984 | Cal St-Northridge | 1995 | Oakland (MI) |

### DIVISION III

| Year | Champion | Year | Champion | Year | Champion |
|------|----------|------|----------|------|----------|
| 1975 | Cal St-Chico | 1982 | Kenyon | 1989 | Kenyon |
| 1976 | St Lawrence | 1983 | Kenyon | 1990 | Kenyon |
| 1977 | Johns Hopkins | 1984 | Kenyon | 1991 | Kenyon |
| 1978 | Johns Hopkins | 1985 | Kenyon | 1992 | Kenyon |
| 1979 | Johns Hopkins | 1986 | Kenyon | 1993 | Kenyon |
| 1980 | Kenyon | 1987 | Kenyon | 1994 | Kenyon |
| 1981 | Kenyon | 1988 | Kenyon | 1995 | Kenyon |

## Women

### DIVISION I

| Year | Champion | Coach | Pts | Runner-Up | Pts |
|------|----------|-------|-----|-----------|-----|
| 1982 | Florida | Randy Reese | 505 | Stanford | 383 |
| 1983 | Stanford | George Haines | 418½ | Florida | 389½ |
| 1984 | Texas | Richard Quick | 392 | Stanford | 324 |
| 1985 | Texas | Richard Quick | 643 | Florida | 400 |
| 1986 | Texas | Richard Quick | 633 | Florida | 586 |
| 1987 | Texas | Richard Quick | 648½ | Stanford | 631½ |
| 1988 | Texas | Richard Quick | 661 | Florida | 542½ |

### Women (Cont.)
#### DIVISION I (Cont.)

| Year | Champion | Coach | Pts | Runner-Up | Pts |
|------|----------|-------|-----|-----------|-----|
| 1989 | Stanford | Richard Quick | 610½ | Texas | 547 |
| 1990 | Texas | Mark Schubert | 632 | Stanford | 622½ |
| 1991 | Texas | Mark Schubert | 746 | Stanford | 653 |
| 1992 | Stanford | Richard Quick | 735½ | Texas | 651 |
| 1993 | Stanford | Richard Quick | 649½ | Florida | 421 |
| 1994 | Stanford | Richard Quick | 512 | Texas | 421 |
| 1995 | Stanford | Richard Quick | 497½ | Michigan | 478½ |

#### DIVISION II

| Year | Champion | Year | Champion | Year | Champion |
|------|----------|------|----------|------|----------|
| 1982 | Cal St-Northridge | 1987 | Cal St-Northridge | 1992 | Oakland (MI) |
| 1983 | Clarion | 1988 | Cal St-Northridge | 1993 | Oakland (MI) |
| 1984 | Clarion | 1989 | Cal St-Northridge | 1994 | Oakland (MI) |
| 1985 | S Florida | 1990 | Oakland (MI) | 1995 | Air Force |
| 1986 | Clarion | 1991 | Oakland (MI) | | |

#### DIVISION III

| Year | Champion | Year | Champion | Year | Champion |
|------|----------|------|----------|------|----------|
| 1982 | Williams | 1987 | Kenyon | 1992 | Kenyon |
| 1983 | Williams | 1988 | Kenyon | 1993 | Kenyon |
| 1984 | Kenyon | 1989 | Kenyon | 1994 | Kenyon |
| 1985 | Kenyon | 1990 | Kenyon | 1995 | Kenyon |
| 1986 | Kenyon | 1991 | Kenyon | | |

## Tennis

### Men
#### INDIVIDUAL CHAMPIONS 1883-1945

| Year | Champion | Year | Champion |
|------|----------|------|----------|
| 1883 | Joseph Clark, Harvard (spring) | 1914 | George Church, Princeton |
| 1883 | Howard Taylor, Harvard (fall) | 1915 | Richard Williams II, Harvard |
| 1884 | W. P. Knapp, Yale | 1916 | G. Colket Caner, Harvard |
| 1885 | W. P. Knapp, Yale | 1917-18 | No tournament |
| 1886 | G. M. Brinley, Trinity (CT) | 1919 | Charles Garland, Yale |
| 1887 | P. S. Sears, Harvard | 1920 | Lascelles Banks, Yale |
| 1888 | P. S. Sears, Harvard | 1921 | Philip Neer, Stanford |
| 1889 | R. P. Huntington, Jr, Yale | 1922 | Lucien Williams, Yale |
| 1890 | Fred Hovey, Harvard | 1923 | Carl Fischer, Philadelphia Osteo |
| 1891 | Fred Hovey, Harvard | 1924 | Wallace Scott, Washington |
| 1892 | William Larned, Cornell | 1925 | Edward Chandler, California |
| 1893 | Malcolm Chace, Brown | 1926 | Edward Chandler, California |
| 1894 | Malcolm Chace, Yale | 1927 | Wilmer Allison, Texas |
| 1895 | Malcolm Chace, Yale | 1928 | Julius Seligson, Lehigh |
| 1896 | Malcolm Whitman, Harvard | 1929 | Berkeley Bell, Texas |
| 1897 | S. G. Thompson, Princeton | 1930 | Clifford Sutter, Tulane |
| 1898 | Leo Ware, Harvard | 1931 | Keith Gledhill, Stanford |
| 1899 | Dwight Davis, Harvard | 1932 | Clifford Sutter, Tulane |
| 1900 | Raymond Little, Princeton | 1933 | Jack Tidball, UCLA |
| 1901 | Fred Alexander, Princeton | 1934 | Gene Mako, Southern Cal |
| 1902 | William Clothier, Harvard | 1935 | Wilbur Hess, Rice |
| 1903 | E. B. Dewhurst, Pennsylvania | 1936 | Ernest Sutter, Tulane |
| 1904 | Robert LeRoy, Columbia | 1937 | Ernest Sutter, Tulane |
| 1905 | E. B. Dewhurst, Pennsylvania | 1938 | Frank Guernsey, Rice |
| 1906 | Robert LeRoy, Columbia | 1939 | Frank Guernsey, Rice |
| 1907 | G. Peabody Gardner, Jr, Harvard | 1940 | Donald McNeil, Kenyon |
| 1908 | Nat Niles, Harvard | 1941 | Joseph Hunt, Navy |
| 1909 | Wallace Johnson, Pennsylvania | 1942 | Frederick Schroeder, Jr, Stanford |
| 1910 | R. A. Holden, Jr, Yale | 1943 | Pancho Segura, Miami (FL) |
| 1911 | E. H. Whitney, Harvard | 1944 | Pancho Segura, Miami (FL) |
| 1912 | George Church, Princeton | 1945 | Pancho Segura, Miami (FL) |
| 1913 | Richard Williams II, Harvard | | |

## Men (Cont.)
### DIVISION I

| Year | Champion | Coach | Pts | Runner-Up | Pts | Individual Champion |
|------|----------|-------|-----|-----------|-----|---------------------|
| 1946 | Southern Cal | William Moyle | 9 | William & Mary | 6 | Robert Falkenburg, Southern Cal |
| 1947 | William & Mary | Sharvey G. Umbeck | 10 | Rice | 4 | Gardner Larned, William & Mary |
| 1948 | William & Mary | Sharvey G. Umbeck | 6 | San Francisco | 5 | Harry Likas, San Francisco |
| 1949 | San Francisco | Norman Brooks | 7 | Rollins/Tulane/ Washington | 4 | Jack Tuero, Tulane |
| 1950 | UCLA | William Ackerman | 11 | California Southern Cal | 5 5 | Herbert Flam, UCLA |
| 1951 | Southern Cal | Louis Wheeler | 9 | Cincinnati | 7 | Tony Trabert, Cincinnati |
| 1952 | UCLA | J. D. Morgan | 11 | California Southern Cal | 5 5 | Hugh Stewart, Southern Cal |
| 1953 | UCLA | J. D. Morgan | 11 | California | 6 | Hamilton Richardson, Tulane |
| 1954 | UCLA | J. D. Morgan | 15 | Southern Cal | 10 | Hamilton Richardson, Tulane |
| 1955 | Southern Cal | George Toley | 12 | Texas | 7 | Jose Aguero, Tulane |
| 1956 | UCLA | J. D. Morgan | 15 | Southern Cal | 14 | Alejandro Olmedo, Southern Cal |
| 1957 | Michigan | William Murphy | 10 | Tulane | 9 | Barry MacKay, Michigan |
| 1958 | Southern Cal | George Toley | 13 | Stanford | 9 | Alejandro Olmedo, Southern Cal |
| 1959 | Notre Dame Tulane | Thomas Fallon Emmet Pare | 8 8 | | | Whitney Reed, San Jose St |
| 1960 | UCLA | J. D. Morgan | 18 | Southern Cal | 8 | Larry Nagler, UCLA |
| 1961 | UCLA | J. D. Morgan | 17 | Southern Cal | 16 | Allen Fox, UCLA |
| 1962 | Southern Cal | George Toley | 22 | UCLA | 12 | Rafael Osuna, Southern Cal |
| 1963 | Southern Cal | George Toley | 27 | UCLA | 19 | Dennis Ralston, Southern Cal |
| 1964 | Southern Cal | George Toley | 26 | UCLA | 25 | Dennis Ralston, Southern Cal |
| 1965 | UCLA | J. D. Morgan | 31 | Miami (FL) | 13 | Arthur Ashe, UCLA |
| 1966 | Southern Cal | George Toley | 27 | UCLA | 23 | Charles Pasarell, UCLA |
| 1967 | Southern Cal | George Toley | 28 | UCLA | 23 | Bob Lutz, Southern Cal |
| 1968 | Southern Cal | George Toley | 31 | Rice | 23 | Stan Smith, Southern Cal |
| 1969 | Southern Cal | George Toley | 35 | UCLA | 23 | Joaquin Loyo-Mayo, Southern Cal |
| 1970 | UCLA | Glenn Bassett | 26 | Trinity (TX) Rice | 22 22 | Jeff Borowiak, UCLA |
| 1971 | UCLA | Glenn Bassett | 35 | Trinity (TX) | 27 | Jimmy Connors, UCLA |
| 1972 | Trinity (TX) | Clarence Mabry | 36 | Stanford | 30 | Dick Stockton, Trinity (TX) |
| 1973 | Stanford | Dick Gould | 33 | Southern Cal | 28 | Alex Mayer, Stanford |
| 1974 | Stanford | Dick Gould | 30 | Southern Cal | 25 | John Whitlinger, Stanford |
| 1975 | UCLA | Glenn Bassett | 27 | Miami (FL) | 20 | Bill Martin, UCLA |
| 1976 | Southern Cal UCLA | George Toley Glenn Bassett | 21 21 | | | Bill Scanlon, Trinity (TX) |
| 1977 | Stanford | Dick Gould | | Trinity (TX) | | Matt Mitchell, Stanford |
| 1978 | Stanford | Dick Gould | | UCLA | | John McEnroe, Stanford |
| 1979 | UCLA | Glenn Bassett | | Trinity (TX) | | Kevin Curren, Texas |
| 1980 | Stanford | Dick Gould | | California | | Robert Van't Hof, Southern Cal |
| 1981 | Stanford | Dick Gould | | UCLA | | Tim Mayotte, Stanford |
| 1982 | UCLA | Glenn Bassett | | Pepperdine | | Mike Leach, Michigan |
| 1983 | Stanford | Dick Gould | | Southern Meth | | Greg Holmes, Utah |
| 1984 | UCLA | Glenn Bassett | | Stanford | | Mikael Pernfors, Georgia |
| 1985 | Georgia | Dan Magill | | UCLA | | Mikael Pernfors, Georgia |
| 1986 | Stanford | Dick Gould | | Pepperdine | | Dan Goldie, Stanford |
| 1987 | Georgia | Dan Magill | | UCLA | | Andrew Burrow, Miami (FL) |
| 1988 | Stanford | Dick Gould | | Louisiana St | | Robby Weiss, Pepperdine |
| 1989 | Stanford | Dick Gould | | Georgia | | Donni Leaycraft, Louisiana St |
| 1990 | Stanford | Dick Gould | | Tennessee | | Steve Bryan, Texas |
| 1991 | Southern Cal | Dick Leach | | Georgia | | Jared Palmer, Stanford |
| 1992 | Stanford | Dick Gould | | Notre Dame | | Alex O'Brien, Stanford |
| 1993 | Southern Cal | Dick Leach | | Georgia | | Chris Woodruff, Tennessee |
| 1994 | Southern Cal | Dick Leach | | Stanford | | Mark Merklein, Florida |
| 1995 | Stanford | Dick Gould | | Mississippi | | Sargis Sargsian, Arizona St |

Note: Prior to 1977, individual wins counted in the team's total points. In 1977, a dual-match single-elimination team championship was initiated, eliminating the point system.

### DIVISION II

| Year | Champion | Year | Champion | Year | Champion |
|------|----------|------|----------|------|----------|
| 1963 | Cal St-LA | 1967 | Long Beach St | 1971 | UC-Irvine |
| 1964 | Cal St-LA/ S Illinois | 1968 | Fresno St | 1972 | UC-Irvine/ Rollins |
| 1965 | Cal St-LA | 1969 | Cal St-Northridge | 1973 | UC-Irvine |
| 1966 | Rollins | 1970 | UC-Irvine | 1974 | San Diego |

## Men (Cont.)

### DIVISION II (Cont.)

| Year | Champion | Year | Champion | Year | Champion |
|------|----------|------|----------|------|----------|
| 1975 | UC-Irvine/ San Diego | 1982 | SIU-Edwardsville | 1989 | Hampton |
| 1976 | Hampton | 1983 | SIU-Edwardsville | 1990 | Cal Poly-SLO |
| 1977 | UC-Irvine | 1984 | SIU-Edwardsville | 1991 | Rollins |
| 1978 | SIU-Edwardsville | 1985 | Chapman | 1992 | UC-Davis |
| 1979 | SIU-Edwardsville | 1986 | Cal Poly-SLO | 1993 | Lander (SC) |
| 1980 | SIU-Edwardsville | 1987 | Chapman | 1994 | Lander (SC) |
| 1981 | SIU-Edwardsville | 1988 | Chapman | 1995 | Lander (SC) |

### DIVISION III

| Year | Champion | Year | Champion | Year | Champion |
|------|----------|------|----------|------|----------|
| 1976 | Kalamazoo | 1982 | Gustavus Adolphus | 1989 | UC-Santa Cruz |
| 1977 | Swarthmore | 1983 | Redlands | 1990 | Swarthmore |
| 1978 | Kalamazoo | 1984 | Redlands | 1991 | Kalamazoo |
| 1979 | Redlands | 1985 | Swarthmore | 1992 | Kalamazoo |
| 1980 | Gustavus Adolphus | 1986 | Kalamazoo | 1993 | Kalamazoo |
| 1981 | Claremont-M-S | 1987 | Kalamazoo | 1994 | Washington (MD) |
|  | Swarthmore | 1988 | Washington & Lee | 1995 | UC-Santa Cruz |

## Women

### DIVISION I

| Year | Champion | Coach | Runner-Up | Individual Champion |
|------|----------|-------|-----------|---------------------|
| 1982 | Stanford | Frank Brennan | UCLA | Alycia Moulton, Stanford |
| 1983 | Southern Cal | Dave Borelli | Trinity (TX) | Beth Herr, Southern Cal |
| 1984 | Stanford | Frank Brennan | Southern Cal | Lisa Spain, Georgia |
| 1985 | Southern Cal | Dave Borelli | Miami (FL) | Linda Gates, Stanford |
| 1986 | Stanford | Frank Brennan | Southern Cal | Patty Fendick, Stanford |
| 1987 | Stanford | Frank Brennan | Georgia | Patty Fendick, Stanford |
| 1988 | Stanford | Frank Brennan | Florida | Shaun Stafford, Florida |
| 1989 | Stanford | Frank Brennan | UCLA | Sandra Birch, Stanford |
| 1990 | Stanford | Frank Brennan | Florida | Debbie Graham, Stanford |
| 1991 | Stanford | Frank Brennan | UCLA | Sandra Birch, Stanford |
| 1992 | Florida | Andy Brandi | Texas | Lisa Raymond, Florida |
| 1993 | Texas | Jeff Moore | Stanford | Lisa Raymond, Florida |
| 1994 | Georgia | Jeff Wallace | Stanford | Angela Lettiere, Georgia |
| 1995 | Texas | Jeff Moore | Florida | Keri Phebus, UCLA |

### DIVISION II

| Year | Champion | Year | Champion | Year | Champion |
|------|----------|------|----------|------|----------|
| 1982 | Cal St-Northridge | 1987 | SIU-Edwardsville | 1992 | Cal Poly-Pomona |
| 1983 | TN-Chattanooga | 1988 | SIU-Edwardsville | 1993 | UC-Davis |
| 1984 | TN-Chattanooga | 1989 | SIU-Edwardsville | 1994 | N Florida |
| 1985 | TN-Chattanooga | 1990 | UC-Davis | 1995 | Armstrong St |
| 1986 | SIU-Edwardsville | 1991 | Cal Poly-Pomona |  |  |

### DIVISION III

| Year | Champion | Year | Champion | Year | Champion |
|------|----------|------|----------|------|----------|
| 1982 | Occidental | 1987 | UC-San Diego | 1992 | Pomona-Pitzer |
| 1983 | Principia | 1988 | Mary Washington | 1993 | Kenyon |
| 1984 | Davidson | 1989 | UC-San Diego | 1994 | UC San Diego |
| 1985 | UC-San Diego | 1990 | Gustavus Adolphus | 1995 | Kenyon |
| 1986 | Trenton St | 1991 | Mary Washington |  |  |

# Indoor Track and Field

## Men

### DIVISION I

| Year | Champion | Coach | Pts | Runner-Up | Pts |
|------|----------|-------|-----|-----------|-----|
| 1965 | Missouri | Tom Botts | 14 | Oklahoma St | 12 |
| 1966 | Kansas | Bob Timmons | 14 | Southern Cal | 13 |
| 1967 | Southern Cal | Vern Wolfe | 26 | Oklahoma | 17 |
| 1968 | Villanova | Jim Elliott | 35 | Southern Cal | 25 |
| 1969 | Kansas | Bob Timmons | 41½ | Villanova | 33 |
| 1970 | Kansas | Bob Timmons | 27½ | Villanova | 26 |

## Men (Cont.)

### DIVISION I (Cont.)

| Year | Champion | Coach | Pts | Runner-Up | Pts |
|------|----------|-------|-----|-----------|-----|
| 1971 | Villanova | Jim Elliott | 22 | UTEP | 19¼ |
| 1972 | Southern Cal | Vern Wolfe | 19 | Bowling Green/ Mich St | 18 |
| 1973 | Manhattan | Fred Dwyer | 18 | Kansas/Kent St/UTEP | 12 |
| 1974 | UTEP | Ted Banks | 19 | Colorado | 18 |
| 1975 | UTEP | Ted Banks | 36 | Kansas | 17½ |
| 1976 | UTEP | Ted Banks | 23 | Villanova | 15 |
| 1977 | Washington St | John Chaplin | 25½ | UTEP | 25 |
| 1978 | UTEP | Ted Banks | 44 | Auburn | 38 |
| 1979 | Villanova | Jim Elliott | 52 | UTEP | 51 |
| 1980 | UTEP | Ted Banks | 76 | Villanova | 42 |
| 1981 | UTEP | Ted Banks | 76 | Southern Meth | 51 |
| 1982 | UTEP | John Wedel | 67 | Arkansas | 30 |
| 1983 | Southern Meth | Ted McLaughlin | 43 | Villanova | 32 |
| 1984 | Arkansas | John McDonnell | 38 | Washington St | 28 |
| 1985 | Arkansas | John McDonnell | 70 | Tennessee | 29 |
| 1986 | Arkansas | John McDonnell | 49 | Villanova | 22 |
| 1987 | Arkansas | John McDonnell | 39 | Southern Meth | 31 |
| 1988 | Arkansas | John McDonnell | 34 | Illinois | 29 |
| 1989 | Arkansas | John McDonnell | 34 | Florida | 31 |
| 1990 | Arkansas | John McDonnell | 44 | Texas A&M | 36 |
| 1991 | Arkansas | John McDonnell | 34 | Georgetown | 27 |
| 1992 | Arkansas | John McDonnell | 53 | Clemson | 46 |
| 1993 | Arkansas | John McDonnell | 66 | Clemson | 30 |
| 1994 | Arkansas | John McDonnell | 83 | UTEP | 45 |
| 1995 | Arkansas | John McDonnell | 59 | GMU/Tennessee | 26 |

### DIVISION II

| Year | Champion | Year | Champion | Year | Champion |
|------|----------|------|----------|------|----------|
| 1985 | SE Missouri St | 1989 | St Augustine's | 1993 | Abilene Christian |
| 1987 | St Augustine's | 1990 | St Augustine's | 1994 | Abilene Christian |
| 1988 | Abilene Christian | 1991 | St Augustine's | 1995 | St Augustine's |
|  | St Augustine's | 1992 | St Augustine's |  |  |

### DIVISION III

| Year | Champion | Year | Champion | Year | Champion |
|------|----------|------|----------|------|----------|
| 1985 | St Thomas (MN) | 1989 | North Central | 1993 | WI-La Crosse |
| 1986 | Frostburg St | 1990 | Lincoln (PA) | 1994 | WI-La Crosse |
| 1987 | WI-La Crosse | 1991 | WI-La Crosse | 1995 | Lincoln (PA) |
| 1988 | WI-La Crosse | 1992 | WI-La Crosse |  |  |

## Women

### DIVISION I

| Year | Champion | Coach | Pts | Runner-Up | Pts |
|------|----------|-------|-----|-----------|-----|
| 1983 | Nebraska | Gary Pepin | 47 | Tennessee | 44 |
| 1984 | Nebraska | Gary Pepin | 59 | Tennessee | 48 |
| 1985 | Florida St | Gary Winckler | 34 | Texas | 32 |
| 1986 | Texas | Terry Crawford | 31 | Southern Cal | 26 |
| 1987 | Louisiana St | Loren Seagrave | 49 | Tennessee | 30 |
| 1988 | Texas | Terry Crawford | 71 | Villanova | 52 |
| 1989 | Louisiana St | Pat Henry | 61 | Villanova | 34 |
| 1990 | Texas | Terry Crawford | 50 | Wisconsin | 26 |
| 1991 | Louisiana St | Pat Henry | 48 | Texas | 39 |
| 1992 | Florida | Bev Kearney | 50 | Stanford | 26 |
| 1993 | Louisiana St | Pat Henry | 49 | Wisconsin | 44 |
| 1994 | Louisiana St | Pat Henry | 48 | Alabama | 29 |
| 1995 | Louisiana St | Pat Henry | 40 | UCLA | 37 |

### DIVISION II

| Year | Champion | Year | Champion | Year | Champion |
|------|----------|------|----------|------|----------|
| 1985 | St Augustine's | 1989 | Abilene Christian | 1993 | Abilene Christian |
| 1986 | not held | 1990 | Abilene Christian | 1994 | Abilene Christian |
| 1987 | St Augustine's | 1991 | Abilene Christian | 1995 | Abilene Christian |
| 1988 | Abilene Christian | 1992 | Alabama A&M |  |  |

### Women (Cont.)

#### DIVISION III

| Year | Champion | Year | Champion | Year | Champion |
|------|----------|------|----------|------|----------|
| 1985 | MA-Boston | 1989 | Christopher Newport | 1993 | Lincoln (PA) |
| 1986 | MA-Boston | 1990 | Christopher Newport | 1994 | WI-Oshkosh |
| 1987 | MA-Boston | 1991 | Cortland St | 1995 | WI-Oshkosh |
| 1988 | Christopher Newport | 1992 | Christopher Newport | | |

## Outdoor Track and Field

### Men

#### DIVISION I

| Year | Champion | Coach | Pts | Runner-Up | Pts |
|------|----------|-------|-----|-----------|-----|
| 1921 | Illinois | Harry Gill | 20† | Notre Dame | 16† |
| 1922 | California | Walter Christie | 28† | Penn St | 19† |
| 1923 | Michigan | Stephen Farrell | 29† | Mississippi St | 16 |
| 1924 | No meet | | | | |
| 1925 | Stanford* | R. L. Templeton | 31† | | |
| 1926 | Southern Cal* | Dean Cromwell | 27† | | |
| 1927 | Illinois* | Harry Gill | 35† | | |
| 1928 | Stanford | R. L. Templeton | 72 | Ohio St | 31 |
| 1929 | Ohio St | Frank Castleman | 50 | Washington | 42 |
| 1930 | Southern Cal | Dean Cromwell | 55† | Washington | 40 |
| 1931 | Southern Cal | Dean Cromwell | 77† | Ohio St | 31† |
| 1932 | Indiana | Billy Hayes | 56 | Ohio St | 49† |
| 1933 | Louisiana St | Bernie Moore | 58 | Southern Cal | 54 |
| 1934 | Stanford | R. L. Templeton | 63 | Southern Cal | 54† |
| 1935 | Southern Cal | Dean Cromwell | 74† | Ohio St | 40† |
| 1936 | Southern Cal | Dean Cromwell | 103† | Ohio St | 73 |
| 1937 | Southern Cal | Dean Cromwell | 62 | Stanford | 50 |
| 1938 | Southern Cal | Dean Cromwell | 67† | Stanford | 38 |
| 1939 | Southern Cal | Dean Cromwell | 86 | Stanford | 44† |
| 1940 | Southern Cal | Dean Cromwell | 47 | Stanford | 28† |
| 1941 | Southern Cal | Dean Cromwell | 81† | Indiana | 50 |
| 1942 | Southern Cal | Dean Cromwell | 85† | Ohio St | 44† |
| 1943 | Southern Cal | Dean Cromwell | 46 | California | 39 |
| 1944 | Illinois | Leo Johnson | 79 | Notre Dame | 43 |
| 1945 | Navy | E. J. Thomson | 62 | Illinois | 48† |
| 1946 | Illinois | Leo Johnson | 78 | Southern Cal | 42† |
| 1947 | Illinois | Leo Johnson | 59† | Southern Cal | 34† |
| 1948 | Minnesota | James Kelly | 46 | Southern Cal | 41† |
| 1949 | Southern Cal | Jess Hill | 55† | UCLA | 31 |
| 1950 | Southern Cal | Jess Hill | 49† | Stanford | 28 |
| 1951 | Southern Cal | Jess Mortenson | 56 | Cornell | 40 |
| 1952 | Southern Cal | Jess Mortenson | 66† | San Jose St | 24† |
| 1953 | Southern Cal | Jess Mortenson | 80 | Illinois | 41 |
| 1954 | Southern Cal | Jess Mortenson | 66† | Illinois | 31† |
| 1955 | Southern Cal | Jess Mortenson | 42 | UCLA | 34 |
| 1956 | UCLA | Elvin Drake | 55† | Kansas | 51 |
| 1957 | Villanova | James Elliott | 47 | California | 32 |
| 1958 | Southern Cal | Jess Mortenson | 48† | Kansas | 40† |
| 1959 | Kansas | Bill Easton | 73 | San Jose St | 48 |
| 1960 | Kansas | Bill Easton | 50 | Southern Cal | 37 |
| 1961 | Southern Cal | Jess Mortenson | 65 | Oregon | 47 |
| 1962 | Oregon | William Bowerman | 85 | Villanova | 40† |
| 1963 | Southern Cal | Vern Wolfe | 61 | Stanford | 42 |
| 1964 | Oregon | William Bowerman | 70 | San Jose St | 40 |
| 1965 | Oregon | William Bowerman | 32 | | |
| | Southern Cal | Vern Wolfe | 32 | | |
| 1966 | UCLA | Jim Bush | 81 | Brigham Young | 33 |
| 1967 | Southern Cal | Vern Wolfe | 86 | Oregon | 40 |
| 1968 | Southern Cal | Vern Wolfe | 58 | Washington St | 57 |
| 1969 | San Jose St | Bud Winter | 48 | Kansas | 45 |
| 1970 | Brigham Young | Clarence Robison | 35 | | |
| | Kansas | Bob Timmons | 35 | | |
| | Oregon | William Bowerman | 35 | | |

## Men (Cont.)

### DIVISION I (Cont.)

| Year | Champion | Coach | Pts | Runner-Up | Pts |
|------|----------|-------|-----|-----------|-----|
| 1971 | UCLA | Jim Bush | 52 | Southern Cal | 41 |
| 1972 | UCLA | Jim Bush | 82 | Southern Cal | 49 |
| 1973 | UCLA | Jim Bush | 56 | Oregon | 31 |
| 1974 | Tennessee | Stan Huntsman | 60 | UCLA | 56 |
| 1975 | UTEP | Ted Banks | 55 | UCLA | 42 |
| 1976 | Southern Cal | Vern Wolfe | 64 | UTEP | 44 |
| 1977 | Arizona St | Senon Castillo | 64 | UTEP | 50 |
| 1978 | UCLA/UTEP | Jim Bush/Ted Banks | 50 | | |
| 1979 | UTEP | Ted Banks | 64 | Villanova | 48 |
| 1980 | UTEP | Ted Banks | 69 | UCLA | 46 |
| 1981 | UTEP | Ted Banks | 70 | Southern Meth | 57 |
| 1982 | UTEP | John Wedel | 105 | Tennessee | 94 |
| 1983 | SMU | Ted McLaughlin | 104 | Tennessee | 102 |
| 1984 | Oregon | Bill Dellinger | 113 | Washington St | 94½ |
| 1985 | Arkansas | John McDonnell | 61 | Washington St | 46 |
| 1986 | Southern Meth | Ted McLaughlin | 53 | Washington St | 52 |
| 1987 | UCLA | Bob Larsen | 81 | Texas | 28 |
| 1988 | UCLA | Bob Larsen | 82 | Texas | 41 |
| 1989 | Louisiana St | Pat Henry | 53 | Texas A&M | 51 |
| 1990 | Louisiana St | Pat Henry | 44 | Arkansas | 36 |
| 1991 | Tennessee | Doug Brown | 51 | Washington St | 42 |
| 1992 | Arkansas | John McDonnell | 60 | Tennessee | 46½ |
| 1993 | Arkansas | John McDonnell | 69 | LSU/Ohio St | 45 |
| 1994 | Arkansas | John McDonnell | 83 | UTEP | 45 |
| 1995 | Arkansas | John McDonnell | 61½ | UCLA | 55 |

*Unofficial championship. †Fraction of a point.

### DIVISION II

| Year | Champion | Year | Champion | Year | Champion |
|------|----------|------|----------|------|----------|
| 1963 | MD-Eastern Shore | 1974 | Eastern Illinois | 1984 | Abilene Christian |
| 1964 | Fresno St | | Norfolk St | 1985 | Abilene Christian |
| 1965 | San Diego St | 1975 | Cal St-Northridge | 1986 | Abilene Christian |
| 1966 | San Diego St | 1976 | UC-Irvine | 1987 | Abilene Christian |
| 1967 | Long Beach St | 1977 | Cal St-Hayward | 1988 | Abilene Christian |
| 1968 | Cal Poly-SLO | 1978 | Cal St-LA | 1989 | St Augustine's |
| 1969 | Cal Poly-SLO | 1979 | Cal Poly-SLO | 1990 | St Augustine's |
| 1970 | Cal Poly-SLO | 1980 | Cal Poly-SLO | 1991 | St Augustine's |
| 1971 | Kentucky St | 1981 | Cal Poly-SLO | 1992 | St Augustine's |
| 1972 | Eastern Michigan | 1982 | Abilene Christian | 1994 | St Augustine's |
| 1973 | Norfolk St | 1983 | Abilene Christian | 1995 | St Augustine's |

### DIVISION III

| Year | Champion | Year | Champion | Year | Champion |
|------|----------|------|----------|------|----------|
| 1974 | Ashland | 1982 | Glassboro St | 1990 | Lincoln (PA) |
| 1975 | Southern-N Orleans | 1983 | Glassboro St | 1991 | WI-La Crosse |
| 1976 | Southern-N Orleans | 1984 | Glassboro St | 1992 | WI-La Crosse |
| 1977 | Southern-N Orleans | 1985 | Lincoln (PA) | 1993 | WI-La Crosse |
| 1978 | Occidental | 1986 | Frostburg St | 1994 | North Central |
| 1979 | Slippery Rock | 1987 | Frostburg St | 1995 | Lincoln (PA) |
| 1980 | Glassboro St | 1988 | WI-La Crosse | | |
| 1981 | Glassboro St | 1989 | North Central | | |

## Women

### DIVISION I

| Year | Champion | Coach | Pts | Runner-Up | Pts |
|------|----------|-------|-----|-----------|-----|
| 1982 | UCLA | Scott Chisam | 153 | Tennessee | 126 |
| 1983 | UCLA | Scott Chisam | 116½ | Florida St | 108 |
| 1984 | Florida St | Gary Winckler | 145 | Tennessee | 124 |
| 1985 | Oregon | Tom Heinonen | 52 | Florida St/LSU | 46 |
| 1986 | Texas | Terry Crawford | 65 | Alabama | 55 |
| 1987 | Louisiana St | Loren Seagrave | 62 | Alabama | 53 |
| 1988 | Louisiana St | Loren Seagrave | 61 | UCLA | 58 |
| 1989 | Louisiana St | Pat Henry | 86 | UCLA | 47 |
| 1990 | Louisiana St | Pat Henry | 53 | UCLA | 46 |
| 1991 | Louisiana St | Pat Henry | 78 | Texas | 67 |
| 1992 | Louisiana St | Pat Henry | 87 | Florida | 81 |
| 1993 | Louisiana St | Pat Henry | 93 | Wisconsin | 44 |
| 1994 | Louisiana St | Pat Henry | 86 | Texas | 43 |
| 1995 | Louisiana St | Pat Henry | 69 | UCLA | 58 |

### Women (Cont.)

#### DIVISION II

| Year | Champion | Year | Champion | Year | Champion |
|------|----------|------|----------|------|----------|
| 1982 | Cal Poly-SLO | 1987 | Abilene Christian | 1992 | Alabama A&M |
| 1983 | Cal Poly-SLO | 1988 | Abilene Christian | 1993 | Alabama A&M |
| 1984 | Cal Poly-SLO | 1989 | Cal Poly-SLO | 1994 | Alabama A&M |
| 1985 | Abilene Christian | 1990 | Cal Poly-SLO | 1995 | Abilene Christian |
| 1986 | Abilene Christian | 1991 | Cal Poly-SLO | | |

#### DIVISION III

| Year | Champion | Year | Champion | Year | Champion |
|------|----------|------|----------|------|----------|
| 1982 | Central (IA) | 1987 | Chris. Newport | 1992 | Chris. Newport |
| 1983 | WI-La Crosse | 1988 | Chris. Newport | 1993 | Lincoln (PA) |
| 1984 | WI-La Crosse | 1989 | Chris. Newport | 1994 | Chris. Newport |
| 1985 | Cortland St | 1990 | WI-Oshkosh | 1995 | WI-Oshkosh |
| 1986 | MA-Boston | 1991 | WI-Oshkosh | | |

## Volleyball

### Men

| Year | Champion | Coach | Score | Runner-Up | Most Outstanding Player |
|------|----------|-------|-------|-----------|-------------------------|
| 1970 | UCLA | Al Scates | 3-0 | Long Beach St | Dane Holtzman, UCLA |
| 1971 | UCLA | Al Scates | 3-0 | UC-Santa Barbara | Kirk Kilgore, UCLA |
| | | | | | Tim Bonynge, UC-Santa Barbara |
| 1972 | UCLA | Al Scates | 3-2 | San Diego St | Dick Irvin, UCLA |
| 1973 | San Diego St | Jack Henn | 3-1 | Long Beach St | Duncan McFarland, San Diego St |
| 1974 | UCLA | Al Scates | 3-2 | UC-Santa Barbara | Bob Leonard, UCLA |
| 1975 | UCLA | Al Scates | 3-1 | UC-Santa Barbara | John Bekins, UCLA |
| 1976 | UCLA | Al Scates | 3-0 | Pepperdine | Joe Mika, UCLA |
| 1977 | Southern Cal | Ernie Hix | 3-1 | Ohio St | Celso Kalache, Southern Cal |
| 1978 | Pepperdine | Marv Dunphy | 3-2 | UCLA | Mike Blanchard, Pepperdine |
| 1979 | UCLA | Al Scates | 3-1 | Southern Cal | Sinjin Smith, UCLA |
| 1980 | Southern Cal | Ernie Hix | 3-1 | UCLA | Dusty Dvorak, Southern Cal |
| 1981 | UCLA | Al Scates | 3-2 | Southern Cal | Karch Kiraly, UCLA |
| 1982 | UCLA | Al Scates | 3-0 | Penn St | Karch Kiraly, UCLA |
| 1983 | UCLA | Al Scates | 3-0 | Pepperdine | Ricci Luyties, UCLA |
| 1984 | UCLA | Al Scates | 3-1 | Pepperdine | Ricci Luyties, UCLA |
| 1985 | Pepperdine | Marv Dunphy | 3-1 | Southern Cal | Bob Ctvrtlik, Pepperdine |
| 1986 | Pepperdine | Rod Wilde | 3-2 | Southern Cal | Steve Friedman, Pepperdine |
| 1987 | UCLA | Al Scates | 3-0 | Southern Cal | Ozzie Volstad, UCLA |
| 1988 | Southern Cal | Bob Yoder | 3-2 | UC-Santa Barbara | Jen-Kai Liu, Southern Cal |
| 1989 | UCLA | Al Scates | 3-0 | Stanford | Matt Sonnichsen, UCLA |
| 1990 | Southern Cal | Jim McLaughlin | 3-1 | Long Beach St | Bryan Ivie, Southern Cal |
| 1991 | Long Beach St | Ray Ratelle | 3-1 | Southern Cal | Brent Hilliard, Long Beach St |
| 1992 | Pepperdine | Marv Dunphy | 3-0 | Stanford | Alon Grinberg, Pepperdine |
| 1993 | UCLA | Al Scates | 3-0 | Cal St-Northridge | Mike Sealy/Jeff Nygaard, UCLA |
| 1994 | Penn St | Tom Peterson | 3-2 | UCLA | Ramon Hernandez, Penn St |
| 1995 | UCLA | Al Scates | 3-0 | Penn St | Jeff Nygaard, UCLA |

### Women

#### DIVISION I

| Year | Champion | Coach | Score | Runner-Up |
|------|----------|-------|-------|-----------|
| 1981 | Southern Cal | Chuck Erbe | 3-2 | UCLA |
| 1982 | Hawaii | Dave Shoji | 3-2 | Southern Cal |
| 1983 | Hawaii | Dave Shoji | 3-0 | UCLA |
| 1984 | UCLA | Andy Banachowski | 3-2 | Stanford |
| 1985 | Pacific | John Dunning | 3-1 | Stanford |
| 1986 | Pacific | John Dunning | 3-0 | Nebraska |
| 1987 | Hawaii | Dave Shoji | 3-1 | Stanford |
| 1988 | Texas | Mick Haley | 3-0 | Hawaii |
| 1989 | Long Beach St | Brian Gimmillaro | 3-0 | Nebraska |
| 1990 | UCLA | Andy Banachowski | 3-0 | Pacific |
| 1991 | UCLA | Andy Banachowski | 3-2 | Long Beach St |
| 1992 | Stanford | Don Shaw | 3-1 | UCLA |
| 1993 | Long Beach St | Brian Gimmillaro | 3-1 | Penn St |
| 1994 | Stanford | Don Shaw | 3-1 | UCLA |

## Women (Cont.)

### DIVISION II

| Year | Champion | Year | Champion | Year | Champion |
|------|----------|------|----------|------|----------|
| 1981 | Cal St-Sacramento | 1986 | UC-Riverside | 1991 | West Texas St |
| 1982 | UC-Riverside | 1987 | Cal St-Northridge | 1992 | Portland St |
| 1983 | Cal St-Northridge | 1988 | Portland St | 1993 | Northern Michigan |
| 1984 | Portland St | 1989 | Cal St-Bakersfield | 1994 | Northern Michigan |
| 1985 | Portland St | 1990 | West Texas St | | |

### DIVISION III

| Year | Champion | Year | Champion | Year | Champion |
|------|----------|------|----------|------|----------|
| 1981 | UC-San Diego | 1986 | UC-San Diego | 1991 | Washington (MO) |
| 1982 | La Verne | 1987 | UC-San Diego | 1992 | Washington (MO) |
| 1983 | Elmhurst | 1988 | UC-San Diego | 1993 | Washington (MO) |
| 1984 | UC-San Diego | 1989 | Washington (MO) | 1994 | Washington (MO) |
| 1985 | Elmhurst | 1990 | UC-San Diego | | |

# Water Polo

| Year | Champion | Coach | Score | Runner-Up |
|------|----------|-------|-------|-----------|
| 1969 | UCLA | Bob Horn | 5-2 | California |
| 1970 | UC-Irvine | Ed Newland | 7-6 (3 OT) | UCLA |
| 1971 | UCLA | Bob Horn | 5-3 | San Jose St |
| 1972 | UCLA | Bob Horn | 10-5 | UC-Irvine |
| 1973 | California | Pete Cutino | 8-4 | UC-Irvine |
| 1974 | California | Pete Cutino | 7-6 | UC-Irvine |
| 1975 | California | Pete Cutino | 9-8 | UC-Irvine |
| 1976 | Stanford | Art Lambert | 13-12 | UCLA |
| 1977 | California | Pete Cutino | 8-6 | UC-Irvine |
| 1978 | Stanford | Dante Dettamanti | 7-6 (3 OT) | California |
| 1979 | UC-Santa Barbara | Pete Snyder | 11-3 | UCLA |
| 1980 | Stanford | Dante Dettamanti | 8-6 | California |
| 1981 | Stanford | Dante Dettamanti | 17-6 | Long Beach St |
| 1982 | UC-Irvine | Ed Newland | 7-4 | Stanford |
| 1983 | California | Pete Cutino | 10-7 | Southern Cal |
| 1984 | California | Pete Cutino | 9-8 | Stanford |
| 1985 | Stanford | Dante Dettamanti | 12-11 (2 OT) | UC-Irvine |
| 1986 | Stanford | Dante Dettamanti | 9-6 | California |
| 1987 | California | Pete Cutino | 9-8 (OT) | Southern Cal |
| 1988 | California | Pete Cutino | 14-11 | UCLA |
| 1989 | UC-Irvine | Ed Newland | 9-8 | California |
| 1990 | California | Steve Heaston | 8-7 | Stanford |
| 1991 | California | Steve Heaston | 7-6 | UCLA |
| 1992 | California | Steve Heaston | 12-11 | Stanford |
| 1993 | Stanford | Dante Dettamanti | 11-9 | Southern Cal |
| 1994 | Stanford | Dante Dettamanti | 14-10 | Southern Cal |

# Wrestling

### DIVISION I

| Year | Champion | Coach | Pts | Runner-Up | Pts | Most Outstanding Wrestler |
|------|----------|-------|-----|-----------|-----|---------------------------|
| 1928 | Oklahoma St* | E. C. Gallagher | | | | |
| 1929 | Oklahoma St* | E. C. Gallagher | 26 | Michigan | 18 | |
| 1930 | Oklahoma St* | E. C. Gallagher | 27 | Illinois | 14 | |
| 1931 | Oklahoma St* | E. C. Gallagher | | Michigan | | |
| 1932 | Indiana* | W. H. Thom | | Oklahoma St | | Edwin Belshaw, Indiana |
| 1933 | Oklahoma St* | E. C. Gallagher | | | | Allan Kelley, Oklahoma St |
| | Iowa St* | Hugo Otopalik | | | | Pat Johnson, Harvard |
| 1934 | Oklahoma St | E. C. Gallagher | 29 | Indiana | 19 | Ben Bishop, Lehigh |
| 1935 | Oklahoma St | E. C. Gallagher | 36 | Oklahoma | 18 | Ross Flood, Oklahoma St |
| 1936 | Oklahoma | Paul Keen | 14 | Central St (OK) | 10 | Wayne Martin, Oklahoma |
| | | | | Oklahoma St | 10 | |
| 1937 | Oklahoma St | E. C. Gallagher | 31 | Oklahoma | 13 | Stanley Henson, Oklahoma St |
| 1938 | Oklahoma St | E. C. Gallagher | 19 | Illinois | 15 | Joe McDaniels, Oklahoma St |

## DIVISION I (Cont.)

| Year | Champion | Coach | Pts | Runner-Up | Pts | Most Outstanding Wrestler |
|---|---|---|---|---|---|---|
| 1939 | Oklahoma St | E. C. Gallagher | 33 | Lehigh | 12 | Dale Hanson, Minnesota |
| 1940 | Oklahoma St | E. C. Gallagher | 24 | Indiana | 14 | Don Nichols, Michigan |
| 1941 | Oklahoma St | Art Griffith | 37 | Michigan St | 26 | Al Whitehurst, Oklahoma St |
| 1942 | Oklahoma St | Art Griffith | 31 | Michigan St | 26 | David Arndt, Oklahoma St |
| 1943-45 | No tournament | | | | | |
| 1946 | Oklahoma St | Art Griffith | 25 | Northern Iowa | 24 | Gerald Leeman, Northern Iowa |
| 1947 | Cornell | Paul Scott | 32 | Northern Iowa | 19 | William Koll, Northern Iowa |
| 1948 | Oklahoma St | Art Griffith | 33 | Michigan St | 28 | William Koll, Northern Iowa |
| 1949 | Oklahoma St | Art Griffith | 32 | Northern Iowa | 27 | Charles Hetrick, Oklahoma St |
| 1950 | Northern Iowa | David McCuskey | 30 | Purdue | 16 | Anthony Gizoni, Waynesburg |
| 1951 | Oklahoma | Port Robertson | 24 | Oklahoma St | 23 | Walter Romanowski, Cornell |
| 1952 | Oklahoma | Port Robertson | 22 | Northern Iowa | 21 | Tommy Evans, Oklahoma |
| 1953 | Penn St | Charles Speidel | 21 | Oklahoma | 15 | Frank Bettucci, Cornell |
| 1954 | Oklahoma St | Art Griffith | 32 | Pittsburgh | 17 | Tommy Evans, Oklahoma |
| 1955 | Oklahoma St | Art Griffith | 40 | Penn St | 31 | Edward Eichelberger, Lehigh |
| 1956 | Oklahoma St | Art Griffith | 65 | Oklahoma | 62 | Dan Hodge, Oklahoma |
| 1957 | Oklahoma | Port Robertson | 73 | Pittsburgh | 66 | Dan Hodge, Oklahoma |
| 1958 | Oklahoma St | Myron Roderick | 77 | Iowa St | 62 | Dick Delgado, Oklahoma |
| 1959 | Oklahoma St | Myron Roderick | 73 | Iowa St | 51 | Ron Gray, Iowa St |
| 1960 | Oklahoma | Thomas Evans | 59 | Iowa St | 40 | Dave Auble, Cornell |
| 1961 | Oklahoma St | Myron Roderick | 82 | Oklahoma | 63 | E. Gray Simons, Lock Haven |
| 1962 | Oklahoma St | Myron Roderick | 82 | Oklahoma | 45 | E. Gray Simons, Lock Haven |
| 1963 | Oklahoma | Thomas Evans | 48 | Iowa St | 45 | Mickey Martin, Oklahoma |
| 1964 | Oklahoma St | Myron Roderick | 87 | Oklahoma | 58 | Dean Lahr, Colorado |
| 1965 | Iowa St | Harold Nichols | 87 | Oklahoma St | 86 | Yojiro Uetake, Oklahoma St |
| 1966 | Oklahoma St | Myron Roderick | 79 | Iowa St | 70 | Yojiro Uetake, Oklahoma St |
| 1967 | Michigan St | Grady Peninger | 74 | Michigan | 63 | Rich Sanders, Portland St |
| 1968 | Oklahoma St | Myron Roderick | 81 | Iowa St | 78 | Dwayne Keller, Oklahoma St |
| 1969 | Iowa St | Harold Nichols | 104 | Oklahoma | 69 | Dan Gable, Iowa St |
| 1970 | Iowa St | Harold Nichols | 99 | Michigan St | 84 | Larry Owings, Washington |
| 1971 | Oklahoma St | Tommy Chesbro | 94 | Iowa St | 66 | Darrell Keller, Oklahoma St |
| 1972 | Iowa St | Harold Nichols | 103 | Michigan St | 72½ | Wade Schalles, Clarion |
| 1973 | Iowa St | Harold Nichols | 85 | Oregon St | 72½ | Greg Strobel, Oregon St |
| 1974 | Oklahoma | Stan Abel | 69½ | Michigan | 67 | Floyd Hitchcock, Bloomsburg |
| 1975 | Iowa | Gary Kurdelmeier | 102 | Oklahoma | 77 | Mike Frick, Lehigh |
| 1976 | Iowa | Gary Kurdelmeier | 123½ | Iowa St | 85¾ | Chuch Yagla, Iowa |
| 1977 | Iowa St | Harold Nichols | 95½ | Oklahoma St | 88¾ | Nick Gallo, Hofstra |
| 1978 | Iowa | Dan Gable | 94½ | Iowa St | 94 | Mark Churella, Michigan |
| 1979 | Iowa | Dan Gable | 122½ | Iowa St | 88 | Bruce Kinseth, Iowa |
| 1980 | Iowa | Dan Gable | 110¾ | Oklahoma St | 87 | Howard Harris, Oregon St |
| 1981 | Iowa | Dan Gable | 129¾ | Oklahoma | 100¼ | Gene Mills, Syracuse |
| 1982 | Iowa | Dan Gable | 131¾ | Iowa St | 111 | Mark Schultz, Oklahoma |
| 1983 | Iowa | Dan Gable | 155 | Oklahoma St | 102 | Mike Sheets, Oklahoma St |
| 1984 | Iowa | Dan Gable | 123¾ | Oklahoma St | 98 | Jim Zalesky, Iowa |
| 1985 | Iowa | Dan Gable | 145¼ | Oklahoma | 98½ | Barry Davis, Iowa |
| 1986 | Iowa | Dan Gable | 158 | Oklahoma | 84¼ | Marty Kistler, Iowa |
| 1987 | Iowa St | Jim Gibbons | 133 | Iowa | 108 | John Smith, Oklahoma St |
| 1988 | Arizona St | Bobby Douglas | 93 | Iowa | 85½ | Scott Turner, N Carolina St |
| 1989 | Oklahoma St | Joe Seay | 91¼ | Arizona St | 70½ | Tim Krieger, Iowa St |
| 1990 | Oklahoma St | Joe Seay | 117¾ | Arizona St | 104¾ | Chris Barnes, Oklahoma St |
| 1991 | Iowa | Dan Gable | 157 | Oklahoma St | 108¾ | Jeff Prescott, Penn St |
| 1992 | Iowa | Dan Gable | 149 | Oklahoma St | 100½ | Tom Brands, Iowa |
| 1993 | Iowa | Dan Gable | 123¾ | Penn St | 87½ | Terry Steiner, Iowa |
| 1994 | Oklahoma St | John Smith | 94¾ | Iowa | 76½ | Pat Smith, Oklahoma St |
| 1995 | Iowa | Dan Gable | 134 | Oregon St | 77½ | T.J. Jaworsky, N Carolina |

*Unofficial champions.

## DIVISION II

| Year | Champion | Year | Champion | Year | Champion |
|---|---|---|---|---|---|
| 1963 | Western St (CO) | 1974 | Cal Poly-SLO | 1985 | SIU-Edwardsville |
| 1964 | Western St (CO) | 1975 | Northern Iowa | 1986 | SIU-Edwardsville |
| 1965 | Mankato St | 1976 | Cal St-Bakersfield | 1987 | Cal St-Bakersfield |
| 1966 | Cal Poly-SLO | 1977 | Cal St-Bakersfield | 1988 | N Dakota St |
| 1967 | Portland St | 1978 | Northern Iowa | 1989 | Portland St |
| 1968 | Cal Poly-SLO | 1979 | Cal St-Bakersfield | 1990 | Portland St |
| 1969 | Cal Poly-SLO | 1980 | Cal St-Bakersfield | 1991 | NE-Omaha |
| 1970 | Cal Poly-SLO | 1981 | Cal St-Bakersfield | 1992 | Central Oklahoma |
| 1971 | Cal Poly-SLO | 1982 | Cal St-Bakersfield | 1993 | Central Oklahoma |
| 1972 | Cal Poly-SLO | 1983 | Cal St-Bakersfield | 1994 | Central Oklahoma |
| 1973 | Cal Poly-SLO | 1984 | SIU-Edwardsville | 1995 | Central Oklahoma |

### DIVISION III

| Year | Champion | Year | Champion | Year | Champion |
|------|----------|------|----------|------|----------|
| 1974 | Wilkes | 1982 | Brockport St | 1990 | Ithaca |
| 1975 | John Carroll | 1983 | Brockport St | 1991 | Augsburg |
| 1976 | Montclair St | 1984 | Trenton St | 1992 | Brockport |
| 1977 | Brockport St | 1985 | Trenton St | 1993 | Augsburg |
| 1978 | Buffalo | 1986 | Montclair St | 1994 | Ithaca |
| 1979 | Trenton St | 1987 | Trenton St | 1995 | Augsburg |
| 1980 | Brockport St | 1988 | St Lawrence | | |
| 1981 | Trenton St | 1989 | Ithaca | | |

# INDIVIDUAL CHAMPIONSHIP
# RECORDS

## Swimming and Diving

### Men

| Event | Time | Record Holder | Date |
|-------|------|---------------|------|
| 50-yard freestyle | 19.14 | David Fox, N Carolina St | 3-25-93 |
| 100-yard freestyle | 41.80 | Matt Biondi, California | 4-4-87 |
| 200-yard freestyle | 1:33.03 | Matt Biondi, California | 4-3-87 |
| 500-yard freestyle | 4:08.75 | Tom Dolan, Michigan | 3-23-95 |
| 1650-yard freestyle | 14:29.31 | Tom Dolan, Michigan | 3-25-95 |
| 100-yard backstroke | 45.43 | Brian Retterer, Stanford | 3-24-95 |
| 200-yard backstroke | 1:40.64 | Jeff Rouse, Stanford | 3-28-92 |
| 100-yard breaststroke | 52.48 | Steve Lundquist, Southern Meth | 3-25-83 |
| 200-yard breaststroke | 1:53.77 | Mike Barrowman, Michigan | 3-24-90 |
| 100-yard butterfly | 46.18 | Lars Frolander, SMU | 3-24-95 |
| 200-yard butterfly | 1:41.78 | Melvin Stewart, Tennessee | 3-30-91 |
| 200-yard individual medley | 1:43.52 | Greg Burgess, Florida | 3-25-93 |
| 400-yard individual medley | 3:38.18 | Tom Dolan, Michigan | 3-24-95 |

### Women

| Event | Time | Record Holder | Date |
|-------|------|---------------|------|
| 50-yard freestyle | 21.77 | Amy Van Dyken, Colorado St | 3-18-94 |
| 100-yard freestyle | 47.61 | Jenny Thompson, Stanford | 3-21-92 |
| 200-yard freestyle | 1:43.28 | Nicole Haislett, Florida | 3-20-92 |
| 500-yard freestyle | 4:34.39 | Janet Evans, Stanford | 3-15-90 |
| 1650-yard freestyle | 15:39.14 | Janet Evans, Stanford | 3-17-90 |
| 100-yard backstroke | 53.98 | Betsy Mitchell, Texas | 3-21-92 |
| 200-yard backstroke | 1:52.98 | Whitney Hedgepeth, Texas | 3-21-87 |
| 100-yard breaststroke | 59.71 | Beata Kaszuba, Arizona St | 3-17-95 |
| 200-yard breaststroke | 2:09.71 | Beata Kaszuba, Arizona St | 3-18-95 |
| 100-yard butterfly | 51.75 | Crissy Ahmann-Leighton, Arizona | 3-20-92 |
| 200-yard butterfly | 1:53.42 | Summer Sanders, Stanford | 3-21-92 |
| 200-yard individual medley | 1:55.54 | Summer Sanders, Stanford | 3-20-92 |
| 400-yard individual medley | 4:02.28 | Summer Sanders, Stanford | 3-20-92 |

## Indoor Track and Field

### Men

| Event | Mark | Record Holder | Date |
|-------|------|---------------|------|
| 55-meter dash | 6.00 | Lee McRae, Pittsburgh | 3-14-86 |
| 55-meter hurdles | 7.07 | Allen Johnson, N Carolina | 3-13-92 |
| 200-meter dash | 20.59 | Michael Johnson, Baylor | 3-10-89 |
| 400-meter dash | 45.79 | Gabriel Luke, Rice | 3-10-90 |
| 800-meter run | 1:46.19 | George Kersh, Mississippi | 3-9-91 |
| Mile run | 3:55.33 | Kevin Sullivan, Michigan | 3-11-95 |
| 3000-meter run | 7:50.90 | Josephat Kapkory, Wash St | 3-11-94 |
| 5000-meter run | 13:37.94 | Jonah Koech, Iowa St | 3-9-90 |
| High jump | 7 ft 9¼ in | Hollis Conway, Southwestern Louisiana | 3-11-89 |
| Pole vault | 19 ft 1½ in | Lawrence Johnson, Tennessee | 3-12-94 |
| Long jump | 27 ft 10 in | Carl Lewis, Houston | 3-13-81 |
| Triple jump | 56 ft 9½ in | Keith Connor, Southern Meth | 3-13-81 |

## Men (Cont.)

| | | | Date |
|---|---|---|---|
| Shot put | 69 ft 8½ in | Michael Carter, SMU | 3-13-81 |
| | | Soren Tallhem, Brigham Young | 3-9-85 |
| 35-pound weight throw | 76 ft 5½ in | Robert Weir, SMU | 3-11-83 |

## Women

| Event | Mark | Record Holder | Date |
|---|---|---|---|
| 55-meter dash | 6.56 | Gwen Torrence, Georgia | 3-14-87 |
| 55-meter hurdles | 7.44 | Lynda Tolbert, Arizona St | 3-9-90 |
| 200-meter dash | 22.90 | Holly Hyche, Indiana St | 3-11-94 |
| 400-meter dash | 51.05 | Maicel Malone, Arizona St | 3-9-91 |
| 800-meter run | 2:02.05 | Amy Wickus, Wisconsin | 3-11-94 |
| Mile run | 4:30.63 | Suzy Favor, Wisconsin | 3-11-89 |
| 3000-meter run | 8:54.98 | Stephanie Herbst, Wisconsin | 3-15-86 |
| 5000-meter run | 15:41.12 | Jennifer Rhines, Villanova | 3-10-95 |
| High jump | 6 ft 5½ in | Amy Acuff, UCLA | 3-11-95 |
| Long jump | 22 ft 1 in | Daphne Saunders, Louisiana St | 3-12-94 |
| Triple jump | 45 ft 9 in | Sheila Hudson, California | 3-10-90 |
| Shot put | 57 ft 11¾ in | Regina Cavanaugh, Rice | 3-14-86 |

## Men

| Event | Mark | Record Holder | Date |
|---|---|---|---|
| 100-meter dash | 10.03 | Stanley Floyd, Houston | 6-5-82 |
| | | Joe DeLoach, Houston | 6-4-88 |
| 200-meter dash | 19.87 | Lorenzo Daniel, Mississippi St | 6-3-88 |
| 400-meter dash | 44.00 | Quincy Watts, Southern Cal | 6-6-92 |
| 800-meter run | 1:44.70 | Mark Everett, Florida | 6-1-90 |
| 1500-meter run | 3:35.30 | Sydney Maree, Villanova | 6-6-81 |
| 3000-meter steeplechase | 8:12.39 | Henry Rono, Washington St | 6-1-78 |
| 5000-meter run | 13:20.63 | Sydney Maree, Villanova | 6-2-79 |
| 10000-meter run | 28:01.30 | Suleiman Nyambui, UTEP | 6-1-79 |
| 110-meter high hurdles | 13.22 | Greg Foster, UCLA | 6-2-78 |
| 400-meter intermediate hurdles | 47.85 | Kevin Young, UCLA | 6-3-88 |
| High jump | 7 ft 9¾ in | Hollis Conway, Southwestern Louisiana | 6-3-89 |
| Pole vault | 19 ft ¼ in | Istvan Bagyula, George Mason | 5-31-91 |
| Long jump | 28 ft | Erick Walder, Arkansas | 6-3-93 |
| Triple jump | 57 ft 7¾ in | Keith Connor, Southern Meth | 6-5-82 |
| Shot put | 72 ft 2¼ in | John Godina, UCLA | 6-3-95 |
| Discus throw | 220 ft | Kamy Keshmiri, Nevada | 6-5-92 |
| Hammer throw | 261 ft 3 in | Balazs Kiss, Southern Cal | 5-31-95 |
| Javelin throw | 266 ft 9 in | Todd Riech, Fresno St | 6-3-94 |
| Decathlon | 8279 pts | Tito Steiner, Brigham Young | 6-2/3-81 |

## Women

| Event | Mark | Record Holder | Date |
|---|---|---|---|
| 100-meter dash | 10.78 | Dawn Sowell, Louisiana St | 6-3-89 |
| 200-meter dash | 22.04 | Dawn Sowell, Louisiana St | 6-2-89 |
| 400-meter dash | 50.18 | Pauline Davis, Alabama | 6-3-89 |
| 800-meter run | 1:59.11 | Suzy Favor, Wisconsin | 6-1-90 |
| 1500-meter run | 4:08.26 | Suzy Favor, Wisconsin | 6-2-90 |
| 3000-meter run | 8:47.35 | Vicki Huber, Villanova | 6-3-88 |
| 5000-meter run | 15:38.47 | Annette Hand, Oregon | 6-4-88 |
| 10000-meter run | 32:28.57 | Sylvia Mosqueda, Cal St-LA | 6-1-88 |
| 100-meter hurdles | 12.70 | Tananjalyn Stanley, Louisiana St | 6-3-89 |
| 400-meter hurdles | 54.64 | Latanya Sheffield, San Diego St | 5-31-85 |
| High jump | 6 ft 5 in | Amy Acuff, UCLA | 6-3-95 |
| Long jump | 22 ft 9¼ in | Sheila Echols, Louisiana St | 6-5-87 |
| Triple jump | 46 ft ¾ in | Sheila Hudson, California | 6-2-90 |
| Shot put | 59 ft 11¾ in | Valeyta Althouse, UCLA | 6-1-95 |
| Discus throw | 209 ft 10 in | Leslie Deniz, Arizona St | 6-4-83 |
| Javelin throw | 206 ft 9 in | Karin Smith, Cal Poly-SLO | 6-4-82 |
| Heptathlon | 6527 pts | Diane Guthrie-Gresham, George Mason | 6-2/3-95 |

# Olympics

**Sports Illustrated**

## The Big Splash

Atlanta gets set to host the
'96 Summer Olympics

# Let the Games Begin

## There was no Olympic competition in 1995 but there *was* plenty of action, and more than a few games being played

### by William Oscar Johnson

NINETEEN-NINETY-five was an off year for the Olympics, and no Games with a capital *G* were played. That, however, is not to say that the Olympic movement was left without a goodly share of lowercase games, gamesmen and gamesmanship.

The biggest little *g* game of the year was the competition to choose a city to host the Winter Olympic Games in 2002. In the beginning no fewer than nine municipalities entered the contest. Some players were better equipped to compete than others.

Sochi on the Black Sea in Russia, a venerable old summer spa, hoped to transform itself into a year-round resort by constructing new Olympic ski runs, ski jumps and a bobsled/luge track in a roadless virgin forest outside town. The International Olympic Committee sent an evaluation commission to inspect Sochi, as it did all the bidding cities, and appalled commission members reported that "a lack of maps" made it all but impossible to locate competition sites in the trackless woods.

Worse, IOC inspectors ruled that the Sochi plan to finance an Olympics would be "burdened with an unbearable amount of risk" due to the wild and crazy state of the Russian economy. Another farfetched—and far-flung—bidder was Jaca, Spain, which called for Games spread over three widely separate venues in the Pyrenees, including one in the tiny land of Andorra, 3½ hours from Jaca. Graz, Austria, included in its Olympic dream a bobsled run that IOC inspectors found to be dangerously "exposed to rockfall." In Tarvisio, Italy, organizers hatched an idealistic blue-sky Olympian political vision that saw the governments of Italy, Slovenia and Austria cooperating as Olympic cohosts—"three countries which historically have not always lived peacefully together," the disbelieving IOC inspectors wisely noted. And in Poprad-Tatry in Slovakia inspectors were shocked to discover that organizers planned to build the media village in a nature reserve, the cross-country and

Alpine race courses in a national park and the Olympic Village in a protected wetlands area.

These five cities were mercifully scrubbed from the list of wannabes in January '95, and that left four in the running—the winner to be chosen at the annual IOC meeting in Budapest in mid-June. The candidates were Sion, Switzerland; Quebec City, Canada; Ostersund, Sweden; and Salt Lake City of the United States. All except one had flaws.

Sion had designed an ungainly, hugely spread-out Olympics with three separate Olympic Villages and the bobsled and luge runs located in St. Moritz—a six-hour train ride from Sion.

Quebec offered a nicely compact Games plan with no venue more than an hour from the city by car. However, the downhill ski course was to start at the top of a mountain whose natural summit stands 100 meters below official height for a world-class course. To bring it up to stan-

**Samaranch may have extended his reign with some crafty politicking.**

dard required an unwieldy height-enhancing pile of landfill, ramps and platforms. A potentially more serious problem: The province of Quebec is run by a secessionist government, which plans to declare independence from Canada someday—preferably soon. What havoc this might wreak on an Olympic bid is hard to predict, although IOC inspectors noted warily that they had been told that "secession is a very remote possibility before 2002."

Ostersund put forth a polished, professional bid, which was not surprising since it was the city's third attempt in nine years to win a Winter Olympics and Sweden's sixth straight. The overall plan was judged "very good" by IOC inspectors, but a major drawback was the IOC's resistance to holding another Olympics in Scandinavia so soon after Lillehammer's masterpiece in 1994.

And then there was long-suffering Salt Lake City. The city had been competing to get a Winter Olympics off and on since 1965, and in 1991 it had lost a perfectly beautiful bid for the 1998 Games to unknown and untested Nagano, Japan. This had happened because Atlanta already owned the '96 Summer Olympics, and the rules of the geopolitical games as played by the IOC didn't allow for two U.S.-based Olympics so close together. This time the outlook looked completely positive. IOC inspectors had given Salt Lake high marks, and European journalists, usually the meanest of nitpickers when it comes to things American, also raved. The Swiss newspaper *Sport* said, "The bid has no weaknesses." And Karl-Heinz Huba, publisher of an Olympic insiders' newsletter out of Musich, said, "Salt Lake has everything in place, the competition sites, the infrastructure, the logistics, the hotels. The setting is beautiful besides."

Still, there was skepticism. Dick Pound, a Montreal lawyer who is also an IOC executive board member warned, "With the IOC you really never know what's going on." Tom Welch, president of the Salt Lake bid committee for 10 years, said worriedly, "I think the winners tend to be everyone's second choice." A loyal Swede agreed: "Being a front-runner is like chewing a wad of gum: After a while you want a new one."

But, no. The IOC stuck with the gum it was chewing, and Salt Lake won on the first secret ballot, taking 54 of the 89 votes cast, while plucky Ostersund tied Sion with 14, and Quebec finished last with seven. Never had there been such a landslide in

**With one year to go, Payne predicted Atlanta would win over the world.**

picking an Olympic city. Welch & Co. estimated the Games would cost $798 million but predicted they would bring Utah some $170 million in tourist dollars and that Olympic-related jobs would generate half a billion dollars. "This is only a beginning," crowed Welch, "but what a beginning."

Picking the site for 2002 was not the only little *g* game underway in Budapest, however. Early in the proceedings the craftiest gamesman of them all, IOC president Juan Antonio Samaranch, entertained a motion to get rid of the IOC's mandatory retirement age of 75, which had been set in 1985. Why? Interestingly enough, the old wizard was to turn 75 soon after the Budapest meeting. He was serving his fourth four-year term as president, and it would expire in 1997. Although he would be allowed to serve to the end of this term, he could not run a fifth time unless the age limit was raised or removed. At the first session Samaranch confidently called for a vote on the age limit. He needed a two-thirds majority, and to his disappointment and surprise, the motion ultimately failed passage by two slim votes. It was judged a stunning defeat for Samaranch, and people began to talk about who might replace him after 1997.

Ah, but the game wasn't over: In the fourth and final session of the meeting, a petition was suddenly introduced bearing the signatures of 70 members. It called for a rule change that would allow IOC delegates to retire at 75 if they wished but to stay on until 80 if they liked. Some members asked for a secret ballot, but Samaranch said that was "nonsense." He quickly called for a show of hands of those opposed to the motion. No more than 10 were counted, the gavel fell, and the new age limit in the IOC was suddenly 80. Did this mean that an octogenarian Juan Antonio would continue to be IOC president on into the 21st century? He was noncommittal at a press conference: "I know my age, and I will take the final decision only at the end of next year, close to the election, some seven months before, I think." Dick Pound, who voted against the age change and is considered a leading contender to replace Samaranch someday, sighed resignedly: "It comes as no surprise when he says he likes the job, and he does a terrific job. If it ain't broke, don't fix it."

There was also in this Olympic off-year a worldwide guessing game about what was going to be broke and what wasn't when the 1996 Summer Games opened in Atlanta next summer. Billy Payne, 48, the former University of Georgia football star who has been the evangelistic leader of the Atlanta Committee for the Olympic Games (ACOG) ever since he had a dream about an Atlanta Olympics eight years ago, has tried to offset any onrushing anxiety by fanning feverish optimism among his followers. He habitually refers to the coming spectacle as "the greatest peacetime gathering of nations in world history," and he promises that July 19, 1996, the first of the 17 days of the Games, "will be the greatest day in my life and in the life of Georgians everywhere. We'll be saying to ourselves at the opening ceremonies: Hey, it's pretty good isn't it? Hey, better than you thought, isn't it? Hey, we couldn't have done it better if we had a thousand years, could we?"

With about one year left to opening day, Payne declared that ACOG had raised 80% of the record-breaking $1.58 billion budgeted for the Games. He said the committee had completed 75% of the $500,000,000 worth of construction on Olympic sites, most of which would be available for local use after the Games were over—including transforming the $170 million, 85,000-seat Olympic Stadium (the first ever with luxury suites) into a new city-owned baseball stadium for the Atlanta Braves, giving five new Olympic Village dormitories to Georgia State University and establishing a permanent $50 million, 21-acre Centennial Olympic Park in downtown Atlanta.

**Ebersol and top Sydney organizer Gary Pemberton (left) celebrate NBC's coup.**

All of this, as Payne & Co. had long promised, was to come to pass without spending any taxpayers' money since all of it was pouring in from corporate sponsors, broadcasters, ticket buyers and merchandise sales. Indeed, if ACOG does reel in all the commercial sponsors it has on the line, it will shatter Olympic corporate funding records, with $500 million contributed by 45 wildly diverse corporations ranging from Coca-Cola to United Parcel to Xerox to Blue Cross and Blue Shield insurance. Individual company fees range as high as $50 million, and sponsors will not be bashful about displaying their wares and their logos. A 92-foot Swatch watch will adorn a downtown building. Coca-Cola will sponsor the Olympic Torch Relay. McDonald's will have six outlets in the athletes' Olympic Village. Daimler-Benz, the German automaker, is going to restore the crum-

bling house where Margaret Mitchell, author of *Gone with the Wind*, was born. Purists (of whom there are not so many these days) complain that such a massive dependence on—and display of—commercial products will make the formerly hallowed ground of the Olympics resemble nothing so much as a gargantuan trade show.

ACOG remains undaunted. "We're proud of what we've done," said Payne. "Even to the cynics it appears we're going to bring this thing in on time and on budget."

Not all cynics were buying the rosy predictions. As a late-summer headline in an Atlanta newspaper declared: DIRE POSSIBILITIES LURK UNDER UPBEAT REPORTS.

Dire indeed: Atlanta traffic is notorious for being a gridlock nightmare—and the city nearly stopped dead during the 1994 Super Bowl. Of course, Atlanta summers are famously scorching and even though ACOG insists that average temperatures over the last 100 years have been about 75° in July, no one can forget the killer heat wave that covered the U.S. in the summer of '95 and sent the mercury above 90° no fewer than 27 times in Atlanta in July alone. Atlanta hotel rooms are none too abundant and with the best ones reserved for the IOC elite, the press and thousands of corporation fat cats, many of the two million Olympic visitors will be forced to commute from far-off places like Chattanooga and Birmingham. Price-gouging has been rampant in the cradle of Southern hospitality: Owners of private homes closed wildly greedy deals with corporate renters, and apartment house owners threatened to bodily evict tenants who refused to pay Olympic-inflated rents of as much as $3,000.

There was also doubt among critics that some of ACOG's more ambitious construction projects will be completed on schedule—including Olympic Stadium itself and the much-ballyhooed Centennial Park, which lay fallow late last summer partly because an ambitious ACOG plan to finance the park by selling two million personalized park-path bricks for $35 each had faltered with a mere 160,000 bricks bought.

There was even bad news at sea for ACOG. The first of the facilities to be tested in a world-class pre-Olympic competition were the yachting venues in Savannah. Some 700 sailors from 53 nations arrived in July to participate in the NationsBank International Regatta. They were, to a man, enraged over the facilities they found. A chief complaint concerned the seemingly endless two- to three-hour motor tow required to bring racing vessels from the Olympic marina to the racing courses in the ocean. And once they had arrived at offshore launching locations, sailors were met with a desperate shortage of toilets, shade and fresh water. Indeed, as the regatta proceeded, the snafus multiplied and, finally, the president of the International Yacht Racing Union suggested the whole Olympic sailing competition be shifted to Miami.

Payne shrugged off all the many complaints with the same game grin: "This is just preliminary criticism, folks. Don't worry. Our friendliness will steal the show when we finally get to '96."

He might be right. For '95, however, the greatest Olympic show stealer of them all proved to be the NBC network. In the wiliest, gutsiest play of Olympic TV gamemanship seen in years, the sharpies at NBC, led by network president Robert Wright and sports president Dick Ebersol, persuaded Samaranch and Pound, the IOC's lead TV negotiator, to secretly accept an unprecedented take-it-or-leave-it, preemptive bid of $1.27 billion to buy the rights to not one but *two* Olympics in the same package. The price was $715 million for the 2000 Summer Games in Sydney (where organizers expected only $500 million from TV) and $555 million for the 2002 Winter Games in Salt Lake City (where just $400 million was budgeted).

No other network was notified, and none was allowed to bring in a competing bid. Ethical or not, it was a monumental achievement for both NBC and the IOC. "It was a helluva deal," said Pound. "We could not let this go." Even the losers had to admire NBC's coup. A spokesman at the Fox network, which happens to be owned by Australian-born Rupert Murdoch, who had wanted the Sydney Games so badly that he had sneaked in his own secret preemptive bid of $701 million, declared coldly, "The Olympics are a great event. We wish NBC well." Later, off the record, he added, "There are many unhappy people here."

And so ended the year of lowercase Olympic games. Next come the big *G*'s of '96 which stand for Games, Georgia and God have mercy on ACOG.

## 1992 Summer Games

### TRACK AND FIELD

#### Men

##### 100 METERS
1. ..Linford Christie, Great Britain — 9.96
2. ..Frank Fredericks, Namibia — 10.02
3. ..Dennis Mitchell, United States — 10.04

##### 200 METERS
1. ..Mike Marsh, United States — 20.01
2. ..Frank Fredericks, Namibia — 20.13
3. ..Michael Bates, United States — 20.38

##### 400 METERS
1. ..Quincy Watts, United States — 43.50OR
2. ..Steve Lewis, United States — 44.21
3. ..Samson Kitur, Kenya — 44.24

##### 800 METERS
1. ..William Tanui, Kenya — 1:43.66
2. ..Nixon Kiprotich, Kenya — 1:43.70
3. ..Johnny Gray, United States — 1:43.97

##### 1500 METERS
1. ..Fermin Cacho, Spain — 3:40.12
2. ..Rachid El-Basir, Morocco — 3:40.62
3. ..Mohamed Ahmed Sulaiman, Qatar — 3:40.69

##### 5000 METERS
1. ..Dieter Baumann, Germany — 13:12.52
2. ..Paul Bitok, Kenya — 13:12.71
3. ..Fita Bayisa, Ethiopia — 13:13.03

##### 10,000 METERS
1. ..Khalid Skah, Morocco — 27:46.70
2. ..Richard Chelimo, Kenya — 27:47.72
3. ..Addis Abebe, Ethiopia — 28.00.07

##### MARATHON
1. ..Hwang Young-Cho, South Korea — 2:13:23
2. ..Koichi Morishita, Japan — 2:13:45
3. ..Stephan Freigang, Germany — 2:14:00

##### 110-METER HURDLES
1. ..Mark McKoy, Canada — 13.12
2. ..Tony Dees, United States — 13.24
3. ..Jack Pierce, United States — 13.26

##### 400-METER HURDLES
1. ..Kevin Young, United States — 46.78WR
2. ..Winthrop Graham, Jamaica — 47.66
3. ..Kriss Akabusi, Great Britain — 47.82

##### 3000-METER STEEPLECHASE
1. ..Mathew Birir, Kenya — 8:08.84
2. ..Patrick Sang, Kenya — 8:09.55
3. ..William Mutwol, Kenya — 8:10.74

##### 4 X 100 METER RELAY
1. ..United States: Mike Marsh, Leroy Burrell, Dennis Mitchell, Carl Lewis — 37.40WR
2. ..Nigeria — 37.98
3. ..Cuba — 38.00

##### 4 X 400 METER RELAY
1. ..United States: Andrew Valmon, Quincy Watts, Michael Johnson, Steve Lewis — 2:55.74 WR
2. ..Cuba — 2:59.51
3. ..Great Britain — 2:59.73

##### 20-KILOMETER WALK
1. ..Daniel Plaza, Spain — 1:21:45
2. ..Guillaume Leblanc, France — 1:22:25
3. ..Giovanni De Benedictis, Italy — 1:23:11

##### 50-KILOMETER WALK
1. ..Andrey Perlov, Unified Team — 3:50:13
2. ..Carlos Mercenario, Mexico — 3:52:09
3. ..Ronald Weigel, Germany — 3:53:45

##### HIGH JUMP
1. ..Javier Sotomayor, Cuba — 7 ft 8 in
2. ..Patrik Sjoberg, Sweden — 7 ft 8 in
3. ..Artur Partyka, Poland — 7 ft 8 in
3. ..Timothy Forsythe, Australia — 7 ft 8 in
3. ..Hollis Conway, United States — 7 ft 8 in

##### POLE VAULT
1. ..Maksim Tarasov, Unified Team — 19 ft ¼ in
2. ..Igor Trandenkov, Unified Team — 19 ft ¼ in
3. ..Javier Garcia, Spain — 18 ft 10¼ in

##### LONG JUMP
1. ..Carl Lewis, United States — 28 ft 5½ in
2. ..Mike Powell, United States — 28 ft 4¼ in
3. ..Joe Greene, United States — 27 ft 4½in

##### TRIPLE JUMP
1. ..Mike Conley, United States — 59 ft 7½ in
2. ..Charles Simpkins, United States — 57 ft 9 in
3. ..Frank Rutherford, Bahamas — 56 ft 11½in

##### SHOT PUT
1. ..Mike Stulce, United States — 71 ft 2½in
2. ..Jim Doehring, United States — 68 ft 9¼ in
3. ..Vyacheslav Lykho, Unified Team — 68 ft 8½in

##### DISCUS THROW
1. ..Romas Ubartas, Lithuania — 213 ft 8 in.
2. ..Jürgen Schult, Germany — 213 ft 1 in
3. ..Roberto Moya, Cuba — 210 ft 4 in

##### HAMMER THROW
1. ..Andrey Abduvaliyev, Unified Team — 270 ft 9 in
2. ..Igor Astapkovich, Unified Team — 268 ft 11 in
3. ..Igor Nikulin, Unified Team — 267 ft

##### JAVELIN
1. ..Jan Zelezny, Czechoslovakia — 294 ft 2 in OR
2. ..Seppo Räty, Finland — 284 ft 1 in
3. ..Steve Backley, Great Britain — 273 ft 7 in

##### DECATHLON
|  | Pts |
| --- | --- |
| 1. ..Robert Zmelik, Czechoslovakia | 8611 |
| 2. ..Antonio Peñalver, Spain | 8412 |
| 3. ..Dave Johnson, United States | 8309 |

Note: OR=Olympic record. WR=world record. EOR=equals Olympic record. EWR=equals world record

## TRACK AND FIELD *(Cont.)*

### Women

#### 100 METERS

1. ..Gail Devers, United States — 10.82
2. ..Juliet Cuthbert, Jamaica — 10.83
3. ..Irina Privalova, Unified Team — 10.84

#### 200 METERS

1. ..Gwen Torrence, United States — 21.81
2. ..Juliet Cuthbert, Jamaica — 22.02
3. ..Merlene Ottey, Jamaica — 22.09

#### 400 METERS

1. ..Marie-Jose Péréc, France — 48.83
2. ..Olga Bryzgina, Unified Team — 49.05
3. ..Ximena Restrepo, Colombia — 49.64

#### 800 METERS

1. ..Ellen Van Langen, The Netherlands — 1:55.54
2. ..Lilia Nurutdinova, Unified Team — 1:55.99
3. ..Ana Fidelia Quirot, Cuba — 1:56.80

#### 1500 METERS

1. ..Hassiba Boulmerka, Algeria — 3:55.30
2. ..Lyudmila Rogacheva, Unified Team — 3:56.91
3. ..Qu Yunxia, China — 3:57.08

#### 3000 METERS

1. ..Elena Romanova, Unified Team — 8:46.04
2. ..Tatiana Dorovskikh, Unified Team — 8:46.85
3. ..Angela Chalmers, Canada — 8:47.22

#### 10,000 METERS

1. ..Derartu Tulu, Ethiopia — 31:06.02
2. ..Elana Meyer, South Africa — 31:11.75
3. ..Lynn Jennings, United States — 31:19.89

#### MARATHON

1. ..Valentina Yegorova, Unified Team — 2:32:41
2. ..Yuko Arimori, Japan — 2:32:49
3. ..Lorraine Moller, New Zealand — 2:33:59

#### 100-METER HURDLES

1. ..Paraskevi Patoulidou, Greece — 12.64
2. ..LaVonna Martin, United States — 12.69
3. ..Yordanka Donkova, Bulgaria — 12.70

#### 400-METER HURDLES

1. ..Sally Gunnell, Great Britain — 53.23
2. ..Sandra Farmer-Patrick, United States — 53.69
3. ..Janeene Vickers, United States — 54.31

#### 4 X 100 METER RELAY

1. ..United States: Evelyn Ashford, Esther Jones, Carlette Guidry, Gwen Torrence — 42.11
2. ..Unified Team — 42.16
3. ..Nigeria — 42.81

#### 4 X 400 METER RELAY

1. ..Unified Team: Yelena Ruzina, Lioudmila Dzhigalova, Olga Nazarova, Olga Bryzgina — 3:20.20
2. ..United States: Natasha Kaiser, Gwen Torrence, Jearl Miles, Rochelle Stevens — 3:20.92
3. ..Great Britain — 3:24.23

#### HIGH JUMP

1. ..Heike Henkel, Germany — 6 ft 7½ in
2. ..Galina Astafei, Romania — 6 ft 6¾ in
3. ..Joanet Quintero, Cuba — 6 ft 5½ in

#### LONG JUMP

1. ..Heike Drechsler, Germany — 23 ft 5¼ in
2. ..Inessa Kravets, Unified Team — 23 ft 4½ in
3. ..Jackie Joyner-Kersee, United States — 23 ft 2½ in

#### SHOT PUT

1. ..Svetlana Kriveleva, Unified Team — 69 ft 1¼ in
2. ..Huang Zhihong, China — 67 ft 2 in
3. ..Kathrin Neimke, Germany — 64 ft 10¾ in

#### DISCUS THROW

1. ..Maritza Martén, Cuba — 229 ft 10 in
2. ..Tzvetanka Mintcheva Khristova, Unified Team — 222 ft 4 in
3. ..Daniela Costian, Australia — 217 ft 4 in

#### JAVELIN

1. ..Silke Renk, Germany — 224 ft 2 in
2. ..Natalia Shikolenka, Unified Team — 223 ft 11 in
3. ..Karen Forkel, Germany — 219 ft 4 in

#### HEPTATHLON

| | Pts |
| --- | --- |
| 1. ..Jackie Joyner-Kersee, United States | 7044 |
| 2. ..Irina Belova, Unified Team | 6845 |
| 3. ..Sabine Braun, Germany | 6649 |

## BADMINTON

### Men

#### SINGLES

1. ..Allan Budikusuma, Indonesia
2. ..Ardy B. Wiranata, Indonesia
3. ..Hermawan Susanto, Indonesia
3. ..Thomas Stuer-Lauridsen, Denmark

#### DOUBLES

1. ..Park Joo-Bong & Kim Moon Soo, South Korea
2. ..Rudy Gunawan & Eddy Hrtona, Indonesia
3. ..Razif Sidek & Jalani Sidek, Malaysia
3. ..Li Yongbo & Tian Bingyi, China

### Women

#### SINGLES

1. ..Susi Susanti, Indonesia
2. ..Bang Soo Hyun, South Korea
3. ..Huang Hua, China
3. ..Tang Jiuhong, China

#### DOUBLES

1. ..Hwang Hye Young & Chung So Young, South Korea
2. ..Guan Weizhen & Nong Qunhua, China
3. ..Lin Yanfen & Yao Fen, China
3. ..Young Ah Gil & Eun Jung Shim, South Korea

## BASEBALL

1. .................................................Cuba
2. .................................................Taiwan
3. .................................................Japan

## CANOE/KAYAK

### Men

#### C-1 FLATWATER 500 METERS

1. ...Nikolai Boukhalov, Bulgaria      1:51.14
2. ...Mikhail Slivinski, Unfied Team      1:51.40
3. ...Olaf Heukrodt, Germany      1:53.00

#### C-1 FLATWATER 1000 METERS

1. ...Nikolai Boukhalov, Bulgaria      4:05.92
2. ...Ivana Klementzjeve, Latvia      4:06.60
3. ...Gyorgy Zala, Hungary      4:07.35

#### C-2 FLATWATER 500 METERS

1. ...A. Maccekov & D. Dovgalenok,      1:41.54
    Unified Team
2. ...U. Papke & I. Spelly, Germany      1:41.68
3. ...M. Marinov & B. Stoyanov, Bulgaria      1:41.94

#### C-2 FLATWATER 1000 METERS

1. ...U. Papke & I. Spelly, Germany      3:37.42
2. ...A. Nielsson & C. Frederiksen, Denmark      3:39.26
3. ...D. Hoyer & O. Bolvin, France      3:39.51

#### C-1 WHITEWATER SLALOM

    **Pts**
1. ...Lukos Pollerr, Czechoslovakia      113.69
2. ...Gareth John Marriott, Great Britain      116.48
3. ...Jacky Avril, France      117.18

#### C-2 WHITEWATER SLALOM

    **Pts**
1. ...S. Strausbaugh & J, Jacobi, U.S.      122.41
2. ...M. Simek & J. Rohan, Czechosolvakia      124.25
3. ...F. Adisson & W. Forgues, France      124.38

#### K-1 FLATWATER 500 METERS

1. ...Mikko Kolehmainen, Finland      1:40.34
2. ...Zaolt Gyulay, Hungary      1:40.64
3. ...Knut Hofmann, Norway      1:40.71

#### K-1 FLATWATER 1000 METERS

1. ...Clint Robinson, Australia      3:37.26
2. ...Knut Hofmann, Norway      3:37.50
3. ...Greg Barton, United States      3:37.93

### Men (Cont.)

#### K-2 FLATWATER 500 METERS

1. ...K. Bluhm & T. Gutsche, Germany      1:28.27
2. ...M. Freimut & W. Kurpiewski, Poland      1:29.84
3. ...A. Rossi & B. Dreossi, Italy      1:30.00

#### K-2 FLATWATER 1000 METERS

1. ...K. Bluhm & T. Gutsche, Germany      3:16.10
2. ...G. Olsson & K. Sundqvist, Sweden      3:17.70
3. ...G. Kotowicz & D. Bielkowski, Poland      3:18.86

#### K-4 FLATWATER 1000 METERS

1. ...Germany      2:54.18
2. ...Hungary      2:54.82
3. ...Australia      2:56.97

### Women

#### K-1 WHITEWATER SLALOM

    **Pts**
1. ...Pierpaolo Ferrazzi, Italy      106.89
2. ...Sylvain Curiruer, France      107.06
3. ...Jochen Lettmann, Germany      108.52

#### K-1 FLATWATER 500 METERS

1. ...Birgit Schmidt, Germany      1:51.60
2. ...Rita Koban, Hungary      1:51.96
3. ...Izabella Dylewska, Poland      1:52.36

#### K-2 FLATWATER 500 METERS

1. ...R. Portwich & A. Von Seck, Germany      1:40.29
2. ...S. Gunnarsson & A. Andersson, Sweden      1:40.41
3. ...R. Koban & E. Donusz, Hungary      1:40.81

#### K-4 FLATWATER 500 METERS

1. ...Hungary      1:38.32
2. ...Germany      1:38.47
3. ...Sweden      1:39.79

#### K-1 WHITEWATER SLALOM

    **Pts**
1. ...Elizabeth Micheler, Germany      126.41
2. ...Danielle Woodward, Australia      128.27
3. ...Dana Chladek, United States      131.75

## BASKETBALL

### Men

Final: United States 117, Croatia 85
Lithuania (3rd)
United States: Christian Laettner, David Robinson, Patrick Ewing, Larry Bird, Scottie Pippen, Michael Jordan, Clyde Drexler, Karl Malone, John Stockton, Chris Mullin, Charles Barkley, Earvin Johnson

### Women

Final: Unified Team 76, China 66
United States (3rd):
Teresa Edwards, Daedra Charles, Clarissa Davis, Tammy Jackson, Teresa Weatherspoon, Vickie Orr, Victoria Bullett, Carolyn Jones, Katrina McClain, Medina Dixon, Cynthia Cooper, Suzanne McConnell

## BOXING

### LIGHT FLYWEIGHT (106 LB)

1. ...................Rogelio Marcelo, Cuba
2. ...................Daniel Bojinov, Bulgaria
3. ...................Jan Quast, Germany
3. ...................Roel Velasco, Philippines

### FLYWEIGHT (112 LB)

1. ...................Su Choi Choi, North Korea
2. ...................Raul Gonzalez, Cuba
3. ...................Timothy Austin, United States
3. ...................Istvan Kovacs, Hungary

### BANTAMWEIGHT (119 LB)

1. ...................Joel Casamayor, Cuba
2. ...................Wayne McCullough, Ireland
3. ...................Li Gwang Sik, North Korea
3. ...................Mohamed Achik, Morocco

### FEATHERWEIGHT (125 LB)

1. ...................Andreas Tews, Germany
2. ...................Faustino Reyes, Spain
3. ...................Hocine Soltani, Algeria
3. ...................Ramazi Paliani, Unified Team

### LIGHTWEIGHT (132 LB)

1. ...................Oscar De La Hoya, United States
2. ...................Marco Rudolph, Germany
3. ...................Hong Sung Sik, North Korea
3. ...................Namjil Bayarsaikhan, Mongolia

### LIGHT WELTERWEIGHT (139 LB)

1. ...................Hector Vinent, Cuba
2. ...................Mark Leduc, Canada
3. ...................Jyri Kjall, Finland
3. ...................Leonard Doroftei, Romania

### WELTERWEIGHT (147 LB)

1. ...................Michael Carruth, Ireland
2. ...................Juan Hernandez, Cuba
3. ...................Aniibal Acevedo Santiago, Puerto Rico
3. ...................Arkom Chenglai, Thailand

### LIGHT MIDDLEWEIGHT (156 LB)

1. ...................Juan Lemus, Cuba
2. ...................Orhan Delibas, Netherlands
3. ...................Gyorgy Mizsei, Hungary
3. ...................Robin Reid, Great Britain

### MIDDLEWEIGHT (165 LB)

1. ...................Ariel Hernandez, Cuba
2. ...................Chris Byrd, United States
3. ...................Chris Johnson, Canada
3. ...................Lee Seung Bae, South Korea

### LIGHT HEAVYWEIGHT (178 LB)

1. ...................Torsten May, Germany
2. ...................Rostislav Zaoulitchnyi, Unified Team
3. ...................Zoltan Beres, Hungary
3. ...................Wojciech Bartnik, Poland

### HEAVYWEIGHT (201 LB)

1. ...................Felix Savon, Cuba
2. ...................David Izonritei, Nigeria
3. ...................Arnold Van Der Lijde, The Netherlands
3. ...................David Tua, New Zealand

### SUPERHEAVYWEIGHT (201+ LB)

1. ...................Roberto Balado, Cuba
2. ...................Richard Igbineghu, Nigeria
3. ...................Brian Nielsen, Denmark
3. ...................Svilen Roussinov, Bulgaria

## GYMNASTICS

### Men

#### ALL-AROUND

| | | Pts |
|---|---|---|
| 1. | Vitaly Scherbo, Unified Team | 59.025 |
| 2. | Grigory Misiutin, Unified Team | 58.925 |
| 3. | Valery Belenki, Unified Team | 58.625 |

#### HORIZONTAL BAR

| | | Pts |
|---|---|---|
| 1. | Trent Dimas, United States | 9.875 |
| 1. | Grigory Misiutin, Unified Team | 9.837 |
| 3. | Andreas Wecker, Germany | 9.837 |

#### PARALLEL BARS

| | | Pts |
|---|---|---|
| 1. | Vitaly Scherbo, Unified Team | 9.900 |
| 2. | Li Jing, China | 9.812 |
| 3. | Guo Linyao, China | 9.800 |
| 3. | Igor Korobchinski, Unified Team | 9.800 |
| 3. | Masayuki Matsunaga, Japan | 9.800 |

#### VAULT

| | | Pts |
|---|---|---|
| 1. | Vitaly Scherbo, Unified Team | 9.856 |
| 2. | Grigory Misiutin, Unified Team | 9.781 |
| 3. | Yoo Ok Ryul, South Korea | 9.762 |

### Women

#### ALL-AROUND

| | | Pts |
|---|---|---|
| 1. | Tatiana Gutsu, Unified Team | 39.737 |
| 2. | Shannon Miller, United States | 39.725 |
| 3. | Lavinia Milosovici, Romania | 39.687 |

#### VAULT

| | | Pts |
|---|---|---|
| 1. | Henrietta Onodi, Hungary | 9.925 |
| 1. | Lavinia Milosovici, Romania | 9.925 |
| 3. | Tatiana Lisenko, Unified Team | 9.912 |

#### UNEVEN BARS

| | | Pts |
|---|---|---|
| 1. | Lu Li, China | 10.000 |
| 2. | Tatiana Gutsu, Unified Team | 9.975 |
| 3. | Shannon Miller, United States | 9.962 |

#### BALANCE BEAM

| | | Pts |
|---|---|---|
| 1. | Tatiana Lisenko, Unified Team | 9.975 |
| 2. | Lu Li, China | 9.912 |
| 2. | Shannon Miller, United States | 9.912 |

## GYMNASTICS (Cont.)

### Men

#### POMMEL HORSE

| | Pts |
|---|---|
| 1. ........Vitaly Scherbo, Unified Team | 9.925 |
| 1. ........Pae Gil Su, North Korea | 9.925 |
| 3. ........Andreas Wecker, Germany | 9.887 |

#### RINGS

| | Pts |
|---|---|
| 1. ........Vitaly Scherbo, Unified Team | 9.937 |
| 1. ........Li Jing, China | 9.875 |
| 3. ........Li Xiaosahuang, China | 9.862 |
| 3. ........Andreas Wecker, Germany | 9.862 |

#### FLOOR EXERCISE

| | Pts |
|---|---|
| 1. ........Li Xizosahuang, China | 9.925 |
| 2. ........Grigory Misiutin, Unified Team | 9.787 |
| 2. ........Yukio Iketani, Japan | 9.787 |

#### TEAM COMBINED EXERCISES

| | Pts |
|---|---|
| 1. ........Unified Team | 585.450 |
| 2. ........China | 580.375 |
| 3. ........Japan | 578.250 |

### Women

#### FLOOR EXERCISE

| | Pts |
|---|---|
| 1. ........Lavinia Milosovici, Romania | 10.000 |
| 2. ........Henrietta Onodi, Hungary | 9.950 |
| 3. ........Shannon Miller, United States | 9.912 |
| 3. ........Cristina Bontas, Romania | 9.912 |
| 3. ........Tatiana Gutsu, Unified Team | 9.912 |

#### TEAM COMBINED EXERCISES

| | Pts |
|---|---|
| 1. ........Unified Team | 395.666 |
| 2. ........Romania | 395.079 |
| 3. ........United States | 394.704 |

#### RHYTHMIC ALL-AROUND

| | Pts |
|---|---|
| 1. ........Aleksandra Timoshenko, Unified Team | 59.037 |
| 2. ........Carolina Pascual Gracia, Spain | 58.100 |
| 3. ........Oksana Skaldina, Unified Team | 57.912 |

## SWIMMING

### Men

#### 50-METER FREESTYLE

| | |
|---|---|
| 1. ..Aleksandr Popov, Unified Team | 21.91 OR |
| 2. ..Matt Biondi, United States | 22.09 |
| 3. ..Tom Jager, Unifed States | 22.30 |

#### 100-METER FREESTYLE

| | |
|---|---|
| 1. ..Aleksandr Popov, Unified Team | 49.02 |
| 2. ..Gustavo Borges, Brazil | 49.43 |
| 3. ..Stephan Caron, France | 49.50 |

#### 200-METER FREESTYLE

| | |
|---|---|
| 1. ..Evgueni Sadovyi, Unified Team | 1:46.70 OR |
| 2. ..Anders Holmertz, Sweden | 1:46.86 |
| 3. ..Antti Kasvio, Finland | 1:47.63 |

#### 400-METER FREESTYLE

| | |
|---|---|
| 1. ..Evgueni Sadovyi, Unified Team | 3:45.00 WR |
| 2. ..Kieren Perkins, Australia | 3:45.16 |
| 3. ..Anders Holmertz, Sweden | 3:46.77 |

#### 1500-METER FREESTYLE

| | |
|---|---|
| 1. ..Kieren Perkins, Australia | 14:43.48 WR |
| 2. ..Glen Housman, Australia | 14:55.29 |
| 3. ..Jörg Hoffmann, Germany | 15:02.29 |

#### 100-METER BACKSTROKE

| | |
|---|---|
| 1. ..Mark Tewksbury, Canada | 53.98 WR |
| 2. ..Jeff Rouse, United States | 54.04 |
| 3. ..David Berkoff, United States | 54.78 |

#### 100-METER BACKSTROKE

| | |
|---|---|
| 1. ..Martin Zubero-Lopez, Spain | 1:58.47 OR |
| 2. ..Vladimir Selkov, Unified Team | 1:58.87 |
| 3. ..Stefano Battistelli, Italy | 1:59.40 |

#### 100-METER BREASTSTROKE

| | |
|---|---|
| 1. ..Nelson Diebel, United States | 1:01.50 OR |
| 2. ..Norbert Rozsa, Hungary | 1:01.68 |
| 3. ..Philip Rogers, Australia | 1:01.76 |

#### 200-METER BREASTSTROKE

| | |
|---|---|
| 1. ..Mike Barrowman, United States | 2:10.16 WR |
| 2. ..Norbert Rozsa, Hungary | 2:11.23 |
| 3. ..Nick Gillingham, Great Britain | 2:11.29 |

#### 100-METER BUTTERFLY

| | |
|---|---|
| 1. ..Pablo Morales, United States | 53.32 |
| 2. ..Rafal Szukala, Poland | 53.35 |
| 3. ..Anthony Nesty, Surinam | 53.41 |

#### 200-METER BUTTERFLY

| | |
|---|---|
| 1. ..Melvin Stewart, United States | 1:56.26 |
| 2. ..Danyon Loader, New Zealand | 1:57.93 |
| 3. ..Franck Esposito, France | 1:58.51 |

#### 200-METER INDIVIDUAL MEDLEY

| | |
|---|---|
| 1. ..Tamas Darnyi, Hungary | 2:00.76 |
| 2. ..Greg Burgess, United States | 2:00.97 |
| 3. ..Attila Czene, Hungary | 2:01.00 |

#### 400-METER INDIVIDUAL MEDLEY

| | |
|---|---|
| 1. ..Tamas Darnyi, Hungary | 4:14.23 OR |
| 2. ..Eric Namesnik, United States | 4:15.57 |
| 3. ..Luca Sacchi, Italy | 4:16.34 |

#### 4 X 100 METER MEDLEY RELAY

| | |
|---|---|
| 1. ..United States: Jeff Rouse, Nelson Diebel, Pablo Morales, Jon Olsen | 3:36.93 WR |
| 2. ..Unified Team | 3:38.56 |
| 3. ..Canada | 3:39.66 |

Note: OR=Olympic record.  WR=world record.  EOR=equals Olympic record.  EWR=equals world record

## SWIMMING (Cont.)

### Men (Cont.)

**4 X 100 METER FREESTYLE RELAY**

1. ..United States: Joe Hudepohl,    3:16.74
   Matt Biondi, Tom Jager,
   Jon Olsen
2. ..Unified Team    3:17.56
3. ..Germany    3:17.90

**4 X 200 METER FREESTYLE RELAY**

1. ..Unified Team: Dimitri Lepikov,    7:11.95 WR
   Vladimir Pychenko, Veniamin Taianovitch,
   Evgueni Sadovyi
2. ..Sweden    7:15.51
3. ..United States    7:16.23

## Women

**50-METER FREESTYLE**

1. ..Yang Wenyi, China    24.79 WR
2. ..Zhuang Yong, China    25.08
3. ..Angel Martino, United States    25.23

**100-METER FREESTYLE**

1. ..Zhuang Yong, China    54.64 OR
2. ..Jenny Thompson, United States    54.84
3. ..Franziska Van Almsick, Germany    54.94

**200-METER FREESTYLE**

1. ..Nicole Haislett, United States    1:57.90
2. ..Franziska Van Almsick, Germany    1:58.00
3. ..Kerstin Kielgass, Germany    1:59.67

**400-METER FREESTYLYE**

1. ..Dagmar Hase, Germany    4:07.18
2. ..Janet Evans, United States    4:07.37
3. ..Hayley Lewis, Australia    4:11.22

**800-METER FREESTYLE**

1. ..Janet Evans, United States    8:25.52
2. ..Hayley Lewis, Australia    8:30.34
3. ..Jana Henke, Germany    8:30.99

**100-METER BACKSTROKE**

1. ..Krisztina Egerszegi, Hungary    1:00.68 OR
2. ..Tunde Szabo, Hungary    1:01.14
3. ..Lea Loveless, United States    1:01.43

**200-METER BACKSTROKE**

1. ..Krisztina Egerszegi, Hungary    2:07.06
2. ..Dagmar Hase, Germany    2:09.46
3. ..Nicole Stevenson, Australia    2:10.20

**100-METER BREASTSTROKE**

1. ..Elena Roudkovskaia, Unified Team    1:08.00
2. ..Anita Nall, United States    1:08.17
3. ..Samantha Riley, Australia    1:09.25

**200-METER BREASTSTROKE**

1. ..Kyoko Iwasaki, Japan    2:26.65 OR
2. ..Lin Li, China    2:26.85
3. ..Anita Nall, United States    2:26.88

**100-METER BUTTERFLY**

1. ..Qian Hong, China    58.62 OR
2. ..Crissy Ahmann-Leighton,    58.74
   United States
3. ..Catherine Plewinski, France    59.01

**200-METER BUTTERFLY**

1. ..Summer Sanders, United States    2:08.67
2. ..Wang Ziaohong, China    2:09.01
3. ..Susan O'Neill, Australia    2:09.03

**200-METER INDIVIDUAL MEDLEY**

1. ..Lin Li, China    2:11.65 WR
2. ..Summer Sanders, United States    2:11.91
3. ..Daniela Hunger, Germany    2:13.92

**400-METER INDIVIDUAL MEDLEY**

1. ..Krisztina Egerszegi, Hungary    4:36.54
2. ..Lin Li, China    4:36.73
3. ..Summer Sanders, United States    4:37.58

**4 X 100 METER MEDLEY RELAY**

1. ..United States: Lea Loveless,    4:02.54 WR
   Anita Nall, Crissy Ahmann-Leighton,
   Jenny Thompson
2. ..Germany    4:05.19
3. ..Unified Team    4:06.44

**4 X 100 METER FREESTYLE RELAY**

1. ..United States: Nicole Haislett,    3:39.46 WR
   Dara Torres, Angel Martino,
   Jenny Thompson
2. ..China    3:40.12
3. ..Germany    3:41.60

# DIVING

## Men

### SPRINGBOARD

| | | Pts |
|---|---|---|
| 1. | ..........Mark Lenzi, United States | 676.53 |
| 2. | ..........Tan Liangde, China | 645.57 |
| 3. | ..........Dmitri Saoutine, Unified Team | 627.78 |

### PLATFORM

| | | Pts |
|---|---|---|
| 1. | ..........Sun Shuwei, China | 677.31 |
| 2. | ..........Scott Donie, United States | 633.63 |
| 3. | ..........Xiong Ni, China | 600.15 |

## Women

### SPRINGBOARD

| | | Pts |
|---|---|---|
| 1. | ..........Gao Min, China | 572.40 |
| 2. | ..........Irina Lachko, Unified Team | 514.14 |
| 3. | ..........Brita Pia Baldus, Germany | 503.07 |

### PLATFORM

| | | Pts |
|---|---|---|
| 1. | ..........Fu Mingxia, China | 461.43 |
| 2. | ..........Yelena Mirochina, Unified Team | 411.63 |
| 3. | ..........Mary Ellen Clark, United States | 401.91 |

Note: OR=Olympic record. WR=world record. EOR=equals Olympic record. EWR=equals world record

## INDIVIDUAL ARCHERY

### Men

1. .........Sebastien Flute, France
2. .........Chung Jae Hun, South Korea
3. .........Simon Terry, Great Britain

### Women

1. .........Cho Youn Jeong, South Korea
2. .........Kim Soo Nyung, South Korea
3. .........Natalia Valeeva, Unified Team

## CYCLING

### Men

#### 100 KM TEAM TIME TRIAL

| | | |
|---|---|---|
| 1. ..Germany: Bernd Dittert, Christian Meyer, Uwe Peschel, Michael Rich | 2:01:39 |
| 2. ..Italy | 2:02:39 |
| 3. ..France | 2:05:25 |

#### 1 KM TIME TRIAL

1. ..Jose Moreno, Spain — 1:03.342 OR
2. ..Shane Kelly, Australia — 1:04.288
3. ..Erin Hartwell, United States — 1:04.753

#### 4000 METER INDIVIDUAL PURSUIT

1. ..Chris Boardman, Great Britain
2. ..Jens Lehmann, Germany
3. ..Gary Anderson, New Zealand

#### 4000 METER TEAM PURSUIT

| | |
|---|---|
| 1. ..Germany: M. Gloeckner, Jens Lehmann, Stefan Steinweg, Guido Fulst | 4:08.791 |
| 2. ..Australia | 4:10.218 |
| 3. ..Denmark | 4:15.860 |

#### POINTS RACE

1. ..Giovanni Lombardi, Italy — 44
2. ..Leon Van Bon, The Netherlands — 43
3. ..Cedric Mathy, Belgium — 41

#### INDIVIDUAL ROAD RACE

1. ..Fabio Casartelli, Italy — 4:35.21
2. ..Erik Dekker, The Netherlands — 4:35.22
3. ..Dainis Ozols, Latvia — 4:35.24

### Women

#### SPRINT

1. ......Erika Saloumiae, Estonia
2. ......Annett Neumann, Germany
3. ......Ingrid Haringa, The Netherlands

#### ROAD RACE

1. ..Kathryn Watt, Australia — 2:04.42
2. ..Jeannie Longo-Ciprelli, France — 2:05.02
3. ..Monique Knol, The Netherlands — 2:05.03

## EQUESTRIAN

#### 3-DAY TEAM

| | |
|---|---|
| 1. ......Australia: David Green, Gillian Rolton, Andrew Hoy, Matthew Ryan | 288.60 |
| 2. ......New Zealand | 290.80 |
| 3. ......Germany | 300.30 |

#### 3-DAY INDIVIDUAL

1. ......Matthew Ryan, Australia — 70.00
2. ......Herbert Blocker, Germany — 81.30
3. ......Blyth Tait, New Zealand — 87.60

#### TEAM DRESSAGE

| | |
|---|---|
| 1. ......Germany: Isabelle Werth, Klaus Balkenhol, Monica Theodorescu, Nicole Uphoff | 5224 |
| 2. ......The Netherlands | 4742 |
| 3. ......United States | 4643 |

#### INDIVIDUAL DRESSAGE

1. ......Nicole Uphoff, Germany — 1768
2. ......Isabelle Werth, Germany — 1762
3. ......Klaus Balkenhol, Germany — 1694

#### TEAM JUMPING

| | |
|---|---|
| 1. ......The Netherlands: Piet Raymakers, Bert Romp, Jan Tops, Jos Lansink | 12.00 |
| 2. ......Austria | 16.75 |
| 3. ......France | 24.75 |

#### INDIVIDUAL JUMPING

1. ......Ludger Beerbaum, Germany — 0.00
2. ......Piet Raymakers, The Netherlands — .25
3. ......Norman Dello Joio, United States — 4.75

Note: OR=Olympic record. WR=world record. EOR=equals Olympic record. EWR=equals world record

## INDIVIDUAL FENCING

### Men

#### FOIL
1. ...................Philippe Omnes, France
2. ...................Sergei Goloubitski, Unified Team
3. ...................Elvis Gregory Gil, Cuba

#### SABRE
1. ...................Bence Szabo, Hungary
2. ...................Marco Marin, Italy
3. ...................Jean-Francois Lamour, France

### Men *(Cont.)*

#### EPEE
1. ...................Eric Srecki, France
2. ...................Pavel Kolobkov, Unified Team
3. ...................Jean-Michel Henry, France

### Women

#### FOIL
1. ...................Giovanna Trillini, Italy
2. ...................Wang Huifeng, China
3. ...................Tatiana Sadovskaia, Unified Team

## FIELD HOCKEY

### Men
1. ...................Germany
2. ...................Australia
3. ...................Pakistan

### Women
1. ...................Spain
2. ...................Germany
3. ...................Great Britain

## TEAM HANDBALL

### Men
1. ...................Unified Team
2. ...................Sweden
3. ...................France

### Women
1. ...................South Korea
2. ...................Norway
3. ...................Unified Team

## JUDO

#### EXTRA-LIGHTWEIGHT
1. ...................Nazim Guseinov, Unified Team
2. ...................Yoon Hyun, South Korea
3. ...................Tadanori Koshino, Japan
3. ...................Richard Trautmann, Germany

#### HALF-LIGHTWEIGHT
1. ...................Rogerio Sampaio Cardoso, Brazil
2. ...................Josef Czak, Hungary
3. ...................Udo Quellmalz, Germany
3. ...................Israel Hernandez Planas, Cuba

#### LIGHTWEIGHT
1. ...................Toshihiko Koga, Japan
2. ...................Bertalan Hajtos, Hungary
3. ...................Chung Hoon, South Korea
3. ...................Shay Oren Smadga, Israel

#### HALF-MIDDLEWEIGHT
1. ...................Hidehiko Yoshida, Japan
2. ...................Jason Morris, United States
3. ...................Bertrand Domaisin, France
3. ...................Kim Byung Joo, South Korea

#### MIDDLEWEIGHT
1. ...................Waldemar Legien, Poland
2. ...................Pascal Tayot, France
3. ...................Hirotaka Okada, Japan
3. ...................Nicolas Gill, Canada

#### HALF-HEAVYWEIGHT
1. ...................Antal Kovacs, Hungary
2. ...................Raymond Stevens, Great Britain
3. ...................Dmitri Sergeev, Unified Team
3. ...................Theo Meijer, The Netherlands

#### HEAVYWEIGHT
1. ...................David Khakaleshvili, Unified Team
2. ...................Naoya Ogowa, Japan
3. ...................David Douillet, France
3. ...................Imre Csosz, Hungary

## MODERN PENTATHLON

#### TEAM
1. ...................Poland
2. ...................Unified Team
3. ...................Italy

#### INDIVIDUAL
1. ...................Arkadiusz Skrzypaszek, Poland
2. ...................Attila Mizser, Hungary
3. ...................Eduard Zenovka, Unified Team

# ROWING

## Men

### SINGLE SCULLS
1. ..Thomas Lange, Germany — 6:51.40
2. ..Vaclav Chalupa, Czechoslovakia — 6:52.93
3. ..Kajetan Broniewski, Poland — 6:56.82

### DOUBLE SCULLS
1. ..Australia — 6:17.32
2. ..Austria — 6:18.42
3. ..The Netherlands — 6:22.82

### COXLESS PAIR
1. ..Great Britain — 6:27.72
2. ..Germany — 6:32.68
3. ..Slovenia — 6:33.43

### COXED FOUR
1. ..Romania — 5:59.37
2. ..Germany — 6:00.34
3. ..Poland — 6:03.27

### COXED PAIR
1. ..Great Britain — 6:49.83
2. ..Italy — 6:50.98
3. ..Romania — 6:51.58

### QUADRUPLE SCULLS
1. ..Germany — 5:45.17
2. ..Norway — 5:47.09
3. ..Italy — 5:47.33

### COXLESS FOUR
1. ..Australia — 5:55.04
2. ..United States — 5:56.68
3. ..Slovenia — 5:58.24

### EIGHT-OARS
1. ..Canada — 5:29.53
2. ..Romania — 5:29.67
3. ..Germany — 5:31.00

## Women

### SINGLE SCULLS
1. ..Elisabeta Lipa, Romania — 7:25.54
2. ..Annelies Bredael, Belgium — 7:26.64
3. ..Silken Suzette Laumann, Canada — 7:28.85

### DOUBLE SCULLS
1. ..Germany — 6:49.00
2. ..Romania — 6:51.47
3. ..China — 6:55.16

### COXLESS PAIR
1. ..Canada — 7:06.22
2. ..Germany — 7:07.96
3. ..United States — 7:08.12

### COXLESS FOUR
1. ..Canada — 6:30.85
2. ..United States — 6:31.86
3. ..Germany — 6:32.34

### QUADRUPLE SCULLS
1. ..Germany — 6:20.18
2. ..Romania — 6:24.34
3. ..Unified Team — 6:25.07

### EIGHT-OARS
1. ..Canada — 6:02.62
2. ..Romania — 6:06.26
3. ..Germany — 6:07.80

# SOCCER
1. ....................................................Spain
2. ....................................................Poland
3. ....................................................Ghana

# SYNCHRONIZED SWIMMING

### SOLO

| | Pts |
|---|---|
| 1. ..........Kristen Babb-Sprague, United States | 191.848 |
| 2. ..........Sylvie Frechette, Canada | 191.717 |
| 3. ..........Fumiko Okuno, Japan | 187.056 |

### DUET

| | Pts |
|---|---|
| 1. ..........Karen & Sarah Josephson, United States | 192.175 |
| 2. ..........Penny & Vicky Vilagos, Canada | 189.394 |
| 3. ..........Fumiko Okuno & Aki Takayama, Japan | 186.868 |

# SHOOTING

## Men

### THREE-POSITION RIFLE

| | Pts |
|---|---|
| 1......Gracha Petikian, Unified Team | 1267.4 |
| 2......Bob Foth, United States | 1266.6 |
| 3......Ryohei Koba, Japan | 1265.9 |

### AIR RIFLE

| | Pts |
|---|---|
| 1......Jury Fedkin, Unified Team | 695.3 |
| 2......Franck Badiou, France | 691.9 |
| 3......Johann Riederer, Germany | 691.7 |

### FREE RIFLE PRONE

| | Pts |
|---|---|
| 1......Eun-Chul Lee, South Korea | 702.5 |
| 2......Harald Stenvaag, Norway | 701.4 |
| 3......Stevan Pletikosic, Independent Team | 701.1 |

### FREE PISTOL

| | Pts |
|---|---|
| 1......Konstantine Loukachik, Unified Team | 658 |
| 2......Yifu Wang, China | 657 |
| 3......Ragnar Skanaker, Sweden | 657 |

## SHOOTING

### Men

#### RAPID-FIRE PISTOL

| | Pts |
|---|---|
| 1......Ralf Schumann, Germany | 885 |
| 2......Afanasij Kusmin, Latvia | 882 |
| 3......Vladimir Vokhmianin, Unified Team | 882 |

#### AIR PISTOL

| | Pts |
|---|---|
| 1......Yifu Wang, China | 684.8 |
| 2......Sergei Pyzhianov, Unified Team | 684.1 |
| 3......Sorin Babii, Romania | 684.1 |

#### RUNNING TARGET

| | Pts |
|---|---|
| 1......Michael Jakosits, Germany | 673 |
| 2......Anatolij Asrabaev, Unified Team | 672 |
| 3......Lubos Racansky, Czechoslovakia | 670 |

#### TRAP

| | Pts |
|---|---|
| 1......Petr Hrdlicka, Czechoslovakia | 219 |
| 2......Kazumi Watanabe, Japan | 219 |
| 3......Marco Venturini, Italy | 218 |

#### SKEET

| | Pts |
|---|---|
| 1......Shan Zhang, China | 223 |
| 2......Juan Giah, Peru | 222 |
| 3......Bruno Rossetti, Italy | 222 |

### Women

#### THREE-POSITION RIFLE

| | Pts |
|---|---|
| 1......Launi Meili, United States | 684.3 |
| 2......Nonca Matova, Bulgaria | 682.7 |
| 3......Malgorzata Ksiazkiewicz, Poland | 681.5 |

#### AIR RIFLE

| | Pts |
|---|---|
| 1......Kab-Soon Yeo, South Korea | 498.2 |
| 2......Vessela Letcheva, Bulgaria | 495.3 |
| 3......Aranka Binder, Independent Team | 495.1 |

#### AIR PISTOL

| | Pts |
|---|---|
| 1......Marina Logvinenko, Unified Team | 486.4 |
| 2......Jasna Sekaric, Independent Team | 486.4 |
| 3......Maria Grousdeva, Bulgaria | 481.6 |

#### SPORT PISTOL

| | Pts |
|---|---|
| 1......Marina Logvinenko, Unified Team | 684 |
| 2......Duihong Li, China | 680 |
| 3......Dorisuren Monchbajar, Mongolia | 679 |

## TABLE TENNIS

### Men

#### SINGLES

1. ....................Jan-Ove Waldner, Sweden
2. ....................Jean Gatien, France
3. ....................Kim Taek Soo, South Korea
3. ....................Ma Wenge, China

#### DOUBLES

1. ....................Lu Lin & Wang Tao, China
2. ..................Steffan Fetzner & Jorg Rosskopf, Germany
3. ....................Kang Hee Chan & Lee Chul Seung, South Korea
3. ....................Kim Taek Soo & Yoo Nam Kyu, South Korea

### Women

#### SINGLES

1. ....................Deng Yaping, China
2. ....................Qiao Hong, China
3. ....................Hyun Jung Hwa, South Korea
3. ....................Li Bun Hui, North Korea

#### DOUBLES

1. ....................Deng Yaping & Qiao Hong, China
2. ..................Chen Zihe & Gao Jun, China
3. ....................Li Bun Hui & Yu Sun Bok, North Korea
3. ....................Hong Cha Ok & Hyun Jung Hwa, South Korea

## TENNIS

### Men

#### SINGLES

1. ....................Marc Rosset, Switzerland
2. ....................Jordi Arrese, Spain
3. ....................Goran Ivanisevic, Croatia
3. ....................Andrei Cherkasov, Unified Team

#### DOUBLES

1. ....................Boris Becker & Michael Stich, Germany
2. ....................Wayne Ferreira & Piet Norval, South Africa
3. ....................Goran Ivanisevic & Goran Prpic, Croatia
3. ....................Javier Frana & Christian Carlos Miniussi, Argentina

### Women

#### SINGLES

1. ....................Jennifer Capriati, United States
2. ....................Steffi Graf, Germany
3. ....................Aranxta Sanchez Vicario, Spain
3. ....................Mary Joe Fernandez, United States

#### DOUBLES

1. ....................Gigi Fernandez & Mary Joe Fernandez, United States
2. ....................Conchita Martinez & Aranxta Sanchez Vicario, Spain
3. ....................Natalya Zvereva & Leila Meskhi, Unified Team
3. ....................Rachel McQuillan & Nicole Provis, Australia

## VOLLEYBALL

### Men

1. ..........Brazil
2. ..........The Netherlands
3. ..........United States: Bob Ctvrtlik, Doug Partie, Steve Timmons, Scott Fortune, Jeff Stork, Eric Sato, Dan Hanan, Dan Greenbaum, Uvaldo Acosta, Bryan Ivie, Bob Samuelson, Javier Gaspar, Trevor Schirman, Carlos Briceno, Nick Becker, Brent Hilliard, Mark Arnold, Allen Allen

### Women

1. ..........Cuba
2. ..........Unified Team
3. ..........United States: Tee Sanders, Yoko Zetterlund, Ann Schirman, Kim Oden, Lori Endicott, Paula Weishoff, Caren Kemner, Tammy Liley, Elaina Oden, Daiva Tomkus, Deitre Collins, Janet Cobbs, Tara Battle, Liane Sato, Ruth Lawanson, Bev Oden

## WATER POLO

1. ............................................Italy
2. ............................................Spain
3. ............................................Unified Team

## WEIGHTLIFTING

### 114 POUNDS

| | | |
|---|---|---|
| 1. ..........Ivan Ivanov, Bulgaria | 584 lb |
| 2. ..........Lin Qisheng, China | 579 lb |
| 3. ..........Traian Ciharean, Romania | 557 lb |

### 123 POUNDS

| | |
|---|---|
| 1. ..........Chun Byun Kwan, South Korea | 634 lb |
| 2. ..........Liu Shoubin, China | 612 lb |
| 3. ..........Luo Jianming, China | 612 lb |

### 132 POUNDS

| | |
|---|---|
| 1. ..........Naim Suleymanoglu, Turkey | 705 lb |
| 2. ..........Nikolai Peshalov, Unified Team | 672 lb |
| 3. ..........He Yingqiang, China | 650 lb |

### 148.5 POUNDS

| | |
|---|---|
| 1. ..........Israel Militossian, Unified Team | 744 lb |
| 2. ..........Yoto Yotov, Bulgaria | 722 lb |
| 3. ..........Andreas Behm, Germany | 706 lb |

### 165 POUNDS

| | |
|---|---|
| 1. ..........Fedor Kassapu, Unified Team | 788 lb |
| 2. ..........Pablo Lara Rodriguez, Cuba | 788 lb |
| 3. ..........Kim Myong Nam, North Korea | 777 lb |

### 181.5 POUNDS

| | |
|---|---|
| 1. ..........Pyrros Dimas, Greece | 816 lb |
| 2. ..........Krzysztof Siemion, Poland | 816 lb |
| 3. ..........Ibragim Samadov, Unified Team | 816 lb |

### 198 POUNDS

| | |
|---|---|
| 1. ..........Kakhi Kakhiachveili, Unified Team | 910 lb OR |
| 2. ..........Sergei Sirtsov, Unified Team | 910 lb OR |
| 3. ..........Sergivsz Wolczanjecki, Poland | 865 lb |

### 220 POUNDS

| | |
|---|---|
| 1. ..........Victor Tregoubov, Unified Team | 904 lb |
| 2. ..........Timour Taimazov, Unified Team | 887 lb |
| 3. ..........Waldemar Malak, Poland | 882 lb |

### 243 POUNDS

| | |
|---|---|
| 1. ..........Ronny Weller, Germany | 953 lb |
| 2. ..........Artur Akoev, Unified Team | 948 lb |
| 3. ..........Stefan Botev, Bulgaria | 920 lb |

### 243+ POUNDS

| | |
|---|---|
| 1. ..........Aleksandr Kurlovich, Unified Team | 992 lb |
| 2. ..........Leonid Taranenko, Unified Team | 937 lb |
| 3. ..........Manfred Nerlinger, Germany | 909 lb |

## FREESTYLE WRESTLING

### 106 POUNDS

1. ....................Kim Il, North Korea
2. ....................Kim Jong, South Korea
3. ....................Vougar Oroudjov, Unified Team

### 115 POUNDS

1. ....................Li Hak Son, North Korea
2. ....................Zeke Jones, United States
3. ....................Valentin Jordanov, Bulgaria

### 126 POUNDS

1. ....................Alejandro Puerto Diaz, Cuba
2. ....................Serguei Smal, Unified Team
3. ....................Kim Yong Sik, North Korea

### 137 POUNDS

1. ....................John Smith, United States
2. ....................Asgari Mohammadian, Iran
3. ....................Lazaro Reinoso, Cuba

### 150 POUNDS

1. ....................Arsen Fadzaev, Unified Team
2. ....................Valentin Getzov, Bulgaria
3. ....................Kosei Akaishi, Japan

### 163 POUNDS

1. ....................Park Jang-Soon, South Korea
2. ....................Kenny Monday, United States
3. ....................Amir Khadem, Iran

### 181 POUNDS

1. ....................Kevin Jackson, United States
2. ....................Elmadi Jabraijlov, Unified Team
3. ....................Rasul Khadem, Iran

### 198 POUNDS

1. ....................Makharbek Khadartsev, Unified Team
2. ....................Kenan Simsek, Turkey
3. ....................Chris Campbell, United States

### 220 POUNDS

1. ....................Leri Khabelov, Unified Team
2. ....................Heiko Balz, Germany
3. ....................Ali Kayali, Turkey

### 286 POUNDS

1. ....................Bruce Baumgartner, United States
2. ....................Jeffrey Thue, Canada
3. ....................David Gobedjichvili, Unified Team

Note: OR=Olympic record.  WR=world record.  EOR=equals Olympic record.  EWR=equals world record

## GRECO-ROMAN WRESTLING

### 106 POUNDS

1. ............Oleg Koutcherenko, Unified Team
2. ............Vincenzo Maenza, Italy
3. ............Wilber Sanchez, Cuba

### 115 POUNDS

1. ............Jon Ronningen, Norway
2. ............Alfred Ter-Mkrtychan, Unified Team
3. ............Min Kyung, South Korea

### 126 POUNDS

1. ............An Han-Bong, South Korea
2. ............Rifat Yildiz, Germany
3. ............Sheng Zetian, China

### 137 POUNDS

1. ............Akif Pirim, Turkey
2. ............Sergei Martynov, Unified Team
3. ............Juan Maren, Cuba

### 150 POUNDS

1. ............Attila Repka, Hungary
2. ............Islam Duguchiev, Unified Team
3. ............Rodney Smith, United States

### 163 POUNDS

1. ............Mnatsakan Iskandarian, Unified Team
2. ............Josef Tracz, Poland
3. ............Torbjoern Korbakk, Sweden

### 181 POUNDS

1. ............Peter Farkas, Hungary
2. ............Piotr Stepien, Poland
3. ............Daulet Tourlykhanov, Unified Team

### 198 POUNDS

1. ............Maik Bullmann, Germany
2. ............Hakki Basar, Turkey
3. ............Gogi Kogouachvili, Unified Team

### 220 POUNDS

1. ............Hector Millian, Cuba
2. ............Dennis Koslowski, United States
3. ............Sergei Demyashkevich, Unified Team

### 286 POUNDS

1. ............Aleksandr Karelin, Unified Team
2. ............Tomas Johansson, Sweden
3. ............Ioan Grigoras, Romania

## YACHTING

### SOLING CLASS

1. ............Denmark
2. ............United States
3. ............Great Britain

### STAR CLASS

1. ............United States
2. ............New Zealand
3. ............Canada

### FLYING DUTCHMAN CLASS

1. ............Spain
2. ............United States
3. ............Denmark

### FINN CLASS

1. ............Jose Van Der Ploeg, Spain
2. ............Brian Ledbetter, United States
3. ............Craig Monk, New Zealand

### TORNADO CLASS

1. ............France
2. ............United States
3. ............Australia

### EUROPE CLASS

1. ............Linda Andersen, Norway
2. ............Natalia Via Dufresne, Spain
3. ............Julia Trotman, United States

### MEN'S 470 CLASS

1. ............Spain
2. ............United States
3. ............Estonia

### WOMEN'S 470 CLASS

1. ............Spain
2. ............New Zealand
3. ............United States

# 1994 Winter Games

## BIATHLON

### Men

#### 10 KILOMETERS

| | | |
|---|---|---|
| 1. | ..Sergei Tchepikov, Russia | 28:07.0 |
| 2. | ..Ricco Gross, Germany | 28:13.0 |
| 3. | ..Sergei Tarasov, Russia | 28:27.4 |

#### 20 KILOMETERS

| | | |
|---|---|---|
| 1. | ..Sergei Tarasov, Russia | 57:25.3 |
| 2. | ..Frank Luck, Germany | 57:28.7 |
| 3. | ..Sven Fischer, Germany | 57:41.9 |

#### 4 X 7.5 KILOMETER RELAY

| | | |
|---|---|---|
| 1. | ............Germany | 1:30:22.1 |
| 2. | ............Russia | 1:31:23.6 |
| 3. | ............France | 1:32:31.3 |

### Women

#### 7.5 KILOMETERS

| | | |
|---|---|---|
| 1. | ..Myriam Bedard, Canada | 26:08.8 |
| 2. | ..Svetlana Paramygina, Belarus | 26:09.9 |
| 3. | ..Valentyna Tserbe, Ukraine | 26:10.0 |

#### 15 KILOMETERS

| | | |
|---|---|---|
| 1. | ..Myriam Bedard, Canada | 52:06.6 |
| 2. | ..Anne Briand, France | 52:53.3 |
| 3. | ..Ursula Disl, Germany | 53:15.3 |

#### 3 X 7.5 KILOMETER RELAY

| | | |
|---|---|---|
| 1. | ............Russia | 1:47:19.5 |
| 2. | ............Germany | 1:51:16.5 |
| 3. | ............France | 1:52:28.3 |

## BOBSLED

### 4-MAN BOB

| | | |
|---|---|---|
| 1. ..........Germany II | 3:27.78 |
| 2. ..........Switzerland | 3:27.84 |
| 3. ..........Germany | 3:28.01 |

### 2-MAN BOB

| | | |
|---|---|---|
| 1. ..........Switzerland | 3:30.81 |
| 2. ..........Switzerland II | 3:30.86 |
| 3. ..........Italy | 3:31.01 |

## ICE HOCKEY

1. ................................................Sweden
2. ................................................Canada
3. ................................................Finland

## LUGE

### Men

#### SINGLES

| | |
|---|---|
| 1. ..........Georg Hackl, Germany | 3:21.571 |
| 2. ..........Markus Prock, Austria | 3:21.584 |
| 3. ..........Armin Zoggeler, Italy | 3:21.833 |

#### DOUBLES

| | |
|---|---|
| 1. ..........K. Brugger and W. Huber, Italy | 1:36.720 |
| 2. ..........H. Raffl and N. Huber, Italy | 1:36.769 |
| 3. ..........S. Krausse and J. Behrendt, Ger. | 1:36.945 |

### Women

#### SINGLES

| | |
|---|---|
| 1. ..........Gerda Weissensteiner, Italy | 3:15.517 |
| 2. ..........Susi Erdmann, Germany | 3:16.276 |
| 3. ..........Andrea Tagwerker, Austria | 3:16.652 |

## FIGURE SKATING

### Men

1. ....................Alexei Urmanov, Russia
2. ....................Elvis Stojko, Canada
3. ....................Philippe Candeloro, France

### Women

1. ....................Oksana Baiul, Ukraine
2. ....................Nancy Kerrigan, United States
3. ....................Chen Lu, China

### Pairs

1. ..Ekaterina Gordeeva and Sergei Grinkov, Russia
2. ..Natalia Mishkutienok and Artur Dmitriev, Russia
3. ..Isabella Brasseur and Lloyd Eisler, Canada

### Ice Dancing

1. ..Oksana Gritschuk and Evgeni Platov, Russia
2. ..Maia Usova and Alexander Zhulin, Russia
3. ..Jayne Torvill and Christopher Dean, Great Britain

## SPEED SKATING

### Men

#### 500 METERS

| | |
|---|---|
| 1. ..Aleksandr Golubev, Russia | 36.33 OR |
| 2. ..Sergei Klevchenya, Russia | 36.39 |
| 3. ..Manabu Horii, Japan | 36.53 |

#### 1000 METERS

| | |
|---|---|
| 1. ....Dan Jansen, United States | 1:12.43 WR |
| 2. ..Igor Zhelezovsky, Belarus | 1:12.72 |
| 3. ..Sergei Klevchenya, Russia | 1:12.85 |

#### 1500 METERS

| | |
|---|---|
| 1. ..Johann Olav Koss, Norway | 1:51.29 WR |
| 2. ..Rintje Ritsma, The Netherlands | 1:54.85 |
| 3. ..Falko Zandstra, The Netherlands | 1:54.90 |

### Women

#### 500 METERS

| | |
|---|---|
| 1. ..Bonnie Blair, United States | 39.25 |
| 2. ..Susan Auch, Canada | 39.61 |
| 3. ..Franziska Schenk, Germany | 39.70 |

#### 1000 METERS

| | |
|---|---|
| 1. ..Bonnie Blair, United States | 1:18.74 |
| 2. ..Anke Baier, Germany | 1:20.12 |
| 3. ..Qiaobo Ye, China | 1:20.22 |

#### 1500 METERS

| | |
|---|---|
| 1. ..Emese Hunyady, Austria | 2:02.19 |
| 2. ..Svetlana Fedotkina, Russia | 2:02.69 |
| 3. ..Seiko Hashimoto, Japan | 2:06.88 |

Note: OR=Olympic Record; WR=World Record; EOR=Equals Olympic Record; EWR=Equals World Record; WB=World Best.

## SPEED SKATING *(Cont.)*

### Men *(Cont.)*

#### 5000 METERS

1. ..Johann Olav Koss, Norway — 6:34.96 WR
2. ..Kjell Storelid, Norway — 6:42.68
3. ..Rintje Ritsma, Netherlands — 6:43.94

#### 10,000 METERS

1. ..Johann Olav Koss, Norway — 13:30.55 WR
2. ..Kjell Storelid, Norway — 13:49.25
3. ..Bart Veldkamp, The Netherlands — 13:56.73

### Women *(Cont.)*

#### 3000 METERS

1. ..Gunda Niemann, Germany — 4:19.90
2. ..Heike Warnicke, Germany — 4:22.88
3. ..Emese Hunyady, Austria — 4:24.64

#### 5000 METERS

1. ..Gunda Niemann, Germany — 7:31.57
2. ..Heike Warnicke, Germany — 7:37.59
3. ..Claudia Pechstein, Germany — 7:39.80

## SHORT TRACK SPEED SKATING

### Men

#### 500 METERS

1. ..Chae Ji-Hoon, South Korea — 43.45
2. ..Mirko Vuillermin, Italy — 43.47
3. ..Nicholas Gooch, Great Britain — 43.68

#### 1000 METERS

1. ...Ki-Hoon Kim, South Korea — 1:34.57
2. ..Ji-Hoon Chae, South Korea — 1:34.92
3. ..Marc Gagnon, Canada — DNF

#### 5000-METER RELAY

1. ...Italy — 7:11.74 OR
2. ..United States — 7:13.37
3. ..Australia — 7:13.68

### Women

#### 500 METERS

1. ..Cathy Turner, United States — 45.98 OR
2. ..Yanmei Zhang, China — 46.44
3. ..Amy Peterson, United States — 46.76

#### 1000 METERS

1. ..Chun Lee-Kyung, South Korea — 1:36.87
2. ..Nathalie Lambert, Canada — 1:36.97
3. ..Kim So-Hee, South Korea — 1:37.09

#### 3000-METER RELAY

1. ...South Korea — 4:26.64 OR
2. ..Canada — 4:32.04
3. ..United States — 4:39.34

## ALPINE SKIING

### Men

#### DOWNHILL

1. ..Tommy Moe, United States — 1:45.75
2. ..Kjetil Andre Aamodt, Norway — 1:45.79
3. ..Edward Podivinsky, Canada — 1:45.87

#### SUPER GIANT SLALOM

1. ..Markus Wasmeier, Germany — 1:32.53
2. ..Tommy Moe, United States — 1:32.61
3. ..Kjetil Andre Aamodt, Norway — 1:32.93

#### GIANT SLALOM

1. ..Markus Wasmeier, Germany — 2:52.46
2. ..Urs Kaelin, Switzerland — 2:52.48
3. ..Christian Mayer, Austria — 2:52.58

#### SLALOM

1. ..Thomas Stangassinger, Austria — 2:02.02
2. ..Alberto Tomba, Italy — 2:02.17
3. ..Jure Kosir, Slovenia — 2:02.53

#### COMBINED

Pts

1. ..Lasse Kjus, Norway — 3:17.53
2. ..Kjell Andre Aamodt, Norway — 3:18.55
3. ..Harald Strand Nilsen, Norway — 3:19.14

### Women

#### DOWNHILL

1. ..Katja Seizinger, Germany — 1:35.93
2. ..Picabo Street, United States — 1:36.59
3. ..Isolde Kostner, Italy — 1:36.85

#### SUPER GIANT SLALOM

1. ..Diann Roffe-Steinrotter, U.S. — 1:22.15
2. ..Svetlana Gladischeva, Russia — 1:22.44
3. ..Isolde Kostner, Italy — 1:22.45

#### GIANT SLALOM

1. ..Deborah Compagnoni, Italy — 2:30.97
2. ..Martina Ertl, Germany — 2:32.19
2. ..Vreni Schneider, Switzerland — 2:32.97

#### SLALOM

1. ..Vreni Schneider, Switzerland — 1:56.01
2. ..Elfriede Eder, Austria — 1:56.35
3. ..Katja Koren, Slovenia — 1:56.61

#### COMBINED

1. ..Pernilla Wiberg, Sweden — 3:05.16
2. ..Vreni Schneider, Switzerland — 3:05.29
3. ..Alenka Dovzan, Slovenia — 3:06.64

Note: OR=Olympic Record; WR=World Record; EOR=Equals Olympic Record; EWR=Equals World Record; WB=World Best; DNF=Did Not Finish.

## ALPINE SKIING *(Cont.)*

### FREESTYLE SKIING

#### Men

##### MOGUL

| | Pts |
|---|---|
| 1. ..Jean-Luc Brassard, Canada | 27.24 |
| 2. ..Sergei Shoupletsov, Russia | 26.90 |
| 3. ..Edgar Grospiron, France | 26.64 |

##### AERIAL

| | Pts |
|---|---|
| 1. ..Andreas Schoenbaechler, Switz. | 234.67 |
| 2. ..Philippe Laroche, Canada | 228.63 |
| 3. ..Lloyd Langlois, Canada | 222.44 |

#### Women

##### MOGUL

| | Pts |
|---|---|
| 1. ..Stine Lise Hattestad, Norway | 25.97 |
| 2. ..Liz McIntyre, United States | 25.89 |
| 3. ..Elizaveta Kojevnikova, Russia | 25.81 |

##### AERIAL

| | Pts |
|---|---|
| 1. ..Lina Cherjazova, Uzbekistan | 166.84 |
| 2. ..Marie Lindgren, Sweden | 165.88 |
| 3. ..Hilde Synnove Lid, Norway | 164.13 |

### NORDIC SKIING

#### Men

##### 10 KILOMETERS (CLASSICAL)

| | |
|---|---|
| 1. ..Bjorn Daehlie, Norway | 24:20.1 |
| 2. ..Vladimir Smirnov, Russia | 24:38.3 |
| 3. ..Marco Albarello, Italy | 24:42.3 |

##### 30 KILOMETERS (CLASSICAL)

| | |
|---|---|
| 1. ..Thomas Alsgaard, Norway | 1:12:26.4 |
| 2. ..Bjorn Daehlie, Norway | 1:13:13.6 |
| 3. ..Myka Myllyla, Finland | 1:14:14.5 |

##### 50 KILOMETERS (FREESTYLE)

| | |
|---|---|
| 1. ..Vladimir Smirnov, Kazakhstan | 2:07:20.3 |
| 2. ..Myka Myllyla, Finland | 2:08:41.9 |
| 3. ..Sture Sivertsen, Norway | 2:08:49.0 |

##### 15 KILOMETERS (FREESTYLE)

| | |
|---|---|
| 1. ..Bjorn Daehlie, Norway | 1:00:08.8 |
| 2. ..Vladimir Smirnov, Kazakhstan | 1:00:38.0 |
| 3. ..Silvio Fauner, Italy | 1:01:48.6 |

##### 4 X 10 KILOMETER RELAY (MIXED)

| | |
|---|---|
| 1.................Italy | 1:41:15.0 |
| 2.................Norway | 1:41:15.4 |
| 3.................Finland | 1:42:15.6 |

##### SKI JUMPING (NORMAL HILL)

| | Pts |
|---|---|
| 1. ..Espen Bredesen, Norway | 282.0 |
| 2. ..Lasse Ottesen, Norway | 268.0 |
| 3. ..Dieter Thoma, Germany | 260.5 |

##### SKI JUMPING (LARGE HILL)

| | Pts |
|---|---|
| 1. ..Jens Weisflogg, Germany | 274.5 |
| 2. ..Espen Bredesen, Norway | 266.5 |
| 3. ..Andreas Goldberger, Austria | 255.0 |

##### TEAM SKI JUMPING

| | Pts |
|---|---|
| 1.................Germany | 970.1 |
| 2.................Japan | 956.9 |
| 3.................Austria | 918.9 |

##### NORDIC COMBINED

| | |
|---|---|
| 1.................Fred B. Lundberg, Norway | 457.970 |
| 2.................Takanori Kono, Japan | 446.345 |
| 3.................Bjarte Engen Vik, Norway | 446.175 |

##### TEAM COMBINED

| | |
|---|---|
| 1.................Japan | 1368.860 |
| 2.................Norway | 1310.940 |
| 3.................Switzerland | 1275.240 |

#### Women

##### 5 KILOMETERS (CLASSICAL)

| | |
|---|---|
| 1. ..Lyubov Egorova, Russia | 14:08.8 |
| 2. ..Manuela Di Centa, Italy | 14:28.3 |
| 3. ..Marja-Liisa Kirvesniemi, Finland | 14:36.0 |

##### 15 KILOMETERS (FREESTYLE)

| | |
|---|---|
| 1. ..Manuela Di Centa, Italy | 39:44.5 |
| 2. ..Lyubov Egorova, Russia | 41:03.0 |
| 3. ..Nina Gavriluk, Russia | 41:10.4 |

##### 10 KILOMETERS (FREESTYLE)

| | |
|---|---|
| 1. ..Lyubov Egorova, Russia | 41:38.1 |
| 2. ..Maunela Di Centa, Italy | 41:46.4 |
| 3. ..Stefania Belmondo, Italy | 42:21.1 |

##### 30 KILOMETERS (CLASSICAL)

| | |
|---|---|
| 1. ..Manuela Di Centa, Italy | 1:25:41.6 |
| 2. ..Marit Wold, Norway | 1:25:57.8 |
| 3. ..Marja-Liisa Kirvesniemi, Finland | 1:26:13.6 |

##### 4 X 5 KILOMETER RELAY (MIXED)

| | |
|---|---|
| 1...................Russia | 57:12.5 |
| 2...................Norway | 57:42.6 |
| 3...................Italy | 58:42.6 |

## Olympic Games Locations and Dates

### Summer

| | Year | Site | Dates | Men | Women | Nations | Most Medals | US Medals |
|---|---|---|---|---|---|---|---|---|
| I | 1896 | Athens, Greece | Apr 6-15 | 311 | 0 | 13 | Greece (10-19-18—47) | 11-6-2—19 (2nd) |
| II | 1900 | Paris, France | May 20-Oct 28 | 1319 | 11 | 22 | France (29-41-32—102) | 20-14-19—53 (2nd) |
| III | 1904 | St Louis, United States | July 1-Nov 23 | 681 | 6 | 12 | United States (80-86-72—238) | |
| — | 1906 | Athens, Greece | Apr 22-May 28 | 77 | 7 | 20 | France (15-9-16—40) | 12-6-5—23 (4th) |
| IV | 1908 | London, Great Britain | Apr 27-Oct 31 | 1999 | 36 | 23 | Britain (56-50-39—145) | 23-12-12—47 (2nd) |
| V | 1912 | Stockholm, Sweden | May 5-July 22 | 2490 | 57 | 28 | Sweden (24-24-17—65) | 23-19-19—61 (2nd) |
| VI | 1916 | Berlin, Germany | Cancelled because of war | | | | | |
| VII | 1920 | Antwerp, Belgium | Apr 20-Sep 12 | 2543 | 64 | 29 | United States (41-27-28—96) | |
| VIII | 1924 | Paris, France | May 4-July 27 | 2956 | 136 | 44 | United States (45-27-27—99) | |
| IX | 1928 | Amsterdam, Netherlands | May 17-Aug 12 | 2724 | 290 | 46 | United States (22-18-16—56) | |
| X | 1932 | Los Angeles, United States | July 30-Aug 14 | 1281 | 127 | 37 | United States (41-32-31—104) | |
| XI | 1936 | Berlin, Germany | Aug 1-16 | 3738 | 328 | 49 | Germany (33-26-30—89) | 24-20-12—56 (2nd) |
| XII | 1940 | Tokyo, Japan | Cancelled because of war | | | | | |
| XIII | 1944 | London, Great Britain | Cancelled because of war | | | | | |
| XIV | 1948 | London, Great Britain | July 29-Aug 14 | 3714 | 385 | 59 | United States (38-27-19—84) | |
| XV | 1952 | Helsinki, Finland | July 19-Aug 3 | 4407 | 518 | 69 | United States (40-19-17—76) | |
| XVI | 1956 | Melbourne, Australia* | Nov 22-Dec 8 | 2958 | 384 | 67 | USSR (37-29-32—98) | 32-25-17—74 (2nd) |
| XVII | 1960 | Rome, Italy | Aug 25-Sep 11 | 4738 | 610 | 83 | USSR (43-29-31—103) | 34-21-16—71 (2nd) |
| XVIII | 1964 | Tokyo, Japan | Oct 10-24 | 4457 | 683 | 93 | United States (36-26-28—90) | |
| XIX | 1968 | Mexico City, Mexico | Oct 12-27 | 4750 | 781 | 112 | United States (45-28-34—107) | |
| XX | 1972 | Munich, West Germany | Aug 26-Sep 10 | 5848 | 1299 | 122 | USSR (50-27-22—99) | 33-31-30—94 (2nd) |
| XXI | 1976 | Montreal, Canada | July 17-Aug 1 | 4834 | 1251 | 92† | USSR (49-41-35—125) | 34-35-25—94 (3rd) |
| XXII | 1980 | Moscow, USSR | July 19-Aug 3 | 4265 | 1088 | 81‡ | USSR (80-69-46—195) | Did not compete |
| XXIII | 1984 | Los Angeles, United States | July 28-Aug 12 | 5458 | 1620 | 141# | United States (83-61-30—174) | |
| XXIV | 1988 | Seoul, South Korea | Sep 17-Oct 2 | 7105 | 2476 | 160 | USSR (55-31-46—132) | 36-31-27—94 (3rd) |
| XXV | 1992 | Barcelona, Spain | July 25-Aug. 9 | 7555 | 3008 | 172 | Unified Team (45-38-29—112) | 37-34-37—108 (2nd) |

*The equestrian events were held in Stockholm, Sweden, June 10-17, 1956.

†This figure includes Cameroon, Egypt, Morocco, and Tunisia, countries that boycotted the 1976 Olympics after some of their athletes had already competed.

‡The US was among 65 countries that refused to participate in the 1980 Summer Games in Moscow.

#The USSR, East Germany, and 14 other countries skipped the Summer Games in Los Angeles.

## Winter

| | Year | Site | Dates | Men | Women | Nations | Most Medals | US Medals |
|---|---|---|---|---|---|---|---|---|
| I | 1924 | Chamonix, France | Jan 25-Feb 4 | 281 | 13 | 16 | Norway (4-7-6—17) | 1-2-1—4 (3rd) |
| II | 1928 | St Moritz, Switzerland | Feb 11-19 | 468 | 27 | 25 | Norway (6-4-5—15) | 2-2-2—6 (2nd) |
| III | 1932 | Lake Placid, United States | Feb 4-15 | 274 | 32 | 17 | United States (6-4-2—12) | |
| IV | 1936 | Garmisch-Partenkirchen, Germany | Feb 6-16 | 675 | 80 | 28 | Norway (7-5-3—15) | 1-0-3—4 (T-5th) |
| — | 1940 | Garmisch-Partenkirchen, Germany | Cancelled because of war | | | | | |
| — | 1944 | Cortina d'Ampezzo, Italy | Cancelled because of war | | | | | |
| V | 1948 | St Moritz, Switzerland | Jan 30-Feb 8 | 636 | 77 | 28 | Norway (4-3-3—10) Sweden (4-3-3—10) Switzerland (3-4-3—10) | 3-4-2—9 (4th) |
| VI | 1952 | Oslo, Norway | Feb 14-25 | 623 | 109 | 30 | Norway (7-3-6—16) | 4-6-1—11 (2nd) |
| VII | 1956 | Cortina d'Ampezzo, Italy | Jan 26-Feb 5 | 686 | 132 | 32 | USSR (7-3-6—16) | 2-3-2—7 (T-4th) |
| VIII | 1960 | Squaw Valley, United States | Feb 18-28 | 521 | 144 | 30 | USSR (7-5-9—21) | 3-4-3—10 (2nd) |
| IX | 1964 | Innsbruck, Austria | Jan 29-Feb 9 | 986 | 200 | 36 | USSR (11-8-6—25) | 1-2-3—6 (7th) |
| X | 1968 | Grenoble, France | Feb 6-18 | 1081 | 212 | 37 | Norway (6-6-2—14) | 1-5-1—7 (T-7th) |
| XI | 1972 | Sapporo, Japan | Feb 3-13 | 1015 | 217 | 35 | USSR (8-5-3—16) | 3-2-3—8 (6th) |
| XII | 1976 | Innsbruck, Austria | Feb 4-15 | 900 | 228 | 37 | USSR (13-6-8—27) | 3-3-4—10 (T-3rd) |
| XIII | 1980 | Lake Placid, United States | Feb 14-23 | 833 | 234 | 37 | USSR (10-6-6—22) | 6-4-2—12 (3rd) |
| XIV | 1984 | Sarajevo, Yugoslavia | Feb 7-19 | 1002 | 276 | 49 | USSR (6-10-9—25) | 4-4-0—8 (T-5th) |
| XV | 1988 | Calgary, Canada | Feb 13-28 | 1128 | 317 | 57 | USSR (11-9-9—29) | 2-1-3—6 (T-8th) |
| XVI | 1992 | Albertville, France | Feb 8-23 | 1318 | 490 | 65 | Germany (10-10-6—26) | 5-4-2—11 (6th) |
| XVII | 1994 | Lillehammer, Norway | Feb 11-27 | 1302 | 542 | | Norway (10-11-5—26) | 6-5-2—13 (T-5th) |

# Summer Games Champions

## TRACK AND FIELD

### Men

#### 100 METERS

| Year | Champion | Time | | Year | Champion | Time |
|---|---|---|---|---|---|---|
| 1896 | Thomas Burke, United States | 12.0 | | 1952 | Lindy Remigino, United States | 10.4 |
| 1900 | Frank Jarvis, United States | 11.0 | | 1956 | Bobby Morrow, United States | 10.5 |
| 1904 | Archie Hahn, United States | 11.0 | | 1960 | Armin Hary, West Germany | 10.2 OR |
| 1906 | Archie Hahn, United States | 11.2 | | 1964 | Bob Hayes, United States | 10.0 EWR |
| 1908 | Reginald Walker, South Africa | 10.8 OR | | 1968 | Jim Hines, United States | 9.95 WR |
| 1912 | Ralph Craig, United States | 10.8 | | 1972 | Valery Borzov, USSR | 10.14 |
| 1920 | Charles Paddock, United States | 10.8 | | 1976 | Hasely Crawford, Trinidad | 10.06 |
| 1924 | Harold Abrahams, Great Britain | 10.6 OR | | 1980 | Allan Wells, Great Britain | 10.25 |
| 1928 | Percy Williams, Canada | 10.8 | | 1984 | Carl Lewis, United States | 9.99 |
| 1932 | Eddie Tolan, United States | 10.3 OR | | 1988 | Carl Lewis, United States* | 9.92 WR |
| 1936 | Jesse Owens, United States | 10.3 | | 1992 | Linford Christie, Great Britain | 9.96 |
| 1948 | Harrison Dillard, United States | 10.3 | | | | |

*Ben Johnson, Canada, disqualified.

## TRACK AND FIELD *(Cont.)*

### Men *(Cont.)*

#### 200 METERS

| | | |
|---|---|---|
| 1900 | John Walter Tewksbury, United States | 22.2 |
| 1904 | Archie Hahn, United States | 21.6 OR |
| 1906 | Not held | |
| 1908 | Robert Kerr, Canada | 22.6 |
| 1912 | Ralph Craig, United States | 21.7 |
| 1920 | Allen Woodring, United States | 22.0 |
| 1924 | Jackson Scholz, United States | 21.6 |
| 1928 | Percy Williams, Canada | 21.8 |
| 1932 | Eddie Tolan, United States | 21.2 OR |
| 1936 | Jesse Owens, United States | 20.7 OR |
| 1948 | Mel Patton, United States | 21.1 |
| 1952 | Andrew Stanfield, United States | 20.7 |
| 1956 | Bobby Morrow, United States | 20.6 OR |
| 1960 | Livio Berruti, Italy | 20.5 EWR |
| 1964 | Henry Carr, United States | 20.3 OR |
| 1968 | Tommie Smith, United States | 19.83 WR |
| 1972 | Valery Borzov, USSR | 20.00 |
| 1976 | Donald Quarrie, Jamaica | 20.23 |
| 1980 | Pietro Mennea, Italy | 20.19 |
| 1984 | Carl Lewis, United States | 19.80 OR |
| 1988 | Joe DeLoach, United States | 19.75 OR |
| 1992 | Mike Marsh, United States | 20.01 |

#### 400 METERS

| | | |
|---|---|---|
| 1896 | Thomas Burke, United States | 54.2 |
| 1900 | Maxey Long, United States | 49.4 OR |
| 1904 | Harry Hillman, United States | 49.2 OR |
| 1906 | Paul Pilgrim, United States | 53.2 |
| 1908 | Wyndham Halswelle, Great Britain | 50.0 |
| 1912 | Charles Reidpath, United States | 48.2 OR |
| 1920 | Bevil Rudd, South Africa | 49.6 |
| 1924 | Eric Liddell, Great Britain | 47.6 OR |
| 1928 | Ray Barbuti, United States | 47.8 |
| 1932 | William Carr, United States | 46.2 WR |
| 1936 | Archie Williams, United States | 46.5 |
| 1948 | Arthur Wint, Jamaica | 46.2 |
| 1952 | George Rhoden, Jamaica | 45.9 |
| 1956 | Charles Jenkins, United States | 46.7 |
| 1960 | Otis Davis, United States | 44.9 WR |
| 1964 | Michael Larrabee, United States | 45.1 |
| 1968 | Lee Evans, United States | 43.86 WR |
| 1972 | Vincent Matthews, United States | 44.66 |
| 1976 | Alberto Juantorena, Cuba | 44.26 |
| 1980 | Viktor Markin, USSR | 44.60 |
| 1984 | Alonzo Babers, United States | 44.27 |
| 1988 | Steve Lewis, United States | 43.87 |
| 1992 | Quincy Watts, United States | 43.50 OR |

#### 800 METERS

| | | |
|---|---|---|
| 1896 | Edwin Flack, Australia | 2:11 |
| 1900 | Alfred Tysoe, Great Britain | 2:01.2 |
| 1904 | James Lightbody, United States | 1:56 OR |
| 1906 | Paul Pilgrim, United States | 2:01.5 |
| 1908 | Mel Sheppard, United States | 1:52.8 WR |
| 1912 | James Meredith, United States | 1:51.9 WR |
| 1920 | Albert Hill, Great Britain | 1:53.4 |
| 1924 | Douglas Lowe, Great Britain | 1:52.4 |
| 1928 | Douglas Lowe, Great Britain | 1:51.8 OR |

#### 800 METERS *(Cont.)*

| | | |
|---|---|---|
| 1932 | Thomas Hampson, Great Britain | 1:49.8 WR |
| 1936 | John Woodruff, United States | 1:52.9 |
| 1948 | Mal Whitfield, United States | 1:49.2 OR |
| 1952 | Mal Whitfield, United States | 1:49.2 EOR |
| 1956 | Thomas Courtney, United States | 1:47.7 OR |
| 1960 | Peter Snell, New Zealand | 1:46.3 OR |
| 1964 | Peter Snell, New Zealand | 1:45.1 OR |
| 1968 | Ralph Doubell, Australia | 1:44.3 EWR |
| 1972 | Dave Wottle, United States | 1:45.9 |
| 1976 | Alberto Juantorena, Cuba | 1:43.50 WR |
| 1980 | Steve Ovett, Great Britain | 1:45.40 |
| 1984 | Joaquim Cruz, Brazil | 1:43.00 OR |
| 1988 | Paul Ereng, Kenya | 1:43.45 |
| 1992 | William Tanui, Kenya | 1:43.66 |

#### 1500 METERS

| | | |
|---|---|---|
| 1896 | Edwin Flack, Australia | 4:33.2 |
| 1900 | Charles Bennett, Great Britain | 4:06.2 WR |
| 1904 | James Lightbody, United States | 4:05.4 WR |
| 1906 | James Lightbody, United States | 4:12.0 |
| 1908 | Mel Sheppard, United States | 4:03.4 OR |
| 1912 | Arnold Jackson, Great Britain | 3:56.8 OR |
| 1920 | Albert Hill, Great Britain | 4:01.8 |
| 1924 | Paavo Nurmi, Finland | 3:53.6 OR |
| 1928 | Harry Larva, Finland | 3:53.2 OR |
| 1932 | Luigi Beccali, Italy | 3:51.2 OR |
| 1936 | Jack Lovelock, New Zealand | 3:47.8 WR |
| 1948 | Henri Eriksson, Sweden | 3:49.8 |
| 1952 | Josef Barthel, Luxemburg | 3:45.1 OR |
| 1956 | Ron Delany, Ireland | 3:41.2 OR |
| 1960 | Herb Elliott, Australia | 3:35.6 WR |
| 1964 | Peter Snell, New Zealand | 3:38.1 |
| 1968 | Kipchoge Keino, Kenya | 3:34.9 OR |
| 1972 | Pekkha Vasala, Finland | 3:36.3 |
| 1976 | John Walker, New Zealand | 3:39.17 |
| 1980 | Sebastian Coe, Great Britain | 3:38.4 |
| 1984 | Sebastian Coe, Great Britain | 3:32.53 OR |
| 1988 | Peter Rono, Kenya | 3:35.96 |
| 1992 | Fermin Cacho, Spain | 3:40.12 |

#### 5000 METERS

| | | |
|---|---|---|
| 1912 | Hannes Kolehmainen, Finland | 14:36.6 WR |
| 1920 | Joseph Guillemot, France | 14:55.6 |
| 1924 | Paavo Nurmi, Finland | 14:31.2 OR |
| 1928 | Villie Ritola, Finland | 14:38 |
| 1932 | Lauri Lehtinen, Finland | 14:30 OR |
| 1936 | Gunnar Höckert, Finland | 14:22.2 OR |
| 1948 | Gaston Reiff, Belgium | 14:17.6 OR |
| 1952 | Emil Zatopek, Czechoslovakia | 14:06.6 OR |
| 1956 | Vladimir Kuts, USSR | 13:39.6 OR |
| 1960 | Murray Halberg, New Zealand | 13:43.4 |
| 1964 | Bob Schul, United States | 13:48.8 |
| 1968 | Mohamed Gammoudi, Tunisia | 14:05.0 |
| 1972 | Lasse Viren, Finland | 13:26.4 OR |
| 1976 | Lasse Viren, Finland | 13:24.76 |
| 1980 | Miruts Yifter, Ethiopia | 13:21.0 |
| 1984 | Said Aouita, Morocco | 13:05.59 OR |
| 1988 | John Ngugi, Kenya | 13:11.70 |
| 1992 | Dieter Baumann, Germany | 13:12.52 |

Note: OR=Olympic Record; WR=World Record; EOR=Equals Olympic Record; EWR=Equals World Record; WB=World Best.

### TRACK AND FIELD (Cont.)

### Men (Cont.)

#### 10,000 METERS

| Year | Champion | Time |
|------|----------|------|
| 1912 | Hannes Kolehmainen, Finland | 31:20.8 |
| 1920 | Paavo Nurmi, Finland | 31:45.8 |
| 1924 | Vilho (Ville) Ritola, Finland | 30:23.2 WR |
| 1928 | Paavo Nurmi, Finland | 30:18.8 OR |
| 1932 | Janusz Kusocinski, Poland | 30:11.4 OR |
| 1936 | Ilmari Salminen, Finland | 30:15.4 |
| 1948 | Emil Zatopek, Czechoslovakia | 29:59.6 OR |
| 1952 | Emil Zatopek, Czechoslovakia | 29:17.0 OR |
| 1956 | Vladimir Kuts, USSR | 28:45.6 OR |
| 1960 | Pyotr Bolotnikov, USSR | 28:32.2 OR |
| 1964 | Billy Mills, United States | 28:24.4 OR |
| 1968 | Naftali Temu, Kenya | 29:27.4 |
| 1972 | Lasse Viren, Finland | 27:38.4 WR |
| 1976 | Lasse Viren, Finland | 27:40.38 |
| 1980 | Miruts Yifter, Ethiopia | 27:42.7 |
| 1984 | Alberto Cova, Italy | 27:47.54 |
| 1988 | Brahim Boutaib, Morocco | 27:21.46 OR |
| 1992 | Khalid Skah, Morocco | 27:46.70 |

#### MARATHON

| Year | Champion | Time |
|------|----------|------|
| 1896 | Spiridon Louis, Greece | 2:58:50 |
| 1900 | Michel Theato, France | 2:59:45 |
| 1904 | Thomas Hicks, United States | 3:28:53 |
| 1906 | William Sherring, Canada | 2:51:23.6 |
| 1908 | John Hayes, United States | 2:55:18.4 OR |
| 1912 | Kenneth McArthur, South Africa | 2:36:54.8 |
| 1920 | Hannes Kolehmainen, Finland | 2:32:35.8 WB |
| 1924 | Albin Stenroos, Finland | 2:41:22.6 |
| 1928 | Boughera El Ouafi, France | 2:32:57 |
| 1932 | Juan Zabala, Argentina | 2:31:36 OR |
| 1936 | Kijung Son, Japan (Korea) | 2:29:19.2 OR |
| 1948 | Delfo Cabrera, Argentina | 2:34:51.6 |
| 1952 | Emil Zatopek, Czechoslovakia | 2:23:03.2 OR |
| 1956 | Alain Mimoun O'Kacha, France | 2:25:00.0 |
| 1960 | Abebe Bikila, Ethiopia | 2:15:16.2 WB |
| 1964 | Abebe Bikila, Ethiopia | 2:12:11.2 WB |
| 1968 | Mamo Wolde, Ethiopia | 2:20:26.4 |
| 1972 | Frank Shorter, United States | 2:12:19.8 |
| 1976 | Waldemar Cierpinski, East Germany | 2:09:55 OR |
| 1980 | Waldemar Cierpinski, East Germany | 2:11:03.0 |
| 1984 | Carlos Lopes, Portugal | 2:09:21.0 OR |
| 1988 | Gelindo Bordin, Italy | 2:10:32 |
| 1992 | Hwang Young-Cho, S Korea | 2:13:23 |

Note: Marathon distances: 1896, 1904—40,000 meters; 1900—40,260 meters; 1906—41,860 meters; 1912—40,200 meters; 1920—42,750 meters; 1908 and since 1924—42,195 meters (26 miles, 385 yards).

#### 110-METER HURDLES

| Year | Champion | Time |
|------|----------|------|
| 1896 | Thomas Curtis, United States | 17.6 |
| 1900 | Alvin Kraenzlein, United States | 15.4 OR |
| 1904 | Frederick Schule, United States | 16.0 |
| 1906 | Robert Leavitt, United States | 16.2 |
| 1908 | Forrest Smithson, United States | 15.0 WR |
| 1912 | Frederick Kelly, United States | 15.1 |
| 1920 | Earl Thomson, Canada | 14.8 WR |
| 1924 | Daniel Kinsey, United States | 15.0 |
| 1928 | Sydney Atkinson, South Africa | 14.8 |
| 1932 | George Saling, United States | 14.6 |
| 1936 | Forrest Towns, United States | 14.2 |
| 1948 | William Porter, United States | 13.9 OR |
| 1952 | Harrison Dillard, United States | 13.7 OR |
| 1956 | Lee Calhoun, United States | 13.5 OR |
| 1960 | Lee Calhoun, United States | 13.8 |
| 1964 | Hayes Jones, United States | 13.6 |
| 1968 | Willie Davenport, United States | 13.3 OR |
| 1972 | Rod Milburn, United States | 13.24 EWR |
| 1976 | Guy Drut, France | 13.30 |
| 1980 | Thomas Munkelt, East Germany | 13.39 |
| 1984 | Roger Kingdom, United States | 13.20 OR |
| 1988 | Roger Kingdom, United States | 12.98 OR |
| 1992 | Mark McKoy, Canada | 13.12 |

#### 400-METER HURDLES

| Year | Champion | Time |
|------|----------|------|
| 1900 | John Walter Tewksbury, United States | 57.6 |
| 1904 | Harry Hillman, United States | 53.0 |
| 1906 | Not held | |
| 1908 | Charles Bacon, United States | 55.0 WR |
| 1912 | Not held | |
| 1920 | Frank Loomis, United States | 54.0 WR |
| 1924 | F. Morgan Taylor, United States | 52.6 |
| 1928 | David Burghley, Great Britain | 53.4 OR |
| 1932 | Robert Tisdall, Ireland | 51.7 |
| 1936 | Glenn Hardin, United States | 52.4 |
| 1948 | Roy Cochran, United States | 51.1 OR |
| 1952 | Charles Moore, United States | 50.8 OR |
| 1956 | Glenn Davis, United States | 50.1 EOR |
| 1960 | Glenn Davis, United States | 49.3 EOR |
| 1964 | Rex Cawley, United States | 49.6 |
| 1968 | Dave Hemery, Great Britain | 48.12 WR |
| 1972 | John Akii-Bua, Uganda | 47.82 WR |
| 1976 | Edwin Moses, United States | 47.64 WR |
| 1980 | Volker Beck, East Germany | 48.70 |
| 1984 | Edwin Moses, United States | 47.75 |
| 1988 | Andre Phillips, United States | 47.19 OR |
| 1992 | Kevin Young, United States | 46.78 WR |

## THEY SAID IT

*Rick Gentile, the senior vice president of CBS Sports, on host Greg Gumbel's Olympic performance at the Lillehammer Winter Games: "He filled the Greg Gumbel role very well."*

## TRACK AND FIELD (Cont.)

### Men (Cont.)

#### 3000-METER STEEPLECHASE

| | | |
|---|---|---|
| 1920 | Percy Hodge, Great Britain | 10:00.4 OR |
| 1924 | Vilho (Ville) Ritola, Finland | 9:33.6 OR |
| 1928 | Toivo Loukola, Finland | 9:21.8 WR |
| 1932 | Volmari Iso-Hollo, Finland | 10:33.4* |
| 1936 | Volmari Iso-Hollo, Finland | 9:03.8 WR |
| 1948 | Thore Sjöstrand, Sweden | 9:04.6 |
| 1952 | Horace Ashenfelter, United States | 8:45.4 WR |
| 1956 | Chris Brasher, Great Britain | 8:41.2 OR |
| 1960 | Zdzislaw Krzyszkowiak, Poland | 8:34.2 OR |
| 1964 | Gaston Roelants, Belgium | 8:30.8 OR |
| 1968 | Amos Biwott, Kenya | 8:51 |
| 1972 | Kipchoge Keino, Kenya | 8:23.6 OR |
| 1976 | Anders Gärderud, Sweden | 8:08.2 WR |
| 1980 | Bronislaw Malinowski, Poland | 8:09.7 |
| 1984 | Julius Korir, Kenya | 8:11.8 |
| 1988 | Julius Kariuki, Kenya | 8:05.51 OR |
| 1992 | Matthew Birir, Kenya | 8:08.84 |

*About 3450 meters; extra lap by error.

#### 4 X 100-METER RELAY

| | | |
|---|---|---|
| 1912 | Great Britain | 42.4 OR |
| 1920 | United States | 42.2 WR |
| 1924 | United States | 41.0 EWR |
| 1928 | United States | 41.0 EWR |
| 1932 | United States | 40.0 EWR |
| 1936 | United States | 39.8 WR |
| 1948 | United States | 40.6 |
| 1952 | United States | 40.1 |
| 1956 | United States | 39.5 WR |
| 1960 | West Germany | 39.5 EWR |
| 1964 | United States | 39.0 WR |
| 1968 | United States | 38.2 WR |
| 1972 | United States | 38.19 EWR |
| 1976 | United States | 38.33 |
| 1980 | USSR | 38.26 |
| 1984 | United States | 37.83 WR |
| 1988 | USSR | 38.19 |
| 1992 | United States | 37.40 WR |

#### 4 X 400-METER RELAY

| | | |
|---|---|---|
| 1908 | United States | 3:29.4 |
| 1912 | United States | 3:16.6 WR |
| 1920 | Great Britain | 3:22.2 |
| 1924 | United States | 3:16.0 WR |
| 1928 | United States | 3:14.2 WR |
| 1932 | United States | 3:08.2 WR |
| 1936 | Great Britain | 3:09.0 |
| 1948 | United States | 3:10.4 WR |
| 1952 | Jamaica | 3:03.9 WR |
| 1956 | United States | 3:04.8 |
| 1960 | United States | 3:02.2 WR |
| 1964 | United States | 3:00.7 WR |
| 1968 | United States | 2:56.16 WR |
| 1972 | Kenya | 2:59.8 |
| 1976 | United States | 2:58.65 |
| 1980 | USSR | 3:01.1 |
| 1984 | United States | 2:57.91 |
| 1988 | United States | 2:56.16 EWR |
| 1992 | United States | 2:55.74 WR |

#### 20-KILOMETER WALK

| | | |
|---|---|---|
| 1956 | Leonid Spirin, USSR | 1:31:27.4 |
| 1960 | Vladimir Golubnichiy, USSR | 1:33:07.2 |
| 1964 | Kenneth Mathews, Great Britain | 1:29:34.0 OR |
| 1968 | Vladimir Golubnichiy, USSR | 1:33:58.4 |
| 1972 | Peter Frenkel, East Germany | 1:26:42.4 OR |
| 1976 | Daniel Bautista, Mexico | 1:24:40.6 OR |
| 1980 | Maurizio Damilano, Italy | 1:23:35.5 OR |
| 1984 | Ernesto Canto, Mexico | 1:23:13.0 OR |
| 1988 | Jozef Pribilinec, Czechoslovakia | 1:19:57.0 OR |
| 1992 | Daniel Plaza, Spain | 1:21:45.0 |

#### 50-KILOMETER WALK

| | | |
|---|---|---|
| 1932 | Thomas Green, Great Britain | 4:50:10 |
| 1936 | Harold Whitlock, Great Britain | 4:30:41.4 OR |
| 1948 | John Ljunggren, Sweden | 4:41:52 |
| 1952 | Giuseppe Dordoni, Italy | 4:28:07.8 OR |
| 1956 | Norman Read, New Zealand | 4:30:42.8 |
| 1960 | Donald Thompson, Great Britain | 4:25:30 OR |
| 1964 | Abdon Parnich, Italy | 4:11:12.4 OR |
| 1968 | Christoph Höhne, East Germany | 4:20:13.6 |
| 1972 | Bernd Kannenberg, West Germany | 3:56:11.6 OR |
| 1980 | Hartwig Gauder, East Germany | 3:49:24.0 OR |
| 1984 | Raul Gonzalez, Mexico | 3:47:26.0 OR |
| 1988 | Viacheslav Ivanenko, USSR | 3:38:29.0 OR |
| 1992 | Andrey Perlov, Unified Team | 3:50:13 |

#### HIGH JUMP

| | | |
|---|---|---|
| 1896 | Ellery Clark, United States | 5 ft 11¼ in |
| 1900 | Irving Baxter, United States | 6 ft 2¾ in OR |
| 1904 | Samuel Jones, United States | 5 ft 11 in |
| 1906 | Cornelius Leahy, Great Britain/Ireland | 5 ft 10 in |
| 1908 | Harry Porter, United States | 6 ft 3 in OR |
| 1912 | Alma Richards, United States | 6 ft 4 in OR |
| 1920 | Richmond Landon, United States | 6 ft 4 in OR |
| 1924 | Harold Osborn, United States | 6 ft 6 in OR |
| 1928 | Robert W. King, United States | 6 ft 4½ in |
| 1932 | Duncan McNaughton, Canada | 6 ft 5½ in |
| 1936 | Cornelius Johnson, United States | 6 ft 8 in OR |
| 1948 | John L. Winter, Australia | 6 ft 6 in |
| 1952 | Walter Davis, United States | 6 ft 8½ in OR |
| 1956 | Charles Dumas, United States | 6 ft 11½ in OR |
| 1960 | Robert Shavlakadze, USSR | 7 ft 1 in OR |
| 1964 | Valery Brumel, USSR | 7 ft 1¾ in OR |
| 1968 | Dick Fosbury, United States | 7 ft 4¼ in OR |
| 1972 | Yuri Tarmak, USSR | 7 ft 3¾ in |
| 1976 | Jacek Wszola, Poland | 7 ft 4½ in OR |
| 1980 | Gerd Wessig, East Germany | 7 ft 8¾ in WR |
| 1984 | Dietmar Mögenburg, West Germany | 7 ft 8½ in |
| 1988 | Gennadiy Avdeyenko, USSR | 7 ft 9¾ in OR |
| 1992 | Javier Sotomayor, Cuba | 7 ft 8 in. |

Note: OR=Olympic Record; WR=World Record; EOR=Equals Olympic Record; EWR=Equals World Record; WB=World Best.

## TRACK AND FIELD *(Cont.)*

### Men *(Cont.)*

#### POLE VAULT

| | | |
|---|---|---|
| 1896 | ...William Hoyt, United States | 10 ft 10 in |
| 1900 | ...Irving Baxter, United States | 10 ft 10 in |
| 1904 | ...Charles Dvorak, United States | 11 ft 5¾ in |
| 1906 | ...Fernand Gonder, France | 11 ft 5¾ in |
| 1908 | ...Alfred Gilbert, United States Edward Cooke, Jr, United States | 12 ft 2 in OR |
| 1912 | ...Harry Babcock, United States | 12 ft 11½ in OR |
| 1920 | ...Frank Foss, United States | 13 ft 5 in WR |
| 1924 | ...Lee Barnes, United States | 12 ft 11½ in |
| 1928 | ...Sabin Carr, United States | 13 ft 9¼ in OR |
| 1932 | ...William Miller, United States | 14 ft 1¾ in OR |
| 1936 | ...Earle Meadows, United States | 14 ft 3¼ in OR |
| 1948 | ...Guinn Smith, United States | 14 ft 1¼ in |
| 1952 | ...Robert Richards, United States | 14 ft 11 in OR |
| 1956 | ...Robert Richards, United States | 14 ft 11½ in OR |
| 1960 | ...Don Bragg, United States | 15 ft 5 in OR |
| 1964 | ...Fred Hansen, United States | 16 ft 8¾ in OR |
| 1968 | ...Bob Seagren, United States | 17 ft 8½ in OR |
| 1972 | ...Wolfgang Nordwig, East Germany | 18 ft ½ in OR |
| 1976 | ...Tadeusz Slusarski, Poland | 18 ft ½ in EOR |
| 1980 | ...Wladyslaw Kozakiewicz, Poland | 18 ft 11½ in WR |
| 1984 | ...Pierre Quinon, France | 18 ft 10¼ in |
| 1988 | ...Sergei Bubka, USSR | 19 ft 9¼ in OR |
| 1992 | ...Maksim Tarasov, Unified Team | 19 ft ¼ in |

#### LONG JUMP

| | | |
|---|---|---|
| 1896 | ...Ellery Clark, United States | 20 ft 10 in |
| 1900 | ...Alvin Kraenzlein, United States | 23 ft 6¾ in OR |
| 1904 | ...Meyer Prinstein, United States | 24 ft 1 in OR |
| 1906 | ...Meyer Prinstein, United States | 23 ft 7½ in |
| 1908 | ...Frank Irons, United States | 24 ft 6½ in OR |
| 1912 | Albert Gutterson, United States | 24 ft 11¼ in OR |
| 1920 | ...William Petersson, Sweden | 23 ft 5½ in |
| 1924 | ...DeHart Hubbard, United States | 24 ft 5 in |
| 1928 | ...Edward B. Hamm, United States | 25 ft 4½ in OR |
| 1932 | ...Edward Gordon, United States | 25 ft ¾ in |
| 1936 | ...Jesse Owens, United States | 26 ft 5½ in OR |
| 1948 | ...William Steele, United States | 25 ft 8 in |
| 1952 | ...Jerome Biffle, United States | 24 ft 10 in |
| 1956 | ...Gregory Bell, United States | 25 ft 8¼ in |
| 1960 | Ralph Boston, United States | 26 ft 7¾ in OR |
| 1964 | ...Lynn Davies, Great Britain | 26 ft 5¾ in |
| 1968 | ...Bob Beamon, United States | 29 ft 2½ in WR |

#### LONG JUMP *(Cont.)*

| | | |
|---|---|---|
| 1972 | ...Randy Williams, United States | 27 ft ½ in |
| 1976 | ...Arnie Robinson, United States | 27 ft 4¾ in |
| 1980 | ...Lutz Dombrowski, East Germany | 28 ft ¼ in |
| 1984 | ...Carl Lewis, United States | 28 ft ¼ in |
| 1988 | ...Carl Lewis, United States | 28 ft 7½ in |
| 1992 | ...Carl Lewis, United States | 28 ft 5½ in |

#### TRIPLE JUMP

| | | |
|---|---|---|
| 1896 | ...James Connolly, United States | 44 ft 11¾ in |
| 1900 | ...Meyer Prinstein, United States | 47 ft 5¾ in OR |
| 1904 | ...Meyer Prinstein, United States | 47 ft 1 in |
| 1906 | ...Peter O'Connor, Great Britain/Ireland | 46 ft 2¼ in |
| 1908 | ...Timothy Ahearne, Great Britain/Ireland | 48 ft 11¼ in OR |
| 1912 | ...Gustaf Lindblom, Sweden | 48 ft 5¼ in |
| 1920 | ...Vilho Tuulos, Finland | 47 ft 7 in |
| 1924 | ...Anthony Winter, Australia | 50 ft 11¼ in WR |
| 1928 | ...Mikio Oda, Japan | 49 ft 11 in |
| 1932 | ...Chuhei Nambu, Japan | 51 ft 7 in WR |
| 1936 | ...Naoto Tajima, Japan | 52 ft 6 in WR |
| 1948 | ...Arne Ahman, Sweden | 50 ft 6¼ in |
| 1952 | ...Adhemar da Silva, Brazil | 53 ft 2¾ in WR |
| 1956 | ...Adhemar da Silva, Brazil | 53 ft 7¾ in OR |
| 1960 | ...Jozef Schmidt, Poland | 55 ft 2 in |
| 1964 | ...Jozef Schmidt, Poland | 55 ft 3½ in OR |
| 1968 | ...Viktor Saneyev, USSR | 57 ft ¾ in WR |
| 1972 | ...Viktor Saneyev, USSR | 56 ft 11¾ in |
| 1976 | ...Viktor Saneyev, USSR | 56 ft 8¾ in |
| 1980 | ...Jaak Uudmae, USSR | 56 ft 11¼ in |
| 1984 | ...Al Joyner, United States | 56 ft 7½ in |
| 1988 | ...Khristo Markov, Bulgaria | 57 ft 9½ in OR |
| 1992 | ...Mike Conley, United States | 59 ft 7½ in |

#### SHOT PUT

| | | |
|---|---|---|
| 1896 | ...Robert Garrett, United States | 36 ft 9¾ in |
| 1900 | ...Richard Sheldon, United States | 46 ft 3¼ in OR |
| 1904 | ...Ralph Rose, United States | 48 ft 7 in WR |
| 1906 | ...Martin Sheridan, United States | 40 ft 5¼ in |
| 1908 | ...Ralph Rose, United States | 46 ft 7½ in |
| 1912 | ...Pat McDonald, United States | 50 ft 4 in OR |
| 1920 | ...Ville Porhola, Finland | 48 ft 7¼ in |
| 1924 | ...Clarence Houser, United States | 49 ft 2¼ in |
| 1928 | ...John Kuck, United States | 52 ft ¾ in WR |
| 1932 | ...Leo Sexton, United States | 52 ft 6 in OR |
| 1936 | ...Hans Woellke, Germany | 53 ft 1¾ in OR |
| 1948 | ...Wilbur Thompson, United States | 56 ft 2 in OR |
| 1952 | ...Parry O'Brien, United States | 57 ft ½ in OR |
| 1956 | ...Parry O'Brien, United States | 60 ft 11¼ in OR |
| 1960 | ...William Nieder, United States | 64 ft 6¾ in OR |

## Summer Games Champions (Cont.)

### TRACK AND FIELD (Cont.)

### Men (Cont.)

#### SHOT PUT (Cont.)

| | | |
|---|---|---|
| 1964 | ...Dallas Long, United States | 66 ft 8½ in OR |
| 1968 | ...Randy Matson, United States | 67 ft 4¾ in |
| 1972 | ...Wladyslaw Komar, Poland | 69 ft 6 in OR |
| 1976 | ...Udo Beyer, East Germany | 69 ft ¾ in |
| 1980 | ...Vladimir Kiselyov, USSR | 70 ft ½ in OR |
| 1984 | ...Alessandro Andrei, Italy | 69 ft 9 in |
| 1988 | ...Ulf Timmermann, East Germany | 73 ft 8¾ in OR |
| 1992 | ...Mike Stulce, United States | 71 ft 2½ in |

#### DISCUS THROW

| | | |
|---|---|---|
| 1896 | ...Robert Garrett, United States | 95 ft 7½ in |
| 1900 | ...Rudolf Bauer, Hungary | 118 ft 3 in OR |
| 1904 | ...Martin Sheridan, United States | 128 ft 10½ in OR |
| 1906 | ...Martin Sheridan, United States | 136 ft |
| 1908 | ...Martin Sheridan, United States | 134 ft 2 in OR |
| 1912 | ...Armas Taipele, Finland | 148 ft 3 in OR |
| 1920 | ...Elmer Niklander, Finland | 146 ft 7 in |
| 1924 | ...Clarence Houser, United States | 151 ft 4 in OR |
| 1928 | ...Clarence Houser, United States | 155 ft 3 in OR |
| 1932 | ...John Anderson, United States | 162 ft 4 in OR |
| 1936 | ...Ken Carpenter, United States | 165 ft 7 in OR |
| 1948 | ...Adolfo Consolini, Italy | 173 ft 2 in OR |
| 1952 | ...Sim Iness, United States | 180 ft 6 in OR |
| 1956 | ...Al Oerter, United States | 184 ft 11 in OR |
| 1960 | ...Al Oerter, United States | 194 ft 2 in OR |
| 1964 | ...Al Oerter, United States | 200 ft 1 in OR |
| 1968 | ...Al Oerter, United States | 212 ft 6 in OR |
| 1972 | ...Ludvik Danek, Czechoslovakia | 211 ft 3 in |
| 1976 | ...Mac Wilkins, United States | 221 ft 5 in OR |
| 1980 | ...Viktor Rashchupkin, USSR | 218 ft 8 in |
| 1984 | ...Rolf Dannenberg, West Germany | 218 ft 6 in |
| 1988 | ...Jürgen Schult, East Germany | 225 ft 9 in OR |
| 1992 | ...Romas Ubartas, Lithuania | 213 ft 8 in |

#### HAMMER THROW

| | | |
|---|---|---|
| 1900 | ...John Flanagan, United States | 163 ft 1 in |
| 1904 | ...John Flanagan, United States | 168 ft 1 in OR |
| 1906 | ...Not held | |
| 1908 | ...John Flanagan, United States | 170 ft 4 in OR |
| 1912 | ...Matt McGrath, United States | 179 ft 7 in OR |
| 1920 | ...Pat Ryan, United States | 173 ft 5 in |
| 1924 | ...Fred Tootell, United States | 174 ft 10 in |
| 1928 | ...Patrick O'Callaghan, Ireland | 168 ft 7 in |
| 1932 | ...Patrick O'Callaghan, Ireland | 176 ft 11 in |
| 1936 | ...Karl Hein, Germany | 185 ft 4 in OR |
| 1948 | ...Imre Nemeth, Hungary | 183 ft 11 in |
| 1952 | ...Jozsef Csermak, Hungary | 197 ft 11 in WR |
| 1956 | ...Harold Connolly, United States | 207 ft 3 in OR |
| 1960 | ...Vasily Rudenkov, USSR | 220 ft 2 in OR |

#### HAMMER THROW (Cont.)

| | | |
|---|---|---|
| 1964 | ...Romuald Klim, USSR | 228 ft 10 in OR |
| 1968 | ...Gyula Zsivotsky, Hungary | 240 ft 8 in OR |
| 1972 | ...Anatoli Bondarchuk, USSR | 247 ft 8 in OR |
| 1976 | ...Yuri Sedykh, USSR | 254 ft 4 in OR |
| 1980 | ...Yuri Sedykh, USSR | 268 ft 4 in WR |
| 1984 | ...Juha Tiainen, Finland | 256 ft 2 in |
| 1988 | ...Sergei Litvinov, USSR | 278 ft 2 in OR |
| 1992 | ...Andrey Abduvaliyev, Unified Team | 270 ft 9 in |

#### JAVELIN

| | | |
|---|---|---|
| 1908 | ...Erik Lemming, Sweden | 179 ft 10 in |
| 1912 | ...Erik Lemming, Sweden | 198 ft 11 in WR |
| 1920 | ...Jonni Myyrä, Finland | 215 ft 10 in OR |
| 1924 | ...Jonni Myyrä, Finland | 206 ft 6 in |
| 1928 | ...Eric Lundkvist, Sweden | 218 ft 6 in OR |
| 1932 | ...Matti Jarvinen, Finland | 238 ft 6 in OR |
| 1936 | ...Gerhard Stöck, Germany | 235 ft 8 in |
| 1948 | ...Kai Rautavaara, Finland | 228 ft 10½ in |
| 1952 | ...Cy Young, United States | 242 ft 1 in OR |
| 1956 | ...Egil Danielson, Norway | 281 ft 2¼ in WR |
| 1960 | ...Viktor Tsibulenko, USSR | 277 ft 8 in |
| 1964 | ...Pauli Nevala, Finland | 271 ft 2 in |
| 1968 | ...Janis Lusis, USSR | 295 ft 7 in OR |
| 1972 | ...Klaus Wolfermann, West Germany | 296 ft 10 in OR |
| 1976 | ...Miklos Nemeth, Hungary | 310 ft 4 in WR |
| 1980 | ...Dainis Kuta, USSR | 299 ft 2⅜ in |
| 1984 | ...Arto Härkönen, Finland | 284 ft 8 in |
| 1988 | ...Tapio Korjus, Finland | 276 ft 6 in |
| 1992 | ...Jan Zelezny, Czechoslovakia | 294 ft 2 in OR |

#### DECATHLON

| | | Pts |
|---|---|---|
| 1904 | ...Thomas Kiely, Ireland | 6036 |
| 1912 | ...Jim Thorpe, United States* | 8412 WR |
| 1920 | ...Helge Lövland, Norway | 6803 |
| 1924 | ...Harold Osborn, United States | 7711 WR |
| 1928 | ...Paavo Yrjölä, Finland | 8053.29 WR |
| 1932 | ...James Bausch, United States | 8462 WR |
| 1936 | ...Glenn Morris, United States | 7900 WR |
| 1948 | ...Robert Mathias, United States | 7139 |
| 1952 | ...Robert Mathias, United States | 7887 WR |
| 1956 | ...Milton Campbell, United States | 7937 OR |
| 1960 | ...Rafer Johnson, United States | 8392 OR |
| 1964 | ...Willi Holdorf, West Germany | 7887 |
| 1968 | ...Bill Toomey, United States | 8193 OR |
| 1972 | ...Nikolai Avilov, USSR | 8454 WR |
| 1976 | ...Bruce Jenner, United States | 8617 WR |
| 1980 | ...Daley Thompson, Great Britain | 8495 |
| 1984 | ...Daley Thompson, Great Britain | 8798 EWR |
| 1988 | ...Christian Schenk, East Germany | 8488 |
| 1992 | ...Robert Zmelik, Czechoslovakia | 8611 |

*In 1913, Thorpe was disqualified for having played professional baseball in 1910. His record was restored in 1982.

Note: OR=Olympic Record; WR=World Record;

EOR=Equals Olympic Record; EWR=Equals World Record; WB=World Best.

### TRACK AND FIELD *(Cont.)*

## Women

### 100 METERS

| | | |
|---|---|---|
| 1928 ...Elizabeth Robinson, United States | 12.2 EWR |
| 1932 ...Stella Walsh, Poland | 11.9 EWR |
| 1936 ...Helen Stephens, United States | 11.5 |
| 1948 ....Francina Blankers-Koen, Netherlands | 11.9 |
| 1952 ...Marjorie Jackson, Australia | 11.5 EWR |
| 1956 ...Betty Cuthbert, Australia | 11.5 EWR |
| 1960 ...Wilma Rudolph, United States | 11.0 |
| 1964 ...Wyomia Tyus, United States | 11.4 |
| 1968 ...Wyomia Tyus, United States | 11.0 WR |
| 1972 ...Renate Stecher, East Germany | 11.07 |
| 1976 ...Annegret Richter, West Germany | 11.08 |
| 1980 ...Lyudmila Kondratyeva, USSR | 11.06 |
| 1984 ...Evelyn Ashford, United States | 10.97 OR |
| 1988 ...Florence Griffith Joyner, United States | 10.54 |
| 1992 ...Gail Devers, United States | 10.82 |

### 200 METERS

| | | |
|---|---|---|
| 1948...Francina Blankers-Koen, Netherlands | 24.4 |
| 1952 ..Marjorie Jackson, Australia | 23.7 |
| 1956 ..Betty Cuthbert, Australia | 23.4 EOR |
| 1960 ..Wilma Rudolph, United States | 24.0 |
| 1964 ..Edith McGuire, United States | 23.0 OR |
| 1968 ..Irena Szewinska, Poland | 22.5 WR |
| 1972 ..Renate Stecher, East Germany | 22.40 EWR |
| 1976 ..Bärbel Eckert, East Germany | 22.37 OR |
| 1980 ..Bärbel Wöckel (Eckert), East Germany | 22.03 OR |
| 1984 ...Valerie Brisco-Hooks, United States | 21.81 OR |
| 1988 ..Florence Griffith Joyner, United States | 21.34 WR |
| 1992 ..Gwen Torrence, United States | 21.81 |

### 400 METERS

| | | |
|---|---|---|
| 1964 ...Betty Cuthbert, Australia | 52.0 OR |
| 1968 ...Colette Besson, France | 52.0 EOR |
| 1972 ...Monika Zehrt, East Germany | 51.08 OR |
| 1976 ...Irena Szewinska, Poland | 49.29 WR |
| 1980 ...Marita Koch, East Germany | 48.88 OR |
| 1984 ...Valerie Brisco-Hooks, United States | 48.83 OR |
| 1988 ...Olga Bryzgina, USSR | 48.65 OR |
| 1992 ...Marie-José Pérec, France | 48.83 |

### 800 METERS

| | | |
|---|---|---|
| 1928 ....Lina Radke, Germany | 2:16.8 WR |
| 1932 ....Not held 1932-1956 | |
| 1960 ....Lyudmila Shevtsova, USSR | 2:04.3 EWR |
| 1964 ....Ann Packer, Great Britain | 2:01.1 OR |
| 1968 ....Madeline Manning, United States | 2:00.9 OR |
| 1972 ....Hildegard Falck, West Germany | 1:58.55 OR |
| 1976 ....Tatyana Kazankina, USSR | 1:54.94 WR |
| 1980 ....Nadezhda Olizarenko, USSR | 1:53.42 WR |
| 1984 ....Doina Melinte, Romania | 1:57.6 |
| 1988 ....Sigrun Wodars, East Germany | 1:56.10 |
| 1992 ....Ellen Van Langen, the Netherlands | 1:55.54 |

### 1500 METERS

| | | |
|---|---|---|
| 1972 ....Lyudmila Bragina, USSR | 4:01.4 WR |
| 1976 ....Tatyana Kazankina, USSR | 4:05.48 |
| 1980 ....Tatyana Kazankina, USSR | 3:56.6 OR |
| 1984 ....Gabriella Dorio, Italy | 4:03.25 |

### 1500 METERS *(Cont.)*

| | | |
|---|---|---|
| 1988 ....Paula Ivan, Romania | 3:53.96 OR |
| 1992 ....Hassiba Boulmerka, Algeria | 3:55.30 |

### 3000 METERS

| | | |
|---|---|---|
| 1984 ....Maricica Puica, Romania | 8:35.96 OR |
| 1988 ....Tatyana Samolenko, USSR | 8:26.53 OR |
| 1992 ....Elena Romanova, Unified Team | 8:46.04 |

### 10,000 METERS

| | | |
|---|---|---|
| 1988 ....Olga Bondarenko, USSR | 31:05.21 OR |
| 1992 ....Derartu Tulu, Ethiopia | 31:06.02 |

### MARATHON

| | | |
|---|---|---|
| 1984 ....Joan Benoit, United States | 2:24:52 |
| 1988 ....Rosa Mota, Portugal | 2:25:40 |
| 1992 ....Valentin Yegorova, Unified Team | 2:32:41 |

### 80-METER HURDLES

| | | |
|---|---|---|
| 1932 ..Babe Didrikson, United States | 11.7 WR |
| 1936 ..Trebisonda Valla, Italy | 11.7 |
| 1948 ..Francina Blankers-Koen, Netherlands | 11.2 OR |
| 1952 ..Shirley Strickland, Australia | 10.9 WR |
| 1956 ..Shirley Strickland, Australia | 10.7 OR |
| 1960 ..Irina Press, USSR | 10.8 |
| 1964 ..Karin Balzer, East Germany | 10.5 |
| 1968 ..Maureen Caird, Australia | 10.3 OR |

### 100-METER HURDLES

| | | |
|---|---|---|
| 1972 ....Annelie Ehrhardt, East Germany | 12.59 WR |
| 1976 ....Johanna Schaller, East Germany | 12.77 |
| 1980 ....Vera Komisova, USSR | 12.56 OR |
| 1984 ....Benita Fitzgerald-Brown, United States | 12.84 |
| 1988 ....Yordanka Donkova, Bulgaria | 12.38 OR |
| 1992 ....Paraskevi Patoulidou, Greece | 12.64 |

### 400-METER HURDLES

| | | |
|---|---|---|
| 1984 ....Nawal el Moutawakel, Morocco | 54.61 OR |
| 1988 ....Debra Flintoff-King, Australia | 53.17 OR |
| 1992 ....Sally Gunnell, Great Britain | 53.23 |

### 4 X 100-METER RELAY

| | | |
|---|---|---|
| 1928 ..............Canada | 48.4 WR |
| 1932 ..............United States | 46.9 WR |
| 1936 ..............United States | 46.9 |
| 1948 ..............Netherlands | 47.5 |
| 1952 ..............United States | 45.9 WR |
| 1956 ..............Australia | 44.5 WR |
| 1960 ..............United States | 44.5 |
| 1964 ..............Poland | 43.6 |
| 1968 ..............United States | 42.8 WR |
| 1972 ..............West Germany | 42.81 EWR |
| 1976 ..............East Germany | 42.55 OR |
| 1980 ..............East Germany | 41.60 WR |
| 1984 ..............United States | 41.65 |
| 1988 ..............United States | 41.98 |
| 1992 ..............United States | 42.11 |

Note: OR=Olympic Record; WR=World Record; EOR=Equals Olympic Record; EWR=Equals World Record; WB=World Best.

## TRACK AND FIELD (Cont.)

### Women (Cont.)

#### 4 X 400-METER RELAY

| | | |
|---|---|---|
| 1972 | East Germany | 3:23 WR |
| 1976 | East Germany | 3:19.23 WR |
| 1980 | USSR | 3:20.02 |
| 1984 | United States | 3:18.29 OR |
| 1988 | USSR | 3:15.18 WR |
| 1992 | Unified Team | 3:20.20 |

#### HIGH JUMP

| | | |
|---|---|---|
| 1928 | Ethel Catherwood, Canada | 5 ft 2½ in |
| 1932 | Jean Shiley, United States | 5 ft 5¼ in WR |
| 1936 | Ibolya Csak, Hungary | 5 ft 3 in |
| 1948 | Alice Coachman, United States | 5 ft 6 in OR |
| 1952 | Esther Brand, South Africa | 5 ft 5¾ in |
| 1956 | Mildred L. McDaniel, United States | 5 ft 9¼ in WR |
| 1960 | Iolanda Balas, Romania | 6 ft ¾ in OR |
| 1964 | Iolanda Balas, Romania | 6 ft 2¾ in OR |
| 1968 | Miloslava Reskova, Czechoslovakia | 5 ft 11½ in |
| 1972 | Ulrike Meyfarth, West Germany | 6 ft 3½ in EWR |
| 1976 | Rosemarie Ackermann, East Germany | 6 ft 4 in OR |
| 1980 | Sara Simeoni, Italy | 6 ft 5½ in OR |
| 1984 | Ulrike Meyfarth, West Germany | 6 ft 7½ in OR |
| 1988 | Louise Ritter, United States | 6 ft 8 in OR |
| 1992 | Heike Henkel, Germany | 6 ft 7½ in |

#### LONG JUMP

| | | |
|---|---|---|
| 1948 | Olga Gyarmati, Hungary | 18 ft 8¼ in |
| 1952 | Yvette Williams, New Zealand | 20 ft 5¾ in OR |
| 1956 | Elzbieta Krzeskinska, Poland | 20 ft 10 in EWR |
| 1960 | Vyera Krepkina, USSR | 20 ft 10¾ in OR |
| 1964 | Mary Rand, Great Britain | 22 ft 2¼ in WR |
| 1968 | Viorica Viscopoleanu, Romania | 22 ft 4½ in WR |
| 1972 | Heidemarie Rosendahl, West Germany | 22 ft 3 in |
| 1976 | Angela Voigt, East Germany | 22 ft ¾ in |
| 1980 | Tatyana Kolpakova, USSR | 23 ft 2 in OR |
| 1984 | Anisoara Stanciu, Romania | 22 ft 10 in |
| 1988 | Jackie Joyner-Kersee, United States | 24 ft 3½ in OR |
| 1992 | Heike Drechsler, Germany | 23 ft 5¼ in |

#### SHOT PUT

| | | |
|---|---|---|
| 1948 | Micheline Ostermeyer, France | 45 ft 1½ in |
| 1952 | Galina Zybina, USSR | 50 ft 1¾ in WR |
| 1956 | Tamara Tyshkevich, USSR | 54 ft 5 in OR |
| 1960 | Tamara Press, USSR | 56 ft 10 in OR |
| 1964 | Tamara Press, USSR | 59 ft 6¼ in OR |
| 1968 | Margitta Gummel, East Germany | 64 ft 4 in WR |
| 1972 | Nadezhda Chizhova, USSR | 69 ft WR |
| 1976 | Ivanka Hristova, Bulgaria | 69 ft 5¼ in OR |
| 1980 | Ilona Slupianek, East Germany | 73 ft 6¼ in |
| 1984 | Claudia Losch, West Germany | 67 ft 2¼ in |

#### SHOT PUT (Cont.)

| | | |
|---|---|---|
| 1988 | Natalya Lisovskaya, USSR | 72 ft 11¾ in |
| 1992 | Svetlana Kriveleva, Unified Team | 69 ft 1¼ in |

#### DISCUS THROW

| | | |
|---|---|---|
| 1928 | Helena Konopacka, Poland | 129 ft 11¾ in WR |
| 1932 | Lillian Copeland, United States | 133 ft 2 in OR |
| 1936 | Gisela Mauermayer, Germany | 156 ft 3 in OR |
| 1948 | Micheline Ostermeyer, France | 137 ft 6 in |
| 1952 | Nina Romaschkova, USSR | 168 ft 8 in OR |
| 1956 | Olga Fikotova, Czechoslovakia | 176 ft 1 in OR |
| 1960 | Nina Ponomaryeva, USSR | 180 ft 9 in OR |
| 1964 | Tamara Press, USSR | 187 ft 10 in OR |
| 1968 | Lia Manoliu, Romania | 191 ft 2 in OR |
| 1972 | Faina Melnik, USSR | 218 ft 7 in OR |
| 1976 | Evelin Schlaak, East Germany | 226 ft 4 in OR |
| 1980 | Evelin Jahl (Schlaak), East Germany | 229 ft 6 in OR |
| 1984 | Ria Stalman, Netherlands | 214 ft 5 in |
| 1988 | Martina Hellmann, East Germany | 237 ft 2 in OR |
| 1992 | Maritza Martén, Cuba | 229 ft 10 in |

#### JAVELIN THROW

| | | |
|---|---|---|
| 1932 | Babe Didrikson, United States | 143 ft 4 in OR |
| 1936 | Tilly Fleischer, Germany | 148 ft 3 in OR |
| 1948 | Herma Bauma, Austria | 149 ft 6 in |
| 1952 | Dana Zatopkova, Czechoslovakia | 165 ft 7 in |
| 1956 | Inese Jaunzeme, USSR | 176 ft 8 in |
| 1960 | Elvira Ozolina, USSR | 183 ft 8 in OR |
| 1964 | Mihaela Penes, Romania | 198 ft 7 in |
| 1968 | Angela Nemeth, Hungary | 198 ft |
| 1972 | Ruth Fuchs, East Germany | 209 ft 7 in OR |
| 1976 | Ruth Fuchs, East Germany | 216 ft 4 in OR |
| 1980 | Maria Colon, Cuba | 224 ft 5 in OR |
| 1984 | Tessa Sanderson, Great Britain | 228 ft 2 in OR |
| 1988 | Petra Felke, East Germany | 245 ft OR |
| 1992 | Silke Renk, Germany | 224 ft 2 in |

#### PENTATHLON

| | | Pts |
|---|---|---|
| 1964 | Irina Press, USSR | 5246 WR |
| 1968 | Ingrid Becker, West Germany | 5098 |
| 1972 | Mary Peters, Great Britain | 4801 WR* |
| 1976 | Siegrun Siegl, East Germany | 4745 |
| 1980 | Nadezhda Tkachenko, USSR | 5083 WR |

*In 1971, 100-meter hurdles replaced 80-meter hurdles, necessitating a change in scoring tables.

#### HEPTATHLON

| | | Pts |
|---|---|---|
| 1984 | Glynis Nunn, Australia | 6390 OR |
| 1988 | Jackie Joyner-Kersee, United States | 7291 WR |
| 1992 | Jackie Joyner-Kersee, United States | 7044 |

# BASKETBALL

## Men

### 1936

Final: United States 19, Canada 8
United States: Ralph Bishop, Joe Fortenberry, Carl Knowles, Jack Ragland, Carl Shy, William Wheatley, Francis Johnson, Samuel Balter, John Gibbons, Frank Lubin, Arthur Mollner, Donald Piper, Duane Swanson, Willard Schmidt

### 1948

Final: United States 65, France 21
United States: Cliff Barker, Don Barksdale, Ralph Beard, Lewis Beck, Vince Boryla, Gordon Carpenter, Alex Groza, Wallace Jones, Bob Kurland, Ray Lumpp, Robert Pitts, Jesse Renick, Bob Robinson, Ken Rollins

### 1952

Final: United States 36, USSR 25
United States: Charles Hoag, Bill Hougland, Melvin Dean Kelley, Bob Kenney, Clyde Lovellette, Marcus Freiberger, Victor Wayne Glasgow, Frank McCabe, Daniel Pippen, Howard Williams, Ronald Bontemps, Bob Kurland, William Lienhard, John Keller

### 1956

Final: United States 89, USSR 55
United States: Carl Cain, Bill Hougland, K. C. Jones, Bill Russell, James Walsh, William Evans, Burdette Haldorson, Ron Tomsic, Dick Boushka, Gilbert Ford, Bob Jeangerard, Charles Darling

### 1960

Final: United States 90, Brazil 63
United States: Jay Arnette, Walt Bellamy, Bob Boozer, Terry Dischinger, Jerry Lucas, Oscar Robertson, Adrian Smith, Burdette Haldorson, Darrall Imhoff, Allen Kelley, Lester Lane, Jerry West

### 1964

Final: United States 73, USSR 59
United States: Jim Barnes, Bill Bradley, Larry Brown, Joe Caldwell, Mel Counts, Richard Davies, Walt Hazzard, Lucius Jackson, John McCaffrey, Jeff Mullins, Jerry Shipp, George Wilson

### 1968

Final: United States 65, Yugoslavia 50
United States: John Clawson, Ken Spain, Jo-Jo White, Michael Barrett, Spencer Haywood, Charles Scott, William Hosket, Calvin Fowler, Michael Silliman, Glynn Saulters, James King, Donald Dee

### 1972

Final: USSR 51, United States 50
United States: Kenneth Davis, Doug Collins, Thomas Henderson, Mike Bantom, Bobby Jones, Dwight Jones, James Forbes, James Brewer, Tom Burleson, Tom McMillen, Kevin Joyce, Ed Ratleff

### 1976

Final: United States 95, Yugoslavia 74
United States: Phil Ford, Steve Sheppard, Adrian Dantley, Walter Davis, Quinn Buckner, Ernie Grunfeld, Kenny Carr, Scott May, Michel Armstrong, Tom La Garde, Phil Hubbard, Mitch Kupchak

### 1980

Final: Yugoslavia 86, Italy 77
U.S. participated in boycott.

### 1984

Final: United States 96, Spain 65
United States: Steve Alford, Leon Wood, Patrick Ewing, Vern Fleming, Alvin Robertson, Michael Jordan, Joe Kleine, Jon Koncak, Wayman Tisdale, Chris Mullin, Sam Perkins, Jeff Turner

### 1988

Final: USSR 76, Yugoslavia 63
United States (3rd): Mitch Richmond, Charles E. Smith, IV, Vernell Coles, Hersey Hawkins, Jeff Grayer, Charles D. Smith, Willie Anderson, Stacey Augmon, Dan Majerle, Danny Manning, J. R. Reid, David Robinson

### 1992

Final: United States 117, Croatia 85
United States: David Robinson, Christian Laettner, Patrick Ewing, Larry Bird, Scottie Pippen, Michael Jordan, Clyde Drexler, Karl Malone, John Stockton, Chris Mullin, Charles Barkley, Earvin Johnson

## Women

### 1976

Gold USSR; Silver, United States*
United States: Cindy Brogdon, Susan Rojcewicz, Ann Meyers, Lusia Harris, Nancy Dunkle, Charlotte Lewis, Nancy Lieberman, Gail Marquis, Patricia Roberts, Mary Anne O'Connor, Patricia Head, Julienne Simpson

*In 1976 the women played a round-robin tournament, with the gold medal going to the team with the best record. The USSR won with a 5-0 record, and the USA, with a 3-2 record, was given the silver by virtue of a 95-79 victory over Bulgaria, which was also 3-2.

### 1980

Final: USSR 104, Bulgaria 73
U.S. participated in boycott.

### 1984

Final: United States 85, Korea 55
United States: Teresa Edwards, Lea Henry, Lynette Woodard, Anne Donovan, Cathy Boswell, Cheryl Miller, Janice Lawrence, Cindy Noble, Kim Mulkey, Denise Curry, Pamela McGee, Carol Menken-Schaudt

## BASKETBALL *(Cont.)*

### Women *(Cont.)*

**1988**

Final: United States 77, Yugoslavia 70
United States: Teresa Edwards, Mary Ethridge, Cynthia Brown, Anne Donovan, Teresa Weatherspoon, Bridgette Gordon, Victoria Bullett, Andrea Lloyd, Katrina McClain, Jennifer Gillom, Cynthia Cooper, Suzanne McConnell

**1992**

Final: Unified Team 76, China 66
United States (3rd): Teresa Edwards, Teresa Weatherspoon, Victoria Bullett, Katrina McClain, Cynthia Cooper, Suzanne McConnell, Daedra Charles, Clarissa Davis, Tammy Jackson, Vickie Orr, Carolyn Jones, Medina Dixon

## BOXING

### LIGHT FLYWEIGHT (106 LB)

| | |
|---|---|
| 1968 | Francisco Rodriguez, Venezuela |
| 1972 | Gyorgy Gedo, Hungary |
| 1976 | Jorge Hernandez, Cuba |
| 1980 | Shamil Sabyrov, USSR |
| 1984 | Paul Gonzalez, United States |
| 1988 | Ivailo Hristov, Bulgaria |
| 1992 | Rogelio Marcelo, Cuba |

### FLYWEIGHT (112 LB)

| | |
|---|---|
| 1904 | George Finnegan, United States |
| 1906-1912 | Not held |
| 1920 | Frank Di Gennara, United States |
| 1924 | Fidel LaBarba, United States |
| 1928 | Antal Kocsis, Hungary |
| 1932 | Istvan Enekes, Hungary |
| 1936 | Willi Kaiser, Germany |
| 1948 | Pascual Perez, Argentina |
| 1952 | Nathan Brooks, United States |
| 1956 | Terence Spinks, Great Britain |
| 1960 | Gyula Torok, Hungary |
| 1964 | Fernando Atzori, Italy |
| 1968 | Ricardo Delgado, Mexico |
| 1972 | Georgi Kostadinov, Bulgaria |
| 1976 | Leo Randolph, United States |
| 1980 | Peter Lessov, Bulgaria |
| 1984 | Steve McCrory, United States |
| 1988 | Kim Kwang Sun, South Korea |
| 1992 | Su Choi Chol, North Korea |

### BANTAMWEIGHT (119 LB)

| | |
|---|---|
| 1904 | Oliver Kirk, United States |
| 1906 | Not held |
| 1908 | A. Henry Thomas, Great Britain |
| 1912 | Not held |
| 1920 | Clarence Walker, South Africa |
| 1924 | William Smith, South Africa |
| 1928 | Vittorio Tamagnini, Italy |
| 1932 | Horace Gwynne, Canada |
| 1936 | Ulderico Sergo, Italy |
| 1948 | Tibor Csik, Hungary |
| 1952 | Pentti Hamalainen, Finland |
| 1956 | Wolfgang Behrendt, East Germany |
| 1960 | Oleg Grigoryev, USSR |
| 1964 | Takao Sakurai, Japan |
| 1968 | Valery Sokolov, USSR |
| 1972 | Orlando Martinez, Cuba |
| 1976 | Yong Jo Gu, North Korea |
| 1980 | Juan Hernandez, Cuba |
| 1984 | Maurizio Stecca, Italy |
| 1988 | Kennedy McKinney, United States |
| 1992 | Joel Casamayor, Cuba |

### FEATHERWEIGHT (125 LB)

| | |
|---|---|
| 1904 | Oliver Kirk, United States |
| 1906 | Not held |
| 1908 | Richard Gunn, Great Britain |
| 1912 | Not held |
| 1920 | Paul Fritsch, France |
| 1924 | John Fields, United States |
| 1928 | Lambertus van Klaveren, Netherlands |
| 1932 | Carmelo Robledo, Argentina |
| 1936 | Oscar Casanovas, Argentina |
| 1948 | Ernesto Formenti, Italy |
| 1952 | Jan Zachara, Czechoslovakia |
| 1956 | Vladimir Safronov, USSR |
| 1960 | Francesco Musso, Italy |
| 1964 | Stanislav Stephashkin, USSR |
| 1968 | Antonio Roldan, Mexico |
| 1972 | Boris Kousnetsov, USSR |
| 1976 | Angel Herrera, Cuba |
| 1980 | Rudi Fink, East Germany |
| 1984 | Meldrick Taylor, United States |
| 1988 | Giovanni Parisi, Italy |
| 1992 | Andreas Tews, Germany |

### LIGHTWEIGHT (132 LB)

| | |
|---|---|
| 1904 | Harry Spanger, United States |
| 1906 | Not held |
| 1908 | Frederick Grace, Great Britain |
| 1912 | Not held |
| 1920 | Samuel Mosberg, United States |
| 1924 | Hans Nielsen, Denmark |
| 1928 | Carlo Orlandi, Italy |
| 1932 | Lawrence Stevens, South Africa |
| 1936 | Imre Harangi, Hungary |
| 1948 | Gerald Dreyer, South Africa |
| 1952 | Aureliano Bolognesi, Italy |
| 1956 | Richard McTaggart, Great Britain |
| 1960 | Kazimierz Pazdzior, Poland |
| 1964 | Jozef Grudzien, Poland |
| 1968 | Ronald Harris, United States |
| 1972 | Jan Szczepanski, Poland |
| 1976 | Howard Davis, United States |
| 1980 | Angel Herrera, Cuba |
| 1984 | Pernell Whitaker, United States |
| 1988 | Andreas Zuelow, East Germany |
| 1992 | Oscar De La Hoya, United States |

### LIGHT WELTERWEIGHT (139 LB)

| | |
|---|---|
| 1952 | Charles Adkins, United States |
| 1956 | Vladimir Yengibaryan, USSR |
| 1960 | Bohumil Nemecek, Czechoslovakia |
| 1964 | Jerzy Kulej, Poland |
| 1968 | Jerzy Kulej, Poland |
| 1972 | Ray Seales, United States |
| 1976 | Ray Leonard, United States |

## BOXING *(Cont.)*

### LIGHT WELTERWEIGHT *(Cont.)*

1980 ...............Patrizio Oliva, Italy
1984 ...............Jerry Page, United States
1988 ...............Viatcheslav Janovski, USSR
1992 ...............Hector Vinent, Cuba

### WELTERWEIGHT (147 LB)

1904 ...............Albert Young, United States
1906-1912 ......Not held
1920 ...............Albert Schneider, Canada
1924 ...............Jean Delarge, Belgium
1928 ...............Edward Morgan, New Zealand
1932 ...............Edward Flynn, United States
1936 ...............Sten Suvio, Finland
1948 ...............Julius Torma, Czechoslovakia
1952 ...............Zygmunt Chychla, Poland
1956 ...............Nicolae Linca, Romania
1960 ...............Giovanni Benvenuti, Italy
1964 ...............Marian Kasprzyk, Poland
1968 ...............Manfred Wolke, East Germany
1972 ...............Emilio Correa, Cuba
1976 ...............Jochen Bachfeld, East Germany
1980 ...............Andres Aldama, Cuba
1984 ...............Mark Breland, United States
1988 ...............Robert Wangila, Kenya
1992 ...............Michael Carruth, Ireland

### LIGHT MIDDLEWEIGHT (156 LB)

1952 ...............Laszlo Papp, Hungary
1956 ...............Laszlo Papp, Hungary
1960 ...............Wilbert McClure, United States
1964 ...............Boris Lagutin, USSR
1968 ...............Boris Lagutin, USSR
1972 ...............Dieter Kottysch, West Germany
1976 ...............Jerzy Rybicki, Poland
1980 ...............Armando Martinez, Cuba
1984 ...............Frank Tate, United States
1988 ...............Park Si-Hun, South Korea
1992 ...............Juan Lemus, Cuba

### MIDDLEWEIGHT (165 LB)

1904 ...............Charles Mayer, United States
1908 ...............John Douglas, Great Britain
1912 ...............Not held
1920 ...............Harry Mallin, Great Britain
1924 ...............Harry Mallin, Great Britain
1928 ...............Piero Toscani, Italy
1932 ...............Carmen Barth, United States
1936 ...............Jean Despeaux, France
1948 ...............Laszlo Papp, Hungary
1952 ...............Floyd Patterson, United States
1956 ...............Gennady Schatkov, USSR
1960 ...............Edward Crook, United States
1964 ...............Valery Popenchenko, USSR
1968 ...............Christopher Finnegan, Great Britain
1972 ...............Vyacheslav Lemechev, USSR
1976 ...............Michael Spinks, United States

### MIDDLEWEIGHT *(Cont.)*

1980 ...............Jose Gomez, Cuba
1984 ...............Shin Joon Sup, South Korea
1988 ...............Henry Maske, East Germany
1992 ...............Ariel Hernandez, Cuba

### LIGHT HEAVYWEIGHT (178 LB)

1920 ...............Edward Eagan, United States
1924 ...............Harry Mitchell, Great Britain
1928 ...............Victor Avendano, Argentina
1932 ...............David Carstens, South Africa
1936 ...............Roger Michelot, France
1948 ...............George Hunter, South Africa
1952 ...............Norvel Lee, United States
1956 ...............James Boyd, United States
1960 ...............Cassius Clay, United States
1964 ...............Cosimo Pinto, Italy
1968 ...............Dan Poznyak, USSR
1972 ...............Mate Parlov, Yugoslavia
1976 ...............Leon Spinks, United States
1980 ...............Slobodan Kacer, Yugoslavia
1984 ...............Anton Josipovic, Yugoslavia
1988 ...............Andrew Maynard, United States
1992 ...............Torsten May, Germany

### HEAVYWEIGHT (OVER 201 LB)

1904 ...............Samuel Berger, United States
1906 ...............Not held
1908 ...............Albert Oldham, Great Britain
1912 ...............Not held
1920 ...............Ronald Rawson, Great Britain
1924 ...............Otto von Porat, Norway
1928 ...............Arturo Rodriguez Jurado, Argentina
1932 ...............Santiago Lovell, Argentina
1936 ...............Herbert Runge, Germany
1948 ...............Rafael Inglesias, Argentina
1952 ...............H. Edward Sanders, United States
1956 ...............T. Peter Rademacher, United States
1960 ...............Franco De Piccoli, Italy
1964 ...............Joe Frazier, United States
1968 ...............George Foreman, United States
1972 ...............Teofilo Stevenson, Cuba
1976 ...............Teofilo Stevenson, Cuba
1980 ...............Teofilo Stevenson, Cuba

### HEAVYWEIGHT (201* LB)

1984 ...............Henry Tillman, United States
1988 ...............Ray Mercer, United States
1992 ...............Felix Savon, Cuba

### SUPER HEAVYWEIGHT (UNLIMITED)

1984 ...............Tyrell Biggs, United States
1988 ...............Lennox Lewis, Canada
1992 ...............Roberto Balado, Cuba

*Until 1984 the heavyweight division was unlimited. With the addition of the super heavyweight division, a limit of 201 pounds was imposed.

## SWIMMING

### Men

#### 50-METER FREESTYLE

| | | |
|---|---|---|
| 1904....Zoltan Halmay, Hungary (50 yds) | 28.0 | |
| 1988....Matt Biondi, United States | 22.14 WR | |
| 1992....Aleksandr Popov, Unified Team | 22.30 | |

#### 100-METER FREESTLYE

| | | |
|---|---|---|
| 1896....Alfred Hajos, Hungary | 1:22.2 OR | |
| 1904....Zoltan Halmay, Hungary (100 yds) | 1:02.8 | |
| 1906....Charles Daniels, United States | 1:13.4 | |
| 1908....Charles Daniels, United States | 1:05.6 WR | |
| 1912....Duke Kahanamoku, United States | 1:03.4 | |
| 1920....Duke Kahanamoku, United States | 1:00.4 WR | |
| 1924....John Weissmuller, United States | 59.0 OR | |
| 1928....John Weissmuller, United States | 58.6 OR | |
| 1932....Yasuji Miyazaki, Japan | 58.2 | |
| 1936....Ferenc Csik, Hungary | 57.6 | |
| 1948....Wally Ris, United States | 57.3 OR | |
| 1952....Clarke Scholes, United States | 57.4 | |
| 1956....Jon Henricks, Australia | 55.4 OR | |
| 1960....John Devitt, Australia | 55.2 OR | |
| 1964....Don Schollander, United States | 53.4 OR | |
| 1968....Mike Wenden, Australia | 52.2 WR | |
| 1972....Mark Spitz, United States | 51.22 WR | |
| 1976....Jim Montgomery, United States | 49.99 WR | |
| 1980....Jörg Woithe, East Germany | 50.40 | |
| 1984....Rowdy Gaines, United States | 49.80 OR | |
| 1988....Matt Biondi, United States | 48.63 OR | |
| 1992....Aleksandr Popov, Unified Team | 49.02 | |

#### 200-METER FREESTYLE

| | | |
|---|---|---|
| 1900....Frederick Lane, Australia | 2:25.2 OR | |
| 1904....Charles Daniels, United States | 2:44.2 | |
| 1906....Not held 1906-1964 | | |
| 1968....Michael Wenden, Australia | 1:55.2 OR | |
| 1972....Mark Spitz, United States | 1:52.78 WR | |
| 1976....Bruce Furniss, United States | 1:50.29 WR | |
| 1980....Sergei Kopliakov, USSR | 1:49.81 WR | |
| 1984....Michael Gross, West Germany | 1:47.44 WR | |
| 1988....Duncan Armstrong, Australia | 1:47.25 WR | |
| 1992....Evgueni Sadovyi, Unified Team | 1:46.70 | |

#### 400-METER FREESTYLE

| | | |
|---|---|---|
| 1896....Paul Neumann, Austria (500 yds) | 8:12.6 | |
| 1904....Charles Daniels, U.S. (440 yds) | 6:16.2 | |
| 1906....Otto Scheff, Austria (440 yds) | 6:23.8 | |
| 1908....Henry Taylor, Great Britain | 5:36.8 | |
| 1912....George Hodgson, Canada | 5:24.4 | |
| 1920....Norman Ross, United States | 5:26.8 | |
| 1924....John Weissmuller, United States | 5:04.2 OR | |
| 1928....Albert Zorilla, Argentina | 5:01.6 OR | |
| 1932....Buster Crabbe, United States | 4:48.4 OR | |
| 1936....Jack Medica, United States | 4:44.5 OR | |
| 1948....William Smith, United States | 4:41.0 OR | |
| 1952....Jean Boiteux, France | 4:30.7 OR | |
| 1956....Murray Rose, Australia | 4:27.3 OR | |
| 1960....Murray Rose, Australia | 4:18.3 OR | |
| 1964....Don Schollander, United States | 4:12.2 WR | |
| 1968....Mike Burton, United States | 4:09.0 OR | |
| 1972....Brad Cooper, Australia | 4:00.27 OR | |
| 1976....Brian Goodell, United States | 3:51.93 WR | |
| 1980....Vladimir Salnikov, USSR | 3:51.31 OR | |
| 1984....George DiCarlo, United States | 3:51.23 OR | |
| 1988....Uwe Dassler, East Germany | 3:46.95 WR | |
| 1992....Evgueni Sadovyi, Unified Team | 3:45.00 WR | |

#### 1500-METER FREESTYLE

| | | |
|---|---|---|
| 1908....Henry Taylor, Great Britain | 22:48.4 WR | |
| 1912....George Hodgson, Canada | 22:00.0 WR | |
| 1920....Norman Ross, United States | 22:23.2 | |
| 1924....Andrew Charlton, Australia | 20:06.6 WR | |
| 1928....Arne Borg, Sweden | 19:51.8 OR | |
| 1932....Kusuo Kitamura, Japan | 19:12.4 OR | |
| 1936....Noboru Terada, Japan | 19:13.7 | |
| 1948....James McLane, United States | 19:18.5 | |
| 1952....Ford Konno, United States | 18:30.3 OR | |
| 1956....Murray Rose, Australia | 17:58.9 | |
| 1960....John Konrads, Australia | 17:19.6 OR | |
| 1964....Robert Windle, Australia | 17:01.7 OR | |
| 1968....Mike Burton, United States | 16:38.9 OR | |
| 1972....Mike Burton, United States | 15:52.58 OR | |
| 1976....Brian Goodell, United States | 15:02.40 WR | |
| 1980....Vladimir Salnikov, USSR | 14:58.27 WR | |
| 1984....Michael O'Brien, United States | 15:05.20 | |
| 1988....Vladimir Salnikov, USSR | 15:00.40 | |
| 1992....Kieren Perkins, Australia | 14:43.48 WR | |

#### 100-METER BACKSTROKE

| | | |
|---|---|---|
| 1904....Walter Brack, Germany (100 yds) | 1:16.8 | |
| 1908....Arno Bieberstein, Germany | 1:24.6 WR | |
| 1912....Harry Hebner, United States | 1:21.2 | |
| 1920....Warren Kealoha, United States | 1:15.2 | |
| 1924....Warren Kealoha, United States | 1:13.2 OR | |
| 1928....George Kojac, United States | 1:08.2 WR | |
| 1932....Masaji Kiyokawa, Japan | 1:08.6 | |
| 1936....Adolph Kiefer, United States | 1:05.9 OR | |
| 1948....Allen Stack, United States | 1:06.4 | |
| 1952....Yoshi Oyakawa, United States | 1:05.4 OR | |
| 1956....David Thiele, Australia | 1:02.2 OR | |
| 1960....David Thiele, Australia | 1:01.9 OR | |
| 1964....Not held | | |
| 1968....Roland Matthes, East Germany | 58.7 OR | |
| 1972....Roland Matthes, East Germany | 56.58 OR | |
| 1976....John Naber, United States | 55.49 WR | |
| 1980....Bengt Baron, Sweden | 56.33 | |
| 1984....Rick Carey, United States | 55.79 | |
| 1988....Daichi Suzuki, Japan | 55.05 | |
| 1992....Mark Tewksbury, Canada | 53.98 WR | |

#### 200-METER BACKSTROKE

| | | |
|---|---|---|
| 1900....Ernst Hoppenberg, Germany | 2:47.0 | |
| 1904....Not held 1904-1960 | | |
| 1964....Jed Graef, United States | 2:10.3 WR | |
| 1968....Roland Matthes, East Germany | 2:09.6 OR | |
| 1972....Roland Matthes, East Germany | 2:02.82 EWR | |
| 1976....John Naber, United States | 1:59.19 WR | |
| 1980....Sandor Wladar, Hungary | 2:01.93 | |
| 1984....Rick Carey, United States | 2:00.23 | |
| 1988....Igor Polianski, USSR | 1:59.37 | |
| 1992....Martin Lopez-Zubero, Spain | 1:58.47 OR | |

#### 100-METER BREASTSTROKE

| | | |
|---|---|---|
| 1968....Don McKenzie, United States | 1:07.7 OR | |
| 1972....Nobutaka Taguchi, Japan | 1:04.94 WR | |
| 1976....John Hencken, United States | 1:03.11 WR | |
| 1980....Duncan Goodhew, Great Britain | 1:03.44 | |
| 1984....Steve Lundquist, United States | 1:01.65 WR | |
| 1988....Adrian Moorhouse, Great Britain | 1:02.04 | |
| 1992....Nelson Diebel, United States | 1:01.50 OR | |

## SWIMMING (Cont.)

### Men (Cont.)

#### 200-METER BREASTSTROKE

| | | |
|---|---|---|
| 1908 | Frederick Holman, Great Britain | 3:09.2 WR |
| 1912 | Walter Bathe, Germany | 3:01.8 OR |
| 1920 | Haken Malmroth, Sweden | 3:04.4 |
| 1924 | Robert Skelton, United States | 2:56.6 |
| 1928 | Yoshiyuki Tsuruta, Japan | 2:48.8 OR |
| 1932 | Yoshiyuki Tsuruta, Japan | 2:45.4 |
| 1936 | Tetsuo Hamuro, Japan | 2:41.5 OR |
| 1948 | Joseph Verdeur, United States | 2:39.3 OR |
| 1952 | John Davies, Australia | 2:34.4 OR |
| 1956 | Masura Furukawa, Japan | 2:34.7 OR |
| 1960 | William Mulliken, United States | 2:37.4 |
| 1964 | Ian O'Brien, Australia | 2:27.8 WR |
| 1968 | Felipe Munoz, Mexico | 2:28.7 |
| 1972 | John Hencken, United States | 2:21.55 WR |
| 1976 | David Wilkie, Great Britain | 2:15.11 WR |
| 1980 | Robertas Zhulpa, USSR | 2:15.85 |
| 1984 | Victor Davis, Canada | 2:13.34 WR |
| 1988 | Jozsef Szabo, Hungary | 2:13.52 |
| 1992 | Mike Barrowman, United States | 2:10.16 WR |

#### 100-METER BUTTERFLY

| | | |
|---|---|---|
| 1968 | Doug Russell, United States | 55.9 OR |
| 1972 | Mark Spitz, United States | 54.27 WR |
| 1976 | Matt Vogel, United States | 54.35 |
| 1980 | Pär Arvidsson, Sweden | 54.92 |
| 1984 | Michael Gross, West Germany | 53.08 WR |
| 1988 | Anthony Nesty, Suriname | 53.00 OR |
| 1992 | Pablo Morales, United States | 53.32 |

#### 200-METER BUTTERFLY

| | | |
|---|---|---|
| 1956 | William Yorzyk, United States | 2:19.3 OR |
| 1960 | Michael Troy, United States | 2:12.8 WR |
| 1964 | Kevin Berry, Australia | 2:06.6 WR |
| 1968 | Carl Robie, United States | 2:08.7 |
| 1972 | Mark Spitz, United States | 2:00.70 WR |
| 1976 | Mike Bruner, United States | 1:59.23 WR |
| 1980 | Sergei Fesenko, USSR | 1:59.76 |
| 1984 | Jon Sieben, Australia | 1:57.04 WR |
| 1988 | Michael Gross, West Germany | 1:56.94 OR |
| 1992 | Melvin Stewart, United States | 1:56.26 OR |

#### 200-METER INDIVIDUAL MEDLEY

| | | |
|---|---|---|
| 1968 | Charles Hickcox, United States | 2:12.0 OR |
| 1972 | Gunnar Larsson, Sweden | 2:07.17 WR |
| 1984 | Alex Baumann, Canada | 2:01.42 WR |
| 1988 | Tamas Darnyi, Hungary | 2:00.17 WR |
| 1992 | Tamas Darnyi, Hungary | 2:00.76 |

#### 400-METER INDIVIDUAL MEDLEY

| | | |
|---|---|---|
| 1964 | Richard Roth, United States | 4:45.4 WR |
| 1968 | Charles Hickcox, United States | 4:48.4 |
| 1972 | Gunnar Larsson, Sweden | 4:31.98 OR |
| 1976 | Rod Strachan, United States | 4:23.68 WR |
| 1980 | Aleksandr Sidorenko, USSR | 4:22.89 OR |
| 1984 | Alex Baumann, Canada | 4:17.41 WR |
| 1988 | Tamas Darnyi, Hungary | 4:14.75 WR |
| 1992 | Tamas Darnyi, Hungary | 4:14.23 OR |

#### 4 X 100-METER MEDLEY RELAY

| | | |
|---|---|---|
| 1960 | United States | 4:05.4 WR |
| 1964 | United States | 3:58.4 WR |
| 1968 | United States | 3:54.9 WR |
| 1972 | United States | 3:48.16 WR |
| 1976 | United States | 3:42.22 WR |
| 1980 | Australia | 3:45.70 |
| 1984 | United States | 3:39.30 WR |
| 1988 | United States | 3:36.93 WR |
| 1992 | United States | 3:36.93 EWR |

#### 4 X 100-METER FREESTYLE RELAY

| | | |
|---|---|---|
| 1964 | United States | 3:32.2 WR |
| 1968 | United States | 3:31.7 WR |
| 1972 | United States | 3:26.42 WR |
| 1976-1980 | Not held | |
| 1984 | United States | 3:19.03 WR |
| 1988 | United States | 3:16.53 WR |
| 1992 | United States | 3:16.74 |

#### 4 X 200-METER FREESTYLE RELAY

| | | |
|---|---|---|
| 1906 | Hungary (1000 m) | 16:52.4 |
| 1908 | Great Britain | 10:55.6 |
| 1912 | Australia/New Zealand | 10:11.6 WR |
| 1920 | United States | 10:04.4 WR |
| 1924 | United States | 9:53.4 WR |
| 1928 | United States | 9:36.2 WR |
| 1932 | Japan | 8:58.4 WR |
| 1936 | Japan | 8:51.5 WR |
| 1948 | United States | 8:46.0 WR |
| 1952 | United States | 8:31.1 OR |
| 1956 | Australia | 8:23.6 WR |
| 1960 | United States | 8:10.2 WR |
| 1964 | United States | 7:52.1 WR |
| 1968 | United States | 7:52.33 |
| 1972 | United States | 7:35.78 WR |
| 1976 | United States | 7:23.22 WR |
| 1980 | USSR | 7:23.50 |
| 1984 | United States | 7:15.69 WR |
| 1988 | United States | 7:12.51 WR |
| 1992 | Unified Team | 7:11.95 WR |

### Women

#### 50-METER FREESTYLE

| | | |
|---|---|---|
| 1988 | Kristin Otto, East Germany | 25.49 OR |
| 1992 | Yang Wenyi, China | 24.79 WR |

#### 100-METER FREESTYLE

| | | |
|---|---|---|
| 1912 | Fanny Durack, Australia | 1:22.2 |
| 1920 | Ethelda Bleibtrey, United States | 1:13.6 WR |
| 1924 | Ethel Lackie, United States | 1:12.4 |
| 1928 | Albina Osipowich, United States | 1:11.0 OR |

#### 100-METER FREESTYLE (Cont.)

| | | |
|---|---|---|
| 1932 | Helene Madison, United States | 1:06.8 OR |
| 1936 | Hendrika Mastenbroek, Netherlands | 1:05.9 OR |
| 1948 | Greta Andersen, Denmark | 1:06.3 |
| 1952 | Katalin Szöke, Hungary | 1:06.8 |
| 1956 | Dawn Fraser, Australia | 1:02.0 WR |
| 1960 | Dawn Fraser, Australia | 1:01.2 OR |
| 1964 | Dawn Fraser, Australia | 59.5 OR |
| 1968 | Jan Henne, United States | 1:00.0 |

## SWIMMING (Cont.)

## Women (Cont.)

### 100-METER FREESTYLE (Cont.)

| | | |
|---|---|---|
| 1972 | Sandra Neilson, United States | 58.59 OR |
| 1976 | Kornelia Ender, East Germany | 55.65 WR |
| 1980 | Barbara Krause, East Germany | 54.79 WR |
| 1984 | Carrie Steinseifer, United States | 55.92 |
| | Nancy Hogshead, United States | 55.92 |
| 1988 | Kristin Otto, East Germany | 54.93 |
| 1992 | Zhuang Yong, China | 54.64 OR |

### 200-METER FREESTYLE

| | | |
|---|---|---|
| 1968 | Debbie Meyer, United States | 2:10.5 OR |
| 1972 | Shane Gould, Australia | 2:03.56 WR |
| 1976 | Kornelia Ender, East Germany | 1:59.26 WR |
| 1980 | Barbara Krause, East Germany | 1:58.33 OR |
| 1984 | Mary Wayte, United States | 1:59.23 |
| 1988 | Heike Friedrich, East Germany | 1:57.65 OR |
| 1992 | Nicole Haislett, United States | 1:57.90 |

### 400-METER FREESTYLE

| | | |
|---|---|---|
| 1924 | Martha Norelius, United States | 6:02.2 OR |
| 1928 | Martha Norelius, United States | 5:42.8 WR |
| 1932 | Helene Madison, United States | 5:28.5 WR |
| 1936 | Hendrika Mastenbroek, Netherlands | 5:26.4 OR |
| 1948 | Ann Curtis, United States | 5:17.8 OR |
| 1952 | Valeria Gyenge, Hungary | 5:12.1 OR |
| 1956 | Lorraine Crapp, Australia | 4:54.6 OR |
| 1960 | Chris von Saltza, United States | 4:50.6 OR |
| 1964 | Virginia Duenkel, United States | 4:43.3 OR |
| 1968 | Debbie Meyer, United States | 4:31.8 OR |
| 1972 | Shane Gould, Australia | 4:19.44 WR |
| 1976 | Petra Thümer, East Germany | 4:09.89 WR |
| 1980 | Ines Diers, East Germany | 4:08.76 WR |
| 1984 | Tiffany Cohen, United States | 4:07.10 OR |
| 1988 | Janet Evans, United States | 4:03.85 WR |
| 1992 | Dagmar Hase, Germany | 4:07.18 |

### 800-METER FREESTYLE

| | | |
|---|---|---|
| 1968 | Debbie Meyer, United States | 9:24.0 OR |
| 1972 | Keena Rothhammer, United States | 8:53.68 WR |
| 1976 | Petra Thümer, East Germany | 8:37.14 WR |
| 1980 | Michelle Ford, Australia | 8:28.90 OR |
| 1984 | Tiffany Cohen, United States | 8:24.95 OR |
| 1988 | Janet Evans, United States | 8:20.20 OR |
| 1992 | Janet Evans, United States | 8:25.52 |

### 100-METER BACKSTROKE

| | | |
|---|---|---|
| 1924 | Sybil Bauer, United States | 1:23.2 OR |
| 1928 | Marie Braun, Netherlands | 1:22.0 |
| 1932 | Eleanor Holm, United States | 1:19.4 |
| 1936 | Dina Senff, Netherlands | 1:18.9 |
| 1948 | Karen Harup, Denmark | 1:14.4 OR |
| 1952 | Joan Harrison, South Africa | 1:14.3 |
| 1956 | Judy Grinham, Great Britain | 1:12.9 OR |
| 1960 | Lynn Burke, United States | 1:09.3 OR |
| 1964 | Cathy Ferguson, United States | 1:07.7 WR |
| 1968 | Kaye Hall, United States | 1:06.2 WR |
| 1972 | Melissa Belote, United States | 1:05.78 OR |
| 1976 | Ulrike Richter, East Germany | 1:01.83 OR |
| 1980 | Rica Reinisch, East Germany | 1:00.86 WR |
| 1984 | Theresa Andrews, United States | 1:02.55 |
| 1988 | Kristin Otto, East Germany | 1:00.89 |
| 1992 | Krisztina Egerszegi, Hungary | 1:00.68 OR |

### 200-METER BACKSTROKE

| | | |
|---|---|---|
| 1968 | Pokey Watson, United States | 2:24.8 OR |
| 1972 | Melissa Belote, United States | 2:19.19 WR |
| 1976 | Ulrike Richter, East Germany | 2:13.43 OR |
| 1980 | Rica Reinisch, East Germany | 2:11.77 WR |
| 1984 | Jolanda De Rover, Netherlands | 2:12.38 |
| 1988 | Krisztina Egerszegi, Hungary | 2:09.29 OR |
| 1992 | Krisztina Egerszegi, Hungary | 2:07.06 |

### 100-METER BREASTSTROKE

| | | |
|---|---|---|
| 1968 | Djurdjica Bjedov, Yugoslavia | 1:15.8 OR |
| 1972 | Catherine Carr, United States | 1:13.58 WR |
| 1976 | Hannelore Anke, East Germany | 1:11.16 |
| 1980 | Ute Geweniger, East Germany | 1:10.22 |
| 1984 | Petra Van Staveren, Netherlands | 1:09.88 OR |
| 1988 | Tania Dangalakova, Bulgaria | 1:07.95 OR |
| 1992 | Elena Roudkovskaia, Unified Team | 1:08.00 |

### 200-METER BREASTSTROKE

| | | |
|---|---|---|
| 1924 | Lucy Morton, Great Britain | 3:33.2 OR |
| 1928 | Hilde Schrader, Germany | 3:12.6 |
| 1932 | Clare Dennis, Australia | 3:06.3 OR |
| 1936 | Hideko Maehata, Japan | 3:03.6 |
| 1948 | Petronella Van Vliet, Netherlands | 2:57.2 |
| 1952 | Eva Szekely, Hungary | 2:51.7 OR |
| 1956 | Ursula Happe, West Germany | 2:53.1 OR |
| 1960 | Anita Lonsbrough, Great Britain | 2:49.5 WR |
| 1964 | Galina Prozumenshikova, USSR | 2:46.4 OR |
| 1968 | Sharon Wichman, United States | 2:44.4 OR |
| 1972 | Beverly Whitfield, Australia | 2:41.71 OR |
| 1976 | Marina Koshevaia, USSR | 2:33.35 WR |
| 1980 | Lina Kaciusyte, USSR | 2:29.54 OR |
| 1984 | Anne Ottenbrite, Canada | 2:30.38 |
| 1988 | Silke Hoerner, East Germany | 2:26.71 WR |
| 1992 | Kyoko Iwasaki, Japan | 2:26.65 OR |

### 100-METER BUTTERFLY

| | | |
|---|---|---|
| 1956 | Shelley Mann, United States | 1:11.0 OR |
| 1960 | Carolyn Schuler, United States | 1:09.5 OR |
| 1964 | Sharon Stouder, United States | 1:04.7 WR |
| 1968 | Lynn McClements, Australia | 1:05.5 |
| 1972 | Mayumi Aoki, Japan | 1:03.34 WR |
| 1976 | Kornelia Ender, East Germany | 1:00.13 EWR |
| 1980 | Caren Metschuck, East Germany | 1:00.42 |
| 1984 | Mary T. Meagher, United States | 59.26 |
| 1988 | Kristin Otto, East Germany | 59.00 OR |
| 1992 | Qian Hong, China | 58.62 OR |

### 200-METER BUTTERFLY

| | | |
|---|---|---|
| 1968 | Ada Kok, Netherlands | 2:24.7 OR |
| 1972 | Karen Moe, United States | 2:15.57 WR |
| 1976 | Andrea Pollack, East Germany | 2:11.41 OR |
| 1980 | Ines Geissler, East Germany | 2:10.44 OR |
| 1984 | Mary T. Meagher, United States | 2:06.90 OR |
| 1988 | Kathleen Nord, East Germany | 2:09.51 |
| 1992 | Summer Sanders, United States | 2:08.67 |

### 200-METER INDIVIDUAL MEDLEY

| | | |
|---|---|---|
| 1968 | Claudia Kolb, United States | 2:24.7 OR |
| 1972 | Shane Gould, Australia | 2:23.07 WR |
| 1976 | Not held 1976-1980 | |
| 1984 | Tracy Caulkins, United States | 2:12.64 OR |

### SWIMMING (Cont.)

### Women (Cont.)

#### 200-METER INDIVIDUAL MEDLEY (Cont.)

| | | |
|---|---|---|
| 1988 | Daniela Hunger, East Germany | 2:12.59 OR |
| 1992 | Lin Li, China | 2:11.65 WR |

#### 400-METER INDIVIDUAL MEDLEY

| | | |
|---|---|---|
| 1964 | Donna de Varona, United States | 5:18.7 OR |
| 1968 | Claudia Kolb, United States | 5:08.5 OR |
| 1972 | Gail Neall, Australia | 5:02.97 WR |
| 1976 | Ulrike Tauber, East Germany | 4:42.77 WR |
| 1980 | Petra Schneider, East Germany | 4:36.29 WR |
| 1984 | Tracy Caulkins, United States | 4:39.24 |
| 1988 | Janet Evans, United States | 4:37.76 |
| 1992 | Krisztina Egerszegi, Hungary | 4:36.54 |

#### 4 X 100-METER MEDLEY RELAY

| | | |
|---|---|---|
| 1960 | United States | 4:41.1 WR |
| 1964 | United States | 4:33.9 WR |
| 1968 | United States | 4:28.3 OR |
| 1972 | United States | 4:20.75 WR |
| 1976 | East Germany | 4:07.95 WR |
| 1980 | East Germany | 4:06.67 WR |
| 1984 | United States | 4:08.34 |
| 1988 | East Germany | 4:03.74 OR |
| 1992 | United States | 4:02.54 WR |

#### 4 X 100-METER FREESTYLE RELAY

| | | |
|---|---|---|
| 1912 | Great Britain | 5:52.8 WR |
| 1920 | United States | 5:11.6 WR |
| 1924 | United States | 4:58.8 WR |
| 1928 | United States | 4:47.6 WR |
| 1932 | United States | 4:38.0 WR |
| 1936 | Netherlands | 4:36.0 OR |
| 1948 | United States | 4:29.2 OR |
| 1952 | Hungary | 4:24.4 WR |
| 1956 | Australia | 4:17.1 WR |
| 1960 | United States | 4:08.9 WR |
| 1964 | United States | 4:03.8 WR |
| 1968 | United States | 4:02.5 OR |
| 1972 | United States | 3:55.19 WR |
| 1976 | United States | 3:44.82 WR |
| 1980 | East Germany | 3:42.71 WR |
| 1984 | United States | 3:43.43 |
| 1988 | East Germany | 3:40.63 OR |
| 1992 | United States | 3:39.46 WR |

Note: OR=Olympic Record; WR=World Record; EOR=Equals Olympic Record; EWR=Equals World Record; WB=World Best.

## DIVING

### Men

#### SPRINGBOARD

| | | Pts |
|---|---|---|
| 1908 | Albert Zürner, Germany | 85.5 |
| 1912 | Paul Günther, Germany | 79.23 |
| 1920 | Louis Kuehn, United States | 675.40 |
| 1924 | Albert White, United States | 97.46 |
| 1928 | Pete DesJardins, United States | 185.04 |
| 1932 | Michael Galitzen, United States | 161.38 |
| 1936 | Richard Degener, United States | 163.57 |
| 1948 | Bruce Harlan, United States | 163.64 |
| 1952 | David Browning, United States | 205.29 |
| 1956 | Robert Clotworthy, United States | 159.56 |
| 1960 | Gary Tobian, United States | 170.00 |
| 1964 | Kenneth Sitzberger, United States | 159.90 |
| 1968 | Bernie Wrightson, United States | 170.15 |
| 1972 | Vladimir Vasin, USSR | 594.09 |
| 1976 | Phil Boggs, United States | 619.05 |
| 1980 | Aleksandr Portnov, USSR | 905.02 |
| 1984 | Greg Louganis, United States | 754.41 |
| 1988 | Greg Louganis, United States | 730.80 |
| 1992 | Mark Lenzi, United States | 676.53 |

#### PLATFORM

| | | Pts |
|---|---|---|
| 1904 | George Sheldon, United States | 12.66 |
| 1906 | Gottlob Walz, Germany | 156.0 |
| 1908 | Hjalmar Johansson, Sweden | 83.75 |
| 1912 | Erik Adlerz, Sweden | 73.94 |
| 1920 | Clarence Pinkston, United States | 100.67 |
| 1924 | Albert White, United States | 97.46 |
| 1928 | Pete DesJardins, United States | 98.74 |
| 1932 | Harold Smith, United States | 124.80 |
| 1936 | Marshall Wayne, United States | 113.58 |
| 1948 | Sammy Lee, United States | 130.05 |
| 1952 | Sammy Lee, United States | 156.28 |
| 1956 | Joaquin Capilla, Mexico | 152.44 |
| 1960 | Robert Webster, United States | 165.56 |
| 1964 | Robert Webster, United States | 148.58 |
| 1968 | Klaus Dibiasi, Italy | 164.18 |
| 1972 | Klaus Dibiasi, Italy | 504.12 |
| 1976 | Klaus Dibiasi, Italy | 600.51 |
| 1980 | Falk Hoffmann, East Germany | 835.65 |
| 1984 | Greg Louganis, United States | 710.91 |
| 1988 | Greg Louganis, United States | 638.61 |
| 1992 | Sun Shuwei, China | 677.31 |

### Women

#### SPRINGBOARD

| | | Pts |
|---|---|---|
| 1920 | Aileen Riggin, United States | 539.90 |
| 1924 | Elizabeth Becker, United States | 474.50 |
| 1928 | Helen Meany, United States | 78.62 |
| 1932 | Georgia Coleman, United States | 87.52 |
| 1936 | Marjorie Gestring, United States | 89.27 |
| 1948 | Victoria Draves, United States | 108.74 |

#### SPRINGBOARD (Cont.)

| | | Pts |
|---|---|---|
| 1952 | Patricia McCormick, United States | 147.30 |
| 1956 | Patricia McCormick, United States | 142.36 |
| 1960 | Ingrid Krämer, East Germany | 155.81 |
| 1964 | Ingrid Engel Krämer, East Germany | 145.00 |
| 1968 | Sue Gossick, United States | 150.77 |

## DIVING *(Cont.)*

### Women *(Cont.)*

#### SPRINGBOARD *(Cont.)*

| | Pts |
|---|---|
| 1972 .....Micki King, United States | 450.03 |
| 1976 .....Jennifer Chandler, United States | 506.19 |
| 1980 .....Irina Kalinina, USSR | 725.91 |
| 1984 .....Sylvie Bernier, Canada | 530.70 |
| 1988 .....Gao Min, China | 580.23 |
| 1992 .....Gao Min, China | 572.40 |

#### PLATFORM

| | Pts |
|---|---|
| 1912 .....Greta Johansson, Sweden | 39.90 |
| 1920 ......Stefani Fryland-Clausen, Denmark | 34.60 |
| 1924 .....Caroline Smith, United States | 33.20 |
| 1928 .......Elizabeth B. Pinkston, United States | 31.60 |

#### PLATFORM *(Cont.)*

| | Pts |
|---|---|
| 1932 .....Dorothy Poynton, United States | 40.26 |
| 1936 ......Dorothy Poynton Hill, United States | 33.93 |
| 1948 ....Victoria Draves, United States | 68.87 |
| 1952 ......Patricia McCormick, United States | 79.37 |
| 1956 ......Patricia McCormick, United States | 84.85 |
| 1960 .....Ingrid Krämer, East Germany | 91.28 |
| 1964 ....Lesley Bush, United States | 99.80 |
| 1968 ......Milena Duchkova, Czechoslovakia | 109.59 |
| 1972 ....Ulrika Knape, Sweden | 390.00 |
| 1976 ....Elena Vaytsekhovskaya, USSR | 406.59 |
| 1980 ....Martina Jäschke, East Germany | 596.25 |
| 1984 ....Zhou Jihong, China | 435.51 |
| 1988 .....Xu Yanmei, China | 445.20 |
| 1992 ....Fu Mingxia, China | 461.43 |

## GYMNASTICS

### Men

#### ALL-AROUND

| | Pts |
|---|---|
| 1900 .....Gustave Sandras, France | 302 |
| 1904 ....Julius Lenhart, Austria | 69.80 |
| 1906 ....Pierre Paysse, France | 97 |
| 1908 .....Alberto Braglia, Italy | 317.0 |
| 1912 .....Alberto Braglia, Italy | 135.0 |
| 1920 ....Giorgio Zampori, Italy | 88.35 |
| 1924 .....Leon Stukelj, Yugoslavia | 110.340 |
| 1928 ....Georges Miez, Switzerland | 247.500 |
| 1932 .....Romeo Neri, Italy | 140.625 |
| 1936 .....Alfred Schwarzmann, Germany | 113.100 |
| 1948 .....Veikko Huhtanen, Finland | 229.70 |
| 1952 .....Viktor Chukarin, USSR | 115.70 |
| 1956 .....Viktor Chukarin, USSR | 114.25 |
| 1960 .....Boris Shakhlin, USSR | 115.95 |
| 1964 .....Yukio Endo, Japan | 115.95 |
| 1968 .....Sawao Kato, Japan | 115.90 |
| 1972 .....Sawao Kato, Japan | 114.65 |
| 1976 .....Nikolai Andrianov, USSR | 116.65 |
| 1980 .....Aleksandr Dityatin, USSR | 118.65 |
| 1984 .....Koji Gushiken, Japan | 118.70 |
| 1988 .....Vladimir Artemov, USSR | 119.125 |
| 1992 .....Vitaly Scherbo, Unified Team | 59.025 |

#### HORIZONTAL BAR

| | Pts |
|---|---|
| 1896 .....Hermann Weingärtner, Germany | — |
| 1900 ....Not held | |
| 1904 .....Anton Heida, United States | 40 |
| 1908-20 .Not held | |
| 1924 ....Leon Stukelj, Yugoslavia | 19.73 |
| 1928 ....Georges Miez, Switzerland | 19.17 |
| 1932 ....Dallas Bixler, United States | 18.33 |
| 1936 ....Aleksanteri Saarvala, Finland | 19.367 |
| 1948 ....Josef Stalder, Switzerland | 19.85 |
| 1952 ....Jack Günthard, Switzerland | 19.55 |
| 1956 ....Takashi Ono, Japan | 19.60 |
| 1960 ....Takashi Ono, Japan | 19.60 |
| 1964 ....Boris Shakhlin, USSR | 19.625 |
| 1968 ....Akinori Nakayama, Japan | 19.55 |
| 1972 .....Mitsuo Tsukahara, Japan | 19.725 |

#### HORIZONTAL BAR *(Cont.)*

| | Pts |
|---|---|
| 1976 ....Mitsuo Tsukahara, Japan | 19.675 |
| 1980 ....Stoyan Deltchev, Bulgaria | 19.825 |
| 1984 ....Shinji Morisue, Japan | 20.00 |
| 1988 ....Vladimir Artemov, USSR | 19.90 |
| 1992 .....Trent Dimas, United States | 9.875 |

#### PARALLEL BARS

| | Pts |
|---|---|
| 1896 .....Alfred Flatow, Germany | — |
| 1900 ....Not held | |
| 1904 .....George Eyser, United States | 44 |
| 1908-20 .Not held | |
| 1924 .....August Güttinger, Switzerland | 21.63 |
| 1928 .....Ladislav Vacha, Czechoslovakia | 18.83 |
| 1932 .....Romeo Neri, Italy | 18.97 |
| 1936 ....Konrad Frey, Germany | 19.067 |
| 1948 .....Michael Reusch, Switzerland | 19.75 |
| 1952 .....Hans Eugster, Switzerland | 19.65 |
| 1956 .....Viktor Chukarin, USSR | 19.20 |
| 1960 .....Boris Shakhlin, USSR | 19.40 |
| 1964 .....Yukio Endo, Japan | 19.675 |
| 1968 .....Akinori Nakayama, Japan | 19.475 |
| 1972 .....Sawao Kato, Japan | 19.475 |
| 1976 .....Sawao Kato, Japan | 19.675 |
| 1980 .....Aleksandr Tkachyov, USSR | 19.775 |
| 1984 .....Bart Conner, United States | 19.95 |
| 1988 .....Vladimir Artemov, USSR | 19.925 |
| 1992 .....Vitaly Scherbo, Unified Team | 9.900 |

#### LONG HORSE VAULT

| | Pts |
|---|---|
| 1896 .....Karl Schumann, Germany | — |
| 1900 .....Not held | |
| 1904 .....George Eyser, United States | 36 |
| 1908-20 .Not held | |
| 1924 .....Frank Kriz, United States | 9.98 |
| 1928 .....Eugen Mack, Switzerland | 9.58 |
| 1932 .....Savino Guglielmetti, Italy | 18.03 |
| 1936 .....Alfred Schwarzmann, Germany | 19.20 |
| 1948 .....Paavo Aaltonen, Finland | 19.55 |

## GYMNASTICS (Cont.)

### Men (Cont.)

#### LONG HORSE VAULT (Cont.)

| | | Pts |
|---|---|---|
| 1952 | Viktor Chukarin, USSR | 19.20 |
| 1956 | Helmut Bantz, Germany | 18.85 |
| 1960 | Takashi Ono, Japan | 19.35 |
| 1964 | Haruhiro Yamashita, Japan | 19.60 |
| 1968 | Mikhail Voronin, USSR | 19.00 |
| 1972 | Klaus Köste, East Germany | 18.85 |
| 1976 | Nikolai Andrianov, USSR | 19.45 |
| 1980 | Nikolai Andrianov, USSR | 19.825 |
| 1984 | Lou Yun, China | 19.95 |
| 1988 | Lou Yun, China | 19.875 |
| 1992 | Vitaly Scherbo, Unified Team | 9.856 |

#### SIDE HORSE

| | | Pts |
|---|---|---|
| 1896 | Louis Zutter, Switzerland | — |
| 1900 | Not held | |
| 1904 | Anton Heida, United States | 42 |
| 1908-20 | Not held | |
| 1924 | Josef Wilhelm, Switzerland | 21.23 |
| 1928 | Hermann Hänggi, Switzerland | 19.75 |
| 1932 | Istvan Pelle, Hungary | 19.07 |
| 1936 | Konrad Frey, Germany | 19.333 |
| 1948 | Paavo Aaltonen, Finland | 19.35 |
| 1952 | Viktor Chukarin, USSR | 19.50 |
| 1956 | Boris Shakhlin, USSR | 19.25 |
| 1960 | Eugen Ekman, Finland | 19.375 |
| 1964 | Miroslav Cerar, Yugoslavia | 19.525 |
| 1968 | Miroslav Cerar, Yugoslavia | 19.325 |
| 1972 | Viktor Klimenko, USSR | 19.125 |
| 1976 | Zoltan Magyar, Hungary | 19.70 |
| 1980 | Zoltan Magyar, Hungary | 19.925 |
| 1984 | Li Ning, China | 19.95 |
| 1988 | Dmitri Bilozerchev, USSR | 19.95 |
| 1992 | Vitaly Scherbo, Unified Team | 9.925 |

#### RINGS

| | | Pts |
|---|---|---|
| 1896 | Ioannis Mitropoulos, Greece | — |
| 1900 | Not held | |
| 1904 | Hermann Glass, United States | 45 |
| 1908-20 | Not held | |
| 1924 | Francesco Martino, Italy | 21.553 |
| 1928 | Leon Stukelj, Yugoslavia | 19.25 |
| 1932 | George Gulack, United States | 18.97 |
| 1936 | Alois Hudec, Czechoslovakia | 19.433 |
| 1948 | Karl Frei, Switzerland | 19.80 |
| 1952 | Grant Shaginyan, USSR | 19.75 |
| 1956 | Albert Azaryan, USSR | 19.35 |
| 1960 | Albert Azaryan, USSR | 19.725 |
| 1964 | Takuji Haytta, Japan | 19.475 |
| 1968 | Akinori Nakayama, Japan | 19.45 |

#### RINGS (Cont.)

| | | Pts |
|---|---|---|
| 1972 | Akinori Nakayama, Japan | 19.35 |
| 1976 | Nikolai Andrianov, USSR | 19.65 |
| 1980 | Aleksandr Dityatin, USSR | 19.875 |
| 1984 | Koji Gushiken, Japan | 19.85 |
| 1988 | Holger Behrendt, East Germany | 19.925 |
| 1992 | Vitaly Scherbo, Unified Team | 9.937 |

#### FLOOR EXERCISES

| | | Pts |
|---|---|---|
| 1896-28 | Not held | |
| 1932 | Istvan Pelle, Hungary | 9.60 |
| 1936 | Georges Miez, Switzerland | 18.666 |
| 1948 | Ferenc Pataki, Hungary | 19.35 |
| 1952 | K. William Thoresson, Sweden | 19.25 |
| 1956 | Valentin Muratov, USSR | 19.20 |
| 1960 | Nobuyuki Aihara, Japan | 19.45 |
| 1964 | Franco Menichelli, Italy | 19.45 |
| 1968 | Sawao Kato, Japan | 19.475 |
| 1972 | Nikolai Andrianov, USSR | 19.175 |
| 1976 | Nikolai Andrianov, USSR | 19.45 |
| 1980 | Roland Brückner, East Germany | 19.75 |
| 1984 | Li Ning, China | 19.925 |
| 1988 | Sergei Kharkov, USSR | 19.925 |
| 1992 | Li Xiaosahuang, China | 9.925 |

#### TEAM COMBINED EXERCISES

| | | Pts |
|---|---|---|
| 1896-00 | Not held | |
| 1904 | Turngemeinde Philadelphia | 374.43 |
| 1906 | Norway | 19.00 |
| 1908 | Sweden | 438 |
| 1912 | Italy | 265.75 |
| 1920 | Italy | 359.855 |
| 1924 | Italy | 839.058 |
| 1928 | Switzerland | 1718.625 |
| 1932 | Italy | 541.850 |
| 1936 | Germany | 657.430 |
| 1948 | Finland | 1358.30 |
| 1952 | USSR | 574.40 |
| 1956 | USSR | 568.25 |
| 1960 | Japan | 575.20 |
| 1964 | Japan | 577.95 |
| 1968 | Japan | 575.90 |
| 1972 | Japan | 571.25 |
| 1976 | Japan | 576.85 |
| 1980 | USSR | 598.60 |
| 1984 | United States | 591.40 |
| 1988 | USSR | 593.35 |
| 1992 | Unified Team | 585.45 |

## GYMNASTICS (Cont.)

### Women

#### ALL-AROUND

| | | Pts |
|---|---|---|
| 1952 | Maria Gorokhovskaya, USSR | 76.78 |
| 1956 | Larissa Latynina, USSR | 74.933 |
| 1960 | Larissa Latynina, USSR | 77.031 |
| 1964 | Vera Caslavska, Czechoslovakia | 77.564 |
| 1968 | Vera Caslavska, Czechoslovakia | 78.25 |
| 1972 | Lyudmila Tousischeva, USSR | 77.025 |
| 1976 | Nadia Comaneci, Romania | 79.275 |
| 1980 | Yelena Davydova, USSR | 79.15 |
| 1984 | Mary Lou Retton, United States | 79.175 |
| 1988 | Yelena Shushunova, USSR | 79.662 |
| 1992 | Tatiana Gutsu, Unified Team | 39.737 |

#### SIDE HORSE VAULT

| | | Pts |
|---|---|---|
| 1952 | Yekaterina Kalinchuk, USSR | 19.20 |
| 1956 | Larissa Latynina, USSR | 18.833 |
| 1960 | Margarita Nikolayeva, USSR | 19.316 |
| 1964 | Vera Caslavska, Czechoslovakia | 19.483 |
| 1968 | Vera Caslavska, Czechoslovakia | 19.775 |
| 1972 | Karin Janz, East Germany | 19.525 |
| 1976 | Nelli Kim, USSR | 19.80 |
| 1980 | Natalya Shaposhnikova, USSR | 19.725 |
| 1984 | Ecaterina Szabo, Romania | 19.875 |
| 1988 | Svetlana Boginskaya, USSR | 19.905 |
| 1992 | Henrietta Onodi, Hungary | 9.925 |
| | Lavinia Milosovici, Romania | 9.925 |

#### UNEVEN BARS

| | | Pts |
|---|---|---|
| 1952 | Margit Korondi, Hungary | 19.40 |
| 1956 | Agnes Keleti, Hungary | 18.966 |
| 1960 | Polina Astakhova, USSR | 19.616 |
| 1964 | Polina Astakhova, USSR | 19.332 |
| 1968 | Vera Caslavska, Czechoslovakia | 19.65 |
| 1972 | Karin Janz, East Germany | 19.675 |
| 1976 | Nadia Comaneci, Romania | 20.00 |
| 1980 | Maxi Gnauck, East Germany | 19.875 |
| 1984 | Ma Yanhong, China | 19.95 |
| 1988 | Daniela Silivas, Romania | 20.00 |
| 1992 | Lu Li, China | 10.00 |

#### BALANCE BEAM

| | | Pts |
|---|---|---|
| 1952 | Nina Bocharova, USSR | 19.22 |
| 1956 | Agnes Keleti, Hungary | 18.80 |
| 1960 | Eva Bosakova, Czechoslovakia | 19.283 |

#### BALANCE BEAM (Cont.)

| | | Pts |
|---|---|---|
| 1964 | Vera Caslavska, Czechoslovakia | 19.449 |
| 1968 | Natalya Kuchinskaya, USSR | 19.65 |
| 1972 | Olga Korbut, USSR | 19.40 |
| 1976 | Nadia Comaneci, Romania | 19.95 |
| 1980 | Nadia Comaneci, Romania | 19.80 |
| 1984 | Simona Pauca, Romania | 19.80 |
| 1988 | Daniela Silivas, Romania | 19.924 |
| 1992 | Tatiana Lisenko, Unified Team | 9.975 |

#### FLOOR EXERCISES

| | | Pts |
|---|---|---|
| 1952 | Agnes Keleti, Hungary | 19.36 |
| 1956 | Agnes Keleti, Hungary | 18.733 |
| 1960 | Larissa Latynina, USSR | 19.583 |
| 1964 | Larissa Latynina, USSR | 19.599 |
| 1968 | Vera Caslavska, Czechoslovakia | 19.675 |
| 1972 | Olga Korbut, USSR | 19.575 |
| 1976 | Nelli Kim, USSR | 19.85 |
| 1980 | Nadia Comaneci, Romania | 19.875 |
| 1984 | Ecaterina Szabo, Romania | 19.975 |
| 1988 | Daniela Silivas, Romania | 19.937 |
| 1992 | Lavinia Milosovici, Romania | 10.00 |

#### TEAM COMBINED EXERCISES

| | | Pts |
|---|---|---|
| 1928 | Holland | 316.75 |
| 1932 | Not held | |
| 1936 | Germany | 506.50 |
| 1948 | Czechoslovakia | 445.45 |
| 1952 | USSR | 527.03 |
| 1956 | USSR | 444.800 |
| 1960 | USSR | 382.320 |
| 1964 | USSR | 280.890 |
| 1968 | USSR | 382.85 |
| 1972 | USSR | 380.50 |
| 1976 | USSR | 466.00 |
| 1980 | USSR | 394.90 |
| 1984 | Romania | 392.02 |
| 1988 | USSR | 395.475 |
| 1992 | Unified Team | 395.666 |

#### RHYTHMIC ALL-AROUND

| | | Pts |
|---|---|---|
| 1984 | Lori Fung, Canada | 57.95 |
| 1988 | Marina Lobach, USSR | 60.00 |
| 1992 | Aleksandra Timoshenko, UTeam | 59.037 |

**Sic Transit Gloria**

The sad story of luge champion Gerda Weissensteiner only went from bad to worse. Within days of her gold-medal performance in the women's singles event at Lillehammer, the newly celebrated Italian star learned that her brother had been killed in a motorcycle accident. Then, while she was attending his funeral, her house was burglarized and her gold medal stolen.

## BIATHLON

### Men

#### 10 KILOMETERS

1980....Frank Ullrich, East Germany    32:10.69
1984....Eirik Kvalfoss, Norway    30:53.8
1988....Frank-Peter Rötsch, W Germany    25:08.1
1992....Mark Kirchner, Germany    26:02.3
1994....Sergei Tchepikov, Russia    28:07.0

#### 20 KILOMETERS

1960....Klas Lestander, Sweden    1:33:21.6
1964....Vladimir Melyanin, Soviet Union    1:20:26.8
1968....Magnar Solberg, Norway    1:13:45.9
1972....Magnar Solberg, Norway    1:15:55.5
1976....Nikolay Kruglov, Soviet Union    1:14:12.26
1980....Anatoliy Alyabiev, Soviet Union    1:08:16.31
1984....Peter Angerer, W Germany    1:11:52.7

#### 20 KILOMETERS (Cont.)

1988....Frank-Peter Rötsch, W Germany    56:33.3
1992....Evgueni Redkine, Unified Team    57:34.4
1994....Sergei Tarasov, Russia    57:25.3

#### 4 X 7.5-KILOMETER RELAY

1968 ...............Soviet Union    2:13:02.4
1972 ...............Soviet Union    1:51:44.92
1976 ...............Soviet Union    1:57:55.64
1980 ...............Soviet Union    1:34:03.27
1984 ...............Soviet Union    1:38:51.7
1988 ...............Soviet Union    1:22:30.0
1992 ...............Germany    1:24:43.5
1994 ...............Germany    1:30:22.1

### Women

#### 7.5 KILOMETERS

1992....Antissa Restzova, Unified Team    24:29.2
1994....Myriam Bedard, Canada    26:08.8

#### 15 KILOMETERS

1992....Antje Misersky, Germany    51:47.2
1994....Myriam Bedard, Canada    52:06.6

#### 3 X 7.5-KILOMETER RELAY

1992....France    1:15:55.6
1994....Russia    1:47:19.5

## BOBSLED

#### 4-MAN BOB

1924....Switzerland (Eduard Scherrer)    5:45.54
1928....United States    3:20.50
    (William Fiske) (5-man)
1932....United States (William Fiske)    7:53.68
1936....Switzerland (Pierre Musy)    5:19.85
1948....United States (Francis Tyler)    5:20.10
1952....Germany (Andreas Ostler)    5:07.84
1956....Switzerland (Franz Kapus)    5:10.44
1960....Not held
1964....Canada (Victor Emery)    4:14.46
1968....Italy (Eugenio Monti) (2 runs)    2:17.39
1972....Switzerland (Jean Wicki)    4:43.07
1976....East Germany    3:40.43
    (Meinhard Nehmer)
1980....East Germany    3:59.92
    (Meinhard Nehmer)
1984.....East Germany (Wolfgang Hoppe)    3:20.22
1988....Switzerland (Ekkehard Fasser)    3:47.51
1992....Austria (Ingo Appelt)    3:53.90
1994....Germany (Harold Czudaj)    3:27.78

Note: Driver in parentheses.

#### 2-MAN BOB

1932....United States (Hubert Stevens)    8:14.74
1936....United States (Ivan Brown)    5:29.29
1948....Switzerland (Felix Endrich)    5:29.20
1952....Germany (Andreas Ostler)    5:24.54
1956....Italy (Lamberto Dalla Costa)    5:30.14
1960....Not held
1964....Great Britain (Anthony Nash)    4:21.90
1968....Italy (Eugenio Monti)    4:41.54
1972....West Germany    4:57.07
    (Wolfgang Zimmerer)
1976....East Germany    3:44.42
    (Meinhard Nehmer)
1980....Switzerland (Erich Schärer)    4:09.36
1984....East Germany (Wolfgang Hoppe)    3:25.56
1988....USSR (Janis Kipours)    3:53.48
1992....Switzerland (Gustav Weder)    4:03.26
1994....Switzerland (Gustav Weder)    3:30.81

Note: Driver in parentheses.

## ICE HOCKEY

1920* ....Canada, United States, Czechoslovakia
1924 .....Canada, United States, Great Britain
1928 .....Canada, Sweden, Switzerland
1932 .....Canada, United States, Germany
1936 .....Great Britain, Canada, United States
1948 .....Canada, Czechoslovakia, Switzerland
1952 .....Canada, United States, Sweden
1956 .....USSR, United States, Canada
1960 .....United States, Canada, USSR
1964 .....USSR, Sweden, Czechoslovakia

1968 .....USSR, Czechoslovakia, Canada
1972 .....USSR, United States, Czechoslovakia
1976 .....USSR, Czechoslovakia, West Germany
1980 .....United States, USSR, Sweden
1984 .....USSR, Czechoslovakia, Sweden
1988 .....USSR, Finland, Sweden
1992 .....Unified Team, Canada, Czechoslovakia
1994 .....Sweden, Canada, Finland

*Competition held at summer games in Antwerp.
Note: Gold, silver, and bronze medals.

## LUGE

### Men

| SINGLES | | | DOUBLES | |
|---|---|---|---|---|
| 1964 | Thomas Köhler, East Germany | 3:26.77 | 1964 ...............Austria | 1:41.62 |
| 1968 | Manfred Schmid, Austria | 2:52.48 | 1968 ...............East Germany | 1:35.85 |
| 1972 | Wolfgang Scheidel, W Germany | 3:27.58 | 1972 ...............East Germany | 1:28.35 |
| 1976 | Detlef Guenther, West Germany | 3:27.688 | 1976 ...............East Germany | 1:25.604 |
| 1980 | Bernhard Glass, West Germany | 2:54.796 | 1980 ...............East Germany | 1:19.331 |
| 1984 | Paul Hildgartner, Italy | 3:04.258 | 1984 ...............West Germany | 1:23.620 |
| 1988 | Jens Müller, West Germany | 3:05.548 | 1988 ...............East Germany | 1:31.940 |
| 1992 | Georg Hackl, Germany | 3:02.363 | 1992 ...............Germany | 1:32.053 |
| 1994 | Georg Hackl, Germany | 3:21.571 | 1994 ...............Italy | 1:36.720 |

### Women

| SINGLES | | | SINGLES *(Cont.)* | |
|---|---|---|---|---|
| 1964 | Ortrun Enderlein, Germany | 3:24.67 | 1984 | Steffi Martin, East Germany | 2:46.570 |
| 1968 | Erica Lechner, Italy | 2:28.66 | 1988 | Steffi Walter (Martin) E Germany | 3:03.973 |
| 1972 | Anna-Maria Müller, East Germany | 2:59.18 | 1992 | Doris Neuner, Austria | 3:06.696 |
| 1976 | Margit Schumann, East Germany | 2:50.621 | 1994 | Gerda Weissensteiner, Italy | 3:15.517 |
| 1980 | Vera Zozulya, USSR | 2:36.537 | | |

## FIGURE SKATING

### Men

| SINGLES | | SINGLES *(Cont.)* | |
|---|---|---|---|
| 1908* | Ulrich Salchow, Sweden | 1968 ...............Wolfgang Schwarz, Austria |
| 1920† | Gillis Grafström, Sweden | 1972 ...............Ondrej Nepela, Czechoslovakia |
| 1924 | Gillis Grafström, Sweden | 1976 ...............John Curry, Great Britain |
| 1928 | Gillis Grafström, Sweden | 1980 ...............Robin Cousins, Great Britain |
| 1932 | Karl Schäfer, Austria | 1984 ...............Scott Hamilton, United States |
| 1936 | Karl Schäfer, Austria | 1988 ...............Brian Boitano, United States |
| 1948 | Dick Button, United States | 1992 ...............Victor Petrenko, Unified Team |
| 1952 | Dick Button, United States | 1994 ...............Alexei Urmanov, Russia |
| 1956 | Hayes Alan Jenkins, United States | |
| 1960 | David Jenkins, United States | *Competition held at summer games in London |
| 1964 | Manfred Schnelldorfer, West Germany | †Competition held at summer games in Antwerp |

### Women

| SINGLES | | SINGLES *(Cont.)* | |
|---|---|---|---|
| 1908* | Madge Syers, Great Britain | 1968 ...............Peggy Fleming, United States |
| 1920† | Magda Julin, Sweden | 1972 ...............Beatrix Schuba, Austria |
| 1924 | Herma Szabo-Planck, Austria | 1976 ...............Dorothy Hamill, United States |
| 1928 | Sonja Henie, Norway | 1980 ...............Anett Pötzsch, East Germany |
| 1932 | Sonja Henie, Norway | 1984 ...............Katarina Witt, East Germany |
| 1936 | Sonja Henie, Norway | 1988 ...............Katarina Witt, East Germany |
| 1948 | Barbara Ann Scott, Canada | 1992 ...............Kristi Yamaguchi, United States |
| 1952 | Jeanette Altwegg, Great Britain | 1994 ...............Oksana Baiul, Ukraine |
| 1956 | Tenley Albright, United States | |
| 1960 | Carol Heiss, United States | *Competition held at summer games in London |
| 1964 | Sjoukje Dijkstra, Netherlands | †Competition held at summer games in Antwerp |

## FIGURE SKATING *(Cont.)*

### Mixed

#### PAIRS

1908* ..Anna Hübler & Heinrich Burger, Germany
1920#..Ludovika & Walter Jakobsson, Finland
1924...Helene Engelmann & Alfred Berger, Austria
1928....Andree Joly & Pierre Brunet, France
1932....Andree Brunet (Joly) & Pierre Brunet, France
1936....Maxi Herber & Ernst Baier, Germany
1948....Micheline Lannoy & Pierre Baugniet, Belgium
1952....Ria Falk and Paul Falk, West Germany
1956....Elisabeth Schwartz & Kurt Oppelt, Austria
1960....Barbara Wagner & Robert Paul, Canada
1964....Lyudmila Beloussova & Oleg Protopopov, USSR
1968....Lyudmila Beloussova & Oleg Protopopov, USSR
1972....Irina Rodnina & Alexei Ulanov, USSR
1976....Irina Rodnina & Aleksandr Zaitsev, USSR
1980....Irina Rodnina & Aleksandr Zaitsev, USSR
1984....Elena Valova & Oleg Vasiliev, USSR
1988....Ekaterina Gordeeva & Sergei Grinkov, USSR

#### PAIRS *(Cont.)*

1992....Natalia Michkouteniok & Artour Dmitriev, Unified Team
1994....Ekaterina Gordeeva and Sergei Grinkov, Russia

#### ICE DANCING

1976....Lyudmila Pakhomova & Aleksandr Gorshkov, USSR
1980....Natalia Linichuk & Gennadi Karponosov, USSR
1984....Jayne Torvill & Christopher Dean, Great Britain
1988....Natalia Bestemianova & Andrei Bukin, USSR
1992....Marina Klimova & Sergei Ponomarenko, Unified Team
1994....Oksana Gritschuk and Evgeni Platov, Russia

*Competition held at summer games in London.
#Competition held at summer games in Antwerp.

## SPEED SKATING

### Men

#### 500 METERS

| | | |
|---|---|---|
| 1924 | Charles Jewtraw, United States | 44.0 |
| 1928 | Clas Thunberg, Finland | 43.4 OR |
| | Bernt Evensen, Norway | 43.4 OR |
| 1932 | John Shea, United States | 43.4 EOR |
| 1936 | Ivar Ballangrud, Norway | 43.4 EOR |
| 1948 | Finn Helgesen, Norway | 43.1 OR |
| 1952 | Kenneth Henry, United States | 43.2 |
| 1956 | Yevgeny Grishin, USSR | 40.2 EWR |
| 1960 | Yevgeny Grishin, USSR | 40.2 EWR |
| 1964 | Terry McDermott, United States | 40.1 OR |
| 1968 | Erhard Keller, West Germany | 40.3 |
| 1972 | Erhard Keller, West Germany | 39.44 OR |
| 1976 | Yevgeny Kulikov, USSR | 39.17 OR |
| 1980 | Eric Heiden, United States | 38.03 OR |
| 1984 | Sergei Fokichev, USSR | 38.19 |
| 1988 | Uwe-Jens Mey, East Germany | 36.45 WR |
| 1992 | Uwe-Jens Mey, East Germany | 37.14 |
| 1994 | Aleksandr Golubev, Russia | 36.33 |

#### 1000 METERS

| | | |
|---|---|---|
| 1976 | Peter Mueller, United States | 1:19.32 |
| 1980 | Eric Heiden, United States | 1:15.18 OR |
| 1984 | Gaetan Boucher, Canada | 1:15.80 |
| 1988 | Nikolai Gulyaev, USSR | 1:13.03 OR |
| 1992 | Olaf Zinke, Germany | 1:14.85 |
| 1994 | Dan Jansen, United States | 1:12.43 WR |

#### 1500 METERS

| | | |
|---|---|---|
| 1924 | Clas Thunberg, Finland | 2:20.8 |
| 1928 | Clas Thunberg, Finland | 2:21.1 |
| 1932 | John Shea, United States | 2:57.5 |
| 1936 | Charles Mathisen, Norway | 2:19.2 OR |
| 1948 | Sverre Farstad, Norway | 2:17.6 OR |

#### 1500 METERS *(Cont.)*

| | | |
|---|---|---|
| 1952 | Hjalmar Andersen, Norway | 2:20.4 |
| 1956 | Yevgeny Grishin, USSR | 2:08.6 WR |
| | Yuri Mikhailov, USSR | 2:08.6 WR |
| 1960 | Roald Aas, Norway | 2:10.4 |
| | Yevgeny Grishin, USSR | 2:10.4 |
| 1964 | Ants Anston, USSR | 2:10.3 |
| 1968 | Cornelis Verkerk, Netherlands | 2:03.4 OR |
| 1972 | Ard Schenk, Netherlands | 2:02.96 OR |
| 1976 | Jan Egil Storholt, Norway | 1:59.38 OR |
| 1980 | Eric Heiden, United States | 1:55.44 OR |
| 1984 | Gaetan Boucher, Canada | 1:58.36 |
| 1988 | Andre Hoffmann, East Germany | 1:52.06 WR |
| 1992 | Johann Olav Koss, Norway | 1:54.81 |
| 1994 | Johann Olav Koss, Norway | 1:51.29 WR |

#### 5000 METERS

| | | |
|---|---|---|
| 1924 | Clas Thunberg, Finland | 8:39.0 |
| 1928 | Ivar Ballangrud, Norway | 8:50.5 |
| 1932 | Irving Jaffee, United States | 9:40.8 |
| 1936 | Ivar Ballangrud, Norway | 8:19.6 OR |
| 1948 | Reidar Liaklev, Norway | 8:29.4 |
| 1952 | Hjalmar Andersen, Norway | 8:10.6 OR |
| 1956 | Boris Shilkov, USSR | 7:48.7 OR |
| 1960 | Viktor Kosichkin, USSR | 7:51.3 |
| 1964 | Knut Johannesen, Norway | 7:38.4 OR |
| 1968 | Fred Anton Maier, Norway | 7:22.4 WR |
| 1972 | Ard Schenk, Netherlands | 7:23.61 |
| 1976 | Sten Stensen, Norway | 7:24.48 |
| 1980 | Eric Heiden, United States | 7:02.29 OR |
| 1984 | Sven Tomas Gustafson, Sweden | 7:12.28 |
| 1988 | Tomas Gustafson, Sweden | 6:44.63 WR |
| 1992 | Geir Karlstad, Norway | 6:59.97 |
| 1994 | Johann Olav Koss, Norway | 6:34.96 WR |

Note: OR=Olympic Record; WR=World Record; EOR=Equals Olympic Record; EWR=Equals World Record; WB=World Best.

## SPEED SKATING (Cont.)

### Men (Cont.)

| 10,000 METERS | | | 10,000 METERS (Cont.) | |
|---|---|---|---|---|
| 1924 | Julius Skutnabb, Finland | 18:04.8 | 1968 | Johnny Höglin, Sweden | 15:23.6 OR |
| 1928 | Not held, thawing of ice | | 1972 | Ard Schenk, Netherlands | 15:01.35 OR |
| 1932 | Irving Jaffee, United States | 19:13.6 | 1976 | Piet Kleine, Netherlands | 14:50.59 OR |
| 1936 | Ivar Ballangrud, Norway | 17:24.3 OR | 1980 | Eric Heiden, United States | 14:28.13 WR |
| 1948 | Ake Seyffarth, Sweden | 17:26.3 | 1984 | Igor Malkov, USSR | 14:39.90 |
| 1952 | Hjalmar Andersen, Norway | 16:45.8 OR | 1988 | Tomas Gustafson, Sweden | 13:48.20 WR |
| 1956 | Sigvard Ericsson, Sweden | 16:35.9 OR | 1992 | Bart Veldkamp, The Netherlands | 14:12.12 |
| 1960 | Knut Johannesen, Norway | 15:46.6 WR | 1994 | Johann Olav Koss, Norway | 13:30.55 WR |
| 1964 | Jonny Nilsson, Sweden | 15:50.1 | | | |

### Women

| 500 METERS | | | 1500 METERS | |
|---|---|---|---|---|
| 1960 | Helga Haase, East Germany | 45.9 | 1960 | Lydia Skoblikova, USSR | 2:25.2 WR |
| 1964 | Lydia Skoblikova, USSR | 45.0 OR | 1964 | Lydia Skoblikova, USSR | 2:22.6 OR |
| 1968 | Lyudmila Titova, USSR | 46.1 | 1968 | Kaija Mustonen, Finland | 2:22.4 OR |
| 1972 | Anne Henning, United States | 43.33 OR | 1972 | Dianne Holum, United States | 2:20.85 OR |
| 1976 | Sheila Young, United States | 42.76 OR | 1976 | Galina Stepanskaya, USSR | 2:16.58 OR |
| 1980 | Karin Enke, East Germany | 41.78 OR | 1980 | Anne Borckink, Netherlands | 2:10.95 OR |
| 1984 | Christa Rothenburger, East Germany | 41.02 OR | 1984 | Karin Enke, East Germany | 2:03.42 WR |
| | | | 1988 | Yvonne van Gennip, Netherlands | 2:00.68 OR |
| 1988 | Bonnie Blair, United States | 39.10 WR | 1992 | Jacqueline Boerner, Germany | 2:05.87 |
| 1992 | Bonnie Blair, United States | 40.33 | 1994 | Emese Hunyady, Austria | 2:02.19 |
| 1994 | Bonnie Blair, United States | 39.25 | | | |

| 1000 METERS | | | 3000 METERS | |
|---|---|---|---|---|
| 1960 | Klara Guseva, USSR | 1:34.1 | 1960 | Lydia Skoblikova, USSR | 5:14.3 |
| 1964 | Lydia Skoblikova, USSR | 1:33.2 OR | 1964 | Lydia Skoblikova, USSR | 5:14.9 |
| 1968 | Carolina Geijssen, Netherlands | 1:32.6 OR | 1968 | Johanna Schut, Netherlands | 4:56.2 OR |
| 1972 | Monika Pflug, West Germany | 1:31.40 OR | 1972 | Christina Baas-Kaiser, Netherlands | 4:52.14 OR |
| 1976 | Tatiana Averina, USSR | 1:28.43 OR | 1976 | Tatiana Averina, USSR | 4:45.19 OR |
| 1980 | Natalya Petruseva, USSR | 1:24.10 OR | 1980 | Bjorg Eva Jensen, Norway | 4:32.13 OR |
| 1984 | Karin Enke, East Germany | 1:21.61 OR | 1984 | Andrea Schöne, East Germany | 4:24.79 OR |
| 1988 | Christa Rothenburger, East Germany | 1:17.65 WR | 1988 | Yvonne van Gennip, Netherlands | 4:11.94 WR |
| | | | 1992 | Gunda Niemann, Germany | 4:19.90 |
| 1992 | Bonnie Blair, United States | 1:21.90 | 1994 | Svetlana Bazhanova, Russia | 4:17.43 |
| 1994 | Bonnie Blair, United States | 1:18.74 | | | |

| 5000 METERS | | |
|---|---|---|
| 1988 | Yvonne van Gennip, Netherlands | 7:14.13 WR |
| 1992 | Gunda Niemann, Germany | 7:31.57 |
| 1994 | Claudia Pechstein, Germany | 7:14.37 |

## SHORT TRACK SPEED SKATING

### Men

#### 500 METERS

| 1994 | Chae Ji-Hoon, South Korea | 43.54 |
|---|---|---|

#### 1000 METERS

| 1992 | Kim Ki-Hoon, South Korea | 1:30.76 WR |
|---|---|---|
| 1994 | Kim Ki-Hoon, South Korea | 1:34.57 |

#### 5000-METER RELAY

| 1992 | Korea | 7:14.02 WR |
|---|---|---|
| 1994 | Italy | 7:11.74 OR |

### Women

#### 500 METERS

| 1992 | Cathy Turner, United States | 47.04 |
|---|---|---|
| 1994 | Cathy Turner, United States | 45.98 OR |

#### 1000 METERS

| 1994 | Chun Lee-Kyung, South Korea | 1:36.87 |
|---|---|---|

#### 3000-METER RELAY

| 1992 | Canada | 4:36.62 |
|---|---|---|
| 1994 | South Korea | 4:26.64 OR |

## ALPINE SKIING

### Men

#### DOWNHILL

| | | |
|---|---|---|
| 1948 | Henri Oreiller, France | 2:55.0 |
| 1952 | Zeno Colo, Italy | 2:30.8 |
| 1956 | Anton Sailer, Austria | 2:52.2 |
| 1960 | Jean Vuarnet, France | 2:06.0 |
| 1964 | Egon Zimmermann, Austria | 2:18.16 |
| 1968 | Jean-Claude Killy, France | 1:59.85 |
| 1972 | Bernhard Russi, Switzerland | 1:51.43 |
| 1976 | Franz Klammer, Austria | 1:45.73 |
| 1980 | Leonhard Stock, Austria | 1:45.50 |
| 1984 | Bill Johnson, United States | 1:45.59 |
| 1988 | Pirmin Zurbriggen, Switzerland | 1:59.63 |
| 1992 | Patrick Ortlieb, Austria | 1:50.37 |
| 1994 | Tommy Moe, United States | 1:45.75 |

#### SUPER GIANT SLALOM

| | | |
|---|---|---|
| 1988 | Franck Piccard, France | 1:39.66 |
| 1992 | Kjetil Andre Aamodt, Norway | 1:13.04 |
| 1994 | Markus Wasmeier, Germany | 1:32.53 |

#### GIANT SLALOM

| | | |
|---|---|---|
| 1952 | Stein Eriksen, Norway | 2:25.0 |
| 1956 | Anton Sailer, Austria | 3:00.1 |
| 1960 | Roger Staub, Switzerland | 1:48.3 |
| 1964 | Francois Bonlieu, France | 1:46.71 |
| 1968 | Jean-Claude Killy, France | 3:29.28 |
| 1972 | Gustav Thöni, Italy | 3:09.62 |
| 1976 | Heini Hemmi, Switzerland | 3:26.97 |
| 1980 | Ingemar Stenmark, Sweden | 2:40.74 |
| 1984 | Max Julen, Switzerland | 2:41.18 |
| 1988 | Alberto Tomba, Italy | 2:06.37 |
| 1992 | Alberto Tomba, Italy | 2:06.98 |
| 1994 | Markus Wasmeier, Germany | 2:52.46 |

#### SLALOM

| | | |
|---|---|---|
| 1948 | Edi Reinalter, Switzerland | 2:10.3 |
| 1952 | Othmar Schneider, Austria | 2:00.0 |
| 1956 | Anton Sailer, Austria | 3:14.7 |
| 1960 | Ernst Hinterseer, Austria | 2:08.9 |
| 1964 | Josef Stiegler, Austria | 2:11.13 |
| 1968 | Jean-Claude Killy, France | 1:39.73 |
| 1972 | Francisco Fernandez Ochoa, Spain | 1:49.27 |
| 1976 | Piero Gros, Italy | 2:03.29 |
| 1980 | Ingemar Stenmark, Sweden | 1:44.26 |
| 1984 | Phil Mahre, United States | 1:39.41 |
| 1988 | Alberto Tomba, Italy | 1:39.47 |
| 1992 | Finn Christian Jagge, Norway | 1:44.39 |
| 1994 | Thomas Stangassinger, Austria | 2:02.02 |

#### *COMBINED

| | | Pts |
|---|---|---|
| 1936 | Franz Pfnür, Germany | 99.25 |
| 1948 | Henri Oreiller, France | 3.27 |
| 1988 | Hubert Strolz, Austria | 36.55 |
| 1992 | Josef Polig, Italy | 14.58 |
| 1994 | Lasse Kjus, Norway | 3:17.53 |

*Beginning in 1994, scoring was based on time.

### Women

#### DOWNHILL

| | | |
|---|---|---|
| 1948 | Hedy Schlunegger, Switzerland | 2:28.3 |
| 1952 | Trude Jochum-Beiser, Austria | 1:47.1 |
| 1956 | Madeleine Berthod, Switzerland | 1:40.7 |
| 1960 | Heidi Biebl, West Germany | 1:37.6 |
| 1964 | Christl Haas, Austria | 1:55.39 |
| 1968 | Olga Pall, Austria | 1:40.87 |
| 1972 | Marie-Theres Nadig, Switzerland | 1:36.68 |
| 1976 | Rosi Mittermaier, West Germany | 1:46.16 |
| 1980 | Annemarie Moser-Pröll, Austria | 1:37.52 |
| 1984 | Michela Figini, Switzerland | 1:13.36 |
| 1988 | Marina Kiehl, West Germany | 1:25.86 |
| 1992 | Kerrin Lee-Gartner, Canada | 1:52.55 |
| 1994 | Katja Seizinger, Germany | 1:35.93 |

#### SUPER GIANT SLALOM

| | | |
|---|---|---|
| 1988 | Sigrid Wolf, Austria | 1:19.03 |
| 1992 | Deborah Compagnoni, Italy | 1:21.22 |
| 1994 | Diann Rolfe-Steinrotter | 1:22.15 |

#### GIANT SLALOM

| | | |
|---|---|---|
| 1952 | Andrea Mead Lawrence, United States | 2:06.8 |
| 1956 | Ossi Reichert, West Germany | 1:56.5 |
| 1960 | Yvonne Rüegg, Switzerland | 1:39.9 |
| 1964 | Marielle Goitschel, France | 1:52.24 |
| 1968 | Nancy Greene, Canada | 1:51.97 |
| 1972 | Marie-Theres Nadig, Switzerland | 1:29.90 |
| 1976 | Kathy Kreiner, Canada | 1:29.13 |
| 1980 | Hanni Wenzel, Liechtenstein (2 runs) | 2:41.66 |
| 1984 | Debbie Armstrong, United States | 2:20.98 |
| 1988 | Vreni Schneider, Switzerland | 2:06.49 |
| 1992 | Pernilla Wiberg, Sweden | 2:12.74 |
| 1994 | Deborah Compagnoni, Italy | 2:30.97 |

#### SLALOM

| | | |
|---|---|---|
| 1948 | Gretchen Fraser, United States | 1:57.2 |
| 1952 | Andrea Mead Lawrence, United States | 2:10.6 |
| 1956 | Renee Colliard, Switzerland | 1:52.3 |
| 1960 | Anne Heggtveigt, Canada | 1:49.6 |
| 1964 | Christine Goitschel, France | 1:29.86 |
| 1968 | Marielle Goitschel, France | 1:25.86 |
| 1972 | Barbara Cochran, United States | 1:31.24 |
| 1976 | Rosi Mittermaier, West Germany | 1:30.54 |
| 1980 | Hanni Wenzel, Liechtenstein | 1:25.09 |
| 1984 | Paoletta Magoni, Italy | 1:36.47 |
| 1988 | Vreni Schneider, Switzerland | 1:36.69 |
| 1992 | Petra Kronberger, Austria | 1:32.68 |
| 1994 | Vreni Schneider, Switzerland | 1:56.01 |

#### *COMBINED

| | | Pts |
|---|---|---|
| 1988 | Anita Wachter, Austria | 29.25 |
| 1992 | Petra Kronberger, Austria | 2.55 |
| 1994 | Pernilla Wiberg, Sweden | 3:05.16 |

## NORDIC SKIING

### Men

#### 15 KILOMETERS (CLASSICAL)

| | | |
|---|---|---|
| *1924 ..Thorlief Haug, Norway | 1:14:31.0 |
| †1928..Johan Gröttumsbraaten, Norway | 1:37:01.0 |
| ‡1932..Sven Utterström, Sweden | 1:23:07.0 |
| *1936 ..Erik-August Larsson, Sweden | 14:38.0 |
| *1948 ..Martin Lundström, Sweden | 13:50.0 |
| *1952 ..Hallgeir Brenden, Norway | 1:34.0 |
| 1956....Hallgeir Brenden, Norway | 49:39.0 |
| 1960....Haakon Brusveen, Norway | 51:55.5 |
| 1964....Eero Mantyränta, Finland | 50:54.1 |
| 1968....Harald Grönningen, Norway | 47:54.2 |
| 1972....Sven-Ake Lundback, Sweden | 45:28.24 |
| 1976....Nikolay Bajukov, Unified Team | 43:58.47 |
| 1980....Thomas Wassberg, Sweden | 41:57.63 |
| 1984....Gunde Swan, Sweden | 41:25.6 |
| 1988....Michael Deviatyarov, USSR | 41:18.9 |
| **1992.Vegard Ulvang, Norway | 27:36.0 |
| **1994.Bjorn Daehlie, Norway | 24:20.1 |

*distance was 18 km; †distance was 19.7 km.;
‡distance was 18.2 km; **distance was 10 km.

#### 30 KILOMETERS (CLASSICAL)

| | |
|---|---|
| 1956....Veikko Hakulinen, Finland | 1:44:06.0 |
| 1960....Sixten Jernberg, Sweden | 1:51:03.9 |
| 1964....Eero Mantyränta, Finland | 1:30:50.7 |
| 1968....Franco Nones, Italy | 1:35:39.2 |
| 1972....Viaceslav Vedenine, USSR | 1:36:31.2 |
| 1976....Sergei Savelyev, USSR | 1:30:29.38 |
| 1980....Nikolai Simyatov, USSR | 1:27:02.80 |
| 1984....Nikolai Simyatov, USSR | 1:28:56.3 |
| 1988....Alexey Prokororov, USSR | 1:24:26.3 |
| 1992....Vegard Ulvang, Norway | 1:22:27.8 |
| 1994....Thomas Alsgaard, Norway | 1:12:26.4 |

#### 50 KILOMETERS (FREESTYLE)

| | |
|---|---|
| 1924....Thorleif Haug, Norway | 3:44:32.0 |
| 1928....Per Erik Hedlund, Sweden | 4:52:03.0 |
| 1932....Veli Saarinen, Finland | 4:28:00.0 |
| 1936....Elis Wiklund, Sweden | 3:30:11.0 |
| 1948....Nils Karlsson, Sweden | 3:47:48.0 |
| 1952....Veikko Hakulinen, Finland | 3:33:33.0 |
| 1956....Sixten Jernberg, Sweden | 2:50:27.0 |
| 1960....Kalevi Hämäläinen, Finland | 2:59:06.3 |
| 1964....Sixten Jernberg, Sweden | 2:43:52.6 |
| 1968....Olle Ellefsaeter, Norway | 2:28:45.8 |
| 1972....Paal Tyldrum, Norway | 2:43:14.75 |
| 1976....Ivar Formo, Norway | 2:37:30.50 |
| 1980....Nikolai Simyatov, USSR | 2:27:24.60 |
| 1984....Thomas Wassberg, Sweden | 2:15:55.8 |
| 1988....Gunde Swan, Sweden | 2:04:30.9 |
| 1992....Bjorn Dählie, Norway | 2:03:41.5 |
| 1994....Vladimir Smirnov, Kazakhstan | 2:07:20.3 |

#### 15 KILOMETERS (FREESTYLE)

| | |
|---|---|
| 1992....Bjorn Daehlie, Norway | 1:05:37.9 |
| 1994....Bjorn Daehlie, Norway | 1:00:08.8 |

#### 4 X 10 KILOMETER RELAY

| | |
|---|---|
| 1936 ...................Finland | 2:41:33.0 |
| 1948 ...................Sweden | 2:32:80.0 |
| 1952 ...................Finland | 2:20:16.0 |
| 1956 ...................USSR | 2:15:30.0 |
| 1960 ...................Finland | 2:18:45.6 |
| 1964 ...................Sweden | 2:18:34.6 |
| 1968 ...................Norway | 2:08:33.5 |
| 1972 ...................USSR | 2:04:47.94 |
| 1976 ...................Finland | 2:07:59.72 |
| 1980 ...................USSR | 1:57:03.46 |
| 1984 ...................Sweden | 1:55:06.3 |
| 1988 ...................Sweden | 1:43:58.6 |
| 1992 ...................Norway | 1:39:26.0 |
| 1994 ...................Italy | 1:41:15.0 |

#### SKI JUMPING (NORMAL HILL)

| | Pts |
|---|---|
| 1964....Veikko Kankkonen, Finland | 229.90 |
| 1968....Jiri Raska, Czechoslovakia | 216.5 |
| 1972....Yukio Kasaya, Japan | 244.2 |
| 1976....Hans-Georg Aschenbach, East Germany | 252.0 |
| 1980....Toni Innauer, Austria | 266.3 |
| 1984....Jens Weissflog, East Germany | 215.2 |
| 1988....Matti Nykänen, Finland | 229.1 |
| 1992....Ernst Vettori, Austria | 222.8 |
| 1994....Espen Bredesen, Norway | 282.0 |

#### SKI JUMPING (LARGE HILL)

| | Pts |
|---|---|
| 1924....Jacob Tullin Thams, Norway | 18.960 |
| 1928....Alf Andersen, Norway | 19.208 |
| 1932....Birger Ruud, Norway | 228.1 |
| 1936....Birger Ruud, Norway | 232.0 |
| 1948....Petter Hugsted, Norway | 228.1 |
| 1952....Arnfinn Bergmann, Norway | 226.0 |
| 1956....Antti Hyvärinen, Finland | 227.0 |
| 1960....Helmut Recknagel, East Germany | 227.2 |
| 1964....Toralf Engan, Norway | 230.70 |
| 1968....Vladimir Beloussov, USSR | 231.3 |
| 1972....Wojciech Fortuna, Poland | 219.9 |
| 1976....Karl Schnabl, Austria | 234.8 |
| 1980....Jouko Tormanen, Finland | 271.0 |
| 1984....Matti Nykänen, Finland | 231.2 |
| 1988....Matti Nykänen, Finland | 224.0 |
| 1992....Toni Nieminen, Finland | 239.5 |
| 1994....Jens Weissflog, Germany | 274.5 |

#### TEAM SKI JUMPING

| | Pts |
|---|---|
| 1988....Finland | 634.4 |
| 1992....Finland | 644.4 |
| 1994....Germany | 970.1 |

#### NORDIC COMBINED

| | Pts |
|---|---|
| *1924 ..Thorleif Haug, Norway | 18.906 |
| *1928 ..Johan Gröttumsbraaten, Norway | 17.833 |
| 1932....Johan Gröttumsbraaten, Norway | 446.0 |
| 1936....Oddbjörn Hagen, Norway | 430.30 |

## NORDIC SKIING (Cont.)

### Men (Cont.)

#### NORDIC COMBINED (Cont.)

| | Pts |
|---|---|
| 1948....Heikki Hasu, Finland | 448.80 |
| 1952....Simon Slattvik, Norway | 451.621 |
| 1956....Sverre Stenersen, Norway | 455.0 |
| 1960....Georg Thoma, West Germany | 457.952 |
| 1964....Tormod Knutsen, Norway | 469.28 |
| 1968....Frantz Keller, West Germany | 449.04 |
| 1972....Ulrich Wehling, East Germany | 413.34 |
| 1976....Ulrich Wehling, East Germany | 423.39 |
| 1980....Ulrich Wehling, East Germany | 432.20 |
| 1984....Tom Sandberg, Norway | 422.595 |
| 1988....Hippolyt Kempf, Switzerland | 432.230 |
| 1992....Fabrice Guy, France | 426.47 |
| 1994....Fred B. Lundberg, Norway | 457.970 |

#### TEAM NORDIC COMBINED

| |
|---|
| 1988....West Germany |
| 1992....Japan |
| 1994....Japan |

*Different scoring system; 1924-1952 distance was 18 km.; 1952-present, 15 km.

### Women

#### 5 KILOMETERS (CLASSICAL)

| 1964....Klaudia Boyarskikh, USSR | 17:50.5 |
|---|---|
| 1968....Toini Gustafsson, Sweden | 16:45.2 |
| 1972....Galina Kulakova, USSR | 17:00.50 |
| 1976....Helena Takalo, Finland | 15:48.69 |
| 1980....Raisa Smetanina, USSR | 15:06.92 |
| 1984....Marja-Liisa Hamalainen, Finland | 17:04.0 |
| 1988....Marjo Matikainen, Finland | 15:04.0 |
| 1992....Marjut Lukkarinen, Finland | 14:13.8 |
| 1994....Lyubova Egorova, Russia | 14:08.8 |

#### 10 KILOMETERS (CLASSICAL)

| 1952....Lydia Widemen, Finland | 41:40.0 |
|---|---|
| 1956....Lyubov Kosyryeva, USSR | 38:11.0 |
| 1960....Maria Gusakova, USSR | 39:46.6 |
| 1964....Klaudia Boyarskikh, USSR | 40:24.3 |
| 1968....Toini Gustafsson, Sweden | 36:46.5 |
| 1972....Galina Kulakova, USSR | 34:17.8 |
| 1976....Raisa Smetanina, USSR | 30:13.41 |
| 1980....Barbara Petzold, East Germany | 30:31.54 |
| 1984....Marja-Lissa Hamalainen, Finland | 31:44.2 |
| 1988....Vida Ventsene, USSR | 30:08.3 |

#### 15 KILOMETERS (CLASSICAL)

| 1992....Lyubov Egorova, Unified Team | 42:20.8 |
|---|---|
| 1994....Manuela Di Centa, Italy | 39:44.5 |

#### 20 KILOMETERS (FREESTYLE)

| 1984....Marja-Liisa Hamalainen, Finland | 1:01:45.0 |
|---|---|
| 1988....Tamara Tikhonova, USSR | 55:53.6 |

#### 30 KILOMETERS (FREESTYLE)

| 1992....Stefania Belmondo, Italy | 1:22:30.1 |
|---|---|
| 1994....Manuela Di Centa, Italy | 1:25:41.6 |

#### 10 KILOMETERS FREESTYLE PURSUIT

| 1992....Lyubov Egorova, Unified Team | 40:07.7 |
|---|---|
| 1994....Lyubov Egorova, Russia | 41:38.1 |

#### 4 X 5-KILOMETER RELAY

| 1956....Finland | 1:9:01.0 |
|---|---|
| 1960....Sweden | 1:4:21.4 |
| 1964....USSR | 59:20.0 |
| 1968....Norway | 57:30.0 |
| 1972....USSR | 48:46.15 |
| 1976....USSR | 1:07:49.75 |
| 1980....East Germany | 1:02:11.10 |
| 1984....Norway | 1:06:49.7 |
| 1988....USSR | 59:51.1 |
| 1992....Unified Team | 59:34.8 |
| 1994....Russia | 57:12.5 |

Note: 10 km. (classical) changed to 15 km. (classical) in 1992; 20 km. (freestyle) changed to 30 km. (freestyle).

## FREESTYLE SKIING

### Men
#### MOGUL

| | Pts |
|---|---|
| 1992....Edgar Grospiron, France | 25.81 |
| 1994....Jean-Luc Brassard, Canada | 27.24 |

#### AERIAL

| | Pts |
|---|---|
| 1994....Andreas Schoenbaechler, SWI | 234.67 |

### Women
#### MOGUL

| | Pts |
|---|---|
| 1992....Donna Weinbrecht, United States | 23.69 |
| 1994....Stine Lise Hattestad, Norway | 25.97 |

#### AERIAL

| | Pts |
|---|---|
| 1994....Lina Cherjazova, Uzbekistan | 166.84 |

# Track and Field

Sports Illustrated

USA TDK 1357 GÖTEBORG '95

## Double Trouble
Michael Johnson strikes twice at the worlds

WALTER IOOSS JR

# Great Leaps Forward

## Records came in bushels in '95, with five men staking claims to athlete of the year honors

### by Merrell Noden

STEVE OVETT, who twice set the world record for the mile in the early '80s, thought that as we inched closer to the limits of human performance, we'd simply carry times out to another decimal place and go bonkers over someone "smashing" a record by .006. Just when it was beginning to look as if Ovett might be right, along comes a startling year like 1995, in which a slew of world records were broken, major barriers fell in the triple jump and the 3,000 steeplechase, and one man lowered the 5,000 record by a truly Beamonesque margin.

The season reached its climax at the fifth I.A.A.F. World Championships, held August 5 through August 13 at Ullevi Stadium in Göteborg, Sweden, where transition, the succession of generations, was the obvious theme. Sergei Bubka alone resisted the youthful tide, winning his fifth world outdoor title in the pole vault. Who would have guessed that Carl Lewis, Jackie Joyner-Kersee and Heike Drechsler—perhaps the sport's three greatest stars over the last dozen years—would come away without a single medal? While Joyner-Kersee and Drechsler competed in Göteborg—finishing sixth and ninth, respectively, in the long jump—Lewis,

feeling a strained left hamstring suffered at the U.S. Olympic Festival in Colorado Springs, went home from Göteborg without making a single attempt in the long jump, which was won easily by 22-year-old Cuban Ivan Pedroso with a leap of 28' 6½".

Instead, Lewis chose to snipe at the meet. "It's boring," said Lewis. "There's no buzz, no passionate missions." Without Lewis, who had failed to qualify for the 100, and the injured pair of world record holder Leroy Burrell and Dennis Mitchell, the top U.S. finisher in the 100 was Mike Marsh, who was fifth, far behind Canada's Donovan Bailey.

Not that the U.S. lacked a sprint star in Göteborg. Michael Johnson has yet to set an outdoor world record but he made history just the same. No one had completed a 200/400 double successfully at the world championship or Olympic level, which is just the kind of incentive Johnson now requires, so thoroughly does he dominate the long sprints. In Göteborg he narrowly missed Butch Reynolds's world record in the 400, clocking 43.39 to win by seven meters; won the 200 by three meters, in 19.79; and anchored the victorious U.S. 4 x 400 team in 44.11.

In most years, Johnson would have been a

shoe-in for athlete of the year honors. But in the annus mirabilis of 1995 four other men had seasons to rival his.

One was Haile Gebrselassie, who for this writer was the track and field athlete of 1995. All year the 22-year-old Ethiopian seemed to be thumbing his nose at the notion of peaking, running fast and frequently from May through September. He set world records for two miles (8:07.46) in May; for 10,000 (26:43.54) in June and for the 5,000 (12:44.39) in August. In Göteborg he won the 10,000 in 27:12.95—a superb time in what was essentially a tactical race—then surprised some people by choosing not to double. That decision looked positively brilliant when, eight days later in Zurich, he ran the last four laps of his 5,000 record in 4:00.4 to leave an excellent field more than a straightaway adrift. The time, 12:44.39, hacked an astonishing 10.91 seconds off the old record.

It's hard to see how Gebrselassie's heroics left room for anyone else in the middle and long distances, but two other men also made history in those events. Moses Kiptanui may have inspired Gebrselassie when on June 8 he broke the Ethiopian's old 5,000 mark, running 12:55.30 in Rome. Like Gebrselassie, Kiptanui held back in Göteborg, winning the 3,000 steeple in 8:04.16. In Zurich he ran the first sub-eight-minute steeple, clocking 7:59.18. Noureddine Morceli broke two world records and would have established more had he not set the world records so high in the middle distances. As it was, the incomparable Algerian, still only 25, became the first man to break 4:50 for the 2,000, clocking 4:47.88 on July 3 in Paris. Nine days later in Nice he broke the 1500 mark by running 3:27.37.

Jonathan Edwards began the year as an unlikely man to revolutionize the triple jump. After winning the bronze medal at the 1993 worlds, the Englishman missed most of 1994 with mononucleosis and decided only last year, at the age of 28, to give up his job as a lab technician to concentrate on the triple jump. After losing three records to trailing winds earlier in the season, Edwards finally nailed Willie Banks's 10-year-old mark of 58' 11½" on July 18 in Salamanca, Spain, bound-

BOB MARTIN

**England's Edwards hopped, skipped and jumped through the 60' barrier.**

ing out 59'. And that was a mere hint of what was to come in Göteborg, where Edwards eclipsed both the 18-meter barrier and 60', jumping 59' 7" (18.16 meters) on his first attempt and 60' ¼" on his second.

Women set world records in five events, four of them relatively minor: the pole vault, the triple jump, the 1,000 and the 5,000. But the best *race* of the year, the women's 400 hurdles in Göteborg, also yeilded a world record when Kim Batten's lunge at the tape beat her U.S. teammate Tonja Buford, 52.61 to 52.62. Both women broke Sally Gunnell's 1993 world record. Batten's performance was all the more remarkable since she had her appendix out on May 21 and had been reduced for a time to just hobbling painfully around the track.

Their rematch should be one of the highlights of next year's Olympic Games in Atlanta. One of many, if 1996 bears any resemblance to its astonishing predecessor.

## U.S. Outdoor Track and Field Championships

### Sacramento, Calif., June 14–18, 1995

### Men

#### 100 METERS

1. .............Mike Marsh, Santa Monica TC     10.23
2. .............Maurice Greene, Powerade AC     10.23
3. .............Dennis Mitchell, Mizuno TC     10.23

#### 200 METERS

1. .............Michael Johnson, Nike Intl     19.83 w
2. .............Kevin Little, US West     20.16
3. .............Jeff Williams, unat     20.20

#### 400 METERS

1. .............Michael Johnson, Nike I     43.66
2. .............Butch Reynolds, Foot Locker AC     44.42
3. .............Darnell Hall, Powerade AC     44.55

#### 800 METERS

1. .............Brandon Rock, U. of Arkansas     1:46.50
2. .............Mark Everett, New Balance TC     1:47.63
3. .............Jose Parilla, adidas     1:48.14

#### 1500 METERS

1. .............Paul McMullen, Asics     3:43.90
2. .............Brian Hyde, William and Mary     3:43.90
3. .............Terrance Herrington, Reebok RC     3:44.03

#### STEEPLECHASE

1. .............Mark Croghan, adidas     8:17.54
2. .............Tom Nohilly, Reebok E     8:26.54
3. .............Karl Van Calcar, Nike     8:27.38

#### 5000 METERS

1. .............Bob Kennedy, Nike I     13:19.99
2. .............Mark Coogan, New Balance     13:23.72
3. .............Matt Giusto, Foot Locker AC     13:27.87

#### 10,000 METERS

1. .............Todd Williams, adidas     28:01.84
2. .............Chris Fox, unat     28:23.94
3. .............Tom Ansberry, Nike     28:27.85

#### 110-METER HURDLES

1. .............Roger Kingdom, Foot Locker AC     13.09 w
2. .............Allen Johnson, Goldwin TC     13.11
3. .............Jack Pierce, Mizuno TC     13.26

#### 400-METER HURDLES

1. .............Derrick Adkins, Reebok RC     48.44
2. .............Ryan Hayden, St Augustine     49.04
3. .............Octavius Terry, Georgia Tech     49.20

#### 20-KILOMETER WALK

1. .............Allen James, Athletes in Action   1:24:46.0
2. .............Herm Nelson, Club NW   1:27:14.8
3. .............Gary Morgan, NYAC   1:28:41.0

#### HIGH JUMP

1. .............Charles Austin, unat     7 ft 6½ in
2T. ...........Tony Barton, adidas     7 ft 5¼ in
2T. ...........Rick Noji, SSTC     7 ft 5¼ in

#### POLE VAULT

1. .............Scott Huffman, Foot Locker RC   19 ft ¼ in
2. .............Dean Starkey, Reebok RC   18 ft 10¼ in
3. .............Bill Payne, unat   18 ft 10¼ in

#### LONG JUMP

1. .............Mike Powell, Foot Locker AC   28 ft ¾ in w
2. .............Carl Lewis, Santa Monica TC   27 ft 8¾ in w
3. .............Kareem Streete-Thompson, unat   27 ft 5¼ in w

#### TRIPLE JUMP

1. .............Mike Conley, Foot Locker AC   56 ft 4½ in
2. .............Ivory Angello, Rice   56 ft 1¼ in
3. .............LaMark Carter, MidA   54 ft 7¼ in w

#### SHOT PUT

1. .............Brent Noon, unat     69 ft 2 in
2. .............John Godina, Reebok RC     68 ft 7 in
3. .............Randy Barnes, Goldwin TC     68 ft 5 in

#### DISCUS THROW

1. .............Mike Buncic, Nike     212 ft 8 in
2. .............John Godina, Reebok RC     211 ft 11 in
3. .............Randy Heisler, Nike Indiana     208 ft 8 in

#### HAMMER THROW

1. .............Lance Deal, NYAC     254 ft 10 in
2. .............David Popejoy, Stanford     240 ft 10 in
3. .............Kevin McMahon, Georgetown   233 ft 11 in

#### JAVELIN THROW

1. .............Tom Pukstys, adidas     267 ft 4 in
2. .............Erik Smith, Bruin     242 ft 11 in
3. .............Jim Connolly, GEO     242 ft 4 in

#### DECATHLON

1. .............Dan O'Brien, Foot Locker AC   8682 pts.
2. .............Chris Huffins, Mizuno   8351 pts.
3. .............Brian Brophy, Reebok RC   8257 pts.

*Meet record.  w=wind aided.  AR=American Record.

## Women

### 100 METERS

1. Gwen Torrence, Mazda TC — 11.04
2. Carlette Guidry, adidas — 11.12
3. Celena Mondie-Milner, MidA — 11.22

### 200 METERS

1. Gwen Torrence, Mazda TC — 22.03 w
2. Carlette Guidry, adidas — 22.57
3. Celena Mondie-Milner, MidA — 22.76

### 400 METERS

1. Jearl Miles, Reebok RC — 50.90
2. Kim Graham, Nike — 51.48
3. Maicel Malone, Asics — 51.56

### 800 METERS

1. Meredith Rainey, Foot Locker AC — 2:00.07
2. Joetta Clark, Foot Locker AC — 2:01.02
3. Amy Wickus, Univ. of Wisconsin — 2:01.26

### 1500 METERS

1. Regina Jacobs, Mizuno TC — 4:05.18
2. Suzy Hamilton, Reebok RC — 4:07.07
3. Sarah Thorsett, Powerade AC — 4:07.49

### 5,000 METERS

1. Gina Procaccio, New Balance — 15:26.34
2. Laura Mykytok, Nike — 15:27.52
3. Libbie Johnson, Mizuno TC — 15:28.27

### 10,000 METERS

1. Lynn Jennings, Nike I — 31:57.19
2. Laurie Henes, adidas — 32:05.32
3. Anne Marie Lauck, Nike — 32:07.43

### 10,000 METER WALK

1. Teresa Vaill, unattached — 45:01.0
2. Michelle Rohl, Brooks — 45:16.2
3. Debbi Lawrence, NS — 45:46.0

### 100-METER HURDLES

1. Gail Devers, Nike I — 12.77
2. Marsha Guialdo, unat — 12.98
3. Doris Williams, Goldwin TC — 13.03

### 400-METER HURDLES

1. Kim Batten, Reebok RC — 54.74
2. Tonja Buford, unat — 54.82
3. Trevaia Williams, Atoms — 55.43

### HIGH JUMP

1. Amy Acuff, UCLA — 6 ft 4¾ in
2. Tisha Waller, Goldwin — 6 ft 3½ in
3. Connie Teabury, Goldwin — 6 ft 3½ in

### LONG JUMP

1. Jackie Joyner-Kersee, Honda — 22 ft 7 in w
2. Marieke Veltman, WC — 22 ft 1½ in w
3. Sharon Couch, Olst — 21 ft 11 in w

### TRIPLE JUMP

1. Sheila Hudson-Strudwick, Reebok RC — 48 ft 1¼ in w
2. Cynthea Rhondes, unat — 46 ft 4 in w
3. Diana Orrange, PT — 45 ft 7 in w

### SHOT PUT

1. Connie Price-Smith, Reebok RC — 62 ft 6 in
2. Ramona Pagel, Nike Coast — 61 ft 2¾ in
3. Eileen Vanisi, Reebok RC — 57 ft 8¼ in

### DISCUS THROW

1. Edie Boyer, unat — 205 ft 4 in
2. Pam Dukes, Nike Coast — 195 ft 0 in
3. Danyel Mitchell, unat — 194 ft 9 in

### JAVELIN

1. Donna Mayhew, Nike Coast — 194 ft 1 in
2. Ashley Selman, Asics — 191 ft 4 in
3. Erica Wheeler, Mizuno — 183 ft 9 in

### HEPTATHLON

1. Jackie Joyner-Kersee, Honda — 6375 pts. w
2. Kym Carter, Nike — 6354 pts.†
3. Kelly Blair, Reebok RC — 6354 pts.†

† Second place awarded to Carter on basis of four-to-three advantage in head-to-head competition.

*Meet record. w=wind aided. AR=American Record.

---

**Still Got a Shot**

Margaret White, who lives in the Oklahoma panhandle town of Turpin, would seem to be perfectly comfortable filling her larder with unripe fruit. She's 100 but in such fine fettle that she put the shot during the Sooner State Games in Oklahoma City last January, setting an age group record with a throw of 11' 4" as the only entrant in the 100–104 division.

Her son Wendell Palmer, 62, is a senior circuit athlete too—a shot-putter, discus thrower and sprinter. But, his mother says, "Wendell is getting of an age that I don't think he ought to do it much longer."

# IAAF World Track and Field Championships

## Göteborg, Sweden, August 5–13, 1995

## Men

### 100 METERS

1. ............Donovan Bailey, Canada — 9.97
2. ............Bruny Surin, Canada — 10.03
3. ............Ato Bolden, Trinidad — 10.03

### 200 METERS

1. ............Michael Johnson, United States — 19.79
2. ............Frank Fredericks, Namibia — 20.12
3. ............Jeff Williams, United States — 20.18

### 400 METERS

1. ............Michael Johnson, United States — 43.39*
2. ............Butch Reynolds, United States — 44.22
3. ............Greg Haughton, Jamaica — 44.56

### 800 METERS

1. ............Wilson Kipketer, Denmark — 1:45.08
2. ............Arthémon Hatungimana, Burundi — 1:45.64
3. ............Vebjørn Rodal, Norway — 1:45.68

### 1,500 METERS

1. ............Noureddine Morceli, Algeria — 3:33.73
2. ............Hicham El Guerrouj, Morocco — 3:35.28
3. ............Vénuste Niyongabo, Burundi — 3:35.56

### STEEPLECHASE

1. ............Moses Kiptanui, Kenya — 8:04.16*
2. ............Christopher Koskei, Kenya — 8:09.30
3. ............S. Shaddad Al-Asmari, Saudi Arabia — 8:12.95

### 5,000 METERS

1. ............Ismael Kirui, Kenya — 13:16.77
2. ............Khalid Boulami, Morocco — 13:17.15
3. ............Shem Kororia, Kenya — 13:17.59

### 10,000 METERS

1. ............Haile Gebrselassie, Ethiopia — 27:12.95*
2. ............Khalid Skah, Morocco — 27:14.53
3. ............Paul Tergat, Kenya — 27:14.70

### MARATHON

1. ............Martin Fiz, Spain — 2:11:41
2. ............Dionisio Ceron, Mexico — 2:12:13
3. ............Luis dos Santos, Brazil — 2:12:49

### 110-METER HURDLES

1. ............Allen Johnson, United States — 13.00
2. ............Tony Jarrett, Great Britain — 13.04
3. ............Roger Kingdom, United States — 13.19

### 400-METER HURDLES

1. ............Derrick Adkins, United States — 47.98
2. ............Samuel Matete, Zambia — 48.03
3. ............Stéphane Diagana, France — 48.14

### 20-KILOMETER WALK

1. ............Michele Didoni, Italy — 1:19:59
2. ............Valentí Massana, Spain — 1:20:23
3. ............Yevgeniy Misyulya, Belarus — 1:20:48

*Meet record. †World record

### 50-KILOMETER WALK

1. ............Valentin Kononen, Finland — 3:43:42
2. ............Giovanni Perricelli, Italy — 3:45:11
3. ............Robert Korzeniowski, Poland — 3:45:57

### 4 X 100 METER RELAY

1. ............Canada — 38.31
2. ............Australia — 38.50
3. ............Italy — 39.07

### 4 X 400 METER RELAY

1. ............United States — 2:57.32
2. ............Jamaica — 2:59.88
3. ............Nigeria — 3:03.18

### HIGH JUMP

1. ............Troy Kemp, Bahamas — 7 ft 9¼ in
2. ............Javier Sotomayor, Cuba — 7 ft 9¼ in
3. ............Artur Partyka, Poland — 7 ft 8½ in

### POLE VAULT

1. ............Sergei Bubka, Ukraine — 19 ft 5 in
2. ............Maksim Tarasov, Russia — 19 ft 2¾ in
3. ............Jean Galfione, France — 19 ft 2¾ in

### LONG JUMP

1. ............Ivan Pedroso, Cuba — 28 ft 6½ in
2. ............James Beckford, Jamaica — 27 ft 2¾ in
3. ............Mike Powell, United States — 27 ft 2½ in

### TRIPLE JUMP

1. ............Jonathan Edwards, Gr Britain — 60 ft ¼ in†
2. ............Brian Wellman, Bermuda — 57 ft 9¾ in w
3. ............Jerome Romain, Dominican R — 57 ft 8½ in w

### SHOT PUT

1. ............John Godina, United States — 70 ft 5¼ in
2. ............Mika Halvari, Finland — 68 ft 8 in
3. ............Randy Barnes, United States — 66 ft 11½ in

### DISCUS

1. ............Lars Reidel, Germany — 225 ft 7 in
2. ............Vladimir Dubrovshchik, Belarus — 216 ft 6 in
3. ............Vasiliy Kaptyukh, Belarus — 216 ft 2 in

### HAMMER

1. ............Andrey Abduvaliyev, Tajikistan — 267 ft 7 in
2. ............Igor Astapkovich, Belarus — 266 ft 1 in
3. ............Tibor Gécsek, Hungary — 265 ft 8 in

### JAVELIN

1. ............Jan Zelezny, Czech Republic — 293 ft 11 in
2. ............Steve Backley, Great Britain — 283 ft 2 in
3. ............Boris Henry, Germany — 282 ft 5 in

### DECATHLON

1. ............Dan O'Brien, United States — 8695 pts
2. ............Eduard Hämäläinen, Belarus — 8489 pts
3. ............Mike Smith, Canada — 8419 pts

## Göteborg, Sweden, August 5–13, 1995

### Women

#### 100 METERS

1. ............Gwen Torrence, United States   10.85
2. ............Merlene Ottey, Jamaica   10.94
3. ............Irina Privalova, Russia   10.96

#### 200 METERS

1. ............Merlene Ottey, Jamaica   22.12
2. ............Irina Privalova, Russia   22.12
3. ............Galina Malchugina, Russia   22.37

#### 400 METERS

1. ............Marie-José Pérec, France   49.28
2. ............Pauline Davis, Bahamas   49.96
3. ............Jearl Miles, United States   50.00

#### 800 METERS

1. ............Ana Quirot, Cuba   1:56.11
2. ............Letitia Vriesde, Suriname   1:56.68
3. ............Kelly Holmes, Great Britain   1:56.95

#### 1,500 METERS

1. ............Hassiba Boulmerka, Algeria   4:02.42
2. ............Kelly Holmes, Great Britain   4:03.04
3. ............Carla Sacramento, Portugal   4:03.79

#### 5,000 METERS

1. ............Sonia O'Sullivan, Ireland   14:46.47*
2. ............Fernanda Ribeiro, Portugal   14:48.54
3. ............Zohra Ouaziz, Morocco   14:53.77

#### 10,000 METERS

1. ............Fernanda Ribeiro, Portugal   31:04.99
2. ............Derartu Tulu, Ethiopia   31:08.10
3. ............Tecla Lorupe, Kenya   31:17.66

#### MARATHON††

1. ............Manuela Machado, Portugal   2:25:39
2. ............Anuta Catuna, Romania   2:26:25
3. ............Ornella Ferrara, Italy   2:30:11

#### 100-METER HURDLES

1. ............Gail Devers, United States   12.68
2. ............Olga Shishigina, Kazakstan   12.80
3. ............Yuliya Graudyn, Russia   12.85

#### 400-METER HURDLES

1. ............Kim Batten, United States   52.61†
2. ............Tonja Buford, United States   52.62
3. ............Deon Hemmings, Jamaica   53.48

#### 10-KILOMETER WALK

1. ............Irina Stankina, Russia   42:13*
2. ............Elisabetta Perrone, Italy   42:16
3. ............Yelena Nikolayeva, Russia   42:20

#### 4 X 100 METER RELAY

1. ............United States   42.12
2. ............Jamaica   42.25
3. ............Germany   43.01

#### 4 X 400 METER RELAY

1. ............United States   3:22.39
2. ............Russia   3:23.98
3. ............Australia   3:25.88

#### HIGH JUMP

1. ............Stefka Kostadinova, Bulgaria   6 ft 7 in
2. ............Alina Astafei, Germany   6 ft 6¼ in
3. ............Inga Babakova, Ukraine   6 ft 6¼ in

#### LONG JUMP

1. ............Fiona May, Italy   22 ft 10¾ in w
2. ............Niurka Montalvo, Cuba   22 ft 6¼ in
3. ............Irina Mushailova, Russia   22 ft 5 in w

#### TRIPLE JUMP

1. ............Inessa Kravets, Ukraine   50 ft 10¼ in†
2. ............Iva Prandzheva, Bulgaria   49 ft 9¾ in
3. ............Ana Biryukova, Russia   49 ft 5¾ in

#### SHOT PUT

1. ............Astrid Kumbernuss, Germany   69 ft 7½ in
2. ............Zhihong Huang, China   65 ft 9 in
3. ............Svetla Mitkova, Bulgaria   64 ft 2¼ in

#### DISCUS

1. ............Ellina Zvereva, Belarus   225 ft 2 in
2. ............Ilke Wyludda, Germany   220 ft 6 in
3. ............Olga Chernyavskaya, Russia   219 ft 4 in

#### JAVELIN

1. ............Natalya Shikolenko, Belarus   221 ft 8 in
2. ............Felicia Tilea, Romania   214 ft 0 in
3. ............Mikaela Ingberg, Finland   213 ft 9 in

#### HEPTATHLON

1. ............Ghada Shouaa, Syria   6651 pts
2. ............Svetlana Moskalets, Russia   6575 pts
3. ............Rita Ináncsi, Hungary   6522 pts

*Meet record. **American record. †World record. †† 400 meters short.

## IAAF World Cross-Country Championships

### Durham, England, March 25, 1995

**MEN (12,020 METERS; 7.41 MILES)**

1. .............Paul Tergat, Kenya — 34:05
2. .............Ismael Kirui, Kenya — 34:13
3. .............Salah Hissou, Morocco — 34:14

**WOMEN (6,470 METERS; 4.00 MILES)**

1. .............Derartu Tulu, Ethiopia — 20:21
2. .............Catherina McKiernan, Ireland — 20:29
3. .............Sally Barsosio, Kenya — 20:39

## Major Marathons

### New York City: November 8, 1994

#### MEN

1. .............German Silva, Mexico — 2:11:21
2. .............Benjamin Paredes, Mexico — 2:11:23
3. .............Arturo Barrios, United States — 2:12:21

#### WOMEN

1. .............Tecla Lorupe, Kenya — 2:27:37
2. .............Madina Biktagirova, Belarus — 2:30:00
3. .............Anne Marie Letko, United States — 2:30:19

### Tokyo: November 20, 1994

#### WOMEN ONLY

1. .............Valentina Yegorova, Russia — 2:30:09
2. .............Sachiyo Seiyama, Japan — 2:30:30
3. .............Lisa Ondieki, Australia — 2:31:01

### Fukuoka, Japan: December 4, 1994

#### MEN ONLY

1. .............Boay Akonay, Tanzania — 2:09:45
2. .............Manuel Matias, Portugal — 2:09:50
3. .............Valdenor dos Santos, Brazil — 2:10:15

### Honolulu: December 11, 1994

#### MEN

1. .............Benson Masya, Kenya — 2:15:04
2. .............Thabiso Mogali, Lesotho — 2:16:52
3. .............Andrew Green, England — 2:16:55

#### WOMEN

1. .............Carla Beurskens, Netherlands — 2:37:06
2. .............Eriko Asai, Japan — 2:38:21
3. .............Lisa Weidenbach, United States — 2:42:44

### Los Angeles: March 5, 1995

#### MEN

1. .............Rolando Vera, Ecuador — 2:11:39
2. .............Bob Kempainen, United States — 2:11:59
3. .............Martin Pitayo, Mexico — 2:12:49

#### WOMEN

1. .............Nadia Prasad, France — 2:29:48
2. .............Anna Rybicka, Poland — 2:32:59
3. .............Lyobov Klochko, Ukraine — 2:33:31

### Rotterdam: April 23, 1995

#### MEN

1. .............Martin Fiz, Spain — 2:08:57
2. .............Bert van Vlaanderen, Netherlands — 2:10:36
3. .............Isaac Garcia, Mexico — 2:10:54

#### WOMEN

1. .............Monica Pont, Spain — 2:30:34
2. .............Carmen de Fuentes, Spain — 2:31:20
3. .............Carla Beurskens, Netherlands — 2:32:39

### London: April 2, 1995

#### MEN

1. .............Dionisio Ceron, Mexico — 2:08:30
2. .............Steve Moneghetti, Australia — 2:08:33
3. .............Antonio Pinto, Portugal — 2:08:48

#### WOMEN

1. .............Malgorzata Sobanska, Poland — 2:27:43
2. .............Manuela Machado, Portugal — 2:27:53
3. .............Ritva Lemettinen, Finland — 2:28:00

### Boston: April 17, 1995

#### MEN

1. .............Cosmas N'Deti, Kenya — 2:09:22
2. .............Moses Tanui, Kenya — 2:10:22
3. .............Luis dos Santos, Brazil — 2:11:02

#### WOMEN

1. .............Uta Pippig, Germany — 2:25:11
2. .............Elana Meyer, South Africa — 2:26:51
3. .............Madina Biktagirova, Belarus — 2:29:00

## TRACK AND FIELD

### World Records

As of September 25, 1995. World outdoor records are recognized by the International Amateur Athletics Federation (IAAF).

## Men

| Event | Mark | Record Holder | Date | Site |
|---|---|---|---|---|
| 100 meters | 9.85 | Leroy Burrell, United States | 7-6-94 | Lausanne, Switzerland |
| 200 meters | 19.72 | Pietro Mennea, Italy | 9-12-79 | Mexico City |
| 400 meters | 43.29 | Butch Reynolds, United States | 8-17-88 | Zurich |
| 800 meters | 1:41.73 | Sebastian Coe, Great Britain | 6-10-81 | Florence |
| 1,000 meters | 2:12.18 | Sebastian Coe, Great Britain | 7-11-81 | Oslo |
| 1,500 meters | 3:27.37 | Noureddine Morceli, Algeria | 7-12-95 | Nice, France |
| Mile | 3:44.29 | Noureddine Morceli, Algeria | 9-5-93 | Rieti, Italy |
| 2,000 meters | 4:47.88 | Noureddine Morceli, Algeria | 7-3-95 | Paris |
| 3,000 meters | 7:25.11 | Noureddine Morceli, Algeria | 8-2-94 | Monte Carlo |
| Steeplechase | 7:59.18 | Moses Kiptanui, Kenya | 8-16-95 | Zurich |
| 5,000 meters | 12:44.39 | Haile Gebrselassie, Ethiopia | 8-16-95 | Zurich |
| 10,000 meters | 26:43.53 | Haile Gebrselassie, Ethiopia | 6-5-95 | Oslo |
| 20,000 meters | 56:55.6 | Arturo Barrios, Mexico | 3-30-91 | La Flâche, France |
| Hour | 21,101 meters | Arturo Barrios, Mexico | 3-30-91 | La Flâche, France |
| 25,000 meters | 1:13:55.8 | Toshihiko Seko, Japan | 3-22-81 | Christchurch, New Zealand |
| 30,000 meters | 1:29:18.8 | Toshihiko Seko, Japan | 3-22-81 | Christchurch, New Zealand |
| Marathon | 2:06:50 | Belayneh Densimo, Ethiopia | 4-17-88 | Rotterdam |
| 110-meter hurdles | 12.91 | Colin Jackson, Great Britain | 8-20-93 | Stuttgart, Germany |
| 400-meter hurdles | 46.78 | Kevin Young, United States | 8-6-92 | Barcelona |
| 20 kilometer walk | 1:17:26 | Bernardo Segura, Mexico | 5-7-94 | Softeland, Norway |
| 30 kilometer walk | 2:01:44.1 | Maurizio Damilano, Italy | 10-3-92 | Cuneo, Italy |
| 50 kilometer walk | 3:41:38.4 | Raul Gonzalez, Mexico | 5-25-79 | Bergen, Norway |
| 4x100-meter relay | 37.40 | United States (Mike Marsh, Leroy Burrell, Dennis Mitchell, Carl Lewis) | 8-8-92 | Barcelona |
| | | United States (Jon Drummond, Andre Cason, Dennis Mitchell, Leroy Burrell) | 8-22-93 | Stuttgart, Germany |
| 4x200-meter relay | 1:18.68 | Santa Monica TC (Mike Marsh, Leroy Burrell, Floyd Heard, Carl Lewis) | 4-17-94 | Walnut, CA |
| 4x400-meter relay | 2:54.29 | United States (Andrew Valmon, Quincy Watts, Butch Reynolds, Michael Johnson) | 8-22-93 | Barcelona |
| 4x800-meter relay | 7:03.89 | Great Britain (Peter Elliott, Garry Cook, Steve Cram, Sebastian Coe) | 8-30-82 | London |
| 4x1500-meter relay | 14:38.8 | West Germany (Thomas Wessinghage, Harald Hudak, Michael Lederer, Karl Fleschen) | 8-17-77 | Cologne |
| High jump | 8 ft ½ in | Javier Sotomayor, Cuba | 7-27-93 | Salamanca, Spain |
| Pole vault | 20 ft 1¾ in | Sergei Bubka, Ukraine | 7-31-94 | Sestriere, Italy |
| Long jump | 29 ft 4½ in | Mike Powell, United States | 8-30-91 | Tokyo |
| Triple jump | 60 ft ¼ in | Jonathan Edwards, Great Britain | 8-7-95 | Göteborg, Sweden |
| Shot put | 75 ft 10¼ in | Randy Barnes, United States | 5-20-90 | Westwood, CA |
| Discus throw | 243 ft 0 in | Jürgen Schult, East Germany | 6-6-86 | Neubrandenburg, Germany |
| Hammer throw | 284 ft 7 in | Yuri Syedikh, USSR | 8-30-86 | Stuttgart, Germany |
| Javelin throw | 313 ft 10 in | Jan Zelezny, Czech Republic | 8-29-93 | Sheffield, England |
| Decathlon | 8891 pts | Dan O'Brien, United States | 9-4/5-92 | Talence, France |

Note: The decathlon consists of 10 events—the 100 meters, long jump, shot put, high jump and 400 meters on the first day; the 110-meter hurdles, discus, pole vault, javelin and 1500 meters on the second.

## Women

| Event | Mark | Record Holder | Date | Site |
|---|---|---|---|---|
| 100 meters | 10.49 | Florence Griffith Joyner, United States | 7-16-88 | Indianapolis |
| 200 meters | 21.34 | Florence Griffith Joyner, United States | 9-29-88 | Seoul |
| 400 meters | 47.60 | Marita Koch, East Germany | 10-6-85 | Canberra, Australia |
| 800 meters | 1:53.28 | Jarmila Kratochvílová, Czechoslovakia | 7-26-83 | Munich |
| 1,000 meters | 2:29.34 | Maria Mutola, Mozambique | 8-25-95 | Brussels |
| 1,500 meters | 3:50.46 | Qu Yunxia, China | 9-11-93 | Beijing |
| Mile | 4:15.61 | Paula Ivan, Romania | 7-10-89 | Nice |
| 2,000 meters | 5:25.36 | Sonia O'Sullivan, Ireland | 7-8-94 | Edinburgh |
| 3,000 meters | 8:06.11 | Wang Junxia, China | 9-13-93 | Beijing |
| 5,000 meters | 14:36.45 | Fernanda Ribeiro, Portugal | 7-22-95 | Hechtel, Belgium |
| 10,000 meters | 29:31.78 | Wang Junxia, China | 9-8-93 | Beijing |
| 25,000 meters | 1:29:29.2 | Karolina Szabó, Hungary | 4-22-88 | Budapest |
| 30,000 meters | 1:49:05.6 | Karolina Szabó, Hungary | 4-22-88 | Budapest |
| Marathon | 2:21:06 | Ingrid Kristiansen, Norway | 4-21-85 | London |
| 100-meter hurdles | 12.21 | Yordanka Donkova, Bulgaria | 8-20-88 | Stara Zagora, Bulgaria |
| 400-meter hurdles | 52.61 | Kim Batten, United States | 8-11-95 | Göteborg, Sweden |
| 5-kilometer walk | 20:17.19 | Kerry Junna-Saxby, Australia | 1-14-90 | Sydney, Australia |
| 10-kilometer walk | 41:56.23 | Nadezhda Ryashkina, USSR | 7-24-90 | Seattle |
| 4x100-meter relay | 41.37 | East Germany (Silke Gladisch, Sabine Reiger, Ingrid Auerswald, Marlies Göhr) | 10-6-85 | Canberra, Australia |
| 4x200-meter relay | 1:28.15 | East Germany (Marlies Göhr, Romy Müller, Bärbel Wöckel, Marita Koch) | 8-9-80 | Jena, East Germany |
| 4x400-meter relay | 3:15.17 | USSR (Tatyana Ledovskaya, Olga Nazarova, Maria Pinigina, Olga Bryzgina) | 10-1-88 | Seoul |
| 4x800-meter relay | 7:50.17 | USSR (Nadezhda Olizarenko, Lyubov Gurina, Lyudmila Borisova, Irina Podyalovskaya) | 8-5-84 | Moscow |
| High jump | 6 ft 10¼ in | Stefka Kostadinova, Bulgaria | 8-30-87 | Rome |
| Pole Vault | 13 ft 9¾ in | Daniella Bartova, Czech Republic | 8-22-95 | Linz, Austria |
| Long jump | 24 ft 8¼ in | Galina Chistyakova, USSR | 6-11-88 | Leningrad |
| Triple Jump | 50 ft 10¼ in | Inessa Kravets, Ukraine | 8-10-95 | Göteborg, Sweden |
| Shot put | 74 ft 3 in | Natalya Lisovskaya, USSR | 6-7-87 | Moscow |
| Discus throw | 252 ft 0 in | Gabriele Reinsch, East Germany | 7-9-88 | Neubrandenburg, Germany |
| Hammer throw | 223 ft 7 in | Olga Kuzenkova, Russia | 6-18-95 | Moscow |
| Javelin throw | 262 ft 5 in | Petra Felke, East Germany | 9-9-88 | Berlin |
| Heptathlon | 7291 pts | Jackie Joyner-Kersee, United States | 9-23/24-88 | Seoul |

Note: The heptathlon consists of 7 events—the 100-meter hurdles, high jump, shot put and 200 meters on the first day; the long jump, javelin and 800 meters on the second.

## On Track Betting

Competitively, the U.S. remains the most powerful track and field nation in the world. Yet when it comes to the interest of the American public, the sport is limping like a sprinter with two torn hamstrings. Attendance at meets is down, long-standing events have been canceled, and media coverage is dwindling. In an effort to turn things around, USA Track & Field (USATF), the sport's national governing body, secured sponsorship from Mobil, Nike and Visa for a series of five indoor meets to be held on consecutive weekends this winter and televised by NBC. Having thus taken a stride toward increasing the sport's exposure, USATF promptly long-jumped into the absurd, announcing just before the second event in the series, last February's Reno Air Games, that it had persuaded the Eldorado Race and Sports Book in Reno to take action on the meet.

"We had to introduce new elements to make track more entertaining to the casual fan," said meet director John Mansoor. After consulting with sports-gambling experts in Las Vegas, the folks at the Eldorado set a line on eight of the meet's 16 events. "To protect the meet's integrity," said Mansoor, the USATF required all athletes to sign a statement saying they would not place any bets, even on themselves.

Despite all the hoopla, gambling on the meet was light, though spectators got a couple of payoffs nonetheless. Michael Johnson, a 1-to-5 favorite, set a world indoor record of 44.97 seconds in the 400 meters, and Jackie Joyner-Kersee, who went off at even money, ran 6.67 to break the U.S. indoor mark for the 50-meter hurdles. Those are the sorts of numbers American track should be betting on.

# American Records

As of September 25, 1995. American outdoor records are recognized by USA Track and Field (USATF). WR=world record.

## Men

| Event | Mark | Record Holder | Date | Site |
|---|---|---|---|---|
| 100 meters | 9.85 WR | Leroy Burrell | 7-6-94 | Lausanne |
| 200 meters | 19.73 | Mike Marsh | 8-5-92 | Barcelona |
| 400 meters | 43.29 WR | Butch Reynolds | 8-17-88 | Zurich |
| 800 meters | 1:42.60 | Johnny Gray | 8-28-85 | Koblenz, Germany |
| 1,000 meters | 2:13.9 | Rick Wohlhuter | 7-30-74 | Oslo |
| 1,500 meters | 3:29.77 | Sydney Maree | 8-25-85 | Cologne |
| Mile | 3:47.69 | Steve Scott | 7-7-82 | Oslo |
| 2,000 meters | 4:52.44 | Jim Spivey | 9-15-87 | Lausanne |
| 3,000 meters | 7:35.33 | Bob Kennedy | 7-18-94 | Nice, France |
| Steeplechase | 8:09.17 | Henry Marsh | 8-28-85 | Koblenz, Germany |
| 5,000 meters | 13:01.15 | Sydney Maree | 7-27-85 | Oslo |
| 10,000 meters | 27:20.56 | Mark Nenow | 9-5-86 | Brussels |
| 20,000 meters | 58:25.0 | Bill Rodgers | 8-9-77 | Boston |
| Hour | 20,547 meters | Bill Rodgers | 8-9-77 | Boston |
| 25,000 meters | 1:14:11.8 | Bill Rodgers | 2-21-79 | Saratoga, CA |
| 30,000 meters | 1:31:49 | Bill Rodgers | 2-21-79 | Saratoga, CA |
| Marathon | 2:10:04 | Pat Petersen | 4-23-89 | London |
| 110-meter hurdles | 12.92 | Roger Kingdom | 8-16-89 | Zurich |
| 400-meter hurdles | 46.78 WR | Kevin Young | 8-6-92 | Barcelona |
| 20-kilometer walk | 1:24:50 | Tim Lewis | 5-7-88 | Seattle |
| 30-kilometer walk | 2:21:40 | Herm Nelson | 9-7-91 | Bellevue, WA |
| 50-kilometer walk | 4:04:23.8 | Herm Nelson | 10-29-89 | Seattle |
| 4x100-meter relay | 37.40 WR | United States (Mike Marsh, Leroy Burrell, Dennis Mitchell, Carl Lewis) | 8-8-92 | Barcelona |
| | | United States (Jon Drummond, Andre Cason, Dennis Mitchell, Leroy Burrell) | 8-22-93 | Stuttgart, Germany |
| 4x200-meter relay | 1:18.68 WR | Santa Monica Track Club (Mike Marsh, Leroy Burrell, Floyd Heard, Carl Lewis) | 4-17-94 | Walnut, CA |
| 4x400-meter relay | 2:54.29 WR | United States (Andrew Valmon, Quincy Watts, Butch Reynolds, Michael Johnson) | 8-22-93 | Stuttgart, Germany |
| 4x800-meter relay | 7:06.5 | Santa Monica Track Club (James Robinson, David Mack, Earl Jones, Johnny Gray) | 4-26-86 | Walnut, CA |
| 4x1500-meter relay | 14:46.3 | National Team (Dan Aldredge, Andy Clifford, Todd Harbour, Tom Duits) | 6-24-79 | Bourges, France |
| High jump | 7 ft 10½ in | Charles Austin | 8-15-91 | Zurich |
| Pole vault | 19 ft 7 in | Scott Huffman | 6-18-94 | Knoxville, TN |
| Long jump | 29 ft 4½ in WR | Mike Powell | 8-30-91 | Tokyo |
| Triple jump | 58 ft 11½ in | Willie Banks | 6-16-85 | Indianapolis |
| Shot put | 75 ft 10¼ in WR | Randy Barnes | 5-20-90 | Westwood, CA |
| Discus throw | 237 ft 4 in | Ben Plucknett | 7-7-81 | Stockholm |
| Hammer throw | 270 ft 8 in | Lance Deal | 6-17-94 | Knoxville, TN |
| Javelin throw | 281 ft 2 in | Tom Pukstys | 6-26-93 | Kuortane, Finland |
| Decathlon | 8891 pts WR | Dan O'Brien | 9-4/5-92 | Talence, France |

# American Records (Cont.)

## Women

| Event | Mark | Record Holder | Date | Site |
|---|---|---|---|---|
| 100 meters | 10.49 WR | Florence Griffith Joyner | 7-16-88 | Indianapolis |
| 200 meters | 21.34 WR | Florence Griffith Joyner | 9-29-88 | Seoul |
| 400 meters | 48.83 | Valerie Brisco-Hooks | 8-6-84 | Los Angeles |
| 800 meters | 1:56.90 | Mary Slaney | 8-16-85 | Bern, Switzerland |
| 1,500 meters | 3:57.12 | Mary Slaney | 7-26-83 | Stockholm |
| Mile | 4:16.71 | Mary Slaney | 8-21-85 | Zurich |
| 2,000 meters | 5:32.7 | Mary Slaney | 8-3-84 | Eugene, OR |
| 3,000 meters | 8:25.83 | Mary Slaney | 9-7-85 | Rome |
| 5,000 meters | 14:56.07 | Annette Peters | 8-27-93 | Berlin |
| 10,000 meters | 31:19.89 | Lynn Jennings | 8-7-92 | Barcelona |
| Marathon | 2:21:21 | Joan Samuelson | 10-20-85 | Chicago |
| 100-meter hurdles | 12.46 | Gail Devers | 8-20-93 | Stuttgart, Germany |
| 400-meter hurdles | 52.61 | Kim Batten | 8-11-95 | Göteborg, Sweden |
| 5,000 meter walk | 21:28.17 | Teresa Vaill | 4-24-93 | Philadelphia |
| 10,000 meter walk | 44:41.9 | Michelle Rohl | 7-26-94 | Moscow |
| 10-kilometer walk road | 44:42 | Debbi Lawrence | 5-16-92 | Kenosha, Wisconsin |
| 4x100-meter relay | 41.49 | National Team (Michelle Finn, Gwen Torrence, Wenda Vereen, Gail Devers) | 8-22-93 | Stuttgart, Germany |
| 4x200-meter relay | 1:32.57 | Louisiana State (Tananjalyn Stanley, Sylvia Brydson, Esther Jones, Dawn Sowell) | 4-28-89 | Des Moines |
| 4x400-meter relay | 3:15.51 | Olympic Team (Denean Howard, Diane Dixon, Valerie Brisco, Florence Griffith Joyner) | 10-1-88 | Seoul |
| 4x800-meter relay | 8:17.09 | Athletics West (Sue Addison, Lee Arbogast, Mary Decker, Chris Mullen) | 4-24-83 | Walnut, CA |
| High jump | 6 ft 8 in | Louise Ritter | 7-8-88 | Austin, TX |
|  |  | Louise Ritter | 9-30-88 | Seoul |
| Pole Vault | 13 ft 1¾ in | Melissa Price | 6-24-95 | Walnut, CA |
| Long jump | 24 ft 7 in | Jackie Joyner-Kersee | 5-22-94 | New York City |
|  |  |  | 7-31-94 | Sestriere, Italy |
| Triple jump | 46 ft 9 in | Sheila Hudson | 7-25-95 | Monaco |
| Shot put | 66 ft 2½ in | Ramona Pagel | 6-25-88 | San Diego |
| Discus throw | 216 ft 10 in | Carol Cady | 5-31-86 | San Jose |
| Javelin throw | 227 ft 5 in | Kate Schmidt | 9-10-77 | Fürth, West Germany |
| Heptathlon | 7291 pts WR | Jackie Joyner-Kersee | 9-23/24-88 | Seoul |

# World and American Indoor Records

## Men

As of September 25, 1995. American indoor records are recognized by USA Track and Field. World Indoor records are recognized by the International Amateur Athletics Federation (IAAF).

| Event | Mark | Record Holder | Date | Site |
|---|---|---|---|---|
| 50 meters | 5.61 | Manfred Kokot, East Germany (W) | 2-4-73 | Berlin |
|  | 5.61 | James Sanford (W, A) | 2-20-81 | San Diego |
| 55 meters* | 6.00 | Lee McRae (A) | 3-14-86 | Oklahoma City |
| 60 meters | 6.41 | Andre Cason (W, A) | 2-14-92 | Madrid |
| 200 meters | 20.25 | Linford Christie, Great Britain (W) | 2-19-95 | Liévin, France |
|  | 20.55 | Michael Johnson (A) | 1-26-91 | Liévin, France |
| 400 meters | 44.63 | Michael Johnson (W, A) | 3-4-95 | Atlanta |
| 800 meters | 1:44.84 | Paul Ereng, Kenya (W) | 3-4-89 | Budapest |
|  | 1:45.00 | Johnny Gray (A) | 3-8-92 | Sindelfingen, Germany |
| 1,000 meters | 2:15.26 | Noureddine Morceli, Algeria (W) | 2-22-92 | Birmingham, England |
|  | 2:18.19 | Ocky Clark (A) | 2-12-89 | Stuttgart |
| 1,500 meters | 3:34.16 | Noureddine Morceli, Algeria (W) | 2-28-91 | Seville |
|  | 3:38.12 | Jeff Atkinson (A) | 3-5-89 | Budapest |
| Mile | 3:49.78 | Eamonn Coughlan, Ireland (W) | 2-27-83 | East Rutherford, NJ |
|  | 3:51.8 | Steve Scott (A) | 2-20-81 | San Diego |

## Men *(Cont.)*

| Event | Mark | Record Holder | Date | Site |
|---|---|---|---|---|
| 3,000 meters | 7:35.15 | Moses Kiptanui, Kenya (W) | 2-12-95 | Ghent, Belgium |
| | 7:39.94 | Steve Scott (A) | 2-10-89 | East Rutherford, NJ |
| 5,000 meters | 13:20.4 | Suleiman Nyambui, Tanzania (W) | 2-6-81 | New York City |
| | 13:20.55 | Doug Padilla (A) | 2-12-82 | Rosemont, Illinois |
| 50-meter hurdles | 6.25 | Mark McKoy, Canada (W) | 3-3-86 | Kobe, Japan |
| | 6.35 | Greg Foster (A) | 1-27-85 | Rosemont, Illinois |
| | 6.35 | Greg Foster (A) | 1-31-87 | Ottawa, Ontario |
| 55-meter hurdles* | 6.82 | Renaldo Nehemiah (A) | 1-30-82 | Dallas |
| 60-meter hurdles | 7.30 | Colin Jackson, Great Britain (W) | 3-6-94 | Sindelfingen, Germany |
| | 7.36 | Greg Foster (A) | 1-16-87 | Los Angeles |
| 5,000-meter walk | 18:07.08 | Mikhail Shchennikov, Russia | 2-14-95 | Moscow |
| 4x200-meter relay | 1:22.11 | Great Britain (W) (Linford Christie, Darren Braithwaite, Ade Mafe, John Regis) | 3-3-91 | Glasgow |
| | 1:22.71 | National Team (Thomas Jefferson, Raymond Pierre, Antonio McKay Kevin Little) | 3-3-91 | Glasgow |
| 4x400-meter relay | 3:03.05 | Germany (W) (Rico Lieder, Jens Carlowitz, Klaus Just, Thomas Schönlebe) | 3-10-91 | Seville |
| | 3:03.24 | National Team (A) (Raymond Pierre, Chip Jenkins, Andrew Valmon, Antonio McKay) | 3-10-91 | Seville |
| 4x800-meter relay | 7:17.8 | Soviet Union (W) (Valeriy Taratynov, Stanislav Meshcherskikh, Aleksey Taranov, Viktor Semyashkin) | 3-14-71 | Sofia |
| | 7:18.23 | University of Florida (A) (Dedric Jones, Lewis Lacy, Stephen Adderly, Scott Peters) | 3-14-92 | Sindelfingen, Germany |
| High jump | 7 ft 11½ in | Javier Sotomayor, Cuba (W) | 3-4-89 | Budapest |
| | 7 ft 10½ in | Hollis Conway (A) | 3-10-91 | Seville |
| Pole vault | 20 ft 2 in | Sergei Bubka, Ukraine (W) | 2-21-93 | Donetsk, Ukraine |
| | 19 ft 3¾ in | Billy Olsen (A) | 1-25-86 | Albuquerque |
| Long jump | 28 ft 10¼ in | Carl Lewis (W, A) | 1-27-84 | New York City |
| Triple jump | 58 ft 3¾ in | Leonid Voloshin (W) | 2-6-94 | Grenoble, France |
| Shot put | 74 ft 4¼ in | Randy Barnes (W, A) | 1-20-89 | Los Angeles |
| Weight Throw | 84 ft 10¼ in | Lance Deal (W, A) | 3-4-95 | Atlanta |
| Pentathlon | 4478 pts | Steve Fritz, United States (W, A) | 1-14-95 | Lawrence, KS |
| Heptathlon | 6476 pts | Dan O'Brien (W, A) | 3-13/14-93 | Toronto |

*No recognized world record

### The Long Race

In 1990 Art Pease, who had been competing in the Special Olympics for three years, decided to enter a five-mile race being run in conjunction with the Portland Marathon. In the confusion at the starting line, however, Pease inadvertently took off with the runners who were competing in the full 26-mile, 385-yarder. It was about an hour later when Pease realized that "it sure seemed like a long race."

Then again, life has always been a long race for Pease, 27, who is mentally retarded. He was born into an abusive household, misdiagnosed as autistic and shuffled through a foster-care system. Things turned around in 1975 when he was taken in by Charles and Virginia Pease of Milton-Freewater, a rural community in northeast Oregon, and adopted by them five years later. Charles is a retired junior high school coach, and his and Virginia's other four sons and their daughter were all active in athletics. Art, too, was expected to be active, so he began running. "I was always pretty good at it," he says. Good enough to earn a varsity letter as a 3,000-meter runner in his hometown. Good enough to run a personal-best of three hours and 14 minutes in a 1993 marathon. Good enough to be named America's Special Olympics Male Athlete of the Year in 1994.

Last July, Pease and 36 other runners ran the streets of New Haven, Conn., in the first full marathon held at the International Special Olympics. As the Special Olympics movement keeps growing—more than 7,000 athletes from 145 countries and every state in the union competed in New Haven—the barriers for mentally challenged athletes keep falling. Nothing demonstrates this as dramatically as the addition of a grueling event like the marathon.

At several points in that 1990 Portland Marathon, officials kept asking Pease if he wanted to pull out. They were concerned since he had set off on the wrong course. It was exactly the right one. "I've finished all 11 marathons I've been in," says Pease. "Once I start, I'm not going to stop."

## Women

| Event | Mark | Record Holder | Date | Site |
|---|---|---|---|---|
| 50 meters | 5.96 | Irina Privolova, Russia (W) | 2-9-95 | Madrid |
| | 6.10 | Gail Devers (A) | 2-20-93 | Los Angeles |
| 55 meters* | 6.56 | Gwen Torrence (A) | 3-14-87 | Oklahoma City |
| 60 meters | 6.92 | Irina Privalova, Russia (W) | 2-11-93 | Madrid |
| | 6.92 | Irina Privalova, Russia (W) | 2-9-95 | Madrid |
| | 6.95 | Gail Devers (A) | 3-12-93 | Toronto |
| 200 meters | 21.87 | Merlene Ottey, Jamaica (W) | 2-13-93 | Liévin, France |
| | 22.73 | Carlette Guidry (A) | 3-4-95 | Atlanta |
| 400 meters | 49.59 | Jarmila Kratochvilová, Czech. | 3-7-82 | Milan |
| | 50.64 | Diane Dixon (A) | 3-10-91 | Seville |
| 800 meters | 1:56.40 | Christine Wachtel, E Germany (W) | 2-14-88 | Vienna |
| | 1:58.9 | Mary Slaney (A) | 2-22-80 | San Diego |
| 1,000 meters | 2:34.41 | Lyubov Kremlyova, Russia (W) | 2-15-95 | Erfurt, Germany |
| | 2:37.60 | Mary Slaney (A) | 1-21-89 | Portland |
| 1,500 meters | 4:00.27 | Doina Melinte, Romania (W) | 2-9-90 | East Rutherford, NJ |
| | 4:00.80 | Mary Slaney (A) | 2-8-80 | New York City |
| Mile | 4:17.14 | Doina Melinte, Romania (W) | 2-9-90 | East Rutherford, NJ |
| | 4:20.5 | Mary Slaney (A) | 2-19-82 | San Diego |
| 3,000 meters | 8:33.82 | Elly van Hulst, Netherlands (W) | 3-4-89 | Budapest |
| | 8:40.45 | Lynn Jennings (A) | 2-23-90 | New York City |
| 5,000 meters | 15:03.17 | Liz McColgan, Scotland (W) | 2-22-92 | Birmingham, England |
| | 15:22.64 | Lynn Jennings (A) | 1-7-90 | Hanover, NH |
| 50-meter hurdles | 6.58 | Cornelia Oschkenat, E Germany (W) | 2-20-88 | Berlin |
| | 6.67 | Jackie Joyner-Kersee (A) | 2-10-95 | Reno, NV |
| 55-meter hurdles* | 7.37 | Jackie Joyner-Kersee (A) | 2-3-89 | New York City |
| 60-meter hurdles | 7.69 | Lyudmila Narozhilenko, Russia (W) | 2-4-90 | Chelyabinsk, Russia |
| | 7.81 | Jackie Joyner-Kersee (A) | 2-5-89 | Fairfax, VA |
| 3,000 meter walk | 11:44.00 | Yelena Ivanova, CIS (W) | 2-7-92 | Moscow |
| | 12:20.42 | Debbi Lawrence (A) | 3-12-93 | Toronto |
| 4x200-meter relay | 1:32.55 | SC Eintracht Hamm, W Gemany (W) (Helga Arendt, Silke-Beate Knoll, Mechthild Kluth, Gisela Kinzel) | 2-20-88 | Dortmund, W Germany |
| | 1:33.24 | National Team (A) (Flirtisha Harris, Chryste Gaines, Terri Dendy, Michele Collins) | 2-12-94 | Glasgow |
| 4x400-meter relay | 3:27.22 | Germany (W) (Sandra Seuser, Annett Hesselbarth, Katrin Schreiter, Grit Breuer) | 3-10-91 | Seville |
| | 3:29.00 | National Team (A) (Terri Dendy, Lillie Leatherwood, Jearl Miles, Diane Dixon) | 3-10-91 | Seville |
| 4x800-meter relay | 8:18.71 | Russia (Natalya Zaytseva, Olga Kuvnetsova, Yelena Afanasyeva, Yekaterina Podkopayeva) | 2-4-94 | Moscow |
| High jump | 6 ft 9½ in | Heike Henkel, Germany (W) | 2-8-92 | Karlsruhe, Germany |
| | 6 ft 6¾ in | Coleen Sommer (A) | 2-13-82 | Ottawa |
| Long jump | 24 ft 2¼ in | Heike Drechsler, E Germany (W) | 2-13-88 | Vienna |
| | 23 ft 4¾ in | Jackie Joyner-Kersee (A) | 3-5-94 | Atlanta |
| Triple jump | 49 ft 3¾ in | Yolanda Chen, Russia (W) | 3-11-95 | Barcelona |
| | 46 ft 8¼ in | Sheila Hudson-Strudwick (A) | 3-4-95 | Atlanta |
| Shot put | 73 ft 10 in | Helena Fibingerová, Czech. (W) | 2-19-77 | Jablonec, Czech. |
| | 65 ft ¾ in | Ramona Pagel (A) | 2-20-87 | Inglewood, California |
| Weight Throw* | 62 ft 10 in | Sonja Fitts (unatt) | 2-28-92 | Princeton, N.J. |
| Pentathlon | 4991 pts | Irina Byelova, CIS (W) | 2-14/15-92 | Berlin |
| | 4632 pts | Kym Carter (A) | 3-10-95 | Barcelona |

*No recognized world record

# World Track and Field Championships

Historically, the Olympics have served as the outdoor world championships for track and field. In 1983 the International Amateur Athletic Federation (IAAF) instituted a separate World Championship meet, to be held every 4 years between the Olympics. The first was held in Helsinki in 1983, the second in Rome in 1987, the third in Tokyo in 1991, the fourth in Stuttgart, Germany, in 1993 and the fifth in Göteborg, Sweden in 1995. In 1993 the IAAF began to hold the meet on a biennial basis.

## Men

### 100 METERS

| | | |
|---|---|---|
| 1983 | Carl Lewis, United States | 10.07 |
| 1987* | Carl Lewis, United States | 9.93 WR |
| 1991 | Carl Lewis, United States | 9.86 WR |
| 1993 | Linford Christie, Great Britain | 9.87 |
| 1995 | Donovan Bailey, Canada | 9.97 |

### 200 METERS

| | | |
|---|---|---|
| 1983 | Calvin Smith, United States | 20.14 |
| 1987 | Calvin Smith United States | 20.16 |
| 1991 | Michael Johnson, United States | 20.01 |
| 1993 | Frank Fredericks, Namibia | 19.85 |
| 1995 | Michael Johnson, United States | 19.79 |

### 400 METERS

| | | |
|---|---|---|
| 1983 | Bert Cameron, Jamaica | 45.05 |
| 1987 | Thomas Schoenlebe, E Germany | 44.33 |
| 1991 | Antonio Pettigrew, United States | 44.57 |
| 1993 | Michael Johnson, United States | 43.65 |
| 1995 | Michael Johnson, United States | 43.39 |

### 800 METERS

| | | |
|---|---|---|
| 1983 | Willi Wulbeck, W Germany | 1:43.65 |
| 1987 | Billy Konchellah, Kenya | 1:43.06 |
| 1991 | Billy Konchellah, Kenya | 1:43.99 |
| 1993 | Paul Ruto, Kenya | 1:44.71 |
| 1995 | Wilson Kipketer, Denmark | 1:45.08 |

### 1500 METERS

| | | |
|---|---|---|
| 1983 | Steve Cram, Great Britain | 3:41.59 |
| 1987 | Abdi Bile, Somalia | 3:36.80 |
| 1991 | Noureddine Morceli, Algeria | 3:32.84 |
| 1993 | Noureddine Morceli, Algeria | 3:34.24 |
| 1995 | Noureddine Morceli, Algeria | 3:33.73 |

### STEEPLECHASE

| | | |
|---|---|---|
| 1983 | Patriz Ilg, W Germany | 8:15.06 |
| 1987 | Francesco Panetta, Italy | 8:08.57 |
| 1991 | Moses Kiptanui, Kenya | 8:12.59 |
| 1993 | Moses Kiptanui, Kenya | 8:06.36 |
| 1995 | Moses Kiptanui, Kenya | 8:04.16 |

### 5000 METERS

| | | |
|---|---|---|
| 1983 | Eamonn Coghlan, Ireland | 13:28.53 |
| 1987 | Said Aouita, Morocco | 13:26.44 |
| 1991 | Yobes Ondieki, Kenya | 13:14.45 |
| 1993 | Ismael Kirui, Kenya | 13:02.75 |
| 1995 | Ismael Kirui, Kenya | 13:16.77 |

### 10,000 METERS

| | | |
|---|---|---|
| 1983 | Alberto Cova, Italy | 28:01.04 |
| 1987 | Paul Kipkoech, Kenya | 27:38.63 |
| 1991 | Moses Tanui, Kenya | 27:38.74 |
| 1993 | Haile Gebrselassie, Ethiopia | 27:46.02 |
| 1995 | Haile Gebrselassie, Ethiopia | 27:12.95 |

### MARATHON

| | | |
|---|---|---|
| 1983 | Rob de Castella, Australia | 2:10:03 |
| 1987 | Douglas Wakiihuri, Kenya | 2:11:48 |
| 1991 | Hiromi Taniguchi, Japan | 2:14:57 |
| 1993 | Mark Plaatjes, United States | 2:13:57 |
| 1995 | Martin Fiz, Spain | 2:11:41 |

### 110-METER HURDLES

| | | |
|---|---|---|
| 1983 | Greg Foster, United States | 13.42 |
| 1987 | Greg Foster, United States | 13.21 |
| 1991 | Greg Foster, United States | 13.06 |
| 1993 | Colin Jackson, Great Britain | 12.91 WR |
| 1995 | Allen Johnson, United States | 13.00 |

### 400-METER HURDLES

| | | |
|---|---|---|
| 1983 | Edwin Moses, United States | 47.50 |
| 1987 | Edwin Moses, United States | 47.46 |
| 1991 | Samuel Matete, Zambia | 47.64 |
| 1993 | Kevin Young, United States | 47.18 |
| 1995 | Derrick Adkins, United States | 47.98 |

### 20-KILOMETER WALK

| | | |
|---|---|---|
| 1983 | Ernesto Canto, Mexico | 1:20:49 |
| 1987 | Maurizio Damilano, Italy | 1:20:45 |
| 1991 | Maurizio Damilano, Italy | 1:19:37 |
| 1993 | Valentin Massana, Spain | 1:22:31 |
| 1995 | Michele Didoni, Italy | 1:19:59 |

### 50-KILOMETER WALK

| | | |
|---|---|---|
| 1983 | Ronald Weigel, E Germany | 3:43:08 |
| 1987 | Hartwig Gauder, E Germany | 3:40:53 |
| 1991 | Aleksandr Potashov, USSR | 3:53:09 |
| 1993 | Jesus Angel Garcia, Spain | 3:41:41 |
| 1995 | Valentin Kononen, Finland | 3:43:42 |

### 4 X 100 METER RELAY

| | | |
|---|---|---|
| 1983 | United States (Emmit King, Willie Gault, Calvin Smith, Carl Lewis) | 37.86 |
| 1987 | United States (Lee McRae, Lee McNeil, Harvey Glance, Carl Lewis) | 37.90 |
| 1991 | United States (Andre Cason Leroy Burrell, Dennis Mitchell, Carl Lewis) | 37.50 WR |
| 1993 | United States (Jon Drummond, Andre Cason, Dennis Mitchell, Leroy Burrell) | 37.48 |
| 1995 | Canada (Robert Esmie, Glenroy Gilbert, Bruny Surin, Donovan Bailey) | 38.31 |

WR=World record.

*Ben Johnson, Canada, disqualified

## Men *(Cont.)*

### 4 X 400 METER RELAY

| | | |
|---|---|---|
| 1983 | USSR (Sergei Lovachev, Alecksandr Troschilo, Nikolay Chernyetski, Viktor Markin) | 3:00.79 |
| 1987 | United States (Danny Everett Rod Haley, Antonio McKay, Butch Reynolds) | 2:57.29 |
| 1991 | Great Britain (Roger Black Derek Redmond, John Regis, Kriss Akabusi) | 2:57.53 |
| 1993 | United States (Andrew Valmon, Quincy Watts, Butch Reynolds, Michael Johnson) | 2:54.29 WR |
| 1995 | United States (Marlon Ramsey, Derek Mills, Butch Reynolds, Michael Johnson) | 2:57.32 |

### HIGH JUMP

| | | |
|---|---|---|
| 1983 | Gennadi Avdeyenko, USSR | 7 ft 7¼ in |
| 1987 | Patrik Sjoberg, Sweden | 7 ft 9¾ in |
| 1991 | Charles Austin, United States | 7 ft 9¾ in |
| 1993 | Javier Sotomayor, Cuba | 7 ft 10½ in |
| 1995 | Troy Kemp, Bahamas | 7 ft 9¼ in |

### POLE VAULT

| | | |
|---|---|---|
| 1983 | Sergei Bubka, USSR | 18 ft 8¼ in |
| 1987 | Sergei Bubka, USSR | 19 ft 2¼ in |
| 1991 | Sergei Bubka, USSR | 19 ft 6¼ in |
| 1993 | Sergei Bubka, Ukraine | 19 ft 8¼ in |
| 1995 | Sergei Bubka, Ukraine | 19 ft 5 in |

### LONG JUMP

| | | |
|---|---|---|
| 1983 | Carl Lewis, United States | 28 ft ¾ in |
| 1987 | Carl Lewis, United States | 28 ft 5¼ in |
| 1991 | Mike Powell, U.S. | 29 ft 4½ in WR |
| 1993 | Mike Powell, United States | 28 ft 2¼ in |
| 1995 | Ivan Pedroso, Cuba | 28 ft 6½ in |

### TRIPLE JUMP

| | | |
|---|---|---|
| 1983 | Zdzislaw Hoffmann, Poland | 57 ft 2 in |
| 1987 | Khristo Markov, Bulgaria | 58 ft 9 ½ in |
| 1991 | Kenny Harrison, United States | 58 ft 4 in |
| 1993 | Mike Conley, United States | 58 ft 7¼ in |
| 1995 | Jonathan Edwards, G.B. | 60 ft ¼ in WR |

### SHOT PUT

| | | |
|---|---|---|
| 1983 | Edward Sarul, Poland | 70 ft 2¼ in |
| 1987 | Werner Günthör, Switzerland | 72 ft 11¼ in |
| 1991 | Werner Günthör, Switzerland | 71 ft 1¼ in |
| 1993 | Werner Günthör, Switzerland | 72 ft 1 in |
| 1995 | John Godina, United States | 70 ft 5¼ in |

### DISCUS THROW

| | | |
|---|---|---|
| 1983 | Imrich Bugar, Czech. | 222 ft 2 in |
| 1987 | Juergen Schult, E Germany | 225 ft 6 in |
| 1991 | Lars Riedel, Germany | 217 ft 2 in |
| 1993 | Lars Riedel, Germany | 222 ft 2 in |
| 1995 | Lars Riedel, Germany | 225 ft 7 in |

### HAMMER THROW

| | | |
|---|---|---|
| 1983 | Sergei Litvinov, USSR | 271 ft 3 in |
| 1987 | Sergei Litvinov, USSR | 272 ft 6 in |
| 1991 | Yuriy Sedykh, USSR | 268 ft |
| 1993 | Andrey Abduvaliyev, Tajikistan | 267 ft 10 in |
| 1995 | Andrey Abduvaliyev, Tajikistan | 267 ft 7 in |

### JAVELIN THROW

| | | |
|---|---|---|
| 1983 | Detlef Michel, E Germany | 293 ft 7 in |
| 1987 | Seppo Räty, Finland | 274 ft 1 in |
| 1991 | Kimmo Kinnunen, Finland | 297 ft 11 in |
| 1993 | Jan Zelezny, Czech Republic | 282 ft 1 in |
| 1995 | Jan Zelezny, Czech Republic | 293 ft 11 in |

### DECATHLON

| | | |
|---|---|---|
| 1983 | Daley Thompson, G Britain | 8666 pts |
| 1987 | Torsten Voss, E Germany | 8680 pts |
| 1991 | Dan O'Brien, United States | 8812 pts |
| 1993 | Dan O'Brien, United States | 8817 pts |
| 1995 | Dan O'Brien, United States | 8695 pts |

## Women

### 100 METERS

| | | |
|---|---|---|
| 1983 | Marlies Gohr, E Germany | 10.97 |
| 1987 | Silke Gladisch, E Germany | 10.90 |
| 1991 | Katrin Krabbe, Germany | 10.99 |
| 1993 | Gail Devers, United States | 10.82 |
| 1995 | Gwen Torrence, United States | 10.85 |

### 200 METERS

| | | |
|---|---|---|
| 1983 | Marita Koch, E Germany | 22.13 |
| 1987 | Silke Gladisch, E Germany | 21.74 |
| 1991 | Katrin Krabbe, Germany | 22.09 |
| 1993 | Merlene Ottey, Jamaica | 21.98 |
| 1995 | Merlene Ottey, Jamaica | 22.12 |

### 400 METERS

| | | |
|---|---|---|
| 1983 | Jarmila Kratochvilova, Czech | 47.99 |
| 1987 | Olga Bryzgina, USSR | 49.38 |
| 1991 | Marie-José Pérec, France | 49.13 |
| 1993 | Jearl Miles, United States | 49.82 |
| 1995 | Marie-José Pérec, France | 49.28 |

### 800 METERS

| | | |
|---|---|---|
| 1983 | Jarmila Kratochvilova, Czech | 1:54.68 |
| 1987 | Sigrun Wodars, E Germany | 1:55.26 |
| 1991 | Lilia Nurutdinova, USSR | 1:57.50 |
| 1993 | Maria Mutola, Mozambique | 1:55.43 |
| 1995 | Ana Quirot, Cuba | 1:56.11 |

### 1500 METERS

| | | |
|---|---|---|
| 1983 | Mary Slaney, United States | 4:00.90 |
| 1987 | Tatyana Samolenko, USSR | 3:58.56 |
| 1991 | Hassiba Boulmerka, Algeria | 4:02.21 |
| 1993 | Dong Liu, China | 4:00.50 |
| 1995 | Hassiba Boulmerka, Algeria | 4:02.42 |

### 3000 METERS*

| | | |
|---|---|---|
| 1983 | Mary Slaney, United States | 8:34.62 |
| 1987 | Tatyana Samolenko, USSR | 8:38.73 |
| 1991 | Tatyana Dorovskikh, USSR | 8:35.82 |
| 1993 | Qu Yunxia, China | 8:28.71 |
| 1995 | Sonia O'Sullivan, Ireland | 14:46.47 |

WR=World record. * contested at 5,000 meters in 1995.

## Women (Cont.)

### 10,000 METERS

| | | |
|---|---|---|
| 1987 | Ingrid Kristiansen, Norway | 31:05.85 |
| 1991 | Liz McColgan, Great Britain | 31:14.31 |
| 1993 | Wang Junxia, China | 30:49:30 |
| 1995 | Fernanda Ribeiro, Portugal | 31:04.99 |

### MARATHON

| | | |
|---|---|---|
| 1983 | Grete Waitz, Norway | 2:28:09 |
| 1987 | Rosa Mota, Portugal | 2:25:17 |
| 1991 | Wanda Panfil, Poland | 2:29:53 |
| 1993 | Junko Asari, Japan | 2:30:03 |
| 1995 | Manuela Machado, Portugal | 2:25:39* |

### 100-METER HURDLES

| | | |
|---|---|---|
| 1983 | Bettine Jahn, E Germany | 12.35 |
| 1987 | Ginka Zagorcheva, Bulgaria | 12.34 |
| 1991 | Lyudmila Narozhilenko, USSR | 12.59 |
| 1993 | Gail Devers, United States | 12.46 |
| 1995 | Gail Devers, United States | 12.68 |

### 400-METER HURDLES

| | | |
|---|---|---|
| 1983 | Yekaterina Fesenko, USSR | 54.14 |
| 1987 | Sabine Busch, E Germany | 53.62 |
| 1991 | Tatyana Ledovskaya, USSR | 53.11 |
| 1993 | Sally Gunnell, Great Britain | 52.74 WR |
| 1995 | Kim Batten, United States | 52.61 |

### 10-KILOMETER WALK

| | | |
|---|---|---|
| 1987 | Irina Strakhova, USSR | 44:12 |
| 1991 | Alina Ivanova, USSR | 42:57 |
| 1993 | Sari Essayah, Finland | 42:59 |
| 1995 | Irina Stankina, Russia | 42:13 |

### 4 X 100 METER RELAY

| | | |
|---|---|---|
| 1983 | East Germany (Silke Gladisch, Marita Koch, Ingrid Auerswald, Marlies Gohr) | 41.76 |
| 1987 | United States (Alice Brown, Diane Williams, Florence Griffith, Pam Marshall) | 41.58 |
| 1991 | Jamaica (Dalia Duhaney, Juliet Cuthbert, Beverley McDonald, Merlene Ottey) | 41.94 |
| 1993 | Russia (Olga Bogoslovskaya, Galina Malchugina, Natalya Voronova, Irina Privalova) | 41.49 |
| 1995 | United States (Celena Mondie-Milner, Carlette Guidry, Chryste Gaines, Gwen Torrence) | 42.12 |

### 4 X 400 METER RELAY

| | | |
|---|---|---|
| 1983 | East Germany (Kerstin Walther, Sabine Busch, Marita Koch, Dagmar Rubsam) | 3:19.73 |
| 1987 | E Germany (Dagmar Neubauer, Kirsten Emmelmann, Petra Müller, Sabine Busch) | 3:18.63 |

### 4 X 400 METER RELAY (Cont.)

| | | |
|---|---|---|
| 1991 | USSR (Tatyana Ledovskaya, Lyudmila Dzhigalova, Olga Nazarova, Olga Bryzgina) | 3:18.43 |
| 1993 | United States (Gwen Torrence, Maicel Malone, Natasha Kaiser-Brown, Jearl Miles) | 3:16.71 |
| 1995 | United States (Kim Graham, Rochelle Stevens, Camara Jones, Jearl Miles) | 3:22.39 |

### HIGH JUMP

| | | |
|---|---|---|
| 1983 | Tamara Bykova, USSR | 6 ft 7 in |
| 1987 | Stefka Kostadinova, Bulgaria | 6 ft 10¼ in |
| 1991 | Heike Henkel, Germany | 6 ft 8¾ in |
| 1993 | Ioamnet Quintero, Cuba | 6 ft 6¼ in |
| 1995 | Stefka Kostadinova, Bulgaria | 6 ft 7 in |

### LONG JUMP

| | | |
|---|---|---|
| 1983 | Heike Daute, E Germany | 23 ft 10¼ in |
| 1987 | Jackie Joyner-Kersee, U.S. | 24 ft 1¾ in |
| 1991 | Jackie Joyner-Kersee, U.S. | 24 ft ¼ in |
| 1993 | Heike Drechsler, Germany | 23 ft 4 in |
| 1995 | Fiona May, Italy | 22 ft 10¾ in w |

### TRIPLE JUMP

| | | |
|---|---|---|
| 1993 | Ana Biryukova, Russia | 49 ft 6 ¼ in WR |
| 1995 | Inessa Kravets, Ukraine | 50 ft 10¼ in WR |

### SHOT PUT

| | | |
|---|---|---|
| 1983 | Helena Fibingerova, Czech. | 69 ft ¾ in |
| 1987 | Natalya Lisovskaya, USSR | 69 ft 8¼ in |
| 1991 | Zhihong Huang, China | 68 ft 4¼ in |
| 1993 | Zhihong Huang, China | 67 ft 6 in |
| 1995 | Astrid Kumbernuss, Germany | 69 ft 7½ in |

### DISCUS THROW

| | | |
|---|---|---|
| 1983 | Martina Opitz, E Germany | 226 ft 2 in |
| 1987 | Martina Hellmann, E Germany | 235 ft |
| 1991 | Tsvetanka Khristova, Bulgaria | 233 ft |
| 1993 | Olga Burova, Russia | 221 ft 1 in |
| 1995 | Ellina Zvereva, Belarus | 225 ft 2 in |

### JAVELIN THROW

| | | |
|---|---|---|
| 1983 | Tiina Lillak, Finland | 232 ft 4 in |
| 1987 | Fatima Whitbread, G Britain | 251 ft 5 in |
| 1991 | Demei Xu, China | 225 ft 8 in |
| 1993 | Trine Hattestad, Finland | 227 ft |
| 1995 | Natalya Shikolenko, Belarus | 221 ft 8 in |

### HEPTATHLON

| | | |
|---|---|---|
| 1983 | Ramona Neubert, E Germany | 6714 pts |
| 1987 | Jackie Joyner-Kersee, U.S. | 7128 pts |
| 1991 | Sabine Braun, Germany | 6672 pts |
| 1993 | Jackie Joyner-Kersee, U.S. | 6837 pts |
| 1995 | Ghada Shouaa, Syria | 6651 pts |

WR=World record. *400 meters short

# Track & Field News Athlete of the Year

Each year (since 1959 for men and since 1974 for women) Track & Field News has chosen the outstanding athlete in the sport.

## Men

| Year | Athlete | Event |
|------|---------|-------|
| 1959 | Martin Lauer, West Germany | 110-meter hurdles/Decathlon |
| 1960 | Rafer Johnson, United States | Decathlon |
| 1961 | Ralph Boston, United States | Long jump |
| 1962 | Peter Snell, New Zealand | 800/1500 meters |
| 1963 | C. K. Yang, Taiwan | Decathlon/Pole vault |
| 1964 | Peter Snell, New Zealand | 800/1500 meters |
| 1965 | Ron Clarke, Australia | 5,000/10,000 meters |
| 1966 | Jim Ryun, United States | 800/1500 meters |
| 1967 | Jim Ryun, United States | 1500 meters |
| 1968 | Bob Beamon, United States | Long jump |
| 1969 | Bill Toomey, United States | Decathlon |
| 1970 | Randy Matson, United States | Shot put |
| 1971 | Rod Milburn, United States | 110-meter hurdles |
| 1972 | Lasse Viren, Finland | 5,000/10,000 meters |
| 1973 | Ben Jipcho, Kenya | 1500/5000 meters/Steeplechase |
| 1974 | Rick Wohlhuter, United States | 800/1500 meters |
| 1975 | John Walker, New Zealand | 800/1500 meters |
| 1976 | Alberto Juantorena, Cuba | 400/800 meters |
| 1977 | Alberto Juantorena, Cuba | 400/800 meters |
| 1978 | Henry Rono, Kenya | 5,000/10,000 meters/Steeplechase |
| 1979 | Sebastian Coe, Great Britain | 800/1500 meters |
| 1980 | Edwin Moses, United States | 400-meter hurdles |
| 1981 | Sebastian Coe, Great Britain | 800/1500 meters |
| 1982 | Carl Lewis, United States | 100/200 meters/Long jump |
| 1983 | Carl Lewis, United States | 100/200 meters/Long jump |
| 1984 | Carl Lewis, United States | 100/200 meters/Long jump |
| 1985 | Said Aouita, Morocco | 1500/5000 meters |
| 1986 | Yuri Syedikh, USSR | Hammer throw |
| 1987 | Ben Johnson, Canada | 100 meters |
| 1988 | Sergei Bubka, USSR | Pole vault |
| 1989 | Roger Kingdom, United States | 110-meter hurdles |
| 1990 | Michael Johnson, United States | 200/400 meters |
| 1991 | Sergei Bubka, CIS | Pole vault |
| 1992 | Kevin Young, United States | 400-meter hurdles |
| 1993 | Noureddine Morceli, Algeria | 1500/mile/3000 |
| 1994 | Noureddine Morceli, Algeria | 1500/mile/3000/5000 |

## Women

| Year | Athlete | Event |
|------|---------|-------|
| 1974 | Irena Szewinska, Poland | 100/200/400 meters |
| 1975 | Faina Melnik, USSR | Shot put/Discus |
| 1976 | Tatyana Kazankina, USSR | 800/1500 meters |
| 1977 | Rosemarie Ackermann, East Germany | High jump |
| 1978 | Marita Koch, East Germany | 100/200/400 meters |
| 1979 | Marita Koch, East Germany | 100/200/400 meters |
| 1980 | Ilona Briesenick, East Germany | Shot put |
| 1981 | Evelyn Ashford, United States | 100/200 meters |
| 1982 | Marita Koch, East Germany | 100/200/400 meters |
| 1983 | Jarmila Kratochvilova, Czechoslovakia | 200/400/800 meters |
| 1984 | Evelyn Ashford, United States | 100 meters |
| 1985 | Marita Koch, East Germany | 100/200/400 meters |
| 1986 | Jackie Joyner-Kersee, United States | Long jump/Heptathlon |
| 1987 | Jackie Joyner-Kersee, United States | 100-meter hurdles/Long jump/Heptathlon |
| 1988 | Florence Griffith Joyner, United States | 100/200 meters |
| 1989 | Ana Quirot, Cuba | 400/800 meters |
| 1990 | Merlene Ottey, Jamaica | 100/200 meters |
| 1991 | Heike Henkel, Germany | High jump |
| 1992 | Heike Drechsler, Germany | Long Jump |
| 1993 | Wang Junxia, China | 1500/3000/10,000/marathon |
| 1994 | Jackie Joyner-Kersee, United States | 100-meter hurdles/Long jump/Heptathlon |

# MARATHON

## World Record Progression

### Men

| Record Holder | Time | Date | Site |
|---|---|---|---|
| John Hayes, United States | 2:55:18.4 | 7-24-08 | Shepherd's Bush, London |
| Robert Fowler, United States | 2:52:45.4 | 1-1-09 | Yonkers, NY |
| James Clark, United States | 2:46:52.6 | 2-12-09 | New York City |
| Albert Raines, United States | 2:46:04.6 | 5-8-09 | New York City |
| Frederick Barrett, Great Britain | 2:42:31 | 5-26-09 | Shepherd's Bush, London |
| Harry Green, Great Britain | 2:38:16.2 | 5-12-13 | Shepherd's Bush, London |
| Alexis Ahlgren, Sweden | 2:36:06.6 | 5-31-13 | Shepherd's Bush, London |
| Johannes Kolehmainen, Finland | 2:32:35.8 | 8-22-20 | Antwerp, Belgium |
| Albert Michelsen, United States | 2:29:01.8 | 10-12-25 | Port Chester, NY |
| Fusashige Suzuki, Japan | 2:27:49 | 3-31-35 | Tokyo |
| Yasuo Ikenaka, Japan | 2:26:44 | 4-3-35 | Tokyo |
| Kitei Son, Japan | 2:26:42 | 11-3-35 | Tokyo |
| Yun Bok Suh, Korea | 2:25:39 | 4-19-47 | Boston |
| James Peters, Great Britain | 2:20:42.2 | 6-14-52 | Chiswick, England |
| James Peters, Great Britain | 2:18:40.2 | 6-13-53 | Chiswick, England |
| James Peters, Great Britain | 2:18:34.8 | 10-4-53 | Turku, Finland |
| James Peters, Great Britain | 2:17:39.4 | 6-26-54 | Chiswick, England |
| Sergei Popov, USSR | 2:15:17 | 8-24-58 | Stockholm |
| Abebe Bikila, Ethiopia | 2:15:16.2 | 9-10-60 | Rome |
| Toru Terasawa, Japan | 2:15:15.8 | 2-17-63 | Beppu, Japan |
| Leonard Edelen, United States | 2:14:28 | 6-15-63 | Chiswick, England |
| Basil Heatley, Great Britain | 2:13:55 | 6-13-64 | Chiswick, England |
| Abebe Bikila, Ethiopia | 2:12:11.2 | 6-21-64 | Tokyo |
| Morio Shigematsu, Japan | 2:12:00 | 6-12-65 | Chiswick, England |
| Derek Clayton, Australia | 2:09:36.4 | 12-3-67 | Fukuoka, Japan |
| Derek Clayton, Australia | 2:08:33.6 | 5-30-69 | Antwerp, Belgium |
| Rob de Castella, Australia | 2:08:18 | 12-6-81 | Fukuoka, Japan |
| Steve Jones, Great Britain | 2:08:05 | 10-21-84 | Chicago |
| Carlos Lopes, Portugal | 2:07:12 | 4-20-85 | Rotterdam, Netherlands |
| Belayneh Densimo, Ethiopia | 2:06:50 | 4-17-88 | Rotterdam, Netherlands |

### Women

| Record Holder | Time | Date | Site |
|---|---|---|---|
| Dale Greig, Great Britain | 3:27:45 | 5-23-64 | Ryde, England |
| Mildred Simpson, New Zealand | 3:19:33 | 7-21-64 | Auckland, New Zealand |
| Maureen Wilton, Canada | 3:15:22 | 5-6-67 | Toronto |
| Anni Pede-Erdkamp, West Germany | 3:07:26 | 9-16-67 | Waldniel, West Germany |
| Caroline Walker, United States | 3:02:53 | 2-28-70 | Seaside, OR |
| Elizabeth Bonner, United States | 3:01:42 | 5-9-71 | Philadelphia |
| Adrienne Beames, Australia | 2:46:30 | 8-31-71 | Werribee, Australia |
| Chantal Langlace, France | 2:46:24 | 10-27-74 | Neuf Brisach, France |
| Jacqueline Hansen, United States | 2:43:54.5 | 12-1-74 | Culver City, CA |
| Liane Winter, West Germany | 2:42:24 | 4-21-75 | Boston |
| Christa Vahlensieck, West Germany | 2:40:15.8 | 5-3-75 | Dülmen, West Germany |
| Jacqueline Hansen, United States | 2:38:19 | 10-12-75 | Eugene, OR |
| Chantal Langlace, France | 2:35:15.4 | 5-1-77 | Oyarzun, France |
| Christa Vahlensieck, West Germany | 2:34:47.5 | 9-10-77 | West Berlin, West Germany |
| Grete Waitz, Norway | 2:32:29.9 | 10-22-78 | New York City |
| Grete Waitz, Norway | 2:27:32.6 | 10-21-79 | New York City |
| Grete Waitz, Norway | 2:25:41.3 | 10-26-80 | New York City |
| Grete Waitz, Norway | 2:25:29 | 4-17-83 | London |
| Joan Benoit Samuelson, United States | 2:22:43 | 4-18-83 | Boston |
| Ingrid Kristiansen, Norway | 2:21:06 | 4-21-85 | London |

# Boston Marathon

The Boston Marathon began in 1897 as a local Patriot's Day event. Run every year but 1918 since then, it has grown into one of the world's premier marathons.

## Men

| Year | Winner | Time | Year | Winner | Time |
|------|--------|------|------|--------|------|
| 1897 | John J. McDermott, United States | 2:55:10 | 1946 | Stylianos Kyriakides, Greece | 2:29:27 |
| 1898 | Ronald J. McDonald, United States | 2:42:00 | 1947 | Yun Bok Suh, Korea | 2:25:39 |
| 1899 | Lawrence J. Brignolia, United States | 2:54:38 | 1948 | Gerard Cote, Canada | 2:31:02 |
| 1900 | James J. Caffrey, Canada | 2:39:44 | 1949 | Karl Gosta Leandersson, Sweden | 2:31:50 |
| 1901 | James J. Caffrey, Canada | 2:29:23 | 1950 | Kee Yong Ham, Korea | 2:32:39 |
| 1902 | Sammy Mellor, United States | 2:43:12 | 1951 | Shigeki Tanaka, Japan | 2:27:45 |
| 1903 | John C. Lorden, United States | 2:41:29 | 1952 | Doroteo Flores, Guatemala | 2:31:53 |
| 1904 | Michael Spring, United States | 2:38:04 | 1953 | Keizo Yamada, Japan | 2:18:51 |
| 1905 | Fred Lorz, United States | 2:38:25 | 1954 | Veikko Karvonen, Finland | 2:20:39 |
| 1906 | Timothy Ford, United States | 2:45:45 | 1955 | Hideo Hamamura, Japan | 2:18:22 |
| 1907 | Tom Longboat, Canada | 2:24:24 | 1956 | Antti Viskari, Finland | 2:14:14 |
| 1908 | Thomas Morrissey, United States | 2:25:43 | 1957 | John J. Kelley, United States | 2:20:05 |
| 1909 | Henri Renaud, United States | 2:53:36 | 1958 | Franjo Mihalic, Yugoslavia | 2:25:54 |
| 1910 | Fred Cameron, Canada | 2:28:52 | 1959 | Eino Oksanen, Finland | 2:22:42 |
| 1911 | Clarence H. DeMar, United States | 2:21:39 | 1960 | Paavo Kotila, Finland | 2:20:54 |
| 1912 | Mike Ryan, United States | 2:21:18 | 1961 | Eino Oksanen, Finland | 2:23:39 |
| 1913 | Fritz Carlson, United States | 2:25:14 | 1962 | Eino Oksanen, Finland | 2:23:48 |
| 1914 | James Duffy, Canada | 2:25:01 | 1963 | Aurele Vandendriessche, Belgium | 2:18:58 |
| 1915 | Edouard Fabre, Canada | 2:31:41 | 1964 | Aurele Vandendriessche, Belgium | 2:19:59 |
| 1916 | Arthur Roth, United States | 2:27:16 | 1965 | Morio Shigematsu, Japan | 2:16:33 |
| 1917 | Bill Kennedy, United States | 2:28:37 | 1966 | Kenji Kimihara, Japan | 2:17:11 |
| 1918 | No race | | 1967 | David McKenzie, New Zealand | 2:15:45 |
| 1919 | Carl Linder, United States | 2:29:13 | 1968 | Amby Burfoot, United States | 2:22:17 |
| 1920 | Peter Trivoulidas, Greece | 2:29:31 | 1969 | Yoshiaki Unetani, Japan | 2:13:49 |
| 1921 | Frank Zuna, United States | 2:18:57 | 1970 | Ron Hill, England | 2:10:30 |
| 1922 | Clarence H. DeMar, United States | 2:18:10 | 1971 | Alvaro Mejia, Colombia | 2:18:45 |
| 1923 | Clarence H. DeMar, United States | 2:23:37 | 1972 | Olavi Suomalainen, Finland | 2:15:39 |
| 1924 | Clarence H. DeMar, United States | 2:29:40 | 1973 | Jon Anderson, United States | 2:16:03 |
| 1925 | Chuck Mellor, United States | 2:33:00 | 1974 | Neil Cusack, Ireland | 2:13:39 |
| 1926 | John C. Miles, Canada | 2:25:40 | 1975 | Bill Rodgers, United States | 2:09:55 |
| 1927 | Clarence H. DeMar, United States | 2:40:22 | 1976 | Jack Fultz, United States | 2:20:19 |
| 1928 | Clarence H. DeMar, United States | 2:37:07 | 1977 | Jerome Drayton, Canada | 2:14:46 |
| 1929 | John C. Miles, Canada | 2:33:08 | 1978 | Bill Rodgers, United States | 2:10:13 |
| 1930 | Clarence H. DeMar, United States | 2:34:48 | 1979 | Bill Rodgers, United States | 2:09:27 |
| 1931 | James (Hinky) Henigan, United States | 2:46:45 | 1980 | Bill Rodgers, United States | 2:12:11 |
| 1932 | Paul de Bruyn, Germany | 2:33:36 | 1981 | Toshihiko Seko, Japan | 2:09:26 |
| 1933 | Leslie Pawson, United States | 2:31:01 | 1982 | Alberto Salazar, United States | 2:08:52 |
| 1934 | Dave Komonen, Canada | 2:32:53 | 1983 | Gregory A. Meyer, United States | 2:09:00 |
| 1935 | John A. Kelley, United States | 2:32:07 | 1984 | Geoff Smith, England | 2:10:34 |
| 1936 | Ellison M. (Tarzan) Brown, United States | 2:33:40 | 1985 | Geoff Smith, England | 2:14:05 |
| 1937 | Walter Young, Canada | 2:33:20 | 1986 | Rob de Castella, Australia | 2:07:51 |
| 1938 | Leslie Pawson, United States | 2:35:34 | 1987 | Toshihiko Seko, Japan | 2:11:50 |
| 1939 | Ellison M. (Tarzan) Brown, United States | 2:28:51 | 1988 | Ibrahim Hussein, Kenya | 2:08:43 |
| 1940 | Gerard Cote, Canada | 2:28:28 | 1989 | Abebe Mekonnen, Ethiopia | 2:09:06 |
| 1941 | Leslie Pawson, United States | 2:30:38 | 1990 | Gelindo Bordin, Italy | 2:08:19 |
| 1942 | Bernard Joseph Smith, United States | 2:26:51 | 1991 | Ibrahim Hussein, Kenya | 2:11:06 |
| 1943 | Gerard Cote, Canada | 2:28:25 | 1992 | Ibrahim Hussein, Kenya | 2:08:14 |
| 1944 | Gerard Cote, Canada | 2:31:50 | 1993 | Cosmas N'Deti, Kenya | 2:09:33 |
| 1945 | John A. Kelley, United States | 2:30:40 | 1994 | Cosmas N'Deti, Kenya | 2:07:15 |
| | | | 1995 | Cosmas N'Deti, Kenya | 2:09:22 |

## Women

| Year | Winner | Time | Year | Winner | Time |
|------|--------|------|------|--------|------|
| 1966 | Roberta Gibb, United States | 3:21:40* | 1976 | Kim Merritt, United States | 2:47:10 |
| 1967 | Roberta Gibb, United States | 3:27:17* | 1977 | Miki Gorman, United States | 2:48:33 |
| 1968 | Roberta Gibb, United States | 3:30:00* | 1978 | Gayle Barron, United States | 2:44:52 |
| 1969 | Sara Mae Berman, United States | 3:22:46* | 1979 | Joan Benoit, United States | 2:35:15 |
| 1970 | Sara Mae Berman, United States | 3:05:07* | 1980 | Jacqueline Gareau, Canada | 2:34:28 |
| 1971 | Sara Mae Berman, United States | 3:08:30* | 1981 | Allison Roe, New Zealand | 2:26:46 |
| 1972 | Nina Kuscsik, United States | 3:10:36 | 1982 | Charlotte Teske, West Germany | 2:29:33 |
| 1973 | Jacqueline A. Hansen, United States | 3:05:59 | 1983 | Joan Benoit, United States | 2:22:43 |
| 1974 | Miki Gorman, United States | 2:47:11 | 1984 | Lorraine Moller, New Zealand | 2:29:28 |
| 1975 | Liane Winter, West Germany | 2:42:24 | 1985 | Lisa Larsen Weidenbach, United States | 2:34:06 |

# Boston Marathon (Cont.)

## Women (Cont.)

| Year | Winner | Time | Year | Winner | Time |
|---|---|---|---|---|---|
| 1986 | Ingrid Kristiansen, Norway | 2:24:55 | 1992 | Olga Markova, Russia | 2:23:43 |
| 1987 | Rosa Mota, Portugal | 2:25:21 | 1993 | Olga Markova, Russia | 2:25:27 |
| 1988 | Rosa Mota, Portugal | 2:24:30 | 1994 | Uta Pippig, Germany | 2:21:45 |
| 1989 | Ingrid Kristiansen, Norway | 2:24:33 | 1995 | Uta Pippig, Germany | 2:25:11* |
| 1990 | Rosa Mota, Portugal | 2:25:24 | | *Unofficial. | |
| 1991 | Wanda Panfil, Poland | 2:24:18 | | | |

Note: Over the years the Boston course has varied in length. The distances have been 24 miles, 1232 yards (1897-1923); 26 miles, 209 yards (1924-1926); 26 miles 385 yards (1927-1952); and 25 miles, 958 yards (1953-1956). Since 1957, the course has been certified to be the standard marathon distance of 26 miles, 385 yards.

# New York City Marathon

From 1970 through 1975 the New York City Marathon was a small local race run in the city's Central Park. In 1976 it was moved to the streets of New York's five boroughs. It has since become one of the biggest and most prestigious marathons in the world.

## Men

| Year | Winner | Time | Year | Winner | Time |
|---|---|---|---|---|---|
| 1970 | Gary Muhrcke, United States | 2:31:38 | 1983 | Rod Dixon, New Zealand | 2:08:59 |
| 1971 | Norman Higgins, United States | 2:22:54 | 1984 | Orlando Pizzolato, Italy | 2:14:53 |
| 1972 | Sheldon Karlin, United States | 2:27:52 | 1985 | Orlando Pizzolato, Italy | 2:11:34 |
| 1973 | Tom Fleming, United States | 2:21:54 | 1986 | Gianni Poli, Italy | 2:11:06 |
| 1974 | Norbert Sander, United States | 2:26:30 | 1987 | Ibrahim Hussein, Kenya | 2:11:01 |
| 1975 | Tom Fleming, United States | 2:19:27 | 1988 | Steve Jones, Great Britain | 2:08:20 |
| 1976 | Bill Rodgers, United States | 2:10:10 | 1989 | Juma Ikangaa, Tanzania | 2:08:01 |
| 1977 | Bill Rodgers, United States | 2:11:28 | 1990 | Douglas Wakiihuri, Kenya | 2:12:39 |
| 1978 | Bill Rodgers, United States | 2:12:12 | 1991 | Salvador Garcia, Mexico | 2:09:28 |
| 1979 | Bill Rodgers, United States | 2:11:42 | 1992 | Willie Mtolo, South Africa | 2:09:29 |
| 1980 | Alberto Salazar, United States | 2:09:41 | 1993 | Andres Espinosa, Mexico | 2:10:04 |
| 1981 | Alberto Salazar, United States | 2:08:13 | 1994 | German Silva, Mexico | 2:11:21 |
| 1982 | Alberto Salazar, United States | 2:09:29 | | | |

## Women

| Year | Winner | Time | Year | Winner | Time |
|---|---|---|---|---|---|
| 1970 | No finisher | | 1983 | Grete Waitz, Norway | 2:27:00 |
| 1971 | Beth Bonner, United States | 2:55:22 | 1984 | Grete Waitz, Norway | 2:29:30 |
| 1972 | Nina Kuscsik, United States | 3:08:41 | 1985 | Grete Waitz, Norway | 2:28:34 |
| 1973 | Nina Kuscsik, United States | 2:57:07 | 1986 | Grete Waitz, Norway | 2:28:06 |
| 1974 | Katherine Switzer, United States | 3:07:29 | 1987 | Priscilla Welch, Great Britain | 2:30:17 |
| 1975 | Kim Merritt, United States | 2:46:14 | 1988 | Grete Waitz, Norway | 2:28:07 |
| 1976 | Miki Gorman, United States | 2:39:11 | 1989 | Ingrid Kristiansen, Norway | 2:25:30 |
| 1977 | Miki Gorman, United States | 2:43:10 | 1990 | Wanda Panfiil, Poland | 2:30:45 |
| 1978 | Grete Waitz, Norway | 2:32:30 | 1991 | Liz McColgan, Scotland | 2:27:23 |
| 1979 | Grete Waitz, Norway | 2:27:33 | 1992 | Lisa Ondieki, Australia | 2:24:40 |
| 1980 | Grete Waitz, Norway | 2:25:41 | 1993 | Uta Pippig, Germany | 2:26:24 |
| 1981 | Allison Roe, New Zealand | 2:25:29 | 1994 | Tecla Lorupe, Kenya | 2:27:37 |
| 1982 | Grete Waitz, Norway | 2:27:14 | | | |

# CROSS COUNTRY

# World Cross-Country Championships

Conducted by the International Amateur Athletic Federation (IAAF), this meet annually brings together the best runners in the world at every distance from the mile to the marathon to compete in the same cross-country race.

## Men

| Year | Winner | Winning Team | Year | Winner | Winning Team |
|---|---|---|---|---|---|
| 1973 | Pekka Paivarinta, Finland | Belgium | 1978 | John Treacy, Ireland | France |
| 1974 | Eric DeBeck, Belgium | Belgium | 1979 | John Treacy, Ireland | England |
| 1975 | Ian Stewart, Scotland | New Zealand | 1980 | Craig Virgin, United States | England |
| 1976 | Carlos Lopes, Portugal | England | 1981 | Craig Virgin, United States | Ethiopia |
| 1977 | Leon Schots, Belgium | Belgium | 1982 | Mohammed Kedir, Ethiopia | Ethiopia |

## Men (Cont.)

| Year | Winner | Winning Team | Year | Winner | Winning Team |
|------|--------|--------------|------|--------|--------------|
| 1983 | Bekele Debele, Ethiopia | Ethiopia | 1990 | Khalid Skah, Morocco | Kenya |
| 1984 | Carlos Lopes, Portugal | Ethiopia | 1991 | Khalid Skah, Morocco | Kenya |
| 1985 | Carlos Lopes, Portugal | Ethiopia | 1992 | John Ngugi, Kenya | Kenya |
| 1986 | John Ngugi, Kenya | Kenya | 1993 | William Sigei, Kenya | Kenya |
| 1987 | John Ngugi, Kenya | Kenya | 1994 | William Sigei, Kenya | Kenya |
| 1988 | John Ngugi, Kenya | Kenya | 1995 | Paul Tergat, Kenya | Kenya |
| 1989 | John Ngugi, Kenya | Kenya | | | |

## Women

| Year | Winner | Winning Team | Year | Winner | Winning Team |
|------|--------|--------------|------|--------|--------------|
| 1973 | Paola Cacchi, Italy | England | 1985 | Zola Budd, England | United States |
| 1974 | Paola Cacchi, Italy | England | 1986 | Zola Budd, England | England |
| 1975 | Julie Brown, United States | United States | 1987 | Annette Sergent, France | United States |
| 1976 | Carmen Valero, Spain | USSR | 1988 | Ingrid Kristiansen, Norway | USSR |
| 1977 | Carmen Valero, Spain | USSR | 1989 | Annette Sergent, France | USSR |
| 1978 | Grete Waitz, Norway | Romania | 1990 | Lynn Jennings, United States | USSR |
| 1979 | Grete Waitz, Norway | United States | 1991 | Lynn Jennings, United States | Kenya |
| 1980 | Grete Waitz, Norway | USSR | 1992 | Lynn Jennings, United States | Kenya |
| 1981 | Grete Waitz, Norway | USSR | 1993 | Albertina Dias, Portugal | Kenya |
| 1982 | Maricica Puica, Romania | USSR | 1994 | Helen Chepngeno, Kenya | Portugal |
| 1983 | Grete Waitz, Norway | United States | 1995 | Derartu Tulu, Ethiopia | Kenya |
| 1984 | Maricica Puica, Romania | United States | | | |

# Notable Achievements

## Longest Winning Streaks

### MEN

| Event | Name and Nationality | Streak | Years |
|-------|---------------------|--------|-------|
| 100-meter dash | Bob Hayes, United States | 49 | 1962–64 |
| 200-meter dash | Manfred Gemar, Germany | 41 | 1956–60 |
| 400-meter run | Michael Johnson, United States | 33 | 1989– |
| 800-meter run | Mal Whitfield, United States | 40 | 1951–54 |
| 1500-meter run | Josy Barthel, Luxembourg | 17 | 1952 |
| 1500-meter run/mile | Steve Ovett, Great Britain | 45 | 1977–80 |
| Mile | Herb Elliott, Australia | 35 | 1957–60 |
| Steeplechase | Gaston Roelants, Belgium | 45 | 1961–66 |
| 5000-meter run | Emil Zátopek, Czechoslovakia | 48 | 1949–52 |
| 10,000-meter run | Emil Zátopek, Czechoslovakia | 38 | 1948–54 |
| Marathon | Frank Shorter, United States | 6 | 1971–73 |
| 110-meter hurdles | Jack Davis, United States | 44 | 1952-55 |
| 400-meter hurdles | Edwin Moses, United States | 107 | 1977–87 |
| High Jump | Ernie Shelton, United States | 46 | 1953–55 |
| Pole Vault | Bob Richards, United States | 50 | 1950–52 |
| Long Jump | Carl Lewis, United States | 65 | 1981–91 |
| Triple Jump | Adhemar da Silva, Brazil | 60 | 1950–56 |
| Shot Put | Parry O'Brien, United States | 116 | 1952–56 |
| Discus Throw | Ricky Bruch, Sweden | 54 | 1972–73 |
| Hammer Throw | Imre Nemeth, Hungary | 73 | 1946–50 |
| Javelin Throw | Janis Lusis, USSR | 41 | 1967–70 |
| Decathlon | Bob Mathias, United States | 11 | 1948–56 |

### WOMEN

| Event | Name and Nationality | Streak | Years |
|-------|---------------------|--------|-------|
| 100-meter dash | Merlene Ottey, Jamaica | 56 | 1987–91 |
| 200-meter dash | Irena Szewinska, Poland | 38 | 1973–75 |
| 400-meter run | Irena Szewinska, Poland | 36 | 1973–78 |
| 800-meter run | Ana Fidelia Quirot, Cuba | 36 | 1987–90 |
| 1500-meter run | Paula Ivan, Romania | 15 | 1988–91 |
| 1500-meter run/mile | Paula Ivan, Romania | 19 | 1988–90 |
| 3000-meter run | Mary Slaney, United States | 10 | 1982–84 |
| 10,000-meter run | Ingrid Kristiansen, Norway | 5 | 1985–87 |

## Longest Winning Streaks *(Cont.)*

### WOMEN *(Cont.)*

| Event | Name and Nationality | Streak | Years |
|---|---|---|---|
| Marathon | Katrin Dörre, East Germany | 10 | 1982–86 |
| 100-meter hurdles | Annelie Ernhardt, East Germany | 44 | 1972–75 |
| 400-meter hurdles | Ann-Louise Skoglund, Sweden | 18 | 1981–83 |
| High Jump | Iolanda Balas, Romania | 140 | 1956–67 |
| Long Jump | Tatyana Shchelkanova, USSR | 19 | 1964–66 |
| Shot Put | Nadezhda Chizhova, USSR | 57 | 1969–73 |
| Discus Throw | Gisela Mauermeyer, Germany | 65 | 1935–42 |
| Javelin Throw | Ruth Fuchs, East Germany | 30 | 1972–73 |
| Multi | Heide Rosendahl, West Germany | 15 | 1969–72 |

## Most Consecutive Years Ranked No. 1 in the World

### MEN

| No. | Name and Nationality | Event | Years |
|---|---|---|---|
| 9 | Victor Saneyev, USSR | Triple Jump | 1968–76 |
| 8 | Bob Richards, United States | Pole Vault | 1949–56 |
| 8 | Ralph Boston, United States | Long Jump | 1960–67 |
| 7 | Emil Zátopek (Czech) | 10,000-meter run | 1948–54 |

### WOMEN

| No. | Name and Nationality | Event | Years |
|---|---|---|---|
| 9 | Iolanda Balas, Romania | High Jump | 1958–66 |
| 8 | Ruth Fuchs, East Germany | Javelin Throw | 1972–79 |
| 7 | Faina Melnick, USSR | Discus Throw | 1971–77 |

## Major Barrier Breakers

### MEN

| Event | Mark | Name and Nationality | Date | Site |
|---|---|---|---|---|
| sub 10-second 100-meter dash | 9.95 | Jim Hines, United States | Oct. 14, 1968 | Mexico City |
| sub 20-second 200-meter dash | 19.83 | Tommie Smith, United States | Oct. 16, 1968 | Mexico City |
| sub 45-second 400-meter run | 44.9 | Otis Davis, United States | Sept. 6, 1960 | Rome |
| sub 1:45 800-meter run | 1:44.3 | Peter Snell, New Zealand | Feb. 3, 1962 | Christchurch, New Zealand |
| sub four minute mile | 3:59.4 | Roger Bannister, Great Britain | May 6, 1954 | Oxford |
| sub 3:50 mile | 3:49.4 | John Walker, New Zealand | Aug. 12, 1975 | Göteborg |
| sub 13-minute 5,000-meter run | 12:58.39 | Said Aouita, Morocco | July 22, 1986 | Rome |
| sub 27:00 10,000-meter run | 26:58.38 | Yobes Ondieki, Kenya | July 10, 1993 | Oslo |
| sub 13-second 110-meter hurdles | 12.93 | Renaldo Nehemiah, United States | Aug. 19, 1981 | Zurich |
| sub 50-second 400-meter hurdles | 49.5 | Glenn Davis, United States | June 29, 1956 | Los Angeles |
| 7' high jump | 7' ⅝" | Charles Dumas, United States | June 29, 1956 | Los Angeles |
| 8' high jump | 8' | Javier Sotomayor, Cuba | July 29, 1989 | San Juan |
| 60' triple jump | 60'¼" | Jonathan Edwards, Great Britain | Aug. 7, 1995 | Göteborg |
| 20' pole vault | 20' | Sergei Bubka, USSR | March 15, 1991 | San Sebastian, Spain |
| 70' shot put | 70' 7¼" | Randy Matson, United States | May 5, 1965 | College Station, Texas |
| 200' discus throw | 200' 5" | Al Oerter, United States | May 18, 1962 | Los Angeles |
| 300' (new) javelin | 300' 1" | Steve Backley, Great Britain | Jan. 25, 1992 | Auckland, New Zealand |

### WOMEN

| Event | Mark | Name and Nationality | Date | Site |
|---|---|---|---|---|
| sub 11-second 100-meter dash | 10.88 | Marlies Oelsner, East Germany | July 1, 1977 | Dresden |
| sub 22-second 200-meter dash | 21.71 | Marita Koch, East Germany | June 10, 1979 | Karl Marx Stadt |
| sub 50-second 400-meter run | 49.9 | Irena Szewinska, Poland | June 22, 1974 | Warsaw |
| sub 2:00 800-meter run | 1:59.1 | Shin Geum Dan, North Korea | Nov. 12, 1963 | Djakarta |
| sub 4:00 1500-meter run | 3:56.0 | Tatyana Kazankina, USSR | June 28, 1976 | Podolsk, USSR |

## Major Barrier Breakers (Cont.)

### WOMEN (Cont.)

| Event | Mark | Name and Nationality | Date | Site |
|---|---|---|---|---|
| sub 4:20 mile | 4:17.55 | Mary Decker, United States | Feb. 16, 1980 | Houston |
| sub 15:00 5,000-meter run | 14:58.89 | Ingrid Kristiansen, Norway | June 28, 1984 | Oslo |
| sub 30:00 10,000-meter run | 29:31.78 | Wang Junxia, China | Sept. 8, 1993 | Beijing |
| sub 2:30 marathon | 2:27:33 | Grete Waitz, Norway | Oct. 21, 1979 | New York City |
| sub 13-second 100-meter hurdles | 12.9 | Karin Balzer, East Germany | Sept. 5, 1969 | Berlin |
| 6' high jump | 6' | Iolanda Balas, Romania | Oct. 18, 1958 | Budapest |
| 70' shot put | 70' 4½" | Nadyezhda Chizhova, USSR | Sept. 29, 1973 | Varna, Bulgaria |
| 200' discus throw | 201' | Liesel Westermann, West Germany | Nov. 5, 1967 | Sao Paulo |
| 200' javelin throw | 201' 4" | Elvira Ozolina, USSR | Aug. 27, 1964 | Kiev |
| first 7,000-point heptathlon | 7,148 | Jackie Joyner-Kersee, United States | July 6–7, 1986 | Moscow |

## Olympic Accomplishments

**Oldest Olympic gold medalist**—Patrick (Babe) McDonald, United States, 42 years, 26 days, 56-pound weight throw, 1920
**Oldest Olympic medalist**—Tebbs Lloyd Johnson, Great Britain, 48 years, 115 days, 1948 (bronze), 50K walk
**Youngest Olympic gold medalist**—Barbara Jones, United States, 15 years 123 days, 1952, 4 x 100 relay
**Youngest gold medalist in individual event**—Ulrike Meyfarth, West Germany, 16 years, 123 days, 1972, high jump

## World Record Accomplishments*

**Most world records equaled or set in a day**—6, Jesse Owens, United States, 5/25/35, (9.4 100-yard dash; 26' 8¼" long jump; 20.3 200-meter dash and 220-yard dash; and 22.6 220-yard hurdles and 200-meter hurdles
**Most records in a year**—10, Gunder Hägg, Sweden, 1941-42, 1500 to 5,000 meters
**Most records in a career**—35, Sergei Bubka, 1983-94, pole vault indoors and out
**Longest span of record setting**—11 years, 20 days, Irena Szewinska, Poland, 1965-76, 200-meter dash
**Youngest person to set a set world record**—Carolina Gisolf, Holland, 15 years, 5 days, 1928, high jump , 5' 3⅜"
**Youngest man to set a world record**—John Thomas, United States, 17 years, 355 days, 1959, high jump, 7' 1¼"
**Oldest person to set world record**—Carlos Lopes, Portugal, 38 years, 59 days, marathon, 2:07:12
**Greatest percentage improvement**—6.59, Bob Beamon, United States, 1968, long jump
**Longest lasting record**—long jump, 26' 8¼", Jesse Owens, United States, 25 years, 79 days (1935-60)
**Highest clearance over head, men**—23¼", Franklin Jacobs United States (5' 8"), 1978
**Highest clearance over head, woman**—12¾", Yolanda Henry, United States (5' 6"), 1990

*Marks sanctioned by the IAAF

### Primo Donna

The 1995 World Indoor Track and Field Championships in Barcelona featured fewer stars than had any of the event's four previous stagings. Among the absent were virually all of the sport's royalty: Jackie Joyner-Kersee, Michael Johnson, Gwen Torrence, Mike Powell, Noureddine Morceli and Carl Lewis. This didn't please Primo Nebiolo, president of the International Amateur Athletic Federation (IAAF), the event's organizer, who reacted like a little boy furious that people wouldn't come to his birthday party.

In his 14 years as head of the IAAF, Nebiolo has never quite accepted that the world doesn't regard his wishes as commands. When Olympic 100-meter champ Linford Christie announced on March 6 that because of fatigue at the end of a long season, he, too, would not be competing in Barcelona, the 71-year-old Nebiolo swung into action. "I appeal to him as a great champion to reconsider," said Nebiolo, hinting that he might grant Christie an unprecedented at-large invitation when Christie insisted that wouldn't be willing to bump Michael Rosswess, who had been awarded his place on the British team. Christie demurred just the same.

One reason so few stars were in Barcelona is the current glut of championships being billed as "major," a situation Nebiolo himself created. In 1987, when the first world indoor meet was held, its outdoor counterpart was contested only quadrenially. Now that each is held every two years,. it's hard to persuade athletes who normally command appearance fees of $25,000 or more that it's worth their while to participate for glory alone. Currently there's only one meet they'll attend without the lure of prize money: the Olympics.

In early March Nebiolo did announce that prize money will be awarded at all IAAF championships after the 1996 Olympics. Providing cash payouts is only fair, given the many lucrative sponsorships the IAAF has, plus the five-year, $92 million TV contract the body signed last year with the European Broadcasting Union. Track's athletes are willing to be led, but they can't be blamed for liking their carrots green.

# Swimming

Sports Illustrated

# Tom Terrific

**Michigan star Tom Dolan shatters three U.S. records at the NCAAs**

# The Next Wave

## Two legends of U.S. swimming saw their Gehrigesque winning streaks ended as new stars swam into the spotlight

### by Gerry Callahan

THEY WERE the Iron Horses of the sport of swimming, and in the summer of 1995, they sank. Janet Evans hadn't lost the 800-meter freestyle in eight years while Melvin Stewart's reign in the 200-meter butterfly dated back even further. No one had outraced Stewart since 1986, and his string of consecutive national titles in the event was up to 12. The last time either Evans or Stewart had suffered a defeat in their respective specialties, Ronald Reagan was running the country and Cal Ripken had a full head of hair and no realistic chance of breaking Lou Gehrig's record.

While baseball celebrated Ripken's 2,131st straight game last summer, the most notable streaks in the sport of swimming were struck down. In August, Evans lost at the national championships in Pasadena, Calif., to Brooke Bennett, a brash 15-year-old who, earlier in the year, had stirred up controversy with some less-than-respectful comments about the legendary Evans. Bennett had said that Evans "gets a little scared" when the two go head-to-head, and then the teen phenom backed up her words with a national champi-

onship in the 800 freestyle. Evans, meanwhile, was not exactly left to lament a split-second defeat—she finished fourth, behind Bennett, Trina Jackson and Christina Teuscher. She also was beaten at the nationals by Bennett in the 400 and 1,500 freestyles.

Stewart's summer wasn't much better. On June 14 the defending Olympic champion in the 200-meter butterfly saw his world record wiped out by Denis Pankratov of Russia, and a few days later his nine-year winning streak was snapped at the Charlotte Ultra Swim. Then things really went south for Stewart: In Pasadena in August, Ray Carey of Stanford knocked off Stewart in the 200 butterfly to snap his national-title streak at an even dozen. Stewart was experimenting with an extended underwater dolphin kick that he had hoped would make him a favorite at the Atlanta Olympics next year. Instead the once untouchable Tennessee native looked like just another swimmer struggling to make the U.S. team.

It was that kind of year in the sport of swimming. Maybe the mighty didn't fall, but they sure did slip a notch. Even the contro-

**After nearly a decade on top, Evans had little to smile about in '95.**

versial Chinese team, which left the '94 world championships with a planeload of world records, seemed to swim off the face of the earth in 1995. The Chinese women, virtually all newcomers to international competition, won 12 of 16 events in Rome and set five world records, and they did it all with charges of drug use swirling above the pool. In '95 the Chinese kept to themselves, revealing little about their national meets to the rest of the world, and no one is quite sure what to expect of them in Atlanta.

For the U.S., the best story to come out of Rome in '94 seemed to get even better back home this year. Tom Dolan, the University of Michigan star who set a world record at the age of 18 in the 400-meter individual medley in '94, won just about everything he entered in '95. At the NCAA championships in Indianapolis in March, Dolan set three U.S. records in three days, and when he reached the end of the pool, no one ever asked for a recount.

Dolan shattered the old NCAA marks in the 500 freestyle (by 2.84 seconds), the 400 individual medley (2.46 seconds) and the 1,650 freestyle (by 5.7 seconds). Dolan also joined three Michigan teammates to capture the 800 freestyle relay as the Wolverines won their first national title in 34 years. For the season at Michigan, Dolan lost only once in his specialty events. At the Pan Pacific Games in Atlanta, he christened the Olympic pool with gold medals in the 200 and 400 individual medleys. USA Swimming named Dolan its Swimmer of the Year for 1995.

"He's the best," says Michigan coach Jon Urbanchek. "He's got the body, the desire, the competitive instinct. Put it all together, and you've got a champion."

You've also got an incredible story. Dolan stands 6'6", weighs 180 pounds and moves through the water like an eel. He appears to be a natural-born swimmer—except for one minor drawback: He can't breathe. At least not as easily as the swimmers in the other lanes. Dolan, 20, has exercise-induced asthma and an unusually narrow windpipe that allows him only 20% of the oxygen intake of the average person. These conditions mean that, for Dolan, swimming is not nearly as difficult as coming up for air. "It can really get bad in our workouts," says Dolan. "There will be some real tightness in my chest, and I won't be able to get a lot of air. But my coach says it actually helps me in meets because it increases my ability to withstand stress."

At the national championships, the Southern California smog caused major problems for Dolan, and he lost out in the 400-meter individual medley to Eric Namesnik, a silver medalist in Barcelona in '92. Depending on the air quality in Atlanta, Dolan could be the United States's best hope for a gold medal in swimming next year.

Another bright spot for the U.S. in an otherwise forgettable '95 was the men's 400-free relay team, which set a world record at the Pan Pac Games. The foursome included David Fox, Joe Huderpohl, Jon Olsen and Gary Hall Jr., whose father broke world records seven times in the late '60s and early '70s. Young Hall also won gold medals at the Pan Pac Games in the 50 freestyle and the 100 freestyle. It wasn't a good year for legends of swimming in the U.S., but it wasn't bad for a son of a legend.

# FOR THE RECORD·1994–1995

## 1995 Major Competitions

### Men

#### U.S. INDOOR CHAMPIONSHIPS
**Minneapolis, Minnesota, March 14-18**

50 free .........David Fox, unattached, 20.23
100 free........David Fox, unattached, 49.43
200 free........David Fox, unattached, 1:51.88
400 free........Reeve Irvin, Charleston, 3:57.11
800 free........Andy Potts, Eastern Express, 8:10.00
1500 free......Reeve Irvin, Charleston, 15:33.49
100 back......Bart Kizierowski, Mission Viejo, 56.83
200 back......Tate Blahnik, NJ Wave, 2:01.18
100 breast....Lief Engstrom, Ft Lauderdale, 1:03.49
200 breast....Lief Engstrom, Ft Lauderdale, 2:18.11
100 fly .........Mel Stewart, Tennessee, 53.90
200 fly .........Mel Stewart, Tennessee, 1:58.24
200 IM .........Sergey Mariniuk, Santa Clara, 2:02.80
400 IM .........Sergey Mariniuk, Santa Clara, 4:18.84
400 m relay ..Ft Lauderdale, 3:48.59
400 f relay ....Ohio State, 3:27.17
800 f relay ....Mission Viejo, 7:36.04
1-m spgbd ...David Pichler, Ft Lauderdale, 390.42
3-m spgbd ...Mark Bradshaw, Ohio State, 646.50
Platform........David Pichler, Ft Lauderdale, 593.13
3-m sync dv..Brian Earley/Kevin McMahon, 329.43
10-m sync plt..Mark Ruiz/Kongzheng Li, 315.99
Diving competitions held in Midland, TX, April 19-23.

#### EUROPEAN CHAMPIONSHIPS
**Vienna, Austria, August 22-29**

50 free .........Alexander Popov, Russia, 22.25
100 free........Alexander Popov, Russia, 49.10
200 free........Jani Sievinen, Finland, 1:48.98
400 free........Steffen Zesner, Germany, 3:50.35
800 free........not held
1500 free......Jorg Hoffmann, Germany, 15:11.25
100 back......Vladimir Selkov, Russia, 55.48
200 back......Vladimir Selkov, Russia, 1:58.48
100 breast....Frederic deBurghgraeve, Belgium, 1:01.12
200 breast....Andrei Korneev, Russia, 2:12.62
100 fly .........Denis Pankratov, Russia, 52.32#
200 fly .........Denis Pankratov, Russia, 1:56.34
200 IM .........Jani Sievinen, Finland, 1:58.61
400 IM .........Jani Sievinen, Finland, 4:14.75
400 m relay ..Russia, 3:38.11
400 f relay ....Russia, 3:18.84
800 f relay ....Germany, 7:18.22

#### WORLD UNIVERSITY GAMES
**Fukuoka, Japan, August 24-29**

50 free .........Fernando Scherer, Brazil, 22.48
100 free........Fernando Scherer, Brazil, 49.89
200 free........Yann deFabrique, France, 1:50.04
400 free........Josh Davis, United States, 3:51.95
800 free........Christian Piper, Germany, 8:04.89
1500 free......Hisato Yasui, Japan, 15:26.81
100 back......Kurt Jachimowski, United States, 56.30
200 back......Sang Joon Ji, Korea, 2:01.19
100 breast....Akira Hayashi, Japan, 1:02.71
200 breast....Alexander Tkatchev, Russia, 2:14.69*
100 fly .........Jason Lancaster, United States, 53.15

#### U.S. OUTDOOR CHAMPIONSHIPS
**Pasadena, California, July 31-August 4**

Jon Olsen, Curl-Burke, 22.42
Jon Olsen, Curl-Burke, 49.44
Chad Carvin, Hilldenbrand Aquatics, 1:48.43
John Piersma, Club Wolverine, 3:49.72
Peter Wright, JW, 8:06.27
Carlton Bruner, Club Wolverine, 15:17.17
Jeff Rouse, Phoenix, 55.29
Tripp Schwenk, SYS, 1:58.33‡
Kurt Grote, Stanford Swimming, 1:01.91
Eric Wunderlich, Napa Valley, 2:15.14
Mark Henderson, Curl-Burke, 53.59
Ray Carey, Stanford Swimming, 1:59.17
Paul Nelsen, FLST, 2:02.11
Eric Namesnik, Club Wolverine, 4:15.57
Phoenix, 3:41.56
Curl-Burke, 3:20.29
Curl-Burke, 7:25.89
David Pichler, Ft Lauderdale Diving, 377.97
Kent Ferguson, Miami Diving, 651.51
Patrick Jeffrey, Team Orlando, 584.16
Brain Earley/Kevin McMahon, 323.34
Chuck Wade/David Pichler, 323.46
Diving competitions held in Bartlesville, OK, August 9-13.

#### PAN PACIFIC CHAMPIONSHIPS
**Atlanta, Georgia, August 10-13**

Gary Hall, United States, 22.30
Gary Hall, United States, 49.47
Danyon Loader, New Zealand, 1:48.72
Daniel Kowalski, Australia, 3:50.01
Daniel Kowalski, Australia, 7:50.28
Kieren Perkins, Australia, 14:58.92
Jeff Rouse, United States, 54.98
Tripp Schwenk, United States, 1:58.87
Eric Wunderlich, United States, 1:01.80
Akira Hayashi, Japan, 2:13.60
Scott Miller, Australia, 53.07
Scott Miller, Australia, 1:57.86
Tom Dolan, United States, 2:00.89
Tom Dolan, United States, 4:14.77
United States, 3:37.04
United States, 3:15.11#
Australia, 7:17.52

#### PAN AMERICAN GAMES
**Mar del Plata, Argentina, March 12-17**

Fernando deQueiroz, Brazil, 22.65
Gustavo Borges, Brazil, 49.31
Gustavo Borges, Brazil, 1:48.49
Josh Davis, United States, 3:55.59
not held
Carlton Bruehner, United States, 15:13.90
Jeff Rouse, United States, 54.74
Brad Bridgewater, United States, 2:00.79
Seth van Nueerden, United States, 1:02.48
Seth van Neerden, United States, 2:16.08
Mark Henderson, United States, 54:11

#World record; ‡American record.

## Men *(Cont.)*

### WORLD UNIVERSITY GAMES *(Cont.)*

| | |
|---|---|
| 200 fly | Tom Malchow, United States, 2:00.78 |
| 200 IM | Tom Wilkins, United States, 2:02.96 |
| 400 IM | Ian Mull, United States, 4:21.41 |
| 400 m relay | United States, 3:42.02* |
| 400 f relay | United States, 3:19.44* |
| 800 f relay | United States, 7:17.83* |
| 1-m spgbd | Zaho Xin, China, 395.37 |
| 3-m spgbd | Fernando Platas, Mexico, 619.20 |
| Platform | Cheng Wei, China, 628.74 |

### PAN AMERICAN GAMES *(Cont.)*

Nelson Molina, Venezuela, 2:00.38
Curtis Myden, Canada, 2:01.70
Curtis Myden, Canada, 4:18.55
United States, 3:41.24
United States, 3:18.60*
United States, 7:21.61*
Dean Panaro, United States, 404.82
Fernando Platas, Mexico, 661.80
Fernando Platas, Mexico, 617.52

### FINA/ALAMO DIVING GRAND PRIX
**Fort Lauderdale, Florida, May 11-14**

| | |
|---|---|
| 1-m spgbd | David Pichler, United States, 386.61 |
| 3-m spgbd | Xiong Ni, China, 666.99 |
| Platform | Jan Hempel, Germany, 663.30 |
| 3-m sync | Pichler/Ferguson, United States, 284.49 |
| 10-m sync | Xu/Tian, China, 313.89 |

### WORLD DIVING CUP
**Atlanta, Georgia, September 5-9**

Yu Zhoucheng, China, 418.50
Dmitry Sautin, Russia, 684.21
Sun Shuwei, China, 681.48
not held
not held

## Women

### U.S. INDOOR CHAMPIONSHIPS
**Minneapolis, Minnesota, March 14-18**

| | |
|---|---|
| 50 free | Ashley Chandler, SwimAtlanta, 25.64 |
| 100 free | Lauren Thies, Multnomah, 56.48 |
| 200 free | Lauren Thies, Multnomah, 2:01.15 |
| 400 free | Janet Evans, Trojan, 4:14.34 |
| 800 free | Janet Evans, Trojan, 8:40.66 |
| 1500 free | Janet Evans, Trojan, 16:34.43 |
| 100 back | Shelly Ripple, Bengal, 1:03.21 |
| 200 back | Beth Botsford, North Baltimore, 2:13.53 |
| 100 breast | A. McReynolds, Scenic, 1:10.93 |
| 200 breast | A. McReynolds, Scenic, 2:29.83 |
| 100 fly | Karen Campbell, SW Michigan, 1:00.89 |
| 200 fly | Collin Sherman, Bolles Sharks, 2:14.69 |
| 200 IM | J. Parmenter, Canyons, 2:27.10 |
| 400 IM | J. Parmenter, Canyons, 4:46.36 |
| 1-m spgbd | Carrie Zarse, unattached, 264.48 |
| 3-m spgbd | Melisa Moses, unattached, 512.52 |
| Platform | Patty Armstrong, Woodlands, 451.74 |
| 3-m sync | Janae Lautenschlager/Amy Sloan, 274.14 |
| 10-m sync | Kristin Ling/Paige Weiskittel, 272.19 |

Diving competitions held in Midland, TX, April 19-23.

### U.S. OUTDOOR CHAMPIONSHIPS
**Pasadena, California, July 31-August 4**

Amy Van Dyken, RNT, 25.13
Angel Martino, Americus, 55.91
Cristina Teuscher, Badger, 2:00.78
Brooke Bennett, BSTC Blue Wave, 4:10.72
Brooke Bennett, BSTC Blue Wave, 8:31.84
Brooke Bennett, BSTC Blue Wave, 16:17.84
Lea Loveless, Badger, 1:02.44
Beth Botsford, North Baltimore, 2:12.82
Amanda Beard, Irvine Novas, 1:10.37
A. McReynolds, Scenic City, 2:28.92
Jenny Thompson, Stanford, 1:00.19
Michelle Griglione, Curl-Burke, 2:11.56
Allison Wagner, Florida Aquatics, 2:15.99
Kristine Quance, Trojan-CA, 4:45.97
Doris Glenn Easterly, Ft Lauderdale, 242.79
Eileen Richetelli, STD, 494.43
Becky Ruehl, Cincinnati Stingrays, 478.47
Jenny Keim/Reyne Borup, 253.56
Patty Armstrong/Laura Wilkinson, 248.85

Diving competitions held in Bartlesville, OK, August 9-13.

### EUROPEAN CHAMPIONSHIPS
**Vienna, Austria, August 22-29**

| | |
|---|---|
| 50 free | Linda Olofsson, Sweden, 25.76 |
| 100 free | Franziska van Almsick, Germany, 55.34 |
| 200 free | Kerstin Kielgass, Germany, 2:00.56 |
| 400 free | Franziska van Almsick, Germany, 4:08.37 |
| 800 free | Julia Jung, Germany, 8:36.08 |
| 1500 free | not held |
| 100 back | Mett Jacobsen, Denmark, 1:02.46 |
| 200 back | Krisztina Egerszegi, Hungary, 2:07.24 |

### PAN PACIFIC CHAMPIONSHIPS
**Atlanta, Georgia, August 10-13**

Amy Van Dyken, United States, 25.03‡
Jenny Thompson, United States, 55.31
Suzu Chiba, Japan, 2:00.00
Brooke Bennett, United States, 4:10.46
Haley Lewis, Australia, 8:28.78
Brooke Bennett, United States, 16:15.58
Noriko Inada, Japan, 1:02.02
Nicole Stevenson, Australia, 2:11.26

*Meet record; ‡American record.

## Women *(Cont.)*

### EUROPEAN CHAMPIONSHIPS *(Cont.)*

| | |
|---|---|
| 100 breast | ...Brigitte Becue, Belgium, 1:09.30 |
| 200 breast | ...Brigitte Becue, Belgium, 2:27.60 |
| 100 fly | ..........Mett Jacobsen, Denmark, 1:00.64 |
| 200 fly | ..........Michelle Smith, Ireland, 2:11.60 |
| 200 IM | ........Michelle Smith, Ireland, 2:15.27 |
| 400 IM | .........Krisztina Egerszegi, Hungary, 4:40.33 |
| 400 m relay | ..Germany, 4:09.97 |
| 400 f relay | ...Germany, 3:43.89 |
| 800 f relay | ...Germany, 8:06.11 |

### PAN PACIFIC CHAMPIONSHIPS *(Cont.)*

Penelope Haynes, South Africa, 1:08.09
Samantha Riley, Australia, 2:24.81
Susan O'Neill, Australia, 59:58
Susan O'Neill, Australia, 2:07.29
Ellie Overton, Australia, 2:14.68
Kumie Kurotori, Japan, 4:44.22
Australia, 4:02.93
United States, 3:41.59
United States, 8:02.68

### WORLD UNIVERSITY GAMES
**Fukuoka, Japan, August 24-29**

| | |
|---|---|
| 50 free | .........Jilin Sun, China, 26.19 |
| 100 free | .......Martina Moravcova, Slovakia, 56.70 |
| 200 free | .......Lisa Jacob, United States, 2:02.03 |
| 400 free | .......Emily Peters, United States, 4:13.89 |
| 800 free | .......Tamako Kihara, Japan, 8:40.68 |
| 1500 free | .....Toby Smith, United States, 16:20.58 |
| 100 back | .....Kristin Heydenek, United States, 1:02.86 |
| 200 back | .....Yoko Koikawa, Japan, 2:14.61 |
| 100 breast | ...Penelope Hines, South Africa, 1:08.47 |
| 200 breast | ...Penelope Hines, South Africa, 2:28.44 |
| 100 fly | ..........Liu Limin, China, 59:74* |
| 200 fly | ..........Tomoko Kunimitsu, Japan, 2:10.29 |
| 200 IM | ........Fumie Kurotori, Japan, 2:17.00 |
| 400 IM | ........Fumie Kurotori, Japan, 4:45.66 |
| 400 m relay | ..United States, 4:10.49* |
| 400 f relay | ...United States, 3:46.68 |
| 800 f relay | ...United States, 8:05.18* |
| 1-m spgbd | ...Dorte Lindner, Germany, 264.54 |
| 3-m spgbd | ...Rao Lang, China, 493.08 |
| Platform | ........Eileen Richetelli, United States, 479.76 |

### PAN AMERICAN GAMES
**Mar del Plata, Argentina, March 12-17**

Angel Martino, United States, 25.40*
Angel Martino, United States, 55.62
Christina Teuscher, United States, 2:01.49
Brooke Bennett, United States, 4:11.78
Trina Jackson, United States, 8:35.42
not held
B.J. Bedford, United States, 1:01.71*
B.J. Bedford, United States, 2:12.98*
Lisa Flood, Canada, 1:10.36
Lisa Flood, Canada, 2:31.33
Amy Van Dyken, United States, 1:00.71
Trina Jackson, United States, 2:12.37
Joanne Malar, Canada, 2:15.66*
Joanne Malar, Canada, 4:43.64
United States, 4:08.17*
United States, 3:44.71*
United States, 8:07.30
Mayte Garbey, Cuba, 270.15
Annie Pelletier, Canada, 519.81
Anne Montminy, Canada, 492.39

### FINA/ALAMO DIVING GRAND PRIX
**Fort Lauderdale, Florida, May 11-14**

| | |
|---|---|
| 1-m spgbd | ...Yuki Motobuchi, Japan, 268.41 |
| 3-m spgbd | ...Tan Shuping, China, 522.03 |
| Platform | ........Svetlana Timoshinina, Russia, 475.20 |
| 3-m sync | ......Fu/Tan, China, 268.02 |
| 10-m sync | ....Guo/Xiong, China, 303.84 |

### WORLD DIVING CUP
**Atlanta, Georgia, September 5-9**

Vera Ilyina, Russia, 287.49
Fu Mingxia, China, 540.63
Chi Bin, China, 512.82
not held
not held

*Meet record

# World and American Records set in 1995

## Men

| Event | Mark | Record Holder | Date | Site |
|---|---|---|---|---|
| 200 backstroke | ..................1:58.33 | Tripp Schwenk (A) | 8-1-95 | Pasadena |
| 100 butterfly | ..........................52.32 | Denis Pankratov, Russia (W) | 8-23-95 | Vienna |
| 200 butterfly | ......................1:55.22 | Denis Pankratov, Russia (W) | 6-14-95 | Canet, France |
| 400 freestyle relay | .............3:43.80 | United States (David Fox, Joe Hudepohl, Jon Olsen, Gary Hall) (W,A) | 8-12-95 | Atlanta |

## Women

| | | | | |
|---|---|---|---|---|
| 50 freestyle | ..........................25.03 | Amy Van Dyken (A) | 8-13-95 | Atlanta |

# FOR THE RECORD·Year by Year

## MEN
### Freestyle

| Event | Time | Record Holder | Date | Site |
|---|---|---|---|---|
| 50 meters | 21.81 | Tom Jager (W,A) | 3-24-90 | Nashville |
| 100 meters | 48.42 | Alexander Popov, Russia (W) | 6-18-94 | Monte Carlo |
| | | Matt Biondi (A) | 8-10-88 | Austin |
| 200 meters | 1:46.69 | Giorgio Lamberti, Italy (W) | 8-15-89 | Bonn |
| | 1:47.72 | Matt Biondi (A) | 8-8-88 | Austin |
| 400 meters | 3:43.80 | Kieran Perkins, Australia (W) | 9-9-94 | Rome |
| | 3:48.06 | Matt Cetlinski (A) | 8-11-88 | Austin |
| 800 meters | 7:46.00 | Kieran Perkins, Australia (W) | 8-24-94 | Vancouver, B.C. |
| | 7:52.45 | Sean Killion (A) | 7-27-87 | Clovis, CA |
| 1500 meters | 14:41.66 | Kieran Perkins, Australia (W) | 8-24-94 | Vancouver, B.C. |
| | 15:01.51 | George DiCarlo (A) | 6-30-84 | Indianapolis |

### Backstroke

| Event | Time | Record Holder | Date | Site |
|---|---|---|---|---|
| 100 meters | 53.86* | Jeff Rouse (W,A) | 7-31-92 | Barcelona |
| 200 meters | 1:56.57 | Martin Zubero, Spain (W) | 11-23-91 | Tuscaloosa, AL |
| | 1:58.33 | Tripp Schwenk (A) | 8-1-95 | Pasadena |

*Set on first leg of relay.

### Breaststroke

| Event | Time | Record Holder | Date | Site |
|---|---|---|---|---|
| 100 meters | 1:00.95 | Karoly Guttler, Hungary (W) | 8-5-93 | Sheffield, England |
| | 1:01.40 | Nelson Diebel (A) | 3-1-92 | Indianapolis |
| | 1:01.40 | Seth Van Neerden (A) | 8-14-94 | Indianapolis |
| 200 meters | 2:10.16 | Mike Barrowman (W,A) | 7-29-92 | Barcelona |

### Butterfly

| Event | Time | Record Holder | Date | Site |
|---|---|---|---|---|
| 100 meters | 52.32 | Denis Pankratov, Russia (W) | 8-23-95 | Vienna |
| | 52.84 | Pablo Morales (A) | 6-23-86 | Orlando, FL |
| 200 meters | 1:55.22 | Denis Pankratov, Russia (W) | 6-14-95 | Canet, France |
| | 1:55.69 | Melvin Stewart (A) | 1-12-91 | Perth, Australia |

### Individual Medley

| Event | Time | Record Holder | Date | Site |
|---|---|---|---|---|
| 200 meters | 1:59.36 | Jani Sievinen, Finland (W) | 9-11-94 | Rome |
| | 2:00.11 | Dave Wharton (A) | 8-20-89 | Tokyo |
| 400 meters | 4:12.30 | Tom Dolan (W,A) | 9-6-94 | Rome |

### Relays

| Event | Time | Record Holder | Date | Site |
|---|---|---|---|---|
| 400-meter medley | 3:36.93 | United States (David Berkoff, Rich Schroeder, Matt Biondi, Chris Jacobs) (W,A) | 9-23-88 | Seoul |
| | 3:36.93 | United States (Jeff Rouse, Nelson Diebel, Pablo Morales, Jon Olsen), (W, A) | 7-31-92 | Barcelona |
| 400-meter freestyle | 3:15.11 | United States (David Fox, Joe Hudepohl, Jon Olsen, Gary Hall) (W) | 8-12-95 | Atlanta |
| 800-meter freestyle | 7:11.95 | EUN (Dmitri Lepikov, Vladimir Taianovitch Veniamin Taianovitch, Yevgeny Sadovyi) (W) | 7-27-92 | Barcelona |
| | 7:12.51 | United States (Troy Dalbey, Matt Cetlinski, Doug Gjertsen, Matt Biondi) (A) | 9-21-88 | Seoul |

## WOMEN

### Freestyle

| Event | Time | Record Holder | Date | Site |
|-------|------|---------------|------|------|
| 50 meters | 24.51 | Li Jingyi, China (W) | 9-11-94 | Rome |
| | 25.03 | Amy Van Dyken (A) | 8-13-95 | Atlanta |
| 100 meters | 54.01 | Li Jingyi, China (W) | 9-5-94 | Rome |
| | 54.48 | Jenny Thompson (A) | 3-1-92 | Indianapolis |
| 200 meters | 1:57.55 | Franziska van Almsick, Germany (W) | 9-6-94 | Rome |
| | 1:57.90 | Nicole Haislett (A) | 7-27-92 | Barcelona |
| 400 meters | 4:03.85 | Janet Evans (W,A) | 9-22-88 | Seoul |
| 800 meters | 8:16.22 | Janet Evans (W,A) | 8-20-89 | Tokyo |
| 1500 meters | 15:52.10 | Janet Evans (W,A) | 3-26-88 | Orlando, FL |

### Backstroke

| Event | Time | Record Holder | Date | Site |
|-------|------|---------------|------|------|
| 100 meters | 1:00.16 | He Cihong, China (W) | 9-10-94 | Rome |
| | 1:00.82† | Lea Loveless (A) | 7-30-92 | Barcelona |
| 200 meters | 2:06.62 | Krisztina Egerszegi, Hungary (W) | 8-26-91 | Athens, Greece |
| | 2:08.60 | Betsy Mitchell (A) | 6-27-86 | Orlando, FL |

### Breaststroke

| Event | Time | Record Holder | Date | Site |
|-------|------|---------------|------|------|
| 100 meters | 1:07.69 | Samantha Riley, Australia (W) | 9-9-94 | Rome |
| | 1:08.17 | Anita Nall (A) | 7-29-92 | Barcelona |
| 200 meters | 2:24.76 | Rebecca Brown (W) | 3-16-94 | Queensland, Aus. |
| | 2:25.35 | Anita Nall (A) | 3-2-92 | Indianapolis |

### Butterfly

| Event | Time | Record Holder | Date | Site |
|-------|------|---------------|------|------|
| 100 meters | 57.93 | Mary T. Meagher (W,A) | 8-16-81 | Brown Deer, WI |
| 200 meters | 2:05.96 | Mary T. Meagher (W,A) | 8-13-81 | Brown Deer, WI |

### Individual Medley

| Event | Time | Record Holder | Date | Site |
|-------|------|---------------|------|------|
| 200 meters | 2:11.65 | Lin Li, China (W) | 7-30-92 | Barcelona |
| | 2:11.91 | Summer Sanders (A) | 7-30-92 | Barcelona |
| 400 meters | 4:36.10 | Petra Schneider, East Germany (W) | 8-1-82 | Guayaquil, Ecuador |
| | 4:37.58 | Summer Sanders (A) | 7-26-92 | Barcelona |

### Relays

| Event | Time | Record Holder | Date | Site |
|-------|------|---------------|------|------|
| 400-meter medley | 4:01.67 | China (He Cihong, Dai Guohong, Liu Limin, Le Jingyi) (W) | 9-10-94 | Rome |
| | 4:02.54 | United States (Lea Loveless, Anita Nall, Crissy Ahmann-Leighton, Jenny Thompson) (A) | 7-30-92 | Barcelona |
| 400-meter freestyle | 3:37.91 | China (Le Jingyi, Ying Shan, Le Ying, Lu Bin) (W) | 9-7-94 | Rome |
| | 3:39.46 | United States (Nicole Haislett, Dara Torres Angel Martino, Jenny Thompson) (A) | 7-28-92 | Barcelona |
| 800-meter freestyle | 7:55.47 | East Germany (Manuela Stellmach, Astrid Strauss, Anke Mohring, Heike Friedrich) (W) | 8-18-87 | Strasbourg, France |
| | 8:02.12 | United States (Betsy Mitchell, Mary T. Meagher, Kim Brown, Mary Wayte) (A) | 8-22-86 | Madrid |

†Time swum on leadoff leg of 400-meter medley relay.

# World Championships

Venues: Belgrade, Sep 4-9, 1973; Cali, Colombia, July 18-27, 1975; West Berlin, Aug 20-28, 1978; Guayaquil, Equador, Aug 1-7, 1982; Madrid, Aug 17-22, 1986; Perth, Australia, Jan 7-13, 1991; Rome, Sep 1-11, 1994.

## MEN

### 50-meter Freestyle

| | | |
|---|---|---|
| 1986 | Tom Jager, United States | 22.49‡ |
| 1991 | Tom Jager, United States | 22.16‡ |
| 1994 | Alexander Popov, Russia | 22.17 |

### 100-meter Freestyle

| | | |
|---|---|---|
| 1973 | Jim Montgomery, United States | 51.70 |
| 1975 | Andy Coan, United States | 51.25 |
| 1978 | David McCagg, United States | 50.24 |
| 1982 | Jorg Woithe, East Germany | 50.18 |
| 1986 | Matt Biondi, United States | 48.94 |
| 1991 | Matt Biondi, United States | 49.18 |
| 1994 | Alexander Popov, Russia | 49.12 |

### 200-meter Freestyle

| | | |
|---|---|---|
| 1973 | Jim Montgomery, United States | 1:53.02 |
| 1975 | Tim Shaw, United States | 1:52.04‡ |
| 1978 | Billy Forrester, United States | 1:51.02‡ |
| 1982 | Michael Gross, West Germany | 1:49.84 |
| 1986 | Michael Gross, West Germany | 1:47.92 |
| 1991 | Giorgio Lamberti, Italy | 1:47.27‡ |
| 1994 | Antti Kasvio, Finland | 1:47.32 |

### 400-meter Freestyle

| | | |
|---|---|---|
| 1973 | Rick DeMont, United States | 3:58.18‡ |
| 1975 | Tim Shaw, United States | 3:54.88‡ |
| 1978 | Vladimir Salnikov, USSR | 3:51.94‡ |
| 1982 | Vladimir Salnikov, USSR | 3:51.30‡ |
| 1986 | Rainer Henkel, West Germany | 3:50.05 |
| 1991 | Joerg Hoffman, Germany | 3:48.04‡ |
| 1994 | Kieran Perkins, Australia | 3:43.80* |

### 1500-meter Freestyle

| | | |
|---|---|---|
| 1973 | Stephen Holland, Australia | 15:31.85 |
| 1975 | Tim Shaw, United States | 15:28.92‡ |
| 1978 | Vladimir Salnikov, USSR | 15:03.99‡ |
| 1982 | Vladimir Salnikov, USSR | 15:01.77‡ |
| 1986 | Rainer Henkel, West Germany | 15:05.31 |
| 1991 | Joerg Hoffman, Germany | 14:50.36* |
| 1994 | Kieran Perkins, Australia | 14:50.52 |

### 100-meter Backstroke

| | | |
|---|---|---|
| 1973 | Roland Matthes, East Germany | 57.47 |
| 1975 | Roland Matthes, East Germany | 58.15 |
| 1978 | Bob Jackson, United States | 56.36‡ |
| 1982 | Dirk Richter, East Germany | 55.95 |
| 1986 | Igor Polianski, USSR | 55.58‡ |
| 1991 | Jeff Rouse, United States | 55.23‡ |
| 1994 | Martin Lopez Zubero, Spain | 55.17‡ |

### 200-meter Backstroke

| | | |
|---|---|---|
| 1973 | Roland Matthes, East Germany | 2:01.87† |
| 1975 | Zoltan Varraszto, Hungary | 2:05.05 |
| 1978 | Jesse Vassallo, United States | 2:02.16 |
| 1982 | Rick Carey, United States | 2:00.82‡ |
| 1986 | Igor Polianski, USSR | 1:58.78‡ |
| 1991 | Martin Zubero, Spain | 1:59.52 |
| 1994 | Vladimir Selkov, Russia | 1:57.42‡ |

### 100-meter Breaststroke

| | | |
|---|---|---|
| 1973 | John Hencken, United States | 1:04.02† |
| 1975 | David Wilkie, Great Britain | 1:04.26† |
| 1978 | Walter Kusch, West Germany | 1:03.56‡ |
| 1982 | Steve Lundquist, United States | 1:02.75‡ |
| 1986 | Victor Davis, Canada | 1:02.71 |
| 1991 | Norbert Rozsa, Hungary | 1:01.45* |
| 1994 | Norbert Rozsa, Hungary | 1:01.24‡ |

### 200-meter Breaststroke

| | | |
|---|---|---|
| 1973 | David Wilkie, Great Britain | 2:19.28† |
| 1975 | David Wilkie, Great Britain | 2:18.23‡ |
| 1978 | Nick Nevid, United States | 2:18.37 |
| 1982 | Victor Davis, Canada | 2:14.77* |
| 1986 | Jozsef Szabo, Hungary | 2:14.27‡ |
| 1991 | Mike Barrowman, United States | 2:11.23* |
| 1994 | Norbert Rozsa, Hungary | 2:12.81 |

### 100-meter Butterfly

| | | |
|---|---|---|
| 1973 | Bruce Robertson, Canada | 55.69 |
| 1975 | Greg Jagenburg, United States | 55.63 |
| 1978 | Joe Bottom, United States | 54.30 |
| 1982 | Matt Gribble, United States | 53.88‡ |
| 1986 | Pablo Morales, United States | 53.54‡ |
| 1991 | Anthony Nesty, Suriname | 53.29‡ |
| 1994 | Rafal Szukala, Poland | 53.51 |

### 200-meter Butterfly

| | | |
|---|---|---|
| 1973 | Robin Backhaus, United States | 2:03.32 |
| 1975 | Bill Forrester, United States | 2:01.95‡ |
| 1978 | Mike Bruner, United States | 1:59.38‡ |
| 1982 | Michael Gross, East Germany | 1:58.85‡ |
| 1986 | Michael Gross, East Germany | 1:56.53‡ |
| 1991 | Melvin Stewart, United States | 1:55.69* |
| 1994 | Denis Pankratov, Russia | 1:56.54 |

### 200-meter Individual Medley

| | | |
|---|---|---|
| 1973 | Gunnar Larsson, Sweden | 2:08.36 |
| 1975 | Andras Hargitay, Hungary | 2:07.72 |
| 1978 | Graham Smith, Canada | 2:03.65* |
| 1982 | Alexander Sidorenko, USSR | 2:03.30‡ |
| 1986 | Tamás Darnyi, Hungary | 2:01.57‡ |
| 1991 | Tamás Darnyi, Hungary | 1:59.36* |
| 1994 | Jani Sievin, Finland | 1:58.16* |

### 400-meter Individual Medley

| | | |
|---|---|---|
| 1973 | Andras Hargitay, Hungary | 4:31.11 |
| 1975 | Andras Hargitay, Hungary | 4:32.57 |
| 1978 | Jesse Vassallo, United States | 4:20.05* |
| 1982 | Ricardo Prado, Brazil | 4:19.78* |
| 1986 | Tamás Darnyi, Hungary | 4:18.98‡ |
| 1991 | Tamás Darnyi, Hungary | 4:12.36* |
| 1994 | Tom Dolan, United States | 4:12.30* |

* World record; ‡ Meet record.

## MEN (Cont.)

### 400-meter Medley Relay

| Year | | Time |
|---|---|---|
| 1973 | United States (Mike Stamm, John Hencken, Joe Bottom, Jim Montgomery) | 3:49.49 |
| 1975 | United States (John Murphy, Rick Colella, Greg Jagenburg, Andy Coan) | 3:49.00 |
| 1978 | United States (Robert Jackson, Nick Nevid, Joe Bottom, David McCagg) | 3:44.63 |
| 1982 | United States (Rick Carey, Steve Lundquist, Matt Gribble, Rowdy Gaines) | 3:40.84* |
| 1986 | United States (Dan Veatch, David Lundberg, Pablo Morales, Matt Biondi) | 3:41.25 |
| 1991 | United States (Jeff Rouse, Eric Wunderlich, Mark Henderson Matt Biondi) | 3:39.66‡ |
| 1994 | United States (Jeff Rouse, Eric Wunderlich, Mark Henderson, Gary Hall) | 3:37.74‡ |

### 400-meter Freestyle Relay

| Year | | Time |
|---|---|---|
| 1973 | United States (Mel Nash, Joe Bottom, Jim Montgomery, John Murphy) | 3:27.18 |
| 1975 | United States (Bruce Furniss, Jim Montgomery, Andy Coan, John Murphy) | 3:24.85 |
| 1978 | United States (Jack Babashoff, Rowdy Gaines, Jim Montgomery, David McCagg) | 3:19.74 |
| 1982 | United States (Chris Cavanaugh, Robin Leamy, David McCagg, Rowdy Gaines) | 3:19.26* |
| 1986 | United States (Tom Jager, Mike Heath, Paul Wallace, Matt Biondi) | 3:19.89 |
| 1991 | United States (Tom Jager, Brent Lang, Doug Gjertsen, Matt Biondi) | 3:17.15‡ |
| 1994 | United States (Jon Olsen, Josh Davis, Ugur Taner, Gary Hall) | 3:16.90‡ |

### 800-meter Freestyle Relay

| Year | | Time |
|---|---|---|
| 1973 | United States (Kurt Krumpholz, Robin Backhaus, Rick Klatt, Jim Montgomery) | 7:33.22* |
| 1975 | West Germany (Klaus Steinbach, Werner Lampe, Hans Joachim Geisler, Peter Nocke) | 7:39.44 |
| 1978 | United States (Bruce Furniss, Billy Forrester, Bobby Hackett, Rowdy Gaines) | 7:20.82 |
| 1982 | United States (Rich Saeger, Jeff Float, Kyle Miller, Rowdy Gaines) | 7:21.09 |
| 1986 | East Germany (Lars Hinneburg, Thomas Flemming, Dirk Richter, Sven Lodziewski) | 7:15.91‡ |
| 1991 | Germany (Peter Sitt, Steffan Zesner, Stefan Pfeiffer, Michael Gross) | 7:13.50‡ |
| 1994 | Sweden (Christer Waller, Tommy Werner, Lars Frolander, Anders Holmertz) | 7:17.34 |

## WOMEN

### 50-meter Freestyle

| Year | | Time |
|---|---|---|
| 1986 | Tamara Costache, Romania | 25.28* |
| 1991 | Zhuang Yong, China | 25.47 |
| 1994 | Le Jingyi, China | 24.51* |

### 100-meter Freestyle

| Year | | Time |
|---|---|---|
| 1973 | Kornelia Ender, East Germany | 57.54 |
| 1975 | Kornelia Ender, East Germany | 56.50 |
| 1978 | Barbara Krause, East Germany | 55.68‡ |
| 1982 | Birgit Meineke, East Germany | 55.79 |
| 1986 | Kristin Otto, East Germany | 55.05‡ |
| 1991 | Nicole Haislett, United States | 55.17 |
| 1994 | Le Jingyi, China | 54.01* |

### 200-meter Freestyle

| Year | | Time |
|---|---|---|
| 1973 | Keena Rothhammer, United States | 2:04.99 |
| 1975 | Shirley Babashoff, United States | 2:02.50 |
| 1978 | Cynthia Woodhead, United States | 1:58.53* |
| 1982 | Annemarie Verstappen, Netherlands | 1:59.53† |
| 1986 | Heike Friedrich, East Germany | 1:58.26‡ |
| 1991 | Hayley Lewis, Australia | 2:00.48 |
| 1994 | Franziska Van Almsick, Germany | 1:56.78* |

### 400-meter Freestyle

| Year | | Time |
|---|---|---|
| 1973 | Heather Greenwood, United States | 4:20.28 |
| 1975 | Shirley Babashoff, United States | 4:22.70 |
| 1978 | Tracey Wickham, Australia | 4:06.28* |
| 1982 | Carmela Schmidt, East Germany | 4:08.98 |
| 1986 | Heike Friedrich, East Germany | 4:07.45 |
| 1991 | Janet Evans, United States | 4:08.63 |
| 1994 | Yang Aihua, China | 4:09.64 |

### 800-meter Freestyle

| Year | | Time |
|---|---|---|
| 1973 | Novella Calligaris, Italy | 8:52.97 |
| 1975 | Jenny Turrall, Australia | 8:44.75‡ |
| 1978 | Tracey Wickham, Australia | 8:24.94‡ |
| 1982 | Kim Linehan, United States | 8:27.48 |
| 1986 | Astrid Strauss, East Germany | 8:28.24 |
| 1991 | Janet Evans, United States | 8:24.05‡ |
| 1994 | Janet Evans, United States | 8:29.85 |

### 100-meter Backstroke

| Year | | Time |
|---|---|---|
| 1973 | Ulrike Richter, East Germany | 1:05.42 |
| 1975 | Ulrike Richter, East Germany | 1:03.30‡ |
| 1978 | Linda Jezek, United States | 1:02.55‡ |

* World record; ‡Meet record.

## WOMEN *(Cont.)*

### 100-meter Backstroke *(Cont.)*

| | | |
|---|---|---|
| 1982 | Kristin Otto, East Germany | 1:01.30‡ |
| 1986 | Betsy Mitchell, United States | 1:01.74 |
| 1991 | Krisztina Egerszegi, Hungary | 1:01.78 |
| 1994 | He Cihong, China | 1:00.57 |

### 200-meter Backstroke

| | | |
|---|---|---|
| 1973 | Melissa Belote, United States | 2:20.52 |
| 1975 | Birgit Treiber, East Germany | 2:15.46* |
| 1978 | Linda Jezek, United States | 2:11.93* |
| 1982 | Cornelia Sirch, East Germany | 2:09.91* |
| 1986 | Cornelia Sirch, East Germany | 2:11.37 |
| 1991 | Krisztina Egerszegi, Hungary | 2:09.15‡ |
| 1994 | He Cihong, China | 2:07.40 |

### 100-meter Breaststroke

| | | |
|---|---|---|
| 1973 | Renate Vogel, East Germany | 1:13.74 |
| 1975 | Hannalore Anke, East Germany | 1:12.72 |
| 1978 | Julia Bogdanova, USSR | 1:10.31* |
| 1982 | Ute Geweniger, East Germany | 1:09.14‡ |
| 1986 | Sylvia Gerasch, East Germany | 1:08.11* |
| 1991 | Linley Frame, Australia | 1:08.81 |
| 1994 | Samantha Riley, Australia | 1:07.96* |

### 200-meter Breaststroke

| | | |
|---|---|---|
| 1973 | Renate Vogel, East Germany | 2:40.01 |
| 1975 | Hannalore Anke, East Germany | 2:37.25‡ |
| 1978 | Lina Kachushite, USSR | 2:31.42* |
| 1982 | Svetlana Varganova, USSR | 2:28.82‡ |
| 1986 | Silke Hoerner, East Germany | 2:27.40* |
| 1991 | Elena Volkova, USSR | 2:29.53 |
| 1994 | Samantha Riley, Australia | 2:26.87‡ |

### 100-meter Butterfly

| | | |
|---|---|---|
| 1973 | Kornelia Ender, East Germany | 1:02.53 |
| 1975 | Kornelia Ender, East Germany | 1:01.24* |
| 1978 | Joan Pennington, United States | 1:00.20‡ |
| 1982 | Mary T. Meagher, United States | 59.41‡ |
| 1986 | Kornelia Gressler, East Germany | 59.51 |
| 1991 | Qian Hong, China | 59.68 |
| 1994 | Liu Limin, China | 58.98‡ |

### 200-meter Butterfly

| | | |
|---|---|---|
| 1973 | Rosemarie Kother, East Germany | 2:13.76† |
| 1975 | Rosemarie Kother, East Germany | 2:15.92 |
| 1978 | Tracy Caulkins, United States | 2:09.87* |
| 1982 | Ines Geissler, East Germany | 2:08.66‡ |
| 1986 | Mary T. Meagher, United States | 2:08.41‡ |
| 1991 | Summer Sanders, United States | 2:09.24 |
| 1994 | Liu Limin, China | 2:07.25‡ |

### 200-meter Individual Medley

| | | |
|---|---|---|
| 1973 | Andrea Huebner, East Germany | 2:20.51 |
| 1975 | Kathy Heddy, United States | 2:19.80 |
| 1978 | Tracy Caulkins, United States | 2:14.07* |
| 1982 | Petra Schneider, East Germany | 2:11.79 |
| 1986 | Kristin Otto, East Germany | 2:15.56 |
| 1991 | Li Lin, China | 2:13.40 |
| 1994 | Lu Bin, China | 2:12.34‡ |

* World record; ‡Meet record

### 400-meter Individual Medley

| | | |
|---|---|---|
| 1973 | Gudrun Wegner, East Germany | 4:57.71 |
| 1975 | Ulrike Tauber, East Germany | 4:52.76‡ |
| 1978 | Tracy Caulkins, United States | 4:40.83* |
| 1982 | Petra Schneider, East Germany | 4:36.10* |
| 1986 | Kathleen Nord, East Germany | 4:43.75 |
| 1991 | Lin Li, China | 4:41.45 |
| 1994 | Dai Guohong, China | 4:39.14 |

### 400-meter Medley Relay

| | | |
|---|---|---|
| 1973 | East Germany (Ulrike Richter, Renate Vogel, Rosemarie Kother, Kornelia Ender) | 4:16.84 |
| 1975 | East Germany (Ulrike Richter, Hannelore Anke, Rosemarie Kother, Kornelia Ender) | 4:14.74 |
| 1978 | United States (Linda Jezek, Tracy Caulkins, Joan Pennington, Cynthia Woodhead) | 4:08.21‡ |
| 1982 | East Germany (Kristin Otto, Ute Geweniger, Ines Geissler, Birgit Meineke) | 4:05.8* |
| 1986 | East Germany (Kathrin Zimmermann, Sylvia Gerasch, Kornelia Gressler, Kristin Otto) | 4:04.82 |
| 1991 | United States (Janie Wagstaff, Tracey McFarlane, Crissy Ahmann-Leighton, Nicole Haislett) | 4:06.51 |
| 1994 | China (He Cihong, Dai Guohong, Liu Limin, Lu Bin) | 4:01.67* |

### 400-meter Freestyle Relay

| | | |
|---|---|---|
| 1973 | East Germany (Kornelia Ender, Andrea Eife, Andrea Huebner, Sylvia Eichner) | 3:52.45 |
| 1975 | East Germany (Kornelia Ender, Barbara Krause, Claudia Hempel, Ute Bruckner) | 3:49.37 |
| 1978 | United States (Tracy Caulkins, Stephanie Elkins, Joan Pennington, Cynthia Woodhead) | 3:43.43* |
| 1982 | East Germany (Birgit Meineke, Susanne Link, Kristin Otto, Caren Metschuk) | 3:43.97 |
| 1986 | East Germany (Kristin Otto, Manuela Stellmach, Sabine Schulze, Heike Friedrich) | 3:40.57* |
| 1991 | United States (Nicole Haislett, Julie Cooper, Whitney Hedgepeth, Jenny Thompson) | 3:43.26 |
| 1994 | China (Le Jingyi, Ying Shan, Le Ying, Lu Bin) | 3:37.91* |

### 800-meter Freestyle Relay

| | | |
|---|---|---|
| 1986 | East Germany (Manuela Stellmach, Astrid Strauss, Nadja Bergknecht, Heike Friedrich) | 7:59.33* |
| 1991 | Germany (Kerstin Kielgass, Manuela Stellmach, Dagmar Hase, Stephanie Ortwig) | 8:02.56 |
| 1994 | China (Le Ying, Yang Alhua, Zhou Guabin, Lu Bin) | 7:57.96 |

# World Diving Championships

## MEN

### 1-meter Springboard

| | | Pts |
|---|---|---|
| 1991 | Edwin Jongejans, Holland | 588.51 |
| 1994 | Evan Stewart, Zimbabwe | 382.14 |

### 3-meter Springboard

| | | Pts |
|---|---|---|
| 1973 | Phil Boggs, United States | 618.57 |
| 1975 | Phil Boggs, United States | 597.12 |
| 1978 | Phil Boggs, United States | 913.95 |
| 1982 | Greg Louganis, United States | 752.67 |
| 1986 | Greg Louganis, United States | 750.06 |
| 1991 | Kent Ferguson, United States | 650.25 |
| 1994 | Wu Zhuocheng, China | 655.44 |

### Platform

| | | Pts |
|---|---|---|
| 1973 | Klaus Dibiasi, Italy | 559.53 |
| 1975 | Klaus Dibiasi, Italy | 547.98 |
| 1978 | Greg Louganis, United States | 844.11 |
| 1982 | Greg Louganis, United States | 634.26 |
| 1986 | Greg Louganis, United States | 668.58 |
| 1991 | Sun Shuwei, China | 626.79 |
| 1994 | Dmitry Sautin, Russia | 634.71 |

## WOMEN

### 1-meter Springboard

| | | Pts |
|---|---|---|
| 1991 | Gao Min, China | 478.26 |
| 1994 | Chen Lixia, China | 279.30 |

### 3-meter Springboard

| | | Pts |
|---|---|---|
| 1973 | Christa Koehler, East Germany | 442.17 |
| 1975 | Irina Kalinina, USSR | 489.81 |
| 1978 | Irina Kalinina, USSR | 691.43 |
| 1982 | Megan Neyer, United States | 501.03 |
| 1986 | Gao Min, China | 582.90 |
| 1991 | Gao Min, China | 539.01 |
| 1994 | Tan Shuping, China | 548.49 |

### Platform

| | | Pts |
|---|---|---|
| 1973 | Ulrike Knape, Sweden | 406.77 |
| 1975 | Janet Ely, United States | 403.89 |
| 1978 | Irina Kalinina, USSR | 412.71 |
| 1982 | Wendy Wyland, United States | 438.79 |
| 1986 | Chen Lin, China | 449.67 |
| 1991 | Fu Mingxia, China | 426.51 |
| 1994 | Fu Mingxia, China | 434.04 |

## Bidding Beijing Adieu

Olympic watchers have assumed that Beijing, disappointed runner-up to Sydney for the right to host the Games in the year 2000, will bid for the 2004 Games. But Chinese Olympic Committee general secretary Wei Jizhong says that two other Chinese citites, Shanghai and Guangzhou, may also mount bid campaigns. What's more, several old China hands tell SI that they wouldn't be surprised to see the country pass on the Games altogether.

One reason is that South Africa was a stout ally of Beijing's unsuccessful bid, and Chinese officials may not want to go up against Cape Town, which is a likely candidate for 2004. The other reason: In Chinese numerology, four is viewed as an inauspicious number; a bid in 2008 would be considered more promising because of the smoothness of the number eight and its intimations of infinity.

## Men

### 50-METER FREESTYLE

| | | |
|---|---|---|
| 1988 | Matt Biondi | 22.14* |

### 100-METER FREESTLYE

| | | |
|---|---|---|
| 1906 | Charles Daniels | 1:13.4 |
| 1908 | Charles Daniels | 1:05.6* |
| 1912 | Duke Kahanamoku | 1:03.4 |
| 1920 | Duke Kahanamoku | 1:00.4 |
| 1924 | John Weissmuller | 59.0‡ |
| 1928 | John Weissmuller | 58.6‡ |
| 1948 | Wally Ris | 57.3‡ |
| 1952 | Clarke Scholes | 57.4 |
| 1964 | Don Schollander | 53.4‡ |
| 1972 | Mark Spitz | 51.22* |
| 1976 | Jim Montgomery | 49.99* |
| 1984 | Rowdy Gaines | 49.80‡ |
| 1988 | Matt Biondi | 48.63‡ |

### 200-METER FREESTYLE

| | | |
|---|---|---|
| 1904 | Charles Daniels | 2:44.2 |
| 1906 | Not held 1906-1964 | |
| 1972 | Mark Spitz | 1:52.78* |
| 1976 | Bruce Furniss | 1:50.29* |

### 400-METER FREESTYLE

| | | |
|---|---|---|
| 1904 | Charles Daniels (440 yds) | 6:16.2 |
| 1920 | Norman Ross | 5:26.8 |
| 1924 | John Weissmuller | 5:04.2‡ |
| 1932 | Buster Crabbe | 4:48.4‡ |
| 1936 | Jack Medica | 4:44.5‡ |
| 1948 | William Smith | 4:41.0‡ |
| 1964 | Don Schollander | 4:12.2* |
| 1968 | Mike Burton | 4:09.0‡ |
| 1976 | Brian Goodell | 3:51.93* |
| 1984 | George DiCarlo | 3:51.23‡ |

### 1500-METER FREESTYLE

| | | |
|---|---|---|
| 1920 | Norman Ross | 22:23.2 |
| 1948 | James McLane | 19:18.5 |
| 1952 | Ford Konno | 18:30.3‡ |
| 1968 | Mike Burton | 16:38.9‡ |
| 1972 | Mlke Burton | 15:52.58‡ |
| 1976 | Brian Goodell | 15:02.40* |
| 1984 | Michael O'Brien | 15:05.20 |

### 100-METER BACKSTROKE

| | | |
|---|---|---|
| 1912 | Harry Hebner | 1:21.2 |
| 1920 | Warren Kealoha | 1:15.2 |
| 1924 | Warren Kealoha | 1:13.2‡ |
| 1928 | George Kojac | 1:08.2* |
| 1936 | Adolph Kiefer | 1:05.9‡ |
| 1948 | Allen Stack | 1:06.4 |
| 1952 | Yoshi Oyakawa | 1:05.4‡ |
| 1976 | John Naber | 55.49* |
| 1984 | Rick Carey | 55.79 |

### 200-METER BACKSTROKE

| | | |
|---|---|---|
| 1964 | Jed Graef | 2:10.3* |
| 1976 | John Naber | 1:59.19* |
| 1984 | Rick Carey | 2:00.23 |

### 100-METER BREASTSTROKE

| | | |
|---|---|---|
| 1968 | Donald McKenzie | 1:07.7‡ |
| 1976 | John Hencken | 1:03.11* |
| 1984 | Steve Lundquist | 1:01.65 * |
| 1992 | Nelson Diebel | 1:01.50‡ |

### 200-METER BREASTSTROKE

| | | |
|---|---|---|
| 1924 | Robert Skelton | 2:56.6 |
| 1948 | Joseph Verdeur | 2:39.3‡ |
| 1960 | William Mulliken | 2:37.4 |
| 1972 | John Hencken | 2:21.55 |
| 1992 | Mike Barrowman | 2:10.16* |

### 100-METER BUTTERFLY

| | | |
|---|---|---|
| 1968 | Douglas Russell | 55.9‡ |
| 1972 | Mark Spitz | 54.27* |
| 1976 | Matt Vogel | 54.35 |
| 1992 | Pablo Morales | 53.32 |

### 200-METER BUTTERFLY

| | | |
|---|---|---|
| 1956 | William Yorzyk | 2:19.3‡ |
| 1960 | Michael Troy | 2:12.8* |
| 1968 | Carl Robie | 2:08.7 |
| 1972 | Mark Spitz | 2:00.70* |
| 1976 | Mike Bruner | 1:59.23* |
| 1992 | Melvin Stewart | 1:56.26 |

### 200-METER INDIVIDUAL MEDLEY

| | | |
|---|---|---|
| 1968 | Charles Hickcox | 2:12.0‡ |

### 400-METER INDIVIDUAL MEDLEY

| | | |
|---|---|---|
| 1964 | Richard Roth | 4:45.4* |
| 1968 | Charles Hickcox | 4:48.4 |
| 1976 | Rod Strachan | 4:23.68* |

### 3-METER SPRINGBOARD DIVING

| | | |
|---|---|---|
| 1920 | Louis Kuehn | 675.4 points |
| 1924 | Albert White | 696.4 |
| 1928 | Pete Desjardins | 185.04 |
| 1932 | Michael Galitzen | 161.38 |
| 1936 | Richard Degener | 163.57 |
| 1948 | Bruce Harlan | 163.64 |
| 1952 | David Browning | 205.29 |
| 1956 | Robert Clotworthy | 159.56 |
| 1960 | Gary Tobian | 170.00 |
| 1964 | Kenneth Sitzberger | 159.90 |
| 1968 | Bernard Wrightson | 170.15 |
| 1976 | Philip Boggs | 619.05 |
| 1984 | Greg Louganis | 754.41 |
| 1988 | Greg Louganis | 730.80 |

### PLATFORM DIVING

| | | |
|---|---|---|
| 1904 | George Sheldon | 12.66 |
| 1920 | Clarence Pinkston | 100.67 |
| 1924 | Albert White | 97.46 |
| 1928 | Pete Desjardins | 98.74 |
| 1932 | Harold Smith | 124.80 |
| 1936 | Marshall Wayne | 113.58 |
| 1948 | Sammy Lee | 130.05 |
| 1952 | Sammy Lee | 156.28 |
| 1960 | Robert Webster | 165.56 |
| 1964 | Robert Webster | 148.58 |
| 1984 | Greg Louganis | 576.99 |
| 1988 | Greg Louganis | 638.61 |

* World record; ‡ Meet (Olympic) record.

## Women

### 100-METER FREESTLYE

| | | |
|---|---|---|
| 1920 | Ethelda Bleibtrey | 1:13.6* |
| 1924 | Ethel Lackie | 1:12.4 |
| 1928 | Albina Osipowich | 1:11.0‡ |
| 1932 | Helene Madison | 1:06.8‡ |
| 1968 | Jan Henne | 1:00.0 |
| 1972 | Sandra Neilson | 58.59‡ |
| 1984 | Carrie Steinseifer | 55.92 |
| | Nancy Hogshead | 55.92 |

### 200-METER FREESTYLE

| | | |
|---|---|---|
| 1968 | Debbie Meyer | 2:10.5‡ |
| 1984 | Mary Wayte | 1:59.23 |
| 1992 | Nicole Haislett | 1:57.90 |

### 400-METER FREESTYLE

| | | |
|---|---|---|
| 1924 | Martha Norelius | 6:02.2‡ |
| 1928 | Martha Norelius | 5:42.8* |
| 1932 | Helene Madison | 5:28.5* |
| 1948 | Ann Curtis | 5:17.8‡ |
| 1960 | Chris von Saltza | 4:50.6 |
| 1964 | Virginia Duenkel | 4:43.3‡ |
| 1968 | Debbie Meyer | 4:31.8‡ |
| 1984 | Tiffany Cohen | 4:07.10‡ |
| 1988 | Janet Evans | 4:03.85* |

### 800-METER FREESTYLE

| | | |
|---|---|---|
| 1968 | Debbie Meyer | 9:24.0‡ |
| 1972 | Keena Rothhammer | 8:53.86* |
| 1984 | Tiffany Cohen | 8:24.95‡ |
| 1988 | Janet Evans | 8:20.20‡ |
| 1992 | Janet Evans | 8:25.52 |

### 100-METER BACKSTROKE

| | | |
|---|---|---|
| 1924 | Sybil Bauer | 1:23.2‡ |
| 1932 | Eleanor Holm | 1:19.4 |
| 1960 | Lynn Burke | 1:09.3‡ |
| 1964 | Cathy Ferguson | 1:07.7* |
| 1968 | Kaye Hall | 1:06.2* |
| 1972 | Melissa Belote | 1:05.78‡ |
| 1984 | Theresa Andrews | 1:02.55 |

### 200-METER BACKSTROKE

| | | |
|---|---|---|
| 1968 | Pokey Watson | 2:24.8‡ |
| 1972 | Melissa Belote | 2:19.19* |

### 100-METER BREASTSTROKE

| | | |
|---|---|---|
| 1972 | Catherine Carr | 1:13.58* |

### 200-METER BREASTSTROKE

| | | |
|---|---|---|
| 1968 | Sharon Wichman | 2:44.4‡ |

### 100-METER BUTTERFLY

| | | |
|---|---|---|
| 1956 | Shelley Mann | 1:11.0‡ |
| 1960 | Carolyn Schuler | 1:09.5‡ |
| 1964 | Sharon Stouder | 1:04.7* |
| 1984 | Mary T. Meagher | 59.26 |

### 200-METER BUTTERFLY

| | | |
|---|---|---|
| 1972 | Karen Moe | 2:15.57* |
| 1984 | Mary T. Meagher | 2:06.90‡ |
| 1992 | Summer Sanders | 2:08.67 |

### 200-METER INDIVIDUAL MEDLEY

| | | |
|---|---|---|
| 1968 | Sharon Wichman | 2:44.4‡ |
| 1984 | Tracy Caulkins | 2:12.64‡ |

### 400-METER INDIVIDUAL MEDLEY

| | | |
|---|---|---|
| 1964 | Donna De Varona | 5:18.7‡ |
| 1968 | Claudia Kolb | 5:08.5‡ |
| 1984 | Tracy Caulkins | 4:39.24 |
| 1988 | Janet Evans | 4:37.76 |

### 3-METER SPRINGBOARD DIVING

| | | |
|---|---|---|
| 1920 | Aileen Riggin | 539.9 points |
| 1924 | Elizabeth Becker | 474.5 |
| 1928 | Helen Meany | 78.62 |
| 1932 | Georgia Coleman | 87.52 |
| 1936 | Marjorie Gestring | 89.27 |
| 1948 | Victoria Draves | 108.74 |
| 1952 | Patricia McCormick | 147.30 |
| 1956 | Patricia McCormick | 142.36 |
| 1968 | Sue Gossick | 150.77 |
| 1972 | Micki King | 450.03 |
| 1976 | Jennifer Chandler | 506.19 |

### PLATFORM DIVING

| | | |
|---|---|---|
| 1924 | Caroline Smith | 33.2 |
| 1928 | Elizabeth Becker Pinkston | 31.6 |
| 1932 | Dorothy Poynton | 40.26 |
| 1936 | Dorothy Poynton Hill | 33.93 |
| 1948 | Victoria Draves | 68.87 |
| 1952 | Patricia McCormick | 79.37 |
| 1956 | Patricia McCormick | 84.85 |
| 1964 | Lesley Bush | 99.80 |

* World record; ‡Meet (Olympic) record.

# Notable Achievements

## Barrier Breakers

### MEN

| Event | Barrier | Athlete and Nation | Time | Date |
|---|---|---|---|---|
| 100 Freestyle | 1:00 | Johnny Weissmuller, United States | 58.6 | 7-9-22 |
| 100 Freestyle | :50 | James Montgomery, United States | 49.99 | 7-25-76 |
| 200 Freestyle | 2:00 | Don Schollander, United States | 1:58.8 | 7-27-63 |
| 200 Freestyle | 1:50 | Sergei Kopliakov, USSR | 1:49.83 | 4-7-79 |
| 400 Freestyle | 4:00 | Rick DeMont, United States | 3:58.18 | 9-6-73 |
| 400 Freestyle | 3:50 | Vladimir Salnikov, USSR | 3:49.57 | 3-12-82 |
| 800 Freestyle | 8:00 | Vladimir Salnikov, USSR | 7:56.49 | 3-23-79 |
| 1500 Freestyle | 15:00 | Vladimir Salnikov, USSR | 14:58.27 | 7-22-80 |
| 100 Backstroke | 1:00 | Thompson Mann, United States | 59.6 | 10-16-64 |
| 200 Backstroke | 2:00 | John Naber, United States | 1:59.19 | 7-24-76 |
| 200 Breaststroke | 2:30 | Chester Jastremski, United States | 2:29.6 | 8-19-61 |
| 100 Butterfly | 1:00 | Lance Larson, United States | 59.0 | 6-29-60 |
| 200 Butterfly | 2:00 | Roger Pyttel, East Germany | 1:59.63 | 6-3-76 |

### WOMEN

| Event | Barrier | Athlete and Nation | Time | Date |
|---|---|---|---|---|
| 100 Freestyle | 1:00 | Dawn Fraser, Australia | 59.9 | 10-27-62 |
| 200 Freestyle | 2:00 | Kornelia Ender, East Germany | 1:59.78 | 6-2-76 |
| 400 Freestyle | 4:30 | Debbie Meyer, United States | 4:29.0 | 8-18-67 |
| 800 Freestyle | 10:00 | Jane Cederqvist, Sweden | 9:55.6 | 8-17-60 |
| 800 Freestyle | 9:00 | Ann Simmons, United States | 8:59.4 | 9-10-71 |
| 1500 Freestyle | 20:00 | Ilsa Konrads, Australia | 19:25.7 | 1-14-60 |
| | 16:00 | Janet Evans, United States | 15:52.10 | 3-26-88 |
| 200 Backstroke | 2:30 | Satoko Tanaka, Japan | 2:29.6 | 2-10-63 |
| 100 Butterfly | 1:00 | Christiane Knacke, East Germany | 59.78 | 8-28-77 |
| 400 Individual Medley | 5:00 | Gudrun Wegner, East Germany | 4:57.51 | 9-6-73 |

## Olympic Achievements

### MOST INDIVIDUAL GOLDS IN SINGLE OLYMPICS

#### MEN

| No. | Athlete and Nation | Olympic Year | Events |
|---|---|---|---|
| 4 | Mark Spitz, United States | 1972 | 100, 200 Free; 100, 200 Fly |

#### WOMEN

| No. | Athlete and Nation | Olympic Year | Events |
|---|---|---|---|
| 4 | Kristin Otto, East Germany | 1988 | 50, 100 Free; 100 Back; 100 Fly |
| 3 | Debbie Meyer, United States | 1968 | 200, 400, 800 Free |
| 3 | Shane Gould, Australia | 1972 | 200, 400 Free; 200 IM |
| 3 | Kornelia Ender, East Germany | 1976 | 100, 200 Free; 100 Fly |
| 3 | Janet Evans, United States | 1988 | 400, 800 Free; 400 IM |
| 3 | Krisztina Egerszegi, Hungary | 1992 | 100, 200 Back; 400 IM |

## Olympic Achievements *(Cont.)*

### MOST INDIVIDUAL OLYMPIC GOLD MEDALS, CAREER

#### MEN

| No. | Athlete and Nation | Olympic Years and Events |
|---|---|---|
| 4 | Charles Meldrum Daniels, United States | 1904 (220, 440 Free); 1906 (100 Free,) 1908 (100 Free) |
| 4 | Roland Matthes, East Germany | 1968 (100, 200 Back); 1972 (100, 200 Back) |
| 4 | Mark Spitz, United States | 1972 (100, 200 Free; 100, 200 Fly) |

#### WOMEN

| | | |
|---|---|---|
| 4 | Kristin Otto, East Germany | 1988 (50 Free; 100 Free, Back and Fly) |

**Most Olympic Gold Medals in a Single Olympics, Men**—7, Mark Spitz, United States, 1972, 100, 200 Free; 100, 200 Fly; 4 x 100, 4 x 200 Free Relays; 4 x 100 Medley

**Most Olympic Gold Medals in a Single Olympics, Women**—6, Kristin Otto, East Germany, 1988, 50, 100 Free; 100 Back; 100 Fly; 4 x 100 Free Relay; 4 x 100 Medley Relay

**Most Olympic Medals in a Career, Men**—
11, Matt Biondi, United States:1984 (one gold), '88 (five gold, one silver, one bronze), 92 (two gold, one silver)
11, Mark Spitz, United States: 1968 (two gold, one silver, one bronze), 1972 (seven gold)

**Most Olympic Medals in Career, Women**—
8, Dawn Fraser, Australia: 1956 (two gold, one silver), '60 (one gold, two silver), '64 (one gold, one silver)
8, Kornelia Ender, East Germany: 1972 (three silver), '76 (four gold, one silver)
8, Shirley Babashoff, United States: 1972 (one gold, two silver), '76 (one gold, four silver)

**Winner, Same Event, Three Consecutive Olympics**—Dawn Fraser, Australia, 100 Freestyle, 1956, '60, '64.

**Youngest Person to Win an Olympic Diving Gold**—Marjorie Gestring, United States, 1936, 13 years, 9 months, springboard diving

**Youngest Person to Win Olympic Swimming Gold**—Krisztina Egerszegi, Hungary, 1988, 14 years, one month, 200 backstroke

## World Record Achievements

**Most World Records, Career, Women**—42, Ragnhild Hveger, Denmark, 1936-42
**Most World Records, Career, Men**—32, Arne Borg, Sweden, 1921-29
**Most Freestyle Records Held Concurrently**—
5, Helene Madison, United States, 1931-33.
5, Shane Gould, Australia, 1972.
**Most Consecutive Lowerings of a Record**—10, Kornelia Ender, East Germany, 100 Freestyle, 7-13-73 to 7-19-76.
**Longest Duration of World Record**—19 years, 359 days, 1:04.6 in 100 Free, Willy den Ouden , the Netherlands

# Skiing

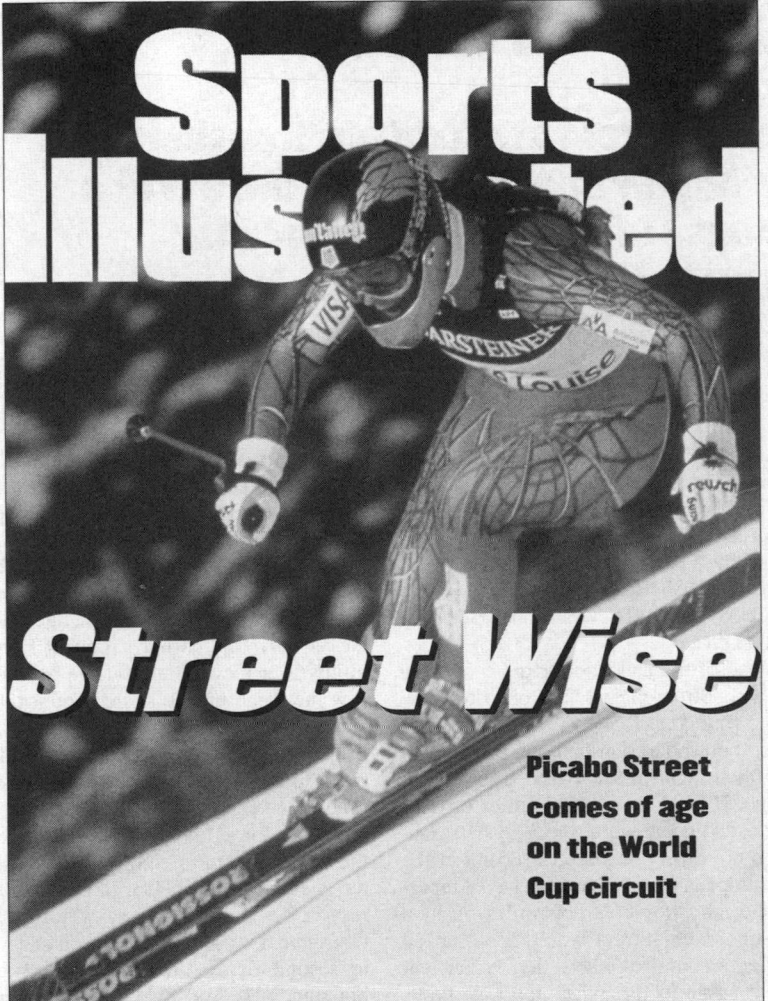

Sports Illustrated

## Street Wise

**Picabo Street comes of age on the World Cup circuit**

# Picabo, We See You

**Picabo Street stepped out from behind her bubbly image and gave the world a glimpse of a champion downhiller**

**by Michael Farber**

PICABO STREET started the 1994–95 Alpine skiing season as a one-race wonder, a fast and frank flibbertigibbet who had squeezed a lot of mileage out of a bubbly personality, a fabulous name and an Olympic silver medal. She left it as a champion, the first U.S. skier to win a World Cup downhill title.

Instead of the childhood game evoked by her name, Street played "last one down the hill is a rotten egg." She won six of the nine women's downhills, finishing the season with her fifth straight at the World Cup final in Bormio. If Michaela Gerg-Leitner of Germany hadn't come out of the 30th start position to nip Street by .02 of a second in the first European downhill in Cortina d'Ampezzo—the only women's downhill won by a non-American—Street would have batted 1.000 on a continent where they usually eat white sausage for breakfast and U.S. skiers for lunch.

After her eye-catching silver medal in the Lillehammer Games, Street made the TV equivalent of the rubber-chicken circuit, showing up on *Sesame Street* and *American Gladiators*. But only the 1994–95 season made her a prime-time star. "This is about greatness, perseverance and consistency," said Street, who had begun the season without a World Cup victory. "That's what I strived for. That's what I thought I had the ability to achieve. Some of the people who saw me come up the skiing ladder thought that if anyone could do it, I could. Then other people looked at me and said, 'No way.' To those people, I say better guess next time."

And as for a 1994 SI story that described the U.S. ski team as "snow plows," well, better guess next time. Hilary Lindh, who is as reserved as Street is brassy, won two of the first three downhills of the season and wound up second to Street in the World Cup downhill standings. And Kyle Rasmussen, whose career was mired on the fringes of the circuit, broke through with a victory at the venerable Lauberhorn in Wengen. At first it seemed

BOB MARTIN

**Tombamania returned to the circuit as La Bomba won seven of nine slaloms.**

like a journeyman shooting four rounds of 68s at Augusta, but Rasmussen proved it was no fluke when he later won at Kvitfjell. "We've dominated the downhill," said Paul Major, the U.S. Alpine program director. "The Europeans are in shock."

Of course the technical disciplines remained the domain of the Europeans, especially the indomitable Alberto Tomba. La Bomba was the only skier who could match results or, for that matter, personalities with Street in 1994–95. Tomba said it would be his last season—"Tomba says a lot of things," said his manager, Paolo Comellini—and then went on to become the first technical skier to win the men's overall World Cup title since Ingemar Stenmark in 1977–78, taking seven of nine slaloms and four giant slaloms. From December until mid February, he won seven straight races. "The most important thing is to be convinced of your chances," Tomba

said. He had been the World Cup runner-up three times, but 1994–95 put this over-the-top Italian truly over the top. Tombamania returned. Despite Street's stunning success, Tomba remains the only global skiing superstar, the eternal center ring in the Great White Circus.

Tomba once said his dream race included downing a glass of wine before the start and stopping midway down for a cigarette before crossing the line in first place. In a giant slalom in Alta Badia, the parallel lines of fact and fantasy seemed to cross. Tomba made a mistake midway down the course that forced him to a dead halt, his skis sideways to the gates. He straightened himself, pointed his skis south and still won the race. This was a quieter, more dedicated Tomba—an extra 25 days in his off-season training regimen helped him lose the suet that creeps on his frame between Olympics—but he had not lost his sense of playfulness. He celebrated the improbable Alta Badia victory by doing a somersault at the finish line, blowing kisses to

**Schneider sails into retirement with
55 career World Cup wins.**

his fans and kneeling to kiss his dog, Yukon.

The other constant of the 1994–95 World Cup season was the weather. "There's a four-letter word to describe the ski weather we've had," said Armin Assinger of Austria, who finished fourth behind men's downhill champion Luc Alphand of France. "Oops." That, too. The World Alpine Championships in Sierra Nevada were postponed until March 1996 because of lack of snow. Through the first week of March 1995, men downhillers had had only seven training runs and seven races.

There should have been an eighth. Thirty-one of the 68 racers were down Aspen Mountain in America's Downhill when a storm hit. AJ Kitt led by a ridiculous .58 of a second, and no one left at the start gate had a prayer of catching him, but he fretted as he waited for officials to declare it a valid race. "I don't want to be the most screwed ski racer in history," said Kitt, who had had two other seeming victories during his career wiped out by weather. Well, he is. On-site officials declared the results official, but a 17-member FIS panel overruled them three days later. Kitt, who now has four firsts but still only one World Cup victory, briefly considered retiring.

Vreni Schneider of Switzerland has 55 World Cup wins and did retire despite being close to the record of 62 victories held by Annemarie Moser-Pröll, the Austrian star of the 1970s. "I decided that now is the right moment to stop," said Schneider, 30. "I've already got enough records." Schneider won her third World Cup overall title—edging Katja Seizinger of Germany by six points with a brilliant slalom performance in Bormio—and the slalom and giant slalom titles, giving her a record 11 championships in individual disciplines. She has also won three world championships and three Olympic gold medals.

No one appreciates the magnitude of these accomplishments better than Schneider's peers, especially those coming up behind her. Of her first World Cup season title Street said, "This puts you in a special, elite category." If she can maintain the standard she set this season, Street will one day reach that next echelon—the one Schneider now exits.

# FOR THE RECORD·1994–1995

## World Cup Season Race Results

### Men

| Date | Event | Site | Winner |
|------|-------|------|--------|
| 12-3-94 | Giant Slalom | Tignes, France | Achim Vogt, Liechtenstein |
| 12-4-94 | Slalom | Tignes, France | Alberto Tomba, Italy |
| 12-11-94 | Super G | Tignes, France | Patrick Ortlieb, Austria |
| 12-12-94 | Slalom | Sestriere, Italy | Alberto Tomba, Italy |
| 12-16-94 | Downhill | Val d'Isere, France | Josef Strobl, Austria |
| 12-17-94 | Downhill | Val d'Isere, France | Armin Assinger, Austria |
| 12-18-94 | Giant Slalom | Val d'Isere, France | Michael vonGruenigen, Switzerland |
| 12-20-94 | Slalom | Lech, Austria | Alberto Tomba, Italy |
| 12-21-94 | Slalom | Lech, Austria | Alberto Tomba, Italy |
| 12-22-94 | Giant Slalom | Alta Badia, Italy | Alberto Tomba, Italy |
| 1-6-95 | Giant Slalom | Kranjska Gora, Slovenia | Alberto Tomba, Italy |
| 1-8-95 | Slalom | Kranjska Gora, Slovenia | Alberto Tomba, Italy |
| 1-14-95 | Downhill | Kitzbuehel, Austria | Luc Alphand, France |
| 1-14-95 | Downhill | Kitzbuehel, Austria | Luc Alphand, France |
| 1-15-95 | Slalom | Kitzbuehel, Austria | Alberto Tomba, Italy |
| 1-14/15-95 | Combined | Kitzbuehel, Austria | Marc Girardelli, Luxembourg |
| 1-16-95 | Super G | Kitzbuehel, Austria | Guenther Mader, Austria |
| 1-20-95 | Downhill | Wengen, Switzerland | Kristian Ghedina, Italy |
| 1-21-95 | Downhill | Wengen, Switzerland | Kyle Rasmussen, United States |
| 1-22-95 | Slalom | Wengen, Switzerland | Alberto Tomba, Italy |
| 1-22-95 | Combined | Wengen, Switzerland | Marc Girardelli, Luxembourg |
| 2-4-95 | Giant Slalom | Adelboden, Switzerland | Alberto Tomba, Italy |
| 2-19-95 | Slalom | Furano, Japan | Michael Tritscher, Austria |
| 2-20-95 | Giant Slalom | Furano, Japan | Mario Reiter, Austria |
| 2-25-95 | Downhill | Whistler, British Columbia | Kristian Ghedina, Italy |
| 2-26-95 | Super G | Whistler, British Columbia | Peter Runggaldier, Italy |
| 3-10-95 | Super G | Kvitfjell, Norway | Werner Perathoner, Italy |
| 3-11-95 | Downhill | Kvitfjell, Norway | Pietro Vitalini, Italy |
| 3-11-95 | Downhill | Kvitfjell, Norway | Kyle Rasmussen, United States |
| 3-15-95 | Downhill | Bormio, Italy | Luc Alphand, France |
| 3-16-95 | Super G | Bormio, Italy | Richard Kroell, Austria |
| 3-18-95 | Giant Slalom | Bormio, Italy | Alberto Tomba, Italy |
| 3-19-95 | Slalom | Bormio, Italy | Ole Christian Furuseth, Norway |

### Women

| Date | Event | Site | Winner |
|------|-------|------|--------|
| 11-26-94 | Giant Slalom | Park City, Utah | Heidi Zeller-Baehler, Switzerland |
| 11-27-94 | Slalom | Park City, Utah | Vreni Schneider, Switzerland |
| 12-2-94 | Downhill | Vail, Colorado | Hilary Lindh, United States |
| 12-3-94 | Super G | Vail, Colorado | Sylvia Eder, Austria |
| 12-4-94 | Giant Slalom | Vail, Colorado | Heidi Zeller-Baehler, Switzerland |
| 12-9-94 | Downhill | Lake Louise, Alberta | Picabo Street, United States |
| 12-10-94 | Downhill | Lake Louise, Alberta | Hilary Lindh, United States |
| 12-11-94 | Super G | Lake Louise, Alberta | Katja Seizinger, Germany |
| 12-18-94 | Slalom | Sestriere, Italy | Vreni Schneider, Switzerland |
| 12-21-94 | Giant Slalom | Alta Badia, Italy | Sabina Panzanini, Italy |
| 12-30-94 | Slalom | Meribel, France | Urska Hrovat, Slovenia |
| 1-7-95 | Super G | Haus, Austria | Anita Wachter, Austria |
| 1-8-95 | Giant Slalom | Haus, Austria | Deborah Compagnoni, Italy |
| 1-10-95 | Super G | Flachau, Austria | Renate Goetschl, Austria |
| 1-14-95 | Super G | Garmisch-Partenkirchen, Germany | Florence Masnada, France |
| 1-15-95 | Slalom | Garmisch-Partenkirchen, Germany | Martina Ertl, Germany |
| 1-20-95 | Downhill | Cortina d'Ampezzo, Italy | Michaela Gerg-Leitner, Germany |
| 1-22-95 | Downhill | Cortina d'Ampezzo, Italy | Picabo Street, United States |
| 1-23-95 | Giant Slalom | Cortina d'Ampezzo, Italy | Anita Wachter, Austria |
| 2-17-95 | Downhill | Are, Sweden | Picabo Street, United States |
| 2-18-95 | Giant Slalom | Are, Sweden | Anita Wachter, Austria |
| 2-25-95 | Giant Slalom | Maribor, Slovenia | Martina Ertl, Germany |
| 2-26/27-95 | Slalom | Maribor, Slovenia | Vreni Schneider, Switzerland |
| 3-5-95 | Downhill | Saalbach, Austria | Picabo Street, United States |
| 3-5-95 | Super G | Saalbach, Austria | Heidi Zeller-Baehler, Switzerland |

## Women *(Cont.)*

| Date | Event | Site | Winner |
|------|-------|------|--------|
| 3-11-95 | Downhill | Lenzerheide, Switzerland | Picabo Street, United States |
| 3-12-95 | Slalom | Lenzerheide, Switzerland | Pernilla Wiberg, Sweden |
| 3-11/12-95 | Combined | Lenzerheide, Switzerland | Pernilla Wiberg, Sweden |
| 3-15-95 | Downhill | Bormio, Italy | Picabo Street, United States |
| 3-16-95 | Super G | Bormio, Italy | Katja Seizinger, Germany |
| 3-18-95 | Giant Slalom | Bormio, Italy | Spela Pretnar, Slovenia |
| 3-19-95 | Slalom | Bormio, Italy | Vreni Schneider, Switzerland |

# World Cup Standings

## Men

### OVERALL

| | Pts |
|---|---|
| Alberto Tomba, Italy | 1150 |
| Günther Mader, Austria | 775 |
| Jure Kosir, Slovenia | 760 |
| Marc Girardelli, Luxembourg | 744 |
| Kjetil Andre Aamodt, Norway | 710 |
| Lasse Kjus, Norway | 665 |
| Kristian Ghedina, Italy | 644 |
| Luc Alphand, France | 609 |

### DOWNHILL

| | Pts |
|---|---|
| Luc Aplhand, France | 484 |
| Kristian Ghedina, Italy | 473 |
| Patrick Ortlieb, Austria | 426 |
| Armin Assinger, Austria | 419 |
| Josef Strobl, Austria | 307 |
| Kyle Rasmussen, United States | 288 |
| Hannes Trinkl, Austria | 273 |
| Werner Perathoner, Italy | 269 |

### SLALOM

| | Pts |
|---|---|
| Alberto Tomba, Italy | 700 |
| Michael Tritscher, Austria | 477 |
| Jure Kosir, Slovenia | 405 |
| Ole Christian Furuseth, Norway | 401 |
| Mario Reiter, Austria | 341 |
| Thomas Sykora, Austria | 302 |
| Michael VonGruenigen, Switz. | 282 |
| Sebastian Amiez, France | 279 |

### GIANT SLALOM

| | Pts |
|---|---|
| Alberto Tomba, Italy | 450 |
| Jure Kosir, Slovenia | 355 |
| Harald Strand Nilsen, Norway | 322 |
| Kjetil Andre Aamodt, Norway | 307 |
| Michael Von Gruenigen, Switz. | 296 |
| Urs Kaelin, Switzerland | 288 |
| Achim Vogt, Liechtenstein | 226 |
| Mario Reiter, Austria | 218 |

### SUPER G

| | Pts |
|---|---|
| Peter Runggaldier, Italy | 332 |
| Günther Mader, Austria | 250 |
| Werner Perathone, Italy | 237 |
| Richard Kroell Austria | 170 |
| Kyle Rasmussen, United States | 148 |
| Atle Skaardal, Norway | 142 |
| Kristian Ghedina, Italy | 126 |
| Armin Assinger, Austria | 123 |

## Women

### OVERALL

| | Pts |
|---|---|
| Vreni Schneider, Switzerland | 1248 |
| Katja Seizinger, Germany | 1242 |
| Heidi Zeller-Baehler, Switz. | 1044 |
| Martina Ertl, Germany | 985 |
| Picabo Street, United States | 905 |
| Pernilla Wiberg, Sweden | 816 |
| Spela Pretnar, Slovenia | 669 |
| Anita Wachter, Austria | 593 |

### DOWNHILL

| | Pts |
|---|---|
| Picabo Street, United States | 709 |
| Hilary Lindh, United States | 493 |
| Katja Seizinger, Germany | 445 |
| Warwara Zelenskaja, Russia | 416 |
| Isolde Kostner, Italy | 310 |
| Babara Merlin, Italy | 304 |
| Michaela Gerg-Leitner, Ger | 262 |
| Heidi Zurbriggen, Switzerland | 252 |

### SLALOM

| | Pts |
|---|---|
| Vreni Schneider, Switzerland | 560 |
| Pernilla Wiberg, Sweden | 355 |
| Martina Ertl, Germany | 278 |
| Urska Hrovat, Slovenia | 275 |
| Kristina Andersson, Sweden | 247 |
| Leila Piccard, France | 222 |
| Patricia Chavet-Blanc, France | 212 |
| Marianne Kjoerstad, Norway | 204 |

### GIANT SLALOM

| | Pts |
|---|---|
| Vreni Schneider, Switzerland | 450 |
| Heidi Zeller-Baehler, Switz | 420 |
| Spela Pretnar, Slovenia | 352 |
| Martina Ertl, Germany | 333 |
| Deborah Compagnoni, Italy | 325 |
| Sabina Panzanini, Italy | 310 |
| Anita Wachter, Austria | 295 |
| Urska Hrovat, Slovenia | 260 |

### SUPER G

| | Pts |
|---|---|
| Katja Seizinger, Germany | 446 |
| Heidi Zeller-Baehler, Switz | 366 |
| Heidi Zurbriggen, Switzerland | 251 |
| Renate Goetschl, Austria | 245 |
| Martina Ertl, Germany | 237 |
| Sylvia Eder, Austria | 230 |
| Florance Masnada, France | 198 |
| Picabo Street, United States | 196 |

# FOR THE RECORD · Year by Year

## Event Descriptions

**Downhill:** A speed event entailing a single run on a course with a minimum vertical drop of 500 meters (800 for Men's World Cup) and very few control gates.
**Slalom:** A technical event in which times for runs on 2 courses are totaled to determine the winner. Skiers must make many quick, short turns through a combination of gates (55-75 gates for men, 40-60 for women) over a short course (140-220-meter vertical drop for men, 120-180 for women).

**Giant Slalom:** A faster technical event with fewer, more broadly spaced gates than in the slalom. Times for runs on 2 courses with vertical drops of 250-400 meters (250-300 for women) are combined to determine the winner.
**Super G:** A speed event that is a cross between the downhill and the giant slalom.
**Combined:** An event in which scores from designated slalom and downhill races are combined to determine finish order.

## FIS World Championships

### Sites

| | |
|---|---|
| 1931 .............................Mürren, Switzerland | 1936 .............................Innsbruck, Austria |
| 1932 .............................Cortina d'Ampezzo, Italy | 1937 .............................Chamonix, France |
| 1933 .............................Innsbruck, Austria | 1938 .............................Engelberg, Switzerland |
| 1934 .............................St Moritz, Switzerland | 1939 .............................Zakopane, Poland |
| 1935 .............................Mürren, Switzerland | |

### Men

#### DOWNHILL

| | |
|---|---|
| 1931 .............................Walter Prager, Switzerland | 1936 .............................Rudolf Rominger, Switzerland |
| 1932 .............................Gustav Lantschner, Austria | 1937 .............................Émile Allais, France |
| 1933 .............................Walter Prager, Switzerland | 1938 .............................James Couttet, France |
| 1934 .............................David Zogg, Switzerland | 1939 .............................Hans Lantschner, Germany |
| 1935 .............................Franz Zingerle, Austria | |

#### SLALOM

| | |
|---|---|
| 1931 .............................David Zogg, Switzerland | 1936 .............................Rudi Matt, Austria |
| 1932 .............................Friedrich Dauber, Germany | 1937 .............................Émile Allais, France |
| 1933 .............................Anton Seelos, Austria | 1938 .............................Rudolf Rominger, Switzerland |
| 1934 .............................Franz Pfnür, Germany | 1939 .............................Rudolf Rominger, Switzerland |
| 1935 .............................Anton Seelos, Austria | |

### Women

#### DOWNHILL

| | |
|---|---|
| 1931 .........................Esme Mackinnon, Great Britain | 1936 .........................Evie Pinching, Great Britain |
| 1932 .........................Paola Wiesinger, Italy | 1937 .........................Christel Cranz, Germany |
| 1933 .........................Inge Wersin-Lantschner, Austria | 1938 .........................Lisa Resch, Germany |
| 1934 .........................Anni Rüegg, Switzerland | 1939 .........................Christel Cranz, Germany |
| 1935 .........................Christel Cranz, Germany | |

#### SLALOM

| | |
|---|---|
| 1931 .........................Esme Mackinnon, Great Britain | 1936 .........................Gerda Paumgarten, Austria |
| 1932 .........................Rösli Streiff, Switzerland | 1937 .........................Christel Cranz, Germany |
| 1933 .........................Inge Wersin-Lantschner, Austria | 1938 .........................Christel Cranz, Germany |
| 1934 .........................Christel Cranz, Germany | 1939 .........................Christel Cranz, Germany |
| 1935 .........................Anni Rüegg, Switzerland | |

# FIS World Alpine Ski Championships

## Sites

1950.............Aspen, Colorado
1954.............Are, Sweden
1958.............Badgastein, Austria
1962.............Chamonix, France
1966.............Portillo, Chile
1970.............Val Gardena, Italy
1974.............St Moritz, Switzerland

1978.............Garmisch-Partenkirchen, West Germany
1982.............Schladming, Austria
1985.............Bormio, Italy
1987.............Crans-Montana, Switzerland
1989.............Vail, Colorado
1991.............Saalbach-Hinterglemm, Austria
1993.............Morioka-Shizukuishi, Japan

## Men

### DOWNHILL

1950.............Zeno Colo, Italy
1954.............Christian Pravda, Austria
1958.............Toni Sailer, Austria
1962.............Karl Schranz, Austria
1966.............Jean-Claude Killy, France
1970.............Bernard Russi, Switzerland
1974.............David Zwilling, Austria

1978.............Josef Walcher, Austria
1982.............Harti Weirather, Austria
1985.............Pirmin Zurbriggen, Switzerland
1987.............Peter Müller, Switzerland
1989.............Hansjörg Tauscher, West Germany
1991.............Franz Heinzer, Switzerland
1993.............Urs Lehmann, Switzerland

### SLALOM

1950.............Georges Schneider, Switzerland
1954.............Stein Eriksen, Norway
1958.............Josl Rieder, Austria
1962.............Charles Bozon, France
1966.............Carlo Senoner, Italy
1970.............Jean-Noël Augert, France
1974.............Gustavo Thoeni, Italy

1978.............Ingemar Stenmark, Sweden
1982.............Ingemar Stenmark, Sweden
1985.............Jonas Nilsson, Sweden
1987.............Frank Wörndl, West Germany
1989.............Rudolf Nierlich, Austria
1991.............Marc Girardelli, Luxembourg
1993.............Kjetil André Aamodt, Norway

### GIANT SLALOM

1950.............Zeno Colo, Italy
1954.............Stein Eriksen, Norway
1958.............Toni Sailer, Austria
1962.............Egon Zimmermann, Austria
1966.............Guy Périllat, France
1970.............Karl Schranz, Austria
1974.............Gustavo Thoeni, Italy

1978.............Ingemar Stenmark, Sweden
1982.............Steve Mahre, United States
1985.............Markus Wasmaier, West Germany
1987.............Pirmin Zurbriggen, Switzerland
1989.............Rudolf Nierlich, Austria
1991.............Rudolf Nierlich, Austria
1993.............Kjetil André Aamodt, Norway

### COMBINED

1982.............Michel Vion, France
1985.............Pirmin Zurbriggen, Switzerland
1987.............Marc Girardelli, Luxembourg

1989.............Marc Girardelli, Luxembourg
1991.............Stefan Eberharter, Austria
1993.............Lasse Kjus, Norway

### SUPER G

1987.............Pirmin Zurbriggen, Switzerland
1989.............Martin Hangl, Switzerland

1991.............Stefan Eberharter, Austria
1993.............Cancelled due to weather

## Women

### DOWNHILL

1950.............Trude Beiser-Jochum, Austria
1954.............Ida Schopfer, Switzerland
1958.............Lucile Wheeler, Canada
1962.............Christl Haas, Austria
1966.............Erika Schinegger, Austria
1970.............Annerösli Zryd, Switzerland
1974.............Annemarie Moser-Pröll, Austria

1978.............Annemarie Moser-Pröll, Austria
1982.............Gerry Sorensen, Canada
1985.............Michela Figini, Switzerland
1987.............Maria Walliser, Switzerland
1989.............Maria Walliser, Switzerland
1991.............Petra Kronberger, Austria
1993.............Kate Pace, Canada

### SLALOM

1950.............Dagmar Rom, Austria
1954.............Trude Klecker, Austria
1958.............Inger Bjornbakken, Norway
1962.............Marianne Jahn, Austria
1966.............Annie Famose, France
1970.............Ingrid Lafforgue, France
1974.............Hanni Wenzel, Liechtenstein

1978.............Lea Sölkner, Austria
1982.............Erika Hess, Switzerland
1985.............Perrine Pelen, France
1987.............Erika Hess, Switzerland
1989.............Mateja Svet, Yugoslavia
1991.............Vreni Schneider, Switzerland
1993.............Karin Buder, Austria

## Women *(Cont.)*

### GIANT SLALOM

| | |
|---|---|
| 1950 .....................Dagmar Rom, Austria | 1978 .....................Maria Epple, West Germany |
| 1954 .....................Lucienne Schmith-Couttet, France | 1982 .....................Erika Hess, Switzerland |
| 1958 .....................Lucile Wheeler, Canada | 1985 .....................Diann Roffe, United States |
| 1962 .....................Marianne Jahn, Austria | 1987 .....................Vreni Schneider, Switzerland |
| 1966 .....................Marielle Goitschel, France | 1989 .....................Vreni Schneider, Switzerland |
| 1970 .....................Betsy Clifford, Canada | 1991 .....................Pernilla Wiberg, Sweden |
| 1974 .....................Fabienne Serrat, France | 1993 .....................Carole Merle, France |

### COMBINED

| | |
|---|---|
| 1982 .....................Erika Hess, Switzerland | 1989 .....................Tamara McKinney, United States |
| 1985 .....................Erika Hess, Switzerland | 1991 .....................Chantal Bournissen, Switzerland |
| 1987 .....................Erika Hess, Switzerland | 1993 .....................Miriam Vogt, Germany |

### SUPER G

| | |
|---|---|
| 1987 .....................Maria Walliser, Switzerland | 1991 .....................Ulrike Maier, Austria |
| 1989 .....................Ulrike Maier, Austria | 1993 .....................Katja Seizinger, Germany |

Note: The 1995 FIS World Championships were cancelled due to the lack of snow.

# World Cup Season Title Holders

## Men
### OVERALL

| | |
|---|---|
| 1967 .....................Jean-Claude Killy, France | 1982 .....................Phil Mahre, United States |
| 1968 .....................Jean-Claude Killy, France | 1983 .....................Phil Mahre, United States |
| 1969 .....................Karl Schranz, Austria | 1984 .....................Pirmin Zurbriggen, Switzerland |
| 1970 .....................Karl Schranz, Austria | 1985 .....................Marc Girardelli, Luxembourg |
| 1971 .....................Gustavo Thoeni, Italy | 1986 .....................Marc Girardelli, Luxembourg |
| 1972 .....................Gustavo Thoeni, Italy | 1987 .....................Pirmin Zurbriggen, Switzerland |
| 1973 .....................Gustavo Thoeni, Italy | 1988 .....................Pirmin Zurbriggen, Switzerland |
| 1974 .....................Piero Gros, Italy | 1989 .....................Marc Girardelli, Luxembourg |
| 1975 .....................Gustavo Thoeni, Italy | 1990 .....................Pirmin Zurbriggen, Switzerland |
| 1976 .....................Ingemar Stenmark, Sweden | 1991 .....................Marc Girardelli, Luxembourg |
| 1977 .....................Ingemar Stenmark, Sweden | 1992 .....................Paul Accola, Switzerland |
| 1978 .....................Ingemar Stenmark, Sweden | 1993 .....................Marc Girardelli, Luxembourg |
| 1979 .....................Peter Lüscher, Switzerland | 1994 .....................Kjetil André Aamodt, Norway |
| 1980 .....................Andreas Wenzel, Liechtenstein | 1995 .....................Alberto Tomba, Italy |
| 1981 .....................Phil Mahre, United States | |

### DOWNHILL

| | |
|---|---|
| 1967 .....................Jean-Claude Killy, France | 1982 .....................Steve Podborski, Canada |
| 1968 .....................Gerhard Nenning, Austria | Peter Müller, Switzerland |
| 1969 .....................Karl Schranz, Austria | 1983 .....................Franz Klammer, Austria |
| 1970 .....................Karl Schranz, Austria | 1984 .....................Urs Raber, Switzerland |
| Karl Cordin, Austria | 1985 .....................Helmut Höflehner, Austria |
| 1971 .....................Bernhard Russi, Switzerland | 1986 .....................Peter Wirnsberger, Austria |
| 1972 .....................Bernhard Russi, Switzerland | 1987 .....................Pirmin Zurbriggen, Switzerland |
| 1973 .....................Roland Collumbin, Switzerland | 1988 .....................Pirmin Zurbriggen, Switzerland |
| 1974 .....................Roland Collumbin, Switzerland | 1989 .....................Marc Girardelli, Luxembourg |
| 1975 .....................Franz Klammer, Austria | 1990 .....................Helmut Höflehner, Austria |
| 1976 .....................Franz Klammer, Austria | 1991 .....................Franz Heinzer, Switzerland |
| 1977 .....................Franz Klammer, Austria | 1992 .....................Franz Heinzer, Switzerland |
| 1978 .....................Franz Klammer, Austria | 1993 .....................Franz Heinzer, Switzerland |
| 1979 .....................Peter Müller, Switzerland | 1994 .....................Marc Girardelli, Luxembourg |
| 1980 .....................Peter Müller, Switzerland | 1995 .....................Luc Alphand, France |
| 1981 .....................Harti Weirather, Austria | |

### SLALOM

| | |
|---|---|
| 1967 .....................Jean-Claude Killy, France | 1973 .....................Gustavo Thoeni, Italy |
| 1968 .....................Domeng Giovanoli, Switzerland | 1974 .....................Gustavo Thoeni, Italy |
| 1969 .....................Jean-Noël Augert, France | 1975 .....................Ingemar Stenmark, Sweden |
| 1970 .....................Patrick Russel, France | 1976 .....................Ingemar Stenmark, Sweden |
| Alain Penz, France | 1977 .....................Ingemar Stenmark, Sweden |
| 1971 .....................Jean-Noël Augert, France | 1978 .....................Ingemar Stenmark, Sweden |
| 1972 .....................Jean-Noël Augert, France | 1979 .....................Ingemar Stenmark, Sweden |

## Men *(Cont.)*

### SLALOM *(Cont.)*

| | |
|---|---|
| 1980 ...............Ingemar Stenmark, Sweden | 1988 ...............Alberto Tomba, Italy |
| 1981 ...............Ingemar Stenmark, Sweden | 1989 ...............Armin Bittner, West Germany |
| 1982 ...............Phil Mahre, United States | 1990 ...............Armin Bittner, West Germany |
| 1983 ...............Ingemar Stenmark, Sweden | 1991 ...............Marc Girardelli, Luxembourg |
| 1984 ...............Marc Girardelli, Luxembourg | 1992 ...............Alberto Tomba, Italy |
| 1985 ...............Marc Girardelli, Luxembourg | 1993 ...............Tomas Fogdof, Sweden |
| 1986 ...............Rok Petrovic, Yugoslavia | 1994 ...............Alberto Tomba, Italy |
| 1987 ...............Bojan Krizaj, Yugoslavia | 1995 ...............Alberto Tomba, Italy |

### GIANT SLALOM

| | |
|---|---|
| 1967 ...............Jean-Claude Killy, France | 1983 ...............Phil Mahre, United States |
| 1968 ...............Jean-Claude Killy, France | 1984 ...............Ingemar Stenmark, Sweden |
| 1969 ...............Karl Schranz, Austria | ..........................Pirmin Zurbriggen, Switzerland |
| 1970 ...............Gustavo Thoeni, Italy | 1985 ...............Marc Girardelli, Luxembourg |
| 1971 ...............Patrick Russel, France | 1986 ...............Joël Gaspoz, Switzerland |
| 1972 ...............Gustavo Thoeni, Italy | 1987 ...............Joël Gaspoz, Switzerland |
| 1973 ...............Hans Hinterseer, Austria | ..........................Pirmin Zurbriggen, Switzerland |
| 1974 ...............Piero Gros, Italy | 1988 ...............Alberto Tomba, Italy |
| 1975 ...............Ingemar Stenmark, Sweden | 1989 ...............Pirmin Zurbriggen, Switzerland |
| 1976 ...............Ingemar Stenmark, Sweden | 1990 ...............Ole-Cristian Furuseth, Norway |
| 1977 ...............Heini Hemmi, Switzerland | ..........................Günther Mader, Austria |
| ..........................Ingemar Stenmark, Sweden | 1991 ...............Alberto Tomba, Italy |
| 1978 ...............Ingemar Stenmark, Sweden | 1992 ...............Alberto Tomba, Italy |
| 1979 ...............Ingemar Stenmark, Sweden | 1993 ...............Kjetil André Aamodt, Norway |
| 1980 ...............Ingemar Stenmark, Sweden | 1994 ...............Christian Mayer, Austria |
| 1981 ...............Ingemar Stenmark, Sweden | 1995 ...............Alberto Tomba, Italy |
| 1982 ...............Phil Mahre, United States | |

### SUPER G

| | |
|---|---|
| 1986 ...............Markus Wasmeier, West Germany | 1991 ...............Franz Heinzer, Switzerland |
| 1987 ...............Pirmin Zurbriggen, Switzerland | 1992 ...............Paul Accola, Switzerland |
| 1988 ...............Pirmin Zurbriggen, Switzerland | 1993 ...............Kjetil André Aamodt, Norway |
| 1989 ...............Pirmin Zurbriggen, Switzerland | 1994 ...............Jan Einar Thorsen, Norway |
| 1990 ...............Pirmin Zurbriggen, Switzerland | 1995 ...............Peter Runggaldier, Italy |

### COMBINED

| | |
|---|---|
| 1979 ...............Andreas Wenzel, Liechtenstein | 1988 ...............Hubert Strolz, Austria |
| 1980 ...............Andreas Wenzel, Liechtenstein | 1989 ...............Marc Girardelli, Luxembourg |
| 1981 ...............Phil Mahre, United States | 1990 ...............Pirmin Zurbriggen, Switzerland |
| 1982 ...............Phil Mahre, United States | 1991 ...............Marc Girardelli, Luxembourg |
| 1983 ...............Phil Mahre, United States | 1992 ...............Paul Accola, Switzerland |
| 1984 ...............Andreas Wenzel, Liechtenstein | 1993 ...............Marc Girardelli, Luxembourg |
| 1985 ...............Andreas Wenzel, Liechtenstein | 1994 ...............Kjetil-André Aamodt, Norway |
| 1986 ...............Markus Wasmeier, West Germany | 1995 ...............Marc Girardelli, Luxembourg |
| 1987 ...............Pirmin Zurbriggen, Switzerland | |

## Women

### OVERALL

| | |
|---|---|
| 1967 ...............Nancy Greene, Canada | 1982 ...............Erika Hess, Switzerland |
| 1968 ...............Nancy Greene, Canada | 1983 ...............Tamara McKinney, United States |
| 1969 ...............Gertrud Gabl, Austria | 1984 ...............Erika Hess, Switzerland |
| 1970 ...............Michèle Jacot, France | 1985 ...............Michela Figini, Switzerland |
| 1971 ...............Annemarie Pröll, Austria | 1986 ...............Maria Walliser, Switzerland |
| 1972 ...............Annemarie Pröll, Austria | 1987 ...............Maria Walliser, Switzerland |
| 1973 ...............Annemarie Pröll, Austria | 1988 ...............Michela Figini, Switzerland |
| 1974 ...............Annemarie Moser-Pröll, Austria | 1989 ...............Vreni Schneider, Switzerland |
| 1975 ...............Annemarie Moser-Pröll, Austria | 1990 ...............Petra Kronberger, Austria |
| 1976 ...............Rosi Mitermaier, West Germany | 1991 ...............Petra Kronberger, Austria |
| 1977 ...............Lise-Marie Morerod, Switzerland | 1992 ...............Petra Kronberger, Austria |
| 1978 ...............Hanni Wenzel, Liechtenstein | 1993 ...............Anita Wachter, Austria |
| 1979 ...............Annemarie Moser-Pröll, Austria | 1994 ...............Vreni Schneider, Switzerland |
| 1980 ...............Hanni Wenzel, Liechtenstein | 1995 ...............Vreni Schneider, Switzerland |
| 1981 ...............Marie-Thérèse Nadig, Switzerland | |

## Women (Cont.)

### DOWNHILL

| | |
|---|---|
| 1967 ...............Marielle Goitschel, France | 1981 ...............Marie-Thérèse Nadig, Switzerland |
| 1968 ...............Isabelle Mir, France | 1982 ...............Marie-Cecile Gros-Gaudenier, France |
|           Olga Pall, Austria | 1983 ...............Doris De Agostini, Switzerland |
| 1969 ...............Wiltrud Drexel, Austria | 1984 ...............Maria Walliser, Switzerland |
| 1970 ...............Isabelle Mir, France | 1985 ...............Michela Figini, Switzerland |
| 1971 ...............Annemarie Pröll, Austria | 1986 ...............Maria Walliser, Switzerland |
| 1972 ...............Annemarie Pröll, Austria | 1987 ...............Michela Figini, Switzerland |
| 1973 ...............Annemarie Pröll, Austria | 1988 ...............Michela Figini, Switzerland |
| 1974 ...............Annemarie Moser-Pröll, Austria | 1989 ...............Michela Figini, Switzerland |
| 1975 ...............Annemarie Moser-Pröll, Austria | 1990 ...............Katrin Gutensohn-Knopf, Germany |
| 1976 ...............Brigitte Totschnig, Austria | 1991 ...............Chantal Bournissen, Switzerland |
| 1977 ...............Brigitte Totschnig-Habersatter, Austria | 1992 ...............Katja Seizinger, Germany |
| 1978 ...............Annemarie Moser-Pröll, Austria | 1993 ...............Katja Seizinger, Germany |
| 1979 ...............Annemarie Moser-Pröll, Austria | 1994 ...............Katja Seizinger, Germany |
| 1980 ...............Marie-Thérèse Nadig, Switzerland | 1995 ...............Picabo Street, United States |

### SLALOM

| | |
|---|---|
| 1967 ...............Marielle Goitschel, France | 1982 ...............Erika Hess, Switzerland |
| 1968 ...............Marielle Goitschel, France | 1983 ...............Erika Hess, Switzerland |
| 1969 ...............Gertrud Gabl, Austria | 1984 ...............Tamara McKinney, United States |
| 1970 ...............Ingrid Lafforgue, France | 1985 ...............Erika Hess, Switzerland |
| 1971 ...............Britt Lafforgue, France | 1986 ...............Roswitha Steiner, Austria |
| 1972 ...............Britt Lafforgue, France |           Erika Hess, Switzerland |
| 1973 ...............Patricia Emonet, France | 1987 ...............Corrine Schmidhauser, Switzerland |
| 1974 ...............Christa Zechmeister, West Germany | 1988 ...............Roswitha Steiner, Austria |
| 1975 ...............Lise-Marie Morerod, Switzerland | 1989 ...............Vreni Schneider, Switzerland |
| 1976 ...............Rosi Mittermaier, West Germany | 1990 ...............Vreni Schneider, Switzerland |
| 1977 ...............Lise-Marie Morerod, Switzerland | 1991 ...............Petra Kronberger, Austria |
| 1978 ...............Hanni Wenzel, Liechtenstein | 1992 ...............Vreni Schneider, Switzerland |
| 1979 ...............Regina Sackl, Austria | 1993 ...............Vreni Schneider, Switzerland |
| 1980 ...............Perrine Pelen, France | 1994 ...............Vreni Schneider, Switzerland |
| 1981 ...............Erika Hess, Switzerland | 1995 ...............Vreni Schneider, Switzerland |

### GIANT SLALOM

| | |
|---|---|
| 1967 ...............Nancy Greene, Canada | 1982 ...............Irene Epple, West Germany |
| 1968 ...............Nancy Greene, Canada | 1983 ...............Tamara McKinney, United States |
| 1969 ...............Marilyn Cochran, United States | 1984 ...............Erika Hess, Switzerland |
| 1970 ...............Michèle Jacot, France | 1985 ...............Maria Keihl, West Germany |
|           Françoise Macchi, France |           Michela Figini, Switzerland |
| 1971 ...............Annemarie Pröll, Austria | 1986 ...............Vreni Schneider, Switzerland |
| 1972 ...............Annemarie Pröll, Austria | 1987 ...............Vreni Schneider, Switzerland |
| 1973 ...............Monika Kaserer, Austria |           Maria Walliser, Switzerland |
| 1974 ...............Hanni Wenzel, Liechtenstein | 1988 ...............Mateja Svet, Yugoslavia |
| 1975 ...............Annemarie Moser-Pröll, Austria | 1989 ...............Vreni Schneider, Switzerland |
| 1976 ...............Lise-Marie Morerod, France | 1990 ...............Anita Wachter, Austria |
| 1977 ...............Lise-Marie Morerod, France | 1991 ...............Vreni Schneider, Switzerland |
| 1978 ...............Lise-Marie Morerod, France | 1992 ...............Carole Merle, France |
| 1979 ...............Christa Kinshofer, West Germany | 1993 ...............Carole Merle, France |
| 1980 ...............Hanni Wenzel, Liechtenstein | 1994 ...............Anita Wachter, Austria |
| 1981 ...............Marie-Thérèse Nadig, Switzerland | 1995 ...............Vreni Schneider, Switzerland |

### SUPER G

| | |
|---|---|
| 1986 ...............Maria Kiehl, West Germany | 1991 ...............Carole Merle, France |
| 1987 ...............Maria Walliser, Switzerland | 1992 ...............Carole Merle, France |
| 1988 ...............Michela Figini, Switzerland | 1993 ...............Katja Seizinger, Germany |
| 1989 ...............Carole Merle, France | 1994 ...............Katja Seizinger, Germany |
| 1990 ...............Carole Merle, France | 1995 ...............Katja Seizinger, Germany |

### COMBINED

| | |
|---|---|
| 1979 ...............Annemarie Moser-Pröll, Austria | 1983 ...............Hanni Wenzel, Liechtenstein |
|           Hanni Wenzel, Liechtenstein | 1984 ...............Erika Hess, Switzerland |
| 1980 ...............Hanni Wenzel, Liechtenstein | 1985 ...............Brigitte Oertli, Switzerland |
| 1981 ...............Marie-Thérèse Nadig, Switzerland | 1986 ...............Maria Walliser, Switzerland |
| 1982 ...............Irene Epple, West Germany | 1987 ...............Brigitte Oertli, Switzerland |

## Women (Cont.)

### COMBINED (Cont.)

| | |
|---|---|
| 1988 ...............Brigitte Oertli, Switzerland | 1992 ...............Sabine Ginther, Austria |
| 1989 ...............Brigitte Oertli, Switzerland | 1993 ...............Anita Wachter, Austria |
| 1990 ...............Anita Wachter, Austria | 1994 ..............Pernilla Wiberg, Sweden |
| 1991 ..............Sabine Ginther, Austria | 1995 ...............Pernilla Wiberg, Sweden |

# World Cup Career Victories

## Men

### DOWNHILL

25............................Franz Klammer, Austria
19............................Peter Müller, Switzerland
15............................Franz Heinzer, Switzerland

### SLALOM

40............................Ingemar Stenmark, Sweden
29............................Alberto Tomba, Italy*
16............................Marc Girardelli, Luxembourg*

### GIANT SLALOM

46............................Ingemar Stenmark, Sweden
15............................Alberto Tomba, Italy*
11............................Gustavo Thoeni, Italy
                    Pirmin Zurbriggen, Switzerland

### SUPER G

10............................Primin Zurbriggen, Switzerland
7...............................Marc Girardelli, Luxembourg*
6............................Markus Wasmeier, Germany

### COMBINED

11............................Phil Mahre, United States
                    Pirmin Zurbriggen, Switzerland
10............................Marc Girardelli, Luxembourg*

*still active

## Women

### DOWNHILL

36............................Annemarie Moser-Pröll, Austria
17............................Michela Figini, Switzerland
14............................Maria Walliser, Switzerland

### SLALOM

33............................Vreni Schneider, Switzerland*
21............................Erika Hess, Switzerland
15............................Perrine Pelen, France

### GIANT SLALOM

21............................Vreni Schneider, Switzerland*
16............................Annemarie Moser-Pröll, Austria
14............................Lise Marie Morerod, France

### SUPER G

12............................Carole Merle, France
7...............................Katja Seizinger, Germany*
3...............................Maria Kiehl, Germany
                    Maria Walliser, Switzerland
                    Sigrid Wolf, Austria

### COMBINED

8...............................Hanni Wenzel, Lichtenstein
7...............................Annemarie Moser-Pröll, Austria
7...............................Brigitte Oertli, Switzerland

*still active

# U.S. Olympic Gold Medalists

## Men

| Year | Winner | Event |
|---|---|---|
| 1980 ..............Phil Mahre | | Combined |
| 1984 ..............Bill Johnson | | Downhill |
| 1984 ..............Phil Mahre | | Slalom |
| 1994 ..............Tommy Moe | | Downhill |

## Women

| Year | Winner | Event |
|---|---|---|
| 1948 ..............Gretchen Fraser | | Slalom |
| 1952 ..............Andrea Mead Lawrence | | Slalom |
| 1952 ..............Andrea Mead Lawrence | | Giant Slalom |
| 1972 ..............Barbara Ann Cochran | | Slalom |
| 1984 ..............Debbie Armstrong | | Giant Slalom |
| 1994 ..............Diann Roffe-Steinrotter | | Super G |

# Figure Skating

## Ice Queen

China's Chen Lu wins the
world figure skating title
in Birmingham, England.

BOB MARTIN

# Goodbye to All That

## With the scandals of '94 forgotten, figure skating enjoyed a banner season

## by Johnette Howard

THERE WAS no more thuggery. No more preoccupation with those four stooges who had ties to Tonya Harding. After the kneecapping of Nancy Kerrigan and Harding's venal sideshow at the 1994 Winter Olympics, the worry inside figure skating was how the dishonored sport would rebound in 1995. And the answer?

Better than anyone dared dream.

Perverse as it sounds, the saturated coverage of the Harding saga had an unexpected good result: The business of figure skating was booming by early 1995. In the U.S. alone, enrollment in basic skating courses jumped 200% to 300% over 1994 levels. TV ratings for figure skating events soared. An unprecedented glut of ersatz competitions, gauzy made-for-TV specials and show tours was spawned. When 1994 Olympic champion Oksana Baiul took the money and ran—forsaking her Olympic eligibility at age 16—some serious fretting began. Would amateur skating be eclipsed by the lucrative and unregulated pro events?

The International Skating Union swiftly announced that it would begin offering prize money at its major events. But in 1995 anyway, there was no need to worry. Olympic-style skating remained the place to go for authentic competition and unimpeachable judging. The major championships proved '95 to be the year of the resurrected star.

Todd Eldredge—a two-time U.S. champion by the age of 19, a feared washout by 21—stopped his three-year title drought with a giant-killing run that included his third national title, then an unforgettable duel with Canada's Elvis Stojko at the March world championships in Birmingham, England.

After seizing the first-day lead at the worlds, Eldredge missed two jumps in his final program that he absolutely had to have—a triple Axel and a triple-triple combination. Suddenly the 23-year-old American was left with a nerve-jangling choice: Should he play it safe in the dying moments of his routine or risk losing everything?

Eldredge went for the win. Improvising boldly now, he first made up the blown combination, then brazenly launched into an unscheduled triple Axel with 20 seconds left in his gutsy, scrambling, crescendoing

**Eldredge (left) upped the ante but Stojko was more than equal to the challenge.**

routine. "I just thought, the hell with it—this is the big time, this is the worlds," Eldredge said later, breaking into a grin.

By daring to be great, Eldredge knew he'd just forced Stojko to do the same. And Stojko, the defending world champion, was more than a match. A gruesome ankle injury kept him out of competition for seven weeks before the worlds. He still hadn't landed three of his five triple jumps until just 72 hours before he had to compete. But skating two spots after Eldredge, Stojko trumped Eldredge's effort with two triple-triple combinations to Eldredge's one, a triple Axel and an attempted quadruple which Stojko missed finishing—though he didn't need the quad to win.

Two nights later Chen Lu became China's first-ever world champion, staving off spirited challenges from Surya Bonaly of France and the U.S.'s Nicole Bobek and Michelle Kwan. Chen withdrew from the '94 worlds in Chiba, Japan, because of a foot stress fracture that didn't respond to the six daily shots of novocaine she took to try to compete. In Birmingham she had to rally to beat Bobek, the free-spirited, wholly unexpected U.S. champion.

Bobek has always been an arresting looking skater. But her halfhearted training habits and balky nerves often doomed her in big competitions. Kwan, just 14 but already a superior jumper, was heavily favored to win the '95 U.S. championships—until Bobek put together back-to-back programs that stopped the show.

In the four-week wait for worlds, Bobek's reputation was clouded again by published reports of a just-dismissed burglary charge against her in Michigan. But Bobek is nothing if not puckish. She shrugged off the uproar and comparisons to Harding by cracking jokes in her first press conference in England, then seizing the first-day lead, then announcing she was beefing up the difficulty in her long program. Like Eldredge, her training partner, Bobek was going for the win.

Though she hit her new move—the first triple-triple combination of her career—Bobek flubbed two subsequent jumps. Still, she left England with the bronze medal and some newfound respect. And Kwan, who finished fourth, gave her older rivals something to worry about in the future. Her closing performance featured seven triple jumps and pulled the Birmingham crowd to its feet with 10 seconds left—an accomplishment that left the 98-pound Kwan sobbing for joy at center ice as raucous cheers and a slanting rain of floral bouquets came down. The scene was among the sweetest moments in a good year—skating's boom year. And it was the sort of pure moment that figure skating craved, and gratefully received, after the embarrassments of '94.

# FOR THE RECORD · 1994-1995

## World Champions

### Women
1........Chen Lu, China
2........Surya Bonaly, France
3........Nicole Bobek, United States

### Men
1.........Elvis Stojko, Canada
2.........Todd Eldredge, United States
3.........Phillippe Candeloro, France

### Pairs
1........Radka Kovarikova and Rene Novotny, Czech
2........Evgenia Shishkova and Vadim Naumov, Russia
3........Jenni Meno and Todd Sand, United States

### Dance
1.........Oksana Gritschuk and Evgeny Platov, Russia
2.........Susanna Rahkamo and Petri Kokko, Finland
3.........Sophie Moniotte and Pascal Lavanchy, France

## World Figure Skating Championships Medal Table

Birmingham, England, March 7–12

| Country | Gold | Silver | Bronze | Total |
|---|---|---|---|---|
| United States | 0 | 1 | 2 | 3 |
| France | 0 | 1 | 2 | 3 |
| Russia | 1 | 1 | 0 | 2 |
| Canada | 1 | 0 | 0 | 1 |
| China | 1 | 0 | 0 | 1 |
| Czech Republic | 1 | 0 | 0 | 1 |
| Finland | 0 | 1 | 0 | 1 |

## Champions of the United States

Providence, Rhode Island, February 7–11

### Women
1..............................Nicole Bobek, Los Angeles FSC
2..............................Michelle Kwan, Los Angeles FSC
3..............................Tonia Kwiatkowski, Winterhurst FSC

### Men
1.......................Todd Elredge, Detroit SC
2.......................Scott Davis, Broadmoor, SC
3.......................Aren Nielsen, Winterhurst FSC

### Pairs
1..............................Jenni Meno and Todd Sand,
Winterhurst FSC/Los Angeles FSC
2..............................Kyoko Ina and Jason Dungjen,
SC of New York/ SC of New York
3..............................Stephanie Stiegler and Lance Travis
Los Angeles FSC/ Los Angeles FSC

### Dance
1.......................Renee Roca and Gorsha Sur
Broadmoor SC/Broadmoor SC
2.......................Elizabeth Punsalan and Jerod Swallow
Detroit SC/Detroit SC
3.......................Amy Webster and Ron Kravette
SC of Boston/SC of Boston

## Special Achievements

Women successfully landing a triple Axel in competition:
Midori Ito, Japan, 1988 free-skating competition at Aichi, Japan.
Tonya Harding, United States, 1991 U.S. Figure Skating Championship.

# FOR THE RECORD·Year by Year

## Skating Terminology*

### Basic Skating Terms

**Edges:** The two sides of the skating blade, on either side of the grooved center. There is an inside edge, on the inner side of the leg; and an outside edge, on the outer side of the leg.

**Free Foot, Hip, Knee, Side, Etc.:** The foot a skater is not skating on at any one time is the free foot; everything on that side of the body is then called "free." (See also "skating foot.")

**Free Skating (Freestyle):** A 4- or 5-minute competition program of free-skating components, choreographed to music, with no set elements. Skating moves include jumps, spins, steps and other linking movements.

**Skating Foot, Hip, Knee, Side, Etc.:** Opposite of the free foot, hip, knee, side, etc. The foot a skater is skating on at any one time is the skating foot; everything on that side of the body is then called "skating."

**Toe Picks (Toe Rakes):** The teeth at the front of the skate blade, used primarily for certain jumps and spins.

**Trace, Tracing:** The line left on the ice by the skater's blade.

### Jumps

**Waltz:** A beginner's jump, involving half a revolution in the air, taken from a forward outside edge and landed on the back outside edge of the other foot.

**Toe Loop:** A one-revolution jump taken off from and landed on the same back outside edge. This jump is similar to the loop jump except that the skater kicks the toe pick of the free leg into the ice upon takeoff, providing added power.

**Toe Walley:** A jump similar to the toe loop, except that the takeoff is from the inside edge.

**Flip:** A jump taken off with the toe pick of the free leg from a back inside edge and landed on a back outside edge, with one in-air revolution.

**Lutz:** A toe jump similar to the flip, taken off with the toe pick of the free leg from a backwrd outside edge. The skater enters the jump skating in one direction, and concludes the jump skating in the opposite direction. Usually performed in the corners of the rink. Named after founder Alois Lutz, who first completed the jump in Vienna, 1918.

**Salchow:** A one-, two- or three-revolution jump. The skater takes off from the back inside edge of one foot and lands backwards on the outside edge of the right foot, the opposite foot from which the skater took off. Named for its originator and first Olympic champion (1908), Sweden's Ulrich Salchow.

**Axel:** A combination of the waltz and loop jumps, including one-and-a-half revolutions. The only jump begun from a forward outside edge, the axel is landed on the back outside edge of the opposite foot. Named for its inventor, Norway's Axel Paulsen.

### Spins

**Spin:** The rotation of the body in one place on the ice. Various spins are the back, fast or scratch, sit, camel, butterfly and layback.

**Camel Spin:** A spin with the skater in an arabesque position (the free leg at right angles to the leg on the ice).

**Flying Camel Spin:** A jump spin ending in the camel-spin position.

**Flying Sit Spin:** A jump spin in which the skater leaps off the ice, assumes a sitting position at the peak of the jump, lands and spins in a similar sitting position.

### Pair Movements/Techniques

**Death Spiral:** One of the most dramatic moves in figure skating. The man, acting as the center of a circle, holds tightly to the hand of his partner and pulls her around him. The woman, gliding on one foot, achieves a position almost horizontal to the ice.

**Lifts:** The most spectacular moves in pairs skating. They involve any maneuver in which the man lifts the woman off the ice. The man often holds his partner above his head with one hand.

**Throws:** The man lifts the woman into the air and throws her away from him. She spins in the air and lands on one foot.

**Twist:** The man throws the woman into the air. She spins in the air (either a double- or triple-twist), and he catches her at the landing.

*Compiled by the United States Figure Skating Assocation.

## World Champions

### Women

| | | | |
|---|---|---|---|
| 1906 | Madge Sayers-Cave, Great Britain | 1931 | Sonja Henie, Norway |
| 1907 | Madge Sayers-Cave, Great Britain | 1932 | Sonja Henie, Norway |
| 1908 | Lily Kronberger, Hungary | 1933 | Sonja Henie, Norway |
| 1909 | Lily Kronberger, Hungary | 1934 | Sonja Henie, Norway |
| 1910 | Lily Kronberger, Hungary | 1935 | Sonja Henie, Norway |
| 1911 | Lily Kronberger, Hungary | 1936 | Sonja Henie, Norway |
| 1912 | Opika von Meray Horvath, Hungary | 1937 | Cecilia Colledge, Great Britain |
| 1913 | Opika von Meray Horvath, Hungary | 1938 | Megan Taylor, Great Britain |
| 1914 | Opika von Meray Horvath, Hungary | 1939 | Megan Taylor, Great Britain |
| 1915-21 | No competition | 1940-46 | No competition |
| 1922 | Herma Plank-Szabo, Austria | 1947 | Barbara Ann Scott, Canada |
| 1923 | Herma Plank-Szabo, Austria | 1948 | Barbara Ann Scott, Canada |
| 1924 | Herma Plank-Szabo, Austria | 1949 | Alena Vrzanova, Czechoslovakia |
| 1925 | Herma Jaross-Szabo, Austria | 1950 | Alena Vrzanova, Czechoslovakia |
| 1926 | Herma Jaross-Szabo, Austria | 1951 | Jeannette Altwegg, Great Britain |
| 1927 | Sonja Henie, Norway | 1952 | Jacqueline duBief, France |
| 1928 | Sonja Henie, Norway | 1953 | Tenley Albright, United States |
| 1929 | Sonja Henie, Norway | 1954 | Gundi Busch, West Germany |
| 1930 | Sonja Henie, Norway | 1955 | Tenley Albright, United States |

## Women (Cont.)

| | |
|---|---|
| 1956 | Carol Heiss, United States |
| 1957 | Carol Heiss, United States |
| 1958 | Carol Heiss, United States |
| 1959 | Carol Heiss, United States |
| 1960 | Carol Heiss, United States |
| 1961 | No competition |
| 1962 | Sjoukje Dijkstra, Netherlands |
| 1963 | Sjoukje Dijkstra, Netherlands |
| 1964 | Sjoukje Dijkstra, Netherlands |
| 1965 | Petra Burka, Canada |
| 1966 | Peggy Fleming, United States |
| 1967 | Peggy Fleming, United States |
| 1968 | Peggy Fleming, United States |
| 1969 | Gabriele Seyfert, East Germany |
| 1970 | Gabriele Seyfert, East Germany |
| 1971 | Beatrix Schuba, Austria |
| 1972 | Beatrix Schuba, Austria |
| 1973 | Karen Magnussen, Canada |
| 1974 | Christine Errath, East Germany |
| 1975 | Dianne DeLeeuw, Netherlands |
| 1976 | Dorothy Hamill, United States |
| 1977 | Linda Fratianne, United States |
| 1978 | Annett Poetzsch, East Germany |
| 1979 | Linda Fratianne, United States |
| 1980 | Annett Poetzsch, East Germany |
| 1981 | Denise Biellmann, Switzerland |
| 1982 | Elaine Zayak, United States |
| 1983 | Rosalynn Sumners, United States |
| 1984 | Katarina Witt, East Germany |
| 1985 | Katarina Witt, East Germany |
| 1986 | Debi Thomas, United States |
| 1987 | Katarina Witt, East Germany |
| 1988 | Katarina Witt, East Germany |
| 1989 | Midori Ito, Japan |
| 1990 | Jill Trenary, United States |
| 1991 | Kristi Yamaguchi, United States |
| 1992 | Kristi Yamaguchi, United States |
| 1993 | Oksana Baiul, Ukraine |
| 1994 | Yuka Sato, Japan |
| 1995 | Chen Lu, China |

## Men

| | |
|---|---|
| 1896 | Gilbert Fuchs, Germany |
| 1897 | Gustav Hugel, Austria |
| 1898 | Henning Grenander, Sweden |
| 1899 | Gustav Hugel, Austria |
| 1900 | Gustav Hugel, Austria |
| 1901 | Ulrich Salchow, Sweden |
| 1902 | Ulrich Salchow, Sweden |
| 1903 | Ulrich Salchow, Sweden |
| 1904 | Ulrich Salchow, Sweden |
| 1905 | Ulrich Salchow, Sweden |
| 1906 | Gilbert Fuchs, Germany |
| 1907 | Ulrich Salchow, Sweden |
| 1908 | Ulrich Salchow, Sweden |
| 1909 | Ulrich Salchow, Sweden |
| 1910 | Ulrich Salchow, Sweden |
| 1911 | Ulrich Salchow, Sweden |
| 1912 | Fritz Kachler, Austria |
| 1913 | Fritz Kachler, Austria |
| 1914 | Gosta Sandhal, Sweden |
| 1915-21 | No competition |
| 1922 | Gillis Grafstrom, Sweden |
| 1923 | Fritz Kachler, Austria |
| 1924 | Gillis Grafstrom, Sweden |
| 1925 | Willy Bockl, Austria |
| 1926 | Willy Bockl, Austria |
| 1927 | Willy Bockl, Austria |
| 1928 | Willy Bockl, Austria |
| 1929 | Gillis Grafstrom, Sweden |
| 1930 | Karl Schafer, Austria |
| 1931 | Karl Schafer, Austria |
| 1932 | Karl Schafer, Austria |
| 1933 | Karl Schafer, Austria |
| 1934 | Karl Schafer, Austria |
| 1935 | Karl Schafer, Austria |
| 1936 | Karl Schafer, Austria |
| 1937 | Felix Kaspar, Austria |
| 1938 | Felix Kaspar, Austria |
| 1939 | Graham Sharp, Great Britain |
| 1940-46 | No competition |
| 1947 | Hans Gerschwiler, Switzerland |
| 1948 | Dick Button, United States |
| 1949 | Dick Button, United States |
| 1950 | Dick Button, United States |
| 1951 | Dick Button, United States |
| 1952 | Dick Button, United States |
| 1953 | Hayes Alan Jenkins, United States |
| 1954 | Hayes Alan Jenkins, United States |
| 1955 | Hayes Alan Jenkins, United States |
| 1956 | Hayes Alan Jenkins, United States |
| 1957 | David W. Jenkins, United States |
| 1958 | David W. Jenkins, United States |
| 1959 | David W. Jenkins, United States |
| 1960 | Alan Giletti, France |
| 1961 | No competition |
| 1962 | Donald Jackson, Canada |
| 1963 | Donald McPherson, Canada |
| 1964 | Manfred Schneldorfer, W Germany |
| 1965 | Alain Calmat, France |
| 1966 | Emmerich Danzer, Austria |
| 1967 | Emmerich Danzer, Austria |
| 1968 | Emmerich Danzer, Austria |
| 1969 | Tim Wood, United States |
| 1970 | Tim Wood, United States |
| 1971 | Andrej Nepela, Czechoslovakia |
| 1972 | Andrej Nepela, Czechoslovakia |
| 1973 | Andrej Nepela, Czechoslovakia |
| 1974 | Jan Hoffmann, East Germany |
| 1975 | Sergei Volkov, USSR |
| 1976 | John Curry, Great Britain |
| 1977 | Vladimir Kovalev, USSR |
| 1978 | Charles Tickner, United States |
| 1979 | Vladimir Kovalev, USSR |
| 1980 | Jan Hoffmann, East Germany |
| 1981 | Scott Hamilton, United States |
| 1982 | Scott Hamilton, United States |
| 1983 | Scott Hamilton, United States |
| 1984 | Scott Hamilton, United States |
| 1985 | Aleksandr Fadeev, USSR |
| 1986 | Brian Boitano, United States |
| 1987 | Brian Orser, Canada |
| 1988 | Brian Boitano, United States |
| 1989 | Kurt Browning, Canada |
| 1990 | Kurt Browning, Canada |
| 1991 | Kurt Browning, Canada |
| 1992 | Viktor Petrenko, CIS |
| 1993 | Kurt Browning, Canada |
| 1994 | Elvis Stojko, Canada |
| 1995 | Elvis Stojko, Canada |

## Pairs

| | |
|---|---|
| 1908.................Anna Hubler, Heinrich Burger, Germany | 1959.................Barbara Wagner, Robert Paul, Canada |
| 1909.................Phyllis Johnson, James H. Johnson, Great Britain | 1960.................Barbara Wagner, Robert Paul, Canada |
| 1910.................Anna Hubler, Heinrich Burger, Germany | 1961.................No competition |
| | 1962.................Maria Jelinek, Otto Jelinek, Canada |
| 1911.................Ludowika Eilers, Walter Jakobsson, Germany/Finland | 1963.................Marika Kilius, Hans-Jurgen Baumler, West Germany |
| 1912.................Phyllis Johnson, James H. Johnson, Great Britain | 1964.................Marika Kilius, Hans-Jurgen Baumler, West Germany |
| 1913.................Helene Engelmann, Karl Majstrik, Germany | 1965.................Ljudmila Protopopov, Oleg Protopopov, USSR |
| 1914.................Ludowika Jakobsson-Eilers, Walter Jakobsson-Eilers, Finland | 1966.................Ljudmila Protopopov, Oleg Protopopov, USSR |
| 1915-21.............No competition | 1967.................Ljudmila Protopopov, Oleg Protopopov, USSR |
| 1922.................Helene Engelmann, Alfred Berger, Germany | 1968.................Ljudmila Protopopov, Oleg Protopopov, USSR |
| 1923.................Ludowika Jakobsson-Eilers, Walter Jakobsson-Eilers, Finland | 1969.................Irina Rodnina, Alexsei Ulanov, USSR |
| 1924.................Helene Engelmann, Alfred Berger, Germany | 1970.................Irina Rodnina, Alexsei Ulanov, USSR |
| | 1971.................Irina Rodnina, Sergei Ulanov, USSR |
| 1925.................Herma Jaross-Szabo, Ludwig Wrede, Austria | 1972.................Irina Rodnina, Sergei Ulanov, USSR |
| 1926.................Andree Joly, Pierre Brunet, France | 1973.................Irina Rodnina, Aleksandr Zaitsev, USSR |
| 1927.................Herma Jaross-Szabo, Ludwig Wrede, Austria | 1974.................Irina Rodnina, Aleksandr Zaitsev, USSR |
| 1928.................Andree Joly, Pierre Brunet, France | 1975.................Irina Rodnina, Aleksandr Zaitsev, USSR |
| 1929.................Lilly Scholz, Otto Kaiser, Austria | |
| 1930.................Andree Brunet-Joly, Pierre Brunet-Joly, France | 1976.................Irina Rodnina, Aleksandr Zaitsev, USSR |
| 1931.................Emilie Rotter, Laszlo Szollas, Hungary | 1977.................Irina Rodnina, Aleksandr Zaitsev, USSR |
| 1932.................Andree Brunet-Joly, Pierre Brunet-Joly, France | 1978.................Irina Rodnina, Aleksandr Zaitsev, USSR |
| 1933.................Emilie Rotter, Laszlo Szollas, Hungary | 1979.................Tai Babilonia, Randy Gardner, United States |
| 1934.................Emilie Rotter, Laszlo Szollas, Hungary | 1980.................Maria Cherkasova, Sergei Shakhrai, USSR |
| 1935.................Emilie Rotter, Laszlo Szollas, Hungary | 1981.................Irina Vorobieva, Igor Lisovsky, USSR |
| | 1982.................Sabine Baess, Tassilio Thierbach, East Germany |
| 1936.................Maxi Herber, Ernst Bajer, Germany | |
| 1937.................Maxi Herber, Ernst Bajer, Germany | 1983.................Elena Valova, Oleg Vasiliev, USSR |
| 1938.................Maxi Herber, Ernst Bajer, Germany | 1984.................Barbara Underhill, Paul Martini, Canada |
| 1939.................Maxi Herber, Ernst Bajer, Germany | |
| 1940-46.............No competition | 1985.................Elena Valova, Oleg Vasiliev, USSR |
| 1947.................Micheline Lannoy, Pierre Baugniet, Belgium | 1986.................Yekaterina Gordeeva, Sergei Grinkov, USSR |
| 1948.................Micheline Lannoy, Pierre Baugniet, Belgium | 1987.................Yekaterina Gordeeva, Sergei Grinkov, USSR |
| 1949.................Andrea Kekessy, Ede Kiraly, Hungary | 1988.................Elena Valova, Oleg Vasiliev, USSR |
| 1950.................Karol Kennedy, Peter Kennedy, United States | 1989.................Yekaterina Gordeeva, Sergei Grinkov, USSR |
| 1951.................Ria Baran, Paul Falk, West Germany | 1990.................Yekaterina Gordeeva, Sergei Grinkov, USSR |
| 1952.................Ria Baran Falk, Paul Falk, West Germany | 1991.................Natalia Mishkutienok, Artur Dmitriev, USSR |
| 1953.................Jennifer Nicks, John Nicks, Great Britain | 1992.................Natalia Mishkutienok, Artur Dmitriev, CIS |
| 1954.................Frances Dafoe, Norris Bowden, Canada | 1993.................Isabelle Brasseur, Lloyd Eisler, Canada |
| 1955.................Frances Dafoe, Norris Bowden, Canada | 1994.................Evgenia Shishkova, Vadim Naumov, Russia |
| 1956.................Sissy Schwarz, Kurt Oppelt, Austria | 1995.................Radka Kovarikova, Rene Novotny, Czech Republic |
| 1957.................Barbara Wagner, Robert Paul, Canada | |
| 1958.................Barbara Wagner, Robert Paul, Canada | |

### Dance

1950 ..................Lois Waring, Michael McGean, U.S.
1951 ..................Jean Westwood, Lawrence Demmy, Great Britain
1952 ..................Jean Westwood, Lawrence Demmy, Great Britain
1953 ..................Jean Westwood, Lawrence Demmy, Great Britain
1954 ..................Jean Westwood, Lawrence Demmy, Great Britain
1955 ..................Jean Westwood, Lawrence Demmy, Great Britain
1956 ..................Pamela Wieght, Paul Thomas, Great Britain
1957 ..................June Markham, Courtney Jones, Great Britain
1958 ..................June Markham, Courtney Jones, Great Britain
1959 ..................Doreen D. Denny, Courtney Jones, Great Britain
1960 ..................Doreen D. Denny, Courtney Jones, Great Britain
1961 ..................No competition
1962 ..................Eva Romanova, Pavel Roman, Czechoslovakia
1963 ..................Eva Romanova, Pavel Roman, Czechoslovakia
1964 ..................Eva Romanova, Pavel Roman, Czechoslovakia
1965 ..................Eva Romanova, Pavel Roman, Czechoslovakia
1966 ..................Diane Towler, Bernard Ford, Great Britain
1967 ..................Diane Towler, Bernard Ford, Great Britain
1968 ..................Diane Towler, Bernard Ford, Great Britain
1969 ..................Diane Towler, Bernard Ford, Great Britain
1970 ..................Ljudmila Pakhomova, Aleksandr Gorshkov, USSR
1971 ..................Ljudmila Pakhomova, Aleksandr Gorshkov, USSR
1972 ..................Ljudmila Pakhomova, Aleksandr Gorshkov, USSR
1973 ..................Ljudmila Pakhomova, Aleksandr Gorshkov, USSR
1974 ..................Ljudmila Pakhomova, Aleksandr Gorshkov, USSR
1975 ..................Irina Moiseeva, Andreij Minenkov, USSR
1976 ..................Ljudmila Pakhomova, Aleksandr Gorshkov, USSR
1977 ..................Irina Moiseeva, Andreij Minenkov, USSR
1978 ..................Natalia Linichuk, Gennadi Karponosov, USSR
1979 ..................Natalia Linichuk, Gennadi Karponosov, USSR
1980 ..................Krisztina Regoeczy, Andras Sallai, Hungary
1981 ..................Jayne Torvill, Christopher Dean, Great Britain
1982 ..................Jayne Torvill, Christopher Dean, Great Britain
1983 ..................Jayne Torvill, Christopher Dean, Great Britain
1984 ..................Jayne Torvill, Christopher Dean, Great Britain
1985 ..................Natalia Bestemianova, Andrei Bukin, USSR
1986 ..................Natalia Bestemianova, Andrei Bukin, USSR
1987 ..................Natalia Bestemianova, Andrei Bukin, USSR
1988 ..................Natalia Bestemianova, Andrei Bukin, USSR
1989 ..................Marina Klimova, Sergei Ponomarenko, USSR
1990 ..................Marina Klimova, Sergei Ponomarenko, USSR
1991 ..................Isabelle Duchesnay, Paul Duchesnay, France
1992 ..................Marina Klimova, Sergei Ponomarenko , CIS
1993 ..................Renee Roca, Gorsha Sur, Broadmoor SC, United States
1994 ..................Oksana Gritschuk, Evgeny Platov, Russia
1995 ..................Oksana Gritschuk, Evgeny Platov, Russia

## Champions of the United States

The championships held in 1914, 1918, 1920 and 1921 under the auspices of the International Skating Union of America were open to Canadians, although they were considered to be United States championships. Beginning in 1922, the championships have been held under the auspices of the United States Figure Skating Association.

### Women

1914 ..........Theresa Weld, SC of Boston
1915-17 ......No competition
1918 ...........Rosemary S. Beresford, New York SC
1919 ..........No competition
1920 ...........Theresa Weld, SC of Boston
1921 ...........Theresa Weld Blanchard, SC of Boston
1922 ...........Theresa Weld Blanchard, SC of Boston
1923 ...........Theresa Weld Blanchard, SC of Boston
1924 ...........Theresa Weld Blanchard, SC of Boston
1925 ...........Beatrix Loughran, New York SC
1926 ...........Beatrix Loughran, New York SC
1927 ...........Beatrix Loughran, New York SC
1928 ...........Maribel Y. Vinson, SC of Boston
1929 ...........Maribel Y. Vinson, SC of Boston
1930 ...........Maribel Y. Vinson, SC of Boston
1931 ...........Maribel Y. Vinson, SC of Boston
1932 ...........Maribel Y. Vinson, SC of Boston
1933 ...........Maribel Y. Vinson, SC of Boston
1934 ...........Suzanne Davis, SC of Boston
1935 ...........Maribel Y. Vinson, SC of Boston
1936 ...........Maribel Y. Vinson, SC of Boston
1937 ...........Maribel Y. Vinson, SC of Boston
1938 ...........Joan Tozzer, SC of Boston
1939 ...........Joan Tozzer, SC of Boston

## Women *(Cont.)*

| | |
|---|---|
| 1940 ..........Joan Tozzer, SC of Boston | 1967 ..........Peggy Fleming, Broadmoor SC |
| 1941 ..........Jane Vaughn, Philadelphia SC & HS | 1968 ..........Peggy Fleming, Broadmoor SC |
| 1942 ..........Jane Vaughn Sullivan, | 1969 ..........Janet Lynn, Wagon Wheel FSC |
| Philadelphia SC & HS | 1970 ..........Janet Lynn, Wagon Wheel FSC |
| 1943..........Gretchen Van Zandt Merrill, SC of Boston | 1971 ..........Janet Lynn, Wagon Wheel FSC |
| 1944..........Gretchen Van Zandt Merrill, SC of Boston | 1972 ..........Janet Lynn, Wagon Wheel FSC |
| 1945..........Gretchen Van Zandt Merrill, SC of Boston | 1973 ..........Janet Lynn, Wagon Wheel FSC |
| 1946..........Gretchen Van Zandt Merrill, SC of Boston | 1974 ..........Dorothy Hamill, SC of New York |
| 1947..........Gretchen Van Zandt Merrill, SC of Boston | 1975 ..........Dorothy Hamill, SC of New York |
| 1948..........Gretchen Van Zandt Merrill, SC of Boston | 1976 ..........Dorothy Hamill, SC of New York |
| 1949 ..........Yvonne Claire Sherman, SC of New York | 1977 ..........Linda Fratianne, Los Angeles FSC |
| 1950 ..........Yvonne Claire Sherman, SC of New York | 1978 ..........Linda Fratianne, Los Angeles FSC |
| 1951 ..........Sonya Klopfer, Junior SC of New York | 1979 ..........Linda Fratianne, Los Angeles FSC |
| 1952 ..........Tenley E. Albright, SC of Boston | 1980 ..........Linda Fratianne, Los Angeles FSC |
| 1953 ..........Tenley E. Albright, SC of Boston | 1981 ..........Elaine Zayak, SC of New York |
| 1954 ..........Tenley E. Albright, SC of Boston | 1982 ..........Rosalynn Sumners, Seattle SC |
| 1955 ..........Tenley E. Albright, SC of Boston | 1983 ..........Rosalynn Sumners, Seattle SC |
| 1956 ..........Tenley E. Albright, SC of Boston | 1984 ..........Rosalynn Sumners, Seattle SC |
| 1957 ..........Carol E. Heiss, SC of New York | 1985 ..........Tiffany Chin, San Diego FSC |
| 1958 ..........Carol E. Heiss, SC of New York | 1986 ..........Debi Thomas, Los Angeles FSC |
| 1959 ..........Carol E. Heiss, SC of New York | 1987 ..........Jill Trenary, Broadmoor SC |
| 1960 ..........Carol E. Heiss, SC of New York | 1988 ..........Debi Thomas, Los Angeles FSC |
| 1961 ..........Laurence R. Owen, SC of Boston | 1989 ..........Jill Trenary, Broadmoor SC |
| 1962 ..........Barbara Roles Pursley, | 1990 ..........Jill Trenary, Broadmoor SC |
| Arctic Blades FSC | 1991 ..........Tonya Harding, Carousel FSC |
| 1963 ..........Lorraine G. Hanlon, SC of Boston | 1992 ..........Kristi Yamaguchi, St Moritz ISC |
| 1964 ..........Peggy Fleming, Arctic Blades FSC | 1993 ..........Nancy Kerrigan, Colonial FSC |
| 1965 ..........Peggy Fleming, Arctic Blades FSC | 1994 ..........Tonya Harding, Portland FSC |
| 1966 ..........Peggy Fleming, City of Colorado Springs | 1995 ..........Nicole Bobek, Los Angeles FSC |

## Men

| | |
|---|---|
| 1914 ..........Norman M. Scott, WC of Montreal | 1951 ......Dick Button, SC of Boston |
| 1915-17 ......No competition | 1952 ......Dick Button, SC of Boston |
| 1918 ..........Nathaniel W. Niles, SC of Boston | 1953 ......Hayes Alan Jenkins, Cleveland SC |
| 1919 ..........No competition | 1954 ......Hayes Alan Jenkins, Broadmoor SC |
| 1920 ..........Sherwin C. Badger, SC of Boston | 1955 ......Hayes Alan Jenkins, Broadmoor SC |
| 1921 ..........Sherwin C. Badger, SC of Boston | 1956 ......Hayes Alan Jenkins, Broadmoor SC |
| 1922 ..........Sherwin C. Badger, SC of Boston | 1957 ......David Jenkins, Broadmoor SC |
| 1923 ..........Sherwin C. Badger, SC of Boston | 1958 ......David Jenkins, Broadmoor SC |
| 1924 ..........Sherwin C. Badger, SC of Boston | 1959 ......David Jenkins, Broadmoor SC |
| 1925 ..........Nathaniel W. Niles, SC of Boston | 1960 ......David Jenkins, Broadmoor SC |
| 1926 ..........Chris I. Christenson, Twin City FSC | 1961 ......Bradley R. Lord, SC of Boston |
| 1927 ..........Nathaniel W. Niles, SC of Boston | 1962 ......Monty Hoyt, Broadmoor SC |
| 1928 ..........Roger F. Turner, SC of Boston | 1963 ......Thomas Litz, Hershey FSC |
| 1929 ..........Roger F. Turner, SC of Boston | 1964 ......Scott Ethan Allen, SC of New York |
| 1930 ..........Roger F. Turner, SC of Boston | 1965 ......Gary C. Visconti, Detroit SC |
| 1931 ..........Roger F. Turner, SC of Boston | 1966 ......Scott Ethan Allen, SC of New York |
| 1932 ..........Roger F. Turner, SC of Boston | 1967 ......Gary C. Visconti, Detroit SC |
| 1933 ..........Roger F. Turner, SC of Boston | 1968 ......Tim Wood, Detroit SC |
| 1934 ..........Roger F. Turner, SC of Boston | 1969 ......Tim Wood, Detroit SC |
| 1935 ..........Robin H. Lee, SC, New York | 1970 ......Tim Wood, City of Colorado Springs |
| 1936 ..........Robin H. Lee, SC, New York | 1971 ......John Misha Petkevich, Great Falls FSC |
| 1937 ..........Robin H. Lee, SC, New York | 1972 ......Kenneth Shelley, Arctic Blades FSC |
| 1938 ..........Robin H. Lee, Chicago FSC | 1973 ......Gordon McKellen, Jr, SC of Lake Placid |
| 1939 ..........Robin H. Lee, St Paul FSC | 1974 ......Gordon McKellen, Jr, SC of Lake Placid |
| 1940 ..........Eugene Turner, Los Angeles FSC | 1975 ......Gordon McKellen, Jr, SC of Lake Placid |
| 1941 ..........Eugene Turner, Los Angeles FSC | 1976 ......Terry Kubicka, Arctic Blades FSC |
| 1942 ..........Robert Specht, Chicago FSC | 1977 ......Charles Tickner, Denver FSC |
| 1943 ..........Arthur R. Vaughn, Jr, | 1978 ......Charles Tickner, Denver FSC |
| Philadelphia SC & HS | 1979 ......Charles Tickner, Denver FSC |
| 1944-45 ......No competition | 1980 ......Charles Tickner, Denver FSC |
| 1946 ..........Dick Button, Philadelphia SC & HS | 1981 ......Scott Hamilton, Philadelphia SC & HS |
| 1947 ..........Dick Button, Philadelphia SC & HS | 1982 ......Scott Hamilton, Philadelphia SC & HS |
| 1948 ..........Dick Button, Philadelphia SC & HS | 1983 ......Scott Hamilton, Philadelphia SC & HS |
| 1949 ..........Dick Button, Philadelphia SC & HS | 1984 ......Scott Hamilton, Philadelphia SC & HS |
| 1950 ..........Dick Button, SC of Boston | 1985 ......Brian Boitano, Peninsula FSC |

## Men *(Cont.)*

1986 ......Brian Boitano, Peninsula FSC
1987 ......Brian Boitano, Peninsula FSC
1988 ......Brian Boitano, Peninsula FSC
1989 ......Christopher Bowman, Los Angeles FSC
1990 ......Todd Eldredge, Los Angeles FSC

1991 ......Todd Eldredge, Los Angeles FSC
1992 ......Christopher Bowman, Los Angeles FSC
1993 ......Scott Davis, Broadmoor SC
1994 ......Scott Davis, Broadmoor SC
1995 ......Todd Eldredge, Detroit SC

## Pairs

1914 ......Jeanne Chevalier, Norman M. Scott,
　　　　　WC of Montreal
1915-17 .No competition
1918 ......Theresa Weld, Nathaniel W. Niles,
　　　　　SC of Boston
1919 ......No competition
1920 ......Theresa Weld, Nathaniel W. Niles,
　　　　　SC of Boston
1921 ......Theresa Weld Blanchard, Nathaniel W.
　　　　　Niles,SC of Boston
1922 ......Theresa Weld Blanchard, Nathaniel W.
　　　　　Niles, SC of Boston
1923 ......Theresa Weld Blanchard, Nathaniel W.
　　　　　Niles, SC of Boston
1924 ......Theresa Weld Blanchard, Nathaniel W.
　　　　　Niles, SC of Boston
1925 ......Theresa Weld Blanchard, Nathaniel W.
　　　　　Niles, SC of Boston
1926 ......Theresa Weld Blanchard, Nathaniel W. Niles
　　　　　SC of Boston
1927 ......Theresa Weld Blanchard, Nathaniel W.
　　　　　Niles, SC of Boston
1928 ......Maribel Y. Vinson, Thornton L. Coolidge,
　　　　　SC of Boston
1929 ......Maribel Y. Vinson, Thornton L. Coolidge,
　　　　　SC of Boston
1930 ......Beatrix Loughran, Sherwin C. Badger,
　　　　　SC of New York
1931 ......Beatrix Loughran, Sherwin C. Badger,
　　　　　SC of New York
1932 ......Beatrix Loughran, Sherwin C. Badger,
　　　　　SC of New York
1933 ......Maribel Y. Vinson, George E. B. Hill,
　　　　　SC of Boston
1934 ......Grace E. Madden, James L. Madden,
　　　　　SC of Boston
1935 ......Maribel Y. Vinson, George E. B. Hill,
　　　　　SC of Boston
1936 ......Maribel Y. Vinson, George E. B. Hill,
　　　　　SC of Boston
1937 ......Maribel Y. Vinson, George E. B. Hill,
　　　　　SC of Boston
1938 ......Joan Tozzer, M. Bernard Fox,
　　　　　SC of Boston
1939 ......Joan Tozzer, M. Bernard Fox,
　　　　　SC of Boston
1940 ......Joan Tozzer, M. Bernard Fox,
　　　　　SC of Boston
1941 ......Donna Atwood, Eugene Turner, Mercury
　　　　　FSC/Los Angeles FSC
1942 ......Doris Schubach, Walter Noffke,
　　　　　Springfield Ice Birds
1943 ......Doris Schubach, Walter Noffke,
　　　　　Springfield Ice Birds
1944 ......Doris Schubach, Walter Noffke,
　　　　　Springfield Ice Birds
1945 ......Donna Jeanne Pospisil, Jean-Pierre Brunet,
　　　　　SC of New York
1946 ......Donna Jeanne Pospisil, Jean-Pierre Brunet,
　　　　　SC of New York

1947 ......Yvonne Claire Sherman, Robert J.
　　　　　Swenning, SC of New York
1948 ......Karol Kennedy, Peter Kennedy,
　　　　　Seattle SC
1949 ......Karol Kennedy, Peter Kennedy,
　　　　　Seattle SC
1950 ......Karol Kennedy, Peter Kennedy,
　　　　　Broadmoor SC
1951 ......Karol Kennedy, Peter Kennedy,
　　　　　Broadmoor SC
1952 ......Karol Kennedy, Peter Kennedy,
　　　　　Broadmoor SC
1953 ......Carole Ann Ormaca, Robin Greiner,
　　　　　SC of Fresno
1954 ......Carole Ann Ormaca, Robin Greiner,
　　　　　SC of Fresno
1955 ......Carole Ann Ormaca, Robin Greiner,
　　　　　St Moritz ISC
1956 ......Carole Ann Ormaca, Robin Greiner,
　　　　　St Moritz ISC
1957 ......Nancy Rouillard Ludington, Ronald
　　　　　Ludington, Commonwealth FSC/
　　　　　SC of Boston
1958 ......Nancy Rouillard Ludington, Ronald
　　　　　Ludington, Commonwealth FSC/
　　　　　SC of Boston
1959 ......Nancy Rouillard Ludington, Ronald
　　　　　Ludington, Commonwealth FSC
1960 ......Nancy Rouillard Ludington, Ronald
　　　　　Ludington, Commonwealth FSC
1961 ......Maribel Y. Owen, Dudley S. Richards,
　　　　　SC of Boston
1962 ......Dorothyann Nelson, Pieter Kollen,
　　　　　Village of Lake Placid
1963 ......Judianne Fotheringill, Jerry J. Fotheringill,
　　　　　Broadmoor SC
1964 ......Judianne Fotheringill, Jerry J. Fotheringill,
　　　　　Broadmoor SC
1965 ......Vivian Joseph, Ronald Joseph,
　　　　　Chicago FSC
1966 ......Cynthia Kauffman, Ronald Kauffman,
　　　　　Seattle SC
1967 ......Cynthia Kauffman, Ronald Kauffman,
　　　　　Seattle SC
1968 ......Cynthia Kauffman, Ronald Kauffman,
　　　　　Seattle SC
1969 ......Cynthia Kauffman, Ronald Kauffman,
　　　　　Seattle SC
1970 ......Jo Jo Starbuck, Kenneth Shelley,
　　　　　Arctic Blades FSC
1971 ......Jo Jo Starbuck, Kenneth Shelley,
　　　　　Arctic Blades FSC
1972 ......Jo Jo Starbuck, Kenneth Shelley,
　　　　　Arctic Blades FSC
1973 ......Melissa Militano, Mark Militano,
　　　　　SC of New York
1974 ......Melissa Militano, Johnny Johns,
　　　　　SC of New York/Detroit SC
1975 ......Melissa Militano, Johnny Johns,
　　　　　SC of New York/Detroit SC

## Pairs *(Cont.)*

1976 ......Tai Babilonia, Randy Gardner,
       Los Angeles FSC
1977 ......Tai Babilonia, Randy Gardner,
       Los Angeles FSC
1978 ......Tai Babilonia, Randy Gardner,
       Los Angeles FSC/Santa Monica FSC
1979 ......Tai Babilonia, Randy Gardner,
       Los Angeles FSC/Santa Monica FSC
1980 ......Tai Babilonia, Randy Gardner,
       Los Angeles FSC/Santa Monica FSC
1981 ......Caitlin Carruthers, Peter Carruthers,
       SC of Wilmington
1982 ......Caitlin Carruthers, Peter Carruthers,
       SC of Wilmington
1983 ......Caitlin Carruthers, Peter Carruthers,
       SC of Wilmington
1984 ......Caitlin Carruthers, Peter Carruthers,
       SC of Wilmington
1985 ......Jill Watson, Peter Oppegard,
       Los Angeles FSC

1986 ......Gillian Wachsman, Todd Waggoner,
       SC of Wilmington
1987 ......Jill Watson, Peter Oppegard,
       Los Angeles FSC
1988 ......Jill Watson, Peter Oppegard,
       Los Angeles FSC
1989 ......Kristi Yamaguchi, Rudi Galindo,
       St Moritz ISC
1990 ......Kristi Yamaguchi, Rudi Galindo,
       St Moritz ISC
1991 ......Natasha Kuchiki, Todd Sand,
       Los Angeles FSC
1992 ......Calla Urbanski, Rocky Marval,
       U of Delaware FSC/SC of New York
1993 ......Calla Urbanski, Rocky Marval,
       U of Delaware FSC/SC of New York
1994 ......Jenni Meno,Todd Sand,
       Winterhurst FSC/Los Angeles FSC
1995 ......Jenni Meno,Todd Sand,
       Winterhurst FSC/Los Angeles FSC

## Dance

1914 ......Waltz
       Theresa Weld, Nathaniel W. Niles,
       SC of Boston
1915-19.No competition
1920 ......Waltz
       Theresa Weld, Nathaniel W. Niles, SC Boston
       Fourteenstep
       Gertrude Cheever Porter, Irving Brokaw,NYSC
1921 ......Waltz and Fourteenstep
       Theresa Weld Blanchard, Nathaniel W.
       Niles, SC of Boston
1922 ......Waltz
       Beatrix Loughran, Edward M. Howland,
       New York SC/SC of Boston
       Fourteenstep
       Theresa Weld Blanchard, Nathaniel W.
       Niles, SC of Boston
1923 ......Waltz
       Mr. & Mrs. Henry W. Howe, New York SC
       Fourteenstep
       Sydney Goode, James B. Greene, NYSC
1924 ......Waltz
       Rosaline Dunn, Frederick Gabel
       New York SC
       Fourteenstep
       Sydney Goode, James B. Greene,
       New York SC
1925 ......Waltz and Fourteenstep
       Virginia Slattery, Ferrier T. Martin,
       New York SC
1926 ......Waltz
       Rosaline Dunn, Joseph K. Savage,
       New York SC
       Fourteenstep
       Sydney Goode, James B. Greene,
       New York SC
1927 ......Waltz and Fourteenstep
       Rosaline Dunn, Joseph K. Savage,
       New York SC
1928 ......Waltz
       Rosaline Dunn, Joseph K. Savage,
       New York SC
       Fourteenstep
       Ada Bauman Kelly, George T. Braakman,
       New York SC

1929 ......Waltz and Original Dance combined
       Edith C. Secord, Joseph K. Savage,
       SC of New York
1930 ......Waltz
       Edith C. Secord, Joseph K. Savage,
       SC of New York
       Original
       Clara Rotch Frothingham, George E. B. Hill,
       SC of Boston
1931 ......Waltz
       Edith C. Secord, Ferrier T. Martin,
       SC of New York
       Original
       Theresa Weld Blanchard, Nathaniel W.
       Niles, SC of Boston
1932 ......Waltz
       Edith C. Secord, Joseph K. Savage,
       SC of New York
       Original
       Clara Rotch Frothingham, George E. B. Hill,
       SC of Boston
1933 ......Waltz
       Ilse Twaroschk, Frederick F. Fleishmann,
       Brooklyn FSC
       Original
       Suzanne Davis, Frederick Goodridge,
       SC of Boston
1934 ......Waltz
       Nettie C. Prantel, Roy Hunt, SC of New York
       Original
       Suzanne Davis, Frederick Goodridge,
       SC of Boston
1935 ......Waltz
       Nettie C. Prantel, Roy Hunt, SC of New York
1936 ......Marjorie Parker, Joseph K. Savage,
       SC of New York
1937 ......Nettie C. Prantel, Harold Hartshorne,
       SC of New York
1938 ......Nettie C. Prantel, Harold Hartshorne,
       SC, of New York
1939 ......Sandy Macdonald, Harold Hartshorne,
       SC of New York
1940 ......Sandy Macdonald, Harold Hartshorne,
       SC of New York
1941 ......Sandy Macdonald, Harold Hartshorne, SCNY

### Dance *(Cont.)*

1942 ......Edith B. Whetstone, Alfred N. Richards, Jr,
          Philadelphia SC & HS
1943 ......Marcella May, James Lochead, Jr,
          Skate & Ski Club
1944 ......Marcella May, James Lochead, Jr,
          Skate & Ski Club
1945 ......Kathe Mehl Williams, Robert J. Swenning,
          SC of New York
1946 ......Anne Davies, Carleton C. Hoffner, Jr,
          Washington FSC
1947 ......Lois Waring, Walter H. Bainbridge, Jr,
          Baltimore FSC/Washigton FSC
1948 ......Lois Waring, Walter H. Bainbridge, Jr,
          Baltimore FSC/Washington FSC
1949 ......Lois Waring, Walter H. Bainbridge, Jr,
          Baltimore FSC/Washington FSC
1950 ......Lois Waring, Michael McGean, Baltimore FSC
1951 ......Carmel Bodel, Edward L. Bodel,
          St Moritz ISC
1952 ......Lois Waring, Michael McGean,
          Baltimore FSC
1953 ......Carol Ann Peters, Daniel C. Ryan,
          Washington FSC
1954 ......Carmel Bodel, Edward L. Bodel, St Moritz ISC
1955 ......Carmel Bodel, Edward L. Bodel,
          St Moritz ISC
1956 ......Joan Zamboni, Roland Junso,
          Arctic Blades FSC
1957 ......Sharon McKenzie, Bert Wright,
          Los Angeles FSC
1958 ......Andree Anderson, Donald Jacoby,
          Buffalo SC
1959 ......Andree Anderson Jacoby, Donald Jacoby,
          Buffalo SC
1960 ......Margie Ackles, Charles W. Phillips, Jr,
          Los Angeles FSC/Arctic Blades FSC
1961 ......Diane C. Sherbloom, Larry Pierce,
          Los Angeles FSC/WC of Indianapolis
1962 ......Yvonne N. Littlefield, Peter F. Betts,
          Arctic Blades FSC/ Paramount, CA
1963 ......Sally Schantz, Stanley Urban,
          SC of Boston/Buffalo SC
1964 ......Darlene Streich, Charles D. Fetter, Jr,
          WC of Indianapolis
1965 ......Kristin Fortune, Dennis Sveum,
          Los Angeles FSC
1966 ......Kristin Fortune, Dennis Sveum,
          Los Angeles FSC
1967 ......Lorna Dyer, John Carrell, Broadmoor SC
1968 ......Judy Schwomeyer, James Sladky,
          WC of Indianapolis/Genesee FSC
1969 ......Judy Schwomeyer, James Sladky,

WC of Indianapolis/Genesee FSC
1970 ......Judy Schwomeyer, James Sladky,
          WC of Indianapolis/Genesee FSC
1971 ......Judy Schwomeyer, James Sladky,
          WC of Indianapolis/Genesee FSC
1972 ......Judy Schwomeyer, James Sladky,
          WC of Indianapolis/Genesee FSC
1973 ......Mary Karen Campbell, Johnny Johns,
          Lansing SC/Detroit SC
1974 ......Colleen O'Connor, Jim Millns,
          Broadmoor SC/City of Colorado Springs
1975 ......Colleen O'Connor, Jim Millns,
          Broadmoor SC
1976 ......Colleen O'Connor, Jim Millns,
          Broadmoor SC
1977 ......Judy Genovesi, Kent Weigle,
          SC of Hartford/Charter Oak FSC
1978 ......Stacey Smith, John Summers,
          SC of Wilmington
1979 ......Stacey Smith, John Summers,
          SC of Wilmington
1980 ......Stacey Smith, John Summers,
          SC of Wilmington
1981 ......Judy Blumberg, Michael Seibert,
          Broadmoor SC/ISC of Indianapolis
1982 ......Judy Blumberg, Michael Seibert,
          Broadmoor SC/ISC of Indianapolis
1983 ......Judy Blumberg, Michael Seibert,
          Pittsburgh FSC
1984 ......Judy Blumberg, Michael Seibert,
          Pittsburgh FSC
1985 ......Judy Blumberg, Michael Seibert,
          Pittsburgh FSC
1986 ......Renee Roca, Donald Adair,
          Genesee FSC/Academy FSC
1987 ......Suzanne Semanick, Scott Gregory,
          U of Delaware SC
1988 ......Suzanne Semanick, Scott Gregory,
          U of Delaware SC
1989 ......Susan Wynne, Joseph Druar,
          Broadmoor SC/Seattle SC
1990 ......Susan Wynne, Joseph Druar,
          Broadmoor SC/Seattle SC
1991 ......Elizabeth Punsalan, Jerod Swallow,
          Broadmoor SC
1992 ......April Sargent, Russ Witherby,
          Ogdensburg FSC/U of Delaware FSC
1993 ......Renee Roca, Gorsha Sur, Broadmoor SC
1994 ......Elizabeth Punsalan, Jerod Swallow,
          Broadmoor SC/Detroit SC
1995 ......Renee Roca, Gorsha Sur,
          Broadmoor SC/ Broadmoor SC

## U.S. Olympic Gold Medalists

### Women

1956 ............................................Tenley Albright
1960 ................................................Carol Heiss
1968 ............................................Peggy Fleming

1976 ............................................Dorothy Hamill
1992 ..........................................Kristi Yamaguchi

### Men

1948 ............................................Richard Button
1952 ............................................Richard Button
1956 ........................................Hayes Alan Jenkins

1960 ..........................................David W. Jenkins
1984 ............................................Scott Hamilton
1988 ..............................................Brian Boitano

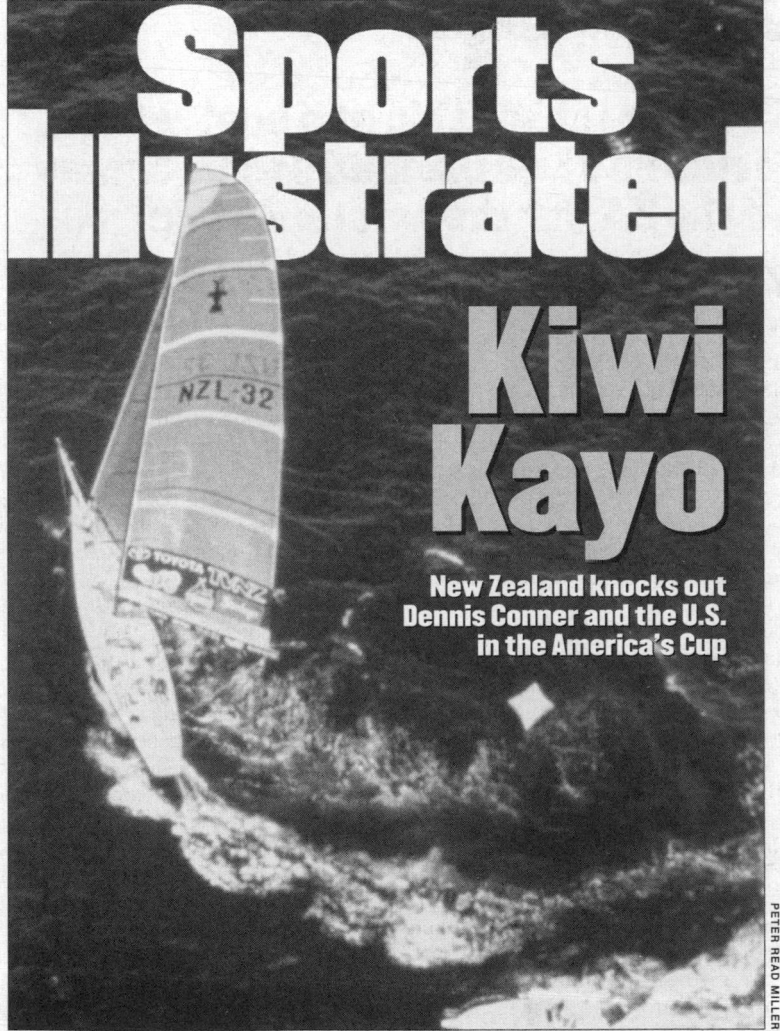

**Sports Illustrated**

**Kiwi Kayo**

New Zealand knocks out
Dennis Conner and the U.S.
in the America's Cup

NZL·32

PETER READ MILLER

# A Clean Sweep

## With their rocket ship of a boat, *Black Magic*, the Kiwis blanked Dennis Conner and the U.S. for the America's Cup

## by E.M. Swift

THIS TIME. That was the motto of Team New Zealand. From the moment the Kiwis arrived in San Diego with a pair of sleek black-hulled International America's Cup Class (IACC) yachts, *Black Magic I* and *Black Magic II*, they were determined that after three previous failures, *this time* they would be carrying the most prestigious trophy in sailing back to Auckland, the city of sails.

The New Zealanders were led by Peter Blake, a rangy, shaggy-haired 47-year-old who in his sailing-mad homeland was already a national hero. In 1989–90 Blake had won the prestigious Whitbread round-the-world race, finishing first on every leg. In '94 he'd taken four days off the record for circumnavigation of the globe, accomplishing the feat in a catamaran in just under 75 days. Blake had logged over a half-million ocean racing miles, yet despite his impressive credentials, he assigned himself the role of the mainsheet traveler aboard *Black Magic*—a lowly grinder of winches. That set the tone for the entire Kiwi campaign: There were no superstars among the New Zealanders. The team came first. And from January to May, in light, fluky breezes or heavy air, in big swells or flat seas, they *finished* first 42 times out of 43 starts. Team New Zealand and its extraordinary black beast skippered by Russell Coutts proved to be in a league of its own.

The event, as usual, was embroiled in nonstop controversy. A new rule, designed to hold down expenses, forbade individual syndicates from building more than two boats for the campaign. Yet both the Australians and the Japanese were accused of circumventing it—a charge that, in the case of the Australians, became moot when its newest and fastest hull, *oneAustralia 95*, sank in midrace on March 5. It was the most visually dramatic moment during the five months of racing: The mast disappeared beneath the waves less than 2½ minutes after a crack split the side of the hull, marking the first time in America's Cup history that a vessel had been lost at sea. No one was hurt, but the disaster was evidence of how far designers were pushing

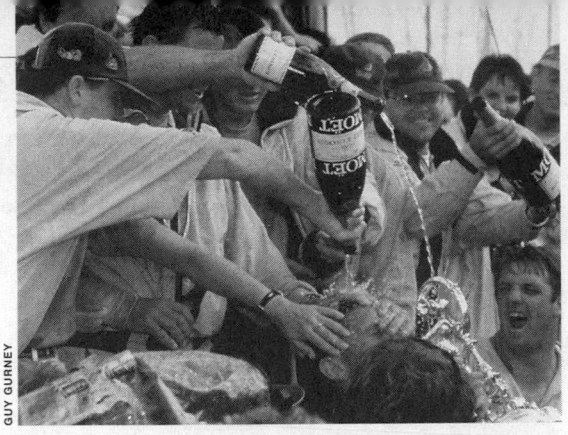

GUY GURNEY

**The Kiwis celebrated the way they won: as a team.**

the envelope on the $3 million to $5 million carbon-fiber IACC yachts, trying to cut weight to optimize speed. The resilient Aussies, led by John Bertrand—who in 1983 became the first foreign skipper to win the America's Cup and hadn't competed in the event since—regrouped and advanced to the challenger finals sailing their older boat, *oneAustralia*. But they were easily eliminated there by their archrivals, the Kiwis, four races to one.

Over on the defender side, the hosts seemed to be doing everything in their power to kill interest in the event. Nineteen ninety-five will be remembered as the year Bill Koch sponsored an all-women's boat, then reneged on his commitment midway through the trials by putting red-whiskered Dave Dellenbaugh aboard as the starter and tactician. Koch's crew thus became known as 15 women and the bearded lady. The credibility of the event was further damaged when Koch, Dennis Conner and PACT 95 chief John Marshall struck an 11th-hour backroom deal that allowed all three boats to advance to the defender finals, rewriting the rules so that no syndicate would have to face the wrath of its corporate sponsors for going home before the races were shown live on ESPN. The 52-year-old Conner, who would have lost out if the original rules had been adhered to, subsequently pulled off one of the most improbable comebacks in Cup history, making up an astonishing five minutes over Koch's *Mighty Mary* in the final three-mile downwind leg, winning the right to defend.

The deal making and finagling wasn't finished. Convinced that his *Stars and Stripes* was the slowest of the three defender boats, Conner jettisoned it and rented PACT 95's *Young America* six days before the showdown with New Zealand. The switch enraged the plain-speaking Blake

and cemented Conner's reputation in New Zealand as "Dirty Den." "If we are fortunate enough to win this event," Blake said, "we're going to clean it up. We're not going to have rules that are different for one side than the other."

Blake will get his chance. *Young America* proved no match for the speedy *Black Magic*. In an anticlimactic best-of-nine series, the Kiwis won all five 18.5-mile races by an average margin of two minutes 51 seconds—roughly two fifths of a mile. They didn't trail at a single rounding mark. "I've never been in a race where I felt I had so little control over the outcome," said Paul Cayard, Team Dennis Conner's helmsman.

"We never guessed the entire defense effort was so far off the pace," said tactician Tom Whidden. "We can't even engage these guys in a race."

It was sweet revenge for the Kiwis, who'd been eliminated in 1987 and '88 by Conner and in '92 by Cayard, who then was sailing for Italy. *This time* was different. Fans of the America's Cup hope that next time the regatta will be different, too. San Diego and the America's Cup proved to be a bad marriage. In the seven years the San Diego Yacht Club held the Cup, it staged three turbulent defenses that were marred by court challenges, insolvency, light winds, boring races, unsportsmanlike conduct and an apathetic local populace. As the Auld Mug leaves San Diego for the bluer waters off Auckland, the chances are it will never return.

## Archery

### National Men's Champions

| | | |
|---|---|---|
| 1879......Will H. Thompson | 1916 ......Dr. Robert Elmer | 1959 ......Wilbert Vetrovsky |
| 1880 ......L. L. Pedinghaus | 1919 ......Dr. Robert Elmer | 1960 ......Robert Kadlec |
| 1881 ......F. H. Walworth | 1920 ......Dr. Robert Elmer | 1961 ......Clayton Sherman |
| 1882 ......D. H. Nash | 1921 ......James Jiles | 1962 ......Charles Sandlin |
| 1883 ......Col. Robert Williams | 1922 ......Dr. Robert Elmer | 1963 ......Dave Keaggy, Jr. |
| 1884 ......Col. Robert Williams | 1923 ......Bill Palmer | 1964 ......Dave Keaggy, Jr. |
| 1885 ......Col. Robert Williams | 1924 ......James Jiles | 1965 ......George Slinzer |
| 1886 ......W. A. Clark | 1925 ......Dr. Paul Crouch | 1966 ......Hardy Ward |
| 1887 ......W. A. Clark | 1926 ......Stanley Spencer | 1967 ......Ray Rogers |
| 1888 ......Lewis Maxson | 1927 ......Dr. Paul Crouch | 1968 ......Hardy Ward |
| 1889 ......Lewis Maxson | 1928 ......Bill Palmer | 1969 ......Ray Rogers |
| 1890 ......Lewis Maxson | 1929 ......Dr. E. K. Roberts | 1970 ......Joe Thornton |
| 1891 ......Lewis Maxson | 1930 ......Russ Hoogerhyde | 1971 ......John Williams |
| 1892 ......Lewis Maxson | 1931 ......Russ Hoogerhyde | 1972 ......Kevin Erlandson |
| 1893 ......Lewis Maxson | 1932 ......Russ Hoogerhyde | 1973 ......Darrell Pace |
| 1894 ......Lewis Maxson | 1933 ......Ralph Miller | 1974 ......Darrell Pace |
| 1895 ......W. B. Robinson | 1934 ......Russ Hoogerhyde | 1975 ......Darrell Pace |
| 1896 ......Lewis Maxson | 1935 ......Gilman Keasey | 1976 ......Darrell Pace |
| 1897 ......W. A. Clark | 1936 ......Gilman Keasey | 1977 ......Rick McKinney |
| 1898 ......Lewis Maxson | 1937 ......Russ Hoogerhyde | 1978 ......Darrell Pace |
| 1899 ......M. C. Howell | 1938 ......Pat Chambers | 1979 ......Rick McKinney |
| 1900 ......A. R. Clark | 1939 ......Pat Chambers | 1980 ......Rick McKinney |
| 1901 ......Will H. Thompson | 1940 ......Russ Hoogerhyde | 1981 ......Rick McKinney |
| 1902 ......Will H. Thompson | 1941 ......Larry Hughes | 1982 ......Rick McKinney |
| 1903 ......Will H. Thompson | 1946 ......Wayne Thompson | 1983 ......Rick McKinney |
| 1904 ......George Bryant | 1947 ......Jack Wilson | 1984 ......Darrell Pace |
| 1905 ......George Bryant | 1948 ......Larry Hughes | 1985 ......Rick McKinney |
| 1906 ......Henry Richardson | 1949 ......Russ Reynolds | 1986 ......Rick McKinney |
| 1907 ......Henry Richardson | 1950 ......Stan Overby | 1987 ......Rick McKinney |
| 1908 ......Will H. Thompson | 1951 ......Russ Reynolds | 1988 ......Jay Barrs |
| 1909 ......George Bryant | 1952 ......Robert Larson | 1989 ......Ed Eliason |
| 1910 ......Henry Richardson | 1953 ......Bill Glackin | 1990 ......Ed Eliason |
| 1911 ......Dr. Robert Elmer | 1954 ......Robert Rhode | 1991 ......Ed Eliason |
| 1912 ......George Bryant | 1955 ......Joe Fries | 1992 ......Alan Rasor |
| 1913 ......George Bryant | 1956 ......Joe Fries | 1993 ......Jay Barrs |
| 1914 ......Dr. Robert Elmer | 1957 ......Joe Fries | 1994 ......Jay Barrs |
| 1915 ......Dr. Robert Elmer | 1958 ......Robert Bitner | 1995 ......Justin Huish |

### National Women's Champions

| | | |
|---|---|---|
| 1879 ......Mrs. S. Brown | 1903 ......Mrs. M. C. Howell | 1929 ......Audrey Grubbs |
| 1880 ......Mrs. T. Davies | 1904 ......Mrs. M. C. Howell | 1930 ......Audrey Grubbs |
| 1881 ......Mrs. A. H. Gibbes | 1905 ......Mrs. M. C. Howell | 1931 ......Dorothy Cummings |
| 1882 ......Mrs. A. H. Gibbes | 1906 ......Mrs. E. C. Cook | 1932 ......Ilda Hanchette |
| 1883 ......Mrs. M. C. Howell | 1907 ......Mrs. M. C. Howell | 1933 ......Madelaine Taylor |
| 1884 ......Mrs. H. Hall | 1908 ......Harriet Case | 1934 ......Desales Mudd |
| 1885 ......Mrs. M. C. Howell | 1909 ......Harriet Case | 1935 ......Ruth Hodgert |
| 1886 ......Mrs. M. C. Howell | 1910 ......J. V. Sullivan | 1936 ......Gladys Hammer |
| 1887 ......Mrs. A. M. Phillips | 1911 ......Mrs. J. S. Taylor | 1937 ......Gladys Hammer |
| 1888 ......Mrs. A. M. Phillips | 1912 ......Mrs. Witwer Tayler | 1938 ......Jean Tenney |
| 1889 ......Mrs. A. M. Phillips | 1913 ......Mrs. P. Fletcher | 1939 ......Belvia Carter |
| 1890 ......Mrs. M. C. Howell | 1914 ......Mrs. B. P. Gray | 1940 ......Ann Weber |
| 1891 ......Mrs. M. C. Howell | 1915 ......Cynthia Wesson | 1941 ......Ree Dillinger |
| 1892 ......Mrs. M. C. Howell | 1916 ......Cynthia Wesson | 1946 ......Ann Weber |
| 1893 ......Mrs. M. C. Howell | 1919 ......Dorothy Smith | 1947 ......Ann Weber |
| 1894 ......Mrs. Albert Kern | 1920 ......Cynthia Wesson | 1948 ......Jean Lee |
| 1895 ......Mrs. M. C. Howell | 1921 ......Mrs. L. C. Smith | 1949 ......Jean Lee |
| 1896 ......Mrs. M. C. Howell | 1922 ......Dorothy Smith | 1950 ......Jean Lee |
| 1897 ......Mrs. J. S. Baker | 1923 ......Norma Pierce | 1951 ......Jean Lee |
| 1898 ......Mrs. M. C. Howell | 1924 ......Dorothy Smith | 1952 ......Ann Weber |
| 1899 ......Mrs. M. C. Howell | 1925 ......Dorothy Smith | 1953 ......Ann Weber |
| 1900 ......Mrs. M. C. Howell | 1926 ......Dorothy Smith | 1954 ......Luarette Young |
| 1901 ......Mrs. C. E. Woodruff | 1927 ......Mrs. R. Johnson | 1955 ......Ann Clark |
| 1902 ......Mrs. M. C. Howell | 1928 ......Beatrice Hodgson | 1956 ......Carole Meinhart |

## Archery (Cont.)

### National Women's Champions (Cont.)

| | | |
|---|---|---|
| 1957 ......Carole Meinhart | 1970 ......Nancy Myrick | 1983 ......Nancy Myrick |
| 1958 ......Carole Meinhart | 1971 ......Doreen Wilber | 1984 ......Ruth Rowe |
| 1959 ......Carole Meinhart | 1972 ......Ruth Rowe | 1985 ......Terri Pesho |
| 1960 ......Ann Clark | 1973 ......Doreen Wilber | 1986 ......Debra Ochs |
| 1961 ......Victoria Cook | 1974 ......Doreen Wilber | 1987 ......Terry Quinn |
| 1962 ......Nancy Vonderheide | 1975 ......Irene Lorensen | 1988 ......Debra Ochs |
| 1963 ......Nancy Vonderheide | 1976 ......Luann Ryon | 1989 ......Debra Ochs |
| 1964 ......Victoria Cook | 1977 ......Luann Ryon | 1990 ......Denise Parker |
| 1965 ......Nancy Pfeiffer | 1978 ......Luann Ryon | 1991 ......Denise Parker |
| 1966 ......Helen Thornton | 1979 ......Lynette Johnson | 1992 ......Sherry Block |
| 1967 ......Ardelle Mills | 1980 ......Judi Adams | 1993 ......Denise Parker |
| 1968 ......Victoria Cook | 1981 ......Debra Metzger | 1994 ......Judy Adams |
| 1969 ......Doreen Wilber | 1982 ......Luann Ryon | 1995 ......Jessica Carlson |

## Chess

### World Champions

#### FIDE

| | |
|---|---|
| 1866-94....................Wilhelm Steinitz, Austria | |
| 1894-1921................Emanuel Lasker, Germany | |
| 1921-27....................Jose Capablanca, Cuba | |
| 1927-35....................Alexander Alekhine, France | |
| 1935-37....................Max Euwe, Holland | |
| 1937-47....................Alexander Alekhine, France | |
| 1948-57....................Mikhail Botvinnik, USSR | |
| 1957-58....................Vassily Smyslov, USSR | |
| 1958-59....................Mikhail Botvinnik, USSR | |
| 1960-61....................Mikhail Tal, USSR | |
| 1961-63....................Mikhail Botvinnik, USSR | |

#### FIDE (Cont.)

| | |
|---|---|
| 1963-69....................Tigran Petrosian, USSR | |
| 1969-72....................Boris Spassky, USSR | |
| 1972-75....................Bobby Fischer, United States | |
| 1975-85....................Anatoly Karpov, USSR | |
| 1985-93....................*Gary Kasparov, USSR | |
| 1993........................vacant | |
| 1994-........................Anatoly Karpov, Russia | |
| *Kasparov stripped of title by FIDE in 1993. | |

#### Professional Chess Association

1993-........................Gary Kasparov

### United States Champions

| | | |
|---|---|---|
| 1857-71........Paul Morphy | 1951-54.......Larry Evans | 1983 .............Larry Christiansen |
| 1871-76........George Mackenzie | 1954-57.......Arthur Bisguier | Walter Browne |
| 1876-80........James Mason | 1957-61.......Bobby Fischer | 1984-85.......Lev Alburt |
| 1880-89........George Mackenzie | 1961-62.......Larry Evans | 1986 .............Yasser Seirawan |
| 1889-90........Samuel Lipschutz | 1962-68.......Bobby Fischer | 1987 .............Joel Benjamin |
| 1890 ............Jackson Showalter | 1968-69.......Larry Evans | Nick DeFirmian |
| 1890-91........Max Judd | 1969-72.......Samuel Reshevsky | 1988 .............Michael Wilder |
| 1891-92........Jackson Showalter | 1972-73.......Robert Byrne | 1989 .............Roman |
| 1892-94........Samuel Lipschutz | 1973-74.......Lubomir Kavale | Dzindzichashvili |
| 1894 ............Jackson Showalter | John Grefe | Stuart Rachels |
| 1894-95........Albert Hodges | 1974-77.......Walter Browne | Yasser Seirawan |
| 1895-97........Jackson Showalter | 1978-80.......Lubomir Kavalek | 1990 .............Lev Alburt |
| 1897-1906....Harry Pillsbury | 1980-81.......Larry Evans | 1991 .............Gata Kamski |
| 1906-09........Vacant | Larry Christiansen | 1992 .............Patrick Wolf |
| 1909-36........Frank Marshall | Walter Browne | 1993 .............A. Yermolinsky |
| 1936-44........Samuel Reshevsky | 1981-83.......Walter Browne | A. Shabalov |
| 1944-46........Arnold Denker | Yasser Seirawan | 1994 .............Boris Gulko |
| 1946-48........Samuel Reshevsky | 1983 ............Roman | 1995 .............Gary Kasparov |
| 1948-51........Herman Steiner | Dzindzichashvili | |

## Curling

### World Men's Champions

| Year | Country, Skip | Year | Country, Skip | Year | Country, Skip |
|---|---|---|---|---|---|
| 1972 | Canada, Crest Melesnuk | 1979 | Norway, Kristian Soerum | 1988 | Norway, Eigil Ramsfjell |
| 1973 | Sweden, Kjell Oscarius | 1980 | Canada, Rich Folk | 1989 | Canada, Pat Ryan |
| 1974 | United States, Bud Somerville | 1981 | Switzerland, Jurg Tanner | 1990 | Canada, Ed Werenich |
| 1975 | Switzerland, Otto Danieli | 1982 | Canada, Al Hackner | 1991 | Scotland, David Smith |
| 1976 | United States, Bruce Roberts | 1983 | Canada, Ed Werenich | 1992 | Switzerland, Markus Eggler |
| 1977 | Sweden, Ragnar Kamp | 1984 | Norway, Eigil Ramsfjell | 1993 | Canada, Russ Howard |
| 1978 | United States, Bob Nichols | 1985 | Canada, Al Hackner | 1994 | Canada, Rick Folk |
| | | 1986 | Canada, Ed Luckowich | 1995 | Canada, Kerry Burtnyk |
| | | 1987 | Canada, Russ Howard | | |

# Curling (Cont.)

## World Women's Champions

| Year | Country, Skip | Year | Country, Skip | Year | Country, Skip |
|------|--------------|------|--------------|------|--------------|
| 1979 | Switzerland, Gaby Casanova | 1983 | Switzerland, Erika Mueller | 1990 | Norway, Dordi Nordby |
| 1980 | Canada, Marj Mitchell | 1984 | Canada, Connie Lallberte | 1991 | Norway, Dordi Nordby |
| 1981 | Sweden, Elisabeth Hogstrom | 1985 | Canada, Linda Moore | 1992 | Sweden, Elisabet Johanssen |
| 1982 | Denmark, Marianne Jorgenson | 1986 | Canada, Marilyn Darte | 1993 | Canada, Sandra Peterson |
| | | 1987 | Canada, Pat Sanders | 1994 | Canada, Sandra Peterson |
| | | 1988 | Germany, Andrea Schopp | 1995 | Sweden, Elisabet Gustafson |
| | | 1989 | Canada, Heather Houston | | |

## U.S. Men's Champions

| Year | Site | Winning Club | Skip |
|------|------|-------------|------|
| 1957 | Chicago, IL | Hibbing, MN | Harold Lauber |
| 1958 | Milwaukee, WI | Detroit, MI | Douglas Fisk |
| 1959 | Green Bay, WI | Hibbing, MN | Fran Kleffman |
| 1960 | Chicago, IL | Grafton, ND | Orvil Gilleshammer |
| 1961 | Grand Forks, ND | Seattle, WA | Frank Crealock |
| 1962 | Detroit, MI | Hibbing, MN | Fran Kleffman |
| 1963 | Duluth, MN | Detroit, MI | Mike Slyziuk |
| 1964 | Utica, NY | Duluth, MN | Robert Magle, Jr. |
| 1965 | Seattle, WA | Superior, WI | Bud Somerville |
| 1966 | Hibbing, MN | Fargo, ND | Joe Zbacnik |
| 1967 | Winchester, MA | Seattle, WA | Bruce Roberts |
| 1968 | Madison, WI | Superior, WI | Bud Somerville |
| 1969 | Grand Forks, ND | Superior, WI | Bud Somerville |
| 1970 | Ardsley, NY | Grafton, ND | Art Tallackson |
| 1971 | Duluth, MN | Edmore, ND | Dale Dalziel |
| 1972 | Wilmette, IL | Grafton, ND | Robert Labonte |
| 1973 | Colorado Springs, CO | Winchester, MA | Charles Reeves |
| 1974 | Schenectady, NY | Superior, WI | Bud Somerville |
| 1975 | Detroit, MI | Seattle, WA | Ed Risling |
| 1976 | Wausau, WI | Hibbing, MN | Bruce Roberts |
| 1977 | Northbrook, IL | Hibbing, MN | Bruce Roberts |
| 1978 | Utica, NY | Superior, WI | Bob Nichols |
| 1979 | Superior, WI | Bemidji, MN | Scott Baird |
| 1980 | Bemidji, MN | Hibbing, MN | Paul Pustovar |
| 1981 | Fairbanks, AK | Superior, WI | Bob Nichols |
| 1982 | Brookline, MA | Madison, WI | Steve Brown |
| 1983 | Colorado Springs, CO | Colorado Springs, CO | Don Cooper |
| 1984 | Hibbing, MN | Hibbing, MN | Bruce Roberts |
| 1985 | Mequon, WI | Wilmette, IL | Tim Wright |
| 1986 | Seattle, WA | Madison, WI | Steve Brown |
| 1987 | Lake Placid, NY | Seattle, WA | Jim Vukich |
| 1988 | St. Paul, MN | Seattle, WA | Doug Jones |
| 1989 | Detroit, MI | Seattle, WA | Jim Vukich |
| 1990 | Superior, WI | Seattle, WA | Doug Jones |
| 1991 | Utica, NY | Madison, WI | Steve Brown |
| 1992 | Grafton, ND | Seattle, WA | Doug Jones |
| 1993 | St Paul, MN | Bemidji, MN | Scott Baird |
| 1994 | Duluth, MN | Bemidji, MN | Scott Baird |
| 1995 | Appleton, WI | Superior, WI | Tim Somerville |

## U.S. Women's Champions

| Year | Site | Winning Club | Skip |
|------|------|-------------|------|
| 1977 | Wilmette, IL | Hastings, NY | Margaret Smith |
| 1978 | Duluth, MN | Wausau, WI | Sandy Robarge |
| 1979 | Winchester, MA | Seattle, WA | Nancy Langley |
| 1980 | Seattle, WA | Seattle, WA | Sharon Kozal |
| 1981 | Kettle Moraine, WI | Seattle, WA | Nancy Langley |
| 1982 | Bowling Green, OH | Oak Park, IL | Ruth Schwenker |
| 1983 | Grafton, ND | Seattle, WA | Nancy Langley |
| 1984 | Wauwatosa, WI | Duluth, MN | Amy Hatten |
| 1985 | Hershey, PA | Fairbanks, AK | Bev Birklid |
| 1986 | Chicago, IL | St. Paul, MN | Gerri Tilden |
| 1987 | St. Paul, MN | Seattle, WA | Sharon Good |
| 1988 | Darien, CT | Seattle, WA | Nancy Langley |
| 1989 | Detroit, MI | Rolla, ND | Jan Lagasse |
| 1990 | Superior, WI | Denver, CO | Bev Behnke |

## Curling (Cont.)

### U.S. Women's Champions (Cont.)

| Year | Site | Winning Club | Skip |
|------|------|--------------|------|
| 1991 | Utica, NY | Houston, TX | Maymar Gemmell |
| 1992 | Grafton, ND | Madison, WI | Lisa Schoeneberg |
| 1993 | St Paul, MN | Denver, CO | Bev Behnke |
| 1994 | Duluth, MN | Denver, CO | Bev Behnke |
| 1995 | Appleton, WI | Madison, WI | Lisa Schoeneberg |

## Cycling

### Professional Road Race World Champions

1927 ....Alfred Binda, Italy
1928 ....George Ronsse, Belgium
1929 ....George Ronsse, Belgium
1930 ....Alfred Binda, Italy
1931 ....Learco Guerra, Italy
1932 ....Alfred Binda, Italy
1933 ....George Speicher, France
1934 ....Karel Kaers, Belgium
1935 ....Jean Aerts, Belgium
1936 ....Antonio Magne, France
1937 ....Elio Meulenberg, Belgium
1938 ....Marcel Kint, Belgium
1939-45.No competition
1946 ....Hans Knecht, Switzerland
1947 ....Theo. Middelkamp, Holland
1948 ....Alberic Schotte, Belgium
1949 ....Henri Van Steenbergen, Belgium
1950 ....Alberic Schotte, Belgium

1951 ....Ferdinand Kubler, Switzerland
1952 ....Heinz Mueller, Germany
1953 ....Fausto Coppi, Italy

1954 ....Louison Bobet, France
1955 ....Stan Ockers, Belgium
1956 ....Rik Van Steenbergen, Belgium
1957 ....Rik Van Steenbergen, Belgium
1958 ....Ercole Baldini, Italy
1959 ....Andre Darrigade, France
1960 ....Rik van Looy, Belgium
1961 ....Rik van Looy, Belgium
1962 ....Jean Stablenski, France
1963 ....Bennoni Beheyt, Belgium
1964 ....Jan Janssen, Holland
1965 ....Tommy Simpson, England
1966 ....Rudi Altig, West Germany
1967 ....Eddy Merckx, Belgium
1968 ....Vittorio Adorni, Italy
1969 ....Harm Ottenbros, Netherlands
1970 ....J.P. Monseré, Belgium
1971 ....Eddy Merckx, Belgium
1972 ....Marino Basso, Italy
1973 ....Felice Gimondi, Italy
1974 ....Eddy Merckx, Belgium

1975 ....Hennie Kuiper, Holland
1976 ....Freddy Maertens, Belgium
1977 ....Francesco Moser, Italy
1978 ....Gerri Knetemann, Holland
1979 ....Jan Raas, Holland
1980 ....Bernard Hinault, France
1981 ....Freddy Maertens, Belgium
1982 ....Giuseppe Saronni, Italy
1983 ....Greg LeMond, United States
1984 ....Claude Criquielion, Belgium
1985 ....Joop Zoetemelk, Holland
1986 ....Moreno Argentin, Italy
1987 ....Stephen Roche, Ireland
1988 ....Maurizio Fondriest, Italy
1989 ....Greg LeMond, United States
1990 ....Rudy Dhaenene, Belgium
1991 ....Gianni Bugno, Italy
1992 ....Gianni Bugno, Italy
1993 ....Lance Armstrong, United States
1994 ....Luc LeBlanc, France
1995 ....Abraham Olano, Spain

### Tour DuPont Winners

| Year | Winner | Time |
|------|--------|------|
| 1989 | Dag Otto Lauritzen, Norway | 33 hrs, 28 min, 48 sec |
| 1990 | Raul Alcala, Mexico | 45 hrs, 20 min, 9 sec |
| 1991 | Erik Breukink, Holland | 48 hrs, 56 min, 53 sec |
| 1992 | Greg LeMond, United States | 44 hrs, 27 min, 43 sec |
| 1993 | Raul Alcala, Mexico | 46 hrs, 42 min, 52 sec |
| 1994 | Viatcheslav Ekimov, Russia | 47 hrs, 14 min, 29 sec |
| 1995 | Lance Armstrong, United States | 46 hrs, 31 min, 16 sec |

### Tour de France Winners

| Year | Winner | Time |
|------|--------|------|
| 1903 | Maurice Garin, France | 94 hrs, 33 min |
| 1904 | Henri Cornet, France | 96 hrs, 5 min, 56 sec |
| 1905 | Louis Trousselier, France | 110 hrs, 26 min, 58 sec |
| 1906 | Rene Pottier, France | Not available |
| 1907 | Lucien Petit-Breton, France | 158 hrs, 54 min, 5 sec |
| 1908 | Lucien Petit-Breton, France | Not available |
| 1909 | Francois Faber, Luxembourg | 157 hrs, 1 min, 22 sec |
| 1910 | Octave Lapize, France | 162 hrs, 41 min, 30 sec |
| 1911 | Gustave Garrigou, France | 195 hrs, 37 min |
| 1912 | Odile Defraye, Belgium | 190 hrs, 30 min, 28 sec |
| 1913 | Philippe Thys, Belgium | 197 hrs, 54 min |
| 1914 | Philippe Thys, Belgium | 200 hrs, 28 min, 48 sec |
| 1915-18 | No race | |
| 1919 | Firmin Lambot, Belgium | 231 hrs, 7 min, 15 sec |
| 1920 | Philippe Thys, Belgium | 228 hrs, 36 min, 13 sec |
| 1921 | Leon Scieur, Belgium | 221 hrs, 50 min, 26 sec |
| 1922 | Firmin Lambot, Belgium | 222 hrs, 8 min, 6 sec |

## Tour de France Winners (Cont.)

| Year | Winner | Time |
|---|---|---|
| 1923 | Henri Pelissier, France | 222 hrs, 15 min, 30 sec |
| 1924 | Ottavio Bottechia, Italy | 226 hrs, 18 min, 21 sec |
| 1925 | Ottavio Bottechia, Italy | 219 hrs, 10 min, 18 sec |
| 1926 | Lucien Buysse, Belgium | 238 hrs, 44 min, 25 sec |
| 1927 | Nicolas Frantz, Luxembourg | 198 hrs, 16 min, 42 sec |
| 1928 | Nicolas Frantz, Luxembourg | 192 hrs, 48 min, 58 sec |
| 1929 | Maurice Dewaele, Belgium | 186 hrs, 39 min, 16 sec |
| 1930 | Andre Leducq, France | 172 hrs, 12 min, 16 sec |
| 1931 | Antonin Magne, France | 177 hrs, 10 min, 3 sec |
| 1932 | Andre Leducq, France | 154 hrs, 12 min, 49 sec |
| 1933 | Georges Speicher, France | 147 hrs, 51 min, 37 sec |
| 1934 | Antonin Magne, France | 147 hrs, 13 min, 58 sec |
| 1935 | Romain Maes, Belgium | 141 hrs, 32 min |
| 1936 | Sylvere Maes, Belgium | 142 hrs, 47 min, 32 sec |
| 1937 | Roger Lapebie, France | 138 hrs, 58 min, 31 sec |
| 1938 | Gino Bartali, Italy | 148 hrs, 29 min, 12 sec |
| 1939 | Sylvere Maes, Belgium | 132 hrs, 3 min, 17 sec |
| 1940-46 | No race | |
| 1947 | Jean Robic, France | 148 hrs, 11 min, 25 sec |
| 1948 | Gino Bartali, Italy | 147 hrs, 10 min, 36 sec |
| 1949 | Fausto Coppi, Italy | 149 hrs, 40 min, 49 sec |
| 1950 | Ferdi Kubler, Switzerland | 145 hrs, 36 min, 56 sec |
| 1951 | Hugo Koblet, Switzerland | 142 hrs, 20 min, 14 sec |
| 1952 | Fausto Coppi, Italy | 151 hrs, 57 min, 20 sec |
| 1953 | Louison Bobet, France | 129 hrs, 23 min, 25 sec |
| 1954 | Louison Bobet, France | 140 hrs, 6 min, 5 sec |
| 1955 | Louison Bobet, France | 130 hrs, 29 min, 26 sec |
| 1956 | Roger Walkowiak, France | 124 hrs, 1 min, 16 sec |
| 1957 | Jacques Anquetil, France | 129 hrs, 46 min, 11 sec |
| 1958 | Charly Gaul, Luxembourg | 116 hrs, 59 min, 5 sec |
| 1959 | Federico Bahamontes, Spain | 123 hrs, 46 min, 45 sec |
| 1960 | Gastone Nencini, Italy | 112 hrs, 8 min, 42 sec |
| 1961 | Jacques Anquetil, France | 122 hrs, 1 min, 33 sec |
| 1962 | Jacques Anquetil, France | 114 hrs, 31 min, 54 sec |
| 1963 | Jacques Anquetil, France | 113 hrs, 30 min, 5 sec |
| 1964 | Jacques Anquetil, France | 127 hrs, 9 min, 44 sec |
| 1965 | Felice Gimondi, Italy | 116 hrs, 42 min, 6 sec |
| 1966 | Lucien Aimar, France | 117 hrs, 34 min, 21 sec |
| 1967 | Roger Pingeon, France | 136 hrs, 53 min, 50 sec |
| 1968 | Jan Janssen, Netherlands | 133 hrs, 49 min, 32 sec |
| 1969 | Eddy Merckx, Belgium | 116 hrs, 16 min, 2 sec |
| 1970 | Eddy Merckx, Belgium | 119 hrs, 31 min, 49 sec |
| 1971 | Eddy Merckx, Belgium | 96 hrs, 45 min, 14 sec |
| 1972 | Eddy Merckx, Belgium | 108 hrs, 17 min, 18 sec |
| 1973 | Luis Ocana, Spain | 122 hrs, 25 min, 34 sec |
| 1974 | Eddy Merckx, Belgium | 116 hrs, 16 min, 58 sec |
| 1975 | Bernard Thevenet, France | 114 hrs, 35 min, 31 sec |
| 1976 | Lucien Van Impe, Belgium | 116 hrs, 22 min, 23 sec |
| 1977 | Bernard Thevenet, France | 115 hrs, 38 min, 30 sec |
| 1978 | Bernard Hinault, France | 108 hrs, 18 min |
| 1979 | Bernard Hinault, France | 103 hrs, 6 min, 50 sec |
| 1980 | Joop Zoetemelk, Netherlands | 109 hrs, 19 min, 14 sec |
| 1981 | Bernard Hinault, France | 96 hrs, 19 min, 38 sec |
| 1982 | Bernard Hinault, France | 92 hrs, 8 min, 46 sec |
| 1983 | Laurent Fignon, France | 105 hrs, 7 min, 52 sec |
| 1984 | Laurent Fignon, France | 112 hrs, 3 min, 40 sec |
| 1985 | Bernard Hinault, France | 113 hrs, 24 min, 23 sec |
| 1986 | Greg LeMond, United States | 110 hrs, 35 min, 19 sec |
| 1987 | Stephen Roche, Ireland | 115 hrs, 27 min, 42 sec |
| 1988 | Pedro Delgado, Spain | 84 hrs, 27 min, 53 sec |
| 1989 | Greg LeMond, United States | 87 hrs, 38 min, 35 sec |
| 1990 | Greg LeMond, United States | 90 hrs, 43 min, 20 sec |
| 1991 | Miguel Induráin, Spain | 101 hrs, 1 min, 20 sec |
| 1992 | Miguel Induráin, Spain | 100 hrs, 49 min, 30 sec |
| 1993 | Miguel Induráin, Spain | 95 hrs, 57 min, 9 sec |
| 1994 | Miguel Induráin, Spain | 103 hrs, 38 min, 38 sec |
| 1995 | Miguel Induráin, Spain | 92 hrs, 44 min, 59 sec |

# Sled Dog Racing

## Iditarod

| Year | Winner | Time | Year | Winner | Time |
|------|--------|------|------|--------|------|
| 1973 | Dick Wilmarth | 20 days, 00:49:41 | 1985 | Libby Riddles | 18 days, 00:20:17 |
| 1974 | Carl Huntington | 20 days, 15:02:07 | 1986 | Susan Butcher | 11 days, 15:06:00 |
| 1975 | Emmitt Peters | 14 days, 14:43:45 | 1987 | Susan Butcher | 11 days, 02:05:13 |
| 1976 | Gerald Riley | 18 days, 22:58:17 | 1988 | Susan Butcher | 11 days, 11:41:40 |
| 1977 | Rick Swenson | 16 days, 16:27:13 | 1989 | Joe Runyan | 11 days, 05:24:34 |
| 1978 | Dick Mackey | 14 days, 18:52:24 | 1990 | Susan Butcher | 11 days, 01:53:23 |
| 1979 | Rick Swenson | 15 days, 10:37:47 | 1991 | Rick Swenson | 12 days, 16:34:39 |
| 1980 | Joe May | 14 days, 07:11:51 | 1992 | Martin Buser | 10 days, 19:17:15 |
| 1981 | Rick Swenson | 12 days, 08:45:02 | 1993 | Jeff King | 10 days, 15:38:15 |
| 1982 | Rick Swenson | 16 days, 04:40:10 | 1994 | Martin Buser | 10 days, 13:02:39 |
| 1983 | Dick Mackey | 12 days, 14:10:44 | 1995 | Doug Swingley | 9 days, 02:42:19 |
| 1984 | Dean Osmar | 12 days, 15:07:33 | | | |

# Fishing

## Saltwater Fishing Records

| Species | Weight | Where Caught | Date | Angler |
|---------|--------|--------------|------|--------|
| Albacore | 88 lb 2 oz | Gran Canaria, Canary Islands | Nov 19, 1977 | Siegfried Dickemann |
| Amberjack, greater | 155 lb 10 oz | Challenger Bank, Bermuda | June 24, 1981 | Joseph Dawson |
| Amberjack, Pacific | 104 lb | Baja California, Mexico | July 4, 1984 | Richard Cresswell |
| Barracuda, great | 85 lb | Christmas Island, Kiribati | April 11, 1992 | John W. Helfrich |
| Barracuda, Mexican | 21 lb | Phantom Isle, Costa Rica | Mar 27, 1987 | E. Greg Kent |
| Barracuda, pickhandle | 17 lb 4 oz | Sitra Channel, Arabian Gulf | Nov 21, 1985 | Roger J. Cranswick |
| Bass, barred sand | 13 lb 3 oz | Huntington Beach, CA | Aug 29, 1988 | Robert Halal |
| Bass, black sea | 9 lb 8 oz | Virginia Beach, VA | Jan 9, 1987 | Joe Mizelle, Jr |
| Bass, European | 20 lb 11 oz | Stes Maries de la Mer, France | May 6, 1986 | Jean Baptiste Bayle |
| Bass, giant sea | 563 lb 8 oz | Anacapa Island, CA | Aug 20, 1968 | James D. McAdam, Jr |
| Bass, redeye | 8 lb 12 oz | Apalatchicola River, FL | Jan 28, 1995 | Carl W. Davis |
| Bass, striped | 78 lb 8 oz | Atlantic City, NJ | Sep 21, 1982 | Albert R. McReynolds |
| Bluefish | 31 lb 12 oz | Hatteras Inlet, NC | Jan 30, 1972 | James M. Hussey |
| Bonefish | 19 lb | Zululand, South Africa | May 26, 1962 | Brian W. Batchelor |
| Bonito, Atlantic | 18 lb 4 oz | Faial Island, Azores | July 8, 1953 | D. G. Higgs |
| Bonito, Pacific | 14 lb 12 oz | Baja California, Mexico | Oct. 12, 1980 | Jerome H. Rilling |
| Cabezon | 23 lb | Juan De Fuca Strait, WA | Aug 4, 1990 | Wesley Hunter |
| Cobia | 135 lb 9 oz | Shark Bay, Australia | July 9, 1985 | Peter W. Goulding |
| Cod, Atlantic | 98 lb 12 oz | Isle of Shoals, NH | June 8, 1969 | Alphonse Bielevich |
| Cod, Pacific | 30 lb | Andrew Bay, AK | July 7, 1984 | Donald R. Vaughn |
| Conger | 133 lb 4 oz | South Devon, England | June 5, 1995 | Vic Evans |
| Dolphin | 87 lb | Papagallo Gulf, Costa Rica | Sep 25, 1976 | Manuel Salazar |
| Drum, black | 113 lb 1 oz | Lewes, DE | Sep 15, 1975 | Gerald M. Townsend |
| Drum, red | 94 lb 2 oz | Avon, NC | Nov 7, 1984 | David Deuel |
| Eel, American | 8 lb 8 oz | Brewster, MA | May 17, 1992 | Gerald G. Lapierre, Sr |
| Eel, marbled | 36 lb 1 oz | Durban, South Africa | June 10, 1984 | Ferdie van Nooten |
| Flounder, southern | 20 lb 9 oz | Nassau Sound, FL | Dec 23, 1983 | Larenza W. Mungin |
| Flounder, summer | 22 lb 7 oz | Montauk, NY | Sep 15, 1975 | Charles Nappi |
| Grouper, warsaw | 436 lb 12 oz | Destin, FL | Dec 22, 1985 | Steve Haeusler |
| Halibut, Atlantic | 255 lb 4 oz | Gloucester, MA | July 28, 1989 | Sonny Manley |
| Halibut, California | 53 lb 4 oz | Santa Rosa Island, CA | July 7, 1988 | Russell J. Harmon |
| Halibut, Pacific | 368 lb | Gustavus, AK | July 5, 1991 | Celia H. Dueitt |
| Jack, crevalle | 57 lb 5 oz | Barra do Kwanza, Angola | Oct 10, 1992 | Cam Nicolson |
| Jack, horse-eye | 24 lb 8 oz | Miami, FL | Dec 20, 1982 | Tilo Schnau |
| Jack, Pacific crevalle | 29 lb 8 oz | Playa Zancudo, Costa Rica | Jan 1, 1994 | Ronald C. Snody |
| Jewfish | 680 lb | Fernandina Beach, FL | May 20, 1961 | Lynn Joyner |
| Kawakawa | 29 lb | Isla Clarion, Mexico | Dec 17, 1986 | Ronald Nakamura |
| Lingcod | 69 lb | Langara Island, B.C. | June 16, 1992 | Murray M. Romer |
| Mackerel, cero | 17 lb 2 oz | Islamorada, FL | Apr 5, 1986 | G. Michael Mills |
| Mackerel, king | 90 lb | Key West, FL | Feb 16, 1976 | Norton I. Thomton |
| Mackerel, narrowbarred | 99 lb | Natal, South Africa | Mar 14, 1982 | Michael J. Wilkinson |
| Mackerel, Spanish | 13 lb | Ocracoke Inlet, NC | Nov 4, 1987 | Robert Cranton |
| Marlin, Atlantic blue | 1402 lb 2 oz | Vitoria, Brazil | Feb. 29, 1992 | Paulo R. A. Amorim |
| Marlin, black | 1560 lb | Cabo Blanco, Peru | Aug 4, 1953 | A. C. Glassell, Jr |
| Marlin, Pacific blue | 1376 lb | Kaaiwi Point, HI | May 31, 1982 | J. W. deBeaubien |
| Marlin, striped | 494 lb | Tutukaka, New Zealand | Jan 16, 1986 | Bill Boniface |
| Marlin, white | 181 lb 14 oz | Vitoria, Brazil | Dec 8, 1979 | Evandro Luiz Caser |

## Saltwater Fishing Records *(Cont.)*

| Species | Weight | Where Caught | Date | Angler |
|---|---|---|---|---|
| Permit | 53 lb 4 oz | Lake Worth, FL | Mar 25, 1994 | Roy Brooker |
| Pollock | 46 lb 10 oz | Ogunquit, ME | Oct. 24, 1990 | Linda M. Paul |
| Pompano, African | 50 lb 8 oz | Daytona Beach, FL | Apr 21, 1990 | Tom Sargent |
| Roosterfish | 114 lb | La Paz, Mexico | June 1, 1960 | Abe Sackheim |
| Runner, blue | 8 lb 7 oz | Port Aransas, TX | Feb 13, 1995 | Allen E. Windecker |
| Runner, rainbow | 37 lb 9 oz | Isla Clarion, Mexico | Nov. 21, 1991 | Tom Pfleger |
| Sailfish, Atlantic | 135 lb 5 oz | Lagos, Nigeria | Nov. 10, 1991 | Ron King |
| Sailfish, Pacific | 221 lb | Santa Cruz Island, Ecuador | Feb 12, 1947 | C. W. Stewart |
| Seabass, white | 83 lb 12 oz | San Felipe, Mexico | Mar 31, 1953 | L. C. Baumgardner |
| Seatrout, spotted | 16 lb | Mason's Beach, VA | May 28, 1977 | William Katko |
| Shark, bigeye thresher | 802 lb | Tutukaka, New Zealand | Feb 8, 1981 | Dianne North |
| Shark, blue | 437 lb | Catherine Bay, NSW, Australia | Oct 2, 1976 | Peter Hyde |
| Shark, grter hammrhd | 991 lb | Sarasota, FL | May 30, 1982 | Allen Ogle |
| Shark, Greenland | 1708 lb 9 oz | Trondheimsfjord, Norway | Oct 18, 1987 | Terje Nordtvedt |
| Shark, porbeagle | 507 lb | Caithness, Scotland | Mar 9, 1993 | Christopher Bennet |
| Shark,shortfin mako | 1115 lb | Black River, Mauritius | Nov 16, 1988 | Patrick Guillanton |
| Shark, tiger | 1780 lb | Cherry Grove, SC | June 14, 1964 | Walter Maxwell |
| Shark, tope | 72 lb 12 oz | Parengarenga Harbor, New Zealand | Dec 19, 1986 | Melanie Feldman |
| Shark, white | 2664 lb | Ceduna, Australia | Apr 21, 1959 | Alfred Dean |
| Skipjack, black | 26 lb | Baja California, Mexico | Oct. 23, 1991 | Clifford K. Hamaishi |
| Snapper, cubera | 121 lb 8 oz | Cameron, LA | July 5, 1982 | Mike Hebert |
| Snook | 53 lb 10 oz | Parismina Ranch, Costa Rica | Oct 18, 1978 | Gilbert Ponzi |
| Spearfish | 90 lb 13 oz | Madeira Island, Portugal | June 2, 1980 | Joseph Larkin |
| Swordfish | 1182 lb | Iquique, Chile | May 7, 1953 | L. Marron |
| Tarpon | 283 lb 4 oz | Sherbro Island, Sierra Leone | April 16, 1991 | Yvon Victor Sebag |
| Tautog | 24 lb | Wachapreague, VA | Aug 25, 1987 | Gregory Bell |
| Tilapia | 6 lb 5 oz | Lake Arenal, Costa Rica | Feb 10, 1995 | Marvin C. Smith |
| Trevally, bigeye | 18 lb 1 oz | Clipperton Island, France | May 12,1990 | Rebecca A. Mills |
| Trevally, giant | 145 lb 8 oz | Maui, HI | Mar 28, 1991 | Russell Mori |
| Tuna, Atlantic bigeye | 375 lb 8 oz | Ocean City, MD | Aug 26, 1977 | Cecil Browne |
| Tuna, blackfin | 42 lb | Bermuda | June 2, 1978 | Alan J. Card |
| Tuna, bluefin | 1496 lb | Challenger Bank, Bermuda | July 18, 1989 | Gilbert C. Pearman |
| | | Aulds Cove, Nova Scotia | Oct 26, 1979 | Ken Fraser |
| Tuna, longtail | 79 lb 2 oz | Montague Island, NSW, Australia | Apr 12, 1982 | Tim Simpson |
| Tuna, Pacific bigeye | 435 lb | Cabo Blanco, Peru | Apr 17, 1957 | Russel Lee |
| Tuna, skipjack | 41 lb 14 oz | Pearl Beach, Mauritius | Nov 12, 1985 | Edmund Heinzen |
| Tuna, southern bluefin | 348 lb 5 oz | Whakatane, New Zealand | Jan 16, 1981 | Rex Wood |
| Tuna, yellowfin | 388 lb 12 oz | San Benedicto Is, Mexico | Apr 1, 1977 | Curt Wiesenhutter |
| Tunny, little | 35 lb 2 oz | Cape de Garde, Algeria | Dec 14, 1988 | Jean Yves Chatard |
| Wahoo | 155 lb 8 oz | San Salvador, Bahamas | Apr 3, 1990 | William Bourne |
| Weakfish | 19 lb 2 oz | Jones Beach Inlet, NY | Oct 11, 1984 | Dennis Rooney |
| | | Delaware Bay, Delaware | May 20, 1989 | William E. Thomas |
| Yellowtail, California | 79 lb 4 oz | Baja California, Mexico | July 2, 1991 | Robert I. Welker |
| Yellowtail, southern | 114 lb 10 oz | Tauranga, New Zealand | Feb 5, 1984 | Mike Godfrey |

## Freshwater Fishing Records

| Species | Weight | Where Caught | Date | Angler |
|---|---|---|---|---|
| Barramundi | 63 lb 2 oz | Queensland, Australia | April 28, 1991 | Scott Barnsley |
| Bass, largemouth | 22 lb 4 oz | Montgomery Lake, GA | June 2, 1932 | George W. Perry |
| Bass, peacock | 27 lb | Rio Negro, Brazil | Dec 4,1994 | Gerald "Doc" Lawson |
| Bass, rock | 3 lb | York River, Ontario | Aug 1, 1974 | Peter Gulgin |
| Bass, smallmouth | 11 lb 15 oz | Dale Hollow Lake, KY | July 9, 1955 | David L. Hayes |
| Bass, Suwannee | 3 lb 14 oz | Suwannee River, FL | Mar 2, 1985 | Ronnie Everett |
| Bass, white | 6 lb 13 oz | Orange, VA | July 31, 1989 | Ronald Sprouse |
| Bass, whiterock | 24 lb 3 oz | Leesville Lake, VA | May 12, 1989 | David Lambert |
| Bass, yellow | 2 lb 4 oz | Lake Monroe, IN | Mar 27, 1977 | Donald L. Stalker |
| Bluegill | 4 lb 12 oz | Ketona Lake, AL | Apr 9, 1950 | T. S. Hudson |
| Bowfin | 21 lb 8 oz | Florence, SC | Jan 29, 1980 | Robert Harmon |
| Buffalo, bigmouth | 70 lb 5 oz | Bastrop, LA | Apr 21, 1980 | Delbert Sisk |
| Buffalo, black | 55 lb 8 oz | Cherokee Lake, TN | May 3, 1984 | Edward McLain |
| Buffalo, smallmouth | 68 lb 8 oz | Lake Hamilton, AR | May 16, 1984 | Jerry Dolezal |
| Bullhead, brown | 5 lb 11oz | Cedar Creek, FL | Mar 28, 1995 | Robert Bengis |
| Bullhead, yellow | 4 lb 4 oz | Mormon Lake, AZ | May 11, 1984 | Emily Williams |

## Freshwater Fishing Records *(Cont.)*

| Species | Weight | Where Caught | Date | Angler |
|---|---|---|---|---|
| Burbot | 18 lb 4 oz | Pickford, MI | Jan 31, 1980 | Thomas Courtemanche |
| Carp | 75 lb 11 oz | Lac de St Cassien, France | May 21, 1987 | Leo van der Gugten |
| Catfish, blue | 109 lb 4 oz | Moncks Corner, SC | Mar 14, 1991 | George A. Lijewski |
| Catfish, channel | 58 lb | Santee-Cooper Reservoir, SC | July 7, 1964 | W. B. Whaley |
| Catfish, flathead | 91 lb 4 oz | Lake Lewisville, TX | Mar 28, 1982 | Mike Rogers |
| Catfish, white | 18 lb 14 oz | Inverness, FL | Sept. 21, 1991 | Jim Miller |
| Char, Arctic | 32 lb 9 oz | Tree River, Canada | July 30, 1981 | Jeffrey Ward |
| Crappie, white | 5 lb 3 oz | Enid Dam, MS | July 31, 1957 | Fred L. Bright |
| Dolly Varden | 18 lb 9 oz | Mashutuk River, AK | July 13, 1993 | Richard B. Evans |
| Dorado | 51 lb 5 oz | Corrientes, Argentina | Sep 27, 1994 | Armando Giudice |
| Drum, freshwater | 54 lb 8 oz | Nickajack Lake, TN | Apr 20, 1972 | Benny E. Hull |
| Gar, alligator | 279 lb | Rio Grande River, TX | Dec 2, 1951 | Bill Valverde |
| Gar, Florida | 21 lb 3 oz | Boca Raton, FL | June 3, 1981 | Jeff Sabol |
| Gar, longnose | 50 lb 5 oz | Trinity River, TX | July 30, 1954 | Townsend Miller |
| Gar, shortnose | 5 lb | Sally Jones Lake, OK | Apr 26, 1985 | Buddy Croslin |
| Gar, spotted | 9 lb 12 oz | Lake Mexia, TX | Apr 7, 1994 | Rick Rivard |
| Grayling, Arctic | 5 lb 15 oz | Katseyedie River, Northwest Territories | Aug 16, 1967 | Jeanne P. Branson |
| Inconnu | 53 lb | Pah River, AK | Aug 20, 1986 | Lawrence Hudnall |
| Kokanee | 9 lb 6 oz | Okanagan Lake, Vernon, BC | June 18, 1988 | Norm Kuhn |
| Muskellunge | 67 lb 8 oz | Hayward, WI | July 24,1949 | Cal Johnson |
| Muskellunge, tiger | 51 lb 3 oz | Lac Vieux-Desert, WI, MI | July 16, 1919 | John Knobla |
| Perch, Nile | 191 lb 8 oz | Lake Victoria, Kenya | Sept. 5, 1991 | Andy Davison |
| Perch, white | 4 lb 12 oz | Messalonskee Lake, ME | June 4, 1949 | Mrs Earl Small |
| Perch, yellow | 4 lb 3 oz | Bordentown, NJ | May 1865 | C. C. Abbot |
| Pickerel, chain | 9 lb 6 oz | Homerville, GA | Feb 17, 1961 | Baxley McQuaig, Jr |
| Pike, northern | 55 lb 1 oz | Lake of Grefeern, West Germany | Oct 16, 1986 | Lothar Louis |
| Redhorse, greater | 9 lb 3 oz | Salmon River, Pulaski, NY | May 11, 1985 | Jason Wilson |
| Redhorse, silver | 11 lb 7 oz | Plum Creek, WI | May 29, 1985 | Neal Long |
| Salmon, Atlantic | 79 lb 2 oz | Tana River, Norway | 1928 | Henrik Henriksen |
| Salmon, chinook | 97 lb 4 oz | Kenai River, AK | May 17, 1985 | Les Anderson |
| Salmon, chum | 32 lb | Behm Canal, AK | June 7, 1985 | Fredrick Thynes |
| Salmon, coho | 33 lb 4 oz | Pulaski, NY | Sept 27, 1989 | Jerry Lifton |
| Salmon, pink | 13 lb 1 oz | Ontario, Canada | Sept. 23, 1992 | Ray Higaki |
| Salmon, sockeye | 15 lb 3 oz | Kenai River, AK | Aug 9, 1987 | Stan Roach |
| Sauger | 8 lb 12 oz | Lake Sakakawea, ND | Oct 6, 1971 | Mike Fischer |
| Shad, American | 11 lb 4 oz | Connecticut River, MA | May 19, 1986 | Bob Thibodo |
| Sturgeon, white | 468 lb | Benicia, CA | July 9, 1983 | Joey Pallotta III |
| Sunfish, green | 2 lb 2 oz | Stockton Lake, MO | June 18, 1971 | Paul M. Dilley |
| Sunfish, redbreast | 1 lb 12 oz | Suwannee River, FL | May 29, 1984 | Alvin Buchanan |
| Sunfish, redear | 5 lb 3 oz | Sacramento, CA | June 27, 1994 | Anthony H. White, Sr |
| Tigerfish, giant | 97 lb | Zaire River, Kinshasa, Zaire | July 9, 1988 | Raymond Houtmans |
| Trout, Apache | 5 lb 3 oz | Apache Reservation, AZ | May 29, 1991 | John Baldwin |
| Trout, brook | 14 lb 8 oz | Nipigon River, Ontario | July 1916 | W. J. Cook |
| Trout, brown | 40 lb 4 oz | Heber Springs, AR | May 9, 1992 | Howard L. Collins |
| Trout, bull | 32 lb | Lake Pond Oreille, ID | Oct 27, 1949 | N. L. Higgins |
| Trout, cutthroat | 41 lb | Pyramid Lake, NV | Dec 1925 | J. Skimmerhorn |
| Trout, golden | 11 lb | Cook's Lake, WY | Aug 5, 1948 | Charles S. Reed |
| Trout, lake | 66 lb 8 oz | Great Bear Lake, Northwest Territories | July 19, 1991 | Rodney Harback |
| Trout, rainbow | 42 lb 2 oz | Bell Island, AK | June 22, 1970 | David Robert White |
| Trout, tiger | 20 lb 13 oz | Lake Michigan, WI | Aug 12, 1978 | Pete M. Friedland |
| Walleye | 25 lb | Old Hickory Lake, TN | Aug 2, 1960 | Mabry Harper |
| Warmouth | 2 lb 7 oz | Yellow River, Holt, FL | Oct 19, 1985 | Tony D. Dempsey |
| Whitefish, lake | 14 lb 6 oz | Meaford, Ontario | May 21, 1984 | Dennis Laycock |
| Whitefish, mountain | 5 lb 6 oz | Rioh River, Saskatchewan, Canada | June 15, 1988 | John Bell |
| Whitefish, broad | 9 lb | Tozitna River, AK | July 17, 1989 | Al Mathews |
| Whitefish, round | 6 lb | Putahow River, Manitoba | June 14, 1984 | Allan J. Ristori |
| Zander | 25 lb 2 oz | Trosa, Sweden | June 12, 1986 | Harry Lee Tennison |

# Greyhound Racing

## Annual Greyhound Race of Champions Winners*

| Year | Winner (Sex) | Affiliation/Owner | Year | Winner | Affiliation/Owner |
|------|--------------|-------------------|------|--------|-------------------|
| 1982 | DD's Jackie (F) | Wonderland Park/R.H. Walters, Jr. | 1988 | BB's Old Yellow (M) | Supplemental (Southland)/ Margie Bonita Hyers |
| 1983 | Comin' Attraction (F) | Rocky Mt Greyhound Park/ Bob Riggin | 1989 | Osh Kosh Juliet (F) | Tampa Greyhound Track/ William F. Pollard |
| 1984 | Fallon (F) | Tampa Greyhound Track/ E.J. Alderson | 1990 | Daring Don (M) | Interstate Kennel Club/ Perry Padrta |
| 1985 | Lady Delight (F) | Lincoln Greyhound Park/ Julian A. Gay | 1991 | Mo Kick (M) | Flagler Greyhound Track/ Eric M. Kennon |
| 1986 | Ben G Speedboat (M) | Multnomah Kennel Club/ Louis Bennett | 1992 | Dicky Vallie (M) | Dairyland Greyhound Track/ George Benjamin |
| 1987 | ET's Pesky (F) | Supplemental (Flagler)/ Emil Tanis | 1993 | Mega Morris (M) | Jacksonville Kennel Club/ Ferrell's Kennel |

* The Greyhound Race of Champions has not been held since 1993.

# Gymnastics

## World Champions
### MEN
### All-Around

| Year | Champion and Nation | Year | Champion and Nation |
|------|---------------------|------|---------------------|
| 1903 | Joseph Martinez, France | 1962 | Yuri Titov, Soviet Union |
| 1905 | Marcel Lalue, France | 1966 | Mikhail Voronin, Soviet Union |
| 1907 | Joseph Czada, Czechoslovakia | 1970 | Eizo Kenmotsu, Japan |
| 1909 | Marcos Torres, France | 1974 | Shigeru Kasamatsu, Japan |
| 1911 | Ferdinand Steiner, Czechoslovakia | 1978 | Nikolai Andrianov, Soviet Union |
| 1913 | Marcos Torres, France | 1979 | Alexander Ditiatin, Soviet Union |
| 1922 | Peter Sumi, Yug./F. Pechacek, Czech. | 1981 | Yuri Korolev, Soviet Union |
| 1926 | Peter Sumi, Yugoslavia | 1983 | Dimitri Bilozertchev, Soviet Union |
| 1930 | Josip Primozic, Yugoslavia | 1985 | Yuri Korolev, Soviet Union |
| 1934 | Eugene Mack, Switzerland | 1987 | Dimitri Bilozertchev, Soviet Union |
| 1938 | Jan Gajdos, Czechoslovakia | 1989 | Igor Korobchinsky, Soviet Union |
| 1950 | Walter Lehmann, Switzerland | 1991 | Grigori Misutin, CIS |
| 1954 | Valentin Mouratov, Soviet Union | 1993 | Vitaly Scherbo, Belarus |
|      | Victor Chukarin, Soviet Union | 1994 | Ivan Ivankov, Belarus |
| 1958 | Boris Shaklin, Soviet Union | 1995 | Li Xiaoshuang, China |

### Pommel Horse

| Year | Champion and Nation | Year | Champion and Nation |
|------|---------------------|------|---------------------|
| 1930 | Josip Primozic, Yugoslavia | 1981 | Michael Mikolai, E Germ/Li Xiaoping, Chi |
| 1934 | Eugene Mack, Switzerland | 1983 | Dmitri Bilozertchev, Soviet Union |
| 1938 | Michael Reusch, Switzerland | 1985 | Valentin Moguilny, Soviet Union |
| 1950 | Josef Stalder, Switzerland | 1987 | Zsolt Borkai, Hungary |
| 1954 | Grant Chaguinjan, Soviet Union |      | Dmitri Bilozertchev, Soviet Union |
| 1958 | Boris Shaklin, Soviet Union | 1989 | Valentin Moguilny, Soviet Union |
| 1962 | Miroslav Cerar, Yugoslavia | 1991 | Valeri Belenki, Soviet Union |
| 1966 | Miroslav Cerar, Yugoslavia | 1992 | Pae Gil Su, North Korea/Vitaly Scherbo, CIS/ Li Jing, China |
| 1970 | Miroslav Cerar, Yugoslavia | 1993 | Pae Gil Su, North Korea |
| 1974 | Zoltan Magyar, Hungary | 1994 | Marius Urzica, Romania |
| 1978 | Zoltan Magyar, Hungary | 1995 | Li Donghua, Switzerland |
| 1979 | Zoltan Magyar, Hungary |      | |

### Floor Exercise

| Year | Champion and Nation | Year | Champion and Nation |
|------|---------------------|------|---------------------|
| 1930 | Josip Primozic, Yugoslavia | 1966 | Akinori Nakayama, Japan |
| 1934 | Georges Miesz, Switzerland | 1970 | Akinori Nakayama, Japan |
| 1938 | Jan Gajdos, Czechoslovakia | 1974 | Shigeru Kasamatsu, Japan |
| 1950 | Josef Stalder, Switzerland | 1978 | Kurt Thomas, United States |
| 1954 | Valentin Mouratov, Soviet Union | 1979 | Kurt Thomas, United States |
|      | Masao Takemoto, Japan |      | Roland Brucker, GDR |
| 1958 | Masao Takemoto, Japan | 1981 | Yuri Korolev, Sov. Union/Li Yuejui, Chi |
| 1962 | Nobuyuki Aihara, Japan | 1983 | Tong Fei, China |
|      | Yukio Endo, Japan | 1985 | Tong Fei, China |

## World Champions (Cont.)

### MEN (Cont.)

### Floor Exercise (Cont.)

| Year | Champion and Nation | Year | Champion and Nation |
|---|---|---|---|
| 1987 | Lou Yun, China | 1993 | Grigori Misutin, Ukraine |
| 1989 | Igor Korobchinsky, Soviet Union | 1994 | Vitaly Scherbo, Belarus |
| 1991 | Igor Korobchinsky, Soviet Union | 1995 | Vitaly Scherbo, Belarus |

### Rings

| Year | Champion and Nation | Year | Champion and Nation |
|---|---|---|---|
| 1930 | Emanuel Loffler, Czechoslovakia | 1979 | Alexander Ditiatin, Soviet Union |
| 1934 | Alois Hudec, Czechoslovakia | 1981 | Alexander Ditiatin, Soviet Union |
| 1938 | Alois Hudec, Czechoslovakia | 1983 | Dimitri Bilozertchev, Soviet Union |
| 1950 | Walter Lehmann, Switzerland | 1985 | Li Ning, China/Yuri Korolev, Sov Union |
| 1954 | Albert Azarian, Soviet Union | 1987 | Yuri Korolev, Soviet Union |
| 1958 | Albert Azarian, Soviet Union | 1989 | Andreas Aguilar, West Germany |
| 1962 | Yuri Titov, Soviet Union | 1991 | Grigory Misutin, Soviet Union |
| 1966 | Mikhail Voronin, Soviet Union | 1992 | Vitaly Scherbo, CIS |
| 1970 | Akinori Nakayama, Japan | 1993 | Yuri Chechi, Italy |
| 1974 | N. Andrianov, Sov Union/D. Grecu, Rom | 1994 | Yuri Chechi, Italy |
| 1978 | Nikolai Andrianov, Soviet Union | 1995 | Yuri Chechi, Italy |

### Parallel Bars

| Year | Champion and Nation | Year | Champion and Nation |
|---|---|---|---|
| 1930 | Josip Primozic, Yugoslavia | 1983 | Vladimir Artemov, Soviet Union |
| 1934 | Eugene Mack, Switzerland | | Lou Yun, China |
| 1938 | Michael Reusch, Switzerland | 1985 | Sylvio Kroll, East Germany |
| 1950 | Hans Eugster, Switzerland | | Valentin Moguilny, Soviet Union |
| 1954 | Victor Chukarin, Soviet Union | 1987 | Vladimir Artemov, Soviet Union |
| 1958 | Boris Shaklin, Soviet Union | 1989 | Li Jing, China |
| 1962 | Miroslav Cerar, Yugoslavia | | Vladimir Artemov, Soviet Union |
| 1966 | Sergei Diamidov, Soviet Union | 1991 | Li Jing, China |
| 1970 | Akinori Nakayama, Japan | 1992 | Li Jin, China |
| 1974 | Eizo Kenmotsu, Japan | | Alexei Voropaev, CIS |
| 1978 | Eizo Kenmotsu, Japan | 1993 | Vitaly Scherbo, Belarus |
| 1979 | Bart Conner, United States | 1994 | Huang Liping, China |
| 1981 | Koji Gushiken, Japan | 1995 | Vitaly Scherbo, Belarus |
| | Alexandr Ditiatin, Soviet Union | | |

### High Bar

| Year | Champion and Nation | Year | Champion and Nation |
|---|---|---|---|
| 1930 | Istvan Pelle, Hungary | 1979 | Kurt Thomas, United States |
| 1934 | Ernst Winter, Germany | 1981 | Alexander Takchev, Soviet Union |
| 1938 | Michael Reusch, Switzerland | 1983 | Dimitri Bilozertchev, Soviet Union |
| 1950 | Paavo Aaltonen, Finland | 1985 | Tong Fei, China |
| 1954 | Valentin Mouratov, Soviet Union | 1987 | Dimitri Bilozertchev, Soviet Union |
| 1958 | Boris Shaklin, Soviet Union | 1989 | Li Chunyang, China |
| 1962 | Takashi Ono, Japan | 1991 | Li Chunyang, China/R. Buechner, Germ |
| 1966 | Akinori Nakayama, Japan | 1992 | Grigori Misutin, CIS |
| 1970 | Eizo Kenmotsu, Japan | 1993 | Sergei Kharkov, Russia |
| 1974 | Eberhard Gienger, West Germany | 1994 | Vitaly Scherbo, Belarus |
| 1978 | Shigeru Kasamatsu, Japan | 1995 | Andreas Wecker, Germany |

### Vault

| Year | Champion and Nation | Year | Champion and Nation |
|---|---|---|---|
| 1934 | Eugene Mack, Switzerland | 1981 | Ralf-Peter Hemmann, East Germany |
| 1938 | Eugene Mack, Switzerland | 1983 | Arthur Akopian, Soviet Union |
| 1950 | Ernst Gebendinger, Switzerland | 1985 | Yuri Korolev, Soviet Union |
| 1954 | Leo Sotornik, Czechoslovakia | 1987 | Lou Yun, China |
| 1958 | Yuri Titov, Soviet Union | | Sylvio Kroll, East Germany |
| 1962 | Premysel Krbec, Czechoslovakia | 1989 | Joreg Behrend, East Germany |
| 1966 | Haruhiro Yamashita, Japan | 1991 | Yoo Ok Youl, South Korea |
| 1970 | Mitsuo Tsukahara, Japan | 1992 | Yoo Ok Youl, South Korea |
| 1974 | Shigeru Kasamatsu, Japan | 1993 | Vitaly Scherbo, Belarus |
| 1978 | Junichi Shimizu, Japan | 1994 | Vitaly Scherbo, Belarus |
| 1979 | Alexander Ditiatin, Soviet Union | 1995 | G. Misutin, Ukraine/A. Nemov Russia |

## World Champions (Cont.)
### WOMEN
### All-Around

| Year | Champion and Nation | Year | Champion and Nation |
|---|---|---|---|
| 1934 | Vlasta Dekanova, Czechoslovakia | 1981 | Olga Bicherova, Soviet Union |
| 1938 | Vlasta Dekanova, Czechoslovakia | 1983 | Natalia Yurchenko, Soviet Union |
| 1950 | Helena Rakoczy, Poland | 1985 | Elena Shoushounova, Soviet Union |
| 1954 | Galina Roudiko, Soviet Union | | Oksana Omeliantchik, Soviet Union |
| 1958 | Larissa Latynina, Soviet Union | 1987 | Aurelia Dobre, Romania |
| 1962 | Larissa Latynina, Soviet Union | 1989 | Svetlana Bouguinskaia, Soviet Union |
| 1966 | Vera Caslavska, Czechoslovakia | 1991 | Kim Zmeskal, United States |
| 1970 | Ludmilla Tourischeva, Soviet Union | 1993 | Shannon Miller, United States |
| 1974 | Ludmilla Tourischeva, Soviet Union | 1994 | Shannon Miller, United States |
| 1978 | Elena Mukhina, Soviet Union | 1995 | Lilia Podkopayeva, Ukraine |
| 1979 | Nelli Kim, Soviet Union | | |

### Floor Exercise

| Year | Champion and Nation | Year | Champion and Nation |
|---|---|---|---|
| 1950 | Helena Rakoczy, Poland | 1985 | Oksana Omeliantchik, Soviet Union |
| 1954 | Tamara Manina, Soviet Union | 1987 | Elena Shoushounova, Soviet Union |
| 1958 | Eva Bosakova, Czechoclovakia | | Daniela Silivas, Romania |
| 1962 | Larissa Latynina, Soviet Union | 1989 | Svetlana Bouguinskaia, Soviet Union |
| 1966 | Natalia Kuchinskaya, Soviet Union | | Daniela Silivas, Romania |
| 1970 | Ludmilla Tourischeva, Soviet Union | 1991 | Cristina Bontas, Romania |
| 1974 | Ludmilla Tourischeva, Soviet Union | | Oksana Tchusovitina, Soviet Union |
| 1978 | Nelli Kim, Soviet Union | 1992 | Kim Zmeskal, United States |
| | Elena Mukhina, Soviet Union | 1993 | Shannon Miller, United States |
| 1979 | Emilia Eberle, Romania | 1994 | Dina Kochetkova, Russia |
| 1981 | Natalia Ilenko, Soviet Union | 1995 | Gina Gogean, Romania |
| 1983 | Ecaterina Szabo, Romania | | |

### Uneven Bars

| Year | Champion and Nation | Year | Champion and Nation |
|---|---|---|---|
| 1950 | Gertchen Kolar, Austria | 1981 | Maxi Gnauck, East Germany |
| | Anna Pettersson, Sweden | 1983 | Maxi Gnauck, East Germany |
| 1954 | Agnes Keleti, Hungary | 1985 | Gabriele Fahrnich, East Germany |
| 1958 | Larissa Latynina, Soviet Union | 1987 | Daniela Silivas, Romania |
| 1962 | Irina Pervuschina, Soviet Union | | Doerte Thuemmler, East Germany |
| 1966 | Natalia Kuchinskaya, Soviet Union | 1989 | Fan Di, China/Daniela Silivas, Rom |
| 1970 | Karin Janz, East Germany | 1991 | Gwang Suk Kim, North Korea |
| 1974 | Annelore Zinke, East Germany | 1992 | Lavinia Milosivici, Romania |
| 1978 | Marcia Frederick, United States | 1993 | Shannon Miller, United States |
| 1979 | Ma Yanhong, China | 1994 | Luo Li, China |
| | Maxi Gnauck, East Germany | 1995 | Svetlana Chorkina, Russia |

### Balance Beam

| Year | Champion and Nation | Year | Champion and Nation |
|---|---|---|---|
| 1950 | Helena Rakoczy, Poland | 1983 | Olga Mostepanova, Soviet Union |
| 1954 | Keiko Tanaka, Japan | 1985 | Daniela Silivas, Romania |
| 1958 | Larissa Latynina, Soviet Union | 1987 | Aurelia Dobre, Romania |
| 1962 | Eva Bosakova, Czechoslovakia | 1989 | Daniela Silivas, Romania |
| 1966 | Natalia Kuchinskaya, Soviet Union | 1991 | Svetlana Boguinskaia, Soviet Union |
| 1970 | Erika Zuchold, East Germany | 1992 | Kim Zmeskal, United States |
| 1974 | Ludmilla Tourischeva, Soviet Union | 1993 | Lavinia Milosovici, Romania |
| 1978 | Nadia Comaneci, Romania | 1994 | Shannon Miller, United States |
| 1979 | Vera Cerna, Czechoslovakia | 1995 | Mo Huilan, China |
| 1981 | Maxi Gnauck, East Germany | | |

### Vault

| Year | Champion and Nation | Year | Champion and Nation |
|---|---|---|---|
| 1950 | Helena Rakoczy, Poland | 1983 | Boriana Stoyanova, Bulgaria |
| 1954 | T Manina, Sov Union/A Pettersson, Swe | 1985 | Elena Shoushounova, Soviet Union |
| 1958 | Larissa Latynina, Soviet Union | 1987 | Elena Shoushounova, Soviet Union |
| 1962 | Vera Caslavska, Czechoslovakia | 1989 | Olesia Durnik, Soviet Union |
| 1966 | Vera Caslavska, Czechoslovakia | 1991 | Lavinia Milosovici, Romania |
| 1970 | Erika Zuchold, East Germany | 1992 | Henrietta Onodi, Hungary |
| 1974 | Olga Korbut, Soviet Union | 1993 | Elena Piskun, Belarus |
| 1978 | Nelli Kim, Soviet Union | 1994 | Gina Gogean, Romania |
| 1979 | Dumitrita Turner, Romania | 1995 | L. Podkopayeva, Ukr./S. Amanar, Rom. |
| 1981 | Maxi Gnauck, East Germany | | |

## National Champions
### MEN
### All-Around

| Year | Champion | Year | Champion | Year | Champion |
|---|---|---|---|---|---|
| 1963 | Art Shurlock | 1974 | John Crosby | 1985 | Brian Babcock |
| 1964 | Rusty Mitchell | 1975 | Tom Beach | 1986 | Tim Daggett |
| 1965 | Rusty Mitchell | | Bart Conner | 1987 | Scott Johnson |
| 1966 | Rusty Mitchell | 1976 | Kurt Thomas | 1988 | Dan Hayden |
| 1967 | Katsuzoki Kanzaki | 1977 | Kurt Thomas | 1989 | Tim Ryan |
| 1968 | Yoshi Hayasaki | 1978 | Kurt Thomas | 1990 | John Roethlisberger |
| 1969 | Steve Hug | 1979 | Bart Conner | 1991 | Chris Waller |
| 1970 | Makoto Sakamoto | 1980 | Peter Vidmar | 1992 | John Roethlisberger |
| | Mas Watanabe | 1981 | Jim Hartung | 1993 | John Roethlisberger |
| 1971 | Yoshi Takei | 1982 | Peter Vidmar | 1994 | Scott Keswick |
| 1972 | Yoshi Takei | 1983 | Mitch Gaylord | 1995 | John Roethlisberger |
| 1973 | Marshall Avener | 1984 | Mitch Gaylord | | |

### Floor Exercise

| Year | Champion | Year | Champion | Year | Champion |
|---|---|---|---|---|---|
| 1963 | Tom Seward | 1973 | John Crosby | 1986 | Robert Sundstrom |
| 1964 | Rusty Mitchell | 1974 | John Crosby | 1987 | John Sweeney |
| 1965 | Rusty Mitchell | 1975 | Peter Korman | 1988 | Mark Oates |
| 1966 | Dan Millman | 1977 | Ron Galimore | | Charles Lakes |
| 1967 | Katsuzoki Kanzaki | 1978 | Kurt Thomas | 1989 | Mike Racanelli |
| | Ron Aure | 1979 | Ron Galimore | 1990 | Bob Stelter |
| 1968 | Katsuzoki Kanzaki | 1980 | Ron Galimore | 1991 | Mike Racanelli |
| 1969 | Steve Hug | 1981 | Jim Hartung | 1992 | Gregg Curtis |
| | Dave Thor | 1982 | Jim Hartung | 1993 | Kerry Huston |
| 1970 | Makoto Sakamoto | 1983 | Mitch Gaylord | 1994 | Jeremy Killen |
| 1971 | John Crosby | 1984 | Peter Vidmar | 1995 | Daniel Stover |
| 1972 | Yoshi Takei | 1985 | Mark Oates | | |

### Pommel Horse

| Year | Champion | Year | Champion | Year | Champion |
|---|---|---|---|---|---|
| 1963 | Larry Spiegel | 1973 | Marshall Avener | 1985 | Phil Cahoy |
| 1964 | Sam Bailie | 1974 | Marshall Avener | 1986 | Phil Cahoy |
| 1965 | Jack Ryan | 1975 | Bart Connor | 1987 | Tim Daggett |
| 1966 | Jack Ryan | 1977 | Gene Whelan | 1988 | Kevin Davis |
| 1967 | Paul Mayer | 1978 | Jim Hartung | 1989 | Kevin Davis |
| | Dave Doty | 1979 | Bart Conner | 1990 | Patrick Kirksey |
| 1968 | Katsuoki Kanzaki | 1980 | Jim Hartung | 1991 | Chris Waller |
| 1969 | Dave Thor | 1981 | Jim Hartung | 1992 | Chris Waller |
| 1970 | Mas Watanabe | 1982 | Jim Hartung | 1993 | Chris Waller |
| 1971 | Leonard Caling | 1983 | Bart Conner | 1994 | Mihai Begiu |
| 1972 | Sadao Hamada | 1984 | Tim Daggett | 1995 | Mark Sohn |

### Rings

| Year | Champion | Year | Champion | Year | Champion |
|---|---|---|---|---|---|
| 1963 | Art Shurlock | 1973 | Jim Ivicek | 1985 | Dan Hayden |
| 1964 | Glen Gailis | 1974 | Tom Weeden | 1986 | Dan Hayden |
| 1965 | Glen Gailis | 1975 | Tom Beach | 1987 | Scott Johnson |
| 1966 | Glen Gailis | 1977 | Kurt Thomas | 1988 | Dan Hayden |
| 1967 | Fred Dennis | 1978 | Mike Silverstein | 1989 | Scott Keswick |
| | Don Hatch | 1979 | Bart Conner | 1990 | Scott Keswick |
| 1968 | Yoshi Hayasaki | 1980 | Jim Hartung | 1991 | Scott Keswick |
| 1969 | Fred Dennis | 1981 | Jim Hartung | 1992 | Tim Ryan |
| | Bob Emery | 1982 | Jim Hartung | 1993 | John Roethlisberger |
| 1970 | Makoto Sakamoto | | Peter Vidmar | 1994 | Scott Keswick |
| 1971 | Yoshi Takei | 1983 | Mitch Gaylord | 1995 | Paul O'Neill |
| 1972 | Yoshi Takei | 1984 | Jim Hartung | | |

## National Champions (Cont.)
### MEN (Cont.)

## Vault

| Year | Champion | Year | Champion | Year | Champion |
|---|---|---|---|---|---|
| 1963 | Art Shurlock | 1974 | John Crosby | 1986 | Scott Wilbanks |
| 1964 | Gary Hery | 1975 | Tom Beach | 1987 | John Sweeney |
| 1965 | Brent Williams | 1977 | Ron Galimore | 1988 | John Sweeney |
| 1966 | Dan Millman | 1978 | Jim Hartung | | Bill Paul |
| 1967 | Jack Kenan | 1979 | Ron Galimore | 1989 | Bill Roth |
| | Sid Jensen | 1980 | Ron Galimore | 1990 | Lance Ringnald |
| 1968 | Rich Scorza | 1981 | Ron Galimore | 1991 | Scott Keswick |
| 1969 | Dave Butzman | 1982 | Jim Hartung | 1992 | Trent Dimas |
| 1970 | Makoto Sakamoto | | Jim Mikus | 1993 | Bill Roth |
| 1971 | Gary Morava | 1983 | Chris Reigel | 1994 | Keith Wiley |
| 1972 | Mike Kelley | 1984 | Chris Reigel | 1995 | David St. Pierre |
| 1973 | Gary Morava | 1985 | Scott Johnson | | |
| | | | Mark Oates | | |

## Parallel Bars

| Year | Champion | Year | Champion | Year | Champion |
|---|---|---|---|---|---|
| 1963 | Tom Seward | 1975 | Bart Conner | 1985 | Tim Daggett |
| 1964 | Rusty Mitchell | 1977 | Kurt Thomas | 1986 | Tim Daggett |
| 1965 | Glen Gailis | 1978 | Bart Conner | 1987 | Scott Johnson |
| 1966 | Ray Hadley | 1979 | Bart Conner | 1988 | Dan Hayden |
| 1967 | Katsuzoki Kanzaki | 1980 | Phil Cahoy | | Kevin Davis |
| | Tom Goldsborough | | Larry Gerard | 1989 | Conrad Voorsanger |
| 1968 | Yoshi Hayasaki | 1981 | Bart Conner | 1990 | Trent Dimas |
| 1969 | Steve Hug | 1982 | Peter Vidmar | 1991 | Scott Keswick |
| 1970 | Makoto Sakamoto | 1983 | Mitch Gaylord | 1992 | Jair Lynch |
| 1971 | Brent Simmons | 1984 | Peter Vidmar | 1993 | Chainey Umphrey |
| 1972 | Yoshi Takei | | Mitch Gaylord | 1994 | Steve McCain |
| 1973 | Marshall Avener | | Tim Daggett | 1995 | John Roethlisberger |
| 1974 | Jim Ivicek | | | | |

## High Bars

| Year | Champion | Year | Champion | Year | Champion |
|---|---|---|---|---|---|
| 1963 | Art Shurlock | 1975 | Tom Beach | 1986 | Dan Hayden |
| 1964 | Glen Gailis | 1977 | Kurt Thomas | | David Moriel |
| 1965 | Rusty Mitchell | 1978 | Kurt Thomas | 1987 | David Moriel |
| 1966 | Katsuzoki Kanzaki | 1979 | Yoichi Tomita | 1988 | Dan Hayden |
| 1967 | Katsuzoki Kanzaki | 1980 | Jim Hartung | 1989 | Tim Ryan |
| | Jerry Fontana | 1981 | Bart Conner | 1990 | Trent Dimas |
| 1968 | Yoshi Hayasaki | 1982 | Mitch Gaylord | | Lance Ringnald |
| 1969 | Rich Grisby | 1983 | Mario McCutcheon | 1991 | Lance Ringnald |
| 1970 | Makoto Sakamoto | 1984 | Peter Vidmar | 1992 | Jair Lynch |
| 1971 | Yoshi Takei | | Tim Daggett | 1993 | Steve McCain |
| 1972 | Tom Lindner | | Mitch Gaylord | 1994 | Scott Keswick |
| 1973 | John Crosby | 1985 | Dan Hayden | 1995 | John Roethlisberger |
| 1974 | Brent Simmons | | | | |

### WOMEN

## All-Around

| Year | Champion | Year | Champion | Year | Champion |
|---|---|---|---|---|---|
| 1963 | Donna Schanezer | 1973 | Joan Moore Gnat | 1985 | Sabrina Mar |
| 1965 | Gail Daley | 1974 | Joan Moore Gnat | 1986 | Jennifer Sey |
| 1966 | Donna Schanezer | 1975 | Tammy Manville | 1987 | Kristie Phillips |
| 1968 | Linda Scott | 1976 | Denise Cheshire | 1988 | Phoebe Mills |
| 1969 | Joyce Tanac | 1977 | Donna Turnbow | 1989 | Brandy Johnson |
| | Schroeder | 1978 | Kathy Johnson | 1990 | Kim Zmeskal |
| 1970 | Cathy Rigby McCoy | 1979 | Leslie Pyfer | 1991 | Kim Zmeskal |
| 1971 | Joan Moore Gnat | 1980 | Julianne McNamara | 1992 | Kim Zmeskal |
| | Linda Metheny | 1981 | Tracee Talavera | 1993 | Shannon Miller |
| | Mulvihill | 1982 | Tracee Talavera | 1994 | Dominique Dawes |
| 1972 | Joan Moore Gnat | 1983 | Dianne Durham | 1995 | Dominique Moceanu |
| | Cathy Rigby McCoy | 1984 | Mary Lou Retton | | |

## National Champions *(Cont.)*
### WOMEN *(Cont.)*

### Vault

| Year | Champion | Year | Champion | Year | Champion |
|---|---|---|---|---|---|
| 1963 | Donna Schanezer | 1974 | Dianne Dunbar | 1985 | Yolanda Mavity |
| 1965 | Gail Daley | 1975 | Kolleen Casey | 1986 | Joyce Wilborn |
| 1966 | Donna Schanezer | 1976 | Debbie Wilcox | 1987 | Rhonda Faehn |
| 1968 | Terry Spencer | 1977 | Lisa Cawthron | 1988 | Rhonda Faehn |
| 1969 | Joyce Tanac | 1978 | Rhonda Schwandt | 1989 | Brandy Johnson |
| | Schroeder | | Sharon Shapiro | 1990 | Brandy Johnson |
| | Cleo Carver | 1979 | Christa Canary | 1991 | Kerri Strug |
| 1970 | Cathy Rigby McCoy | 1980 | Julianne McNamara | 1992 | Kerri Strug |
| 1971 | Joan Moore Gnat | | Beth Kline | 1993 | Dominique Dawes |
| | Adele Gleaves | 1981 | Kim Neal | 1994 | Dominique Dawes |
| 1972 | Cindy Eastwood | 1982 | Yumi Mordre | 1995 | Shannon Miller |
| 1973 | Roxanne Pierce | 1983 | Dianne Durham | | |
| | Mancha | 1984 | Mary Lou Retton | | |

### Uneven Bars

| Year | Champion | Year | Champion | Year | Champion |
|---|---|---|---|---|---|
| 1963 | Donna Schanezer | 1973 | Roxanne Pierce | 1984 | Julianne McNamara |
| 1965 | Irene Haworth | | Mancha | 1985 | Sabrina Mar |
| 1966 | Donna Schanezer | 1974 | Diane Dunbar | 1986 | Marie Roethlisberger |
| 1968 | Linda Scott | 1975 | Leslie Wolfsberger | 1987 | Melissa Marlowe |
| 1969 | Joyce Tanac | 1976 | Leslie Wolfsberger | 1988 | Chelle Stack |
| | Schroeder | 1977 | Donna Turnbow | 1989 | Chelle Stack |
| | Lisa Nelson | 1978 | Marcia Frederick | 1990 | Sandy Woolsey |
| 1970 | Roxanne Pierce | 1979 | Marcia Frederick | 1991 | Elisabeth Crandall |
| | Mancha | 1980 | Marcia Frederick | 1992 | Dominique Dawes |
| 1971 | Joan Moore Gnat | 1981 | Julianne McNamara | 1993 | Shannon Miller |
| 1972 | Cathy Rigby McCoy | 1982 | Marie Roethlisberger | 1994 | Dominique Dawes |
| | | 1983 | Julianne McNamara | 1995 | Dominique Dawes |

### Balance Beam

| Year | Champion | Year | Champion | Year | Champion |
|---|---|---|---|---|---|
| 1963 | Leissa Krol | 1975 | Kyle Gayner | 1985 | Kelly Garrison-Steves |
| 1965 | Gail Daley | 1976 | Carrie Englert | 1988 | Kelly Garrison-Steves |
| 1966 | Irene Haworth | 1977 | Donna Turnbow | 1989 | Brandy Johnson |
| | Linda Scott | 1978 | Christa Canary | 1990 | Betty Okino |
| 1968 | Linda Scott | 1979 | Heidi Anderson | 1991 | Shannon Miller |
| 1969 | Lonna Woodward | 1980 | Kelly Garrison-Steves | 1992 | Kerri Strug |
| 1970 | Joyce Tanac | 1981 | Tracee Talavera | | Kim Zmeskal |
| | Schroeder | 1982 | Julianne McNamara | 1993 | Dominique Dawes |
| 1971 | Linda Metheny | 1983 | Dianne Durham | 1994 | Dominique Dawes |
| | Mulvihill | 1984 | Pam Bileck | 1995 | Doni Thompson |
| 1972 | Kim Chace | | Tracee Talavera | | Monica Flammer |
| 1973 | Nancy Thies Marshall | 1986 | Angie Denkins | | |
| 1974 | Joan Moore Gnat | 1987 | Kristie Phillips | | |

### Floor Exercise

| Year | Champion | Year | Champion | Year | Champion |
|---|---|---|---|---|---|
| 1963 | Donna Schanezer | 1975 | Kathy Howard | 1986 | Yolanda Mavity |
| 1965 | Gail Daley | 1976 | Carrie Englert | 1987 | Kristie Phillips |
| 1966 | Donna Schanezer | 1977 | Kathy Johnson | 1988 | Phoebe Mills |
| 1968 | Linda Scott | 1978 | Kathy Johnson | 1989 | Brandy Johnson |
| 1970 | Cathy Rigby McCoy | 1979 | Heidi Anderson | 1990 | Brandy Johnson |
| 1971 | Joan Moore Gnat | 1980 | Beth Kline | 1991 | Kim Zmeskal |
| | Linda Metheny | 1981 | Michelle Goodwin | | Dominique Dawes |
| | Mulvihill | 1982 | Amy Koopman | 1992 | Kim Zmeskal |
| 1972 | Joan Moore Gnat | 1983 | Dianne Durham | 1993 | Shannon Miller |
| 1973 | Joan Moore Gnat | 1984 | Mary Lou Retton | 1994 | Dominique Dawes |
| 1974 | Joan Moore Gnat | 1985 | Sabrina Mar | 1995 | Dominique Dawes |

# Handball

## National Four-Wall Champions
### MEN

| | | | |
|---|---|---|---|
| 1919 .....Bill Ranft | 1939 .....Joe Platak | 1959 .....John Sloan | 1979 .....Naty Alvarado |
| 1920 .....Max Gold | 1940 .....Joe Platak | 1960 .....Jimmy Jacobs | 1980 .....Naty Alvarado |
| 1921 .....Carl Haedge | 1941 .....Joe Platak | 1961 .....John Sloan | 1981 .....Fred Lewis |
| 1922 .....Art Shinners | 1942 .....Jack Clemente | 1962 .....Oscar Obert | 1982 .....Naty Alvarado |
| 1923 .....Joe Murray | 1943 .....Joe Platak | 1963 .....Oscar Obert | 1983 .....Naty Alvarado |
| 1924 .....Maynard Laswe | 1944 .....Frank Coyle | 1964 .....Jimmy Jacobs | 1984 .....Naty Alvarado |
| 1925 .....Maynard Laswe | 1945 .....Joe Platak | 1965 .....Jimmy Jacobs | 1985 .....Naty Alvarado |
| 1926 .....Maynard Laswe | 1946 .....Angelo Trutio | 1966 .....Paul Haber | 1986 .....Naty Alvarado |
| 1927 .....George Nelson | 1947 .....Gus Lewis | 1967 .....Paul Haber | 1987 .....Naty Alvarado |
| 1928 .....Joe Griffin | 1948 .....Gus Lewis | 1968 .....Stuffy Singer | 1988 .....Naty Alvarado |
| 1919 .....Al Banuet | 1949 .....Vic Hershkowitz | 1969 .....Paul Haber | 1989 .....Poncho Monreal |
| 1930 .....Al Banuet | 1950 .....Ken Schneider | 1970 .....Paul Haber | 1990 .....Naty Alvarado |
| 1931 .....Al Banuet | 1951 .....Walter Plakan | 1971 .....Paul Haber | 1991 .....John Bike |
| 1932 .....Angelo Trutio | 1952 .....Vic Hershkowitz | 1972 .....Fred Lewis | 1992 .....Octavio Silveyra |
| 1933 .....Sam Atcheson | 1953 .....Bob Brady | 1973 .....Terry Muck | 1993 .....David Chapman |
| 1934 .....Sam Atcheson | 1954 .....Vic Hershkowitz | 1974 .....Fred Lewis | 1994 .....Octavio Silveyra |
| 1935 .....Joe Platak | 1955 .....Jimmy Jacobs | 1975 .....Fred Lewis | 1995 .....David Chapman |
| 1936 .....Joe Platak | 1956 .....Jimmy Jacobs | 1976 .....Fred Lewis | |
| 1937 .....Joe Platak | 1957 .....Jimmy Jacobs | 1977 .....Naty Alvarado | |
| 1938 .....Joe Platak | 1958 .....John Sloan | 1978 .....Fred Lewis | |

### WOMEN

| | | | |
|---|---|---|---|
| 1980 .....Rosemary Bellini | 1984 .....Rosemary Bellini | 1988 .....Rosemary Bellini | 1992 .....Lisa Fraser |
| 1981 .....Rosemary Bellini | 1985 .....Peanut Motal | 1989 .....Anna Engele | 1993 .....Anna Engele |
| 1982 .....Rosemary Bellini | 1986 .....Peanut Motal | 1990 .....Anna Engele | 1994 .....Anna Engele |
| 1983 .....Diane Harmon | 1987 .....Rosemary Bellini | 1991 .....Anna Engele | 1995 .....Anna Engele |

## National Three-Wall Champions
### MEN

| | | | |
|---|---|---|---|
| 1950 .....Vic Hershkowitz | 1962 .....Oscar Obert | 1974 .....Fred Lewis | 1986 .....Vern Roberts |
| 1951 .....Vic Hershkowitz | 1963 .....Marty Decatur | 1975 .....Lou Russo | 1987 .....Vern Roberts |
| 1952 .....Vic Hershkowitz | 1964 .....Marty Decatur | 1976 .....Lou Russo | 1988 .....Jon Kendler |
| 1953 .....Vic Herskkowitz | 1965 .....Carl Obert | 1977 .....Fred Lewis | 1989 .....John Bike |
| 1954 .....Vic Hershkowitz | 1966 .....Marty Decatur | 1978 .....Fred Lewis | 1990 .....Vince Munoz |
| 1955 .....Vic Hershkowitz | 1967 .....Carl Obert | 1979 .....Naty Alvarado | 1991 .....John Bike |
| 1956 .....Vic Hershkowitz | 1968 .....Marty Decatur | 1980 .....Lou Russo | 1992 .....John Bike |
| 1957 .....Vic Hershkowitz | 1969 .....Marty Decatur | 1981 .....Naty Alvarado | 1993 .....Eric Klarman |
| 1958 .....Vic Hershkowitz | 1970 .....Steve August | 1982 .....Naty Alvarado | 1994 .....David Chapman |
| 1959 .....Jimmy Jacobs | 1971 .....Lou Russo | 1983 .....Naty Alvarado | 1995 .....David Chapman |
| 1960 .....Jimmy Jacobs | 1972 .....Lou Russo | 1984 .....Naty Alvarado | |
| 1961 .....Jimmy Jacobs | 1973 .....Paul Haber | 1985 .....Vern Roberts | |

### WOMEN

| | | | |
|---|---|---|---|
| 1981 .....Allison Roberts | 1985 .....Rosemary Bellini | 1989 .....Rosemary Bellini | 1993 .....Anna Engele |
| 1982 .....Allison Roberts | 1986 .....Rosemary Bellini | 1990 .....Rosemary Bellini | 1994 .....Anna Engele |
| 1983 .....Allison Roberts | 1987 .....Rosemary Bellini | 1991 .....Rosemary Bellini | 1995 .....Allison Roberts |
| 1984 .....Rosemary Bellini | 1988 .....Rosemary Bellini | 1992 .....Anna Engele | |

## World Four-Wall Champions

| | |
|---|---|
| 1984 ...................Merv Deckert, Canada | 1991 ...................Pancho Monreal, United States |
| 1986 ...................Vern Roberts, United States | 1994 ...................David Chapman, United States |
| 1988 ...................Naty Alvarado, United States | |

# Lacrosse

## United States Club Lacrosse Association Champions

| | | |
|---|---|---|
| 1960 ......Mt Washington Club | 1972 ......Carling | 1984 ......Maryland Lacrosse Club |
| 1961 ......Baltimore Lacrosse Club | 1973 ......Long Island Athletic Club | 1985 ......LI-Hofstra Lacrosse Club |
| 1962 ......Mt Washington Club | 1974 ......Long Island Athletic Club | 1986 ......LI-Hofstra Lacrosse Club |
| 1963 ......University Club | 1975 ......Mt Washington Club | 1987 ......LI-Hofstra Lacrosse Club |
| 1964 ......Mt Washington Club | 1976 ......Mt Washington Club | 1988 ......Maryland Lacrosse Club |
| 1965 ......Mt Washington Club | 1977 ......Mt Washington Club | 1989 ......LI-Hofstra Lacrosse Club |
| 1966 ......Mt Washington Club | 1978 ......Long Island Athletic Club | 1990 ......Mt Washington Club |
| 1967 ......Mt Washington Club | 1979 ......Maryland Lacrosse Club | 1991 ......Mt Washington Club |
| 1968 ......Long Island Athletic Club | 1980 ......Long Island Athletic Club | 1992 ......Maryland Lacrosse Club |
| 1969 ......Long Island Athletic Club | 1981 ......Long Island Athletic Club | 1993 ......Mt Washington Club |
| 1970 ......Long Island Athletic Club | 1982 ......Maryland Lacrosse Club | 1994 ......LI-Hofstra Lacrosse Club |
| 1971 ......Long Island Athletic Club | 1983 ......Maryland Lacrosse Club | 1995 ......Mt Washington Club |

# Little League Baseball

## Little League World Series Champions

| Year | Champion | Runner-Up | Score | Year | Champion | Runner-Up | Score |
|------|----------|-----------|-------|------|----------|-----------|-------|
| 1947 | ..Williamsport, PA | Lock Haven, PA | 16-7 | 1972 | ..Taipei, Taiwan | Hammond, IN | 6-0 |
| 1948 | ..Lock Haven, PA | St. Petersburg, FL | 6-5 | 1973 | ..Tainan City, Taiwan | Tucson, AZ | 12-0 |
| 1949 | ..Hammonton, NJ | Pensacola, FL | 5-0 | 1974 | ..Kao Hsiung, Taiwan | El Cajun, CA | 7-2 |
| 1950 | ..Houston, TX | Bridgeport, CT | 2-1 | 1975 | ..Lakewood, NJ | Tampa, FL | 4-3 |
| 1951 | ..Stamford, CT | Austin, TX | 3-0 | 1976 | ..Tokyo, Japan | Campbell, CA | 10-3 |
| 1952 | ..Norwalk, CT | Monongahela, PA | 4-3 | 1977 | ..Kao Hsiung, Taiwan | El Cajun, CA | 7-2 |
| 1953 | ..Birmingham, AL | Schenectady, NY | 1-0 | 1978 | ..Pin-Tung, Taiwan | Danville, CA | 11-1 |
| 1954 | ..Schenectady, NY | Colton, CA | 7-5 | 1979 | ..Hsien, Taiwan | Campbell, CA | 2-1 |
| 1955 | ..Morrisville, PA | Merchantville, NJ | 4-3 | 1980 | ..Hua Lian, Taiwan | Tampa, FL | 4-3 |
| 1956 | ..Roswell, NM | Merchantville, NJ | 3-1 | 1981 | ..Tai-Chung, Taiwan | Tampa, FL | 4-2 |
| 1957 | ..Monterrrey, Mex. | LaMesa, CA | 4-0 | 1982 | ..Kirkland, WA | Hsien, Taiwan | 6-0 |
| 1958 | ..Monterrey, Mex. | Kankakee, IL | 10-1 | 1983 | ..Marietta, GA | Barahona, D.Rep. | 3-1 |
| 1959 | ..Hamtramck, MI | Auburn, CA | 12-0 | 1984 | ..Seoul, S. Korea | Altamonte Sgs, FL | 6-2 |
| 1960 | ..Levittown, PA | Ft. Worth, TX | 5-0 | 1985 | ..Seoul, S. Korea | Mexicali, Mex. | 7-1 |
| 1961 | ..El Cajon, CA | El Campo, TX | 4-2 | 1986 | ..Tainan Park, Taiwan | Tucson, AZ | 12-0 |
| 1962 | ..San Jose, CA | Kankakee, IL | 3-0 | 1987 | ..Hua Lian, Taiwan | Irvine, CA | 21-1 |
| 1963 | ..Granada Hills, CA | Stratford, CT | 2-1 | 1988 | ..Tai-Chung, Taiwan | Pearl City, HI | 10-0 |
| 1964 | ..Staten Island, NY | Monterrey, Mex. | 4-0 | 1989 | ..Trumbull, CT | Kaohsiung, Taiwan | 5-2 |
| 1965 | ..Windsor Locks, CT | Stoney Creek, Can. | 3-1 | 1990 | ..Taipei, Taiwan | Shippensburg, PA | 9-0 |
| 1966 | ..Houston, TX | W.New York, NJ | 8-2 | 1991 | ..Tai-Chung, Taiwan | San Ramon Vly, CA | 11-0 |
| 1967 | ..West Tokyo, Japan | Chicago, IL | 4-1 | 1992* | ..Long Beach, CA | Zamboanga, Phil. | 6-0 |
| 1968 | ..Osaka, Japan | Richmond, VA | 1-0 | 1993 | ..Long Beach, CA | David Chiriqui, Pan. | 3-2 |
| 1969 | ..Taipei, Taiwan | Santa Clara, CA | 5-0 | 1994 | ..Maracaibo, Venez | Northridge, CA | 4-3 |
| 1970 | ..Wayne, NJ | Campbell, CA | 2-0 | 1995 | ..Tainan, Taiwan | Sprint, TX | 17-3 |
| 1971 | ..Tainan, Taiwan | Gary, IN | 12-3 | | | | |

*Long Beach declared a 6-0 winner after the international tournament committee determined that Zamboanga City had used players that were not within its city limits.

# Motor Boat Racing

## American Power Boat Association Gold Cup Champions

| Year | Boat | Driver | Avg MPH | Year | Boat | Driver | Avg MPH |
|------|------|--------|---------|------|------|--------|---------|
| 1904 | ....Standard (June) | Carl Riotte | 23.160 | 1930 | ....Hotsy Totsy | Vic Kliesrath | 52.673 |
| 1904 | ....Vingt-et-Un II (Sep) | W. Sharpe Kilmer | 24.900 | 1931 | ....Hotsy Totsy | Vic Kliesrath | 53.602 |
| 1905 | ....Chip I | J. Wainwright | 15.000 | 1932 | ....Delphine IV | Bill Horn | 57.775 |
| 1906 | ....Chip II | J. Wainwright | 25.000 | 1933 | ....El Lagarto | George Reis | 56.260 |
| 1907 | ....Chip II | J. Wainwright | 23.903 | 1934 | ....El Lagarto | George Reis | 55.000 |
| 1908 | ....Dixie II | E. J. Schroeder | 29.938 | 1935 | ....El Lagarto | George Reis | 55.056 |
| 1909 | ....Dixie II | E. J. Schroeder | 29.590 | 1936 | ....Impshi | Kaye Don | 45.735 |
| 1910 | ....Dixie III | F. K. Burnham | 32.473 | 1937 | ....Notre Dame | Clell Perry | 63.675 |
| 1911 | ....MIT II | J. H. Hayden | 37.000 | 1938 | ....Alagi | Theo Rossi | 64.340 |
| 1912 | ....P.D.Q. II | A. G. Miles | 39.462 | 1939 | ....My Sin | Z. G. Simmons, Jr | 66.133 |
| 1913 | ....Ankle Deep | Cas Mankowski | 42.779 | 1940 | ....Hotsy Totsy III | Sidney Allen | 48.295 |
| 1914 | ....Baby Speed Demon II | Jim Blackton & Bob Edgren | 48.458 | 1941 | ....My Sin | Z. G. Simmons, Jr | 52.509 |
| | | | | 1942-45 | | No race | |
| 1915 | ....Miss Detroit | Johnny Milot & Jack Beebe | 37.656 | 1946 | ....Tempo VI | Guy Lombardo | 68.132 |
| | | | | 1947 | ....Miss Peps V | Danny Foster | 57.000 |
| 1916 | ....Miss Minneapolis | Bernard Smith | 48.860 | 1948 | ....Miss Great Lakes | Danny Foster | 46.845 |
| 1917 | ....Miss Detroit II | Gar Wood | 54.410 | 1949 | ....My Sweetie | Bill Cantrell | 73.612 |
| 1918 | ....Miss Detroit II | Gar Wood | 51.619 | 1950 | ....Slo-Mo-Shun IV | Ted Jones | 78.216 |
| 1919 | ....Miss Detroit III | Gar Wood | 42.748 | 1951 | ....Slo-Mo-Shun V | Lou Fageol | 90.871 |
| 1920 | ....Miss America I | Gar Wood | 62.022 | 1952 | ....Slo-Mo-Shun IV | Stan Dollar | 79.923 |
| 1921 | ....Miss America I | Gar Wood | 52.825 | 1953 | ....Slo-Mo-Shun IV | Joe Taggart & Lou Fageol | 99.108 |
| 1922 | ....Packard Chriscraft | J. G. Vincent | 40.253 | | | | |
| 1923 | ....Packard Chriscraft | Caleb Bragg | 43.867 | 1954 | ....Slo-Mo-Shun IV | Joe Taggart & Lou Fageol | 92.613 |
| 1924 | ....Baby Bootlegger | Caleb Bragg | 45.302 | | | | |
| 1925 | ....Baby Bootlegger | Caleb Bragg | 47.240 | 1955 | ....Gale V | Lee Schoenith | 99.552 |
| 1926 | ....Greenwich Folly | George Townsend | 47.984 | 1956 | ....Miss Thriftaway | Bill Muncey | 96.552 |
| | | | | 1957 | ....Miss Thriftaway | Bill Muncey | 101.787 |
| 1927 | ....Greenwich Folly | George Townsend | 47.662 | 1958 | ....Hawaii Kai III | Jack Regas | 103.000 |
| | | | | 1959 | ....Maverick | Bill Stead | 104.481 |
| 1928 | ....No race | | | 1960 | | No race | |
| 1929 | ....Imp | Richard Hoyt | 48.662 | 1961 | ....Miss Century 21 | Bill Muncey | 99.678 |

### American Power Boat Association Gold Cup Champions *(Cont.)*

| Year | Boat | Driver | Avg MPH | Year | Boat | Driver | Avg MPH |
|---|---|---|---|---|---|---|---|
| 1962 | Miss Century 21 | Bill Muncey | 100.710 | 1980 | Miss Budweiser | Dean Chenoweth | 106.932 |
| 1963 | Miss Bardahl | Ron Musson | 105.124 | | | | |
| 1964 | Miss Bardahl | Ron Musson | 103.433 | 1981 | Miss Budweiser | Dean Chenoweth | 116.932 |
| 1965 | Miss Bardahl | Ron Musson | 103.132 | | | | |
| 1966 | Tahoe Miss | Mira Slovak | 93.019 | 1982 | Atlas Van Lines | Chip Hanauer | 120.050 |
| 1967 | Miss Bardahl | Bill Shumacher | 101.484 | 1983 | Atlas Van Lines | Chip Hanauer | 118.507 |
| 1968 | Miss Bardahl | Bill Shumacher | 108.173 | 1984 | Atlas Van Lines | Chip Hanauer | 130.175 |
| 1969 | Miss Budweiser | Bill Sterett | 98.504 | 1985 | Miller American | Chip Hanauer | 120.643 |
| 1970 | Miss Budweiser | Dean Chenoweth | 99.562 | 1986 | Miller American | Chip Hanauer | 116.523 |
| | | | | 1987 | Miller American | Chip Hanauer | 127.620 |
| 1971 | Miss Madison | Jim McCormick | 98.043 | 1988 | Miss Circus Circus | Chip Hanauer & Jim Prevost | 123.756 |
| 1972 | Atlas Van Lines | Bill Muncey | 104.277 | | | | |
| 1973 | Atlas Van Lines | Dean Chenoweth | 99.043 | 1989 | Miss Budweiser | Tom D'Eath | 131.209 |
| | | | | 1990 | Miss Budweiser | Tom D'Eath | 143.176 |
| 1974 | Pay 'n Pak | George Henley | 104.428 | 1991 | Winston Eagle | Mark Tate | 137.771 |
| 1975 | Pay 'n Pak | George Henley | 108.921 | 1992 | Miss Budweiser | Chip Hanauer | 136.282 |
| 1976 | Miss U.S. | Tom D'Eath | 100.412 | 1993 | Miss Budweiser | Chip Hanauer | 141.195 |
| 1977 | Atlas Van Lines | Bill Muncey | 111.822 | 1994 | Smokin' Joe Camel | Mark Tate | 145.260 |
| 1978 | Atlas Van Lines | Bill Muncey | 111.412 | 1995 | Miss Budweiser | Chip Hanauer | 149.160 |
| 1979 | Atlas Van Lines | Bill Muncey | 100.765 | | | | |

### American Power Boat Association Annual Champion Drivers

| Year | Driver | Boats | Wins | Year | Driver | Boats | Wins |
|---|---|---|---|---|---|---|---|
| 1947 | Danny Foster | Miss Peps V | 6 | 1971 | Dean Chenoweth | Miss Budweiser | 2 |
| 1948 | Dan Arena | Such Crust | 2 | 1972 | Bill Muncey | Atlas Van Lines | 6 |
| 1949 | Bill Cantrell | My Sweetie | 7 | 1973 | Mickey Remund | Pay 'n Pack | 4 |
| 1950 | Dan Foster | Such Crust/DaphneX | 2 | 1974 | George Henley | Pay 'n Pack | 7 |
| 1951 | Chuck Thompson | Miss Pepsi | 2 | 1975 | Billy Schumacher | Weisfleld's | 2 |
| 1952 | Chuck Thompson | Miss Pepsi | 3 | 1976 | Bill Muncey | Atlas Van Lines | 5 |
| 1953 | Lee Schoenith | Gale II | 1 | 1977 | Mickey Remund | Miss Budweiser | 3 |
| 1954 | Lee Schoenith | Gale V | 4 | 1978 | Bill Muncey | Atlas Van Lines | 6 |
| 1955 | Lee Schoenith | Gale V/Wha Hoppen | 1 | 1979 | Bill Muncey | Atlas Van Lines | 7 |
| 1956 | Russ Schleeh | Shanty I | 3 | 1980 | Dean Chenoweth | Miss Budweiser | 5 |
| 1957 | Jack Regas | Hawaii Kai III | 4 | 1981 | Dean Chenoweth | Miss Budweiser | 6 |
| 1958 | Mira Slovak | Bardah/Miss Buren | 3 | 1982 | Chip Hanauer | Atlas Van Lines | 5 |
| 1959 | Bill Stead | Maverick | 5 | 1983 | Chip Hanauer | Atlas Van Lines | 3 |
| 1960 | Bill Muncey | Miss Thriftway | 4 | 1984 | Jim Kropfeld | Miss Budweiser | 6 |
| 1961 | Bill Muncey | Miss Century 21 | 4 | 1985 | Chip Hanauer | Miller American | 5 |
| 1962 | Bill Muncey | Miss Century 21 | 5 | 1986 | Jim Kropfeld | Miss Budweiser | 3 |
| 1963 | Bill Cantrell | Gale V | 0 | 1987 | Jim Kropfeld | Miss Budweiser | 5 |
| 1964 | Ron Musson | Miss Bardahl | 4 | 1988 | Tom D'Eath | Miss Budweiser | 4 |
| 1965 | Ron Musson | Miss Bardahl | 4 | 1989 | Chip Hanauer | Miss Circus Circus | 3 |
| 1966 | Mira Slovak | Tahoe Miss | 4 | 1990 | Chip Hanauer | Miss Circus Circus | 6 |
| 1967 | Bill Schumacher | Miss Bardahl | 6 | 1991 | Mark Tate | Winston/Oberto | 3 |
| 1968 | Bill Schumacher | Miss Bardahl | 4 | 1992 | Chip Hanauer | Miss Budweiser | 7 |
| 1969 | Bill Sterett, Sr. | Miss Budweiser | 4 | 1993 | Chip Hanauer | Miss Budweiser | 7 |
| 1970 | Dean Chenoweth | Miss Budweiser | 4 | 1994 | Mark Tate | Smokin' Joe Camel | 2 |

### American Power Boat Association Annual Champion Boats

| Year | Boat | Owner | Wins | Year | Boat | Owner | Wins |
|---|---|---|---|---|---|---|---|
| 1970 | Miss Budweiser | Little-Friedkin | 4 | 1983 | Atlas Van Lines | Muncey-Lucero | 3 |
| 1971 | Miss Budweiser | Little-Friedkin | 2 | 1984 | Miss Budweiser | Bernie Little | 6 |
| 1972 | Atlas Van Lines | Joe Schoenith | 6 | 1985 | Miller American | Muncey-Lucero | 5 |
| 1973 | Pay 'n Pak | Dave Heerensperger | 4 | 1986 | Miss Budweiser | Bernie Little | 3 |
| 1974 | Pay 'n Pak | Dave Heerensperger | 7 | 1987 | Miss Budweiser | Bernie Little | 5 |
| 1975 | Pay 'n Pak | Dave Heerensperger | 5 | 1988 | Miss Budweiser | Bernie Little | 4 |
| 1976 | Atlas Van Lines | Bill Muncey | 5 | 1989 | Miss Budweiser | Bernie Little | 4 |
| 1977 | Miss Budweiser | Bernie Little | 3 | 1990 | Circus Circus | Bill Bennett | 6 |
| 1978 | Atlas Van Lines | Bill Muncey | 6 | 1991 | Miss Budweiser | Bernie Little | 4 |
| 1979 | Atlas Van Lines | Bill Muncey | 7 | 1992 | Miss Budweiser | Bernie Little | 7 |
| 1980 | Miss Budweiser | Bernie Little | 5 | 1993 | Miss Budweiser | Bernie Little | 7 |
| 1981 | Miss Budweiser | Bernie Little | 6 | 1994 | Miss Budweiser | Bernie Little | 4 |
| 1982 | Atlas Van Lines | Fran Muncey | 5 | | | | |

# Polo

## United States Open Polo Champions

| | | | |
|---|---|---|---|
| 1904 ......Wanderers | 1932 ......Templeton | 1958 ......Dallas | 1978 ......Abercrombie & |
| 1905-09..Not contested | 1933 ......Aurora | 1959 ......Circle F | Kent |
| 1910 ..... Ranelagh | 1934 ......Templeton | 1960 ......Oak Brook— | 1979 ......Retama |
| 1911 ......Not contested | 1935 ......Greentree | C.C.C. | 1980 ......Southern Hills |
| 1912 ......Cooperstown | 1936 ......Greentree | 1961 ......Milwaukee | 1981 ......Rolex A & K |
| 1913 ......Cooperstown | 1937 ......Old Westbury | 1962 ......Santa Barbara | 1982 ......Retama |
| 1914 ......Meadow Brook | 1938 ......Old Westbury | 1963 ......Tulsa | 1983 ......Ft. Lauderdale |
| Magpies | 1939 ......Bostwick Field | 1964 ......Concar Oak | 1984 ......Retama |
| 1915 ......Not contested | 1940 ......Aknusti | Brook | 1985 ......Carter Ranch |
| 1916 ......Meadow Brook | 1941 ......Gulf Stream | 1965 ......Oak Brook— | 1986 ......Retama II |
| 1917-18..Not contested | 1942-45..Not contested | Santa Barbara | 1987 ......Aloha |
| 1919 ......Meadow Brook | 1946 ......Mexico | 1966 ......Tulsa | 1988 ......Les Diables |
| 1920 ......Meadow Brook | 1947 ......Old Westbury | 1967 ......Bunntyco—- | Bleus |
| 1921 ......Great Neck | 1948 ......Hurricanes | Oak Brook | 1989 ......Les Diables |
| 1922 ......Argentine | 1949 ......Hurricanes | 1968 ......Midland | Bleus |
| 1923 ......Meadow Brook | 1950 ......Bostwick | 1969 ......Tulsa Greenhill | 1990 ......Les Diables |
| 1924 ......Midwick | 1951 ......Milwaukee | 1970 ......Tulsa Greenhill | Bleus |
| 1925 ......Orange County | 1952 ......Beverly Hills | 1971 ......Oak Brook | 1991 ......Grant's Farm |
| 1926 ......Hurricanes | 1953 ......Meadow Brook | 1972 ......Milwaukee | Manor |
| 1927 ......Sands Point | 1954 ......C.C.C.— | 1973 ......Oak Brook | 1992 ......Hanalei Bay |
| 1928 ......Meadow Brook | Meadow Brook | 1974 ......Milwaukee | 1993 ......Gehache |
| 1929 ......Hurricanes | 1955 ......C.C.C. | 1975 ......Milwaukee | 1994 ......Aspen |
| 1930 ......Hurricanes | 1956 ......Brandywine | 1976 ......Willow Bend | 1995 ......Outback |
| 1931 ......Santa Paula | 1957 ......Detroit | 1977 ......Retama | |

## Top-Ranked Players

The United States Polo Association ranks its registered players from minus 2 to plus 10 goals, with 10 Goal players being the game's best. At present, the USPA recognizes thirteen 10-Goal and nine 9-Goal players:

| 10-GOAL | 9-GOAL |
|---|---|
| Mariano Aguerre (Greenwich) | A.D. Alberdi (Palm Beach) |
| Adolfo Cambiaso (Palm Beach) | Benjamin Araya (Palm Beach) |
| Carlos Gracida (San Antonio) | Michael Vincen Azzaro (San Antonio) |
| Guillermo Gracida, Jr (Palm Beach) | T. Fernandez-Llorente (Palm Beach) |
| Bautista Heguy (Palm Beach) | Ignacio Heguy (Palm Beach) |
| Eduardo Heguy (Palm Beach) | Esteban Panelo (Hidden Pond) |
| Gonzalo Heguy (Myopia) | Gonzalo Pieres (Palm Beach) |
| Marcos Heguy (Palm Beach) | Owen R. Rinehart (Palm Beach) |
| Alberto Heguy, Jr (Palm Beach) | Martin Zubia (Palm Beach) |
| Christian LaPrida (Palm Beach) | |
| Juan Ignacio Merlos (Palm Beach) | |
| Sebastian Merlos (Aiken) | |
| Ernesto Trotz (Palm Beach) | |

# Rodeo

## All-Around

| | | | |
|---|---|---|---|
| 1929....Earl Thode | 1947....Todd Whatley | 1963....Dean Oliver | 1979....Tom Ferguson |
| 1930....Clay Carr | 1948....Gerald Roberts | 1964....Dean Oliver | 1980....Paul Tierney |
| 1931....John Schneider | 1949....Jim Shoulders | 1965....Dean Oliver | 1981....Jimmie Cooper |
| 1932....Donald Nesbit | 1950....Bill Linderman | 1966....Larry Mahan | 1982....Chris Lybbert |
| 1933....Clay Carr | 1951....Casey Tibbs | 1967....Larry Mahan | 1983....Roy Cooper |
| 1934....Leonard Ward | 1952....Harry Tompkins | 1968....Larry Mahan | 1984....Dee Picket |
| 1935....Everett Bowman | 1953....Bill Linderman | 1969....Larry Mahan | 1985....Lewis Feild |
| 1936....John Bowman | 1954....Buck Rutherford | 1970....Larry Mahan | 1986....Lewis Feild |
| 1937....Everett Bowman | 1955....Casey Tibbs | 1971....Phil Lyne | 1987....Lewis Feild |
| 1938....Burel Mulkey | 1956....Jim Shoulders | 1972....Phil Lyne | 1988....Dave Appleton |
| 1939....Paul Carney | 1957....Jim Shoulders | 1973....Larry Mahan | 1989....Ty Murray |
| 1940....Fritz Truan | 1958....Jim Shoulders | 1974....Tom Ferguson | 1990....Ty Murray |
| 1941....Homer Pettigrew | 1959....Jim Shoulders | 1975....Tom Ferguson | 1991....Ty Murray |
| 1942....Gerald Roberts | 1960....Harry Tompkins | 1976....Tom Ferguson | 1992....Ty Murray |
| 1943....Louis Brooks | 1961....Benny Reynolds | 1977....Tom Ferguson | 1993....Ty Murray |
| 1944....Louis Brooks | 1962....Tom Nesmith | 1978....Tom Ferguson | 1994....Ty Murray |

## Saddle Bronc Riding

| | | | |
|---|---|---|---|
| 1929....Earl Thode | 1947....Carl Olson | 1963....Guy Weeks | 1979....Bobby Berger |
| 1930....Clay Carr | 1948....Gene Pruett | 1964....Marty Wood | 1980....Clint Johnson |
| 1931....Earl Thode | 1949....Casey Tibbs | 1965....Shawn Davis | 1981....B. Gjermundson |
| 1932....Peter Knight | 1950....Bill Linderman | 1966....Marty Wood | 1982....Monty Henson |
| 1933....Peter Knight | 1951....Casey Tibbs | 1967....Shawn Davis | 1983....B. Gjermundson |
| 1934....Leonard Ward | 1952....Casey Tibbs | 1968....Shawn Davis | 1984....B. Gjermundson |
| 1935....Peter Knight | 1953....Casey Tibbs | 1969....Bill Smith | 1985....B. Gjermundson |
| 1936....Peter Knight | 1954....Casey Tibbs | 1970....Dennis Reiners | 1986....Bud Munroe |
| 1937....Burel Mulkey | 1955....DebCopenhaver | 1971....Bill Smith | 1987....Clint Johnson |
| 1938....Burel Mulkey | 1956....DebCopenhaver | 1972....Mel Hyland | 1988....Clint Johnson |
| 1939....Fritz Truan | 1957....Alvin Nelson | 1973....Bill Smith | 1989....Clint Johnson |
| 1940....Fritz Truan | 1958....Marty Wood | 1974....John McBeth | 1990....Robert Etbauer |
| 1941....Doff Aber | 1959....Casey Tibbs | 1975....Monty Henson | 1991....Robert Etbauer |
| 1942....Doff Aber | 1960....Enoch Walker | 1976....Monty Henson | 1992....Billy Etbauer |
| 1943....Louis Brooks | 1961....Winston Bruce | 1977....Bobby Berger | 1993....Dan Mortensen |
| 1944....Louis Brooks | 1962....Kenny McLean | 1978....Joe Marvel | 1994....Dan Mortensen |

## Bareback Riding

| | | | |
|---|---|---|---|
| 1932....Smoky Snyder | 1950....Jim Shoulders | 1966....Paul Mayo | 1982....Bruce Ford |
| 1933....Nate Waldrum | 1951....Casey Tibbs | 1967....Clyde Varnvoras | 1983....Bruce Ford |
| 1934....Leonard Ward | 1952....Harry Tompkins | 1968....Clyde Vamvoras | 1984....Larry Peabody |
| 1935....Frank Schneider | 1953....Eddy Akridge | 1969....Gary Tucker | 1985....Lewis Feild |
| 1936....Smoky Snyder | 1954....Eddy Akridge | 1970....Paul Mayo | 1986....Lewis Feild |
| 1937....Paul Carney | 1955....Eddy Adridge | 1971....Joe Alexander | 1987....Bruce Ford |
| 1938....Pete Grubb | 1956....Jim Shoulders | 1972....Joe Alexander | 1988....Marvin Garrett |
| 1939....Paul Carney | 1957....Jim Shoulders | 1973....Joe Alexander | 1989....Marvin Garrett |
| 1940....Carl Dossey | 1958....Jim Shoulders | 1974....Joe Alexander | 1990....Chuck Logue |
| 1941....George Mills | 1959....Jack Buschbom | 1975....Joe Alexander | 1991....Clint Corey |
| 1942....Louis Brooks | 1960....Jack Buschbom | 1976....Joe Alexander | 1992....Wayne Herman |
| 1943....Bill Linderman | 1961....Eddy Akridge | 1977....Joe Alexander | 1993....Deb Greenough |
| 1944....Louis Brooks | 1962....Ralph Buell | 1978....Bruce Ford | 1994....Marvin Garrett |
| 1947....Larry Finley | 1963....John Hawkins | 1979....Bruce Ford | |
| 1948....Sonny Tureman | 1964....Jim Houston | 1980....Bruce Ford | |
| 1949....Jack Buschbom | 1965....Jim Houston | 1981....J.C. Trujillo | |

## Bull Riding

| | | | |
|---|---|---|---|
| 1929....John Schneider | 1944....Ken Roberts | 1963....Bill Kornell | 1980....Don Gay |
| 1930....John Schneider | 1947....Wag Blessing | 1964....Bob Wegner | 1981....Don Gay |
| 1931....Smokey Snyder | 1948....Harry Tompkins | 1965....Larry Mahan | 1982.....Charles Sampson |
| 1932....John Schneider | 1949....Harry Tompkins | 1966....Ronnie Rossen | 1983....Cody Snyder |
| 1932....Smokey Snyder | 1950....Harry Tompkins | 1967....Larry Mahan | 1984....Don Gay |
|         John Schneider | 1951....Jim Shoulders | 1968....George Paul | 1985....Ted Nuce |
| 1933....Frank Schneider | 1952....Harry Tompkins | 1969....Doug Brown | 1986....Tuff Hedeman |
| 1934....Frank Schneider | 1953....Todd Whatley | 1970....Gary Leffew | 1987....Lane Frost |
| 1935....Smokey Snyder | 1954....Jim Shoulders | 1971....Bill Nelson | 1988....Jim Sharp |
| 1936....Smokey Snyder | 1955....Jim Shoulders | 1972....John Quintana | 1989....Tuff Hedeman |
| 1937....Smokey Snyder | 1956....Jim Shoulders | 1973....Bobby Steiner | 1990....Jim Sharp |
| 1938....Kid Fletcher | 1957....Jim Shoulders | 1974....Don Gay | 1991....Tuff Hedeman |
| 1939....Dick Griffith | 1958....Jim Shoulders | 1975....Don Gay | 1992....Cody Custer |
| 1940....Dick Griffith | 1959....Jim Shoulders | 1976....Don Gay | 1993....Ty Murray |
| 1941....Dick Griffith | 1960....Harry Tompkins | 1977....Don Gay | 1994....Daryl Mills |
| 1942....Dick Griffith | 1961....Ronnie Rossen | 1978....Don Gay | |
| 1943....Ken Roberts | 1962....Freckles Brown | 1979....Don Gay | |

## Calf Roping

| | | | |
|---|---|---|---|
| 1929....Everett Bowman | 1939....Toots Mansfield | 1951....Don McLaughlin | 1961....Dean Oliver |
| 1930....Jake McClure | 1940....Toots Mansfield | 1952....Don McLaughlin | 1962....Dean Oliver |
| 1931....Herb Meyers | 1941....Toots Mansfield | 1953....Don McLaughlin | 1963....Dean Oliver |
| 1932.....Richard Merchant | 1942....Clyde Burk | 1954....Don McLaughlin | 1964....Dean Oliver |
| 1933....Bill McFarlane | 1943....Toots Mansfield | 1955....Dean Oliver | 1965....Glen Franklin |
| 1934....Irby Mundy | 1944....Clyde Burk | 1956....Ray Wharton | 1966....Junior Garrison |
| 1935....Everett Bowman | 1947....Troy Fort | 1957....Don McLaughlin | 1967....Glen Franklin |
| 1936....Clyde Burk | 1948....Toots Mansfield | 1958....Dean Oliver | 1968....Glen Franklin |
| 1937....Everett Bowman | 1949....Troy Fort | 1959....Jim Bob Altizer | 1969....Dean Oliver |
| 1938....Burel Mulkey | 1950....Toots Mansfield | 1960....Dean Oliver | |

## Calf Roping *(Cont.)*

| | | | |
|---|---|---|---|
| 1970....Junior Garrison | 1977....Roy Cooper | 1984....Roy Cooper | 1991....Fred Whitfield |
| 1971....Phil Lyne | 1978....Roy Cooper | 1985....Joe Beaver | 1992....Joe Beaver |
| 1972....Phil Lyne | 1979....Paul Tierney | 1986....Chris Lybbert | 1993....Joe Beaver |
| 1973....Ernie Taylor | 1980....Roy Cooper | 1987....Joe Beaver | 1994....Herbert Theriot |
| 1974....Tom Ferguson | 1981....Roy Cooper | 1988....Joe Beaver | |
| 1975....Jeff copenhaver | 1982....Roy Cooper | 1989....Rabe Rabon | |
| 1976....Roy Cooper | 1983....Roy Cooper | 1990....Troy Pruitt | |

## Steer Wrestling

| | | | |
|---|---|---|---|
| 1929....Gene Ross | 1947....Todd Whatley | 1963....Jim Bynum | 1979....Stan Williamson |
| 1930....Everett Bowman | 1948....Homer Pettigrew | 1964....C.R. Boucher | 1980....Butch Myers |
| 1931....Gene Ross | 1949....Bill McGuire | 1965....Harley May | 1981....Byron Walker |
| 1932....Hugh Bennett | 1950....Bill Linderman | 1966....Jack Roddy | 1982....Stan Williamson |
| 1933....Everett Bowman | 1951....Dub Phillips | 1967....Roy Duvall | 1983....Joel Edmondson |
| 1934....Shorty Ricker | 1952....Harley May | 1968....Jack Roddy | 1984....John W. Jones |
| 1935....Everett Bowman | 1953....Ross Dollarhide | 1969....Roy Duvall | 1985....Ote Berry |
| 1936....Jack Kerschner | 1954....James Bynum | 1970....John W. Jones | 1986....Steve Duhon |
| 1937....Gene Ross | 1955....Benny Combs | 1971....Billy Hale | 1987....Steve Duhon |
| 1938....Everett Bowman | 1956....Harley May | 1972....Roy Duvall | 1988....John W. Jones |
| 1939....Harry Hart | 1957....Clark McEntire | 1973....Bob Marshall | 1989....John W. Jones |
| 1940....Homer Pettigrew | 1958....James Bynum | 1974....Tommy Puryear | 1990....Ote Berry |
| 1941....Hub Whiteman | 1959....Harry Charters | 1975....F. Shepperson | 1991....Ote Berry |
| 1942....Homer Pettigrew | 1960....Bob A. Robinson | 1976....Tom Ferguson | 1992....Mark Roy |
| 1943....Homer Pettigrew | 1961....Jim Bynum | 1977....Larry Ferguson | 1993....Steve Duhon |
| 1944....Homer Pettigrew | 1962....Tom Nesmith | 1978....Byron Walker | 1994....Blaine Pederson |

## Team Roping

| | | | |
|---|---|---|---|
| 1929....Charles Maggini | 1944....Murphy Chaney | 1963....Les Hirdes | 1980....Tee Woolman |
| 1930....Norman Cowan | 1947....Jim Brister | 1964....Bill Hamilton | 1981....Walt Woodard |
| 1931....Arthur Beloat | 1948....Joe Glenn | 1965....Jim Rodriguez Jr. | 1982....Tee Woolman |
| 1932....Ace Gardner | 1949....Ed Yanez | 1966....Ken Luman | 1983....Leo Camarillo |
| 1933....Roy Adams | 1950....Buck Sorrels | 1967....Joe Glenn | 1984....Dee Pickett |
| 1934....Andy Jauregui | 1951....Olan Sims | 1968....Art Arnold | 1985....Jake Barnes |
| 1935....Lawrence Conltk | 1952....Asbury Schell | 1969....Jerold Camarillo | 1986....Clay O. Cooper |
| 1936....John Rhodes | 1953....Ben Johnson | 1970....John Miller | 1987....Clay O. Cooper |
| 1937....Asbury Schell | 1954....Eddie Schell | 1971....John Miller | 1988....Jake Barnes |
| 1938....John Rhodes | 1955....Vern Castro | 1972....Leo Camarillo | 1989....Jake Barnes |
| 1939....Asbury Schell | 1956....Dale Smith | 1973....Leo Camarillo | 1990....Allen Bach |
| 1940....Pete Grubb | 1957....Dale Smith | 1974....H.P. Evetts | 1991....Bob Harris |
| 1941....Jim Hudson | 1958....Ted Ashworth | 1975....Leo Camarillo | 1992....Clay O. Cooper |
| 1942....Verne Castro | 1959....Jim Rodriguez Jr. | 1976....Leo Camarillo | 1993....Bobby Hurley |
| ........Vic Castro | 1960....Jim Rodriguez Jr. | 1977....Jerold Camarillo | 1994....Jake Barnes |
| 1943....Mark Hull | 1961....Al Hooper | 1978....Doyle Gellerman | ........Clay O. Cooper |
| ........Leonard Block | 1962....Jim Rodriguez Jr. | 1979....Allen Bach | |

## Steer Roping

| | | | |
|---|---|---|---|
| 1929....Charles Maggini | 1946....Everett Shaw | 1963....Don McLaughlin | 1980....Guy Allen |
| 1930....Clay Carr | 1947....Ike Rude | 1964....Sonny Davis | 1981....Arnold Felts |
| 1931....Andy Jauregui | 1948....Everett Shaw | 1965....Sonney Wright | 1982....Guy Allen |
| 1932....George Weir | 1949....Shoat Webster | 1966....Sonny Davis | 1983....Roy Cooper |
| 1933....John Bowman | 1950....Shoat Webster | 1967....Jim Bob Altizer | 1984....Guy Allen |
| 1934....John McEntire | 1951....Everett Shaw | 1968....Sonny Davis | 1985....Jim Davis |
| 1935....Richard Merchant | 1952....Buddy Neal | 1969....Walter Arnold | 1986....Jim Davis |
| 1936....John Bowman | 1953....Ike Rude | 1970....Don McLaughlin | 1987....Shaun Burchett |
| 1937....Everett Bowman | 1954....Shoat Webster | 1971....Olin Young | 1988....Shaun Burchett |
| 1938....Hugh Bennett | 1955....Shoat Webster | 1972....Allen Keller | 1989....Guy Allen |
| 1939....Dick Truitt | 1956....Jim Snively | 1973....Roy Thompson | 1990....Phil Lyne |
| 1940....Clay Carr | 1957....Clark McEntire | 1974....Olin Young | 1991....Guy Allen |
| 1941....Ike Rude | 1958....Clark McEntire | 1975....Roy Thompson | 1992....Guy Allen |
| 1942....King Merrit | 1959....Everett Shaw | 1976....Marvin Cantrell | 1993....Guy Allen |
| 1943....Tom Rhodes | 1960....Don McLaughlin | 1977....Buddy Cockrell | 1994....Guy Allen |
| 1944....Tom Rhodes | 1961....Clark McEntire | 1978....Sonny Worrell | |
| 1945....Everett Shaw | 1962....Everett Shaw | 1979....Gary Good | |

Note: In 1945-46 champions were crowned only in Steer Roping.

# Rowing

## National Collegiate Rowing Champions
### MEN'S EIGHT

| | | |
|---|---|---|
| 1982 ...............Yale | 1987 ...............Harvard | 1992 ...............Harvard |
| 1983 ...............Harvard | 1988 ...............Harvard | 1993 ...............Brown |
| 1984 ...............Washington | 1989 ...............Harvard | 1994 ...............Brown |
| 1985 ...............Harvard | 1990 ...............Wisconsin | 1995 ...............Brown |
| 1986 ...............Wisconsin | 1991 ...............Pennsylvania | |

### WOMEN'S EIGHT

| | | |
|---|---|---|
| 1979 ...............Yale | 1985 ...............Washington | 1991 ...............Boston University |
| 1980 ...............California | 1986 ...............Wisconsin | 1992 ...............Boston University |
| 1981 ...............Washington | 1987 ...............Washington | 1993 ...............Princeton |
| 1982 ...............Washington | 1988 ...............Washington | 1994 ...............Princeton |
| 1983 ...............Washington | 1989 ...............Cornell | 1995 ...............Princeton |
| 1984 ...............Washington | 1990 ...............Princeton | |

# Rugby

## National Men's Club Championship

| Year | Winner | Runner-Up | Year | Winner | Runner-Up |
|---|---|---|---|---|---|
| 1979 .......Old Blues (Calif.) | St Louis Falcons | | 1988 .......Old Mission Beach AC | Milwaukee | |
| 1980 .......Old Blues (Calif.) | St. Louis Falcons | | 1989 .......Old Mission Beach AC | Philly/Whitemarsh | |
| 1981 .......Old Blues (Calif.) | Old Blue (NY) | | 1990 .......Denver Barbos | Old Blues (CA) | |
| 1982 .......Old Blues (Calif.) | Denver Barbos | | 1991 .......Old Mission Beach AC | Washington | |
| 1983 .......Old Blues (Calif.) | Dallas Harlequins | | 1992 .......Old Blues (Calif.) | Mystic River (MA) | |
| 1984 .......Dallas Harlequins | Los Angeles | | 1993 .......Old Mission Beach AC | Milwaukee | |
| 1985 .......Milwaukee | Denver Barbos | | 1994 .......Old Mission Beach AC | Life College (GA) | |
| 1986 .......Old Blues (Calif.) | Old Blue (NY) | | 1995 .......Potomac Athletic Club | Old Mission Beach | |
| 1987 .......Old Blues (Calif.) | Pittsburgh | | | | |

## National Men's Collegiate Championship

| Year | Winner | Runner-Up | Year | Winner | Runner-Up |
|---|---|---|---|---|---|
| 1980 .......California | Air Force | | 1988 .......California | Dartmouth | |
| 1981 .......California | Harvard | | 1989 .......Air Force | Long Beach | |
| 1982 .......California | Life College | | 1990 .......Air Force | Army | |
| 1983 .......California | Air Force | | 1991 .......California | Army | |
| 1984 .......Harvard | Colorado | | 1992 .......California | Army | |
| 1985 .......California | Maryland | | 1993 .......California | Air Force | |
| 1986 .......California | Dartmouth | | 1994 .......California | Navy | |
| 1987 .......San Diego State | Air Force | | 1995 .......California | Air Force | |

## World Cup Championship

| Year | Winner | Runner-Up | Year | Winner | Runner-Up |
|---|---|---|---|---|---|
| 1987 .......New Zealand | France | | 1995 .......South Africa | New Zealand | |
| 1991 .......Australia | England | | | | |

# Sailing

## America's Cup Champions
### SCHOONERS AND J-CLASS BOATS

| Year | Winner | Skipper | Series | Loser | Skipper |
|---|---|---|---|---|---|
| 1851.......America | Richard Brown | | | | |
| 1870.......Magic | Andrew Comstock | 1-0 | Cambria, Great Britain | J. Tannock |
| 1871.......Columbia (2-1) | Nelson Comstock | 4-1 | Livonia, Great Britain | J. R. Woods |
| Sappho (2-0) | Sam Greenwood | | | | |
| 1876.......Madeleine | Josephus Williams | 2-0 | Countess of Dufferin, Canada | J. E. Ellsworth |
| 1881.......Mischief | Nathanael Clock | 2-0 | Atalanta, Canada | Alexander Cuthbert |
| 1885.......Puritan | Aubrey Crocker | 2-0 | Genesta, Great Britain | John Carter |
| 1886.......Mayflower | Martin Stone | 2-0 | Galatea, Great Britain | Dan Bradford |
| 1887.......Volunteer | Henry Haff | 2-0 | Thistle, Great Britain | John Barr |
| 1893.......Vigilant | William Hansen | 3-0 | Valkyrie II, Great Britain | William Granfield |
| 1895.......Defender | Henry Haff | 3-0 | Valkyrie III, Great Britain | William Granfield |
| 1899.......Columbia | Charles Barr | 3-0 | Shamrock I, Great Britain | Archie Hogarth |
| 1901.......Columbia | Charles Barr | 3-0 | Shamrock II, Great Britain | E. A. Sycamore |

## America's Cup Champions *(Cont.)*

### SCHOONERS AND J-CLASS BOATS *(Cont.)*

| Year | Winner | Skipper | Series | Loser | Skipper |
|------|--------|---------|--------|-------|---------|
| 1903 | Reliance | Charles Barr | 3-0 | Shamrock III, Great Britain | Bob Wringe |
| 1920 | Resolute | Charles F. Adams | 3-2 | Shamrock IV, Great Britain | William Burton |
| 1930 | Enterprise | Harold Vanderbilt | 4-0 | Shamrock V, Great Britain | Ned Heard |
| 1934 | Rainbow | Harold Vanderbilt | 4-2 | Endeavour, Great Britain | T. O. M. Sopwith |
| 1937 | Ranger | Harold Vanderbilt | 4-0 | Endeavour II, Great Britain | T. O. M. Sopwith |

### 12-METER BOATS

| Year | Winner | Skipper | Series | Loser | Skipper |
|------|--------|---------|--------|-------|---------|
| 1958 | Columbia | Briggs Cunningham | 4-0 | Sceptre, Great Britain | Graham Mann |
| 1962 | Weatherly | Bus Mosbacher | 4-1 | Gretel, Australia | Jock Sturrock |
| 1964 | Constellation | Bob Bavier & Eric Ridder | 4-0 | Sovereign, Australia | Peter Scott |
| 1967 | Intrepid | Bus Mosbacher | 4-0 | Dame Pattie, Australia | Jock Sturrock |
| 1970 | Intrepid | Bill Ficker | 4-1 | Gretel II, Australia | Jim Hardy |
| 1974 | Courageous | Ted Hood | 4-0 | Southern Cross, Australia | John Cuneo |
| 1977 | Courageous | Ted Turner | 4-0 | Australia | Noel Robins |
| 1980 | Freedom | Dennis Conner | 4-1 | Australia | Jim Hardy |
| 1983 | Australia II | John Bertrand | 4-3 | Liberty, United States | Dennis Conner |
| 1987 | Stars & Stripes | Dennis Conner | 4-0 | Kookaburra III, Australia | Iain Murray |

### 60-FOOT CATAMARAN VS 133-FOOT MONOHULL

| Year | Winner | Skipper | Series | Loser | Skipper |
|------|--------|---------|--------|-------|---------|
| 1988 | Stars & Stripes | Dennis Conner | 2-0 | New Zealand | David Barnes |

### 75-FOOT MONOHULL (IACC)

| Year | Winner | Skipper | Series | Loser | Skipper |
|------|--------|---------|--------|-------|---------|
| 1992 | America[3] | Bill Koch | 4-1 | Il Moro di Vinezia, Italy | Paul Cayard |
| 1995 | Black Magic I | Russell Coutts | 5-0 | Young America, United States | Dennis Conner |

Note: Winning entries have been from the United States every year but two; in 1983 an Australian vessel won, and in 1995 a vessel from New Zealand won.

## Shooting World Champions

### Men

#### 50M FREE RIFLE PRONE

1947 .....O. Sannes, Norway
1949 .....A.C. Jackson, United States
1952 .....A.C. Jackson, United States
1954 .....G. Boa, Canada
1958 .....M. Nordquist
1962 .....K. Wenk, West Germany
1966 .....D. Boyd, United States
1970 .....M. Fiess, S. Africa
1974 .....K. Bulan, Czech.
1978 .....A. Allan, Great Britain
1982 .....V. Danilschenko, Soviet Union
1986 .....S. Bereczky, Hungary
1990 .....V. Bochkarev, Sov Union
1994 .....Venjie Li, China

#### AIR RIFLE

1966 .....G. Kümmet, W. Germany
1970 .....G. Kusterman, W. Germ.
1974 .....E. Pedzisz, Poland
1978 .....O. Schlipf, W. Germany
1979 .....K. Hillenbrand
1981 .....F. Bessy, France
1982 .....F. Rettkowski, E. Germ.
1983 .....P. Heberle, France
1985 .....P. Heberle, France
1986 .....H. Riederer, W. Germany
1987 .....K. Ivanov, Soviet Union

#### AIR RIFLE *(Cont.)*

1989 .....J. P. Amet, France
1990 .....H. Riederer, W. Germany
1994 .....Boris Polak, Israel

#### MEN'S TRAP

1929 .....De Lumniczer, Hungary
1930 .....M. Arie, United States
1931 .....Kiszkurno, Poland
1933 .....De Lumniczer, Hungary
1934 .....A. Montagh, Hungary
1935 .....R. Sack, W. Germany
1936 .....Kiszkurno, Poland
1937 .....K. Huber, Finland
1938 .....I. Strassburger, Hungary
1939 .....De Lumniczer, Hungary
1947 .....H. Liljedahl, Sweden
1949 .....F. Rocchi, Argentina
1950 .....C. Sala, Italy
1952 .....P.J. Grossi, Argentina
1954 .....C. Merlo, Italy
1958 .....F. Eisenlauer, United States
1959 .....H. Badravi, Egypt
1961 .....E. Mattarelli, Italy
1962 .....W. Zimenko, Soviet Union
1965 .....J.E. Lire, Chile
1966 .....K. Jones, United States
1967 .....G. Rennard, Belgium
1969 .....E. Mattarelli, Italy
1970 .....M. Carrega, France

#### MEN'S TRAP *(Cont.)*

1971 .....M. Carrega, France
1973 .....A. Andrushkin, Soviet Union
1974 .....M. Carrega, France
1975 .....J. Primrose, Canada
1977 .....E. Azkue, Spain
1978 .....E. Vallduvi, Spain
1979 .....M. Carrega, France
1981 .....A. Asanov, Soviet Union
1982 .....L. Giovonnetti, Italy
1983 .....J. Primrose, Canada
1985 .....M. Bednarik, Czech.
1986 .....M. Benarik, Czech.
1987 .....D. Monakov, Soviet Union
1989 .....M. Venturini, Italy
1990 .....J. Damne, E. Germany
1994 .....Dmitriy Monakov, Ukraine
1995 .....G. Pellielo, Italy

#### THREE POSITION RIFLE

1929 .....O. Ericsson, Sweden
1930 .....Petersen, Denmark
1931 .....Amundson, Norway
1933 .....De Lisle, France
1935 .....Leskinnen, Finland
1937 .....Mazoyer, France
1939 .....Steigelmann, Germany
1947 .....I. H. Erben, Sweden
1949 .....P. Janhonen, Finland
1952 .....Kongshaug, Norway

## Men *(Cont.)*

### THREE POSITION RIFLE *(Cont.)*
1954 .....A. Bugdanov,
Soviet Union
1958 .....Itkis, Soviet Union
1962 .....G. Anderson,
United States

### THREE POSITION RIFLE *(Cont.)*
1966 .....G. Anderson,
United States
1970 .....Parkhimovitch,
Soviet Union
1974 .....L. Wigger, United States

### THREE POSITION RIFLE *(Cont.)*
1978 .....E. Svensson, Sweden
1982 .....K. Ivanov, Soviet Union
1986 .....P. Heinz, W. Germany
1990 .....E. C. Lee, S. Korea
1994 .....Petr Kurka, Czech Republic

## Women

### THREE POSITION RIFLE
1966 .....M. Thompson,
United States
1970 .....M. Thompson Murdock,
United States
1974 .....A. Pelova, Bulgaria
1978 .....W. Oliver, United States
1982 .....M. Helbig, E. Germany
1986 .....V. Letcheva, Bulgaria
1990 .....V. Letcheva, Bulgaria
1994 .....A. Maloukhina, Russia

### AIR RIFLE
1970 .......V. Cherkasque, Soviet Union
1974 .....T. Ratkinova, Soviet Union
1978 .....W. Oliver, United States
1979 .....K. Monez, United States
1981 .....S. Romaristova,
Soviet Union

### AIR RIFLE *(Cont.)*
1982 .....S. Lang, W. Germany
1983 .....M. Helbig, E. Germany
1985 .....E. Forian, Hungary
1986 .....V. Letcheva, Bulgaria
1987 .....V. Letcheva, Bulgaria
1989 .....V. Letcheva, Bulgaria
1990 .....E.Joc, Hungary
1994 .....S. Pfeilschifter, Germany

### SPORT PISTOL
1966 .....N. Rasskazova,
Soviet Union
1970.....N. Stoljarova, Soviet Union
1974.....N. Stoljarova, Soviet Union
1978 .....K. Dyer, United States
1982 .....P. Balogh, Hungary
1986 .....M. Dobrantcheva,
Soviet Union

### SPORT PISTOL *(Cont.)*
1990 .....M. Logvinenko, Sov Union
1994 .....Soon Hee Boo, S. Korea

### AIR PISTOL
1970 .....S. Carroll, United States
1974 .....Z. Simonian, Soviet Union
1978 .....K. Hansson, Sweden
1979 .....R. Fox, United States
1981 .....N. Kalinina, Soviet Union
1982 .....M. Dobrantcheva,
Soviet Union
1983 .....K. Bodin, Sweden
1985 .....M. Dobrantcheva, Sov Union
1986 .....A. Völker, E. Germany
1987 .....J. Brajkovic, Yugoslavia
1989 .....N. Salukvadse,
Soviet Union
1990 .....Jasna Sekaric, Yugoslavia
1994 .....Jasna Sekaric, IOP

## Men
### MAJOR FAST PITCH

| | | | |
|---|---|---|---|
| 1933 | J. L. Gill Boosters, Chicago | 1965 | Sealmasters, Aurora, IL |
| 1934 | Ke-Nash-A, Kenosha, WI | 1966 | Clearwater (FL) Bombers |
| 1935 | Crimson Coaches, Toledo, OH | 1967 | Sealmasters, Aurora, IL |
| 1936 | Kodak Park, Rochester, NY | 1968 | Clearwater (FL) Bombers |
| 1937 | Briggs Body Team, Detroit | 1969 | Raybestos Cardinals, Stratford, CT |
| 1938 | The Pohlers, Cincinnati | 1970 | Raybestos Cardinals, Stratford, CT |
| 1939 | Carr's Boosters, Covington, KY | 1971 | Welty Way, Cedar Rapids, IA |
| 1940 | Kodak Park, Rochester, NY | 1972 | Raybestos Cardinals, Stratford, CT |
| 1941 | Bendix Brakes, South Bend, IN | 1973 | Clearwater (FL) Bombers |
| 1942 | Deep Rock Oilers, Tulsa | 1974 | Gianella Bros, Santa Rosa, CA |
| 1943 | Hammer Air Field, Fresno | 1975 | Rising Sun Hotel, Reading, PA |
| 1944 | Hammer Air Field, Fresno | 1976 | Raybestos Cardinals, Stratford, CT |
| 1945 | Zollner Pistons, Fort Wayne, IN | 1977 | Billard Barbell, Reading, PA |
| 1946 | Zollner Pistons, Fort Wayne, IN | 1978 | Billard Barbell, Reading, PA |
| 1947 | Zollner Pistons, Fort Wayne, IN | 1979 | McArdle Pontiac/Cadillac, Midland, MI |
| 1948 | Briggs Beautyware, Detroit | 1980 | Peterbilt Western, Seattle |
| 1949 | Tip Top Tailors, Toronto | 1981 | Archer Daniels Midland, Decatur, IL |
| 1950 | Clearwater (FL) Bombers | 1982 | Peterbilt Western, Seattle |
| 1951 | Dow Chemical, Midland, MI | 1983 | Franklin Cardinals, Stratford, CT |
| 1952 | Briggs Beautyware, Detroit | 1984 | California Kings, Merced, CA |
| 1953 | Briggs Beautyware, Detroit | 1985 | Pay'n Pak, Seattle |
| 1954 | Clearwater (FL) Bombers | 1986 | Pay'n Pak, Seattle |
| 1955 | Raybestos Cardinals, Stratford, CT | 1987 | Pay'n Pak, Seattle |
| 1956 | Clearwater (FL) Bombers | 1988 | TransAire, Elkhart, IN |
| 1957 | Clearwater (FL) Bombers | 1989 | Penn Corp, Sioux City, IA |
| 1958 | Raybestos Cardinals, Stratford, CT | 1990 | Penn Corp, Sioux City, IA |
| 1959 | Sealmasters, Aurora, IL | 1991 | Guanella Brothers, Rohnert Park, CA |
| 1960 | Clearwater (FL) Bombers | 1992 | Natl Health Care Disc, Sioux City, IA |
| 1961 | Sealmasters, Aurora, IL | 1993 | Natl Health Care Disc, Sioux City, IA |
| 1962 | Clearwater (FL) Bombers | 1994 | Decatur Pride, Decatur, IL |
| 1963 | Clearwater (FL) Bombers | 1995 | Decatur Pride, Decatur, IL |
| 1964 | Burch Tool, Detroit | | |

# Softball

## Men *(Cont.)*
### SUPER SLOW PITCH

1981...............Howard's/Western Steer, Denver, NC
1982...............Jerry's Catering, Miami, Fla.
1983...............Howard's/Western Steer, Denver, NC
1984...............Howard's/Western Steer, Denver, NC
1985...............Steele's Sports, Grafton, OH
1986...............Steele's Sports, Grafton, OH
1987...............Steele's Sports, Grafton, OH
1988...............Starpath, Monticello, KY

1989...............Ritch's Salvage, Harrisburg, NC
1990...............Steele's Silver Bullets, Grafton, OH
1991...............Sunbelt/Worth, Centerville, GA
1992...............Ritch's/Superior, Windsor Locks, CT
1993...............Ritch's/Superior, Windsor Locks, CT
1994...............Bell Corp, Tampa, Fla.
1995...............Lighthouse Worth, Stone Mtn., GA

### MAJOR SLOW PITCH

1953...............Shields Construction, Newport, KY
1954...............Waldneck's Tavern, Cincinnati
1955...............Lang Pet Shop, Covington, KY
1956...............Gatliff Auto Sales, Newport, KY
1957...............Gatliff Auto Sales, Newport, KY
1958...............East Side Sports, Detroit
1959...............Yorkshire Restaurant, Newport, KY
1960...............Hamilton Tailoring, Cincinnati
1961...............Hamilton Tailoring, Cincinnati
1962...............Skip Hogan A.C., Pittsburgh
1963...............Gatliff Auto Sales, Newport, KY
1964...............Skip Hogan A.C., Pittsburgh
1965...............Skip Hogan A.C., Pittsburgh
1966...............Michael's Lounge, Detroit
1967...............Jim's Sport Shop, Pittsburgh
1968...............County Sports, Levittown, NY
1969...............Copper Hearth, Milwaukee
1970...............Little Caesar's, Southgate, MI
1971...............Pile Drivers, Virginia Beach, VA
1972...............Jiffy Club, Louisville, KY
1973...............Howard's Furniture, Denver, NC
1974...............Howard's Furniture, Denver, NC

1975..........Pyramid Cafe, Lakewood, OH
1976..........Warren Motors, Jacksonville, FL
1977..........Nelson Painting, Oklahoma City
1978..........Campbell Carpets, Concord, CA
1979..........Nelco Mfg Co, Oklahoma City
1980..........Campbell Carpets, Concord, CA
1981..........Elite Coating, Gordon, CA
1982..........Triangle Sports, Minneapolis
1983..........No. 1 Electric & Heating, Gastonia, NC
1984..........Lilly Air Systems, Chicago
1985..........Blanton's, Fayetteville, NC
1986..........Non-Ferrous Metals, Cleveland
1987..........Starpath, Monticello, KY
1988..........Bell Corp/FAF, Tampa, FL
1989..........Ritch's Salvage, Harrisburg, NC
1990..........New Construction, Shelbyville, IN
1991..........Riverside Paving, Louisville, KY
1992..........Vernon's, Jacksonville, FL
1993..........Back Porch/Destin Roofing, Destin, FL
1994..........Riverside RAM/Taylor Bros., Louisville, KY
1995..........Riverside/RAM/Taylor/TPS, Louisville, KY

## Women
### MAJOR FAST PITCH

1933..........Great Northerns, Chicago
1934..........Hart Motors, Chicago
1935..........Bloomer Girls, Cleveland
1936..........Nat'l Screw & Mfg, Cleveland
1937..........Nat'l Screw & Mfg, Cleveland
1938..........J. J. Krieg's, Alameda, CA
1939..........J. J. Krieg's, Alameda, CA
1940..........Arizona Ramblers, Phoenix
1941..........Higgins Midgets, Tulsa
1942..........Jax Maids, New Orleans
1943..........Jax Maids, New Orleans
1944..........Lind & Pomeroy, Portland, OR
1945..........Jax Maids, New Orleans
1946..........Jax Maids, New Orleans
1947..........Jax Maids, New Orleans
1948..........Arizona Ramblers, Phoenix
1949..........Arizona Ramblers, Phoenix
1950..........Orange (CA) Lionettes
1951..........Orange (CA) Lionettes
1952..........Orange (CA) Lionettes
1953..........Betsy Ross Rockets, Fresno
1954..........Leach Motor Rockets, Fresno
1955..........Orange (CA) Lionettes
1956..........Orange (CA) Lionettes
1957..........Hacienda Rockets, Fresno
1958..........Raybestos Brakettes, Stratford, CT
1959..........Raybestos Brakettes, Stratford, CT
1960..........Raybestos Brakettes, Stratford, CT
1961..........Gold Sox, Whittier, CA
1962..........Orange (CA) Lionettes
1963..........Raybestos Brakettes, Stratford, CT
1964..........Erv Lind Florists, Portland, OR

1965..........Orange (CA) Lionettes
1966..........Raybestos Brakettes, Stratford, CT
1967..........Raybestos Brakettes, Stratford, CT
1968..........Raybestos Brakettes, Stratford, CT
1969..........Orange (CA) Lionettes
1970..........Orange (CA) Lionettes
1971..........Raybestos Brakettes, Stratford, CT
1972..........Raybestos Brakettes, Stratford, CT
1973..........Raybestos Brakettes, Stratford, CT
1974..........Raybestos Brakettes, Stratford, CT
1975..........Raybestos Brakettes, Stratford, CT
1976..........Raybestos Brakettes, Stratford, CT
1977..........Raybestos Brakettes, Stratford, CT
1978..........Raybestos Brakettes, Stratford, CT
1979..........Sun City (AZ) Saints
1980..........Raybestos Brakettes, Stratford, CT
1981..........Orlando (FL) Rebels
1982..........Raybestos Brakettes, Stratford, CT
1983..........Raybestos Brakettes, Stratford, CT
1984..........Los Angeles Diamonds
1985..........Hi-Ho Brakettes, Stratford, CT
1986..........Southern California Invasion, Los Angeles
1987..........Orange County Majestics, Anaheim, CA
1988..........Hi-Ho Brakettes, Stratford, CT
1989..........Whittier (CA) Raiders
1990..........Raybestos Brakettes, Stratford, CT
1991..........Raybestos Brakettes, Stratford, CT
1992..........Raybestos Brakettes, Stratford, CT
1993..........Redding Rebels, Redding, CA
1994..........Redding Rebels, Redding, CA
1995..........Redding Rebels, Redding, CA

# Softball (Cont.)

## Women (Cont.)

### MAJOR SLOW PITCH

| | |
|---|---|
| 1959..........Pearl Laundry, Richmond, VA | 1978..........Bob Hoffman's Dots, Miami |
| 1960..........Carolina Rockets, High Pt, NC | 1979..........Bob Hoffman's Dots, Miami |
| 1961..........Dairy Cottage, Covington, KY | 1980..........Howard's Rubi-Otts, Graham, NC |
| 1962..........Dana Gardens, Cincinnati | 1981..........Tifton (GA) Tomboys |
| 1963..........Dana Gardens, Cincinnati | 1982..........Richmond (VA) Stompers |
| 1964..........Dana Gardens, Cincinnati | 1983..........Spooks, Anoka, MN |
| 1965..........Art's Acres, Omaha | 1984..........Spooks, Anoka, MN |
| 1966..........Dana Gardens, Cincinnati | 1985..........Key Ford Mustangs, Pensacola, FL |
| 1967..........Ridge Maintenance, Cleveland | 1986..........Sur-Way Tomboys, Tifton, GA |
| 1968..........Escue Pontiac, Cincinnati | 1987..........Key Ford Mustangs, Pensacola, FL |
| 1969..........Converse Dots, Hialeah, FL | 1988..........Spooks, Anoka, MN |
| 1970..........Rutenschruder Floral, Cincinnati | 1989..........Canaan's Illusions, Houston |
| 1971..........Gators, Ft Lauderdale, FL | 1990..........Spooks, Anoka, MN |
| 1972..........Riverside Ford, Cincinnati | 1991..........Kannan's Illusions, San Antonio, TX |
| 1973..........Sweeney Chevrolet, Cincinnati | 1992..........Universal Plastics, Cookeville, TN |
| 1974..........Marks Brothers Dots, Miami | 1993..........Universal Plastics, Cookeville, TN |
| 1975..........Marks Brothers Dots, Miami | 1994..........Universal Plastics, Cookeville, TN |
| 1976..........Sorrento's Pizza, Cincinnati | 1995..........Armed Forces, Sacramento, CA |
| 1977..........Fox Valley Lassies, St Charles, IL | |

# Speed Skating

## All-Round World Champions

### MEN

| | | |
|---|---|---|
| 1891.....Joseph F. Donoghue, US | 1933.....Hans Engnestangen, Nor | 1969.....Dag Fornaes, Norway |
| 1893.....Jaap Eden, Holland | 1934.....Bernt Evensen, Norway | 1970.....Ard Schenk, Holland |
| 1895.....Jaap Eden, Holland | 1935.....Michael Staksrud, Nor. | 1971.....Ard Schenk, Holland |
| 1896.....Jaap Eden, Holland | 1936.....Ivar Ballangrud, Norway | 1972.....Ard Schenk, Holland |
| 1897.....Jack K. McCulloch, Can. | 1937.....Michael Staksrud, Nor. | 1973.....Göran Claeson, Sweden |
| 1898.....Peder Ostlund, Norway | 1938.....Ivar Ballangrud, Norway | 1974.....Sten Stensen, Norway |
| 1899.....Peder Ostlund, Norway | 1939.....Birger Wasenius, Finland | 1975.....Harm Kuipers, Holland |
| 1900.....Edvard Engelsaas, Nor. | 1947.....Lassi Parkkinen, Finland | 1976.....Piet Kleine, Holland |
| 1901.....Franz F. Wathan, Finland | 1948.....Odd Lundberg, Norway | 1977.....Eric Heiden, USA |
| 1904.....Sigurd Mathisen, Norway | 1949.....Kornel Pajor, Hungary | 1978.....Eric Heiden, USA |
| 1905.....C. Coen de Koning, Holl. | 1950.....Hjalmar Andersen, Nor. | 1979.....Eric Heiden, USA |
| 1908.....Oscar Mathisen, Norway | 1951.....Hjalmar Andersen, Nor. | 1980.....Hilbert van der Duin, Holl. |
| 1909.....Oscar Mathisen, Norway | 1952.....Hjalmar Andersen, Nor. | 1981.....Amund Sjobrand, Norway |
| 1910.....Nikolai Strunnikov, Russia | 1953.....Oleg Goncharenko, Sov U | 1982.....Hilbert van der Duin, Holl |
| 1911.....Nikolai Strunnikov, Russia | 1954.....Boris Shilkov, Sov U | 1983.....Rolf Falk-Larssen, Nor. |
| 1912.....Oscar Mathisen, Norway | 1955.....Sigvard Ericsson, Swe. | 1984.....Oleg Bozhev, Sov U |
| 1913.....Oscar Mathisen, Norway | 1956.....Oleg Goncharenko, Sov U | 1985.....Hein Vergeer, Holland |
| 1914.....Oscar Mathisen, Norway | 1957.....Knut Johannesen, Nor. | 1986.....Hein Vergeer, Holland |
| 1922.....Harald Strom, Norway | 1958.....Oleg Goncharenko, Sov U | 1987.....Nikolai Guliaev, Sov U |
| 1923.....Klas Thunberg, Finland | 1959.....Juhani Järvinen, Finland | 1988.....Eric Flaim, USA |
| 1924.....Roald Larsen, Norway | 1960.....Boris Stenin, Sov U | 1989.....Leo Visser, Holland |
| 1925.....Klas Thunberg, Finland | 1961.....Henk van der Grift, Holl. | 1990.....Johann Olav Koss, Nor. |
| 1926.....Ivar Ballangrud, Norway | 1962.....Viktor Kosichkin, Sov U | 1991.....Johann Olav Koss, Nor. |
| 1927.....Bernt Evensen, Norway | 1963.....Jonny Nilsson, Sweden | 1992.....Roberto Sighel, Italy |
| 1928.....Klas Thunberg, Finland | 1964.....Knut Johannesen, Nor. | 1993.....Falko Zandstra, Holland |
| 1929.....Klas Thunberg, Finland | 1965.....Per Ivar Moe, Norway | 1994.....Johann Olav Koss, Nor. |
| 1930.....Michael Staksrud, Nor. | 1966.....Kees Verkerk, Holland | 1995.....Rintje Ritsma, Holland |
| 1931.....Klas Thunberg, Finland | 1967.....Kees Verkerk, Holland | |
| 1932.....Ivar Ballangrud, Norway | 1968.....Fred Anton Maier, Nor. | |

### WOMEN

| | | |
|---|---|---|
| 1936.....Kit Klein, USA | 1951.....Eevi Huttunen, Finland | 1958.....Inga Artamonova, Sov U |
| 1937.....Laila Schou Nilsen, Nor. | 1952.....Lidia Selikhova, Sov U | 1959.....Tamara Rylova, Sov U |
| 1938.....Laila Schou Nilsen, Nor. | 1953.....Khalida Shchegoleeva, | 1960.....Valentina Stenina, Sov U |
| 1939.....Verné Lesche, Finland | Soviet Union | 1961.....Valentina Stenina, Sov U |
| 1947.....Verné Lesche, Finland | 1954.....Lidia Selikhova, Sov U | 1962.....Inga Artamonova, Sov U |
| 1948.....Maria Isakova, Sov U | 1955.....Rimma Zhukova, Sov U | 1963.....Lidia Skoblikova, Sov U |
| 1949.....Maria Isakova, Sov U | 1956.....Sofia Kondakova, Sov U | 1964.....Lidia Skoblikova, Sov U |
| 1950.....Maria Isakova, Sov U | 1957.....Inga Artamonova, Sov U | 1965.....Inga Artamonova, Sov U |

## All-Round World Champions *(Cont.)*
### WOMEN *(Cont.)*

| | | |
|---|---|---|
| 1966 .....Valentina Stenina, Sov U | 1977 .....Vera Bryndzej, Sov U | 1988 .....Karin Kania, GDR |
| 1967 .....Stien Kaiser, Holland | 1978 .....Tatiana Averina, Sov U | 1989 .....Constanze Moser, GDR |
| 1968 .....Stien Kaiser, Holland | 1979 .....Beth Heiden, USA | 1990 .....Jacqueline Börner, GDR |
| 1969 .....Lasma Kauniste, Sov U | 1980 .....Natalia Petruseva, Sov U | 1991 .....Gunda Kleemann, Ger. |
| 1970 .....Atje Keulen-Deelstra, Holl. | 1981 .....Natalia Petruseva, Sov U | 1992 .....Gunda Niemann- |
| 1971 .....Nina Statkevich, Sov U | 1982 .....Karin Busch, GDR | Kleemann, Germany |
| 1972 .....Atje Keulen-Deelstra, Holl. | 1983 .....Andrea Schöne, GDR | 1993 .....Gunda Niemann, Germany |
| 1973 .....Atje Keulen-Deelstra, Holl. | 1984 .....Karin Enke-Busch, GDR | 1994 .....Emese Hunyady, Austria |
| 1974 .....Atje Keulen-Deelstra, Holl. | 1985 .....Andrea Schöne, GDR | 1995 .....Gunda Niemann, Germany |
| 1975 .....Karin Kessow, GDR | 1986 .....Karin Kania-Enke, GDR | |
| 1976 .....Sylvia Burka, Canada | 1987 .....Karin Kania, GDR | |

# Squash

## National Men's Champions

| HARD BALL | | HARD BALL *(Cont.)* | | HARD BALL *(Cont.)* | |
|---|---|---|---|---|---|
| **Year** | **Champion** | **Year** | **Champion** | **Year** | **Champion** |
| 1907 | John A. Miskey | 1943-45 | No tournament | 1978 | Michael Desaulniers |
| 1908 | John A. Miskey | 1946 | Charles M. P. Britton | 1979 | Mario Sanchez |
| 1909 | William L. Freeland | 1947 | Charles M. P. Britton | 1980 | Michael Desaulniers |
| 1910 | John A. Miskey | 1948 | Stanley W. Pearson Jr. | 1981 | Mark Alger |
| 1911 | Francis S. White | 1949 | H. Hunter Lott Jr. | 1982 | John Nimick |
| 1912 | Constantine Hutchins | 1950 | Edward J. Hahn | 1983 | Kenton Jernigan |
| 1913 | Morton L. Newhall | 1951 | Edward J. Hahn | 1984 | Kenton Jernigan |
| 1914 | Constantine Hutchins | 1952 | Harry B. Conlon | 1985 | Kenton Jernigan |
| 1915 | Stanley W. Pearson | 1953 | Ernest Howard | 1986 | Hugh LaBossier |
| 1916 | Stanley W. Pearson | 1954 | G. Diehl Mateer Jr. | 1987 | Frank J. Stanley IV |
| 1917 | Stanley W. Pearson | 1955 | Henri R. Salaun | 1988 | Scott Dulmage |
| 1918-19 | No tournament | 1956 | G. Diehl Mateer Jr. | 1989 | Rodolfo Rodriquez |
| 1920 | Charles C. Peabody | 1957 | Henri R. Salaun | 1990 | Hector Barragan |
| 1921 | Stanley W. Pearson | 1958 | Henri R. Salaun | 1991 | Hector Barragan |
| 1922 | Stanley W. Pearson | 1959 | Benjamin H. | 1992 | Hector Barragan |
| 1923 | Stanley W. Pearson | | Heckscher | 1993 | Hector Barragan |
| 1924 | Gerald Roberts | 1960 | G. Diehl Mateer Jr | 1994 | Hector Barragan |
| 1925 | W. Palmer Dixon | 1961 | Henri R. Salaun | 1995 | W. Keen Butcher |
| 1926 | W. Palmer Dixon | 1962 | Samuel P. Howe III | | |
| 1927 | Myles Baker | 1963 | Benjamin H. | **SOFT BALL** | |
| 1928 | Herbert N. Rawlins Jr. | | Heckscher | **Year** | **Champion** |
| 1929 | J. Lawrence Pool | 1964 | Ralph E. Howe | 1983 | Kenton Jernigan |
| 1930 | Herbert N. Rawlins Jr. | 1965 | Stephen T. Vehslage | 1984 | Kenton Jernigan |
| 1931 | J. Lawrence Pool | 1966 | Victor Niederhoffer | 1985 | Kenton Jernigan |
| 1932 | Beckman H. Pool | 1967 | Samuel P. Howe III | 1986 | Darius Pandole |
| 1933 | Beckman H. Pool | 1968 | Colin Adair | 1987 | Richard Hashim |
| 1934 | Neil J. Sullivan II | 1969 | Anil Nayar | 1988 | John Phelan |
| 1935 | Donald Strachan | 1970 | Anil Nayar | 1989 | Will Carlin |
| 1936 | Germain G. Glidden | 1971 | Colin Adair | 1990 | Syed Jafry |
| 1937 | Germain G. Glidden | 1972 | Victor Niederhoffer | 1991 | Hector Barragan |
| 1938 | Germain G. Glidden | 1973 | Victor Niederhoffer | 1992 | Phil Yarrow |
| 1939 | Donald Strachan | 1974 | Victor Niederhoffer | 1993 | Phil Yarrow |
| 1940 | A. Willing Patterson | 1975 | Victor Niederhoffer | 1994 | Roberto Rosales |
| 1941 | Charles M. P. Britton | 1976 | Peter Briggs | 1995 | A. Martin Clark |
| 1942 | Charles M. P. Britton | 1977 | Thomas E. Page | | |

## National Women's Champions

| Year | Champion | Year | Champion | Year | Champion |
|---|---|---|---|---|---|
| **HARD BALL** | | **HARD BALL (Cont.)** | | **HARD BALL (Cont.)** | |
| 1928 | Eleanora Sears | 1961 | Margaret Varner | 1990 | Demer Holleran |
| 1929 | Margaret Howe | 1962 | Margaret Varner | 1991 | Demer Holleran |
| 1930 | Hazel Wightman | 1963 | Margaret Varner | 1992 | Demer Holleran |
| 1931 | Ruth Banks | 1964 | Ann Wetzel | 1993 | Demer Holleran |
| 1932 | Margaret Howe | 1965 | Joyce Davenport | 1994 | Demer Holleran |
| 1933 | Susan Noel | 1966 | Betty Meade | 1995 | Not held |
| 1934 | Margaret Howe | 1967 | Betty Meade | **SOFT BALL** | |
| 1935 | Margot Lumb | 1968 | Betty Meade | Year | Champion |
| 1936 | Anne Page | 1969 | Joyce Davenport | 1983 | Alicia McConnell |
| 1937 | Anne Page | 1970 | Nina Moyer | 1984 | Julie Harris |
| 1938 | Cecile Bowes | 1971 | Carol Thesieres | 1985 | Sue Clinch |
| 1939 | Anne Page | 1972 | Nina Moyer | 1986 | Julie Harris |
| 1940 | Cecile Bowes | 1973 | Gretchen Spruance | 1987 | Diana Staley |
| 1941 | Cecile Bowes | 1974 | Gretchen Spruance | 1988 | Sara Luther |
| 1942-46 | No tournament | 1975 | Ginny Akabane | 1989 | Nancy Gengler |
| 1947 | Anne Page Homer | 1976 | Gretchen Spruance | 1990 | Joyce Maycock |
| 1948 | Cecile Bowes | 1977 | Gretchen Spruance | 1991 | Ellie Pierce |
| 1949 | Janet Morgan | 1978 | Gretchen Spruance | 1992 | Demer Holleran |
| 1950 | Betty Howe | 1979 | Heather McKay | 1993 | Demer Holleran |
| 1951 | Jane Austin | 1980 | Barbara Maltby | 1994 | Demer Holleran |
| 1952 | Margaret Howe | 1981 | Barbara Maltby | 1995 | Ellie Pierce |
| 1953 | Margaret Howe | 1982 | Alicia McConnell | | |
| 1954 | Lois Dilks | 1983 | Alicia McConnell | | |
| 1955 | Janet Morgan | 1984 | Alicia McConnell | | |
| 1956 | Betty Howe Constable | 1985 | Alicia McConnell | | |
| 1957 | Betty Howe Constable | 1986 | Alicia McConnell | | |
| 1958 | Betty Howe Constable | 1987 | Alicia McConnell | | |
| 1959 | Betty Howe Constable | 1988 | Alicia McConnell | | |
| 1960 | Margaret Varner | 1989 | Demer Holleran | | |

# Triathlon

## Ironman Championship

### MEN

| Date | Winner | Time | Site |
|---|---|---|---|
| 1978 | Gordon Haller | 11:46 | Waikiki Beach |
| 1979 | Tom Warren | 11:15:56 | Waikiki Beach |
| 1980 | Dave Scott | 9:24:33 | Ala Moana Park |
| 1981 | John Howard | 9:38:29 | Kailua-Kona |
| 1982 | Scott Tinley | 9:19:41 | Kailua-Kona |
| 1982 | Dave Scott | 9:08:23 | Kailua-Kona |
| 1983 | Dave Scott | 9:05:57 | Kailua-Kona |
| 1984 | Dave Scott | 8:54:20 | Kailua-Kona |
| 1985 | Scott Tinley | 8:50:54 | Kailua-Kona |
| 1986 | Dave Scott | 8:28:37 | Kailua-Kona |
| 1987 | Dave Scott | 8:34:13 | Kailua-Kona |
| 1988 | Scott Molina | 8:31:00 | Kailua-Kona |
| 1989 | Mark Allen | 8:09:15 | Kailua-Kona |
| 1990 | Mark Allen | 8:28:17 | Kailua-Kona |
| 1991 | Mark Allen | 8:18:32 | Kailua-Kona |
| 1992 | Mark Allen | 8:09:09 | Kailua-Kona |
| 1993 | Mark Allen | 8:07:46 | Kailua-Kona |
| 1994 | Greg Welch | 8:20:27 | Kailua-Kona |
| 1995 | Mark Allen | 8:20:34 | Kailua-Kona |

### WOMEN

| Date | Winner | Time | Site |
|---|---|---|---|
| 1978 | No finishers | | |
| 1979 | Lyn Lemaire | 12:55 | Waikiki Beach |
| 1980 | Robin Beck | 11:21:24 | Ala Moana Park |
| 1981 | Linda Sweeney | 12:00:32 | Kailua-Kona |
| 1982 | Kathleen McCartney | 11:09:40 | Kailua-Kona |
| 1982 | Julie Leach | 10:54:08 | Kailua-Kona |
| 1983 | Sylviane Puntous | 10:43:36 | Kailua-Kona |

## Ironman Championship (Cont.)
### WOMEN (Cont.)

| Date | Winner | Time | Site |
|------|--------|------|------|
| 1984 | Sylviane Puntous | 10:25:13 | Kailua-Kona |
| 1985 | Joanne Ernst | 10:25:22 | Kailua-Kona |
| 1986 | Paula Newby-Fraser | 9:49:14 | Kailua-Kona |
| 1987 | Erin Baker | 9:35:25 | Kailua-Kona |
| 1988 | Paula Newby-Fraser | 9:01:01 | Kailua-Kona |
| 1989 | Paula Newby-Fraser | 9:00:56 | Kailua-Kona |
| 1990 | Erin Baker | 9:13:42 | Kailua-Kona |
| 1991 | Paula Newby-Fraser | 9:07:52 | Kailua-Kona |
| 1992 | Paula Newby-Fraser | 8:55:29 | Kailua-Kona |
| 1993 | Paula Newby-Fraser | 8:58:23 | Kailua-Kona |
| 1994 | Paula Newby-Fraser | 9:20:14 | Kailua-Kona |
| 1995 | Karen Smyers | 9:16:46 | Kailua-Kona |

Note: The Ironman Championship was contested twice in 1982.

# Volleyball

## World Champions
### MEN

| Year | Winner | Runnerup | Site |
|------|--------|----------|------|
| 1949 | Soviet Union | Czechoslovakia | Prague, Czechoslovakia |
| 1952 | Soviet Union | Czechoslovakia | Moscow, Soviet Union |
| 1956 | Czechoslovakia | Soviet Union | Paris, France |
| 1960 | Soviet Union | Czechoslovakia | Rio de Janeiro, Brazil |
| 1962 | Soviet Union | Czechoslovakia | Moscow, Soviet Union |
| 1966 | Czechoslovakia | Romania | Prague, Czechoslovakia |
| 1970 | East Germany | Bulgaria | Sofia, Bulgaria |
| 1974 | Poland | Soviet Union | Mexico City |
| 1978 | Soviet Union | Italy | Rome, Italy |
| 1982 | Soviet Union | Brazil | Buenos Aires, Argentina |
| 1986 | United States | Soviet Union | Paris, France |
| 1990 | Italy | Cuba | Rio de Janeiro, Brazil |
| 1994 | Italy | Netherlands | Athens, Greece |

### WOMEN

| Year | Winner | Runnerup | Site |
|------|--------|----------|------|
| 1952 | Soviet Union | Poland | Moscow, Soviet Union |
| 1956 | Soviet Union | Romania | Paris, France |
| 1960 | Soviet Union | Japan | Rio de Janeiro, Brazil |
| 1962 | Japan | Soviet Union | Moscow, Soviet Union |
| 1966 | Japan | United States | Prague, Czechoslovakia |
| 1970 | Soviet Union | Japan | Sofia, Bulgaria |
| 1974 | Japan | Soviet Union | Mexico City |
| 1978 | Cuba | Japan | Rome, Italy |
| 1982 | China | Peru | Lima, Peru |
| 1986 | China | Cuba | Prague, Czechoslovakia |
| 1990 | Soviet Union | China | Beijing, China |
| 1994 | Cuba | Brazil | Sao Paulo, Brazil |

## U.S. Men's Open Champions—Gold Division

| | |
|---|---|
| 1928 | Germantown, PA YMCA |
| 1929 | Hyde Park YMCA, IL |
| 1930 | Hyde Park YMCA, IL |
| 1931 | San Antonio, TX YMCA |
| 1932 | San Antonio, TX YMCA |
| 1933 | Houston, TX YMCA |
| 1934 | Houston, TX YMCA |
| 1935 | Houston, TX YMCA |
| 1936 | Houston, TX YMCA |
| 1937 | Duncan YMCA, IL |
| 1938 | Houston, TX YMCA |
| 1939 | Houston, TX YMCA |
| 1940 | Los Angeles AC, CA |
| 1941 | North Ave. YMCA, IL |
| 1942 | North Ave. YMCA, IL |
| 1943-44 | No championships |
| 1945 | North Ave. YMCA, IL |
| 1946 | Pasadena, CA YMCA |
| 1947 | North Ave. YMCA, IL |
| 1948 | Hollywood, CA YMCA |
| 1949 | Downtown YMCA, CA |
| 1950 | Long Beach, CA YMCA |
| 1951 | Hollywood, CA YMCA |
| 1952 | Hollywood, CA YMCA |
| 1953 | Hollywood, CA YMCA |
| 1954 | Stockton, CA YMCA |
| 1955 | Stockton, CA YMCA |
| 1956 | Hollywood, CA YMCA Stars |
| 1957 | Hollywood, CA YMCA Stars |
| 1958 | Hollywood, CA YMCA Stars |
| 1959 | Hollywood, CA YMCA Stars |
| 1960 | Westside JCC, CA |

## U.S. Men's Open Champions—Gold Division (Cont.)

| | |
|---|---|
| 1961 | Hollywood, CA YMCA |
| 1962 | Hollywood, CA YMCA |
| 1963 | Hollywood, CA YMCA |
| 1964 | Hollywood, CA YMCA Stars |
| 1965 | Westside JCC, CA |
| 1966 | Sand & Sea Club, CA |
| 1967 | Fresno, CA VBC |
| 1968 | Westside JCC, L.A., CA |
| 1969 | Los Angeles, CA YMCA |
| 1970 | Chart House, San Diego |
| 1971 | Santa Monica, CA YMCA |
| 1972 | Chart House, San Diego |
| 1973 | Chuck's Steak, L.A., CA |
| 1974 | Un of CA Santa Barbara |
| 1975 | Chart House, San Diego |
| 1976 | Maliabu, L.A., CA |
| 1977 | Chuck's, Santa Barbara |
| 1978 | Chuck's, Los Angeles |
| 1979 | Nautilus, Long Beach |
| 1980 | Olympic Club, San Francisco |
| 1981 | Nautilus, Long Beach |
| 1982 | Chuck's, Los Angeles |
| 1983 | Nautilus Pacifica, CA |
| 1984 | Nautilus Pacifica, CA |
| 1985 | Molten/SSI Torrance, CA |
| 1986 | Molten, Torrance, CA |
| 1987 | Molten, Torrance, CA |
| 1988 | Molten, Torrance, CA |
| 1989 | Not held |
| 1990 | Nike, Carson, CA |
| 1991 | Offshore, Woodland Hills, CA |
| 1992 | Creole Six Pack, Elmhurst, NY |
| 1993 | Asics, Huntington Beach, CA |
| 1994 | Asics/Paul Mitchell, Hunt. Beach, CA |
| 1995 | Shakter, Belagarad, Ukraine |

## U.S. Women's Open Champions—Gold Division

| | |
|---|---|
| 1949 | Eagles, Houston TX |
| 1950 | Voit #1, Santa Monica, CA |
| 1951 | Eagles, Houston, TX |
| 1952 | Voit #1, Santa Monica, CA |
| 1953 | Voit #1, Los Angeles, CA |
| 1954 | Houstonettes, Houston, TX |
| 1955 | Mariners, Santa Monica, CA |
| 1956 | Mariners, Santa Monica, CA |
| 1957 | Mariners, Santa Monica, CA |
| 1958 | Mariners, Santa Monica, CA |
| 1959 | Mariners, Santa Monica, CA |
| 1960 | Mariners, Santa Monica, CA |
| 1961 | Breakers, Long Beach, CA |
| 1962 | Shamrocks, Long Beach, CA |
| 1963 | Shamrocks, Long Beach, CA |
| 1964 | Shamrocks, Long Beach, CA |
| 1965 | Shamrocks, Long Beach, CA |
| 1966 | Renegades, Los Angeles, CA |
| 1967 | Shamrocks, Long Beach, CA |
| 1968 | Shamrocks, Long Beach, CA |
| 1969 | Shamrocks, Long Beach, CA |
| 1970 | Shamrocks, Long Beach, CA |
| 1971 | Renegades, Los Angeles, CA |
| 1972 | E Pluribus Unum, Houston |
| 1973 | E Pluribus Unum, Houston |
| 1974 | Renegades, Los Angeles, CA |
| 1975 | Adidas, Norwalk, CA |
| 1976 | Pasadena, TX |
| 1977 | Spoilers, Hermosa, CA |
| 1978 | Nick's, Los Angeles, CA |
| 1979 | Mavericks, Los Angeles, CA |
| 1980 | NAVA, Fountain Valley, CA |
| 1981 | Utah State, Logan, UT |
| 1982 | Monarchs, Hilo, HI |
| 1983 | Syntex, Stockton, CA |
| 1984 | Chrysler, Palo Alto, CA |
| 1985 | Merrill Lynch, Arizona |
| 1986 | Merrill Lynch, Arizona |
| 1987 | Chrysler, Pleasanton, CA |
| 1988 | Chrysler, Hayward, CA |
| 1989 | Plymouth, Hayward, CA |
| 1990 | Plymouth, Hayward, CA |
| 1991 | Fitness, Champaign, IL |
| 1992 | Nick's Kronies, Chicago, IL |
| 1993 | Nick's Fishmarket, Chicago, IL |
| 1994 | Nick's Fishmarket, Chicago, IL |
| 1995 | Kittleman Assoc./Rudi's/Nick's, Chicago, IL |

# Wrestling

## United States National Champions

### 1983

**FREESTYLE**

| | |
|---|---|
| 105.5 | Rich Salamone |
| 114.5 | Joe Gonzales |
| 125.5 | Joe Corso |
| 136.5 | Rich Dellagatta* |
| 149.5 | Bill Hugent |
| 163 | Lee Kemp |
| 180.5 | Chris Campbell |
| 198 | Pete Bush |

**FREESTYLE (Cont.)**

| | |
|---|---|
| 220 | Greg Gibson |
| Hvy | Bruce Baumgartner |
| Team | Sunkist Kids |

**GRECO-ROMAN**

| | |
|---|---|
| 105.5 | T. J. Jones |
| 114.5 | Mark Fuller |
| 125.5 | Rob Hermann |
| 136.5 | Dan Mello |

**GRECO-ROMAN (Cont.)**

| | |
|---|---|
| 149.5 | Jim Martinez |
| 163 | James Andre |
| 180.5 | Steve Goss |
| 198 | Steve Fraser* |
| 220 | Dennis Koslowski |
| Hvy | No champion |
| Team | Minnesota Wrestling Club |

### 1984

**FREESTYLE**

| | |
|---|---|
| 105.5 | Rich Salamone |
| 114.5 | Charlie Heard |
| 125.5 | Joe Corso |
| 136.5 | Rich Dellagatta* |
| 149.5 | Andre Metzger |

**FREESTYLE (Cont.)**

| | |
|---|---|
| 163 | Dave Schultz* |
| 180.5 | Mark Schultz |
| 198 | Steve Fraser |
| 220 | Harold Smith |
| Hvy | Bruce Baumgartner |

**FREESTYLE (Cont.)**

| | |
|---|---|
| Team | Sunkist Kids |

**GRECO-ROMAN**

| | |
|---|---|
| 105.5 | T. J. Jones |
| 114.5 | Mark Fuller |

## United States National Champions (Cont.)

### 1984 (Cont.)

**GRECO-ROMAN (Cont.)**
136.5 ......Dan Mello
149.5 ......Jim Martinez*
163 .........John Matthews

**GRECO-ROMAN (Cont.)**
180.5 ......Tom Press
198 ..........Mike Houck
220 ..........No champion

**GRECO-ROMAN (Cont.)**
Hvy ..........No champion
Team............Adirondack Three-Style, WA

### 1985

**FREESTYLE**
105.5 ......Tim Vanni
114.5 ......Jim Martin
125.5 ......Charlie Heard
136.5 ......Darryl Burley
149.5 ......Bill Nugent*
163 .........Kenny Monday
180.5 ......Mike Sheets
198 .........Mark Schultz

**FREESTYLE (Cont.)**
220 ..........Greg Gibson
286 ..........Bruce Baumgartner
Team .......Sunkist Kids

**GRECO-ROMAN**
105.5 ......T. J. Jones
114.5 ......Mark Fuller
125.5 ......Eric Seward*

**GRECO-ROMAN (Cont.)**
136.5 ......Buddy Lee
149.5 ......Jim Martinez
163 ..........David Butler
180.5 ......Chris Catallo
198 ..........Mike Houck
220 ..........Greg Gibson
286 ..........Dennis Koslowski
Team .......U.S. Marine Corps

### 1986

**FREESTYLE**
105.5 .....Rich Salamone
114.5 ......Joe Gonzales
125.5 ......Kevin Darkus
136.5 ......John Smith
149.5 ......Andre Metzger*
163 .........Dave Schultz
180.5 ......Mark Schultz
198 ..........Jim Scherr
220 .........Dan Severn

**FREESTYLE (Cont.)**
286 ..........Bruce Baumgartner
Team .......Sunkist Kids (Div. I)
.............Hawkeye Wrestling
.............Club (Div. II)

**GRECO-ROMAN**
105.5 ......Eric Wetzel
114.5 ......Shawn Sheldon
125.5 ......Anthony Amado

**GRECO-ROMAN (Cont.)**
136.5 ......Frank Famiano
149.5 ......Jim Martinez
163 ..........David Butler*
180.5 ......Darryl Gholar
198 ..........Derrick Waldroup
220 ..........Dennis Koslowski
286 ..........Duane Koslowski
Team .......U.S. Marine Corps (Div. I)
.............U.S. Navy (Div. II)

### 1987

**FREESTYLE**
105.5 ......Takashi Irie
114.5 ......Mitsuru Sato
125.5 ......Barry Davis
136.5 ......Takumi Adachi
149.5 ......Andre Metzger
163 .........Dave Schultz*
180.5 ......Mark Schultz
198 .........Jim Scherr
220 .........Bill Scherr

**FREESTYLE (Cont.)**
286 ..........Bruce Baumgartner
Team .......Sunkist Kids (Div. I)
.............Team Foxcatcher (Div. II)

**GRECO-ROMAN**
105.5 ......Eric Wetzel
114.5 ......Shawn Sheldon
125.5 ......Eric Seward
136.5 ......Frank Famiano

**GRECO-ROMAN (Cont.)**
149.5 ......Jim Martinez
163 ..........David Butler
180.5 ......Chris Catallo
198 ..........Derrick Waldroup*
220 ..........Dennis Koslowski
286 ..........Duane Koslowski
Team........U.S. Marine Corp (Div. I)
.............U.S. Army (Div. II)

### 1988

**FREESTYLE**
105.5 ......Tim Vanni
114.5 ......Joe Gonzales
125.5 ......Kevin Darkus
136.5 ......John Smith*
149.5 ......Nate Carr
163 .........Kenny Monday
180.5 ......Dave Schultz
198 ..........Melvin Douglas III
220 ..........Bill Scherr

**FREESTYLE (Cont.)**
286 ..........Bruce Baumgartner
Team .......Sunkist Kids (Div. I)
.............Team Foxcatcher (Div. II)

**GRECO-ROMAN**
105.5 ......T. J. Jones
114.5 ......Shawn Sheldon
125.5 ......Gogi Parseghian*
136.5 ......Dalen Wasmund

**GRECO-ROMAN (Cont.)**
149.5 ......Craig Pollard
163 .........Tony Thomas
180.5 ......Darryl Gholar
198 ..........Mike Carolan
220 ..........Dennis Koslowski
286 ..........Duane Koslowski
Team .......U.S. Marine Corps (Div. I)
.............Sunkist Kids (Div. II)

### 1989

**FREESTYLE**
105.5 ......Tim Vanni
114.5 ......Zeke Jones
125.5 ......Brad Penrith
136.5 ......John Smith
149.5 ......Nate Carr
163 .........Rob Koll
180.5 ......Rico Chiapparelli
198 ..........Jim Scherr*
220 ..........Bill Scherr

**FREESTYLE (Cont.)**
286 ..........Bruce Baumgartner
Team .......Sunkist Kids (Div. I)
.............Team Foxcatcher (Div. II)

**GRECO-ROMAN**
105.5 ......Lew Dorrance
114.5 ......Mark Fuller
125.5 ......Gogi Parseghian
136.5 ......Isaac Anderson

**GRECO-ROMAN (Cont.)**
149.5 ......Andy Seras*
163 ..........David Butler
180.5 ......John Morgan
198 ..........Michial Foy
220 ..........Steve Lawson
286 ..........Craig Pittman
Team .......U.S. Marine Corps (Div. I)
.............Jets USA (Div. II)

### 1990

**FREESTYLE**
105.5 ......Rob Eiter
114.5 ......Zeke Jones

**FREESTYLE (Cont.)**
125,5 ......Joe Melchiore
136.5 ......John Smith

**FREESTYLE (Cont.)**
149.5 ......Nate Carr
163 ..........Rob Koll

## United States National Champions (Cont.)

### 1990 (Cont.)

#### FREESTYLE (Cont.)
180.5 .......Royce Alger
198 ..........Chris Campbell*
220 ..........Bill Scherr
286 ..........Bruce Baumgartner
Team .......Sunkist Kids (Div. I)
        Team Foxcatcher (Div. II)

#### GRECO-ROMAN
105.5 .......Lew Dorrance
114.5 .......Sam Henson
125.5 .......Mark Pustelnik
136.5 .......Isaac Anderson
149.5 .......Andy Seras
163 ..........David Butler

#### GRECO-ROMAN (Cont.)
180.5 .......Derrick Waldroup
198 ..........Randy Couture*
220 ..........Chris Tironi
286 ..........Matt Ghaffari
Team .......Jets USA (Div. I)
        California Jets (Div. II)

### 1991

#### FREESTYLE
105.5 .......Tim Vanni
114.5 .......Zeke Jones
125.5 .......Brad Penrith
136.5 .......John Smith*
149.5 .......Townsend Saunders
163 ..........Kenny Monday
180.5 .......Kevin Jackson
198 ..........Chris Campbell

#### FREESTYLE (Cont.)
220 ..........Mark Coleman
286 ..........Bruce Baumgartner
Team .......Sunkist Kids (Div. I)
        Jets USA (Div. II)

#### GRECO-ROMAN
105.5 .......Eric Wetzel
114.5 .......Shawn Sheldon
125.5 .......Frank Famiano

#### GRECO-ROMAN (Cont.)
136.5 .......Buddy Lee
149.5 .......Andy Seras
163 ..........Gordy Morgan
180.5 .......John Morgan*
198 ..........Michial Foy
220 ..........Dennis Koslowski
286 ..........Craig Pittman
Team .......Jets USA (Div. I)
        Sunkist Kids (Div. II)

### 1992

#### FREESTYLE
105.5 .......Rob Eiter
114.5 .......Jack Griffin
125.5 .......Kendall Cross*
136.5 .......John Fisher
149.5 .......Matt Demaray
163 ..........Greg Elinsky
180.5 .......Royce Alger
198 ..........Dan Chaid
220 ..........Bill Scherr

#### FREESTYLE (Cont.)
286 ..........Bruce Baumgartner
Team .......Sunkist Kids (Div. I)
        Team Foxcatcher (Div. II)

#### GRECO-ROMAN
105.5 .......Eric Wetzel
114.5 .......Mark Fuller
125.5 .......Dennis Hall
136.5 .......Buddy Lee*

#### GRECO-ROMAN (Cont.)
149.5 .......Rodney Smith
163 ..........Travis West
180.5 .......John Morgan
198 ..........Michial Foy
220 ..........Dennis Koslowski
286 ..........Matt Ghaffari
Team .......NY Athletic Club (Div. I)
        Sunkist Kids (Div. II)

### 1993

#### FREESTYLE
105.5 .......Rob Eiter
114.5 .......Zeke Jones
125.5 .......Brad Penrith
136.5 .......Tom Brands
149.5 .......Matt Demaray
163 ..........Dave Schultz*
180.5 .......Kevin Jackson
198 ..........Melvin Douglas
220 ..........Kirk Trost

#### FREESTYLE (Cont.)
286 ..........Bruce Baumgartner
Team .......Sunkist Kids (Div. I)
        Team Foxcatcher (Div. II)

#### GRECO-ROMAN
105.5 .......Eric Wetzel
114.5 .......Shawn Sheldon
125.5 .......Dennis Hall*
136.5 .......Shon Lewis

#### GRECO-ROMAN (Cont.)
149.5 .......Andy Seras
163 ..........Gordy Morgan
180.5 .......Dan Henderson
198 ..........Randy Couture
220 ..........James Johnson
286 ..........Matt Ghaffari
Team .......NY Athletic Club (Div. I)
        Sunkist Kids (Div. II)

### 1994

#### FREESTYLE
105.5 .......Tim Vanni
114.5 .......Zeke Jones
125.5 .......Terry Brands
136.5 .......Tom Brands
149.5 .......Matt Demaray
163 ..........Dave Schultz
180.5 .......Royce Alger
198 ..........Melvin Douglas
220 ..........Mark Kerr

#### FREESTYLE (Cont.)
286 ..........Bruce Baumgartner*
Team .......Sunkist Kids (Div. I)
        Team Foxcatcher (Div. II)

#### GRECO-ROMAN
105.5 .......Isaac Ramaswamy
114.5 .......Shawn Sheldon
125.5 .......Dennis Hall
136.5 .......Shon Lewis

#### GRECO-ROMAN (Cont.)
149.5 .......Andy Seras*
163 ..........Gordy Morgan
180.5 .......Dan Henderson
198 ..........Derrick Waldroup
220 ..........James Johnson
286 ..........Matt Ghaffari
Team .......Armed Forces (Div. I)
        NY Athletic Club (Div. II)

### 1995

#### FREESTYLE
105.5 .......Rob Eiter
114.5 .......Lou Rosselli
125.5 .......Kendall Cross*
136.5 .......Tom Brands
149.5 .......Matt Demaray
163 ..........Dave Schultz
180.5 .......Kevin Jackson
198 ..........Melvin Douglas
220 ..........Kurt Angle

#### FREESTYLE (Cont.)
286 ..........Bruce Baumgartner
Team .......Sunkist Kids (Div. I)
        Team Foxcatcher (Div. II)

#### GRECO-ROMAN
105.5 .......Isaac Ramaswamy
114.5 .......Shawn Sheldon
125.5 .......Dennis Hall*
136.5 .......Van Fronhofer

#### GRECO-ROMAN (Cont.)
149.5 .......Heath Sims
163 ..........Matt Lindland
180.5 .......Marty Morgan
198 ..........Michial Foy
220 ..........James Johnson
286 ..........Rulon Gardner
Team .......Armed Forces (Div. I)
        Sunkist Kids (Div. II)

*Outstanding wrestler

# The Sports Market

Why Is This Man Worth $35 Million?

OCTOBER 9, 1995
$2.95 (CAN. $3.95)

*Sports Illustrated*

NFL players and
coaches tell
us what makes
Deion great

GEORGE LANGE

# Same Changes

## Despite a flurry of lockouts and lawsuits the business of sports was fundamentally unchanged

## by John Steinbreder

IT WAS the French journalist Alphonse Karr who said, "The more things change, the more they remain the same," and though those words were uttered more than a century ago, they give a good idea of what went on in the sports market in 1995. A lot transpired during the year, but it seems that the core issues and headlines were not much different from those that dominated the scene in 1994.

Labor problems continued to plague Major League Baseball, and though the players and owners did get in an abbreviated season, they still weren't able to craft a new collective bargaining agreement and appeared as far apart on most issues as they were when the players first went on strike. The National Hockey League season resumed last January after a 103-day lockout, but five months later that bastion of tranquillity known as the National Basketball Association started having serious problems of its own. The owners locked out the players when they balked at approving a new labor pact, and then the players sued and threatened to decertify their union. The National Football League enjoyed a reasonably peaceful off-season, but at the end of the summer a fierce battle broke out among the owners when Jerry Jones of the Dallas Cowboys began to challenge the NFL's authority over licensing and marketing deals.

Baseball had a strange year. The players and owners bickered for most of the winter and still hadn't agreed on a new contract when it came time to start spring training. But instead of bringing in their regular players, who could have worked out while the two sides negotiated, the owners decided to field replacement squads and began playing exhibition games with ragtag units of beer league rejects, major league has-beens and minor league never-will-bes. The owners were ready to start the regular season with their replacement teams, but just

DAVID LIAM KYLE

Inspired by Abbie Hoffman's sprinkling of money on the floor of the New York Stock Exchange in 1967, a trio of New Yorkers wearing T-shirts that spelled GREED across their chests dashed onto the field at Shea Stadium one night and tossed 150 $1 bills around the infield.

The stellar play of teams such as the Cleveland Indians and the Boston Red Sox made it a little easier for some fans to forgive and forget as the season progressed, but bad feelings toward the game lingered, and people stayed away from the ballparks in droves. As of mid-August, for example, average attendance for the majors was down 19% from the previous year. Of baseball's 28 teams, only two recorded increases, while the rest posted drop-offs that in all but a couple of cases were greater than 10% and in some instances rose above 30%. Sales of licensed merchandise slumped, and the collectibles market fell off. In addition, ABC and NBC announced last July that due to financial losses and the generally sorry state of the game, they would abandon the Baseball Network partnership they had formed with team owners only two years before and forsake any involvement in the sport after the 1995 season.

Given baseball's rich heritage, it's sad to think of both the fans and the television networks turning their backs on what once truly was the national pastime. But until a new contract is signed and some semblance of trust restored, baseball will be a sport that evokes as much disdain among its fans as it does affection. And it will continue to suffer as a result.

before the first pitch was to be thrown, U.S. District Court Judge Sonia Sotomayor granted a National Labor Relations Board request for a preliminary injunction against the owners for unilaterally rescinding several provisions from the old labor pact and ordered them restored until a new deal was cut. Rather than appealing the decision or running the legal risk of locking out players who had said they would report to camp if the judge ruled in their favor, the owners agreed to invite their regulars to a shortened spring training. And even though the two sides still didn't have a new collective bargaining agreement, the 1995 season was on.

The 144-game schedule began on April 26, and not surprisingly, neither the players nor the owners were welcomed back with open arms. A plane flew over Riverfront Stadium in Cincinnati during the first game pulling a a banner reading: OWNERS & PLAYERS: TO HELL WITH ALL OF YOU.

KEVIN LARKIN/AP

**Bob Goodenow led the players back to the ice, where they were warmly welcomed.**

Hockey had a much easier time recovering from its labor problems. As soon as NHL players and owners ended the three-month lockout last winter and agreed to a new, six-year deal, fans began storming the ticket windows. More than 12,000 people crammed into the Spectrum in Philadelphia a few days after the settlement was announced to watch the Flyers scrimmage; and the New York Islanders, who have been struggling in the standings and at the box office the past several years, sold 15,000 tickets in one day, about five times what they expected to move. The Tampa Bay Lightning entertained crowds of more than 20,000 for their first two home games, and the Hartford Whalers reported more media and fan interest in their team than they have seen in five years.

Fortunately for the league, that enthusiasm continued throughout the year. Though total attendance numbers were down as a result of the shortened season, the average attendance per game was up. In addition, more people watched Games 1 and 4 of the Stanley Cup finals than had ever seen an NHL contest on TV before.

Why did hockey rebound so well? For one thing, labor disputes have not been a recurring problem for the sport, and its fans didn't feel nearly as betrayed or frustrated as their baseball brethren. Also, the league's labor problems happened to coincide with hockey's wild surge in popularity. Fueled in large part by a greater appreciation of the sport, better marketing by the league and a growing participation among weekend athletes not only in ice hockey but also in street versions of the game, the NHL has scarcely been more popular.

Largely as a result of those factors, the NHL has been able to attract the attention of corporate heavyweights who now see it as a terrific promotional vehicle for their products. Last year Anheuser-Busch decided to market its Bud Ice brand primarily through the league. And then Nike got into the game. In addition to signing a marketing agreement with the NHL, the Oregon-based footwear giant developed a street hockey shoe and cosponsored a national street hockey program that the league created in an effort to boost grass-roots interest in the game. Nike also demonstrated its faith in hockey's future by buying Canstar Sports, which makes Bauer skates and Cooper protective gear, and adding Red Wing star forward Sergei Federov to its stable of national spokesmen.

Basketball continues to prosper though it came perilously close this past year to suffering through the first work stoppage in its history. The problems began in June when NBA commissioner David Stern negotiated a new labor pact with Simon Gourdine, the head of the players' union. An agreement was announced just as the Houston Rockets were wrapping up their second NBA title, and it seemed that the NBA, which had played the previous season without a contract between its players and the owners, would once again avoid the sorts of labor troubles that have marred the other major sports leagues.

DAVID E. KLUTHO

would effectively limit what veterans could be paid when re-signing with their teams. A number of players, including Michael Jordan and Patrick Ewing, were so incensed at the deal that they called for decertification of the union. They quickly gathered more than the required number of signatures to force a vote on the matter and then began a vigorous campaign to take down the union. Faced with the threat of decertification, Gourdine and Stern, who had imposed a lockout on all NBA players when they chose not to ratify the first deal, went back to the table and worked out a new contract, this one without the luxury tax. That seemed to mollify many of the players, but the league and the union had to wait for the decertification vote before either side

But then the players got a look at what their union head had negotiated. Many thought that Gourdine, who had once worked for the NBA and served for a time as deputy commissioner, had sold out to the owners. Of particular concern was the inclusion of a luxury tax that could act on the new deal.

The vote was held on two separate days at the end of the summer, and in the end the union prevailed, with 226 players electing to keep it intact and 134 moving to decertify. With that out of the way, the player representatives from all NBA

**Jones pushed the envelope of NFL regulations with his marketing deals.**

teams got together and approved the revised contract by a vote of 25–2. Shortly afterward the owners approved the pact themselves, and Stern lifted the lockout.

Fortunately for the NBA, its 1995–96 season started on time. But while it narrowly averted a long and ugly labor battle, the league did not emerge completely unscathed. Divisions were sown among players, and the league's carefully nurtured image of order and prosperity has been tainted by the sight of extraordinarily wealthy athletes, owners and agents haggling over hundreds of millions of dollars in revenues.

A similar battle over money broke out in the NFL last summer, pitting Dallas Cowboy owner Jerry Jones against the league. At issue was the concept of shared revenues. Traditionally the profits earned from the sale of NFL licensed merchandise are divided equally among all franchises. But that had begun to irk Jones, who took in the same $3 million that every other team got last year even though Cowboy-oriented apparel accounted for 24% of all sales. So in an effort to further capitalize on his team's logo, he began to do some marketing of his own. First he signed a 10-year, $25 million contract with Pepsi, making it the official soft drink of Texas Stadium. Then Jones signed a $2.5 million deal with Nike to make apparel for all Cowboy sideline personnel and help develop a theme park at the stadium. The problem was, many NFL officials and team

owners felt that those arrangements not only threatened a longstanding business philosophy that had brought great riches to all teams but also undermined lucrative marketing deals the NFL had already signed with Coca-Cola and Reebok, who just happen to be Pepsi's and Nike's biggest competitors. So when Jones was about to announce another marketing agreement, this time with American Express, the NFL filed a $300 million suit against the Cowboys' owner, seeking damages for his "ambush" contracts and demanding that he not sign any others.

A number of owners have spoken out against Jones's moves, saying that they will weaken the collective strength of the NFL. But some privately support his actions, believing it is only right that Jones, or any other owner, should be able to garner whatever outside revenues he can. What happens next is anybody's guess, but it seems likely that the suit will be settled out of court and a compromise reached, probably one that preserves the revenue-sharing ideals of the NFL but

**NBC's Dick Ebersol (right) and Sydney rep Gary Pemberton inked a record deal.**

also gives teams more of a right to make some extra money on the side.

Things on the Olympic front were much less contentious. As Atlanta continued to prepare itself for the 1996 Summer Games, the International Olympic Committee awarded the 2002 Winter Games to Salt Lake City. And shortly afterward NBC agreed to pay a record $1.27 billion for the right to televise the Summer Olympics from Sydney, Australia, in 2000 and the Salt Lake Games two years later.

That's just the way it seems to be with sports these days. Labor disputes shut down seasons, players complain about being underpaid, and owners cry poverty. But vast amounts of money keep flowing in, and in spite of all its perceived problems, the world of sports keeps getting stronger and stronger financially. Alphonse Karr would have appreciated the irony. The more things change, the more they remain the same.

# Baseball Directory

## Major League Baseball
Address: 350 Park Avenue
New York, NY 10022
Telephone: (212) 339-7800
Acting Commissioner and Chairman of the Executive
Council: Bud Selig
Executive Director: Richard Levin

## Major League Baseball Players Association
Address: 12 East 49th Street 24th Floor
New York, NY 10017
Telephone: (212) 826-0808
Executive Director: Donald Fehr
Director of Marketing: Judy Heeter

## American League

### American League Office
Address: 350 Park Avenue
New York, NY 10022
Telephone: (212) 339-7600
President: Dr. Gene Budig
VP of Media Affairs and Administration: Phyllis
Merhige

### Baltimore Orioles
Address: Oriole Park at Camden Yards
333 W Camden Street
Baltimore, MD 21201
Telephone: (410) 685-9800
Stadium (Capacity): Camden Yards (48,262)
Managing Partner/Owner: Peter G. Angelos
Vice Chairmen: Thomas Clancy and Joseph Foss
Manager: Phil Regan
Director of Public Relations: John Maroon

### Boston Red Sox
Address: 4 Yawkey Way
Fenway Park
Boston, MA 02215
Telephone: (617) 267-9440
Stadium (Capacity): Fenway Park (33,871)
Majority Owner/Chairman of the Board: John Harrington
Executive VP of Baseball Operations: Lou Gorman
Executive VP and GM: Daniel F. Duquette
Manager: Kevin Kennedy
Vice President, Public Relations: Dick Bresciani

### California Angels
Address: P.O. Box 2000
Anaheim Stadium
Anaheim, CA 92803
Telephone: (714) 937-7200 or (213) 625-1123
Stadium (Capacity): Anaheim Stadium (64,573)
Chairman of the Board: Gene Autry
General Manager: Bill Bavasi
Manager: Marcel Lachemann
Assistant VP of Media Relations: John Sevano

### Chicago White Sox
Address: Comiskey Park
Chicago, IL 60616
Telephone: (312) 924-1000
Stadium (Capacity): Comiskey Park (44,321)
Chairman: Jerry Reinsdorf
General Manager: Ron Schueler
Manager: Terry Bevington
Director of Publc Relations: Doug Abel

### Cleveland Indians
Address: Jacobs Field
2401 Ontario Street
Cleveland, OH 44115-4003
Telephone: (216) 861-1200
Stadium (Capacity): Jacobs Field (74,483)
Chairman of the Board and CEO: Richard Jacobs
Executive VP and General Manager: John Hart
Manager: Mike Hargrove
Vice President, Public Relations: Bob DiBiasio

### Detroit Tigers
Address: 2121 Trumbull Ave.
Tiger Stadium
Detroit, MI 48216
Telephone: (313) 962-4000
Stadium (Capacity): Tiger Stadium (52,416)
Owner: Mike Ilitch
CEO and President: John McHale
Manager: Sparky Anderson
Vice President, Media and Public Relations: Dan
Ewald

### Kansas City Royals
Address: P.O. Box 419969
Kansas City, MO 64141
Telephone: (816) 921-2200
Stadium (Capacity): Kauffman Stadium (40,625)
Chairman of the Board and CEO: David D. Glass
General Manager: Herk Robinson
Manager: Bob Boone
Vice President, Public Relations: Dean Vogelaar

### Milwaukee Brewers
Address: P.O. Box 3099
Milwaukee, WI 53201-3099
Telephone: (414) 933-4114
Stadium (Capacity): Milwaukee County Stadium
(53,192)
President and Chief Executive Officer: Bud Selig
Senior VP, Baseball Operations: Sal Bando
Manager: Phil Garner
Media Relations: Jon Greenberg

### Minnesota Twins
Address: 501 Chicago Avenue South
Hubert H. Humphrey Metrodome
Minneapolis, MN 55415
Telephone: (612) 375-1366
Stadium (Capacity): Hubert H. Humphrey Metrodome
(56,144)
Owner: Carl Pohlad
General Manager: Terry Ryan
Manager: Tom Kelly
Director of Media Relations: Rob Antony

### New York Yankees
Address: Yankee Stadium
Bronx, NY 10451
Telephone: (718) 293-4300
Stadium (Capacity): Yankee Stadium (57,545)
Principal Owner: George Steinbrenner
VP and Executive Consul: David Sussman
General Manager: Gene Michael
Manager: Buck Showalter
Director of Media Relations and Publicity: Rob
Butcher

## American League *(Cont.)*

### Oakland Athletics
Address:    Oakland-Alameda County Coliseum
              Oakland, CA 94621
Telephone: (510) 638-4900
Stadium (Capacity): Oakland-Alameda County
  Coliseum (46,990)
Owner/Managing General Partner: Walter Haas
President and General Manager: Sandy Alderson
Manager: Tony LaRussa
Director of Baseball Information: Jay Alves

### Seattle Mariners
Address:    P.O. Box 4100
              Seattle, WA 98104
Telephone: (206) 628-3555
Stadium (Capacity): The Kingdome (59,166)
Chairman: John Ellis
General Manager: Woody Woodward
Manager: Lou Piniella
Director of Public Relations: Dave Aust

### Texas Rangers
Address:    P.O. Box 90111
              Arlington, TX 76004
Telephone: (817) 273-5222
Stadium (Capacity): The Ballpark in Arlington (49,178)
General Partners: Rusty Rose and Thomas Schieffer
General Manager: Doug Melvin
Manager: Johnny Oates
Vice President, Public Relations: John Blake

### Toronto Blue Jays
Address:    SkyDome
              1 Blue Jays Way, Suite 3200
              Toronto, Ontario, Canada M5V 1J1
Telephone: (416) 341-1000
Stadium (Capacity): SkyDome (50,516)
Chairman of the Board: Peter N.T. Widdrington
President and CEO: Paul Beeston
Executive VP of Baseball Operations: Pat Gillick
Manager: Cito Gaston
Director of Public Relations: Howard Starkman

## National League

### National League Office
Address:    350 Park Avenue
              New York, NY 10022
Telephone: (212) 339-7700
President: Leonard Coleman
Director of Public Relations: Ricky Clemons

### Atlanta Braves
Address:    P.O. Box 4064
              Atlanta, GA 30302
Telephone: (404) 522-7630
Stadium (Capacity): Atlanta-Fulton County Stadium
  (52,007)
Owner: Ted Turner
General Manager: John Schuerholz
Manager: Bobby Cox
Director of Public Relations: Jim Schultz

### Chicago Cubs
Address:    Wrigley Field
              1060 West Addison
              Chicago, IL 60613
Telephone: (312) 404-2827
Stadium (Capacity): Wrigley Field (38,765)
President and CEO: Andrew B. MacPhail
Executive VP of Business Operations: Mark McGuire
General Manager: Ed Lynch
Manager: Jim Riggleman
Director of Media Relations: Sharon Panozzo

### Cincinnati Reds
Address:    100 Riverfront Stadium
              Cincinnati, OH 45202
Telephone: (513) 421-4510
Stadium (Capacity): Riverfront Stadium (52,952)
General Partner: Marge Schott
General Manager: James G. Bowden
Manager: Davey Johnson
Publicity Director: Mike Ringering

### Colorado Rockies
Address:    2001 Blake Street
              Denver, CO 80205
Telephone: (303) 292-0200
Stadium (Capacity): Coors Field (50,249)
President: Jerry McMorris
Executive VP of Baseball Operations: Keli McGregor
Manager: Don Baylor
Director of Public Relations: Mike Swanson

### Florida Marlins
Address:    2267 N.W. 199th Street
              Miami, FL 33056
Telephone: (305) 626-7400
Stadium (Capacity): Joe Robbie Stadium (46,000)
Owner: H. Wayne Huizenga
Vice President and General Manager: David
  Dombrowski
Manager: Rene Lachemann
Director of Media Relations: Chuck Pool

### Houston Astros
Address:    P.O. Box 288
              Houston, TX 77001
Telephone: (713) 799-9500
Stadium (Capacity): Astrodome (54,313)
Chairman: Drayton McLane Jr.
General Manager: Bob Watson
Manager: Terry Collins
Director of Media Relations: Rob Matwick

### Los Angeles Dodgers
Address:    1000 Elysian Park Avenue
              Los Angeles, CA 90012-1199
Telephone: (213) 224-1500
Stadium (Capacity): Dodger Stadium (56,000)
President: Peter O'Malley
Executive Vice President: Fred Claire
Manager: Tom Lasorda
Director of Publicity: Jay Lucas

### Montreal Expos
Address:    P.O. Box 500
              Station M
              Montreal
              Quebec, Canada H1V 3P2
Telephone: (514) 253-3434
Stadium (Capacity): Olympic Stadium (46,500)
President: Claude Brochu
Vice President and General Manager: Kevin Malone
Manager: Felipe Alou
Director, Media Relations: Pete Loyello

## National League *(Cont.)*

**New York Mets**
Address:     Shea Stadium
             Flushing, NY 11368
Telephone: (718) 507-6387
Stadium (Capacity): Shea Stadium (55,601)
Chairman: Nelson Doubleday
President and CEO: Fred Wilpon
Executive VP of Baseball Operations: Joe McIlvaine
Manager: Dallas Green
Director of Media Relations: Jay Horwitz

**Philadelphia Phillies**
Address:     P.O. Box 7575
             Philadelphia, PA 19101-7575
Telephone: (215) 463-6000
Stadium (Capacity): Veterans Stadium (62,238)
President: Bill Giles
General Manager: Lee Thomas
Manager: Jim Fregosi
Vice President, Public Relations: Larry Shenk

**Pittsburgh Pirates**
Address:     P.O. Box 7000
             Pittsburgh, PA 15212
Telephone: (412) 323-5000
Stadium (Capacity): Three Rivers Stadium (58,729)
President and CEO: Mark Sauer
General Manager: Cam Bonifay
Manager: Jim Leyland
Director of.Media Relations: Jim Trdinich

**St. Louis Cardinals**
Address:     250 Stadium Plaza
             Busch Stadium
             St. Louis, MO 63102
Telephone: (314) 421-3060
Stadium (Capacity): Busch Stadium (57,001)
Chairman of the Board: August A. Busch III
General Manager: Walt Jocketty
Manager: Mike Jorgensen
Director of Public Relations: Brian Bartow

**San Diego Padres**
Address:     P.O. Box 2000
             San Diego, CA 92112
Telephone: (619) 283-4494
Stadium (Capacity): San Diego/Jack Murphy Stadium
  (60,000)
Chairman: John Moores
General Manager: TBA
Manager: Bruce Botchy
Director of Media Relations: Dennis Smythe

**San Francisco Giants**
Address:     Candlestick Park
             San Francisco, CA 94124
Telephone: (415) 468-3700
Stadium (Capacity): Candlestick Park (63,000)
Chairman: Peter Magowan
General Manager: Bob Quinn
Manager: Dusty Baker
Director of Public Relations: Bob Rose

# Pro Football Directory

**National Football League**
Address:     410 Park Avenue
             New York, New York 10022
Telephone: (212) 758-1500
Commissioner: Paul Tagliabue
Director of Communications: Greg Aiello

**National Football League Players Association**
Address:     2021 L Street, N.W.
             Washington, D.C. 20036
Telephone: (202) 463-2200
Executive Director: Gene Upshaw
Director, Public Relations: Frank Woschitz

## National Conference

**Arizona Cardinals**
Address:     P.O. Box 888
             Phoenix, AZ 85001
Telephone: (602) 379-0101
Stadium (Capacity): Sun Devil Stadium (73,377)
President and Owner: Bill Bidwill
Coach and General Manager: Buddy Ryan
Vice President: Larry Wilson
Director of Public Relations: Paul Jensen

**Atlanta Falcons**
Address:     1 Falcon Place
             Suwanee, GA 30174
Telephone: (404) 945-1111
Stadium (Capacity): Georgia Dome (71,228)
Chairman of the Board: Rankin M. Smith Sr.
President: Taylor W. Smith
Director of Player Personnel: Ken Herock
Coach: June Jones
Publicity Director: Charlie Taylor

**Carolina Panthers**
Address:     227 West Trade Street, Suite 1600
             Charlotte, NC 28202
Telephone: (803) 372-5116
Stadium (Capacity): Clemson Memorial Stadium
  (76, 055)
Founder and Owner: Jerry Richardson
President: Mike McCormack
General Manager: Bill Polian
Coach: Dom Capers
Director of Communications: Charlie Dayton

**Chicago Bears**
Address:     250 N. Washington Road
             Lake Forest, IL 60045
Telephone: (708) 295-6600
Stadium (Capacity): Soldier Field (66,946)
President: Michael McCaskey
Coach: Dave Wannstedt
Director of Public Relations: Bryan Harlan

## National Conference *(Cont.)*

### Dallas Cowboys
Address:    One Cowboys Parkway
              Irving, TX 75063
Telephone: (214) 556-9900
Stadium (Capacity): Texas Stadium (65,024)
Owner, President, and General Manager: Jerry Jones
Coach: Barry Switzer
Public Relations Director: Rich Dalrymple

### Detroit Lions
Address:    1200 Featherstone Road
              Pontiac, MI 48342
Telephone: (810) 335-4131
Stadium (Capacity): Pontiac Silverdome (80,500)
President and Owner: William Clay Ford
Executive Vice President: Chuck Schmidt
Coach: Wayne Fontes
Media Relations Director: Mike Murray

### Green Bay Packers
Address:    1265 Lombardi Avenue
              Green Bay, WI 54304
Telephone: (414) 496-5700
Stadium (Capacity): Lambeau Field (60,790)
President: Bob Harlan
General Manager: Ron Wolf
Coach: Mike Holmgren
Public Relations Director: Lee Remmel

### Minnesota Vikings
Address:    9520 Viking Drive
              Eden Prairie, MN 55344
Telephone: (612) 828-6500
Stadium (Capacity): HHH Metrodome (63,000)
President: Roger L. Headrick
VP of Administrative and Team Operations: Jeff Diamond
Coach: Dennis Green
Public Relations Director: David Pelletier

### New Orleans Saints
Address:    6928 Saints Drive
              Metairie, LA 70003
Telephone: (504) 733-0255
Stadium (Capacity): Louisiana Superdome (69,065)
Owner: Tom Benson
VP of Football Operations: Bill Kuharich
Executive VP of Administration: Jim Miller
VP/Head Coach: Jim Mora
Director of Media Relations: Rusty Kasmiersky

### New York Giants
Address:    Giants Stadium
              East Rutherford, NJ 07073
Telephone: (201) 935-8111
Stadium (Capacity): Giants Stadium (77,311)
President and co-CEO: Wellington T. Mara
Chairman and co-CEO: Preston Robert Tisch
General Manager: George Young
Coach: Dan Reeves
Director of Public Relations: Pat Hanlon

### Philadelphia Eagles
Address:    Veterans Stadium
              Broad Street and Pattison Avenue
              Philadelphia, PA 19148
Telephone: (215) 463-2500
Stadium (Capacity): Veterans Stadium (65,178)
Owner: Jeffrey Lurie
President and COO: TBA
Coach: Ray Rhodes
Director of Public Relations: Ron Howard

### St. Louis Rams
Address:    Matthews Dickey Building
              4245 North Kings Highway
              St. Louis, MO 63115
Telephone: (314) 877-3700
Stadium (Capacity): Busch Stadium (57,191);
 TWA Dome (65,000)
Owner and Chairman: Georgia Frontiere
President: John Shaw
Coach: Rich Brooks
Director of Public Relations: Rick Smith

### San Francisco 49ers
Address:    4949 Centennial Boulevard
              Santa Clara, CA 95054
Telephone: (408) 562-4949
Stadium (Capacity): Candlestick Park (66,455)
Owner: Edward J. DeBartolo Jr.
General Manager: Dwight Clark
Coach: George Seifert
Public Relations Director: Rodney Knox

### Tampa Bay Buccaneers
Address:    One Buccaneer Place
              Tampa, FL 33607
Telephone: (813) 870-2700
Stadium (Capacity): Tampa Stadium (74,321)
Owner: Malcolm Glazer
Director of Football Operations and Coach: Sam
 Wyche
Director of Public Relations: Chip Namias

### Washington Redskins
Address:    21300 Redskin Park Drive
              Ashburn, VA 22011
Telephone: (703) 478-8900
Stadium (Capacity): RFK Memorial Stadium (55,454)
Owner: Jack Kent Cooke
General Manager: Charley Casserly
Coach: Norv Turner
Director of Communications: Rick Vaughn

## American Conference

### Buffalo Bills
Address:    One Bills Drive
              Orchard Park, NY 14127
Telephone: (716) 648-1800
Stadium (Capacity): Rich Stadium (80,024)
President: Ralph C. Wilson Jr.
Executive VP/General Manager: John Butler
Coach: Marv Levy
Director of Media Relations: Scott Berchtold

### Cincinnati Bengals
Address:    200 Riverfront Stadium
              Cincinnati, OH 45202
Telephone: (513) 621-3550
Stadium (Capacity): Riverfront Stadium (60,389)
President and General Manager: Mike Brown
Vice President: John Sawyer
Coach: Dave Shula
Director of Public Relations: Jack Brennan

# Pro Football Directory *(Cont.)*

## American Conference *(Cont.)*

### Cleveland Browns
Address:    80 First Avenue
             Berea, OH 44017
Telephone: (216) 891-5000
Stadium (Capacity): Cleveland Stadium (78,512)
President: Art Modell
Coach: Bill Belichick
VP and Director of Public Relations: Kevin Byrne

### Denver Broncos
Address:    13655 Broncos Parkway
             Englewood, CO 80112
Telephone: (303) 649-9000
Stadium (Capacity): Mile High Stadium (76,273)
President/CEO: Pat Bowlen
General Manager: John Beake
Coach: Mike Shanahan
Director of Media Relations: Jim Saccomano

### Houston Oilers
Address:    6910 Fannin Street
             Houston, TX 77030
Telephone: (713) 797-9111
Stadium (Capacity): Astrodome (59,969)
President: K. S. (Bud) Adams Jr.
General Manager: Floyd Reese
Coach: Jeff Fisher
Director of Media Relations: Dave Pearson

### Indianapolis Colts
Address:    P.O. Box 535000
             Indianapolis, IN 46253
Telephone: (317) 297-2658
Stadium (Capacity): RCA Dome (60,129)
Owner: Robert Irsay
VP and General Manager: Jim Irsay
Coach: Ted Marchibroda
Public Relations Director: Craig Kelley

### Jacksonville Jaguars
Address:    One Stadium Place
             Jacksonville, FL 32202
Telephone: (904) 633-6000
Stadium (Capacity): Jacksonville Municipal Stadium (93,000)
Owner: J. Wayne Weaver
President and COO: David Seldin
Coach: Tom Coughlin
Executive Director of Communications: Dan Edwards

### Kansas City Chiefs
Address:    One Arrowhead Drive
             Kansas City, MO 64129
Telephone: (816) 924-9300
Stadium (Capacity): Arrowhead Stadium (79,101)
Founder: Lamar Hunt
President and General Manager: Carl Peterson
Coach: Marty Schottenheimer
Public Relations Director: Bob Moore

### Miami Dolphins
Address:    Joe Robbie Stadium
             7500 S.W. 30th Street
             Davie, FL 33314
Telephone: (305) 452-7000
Stadium (Capacity): Joe Robbie Stadium (74,916)
Chairman of the Board/Owner: H. Wayne Huizenga
Executive VP/General Manager: Eddie J. Jones
Coach: Don Shula
Media Relations Director: Harvey Greene

### New England Patriots
Address:    Foxboro Stadium
             60 Washington St.
             Foxboro, MA 02035
Telephone: (508) 543-8200
Stadium (Capacity): Foxboro Stadium (60,292)
President and CEO: Robert K. Kraft
VP Owners Representative: Jonathan Kraft
VP Business Operations: Andy Wasynczuk
Coach: Bill Parcells
Dir. of Public and Community Relations: Donald Lowery

### New York Jets
Address:    1000 Fulton Avenue
             Hempstead, NY 11550
Telephone: (516) 538-6600
Stadium (Capacity): Giants Stadium (77,716)
Chairman of the Board: Leon Hess
Director of Player Personnel: Dick Haley
Coach: Rich Kotite
Director of Public Relations: Frank Ramos

### Oakland Raiders
Address:    332 Center Street
             El Segundo, CA 90245
Telephone: (310) 322-3451
Stadium (Capacity): Oakland-Alameda County Coliseum (54,444)
President of the General Partner: Al Davis
Coach: Mike White
Executive Assistant: Al LoCasale

### Pittsburgh Steelers
Address:    Three Rivers Stadium
             300 Stadium Circle
             Pittsburgh, PA 15212
Telephone: (412) 323-1200
Stadium (Capacity): Three Rivers Stadium (59,600)
President: Dan Rooney
Director of Football Operations: Tom Donahoe
Coach: Bill Cowher
Media Relations Coordinator: Rob Boulware

### San Diego Chargers
Address:    San Diego Jack Murphy Stadium
             P.O. Box 609609
             San Diego, CA 92160
Telephone: (619) 280-2111
Stadium (Capacity): San Diego Jack Murphy Stadium (61,863)
Chairman of the Board/President: Alex G. Spanos
General Manager: Bobby Beathard
Coach: Bobby Ross
Director of Public Relations: Bill Johnston

### Seattle Seahawks
Address:    11220 N.E. 53rd Street
             Kirkland, WA 98033
Telephone: (206) 827-9777
Stadium (Capacity): The Kingdome (66,400)
Owner: Ken Behring
President: David Behring
GM: Tom Flores
Coach: Dennis Erickson
VP of Administration and Communications: Gary Wright
Director of Public Relations: Dave Neubert

# Pro Football Directory *(Cont.)*

## Other Leagues

### Canadian Football League
Address:    110 Eglinton Avenue West, 5th floor
           Toronto, Ontario M4R 1A3, Canada
Telephone: (416) 322-9650
Commissioner: Larry Smith
Communications Director: Michael Murray

### World League of American Football
Address:    410 Park Avenue
           New York, NY 10022
Telephone: (212) 758-1500
President: Oliver Luck (London)
Chief Operating Officer: Dick Regan (London)
Director of Communications: Pete Abitante

# Pro Basketball Directory

### National Basketball Association
Address:    645 Fifth Avenue
           New York, NY 10022
Telephone: (212) 826-7000
Commissioner: David Stern
Deputy Commissioner: Russell Granik
Group VP and GM, Communications Group: Brian McIntyre

### National Basketball Association Players Association
Address:    1775 Broadway
           Suite 2401
           New York, NY 10019
Telephone: (212) 333-7510
Executive Director: Simon Gourdine

### Atlanta Hawks
Address:    One CNN Center, South Tower
           Suite 405
           Atlanta, GA 30303
Telephone: (404) 827-3800
Arena (Capacity): The Omni (16,378)
Owner: Ted Turner
President: Stan Kasten
General Manager: Pete Babcock
Coach: Lenny Wilkens
Director of Media Relations: Arthur Triche

### Boston Celtics
Address:    151 Merrimac Street
           Boston, MA 02114
Telephone: (617) 523-6050
Arena (Capacity): FleetCenter (18,600)
Owner and Chairman of the Board: Paul Gaston
President: Arnold (Red) Auerbach
Executive VP & General Manager: Jan Volk
Coach: M. L. Carr
Director of Public Relations: R. Jeffrey Twiss

### Charlotte Hornets
Address:    100 Hive Drive
           Charlotte, NC 28217
Telephone: (704) 357-0252
Arena (Capacity): Charlotte Coliseum (24,042)
Owner: George Shinn
President: Spencer Stolpen
Coach: Allan Bristow
Director of Media Relations: Harold Kaufman

### Chicago Bulls
Address:    1901 W. Madison
           Chicago, IL 60612
Telephone: (312) 455-4000
Arena (Capacity): United Center (21,711)
Chairman: Jerry Reinsdorf
General Manager: Jerry Krause
Coach: Phil Jackson
Director of Media Services: Tim Hallam

### Cleveland Cavaliers
Address:    One Center Court
           Cleveland, OH 44115
Telephone: (216) 420-2262
Arena (Capacity): Gund Arena (20,562)
Chairman of the Board: Gordon Gund
President/COO, Team Division: Wayne Embry
Coach: Mike Fratello
Director of Public Relations: Bob Zink

### Dallas Mavericks
Address:    Reunion Arena
           777 Sports Street
           Dallas, TX 75207
Telephone: (214) 748-1808
Arena (Capacity): Reunion Arena (17,502)
Owner and Chairman of the Board: Donald Carter
President and General Manager: Norm Sonju
Coach: Dick Motta
Director of Media Services: Kevin Sullivan

### Denver Nuggets
Address:    McNichols Sports Arena
           1635 Clay Street
           Denver, CO 80204
Telephone: (303) 893-6700
Arena (Capacity): McNichols Sports Arena (17,171)
Owners: Comsat Entertainment Group
General Manager and Coach: Bernie Bickerstaff
Media Relations Director: Tommy Sheppard

### Detroit Pistons
Address:    The Palace of Auburn Hills
           Two Championship Drive
           Auburn Hills, MI 48326
Telephone: (810) 377-0100
Arena (Capacity): The Palace of Auburn Hills (21,454)
Owner: William M. Davidson
VP of Player Personnel: Rick Sund
Coach: Doug Collins
VP, Public Relations: Matt Dobek

### Golden State Warriors
Address:    7000 Coliseum Way
           Oakland Coliseum Arena
           Oakland, CA 94621
Telephone: (510) 638-6300
Arena (Capacity): Oakland Coliseum Arena (15,025)
Owner: Christopher Cohan
Chairman: James F. Fitzgerald
General Manager: Dave Twardzik
Coach: Rick Adelman
Director of Communications: Julie Marvel

### Houston Rockets

Address:   The Summit
Ten Greenway Plaza
Houston, TX 77046
Telephone: (713) 627-3865
Arena (Capacity): The Summit (16,611)
Owner: Leslie Alexander
Executive Vice-President: John Thomas
General Manager: Bob Weinhauer
Coach: Rudy Tomjanovich
Director of Media Information: Robert Falkoff

### Indiana Pacers

Address:   300 E. Market Street
Indianapolis, IN 46204
Telephone: (317) 263-2100
Arena (Capacity): Market Square Arena (16,530)
Owners: Melvin Simon and Herbert Simon
President: Donnie Walsh
Coach: Larry Brown
Media Relations Director: David Benner

### Los Angeles Clippers

Address:   L.A. Memorial Sports Arena
3939 S. Figueroa Street
Los Angeles, CA 90037
Telephone: (213) 748-8000
Arena (Capacity): L.A. Memorial Sports Arena (16,021)
Owner: Donald T. Sterling
VP of Basketball Operations: Elgin Baylor
Coach: Bill Fitch
VP of Communications: Joe Safety

### Los Angeles Lakers

Address:   Great Western Forum
3900 West Manchester Boulevard
Inglewood, CA 90306
Telephone: (310) 419-3100
Arena (Capacity): The Great Western Forum (17,505)
Owner: Dr. Jerry Buss
General Manager: Jerry West
Coach: Del Harris
Director of Public Relations: John Black

### Miami Heat

Address:   Sun Trust International Center
One S.E. 3rd Ave., Suite 2300
Miami, FL 33131
Telephone: (305) 577-4328
Arena (Capacity): Miami Arena (15,200)
Managing Partner: Mickey Arison
Executive VP/Business Operations: Pauline Winick
Executive VP/Basketball Operations: Dave Wohl
President and Coach: Pat Riley
Director of Public Relations: Wayne Witt

### Milwaukee Bucks

Address:   The Bradley Center
1001 N. Fourth Street
Milwaukee, WI 53203
Telephone: (414) 227-0500
Arena (Capacity): The Bradley Center (18,633)
Owner: Herb Kohl
Coach and VP of Bask. Operations: Mike Dunleavy
Public Relations Director: Bill King II

### Minnesota Timberwolves

Address:   600 First Avenue North
Minneapolis, MN 55403
Telephone: (612) 673-1602
Arena (Capacity): Target Center (19,006)
Owner: Glen Taylor
VP of Basketball Operations: Kevin McHale
Coach: Bill Blair
Manager of PR/Communications: Kent Wipf

### New Jersey Nets

Address:   405 Murray Hill Parkway
East Rutherford, NJ 07073
Telephone: (201) 935-8888
Arena (Capacity): Meadowlands Arena (20,029)
Chairman/CEO: Alan L. Aufzien
Vice President of Basketball Operations: Willis Reed
Coach: Butch Beard
Director of Public Relations: John Mertz

### New York Knickerbockers

Address:   Madison Square Garden
Two Pennsylvania Plaza
New York, NY 10121
Telephone: (212) 465-6499
Arena (Capacity): Madison Square Garden (19,763)
Owner: ITT/Sheraton and Cablevision
President: David Checketts
General Manager: Ernie Grunfeld
Coach: Don Nelson
Director of Public Relations: Josh Rosenfeld

### Orlando Magic

Address:   P.O. Box 76
Orlando, FL 32802
Telephone: (407) 649-3200
Arena (Capacity): Orlando Arena (17,248)
Owner: Rich DeVos
General Manager: Pat Williams
Coach: Brian Hill
Director of Publicity/Media Relations: Alex Martins

### Philadelphia 76ers

Address:   Veterans Stadium
P.O. Box 25040
Broad Street and Pattison Avenue
Philadelphia, PA 19147
Telephone: (215) 339-7600
Arena (Capacity): CoreStates Spectrum (18,168)
Owner and President: Harold Katz
General Manager and Coach: John Lucas
Public Relations Director: Joe Favorito

### Phoenix Suns

Address:   P.O. Box 1369
Phoenix, AZ 85001
Telephone: (602) 379-7867
Arena (Capacity): America West Arena (19,023)
Owner: Jerry Colangelo
Coach: Paul Westphal
Media Relations Director: Julie Fie

### Portland Trail Blazers

Address:   One Center Court
Suite 200
Portland, OR 97227
Telephone: (503) 234-9291
Arena (Capacity): Rose Garden Arena (21,500)
Chairman of the Board: Paul Allen
President and GM of Blazers Basketball, Inc.: Bob Whitsitt
President of Trailblazers, Inc.: Marshall Glickman
Coach: P.J. Carlesimo
Director of Sports Communication: John Christiansen

# Pro Basketball Directory (Cont.)

## Sacramento Kings
Address:    One Sports Parkway
            Sacramento, CA 95834
Telephone: (916) 928-0000
Arena (Capacity): ARCO Arena (17,317)
Managing General Partner: Jim Thomas
VP of Basketball Operations: Geoff Petrie
Coach: Garry St. Jean
Director of Media Relations: Travis Stanley

## San Antonio Spurs
Address:    AlamoDome
            100 Montana
            San Antonio, TX 78203
Telephone: (210) 554-7787
Arena (Capacity): AlamoDome (20,662)
Chairman: General Robert McDermott
President and CEO: John C. Diller
Coach: Bob Hill
Director of Media Services: Tom James

## Seattle Supersonics
Address:    190 Queen Anne Avenue North
            Suite 200
            Seattle, WA 98109
Telephone: (206) 281-5800
Arena (Capacity): KeyArena (17,100)
Owner: Barry Ackerley
President and General Manager: Wally Walker
Coach: George Karl
Director of Public/Media Relations: Cheri White

## Toronto Raptors
Address:    20 Bay Street, Suite 1702
            Toronto, Ontario, Canada M5J 2N8
Telephone: (416) 214-2255
Arena (Capacity): SkyDome (22,911)
Owner: Bitove Investments, Inc., Slaight Investments
    Inc., Bank of Nova Scotia, Phil Granovsky, David
    Peterson, Isiah Thomas
VP, Basketball Operations: Isiah Thomas
Coach: Brendan Malone
Director of Media Relations: John Lashway

## Utah Jazz
Address:    301 West So. Temple
            Salt Lake City, UT 84101
Telephone: (801) 575-7800
Arena (Capacity): Delta Center (20,600)
Owner: Larry H. Miller
General Manager: R. Tim Howells
Coach: Jerry Sloan
Director of Media Services/Special Events: Kim Turner

## Washington Bullets
Address:    One Harry S. Truman Drive
            Landover, MD 20785
Telephone: (301) 773-2255
Arena (Capacity): USAir Arena (18,756)
Owner: Abe Pollin
General Manager and Vice President: John Nash
Coach: Jim Lynam
Director of Public Relations: Maureen Lewis

### Other League

## Continental Basketball Association
Address:    701 Market Street, Suite 140
            St. Louis, MO 63101
Telephone: (314) 621-7222
Commissioner: Tom Valdiserri
VP of Public Relations: Brett Meister

# Hockey Directory

## National Hockey League
Address:    1251 Avenue of Americas
            47th floor
            New York, NY 10020-1198
Telephone: (212) 789-2000
Commissioner: Gary Bettman
Senior VP and Chief Operating Officer: Steven Solomon
Vice President, Public Relations: Arthur Pincus

## National Hockey League Players Association
Address:    One Dundas Street West
            Suite 2300
            Toronto, Ontario
            Canada M5G 1Z3
Telephone: (416) 408-4040
Executive Director: Bob Goodenow

## Mighty Ducks of Anaheim
Address:    P.O. Box 61077
            Anaheim, CA 92803-6177
Telephone: (714) 704-2700
Arena (Capacity): Arrowhead Pond of Anaheim (17,174)
Owner: Disney Sports Enterprises
General Manager: Jack Ferreira
Coach: Ron Wilson
Director of Media Relations: Bill Robertson

## Boston Bruins
Address:    One FleetCenter
            Suite 250
            Boston, MA 02114
Telephone: (617) 624-1909
Arena (Capacity): FleetCenter (17,565)
Owner and Governor: Jeremy M. Jacobs
Alternative Governor, President and General
    Manager: Harry Sinden
Coach: Steve Kasper
Director of Media Relations: Heidi Holland

## Buffalo Sabres
Address:    Memorial Auditorium
            140 Main Street
            Buffalo, NY 14202
Telephone: (716) 856-7300
Arena (Capacity): Memorial Auditorium (16,230)
Chairman of the Board: Seymour H. Knox III
President and CEO: Douglas G. Moss
General Manager: John Muckler
Coach: Ted Nolan
Director of Public Relations: Jeff Holbrook

## Calgary Flames
Address:    Canadian Airlines Saddledome
        P.O. Box 1540, Station M
        Calgary, Alberta T2P 3B9
Telephone: (403) 777-2177
Arena (Capacity): Canadian Airlines Saddledome
  (20,000)
Owners: Grant A. Bartlett, Harley N. Hotchkiss, N.
  Murray Edwards, Ronald V. Joyce, Alvin G. Libin,
  Allan P. Markin, J.R. McCaig, Byron J. Seaman, and
  Daryl K. Seaman
Executive VP and Alternate Governor: Al Coates
Director of Hockey Operations: Al MacNeil
VP/General Manager: Doug Risebrough
Coach: Pierre Page
Director of Public Relations: Rick Skaggs

## Chicago Blackhawks
Address:    United Center
        1901 W. Madison Street
        Chicago, IL 60612
Telephone: (312) 455-7000
Arena (Capacity): United Center (20,500)
President: William W. Wirtz
General Manager: Robert Pulford
Coach: Craig Hartsburg
Public Relations Director: Jim DeMaria

## Colorado Avalanche
Address:    McNichols Sports Arena
        1635 Clay Street
        Denver, CO 80204
Telephone: (303) 893-6700
Arena (Capacity): McNichols Sports Arena (16,061)
Owner: Comsat Entertainment Group
General Manager: Pierre Lacroix
Coach: Marc Crawford
Director of Press Relations: Jean Martineau

## Dallas Stars
Address:    211 Cowboys Parkway
        Irving, TX 75063
Telephone: (214) 712-2890
Arena (Capacity): Reunion Arena (16,924)
Owner: Norman N. Green
General Manager and Coach: Bob Gainey
Director of Public Relations: Larry Kelly

## Detroit Red Wings
Address:    Joe Louis Sports Arena
        600 Civic Center Drive
        Detroit, MI 48226
Telephone: (313) 396-7544
Arena (Capacity): Joe Louis Sports Arena (19,275)
Senior Vice President: Jim Devellano
Director of Player Personnel and Head Coach: Scott
  Bowman
Assistant General Manager: Ken Holland
Director of Public Relations: Bill Jamieson

## Edmonton Oilers
Address:    Edmonton Coliseum
        Edmonton, Alberta T5B 4M9
Telephone: (403) 474-8561
Arena (Capacity): Edmonton Coliseum
  (17,103)
Owner and Governor: Peter Pocklington
General Manager: Glen Sather
Coach: Ron Low
Director of Public Relations: Bill Tuele

## Florida Panthers
Address:    100 Northeast Third Avenue, 10th floor
        Fort Lauderdale, FL 33301
Telephone: (305) 768-1900
Arena (Capacity): Miami Arena (14,703)
Owner: H. Wayne Huizenga
General Manager: Bryan Murray
Coach: Doug MacLean
Director of Media Relations: Greg Bouris

## Hartford Whalers
Address:    242 Trumbull Street, 8th floor
        Hartford, CT 06103
Telephone: (203) 728-3366
Arena (Capacity): Hartford Civic Center Coliseum
  (15,635)
Owner: KTR Hockey Ltd. Partnership
President and General Manager: Jim Rutherford
Assistant General Manager: Terry McDonnell
Coach: Paul Holmgren
Director of Public Relations: Chris Brown

## Los Angeles Kings
Address:    The Great Western Forum
        3900 West Manchester Boulevard
        P.O. Box 17013
        Inglewood, CA 90308
Telephone: (310) 419-3160
Arena (Capacity): The Great Western Forum (16,005)
President: Rogie Vachonl
General Manager: Sam McMaster
Coach: Larry Robinson
Media Relations: Rick Minch

## Montreal Canadiens
Address:    Montreal Forum
        2313 St. Catherine Street West
        Montreal, Quebec H3H 1N2
Telephone: (514) 932-2582
Arena (Capacity): Montreal Forum (16,259; standing:
  1,700)
Chairman of the Board, President and Governor:
  Ronald Corey
General Manager: Serge A. Savard
Coach: Jacques Demers
Director of Communications: Donald Beauchamp

## New Jersey Devils
Address:    Byrne Meadowlands Arena
        P.O. Box 504
        East Rutherford, NJ 07073
Telephone: (201) 935-6050
Arena (Capacity): Byrne Meadowlands Arena
  (19,040)
Chairman: John J. McMullen
President and General Manager: Lou Lamoriello
Coach: Jacques Lemaire
Director of Information and Publications: Mike Levine

## New York Islanders
Address:    Nassau Veterans' Memorial Coliseum
        Uniondale, NY 11553
Telephone: (516) 794-4100
Arena (Capacity): Nassau Veterans' Memorial
  Coliseum (16,297)
Co-Chairmen: Robert Rosenthal, Stephen Walsh
General Manager: Don Maloney
Coach: Mike Milbury
Media Relations Director: Ginger Killian

## New York Rangers

Address: Madison Square Garden
2 Pennsylvania Plaza
New York, NY 10121
Telephone: (212) 465-6000
Arena (Capacity): Madison Square Garden (18,200)
Owner: ITT Cablevision
President and General Manager: Neil Smith
Coach: Colin Campbell
Director of Communications: Brooks Thomas

## Ottawa Senators

Address: 301 Moodie Drive
Suite 200
Nepean, Ontario K2H 9C4
Telephone: (613) 721-0115
Arena (Capacity): The Palladium (18,500)
Founder: Bruce M. Firestone
Chairman and Governor: Rod Bryden
President and General Manager: Randy Sexton
Coach: Rick Bowness
Director, Media Relations: Laurent Benoit

## Philadelphia Flyers

Address: CoreStates Spectrum
3601 S. Broad Street
Philadelphia, PA 19148
Telephone: (215) 465-4500
Arena (Capacity): CoreStates Spectrum (17,380)
Majority Owners: Ed Snider and family
Limited Partners: Sylvan and Fran Tobin
President and General Manager: Bob Clarke
Coach: Terry Murray
Vice President of Public Relations: Mark Piazza

## Pittsburgh Penguins

Address: Civic Arena
300 Auditorium Place, Gate 9
Pittsburgh, PA 15219
Telephone: (412) 642-1800
Arena (Capacity): Civic Arena (17,189)
Ownership: Howard Baldwin, Morris Belzberg,
Thomas Ruta
General Manager: Craig Patrick
Coach: Eddie Johnston
Director of Media Relations: Harry Sanders

## St. Louis Blues

Address: Kiel Center
P.O. Box 66792
St. Louis, MO 63166-6792
Telephone: (314) 622-2500
Arena (Capacity): Kiel Center (19,260)
President and CEO: Jack Quinn
General Manager and Coach: Mike Keenan
Director of Public Relations: Adam Fell

## San Jose Sharks

Address: San Jose Arena
525 West Santa Clara Street
San Jose, CA 95113
Telephone: (408) 287-7070
Arena (Capacity): San Jose Arena (17,190)
Owners: George and Gordon Gund
Vice President and General Manager: Dean Lombardi
Coach: Kevin Constantine
Director of Media Relations: Ken Arnold

## Tampa Bay Lightning

Address: 501 East Kennedy Boulvard
Suite 175
Tampa, FL 33602
Telephone: (813) 229-2658
Arena (Capacity): The Thunderdome (27,000)
President: Steve Oto
General Manager and President: Phil Esposito
Coach: Terry Crisp
Media Relations Manager: Gerry Helper

## Toronto Maple Leafs

Address: Maple Leaf Gardens
60 Carlton Street
Toronto, Ontario M5B 1L1
Telephone: (416) 977-1641
Arena (Capacity): Maple Leaf Gardens (15,720)
CEO: Steve A. Stavro
General Manager: Cliff Fletcher
Coach: Pat Burns
Director of Business Operations and Communications:
Bob Stellick

## Vancouver Canucks

Address: General Motors Place
800 Griffiths Way
Vancouver, B.C. V6B 6G1
Telephone: (604) 899-4600
Arena (Capacity): General Motors Place (19,056)
Chairman and CEO: Arthur Griffiths
Vice Chairman: John E. McCaw Jr
President and C.O.O.: John Chaple
President, GM, and Alternate Governor: Pat Quinn
Coach: Rick Lee
Mgr. of Hockey Information: Devin Smith
Public and Community Relations Coordinator:
Veronica Varhaug

## Washington Capitals

Address: USAir Arena
Landover, MD 20785
Telephone: (301) 386-7000
Arena (Capacity): USAir Arena (18,130)
Board of Directors: Abe Pollin, David P. Binderman,
Stewart L. Binderman, James E. Cafritz, A. James
Clark, Albert Cohen, J. Martin Irving, James T.
Lewis, R. Robert Linowes, Arthur K. Mason, Dr.
Jack Meshel, David M. Osnos, Richard M. Patrick
VP and General Manager: Dave Poile
Coach: Jim Schoenteld
VP of Communications: Matt Williams

## Winnipeg Jets

Address: 10th Floor
1661 Portaze Avenue
Winnipeg, Manitoba R3J 3T7
Telephone: (204) 982-5387
Arena (Capacity): Winnipeg Arena (15,393)
President and Governor: Barry L. Shenkarow
Alternate Governor: Bill Davis
Board of Directors: Barry L. Shenkarow, Dick Archer,
Barry McQueen, Marvin Shenkarow, Steve
Bannatyne, Harvey Secter, Bill Davis
General Manager: John Paddock
Coach: Terry Simpson
Director of Communications: Richard Nairn

# College Sports Directory

## NATIONAL COLLEGIATE ATHLETIC ASSOCIATION (NCAA)
Address: 6201 College Boulevard
Overland Park, KS 66211
Telephone: (913) 339-1906
Executive Director: Cedric Dempsey
Director of Public Information: Kathryn Reith

## ATLANTIC COAST CONFERENCE
Address: P.O. Drawer ACC
Greensboro, NC 27419-6999
Telephone: (910) 854-8787
Commissioner: Eugene F. Corrigan
Director of Media Relations: Brian Morrison

### Clemson University
Address: Clemson, SC 29633
Nickname: Tigers
Telephone: (803) 656-2114
Football Stadium (Capacity): Clemson Memorial Stadium (81,473)
Basketball Arena (Capacity): Littlejohn Coliseum (11,020)
President: Constantine Curris
Athletic Director: Bobby Robinson
Football Coach: Tommy West
Basketball Coach: Rick Barnes
Sports Information Director: Tim Bourret

### Duke University
Address: Durham, NC 27708
Nickname: Blue Devils
Telephone: (919) 684-2633
Football Stadium (Capacity): Wallace Wade Stadium (33,941)
Basketball Arena (Capacity): Cameron Indoor Stadium (9,314)
President: Nan Keohane
Athletic Director: Tom Butters
Football Coach: Fred Goldsmith
Basketball Coach: Mike Krzyzewski
Sports Information Director: Mike Cragg

### Florida State University
Address: P.O. Box 2195
Tallahassee, FL 32316
Nickname: Seminoles
Telephone: (904) 644-1403
Football Stadium (Capacity): Doak S. Campbell Stadium (77,500)
Basketball Arena (Capacity): Leon County Civic Center (12,500)
President: Sandy D'Alemberte
Athletic Director: Dave Hart
Football Coach: Bobby Bowden
Basketball Coach: Pat Kennedy
Sports Information Director: Rob Wilson

### Georgia Tech
Address: 150 Bobby Dodd Way
Atlanta, GA 30332
Nickname: Yellow Jackets
Telephone: (404) 894-5445
Football Stadium (Capacity): Bobby Dodd Stadium/Grant Field (46,000)
Basketball Arena (Capacity): Alexander Memorial Coliseum at McDonald's Center (10,000)
President: G. Wayne Clough
Athletic Director: Dr. Homer Rice
Football Coach: George O'Leary
Basketball Coach: Bobby Cremins
Sports Information Director: Mike Finn

### University of Maryland
Address: P.O. Box 295
College Park, MD 20741
Nickname: Terrapins
Telephone: (301) 314-7064
Football Stadium (Capacity): Byrd Stadium (48,055)
Basketball Arena (Capacity): Cole Fieldhouse (14,500)
President: Dr. William E. Kirwin
Athletic Director: Deborah Yow
Football Coach: Mark Duffner
Basketball Coach: Gary Williams
Sports Information Director: Herb Hartnett

### University of North Carolina
Address: P.O. Box 2126
Chapel Hill, NC 27514
Nickname: Tar Heels
Telephone: (919) 962-2123
Football Stadium (Capacity): Kenan Memorial Stadium (52,000)
Basketball Arena (Capacity): Dean E. Smith Center (21,572)
Chancellor: Dr. Michael K. Hooker
Athletic Director: John Swofford
Football Coach: Mack Brown
Basketball Coach: Dean Smith
Sports Information Director: Rick Brewer

### North Carolina State University
Address: Box 8501
Raleigh, NC 27695
Nickname: Wolfpack
Telephone: (919) 515-2102
Football Stadium (Capacity): Carter-Finley Stadium (51,500)
Basketball Arena (Capacity): Reynolds Coliseum (12,400)
Chancellor: Dr. Larry K. Monteith
Athletic Director: Todd Turner
Football Coach: Mike O'Cain
Basketball Coach: Les Robinson
Sports Information Director: Mark Bockelman

### University of Virginia
Address: P.O. Box 3785
Charlottesville, VA 22903
Nickname: Cavaliers
Telephone: (804) 982-5151
Football Stadium (Capacity): Scott Stadium (42,000)
Basketball Arena (Capacity): University Hall (8,500)
President: John Casteen III
Athletic Director: Terry Holland
Football Coach: George Welsh
Basketball Coach: Jeff Jones
Sports Information Director: Rich Murray

### Wake Forest University
Address: P.O. Box 7426
Winston-Salem, NC 27109
Nickname: Demon Deacons
Telephone: (910) 759-5640
Football Stadium (Capacity): Groves Stadium (31,500)
Basketball Arena (Capacity): Lawrence Joel Memorial Coliseum (14,407)
President: Dr. Thomas K. Hearn Jr.
Athletic Director: Ron Wellman
Football Coach: Jim Caldwell
Basketball Coach: Dave Odom
Sports Information Director: John Justus

## BIG EAST CONFERENCE

Address: 56 Exchange Terrace, 5th floor
Providence, RI 02903
Telephone: (401) 272-9108
Commissioner: Michael A. Tranghese
Ass't Commissioner for Public Relations: John
Paquette

## Boston College

Address: Chestnut Hill, MA 02167
Nickname: Eagles
Telephone: (617) 552-3004
Football Stadium (Capacity): Alumni Stadium (44,500)
Basketball Arena (Capacity): Silvio O. Conte Forum
(8,604)
President: Rev. J. Donald Monan, S.J.
Athletic Director: Chet Gladchuk
Football Coach: Dan Henning
Basketball Coach: Jim O'Brien
Sports Information Director: Reid Oslin

## University of Connecticut

Address: 2095 Hillside Road
Storrs, CT 06269-3078
Nickname: Huskies
Telephone: (203) 486-2725
Football Stadium (Capacity): Memorial Stadium
(16,200)
Basketball Arena (Capacity): Gampel Pavilion (8,241)
President: Dr. Harry J. Hartley
Athletic Director: Lew Perkins
Football Coach: Skip Holtz
Basketball Coach: Jim Calhoun
Sports Information Director: Tim Tolokan
Note: Division I-AA football

## Georgetown University

Address: McDonough Arena
Box 571124
Washington, DC 20057-1124
Nickname: Hoyas
Telephone: (202) 687-2435
Football Stadium (Capacity): Kehoe Field (2,000)
Basketball Arena (Capacity): USAir Arena (19,035)
President: Rev. Leo J. O'Donovan, S.J.
Senior Athletic Director: Francis X. Rienzo
Athletic Director: Joseph Lang
Football Coach: Robert Benson
Basketball Coach: John Thompson
Sports Information Director: Bill Shapland (basketball),
Bill Hurd
Note: Division I-AA football

## University of Miami

Address: One Hurricane Drive
Coral Gables, FL 33146
Nickname: Hurricanes
Telephone: (305) 284-3822
Football Stadium (Capacity): Orange Bowl (74,476)
Basketball Arena (Capacity): Miami Arena (15,388)
President: Edward Foote II
Athletic Director: Paul Dee
Football Coach: Butch Davis
Basketball Coach: Leonard Hamilton
Sports Information Director: John Hahn

## University of Pittsburgh

Address: Dept. of Athletics, P.O. Box 7436
Pittsburgh, PA 15213
Nickname: Panthers
Telephone: (412) 648-8240
Football Stadium (Capacity): Pitt Stadium (56,500)
Basketball Arena (Capacity): Fitzgerald Field House
(6,798), Pittsburgh Civic Arena (16,798)
Chancellor: J. Dennis O'Connor
Athletic Director: Oval Jaynes
Football Coach: Johnny Majors
Basketball Coach: Ralph Willard
Sports Information Director: Ron Wall

## Providence College

Address: River Avenue
Providence, RI 02918
Nickname: Friars
Telephone: (401) 865-2265
Basketball Arena (Capacity): Providence Civic Center
(13,410)
President: Rev. Philip A. Smith, O.P.
Athletic Director: John Marinatto
Basketball Coach: Pete Gillen
Sports Information Director: Tim Connor
Note: No football program

## Rutgers University

Address: P.O. Box 1149
Piscataway, NJ 08855-1149
Nickname: Scarlet Knights
Telephone: (908) 445-4200
Football Stadium (Capacity): Rutgers Stadium
(42,000), Giants Stadium (76,000)
Basketball Arena (Capacity): Louis Brown Athletic
Center (9,000)
President: Dr. Francis L. Lawrence
Athletic Director: Frederick Gruninger
Football Coach: Doug Graber
Basketball Coach: Bob Wenzel
Sports Information Director: Peter Kowalski

## St. John's University

Address: 8000 Utopia Parkway
Jamaica, NY 11439
Nickname: Red Storm
Telephone: (718) 990-6367
Football Stadium (Capacity): St. John's Stadium (3,000)
Basketball Arena (Capacity): Alumni Hall (6,008),
Madison Square Garden (19,876)
President: Very Rev. Donald J. Harrington, C.M.
Athletic Director: Edward J. Manetta Jr.
Football Coach: Bob Ricca
Basketball Coach: Brian Mahoney
Sports Information Director: Frank Racaniello
Note: Division I-AA football

## Seton Hall University

Address: 400 South Orange Avenue
South Orange, NJ 07079
Nickname: Pirates
Telephone: (201) 761-9497
Basketball Arena (Capacity): Walsh Auditorium
(3,200), The Meadowlands (20,029)
President: Rev. Thomas R. Peterson
Athletic Director: Larry Keating
Basketball Coach: George Blaney
Sports Information Director: John Wooding
Note: No football program

## Syracuse University

Address: Manley Field House
Syracuse, NY 13244-5020
Nickname: Orangemen
Telephone: (315) 443-2608
Football Stadium (Capacity): Carrier Dome (50,000)
Basketball Arena (Capacity): Carrier Dome (33,000)
Chancellor: Dr. Kenneth Shaw
Athletic Director: Jake Crouthamel
Football Coach: Paul Pasqualoni
Basketball Coach: Jim Boeheim
Sports Information Director: Larry Kimball

## Temple University

Address: McGonigle Hall
Philadelphia, PA 19122
Nickname: Owls
Telephone: (215) 204-7445
Football Stadium (Capacity): Veterans Stadium
(66,592)
Basketball Arena (Capacity): McGonigle Hall (3,900)
President: Peter J. Liacouras
Athletic Director: R. C. Johnson
Football Coach: Ron Dickerson
Basketball Coach: John Chaney
Sports Information Director: Gerry Emig
Note: Plays football in Big East, basketball in Atlantic 10
Conference.

## Villanova University

Address: 800 Lancaster Avenue
Villanova, PA 19085
Nickname: Wildcats
Telephone: (610) 519-4110
Football Stadium (Capacity): Villanova Stadium (13,400)
Basketball Arena (Capacity): duPont Pavilion (6,500),
CoreStates Spectrum (18,497)
President: Rev. Edmund Dobbin, O.S.A.
Athletic Director: Gene DeFilippo
Football Coach: Andy Talley
Basketball Coach: Steve Lappas
Sports Information Director: Karen Frascona
Note: Division I-AA football

## Virginia Tech

Address: Jamerson Athletic Center
Blacksburg, VA 24061
Nickname: Hokies
Telephone: (703) 231-6726
Football Stadium (Capacity): Lane Stadium/Worsham
Field (51,000)
Basketball Arena (Capacity): Cassell Coliseum (9,971)
President: Dr. Paul Torgersen
Athletic Director: Dave Braine
Football Coach: Frank Beamer
Basketball Coach: Bill Foster
Sports Information Director: Dave Smith
Note: Plays football in Big East, basketball in Atlantic 10.

## West Virginia University

Address: P.O. Box 0877
Morgantown, WV 26507-0877
Nickname: Mountaineers
Telephone: (304) 293-2821
Football Stadium (Capacity): Mountaineer Field
(63,500)
Basketball Arena (Capacity): WVU Coliseum (14,000)
President: David Hardesty
Athletic Director: Ed Pastilong
Football Coach: Don Nehlen
Basketball Coach: Gale Catlett
Sports Information Director: Shelley Poe

## BIG EIGHT CONFERENCE

Address: 104 West Ninth Street, Suite 408
Kansas City, MO 64105
Telephone: (816) 471-5088
Commissioner: Carl C. James
Publicity Director: Jeff Bollig

## University of Colorado

Address: Campus Box 357
Boulder, CO 80309
Nickname: Buffaloes
Telephone: (303) 492-5626
Football Stadium (Capacity): Folsom Field (51,748)
Basketball Arena (Capacity): Coors Event Center
(11,199)
President: Dr. Judith Albino
Athletic Director: Bill Marolt
Football Coach: Rick Neuheisel
Basketball Coach: Joe Harrington
Sports Information Director: David Plati

## Iowa State University

Address: 1802 S. Fourth
Olsen Annex
Ames, IA 50011
Nickname: Cyclones
Telephone: (515) 294-3372
Football Stadium (Capacity): Cyclone Stadium-Jack
Trice Field (43,000)
Basketball Arena (Capacity): Hilton Coliseum
(14,020)
President: Dr. Martin C. Jischke
Athletic Director: Gene Smith
Football Coach: Dan McCarney
Basketball Coach: Tim Floyd
Sports Information Director: Tom Kroeschell

## University of Kansas

Address: Allen Field House, Room 104
Lawrence, KS 66045
Nickname: Jayhawks
Telephone: (913) 864-3417
Football Stadium (Capacity): Memorial Stadium
(50,250)
Basketball Arena (Capacity): Allen Field House
(16,300)
Chancellor: Robert Hemenway
Athletic Director: Dr. Bob Fredrick
Football Coach: Glen Mason
Basketball Coach: Roy Williams
Sports Information Director: Doug Vance

## Kansas State University
Address: Manhattan, KS 66502
Nickname: Wildcats
Telephone: (913) 532-6011
Football Stadium (Capacity): KSU Stadium (45,000)
Basketball Arena (Capacity): Bramlage Coliseum
  (13,500)
President: Dr. Jon Wefald
Athletic Director: Max Urick
Football Coach: Bill Snyder
Basketball Coach: Tom Asbury
Sports Information Director: Ben Boyle

## University of Missouri
Address:     P.O. Box 677
             Columbia, MO 65205
Nickname: Tigers
Telephone: (314) 882-3241
Football Stadium (Capacity): Faurot Field/Memorial
  Stadium (62,000)
Basketball Arena (Capacity): Hearnes Center (13,349)
Chancellor: Dr. Charles Kiesler
Athletic Director: Joe Castiglione
Football Coach: Larry Smith
Basketball Coach: Norm Stewart
Sports Information Director: Bob Brendel

## University of Nebraska
Address:     116 South Stadium
             Lincoln, NE 68588
Nickname: Cornhuskers
Telephone: (402) 472-2263
Football Stadium (Capacity): Memorial Stadium
  (72,700)
Basketball Arena (Capacity): Bob Devaney Sports
  Center (14,302)
President: L. Dennis Smith
Athletic Director: Bill Byrne
Football Coach: Tom Osborne
Basketball Coach: Danny Nee
Sports Information Director: Chris Anderson

## University of Oklahoma
Address:     180 W. Brooks, Room 235
             Norman, OK 73019
Nickname: Sooners
Telephone: (405) 325-8231
Football Stadium (Capacity): Memorial Stadium/Owen
  Field (75,004)
Basketball Arena (Capacity): Lloyd Noble Center
  (11,100)
President: David Boren
Athletic Director: Donnie Duncan
Football Coach: Howard Schnellenberger
Basketball Coach: Kelvin Sampson
Sports Information Director: Mike Prusinski

## Oklahoma State University
Address:     202 Gallagher-Iba Arena
             Stillwater, OK 74078
Nickname: Cowboys
Telephone: (405) 744-5749
Football Stadium (Capacity): Lewis Field (50,614)
Basketball Arena (Capacity): Gallagher-Iba Arena
  (6,381)
President: Dr. James Halligan
Athletic Director: Terry Don Phillips
Football Coach: Bob Simmons
Basketball Coach: Eddie Sutton
Sports Information Director: Steve Buzzard

## BIG TEN CONFERENCE
Address:     1500 West Higgins Road
             Park Ridge, IL 60068
Telephone: (708) 696-1010
Commissioner: James E. Delany
Assistant Commissioner: Mark Rudner

## University of Illinois
Address:     1817 S. Neil Street, Suite 201
             Champaign, IL 61820
Nickname: Fighting Illini
Telephone: (217) 333-1390
Football Stadium (Capacity): Memorial Stadium (72,292)
Basketball Arena (Capacity): Assembly Hall (16,153)
President: James Stukel
Athletic Director: Ronald Guenther
Football Coach: Lou Tepper
Basketball Coach: Lou Henson
Sports Information Director: Mike Pearson

## Indiana University
Address:     17th Street and Fee Lane/Assembly Hall
             Bloomington, IN 47405
Nickname: Hoosiers
Telephone: (812) 855-2421
Football Stadium (Capacity): Memorial Stadium
  (52,354)
Basketball Arena (Capacity): Assembly Hall (17,357)
President: Myles Brand
Athletic Director: Clarence Doninger
Football Coach: Bill Mallory
Basketball Coach: Bob Knight
Sports Information Director: Kit Klingelhoffer

## University of Iowa
Address:     205 Carver-Hawkeye Arena
             Iowa City, IA 52242
Nickname: Hawkeyes
Telephone: (319) 335-9411
Football Stadium (Capacity): Kinnick Stadium (70,397)
Basketball Arena (Capacity): Carver-Hawkeye Arena
  (15,500)
President: Mary Sue Coleman
Athletic Director: Robert Bowlsby
Football Coach: Hayden Fry
Basketball Coach: Tom Davis
Sports Information Director: Phil Haddy

## University of Michigan
Address:     1000 S. State Street
             Ann Arbor, MI 48109
Nickname: Wolverines
Telephone: (313) 763-4423
Football Stadium (Capacity): Michigan Stadium
  (102,501)
Basketball Arena (Capacity): Crisler Arena (13,562)
President: James Duderstadt
Athletic Director: Dr. Joseph Roberson
Football Coach: Lloyd Carr
Basketball Coach: Steve Fisher
Sports Information Director: Bruce Madej

## Michigan State University

Address: East Lansing, MI 48824
Nickname: Spartans
Telephone: (517) 355-2271
Football Stadium (Capacity): Spartan Stadium (72,027)
Basketball Arena (Capacity): Jack Breslin Student Events Center (15,138)
President: M. Peter McPherson
Athletic Director: Merritt J. Norvell Jr., Ph.D.
Football Coach: Nick Saban
Basketball Coach: Tom Izzo
Sports Information Director: Ken Hoffman

## University of Minnesota

Address: 516 15th Avenue S.E.
Minneapolis, MN 55455
Nickname: Golden Gophers
Telephone: (612) 625-4090
Football Stadium (Capacity): Hubert H. Humphrey Metrodome (63,669)
Basketball Arena (Capacity): Williams Arena (14,300)
President: Nils Hasselmo
Athletic Director: McKinley Boston
Football Coach: Jim Wacker
Basketball Coach: Clem Haskins
Sports Information Director: Marc Ryan

## Northwestern University

Address: 1501 Central Street
Evanston, IL 60208
Nickname: Wildcats
Telephone: (708) 491-3205
Football Stadium (Capacity): Dyche Stadium (49,256)
Basketball Arena (Capacity): Welsh-Ryan Arena (8,117)
President: Henry S. Bienen
Athletic Director: Rick Taylor
Football Coach: Gary Barnett
Basketball Coach: Ricky Byrdsong
Director of Media Services: Brad Hurlbut

## Ohio State University

Address: 410 Woody Hayes Drive, Room 124
Columbus, OH 43210
Nickname: Buckeyes
Telephone: (614) 292-6861
Football Stadium (Capacity): Ohio Stadium (89,542)
Basketball Arena (Capacity): St. John Arena (13,276)
President: Dr. E. Gordon Gee
Athletic Director: Andy Geiger
Football Coach: John Cooper
Basketball Coach: Randy Ayers
Sports Information Director: Steve Snapp

## Penn State University

Address: Recreation Building
University Park, PA 16802
Nickname: Nittany Lions
Telephone: (814) 865-1757
Football Stadium (Capacity): Beaver Stadium (93,967)
Basketball Arena (Capacity): Recreation Hall (6,846)
President: Dr. Graham Spanier
Athletic Director: Tim Curley
Football Coach: Joe Paterno
Basketball Coach: Jerry Dunn
Sports Information Director: Jeff Nelson

## Purdue University

Address: Mackey Arena, Room 15
West Lafayette, IN 47907
Nickname: Boilermakers
Telephone: (317) 494-3200
Football Stadium (Capacity): Ross-Ade Stadium (67,861)
Basketball Arena (Capacity): Mackey Arena (14,123)
President: Dr. Steven C. Beering
Athletic Director: Morgan Burke
Football Coach: Jim Colletto
Basketball Coach: Gene Keady
Sports Information Director: Mark Adams

## University of Wisconsin

Address: 1440 Monroe Street
Madison, WI 53711
Nickname: Badgers
Telephone: (608) 262-1811
Football Stadium (Capacity): Camp Randall Stadium (77,745)
Basketball Arena (Capacity): UW Fieldhouse (11,895)
Chancellor: David Ward
Athletic Director: Pat Richter
Football Coach: Barry Alvarez
Basketball Coach: Dick Bennett
Sports Information Director: Steve Malchow

## BIG WEST CONFERENCE

Address: 2 Corporate Park
Suite 206
Irvine, CA 92714
Telephone: (714) 261-2525
Commissioner: Dennis Farrell
Publicity Director: Dennis Bickmeyer

## California State University–Fullerton

Address: 800 North State College Boulevard
P.O. Box 34080
Fullerton, CA 92634-9480
Nickname: Titans
Telephone: (714) 773-2677
Basketball Arena (Capacity): Titan Gym (4,000)
President: Dr. Milton A. Gordon
Athletic Director: John Easterbrook
Basketball Coach: Bob Hawking
Sports Information Director: Mel Franks
Note: No football program in 1995.

## Fresno State University

Address: 5305 N. Campus Drive, Room 153
Fresno, CA 93740-0027
Nickname: Bulldogs
Telephone: (209) 278-2643
Football Stadium (Capacity): Bulldog Stadium (41,031)
Basketball Arena (Capacity): Selland Arena (10,159)
President: Dr. John Welty
Interim Athletic Director: Dr. Benjamin Quillian
Football Coach: Jim Sweeney
Basketball Coach: Jerry Tarkanian
Sports Information Director: Scott Johnson

## Long Beach State University

Address: 1250 Bellflower Boulevard
Long Beach, CA 90840
Nickname: 49ers
Telephone: (310) 985-4655
Basketball Arena (Capacity): The Pyramid (5,000)
President: Dr. Robert C. Maxson
Athletic Director: David O'Brien
Basketball Coach: Seth Greenberg
Sports Information Director: Scott Cathcart

## University of Nevada at Las Vegas

Address: 4505 Maryland Parkway
Las Vegas, NV 89154
Nickname: Rebels
Telephone: (702) 895-3207
Football Stadium (Capacity): Sam Boyd Stadium
(32,000)
Basketball Arena (Capacity): Thomas and Mack
Center (18,500)
President: Carol C. Harter
Athletic Director: Charles Cavagnaro
Football Coach: Jeff Horton
Basketball Coach: Bill Bayno
Sports Information Director: Jim Gemma

## New Mexico State University

Address: Box 30001, Dept. 3145
Las Cruces, NM 88003
Nickname: Aggies
Telephone: (505) 646-4126
Football Stadium (Capacity): Aggie Memorial Stadium
(30,343)
Basketball Arena (Capacity): Pan American Center
(13,007)
President: Michael J. Orenduff
Athletic Director: Al Gonzales
Football Coach: Jim Hess
Basketball Coach: Neil McCarthy
Sports Information Director: Steve Shutt

## University of the Pacific

Address: 3601 Pacific Avenue
Stockton, CA 95211
Nickname: Tigers
Telephone: (209) 946-2479
Football Stadium (Capacity): Amos Alonzo Stagg
Memorial Stadium (30,000)
Basketball Arena (Capacity): A.G. Spanos Center
(6,150)
President: Dr. Donald DeRosa
Athletic Director: Bob Lee
Football Coach: Chuck Shelton
Basketball Coach: Bob Thomason
Sports Information Director: Mike Millerick

## San Jose State University

Address: One Washington Square
San Jose, CA 95192-0062
Nickname: Spartans
Telephone: (408) 924-1200
Football Stadium (Capacity): Spartan Stadium
(31,218)
Basketball Arena (Capacity): Event Center (4,600)
President: Dr. Robert L. Caret
Athletic Director: Dr. Tom Brennan
Football Coach: John Ralston
Basketball Coach: Stan Morrison
Sports Information Director: Lawrence Fan

## Utah State University

Address: Logan, UT 84322-7400
Nickname: Aggies
Telephone: (801) 797-1850
Football Stadium (Capacity): Romney Stadium
(30,000)
Basketball Arena (Capacity): The Smith Spectrum
(10,270)
President: Dr. George H. Emert
Athletic Director: Chuck Bell
Football Coach: John L. Smith
Basketball Coach: Larry Eustachy
Sports Information Director: John Lewandowski

## CONFERENCE USA

Address: 35 East Wacker Drive, Suite 650
Chicago, IL 60601
Telephone: (312) 553-0483
Comissioner: Michael Slive
Media Relations Director: Brian Teter

## University of Alabama-Birmingham

Address: UAB Arena
617 13th Street South
Birmingham, AL 35294
Nickname: Blazers
Telephone: (205) 934-7252
Football Stadium (Capacity): Legion Field (83,091)
Basketball Arena (Capacity): UAB Arena (8,500)
President: Dr. J. Claude Bennett
Athletic Director: Gene Bartow
Football Coach: Watson Brown
Basketball Coach: Gene Brown
Sports Information Director: Grant Shingleton
Note: Will begin conference play in football in 1996-97.

## University of Cincinnati

Address: Cincinnati, OH 45221-0021
Nickname: Bearcats
Telephone: (513) 556-5601
Football Stadium (Capacity): Nippert Stadium (35,500)
Basketball Arena (Capacity): Myrl Shoemaker Center
(13,176)
President: Dr. Joseph A. Steger
Athletic Director: Gerald O'Dell
Football Coach: Rick Minter
Basketball Coach: Bob Huggins
Sports Information Director: Tom Hathaway
Note: Will begin conference play in football in 1996-97.

## DePaul University

Address: 1011 West Belden Avenue
Chicago, IL 60614
Nickname: Blue Demons
Telephone: (312) 325-7526
Basketball Arena (Capacity): Rosemont Horizon
(17,500)
President: Rev. John P. Minogue, C.M.
Athletic Director: Bill Bradshaw
Basketball Coach: Joey Meyer
Sports Information Director: John Lanctot
Note: No football program.

## University of Houston
Address:    3100 Cullen Boulevard
            Houston, TX 77004
Nickname: Cougars
Telephone: (713) 743-9370
Football Stadium (Capacity): Astrodome (65,000)
Basketball Arena (Capacity): Hofheinz Pavilion
  (10,060)
President: Dr. Glenn Goerke
Athletic Director: William C. Carr
Football Coach: Kim Helton
Basketball Coach: Alvin Brooks
Sports Information Director: Donna Turner
Note: Will begin conference play in 1996-97.

## University of Louisville
Address: Louisville, KY 40292
Nickname: Cardinals
Telephone: (502) 852-5732
Football Stadium (Capacity): Cardinal Stadium
  (37,500)
Basketball Arena (Capacity): Freedom Hall (19,000)
President: Dr. John Schumaker
Athletic Director: William Olsen
Football Coach: Ron Cooper
Basketball Coach: Denny Crum
Sports Information Director: Kenny Klein
Note: Will begin conference play in football in 1996-97.

## Marquette University
Address:    P.O. Box 1881
            Milwaukee, WI 53201-1881
Nickname: Golden Eagles
Telephone: (414) 288-7447
Basketball Arena (Capacity): Bradley Center (18,592)
President: Rev. Albert J. DiUlio, S.J.
Athletic Director: Bill Cords
Basketball Coach: Mike Deane
Sports Information Director: Kathleen Hohl
Note: No football program.

## University of Memphis
Address: Memphis, TN 38152
Nickname: Tigers
Telephone: (901) 678-2337
Football Stadium (Capacity): Liberty Bowl Memorial
  Stadium/Rex Dockery Field (62,380)
Basketball Arena (Capacity): The Pyramid (20,142)
President: Dr. V. Lane Rawlins
Interim Athletic Director: Dr. Don Carson
Football Coach: Rip Scherer
Basketball Coach: Larry Finch
Sports Information Director: Bob Winn
Note: Will begin conference play in football in 1996-97.

## University of North Carolina-Charlotte
Address:    9201 University City Boulevard
            UNC-Charlotte
            Belk Gymnasium
            Charlotte, NC 28223-0001
Nickname: 49ers
Telephone: (704) 547-4937
Basketball Arena (Capacity): Independence Arena
  (9,575)
Chancellor: James H. Woodward
Athletic Director: Judy W. Rose
Basketball Coach: Jeff Mullins
Sports Information Director: Mark Colone
Note: No football program.

## Saint Louis University
Address:    3672 West Pine Boulevard
            St. Louis, MO 63108
Nickname: Billikens
Telephone: (314) 977-3177
Basketball Arena (Capacity): Kiel Center (20,000)
President: Rev. Lawrence Biondi, S.J.
Athletic Director: Doug Woolard
Basketball Coach: Charlie Spoonhour
Sports Information Director: Doug McIlhagga
Note: No football program.

## University of South Florida
Address:    4202 East Fowler Ave., PED 214
            Tampa, FL 33620
Nickname: Bulls
Telephone: (813) 974-2125
Basketball Arena (Capacity): Sun Dome (11,000)
President: Betty Castor
Athletic Director: Paul Griffin
Basketball Coach: Bobby Paschal
Sports Information Director: John Gerdes
Note: The football program will begin with the 1997 season.

## University of Southern Mississippi
Address:    P.O. Box 5161
            Hattiesburg, MS 39406
Nickname: Golden Eagles
Telephone: (601) 266-5017
Football Stadium (Capacity): M. M. Roberts Stadium
  (33,000)
Basketball Arena (Capacity): Reed Green Coliseum
  (8,095)
President: Dr. Aubrey K. Lucas
Athletic Director: H. C. Bill McLellan
Football Coach: Jeff Bower
Basketball Coach: M. K. Turk
Sports Information Director: Regiel Napier
Note: Will begin conference play in football in 1996-97.

## Tulane University
Address:    James Wilson Jr. Center for
            Intercollegiate Athletics
            New Orleans, LA 70118
Nickname: Green Wave
Telephone: (504) 865-5501
Football Stadium (Capacity): Louisiana Superdome
  (71,000)
Basketball Arena (Capacity): Fogelman Arena (5,000)
President: Dr. Eamon Kelly
Athletic Director: Dr. Kevin White
Football Coach: Eugene (Buddy) Teevens
Basketball Coach: Perry Clark
Sports Information Director: Lenny Vangilder
Note: Will begin conference play in football in 1996-97.

## IVY LEAGUE
Address: 120 Alexander Street, Princeton, NJ 08544
Telephone: (609) 258-6426
Executive Director: Jeff Orleans
Publicity Director: Chuck Yrigoyen

### Brown University
Address: Hope Street, Providence, RI 02912
Nickname: Bears
Telephone: (401) 863-2211
Football Stadium (Capacity): Brown Stadium (20,000)
Basketball Arena (Capacity): Paul Bailey Pizzitola
  Memorial Sports Center (2,500)
President: Vartan Gregorian
Athletic Director: David Roach
Football Coach: Mark Whipple
Basketball Coach: Franklin Dobbs
Sports Information Director: Christopher Humm

### Columbia University
Address: Dodge Physical Fitness Center,
  New York, NY 10027
Nickname: Lions
Telephone: (212) 854-2538
Football Stadium (Capacity): Lawrence A. Wien
  Stadium at Baker Field (17,000)
Basketball Arena (Capacity): Levien Gymnasium (3,400)
President: Dr. George Rupp
Athletic Director: Dr. John Reeves
Football Coach: Ray Tellier
Basketball Coach: Armond Hill
Sports Information Director: William C. Steinman

### Cornell University
Address: Teagle Hall, Campus Road
  Ithaca, NY 14853
Nickname: Big Red
Telephone: (607) 255-5220
Football Stadium (Capacity): Schoellkopf Field (27,000)
Basketball Arena (Capacity): Newman Arena (4,750)
President: Hunter R. Rawlings III
Athletic Director: Charles Moore
Football Coach: Jim Hofher
Basketball Coach: Al Walker
Sports Information Director: Dave Wohlhueter

### Dartmouth College
Address: 6083 Alumni Gym
  Hanover, NH 03755-3512
Nickname: Big Green
Telephone: (603) 646-2465
Football Stadium (Capacity): Memorial Field (20,416)
Basketball Arena (Capacity): Leede Arena (2,100)
President: James Freedman
Athletic Director: Richard G. Jaeger
Football Coach: John Lyons
Basketball Coach: Dave Faucher
Sports Information Director: Kathy Slattery

### Harvard University
Address: 60 John F. Kennedy St.
  Cambridge, MA 02138
Nickname: Crimson
Telephone: (617) 495-2206
Football Stadium (Capacity): Harvard Stadium (37,967)
Basketball Arena (Capacity): Briggs Athletic Center
  (2,083)
President: Neil L. Rudentsine
Athletic Director: William J. Cleary Jr.
Football Coach: Tim Murphy
Basketball Coach: Frank Sullivan
Sports Information Director: John Veneziano

### University of Pennsylvania
Address: Weightman Hall North
  235 South 33rd Street
  Philadelphia, PA 19104-6322
Nickname: Quakers
Telephone: (215)898-6121
Football Stadium (Capacity): Franklin Field (60,546)
Basketball Arena (Capacity): Palestra Arena (8,700)
President: Dr. Judith Rodin
Athletic Director: Steven Bilsky
Football Coach: Al Bagnoli
Basketball Coach: Fran Dunphy
Director, Media Relations: Gail Stasulli Zachary
Director, Athletic Communications: Shaun May

### Princeton University
Address: P.O. Box 71
  Jadwin Gym
  Princeton, NJ 08544
Nickname: Tigers
Telephone: (609) 258-3568
Football Stadium (Capacity): Palmer Stadium (45,725)
Basketball Arena (Capacity): Jadwin Gym (7,550)
President: Harold Shapiro
Athletic Director: Gary D. Walters
Football Coach: Steve Tosches
Basketball Coach: Pete Carril
Sports Information Director: Kurt Kehl

### Yale University
Address: Box 208216
  New Haven, CT 06520
Nickname: Bulldogs, Elis
Telephone: (203) 432-1456
Football Stadium (Capacity): Yale Bowl (64,269)
Basketball Arena (Capacity): Payne Whitney Gym
  (3,100)
President: Richard C. Levin
Athletic Director: Tom Beckett
Football Coach: Carmen Cozza
Basketball Coach: Dick Kuchen
Sports Information Director: Steve Conn

## MID-AMERICAN CONFERENCE
Address: Four Seagate, Suite 102
  Toledo, OH 43604
Telephone: (419) 249-7177
Commissioner: Jerry Ippoliti
Publicity Director: Tom Lessig

### Ball State University
Address: 2000 University Avenue
  Muncie, IN 47306
Nickname: Cardinals
Telephone: (317) 285-8225
Football Stadium (Capacity): Ball State University
  Stadium (16,319)
Basketball Arena (Capacity): University Arena
  (11,500)
President: Dr. John E. Worthen
Athletic Director: Andrea Seger
Football Coach: Bill Lynch
Basketball Coach: Ray McCallum
Sports Information Director: Joe Hernandez

## Bowling Green University
Address: Bowling Green, OH 43403
Nickname: Falcons
Telephone: (419) 372-2401
Football Stadium (Capacity): Doyt L. Perry Stadium (30,599)
Basketball Arena (Capacity): Anderson Arena (5,000)
President: Dr. Sidney A. Ribeau
Athletic Director: Ron Zwierlein
Football Coach: Gary Blackney
Basketball Coach: Jim Larranga
Sports Information Director: Steve Barr

## Central Michigan University
Address: Rose Center
Mount Pleasant, MI 48859
Nickname: Chippewas
Telephone: (517) 774-3041
Football Stadium (Capacity): Kelly/Shorts Stadium (20,083)
Basketball Arena (Capacity): Rose Arena (6,000)
President: Leonard Plachta
Athletic Director: Herb Deromedi
Football Coach: Dick Flynn
Basketball Coach: Leonard Drake
Sports Information Director: Fred Stabley, Jr.

## Eastern Michigan University
Address: Bowen Fieldhouse
Ypsilanti, MI 48197
Nickname: Eagles
Telephone: (313) 487-0317
Football Stadium (Capacity): Rynearson Stadium (30,200)
Basketball Arena (Capacity): Bowen Arena (5,600)
President: Dr. William Shelton
Athletic Director: Tim Weiser
Football Coach: Rick Rasnick
Basketball Coach: Ben Braun
Sports Information Director: James Streeter

## Kent State University
Address: Kent, OH 44242
Nickname: Golden Flashes
Telephone: (216) 672-3120
Football Stadium (Capacity): Dix Stadium (30,520)
Basketball Arena (Capacity): Memorial Athletic and Convocation Center (6,034)
President: Dr. Carol A. Cartwright
Athletic Director: Laing Kennedy
Football Coach: Jim Corrigall
Basketball Coach: Dave Grube
Sports Information Director: Dale Gallagher

## Miami University
Address: Millett Hall
Oxford, OH 45056
Nickname: Redskins
Telephone: (513) 529-3113
Football Stadium (Capacity): Yager Stadium (25,183)
Basketball Arena (Capacity): Millett Hall (9,200)
President: Dr. Paul G. Risser
Athletic Director: Eric Hyman
Football Coach: Randy Walker
Basketball Coach: Herb Sendek
Sports Information Director: John Estes

## Ohio University
Address: P.O. Box 689
Convocation Center
Athens, OH 45701-2979
Nickname: Bobcats
Telephone: (614) 593-1174
Football Stadium (Capacity): Don Peden Stadium (20,000)
Basketball Arena (Capacity): Convocation Center (13,000)
President: Dr. Robert Glidden
Athletic Director: Thomas Boeh
Football Coach: Jim Grobe
Basketball Coach: Larry Hunter
Director of Media Services: George Mauzy

## University of Toledo
Address: 2801 W. Bancroft St.
Toledo, OH 43606
Nickname: Rockets
Telephone: (419) 537-4184
Football Stadium (Capacity): Glass Bowl (26,248)
Basketball Arena (Capacity): Savage Hall (9,000)
President: Dr. Frank E. Horton
Athletic Director: Dr. Allen R. Bohl
Football Coach: Gary Pinkel
Basketball Coach: Larry Gipson
Sports Information Director: Rod Brandt

## Western Michigan University
Address: Kalamazoo, MI 49008
Nickname: Broncos
Telephone: (616) 387-4138
Football Stadium (Capacity): Waldo Stadium (30,062)
Basketball Arena (Capacity): University Arena (5,800)
President: Dr. D. H. Haenicke
Interim Athletic Director: Charles Elliott
Football Coach: Al Molde
Basketball Coach: Bob Donewald
Sports Information Director: John Beatty

## PACIFIC-10 CONFERENCE
Address: 800 S. Broadway, Suite 400
Walnut Creek, CA 94596
Telephone: (510) 932-4411
Commissioner: Thomas C. Hansen
Publicity Director: Jim Muldoon

## University of Arizona
Address: 229 McHale Center
Tuscon, AZ 85721
Nickname: Wildcats
Telephone: (602) 621-2211
Football Stadium (Capacity): Arizona Stadium (56,167)
Basketball Arena (Capacity): McHale Center (13,447)
President: Dr. Manuel Pacheco
Athletic Director: Jim Livengood
Football Coach: Dick Tomey
Basketball Coach: Lute Olson
Sports Information Director: Tom Duddleston

## Arizona State University
Address: Tempe, AZ 85287
Nickname: Sun Devils
Telephone: (602) 965-6592
Football Stadium (Capacity): Sun Devil Stadium (73,656)
Basketball Arena (Capacity): University Activity Center (14,287)
President: Lattie Coor
Interim Athletic Director: Christine Wilkinson
Football Coach: Bruce Snyder
Basketball Coach: Bill Frieder
Sports Information Director: Mark Brand

## University of California
Address: Berkeley, CA 94720
Nickname: Golden Bears
Telephone: (510) 642-5363
Football Stadium (Capacity): Memorial Stadium (75,662)
Basketball Arena (Capacity): Harmon Gym (6,578),
  Oakland-Alameda County Coliseum Arena (15,039)
Chancellor: Chang-Lin Tien
Athletic Director: John Kasser
Football Coach: Keith Gilbertson
Basketball Coach: Todd Bozeman
Sports Information Director: Kevin Reneau

## University of California at Los Angeles
Address:    P.O. Box 24044
            Los Angeles, CA 90024
Nickname: Bruins
Telephone: (310) 206-6831
Football Stadium (Capacity): Rose Bowl (102,083)
Basketball Arena (Capacity): Pauley Pavilion (12,819)
Chancellor: Dr. Charles Young
Athletic Director: Peter T. Dalis
Football Coach: Terry Donahue
Basketball Coach: Jim Harrick
Sports Information Director: Marc Dellins

## University of Oregon
Address:    Len Casanova Athletic Center
            2727 Leo Harris Parkway
            Eugene, OR 97401
Nickname: Ducks
Telephone: (503) 346-4481
Football Stadium (Capacity): Autzen Stadium (41,698)
Basketball Arena (Capacity): McArthur Court (10,063)
President: David Frohnmayer
Athletic Director: William Moos
Football Coach: Mike Bellotti
Basketball Coach: Jerry Green
Sports Information Director: Steve Hellyer

## Oregon State University
Address:    Gill Coliseum
            Corvallis, OR 97331
Nickname: Beavers
Telephone: (503) 737-3720
Football Stadium (Capacity): Parker Stadium (36,345)
Basketball Arena (Capacity): Gill Coliseum (10,400)
President: Dr. John V. Byrne
Athletic Director: Dutch Baughman
Football Coach: Jerry Pettibone
Basketball Coach: Eddie Payne
Sports Information Director: Hal Cowan

## University of Southern California
Address: Los Angeles, CA 90089
Nickname: Trojans
Telephone: (213) 740-8480
Football Stadium (Capacity): Los Angeles Memorial
  Coliseum (94,159)
Basketball Arena (Capacity): Los Angeles Sports
  Arena (15,509)
President: Dr. Steven Sample
Athletic Director: Mike Garrett
Football Coach: John Robinson
Basketball Coach: Charlie Parker
Sports Information Director: Tim Tessalone

## Stanford University
Address: Stanford, CA 94305
Nickname: Cardinal
Telephone: (415) 723-4418
Football Stadium (Capacity): Stanford Stadium (85,500)
Basketball Arena (Capacity): Maples Pavilion (7,500)
President: Gerhard Casper
Athletic Director: Dr. Ted Leland
Football Coach: Tyrone Willingham
Basketball Coach: Mike Montgomery
Sports Information Director: Gary Migdol

## University of Washington
Address:    UW Media Relations
            Graves Building, Box 354070
            Seattle, WA 98195-4070
Nickname: Huskies
Telephone: (206) 543-2230
Football Stadium (Capacity): Husky Stadium (72,500)
Basketball Arena (Capacity): Hec Edmundson
  Pavilion (8,000)
President: Richard L. McCormick
Athletic Director: Barbara Hedges
Football Coach: Jim Lambright
Basketball Coach: Bob Bender
Sports Information Director: Jim Daves

## Washington State University
Address:    107 Bohler Gym
            Pullman, WA 99164-1610
Nickname: Cougars
Telephone: (509) 335-0270
Football Stadium (Capacity): Martin Stadium (40,000)
Basketball Arena (Capacity): Friel Court (12,058)
President: Dr. Samuel H. Smith
Athletic Director: Rick Dickson
Football Coach: Mike Price
Basketball Coach: Kevin Eastman
Sports Information Director: Rod Commons

## SOUTHEASTERN CONFERENCE
Address:    2201 Civic Center Boulevard
            Birmingham, AL 35203
Telephone: (205) 458-3000
Commissioner: Roy Kramer
Publicity Director: Mark Whitworth

## University of Alabama
Address:    P.O. Box 870323
            Paul Bryant Drive
            Tuscaloosa, AL 35487
Nickname: Crimson Tide
Telephone: (205) 348-3600
Football Stadium (Capacity): Bryant-Denny Stadium
  (70,123)
Basketball Arena (Capacity): Coleman Coliseum
  (15,043)
President: Dr. Roger Sayers
Interim Athletic Director: Glen Tuckett
Football Coach: Gene Stallings
Basketball Coach: David Hobbs
Sports Information Director: Larry White

## University of Arkansas
Address:     Broyles Athletic Center
             Fayetteville, AR 72701
Nickname: Razorbacks
Telephone: (501) 575-2751
Football Stadium (Capacity): Razorback Stadium
  (51,000)
Basketball Arena (Capacity): Bud Walton Arena
  (19,002)
Chancellor: Dr. Dan Ferritor
Athletic Director: Frank Broyles
Football Coach: Danny Ford
Basketball Coach: Nolan Richardson
Sports Information Director: Rick Schaeffer

## Auburn University
Address:     P.O. Box 351
             Auburn, AL 36831-0351
Nickname: Tigers
Telephone: (334) 844-9800
Football Stadium (Capacity): Jordan Hare Stadium
  (85,214)
Basketball Arena (Capacity): Beard-Eaves Memorial
  Coliseum (13,500)
President: Dr. William V. Muse
Athletic Director: David Housel
Football Coach: Terry Bowden
Basketball Coach: Cliff Ellis
Sports Information Director: Kent Partridge

## University of Florida
Address:     P.O. Box 14485
             Gainesville, FL 32604
Nickname: Gators
Telephone: (904) 375-4683
Football Stadium (Capacity): Ben Hill Griffin Stadium
  at Florida Field (83,000)
Basketball Arena (Capacity): Stephen C. O'Connell
  Center (12,000)
President: Dr. John Lombardi
Athletic Director: Jeremy Foley
Football Coach: Steve Spurrier
Basketball Coach: Lon Kruger
Sports Information Director: John Humenik

## University of Georgia
Address:     P.O. Box 1472
             Athens, GA 30603-1472
Nickname: Bulldogs
Telephone: (706) 542-1621
Football Stadium (Capacity): Sanford Stadium (86,117)
Basketball Arena (Capacity): The Coliseum (10,512)
President: Dr. Charles Knapp
Athletic Director: Vince Dooley
Football Coach: Ray Goff
Basketball Coach: Tubby Smith
Sports Information Director: Claude Felton

## University of Kentucky
Address:     Memorial Coliseum
             Lexington, KY 40506
Nickname: Wildcats
Telephone: (606) 257-3838
Football Stadium (Capacity): Commonwealth Stadium
  (57,800)
Basketball Arena (Capacity): Rupp Arena (23,000)
President: Dr. Charles Wethington Jr.
Athletic Director: C. M. Newton
Football Coach: Bill Curry
Basketball Coach: Rick Pitino
Sports Information Director: Tony Neeley

## Louisiana State University
Address:     P.O. Box 25095
             Baton Rouge, LA 70894
Nickname: Fighting Tigers
Telephone: (504) 388-8226
Football Stadium (Capacity): Tiger Stadium (79,940)
Basketball Arena (Capacity): Pete Maravich
  Assembly Center (14,164)
Chancellor: Dr. William E. Davis
Athletic Director: Joe Dean
Football Coach: Gerry DiNardo
Basketball Coach: Dale Brown
Sports Information Director: Herb Vincent

## University of Mississippi
Address:     P.O. Box 217
             University, MS 38677
Nickname: Rebels
Telephone: (601) 232-7522
Football Stadium (Capacity): Vaught-Hemingway
  Stadium (42,577)
Basketball Arena (Capacity): C. M. (Tad) Smith
  Coliseum (8,135)
Chancellor: Dr. Robert C. Khayat
Athletic Director: Pete Boone
Football Coach: Tommy Tuberville
Basketball Coach: Robert Evans
Sports Information Director: Langston Rogers

## Mississippi State University
Address:     P.O. Drawer 5308
             Mississippi St., MS 39762
Nickname: Bulldogs
Telephone: (601) 325-2703
Football Stadium (Capacity): Scott Field (41,200)
Basketball Arena (Capacity): Humphrey Coliseum
  (9,149)
President: Dr. Donald Zacharias
Athletic Director: Larry Templeton
Football Coach: Jackie Sherrill
Basketball Coach: Richard Williams
Sports Information Director: Mike Nemeth

## University of South Carolina
Address:     Rex Enright Athletic Center
             1300 Rosewood Drive
             Columbia, SC 29208
Nickname: Gamecocks
Telephone: (803) 777-5204
Football Stadium (Capacity): Williams-Brice Stadium
  (72,400)
Basketball Arena (Capacity): Frank McGuire Arena
  (12,401)
President: Dr. John Palms
Athletic Director: Dr. Mike McGee
Football Coach: Brad Scott
Basketball Coach: Eddie Fogler
Sports Information Director: Kerry Tharp

## University of Tennessee
Address:     P.O. Box 15016
             Knoxville, TN 37901
Nickname: Volunteers
Telephone: (615) 974-1212
Football Stadium (Capacity): Neyland Stadium (91,902)
Basketball Arena (Capacity): Thompson Boling Arena
  and Assembly Center (24,535)
President: Dr. Joseph E. Johnson
Athletic Director: Doug Dickey
Football Coach: Phillip Fulmer
Basketball Coach: Kevin O'Neill
Sports Information Director: Bud Ford

## Vanderbilt University

Address:　P.O. Box 120158
　　　　　Nashville, TN 37212
Nickname: Commodores
Telephone: (615) 322-4121
Football Stadium (Capacity): Vanderbilt Stadium (41,000)
Basketball Arena (Capacity): Memorial Gym (15,311)
Chancellor: Joe B. Wyatt
Athletic Director: Paul Hoolahan
Football Coach: Rod Dowhower
Basketball Coach: Jan Van Breda Kolff
Sports Information Director: Rod Williamson

## SOUTHWEST ATHLETIC CONFERENCE

Address:　P.O. Box 569420
　　　　　Dallas, TX 75356
Telephone: (214) 634-7353
Commissioner: Kyle Kallander
Director of Media Relations: Bo Carter

## Baylor University

Address:　150 Bear Run
　　　　　Waco, TX 76711
Nickname: Bears
Telephone: (817) 755-1234
Football Stadium (Capacity): Floyd Casey Stadium (48,500)
Basketball Arena (Capacity): Ferrell Center (10,080)
President: Dr. Herbert H. Reynolds
Athletic Director: Dr. Dick Ellis
Football Coach: Chuck Reedy
Basketball Coach: Darrel Johnson
Sports Information Director: Maxey Parrish

## Rice University

Address:　6100 Main, MS548
　　　　　Houston, TX 77005-1892
Nickname: Owls
Telephone: (713) 527-4034
Football Stadium (Capacity): Rice Stadium (70,000)
Basketball Arena (Capacity): Autry Court (5,000)
President: Malcolm Gillis
Athletic Director: Bobby May
Football Coach: Ken Hatfield
Basketball Coach: Willis Wilson
Sports Information Director: Bill Cousins

## Southern Methodist University

Address:　SMU Box 216
　　　　　Dallas, TX 75275
Nickname: Mustangs
Telephone: (214) 768-2883
Football Stadium (Capacity): Cotton Bowl (68,252)
Basketball Arena (Capacity): Moody Coliseum (9,007)
President: R. Gerald Turner
Athletic Director: Jim Copeland
Football Coach: Tom Rossley
Basketball Coach: Mike Dement
Sports Information Director: Jon Jackson

## University of Texas

Address:　P.O. Box 7399
　　　　　Austin, TX 78713
Nickname: Longhorns
Telephone: (512) 471-7437
Football Stadium (Capacity): Memorial Stadium (75,512)
Basketball Arena (Capacity): Erwin Special Events Center (16,231)
Chancellor: Dr. William Cunningham
Athletic Director: DeLoss Dodds
Football Coach: John Mackovic
Basketball Coach: Tom Penders
Sports Information Director: Dave Saba

## Texas A&M University

Address:　John Koldus Building
　　　　　College Station, TX 77843
Nickname: Aggies
Telephone: (409) 845-3218
Football Stadium (Capacity): Kyle Field (72,387)
Basketball Arena (Capacity): G. Rollie White Coliseum (7,800)
President: Dr. Ray Bowen
Athletic Director: Wally Groff
Football Coach: R. C. Slocum
Basketball Coach: Tony Barone
Sports Information Director: Alan Cannon

## Texas Christian University

Address:　P.O. Box 32924
　　　　　Fort Worth, TX 76129
Nickname: Horned Frogs
Telephone: (817) 921-7969
Football Stadium (Capacity): Amon G. Carter Stadium (46,000)
Basketball Arena (Capacity): Daniel-Meyer Coliseum (7,166)
Chancellor: Dr. William E. Tucker
Athletic Director: Frank Windegger
Football Coach: Pat Sullivan
Basketball Coach: Billy Tubbs
Sports Information Director: Glen Stone

## Texas Tech University

Address:　Box 43021
　　　　　Lubbock, TX 79409
Nickname: Red Raiders
Telephone: (806) 742-2770
Football Stadium (Capacity): Jones Stadium (50,500)
Basketball Arena (Capacity): Lubbock Municipal Coliseum (8,174)
President: Dr. Robert Lawless
Athletic Director: Bob Bockrath
Football Coach: Spike Dykes
Basketball Coach: James Dickey
Sports Information Director: Joe Hornaday

## WESTERN ATHLETIC CONFERENCE
Address:     14 West Dry Creek Circle
             Littleton, CO 80120
Telephone: (303) 795-1962
Commissioner: Karl Benson
Publicity Director: Jeff Hurd

### Air Force
Address: USAF Academy, CO 80840-9500
Nickname: Falcons
Telephone: (719) 472-4008
Football Stadium (Capacity): Falcon Stadium (50,126)
Basketball Arena (Capacity): Clune Arena (6,007)
President: Lt. Gen. Paul E. Stein
Athletic Director: Col. Kenneth L. Schweitzer
Football Coach: Fisher DeBerry
Basketball Coach: Reggie Minton
Sports Information Director: David Kellogg

### Brigham Young University
Address:     30 Smith Field House
             Provo, UT 84602
Nickname: Cougars
Telephone: (801) 378-4911
Football Stadium (Capacity): Cougar Stadium (65,000)
Basketball Arena (Capacity): Marriott Center (23,000)
President: Robert B. Sloan
Athletic Director: Rondo Fehlberg
Football Coach: LaVell Edwards
Basketball Coach: Harry Miller
Sports Information Director: Ralph Zobell

### Colorado State University
Address:     Moby Arena
             Fort Collins, CO 80523
Nickname: Rams
Telephone: (303) 491-5300
Football Stadium (Capacity): Hughes Stadium (30,000)
Basketball Arena (Capacity): Moby Arena (9,001)
President: Dr. Albert C. Yates
Athletic Director: Tom Jurich
Football Coach: Sonny Lubick
Basketball Coach: Stew Morrill
Sports Information Director: Gary Ozello

### University of Hawaii
Address:     1335 Lower Campus Road
             Honolulu, HI 96822-2370
Nickname: Rainbow Warriors
Telephone: (808) 956-8111
Football Stadium (Capacity): Aloha Stadium (50,000)
Basketball Arena (Capacity): Special Events Arena
  (10,225)
President: Dr. Kenneth Mortimer
Athletic Director: Hugh Yoshida
Football Coach: Bob Wagner
Basketball Coach: Riley Wallace
Interim Sports Information Director: Lois Manin

### University of New Mexico
Address:     1414 University S.E.
             Albuquerque, NM 87131
Nickname: Lobos
Telephone: (505) 277-6375
Football Stadium (Capacity): University Stadium (30,646)
Basketball Arena (Capacity): University Arena—The
  Pit (18,100)
President: Dr. Richard Peck
Athletic Director: Rudy Davalos
Football Coach: Dennis Franchione
Basketball Coach: Dave Bliss
Sports Information Director: Greg Remington

### San Diego State University
Address: San Diego, CA 92182
Nickname: Aztecs
Telephone: (619) 594-5163
Football Stadium (Capacity): San Diego Jack Murphy
  Stadium (61,104)
Basketball Arena (Capacity): San Diego Sports
  Arena (13,741)
President: Dr. Thomas B. Day
Athletic Director: Rick Bay
Football Coach: Ted Tollner
Basketball Coach: Fred Trenkle
Sports Information Director: John Rosenthal

### University of Texas at El Paso
Address:     201 Baltimore
             El Paso, TX 79902
Nickname: Miners
Telephone: (915) 747-5347
Football Stadium (Capacity): Sun Bowl (53,000)
Basketball Arena (Capacity): Special Events Center
  (12,222)
President: Dr. Diana Natalicio
Athletic Director: John Thompson
Football Coach: Charlie Bailey
Basketball Coach: Don Haskins
Sports Information Director: Eddie Mullens

### University of Utah
Address:     Huntsman Center
             Salt Lake City, UT 84112
Nickname: Utes
Telephone: (801) 581-8171
Football Stadium (Capacity): Rice Stadium (35,000)
Basketball Arena (Capacity): Huntsman Center
  (15,000)
President: Dr. Arthur K. Smith
Athletic Director: Dr. Chris Hill
Football Coach: Ron McBride
Basketball Coach: Rick Majerus
Sports Information Director: Bruce Woodbury

### University of Wyoming
Address:     P.O. Box 3414
             Laramie, WY 82071-3414
Nickname: Cowboys
Telephone: (307) 766-2292
Football Stadium (Capacity): War Memorial Stadium
  (33,500)
Basketball Arena (Capacity): Arena-Auditorium (15,028)
President: Dr. Terry Roark
Athletic Director: Paul Roach
Football Coach: Joe Tiller
Basketball Coach: Joby Wright
Sports Information Director: Kevin McKinney

## INDEPENDENTS

### Army
Address: West Point, NY 10996
Nickname: Cadets/Black Knights
Telephone: (914) 938-3303
Football Stadium (Capacity): Michie Stadium (39,929)
Basketball Arena (Capacity): Cristl Arena (5,043)
Superintendent: Lt. Gen. Howard D. Graves
Athletic Director: Al Vanderbush
Football Coach: Bob Sutton
Basketball Coach: Dino Gaudio
Sports Information Director: Bob Peretta

Note: Plays football as indep., basketball in Patriot League.

### East Carolina University
Address: Greenville, NC 27858-4353
Nickname: Pirates
Telephone: (919) 328-4600
Football Stadium (Capacity): Dowdy-Ficklen Stadium (35,000)
Basketball Arena (Capacity): Williams Arena (7,500)
Chancellor: Dr. Richard R. Eakin
Athletic Director: Michael A. Hamrick
Football Coach: Steve Logan
Basketball Coach: Joe Dooley
Sports Information Director: Norm Reilly

### Navy
Address:     566 Brownson Road, Ricketts Hall
                 Annapolis, MD 21402
Nickname: Midshipmen
Telephone: (410) 268-6220
Football Stadium (Capacity): Navy-Marine Corps Memorial Stadium (30,000)
Basketball Arena (Capacity): Alumni Hall (5,710)
Superintendent: Adm. Charles A. Larson, USN
Athletic Director: Jack Lengyel
Football Coach: Charlie Weatherby
Basketball Coach: Don DeVoe
Sports Information Director: Thomas Bates

Note: Plays football as indep., basketball in Patriot League.

### University of Notre Dame
Address: Notre Dame, IN 46556
Nickname: Fighting Irish
Telephone: (219) 631-6107
Football Stadium (Capacity): Notre Dame Stadium (59,075)
Basketball Arena (Capacity): Joyce Athletic and Convocation Center (11,418)
President: Rev. Edward A. Malloy, CSC
Athletic Director: Michael Wadsworth
Football Coach: Lou Holtz
Basketball Coach: John MacLeod
Sports Information Director: John Heisler

### University of Tulsa
Address:     600 S. College
                 Tulsa, OK 74104
Nickname: Golden Hurricane
Telephone: (918) 631-2395
Football Stadium (Capacity): Skelley Stadium (40,385)
Basketball Arena (Capacity): Tulsa Convention Center (8,659)
President: Dr. Robert H. Donaldson
Interim Athletic Director: Judy MacLeod
Football Coach: Dave Rader
Basketball Coach: Steve Robinson
Sports Information Director: Don Tomkalski

# Olympic Sports Directory

### United States Olympic Committee
Address:     Olympic House
                 1 Olympic Plaza
                 Colorado Springs, CO 80909
Telephone: (719) 632-5551
Executive Director: Dick Schultz
Director of Media Relations: Mike Moran

### U.S. Olympic Training Center
Address:     1 Olympic Plaza
                 Colorado Springs, CO 80909
Telephone: (719) 578-4500
Director: John Smith

### U.S. Olympic Training Center
Address:     421 Old Military Road
                 Lake Placid, NY 12946
Telephone: (518) 523-2600
Associate Director: Jack Favro

### International Olympic Committee
Address:     Chateau de Vidy
                 CH-1007 Lausanne
                 Switzerland
Telephone: (41.21) 25 3271/3272
President: Juan Antonio Samaranch
Director General: Francois Carrard
Public Relations Officer: Michele Verdier

### Atlanta Olympic Organizing Committee
Address:     P.O. Box 1996
                 Atlanta, GA 30301
Telephone: (404) 224-1996
Co-Chairman: Hon. Andrew Young
President: William Porter Payne
Executive Director: Doug Gatlin
(Games of the XXVIth Olympiad; Dates: July 19-August 4, 1996)

## U.S. Olympic Organizations

### Archery

**National Archery Association (NAA)**
Address: 1 Olympic Plaza
Colorado Springs, CO 80909
Telephone: (719) 578-4576
President: Tom Stevenson, Jr.
Executive Director: Robert C. Balink

### Athletics (Track & Field)

**USA Track & Field (formerly TAC)**
Address: P.O. Box 120
Indianapolis, IN 46206
Telephone: (317) 261-0500
President: Larry Ellis
Executive Director: Ollan Cassell
Press Information Director: Pete Cava

### Badminton

**U.S. Badminton Association (USBA)**
Address: 1 Olympic Plaza
Colorado Springs, CO 80909
Telephone: (719) 578-4808
President: Diane Cornell
Executive Director: TBA

### Baseball

**U.S. Baseball Federation (USBF)**
Address: 2160 Greenwood Avenue
Trenton, NJ 08609
Telephone: (609) 586-2381
President: Mark Marquess
Executive Director: Richard Case
Communications Director: George Doig

### Basketball

**USA Basketball**
Address: 5465 Mark Dabling Blvd.
Colorado Springs, CO 80918
Telephone: (719) 590-4800
President: C.M. Newton
Executive Director: Warren Brown
Assistant Executive Director for Public Relations:
Craig Miller

### Biathlon

**U.S. Biathlon Association (USBA)**
Address: 421 Old Military Road
Lake Placid, NY 12946
Telephone: (518) 523-3836
President: Don Edwards
Executive Director: Dusty Johnstone

### Bobsled

**U.S. Bobsled and Skeleton Federation**
Address: P.O. Box 828
Lake Placid, NY 12946
Telephone: (518) 523-1842
President: Jim Morris
Executive Director: Matt Roy
Marketing and Communications Director: Terry Kent

### Bowling

**U.S. Tenpin Bowling Federation**
Address: 5301 South 76th Street
Greendale, WI 53129
Telephone: (414) 421-9008
President: Max Skelton
Executive Director: Gerald Koenig
Communications Director: Christine Krebs

### Boxing

**USA Boxing**
Address: 1 Olympic Plaza
Colorado Springs, CO 80909
Telephone: (719) 578-4506
President: Jerry Dusenberry
Executive Director: Bruce Mathis
Director of Communications: Kurt Stenerson

### Canoe/Kayak

**U.S. Canoe and Kayak Team**
Address: Pan American Plaza, Suite 610
201 South Capitol Avenue
Indianapolis, IN 46225
Telephone: (317) 237-5690
Chairman: Lamar Sims
Executive Director: Chuck Wielgus
Director of Comm. and Marketing: Craig Bohnert

### Cycling

**U.S. Cycling Federation (USCF)**
Address: 1 Olympic Plaza
Colorado Springs, CO 80909
Telephone: (719) 578-4581
President: Mike Fraysse
Executive Director: Lisa Voight
Media and Public Relations Director: Steve Penny

### Diving

**United States Diving, Inc. (USD)**
Address: Pan American Plaza, Suite 430
201 South Capitol Avenue
Indianapolis, IN 46225
Telephone: (317) 237-5252
President: Steve McFarland
Executive Director: Todd Smith
Director of Communications: Dave Shatkowski

### Equestrian

**U.S. Equestrian Team (USET)**
Address: Gladstone, NJ 07934
Telephone: (908) 234-0155
Executive Director: Robert C. Standish
Director of Public Relations: Marty Bauman

## Fencing

**U.S. Fencing Association (USFA)**
Address:     1 Olympic Plaza
               Colorado Springs, CO 80909
Telephone: (719) 578-4511
President: Stephen Sobel
Executive Director: TBA
Media Relations Director: TBA

## Field Hockey

**U.S. Field Hockey Association (USFHA)**
**(Women)**
Address:     1 Olympic Plaza
               Colorado Springs, CO 80909
Telephone: (719) 578-4567
President: Jenepher Shillingford
Executive Director: Carrie Haag
Director of Public Relations: Mark Whitney

## Figure Skating

**U.S. Figure Skating Association (USFSA)**
Address:     20 First Street
               Colorado Springs, CO 80906
Telephone: (719) 635-5200
President: Morry Stillwell
Executive Director: Jerry Lace
Communications Director: Kristin Matta

## Gymnastics

**U.S. Gymnastics Federation (USGF)**
Address:     Pan American Plaza, Suite 300
               201 South Capitol Avenue
               Indianapolis, IN 46225
Telephone: (317) 237-5050
Chairman of the Board: Sandy Knapp
President: Kathy Scanlan
Director of Public Relations: Luan Peszek

## Hockey

**USA Hockey**
Address:     4965 North 30th Street
               Colorado Springs, CO 80919
Telephone: (719) 599-5500
President: Walter Bush
Executive Director: Dave Ogrean
Public Relations Coordinator: Darryl Sibel

## Judo

**United States Judo, Inc. (USJ)**
Address:     P.O. Box 10013
               El Paso, TX 79991
Telephone: (915) 565-8754
President and Media Contact: Frank Fullerton

## Luge

**U.S. Luge Association (USLA)**
Address:     P.O. Box 651
               Lake Placid, NY 12946
Telephone: (518) 523-2071
President: Dwight Bell
Executive Director: Ron Rossi
Public Relations Coordinator: Sandy Caligiore

## Modern Pentathlon

**U.S. Modern Pentathlon Association**
**(USMPA)**
Address:     530 McCullough Avenue, Suite 619
               San Antonio, TX 78215
Telephone: (210) 246-3000
President: Robert Marbut
Executive Director: W. Dean Billick

## Racquetball

**American Amateur Racquetball**
**Association (AARA)**
Address:     1685 West Uintah
               Colorado Springs, CO 80904
Telephone: (719) 635-5396
President: Van Dubolsky
Executive Director: Luke St. Onge
Public Relations Director: Linda Mojer

## Roller Skating

**U.S. Amateur Confederation of Roller**
**Skating (USAC/RS)**
Address:     4730 South Street
               P.O. Box 6579
               Lincoln, NE 68506
Telephone: (402) 483-7551
President: Betty Ann Danna
Executive Director: George H. Pickard
Sports Information Director: Andy Seeley

## Rowing

**U.S. Rowing Association (USRA)**
Address:     Pan American Plaza, Suite 400
               201 South Capitol Avenue
               Indianapolis, IN 46225
Telephone: (317) 237-5656
President: Dave Vogel
Executive Director: Frank J. Coyle
Director of Communications: Maureen Merhoff

## Shooting

**USA Shooting Association**
Address:     1 Olympic Plaza
               Colorado Springs, CO  80909
Telephone: (719) 578-4670
President: Stevan B. Richards
Executive Director: Robert L. Jursnick
Director of Public Relations: Nancy Moore
Program Administrator: Stephen Ducoff

## Skiing

**U.S. Skiing**
Address:     P.O. Box 100
               Park City, UT 84060
Telephone: (801) 649-9090
Chairman: Nick Badami
President and CEO: Tim Leiweki
Vice-Chairman: Suzette Cantin
President, U.S. Ski Team Foundation:
   Vinton Sommerville
Director of Communications: Tom Kelly
Media Services Coordinator: Deborah Engen

## Soccer

**U.S. Soccer Federation (USSF)**
Address:     1801-1811 South Prairie Avenue
             Chicago, IL  60616
Telephone: (312) 808-1300
President: Alan Rothenberg
Executive Director: Hank Steinbrecher
Director of Communications: Tom Lang

## Softball

**Amateur Softball Association (ASA)**
Address:     2801 N.E. 50th Street
             Oklahoma City, OK 73111
Telephone: (405) 424-5266
President: Wayne Myers
Executive Director: Don Porter
Director of Communications: Ron Babb

## Speedskating

**U.S. International Speedskating Association (USISA)**
Address:     P.O. Box 16157
             Rocky River, OH 44116
Telephone: (216) 899-0128
President: Bill Cushman
Executive Director: Katie Marquard
Media Contact: Susan Polakoff-Shaw

## Swimming

**U.S. Swimming, Inc. (USS)**
Address:     1 Olympic Plaza
             Colorado Springs, CO  80909
Telephone: (719) 578-4578
President: Carol Zaleski
Executive Director: Ray Essick
Communications Director: Charlie Snyder

## Synchronized Swimming

**U.S. Synchronized Swimming, Inc. (USSS)**
Address:     Pan American Plaza, Suite 510
             201 South Capitol Avenue
             Indianapolis, IN 46225
Telephone: (317) 237-5700
President: Nancy Wichtman
Executive Director: Debbie Hesse
Membership and Communications: Laura LaMarca

## Table Tennis

**U.S. Table Tennis Association (USTTA)**
Address:     1 Olympic Plaza
             Colorado Springs, CO 80909
Telephone: (719) 578-4583
Executive Director: Paul Montville
President: Terry Timmins
Deputy Executive Director: Linda Gleeson

## Taekwondo

**U.S. Taekwondo Union (USTU)**
Address:     1 Olympic Plaza, Suite 405
             Colorado Springs, CO  80909
Telephone: (719) 578-4632
President: Hwa Chong
Executive Director: Robert Fujimura

## Team Handball

**U.S. Team Handball Federation (USTHF)**
Address:     1 Olympic Plaza
             Colorado Springs, CO  80909
Telephone: (719) 578-4582
President: Dr. Thomas Rosandich
Executive Director: Michael D. Cavanaugh

## Tennis

**U.S. Tennis Association**
Address:     70 West Red Oak Lane
             White Plains, NY 10604
Telephone: (914) 696-7000
President: Dr. Lester Snyder
Executive Director: TBA
Director of Communications: Page Crosland

## Volleyball

**U.S. Volleyball Association (USVBA)**
Address:     3595 East Fountain Boulevard, Suite I-2
             Colorado Springs, CO 80910-1740
Telephone: (719) 637-8300
President: Jerry Sherman
Executive Director: John Carroll

## Water Polo

**United States Water Polo (USWP)**
Address:     Pan American Plaza, Suite 520
             201 South Capitol Avenue
             Indianapolis, IN 46225
Telephone: (317) 237-5599
President: Richard Foster
Executive Director: Bruce J. Wigo
Communications Director: Kevin Messenger

## Weightlifting

**U.S. Weightlifting Federation (USWF)**
Address:     1 Olympic Plaza
             Colorado Springs, CO  80909
Telephone: (719) 578-4508
President: Jim Schmitz
Executive Director: George Greenway
Communications Director: John Halpin

## Wrestling

**USA Wrestling**
Address:     6155 Lehman
             Colorado Springs, CO  80918
Telephone: (719) 598-8181
President: Larry Sciacchetano
Executive Director: Jim Scherr
Director of Communications: Gary Abbott

## Yachting

**U.S. Yacht Racing Union (USYRU)**
Address:     P.O. Box 1260
             Portsmouth, RI 02871
Telephone: (401) 683-0800
President: David Irish
Executive Director: Terry Hopper
Communications Director: Dana Marnane
Olympic Yachting Director: Jonathan R. Harley

## Affiliated Sports Organizations

### Amateur Athletic Union (AAU)
Address:     3400 West 86th Street
             P.O. Box 68207
             Indianapolis, IN 46268
Telephone: (317) 872-2900
President: Bobby Dodd
Associate Operations Directors: Bruce Hopp and
  Tom Leix

### Curling

### U.S. Curling Association (USCA)
Address:     1100 Center Point Drive
             Box 866
             Stevens Point, WI 54481
Telephone: (715) 344-1199
President: Warren Lowe
Executive Director: David Garber

### Karate

### USA Karate Federation
Address:     1300 Kenmore Boulevard
             Akron, OH 44314
Telephone: (216) 753-3114
President: George Anderson

### Orienteering

### U.S. Orienteering Federation
Address:     P.O. Box 1444
             Forest Park, GA 30051
Telephone: (404) 363-2110
President: Rick Worner
Executive Director: Robin Shannonhouse
Media and Publicity Contact: John Nash
Publicity telephone: (207) 439-7096

### Squash

### U.S. Squash Racquets Association
Address:     23 Cynwyd Road
             P.O. Box 1216
             Bala Cynwyd, PA 19004
Telephone: (610) 667-4006
President: Andre Naniche
Executive Director: Craig Brand

### Trampoline and Tumbling

### American Trampoline and Tumbling Association
Address:     400 West Broadway, Suite 207
             or P.O. Box 306
             Brownfield, TX 79316-0306
Telephone: (806) 637-8670
President: Chris Sans
Executive Director: Ann Sims

### Triathlon

### Triathlon Federation USA
Address:     3595 East Fountain Boulevard, Suite F-1
             Colorado Springs, CO 80910
Telephone: (719) 597-9090
President: Rick Margiotta
Executive Director: Steve Locke
Deputy Director and Media Contact: Tim Yount

### Underwater Swimming

### Underwater Society of America
Address:     849 West Orange Avenue
             No. 1002
             South San Francisco, CA 94080
Telephone: (415) 583-8492
President: George Rose

### Water Skiing

### American Water Ski Association
Address:     799 Overlook Drive, S.E.
             Winter Haven, FL 33884
Telephone: (813) 324-4341
President: Andrea Plough
Executive Director: Duke Waldrop
Public Relations Manager: Don Cullimore

# Miscellaneous Sports Directory

### American Professional Soccer League
Address:     2 Village Road, Suite 5
             Horsham, PA 19044
Telephone: (215) 657-7440
Chairman of the Board: Scott Oki
Commissioner: Richard Groff
Director of Operations: Chris Branscome

### Continental Indoor Soccer League
Address:     16027 Ventura Boulevard, Suite 605
             Encino, CA 91436
Telephone: (818) 906-7627
Commissioner: Ron Weinstein
Director of Public Relations: Dan Courtemanche

### National Professional Soccer League
Address:     229 Third Street NW
             Canton, OH 44702
Telephone: (216) 455-4625
Commissioner: Steve Paxos
Director of Operations: Paul Luchowski

### Ladies Professional Golf Association
Address:     2570 W International Speedway
             Boulevard, Suite B
             Daytona Beach, FL 32114
Telephone: (904) 254-8800
Commissioner: Charles S. Mechem Jr.
Commissioner/elect: Jim Ritts
Director of Communications: Elaine Scott

## Professional Golfers Association
Address:    112 TPC Boulevard
            Ponte Vedra, FL 32082
Telephone: (904) 285-3700
Commissioner: Ken Finchem
Director of Public Relations: John Morris

## United States Golf Association
Address:    P.O. Box 708, Golf House
            Liberty Corner Road
            Far Hills, NJ 07931-0708
Telephone: (908) 234-2300
President: Reg Murphy

## Association of Tennis Professionals Tour
Address:    200 ATP Tour Boulevard
            Ponte Vedra Beach, FL 32082
Telephone: (904) 285-8000
Chief Executive Officer: Mark Miles
Director of Communications: Pete Alfano

## Women's Tennis Association
Address:    133 First Street N.E.
            St. Petersburg, FL 33701
Telephone: (813) 895-5000
Chief Executive Officer: Anne Person-Worcester
Director of Public Relations: TBA

## United States Tennis Association
Address:    70 West Red Oak Lane
            White Plains, NY 10604
Telephone: (914) 696-7000
President: Dr. Lester Snyder
Executive Director: TBA
Director of Communications: Page Crosland

## National Association for Stock Car Auto Racing (NASCAR)
Address:    P.O. Box 2875, 1801 W International
            Speedway Boulevard
            Daytona Beach, FL 32120
Telephone: (904) 253-0611
President: Bill France Jr.
Director of Public Relations: Andy Hall

## Championship Auto Racing Teams (CART)
Address:    755 West Big Beaver Road, Suite 800
            Troy, MI  48084
Telephone: (810) 362-8800
President/CEO: Andrew Craig
Director of Publicity: Adam Sall

## National Hot Rod Association
Address:    2035 East Financial Way
            Glendora, CA  91741
Telephone: (818) 914-4761
President: Dallas Gardner
Director of Communications: Denny Darnell

## International Motor Sports Association
Address:    3502 Henderson Boulevard
            Tampa, FL 33609
Telephone: (813) 877-4672
President: George Silberman
Communications Director: Lynn Myfelt

## Professional Rodeo Cowboys Association
Address:    101 Pro Rodeo Drive
            Colorado Springs, CO 80919
Telephone: (719) 593-8840
Commissioner: Lewis Cryer
Director of Communications: Steve Fleming

## Thoroughbred Racing Associations of America
Address:    420 Fair Hill Drive, Suite 1
            Elkton, MD  21921
Telephone: (410) 392-9200
President: Clifford C. Goodrich
Director of Service Bureau: Conrad Sobkowiak

## Thoroughbred Racing Communications, Inc.
Address:    40 East 52nd Street
            New York, NY 10022
Telephone: (212) 371-5910
Executive Director: Tom Merritt
Director of Media Relations and Development:
Bob Curran

## Breeders' Cup Limited
Address:    2525 Harrodsburg Road
            Lexington, KY 40544-4230
Telephone: (606) 223-5444
President: James Bassett
Media Relations Directors: Ben Metzger and James
Gluckson

## The Jockeys' Guild, Inc.
Address:    250 West Main Street, Suite 1820
            Lexington, KY 40507
Telephone: (606) 259-3211
President: Jerry Bailey
National Manager/Secretary: John Giovanni

## United States Trotting Association
Address:    750 Michigan Avenue
            Columbus, OH 43215
Telephone: (614) 224-2291
President: Corwin Nixon
Publicity Department: John Pawlak

## Professional Bowlers Association
Address:    1720 Merriman Road, P.O. Box 5118
            Akron, OH 44334-0118
Telephone: (216) 836-5568
Commissioner: Michael Connor
Public Relations Director: Kevin Shippy

## Ladies Pro Bowlers Tour
Address:    7171 Cherryvale Boulevard
            Rockford, IL 61112
Telephone: (815) 332-5756
Executive Tournament Director: TBA
Media Director: Lennie Gessler

## Women's International Bowling Congress
Address:    5301 South 76th Street
            Greendale, WI 53129-1191
Telephone: (414) 421-9000
President: Joyce Deitch
Public Relations Manager: Dave DeLorenzo

## American Bowling Congress
Address:    5301 South 76th Street
            Greendale, WI  53129
Telephone: (414) 421-6400
President: Ben Palumbo
Communications Executive: Steve James

## Association of Volleyball Professionals
Address:    15260 Ventura Blvd., Suite #2250
            Sherman Oaks, CA 91403
Telephone: (818) 386-2486
President: Jon Stevenson
VP of Sales and Marketing: Alison Canfield

## U.S. Chess Federation
Address:    186 Route 9W
              New Windsor, NY 12553
Telephone: (914) 562-8350
Executive Director: Al Lawrence
Director of Operations: George Filippone

## Iditarod Trail Committee
Address:    P.O. Box 870800
              Wasilla, AK 99687
Telephone: (907) 376-5155
Executive Director: Stan Hooley
Race Director: Joanne Potts

## International Game Fish Association
Address:    1301 East Atlantic Boulevard
              Pompano Beach, FL 33060
Telephone: (305) 941-3474
President: Mike Leech

## American Greyhound Track Operators Association
Address:    1065 Northeast 125th Street, Suite 219
              North Miami, FL 33161
Telephone: (305) 893-2101
President: Stanley S. Phillips
Secretary/Executive Director: Patrick E. Winters

## U.S. Handball Association
Address:    2333 North Tucson Boulevard
              Tucson, AZ 85716
Telephone: (602) 795-0434
Executive Director: Vern Roberts
Director of Public Relations: Cheri Beltramo

## U.S. Club Lacrosse Association
Address:    c/o Lacrosse Foundation
              113 W University Parkway
              Baltimore, MD 21210
Telephone: (410) 235-6882
Executive Director: Steven B. Stenersen

## Little League Baseball, Inc.
Address:    P.O. Box 3485
              Williamsport, PA 17701
Telephone: (717) 326-1921
President: Stephen Keener
Communications Director: Dennis Sullivan

## American Powerboating Association
Address:    P.O. Box 377
              Eastpointe, MI 48021
Telephone: (810) 773-9700
Executive Administrator: Gloria Urbin

## U.S. Polo Association
Address:    4059 Iron Works Pike
              Lexington, KY 40511
Telephone: (606) 255-0593
Executive Director: George Alexander, Jr.

## U.S. Rugby Football Union
Address:    3595 East Fountain Boulevard
              Colorado Springs, CO 80910
Telephone: (719) 637-1022
Executive Director: TBA

# MINOR LEAGUES

## Baseball (AAA)

### American Association
Address:    6801 Miami Ave., Suite 3
              Cincinnati, OH 45243
Telephone: (513) 271-4800
President: Branch B. Rickey

### International League
Address:    55 South High Street, Suite 202
              Dublin, OH 43017
Telephone: (614) 791-9300
President: Randy Mobley

### Mexican League
Address:    Angela Pola #16
              Col. Periodista, C.P. 11220
              Mexico D.F.
Telephone: 011-525-557-10-07
President: Pedro Cisneros

### Pacific Coast League
Address:    2345 South Alma School Rd., Suite 110
              Mesa, AZ 85210
Telephone: (602) 838-2171
President: Bill Cutler

## Hockey

### American Hockey League
Address:    425 Union Street
              West Springfield, MA 01089
Telephone: (413) 781-2030
President: David Andrews
Senior VP of Hockey Operations: Gordon Anziano

### International Hockey League
Address:    1577 North Woodward Ave., Suite 212
              Bloomfield Hills, MI 48304
Telephone: (810) 258-0580
Commissioner: Robert P. Ufer
VP of Public Relations: Tim Bryant

# Hall of Fame Directory

## National Baseball Hall of Fame and Museum
Address:      P.O. Box 590
               Cooperstown, NY 13326
Telephone: (607) 547-9114
Vice President: Bill Guilfoile
Director of Public Relations: Jeff Idelson

## Naismith Memorial Basketball Hall of Fame
Address:      1150 West Columbus Avenue
               Springfield, MA 01101
Telephone: (413) 781-6500
President: Joseph O'Brien
Director of Public Relations: Robin Deutsch

## National Bowling Hall of Fame and Museum
Address:      111 Stadium Plaza
               St Louis, MO 63102
Telephone: (314) 231-6340
Executive Director: Gerald Baltz
Director of Marketing: Raleigh Ragan

## National Boxing Hall of Fame
Address:      1 Hall of Fame Drive
               Canastota, NY 13032
Telephone: (315) 697-7095
President: Donald Ackerman
Executive Director: Edward Brophy

## Professional Football Hall of Fame
Address:      2121 George Halas Drive NW
               Canton, OH 44708
Telephone: (216) 456-8207
Executive Director: Pete Elliott
Vice President, Public Relations: Don Smith

## LPGA Hall of Fame
Address:      2570 West International Speedway
               Boulevard, Suite B
               Daytona Beach, FL 32114
Telephone: (904) 254-8800
Commissioner: Charles S. Mechem
Commissioner/elect: Jim Ritts
Communications Director: Elaine Scott

## Professional Hockey Hall of Fame
Address:      30 Young Street BCE Place
               Toronto, Ontario Canada M5E 1X8
Telephone: (416) 360-7735
VP of Marketing and Communications: Bryan Blanc
VP of Finance: Jeff Denomme

## National Museum of Racing and Hall of Fame
Address:      191 Union Avenue
               Saratoga Springs, NY 12866
Telephone: (518) 584-0400
Executive Director: Peter Hammell
Assistant Director: Catherine Maguire

## National Soccer Hall of Fame
Address:      5-11 Ford Avenue
               Oneonta, NY 13820
Telephone: (607) 432-3351
Executive Director: Albert Colone
External Affairs: Will Lunn

## International Swimming Hall of Fame
Address:      1 Hall of Fame Drive
               Fort Lauderdale, FL 33316
Telephone: (305) 462-6536
President: Dr. Samuel J. Freas
Director of Marketing: Michelle Mitchell-Rocha

## International Tennis Hall of Fame
Address:      194 Bellevue Avenue
               Newport, RI 02840
Telephone: (401) 849-3990
Executive Director: Mark Stenning
Director of Public Relations: Linda Johnson

## National Track & Field Hall of Fame
Address:      1 RCA Dome, Suite 140
               Indianapolis, IN 46225
Telephone: (317) 261-0500
Historian: Hal Bateman
Director of Media Relations: Pete Cava

# Awards

sportswoman and sportsman of the year

**Sports Illustrated**

olympians
bonnie blair
and
johann olav koss

## Athlete Awards

### Sports Illustrated Sportsman of the Year

| | |
|---|---|
| 1954 | Roger Bannister, Track |
| 1955 | Johnny Podres, Baseball |
| 1956 | Bobby Morrow, Track |
| 1957 | Stan Musial, Baseball |
| 1958 | Rafer Johnson, Track |
| 1959 | Ingemar Johansson, Boxing |
| 1960 | Arnold Palmer, Golf |
| 1961 | Jerry Lucas, Basketball |
| 1962 | Terry Baker, Football |
| 1963 | Pete Rozelle, Pro Football |
| 1964 | Ken Venturi, Golf |
| 1965 | Sandy Koufax, Baseball |
| 1966 | Jim Ryun, Track |
| 1967 | Carl Yastrzemski, Baseball |
| 1968 | Bill Russell, Pro Basketball |
| 1969 | Tom Seaver, Baseball |
| 1970 | Bobby Orr, Hockey |
| 1971 | Lee Trevino, Golf |
| 1972 | Billie Jean King, Tennis |
| | John Wooden, Basketball |
| 1973 | Jackie Stewart, Auto Racing |
| 1974 | Muhammad Ali, Boxing |
| 1975 | Pete Rose, Baseball |
| 1976 | Chris Evert, Tennis |
| 1977 | Steve Cauthen, Horse Racing |
| 1978 | Jack Nicklaus, Golf |
| 1979 | Terry Bradshaw, Pro Football |
| | Willie Stargell, Baseball |
| 1980 | US Olympic Hockey Team |
| 1981 | Sugar Ray Leonard, Boxing |
| 1982 | Wayne Gretzky, Hockey |
| 1983 | Mary Decker, Track |
| 1984 | Mary Lou Retton, Gymnastics |
| | Edwin Moses, Track |
| 1985 | Kareem Abdul-Jabbar, Pro Basketball |
| 1986 | Joe Paterno, Football |
| 1987 | Athletes Who Care |
| | Bob Bourne, Hockey |
| | Kip Keino, Track |
| | Judi Brown King, Track |
| | Dale Murphy, Baseball |
| | Chip Rives, Football |
| | Patty Sheehan, Golf |
| | Rory Sparrow, Pro Basketball |
| | Reggie Williams, Pro Football |
| 1988 | Orel Hershiser, Baseball |
| 1989 | Greg LeMond, Cycling |
| 1990 | Joe Montana, Pro Football |
| 1991 | Michael Jordan, Pro Basketball |
| 1992 | Arthur Ashe |
| 1993 | Don Shula, Pro Football |
| 1994 | Bonnie Blair, Speed Skating |
| | Johann Olav Koss, Speed Skating |

### Associated Press Athletes of the Year

| | MEN | WOMEN |
|---|---|---|
| 1931 | Pepper Martin, Baseball | Helene Madison, Swimming |
| 1932 | Gene Sarazen, Golf | Babe Didrikson, Track |
| 1933 | Carl Hubbell, Baseball | Helen Jacobs, Tennis |
| 1934 | Dizzy Dean, Baseball | Virginia Van Wie, Golf |
| 1935 | Joe Louis, Boxing | Helen Wills Moody, Tennis |
| 1936 | Jesse Owens, Track | Helen Stephens, Track |
| 1937 | Don Budge, Tennis | Katherine Rawls, Swimming |
| 1938 | Don Budge, Tennis | Patty Berg, Golf |
| 1939 | Nile Kinnick, Football | Alice Marble, Tennis |
| 1940 | Tom Harmon, Football | Alice Marble, Tennis |
| 1941 | Joe DiMaggio, Baseball | Betty Hicks Newell, Golf |
| 1942 | Frank Sinkwich, Football | Gloria Callen, Swimming |
| 1943 | Gunder Haegg, Track | Patty Berg, Golf |
| 1944 | Byron Nelson, Golf | Ann Curtis, Swimming |
| 1945 | Bryon Nelson, Golf | Babe Didrikson Zaharias, Golf |
| 1946 | Glenn Davis, Football | Babe Didrikson Zaharias, Golf |
| 1947 | Johnny Lujack, Football | Babe Didrikson Zaharias, Golf |
| 1948 | Lou Boudreau, Baseball | Fanny Blankers-Koen, Track |
| 1949 | Leon Hart, Football | Marlene Bauer, Golf |
| 1950 | Jim Konstanty, Baseball | Babe Didrikson Zaharias, Golf |
| 1951 | Dick Kazmaier, Football | Maureen Connolly, Tennis |
| 1952 | Bob Mathias, Track | Maureen Connolly, Tennis |
| 1953 | Ben Hogan, Golf | Maureen Connolly, Tennis |
| 1954 | Willie Mays, Baseball | Babe Didrikson Zaharias, Golf |
| 1955 | Hopalong Cassidy, Football | Patty Berg, Golf |
| 1956 | Mickey Mantle, Baseball | Pat McCormick, Diving |
| 1957 | Ted Williams, Baseball | Althea Gibson, Tennis |
| 1958 | Herb Elliott, Track | Althea Gibson, Tennis |
| 1959 | Ingemar Johansson, Boxing | Maria Bueno, Tennis |
| 1960 | Rafer Johnson, Track | Wilma Rudolph, Track |
| 1961 | Roger Maris, Baseball | Wilma Rudolph, Track |
| 1962 | Maury Wills, Baseball | Dawn Fraser, Swimming |
| 1963 | Sandy Koufax, Baseball | Mickey Wright, Golf |

## Associated Press Athletes of the Year *(Cont.)*

| | MEN | WOMEN |
|---|---|---|
| 1964 | Don Schollander, Swimming | Mickey Wright, Golf |
| 1965 | Sandy Koufax, Baseball | Kathy Whitworth, Golf |
| 1966 | Frank Robinson, Baseball | Kathy Whitworth, Golf |
| 1967 | Carl Yastrzemski, Baseball | Billie Jean King, Tennis |
| 1968 | Denny McLain, Baseball | Peggy Fleming, Skating |
| 1969 | Tom Seaver, Baseball | Debbie Meyer, Swimming |
| 1970 | George Blanda, Pro Football | Chi Cheng, Track |
| 1971 | Lee Trevino, Golf | Evonne Goolagong, Tennis |
| 1972 | Mark Spitz, Swimming | Olga Korbut, Gymnastics |
| 1973 | O. J. Simpson, Pro Football | Billie Jean King, Tennis |
| 1974 | Muhammad Ali, Boxing | Chris Evert, Tennis |
| 1975 | Fred Lynn, Baseball | Chris Evert, Tennis |
| 1976 | Bruce Jenner, Track | Nadia Comaneci, Gymnastics |
| 1977 | Steve Cauthen, Horse Racing | Chris Evert, Tennis |
| 1978 | Ron Guidry, Baseball | Nancy Lopez, Golf |
| 1979 | Willie Stargell, Baseball | Tracy Austin, Tennis |
| 1980 | US Olympic Hockey Team | Chris Evert Lloyd, Tennis |
| 1981 | John McEnroe, Tennis | Tracy Austin, Tennis |
| 1982 | Wayne Gretzky, Hockey | Mary Decker, Track |
| 1983 | Carl Lewis, Track | Martina Navratilova, Tennis |
| 1984 | Carl Lewis, Track | Mary Lou Retton, Gymnastics |
| 1985 | Dwight Gooden, Baseball | Nancy Lopez, Golf |
| 1986 | Larry Bird, Pro Basketball | Martina Navratilova, Tennis |
| 1987 | Ben Johnson, Track | Jackie Joyner-Kersee, Track |
| 1988 | Orel Hershiser, Baseball | Florence Griffith Joyner, Track |
| 1989 | Joe Montana, Pro Football | Steffi Graf, Tennis |
| 1990 | Joe Montana, Pro Football | Beth Daniel, Golf |
| 1991 | Michael Jordan, Pro Basketball | Monica Seles, Tennis |
| 1992 | Michael Jordan, Pro Basketball | Monica Seles, Tennis |
| 1993 | Michael Jordan, Pro Basketball | Sheryl Swoopes, College Basketball |
| 1994 | George Foreman, Boxing | Bonnie Blair, Speed Skating |

## James E. Sullivan Award

Presented annually by the Amateur Athletic Union to the athlete who "by his or her performance, example and influence as an amateur, has done the most during the year to advance the cause of sportsmanship."

| | | | |
|---|---|---|---|
| 1930 | Bobby Jones, Golf | 1960 | Rafer Johnson, Track |
| 1931 | Barney Berlinger, Track | 1961 | Wilma Rudolph, Track |
| 1932 | Jim Rausch, Track | 1962 | Jim Beatty, Track |
| 1933 | Glenn Cunningham, Track | 1963 | John Pennel, Track |
| 1934 | Bill Bonthron, Track | 1964 | Don Schollander, Swimming |
| 1935 | Lawson Little, Golf | 1965 | Bill Bradley, Basketball |
| 1936 | Glenn Morris, Track | 1966 | Jim Ryun, Track |
| 1937 | Don Budge, Tennis | 1967 | Randy Matson, Track |
| 1938 | Don Lash, Track | 1968 | Debbie Meyer, Swimming |
| 1939 | Joe Burk, Rowing | 1969 | Bill Toomey, Track |
| 1940 | Greg Rice, Track | 1970 | John Kinsella, Swimming |
| 1941 | Leslie MacMitchell, Track | 1971 | Mark Spitz, Swimming |
| 1942 | Cornelius Warmerdam, Track | 1972 | Frank Shorter, Track |
| 1943 | Gilbert Dodds, Track | 1973 | Bill Walton, Basketball |
| 1944 | Ann Curtis, Swimming | 1974 | Rich Wohlhuter, Track |
| 1945 | Doc Blanchard, Football | 1975 | Tim Shaw, Swimming |
| 1946 | Arnold Tucker, Football | 1976 | Bruce Jenner, Track |
| 1947 | John B. Kelly, Jr, Rowing | 1977 | John Naber, Swimming |
| 1948 | Bob Mathias, Track | 1978 | Tracy Caulkins, Swimming |
| 1949 | Dick Button, Skating | 1979 | Kurt Thomas, Gymnastics |
| 1950 | Fred Wilt, Track | 1980 | Eric Heiden, Speed Skating |
| 1951 | Bob Richards, Track | 1981 | Carl Lewis, Track |
| 1952 | Horace Ashenfelter, Track | 1982 | Mary Decker, Track |
| 1953 | Sammy Lee, Diving | 1983 | Edwin Moses, Track |
| 1954 | Mal Whitfield, Track | 1984 | Greg Louganis, Diving |
| 1955 | Harrison Dillard, Track | 1985 | Joan B. Samuelson, Track |
| 1956 | Pat McCormick, Diving | 1986 | Jackie Joyner-Kersee, Track |
| 1957 | Bobby Morrow, Track | 1987 | Jim Abbott, Baseball |
| 1958 | Glenn Davis, Track | 1988 | Florence Griffith Joyner, Track |
| 1959 | Parry O'Brien, Track | 1989 | Janet Evans, Swimming |

## James E. Sullivan Award (Cont.)

| | |
|---|---|
| 1990 | John Smith, Wrestling |
| 1991 | Mike Powell, Track |
| 1992 | Bonnie Blair, Speed Skating |
| 1993 | Charlie Ward, College Football, Basketball |
| 1994 | Dan Jansen, Speed Skating |

## The Sporting News Man of the Year

| | |
|---|---|
| 1968 | Denny McLain, Baseball |
| 1969 | Tom Seaver, Baseball |
| 1970 | John Wooden, Basketball |
| 1971 | Lee Trevino, Golf |
| 1972 | Charles O. Finley, Baseball |
| 1973 | O. J. Simpson, Pro Football |
| 1974 | Lou Brock, Baseball |
| 1975 | Archie Griffin, Football |
| 1976 | Larry O'Brien, Pro Basketball |
| 1977 | Steve Cauthen, Horse Racing |
| 1978 | Ron Guidry, Baseball |
| 1979 | Willie Stargell, Baseball |
| 1980 | George Brett, Baseball |
| 1981 | Wayne Gretzky, Hockey |
| 1982 | Whitey Herzog, Baseball |
| 1983 | Bowie Kuhn, Baseball |
| 1984 | Peter Ueberroth, LA Olympics |
| 1985 | Pete Rose, Baseball |
| 1986 | Larry Bird, Pro Basketball |
| 1987 | No award |
| 1988 | Jackie Joyner-Kersee, Track |
| 1989 | Joe Montana, Pro Football |
| 1990 | Nolan Ryan, Baseball |
| 1991 | Michael Jordan, Pro Basketball |
| 1992 | Mike Krzyzewski, College Basketball Coach |
| 1993 | Pat Gillick and Cito Gaston, Baseball |
| 1994 | Emmitt Smith, Pro Football |

## United Press International Male and Female Athlete of the Year

| | MEN | WOMEN |
|---|---|---|
| 1974 | Muhammad Ali, Boxing | Irena Szewinska, Track and Field |
| 1975 | Joao Oliveira, Track and Field | Nadia Comaneci, Gymnastics |
| 1976 | Alberto Juantorena, Track and Field | Nadia Comaneci, Gymnastics |
| 1977 | Alberto Juantorena, Track and Field | Rosie Ackermann, Track and Field |
| 1978 | Henry Rono, Track and Field | Tracy Caulkins, Swimming |
| 1979 | Sebastian Coe, Track and Field | Marita Koch, Track and Field |
| 1980 | Eric Heiden, Speed Skating | Hanni Wenzel, Alpine Skiing |
| 1981 | Sebastian Coe, Track and Field | Chris Evert Lloyd, Tennis |
| 1982 | Daley Thompson, Track and Field | Marita Koch, Track and Field |
| 1983 | Carl Lewis, Track and Field | Jarmila Kratochvilova, Track and Field |
| 1984 | Carl Lewis, Track and Field | Martina Navratilova, Tennis |
| 1985 | Steve Cram, Track and Field | Mary Decker Slaney, Track and Field |
| 1986 | Diego Maradona, Soccer | Heike Drechsler, Track and Field |
| 1987 | Ben Johnson, Track and Field | Steffi Graf, Tennis |
| 1988 | Matt Biondi, Swimming | Florence Griffith Joyner, Track and Field |
| 1989 | Boris Becker, Tennis | Steffi Graf, Tennis |
| 1990 | Stefan Edberg, Tennis | Merlene Ottey, Track and Field |
| 1991 | Michael Jordan, Pro Basketball | Monica Seles, Tennis |
| 1992 | Mario Lemieux, Hockey | Monica Seles, Tennis |
| 1993 | Michael Jordan, Pro Basketball | Steffi Graf, Tennis |
| 1994 | Nick Price, Golf | Bonnie Blair, Speed Skating |

## Dial Award

Presented annually by the Dial Corporation to the male and female national high school athlete/scholar of the year.

| | MEN | WOMEN |
|---|---|---|
| 1979 | Herschel Walker, Football | No award |
| 1980 | Bill Fralic, Football | Carol Lewis, Track |
| 1981 | Kevin Willhite, Football | Cheryl Miller, Basketball |
| 1982 | Mike Smith, Basketball | Elaine Zayak, Skating |
| 1983 | Chris Spielman, Football | Melanie Buddemeyer, Swimming |
| 1984 | Hart Lee Dykes, Football | Nora Lewis, Basketball |
| 1985 | Jeff George, Football | Gea Johnson, Track |
| 1986 | Scott Schaffner, Football | Mya Johnson, Track |
| 1987 | Todd Marinovich, Football | Kristi Overton, Water Skiing |
| 1988 | Carlton Gray, Football | Courtney Cox, Basketball |
| 1989 | Robert Smith, Football | Lisa Leslie, Basketball |
| 1990 | Derrick Brooks, Football | Vicki Goetze, Golf |
| 1991 | Jeff Buckey, Football, Track | Katie Smith, Basketball, Volleyball, Track |
| 1992 | Jacque Vaughn, Basketball | Amanda White, Track, Swimming |
| 1993 | Tiger Woods, Golf | Kristin Folkl, Basketball |
| 1994 | Taymon Domzalski, Basketball | Shannon Miller, Gymnastics |

# Profiles

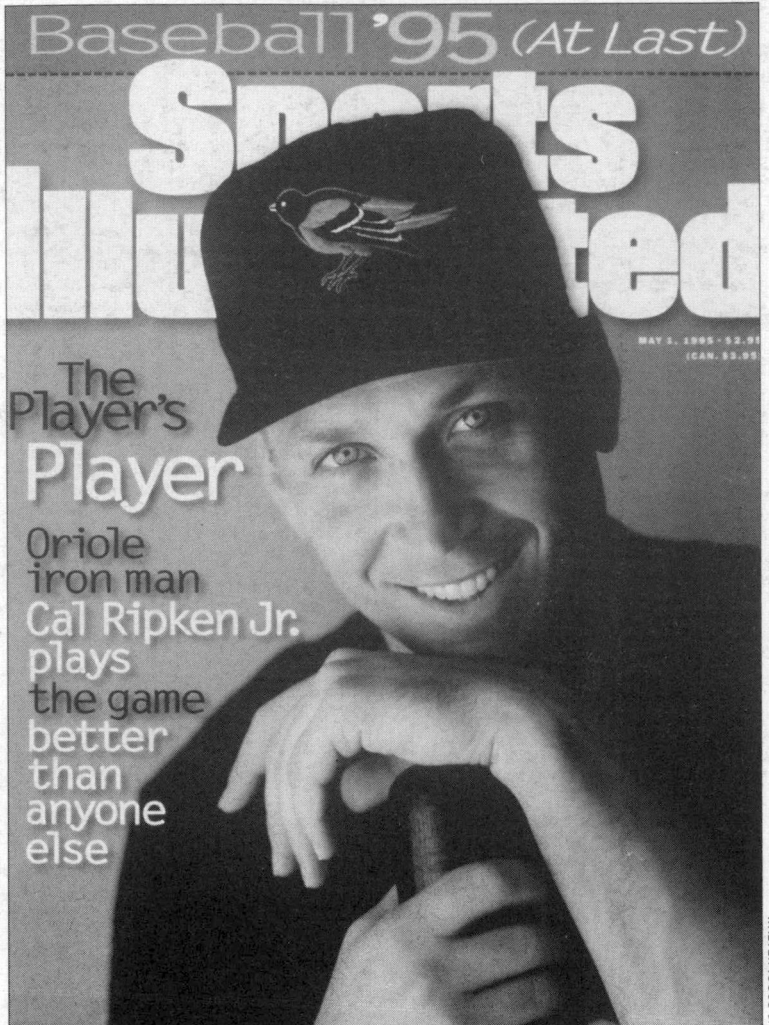

Baseball '95 *(At Last)*

Sports Illustrated

MAY 1, 1995 · $2.95
(CAN. $3.95)

The Player's **Player**

Oriole iron man Cal Ripken Jr. plays the game better than anyone else

WALTER IOOSS JR.

# Profiles

**Henry Aaron** (b. 2-5-34): Baseball OF. "Hammerin' Hank." Alltime leader in HR (755) and RBI (2,297); third in hits (3,771). 1957 MVP. Led league in HR and RBI 4 times each, runs scored 3 times, hits and batting average 2 times. No. 44, he had 44 homers 4 times. Had 40+ HR 8 times; 100+ RBI 11 times; .300+ average 14 times. 24-time All-Star. Career span 1954–76; jersey number retired by Atlanta and Milwaukee.

**Kareem Abdul-Jabbar** (b. 4-16-47): Born Lew Alcindor. Basketball C. All-time leader points scored (38,387), field goals attempted (28,307), field goals made (15,837), blocked shots (3,189), games played (1,560), and years played (20); third all-time rebounds (17,440). Won 6 MVP awards (1971–72, 1974, 1976–77, 1980). Career scoring average was 24.6, rebounding average 11.2. 10-time All-Star, All-Defensive team 5 times. 1970 Rookie of the Year. Played on 6 championship teams; was playoff MVP in 1971, 1985. Career span 1969–88 with Milwaukee, Los Angeles. Also played on 3 NCAA championship teams with UCLA; tournament MVP 1967–69; Player of the Year 2 times.

**Affirmed** (b. 2-21-75): Thoroughbred race horse. Triple Crown winner in 1978 with jockey Steve Cauthen aboard. Trained by Laz Barrera.

**Troy Aikman** (b. 11-21-66): Football QB. MVP of Super Bowl XXVII, in which he completed 22 of 30 passes for 273 yards and four TDs with no interceptions. Led Cowboys to Super Bowl XXVIII victory. Career span since 1989 with Dallas Cowboys.

**Tenley Albright** (b. 7-18-35): Figure skater. Gold medalist at 1956 Olympics, silver medalist at 1952 Olympics. World champion 2 times (1953, 1955) and U.S. champion 5 consecutive years (1952–56).

**Grover Cleveland Alexander** (b. 2-26-1887, d. 11-4-50): Baseball RHP. Third alltime most wins (373), second most shutouts (90). Won 30+ games 3 times, 20+ games 6 other times. Set rookie record with 28 wins in 1911. Career span 1911–30 with Philadelphia (NL), Chicago (NL), St Louis (NL).

**Vasili Alexeyev** (b. 1942): Soviet weightlifter. Gold medalist at 2 consecutive Olympics in 1972, 1976. World champion 8 times.

**Muhammad Ali** (b. 1-17-42): Born Cassius Clay. Boxer. Heavyweight champion 3 times (1964–67, 1974–78, 1978–79). Stripped of title in 1967 because he refused to serve in the Vietnam War. Career record 56–5 with 37 KOs. Defended title 19 times. Also light heavyweight gold medalist at 1960 Olympics.

**Phog Allen** (b. 11-18-1885, d. 9-16-74): College basketball coach. Fifth alltime most wins (746); .739 career winning percentage. Won 1952 NCAA championship. Most of career, 1920–56, with Kansas.

**Bobby Allison** (b. 12-3-37): Auto racer. Third all-time in NASCAR victories (84) at the time of his retirement. Won Daytona 500 3 times (1978, 1982, 1988). Also NASCAR champion in 1983.

**Naty Alvarado** (b. 7-25-55): Mexican-born handball player. "El Gato (The Cat)". Won a record 11 U.S. pro four-wall handball titles starting in 1977.

**Lance Alworth** (b. 8-3-40): Football WR. "Bambi" led NFL in receiving in 1966, '68 and '69. 200+ yards in a game 5 times in career, a record. Gained 100+ yards

in game 41 times. In 1965 gained 1,602 yards, still second highest seasonal yardage ever. Career span 1962–70 with San Diego and 1971–72 with Dallas. Elected to Pro Football Hall of Fame 1978.

**Sparky Anderson** (b. 2-22-34): Baseball manager. Only manager to win World Series in both leagues (Detroit, 1984, Cincinnati, 1975–76); only manager to win 100 games in both leagues.

**Willie Anderson** (b. 1880, d. 1910): Scottish golfer. Won U.S. Open 4 times (1901 and an unmatched three straight, 1903–05). Also won 4 Western Opens between 1902 and 1909.

**Mario Andretti** (b. 2-28-40): Auto racer. The only driver in history to win Daytona 500 (1967), Indy 500 (1969) and Formula One world championship (1978). Second alltime in CART victories (52) as of retirement in Oct. 1994. Also 12 career Formula One victories. USAC/CART champion 4 times (consecutively 1965–66, 1969, 1984). Named Indy 500 Rookie of the Year in 1965.

**Earl Anthony** (b. 4-27-38): Bowler. Won PBA National Championship 6 times, more than any other bowler (consecutively 1973–75, 1981–83) and Tournament of Champions 2 times (1974, 1978). First bowler to top $1 million in career earnings. Bowler of the Year 6 times (consecutively 1974–76, 1981–83). Has won 45 career PBA titles since 1970.

**Said Aouita** (b. 11-2-60): Track and field. Moroccan set world records in 2,000 meters (4:50.81 in 1987), and 5,000 meters (12:58.39 in 1987). 1984 Olympic champion in 5,000; 1988 Olympic third place in 800.

**Al Arbour** (b. 11-1-32): Hockey D-coach. Led NY Islanders to 4 consecutive Stanley Cup championships (1980–83). Also played on 3 Stanley Cup champions: Detroit, Chicago and Toronto, from 1953 to 1971.

**Eddie Arcaro** (b. 2-19-16): Horse racing jockey. The only jockey to win the Triple Crown 2 times (aboard Whirlaway in 1941, Citation in 1948). Rode Preakness Stakes winner (1941, 1948, consecutively 1950–51, 1955, 1957) and Belmont Stakes winner (consecutively 1941–42, 1945, 1948, 1952, 1955) 6 times each and Kentucky Derby winner 5 times (1938, 1941, 1945, 1948, 1952). 4,779 career wins.

**Nate Archibald** (b. 9-2-48): Basketball player. "Tiny" only by NBA standards at 6' 1", 160 pounds. Drafted by Cincinnati in 1970. Averaged 34 points per game for K.C.-Omaha in 1972–73. Led NBA in scoring (34.0) and assists (910) in 1972–73. First team, all-NBA in 1973, '75 and '76. MVP of NBA All Star game in 1981. Retired in 1984.

**Alexis Arguello** (b. 4-19-52): Nicaraguan Boxer. Won world titles in three weight classes— featherweight, super featherweight and lightweight. Won first title, WBA featherweight, on 11-23-74 when he KO'd Ruben Olivares in 13. Won last title, vacant WBC lightweight, on 5-22-82 when he KO'd Andrew Ganigan in 5. Career record: 86 bouts; won 65 by KO, 15 by decision; lost 6, three by KO.

**Henry Armstrong** (b. 12-12-12): Boxer. Champion in 3 different weight classes: featherweight (1937—relinquished 1938), welterweight (1938–40) and lightweight (1938–39). Career record 145-20-9 with 98 KOs (27 consecutively, 1937–38) from 1931 to 1945.

**Arthur Ashe** (b. 7-10-43; d. 2-6-93): Tennis player. First black man to win U.S. Open (1968, as an amateur), Australian Open (1970) and Wimbledon singles titles (1975). 33 career tournament victories. Member of Davis Cup team 1963–78; captain 1980–85. Died of AIDS-related pneumonia.

**Assault** (b. 1943): Thoroughbred race horse. Horse of the Year for 1946; won Triple Crown that year. Won Kentucky Derby by 8 lengths; Preakness by a neck over Lord Boswell; and the Belmont by 3 lengths from Natchez. Trained by Max Hirsch.

**Red Auerbach** (b. 9-20-17): Basketball coach-executive.Second in wins (938). Coached Boston from 1946 to 1965, winning 9 championships, 8 consecutively. Had .662 career winning percentage, with 50+ wins 8 consecutive seasons. Also won 7 championships as general manager.

**Hobey Baker** (b. 1-15-1892, d. 12-21-18): Sportsman. Member of both college football and hockey Halls of Fame. College hockey and football star with Princeton, 1911–14. Fighter pilot in World War I, died in plane crash. College hockey Player of the Year award named in his honor.

**Seve Ballesteros** (b. 4-9-57): Spanish golfer. Notorious scrambler. Won British Opens in 1979, '84 and '88. Won Masters in 1980 and '83.

**Ernie Banks** (b. 1-31-31): Baseball SS-1B. "Mr. Cub." Won 2 consecutive MVP awards, in 1958–59. 512 career HR. League leader in HR, RBI 2 times each; career batting average of .274; 40+ HR 5 times; 100+ RBI 8 times. Most HR by a shortstop with 47 in 1958. Career span 1953–71 with Chicago.

**Roger Bannister** (b. 3-23-29): Track and field. British runner broke the 4-minute mile barrier, running 3:59.4 on May 6, 1954.

**Red Barber** (b. 2-17-08, d. 10-22-92): Sportscaster. TV-radio baseball announcer was the voice of Cincinnati, Brooklyn and NY Yankees. His expressions, such as "sitting in the catbird seat," "pea patch" and "rhubarb" captivated audiences from 1934 to 1966.

**Charles Barkley** (b. 2-20-63): Basketball F. Five-time first-team All-Star. All-Rookie team, 1985. Led NBA in rebounding, 1987. Averaged 20+ points in seven of 8 seasons with Philadelphia. 1992 Olympic team leading scorer. Traded to Phoenix before 1992-93 season. League MVP for 1992-93 season.

**Rick Barry** (b. 3-28-44): Basketball F. Only player in history to win scoring titles in NBA (San Francisco, 1967) and ABA (Oakland, 1969). Second alltime highest free throw percentage (.900). Career scoring average 23.2. Led league in free throw percentage 6 times, steals and scoring 1 time each. Averaged 30+ points 2 times, 20+ points 6 other times. 5-time All-Star. 1975 playoff MVP with Golden State. 1966 Rookie of the Year. Career span 1967–79.

**Carmen Basilio** (b. 4-2-27): Boxer. Won titles in two weight classes, welter and middle. Lost first welter title bid to Kid Gavilan on 9-18-53. Won world welter title by TKO of Tony DeMarco in 12 rounds on 6-10-55. Lost, regained and retained welter title in three fights with Johnny Saxton. Won and then lost middleweight title in two 15 round fights with Ray Robinson. Made three unsuccessful bids to regain middle title. *The Ring* Fighter of the Year for 1957. Career record: 78 bouts; won 26 by KO and 29 by decision; drew 7; lost 16, two by KO. Elected to Boxing Hall of Fame in 1969.

**Sammy Baugh** (b. 3-17-14): Football QB-P. Set records by leading league in passing 6 times and punting 4 times. Also holds record for highest career punting average (45.1) and highest season average (51.0 in 1940). Career span 1937–52 with Washington. Also All-America with Texas Christian 3 consecutive seasons.

**Elgin Baylor** (b. 9-16-34): Basketball F. Third alltime highest scoring average (27.4), scored 23,149 points. Averaged 30+ points 3 consecutive seasons, 20+ points 8 other times. 10-time All-Star. 1962 Rookie of the Year. Played in 8 finals without winning championship. Career span 1958–71 with Los Angeles. Also 1958 MVP in NCAA tournament with Seattle.

**Bob Beamon** (b. 8-29-46): Track and field. Gold medalist in long jump at 1968 Olympics with world record jump of 29' 2½" that stood until 1991.

**Franz Beckenbauer** (b. 1945): West German soccer player. Captain of 1974 World Cup champions and coach of 1990 champions. Also played for NY Cosmos from 1977 to 1980.

**Boris Becker** (b. 11-22-67): German tennis player. The youngest male player to win a Wimbledon singles title at age 17 in 1985. Has won 3 Wimbledon titles (consecutively 1985–86, 1989), 1 U.S. Open (1989) and 1 Australian Open title (1991). Led West Germany to 2 consecutive Davis Cup victories (1988–89).

**Chuck Bednarik** (b. 5-1-25): Football C-LB. Last of the great two-way players, was named All-Pro at both center and linebacker. Missed only 3 games in 14 seasons with Philadelphia from 1949–62. Also All-America 2 times at Pennsylvania.

**Clair Bee** (b. 3-2-1896, d. 5-20-83): Basketball coach. Originated 1-3-1 defense, helped develop three-second rule, 24-second clock. Won 82.7 percent of games as coach for Rider College and Long Island University. Coach Baltimore Bullets, 1952–54. Author, 23-volume Chip Hilton series for children, 21 nonfiction sports books.

**Jean Beliveau** (b. 8-31-31): Hockey C. Won MVP award 2 times (1956, 1964), playoff MVP in 1965. Led league in assists 3 times, goals 2 times and points 1 time. 507 career goals, 712 assists. All-Star 6 times. Played on 10 Stanley Cup champions with Montreal from 1950 to 1971.

**Bert Bell** (b. 2-25-1895, d. 10-11-59): Football executive. Second NFL commissioner (1946–59). Also owner of Philadelphia (1933–40) and Pittsburgh (1941–46). Proposed the first college draft in 1936.

**James "Cool Papa" Bell** (b. 5-17-03): Baseball OF. Legendary foot speed—according to Satchel Paige could flip light switch and be in bed before room was dark. Hit .392 in games against white major leaguers. Career span 1922–46 with many teams of the Negro Leagues, including the Pittsburgh Crawfords and the Homestead Grays. Inducted in the Hall of Fame in 1974.

**Lyudmila Belousova/Oleg Protopov** (no dates of birth available): Soviet figure skaters. Won Olympic gold medal in pairs competition in 1964 and 1968. Won four consecutive World and European championships (1965–68) and eight consecutive Soviet titles (1961–68).

**Deane Beman** (b. 4-22-38): Commissioner of the PGA Tour 1974–94. Won British Amateur title in 1959 and U.S. Amateur titles in 1960 and 1963.

**Johnny Bench** (b. 12-7-47): Baseball C. MVP in 1970, 1972; World Series MVP in 1976; Rookie of the Year in 1968. 389 career HR. League leader in HR 2 times, RBI 3 times. Career span 1967–83 with Cincinnati.

**Patty Berg** (b. 2-13-18): Golfer. Alltime women's leader in major championships (16), third alltime in career wins (57). Won Titleholders Championship (1937–39, 1948, 1953–54, 1957) and Western Open (1941, 1943, 1948, 1951, 1955, 1957–58) 7 times each, the most of any golfer. Also won U.S. Women's Amateur (1938) and U.S. Women's Open (1946).

**Yogi Berra** (b. 5-12-25): Baseball C. Played on 10 World Series winners. All-time Series leader in games, at bats, hits and doubles. MVP in 1951 and consecutively 1954–55. 358 career HR. Career span 1946–65. Also managed pennant-winning Yankees (1964) and NY Mets (1973).

**Jay Berwanger** (b. 3-19-14): College football RB. Won the first Heisman Trophy and named All-America with Chicago in 1935.

**Raymond Berry** (b. 2-27-33): Football E. Led NFL in receiving 1958–60. In 13-season career, caught 631 passes, 68 for TDs. Career span 1955–67, all with Baltimore Colts. Later coached New England Patriots from 1984–89 with 51–41 record.

**George Best** (b. 5-22-46): Irish soccer player. Led Manchester United to European Cup title in 1968. Named England's and Europe's Player of the Year in 1968. Played in North American Soccer League for Los Angeles (1976–78), Fort Lauderdale (1978–79) and San Jose (1980–81). Frequent troubles with alcohol and gambling overshadowed career.

**Abebe Bikila** (b. 8-7-32, d. 10-25-73): Track and field. Ethiopian barefoot runner won consecutive gold medals in the marathon at Olympics, in 1960 and 1964.

**Fred Biletnikoff** (b. 2-23-43): Football WR. In 14 pro seasons caught 589 passes for 8,974 yards and 76 TDs. In 1961 led NFL receivers with 61 catches; in '62 led AFC with 58. Career span 1965–78, all with Raiders. Elected to Pro Football Hall of Fame in 1988.

**Dmitri Bilozerchev** (b. 12-22-66): Soviet gymnast. Won 3 gold medals at 1988 Olympics. Made comeback after shattering his left leg into 44 pieces in 1985. Two-time world champion (1983, 1987). At 16, became youngest to win all-around world championship title in 1983.

**Dave Bing** (b. 11-24-43): Basketball G. Averaged 24.8 points a game in four years at Syracuse. NBA Rookie of Year in 1967. Led NBA in scoring (27.1) in 1968. MVP NBA All Star game in 1976. In 12 year career from 1967–78, most of it with Detroit Pistons, averaged 20.3 points.

**Matt Biondi** (b. 10-8-65): Swimmer. Winner of 5 gold medals, 1 silver medal and 1 bronze medal at 1988 Olympics. Won one gold and one silver at 1992 Olympics.

**Larry Bird** (b. 12-7-56): Basketball F. Won 3 consecutive MVP awards (1984–86) and 2 playoff MVP awards (1984, 1986). Also Rookie of the Year (1980) and All-Star 9 consecutive seasons. Has led league in free throw percentage 4 times. Averaged 20+ points 10 times. Career span 1979-1992 with Boston. Named College Player of the Year in 1979 with Indiana State.

**Bonnie Blair** (b. 3-18-64): Speed skater. Won gold medal in 500 meters and bronze medal in 1,000 meters

at 1988 Olympics and gold medals in both events in 1992 and '94. Also 1989 World Sprint champion. Winner of 1992 Sullivan Award.

**Toe Blake** (b. 8-21-12, d. 5-17-95): Hockey LW and coach. Second alltime highest winning percentage (.634) and fifth in wins (500). Led Montreal to 8 Stanley Cup championships from 1955 to 1968 (consecutively 1956–60, 1965–66, 1968). Also MVP and scoring leader in 1939. Played on 2 Stanley Cup champions with Montreal from 1932 to 1948.

**Doc Blanchard** (b. 12-11-24): College football FB. "Mr. Inside." Teamed with Glenn Davis to lead Army to 3 consecutive undefeated seasons (1944–46) and 2 consecutive national championships (1944–45). Won Heisman Trophy and Sullivan Award in 1945. Also All-America 3 times.

**George Blanda** (b. 9-17-27): Football QB-K. Alltime leader in seasons played (26), games played (340), points scored (2,002) and points after touchdown (943); third in field goals (335). Also passed for 26,920 career yards and 236 touchdowns. Tied record with 7 touchdown passes on Nov. 19, 1961. Player of the Year 2 times (1961, 1970). Retired at age 48, the oldest to ever play. Career span 1949–75 with Chicago, Houston, Oakland.

**Fanny Blankers-Koen** (b. 4-26-18): Track and field. Dutch athlete won four gold medals at 1948 Olympics, in 100-meters; 200 meters; 80-meter hurdles; and 400-meter relay. Versatile, she also set world records in high jump (5' 7-1/4" in 1943), long jump (20' 6" in 1943) and pentathlon (4,692 points in 1951).

**Wade Boggs** (b. 6-15-58): Baseball 3B. Won 5 batting titles (1983, consecutively 1985–88); has had .350+ average 5 times, 200+ hits 7 times. Career span 1982–92 with Boston, 1993- with New York Yankees.

**Nick Bolletieri** (b. 7-31-31): Tennis coach. Since 1976, has run Nick Bolletieri Tennis Academy in Bradenton, Fla. Former residents of the academy include Andre Agassi, Monica Seles and Jim Courier.

**Barry Bonds** (b. 7-24-64): Baseball OF. Three-time National League MVP (1990, '92, '93); Career span 1986 to '92, with Pirates; 1993- with Giants.

**Bjorn Borg** (b. 6-6-56): Swedish tennis player. Second alltime men's leader in Grand Slam singles titles (11—tied with Rod Laver). Set modern record by winning 5 consecutive Wimbledon titles (1976–80). Won 6 French Open titles (consecutively 1974–75, 1978–81). Reached U.S. Open final 4 times, but title eluded him. 65 career tournament victories. Led Sweden to Davis Cup win in 1975.

**Julius Boros** (b. 3-3-20): Golfer. Won US. Opens in 1952 at Northwood CC in Dallas and in 1963 at The Country Club in Brookline, Mass. Also won 1968 PGA Championship at Pecan Valley CC, San Antonio, when 48 years old, making him oldest winner of a major ever. Led PGA money list in 1952 and '55.

**Mike Bossy** (b. 1-22-57): Hockey RW. In 1978 set NHL rookie scoring record of 54 goals, broken in 1993. Scored 50 or more each of first nine seasons, totaling 573 goals and 1,126 points in 10 seasons (1977–78 through 1986–87) with New York Islanders. Elected to Hall of Fame in 1991.

**Ralph Boston** (b. 5-9-39): Track and field. Long jumper won medals at 3 consecutive Olympics; gold in 1960, silver in 1964, bronze in 1968.

**Ray Bourque** (b. 12-28-60): Hockey D. Won Norris Trophy as NHL's top defenseman five times. Career span since 1979 with Boston Bruins.

**Scotty Bowman** (b. 9-18-33): Hockey coach. Entered 1995–96 season as alltime leader in regular season wins (913) and in regular season winning percentage (.657). Also alltime leader in playoff wins (152). Led Montreal to 5 Stanley Cups, and has also coached St Louis and Buffalo. Won Jack Adams Award, Coach of the Year, 1976–77.

**Bill Bradley** (b. 7-28-43): Basketball F. Played on 2 NBA championship teams with New York from 1967 to 1977. Player of the Year and NCAA tournament MVP in 1965 with Princeton; All-America 3 times; Sullivan Award winner in 1965. Rhodes scholar. U.S. Senator (D-NJ) since 1979.

**Terry Bradshaw** (b. 9-2-48): Football QB. Played on 4 Super Bowl champions (consecutively 1974–75, 1978–79); named Super Bowl MVP 2 consecutive seasons (1978–79). 212 career touchdown passes; 27,989 yards passing. Player of the Year in 1978. Career span 1970–83 with Pittsburgh.

**George Brett** (b. 5-15-53): Baseball 3B-1B. MVP in 1980 with .390 batting average; 3 batting titles, in 1976, 1980, 1990; and .300+ average 11 times. Led league in hits and triples 3 times. Reached 3,000-hit mark in 1992. Career span 1973–93, with Kansas City. Career totals: 3,153 hits; 317 HR; 1,595 RBIs; batting average .305.

**Bret Hanover** (b. 5-19-62): Horse. Son of Adios. Won 62 of 68 harness races and earned $922,616. Undefeated as two-year-old. From total of 1,694 foals, he sired winners of $61 million and 511 horses which have recorded sub-2:00 performances.

**Lou Brock** (b. 6-18-39): Baseball OF. Second alltime most stolen bases (938); second most season steals (118). Led league in steals 8 times, with 50+ steals 12 consecutive seasons. Alltime World Series leader in steals (14—tied with Eddie Collins); third in Series batting average (.391). 3,023 career hits. Career span 1961–79 with St Louis.

**Jim Brown** (b. 2-17-36): Football FB. Second alltime in touchdowns (126); and fourth in yards rushing (12,312). Led league in rushing a record 8 times. His 5.22-yards per carry average is also the best ever. Player of the Year 4 times (consecutively 1957–58, 1963, 1965) and Rookie of the Year in 1957. Rushed for 1,000+ yards in 7 seasons, 200+ yards in 4 games, 100+ yards in 54 other games. Career span 1957–65 with Cleveland; never missed a game. Also All-America with Syracuse.

**Paul Brown** (b. 9-7-08, d. 8-5-91): Football coach. Led Cleveland to 10 consecutive championship games. Won 4 consecutive AAFC titles (1946–49) and 3 NFL titles (1950, consecutively 1954–55). Coached Cleveland from 1946 to 1962; became first coach of Cincinnati, 1968–75, and then general manager. Career coaching record 222-113-9. Also won national championship with Ohio State in 1942.

**Avery Brundage** (b. 9-28-1887, d. 5-5-75): Amateur sports executive. President of International Olympic Committee 1952–72. Served as president of U.S. Olympic Committee 1929–53. Also president of Amateur Athletic Union 1928–35. Member of 1912 U.S. Olympic track and field team.

**Paul "Bear" Bryant** (b. 9-11-13, d. 1-26-83): College football coach. Alltime Division I-A leader in wins (323). Won 6 national championships (1961, consecutively 1964–65, 1973, consecutively 1978–79) with Alabama. Career record 323–85–17, including 4 undefeated seasons. Also won 15 bowl games. Career span 1945–82 with Maryland, Kentucky, Texas A&M, Alabama.

**Sergei Bubka** (b. 12-4-63): Track and field. Ukrainian pole vaulter was gold medalist at 1988 Olympics. Only five-time world outdoor champion in any event (1983, 1987, 1991, 1993, 1995). First man to vault 20 feet, set world indoor record of 20' 2" on 2-21-93 and world outdoor record of 20' 1½", set on 9-20-92.

**Buck Buchanan** (b. 9-10-40): Football DT. Career span 1963–75 with Kansas City Chiefs. Elected to Pro Football Hall of Fame 1990.

**Don Budge** (b. 6-13-15): Tennis player. First player to achieve the Grand Slam, in 1938. Won 2 consecutive Wimbledon and U.S. singles titles (1937–38), 1 French and 1 Australian title (1938).

**Dick Butkus** (b. 12-9-42): Football LB. Recovered 25 opponents' fumbles, second most in history. Selected for Pro Bowl 8 times. Career span 1965–73 with Chicago. Also All-America 2 times with Illinois. Award recognizing the outstanding college linebacker named in his honor.

**Dick Button** (b. 7-18-29): Figure skater. Gold medalist at 2 consecutive Olympics in 1948, 1952. World champion 5 consecutive years (1948–52) and U.S. champion 7 consecutive years (1946–52). Sullivan Award winner in 1949.

**Walter Byers** (b. 3-13-22): Amateur sports executive. First executive director of NCAA, served from 1952 to 1987.

**Frank Calder** (b. 11-17-1877, d. 2-4-43): Hockey executive. First commissioner of NHL, served from 1917 to 1943. Rookie of the Year award named in his honor.

**Walter Camp** (b. 4-7-1859, d. 3-14-25): Football pioneer. Played for Yale in its first football game vs. Harvard on Nov. 17, 1876. Proposed rules such as 11 men per side, scrimmage line, center snap, yards and downs. Founded the All-America selections in 1889.

**Roy Campanella** (b. 11-19-21; d. 6-26-93): Baseball C. Career span 1948–57, ended when paralyzed in car crash. MVP in 1951, 1953, 1955. Played on 5 pennant winners; 1955 World Series winner with Brooklyn Dodgers.

**Earl Campbell** (b. 3-29-55): Football RB. Tenth alltime yards rushing (9,407); third alltime in season yards rushing (1,934 in 1980) and fourth in TDs rushing (19 in 1979). Led league in rushing 3 consecutive seasons. Rushed for 1,000+ yards in 5 seasons. Scored 74 career touchdowns. Player of the Year 2 consecutive seasons (1978–79). Rookie of the Year in 1978. Career span 1978–85 with Houston, New Orleans. Won Heisman Trophy with Texas in 1977.

**John Campbell** (b. 4-8-55): Canadian harness racing driver. Alltime leading money winner with over $100 million in earnings. Leading money winner 1986–90. Has more than 5,500 career wins.

**Billy Cannon** (b. 2-8-37): Football RB. Led Louisiana State to national championship in 1958 and won Heisman Trophy in 1959. Signed contract in both NFL (Los Angeles) and AFL (Houston). Houston won lawsuit for his services. Played in 6 AFL championship games with Houston, Oakland, Kansas City. Career span

1960–70. Served three-year jail term for 1983 conviction on counterfeiting charges.

**Jose Canseco** (b. 7-2-64): Baseball OF. Only player to top 40 homers (42) and 40 (40) steals in same season (1988). AL MVP in 1988, when he also batted .307 with 124 RBIs. Career span 1985–1992 with Oakland and since 1992 with Texas Rangers.

**Harry Caray** (b. 3-1-17): Sportscaster. TV-radio baseball announcer since 1945 with St Louis (NL), Oakland, Chicago (AL) and Chicago (NL). Achieved celebrity status on Cubs' superstation WGN by singing "Take Me Out to the Ballgame" with Wrigley Field fans.

**Rod Carew** (b. 10-1-45): Baseball 2B-1B. Won 7 batting titles (1969, consecutively 1972–75, 1977–78). Had .328 career average, 3,053 career hits, and .300+ average 15 times. 1977 MVP; 1967 Rookie of the Year. Career span 1967–85; jersey number (29) retired by Minnesota and California.

**Steve Carlton** (b. 12-22-44): Baseball LHP. Second alltime most strikeouts (4,136). 4 Cy Young awards (1972, 1977, 1980, 1982). 329 career wins; won 20+ games 6 times. League leader in wins 4 times, innings pitched and strikeouts 5 times each. Struck out 19 batters in 1 game in 1969. Career span 1965–88 with St. Louis, Philadelphia and four other teams in last two years.

**JoAnne Carner** (b. 4-21-39): Golfer. Won 42 titles, including US Women's Opens in 1971 and '76 and du Maurier Classic in 1975 and '78. LPGA top earner in 1974 and 1982–83. LPGA Player of the Year in 1974 and 1981–82. Won five Vare Trophies (1974–75 and 1981–83).

**Joe Carr** (b. 10-22-1880; d. 5-20-39): Football administrator. Instrumental in forming American Professional Football Association in 1920. President of AAFA from 1922 to '39.

**Don Carter** (b. 7-29-26): Bowler. Won All-Star Tournament 4 times (1952, 1954, 1956, 1958) and PBA National Championship in 1960. Voted Bowler of the Year 6 times (consecutively 1953–54, 1957–58, 1960, 1962).

**Alexander Cartwright** (b. 4-17-1820, d. 7-12-1892): Baseball pioneer. Organized the first baseball game on June 19, 1846, and set the basic rules of bases 90 feet apart, 9 men per side, 3 strikes per out and 3 outs per inning. In that first game his New York Knickerbockers lost to the New York Nine 23–1 at Elysian Fields in Hoboken, NJ.

**Billy Casper** (b. 6-24-31): Golfer. Famed putter. Won 51 PGA tournaments. PGA Player of Year in both 1966 and '70. Won Vardon Trophy in 1960, '63, '64, '65 and '68. Won the US Open twice, in 1959 at Winged Foot in Mamaronek, New York, and in 1966 in 18-hole playoff over Arnold Palmer at Olympic Club, San Francisco. Beat Gene Littler in 18 hole playoff to win 1970 Masters.

**Tracy Caulkins** (b. 1-11-63): Swimmer. Won 3 gold medals at 1984 Olympics. Won 48 U.S. national titles, more than any other swimmer, from 1978 to 1984. Also won Sullivan Award in 1978.

**Steve Cauthen** (b. 5-1-60): Jockey. In 1978 became youngest jockey to win Triple Crown, aboard Affirmed. First jockey to top $6 million in season earnings (1977). *Sports Illustrated* Sportsman of Year for 1977. Moved to England in 1979. Among the 1,389 winners he had ridden in England through end of 1990 were two winners of Epsom Derby—Slip Anchor in 1985 and Reference Point in 1987.

**Evonne Goolagong Cawley** (b. 7-31-51): Tennis. Won 4 Australian Open titles from 1974 through '77; won '71 French Open; Wimbledon in 1971 and '80, Runnerup four straight years at U.S. Open (1973–76) which she never won.

**Bill Chadwick** (b. 10-10-15): Hockey referee. Spent 16 years as a referee despite vision in only one eye. Developed hand signals to signify penalties. Also former television announcer for the New York Rangers.

**Wilt Chamberlain** (b. 8-21-36): Basketball C. Alltime leader in rebounds (23,924) and rebounding average (22.9). Alltime season leader in points scored (4,029 in 1962), scoring average (50.4 in 1962), rebounding average (27.2 in 1961) and field goal percentage (.727 in 1973). Alltime single-game most points scored (100 in 1962) and most rebounds (55 in 1960). Second alltime most points scored (31,419) and most field goals made (12,681). 4 MVP awards (1960, consecutively 1966–68); playoff MVP in 1972 and 1960 Rookie of the Year. 7-time All-Star. 30.1 career scoring average. Career span 1959–72 with Philadelphia, Los Angeles. Also named College Player of the Year in 1957 at Kansas.

**Colin Chapman** (b. 1928, d. 12-16-83): Auto racing engineer. Founded Lotus race and street cars, designing the first Lotus racer in 1948. Introduced the monocoque design for Formula One cars in 1962 and ground effects in 1978. Four of his drivers, including Mario Andretti, won Formula One world championships.

**Julio Cesar Chavez** (b. 7-12-62): Boxer. Through 10-1-95 the current WBC junior welterweight champion. But many thought he lost fight against Pernell Whitaker on 9-10-93 in Alamodome which ended officially as a "majority draw". Also won titles as super featherweight (1984–87) and lightweight (1987–89).

**Gerry Cheevers** (b. 12-7-40): Hockey goalie. Goaltender for Stanley Cup-winning Boston Bruins teams of 1970 and '72. In 12 seasons with Boston had 230-94-74 record with a goals against average of 2.89. Also coached Bruins from 1980–84, with 204-126-46 record. Elected to Hall of Fame 1985.

**Citation** (b. 4-11-45, d. 8-8-70): Thoroughbred race horse. Triple Crown winner in 1948 with jockey Eddie Arcaro aboard. Trained by Ben A. Jones.

**King Clancy** (b. 2-25-03, d. 11-6-86): Hockey D. Four-time All-Star. Coach, Montreal Maroons, Toronto. Referee. Trophy named in his honor, recognizing leadership qualities and contribution to community.

**Jim Clark** (b. 3-4-36, d. 4-7-68): Scottish auto racer. Fifth alltime in Formula 1 victories (25—tied with Niki Lauda). Formula 1 champion 2 times (1963, 1965). Won Indy 500 1 time (1965). Named Indy 500 Rookie of the Year in 1963. Killed during competition in 1968 at age 32.

**Bobby Clarke** (b. 8-13-49): Hockey C. Won MVP award 3 times (1973, consecutively 1975–76). 358 career goals, 852 assists. Led league in assists 2 consecutive seasons and scored 100+ points 3 times. Played on 2 consecutive Stanley Cup champions (1974–75) with Philadelphia. Career span 1969 to 1984. Also general manager with Philadelphia from 1984 to 1990, Minnesota 1991-92, Florida 1993-94, and Philadelphia since 1994.

**Roger Clemens** (b. 8-4-62): Baseball RHP. Record 20 strikeouts in 1 game. Won 2 consecutive Cy Young Awards in 1986, 1987. Also 1986 MVP. League leader in ERA 4 times, wins and strikeouts 2 times each. Career span since 1984 with Boston.

**Roberto Clemente** (b. 8-18-34, d. 12-31-72): Baseball OF. Killed in plane crash while still an active player. Had 3,000 career hits and .317 career average. 4 batting titles; .300+ average 13 times. 1966 MVP; 1971 World Series MVP. 12 consecutive Gold Gloves; led league in assists 5 times. Career span 1955–72 with Pittsburgh.

**Ty Cobb** (b. 12-18-1886, d. 7-17-61): Baseball OF. Alltime leader in batting average (.367) and runs scored (2,245); second most hits (4,191); fourth most stolen bases (892). 1911 MVP and 1909 Triple Crown winner. 12 batting titles. Had .400+ average 3 times, .350+ average 13 other times; 200+ hits 9 times. Led league in hits 7 times, steals 6 times and runs scored 5 times. Career span 1905–28 with Detroit.

**Mickey Cochrane** (b. 4-6-03, d. 6-28-62): Baseball C. Alltime highest career batting average among catchers (.320). MVP in 1928, 1934. Had .300+ average 8 times. Career span 1925–37 with Philadelphia, Detroit.

**Sebastian Coe** (b. 9-29-56): Track and field. British runner was gold medalist in 1,500 meters and silver medalist in 800 meters at 2 consecutive Olympics in 1980, 1984. World record holder in 800 meters (1:41.73 set in 1981) and 1,000 meters (2:12.18 set in 1981). Now a member of parliament.

**Eddie Collins** (b. 5-2-1887, d. 3-25-51): Baseball 2B. Alltime leader among 2nd basemen in games, chances and assists; led league in fielding 9 times. 3,311 career hits; .333 career average; .330+ average 12 times. Fifth alltime most stolen bases (743—tied with Tim Raines); alltime most World Series steals (14—tied with Lou Brock); alltime leader in single-game steals (6, twice). 1914 MVP. Career span 1906–30 with Philadelphia, Chicago.

**Nadia Comaneci** (b. 11-12-61): Romanian gymnast. First ever to score a perfect 10 at Olympics (on uneven parallel bars in 1976). Won 3 gold, 2 silver and 1 bronze medal at 1976 Olympics. Also won 2 gold and 2 silver medals at 1980 Olympics.

**Dennis Conner** (b. 9-16-42): Sailing. Captain of America's Cup winner 3 times (1980, '87,'88).

**Maureen Connolly** (b. 9-17-34, d. 6-21-69): Tennis player. "Little Mo" first woman to achieve the Grand Slam, in 1953. Won the U.S. singles title in 1951 at age 16. Thereafter lost only 4 matches before retiring in 1954 because of a broken leg caused by a riding accident. Was never beaten in singles at Wimbledon, winning 3 consecutive titles (1952–54). Won 3 consecutive U.S. singles titles (1951–53) and 2 consecutive French titles (1953–54). Also won 1 Australian title (1953).

**Jimmy Connors** (b. 9-2-52): Tennis player. Alltime men's leader in tournament victories (109). Held men's #1 ranking a record 159 consecutive weeks, July 29, 1974 through Aug. 16, 1977. Won 5 U.S. Open singles titles on 3 different surfaces (grass 1974, clay 1976, hard 1978, consecutively 1982–83). Won 2 Wimbledon singles titles (1974, 1982) farther apart than anyone since Bill Tilden. Also won 1974 Australian Open title. Reached Grand Slam final 7 other times.

**Jim Corbett** (b. 9-1-1866; d. 2-18-33): Boxer. "Gentleman Jim". Invented jab. Fight with Australian Peter Jackson on 5-21-91 ruled no contest when neither could continue into 62nd round. Won heavyweight title on 9-7-92 with a KO of John Sullivan in 21 rounds; it was first heavyweight title fight using gloves. Retained title with KO of British champ Charley Mitchell. Lost title when KO'd by Bob Fitzsimmons in 14 on 3-17-1897, then lost two bids to regain it against Jim Jeffries. Career record: 19 fights; won 7 by KO and 4 by decision; drew 2; lost 4; 2 no decision. Elected to Boxing Hall of Fame in 1954.

**Angel Cordero** (b. 11-8-42): Jockey. At end of 1994 third alltime in wins (7,057) and earnings ($164,526,217). Led yearly earnings three times, in 1976 and 1982–83, winning Eclipse Awards in the last two years.

**Howard Cosell** (b. 3-25-18, d. 4-23-95): Sportscaster. Lawyer turned TV-radio sports commentator in 1953. Best known for his work on "Monday Night Football." His nasal voice and "tell it like it is" approach made him a controversial figure.

**James "Doc" Counsilman** (b. 12-28-20): Swimming coach. Coached Indiana from 1957 to 1990. Won 6 consecutive NCAA championships (1968–73). Career record 287–36–1. Coached U.S. men's team at Olympics in 1964, 1976. Also oldest person to swim English Channel (58 in 1979).

**Count Fleet** (b. 3-24-40, d. 12-3-73): Thoroughbred race horse. Triple Crown winner in 1943 with jockey Johnny Longden aboard. Trained by Don Cameron.

**Yvan Cournoyer** (b. 11-22-43): Hockey RW. "The Roadrunner" had 428 goals and 435 assists during his 15 season career with the Montreal Canadiens. Had 25 or more goals in 12 straight seasons. Played on 10 Stanley Cup championship teams. Elected to Hall of Fame in 1982.

**Margaret Smith Court** (b. 7-16-42): Australian tennis player. Alltime leader in Grand Slam singles titles (26) and total Grand Slam titles (66). Achieved Grand Slam in 1970 and mixed doubles Grand Slam in 1963 with Ken Fletcher. Won 11 Australian singles titles (consecutively 1960–66, 1969–71, 1973), 5 French titles (1962, 1964, consecutively 1969–70, 1973), 7 U.S. titles (1962, 1965, consecutively 1969–70, 1973) and 3 Wimbledon titles (1963, 1965, 1970). Also won 19 Grand Slam doubles titles and 19 mixed doubles titles.

**Bob Cousy** (b. 8-9-28): Basketball G. Finished career with 6,955 assists, second alltime most assists in a game (28 in 1958). League leader in assists 8 consecutive seasons. Averaged 18+ points and named to All-Star team 10 consecutive seasons. 1957 MVP. Played on 6 championship teams with Boston from 1950 to 1969. Also played on NCAA championship team in 1947 with Holy Cross.

**Dave Cowens** (b. 10-25-48): Basketball C. After college career at Florida State, NBA co-Rookie of Year in 1971. NBA MVP for 1973. All-Star game MVP in 1973. Career span 1970–71 through 1982–83, all but the last year with the Boston Celtics. Elected to Hall of Fame in 1991.

**Ben Crenshaw** (b. 1-11-52): Golfer. Legendary putter. Won 1984 Masters.

**Larry Csonka** (b. 12-25-46): Football RB. In 11 seasons rushed 1,891 times for 8,081 yards (4.3 per carry) and 64 TDs. MVP of Super Bowl VIII, when he rushed 33 times for a then Super Bowl record 145 yards in Miami's 24–7 defeat of Minnesota. Career span 1968–74, 1979 with Miami Dolphins; 1976–78 with New York Giants. Elected to Hall of Fame in 1987.

**Billy Cunningham** (b. 6-3-43): Basketball player and coach. Averaged 24.8 points a game at North Carolina. In nine seasons (1965–66 through 1975–76) with Philadelphia 76ers, averaged 20.8 points per game. All NBA first team 1969, '70 and '71. In 8 seasons as Sixer coach went 454–196 in season, 66–39 in playoffs and won NBA title in 1983. Elected to Hall of Fame in 1985.

**Chuck Daly** (b. 7-20-30): Basketball coach. Won 2 consecutive championships with Detroit (1989–90). Won 50+ games 4 consecutive seasons. Coach of 1992 Olympic team. Career span as pro coach 1983–92 with Pistons; 1992–94 with New Jersey Nets.

**Damascus** (b. 1964): Thoroughbred race horse. After finishing 3rd in 1967 Kentucky Derby, won the Preakness, the Belmont, the Dwyer, the American Derby, the Travers, the Woodward and others—12 of 16 starts. Unanimous Horse of the Year for 1967.

**Stanley Dancer** (b. 7-25-27): Harness racing driver. Only driver to win the Trotting Triple Crown 2 times (Nevele Pride in 1968, Super Bowl in 1972). Also won Pacing Triple Crown driving Most Happy Fella in 1970. Won The Hambletonian 4 times (1968, 1972, 1975, 1983). Driver of the Year in 1968.

**Tamas Darnyi** (b. 6-3-67): Hungarian swimmer. Gold medalist in 200-meter and 400-meter individual medleys at 1988 and 1992 Olympics. Also won both events at World Championships in 1986 and 1991. Set world records in these events at 1991 Championships (1:59.36 and 4:12.36).

**Al Davis** (b. 7-4-29): Football executive. Owner and general manager of Oakland-LA Raiders since 1963. Built winningest franchise in sports history (313-192-11—a .617 winning percentage entering the 1995 season). Team has won 3 Super Bowl championships (1976, 1980, 1983). Also served as AFL commissioner in 1966, helped negotiate AFL–NFL merger.

**Ernie Davis** (b. 12-14-39, d. 5-18-63): Football RB. Won Heisman Trophy in 1961, the first black man to win the award. All-America 3 times at Syracuse. First selection in 1962 NFL draft, but became fatally ill with leukemia and never played professionally.

**Glenn Davis** (b. 12-26-24): College football HB. "Mr. Outside." Teamed with Doc Blanchard to lead Army to 3 consecutive undefeated seasons (1944–46) and 2 consecutive national championships (1944–45). Won Heisman Trophy in 1946. Also named All-America 3 times.

**John Davis** (b. 1-12-21, d. 7-13-84): Weightlifter. Gold medalist at 2 consecutive Olympics in 1948, 1952. World champion 6 times.

**Pete Dawkins** (b. 3-8-38): Football RB. Starred at Army 1956–58. Won Heisman Trophy 1958. Was first captain of cadets, class president, top 5 percent of class academically, and football team captain; first man to do all four at West Point. Did not play pro football. Attended Oxford on Rhodes scholarship, won two Bronze Stars in Vietnam, rose to brigadier general before leaving Army to become investment banker. Made unsuccessful run for Senate from New Jersey in 1988.

**Len Dawson** (b. 6-20-35): Football QB. Completed 2,136 of 3,741 pass attempts with 239 TDs. In first

Super Bowl threw for one TD in 35–10 loss to Green Bay. MVP of Super Bowl IV, which Kansas City won 23–7 over Minnesota. Career span 1957–75, the last 13 seasons with Kansas City Chiefs. Elected to Hall of Fame in 1987.

**Dizzy Dean** (b. 1-16-11, d. 7-17-74): Baseball RHP. 1934 MVP with 30 wins. League leader in strikeouts, complete games 4 times each. 150 career wins. Arm trouble shortened career after 134 wins by age 26. Career span 1930–41 and 1947 with St Louis and Chicago Cubs.

**Dave DeBusschere** (b. 10-16-40): Basketball F. NBA First Team Defense six straight seasons, 1969–74. Member of NBA champion New York Knicks in 1970 and '73. Career span 1962–63 through middle of 1968–69 season with Detroit Pistons; through 1973–74 with Knicks. Youngest coach (24) in NBA history. Elected to NBA Hall of Fame in 1982.

**Pierre de Coubertin** (b. 1-1-1863, d. 9-2-37): Frenchman called the father of the Modern Olympics. President of International Olympic Committee from 1896 to 1925.

**Jack Dempsey** (b. 6-24-1895, d. 5-31-83): Boxer. Heavyweight champion (1919–26), lost title to Gene Tunney and rematch in the famous "long count" bout in 1927. Career record 62-6-10 with 49 KOs from 1914 to 1928.

**Gail Devers** (b. 11-19-66): Track and field sprinter/hurdler. Won 100 at 1992 Olympics; leading 100 hurdles when she tripped over final hurdle and finished fifth. Successfully completed same double at 1993 World Championships, winning 100 in 10.82 and 100 hurdles in American record 12.46. Also won world indoor title in 60 (6.95). Battled Graves Disease.

**Klaus Dibiasi** (b. 10-6-47): Italian diver. Gold medalist in platform at 3 consecutive Olympics (1968, 1972, 1976) and silver medalist at 1964 Olympics.

**Eric Dickerson** (b. 9-2-60): Football RB. Alltime season leader in yards rushing (2,105 in 1984), second alltime most career yards rushing (13,259). Rushed for 1,000+ yards a record 7 consecutive seasons; 100+ yards in 61 games, including 12 times in 1984. Led league in rushing 4 times. Rookie of the Year in 1983. Career span 1983–93 with Los Angeles Rams, Indianapolis, L.A. Raiders and Atlanta Falcons.

**Bill Dickey** (b. 6-6-07): Baseball C. Lifetime average .313. Hit 202 home runs. Played on 11 AL All-Star teams. In eight World Series, hit five homers and 24 RBIs. Career span 1928–43 and 1946, all with the New York Yankees. Inducted to Hall of Fame 1954.

**Harrison Dillard** (b. 7-8-23): Track and field. Only man to win Olympic gold medal in sprint (100 meters in 1948) and hurdles (110 meters in 1952). Sullivan Award winner in 1955.

**Joe DiMaggio** (b. 11-25-14): Baseball OF. Voted baseball's greatest living player. Record 56-game hitting streak in 1941. MVP in 1939, 1941, 1947. Had .325 career batting average; .300+ average 11 times; 100+ RBI 9 times. League leader in batting average, HR, and RBI 2 times each. Played on 10 World Series winners with NY Yankees. Career span 1936–51.

**Mike Ditka** (b. 10-18-39): Football TE-Coach. NFL Rookie of the Year in 1961. Named to Pro Bowl five times. Made 427 catches for 5,812 yards and 43 TDs.

Career span 1961 to '72 with Bears, Eagles and Cowboys. Coach of Bears from 1982–92 with 112–68 overall record. Coach of Bear team that won Super Bowl XX, 46–10 over New England. Elected to Hall of Fame 1988.

**Tony Dorsett** (b. 4-7-54): Football RB. Third alltime in yards rushing (12,739), fourth in attempts (2,936). Rushed for 1,000+ yards in 8 seasons. Set record for longest run from scrimmage with 99-yard touchdown run on January 3, 1983. Scored 91 career touchdowns. Named Rookie of the Year in 1977. Career span 1977–88 with Dallas, Denver. Also won Heisman Trophy in 1976, leading Pittsburgh to national championship. Alltime NCAA leader in yards rushing and only man to break 6,000-yard barrier (6,082).

**Abner Doubleday** (b. 6-26-1819, d. 1-26-1893): Civil War hero incorrectly credited as the inventor of baseball in Cooperstown, New York, in 1839. More recent research calls Alexander Cartwright the true father of the game.

**Clyde Drexler** (b. 6-22-62): Basketball G. Nicknamed "The Glide" for his smooth play. Member of U.S. "Dream Team" that won 1992 Olympic gold medal. Career span 1984–1994 with Portland Trail Blazers and 1995– with Houston Rockets, with whom he won his first NBA title in 1995.

**Ken Dryden** (b. 8-8-47): Hockey G. Goaltender of the Year 5 times (1973, consecutively 1976–79). Playoff MVP as a rookie in 1971, maintained rookie status and named Rookie of the Year in 1972. Led league in goals against average 5 times, wins and shutouts 4 times each. Career record 258-57-74, including 46 shutouts. Career 2.24 goals against average is the modern record. Second alltime in playoff wins (80). Tied record of 4 playoff shutouts in 1977. Played on 6 Stanley Cup champions with Montreal from 1970 to 1979.

**Don Drysdale** (b. 7-23-36, d. 7-3-93): Baseball RHP. Led NL three times in strikeouts (1959, '60, '62) and once in wins (1962). Won 1962 Cy Young Award with 25–9 mark. In 1968 pitched six straight shutouts en route to major league record—broken in 1988 by Orel Hershiser—of 58 consecutive scoreless innings. Career record of 209–166, with 2,484 K's and ERA of 2.95. Career span 1956–69, all with Dodgers. Inducted into Hall of Fame 1984.

**Roberto Duran** (b. 6-16-51): Panamanian boxer. Champion in 3 different weight classes: lightweight (1972–79), welterweight (1980, lost rematch to Sugar Ray Leonard in famous "no mas" bout) and junior middleweight (1983–84). Career record 90–9 with 62 KOs since 1967.

**Leo Durocher** (b. 7-27-05, d. 10-7-91): Baseball manager. "Leo the Lip." Said "Nice guys finish last." Managed 3 pennant winners and 1954 World Series winner. Won 2,008 games in 24 years. Led Brooklyn 1939–48; New York 1948–55; Chicago 1966–72; and Houston 1972–73.

**Eddie Eagan** (b. 4-26-1898, d. 6-14-67): Only American athlete to win gold medal at Summer and Winter Olympic Games (boxing 1920, bobsled 1932).

**Alan Eagleson** (b. 4-24-33): Hockey labor leader. Founder of NHL Players' Association and its executive director from 1967–92.

**Dale Earnhardt** (b. 4-29-52): Auto racer. NASCAR champion 7 times (1980, 1986–87, 1990–91, 1993-94). 66 career NASCAR victories through 9-17-95.

**Stefan Edberg** (b. 1-19-66): Swedish tennis player. Has won 2 Wimbledon singles titles (1988, 1990), 2 Australian Open titles (1985, 1987) and 2 U.S. Open titles (1991, 1992). Led Sweden to 3 Davis Cup victories (consecutively 1984–85, 1987).

**Gertrude Ederle** (b. 10-23-06): Swimmer. First woman to swim the English Channel, in 1926. Swam 21 miles from France to England in 14:39. Also won 3 medals at the 1924 Olympics.

**Herb Elliott** (b. 2-25-38): Track and field. Australian runner was gold medalist in 1960 Olympic 1,500 meters in world record 3:35.6. Also set world mile record of 3:54.5 in 1958. Undefeated at 1500 meters/mile in international competition. Retired at 21.

**John Elway** (b. 6-28-60): Football QB. First player taken in 1983 NFL draft. Topped 3,000 yards passing every season from 1985–91. Through '94 season had thrown for 37,736 yards, 199 TDs. Famous for last minute drives. Career span since 1983 with Denver Broncos.

**Roy Emerson** (b. 11-3-36): Australian tennis player. Alltime men's leader in Grand Slam singles titles (12). Won 6 Australian titles, 5 consecutively (1961, 1963–67), 2 consecutive Wimbledon titles (1964–65), 2 U.S. titles (1961, 1964) and 2 French titles (1963, 1967). Also won 13 Grand Slam doubles titles.

**Kornelia Ender** (b. 10-25-58): East German swimmer. Won 4 gold medals at 1976 Olympics and 3 silver medals at 1972 Olympics.

**Julius Erving** (b. 2-22-50): "Dr. J." Basketball F. Third alltime most points scored for combined ABA and NBA career (30,026). 24.2 scoring average. Averaged 20+ points 14 consecutive seasons. 4 MVP awards, consecutively 1974–76, 1981; playoff MVP 1974, 1976. All-Star 9 times. Led league in scoring 3 times. Played on 3 championship teams, with New York (ABA) and Philadelphia (NBA). Career span 1971 to 1986.

**Phil Esposito** (b. 2-20-42): Hockey C. "Espo." First to break the 100-point barrier (126 in 1969). Fourth alltime in points (1,590) and goals (717), ninth in assists (873). Led league in goals 6 consecutive seasons, points 5 times and assists 3 times. Won MVP award 2 times (1969, 1974). Scored 30+ goals 13 consecutive seasons and 100+ points 6 times. All-Star 6 times. Career span 1963–81 with Chicago, Boston, NY Rangers. Also general manager of NY Rangers from 1986 to 1989. Currently general manager of Tampa Bay.

**Tony Esposito** (b. 4-23-43): Hockey goalie. Brother of Phil. A five-time All Star during 16-season NHL career, almost all of it with the Chicago Blackhawks. In 886 games gave up 2,563 goals, an average of 2.92 per game. Won or shared Vezina Trophy three times. Elected to Hall of Fame in 1988.

**Janet Evans** (b. 8-28-71): Swimmer. Won 3 gold medals at 1988 Olympics and 1 at 1992 Olympics. Set world record in 400-meter freestyle (4:03.85 in 1988), 800-meter freestyle (8:16.22 in 1989) and 1,500-meter freestyle (15:52.10 in 1988). Sullivan Award winner in 1989.

**Lee Evans** (b. 2-25-47): Track and field. Gold medalist in 400 meters at 1968 Olympics with world record time of 43.86 that stood until 1988.

**Chris Evert** (b. 12-21-54): Also Chris Evert Lloyd. Tennis player. Second alltime in tournament victories

(157). Third alltime in women's Grand Slam singles titles (18—tied with Martina Navratilova). Won at least 1 Grand Slam singles title every year from 1974 to 1986. Won 7 French Open titles (1974–75, 1979–1980, 1983, 1985–86), 6 U.S. Open titles (1975–77, 1978, 1980, 1982), 3 Wimbledon titles (1974, 1976, 1981) and 2 Australian Open titles (1982, 1984). Reached Grand Slam finals 16 other times. Reached semifinals at 52 of her last 56 Grand Slam tournaments.

**Weeb Ewbank** (b. 5-6-07): Football coach. Only coach to win titles in both the NFL and AFL. Coached Baltimore Colts to classic overtime defeat of New York Giants in 1958 and New York Jets to their stunning 16–7 win over Baltimore in Super Bowl III. Career record of 134-130-7. Career span 1954–62 with Colts and 1963–73 with Jets. Elected to Hall of Fame in 1978.

**Patrick Ewing** (b. 8-5-62): Basketball C. 1986 Rookie of the Year with New York. 20+ points average in all 10 seasons with Knicks. All-NBA first team 1990. Played on 3 NCAA final teams with Georgetown (1982, 1984–85); tournament MVP in 1984. All-America 3 times.

**Nick Faldo** (b. 7-18-57): British golfer. Winner of the Masters 2 consecutive years (1989–90) and British Open 3 times (1987, 1990, 1992).

**Juan Manuel Fangio** (b. 6-24-11, d. 7-17-95): Argentinian auto racer. Seventh all-time in Formula 1 victories (24, but in just 51 starts). Formula 1 champion 5 times, the most of any driver (1951, consecutively 1954–57). Retired in 1958.

**Bob Feller** (b. 11-3-18): Baseball RHP. League leader in wins 6 times, strikeouts 7 times, innings pitched 5 times. Pitched 3 no-hitters and 12 one-hitters. 266 career wins; 2,581 career strikeouts. Won 20+ games 6 times. Served 4 years in military during career. Career span 1936–41, 1945–56 with Cleveland.

**Tom Ferguson** (b. 12-20-50): Rodeo. First to top $1 million in career earnings. All-Around champion 6 consecutive years (1974–79).

**Enzo Ferrari** (b. 2-8-1898, d. 8-14-88): Auto racing engineer. Team owner since 1929, he built first Ferrari race car in Italy in 1947 and continued to preside over Ferrari race and street cars until his death. In 61 years of competition, Ferrari's cars have won over 5,000 races.

**Mark Fidrych** (b. 8-14-54): Baseball RHP. "The Bird." Rookie of the Year in 1976 with Detroit. Had 19–9 record with league-best 2.39 ERA and 24 complete games. Habit of talking to the ball on the mound made him a cult hero. Arm injuries curtailed career.

**Cecil Fielder** (b. 9-21-63): Baseball 1B. The last man to hit 50+ HR (51 in 1990). Has led the major leagues in HR twice and RBI 3 consecutive seasons (1990–92) after spending 1989 season in Japanese league. Career span since 1985 with Toronto, Detroit.

**Herve Filion** (b. 2-1-40): Harness racing driver. Alltime leader in career wins (more than 13,000). Driver of the Year 10 times, more than any other driver (consecutively 1969–74, 1978, 1981, 1989).

**Rollie Fingers** (b. 8-25-46): Baseball RHP. Third alltime in saves (341); third in relief wins (107); fifth in appearances (944). 1981 Cy Young and MVP winner; 1974 World Series MVP. Alltime Series leader in saves (6). Career span 1968–85 with Oakland, San Diego, Milwaukee.

**Bobby Fischer** (b. 3-9-43): Chess. World champion from 1972 to 1975, the only American to hold title. Never played competitive chess during his reign. Forfeited title to Anatoly Karpov by refusing to play him.

**Carlton Fisk** (b. 12-26-47): Baseball C. Alltime HR leader among catchers (352) and second in games caught (2,226). 376 career HR, including a record 75 after age 40. Rookie of the Year in 1972 and All-Star 11 times. Hit dramatic 12th-inning HR to win Game 6 of 1975 World Series. Career span 1969-93 with Boston, Chicago (AL).

**Emerson Fittipaldi** (b. 12-12-46): Brazilian auto racer. Won Indy 500 in 1989 and '93. Won CART championship in 1989. Formula 1 champion 2 times (1972, 1974).

**James Fitzsimmons** (b. 7-23-1874, d. 3-11-66): Horse racing trainer. "Sunny Jim." Trained Triple Crown winner 2 times (Gallant Fox in 1930, Omaha in 1935). Trained Belmont Stakes winner 6 times (1930, 1932, consecutively 1935–36, 1939, 1955), Preakness Stakes winner 4 times (1930, 1935, 1955, 1957) and Kentucky Derby winner 3 times (1930, 1935, 1939).

**Peggy Fleming** (b. 7-27-48): Figure skater. Gold medalist at 1968 Olympics. World champion 3 consecutive years (1966–68) and U.S. champion 5 consecutive years (1964–68).

**Curt Flood** (b. 1-18-38): Baseball OF. Won 7 consecutive Gold Gloves from 1963 to 1969. Career batting average of .293. Refused to be traded after 1969 season, challenging baseball's reserve clause. Supreme Court rejected his plea, but baseball was eventually forced to adopt free agency system. Career span 1956–69 with St. Louis.

**Whitey Ford** (b. 10-21-26): Baseball LHP. All-time World Series leader in wins, losses, games started, innings pitched, hits allowed, walks and strikeouts. 236 career wins, 2.75 ERA. Third alltime best career winning percentage (.690). Led league in wins and winning percentage 3 times each; ERA, shutouts, innings pitched 2 times each. 1961 Cy Young winner and World Series MVP. Career span 1950, 1953–67 with New York Yankees.

**Forego** (b. 1970): Thoroughbred race horse. Horse of the Year in 1974 (won 8 of 13 starts); '75 (won 6 of 9); and '76 (won 6 of 8). Finished fourth in 1973 Kentucky Derby. Over six years won 34 of 57 starts and $1,938,957.

**George Foreman** (b. 1-22-48): Boxer. Heavyweight champion (1973–74). Retired in 1977, but returned to the ring in 1987. Lost 12-round decision to champion Evander Holyfield in 1991. Retired after losing to Tommy Morrison 6-7-93. Career record 72–4 with 67 KOs since 1969. Also heavyweight gold medalist at 1968 Olympics.

**Dick Fosbury** (b. 3-6-47): Track and field. Gold medalist in high jump at 1968 Olympics. Introduced back-to-the-bar style of high jumping, called the "Fosbury Flop."

**Jimmie Foxx** (b. 10-22-07, d. 7-21-67): Baseball 1B. Won 3 MVP awards, consecutively 1932–33, 1938. Fourth alltime highest slugging average (.609), with 534 career HR; hit 30+ HR 12 consecutive seasons, 100+ RBI 13 consecutive seasons. Won Triple Crown in 1933. Led league in HR 4 times, batting average 2 times. Career span 1925–45 with Philadelphia, Boston.

**A. J. Foyt** (b. 1-16-35): Auto racer. Alltime leader in Indy Car victories (67). Won Indy 500 4 times (1961, 1964, 1967, 1977), Daytona 500 1 time (1972), 24 Hours of Daytona 2 times (1983, 1985) and 24 Hours of LeMans 1 time (1967). USAC champion 7 times, more than any other driver (consecutively 1960–61, 1963–64, 1967, 1975, 1979).

**William H. G. France** (b. 9-26-09): Auto racing executive. Founder of NASCAR and president from 1948 to 1972, succeeded by his son Bill Jr. Builder of Daytona and Talladega speedways.

**Dawn Fraser** (b. 9-4-37): Australian swimmer. Only swimmer to win gold medal in same event at 3 consecutive Olympics (100-meter freestyle in 1956, 1960, 1964). First woman to break the 1-minute barrier at 100 meters (59.9 in 1962).

**Joe Frazier** (b. 1-12-44): Boxer. "Smokin' Joe." Heavyweight champion (1970–73). Best known for his 3 epic bouts with Muhammad Ali. Career record 32-4-1 with 27 KOs from 1965 to 1976. Also heavyweight gold medalist at 1964 Olympics.

**Walt Frazier** (b. 3-29-45): Basketball G. Point guard on championship Knick teams of 1970 and '73. First team All Star in 1970, '72, '74 and '75. First team All Defense every year from 1969–1975. Averaged 18.9 points per game in 13-season NBA career. Elected to Hall of Fame in 1986.

**Frankie Frisch** (b. 9-9-98, d. 3-12-73): Baseball IN. "The Fordham Flash." Led NL in hits in 1923 (223). Hit over .300 13 seasons. Scored 100+ runs 7 times. Drove in 100+ runs three times. Career .316 batting average. Career span 1919–26 with New York Giants and 1927–37 with St. Louis Cardinals "Gashouse Gang." NL MVP in 1931. Elected to Hall of Fame in 1947.

**Dan Gable** (b. 10-25-48): Wrestler. Gold medalist in 149–pound division at 1972 Olympics. Also NCAA champion 2 times (in 1968 at 130 pounds, in 1969 at 137 pounds). Coached Iowa to NCAA championship 13 years (consecutively 1978–86, 1991–93 and 1995).

**Clarence Gaines** (b. 5-21-23): College basketball coach. "Bighouse." Retired after 1992-93 season with 828 career wins in 46 seasons at Division II Winston-Salem State since 1947.

**John Galbreath** (b. 8-10-1897, d. 7-20-88): Horse racing owner. Owner of Darby Dan Farms from 1935 until his death and of baseball's Pittsburgh Pirates from 1946 to 1985. Only man to breed and own winners of both the Kentucky Derby (Chateaugay in 1963 and Proud Clarion in 1967) and the Epsom Derby (Roberto in 1972).

**Gallant Fox** (b. 3-23-27, d. 11-13-54): Thoroughbred race horse. Triple Crown winner in 1930 with jockey Earle Sande aboard. Trained by James Fitzsimmons. The only Triple Crown winner to sire another Triple Crown winner (Omaha in 1935).

**Don Garlits** (b. 1-14-32): Auto racer. "Big Daddy." Has won 35 National Hot Rod Association top fuel events. Won 3 NHRA top fuel points titles (1975, 1985–86). First top fuel driver to surpass 190 mph (1963), 200 mph (1964), 240 mph (1973), 250 mph (1975) and 270 mph (1986). Credited with developing rear engine dragster.

**Lou Gehrig** (b. 6-19-03, d. 6-2-41): Baseball 1B. "The Iron Horse." Second alltime in consecutive games played (2,130), leader in grand slam HR (23), third in

RBI (1,990) and slugging average (.632). MVP in 1927, 1936; won Triple Crown in 1934. .340 career average; 493 career HR. 100+ RBI 13 consecutive seasons. Led league in RBI 5 times and HR 3 times. Played on 7 World Series winners with New York Yankees. Died of disease since named for him. Career span 1923–39.

**Bernie Geoffrion** (b. 2-16-31): Hockey RW. "Boom Boom" for his powerful slapshot. Won Hart Memorial Trophy for 1960–61. Scored 393 goals and 429 assists in 16 seasons (1950–51 through 1967–68), the first 14 with the Montreal Canadiens, the final two with the New York Rangers. Elected to Hall of Fame 1972.

**Eddie Giacomin** (b. 6-6-39): Hockey goalie. "Fast Eddie" led NHL goalies in games won for three straight seasons. Shared Vezina Trophy for 1970–71. In 610 games gave up 1,675 goals, a goals against average of 2.82. Career span 1965–75 with the New York Rangers and 1975–78 with Detroit Red Wings.

**Althea Gibson** (b. 8-25-27): Tennis player. Won 2 consecutive Wimbledon and U.S. singles titles (1957–58), the first black player to win these tournaments. Also won 1 French title (1956).

**Bob Gibson** (b. 11-9-35): Baseball RHP. 1968 Cy Young and MVP award winner with alltime National League best in ERA (1.12) and second most shutouts (13). Also 1970 Cy Young award winner. Record holder for most strikeouts in a World Series game (17); Series MVP in 1964, 1967. Won 20+ games 5 times. 251 career wins; 3,117 strikeouts. Pitched no-hitter in 1971. Career span 1959–75 with St. Louis.

**Josh Gibson** (b. 12-21-11, d. 1-20-47): Baseball C in Negro leagues. "The Black Babe Ruth." Couldn't play in major leagues because of color. Credited with 950 HR (75 in 1931, 69 in 1934) and .350 batting average. Had .400+ average 2 times. Career span 1930–46 with Homestead Grays, Pittsburgh Crawfords.

**Kirk Gibson** (b. 5-28-57): Baseball OF. Played on 2 World Series champions (Detroit in 1984 and Los Angeles in 1988). Hit dramatic pinch-hit HR in 9th inning to win Game 1 of 1988 series. MVP in 1988. Career span since 1979, currently with Detroit. Also starred in baseball and football at Michigan State.

**Frank Gifford** (b. 8-16-30): Football RB. NFL Player of Year in 1956 when he rushed for 819 yards and caught 51 passes. Played in seven Pro Bowls. Retired for one season after ferocious hit by Chuck Bednarik. Career span 1952–60 and 1962–64, all with New York Giants. Elected to Hall of Fame in 1977.

**Rod Gilbert** (b. 7-1-41): Hockey RW. Played 16 seasons, all with the New York Rangers (1960–61 through 1977–78), and had 406 goals and 615 assists. Elected to Hall of Fame 1982.

**Sid Gillman** (b. 10-26-11): Football coach. Developed wide-open, pass-oriented style of offense, introduced techniques for situational player substitutions and the study of game films. Won one division title with Los Angeles Rams and five division titles and one AFL championship (1963) with Los Angeles/San Diego Chargers. Career span 1955–59 Los Angeles Rams; 1960 Los Angeles Chargers; 1961–69 San Diego; 1973–74 Houston. Lifetime record 124-101-7. Also general manager in San Diego and Houston.

**Pancho Gonzales** (b. 5-9-28, d. 7-3-95): Tennis player. Won 2 consecutive U.S. singles titles (1948–49). In 1969, at age 41, beat Charlie Pasarell

22–24, 1–6, 16–14, 6–3, 11–9 in longest Wimbledon match ever (5:12).

**Shane Gould** (b. 11-23-56): Australian swimmer. Won 3 gold medals, 1 silver and 1 bronze at 1972 Olympics. Set 11 world records over 23-month period beginning in 1971. Held world record in 5 freestyle distances ranging from 100 meters to 1,500 meters in late 1971 and 1972. Retired at age 16.

**Steffi Graf** (b. 6-14-69): German tennis player. Achieved the Grand Slam in 1988. Has won 4 Australian Open singles titles (1988–90, '94), 6 Wimbledon titles (1988–89, 1991–93, '95), 4 French Open titles (1987–88, '93 and '95) and 4 U.S. Open titles (1988–89, '93 and '95). Held the #1 ranking a record 186 weeks; Aug. 17, 1987 through March 10, 1991. Gold medalist at 1988 Olympics.

**Otto Graham** (b. 12-6-21): Football QB. Led Cleveland to 10 championship games in his 10-year career. Played on 4 consecutive AAFC champions (1946–49) and 3 NFL champions (1950, consecutively 1954–55). Combined league totals: 23,584 yards passing, 174 touchdown passes. Player of the Year 2 times (1953, 1955). Led league in passing 6 times. Career span 1946–55.

**Red Grange** (b. 6-13-03, d. 1-28-91): Football HB. "The Galloping Ghost." All-America 3 consecutive seasons with Illinois (1923–25), scoring 31 touchdowns in 20–game collegiate career. Signed by George Halas of Chicago in 1925, attracted sellout crowds across the country. Established the first AFL with manager C. C. Pyle in 1926, but league folded after 1 year. Career span 1925–34 with Chicago, New York.

**Rocky Graziano** (b. 6-7-22, d. 5-22-90): Boxer. Middleweight champion from 1947 to 1948. Career record 67–13. Endured 3 brutal title fights against Tony Zale, with Zale winning by KO in 1946 and 1948, and Graziano winning by KO in 1947.

**Hank Greenberg** (b. 1-1-11, d. 9-4-86): Baseball 1B. 331 career HR (58 in 1938). MVP in 1935, 1940. League leader in HR and RBI 4 times each. Fifth alltime highest slugging average (.605). 100+ RBI 7 times. Career span 1933-41, 1945-47 with Detroit, Pittsburgh.

**Joe Greene** (b. 9-24-46): Football DT. "Mean Joe." Anchored Pittsburgh's famed "Steel Curtain" defense. Selected for Pro Bowl 10 times. Played on 4 Super Bowl champions (consecutively 1974-75, 1978-79). Career span 1969 to 1981.

**Forrest Gregg** (b. 10-18-33): Football OT/G. Played in then-record 188 straight games from 1956 through 1971. Named all-NFL eight straight years starting in 1960. Career span 1956–71, most of it with Green Bay Packers. Played on winning Packer team in first two Super Bowls. Inducted into Hall of Fame in 1977.

**Wayne Gretzky** (b. 1-26-61): Hockey C. "The Great One." Most dominant player in history. Alltime scoring leader in points (2,506), assists (1,692), and goals (814). Alltime single season scoring leader in points (215 in 1986), goals (92 in 1982) and assists (163 in 1986). Has won MVP award 9 times, more than any other player (consecutively 1980-87, 1989). Led league in assists 14 times, scoring 11 times, goals 5 times. Scored 200+ points 4 times, 100+ points 9 other times; 70+ goals 4 consecutive seasons, 50+ goals 5 other times; 100+ assists 11 consecutive seasons. Also alltime playoff scoring leader in points (346), goals (110) and assists (236). Playoff MVP 2 times (1985, 1988). All-Star 8 times. Played on 5

Stanley Cup champions with Edmonton from 1978 to 1988. Traded to Los Angeles on Aug. 9, 1988.

**Bob Griese** (b. 2-3-45): Football QB. Career span 1967–80 with Miami Dolphins. Played in three straight Super Bowls, 1971–73. Quarterback of 1972 Dolphin team that went 17–0. Won Super Bowl VII and VIII. In 14 seasons completed 1,926 passes for 25,092 yards and 192 TDs. Elected to Hall of Fame in 1990.

**Archie Griffin** (b. 8-21-54): College football RB. Only player to win the Heisman Trophy 2 times (consecutively 1974-75), with Ohio State. Fourth alltime NCAA most yards rushing (5,177), his 6.13 yards per carry is the collegiate record. Professional career span 1976-83 with Cincinnati; totaled 2,808 yards rushing and 192 receptions.

**Lefty Grove** (b. 3-6-00, d. 5-22-75): Baseball LHP. 300 career wins and fourth alltime highest winning percentage (.680). League leader in ERA 9 times, strikeouts 7 consecutive seasons. Won 20+ games 8 times. 1931 MVP. Career span 1925-41 with Philadelphia, Boston.

**Tony Gwynn** (b. 5-9-60): Baseball OF. 6 batting titles (1984, consecutively 1987-89, 1994-95). League leader in hits 6 times, with .300+ average 11 times, 200+ hits 4 times. Career span since 1982 with San Diego.

**Walter Hagen** (b. 12-21-1892, d. 10-5-69): Golfer. Third alltime leader in major championships (11). Won PGA Championship 5 times (1921, consecutively 1924-27), British Open 4 times (1922, 1924, consecutively 1928-29) and U.S. Open 2 times (1914, 1919). Won 40 career tournaments.

**Marvin Hagler** (b. 5-23-54): Boxer. "Marvelous." Middleweight champion (1980-87). Career record 62-3-2 with 52 KOs from 1973 to 1987. Defended title 13 times.

**George Halas** (b. 2-2-1895, d. 10-31-83): Football owner and coach. "Papa Bear." Alltime leader in seasons coaching (40) and second in wins (324). Career record 324-151-31 intermittently from 1920 to 1967. Remained as owner until his death. Chicago won a record 7 NFL championships during his tenure.

**Glenn Hall** (b. 10-3-31): Hockey goalie. "Mr. Goalie" was an All-Star goalie in 11 of his 18 seasons. Set record for consecutive games by a goaltender, with 502, and ended career with goals against average of 2.51. Won or shared Vezina Trophy three times. Career span 1952–53 through 1970–71.

**Arthur B. "Bull" Hancock** (b. 1-24-10, d. 9-14-72): Horse racing owner. Owner of Claiborne Farm and arguably the greatest breeder in history. For 15 straight years, from 1955 to 1969, a Claiborne stallion led the sire list. Foaled at Claiborne Farm were 4 Horses of the Year (Kelso, Round Table, Bold Ruler and Nashua).

**Tom Harmon** (b. 9-28-19, d. 3-17-90): Football RB. Won Heisman Trophy in 1940 with Michigan. Triple-threat back led nation in scoring and named All-America 2 consecutive seasons (1939-40). Awarded Silver Star and Purple Heart in World War II. Played in NFL with Los Angeles (1946-47).

**Franco Harris** (b. 3-7-50): Football RB. Fifth alltime most rushing yards (12,120) and fifth in rushing touchdowns (91). Rushed for 1,000+ yards in 8 seasons. 100+ yards in 47 games. Scored 100 career touchdowns. Selected for Pro Bowl 9 times. Rookie of the Year in 1972. Played on 4 Super Bowl champions (consecutively 1974-75, 1978-79) with Pittsburgh. Super Bowl MVP in 1974. Holds Super Bowl record for most rushing yards (354) and tied for most rushing touchdowns (4). Made the "Immaculate Reception" to win 1972 playoff game against Oakland. Career span 1972-83 with Pittsburgh.

**Leon Hart** (b. 11-2-28): Football DE. Won Heisman Trophy in 1949, the last lineman to win the award. Played on 3 national champions with Notre Dame (consecutively 1946–47, 1949) and the Irish went undefeated during his 4 years (36-0-2). Also played on 3 NFL champions with Detroit. Career span 1950-57.

**Bill Hartack** (b. 12-9-32): Horse racing jockey. Rode Kentucky Derby winner 5 times (1957, 1960, 1962, 1964, 1969), Preakness Stakes winner 3 times (1956, 1964, 1969) and Belmont Stakes winner 1 time (1960).

**Doug Harvey** (b. 12-19-24, d. 12-26-90): Hockey D. Defensive Player of the Year 7 times (consecutively 1954-57, 1959-61). Led league in assists in 1954. All-Star 10 times. Played on 6 Stanley Cup champions with Montreal from 1947 to 1968.

**Billy Haughton** (b. 11-2-23, d. 7-15-86): Harness racing driver. Won the Pacing Triple Crown driving Rum Customer in 1968. Won The Hambletonian 4 times (1974, consecutively 1976-77, 1980).

**John Havlicek** (b. 4-8-40): Basketball F/G. Member of Ohio State team that won 1960 NCAA title. "Hondo" averaged 20.8 points per game over 16-season NBA career, all with Boston. First team NBA All Star in 1971, '72, '73 and '74. Member of eight Celtic teams that won NBA title. Playoff MVP 1974. Elected to Hall of Fame in 1983.

**Elvin Hayes** (b. 11-17-45): Basketball C. 1968 *Sporting News* College Player of Year as Houston senior. Averaged 21.0 points per game over 16-season NBA career. Led NBA in scoring (28.4) in 1969 and in rebounding in 1970 (16.9 per game) and '74 (18.1). First team All NBA in 1975, '77 and '79. Elected to Hall of Fame in 1989.

**Woody Hayes** (b. 2-14-13, d. 3-12-87): College football coach. Sixth alltime in wins (238). Won national championship 3 times (1954, 1957, 1968) and Rose Bowl 4 times. Career record 238-72-10, including 4 undefeated seasons, with Ohio State from 1951 to 1978. Forced to resign after striking an opposing player during 1978 Gator Bowl.

**Marques Haynes** (b. 10-3-26): Basketball G. Known as "The World's Greatest Dribbler." Since 1946 has barnstormed more than 4 million miles throughout 97 countries for the Harlem Globetrotters, Harlem Magicians, Meadowlark Lemon's Bucketeers, Harlem Wizards.

**Thomas Hearns** (b. 10-18-58): Boxer. "Hit Man." Champion in 5 different weight classes: junior middleweight, light heavyweight, middleweight, super middleweight, and light heavyweight.

**Eric Heiden** (b. 6-14-58): Speed skater. Won 5 gold medals at 1980 Olympics. World champion 3 consecutive years (1977-79). Also won Sullivan Award in 1980.

**Carol Heiss** (b. 1-20-40): Figure skater. Gold medalist at 1960 Olympics, silver medalist at 1956 Olympics. World champion 5 consecutive years (1956-60) and U.S. champion 4 consecutive years (1957-60). Married 1956 gold medalist Hayes Jenkins.

**Rickey Henderson** (b. 12-25-57): Baseball OF. Alltime career stolen base leader (1117); alltime season stolen base record holder (130) in 1982. Led league in steals 11 times. Scored 100+ runs 11 times. 1990 MVP. Alltime most HR leading off game. Career span since 1979 with Oakland, New York and Toronto.

**Sonja Henie** (b. 4-8-12, d. 10-12-69): Norwegian figure skater. Gold medalist at 3 consecutive Olympics (1928, 1932, 1936). World champion 10 consecutive years (1927-36).

**Orel Hershiser** (b. 9-16-58): Baseball RHP. Alltime leader most consecutive scoreless innings pitched (59 in 1988). Cy Young Award winner in 1988 and World Series MVP. Career span since 1983 with Los Angeles.

**Foster Hewitt** (b. 11-21-02, d. 4-22-85): Hockey sportscaster. In 1923, aired one of hockey's first radio broadcasts. Became the voice of hockey in Canada on radio and later television. Famous for the phrase, "He shoots ... he scores!"

**Tommy Hitchcock** (b. 2-11-00, d. 4-19-44): Polo. 10-goal rating 18 times in his 19-year career from 1922 to 1940. Killed in plane crash in World War II.

**Lew Hoad** (b. 11-23-34): Australian tennis player. Won 2 consecutive Wimbledon singles titles (1956-57). Also won French title and Australian title in 1956, but failed to achieve the Grand Slam when defeated at Forest Hills by countryman Ken Rosewall.

**Ben Hogan** (b. 8-13-12): Golfer. Third alltime in career wins (63). Won U.S. Open 4 times (1948, consecutively 1950-51, 1953), the Masters (1951, 1953) and PGA Championship (1946, 1948) 2 times each and British Open once (1953). PGA Player of the Year 4 times (1948, consecutively 1950-51, 1953).

**Marshall Holman** (b. 9-29-54): Bowler. Won 21 PBA titles between 1975 and 1988. Had leading average in 1987 (213.54) and was named PBA Bowler of the Year.

**Nat Holman** (b. 10-18-1896, d. 2-12-95): College basketball coach. Only coach in history to win NCAA and NIT championships in same season in 1950 with CCNY. 423 career wins, a .689 winning percentage.

**Larry Holmes** (b. 11-3-49): Boxer. Heavyweight champion (1978-85). Career record 53–3 with 37 KOs from 1973 to 1991. Defended title 21 times.

**Lou Holtz** (b. 1-6-37): Football coach. Coached Notre Dame to national championship in 1988 with 12–0 record and a 34–21 win over West Virginia in Fiesta Bowl. At start of '95 season had 199-89-7 career record. 10-7-2 career record in bowl games. Career span 1969–71 at William & Mary (13–20); 1972–75 at N.C. State (33-12-3); 1977–83 at Arkansas (60-21-2); 1984–85 at Minnesota 10–12); and since 1986 at Notre Dame (77-19-1).

**Evander Holyfield** (b. 10-19-62): Boxer. Won heavyweight crown Oct. 25, 1990 when he beat James "Buster" Douglas in Las Vegas. Lost title to Riddick Bowe in Las Vegas on 11-13-92, regained it from Bowe one year later, then lost to Michael Moorer on 4-22-94.

**Red Holzman** (b. 8-10-20): Basketball coach. Led New York Knicks to NBA title in 1970 and '73. NBA coach of the Year in 1970. Member of Rochester team that won NBA title in both 1946 (in NBL) and '51. After two-year coaching stints with Milwaukee and St. Louis, coached New York Knicks from 1968–82. Elected to Hall of Fame in 1985.

**Harry Hopman** (b. 8-12-06, d. 12-27-85): Australian tennis coach. As nonplaying captain, led Australia to 15 Davis Cup titles between 1950 and 1969. Mentor to Lew Hoad, Ken Rosewall, Rod Laver and John Newcombe.

**Willie Hoppe** (b. 10-11-1887, d. 2-1-59): Billiards. Won 51 world championship matches from 1904 to 1952.

**Rogers Hornsby** (b. 4-27-1896, d. 1-5-63): Baseball 2B. Second all-time highest career batting average (.358) and 7 batting titles, including .424 average in 1924. 200+ hits 7 times; .400+ average 3 times and .300+ average 12 other times. Led league in slugging average 9 times. Triple Crown winner in 1922, 1925; MVP award winner in 1925, 1929. Career span 1915-37 with St Louis (NL), New York (NL), Boston, Chicago (NL).

**Paul Hornung** (b. 12-23-35): Football RB-K. Led league in scoring 3 consecutive seasons, including a record 176 points in 1960 (15 touchdowns, 15 field goals, 41 extra points). Player of the Year in 1961. Career span 1957-66 with Green Bay. Suspended for 1963 season by Pete Rozelle for gambling. Also won Heisman Trophy in 1956 with Notre Dame.

**Gordie Howe** (b. 3-31-28): Hockey RW. Second alltime in goals (801), first in years played (26) and games (1,767). Second alltime in points (1,850) and assists (1,049). Won MVP award 6 times (consecutively 1952-53, 1957-58, 1960, 1963). Led league in scoring 6 times, goals 5 times and assists 3 times. Scored 40+ goals 5 times, 30+ goals 13 other times, 100+ points 3 times. All-Star 12 times. Played on 4 Stanley Cup champions with Detroit from 1946 to 1971. Teamed with sons Mark and Marty in the WHA with Houston and New England from 1973 to 1979, in NHL with Hartford in 1980.

**Carl Hubbell** (b. 6-22-03, d. 11-21-88): Baseball LHP. 253 career wins. MVP in 1933, 1936. League leader in wins and ERA 3 times each. Won 24 consecutive games from 1936 to 1937. Struck out Ruth, Gehrig, Foxx, Simmons and Cronin consecutively in 1934 All-Star game. Pitched no-hitter in 1929. Career span 1928-43 with New York.

**Sam Huff** (b. 10-4-34): Football LB. Made 30 interceptions. Career span 1956–69 with New York Giants and Washington Redskins. Elected to Hall of Fame in 1982.

**Bobby Hull** (b. 1-3-39): Hockey LW. "The Golden Jet." Sixth alltime in goals scored (610). Led league in goals 7 times and points 3 times. Scored 50+ goals 5 times, 30+ goals 8 other times. Won MVP award 2 consecutive seasons (1965-66). Son Brett won MVP award in 1991, the only father and son to be so honored. All-Star 10 times. Career span 1957-72 with Chicago, 1973-80 with Winnipeg of WHA.

**Brett Hull** (b. 8-9-64): Hockey RW. Son of Bobby Hull. Won Hart Memorial Trophy for 1990–91 season. Career span 1986–87 with Calgary Flames; since 1987 with St. Louis Blues.

**Jim "Catfish" Hunter** (b. 4-8-46): Baseball RHP. 1974 Cy Young award winner. Won 20+ games 5 consecutive seasons. Led league in wins and winning percentage 2 times each, ERA 1 time. 250+ innings pitched 8 times. Pitched perfect game in 1968. Member of 5 World Series champions for Oakland and New York Yankees. Career span 1965-79.

**Don Hutson** (b. 1-31-13): Football WR. Third alltime in touchdown receptions (99). Led league in pass receptions 8 times, receiving yards 7 times and scoring 5 consecutive seasons. Caught at least 1 pass in 95 consecutive games. Player of the Year 2 consecutive seasons (1941-42). Career span 1935-45 with Green Bay.

**Hank Iba** (b. 8-6-04; d. 1-15-93): College basketball coach. Coached Oklahoma A&M (which became Oklahoma State) from 1934 to 1970. Team won NCAA titles in 1945 and '46. 767 career wins is third alltime behind Adolph Rupp and Dean Smith.

**Jackie Ickx** (b. 1-1-45): Belgian auto racer. Won the 24 Hours of LeMans a record six times (1969, consecutively 1975-77, 1981-82) before retiring in 1985.

**Punch Imlach** (b. 3-15-18, d. 12-1-87): Hockey coach. 467 wins. With Toronto from 1958 to 1969. Won 4 Stanley Cup championships (consecutively 1962-64, 1967).

**Bo Jackson** (b. 11-30-62): Baseball OF and Football RB. Only person in history to be named to baseball All-Star game and football Pro Bowl game. 1985 Heisman Trophy winner at Auburn. First pick in 1986 NFL draft by Tampa Bay, but opted to play baseball at Kansas City. 1989 All-Star game MVP. Signed with football's LA Raiders in 1988. Sustained football injury in 1990, released from baseball contract by KC, signed by Chicago and returned from injury in early September 1991, but comeback failed at first. Had hip replacement surgery and hit homer in first at bat afterwards.

**Joe Jackson** (b. 7-16-1889, d. 12-5-51): Baseball OF. "Shoeless Joe." Third alltime highest career batting average (.356), with .300+ average 11 times. One of the "8 men out" banned from baseball for throwing 1919 World Series. Career span 1908-20 with Cleveland, Chicago.

**Reggie Jackson** (b. 5-18-46): Baseball OF. "Mr. October." Alltime leader in World Series slugging average (.755). 1977 Series MVP, hit 3 HR in final game on 3 consecutive pitches. 563 career HR total is sixth best alltime. Led league in HR 4 times. 1973 MVP. Alltime strikeout leader (2,597). In a 12-year period played on 10 first-place teams, 5 World Series winners. Career span 1967-87 with Oakland, New York, California. Inducted into baseball Hall of Fame in 1993.

**Bruce Jenner** (b. 10-28-49): Track and Field. Set world decathlon record (8,634) in winning gold medal at 1976 Olympics. Sullivan Award winner in 1976.

**John Henry** (b. 1975): Thoroughbred race horse. Sold as yearling for $1,100, the gelding was Horse of the Year in 1981 and in 1984 and retired with then-record $6,597,947 in winnings.

**Ben Johnson** (b. 12-30-61): Track and field. Canadian sprinter set world record in 100 meters (9.83 in 1987). Won event at 1988 Olympics in 9.79, but gold medal revoked for failing drug test. Both world records revoked for steroid usage. Suspended for life after testing positive for elevated testosterone level at an indoor meet in Montreal on 1-17-93.

**Earvin "Magic" Johnson** (b. 8-14-59): Basketball G. Retired Nov. 7, 1991 after being diagnosed with HIV, the virus that causes AIDS. Second alltime in assists (9,921); alltime playoff leader in assists (2,320) and steals (358). MVP award 3 times (1987, consecutively 1989-90) and playoff MVP 1980, 1982, 1987. Played on 5 championship teams with Los Angeles since 1979. All-Star 8 consecutive seasons.

League leader in assists 4 times, steals 2 times, free throw percentage 1 time. Also won NCAA championship and named tournament MVP in 1979 with Michigan State.

**Jack Johnson** (b. 3-31-1878, d. 6-10-46): Boxer. First black heavyweight champion (1908-15). Career record 78-8-12 with 45 KOs from 1897 to 1928.

**Jimmy Johnson** (b. 7-16-43): Football coach. Led the Cowboys from 1–15 in 1989, his first season in Dallas, to a 52–17 win over the Buffalo Bills in the Super Bowl XXVII just four seasons later. Also coached Super Bowl XXVIII champion Cowboys before resigning because of a dispute with owner Jerry Jones. Head coach at Oklahoma State from 1979–83 and Univ. of Miami 1984–88 with career collegiate record of 81-34-3. Johnson's Hurricanes won national championship in 1987.

**Michael Johnson** (b. 9-13-67): Track and field sprinter. Only person ever to break 44 seconds for 400 (best of 43.65) and 20 seconds for 200 (19.79). Won 200 at 1991 World Championships, 400 at '93 worlds and both events at the '95 worlds. Anchored US 4 x 400 team at 1993 World Championship to world record of 2:54.29 with fastest meal relay carry of 42.97.

**Walter Johnson** (b. 11-6-1887, d. 12-10-46): Baseball RHP. "Big Train." Alltime leader in shutouts (110), second in wins (416), fourth in losses (279) and third in innings pitched (5,923). His 2.17 career ERA and 3,508 career strikeouts are seventh best alltime. MVP in 1913, 1924. Won 20+ games 12 times. League leader in strikeouts 12 times, ERA 5 times, wins 6 times. Pitched no-hitter in 1920. Career span 1907-27 with Washington.

**Ben A. Jones** (b. 12-31-1882, d. 6-13-61): Horse racing trainer. Trained Triple Crown winner 2 times (Whirlaway in 1941, Citation in 1948). Trained Kentucky Derby winner 6 times, more than any other trainer (1938, 1941, 1944, consecutively 1948-49, 1952), Preakness Stakes winner 2 times (1941, 1944) and Belmont Stakes winner 1 time (1941).

**Bobby Jones** (b. 3-17-02, d. 12-18-71): Golfer. Achieved golf's only recognized Grand Slam in 1930. Second alltime in major championships (13). Won U.S. Amateur 5 times, more than any golfer (consecutively 1924-25, 1927-28, 1930), U.S. Open 4 times (1923, 1926, consecutively 1929-30), British Open 3 times (consecutively 1926-27, 1930) and British Amateur (1930). Also designed Augusta National course, site of the Masters, and founded the tournament. Winner of Sullivan Award in 1930.

**K.C. Jones** (b. 5-25-32): Basketball G-coach. Member of 8 straight NBA-championship Boston Celtic teams in his nine season career from 1958–59 through 1966–67. Averaged 7.4 points and 4.3 assists per game. Coached Celtics from 1983–84 through 1987–88, with 308–102 regular season record and 65–37 playoff record with NBA titles in 1984 and '86.

**Robert Trent Jones** (b. 6-20-06): English-born golf course architect designed or remodelled over 400 courses, including Baltusrol, Hazeltine, Oak Hill and Winged Foot. In the mid-60s five straight U.S. Opens were played on courses designed or remodelled by Jones.

**Sam Jones** (b. 6-24-33): Basketball G. Played 12 seasons with Boston Celtics (1958–69) and made the playoffs every year, winning NBA title every year from 1959–66 plus 1968 and '69. Averaged 17.7 points per game for career. Elected to Hall of Fame in 1983.

**Michael Jordan** (b. 2-17-63): Basketball G. "Air." After 1994-95 season, alltime highest regular season scoring average (32.2) and most points scored in a playoff game (63 in 1986). Led league in scoring 7 consecutive seasons, steals 3 times. MVP in 1988, 1991-92; playoff MVP in 1991-93; Rookie of the Year in 1985. All-Star team 6 consecutive seasons, All-Defensive team 5 consecutive seasons. Career span 1984–93, 1995- with Chicago. Announced retirement on 10-6-93, returned in March 1995. Also College Player of the Year in 1984. Played on NCAA championship team with North Carolina in 1982. Member of gold medal-winning 1984 and '92 Olympic teams.

**Florence Griffith Joyner** (b. 12-21-59): Track and field. Won 3 gold medals (100 meters, 200 meters, 4x100-meter relay) at 1988 Olympics; silver medalist at 1984 Olympics. Set world record in 100 (10.49) in 1988 and in 200 (21.34) at the 1988 Olympics. Sullivan Award winner in 1988.

**Jackie Joyner-Kersee** (b. 3-3-62): Track and field. Gold medalist in heptathlon and long jump at 1988 Olympics and in the former at the 1992 Olympics. Set heptathlon world record (7,291 points) at 1988 Olympics. Also won silver medal in heptathlon at 1984 Olympics and bronze in long jump at 1992 Olympics. Sullivan Award winner in 1986.

**Alberto Juantorena** (b. 3-12-51): Track and field. Cuban was gold medalist in 400 meters and 800 meters at 1976 Olympics.

**Sonny Jurgensen** (b. 8-23-34): Football QB. In 18 seasons completed 2,433 of 4,262 pass attempts for 32,224 yards and 255 TDs. Led NFL in passing both 1967 and '69. Career span 1957–1974 with Philadelphia Eagles and Washington Redskins. Elected to Hall of Fame in 1983.

**Duke Kahanamoku** (b. 8-24-1890, d. 1-22- 68): Swimmer. Won a total of 5 medals (3 gold and 2 silver) at 3 Olympics in 1912, 1920, 1924. Introduced the crawl stroke to America. Surfing pioneer and water polo player. Later sheriff of Honolulu.

**Al Kaline** (b. 12-19-34): Baseball OF. 3,007 career hits and 399 career HR. Youngest player to win batting title with .340 average as a 20-year-old in 1955. Had .300+ average 9 times. Played in 18 All-Star games. Career span 1953-74 with Detroit.

**Anatoly Karpov** (b. 5-23-61): Soviet chess player. First world champion to receive title by default, in 1975, when Bobby Fischer chose not to defend his crown. Champion until 1985 when beaten by Gary Kasparov. Recognized by FIDE as champion in 1994.

**Gary Kasparov** (b. 4-13-63): Born Harry Weinstein. Chess player. World champion from 1985 to 1993 when stripped of title by FIDE.

**Kip Keino** (b. 1-17-40): Track and field. Kenyan was gold medalist in 1,500 meters at 1968 Olympics and in steeplechase at 1972 Olympics.

**Jim Kelly** (b. 2-14-60): Football QB. Led NFL in passing in 1990 (219 of 346 for 2,829 yards and 24 TDs). Led AFC in passing in 1991. In nine seasons through '94 completed 2,397 of 3,942 attempts for 29,527 yards and 201 TDs. Career span 1983-85 with New Jersey Generals (USFL), since 1986 with

Buffalo Bills. Led Bills to four straight Super Bowls, all losses.

**Kelso** (b. 1957, d. 1983): Thoroughbred race horse. Gelding was Horse of the Year 5 straight years (1960-64). Finished in the money in 53 of 63 races. Career earnings $1,977,896.

**Harmon Killebrew** (b. 6-29-36): Baseball 3B-1B. 573 career HR total is fifth most alltime. 100+ RBI 9 times, 40+ HR 8 times. League leader in HR 6 times and RBI 4 times. 1969 MVP. 100+ walks and strikeouts 7 times each. Career span 1954-75 with Washington, Minnesota.

**Jean Claude Killy** (b. 8-30-43): French skier. Won 3 gold medals at 1968 Olympics. World Cup overall champion 2 consecutive years (1967-68).

**Ralph Kiner** (b. 10-27-22): Baseball OF. Second to Babe Ruth in alltime HR frequency (7.1 HR every 100 at bats). 369 career HR. Led league in HR 7 consecutive seasons, with 50+ HR 2 times; 100+ RBI and runs scored in same season 6 times; 100+ walks 6 times. Career span 1946-55 with Pittsburgh.

**Billie Jean King** (b. 11-22-43): Tennis player. Won a record 20 Wimbledon titles, including 6 singles titles (consecutively 1966-68, 1972-73, 1975). Won 4 U.S. singles titles (1967, consecutively 1971-72, 1974), and singles titles at Australian Open (1968) and French Open (1972). Won 27 Grand Slam doubles titles—total of 39 Grand Slam titles is third alltime. Helped found the women's pro tour in 1970, serving as president of the Women's Tennis Association 2 times. Helped form Team Tennis.

**Nile Kinnick** (b. 7-9-18, d. 6-2-43): College football RB. Won the Heisman Trophy in 1939 with Iowa. Premier runner, passer and punter was killed in plane crash during routine Navy training flight. Stadium in Iowa City named in his honor.

**Tom Kite** (b. 12-9-49): Golfer. PGA alltime money leader, with $9,159,418 through end of '94 season. Led PGA in scoring average in 1981 (69.80) and '82 (70.21). PGA Player of Year in 1989, when he won a then-record $1,395,278. Shook reputation for failing to win the big ones by winning 1992 US Open at windy Pebble Beach.

**Franz Klammer** (b. 12-3-54): Austrian alpine skier. Greatest downhiller ever. Gold medalist in downhill at 1976 Olympics. Also won four World Cup downhill titles (1975-78).

**Bob Knight** (b. 10-25-40): College basketball coach. Won 3 NCAA championships with Indiana in 1976, 1981, 1987. Coached U.S. team to gold medal in 1984. 659 career wins and .737 career winning percentage entering 1995-96 season. Career span since 1966.

**Olga Korbut** (b. 5-16-55): Soviet gymnast. First ever to complete backward somersault on balance beam. Won 3 gold medals at 1972 Olympics.

**Sandy Koufax** (b. 12-30-35): Baseball LHP. Cy Young Award winner 3 times (1963, consecutively 1965-66); and MVP in 1963; World Series MVP in 1963, 1965. Pitched 1 perfect game, 3 no-hitters. League leader in ERA 5 consecutive seasons, strikeouts 4 times. Won 25+ games 3 times. Career record 165-87, with 2.76 ERA. Career span 1955-66 with Brooklyn/Los Angeles.

**Jack Kramer** (b. 8-1-21): Tennis player. Won 2 consecutive U.S. singles titles (1946-47) and 1

Wimbledon title (1947). Also won 6 Grand Slam doubles titles. Served as executive director of Association of Tennis Professionals from 1972 to 1975.

**Ingrid Kristiansen** (b. 3-21-56): Track and field. Norwegian runner is only person—male or female—to hold world records in 5,000 meters (14:37.33 set in 1986), 10,000 meters (30:13.74 set in 1986) and marathon (2:21:06 set in 1985). Also won Boston Marathon 2 times (1986, 1989).

**Bob Kurland** (b. 12-23-24): College basketball player. 6' 10¼" center on Oklahoma A&M teams that won NCAA titles in 1945 and '46. Consensus All America and NCAA tournament MVP in both 1945 and '46. Led nation in scoring in '46. His habit of swatting shots off rim led to creation of goaltending rule in 1945. Won gold medals in both 1948 and '52 Olympics. Turned down lucrative pro offers, playing instead for Phillips 66 Oilers AAU team.

**Rene Lacoste** (b. 7-2-05): French tennis player. "The Crocodile." One of France's "Four Musketeers" of the 1920s. Won 3 French singles titles (1925, 1927, 1929), 2 consecutive U.S. titles (1926-27) and 2 Wimbledon titles (1925, 1928). Also designed casual shirt with embroidered crocodile that bears his name.

**Marion Ladewig** (b. 10-30-14): Bowler. Won All-Star Tournament 8 times (consecutively 1949-52, 1954, 1956, 1959, 1963) and WPBA National Championship once (1960). Also voted Bowler of the Year 9 times (consecutively 1950-54, 1957-59, 1963).

**Guy Lafleur** (b. 9-20-51): Hockey RW. Won MVP award 2 consecutive seasons (1977-78), playoff MVP in 1977. Scored 50+ goals and 100+ points 6 consecutive seasons. Led league in points scored 3 consecutive seasons, goals and assists 1 time each. 560 career goals, 793 assists. Played on 5 Stanley Cup champions with Montreal from 1971 to 1985.

**Curly Lambeau** (b. 4-9-1898; d. 6-1-65): Football QB and coach. Quarterback for Packer team in early 20's. Record of 212-106-21 in his 29 seasons (1921-49) as Packer coach, winning three NFL titles in 1929-31.

**Jack Lambert** (b. 7-8-52): Football LB. Anchored Pittsburgh's famed "Steel Curtain" defense. Selected for Pro Bowl 9 times. Played on 4 Super Bowl champions (consecutively 1974-75, 1978-79) with Pittsburgh from 1974 to 1984.

**Jake LaMotta** (b. 7-10-21): Boxer. "The Bronx Bull." Subject of *Raging Bull*, movie by Martin Scorcese, starring Robert DeNiro. Won middleweight title by knocking out Marcel Cerdan in 10 on 6-16-49. Lost title to Ray Robinson, who KO'd him in 13 on 2-13-51. Career record: 106 bouts; won 30 by KO and 53 by decision; drew 4; and lost 19, 4 by KO.

**Kenesaw Mountain Landis** (b. 11-20-1866, d. 11-25-44): Baseball's first and most powerful commissioner from 1920 to 1944. By banning the 8 "Black Sox" involved in the fixing of the 1919 World Series, he restored public confidence in the integrity of baseball.

**Tom Landry** (b. 9-11-24): Football coach. Third alltime in wins (270). The first coach in Dallas history, from 1960 to 1988. Led team to 13 division titles, 7 championship games and 5 Super Bowls. Won 2 Super Bowl championships (1971, 1977). Career record 270-178-6.

**Dick "Night Train" Lane** (b. 4-16-28): Football DB. Third alltime in interceptions (68) and second in interception yardage (1,207). Set record with 14 interceptions as a rookie in 1952. Career span 1952-65 with Los Angeles, Chicago Cardinals, Detroit.

**Joe Lapchick** (b. 4-12-00, d. 8-10-70): Basketball C-coach. One of the first big men in basketball, member of New York's Original Celtics. Coached St. John's (1936-47, 1956-65) winning four NIT Tournaments. Coached New York Knicks, 1947-56.

**Steve Largent** (b. 9-28-54): Football WR. Third alltime in pass receptions (819), second in TD receptions (100). 177 consecutive games with reception, 10 seasons with 50+ receptions and 8 seasons with 1,000+ yards receiving. Career span 1976-89 with Seattle.

**Don Larsen** (b. 8-7-29): Baseball RHP. Pitched only perfect game in World Series history for the NY Yankees on Oct. 8, 1956, beating the Dodgers 2-0; named World Series MVP. Career span 1953-67 for many teams.

**Tommy Lasorda** (b. 9-22-27): Baseball manager. Has spent nearly his entire minor and major league career in Dodgers organization as a pitcher, coach and manager. Has managed Dodgers since 1977, winning 4 pennants and 2 World Series (1981, 1988).

**Rod Laver** (b. 8-9-38): Australian tennis player. "Rocket." Only player to achieve the Grand Slam twice (as an amateur in 1962 and as a pro in 1969). Second alltime in men's Grand Slam singles titles (11—tied with Bjorn Borg). Won 4 Wimbledon titles (consecutively 1961-62, 1968-69), 3 Australian titles (1960, 1962, 1969), 2 U.S. titles (1962, 69) and 2 French titles (1962, 1969). Also won 8 Grand Slam doubles titles. First player to earn $1 million in prize money. 47 career tournament victories. Member of undefeated Australian Davis Cup team from 1959 to 1962.

**Andrea Mead Lawrence** (b. 4-19-32): Skier. Gold medalist in slalom and giant slalom at 1952 Olympics.

**Bobby Layne** (b. 12-19-26; d. 12-1-86): Football QB. Led Detroit Lions to NFL championships in both 1952 and '53. In 1952 led NFL in every passing category. Career span 1948-62, most with the Detroit Lions. Elected to Hall of Fame in 1967.

**Sammy Lee** (b. 8-1-20): Diver. Gold medalist at 2 consecutive Olympics (highboard in 1948, 1952); bronze medalist in springboard at 1948 Olympics. Won the 1953 Sullivan Award. Also 1960 U.S. Olympic diving coach.

**Jacques Lemaire** (b. 9-7-45): Hockey C-Coach. As center for Montreal Canadiens from 1967–68 through 1978–79 was part of eight Stanley Cup winning teams. Over 12 seasons, all with Montreal, scored 366 goals and had 469 assists. Elected to Hall of Fame in 1984. Coached Canadiens 1983-85 and N.J. Devils since 1993.

**Mario Lemieux** (b. 10-5-65): Hockey C. Won MVP award in 1988, playoff MVP in 1991. Led league in most points 4 seasos and goals scored 2 consecutive seasons, assists 1 season. Scored 40+ goals and 100+ points 6 consecutive seasons, including 85 goals and 199 points in 1989. Rookie of the Year in 1985. Won 1992-93 scoring title despite sitting out six weeks to receive treatment for Hodgkin's disease, a form of cancer. Career span since 1984 with Pittsburgh.

**Greg LeMond** (b. 6-26-61): Cyclist. Only American to win Tour de France; won event 3 times (1986,

consecutively 1989-90). Recovered from hunting accident to win in 1989.

**Ivan Lendl** (b. 3-7-60): Tennis player. Second alltime men's most career tournament victories (94). Won 3 consecutive U.S. Open singles titles (1985-87) and 3 French Open titles (1984, consecutively 1985-86). Also won 2 consecutive Australian Open titles (1989-90). Reached Grand Slam final 9 other times. Alltime leader in prize money, with more than $20 million.

**Suzanne Lenglen** (b. 5-24-1899, d. 7-4-38): French tennis player. Lost only 1 match from 1919 to her retirement in 1926. Won 6 Wimbledon singles and doubles titles (consecutively 1919-23, 1925). Won 6 French singles and doubles titles (consecutively 1920-23, 1925-26).

**Sugar Ray Leonard** (b. 5-17-56): Boxer. Champion in 5 different weight classes: welterweight, junior middleweight, middleweight, light heavyweight and super middleweight. Career record 36-2-1 with 25 KOs from 1977 to 1991. Also light welterweight gold medalist at 1976 Olympics.

**Carl Lewis** (b. 7-1-61): Track and field. Held world record for 100 meters 9.86; set on 8-25-91 at World Championships in Tokyo. Duplicated Jesse Owens's feat by winning 4 gold medals at 1984 Olympics (100 and 200 meters, 4x100-meter relay and long jump). Also won 2 gold medals (100 meters, long jump) and 1 silver (200 meters) at 1988 Olympics and two gold medals (long jump, 4x100 relay) at 1992 Olympics. Sullivan Award winner in 1981.

**Nancy Lieberman** (b. 7-1-58): Basketball G. Three-time All-America at Old Dominion. Player of the Year (1979, 1980). Olympian, 1976, and selected for 1980 team, but quit because of Moscow boycott. Promoter of women's basketball, played in WPBL, WABA. First woman to play basketball in a men's professional league (USBL) in 1986.

**Bob Lilly** (b. 7-26-39): Football DT. Dallas Cowboys' first ever draft pick, first Pro Bowl player and first all-NFL choice. Made all-NFL eight times. Career span 1961–74, all with Cowboys. Elected to Hall of Fame in 1980.

**Sonny Liston** (b. 5-8-32, d. 12-30-70): Boxer. Heavyweight champion from 1962 to 1964. Won title by KO of Floyd Patterson on 9-25-62. Lost title when TKO'd by Cassius Clay (Muhammad Ali) on 2-25-64 and then lost rematch on 5-25-65 when KO'd in first round. Career record: 54 fights; won 39 by KO and 11 by decision; lost 4, three by KO.

**Vince Lombardi** (b. 6-11-13, d. 9-3-70): Football coach. Alltime highest winning percentage (.740). Career record 105-35-6. Won 5 NFL championships and 2 consecutive Super Bowl titles with Green Bay from 1959 to 1967. Coached Washington in 1969. Super Bowl trophy named in his honor.

**Johnny Longden** (b. 2-14-07): Horse racing jockey. Rode Triple Crown winner Count Fleet in 1943. 6,032 wins.

**Nancy Lopez** (b. 1-6-57): Golfer. LPGA Player of the Year 4 times (consecutively 1978-79, 1985, 1988). Winner of LPGA Championship 3 times (1978, 1985, 1989). Member of the LPGA Hall of Fame.

**Greg Louganis** (b. 1-29-60): Diver. Gold medalist in platform and springboard at 2 consecutive Olympics in 1984, 1988. World champion 5 times (platform in 1978, 1982, 1986; springboard in 1982, 1986). Also Sullivan Award winner in 1984.

**Joe Louis** (b. 5-13-14, d. 4-12-81): Boxer. "The Brown Bomber." Longest title reign of any heavyweight champion (11 years, 9 months) from June 1937 through March 1949. Career record 63-3 with 49 KOs from 1934 to 1951. Defended title 25 times.

**Jerry Lucas** (b. 3-30-40): Basketball F. Star at Ohio State. *Sporting News* College Player of Year in both 1961 and '62. In 1960 member of both NCAA championship team and gold-medal winning U.S. Olympic team. Averaged over 20 points and 20 rebounds a game for college career. NBA Rookie of Year in 1964. In 11 NBA seasons averaged 17 points a game. Elected to Hall of Fame in 1979.

**Sid Luckman** (b. 11-21-16): Football QB. Played on 4 NFL champions (consecutively 1940-41, 1943, 1946) with Chicago. Player of the Year in 1943. Tied record with 7 touchdown passes on Nov. 14, 1943. All-Pro 6 times. 137 career touchdown passes. Career span 1939-50. Also All-America with Columbia.

**Jon Lugbill** (b. 5-27-61): White water canoe racer. Won 5 world singles titles from 1979 to 1989.

**Hank Luisetti** (b. 6-16-16): Basketball F. The first player to use the one-handed shot. All-America at Stanford 3 consecutive years from 1936-38.

**D. Wayne Lukas** (b. 9-2-35): Horse racing trainer. Former college basketball coach and quarter horse trainer takes mass production approach with stables at most major tracks around country. Trained two Horses of the Year, Lady's Secret in 1986 and Criminal Type in 1990. Won 1988 Kentucky Derby with a filly, Winning Colors. Won 1994 Preakness and Belmont with Tabasco Cat. Won all three Triple Crown races in 1995, with Thunder Gulch (Kentucky Derby and Belmont) and Timber County (Preakness).

**Connie Mack** (b. 2-22-1862, d. 2-8-56): Born Cornelius McGillicuddy. Baseball manager. Managed Philadelphia for 50 years (1901-50) until age 87. All-time leader in games (7,755), wins (3,731) and losses (3,948). Won 9 pennants and 5 World Series (1910-11, 1913, 1929-30).

**Larry Mahan** (b. 11-21-43): Rodeo. All-Around champion 6 times (consecutively 1966-70, 1973).

**Frank Mahovlich** (b. 1-10-38): Hockey LW. Winner of Calder Trophy for top rookie for 1957–58 season. In 18 NHL seasons with Toronto Maple Leafs, Detroit Red Wings and Montreal Canadiens, had 533 goals and 570 assists. Played for six Stanley Cup winners. Elected to Hall of Fame 1981.

**Phil Mahre** (b. 5-10-57): Skier. Gold medalist in slalom at 1984 Olympics (twin brother Steve won silver medal). World Cup champion 3 consecutive years (1981-83).

**Joe Malone** (b. 2-28-1890, d. 5-15-69): Hockey F. "Phantom Joe." Led the NHL in its first season, 1917-18, with 44 goals in 20 games with Montreal. Led league in scoring 2 times (1918, 1920). Holds NHL record with most goals scored, single game (7) in 1920.

**Karl Malone** (b. 7-24-63): Basketball F. "The Mailman." Five-time first-team All-Star. All-Star MVP, 1989. All-Rookie team, 1986. Scored 20+ points per game in 10 of 11 seasons with Utah. Member of 1992 Olympic team. Career span since 1985 with Utah.

**Moses Malone** (b. 3-23-55): Basketball C. Entering 1995-96 season alltime leader free throws made (8,568), fifth in rebounds (16,212) and third in points scored (27,409). 3 MVP awards in 1979, consecutively 1982-83; playoff MVP in 1983. 4-time All-Star. Led league in rebounding 6 times, 5 consecutively. Career span since 1976 with Houston, Philadelphia, Washington, Atlanta, Milwaukee.

**Man o' War** (b. 1917, d. 1947): Thoroughbred race horse. Won 20 of 21 races from 1919 to 1920. Only loss was in 1919 in Sanford Stakes to Upset. Passed up Derby but won both Preakness and Belmont. Winner of $249,465. Sire of War Admiral, 1937 Triple Crown winner.

**Mickey Mantle** (b. 10-20-31, d. 8-13-95): Baseball OF. Won 3 MVP awards, consecutively 1956-57 and 1962; won Triple Crown in 1956. 536 career HR. Greatest switch hitter in history. Played in 20 All-Star games. Alltime World Series leader in HR (18), RBI (40) and runs scored (42). No. 7 was a member of 7 World Series winners with NY Yankees. Career span 1951-68.

**Diego Maradona** (b. 10-30-60): Argentine soccer player. Led Argentina to 1986 World Cup victory and to 1990 World Cup finals. Led Naples to Italian League titles (1987, 1990), Italian Cup (1987) and to European Champion Clubs' Cup title (1989). Throughout 1980s often acknowledged as best player in the world. Tested positive for cocaine and suspended by FIFA and Italian Soccer Federation for 15 months in March 1991. Also failed drug test in 1994 World Cup and suspended before second round.

**Pete Maravich** (b. 6-22-47, d. 1-5-88): Basketball G. "Pistol Pete." Alltime NCAA leader in points scored (3,667), scoring average (44.2) and games scoring 50+ points (28, including then Division I record 69 points in 1970). Alltime season leader in points scored (1,381) and scoring average (44.5) in 1970. College Player of the Year in 1970. NCAA scoring leader and All-America 3 consecutive seasons from 1968 to 1970 with Louisiana State. Also led NBA in scoring in 1977. Averaged 20+ points 8 times. All-Star 2 times. Career span 1970-79 with Atlanta, New Orleans/Utah, Boston.

**Gino Marchetti** (b. 1-2-27): Football DE. Played in Pro Bowl every year from 1955 to '65, except 1958 when he broke right ankle tackling Frank Gifford in Colts' 23–17 win over the Giants. Career span 1952–66, almost all with Baltimore Colts. Inducted into Hall of Fame in 1972.

**Rocky Marciano** (b. 9-1-23, d. 8-31-69): Boxer. Heavyweight champion (1952-56). Career record 49-0 with 43 KOs from 1947 to 1956. Retired as undefeated champion.

**Juan Marichal** (b. 10-24-37): Baseball RHP. 243 career wins, 2.89 career ERA. Won 20+ games 6 times; 250+ innings pitched 8 times; 200+ strikeouts 6 times. Pitched no-hitter in 1963. Career span 1960-75, mostly with San Francisco.

**Dan Marino** (b. 9-15-61): Football QB. Set alltime season record for yards passing (5,084) and touchdown passes (48) in 1984. Prior to 1995-96 season had passed for 4,000+ yards 5 other seasons. Player of the Year in 1984. Career totals through 1994-95 season: 45,173 yards passing, 328 touchdown passes, second alltime in both categories. Career span since 1983 with Miami.

**Roger Maris** (b. 9-10-34, d. 12-14-85): Baseball OF. Broke Babe Ruth's alltime season HR record with 61 in

1961. Won consecutive MVP awards and led league in RBI 1960-61. Career span 1957-68 with Kansas City, New York (AL), St Louis.

**Billy Martin** (b. 5-16-28, d. 12-25-89): Baseball 2B-manager. Volatile manager was hired and fired by Minnesota, Detroit, Texas, New York Yankees (5 times!) and Oakland from 1969 to 1988. Won World Series with Yankees as manager in 1977 and as player 4 times.

**Eddie Mathews** (b. 10-13-31): Baseball 3B. 512 career HR and 30+ HR 9 consecutive seasons. League leader in HR 2 times, walks 4 times. Career span 1952-68 with Milwaukee.

**Christy Mathewson** (b. 8-12-1880, d. 10-7-25): Baseball RHP. Third alltime most wins (373) and shutouts (80); fifth alltime best ERA (2.13). Led league in wins 5 times; won 30+ games 4 times and 20+ games 9 other times. Led league in ERA and strikeouts 5 times each. 300+ innings pitched 11 times. Pitched 2 no-hitters. Pitched 3 shutouts in 1905 World Series. Career span 1900-16 with New York.

**Bob Mathias** (b. 11-17-30): Track and field. At age 17, youngest to win gold medal in decathlon at 1948 Olympics. First decathlete to win gold medal at consecutive Olympics (1948, 1952). Also won Sullivan Award in 1948.

**Ollie Matson** (b. 5-1-30): Football RB. Versatile runner totalled 12,884 combined yards rushing, receiving and kick returning. Scored 73 career touchdowns, including a 105-yard kickoff return on Oct. 14, 1956, the second longest ever. Career span 1952-66 with Chicago Cardinals, Los Angeles, Detroit, Philadelphia. Also won bronze medal in 400-meters at 1952 Olympics.

**Roland Matthes** (b. 11-17-50): German swimmer. Gold medalist in 100-meter and 200-meter backstroke at 2 consecutive Olympics (1968, 1972). Set 16 world records from 1967 to 1973.

**Don Maynard** (b. 1-25-37): Football WR. Retired in 1973 as the NFL's alltime leading receiver. In 15 seasons, 10 with the New York Jets, caught 633 passes for 11,834 yards and 88 TDs. Averaged 18.7 yards per catch for career. In 1967 and '68 led AFL with average of 20.2 and 22.8 yards per catch. Elected to Hall of Fame in 1987.

**Willie Mays** (b. 5-6-31): Baseball OF. "Say Hey Kid." MVP in 1954, 1965; Rookie of the Year in 1951. Third alltime most HR (660), with 50+ HR 2 times, 30+ HR 9 other times. Led league in HR 4 times. 100+ RBI 10 times; 100+ runs scored 12 consecutive seasons. 3,283 career hits. Led league in stolen bases 4 consecutive seasons. 30 HR and 30 steals in same season 2 times and first man in history to hit 300+ HR and steal 300+ bases. Won 11 consecutive Gold Gloves; set record for career putouts by an outfielder and league record for total chances. His catch in the 1954 World Series off the bat of Vic Wertz called the greatest ever. Career span 1951-73 with New York and San Francisco Giants, New York Mets.

**Bill Mazeroski** (b. 9-5-36): Baseball 2B. Hit dramatic 9th-inning home run in Game 7 to win 1960 World Series, first of only two Series' to end on a home run. Also a great fielder, won Gold Glove 8 times. Led league in assists 9 times, double plays 8 times and putouts 5 times.

**Joe McCarthy** (b. 4-21-1887, d. 1-3-78): Baseball manager. Alltime highest winning percentage among

managers for regular season (.615) and World Series (.763). First manager to win pennants in both leagues (Chicago (NL), 1929, New York (AL), 1932). From 1926 to 1950 his teams won 7 World Series and 9 pennants.

**Mark McCormack** (b. 11-6-30): Sports marketing agent. Founded International Management Group in 1962. Also author of best-selling business advice books.

**Pat McCormick** (b. 5-12-30): Diver. Gold medalist in platform and springboard at 2 consecutive Olympics (1952, 1956). Also won Sullivan Award in 1956.

**Willie McCovey** (b. 1-10-38): Baseball 1B. Led NL in homers three times (1963, '68, '69) and in RBIs twice (1968-69). 521 career homers. .270 career batting average. Hit 18 grand slams. Rookie of Year 1959. NL MVP in 1969. Career span 1959-73 and 1977-80 with San Francisco Giants, 1974-76 with San Diego Padres and 1976 with Oakland A's. Elected to Hall of Fame in 1986.

**John McEnroe** (b. 2-26-59): Tennis player. Has won 4 U.S. Open singles titles (consecutively 1979-81, 1984) and 3 Wimbledon titles (1981, consecutively 1983-84). Also won 8 Grand Slam doubles titles. Third alltime men's most career tournament victories (77). Led U.S. to 5 Davis Cup victories (1978-79, 1981-82, 1992).

**John McGraw** (b. 4-7-1873, d. 2-25-34): Baseball manager. Second alltime most games (4,801) and wins (2,784). Guided New York Giants to 3 World Series titles and 10 pennants from 1902 to 1932.

**Denny McLain** (b. 3-29-44): Baseball RHP. Last pitcher to win 30+ games in a season (Detroit, 1968); won 20+ games 2 other times. Won 2 consecutive Cy Young Awards (1968-69). Led league in innings pitched 2 times. Served 2½-year jail term for 1985 conviction of extortion, racketeering and drug possession. Career span 1963-72.

**Mary T. Meagher** (b. 10-27-64): Swimmer. "Madame Butterfly." Won 3 gold medals at 1984 Olympics (100-meter butterfly, 200-meter butterfly and 400-medley relay). In 1981 set world records in 100-meter butterfly (57.93) and 200-meter butterfly (2:05.96).

**Rick Mears** (b. 12-3-51): Auto racer. Has won Indy 500 4 times (1979, 1984, 1988, 1991) and been CART champion 3 times (1979, consecutively 1981-82). Named Indy 500 Rookie of the Year in 1978.

**Cary Middlecoff** (b. 1-6-21): Golfer. Also a dentist. Won 40 PGA tournaments, including 1955 Masters and US Opens in 1949 and '56. Won 1956 Vardon Trophy.

**George Mikan** (b. 6-18-24): Basketball C. Averaged 20+ points per game and named to All-Star team 6 consecutive seasons. Led league in scoring 3 times, rebounding 1 time. Played on 5 championship teams in 6 years (1949-54) with Minneapolis. Also played on 1945 NIT championship team with DePaul. All-America 3 times. Served as ABA Commissioner from 1968 to 1969.

**Stan Mikita** (b. 5-20-40): Hockey C. Won MVP award 2 consecutive seasons (1967-68). Fifth alltime in assists (926); fifth alltime in points (1,467). Led league in assists 4 consecutive seasons and points 4 times. 541 career goals. All-Star 6 times. Career span 1958-80 with Chicago.

**Del Miller** (b. 7-5-13): Harness racing driver. Has raced in 8 decades since 1929, the longest career of any athlete. Won The Hambletonian in 1950.

**Marvin Miller** (b. 4-14-17): Labor negotiator. Union chief of Major League Baseball Players Association from 1966 to 1984. Led strikes in 1972 and 1981. Negotiated 5 labor contracts with owners that increased minimum salary and pension fund, allowed for agents and arbitration, and brought about the end of the reserve clause and the beginning of free agency.

**Art Monk** (b. 12-5-57): Football WR. Caught more passes than anyone in NFL history (934 for 12,607 and 68 TDs through end of 1994-95 season). 106 catches in 1984 was then NFL single season record. Twice caught 13 passes in single game. Career span 1980–93 with Redskins, since 1993 with New York Jets.

**Earl Monroe** (b. 11-21-44): Basketball G. "The Pearl" played 13 seasons (1968–80) with the Baltimore Bullets and New York Knicks. NBA Rookie of Year in 1968. Member of 1973 NBA championship Knicks team. Averaged 18.8 points a game. Elected to Hall of Fame 1989.

**Joe Montana** (b. 6-11-56): Football QB. Second alltime highest-rated passer (92.3), third in completions (3,409), fourth in passing yards (40,551) and fourth in touchdown passes (273). Won 4 Super Bowl championships (1981, 1984, consecutively 1988-89) with San Francisco since 1979. Named Super Bowl MVP 3 times (1981, 1984, 1989). Player of the Year in 1989. Also led Notre Dame to national championship in 1977.

**Carlos Monzon** (b. 8-7-42, d. 1-8-95): Argentine boxer. Longest title reign of any middleweight champion (6 years, 9 months) from Nov. 1970 through Aug. 1977. Career record 89-3-9 with 61 KOs from 1963 to 1977. Won 82 consecutive bouts from 1964 to 1977. Defended title 14 times. Retired as champion.

**Helen Wills Moody** (b. 10-6-05): Tennis player. Second alltime most women's Grand Slam singles titles (19). Her 8 Wimbledon titles are second most alltime (consecutively 1927-30, 1932-33, 1935, 1938). Won 7 U.S. titles (consecutively 1923-25, 1927-29, 1931) and 4 French titles (consecutively 1928-30, 1932). Also won 12 Grand Slam doubles titles.

**Archie Moore** (b. 12-13-16): Boxer. Longest title reign of any light heavyweight champion (9 years, 1 month) from Dec. 1952 through Feb. 1962. Career record 199-26-8 with an alltime record 145 KOs from 1935 to 1965. Retired at age 52.

**Davey Moore** (b. 11-1-33; d. 3-23-63): Boxer. Won featherweight title by KO of Kid Bassey in 13 on 3-18-59. Five successful defenses of title, before losing it on 3-21-63 to Sugar Ramos who KO'd him in 10. Died two days after fight of brain damage suffered during fight. Career record: 67 bouts; won 30 by KO, 28 by decision, 1 because of foul; drew 1; lost 7, two by KO.

**Noureddine Morceli** (b. 2-20-70). Algerian track and field middle distance runner. Set world record for mile (3:44.39) in Rieti, Italy, on 9-5-93. Set world record for 1,500 (3:28.86) on 9-5-92. World champion at 1,500 in both 1991 and '93. Finished a shocking seventh at 1992 Olympics. Only man ever to rank first in the world at 1,500/mile four straight years (1990–93).

**Joe Morgan** (b. 9-19-43): Baseball 2B. Won 2 consecutive MVP awards in 1975-76. Third alltime most walks (1,865). 689 stolen bases. Led league in walks 4 times. 100+ walks and runs scored 8 times each; 40+ stolen bases 9 times. Won 5 Gold Gloves. Second

alltime most games played by 2nd baseman (2,527). Career span 1963-84 with Houston, Cincinnati.

**Willie Mosconi** (b. 6-27-13; d. 9-16-93): Pocket billiards player. Won world title a record 15 straight times between 1941 and 1957. Once pocketed 526 balls without a miss.

**Edwin Moses** (b. 8-31-55): Track and field. Gold medalist in 400-meter hurdles at 2 Olympics, in 1976, 1984 (U.S. boycotted 1980 Games); bronze medalist at 1988 Olympics. Set four world records in 400-meter hurdles (best of 47.02 set on 8-31-83). Won 122 consecutive races from 1977 to 1987. Won Sullivan Award in 1983.

**Marion Motley** (b. 6-5-20): Football FB. All-time AAFC leader in yards rushing (3,024). Also led NFL in rushing 1 time. Combined league totals: 4,712 yards rushing, 39 touchdowns. Played on 4 consecutive AAFC champions (1946-49), 1 NFL champion (1950) with Cleveland from 1946 to 1953.

**Shirley Muldowney** (b. 6-19-40): Drag racer. First woman to win the Top Fuel championship, which she won 3 times (1977, 1980, 1982).

**Anthony Munoz** (b. 8-19-58): Football OT. Probably the greatest tackle ever. Made Pro Bowl a record-tying 11 times. Career span 1980–92 with the Cincinnati Bengals.

**Isaac Murphy** (b. 4-16-1861, d. 2-12-1896): Horse racing jockey. Top jockey of his era, Murphy, who was black, won 3 Kentucky Derbys (aboard Buchanan in 1884, Riley in 1890 and Kingman in 1891).

**Eddie Murray** (b. 2-24-56): Baseball 1B. 100+ RBIs 6 seasons and 30+ HRs five seasons. Through '94 season had 2,930 hits, 458 HRs and 1,738 RBI. Alltime leader in RBI by switch hitter. Career span 1977–88 with Baltimore Orioles; 1989–91 with LA Dodgers; 1992–93 with New York Mets, since 1994 with Cleveland Indians.

**Jim Murray** (b. 12-29-19): Sportswriter. Won Pulitzer Prize in 1990. Named Sportswriter of the Year 14 times. Columnist for *Los Angeles Times* since 1961.

**Ty Murray** (b. 10-11-69): Rodeo cowboy. All-Around world champion, 1989-93. Set single-season earnings record, 1990 ($213,771). Rookie of the Year, 1988. At 20 in 1989, became youngest man ever to win national all-around title.

**Stan Musial** (b. 11-21-20): Baseball OF-1B. "Stan the Man." Had .331 career batting average and 475 career HR. MVP award winner 1943, 1946, 1948. Fourth alltime in hits (3,630) and third in doubles (725). Won 7 batting titles. Led league in hits 6 times, slugging average 5 times, doubles 8 times. Had .300+ batting average 17 times, 200+ hits 6 times, 100+ RBI 10 times, and 100+ runs scored 11 times. 24-time All-Star. Career span 1941-63 with St. Louis.

**John Naber** (b. 1-20-56): Swimmer. Won 4 gold medals and 1 silver medal at 1976 Olympics. Sullivan Award winner in 1977.

**Bronko Nagurski** (b. 11-3-08, d. 1-7-90): Football FB. Punishing runner played on 3 NFL champions (consecutively 1932-33, 1943) with Bears. Rushed for 2,778 career yards, 1930-37 and 1943 with Chicago. Also All-America with Minnesota.

**James Naismith** (b. 11-6-1861, d. 11-28-39): Invented basketball in 1891 while an instructor at YMCA Training School in Springfield, Mass. Refined the game while a professor at Kansas from 1898 to 1937. Hall of Fame is named in his honor.

**Joe Namath** (b. 5-31-43): Football QB. "Broadway Joe." Super Bowl MVP in 1968 after he guaranteed victory for AFL. 173 career touchdown passes. Led league in yards passing 3 times, including 4,007 yards in 1967. Player of the Year in 1968, Rookie of the Year in 1965. Career span 1965-77 with NY Jets, LA Rams.

**Ilie Nastase** (b. 7-19-46): Romanian tennis player. "Nasty" for his unruly deportment on court. Beat Arthur Ashe to win 1972 US Open title. Won 1973 French Open. Twice Wimbledon runnerup (to Stan Smith in 1972 and Bjorn Borg in '76).

**Martina Navratilova** (b. 10-18-56): Tennis player. Third alltime most women's Grand Slam singles titles (18—tied with Chris Evert). Won a record 9 Wimbledon titles, including 6 consecutively (1978-79, 1982-87, 1990). Won 4 U.S. Open titles (consecutively 1983-84, 1986-87), 3 Australian Open titles (1981, 1983, 1985) and 2 French Open titles (1982, 1984). Reached Grand Slam final 13 other times. Also won 37 Grand Slam doubles titles. Her total of 55 Grand Slam titles is second alltime to Margaret Court's. Completed a non-calendar year Grand Slam in 1984-85. Set mark for longest winning streak with 74 matches in 1984. Also won the doubles Grand Slam in 1984 with Pam Shriver. Won 109 consecutive matches with Shriver from 1983 to 1985. Retired after 1994 season.

**Byron Nelson** (b. 2-14-12): Golfer. Won the Masters (1937, 1942) and PGA Championship (1940, 1945) 2 times each and U.S. Open once (1939). Won 52 career tournaments, including 11 consecutively in 1945.

**Ernie Nevers** (b. 6-11-03, d. 5-3-76): Football FB. Set alltime pro single game record for points scored (40) and touchdowns (6) on Nov. 28, 1929. Career span 1926-31 with Duluth, Chicago. Also a pitcher with St. Louis, surrendered 2 of Babe Ruth's 60 HR in 1927. All-America at Stanford, earned 11 letters in 4 sports.

**John Newcombe** (b. 5-23-44): Australian tennis player. Won 3 Wimbledon singles titles (1967, consecutively 1970-71), 2 U.S. titles (1967, 1973) and 2 Australian Open titles (1973, 1975). Also won 17 Grand Slam doubles titles.

**Pete Newell** (b. 8-31-15): College basketball coach. Despite coaching only 13 seasons, 1947 through 1960, was first coach to win NIT, NCAA and Olympic crowns. Led Univ. of San Francisco to 1949 NIT title, Cal to 1959 NCAA title, and the 1960 U.S. Olympic basketball team that included Jerry Lucas, Oscar Robertson and Jerry West to gold medal. Overall collegiate coaching record of 234–123.

**Jack Nicklaus** (b. 1-21-40): Golfer. "The Golden Bear." Alltime leader in major championships (20). Second alltime in career wins (70). Winner of the Masters 6 times, more than any golfer (1963, consecutively 1965-66, 1972, 1975, 1986—at age 46, the oldest player to win event), PGA Championship 5 times (1963, 1971, 1973, 1975, 1980), U.S. Open 4 times (1962, 1967, 1972, 1980), British Open 3 times (1966, 1970, 1978) and U.S. Amateur 2 times (1959, 1961). PGA Player of the Year 5 times (1967, consecutively 1972-73, 1975-76). Also NCAA champion with Ohio State in 1961.

**Ray Nitschke** (b. 12-29-36): Football LB. Defensive signal caller for the great Packer teams of the '60s.

Voted Packer MVP by teammates after 1967 season. MVP of the 1962 NFL title game. Career span 1958–72 with Green Bay Packers.

**Greg Norman** (b. 2-10-55): Golfer. "The Shark" led PGA in winnings in 1986 and '90. Won Vardon Trophy twice, 1989–90. Won two British Opens—in 1986 at Turnberry and in '93 at Royal St. George's—but is almost as famous for his heartbreaking misses. Beaten at the 1986 PGA when Bob Tway holed out a sand shot and at the 1987 Masters when Larry Mize chipped in from a tough downhill lie.

**James D. Norris** (b. 11-6-06, d. 2-25-66): Hockey executive. Owner of Detroit from 1933 to 1943 and Chicago from 1946 to 1966. Teams won 4 Stanley Cup championships (consecutively 1936-37, 1943, 1961). Defensive Player of the Year award named in his honor. Also a boxing promoter, operated International Boxing Club from 1949 to 1958.

**Paavo Nurmi** (b. 6-13-1897, d. 10-2-73): Track and field. Finnish middle- and long-distance runner won a total of 9 gold medals at 3 Olympics in 1920, 1924, 1928

**Matti Nykänen** (b. 7-17-63): Finnish ski jumper. Three-time Olympic gold medalist. Won 90-meter jump (1984, 1988) and 70-meter jump (1988). World champion on 90-meter jump in 1982. Won four World Cups (1983, 1985, 1986, 1988).

**Dan O'Brien** (b. 7-18-66): Track and field decathlete. Won world decathlon title in 1991, '93 and '95. Set world decathlon record of 8,891 in Talence, France, on 9-4/5-92. Heavily favored to win 1992 Olympic decathlon but missed making U.S. team when he no heighted in pole vault at U.S. Olympic Trials.

**Parry O'Brien** (b. 1-28-32): Track and field. Shot putter who revolutionized the event with his "glide" technique and won Olympic gold medals in 1952 and 1956, silver in 1960. Set 10 world records from 1953 to 1959, topped by a put of 63' 4" in 1959. Sullivan Award winner in 1959.

**Al Oerter** (b. 8-19-36): Track and field. Gold medalist in discus at 4 consecutive Olympics (1956, 1960, 1964, 1968), setting Olympic record each time. First to break the 200-foot barrier, throwing 200' 5" in 1962.

**Sadaharu Oh** (b. 5-20-40): Baseball 1B in Japanese league. 868 career HR in 22 seasons for the Tokyo Giants. Led league in HR 15 times, RBI 13 times, batting 5 times and runs 13 consecutive seasons. Awarded MVP 9 times; won 2 consecutive Triple Crowns and 9 Gold Gloves.

**Hakeem Olajuwon** (b. 1-21-63): Basketball C. From Nigeria. As part of the University of Houston's "Phi Slamma Jamma" his senior year led NCAA in field goal percentage, rebounding and blocked shots in 1984. All-NBA First Team 1987, '88, '89, '93, 94. Led NBA in rebounding in both 1989 (13.5 per game) and '90 (14.0). League MVP in 1994 as he led Houston to NBA title. Career span since 1985 with the Rockets.

**Merlin Olsen** (b. 9-15-40): Fooball DT. Part of L.A. Rams "Fearsome Foursome" defensive line. Named to Pro Bowl 14 straight times. Career span 1962–76, all with L.A. Rams. Elected to Hall of Fame 1982.

**Omaha** (b. 1932): Thoroughbred race horse. In 1935 third horse to win Triple Crown. Won Kentucky Derby by 1½ lengths over Roman Soldier; Preakness by 6 over Firethorn; and the Belmont by 1½ from Firethorn. Trained by Sunny Jim Fitzsimmons.

**Shaquille O'Neal** (b. 3-6-72): Basketball C. As LSU junior led NCAA in blocked shots in 1992, with 5.23 a game, and averaged 4.58 over his 90-game, three-year career. Top pick of Orlando Magic in 1992 NBA draft. Almost unanimous NBA Rookie of the Year 1993. Averaged 23.4 points, 13.9 rebounds and 3.5 blocked shots in first NBA season. Led Magic to first ever playoff appearance in 1994. Led league in scoring with 29.3 average in 1994-95.

**Bobby Orr** (b. 3-20-48): Hockey D. Defensive Player of the Year more than any other player, 8 consecutive seasons (1968-75). Won MVP award 3 consecutive seasons (1970-72), playoff MVP 2 times (1970, 1972). Also Rookie of the Year in 1967. Led league in assists 5 times and scoring 2 times. Career span 1966-77 with Boston.

**Mel Ott** (b. 3-2-09, d. 11-21-58): Baseball OF. 511 career HR, 1,861 RBI, .304 batting average. League leader in HR and walks 6 times each. 100+ RBI 9 times and 100+ walks 10 times. Career span 1926-47 with New York.

**Jim Otto** (b. 1-5-38): Football C. Number 00 started every game (308) in his 15 year career (1960-74) with the Oakland Raiders. Inducted into Hall of Fame in 1980.

**Kristin Otto** (b. 1966): German swimmer. Won 6 gold medals for East Germany at 1988 Olympics.

**Jesse Owens** (b. 9-12-13, d. 3-31-80): Track and field. Gold medalist in 4 events (100 meters and 200 meters; 4x100-meter relay and long jump) at 1936 Olympics. At the 1935 Big 10 championship set or equaled 4 world record in 70 minutes, including 100 yards, long jump, 220-yard low hurdles and 220 dash.

**Alan Page** (b. 8-7-45): Football DT. First defensive player to be named NFL Player of the Year, in 1972. Career span 1967-78 with Minnesota Vikings and 1978-81 with Chicago Bears. Now sits on Minnesota Supreme Court.

**Satchel Paige** (b. 7-7-06, d. 6-8-82): Baseball RHP. Alltime greatest black pitcher, didn't pitch in major leagues until 1948 at age 42 with Cleveland. Oldest pitcher in major league history at age 59 with Kansas City in 1965. Pitched in the Negro leagues from 1926 to 1950 with Birmingham Black Barons, Pittsburgh Crawfords and Kansas City Monarchs. Estimated career record is 2,000 wins, 250 shutouts, 30,000 strikeouts, 45 no-hitters. Said "Don't look back. Something may be gaining on you."

**Arnold Palmer** (b. 9-10-29): Golfer. Fourth alltime in career wins (60). Won the Masters 4 times (1958, 1960, 1962, 1964), British Open 2 consecutive years (1961-62) and U.S. Open (1960) and U.S. Amateur (1954) once each. PGA Player of the Year 2 times (1960, 1962). The first golfer to surpass $1 million in career earnings. Also won Seniors Championship 2 times (1980, 1984) and U.S. Senior Open once (1981).

**Jim Palmer** (b. 10-15-45): Baseball RHP. 268 career wins, 2.86 ERA. Won 3 Cy Young Awards (1973, consecutively 1975-76). Won 20+ games 8 times. Led league in wins 3 times, innings pitched 4 times, ERA 2 times. Never allowed a grand slam HR. Pitched on 6 World Series teams with Baltimore, including shutout at 20 years old in 1966. Pitched no-hitter in 1969. Jockey underwear pitchman. Career span 1965-84.

**Bernie Parent** (b. 4-3-45): Hockey G. Alltime leader for wins in a season (47 in 1974). Goaltender of the Year, playoff MVP, league leader in wins, goals against average and shutouts 2 consecutive seasons

(1974-75). Career record 270-197-121, including 55 shutouts. Career 2.55 goals against average. Tied record of 4 playoff shutouts in 1975. Played on 2 consecutive Stanley Cup champions (1974-75). Career span 1965 to 1979 with Philadelphia. Also the first NHL player to sign with the WHA in 1972, with Philadelphia.

**Brad Park** (b. 7-6-48): Hockey D. Seven-time All Star. In 17 seasons with the New York Rangers, Boston Bruins and Detroit Red Wings (1968-69 through 1984-85) scored 213 goals and had 683 assists. Elected to Hall of Fame 1988.

**Jim Parker** (b. 4-3-34): Football T/G. Winner of 1956 Outland Trophy as Ohio State senior. Blocked for Johnny Unitas. All-NFL four times at guard, four times at tackle. Career span 1957-67, all with Baltimore Colts. Inducted to Hall of Fame in 1973.

**Joe Paterno** (b. 12-21-26): College football coach. Fourth alltime in wins in Division I-A (269—the most of any active coach at that level). Has won 2 national championships (1982, 1986) with Penn State since 1966. Career record 269-69-3, including 5 undefeated seasons. Has also won 16 bowl games.

**Lester Patrick** (b. 12-30-1883, d. 6-1-60): Hockey coach. Led NY Rangers to three Stanley Cup championships (1928, 1933, 1940). Originated the NHL's farm system and developed playoff format.

**Floyd Patterson** (b. 1-4-35): Boxer. Heavyweight champion 2 times (1956-59, 1960-62). First heavyweight to regain title, in rematch with Ingemar Johansson. Career record 55-8-1 with 40 KOs from 1952 to 1972. Also middleweight gold medalist at 1952 Olympics.

**Walter Payton** (b. 7-25-54): Football RB. Alltime leader in yards rushing (16,726), rushing attempts (3,838), seasons gaining 1,000+ yards rushing (10) and rushing touchdowns (110). His 125 total touchdowns rank third. Rushed for a record 275 yards on Nov. 20, 1977. Selected for Pro Bowl 9 times. Player of the Year 2 times (1977, 1985). Led league in rushing 5 consecutive seasons. Career span 1975-87 with Chicago.

**Pele** (b. 10-23-40): Born Edson Arantes do Nascimento. Brazilian soccer player. Soccer's great ambassador. Played on 3 World Cup winners with Brazil (1958, 1962, 1970). Helped promote soccer in U.S. by playing with NY Cosmos from 1975 to 1977. Scored 1,281 goals in 22 years.

**Willie Pep** (b. 9-19-22): Boxer. Featherweight champion 2 times (1942-48, 1949-50). Lost title to Sandy Saddler, won it back in rematch, then lost it to Saddler again. Career record 230-11-1 with 65 KOs from 1940 to 1966. Won 73 consecutive bouts from 1940 to 1943. Defended title 9 times.

**Gil Perreault** (b. 11-13-50): Hockey C. Won Calder Trophy as NHL's top rookie for 1970-71 season. Played 17 seasons (1970-71 through 1986-87), all with Buffalo Sabres. Scored 512 goals and had 814 assists in career. Elected to Hall of Fame in 1990.

**Fred Perry** (b. 5-18-09, d. 2-2-95): British tennis player. Won 3 consecutive Wimbledon singles titles (1934-36), the last British man to win the tournament. Also won 3 U.S. titles (consecutively 1933-34, 1936), 1 French title (1935) and 1 Australian title (1934).

**Gaylord Perry** (b. 9-15-38): Baseball RHP. Only pitcher to win Cy Young Award in both leagues (Cleveland 1972, San Diego 1978). 314 career wins,

3,534 strikeouts. 20+ wins 5 times; 200+ strikeouts 8 times; 250+ innings pitched 12 times. Pitched no-hitter in 1968. Admitted to throwing a spitter. Career span 1962-83 with San Francisco, Cleveland, San Diego.

**Bob Pettit** (b. 12-12-32): Basketball F. First player in history to break 20,000-point barrier (20,880 career points scored). Fifth alltime highest scoring average (26.4) and seventh most free throws made (6,182). Also grabbed 12,849 rebounds for 16.2 average. MVP in 1956, 1959; Rookie of the Year in 1955. All-Star 10 consecutive seasons. Led league in scoring 2 times, rebounding 1 time. Career span 1954-64 with St Louis.

**Richard Petty** (b. 7-2-37): Auto racer. Alltime leader in NASCAR victories (200). Daytona 500 winner (1964, 1966, 1971, consecutively 1973-74, 1979, 1981) and NASCAR champion (1964, 1967, consecutively 1971-72, 1974-75, 1979) 7 times each, the most of any driver. First stock car racer to reach $1 million in earnings. Son of Lee Petty, 3-time NASCAR champion (1954, consecutively 1958-59). Retired after 1992 season.

**Laffit Pincay Jr.** (b. 12-29-46): Jockey. Through 1994 had won more money than any other jockey ($183,910,301) and was second only to Bill Shoemaker in wins, with 8,213. Won 5 Eclipse Awards as outstanding jockey. Rode 3 Kentucky Derby winners; 2 Preakness winners; and 1 Belmont winner.

**Jacques Plante** (b. 1-17-29, d. 2-27-86): Hockey G. First goalie to wear a mask. Second alltime in wins (434) and second lowest modern goals against average (2.38). Goaltender of the Year 7 times, more than any other goalie (consecutively 1955-59, 1961, 1968). Won MVP award in 1961. Led league in goals against average 8 times, wins 6 times and shutouts 4 times. Was on 6 Stanley Cup champions with Montreal from 1952 to 1962 and played for 4 other teams until retirement in 1972.

**Gary Player** (b. 11-1-35): South African golfer. Won the Masters (1961, 1974, 1978) and British Open (1959, 1968, 1974) 3 times each, PGA Championship 2 times (1962, 1972) and U.S. Open (1965). Also won Seniors Championship 3 times (1986, 1988, 1990) and U.S. Senior Open 2 consecutive years (1987-88).

**Sam Pollock** (b. 12-15-25): Hockey executive. As general manager of Montreal from 1964 to 1978 won 9 Stanley Cup championships (1965-66, 1968-69, 1971, 1973, 1976-78).

**Denis Potvin** (b. 10-29-53): Hockey D. Seven time All Star during 15 season career (1973-74 through 1987-88), all with New York Islanders. Won Calder Trophy for 1973-74 season. Won Norris Trophy three times. Captained Islanders to four Stanley Cup championships. Elected to Hall of Fame in 1991.

**Mike Powell** (b. 11-10-63): Track and field. Long jumper broke Bob Beamon's 23-year-old world record at 1991 World Championships in Tokyo with a jump of 29' 4½".

**Annemarie Moser-Pröll** (b. 3-27-53): Austrian skier. Gold medalist in downhill at 1980 Olympics. World Cup overall champion 6 times, more than any other skier (consecutively 1971-75, 1979).

**Alain Prost** (b. 2-24-55): French auto racer. Alltime leader in Formula 1 victories. Formula 1 champion 4 times (consecutively 1985-86, 1989, 1993).

**Jack Ramsay** (b. 2-21-25): Basketball coach. Never played in NBA. Coached 11 seasons at St. Joseph's University, with 234–72 record. Overall record of

864–783 as NBA coach. Coach of NBA champion 1977 Portland Trail Blazers. Elected to Hall of Fame 1992.

**Jean Ratelle** (b. 10-3-40): Hockey C. In 21 season career (1960–61 through 1980–81) with the New York Rangers and Boston Bruins, scored 491 goals and had 776 assists. Twice won Lady Byng Trophy. Elected to Hall of Fame in 1985.

**Willis Reed** (b. 6-25-42): Basketball C. Played 10 seasons (1965–74), all with the New York Knicks. Career average of 18.7 points a game. NBA Rookie of Year in 1965. Playoff MVP of both Knick championship teams, in 1970 and '73. NBA MVP in 1970. Elected to Hall of Fame in 1970.

**Harold Henry "Pee Wee" Reese** (b. 7-23-18): Baseball SS. Played on 7 pennant-winning Dodger teams. Led NL in runs scored in 1949, with 132. Elected to Hall of Fame in 1984.

**Mary Lou Retton** (b. 1-24-68): Gymnast. Won 1 gold, 1 silver and 2 bronze medals at 1984 Olympics.

**Grantland Rice** (b. 11-1-1880, d. 7-13-54): Sportswriter. Legendary figure during sport's Golden Age of the 1920s. Wrote "When the Last Great Scorer comes / To mark against your name, / He'll write not 'won' or 'lost' / But how you played the game." Also named the 1924-25 Notre Dame backfield the "Four Horsemen."

**Jerry Rice** (b. 10-13-62): Football WR. Entering 1995 season, alltime leader in touchdowns (139), touchdown receptions (131) and in consecutive games with a TD reception (13 in 1988). Player of the Year in 1987 and led league in scoring (138 points on 23 touchdowns). Super Bowl MVP in 1989 with record 215 receiving yards on 11 catches. Also set Super Bowl record with 3 touchdown receptions in 1990. Career span since 1985 with San Francisco 49ers.

**Henri Richard** (b. 2-29-36): Hockey C. "The Pocket Rocket." Played on 11 Stanley Cup champions with Montreal. Four-time All-Star. Career span from 1955 to 1975.

**Maurice Richard** (b. 8-4-21): Hockey RW. "The Rocket." First player ever to score 50 goals in a season, in 1945. Led league in goals 5 times. 544 career goals. Won MVP award in 1947. All-Star 8 times. Tied playoff game record for most goals (5 on March 23, 1944). Played on 8 Stanley Cup champions with Montreal from 1942 to 1959.

**Bob Richards** (b. 2-2-26): Track and field. The only pole vaulter to win gold medal at 2 consecutive Olympics (1952, 1956). Also won Sullivan Award in 1951.

**Branch Rickey** (b. 12-20-1881, d. 12-9-65): Baseball executive. Integrated major league baseball in 1947 by signing Jackie Robinson to contract with Brooklyn Dodgers. Conceived minor league farm system in 1919 at St Louis; instituted batting cage and sliding pit.

**Pat Riley** (b. 3-20-45): Basketball coach. Going into 1995-96 season most playoff wins (137). Coached Los Angeles to 4 championships, 2 consecutively, from 1981 to 1989. 60+ wins 6 times (4 times consecutively), 50+ wins 4 other times. Led New York Knicks to NBA Finals in 1994.

**Cal Ripken Jr** (b. 8-24-60): Baseball SS. Enters 1996 season with longest consecutive game streak (2,153 since May 29, 1982). Set record for consecutive errorless games by a shortstop (95 in 1990). MVP in 1983 and Rookie of the Year in 1982. Hit 20+ HRs in

11 consecutive seasons and started in 11 consecutive All-Star games.

**Glenn "Fireball" Roberts** (b. 1-20-31, d. 7-2-64): Auto racer. Won 34 NASCAR races. Died as a result of fiery accident in World 600 at Charlotte Motor Speedway in May 1964. At time of his death had won more major races than any other driver in NASCAR history.

**Oscar Robertson** (b. 11-24-38): Basketball G. "The Big O." Third alltime in assists (9,887) second in free throws made (7,694) and fifth in points scored (26,710). 9,508 field goals made, 25.7 scoring average. MVP in 1964, All-Star 9 consecutive seasons and 1961 Rookie of the Year. Led league in assists 6 times, free throw percentage 2 times. Averaged 30+ points 6 times in 7 seasons, 20+ points 4 other times. Only player in history to average a season triple-double (1961). Career span 1960-72 with Cincinnati, Milwaukee. Also College Player of the Year, All-America and NCAA scoring leader 3 consecutive seasons from 1958 to 1960 with Cincinnati. Third all-time NCAA highest scoring average (33.8); seventh most points scored (2,973).

**Brooks Robinson** (b. 5-18-37): Baseball 3B. Alltime leader in assists, putouts, double plays and fielding average among 3rd baseman. Won 16 consecutive Gold Gloves. Led league in fielding average a record 11 times. MVP in 1964—led league in RBI—and MVP in 1970 World Series. Career span 1955-77 with Baltimore.

**David Robinson** (b. 8-6-65): Basketball C. *Sporting News* Player of the Year for 1987. Led college players in 1986 in both rebounding (13.0) and blocked shots (5.91, a record that still stands). NBA Rookie of Year in 1990. Led NBA in rebounding 1991 (13.0) and in blocked shots in 1992, when he was named Defensive Player of the Year. Named NBA MVP in 1995.

**Eddie Robinson** (b. 2-13-19): College football coach. Has had alltime college record 388 career wins at Division I-AA Grambling State since 1941.

**Frank Robinson** (b. 8-31-35): Baseball OF-manager. Only player to win MVP awards in both leagues (Cincinnati, 1961, Baltimore, 1966). Won Triple Crown and World Series MVP in 1966. Rookie of the Year in 1956. Fourth alltime most HR (586). 30+ HR 11 times; 100+ RBI 6 times; 100+ runs scored 8 times (led league 3 times). Had .300+ batting average 9 times. Became first black manager in major leagues, with Cleveland in 1975. Career span as player 1956-76. Career span as manager 1975-77 with Cleveland; 1981-84 with San Francisco; 1988-91 with Baltimore.

**Jackie Robinson** (b. 1-13-19, d. 10-24-72): Baseball 2B. Broke the color barrier as first black player in major leagues in 1947 with Brooklyn Dodgers. 1947 Rookie of the Year; 1949 MVP with .342 batting average to lead league. Had .311 career batting average. Led league in stolen bases 2 times; stole home 19 times. Played on 6 pennant winners in 10 years with Brooklyn.

**Larry Robinson** (b. 6-2-51): Hockey D. Twice won Norris Trophy as NHL's top defenseman. Career span 1972–73 through 1991–92, all but the last three with the Montreal Canadiens. Member of six Montreal teams that won Stanley Cup. Awarded Conn Smythe Trophy as MVP of 1978 Stanley Cup.

**Sugar Ray Robinson** (b. 5-3-21, d. 4-12-89): Born Walker Smith, Jr. Boxer. Called best pound-for-pound boxer in history. Welterweight champion (1946-51) and middleweight champion 5 times. Career record 174-19-6 with 109 KOs from 1940 to 1965. Won 91 consecutive bouts from 1943 to 1951. 15 of his 19 losses came after age 35. Retired at age 45.

**Knute Rockne** (b. 3-4-1888, d. 3-31-31): College football coach. Won national championship 3 times (1924, consecutively 1929-30). Alltime highest winning percentage (.881). Career record 105-12-5, including 5 undefeated seasons, with Notre Dame from 1918 to 1930.

**Bill Rodgers** (b. 12-23-47): Track and field. Won the Boston and New York City marathons 4 times each between 1975 and 1980.

**Chi Chi Rodriguez** (b. 10-23-35): Golfer. Led senior money list for 1987 ($509,145). Won 8 events during PGA career that began in 1960.

**Art Rooney** (b. 1-27-01; d. 8-25-88): Owner of Pittsburgh Steelers. Bought team in 1933 and ran it until his death in 1988. Elected to Hall of Fame in 1964.

**Murray Rose** (b. 1-6-39) Australian swimmer. Won 3 gold medals (including 400- and 1500-meter freestyle) at 1956 Olympics. Also won 1 gold, 1 silver and 1 bronze medal at 1960 Olympics.

**Pete Rose** (b. 4-14-41): Baseball OF-IF. "Charlie Hustle." Alltime leader in hits (4,256), games played (3,562) and at bats (14,053); second in doubles (746); fourth in runs scored (2,165). Had .303 career average and won 3 batting titles. Averaged .300+ 15 times, 200+ hits and 100+ runs scored each 10 times. Led league in hits 7 times, runs scored 4 times, doubles 5 times. 1963 Rookie of the Year; 1973 MVP; 1975 World Series MVP. Had 44-game hitting streak in 1978. Played in 17 All-Star games, starting at 5 different positions. Career span 1963-86 with Cincinnati, Philadelphia. Manager of Cincinnati from 1984 to 1989. Banned from baseball for life by Commissioner Bart Giamatti in 1989 for betting activities. Served 5-month jail term for tax evasion in 1990. Ineligible for Hall of Fame.

**Ken Rosewall** (b. 11-2-34): Australian tennis player. Won Grand Slam singles titles at ages 18 and 35. Won 4 Australian titles (1953, 1955, consecutively 1971-72), 2 French titles (1953, 1968) and 2 U.S. titles (1956, 1970). Reached 4 Wimbledon finals, but title eluded him.

**Art Ross** (b. 1-13-1886, d. 8-5-64): Hockey D-coach. Improved design of puck and goal net. Manager-coach of Boston, 1924-45, won Stanley Cup, 1938-39. The Art Ross Trophy is awarded to the NHL scoring champion.

**Donald Ross** (b. 1873, d. 4-26-48): Scottish-born golf course architect. Trained at St. Andrews under Old Tom Morris. Designed over 500 courses, including Pinehurst No. 2 course and Oakland Hills.

**Patrick Roy** (b. 10-5-65): Hockey G. Won Vezina Trophy as NHL's top goalie three times. Won Conn Smythe Trophy as MVP of 1993 Stanley Cup. Career span since 1984 with Montreal.

**Pete Rozelle** (b. 3-1-26): Football executive. Fourth NFL commissioner, served from 1960 to 1989. During his term, league expanded from 12 to 28 teams. Created Super Bowl in 1966 and negotiated merger with AFL. Devised plan for revenue sharing of lucrative TV monies among owners. Presided during players' strikes of 1982, 1987.

**Wilma Rudolph** (b. 6-23-40, d. 11-12-94): Track and field. Gold medalist in 3 events (100-, 200- and 4x100-meter relay) at 1960 Olympics. Also won Sullivan Award in 1961.

**Adolph Rupp** (b. 9-2-01, d. 12-10-77): College basketball coach. Alltime NCAA leader in wins (875) and third highest winning percentage (.822). Won 4 NCAA championships consecutively 1948-49, 1951, 1958. Career span 1930-72 with Kentucky.

**Amos Rusie** (b. 5-3-1871, d. 12-6-42): Baseball RHP. Fastball was so intimidating that in 1893 the pitching mound was moved back 5' 6" to its present distance of 60' 6." Led league in strikeouts and walks 5 times each. Career record 246-174, 3.07 ERA with New York (NL) from 1889-1901.

**Bill Russell** (b. 2-12-34): Basketball C. Won MVP award 5 times (1958, consecutively 1961-63, 1965). Played on 11 championship teams, 8 consecutively, with Boston (1957, 1959-66, 1968-69). Player-coach 1968-69 (league's first black coach). Second alltime most rebounds (21,620) and second highest rebounding average (22.5); second most rebounds in a game (51 in 1960). Led league in rebounding 4 times. Also played on 2 consecutive NCAA championship teams with San Francisco in 1955-56; tournament MVP in 1955. Member of gold medal-winning 1956 Olympic team.

**Babe Ruth** (b. 2-6-1895, d. 8-16-48): Born George Herman Ruth. Baseball P-OF. Most dominant player in history. Alltime leader in slugging average (.690), HR frequency (8.5 HR every 100 at bats) and walks (2,056); second alltime most HR (714), RBI (2,211) and runs scored (2,174). Holds season record highest slugging average (.847 in 1920). 1923 MVP. Had .342 career batting average and 2,873 hits. 60 HR in 1927, 50+ HR 3 other times and 40+ HR 7 other times; 100+ RBI and 100+ walks 13 times each; 100+ runs scored 12 times. Second alltime most World Series HR (15), including his "called shot" off Charlie Root in 1932. Began career as a pitcher for Boston Red Sox: 94 career wins and 2.28 ERA. Won 20+ games 2 times; ERA leader in 1916. Played on 10 pennant winners, 7 World Series winners (3 with Boston, 4 with New York). Sold to Yankees in 1920 (Boston hasn't won World Series since). Career span 1914-35.

**Nolan Ryan** (b. 1-31-47): Baseball RHP. Pitched record 7th no hitter on May 1, 1991. Alltime leader in strikeouts (5,714), walks (2,795). League leader in strikeouts 11 times, walks 8 times, shutouts 3 times, ERA 2 times. 300+ strikeouts 6 times, including season record of 383 in 1973. 324 career wins. Career span 1966–93 with New York (NL), California, Houston, Texas.

**Jim Ryun** (b. 4-29-47): Track and field. Youngest ever to run under four minutes for the mile (3:59.0 at 17 years, 37 days). Set two world records in mile (3:51.3 in 1966 and 3:51.1 in 1967) and one in 1,500 (3:33.1 in 1967). Plagued by bad luck at Olympics; won silver medal in 1968 1,500 meters despite mononucleosis; was bumped and fell in 1972. Won Sullivan Award in 1967.

**Toni Sailer** (b. 11-17-35): Austrian skier. Won gold medals in 1956 Olympics in slalom, giant slalom and downhill, the first skier to accomplish the feat.

**Juan Antonio Samaranch** (b. 7-17-20): Amateur sports executive. Since 1980, Spaniard has served as president of International Olympic Committee.

**Joan Benoit Samuelson** (b. 5-16-57): Track and field. Gold medalist in first ever women's Olympic marathon (1984). Won Boston Marathon 2 times (1979, 1983). Sullivan Award winner in 1985.

**Barry Sanders** (b. 7-16-68): Football RB. Alltime NCAA season leader in yards rushing (2,628 in 1988).

Won Heisman Trophy in 1988 at Oklahoma State. Entered NFL in 1989 with Detroit and named Rookie of the Year. Gained 1,000+ yards rushing and named to Pro Bowl each of his first 6 seasons. Led league in rushing in 1990 and '94.

**Gene Sarazen** (b. 2-27-02): Golfer. Won PGA Championship 3 times (consecutively 1922-23, 1933), U.S. Open 2 times (1922, 1932), British Open once (1932) and the Masters once (1935). His win at the Masters included golf's most famous shot, a double eagle on the 15th hole of the final round to tie Craig Wood (Sarazen then won the playoff). Won 38 career tournaments. Also won Seniors Championship 2 times (1954, 1958). Pioneered the sand wedge in 1930.

**Glen Sather** (b. 9-2-43): Hockey coach and general manager. As coach, third alltime highest winning percentage (.616). 464 regular season wins. Led Edmonton to 4 Stanley Cup championships (consecutively 1984-85, 1987-88) from 1979 to 1989 and 1993-94. Also played for 6 teams from 1966 to 1976.

**Terry Sawchuk** (b. 12-28-29): Hockey G. All-time leader in wins (435) and shutouts (103). Career 2.52 goals against average. Goaltender of the Year 4 times (consecutively 1951-52, 1954, 1964). Led league in wins and shutouts 3 times and goals against average 2 times. Rookie of the Year in 1950. Tied record of 4 playoff shutouts in 1952. Played on 4 Stanley Cup champions with Detroit and Toronto from 1949 to 1969.

**Gale Sayers** (b. 5-30-43): Football RB. Alltime leader in kickoff return average (30.6). Scored 56 career touchdowns, including a rookie record 22 in 1965. Led league in rushing and gained 1,000+ yards rushing 2 times. Averaged 5 yards per carry. Rookie of the Year in 1965. Tied record with 6 rushing touchdowns on Dec. 12, 1965. Career span 1965-71 with Chicago cut short due to knee injury. Also All-America 2 times with Kansas.

**Dolph Schayes** (b. 5-19-28): Basketball player. College star at NYU. In 1960 became first NBA player to reach 15,000 career points. Also first NBA player to play in 1,000 games. Led NBA in free throw percentage three times, and averaged .843 for his career. Over stretch of 10 years played in 706 consecutive games. Elected to Hall of Fame 1972.

**Bo Schembechler** (b. 4-1-29): Football coach. In 21 seasons at Michigan from 1969–89, had a 194-48-5 record. Overall college coaching record 234-65-8.

**Mike Schmidt** (b. 9-27-49): Baseball 3B. Won 3 MVP awards (consecutively 1980-81, 1986). 548 career HR. Led league in HR 8 times, slugging average 5 times and RBI, walks and strikeouts 4 times each. 40+ HR 3 times, 30+ HR 10 other times; 100+ RBI 9 times, 100+ runs scored 7 times, 100+ strikeouts 12 times and third alltime most strikeouts (1,883). 100+ walks 7 times. Won 10 Gold Gloves. Career span 1972-89 with Philadelphia.

**Don Schollander** (b. 4-30-46): Swimmer. Won 4 gold medals (including 100- and 400-meter freestyle) at 1964 Olympics; won 1 gold and 1 silver medal at 1968 Olympics. Also won Sullivan Award in 1964.

**Dick Schultz** (b. 9-5-29): Amateur sports executive. Second executive director of the NCAA, served from 1987 to '93. Also served as athletic director at Cornell (1976-81) and Virginia (1981-87).

**Seattle Slew** (b. 1974): Thoroughbred race horse. Horse of the Year for 1977, when he won the Triple Crown, winning the Kentucky Derby by 1¾ lengths; the Preakness by 1½; and the Belmont by 4. In three year career from 1976–78, won 14 of 17 starts.

**Tom Seaver** (b. 11-17-44): Baseball RHP. "Tom Terrific." 311 career wins, 2.86 ERA. Cy Young Award winner 3 times (1969, 1973, 1975) and Rookie of the Year 1967. Fourth alltime most strikeouts (3,640). Led league in strikeouts 5 times, winning percentage 4 times and wins and ERA 3 times each. Won 20+ games 5 times; 200+ strikeouts 10 times. Struck out 19 batters in 1 game in 1970, including the final 10 in succession. Pitched no-hitter in 1978. Career span 1967-86 with New York (NL), Cincinnati, Chicago (AL), Boston.

**Secretariat** (b. 3-30-70, d. 10-4-89): Thoroughbred race horse. Triple Crown winner in 1973 with jockey Ron Turcotte aboard. Trained by Lucien Laurin.

**Monica Seles** (b. 12-2-73): Tennis player. Has won 3 consecutive French Open singles titles (1990-92), 3 Australian Open titles (1991-93) and 2 U.S. Open titles (1991-92). Seles' 1993 season ended on 4-30 when she was stabbed in the back by Gunther Parche while seated during a changeover in a tournament in Hamburg, Germany; also missed 1994 season.

**Bill Sharman** (b. 5-25-26): Basketball G. First team All Star four straight years 1956–59. Led NBA in free throw percentage every year from 1953–57, and in 1959 and '61. All Star Game MVP in 1955. NBA Coach of the Year in 1972, when his Lakers won NBA title. Elected to Hall of Fame in 1974.

**Wilbur Shaw** (b. 10-31-02, d. 10-30-54): Auto racer. Won Indy 500 3 times in 4 years (1937, consecutively 1939-40). AAA champion 2 times (1937, 1939). Also pioneered the use of the crash helmet after suffering skull fracture in 1923 crash.

**Patty Sheehan** (b. 10-27-57): Golfer. Won back-to-back LPGA championships, 1983–84. Won 1992 US Women's Open. 1983 LPGA Player of Year. Vare Trophy winner in 1984. Through '93 season, 31 career wins on LPGA tour; third alltime in earnings, with $4,131,837.01.

**Fred Shero** (b. 10-23-25, d. 11-24-90): Hockey coach. Fourth all-time highest winning percentage (.612, regular season). Led Philadelphia to 2 Stanley Cup championships (1974-75). Also coached NY Rangers. Played defense for NY Rangers, 1947-50.

**Bill Shoemaker** (b. 8-19-31): Horse racing jockey. Through 1994, alltime leader in wins (8,833). Rode Belmont Stakes winner 5 times (1957, 1959, 1962, 1967, 1975), Kentucky Derby winner 4 times (1955, 1959, 1965, 1986--at age 54, the oldest jockey to win Derby) and Preakness Stakes winner 2 times (1963, 1967). Also won Eclipse Award in 1981.

**Eddie Shore** (b. 11-25-02, d. 3-16-85): Hockey D. Won MVP award 4 times (1933, consecutively 1935-36, 1938). All-Star 7 times. Played on 2 Stanley Cup champions with Boston from 1926 to 1940.

**Frank Shorter** (b. 10-31-47): Track and field. Gold medalist in marathon at 1972 Olympics, the first American to win the event since 1908. Olympic silver medalist in 1976 marathon. Sullivan Award winner in 1972.

**Jim Shoulders** (b. 5-13-28): Rodeo. Alltime leader in career titles (16). All-Around champion 5 times (1949, consecutively 1956-59).

**Don Shula** (b. 1-4-30): Football coach. Alltime leader in wins (338 through 1994-95 season). Won 2 consecutive Super Bowl championships (1972-73) with Miami, including NFL's only undefeated season in 1972. Also reached Super Bowl 4 other times. Career span since 1963 with Baltimore and Miami.

**Al Simmons** (b. 5-22-02; d. 5-26-56): Baseball OF. "Bucketfoot Al" for hitting stance. Named AL MVP for 1929, when he led league 157 RBIs. Led league in batting average in 1930 (.381) and '31 (.390). Lifetime average of .334 with 307 homers. Career span 1924–44 with a variety of teams, but mostly Philadelphia A's. Elected to Hall of Fame in 1953.

**O. J. Simpson** (b. 7-9-47): Given name Orenthal James. Football RB. Seventh alltime in yards rushing (11,236). Gained 1,000+ yards rushing 5 consecutive seasons, including then-record 2,003 yards in 1973. Player of the Year 3 times (consecutively 1972-73, 1975). Led league in rushing 4 times. Gained 200+ yards rushing in a game a record 6 times, including 273 yards on Nov. 25, 1976. Scored 61 career touchdowns, including 23 in 1975. Also won Heisman Trophy with USC in 1968.

**Sir Barton** (b. 1916): Thoroughbred race horse. In 1919, before they were linked as the Triple Crown, became first horse to win the Kentucky Derby, the Preakness and the Belmont Stakes. Won 8 of 13 starts as 3-year-old.

**George Sisler** (b. 3-24-1893, d. 3-26-73): Baseball 1B. Alltime most hits in a season (257 in 1920). League leader in hits 2 times, with 200+ hits 6 times. Won 2 batting titles, including .420 average in 1922; averaged .400+ 2 times and .300+ 11 other times. Had 2,812 career hits and .340 average. Career span 1915-30 with St Louis.

**Mary Decker Slaney** (b. 8-4-58): Track and field. American record holder in 5 events ranging from 800 to 3,000 meters. Won 1,500 and 3,000 meters at World Championships in 1983. Lost chance for medal at 1984 Olympics when she tripped and fell after contact with Zola Budd. Won Sullivan Award in 1982.

**Dean Smith** (b. 2-28-31): College basketball coach. Entered 1995-96 season second alltime in wins (830), the most among active coaches; fifth alltime highest winning percentage (.779). Alltime most NCAA tournament appearances (25), reached Final Four 10 times. Won NCAA championship in 1982 and '93. Coached 1976 Olympic team to gold medal. Career span since 1962 with North Carolina.

**Emmitt Smith** (b. 5-15-69): Football RB. Led NFL in rushing in 1991 (1,563 yards) and '92 (1,713 and 18 TDs). Rushed for 108 yards in 52–17 Cowboy win over Bills in Super Bowl XXVII. Rushed for 132 yards and named MVP of Super Bowl XXVIII, a 30–13 Dallas victory over Buffalo. Career span since 1990 with Cowboys.

**Ozzie Smith** (b. 12-26-54): Baseball SS. "The Wizard of Oz." May be the best defensive shortstop in history. Holds alltime record for most assists in a season among shortstops (621 in 1980). 10 consecutive starts in All-Star game. Won 13 consecutive Gold Gloves. Career span since 1978 with San Diego, St Louis.

**Red Smith** (b. 9-25-05, d. 1-15-82): Sportswriter. Won Pulitzer Prize in 1976. After Grantland Rice, the most widely syndicated sports columnist. His literate essays appeared in the *NY Herald Tribune* from 1945 to 1971 and the *NY Times* from 1971 to 1982.

**Stan Smith** (b. 12-14-46): Tennis. Won 39 tournaments in career, including 1972 Wimbledon in 5 sets over Ilie Nastase. Won 1971 US Open over Jan Kodes and amateur version of U.S. Open in 1969. 1970 won inaugural Grand Prix Masters. Inducted to Tennis Hall of Fame in 1987.

**Tommy Smith** (b. 6-5-44): Track and field. Sprinter won 1968 Olympic 200 meters in world record of 19.83, then was expelled from Olympic Village, along with bronze medalist John Carlos, for raising black-gloved fist and bowing head during playing of national anthem to protest racism in U.S.

**Conn Smythe** (b. 2-1-1895, d. 11-18-80): Hockey executive. As general manager with Toronto from 1929 to 1961 won 7 Stanley Cup championships (1932, 1942, 1945, consecutively 1947-49, 1951). Award for playoff MVP named in his honor.

**Sam Snead** (b. 5-27-12): Golfer. Alltime leader in career wins (81). Won the Masters (1949, 1952, 1954) and PGA Championship (1942, 1949, 1951) 3 times each and British Open (1946). Runner-up at U.S. Open 4 times, but title eluded him. PGA Player of the Year in 1949. Won Seniors Championship 6 times, more than any golfer (1964-65, 1967, 1970, 1972-73).

**Peter Snell** (b. 12-17-38): Track and field. New Zealand runner was gold medalist in 800 meters at 2 consecutive Olympics in 1960, 1964. Also gold medalist in 1,500 meters at 1964 Olympics. Twice broke world mile record; broke world 800 record once.

**Duke Snider** (b. 9-19-26): Baseball OF. Career .295 average, 407 HR and 1,333 RBIs. Hit 40+ HR 5 consecutive seasons and 100+ RBIs 6 times. Also led league in runs scored 3 consecutive seasons. Played on 6 pennant winners with the Brooklyn Dodgers. World Series total of 11 HR and 26 RBIs are NL best. Career span from 1947-64.

**Javier Sotomayor** (b. 10-13-67): Track and field. Cuban high jumper broke the 8-foot barrier with world record jump of 8' 0" in 1989. Set current record of 8' ½" in 7-27-93 in Salamanca, Spain.

**Warren Spahn** (b. 4-23-21): Baseball LHP. Alltime leader in games won for a lefthander (363): 20+ wins 13 times. League leader in wins 8 times (5 seasons consecutively), complete games 9 times (7 seasons consecutively), strikeouts 4 consecutive seasons, innings pitched 4 times and ERA 3 times. 1957 Cy Young award. 63 career shutouts. Pitched 2 no-hitters after age 39. Career span 1942-65, all but last year with Boston (NL), Milwaukee.

**Tris Speaker** (b. 4-4-1888, d. 12-8-58): Baseball OF. Alltime leader in doubles (792), fifth in hits (3,514) and fifth in batting average (.345). 1 batting title (.386 in 1916), but .375+ average 6 times and .300+ average 12 other times. League leader in doubles 8 times, hits 2 times and HR and RBI 1 time each. 200+ hits 4 times, 40+ doubles 10 times and 100+ runs scored 7 times. MVP in 1912. Career span 1907-28 with Boston, Cleveland.

**Michael Spinks** (b. 7-13-56): Boxer. 1976 Olympic middleweight champion. Brother Leon was heavyweight champ. Won world light heavyweight title by decision over Mustafa Muhammad on 7-18-81. Defended it 5 times and then consolidated light heavy titles with decision over Dwight Braxton on 3-18-83. Defended four more times. Won heavyweight title on 9-22-85 in decision over Larry Holmes. Lost title to Mike Tyson in 91 seconds on 6-27-88.

**Mark Spitz** (b. 2-10-50): Swimmer. Won a record 7 gold medals (2 in freestyle, 2 in butterfly, 3 in relays) at 1972 Olympics, setting world record in each event. Also won 2 gold medals and 1 silver and 1 bronze medal at 1968 Olympics. Sullivan Award winner in 1971.

**Amos Alonzo Stagg** (b. 8-16-1862, d. 3-17-65): College football coach. Third alltime in wins (314). Won national championship with Chicago in 1905. Coach of the Year with Pacific in 1943 at age 81. Career record 314-199-35, including 5 undefeated seasons, from 1892 to 1946. Only person elected to both college football and basketball Halls of Fame. Played in the first basketball game in 1891.

**Willie Stargell** (b. 3-6-40): Baseball OF/1B. "Pops" achieved a 1979 MVP triple crown, winning NL regular season, playoff and World Series MVP awards. Led NL in homers in 1971 and '73. Hit 475 career homers. Drove in 1,540 runs. Had .282 career batting average. Played all 21 seasons with the Pirates. Elected to Hall of Fame in 1988.

**Bart Starr** (b. 1-9-34): Football QB. Played on 3 NFL champions (consecutively 1961-62, 1965) and first two Super Bowl champions (1966-67) with Green Bay. Also named MVP of first two Super Bowls. Player of the Year in 1966. Led league in passing 3 times. Also coached Green Bay to 53-77-3 record from 1975 to 1983.

**Roger Staubach** (b. 2-5-42): Football QB. Won Heisman Trophy with Navy as a junior in 1963. Served 4-year military obligation before turning pro. Led Dallas to 6 NFC Championships, 4 Super Bowls and 2 Super Bowl titles (1971, 1977). Player of the Year and Super Bowl MVP in 1971. Also led league in passing 4 times. Career span 1969-79.

**Jan Stenerud** (b. 11-26-42): Football K. Second to George Blanda on NFL scoring list, with 1,699 points. Converted an NFL record 373 field goals in 558 attempts. Career span 1967–79 with Kansas City Chiefs, 1980–83 with Green Bay Packers and 1984-85 with Minnesota Vikings. First pure kicker inducted to Hall of Fame 1991.

**Casey Stengel** (b. 7-30-1890, d. 9-29-75): Baseball manager. "The Ol' Perfesser." Managed New York Yankees to 10 pennants and 7 World Series titles (5 consecutively) in 12 years from 1949 to 1960. Alltime leader in World Series games (63), wins (37) and losses (26). Platoon system was his trademark strategy, Stengelese his trademark language ("You could look it up"). Managed New York Mets from 1962 to 1965. Jersey number (37) retired by Yankees and Mets.

**Ingemar Stenmark** (b. 3-18-56): Swedish skier. Gold medalist in slalom and giant slalom at 1980 Olympics. World Cup overall champion 3 consecutive years (1976-78).

**Woody Stephens** (b. 9-1-13): Horse racing trainer. Trained 2 Kentucky Derby winners (Cannonade, who won the 100th Derby in 1974 and Swale in 1984) and 5 straight Belmont winners from 1982-86, starting with 1982 Horse of the Year Conquistador Cielo.

**David Stern** (b. 9-22-42): Fourth NBA commissioner. Served since 1984. Average worth of a franchise has tripled from $20 million to $65 million. Owners rewarded him with 5-year, $27.5 million contract extension in 1990.

**Jackie Stewart** (b. 6-11-39): Scottish auto racer. Fourth alltime in Formula 1 victories (27); Formula 1 champion 3 times (1969, 1971, 1973). Also Indy 500 Rookie of the Year in 1966. Retired in 1973.

**John L. Sullivan** (b. 10-15-1858, d. 2-2-18): Boxer. Last bare knuckle champion. Heavyweight title holder (1882-92), lost to Jim Corbett. Career record 38-1-3 with 33 KOs from 1878 to 1892.

**Paul Tagliabue** (b. 11-24-40): Football executive. Fifth NFL commissioner, has served since 1989.

**Anatoli Tarasov** (b. 1918): Hockey coach. Orchestrated Soviet Union's emergence as a hockey power. Won 9 consecutive world amateur championships (1963-71) and 3 Olympic gold medals in 1964, 1968, 1972.

**Fran Tarkenton** (b. 2-3-40): Football QB. Through 1994-95 season, alltime leader in touchdown passes (342), yards passing (47,003), pass attempts (6,467) and pass completions (3,686). Player of the Year in 1975. Career span 1961-78 with Minnesota, NY Giants.

**Lawrence Taylor** (b. 2-4-59): Football LB. Revolutionized the linebacker position. Ended 1993 season as the alltime leader in sacks. Also named to Pro Bowl a record 10 consecutive seasons. Player of the Year in 1986. Has played on 2 Super Bowl champions with New York Giants (1986, 1990). Career span 1981-93 with Giants.

**Isiah Thomas** (b. 4-30-61): Basketball G. Member of Indiana University team that won 1981 NCAA title. Point guard for Detroit Pistons 1982–94. All-NBA First Team 1984, '85 and '86. NBA All Star Game MVP both 1984 and '86. Led NBA in assists (13.9) in 1984–85. Fourth alltime in assists (9,061). Member of Piston team that won NBA title in both 1989 and '90.

**Thurman Thomas** (b. 5-15-66): Football RB. Led AFC in rushing both 1990 (1,297 yards) and '91 (1,407). Career span since 1988 with Buffalo Bills.

**Daley Thompson** (b. 7-30-58): Track and field. British decathlete was gold medalist at 2 consecutive Olympics in 1980, 1984. At 1984 Olympics set world record (8,847 points) that lasted eight years.

**John Thompson** (b. 9-2-41): College basketball coach. From 1973 to present, head coach at Georgetown, where he taught Patrick Ewing, Alonzo Mourning and Dikembe Mutombo to play center. Won NCAA title in 1984, beating Houston 84–75. NCAA runnerup in 1982 and '85.

**Bobby Thomson** (b. 10-25-23): Baseball OF. Hit dramatic 9th-inning playoff home run to win NL pennant for New York Giants on Oct. 3, 1951. The Giants came from 13½ games behind the Brooklyn Dodgers on Aug. 11 to win the pennant on Thomson's 3-run homer off Ralph Branca in the final game of the 3-game playoff.

**Jim Thorpe** (b. 5-28-1888, d. 3-28-53): Sportsman. Gold medalist in decathlon and pentathlon at 1912 Olympics. Played pro baseball with New York (NL) and Cincinnati from 1913 to 1919, and pro football with several teams from 1919 to 1926. Also All-America 2 times with Carlisle.

**Dick Tiger** (b. 8-14-29; d. 12-14-71): Nigerian Boxer. Born Richard Ihetu. Won middleweight title by decision over Gene Fullmer on 10-23-62. Lost middle title to Joey Giardello on 12-7-63, then regained it from Giardello on 10-21-65. Won world light heavyweight title by decision over Jose Torres on 12-16-66, then lost it when KO'd by Bob Foster in 4 on 5-24-68. *The Ring* Fighter of the Year for 1962 and '65. Career record: 61-17-3. Elected to Boxing Hall of Fame 1974.

**Bill Tilden** (b. 2-10-1893, d. 6-5-53): Tennis player. "Big Bill." Won 7 U.S. singles titles, 6 consecutively (1920-25, 1929) and 3 Wimbledon titles (consecutively 1920-21, 1930). Also won 6 Grand Slam doubles titles. Led U.S. to 7 consecutive Davis Cup victories (1920-26).

**Ted Tinling** (b. 6-23-10, d. 5-23-90): British tennis couturier. The premier source on women's tennis from Suzanne Lenglen to Steffi Graf. Also designed tennis clothes, most notably the frilled lace panties worn by Gorgeous Gussy Moran at Wimbledon in 1949.

**Y.A. Tittle** (b. 10-24-26): Football QB. Threw 33 TD passes in 1962 and in '63 led league in passing, completing 221 of 367 attempts for 3,145 yards and 36 TDs. Career span 1948–64, mostly with San Francisco 49ers and New York Giants. Inducted into Hall of Fame 1971.

**Jayne Torvill/Christopher Dean** (b. 10-7-57/ b. 7-27-58): British figure skaters. Won 4 consecutive ice dancing world championships (1981-84) and Olympic ice dancing gold medal (1984). Won world professional championships in 1985. Won Olympic ice dancing bronze in 1994.

**Vladislav Tretiak** (b. 4-25-52): Hockey G. Led Soviet Union to 3 gold medals at Olympics in 1972, 1976, 1984. Played on 13 world amateur champions from 1970 to 1984.

**Lee Trevino** (b. 12-1-39): Golfer. Won U.S. Open (1968, 1971), British Open (consecutively 1971-72) and PGA Championship (1974, 1984) 2 times each. PGA Player of the Year in 1971. Also won U.S. Senior Open in 1990. First Senior $1 million season.

**Emlen Tunnell** (b. 3-29-25, d. 7-23-75): Football S. Alltime leader in interception yardage (1,282) and second in interceptions (79). All-Pro 9 times. Career span 1948-61 with New York Giants and Green Bay.

**Gene Tunney** (b. 5-25-1897, d. 11-7-78): Boxer. Heavyweight champion (1926-28). Defeated Jack Dempsey 2 times, including famous "long count" bout. Career record 65-2-1 with 43 KOs from 1915 to 1928. Retired as champion.

**Ted Turner** (b. 11-19-38): Sportsman. Skipper who successfully defended the America's Cup in 1977. Also owner of the Atlanta Braves since 1976 and Hawks since 1977. Founded the Goodwill Games in 1986.

**Mike Tyson** (b. 6-30-66): Boxer. Youngest heavyweight champion at 19 years old in 1986. Held title until knocked out by James "Buster" Douglas in Tokyo on Feb. 10, 1990. Career record as of 10-1-95 42–1 with 37 KOs since 1985. Convicted of rape in 1992, released from prison in 1995.

**Johnny Unitas** (b. 5-7-33): Football QB. 47 consecutive games throwing touchdown pass (1956-60), third alltime touchdown passes (290), fifth alltime yards passing (40,239). Led league in touchdown passes 4 consecutive seasons. Player of the Year 3 times (1959, 1964, 1967). Career span 1956-72 with Baltimore, San Diego.

**Al Unser Sr.** (b. 5-29-39): Auto racer. Won Indy 500 4 times (consecutively 1970-71, 1978, 1987). Third alltime in CART victories (39). USAC/CART champion 3 times (1970, 1983, 1985). Brother of Bobby.

**Bobby Unser** (b. 2-20-34): Auto racer. Won Indy 500 3 times (1968, 1975, 1981). Fourth alltime in CART victories (35). USAC champion 2 times (1968, 1974). Brother of Al, Sr.

**Harold S. Vanderbilt** (b. 7-6-1884, d. 7-4-70): Sailer. Owner and skipper who successfully defended the America's Cup 3 consecutive times (1930, 1934, 1937).

**Glenna Collett Vare** (b. 6-20-03, d. 2-2-89): Golfer. Won U.S. Women's Amateur 6 times, more than any golfer (1922, 1925, consecutively 1928-30, 1935).

**Bill Veeck** (b. 2-9-14, d. 1-2-86): Baseball owner. From 1946 to 1980, owned ballclubs in Cleveland, St Louis (AL), Chicago (AL). In 1948, Cleveland became baseball's first team to draw 2 million in attendance. That year Veeck integrated AL by signing Larry Doby and then Satchel Paige. A brilliant promoter, Veeck sent midget Eddie Gaedel up to bat for St Louis in 1951. Brought exploding scoreboard to stadiums and put players' names on uniforms.

**Guillermo Vilas** (b. 8-17-52): Tennis. Argentine won 50 straight matches in 1977. In '77 won French Open, where he beat Brian Gottfried, and the U.S. Open, where he beat Jimmy Connors. Also won Australian Open twice, 1978–79.

**Lasse Viren** (b. 7-22-49): Track and field. Finnish runner was gold medalist in 5,000 and 10,000 meters at 2 consecutive Olympics (1972, 1976).

**Virginia Wade** (b. 7-10-45): Tennis. Beloved in Britain, Wade won four major titles, most notably Wimbledon in 1977, its centenary year, where she triumphed over Betty Stove. Also won 1968 U.S. Open and '72 Australian Open.

**Honus Wagner** (b. 2-24-1874, d. 12-6-55): Baseball SS. Had .327 career batting average, 3,415 hits and 8 batting titles. Averaged .300+ 15 consecutive seasons. Led league in RBI 4 times, with 100+ RBI 9 times. Third alltime in triples (252) and league leader in doubles 8 times. 703 career stolen bases, league leader in steals 5 times. Career span 1897-1917 with Pittsburgh.

**Grete Waitz** (b. 10-1-53): Track and field. Norwegian runner has won New York City Marathon a record 9 times (consecutively 1978-80, 1982-86, 1988). Won the women's marathon at the 1983 World Championship.

**Jersey Joe Walcott** (b. 10-31-14): Boxer. Heavyweight champion from 1951 to 1952. Won title at age 37 on fifth attempt before surrendering it to Rocky Marciano. Later became sheriff of Camden, NJ.

**Doak Walker** (b. 1-1-27): Football HB. Led league in scoring 2 times, his first and final seasons. All-Pro 5 times. Played on 2 consecutive NFL champions (1952-53) with Detroit. Career span 1950 to 1955. Also won Heisman Trophy as a junior in 1948. All-America 3 consecutive seasons with SMU.

**Herschel Walker** (b. 3-3-62): Football RB. Won Heisman Trophy in 1982 with Georgia. Turned pro by entering USFL with New Jersey. Gained 7,000+ rushing yards and scored 61 touchdowns in 3 seasons before league folded. Entered NFL in 1986 with Dallas and led league in rushing yards (1,514 in 1988).

**Bill Walsh** (b. 11-30-31): Football coach. Led the San Francisco 49ers to four Super Bowl wins, after the 1981, '84, '88 and '89 seasons. Career record with 49ers 102-63-1. Developed short-passing game. Returned to Stanford University for 1992 season.

**Bill Walton** (b. 11-5-52): Basketball C. MVP in 1978, playoff MVP in 1977. Led league in rebounding and blocks in 1977. Career span 1974-86 with Portland, San Diego, Boston. Also College Player of the Year 3 consecutive seasons (1972-74). Played on 2

consecutive NCAA championship teams (1972-73) with UCLA; tournament MVP twice (1972-73). Sullivan Award winner in 1973.

**Junxia Wang** (b. 1963): Chinese distance runner. Broke four existing world records over six days in Sept. 1993. Broke 10,000 (29:31.78) on 9-8; ran 1500 in 3:51.92 in finishing second to countrywoman Qu Yunxia's world record of 3:50.46 on 9-11; ran 3,000 record of 8:12.19 in heats on 9-12 and lowered it to 8:06.11 on 9-13.

**War Admiral** (b. 1934): Thoroughbred race horse. A son of Man o' War, won Triple Crown and Horse of the Year honors in 1937.

**Paul Warfield** (b. 11-28-42): Football WR. Caught 427 passes for 8,565 yards and 85 TDs. Played on two Super Bowl-winning Miami Dolphin teams. Career span 1964–77, all with Cleveland Browns except for 1970–74 with Miami Dolphins. Inducted to Hall of Fame 1983.

**Glenn "Pop" Warner** (b. 4-5-1871, d. 9-7-54): College football coach. Second alltime in wins (319). Won 3 national championships with Pittsburgh (1916, 1918) and Stanford (1926). Career record 319-106-32 with 6 teams from 1896 to 1938.

**Tom Watson** (b. 9-4-49): Golfer. Winner of British Open 5 times (1975, 1977, 1980, consecutively 1982-83), the Masters 2 times (1977, 1981) and U.S. Open once (1982). PGA Player of the Year 6 times, more than any golfer (consecutively 1977-80, 1982, 1984).

**Dick Weber** (b. 12-23-29): Bowler. Won All-Star Tournament 4 times (consecutively 1962-63, 1965-66). Voted Bowler of the Year 3 times (1961, 1963, 1965). Won 31 career PBA titles.

**Johnny Weismuller** (b. 6-2-04, d. 1-21-84): Swimmer. Won 3 gold medals (including 100- and 400-meter freestyle) at 1924 Olympics and 2 gold medals at 1928 Olympics. Also played Tarzan in the movies.

**Jerry West** (b. 5-28-38): Basketball G. 10 time All-Star; All-Defensive Team 4 times; 1969 playoff MVP. Led league in assists and scoring 1 time each. Career span 1960-72 with Los Angeles. Currently general manager. Also NCAA tournament MVP in 1959. All-America 2 times with West Virginia. Played on 1960 gold medal-winning Olympic team.

**Whirlaway** (b. 4-2-38, d. 4-6-53): Thoroughbred race horse. Triple Crown winner in 1941 with jockey Eddie Arcaro aboard. Trained by Ben A. Jones.

**Byron "Whizzer" White** (b. 6-8-17): Football RB. Led NFL in rushing 2 times (Pittsburgh in 1938, Detroit in 1940). Led NCAA in scoring and rushing with Colorado in 1937; named All-America. Supreme Court justice from 1962 to '93.

**Reggie White** (b. 12-19-62): Football DE. Fearsome pass rusher. Winner in new era of free agency, signed with Green Bay Packers in 1993 for $17 million over four years. Career span: 1984 with Memphis Showboats, 1985–92 with Philadelphia Eagles and since 1993 with Green Bay.

**Charles Whittingham** (b. 4-13-13): Thoroughbred race horse trainer. "Bald Eagle" after losing hair to tropical disease in World War II. In 1986 became the oldest trainer to win Kentucky Derby, with Ferdinand. Led yearly earnings list for trainers from 1970–73 consecutively; in 1975; and in 1981–82 consecutively. Won three Eclipse Awards and trained two Horses of the Year (Ack Ack in 1971 and Ferdinand in 1987).

**Kathy Whitworth** (b. 9-27-39): Golfer. Alltime LPGA leader with 88 tour victories, including six majors. Won LPGA Championship in 1967, '71 and '75. Won 1977 Dinah Shore. Won Titleholders Championship (extinct major) in 1965 and '66. Won Western Open (extinct major) in 1967. Won Vare Trophy every year from 1965–72, except 1968. LPGA Player of Year from 1966–69 and 1971–73.

**Hoyt Wilhelm** (b. 7-26-23): Baseball RHP. Hall of Famer. Threw knuckleball until age 48. Alltime pitching leader in games (1,070). Career record: 143-122, 2.52 ERA, 227 saves. Hit home run in his first at bat (never hit another) and pitched no-hitter in 1958. Career span with 9 teams from 1952-72.

**Bud Wilkinson** (b. 4-23-15 d. 2-9-94): Football coach. Alltime NCAA leader in consecutive wins (47, 1953-57). Won 3 national championships (1950, consecutively 1955-56) with Oklahoma, where he coached from 1947 to 1963. Won Orange Bowl 4 times and Sugar Bowl 2 times. Career record 145-29-4, including 4 undefeated seasons. Also coached with St Louis of NFL in 1978-79.

**Billy Williams** (b. 6-15-38): Baseball OF. Nicknamed "Sweet Swinging". NL Rookie of the Year for 1961. Hit 426 career home runs. Drove in 1,475 runs. Lifetime averge of .290. Named to six NL All Star teams. Career span 1959–74 with Chicago Cubs, 1975–76 with Oakland A's. Elected to Hall of Fame in 1987.

**Ted Williams** (b. 8-30-18): Baseball OF. "The Splendid Splinter." Last player to hit .400 (.406 in 1941). MVP in 1946, 1949 and Triple Crown winner in 1942, 1947. Sixth alltime highest batting average (.344), second most walks (2,019) and second highest slugging average (.634). 521 career HR, 1,839 career RBIs. League leader in batting average and runs scored 6 times each, RBI and HR 4 times each, walks 8 times and doubles 2 times. Had .300+ average 15 consecutive seasons; 100+ RBI and runs scored 9 times each; 30+ HR 8 times; and 100+ walks 11 times. Lost nearly 5 seasons to military service. Career span 1939-42 and 1946-60 with Boston.

**Hack Wilson** (b. 4-26-00; d. 11-23-48): Baseball OF. Stood 5' 6" but weighed 210. Had five incredible seasons 1926–30. Best was 1930 when he hit .356, scored 146 runs, hit a NL record 56 homers and drove in 190, which is still the major league record. Declined through drinking. Career span 1923–34 with several teams. Elected to Hall of Fame in 1979.

**Dave Winfield** (b. 10-3-51): Baseball OF. Also drafted out of Univ. of Minnesota for both pro basketball and football. Led NL in RBIs in 1979 (118). In 1992, first 40-year-old to get 100+ RBIs, with 108. Had clutch double to win 1992 World Series. Got 3,000th hit, off Dennis Eckersley, on 9-16-93. Career span 1973–80 with San Diego; 1981–90 with Yankees; 1990–91 with California; 1992 with Toronto; 1993-94 with Minnesota; and 1995 with Cleveland.

**Major W. C. Wingfield** (b. 19-16-1833, d. 4-18-12): British tennis pioneer. Credited with inventing the game of tennis, which he called "Sphairistike" or "sticky" and patented in February 1874.

**Colonel Matt Winn** (b. 6-30-1861, d. 10-6-49): As general manager of Churchill Downs from 1904 until his death, promoted the Kentucky Derby into the premier race in the country.

**Katarina Witt** (b. 12-3-65): East German figure skater. Gold medalist at 2 consecutive Olympics in 1984, 1988. Also world champion 4 times (consecutively 1984-85, 1987-88).

**John Wooden** (b. 10-14-10): College basketball coach. Only member of basketball Hall of Fame as coach and player. Coached UCLA to 10 NCAA championships in 12 years (consecutively 1964-65, 1967-73, 1975). Alltime winning streak 88 games (1971-74). 664 career wins and fourth alltime highest winning percentage (.804). Career span 1949-75 with UCLA. Also 1932 College Player of the Year at Purdue.

**Mickey Wright** (b. 2-14-35): Golfer. Second alltime in career wins (82) and major championships (13—tied with Louise Suggs). Won U.S. Open 4 times (consecutively 1958-59, 1961, 1964), LPGA Championship 4 times (1958, consecutively 1960-61, 1963), Western Open 3 times (consecutively 1962-63, 1966) and Titleholders Championship twice (1961-62).

**Cale Yarborough** (b. 3-27-40): Auto racer. Won Daytona 500 4 times (1968, 1977, consecutively 1983-84). Fifth alltime in NASCAR victories (83). Also NASCAR champion 3 consecutive years (1976-78).

**Carl Yastrzemski** (b. 8-22-39): Baseball OF. "Yaz." 3,419 career hits, 452 HR. 1967 MVP and Triple Crown winner. 3 batting titles, including .301 in 1968, the lowest ever to win. Second alltime in games played (3,308) and fourth in walks (1,845). Career span 1961-83 with Boston.

**Cy Young** (b. 3-29-1867, d. 11-4-55): Baseball RHP. Alltime leader in wins (511), losses (315), innings pitched (7,354.2) and complete games (749); fourth in shutouts (76). Had 2.63 career ERA. Pitched 3 no-hitters, including a perfect game in 1904. Pitching award named in his honor. Career span 1890-1911 with Cleveland, Boston.

**Robin Yount** (b. 9-16-55): Baseball OF/SS. Became Brewer shortstop at 18. Landslide winner of 1982 AL MVP in 1982 when he hit .331 with 29 homers. Hit .414 in Brewers' 1982 Series loss to Cardinals. 3,142 hits. Shoulder injury made Yount move to outfield in 1984. Career span 1974–93, all with the Brewers.

**Babe Didrikson Zaharias** (b. 6-26-14, d. 9-27-56): Sportswoman. Gold medalist in 80-meter hurdles and javelin throw at 1932 Olympics; also won silver medal in high jump (her gold medal jump was disallowed for using the then-illegal western roll). Became a golfer in 1935 and won 12 major titles, including U.S. Open 3 times (1948, 1950, 1954—a year after cancer surgery). Also helped found the LPGA in 1949.

**Tony Zale** (b. 5-29-13): Boxer. Born Anthony Zaleski. "The Man of Steel." Won vacant middleweight title by decision over Georgie Abrams on 7-28-41. Lost title to Billy Conn on 2-13-42. Spent almost 4 years in Navy. In sensational 3 fight series with Rocky Graziano, retained title with KO in 6 on 9-27-46; lost it to Graziano by KO in 6 on 7-17-47; and then reclaimed it by KOing Graziano in 3 on 6-10-48. Lost title to Marcel Cerdan, who KO'd him in 12 on 9-21-48. Career record: 88 bouts; won 46 by KO and 24 by decision; drew 2; lost 16, 4 by KO. Elected to Boxing Hall of Fame 1958.

**Emil Zatopek** (b. 9-19-22): Track and field. Czechoslovakian runner became only athlete to win gold medal in 5,000 and 10,000 meters and marathon, at 1952 Olympics. Also gold medalist in 10,000 meters at 1948 Olympics.

# Obituaries

AUGUST 21, 1995 • $2.95 (CAN. $3.95)

GEORGE SILK

# Obituaries

**Johnny Adams, 79, horse racing trainer.**
Adams's riding career began in the early 1930's. As a jockey, he rode 3,270 winners, which earned more than $9.7 million, and won the 1954 Preakness aboard Hasty Road. After retiring from riding in 1958, Adams became a trainer. One of the horses he trained, J.O. Tobin, beat the previously undefeated Seattle Slew, a Triple Crown winner, in the 1977 Swaps Stakes. In Arcadia, Calif., after a lengthy illness, August 19.

**Bob Allison, 60, baseball player.** The American League Rookie of the Year in 1959 with the Washington Senators, Allison was diagnosed five years ago with ataxia, a neurodegenerative disorder that affects nerve cells in the brain and impairs coordination. He and his family then founded the Bob Allison Ataxia Research Center at the University of Minnesota. He had been in a wheelchair for the last year and had difficulty reading, swallowing, and speaking. A two-time All-Star, Allison was one of the early stars of the Minnesota Twins and spent 13 years in the majors. His career batting average was .255, with 256 home runs and 769 RBIs. He twice topped 100 RBIs, and his 99 runs scored led the AL in 1963. In Rio Verde, Ariz., of aspiration in the lungs related to ataxia, April 9.

**Francis "Reds" Bagnell, 66, football player.** A fiery red-head, Bagnell anchored the powerful single-wing offense of the University of Pennsylvania football team from 1948 to 1950. He won the Maxwell Award and the Helms Athletic Award and finished third in the Heisman Trophy balloting in 1950, when he threw 88 passes without an interception. In a victory that fall over Dartmouth, Bagnell amassed 490 yards to establish the single-game collegiate record for total yardage. He earned nine varsity letters at Penn, three each in football, baseball and basketball. In 1990, he was elected president of the National Football Foundation and College Hall of Fame Board. In Philadelphia, of heart failure, July 10.

**Sally Baile, 58, horse racing trainer.** Baile was one of the first women to train thoroughbred race horses to victory in major U.S. stakes races. Her best-known horse was probably Win, whose victories included the 1985 Man o' War. In Mineola, Long Island, of cancer, August 21.

**Gus Bell, 66, baseball player.** The oldest member of a three-generation baseball family, Bell was an outfielder with the Cincinnati Reds for nine (1953-61) of his 15 seasons. His best years were 1953, when he batted .300 with 30 homers, and 1955, when he hit .308 with 27 home runs. Four times, the left-handed hitter knocked in more than 100 runs in a season. Bell was the Mets' right fielder in their first game on April 11, 1962, and got their first hit. His son Buddy and grandson David have also played in the major leagues. In Cincinnati, of a heart attack, May 7.

**Hector "Toe" Blake, 83, hockey coach.** During a 28-year NHL career, Blake won three Stanley Cups as a player and eight as a coach. During his playing years with the Montreal Maroons and Canadiens, the left wing appeared in 578 games and had 235 goals and 292 assists for 527 points. Blake won scoring and MVP honors in 1938-39, and was awarded the Lady Byng trophy for sportsmanship in 1945-46. As the Canadiens' coach for 13 seasons, he was 500-255-129. In Montreal, of Alzheimer's disease, May 17.

**Glenn Burke, 42, baseball player.** Burke was the first major league baseball player to publicly acknowledge his homosexuality. He played for the Los Angeles Dodgers and the Oakland Athletics for four and a half seasons, batting .237 and stealing 35 bases, but he left the game at the age of 27 in 1980. "Prejudice drove me out of baseball sooner than I should have," he said. "But I wasn't changing." In 1987, his right leg and foot were shattered when he was hit by a car in San Francisco. After the accident, his years-long drug use increased, and he served prison time for grand theft and possession of drugs. He was sometimes seen panhandling and wandering in the Castro district of San Francisco. In San Leandro, Calif., of complications from AIDS, May 30.

**Fabio Casartelli, 24, cyclist.** The third rider to die during the 92-year history of the Tour de France, Casartelli fractured his skull in a crash on a mountain bend. The Italian racer failed to negotiate a curve and appeared to hit a concrete block on the side of the road. Like most of the other riders, Casartelli rode without a helmet, and his death renewed debate about the cyclists' safety. Tour riders observed a minute of silence in Casartelli's memory at the start of the 16th stage, the day after his death. In Tarbes, France, of head injuries, July 18.

**Howard Cosell, 77, broadcaster.** The trailblazing journalist introduced sports journalism to television and brought entertainment to prime-time football. Cosell gave up a law career in the 1950s to go into broadcasting, where he stirred up controversy wherever he went. "Telling it like it is," Cosell once wrote, "I've had a remarkable life."

William Nack writes:

"On a winter night in 1983, in a dining room of the Ritz-Carlton Hotel in New York City, the face that had launched a thousand quips was up now and floating among the tables of network talking heads and sports celebrities.

"It was a dinner for the Special Olympics, and no one navigated such an occasion more noisily than Howard Cosell, particularly when he was fondling his ninth vodka martini. And suddenly there he was across the room, hovering over one table, scolding and sarcastic, loud and bombastic—the familiar cigar jabbing at the air, the voice growing louder as the Havana grew shorter. Howard was Coselling again, speaking of sports, of broadcasting, of anything that came to mind. Finally the rest of the room fell silent, and all to be heard was the voice of Howard, America's voice. During the lull, Howard's wife, Emmy, sitting across the room, summoned her husband back to earth with a voice that went boom in the night.

" 'Howard, shut up! Nobody cares.' "

"After it was announced on Sunday that Cosell had died of a heart embolism at 4 a.m. in a Manhattan hospital, the thought of that old rebuke came back again with a kind of eerie resonance. Of all the figures in modern American sport, none inspired a sense of ambivalence that ran quite as deep and powerful as did Howard Cosell, in life and in death, and this was nowhere more evident than in the eulogies served up on Sunday with a side of ice. Bob Costa's piece on NBC was delivered with a very dry eye, and even Cosell's former boss at ABC Sports, Roone Arledge, could summon nothing that could be properly described as emotion. 'Howard Cosell was one of the most original people ever to appear on American television,' Arledge said. 'He became a giant by telling the truth in an industry that was not used to hearing it and considered it revolutionary.'

"It all rang, in a rather unsettling way, as though nobody really gave a damn. It has been 10 years since Cosell left TV broadcasting, a dozen since he abandoned the book on *Monday Night Football*, and there is a whole new generation out there that has missed the gaudiest, smartest and most entertaining and unforgettable television broadcaster in the history of sports—a superb reporter who worked harder and asked better questions than anyone else who'd ever worn earphones. They also have missed a man who was, by turns, well.... Let him tell it like it was: 'Arrogant, pompous, obnoxious, vain, cruel, verbose, a showoff. I have been called all of these. Of course, I am.' All he forgot was irritating, generous, egomaniacal, funny, paranoid, charming, insecure and.... 'If Howard Cosell were a sport, he'd be roller derby,' said columnist Jimmy Cannon.

"Above all, he was sui generis, an unalloyed original who, as a homely Jewish lawyer from Brooklyn, brought to television what one writer called 'the grand slam of network liabilities.' Upon arriving on the national scene in the 1960s, Cosell got swept up in the political currents quickened by the civil rights movement and the Vietnam War. Unlike his buttoned-down peers, who ducked social issues and fled at the first whiff of controversy, Cosell waded into every major battle of his time, cutting his way against the grain. He allied himself with Curt Flood in the player's challenge to baseball's hoary reserve clause, and he championed Muhammad Ali in his fight against the draft, setting fire to the national shirt by insisting on calling Ali by his Muslim name. Many of his pen pals remained anonymous when they addressed him 'You nigger-loving Jew bastard....'

"If his alliance with Ali launched him as a social force—a regular in front of congressional committees and college classrooms—his 14 years on *Monday Night Football* made him an enduring celebrity, at once the most loved and the most reviled of broadcasters. On Monday nights bar owners all over America held contests in which the winner got to heave a brick at How-wud's visage on a television screen. One night in the 1970s, as he left the broadcast booth following a game in Baltimore, the crowd around him grew so menacing, pressing in and shouting obscenities, that policemen formed a wedge to shield him. Stepping onto the elevator, Cosell adjusted his tie and sniffed, 'Have you ever seen such *animals*?' By then, of course, the game had become the undercard to the main event. Cosell was the show.

"When his television career ended in the mid-1980s, he left as one of the most influential figures in sports, and very much in the Cosellian tradition, he did not leave quietly. He wrote two books attacking just about everything in sports, including a number of his former colleagues on *Monday Night Football*, leaving behind a bitter and angry history of his life and times in the world of games. Cosell was too much of an original to leave heirs, and the landscape of broadcast journalism that he left on Sunday looks much the way he found it 35 years ago. Once again the waves are filled with talking heads and apologists, with hometown cheerleaders and mindless drones. No one is asking the questions that he asked. And Emmy was right—nobody cares."

In New York City, of a heart embolism, April 23.

**Leon Day, 78, baseball player.** Day died just six days after he achieved his lifelong dream, being elected into baseball's Hall of Fame. He was considered one of the best pitchers in the Negro Leagues. Playing mainly for the Newark (N.J.) Eagles, Day pitched in a record seven All-Star games from 1934-50. In Baltimore, of a heart condition, March 13.

**Edward J. DeBartolo, Sr., 85, team owner.** DeBartolo, one of the country's richest businessmen, owned the San Francisco's 49ers and, for a time, the Pittsburgh Penguins (which he sold in 1991). He earned his fortune by parlaying a real estate business into one of the world's largest shopping center and development firms. DeBartolo also served as president of three horse tracks—Louisiana Downs, Thistledown in Cleveland and Remington Park in Oklahoma City. His son, Edward Jr., runs the 49ers. In Youngstown, Ohio, of complications from pneumonia, December 19, 1994.

**Juan Manuel Fangio, 84, race car driver.** Fangio dominated Grand Prix racing in the 1950s by winning 24 of the 51 world championship races he contested for the Mercedes-Benz, Alfa Romeo, Ferrari and Maserati teams. The world driving champion in 1951 and from 1954 through 1957, Fangio ranks seventh among alltime Grand Prix winners.

SI writes:

"During his brief, spectacular Formula One racing career, Argentina's Juan Manuel Fangio, who died last week of kidney failure at the age of 84, maintained a presence befitting so imperial a sport. The epitome of the old school driver, looking dashing in the cockpit of the elegant front-engined cars whose sleek bodywork was uncluttered by sponsor logos, Fangio was the standard by which all Grand Prix drivers measure themselves. Yet he somehow never lost the unassuming sensibilities of the common man.

"Even during the 1950s, one of the most volatile and divisive political decades in Latin American history, right-wing dictators and Marxist revolutionaries could agree on at least one thing: Fangio's greatness. Friends of the Maestro like to recall the time when, before a minor F/1 race in Havana in 1958, Fangio was captured by a group of pro-Castro insurgents hostile to the rightist Batista regime. The revolutionaries were so in awe of their hostage that they brought him breakfast in bed and watched the race with him before releasing him that night. When Fangio was buried last week in his birthplace of Balcarce, his open casket was surrounded by two enormous funeral wreaths, one from Fidel Castro and another from Arnold Rodriguez, the man who led the group that had kidnapped him from his Havana hotel.

"Although Fangio was already 37 when he began his Grand Prix career, he won an astounding 24 of 51 races in his 10 years on the F/1 circuit before retiring in 1958, citing his belief that champions, like actors and dictators, should go out while still on top. Yet in retirement the Maestro never failed to carry himself with the forbearance and humility that had defined him during his racing career. 'When one runs the risk of losing a sense of proportion,' he once said, 'it's time to go home, sleep in the same bed in which one dreamed while still a nobody and to eat the simple, healthy dishes of one's childhood.' "

In Buenos Aires, of pneumonia, July 17.

**Richard "Pancho" Gonzales, 67, tennis player.** A two-time national champion, the 6'3" Gonzales dominated the court with his powerful right-handed serve and precise, versatile ground strokes. He never won Wimbledon, although as a 41-year-old grandfather he won the longest match in Wimbledon history, a first-round bout that lasted 5 hours and 12 minutes and spanned two days. Gonzalez, who taught himself to play on the public courts in Los Angeles, turned pro in 1949 in the days before open (pro and amateur) tournaments, and spent his prime playing in Jack Kramer's "circus" tour. "He was a great competitor," said Kramer. "He would have won several Wimbledons if he hadn't turned professional. The records of Richard Gonzalez are obscured because of that. He never showed up at Wimbledon and Forest Hills until 1968...."

SI writes:

"A recurring theme in the obituaries of Richard (Pancho) Gonzales last week was that this great player was tennis's first enfant terrible, the progenitor of a generation of boors. Gonzales, in fact, did complain from time to time about questionable calls and even whacked an occasional ball into the seats in a fit of pique. He responded, often heatedly, to hecklers. He was not above teasing an opponent if he thought it might give him an edge. And once he even threw a courtside chair at a tournament referee whom he considered negligent.

"In his day such behavior was considered abhorrent. Now it is merely the norm. Or did you miss the farcical goings-on at Wimbledon, where not one player but three got the boot, and the wife of one of them took a poke at a chair umpire? If these churls are the inheritors of the Gonzales legacy, then poor Pancho ought to be committed immediately and without clemency to purgatory.

"Gonzales did have a chip on his shoulder. His court ferocity was fed in no small part by a sense of social inferiority that was accentuated in a sport then considered upper crust. No country-club kid, he learned his game on the public courts as an urban warrior. And if he behaved badly at times, it was not out of petulance, but out of a deep-seated dread of failure. Mostly, he was an imposing and even dignified presence on the court.

"Gonzales would certainly have resented suggestions that he had anything at all in common with the Visigoths who have succeeded him on the courts. And we agree. After all, in his lifetime he had five wives—including an older sister of Andre Agassi—and none of them ever slugged a chair umpire."

In Las Vegas, of stomach cancer, July 3.

**David Griggs, 28, football player.** Griggs was killed when he apparently lost control of his car on an expressway ramp. After five seasons with the Miami Dolphins, the linebacker had joined the San Diego Chargers as a free agent in 1994 and helped them win the AFC title. In Fort Lauderdale, of injuries sustained in a car accident, June 19.

**Alex Groza, 68, basketball player.** Groza, an all-America center for the championship Kentucky basketball teams of the late 1940's, played a prominent role in the game's biggest betting scandal. At 6'7", Groza parlayed size with quickness and finished with 1,744 points, which topped the Kentucky career list for 15 years after he left and still ranks seventh in school history. Groza went on to play for the NBA's Indianapolis Olympians, where he was second in scoring behind George Mikan in his two seasons. Before the start of the 1952 season, he and former teammates Ralph Beard and Dale Barnstable admitted to conspiring to shave points in return for bribes from gamblers while at Kentucky. They received suspended sentences and their professional careers were ended. Groza later became general manager and coach of the Kentucky Colonels and general manager of the San Diego Conquistadores of the ABA. He was the younger

brother of Lou, a Hall of Fame tackle and place-kicker who starred for the Cleveland Browns. In San Diego, of cancer, January 21.

**Pat Haggerty, 67, football referee.** Haggerty's career as an NFL referee spanned 28 years and three Super Bowls. In Greeley, Colo., of prostate and bone cancer, December 9, 1994.

**Nat Holman, 98, basketball coach.** Holman, one of the greatest basketball players of the 1920's, coached the 1950 City College of New York team to victories in both the NCAA and the NIT championships, a feat that can no longer be duplicated because the tournaments are now held at the same time. A year later, several of his key players were arrested for point-shaving—trying to win a game by fewer points than the margin predicted by bookmakers. Holman knew nothing of the players' deceit, however. He was one of the few men who played both pro basketball and coached a college team at the same time. From 1921-27, he played with the Original Celtics, the famous barnstorming team that helped legitimize pro basketball, and was billed by the team as "the world's greatest basketball player." In Riverdale, Bronx, of natural causes, February 12.

**Jim Lee Howell, 80, football coach.** Howell, a stalwart on the Steve Owen Giants' teams that played in four NFL championship games from 1937 to 1948, is best remembered as Owen's successor as head coach. During that seven year span, from 1954 to 1960, Howell never had a losing season. His overall record of 55-29-4, for a winning percentage of .663, is the best of any Giant coach of comparable tenure. He coached some of the team's most acclaimed players, including Charley Conerly, Frank Gifford, Kyle Rote and Sam Huff. After leaving the head-coach position, he spent 19 years as the Giants' director of player personnel and seven as a special scout and consultant. During his playing days, the Arkansas native also served in his home state's Legislature. In Lonoke, Ark., of natural causes, January 4.

**Jim Katcavage, 60, football player.** A defensive end for the New York Giants, Katcavage began his career on the famous 1956 championship team, the first Giants team to win an NFL championship in 18 years (it would be another 30 years before the feat was duplicated). The title was won when the Giants, wearing basketball shoes on a frozen field, rolled to a 47-7 victory over the Chicago Bears. In his 13-year career, Katcavage was an All-Pro three times and scored a total of three safeties, tying for second on the league career list. In the 14-game 1963 season, 19 years before the league started keeping official sack records, he was credited with 25 sacks, three more than the official 16-game season record. In Maple Glen, Penn., of a heart attack, February 22.

**Irving S. Kosloff, 82, team owner.** Kosloff owned the Philadelphia 76ers teams that set NBA records for both the best (1966-67) and the worst (1972-73) seasons. During the period of his ownership, from 1963 to '76, the 76ers made the playoffs nine times, reached the Eastern Conference final three times and won the NBA championship in 1967 with Wilt Chamberlain at center. In Merion, Pa., of undisclosed causes, February 19.

**Millicent Lang, 78, tennis player.** Lang, a Bronx native, won her first public tournament at age 11. She captured three titles as a junior player in the 1930's and was a veteran player on the women's tennis circuit by the time she was 19. In the early 1940's, Lang was ranked 14th in the United States women's singles and No. 1 in the Eastern states. In Boca Raton, Fla., of a stroke, February 10.

**Ron Luciano, 57, umpire.** An American League umpire from 1968-79, Luciano was known for his wise-cracks and arm-waving antics. After retiring from baseball, Luciano worked as a commentator for NBC, wrote four books about his umpiring exploits and became a hit on the talk-show circuit.

SI writes:

"It wasn't so much the things he did and said, but the way he did and said them. Ron Luciano, the umpire who struck back, made his calls with great histrionics and made his opinions known with similar flair. Anything refracted through his world view, an outlook that was equal parts Berra and Berle, came out so skewed that it somehow made perfect sense. 'When I started, baseball was played by nine tough competitors on grass in graceful ballparks,' he once said of the 11 years he spent wearing American League blue. 'By the time I finished, there were 10 men on a side, the game was played indoors on plastic, and I spent half my time watching out for a man dressed in a chicken suit who kept trying to kiss me.'

"Luciano said much more before last week when, at 57, perhaps out of loneliness, perhaps out of depression over his mother's Alzheimer's disease, he asphyxiated himself in his garage in Endicott, N.Y.

"*On himself*: 'I like to hunt, but I never hit anything. I don't see too well.'

" 'A double play takes 3.8 seconds. Even as dumb as I am, I can concentrate that long.'

" 'I never called a balk in my life. I didn't understand the rule.'

"*On his craft*: 'Umpiring is best described as the profession of standing between two seven-year-olds with one ice-cream cone.'

" 'There are a lot of salls and brikes that I have to call balls and strikes.'

" 'An indecisive umpire is as vulnerable as the rich sky diver who allows his only heir to pack his parachute.'

" 'When you're wrong, and you call something and they still believe you, that makes a great umpire.'

"*Upon being asked by Larry King if there are natural umpires*: 'Yeah, there really are, but nobody starts out that way.'

"*And*: 'Umpires never win.' "

In Endicott, N.Y., of carbon monoxide poisoning, January 18.

**Mickey Mantle, 63, baseball player.** His career with the New York Yankees spanned 18 seasons (1951-68); his hold on the nation's affections lasted even longer. Mantle, perhaps the most powerful switch-hitter ever, twice topped 50 homers, led the AL in home runs four times and finished with a total of 536. He achieved the Triple Crown in 1956, played in 20 All-Star games and earned three MVP Awards (in 1956, '57, and '62). Mantle's death two months after a much-publicized liver transplant prompted an effort to understand his place in American lore. Richard Hoffer offers this provocative essay on Mantle as man and myth:

"Mickey Mantle, with his death at 63, passes from these pages forever and becomes the property of anthropologists, people who can more properly put the calipers to celebrity, who can more accurately track the force of personality. We can't do it anymore, couldn't really do it to begin with. He batted this, hit that. You can look it up. Hell, we do all the time. But there's

nothing in our library, in all those numbers, that explains how Mantle moves so smoothly from baseball history into national legend, a country's touchstone, the lopsided grin on our society.

"He wasn't the greatest player who ever lived, not even of his time perhaps. He was a centerfielder of surprising swiftness, a switch-hitter of heart-stopping power, and he was given to spectacle: huge home runs (his team, the New York Yankees, invented the tape-measure home run for him); huge seasons (.353, 52 HRs, 130 RBIs to win the Triple Crown in 1956); one World Series after another (12 in his first 14 seasons). Yet, for one reason or another, he never became Babe Ruth or Joe DiMaggio—or, arguably, even Willie Mays, his exact contemporary.

"But for generations of men, he's the guy, has been the guy, will be the guy. And what does that mean exactly? A woman beseeches Mantle, who survived beyond his baseball career as a kind of corporate greeter, to make an appearance, to surprise her husband. Mantle materializes at some cocktail party, introductions are made, and the husband weeps in the presence of such fantasy made flesh. It means that, exactly.

"It's easy to account, at least partly, for the durability and depth of his fame: He played on baseball's most famous team during the game's final dominant era. From Mantle's rookie season in 1951—the lead miner's son signed out of Commerce, Oklahoma, for $1,100—to his injury-racked final year in 1968, baseball was still the preeminent game in the country. This was baseball B.C. (Before Cable), and a nation's attention was not scattered come World Series time. Year in, year out, men and boys in every corner of the country were given to understand during this autumnal rite that there really was only one baseball team and that there really was only one player: No. 7, talked with a twang, knocked the ball a country mile. But it was more than circumstance that fixed Mantle in the national psyche; he did hit 18 World Series home runs, a record, over the course of 65 of the most watched games of our lives.

"Even knowing that, acknowledging the pin-striped pedigree, the fascination still doesn't add up. If he was a pure talent, he was not, as we found out, a pure spirit. But to look upon his youthful mug today, three decades after he played, is to realize how uncluttered our memories of him are. Yes, he was a confessed drunk; yes, he shorted his potential—he himself said so. And still, looking at the slightly uplifted square jaw, all we see is America's romance with boldness, its celebration of muscle, a continent's comfort in power during a time when might did make right. Mantle was the last great player on the last great team in the last great country, a postwar civilization that was booming and confident, not a trouble in the world.

"Of course, even had he not reflected the times, Mantle would have been walking Americana. His career was storybook stuff, hewing more to our ideas of myth than any player's since Ruth. Spotted playing shortstop on the Baxter Springs Whiz Kids, he was delivered from a rural obscurity into America's distilled essence of glamour. One year Mantle is dropping 400 feet into the earth, very deep into Oklahoma, to mine lead on his father's crew, another he's spilling drinks with Whitey Ford and Billy Martin at the Copa.

"A lesson reaffirmed: Anything can happen to anybody in this country, so long as they're daring in their defeats and outsized in victory. Failure is forgiven of the big swingers, in whom even foolishness is flamboyant. Do you remember Mantle in Pittsburgh in the 1960 Series, twice whiffing in Game 1 and then, the next day, crushing two? Generations of men still do. The world will always belong to those who swing from the heels.

"Still, Mantle's grace was mostly between the lines; he developed no particular bonds beyond his teammates, and he established no popularity outside of baseball. As he was dying from liver cancer, none of the pre-tributes remarked much on his charm. And, as he was dying from a disease that many have presumed was drinking-related, there was a revisionist cast to the remembrances. Maybe he wasn't so much fun after all.

"But, back then, he most certainly was. Drunkenness had a kind of high-life cachet in the '50s: It was manly, inasmuch as you were a stand-up guy who could be counted on to perform the next afternoon, and it was glamorous. Down the road, as Mantle would later confess from the other side of rehabilitation, it was merely stupid. But palling around with Billy and Whitey—just boys, really, they all had little boys' names—it amounted to low grade mischief. Whatever harm was being done to families and friends, it was a small price to pay for the excitement conferred upon a workaday nation.

"In any event, we don't mind our heroes flawed, or even doomed. Actually, our interest in Mantle was probably piqued by his obvious destiny, the ruin he often foretold. As a Yankee he was never a whole person, having torn up his knee for the first first time in his first World Series in '51. Thereafter, increasingly, he played in gauze and pain, his prodigal blasts heroically backlit by chronic injury. But more: At the hospital after that '51 incident, Mantle learned that his father, Mutt, admitted to the same hospital that same day, was dying of Hodgkin's disease. It was a genetic devastation that had claimed every Mantle male before the age of 40. The black knowledge of this looming end informed everything Mickey did; there was little time, and every event had to be performed on a grand scale, damn the consequences. Everything was excused.

"As we all know, having participated in this gloomy death watch, it didn't end with that kind of drama. It was Billy, the third of Mantles' four sons, who came down with Hodgkin's, and who later died of a heart attack at 36. Mickey lived much longer, prospering in an era of nostalgia, directionless in golf and drinking, coasting on a fame that confounded him (Why was this man, just introduced to him, weeping?).

"Then Mantle, who might forever have been embedded in a certain culture, square-jawed and unchanged, did a strange thing. Having failed to die in a way that might have satisfied mythmakers, he awoke with a start and checked himself into the Betty Ford Center. This was only a year and a half ago, and, of course, it was way too late almost any way you figure it. Still, his remorse seemed genuine. The waste seemed to gall him, and his anger shook the rest of us.

"The generation of men who watched him play baseball, flipped for his cards or examined every box score must now puzzle out the attraction he held. The day he died there was the usual rush for perspective and the expected sweep through the Yankee organization. They said the usual things. But former teammate Bobby Murcer reported that he had talked to the Mick before he had gone into the hospital the final time—neither a liver transplant nor chemotherapy could arrest the cancer or stop his pain—and Mantle, first thing, asked how a fund-raiser for children affected by the Oklahoma City bombing was going, something he and Murcer, also from Oklahoma, were involved in. It was odd, like the sudden decision to enter rehab and

rescue his and his family's life, and it didn't really square with our idea of Mantle.

"But let's just say you were of this generation of men, that you once had been a kid growing up in the '50s, on some baseball team in Indiana, and you remember stitching a No. 7 on the back of your KIRCHNER'S PHARMACY T-shirt, using red thread and having no way of finishing off a stitch, meaning your hero's number would unravel indefinitely and you would have to do it over and over, stupid and unreformed in your idolatry. And today here's this distant demigod, in his death, taking human shape. What would you think now?"

In Dallas, of cancer, August 13, 1995.

**Timothy J. Mara, 59, team owner.** Mara, the grandson of the New York Giants' founder, was a co-owner of the team with his uncle Wellington Mara from 1965 until 1990. Tim Mara grew up on the Giants' sidelines, and was a close friend of Frank Gifford in his rookie days. Conflict with his uncle over personnel and coaching selections led to a long family feud. The two co-owners sat in separate owner's boxes at home games and communicated mostly through the general manager. After the 1990 season, Tim, representing his mother and his sister, sold their half-interest in the team to Preston Robert Tisch of the Loews Corporation. In Florida, of Hodgkins disease, May 1.

**Carlos Monzon, 52, boxer.** Monzon won the middleweight crown in 1970 on a 12th-round knockout of Nino Benvenutti. In 1988, he was convicted of killing his estranged lover, 32-year-old Alicia Muniz, when an autopsy revealed that she had been strangled to the point of unconsciousness before being hurled from a second-story balcony. The killing gripped Argentina, where Monzon was a hero. The boxer was sentenced to 11 years in prison but was free on a furlough program when he was killed in a car crash. In Santa Rosa de Calchines, Argentina, of injuries sustained in a car accident, January 8.

**Lindsey Nelson, 76, broadcaster.** Known for his collection of garish sports jackets and his erudition in the booth, Nelson was one of the New York Mets' three original announcers. He also covered the NFL, the Cotton Bowl, the San Francisco Giants and called 13 years of Notre Dame football. Nelson (who donated one of his jackets for display) was inducted into the broadcasters' wing of baseball's Hall of Fame in 1988. About 1962, his first year with the Mets, Nelson said in the book *Voices of the Game*: "Ralph [Kiner], Bob [Murphy] and I sat down and decided we were going to level and be straightforward; we had a bad club and we had to say so. And it seemed to work. The Yankees were winners, we were losers, and yet by July 1963, we passed them in radio and TV ratings." Nelson spent 17 years with the team and then called San Francisco Giants games for three seasons. In Atlanta, of complications of Parkinson's disease and pneumonia, June 10.

**Ralph Neves, 78, jockey.** Neves made headlines in 1936 when he walked out of a mortuary after being declared dead in a track accident. He was riding at Bay Meadows in San Mateo, Calif., when his horse threw him into a wooden rail. He was trampled by other horses and pronounced dead. At the mortuary, a doctor friend gave him a shot of adrenaline in the heart. Neves awoke and, half-conscious, wandered to a cab stand where he got a ride back to the track. He was not allowed to race until the next day. Neves won 3,771 races, including 173 stakes, before retiring in 1964. In San Marcos, Calif., of lung cancer, July 7.